image comics presents

THE WALKING DEAD

COMPENDIUM ONE

ROBERT KIRKMAN
creator, writer,
letterer (chapters 1-3)

TONY MOORE
penciler, inker, gray tones (chapter 1)

CHARLIE ADLARD
penciler, inker (chapters 2-8)

CLIFF RATHBURN
gray tones (chapters 2-8)

RUS WOOTON
letterer (chapter 4-8)

SINA GRACE
editor

CHARLIE ADLARD & CLIFF RATHBURN
cover

For SKYBOUND ENTERTAINMENT

Robert Kirkman - CEO
J.J. Didde - President
Sean Mackiewicz - Editorial Director
Shawn Kirkham - Director of Business Development
Helen Leigh - Office Manager
Brandon West - Inventory Control
Feldman Public Relations LA - Public Relations

For international rights inquiries,
please contact: foreign@skybound.com
WWW.SKYBOUND.COM

IMAGE COMICS, INC.
Robert Kirkman - chief operating officer
Erik Larsen - chief financial officer
Todd McFarlane - president
Marc Silvestri - chief executive officer
Jim Valentino - vice-president
Eric Stephenson - publisher
Todd Martinez - sales & licensing coordinator
Jennifer de Guzman - pr & marketing director
Branwyn Bigglestone - accounts manager
Emily Miller - accounting assistant
Jamie Parreno - marketing assistant
Jenna Savage - administrative assistant
Sarah deLaine - events coordinator
Kevin Yuen - digital rights coordinator
Jonathan Chan - production manager
Drew Gill - art director
Monica Garcia - production artist
Vincent Kukua - production artist
Jana Cook - production artist
www.imagecomics.com

Chapter One:
Days Gone Bye

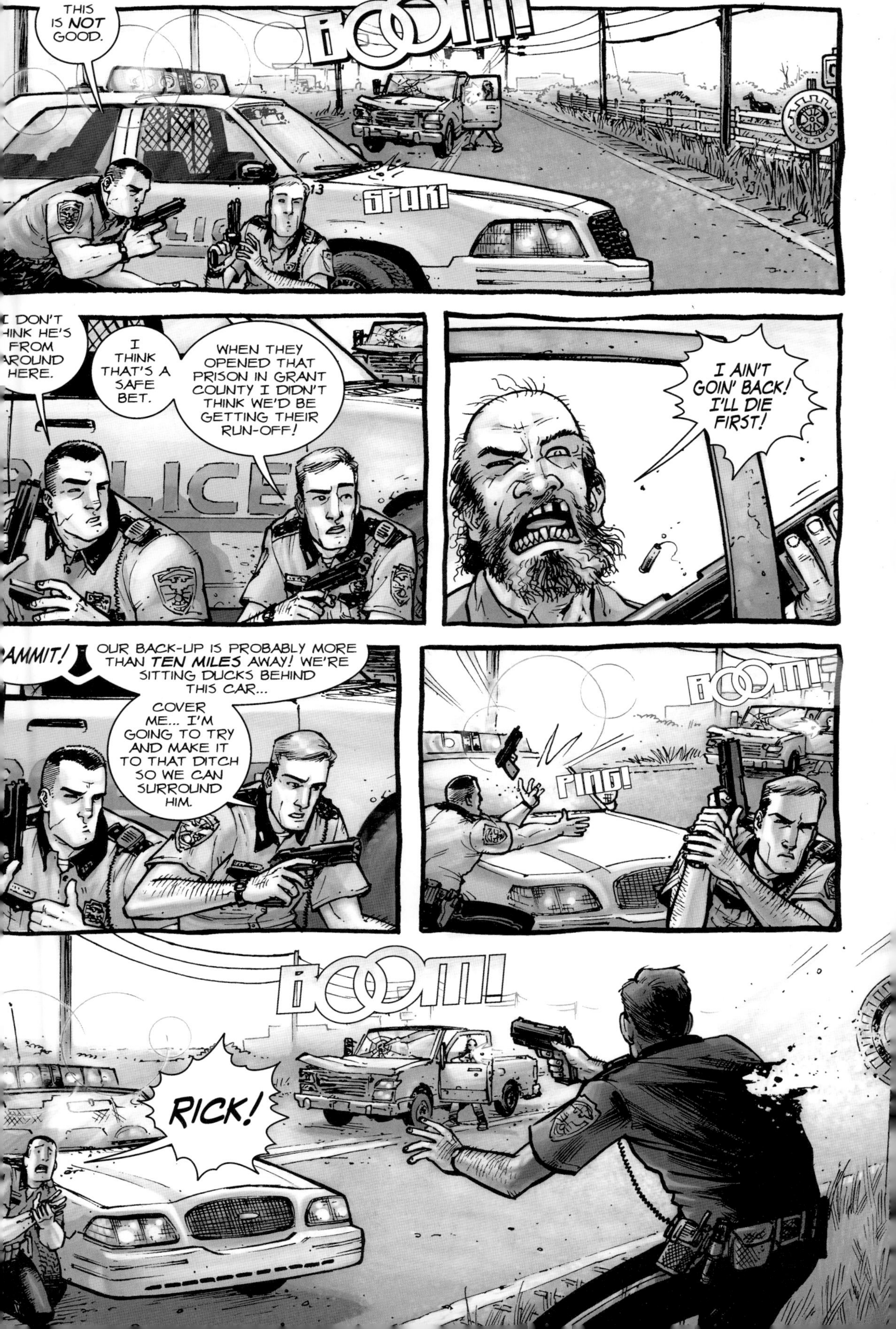
THIS IS NOT GOOD.
BOOM!
SPAK!
I DON'T THINK HE'S FROM AROUND HERE.
I THINK THAT'S A SAFE BET.
WHEN THEY OPENED THAT PRISON IN GRANT COUNTY I DIDN'T THINK WE'D BE GETTING THEIR RUN-OFF!
I AIN'T GOIN' BACK! I'LL DIE FIRST!
DAMMIT!
OUR BACK-UP IS PROBABLY MORE THAN TEN MILES AWAY! WE'RE SITTING DUCKS BEHIND THIS CAR...
COVER ME... I'M GOING TO TRY AND MAKE IT TO THAT DITCH SO WE CAN SURROUND HIM.
BOOM!
PING!
BOOM!
RICK!

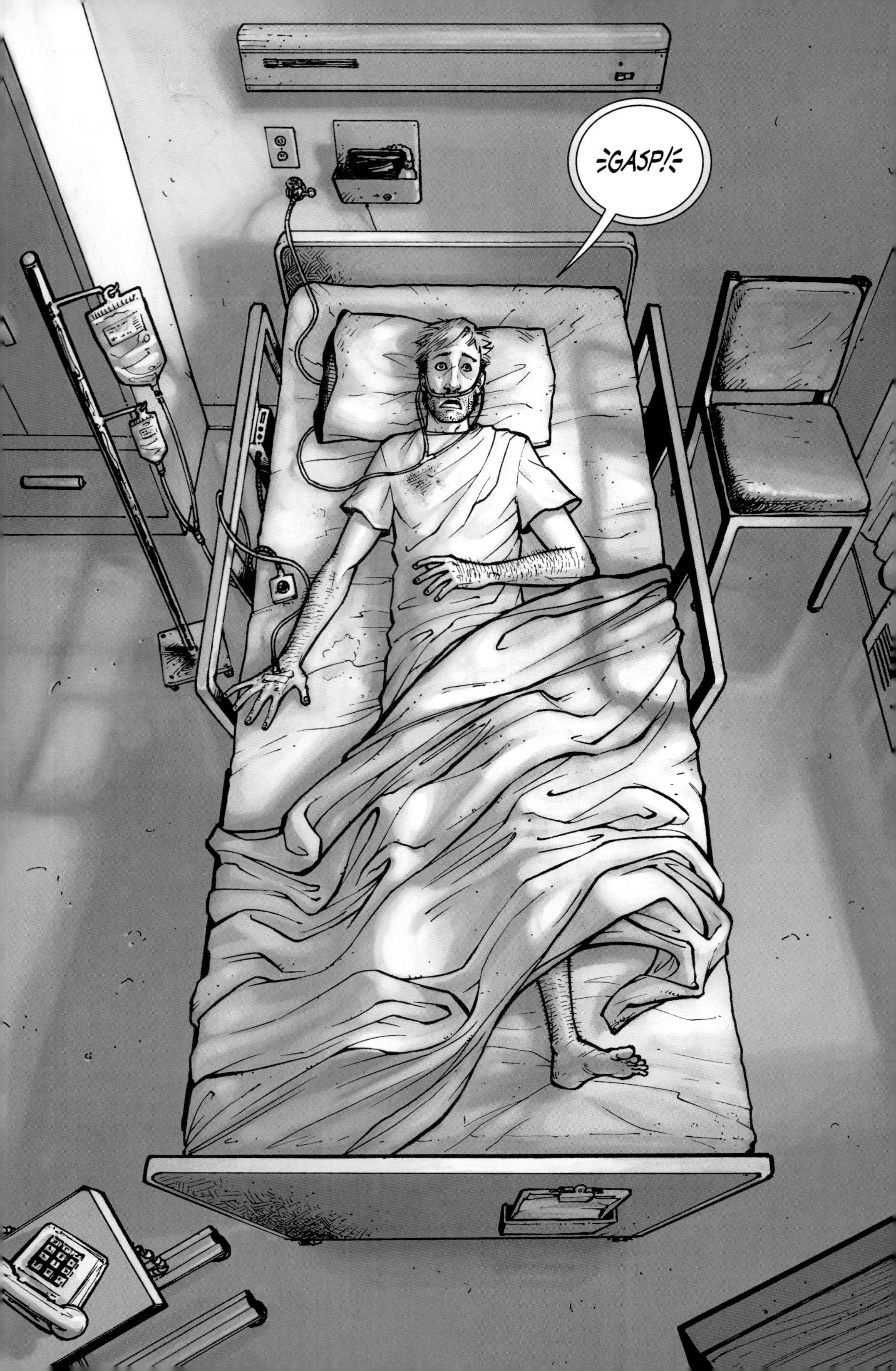
GASP!

NURSE!

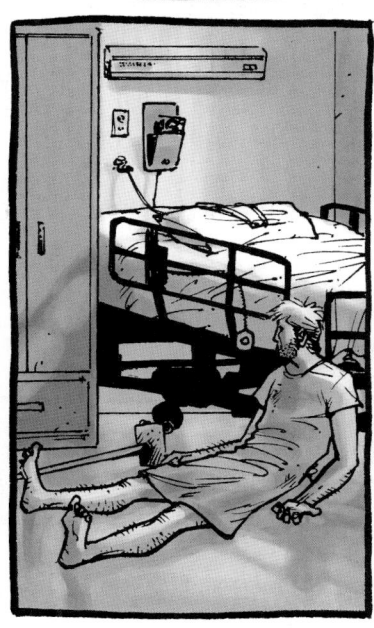

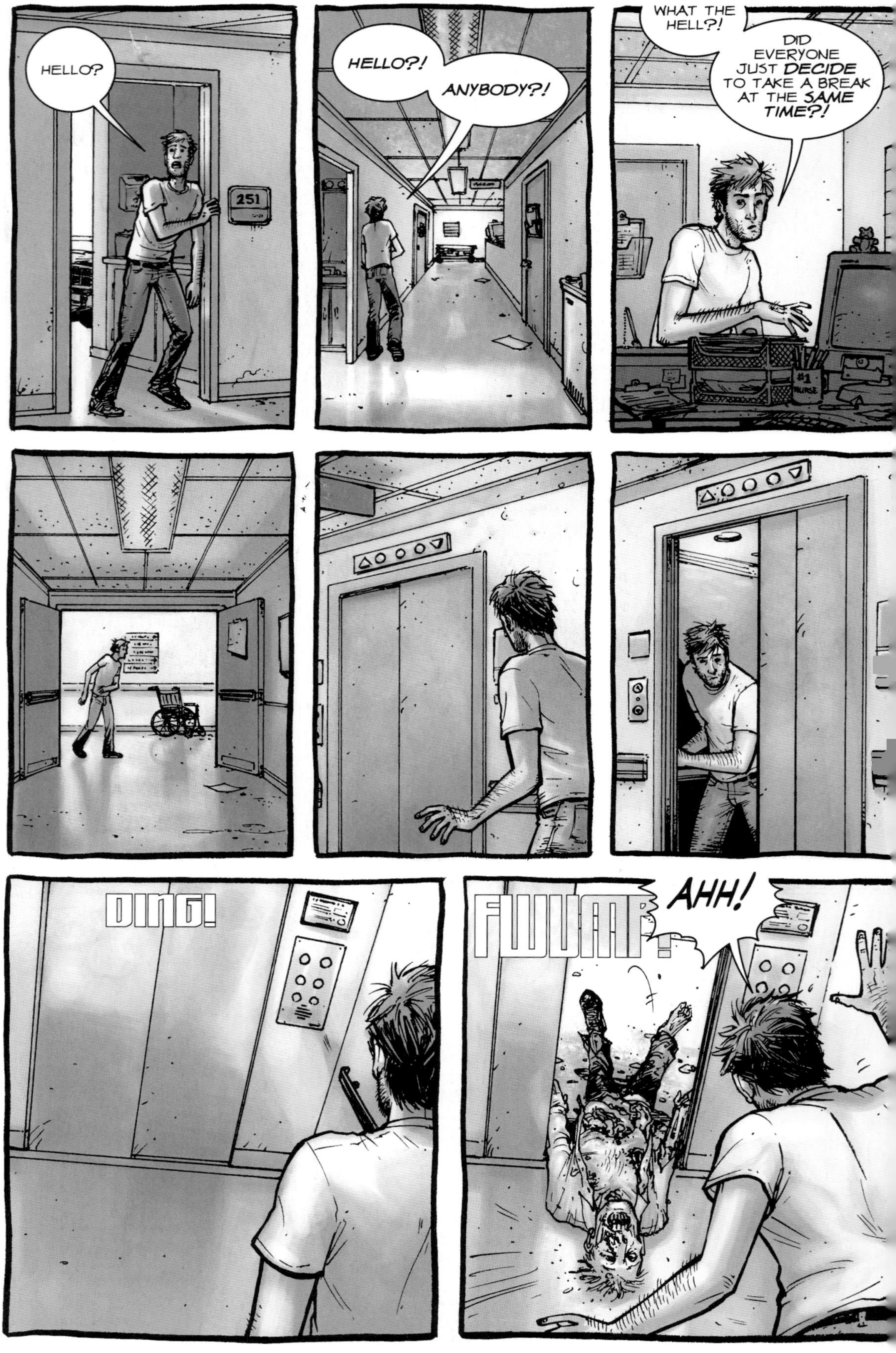
HELLO?
HELLO?!
ANYBODY?!
WHAT THE HELL?!
DID EVERYONE JUST DECIDE TO TAKE A BREAK AT THE SAME TIME?!
DING!
FWUMP!
AHH!

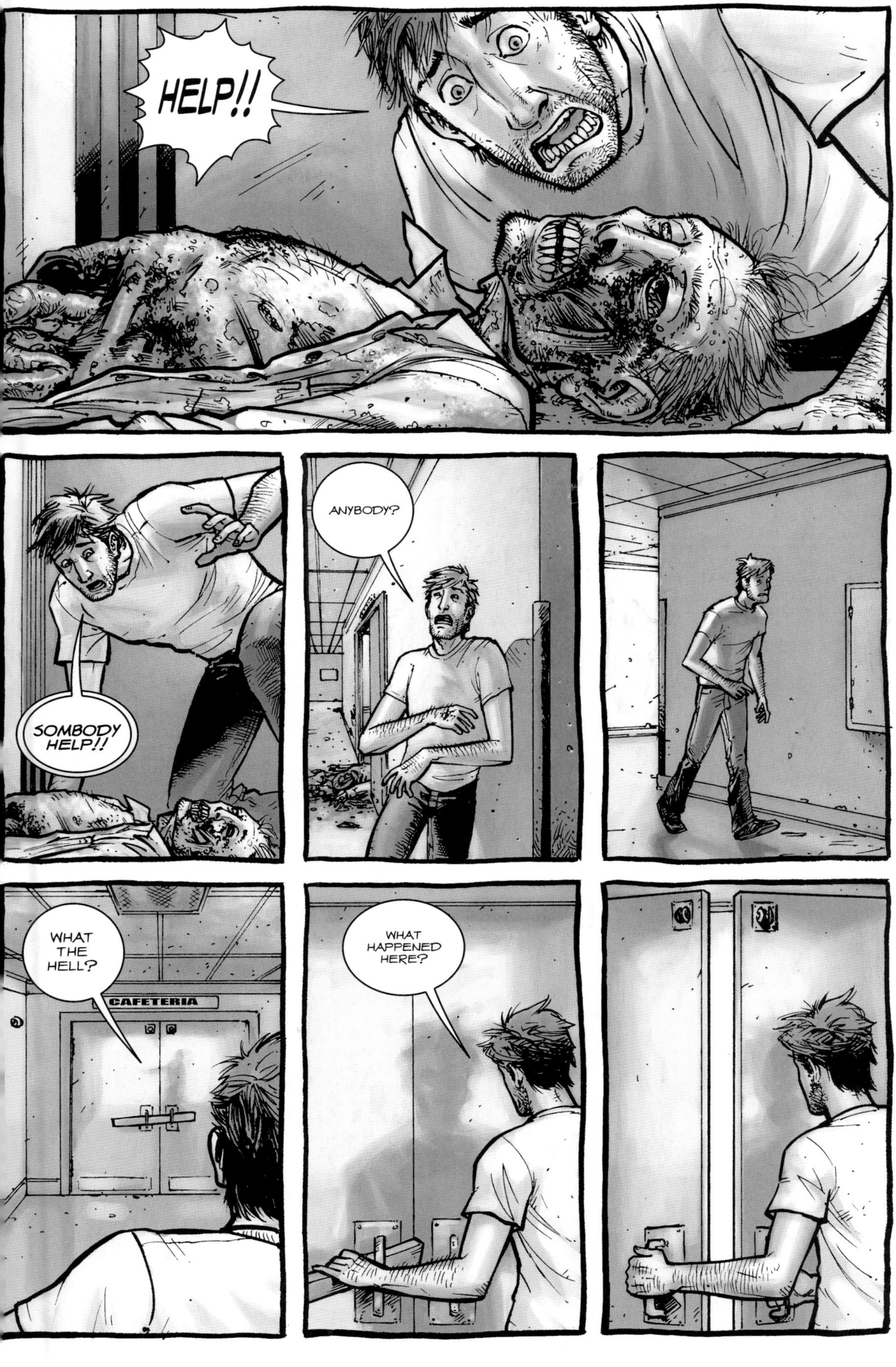
HELP!!
SOMBODY HELP!!
ANYBODY?
WHAT THE HELL?
CAFETERIA
WHAT HAPPENED HERE?

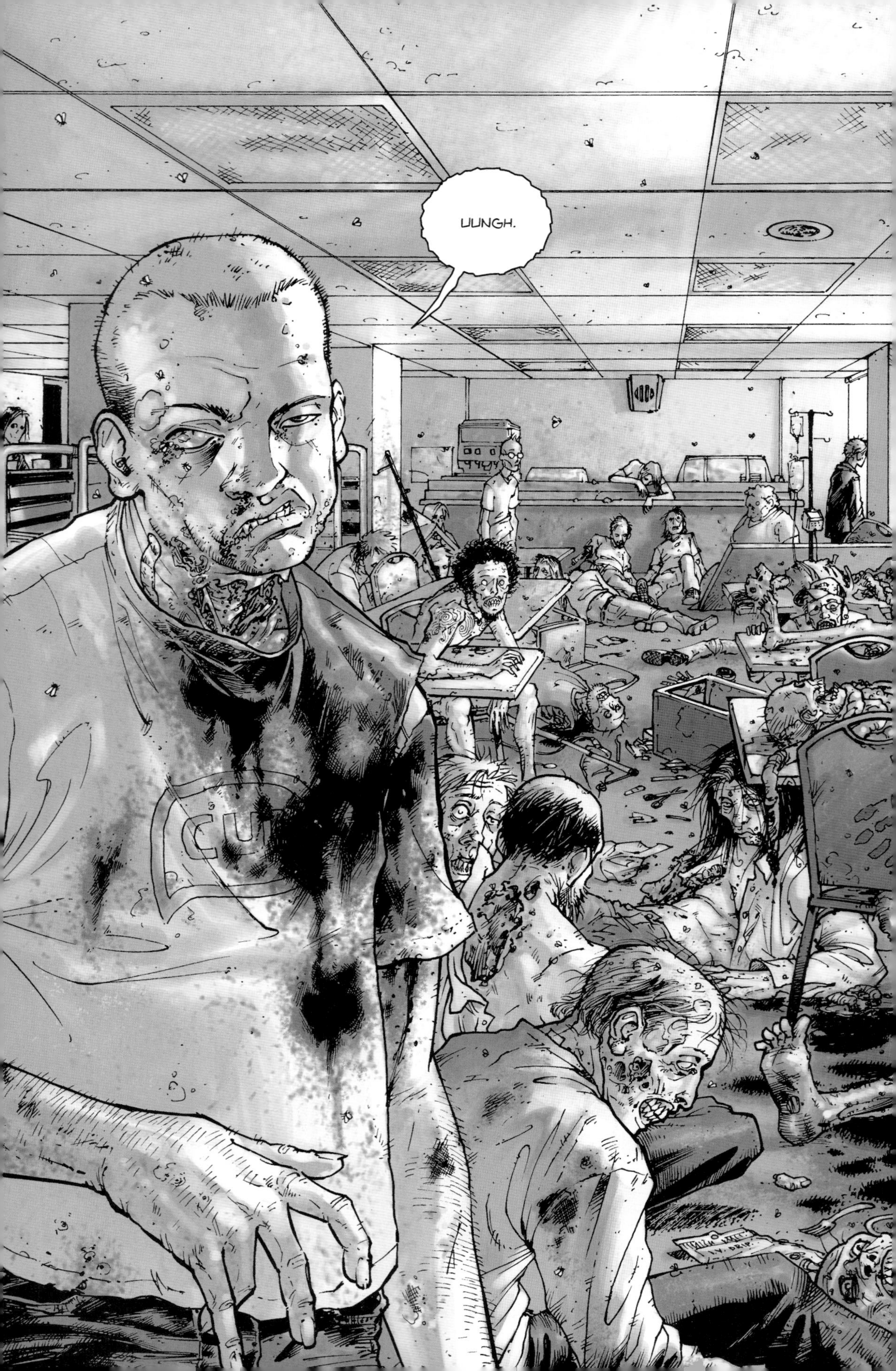
UUNGH.

UH.
UH.
UH.
UFF!
THAP!
STOP!
EXIT
GET AWAY FROM ME!
CAN'T YOU UNDER-STAND?!
FWUMP!
PLEASE!
WHUMP!
SNAP!

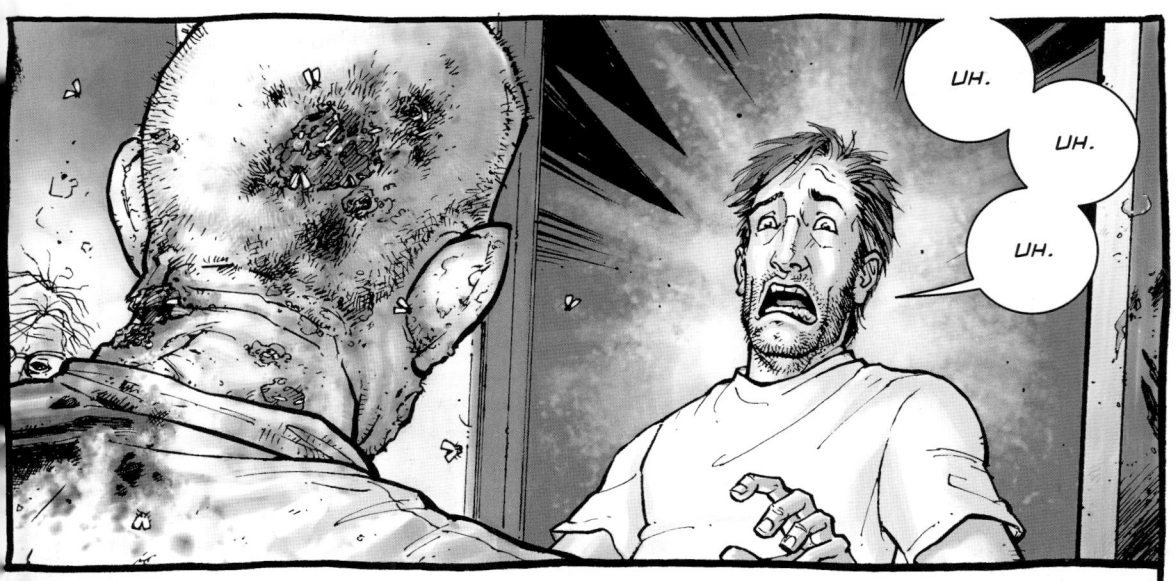

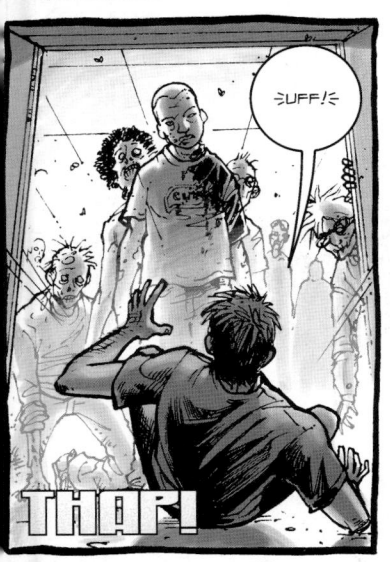

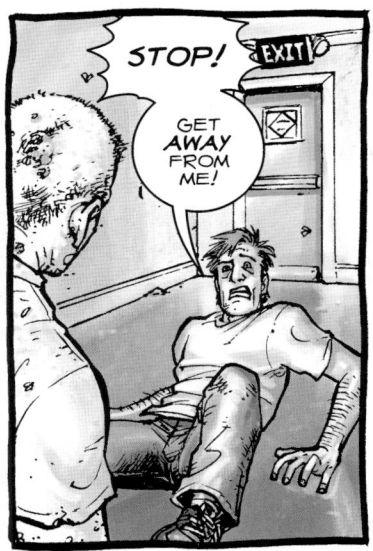

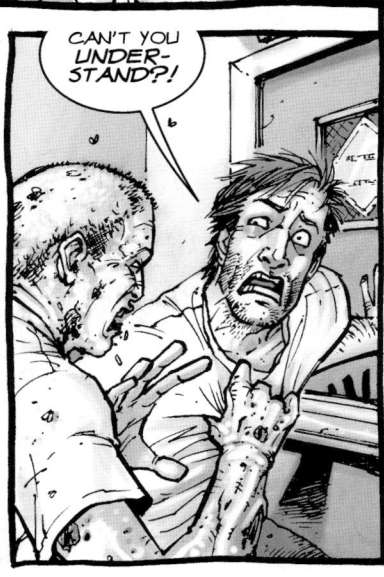

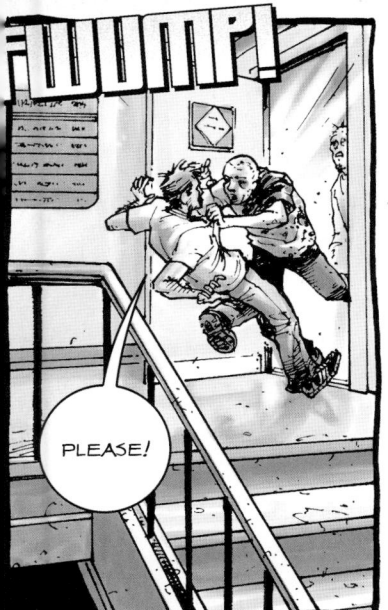

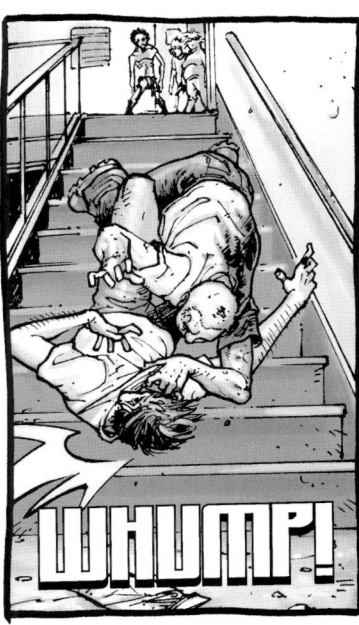

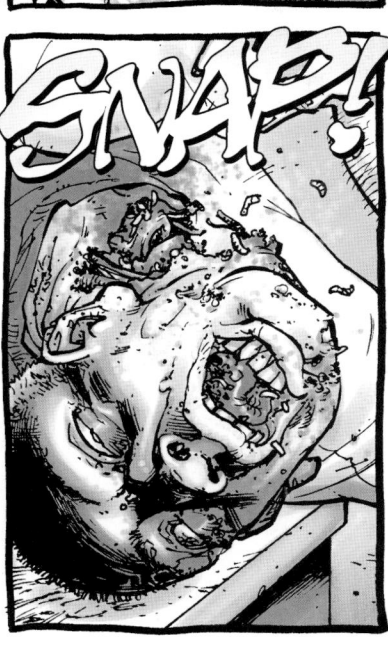

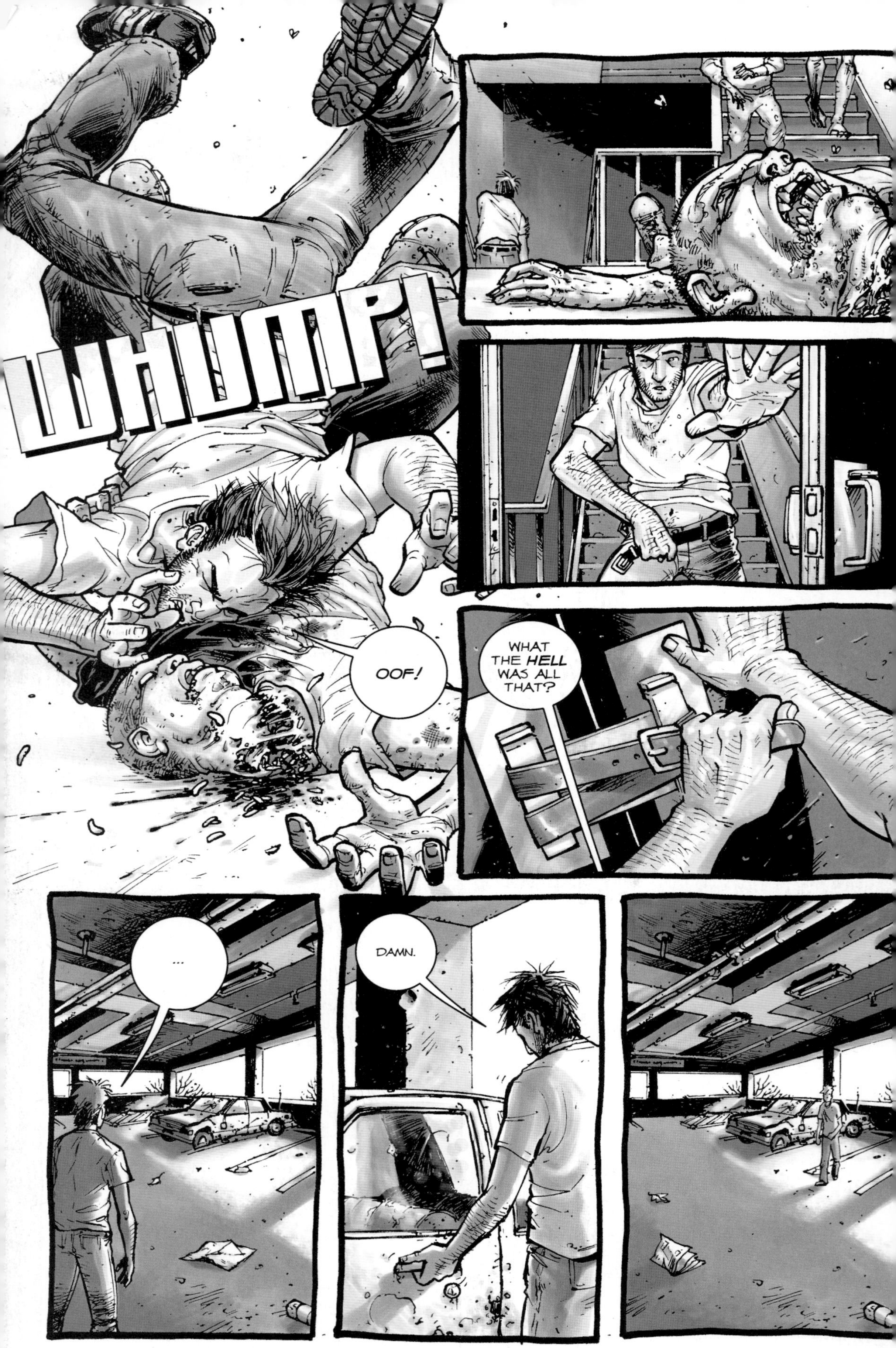
WHUMP!
OOF!
WHAT THE HELL WAS ALL THAT?
...
DAMN.

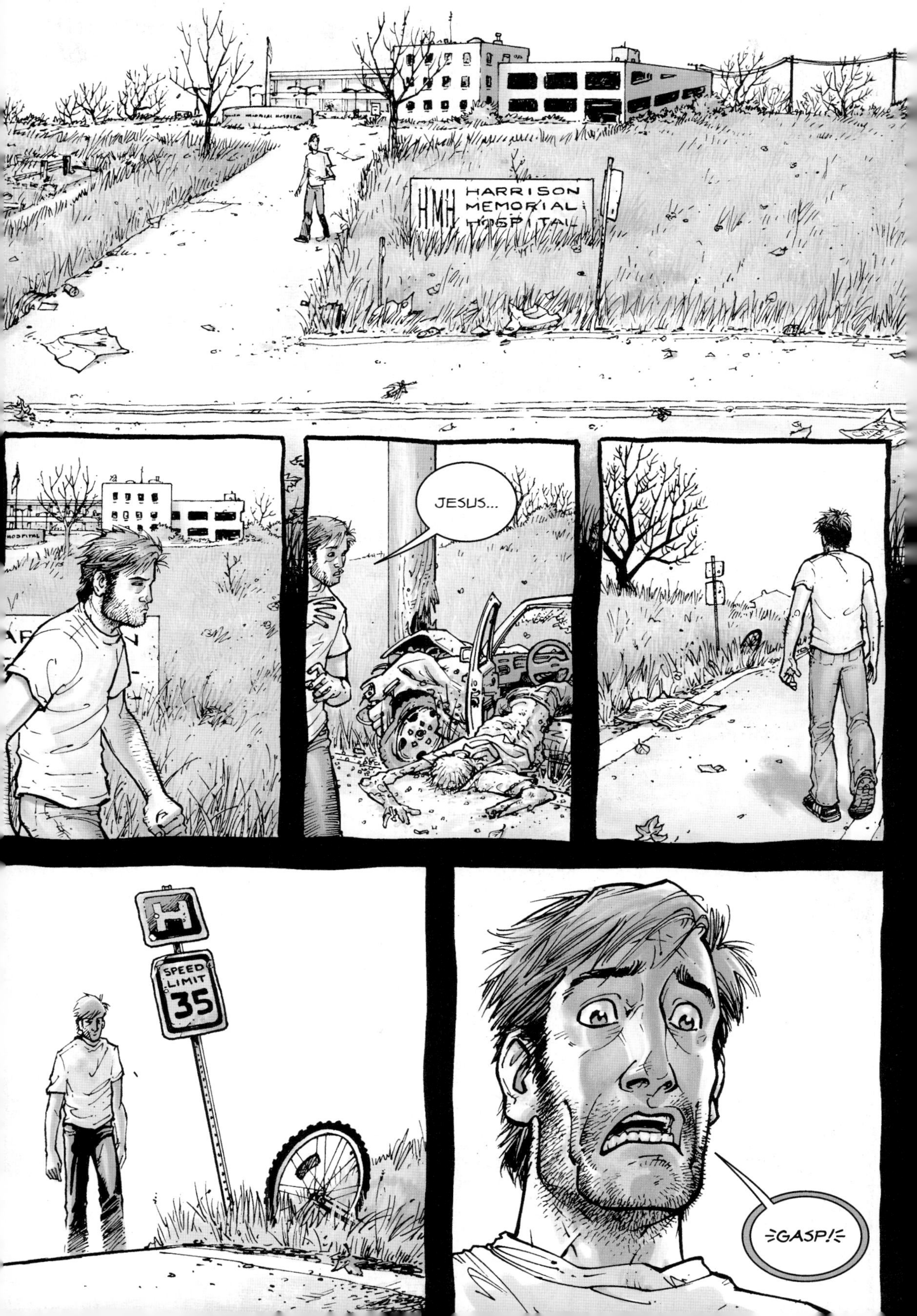
HARRISON MEMORIAL HOSPITAL
HMH
JESUS...
SPEED LIMIT 35
GASP!

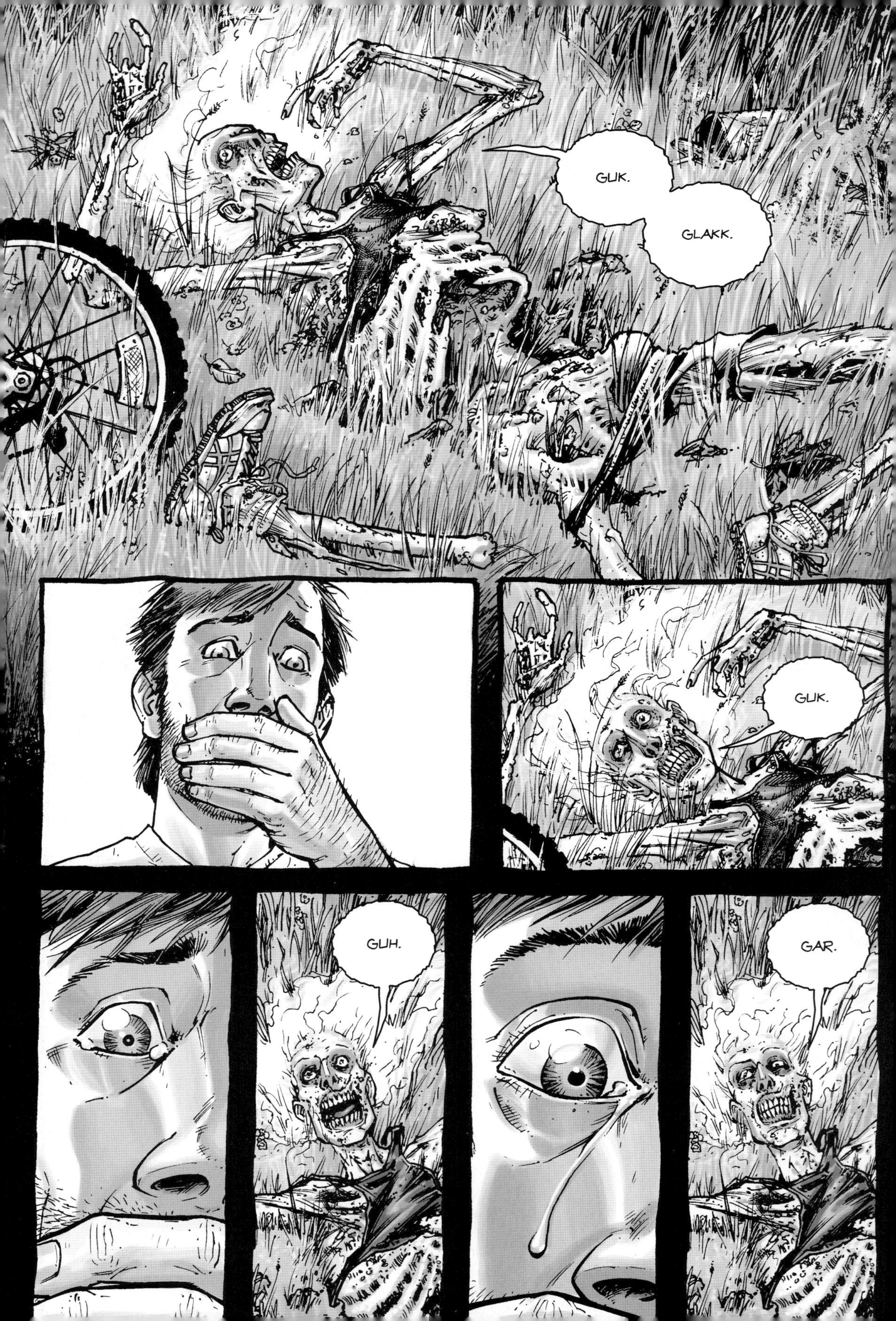
GUK.
GLAKK.
GUK.
GUH.
GAR.

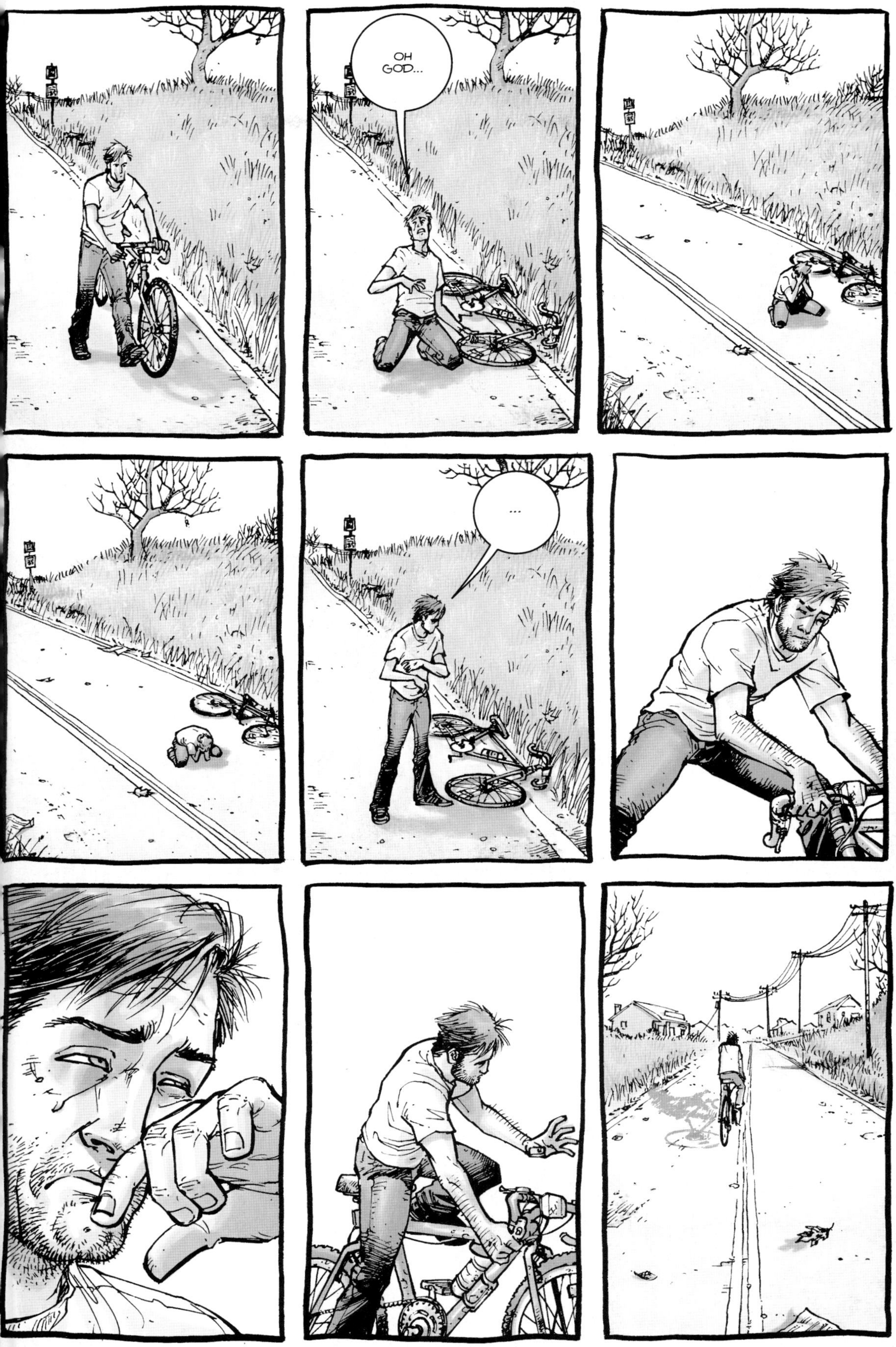
OH GOD...
...

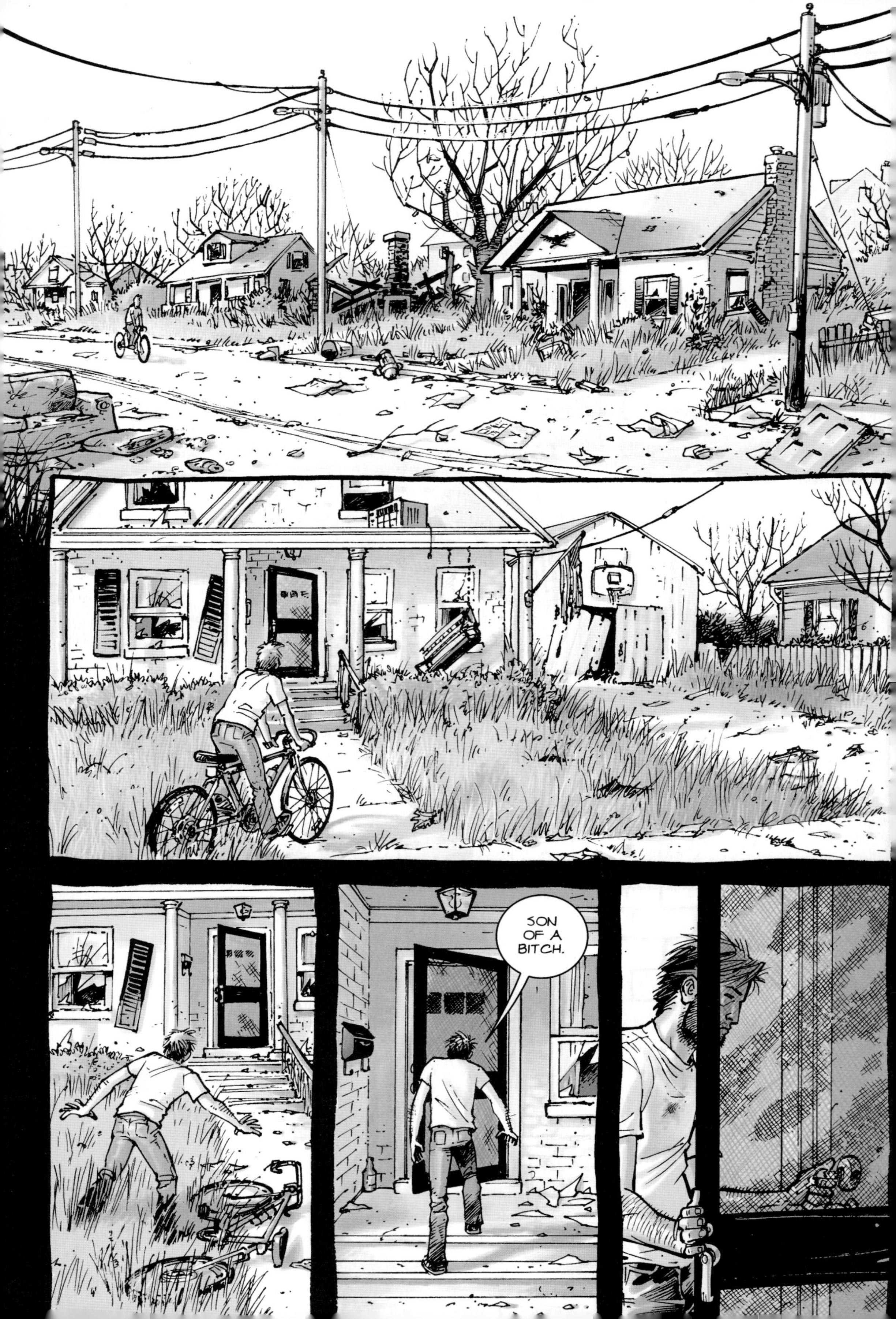
SON OF A BITCH.

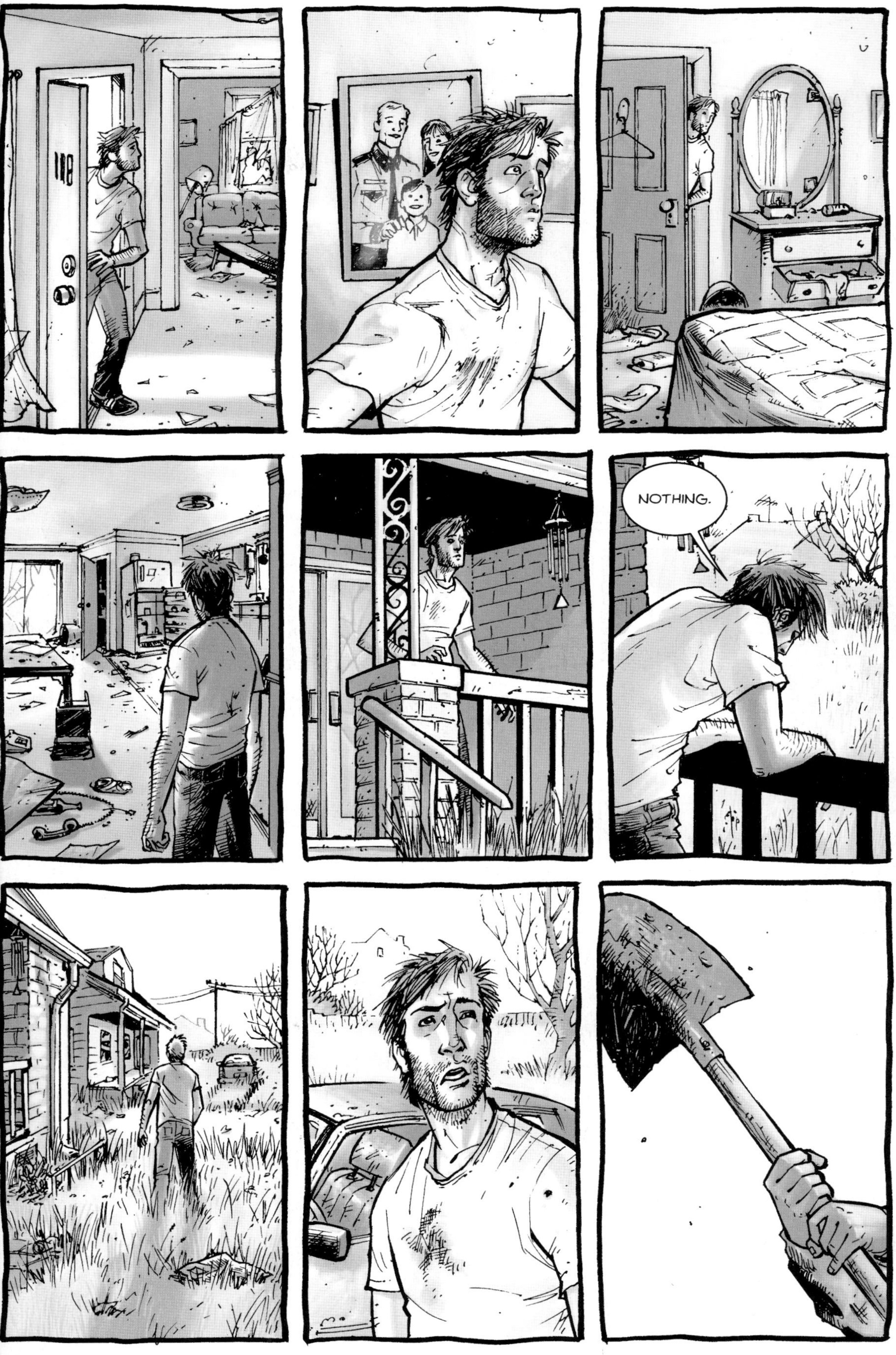
NOTHING.

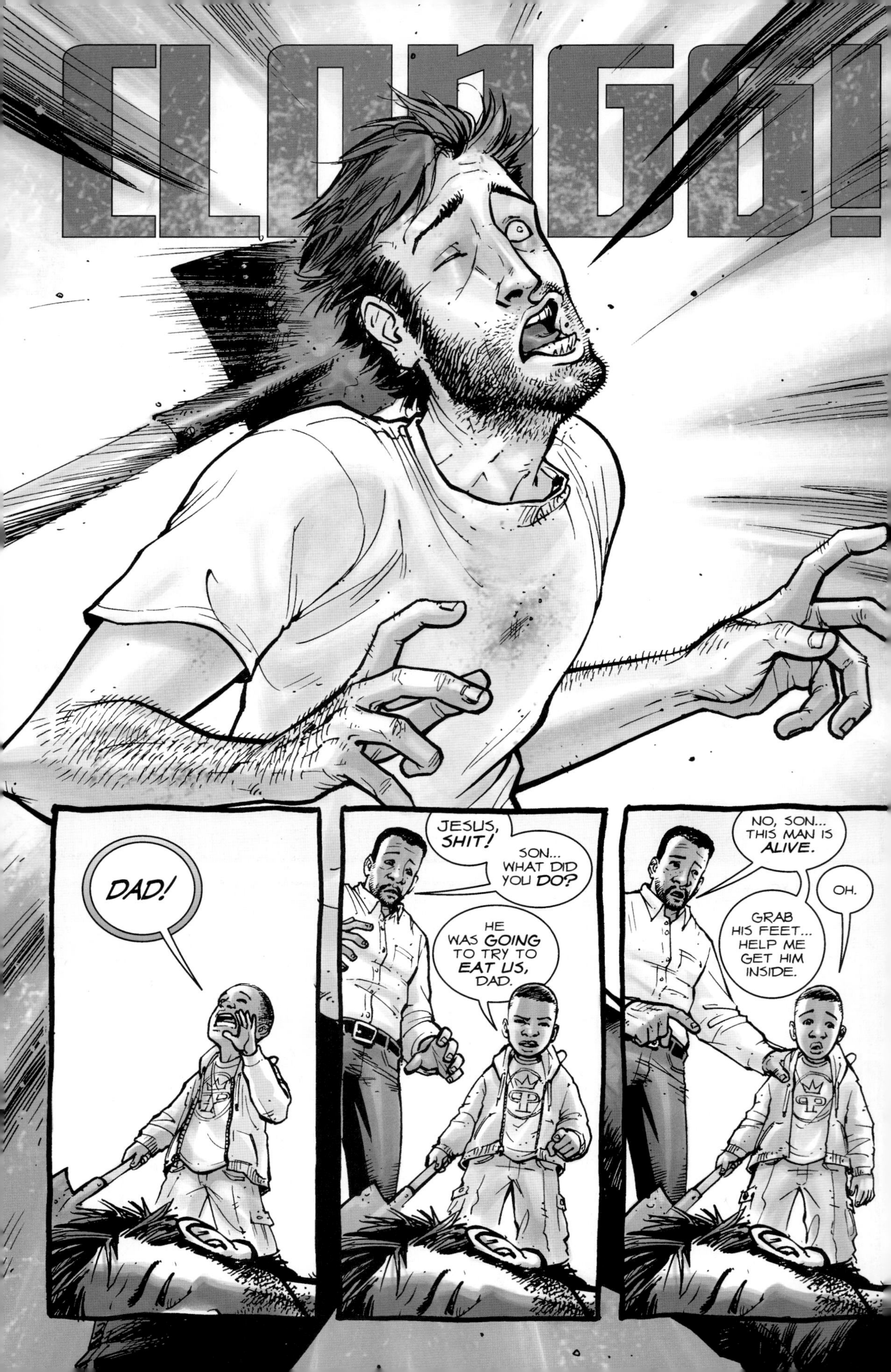
CLONGG!
DAD!
JESUS, SHIT!
SON... WHAT DID YOU DO?
HE WAS GOING TO TRY TO EAT US, DAD.
NO, SON... THIS MAN IS ALIVE.
OH.
GRAB HIS FEET... HELP ME GET HIM INSIDE.

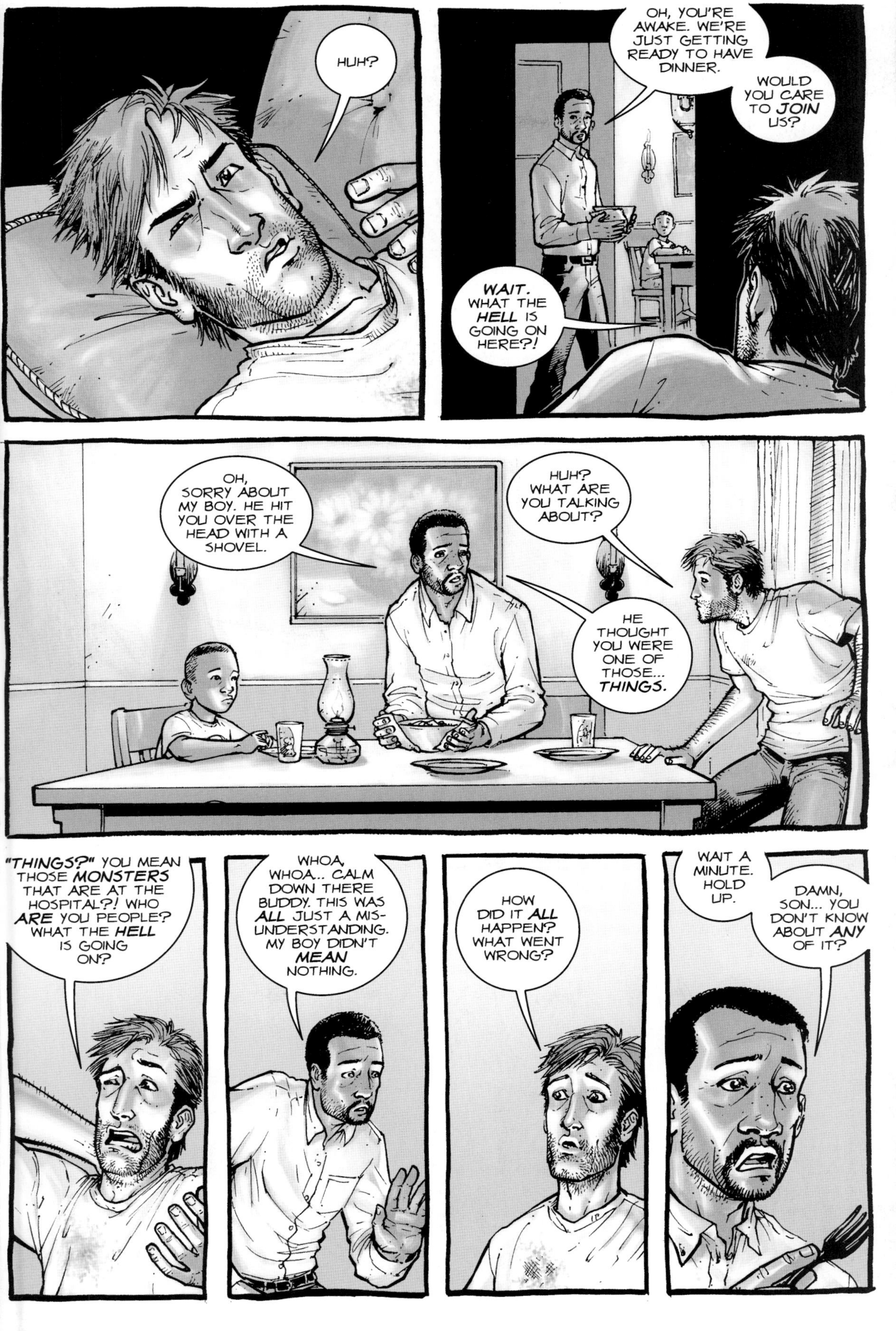
HUH?
OH, YOU'RE AWAKE. WE'RE JUST GETTING READY TO HAVE DINNER.
WOULD YOU CARE TO JOIN US?
WAIT. WHAT THE HELL IS GOING ON HERE?!
OH, SORRY ABOUT MY BOY. HE HIT YOU OVER THE HEAD WITH A SHOVEL.
HUH? WHAT ARE YOU TALKING ABOUT?
HE THOUGHT YOU WERE ONE OF THOSE... THINGS.
"THINGS?" YOU MEAN THOSE MONSTERS THAT ARE AT THE HOSPITAL?! WHO ARE YOU PEOPLE? WHAT THE HELL IS GOING ON?
WHOA, WHOA... CALM DOWN THERE BUDDY. THIS WAS ALL JUST A MIS-UNDERSTANDING. MY BOY DIDN'T MEAN NOTHING.
HOW DID IT ALL HAPPEN? WHAT WENT WRONG?
WAIT A MINUTE. HOLD UP.
DAMN, SON... YOU DON'T KNOW ABOUT ANY OF IT?

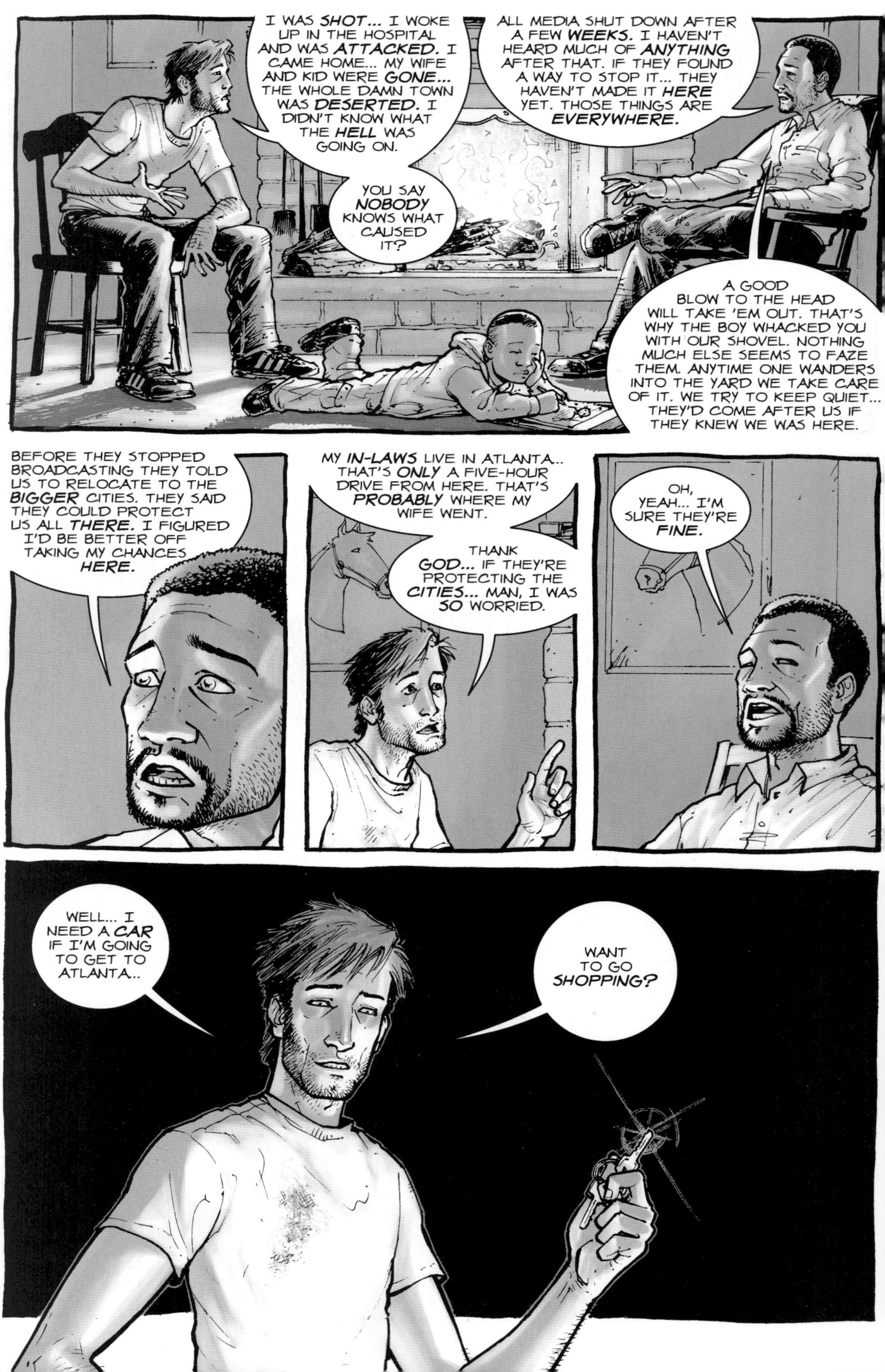

I WAS SHOT... I WOKE UP IN THE HOSPITAL AND WAS ATTACKED. I CAME HOME... MY WIFE AND KID WERE GONE... THE WHOLE DAMN TOWN WAS DESERTED. I DIDN'T KNOW WHAT THE HELL WAS GOING ON.
ALL MEDIA SHUT DOWN AFTER A FEW WEEKS. I HAVEN'T HEARD MUCH OF ANYTHING AFTER THAT. IF THEY FOUND A WAY TO STOP IT... THEY HAVEN'T MADE IT HERE YET. THOSE THINGS ARE EVERYWHERE.
YOU SAY NOBODY KNOWS WHAT CAUSED IT?
A GOOD BLOW TO THE HEAD WILL TAKE 'EM OUT. THAT'S WHY THE BOY WHACKED YOU WITH OUR SHOVEL. NOTHING MUCH ELSE SEEMS TO FAZE THEM. ANYTIME ONE WANDERS INTO THE YARD WE TAKE CARE OF IT. WE TRY TO KEEP QUIET... THEY'D COME AFTER US IF THEY KNEW WE WAS HERE.
BEFORE THEY STOPPED BROADCASTING THEY TOLD US TO RELOCATE TO THE BIGGER CITIES. THEY SAID THEY COULD PROTECT US ALL THERE. I FIGURED I'D BE BETTER OFF TAKING MY CHANCES HERE.
MY IN-LAWS LIVE IN ATLANTA.. THAT'S ONLY A FIVE-HOUR DRIVE FROM HERE. THAT'S PROBABLY WHERE MY WIFE WENT.
THANK GOD... IF THEY'RE PROTECTING THE CITIES... MAN, I WAS SO WORRIED.
OH, YEAH... I'M SURE THEY'RE FINE.
WELL... I NEED A CAR IF I'M GOING TO GET TO ATLANTA..
WANT TO GO SHOPPING?

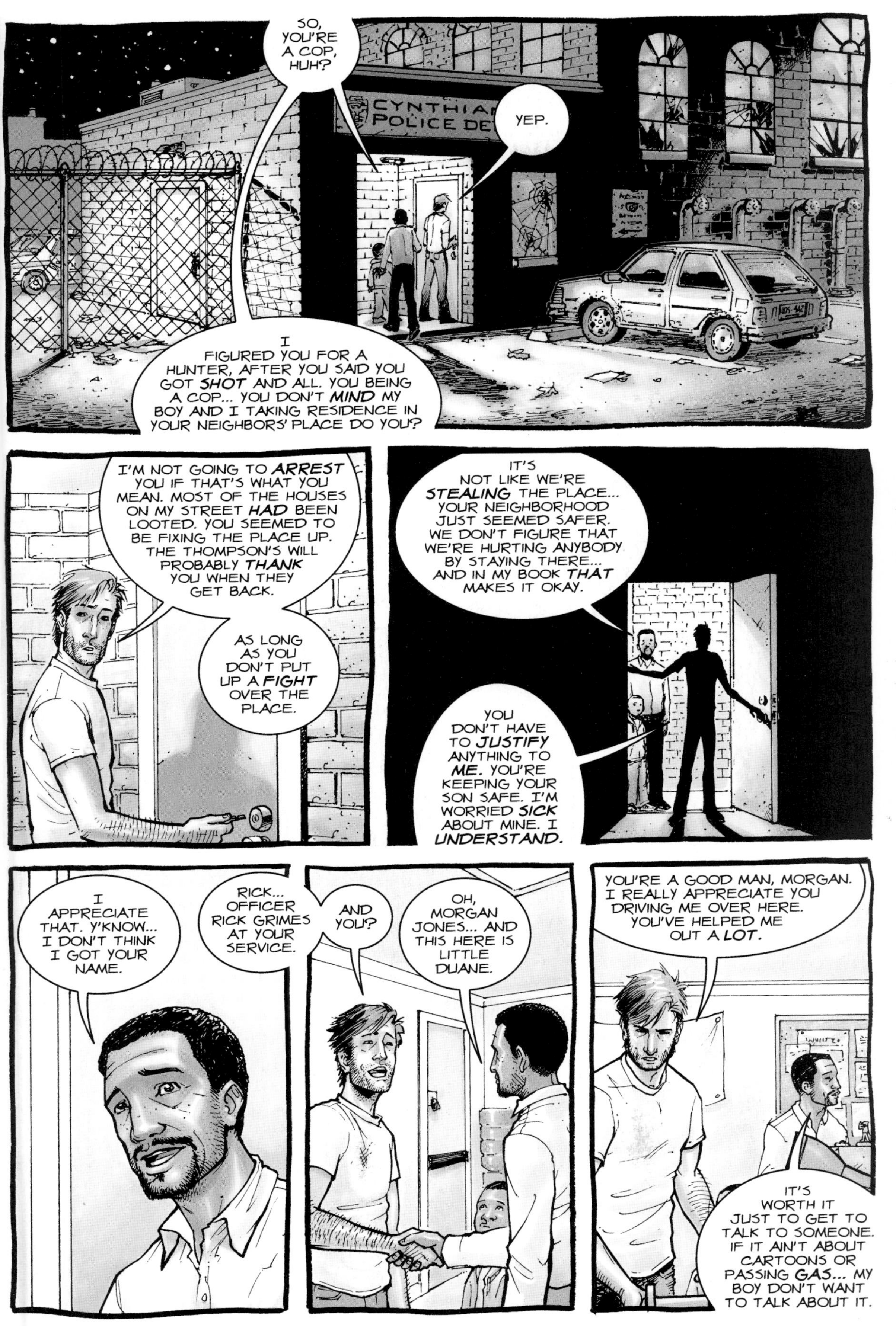
CYNTHIAN
POLICE DE
SO, YOU'RE A COP, HUH?
YEP.
I FIGURED YOU FOR A HUNTER, AFTER YOU SAID YOU GOT SHOT AND ALL. YOU BEING A COP... YOU DON'T MIND MY BOY AND I TAKING RESIDENCE IN YOUR NEIGHBORS' PLACE DO YOU?
I'M NOT GOING TO ARREST YOU IF THAT'S WHAT YOU MEAN. MOST OF THE HOUSES ON MY STREET HAD BEEN LOOTED. YOU SEEMED TO BE FIXING THE PLACE UP. THE THOMPSON'S WILL PROBABLY THANK YOU WHEN THEY GET BACK.
AS LONG AS YOU DON'T PUT UP A FIGHT OVER THE PLACE.
IT'S NOT LIKE WE'RE STEALING THE PLACE... YOUR NEIGHBORHOOD JUST SEEMED SAFER. WE DON'T FIGURE THAT WE'RE HURTING ANYBODY BY STAYING THERE... AND IN MY BOOK THAT MAKES IT OKAY.
YOU DON'T HAVE TO JUSTIFY ANYTHING TO ME. YOU'RE KEEPING YOUR SON SAFE. I'M WORRIED SICK ABOUT MINE. I UNDERSTAND.
I APPRECIATE THAT. Y'KNOW... I DON'T THINK I GOT YOUR NAME.
RICK... OFFICER RICK GRIMES AT YOUR SERVICE.
AND YOU?
OH, MORGAN JONES... AND THIS HERE IS LITTLE DUANE.
YOU'RE A GOOD MAN, MORGAN. I REALLY APPRECIATE YOU DRIVING ME OVER HERE. YOU'VE HELPED ME OUT A LOT.
IT'S WORTH IT JUST TO GET TO TALK TO SOMEONE. IF IT AIN'T ABOUT CARTOONS OR PASSING GAS... MY BOY DON'T WANT TO TALK ABOUT IT.

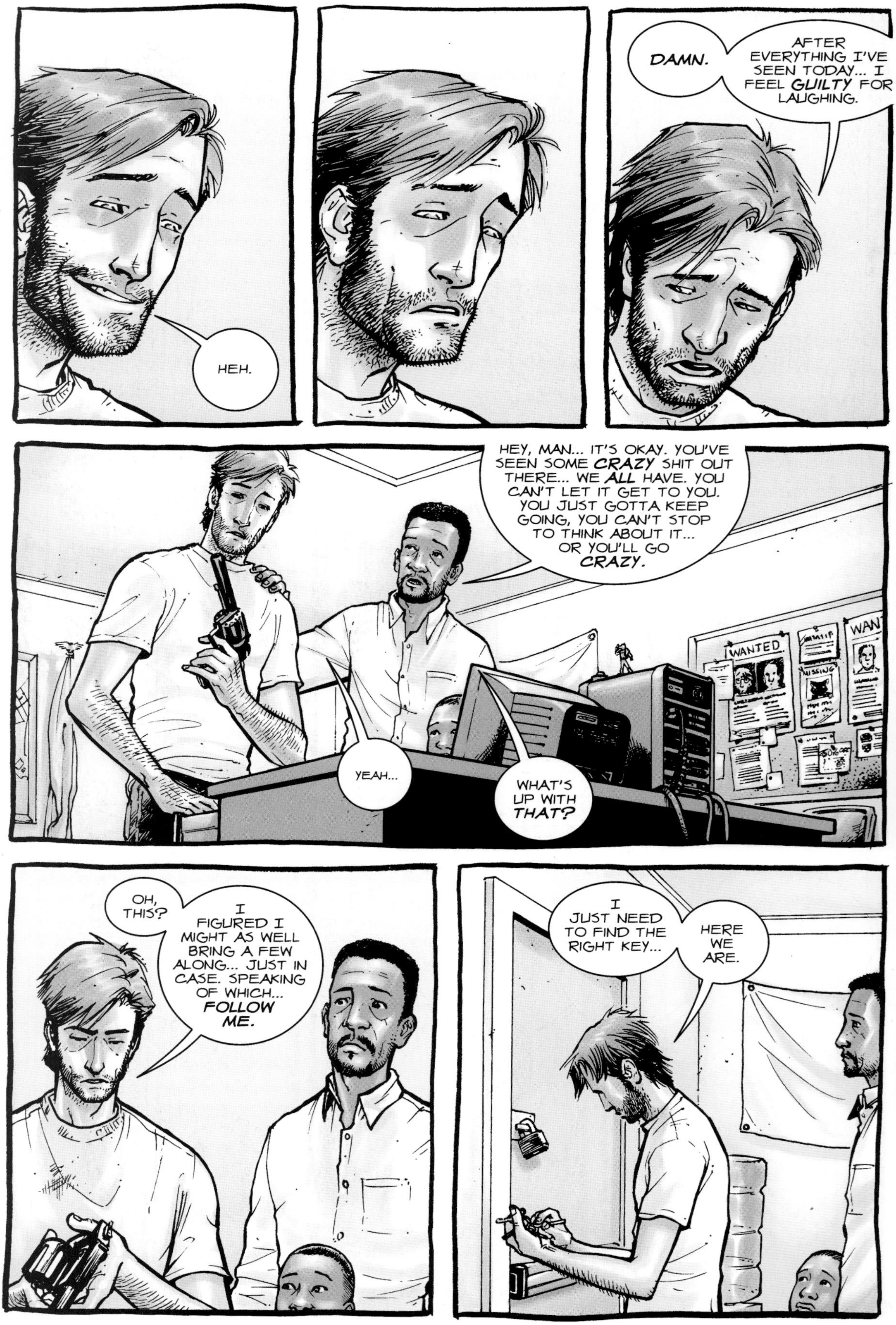
HEH.
DAMN.
AFTER EVERYTHING I'VE SEEN TODAY... I FEEL GUILTY FOR LAUGHING.
HEY, MAN... IT'S OKAY. YOU'VE SEEN SOME CRAZY SHIT OUT THERE... WE ALL HAVE. YOU CAN'T LET IT GET TO YOU. YOU JUST GOTTA KEEP GOING, YOU CAN'T STOP TO THINK ABOUT IT... OR YOU'LL GO CRAZY.
YEAH...
WHAT'S UP WITH THAT?
WANTED
MISSING
OH, THIS?
I FIGURED I MIGHT AS WELL BRING A FEW ALONG... JUST IN CASE. SPEAKING OF WHICH... FOLLOW ME.
I JUST NEED TO FIND THE RIGHT KEY...
HERE WE ARE.

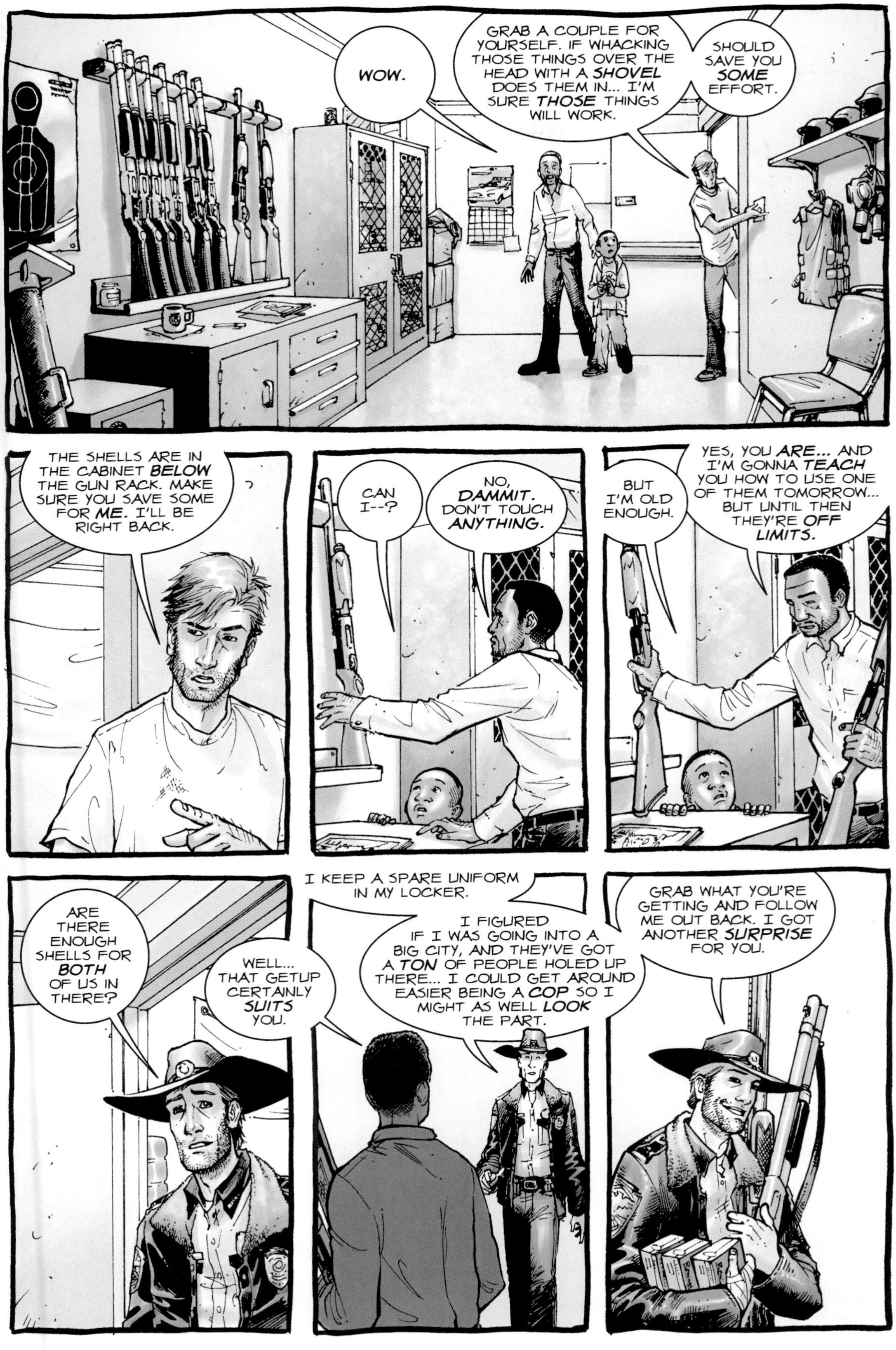
WOW.
GRAB A COUPLE FOR YOURSELF. IF WHACKING THOSE THINGS OVER THE HEAD WITH A SHOVEL DOES THEM IN... I'M SURE THOSE THINGS WILL WORK.
SHOULD SAVE YOU SOME EFFORT.
THE SHELLS ARE IN THE CABINET BELOW THE GUN RACK. MAKE SURE YOU SAVE SOME FOR ME. I'LL BE RIGHT BACK.
CAN I--?
NO, DAMMIT. DON'T TOUCH ANYTHING.
BUT I'M OLD ENOUGH.
YES, YOU ARE... AND I'M GONNA TEACH YOU HOW TO USE ONE OF THEM TOMORROW... BUT UNTIL THEN THEY'RE OFF LIMITS.
ARE THERE ENOUGH SHELLS FOR BOTH OF US IN THERE?
WELL... THAT GETUP CERTAINLY SUITS YOU.
I KEEP A SPARE UNIFORM IN MY LOCKER.
I FIGURED IF I WAS GOING INTO A BIG CITY, AND THEY'VE GOT A TON OF PEOPLE HOLED UP THERE... I COULD GET AROUND EASIER BEING A COP SO I MIGHT AS WELL LOOK THE PART.
GRAB WHAT YOU'RE GETTING AND FOLLOW ME OUT BACK. I GOT ANOTHER SURPRISE FOR YOU.

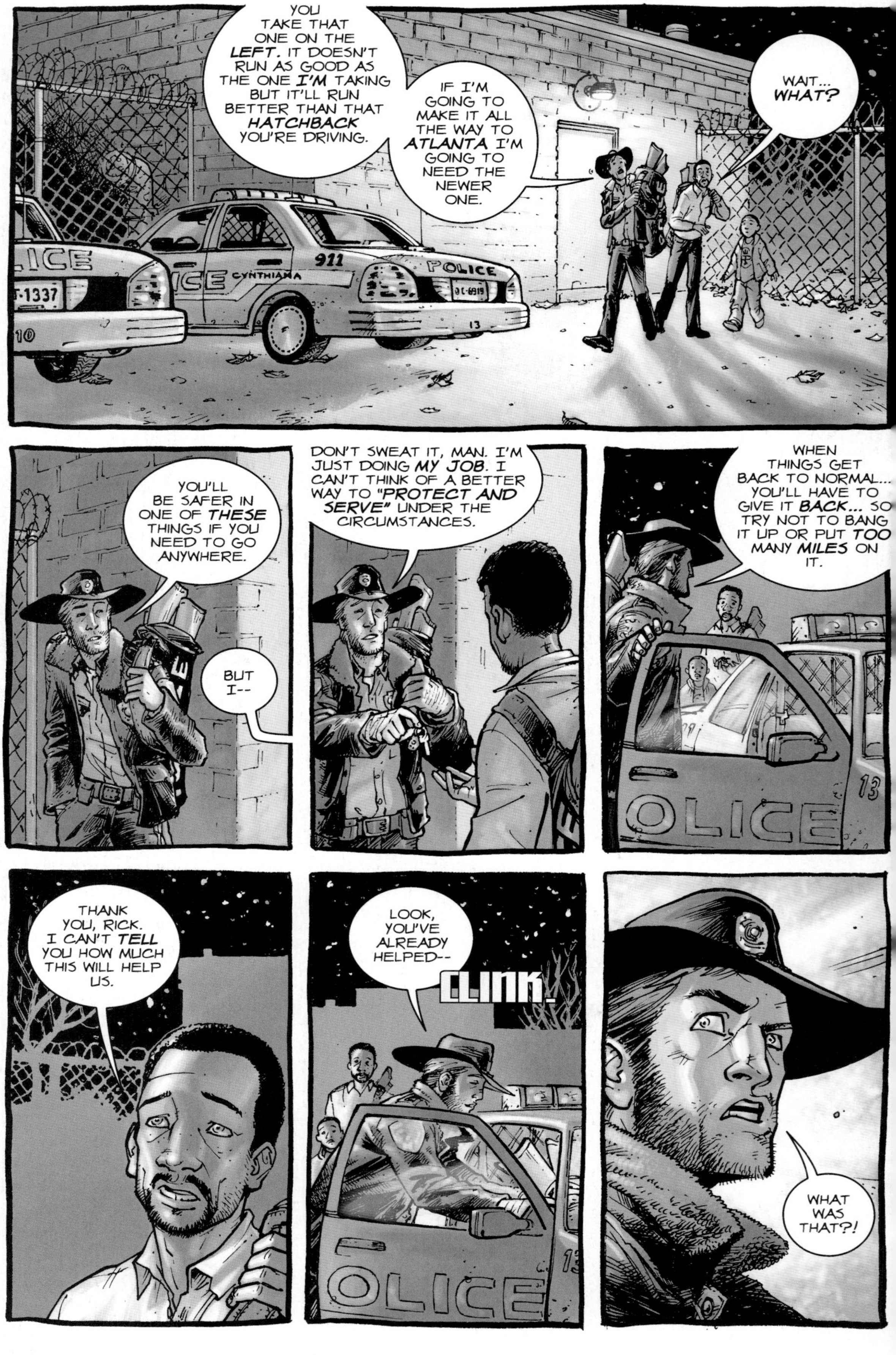
YOU TAKE THAT ONE ON THE LEFT. IT DOESN'T RUN AS GOOD AS THE ONE I'M TAKING BUT IT'LL RUN BETTER THAN THAT HATCHBACK YOU'RE DRIVING.
IF I'M GOING TO MAKE IT ALL THE WAY TO ATLANTA I'M GOING TO NEED THE NEWER ONE.
WAIT... WHAT?
POLICE
911
CYNTHIANA
YOU'LL BE SAFER IN ONE OF THESE THINGS IF YOU NEED TO GO ANYWHERE.
BUT I--
DON'T SWEAT IT, MAN. I'M JUST DOING MY JOB. I CAN'T THINK OF A BETTER WAY TO "PROTECT AND SERVE" UNDER THE CIRCUMSTANCES.
WHEN THINGS GET BACK TO NORMAL... YOU'LL HAVE TO GIVE IT BACK... SO TRY NOT TO BANG IT UP OR PUT TOO MANY MILES ON IT.
THANK YOU, RICK. I CAN'T TELL YOU HOW MUCH THIS WILL HELP US.
LOOK, YOU'VE ALREADY HELPED--
CLINK.
WHAT WAS THAT?!

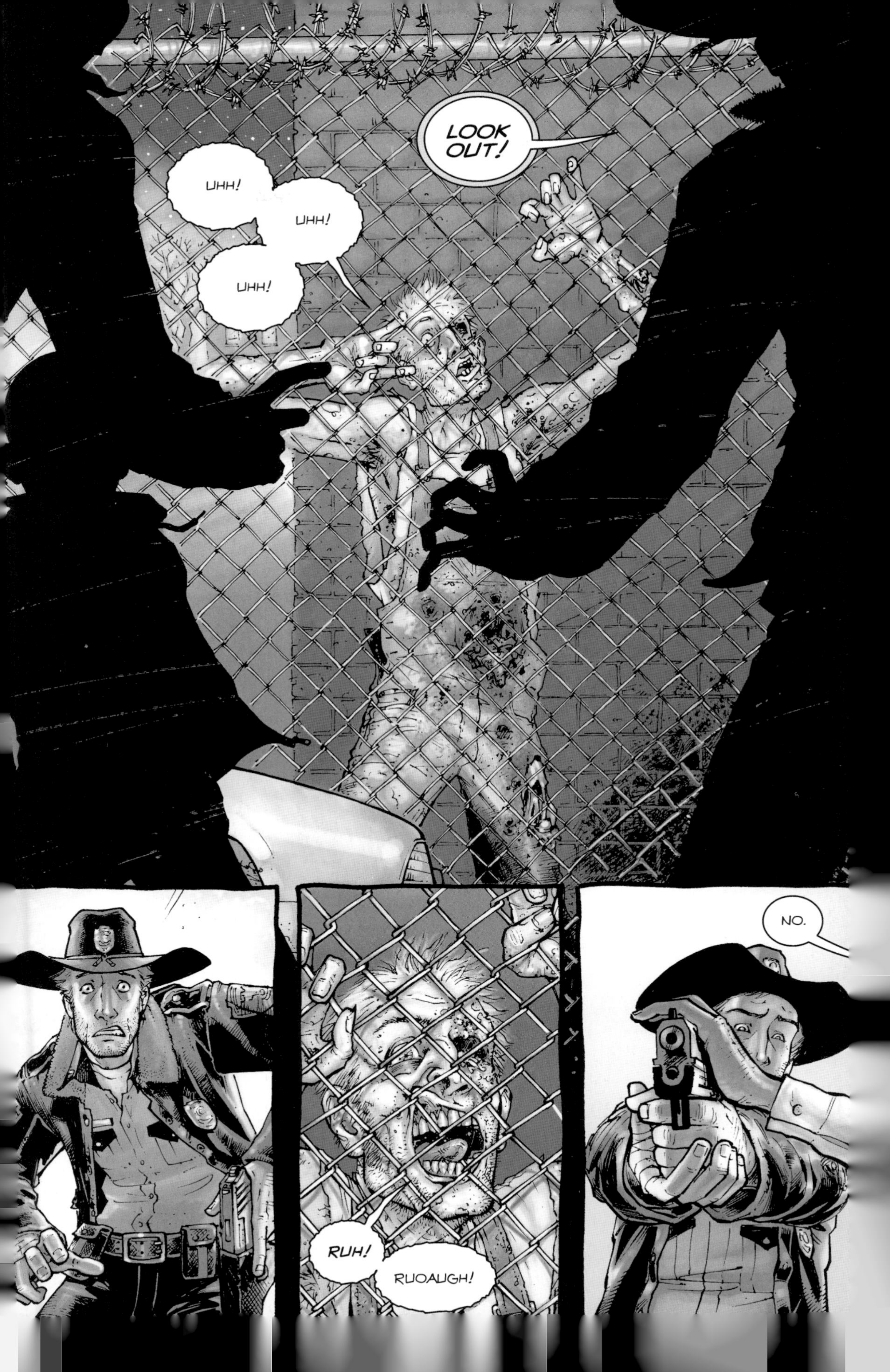

UHH!
UHH!
UHH!
LOOK OUT!
RUH!
RUOAUGH!
NO.

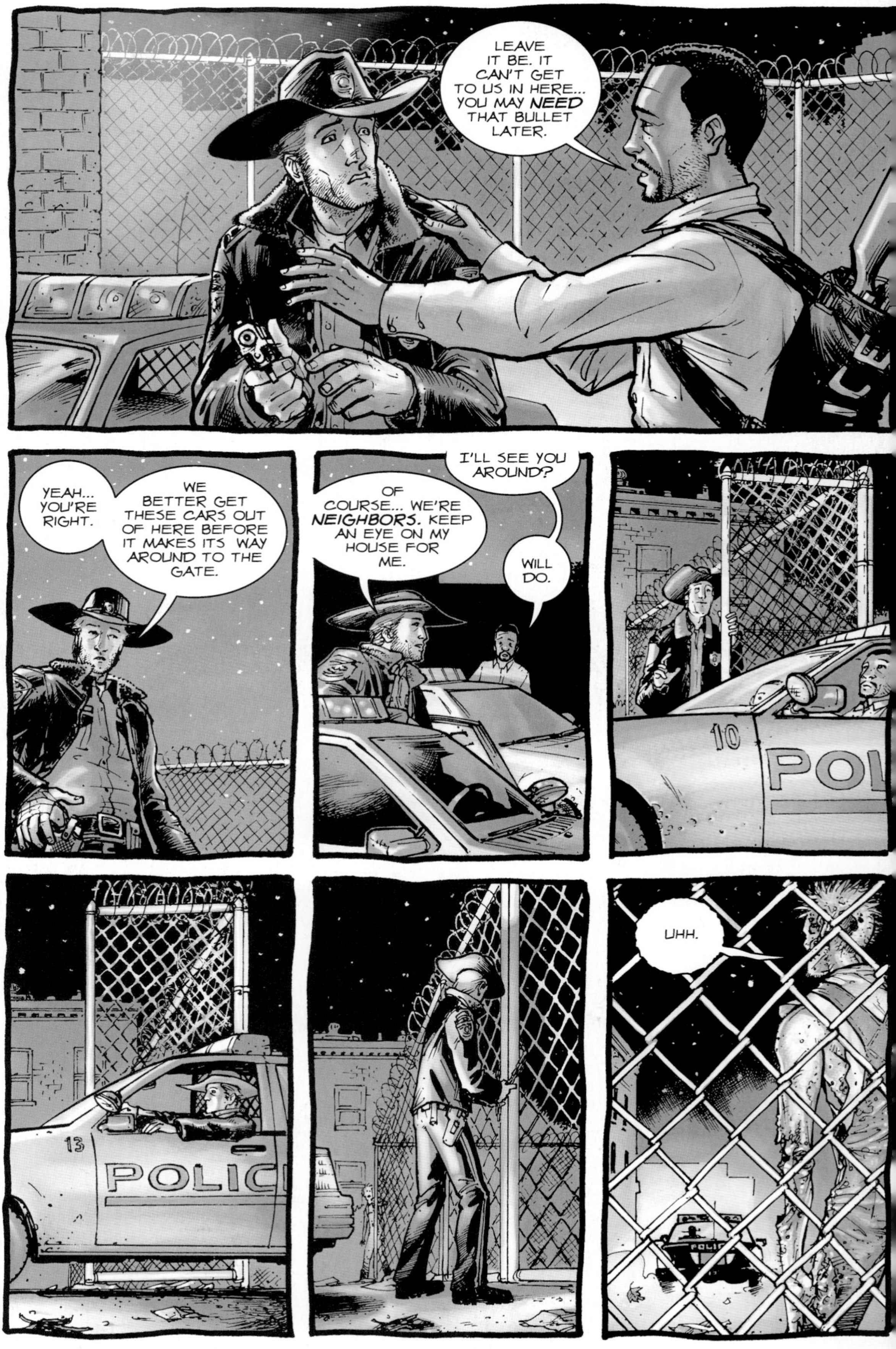
LEAVE IT BE. IT CAN'T GET TO US IN HERE... YOU MAY NEED THAT BULLET LATER.
YEAH... YOU'RE RIGHT.
WE BETTER GET THESE CARS OUT OF HERE BEFORE IT MAKES ITS WAY AROUND TO THE GATE.
I'LL SEE YOU AROUND?
OF COURSE... WE'RE NEIGHBORS. KEEP AN EYE ON MY HOUSE FOR ME.
WILL DO.
10
POLI
13
POLIC
UHH.

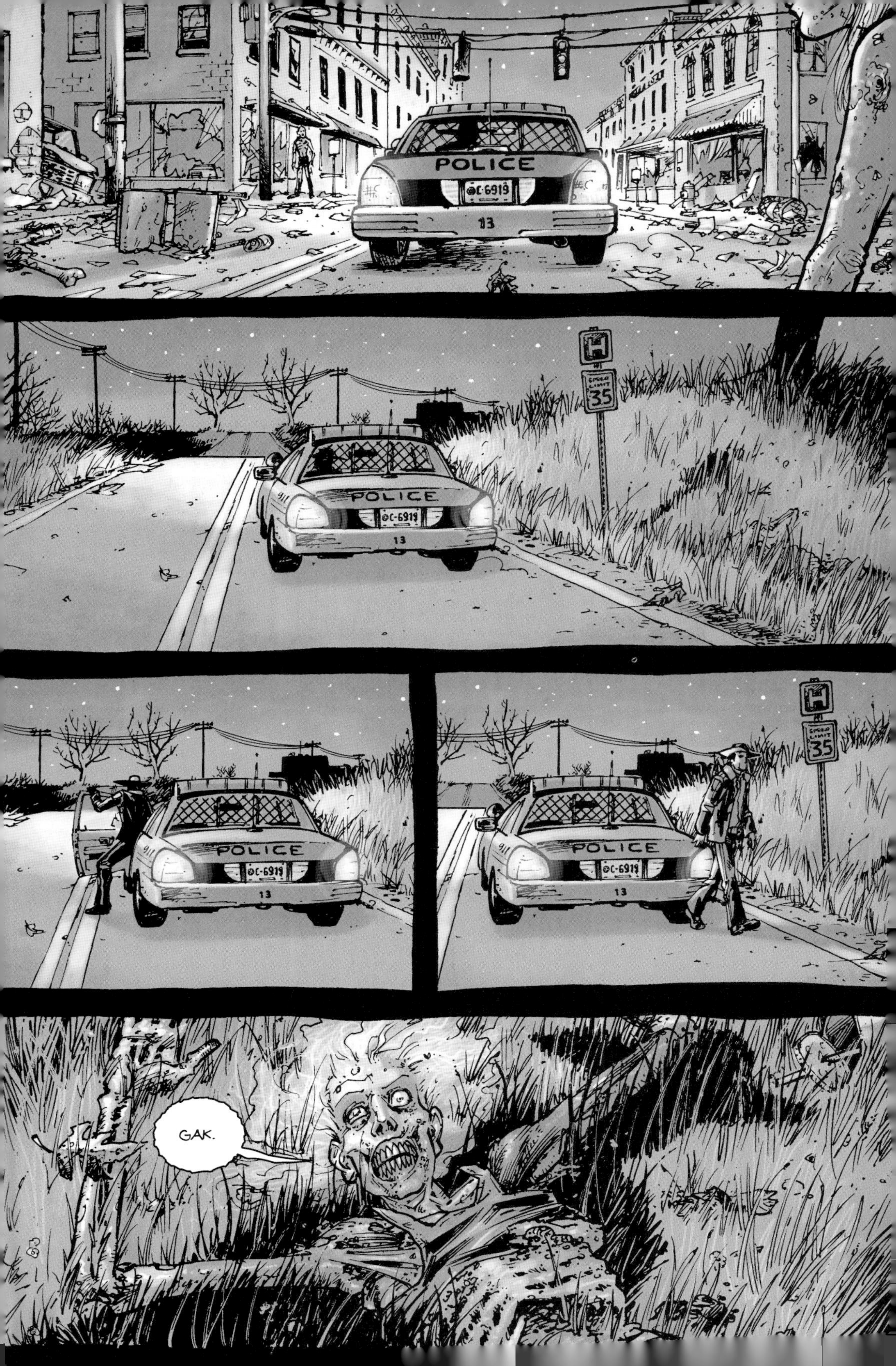
POLICE
C-6919
13
SPEED LIMIT 35
GAK.

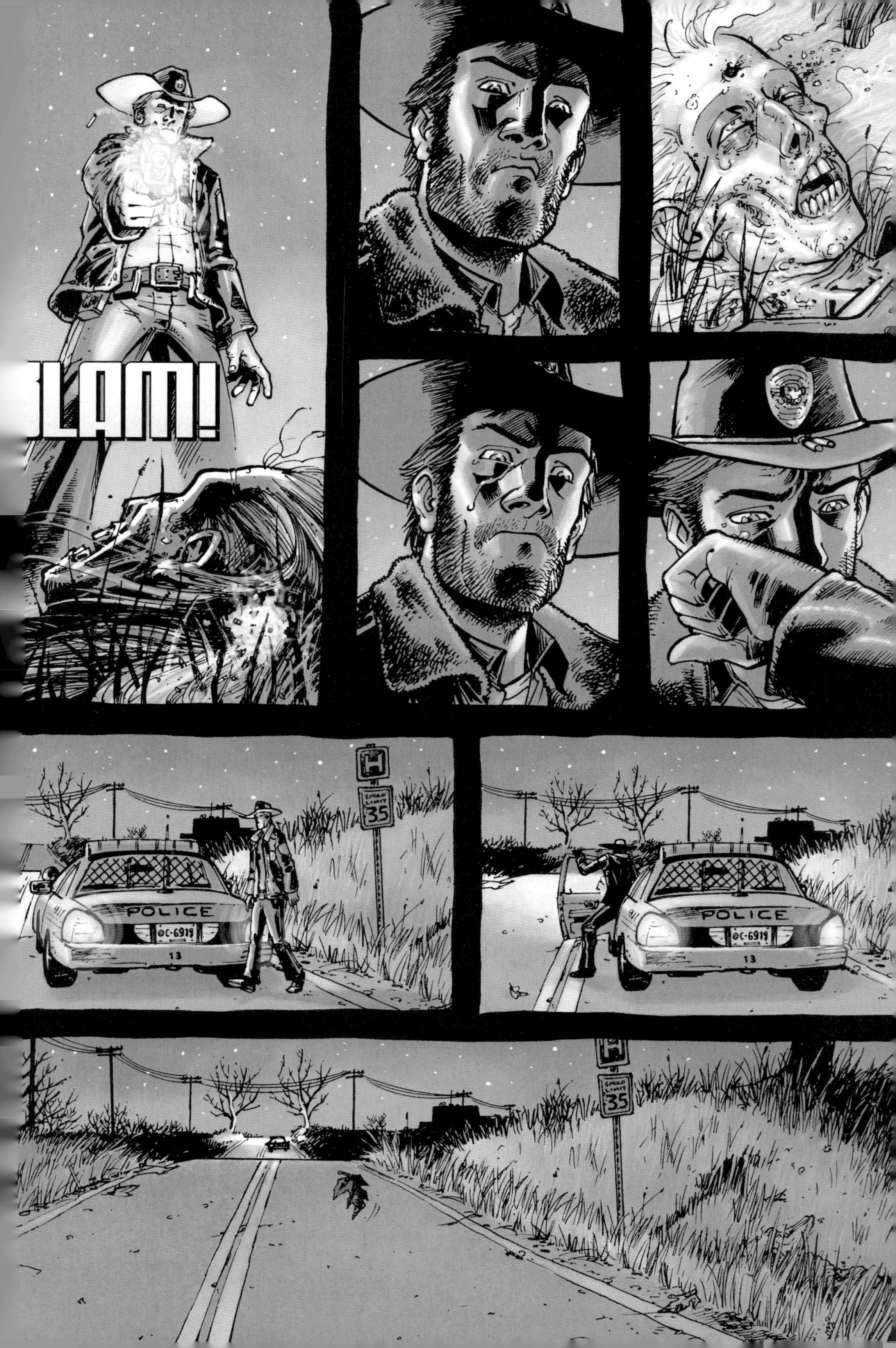
BLAM!
H
SPEED LIMIT 35
POLICE
C-6919
13

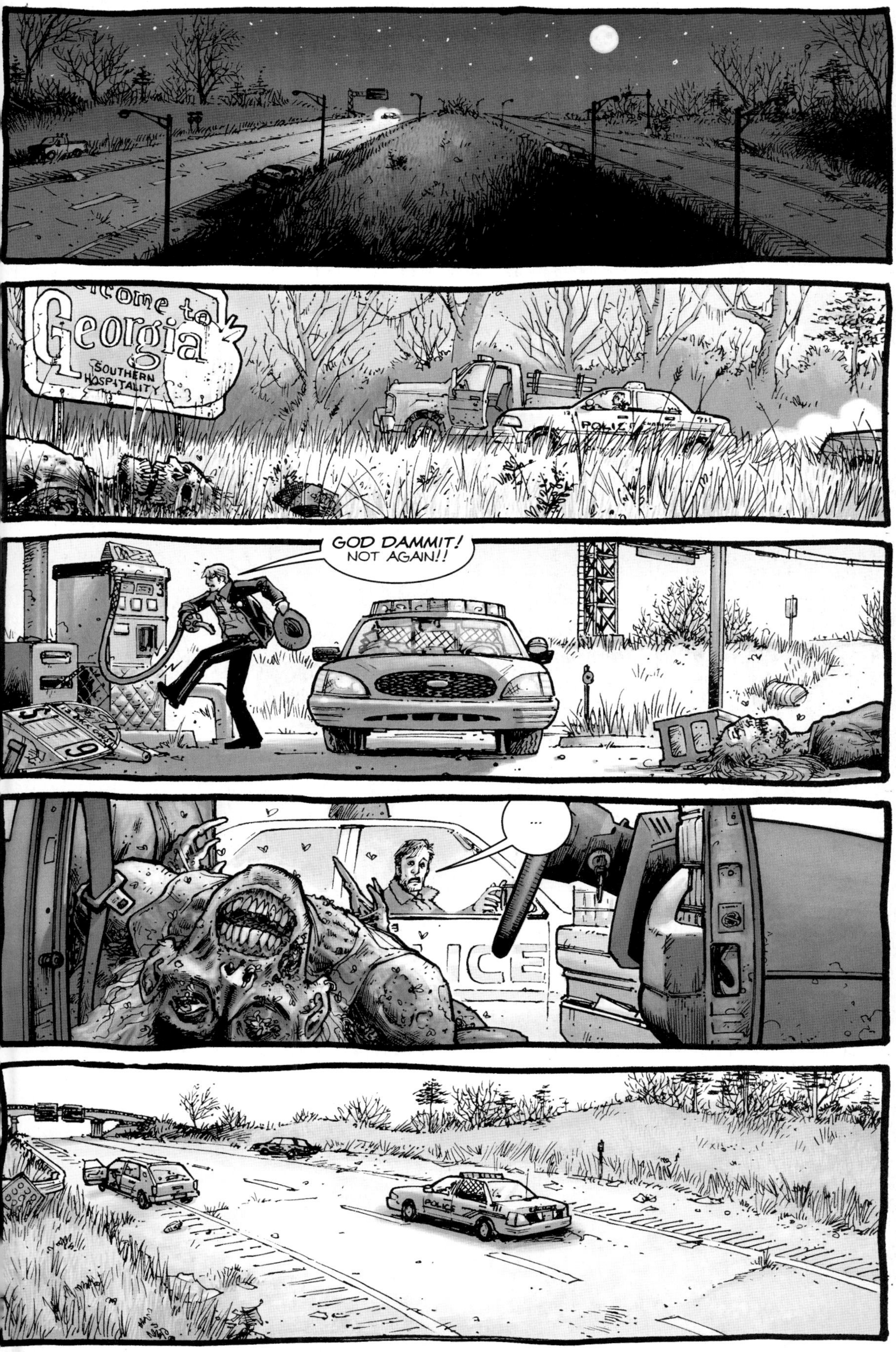
Welcome to Georgia
SOUTHERN HOSPITALITY
GOD DAMMIT! NOT AGAIN!!
...
ICE
POLICE

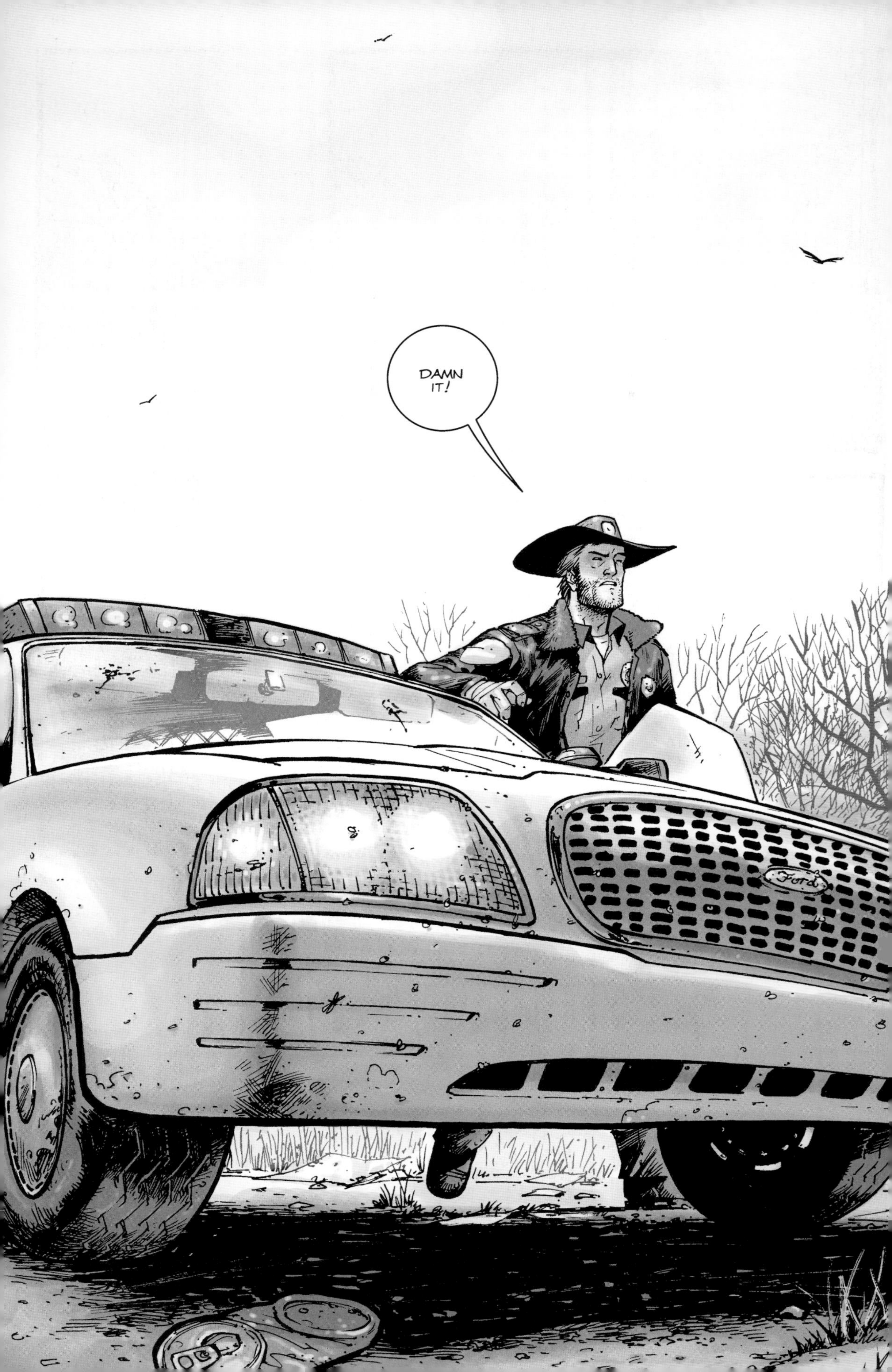
DAMN IT!

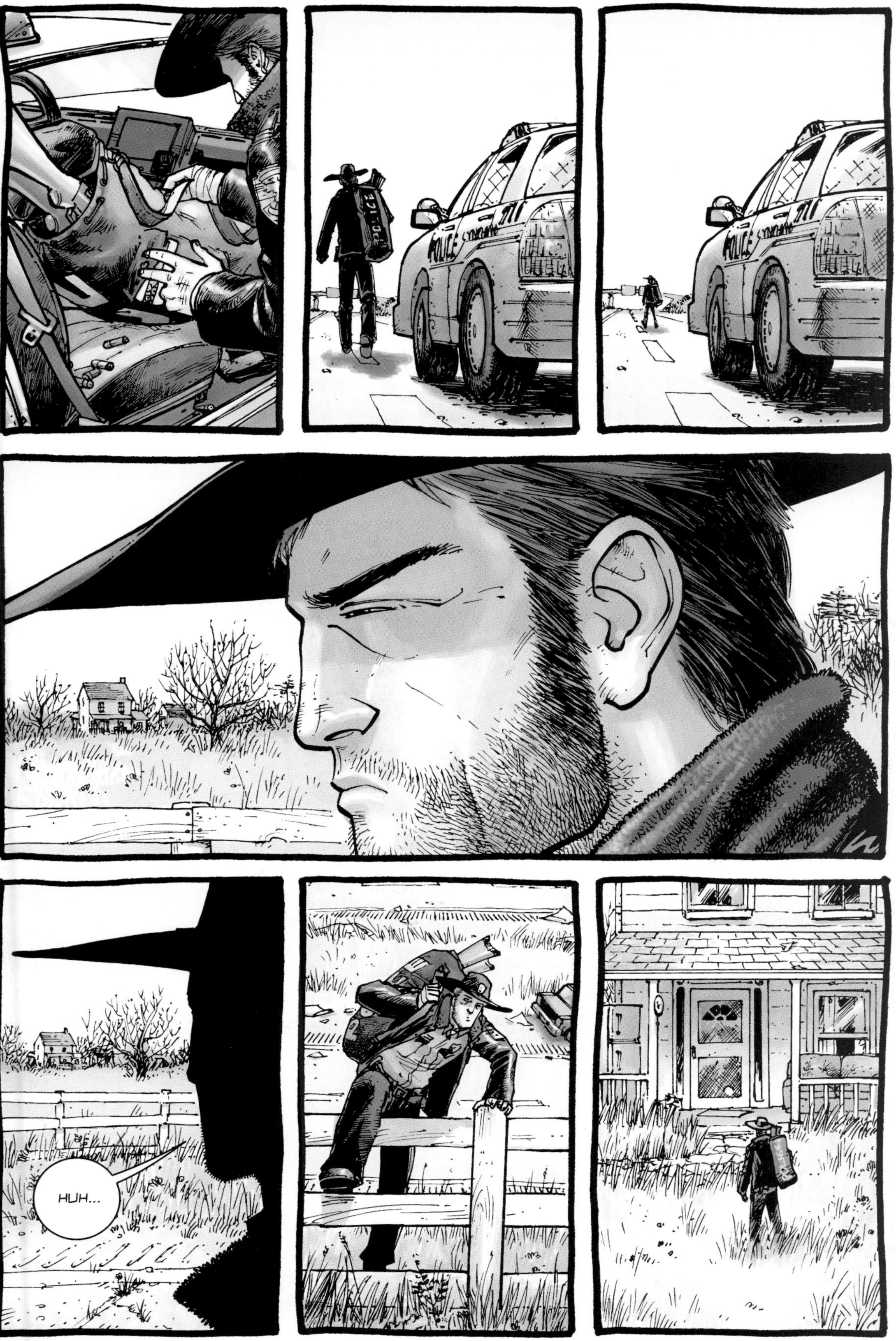

HUH...

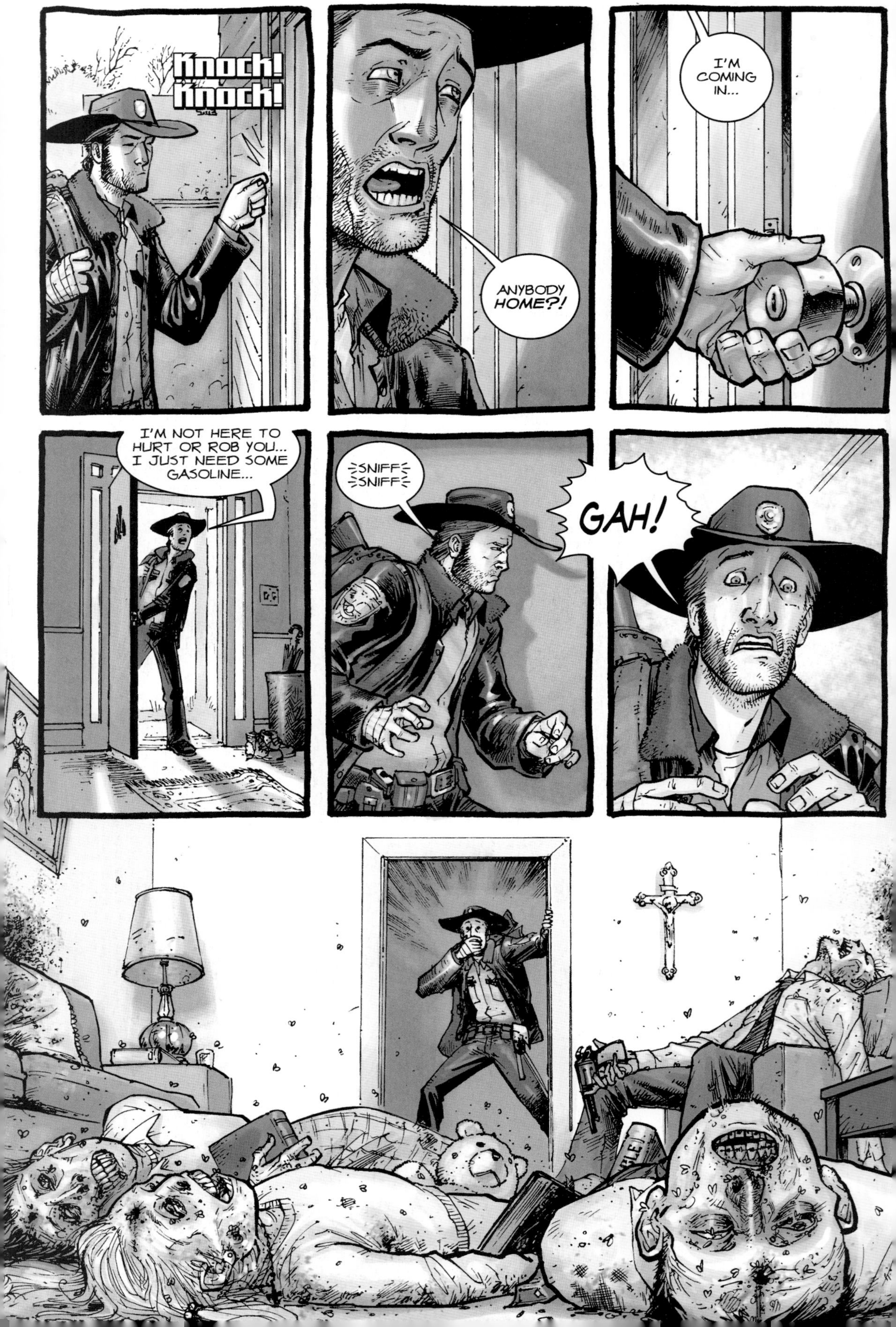
KNOCK! KNOCK!
ANYBODY HOME?!
I'M COMING IN...
I'M NOT HERE TO HURT OR ROB YOU... I JUST NEED SOME GASOLINE...
SNIFF SNIFF
GAH!

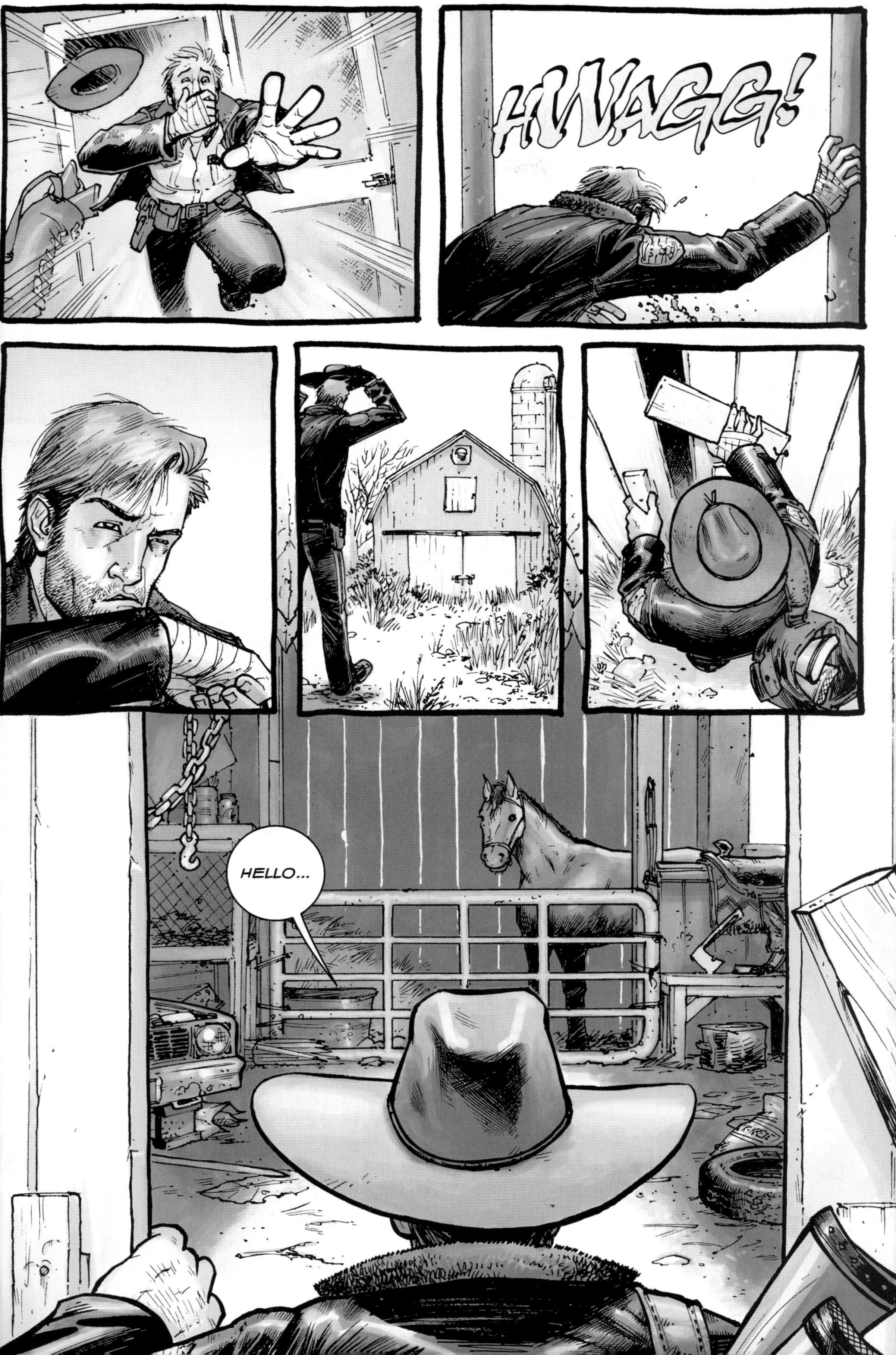
HWAGG!
HELLO...

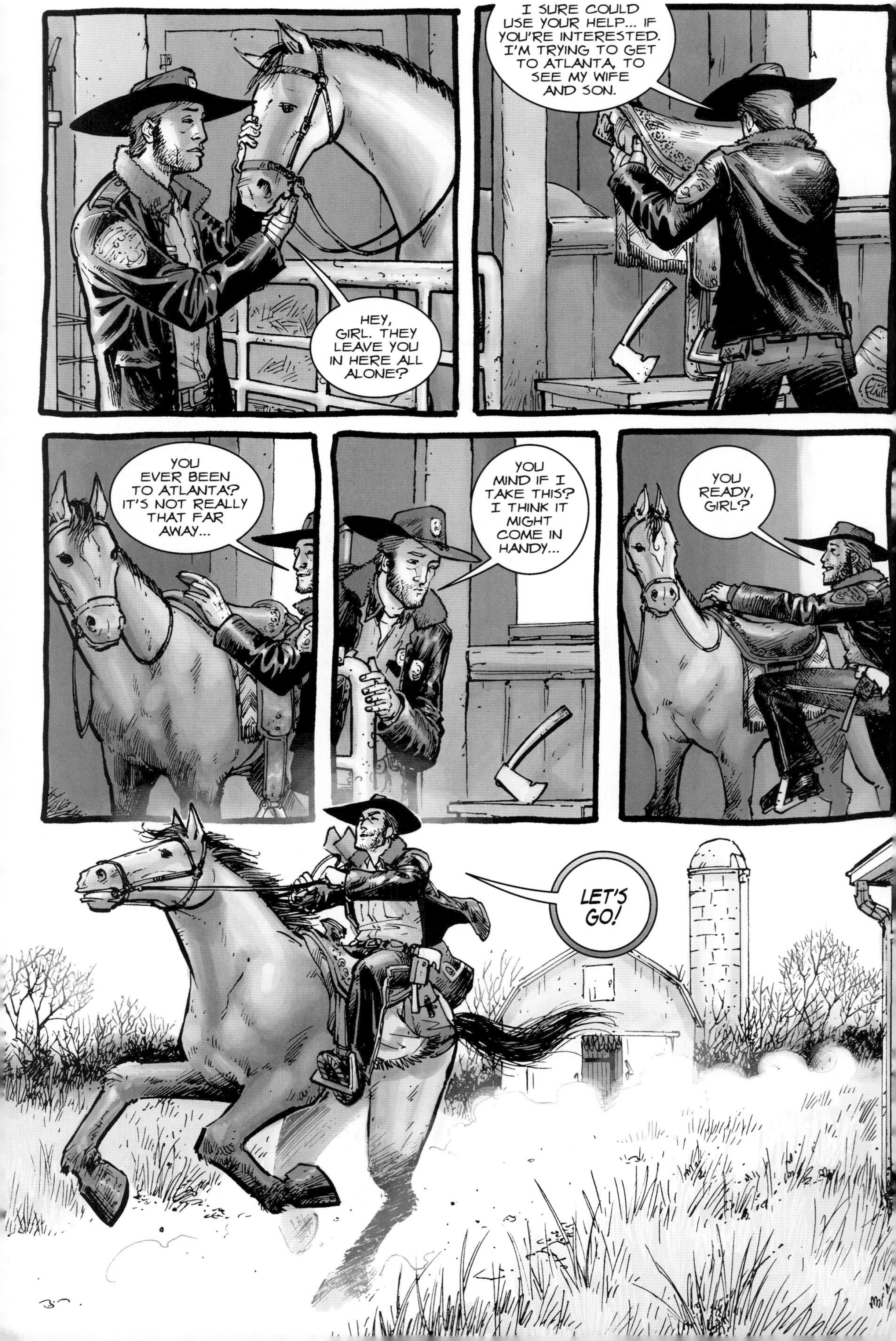
HEY, GIRL. THEY LEAVE YOU IN HERE ALL ALONE?
I SURE COULD USE YOUR HELP... IF YOU'RE INTERESTED. I'M TRYING TO GET TO ATLANTA, TO SEE MY WIFE AND SON.
YOU EVER BEEN TO ATLANTA? IT'S NOT REALLY THAT FAR AWAY...
YOU MIND IF I TAKE THIS? I THINK IT MIGHT COME IN HANDY...
YOU READY, GIRL?
LET'S GO!

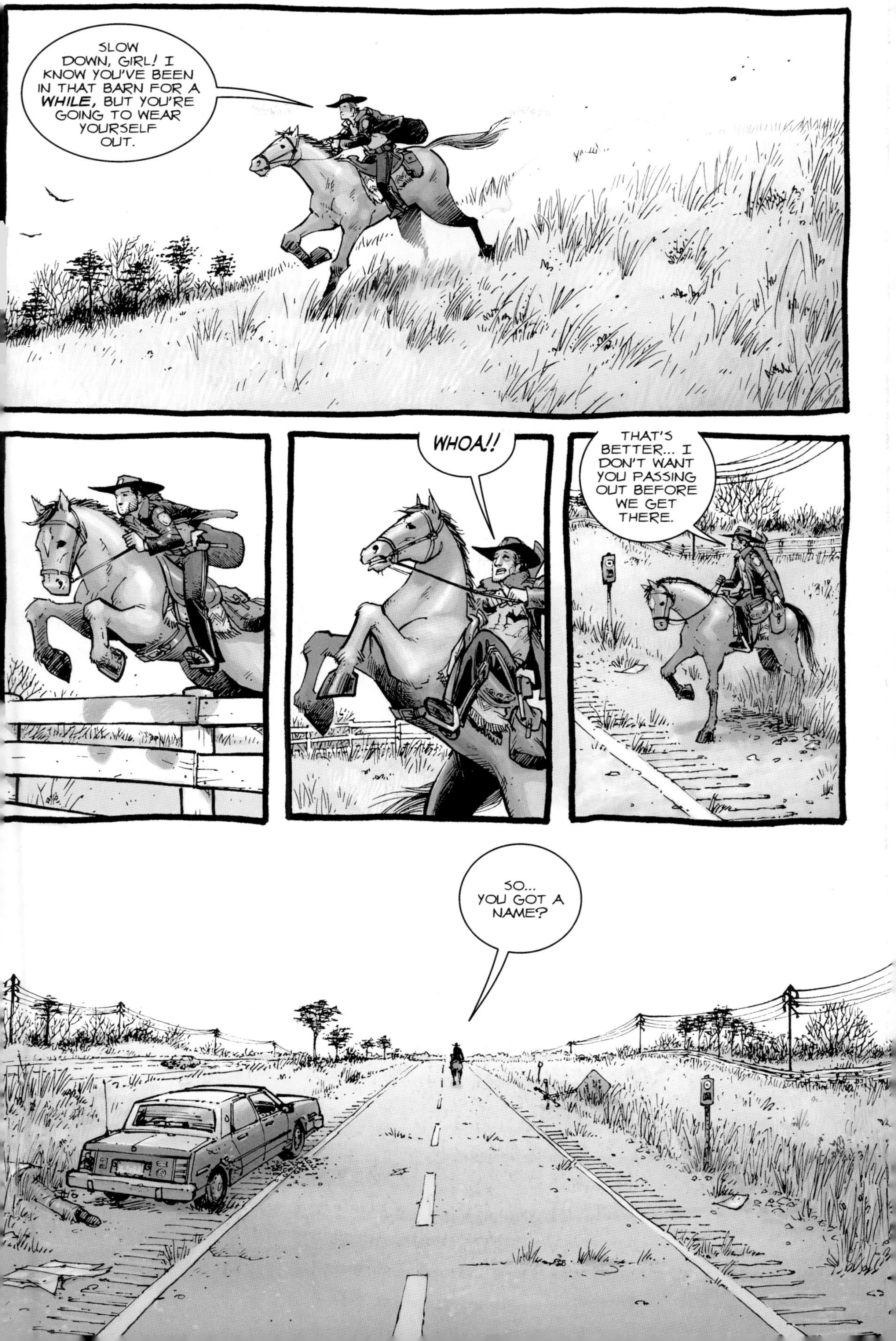

SLOW DOWN, GIRL! I KNOW YOU'VE BEEN IN THAT BARN FOR A WHILE, BUT YOU'RE GOING TO WEAR YOURSELF OUT.
WHOA!!
THAT'S BETTER... I DON'T WANT YOU PASSING OUT BEFORE WE GET THERE.
SO... YOU GOT A NAME?

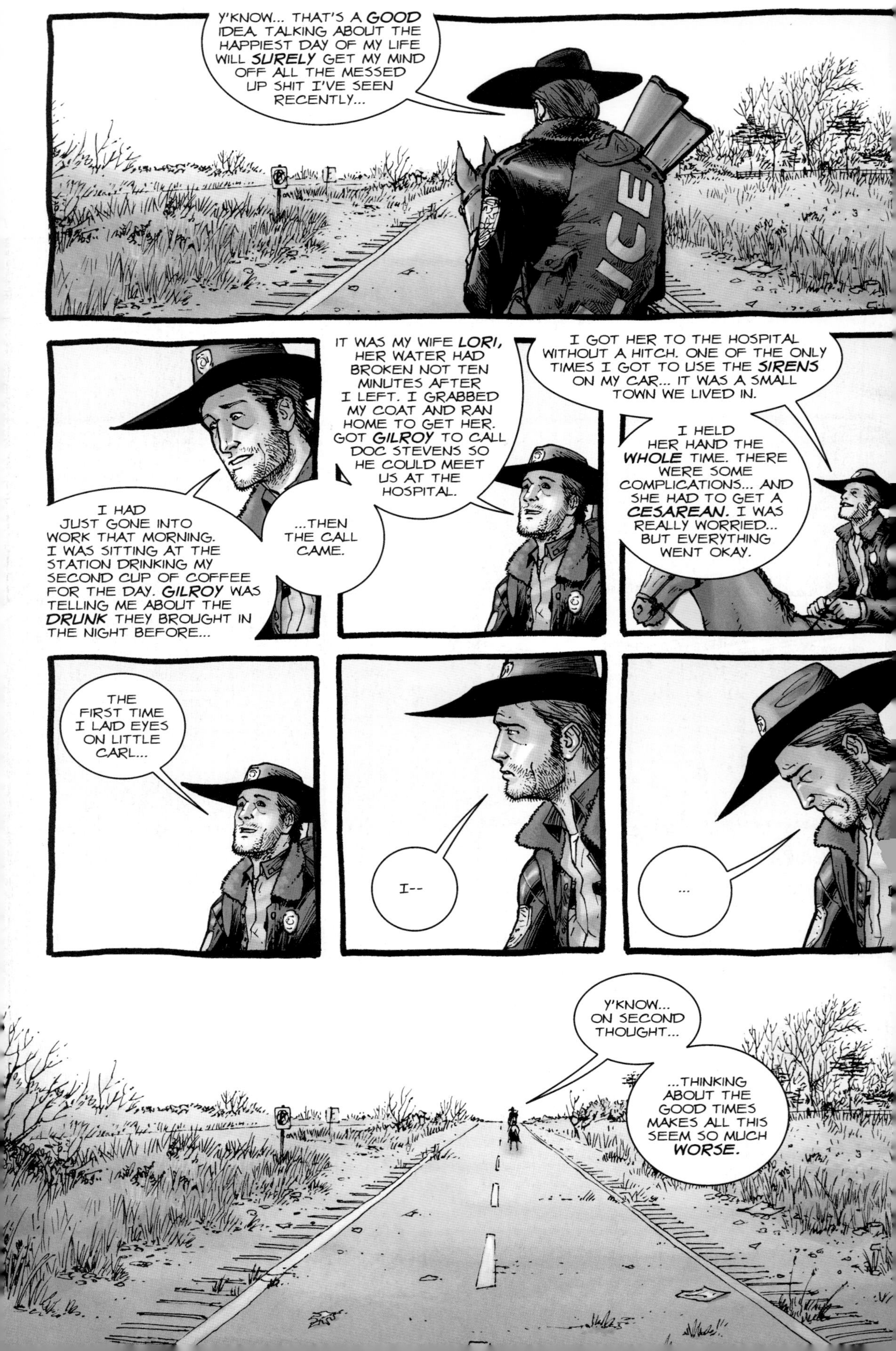
Y'KNOW... THAT'S A GOOD IDEA. TALKING ABOUT THE HAPPIEST DAY OF MY LIFE WILL SURELY GET MY MIND OFF ALL THE MESSED UP SHIT I'VE SEEN RECENTLY...
I HAD JUST GONE INTO WORK THAT MORNING. I WAS SITTING AT THE STATION DRINKING MY SECOND CUP OF COFFEE FOR THE DAY. GILROY WAS TELLING ME ABOUT THE DRUNK THEY BROUGHT IN THE NIGHT BEFORE...
...THEN THE CALL CAME.
IT WAS MY WIFE LORI, HER WATER HAD BROKEN NOT TEN MINUTES AFTER I LEFT. I GRABBED MY COAT AND RAN HOME TO GET HER. GOT GILROY TO CALL DOC STEVENS SO HE COULD MEET US AT THE HOSPITAL.
I GOT HER TO THE HOSPITAL WITHOUT A HITCH. ONE OF THE ONLY TIMES I GOT TO USE THE SIRENS ON MY CAR... IT WAS A SMALL TOWN WE LIVED IN.
I HELD HER HAND THE WHOLE TIME. THERE WERE SOME COMPLICATIONS... AND SHE HAD TO GET A CESAREAN. I WAS REALLY WORRIED... BUT EVERYTHING WENT OKAY.
THE FIRST TIME I LAID EYES ON LITTLE CARL...
I--
...
Y'KNOW... ON SECOND THOUGHT...
...THINKING ABOUT THE GOOD TIMES MAKES ALL THIS SEEM SO MUCH WORSE.

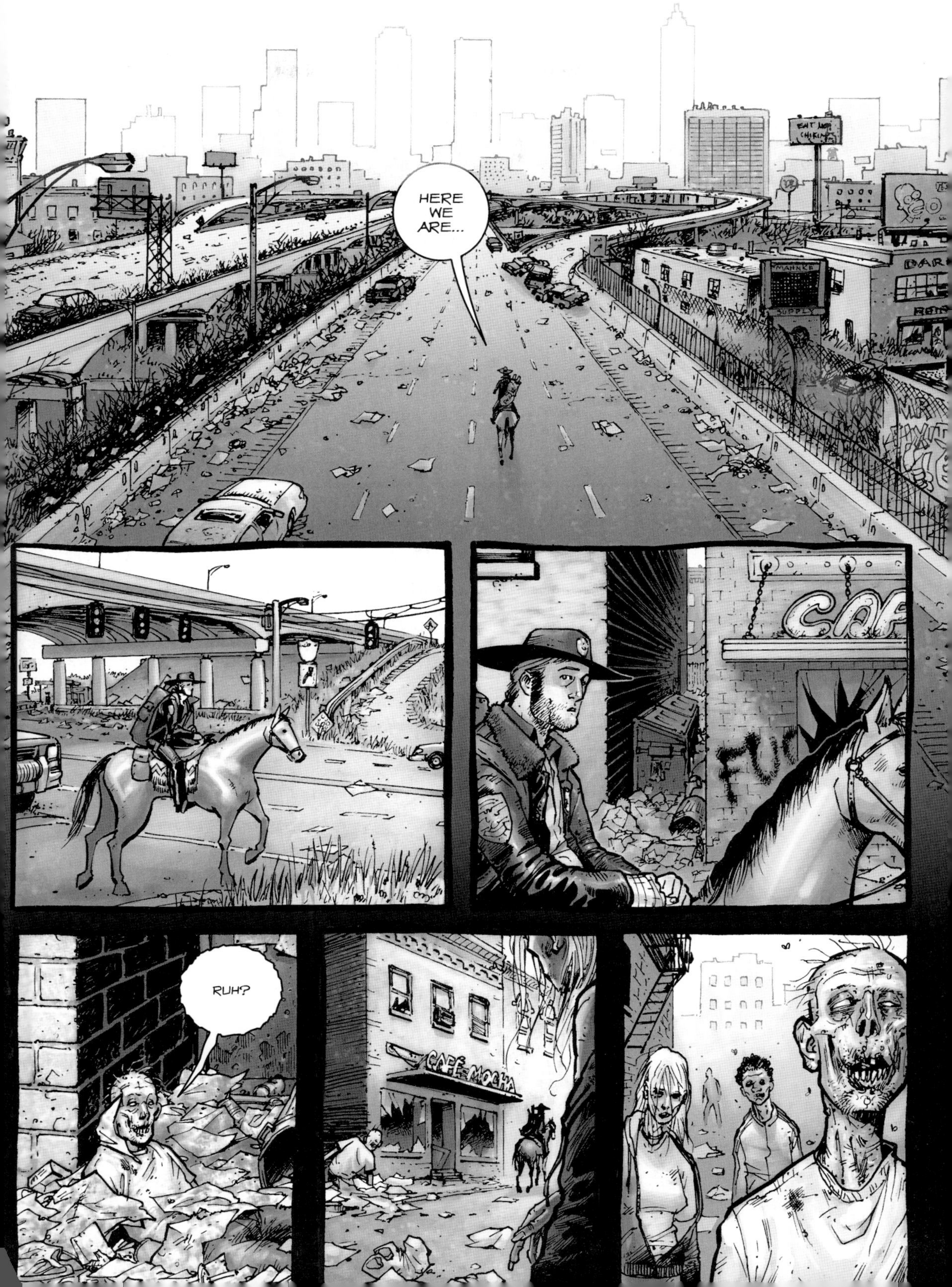
HERE WE ARE...
RUH?
CAFÉ MOCHA

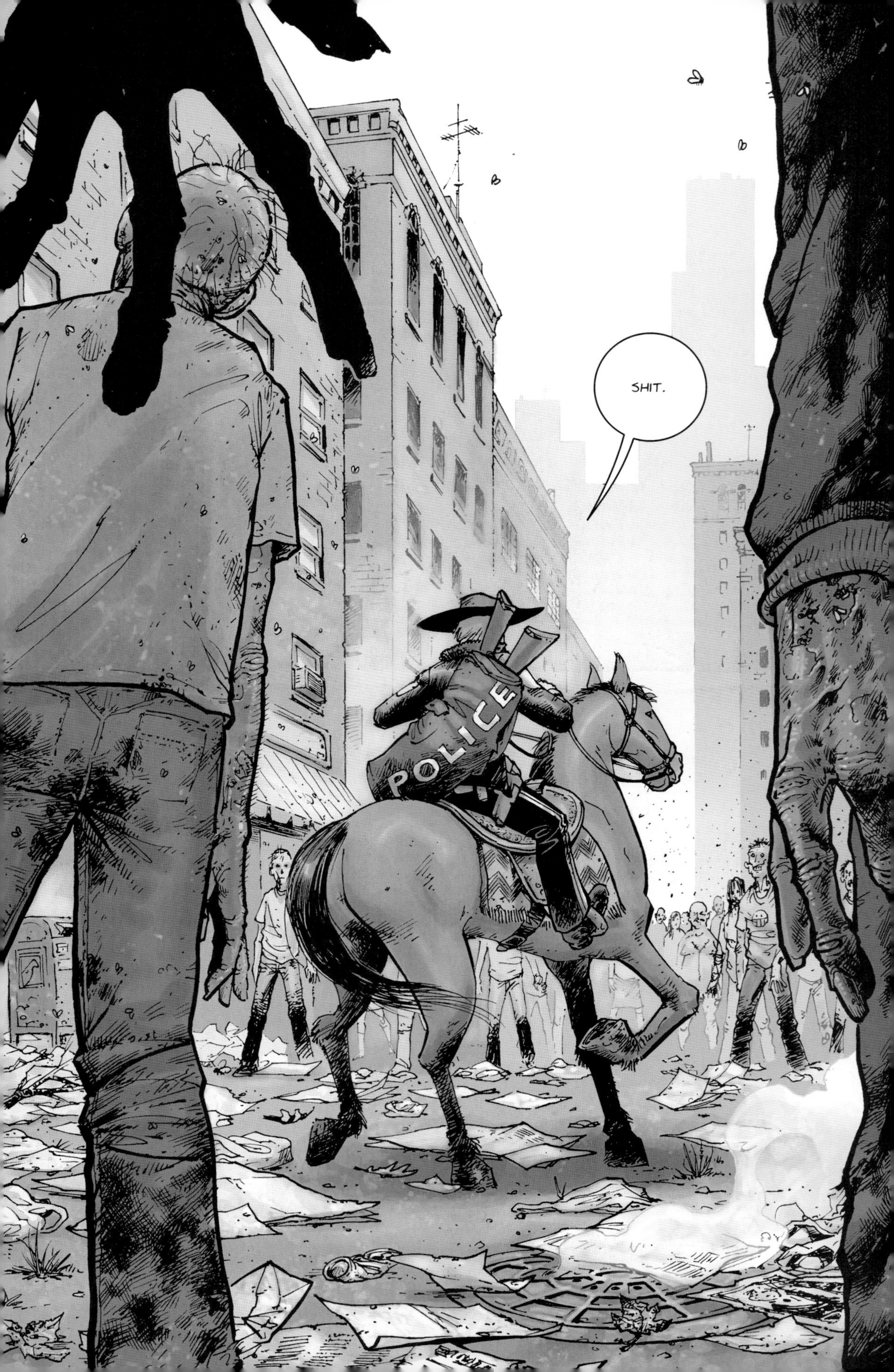
SHIT.
POLICE

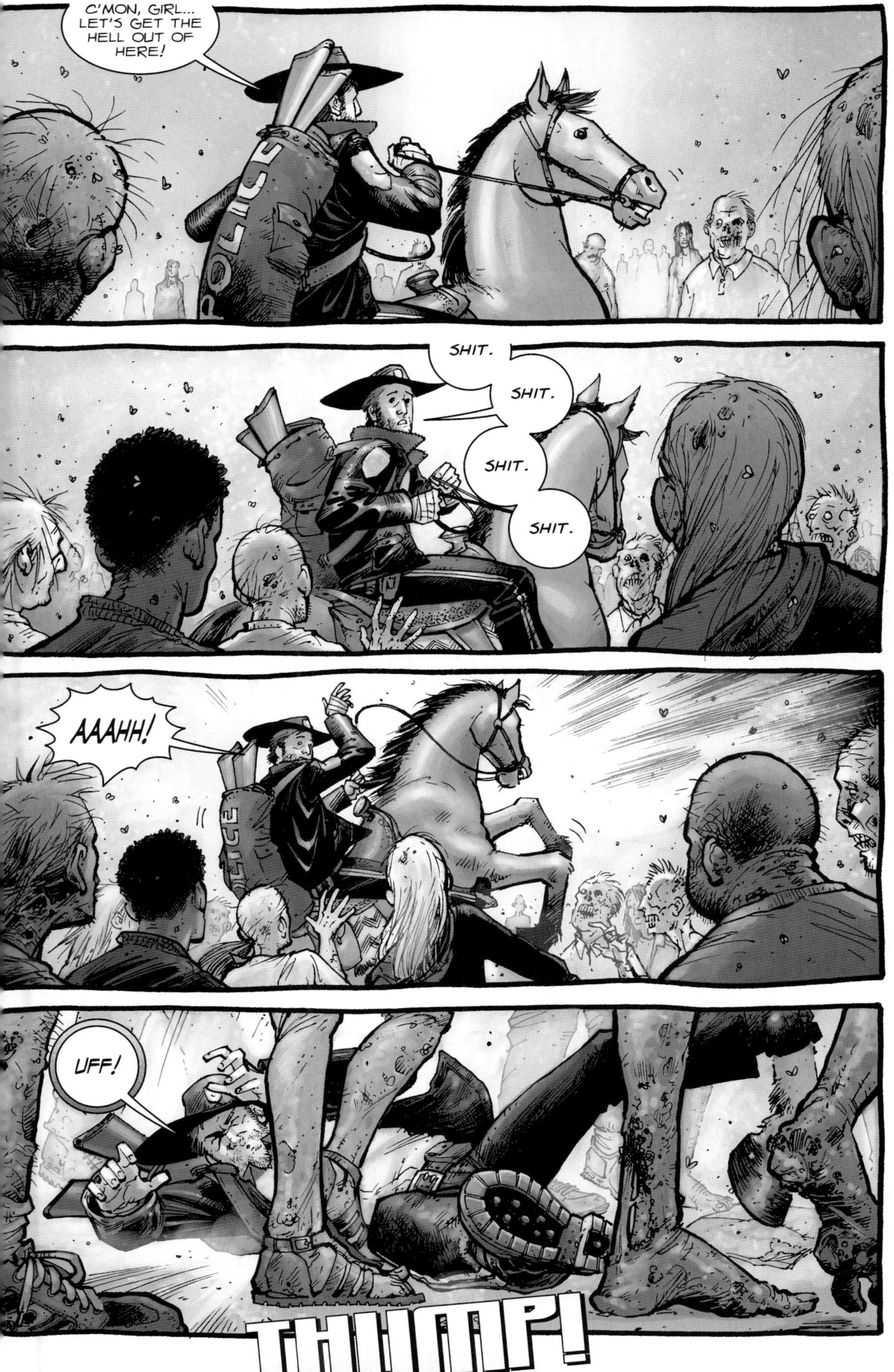
C'MON, GIRL... LET'S GET THE HELL OUT OF HERE!
SHIT.
SHIT.
SHIT.
SHIT.
AAAHH!
UFF!
THUMP!

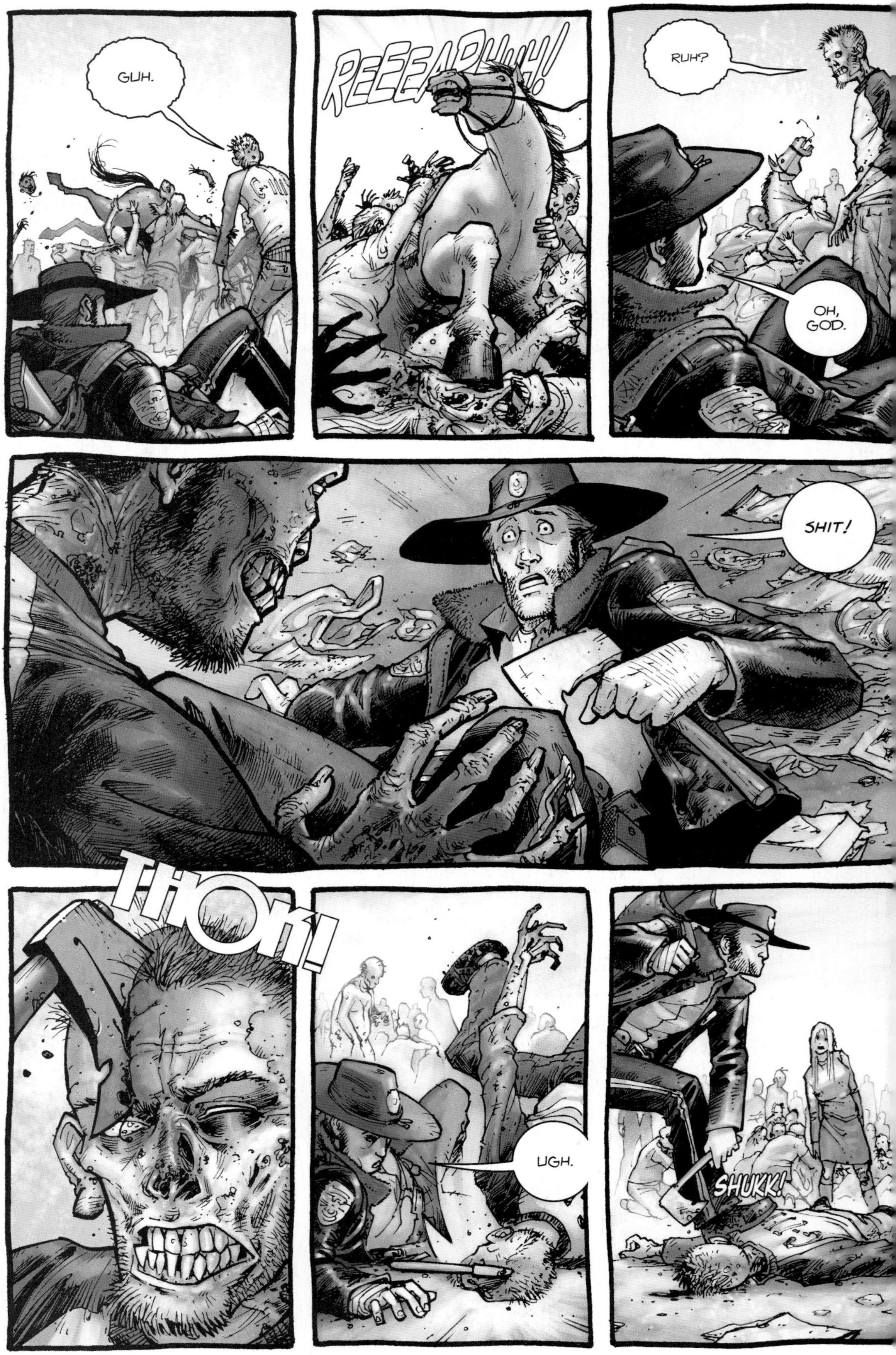
GUH.
REEEEARHHH!
RUH?
OH, GOD.
SHIT!
THOK!
UGH.
SHUKK!

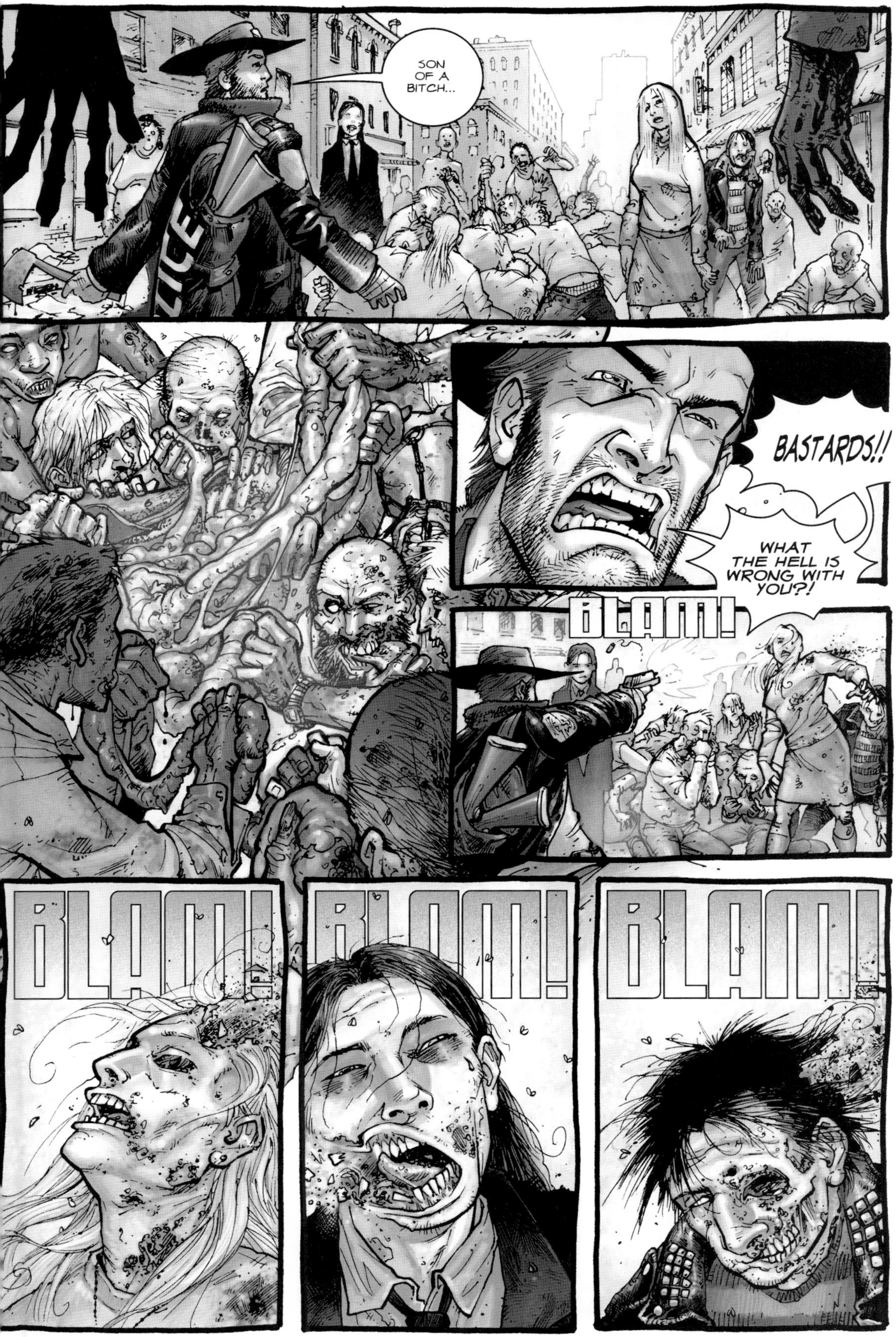
SON OF A BITCH...
BASTARDS!!
WHAT THE HELL IS WRONG WITH YOU?!
BLAM!
BLAM!
BLAM!
BLAM!

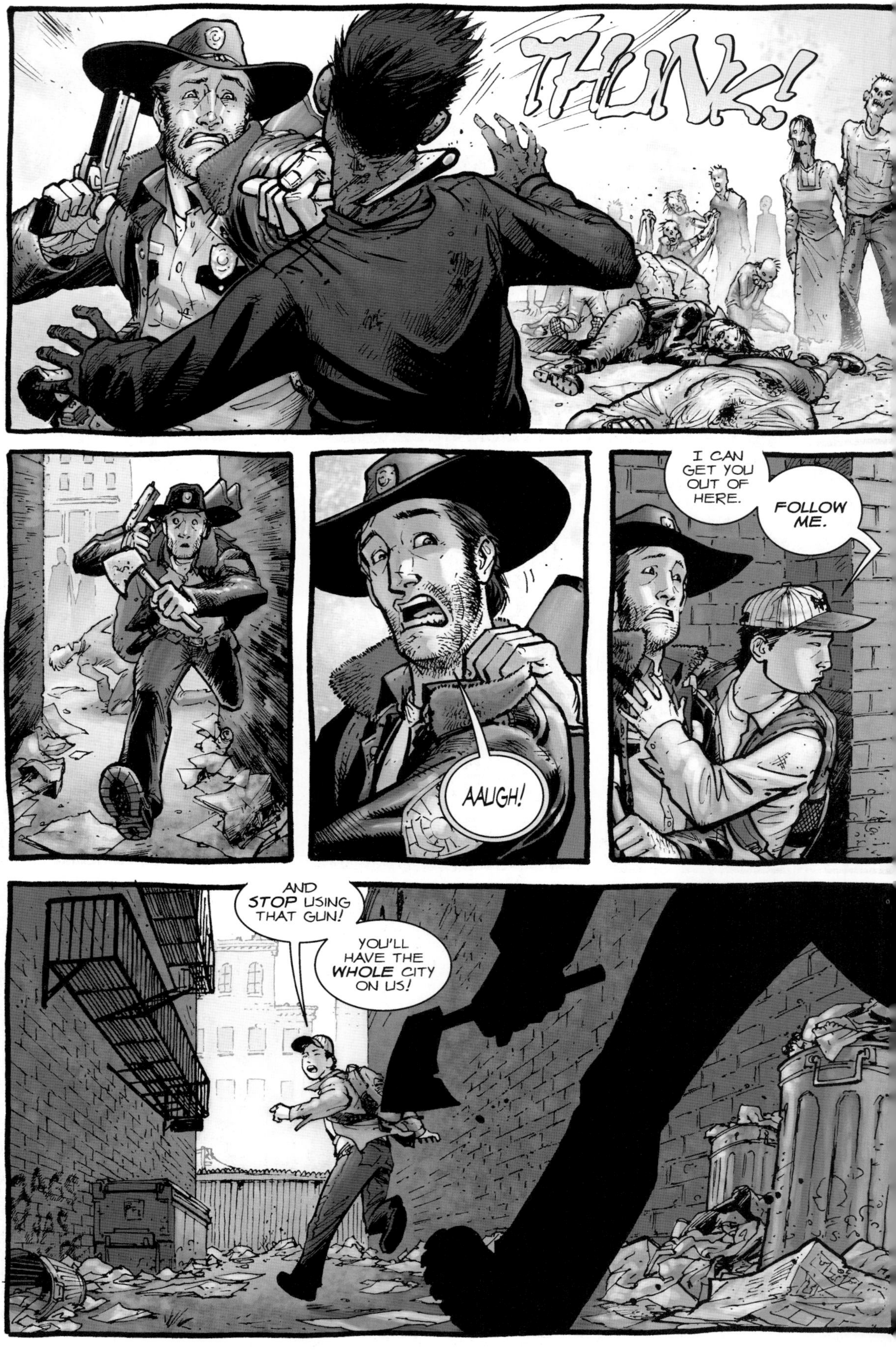
THUNK!
AAUGH!
I CAN GET YOU OUT OF HERE.
FOLLOW ME.
AND STOP USING THAT GUN!
YOU'LL HAVE THE WHOLE CITY ON US!

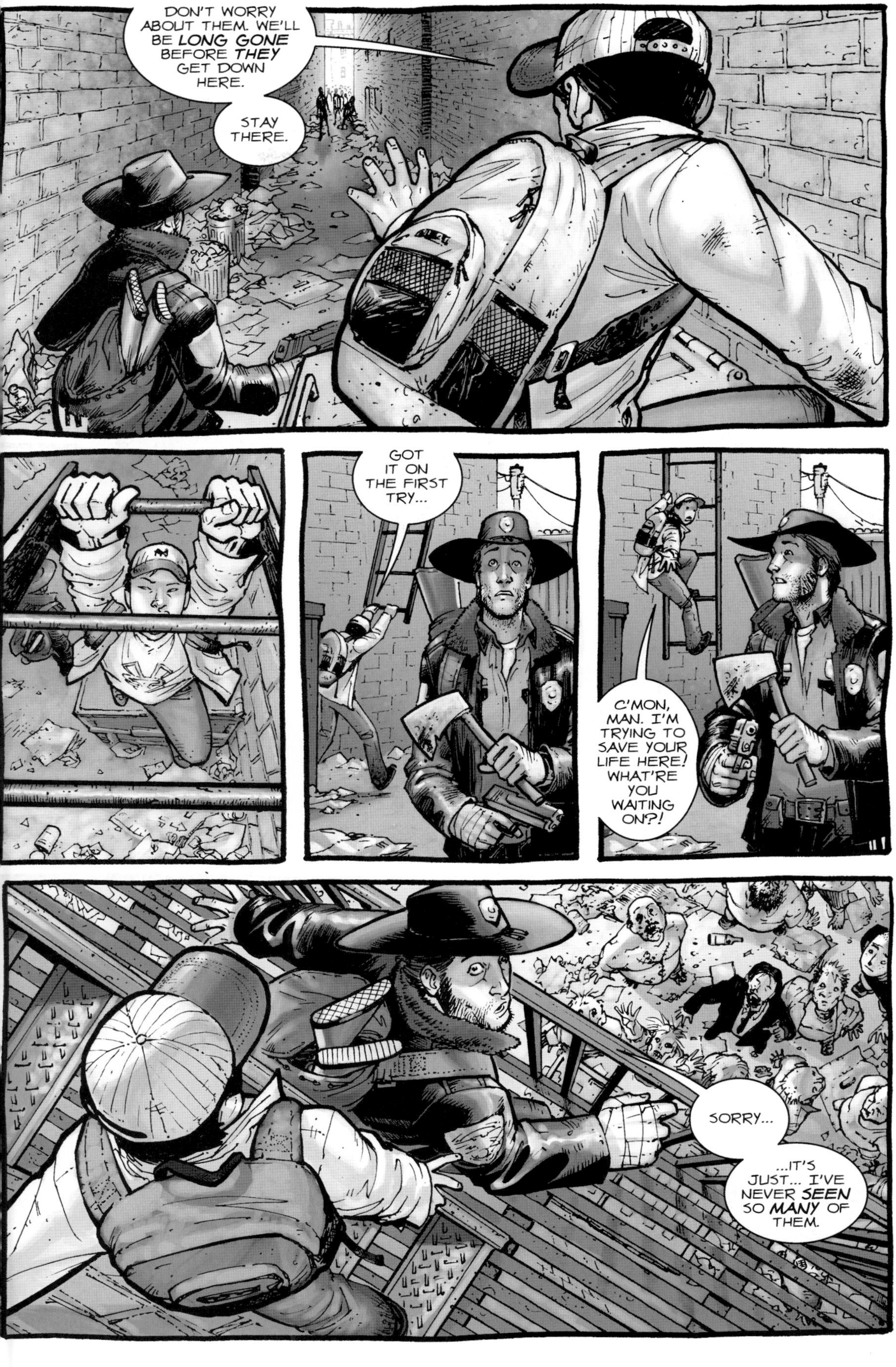

DON'T WORRY ABOUT THEM. WE'LL BE LONG GONE BEFORE THEY GET DOWN HERE.
STAY THERE.
GOT IT ON THE FIRST TRY...
C'MON, MAN. I'M TRYING TO SAVE YOUR LIFE HERE! WHAT'RE YOU WAITING ON?!
SORRY...
...IT'S JUST... I'VE NEVER SEEN SO MANY OF THEM.

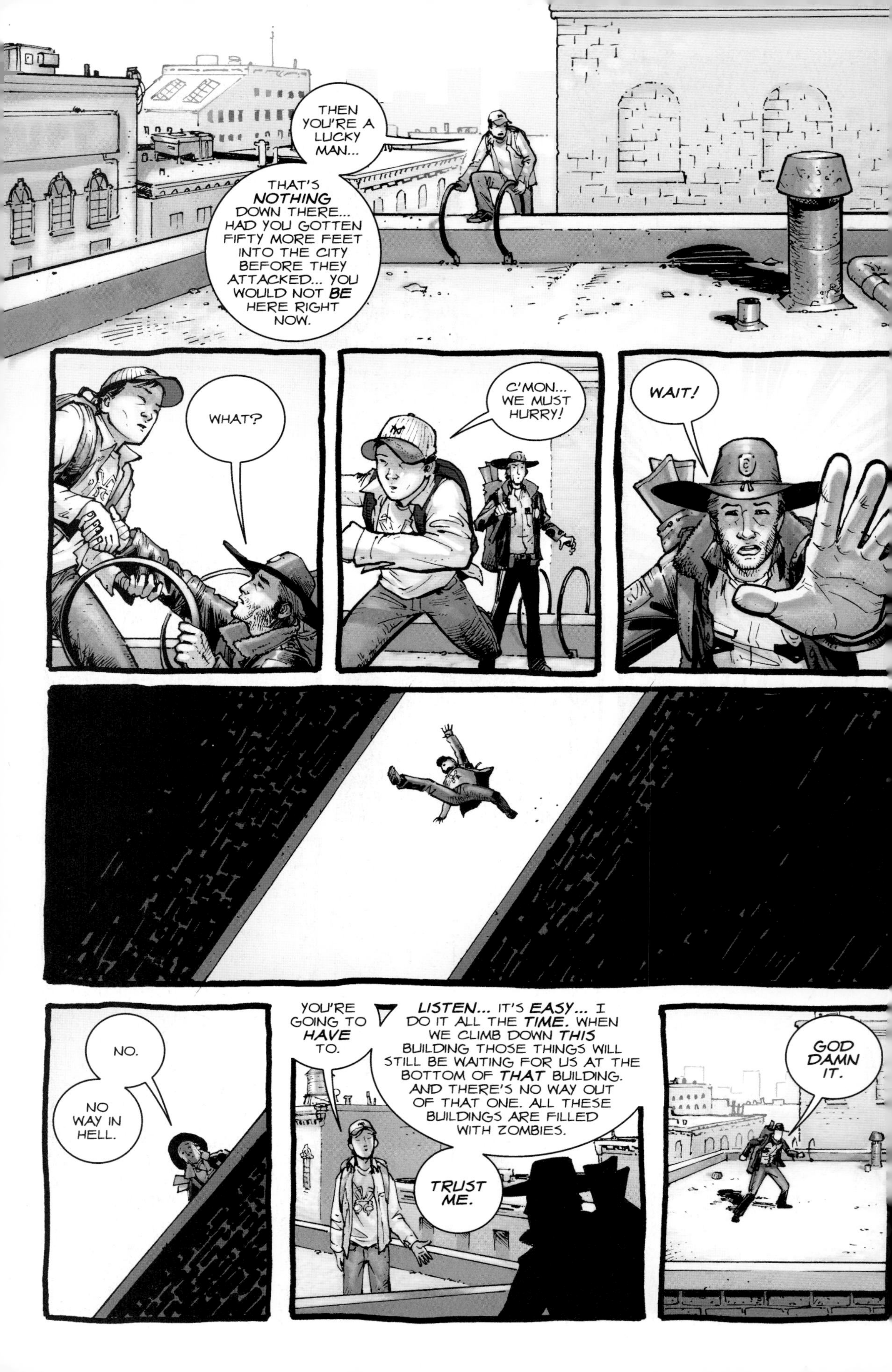
THEN YOU'RE A LUCKY MAN...
THAT'S NOTHING DOWN THERE... HAD YOU GOTTEN FIFTY MORE FEET INTO THE CITY BEFORE THEY ATTACKED... YOU WOULD NOT BE HERE RIGHT NOW.
WHAT?
C'MON... WE MUST HURRY!
WAIT!
NO.
NO WAY IN HELL.
YOU'RE GOING TO HAVE TO.
LISTEN... IT'S EASY... I DO IT ALL THE TIME. WHEN WE CLIMB DOWN THIS BUILDING THOSE THINGS WILL STILL BE WAITING FOR US AT THE BOTTOM OF THAT BUILDING. AND THERE'S NO WAY OUT OF THAT ONE. ALL THESE BUILDINGS ARE FILLED WITH ZOMBIES.
TRUST ME.
GOD DAMN IT.

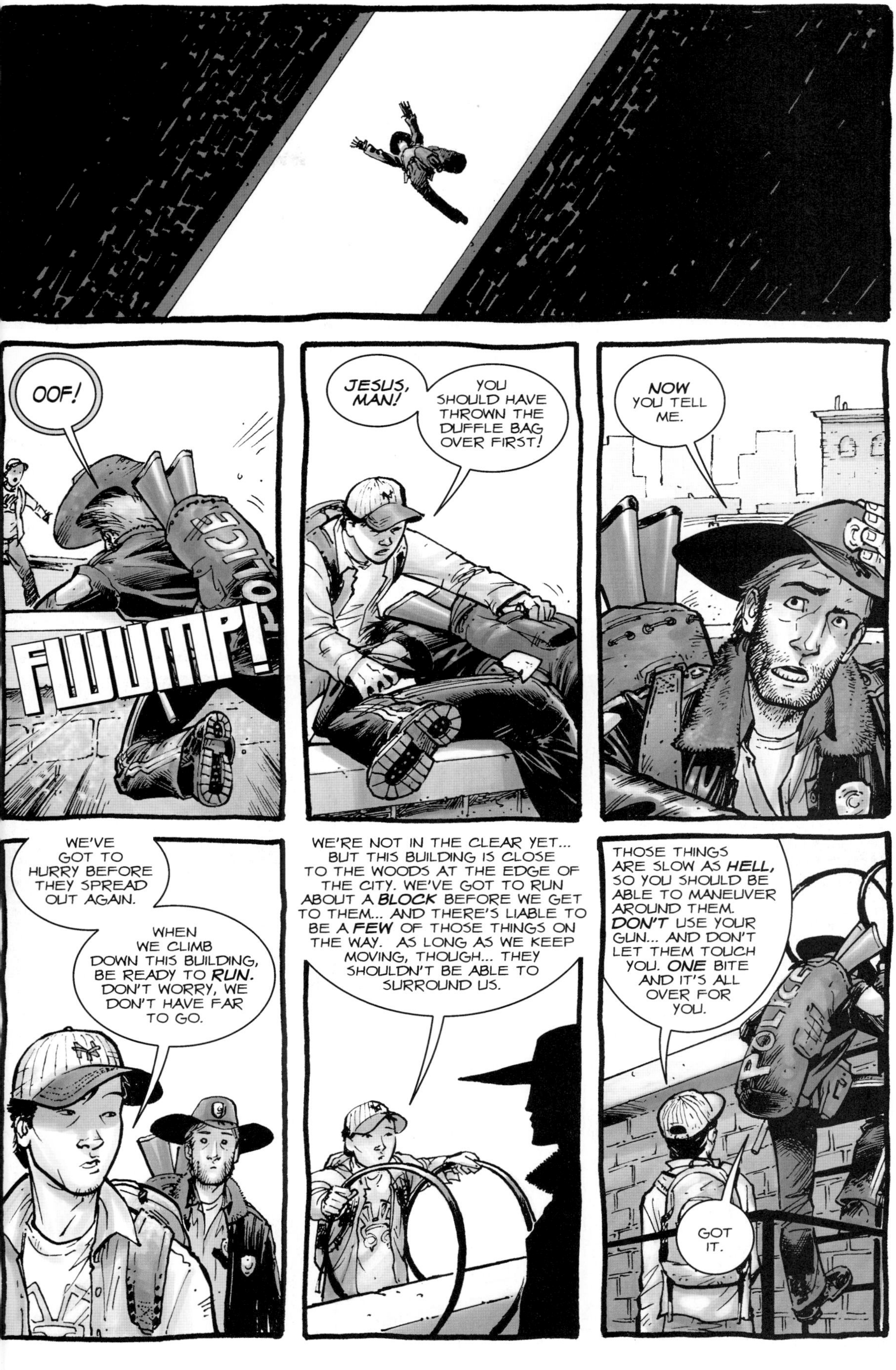
OOF!
FWUMP!
JESUS, MAN!
YOU SHOULD HAVE THROWN THE DUFFLE BAG OVER FIRST!
NOW YOU TELL ME.
WE'VE GOT TO HURRY BEFORE THEY SPREAD OUT AGAIN.
WHEN WE CLIMB DOWN THIS BUILDING, BE READY TO RUN. DON'T WORRY, WE DON'T HAVE FAR TO GO.
WE'RE NOT IN THE CLEAR YET... BUT THIS BUILDING IS CLOSE TO THE WOODS AT THE EDGE OF THE CITY. WE'VE GOT TO RUN ABOUT A BLOCK BEFORE WE GET TO THEM... AND THERE'S LIABLE TO BE A FEW OF THOSE THINGS ON THE WAY. AS LONG AS WE KEEP MOVING, THOUGH... THEY SHOULDN'T BE ABLE TO SURROUND US.
THOSE THINGS ARE SLOW AS HELL, SO YOU SHOULD BE ABLE TO MANEUVER AROUND THEM. DON'T USE YOUR GUN... AND DON'T LET THEM TOUCH YOU. ONE BITE AND IT'S ALL OVER FOR YOU.
GOT IT.

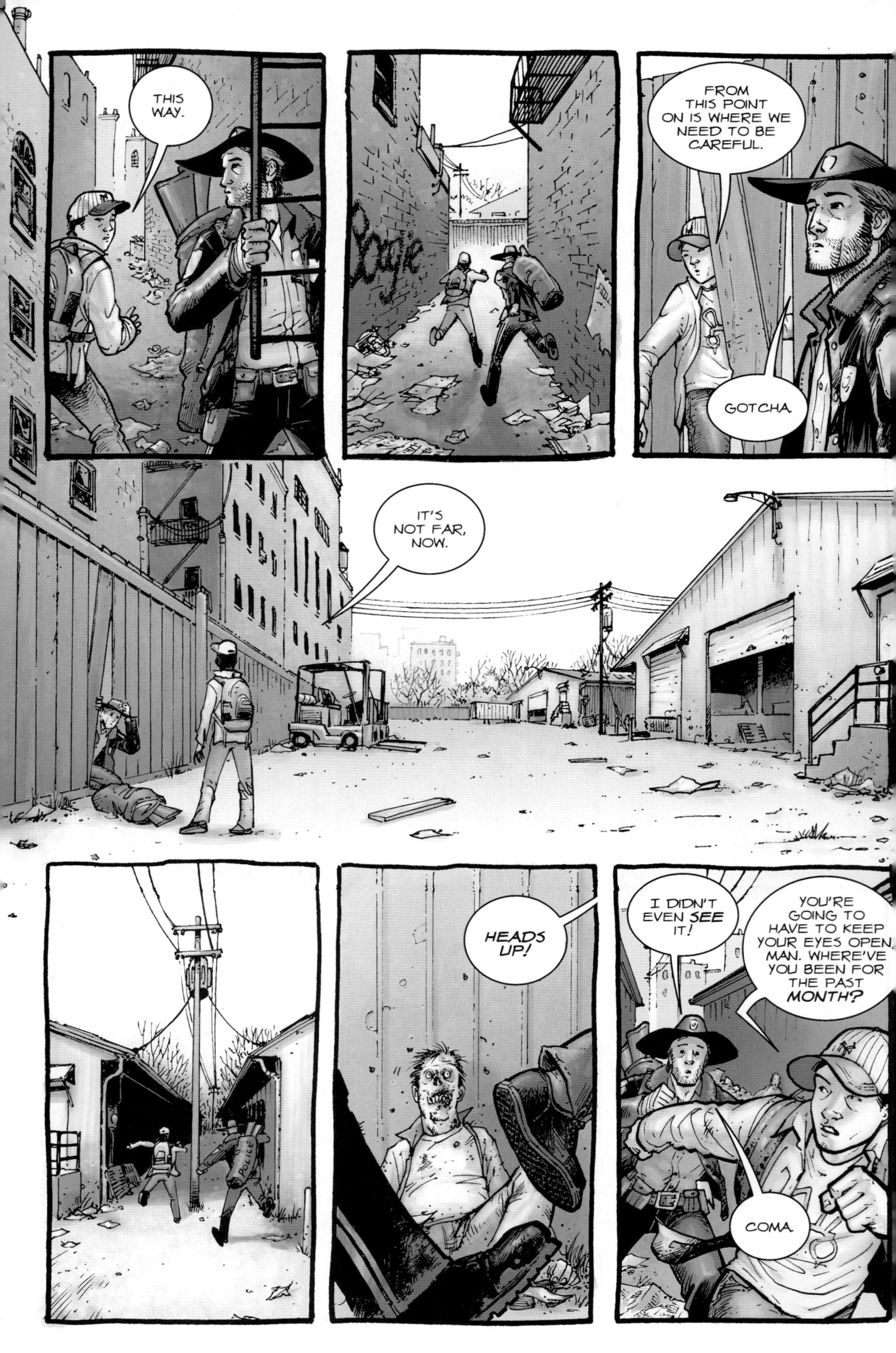
THIS WAY.
FROM THIS POINT ON IS WHERE WE NEED TO BE CAREFUL.
GOTCHA
IT'S NOT FAR, NOW.
POLICE
HEADS UP!
I DIDN'T EVEN SEE IT!
YOU'RE GOING TO HAVE TO KEEP YOUR EYES OPEN MAN. WHERE'VE YOU BEEN FOR THE PAST MONTH?
COMA

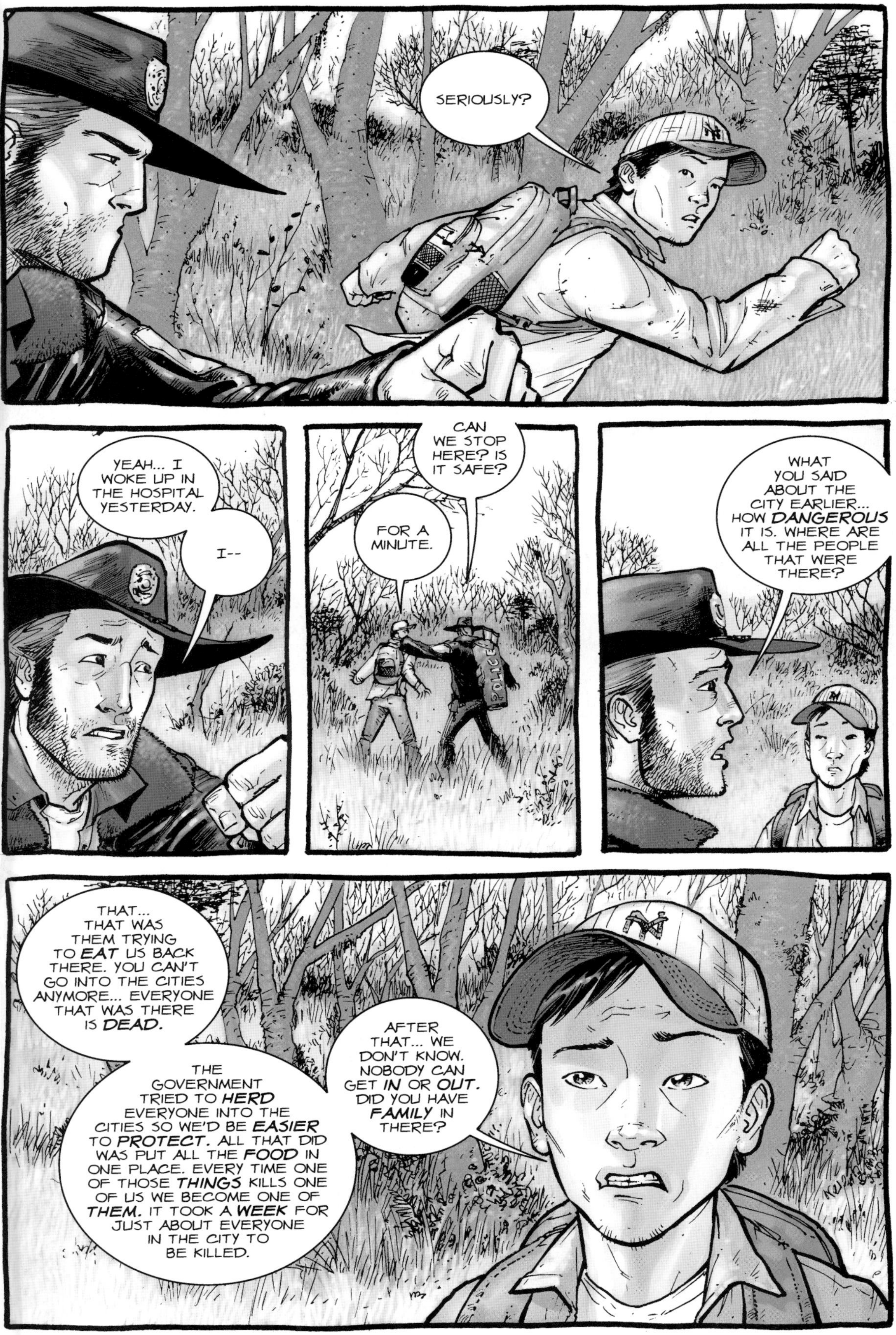
SERIOUSLY?
YEAH... I WOKE UP IN THE HOSPITAL YESTERDAY.
I--
CAN WE STOP HERE? IS IT SAFE?
FOR A MINUTE.
POLICE
WHAT YOU SAID ABOUT THE CITY EARLIER... HOW DANGEROUS IT IS. WHERE ARE ALL THE PEOPLE THAT WERE THERE?
THAT... THAT WAS THEM TRYING TO EAT US BACK THERE. YOU CAN'T GO INTO THE CITIES ANYMORE... EVERYONE THAT WAS THERE IS DEAD.
THE GOVERNMENT TRIED TO HERD EVERYONE INTO THE CITIES SO WE'D BE EASIER TO PROTECT. ALL THAT DID WAS PUT ALL THE FOOD IN ONE PLACE. EVERY TIME ONE OF THOSE THINGS KILLS ONE OF US WE BECOME ONE OF THEM. IT TOOK A WEEK FOR JUST ABOUT EVERYONE IN THE CITY TO BE KILLED.
AFTER THAT... WE DON'T KNOW. NOBODY CAN GET IN OR OUT. DID YOU HAVE FAMILY IN THERE?

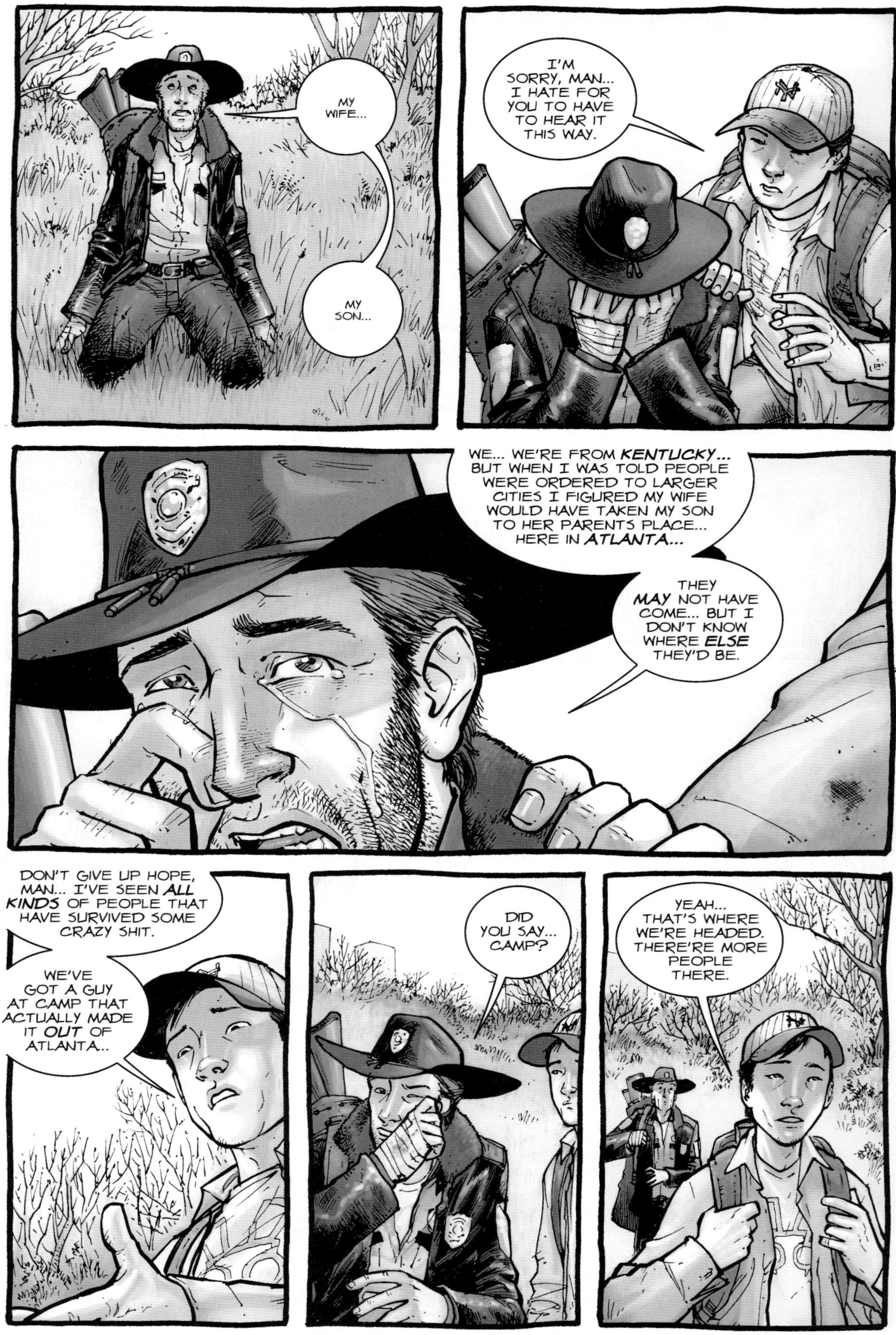
MY WIFE...
MY SON...
I'M SORRY, MAN... I HATE FOR YOU TO HAVE TO HEAR IT THIS WAY.
WE... WE'RE FROM KENTUCKY... BUT WHEN I WAS TOLD PEOPLE WERE ORDERED TO LARGER CITIES I FIGURED MY WIFE WOULD HAVE TAKEN MY SON TO HER PARENTS PLACE... HERE IN ATLANTA...
THEY MAY NOT HAVE COME... BUT I DON'T KNOW WHERE ELSE THEY'D BE.
DON'T GIVE UP HOPE, MAN... I'VE SEEN ALL KINDS OF PEOPLE THAT HAVE SURVIVED SOME CRAZY SHIT.
WE'VE GOT A GUY AT CAMP THAT ACTUALLY MADE IT OUT OF ATLANTA...
DID YOU SAY... CAMP?
YEAH... THAT'S WHERE WE'RE HEADED. THERE'RE MORE PEOPLE THERE.

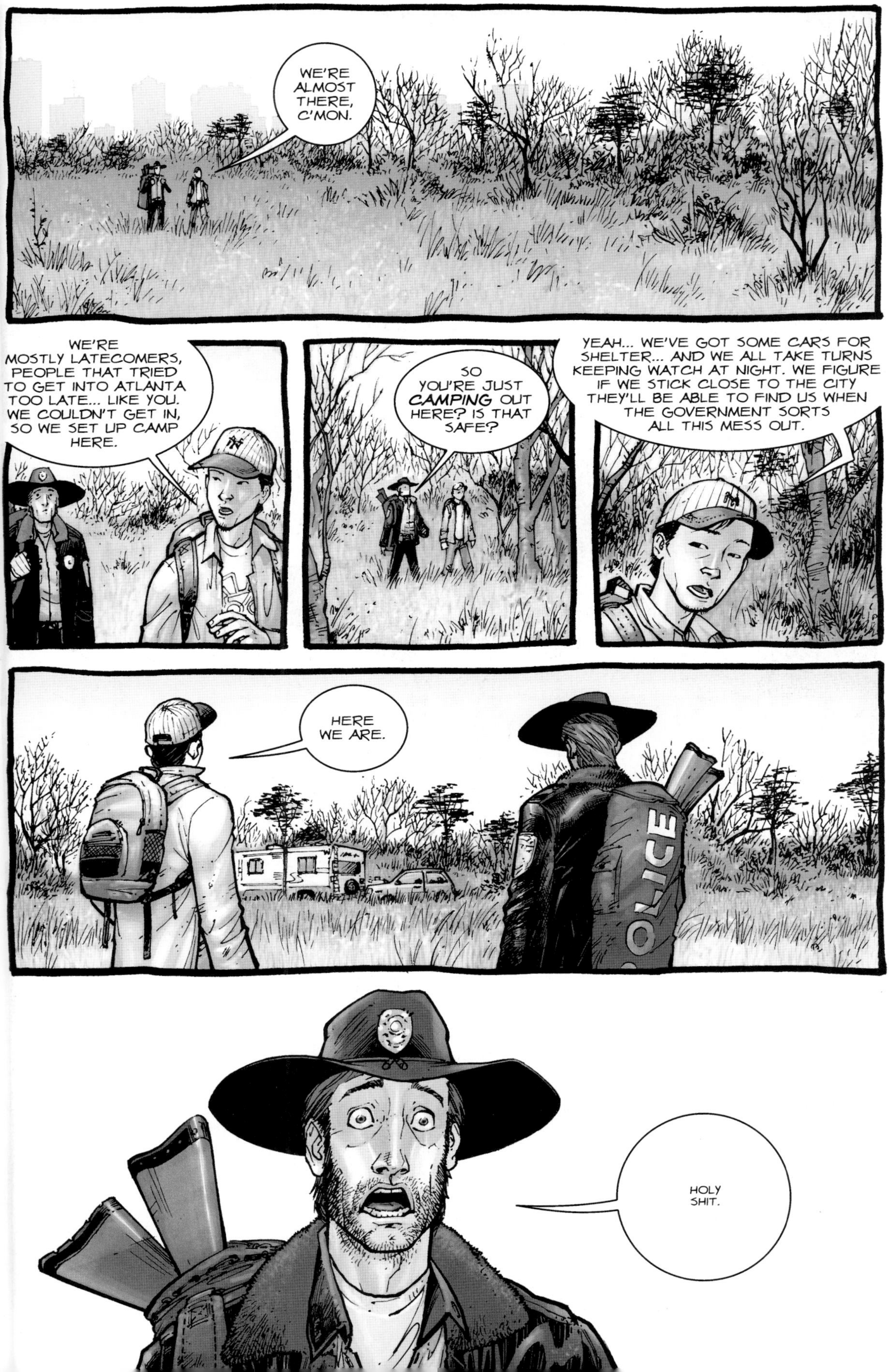
WE'RE ALMOST THERE, C'MON.
WE'RE MOSTLY LATECOMERS, PEOPLE THAT TRIED TO GET INTO ATLANTA TOO LATE... LIKE YOU. WE COULDN'T GET IN, SO WE SET UP CAMP HERE.
SO YOU'RE JUST CAMPING OUT HERE? IS THAT SAFE?
YEAH... WE'VE GOT SOME CARS FOR SHELTER... AND WE ALL TAKE TURNS KEEPING WATCH AT NIGHT. WE FIGURE IF WE STICK CLOSE TO THE CITY THEY'LL BE ABLE TO FIND US WHEN THE GOVERNMENT SORTS ALL THIS MESS OUT.
HERE WE ARE.
POLICE
HOLY SHIT.

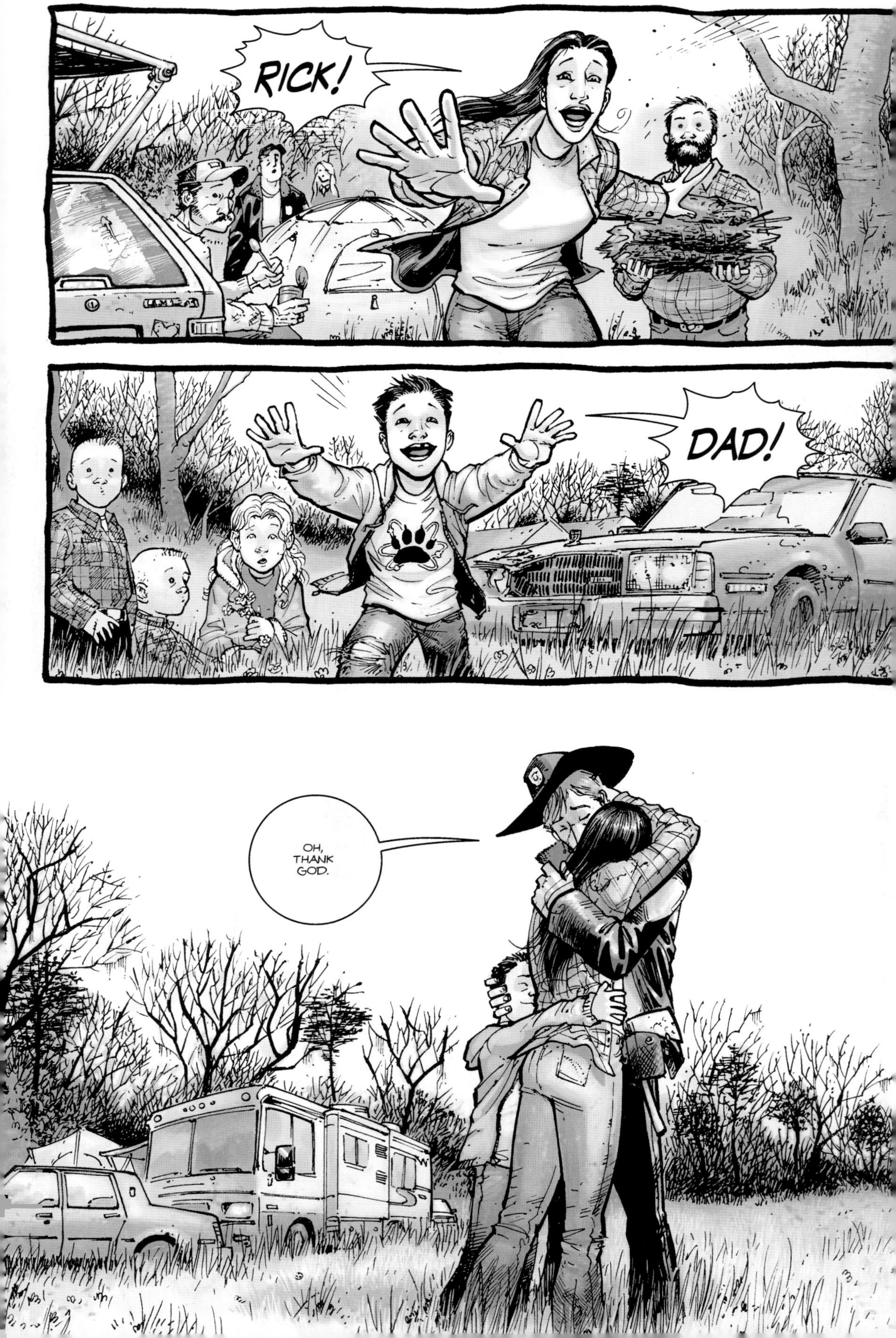
RICK!
DAD!
OH, THANK GOD.

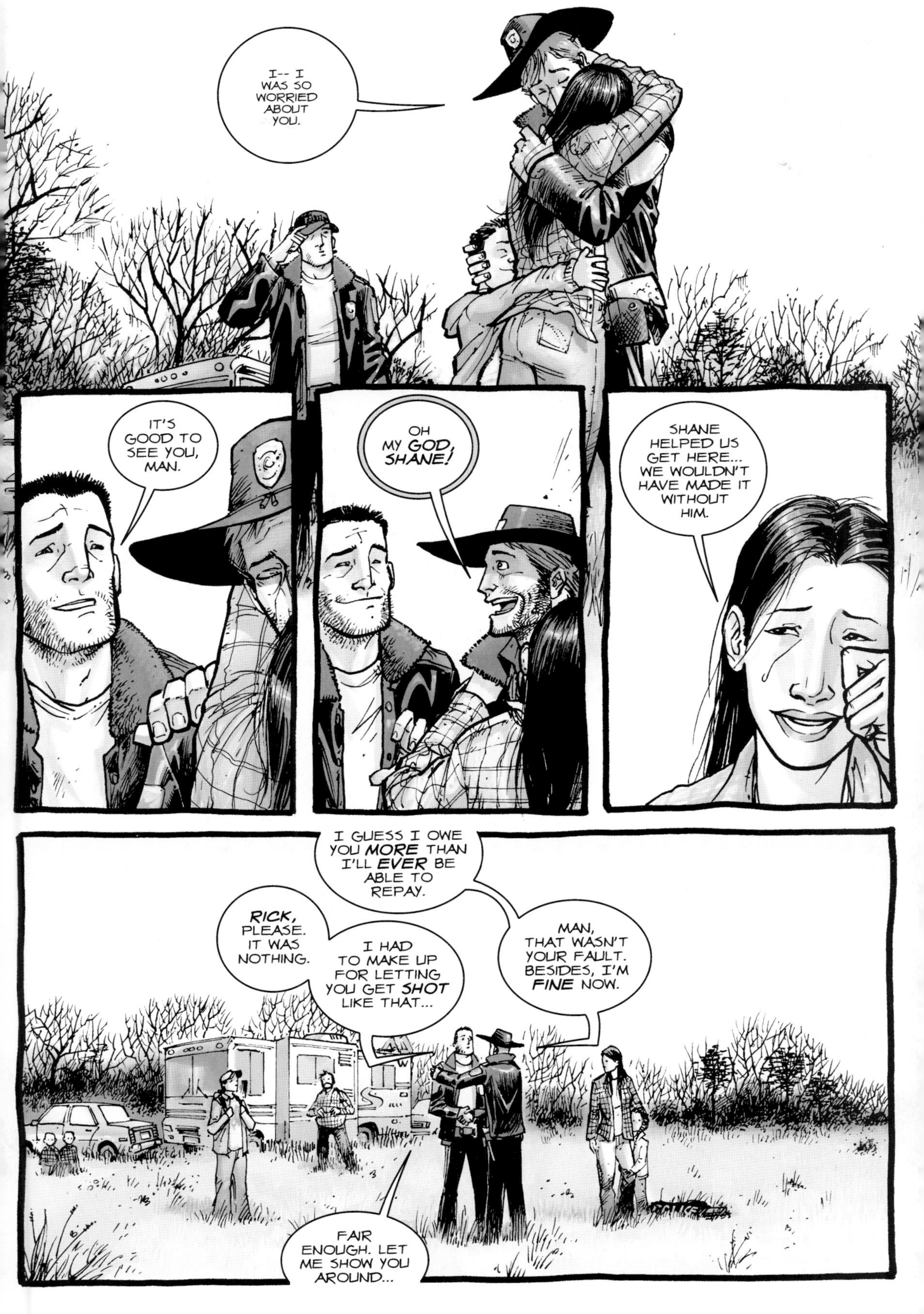
I-- I WAS SO WORRIED ABOUT YOU.
IT'S GOOD TO SEE YOU, MAN.
OH MY GOD, SHANE!
SHANE HELPED US GET HERE... WE WOULDN'T HAVE MADE IT WITHOUT HIM.
I GUESS I OWE YOU MORE THAN I'LL EVER BE ABLE TO REPAY.
RICK, PLEASE. IT WAS NOTHING.
I HAD TO MAKE UP FOR LETTING YOU GET SHOT LIKE THAT...
MAN, THAT WASN'T YOUR FAULT. BESIDES, I'M FINE NOW.
FAIR ENOUGH. LET ME SHOW YOU AROUND...

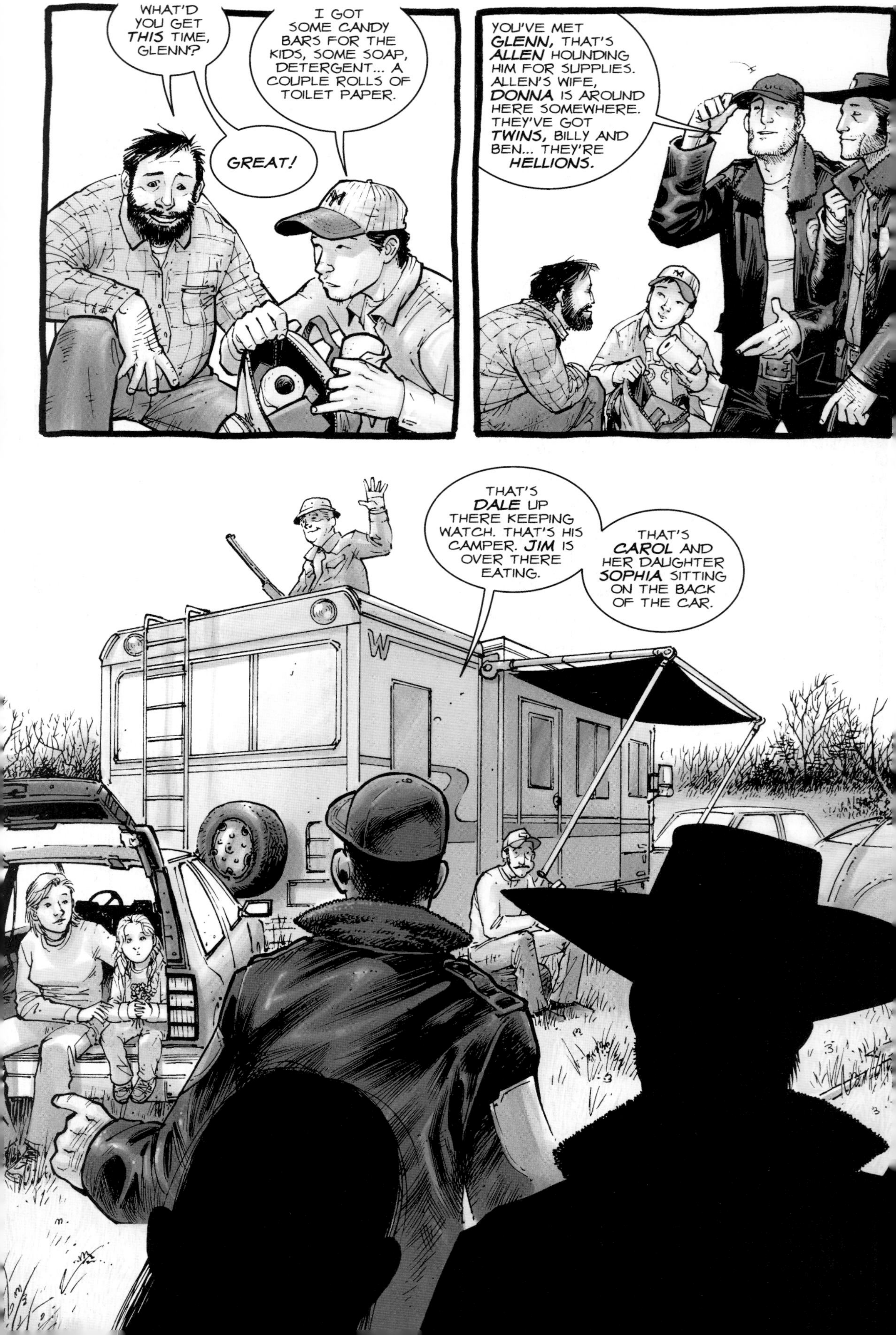

WHAT'D YOU GET THIS TIME, GLENN?
I GOT SOME CANDY BARS FOR THE KIDS, SOME SOAP, DETERGENT... A COUPLE ROLLS OF TOILET PAPER.
GREAT!
YOU'VE MET GLENN, THAT'S ALLEN HOUNDING HIM FOR SUPPLIES. ALLEN'S WIFE, DONNA IS AROUND HERE SOMEWHERE. THEY'VE GOT TWINS, BILLY AND BEN... THEY'RE HELLIONS.
THAT'S DALE UP THERE KEEPING WATCH. THAT'S HIS CAMPER. JIM IS OVER THERE EATING.
THAT'S CAROL AND HER DAUGHTER SOPHIA SITTING ON THE BACK OF THE CAR.

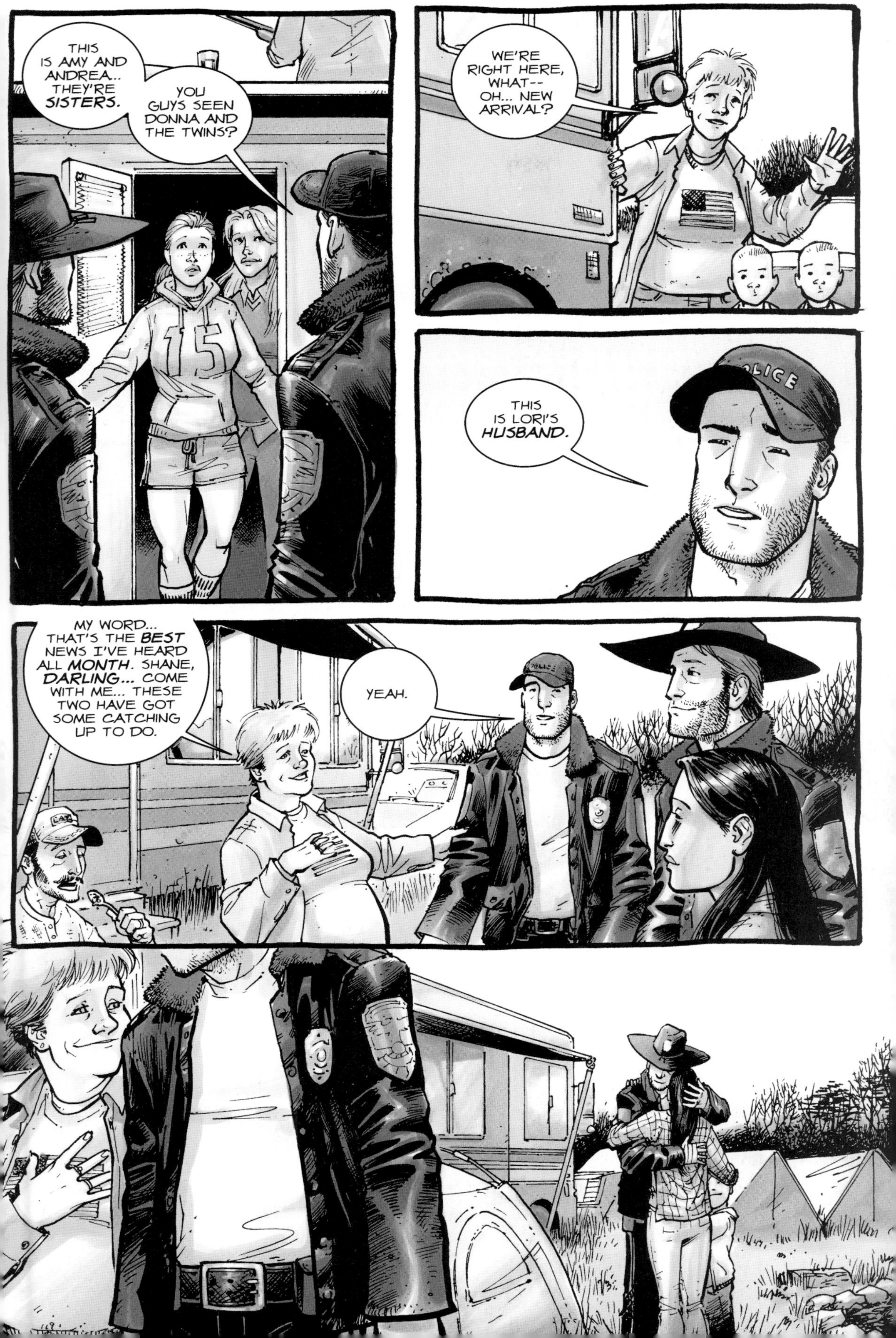
THIS IS AMY AND ANDREA.. THEY'RE SISTERS.
YOU GUYS SEEN DONNA AND THE TWINS?
WE'RE RIGHT HERE, WHAT-- OH... NEW ARRIVAL?
THIS IS LORI'S HUSBAND.
MY WORD... THAT'S THE BEST NEWS I'VE HEARD ALL MONTH. SHANE, DARLING... COME WITH ME... THESE TWO HAVE GOT SOME CATCHING UP TO DO.
YEAH.

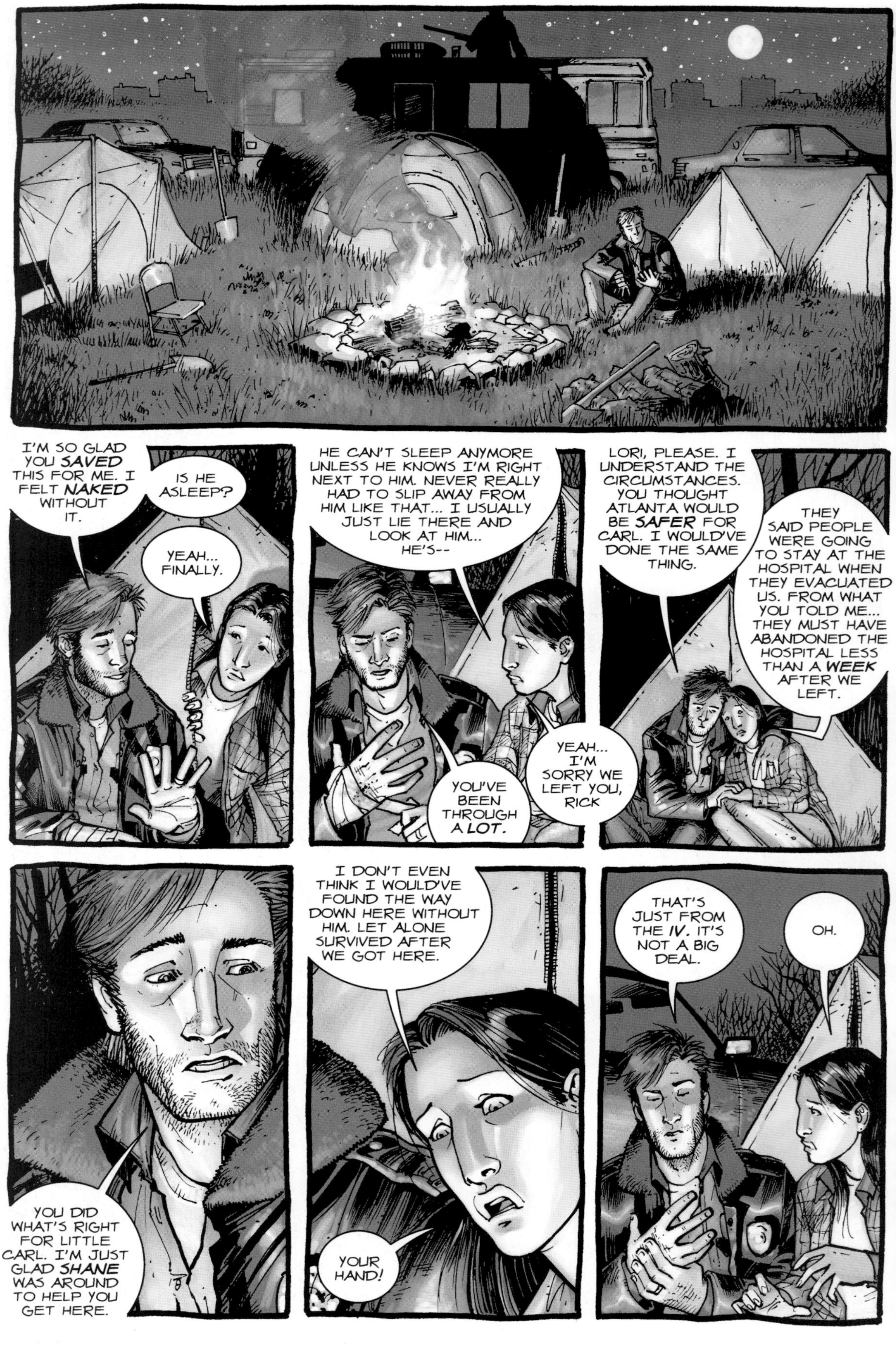
I'M SO GLAD YOU SAVED THIS FOR ME. I FELT NAKED WITHOUT IT.
IS HE ASLEEP?
YEAH... FINALLY.
HE CAN'T SLEEP ANYMORE UNLESS HE KNOWS I'M RIGHT NEXT TO HIM. NEVER REALLY HAD TO SLIP AWAY FROM HIM LIKE THAT... I USUALLY JUST LIE THERE AND LOOK AT HIM... HE'S--
YOU'VE BEEN THROUGH A LOT.
YEAH... I'M SORRY WE LEFT YOU, RICK
LORI, PLEASE. I UNDERSTAND THE CIRCUMSTANCES. YOU THOUGHT ATLANTA WOULD BE SAFER FOR CARL. I WOULD'VE DONE THE SAME THING.
THEY SAID PEOPLE WERE GOING TO STAY AT THE HOSPITAL WHEN THEY EVACUATED US. FROM WHAT YOU TOLD ME... THEY MUST HAVE ABANDONED THE HOSPITAL LESS THAN A WEEK AFTER WE LEFT.
YOU DID WHAT'S RIGHT FOR LITTLE CARL. I'M JUST GLAD SHANE WAS AROUND TO HELP YOU GET HERE.
I DON'T EVEN THINK I WOULD'VE FOUND THE WAY DOWN HERE WITHOUT HIM. LET ALONE SURVIVED AFTER WE GOT HERE.
YOUR HAND!
THAT'S JUST FROM THE IV. IT'S NOT A BIG DEAL.
OH.

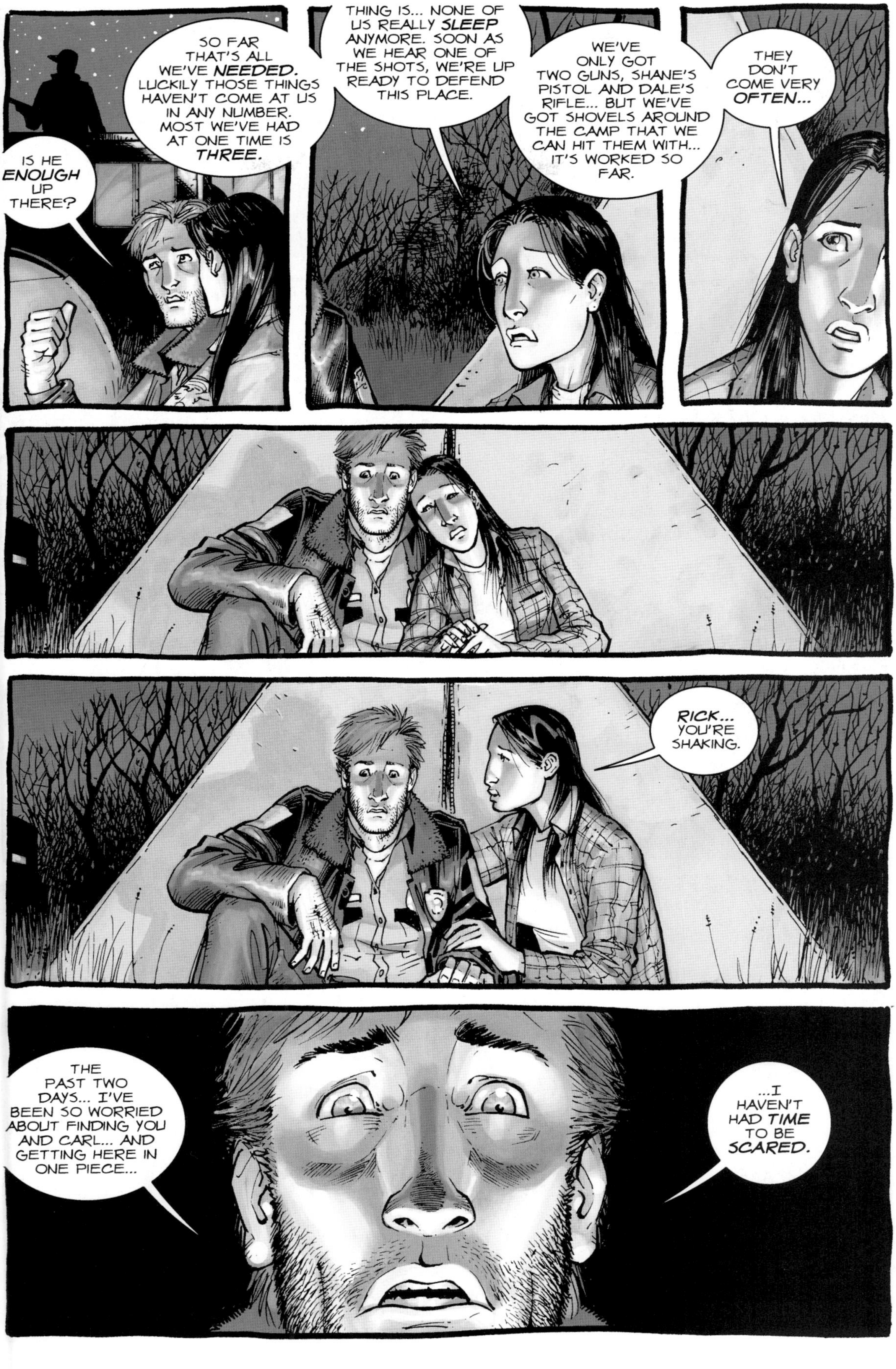
IS HE ENOUGH UP THERE?
SO FAR THAT'S ALL WE'VE NEEDED. LUCKILY THOSE THINGS HAVEN'T COME AT US IN ANY NUMBER. MOST WE'VE HAD AT ONE TIME IS THREE.
THING IS... NONE OF US REALLY SLEEP ANYMORE. SOON AS WE HEAR ONE OF THE SHOTS, WE'RE UP READY TO DEFEND THIS PLACE.
WE'VE ONLY GOT TWO GUNS, SHANE'S PISTOL AND DALE'S RIFLE... BUT WE'VE GOT SHOVELS AROUND THE CAMP THAT WE CAN HIT THEM WITH... IT'S WORKED SO FAR.
THEY DON'T COME VERY OFTEN...
RICK... YOU'RE SHAKING.
THE PAST TWO DAYS... I'VE BEEN SO WORRIED ABOUT FINDING YOU AND CARL... AND GETTING HERE IN ONE PIECE...
...I HAVEN'T HAD TIME TO BE SCARED.

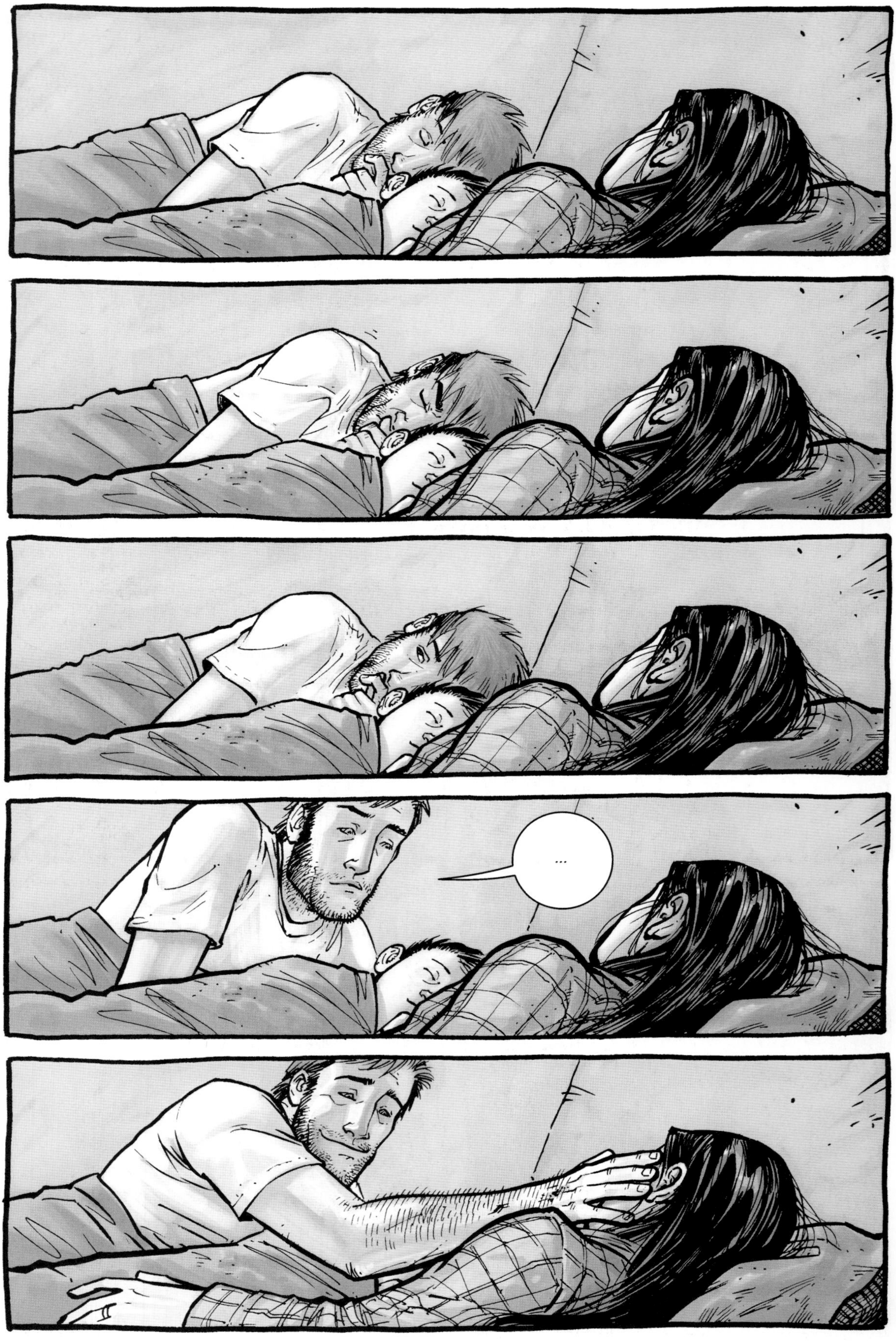
...

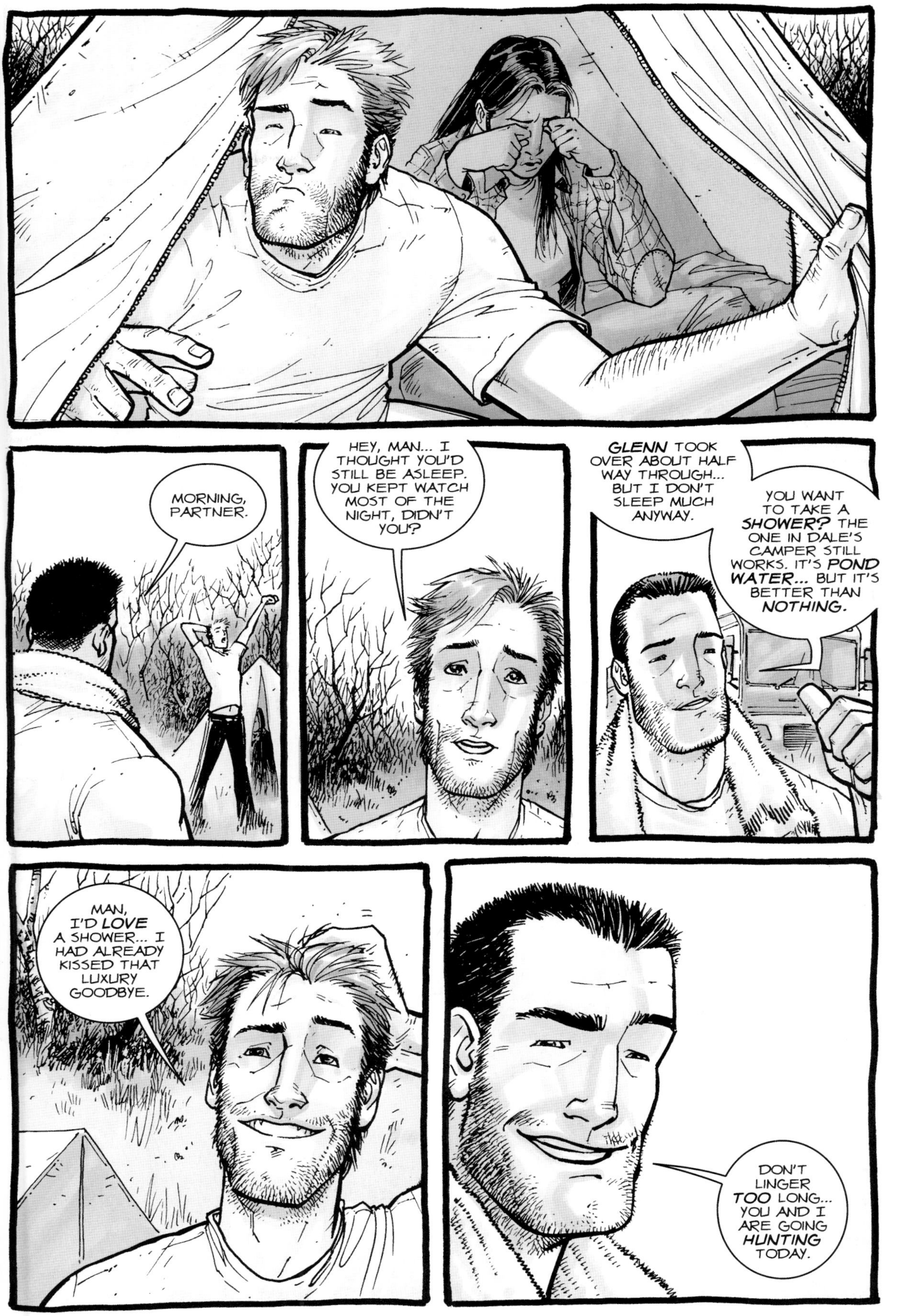

MORNING, PARTNER.
HEY, MAN... I THOUGHT YOU'D STILL BE ASLEEP. YOU KEPT WATCH MOST OF THE NIGHT, DIDN'T YOU?
GLENN TOOK OVER ABOUT HALF WAY THROUGH... BUT I DON'T SLEEP MUCH ANYWAY.
YOU WANT TO TAKE A SHOWER? THE ONE IN DALE'S CAMPER STILL WORKS. IT'S POND WATER... BUT IT'S BETTER THAN NOTHING.
MAN, I'D LOVE A SHOWER... I HAD ALREADY KISSED THAT LUXURY GOODBYE.
DON'T LINGER TOO LONG... YOU AND I ARE GOING HUNTING TODAY.

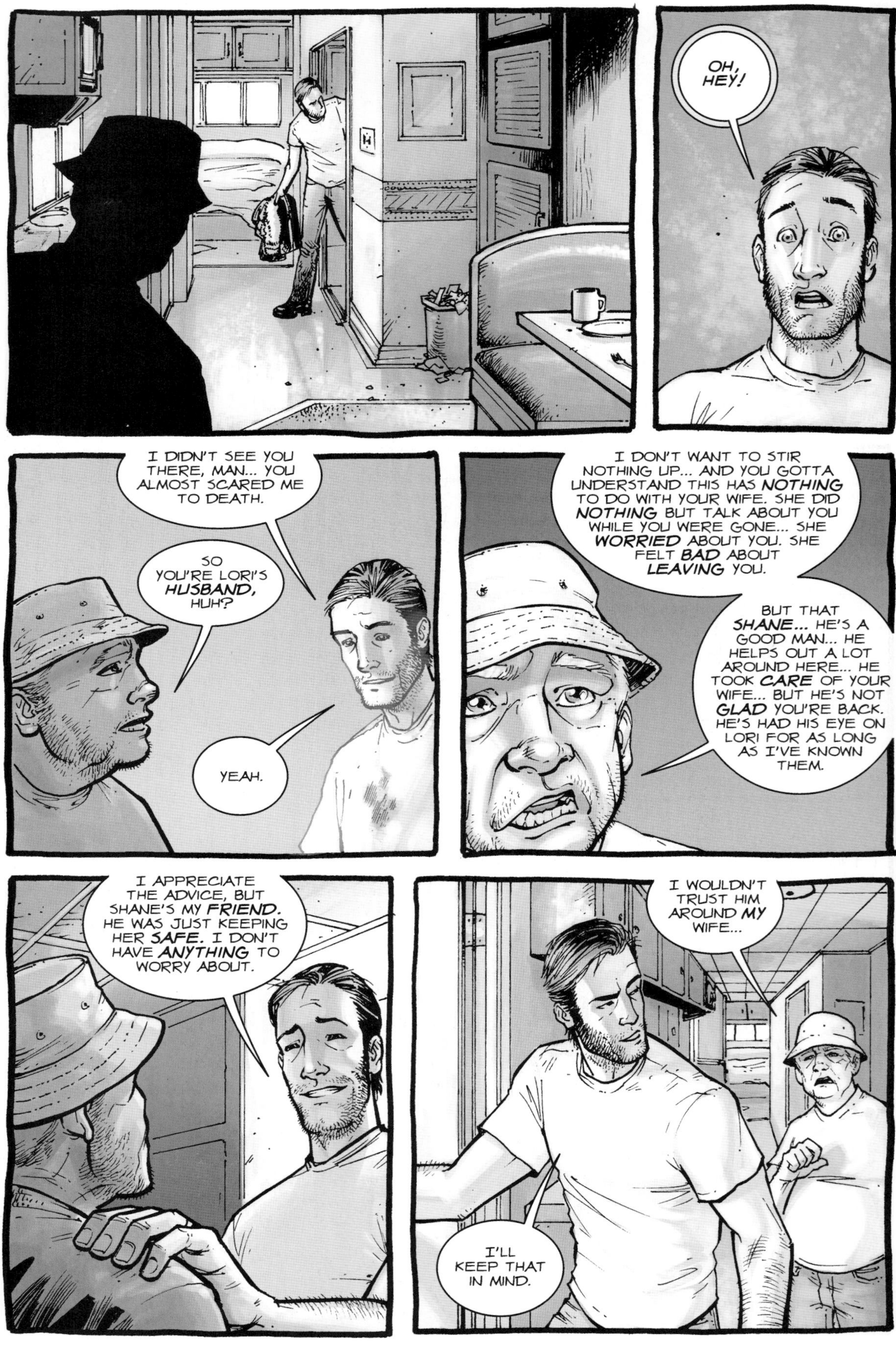
OH, HEY!
I DIDN'T SEE YOU THERE, MAN... YOU ALMOST SCARED ME TO DEATH.
SO YOU'RE LORI'S HUSBAND, HUH?
YEAH.
I DON'T WANT TO STIR NOTHING UP... AND YOU GOTTA UNDERSTAND THIS HAS NOTHING TO DO WITH YOUR WIFE. SHE DID NOTHING BUT TALK ABOUT YOU WHILE YOU WERE GONE... SHE WORRIED ABOUT YOU. SHE FELT BAD ABOUT LEAVING YOU.
BUT THAT SHANE... HE'S A GOOD MAN... HE HELPS OUT A LOT AROUND HERE... HE TOOK CARE OF YOUR WIFE... BUT HE'S NOT GLAD YOU'RE BACK. HE'S HAD HIS EYE ON LORI FOR AS LONG AS I'VE KNOWN THEM.
I APPRECIATE THE ADVICE, BUT SHANE'S MY FRIEND. HE WAS JUST KEEPING HER SAFE. I DON'T HAVE ANYTHING TO WORRY ABOUT.
I WOULDN'T TRUST HIM AROUND MY WIFE...
I'LL KEEP THAT IN MIND.

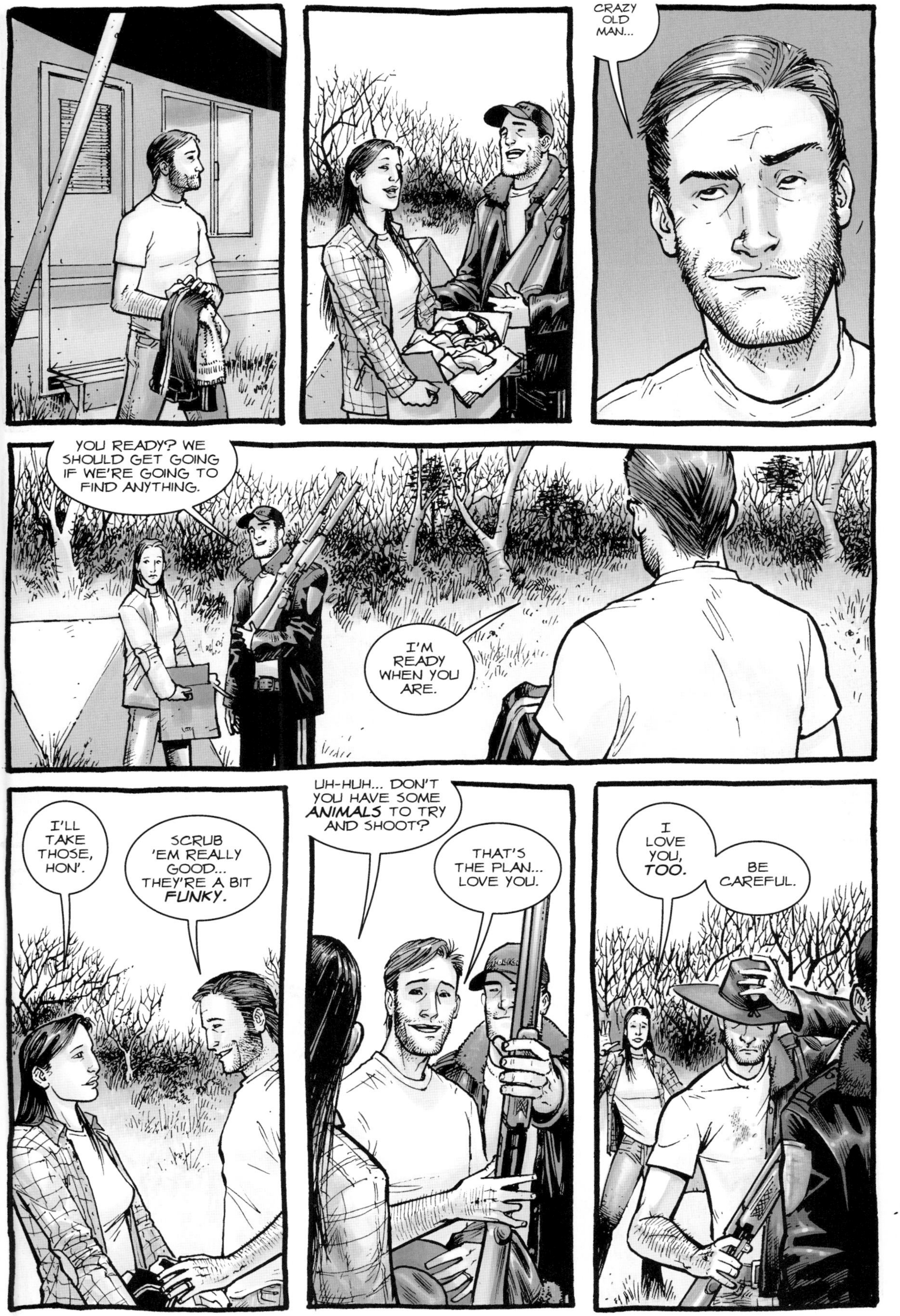
CRAZY OLD MAN...
YOU READY? WE SHOULD GET GOING IF WE'RE GOING TO FIND ANYTHING.
I'M READY WHEN YOU ARE.
I'LL TAKE THOSE, HON'.
SCRUB 'EM REALLY GOOD... THEY'RE A BIT FUNKY.
UH-HUH... DON'T YOU HAVE SOME ANIMALS TO TRY AND SHOOT?
THAT'S THE PLAN... LOVE YOU.
I LOVE YOU, TOO.
BE CAREFUL.

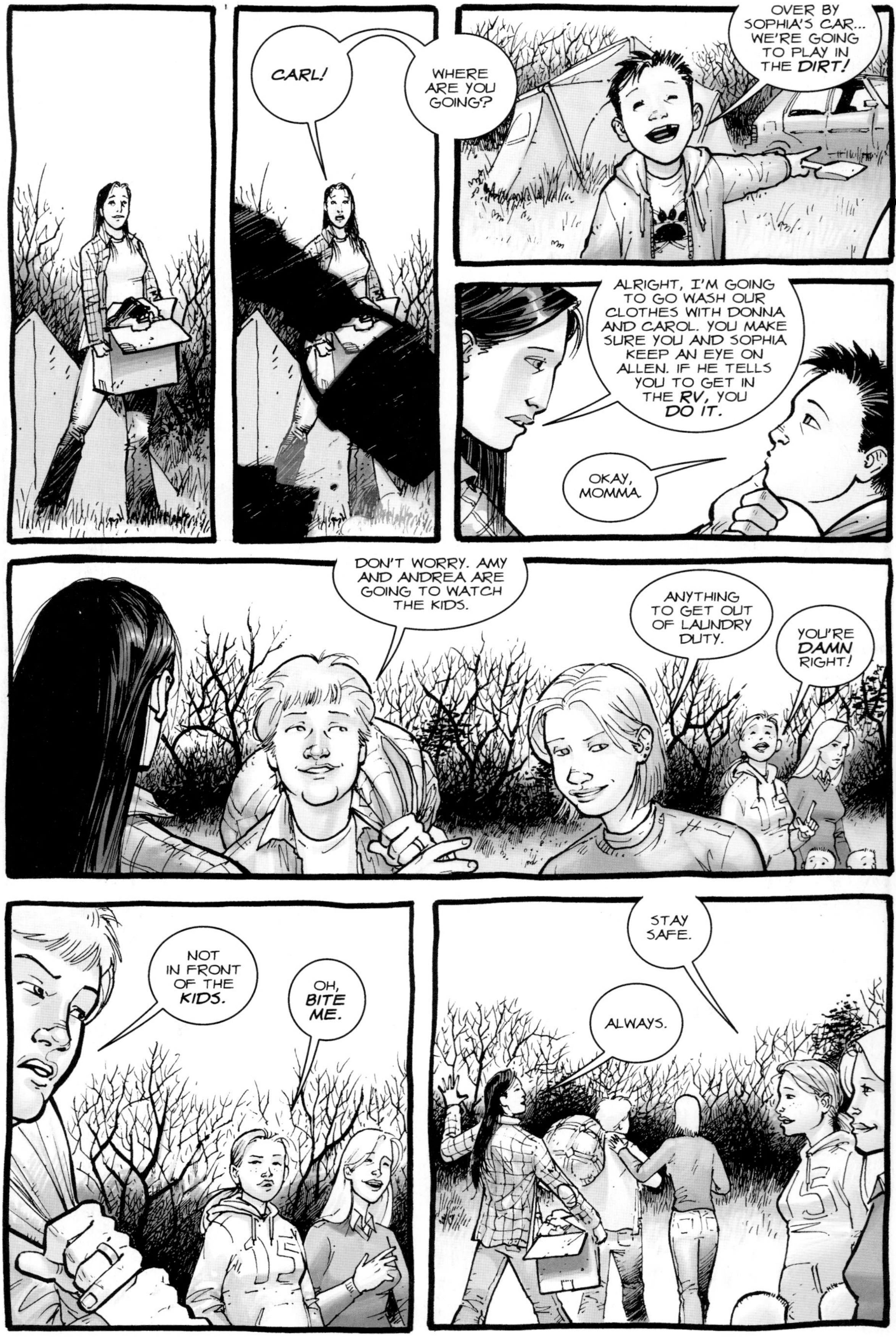
CARL!
WHERE ARE YOU GOING?
OVER BY SOPHIA'S CAR... WE'RE GOING TO PLAY IN THE DIRT!
ALRIGHT, I'M GOING TO GO WASH OUR CLOTHES WITH DONNA AND CAROL. YOU MAKE SURE YOU AND SOPHIA KEEP AN EYE ON ALLEN. IF HE TELLS YOU TO GET IN THE RV, YOU DO IT.
OKAY, MOMMA.
DON'T WORRY. AMY AND ANDREA ARE GOING TO WATCH THE KIDS.
ANYTHING TO GET OUT OF LAUNDRY DUTY.
YOU'RE DAMN RIGHT!
NOT IN FRONT OF THE KIDS.
OH, BITE ME.
STAY SAFE.
ALWAYS.

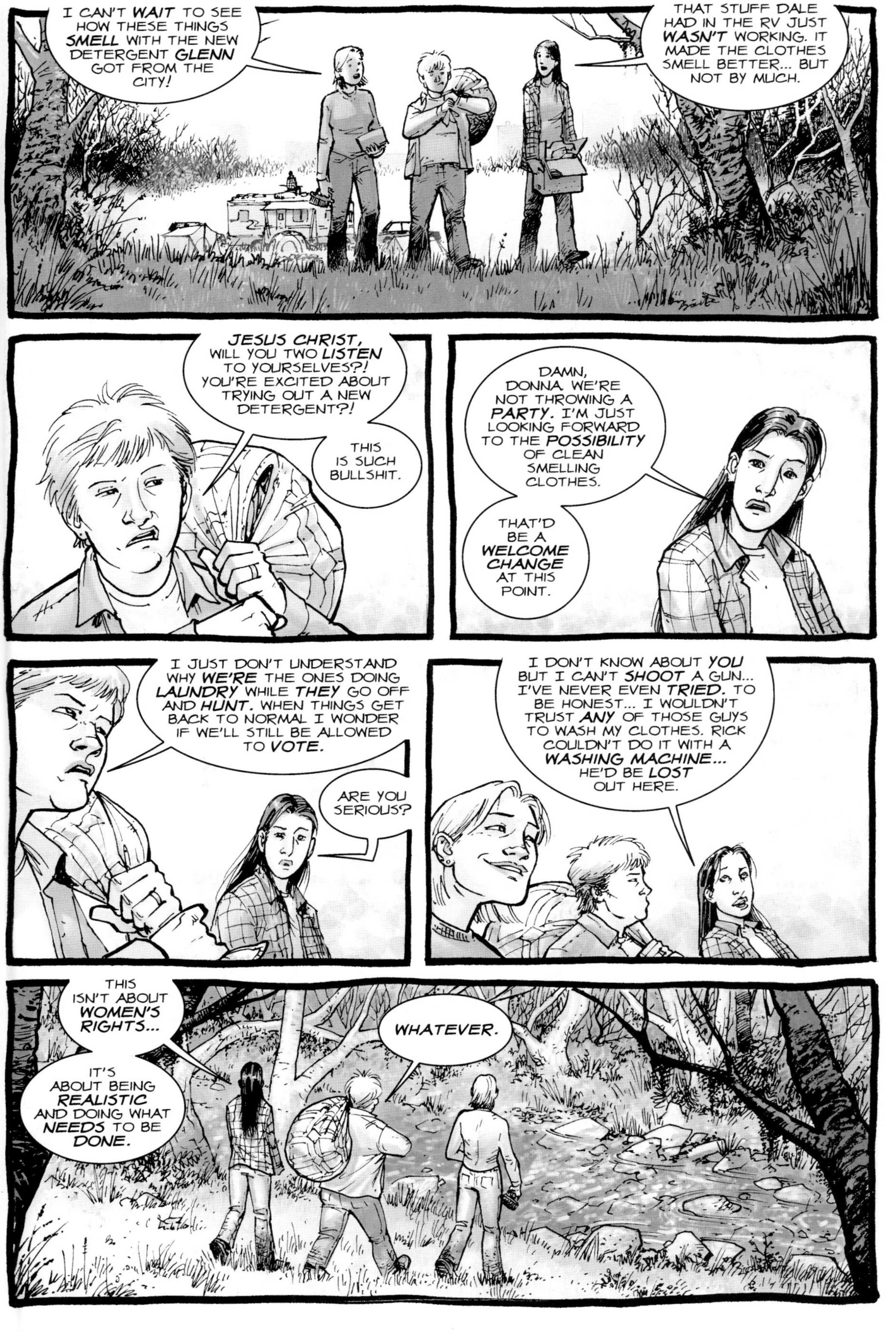

I CAN'T WAIT TO SEE HOW THESE THINGS SMELL WITH THE NEW DETERGENT GLENN GOT FROM THE CITY!
THAT STUFF DALE HAD IN THE RV JUST WASN'T WORKING. IT MADE THE CLOTHES SMELL BETTER... BUT NOT BY MUCH.
JESUS CHRIST, WILL YOU TWO LISTEN TO YOURSELVES?! YOU'RE EXCITED ABOUT TRYING OUT A NEW DETERGENT?!
THIS IS SUCH BULLSHIT.
DAMN, DONNA WE'RE NOT THROWING A PARTY. I'M JUST LOOKING FORWARD TO THE POSSIBILITY OF CLEAN SMELLING CLOTHES.
THAT'D BE A WELCOME CHANGE AT THIS POINT.
I JUST DON'T UNDERSTAND WHY WE'RE THE ONES DOING LAUNDRY WHILE THEY GO OFF AND HUNT. WHEN THINGS GET BACK TO NORMAL I WONDER IF WE'LL STILL BE ALLOWED TO VOTE.
ARE YOU SERIOUS?
I DON'T KNOW ABOUT YOU BUT I CAN'T SHOOT A GUN... I'VE NEVER EVEN TRIED. TO BE HONEST... I WOULDN'T TRUST ANY OF THOSE GUYS TO WASH MY CLOTHES. RICK COULDN'T DO IT WITH A WASHING MACHINE... HE'D BE LOST OUT HERE.
THIS ISN'T ABOUT WOMEN'S RIGHTS...
IT'S ABOUT BEING REALISTIC AND DOING WHAT NEEDS TO BE DONE.
WHATEVER.

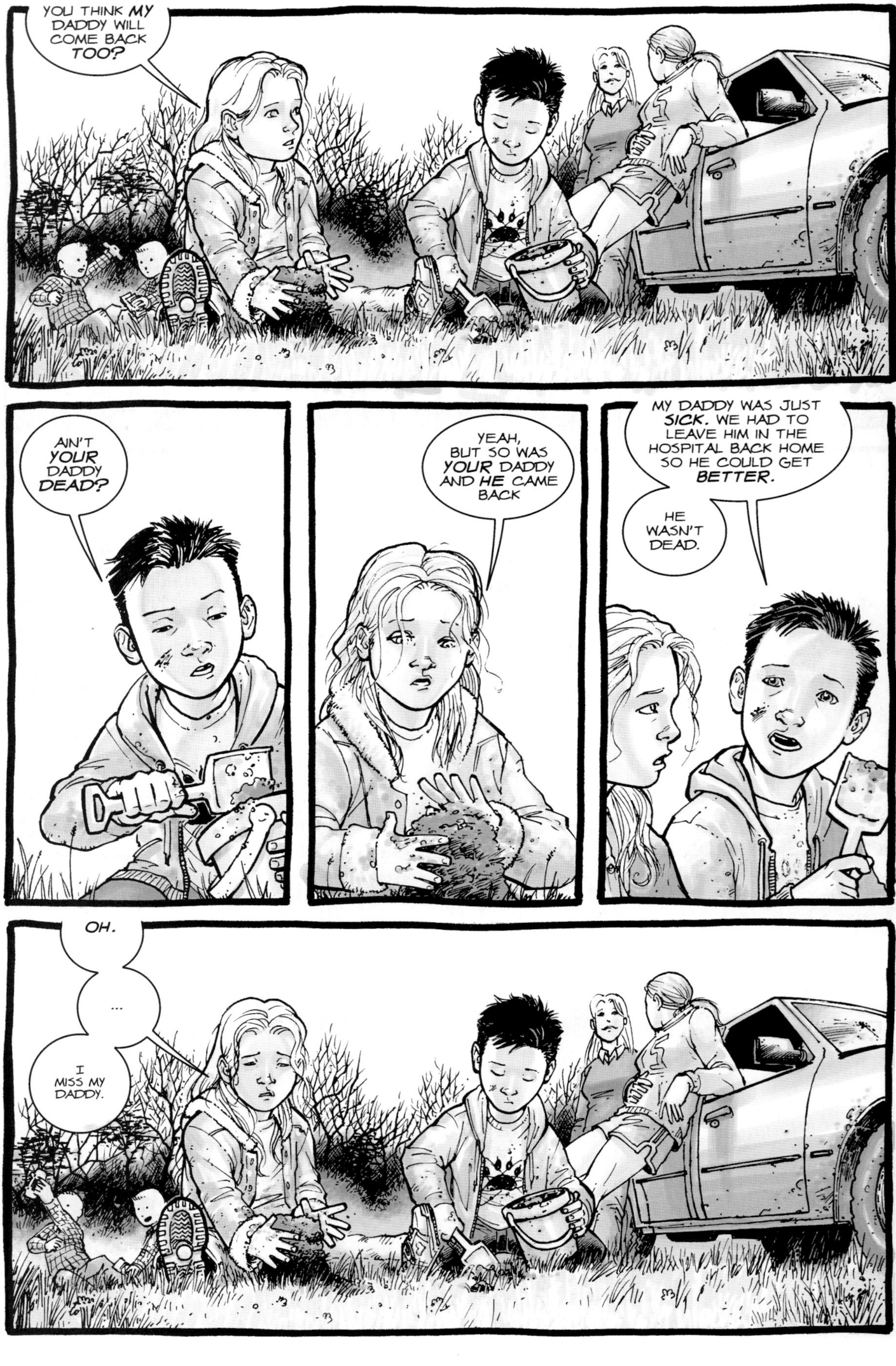
YOU THINK MY DADDY WILL COME BACK TOO?
AIN'T YOUR DADDY DEAD?
YEAH, BUT SO WAS YOUR DADDY AND HE CAME BACK
HE WASN'T DEAD.
MY DADDY WAS JUST SICK. WE HAD TO LEAVE HIM IN THE HOSPITAL BACK HOME SO HE COULD GET BETTER.
OH.
...
I MISS MY DADDY.

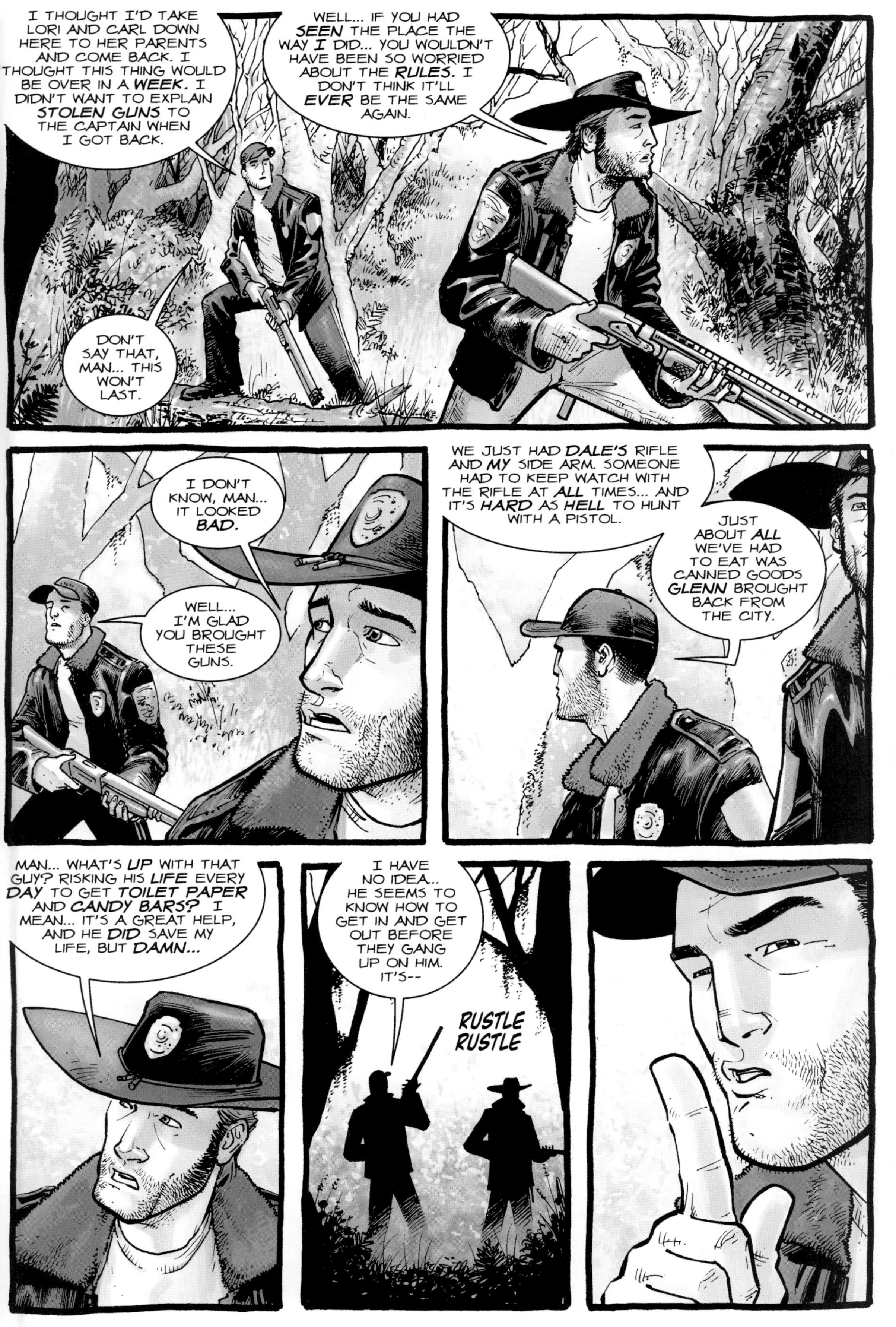
I THOUGHT I'D TAKE LORI AND CARL DOWN HERE TO HER PARENTS AND COME BACK. I THOUGHT THIS THING WOULD BE OVER IN A WEEK. I DIDN'T WANT TO EXPLAIN STOLEN GUNS TO THE CAPTAIN WHEN I GOT BACK.
WELL... IF YOU HAD SEEN THE PLACE THE WAY I DID... YOU WOULDN'T HAVE BEEN SO WORRIED ABOUT THE RULES. I DON'T THINK IT'LL EVER BE THE SAME AGAIN.
DON'T SAY THAT, MAN... THIS WON'T LAST.
I DON'T KNOW, MAN... IT LOOKED BAD.
WELL... I'M GLAD YOU BROUGHT THESE GUNS.
WE JUST HAD DALE'S RIFLE AND MY SIDE ARM. SOMEONE HAD TO KEEP WATCH WITH THE RIFLE AT ALL TIMES... AND IT'S HARD AS HELL TO HUNT WITH A PISTOL.
JUST ABOUT ALL WE'VE HAD TO EAT WAS CANNED GOODS GLENN BROUGHT BACK FROM THE CITY.
MAN... WHAT'S UP WITH THAT GUY? RISKING HIS LIFE EVERY DAY TO GET TOILET PAPER AND CANDY BARS? I MEAN... IT'S A GREAT HELP, AND HE DID SAVE MY LIFE, BUT DAMN...
I HAVE NO IDEA.. HE SEEMS TO KNOW HOW TO GET IN AND GET OUT BEFORE THEY GANG UP ON HIM. IT'S--
RUSTLE RUSTLE

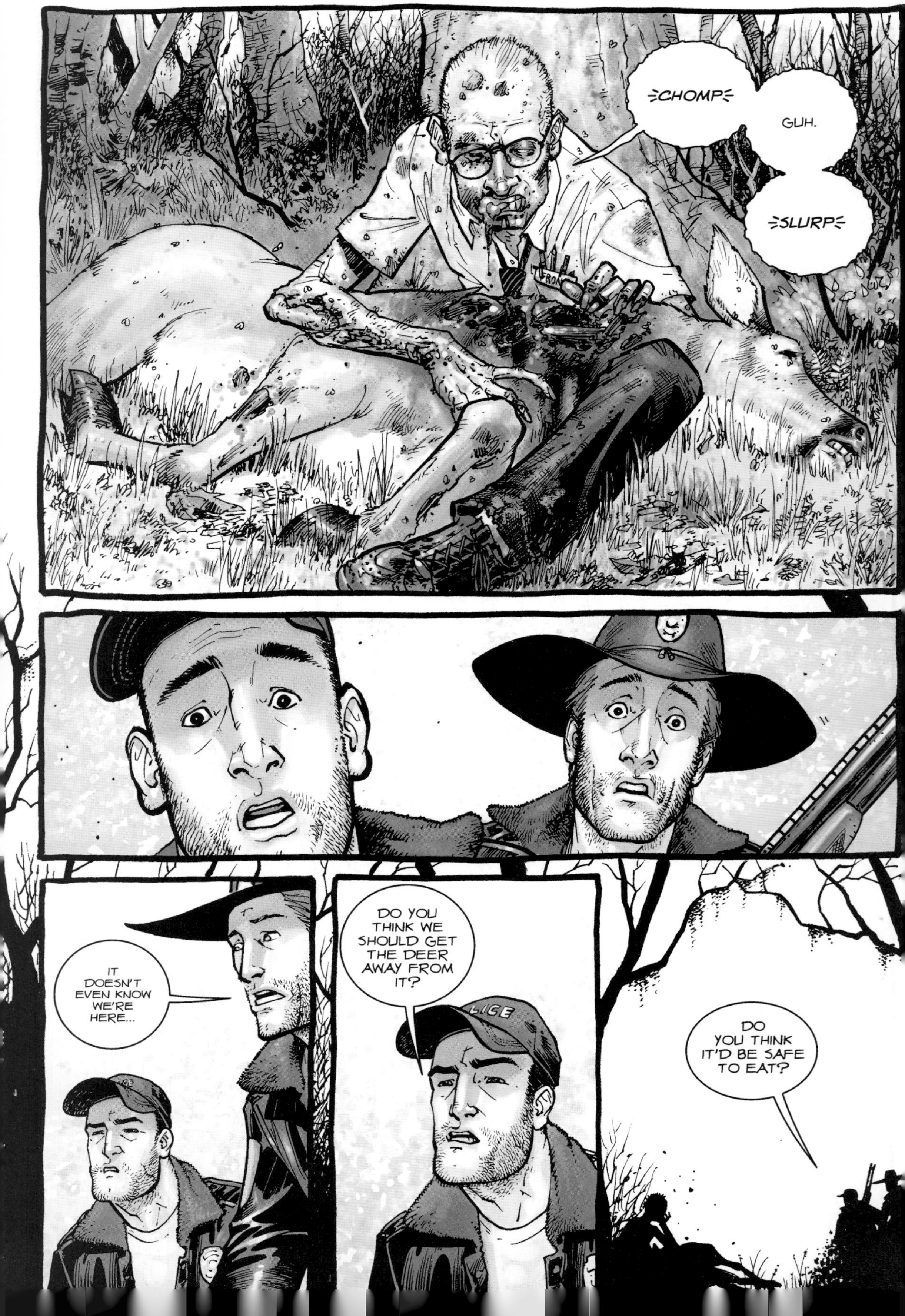

CHOMP
GUH.
SLURP
IT DOESN'T EVEN KNOW WE'RE HERE...
DO YOU THINK WE SHOULD GET THE DEER AWAY FROM IT?
DO YOU THINK IT'D BE SAFE TO EAT?

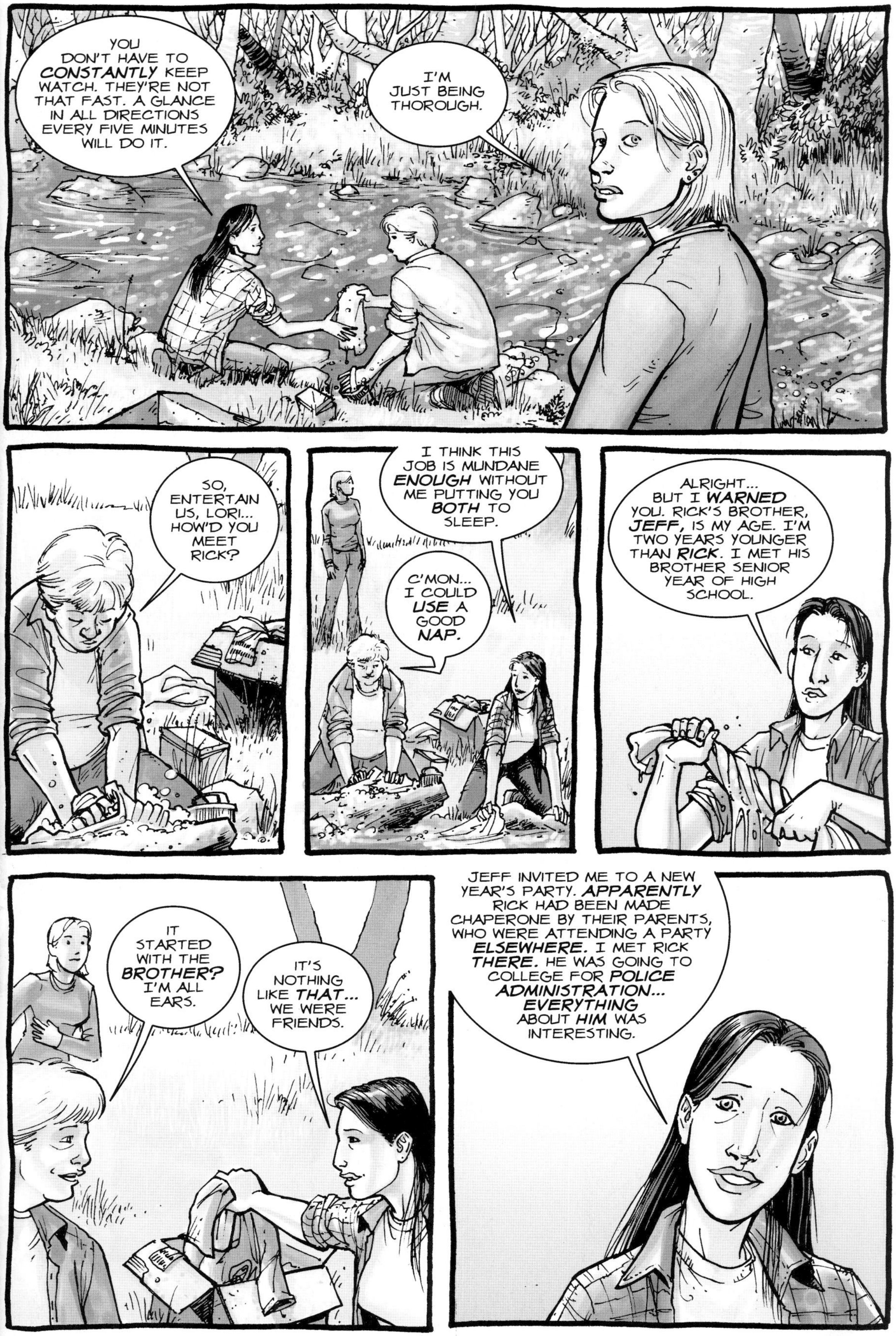
YOU DON'T HAVE TO CONSTANTLY KEEP WATCH. THEY'RE NOT THAT FAST. A GLANCE IN ALL DIRECTIONS EVERY FIVE MINUTES WILL DO IT.
I'M JUST BEING THOROUGH.
SO, ENTERTAIN US, LORI... HOW'D YOU MEET RICK?
I THINK THIS JOB IS MUNDANE ENOUGH WITHOUT ME PUTTING YOU BOTH TO SLEEP.
C'MON... I COULD USE A GOOD NAP.
ALRIGHT... BUT I WARNED YOU. RICK'S BROTHER, JEFF, IS MY AGE. I'M TWO YEARS YOUNGER THAN RICK. I MET HIS BROTHER SENIOR YEAR OF HIGH SCHOOL.
IT STARTED WITH THE BROTHER? I'M ALL EARS.
IT'S NOTHING LIKE THAT... WE WERE FRIENDS.
JEFF INVITED ME TO A NEW YEAR'S PARTY. APPARENTLY RICK HAD BEEN MADE CHAPERONE BY THEIR PARENTS, WHO WERE ATTENDING A PARTY ELSEWHERE. I MET RICK THERE. HE WAS GOING TO COLLEGE FOR POLICE ADMINISTRATION... EVERYTHING ABOUT HIM WAS INTERESTING.

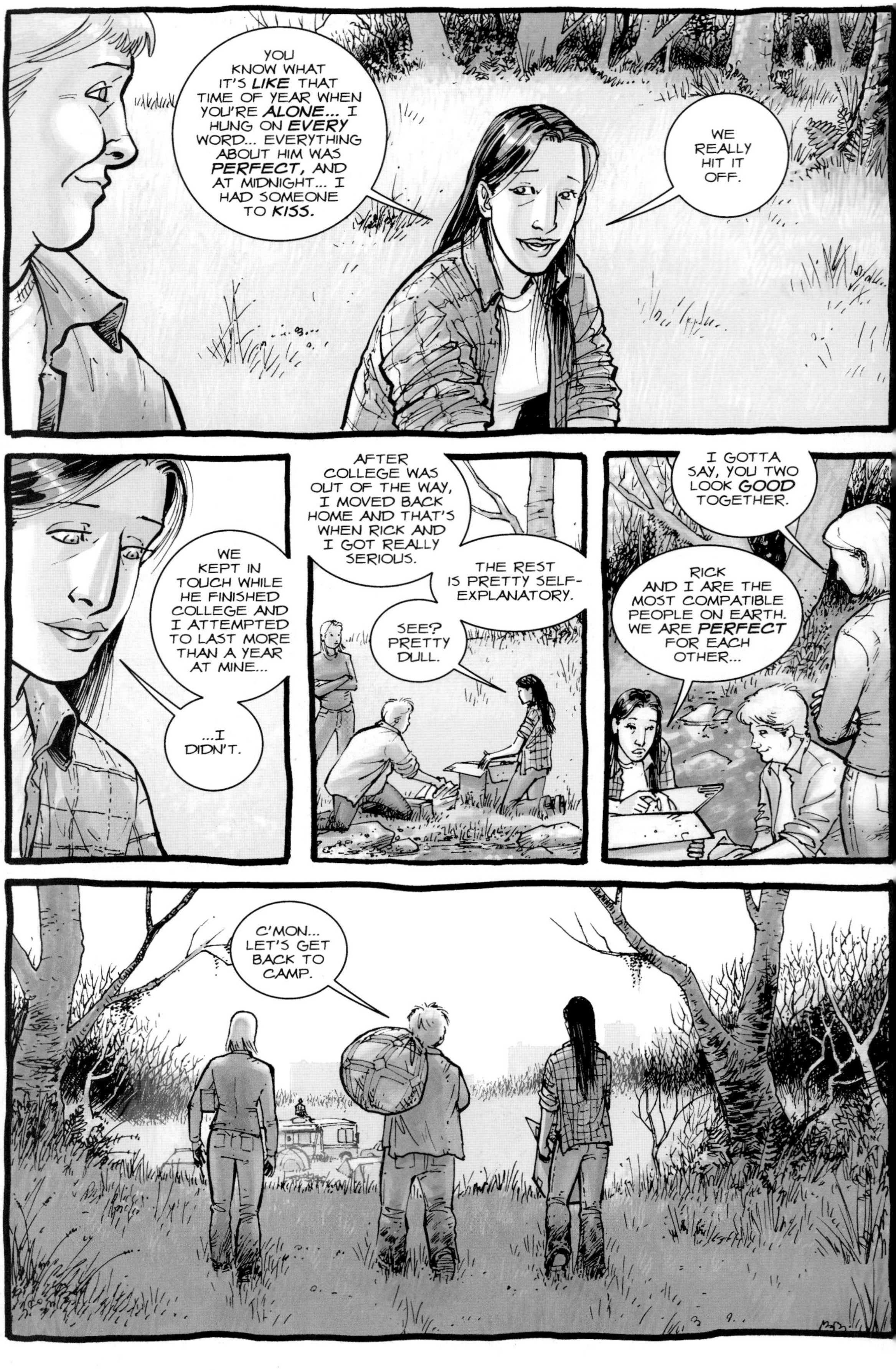
YOU KNOW WHAT IT'S LIKE THAT TIME OF YEAR WHEN YOU'RE ALONE... I HUNG ON EVERY WORD... EVERYTHING ABOUT HIM WAS PERFECT, AND AT MIDNIGHT... I HAD SOMEONE TO KISS.
WE REALLY HIT IT OFF.
WE KEPT IN TOUCH WHILE HE FINISHED COLLEGE AND I ATTEMPTED TO LAST MORE THAN A YEAR AT MINE...
...I DIDN'T.
AFTER COLLEGE WAS OUT OF THE WAY, I MOVED BACK HOME AND THAT'S WHEN RICK AND I GOT REALLY SERIOUS.
THE REST IS PRETTY SELF-EXPLANATORY.
SEE? PRETTY DULL.
I GOTTA SAY, YOU TWO LOOK GOOD TOGETHER.
RICK AND I ARE THE MOST COMPATIBLE PEOPLE ON EARTH. WE ARE PERFECT FOR EACH OTHER...
C'MON... LET'S GET BACK TO CAMP.

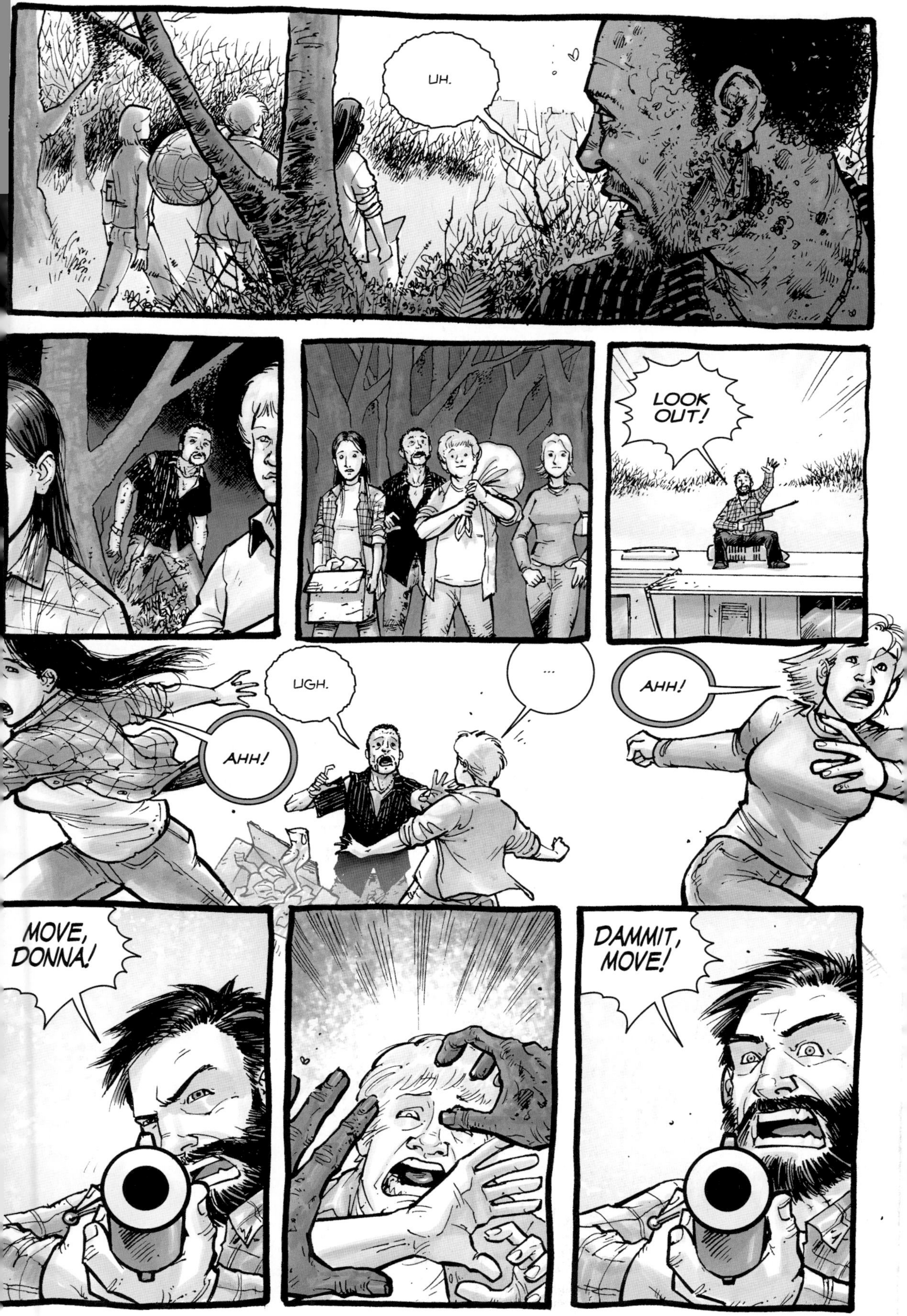
UH.
LOOK OUT!
AHH!
UGH.
...
AHH!
MOVE, DONNA!
DAMMIT, MOVE!

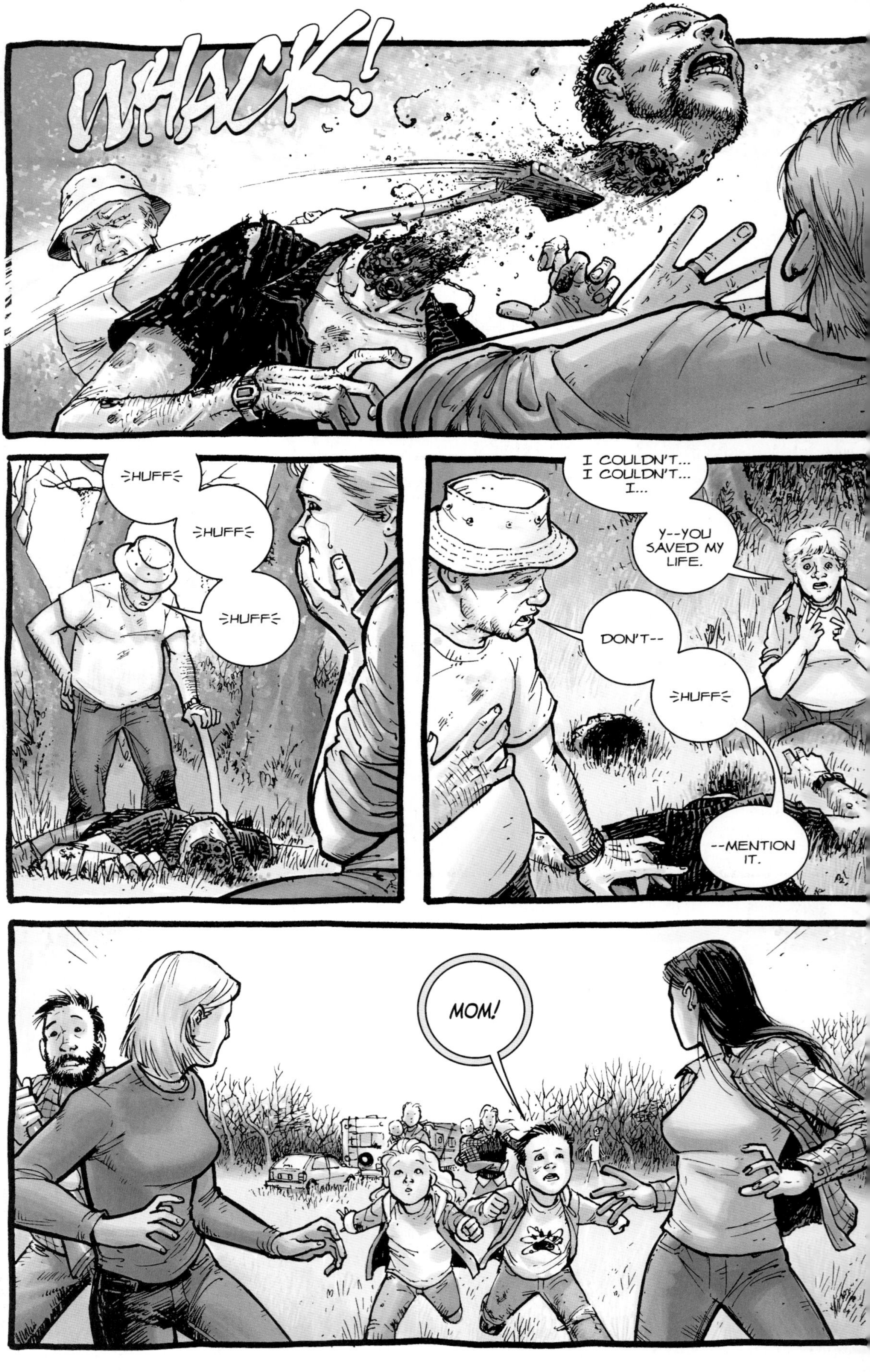
WHACK!
HUFF
HUFF
HUFF
I COULDN'T... I COULDN'T... I...
Y--YOU SAVED MY LIFE.
DON'T--
HUFF
--MENTION IT.
MOM!

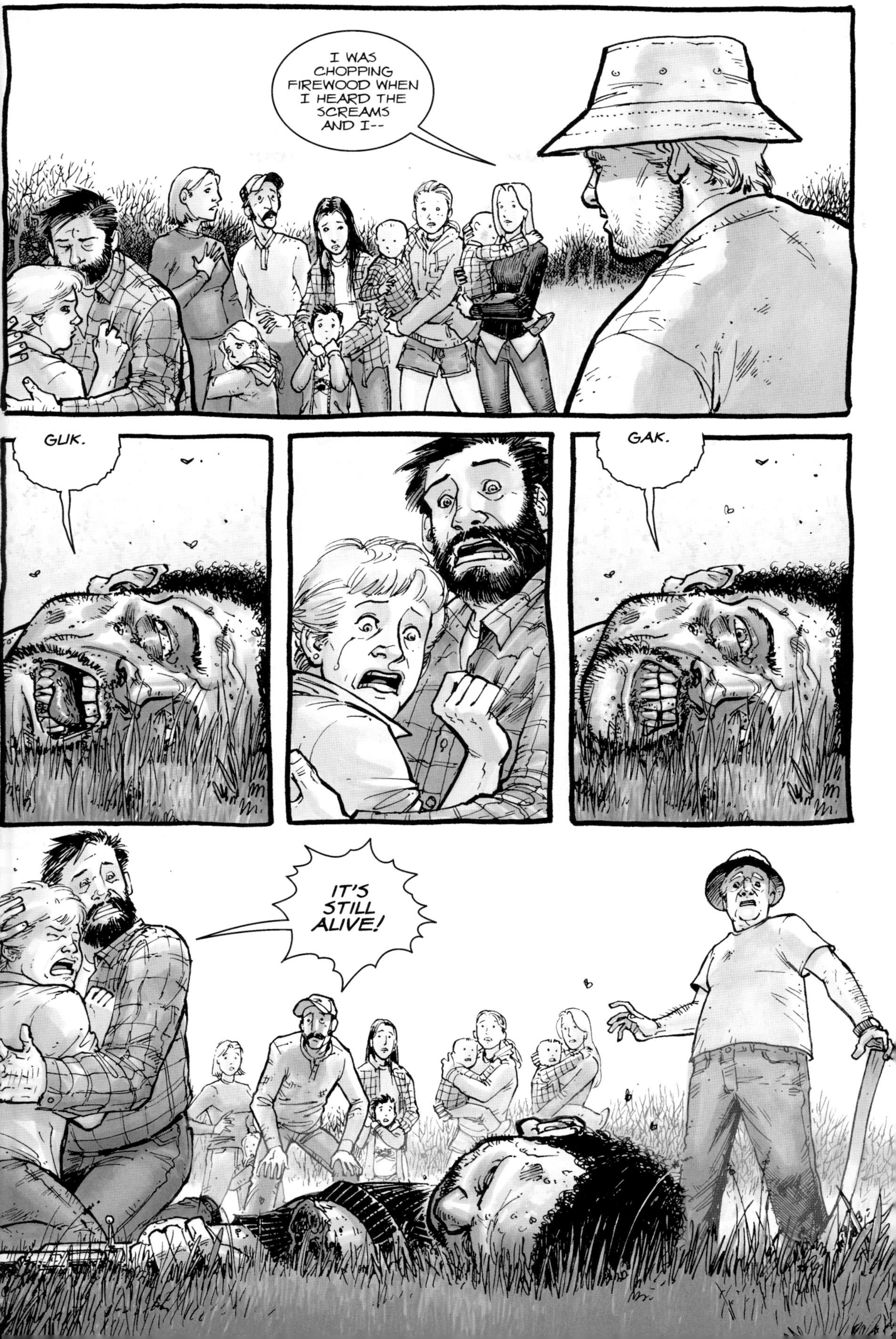
I WAS CHOPPING FIREWOOD WHEN I HEARD THE SCREAMS AND I--
GUK.
GAK.
IT'S STILL ALIVE!

I DON'T EVEN WANT TO *THINK* ABOUT THE DISEASES THESE THINGS MUST CARRY. *I'M* NOT EATING ANY OF THAT DEER... AND NEITHER IS MY *FAMILY.*

YEAH... I THINK YOU'RE RIGHT.

YOU EVER SEEN ONE *UP CLOSE* LIKE THIS?

COUPLE TIMES... BUT NOT FOR THIS LONG WITHOUT IT ATTACKING ME.

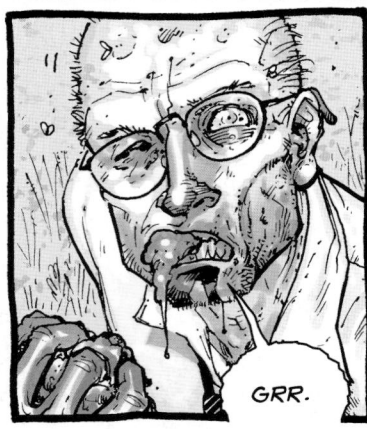

GRR.

THAT'S NO GOOD!

RRGH!

RLAM!

I WASN'T GOING TO WAIT FOR HIM TO COME AFTER US.

THE CAMP!

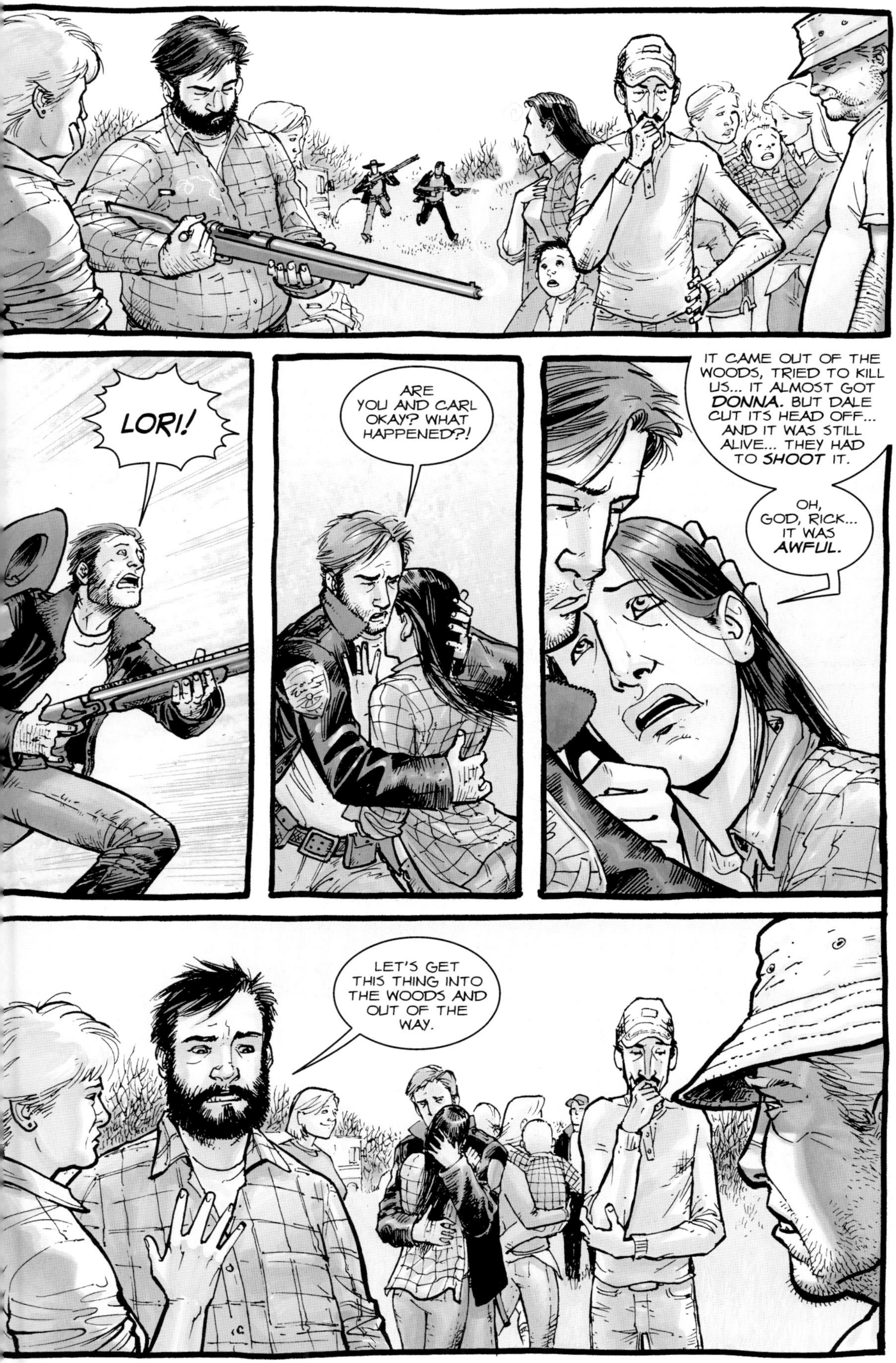
LORI!
ARE YOU AND CARL OKAY? WHAT HAPPENED?!
IT CAME OUT OF THE WOODS, TRIED TO KILL US... IT ALMOST GOT DONNA. BUT DALE CUT ITS HEAD OFF... AND IT WAS STILL ALIVE... THEY HAD TO SHOOT IT.
OH, GOD, RICK... IT WAS AWFUL.
LET'S GET THIS THING INTO THE WOODS AND OUT OF THE WAY.

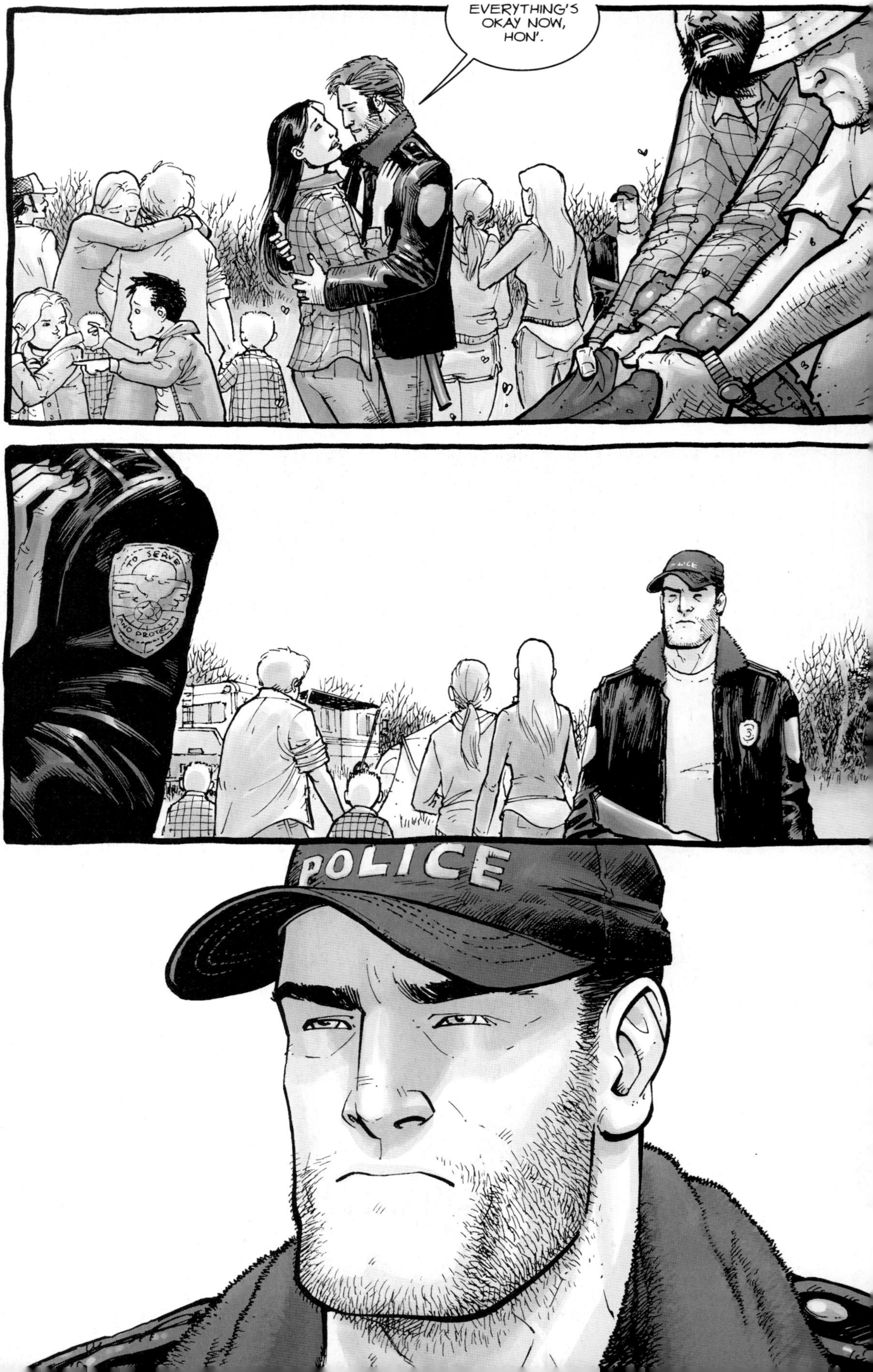
EVERYTHING'S OKAY NOW, HON'.
TO SERVE AND PROTECT
POLICE

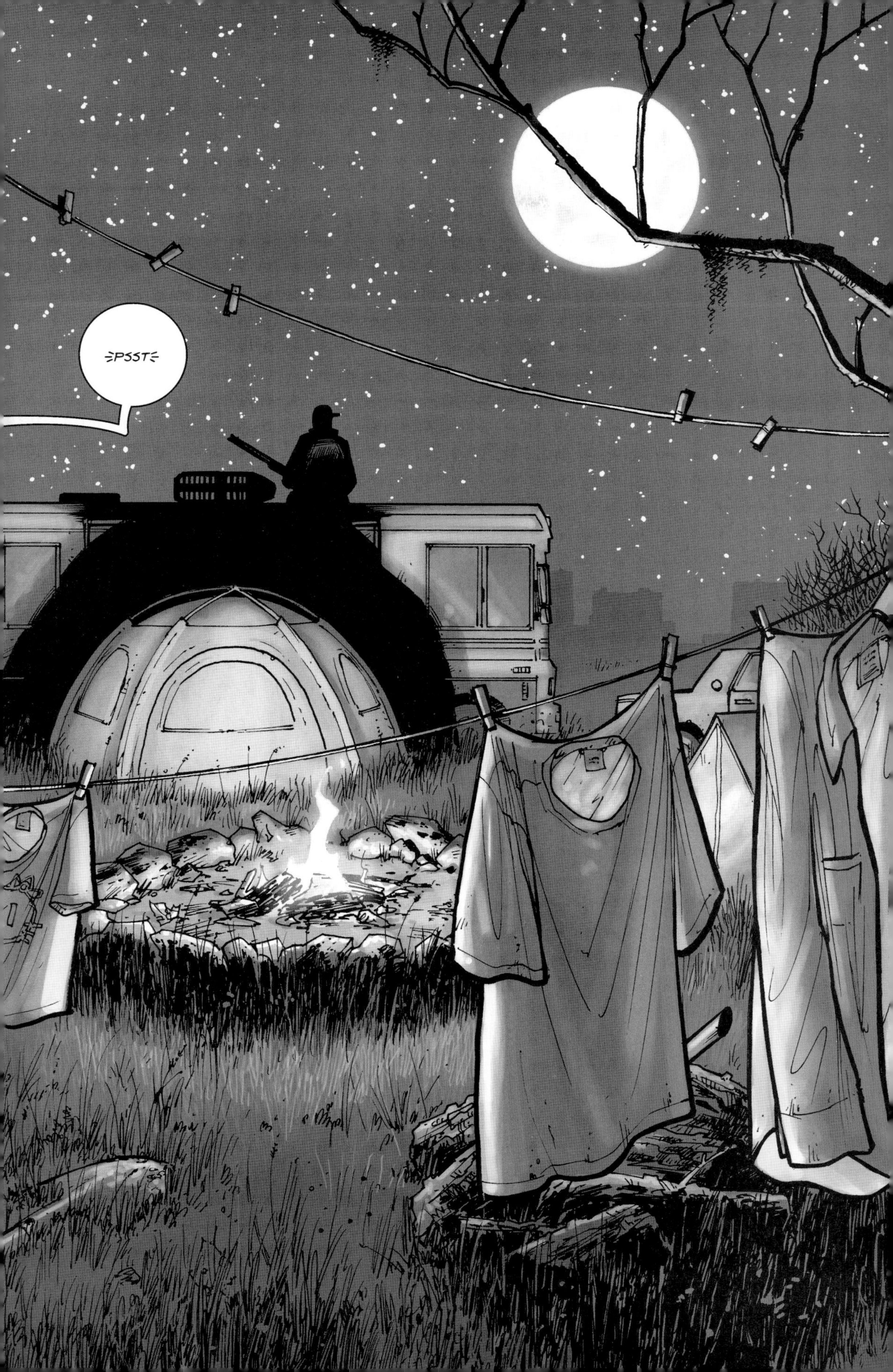
PSST

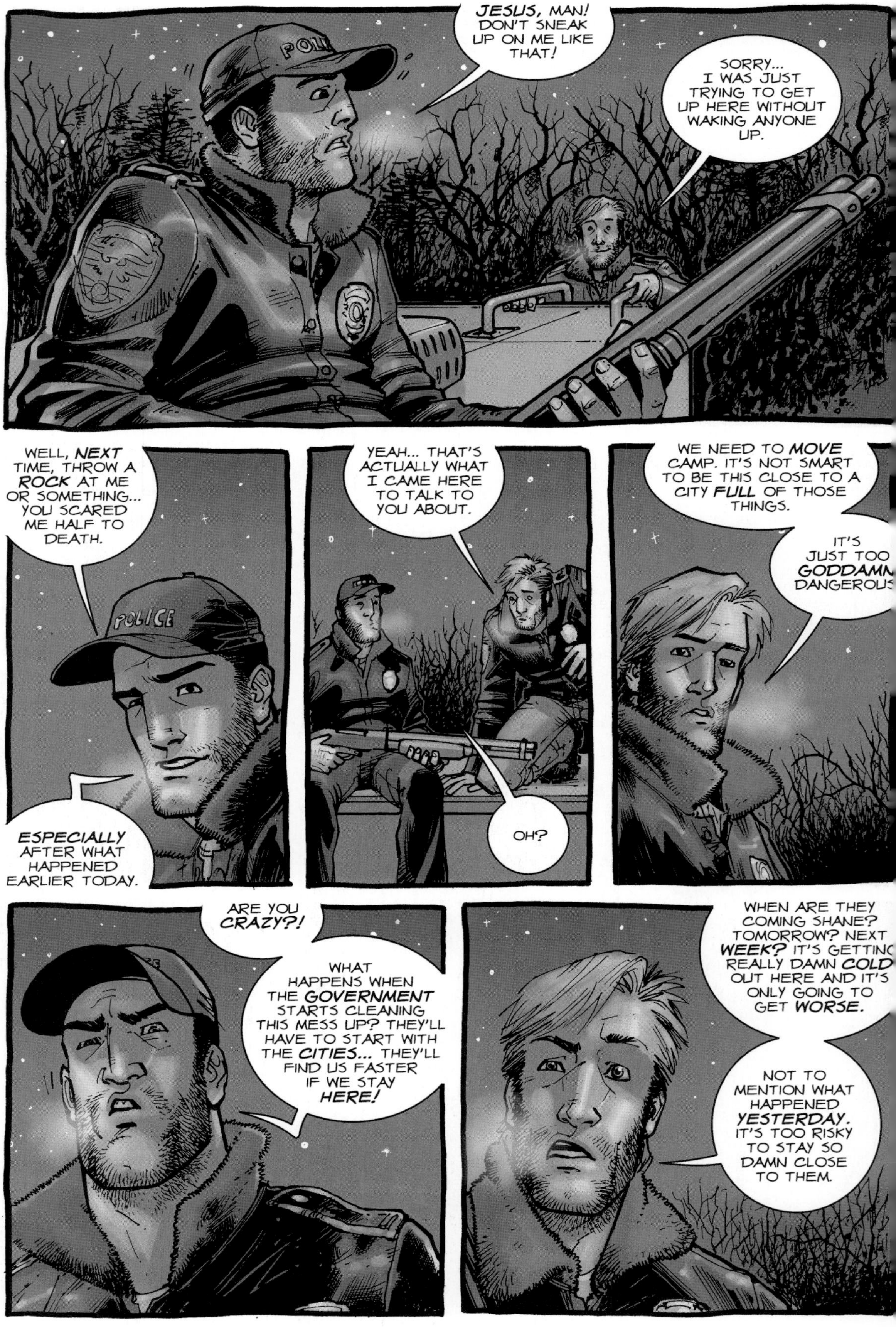
JESUS, MAN! DON'T SNEAK UP ON ME LIKE THAT!
SORRY... I WAS JUST TRYING TO GET UP HERE WITHOUT WAKING ANYONE UP.
POLICE
WELL, NEXT TIME, THROW A ROCK AT ME OR SOMETHING... YOU SCARED ME HALF TO DEATH.
ESPECIALLY AFTER WHAT HAPPENED EARLIER TODAY.
YEAH... THAT'S ACTUALLY WHAT I CAME HERE TO TALK TO YOU ABOUT.
OH?
WE NEED TO MOVE CAMP. IT'S NOT SMART TO BE THIS CLOSE TO A CITY FULL OF THOSE THINGS.
IT'S JUST TOO GODDAMN DANGEROUS
ARE YOU CRAZY?!
WHAT HAPPENS WHEN THE GOVERNMENT STARTS CLEANING THIS MESS UP? THEY'LL HAVE TO START WITH THE CITIES... THEY'LL FIND US FASTER IF WE STAY HERE!
WHEN ARE THEY COMING SHANE? TOMORROW? NEXT WEEK? IT'S GETTING REALLY DAMN COLD OUT HERE AND IT'S ONLY GOING TO GET WORSE.
NOT TO MENTION WHAT HAPPENED YESTERDAY. IT'S TOO RISKY TO STAY SO DAMN CLOSE TO THEM.

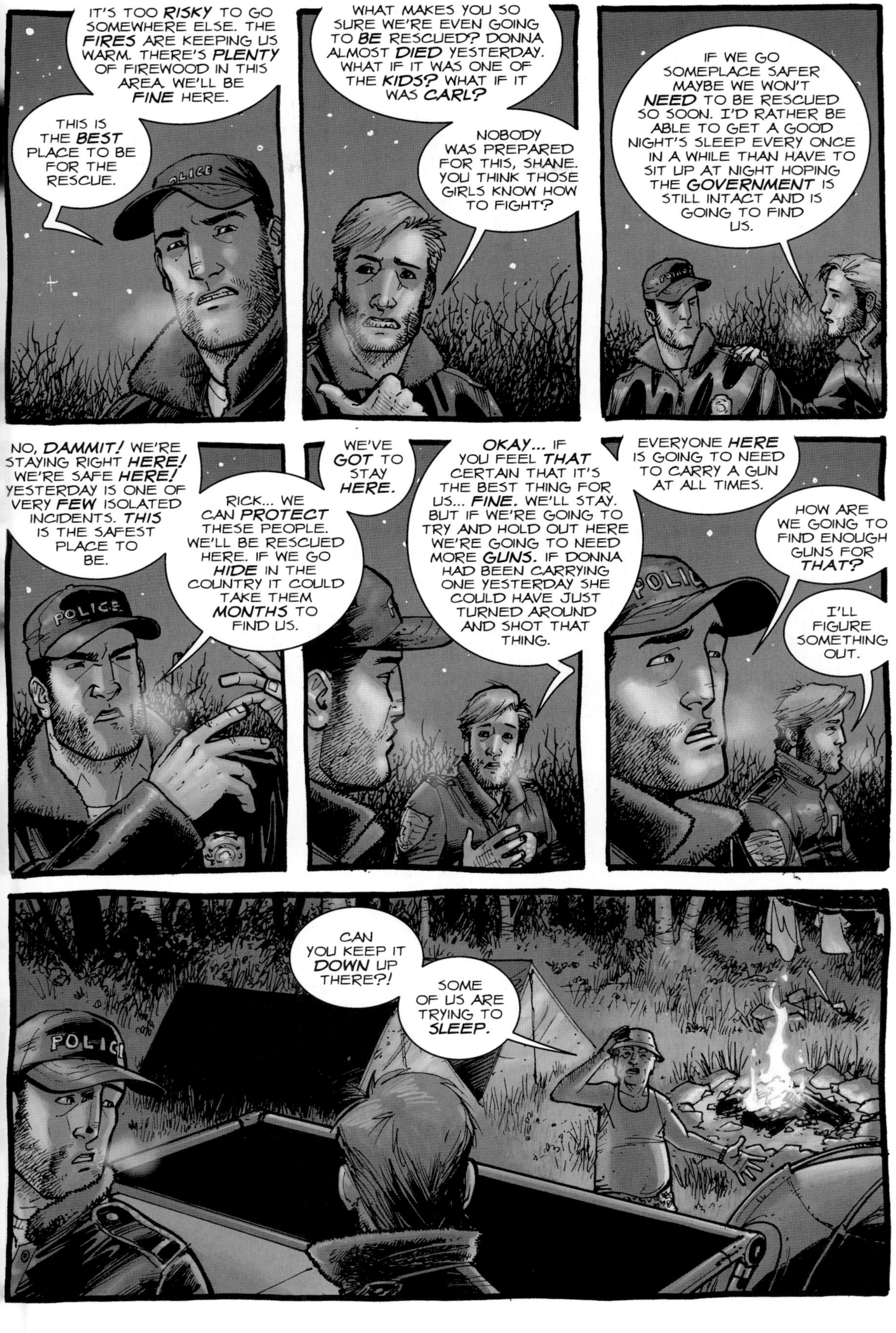
IT'S TOO RISKY TO GO SOMEWHERE ELSE. THE FIRES ARE KEEPING US WARM. THERE'S PLENTY OF FIREWOOD IN THIS AREA. WE'LL BE FINE HERE.
THIS IS THE BEST PLACE TO BE FOR THE RESCUE.
POLICE
WHAT MAKES YOU SO SURE WE'RE EVEN GOING TO BE RESCUED? DONNA ALMOST DIED YESTERDAY. WHAT IF IT WAS ONE OF THE KIDS? WHAT IF IT WAS CARL?
NOBODY WAS PREPARED FOR THIS, SHANE. YOU THINK THOSE GIRLS KNOW HOW TO FIGHT?
IF WE GO SOMEPLACE SAFER MAYBE WE WON'T NEED TO BE RESCUED SO SOON. I'D RATHER BE ABLE TO GET A GOOD NIGHT'S SLEEP EVERY ONCE IN A WHILE THAN HAVE TO SIT UP AT NIGHT HOPING THE GOVERNMENT IS STILL INTACT AND IS GOING TO FIND US.
NO, DAMMIT! WE'RE STAYING RIGHT HERE! WE'RE SAFE HERE! YESTERDAY IS ONE OF VERY FEW ISOLATED INCIDENTS. THIS IS THE SAFEST PLACE TO BE.
RICK... WE CAN PROTECT THESE PEOPLE. WE'LL BE RESCUED HERE. IF WE GO HIDE IN THE COUNTRY IT COULD TAKE THEM MONTHS TO FIND US.
POLICE
WE'VE GOT TO STAY HERE.
OKAY... IF YOU FEEL THAT CERTAIN THAT IT'S THE BEST THING FOR US... FINE. WE'LL STAY. BUT IF WE'RE GOING TO TRY AND HOLD OUT HERE WE'RE GOING TO NEED MORE GUNS. IF DONNA HAD BEEN CARRYING ONE YESTERDAY SHE COULD HAVE JUST TURNED AROUND AND SHOT THAT THING.
EVERYONE HERE IS GOING TO NEED TO CARRY A GUN AT ALL TIMES.
HOW ARE WE GOING TO FIND ENOUGH GUNS FOR THAT?
I'LL FIGURE SOMETHING OUT.
CAN YOU KEEP IT DOWN UP THERE?!
SOME OF US ARE TRYING TO SLEEP.
POLICE

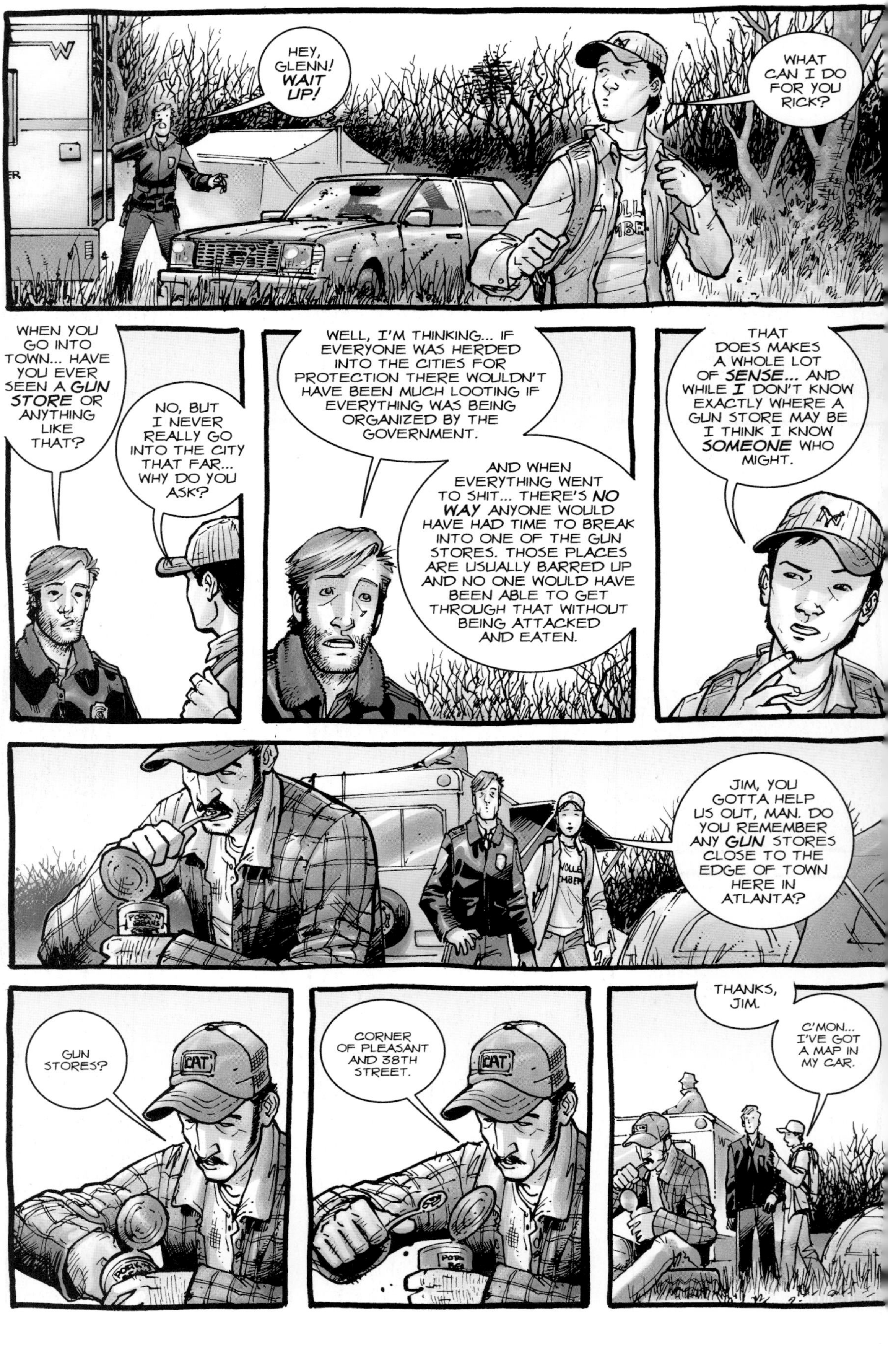
HEY, GLENN! WAIT UP!
WHAT CAN I DO FOR YOU RICK?
WHEN YOU GO INTO TOWN... HAVE YOU EVER SEEN A GUN STORE OR ANYTHING LIKE THAT?
NO, BUT I NEVER REALLY GO INTO THE CITY THAT FAR... WHY DO YOU ASK?
WELL, I'M THINKING... IF EVERYONE WAS HERDED INTO THE CITIES FOR PROTECTION THERE WOULDN'T HAVE BEEN MUCH LOOTING IF EVERYTHING WAS BEING ORGANIZED BY THE GOVERNMENT.
AND WHEN EVERYTHING WENT TO SHIT... THERE'S NO WAY ANYONE WOULD HAVE HAD TIME TO BREAK INTO ONE OF THE GUN STORES. THOSE PLACES ARE USUALLY BARRED UP AND NO ONE WOULD HAVE BEEN ABLE TO GET THROUGH THAT WITHOUT BEING ATTACKED AND EATEN.
THAT DOES MAKES A WHOLE LOT OF SENSE... AND WHILE I DON'T KNOW EXACTLY WHERE A GUN STORE MAY BE I THINK I KNOW SOMEONE WHO MIGHT.
JIM, YOU GOTTA HELP US OUT, MAN. DO YOU REMEMBER ANY GUN STORES CLOSE TO THE EDGE OF TOWN HERE IN ATLANTA?
GUN STORES?
CORNER OF PLEASANT AND 38TH STREET.
THANKS, JIM.
C'MON... I'VE GOT A MAP IN MY CAR.

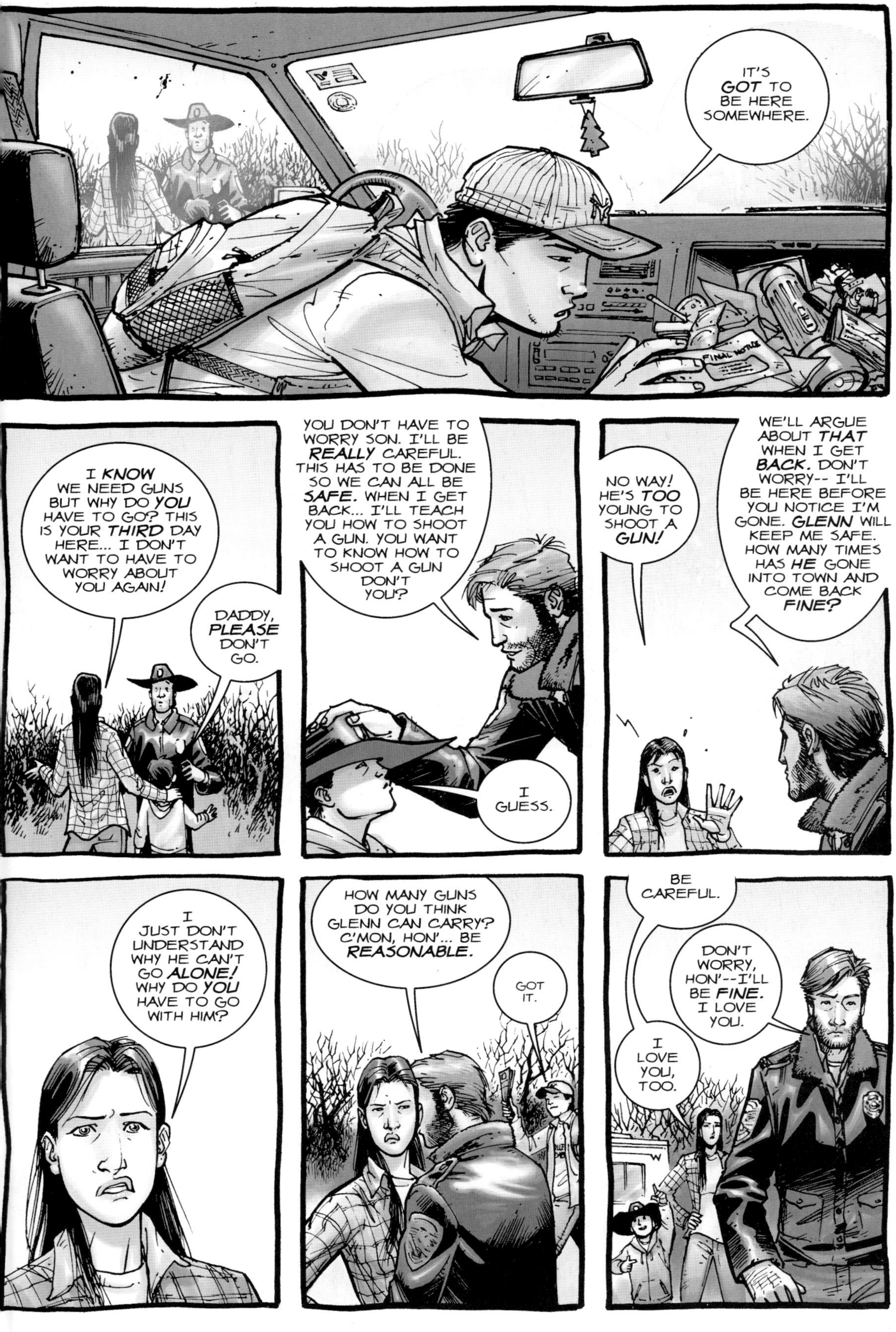
IT'S GOT TO BE HERE SOMEWHERE.
FINAL NOTICE
I KNOW WE NEED GUNS BUT WHY DO YOU HAVE TO GO? THIS IS YOUR THIRD DAY HERE... I DON'T WANT TO HAVE TO WORRY ABOUT YOU AGAIN!
DADDY, PLEASE DON'T GO.
YOU DON'T HAVE TO WORRY SON. I'LL BE REALLY CAREFUL. THIS HAS TO BE DONE SO WE CAN ALL BE SAFE. WHEN I GET BACK... I'LL TEACH YOU HOW TO SHOOT A GUN. YOU WANT TO KNOW HOW TO SHOOT A GUN DON'T YOU?
I GUESS.
NO WAY! HE'S TOO YOUNG TO SHOOT A GUN!
WE'LL ARGUE ABOUT THAT WHEN I GET BACK. DON'T WORRY-- I'LL BE HERE BEFORE YOU NOTICE I'M GONE. GLENN WILL KEEP ME SAFE. HOW MANY TIMES HAS HE GONE INTO TOWN AND COME BACK FINE?
I JUST DON'T UNDERSTAND WHY HE CAN'T GO ALONE! WHY DO YOU HAVE TO GO WITH HIM?
HOW MANY GUNS DO YOU THINK GLENN CAN CARRY? C'MON, HON'... BE REASONABLE.
GOT IT.
BE CAREFUL.
DON'T WORRY, HON'--I'LL BE FINE. I LOVE YOU.
I LOVE YOU, TOO.

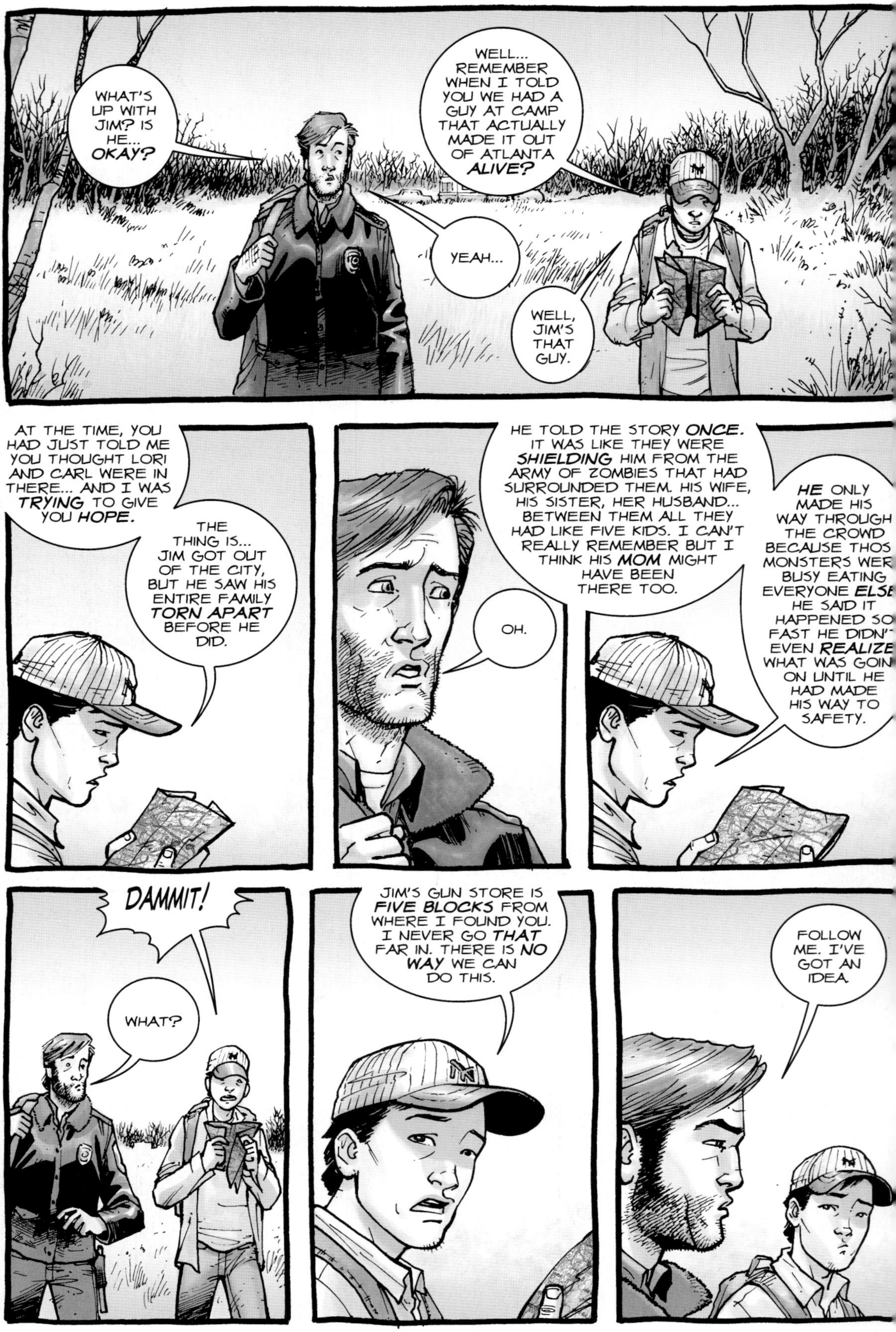

WHAT'S UP WITH JIM? IS HE... OKAY?
WELL... REMEMBER WHEN I TOLD YOU WE HAD A GUY AT CAMP THAT ACTUALLY MADE IT OUT OF ATLANTA ALIVE?
YEAH...
WELL, JIM'S THAT GUY.
AT THE TIME, YOU HAD JUST TOLD ME YOU THOUGHT LORI AND CARL WERE IN THERE... AND I WAS TRYING TO GIVE YOU HOPE.
THE THING IS... JIM GOT OUT OF THE CITY, BUT HE SAW HIS ENTIRE FAMILY TORN APART BEFORE HE DID.
OH.
HE TOLD THE STORY ONCE. IT WAS LIKE THEY WERE SHIELDING HIM FROM THE ARMY OF ZOMBIES THAT HAD SURROUNDED THEM. HIS WIFE, HIS SISTER, HER HUSBAND... BETWEEN THEM ALL THEY HAD LIKE FIVE KIDS. I CAN'T REALLY REMEMBER BUT I THINK HIS MOM MIGHT HAVE BEEN THERE TOO.
HE ONLY MADE HIS WAY THROUGH THE CROWD BECAUSE THOS MONSTERS WER BUSY EATING EVERYONE ELSE HE SAID IT HAPPENED SO FAST HE DIDN' EVEN REALIZE WHAT WAS GOIN ON UNTIL HE HAD MADE HIS WAY TO SAFETY.
DAMMIT!
WHAT?
JIM'S GUN STORE IS FIVE BLOCKS FROM WHERE I FOUND YOU. I NEVER GO THAT FAR IN. THERE IS NO WAY WE CAN DO THIS.
FOLLOW ME. I'VE GOT AN IDEA.

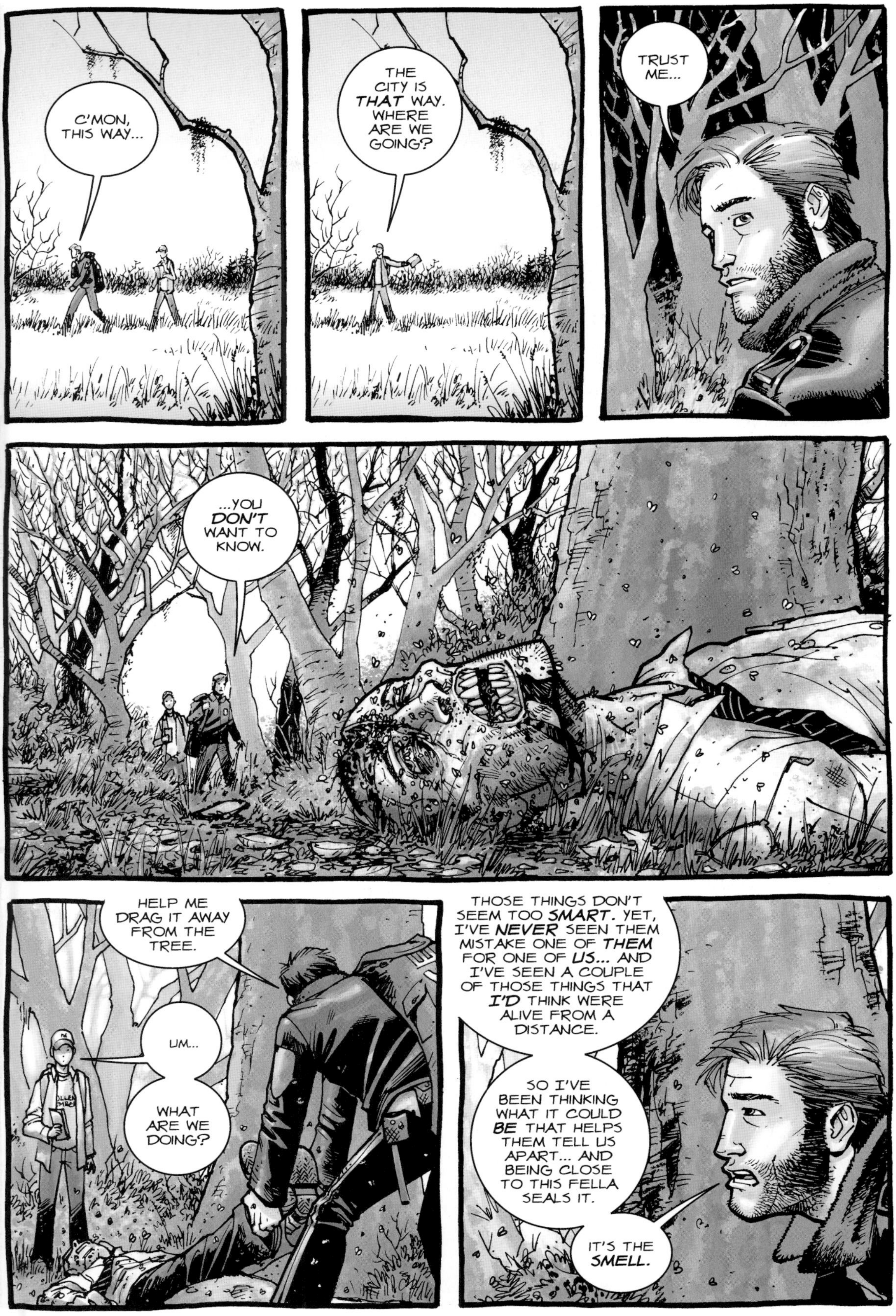
C'MON, THIS WAY...
THE CITY IS THAT WAY. WHERE ARE WE GOING?
TRUST ME...
...YOU DON'T WANT TO KNOW.
HELP ME DRAG IT AWAY FROM THE TREE.
UM...
WHAT ARE WE DOING?
THOSE THINGS DON'T SEEM TOO SMART. YET, I'VE NEVER SEEN THEM MISTAKE ONE OF THEM FOR ONE OF US... AND I'VE SEEN A COUPLE OF THOSE THINGS THAT I'D THINK WERE ALIVE FROM A DISTANCE.
SO I'VE BEEN THINKING WHAT IT COULD BE THAT HELPS THEM TELL US APART... AND BEING CLOSE TO THIS FELLA SEALS IT.
IT'S THE SMELL.

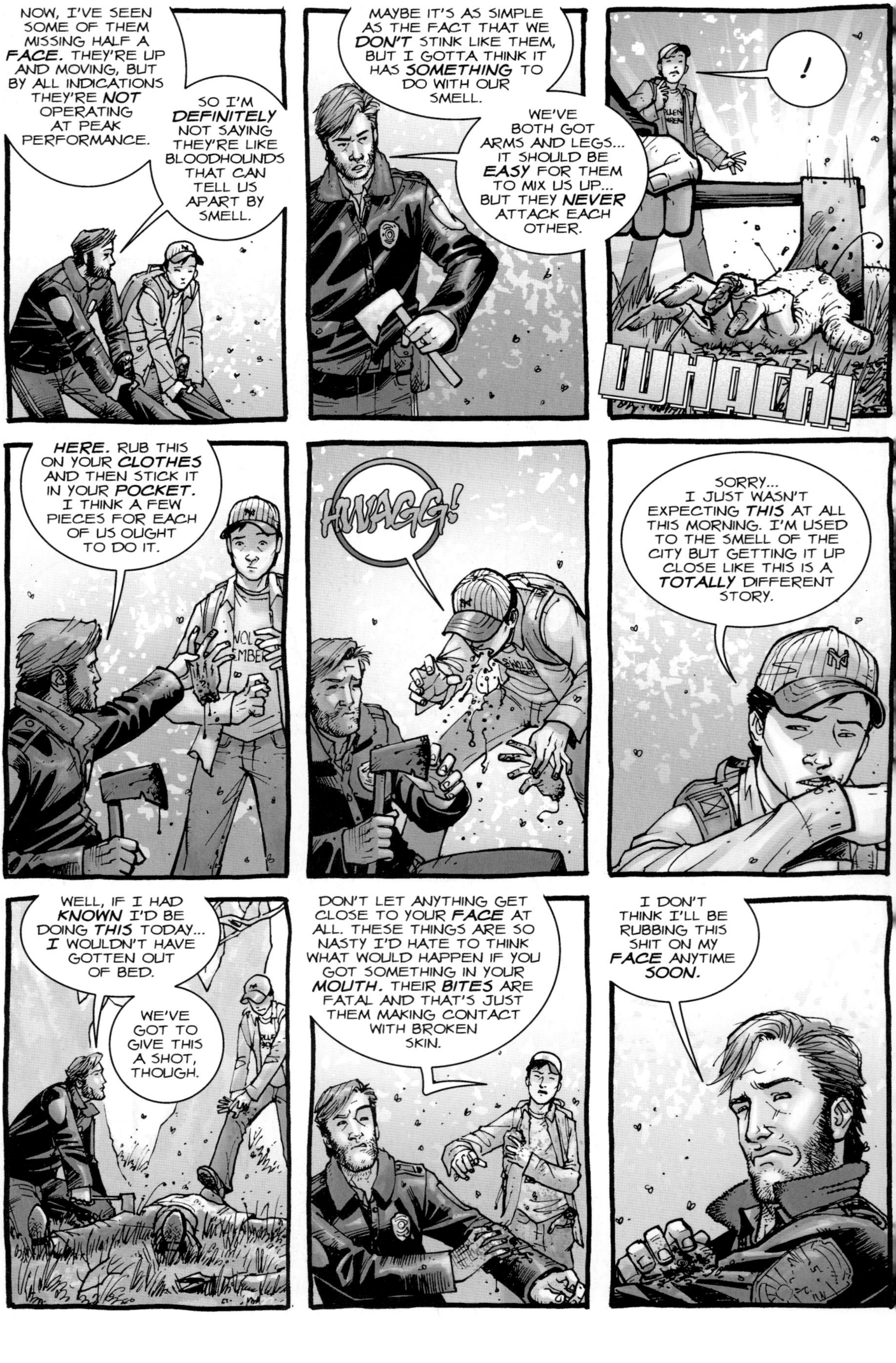
NOW, I'VE SEEN SOME OF THEM MISSING HALF A FACE. THEY'RE UP AND MOVING, BUT BY ALL INDICATIONS THEY'RE NOT OPERATING AT PEAK PERFORMANCE.
SO I'M DEFINITELY NOT SAYING THEY'RE LIKE BLOODHOUNDS THAT CAN TELL US APART BY SMELL.
MAYBE IT'S AS SIMPLE AS THE FACT THAT WE DON'T STINK LIKE THEM, BUT I GOTTA THINK IT HAS SOMETHING TO DO WITH OUR SMELL.
WE'VE BOTH GOT ARMS AND LEGS... IT SHOULD BE EASY FOR THEM TO MIX US UP... BUT THEY NEVER ATTACK EACH OTHER.
!
WHACK!
HERE. RUB THIS ON YOUR CLOTHES AND THEN STICK IT IN YOUR POCKET. I THINK A FEW PIECES FOR EACH OF US OUGHT TO DO IT.
HWAGG!
SORRY... I JUST WASN'T EXPECTING THIS AT ALL THIS MORNING. I'M USED TO THE SMELL OF THE CITY BUT GETTING IT UP CLOSE LIKE THIS IS A TOTALLY DIFFERENT STORY.
WELL, IF I HAD KNOWN I'D BE DOING THIS TODAY... I WOULDN'T HAVE GOTTEN OUT OF BED.
WE'VE GOT TO GIVE THIS A SHOT, THOUGH.
DON'T LET ANYTHING GET CLOSE TO YOUR FACE AT ALL. THESE THINGS ARE SO NASTY I'D HATE TO THINK WHAT WOULD HAPPEN IF YOU GOT SOMETHING IN YOUR MOUTH. THEIR BITES ARE FATAL AND THAT'S JUST THEM MAKING CONTACT WITH BROKEN SKIN.
I DON'T THINK I'LL BE RUBBING THIS SHIT ON MY FACE ANYTIME SOON.

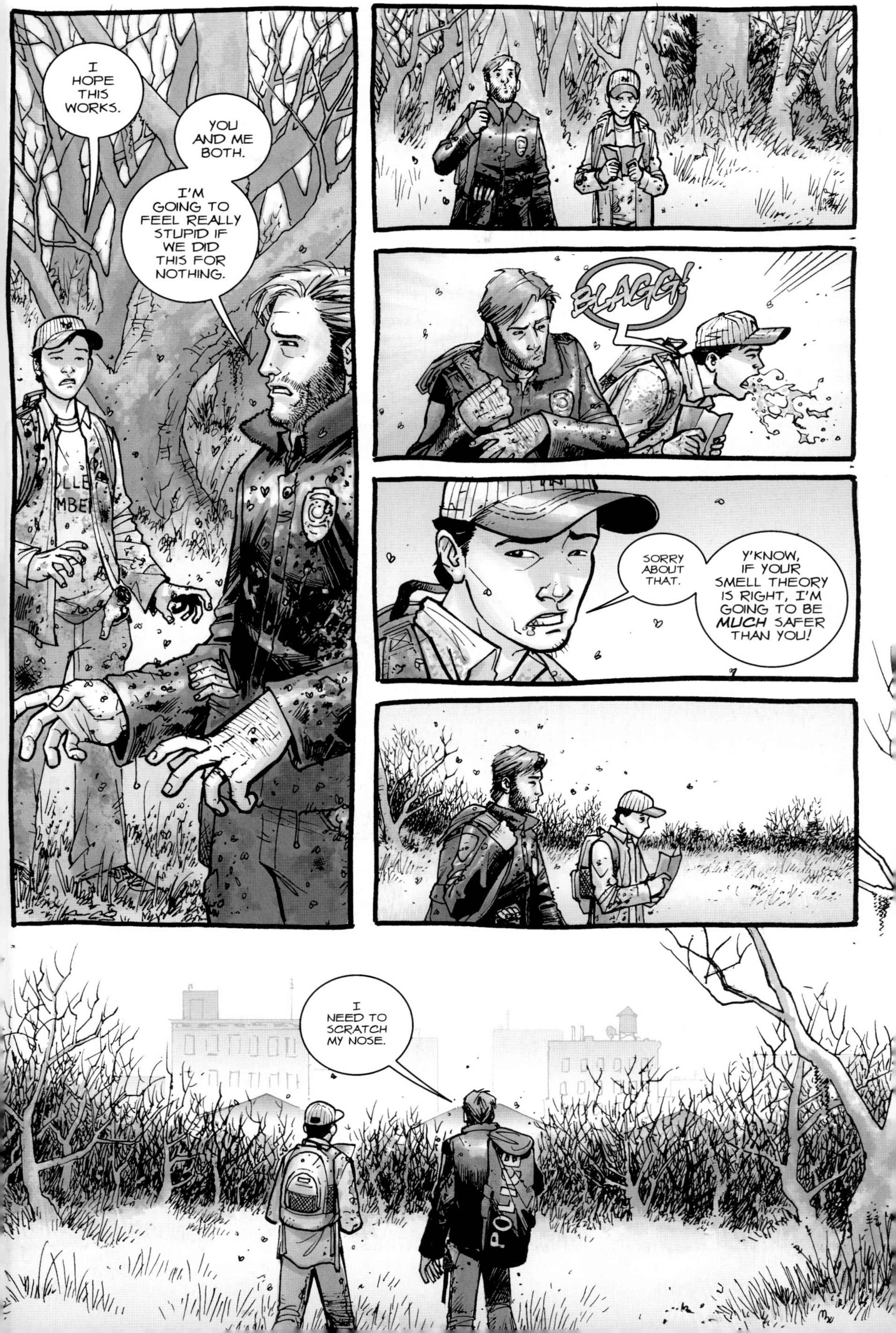
I HOPE THIS WORKS.
YOU AND ME BOTH.
I'M GOING TO FEEL REALLY STUPID IF WE DID THIS FOR NOTHING.
BLAGG!
SORRY ABOUT THAT.
Y'KNOW, IF YOUR SMELL THEORY IS RIGHT, I'M GOING TO BE *MUCH* SAFER THAN YOU!
I NEED TO SCRATCH MY NOSE.
POLICE

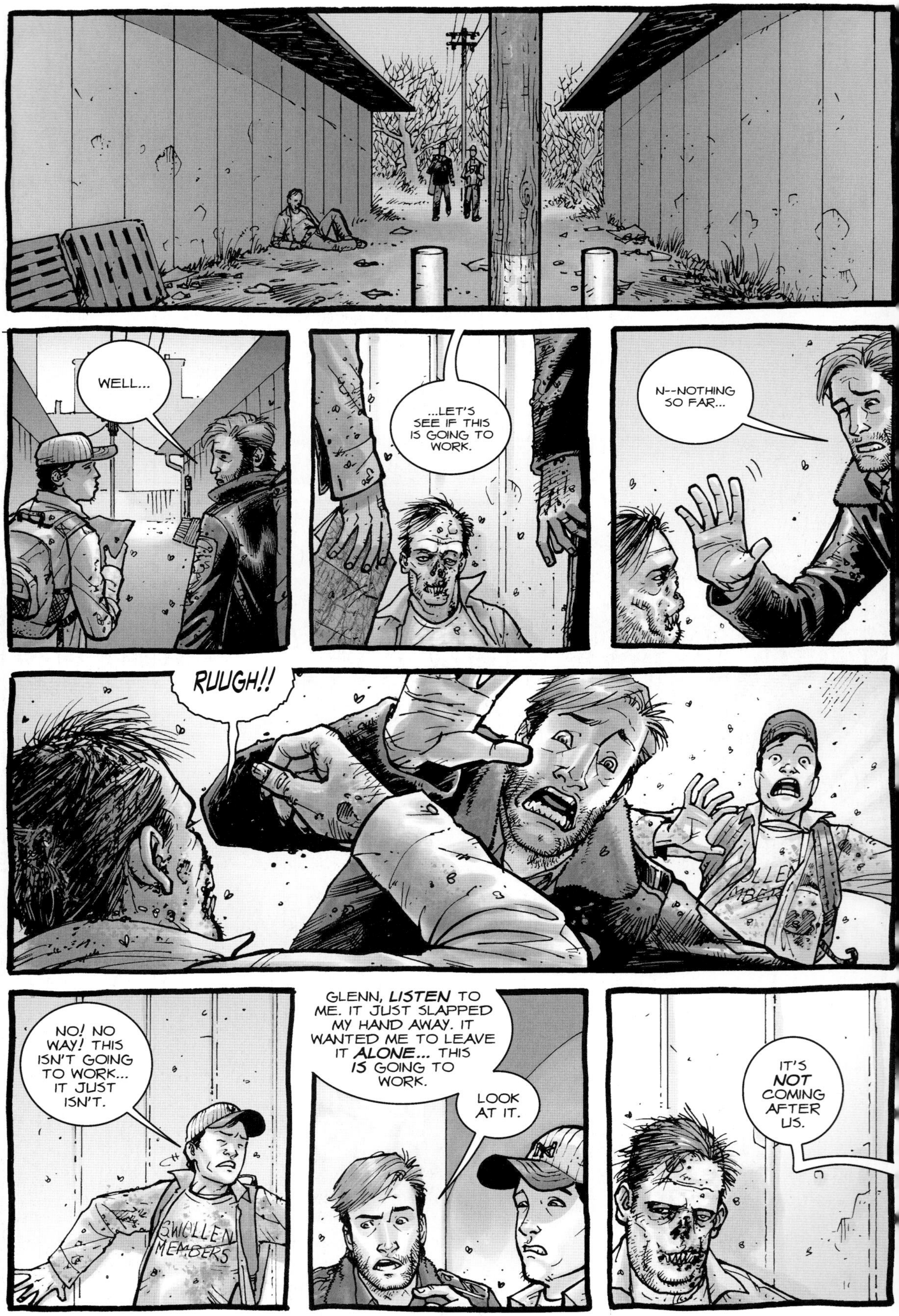
WELL...
...LET'S SEE IF THIS IS GOING TO WORK.
N--NOTHING SO FAR...
RUUGH!!
NO! NO WAY! THIS ISN'T GOING TO WORK... IT JUST ISN'T.
GLENN, LISTEN TO ME. IT JUST SLAPPED MY HAND AWAY. IT WANTED ME TO LEAVE IT ALONE... THIS IS GOING TO WORK.
LOOK AT IT.
IT'S NOT COMING AFTER US.
SWOLLEN MEMBERS

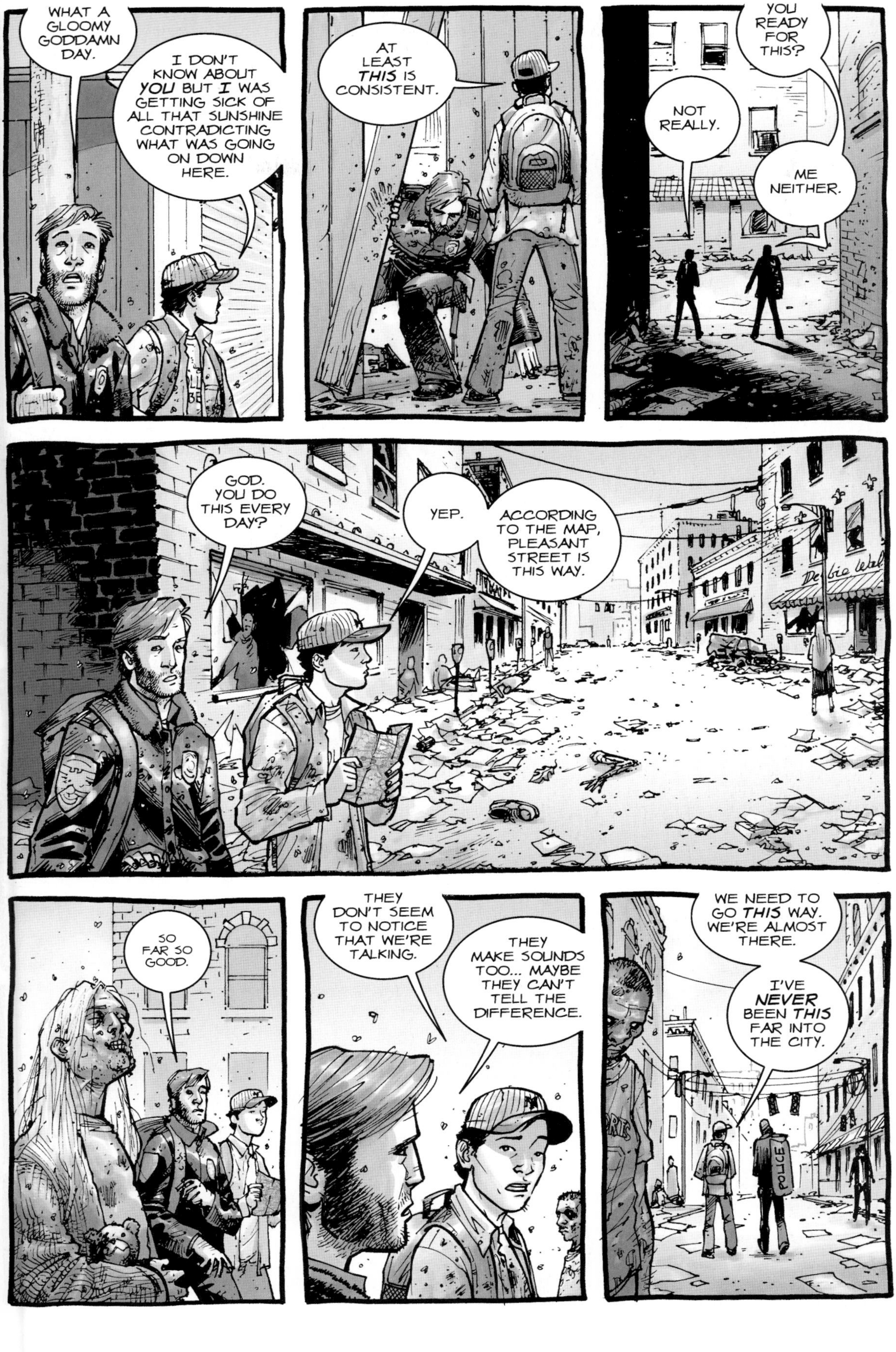

WHAT A GLOOMY GODDAMN DAY.
I DON'T KNOW ABOUT YOU BUT I WAS GETTING SICK OF ALL THAT SUNSHINE CONTRADICTING WHAT WAS GOING ON DOWN HERE.
AT LEAST THIS IS CONSISTENT.
YOU READY FOR THIS?
NOT REALLY.
ME NEITHER.
GOD. YOU DO THIS EVERY DAY?
YEP.
ACCORDING TO THE MAP, PLEASANT STREET IS THIS WAY.
SO FAR SO GOOD.
THEY DON'T SEEM TO NOTICE THAT WE'RE TALKING.
THEY MAKE SOUNDS TOO... MAYBE THEY CAN'T TELL THE DIFFERENCE.
WE NEED TO GO THIS WAY. WE'RE ALMOST THERE.
I'VE NEVER BEEN THIS FAR INTO THE CITY.
POLICE

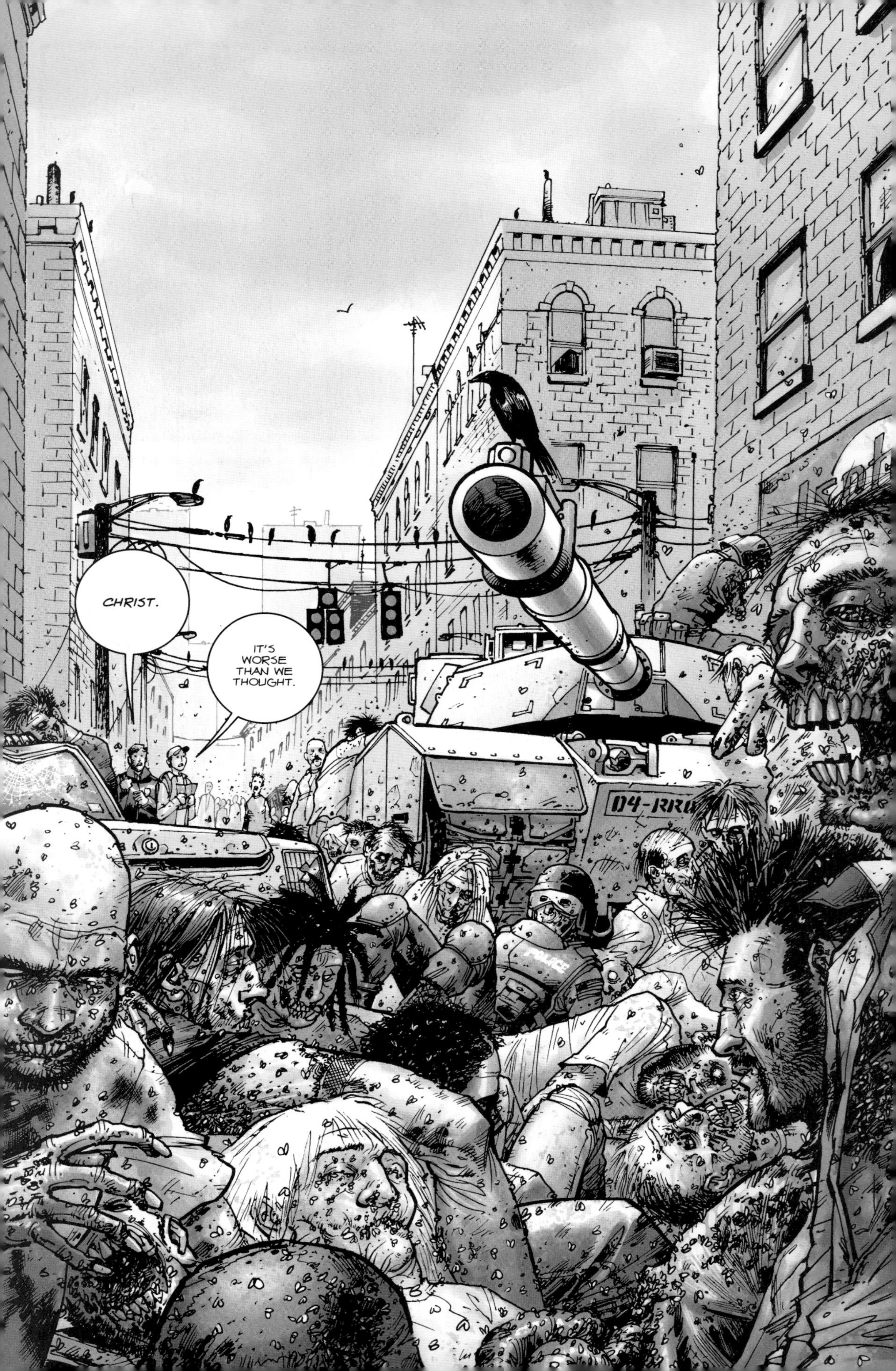
CHRIST.
IT'S WORSE THAN WE THOUGHT.
D4-RRO
POLICE

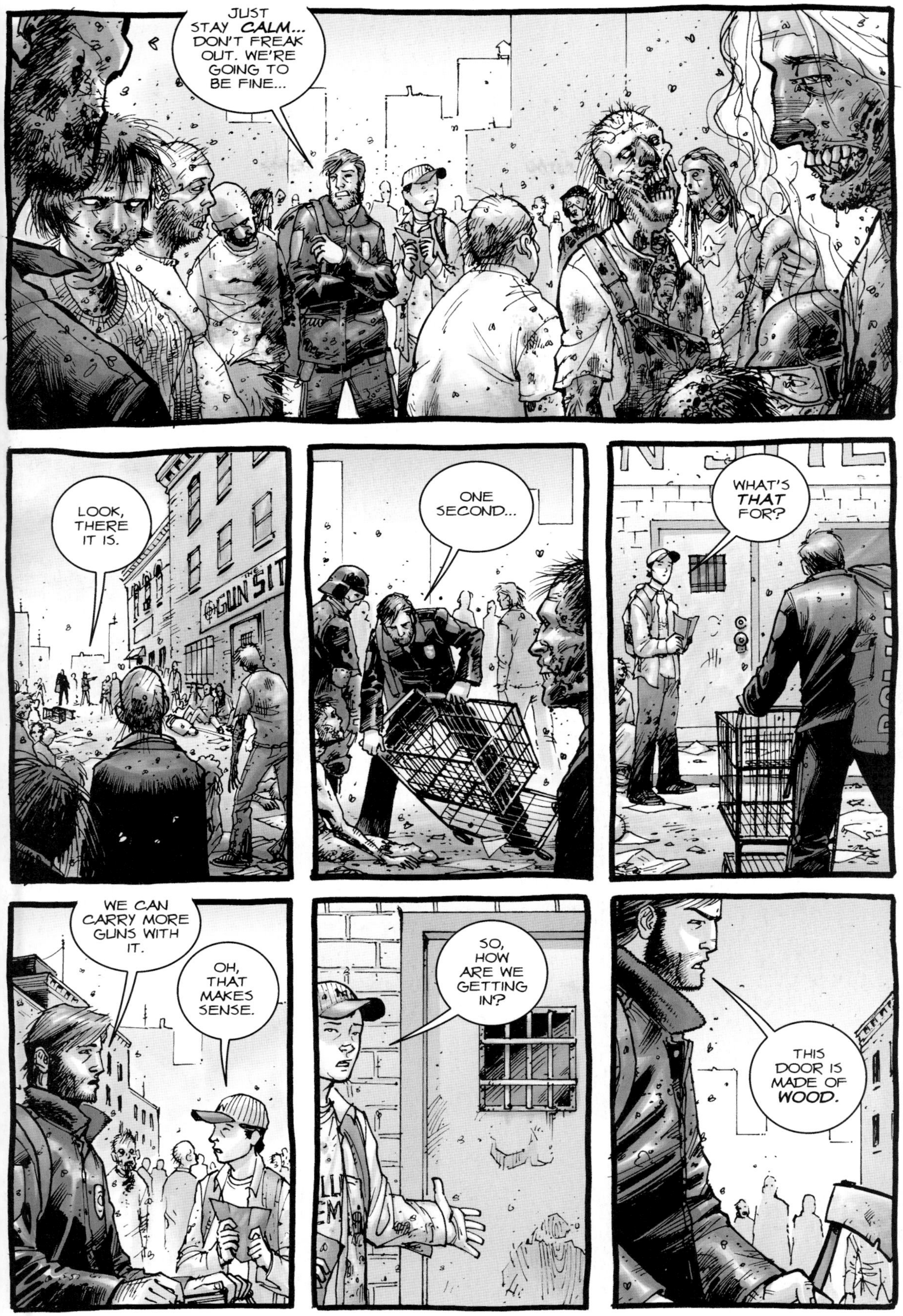
JUST STAY CALM... DON'T FREAK OUT. WE'RE GOING TO BE FINE...
LOOK, THERE IT IS.
THE GUN SIT
ONE SECOND...
WHAT'S THAT FOR?
WE CAN CARRY MORE GUNS WITH IT.
OH, THAT MAKES SENSE.
SO, HOW ARE WE GETTING IN?
THIS DOOR IS MADE OF WOOD.

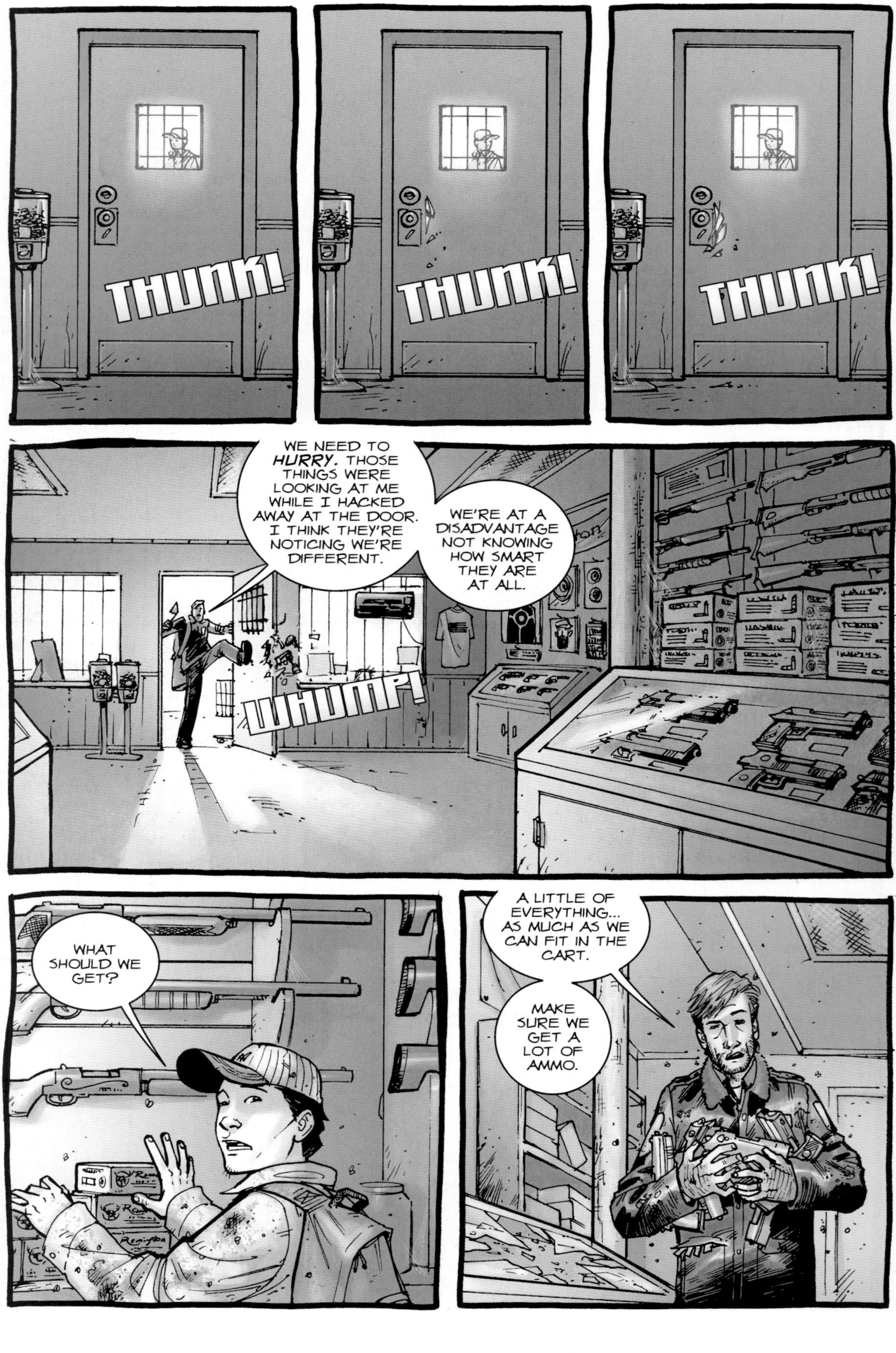
THUNK!
THUNK!
THUNK!
WE NEED TO HURRY. THOSE THINGS WERE LOOKING AT ME WHILE I HACKED AWAY AT THE DOOR. I THINK THEY'RE NOTICING WE'RE DIFFERENT.
WE'RE AT A DISADVANTAGE NOT KNOWING HOW SMART THEY ARE AT ALL.
WHUMP!
WHAT SHOULD WE GET?
A LITTLE OF EVERYTHING... AS MUCH AS WE CAN FIT IN THE CART.
MAKE SURE WE GET A LOT OF AMMO.

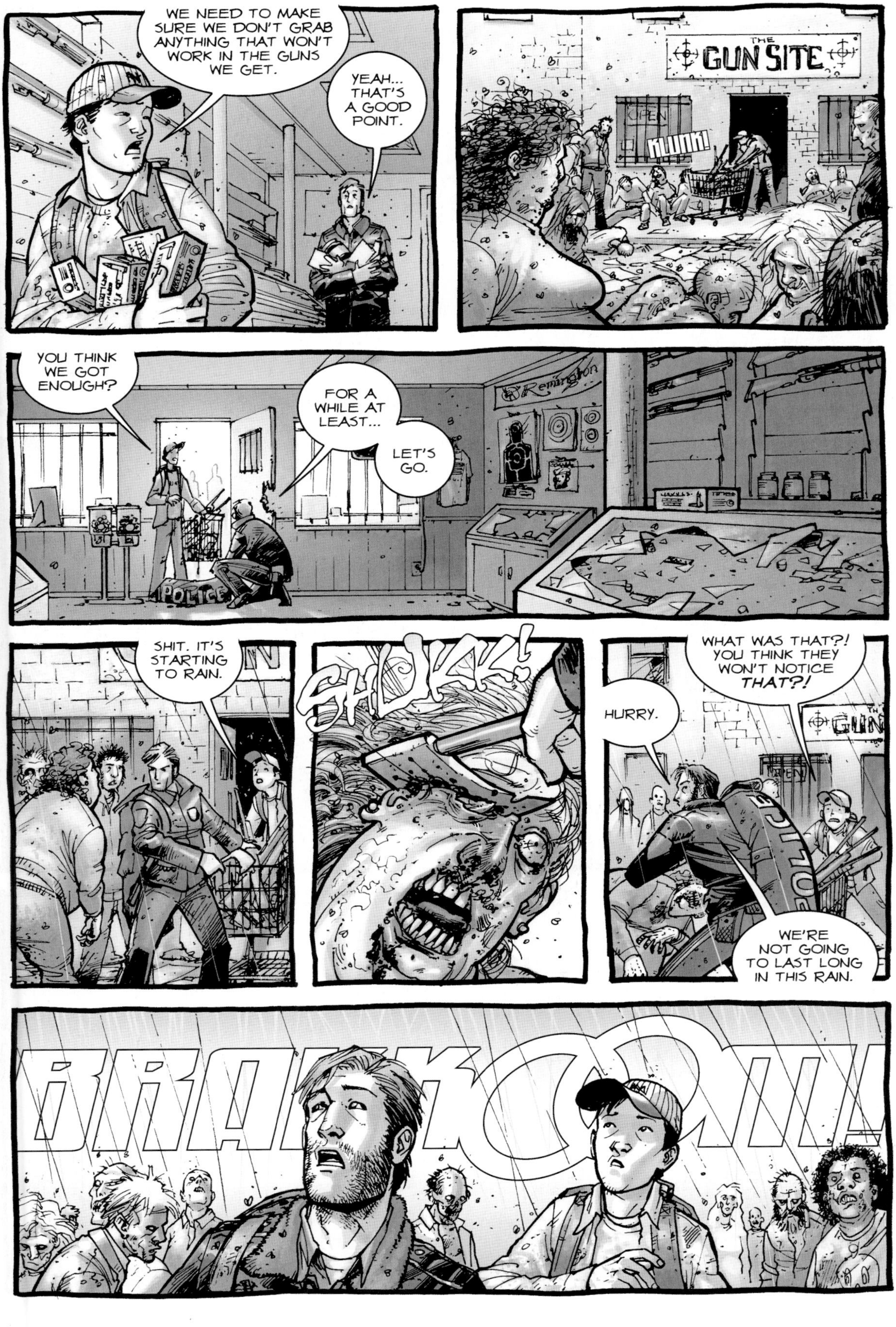
WE NEED TO MAKE SURE WE DON'T GRAB ANYTHING THAT WON'T WORK IN THE GUNS WE GET.
YEAH... THAT'S A GOOD POINT.
THE GUN SITE
OPEN
KLUNK!
YOU THINK WE GOT ENOUGH?
FOR A WHILE AT LEAST...
LET'S GO.
Remington
POLICE
SHIT. IT'S STARTING TO RAIN.
SHUKK!
WHAT WAS THAT?! YOU THINK THEY WON'T NOTICE *THAT?!*
HURRY.
WE'RE NOT GOING TO LAST LONG IN THIS RAIN.

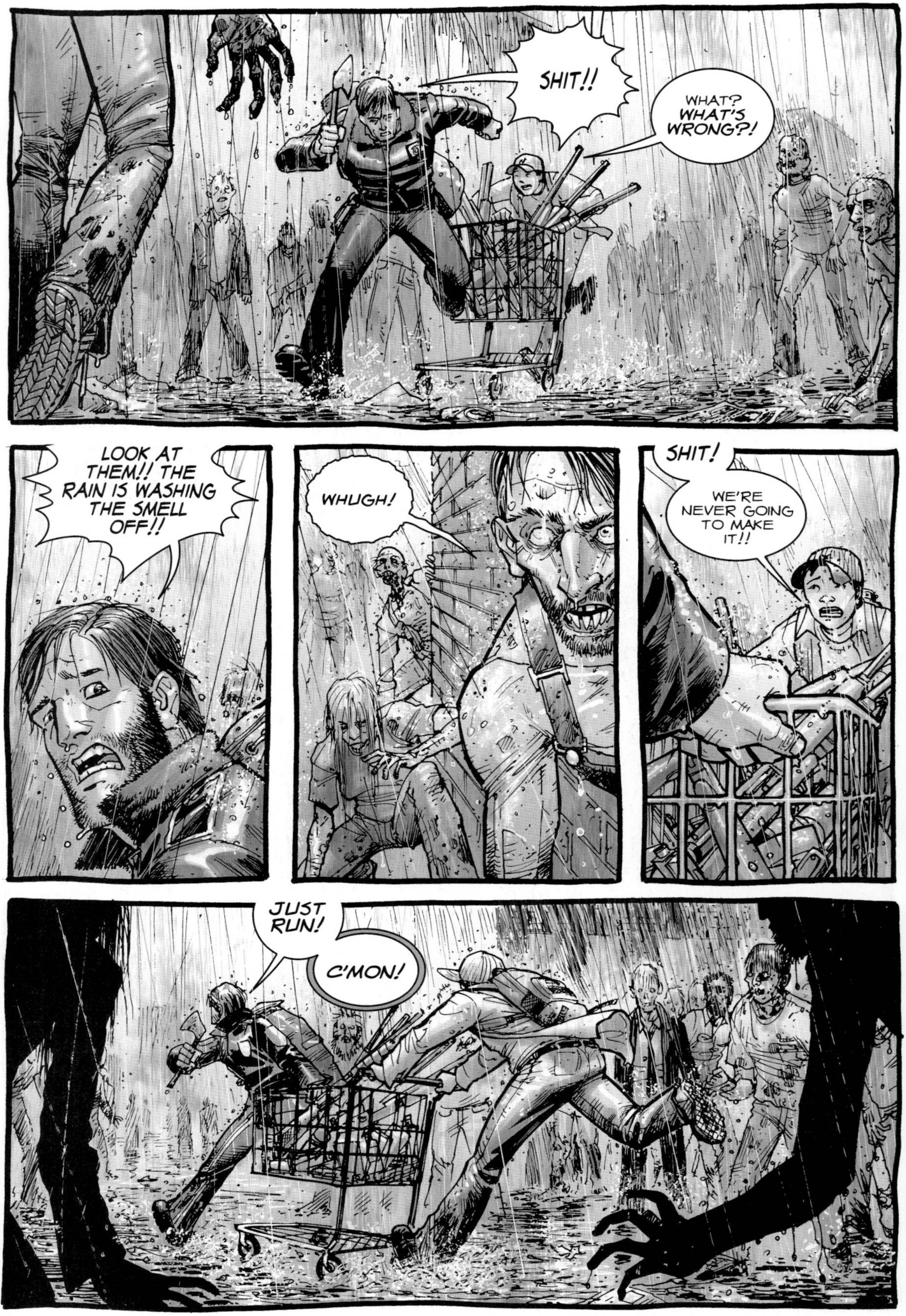

SHIT!!
WHAT? WHAT'S WRONG?!
LOOK AT THEM!! THE RAIN IS WASHING THE SMELL OFF!!
WHUGH!
SHIT!
WE'RE NEVER GOING TO MAKE IT!!
JUST RUN!
C'MON!

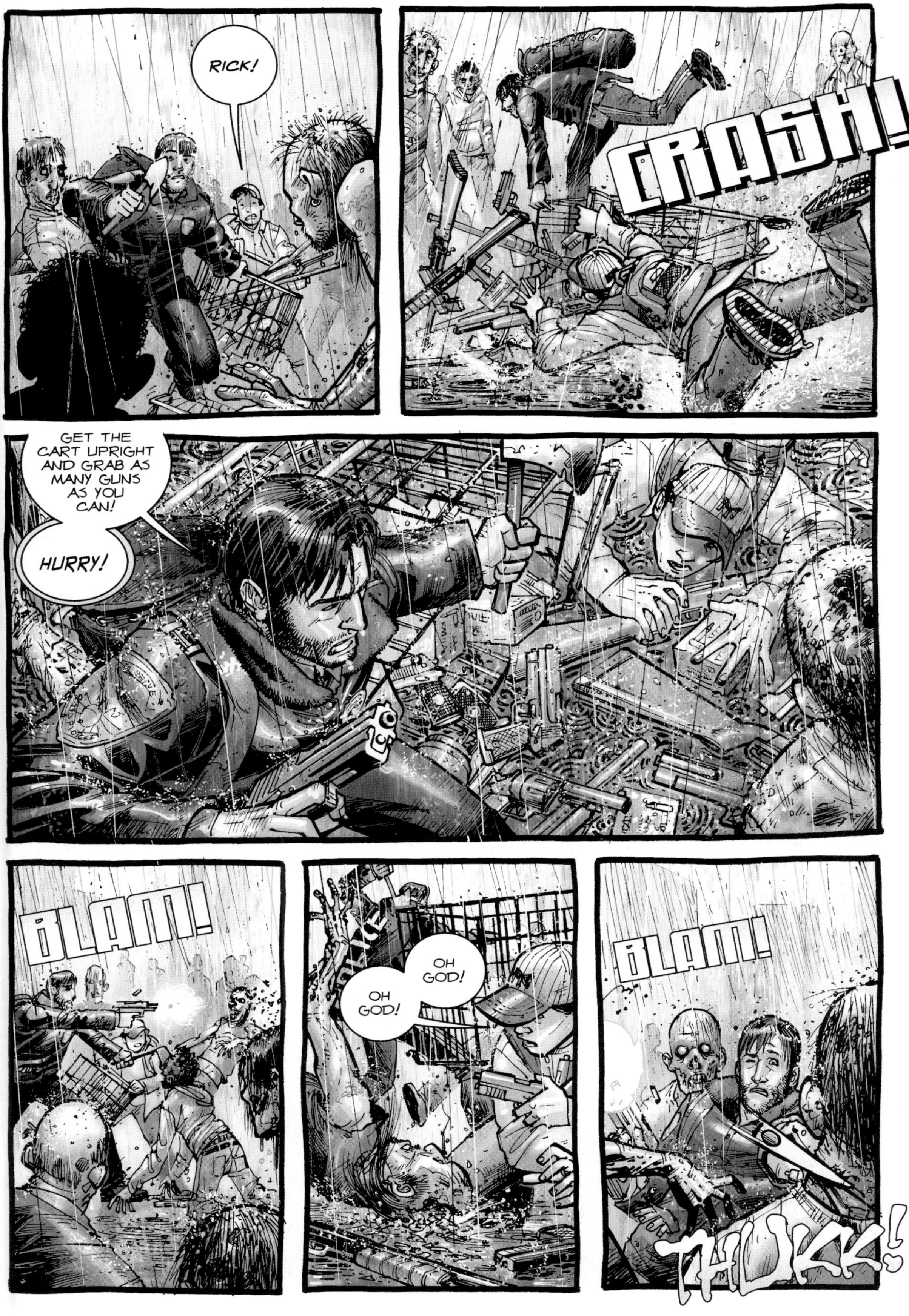
RICK!
CRASH!
GET THE CART UPRIGHT AND GRAB AS MANY GUNS AS YOU CAN!
HURRY!
BLAM!
OH GOD!
OH GOD!
BLAM!
THUKK!

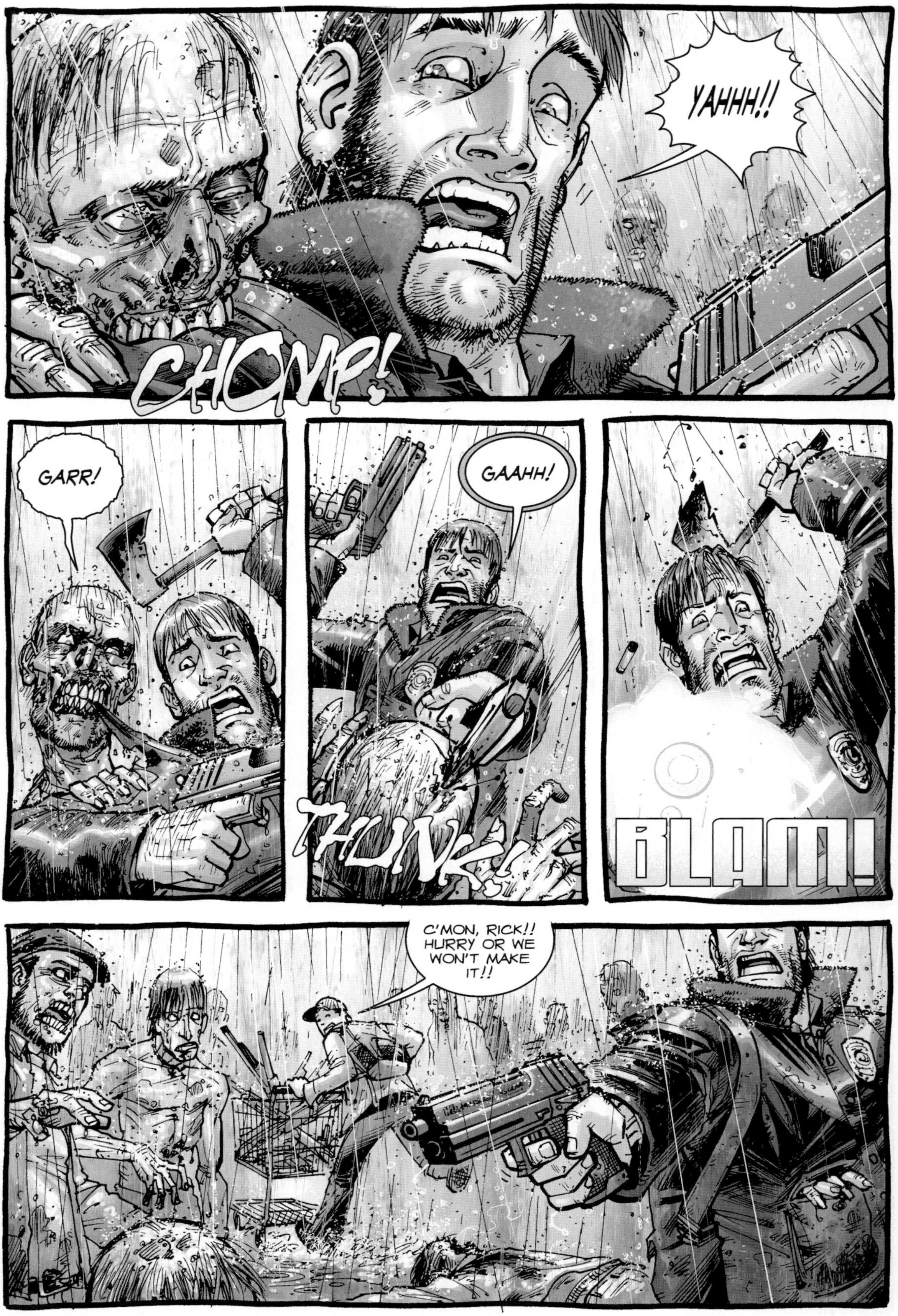
YAHHH!!
CHOMP!
GARR!
GAAHH!
THUNK!
BLAM!
C'MON, RICK!! HURRY OR WE WON'T MAKE IT!!

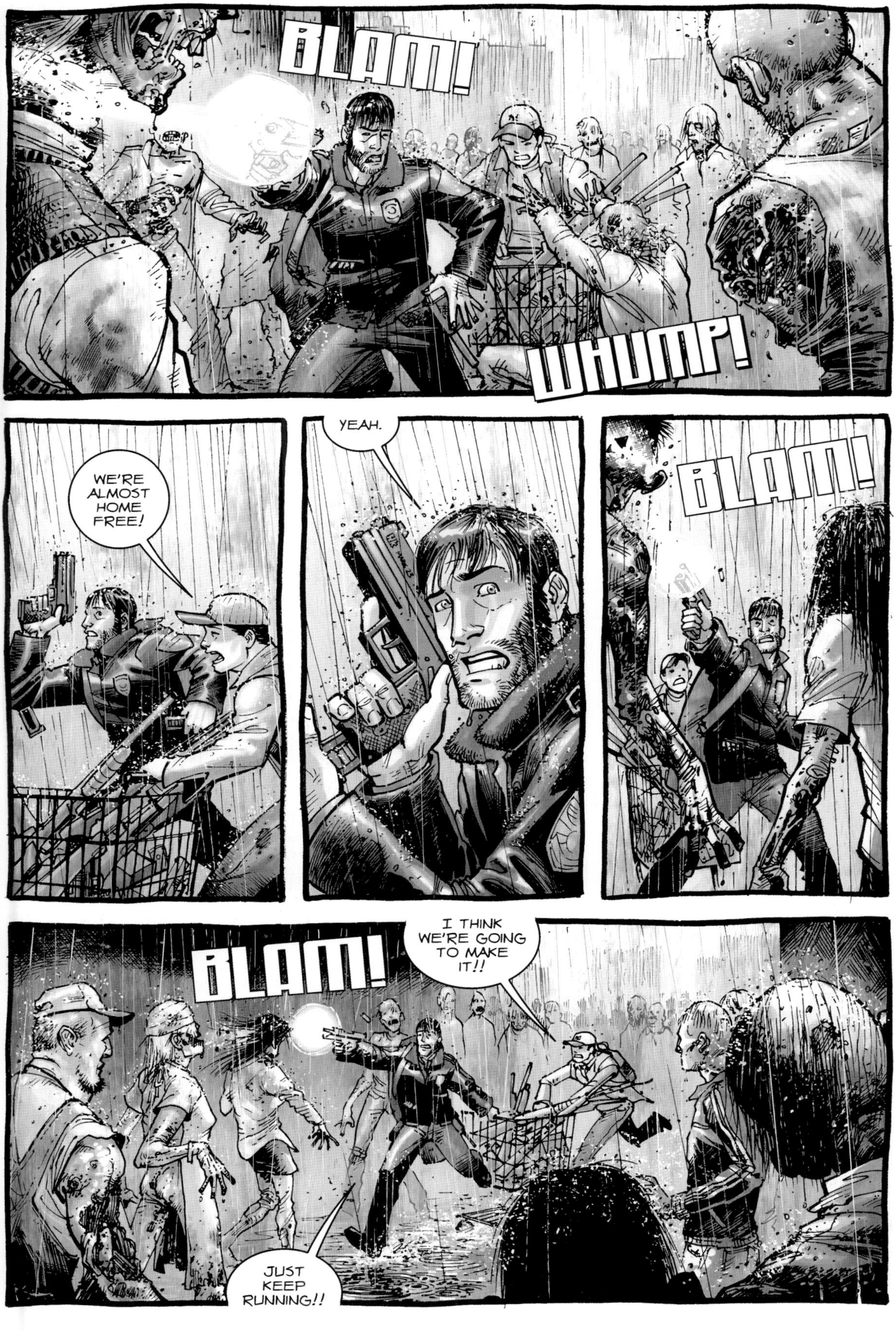
BLAM!
WHUMP!
WE'RE ALMOST HOME FREE!
YEAH.
BLAM!
BLAM!
I THINK WE'RE GOING TO MAKE IT!!
JUST KEEP RUNNING!!

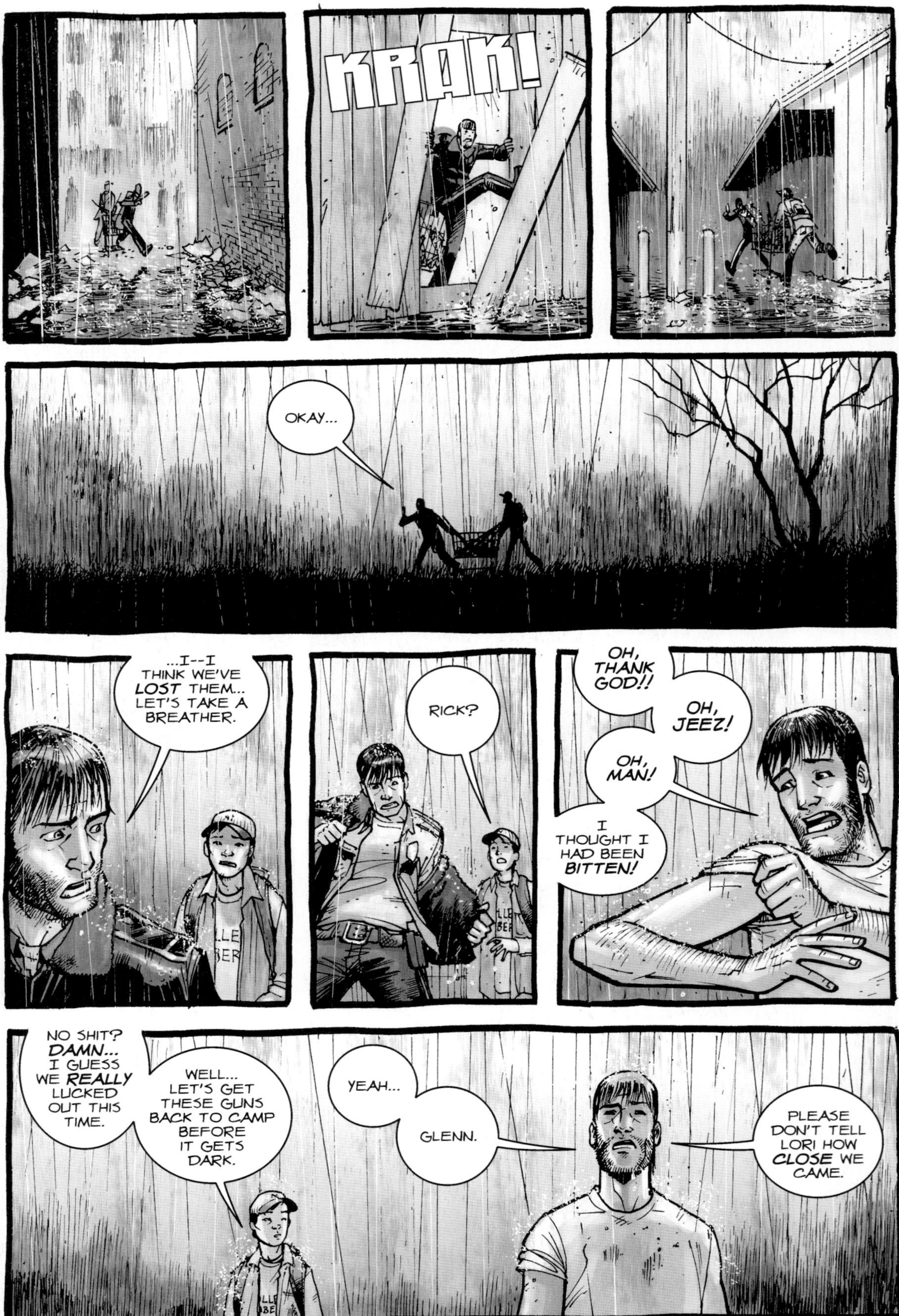
KRAK!
OKAY...
...I--I THINK WE'VE LOST THEM... LET'S TAKE A BREATHER.
RICK?
OH, THANK GOD!!
OH, JEEZ!
OH, MAN!
I THOUGHT I HAD BEEN BITTEN!
NO SHIT? DAMN... I GUESS WE REALLY LUCKED OUT THIS TIME.
WELL... LET'S GET THESE GUNS BACK TO CAMP BEFORE IT GETS DARK.
YEAH...
GLENN.
PLEASE DON'T TELL LORI HOW CLOSE WE CAME.

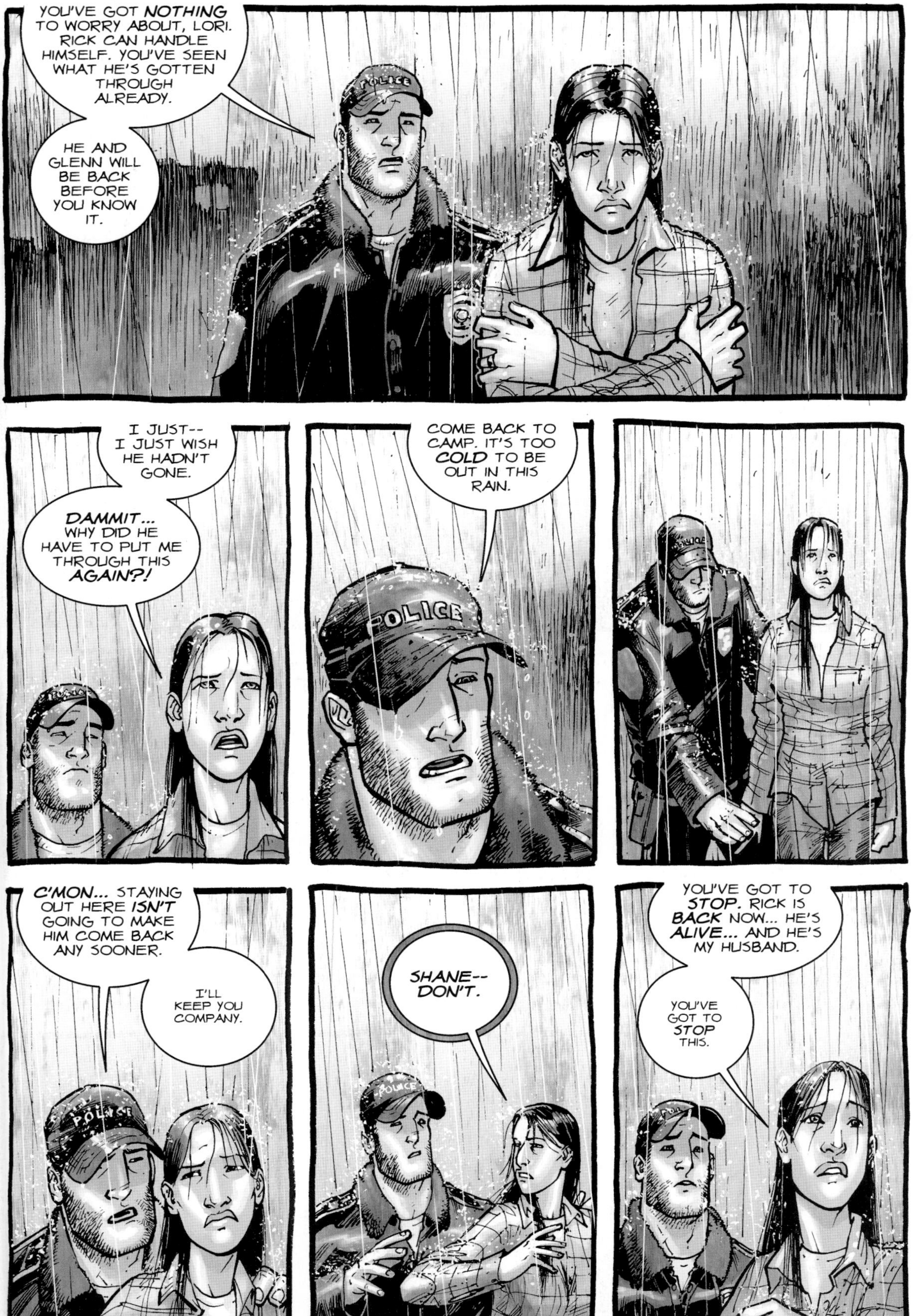
YOU'VE GOT NOTHING TO WORRY ABOUT, LORI. RICK CAN HANDLE HIMSELF. YOU'VE SEEN WHAT HE'S GOTTEN THROUGH ALREADY.
HE AND GLENN WILL BE BACK BEFORE YOU KNOW IT.
POLICE
I JUST-- I JUST WISH HE HADN'T GONE.
DAMMIT... WHY DID HE HAVE TO PUT ME THROUGH THIS AGAIN?!
COME BACK TO CAMP. IT'S TOO COLD TO BE OUT IN THIS RAIN.
POLICE
C'MON... STAYING OUT HERE ISN'T GOING TO MAKE HIM COME BACK ANY SOONER.
I'LL KEEP YOU COMPANY.
POLICE
SHANE-- DON'T.
POLICE
YOU'VE GOT TO STOP. RICK IS BACK NOW... HE'S ALIVE... AND HE'S MY HUSBAND.
YOU'VE GOT TO STOP THIS.

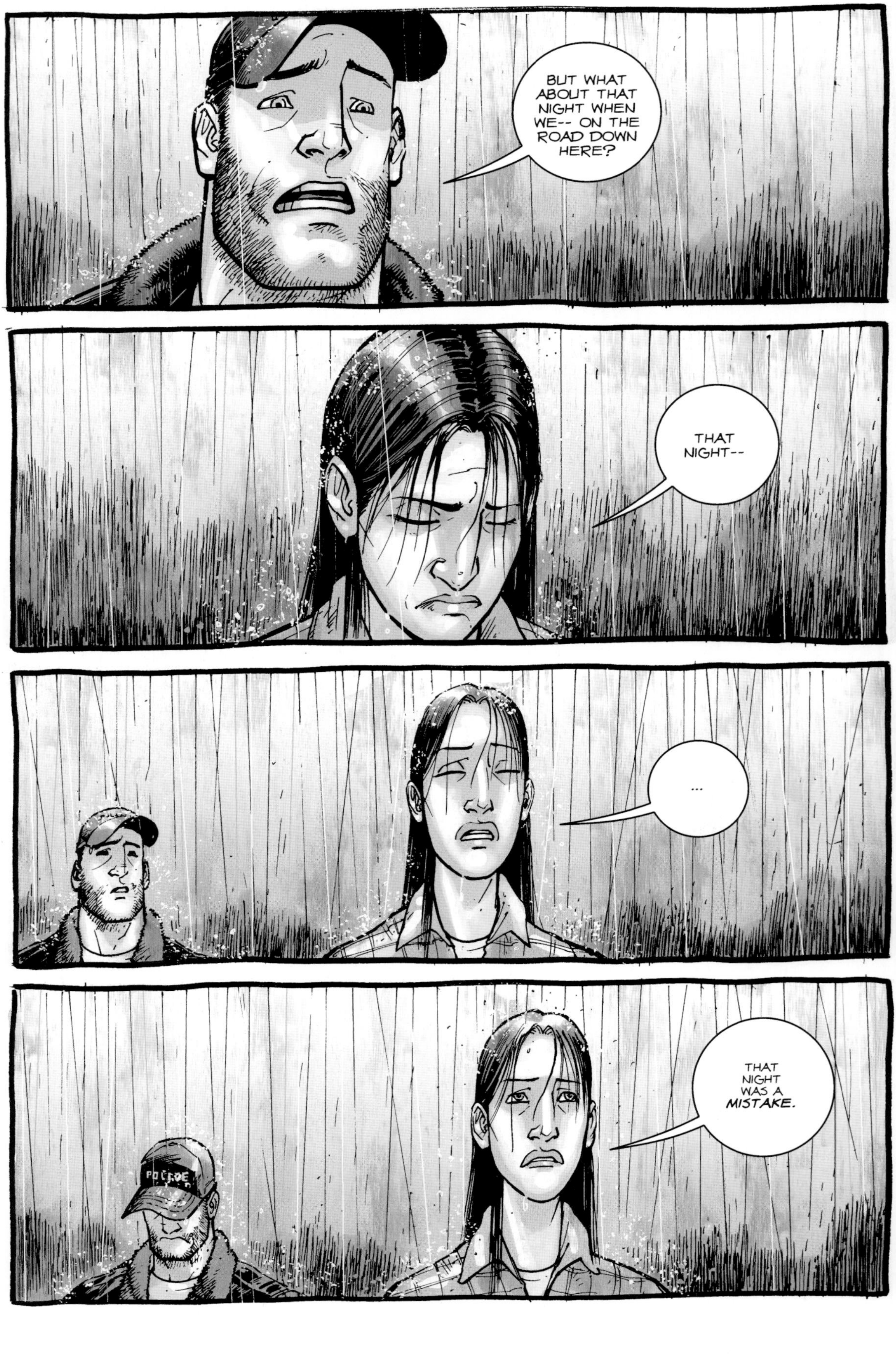
BUT WHAT ABOUT THAT NIGHT WHEN WE-- ON THE ROAD DOWN HERE?
THAT NIGHT--
...
POLICE
THAT NIGHT WAS A *MISTAKE.*

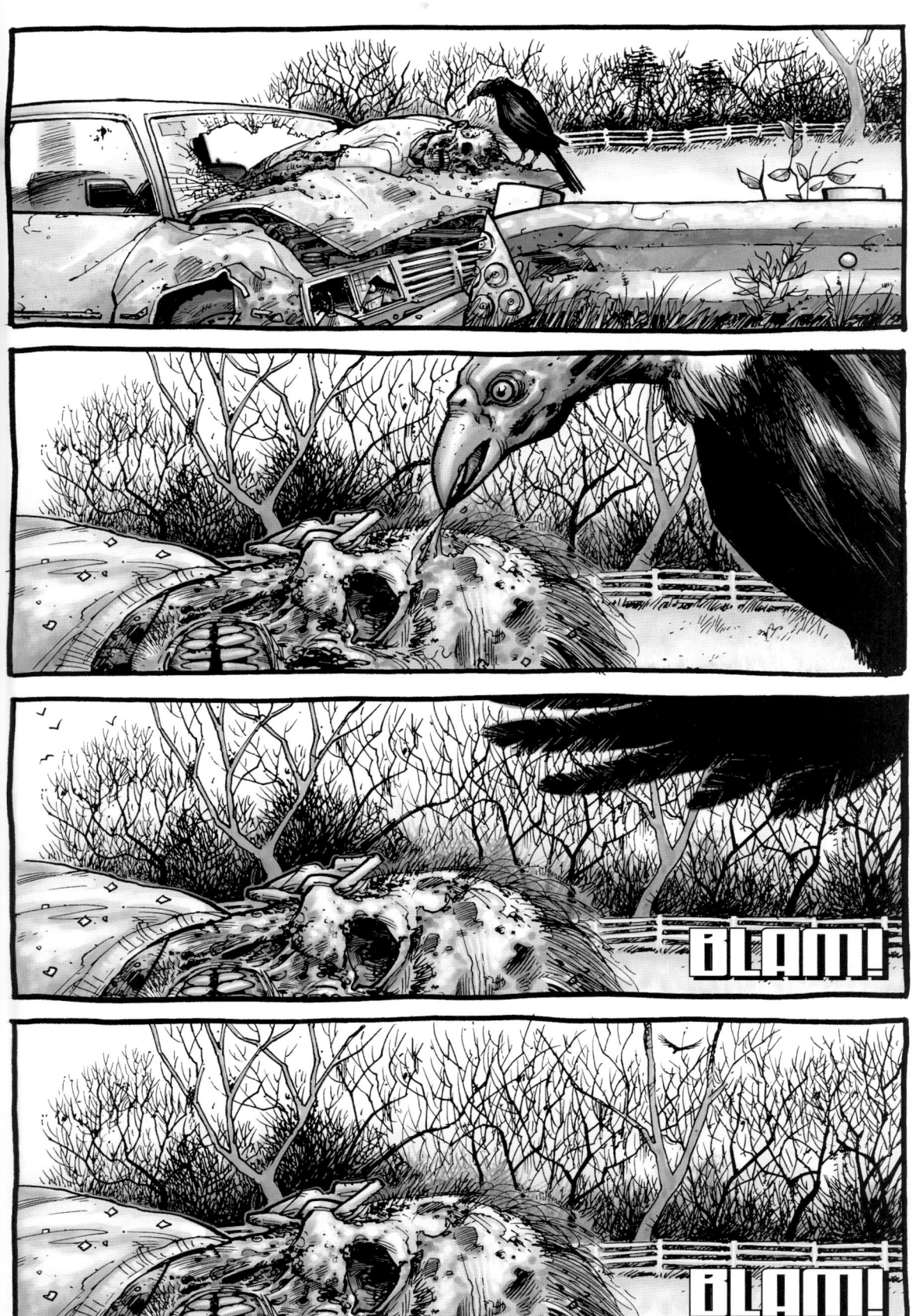

BLAM!

BLAM!

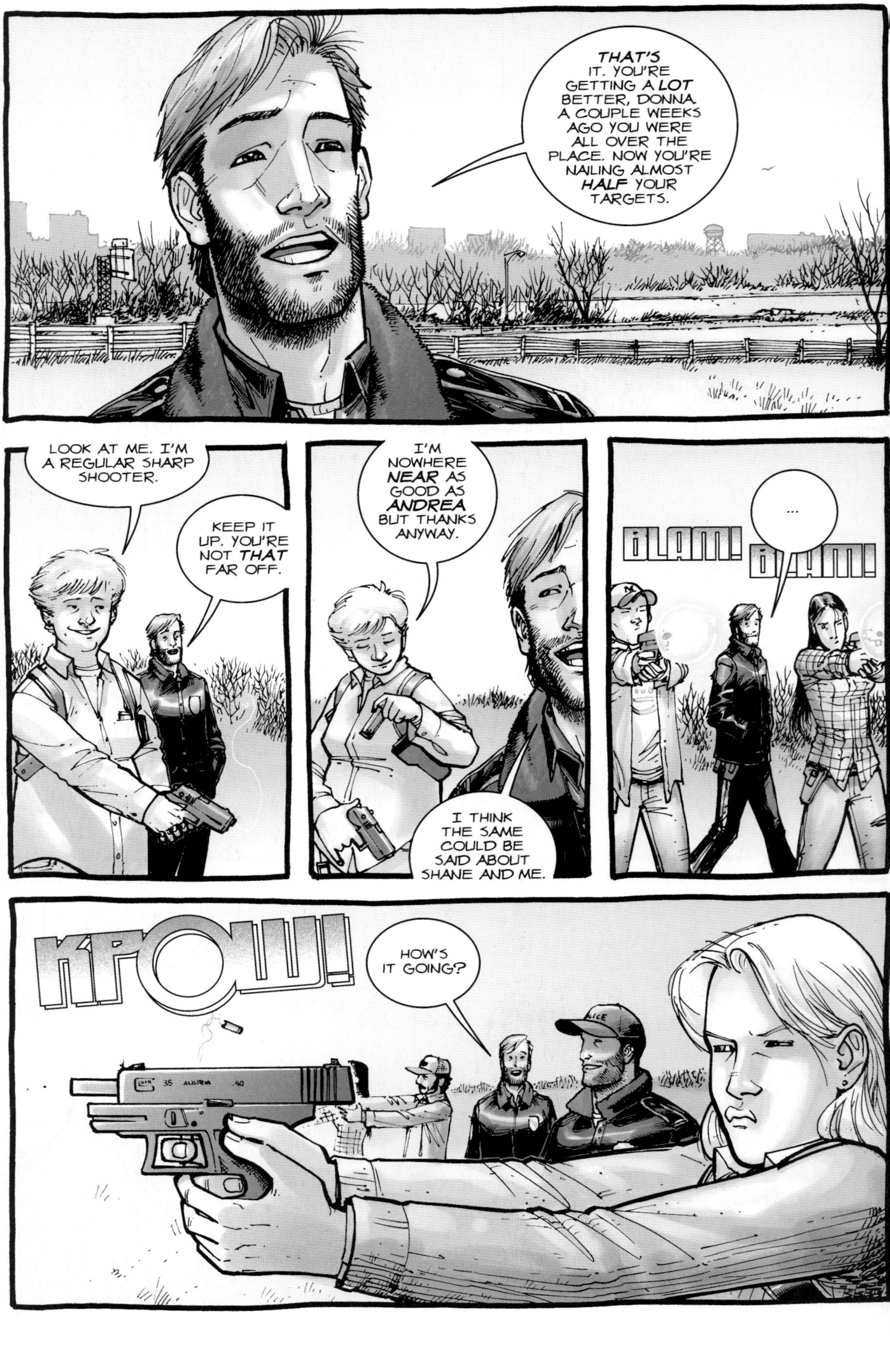
THAT'S IT. YOU'RE GETTING A LOT BETTER, DONNA. A COUPLE WEEKS AGO YOU WERE ALL OVER THE PLACE. NOW YOU'RE NAILING ALMOST HALF YOUR TARGETS.
LOOK AT ME. I'M A REGULAR SHARP SHOOTER.
KEEP IT UP. YOU'RE NOT THAT FAR OFF.
I'M NOWHERE NEAR AS GOOD AS ANDREA BUT THANKS ANYWAY.
I THINK THE SAME COULD BE SAID ABOUT SHANE AND ME.
BLAM! BLAM!
...
KPOW!
HOW'S IT GOING?

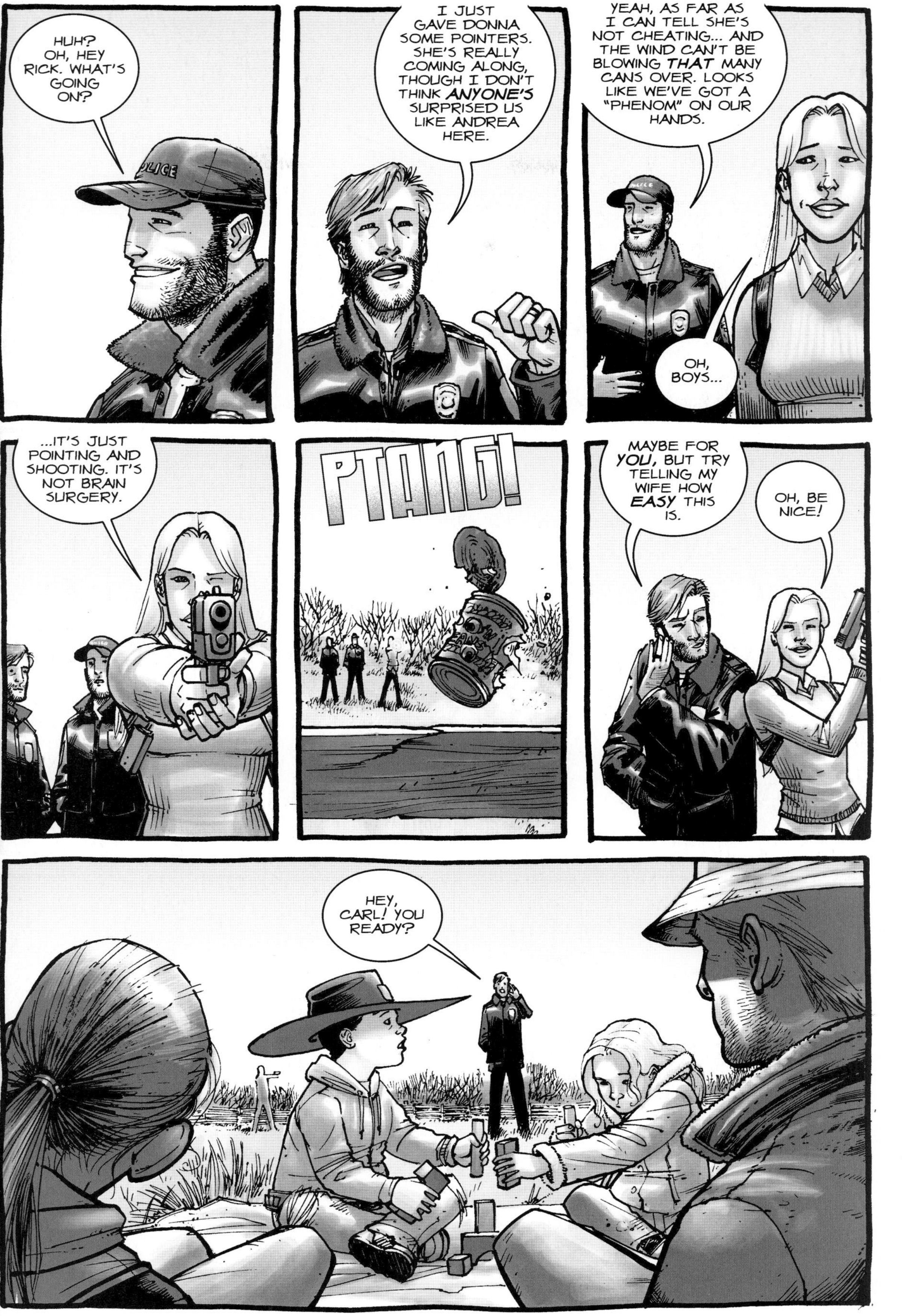
HUH? OH, HEY RICK. WHAT'S GOING ON?
I JUST GAVE DONNA SOME POINTERS. SHE'S REALLY COMING ALONG, THOUGH I DON'T THINK ANYONE'S SURPRISED US LIKE ANDREA HERE.
YEAH, AS FAR AS I CAN TELL SHE'S NOT CHEATING... AND THE WIND CAN'T BE BLOWING THAT MANY CANS OVER. LOOKS LIKE WE'VE GOT A "PHENOM" ON OUR HANDS.
OH, BOYS...
...IT'S JUST POINTING AND SHOOTING. IT'S NOT BRAIN SURGERY.
PTANG!
MAYBE FOR YOU, BUT TRY TELLING MY WIFE HOW EASY THIS IS.
OH, BE NICE!
HEY, CARL! YOU READY?

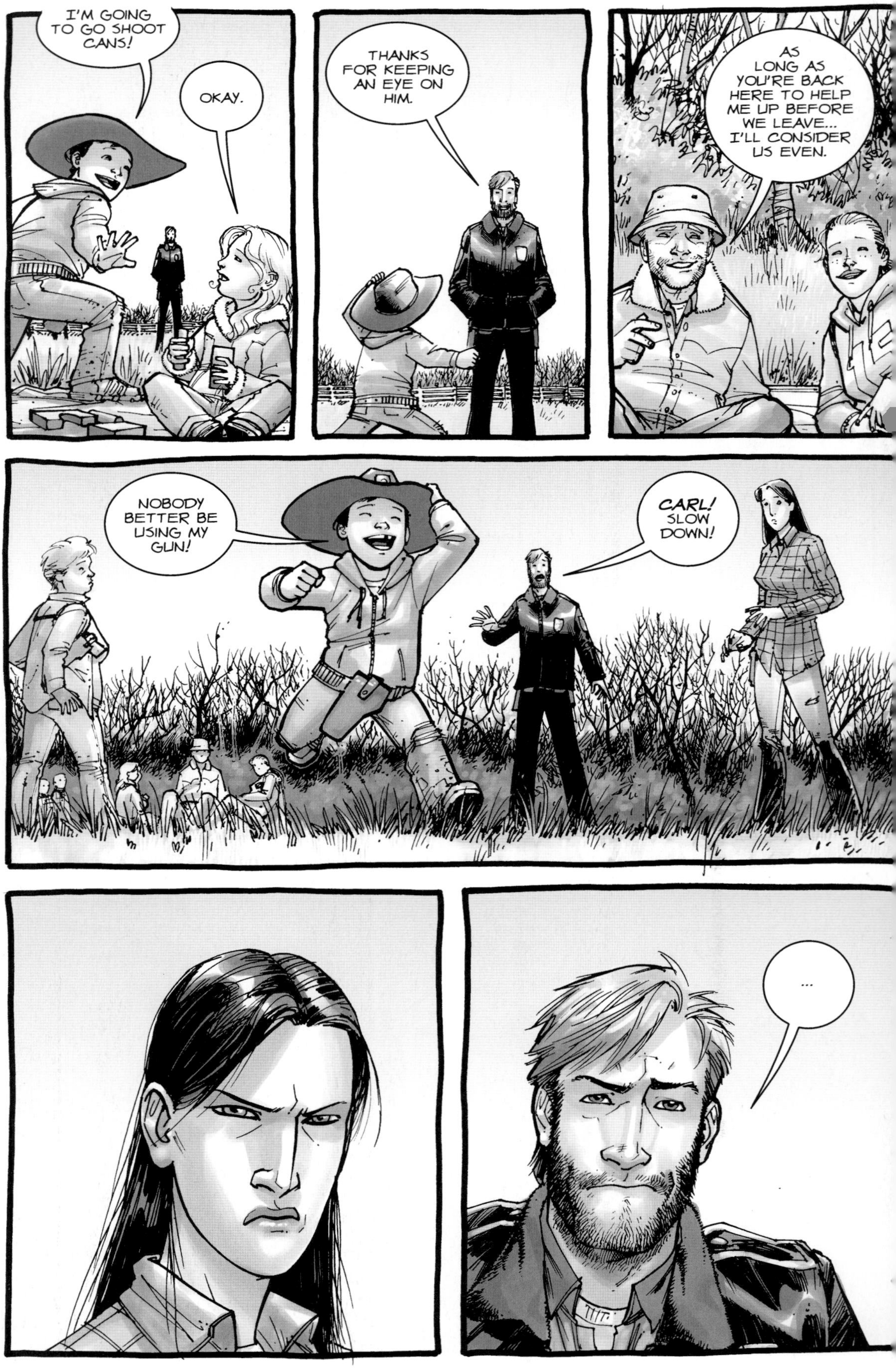
I'M GOING TO GO SHOOT CANS!
OKAY.
THANKS FOR KEEPING AN EYE ON HIM.
AS LONG AS YOU'RE BACK HERE TO HELP ME UP BEFORE WE LEAVE... I'LL CONSIDER US EVEN.
NOBODY BETTER BE USING MY GUN!
CARL! SLOW DOWN!
...

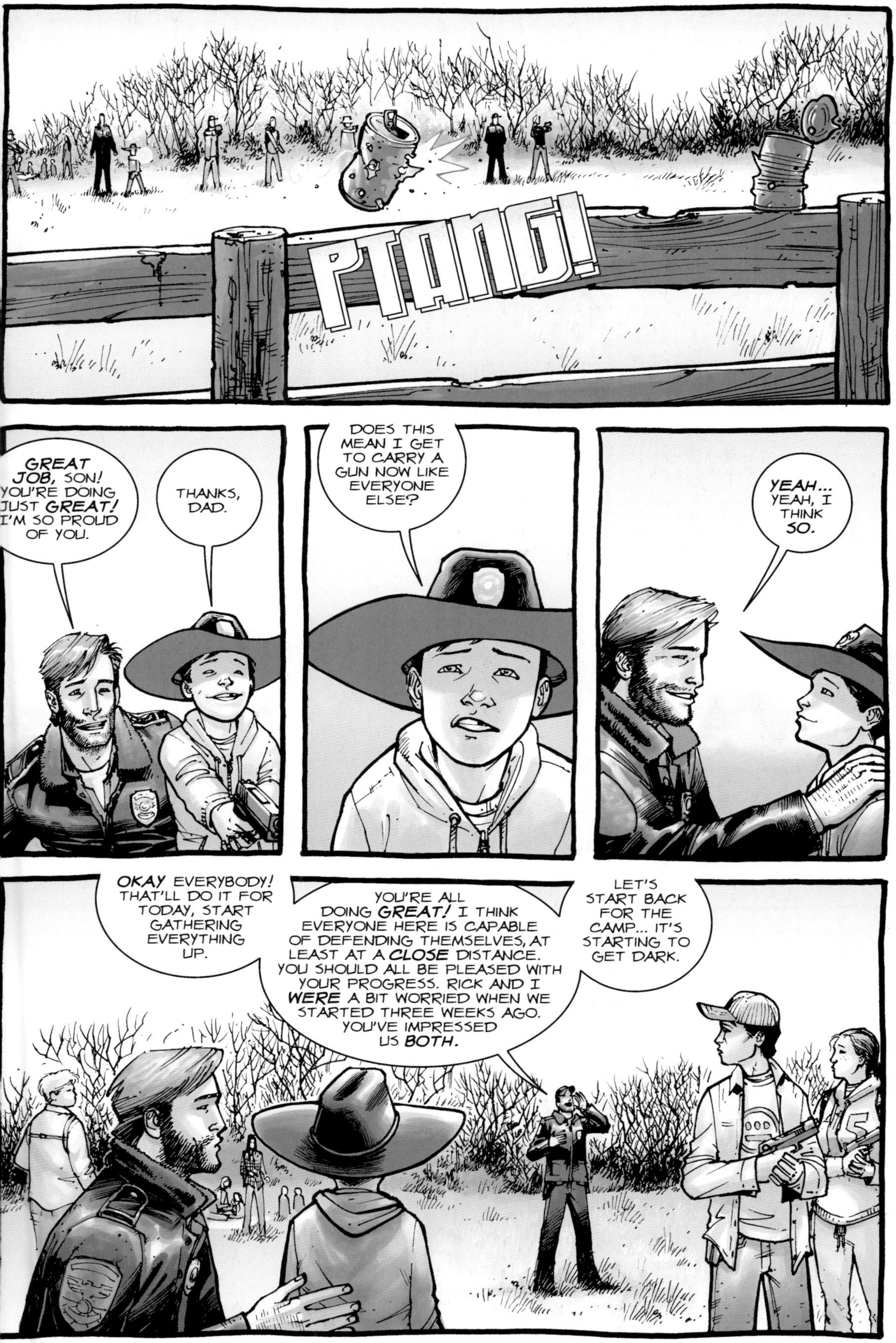
PTANG!
GREAT JOB, SON! YOU'RE DOING JUST GREAT! I'M SO PROUD OF YOU.
THANKS, DAD.
DOES THIS MEAN I GET TO CARRY A GUN NOW LIKE EVERYONE ELSE?
YEAH... YEAH, I THINK SO.
OKAY EVERYBODY! THAT'LL DO IT FOR TODAY, START GATHERING EVERYTHING UP.
YOU'RE ALL DOING GREAT! I THINK EVERYONE HERE IS CAPABLE OF DEFENDING THEMSELVES, AT LEAST AT A CLOSE DISTANCE. YOU SHOULD ALL BE PLEASED WITH YOUR PROGRESS. RICK AND I WERE A BIT WORRIED WHEN WE STARTED THREE WEEKS AGO. YOU'VE IMPRESSED US BOTH.
LET'S START BACK FOR THE CAMP... IT'S STARTING TO GET DARK.

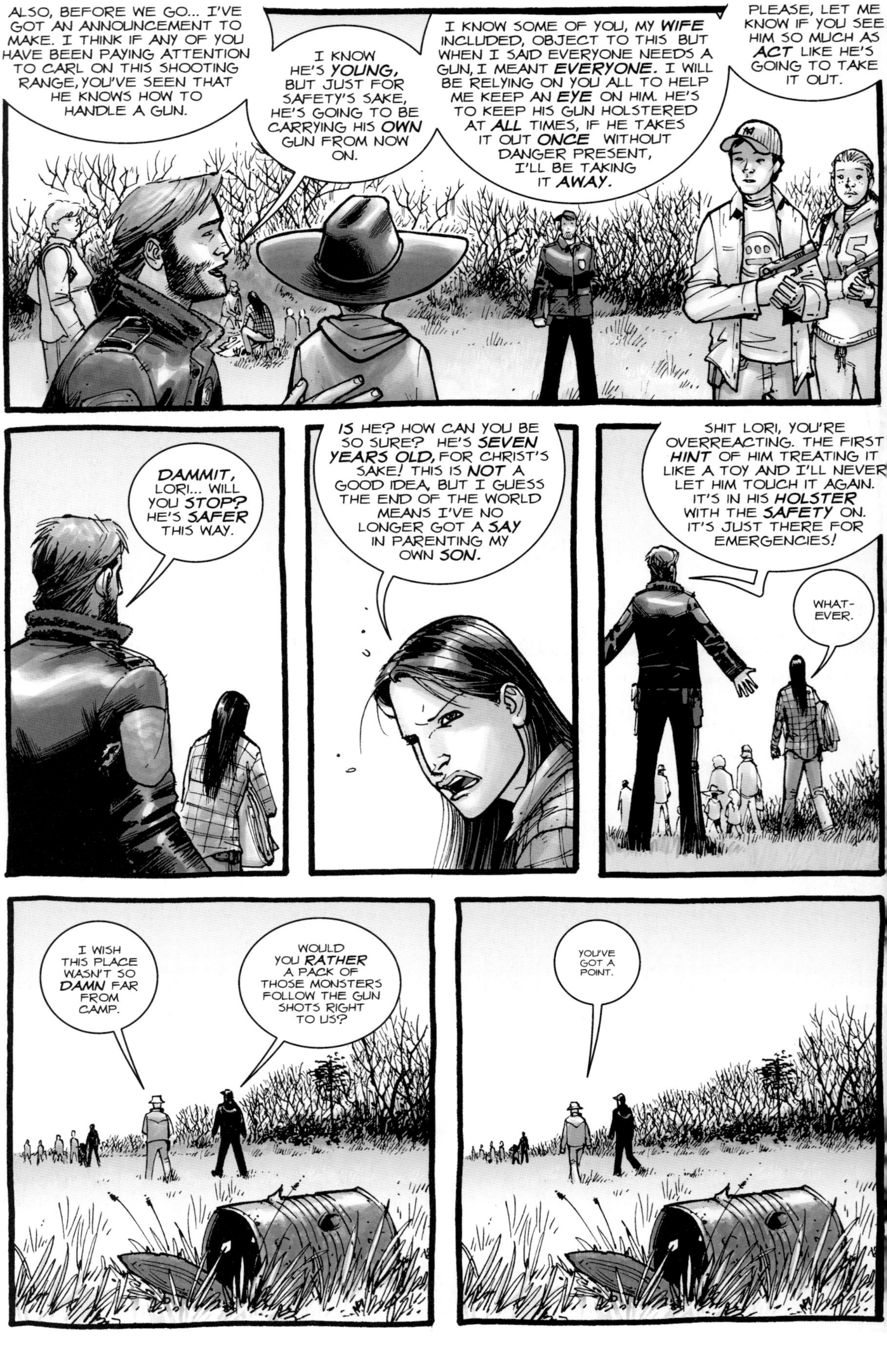

ALSO, BEFORE WE GO... I'VE GOT AN ANNOUNCEMENT TO MAKE. I THINK IF ANY OF YOU HAVE BEEN PAYING ATTENTION TO CARL ON THIS SHOOTING RANGE, YOU'VE SEEN THAT HE KNOWS HOW TO HANDLE A GUN.
I KNOW HE'S YOUNG, BUT JUST FOR SAFETY'S SAKE, HE'S GOING TO BE CARRYING HIS OWN GUN FROM NOW ON.
I KNOW SOME OF YOU, MY WIFE INCLUDED, OBJECT TO THIS BUT WHEN I SAID EVERYONE NEEDS A GUN, I MEANT EVERYONE. I WILL BE RELYING ON YOU ALL TO HELP ME KEEP AN EYE ON HIM. HE'S TO KEEP HIS GUN HOLSTERED AT ALL TIMES, IF HE TAKES IT OUT ONCE WITHOUT DANGER PRESENT, I'LL BE TAKING IT AWAY.
PLEASE, LET ME KNOW IF YOU SEE HIM SO MUCH AS ACT LIKE HE'S GOING TO TAKE IT OUT.
DAMMIT, LORI... WILL YOU STOP? HE'S SAFER THIS WAY.
IS HE? HOW CAN YOU BE SO SURE? HE'S SEVEN YEARS OLD, FOR CHRIST'S SAKE! THIS IS NOT A GOOD IDEA, BUT I GUESS THE END OF THE WORLD MEANS I'VE NO LONGER GOT A SAY IN PARENTING MY OWN SON.
SHIT LORI, YOU'RE OVERREACTING. THE FIRST HINT OF HIM TREATING IT LIKE A TOY AND I'LL NEVER LET HIM TOUCH IT AGAIN. IT'S IN HIS HOLSTER WITH THE SAFETY ON. IT'S JUST THERE FOR EMERGENCIES!
WHAT-EVER.
I WISH THIS PLACE WASN'T SO DAMN FAR FROM CAMP.
WOULD YOU RATHER A PACK OF THOSE MONSTERS FOLLOW THE GUN SHOTS RIGHT TO US?
YOU'VE GOT A POINT.

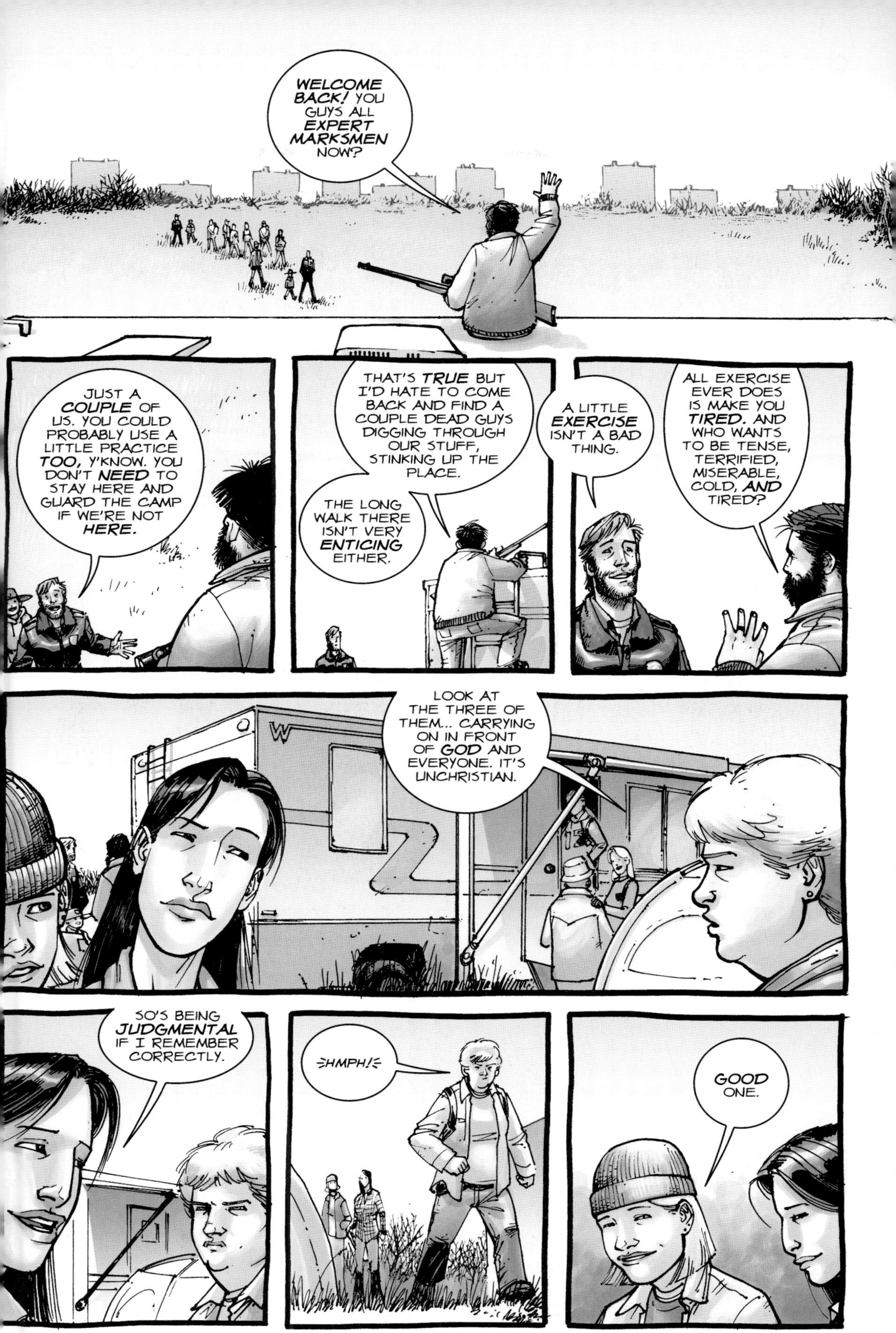
WELCOME BACK! YOU GUYS ALL EXPERT MARKSMEN NOW?
JUST A COUPLE OF US. YOU COULD PROBABLY USE A LITTLE PRACTICE TOO, Y'KNOW. YOU DON'T NEED TO STAY HERE AND GUARD THE CAMP IF WE'RE NOT HERE.
THAT'S TRUE BUT I'D HATE TO COME BACK AND FIND A COUPLE DEAD GUYS DIGGING THROUGH OUR STUFF, STINKING UP THE PLACE.
THE LONG WALK THERE ISN'T VERY ENTICING EITHER.
A LITTLE EXERCISE ISN'T A BAD THING.
ALL EXERCISE EVER DOES IS MAKE YOU TIRED. AND WHO WANTS TO BE TENSE, TERRIFIED, MISERABLE, COLD, AND TIRED?
LOOK AT THE THREE OF THEM... CARRYING ON IN FRONT OF GOD AND EVERYONE. IT'S UNCHRISTIAN.
SO'S BEING JUDGMENTAL IF I REMEMBER CORRECTLY.
HMPH!
GOOD ONE.

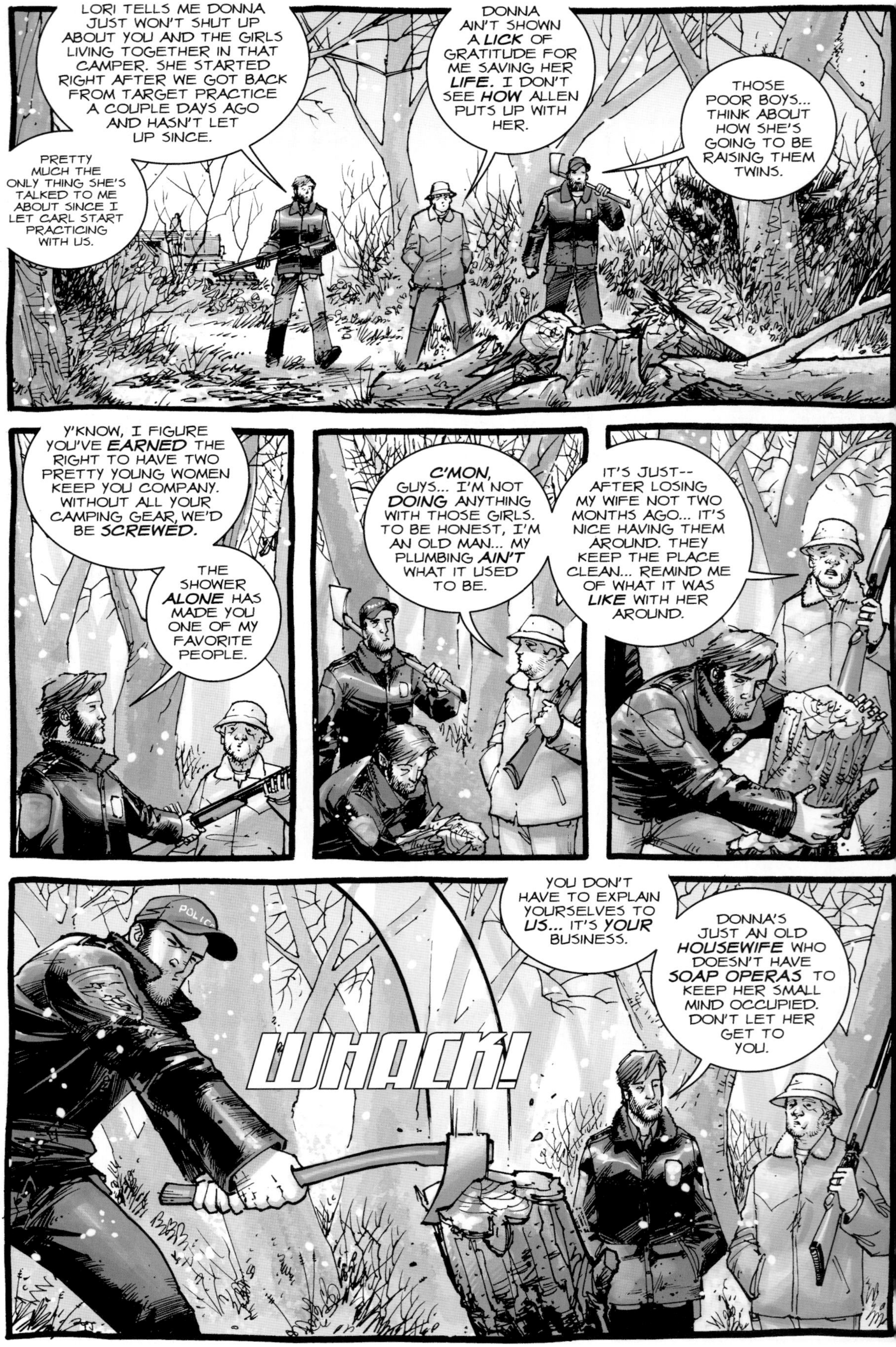
LORI TELLS ME DONNA JUST WON'T SHUT UP ABOUT YOU AND THE GIRLS LIVING TOGETHER IN THAT CAMPER. SHE STARTED RIGHT AFTER WE GOT BACK FROM TARGET PRACTICE A COUPLE DAYS AGO AND HASN'T LET UP SINCE.
PRETTY MUCH THE ONLY THING SHE'S TALKED TO ME ABOUT SINCE I LET CARL START PRACTICING WITH US.
DONNA AIN'T SHOWN A LICK OF GRATITUDE FOR ME SAVING HER LIFE. I DON'T SEE HOW ALLEN PUTS UP WITH HER.
THOSE POOR BOYS... THINK ABOUT HOW SHE'S GOING TO BE RAISING THEM TWINS.
Y'KNOW, I FIGURE YOU'VE EARNED THE RIGHT TO HAVE TWO PRETTY YOUNG WOMEN KEEP YOU COMPANY. WITHOUT ALL YOUR CAMPING GEAR, WE'D BE SCREWED.
THE SHOWER ALONE HAS MADE YOU ONE OF MY FAVORITE PEOPLE.
C'MON, GUYS... I'M NOT DOING ANYTHING WITH THOSE GIRLS. TO BE HONEST, I'M AN OLD MAN... MY PLUMBING AIN'T WHAT IT USED TO BE.
IT'S JUST-- AFTER LOSING MY WIFE NOT TWO MONTHS AGO... IT'S NICE HAVING THEM AROUND. THEY KEEP THE PLACE CLEAN... REMIND ME OF WHAT IT WAS LIKE WITH HER AROUND.
WHACK!
YOU DON'T HAVE TO EXPLAIN YOURSELVES TO US... IT'S YOUR BUSINESS.
DONNA'S JUST AN OLD HOUSEWIFE WHO DOESN'T HAVE SOAP OPERAS TO KEEP HER SMALL MIND OCCUPIED. DON'T LET HER GET TO YOU.

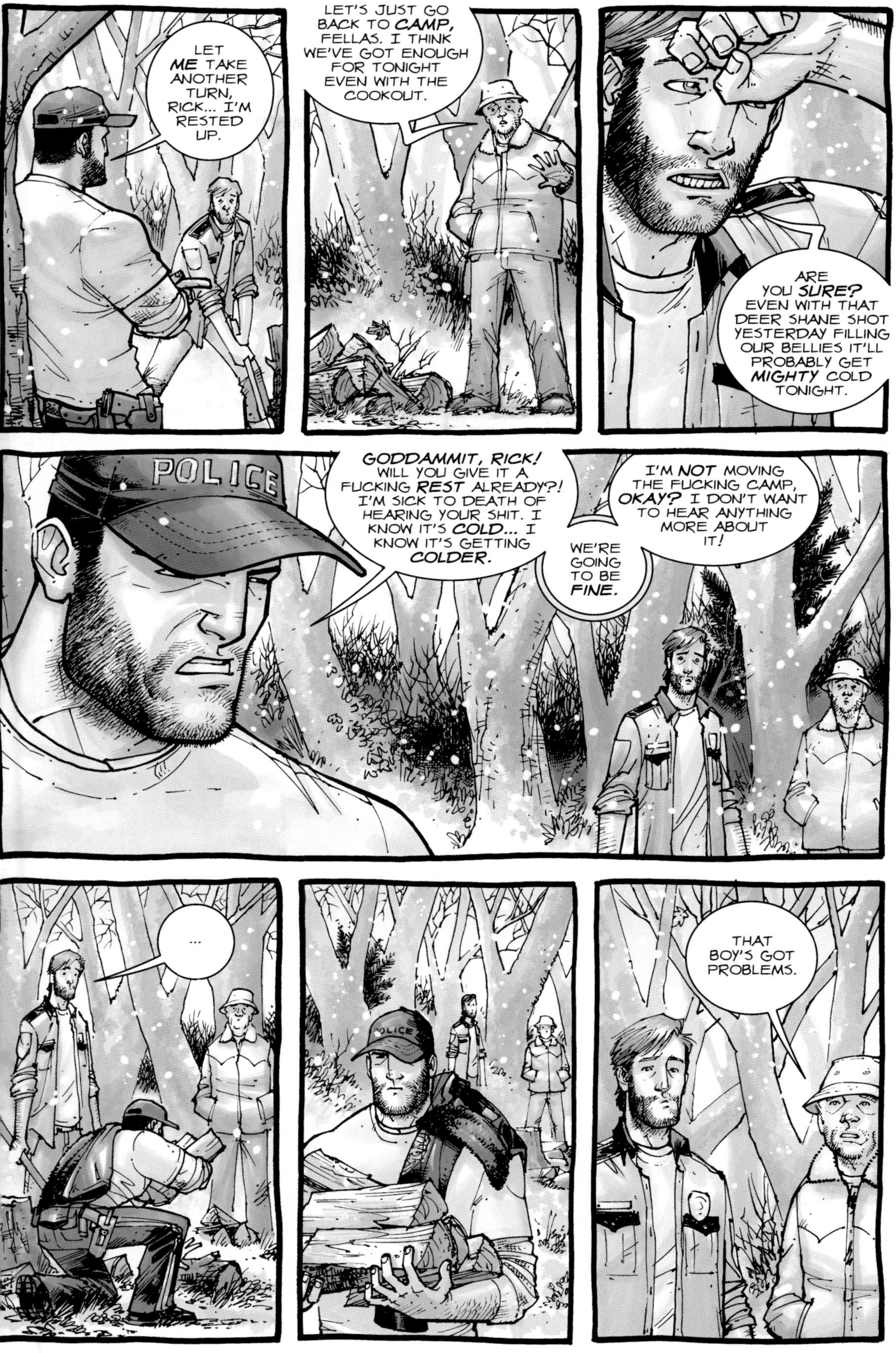
LET ME TAKE ANOTHER TURN, RICK... I'M RESTED UP.
LET'S JUST GO BACK TO CAMP, FELLAS. I THINK WE'VE GOT ENOUGH FOR TONIGHT EVEN WITH THE COOKOUT.
ARE YOU SURE? EVEN WITH THAT DEER SHANE SHOT YESTERDAY FILLING OUR BELLIES IT'LL PROBABLY GET MIGHTY COLD TONIGHT.
POLICE
GODDAMMIT, RICK! WILL YOU GIVE IT A FUCKING REST ALREADY?! I'M SICK TO DEATH OF HEARING YOUR SHIT. I KNOW IT'S COLD... I KNOW IT'S GETTING COLDER.
WE'RE GOING TO BE FINE.
I'M NOT MOVING THE FUCKING CAMP, OKAY? I DON'T WANT TO HEAR ANYTHING MORE ABOUT IT!
...
POLICE
THAT BOY'S GOT PROBLEMS.

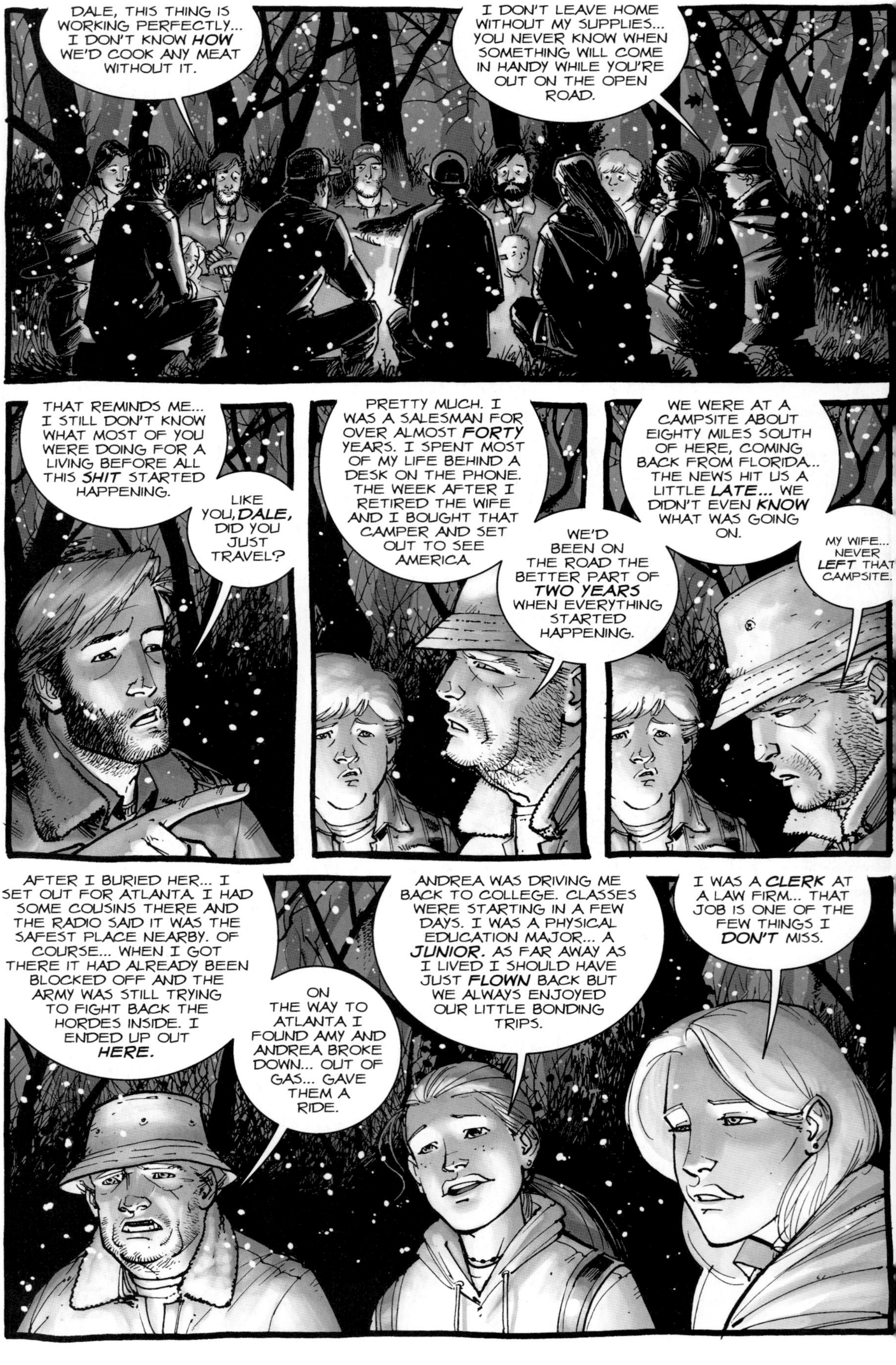
DALE, THIS THING IS WORKING PERFECTLY... I DON'T KNOW HOW WE'D COOK ANY MEAT WITHOUT IT.
I DON'T LEAVE HOME WITHOUT MY SUPPLIES... YOU NEVER KNOW WHEN SOMETHING WILL COME IN HANDY WHILE YOU'RE OUT ON THE OPEN ROAD.
THAT REMINDS ME... I STILL DON'T KNOW WHAT MOST OF YOU WERE DOING FOR A LIVING BEFORE ALL THIS SHIT STARTED HAPPENING.
LIKE YOU, DALE, DID YOU JUST TRAVEL?
PRETTY MUCH. I WAS A SALESMAN FOR OVER ALMOST FORTY YEARS. I SPENT MOST OF MY LIFE BEHIND A DESK ON THE PHONE. THE WEEK AFTER I RETIRED THE WIFE AND I BOUGHT THAT CAMPER AND SET OUT TO SEE AMERICA.
WE'D BEEN ON THE ROAD THE BETTER PART OF TWO YEARS WHEN EVERYTHING STARTED HAPPENING.
WE WERE AT A CAMPSITE ABOUT EIGHTY MILES SOUTH OF HERE, COMING BACK FROM FLORIDA.. THE NEWS HIT US A LITTLE LATE... WE DIDN'T EVEN KNOW WHAT WAS GOING ON.
MY WIFE... NEVER LEFT THAT CAMPSITE.
AFTER I BURIED HER... I SET OUT FOR ATLANTA. I HAD SOME COUSINS THERE AND THE RADIO SAID IT WAS THE SAFEST PLACE NEARBY. OF COURSE... WHEN I GOT THERE IT HAD ALREADY BEEN BLOCKED OFF AND THE ARMY WAS STILL TRYING TO FIGHT BACK THE HORDES INSIDE. I ENDED UP OUT HERE.
ON THE WAY TO ATLANTA I FOUND AMY AND ANDREA BROKE DOWN... OUT OF GAS... GAVE THEM A RIDE.
ANDREA WAS DRIVING ME BACK TO COLLEGE. CLASSES WERE STARTING IN A FEW DAYS. I WAS A PHYSICAL EDUCATION MAJOR... A JUNIOR. AS FAR AWAY AS I LIVED I SHOULD HAVE JUST FLOWN BACK BUT WE ALWAYS ENJOYED OUR LITTLE BONDING TRIPS.
I WAS A CLERK AT A LAW FIRM... THAT JOB IS ONE OF THE FEW THINGS I DON'T MISS.

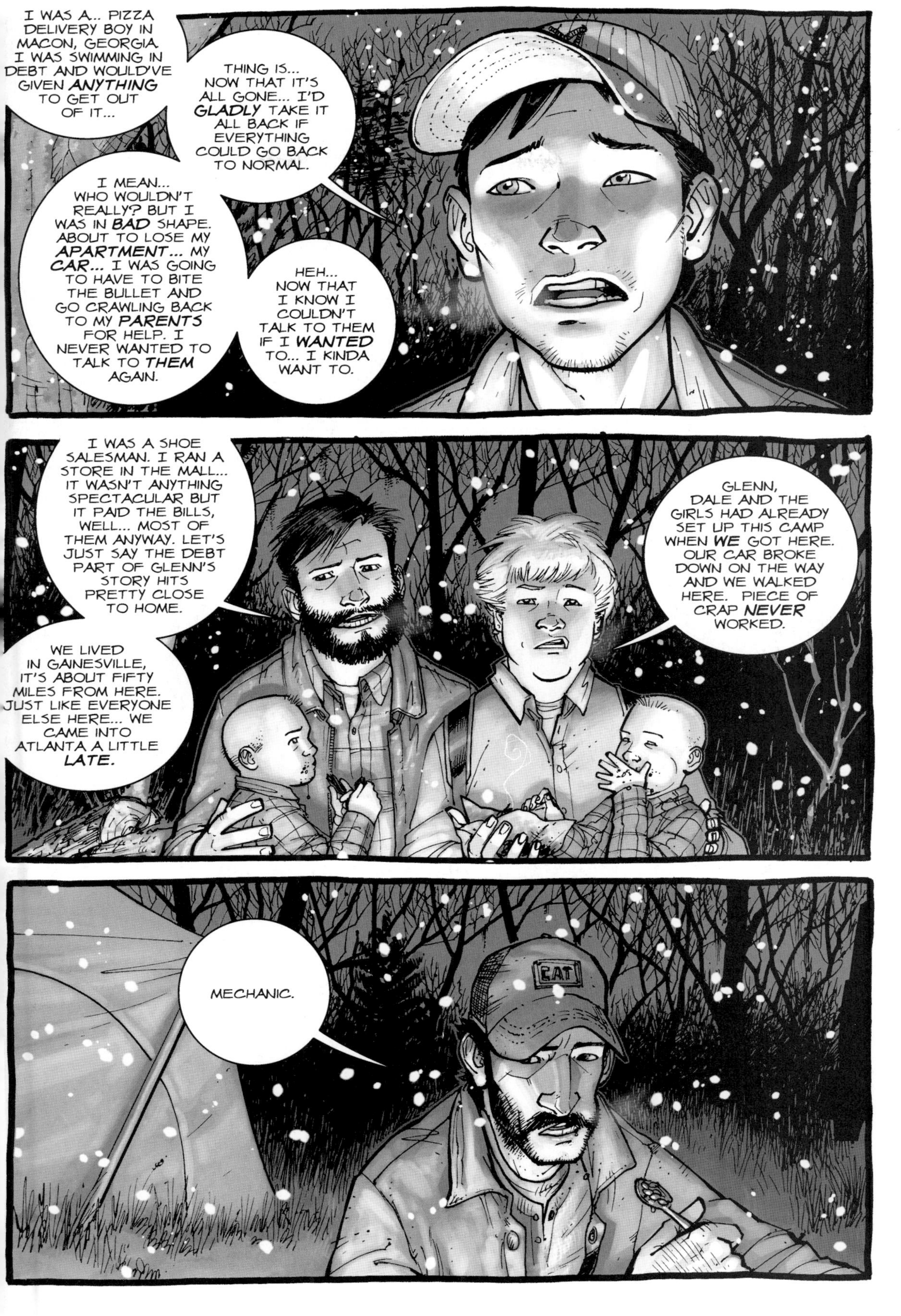
I WAS A... PIZZA DELIVERY BOY IN MACON, GEORGIA I WAS SWIMMING IN DEBT AND WOULD'VE GIVEN ANYTHING TO GET OUT OF IT...
THING IS... NOW THAT IT'S ALL GONE... I'D GLADLY TAKE IT ALL BACK IF EVERYTHING COULD GO BACK TO NORMAL.
I MEAN... WHO WOULDN'T REALLY? BUT I WAS IN BAD SHAPE. ABOUT TO LOSE MY APARTMENT... MY CAR... I WAS GOING TO HAVE TO BITE THE BULLET AND GO CRAWLING BACK TO MY PARENTS FOR HELP. I NEVER WANTED TO TALK TO THEM AGAIN.
HEH... NOW THAT I KNOW I COULDN'T TALK TO THEM IF I WANTED TO... I KINDA WANT TO.
I WAS A SHOE SALESMAN. I RAN A STORE IN THE MALL... IT WASN'T ANYTHING SPECTACULAR BUT IT PAID THE BILLS, WELL... MOST OF THEM ANYWAY. LET'S JUST SAY THE DEBT PART OF GLENN'S STORY HITS PRETTY CLOSE TO HOME.
WE LIVED IN GAINESVILLE, IT'S ABOUT FIFTY MILES FROM HERE. JUST LIKE EVERYONE ELSE HERE... WE CAME INTO ATLANTA A LITTLE LATE.
GLENN, DALE AND THE GIRLS HAD ALREADY SET UP THIS CAMP WHEN WE GOT HERE. OUR CAR BROKE DOWN ON THE WAY AND WE WALKED HERE. PIECE OF CRAP NEVER WORKED.
MECHANIC.
CAT

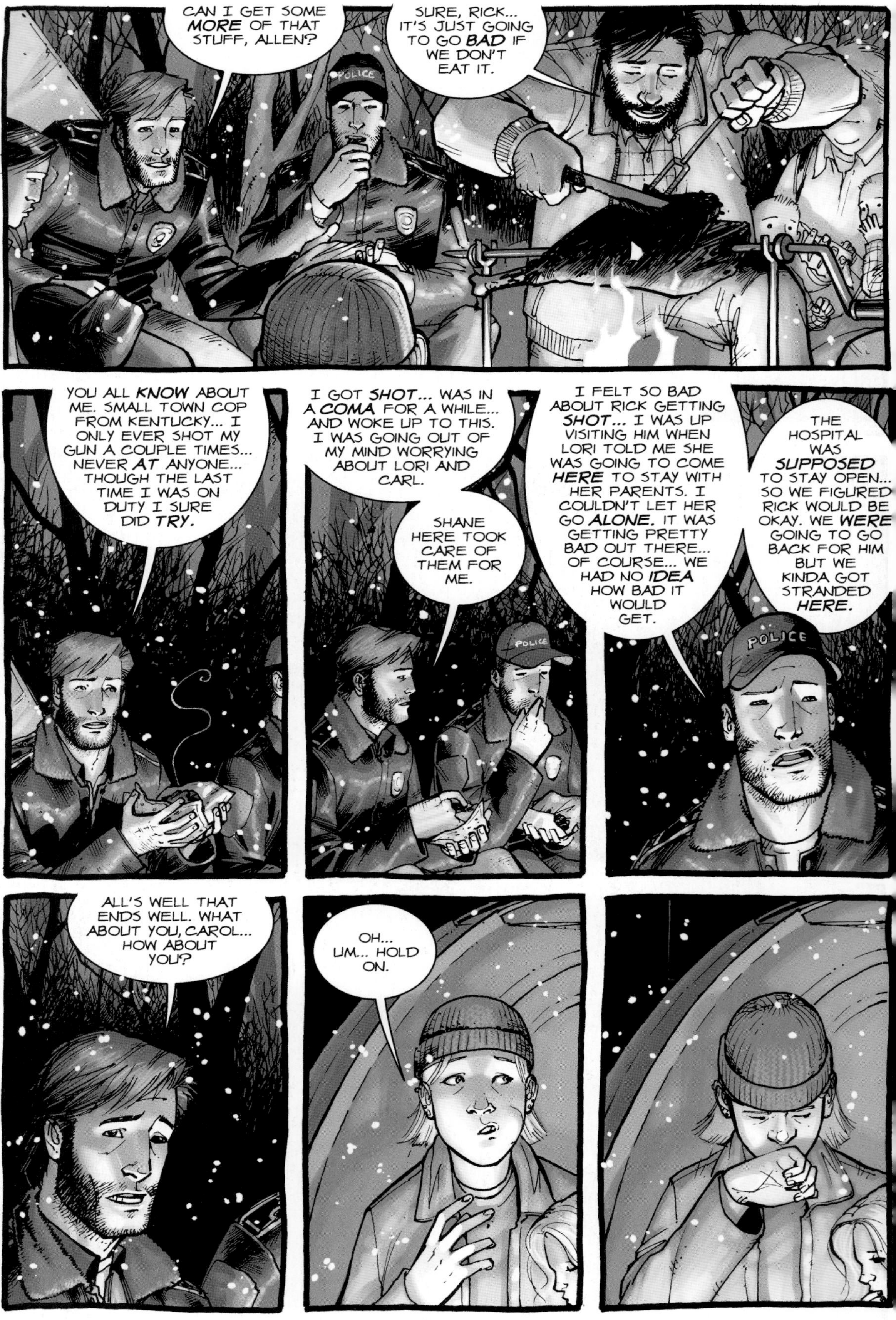
CAN I GET SOME MORE OF THAT STUFF, ALLEN?
SURE, RICK... IT'S JUST GOING TO GO BAD IF WE DON'T EAT IT.
POLICE
YOU ALL KNOW ABOUT ME. SMALL TOWN COP FROM KENTUCKY... I ONLY EVER SHOT MY GUN A COUPLE TIMES... NEVER AT ANYONE... THOUGH THE LAST TIME I WAS ON DUTY I SURE DID TRY.
I GOT SHOT... WAS IN A COMA FOR A WHILE... AND WOKE UP TO THIS. I WAS GOING OUT OF MY MIND WORRYING ABOUT LORI AND CARL.
SHANE HERE TOOK CARE OF THEM FOR ME.
POLICE
I FELT SO BAD ABOUT RICK GETTING SHOT... I WAS UP VISITING HIM WHEN LORI TOLD ME SHE WAS GOING TO COME HERE TO STAY WITH HER PARENTS. I COULDN'T LET HER GO ALONE. IT WAS GETTING PRETTY BAD OUT THERE... OF COURSE... WE HAD NO IDEA HOW BAD IT WOULD GET.
THE HOSPITAL WAS SUPPOSED TO STAY OPEN... SO WE FIGURED RICK WOULD BE OKAY. WE WERE GOING TO GO BACK FOR HIM BUT WE KINDA GOT STRANDED HERE.
POLICE
ALL'S WELL THAT ENDS WELL. WHAT ABOUT YOU, CAROL... HOW ABOUT YOU?
OH... UM... HOLD ON.

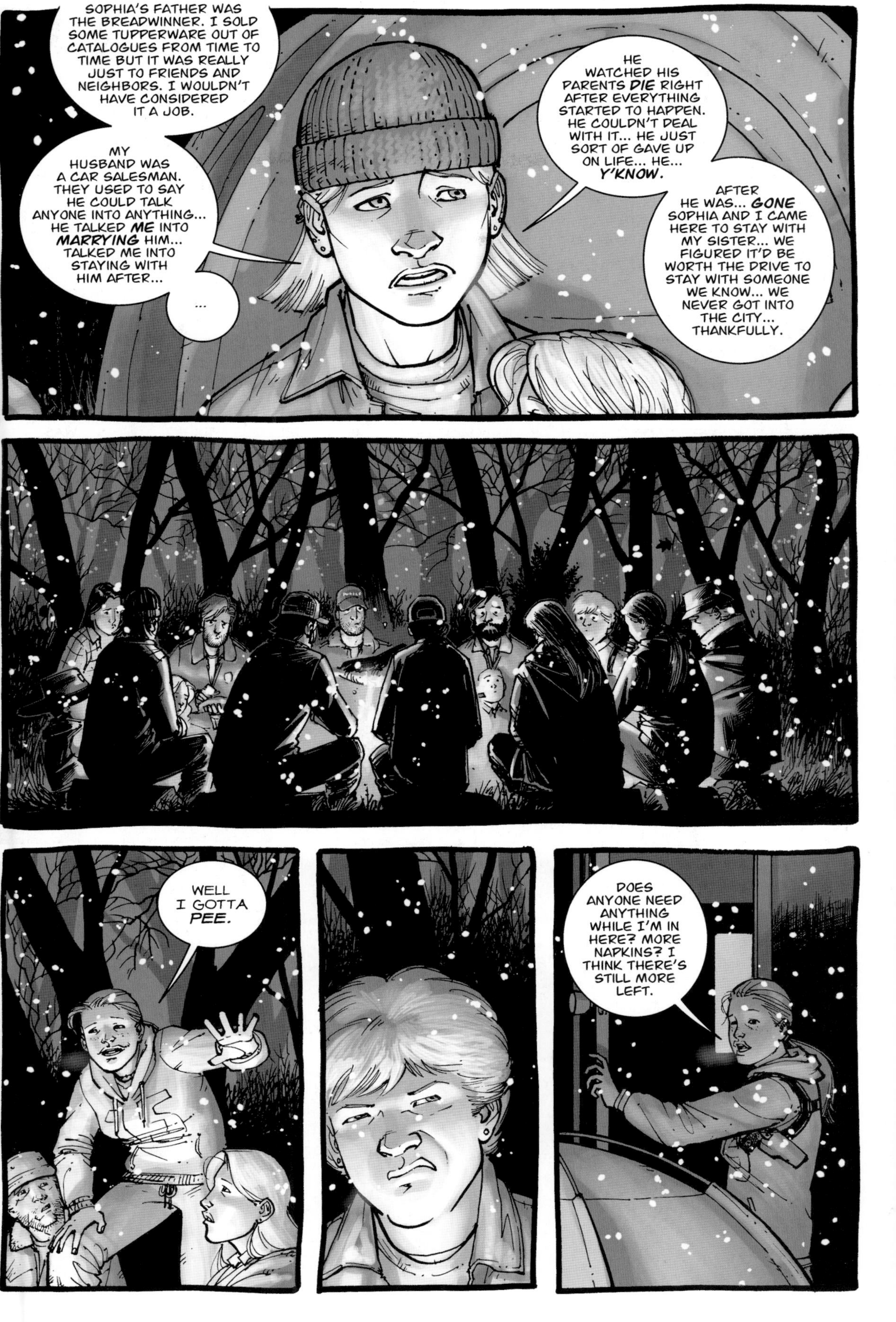
SOPHIA'S FATHER WAS THE BREADWINNER. I SOLD SOME TUPPERWARE OUT OF CATALOGUES FROM TIME TO TIME BUT IT WAS REALLY JUST TO FRIENDS AND NEIGHBORS. I WOULDN'T HAVE CONSIDERED IT A JOB.
MY HUSBAND WAS A CAR SALESMAN. THEY USED TO SAY HE COULD TALK ANYONE INTO ANYTHING... HE TALKED ME INTO MARRYING HIM... TALKED ME INTO STAYING WITH HIM AFTER...
...
HE WATCHED HIS PARENTS DIE RIGHT AFTER EVERYTHING STARTED TO HAPPEN. HE COULDN'T DEAL WITH IT... HE JUST SORT OF GAVE UP ON LIFE... HE... Y'KNOW.
AFTER HE WAS... GONE SOPHIA AND I CAME HERE TO STAY WITH MY SISTER... WE FIGURED IT'D BE WORTH THE DRIVE TO STAY WITH SOMEONE WE KNOW... WE NEVER GOT INTO THE CITY... THANKFULLY.
WELL I GOTTA PEE.
DOES ANYONE NEED ANYTHING WHILE I'M IN HERE? MORE NAPKINS? I THINK THERE'S STILL MORE LEFT.

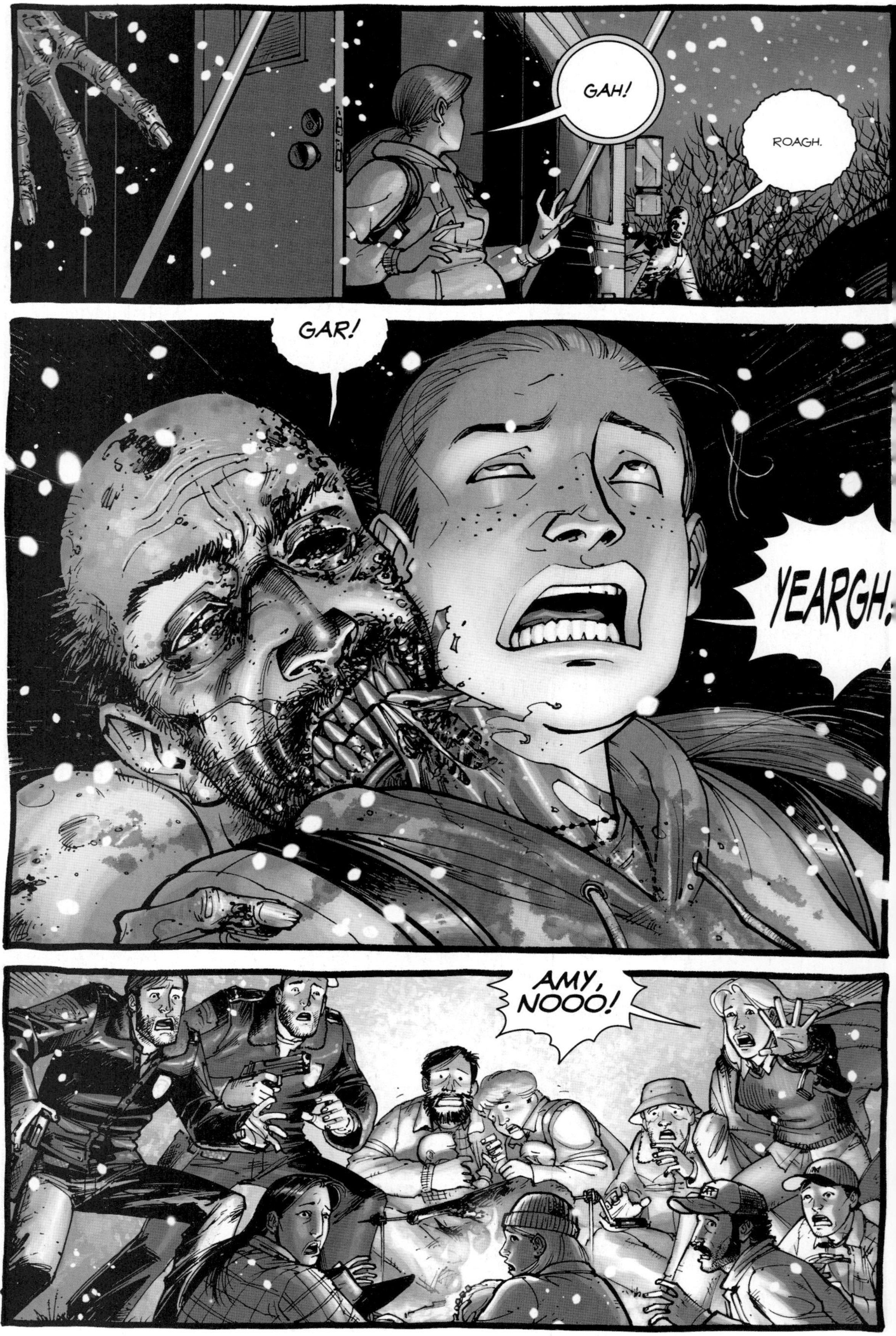
GAH!
ROAGH.
GAR!
YEARGH!
AMY, NOOO!

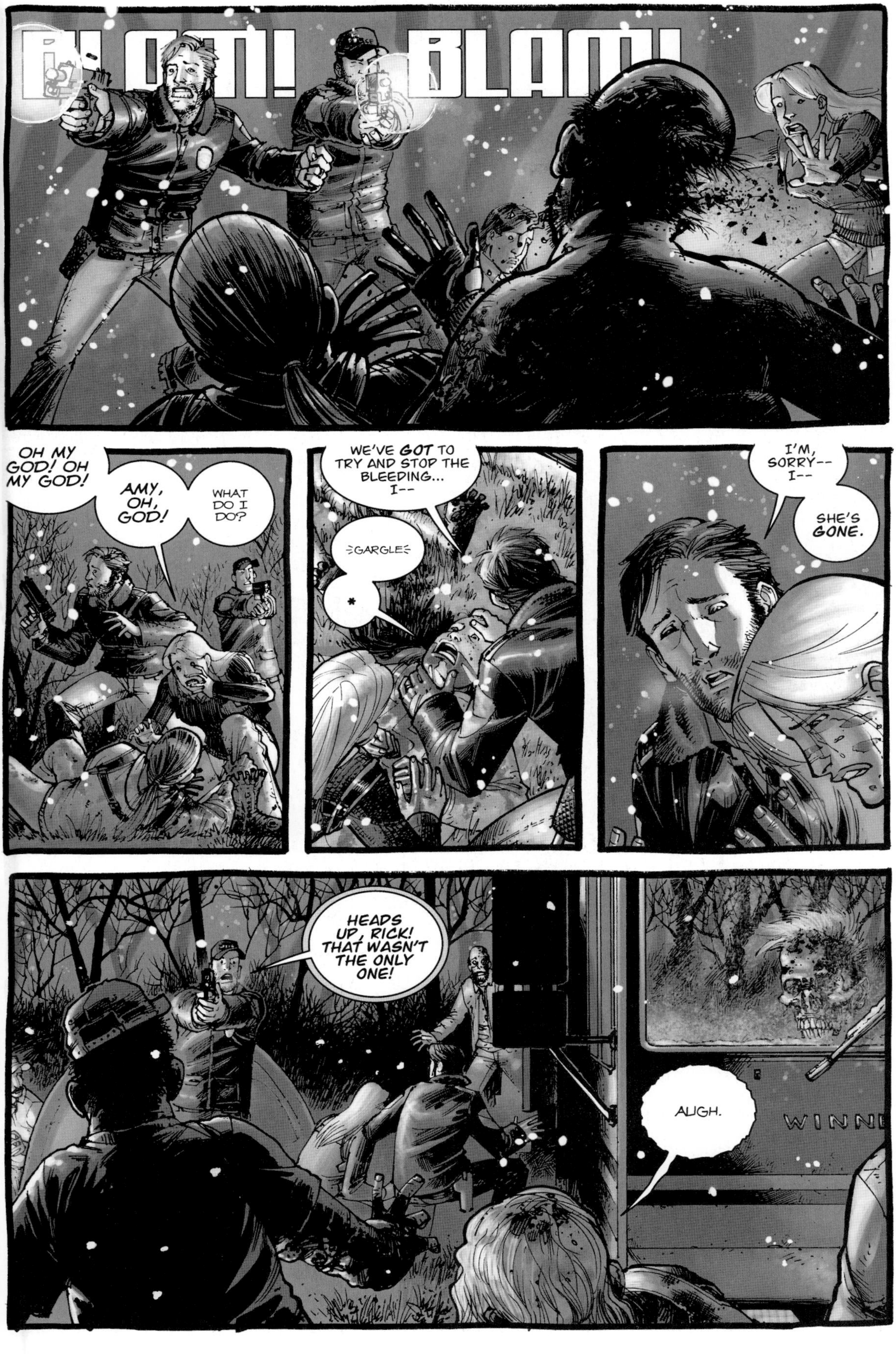
BLAM! BLAM!
OH MY GOD! OH MY GOD!
AMY, OH, GOD!
WHAT DO I DO?
WE'VE GOT TO TRY AND STOP THE BLEEDING... I--
GARGLE
*
I'M, SORRY-- I--
SHE'S GONE.
HEADS UP, RICK! THAT WASN'T THE ONLY ONE!
AUGH.
WINNE

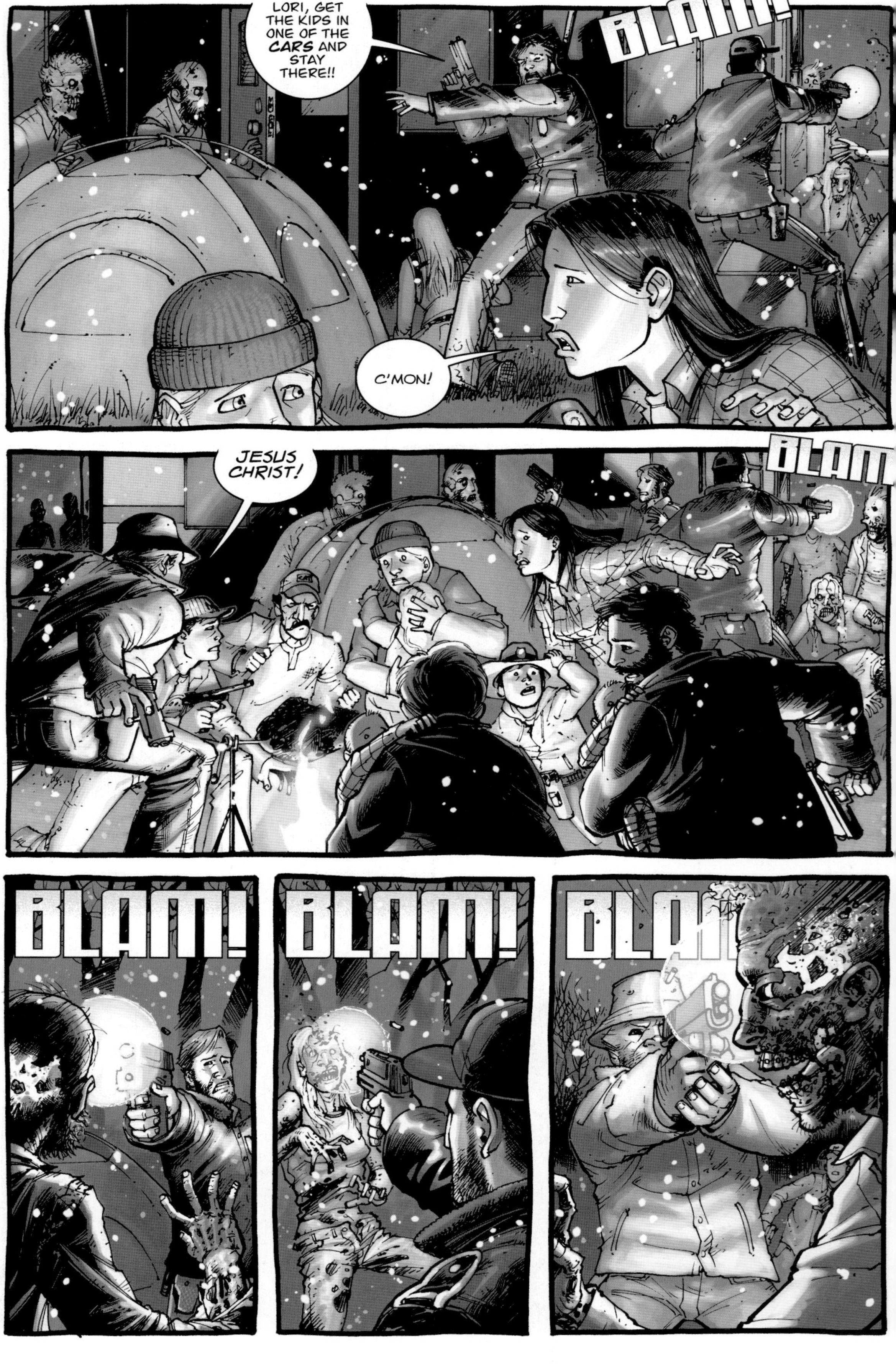
LORI, GET THE KIDS IN ONE OF THE CARS AND STAY THERE!!
BLAM!
C'MON!
JESUS CHRIST!
BLAM
BLAM!
BLAM!
BLA

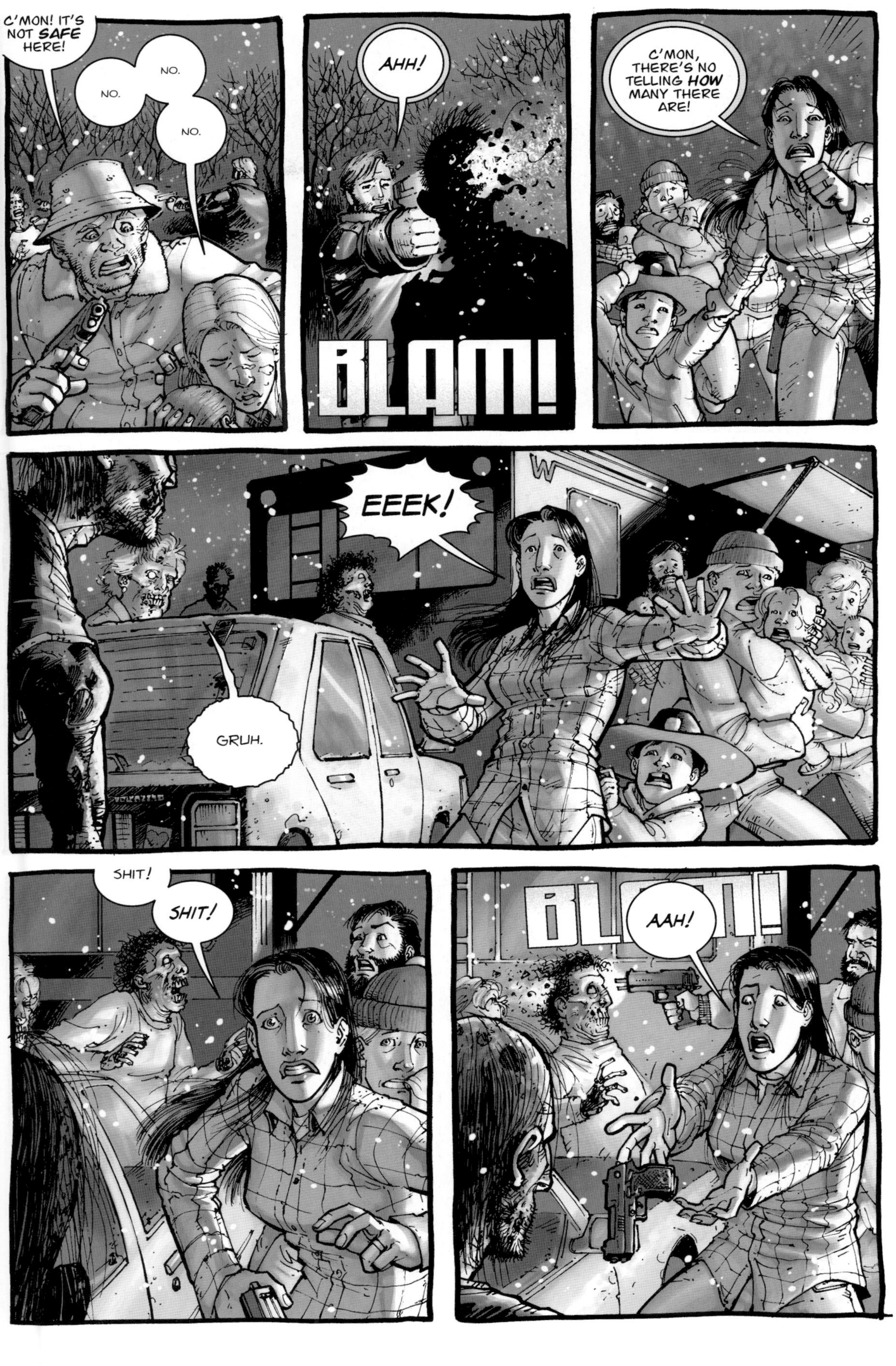
C'MON! IT'S NOT SAFE HERE!
NO.
NO.
NO.
AHH!
BLAM!
C'MON, THERE'S NO TELLING HOW MANY THERE ARE!
EEEK!
GRUH.
SHIT!
SHIT!
AAH!

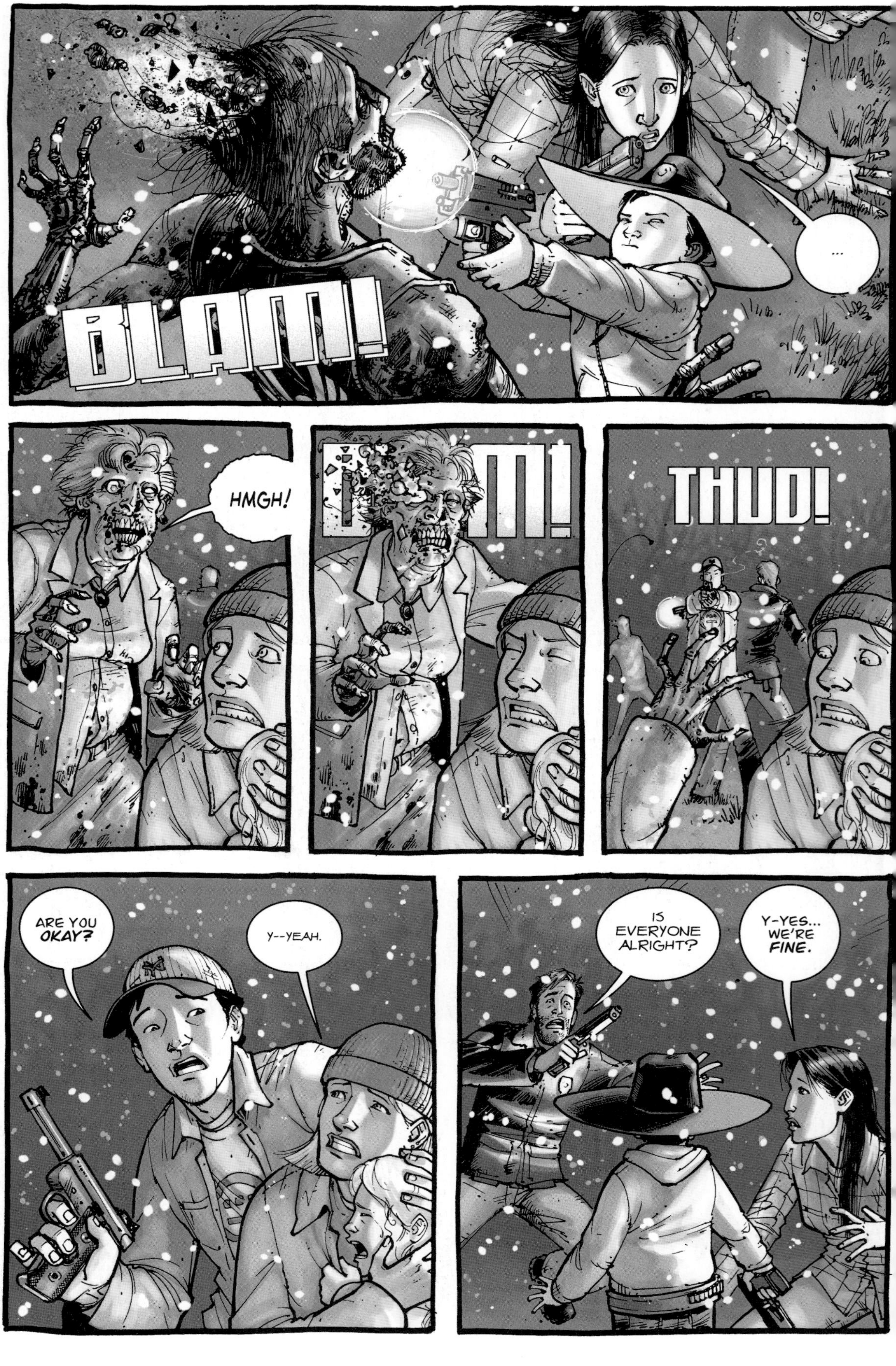
BLAM!
...
HMGH!
M!
THUD!
ARE YOU OKAY?
Y--YEAH.
IS EVERYONE ALRIGHT?
Y-YES... WE'RE FINE.

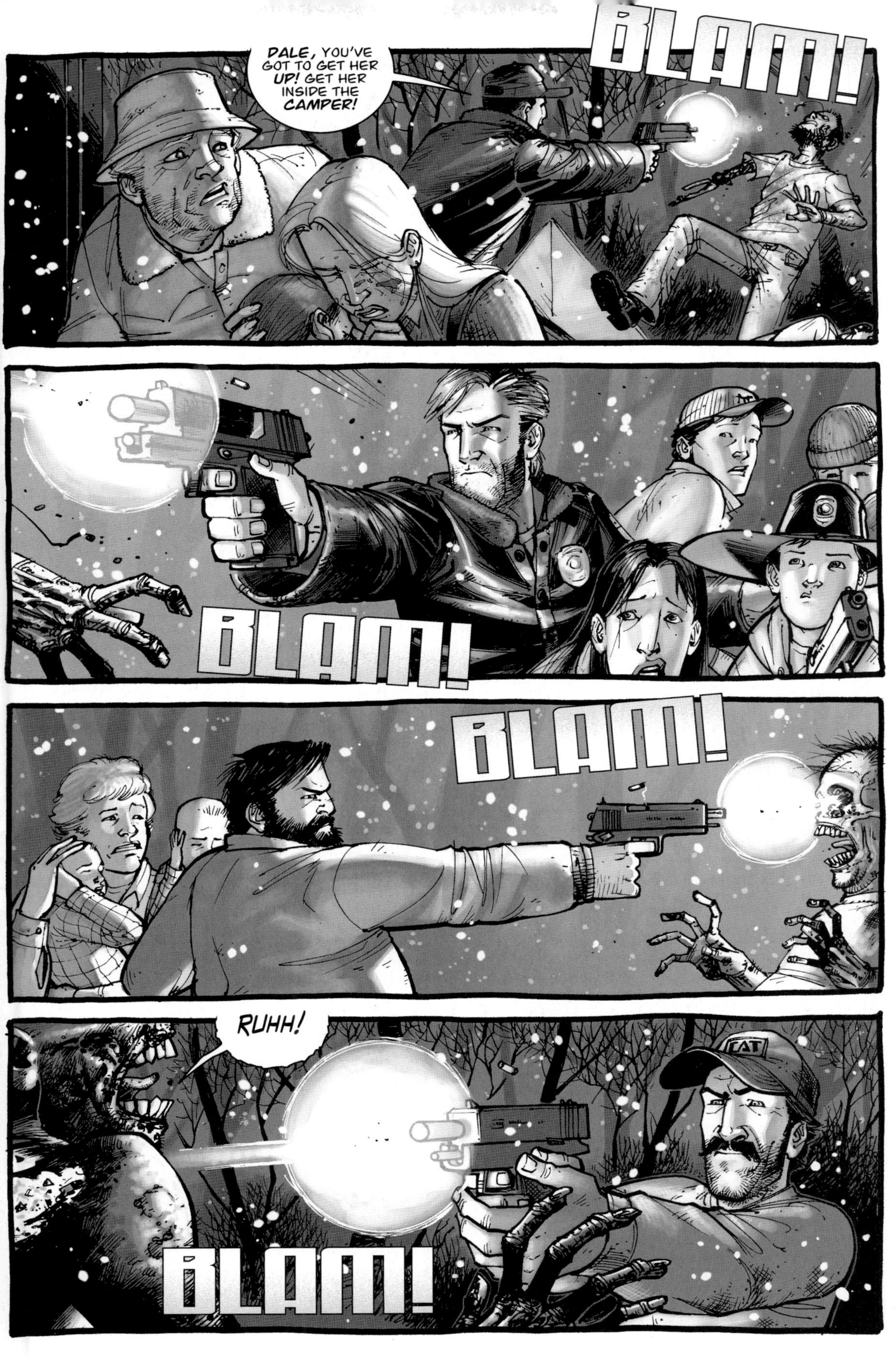
DALE, YOU'VE GOT TO GET HER UP! GET HER INSIDE THE CAMPER!
BLAM!
BLAM!
BLAM!
RUHH!
BLAM!

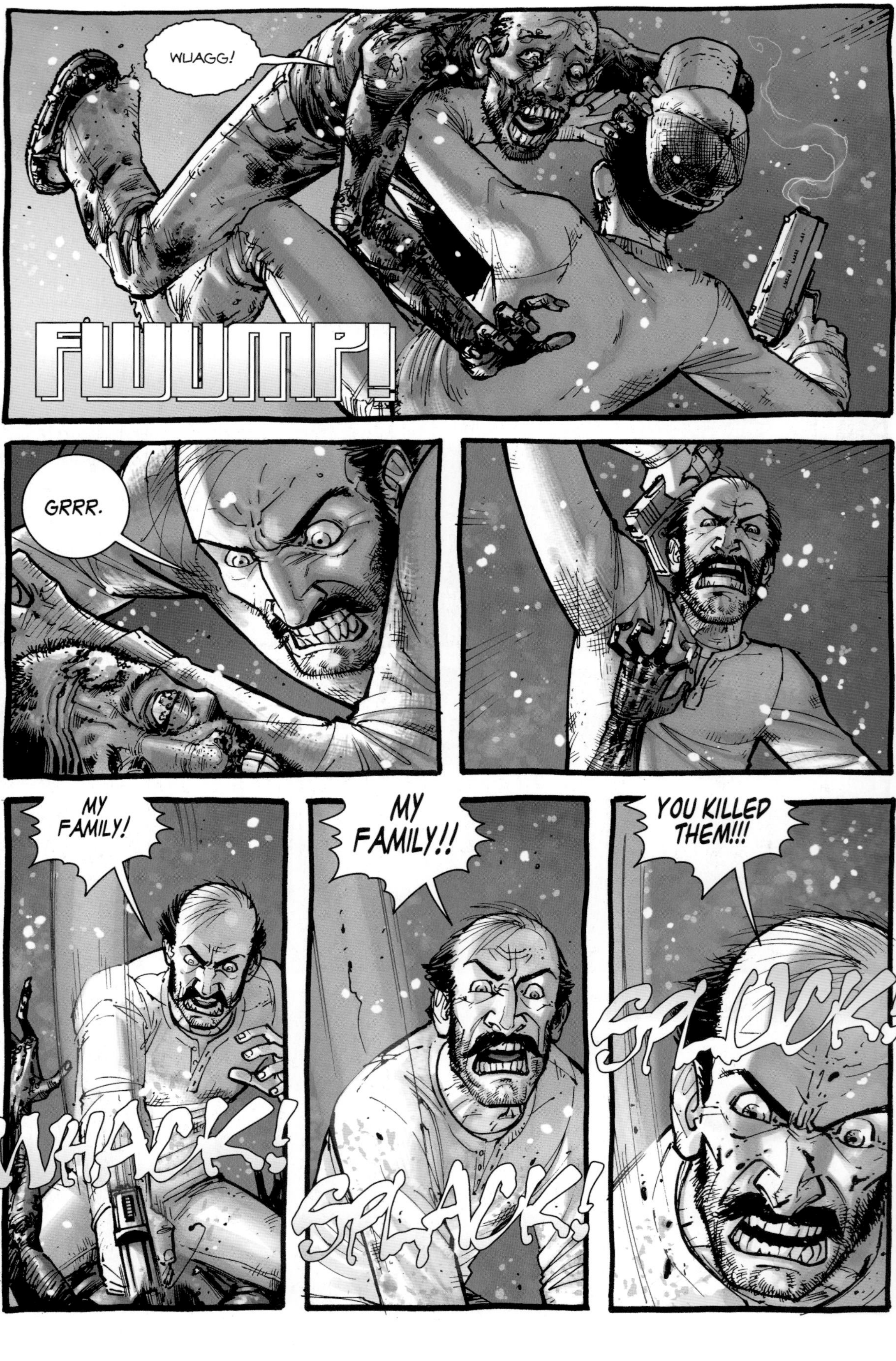
WUAGG!
FWUMP!
GRRR.
MY FAMILY!
WHACK!
MY FAMILY!!
SPLACK!
YOU KILLED THEM!!!
SPLUCK!

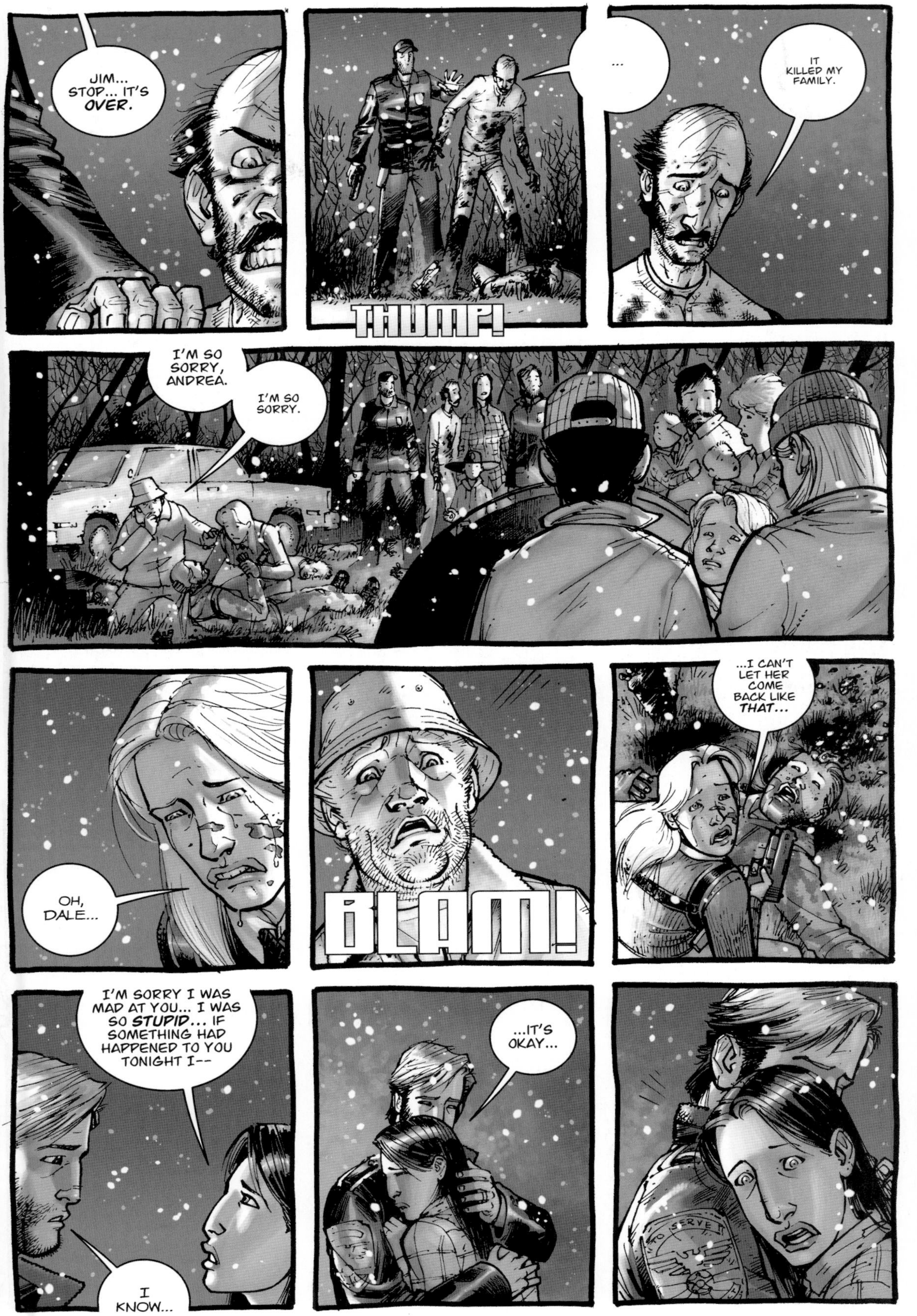
JIM... STOP... IT'S OVER.
THUMP!
...
IT KILLED MY FAMILY.
I'M SO SORRY, ANDREA.
I'M SO SORRY.
OH, DALE...
BLAM!
...I CAN'T LET HER COME BACK LIKE THAT...
I'M SORRY I WAS MAD AT YOU... I WAS SO STUPID... IF SOMETHING HAD HAPPENED TO YOU TONIGHT I--
I KNOW...
...IT'S OKAY...

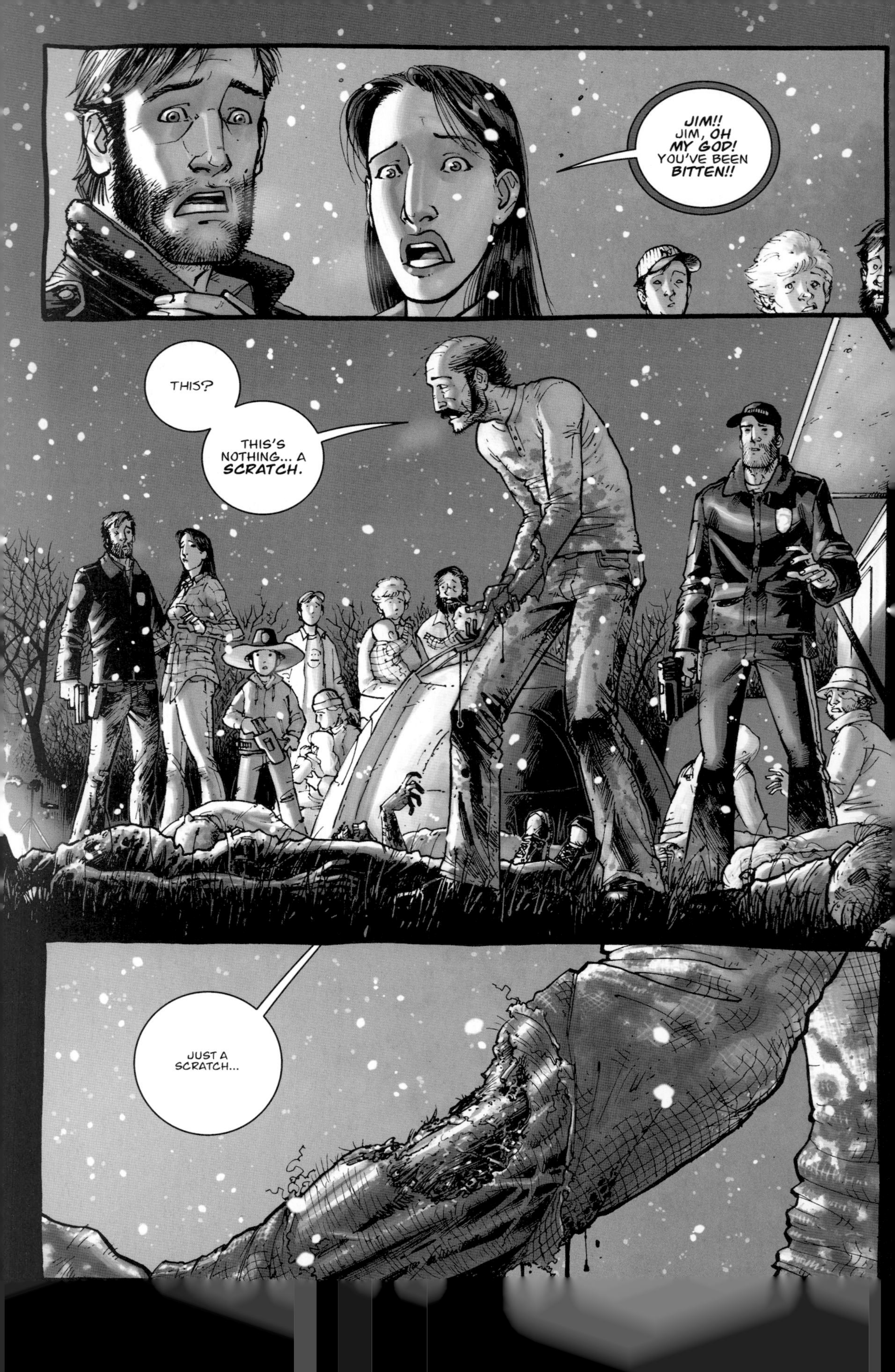
JIM!! JIM, OH MY GOD! YOU'VE BEEN BITTEN!!
THIS?
THIS'S NOTHING... A SCRATCH.
JUST A SCRATCH...

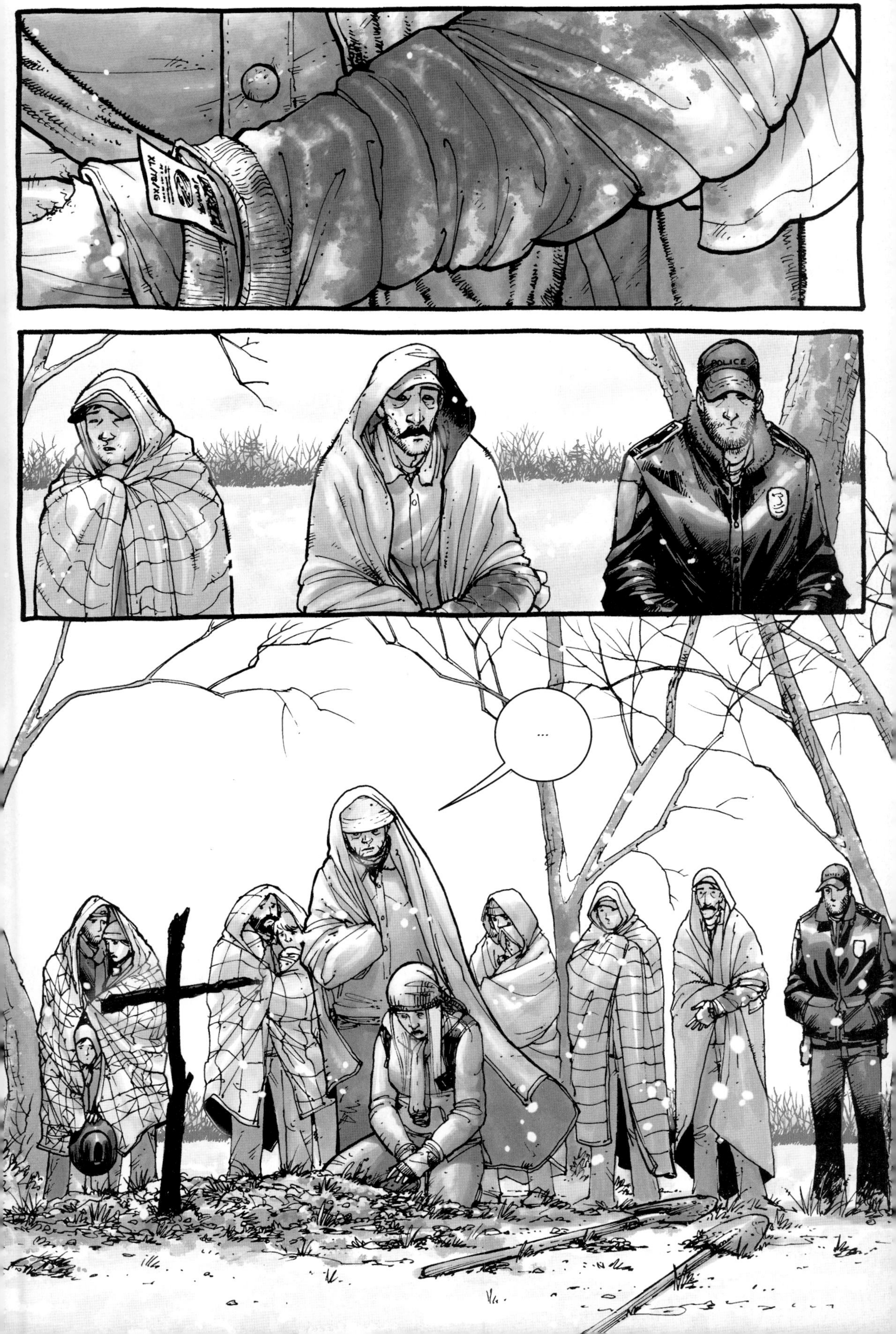
POLICE
...

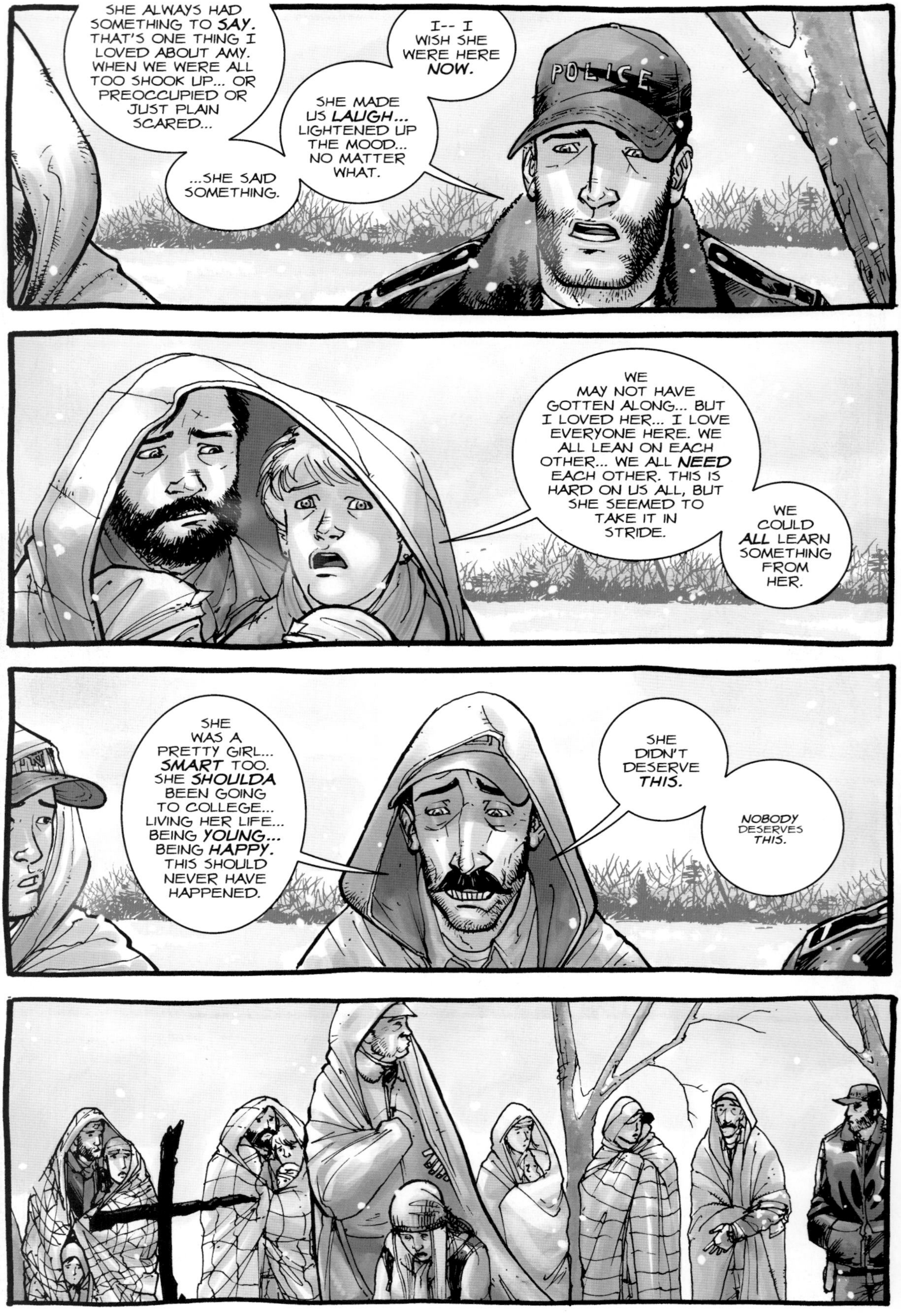
SHE ALWAYS HAD SOMETHING TO SAY. THAT'S ONE THING I LOVED ABOUT AMY. WHEN WE WERE ALL TOO SHOOK UP... OR PREOCCUPIED OR JUST PLAIN SCARED...
...SHE SAID SOMETHING.
SHE MADE US LAUGH... LIGHTENED UP THE MOOD... NO MATTER WHAT.
I-- I WISH SHE WERE HERE NOW.
WE MAY NOT HAVE GOTTEN ALONG... BUT I LOVED HER... I LOVE EVERYONE HERE. WE ALL LEAN ON EACH OTHER... WE ALL NEED EACH OTHER. THIS IS HARD ON US ALL, BUT SHE SEEMED TO TAKE IT IN STRIDE.
WE COULD ALL LEARN SOMETHING FROM HER.
SHE WAS A PRETTY GIRL... SMART TOO. SHE SHOULDA BEEN GOING TO COLLEGE... LIVING HER LIFE... BEING YOUNG... BEING HAPPY. THIS SHOULD NEVER HAVE HAPPENED.
SHE DIDN'T DESERVE THIS.
NOBODY DESERVES THIS.

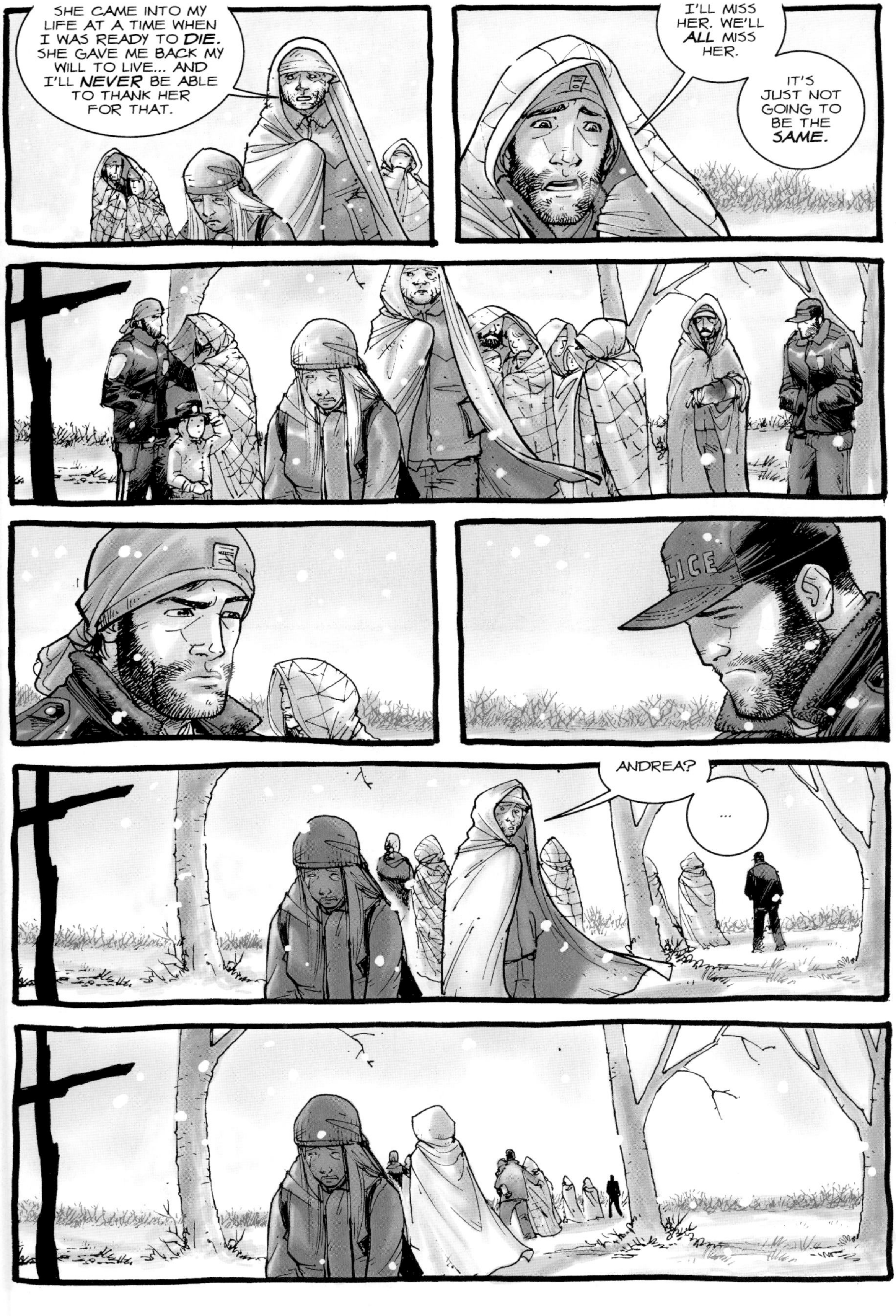
SHE CAME INTO MY LIFE AT A TIME WHEN I WAS READY TO DIE. SHE GAVE ME BACK MY WILL TO LIVE... AND I'LL NEVER BE ABLE TO THANK HER FOR THAT.
I'LL MISS HER. WE'LL ALL MISS HER.
IT'S JUST NOT GOING TO BE THE SAME.
LICE
ANDREA?
...

DO YOU NEED MORE BLANKETS?
NO...
...I'M FINE.
THIS SHOULD COOL YOUR FACE DOWN A LITTLE.
THANKS...
BOSS AT MY GARAGE... FIRST GUY I SAW ATTACKED. HE TURNED IN A COUPLE HOURS. NO ONE'S EVER LASTED MORE THAN A DAY... NOT AFTER BEING BITTEN.
GUESS I'M LUCKY.
MAYBE YOU WON'T TURN. NOBODY KNOWS ANYTHING FOR SURE.
YEAH...
IF YOU NEED ANYTHING... JUST GIVE US A YELL. SOMEONE WILL COME GET ME IF I DON'T HEAR.

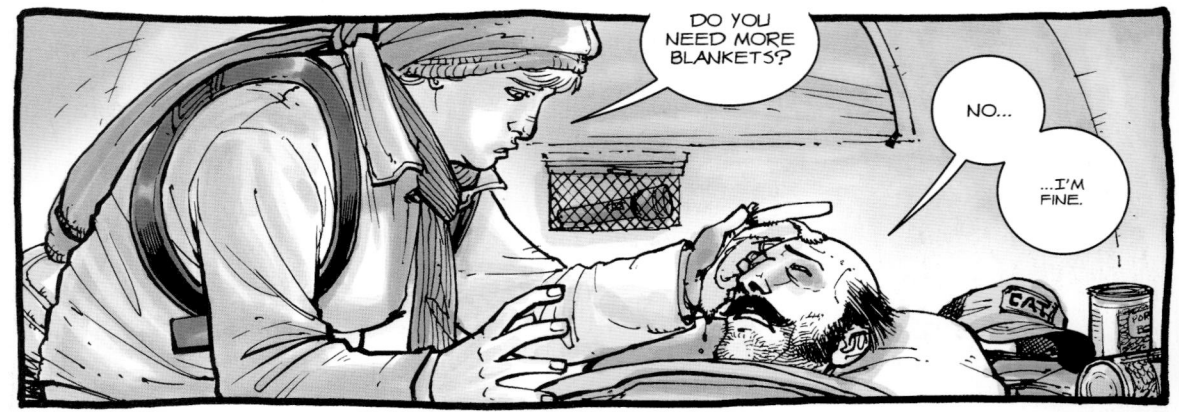

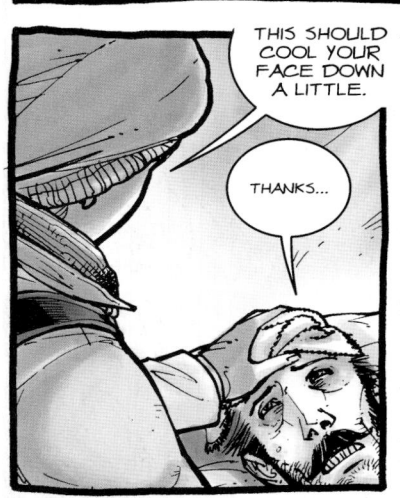

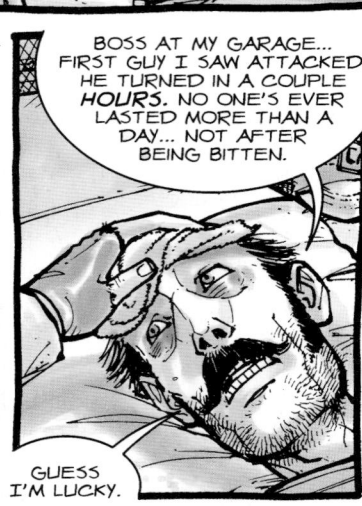

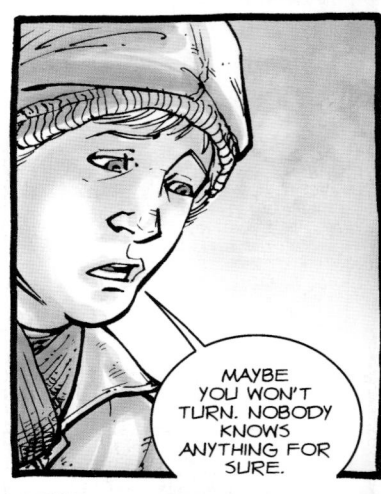

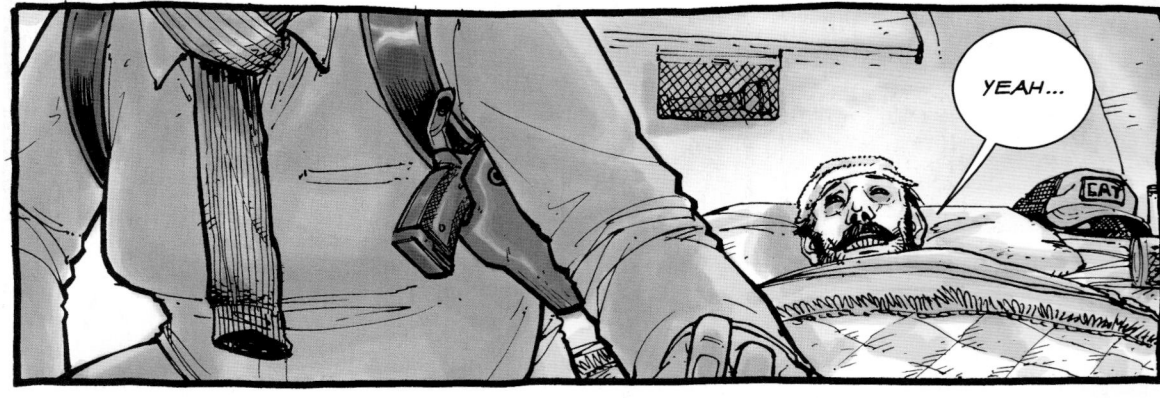

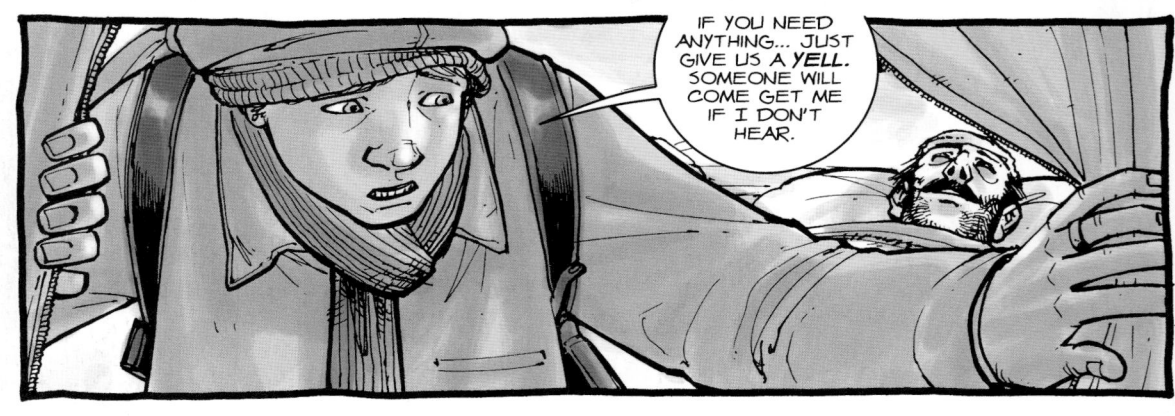

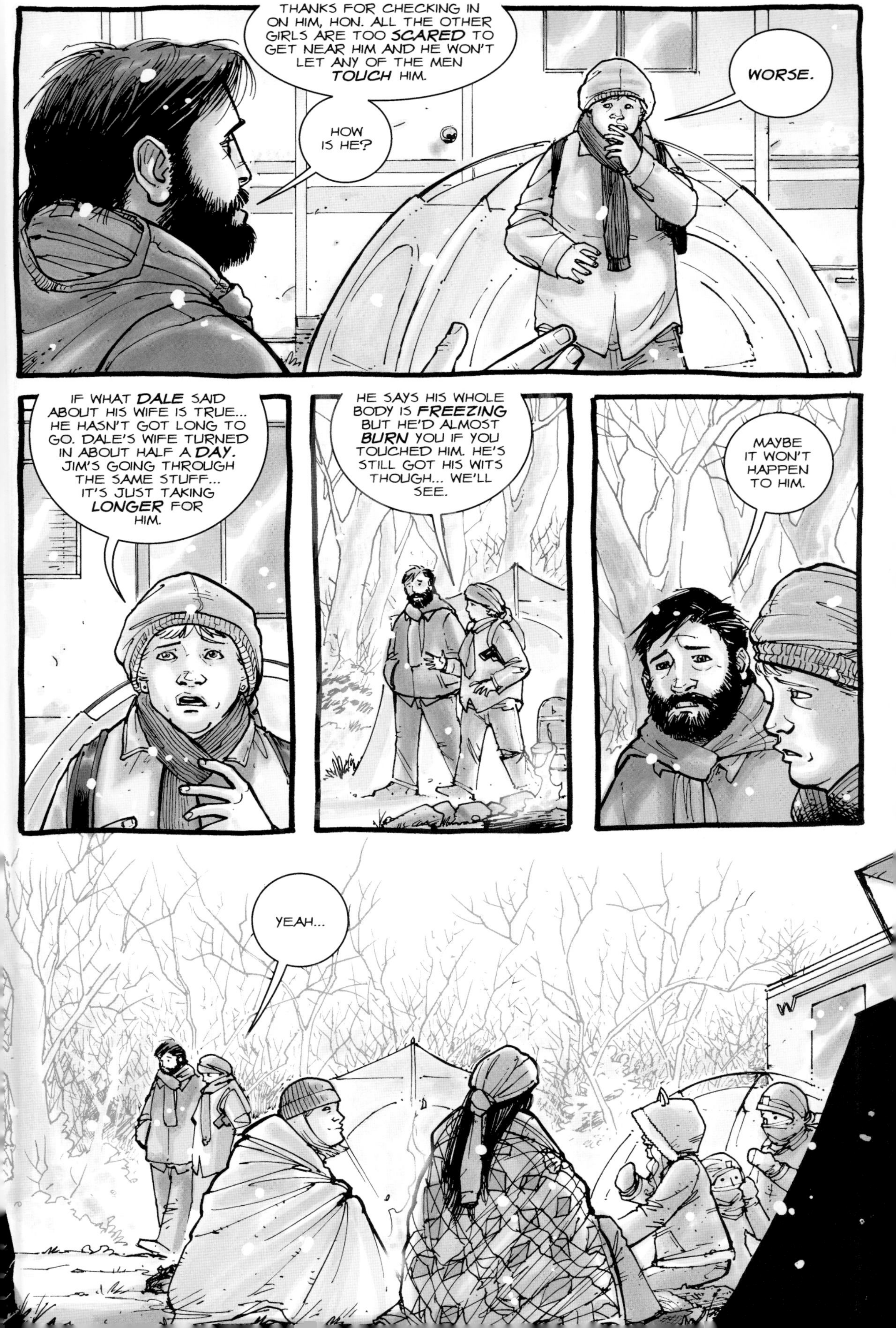
THANKS FOR CHECKING IN ON HIM, HON. ALL THE OTHER GIRLS ARE TOO SCARED TO GET NEAR HIM AND HE WON'T LET ANY OF THE MEN TOUCH HIM.
HOW IS HE?
WORSE.
IF WHAT DALE SAID ABOUT HIS WIFE IS TRUE... HE HASN'T GOT LONG TO GO. DALE'S WIFE TURNED IN ABOUT HALF A DAY. JIM'S GOING THROUGH THE SAME STUFF... IT'S JUST TAKING LONGER FOR HIM.
HE SAYS HIS WHOLE BODY IS FREEZING BUT HE'D ALMOST BURN YOU IF YOU TOUCHED HIM. HE'S STILL GOT HIS WITS THOUGH... WE'LL SEE.
MAYBE IT WON'T HAPPEN TO HIM.
YEAH...

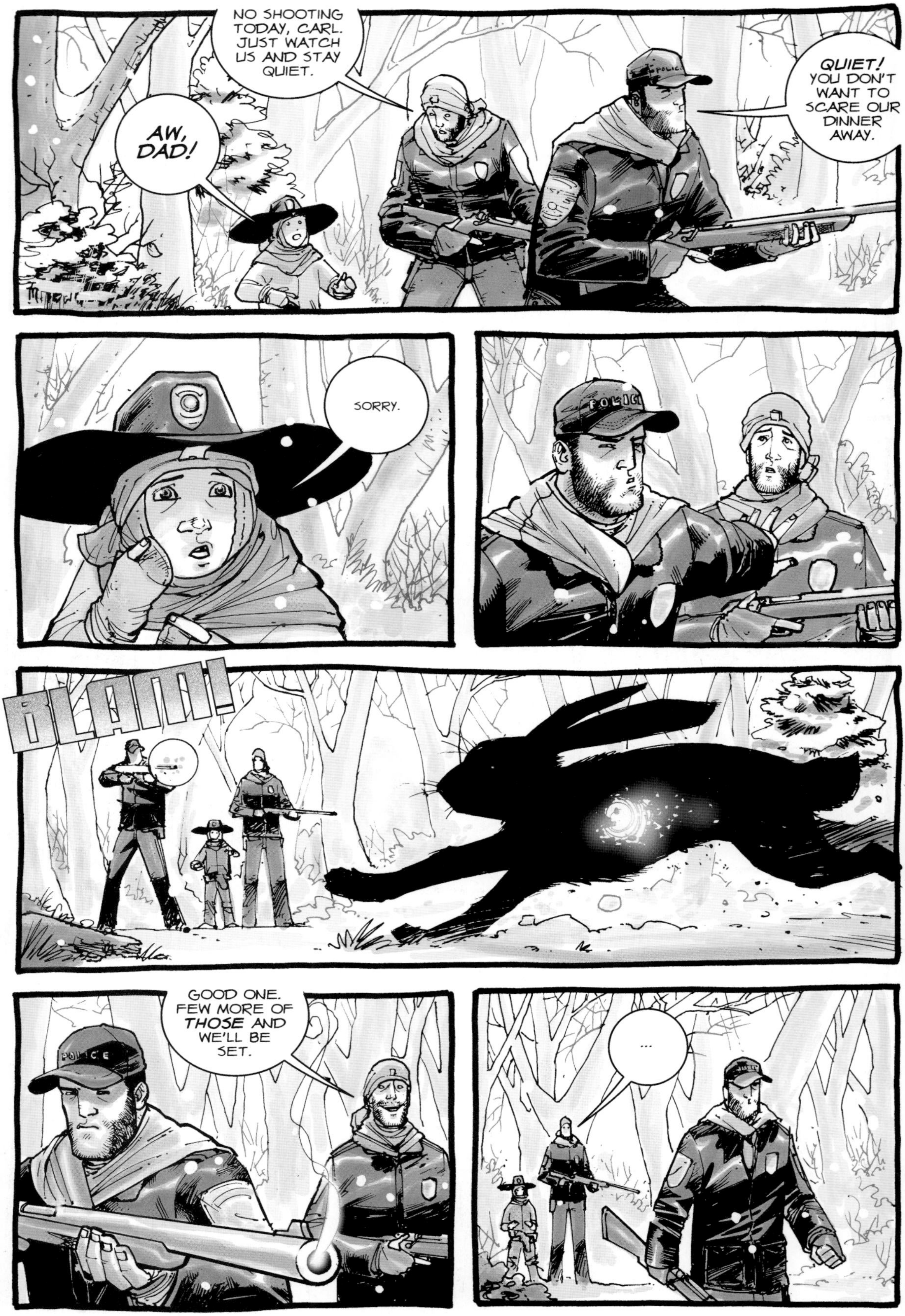
NO SHOOTING TODAY, CARL. JUST WATCH US AND STAY QUIET.
AW, DAD!
QUIET! YOU DON'T WANT TO SCARE OUR DINNER AWAY.
SORRY.
BLAM!
GOOD ONE. FEW MORE OF THOSE AND WE'LL BE SET.
...

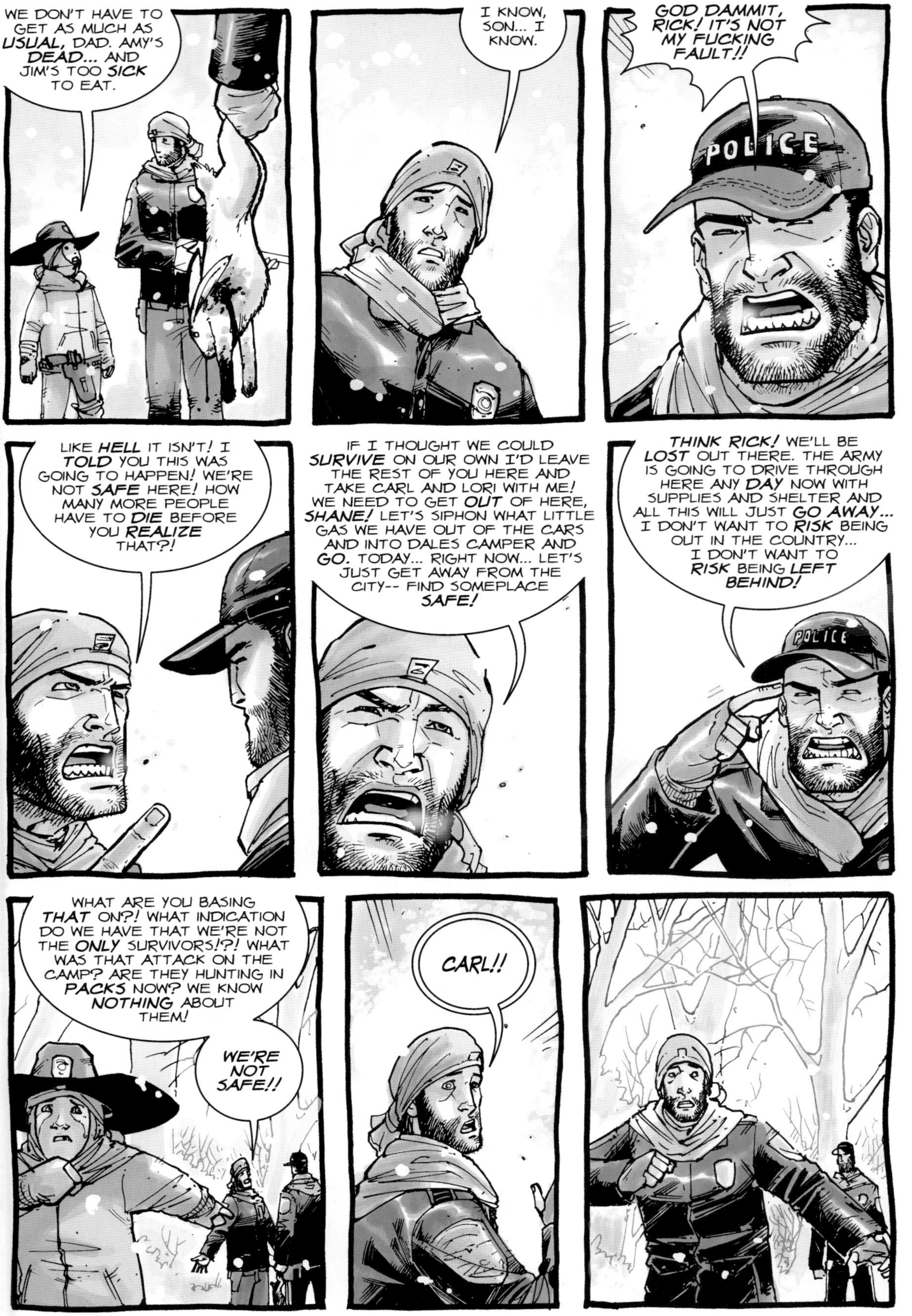
WE DON'T HAVE TO GET AS MUCH AS USUAL, DAD. AMY'S DEAD... AND JIM'S TOO SICK TO EAT.
I KNOW, SON... I KNOW.
GOD DAMMIT, RICK! IT'S NOT MY FUCKING FAULT!!
LIKE HELL IT ISN'T! I TOLD YOU THIS WAS GOING TO HAPPEN! WE'RE NOT SAFE HERE! HOW MANY MORE PEOPLE HAVE TO DIE BEFORE YOU REALIZE THAT?!
IF I THOUGHT WE COULD SURVIVE ON OUR OWN I'D LEAVE THE REST OF YOU HERE AND TAKE CARL AND LORI WITH ME! WE NEED TO GET OUT OF HERE, SHANE! LET'S SIPHON WHAT LITTLE GAS WE HAVE OUT OF THE CARS AND INTO DALES CAMPER AND GO. TODAY... RIGHT NOW... LET'S JUST GET AWAY FROM THE CITY-- FIND SOMEPLACE SAFE!
THINK RICK! WE'LL BE LOST OUT THERE. THE ARMY IS GOING TO DRIVE THROUGH HERE ANY DAY NOW WITH SUPPLIES AND SHELTER AND ALL THIS WILL JUST GO AWAY... I DON'T WANT TO RISK BEING OUT IN THE COUNTRY... I DON'T WANT TO RISK BEING LEFT BEHIND!
WHAT ARE YOU BASING THAT ON?! WHAT INDICATION DO WE HAVE THAT WE'RE NOT THE ONLY SURVIVORS!?! WHAT WAS THAT ATTACK ON THE CAMP? ARE THEY HUNTING IN PACKS NOW? WE KNOW NOTHING ABOUT THEM!
WE'RE NOT SAFE!!
CARL!!

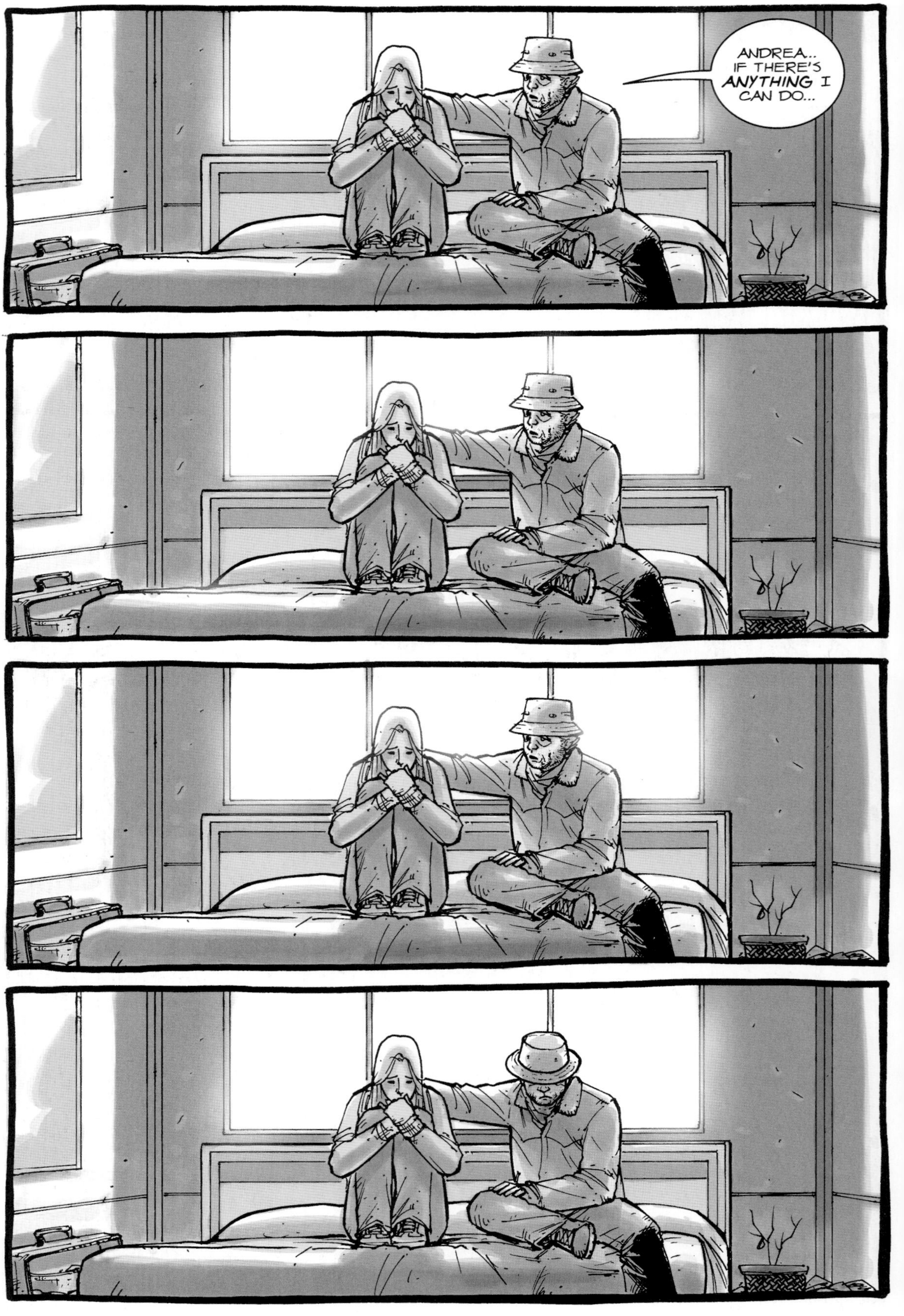
ANDREA.. IF THERE'S ANYTHING I CAN DO...

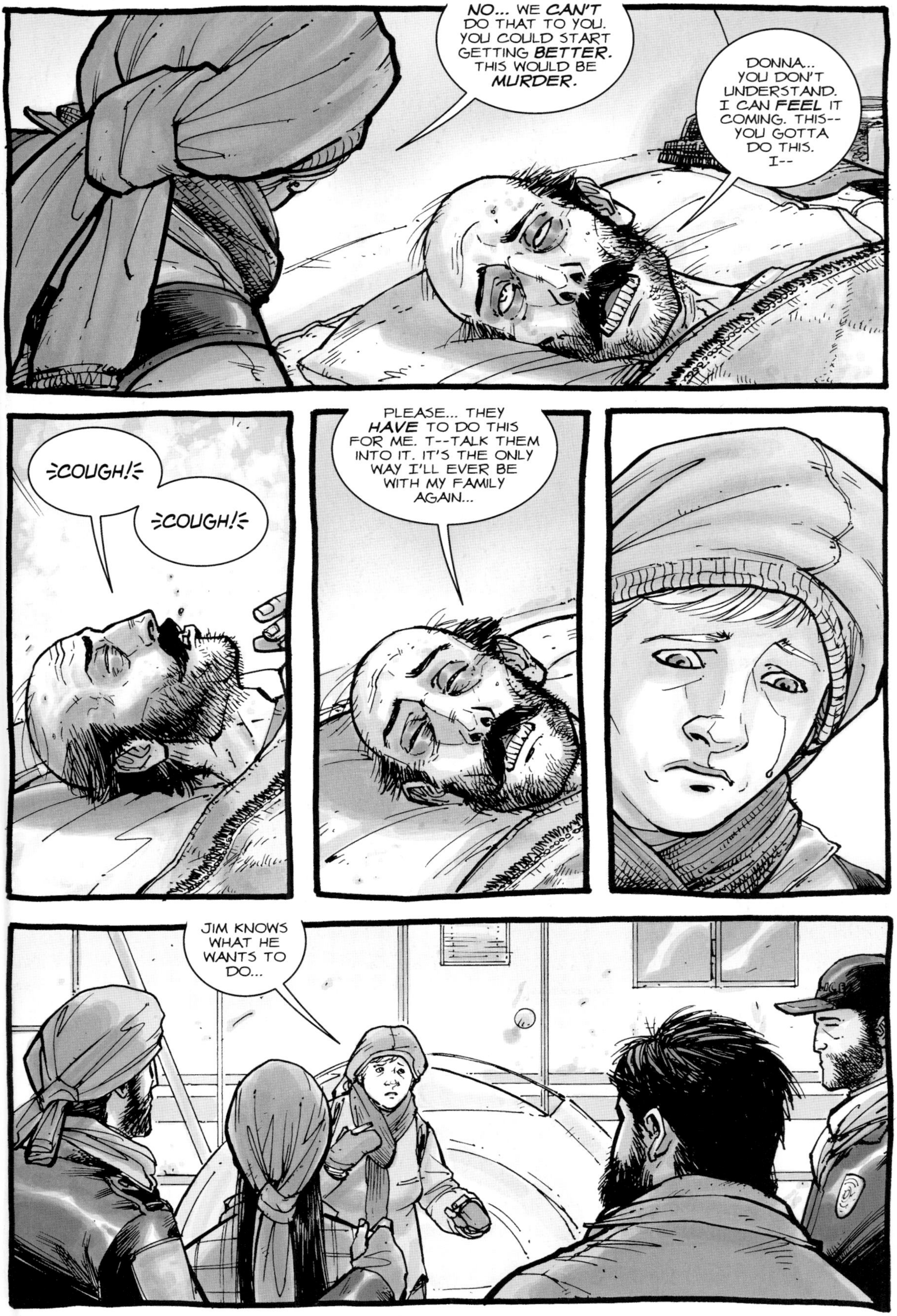
NO... WE CAN'T DO THAT TO YOU. YOU COULD START GETTING BETTER. THIS WOULD BE MURDER.
DONNA... YOU DON'T UNDERSTAND. I CAN FEEL IT COMING. THIS-- YOU GOTTA DO THIS. I--
COUGH!
COUGH!
PLEASE... THEY HAVE TO DO THIS FOR ME. T--TALK THEM INTO IT. IT'S THE ONLY WAY I'LL EVER BE WITH MY FAMILY AGAIN...
JIM KNOWS WHAT HE WANTS TO DO...

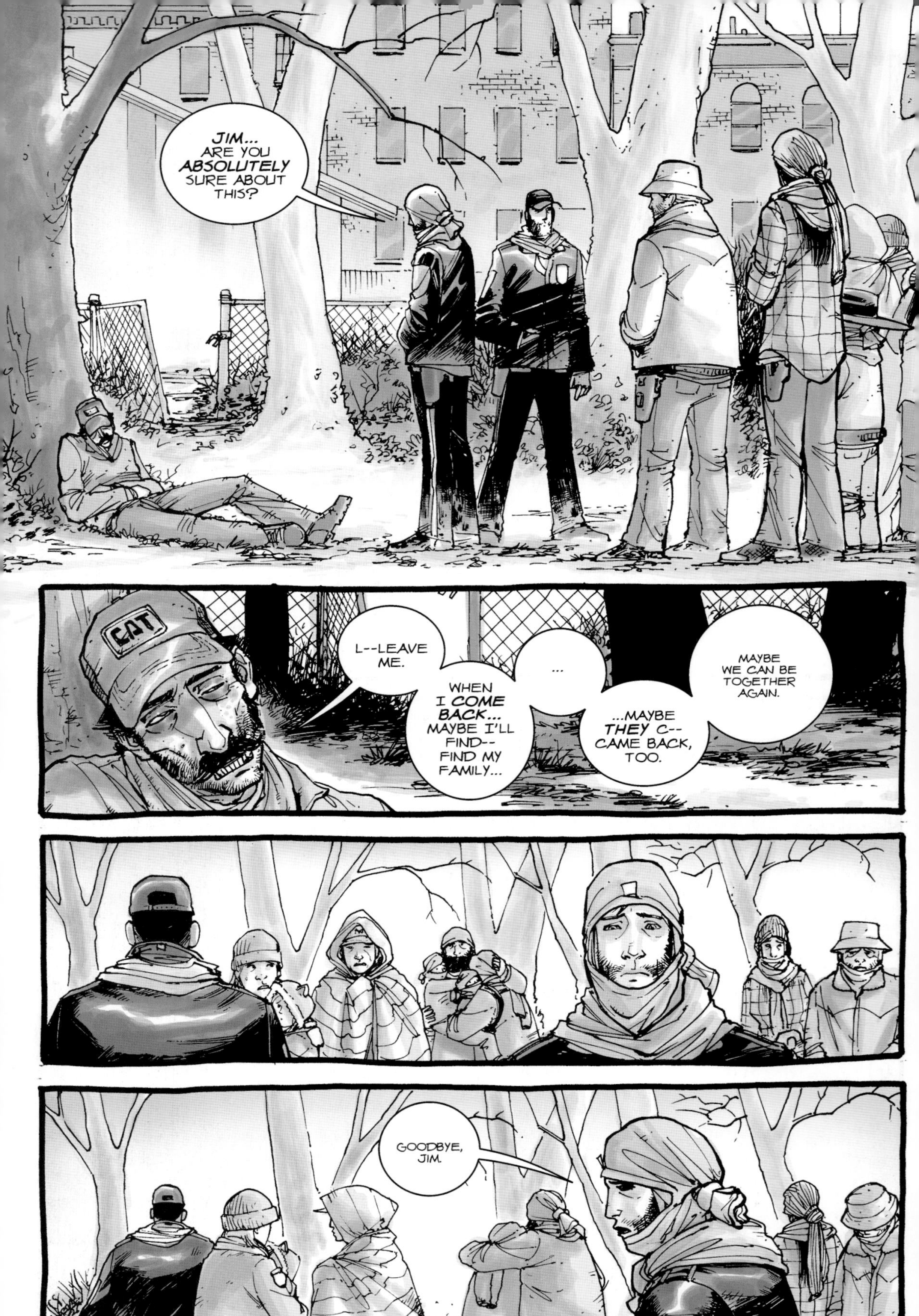

JIM... ARE YOU ABSOLUTELY SURE ABOUT THIS?
L--LEAVE ME.
WHEN I COME BACK... MAYBE I'LL FIND-- FIND MY FAMILY...
...
...MAYBE THEY C-- CAME BACK, TOO.
MAYBE WE CAN BE TOGETHER AGAIN.
GOODBYE, JIM.

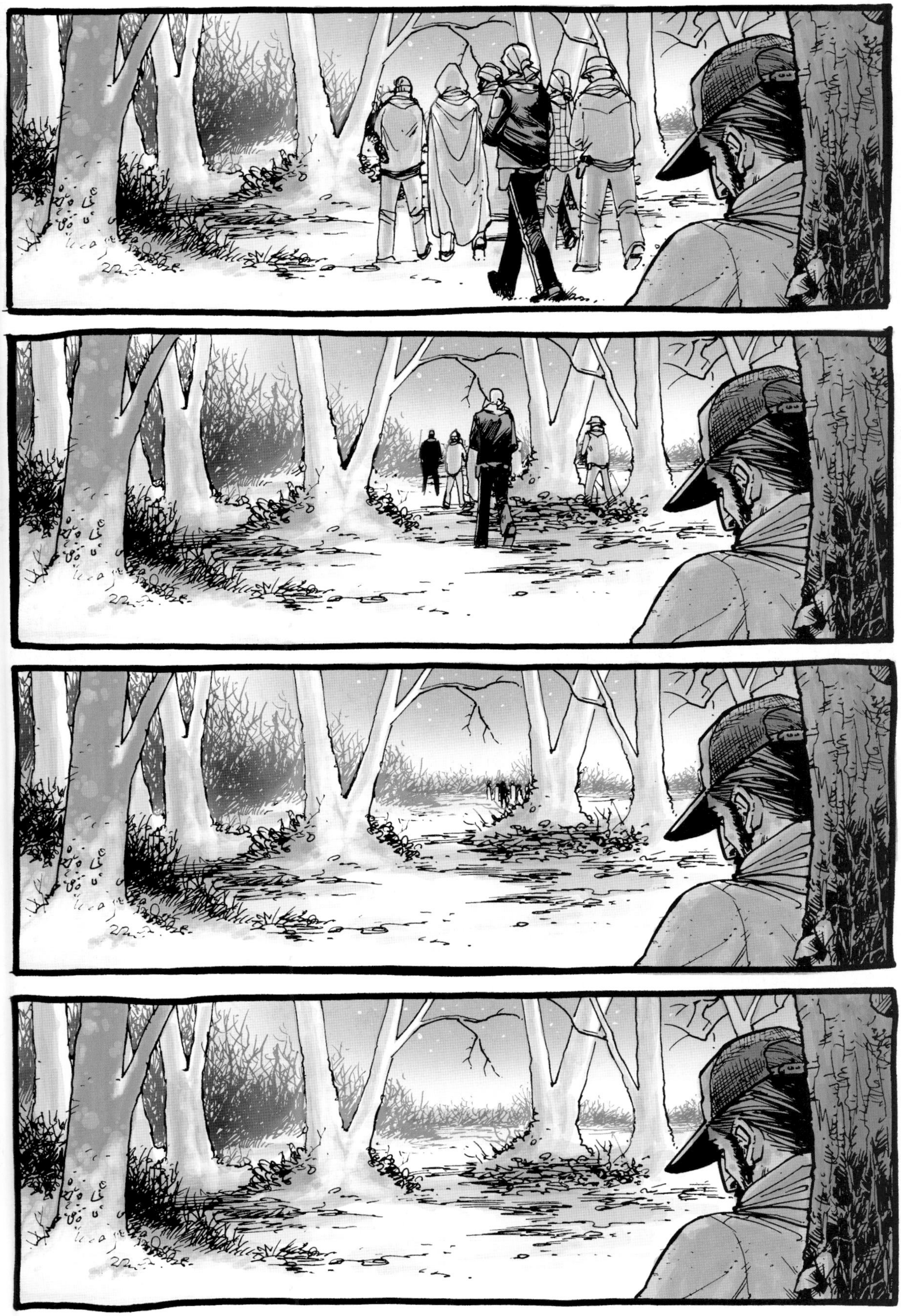

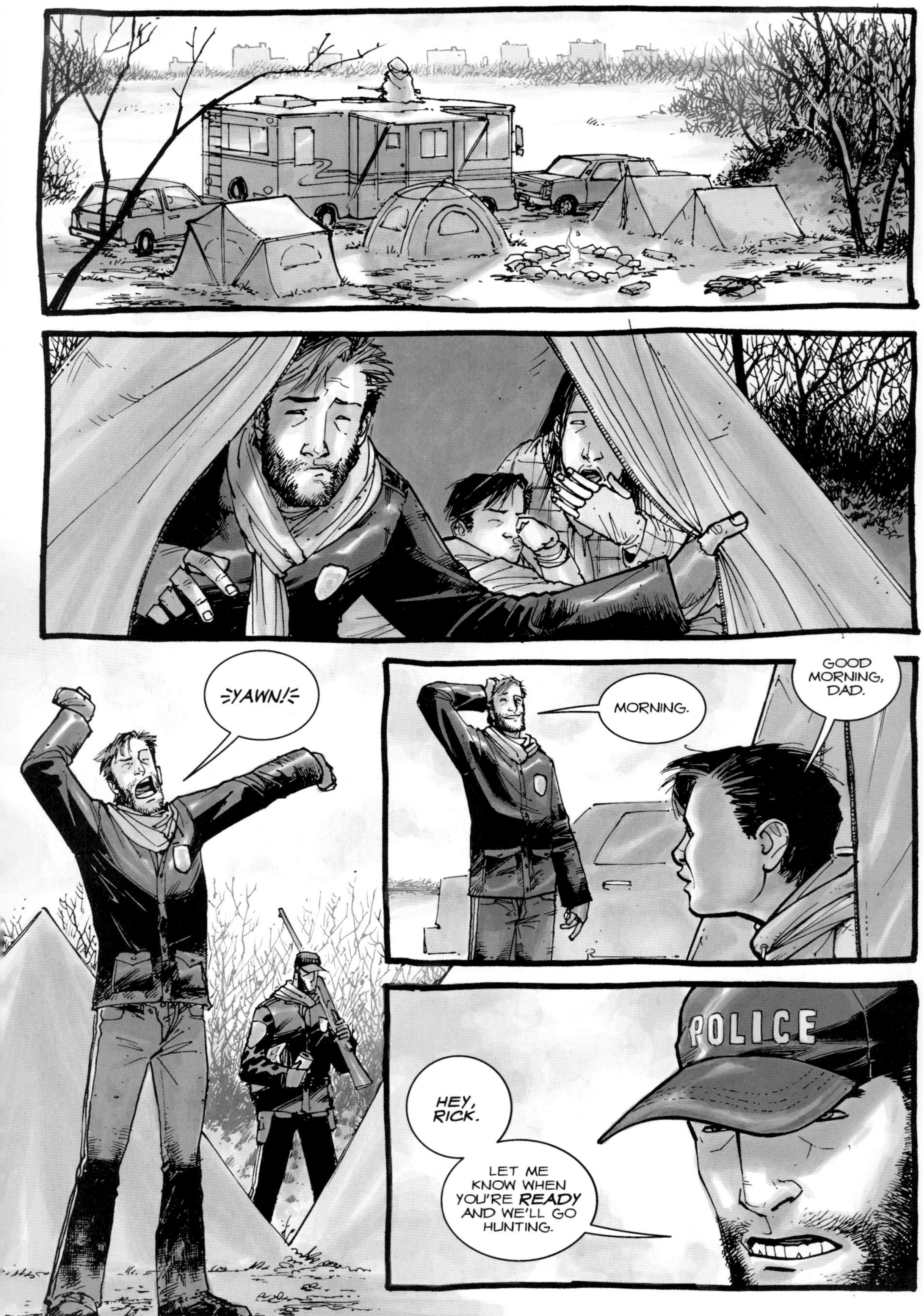
YAWN!
MORNING.
GOOD MORNING, DAD.
POLICE
HEY, RICK.
LET ME KNOW WHEN YOU'RE READY AND WE'LL GO HUNTING.

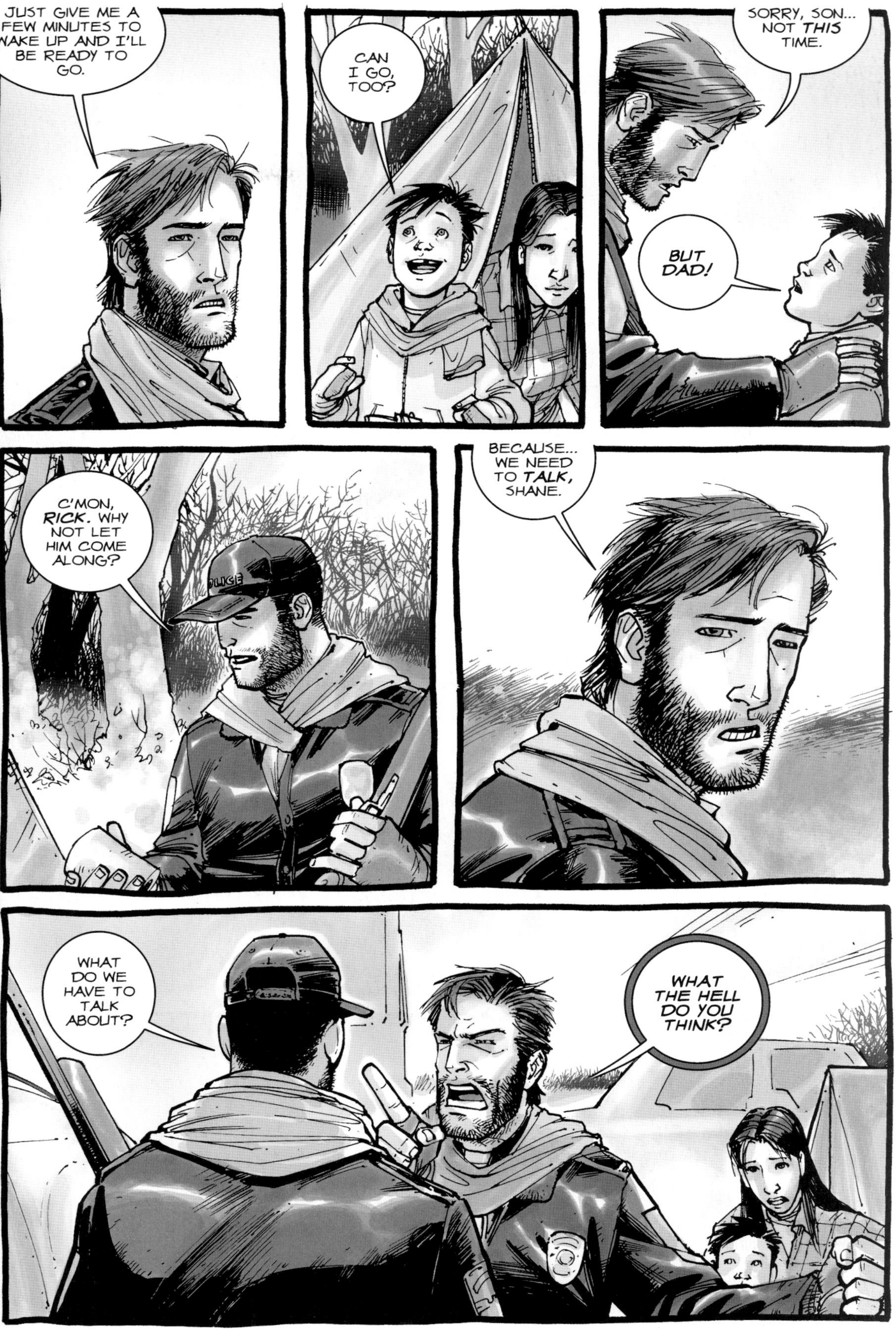
JUST GIVE ME A FEW MINUTES TO WAKE UP AND I'LL BE READY TO GO.
CAN I GO, TOO?
SORRY, SON... NOT *THIS* TIME.
BUT DAD!
C'MON, *RICK.* WHY NOT LET HIM COME ALONG?
BECAUSE... WE NEED TO *TALK,* SHANE.
WHAT DO WE HAVE TO TALK ABOUT?
WHAT THE HELL DO YOU THINK?

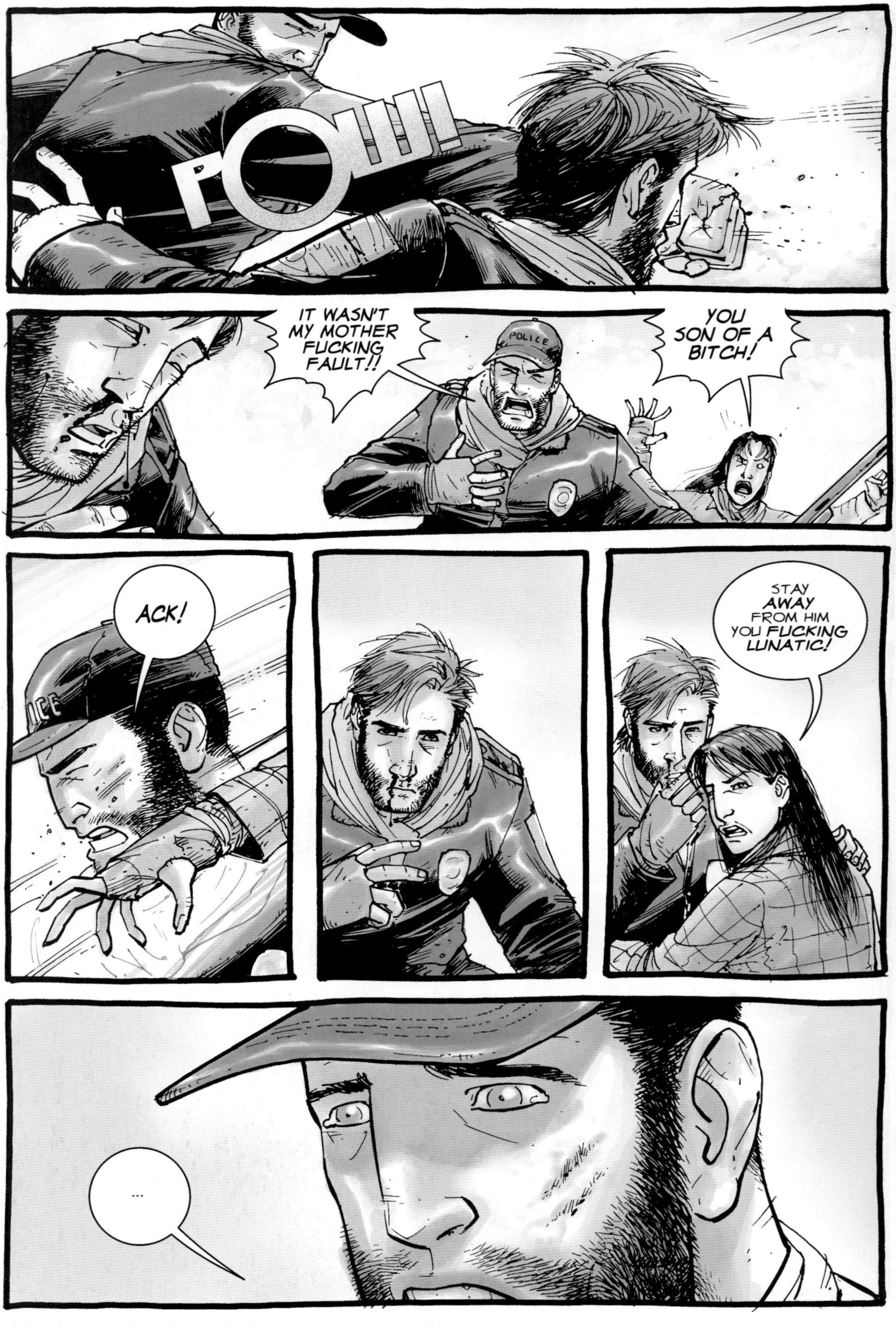
POW!
IT WASN'T MY MOTHER FUCKING FAULT!!
YOU SON OF A BITCH!
ACK!
STAY AWAY FROM HIM YOU FUCKING LUNATIC!
...

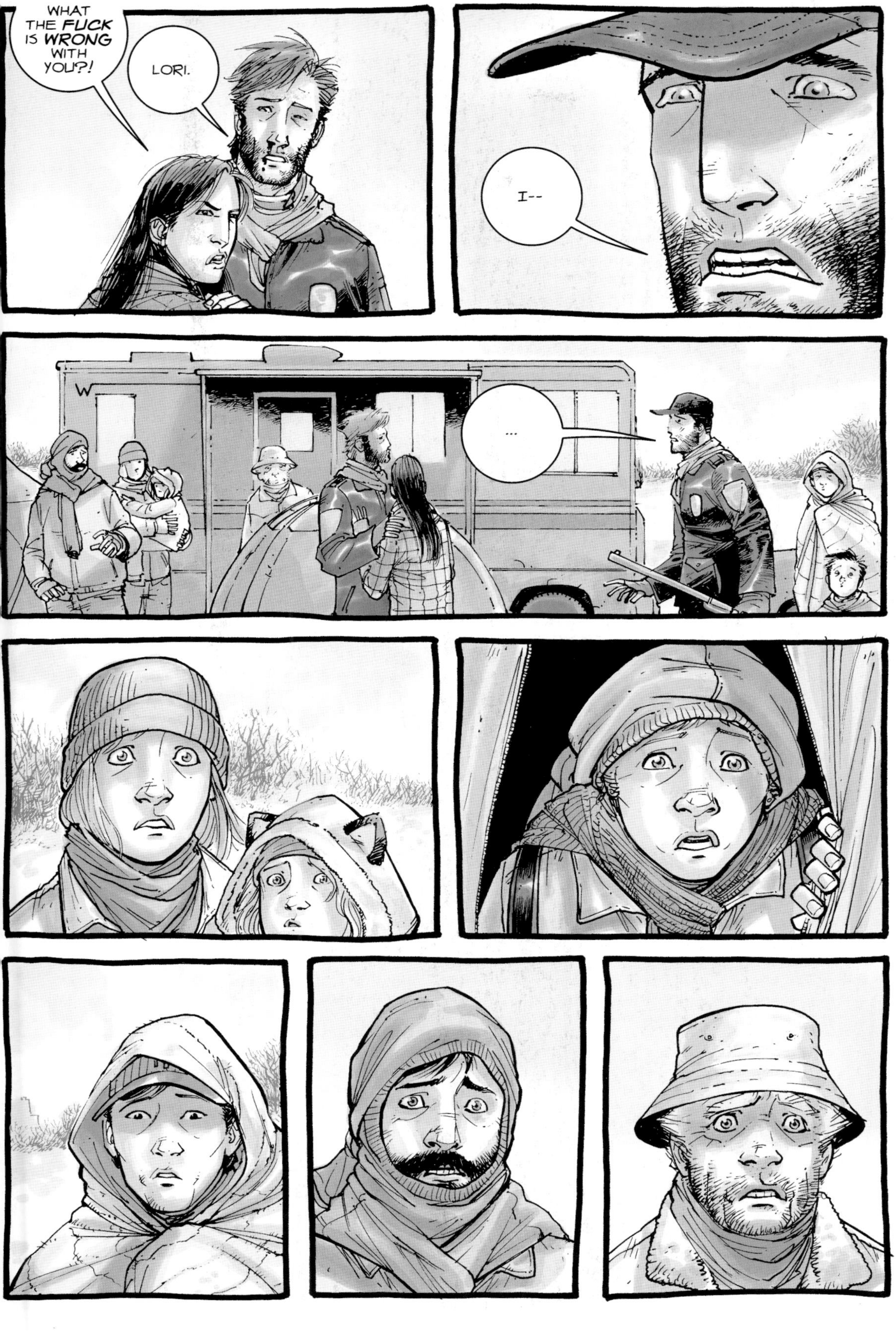
WHAT THE FUCK IS WRONG WITH YOU?!
LORI.
I--
...

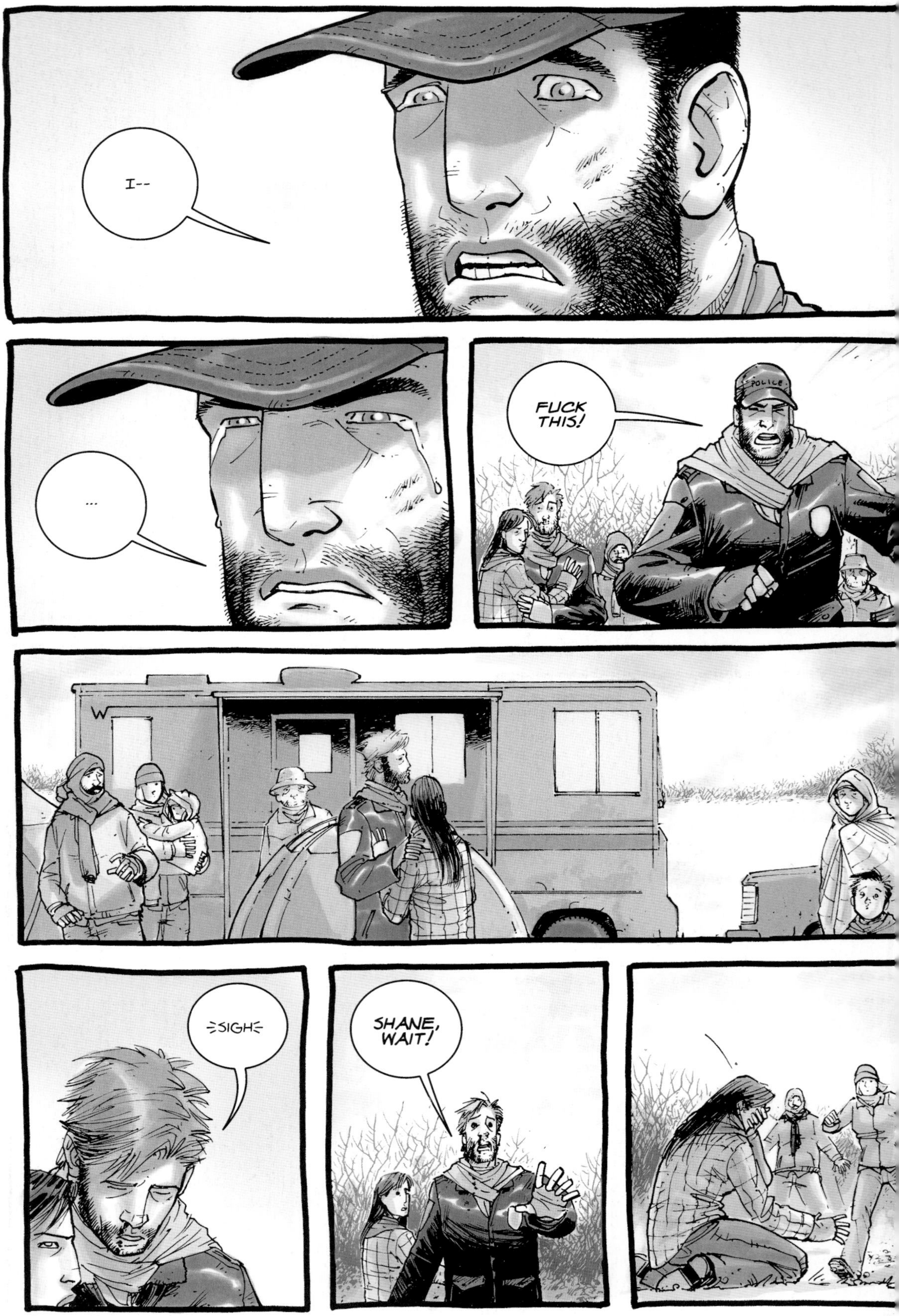
I--
...
FUCK THIS!
=SIGH=
SHANE, WAIT!

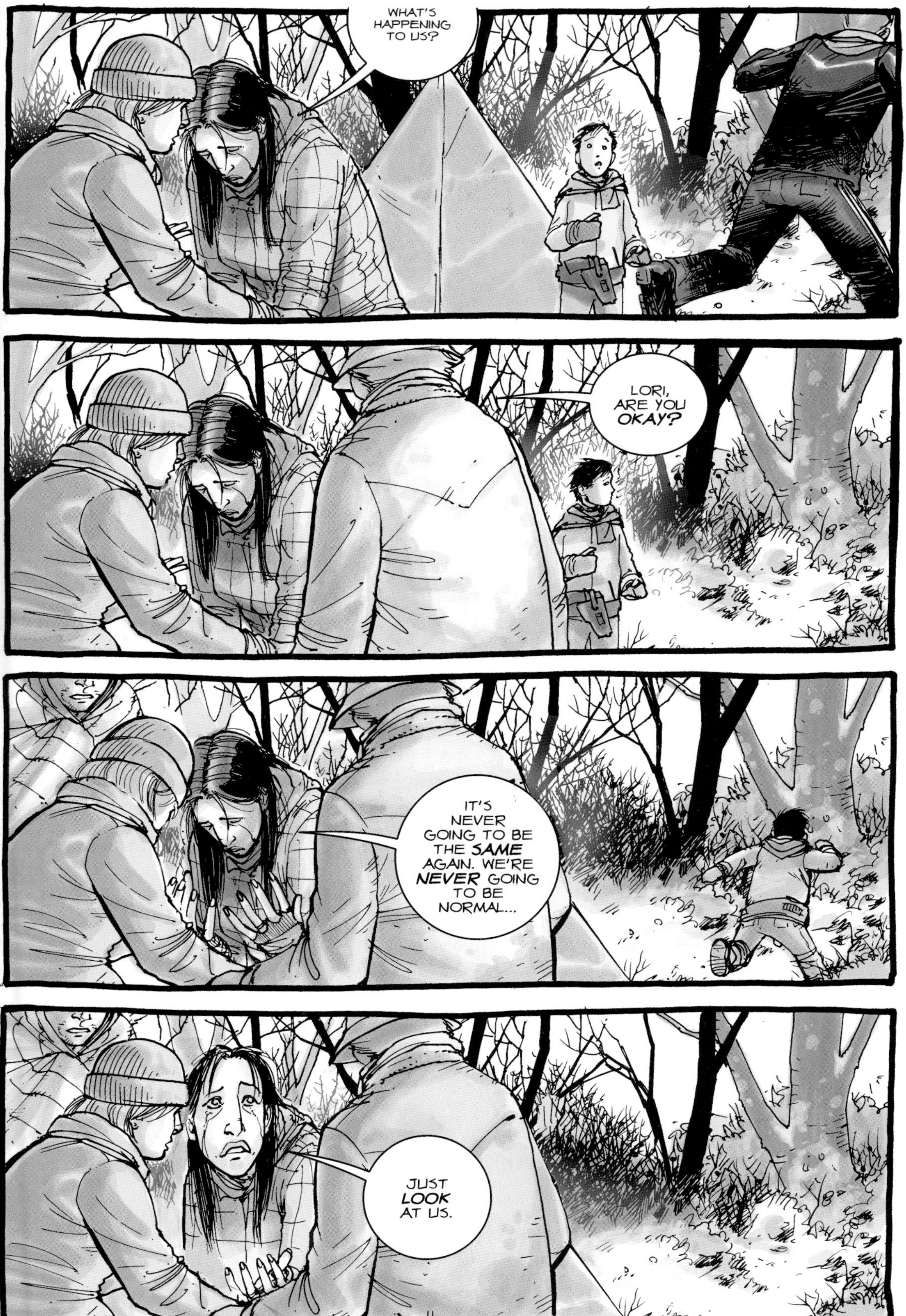
WHAT'S HAPPENING TO US?
LORI, ARE YOU OKAY?
IT'S NEVER GOING TO BE THE SAME AGAIN. WE'RE NEVER GOING TO BE NORMAL...
JUST LOOK AT US.

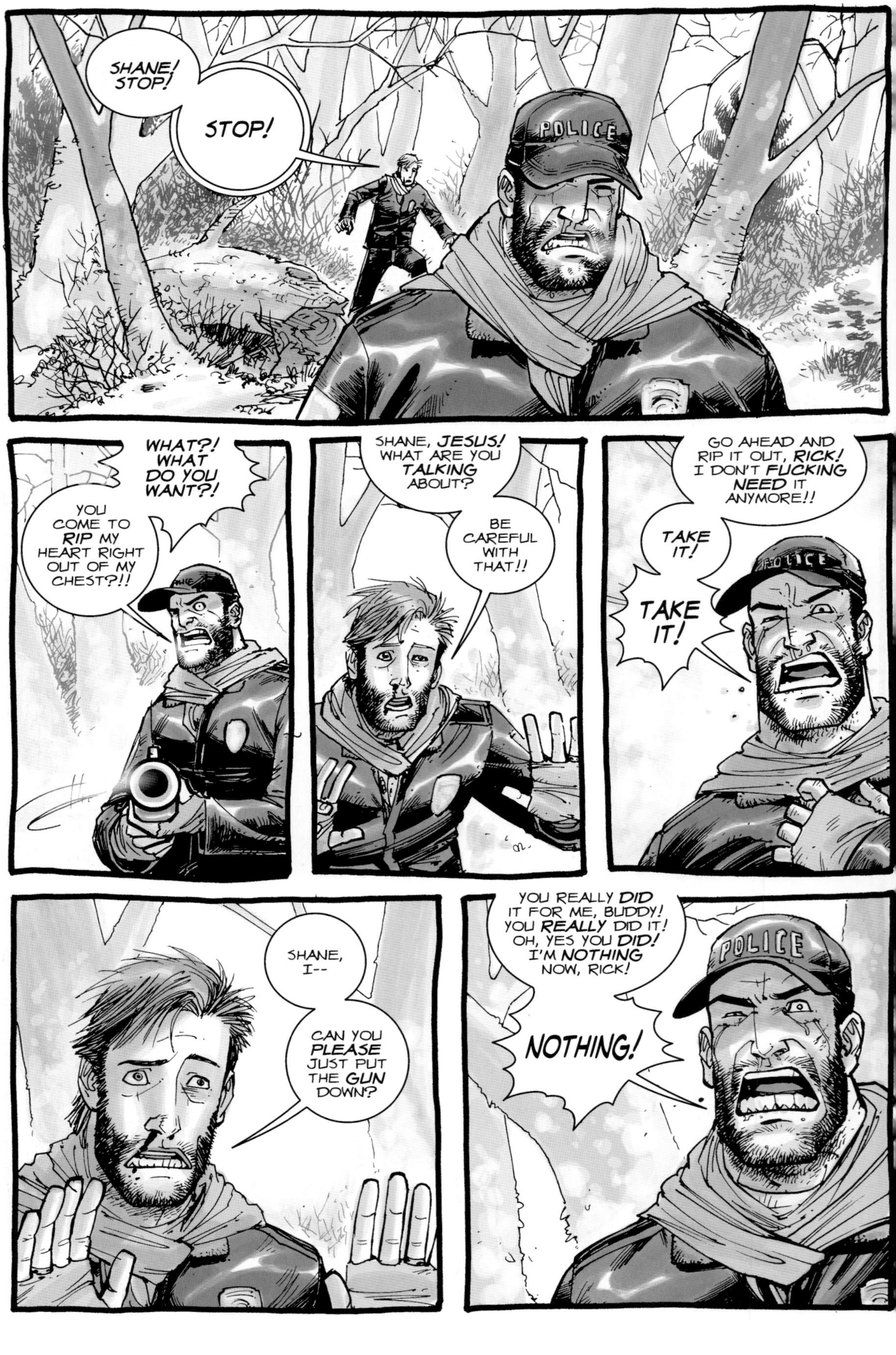
SHANE! STOP!
STOP!
WHAT?! WHAT DO YOU WANT?!
YOU COME TO RIP MY HEART RIGHT OUT OF MY CHEST?!!
SHANE, JESUS! WHAT ARE YOU TALKING ABOUT?
BE CAREFUL WITH THAT!!
GO AHEAD AND RIP IT OUT, RICK! I DON'T FUCKING NEED IT ANYMORE!!
TAKE IT!
TAKE IT!
SHANE, I--
CAN YOU PLEASE JUST PUT THE GUN DOWN?
YOU REALLY DID IT FOR ME, BUDDY! YOU REALLY DID IT! OH, YES YOU DID! I'M NOTHING NOW, RICK!
NOTHING!

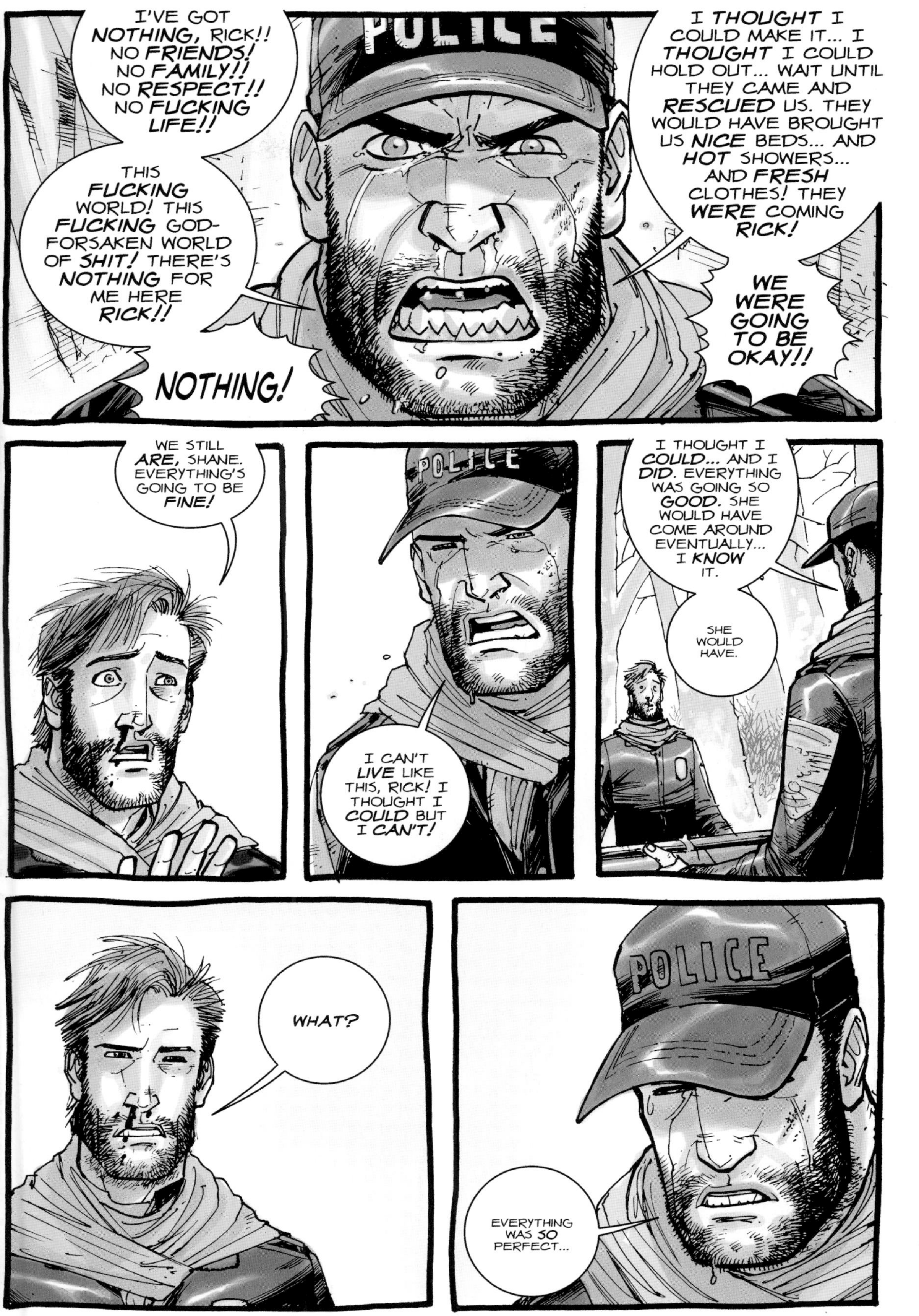

I'VE GOT NOTHING, RICK!! NO FRIENDS! NO FAMILY!! NO RESPECT!! NO FUCKING LIFE!!
THIS FUCKING WORLD! THIS FUCKING GOD-FORSAKEN WORLD OF SHIT! THERE'S NOTHING FOR ME HERE RICK!!
NOTHING!
I THOUGHT I COULD MAKE IT... I THOUGHT I COULD HOLD OUT... WAIT UNTIL THEY CAME AND RESCUED US. THEY WOULD HAVE BROUGHT US NICE BEDS... AND HOT SHOWERS... AND FRESH CLOTHES! THEY WERE COMING RICK!
WE WERE GOING TO BE OKAY!!
WE STILL ARE, SHANE. EVERYTHING'S GOING TO BE FINE!
I CAN'T LIVE LIKE THIS, RICK! I THOUGHT I COULD BUT I CAN'T!
I THOUGHT I COULD... AND I DID. EVERYTHING WAS GOING SO GOOD. SHE WOULD HAVE COME AROUND EVENTUALLY... I KNOW IT.
SHE WOULD HAVE.
WHAT?
EVERYTHING WAS SO PERFECT...

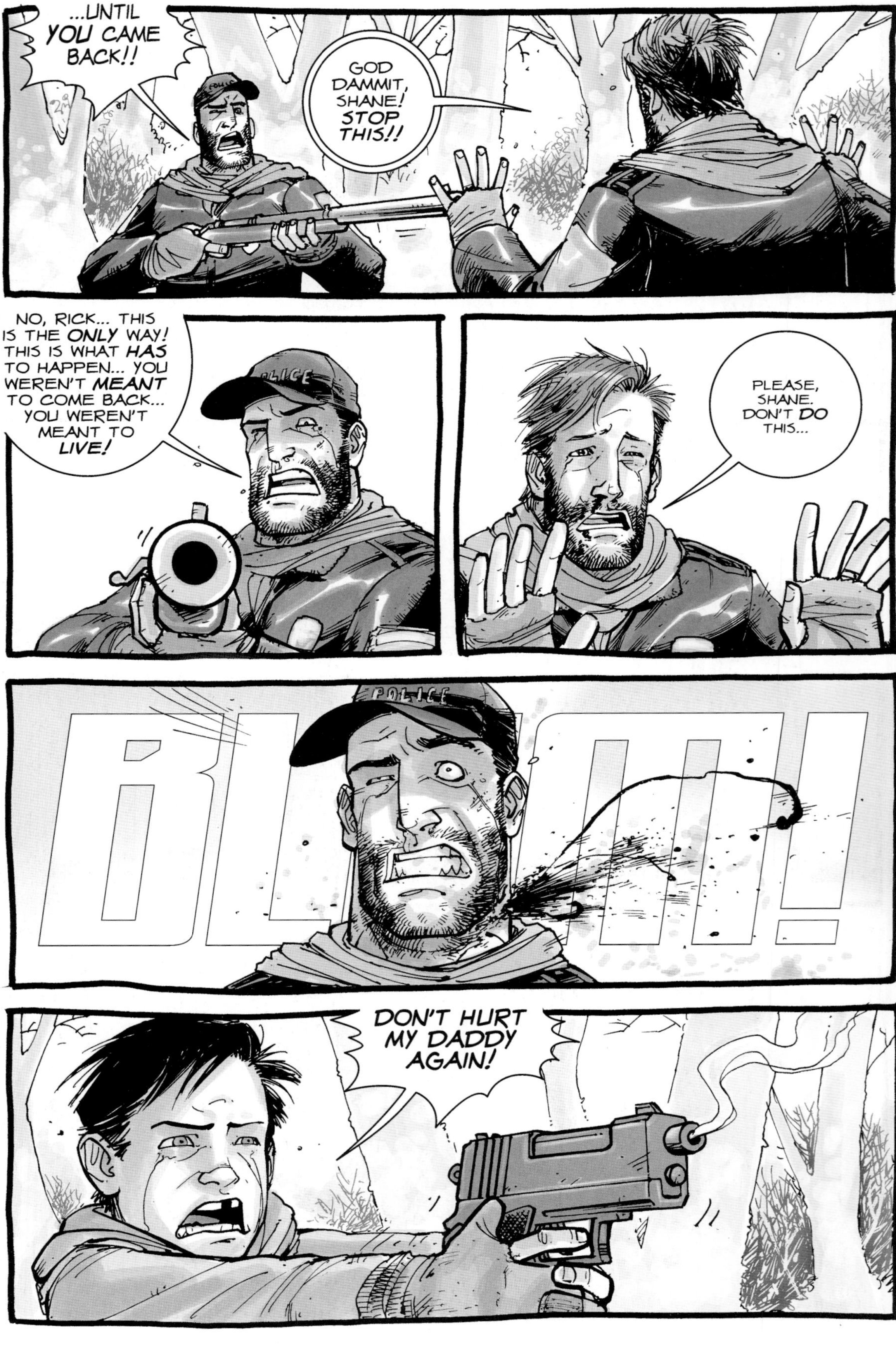
...UNTIL YOU CAME BACK!!
GOD DAMMIT, SHANE! STOP THIS!!
NO, RICK... THIS IS THE ONLY WAY! THIS IS WHAT HAS TO HAPPEN... YOU WEREN'T MEANT TO COME BACK... YOU WEREN'T MEANT TO LIVE!
PLEASE, SHANE. DON'T DO THIS...
POLICE
DON'T HURT MY DADDY AGAIN!

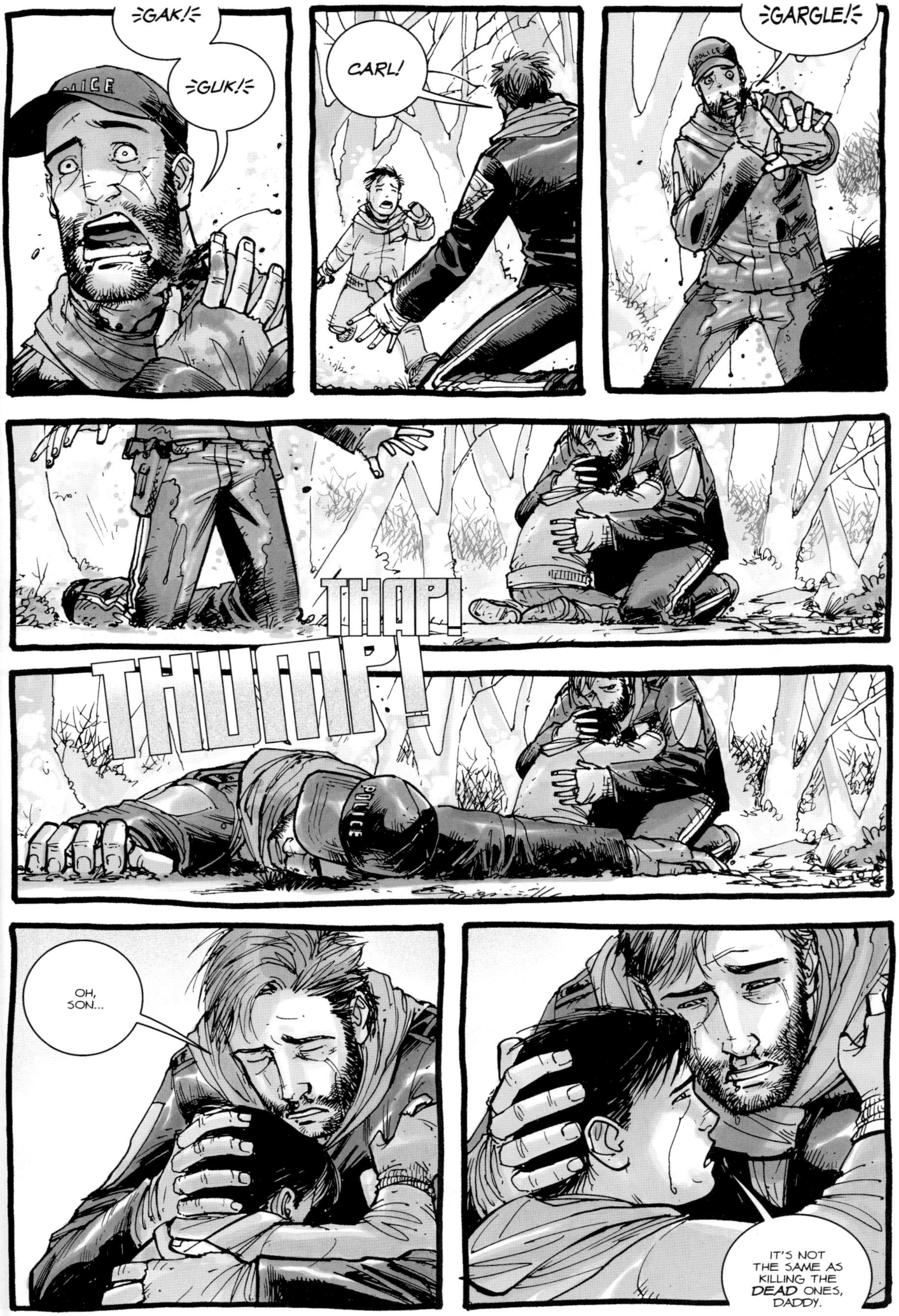

GAK!
GUK!
CARL!
GARGLE!
THAP!
THUMP!
OH, SON...
IT'S NOT THE SAME AS KILLING THE *DEAD* ONES, DADDY.

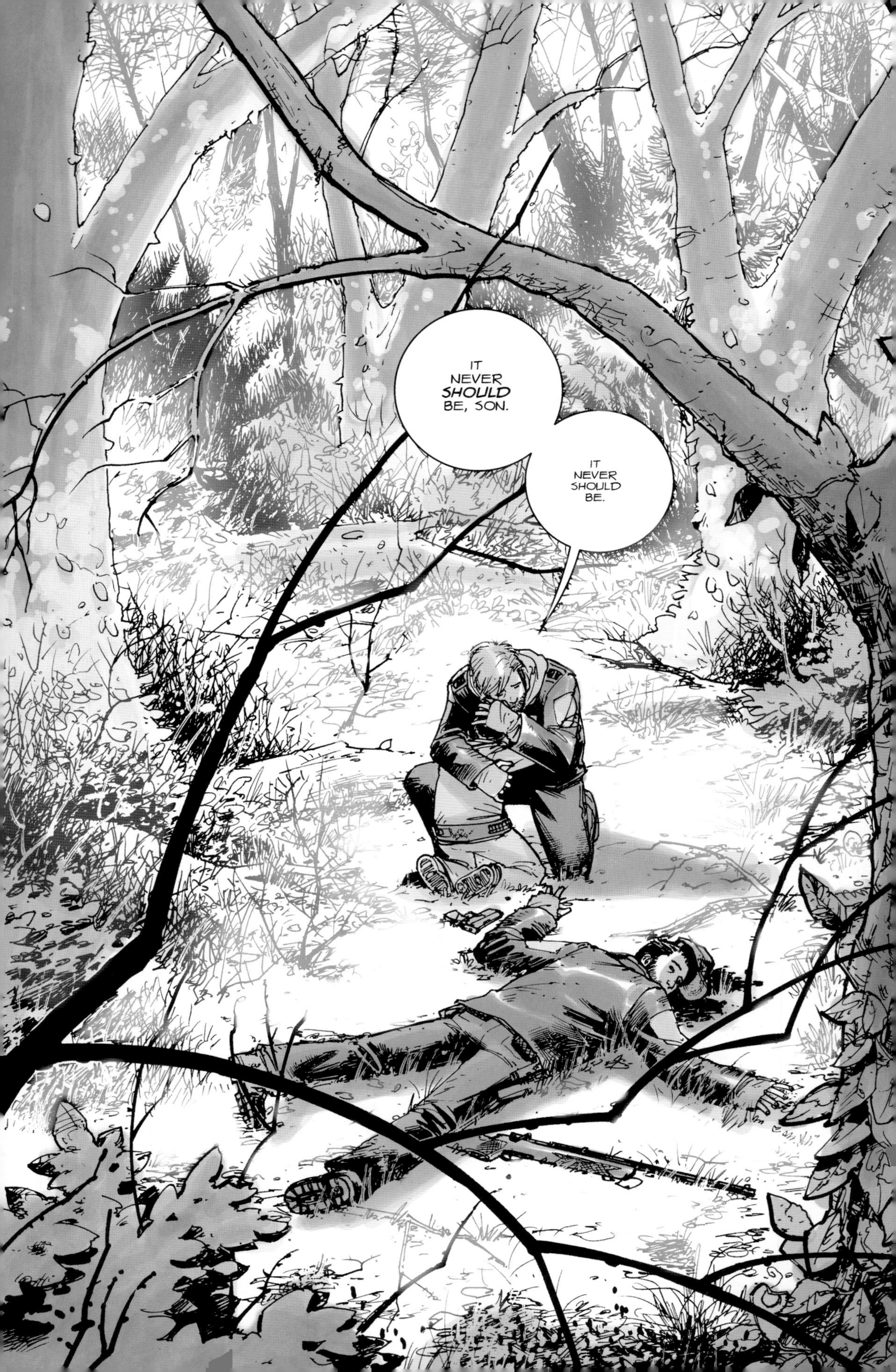
IT NEVER *SHOULD* BE, SON.
IT NEVER SHOULD BE.

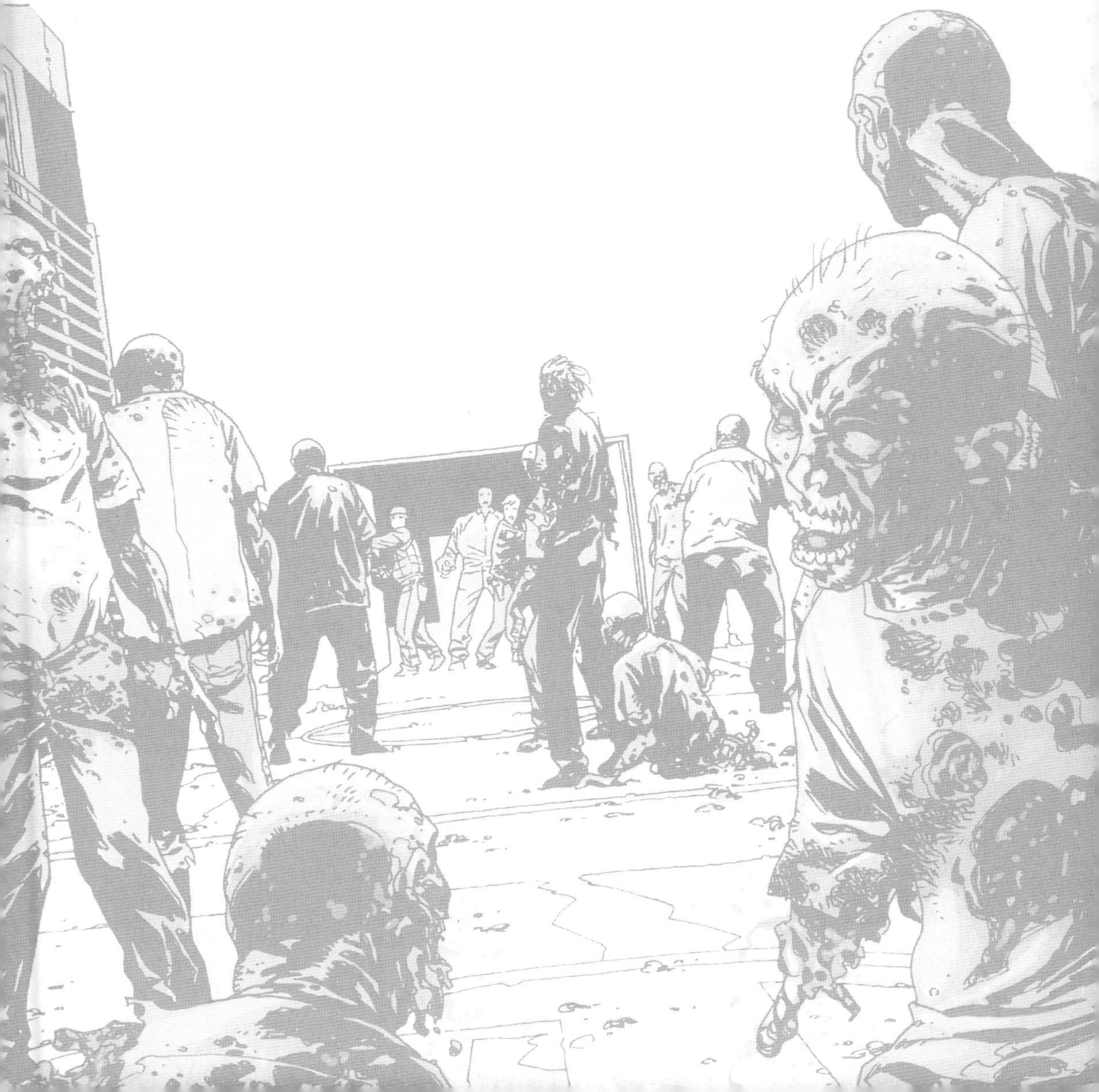

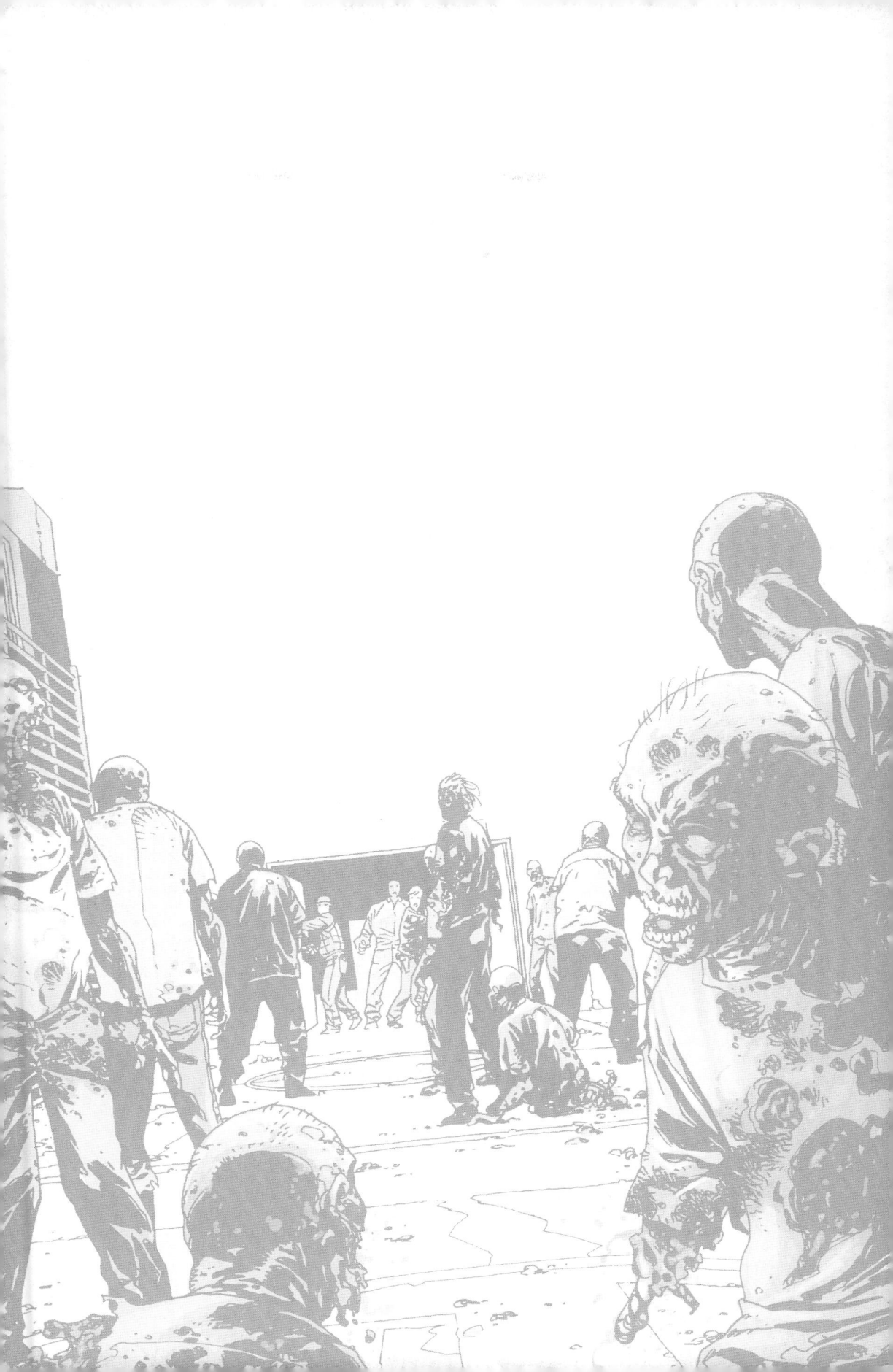

Chapter Two:
Miles Behind Us

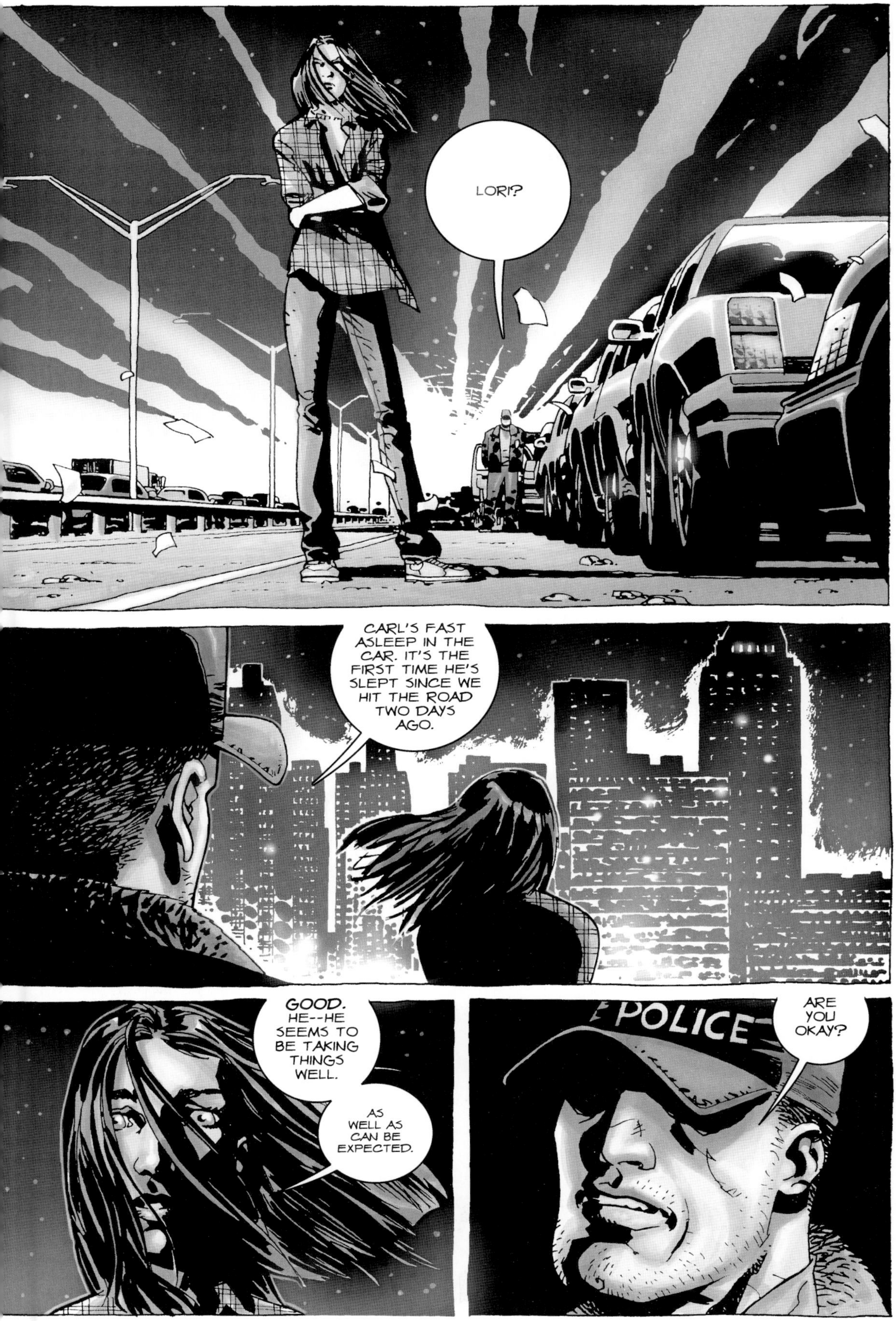
LORI?
CARL'S FAST ASLEEP IN THE CAR. IT'S THE FIRST TIME HE'S SLEPT SINCE WE HIT THE ROAD TWO DAYS AGO.
GOOD. HE--HE SEEMS TO BE TAKING THINGS WELL.
AS WELL AS CAN BE EXPECTED.
POLICE
ARE YOU OKAY?

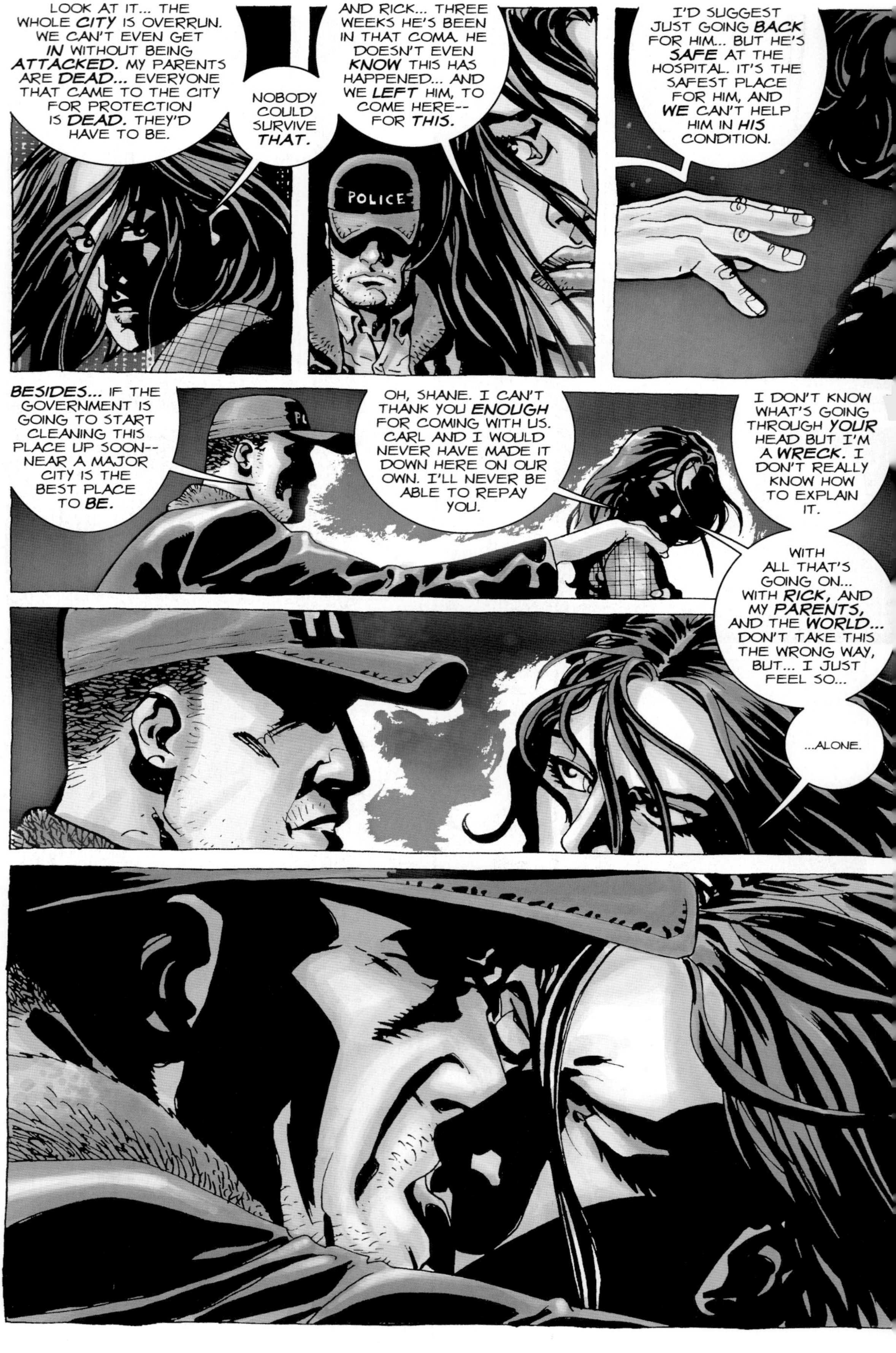

LOOK AT IT... THE WHOLE CITY IS OVERRUN. WE CAN'T EVEN GET IN WITHOUT BEING ATTACKED. MY PARENTS ARE DEAD... EVERYONE THAT CAME TO THE CITY FOR PROTECTION IS DEAD. THEY'D HAVE TO BE.
NOBODY COULD SURVIVE THAT.
AND RICK... THREE WEEKS HE'S BEEN IN THAT COMA. HE DOESN'T EVEN KNOW THIS HAS HAPPENED... AND WE LEFT HIM, TO COME HERE-- FOR THIS.
POLICE
I'D SUGGEST JUST GOING BACK FOR HIM... BUT HE'S SAFE AT THE HOSPITAL. IT'S THE SAFEST PLACE FOR HIM, AND WE CAN'T HELP HIM IN HIS CONDITION.
BESIDES... IF THE GOVERNMENT IS GOING TO START CLEANING THIS PLACE UP SOON-- NEAR A MAJOR CITY IS THE BEST PLACE TO BE.
OH, SHANE. I CAN'T THANK YOU ENOUGH FOR COMING WITH US. CARL AND I WOULD NEVER HAVE MADE IT DOWN HERE ON OUR OWN. I'LL NEVER BE ABLE TO REPAY YOU.
I DON'T KNOW WHAT'S GOING THROUGH YOUR HEAD BUT I'M A WRECK. I DON'T REALLY KNOW HOW TO EXPLAIN IT.
WITH ALL THAT'S GOING ON... WITH RICK, AND MY PARENTS, AND THE WORLD... DON'T TAKE THIS THE WRONG WAY, BUT... I JUST FEEL SO...
...ALONE.

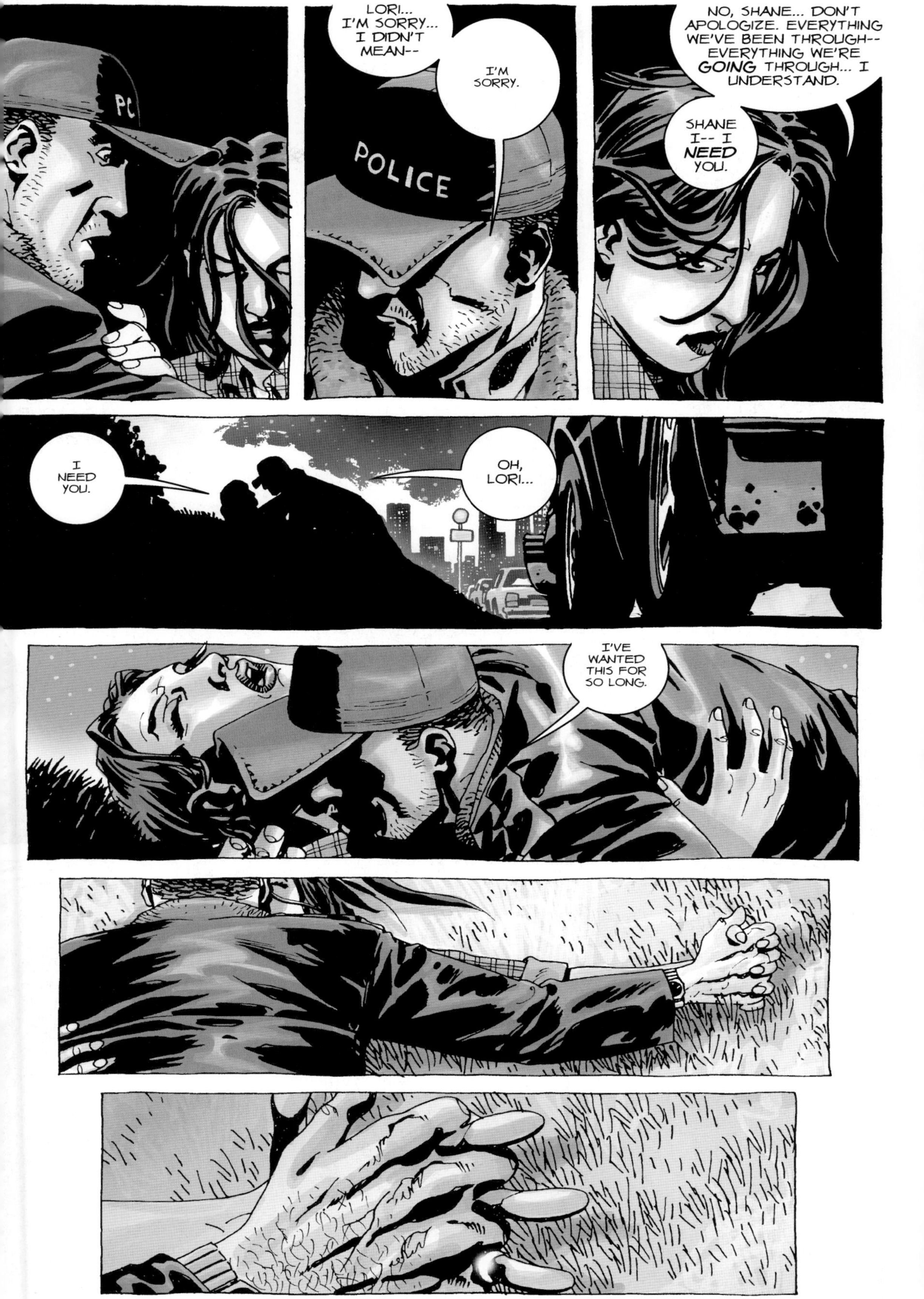
LORI... I'M SORRY... I DIDN'T MEAN--
I'M SORRY.
NO, SHANE... DON'T APOLOGIZE. EVERYTHING WE'VE BEEN THROUGH-- EVERYTHING WE'RE GOING THROUGH... I UNDERSTAND.
SHANE I-- I NEED YOU.
I NEED YOU.
OH, LORI...
I'VE WANTED THIS FOR SO LONG.

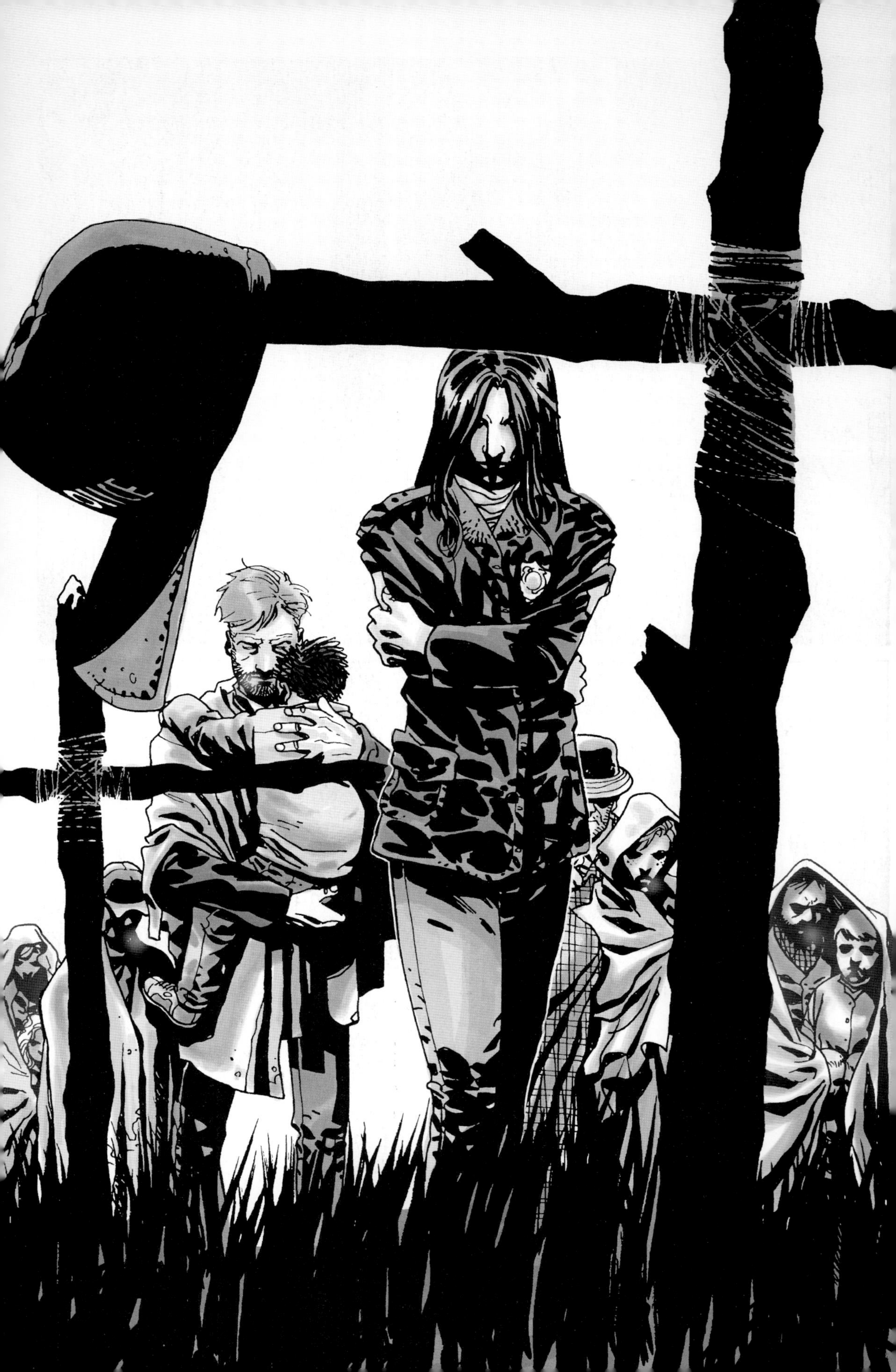

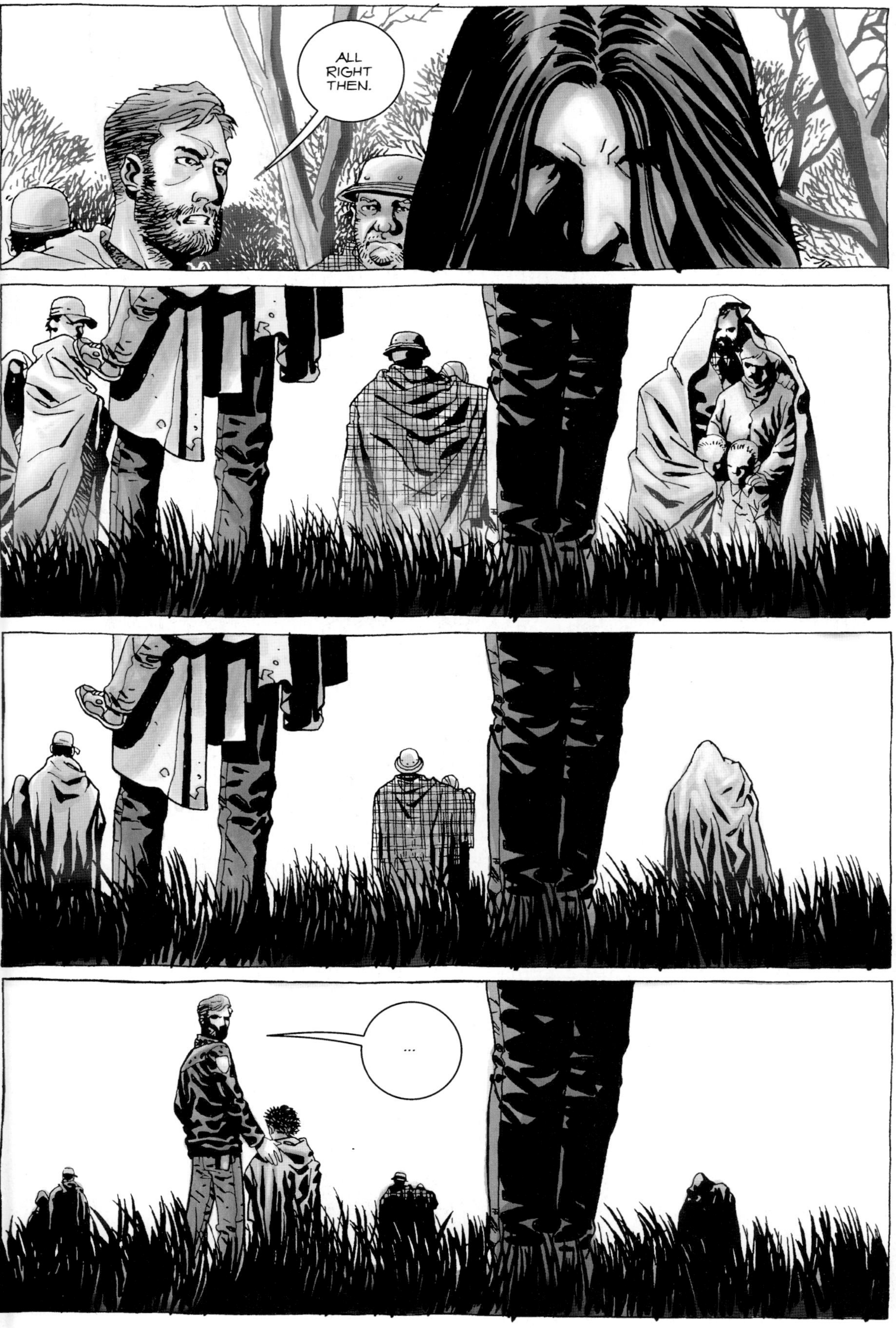
ALL RIGHT THEN.
...

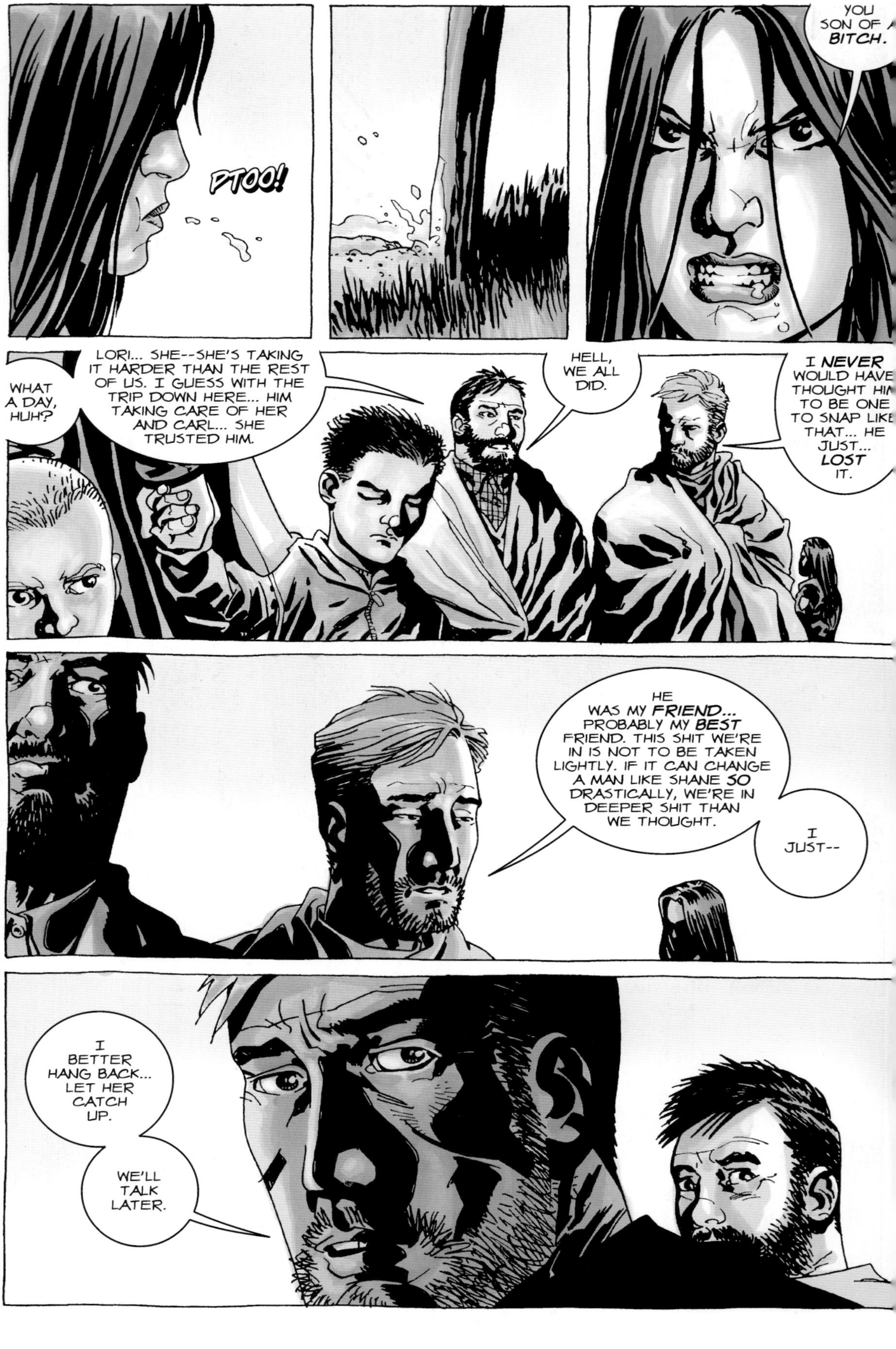

PTOO!
YOU SON OF A BITCH.
WHAT A DAY, HUH?
LORI... SHE--SHE'S TAKING IT HARDER THAN THE REST OF US. I GUESS WITH THE TRIP DOWN HERE... HIM TAKING CARE OF HER AND CARL... SHE TRUSTED HIM.
HELL, WE ALL DID.
I NEVER WOULD HAVE THOUGHT HIM TO BE ONE TO SNAP LIKE THAT... HE JUST... LOST IT.
HE WAS MY FRIEND... PROBABLY MY BEST FRIEND. THIS SHIT WE'RE IN IS NOT TO BE TAKEN LIGHTLY. IF IT CAN CHANGE A MAN LIKE SHANE SO DRASTICALLY, WE'RE IN DEEPER SHIT THAN WE THOUGHT.
I JUST--
I BETTER HANG BACK... LET HER CATCH UP.
WE'LL TALK LATER.

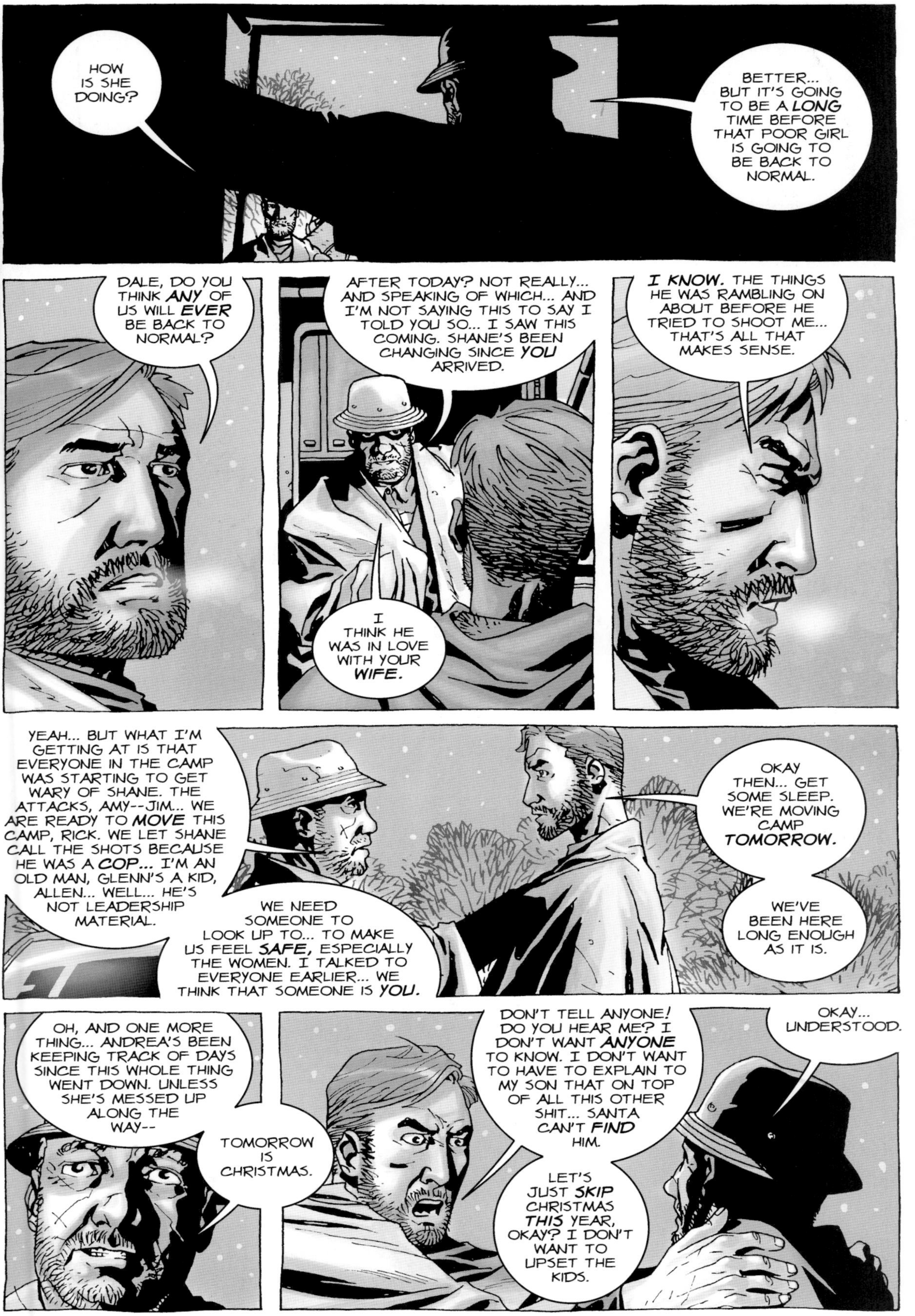
HOW IS SHE DOING?
BETTER... BUT IT'S GOING TO BE A LONG TIME BEFORE THAT POOR GIRL IS GOING TO BE BACK TO NORMAL.
DALE, DO YOU THINK ANY OF US WILL EVER BE BACK TO NORMAL?
AFTER TODAY? NOT REALLY... AND SPEAKING OF WHICH... AND I'M NOT SAYING THIS TO SAY I TOLD YOU SO... I SAW THIS COMING. SHANE'S BEEN CHANGING SINCE YOU ARRIVED.
I THINK HE WAS IN LOVE WITH YOUR WIFE.
I KNOW. THE THINGS HE WAS RAMBLING ON ABOUT BEFORE HE TRIED TO SHOOT ME... THAT'S ALL THAT MAKES SENSE.
YEAH... BUT WHAT I'M GETTING AT IS THAT EVERYONE IN THE CAMP WAS STARTING TO GET WARY OF SHANE. THE ATTACKS, AMY--JIM... WE ARE READY TO MOVE THIS CAMP, RICK. WE LET SHANE CALL THE SHOTS BECAUSE HE WAS A COP... I'M AN OLD MAN, GLENN'S A KID, ALLEN... WELL... HE'S NOT LEADERSHIP MATERIAL.
WE NEED SOMEONE TO LOOK UP TO... TO MAKE US FEEL SAFE, ESPECIALLY THE WOMEN. I TALKED TO EVERYONE EARLIER... WE THINK THAT SOMEONE IS YOU.
OKAY THEN... GET SOME SLEEP. WE'RE MOVING CAMP TOMORROW.
WE'VE BEEN HERE LONG ENOUGH AS IT IS.
OH, AND ONE MORE THING... ANDREA'S BEEN KEEPING TRACK OF DAYS SINCE THIS WHOLE THING WENT DOWN. UNLESS SHE'S MESSED UP ALONG THE WAY--
TOMORROW IS CHRISTMAS.
DON'T TELL ANYONE! DO YOU HEAR ME? I DON'T WANT ANYONE TO KNOW. I DON'T WANT TO HAVE TO EXPLAIN TO MY SON THAT ON TOP OF ALL THIS OTHER SHIT... SANTA CAN'T FIND HIM.
LET'S JUST SKIP CHRISTMAS THIS YEAR, OKAY? I DON'T WANT TO UPSET THE KIDS.
OKAY... UNDERSTOOD.

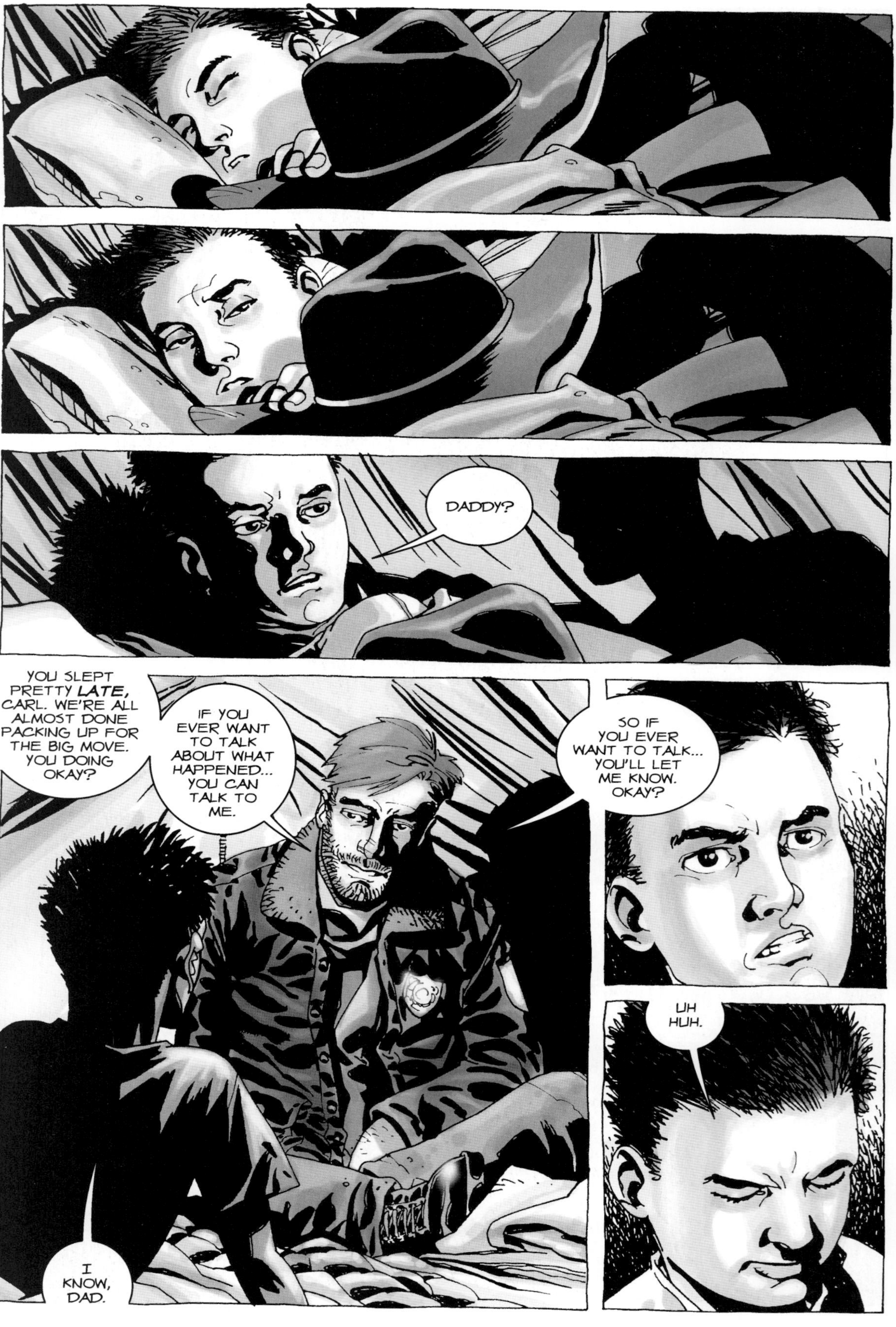
DADDY?
YOU SLEPT PRETTY *LATE,* CARL. WE'RE ALL ALMOST DONE PACKING UP FOR THE BIG MOVE. YOU DOING OKAY?
IF YOU EVER WANT TO TALK ABOUT WHAT HAPPENED... YOU CAN TALK TO ME.
I KNOW, DAD.
SO IF YOU EVER WANT TO TALK... YOU'LL LET ME KNOW. OKAY?
UH HUH.

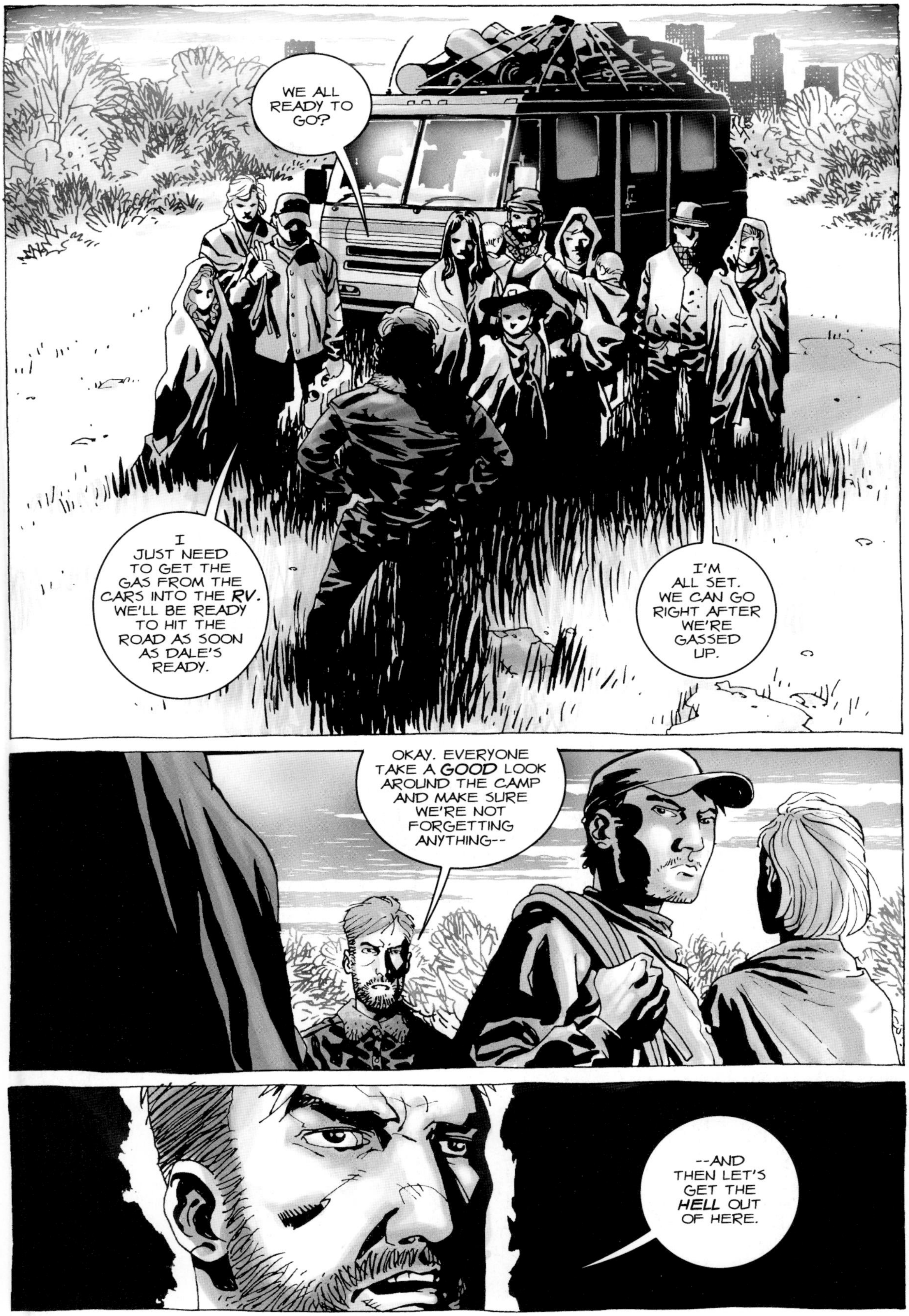
WE ALL READY TO GO?
I JUST NEED TO GET THE GAS FROM THE CARS INTO THE RV. WE'LL BE READY TO HIT THE ROAD AS SOON AS DALE'S READY.
I'M ALL SET. WE CAN GO RIGHT AFTER WE'RE GASSED UP.
OKAY. EVERYONE TAKE A GOOD LOOK AROUND THE CAMP AND MAKE SURE WE'RE NOT FORGETTING ANYTHING--
--AND THEN LET'S GET THE HELL OUT OF HERE.

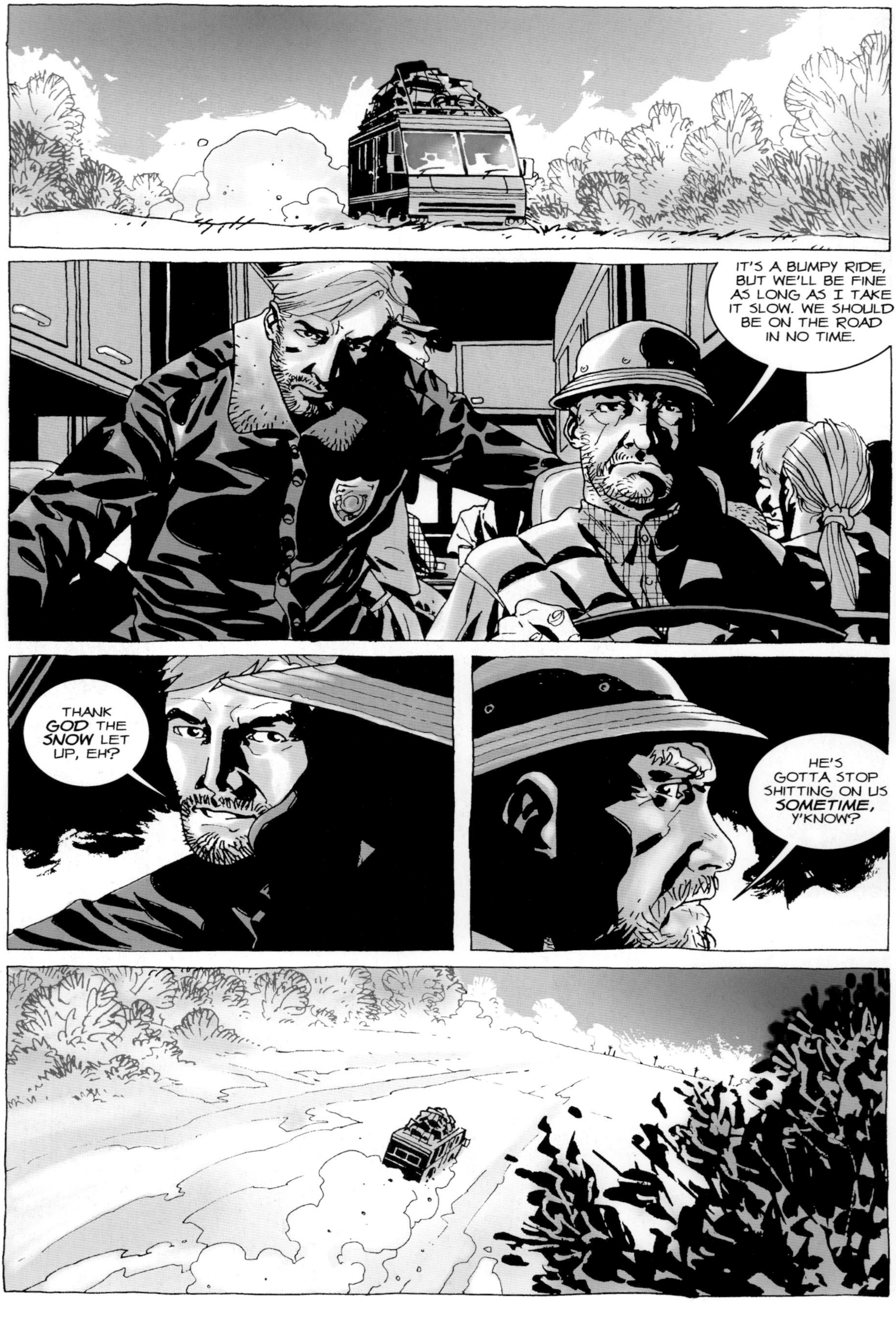
IT'S A BUMPY RIDE, BUT WE'LL BE FINE AS LONG AS I TAKE IT SLOW. WE SHOULD BE ON THE ROAD IN NO TIME.
THANK GOD THE SNOW LET UP, EH?
HE'S GOTTA STOP SHITTING ON US SOMETIME, Y'KNOW?

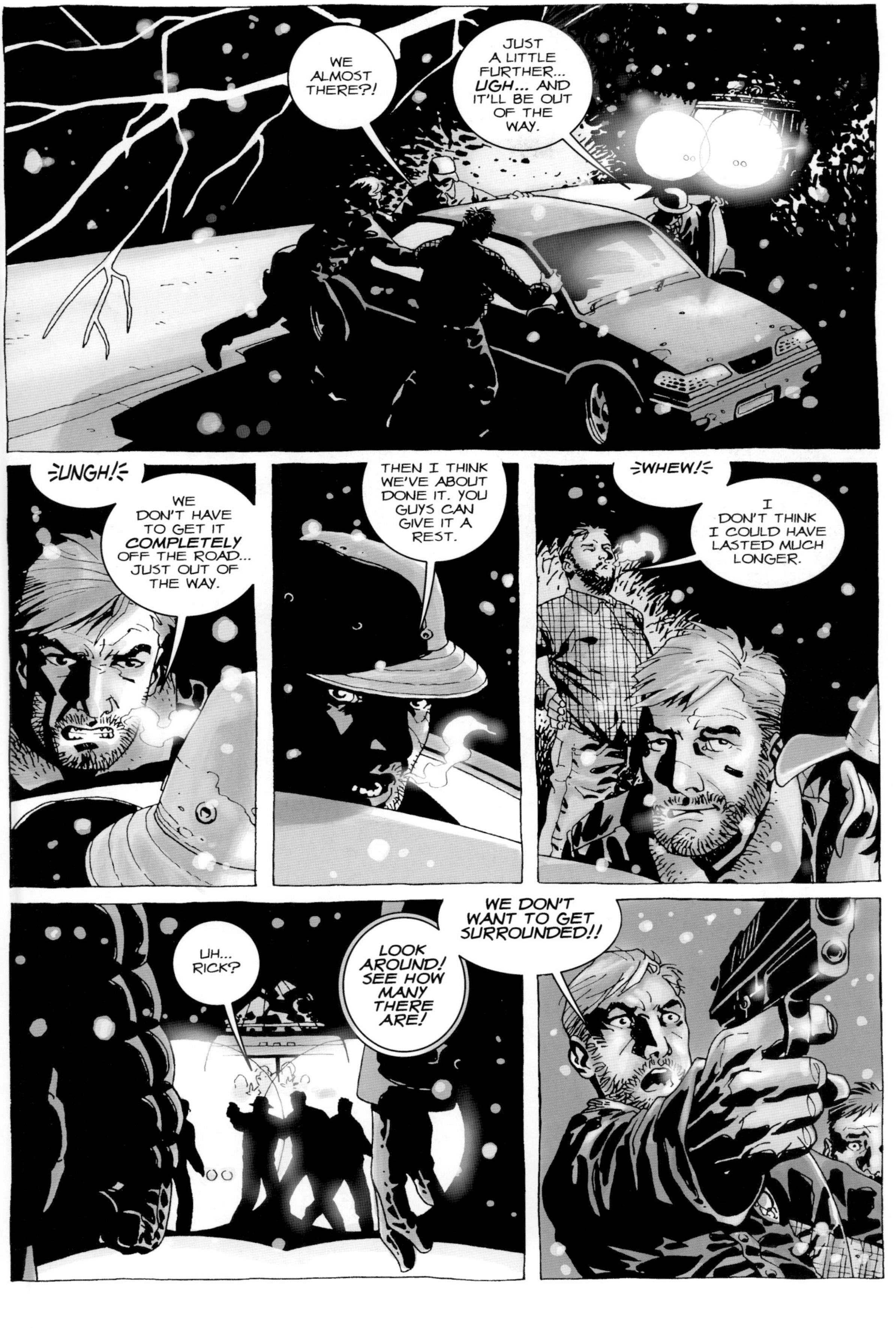
WE ALMOST THERE?!
JUST A LITTLE FURTHER... UGH... AND IT'LL BE OUT OF THE WAY.
UNGH!
WE DON'T HAVE TO GET IT COMPLETELY OFF THE ROAD... JUST OUT OF THE WAY.
THEN I THINK WE'VE ABOUT DONE IT. YOU GUYS CAN GIVE IT A REST.
WHEW!
I DON'T THINK I COULD HAVE LASTED MUCH LONGER.
UH... RICK?
LOOK AROUND! SEE HOW MANY THERE ARE!
WE DON'T WANT TO GET SURROUNDED!!

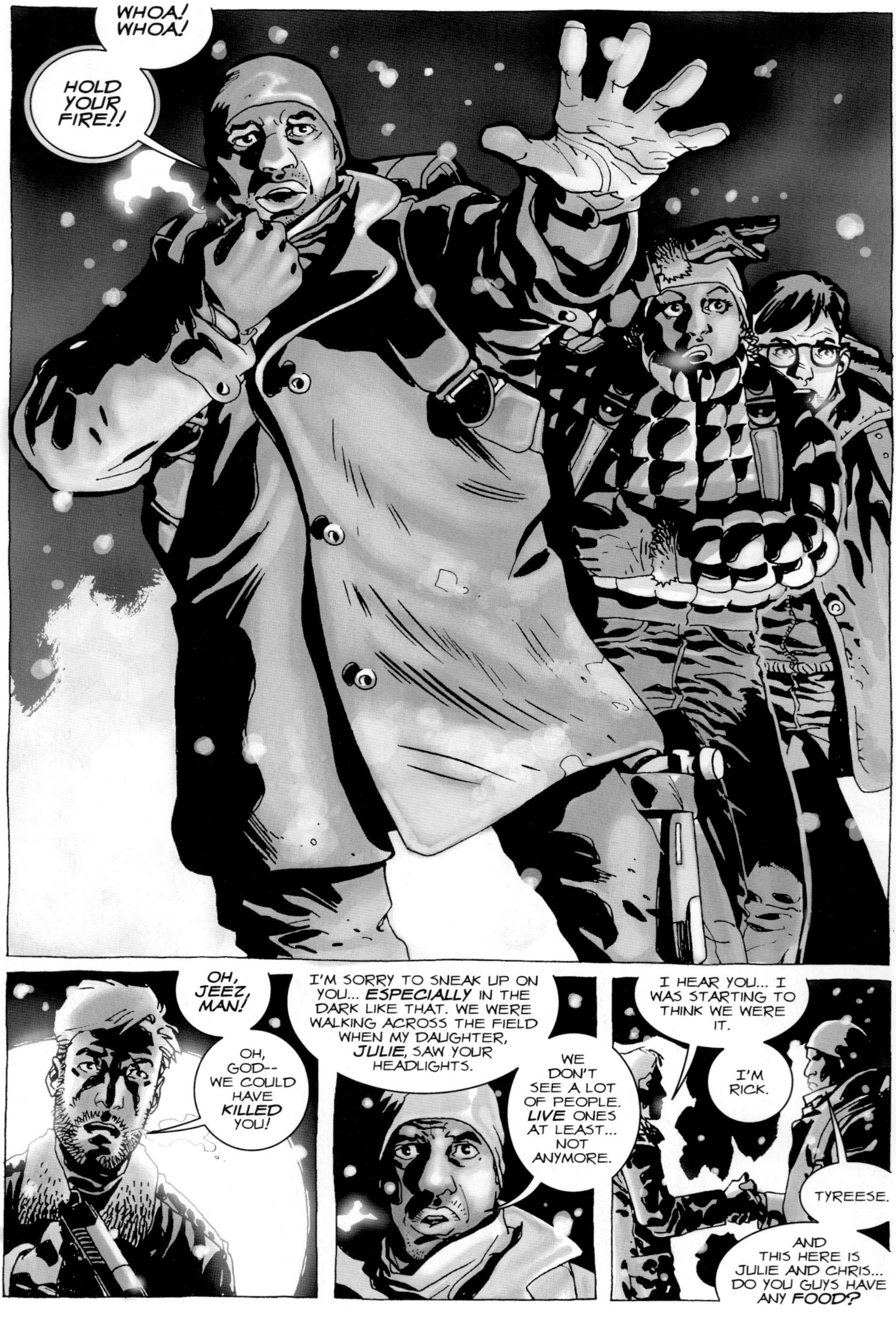
WHOA! WHOA!
HOLD YOUR FIRE!!
OH, JEEZ, MAN!
OH, GOD-- WE COULD HAVE KILLED YOU!
I'M SORRY TO SNEAK UP ON YOU... ESPECIALLY IN THE DARK LIKE THAT. WE WERE WALKING ACROSS THE FIELD WHEN MY DAUGHTER, JULIE, SAW YOUR HEADLIGHTS.
WE DON'T SEE A LOT OF PEOPLE. LIVE ONES AT LEAST... NOT ANYMORE.
I HEAR YOU... I WAS STARTING TO THINK WE WERE IT.
I'M RICK.
TYREESE.
AND THIS HERE IS JULIE AND CHRIS... DO YOU GUYS HAVE ANY FOOD?

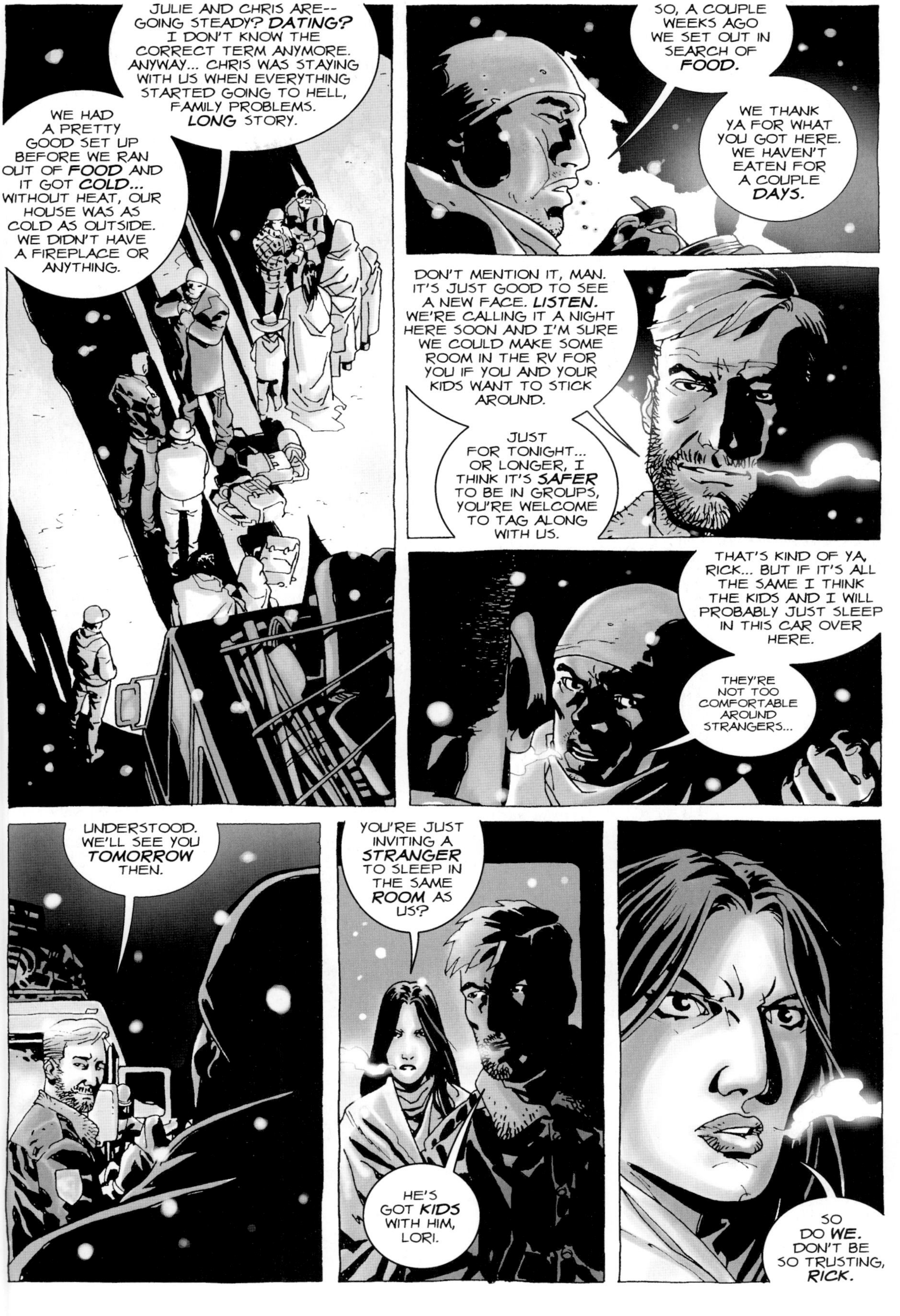
JULIE AND CHRIS ARE-- GOING STEADY? DATING? I DON'T KNOW THE CORRECT TERM ANYMORE. ANYWAY... CHRIS WAS STAYING WITH US WHEN EVERYTHING STARTED GOING TO HELL, FAMILY PROBLEMS. LONG STORY.
WE HAD A PRETTY GOOD SET UP BEFORE WE RAN OUT OF FOOD AND IT GOT COLD... WITHOUT HEAT, OUR HOUSE WAS AS COLD AS OUTSIDE. WE DIDN'T HAVE A FIREPLACE OR ANYTHING.
SO, A COUPLE WEEKS AGO WE SET OUT IN SEARCH OF FOOD.
WE THANK YA FOR WHAT YOU GOT HERE. WE HAVEN'T EATEN FOR A COUPLE DAYS.
DON'T MENTION IT, MAN. IT'S JUST GOOD TO SEE A NEW FACE. LISTEN. WE'RE CALLING IT A NIGHT HERE SOON AND I'M SURE WE COULD MAKE SOME ROOM IN THE RV FOR YOU IF YOU AND YOUR KIDS WANT TO STICK AROUND.
JUST FOR TONIGHT... OR LONGER, I THINK IT'S SAFER TO BE IN GROUPS, YOU'RE WELCOME TO TAG ALONG WITH US.
THAT'S KIND OF YA, RICK... BUT IF IT'S ALL THE SAME I THINK THE KIDS AND I WILL PROBABLY JUST SLEEP IN THIS CAR OVER HERE.
THEY'RE NOT TOO COMFORTABLE AROUND STRANGERS...
UNDERSTOOD. WE'LL SEE YOU TOMORROW THEN.
YOU'RE JUST INVITING A STRANGER TO SLEEP IN THE SAME ROOM AS US?
HE'S GOT KIDS WITH HIM, LORI.
SO DO WE. DON'T BE SO TRUSTING, RICK.

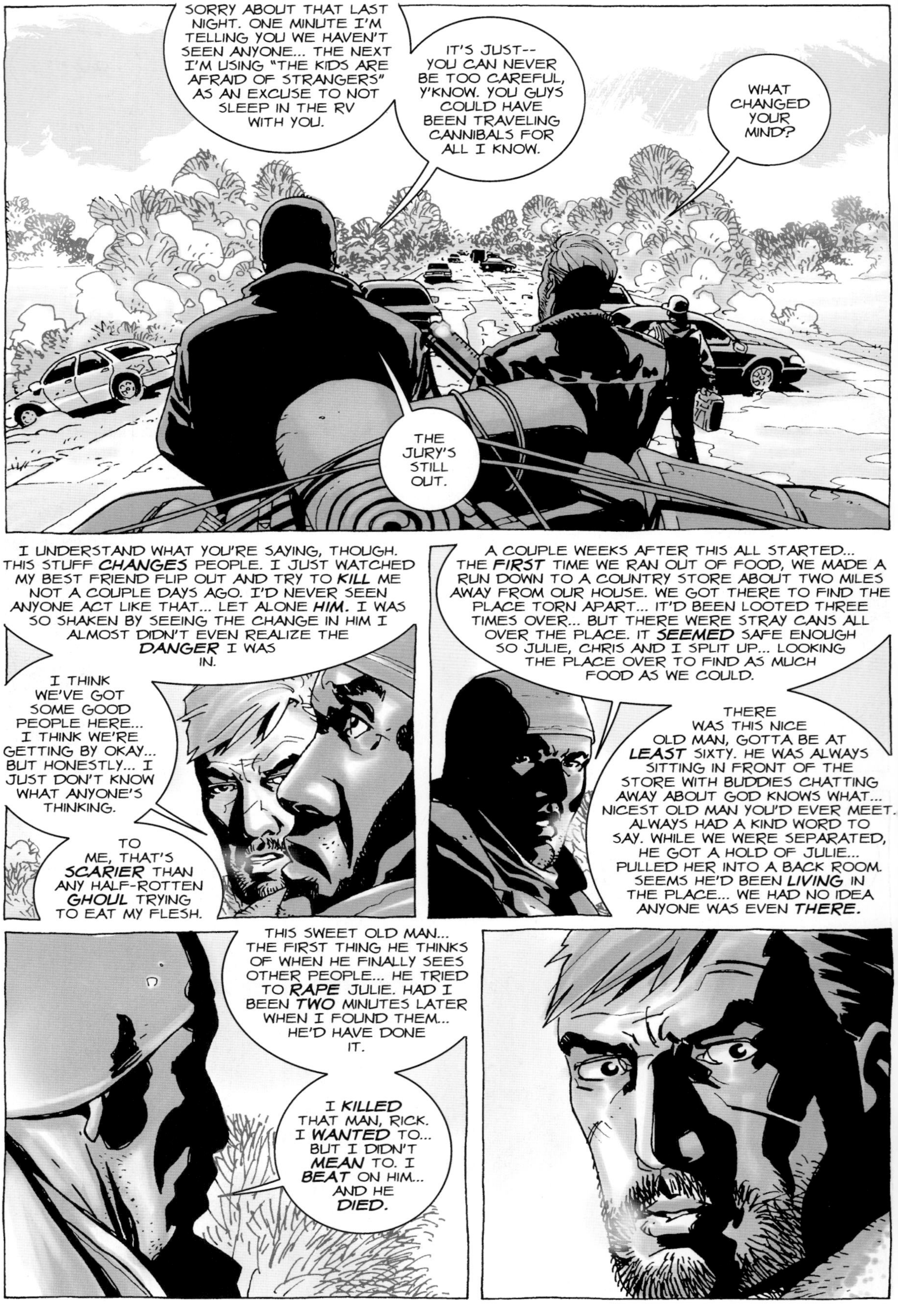

SORRY ABOUT THAT LAST NIGHT. ONE MINUTE I'M TELLING YOU WE HAVEN'T SEEN ANYONE... THE NEXT I'M USING "THE KIDS ARE AFRAID OF STRANGERS" AS AN EXCUSE TO NOT SLEEP IN THE RV WITH YOU.
IT'S JUST-- YOU CAN NEVER BE TOO CAREFUL, Y'KNOW. YOU GUYS COULD HAVE BEEN TRAVELING CANNIBALS FOR ALL I KNOW.
WHAT CHANGED YOUR MIND?
THE JURY'S STILL OUT.
I UNDERSTAND WHAT YOU'RE SAYING, THOUGH. THIS STUFF CHANGES PEOPLE. I JUST WATCHED MY BEST FRIEND FLIP OUT AND TRY TO KILL ME NOT A COUPLE DAYS AGO. I'D NEVER SEEN ANYONE ACT LIKE THAT... LET ALONE HIM. I WAS SO SHAKEN BY SEEING THE CHANGE IN HIM I ALMOST DIDN'T EVEN REALIZE THE DANGER I WAS IN.
I THINK WE'VE GOT SOME GOOD PEOPLE HERE... I THINK WE'RE GETTING BY OKAY... BUT HONESTLY... I JUST DON'T KNOW WHAT ANYONE'S THINKING.
TO ME, THAT'S SCARIER THAN ANY HALF-ROTTEN GHOUL TRYING TO EAT MY FLESH.
A COUPLE WEEKS AFTER THIS ALL STARTED... THE FIRST TIME WE RAN OUT OF FOOD, WE MADE A RUN DOWN TO A COUNTRY STORE ABOUT TWO MILES AWAY FROM OUR HOUSE. WE GOT THERE TO FIND THE PLACE TORN APART... IT'D BEEN LOOTED THREE TIMES OVER... BUT THERE WERE STRAY CANS ALL OVER THE PLACE. IT SEEMED SAFE ENOUGH SO JULIE, CHRIS AND I SPLIT UP... LOOKING THE PLACE OVER TO FIND AS MUCH FOOD AS WE COULD.
THERE WAS THIS NICE OLD MAN, GOTTA BE AT LEAST SIXTY. HE WAS ALWAYS SITTING IN FRONT OF THE STORE WITH BUDDIES CHATTING AWAY ABOUT GOD KNOWS WHAT... NICEST OLD MAN YOU'D EVER MEET. ALWAYS HAD A KIND WORD TO SAY. WHILE WE WERE SEPARATED, HE GOT A HOLD OF JULIE... PULLED HER INTO A BACK ROOM. SEEMS HE'D BEEN LIVING IN THE PLACE... WE HAD NO IDEA ANYONE WAS EVEN THERE.
THIS SWEET OLD MAN... THE FIRST THING HE THINKS OF WHEN HE FINALLY SEES OTHER PEOPLE... HE TRIED TO RAPE JULIE. HAD I BEEN TWO MINUTES LATER WHEN I FOUND THEM... HE'D HAVE DONE IT.
I KILLED THAT MAN, RICK. I WANTED TO... BUT I DIDN'T MEAN TO. I BEAT ON HIM... AND HE DIED.

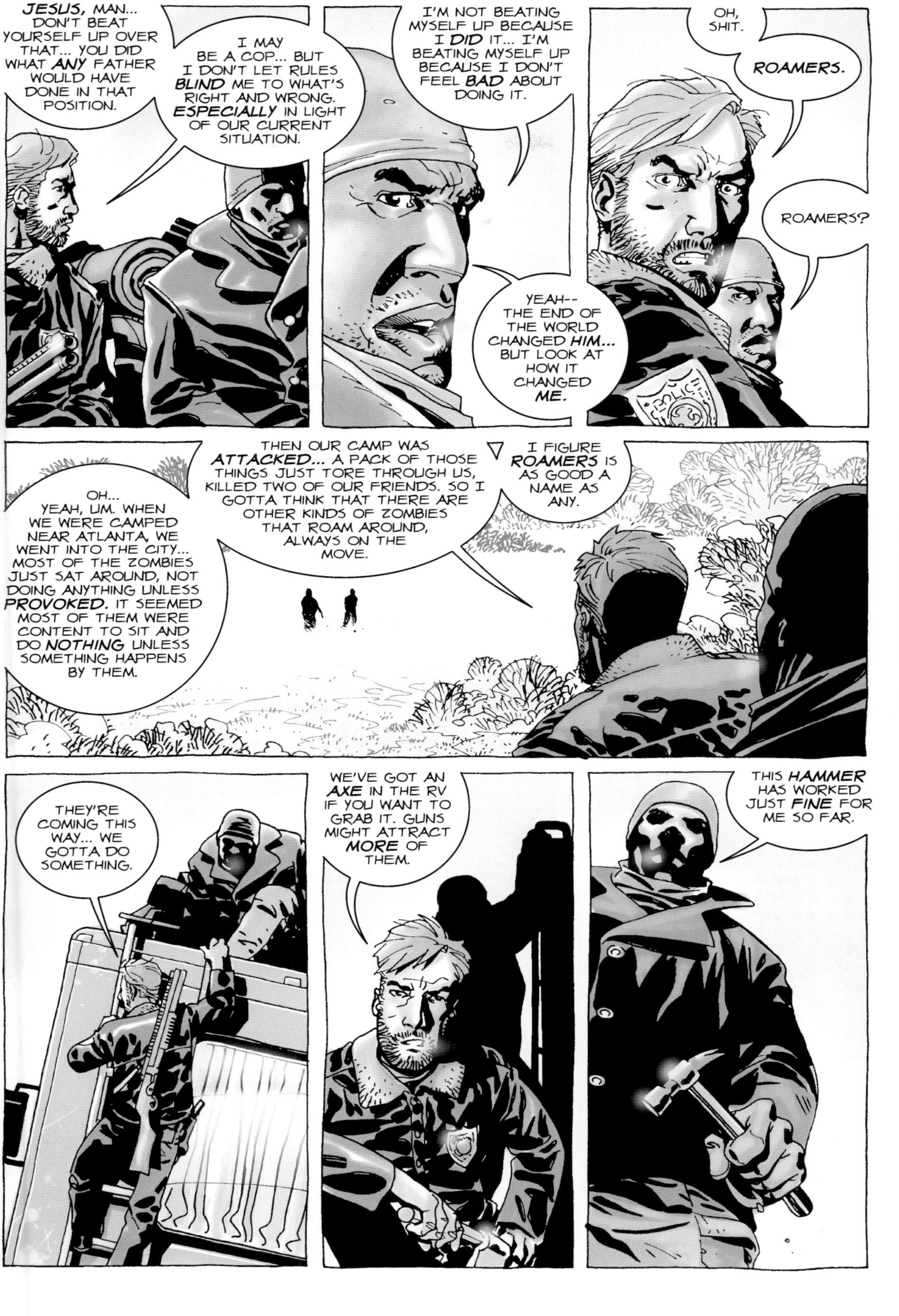
JESUS, MAN... DON'T BEAT YOURSELF UP OVER THAT... YOU DID WHAT ANY FATHER WOULD HAVE DONE IN THAT POSITION.
I MAY BE A COP... BUT I DON'T LET RULES BLIND ME TO WHAT'S RIGHT AND WRONG. ESPECIALLY IN LIGHT OF OUR CURRENT SITUATION.
I'M NOT BEATING MYSELF UP BECAUSE I DID IT... I'M BEATING MYSELF UP BECAUSE I DON'T FEEL BAD ABOUT DOING IT.
YEAH-- THE END OF THE WORLD CHANGED HIM... BUT LOOK AT HOW IT CHANGED ME.
OH, SHIT.
ROAMERS.
ROAMERS?
OH... YEAH, UM. WHEN WE WERE CAMPED NEAR ATLANTA, WE WENT INTO THE CITY... MOST OF THE ZOMBIES JUST SAT AROUND, NOT DOING ANYTHING UNLESS PROVOKED. IT SEEMED MOST OF THEM WERE CONTENT TO SIT AND DO NOTHING UNLESS SOMETHING HAPPENS BY THEM.
THEN OUR CAMP WAS ATTACKED... A PACK OF THOSE THINGS JUST TORE THROUGH US, KILLED TWO OF OUR FRIENDS. SO I GOTTA THINK THAT THERE ARE OTHER KINDS OF ZOMBIES THAT ROAM AROUND, ALWAYS ON THE MOVE.
I FIGURE ROAMERS IS AS GOOD A NAME AS ANY.
THEY'RE COMING THIS WAY... WE GOTTA DO SOMETHING.
WE'VE GOT AN AXE IN THE RV IF YOU WANT TO GRAB IT. GUNS MIGHT ATTRACT MORE OF THEM.
THIS HAMMER HAS WORKED JUST FINE FOR ME SO FAR.

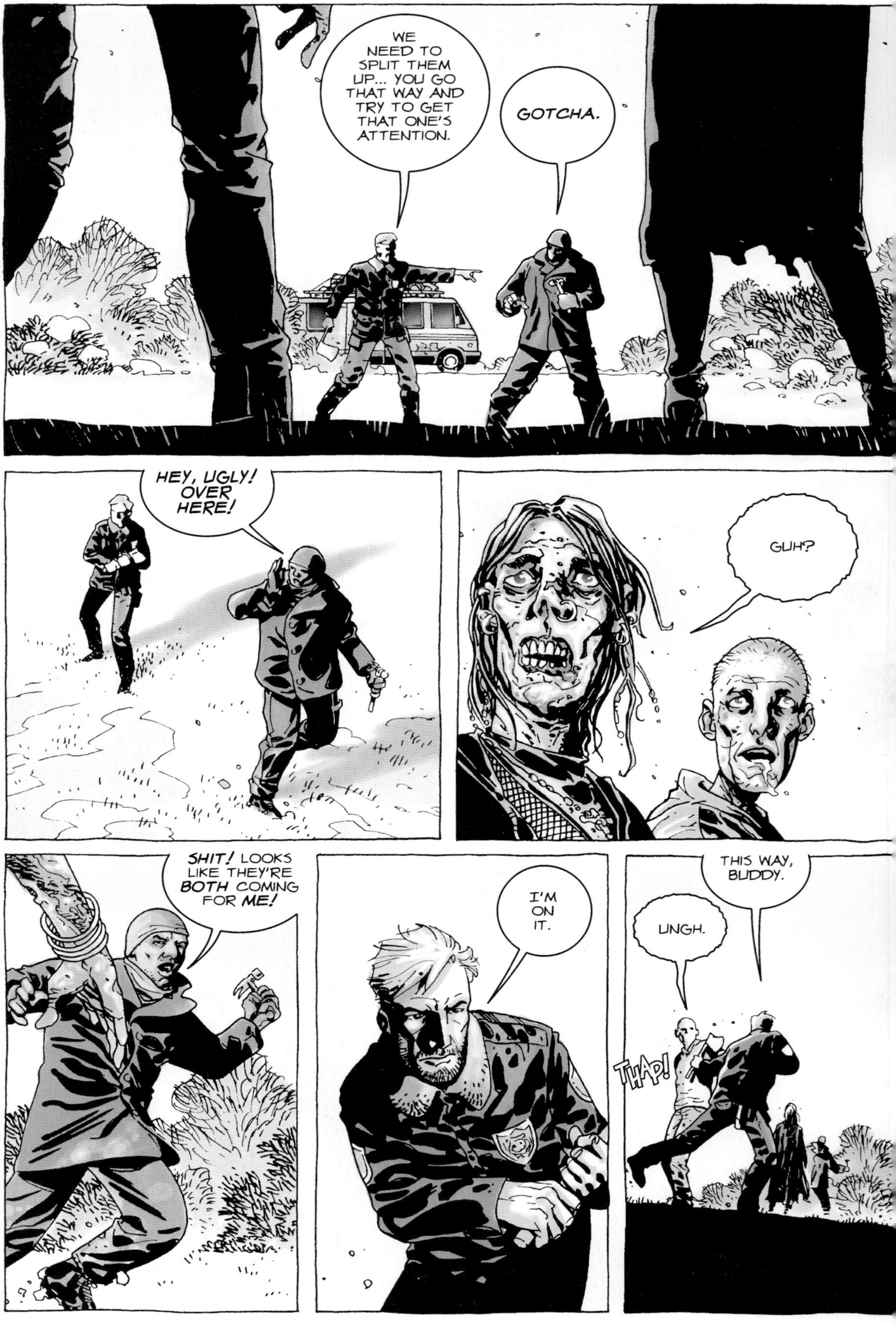
WE NEED TO SPLIT THEM UP... YOU GO THAT WAY AND TRY TO GET THAT ONE'S ATTENTION.
GOTCHA.
HEY, UGLY! OVER HERE!
GUH?
SHIT! LOOKS LIKE THEY'RE BOTH COMING FOR ME!
I'M ON IT.
THIS WAY, BUDDY.
UNGH.
THAP!

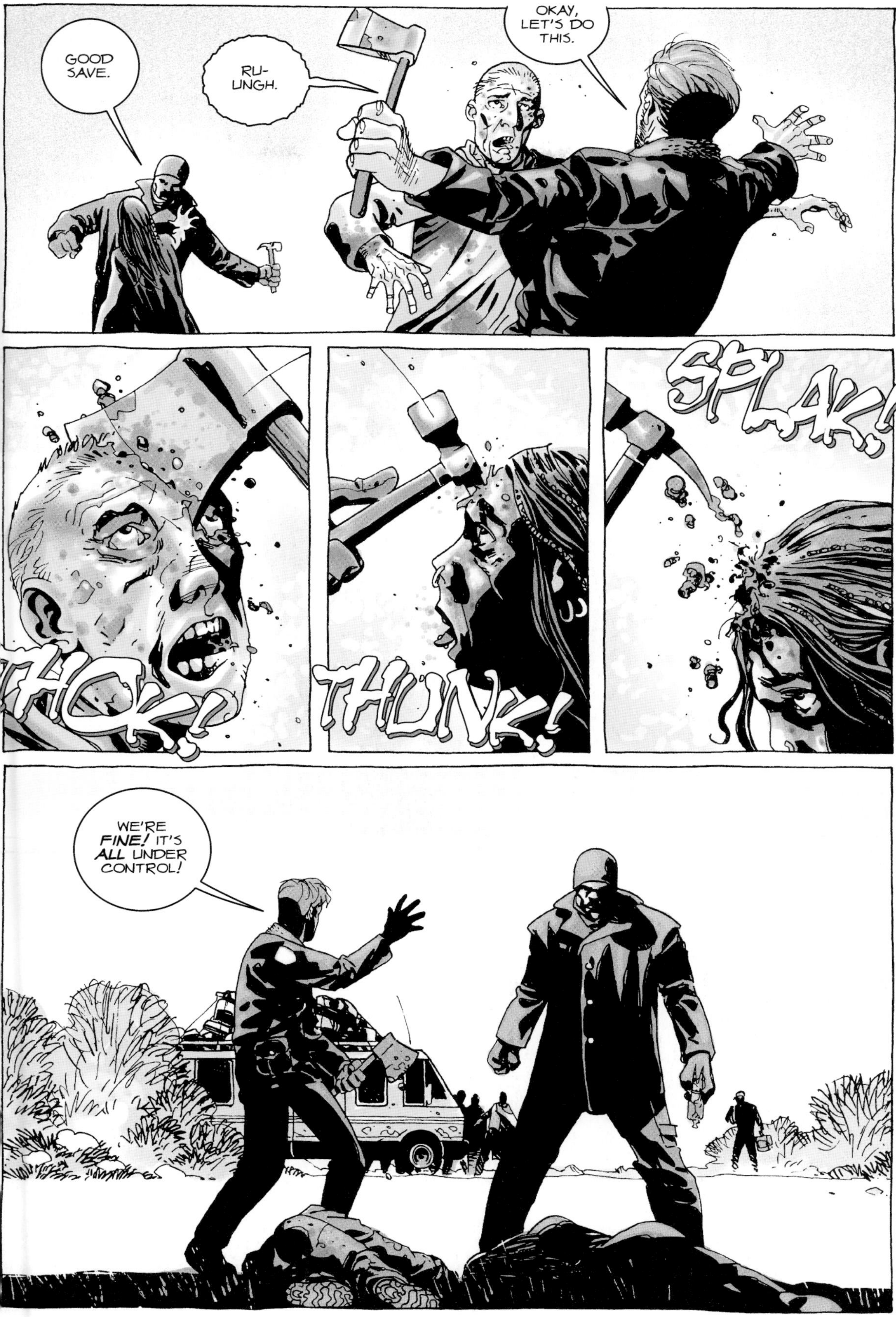
GOOD SAVE.
RU-UNGH.
OKAY, LET'S DO THIS.
THUNK!
SPLAK!
WE'RE FINE! IT'S ALL UNDER CONTROL!

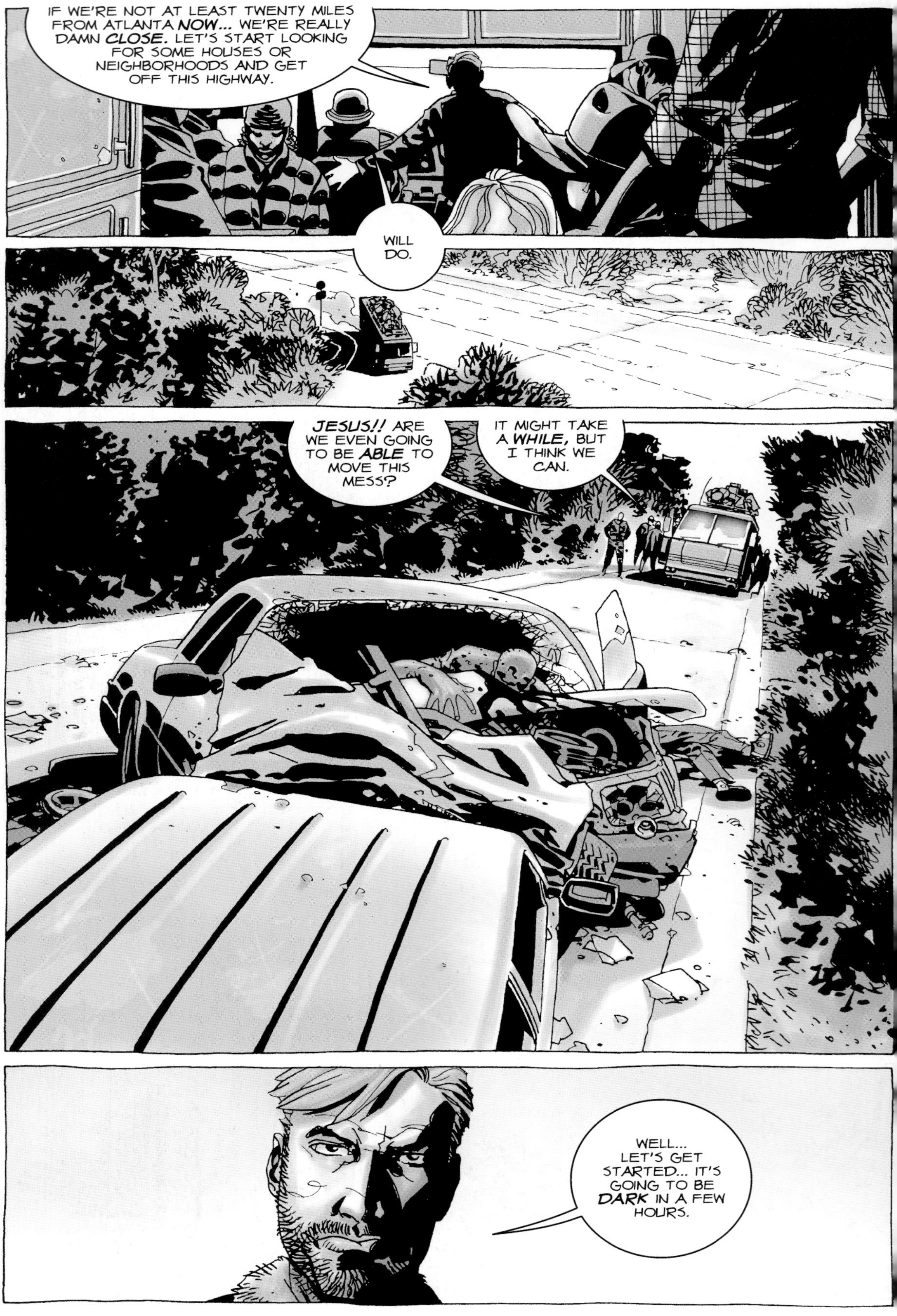
IF WE'RE NOT AT LEAST TWENTY MILES FROM ATLANTA NOW... WE'RE REALLY DAMN CLOSE. LET'S START LOOKING FOR SOME HOUSES OR NEIGHBORHOODS AND GET OFF THIS HIGHWAY.
WILL DO.
JESUS!! ARE WE EVEN GOING TO BE ABLE TO MOVE THIS MESS?
IT MIGHT TAKE A WHILE, BUT I THINK WE CAN.
WELL... LET'S GET STARTED... IT'S GOING TO BE DARK IN A FEW HOURS.

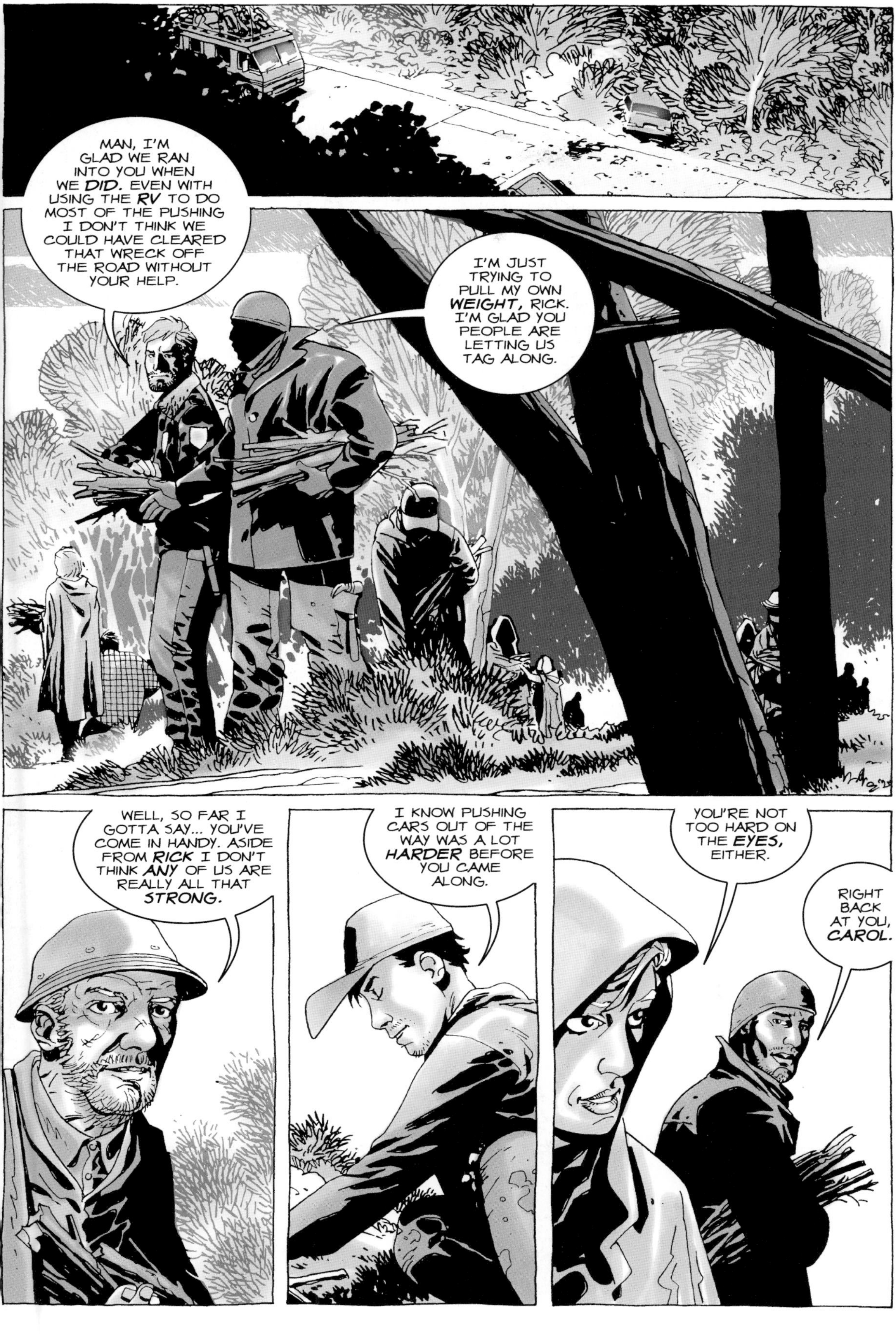

MAN, I'M GLAD WE RAN INTO YOU WHEN WE DID. EVEN WITH USING THE RV TO DO MOST OF THE PUSHING I DON'T THINK WE COULD HAVE CLEARED THAT WRECK OFF THE ROAD WITHOUT YOUR HELP.
I'M JUST TRYING TO PULL MY OWN WEIGHT, RICK. I'M GLAD YOU PEOPLE ARE LETTING US TAG ALONG.
WELL, SO FAR I GOTTA SAY... YOU'VE COME IN HANDY. ASIDE FROM RICK I DON'T THINK ANY OF US ARE REALLY ALL THAT STRONG.
I KNOW PUSHING CARS OUT OF THE WAY WAS A LOT HARDER BEFORE YOU CAME ALONG.
YOU'RE NOT TOO HARD ON THE EYES, EITHER.
RIGHT BACK AT YOU, CAROL.

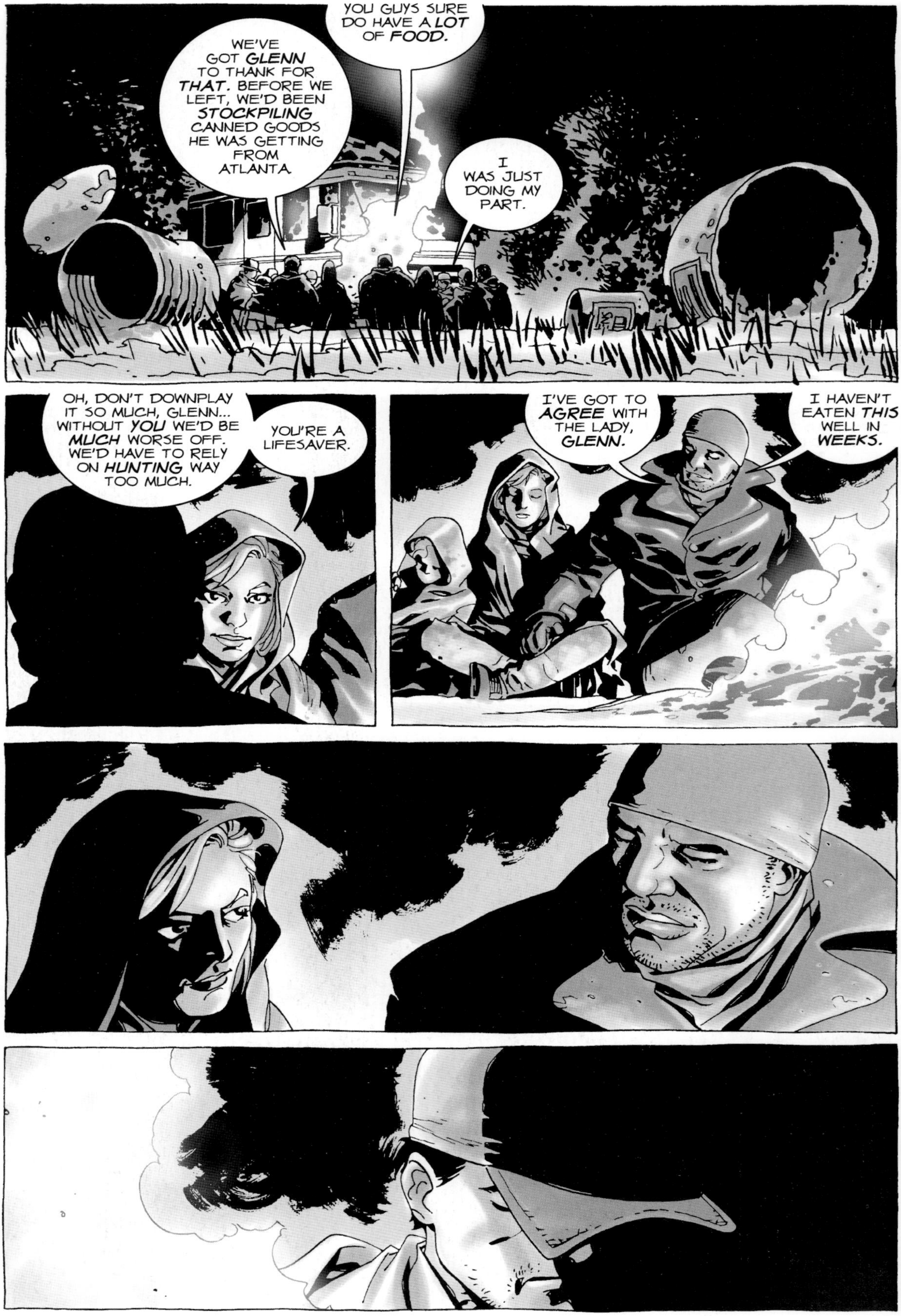
YOU GUYS SURE DO HAVE A LOT OF FOOD.
WE'VE GOT GLENN TO THANK FOR THAT. BEFORE WE LEFT, WE'D BEEN STOCKPILING CANNED GOODS HE WAS GETTING FROM ATLANTA.
I WAS JUST DOING MY PART.
OH, DON'T DOWNPLAY IT SO MUCH, GLENN... WITHOUT YOU WE'D BE MUCH WORSE OFF. WE'D HAVE TO RELY ON HUNTING WAY TOO MUCH.
YOU'RE A LIFESAVER.
I'VE GOT TO AGREE WITH THE LADY, GLENN.
I HAVEN'T EATEN THIS WELL IN WEEKS.

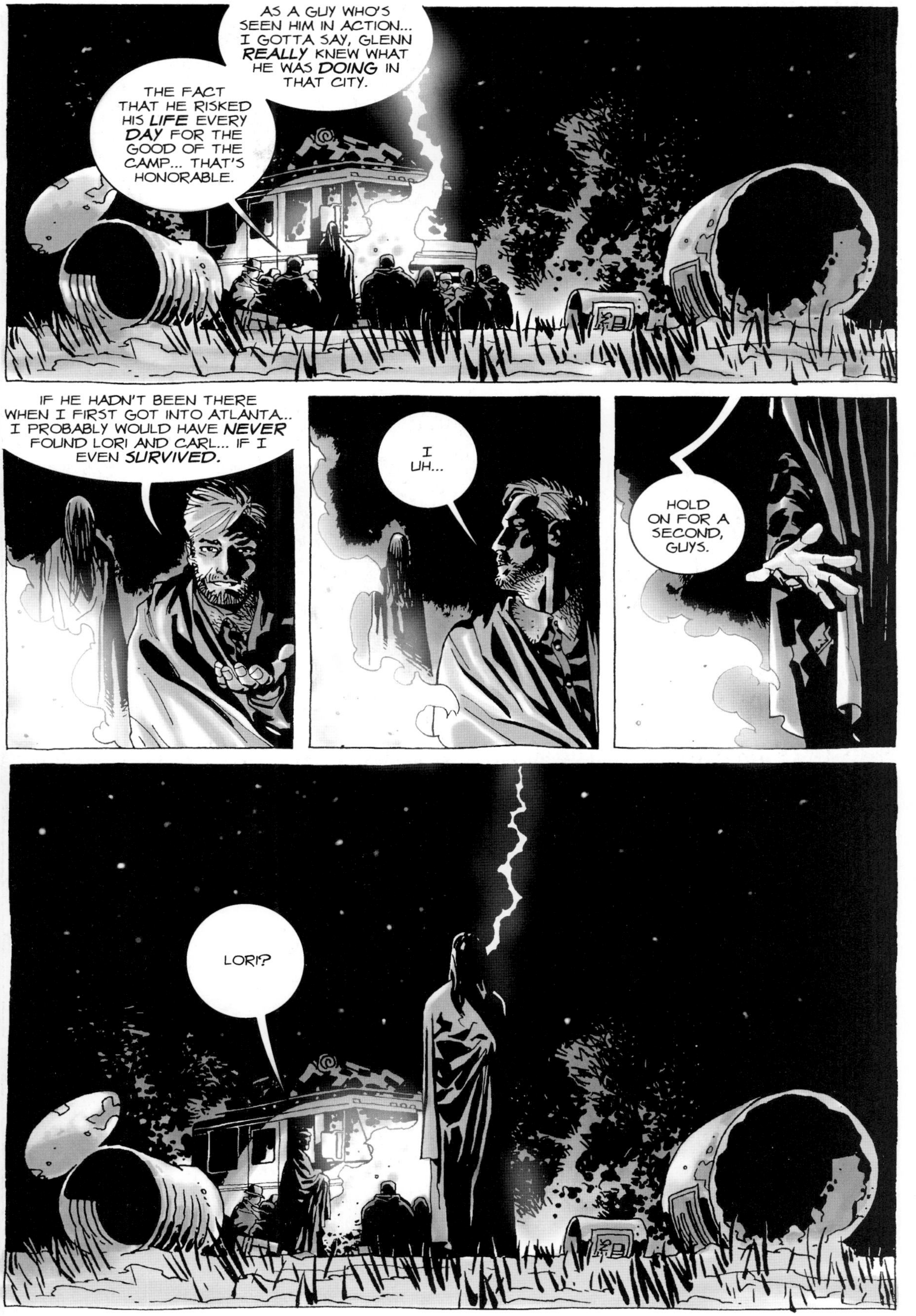
AS A GUY WHO'S SEEN HIM IN ACTION... I GOTTA SAY, GLENN REALLY KNEW WHAT HE WAS DOING IN THAT CITY.
THE FACT THAT HE RISKED HIS LIFE EVERY DAY FOR THE GOOD OF THE CAMP... THAT'S HONORABLE.
IF HE HADN'T BEEN THERE WHEN I FIRST GOT INTO ATLANTA... I PROBABLY WOULD HAVE NEVER FOUND LORI AND CARL... IF I EVEN SURVIVED.
I UH...
HOLD ON FOR A SECOND, GUYS.
LORI?

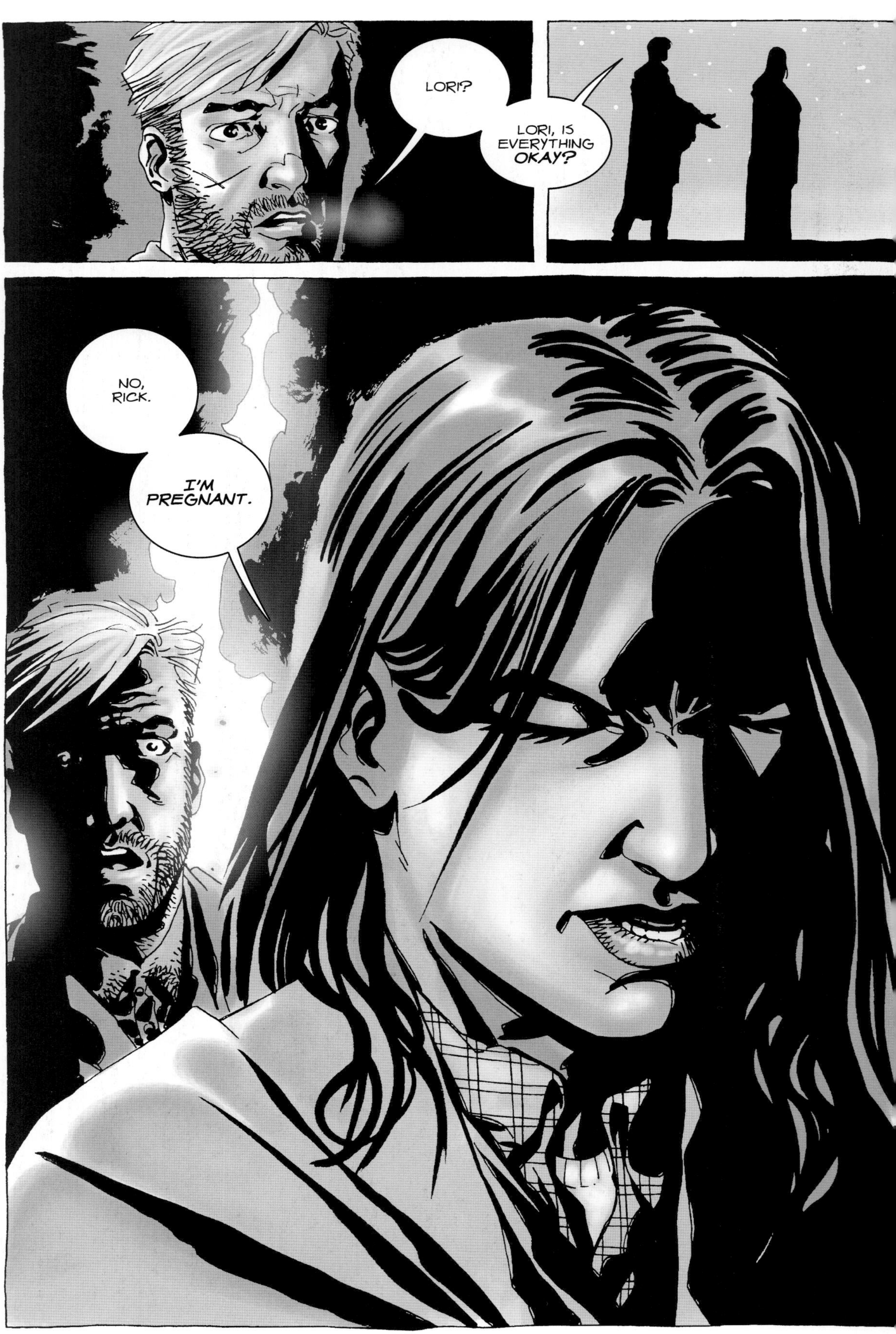
LORI!?
LORI, IS EVERYTHING OKAY?
NO, RICK.
I'M PREGNANT.

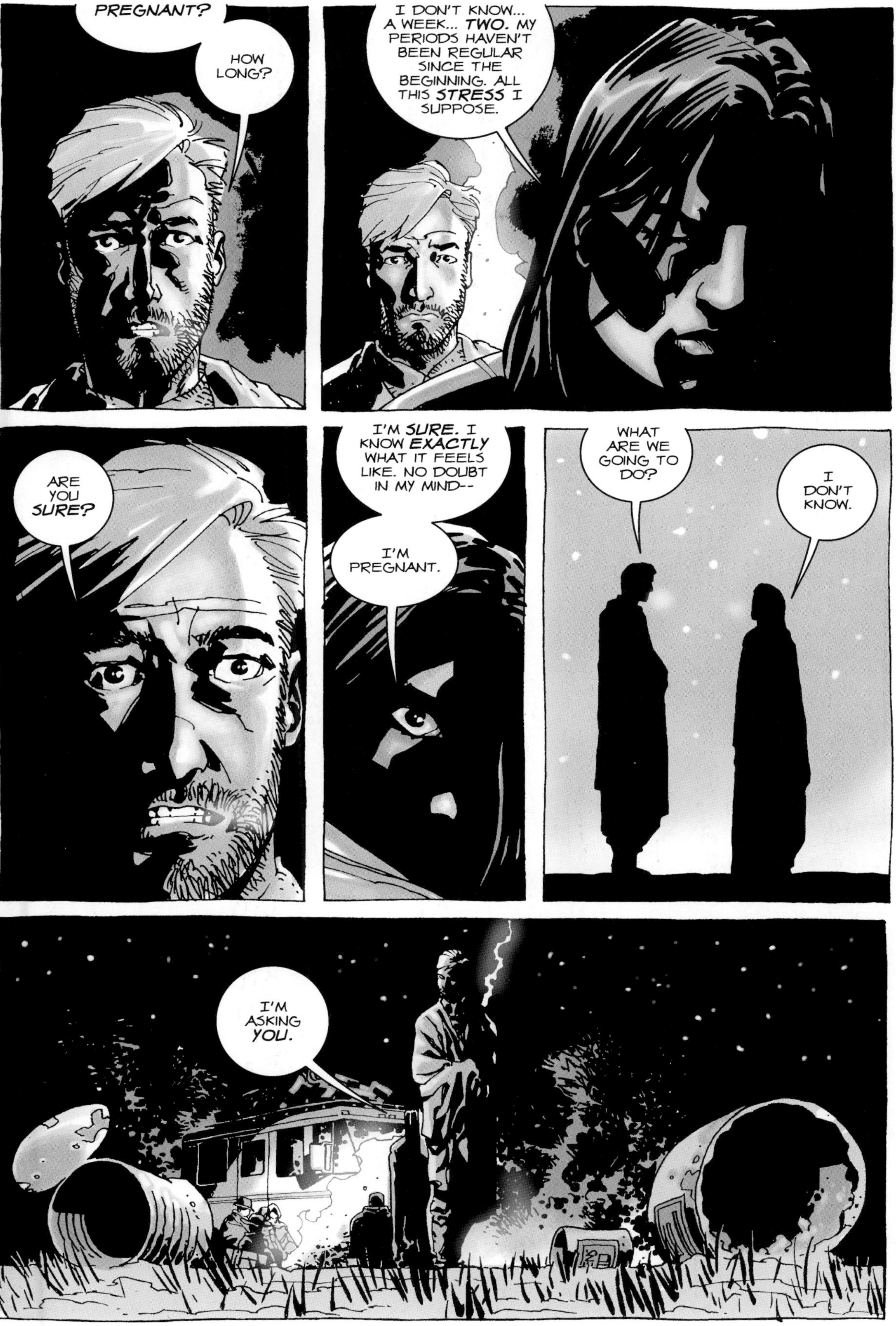
PREGNANT?
HOW LONG?
I DON'T KNOW... A WEEK... TWO. MY PERIODS HAVEN'T BEEN REGULAR SINCE THE BEGINNING. ALL THIS STRESS I SUPPOSE.
ARE YOU SURE?
I'M SURE. I KNOW EXACTLY WHAT IT FEELS LIKE. NO DOUBT IN MY MIND--
I'M PREGNANT.
WHAT ARE WE GOING TO DO?
I DON'T KNOW.
I'M ASKING YOU.

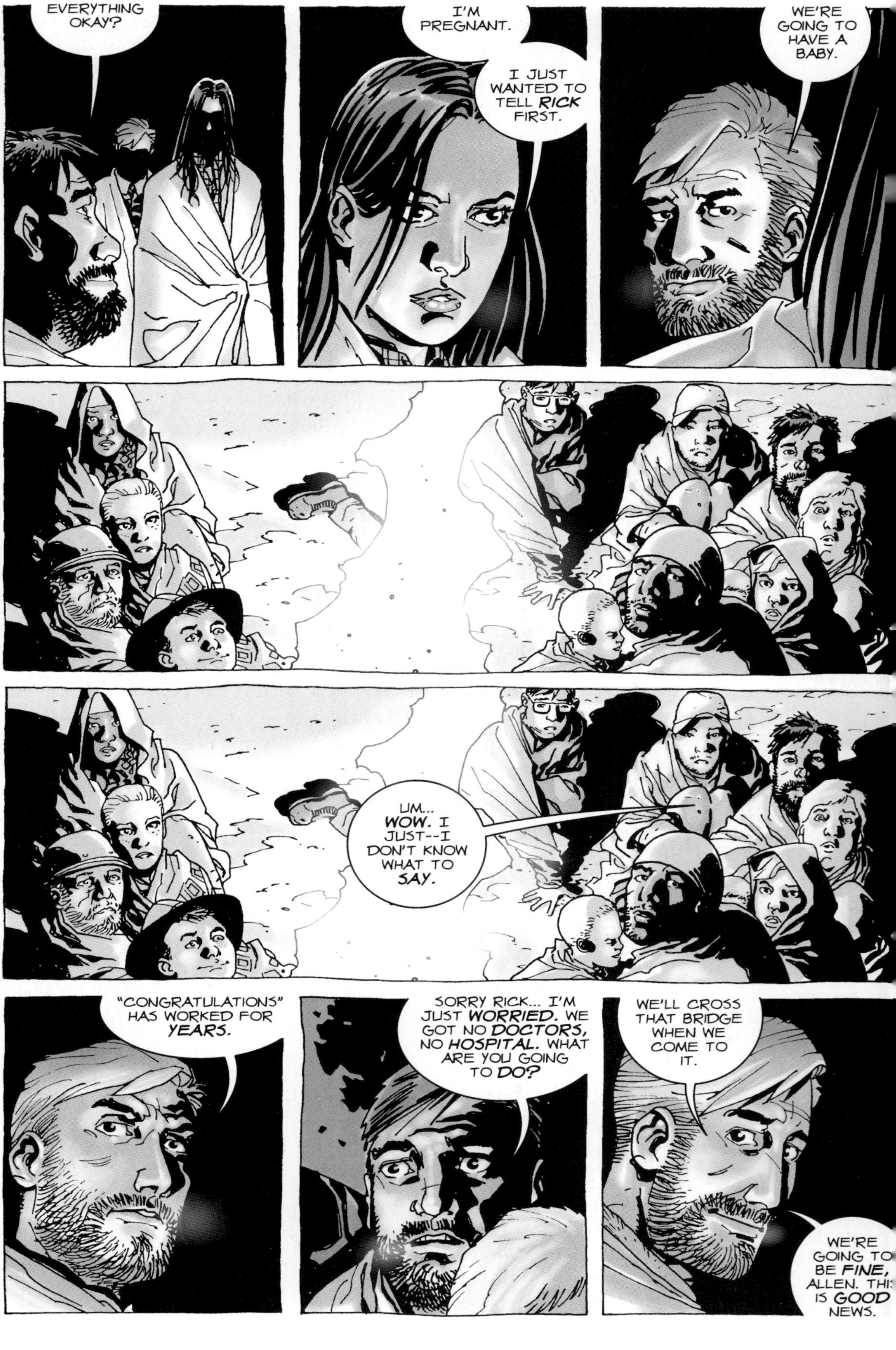
EVERYTHING OKAY?
I'M PREGNANT.
I JUST WANTED TO TELL RICK FIRST.
WE'RE GOING TO HAVE A BABY.
UM... WOW. I JUST--I DON'T KNOW WHAT TO SAY.
"CONGRATULATIONS" HAS WORKED FOR YEARS.
SORRY RICK... I'M JUST WORRIED. WE GOT NO DOCTORS, NO HOSPITAL. WHAT ARE YOU GOING TO DO?
WE'LL CROSS THAT BRIDGE WHEN WE COME TO IT.
WE'RE GOING TO BE FINE, ALLEN. THIS IS GOOD NEWS.

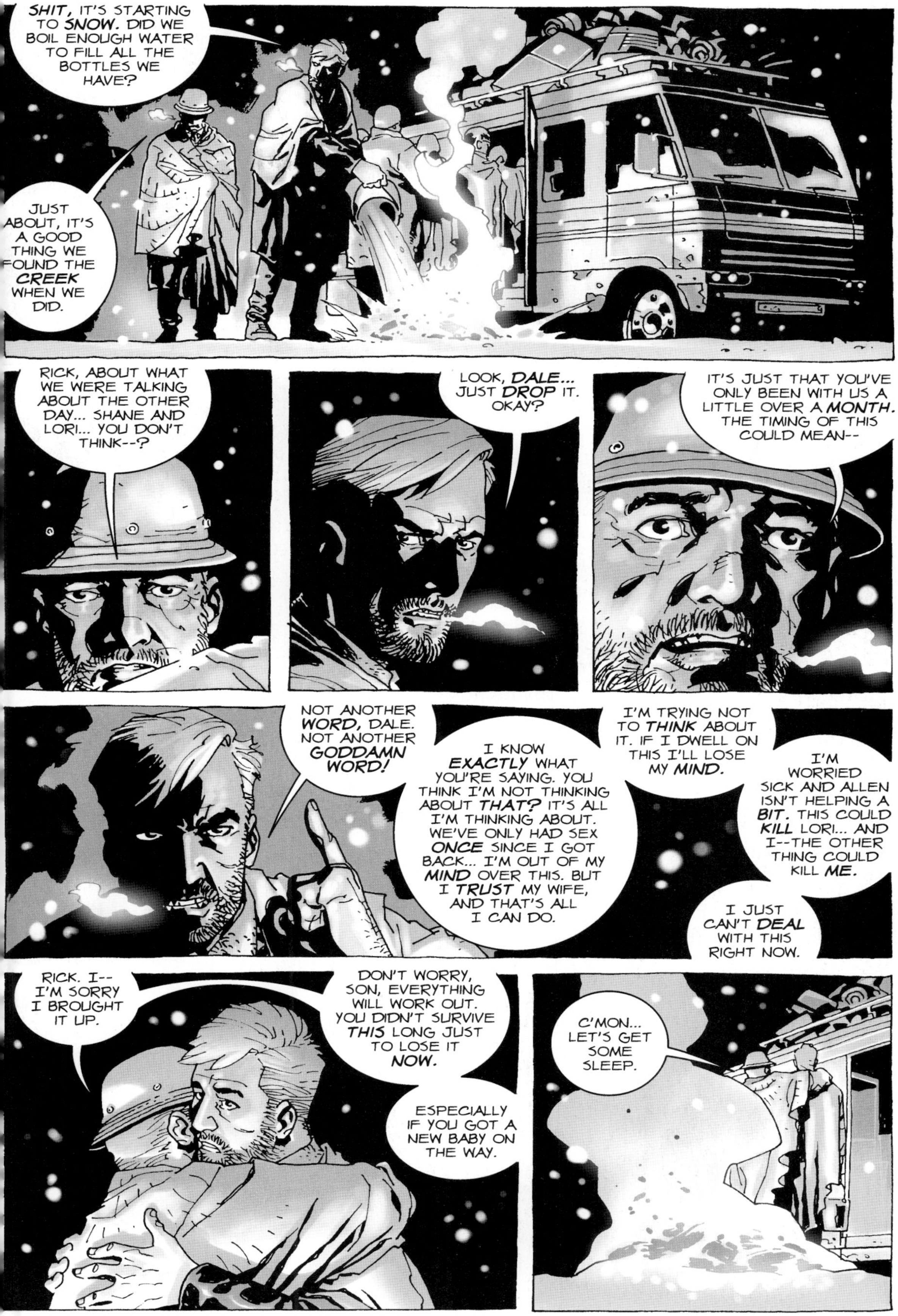
SHIT, IT'S STARTING TO SNOW. DID WE BOIL ENOUGH WATER TO FILL ALL THE BOTTLES WE HAVE?
JUST ABOUT, IT'S A GOOD THING WE FOUND THE CREEK WHEN WE DID.
RICK, ABOUT WHAT WE WERE TALKING ABOUT THE OTHER DAY... SHANE AND LORI... YOU DON'T THINK--?
LOOK, DALE... JUST DROP IT. OKAY?
IT'S JUST THAT YOU'VE ONLY BEEN WITH US A LITTLE OVER A MONTH. THE TIMING OF THIS COULD MEAN--
NOT ANOTHER WORD, DALE. NOT ANOTHER GODDAMN WORD!
I KNOW EXACTLY WHAT YOU'RE SAYING. YOU THINK I'M NOT THINKING ABOUT THAT? IT'S ALL I'M THINKING ABOUT. WE'VE ONLY HAD SEX ONCE SINCE I GOT BACK... I'M OUT OF MY MIND OVER THIS. BUT I TRUST MY WIFE, AND THAT'S ALL I CAN DO.
I'M TRYING NOT TO THINK ABOUT IT. IF I DWELL ON THIS I'LL LOSE MY MIND.
I'M WORRIED SICK AND ALLEN ISN'T HELPING A BIT. THIS COULD KILL LORI... AND I--THE OTHER THING COULD KILL ME.
I JUST CAN'T DEAL WITH THIS RIGHT NOW.
RICK. I-- I'M SORRY I BROUGHT IT UP.
DON'T WORRY, SON, EVERYTHING WILL WORK OUT. YOU DIDN'T SURVIVE THIS LONG JUST TO LOSE IT NOW.
ESPECIALLY IF YOU GOT A NEW BABY ON THE WAY.
C'MON... LET'S GET SOME SLEEP.

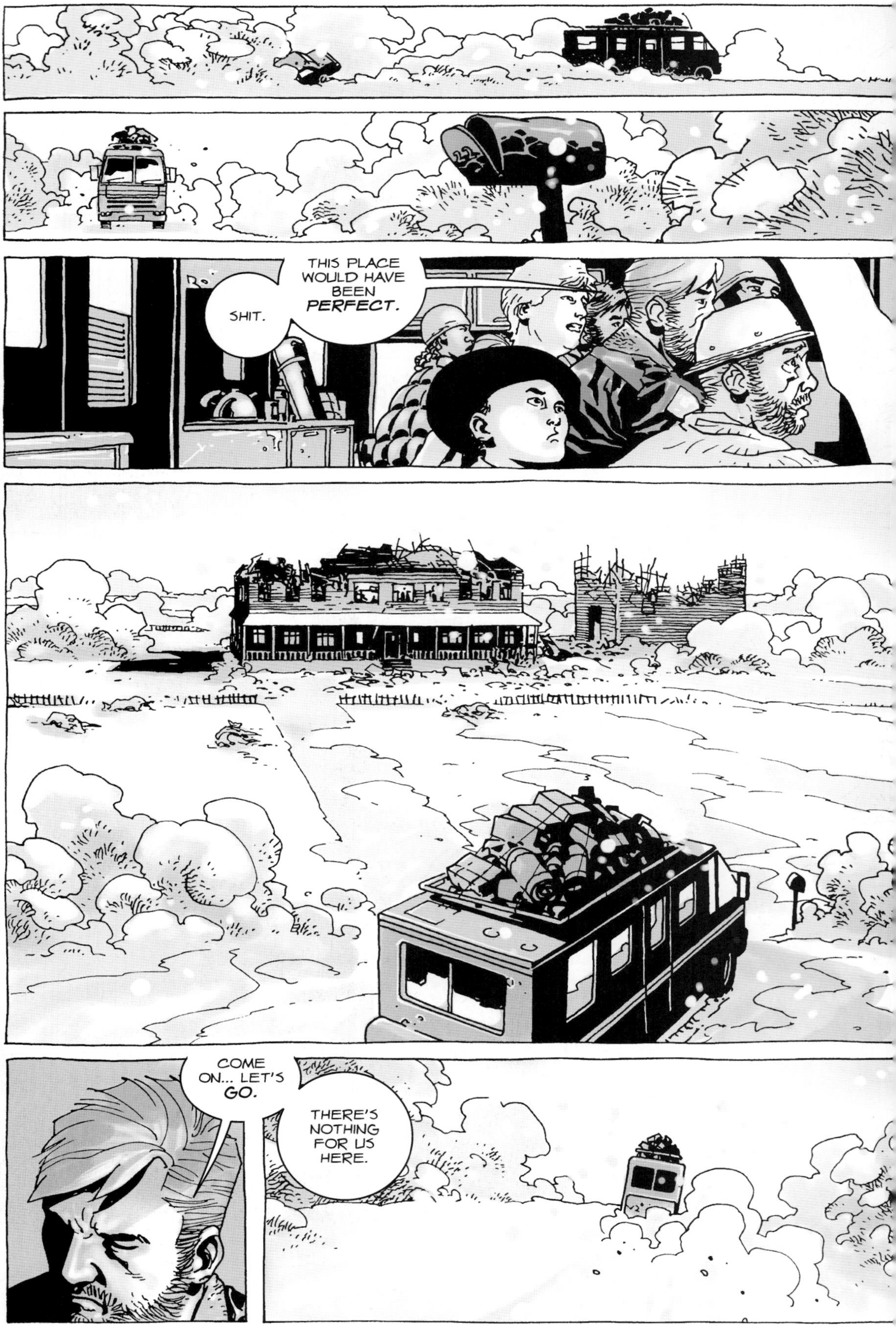
SHIT.
THIS PLACE WOULD HAVE BEEN PERFECT.
COME ON... LET'S GO.
THERE'S NOTHING FOR US HERE.

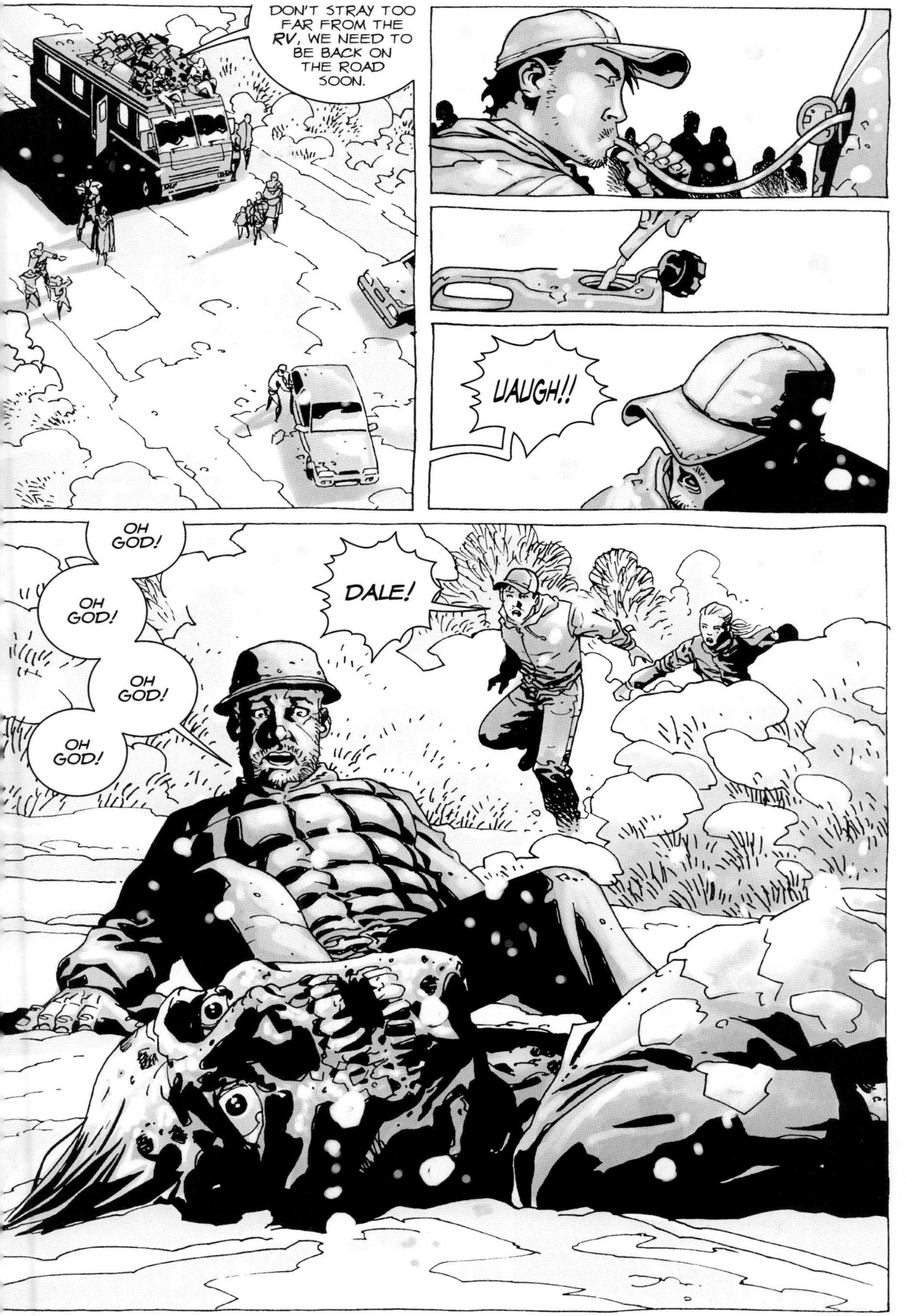
DON'T STRAY TOO FAR FROM THE RV, WE NEED TO BE BACK ON THE ROAD SOON.
UAUGH!!
OH GOD!
OH GOD!
OH GOD!
OH GOD!
DALE!

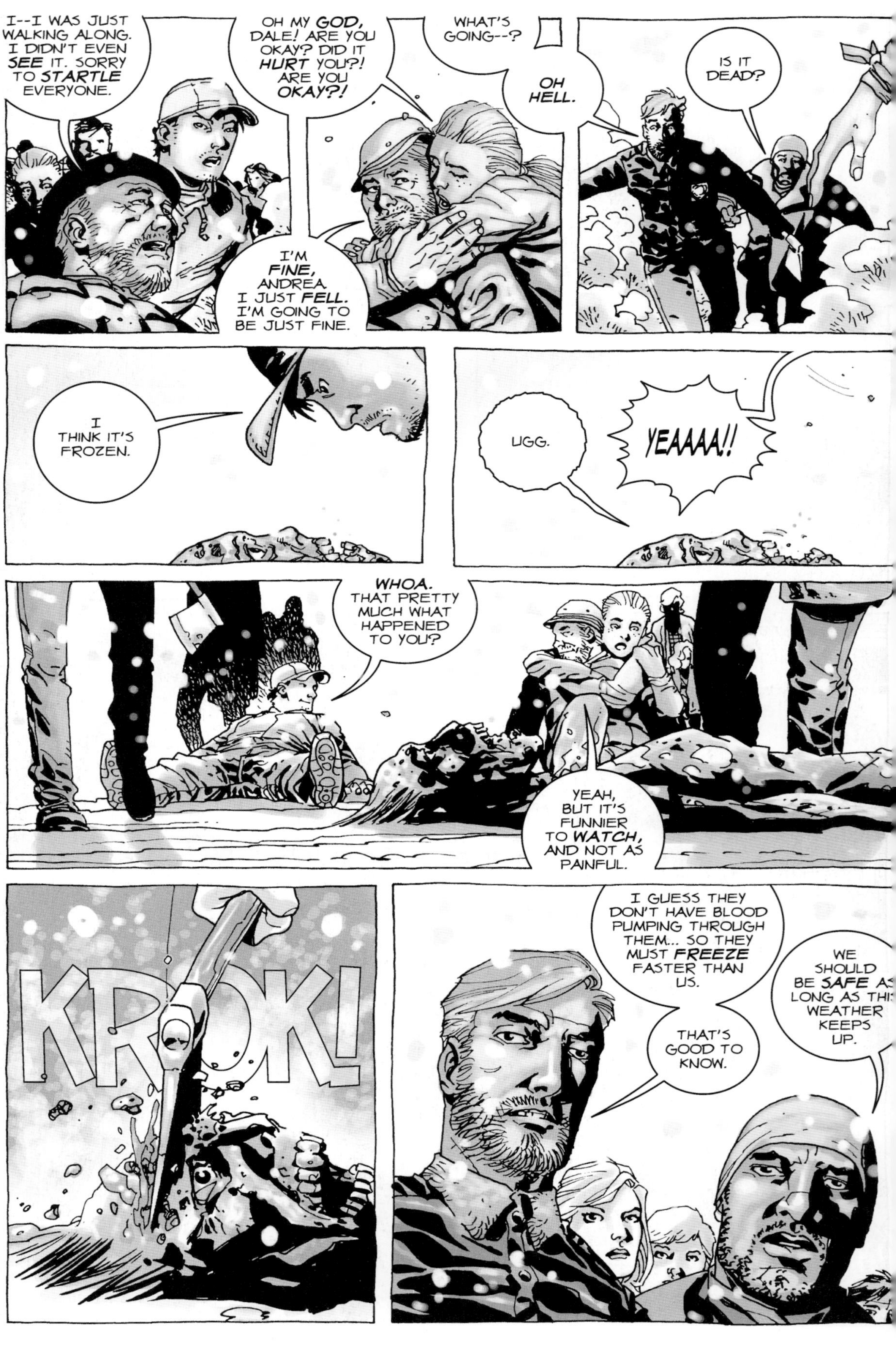
I--I WAS JUST WALKING ALONG. I DIDN'T EVEN SEE IT. SORRY TO STARTLE EVERYONE.
OH MY GOD, DALE! ARE YOU OKAY? DID IT HURT YOU?! ARE YOU OKAY?!
I'M FINE, ANDREA. I JUST FELL. I'M GOING TO BE JUST FINE.
WHAT'S GOING--?
OH HELL.
IS IT DEAD?
I THINK IT'S FROZEN.
UGG.
YEAAAA!!
WHOA. THAT PRETTY MUCH WHAT HAPPENED TO YOU?
YEAH, BUT IT'S FUNNIER TO WATCH, AND NOT AS PAINFUL.
KROK!
I GUESS THEY DON'T HAVE BLOOD PUMPING THROUGH THEM... SO THEY MUST FREEZE FASTER THAN US.
THAT'S GOOD TO KNOW.
WE SHOULD BE SAFE AS LONG AS THIS WEATHER KEEPS UP.

ARE WE OUT OF CANNED PEARS?

LAST TIME I CHECKED I DIDN'T SEE *ANY*. WE'VE GOT ABOUT THREE MORE CANS OF PEACHES THOUGH. OTHER THAN THAT, THE FRUIT IS ALMOST GONE.

CRAP... I REALLY *LIKED* THE PEARS. AND I *HATE* PEACHES.

ARE YOU WORRIED?

ABOUT THE *BABY*, I MEAN.

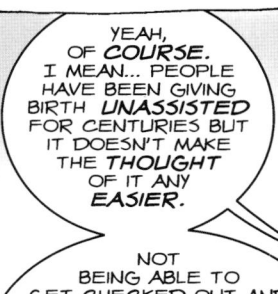

YEAH, OF *COURSE*. I MEAN... PEOPLE HAVE BEEN GIVING BIRTH *UNASSISTED* FOR CENTURIES BUT IT DOESN'T MAKE THE *THOUGHT* OF IT ANY *EASIER*.

NOT BEING ABLE TO GET CHECKED OUT AND MAKE SURE EVERYTHING IS *OKAY* ISN'T TOO DESIRABLE EITHER. I COULD BE HAVING *TWINS* AND NOT EVEN *KNOW* IT.

AND *MORPHINE*. YOU'RE NOT GOING TO HAVE ANY *MORPHINE*.

SHIT. I HADN'T THOUGHT OF *THAT*.

AW, *MOM!* YOU SAID A *BAD WORD*. YOU OWE ME A QUARTER!

TEE HEE!

OH, *CARL*. PUT IT ON MY *TAB*.

OVER THERE! *STOP!* PULL OVER!

I SEE IT!

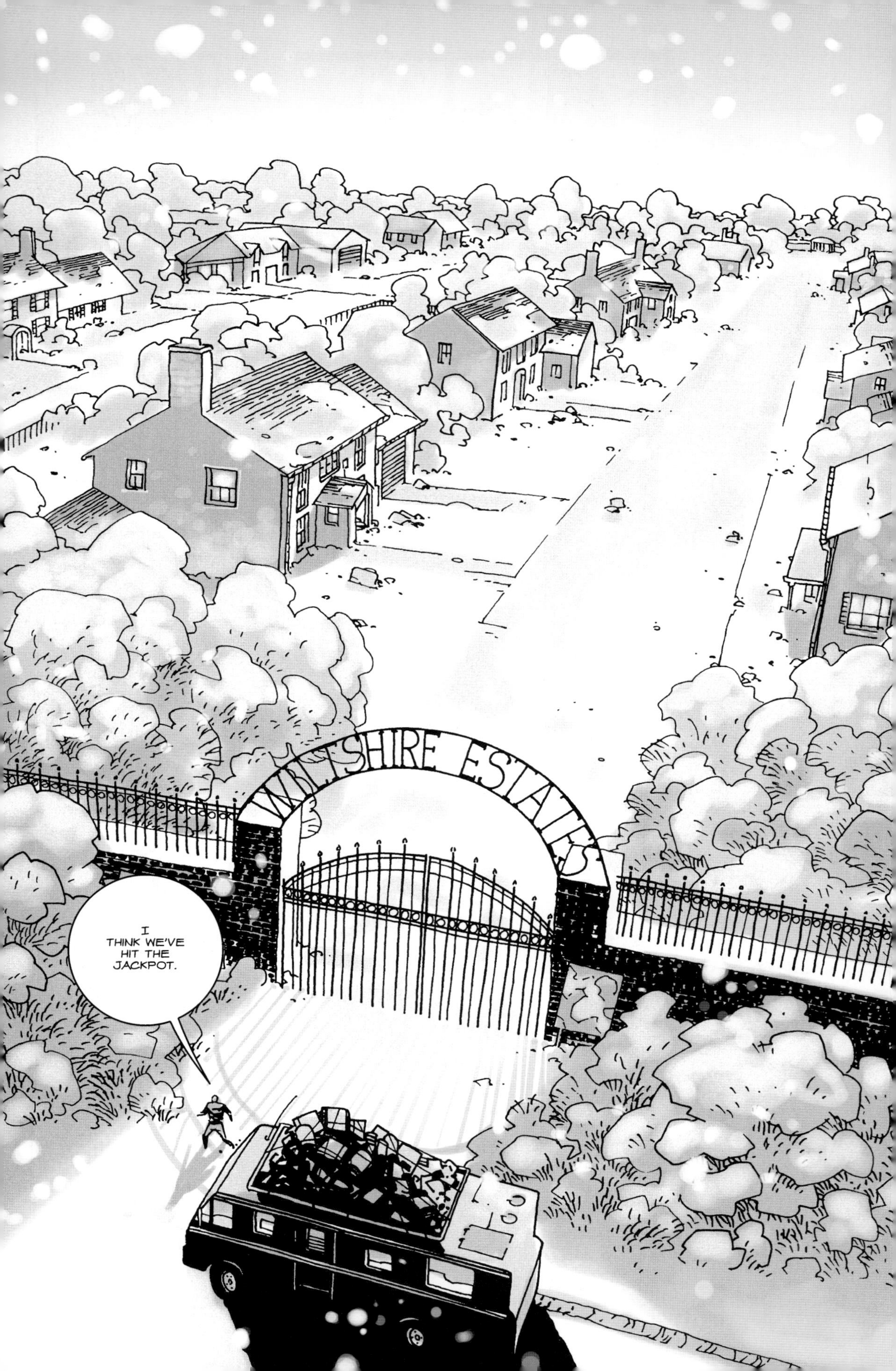
I THINK WE'VE HIT THE JACKPOT.

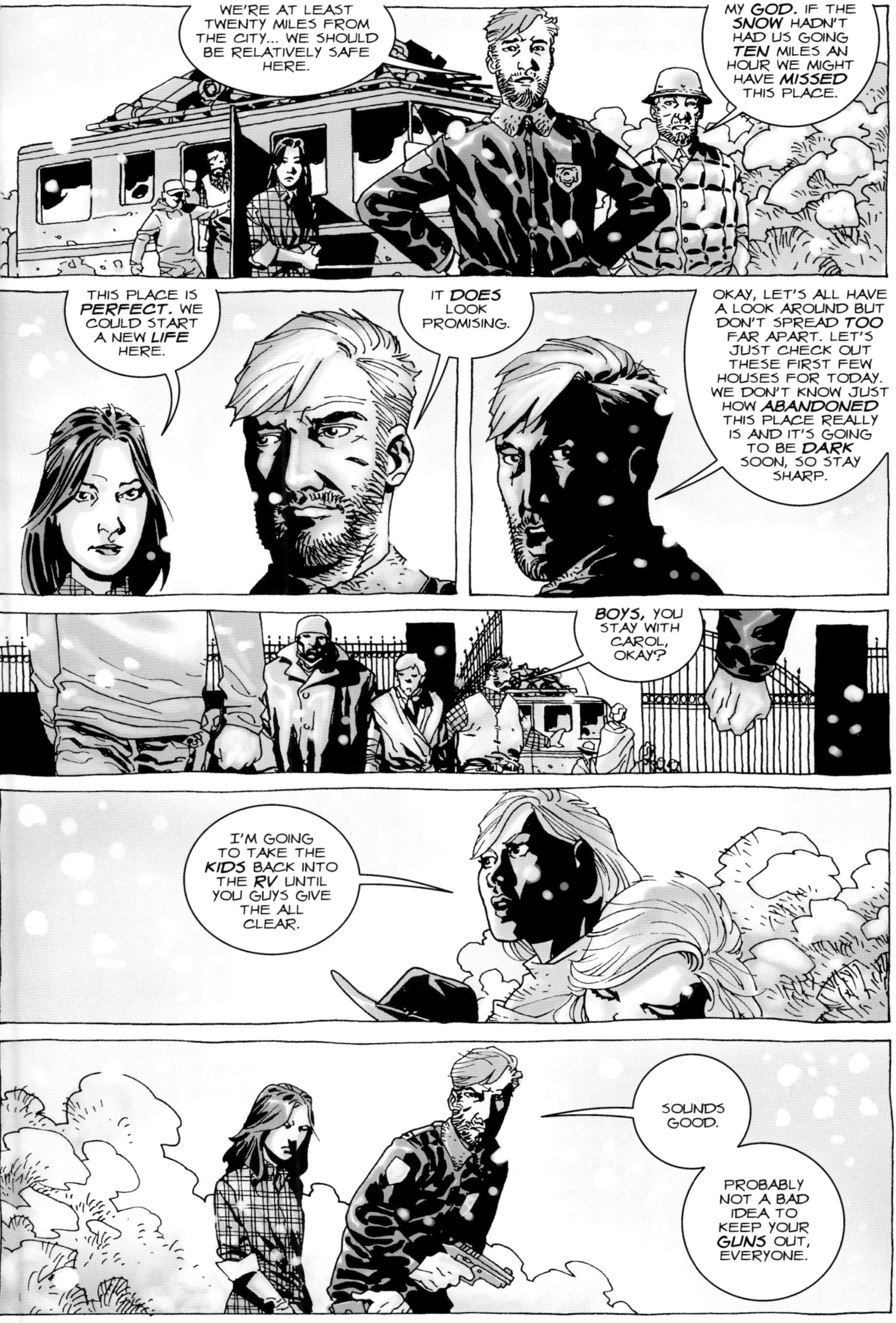
WE'RE AT LEAST TWENTY MILES FROM THE CITY... WE SHOULD BE RELATIVELY SAFE HERE.
MY GOD. IF THE SNOW HADN'T HAD US GOING TEN MILES AN HOUR WE MIGHT HAVE MISSED THIS PLACE.
THIS PLACE IS PERFECT. WE COULD START A NEW LIFE HERE.
IT DOES LOOK PROMISING.
OKAY, LET'S ALL HAVE A LOOK AROUND BUT DON'T SPREAD TOO FAR APART. LET'S JUST CHECK OUT THESE FIRST FEW HOUSES FOR TODAY. WE DON'T KNOW JUST HOW ABANDONED THIS PLACE REALLY IS AND IT'S GOING TO BE DARK SOON, SO STAY SHARP.
BOYS, YOU STAY WITH CAROL, OKAY?
I'M GOING TO TAKE THE KIDS BACK INTO THE RV UNTIL YOU GUYS GIVE THE ALL CLEAR.
SOUNDS GOOD.
PROBABLY NOT A BAD IDEA TO KEEP YOUR GUNS OUT, EVERYONE.

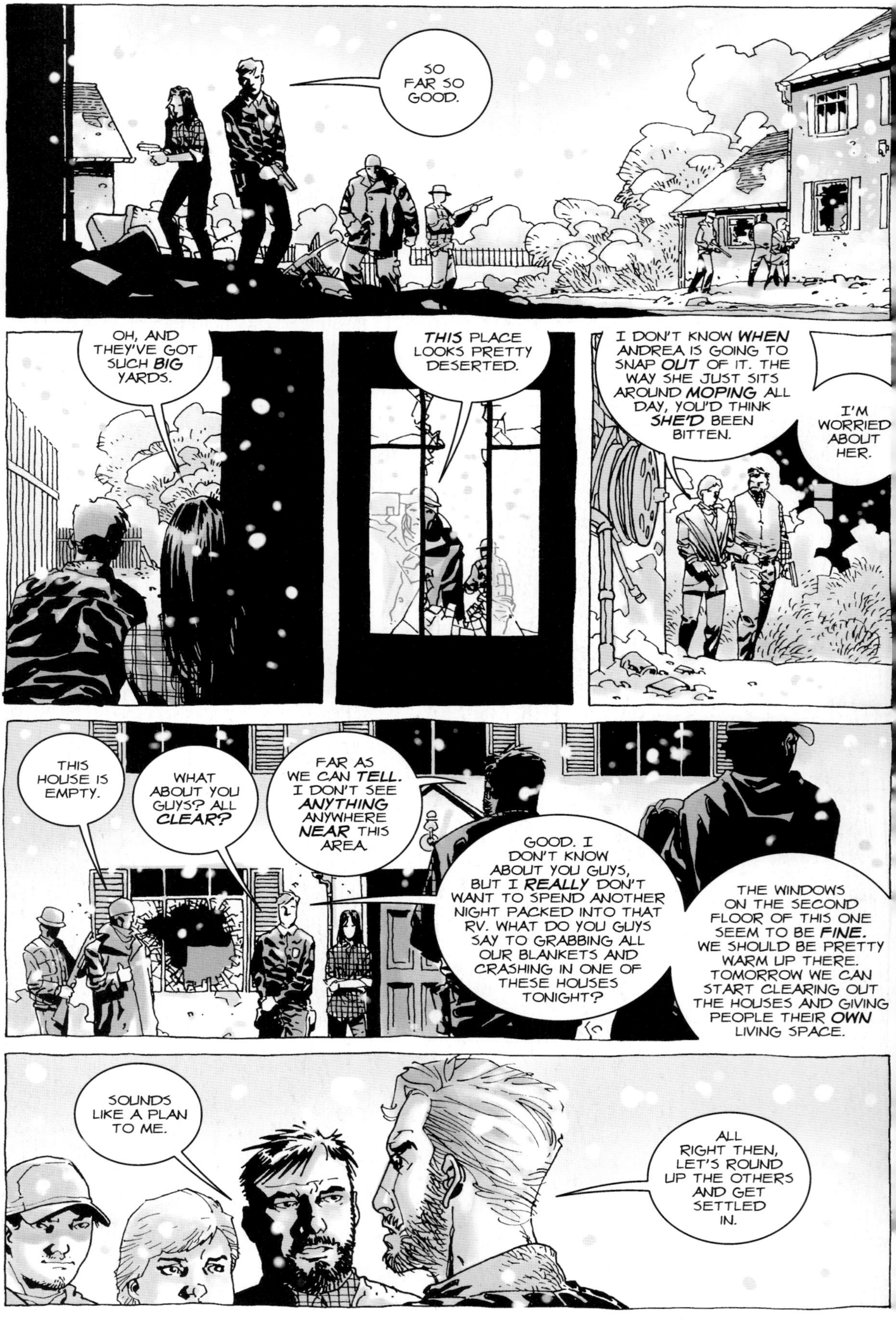
SO FAR SO GOOD.
OH, AND THEY'VE GOT SUCH BIG YARDS.
THIS PLACE LOOKS PRETTY DESERTED.
I DON'T KNOW WHEN ANDREA IS GOING TO SNAP OUT OF IT. THE WAY SHE JUST SITS AROUND MOPING ALL DAY, YOU'D THINK SHE'D BEEN BITTEN.
I'M WORRIED ABOUT HER.
THIS HOUSE IS EMPTY.
WHAT ABOUT YOU GUYS? ALL CLEAR?
FAR AS WE CAN TELL. I DON'T SEE ANYTHING ANYWHERE NEAR THIS AREA.
GOOD. I DON'T KNOW ABOUT YOU GUYS, BUT I REALLY DON'T WANT TO SPEND ANOTHER NIGHT PACKED INTO THAT RV. WHAT DO YOU GUYS SAY TO GRABBING ALL OUR BLANKETS AND CRASHING IN ONE OF THESE HOUSES TONIGHT?
THE WINDOWS ON THE SECOND FLOOR OF THIS ONE SEEM TO BE FINE. WE SHOULD BE PRETTY WARM UP THERE. TOMORROW WE CAN START CLEARING OUT THE HOUSES AND GIVING PEOPLE THEIR OWN LIVING SPACE.
SOUNDS LIKE A PLAN TO ME.
ALL RIGHT THEN, LET'S ROUND UP THE OTHERS AND GET SETTLED IN.

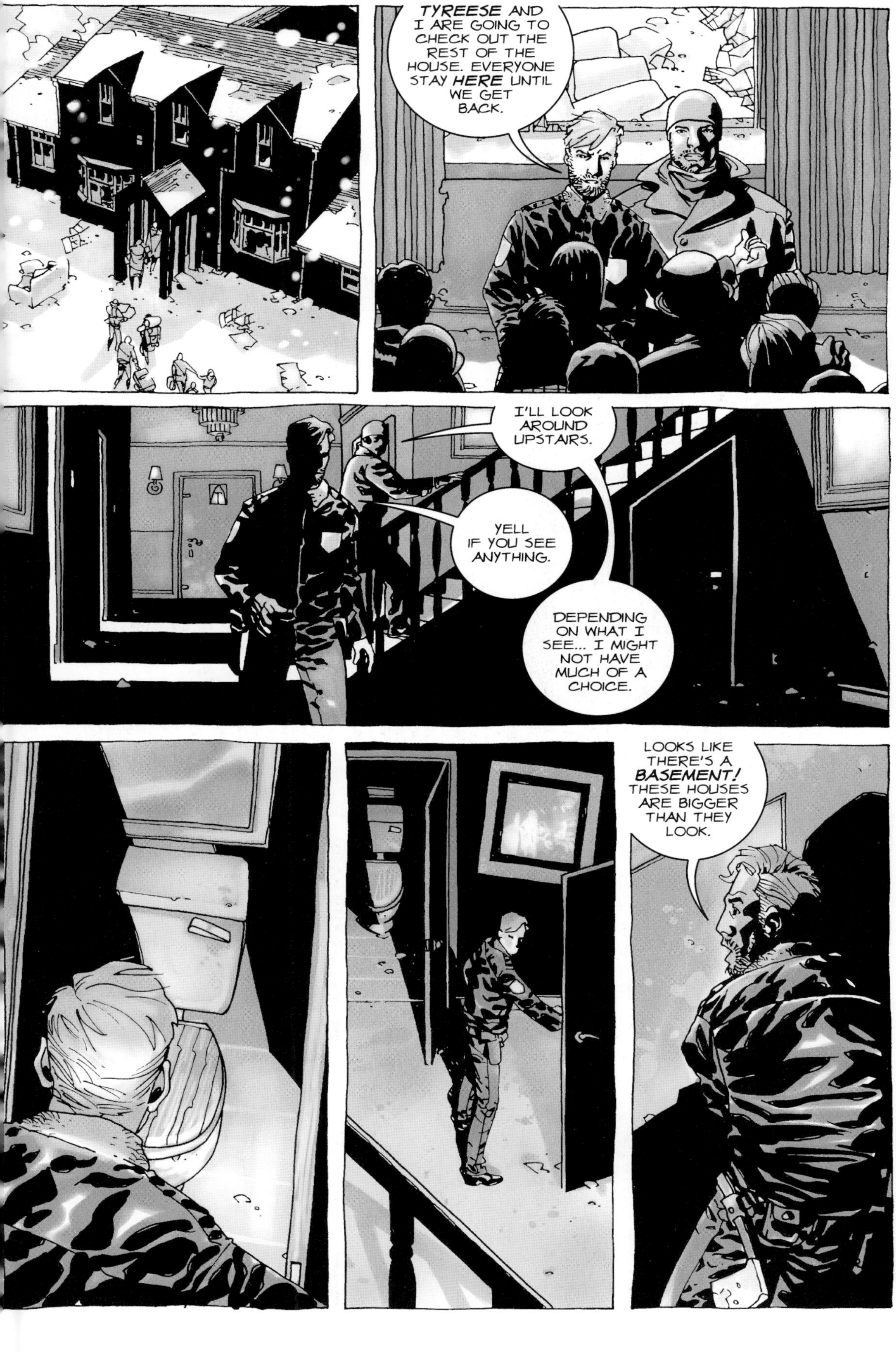
TYREESE AND I ARE GOING TO CHECK OUT THE REST OF THE HOUSE. EVERYONE STAY HERE UNTIL WE GET BACK.
I'LL LOOK AROUND UPSTAIRS.
YELL IF YOU SEE ANYTHING.
DEPENDING ON WHAT I SEE... I MIGHT NOT HAVE MUCH OF A CHOICE.
LOOKS LIKE THERE'S A BASEMENT! THESE HOUSES ARE BIGGER THAN THEY LOOK.

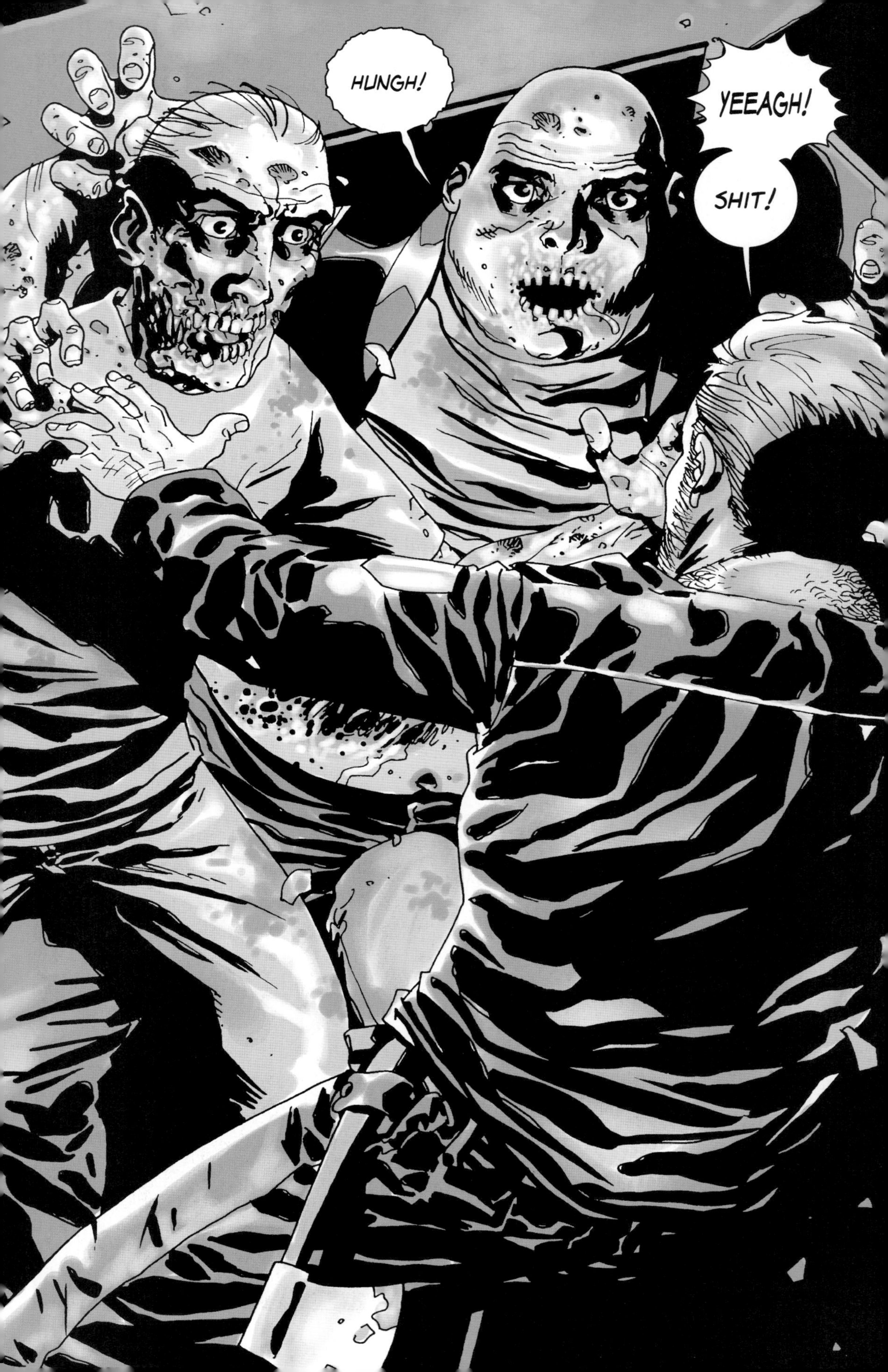
HUNGH!
YEEAGH!
SHIT!

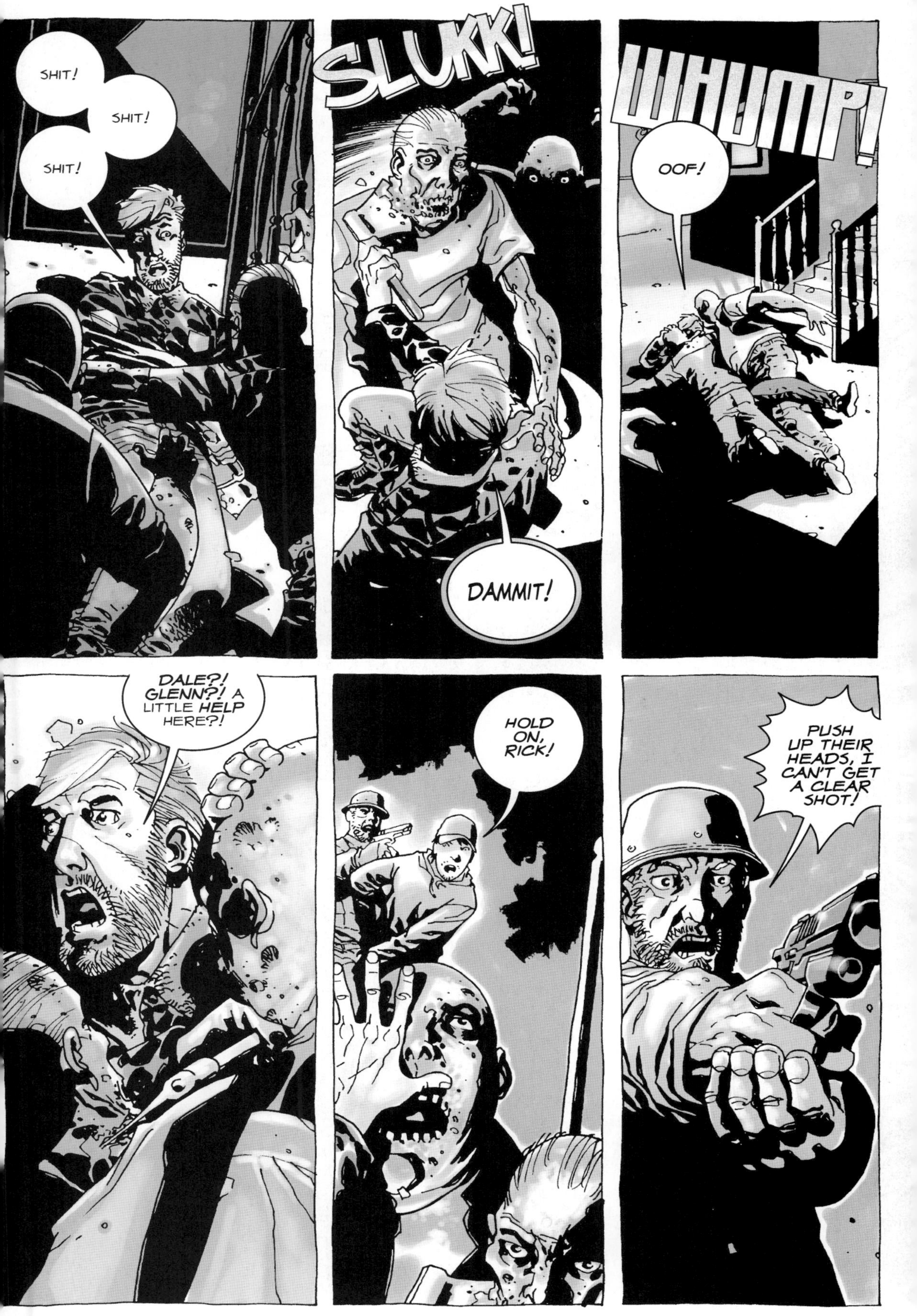
SHIT!
SHIT!
SHIT!
SLUKK!
DAMMIT!
WHUMP!
OOF!
DALE?! GLENN?! A LITTLE HELP HERE?!
HOLD ON, RICK!
PUSH UP THEIR HEADS, I CAN'T GET A CLEAR SHOT!

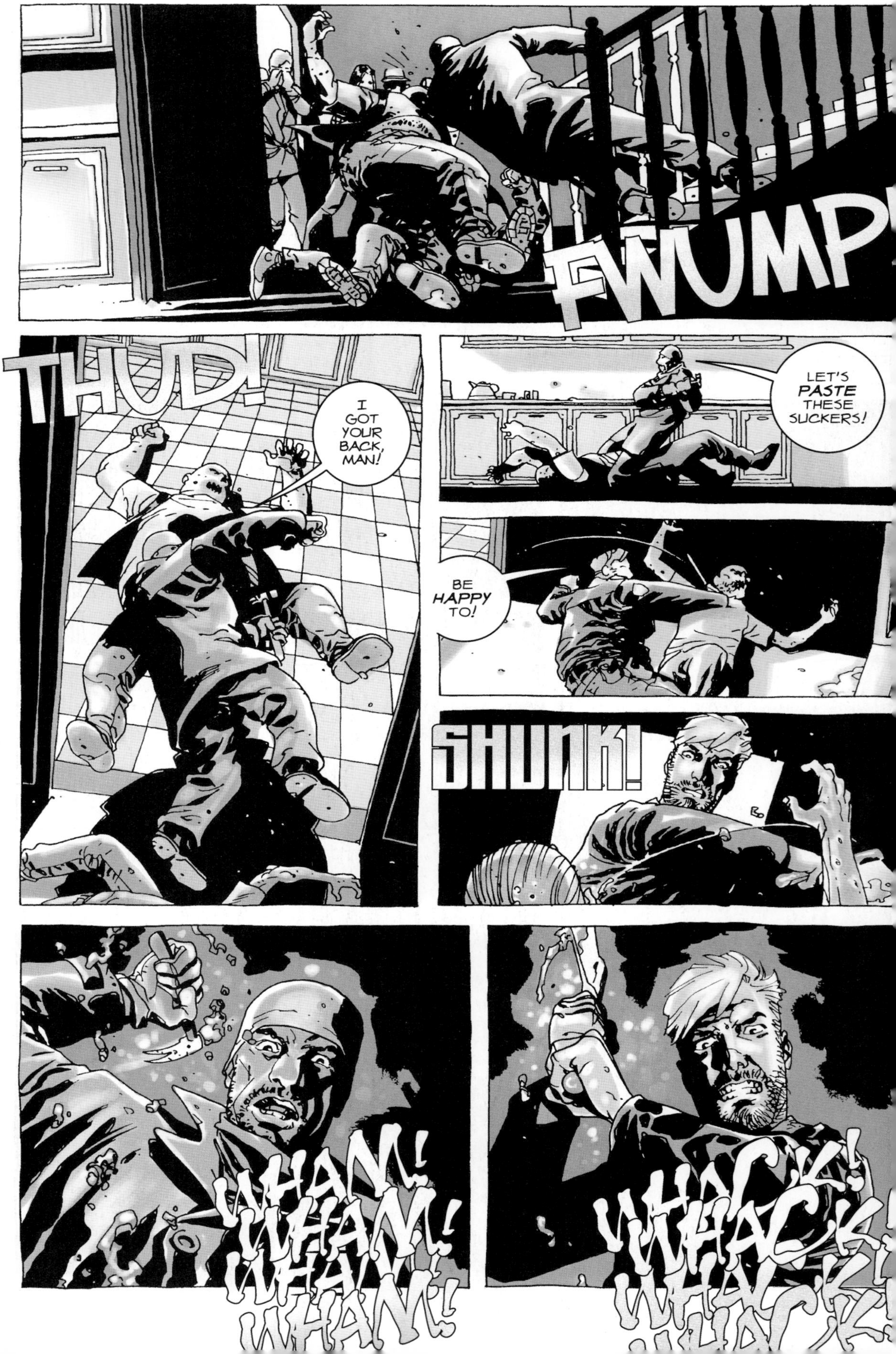
FWUMP
THUD!
I GOT YOUR BACK, MAN!
LET'S PASTE THESE SUCKERS!
BE HAPPY TO!
SHUNK!
WHAM! WHAM! WHAM! WHAM!
WHACK! WHACK!

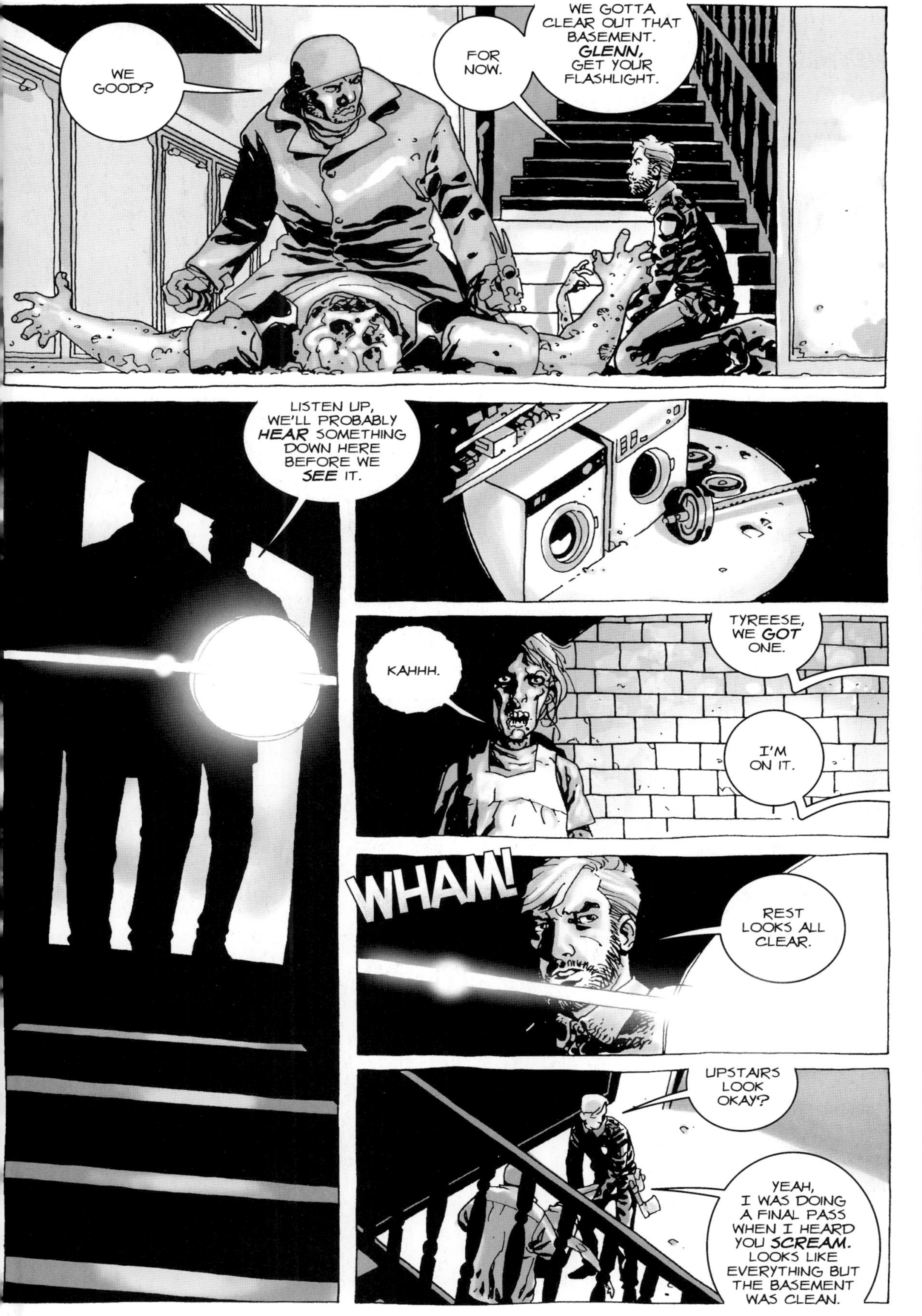
WE GOOD?
FOR NOW.
WE GOTTA CLEAR OUT THAT BASEMENT. GLENN, GET YOUR FLASHLIGHT.
LISTEN UP, WE'LL PROBABLY HEAR SOMETHING DOWN HERE BEFORE WE SEE IT.
KAHHH.
TYREESE, WE GOT ONE.
I'M ON IT.
WHAM!
REST LOOKS ALL CLEAR.
UPSTAIRS LOOK OKAY?
YEAH, I WAS DOING A FINAL PASS WHEN I HEARD YOU SCREAM. LOOKS LIKE EVERYTHING BUT THE BASEMENT WAS CLEAN.

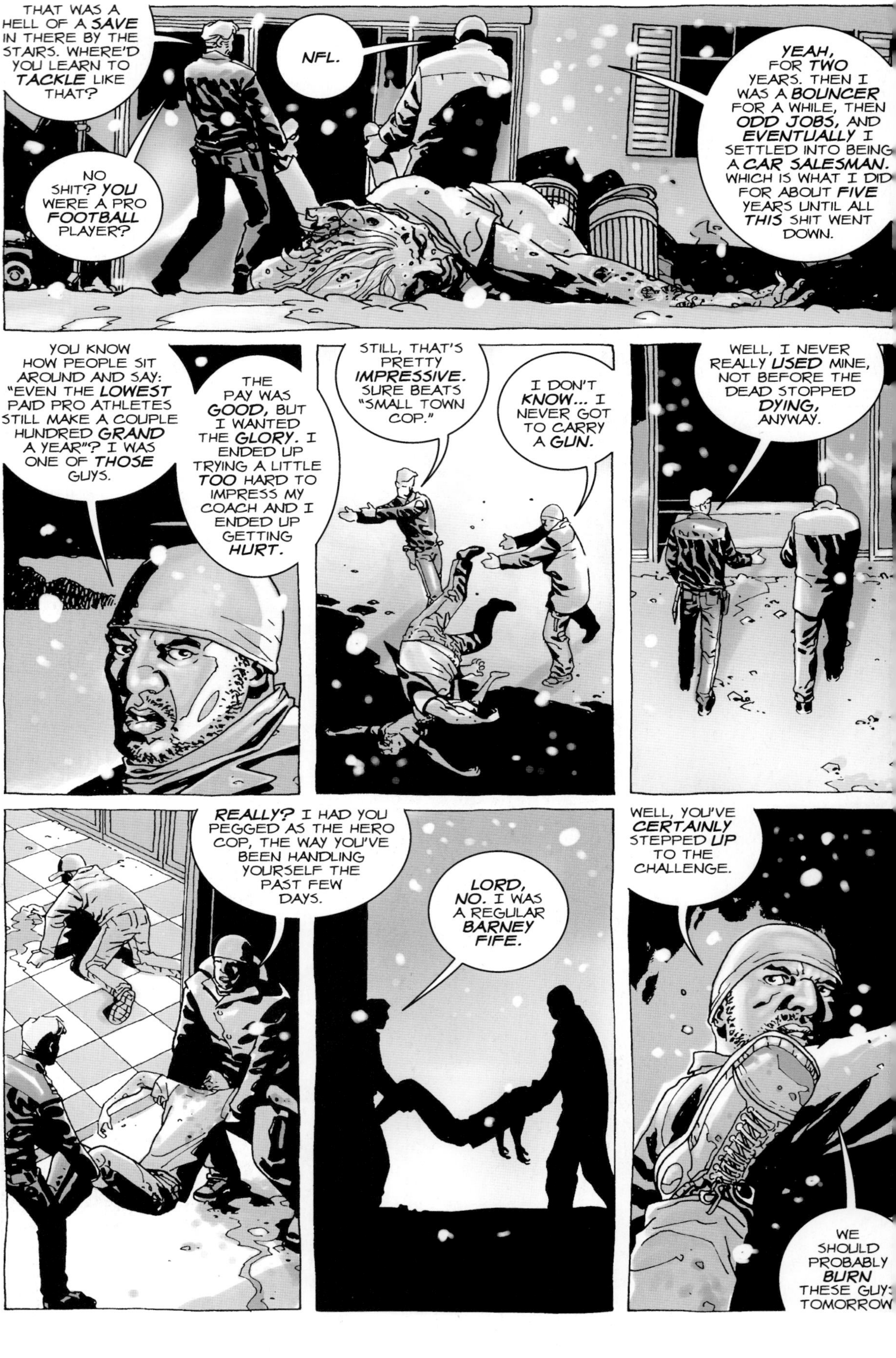
THAT WAS A HELL OF A SAVE IN THERE BY THE STAIRS. WHERE'D YOU LEARN TO TACKLE LIKE THAT?
NFL.
NO SHIT? YOU WERE A PRO FOOTBALL PLAYER?
YEAH, FOR TWO YEARS. THEN I WAS A BOUNCER FOR A WHILE, THEN ODD JOBS, AND EVENTUALLY I SETTLED INTO BEING A CAR SALESMAN. WHICH IS WHAT I DID FOR ABOUT FIVE YEARS UNTIL ALL THIS SHIT WENT DOWN.
YOU KNOW HOW PEOPLE SIT AROUND AND SAY: "EVEN THE LOWEST PAID PRO ATHLETES STILL MAKE A COUPLE HUNDRED GRAND A YEAR"? I WAS ONE OF THOSE GUYS.
THE PAY WAS GOOD, BUT I WANTED THE GLORY. I ENDED UP TRYING A LITTLE TOO HARD TO IMPRESS MY COACH AND I ENDED UP GETTING HURT.
STILL, THAT'S PRETTY IMPRESSIVE. SURE BEATS "SMALL TOWN COP."
I DON'T KNOW... I NEVER GOT TO CARRY A GUN.
WELL, I NEVER REALLY USED MINE, NOT BEFORE THE DEAD STOPPED DYING, ANYWAY.
REALLY? I HAD YOU PEGGED AS THE HERO COP, THE WAY YOU'VE BEEN HANDLING YOURSELF THE PAST FEW DAYS.
LORD, NO. I WAS A REGULAR BARNEY FIFE.
WELL, YOU'VE CERTAINLY STEPPED UP TO THE CHALLENGE.
WE SHOULD PROBABLY BURN THESE GUYS TOMORROW

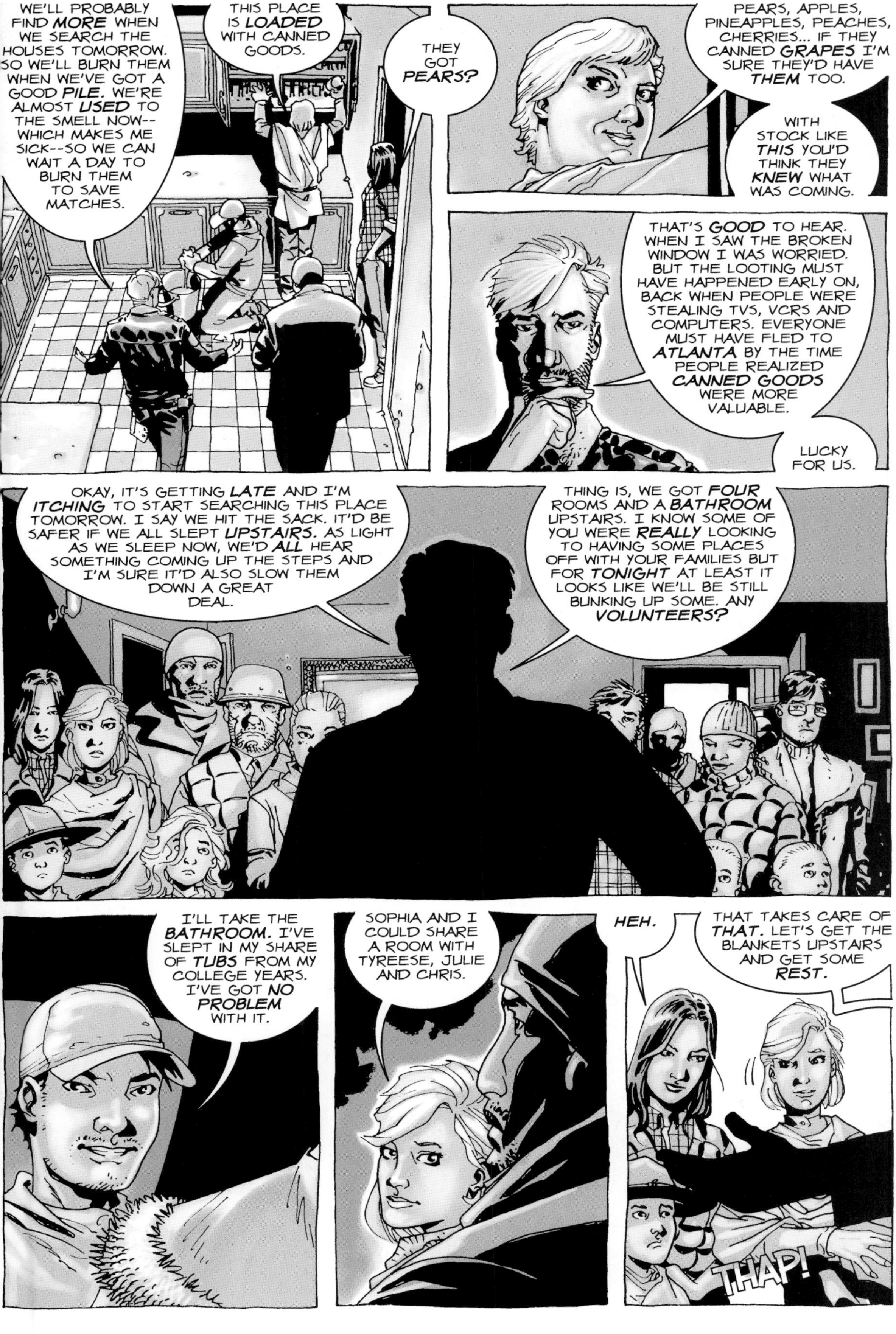
WE'LL PROBABLY FIND MORE WHEN WE SEARCH THE HOUSES TOMORROW. SO WE'LL BURN THEM WHEN WE'VE GOT A GOOD PILE. WE'RE ALMOST USED TO THE SMELL NOW--WHICH MAKES ME SICK--SO WE CAN WAIT A DAY TO BURN THEM TO SAVE MATCHES.
THIS PLACE IS LOADED WITH CANNED GOODS.
THEY GOT PEARS?
PEARS, APPLES, PINEAPPLES, PEACHES, CHERRIES... IF THEY CANNED GRAPES I'M SURE THEY'D HAVE THEM TOO.
WITH STOCK LIKE THIS YOU'D THINK THEY KNEW WHAT WAS COMING.
THAT'S GOOD TO HEAR. WHEN I SAW THE BROKEN WINDOW I WAS WORRIED. BUT THE LOOTING MUST HAVE HAPPENED EARLY ON, BACK WHEN PEOPLE WERE STEALING TVS, VCRS AND COMPUTERS. EVERYONE MUST HAVE FLED TO ATLANTA BY THE TIME PEOPLE REALIZED CANNED GOODS WERE MORE VALUABLE.
LUCKY FOR US.
OKAY, IT'S GETTING LATE AND I'M ITCHING TO START SEARCHING THIS PLACE TOMORROW. I SAY WE HIT THE SACK. IT'D BE SAFER IF WE ALL SLEPT UPSTAIRS. AS LIGHT AS WE SLEEP NOW, WE'D ALL HEAR SOMETHING COMING UP THE STEPS AND I'M SURE IT'D ALSO SLOW THEM DOWN A GREAT DEAL.
THING IS, WE GOT FOUR ROOMS AND A BATHROOM UPSTAIRS. I KNOW SOME OF YOU WERE REALLY LOOKING TO HAVING SOME PLACES OFF WITH YOUR FAMILIES BUT FOR TONIGHT AT LEAST IT LOOKS LIKE WE'LL BE STILL BUNKING UP SOME. ANY VOLUNTEERS?
I'LL TAKE THE BATHROOM. I'VE SLEPT IN MY SHARE OF TUBS FROM MY COLLEGE YEARS. I'VE GOT NO PROBLEM WITH IT.
SOPHIA AND I COULD SHARE A ROOM WITH TYREESE, JULIE AND CHRIS.
HEH.
THAT TAKES CARE OF THAT. LET'S GET THE BLANKETS UPSTAIRS AND GET SOME REST.
THAP!

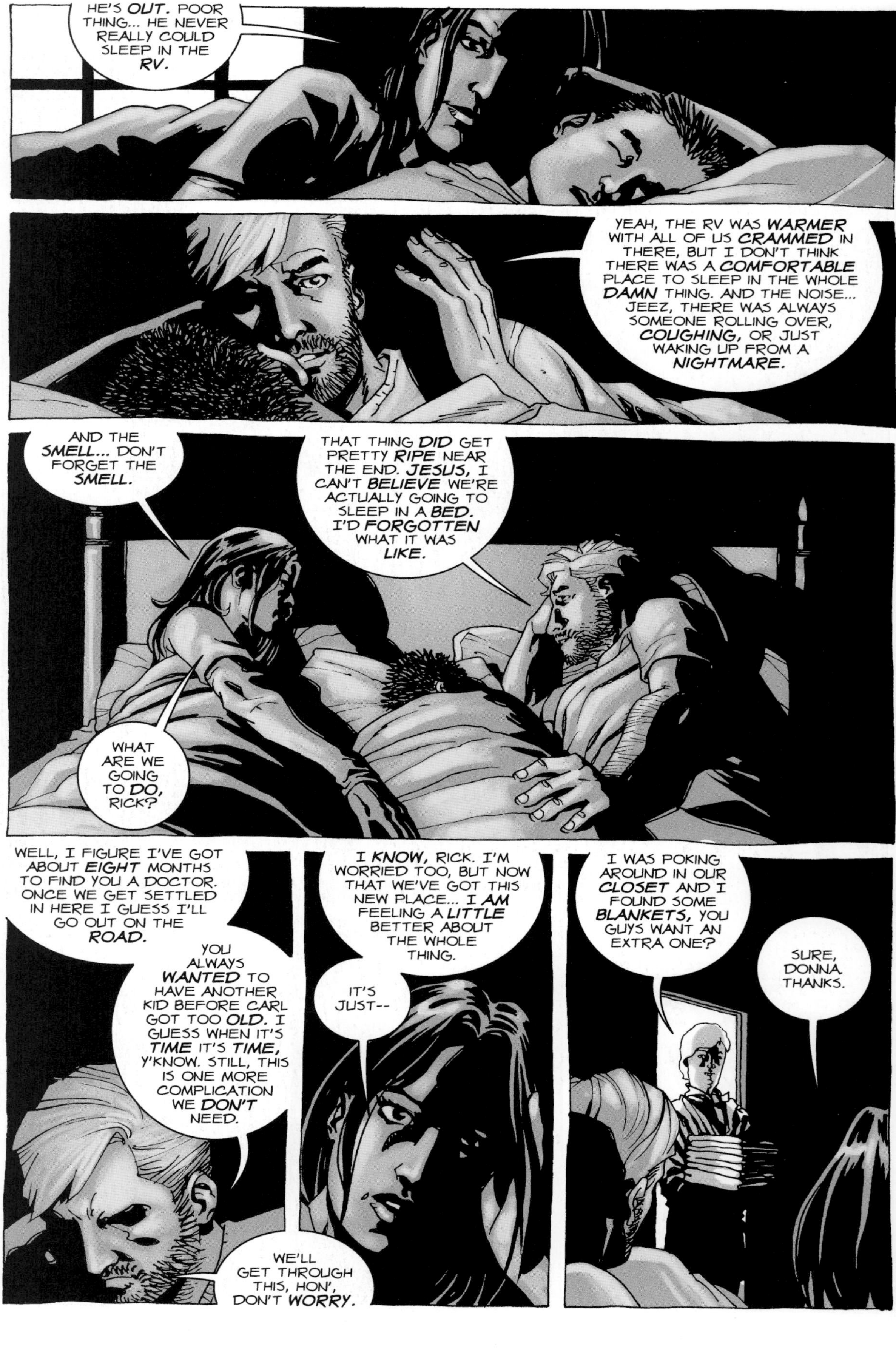
HE'S OUT. POOR THING... HE NEVER REALLY COULD SLEEP IN THE RV.
YEAH, THE RV WAS WARMER WITH ALL OF US CRAMMED IN THERE, BUT I DON'T THINK THERE WAS A COMFORTABLE PLACE TO SLEEP IN THE WHOLE DAMN THING. AND THE NOISE... JEEZ, THERE WAS ALWAYS SOMEONE ROLLING OVER, COUGHING, OR JUST WAKING UP FROM A NIGHTMARE.
AND THE SMELL... DON'T FORGET THE SMELL.
THAT THING DID GET PRETTY RIPE NEAR THE END. JESUS, I CAN'T BELIEVE WE'RE ACTUALLY GOING TO SLEEP IN A BED. I'D FORGOTTEN WHAT IT WAS LIKE.
WHAT ARE WE GOING TO DO, RICK?
WELL, I FIGURE I'VE GOT ABOUT EIGHT MONTHS TO FIND YOU A DOCTOR. ONCE WE GET SETTLED IN HERE I GUESS I'LL GO OUT ON THE ROAD.
YOU ALWAYS WANTED TO HAVE ANOTHER KID BEFORE CARL GOT TOO OLD. I GUESS WHEN IT'S TIME IT'S TIME, Y'KNOW. STILL, THIS IS ONE MORE COMPLICATION WE DON'T NEED.
WE'LL GET THROUGH THIS, HON', DON'T WORRY.
I KNOW, RICK. I'M WORRIED TOO, BUT NOW THAT WE'VE GOT THIS NEW PLACE... I AM FEELING A LITTLE BETTER ABOUT THE WHOLE THING.
IT'S JUST--
I WAS POKING AROUND IN OUR CLOSET AND I FOUND SOME BLANKETS, YOU GUYS WANT AN EXTRA ONE?
SURE, DONNA. THANKS.

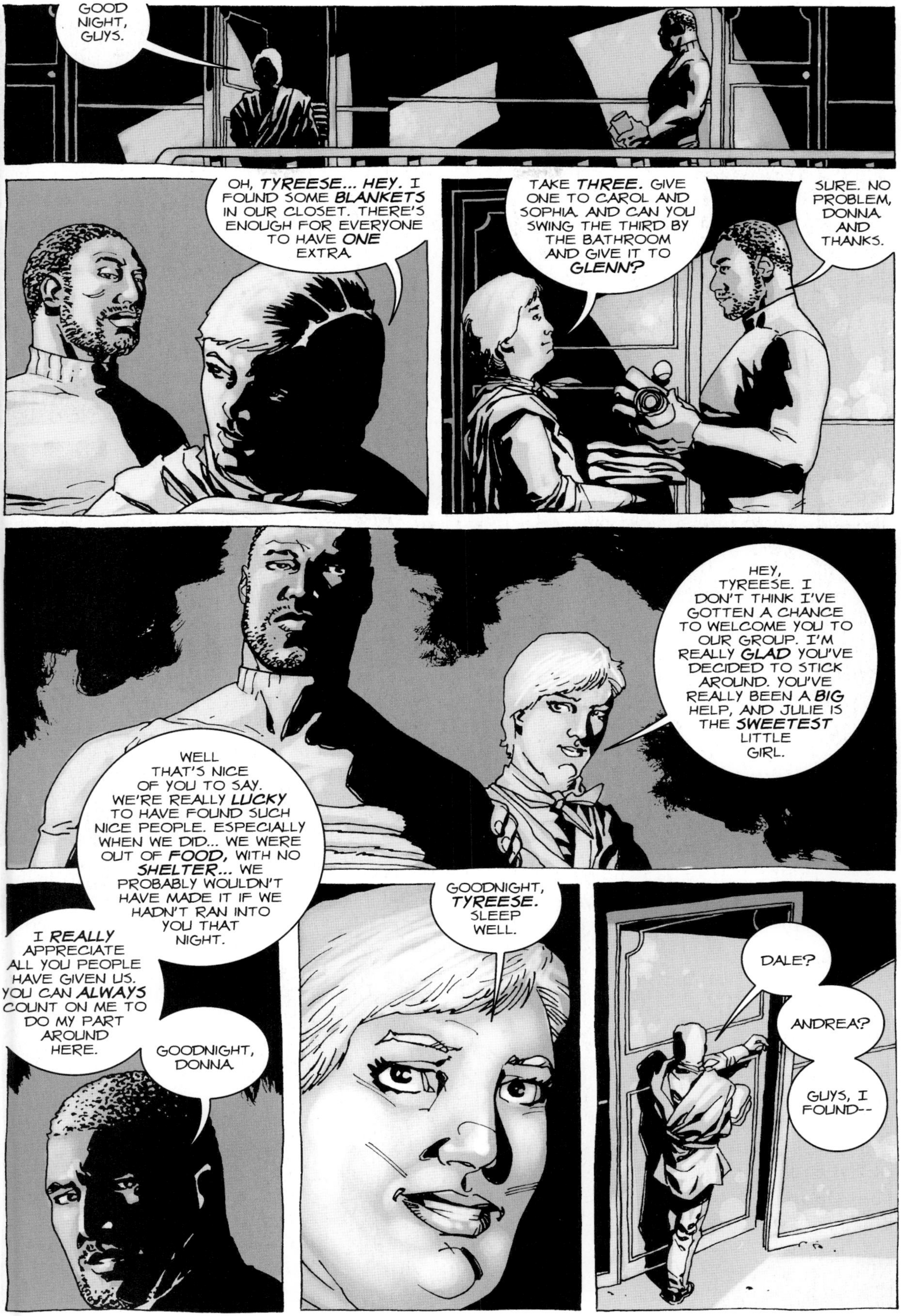

GOOD NIGHT, GUYS.
OH, TYREESE... HEY. I FOUND SOME BLANKETS IN OUR CLOSET. THERE'S ENOUGH FOR EVERYONE TO HAVE ONE EXTRA.
TAKE THREE. GIVE ONE TO CAROL AND SOPHIA. AND CAN YOU SWING THE THIRD BY THE BATHROOM AND GIVE IT TO GLENN?
SURE. NO PROBLEM, DONNA. AND THANKS.
HEY, TYREESE. I DON'T THINK I'VE GOTTEN A CHANCE TO WELCOME YOU TO OUR GROUP. I'M REALLY GLAD YOU'VE DECIDED TO STICK AROUND. YOU'VE REALLY BEEN A BIG HELP, AND JULIE IS THE SWEETEST LITTLE GIRL.
WELL THAT'S NICE OF YOU TO SAY. WE'RE REALLY LUCKY TO HAVE FOUND SUCH NICE PEOPLE. ESPECIALLY WHEN WE DID... WE WERE OUT OF FOOD, WITH NO SHELTER... WE PROBABLY WOULDN'T HAVE MADE IT IF WE HADN'T RAN INTO YOU THAT NIGHT.
I REALLY APPRECIATE ALL YOU PEOPLE HAVE GIVEN US. YOU CAN ALWAYS COUNT ON ME TO DO MY PART AROUND HERE.
GOODNIGHT, DONNA.
GOODNIGHT, TYREESE. SLEEP WELL.
DALE?
ANDREA?
GUYS, I FOUND--

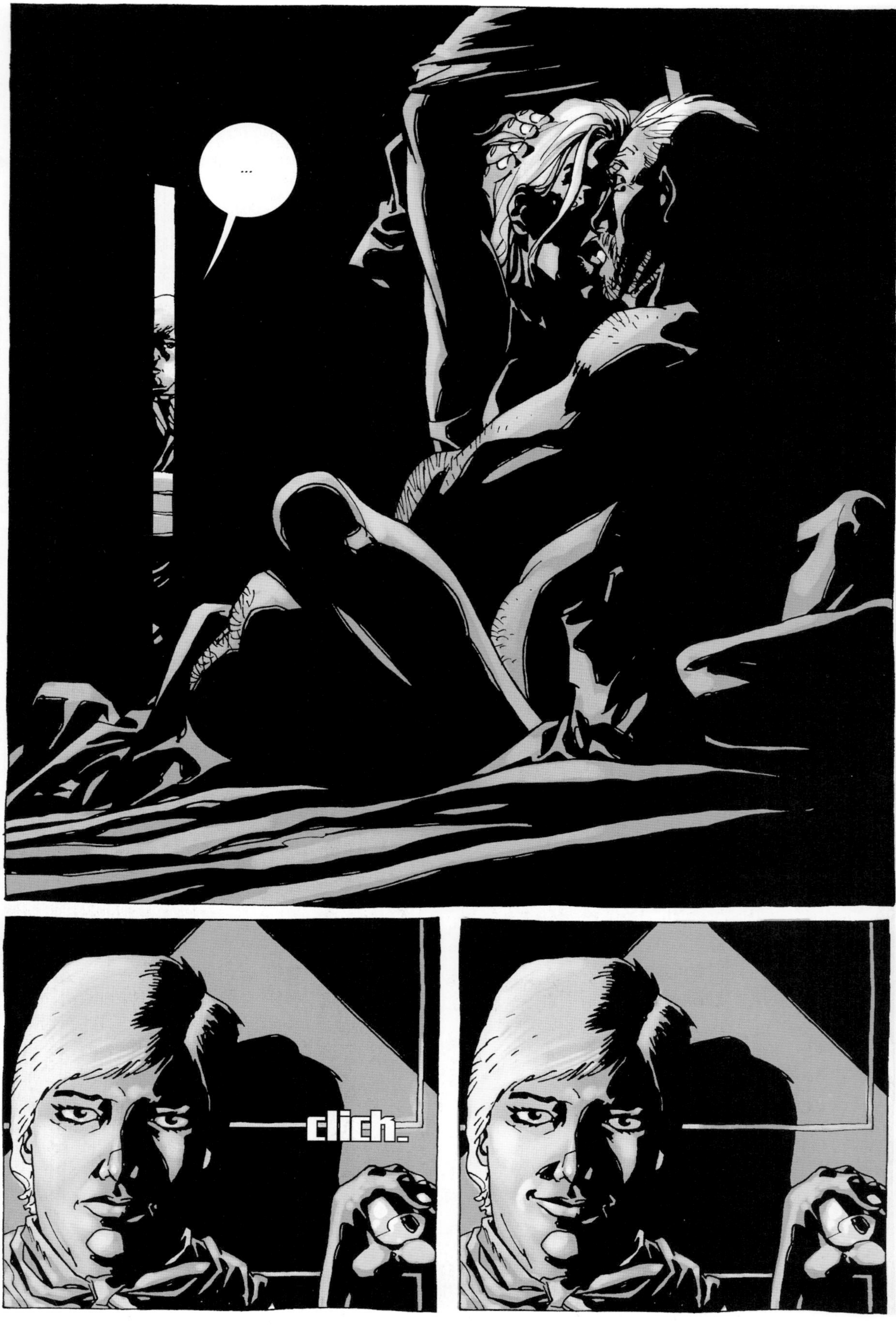
...
click.

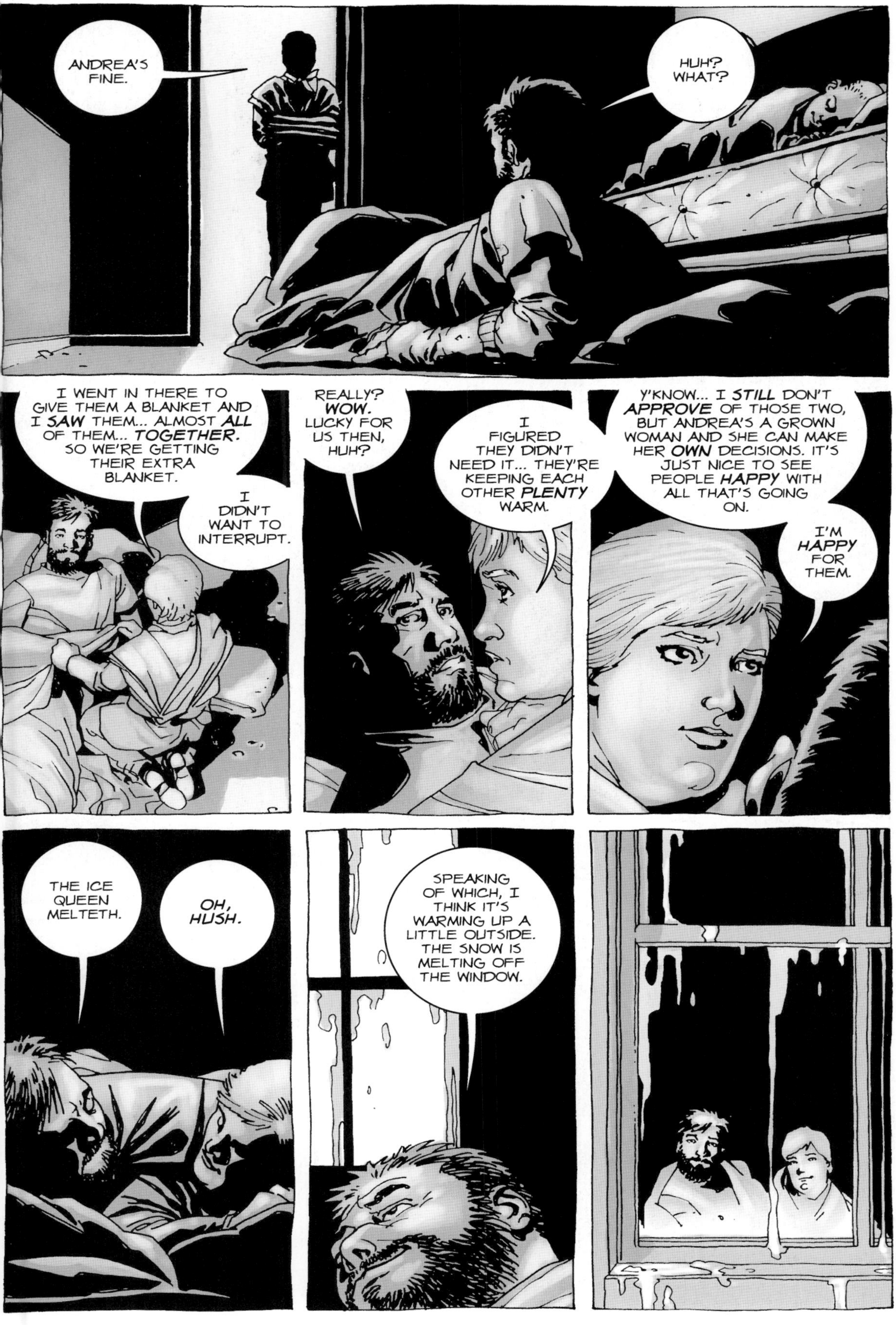
ANDREA'S FINE.
HUH? WHAT?
I WENT IN THERE TO GIVE THEM A BLANKET AND I SAW THEM... ALMOST ALL OF THEM... TOGETHER. SO WE'RE GETTING THEIR EXTRA BLANKET.
I DIDN'T WANT TO INTERRUPT.
REALLY? WOW. LUCKY FOR US THEN, HUH?
I FIGURED THEY DIDN'T NEED IT... THEY'RE KEEPING EACH OTHER PLENTY WARM.
Y'KNOW... I STILL DON'T APPROVE OF THOSE TWO, BUT ANDREA'S A GROWN WOMAN AND SHE CAN MAKE HER OWN DECISIONS. IT'S JUST NICE TO SEE PEOPLE HAPPY WITH ALL THAT'S GOING ON.
I'M HAPPY FOR THEM.
THE ICE QUEEN MELTETH.
OH, HUSH.
SPEAKING OF WHICH, I THINK IT'S WARMING UP A LITTLE OUTSIDE. THE SNOW IS MELTING OFF THE WINDOW.

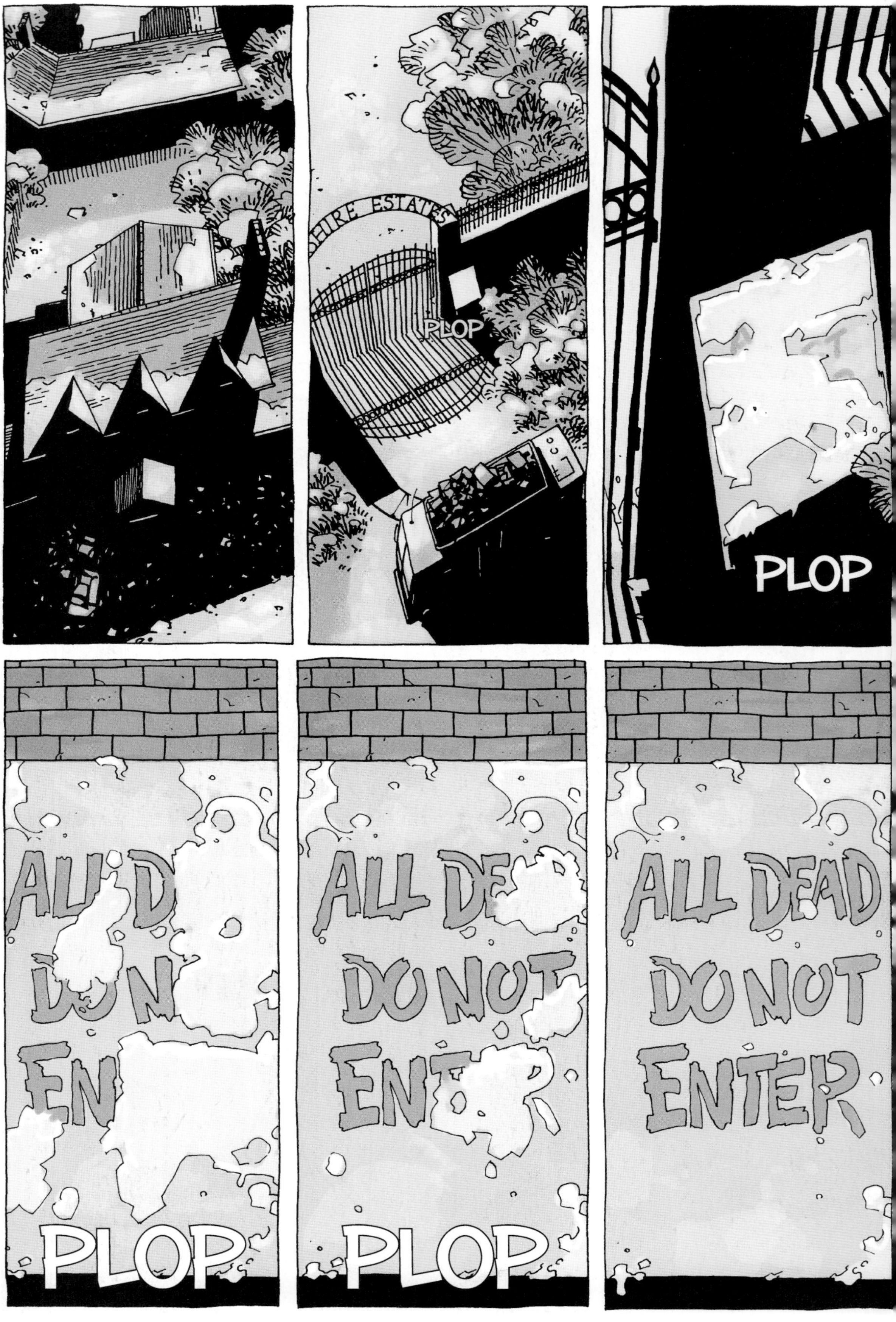

ESTATES
PLOP
PLOP
PLOP
PLOP
ALL DEAD
DO NOT
ENTER

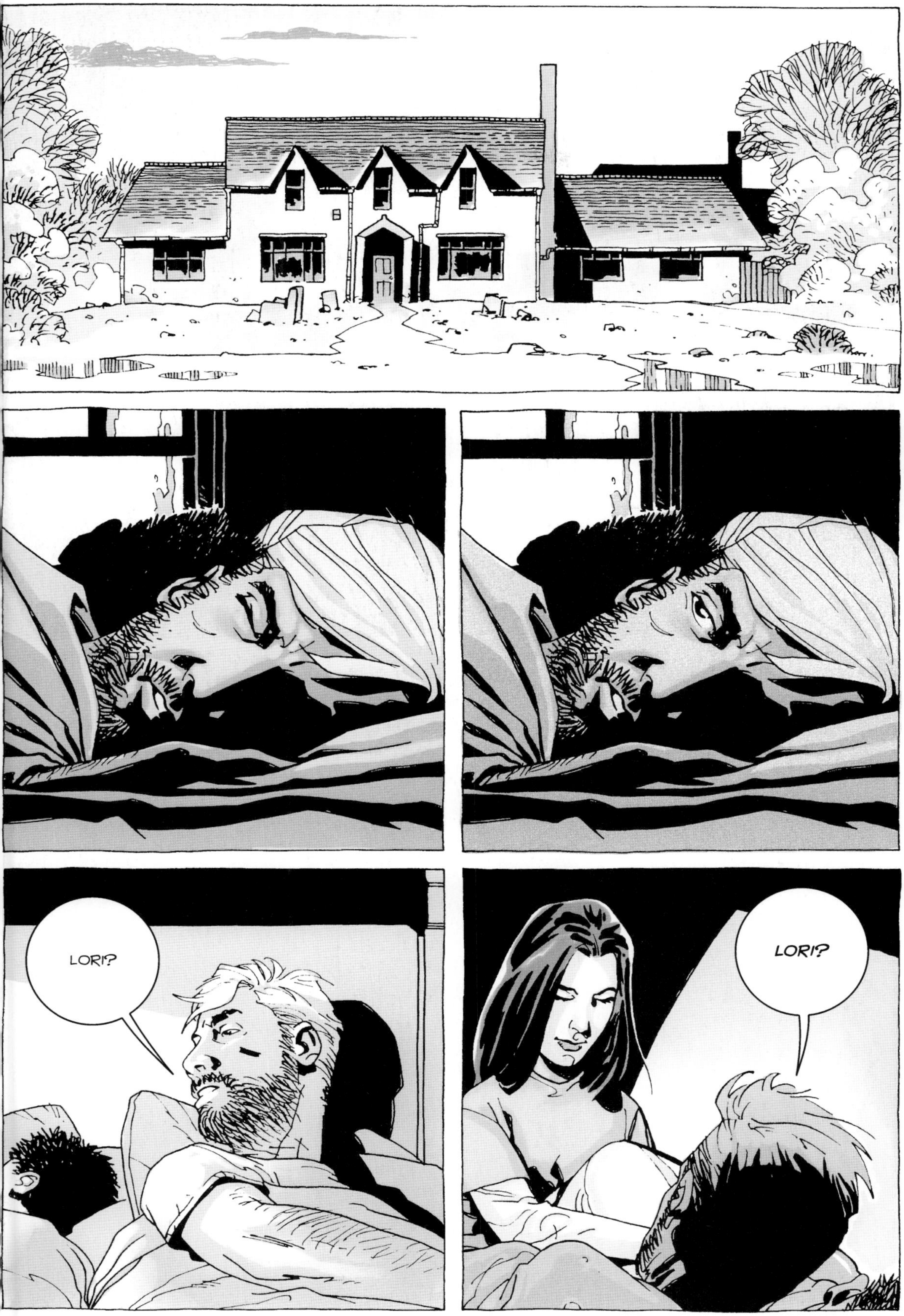
LORI?
LORI?

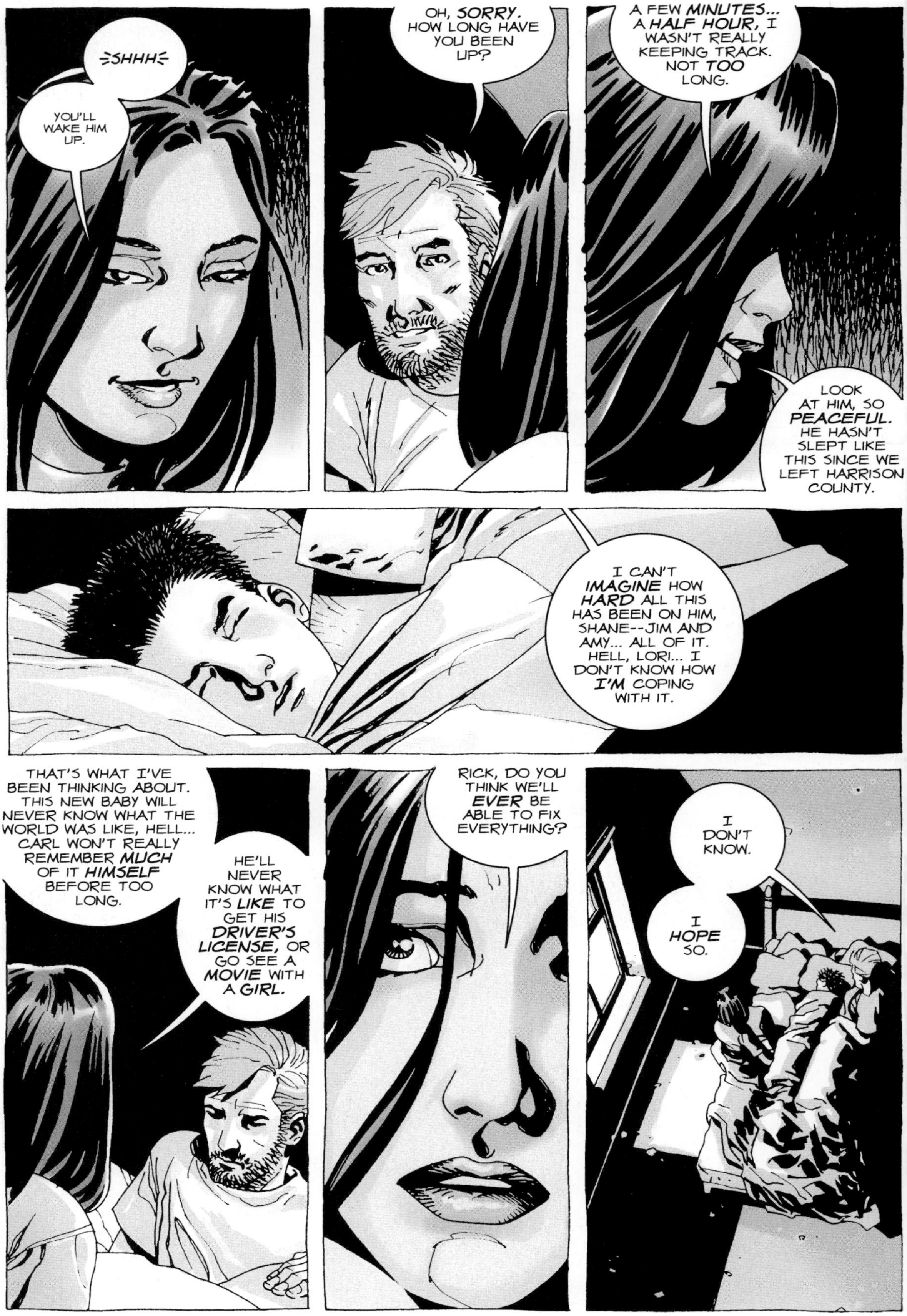

SHHH
YOU'LL WAKE HIM UP.
OH, SORRY. HOW LONG HAVE YOU BEEN UP?
A FEW MINUTES... A HALF HOUR, I WASN'T REALLY KEEPING TRACK. NOT TOO LONG.
LOOK AT HIM, SO PEACEFUL. HE HASN'T SLEPT LIKE THIS SINCE WE LEFT HARRISON COUNTY.
I CAN'T IMAGINE HOW HARD ALL THIS HAS BEEN ON HIM, SHANE--JIM AND AMY... ALL OF IT. HELL, LORI... I DON'T KNOW HOW I'M COPING WITH IT.
THAT'S WHAT I'VE BEEN THINKING ABOUT. THIS NEW BABY WILL NEVER KNOW WHAT THE WORLD WAS LIKE, HELL... CARL WON'T REALLY REMEMBER MUCH OF IT HIMSELF BEFORE TOO LONG.
HE'LL NEVER KNOW WHAT IT'S LIKE TO GET HIS DRIVER'S LICENSE, OR GO SEE A MOVIE WITH A GIRL.
RICK, DO YOU THINK WE'LL EVER BE ABLE TO FIX EVERYTHING?
I DON'T KNOW.
I HOPE SO.

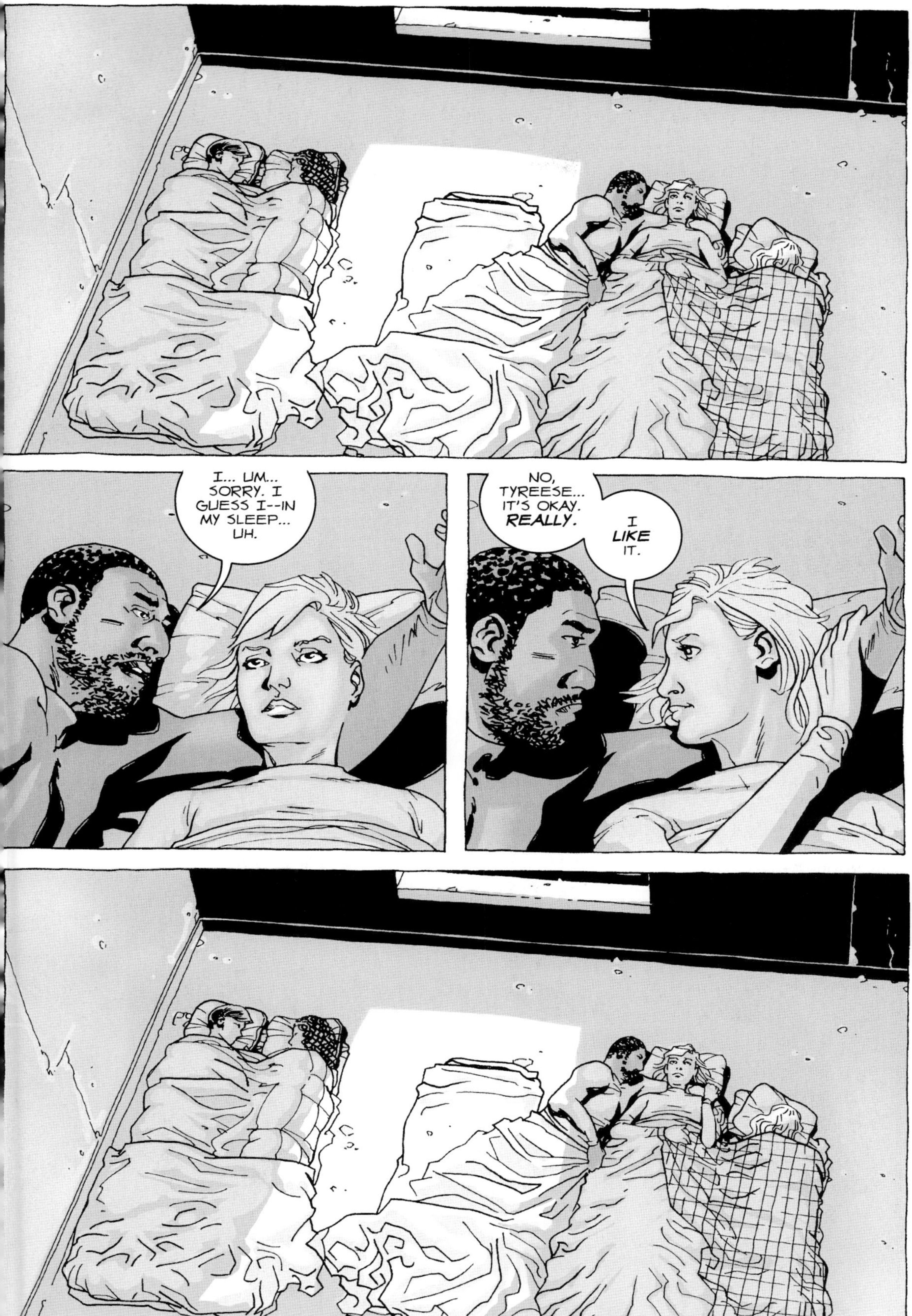
I... UM... SORRY. I GUESS I--IN MY SLEEP... UH.
NO, TYREESE... IT'S OKAY. REALLY.
I LIKE IT.

WHAT ARE YOU *THINKING*?

I DIDN'T KNOW YOU WERE AWAKE.

SURPRISE.

I WAS JUST THINKING ABOUT ANDREA AND DALE... THEY BOTH LOST SOMEONE THEY *LOVED*... SOMEONE VERY *CLOSE* TO THEM. IT HIT THEM HARD, WE SAW THAT... BUT THEY EVENTUALLY PULLED OUT OF IT. SEEING THEM *TOGETHER* LAST NIGHT-- THEY'RE *HAPPY*.

SEEING THEM--KNOWING THAT THEY CAN PUT THEIR LIVES BACK TOGETHER... IT GIVES ME *HOPE*.

AND THEN THERE'S *THIS* PLACE... A CHANCE TO *START OVER*. A NEW PLACE... ALL TO OURSELVES, AND IF *HALF* OF THE HOUSES IN THIS NEIGHBORHOOD ARE A NICE AS THIS ONE WE'LL *ALL* BE HAPPY. THIS PLACE--IT'S *PERFECT*.

I THINK WE CAN BE *HAPPY* HERE.

...AND EVERYONE WE'RE WITH. THEY'RE *GOOD PEOPLE*. I CAN'T *BELIEVE* WE STUMBLED INTO FINDING PEOPLE LIKE THEM. WE COULDN'T *ASK* FOR BETTER NEIGHBORS.

WE'RE *REALLY* LUCKY.

YOU'RE *RIGHT*. IF THIS WORKS OUT WE'VE GOT IT *MADE*. IT'S BEEN A WHILE SINCE I'VE SEEN YOU THIS HAPPY, *DONNA*.

YOU WANT TO HAVE *SEX*?

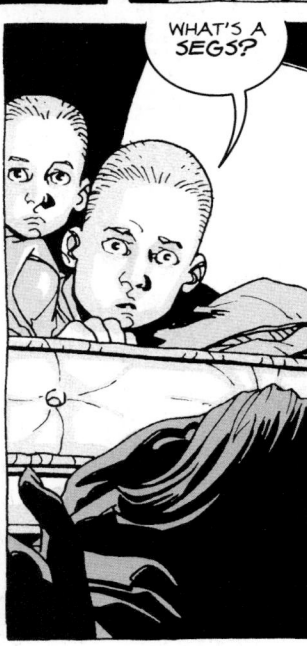

WHAT'S A *SEGS*?

THAT ANSWER YOUR QUESTION?

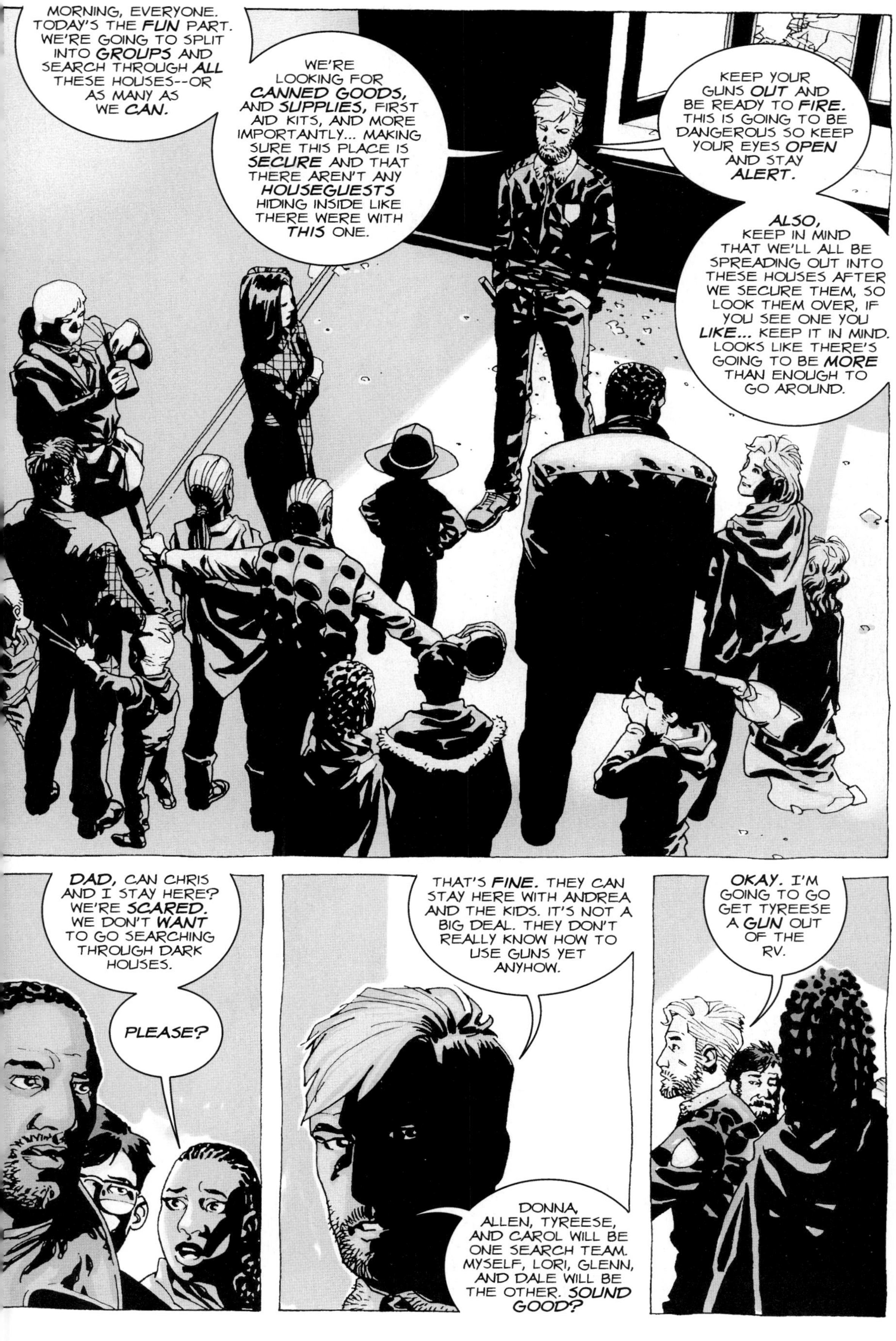
MORNING, EVERYONE. TODAY'S THE FUN PART. WE'RE GOING TO SPLIT INTO GROUPS AND SEARCH THROUGH ALL THESE HOUSES--OR AS MANY AS WE CAN.
WE'RE LOOKING FOR CANNED GOODS, AND SUPPLIES, FIRST AID KITS, AND MORE IMPORTANTLY... MAKING SURE THIS PLACE IS SECURE AND THAT THERE AREN'T ANY HOUSEGUESTS HIDING INSIDE LIKE THERE WERE WITH THIS ONE.
KEEP YOUR GUNS OUT AND BE READY TO FIRE. THIS IS GOING TO BE DANGEROUS SO KEEP YOUR EYES OPEN AND STAY ALERT.
ALSO, KEEP IN MIND THAT WE'LL ALL BE SPREADING OUT INTO THESE HOUSES AFTER WE SECURE THEM, SO LOOK THEM OVER, IF YOU SEE ONE YOU LIKE... KEEP IT IN MIND. LOOKS LIKE THERE'S GOING TO BE MORE THAN ENOUGH TO GO AROUND.
DAD, CAN CHRIS AND I STAY HERE? WE'RE SCARED. WE DON'T WANT TO GO SEARCHING THROUGH DARK HOUSES.
PLEASE?
THAT'S FINE. THEY CAN STAY HERE WITH ANDREA AND THE KIDS. IT'S NOT A BIG DEAL. THEY DON'T REALLY KNOW HOW TO USE GUNS YET ANYHOW.
DONNA, ALLEN, TYREESE, AND CAROL WILL BE ONE SEARCH TEAM. MYSELF, LORI, GLENN, AND DALE WILL BE THE OTHER. SOUND GOOD?
OKAY. I'M GOING TO GO GET TYREESE A GUN OUT OF THE RV.

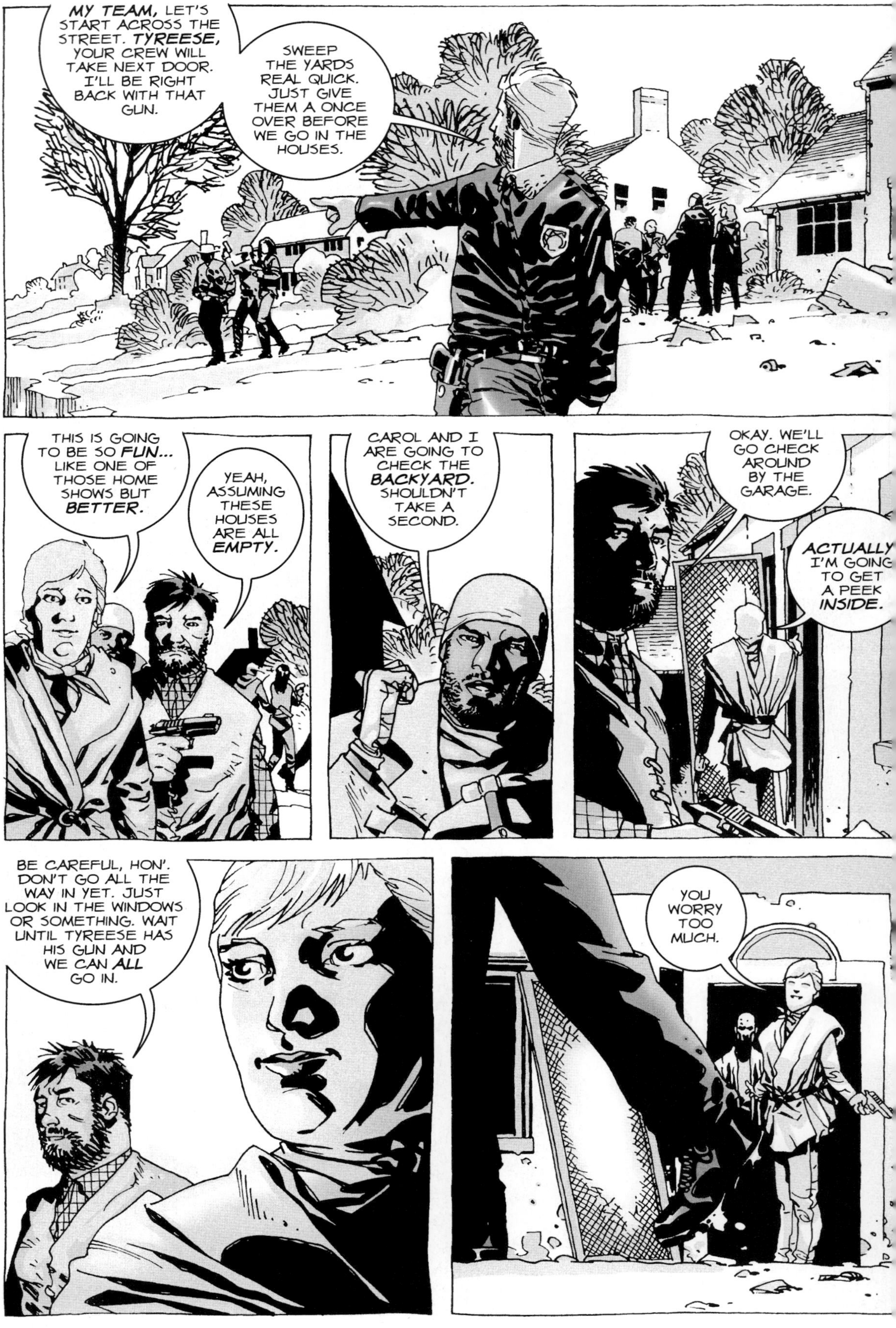
MY TEAM, LET'S START ACROSS THE STREET. TYREESE, YOUR CREW WILL TAKE NEXT DOOR. I'LL BE RIGHT BACK WITH THAT GUN.
SWEEP THE YARDS REAL QUICK. JUST GIVE THEM A ONCE OVER BEFORE WE GO IN THE HOUSES.
THIS IS GOING TO BE SO FUN... LIKE ONE OF THOSE HOME SHOWS BUT BETTER.
YEAH, ASSUMING THESE HOUSES ARE ALL EMPTY.
CAROL AND I ARE GOING TO CHECK THE BACKYARD. SHOULDN'T TAKE A SECOND.
OKAY. WE'LL GO CHECK AROUND BY THE GARAGE.
ACTUALLY I'M GOING TO GET A PEEK INSIDE.
BE CAREFUL, HON'. DON'T GO ALL THE WAY IN YET. JUST LOOK IN THE WINDOWS OR SOMETHING. WAIT UNTIL TYREESE HAS HIS GUN AND WE CAN ALL GO IN.
YOU WORRY TOO MUCH.

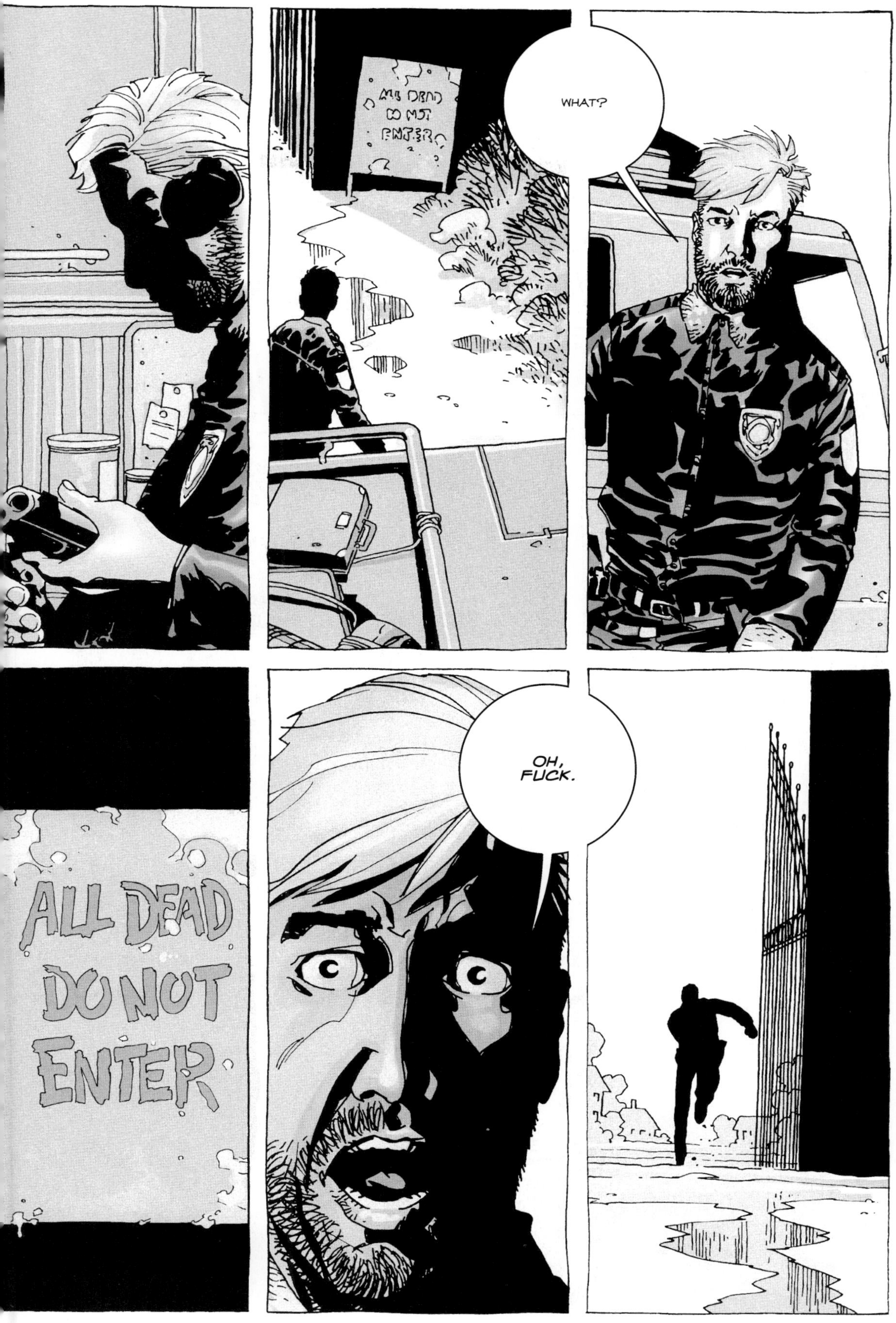

ALL DEAD DO NOT ENTER
WHAT?
ALL DEAD DO NOT ENTER
OH, FUCK.

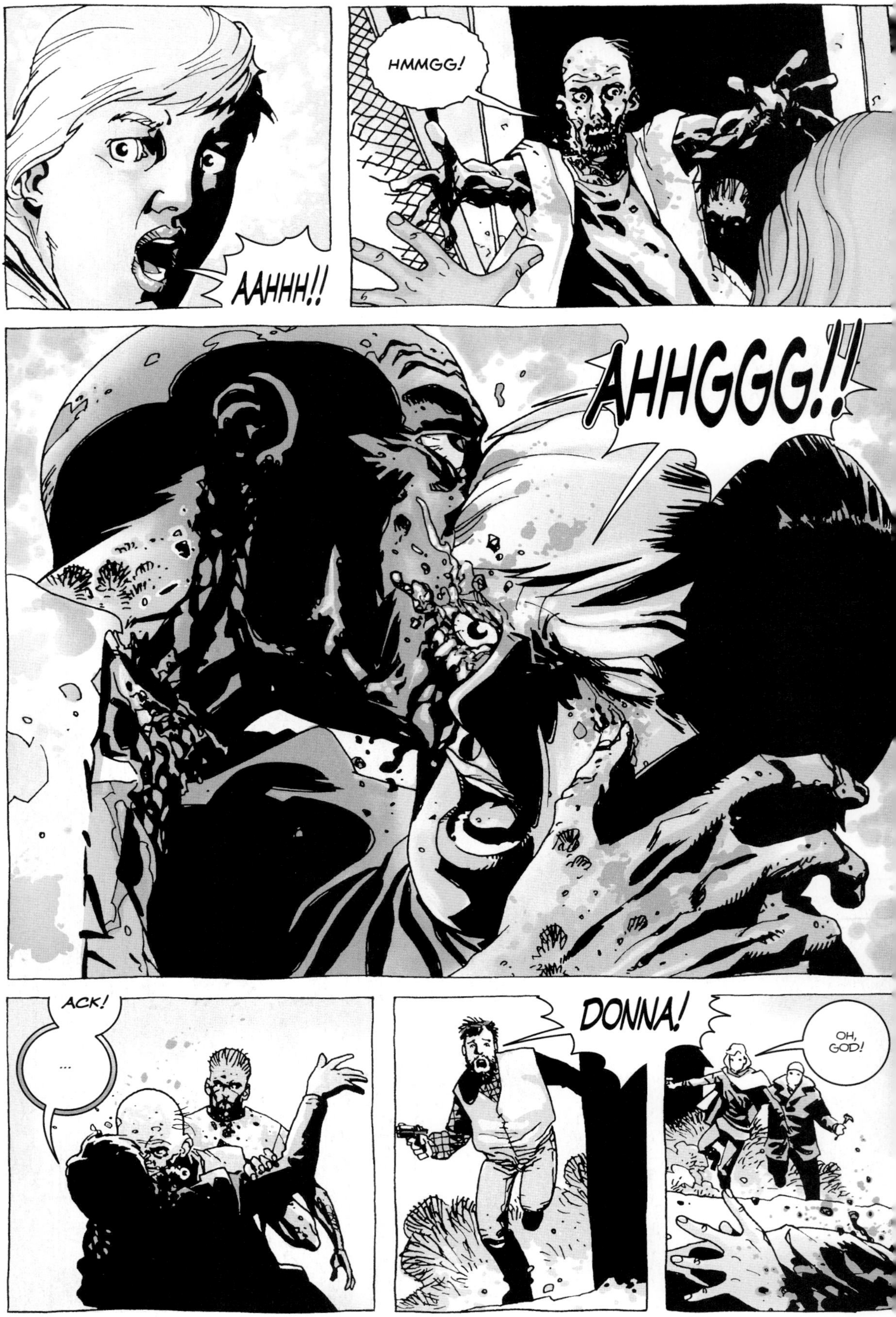
AAHHH!!
HMMGG!
AHHGGG!!
ACK!
...
DONNA!
OH, GOD!

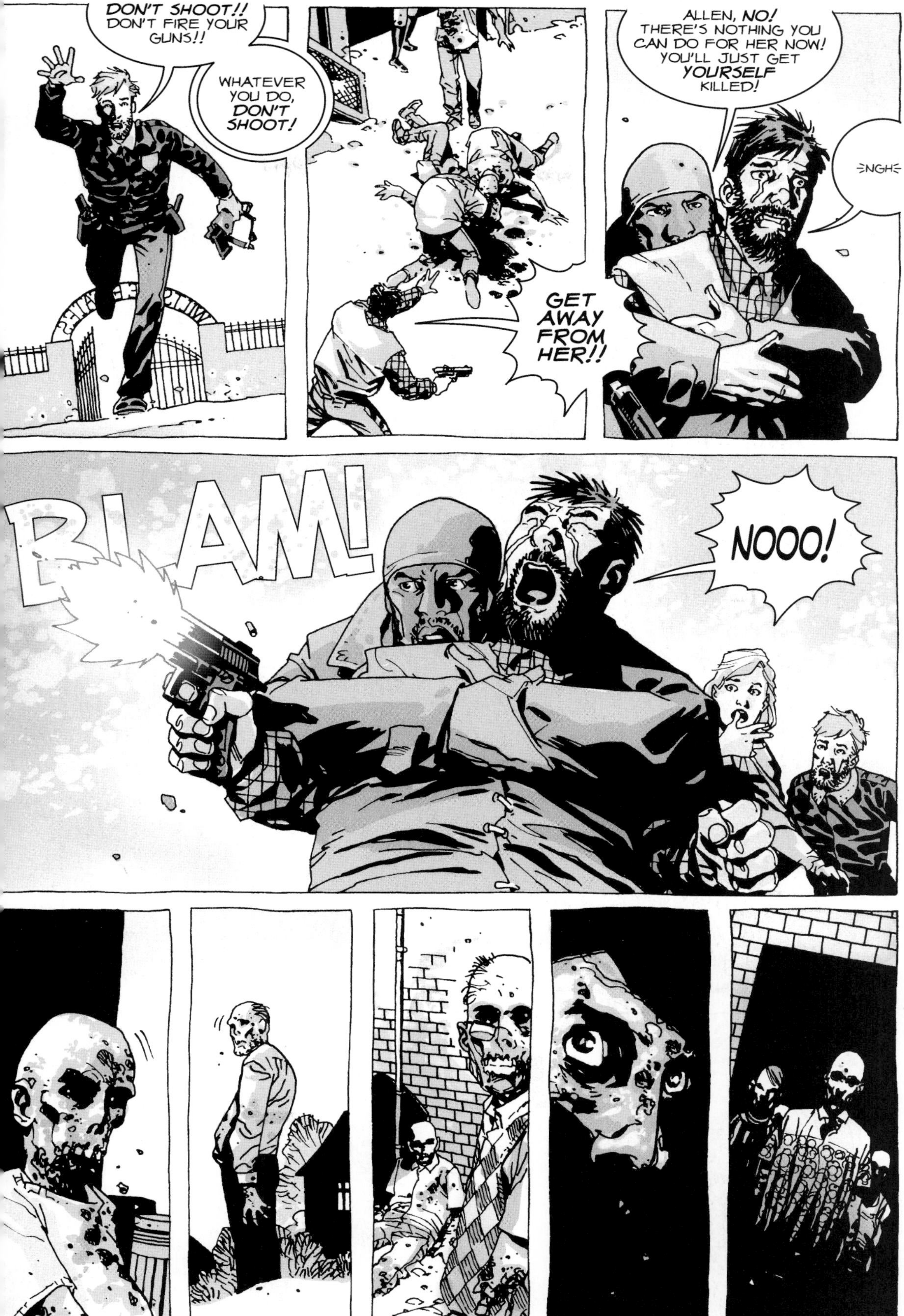

DON'T SHOOT!! DON'T FIRE YOUR GUNS!!
WHATEVER YOU DO, DON'T SHOOT!
GET AWAY FROM HER!!
ALLEN, NO! THERE'S NOTHING YOU CAN DO FOR HER NOW! YOU'LL JUST GET YOURSELF KILLED!
NGH
BLAM!
NOOO!

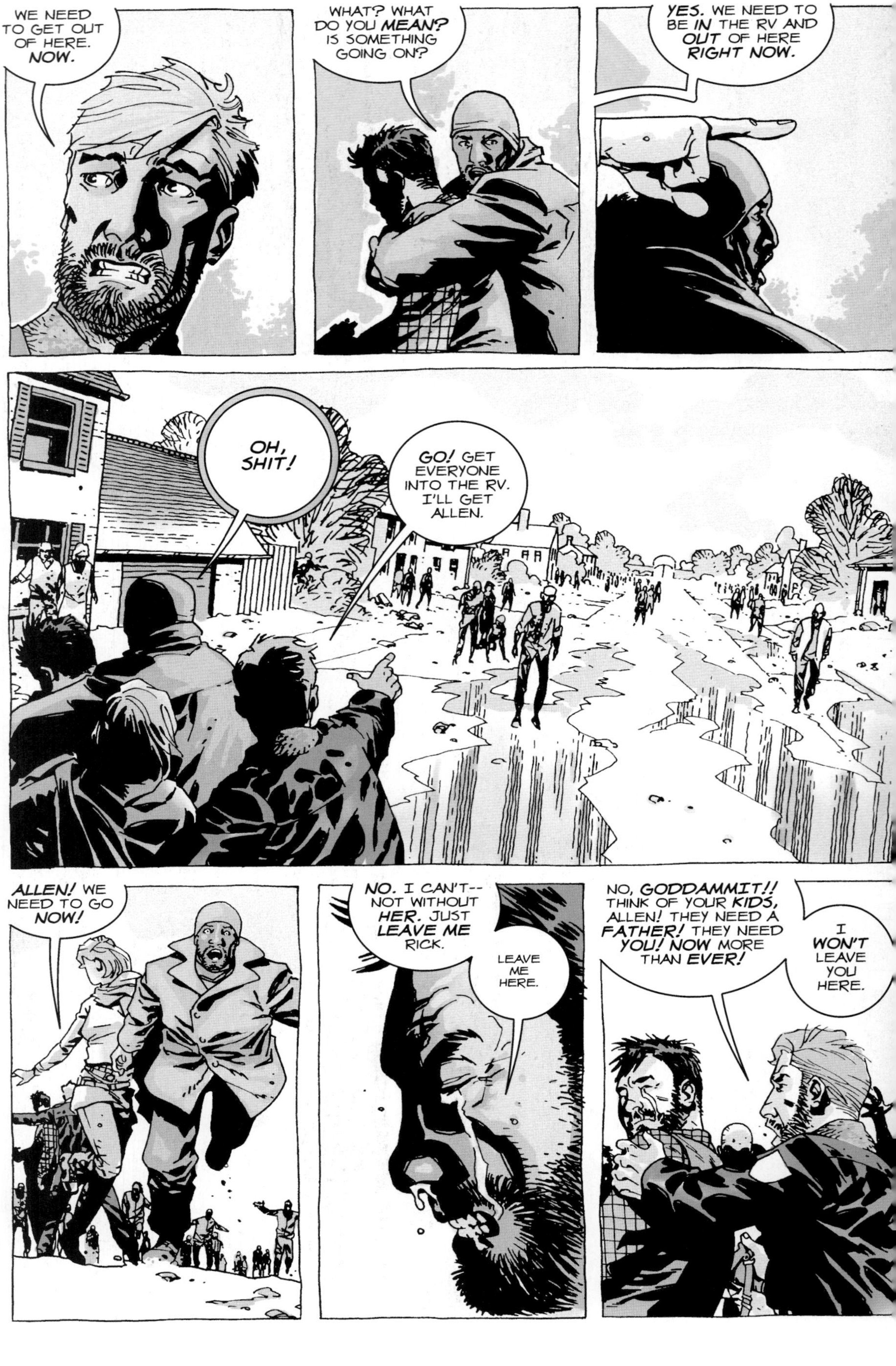

WE NEED TO GET OUT OF HERE. NOW.
WHAT? WHAT DO YOU MEAN? IS SOMETHING GOING ON?
YES. WE NEED TO BE IN THE RV AND OUT OF HERE RIGHT NOW.
OH, SHIT!
GO! GET EVERYONE INTO THE RV. I'LL GET ALLEN.
ALLEN! WE NEED TO GO NOW!
NO. I CAN'T-- NOT WITHOUT HER. JUST LEAVE ME RICK.
LEAVE ME HERE.
NO, GODDAMMIT!! THINK OF YOUR KIDS, ALLEN! THEY NEED A FATHER! THEY NEED YOU! NOW MORE THAN EVER!
I WON'T LEAVE YOU HERE.

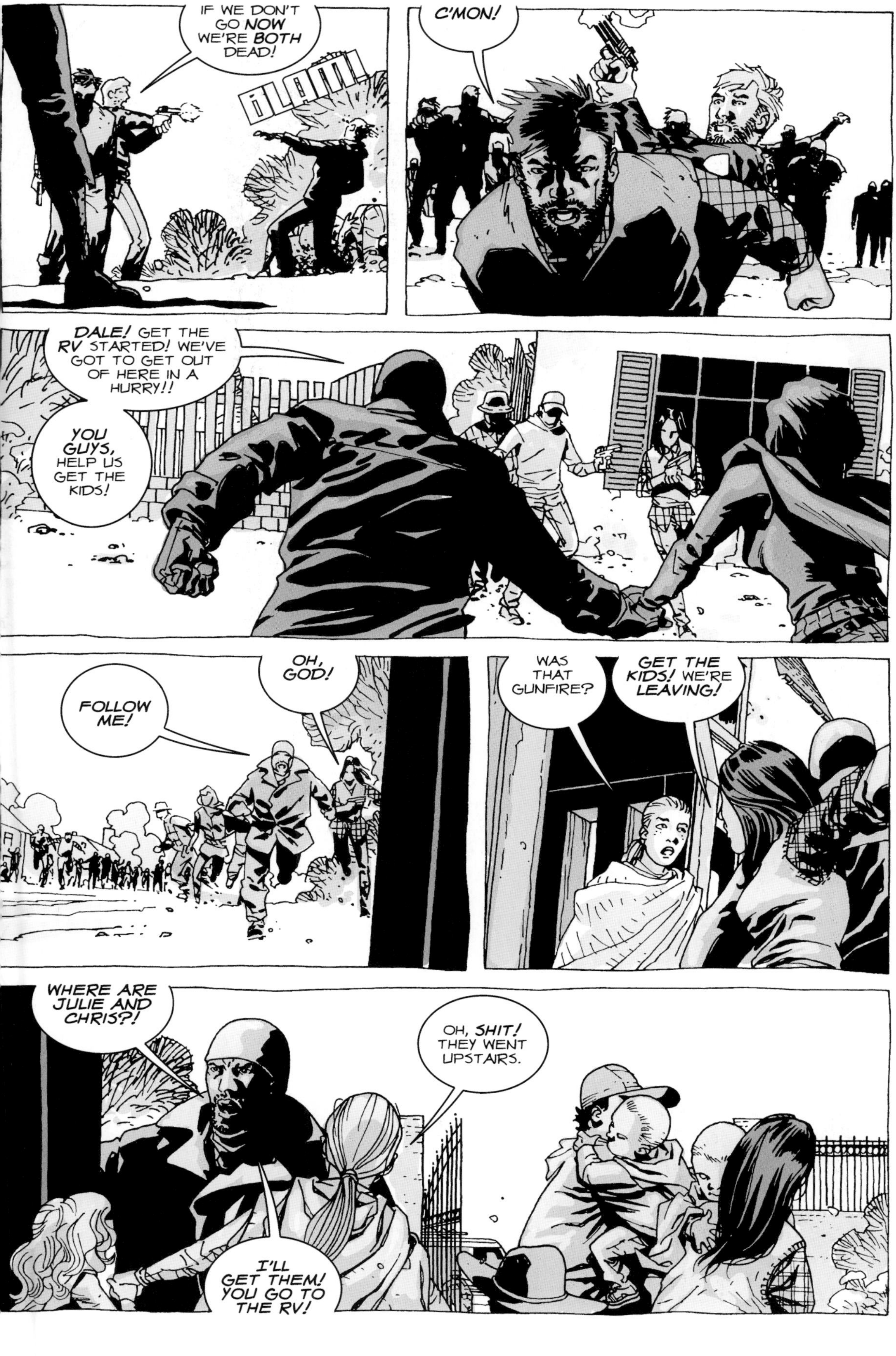

IF WE DON'T GO NOW WE'RE BOTH DEAD!
BLAM
C'MON!
DALE! GET THE RV STARTED! WE'VE GOT TO GET OUT OF HERE IN A HURRY!!
YOU GUYS, HELP US GET THE KIDS!
FOLLOW ME!
OH, GOD!
WAS THAT GUNFIRE?
GET THE KIDS! WE'RE LEAVING!
WHERE ARE JULIE AND CHRIS?!
OH, SHIT! THEY WENT UPSTAIRS.
I'LL GET THEM! YOU GO TO THE RV!

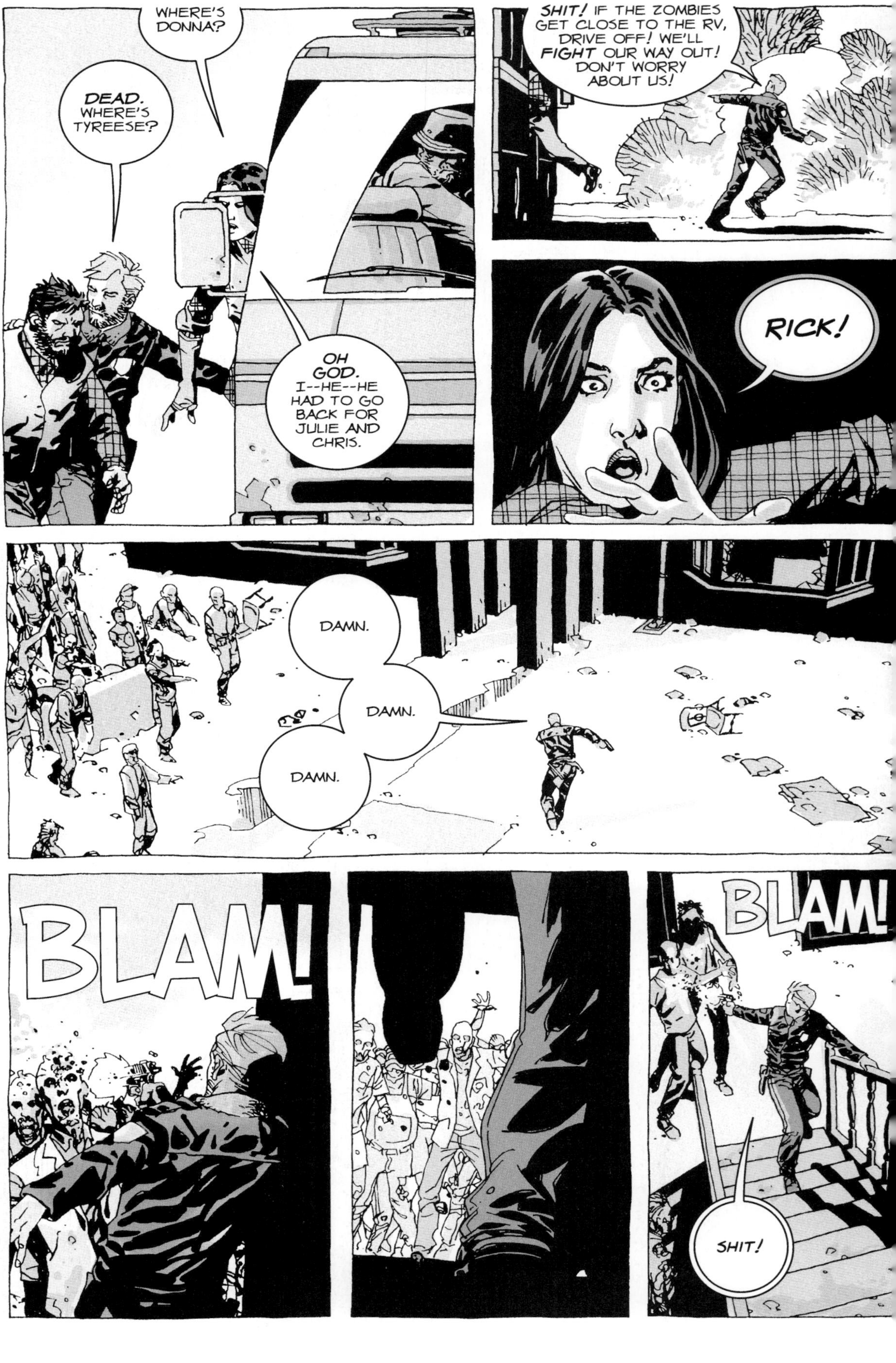
WHERE'S DONNA?
DEAD. WHERE'S TYREESE?
OH GOD. I--HE--HE HAD TO GO BACK FOR JULIE AND CHRIS.
SHIT! IF THE ZOMBIES GET CLOSE TO THE RV, DRIVE OFF! WE'LL FIGHT OUR WAY OUT! DON'T WORRY ABOUT US!
RICK!
DAMN.
DAMN.
DAMN.
BLAM!
BLAM!
SHIT!

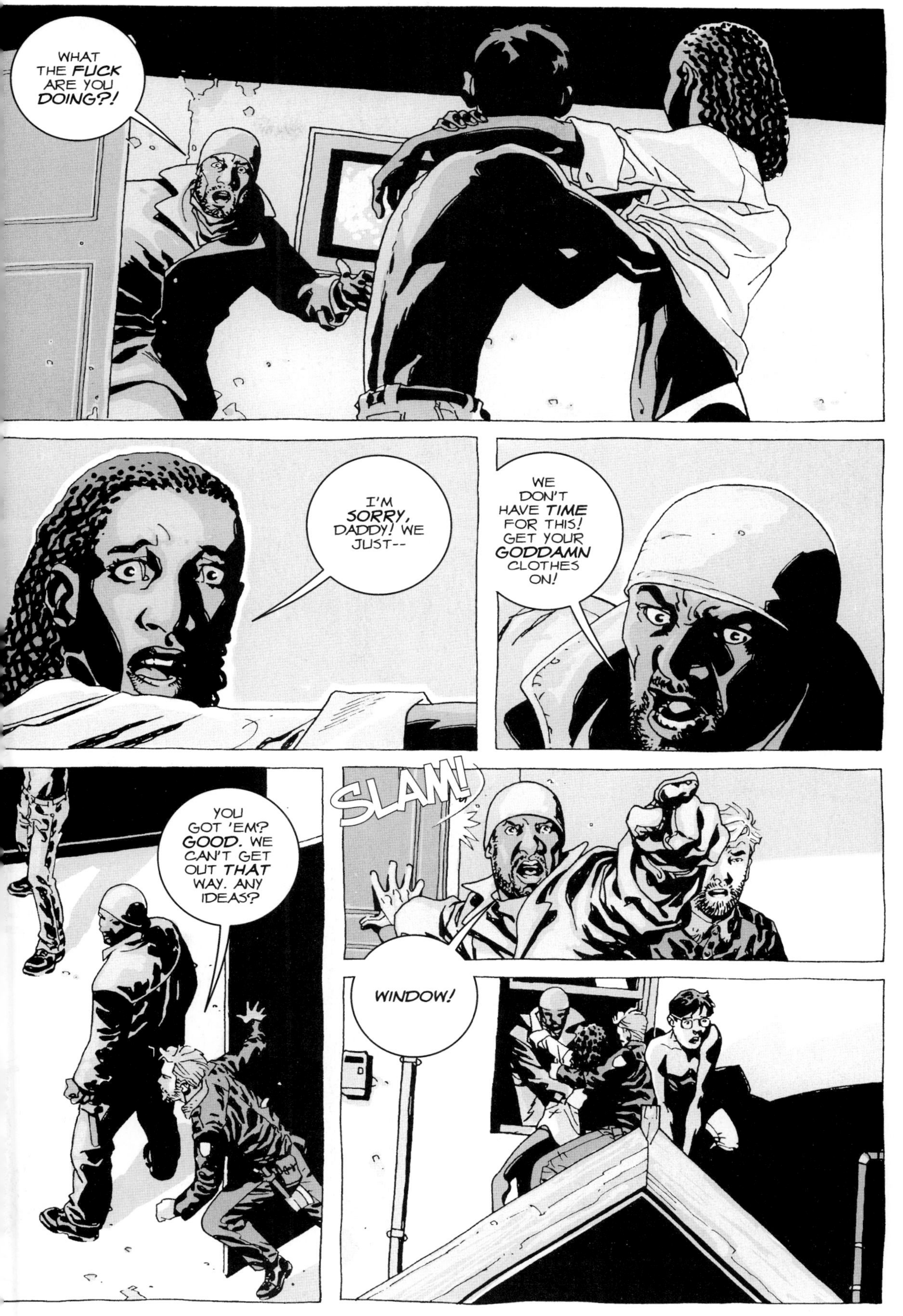
WHAT THE FUCK ARE YOU DOING?!
I'M SORRY, DADDY! WE JUST--
WE DON'T HAVE TIME FOR THIS! GET YOUR GODDAMN CLOTHES ON!
YOU GOT 'EM? GOOD. WE CAN'T GET OUT THAT WAY. ANY IDEAS?
SLAM!
WINDOW!

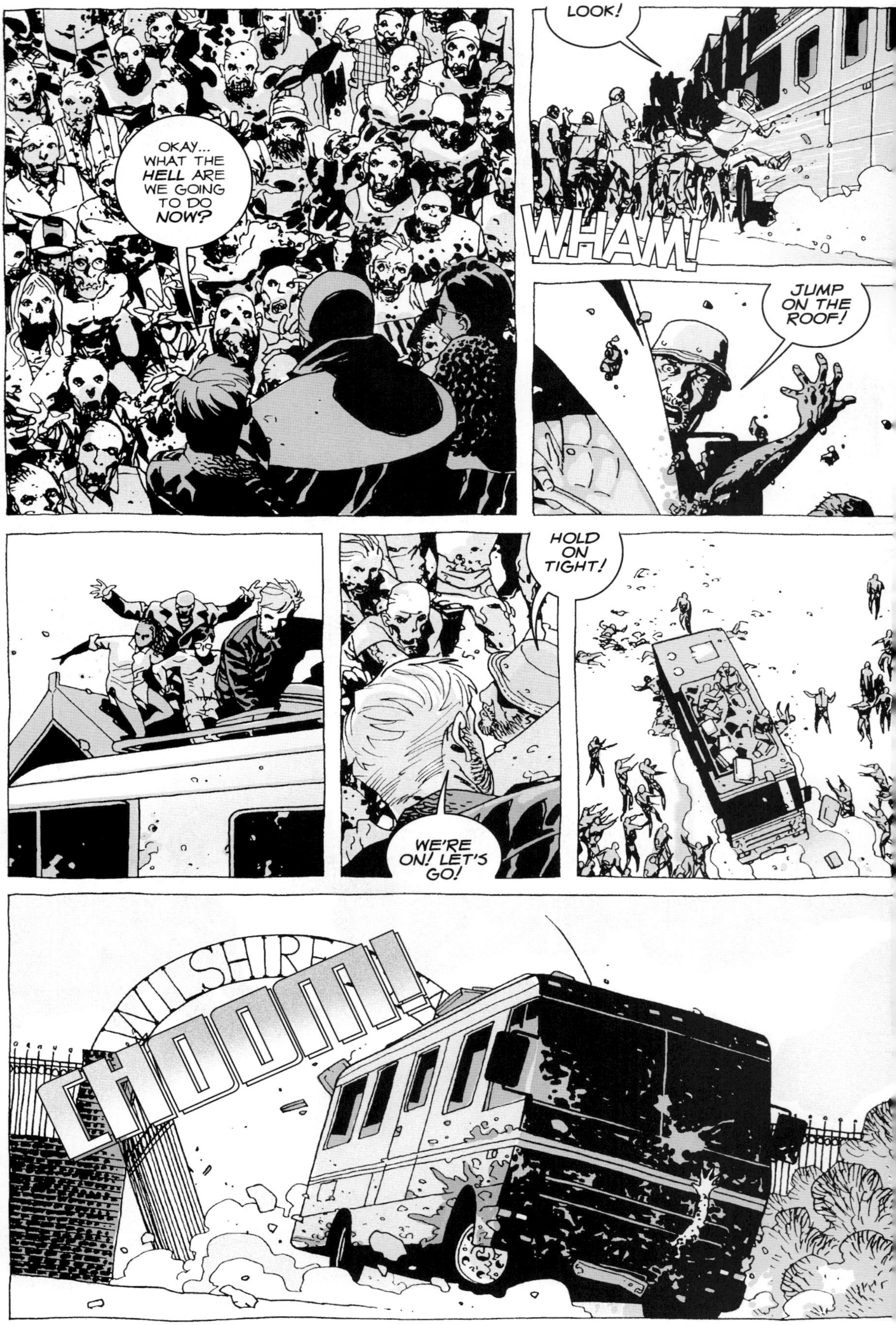

OKAY... WHAT THE HELL ARE WE GOING TO DO NOW?
LOOK!
WHAM!
JUMP ON THE ROOF!
HOLD ON TIGHT!
WE'RE ON! LET'S GO!
CHOOM!

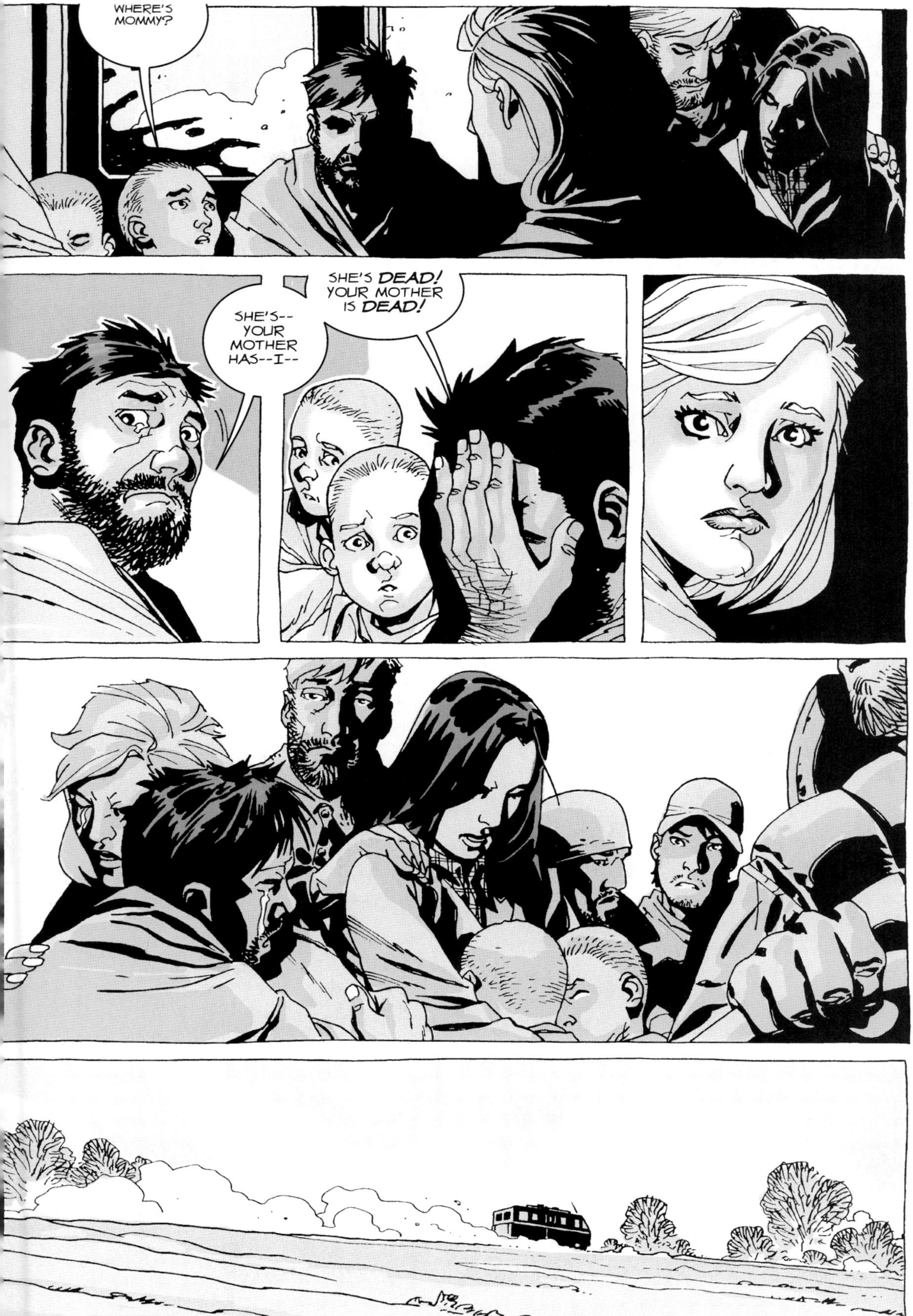
WHERE'S MOMMY?
SHE'S-- YOUR MOTHER HAS--I--
SHE'S DEAD! YOUR MOTHER IS DEAD!

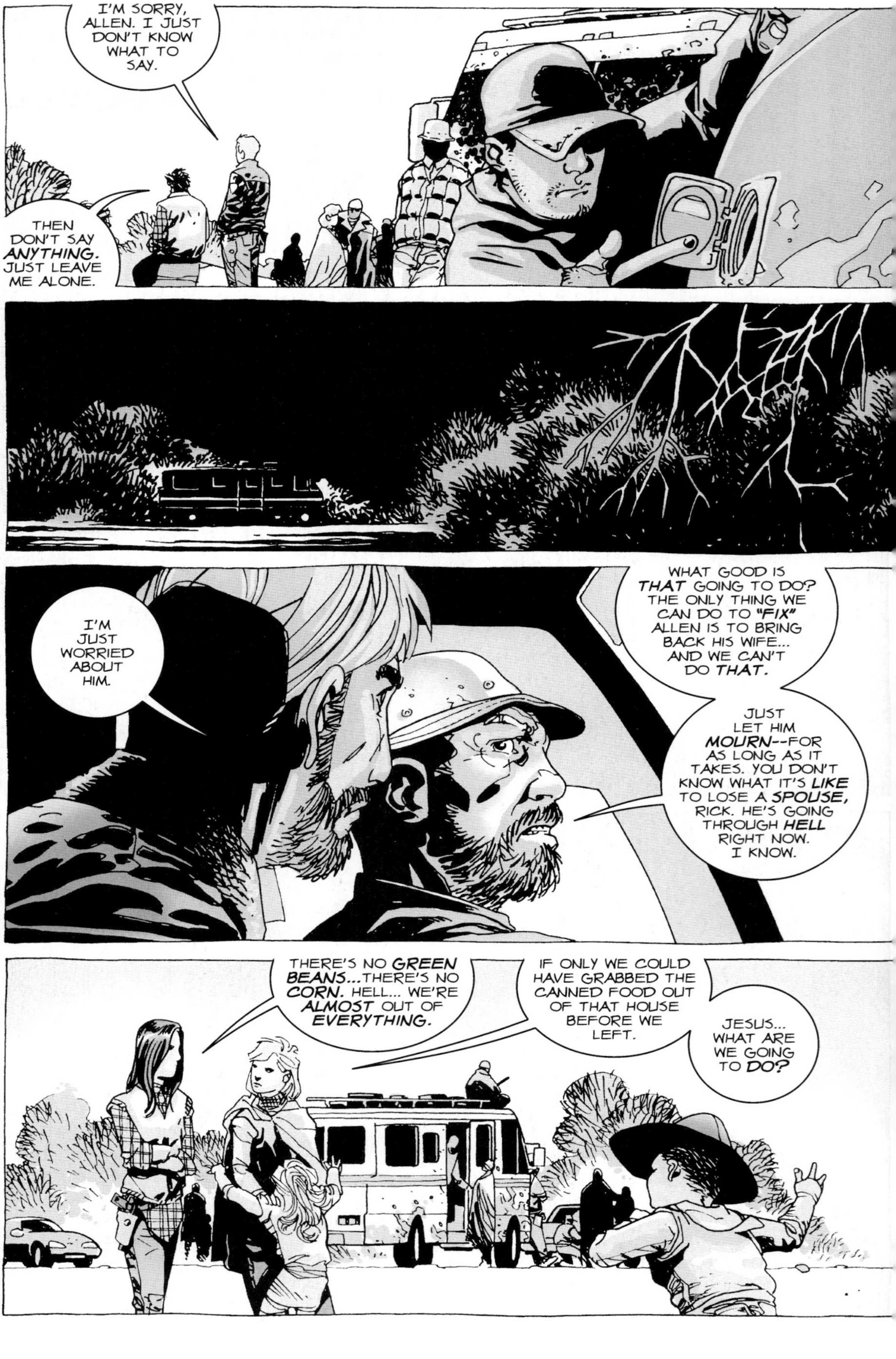

I'M SORRY, ALLEN. I JUST DON'T KNOW WHAT TO SAY.
THEN DON'T SAY **ANYTHING.** JUST LEAVE ME ALONE.
I'M JUST WORRIED ABOUT HIM.
WHAT GOOD IS **THAT** GOING TO DO? THE ONLY THING WE CAN DO TO **"FIX"** ALLEN IS TO BRING BACK HIS WIFE... AND WE CAN'T DO **THAT.**
JUST LET HIM **MOURN**--FOR AS LONG AS IT TAKES. YOU DON'T KNOW WHAT IT'S **LIKE** TO LOSE A **SPOUSE,** RICK. HE'S GOING THROUGH **HELL** RIGHT NOW. I KNOW.
THERE'S NO **GREEN BEANS...**THERE'S NO **CORN.** HELL... WE'RE **ALMOST** OUT OF **EVERYTHING.**
IF ONLY WE COULD HAVE GRABBED THE CANNED FOOD OUT OF THAT HOUSE BEFORE WE LEFT.
JESUS... WHAT ARE WE GOING TO **DO?**

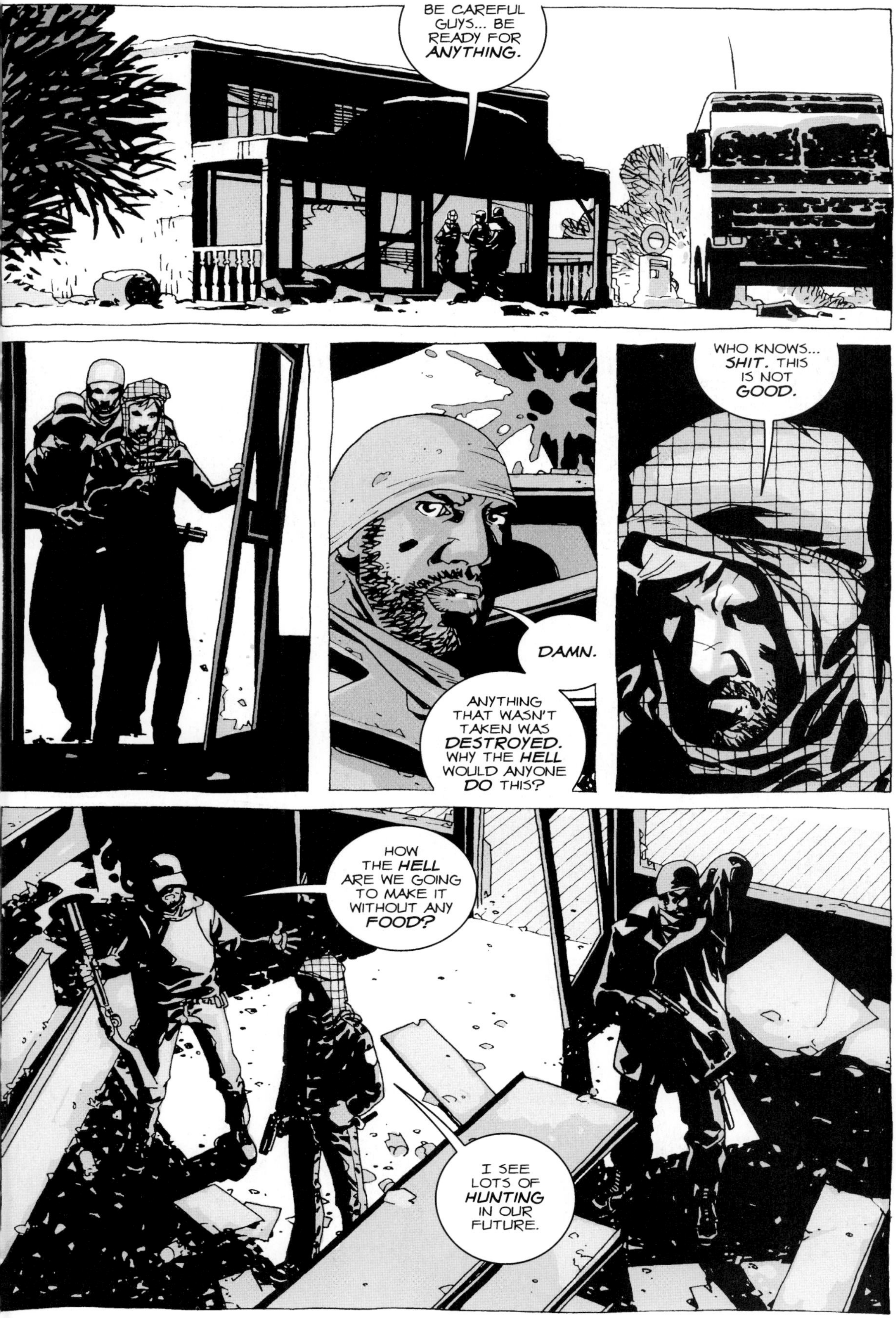
BE CAREFUL GUYS... BE READY FOR ANYTHING.
WHO KNOWS... SHIT. THIS IS NOT GOOD.
DAMN.
ANYTHING THAT WASN'T TAKEN WAS DESTROYED. WHY THE HELL WOULD ANYONE DO THIS?
HOW THE HELL ARE WE GOING TO MAKE IT WITHOUT ANY FOOD?
I SEE LOTS OF HUNTING IN OUR FUTURE.

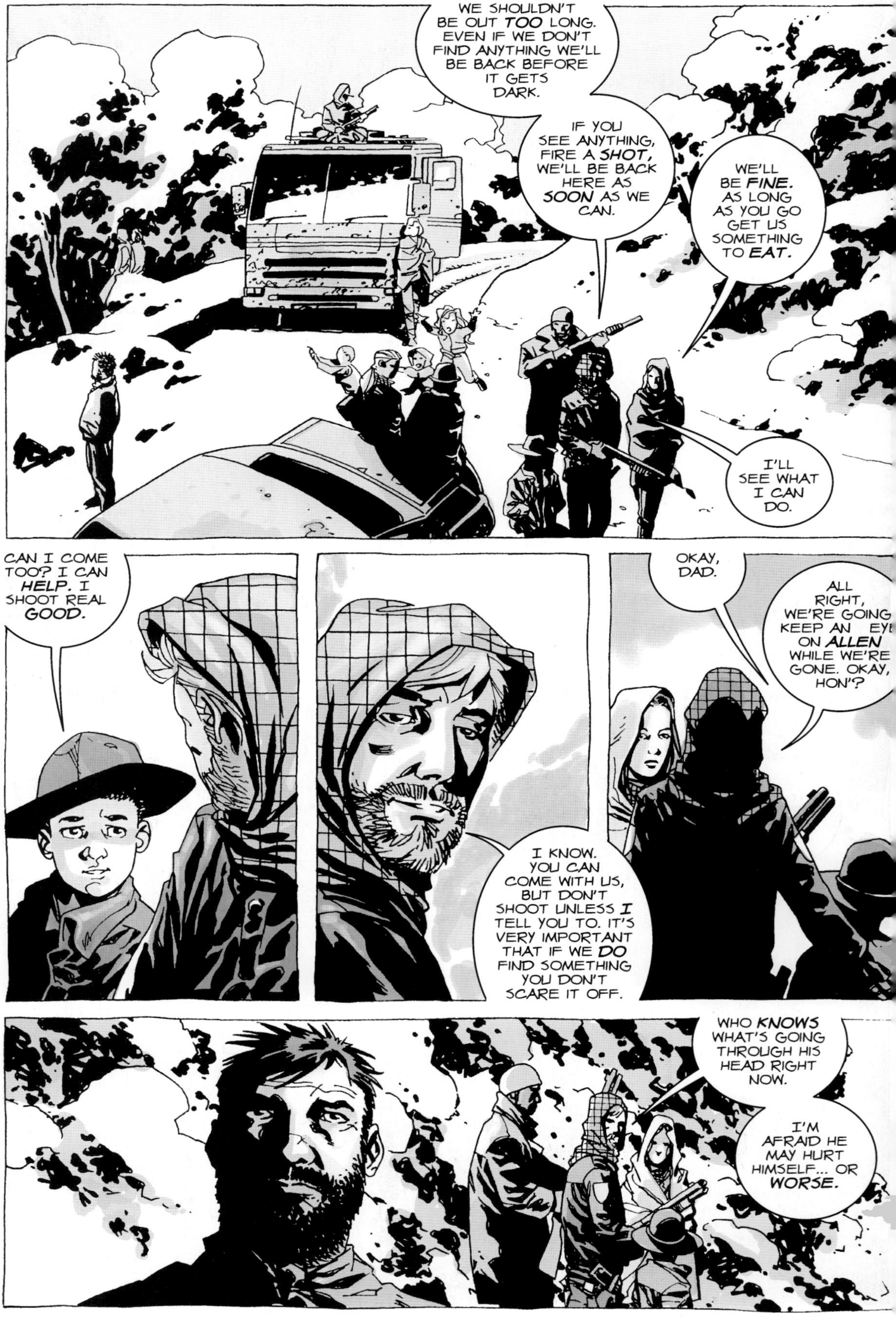
WE SHOULDN'T BE OUT TOO LONG. EVEN IF WE DON'T FIND ANYTHING WE'LL BE BACK BEFORE IT GETS DARK.
IF YOU SEE ANYTHING, FIRE A SHOT, WE'LL BE BACK HERE AS SOON AS WE CAN.
WE'LL BE FINE. AS LONG AS YOU GO GET US SOMETHING TO EAT.
I'LL SEE WHAT I CAN DO.
CAN I COME TOO? I CAN HELP. I SHOOT REAL GOOD.
I KNOW. YOU CAN COME WITH US, BUT DON'T SHOOT UNLESS I TELL YOU TO. IT'S VERY IMPORTANT THAT IF WE DO FIND SOMETHING YOU DON'T SCARE IT OFF.
OKAY, DAD.
ALL RIGHT, WE'RE GOING KEEP AN EYE ON ALLEN WHILE WE'RE GONE. OKAY, HON'?
WHO KNOWS WHAT'S GOING THROUGH HIS HEAD RIGHT NOW.
I'M AFRAID HE MAY HURT HIMSELF... OR WORSE.

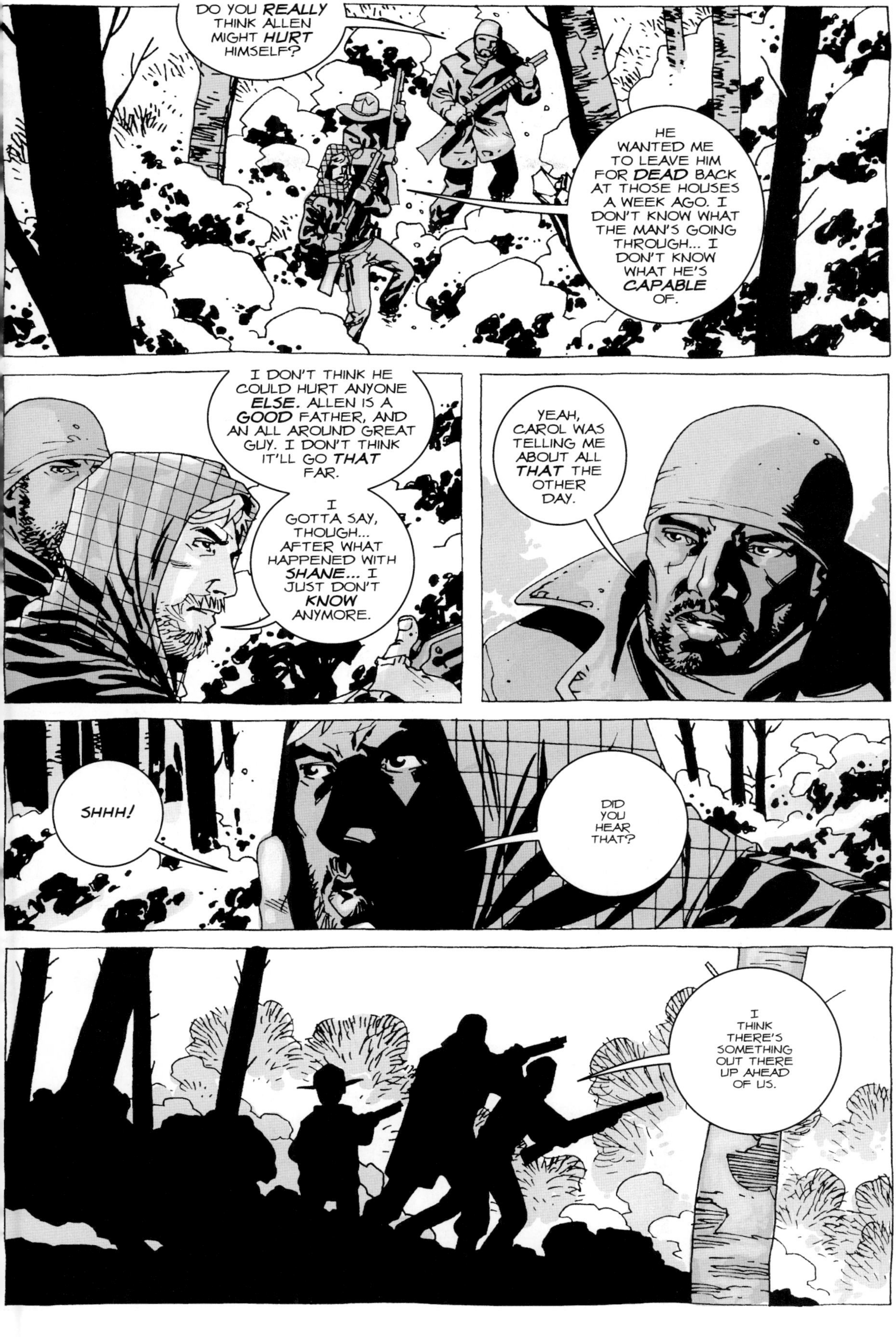
DO YOU REALLY THINK ALLEN MIGHT HURT HIMSELF?
HE WANTED ME TO LEAVE HIM FOR DEAD BACK AT THOSE HOUSES A WEEK AGO. I DON'T KNOW WHAT THE MAN'S GOING THROUGH... I DON'T KNOW WHAT HE'S CAPABLE OF.
I DON'T THINK HE COULD HURT ANYONE ELSE. ALLEN IS A GOOD FATHER, AND AN ALL AROUND GREAT GUY. I DON'T THINK IT'LL GO THAT FAR.
I GOTTA SAY, THOUGH... AFTER WHAT HAPPENED WITH SHANE... I JUST DON'T KNOW ANYMORE.
YEAH, CAROL WAS TELLING ME ABOUT ALL THAT THE OTHER DAY.
SHHH!
DID YOU HEAR THAT?
I THINK THERE'S SOMETHING OUT THERE UP AHEAD OF US.

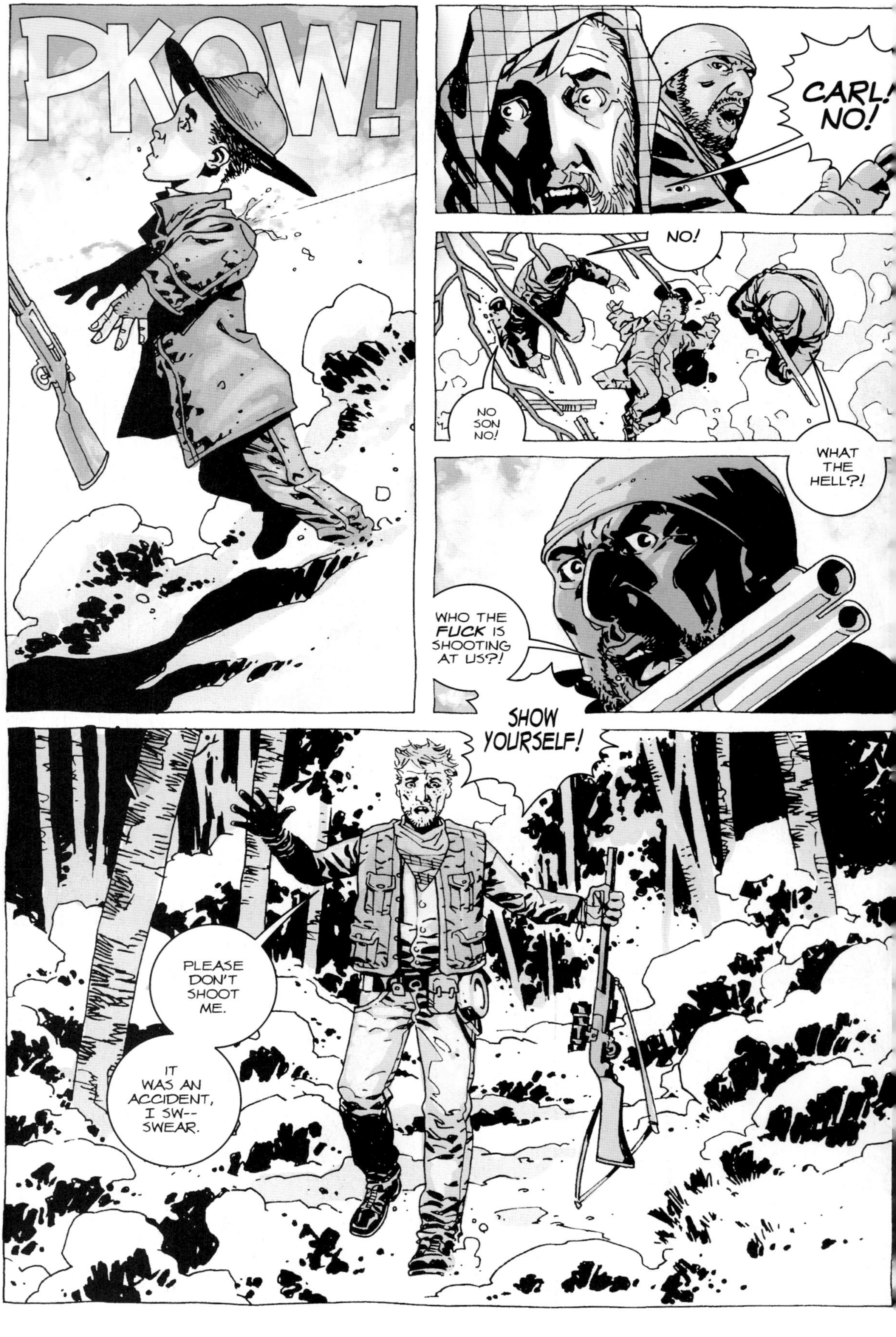
PKOW!
CARL! NO!
NO!
NO SON NO!
WHAT THE HELL?!
WHO THE *FUCK* IS SHOOTING AT US?!
SHOW YOURSELF!
PLEASE DON'T SHOOT ME.
IT WAS AN ACCIDENT, I SW-- SWEAR.

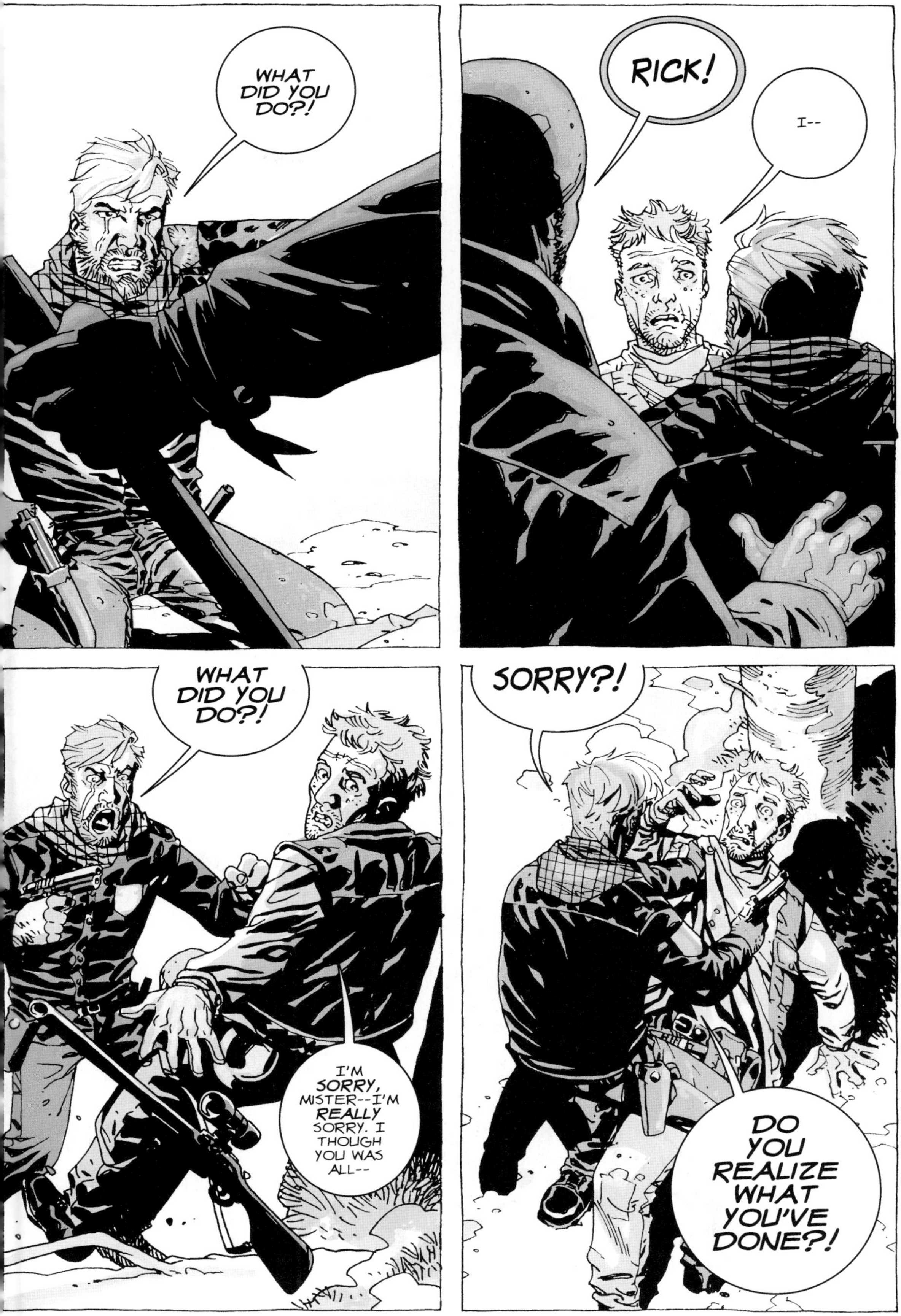
WHAT DID YOU DO?!
RICK!
I--
WHAT DID YOU DO?!
I'M SORRY, MISTER--I'M REALLY SORRY. I THOUGH YOU WAS ALL--
SORRY?!
DO YOU REALIZE WHAT YOU'VE DONE?!

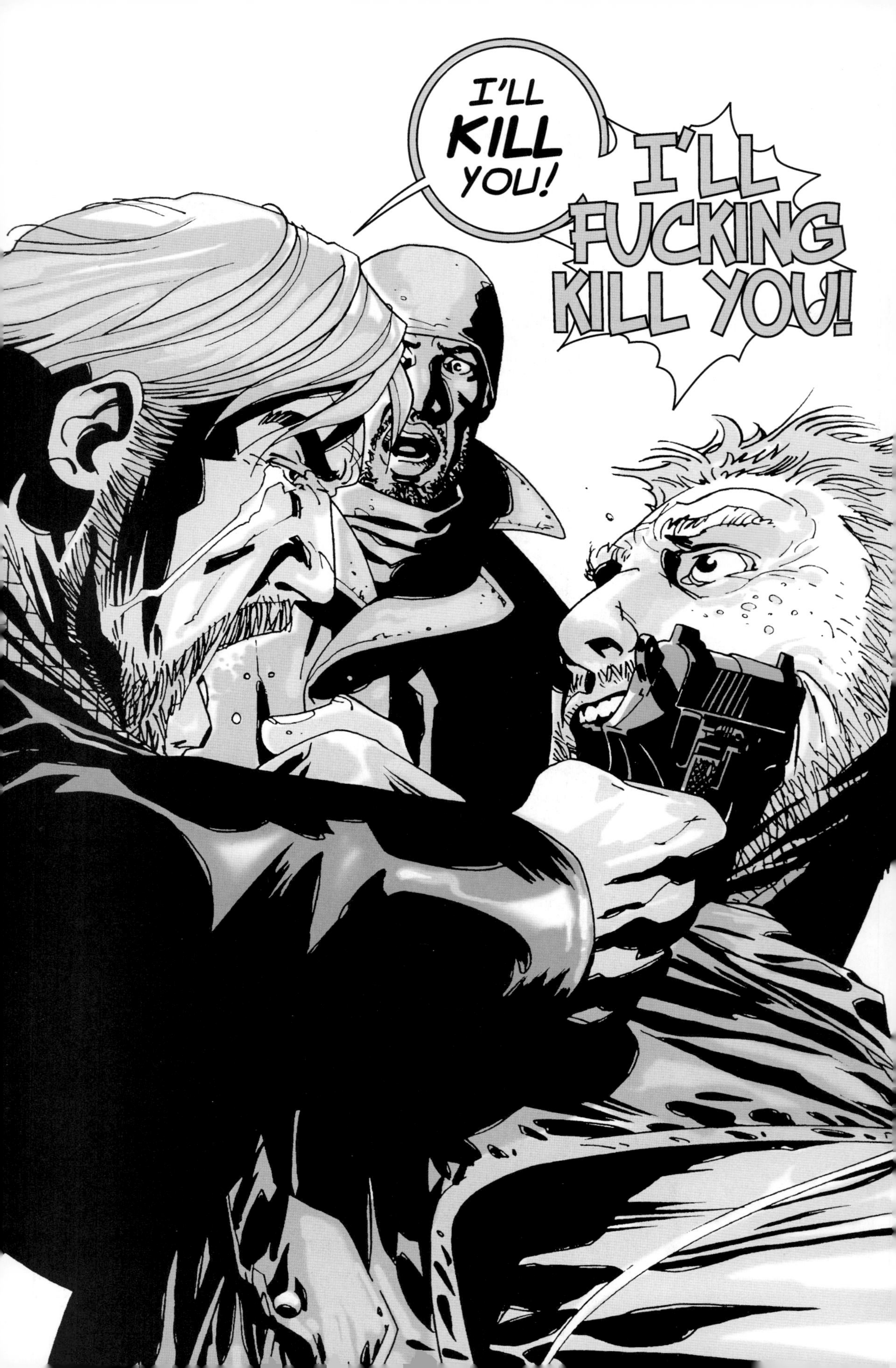
I'LL KILL YOU!
I'LL FUCKING KILL YOU!

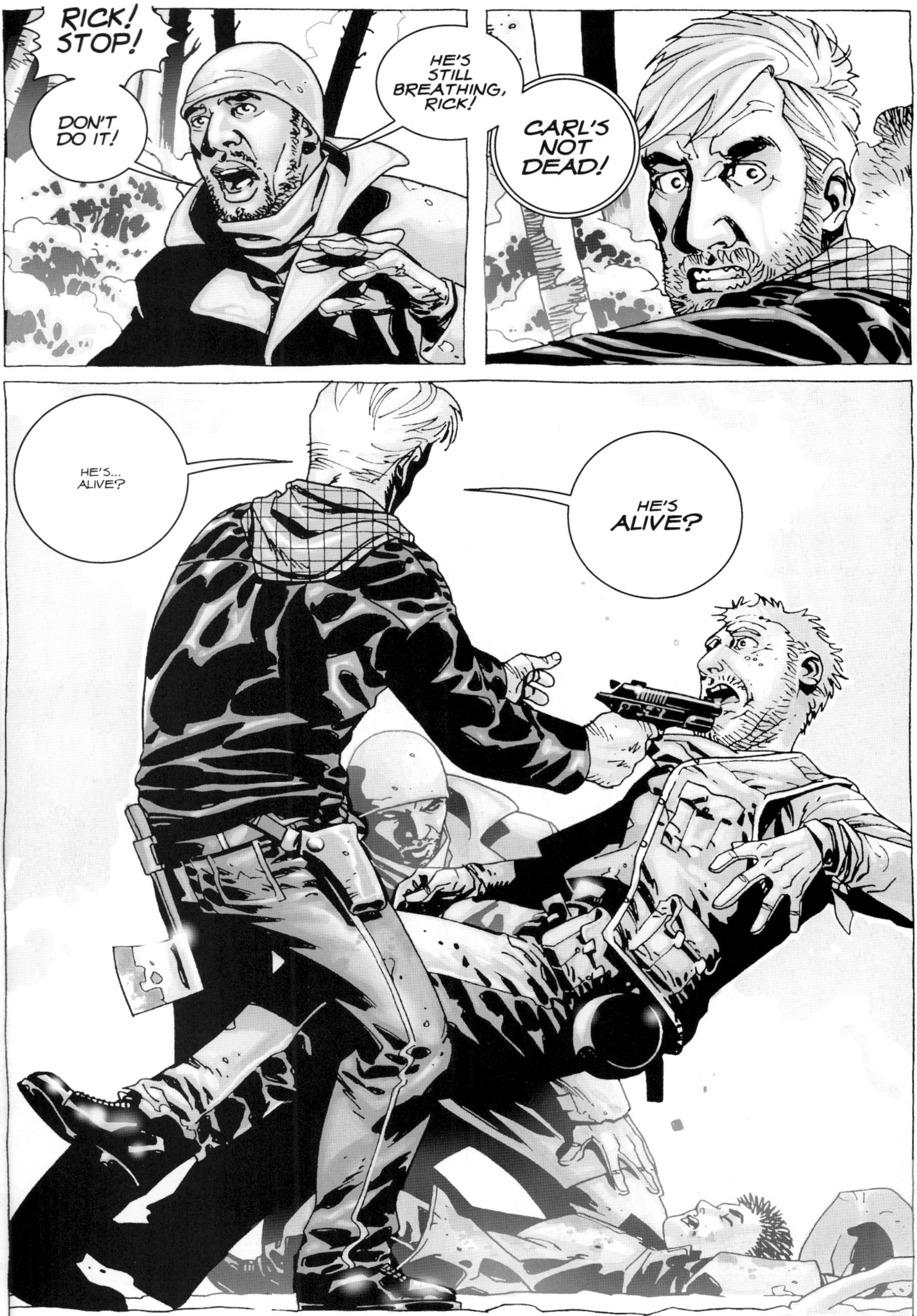
RICK! STOP!
DON'T DO IT!
HE'S STILL BREATHING, RICK!
CARL'S NOT DEAD!
HE'S... ALIVE?
HE'S ALIVE?

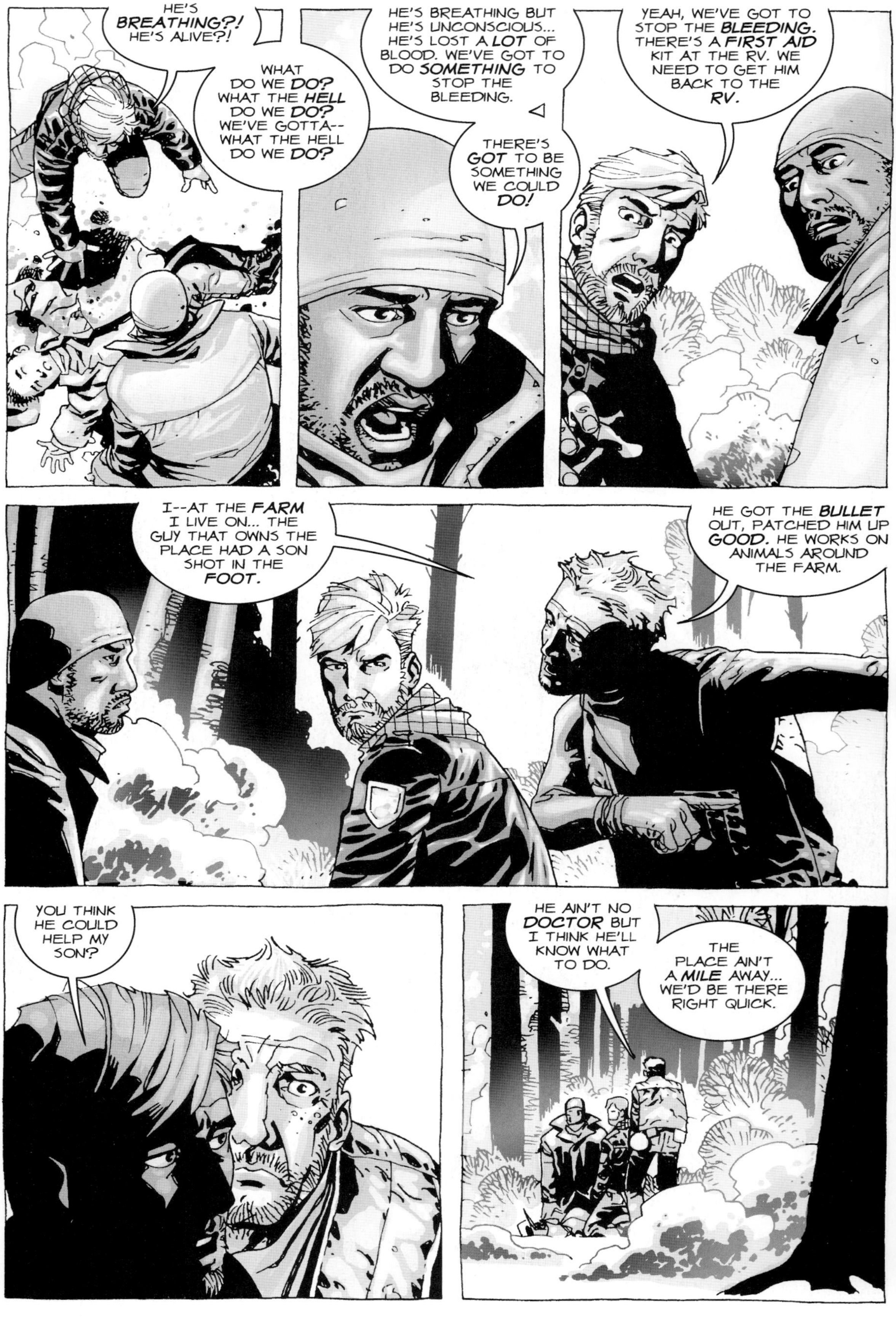
HE'S BREATHING?! HE'S ALIVE?!
WHAT DO WE DO? WHAT THE HELL DO WE DO? WE'VE GOTTA-- WHAT THE HELL DO WE DO?
HE'S BREATHING BUT HE'S UNCONSCIOUS... HE'S LOST A LOT OF BLOOD. WE'VE GOT TO DO SOMETHING TO STOP THE BLEEDING.
THERE'S GOT TO BE SOMETHING WE COULD DO!
YEAH, WE'VE GOT TO STOP THE BLEEDING. THERE'S A FIRST AID KIT AT THE RV. WE NEED TO GET HIM BACK TO THE RV.
I--AT THE FARM I LIVE ON... THE GUY THAT OWNS THE PLACE HAD A SON SHOT IN THE FOOT.
HE GOT THE BULLET OUT, PATCHED HIM UP GOOD. HE WORKS ON ANIMALS AROUND THE FARM.
YOU THINK HE COULD HELP MY SON?
HE AIN'T NO DOCTOR BUT I THINK HE'LL KNOW WHAT TO DO.
THE PLACE AIN'T A MILE AWAY... WE'D BE THERE RIGHT QUICK.

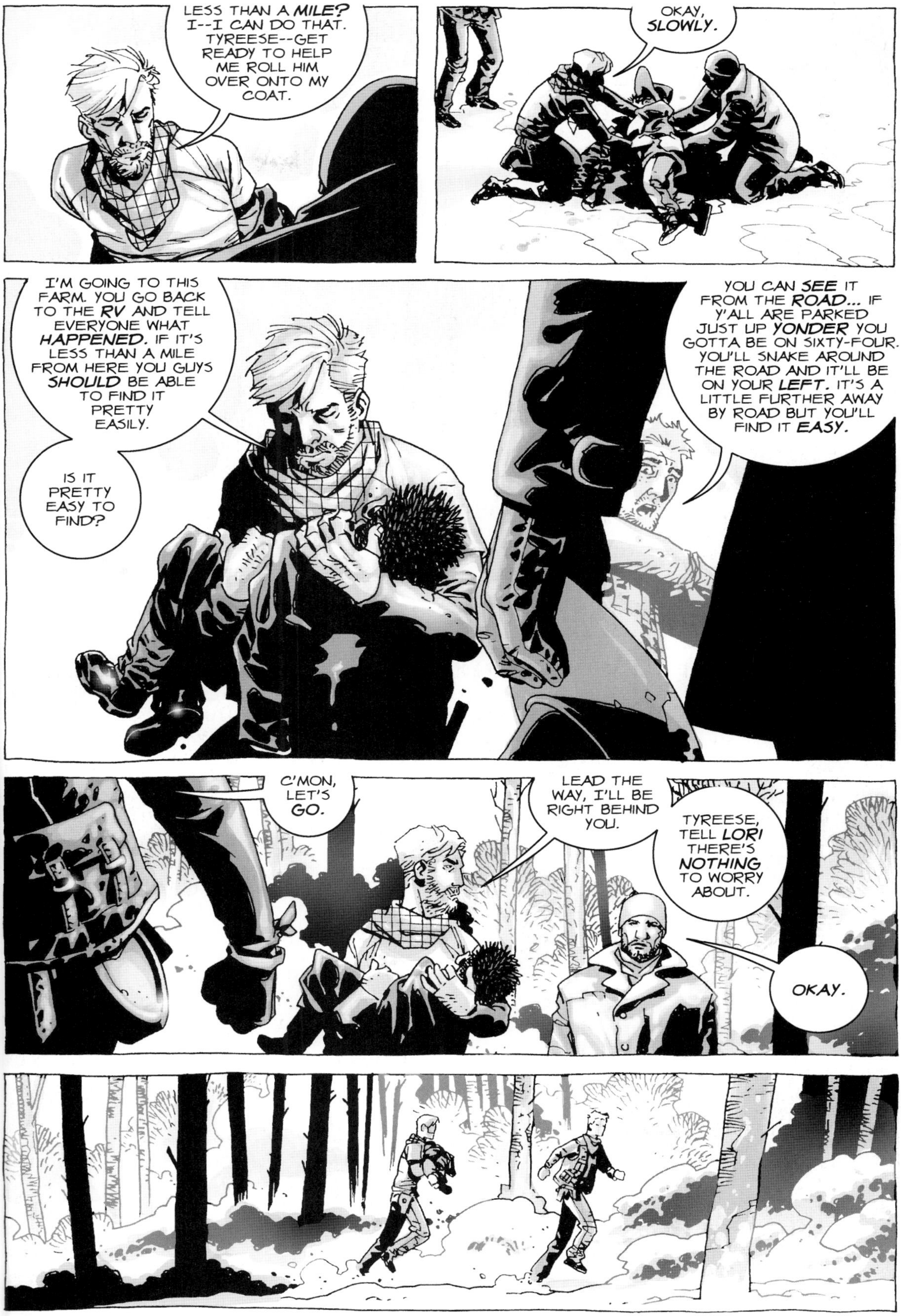
LESS THAN A MILE? I--I CAN DO THAT. TYREESE--GET READY TO HELP ME ROLL HIM OVER ONTO MY COAT.
OKAY, SLOWLY.
I'M GOING TO THIS FARM. YOU GO BACK TO THE RV AND TELL EVERYONE WHAT HAPPENED. IF IT'S LESS THAN A MILE FROM HERE YOU GUYS SHOULD BE ABLE TO FIND IT PRETTY EASILY.
IS IT PRETTY EASY TO FIND?
YOU CAN SEE IT FROM THE ROAD... IF Y'ALL ARE PARKED JUST UP YONDER YOU GOTTA BE ON SIXTY-FOUR. YOU'LL SNAKE AROUND THE ROAD AND IT'LL BE ON YOUR LEFT. IT'S A LITTLE FURTHER AWAY BY ROAD BUT YOU'LL FIND IT EASY.
C'MON, LET'S GO.
LEAD THE WAY, I'LL BE RIGHT BEHIND YOU.
TYREESE, TELL LORI THERE'S NOTHING TO WORRY ABOUT.
OKAY.

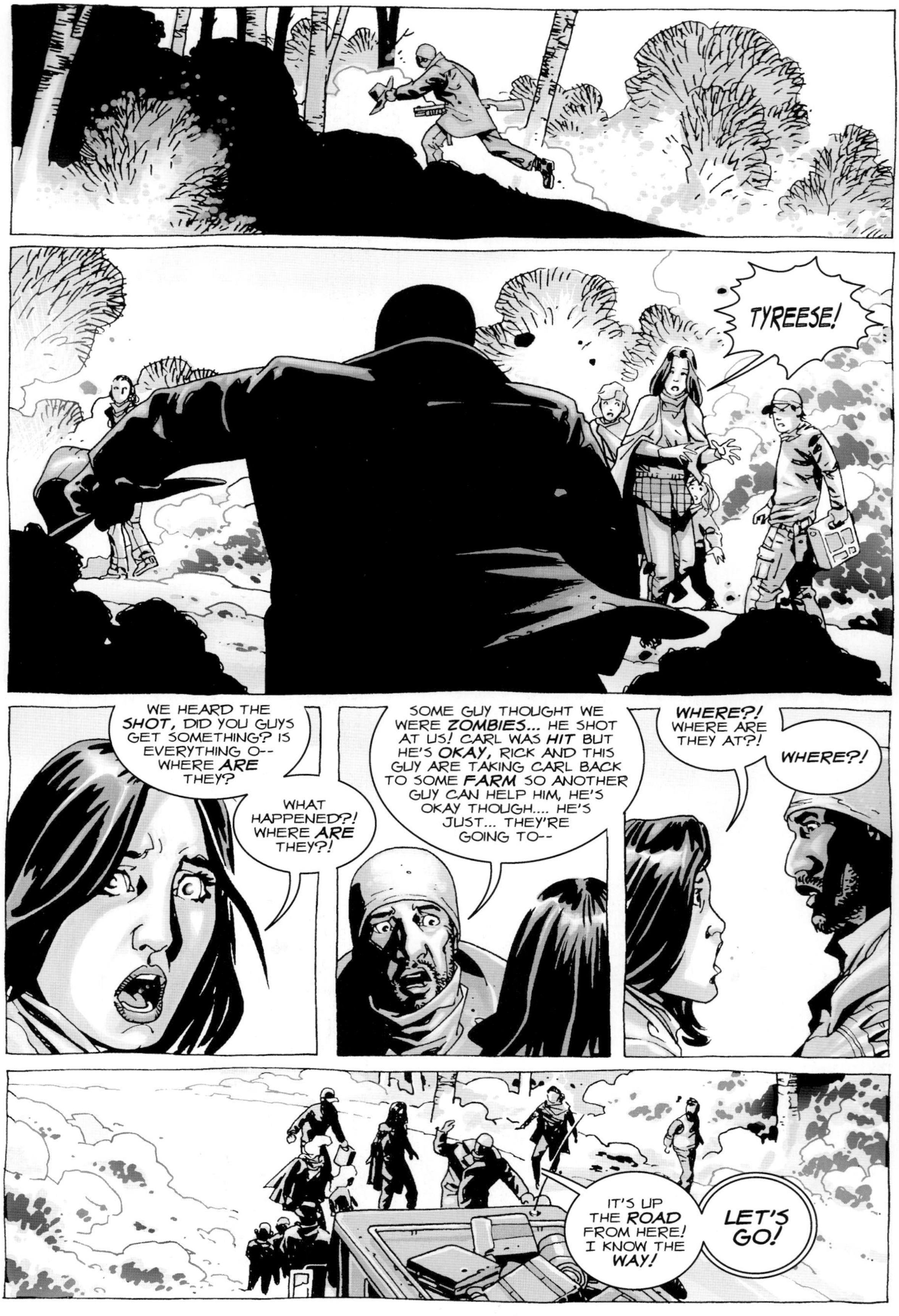
TYREESE!
WE HEARD THE SHOT, DID YOU GUYS GET SOMETHING? IS EVERYTHING O-- WHERE ARE THEY?
WHAT HAPPENED?! WHERE ARE THEY?!
SOME GUY THOUGHT WE WERE ZOMBIES... HE SHOT AT US! CARL WAS HIT BUT HE'S OKAY, RICK AND THIS GUY ARE TAKING CARL BACK TO SOME FARM SO ANOTHER GUY CAN HELP HIM, HE'S OKAY THOUGH.... HE'S JUST... THEY'RE GOING TO--
WHERE?! WHERE ARE THEY AT?!
WHERE?!
IT'S UP THE ROAD FROM HERE! I KNOW THE WAY!
LET'S GO!

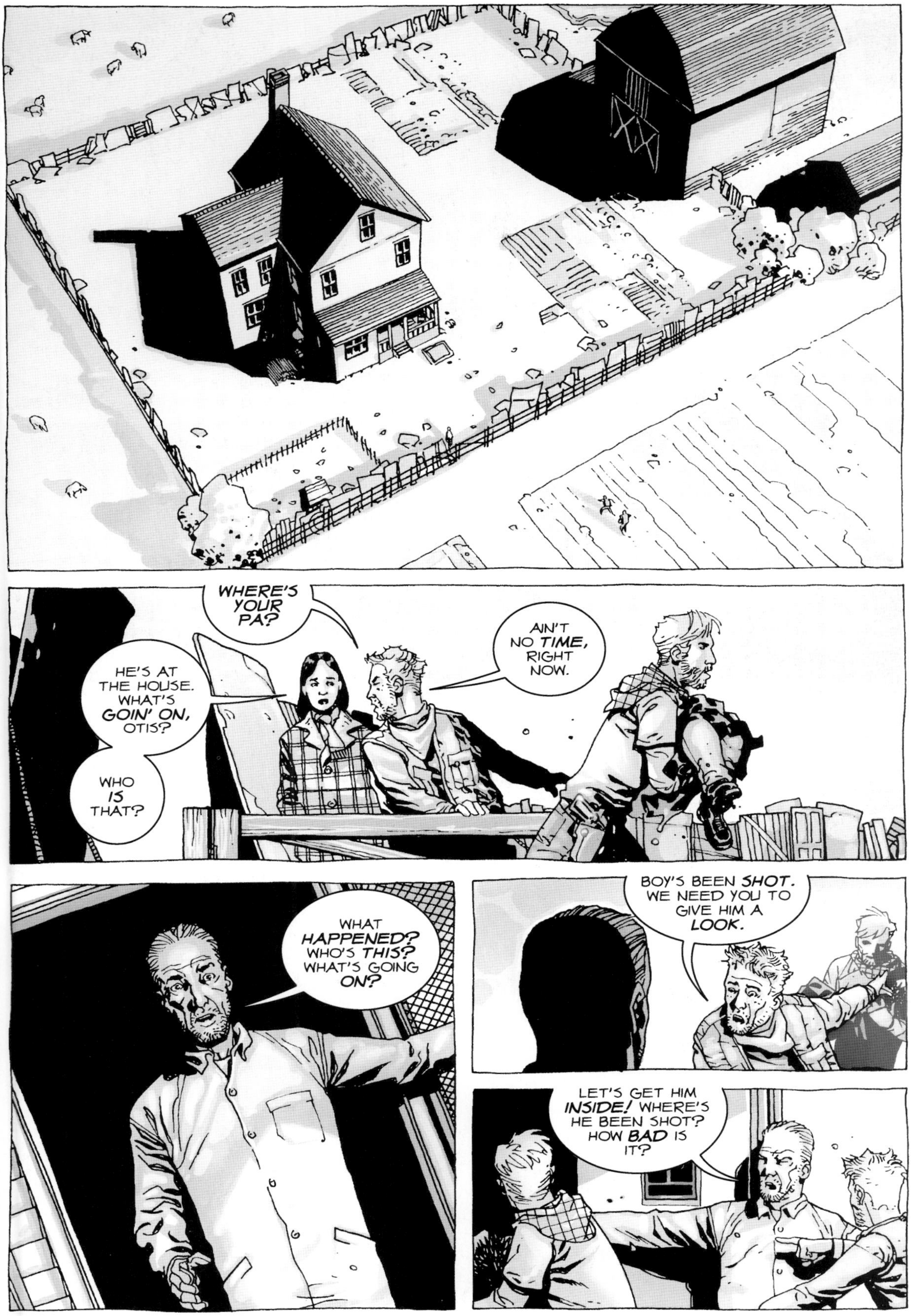
WHERE'S YOUR PA?
HE'S AT THE HOUSE. WHAT'S GOIN' ON, OTIS?
WHO IS THAT?
AIN'T NO TIME, RIGHT NOW.
WHAT HAPPENED? WHO'S THIS? WHAT'S GOING ON?
BOY'S BEEN SHOT. WE NEED YOU TO GIVE HIM A LOOK.
LET'S GET HIM INSIDE! WHERE'S HE BEEN SHOT? HOW BAD IS IT?

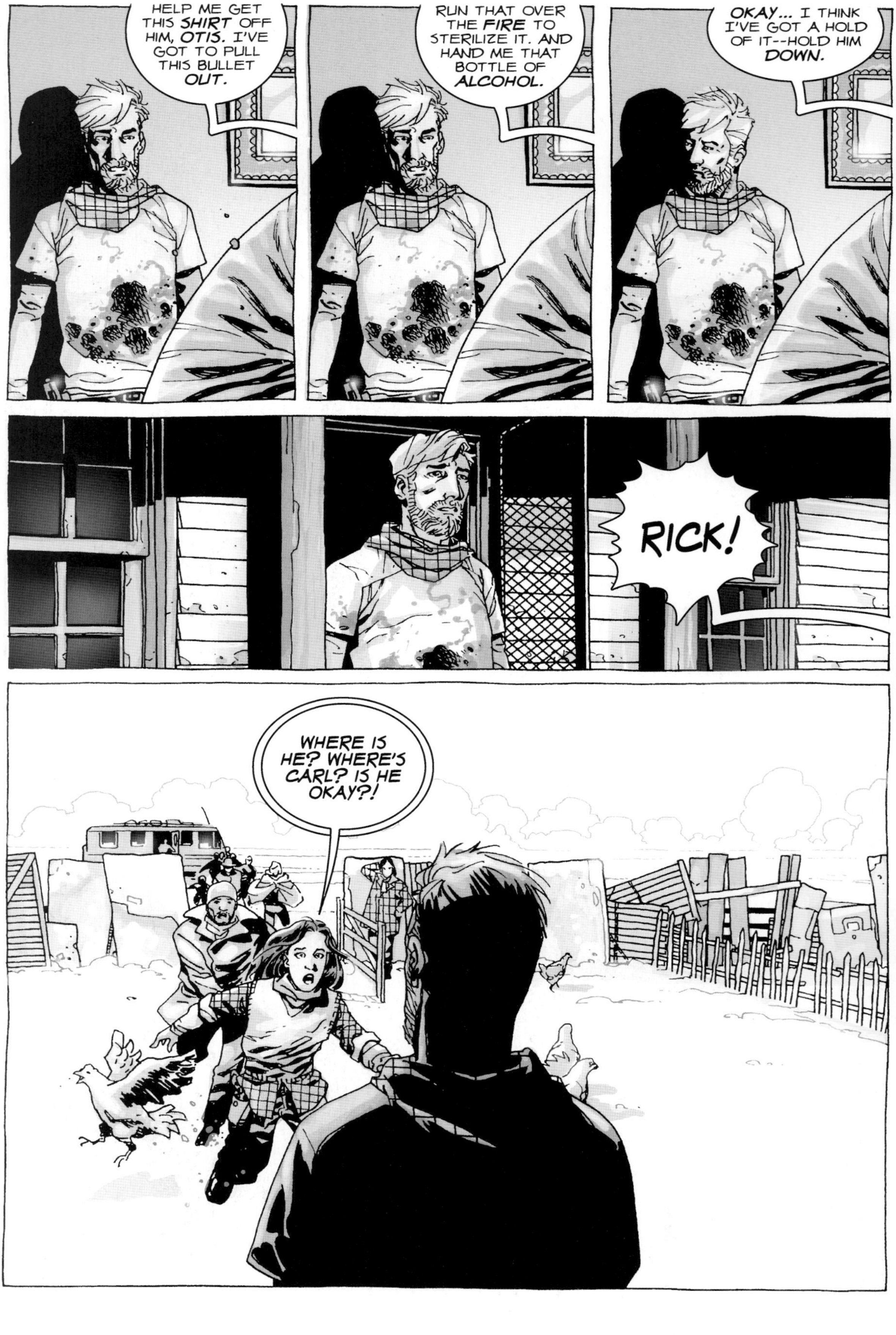
HELP ME GET THIS SHIRT OFF HIM, OTIS. I'VE GOT TO PULL THIS BULLET OUT.
RUN THAT OVER THE FIRE TO STERILIZE IT. AND HAND ME THAT BOTTLE OF ALCOHOL.
OKAY... I THINK I'VE GOT A HOLD OF IT--HOLD HIM DOWN.
RICK!
WHERE IS HE? WHERE'S CARL? IS HE OKAY?!

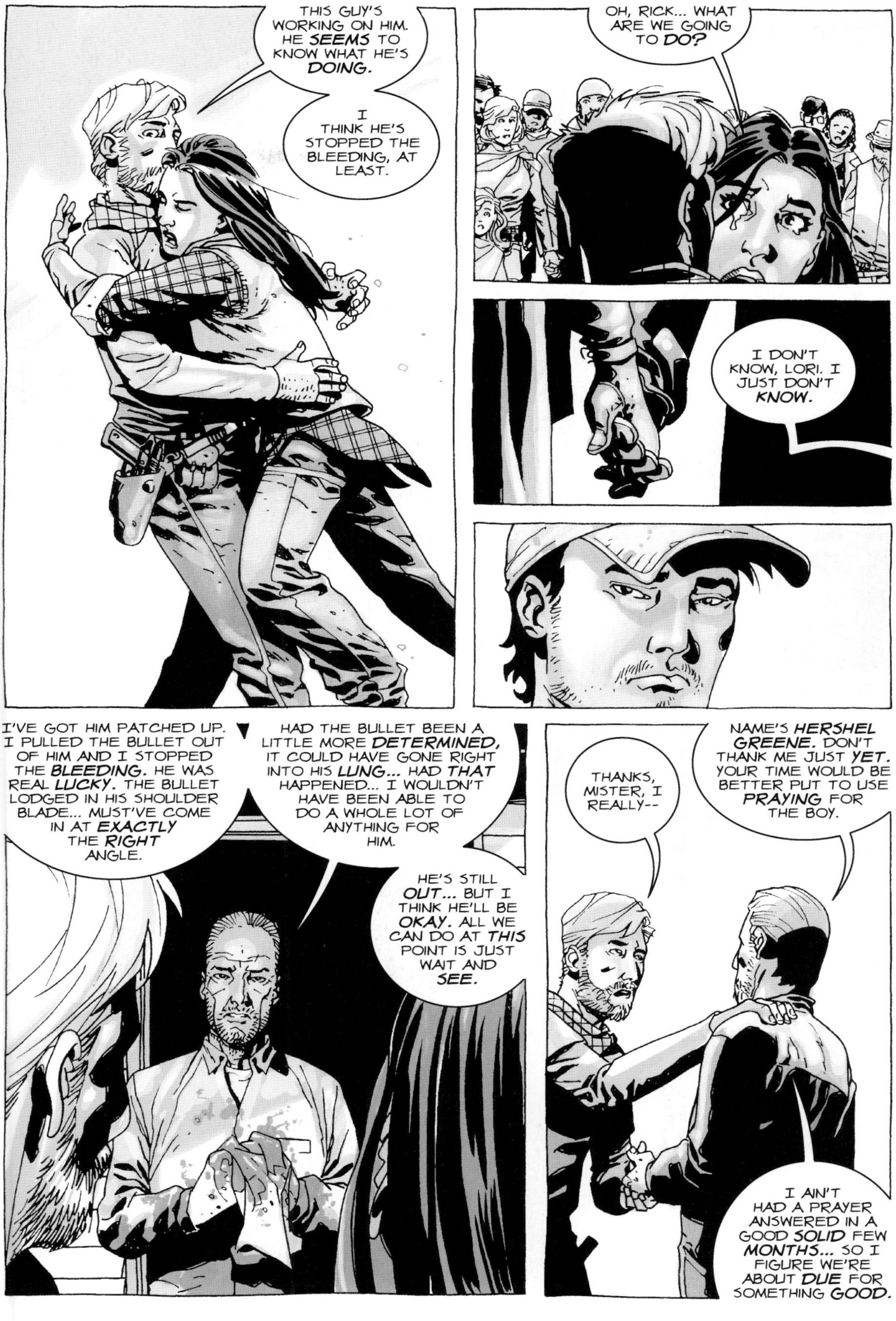
THIS GUY'S WORKING ON HIM. HE SEEMS TO KNOW WHAT HE'S DOING.
I THINK HE'S STOPPED THE BLEEDING, AT LEAST.
OH, RICK... WHAT ARE WE GOING TO DO?
I DON'T KNOW, LORI. I JUST DON'T KNOW.
I'VE GOT HIM PATCHED UP. I PULLED THE BULLET OUT OF HIM AND I STOPPED THE BLEEDING. HE WAS REAL LUCKY. THE BULLET LODGED IN HIS SHOULDER BLADE... MUST'VE COME IN AT EXACTLY THE RIGHT ANGLE.
HAD THE BULLET BEEN A LITTLE MORE DETERMINED, IT COULD HAVE GONE RIGHT INTO HIS LUNG... HAD THAT HAPPENED... I WOULDN'T HAVE BEEN ABLE TO DO A WHOLE LOT OF ANYTHING FOR HIM.
HE'S STILL OUT... BUT I THINK HE'LL BE OKAY. ALL WE CAN DO AT THIS POINT IS JUST WAIT AND SEE.
THANKS, MISTER, I REALLY--
NAME'S HERSHEL GREENE. DON'T THANK ME JUST YET. YOUR TIME WOULD BE BETTER PUT TO USE PRAYING FOR THE BOY.
I AIN'T HAD A PRAYER ANSWERED IN A GOOD SOLID FEW MONTHS... SO I FIGURE WE'RE ABOUT DUE FOR SOMETHING GOOD.

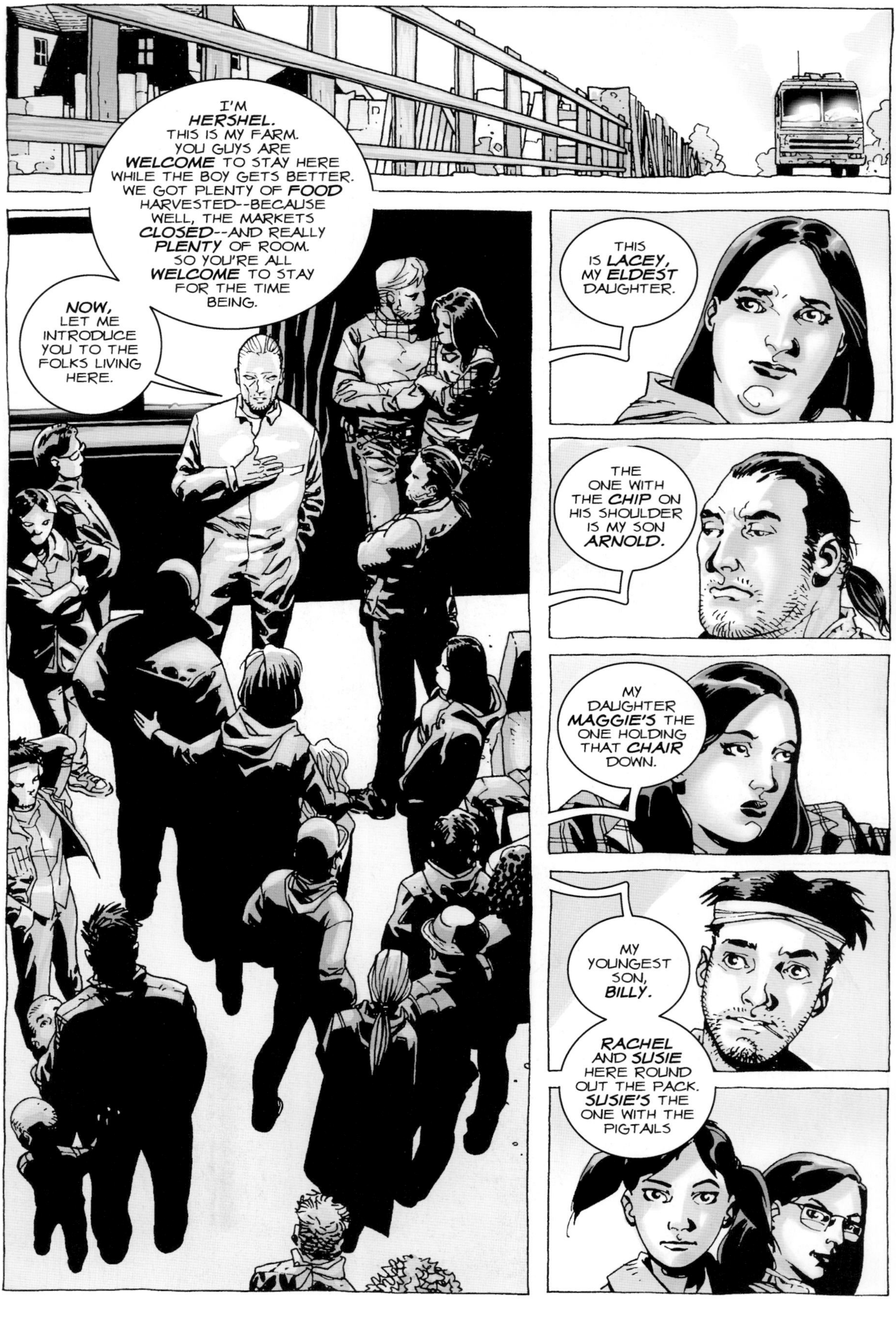
I'M HERSHEL. THIS IS MY FARM. YOU GUYS ARE WELCOME TO STAY HERE WHILE THE BOY GETS BETTER. WE GOT PLENTY OF FOOD HARVESTED--BECAUSE WELL, THE MARKETS CLOSED--AND REALLY PLENTY OF ROOM. SO YOU'RE ALL WELCOME TO STAY FOR THE TIME BEING.
NOW, LET ME INTRODUCE YOU TO THE FOLKS LIVING HERE.
THIS IS LACEY, MY ELDEST DAUGHTER.
THE ONE WITH THE CHIP ON HIS SHOULDER IS MY SON ARNOLD.
MY DAUGHTER MAGGIE'S THE ONE HOLDING THAT CHAIR DOWN.
MY YOUNGEST SON, BILLY.
RACHEL AND SUSIE HERE ROUND OUT THE PACK. SUSIE'S THE ONE WITH THE PIGTAILS

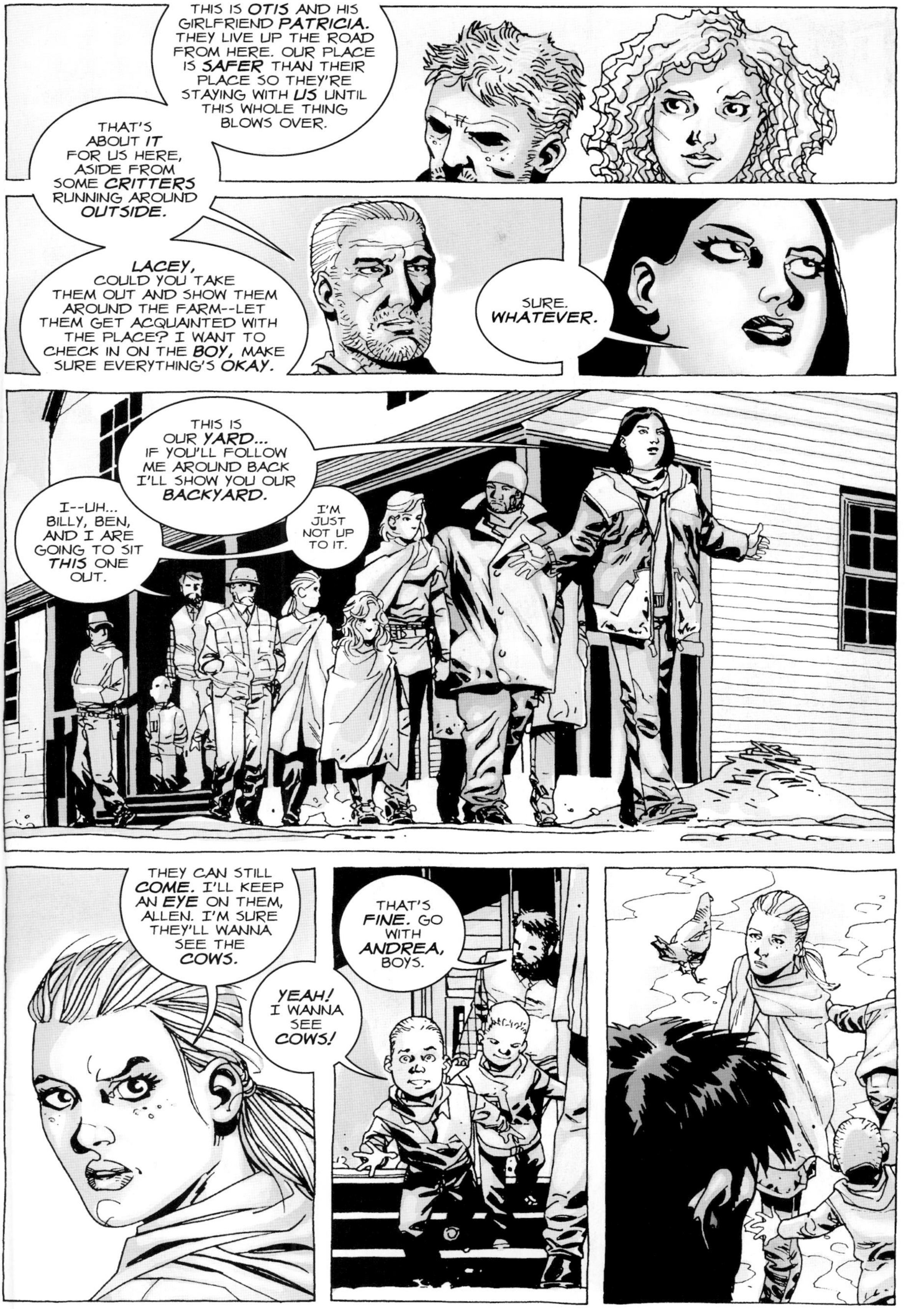
THIS IS OTIS AND HIS GIRLFRIEND PATRICIA. THEY LIVE UP THE ROAD FROM HERE. OUR PLACE IS SAFER THAN THEIR PLACE SO THEY'RE STAYING WITH US UNTIL THIS WHOLE THING BLOWS OVER.
THAT'S ABOUT IT FOR US HERE, ASIDE FROM SOME CRITTERS RUNNING AROUND OUTSIDE.
LACEY, COULD YOU TAKE THEM OUT AND SHOW THEM AROUND THE FARM--LET THEM GET ACQUAINTED WITH THE PLACE? I WANT TO CHECK IN ON THE BOY, MAKE SURE EVERYTHING'S OKAY.
SURE. WHATEVER.
THIS IS OUR YARD... IF YOU'LL FOLLOW ME AROUND BACK I'LL SHOW YOU OUR BACKYARD.
I--UH... BILLY, BEN, AND I ARE GOING TO SIT THIS ONE OUT.
I'M JUST NOT UP TO IT.
THEY CAN STILL COME. I'LL KEEP AN EYE ON THEM, ALLEN. I'M SURE THEY'LL WANNA SEE THE COWS.
THAT'S FINE. GO WITH ANDREA, BOYS.
YEAH! I WANNA SEE COWS!

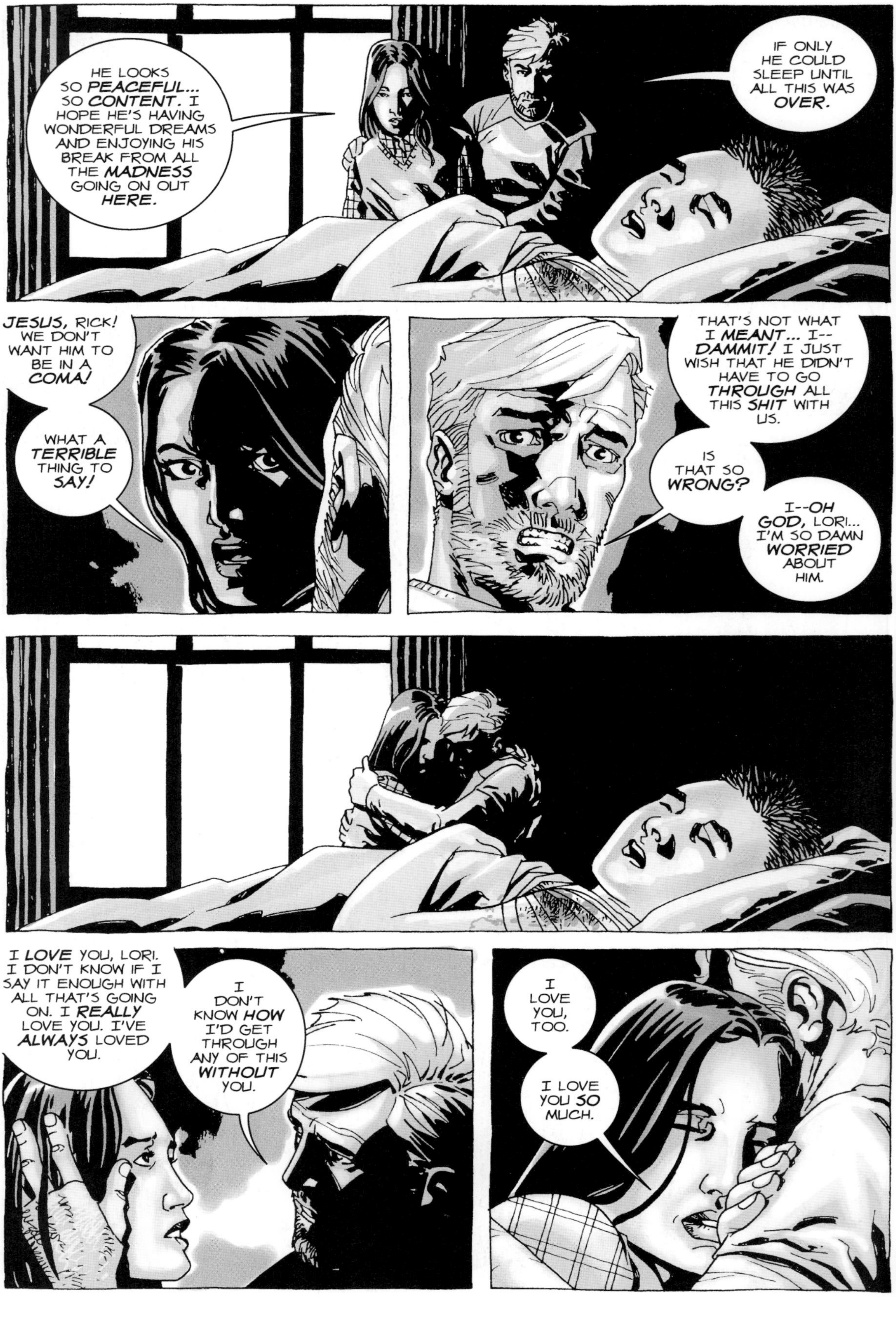

HE LOOKS SO PEACEFUL... SO CONTENT. I HOPE HE'S HAVING WONDERFUL DREAMS AND ENJOYING HIS BREAK FROM ALL THE MADNESS GOING ON OUT HERE.
IF ONLY HE COULD SLEEP UNTIL ALL THIS WAS OVER.
JESUS, RICK! WE DON'T WANT HIM TO BE IN A COMA!
WHAT A TERRIBLE THING TO SAY!
THAT'S NOT WHAT I MEANT... I--DAMMIT! I JUST WISH THAT HE DIDN'T HAVE TO GO THROUGH ALL THIS SHIT WITH US.
IS THAT SO WRONG?
I--OH GOD, LORI... I'M SO DAMN WORRIED ABOUT HIM.
I LOVE YOU, LORI. I DON'T KNOW IF I SAY IT ENOUGH WITH ALL THAT'S GOING ON. I REALLY LOVE YOU. I'VE ALWAYS LOVED YOU.
I DON'T KNOW HOW I'D GET THROUGH ANY OF THIS WITHOUT YOU.
I LOVE YOU, TOO.
I LOVE YOU SO MUCH.

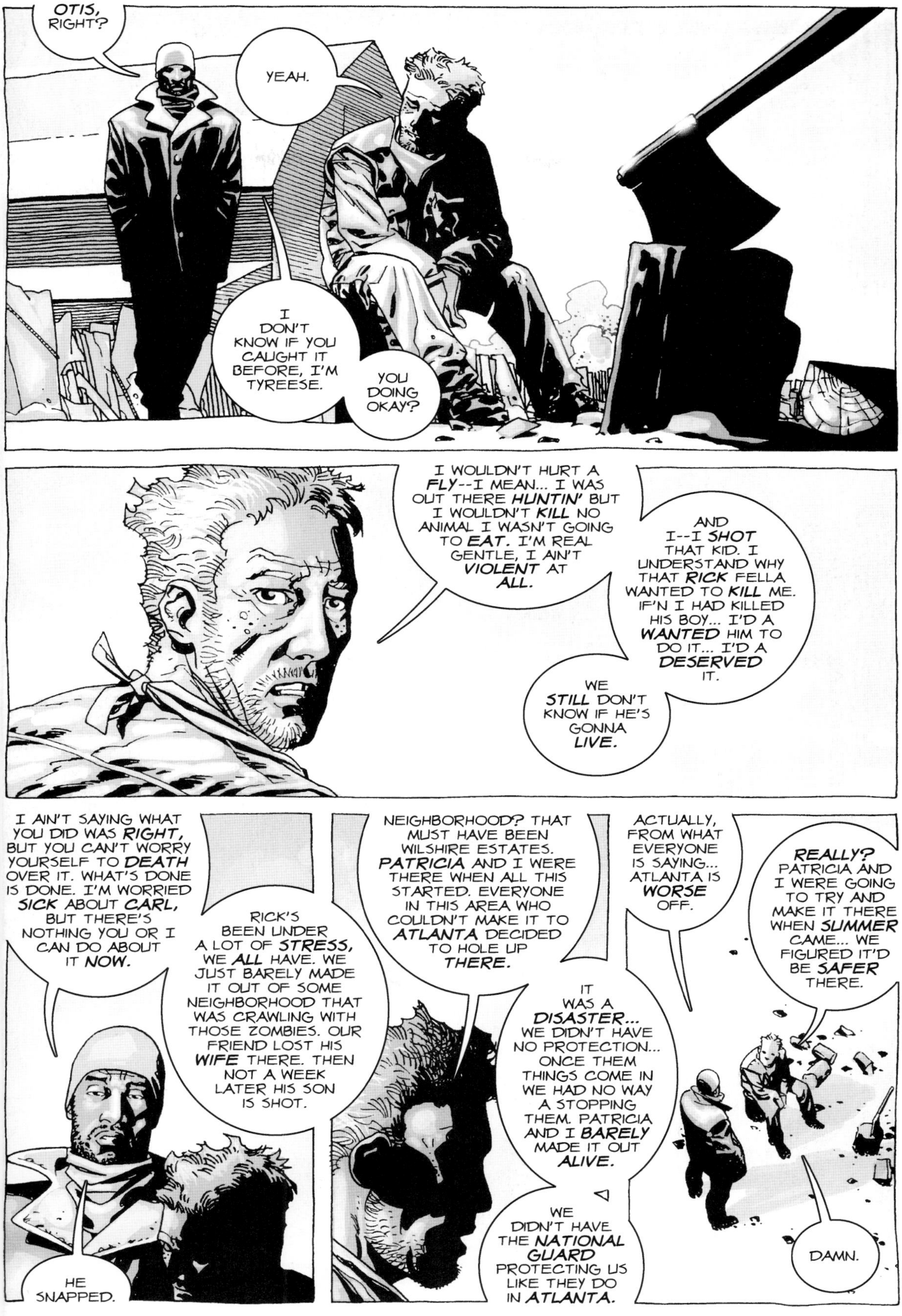
OTIS, RIGHT?
YEAH.
I DON'T KNOW IF YOU CAUGHT IT BEFORE, I'M TYREESE.
YOU DOING OKAY?
I WOULDN'T HURT A FLY--I MEAN... I WAS OUT THERE HUNTIN' BUT I WOULDN'T KILL NO ANIMAL I WASN'T GOING TO EAT. I'M REAL GENTLE, I AIN'T VIOLENT AT ALL.
AND I--I SHOT THAT KID. I UNDERSTAND WHY THAT RICK FELLA WANTED TO KILL ME. IF'N I HAD KILLED HIS BOY... I'D A WANTED HIM TO DO IT... I'D A DESERVED IT.
WE STILL DON'T KNOW IF HE'S GONNA LIVE.
I AIN'T SAYING WHAT YOU DID WAS RIGHT, BUT YOU CAN'T WORRY YOURSELF TO DEATH OVER IT. WHAT'S DONE IS DONE. I'M WORRIED SICK ABOUT CARL, BUT THERE'S NOTHING YOU OR I CAN DO ABOUT IT NOW.
RICK'S BEEN UNDER A LOT OF STRESS, WE ALL HAVE. WE JUST BARELY MADE IT OUT OF SOME NEIGHBORHOOD THAT WAS CRAWLING WITH THOSE ZOMBIES. OUR FRIEND LOST HIS WIFE THERE. THEN NOT A WEEK LATER HIS SON IS SHOT.
HE SNAPPED.
NEIGHBORHOOD? THAT MUST HAVE BEEN WILSHIRE ESTATES. PATRICIA AND I WERE THERE WHEN ALL THIS STARTED. EVERYONE IN THIS AREA WHO COULDN'T MAKE IT TO ATLANTA DECIDED TO HOLE UP THERE.
IT WAS A DISASTER... WE DIDN'T HAVE NO PROTECTION... ONCE THEM THINGS COME IN WE HAD NO WAY A STOPPING THEM. PATRICIA AND I BARELY MADE IT OUT ALIVE.
WE DIDN'T HAVE THE NATIONAL GUARD PROTECTING US LIKE THEY DO IN ATLANTA.
ACTUALLY, FROM WHAT EVERYONE IS SAYING... ATLANTA IS WORSE OFF.
REALLY? PATRICIA AND I WERE GOING TO TRY AND MAKE IT THERE WHEN SUMMER CAME... WE FIGURED IT'D BE SAFER THERE.
DAMN.

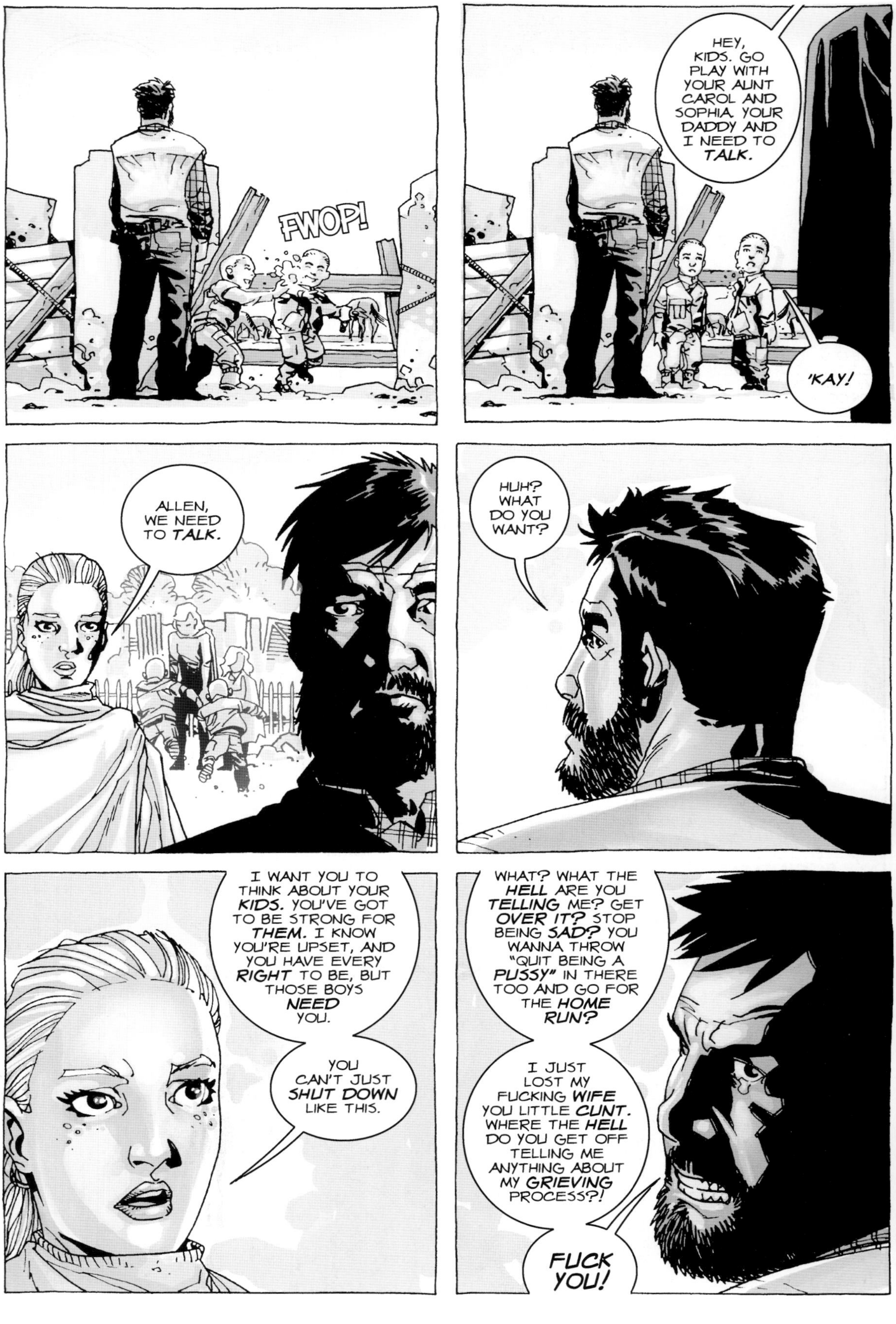
FWOP!
HEY, KIDS. GO PLAY WITH YOUR AUNT CAROL AND SOPHIA. YOUR DADDY AND I NEED TO TALK.
'KAY!
ALLEN, WE NEED TO TALK.
HUH? WHAT DO YOU WANT?
I WANT YOU TO THINK ABOUT YOUR KIDS. YOU'VE GOT TO BE STRONG FOR THEM. I KNOW YOU'RE UPSET, AND YOU HAVE EVERY RIGHT TO BE, BUT THOSE BOYS NEED YOU.
YOU CAN'T JUST SHUT DOWN LIKE THIS.
WHAT? WHAT THE HELL ARE YOU TELLING ME? GET OVER IT? STOP BEING SAD? YOU WANNA THROW "QUIT BEING A PUSSY" IN THERE TOO AND GO FOR THE HOME RUN?
I JUST LOST MY FUCKING WIFE YOU LITTLE CUNT. WHERE THE HELL DO YOU GET OFF TELLING ME ANYTHING ABOUT MY GRIEVING PROCESS?!
FUCK YOU!

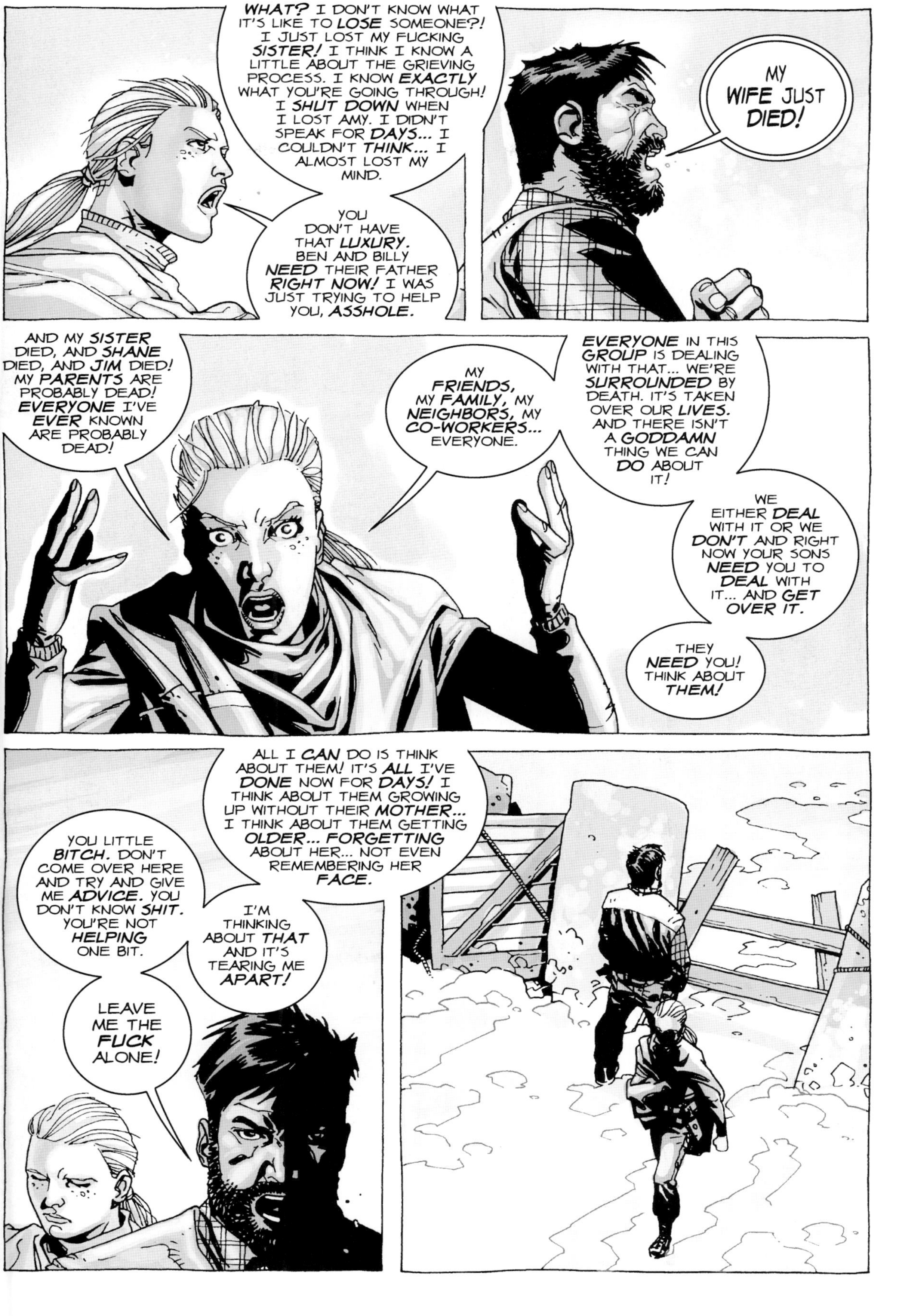
WHAT? I DON'T KNOW WHAT IT'S LIKE TO LOSE SOMEONE?! I JUST LOST MY FUCKING SISTER! I THINK I KNOW A LITTLE ABOUT THE GRIEVING PROCESS. I KNOW EXACTLY WHAT YOU'RE GOING THROUGH! I SHUT DOWN WHEN I LOST AMY. I DIDN'T SPEAK FOR DAYS... I COULDN'T THINK... I ALMOST LOST MY MIND.
YOU DON'T HAVE THAT LUXURY. BEN AND BILLY NEED THEIR FATHER RIGHT NOW! I WAS JUST TRYING TO HELP YOU, ASSHOLE.
MY WIFE JUST DIED!
AND MY SISTER DIED, AND SHANE DIED, AND JIM DIED! MY PARENTS ARE PROBABLY DEAD! EVERYONE I'VE EVER KNOWN ARE PROBABLY DEAD!
MY FRIENDS, MY FAMILY, MY NEIGHBORS, MY CO-WORKERS... EVERYONE.
EVERYONE IN THIS GROUP IS DEALING WITH THAT... WE'RE SURROUNDED BY DEATH. IT'S TAKEN OVER OUR LIVES. AND THERE ISN'T A GODDAMN THING WE CAN DO ABOUT IT!
WE EITHER DEAL WITH IT OR WE DON'T AND RIGHT NOW YOUR SONS NEED YOU TO DEAL WITH IT... AND GET OVER IT.
THEY NEED YOU! THINK ABOUT THEM!
ALL I CAN DO IS THINK ABOUT THEM! IT'S ALL I'VE DONE NOW FOR DAYS! I THINK ABOUT THEM GROWING UP WITHOUT THEIR MOTHER... I THINK ABOUT THEM GETTING OLDER... FORGETTING ABOUT HER... NOT EVEN REMEMBERING HER FACE.
YOU LITTLE BITCH. DON'T COME OVER HERE AND TRY AND GIVE ME ADVICE. YOU DON'T KNOW SHIT. YOU'RE NOT HELPING ONE BIT.
I'M THINKING ABOUT THAT AND IT'S TEARING ME APART!
LEAVE ME THE FUCK ALONE!

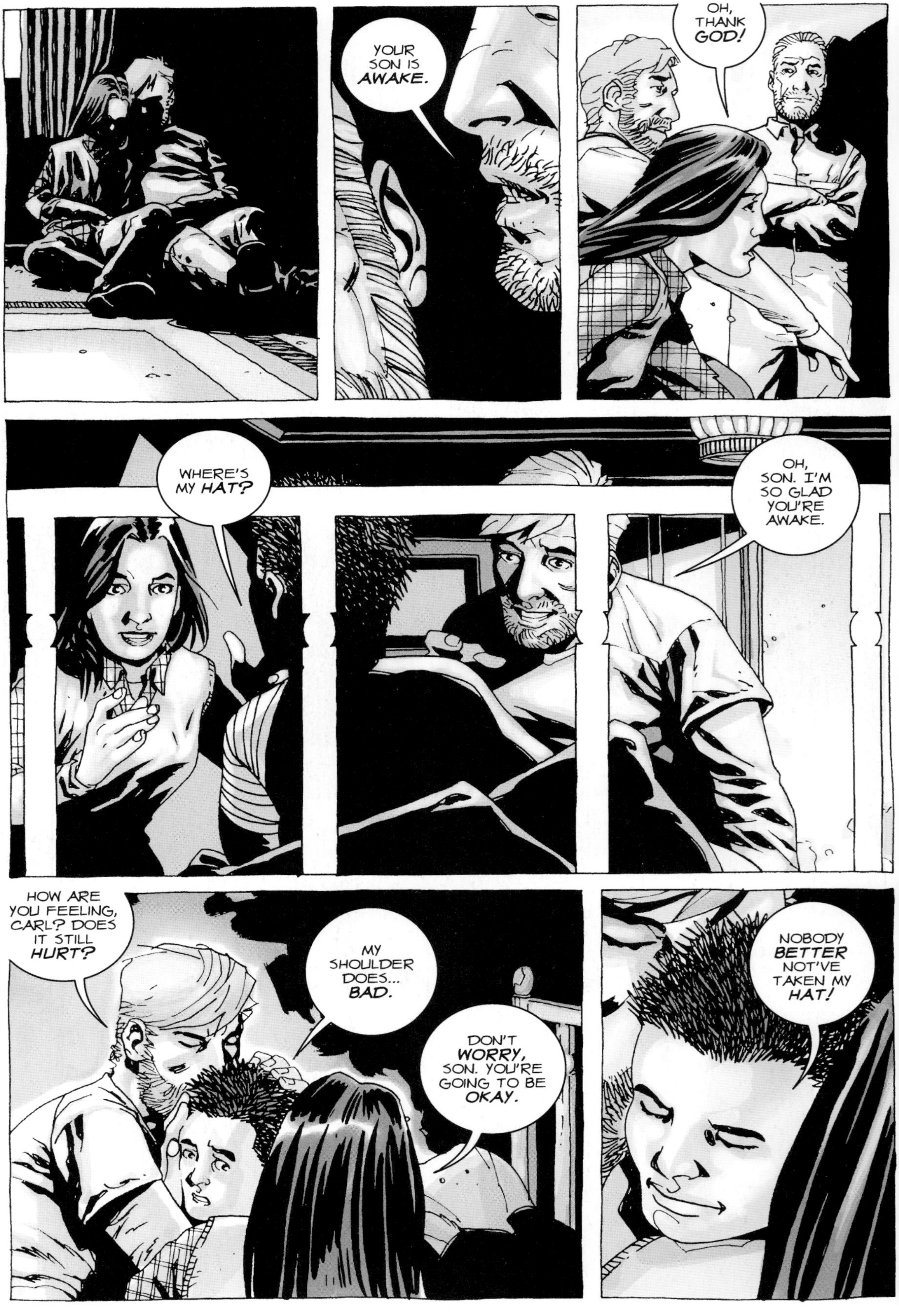

YOUR SON IS AWAKE.
OH, THANK GOD!
WHERE'S MY HAT?
OH, SON. I'M SO GLAD YOU'RE AWAKE.
HOW ARE YOU FEELING, CARL? DOES IT STILL HURT?
MY SHOULDER DOES... BAD.
DON'T WORRY, SON. YOU'RE GOING TO BE OKAY.
NOBODY BETTER NOT'VE TAKEN MY HAT!

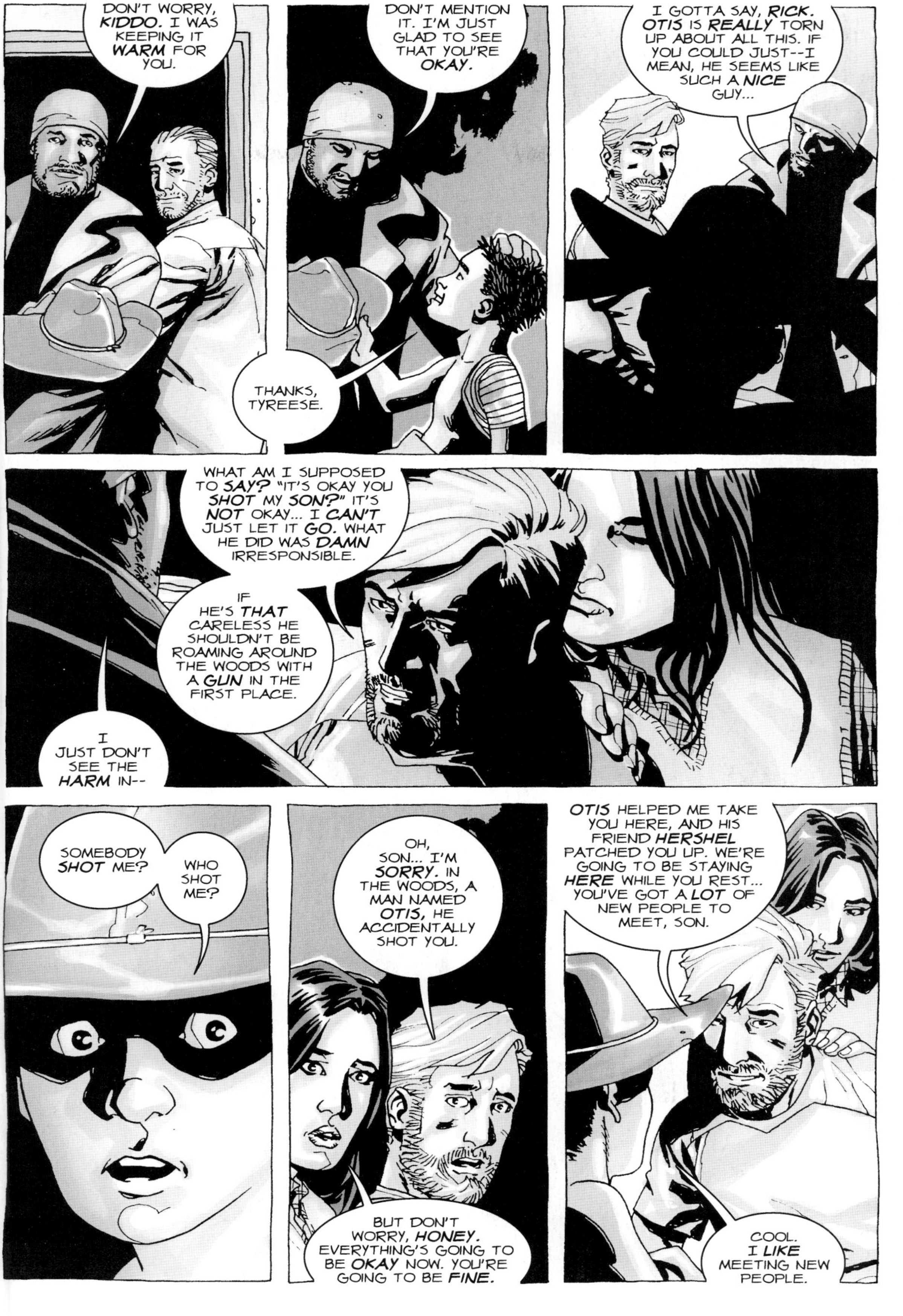
DON'T WORRY, KIDDO. I WAS KEEPING IT WARM FOR YOU.
DON'T MENTION IT. I'M JUST GLAD TO SEE THAT YOU'RE OKAY.
THANKS, TYREESE.
I GOTTA SAY, RICK. OTIS IS REALLY TORN UP ABOUT ALL THIS. IF YOU COULD JUST--I MEAN, HE SEEMS LIKE SUCH A NICE GUY...
WHAT AM I SUPPOSED TO SAY? "IT'S OKAY YOU SHOT MY SON?" IT'S NOT OKAY... I CAN'T JUST LET IT GO. WHAT HE DID WAS DAMN IRRESPONSIBLE.
IF HE'S THAT CARELESS HE SHOULDN'T BE ROAMING AROUND THE WOODS WITH A GUN IN THE FIRST PLACE.
I JUST DON'T SEE THE HARM IN--
SOMEBODY SHOT ME?
WHO SHOT ME?
OH, SON... I'M SORRY. IN THE WOODS, A MAN NAMED OTIS, HE ACCIDENTALLY SHOT YOU.
BUT DON'T WORRY, HONEY. EVERYTHING'S GOING TO BE OKAY NOW. YOU'RE GOING TO BE FINE.
OTIS HELPED ME TAKE YOU HERE, AND HIS FRIEND HERSHEL PATCHED YOU UP. WE'RE GOING TO BE STAYING HERE WHILE YOU REST... YOU'VE GOT A LOT OF NEW PEOPLE TO MEET, SON.
COOL. I LIKE MEETING NEW PEOPLE.

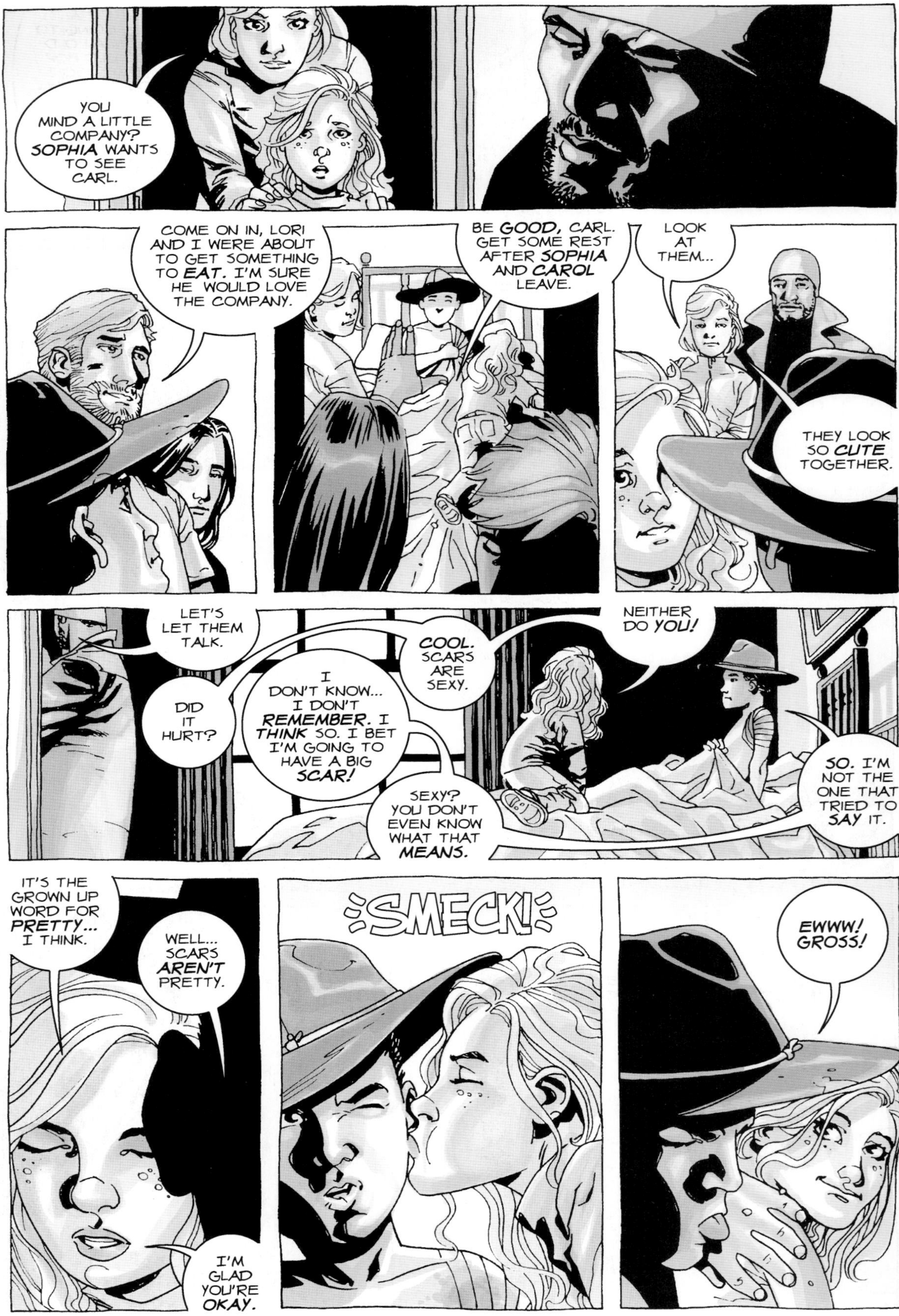

YOU MIND A LITTLE COMPANY? SOPHIA WANTS TO SEE CARL.
COME ON IN, LORI AND I WERE ABOUT TO GET SOMETHING TO EAT. I'M SURE HE WOULD LOVE THE COMPANY.
BE GOOD, CARL. GET SOME REST AFTER SOPHIA AND CAROL LEAVE.
LOOK AT THEM...
THEY LOOK SO CUTE TOGETHER.
LET'S LET THEM TALK.
DID IT HURT?
I DON'T KNOW... I DON'T REMEMBER. I THINK SO. I BET I'M GOING TO HAVE A BIG SCAR!
COOL. SCARS ARE SEXY.
SEXY? YOU DON'T EVEN KNOW WHAT THAT MEANS.
NEITHER DO YOU!
SO. I'M NOT THE ONE THAT TRIED TO SAY IT.
IT'S THE GROWN UP WORD FOR PRETTY... I THINK.
WELL... SCARS AREN'T PRETTY.
I'M GLAD YOU'RE OKAY.
SMECK!
EWWW! GROSS!

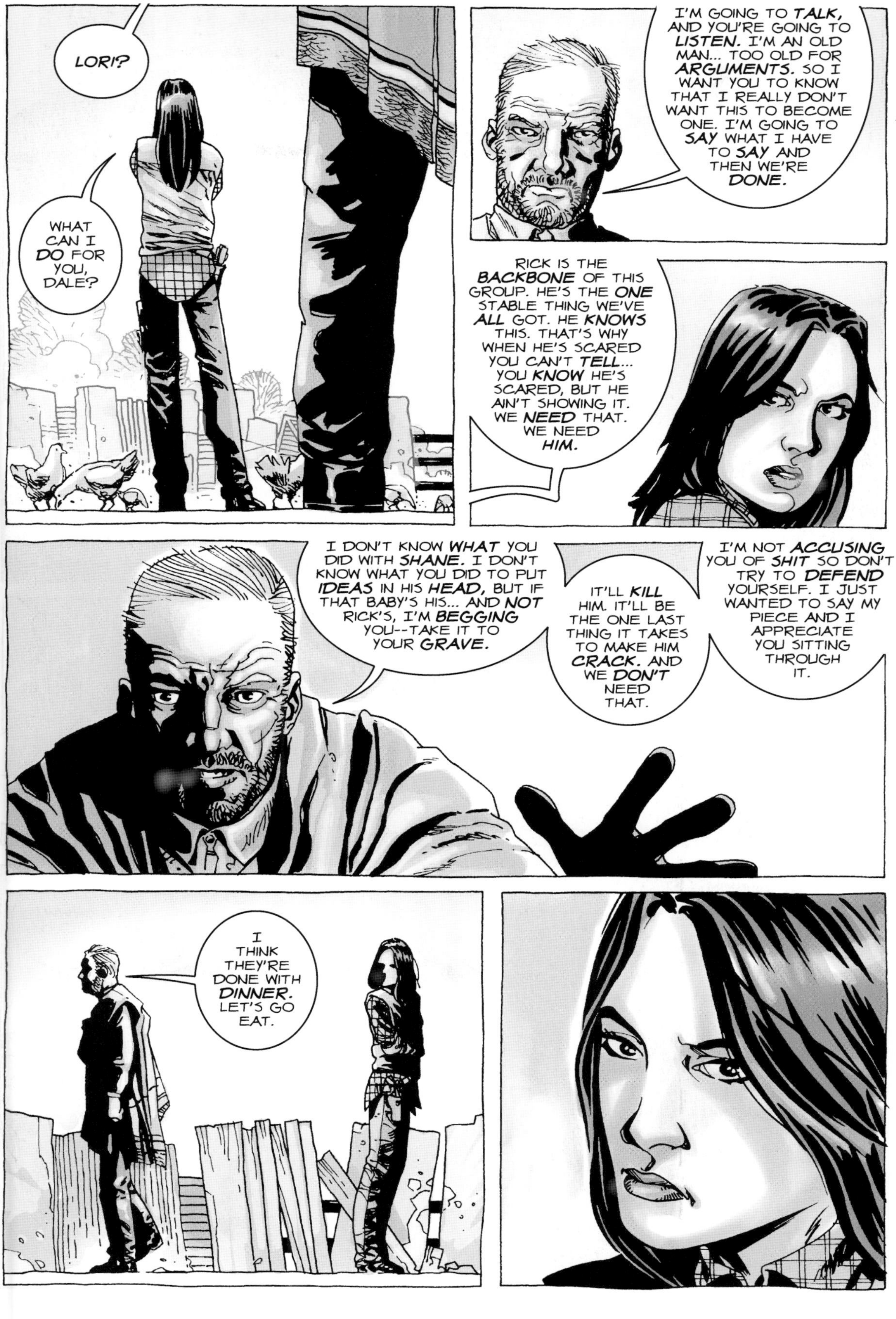
LORI?
WHAT CAN I DO FOR YOU, DALE?
I'M GOING TO TALK, AND YOU'RE GOING TO LISTEN. I'M AN OLD MAN... TOO OLD FOR ARGUMENTS. SO I WANT YOU TO KNOW THAT I REALLY DON'T WANT THIS TO BECOME ONE. I'M GOING TO SAY WHAT I HAVE TO SAY AND THEN WE'RE DONE.
RICK IS THE BACKBONE OF THIS GROUP. HE'S THE ONE STABLE THING WE'VE ALL GOT. HE KNOWS THIS. THAT'S WHY WHEN HE'S SCARED YOU CAN'T TELL... YOU KNOW HE'S SCARED, BUT HE AIN'T SHOWING IT. WE NEED THAT. WE NEED HIM.
I DON'T KNOW WHAT YOU DID WITH SHANE. I DON'T KNOW WHAT YOU DID TO PUT IDEAS IN HIS HEAD, BUT IF THAT BABY'S HIS... AND NOT RICK'S, I'M BEGGING YOU--TAKE IT TO YOUR GRAVE.
IT'LL KILL HIM. IT'LL BE THE ONE LAST THING IT TAKES TO MAKE HIM CRACK. AND WE DON'T NEED THAT.
I'M NOT ACCUSING YOU OF SHIT SO DON'T TRY TO DEFEND YOURSELF. I JUST WANTED TO SAY MY PIECE AND I APPRECIATE YOU SITTING THROUGH IT.
I THINK THEY'RE DONE WITH DINNER. LET'S GO EAT.

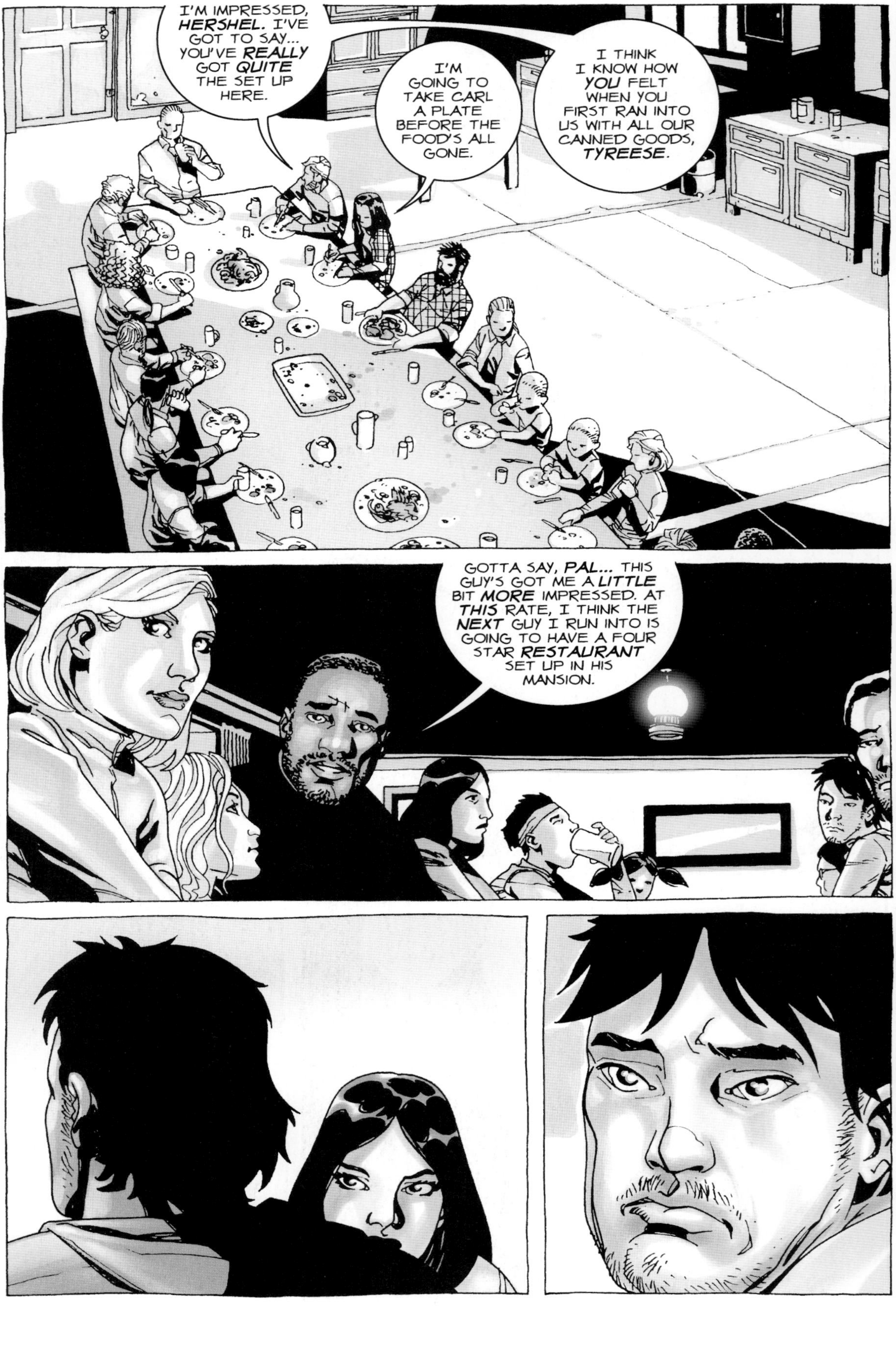
I'M IMPRESSED, HERSHEL. I'VE GOT TO SAY... YOU'VE REALLY GOT QUITE THE SET UP HERE.
I'M GOING TO TAKE CARL A PLATE BEFORE THE FOOD'S ALL GONE.
I THINK I KNOW HOW YOU FELT WHEN YOU FIRST RAN INTO US WITH ALL OUR CANNED GOODS, TYREESE.
GOTTA SAY, PAL... THIS GUY'S GOT ME A LITTLE BIT MORE IMPRESSED. AT THIS RATE, I THINK THE NEXT GUY I RUN INTO IS GOING TO HAVE A FOUR STAR RESTAURANT SET UP IN HIS MANSION.

GLENN, RIGHT? SO, UM... WHY YOU STARIN' AT THAT BLACK GUY'S GIRLFRIEND ALL THE TIME?
YOU DIDN'T TAKE YOUR EYES OFF HER ALL THROUGH DINNER.
HUH?
I SAW YOU LOOKING AT HER... WHAT'S UP WITH THAT?
BEFORE TYREESE CAME... I GUESS I HAD MY EYE ON CAROL... SHE'S A BIT OLDER THAN ME... BUT I LIKED HER.
I GUESS I'M JUST A LITTLE PISSED THAT I NEVER MADE MY MOVE.
YEAH, I GUESS SHE'S PRETTY.
IT'S NOT EVEN THAT... I MEAN... SHE IS PRETTY, BUT... I DON'T KNOW. EVERYONE AROUND ME IS PAIRING OFF. THERE'S JUST NOT THAT MANY WOMEN TO GO AROUND.
ON TOP OF ALL THAT'S GOING ON AROUND ME... I JUST DON'T WANT TO END UP ALONE TOO. I MEAN... I WANT TO HAVE SEX AT LEAST A COUPLE MORE TIMES BEFORE I DIE.
JESUS. I DON'T EVEN KNOW YOU. I'M SORRY. I DON'T MEAN TO SPILL MY GUTS LIKE THIS.
I'LL FUCK YOU.
WHAT?
IF THAT'S WHAT YOU'RE AFTER, I'LL FUCK YOU.
MY BOYFRIEND'S GONE-- PROBABLY DEAD. TO BE HONEST, HE WAS A BIT OF A JERK ANYWAY. YOU'RE THE FIRST GUY I'VE SEEN IN MONTHS THAT'S NOT RELATED TO ME OR THAT OTIS IDIOT. IT'S LIKE YOU SAID--OUR CHOICES AREN'T VERY BROAD.
WE'VE GOTTA BE PROACTIVE... OR WE'RE GOING TO END UP ALONE.
THAT DOES MAKE SENSE.
SO LET'S FUCK THEN. YOU WANNA DO THAT?
YEAH. SURE.

OKAY, GUYS. WE NEED TO *TALK*.

DAAAD!

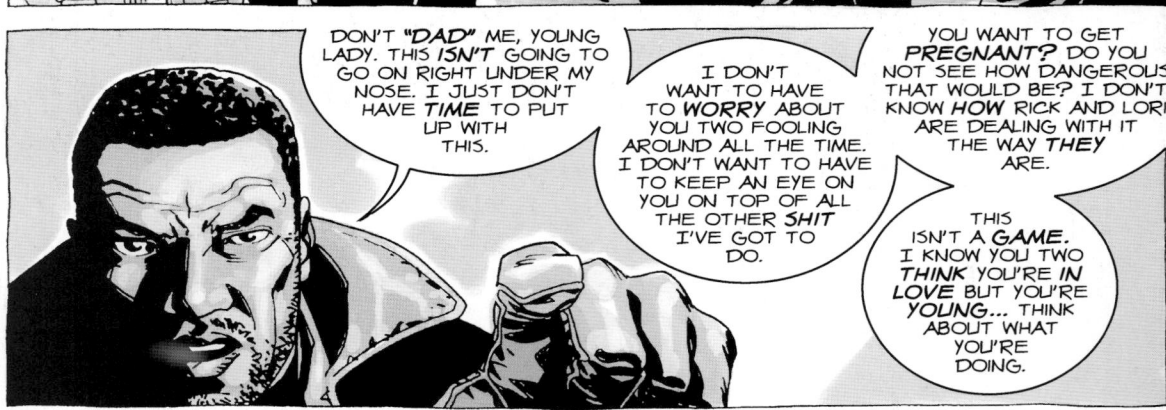

DON'T *"DAD"* ME, YOUNG LADY. THIS *ISN'T* GOING TO GO ON RIGHT UNDER MY NOSE. I JUST DON'T HAVE *TIME* TO PUT UP WITH THIS.

I DON'T WANT TO HAVE TO *WORRY* ABOUT YOU TWO FOOLING AROUND ALL THE TIME. I DON'T WANT TO HAVE TO KEEP AN EYE ON YOU ON TOP OF ALL THE OTHER *SHIT* I'VE GOT TO DO.

YOU WANT TO GET *PREGNANT?* DO YOU NOT SEE HOW DANGEROUS THAT WOULD BE? I DON'T KNOW *HOW* RICK AND LORI ARE DEALING WITH IT THE WAY *THEY* ARE.

THIS ISN'T A *GAME.* I KNOW YOU TWO *THINK* YOU'RE *IN LOVE* BUT YOU'RE *YOUNG...* THINK ABOUT WHAT YOU'RE DOING.

=SIGH=

JUST KEEP YOUR *HANDS* TO YOURSELVES.

SEE? I TOLD YOU WE NEEDED TO GO AHEAD AND *DO* IT. I WANT TO BE *TOGETHER* WITH YOU FOR THE REST OF *ETERNITY.* I DON'T WANT YOUR *FATHER* TO STAND IN THE WAY OF *THAT.*

I *KNOW...* I JUST DON'T WANT TO DO IT UNTIL THE TIME IS *RIGHT.* WE HAVE TO WAIT.

FINE, JULIE. WE'LL PLAY IT *YOUR* WAY... BUT I DON'T WANT TO WAIT *FOREVER.*

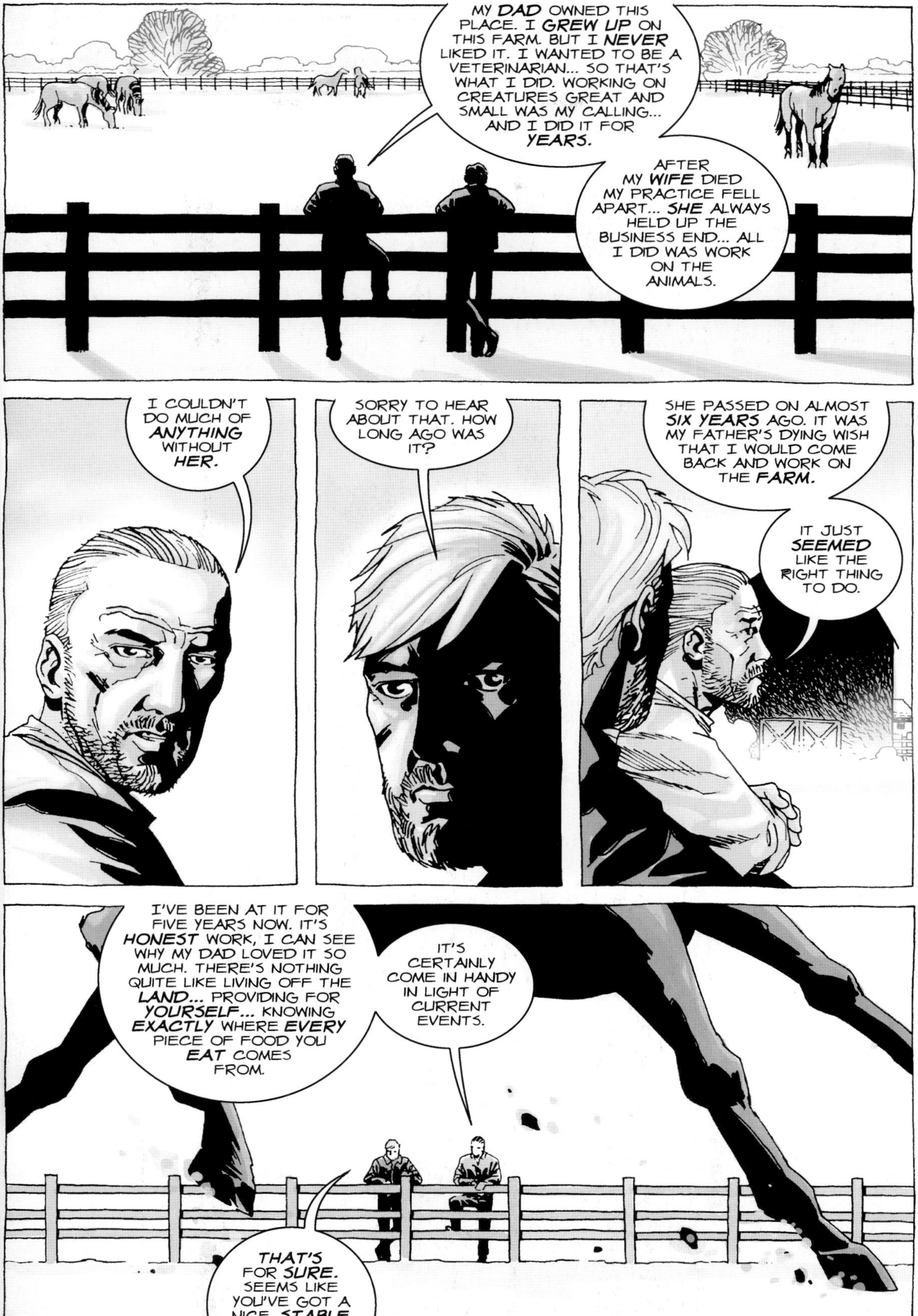

MY DAD OWNED THIS PLACE. I GREW UP ON THIS FARM. BUT I NEVER LIKED IT. I WANTED TO BE A VETERINARIAN... SO THAT'S WHAT I DID. WORKING ON CREATURES GREAT AND SMALL WAS MY CALLING... AND I DID IT FOR YEARS.
AFTER MY WIFE DIED MY PRACTICE FELL APART... SHE ALWAYS HELD UP THE BUSINESS END... ALL I DID WAS WORK ON THE ANIMALS.
I COULDN'T DO MUCH OF ANYTHING WITHOUT HER.
SORRY TO HEAR ABOUT THAT. HOW LONG AGO WAS IT?
SHE PASSED ON ALMOST SIX YEARS AGO. IT WAS MY FATHER'S DYING WISH THAT I WOULD COME BACK AND WORK ON THE FARM.
IT JUST SEEMED LIKE THE RIGHT THING TO DO.
I'VE BEEN AT IT FOR FIVE YEARS NOW. IT'S HONEST WORK, I CAN SEE WHY MY DAD LOVED IT SO MUCH. THERE'S NOTHING QUITE LIKE LIVING OFF THE LAND... PROVIDING FOR YOURSELF... KNOWING EXACTLY WHERE EVERY PIECE OF FOOD YOU EAT COMES FROM.
IT'S CERTAINLY COME IN HANDY IN LIGHT OF CURRENT EVENTS.
THAT'S FOR SURE. SEEMS LIKE YOU'VE GOT A NICE, STABLE SET UP HERE.

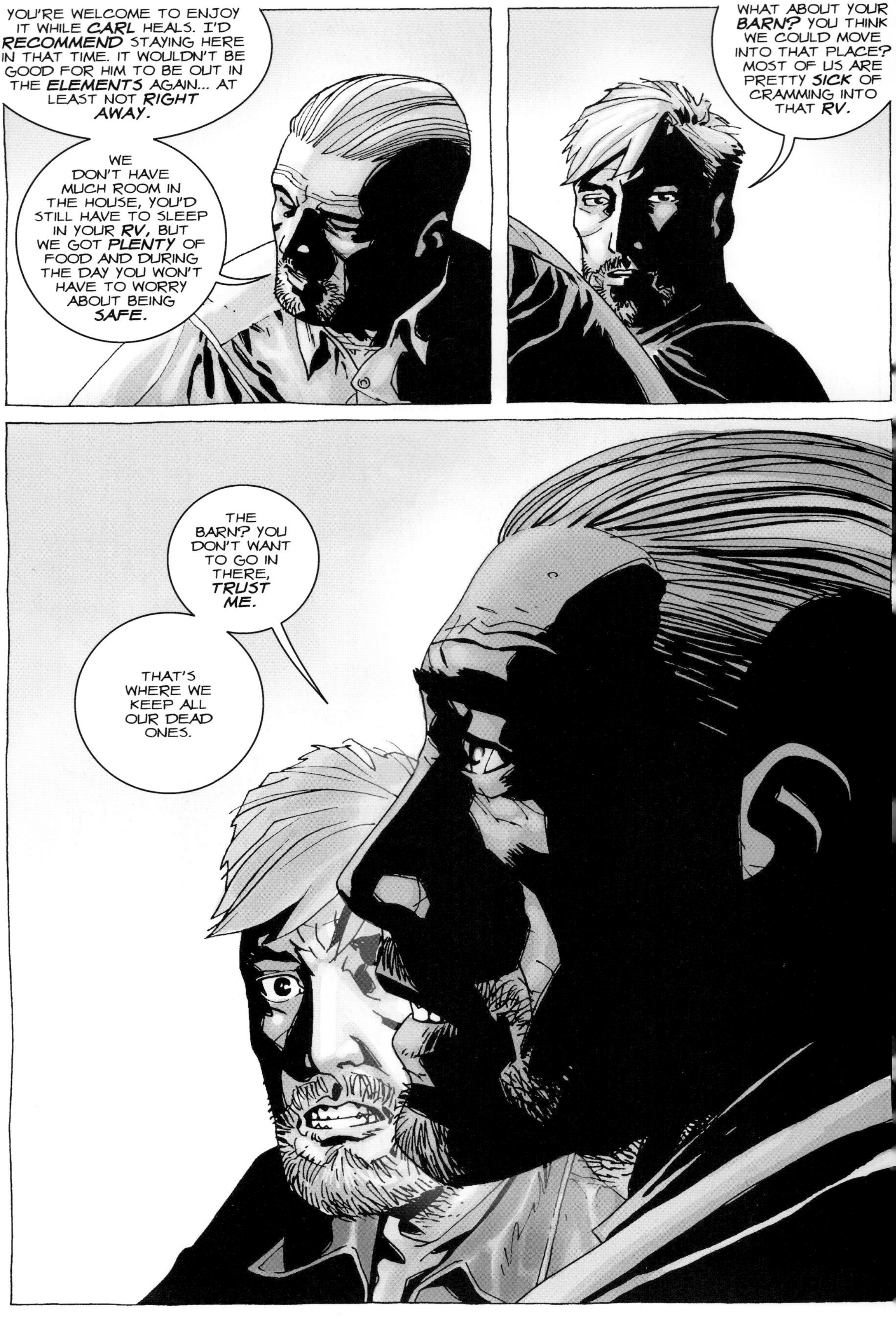
YOU'RE WELCOME TO ENJOY IT WHILE CARL HEALS. I'D RECOMMEND STAYING HERE IN THAT TIME. IT WOULDN'T BE GOOD FOR HIM TO BE OUT IN THE ELEMENTS AGAIN... AT LEAST NOT RIGHT AWAY.
WE DON'T HAVE MUCH ROOM IN THE HOUSE, YOU'D STILL HAVE TO SLEEP IN YOUR RV, BUT WE GOT PLENTY OF FOOD AND DURING THE DAY YOU WON'T HAVE TO WORRY ABOUT BEING SAFE.
WHAT ABOUT YOUR BARN? YOU THINK WE COULD MOVE INTO THAT PLACE? MOST OF US ARE PRETTY SICK OF CRAMMING INTO THAT RV.
THE BARN? YOU DON'T WANT TO GO IN THERE, TRUST ME.
THAT'S WHERE WE KEEP ALL OUR DEAD ONES.

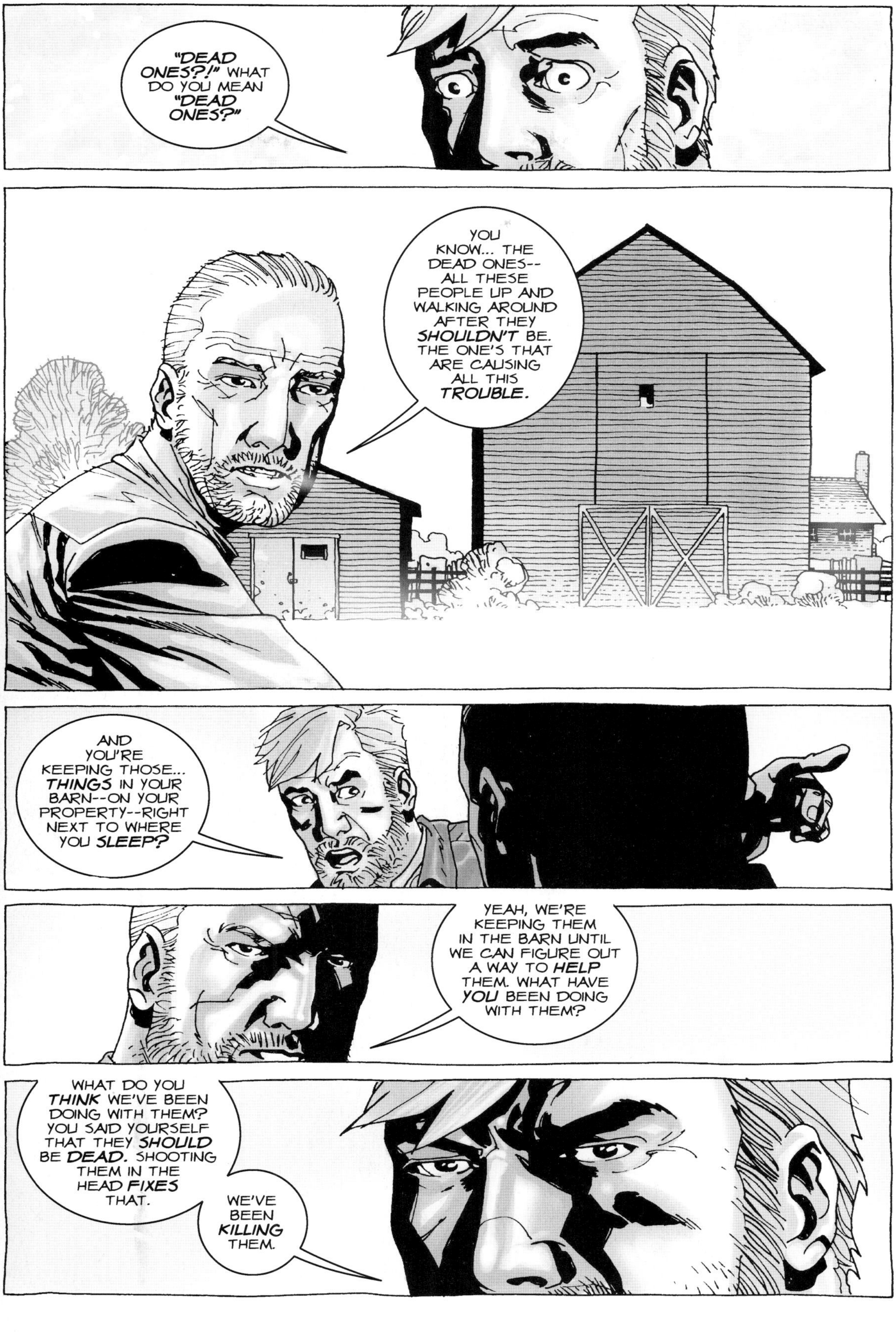
"DEAD ONES?!" WHAT DO YOU MEAN "DEAD ONES?"
YOU KNOW... THE DEAD ONES-- ALL THESE PEOPLE UP AND WALKING AROUND AFTER THEY SHOULDN'T BE. THE ONE'S THAT ARE CAUSING ALL THIS TROUBLE.
AND YOU'RE KEEPING THOSE... THINGS IN YOUR BARN--ON YOUR PROPERTY--RIGHT NEXT TO WHERE YOU SLEEP?
YEAH, WE'RE KEEPING THEM IN THE BARN UNTIL WE CAN FIGURE OUT A WAY TO HELP THEM. WHAT HAVE YOU BEEN DOING WITH THEM?
WHAT DO YOU THINK WE'VE BEEN DOING WITH THEM? YOU SAID YOURSELF THAT THEY SHOULD BE DEAD. SHOOTING THEM IN THE HEAD FIXES THAT.
WE'VE BEEN KILLING THEM.

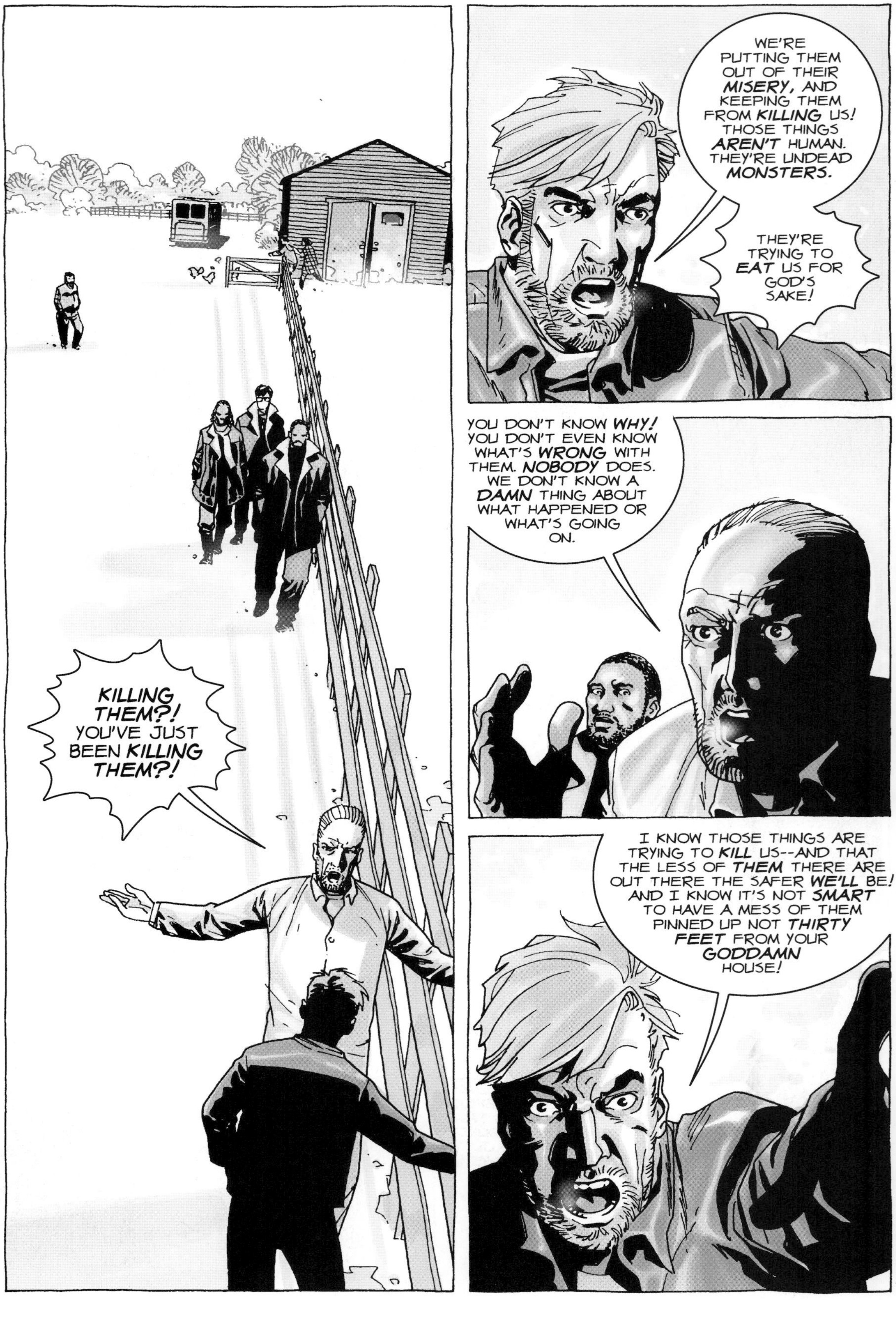
KILLING THEM?! YOU'VE JUST BEEN KILLING THEM?!
WE'RE PUTTING THEM OUT OF THEIR MISERY, AND KEEPING THEM FROM KILLING US! THOSE THINGS AREN'T HUMAN. THEY'RE UNDEAD MONSTERS.
THEY'RE TRYING TO EAT US FOR GOD'S SAKE!
YOU DON'T KNOW WHY! YOU DON'T EVEN KNOW WHAT'S WRONG WITH THEM. NOBODY DOES. WE DON'T KNOW A DAMN THING ABOUT WHAT HAPPENED OR WHAT'S GOING ON.
I KNOW THOSE THINGS ARE TRYING TO KILL US--AND THAT THE LESS OF THEM THERE ARE OUT THERE THE SAFER WE'LL BE! AND I KNOW IT'S NOT SMART TO HAVE A MESS OF THEM PINNED UP NOT THIRTY FEET FROM YOUR GODDAMN HOUSE!

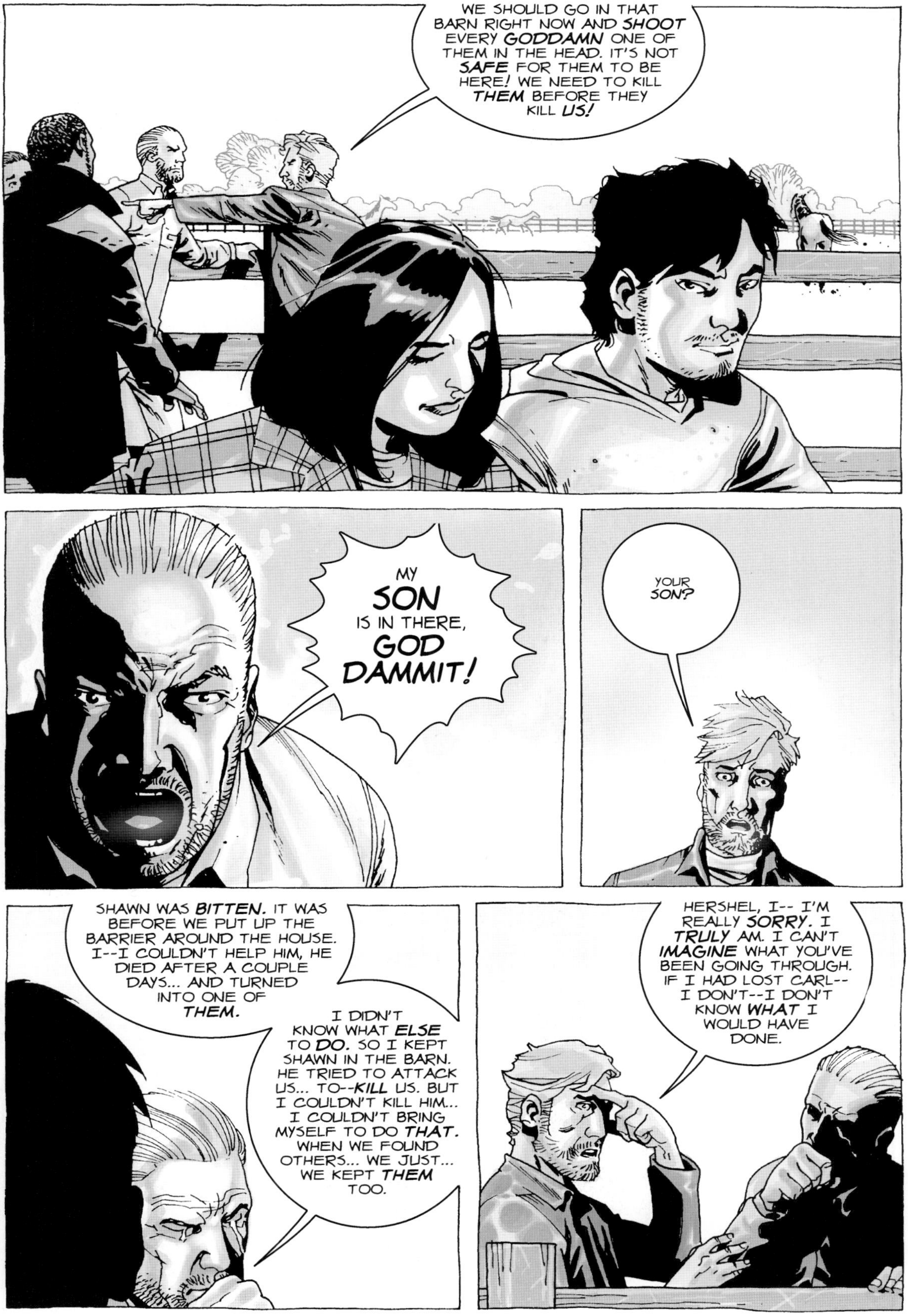

WE SHOULD GO IN THAT BARN RIGHT NOW AND SHOOT EVERY GODDAMN ONE OF THEM IN THE HEAD. IT'S NOT SAFE FOR THEM TO BE HERE! WE NEED TO KILL THEM BEFORE THEY KILL US!
MY SON IS IN THERE, GOD DAMMIT!
YOUR SON?
SHAWN WAS BITTEN. IT WAS BEFORE WE PUT UP THE BARRIER AROUND THE HOUSE. I--I COULDN'T HELP HIM, HE DIED AFTER A COUPLE DAYS... AND TURNED INTO ONE OF THEM.
I DIDN'T KNOW WHAT ELSE TO DO. SO I KEPT SHAWN IN THE BARN. HE TRIED TO ATTACK US... TO--KILL US. BUT I COULDN'T KILL HIM... I COULDN'T BRING MYSELF TO DO THAT. WHEN WE FOUND OTHERS... WE JUST... WE KEPT THEM TOO.
HERSHEL, I-- I'M REALLY SORRY. I TRULY AM. I CAN'T IMAGINE WHAT YOU'VE BEEN GOING THROUGH. IF I HAD LOST CARL-- I DON'T--I DON'T KNOW WHAT I WOULD HAVE DONE.

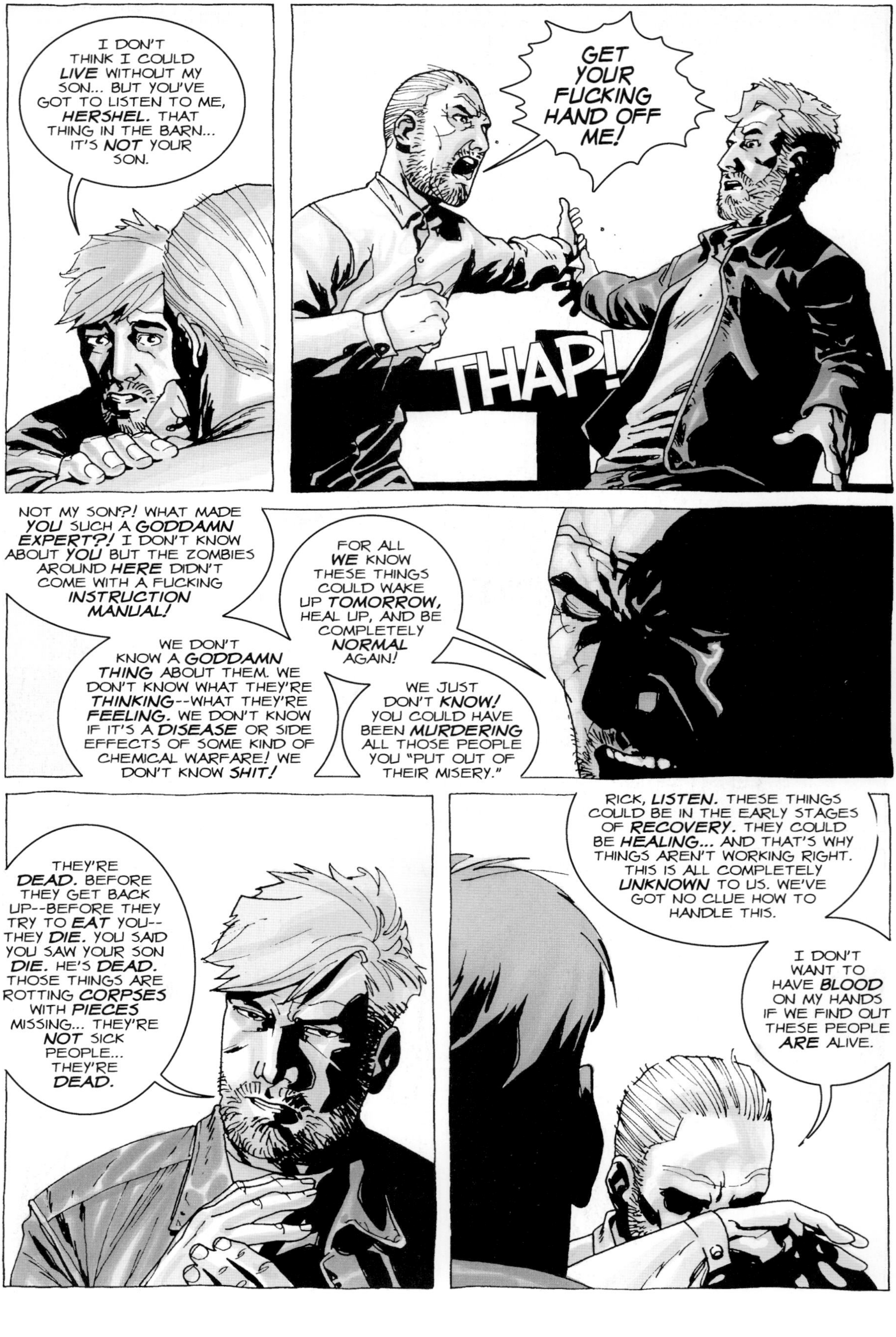
I DON'T THINK I COULD LIVE WITHOUT MY SON... BUT YOU'VE GOT TO LISTEN TO ME, HERSHEL. THAT THING IN THE BARN... IT'S NOT YOUR SON.
GET YOUR FUCKING HAND OFF ME!
THAP!
NOT MY SON?! WHAT MADE YOU SUCH A GODDAMN EXPERT?! I DON'T KNOW ABOUT YOU BUT THE ZOMBIES AROUND HERE DIDN'T COME WITH A FUCKING INSTRUCTION MANUAL!
WE DON'T KNOW A GODDAMN THING ABOUT THEM. WE DON'T KNOW WHAT THEY'RE THINKING--WHAT THEY'RE FEELING. WE DON'T KNOW IF IT'S A DISEASE OR SIDE EFFECTS OF SOME KIND OF CHEMICAL WARFARE! WE DON'T KNOW SHIT!
FOR ALL WE KNOW THESE THINGS COULD WAKE UP TOMORROW, HEAL UP, AND BE COMPLETELY NORMAL AGAIN!
WE JUST DON'T KNOW! YOU COULD HAVE BEEN MURDERING ALL THOSE PEOPLE YOU "PUT OUT OF THEIR MISERY."
THEY'RE DEAD. BEFORE THEY GET BACK UP--BEFORE THEY TRY TO EAT YOU--THEY DIE. YOU SAID YOU SAW YOUR SON DIE. HE'S DEAD. THOSE THINGS ARE ROTTING CORPSES WITH PIECES MISSING... THEY'RE NOT SICK PEOPLE... THEY'RE DEAD.
RICK, LISTEN. THESE THINGS COULD BE IN THE EARLY STAGES OF RECOVERY. THEY COULD BE HEALING... AND THAT'S WHY THINGS AREN'T WORKING RIGHT. THIS IS ALL COMPLETELY UNKNOWN TO US. WE'VE GOT NO CLUE HOW TO HANDLE THIS.
I DON'T WANT TO HAVE BLOOD ON MY HANDS IF WE FIND OUT THESE PEOPLE ARE ALIVE.

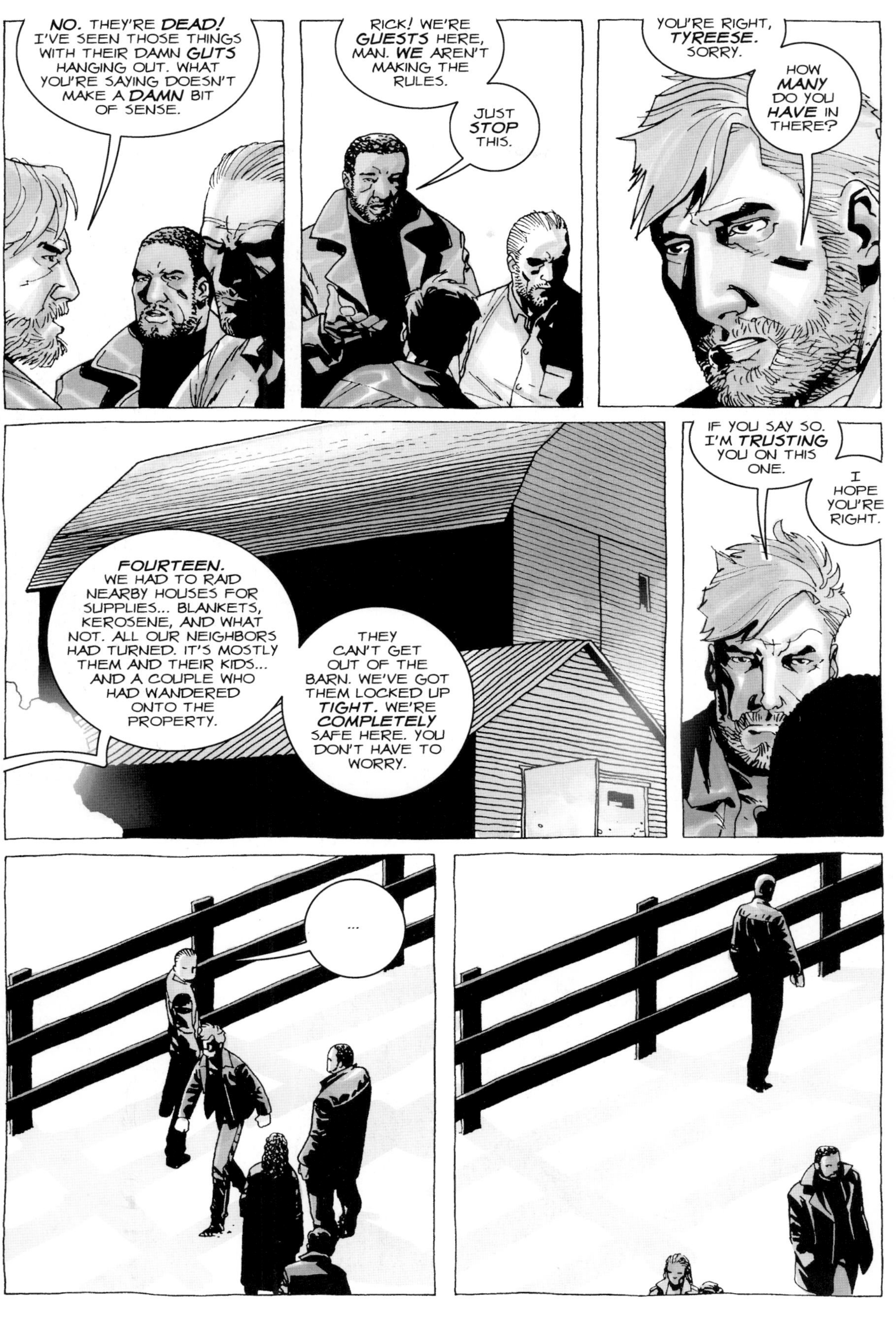
NO. THEY'RE DEAD! I'VE SEEN THOSE THINGS WITH THEIR DAMN GUTS HANGING OUT. WHAT YOU'RE SAYING DOESN'T MAKE A DAMN BIT OF SENSE.
RICK! WE'RE GUESTS HERE, MAN. WE AREN'T MAKING THE RULES.
JUST STOP THIS.
YOU'RE RIGHT, TYREESE. SORRY.
HOW MANY DO YOU HAVE IN THERE?
FOURTEEN. WE HAD TO RAID NEARBY HOUSES FOR SUPPLIES... BLANKETS, KEROSENE, AND WHAT NOT. ALL OUR NEIGHBORS HAD TURNED. IT'S MOSTLY THEM AND THEIR KIDS... AND A COUPLE WHO HAD WANDERED ONTO THE PROPERTY.
THEY CAN'T GET OUT OF THE BARN. WE'VE GOT THEM LOCKED UP TIGHT. WE'RE COMPLETELY SAFE HERE. YOU DON'T HAVE TO WORRY.
IF YOU SAY SO. I'M TRUSTING YOU ON THIS ONE.
I HOPE YOU'RE RIGHT.
...

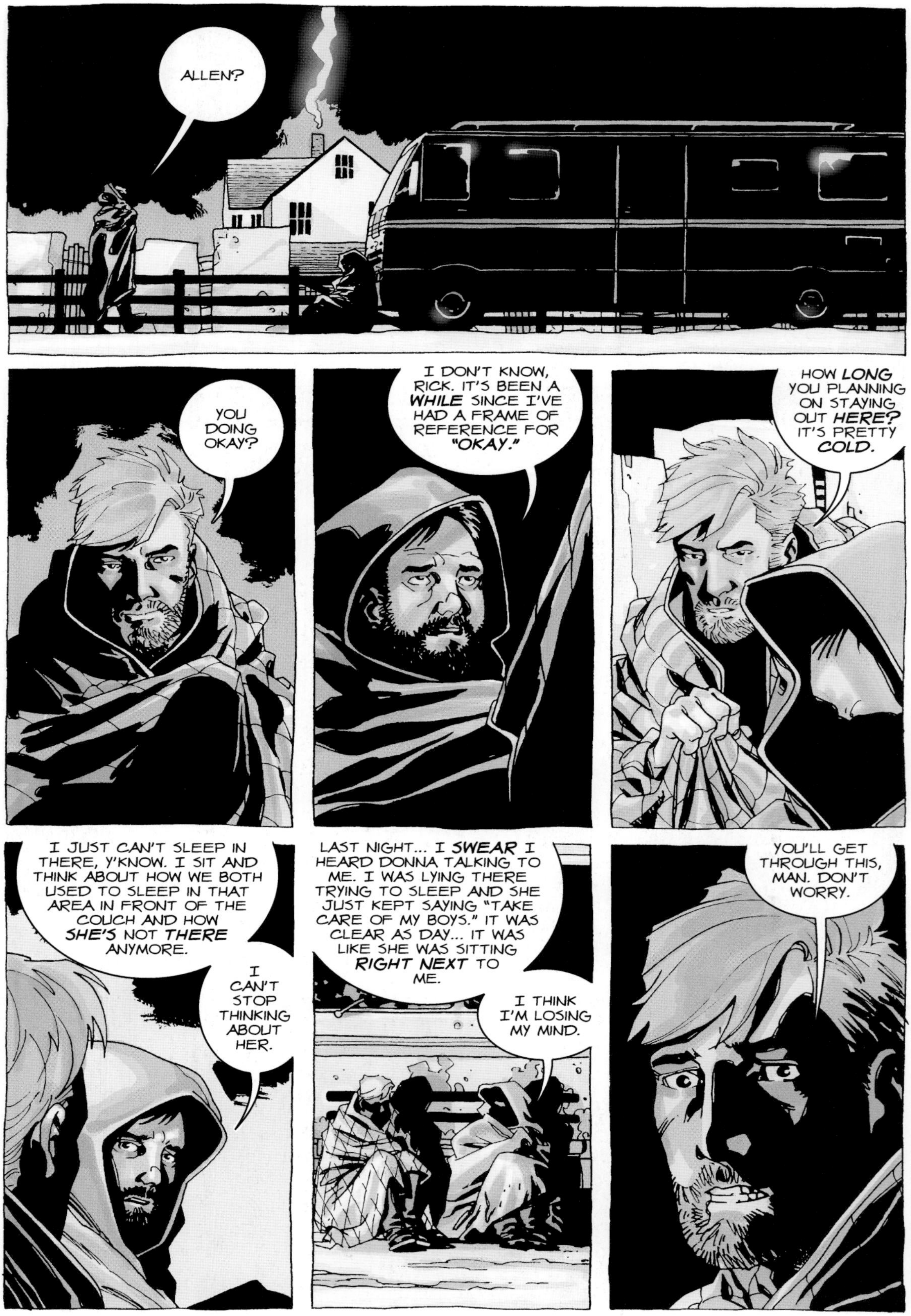
ALLEN?
YOU DOING OKAY?
I DON'T KNOW, RICK. IT'S BEEN A WHILE SINCE I'VE HAD A FRAME OF REFERENCE FOR "OKAY."
HOW LONG YOU PLANNING ON STAYING OUT HERE? IT'S PRETTY COLD.
I JUST CAN'T SLEEP IN THERE, Y'KNOW. I SIT AND THINK ABOUT HOW WE BOTH USED TO SLEEP IN THAT AREA IN FRONT OF THE COUCH AND HOW SHE'S NOT THERE ANYMORE.
I CAN'T STOP THINKING ABOUT HER.
LAST NIGHT... I SWEAR I HEARD DONNA TALKING TO ME. I WAS LYING THERE TRYING TO SLEEP AND SHE JUST KEPT SAYING "TAKE CARE OF MY BOYS." IT WAS CLEAR AS DAY... IT WAS LIKE SHE WAS SITTING RIGHT NEXT TO ME.
I THINK I'M LOSING MY MIND.
YOU'LL GET THROUGH THIS, MAN. DON'T WORRY.

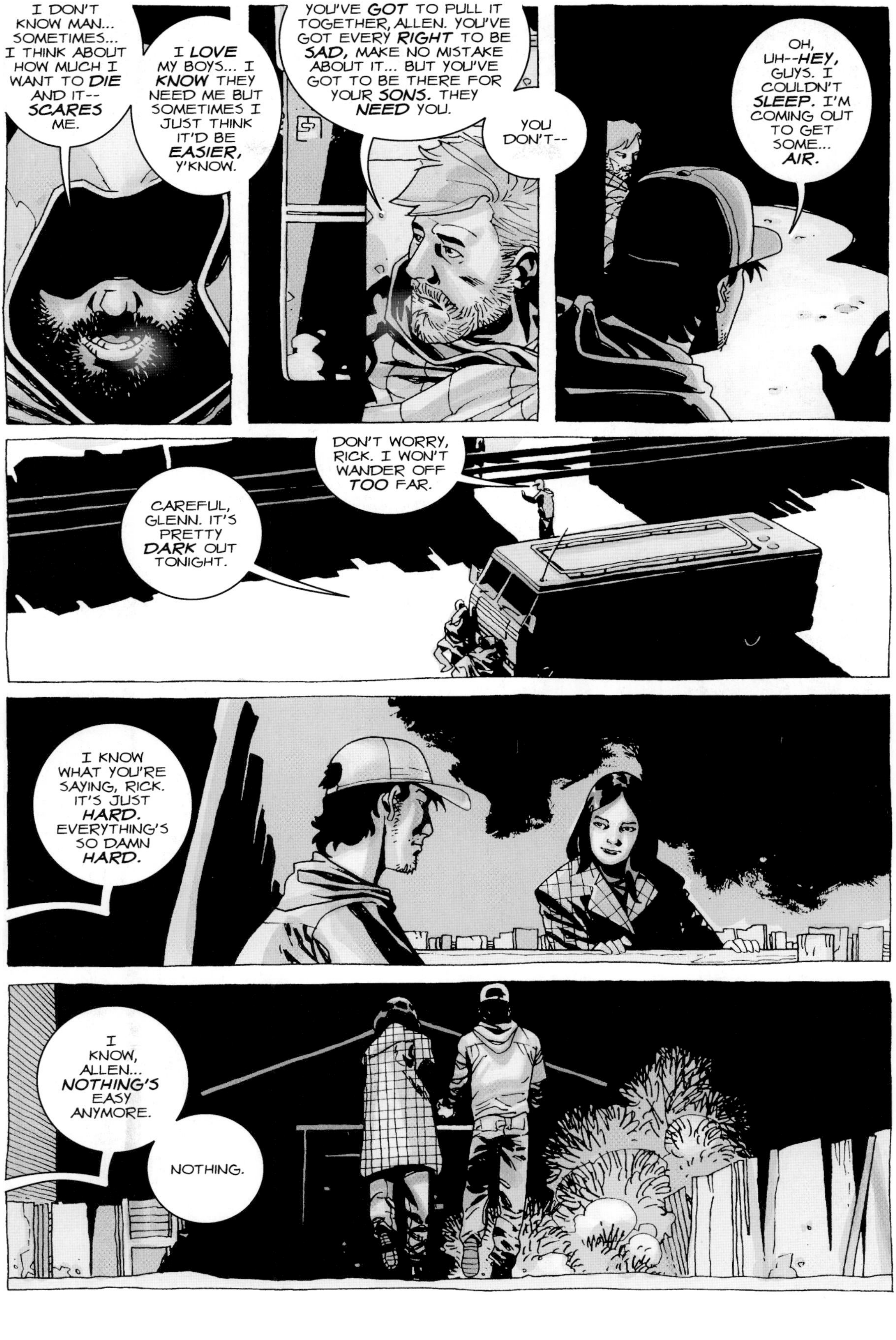
I DON'T KNOW MAN... SOMETIMES... I THINK ABOUT HOW MUCH I WANT TO DIE AND IT-- SCARES ME.
I LOVE MY BOYS... I KNOW THEY NEED ME BUT SOMETIMES I JUST THINK IT'D BE EASIER, Y'KNOW.
YOU'VE GOT TO PULL IT TOGETHER, ALLEN. YOU'VE GOT EVERY RIGHT TO BE SAD, MAKE NO MISTAKE ABOUT IT... BUT YOU'VE GOT TO BE THERE FOR YOUR SONS. THEY NEED YOU.
YOU DON'T--
OH, UH--HEY, GUYS. I COULDN'T SLEEP. I'M COMING OUT TO GET SOME... AIR.
CAREFUL, GLENN. IT'S PRETTY DARK OUT TONIGHT.
DON'T WORRY, RICK. I WON'T WANDER OFF TOO FAR.
I KNOW WHAT YOU'RE SAYING, RICK. IT'S JUST HARD. EVERYTHING'S SO DAMN HARD.
I KNOW, ALLEN... NOTHING'S EASY ANYMORE.
NOTHING.

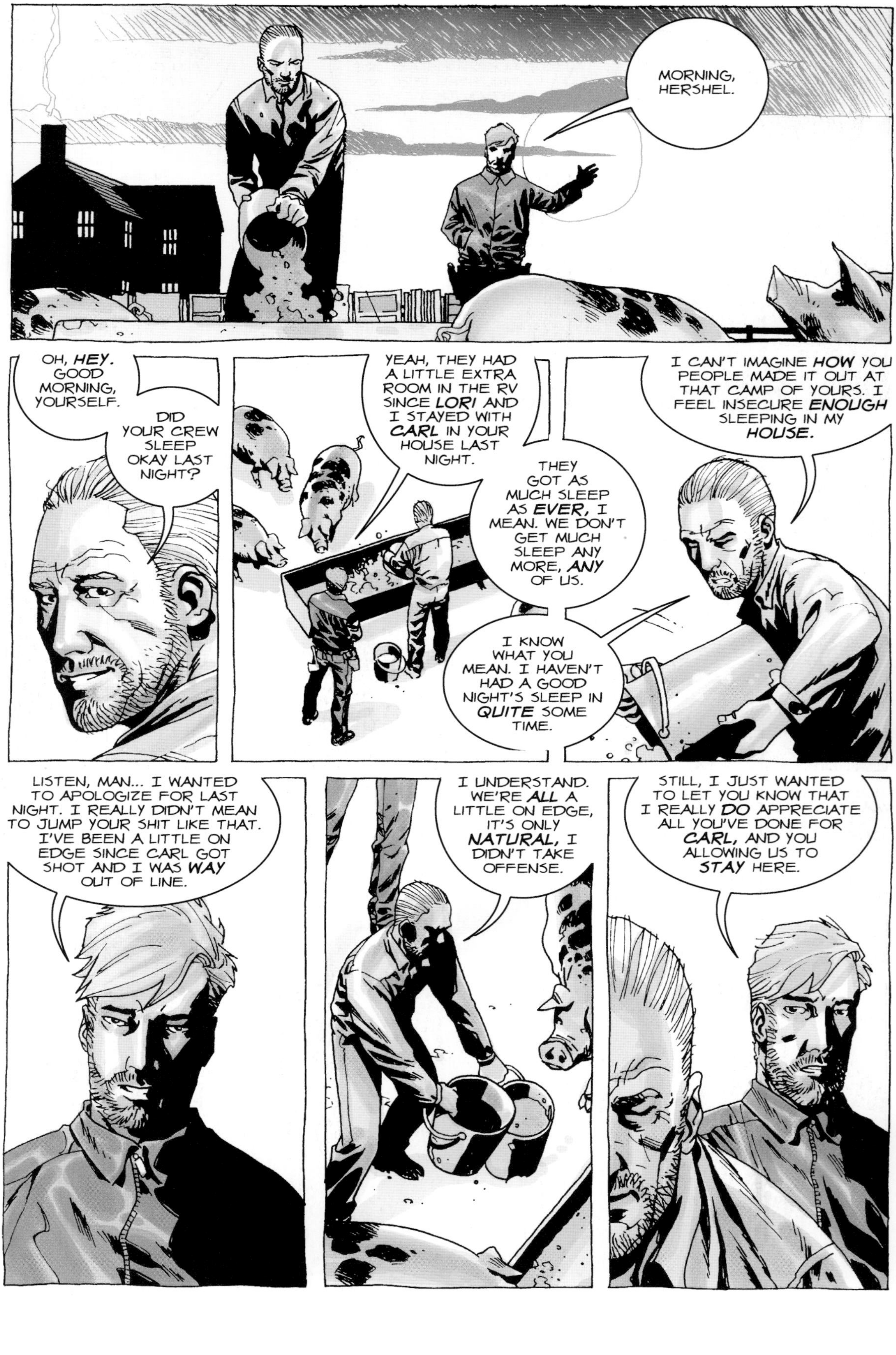
MORNING, HERSHEL.
OH, HEY. GOOD MORNING, YOURSELF.
DID YOUR CREW SLEEP OKAY LAST NIGHT?
YEAH, THEY HAD A LITTLE EXTRA ROOM IN THE RV SINCE LORI AND I STAYED WITH CARL IN YOUR HOUSE LAST NIGHT.
THEY GOT AS MUCH SLEEP AS EVER, I MEAN. WE DON'T GET MUCH SLEEP ANY MORE, ANY OF US.
I CAN'T IMAGINE HOW YOU PEOPLE MADE IT OUT AT THAT CAMP OF YOURS. I FEEL INSECURE ENOUGH SLEEPING IN MY HOUSE.
I KNOW WHAT YOU MEAN. I HAVEN'T HAD A GOOD NIGHT'S SLEEP IN QUITE SOME TIME.
LISTEN, MAN... I WANTED TO APOLOGIZE FOR LAST NIGHT. I REALLY DIDN'T MEAN TO JUMP YOUR SHIT LIKE THAT. I'VE BEEN A LITTLE ON EDGE SINCE CARL GOT SHOT AND I WAS WAY OUT OF LINE.
I UNDERSTAND. WE'RE ALL A LITTLE ON EDGE, IT'S ONLY NATURAL, I DIDN'T TAKE OFFENSE.
STILL, I JUST WANTED TO LET YOU KNOW THAT I REALLY DO APPRECIATE ALL YOU'VE DONE FOR CARL, AND YOU ALLOWING US TO STAY HERE.

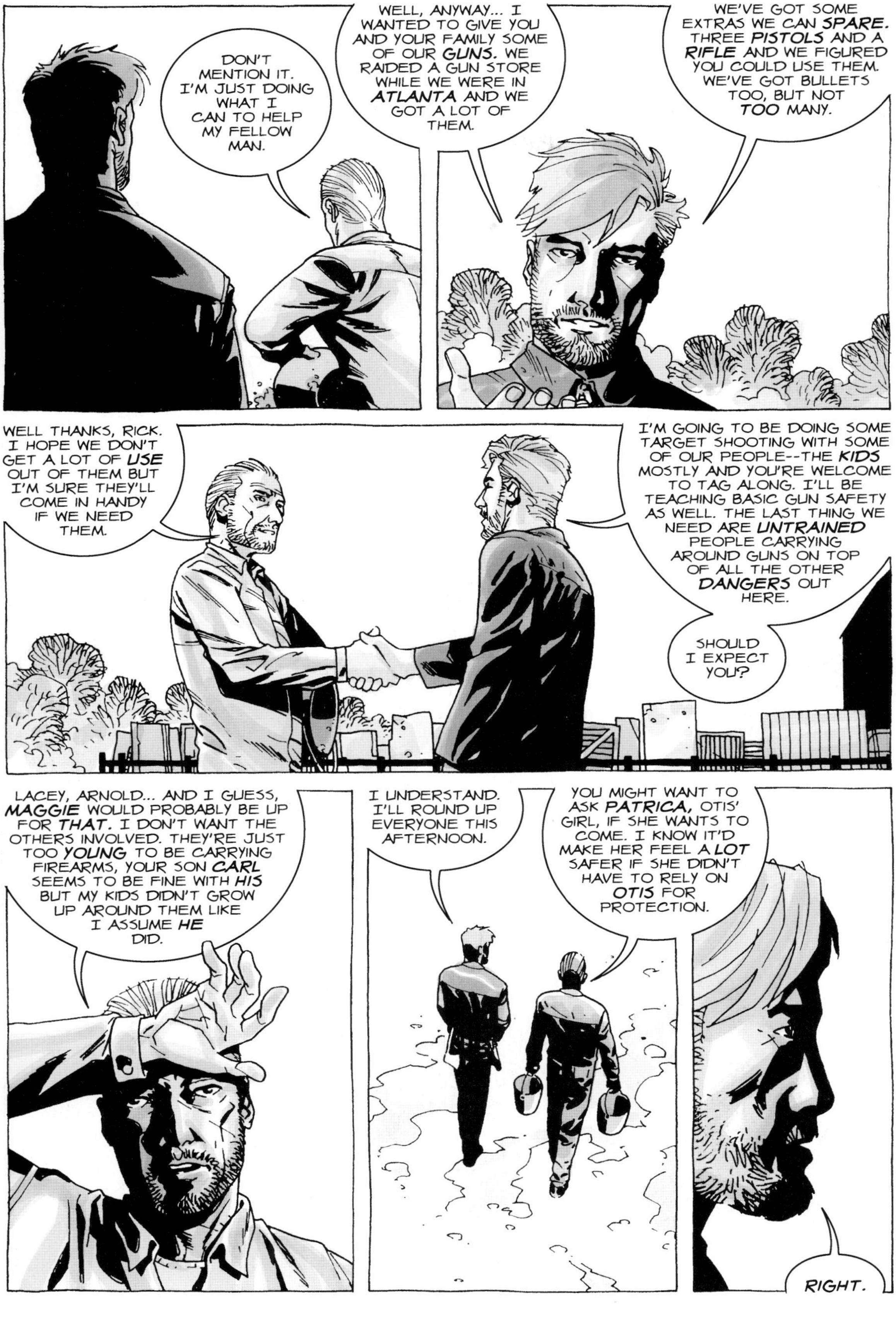
DON'T MENTION IT. I'M JUST DOING WHAT I CAN TO HELP MY FELLOW MAN.
WELL, ANYWAY... I WANTED TO GIVE YOU AND YOUR FAMILY SOME OF OUR GUNS. WE RAIDED A GUN STORE WHILE WE WERE IN ATLANTA AND WE GOT A LOT OF THEM.
WE'VE GOT SOME EXTRAS WE CAN SPARE. THREE PISTOLS AND A RIFLE AND WE FIGURED YOU COULD USE THEM. WE'VE GOT BULLETS TOO, BUT NOT TOO MANY.
WELL THANKS, RICK. I HOPE WE DON'T GET A LOT OF USE OUT OF THEM BUT I'M SURE THEY'LL COME IN HANDY IF WE NEED THEM.
I'M GOING TO BE DOING SOME TARGET SHOOTING WITH SOME OF OUR PEOPLE--THE KIDS MOSTLY AND YOU'RE WELCOME TO TAG ALONG. I'LL BE TEACHING BASIC GUN SAFETY AS WELL. THE LAST THING WE NEED ARE UNTRAINED PEOPLE CARRYING AROUND GUNS ON TOP OF ALL THE OTHER DANGERS OUT HERE.
SHOULD I EXPECT YOU?
LACEY, ARNOLD... AND I GUESS, MAGGIE WOULD PROBABLY BE UP FOR THAT. I DON'T WANT THE OTHERS INVOLVED. THEY'RE JUST TOO YOUNG TO BE CARRYING FIREARMS, YOUR SON CARL SEEMS TO BE FINE WITH HIS BUT MY KIDS DIDN'T GROW UP AROUND THEM LIKE I ASSUME HE DID.
I UNDERSTAND. I'LL ROUND UP EVERYONE THIS AFTERNOON.
YOU MIGHT WANT TO ASK PATRICA, OTIS' GIRL, IF SHE WANTS TO COME. I KNOW IT'D MAKE HER FEEL A LOT SAFER IF SHE DIDN'T HAVE TO RELY ON OTIS FOR PROTECTION.
RIGHT.

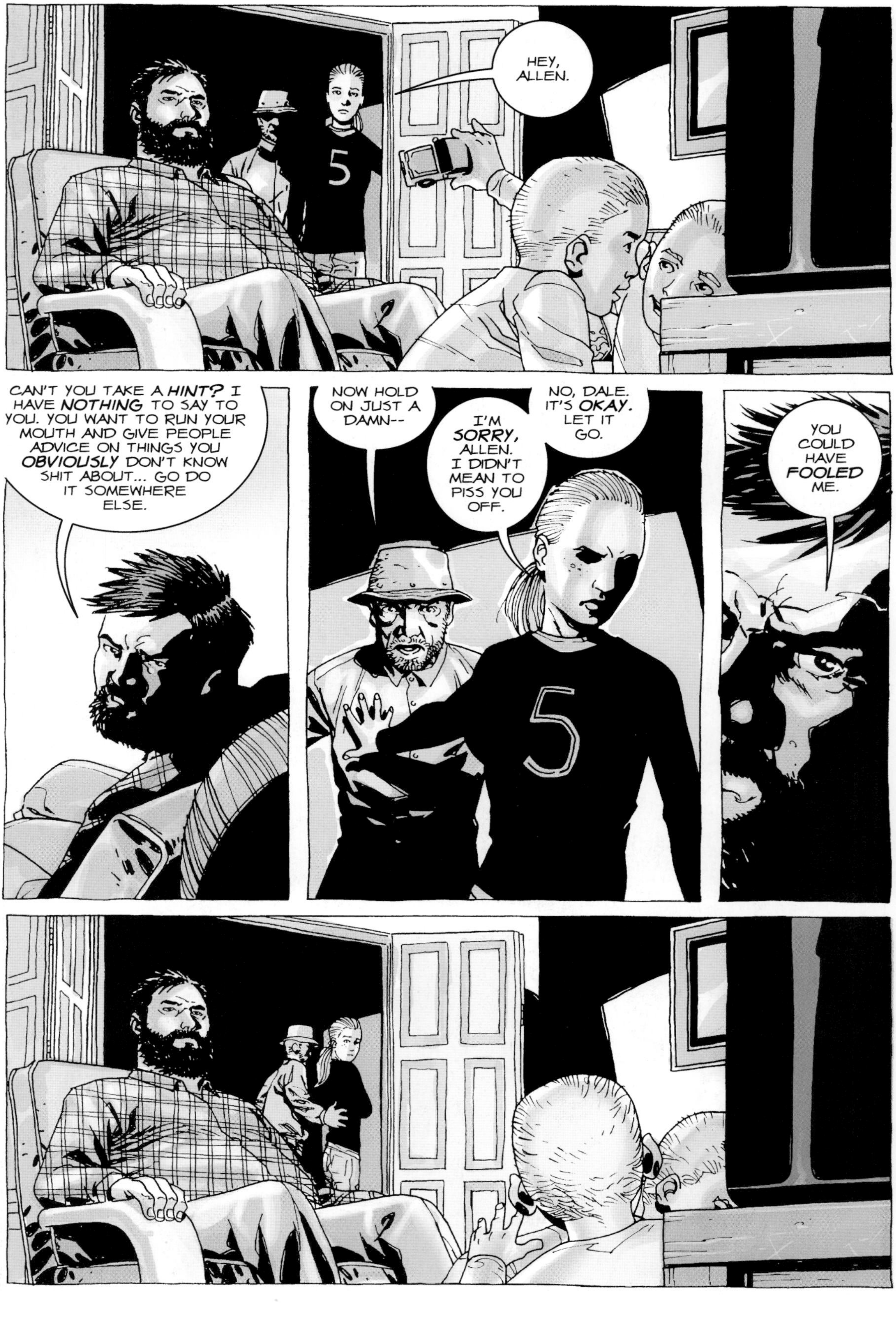
HEY, ALLEN.
CAN'T YOU TAKE A HINT? I HAVE NOTHING TO SAY TO YOU. YOU WANT TO RUN YOUR MOUTH AND GIVE PEOPLE ADVICE ON THINGS YOU OBVIOUSLY DON'T KNOW SHIT ABOUT... GO DO IT SOMEWHERE ELSE.
NOW HOLD ON JUST A DAMN--
NO, DALE. IT'S OKAY. LET IT GO.
I'M SORRY, ALLEN. I DIDN'T MEAN TO PISS YOU OFF.
YOU COULD HAVE FOOLED ME.

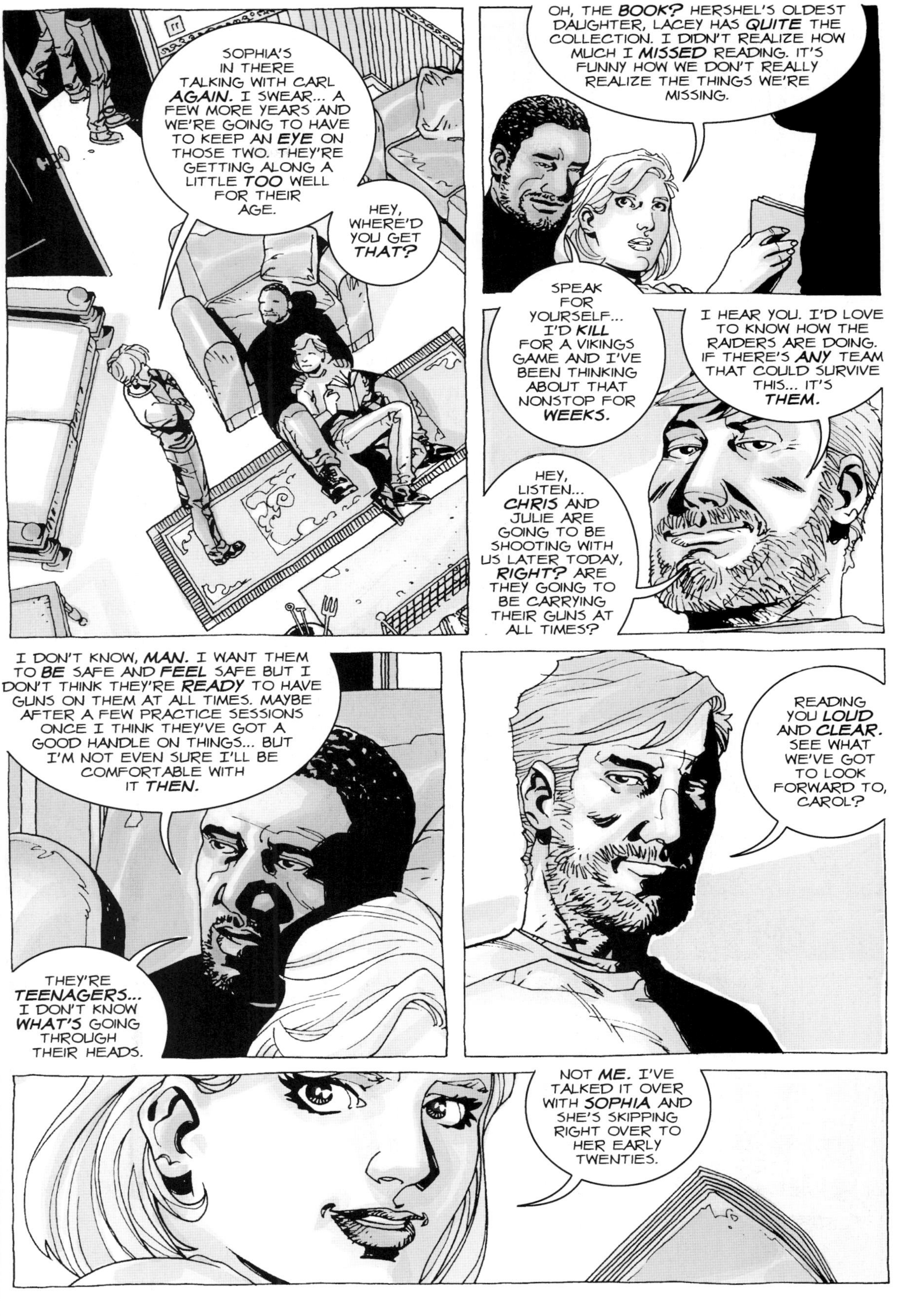
SOPHIA'S IN THERE TALKING WITH CARL AGAIN. I SWEAR... A FEW MORE YEARS AND WE'RE GOING TO HAVE TO KEEP AN EYE ON THOSE TWO. THEY'RE GETTING ALONG A LITTLE TOO WELL FOR THEIR AGE.
HEY, WHERE'D YOU GET THAT?
OH, THE BOOK? HERSHEL'S OLDEST DAUGHTER, LACEY HAS QUITE THE COLLECTION. I DIDN'T REALIZE HOW MUCH I MISSED READING. IT'S FUNNY HOW WE DON'T REALLY REALIZE THE THINGS WE'RE MISSING.
SPEAK FOR YOURSELF... I'D KILL FOR A VIKINGS GAME AND I'VE BEEN THINKING ABOUT THAT NONSTOP FOR WEEKS.
I HEAR YOU. I'D LOVE TO KNOW HOW THE RAIDERS ARE DOING. IF THERE'S ANY TEAM THAT COULD SURVIVE THIS... IT'S THEM.
HEY, LISTEN... CHRIS AND JULIE ARE GOING TO BE SHOOTING WITH US LATER TODAY, RIGHT? ARE THEY GOING TO BE CARRYING THEIR GUNS AT ALL TIMES?
I DON'T KNOW, MAN. I WANT THEM TO BE SAFE AND FEEL SAFE BUT I DON'T THINK THEY'RE READY TO HAVE GUNS ON THEM AT ALL TIMES. MAYBE AFTER A FEW PRACTICE SESSIONS ONCE I THINK THEY'VE GOT A GOOD HANDLE ON THINGS... BUT I'M NOT EVEN SURE I'LL BE COMFORTABLE WITH IT THEN.
THEY'RE TEENAGERS... I DON'T KNOW WHAT'S GOING THROUGH THEIR HEADS.
READING YOU LOUD AND CLEAR. SEE WHAT WE'VE GOT TO LOOK FORWARD TO, CAROL?
NOT ME. I'VE TALKED IT OVER WITH SOPHIA AND SHE'S SKIPPING RIGHT OVER TO HER EARLY TWENTIES.

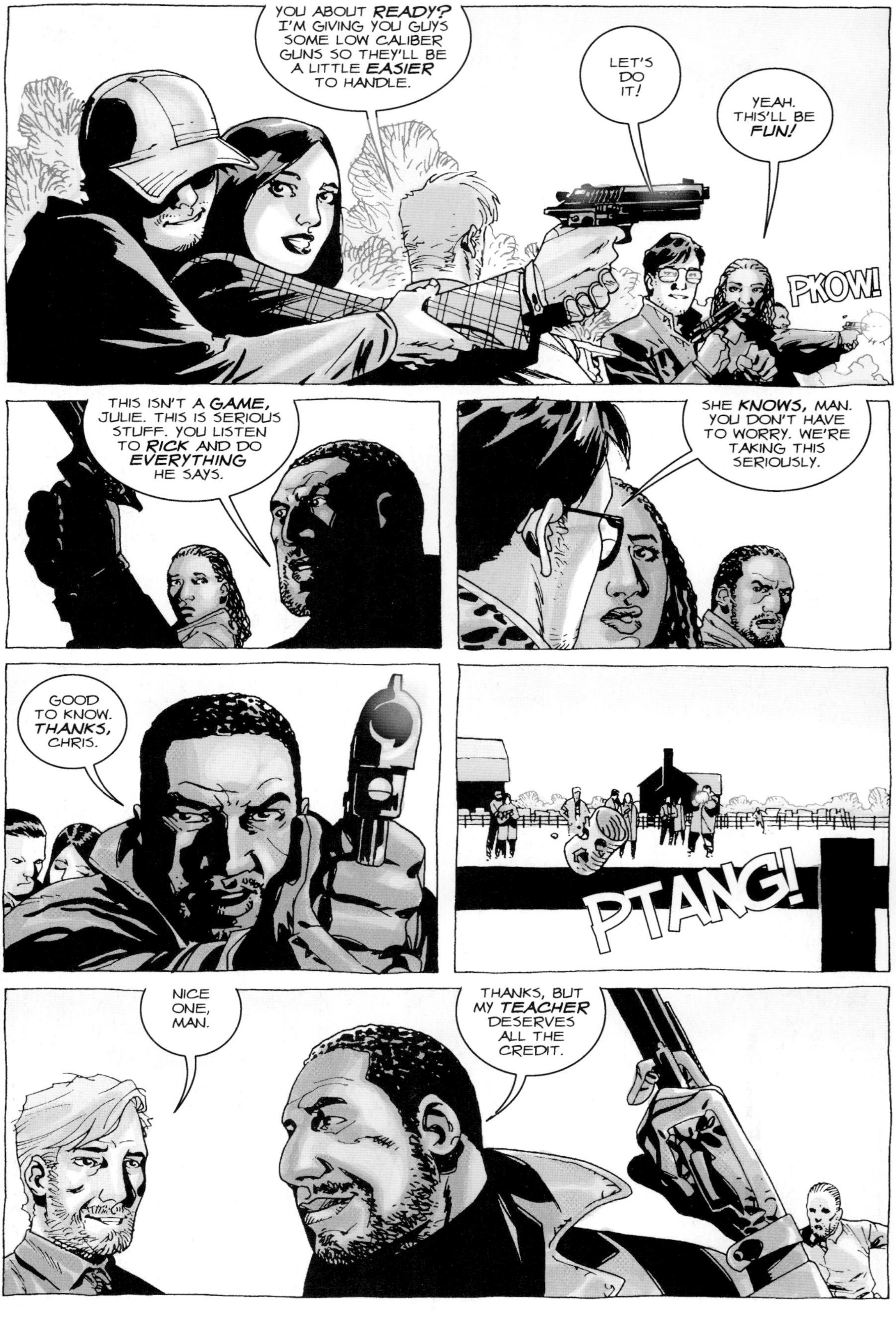

YOU ABOUT **READY?** I'M GIVING YOU GUYS SOME LOW CALIBER GUNS SO THEY'LL BE A LITTLE **EASIER** TO HANDLE.
LET'S DO IT!
YEAH. THIS'LL BE **FUN!**
PKOW!
THIS ISN'T A **GAME,** JULIE. THIS IS SERIOUS STUFF. YOU LISTEN TO **RICK** AND DO **EVERYTHING** HE SAYS.
SHE **KNOWS,** MAN. YOU DON'T HAVE TO WORRY. WE'RE TAKING THIS SERIOUSLY.
GOOD TO KNOW. **THANKS,** CHRIS.
PTANG!
NICE ONE, MAN.
THANKS, BUT MY **TEACHER** DESERVES ALL THE CREDIT.

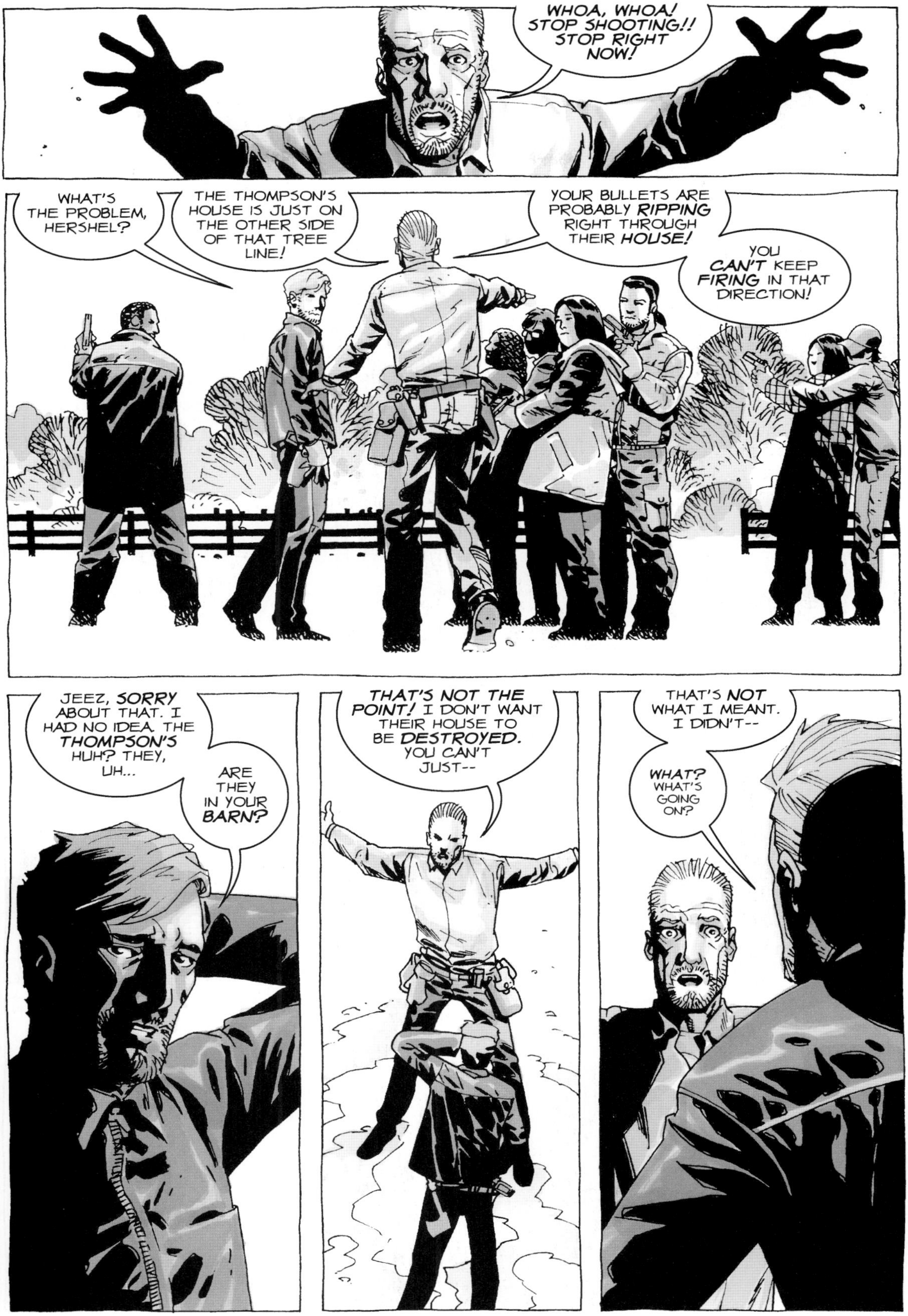

WHOA, WHOA! STOP SHOOTING!! STOP RIGHT NOW!
WHAT'S THE PROBLEM, HERSHEL?
THE THOMPSON'S HOUSE IS JUST ON THE OTHER SIDE OF THAT TREE LINE!
YOUR BULLETS ARE PROBABLY RIPPING RIGHT THROUGH THEIR HOUSE!
YOU CAN'T KEEP FIRING IN THAT DIRECTION!
JEEZ, SORRY ABOUT THAT. I HAD NO IDEA THE THOMPSON'S HUH? THEY, UH...
ARE THEY IN YOUR BARN?
THAT'S NOT THE POINT! I DON'T WANT THEIR HOUSE TO BE DESTROYED. YOU CAN'T JUST--
THAT'S NOT WHAT I MEANT. I DIDN'T--
WHAT? WHAT'S GOING ON?

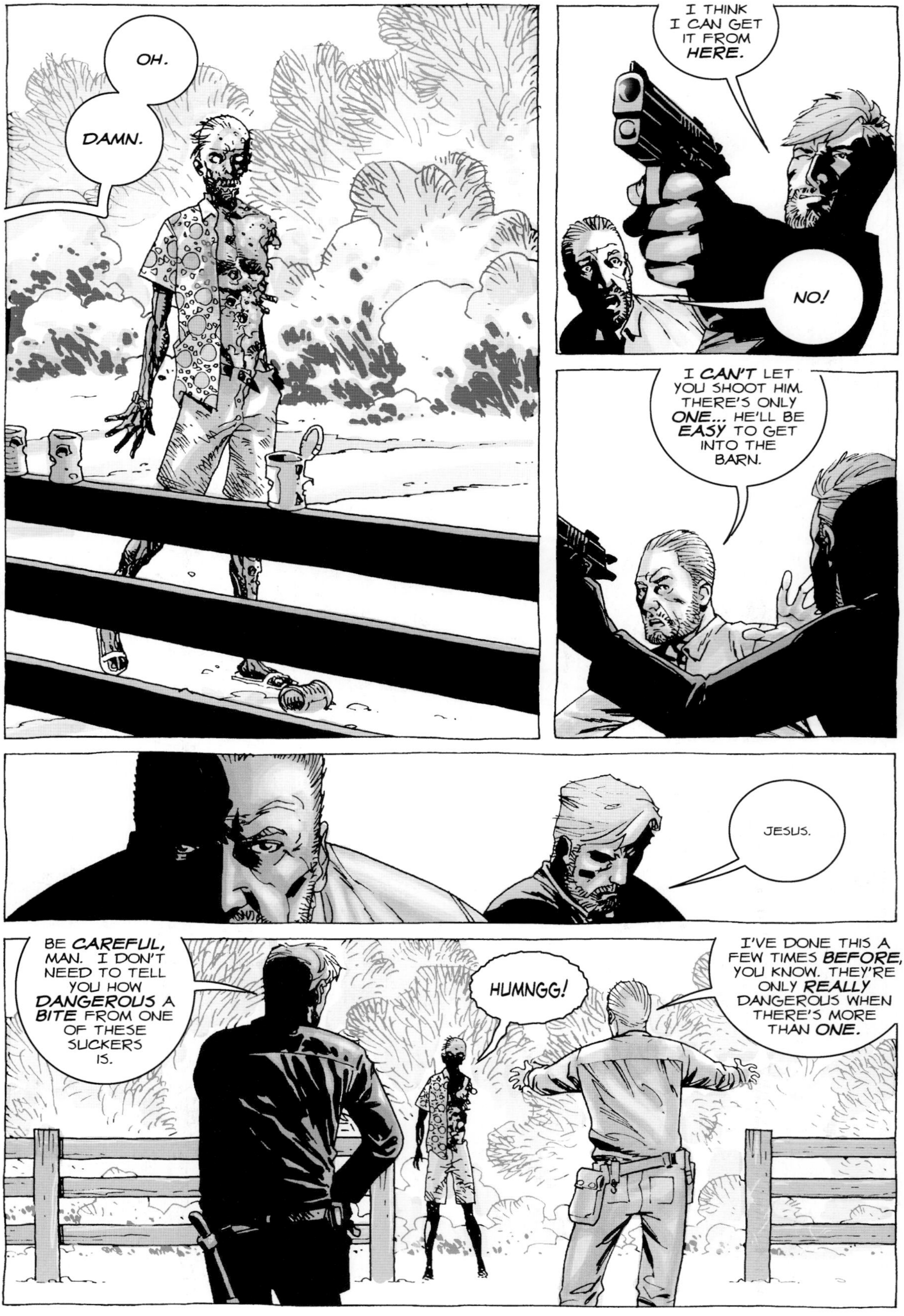
OH.
DAMN.
I THINK I CAN GET IT FROM HERE.
NO!
I CAN'T LET YOU SHOOT HIM. THERE'S ONLY ONE... HE'LL BE EASY TO GET INTO THE BARN.
JESUS.
BE CAREFUL, MAN. I DON'T NEED TO TELL YOU HOW DANGEROUS A BITE FROM ONE OF THESE SUCKERS IS.
HUMNGG!
I'VE DONE THIS A FEW TIMES BEFORE, YOU KNOW. THEY'RE ONLY REALLY DANGEROUS WHEN THERE'S MORE THAN ONE.

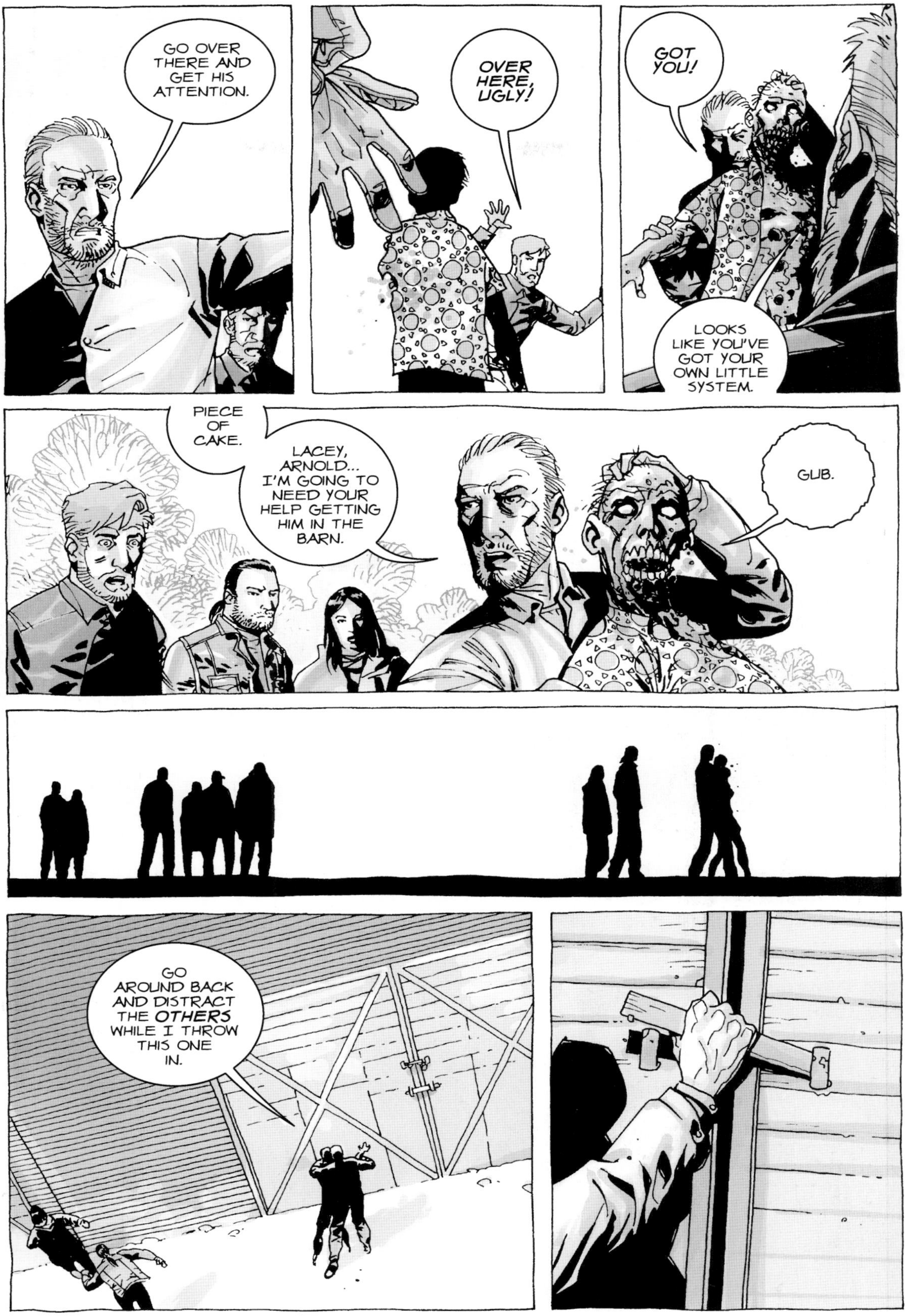
GO OVER THERE AND GET HIS ATTENTION.
OVER HERE, UGLY!
GOT YOU!
LOOKS LIKE YOU'VE GOT YOUR OWN LITTLE SYSTEM.
PIECE OF CAKE.
LACEY, ARNOLD... I'M GOING TO NEED YOUR HELP GETTING HIM IN THE BARN.
GUB.
GO AROUND BACK AND DISTRACT THE OTHERS WHILE I THROW THIS ONE IN.

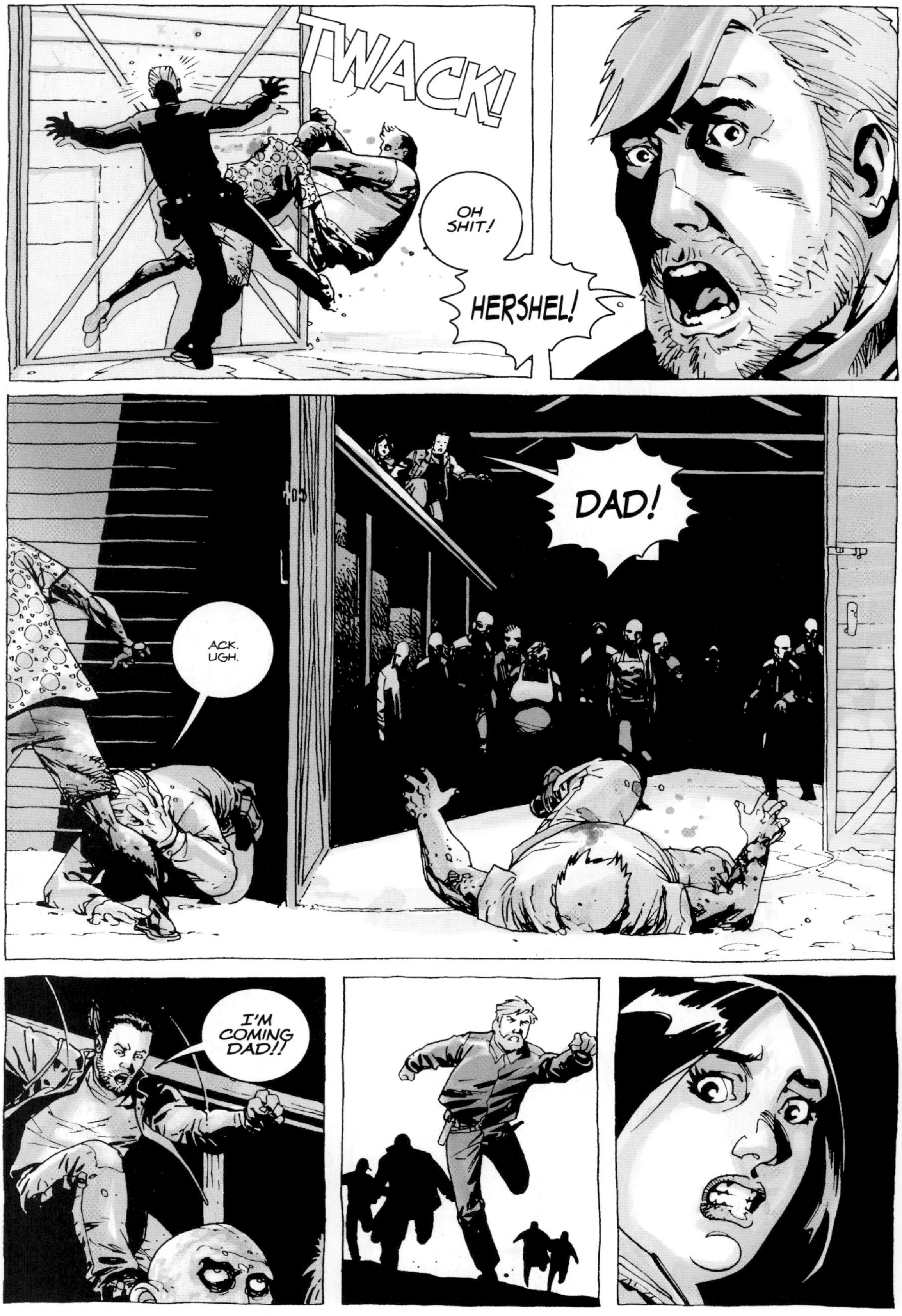
TWACK!
OH SHIT!
HERSHEL!
DAD!
ACK. UGH.
I'M COMING DAD!!

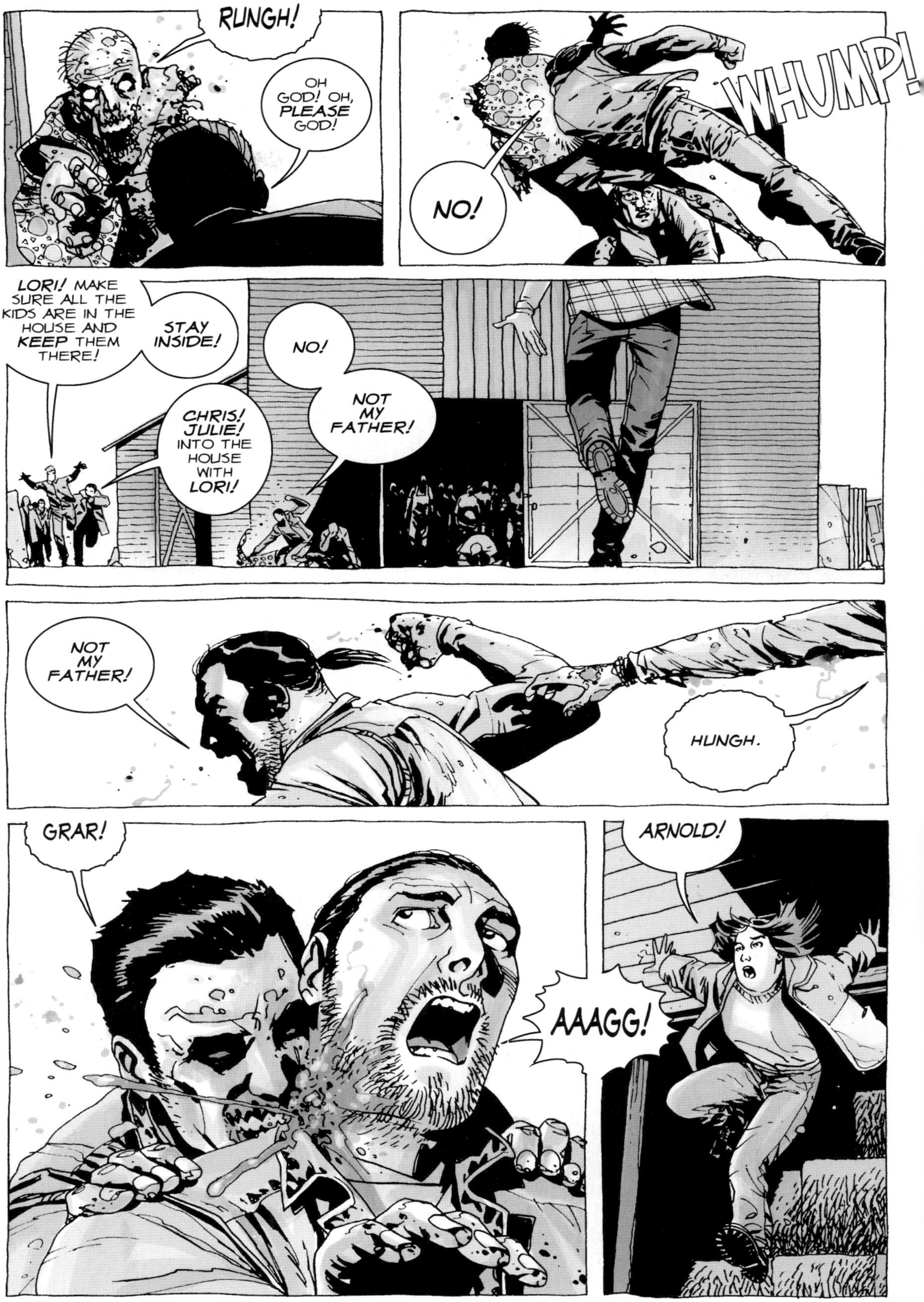
RUNGH!
OH GOD! OH, PLEASE GOD!
NO!
WHUMP!
LORI! MAKE SURE ALL THE KIDS ARE IN THE HOUSE AND KEEP THEM THERE!
STAY INSIDE!
CHRIS! JULIE! INTO THE HOUSE WITH LORI!
NO!
NOT MY FATHER!
NOT MY FATHER!
HUNGH.
GRAR!
AAAGG!
ARNOLD!

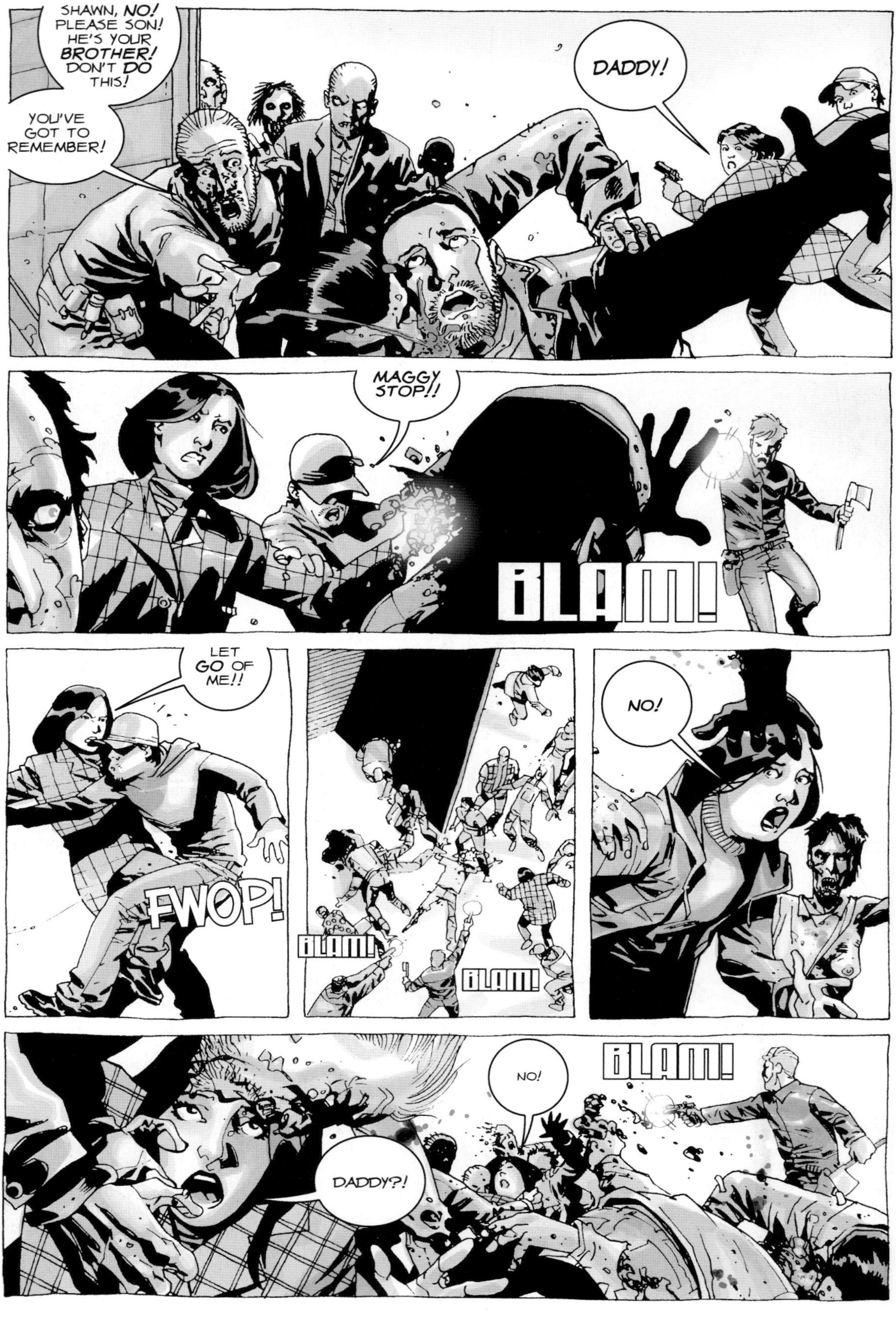
SHAWN, NO! PLEASE SON! HE'S YOUR BROTHER! DON'T DO THIS!
YOU'VE GOT TO REMEMBER!
DADDY!
MAGGY STOP!!
BLAM!
LET GO OF ME!!
FWOP!
BLAM!
BLAM!
NO!
BLAM!
NO!
DADDY?!

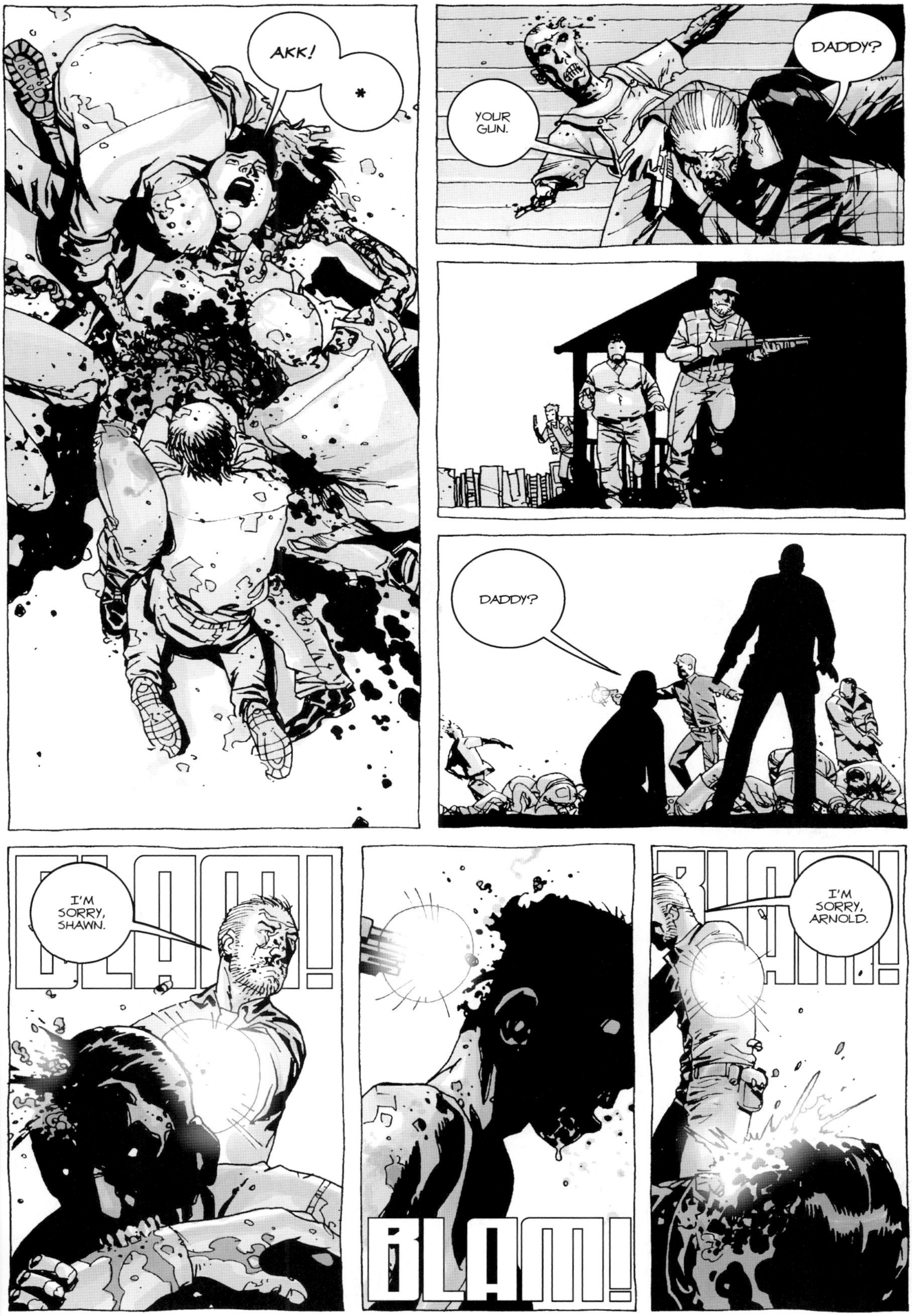
AKK!
*
DADDY?
YOUR GUN.
DADDY?
BLAM!
I'M SORRY, SHAWN.
BLAM!
BLAM!
I'M SORRY, ARNOLD.

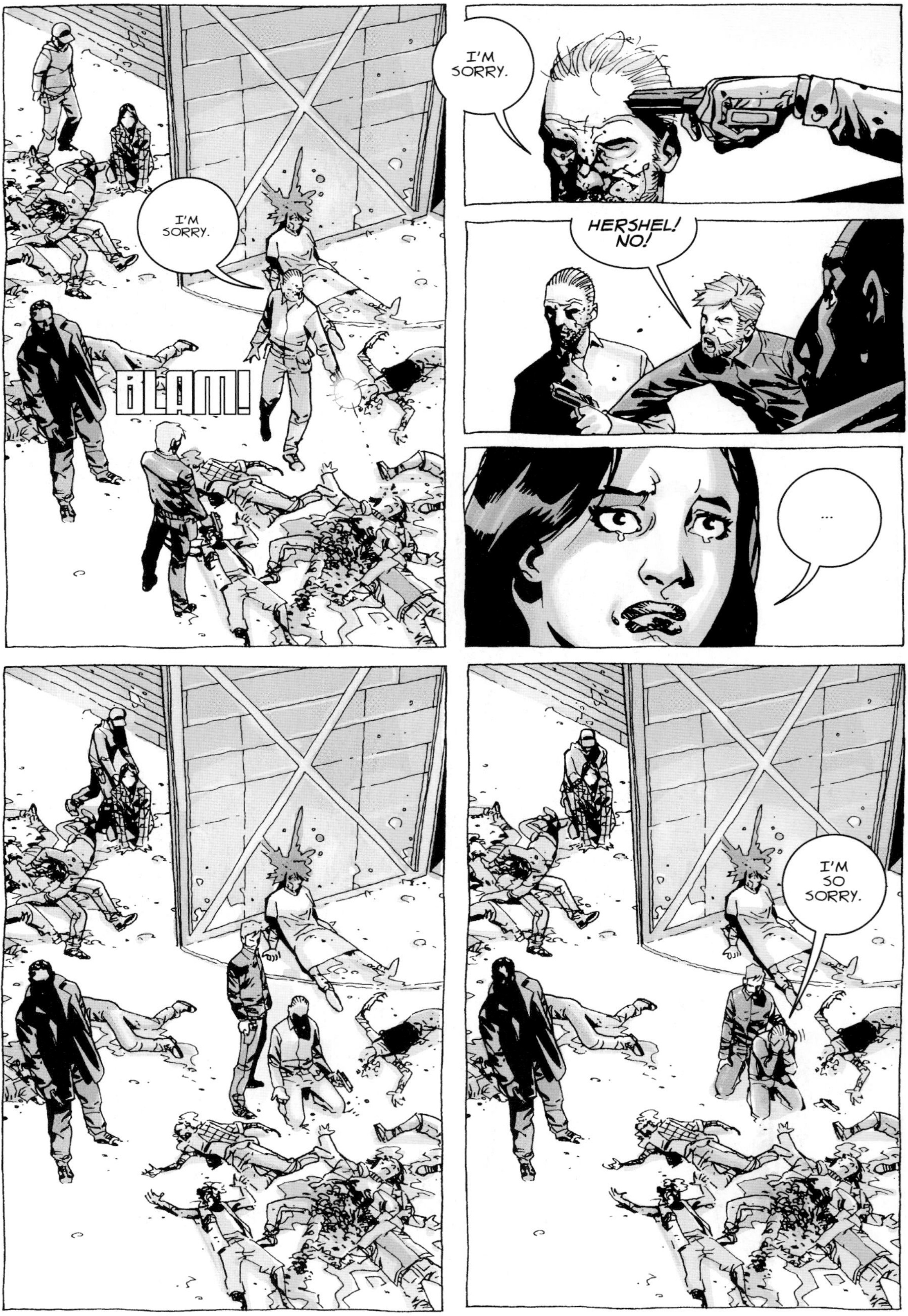
I'M SORRY.
BLAM!
I'M SORRY.
HERSHEL! NO!
...
I'M SO SORRY.

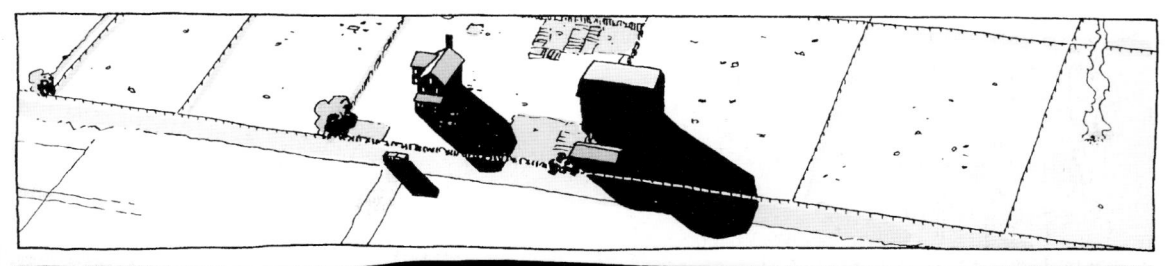

YOU
WERE
RIGHT.

DAD. MISTER *GRIMES* NEVER TOOK OUR GUNS BACK AFTER TARGET PRACTICE. I DON'T WANT YOU TO GET *MAD* AT US FOR STILL HAVING THEM LATER... SO WE'RE GIVING THEM TO *YOU.*

RICK'S HAD A LOT ON HIS HANDS TODAY, JULIE. I'LL JUST--

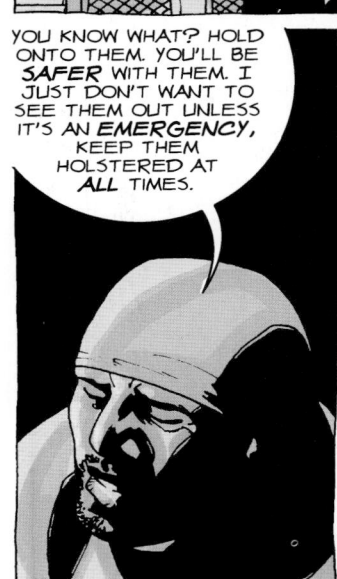

YOU KNOW WHAT? HOLD ONTO THEM. YOU'LL BE *SAFER* WITH THEM. I JUST DON'T WANT TO SEE THEM OUT UNLESS IT'S AN *EMERGENCY,* KEEP THEM HOLSTERED AT *ALL* TIMES.

OKAY.

FINALLY. I THOUGHT THAT *BASTARD* WOULD *NEVER* LET US HAVE GUNS.

IT'S GOING TO BE SO MUCH *EASIER* NOW.

YES. WE'LL DO IT AS SOON AS THE TIME IS RIGHT. I *LOVE* YOU, CHRIS.

I LOVE YOU, TOO.

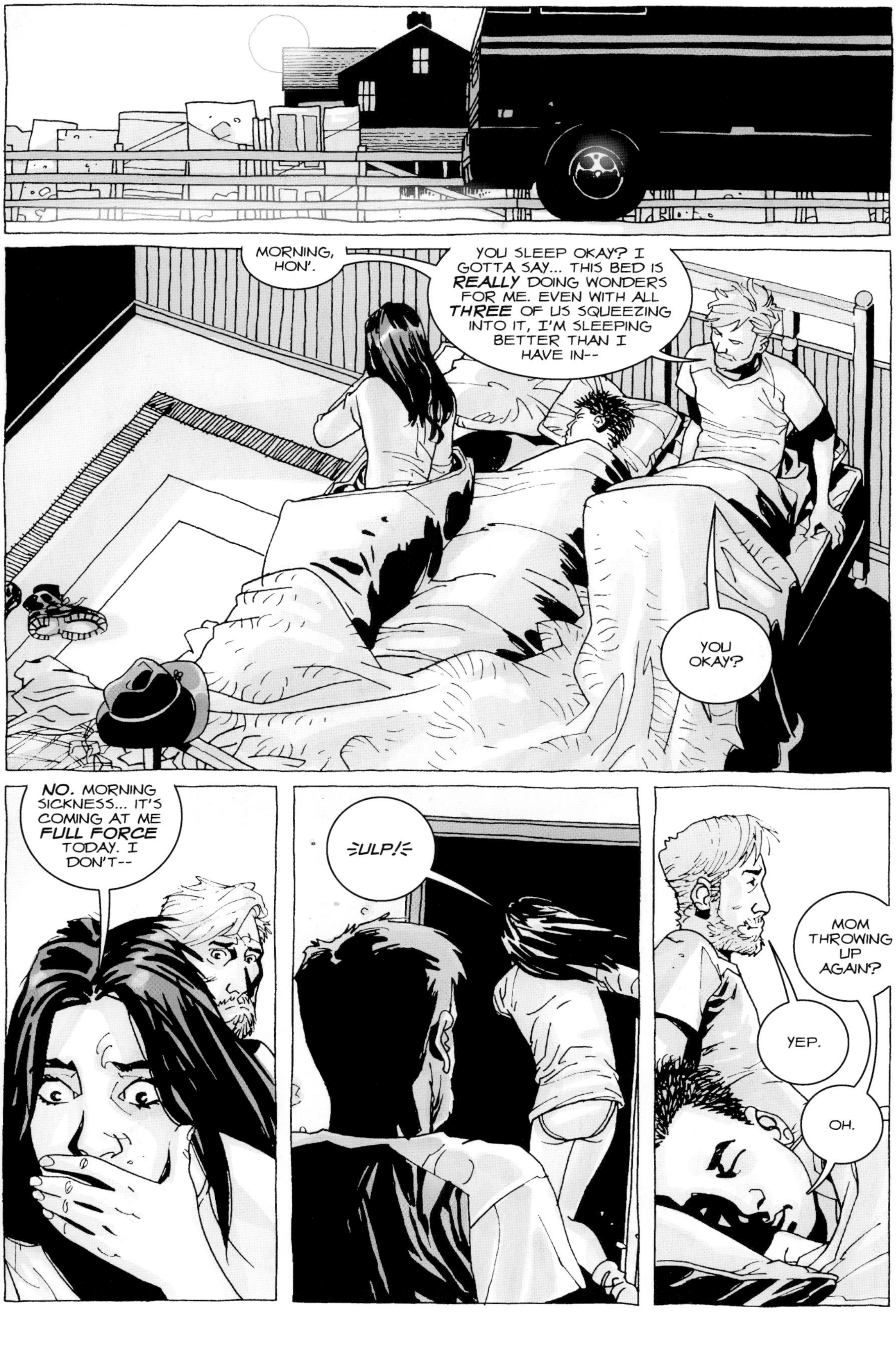
MORNING, HON'.
YOU SLEEP OKAY? I GOTTA SAY... THIS BED IS REALLY DOING WONDERS FOR ME. EVEN WITH ALL THREE OF US SQUEEZING INTO IT, I'M SLEEPING BETTER THAN I HAVE IN--
YOU OKAY?
NO. MORNING SICKNESS... IT'S COMING AT ME FULL FORCE TODAY. I DON'T--
ULP!
MOM THROWING UP AGAIN?
YEP.
OH.

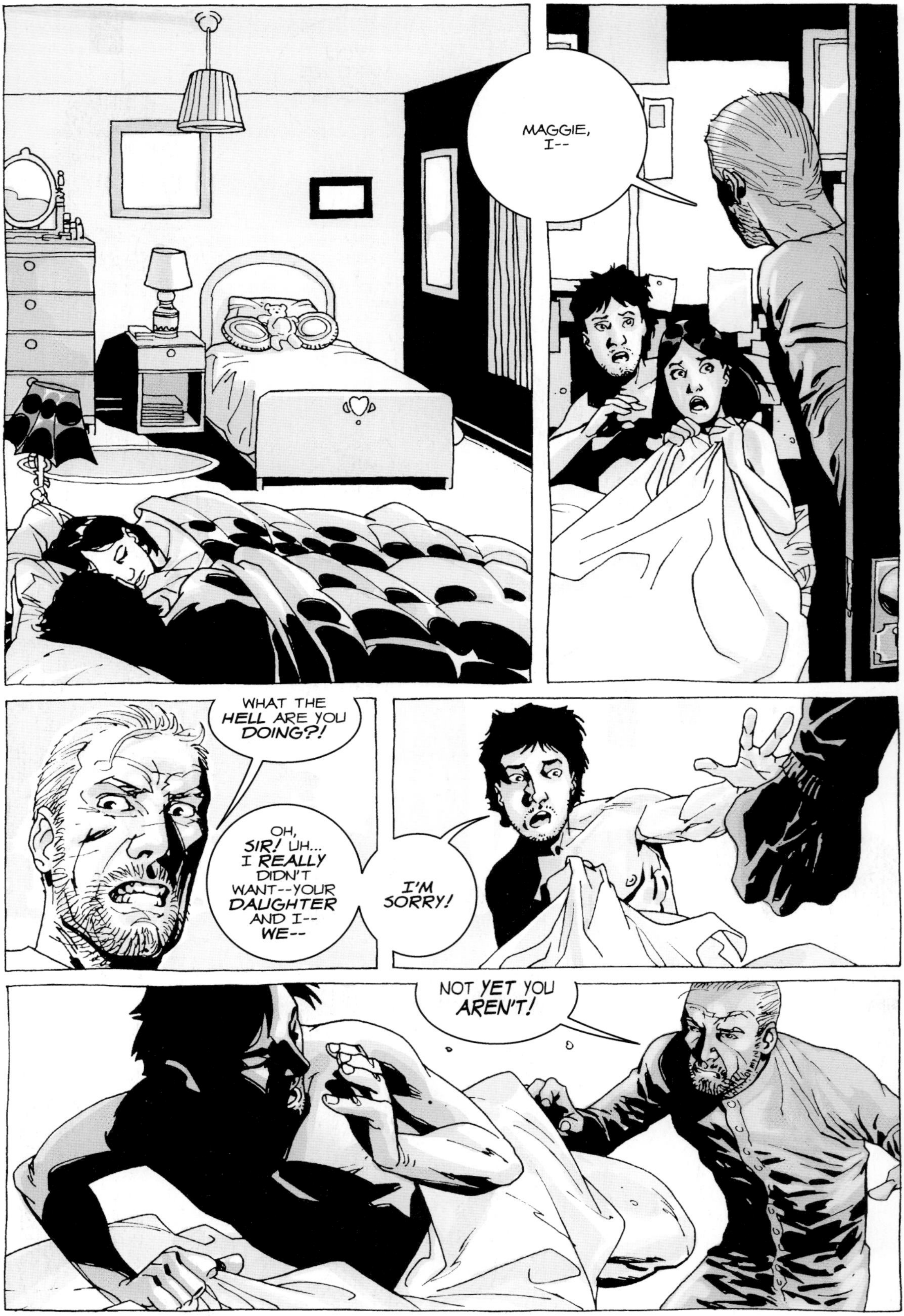
MAGGIE, I--
WHAT THE HELL ARE YOU DOING?!
OH, SIR! UH... I REALLY DIDN'T WANT--YOUR DAUGHTER AND I-- WE--
I'M SORRY!
NOT YET YOU AREN'T!

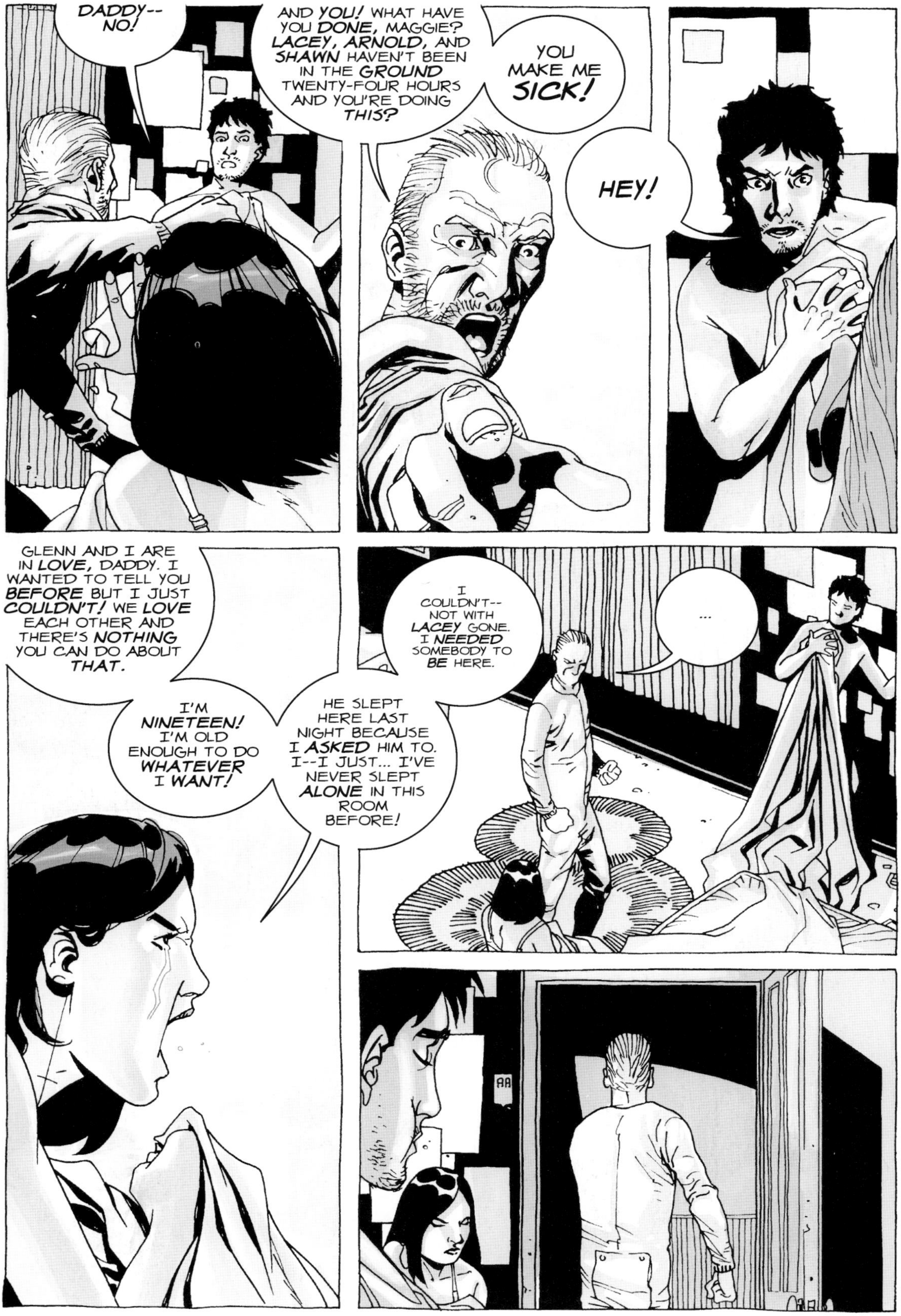

DADDY-- NO!
AND YOU! WHAT HAVE YOU DONE, MAGGIE? LACEY, ARNOLD, AND SHAWN HAVEN'T BEEN IN THE GROUND TWENTY-FOUR HOURS AND YOU'RE DOING THIS?
YOU MAKE ME SICK!
HEY!
GLENN AND I ARE IN LOVE, DADDY. I WANTED TO TELL YOU BEFORE BUT I JUST COULDN'T! WE LOVE EACH OTHER AND THERE'S NOTHING YOU CAN DO ABOUT THAT.
I'M NINETEEN! I'M OLD ENOUGH TO DO WHATEVER I WANT!
HE SLEPT HERE LAST NIGHT BECAUSE I ASKED HIM TO. I--I JUST... I'VE NEVER SLEPT ALONE IN THIS ROOM BEFORE!
I COULDN'T-- NOT WITH LACEY GONE. I NEEDED SOMEBODY TO BE HERE.
...

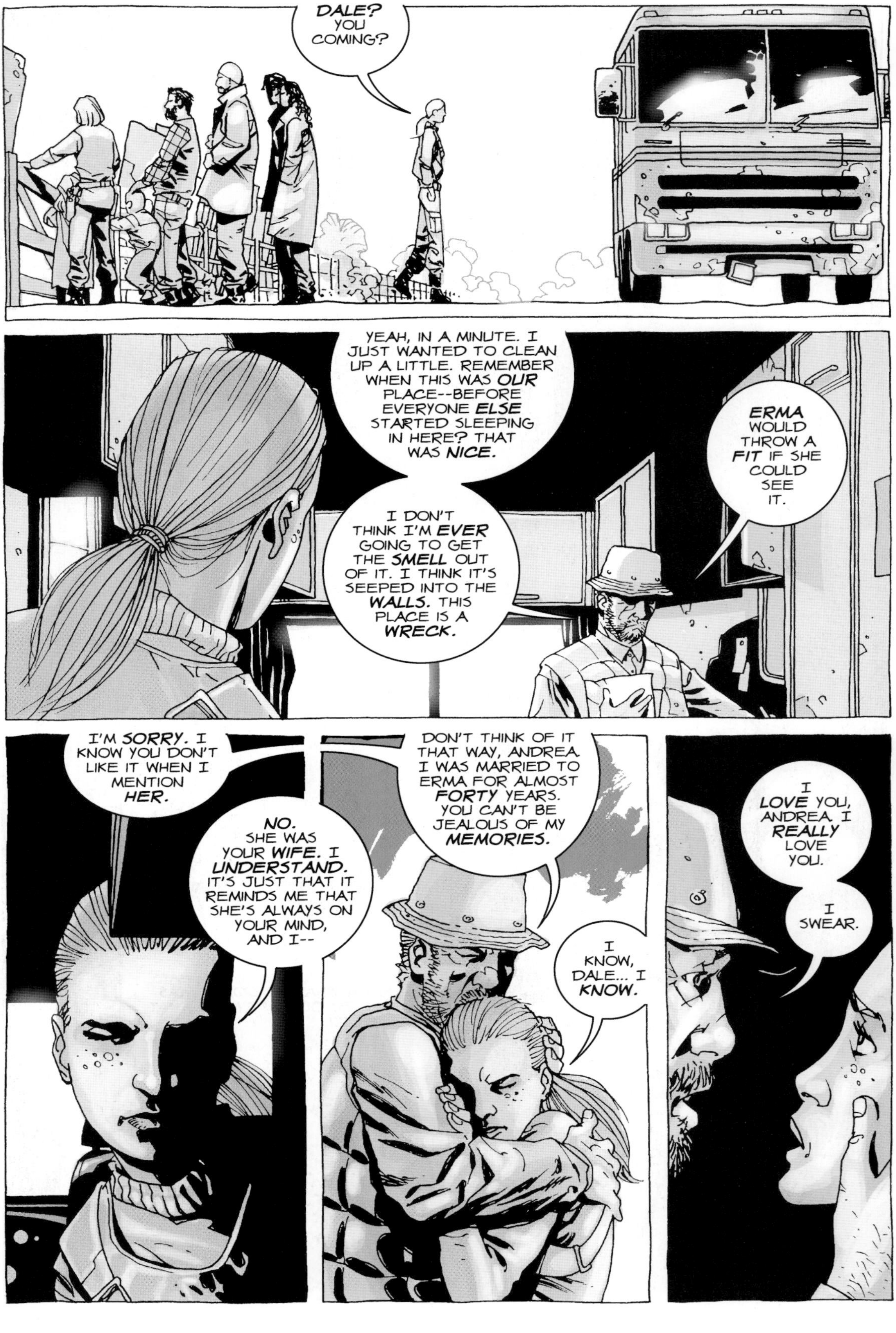

DALE? YOU COMING?
YEAH, IN A MINUTE. I JUST WANTED TO CLEAN UP A LITTLE. REMEMBER WHEN THIS WAS OUR PLACE--BEFORE EVERYONE ELSE STARTED SLEEPING IN HERE? THAT WAS NICE.
I DON'T THINK I'M EVER GOING TO GET THE SMELL OUT OF IT. I THINK IT'S SEEPED INTO THE WALLS. THIS PLACE IS A WRECK.
ERMA WOULD THROW A FIT IF SHE COULD SEE IT.
I'M SORRY. I KNOW YOU DON'T LIKE IT WHEN I MENTION HER.
NO. SHE WAS YOUR WIFE. I UNDERSTAND. IT'S JUST THAT IT REMINDS ME THAT SHE'S ALWAYS ON YOUR MIND, AND I--
DON'T THINK OF IT THAT WAY, ANDREA. I WAS MARRIED TO ERMA FOR ALMOST FORTY YEARS. YOU CAN'T BE JEALOUS OF MY MEMORIES.
I KNOW, DALE... I KNOW.
I LOVE YOU, ANDREA. I REALLY LOVE YOU.
I SWEAR.

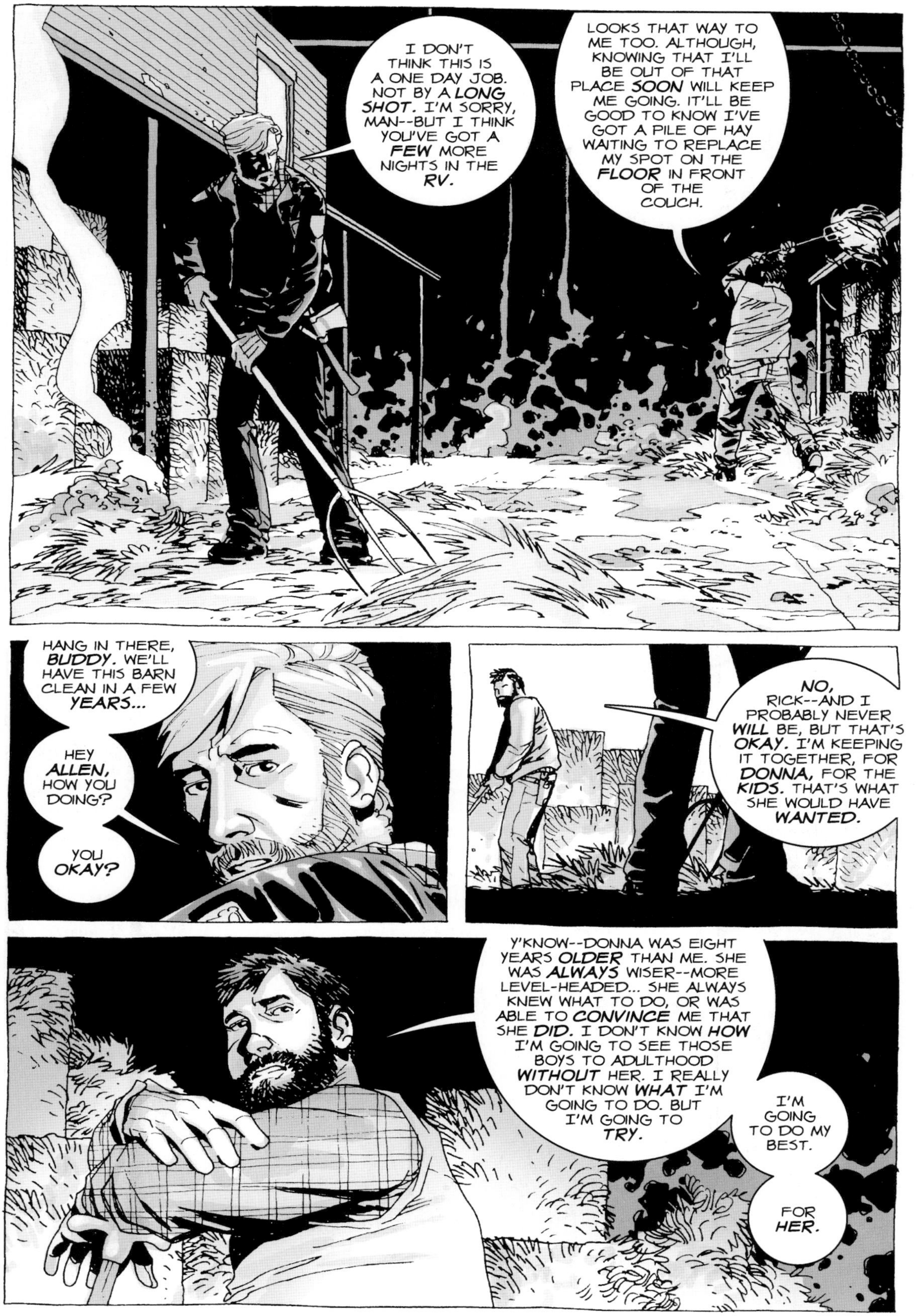
I DON'T THINK THIS IS A ONE DAY JOB. NOT BY A LONG SHOT. I'M SORRY, MAN--BUT I THINK YOU'VE GOT A FEW MORE NIGHTS IN THE RV.
LOOKS THAT WAY TO ME TOO. ALTHOUGH, KNOWING THAT I'LL BE OUT OF THAT PLACE SOON WILL KEEP ME GOING. IT'LL BE GOOD TO KNOW I'VE GOT A PILE OF HAY WAITING TO REPLACE MY SPOT ON THE FLOOR IN FRONT OF THE COUCH.
HANG IN THERE, BUDDY. WE'LL HAVE THIS BARN CLEAN IN A FEW YEARS...
HEY ALLEN, HOW YOU DOING?
YOU OKAY?
NO, RICK--AND I PROBABLY NEVER WILL BE, BUT THAT'S OKAY. I'M KEEPING IT TOGETHER, FOR DONNA, FOR THE KIDS. THAT'S WHAT SHE WOULD HAVE WANTED.
Y'KNOW--DONNA WAS EIGHT YEARS OLDER THAN ME. SHE WAS ALWAYS WISER--MORE LEVEL-HEADED... SHE ALWAYS KNEW WHAT TO DO, OR WAS ABLE TO CONVINCE ME THAT SHE DID. I DON'T KNOW HOW I'M GOING TO SEE THOSE BOYS TO ADULTHOOD WITHOUT HER. I REALLY DON'T KNOW WHAT I'M GOING TO DO. BUT I'M GOING TO TRY.
I'M GOING TO DO MY BEST.
FOR HER.

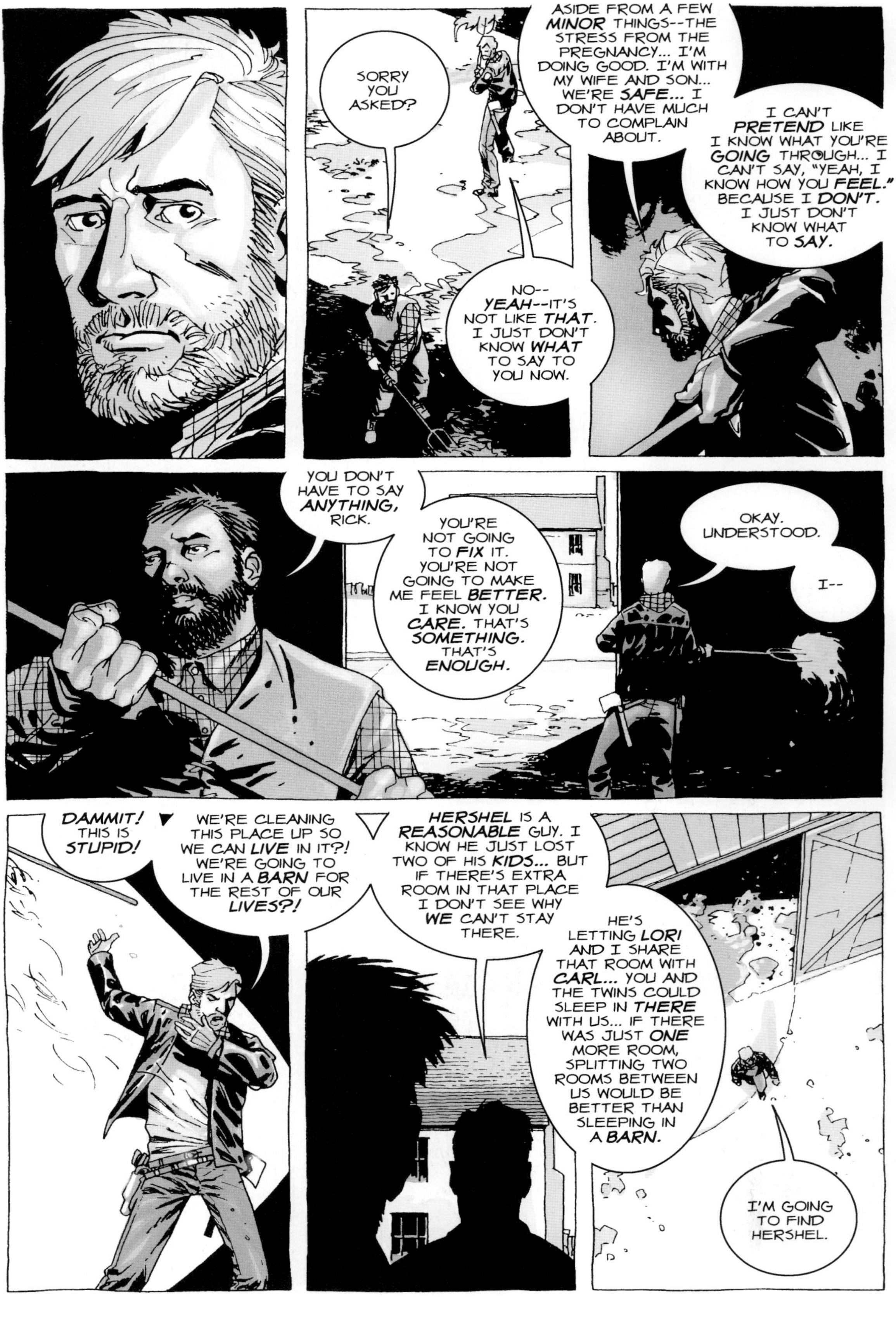
SORRY YOU ASKED?
ASIDE FROM A FEW MINOR THINGS--THE STRESS FROM THE PREGNANCY... I'M DOING GOOD. I'M WITH MY WIFE AND SON... WE'RE SAFE... I DON'T HAVE MUCH TO COMPLAIN ABOUT.
NO-- YEAH--IT'S NOT LIKE THAT. I JUST DON'T KNOW WHAT TO SAY TO YOU NOW.
I CAN'T PRETEND LIKE I KNOW WHAT YOU'RE GOING THROUGH... I CAN'T SAY, "YEAH, I KNOW HOW YOU FEEL." BECAUSE I DON'T. I JUST DON'T KNOW WHAT TO SAY.
YOU DON'T HAVE TO SAY ANYTHING, RICK.
YOU'RE NOT GOING TO FIX IT. YOU'RE NOT GOING TO MAKE ME FEEL BETTER. I KNOW YOU CARE. THAT'S SOMETHING. THAT'S ENOUGH.
OKAY. UNDERSTOOD.
I--
DAMMIT! THIS IS STUPID!
WE'RE CLEANING THIS PLACE UP SO WE CAN LIVE IN IT?! WE'RE GOING TO LIVE IN A BARN FOR THE REST OF OUR LIVES?!
HERSHEL IS A REASONABLE GUY. I KNOW HE JUST LOST TWO OF HIS KIDS... BUT IF THERE'S EXTRA ROOM IN THAT PLACE I DON'T SEE WHY WE CAN'T STAY THERE.
HE'S LETTING LORI AND I SHARE THAT ROOM WITH CARL... YOU AND THE TWINS COULD SLEEP IN THERE WITH US... IF THERE WAS JUST ONE MORE ROOM, SPLITTING TWO ROOMS BETWEEN US WOULD BE BETTER THAN SLEEPING IN A BARN.
I'M GOING TO FIND HERSHEL.

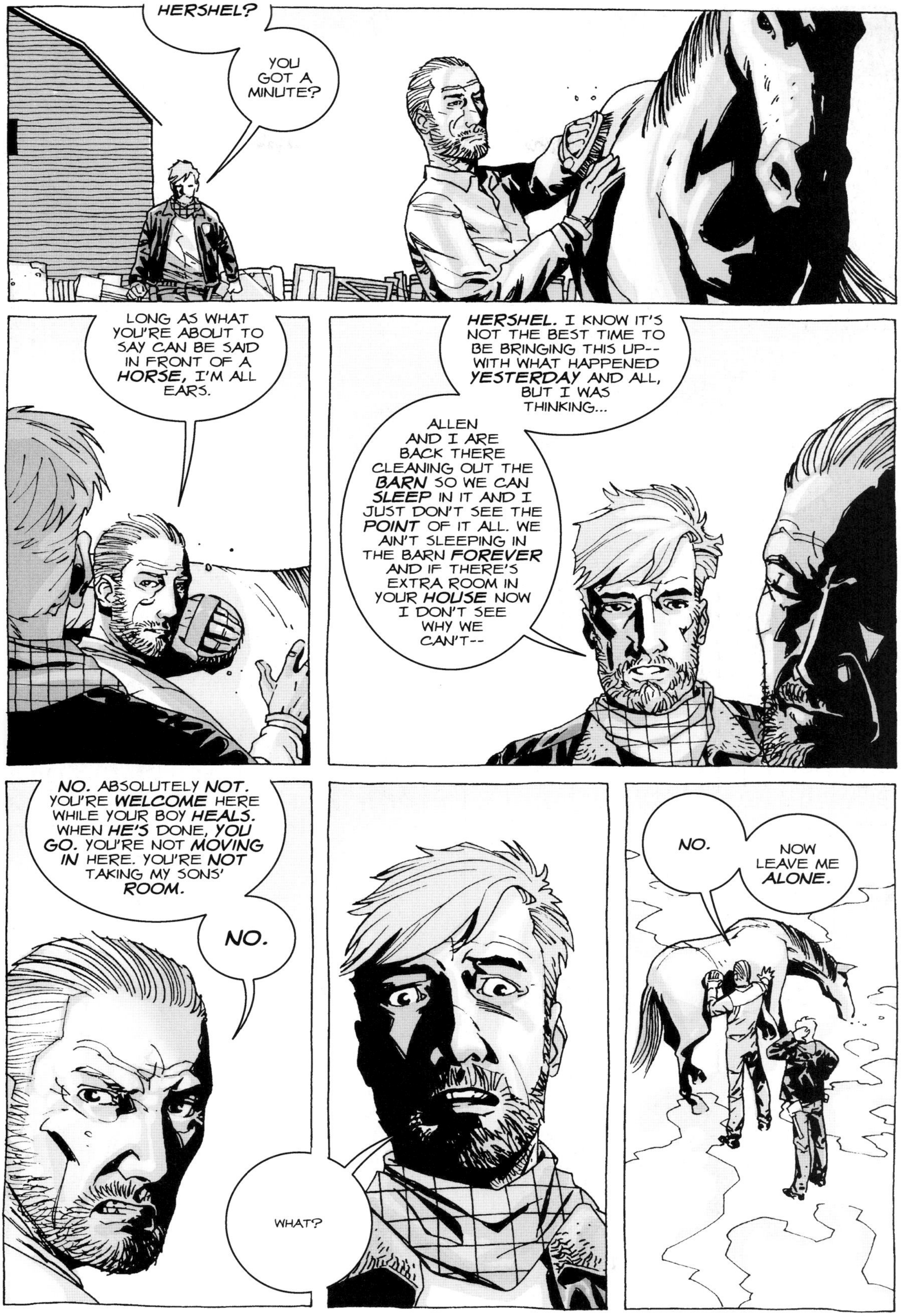
HERSHEL?
YOU GOT A MINUTE?
LONG AS WHAT YOU'RE ABOUT TO SAY CAN BE SAID IN FRONT OF A HORSE, I'M ALL EARS.
HERSHEL. I KNOW IT'S NOT THE BEST TIME TO BE BRINGING THIS UP-- WITH WHAT HAPPENED YESTERDAY AND ALL, BUT I WAS THINKING...
ALLEN AND I ARE BACK THERE CLEANING OUT THE BARN SO WE CAN SLEEP IN IT AND I JUST DON'T SEE THE POINT OF IT ALL. WE AIN'T SLEEPING IN THE BARN FOREVER AND IF THERE'S EXTRA ROOM IN YOUR HOUSE NOW I DON'T SEE WHY WE CAN'T--
NO. ABSOLUTELY NOT. YOU'RE WELCOME HERE WHILE YOUR BOY HEALS. WHEN HE'S DONE, YOU GO. YOU'RE NOT MOVING IN HERE. YOU'RE NOT TAKING MY SONS' ROOM.
NO.
WHAT?
NO.
NOW LEAVE ME ALONE.

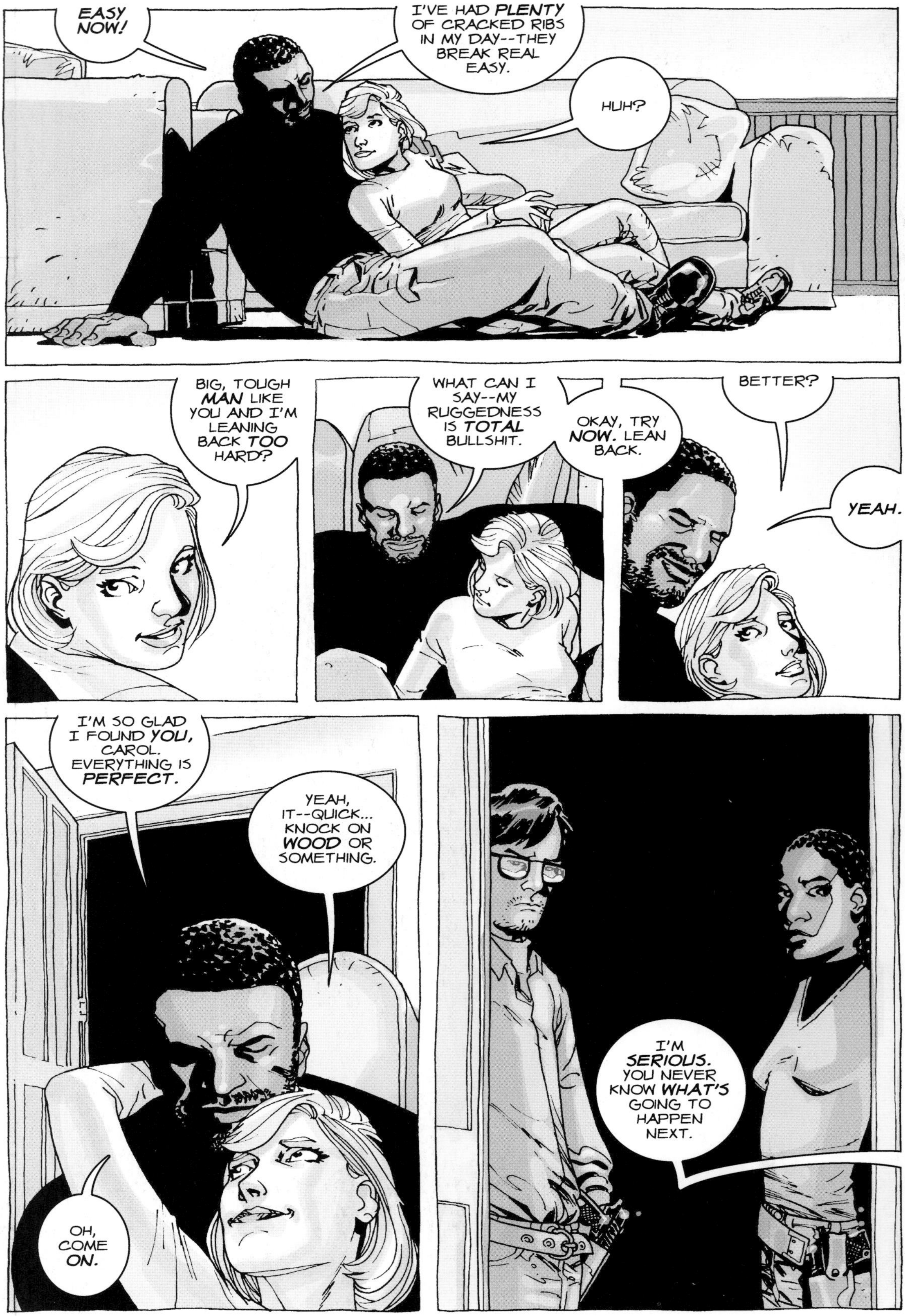
EASY NOW!
I'VE HAD PLENTY OF CRACKED RIBS IN MY DAY--THEY BREAK REAL EASY.
HUH?
BIG, TOUGH MAN LIKE YOU AND I'M LEANING BACK TOO HARD?
WHAT CAN I SAY--MY RUGGEDNESS IS TOTAL BULLSHIT.
OKAY, TRY NOW. LEAN BACK.
BETTER?
YEAH.
I'M SO GLAD I FOUND YOU, CAROL. EVERYTHING IS PERFECT.
YEAH, IT--QUICK... KNOCK ON WOOD OR SOMETHING.
OH, COME ON.
I'M SERIOUS. YOU NEVER KNOW WHAT'S GOING TO HAPPEN NEXT.

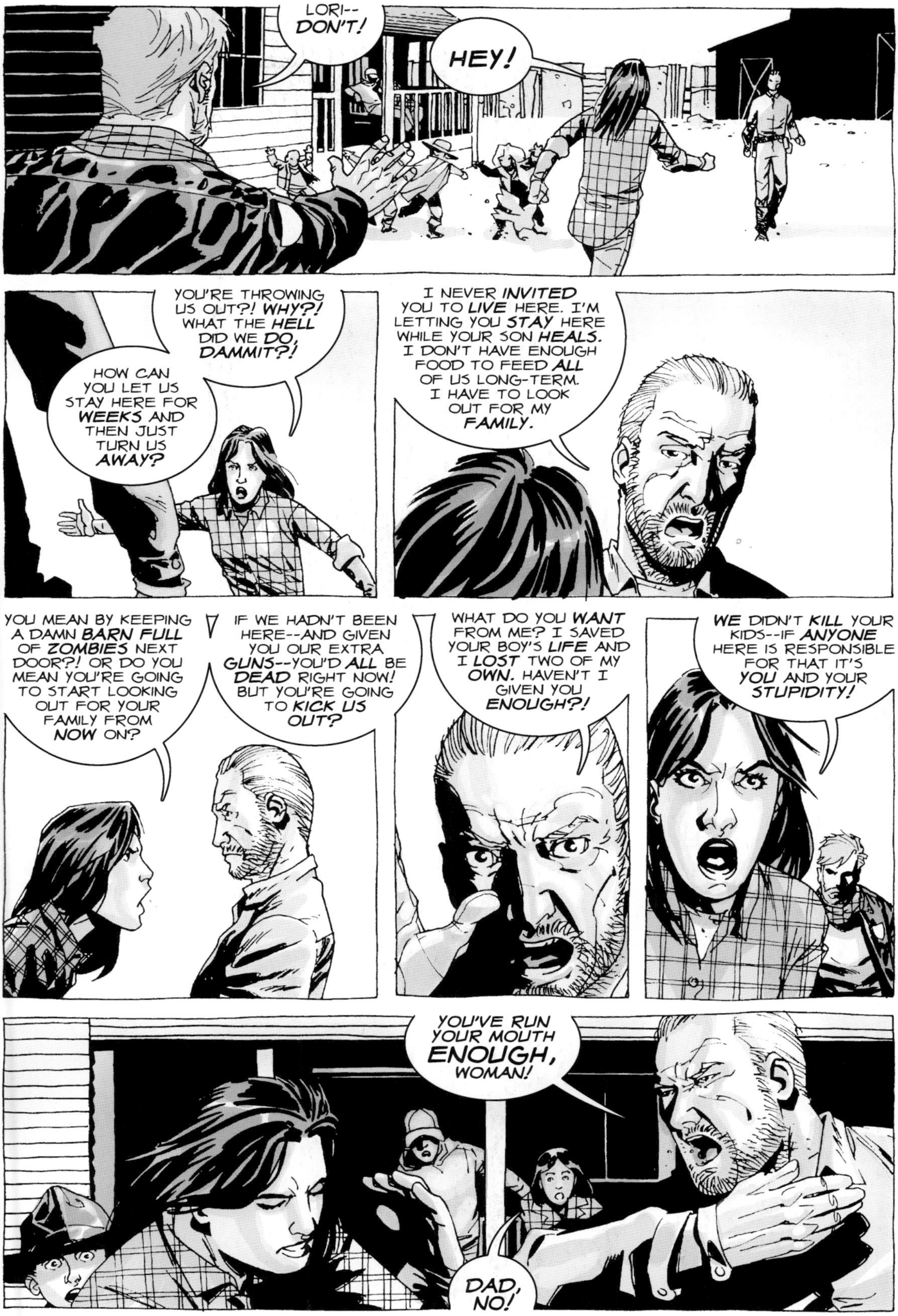

LORI-- DON'T!
HEY!
YOU'RE THROWING US OUT?! WHY?! WHAT THE HELL DID WE DO, DAMMIT?!
HOW CAN YOU LET US STAY HERE FOR WEEKS AND THEN JUST TURN US AWAY?
I NEVER INVITED YOU TO LIVE HERE. I'M LETTING YOU STAY HERE WHILE YOUR SON HEALS. I DON'T HAVE ENOUGH FOOD TO FEED ALL OF US LONG-TERM. I HAVE TO LOOK OUT FOR MY FAMILY.
YOU MEAN BY KEEPING A DAMN BARN FULL OF ZOMBIES NEXT DOOR?! OR DO YOU MEAN YOU'RE GOING TO START LOOKING OUT FOR YOUR FAMILY FROM NOW ON?
IF WE HADN'T BEEN HERE--AND GIVEN YOU OUR EXTRA GUNS--YOU'D ALL BE DEAD RIGHT NOW! BUT YOU'RE GOING TO KICK US OUT?
WHAT DO YOU WANT FROM ME? I SAVED YOUR BOY'S LIFE AND I LOST TWO OF MY OWN. HAVEN'T I GIVEN YOU ENOUGH?!
WE DIDN'T KILL YOUR KIDS--IF ANYONE HERE IS RESPONSIBLE FOR THAT IT'S YOU AND YOUR STUPIDITY!
YOU'VE RUN YOUR MOUTH ENOUGH, WOMAN!
DAD, NO!

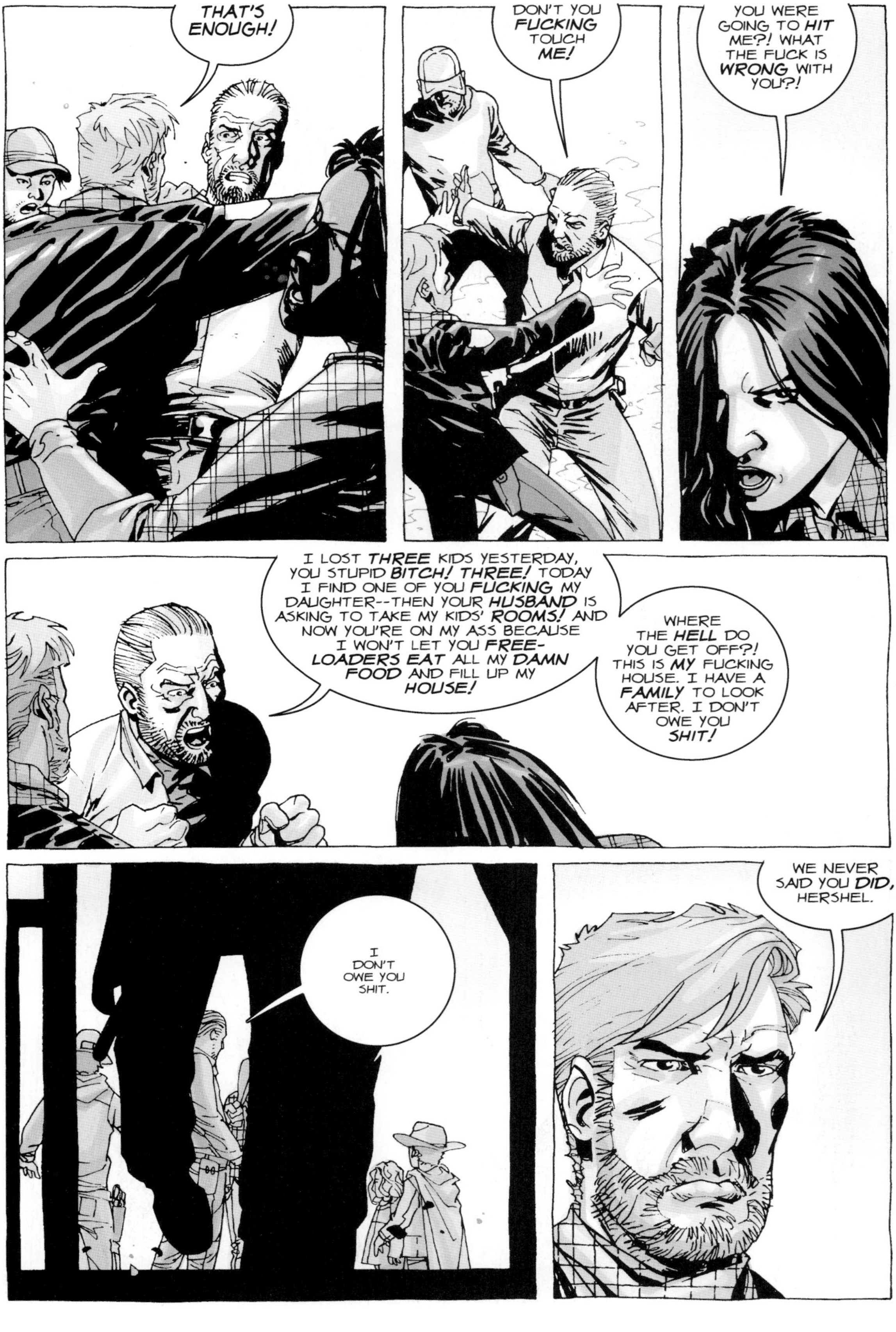
THAT'S ENOUGH!
DON'T YOU FUCKING TOUCH ME!
YOU WERE GOING TO HIT ME?! WHAT THE FUCK IS WRONG WITH YOU?!
I LOST THREE KIDS YESTERDAY, YOU STUPID BITCH! THREE! TODAY I FIND ONE OF YOU FUCKING MY DAUGHTER--THEN YOUR HUSBAND IS ASKING TO TAKE MY KIDS' ROOMS! AND NOW YOU'RE ON MY ASS BECAUSE I WON'T LET YOU FREE-LOADERS EAT ALL MY DAMN FOOD AND FILL UP MY HOUSE!
WHERE THE HELL DO YOU GET OFF?! THIS IS MY FUCKING HOUSE. I HAVE A FAMILY TO LOOK AFTER. I DON'T OWE YOU SHIT!
I DON'T OWE YOU SHIT.
WE NEVER SAID YOU DID, HERSHEL.

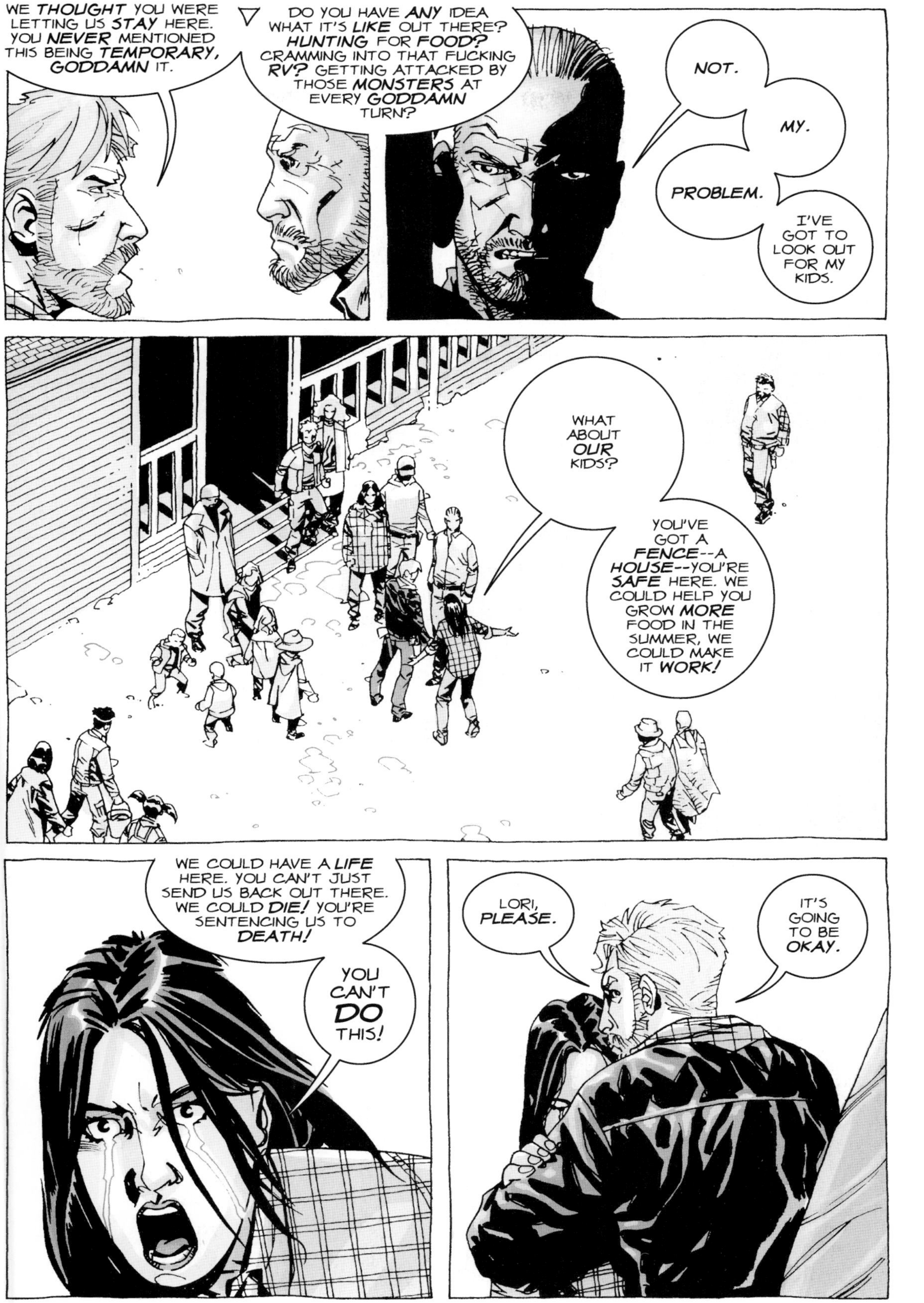
WE THOUGHT YOU WERE LETTING US STAY HERE. YOU NEVER MENTIONED THIS BEING TEMPORARY, GODDAMN IT.
DO YOU HAVE ANY IDEA WHAT IT'S LIKE OUT THERE? HUNTING FOR FOOD? CRAMMING INTO THAT FUCKING RV? GETTING ATTACKED BY THOSE MONSTERS AT EVERY GODDAMN TURN?
NOT.
MY.
PROBLEM.
I'VE GOT TO LOOK OUT FOR MY KIDS.
WHAT ABOUT OUR KIDS?
YOU'VE GOT A FENCE--A HOUSE--YOU'RE SAFE HERE. WE COULD HELP YOU GROW MORE FOOD IN THE SUMMER, WE COULD MAKE IT WORK!
WE COULD HAVE A LIFE HERE. YOU CAN'T JUST SEND US BACK OUT THERE. WE COULD DIE! YOU'RE SENTENCING US TO DEATH!
YOU CAN'T DO THIS!
LORI, PLEASE.
IT'S GOING TO BE OKAY.

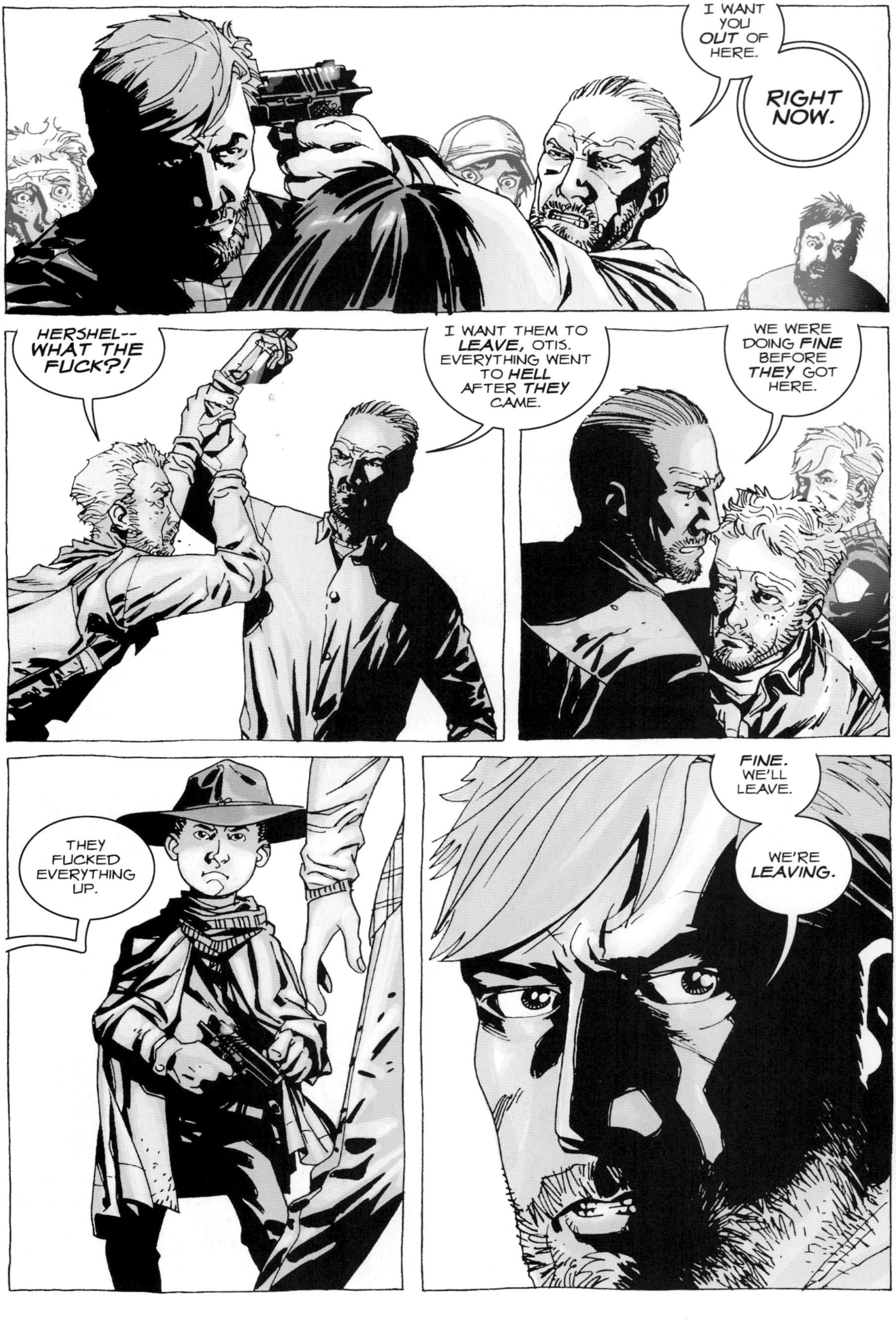
I WANT YOU OUT OF HERE.
RIGHT NOW.
HERSHEL-- WHAT THE FUCK?!
I WANT THEM TO LEAVE, OTIS. EVERYTHING WENT TO HELL AFTER THEY CAME.
WE WERE DOING FINE BEFORE THEY GOT HERE.
THEY FUCKED EVERYTHING UP.
FINE. WE'LL LEAVE.
WE'RE LEAVING.

HERSHEL? YOU IN THERE? I WANNA *TALK* TO YOU.

I AIN'T GOT NO *CLUE* WHAT'S RUNNING AROUND IN YOUR HEAD, MAN--BUT YOU COULDA *SHOT* THAT MAN.

YOU *HEAR* ME IN THERE?

MAN, I UNDERSTAND YOU WANTING THEM TO *GO*--BUT THAT AIN'T *NO WAY* TO BE TREATIN' *ANYBODY.* YOU GOTTA *APOLOGIZE* TO RICK BEFORE HE GOES, MAN.

YOU *GOTTA*--

YOU *IN* THERE?

HERSHEL?

HERSHEL!

I WAS GOING TO *SHOOT* THAT MAN, *OTIS.* I WAS GOING TO PULL THAT *TRIGGER* IF HE RESISTED IN *ANY* WAY. I WANTED THEM TO LEAVE *THAT* BAD.

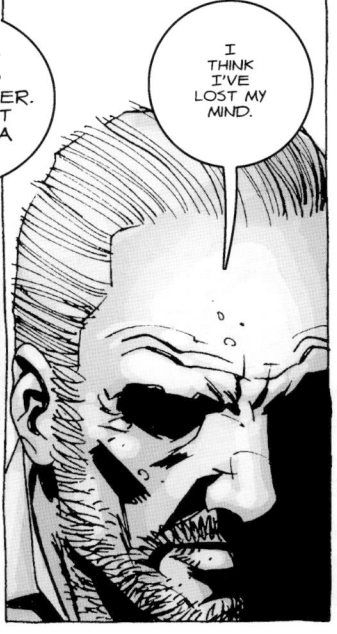

I *ALMOST* PULLED THE TRIGGER. I ALMOST *KILLED* A MAN.

I THINK I'VE LOST MY MIND.

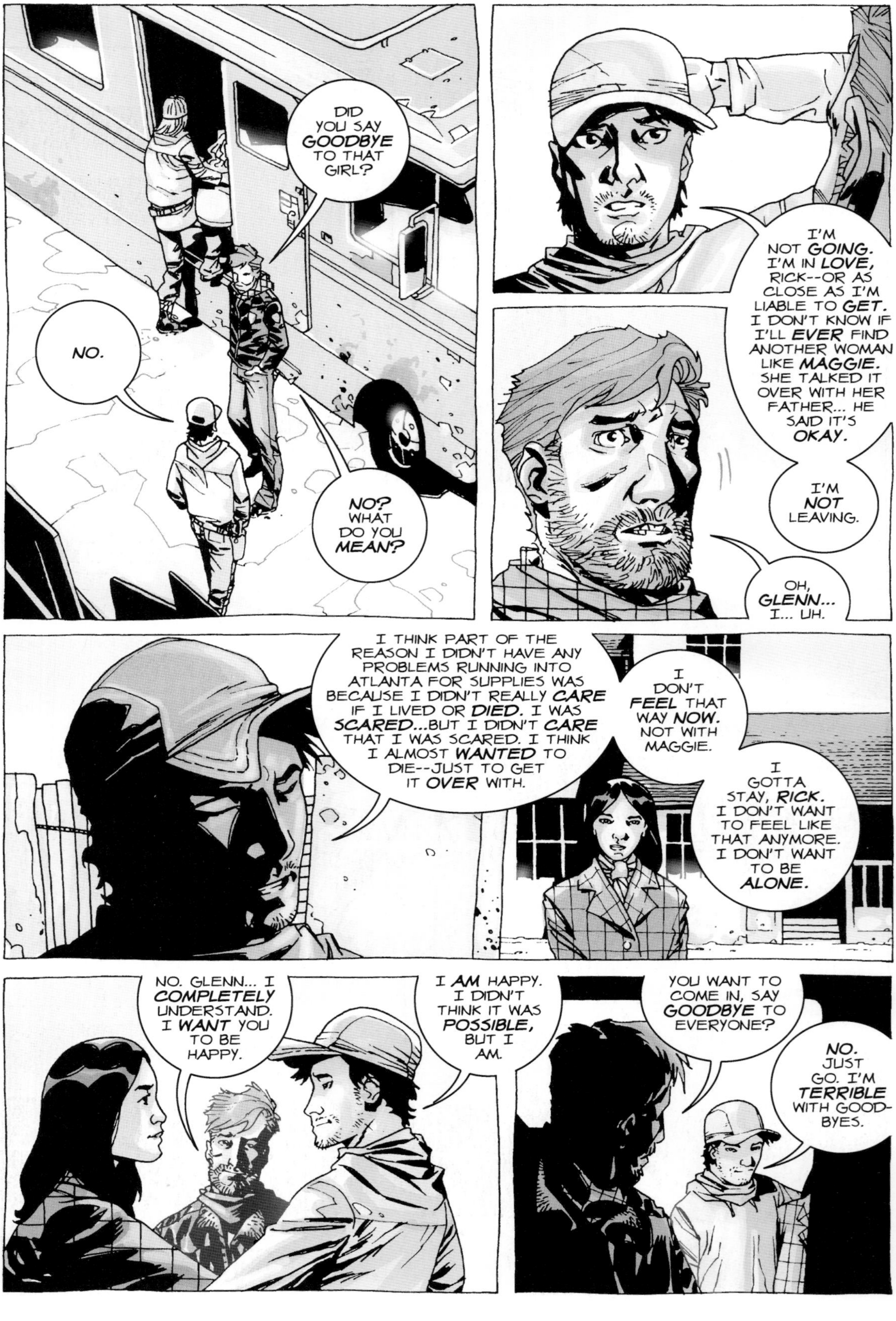
DID YOU SAY GOODBYE TO THAT GIRL?
NO.
NO? WHAT DO YOU MEAN?
I'M NOT GOING. I'M IN LOVE, RICK--OR AS CLOSE AS I'M LIABLE TO GET. I DON'T KNOW IF I'LL EVER FIND ANOTHER WOMAN LIKE MAGGIE. SHE TALKED IT OVER WITH HER FATHER... HE SAID IT'S OKAY.
I'M NOT LEAVING.
OH, GLENN... I... UH.
I THINK PART OF THE REASON I DIDN'T HAVE ANY PROBLEMS RUNNING INTO ATLANTA FOR SUPPLIES WAS BECAUSE I DIDN'T REALLY CARE IF I LIVED OR DIED. I WAS SCARED...BUT I DIDN'T CARE THAT I WAS SCARED. I THINK I ALMOST WANTED TO DIE--JUST TO GET IT OVER WITH.
I DON'T FEEL THAT WAY NOW. NOT WITH MAGGIE.
I GOTTA STAY, RICK. I DON'T WANT TO FEEL LIKE THAT ANYMORE. I DON'T WANT TO BE ALONE.
NO. GLENN... I COMPLETELY UNDERSTAND. I WANT YOU TO BE HAPPY.
I AM HAPPY. I DIDN'T THINK IT WAS POSSIBLE, BUT I AM.
YOU WANT TO COME IN, SAY GOODBYE TO EVERYONE?
NO. JUST GO. I'M TERRIBLE WITH GOOD-BYES.

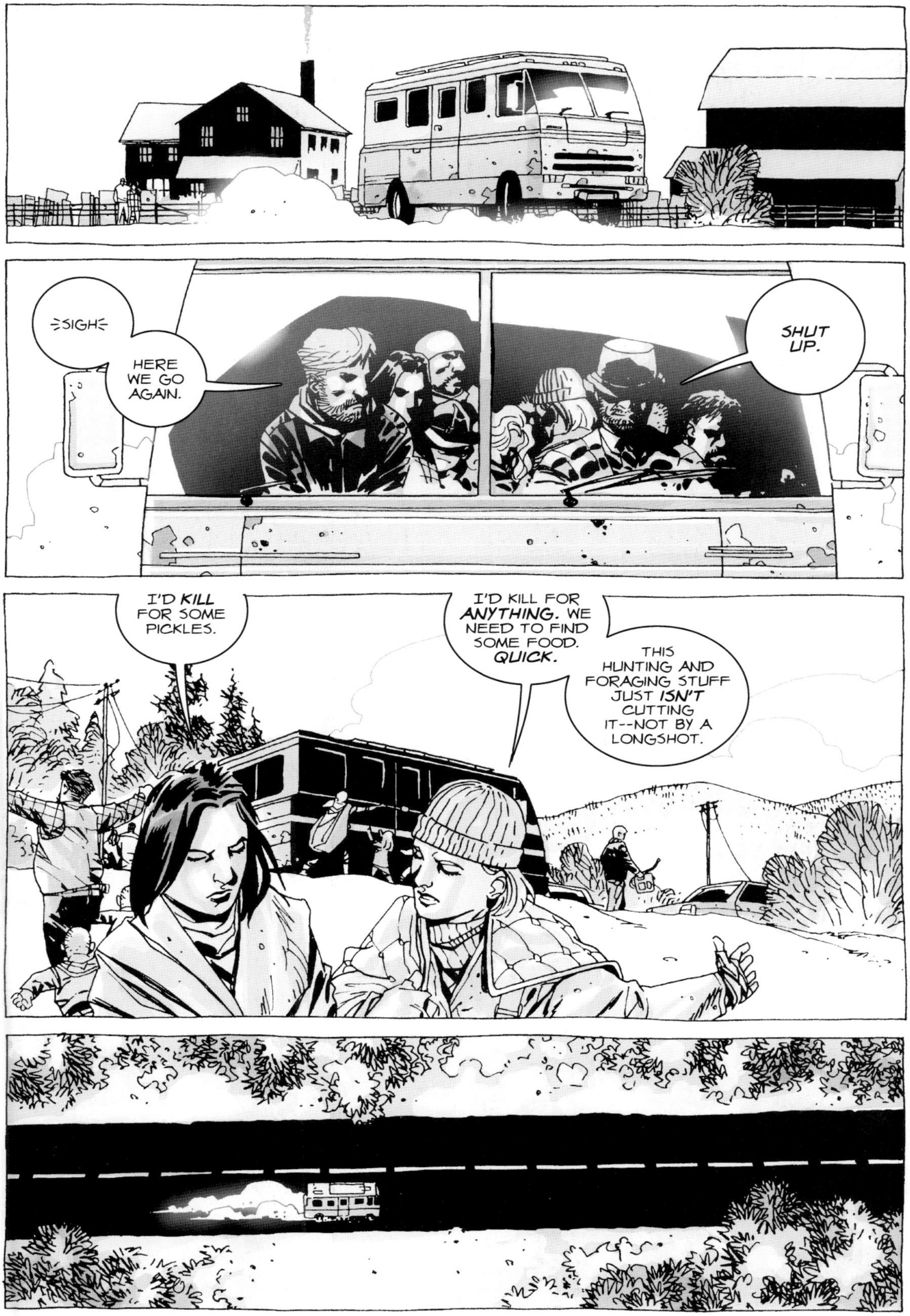

SIGH
HERE WE GO AGAIN.
SHUT UP.
I'D KILL FOR SOME PICKLES.
I'D KILL FOR ANYTHING. WE NEED TO FIND SOME FOOD. QUICK.
THIS HUNTING AND FORAGING STUFF JUST ISN'T CUTTING IT--NOT BY A LONGSHOT.

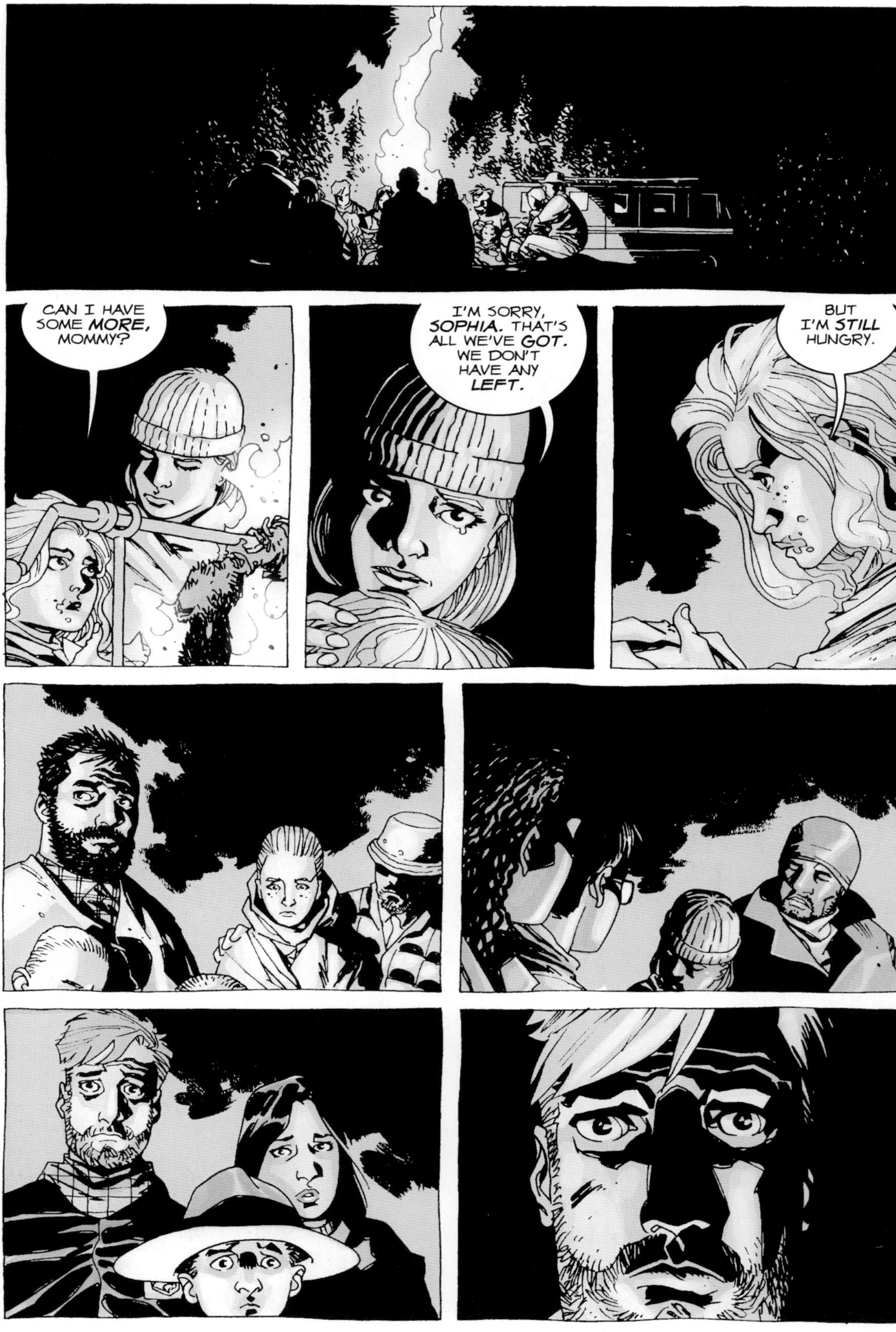
CAN I HAVE SOME MORE, MOMMY?
I'M SORRY, SOPHIA. THAT'S ALL WE'VE GOT. WE DON'T HAVE ANY LEFT.
BUT I'M STILL HUNGRY.

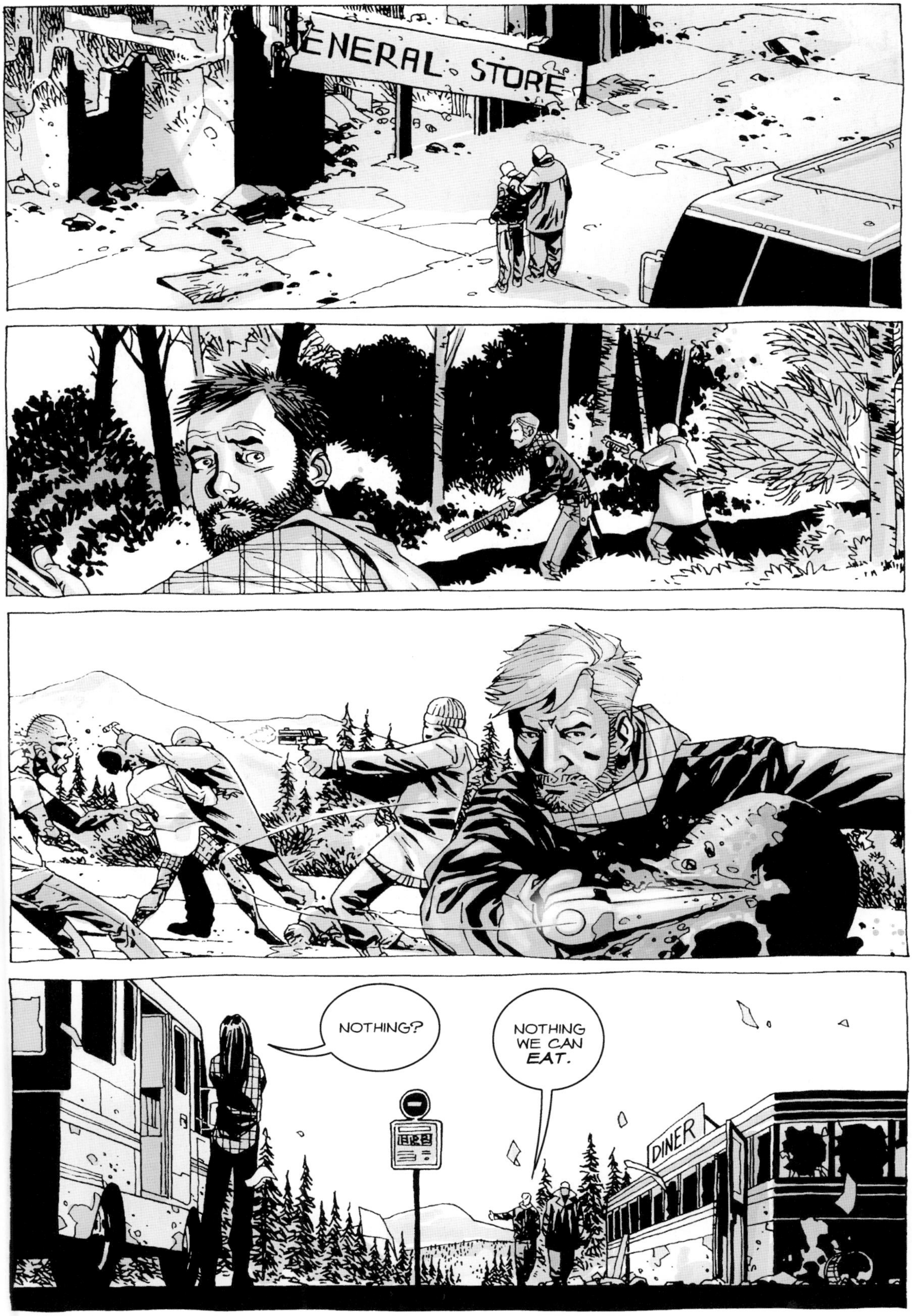
ENERAL STORE
NOTHING?
NOTHING WE CAN EAT.
DINER

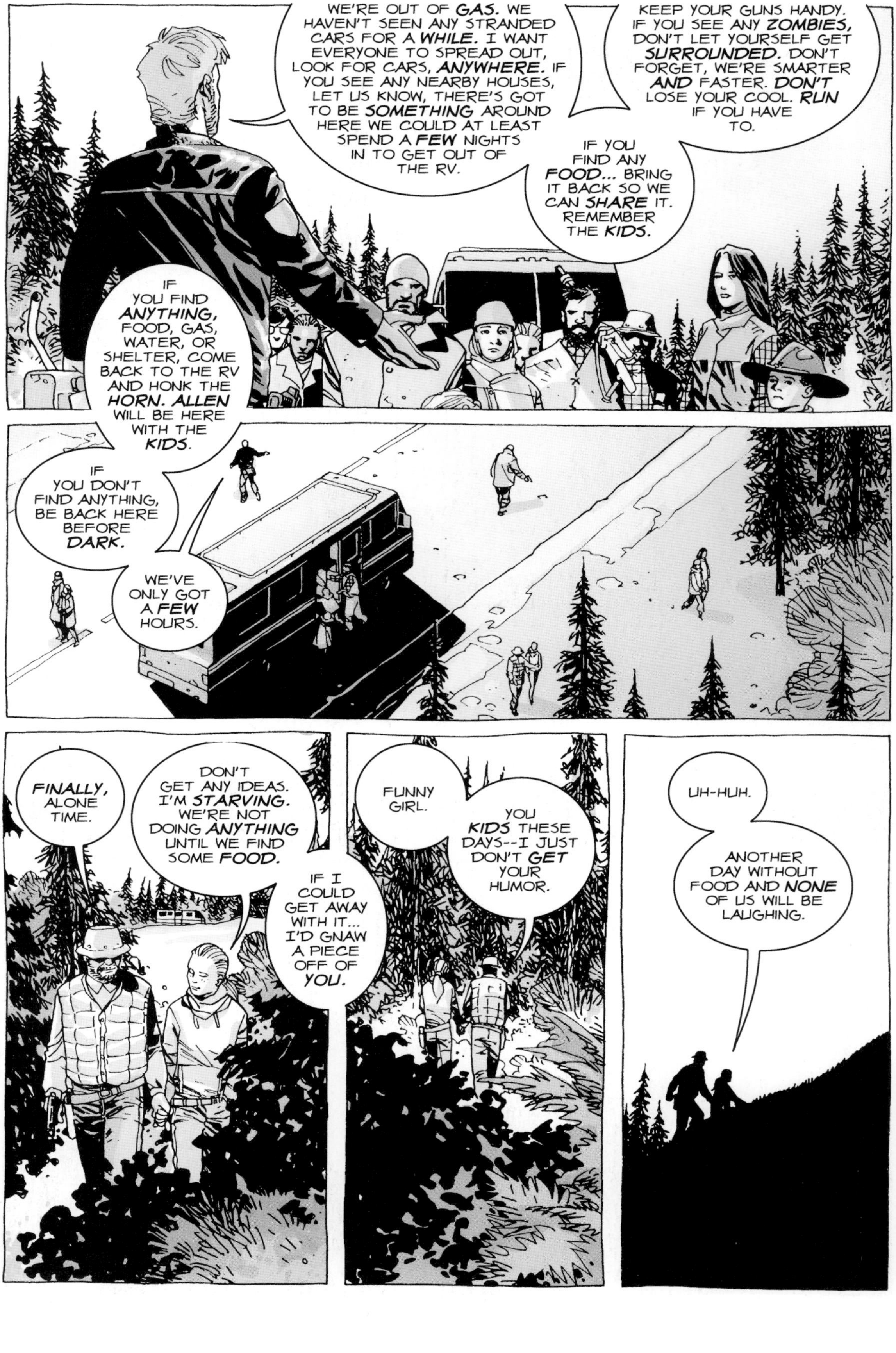

WE'RE OUT OF GAS. WE HAVEN'T SEEN ANY STRANDED CARS FOR A WHILE. I WANT EVERYONE TO SPREAD OUT, LOOK FOR CARS, ANYWHERE. IF YOU SEE ANY NEARBY HOUSES, LET US KNOW, THERE'S GOT TO BE SOMETHING AROUND HERE WE COULD AT LEAST SPEND A FEW NIGHTS IN TO GET OUT OF THE RV.
KEEP YOUR GUNS HANDY. IF YOU SEE ANY ZOMBIES, DON'T LET YOURSELF GET SURROUNDED. DON'T FORGET, WE'RE SMARTER AND FASTER. DON'T LOSE YOUR COOL. RUN IF YOU HAVE TO.
IF YOU FIND ANY FOOD... BRING IT BACK SO WE CAN SHARE IT. REMEMBER THE KIDS.
IF YOU FIND ANYTHING, FOOD, GAS, WATER, OR SHELTER, COME BACK TO THE RV AND HONK THE HORN. ALLEN WILL BE HERE WITH THE KIDS.
IF YOU DON'T FIND ANYTHING, BE BACK HERE BEFORE DARK.
WE'VE ONLY GOT A FEW HOURS.
FINALLY, ALONE TIME.
DON'T GET ANY IDEAS. I'M STARVING. WE'RE NOT DOING ANYTHING UNTIL WE FIND SOME FOOD.
IF I COULD GET AWAY WITH IT... I'D GNAW A PIECE OFF OF YOU.
FUNNY GIRL.
YOU KIDS THESE DAYS--I JUST DON'T GET YOUR HUMOR.
UH-HUH.
ANOTHER DAY WITHOUT FOOD AND NONE OF US WILL BE LAUGHING.

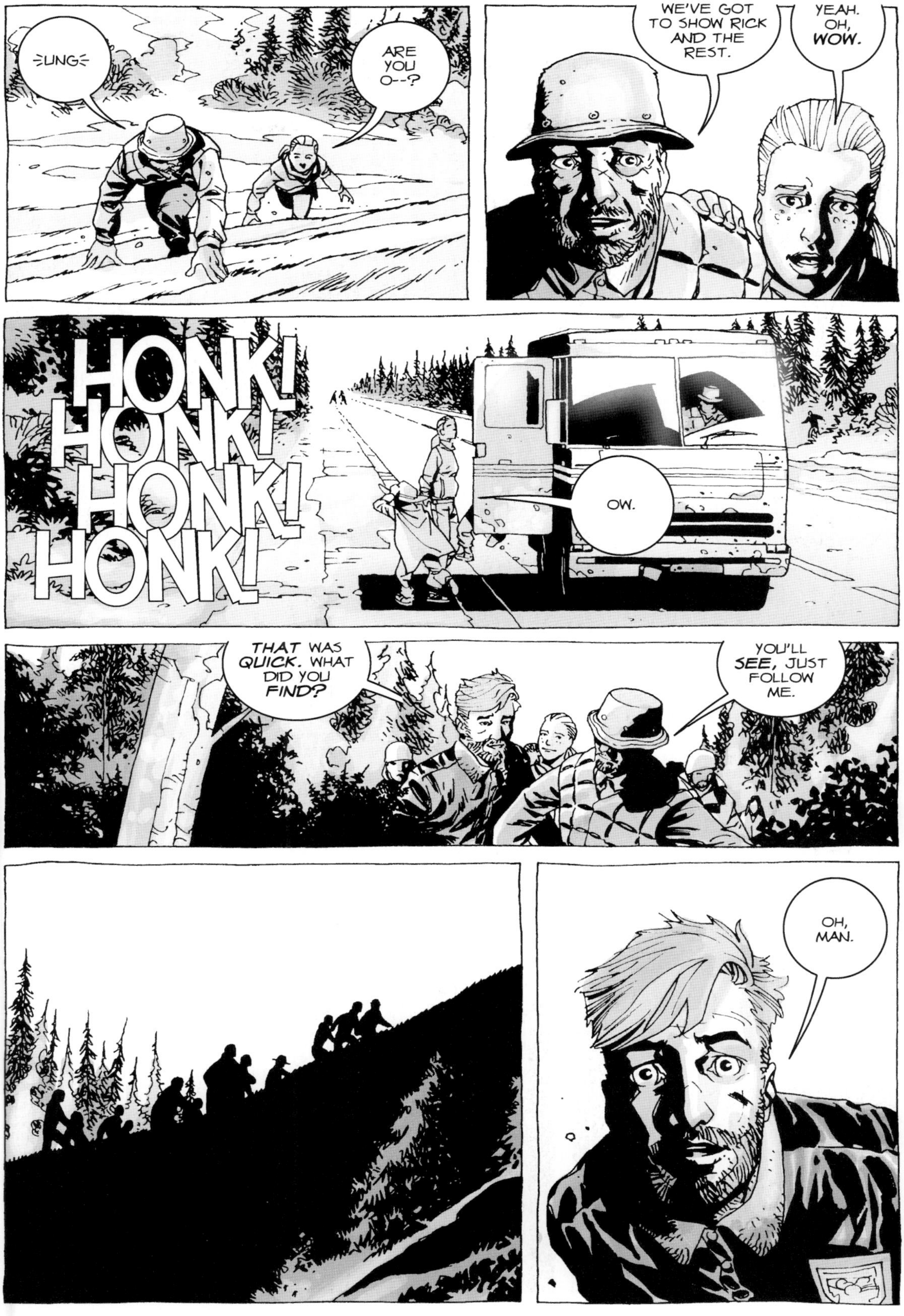

≡UNG≡
ARE YOU O--?
WE'VE GOT TO SHOW RICK AND THE REST.
YEAH. OH, WOW.
HONK! HONK! HONK! HONK!
OW.
THAT WAS QUICK. WHAT DID YOU FIND?
YOU'LL SEE, JUST FOLLOW ME.
OH, MAN.

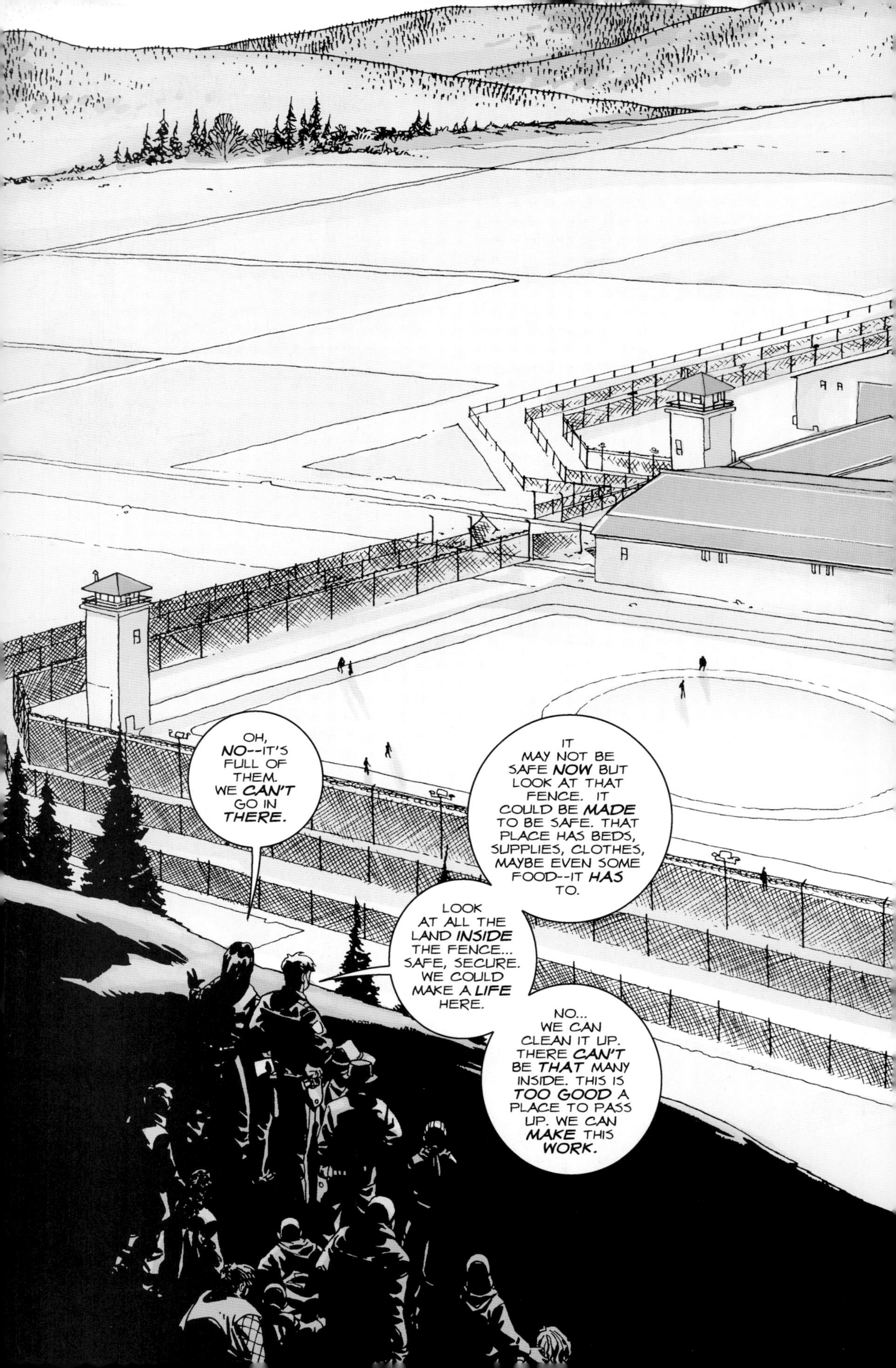
OH, NO--IT'S FULL OF THEM. WE CAN'T GO IN THERE.
IT MAY NOT BE SAFE NOW BUT LOOK AT THAT FENCE. IT COULD BE MADE TO BE SAFE. THAT PLACE HAS BEDS, SUPPLIES, CLOTHES, MAYBE EVEN SOME FOOD--IT HAS TO.
LOOK AT ALL THE LAND INSIDE THE FENCE... SAFE, SECURE. WE COULD MAKE A LIFE HERE.
NO... WE CAN CLEAN IT UP. THERE CAN'T BE THAT MANY INSIDE. THIS IS TOO GOOD A PLACE TO PASS UP. WE CAN MAKE THIS WORK.

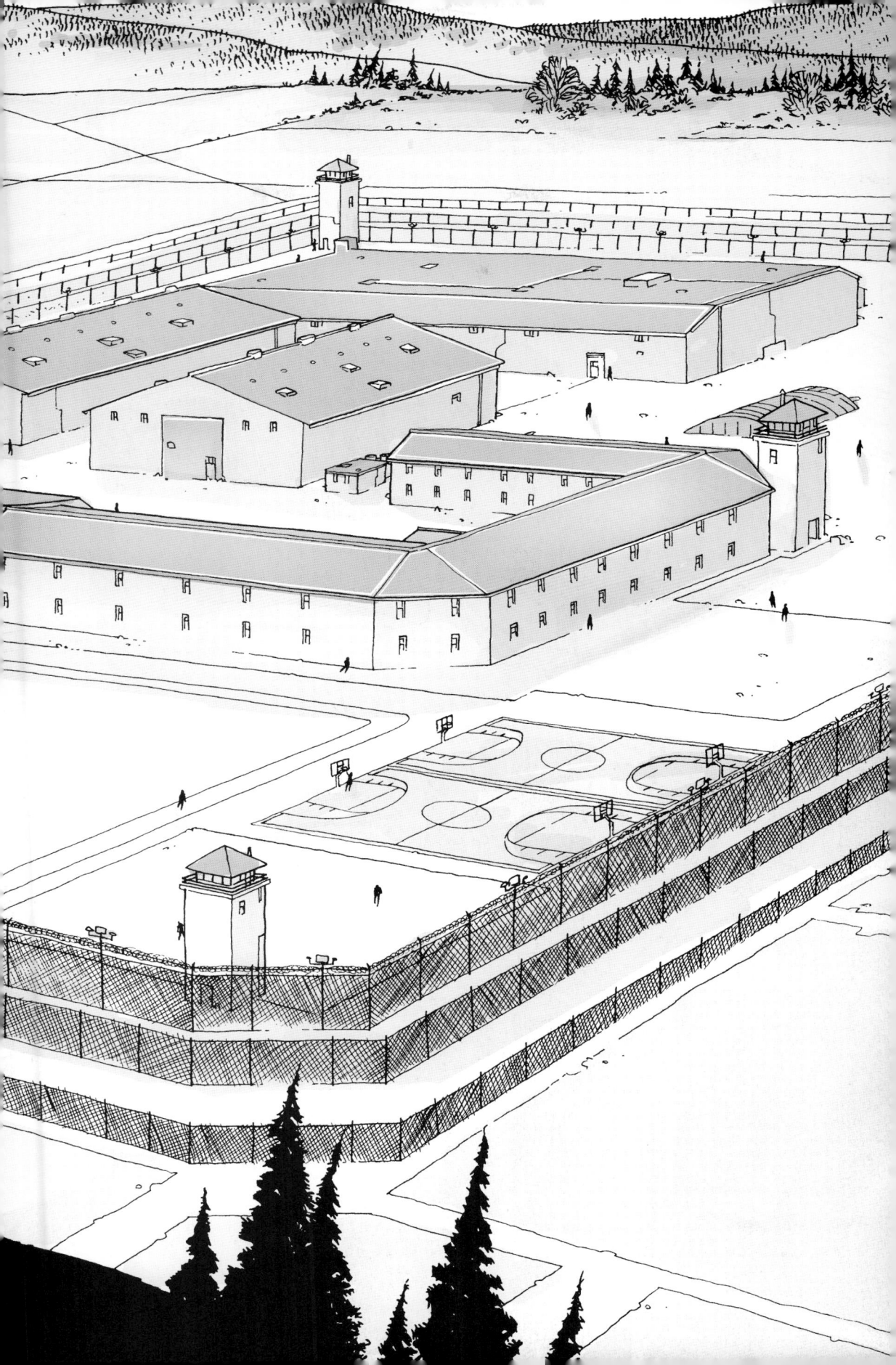

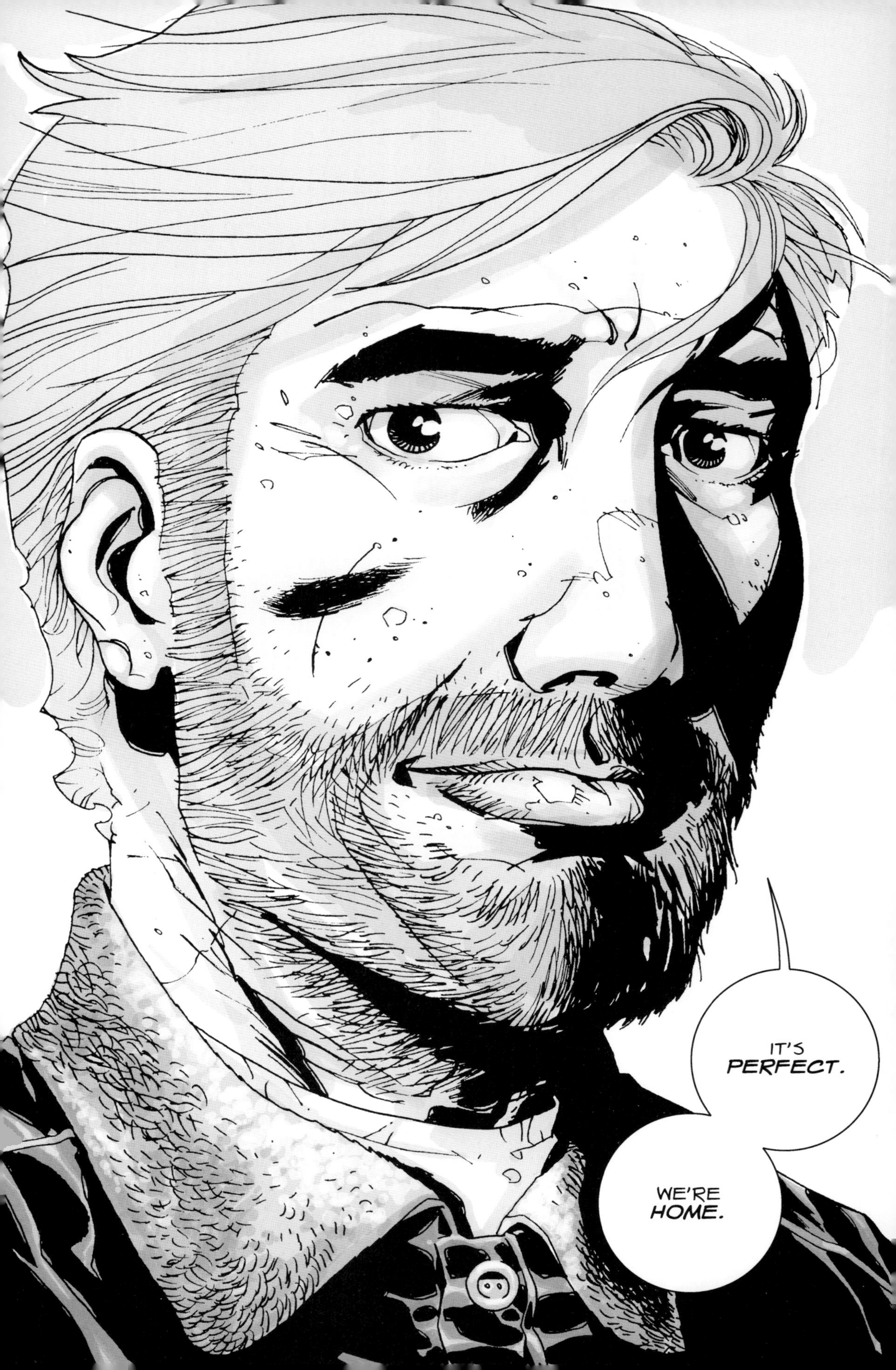
IT'S PERFECT.
WE'RE HOME.

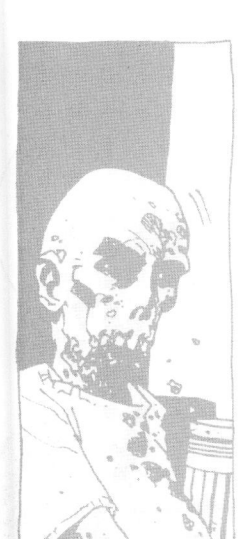

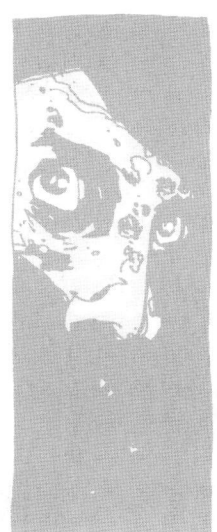

Chapter Three:
Safety Behind Bars

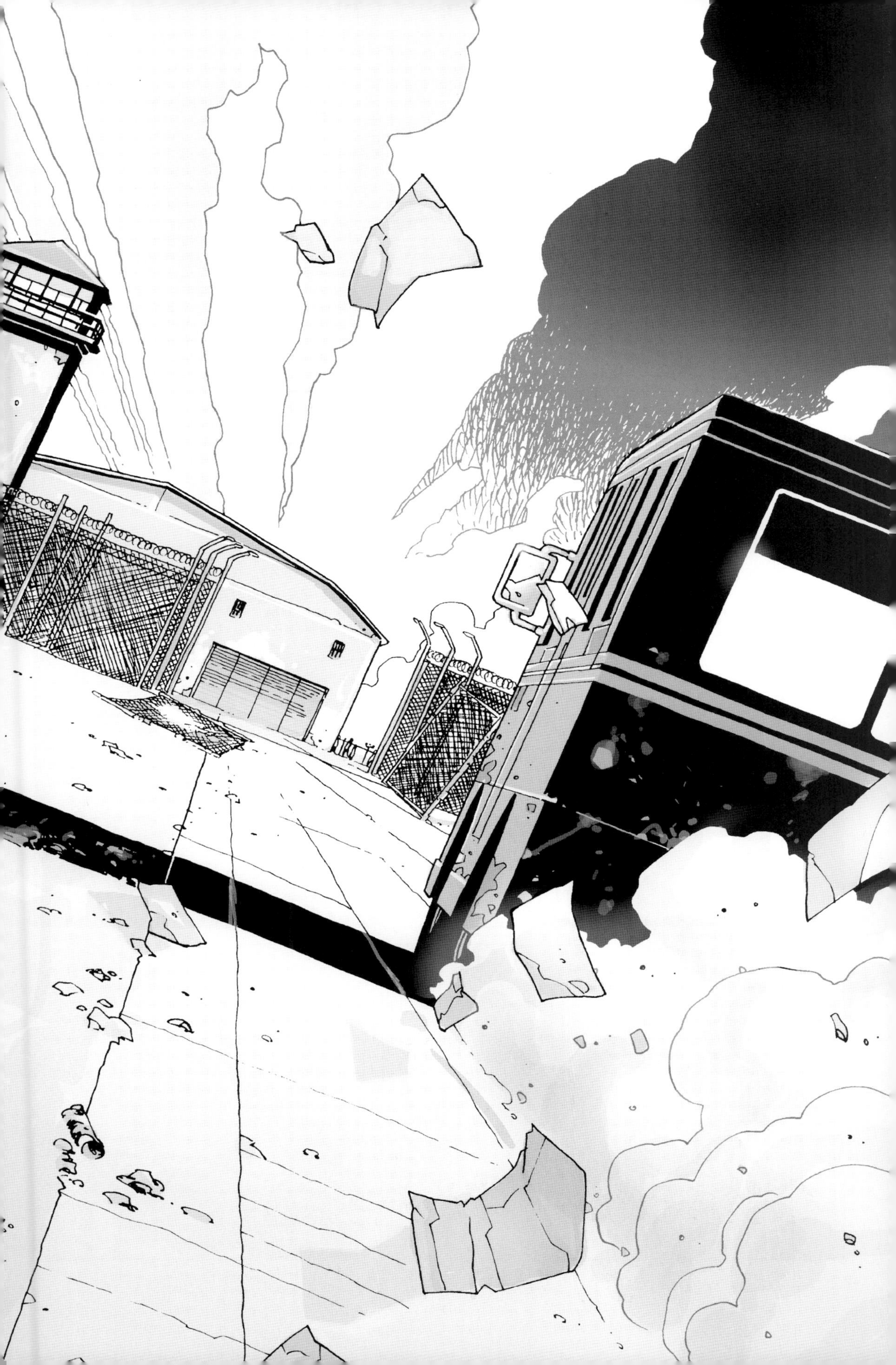

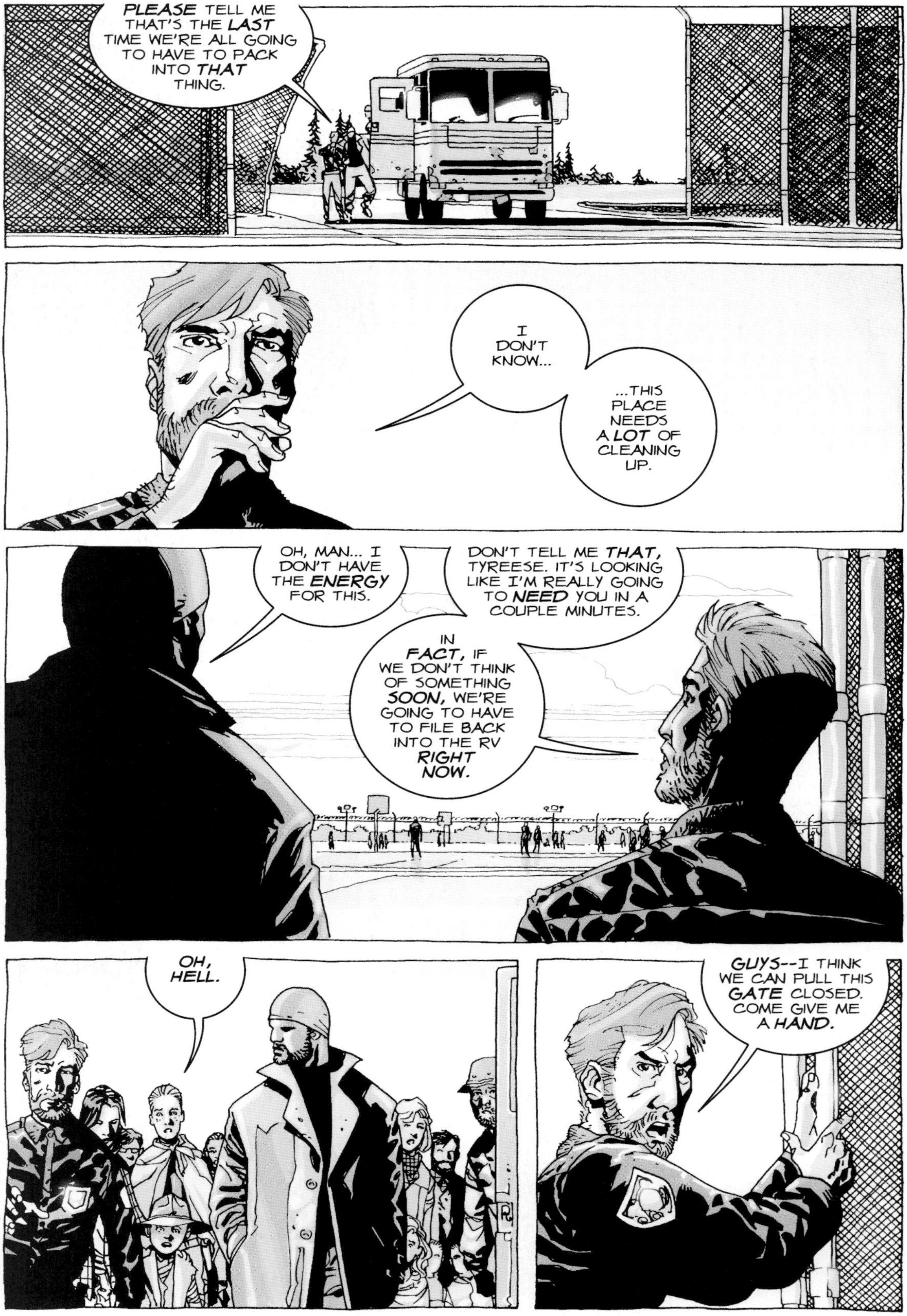
PLEASE TELL ME THAT'S THE LAST TIME WE'RE ALL GOING TO HAVE TO PACK INTO THAT THING.
I DON'T KNOW...
...THIS PLACE NEEDS A LOT OF CLEANING UP.
OH, MAN... I DON'T HAVE THE ENERGY FOR THIS.
DON'T TELL ME THAT, TYREESE. IT'S LOOKING LIKE I'M REALLY GOING TO NEED YOU IN A COUPLE MINUTES.
IN FACT, IF WE DON'T THINK OF SOMETHING SOON, WE'RE GOING TO HAVE TO FILE BACK INTO THE RV RIGHT NOW.
OH, HELL.
GUYS--I THINK WE CAN PULL THIS GATE CLOSED. COME GIVE ME A HAND.

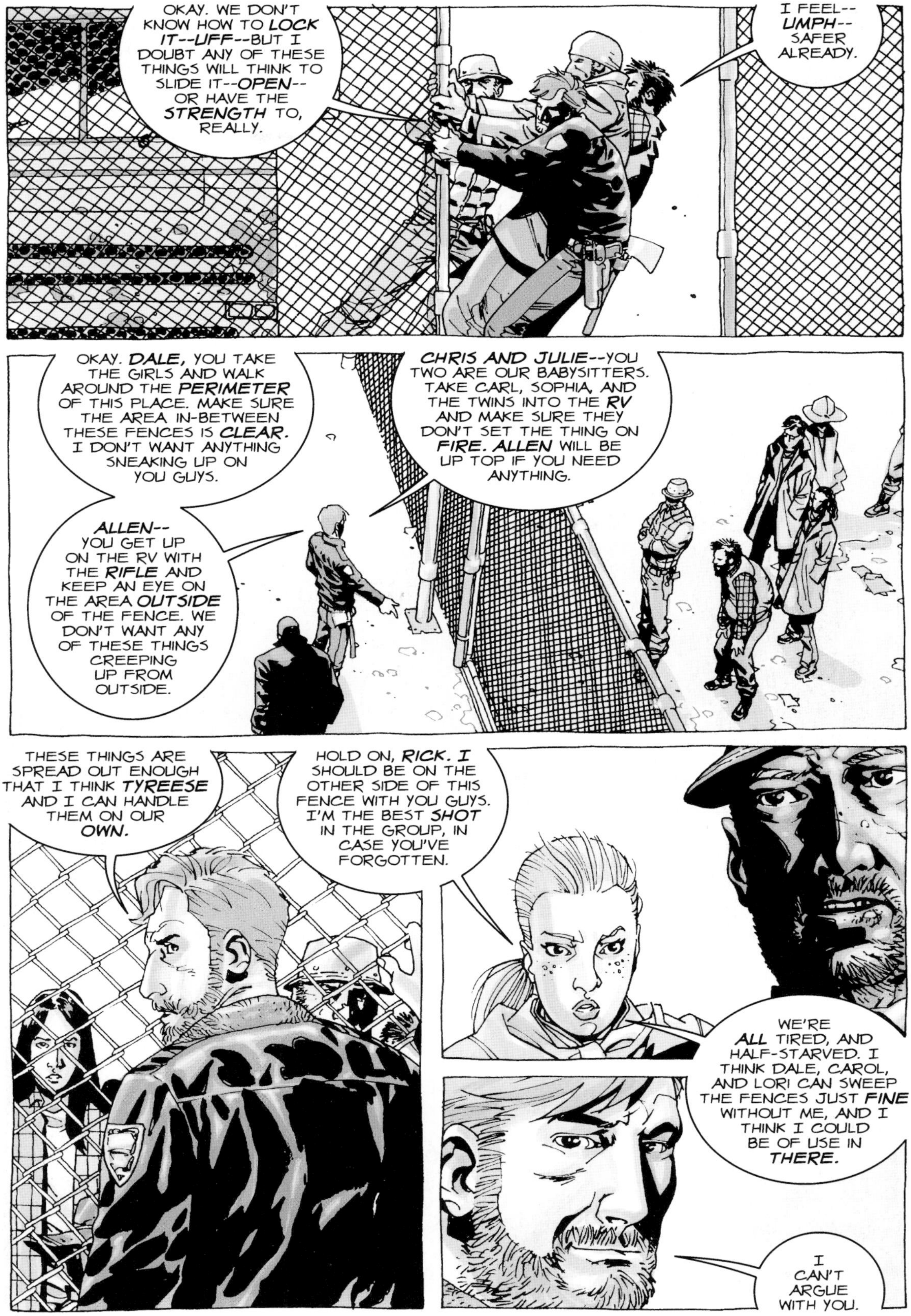

OKAY. WE DON'T KNOW HOW TO LOCK IT--UFF--BUT I DOUBT ANY OF THESE THINGS WILL THINK TO SLIDE IT--OPEN--OR HAVE THE STRENGTH TO, REALLY.
I FEEL--UMPH--SAFER ALREADY.
OKAY. DALE, YOU TAKE THE GIRLS AND WALK AROUND THE PERIMETER OF THIS PLACE. MAKE SURE THE AREA IN-BETWEEN THESE FENCES IS CLEAR. I DON'T WANT ANYTHING SNEAKING UP ON YOU GUYS.
ALLEN--YOU GET UP ON THE RV WITH THE RIFLE AND KEEP AN EYE ON THE AREA OUTSIDE OF THE FENCE. WE DON'T WANT ANY OF THESE THINGS CREEPING UP FROM OUTSIDE.
CHRIS AND JULIE--YOU TWO ARE OUR BABYSITTERS. TAKE CARL, SOPHIA, AND THE TWINS INTO THE RV AND MAKE SURE THEY DON'T SET THE THING ON FIRE. ALLEN WILL BE UP TOP IF YOU NEED ANYTHING.
THESE THINGS ARE SPREAD OUT ENOUGH THAT I THINK TYREESE AND I CAN HANDLE THEM ON OUR OWN.
HOLD ON, RICK. I SHOULD BE ON THE OTHER SIDE OF THIS FENCE WITH YOU GUYS. I'M THE BEST SHOT IN THE GROUP, IN CASE YOU'VE FORGOTTEN.
WE'RE ALL TIRED, AND HALF-STARVED. I THINK DALE, CAROL, AND LORI CAN SWEEP THE FENCES JUST FINE WITHOUT ME, AND I THINK I COULD BE OF USE IN THERE.
I CAN'T ARGUE WITH YOU.

WOW--FEELS A LOT DIFFERENT ON *THIS* SIDE OF THE FENCE.

DON'T FORGET HOW MUCH *FASTER* WE ARE THAN THESE GUYS. JUST DON'T LET YOURSELF GET SURROUNDED.

IF YOU HAVE TO RUN--*RUN*.

OKAY... LET'S *DO* THIS, PEOPLE.

TYREESE AND I WILL DO THE *DIRTY* WORK. YOU HANG BACK AND IF WE LOOK LIKE WE'VE GOT *TOO MANY* OF THEM COMING AT US AT ONE TIME, PICK THEM *OFF*.

I WANT TO KEEP THE SHOTS FIRED TO A *MINIMUM*. I DON'T WANT TO CAUSE THEM TO SWARM US.

THIS IS GOING TO *SUCK*.

JUST *LOOK* AT THIS PLACE, IT'LL BE *WORTH* IT.

THUKK!

IT *BETTER* BE.

THWAK!

SHUKK!

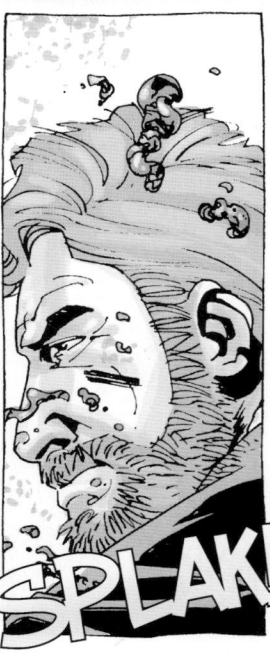

SPLAK!

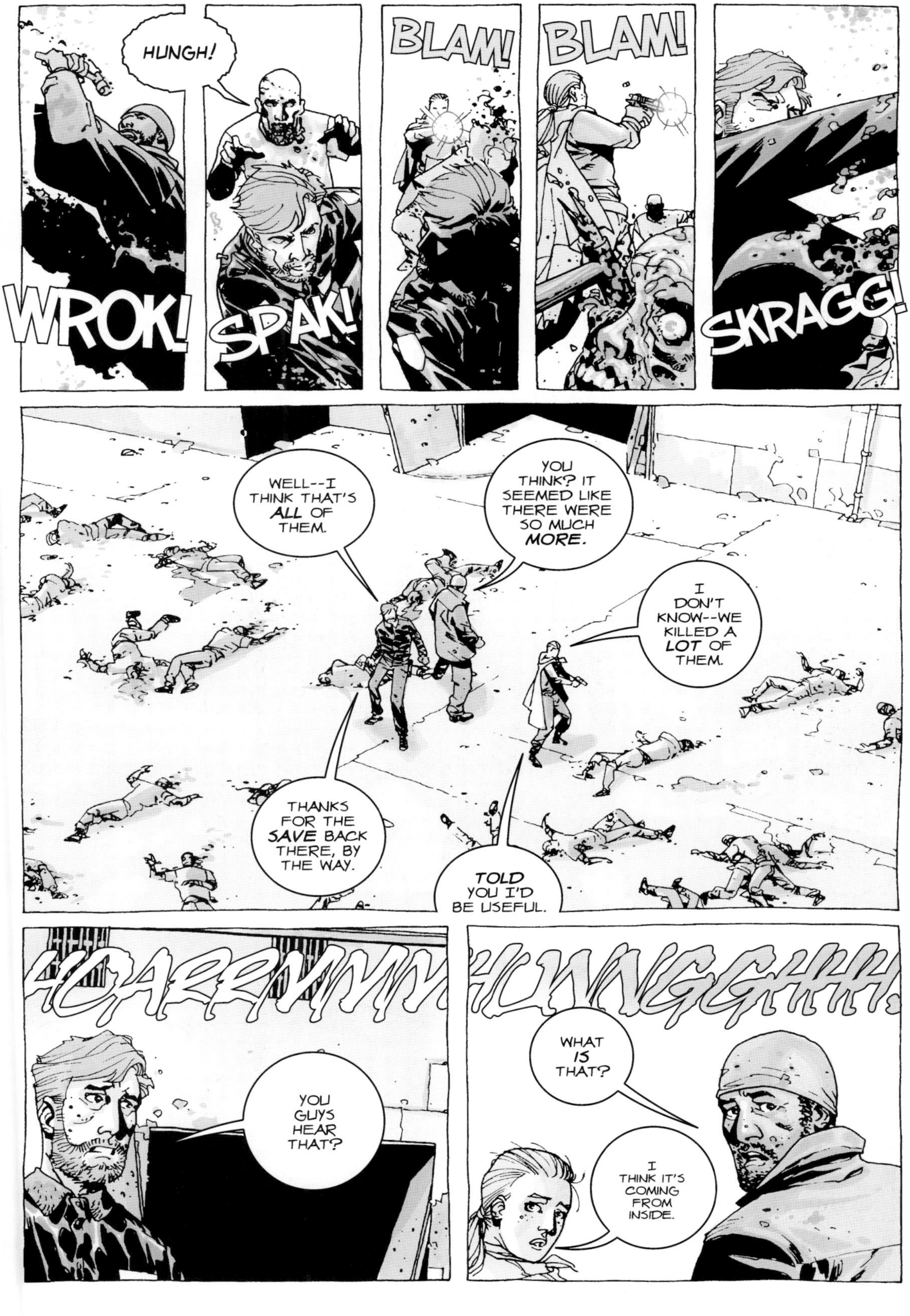
HUNGH!
WROK!
SPAK!
BLAM!
BLAM!
SKRAGG!
WELL--I THINK THAT'S ALL OF THEM.
YOU THINK? IT SEEMED LIKE THERE WERE SO MUCH MORE.
I DON'T KNOW--WE KILLED A LOT OF THEM.
THANKS FOR THE SAVE BACK THERE, BY THE WAY.
TOLD YOU I'D BE USEFUL.
YOU GUYS HEAR THAT?
WHAT IS THAT?
I THINK IT'S COMING FROM INSIDE.

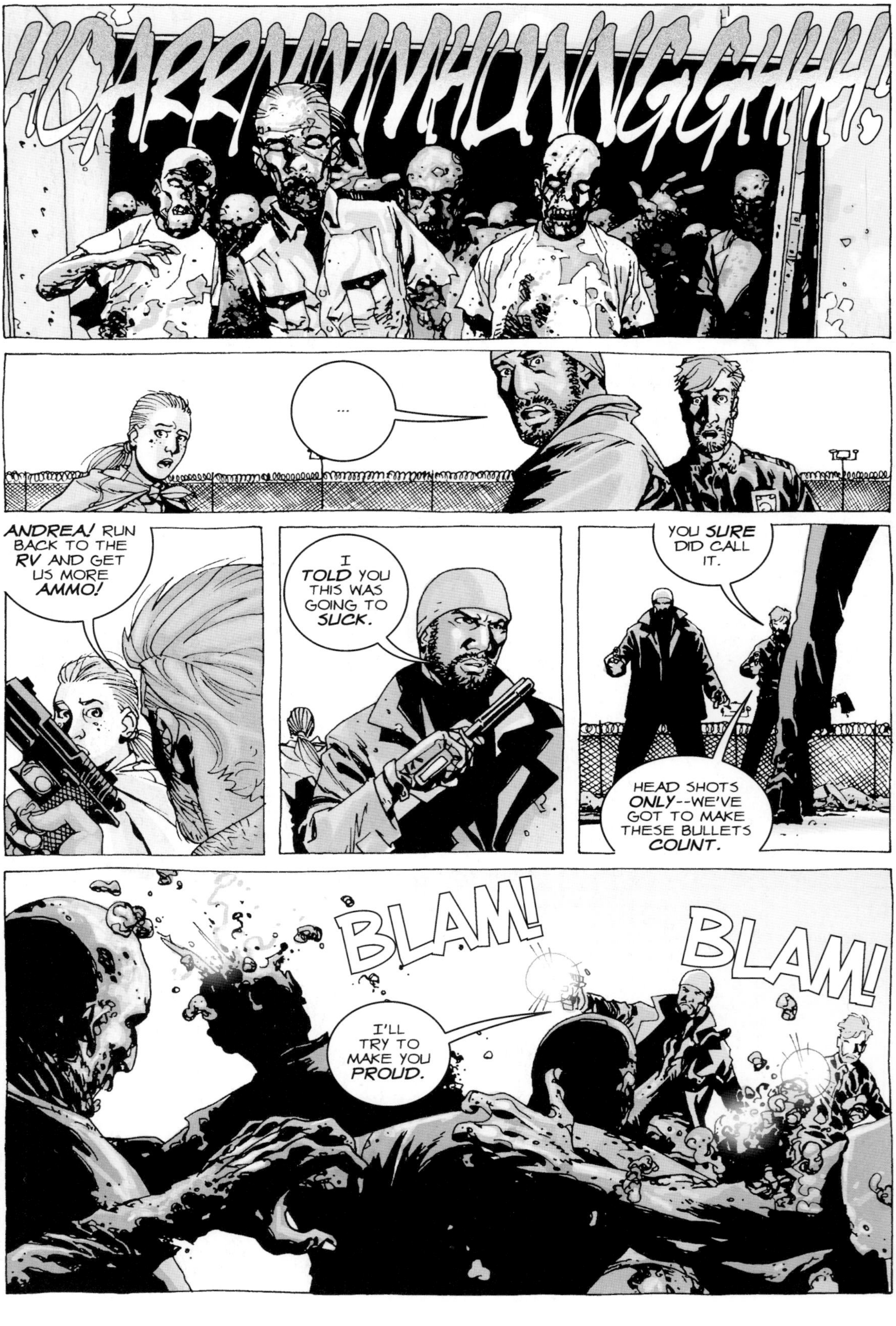
...
ANDREA! RUN BACK TO THE RV AND GET US MORE AMMO!
I TOLD YOU THIS WAS GOING TO SUCK.
YOU SURE DID CALL IT.
HEAD SHOTS ONLY--WE'VE GOT TO MAKE THESE BULLETS COUNT.
BLAM!
I'LL TRY TO MAKE YOU PROUD.
BLAM!

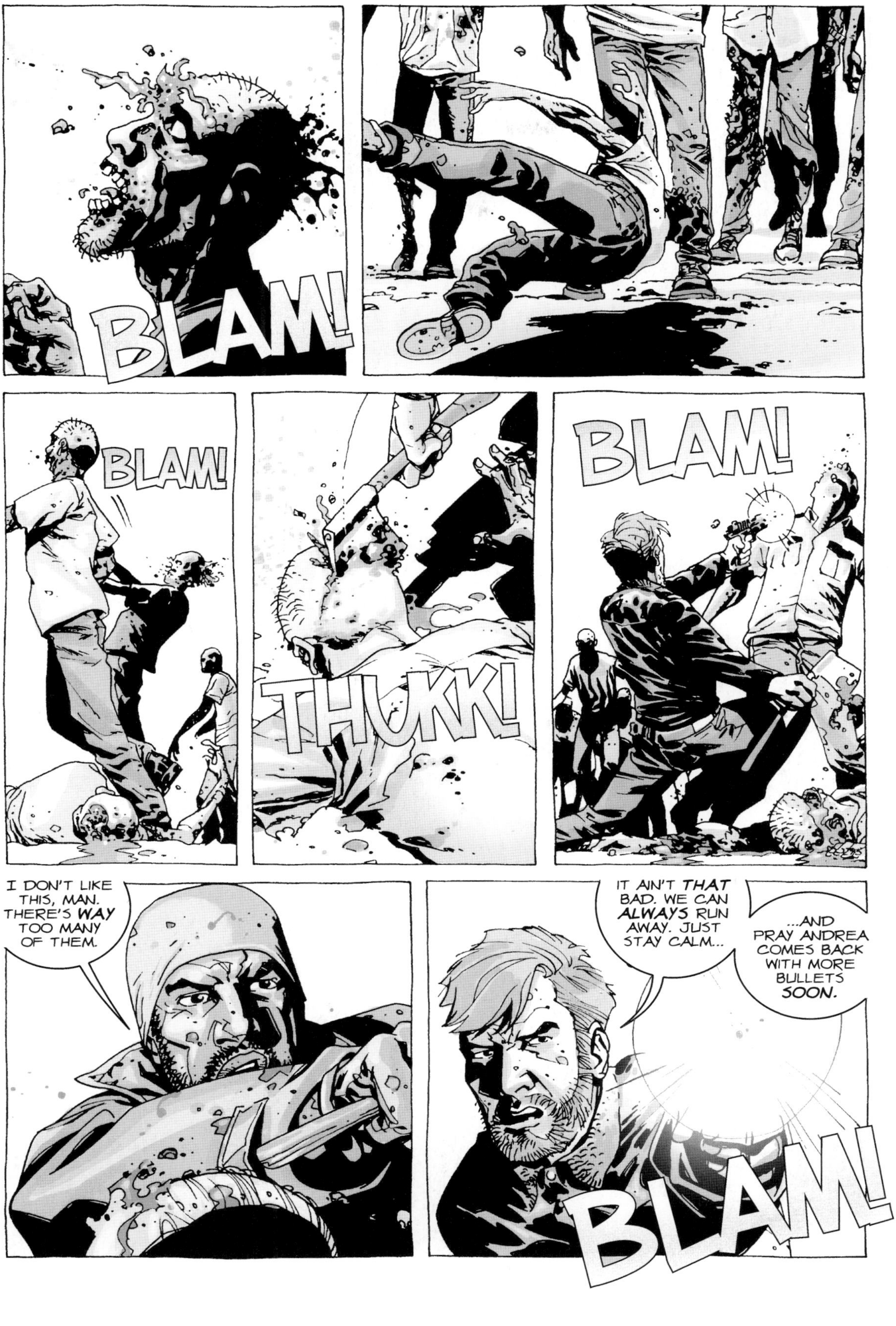
BLAM!
BLAM!
THUKK!
BLAM!
I DON'T LIKE THIS, MAN. THERE'S WAY TOO MANY OF THEM.
IT AIN'T THAT BAD. WE CAN ALWAYS RUN AWAY. JUST STAY CALM...
...AND PRAY ANDREA COMES BACK WITH MORE BULLETS SOON.
BLAM!

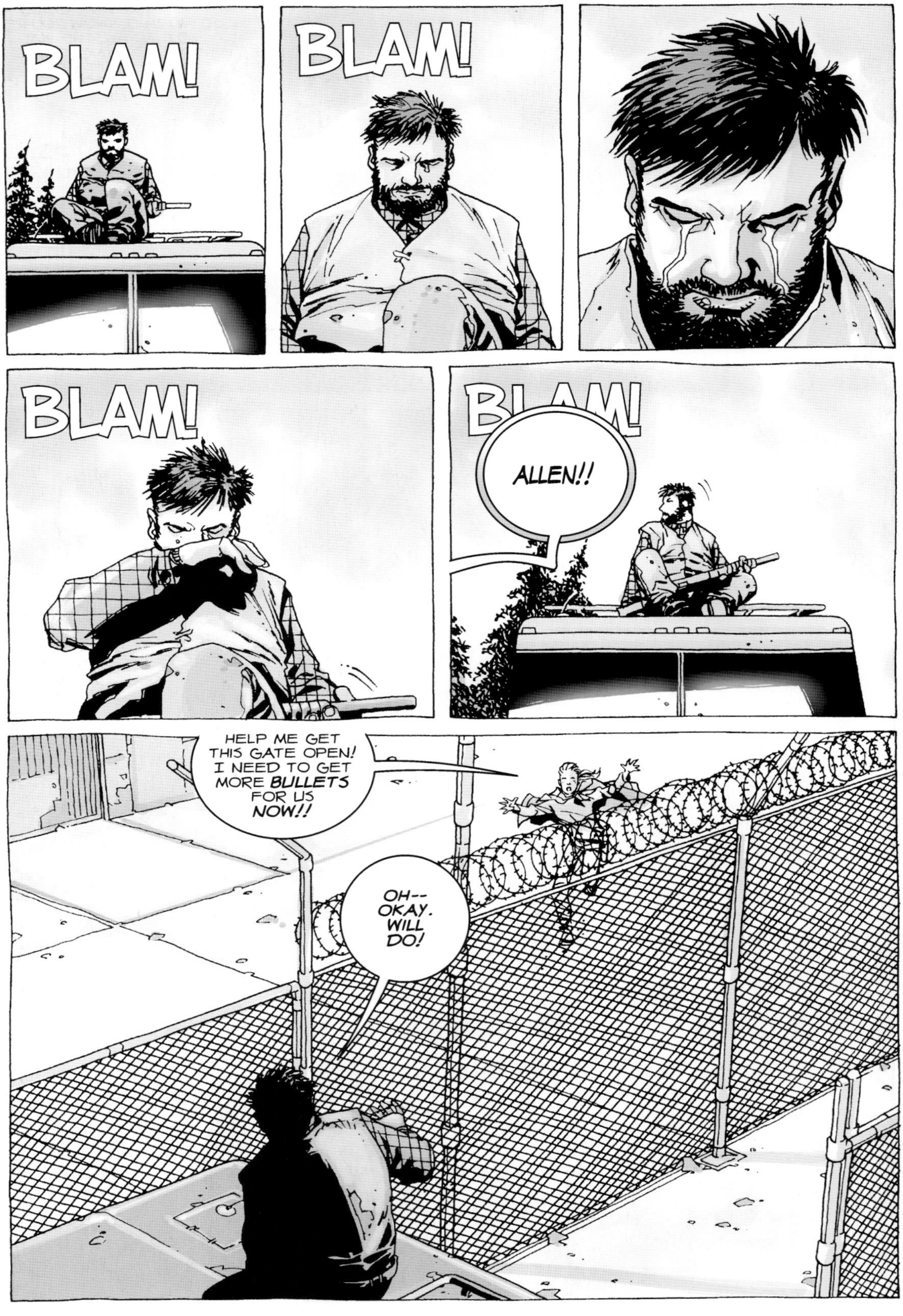
BLAM!
BLAM!
BLAM!
BLAM!
ALLEN!!
HELP ME GET THIS GATE OPEN! I NEED TO GET MORE BULLETS FOR US NOW!!
OH-- OKAY. WILL DO!

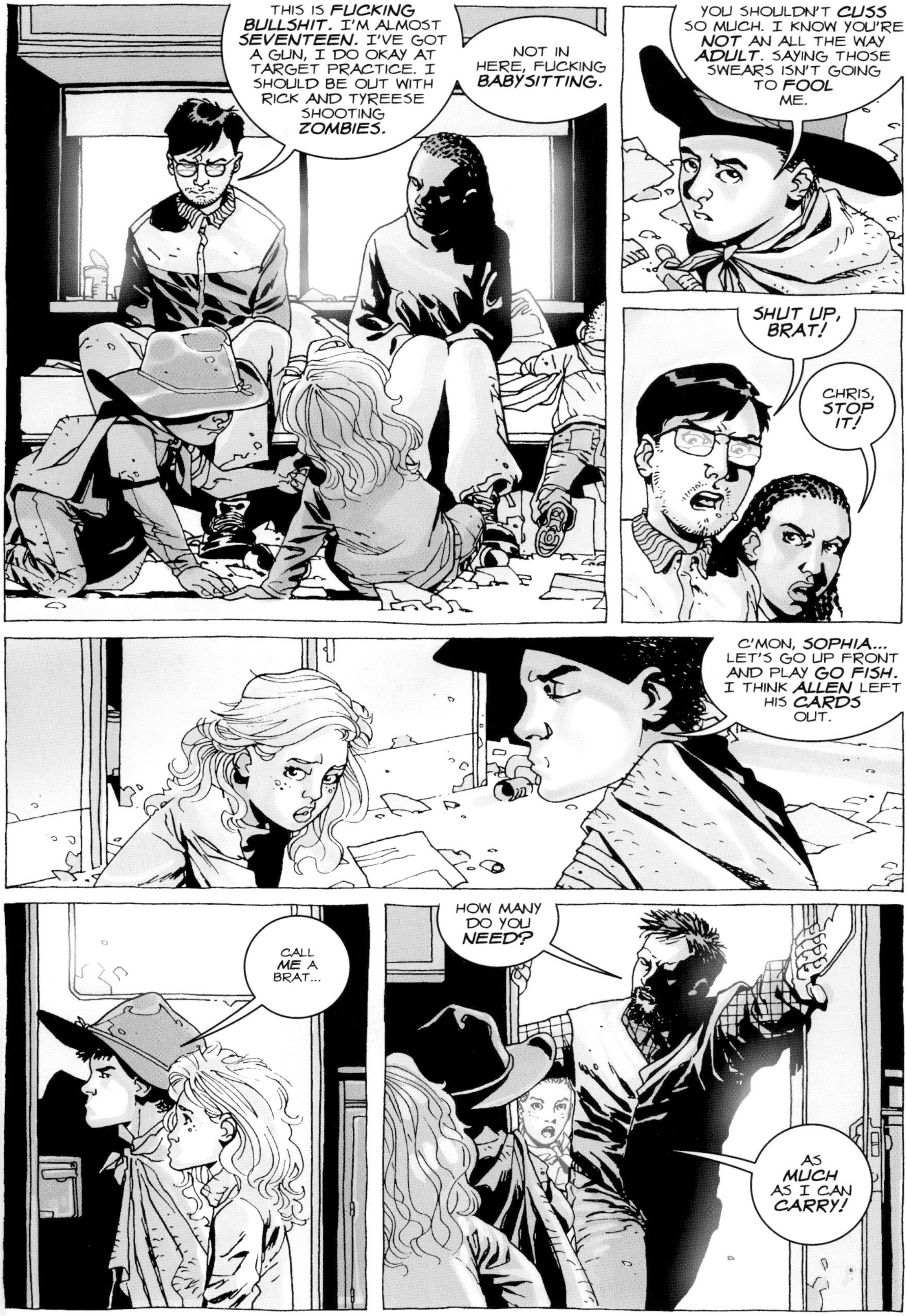
THIS IS FUCKING BULLSHIT. I'M ALMOST SEVENTEEN. I'VE GOT A GUN, I DO OKAY AT TARGET PRACTICE. I SHOULD BE OUT WITH RICK AND TYREESE SHOOTING ZOMBIES.
NOT IN HERE, FUCKING BABYSITTING.
YOU SHOULDN'T CUSS SO MUCH. I KNOW YOU'RE NOT AN ALL THE WAY ADULT. SAYING THOSE SWEARS ISN'T GOING TO FOOL ME.
SHUT UP, BRAT!
CHRIS, STOP IT!
C'MON, SOPHIA... LET'S GO UP FRONT AND PLAY GO FISH. I THINK ALLEN LEFT HIS CARDS OUT.
CALL ME A BRAT...
HOW MANY DO YOU NEED?
AS MUCH AS I CAN CARRY!

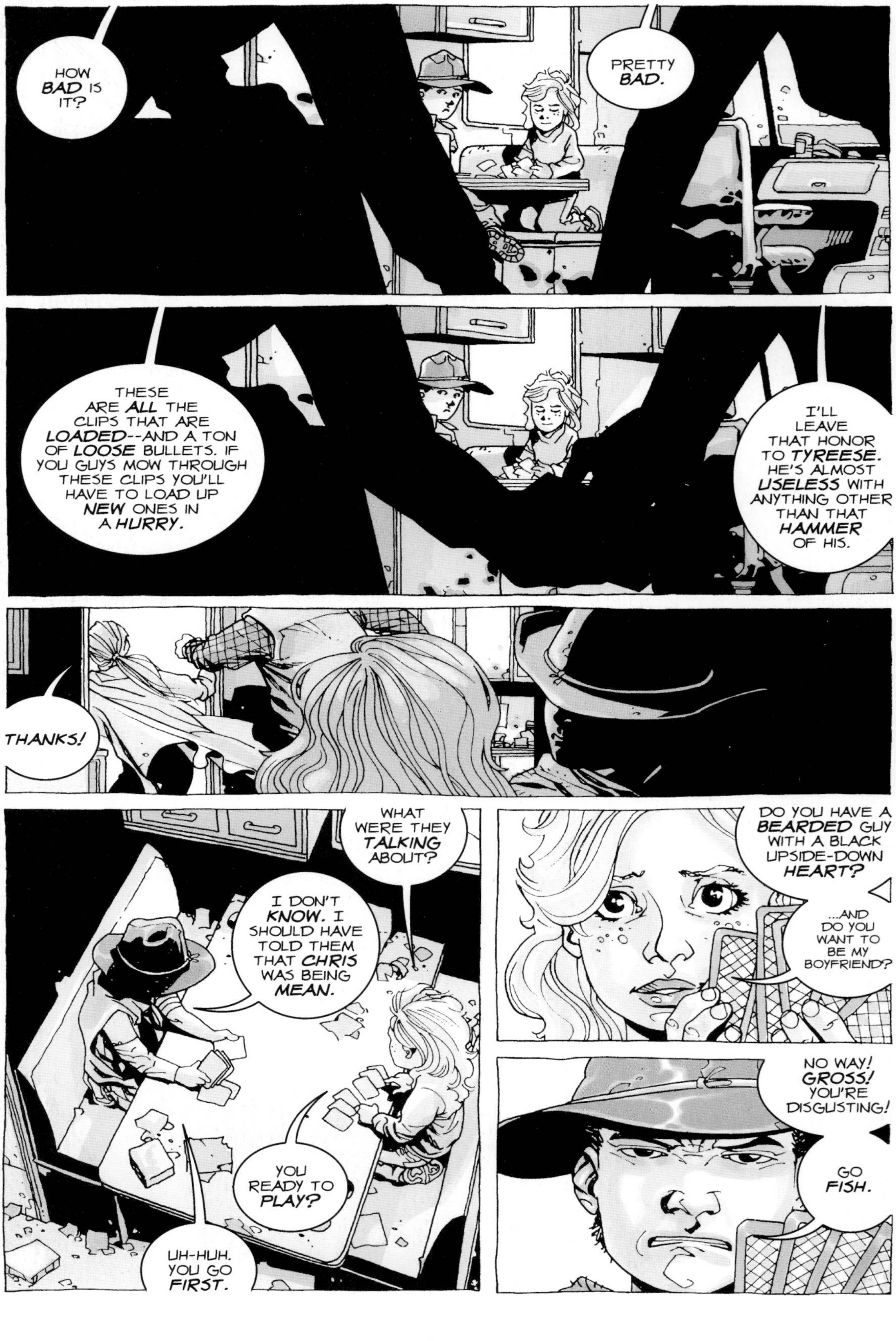

HOW BAD IS IT?
PRETTY BAD.
THESE ARE ALL THE CLIPS THAT ARE LOADED--AND A TON OF LOOSE BULLETS. IF YOU GUYS MOW THROUGH THESE CLIPS YOU'LL HAVE TO LOAD UP NEW ONES IN A HURRY.
I'LL LEAVE THAT HONOR TO TYREESE. HE'S ALMOST USELESS WITH ANYTHING OTHER THAN THAT HAMMER OF HIS.
THANKS!
WHAT WERE THEY TALKING ABOUT?
I DON'T KNOW. I SHOULD HAVE TOLD THEM THAT CHRIS WAS BEING MEAN.
YOU READY TO PLAY?
UH-HUH. YOU GO FIRST.
DO YOU HAVE A BEARDED GUY WITH A BLACK UPSIDE-DOWN HEART?
...AND DO YOU WANT TO BE MY BOYFRIEND?
NO WAY! GROSS! YOU'RE DISGUSTING!
GO FISH.

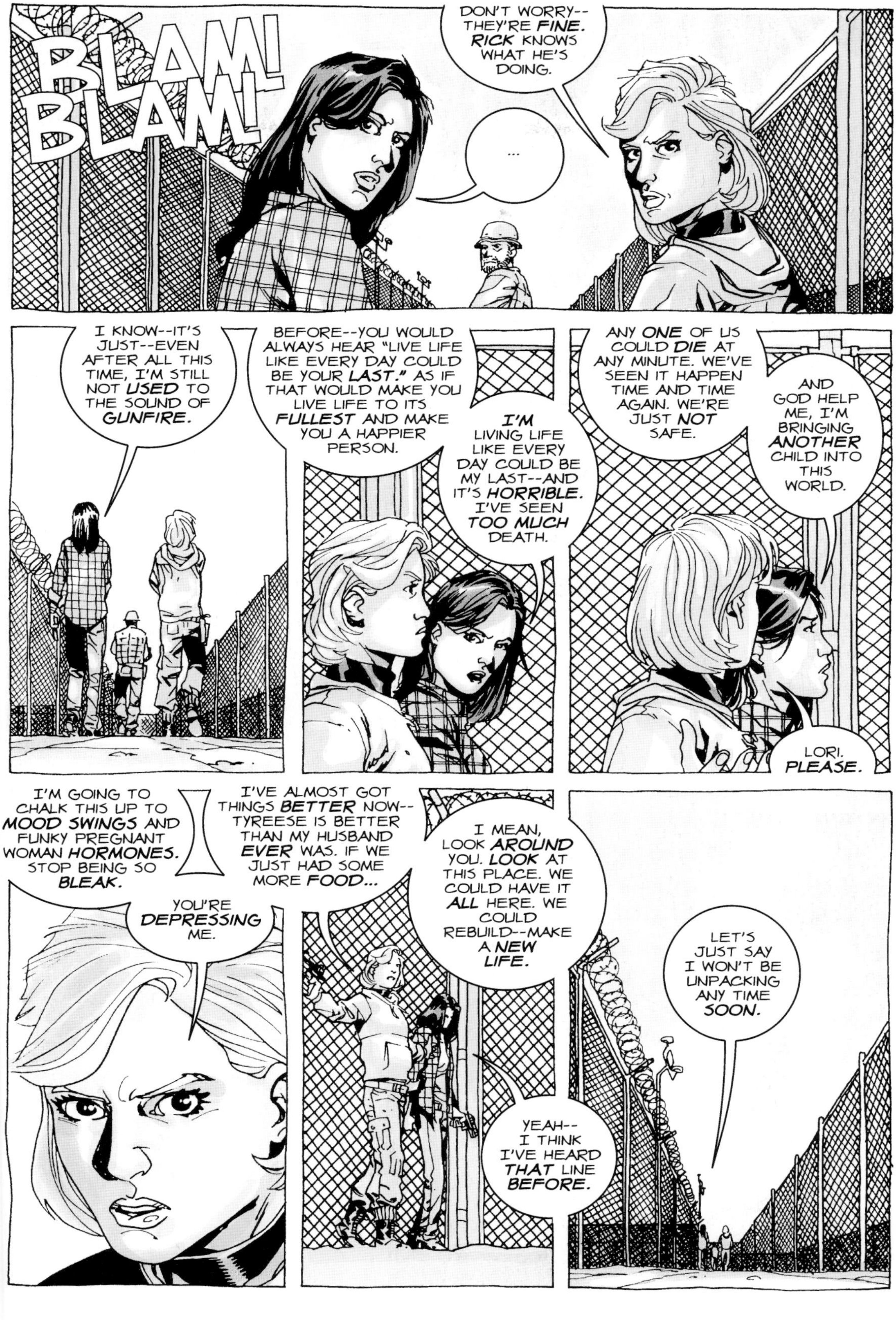
BLAM! BLAM!
DON'T WORRY-- THEY'RE FINE. RICK KNOWS WHAT HE'S DOING.
...
I KNOW--IT'S JUST--EVEN AFTER ALL THIS TIME, I'M STILL NOT USED TO THE SOUND OF GUNFIRE.
BEFORE--YOU WOULD ALWAYS HEAR "LIVE LIFE LIKE EVERY DAY COULD BE YOUR LAST." AS IF THAT WOULD MAKE YOU LIVE LIFE TO ITS FULLEST AND MAKE YOU A HAPPIER PERSON.
I'M LIVING LIFE LIKE EVERY DAY COULD BE MY LAST--AND IT'S HORRIBLE. I'VE SEEN TOO MUCH DEATH.
ANY ONE OF US COULD DIE AT ANY MINUTE. WE'VE SEEN IT HAPPEN TIME AND TIME AGAIN. WE'RE JUST NOT SAFE.
AND GOD HELP ME, I'M BRINGING ANOTHER CHILD INTO THIS WORLD.
LORI. PLEASE.
I'M GOING TO CHALK THIS UP TO MOOD SWINGS AND FUNKY PREGNANT WOMAN HORMONES. STOP BEING SO BLEAK.
YOU'RE DEPRESSING ME.
I'VE ALMOST GOT THINGS BETTER NOW-- TYREESE IS BETTER THAN MY HUSBAND EVER WAS. IF WE JUST HAD SOME MORE FOOD...
I MEAN, LOOK AROUND YOU. LOOK AT THIS PLACE. WE COULD HAVE IT ALL HERE. WE COULD REBUILD--MAKE A NEW LIFE.
YEAH-- I THINK I'VE HEARD THAT LINE BEFORE.
LET'S JUST SAY I WON'T BE UNPACKING ANY TIME SOON.

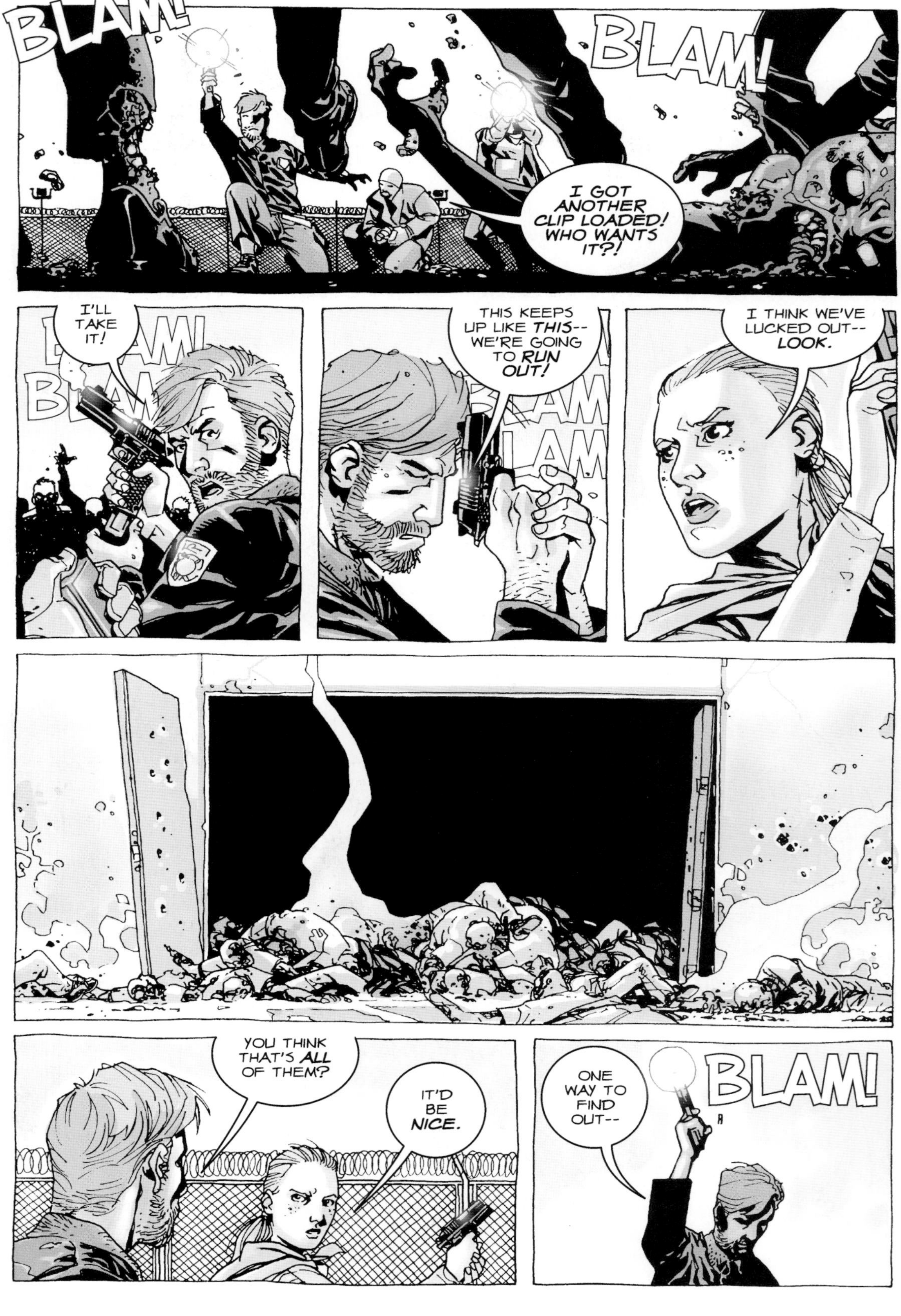
BLAM!
BLAM!
I GOT ANOTHER CLIP LOADED! WHO WANTS IT?!
I'LL TAKE IT!
BLAM!
BLAM!
THIS KEEPS UP LIKE THIS-- WE'RE GOING TO RUN OUT!
I THINK WE'VE LUCKED OUT-- LOOK.
YOU THINK THAT'S ALL OF THEM?
IT'D BE NICE.
ONE WAY TO FIND OUT--
BLAM!

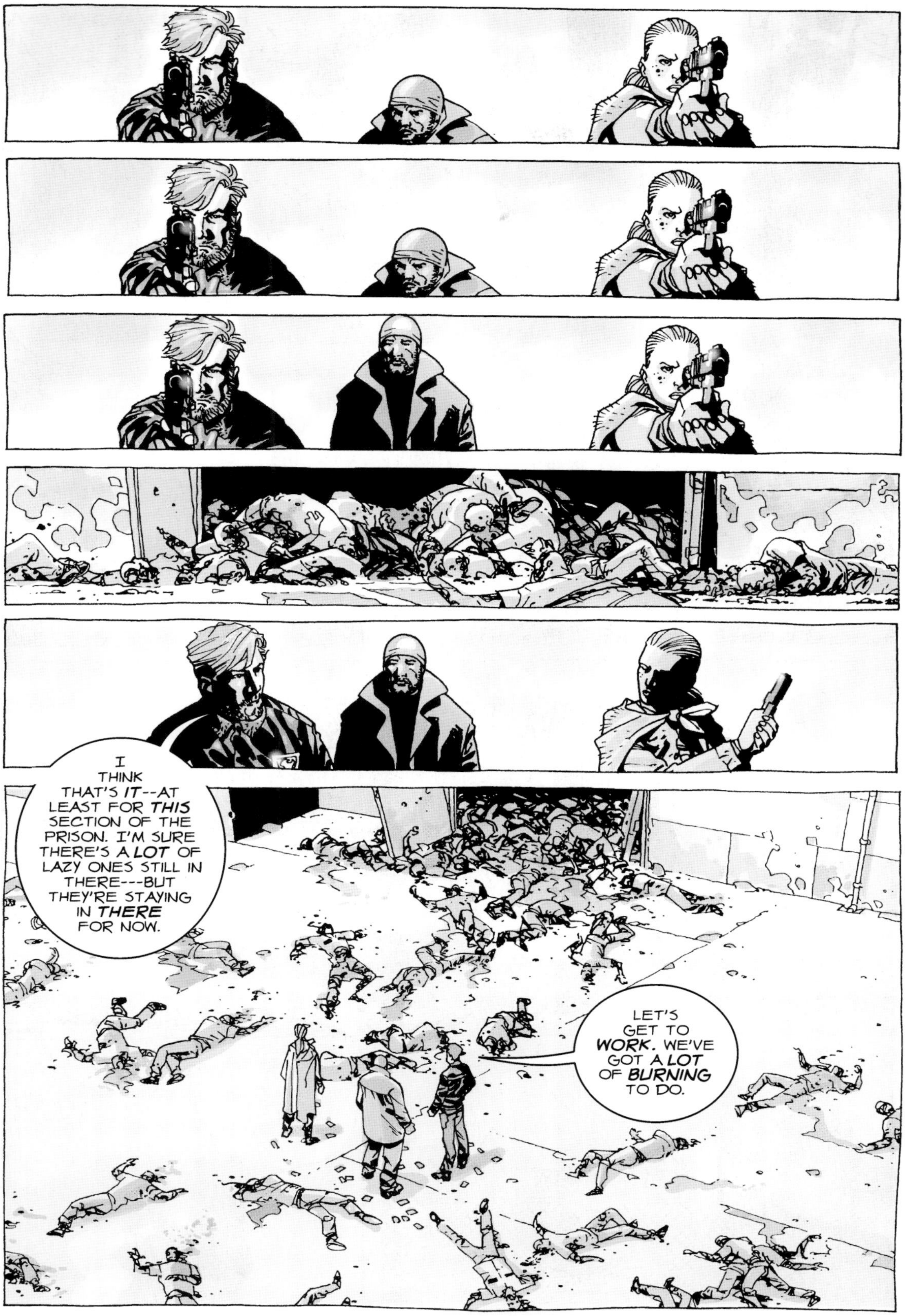
I THINK THAT'S IT--AT LEAST FOR THIS SECTION OF THE PRISON. I'M SURE THERE'S A LOT OF LAZY ONES STILL IN THERE---BUT THEY'RE STAYING IN THERE FOR NOW.
LET'S GET TO WORK. WE'VE GOT A LOT OF BURNING TO DO.

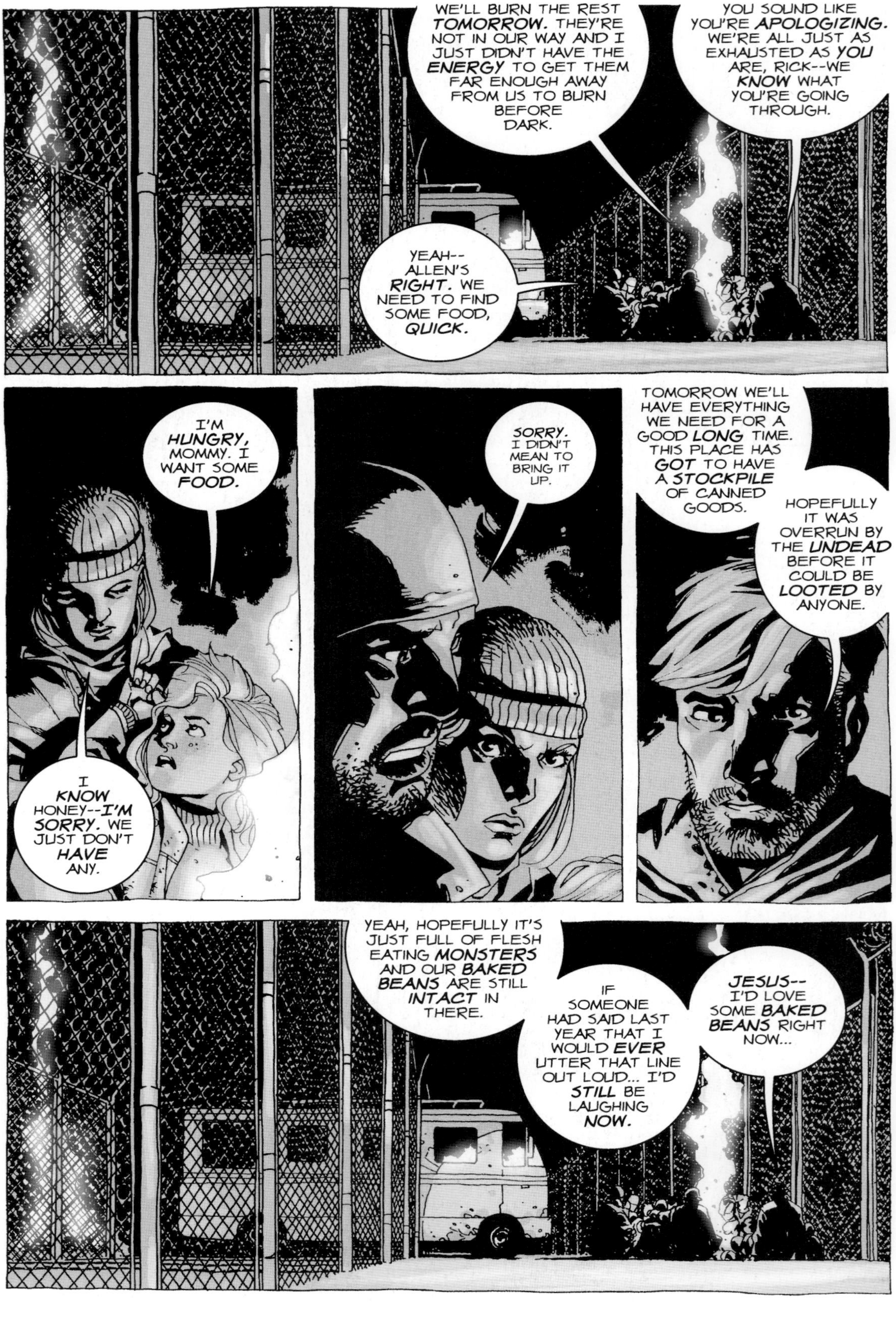
WE'LL BURN THE REST TOMORROW. THEY'RE NOT IN OUR WAY AND I JUST DIDN'T HAVE THE ENERGY TO GET THEM FAR ENOUGH AWAY FROM US TO BURN BEFORE DARK.
YOU SOUND LIKE YOU'RE APOLOGIZING. WE'RE ALL JUST AS EXHAUSTED AS YOU ARE, RICK--WE KNOW WHAT YOU'RE GOING THROUGH.
YEAH-- ALLEN'S RIGHT. WE NEED TO FIND SOME FOOD, QUICK.
I'M HUNGRY, MOMMY. I WANT SOME FOOD.
I KNOW HONEY--I'M SORRY. WE JUST DON'T HAVE ANY.
SORRY. I DIDN'T MEAN TO BRING IT UP.
TOMORROW WE'LL HAVE EVERYTHING WE NEED FOR A GOOD LONG TIME. THIS PLACE HAS GOT TO HAVE A STOCKPILE OF CANNED GOODS.
HOPEFULLY IT WAS OVERRUN BY THE UNDEAD BEFORE IT COULD BE LOOTED BY ANYONE.
YEAH, HOPEFULLY IT'S JUST FULL OF FLESH EATING MONSTERS AND OUR BAKED BEANS ARE STILL INTACT IN THERE.
IF SOMEONE HAD SAID LAST YEAR THAT I WOULD EVER UTTER THAT LINE OUT LOUD... I'D STILL BE LAUGHING NOW.
JESUS-- I'D LOVE SOME BAKED BEANS RIGHT NOW...

OH! THAT TIME ALREADY?

YEP. I'M TAKING OVER FOR YOU. YOU REGRETTING SLEEPING ON *THIS* SIDE OF THE FENCE JUST YET?

I KNOW *I* WILL IN ABOUT AN HOUR.

I'M STILL NOT SURE IT'S ANY *SAFER* ON THE *OTHER* SIDE. WE KILLED A LOT OF ZOMBIES IN THERE TODAY BUT THAT'S A *BIG* PLACE--I'M SURE THERE'S *MORE*.

THAT'S SOMETHING WE NEED TO DO IF WE END UP *STAYING* HERE--FIX THESE GATES. IT'S NO GOOD TO HAVE *THREE* FENCES IF ONLY *ONE* OF THEM HAS A *GATE* WE CAN CLOSE.

OF COURSE, IF THE GATE WAS WORKING ON THIS *SECOND* FENCE WE COULD CLOSE OURSELVES IN WITH A FENCE ON *EITHER* SIDE.

RICK, IF WE DON'T END UP STAYING HERE, I'M SHOOTING MYSELF IN THE *FACE*. I'M *NOT* SPENDING ANOTHER *NIGHT* IN THIS *RV*.

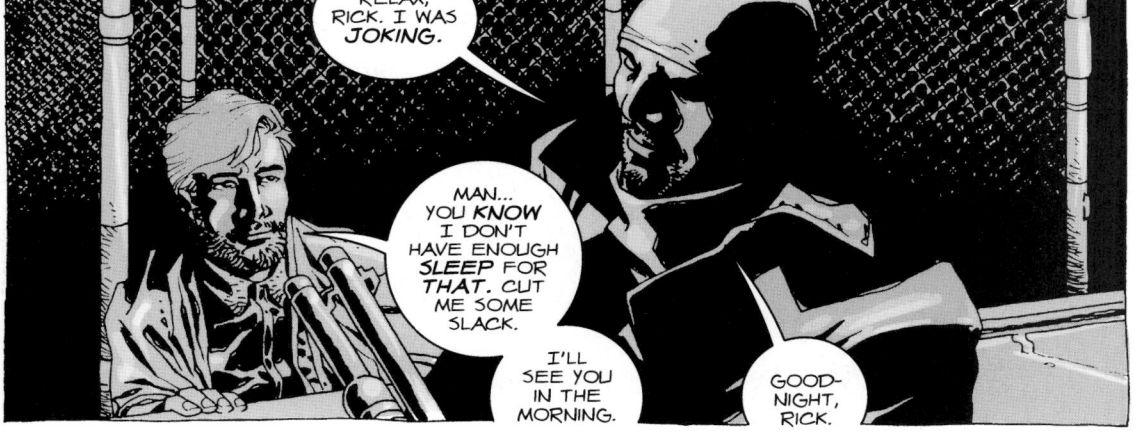

RELAX, RICK. I WAS *JOKING*.

MAN... YOU *KNOW* I DON'T HAVE ENOUGH *SLEEP* FOR *THAT*. CUT ME SOME SLACK.

I'LL SEE YOU IN THE MORNING.

GOOD-NIGHT, RICK.

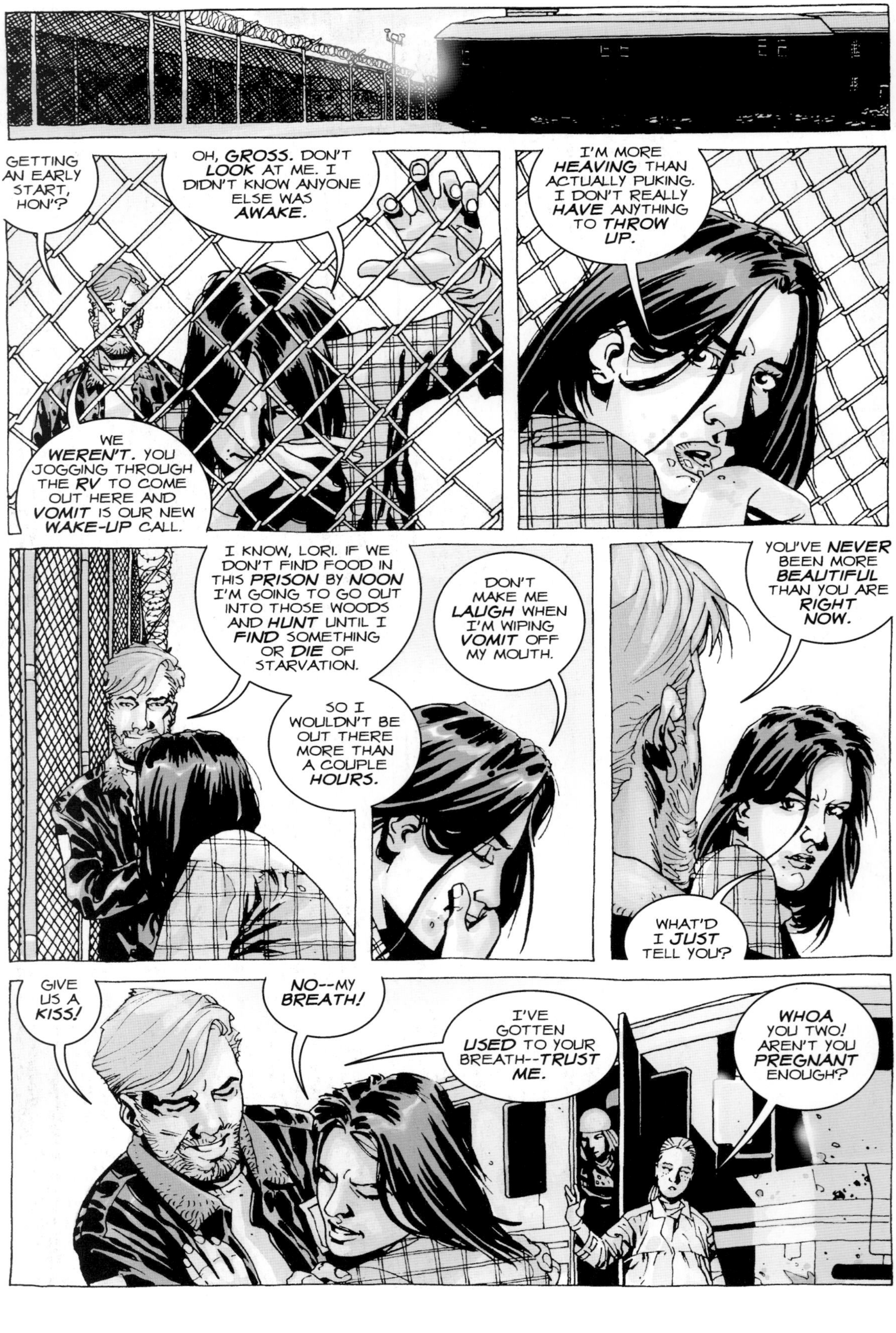
GETTING AN EARLY START, HON'?
OH, GROSS. DON'T LOOK AT ME. I DIDN'T KNOW ANYONE ELSE WAS AWAKE.
WE WEREN'T. YOU JOGGING THROUGH THE RV TO COME OUT HERE AND VOMIT IS OUR NEW WAKE-UP CALL.
I'M MORE HEAVING THAN ACTUALLY PUKING. I DON'T REALLY HAVE ANYTHING TO THROW UP.
I KNOW, LORI. IF WE DON'T FIND FOOD IN THIS PRISON BY NOON I'M GOING TO GO OUT INTO THOSE WOODS AND HUNT UNTIL I FIND SOMETHING OR DIE OF STARVATION.
SO I WOULDN'T BE OUT THERE MORE THAN A COUPLE HOURS.
DON'T MAKE ME LAUGH WHEN I'M WIPING VOMIT OFF MY MOUTH.
YOU'VE NEVER BEEN MORE BEAUTIFUL THAN YOU ARE RIGHT NOW.
WHAT'D I JUST TELL YOU?
GIVE US A KISS!
NO--MY BREATH!
I'VE GOTTEN USED TO YOUR BREATH--TRUST ME.
WHOA YOU TWO! AREN'T YOU PREGNANT ENOUGH?

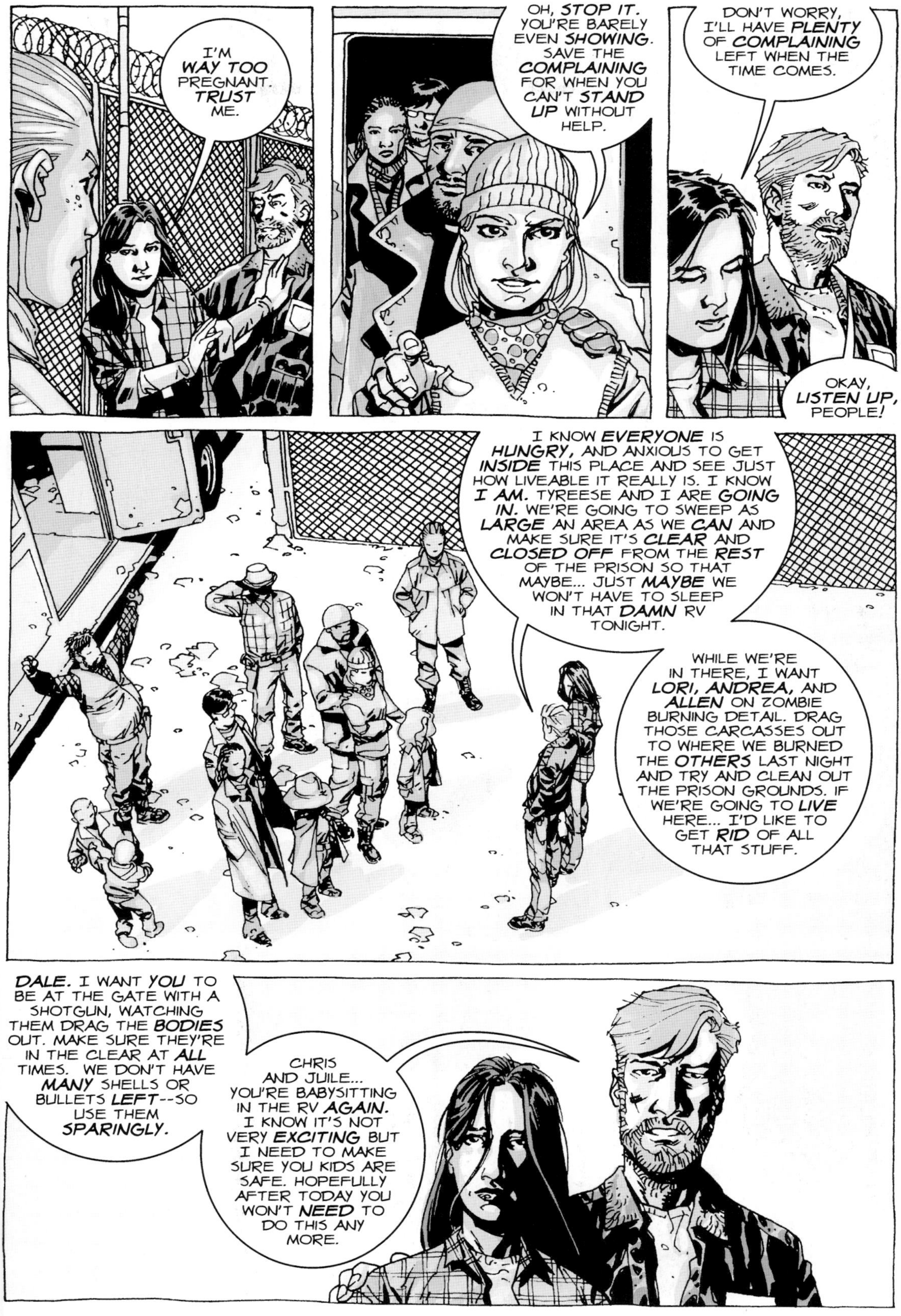

I'M WAY TOO PREGNANT. TRUST ME.
OH, STOP IT. YOU'RE BARELY EVEN SHOWING. SAVE THE COMPLAINING FOR WHEN YOU CAN'T STAND UP WITHOUT HELP.
DON'T WORRY, I'LL HAVE PLENTY OF COMPLAINING LEFT WHEN THE TIME COMES.
OKAY, LISTEN UP, PEOPLE!
I KNOW EVERYONE IS HUNGRY, AND ANXIOUS TO GET INSIDE THIS PLACE AND SEE JUST HOW LIVEABLE IT REALLY IS. I KNOW I AM. TYREESE AND I ARE GOING IN. WE'RE GOING TO SWEEP AS LARGE AN AREA AS WE CAN AND MAKE SURE IT'S CLEAR AND CLOSED OFF FROM THE REST OF THE PRISON SO THAT MAYBE... JUST MAYBE WE WON'T HAVE TO SLEEP IN THAT DAMN RV TONIGHT.
WHILE WE'RE IN THERE, I WANT LORI, ANDREA, AND ALLEN ON ZOMBIE BURNING DETAIL. DRAG THOSE CARCASSES OUT TO WHERE WE BURNED THE OTHERS LAST NIGHT AND TRY AND CLEAN OUT THE PRISON GROUNDS. IF WE'RE GOING TO LIVE HERE... I'D LIKE TO GET RID OF ALL THAT STUFF.
DALE. I WANT YOU TO BE AT THE GATE WITH A SHOTGUN, WATCHING THEM DRAG THE BODIES OUT. MAKE SURE THEY'RE IN THE CLEAR AT ALL TIMES. WE DON'T HAVE MANY SHELLS OR BULLETS LEFT--SO USE THEM SPARINGLY.
CHRIS AND JUILE... YOU'RE BABYSITTING IN THE RV AGAIN. I KNOW IT'S NOT VERY EXCITING BUT I NEED TO MAKE SURE YOU KIDS ARE SAFE. HOPEFULLY AFTER TODAY YOU WON'T NEED TO DO THIS ANY MORE.

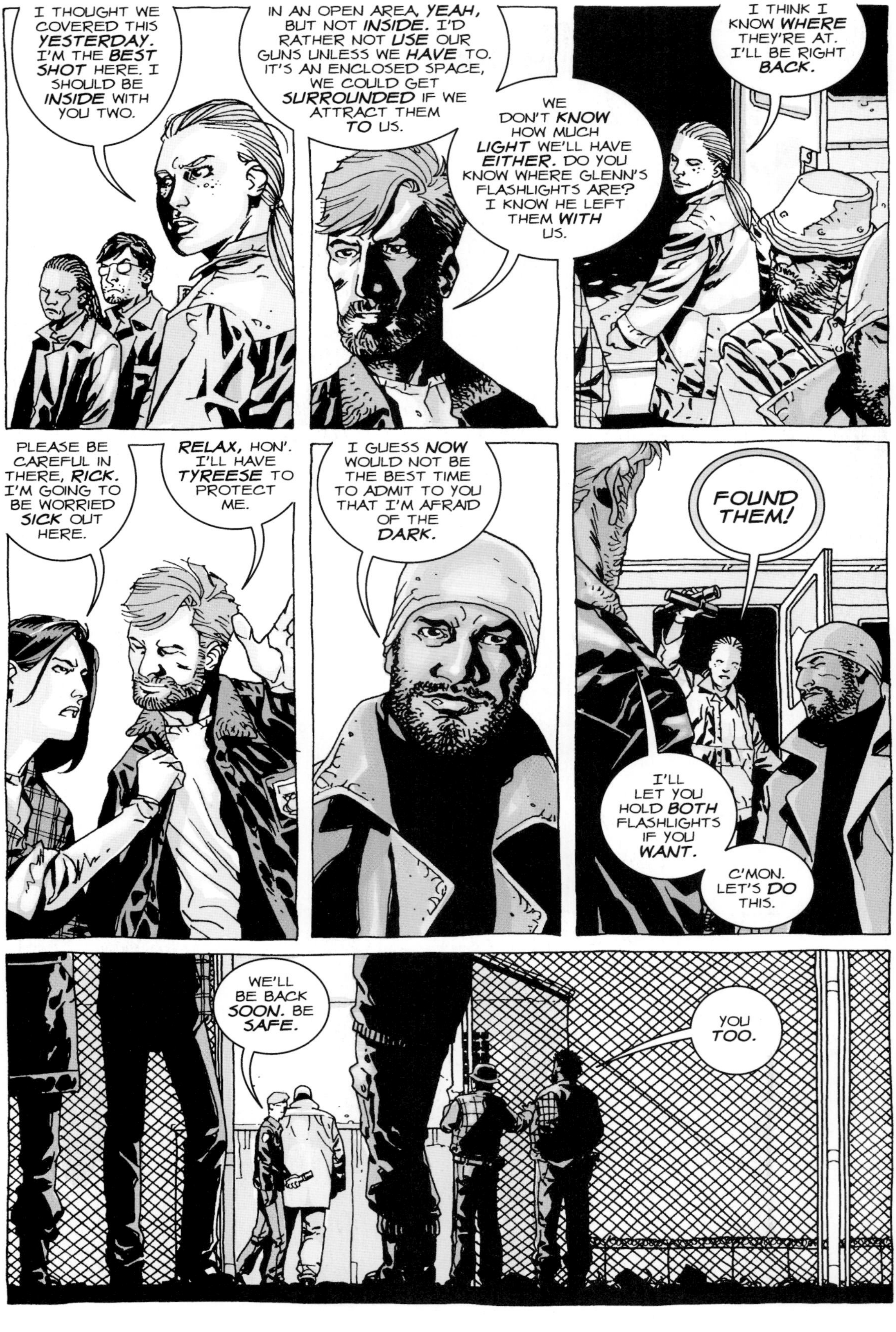
I THOUGHT WE COVERED THIS YESTERDAY. I'M THE BEST SHOT HERE. I SHOULD BE INSIDE WITH YOU TWO.
IN AN OPEN AREA, YEAH, BUT NOT INSIDE. I'D RATHER NOT USE OUR GUNS UNLESS WE HAVE TO. IT'S AN ENCLOSED SPACE, WE COULD GET SURROUNDED IF WE ATTRACT THEM TO US.
WE DON'T KNOW HOW MUCH LIGHT WE'LL HAVE EITHER. DO YOU KNOW WHERE GLENN'S FLASHLIGHTS ARE? I KNOW HE LEFT THEM WITH US.
I THINK I KNOW WHERE THEY'RE AT. I'LL BE RIGHT BACK.
PLEASE BE CAREFUL IN THERE, RICK. I'M GOING TO BE WORRIED SICK OUT HERE.
RELAX, HON'. I'LL HAVE TYREESE TO PROTECT ME.
I GUESS NOW WOULD NOT BE THE BEST TIME TO ADMIT TO YOU THAT I'M AFRAID OF THE DARK.
FOUND THEM!
I'LL LET YOU HOLD BOTH FLASHLIGHTS IF YOU WANT.
C'MON. LET'S DO THIS.
WE'LL BE BACK SOON. BE SAFE.
YOU TOO.

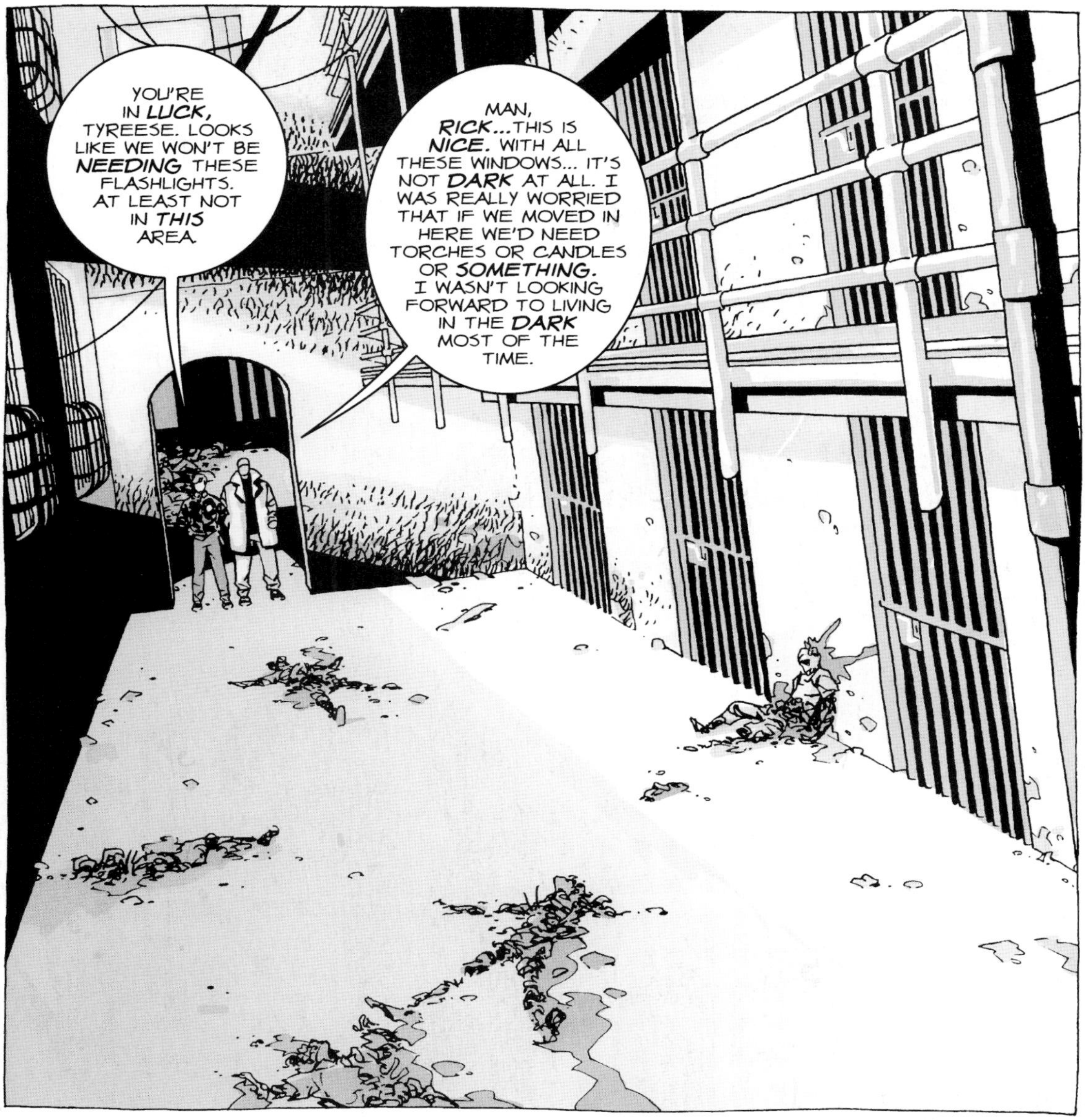
YOU'RE IN LUCK, TYREESE. LOOKS LIKE WE WON'T BE NEEDING THESE FLASHLIGHTS. AT LEAST NOT IN THIS AREA.
MAN, RICK...THIS IS NICE. WITH ALL THESE WINDOWS... IT'S NOT DARK AT ALL. I WAS REALLY WORRIED THAT IF WE MOVED IN HERE WE'D NEED TORCHES OR CANDLES OR SOMETHING. I WASN'T LOOKING FORWARD TO LIVING IN THE DARK MOST OF THE TIME.

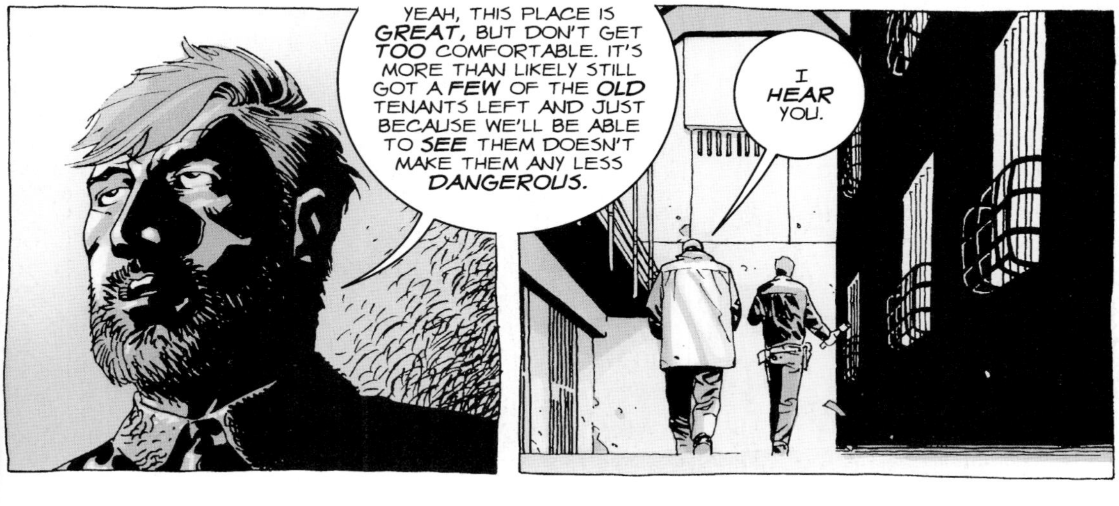
YEAH, THIS PLACE IS GREAT, BUT DON'T GET TOO COMFORTABLE. IT'S MORE THAN LIKELY STILL GOT A FEW OF THE OLD TENANTS LEFT AND JUST BECAUSE WE'LL BE ABLE TO SEE THEM DOESN'T MAKE THEM ANY LESS DANGEROUS.
I HEAR YOU.

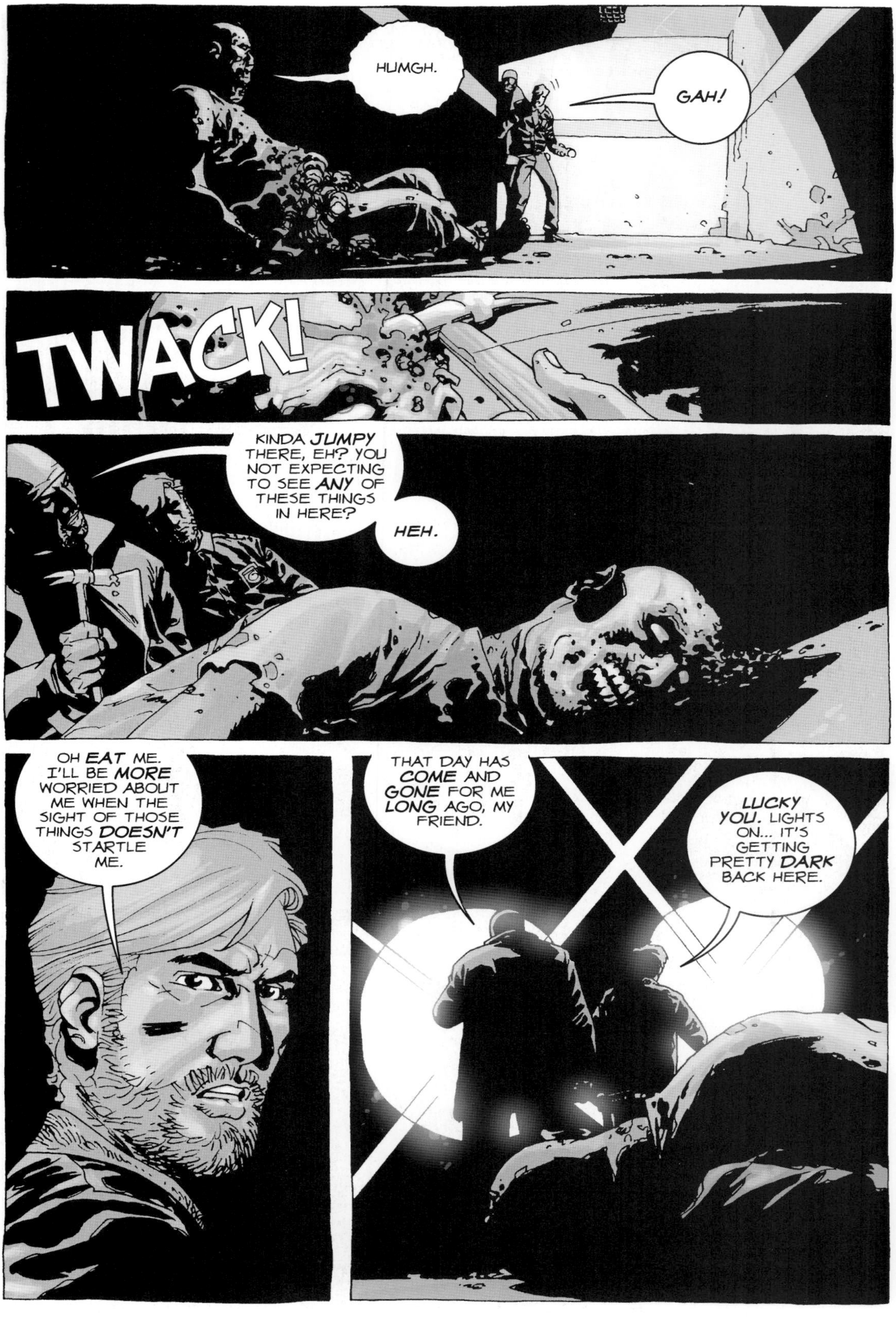
HUMGH.
GAH!
TWACK!
KINDA JUMPY THERE, EH? YOU NOT EXPECTING TO SEE ANY OF THESE THINGS IN HERE?
HEH.
OH EAT ME. I'LL BE MORE WORRIED ABOUT ME WHEN THE SIGHT OF THOSE THINGS DOESN'T STARTLE ME.
THAT DAY HAS COME AND GONE FOR ME LONG AGO, MY FRIEND.
LUCKY YOU. LIGHTS ON... IT'S GETTING PRETTY DARK BACK HERE.

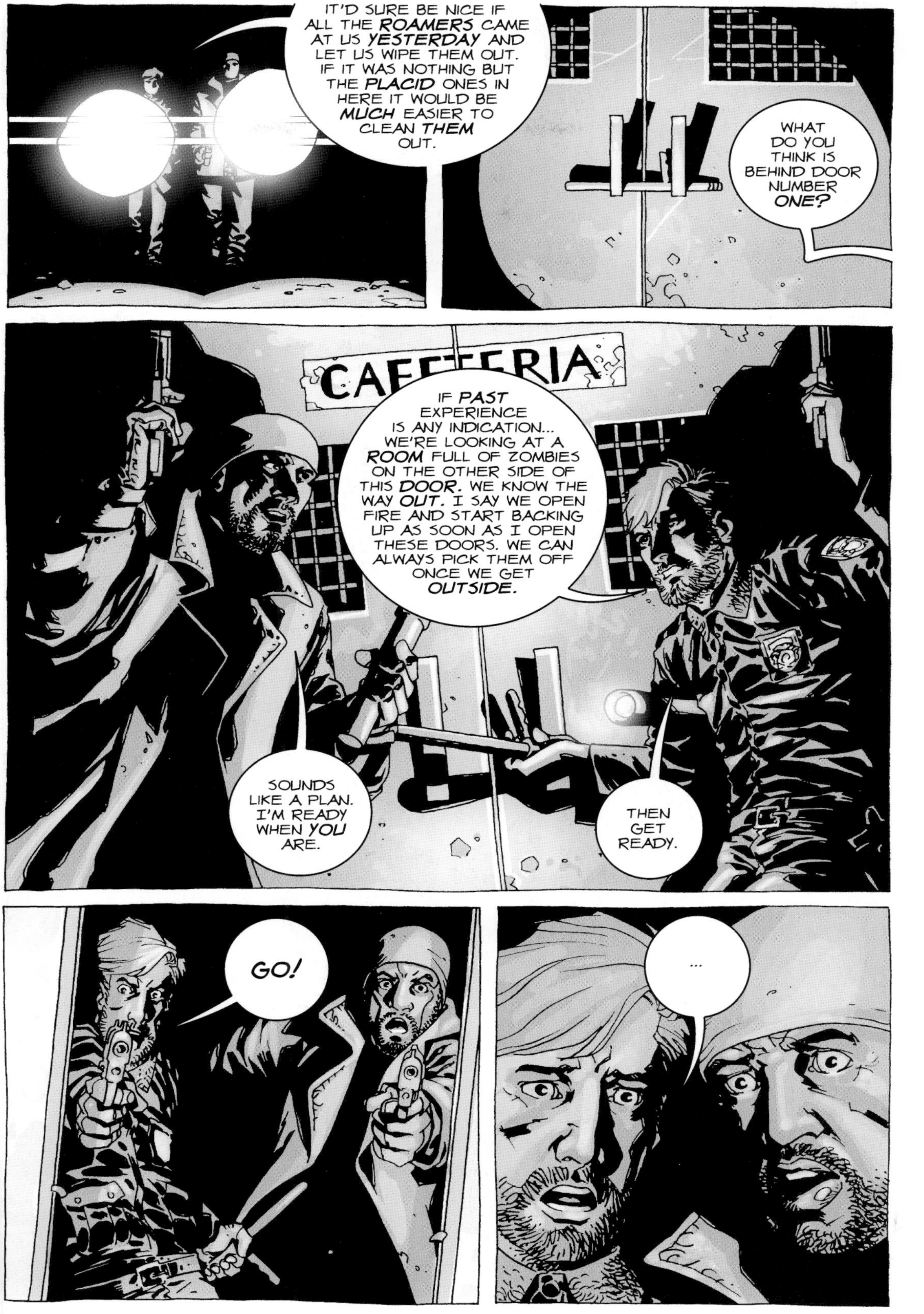
IT'D SURE BE NICE IF ALL THE ROAMERS CAME AT US YESTERDAY AND LET US WIPE THEM OUT. IF IT WAS NOTHING BUT THE PLACID ONES IN HERE IT WOULD BE MUCH EASIER TO CLEAN THEM OUT.
WHAT DO YOU THINK IS BEHIND DOOR NUMBER ONE?
CAFETERIA
IF PAST EXPERIENCE IS ANY INDICATION... WE'RE LOOKING AT A ROOM FULL OF ZOMBIES ON THE OTHER SIDE OF THIS DOOR. WE KNOW THE WAY OUT. I SAY WE OPEN FIRE AND START BACKING UP AS SOON AS I OPEN THESE DOORS. WE CAN ALWAYS PICK THEM OFF ONCE WE GET OUTSIDE.
SOUNDS LIKE A PLAN. I'M READY WHEN YOU ARE.
THEN GET READY.
GO!
...

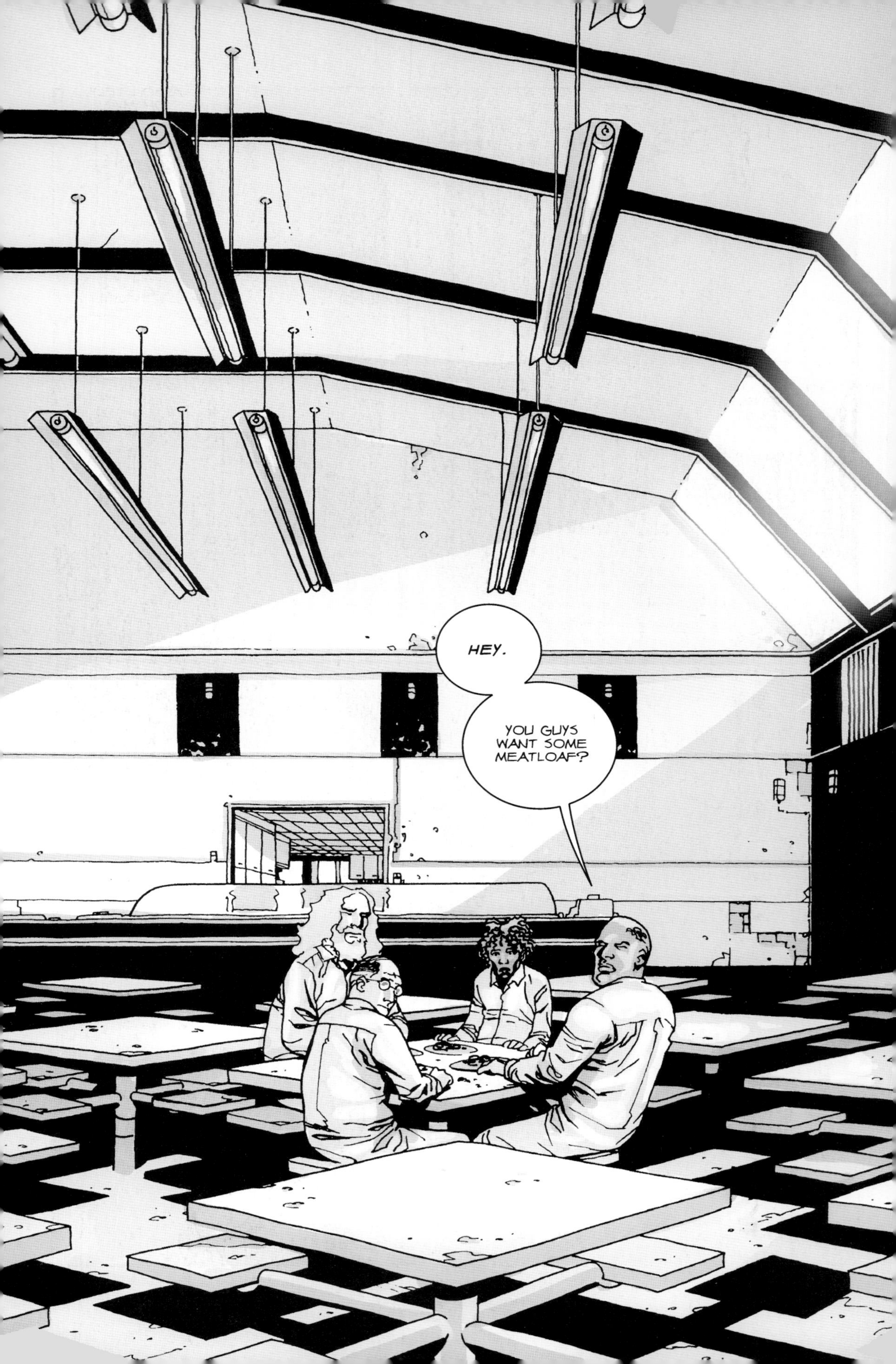
HEY.
YOU GUYS WANT SOME MEATLOAF?

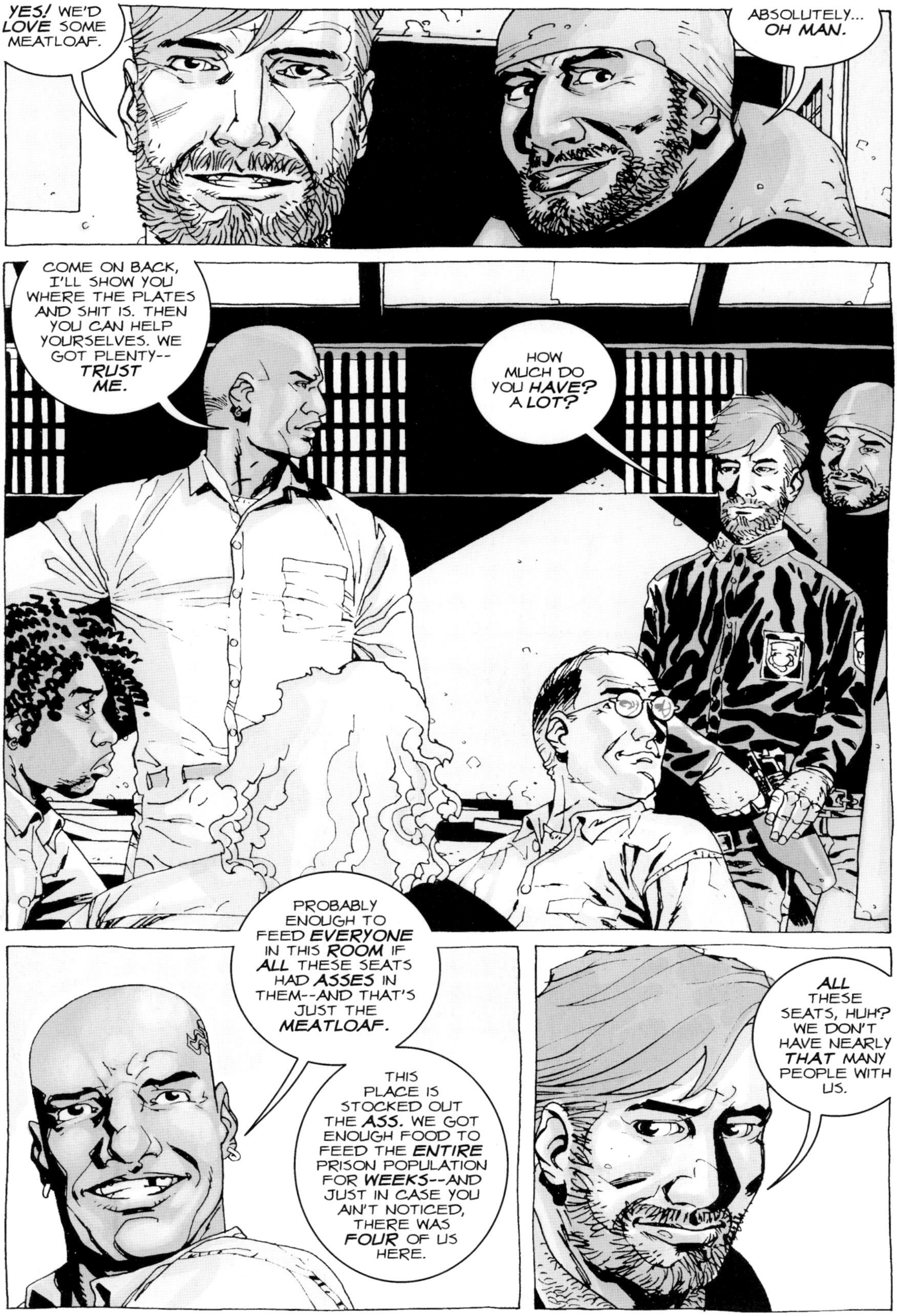
YES! WE'D LOVE SOME MEATLOAF.
ABSOLUTELY... OH MAN.
COME ON BACK, I'LL SHOW YOU WHERE THE PLATES AND SHIT IS. THEN YOU CAN HELP YOURSELVES. WE GOT PLENTY-- TRUST ME.
HOW MUCH DO YOU HAVE? A LOT?
PROBABLY ENOUGH TO FEED EVERYONE IN THIS ROOM IF ALL THESE SEATS HAD ASSES IN THEM--AND THAT'S JUST THE MEATLOAF.
THIS PLACE IS STOCKED OUT THE ASS. WE GOT ENOUGH FOOD TO FEED THE ENTIRE PRISON POPULATION FOR WEEKS--AND JUST IN CASE YOU AIN'T NOTICED, THERE WAS FOUR OF US HERE.
ALL THESE SEATS, HUH? WE DON'T HAVE NEARLY THAT MANY PEOPLE WITH US.

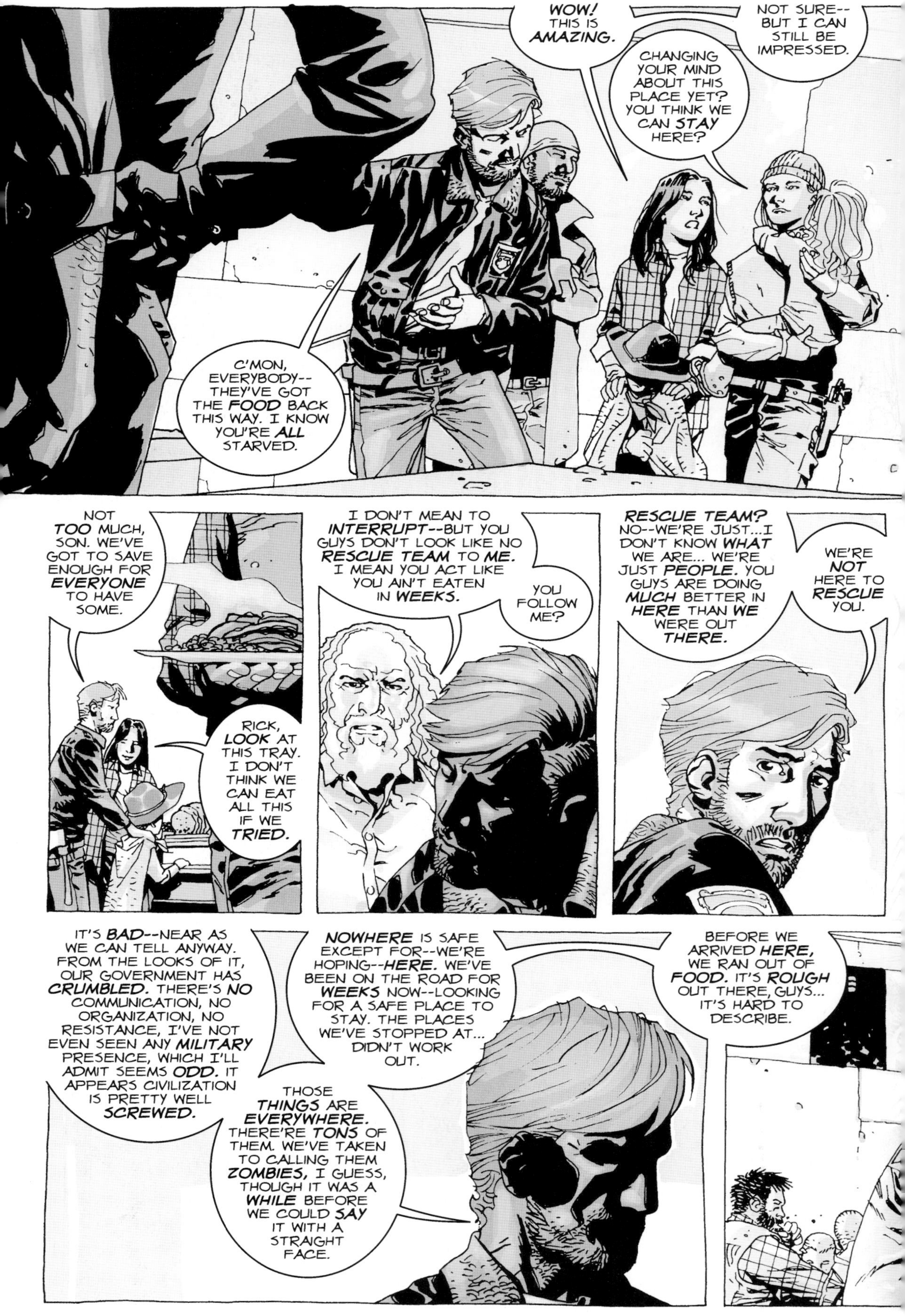

WOW! THIS IS AMAZING.
NOT SURE-- BUT I CAN STILL BE IMPRESSED.
CHANGING YOUR MIND ABOUT THIS PLACE YET? YOU THINK WE CAN STAY HERE?
C'MON, EVERYBODY-- THEY'VE GOT THE FOOD BACK THIS WAY. I KNOW YOU'RE ALL STARVED.
NOT TOO MUCH, SON. WE'VE GOT TO SAVE ENOUGH FOR EVERYONE TO HAVE SOME.
RICK, LOOK AT THIS TRAY. I DON'T THINK WE CAN EAT ALL THIS IF WE TRIED.
I DON'T MEAN TO INTERRUPT--BUT YOU GUYS DON'T LOOK LIKE NO RESCUE TEAM TO ME. I MEAN YOU ACT LIKE YOU AIN'T EATEN IN WEEKS.
YOU FOLLOW ME?
WE'RE NOT HERE TO RESCUE YOU.
RESCUE TEAM? NO--WE'RE JUST...I DON'T KNOW WHAT WE ARE... WE'RE JUST PEOPLE. YOU GUYS ARE DOING MUCH BETTER IN HERE THAN WE WERE OUT THERE.
IT'S BAD--NEAR AS WE CAN TELL ANYWAY. FROM THE LOOKS OF IT, OUR GOVERNMENT HAS CRUMBLED. THERE'S NO COMMUNICATION, NO ORGANIZATION, NO RESISTANCE, I'VE NOT EVEN SEEN ANY MILITARY PRESENCE, WHICH I'LL ADMIT SEEMS ODD. IT APPEARS CIVILIZATION IS PRETTY WELL SCREWED.
NOWHERE IS SAFE EXCEPT FOR--WE'RE HOPING--HERE. WE'VE BEEN ON THE ROAD FOR WEEKS NOW--LOOKING FOR A SAFE PLACE TO STAY. THE PLACES WE'VE STOPPED AT... DIDN'T WORK OUT.
THOSE THINGS ARE EVERYWHERE. THERE'RE TONS OF THEM. WE'VE TAKEN TO CALLING THEM ZOMBIES, I GUESS, THOUGH IT WAS A WHILE BEFORE WE COULD SAY IT WITH A STRAIGHT FACE.
BEFORE WE ARRIVED HERE, WE RAN OUT OF FOOD. IT'S ROUGH OUT THERE, GUYS... IT'S HARD TO DESCRIBE.

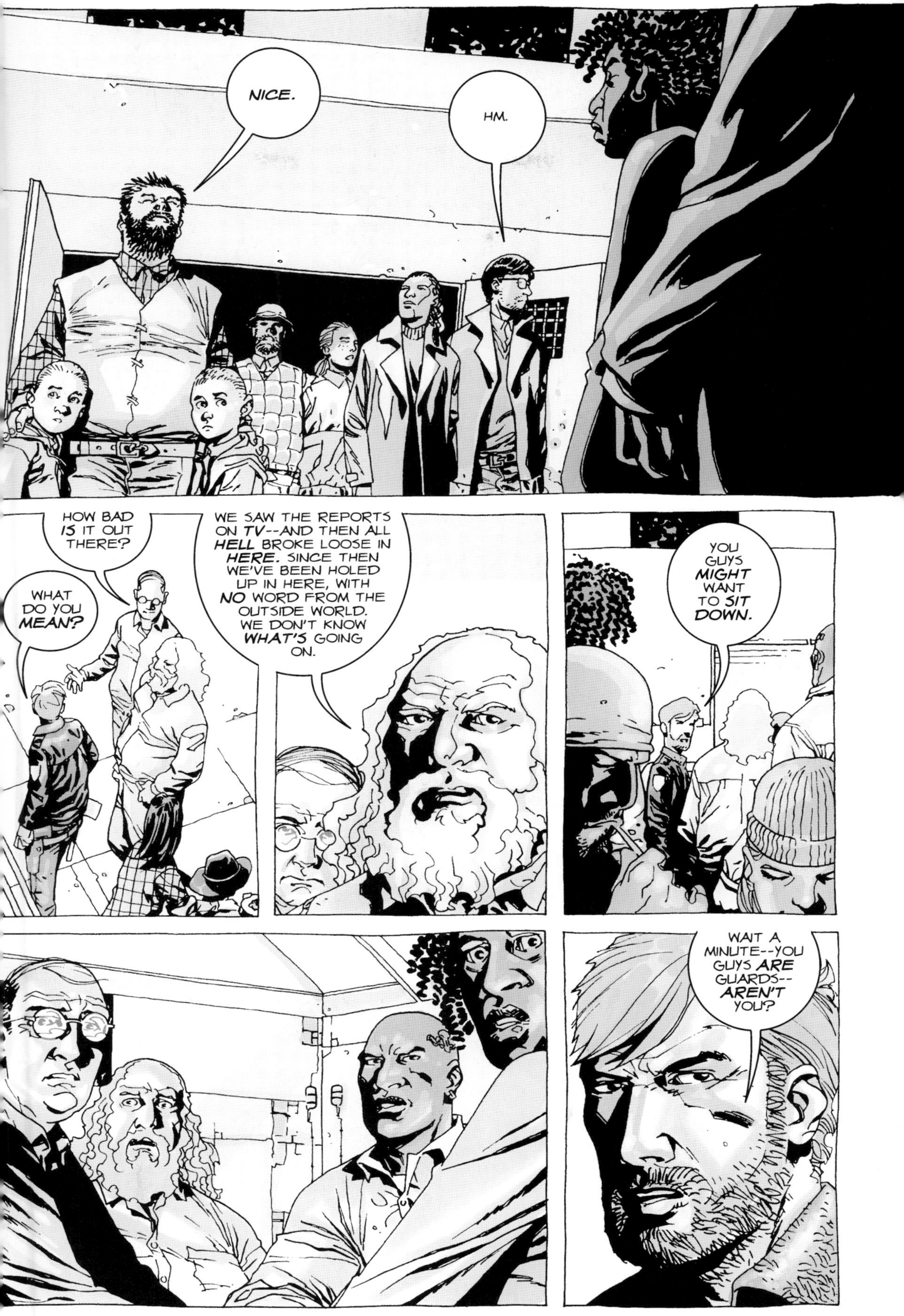
NICE.
HM.
HOW BAD IS IT OUT THERE?
WHAT DO YOU MEAN?
WE SAW THE REPORTS ON TV--AND THEN ALL HELL BROKE LOOSE IN HERE. SINCE THEN WE'VE BEEN HOLED UP IN HERE, WITH NO WORD FROM THE OUTSIDE WORLD. WE DON'T KNOW WHAT'S GOING ON.
YOU GUYS MIGHT WANT TO SIT DOWN.
WAIT A MINUTE--YOU GUYS ARE GUARDS-- AREN'T YOU?

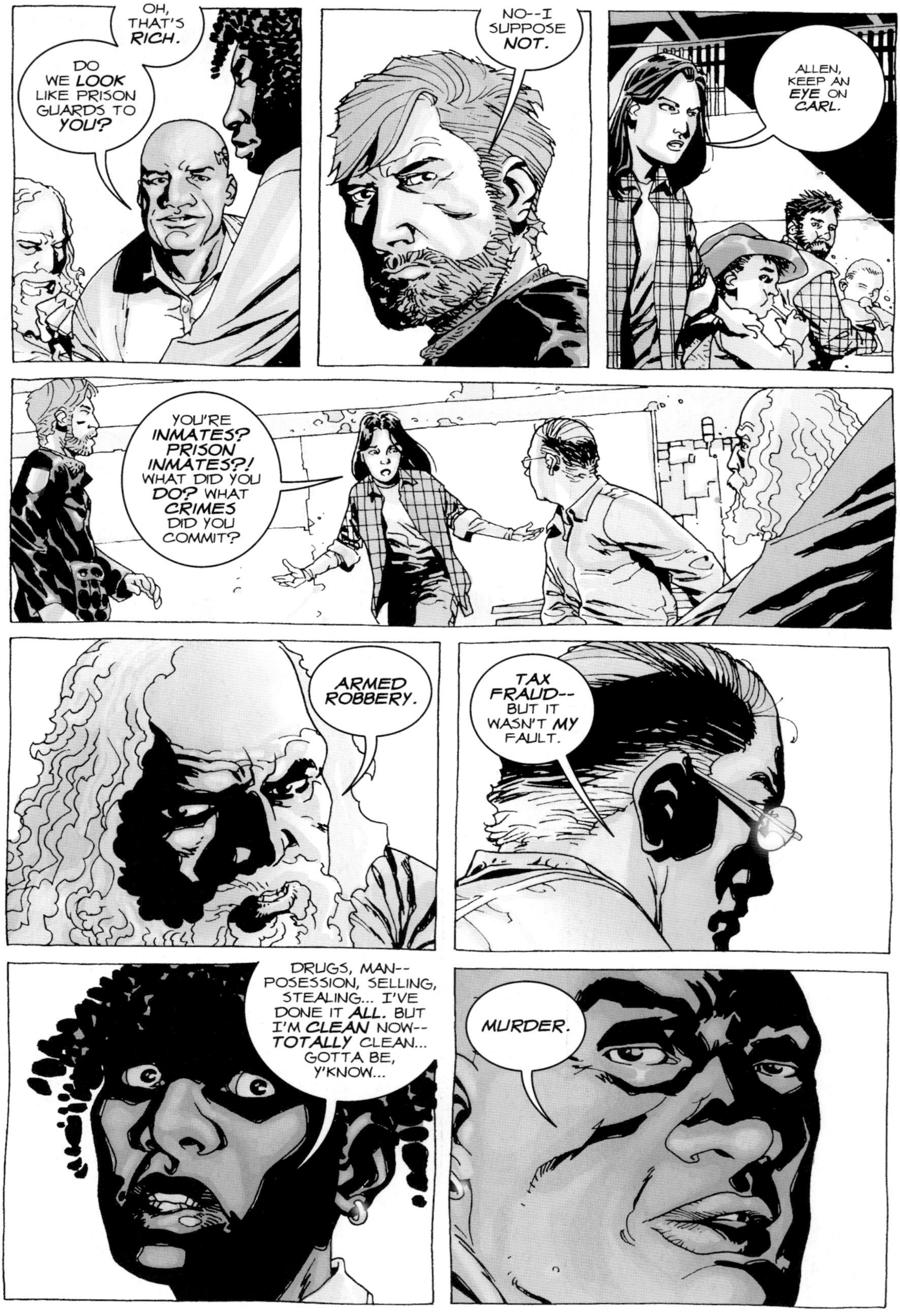

OH, THAT'S RICH.
DO WE LOOK LIKE PRISON GUARDS TO YOU?
NO--I SUPPOSE NOT.
ALLEN, KEEP AN EYE ON CARL.
YOU'RE INMATES? PRISON INMATES?! WHAT DID YOU DO? WHAT CRIMES DID YOU COMMIT?
ARMED ROBBERY.
TAX FRAUD-- BUT IT WASN'T MY FAULT.
DRUGS, MAN-- POSESSION, SELLING, STEALING... I'VE DONE IT ALL. BUT I'M CLEAN NOW-- TOTALLY CLEAN... GOTTA BE, Y'KNOW...
MURDER.

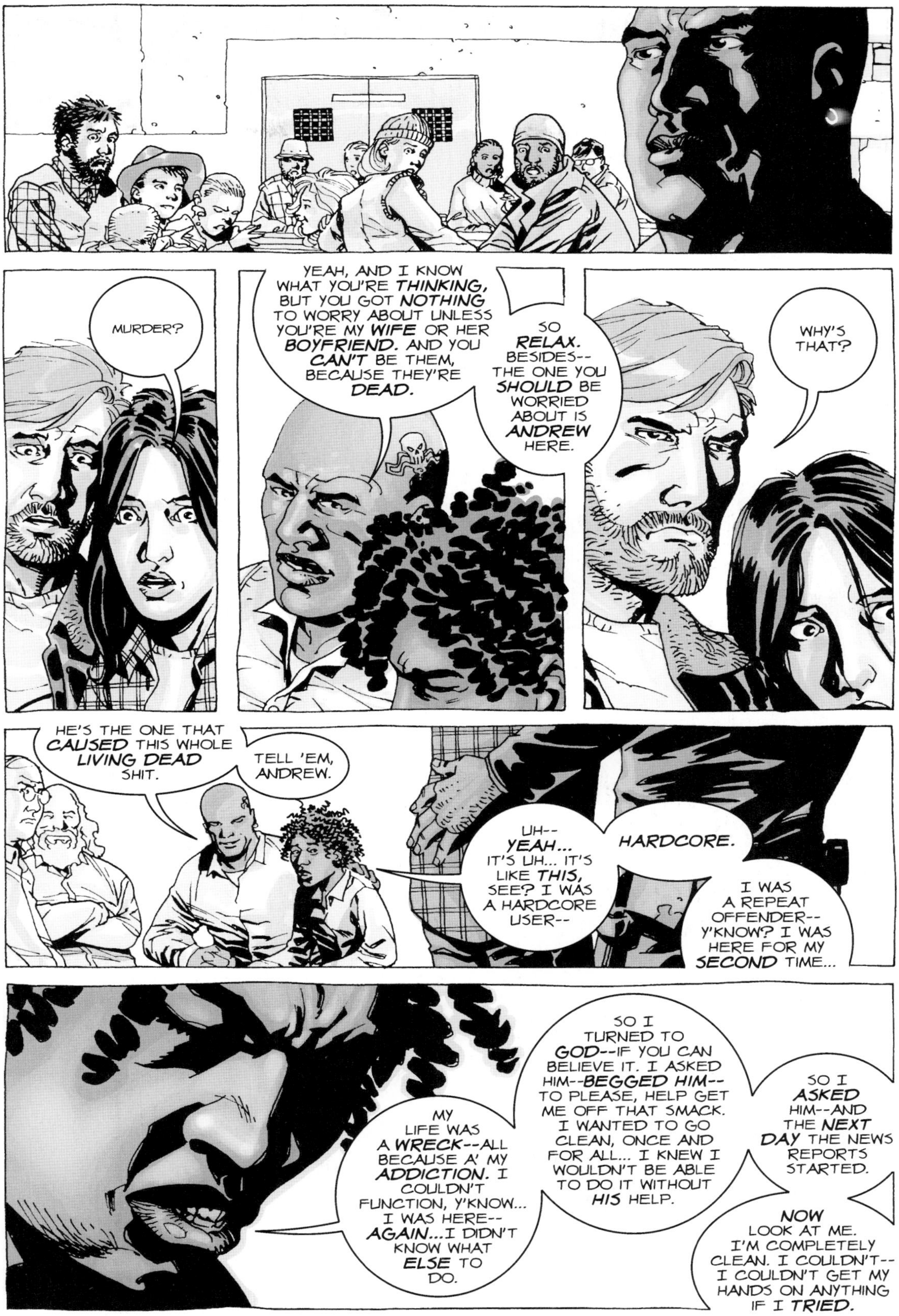
MURDER?
YEAH, AND I KNOW WHAT YOU'RE THINKING, BUT YOU GOT NOTHING TO WORRY ABOUT UNLESS YOU'RE MY WIFE OR HER BOYFRIEND. AND YOU CAN'T BE THEM, BECAUSE THEY'RE DEAD.
SO RELAX. BESIDES-- THE ONE YOU SHOULD BE WORRIED ABOUT IS ANDREW HERE.
WHY'S THAT?
HE'S THE ONE THAT CAUSED THIS WHOLE LIVING DEAD SHIT.
TELL 'EM, ANDREW.
UH-- YEAH... IT'S UH... IT'S LIKE THIS, SEE? I WAS A HARDCORE USER--
HARDCORE.
I WAS A REPEAT OFFENDER-- Y'KNOW? I WAS HERE FOR MY SECOND TIME...
MY LIFE WAS A WRECK--ALL BECAUSE A' MY ADDICTION. I COULDN'T FUNCTION, Y'KNOW... I WAS HERE-- AGAIN...I DIDN'T KNOW WHAT ELSE TO DO.
SO I TURNED TO GOD--IF YOU CAN BELIEVE IT. I ASKED HIM--BEGGED HIM-- TO PLEASE, HELP GET ME OFF THAT SMACK. I WANTED TO GO CLEAN, ONCE AND FOR ALL... I KNEW I WOULDN'T BE ABLE TO DO IT WITHOUT HIS HELP.
SO I ASKED HIM--AND THE NEXT DAY THE NEWS REPORTS STARTED.
NOW LOOK AT ME. I'M COMPLETELY CLEAN. I COULDN'T-- I COULDN'T GET MY HANDS ON ANYTHING IF I TRIED.

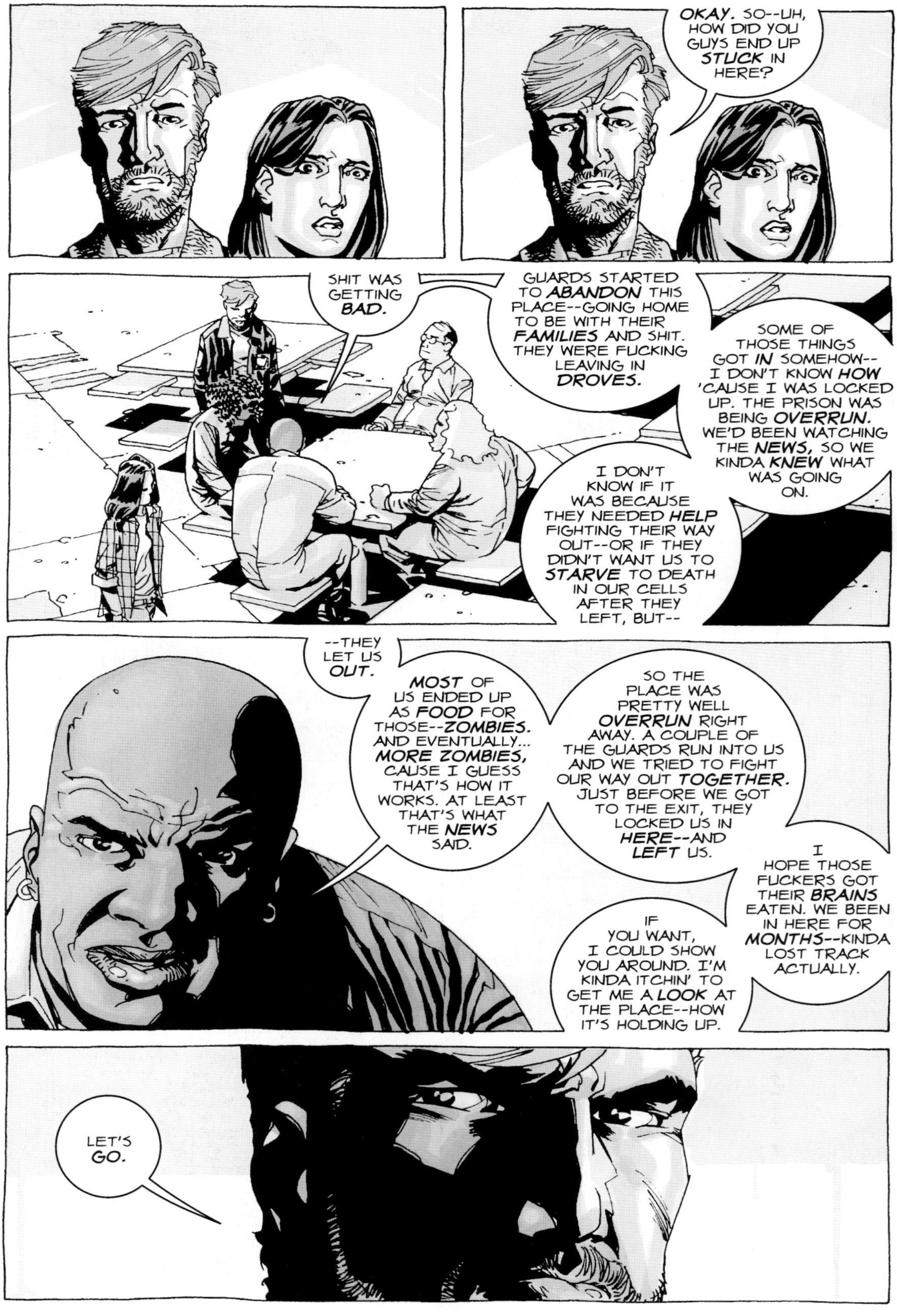
OKAY. SO--UH, HOW DID YOU GUYS END UP STUCK IN HERE?
SHIT WAS GETTING BAD.
GUARDS STARTED TO ABANDON THIS PLACE--GOING HOME TO BE WITH THEIR FAMILIES AND SHIT. THEY WERE FUCKING LEAVING IN DROVES.
SOME OF THOSE THINGS GOT IN SOMEHOW-- I DON'T KNOW HOW 'CAUSE I WAS LOCKED UP. THE PRISON WAS BEING OVERRUN. WE'D BEEN WATCHING THE NEWS, SO WE KINDA KNEW WHAT WAS GOING ON.
I DON'T KNOW IF IT WAS BECAUSE THEY NEEDED HELP FIGHTING THEIR WAY OUT--OR IF THEY DIDN'T WANT US TO STARVE TO DEATH IN OUR CELLS AFTER THEY LEFT, BUT--
--THEY LET US OUT.
MOST OF US ENDED UP AS FOOD FOR THOSE--ZOMBIES. AND EVENTUALLY... MORE ZOMBIES, CAUSE I GUESS THAT'S HOW IT WORKS. AT LEAST THAT'S WHAT THE NEWS SAID.
SO THE PLACE WAS PRETTY WELL OVERRUN RIGHT AWAY. A COUPLE OF THE GUARDS RUN INTO US AND WE TRIED TO FIGHT OUR WAY OUT TOGETHER. JUST BEFORE WE GOT TO THE EXIT, THEY LOCKED US IN HERE--AND LEFT US.
I HOPE THOSE FUCKERS GOT THEIR BRAINS EATEN. WE BEEN IN HERE FOR MONTHS--KINDA LOST TRACK ACTUALLY.
IF YOU WANT, I COULD SHOW YOU AROUND. I'M KINDA ITCHIN' TO GET ME A LOOK AT THE PLACE--HOW IT'S HOLDING UP.
LET'S GO.

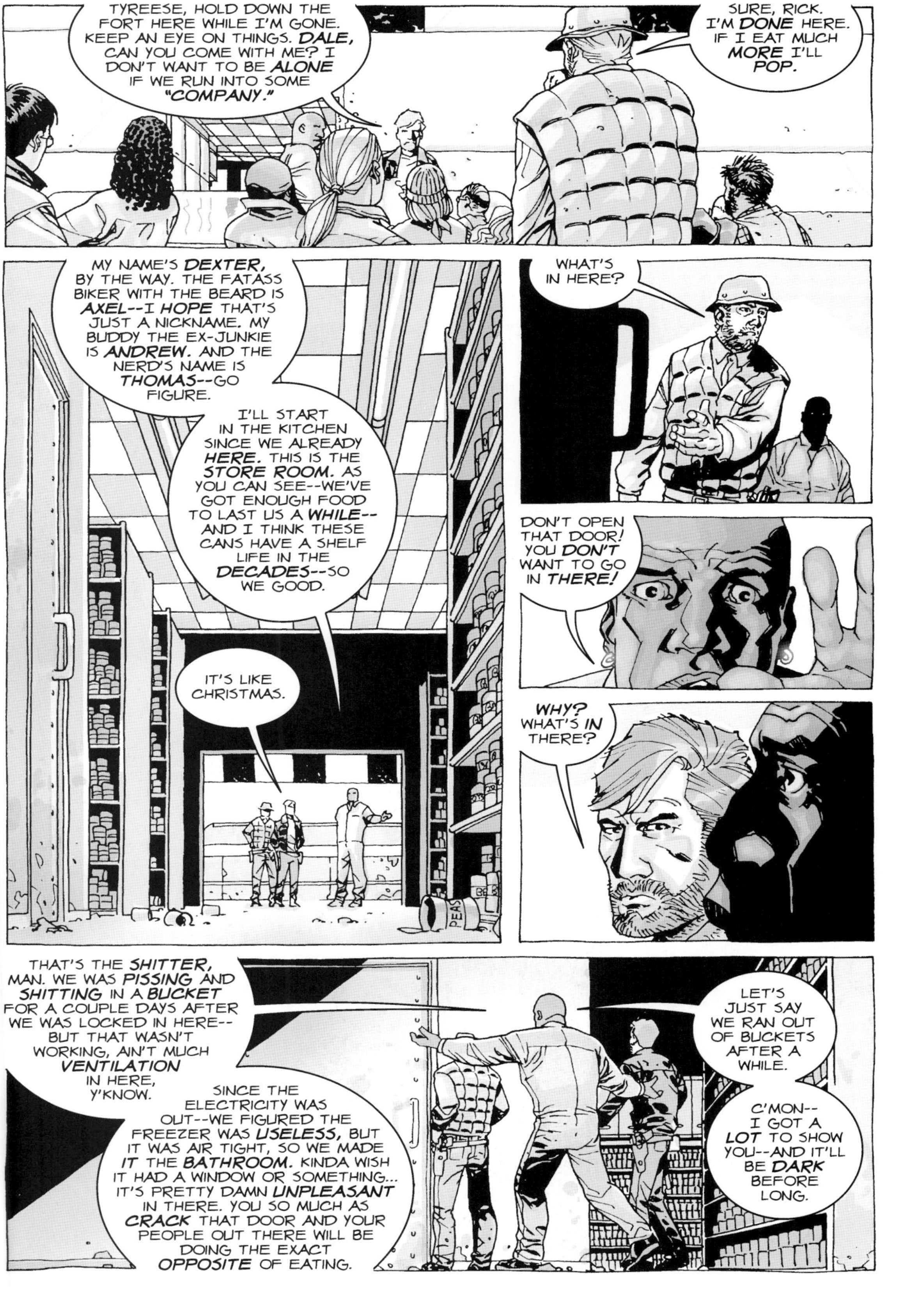
TYREESE, HOLD DOWN THE FORT HERE WHILE I'M GONE. KEEP AN EYE ON THINGS. DALE, CAN YOU COME WITH ME? I DON'T WANT TO BE ALONE IF WE RUN INTO SOME "COMPANY."
SURE, RICK. I'M DONE HERE. IF I EAT MUCH MORE I'LL POP.
MY NAME'S DEXTER, BY THE WAY. THE FATASS BIKER WITH THE BEARD IS AXEL--I HOPE THAT'S JUST A NICKNAME. MY BUDDY THE EX-JUNKIE IS ANDREW. AND THE NERD'S NAME IS THOMAS--GO FIGURE.
I'LL START IN THE KITCHEN SINCE WE ALREADY HERE. THIS IS THE STORE ROOM. AS YOU CAN SEE--WE'VE GOT ENOUGH FOOD TO LAST US A WHILE--AND I THINK THESE CANS HAVE A SHELF LIFE IN THE DECADES--SO WE GOOD.
IT'S LIKE CHRISTMAS.
WHAT'S IN HERE?
DON'T OPEN THAT DOOR! YOU DON'T WANT TO GO IN THERE!
WHY? WHAT'S IN THERE?
THAT'S THE SHITTER, MAN. WE WAS PISSING AND SHITTING IN A BUCKET FOR A COUPLE DAYS AFTER WE WAS LOCKED IN HERE--BUT THAT WASN'T WORKING, AIN'T MUCH VENTILATION IN HERE, Y'KNOW.
SINCE THE ELECTRICITY WAS OUT--WE FIGURED THE FREEZER WAS USELESS, BUT IT WAS AIR TIGHT, SO WE MADE IT THE BATHROOM. KINDA WISH IT HAD A WINDOW OR SOMETHING... IT'S PRETTY DAMN UNPLEASANT IN THERE. YOU SO MUCH AS CRACK THAT DOOR AND YOUR PEOPLE OUT THERE WILL BE DOING THE EXACT OPPOSITE OF EATING.
LET'S JUST SAY WE RAN OUT OF BUCKETS AFTER A WHILE.
C'MON--I GOT A LOT TO SHOW YOU--AND IT'LL BE DARK BEFORE LONG.

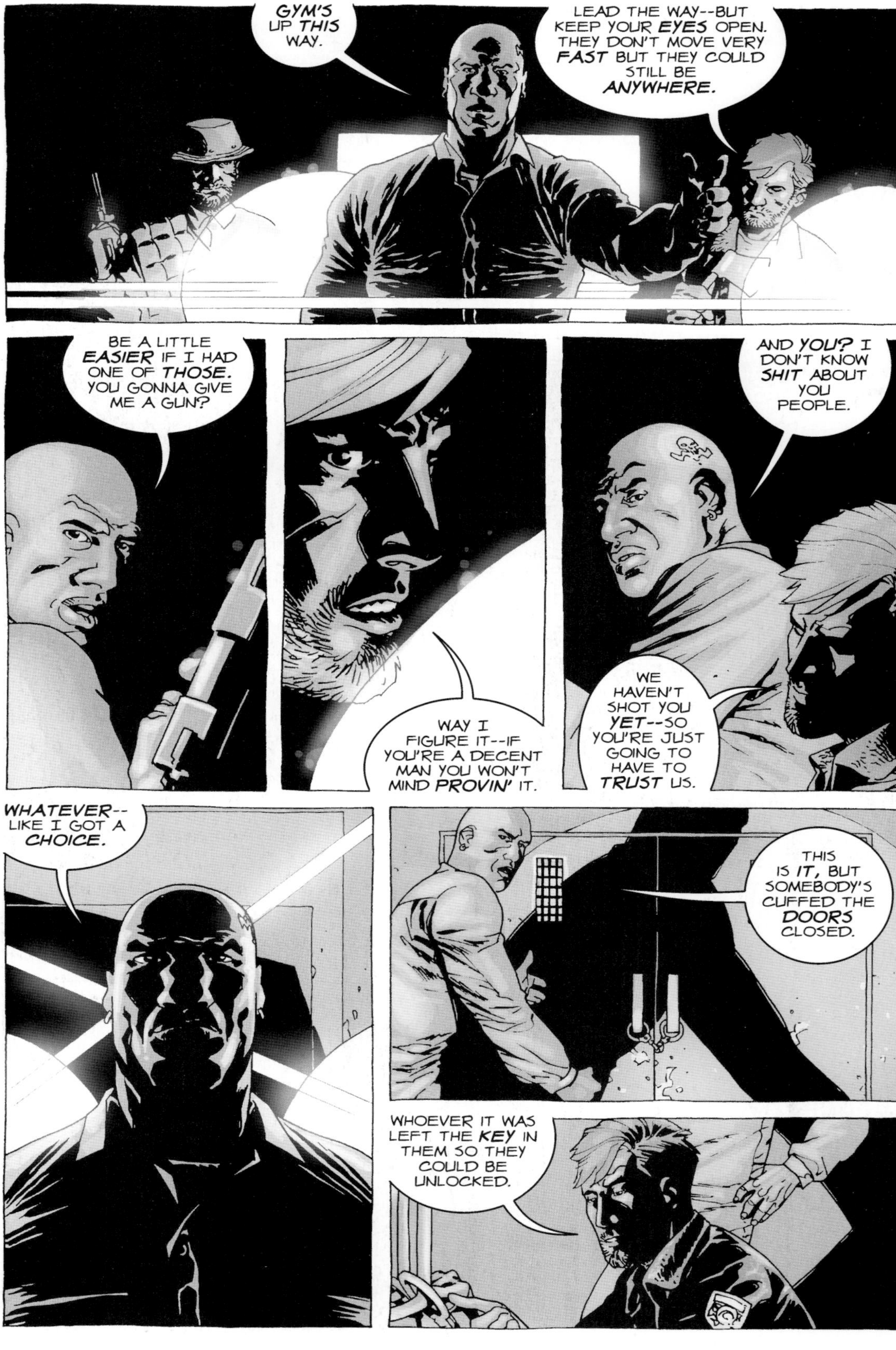
GYM'S UP THIS WAY.
LEAD THE WAY--BUT KEEP YOUR EYES OPEN. THEY DON'T MOVE VERY FAST BUT THEY COULD STILL BE ANYWHERE.
BE A LITTLE EASIER IF I HAD ONE OF THOSE. YOU GONNA GIVE ME A GUN?
WAY I FIGURE IT--IF YOU'RE A DECENT MAN YOU WON'T MIND PROVIN' IT.
AND YOU? I DON'T KNOW SHIT ABOUT YOU PEOPLE.
WE HAVEN'T SHOT YOU YET--SO YOU'RE JUST GOING TO HAVE TO TRUST US.
WHATEVER-- LIKE I GOT A CHOICE.
THIS IS IT, BUT SOMEBODY'S CUFFED THE DOORS CLOSED.
WHOEVER IT WAS LEFT THE KEY IN THEM SO THEY COULD BE UNLOCKED.

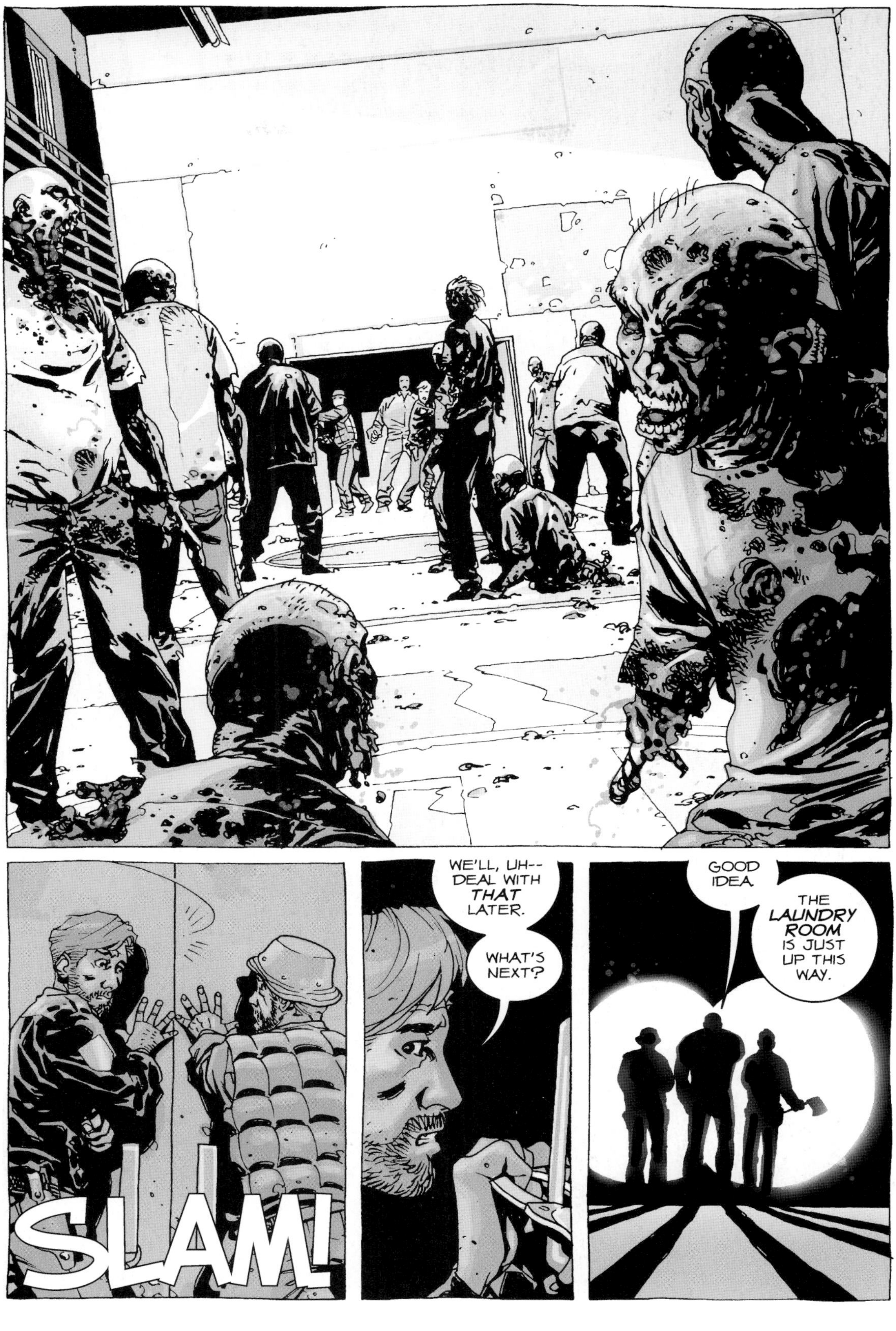
SLAM!
WE'LL, UH-- DEAL WITH THAT LATER.
WHAT'S NEXT?
GOOD IDEA.
THE LAUNDRY ROOM IS JUST UP THIS WAY.

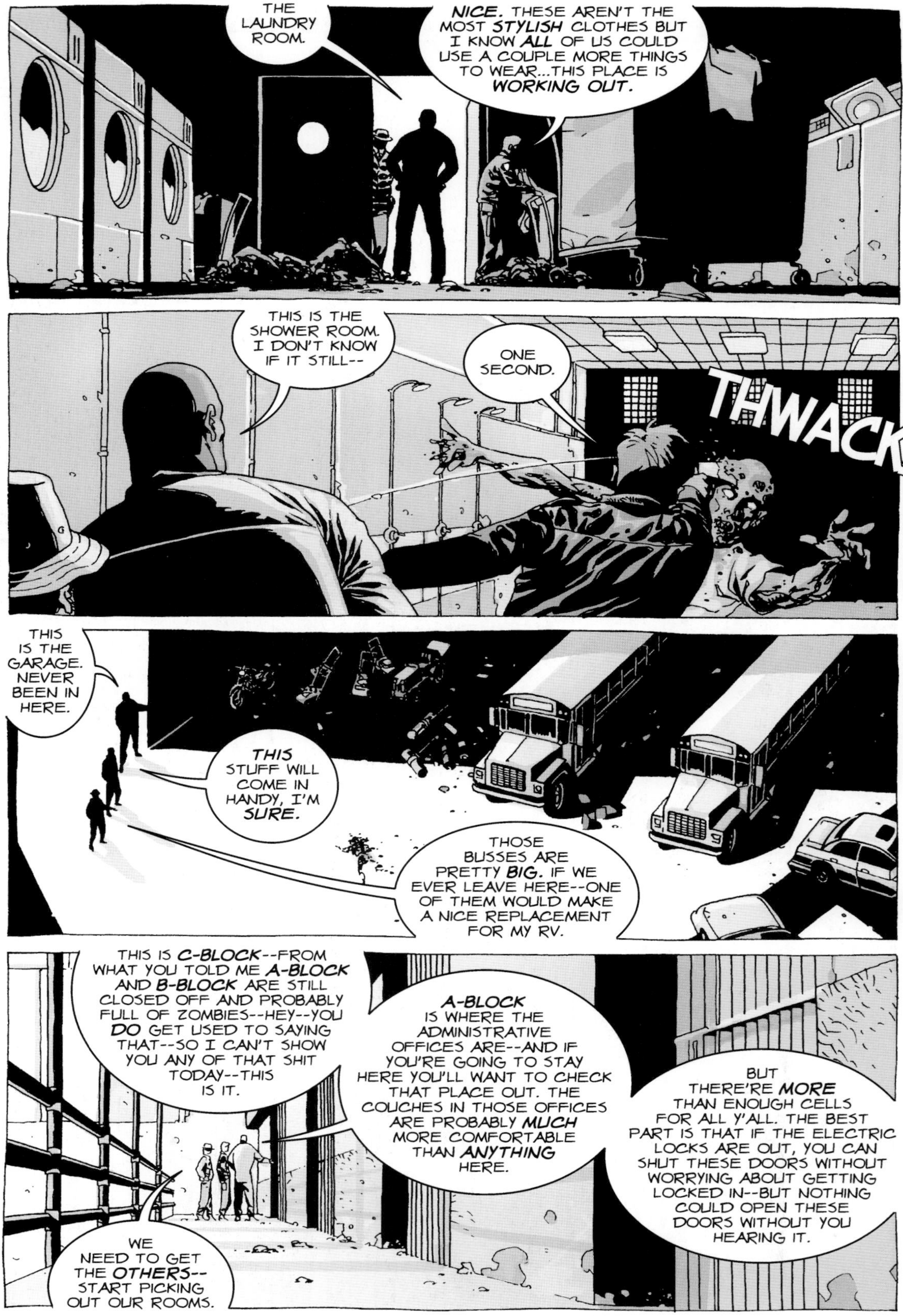
THE LAUNDRY ROOM.
NICE. THESE AREN'T THE MOST STYLISH CLOTHES BUT I KNOW ALL OF US COULD USE A COUPLE MORE THINGS TO WEAR...THIS PLACE IS WORKING OUT.
THIS IS THE SHOWER ROOM. I DON'T KNOW IF IT STILL--
ONE SECOND.
THWACK!
THIS IS THE GARAGE. NEVER BEEN IN HERE.
THIS STUFF WILL COME IN HANDY, I'M SURE.
THOSE BUSSES ARE PRETTY BIG. IF WE EVER LEAVE HERE--ONE OF THEM WOULD MAKE A NICE REPLACEMENT FOR MY RV.
THIS IS C-BLOCK--FROM WHAT YOU TOLD ME A-BLOCK AND B-BLOCK ARE STILL CLOSED OFF AND PROBABLY FULL OF ZOMBIES--HEY--YOU DO GET USED TO SAYING THAT--SO I CAN'T SHOW YOU ANY OF THAT SHIT TODAY--THIS IS IT.
A-BLOCK IS WHERE THE ADMINISTRATIVE OFFICES ARE--AND IF YOU'RE GOING TO STAY HERE YOU'LL WANT TO CHECK THAT PLACE OUT. THE COUCHES IN THOSE OFFICES ARE PROBABLY MUCH MORE COMFORTABLE THAN ANYTHING HERE.
BUT THERE'RE MORE THAN ENOUGH CELLS FOR ALL Y'ALL. THE BEST PART IS THAT IF THE ELECTRIC LOCKS ARE OUT, YOU CAN SHUT THESE DOORS WITHOUT WORRYING ABOUT GETTING LOCKED IN--BUT NOTHING COULD OPEN THESE DOORS WITHOUT YOU HEARING IT.
WE NEED TO GET THE OTHERS--START PICKING OUT OUR ROOMS.

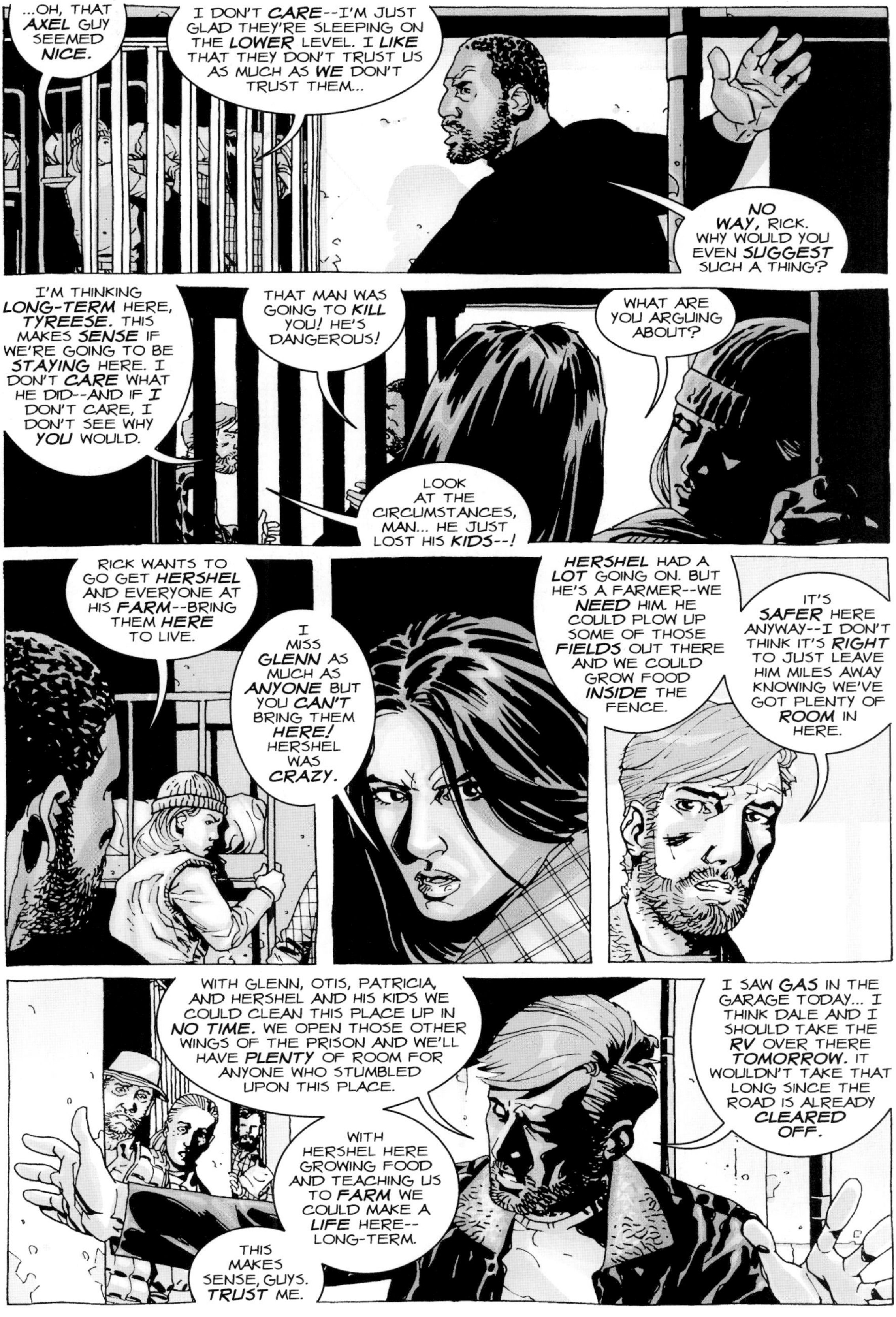
...OH, THAT AXEL GUY SEEMED NICE.
I DON'T CARE--I'M JUST GLAD THEY'RE SLEEPING ON THE LOWER LEVEL. I LIKE THAT THEY DON'T TRUST US AS MUCH AS WE DON'T TRUST THEM...
NO WAY, RICK. WHY WOULD YOU EVEN SUGGEST SUCH A THING?
I'M THINKING LONG-TERM HERE, TYREESE. THIS MAKES SENSE IF WE'RE GOING TO BE STAYING HERE. I DON'T CARE WHAT HE DID--AND IF I DON'T CARE, I DON'T SEE WHY YOU WOULD.
THAT MAN WAS GOING TO KILL YOU! HE'S DANGEROUS!
WHAT ARE YOU ARGUING ABOUT?
LOOK AT THE CIRCUMSTANCES, MAN... HE JUST LOST HIS KIDS--!
RICK WANTS TO GO GET HERSHEL AND EVERYONE AT HIS FARM--BRING THEM HERE TO LIVE.
I MISS GLENN AS MUCH AS ANYONE BUT YOU CAN'T BRING THEM HERE! HERSHEL WAS CRAZY.
HERSHEL HAD A LOT GOING ON. BUT HE'S A FARMER--WE NEED HIM. HE COULD PLOW UP SOME OF THOSE FIELDS OUT THERE AND WE COULD GROW FOOD INSIDE THE FENCE.
IT'S SAFER HERE ANYWAY--I DON'T THINK IT'S RIGHT TO JUST LEAVE HIM MILES AWAY KNOWING WE'VE GOT PLENTY OF ROOM IN HERE.
WITH GLENN, OTIS, PATRICIA, AND HERSHEL AND HIS KIDS WE COULD CLEAN THIS PLACE UP IN NO TIME. WE OPEN THOSE OTHER WINGS OF THE PRISON AND WE'LL HAVE PLENTY OF ROOM FOR ANYONE WHO STUMBLED UPON THIS PLACE.
WITH HERSHEL HERE GROWING FOOD AND TEACHING US TO FARM WE COULD MAKE A LIFE HERE--LONG-TERM.
THIS MAKES SENSE, GUYS. TRUST ME.
I SAW GAS IN THE GARAGE TODAY... I THINK DALE AND I SHOULD TAKE THE RV OVER THERE TOMORROW. IT WOULDN'T TAKE THAT LONG SINCE THE ROAD IS ALREADY CLEARED OFF.

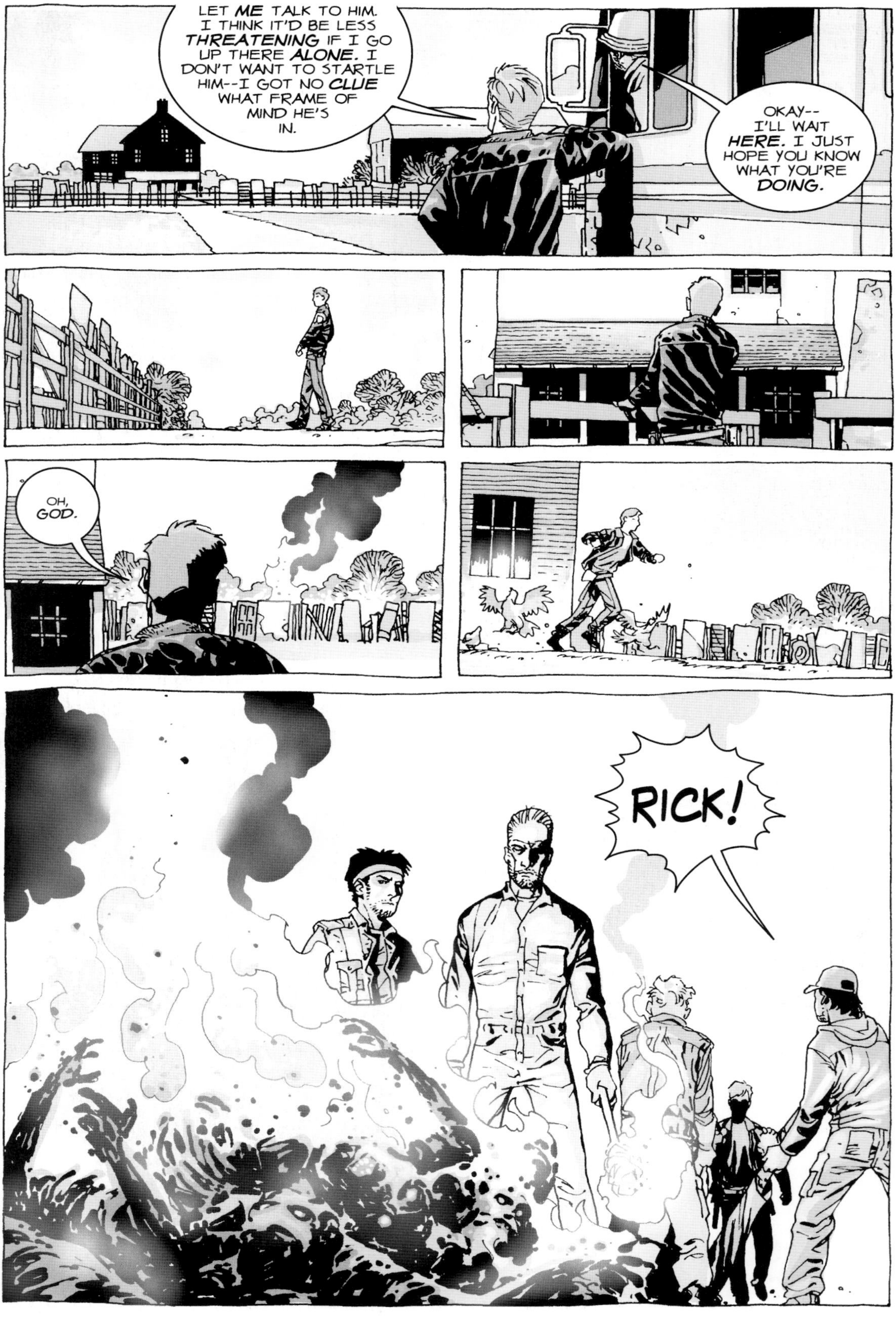
LET ME TALK TO HIM. I THINK IT'D BE LESS THREATENING IF I GO UP THERE ALONE. I DON'T WANT TO STARTLE HIM--I GOT NO CLUE WHAT FRAME OF MIND HE'S IN.
OKAY-- I'LL WAIT HERE. I JUST HOPE YOU KNOW WHAT YOU'RE DOING.
OH, GOD.
RICK!

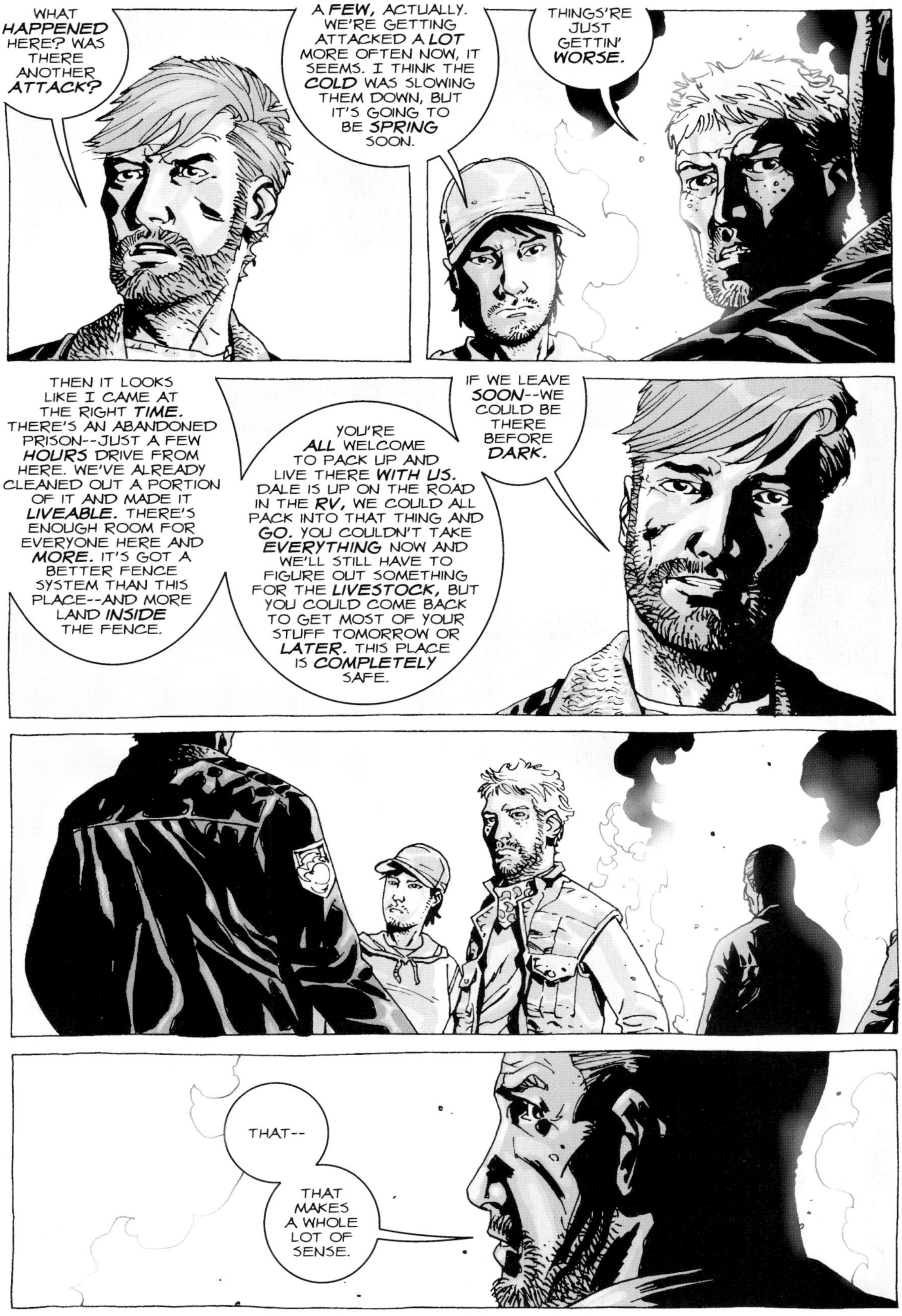
WHAT HAPPENED HERE? WAS THERE ANOTHER ATTACK?
A FEW, ACTUALLY. WE'RE GETTING ATTACKED A LOT MORE OFTEN NOW, IT SEEMS. I THINK THE COLD WAS SLOWING THEM DOWN, BUT IT'S GOING TO BE SPRING SOON.
THINGS'RE JUST GETTIN' WORSE.
THEN IT LOOKS LIKE I CAME AT THE RIGHT TIME. THERE'S AN ABANDONED PRISON--JUST A FEW HOURS DRIVE FROM HERE. WE'VE ALREADY CLEANED OUT A PORTION OF IT AND MADE IT LIVEABLE. THERE'S ENOUGH ROOM FOR EVERYONE HERE AND MORE. IT'S GOT A BETTER FENCE SYSTEM THAN THIS PLACE--AND MORE LAND INSIDE THE FENCE.
YOU'RE ALL WELCOME TO PACK UP AND LIVE THERE WITH US. DALE IS UP ON THE ROAD IN THE RV, WE COULD ALL PACK INTO THAT THING AND GO. YOU COULDN'T TAKE EVERYTHING NOW AND WE'LL STILL HAVE TO FIGURE OUT SOMETHING FOR THE LIVESTOCK, BUT YOU COULD COME BACK TO GET MOST OF YOUR STUFF TOMORROW OR LATER. THIS PLACE IS COMPLETELY SAFE.
IF WE LEAVE SOON--WE COULD BE THERE BEFORE DARK.
THAT--
THAT MAKES A WHOLE LOT OF SENSE.

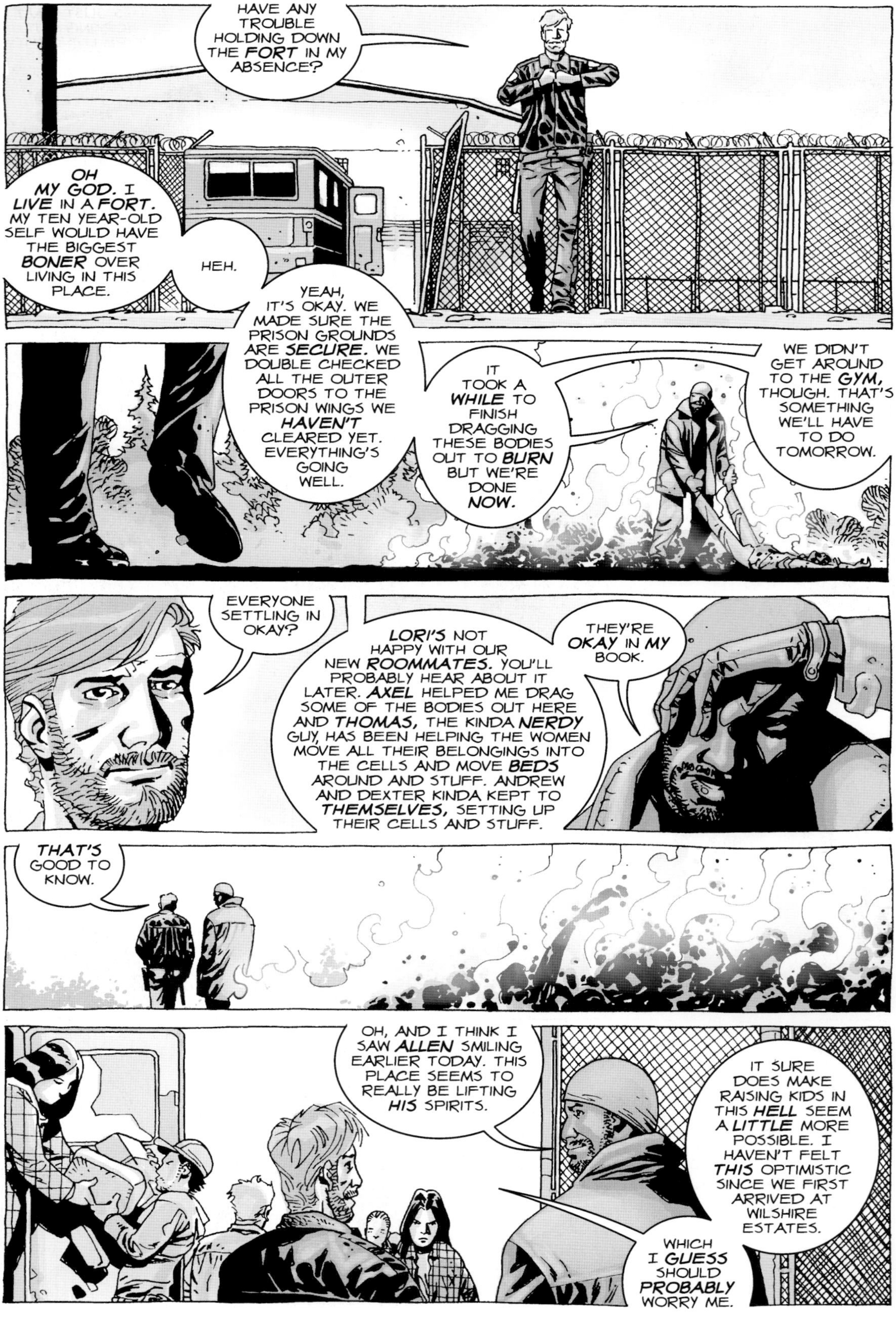
HAVE ANY TROUBLE HOLDING DOWN THE FORT IN MY ABSENCE?
OH MY GOD. I LIVE IN A FORT. MY TEN YEAR-OLD SELF WOULD HAVE THE BIGGEST BONER OVER LIVING IN THIS PLACE.
HEH.
YEAH, IT'S OKAY. WE MADE SURE THE PRISON GROUNDS ARE SECURE. WE DOUBLE CHECKED ALL THE OUTER DOORS TO THE PRISON WINGS WE HAVEN'T CLEARED YET. EVERYTHING'S GOING WELL.
IT TOOK A WHILE TO FINISH DRAGGING THESE BODIES OUT TO BURN BUT WE'RE DONE NOW.
WE DIDN'T GET AROUND TO THE GYM, THOUGH. THAT'S SOMETHING WE'LL HAVE TO DO TOMORROW.
EVERYONE SETTLING IN OKAY?
THEY'RE OKAY IN MY BOOK.
LORI'S NOT HAPPY WITH OUR NEW ROOMMATES. YOU'LL PROBABLY HEAR ABOUT IT LATER. AXEL HELPED ME DRAG SOME OF THE BODIES OUT HERE AND THOMAS, THE KINDA NERDY GUY, HAS BEEN HELPING THE WOMEN MOVE ALL THEIR BELONGINGS INTO THE CELLS AND MOVE BEDS AROUND AND STUFF. ANDREW AND DEXTER KINDA KEPT TO THEMSELVES, SETTING UP THEIR CELLS AND STUFF.
THAT'S GOOD TO KNOW.
OH, AND I THINK I SAW ALLEN SMILING EARLIER TODAY. THIS PLACE SEEMS TO REALLY BE LIFTING HIS SPIRITS.
IT SURE DOES MAKE RAISING KIDS IN THIS HELL SEEM A LITTLE MORE POSSIBLE. I HAVEN'T FELT THIS OPTIMISTIC SINCE WE FIRST ARRIVED AT WILSHIRE ESTATES.
WHICH I GUESS SHOULD PROBABLY WORRY ME.

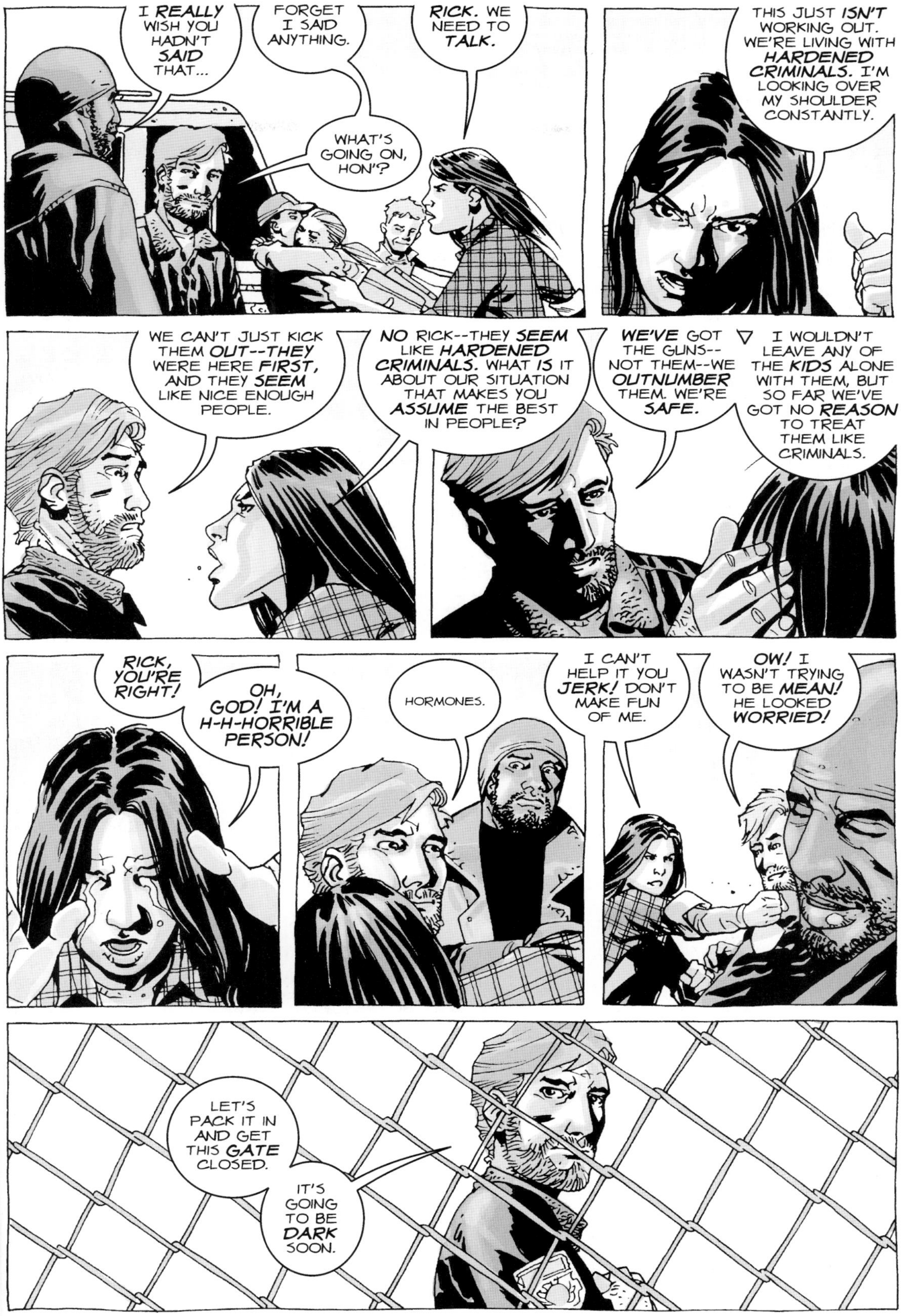
I REALLY WISH YOU HADN'T SAID THAT...
FORGET I SAID ANYTHING.
WHAT'S GOING ON, HON'?
RICK. WE NEED TO TALK.
THIS JUST ISN'T WORKING OUT. WE'RE LIVING WITH HARDENED CRIMINALS. I'M LOOKING OVER MY SHOULDER CONSTANTLY.
WE CAN'T JUST KICK THEM OUT--THEY WERE HERE FIRST, AND THEY SEEM LIKE NICE ENOUGH PEOPLE.
NO RICK--THEY SEEM LIKE HARDENED CRIMINALS. WHAT IS IT ABOUT OUR SITUATION THAT MAKES YOU ASSUME THE BEST IN PEOPLE?
WE'VE GOT THE GUNS--NOT THEM--WE OUTNUMBER THEM. WE'RE SAFE.
I WOULDN'T LEAVE ANY OF THE KIDS ALONE WITH THEM, BUT SO FAR WE'VE GOT NO REASON TO TREAT THEM LIKE CRIMINALS.
RICK, YOU'RE RIGHT!
OH, GOD! I'M A H-H-HORRIBLE PERSON!
HORMONES.
I CAN'T HELP IT YOU JERK! DON'T MAKE FUN OF ME.
OW! I WASN'T TRYING TO BE MEAN! HE LOOKED WORRIED!
LET'S PACK IT IN AND GET THIS GATE CLOSED.
IT'S GOING TO BE DARK SOON.

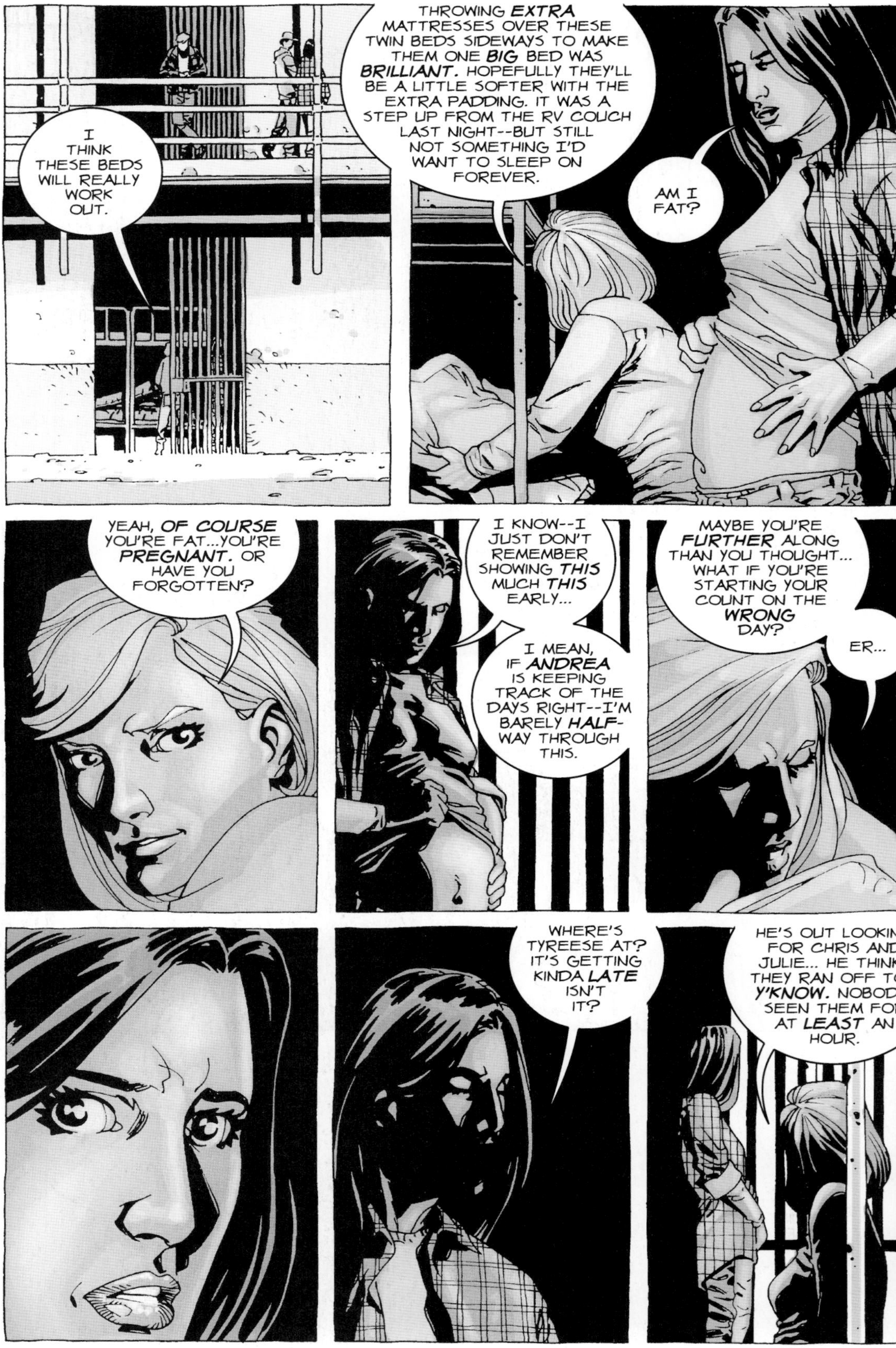
I THINK THESE BEDS WILL REALLY WORK OUT.
THROWING **EXTRA** MATTRESSES OVER THESE TWIN BEDS SIDEWAYS TO MAKE THEM ONE **BIG** BED WAS **BRILLIANT.** HOPEFULLY THEY'LL BE A LITTLE SOFTER WITH THE EXTRA PADDING. IT WAS A STEP UP FROM THE RV COUCH LAST NIGHT--BUT STILL NOT SOMETHING I'D WANT TO SLEEP ON FOREVER.
AM I FAT?
YEAH, **OF COURSE** YOU'RE FAT...YOU'RE **PREGNANT.** OR HAVE YOU FORGOTTEN?
I KNOW--I JUST DON'T REMEMBER SHOWING **THIS** MUCH **THIS** EARLY...
I MEAN, IF **ANDREA** IS KEEPING TRACK OF THE DAYS RIGHT--I'M BARELY **HALF-**WAY THROUGH THIS.
MAYBE YOU'RE **FURTHER** ALONG THAN YOU THOUGHT... WHAT IF YOU'RE STARTING YOUR COUNT ON THE **WRONG** DAY?
ER...
WHERE'S TYREESE AT? IT'S GETTING KINDA **LATE** ISN'T IT?
HE'S OUT LOOKING FOR CHRIS AND JULIE... HE THINKS THEY RAN OFF TO... **Y'KNOW.** NOBODY'S SEEN THEM FOR AT **LEAST** AN HOUR.

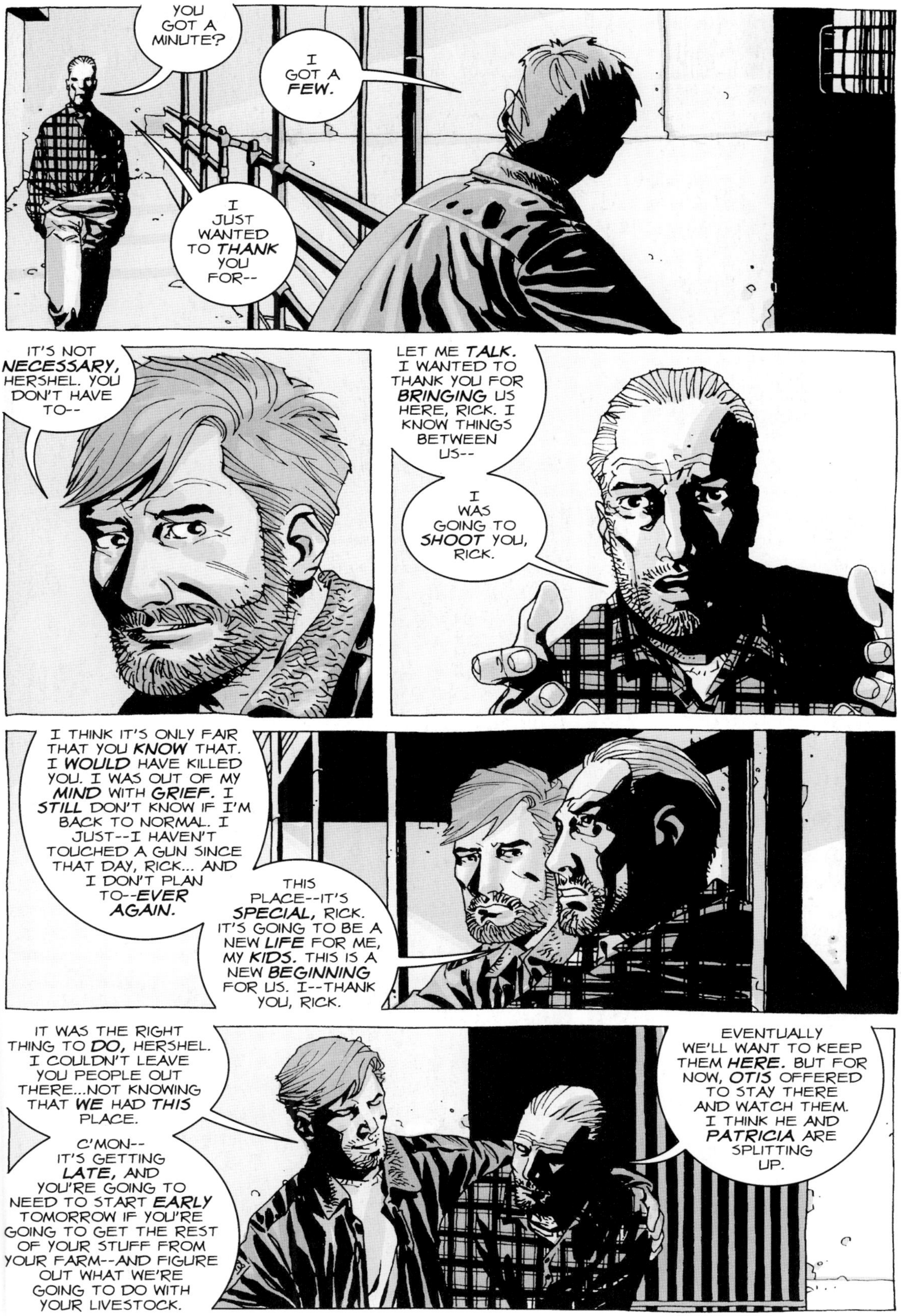
YOU GOT A MINUTE?
I GOT A FEW.
I JUST WANTED TO THANK YOU FOR--
IT'S NOT NECESSARY, HERSHEL. YOU DON'T HAVE TO--
LET ME TALK. I WANTED TO THANK YOU FOR BRINGING US HERE, RICK. I KNOW THINGS BETWEEN US--
I WAS GOING TO SHOOT YOU, RICK.
I THINK IT'S ONLY FAIR THAT YOU KNOW THAT. I WOULD HAVE KILLED YOU. I WAS OUT OF MY MIND WITH GRIEF. I STILL DON'T KNOW IF I'M BACK TO NORMAL. I JUST--I HAVEN'T TOUCHED A GUN SINCE THAT DAY, RICK... AND I DON'T PLAN TO--EVER AGAIN.
THIS PLACE--IT'S SPECIAL, RICK. IT'S GOING TO BE A NEW LIFE FOR ME, MY KIDS. THIS IS A NEW BEGINNING FOR US. I--THANK YOU, RICK.
IT WAS THE RIGHT THING TO DO, HERSHEL. I COULDN'T LEAVE YOU PEOPLE OUT THERE...NOT KNOWING THAT WE HAD THIS PLACE.
C'MON-- IT'S GETTING LATE, AND YOU'RE GOING TO NEED TO START EARLY TOMORROW IF YOU'RE GOING TO GET THE REST OF YOUR STUFF FROM YOUR FARM--AND FIGURE OUT WHAT WE'RE GOING TO DO WITH YOUR LIVESTOCK.
EVENTUALLY WE'LL WANT TO KEEP THEM HERE. BUT FOR NOW, OTIS OFFERED TO STAY THERE AND WATCH THEM. I THINK HE AND PATRICIA ARE SPLITTING UP.

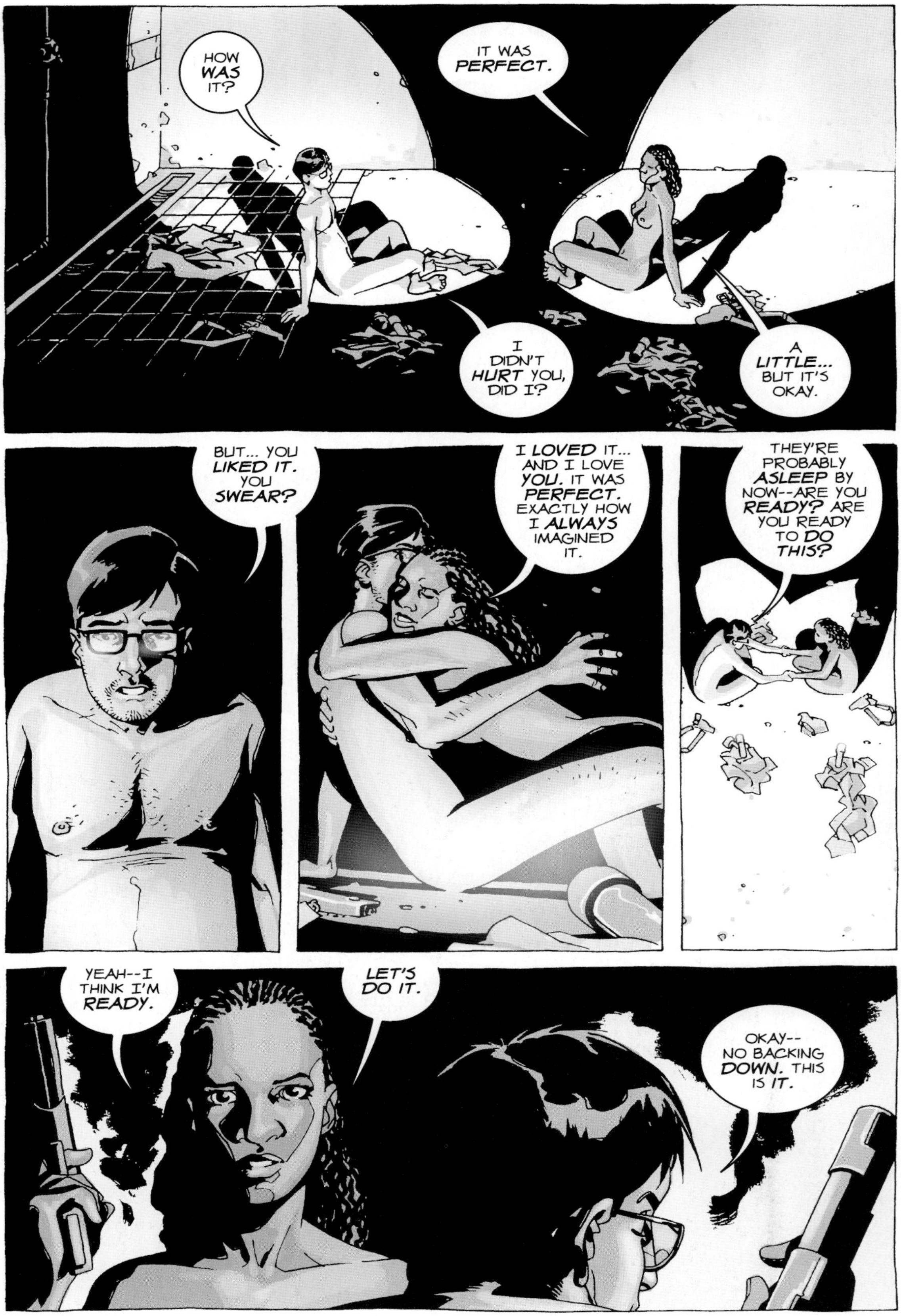
HOW WAS IT?
IT WAS PERFECT.
I DIDN'T HURT YOU, DID I?
A LITTLE... BUT IT'S OKAY.
BUT... YOU LIKED IT. YOU SWEAR?
I LOVED IT... AND I LOVE YOU. IT WAS PERFECT. EXACTLY HOW I ALWAYS IMAGINED IT.
THEY'RE PROBABLY ASLEEP BY NOW--ARE YOU READY? ARE YOU READY TO DO THIS?
YEAH--I THINK I'M READY.
LET'S DO IT.
OKAY-- NO BACKING DOWN. THIS IS IT.

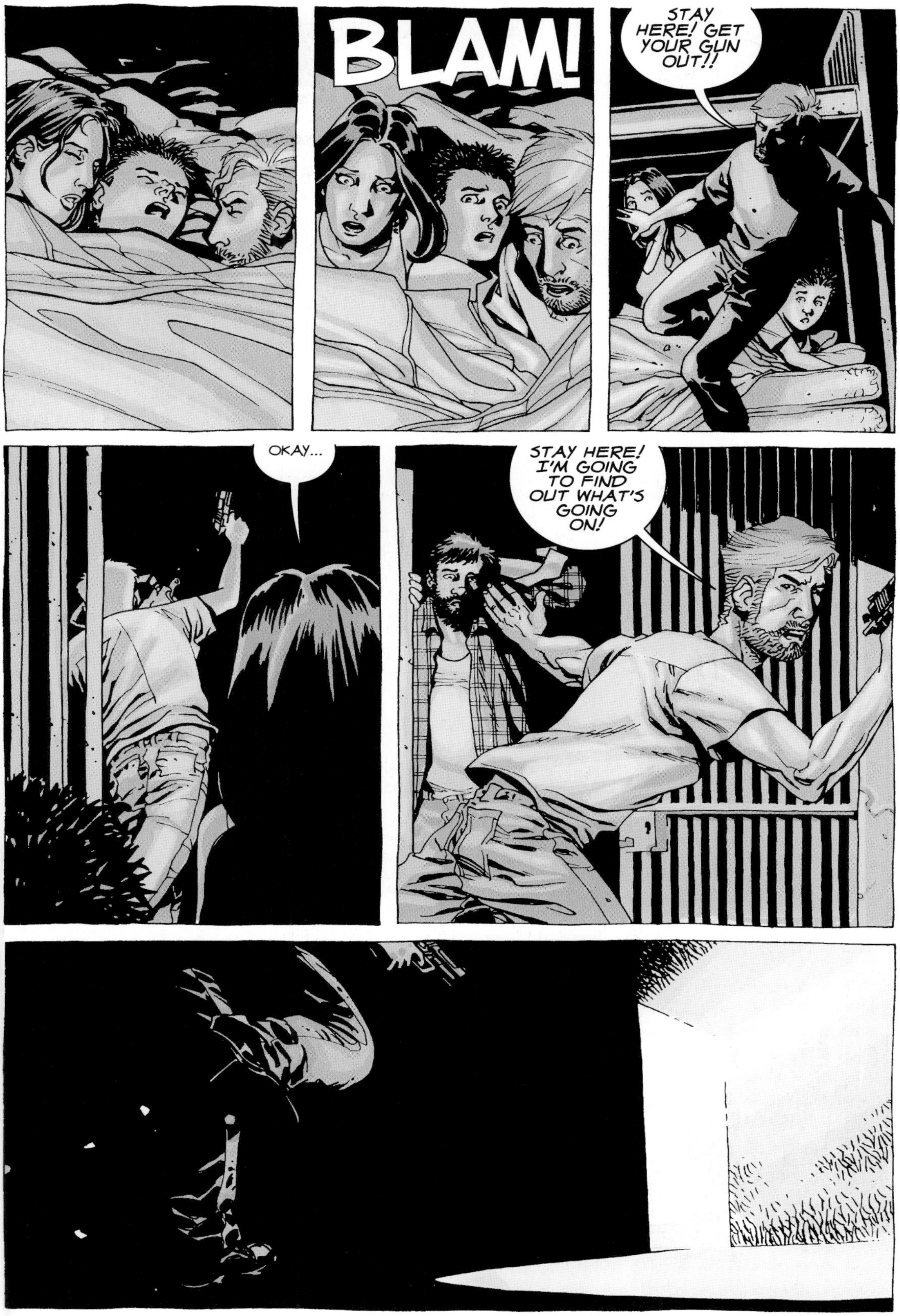
BLAM!
STAY HERE! GET YOUR GUN OUT!!
OKAY...
STAY HERE! I'M GOING TO FIND OUT WHAT'S GOING ON!

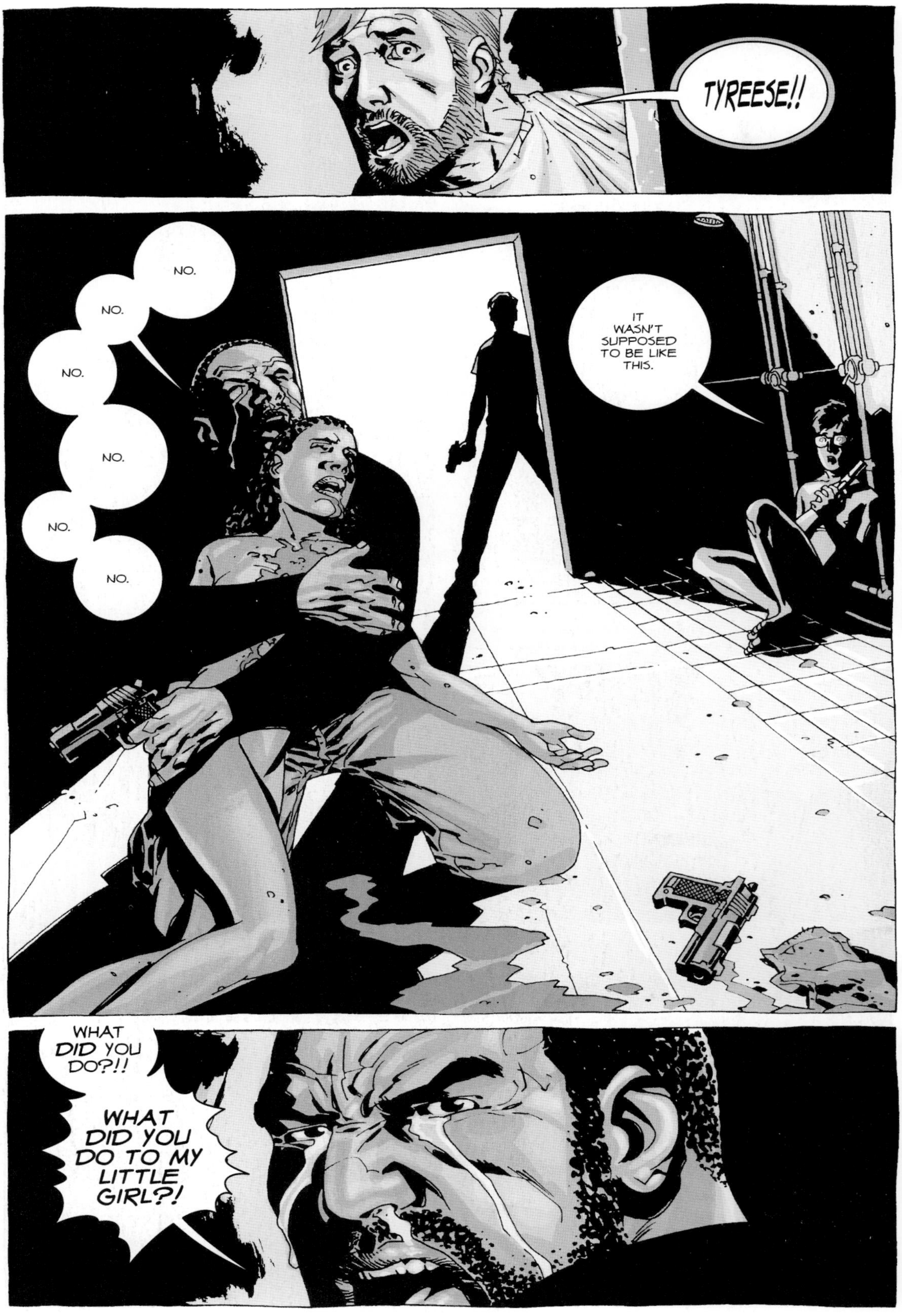
TYREESE!!
NO.
NO.
NO.
NO.
NO.
NO.
IT WASN'T SUPPOSED TO BE LIKE THIS.
WHAT DID YOU DO?!!
WHAT DID YOU DO TO MY LITTLE GIRL?!

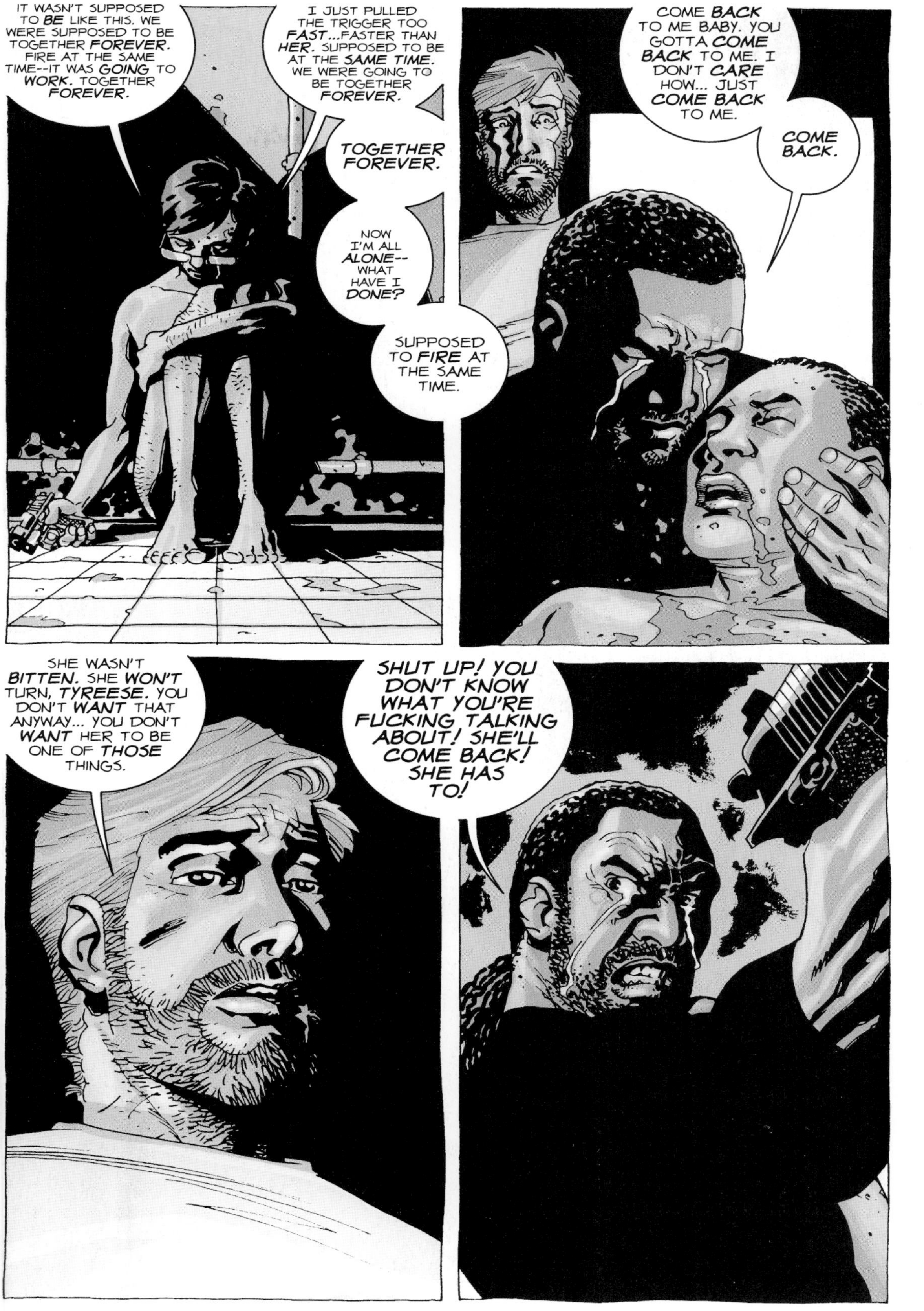

IT WASN'T SUPPOSED TO BE LIKE THIS. WE WERE SUPPOSED TO BE TOGETHER FOREVER. FIRE AT THE SAME TIME--IT WAS GOING TO WORK. TOGETHER FOREVER.
I JUST PULLED THE TRIGGER TOO FAST...FASTER THAN HER. SUPPOSED TO BE AT THE SAME TIME. WE WERE GOING TO BE TOGETHER FOREVER.
TOGETHER FOREVER.
NOW I'M ALL ALONE--WHAT HAVE I DONE?
SUPPOSED TO FIRE AT THE SAME TIME.
COME BACK TO ME BABY. YOU GOTTA COME BACK TO ME. I DON'T CARE HOW... JUST COME BACK TO ME.
COME BACK.
SHE WASN'T BITTEN. SHE WON'T TURN, TYREESE. YOU DON'T WANT THAT ANYWAY... YOU DON'T WANT HER TO BE ONE OF THOSE THINGS.
SHUT UP! YOU DON'T KNOW WHAT YOU'RE FUCKING TALKING ABOUT! SHE'LL COME BACK! SHE HAS TO!

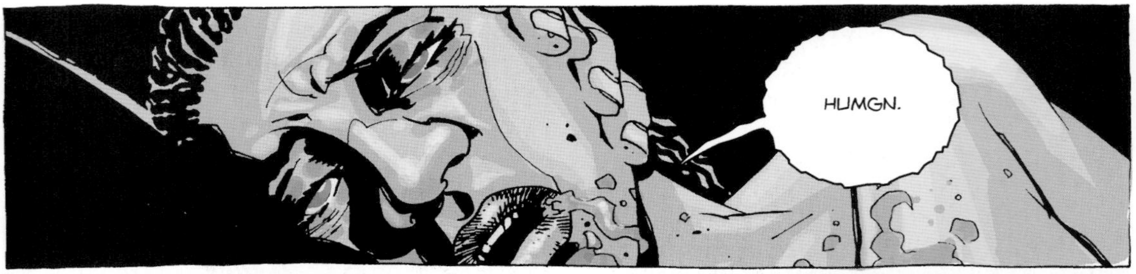
HUMGN.

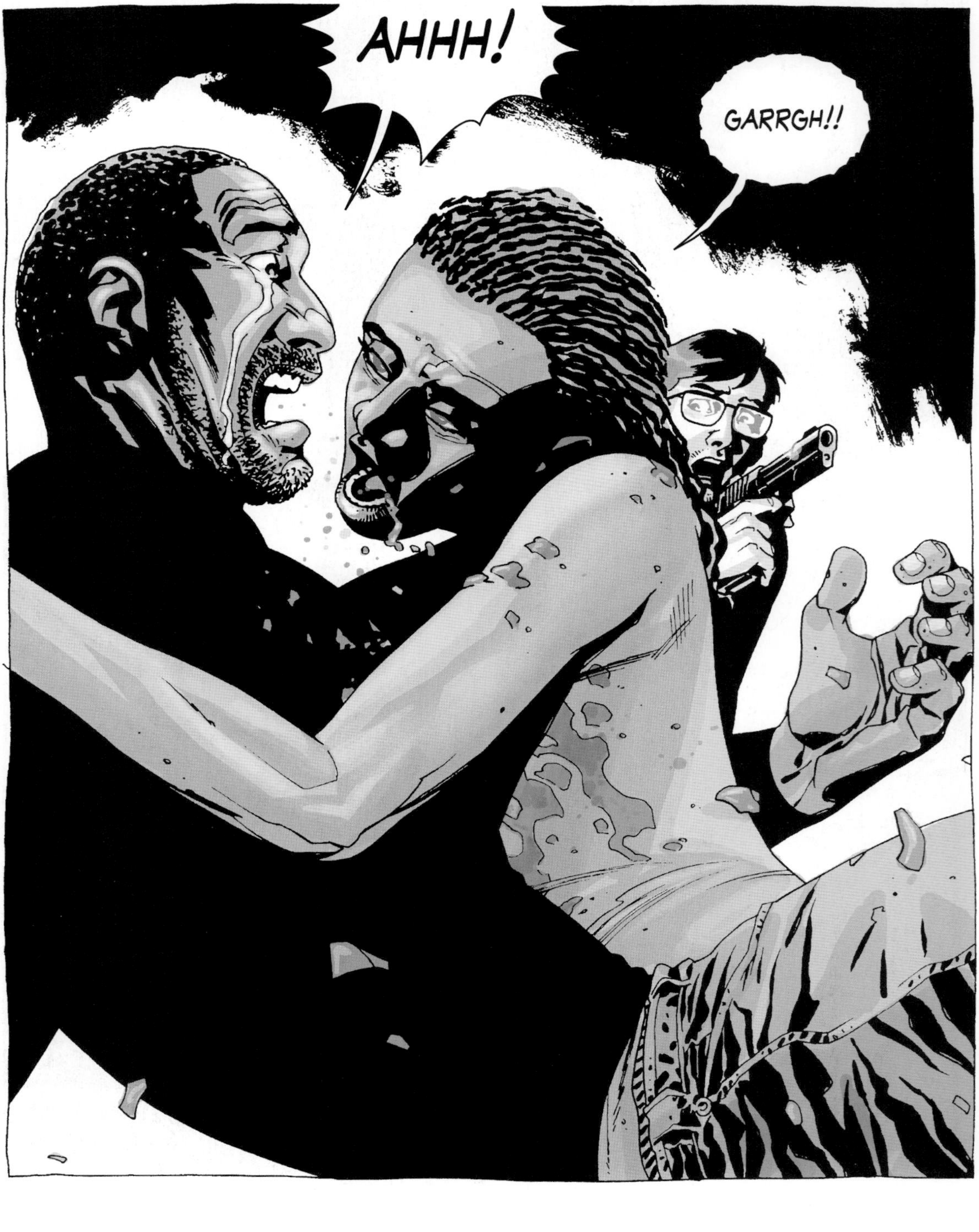
AHHH!
GARRGH!!

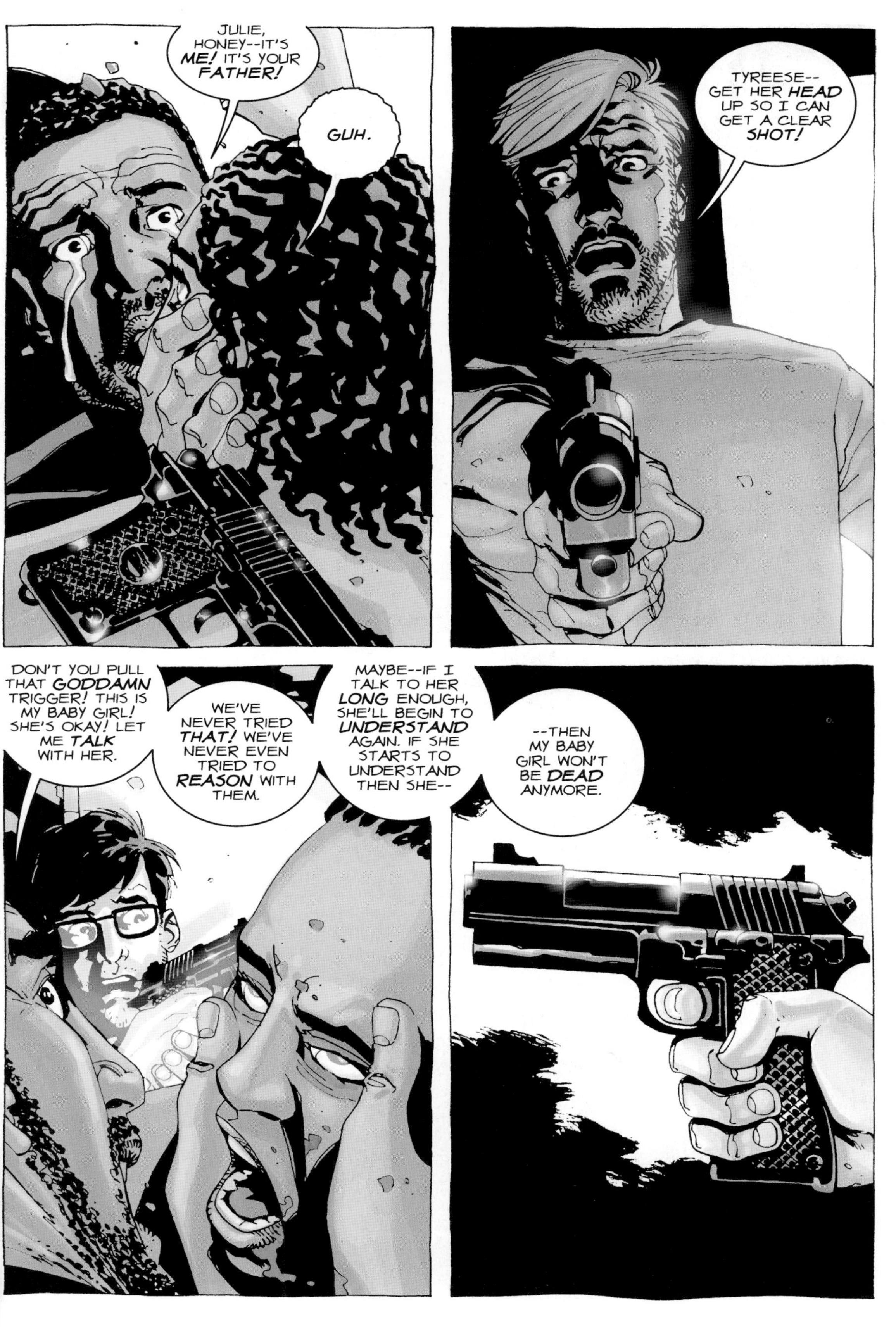
JULIE, HONEY--IT'S *ME!* IT'S YOUR *FATHER!*
GUH.
TYREESE--GET HER *HEAD* UP SO I CAN GET A CLEAR *SHOT!*
DON'T YOU PULL THAT *GODDAMN* TRIGGER! THIS IS MY BABY GIRL! SHE'S OKAY! LET ME *TALK* WITH HER.
WE'VE NEVER TRIED *THAT!* WE'VE NEVER EVEN TRIED TO *REASON* WITH THEM.
MAYBE--IF I TALK TO HER *LONG* ENOUGH, SHE'LL BEGIN TO *UNDERSTAND* AGAIN. IF SHE STARTS TO UNDERSTAND THEN SHE--
--THEN MY BABY GIRL WON'T BE *DEAD* ANYMORE.

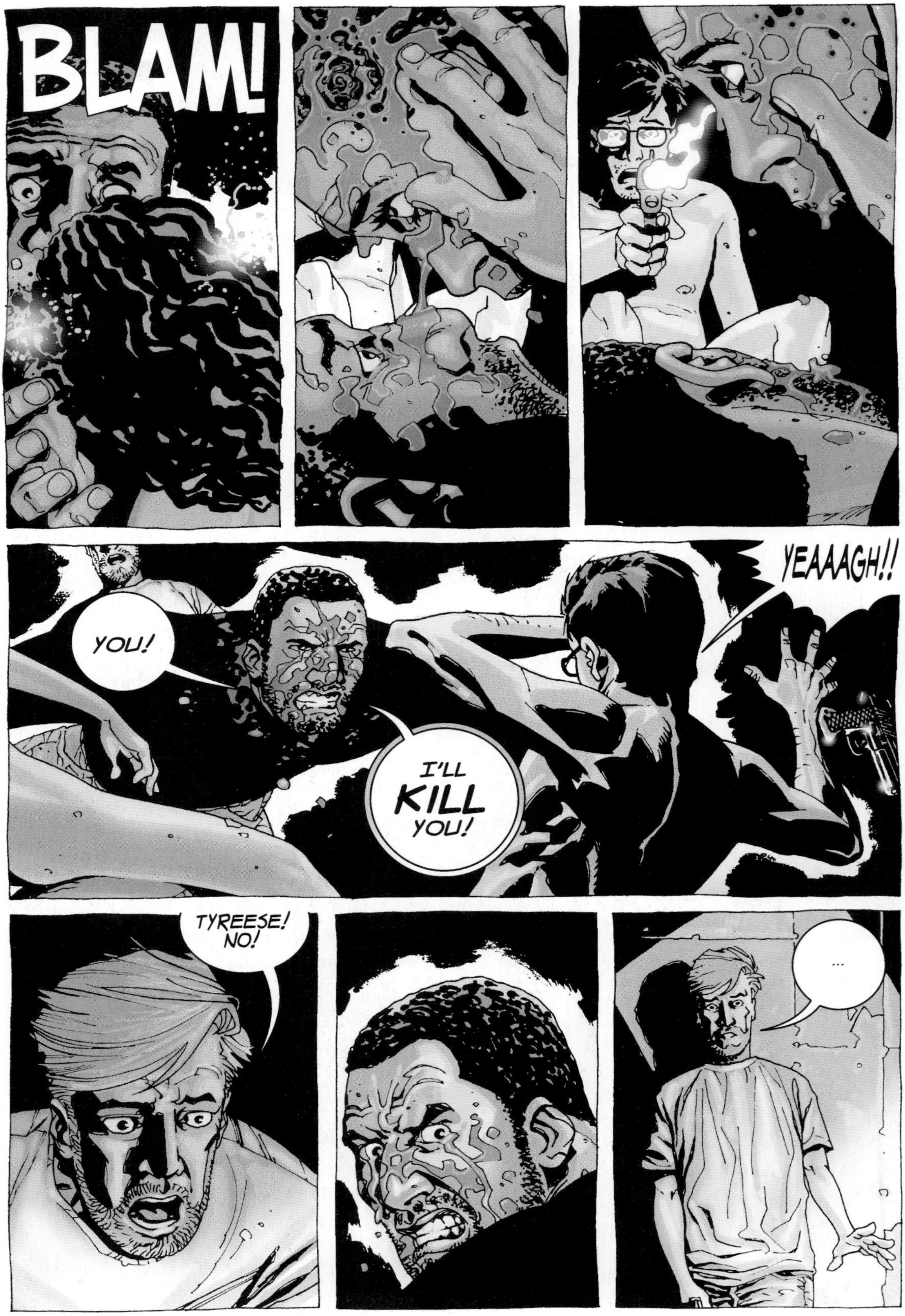
BLAM!
YOU!
I'LL KILL YOU!
YEAAAGH!!
TYREESE! NO!
...

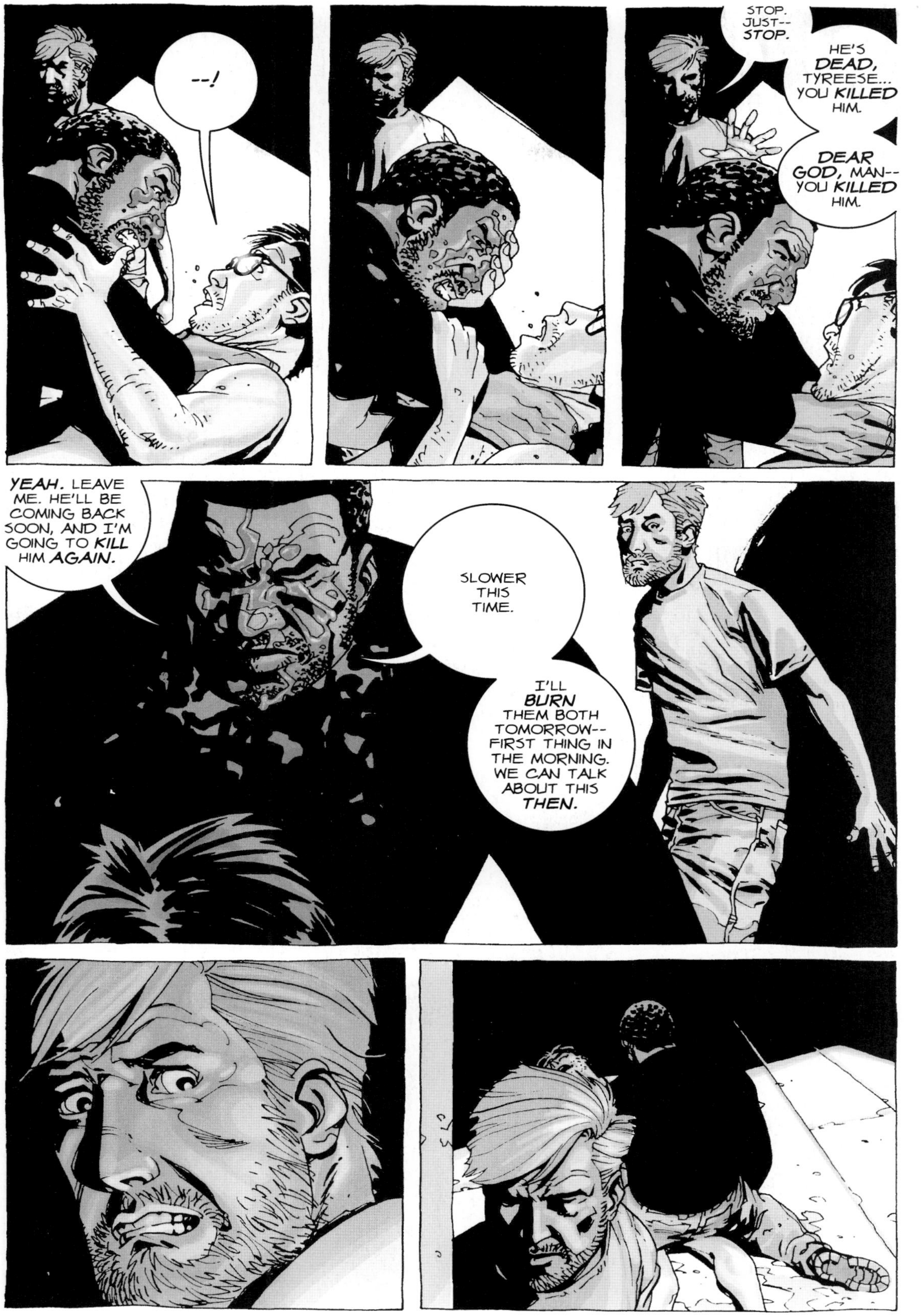
--!
STOP. JUST-- STOP.
HE'S DEAD, TYREESE... YOU KILLED HIM.
DEAR GOD, MAN-- YOU KILLED HIM.
YEAH. LEAVE ME. HE'LL BE COMING BACK SOON, AND I'M GOING TO KILL HIM AGAIN.
SLOWER THIS TIME.
I'LL BURN THEM BOTH TOMORROW-- FIRST THING IN THE MORNING. WE CAN TALK ABOUT THIS THEN.

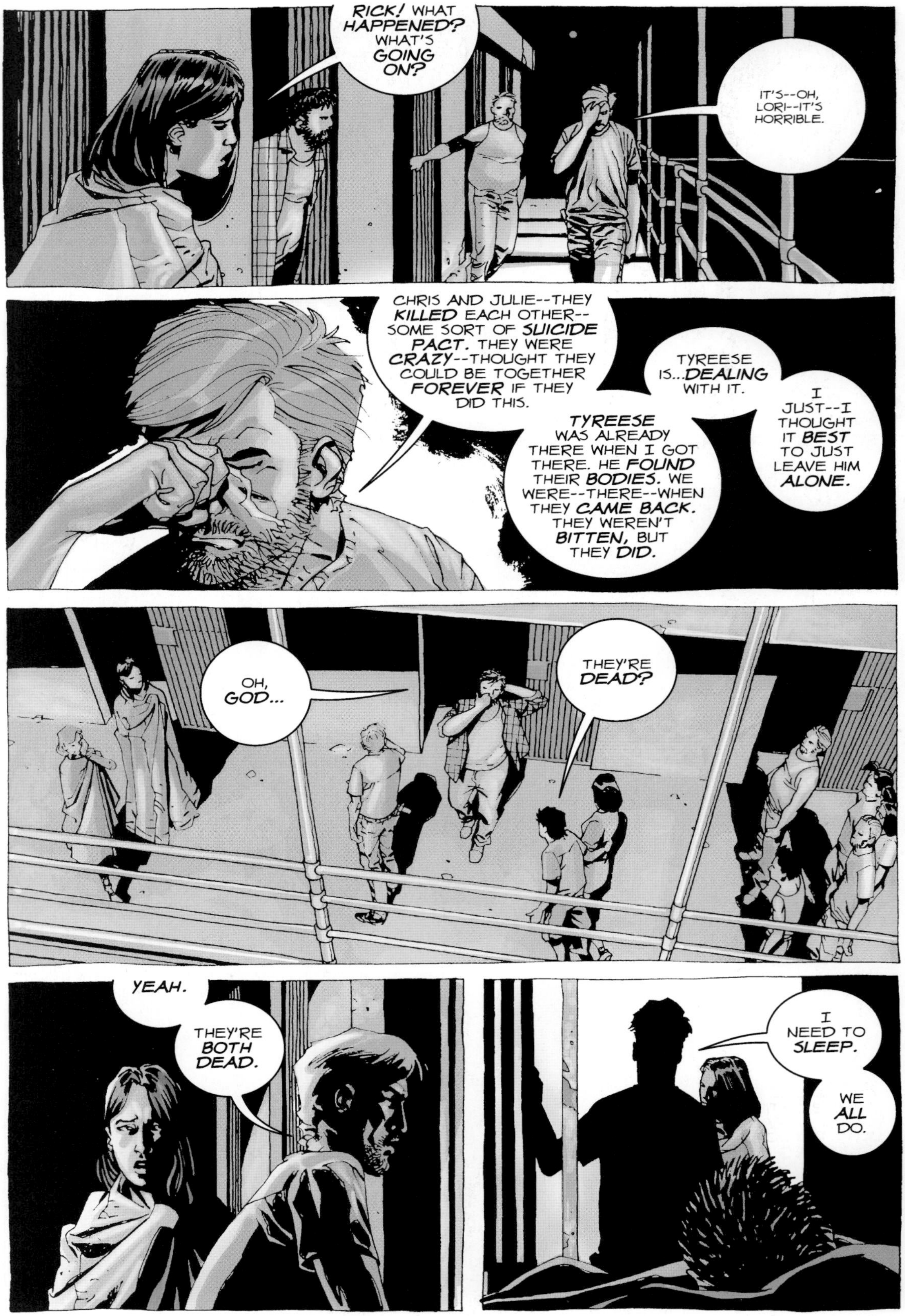
RICK! WHAT HAPPENED? WHAT'S GOING ON?
IT'S--OH, LORI--IT'S HORRIBLE.
CHRIS AND JULIE--THEY KILLED EACH OTHER--SOME SORT OF SUICIDE PACT. THEY WERE CRAZY--THOUGHT THEY COULD BE TOGETHER FOREVER IF THEY DID THIS.
TYREESE WAS ALREADY THERE WHEN I GOT THERE. HE FOUND THEIR BODIES. WE WERE--THERE--WHEN THEY CAME BACK. THEY WEREN'T BITTEN, BUT THEY DID.
TYREESE IS...DEALING WITH IT.
I JUST--I THOUGHT IT BEST TO JUST LEAVE HIM ALONE.
OH, GOD...
THEY'RE DEAD?
YEAH.
THEY'RE BOTH DEAD.
I NEED TO SLEEP.
WE ALL DO.

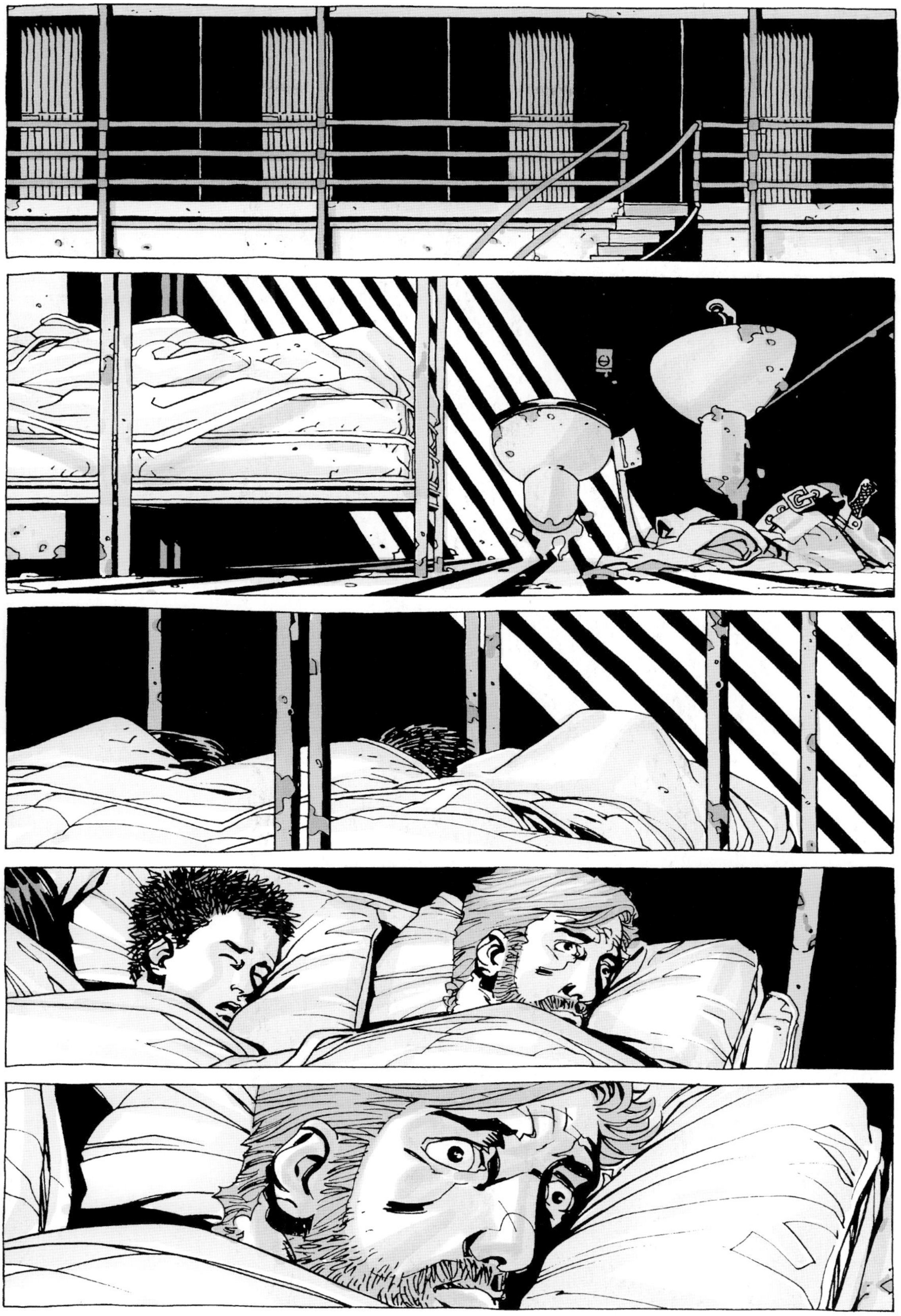

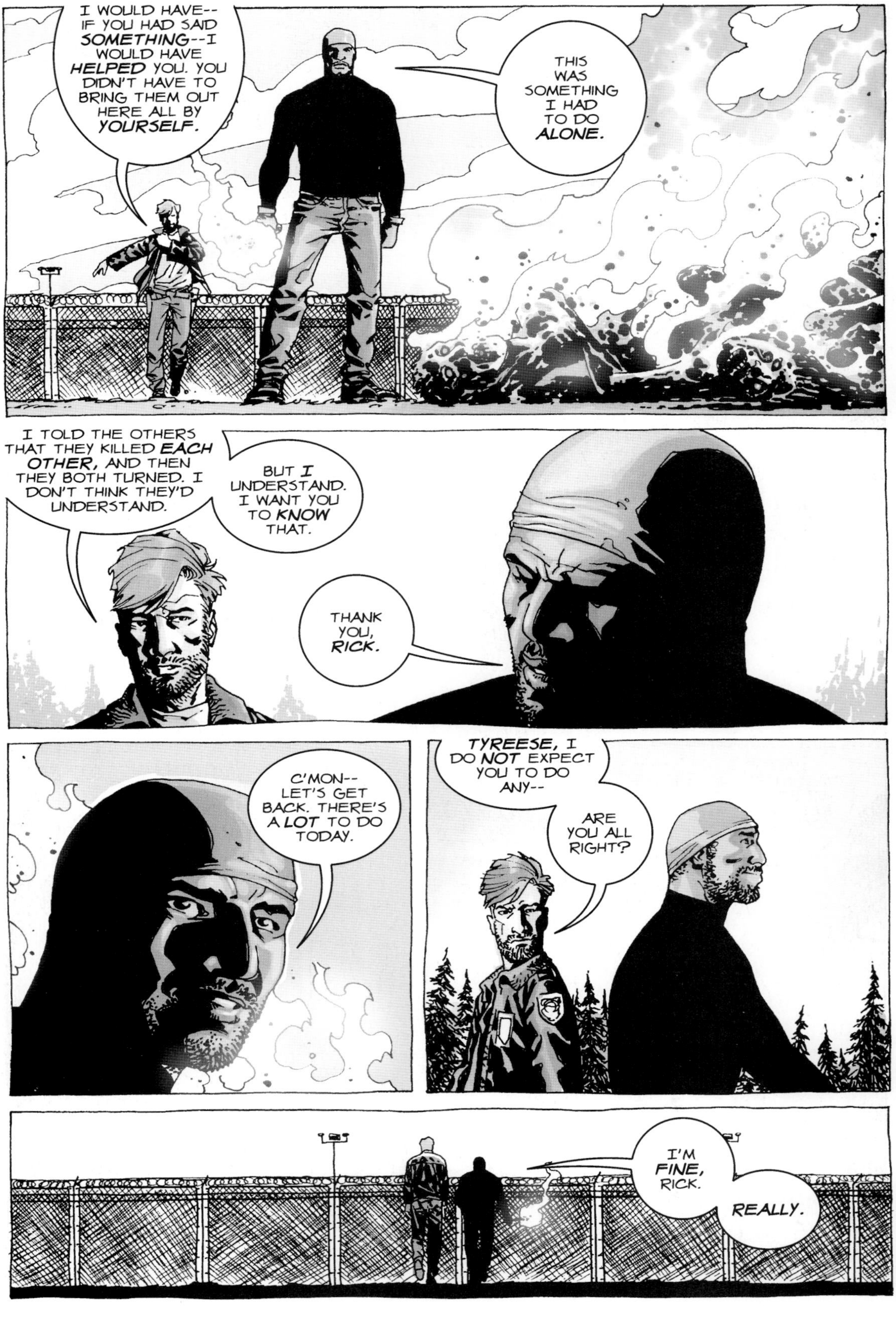

I WOULD HAVE-- IF YOU HAD SAID SOMETHING--I WOULD HAVE HELPED YOU. YOU DIDN'T HAVE TO BRING THEM OUT HERE ALL BY YOURSELF.
THIS WAS SOMETHING I HAD TO DO ALONE.
I TOLD THE OTHERS THAT THEY KILLED EACH OTHER, AND THEN THEY BOTH TURNED. I DON'T THINK THEY'D UNDERSTAND.
BUT I UNDERSTAND. I WANT YOU TO KNOW THAT.
THANK YOU, RICK.
C'MON-- LET'S GET BACK. THERE'S A LOT TO DO TODAY.
TYREESE, I DO NOT EXPECT YOU TO DO ANY--
ARE YOU ALL RIGHT?
I'M FINE, RICK.
REALLY.

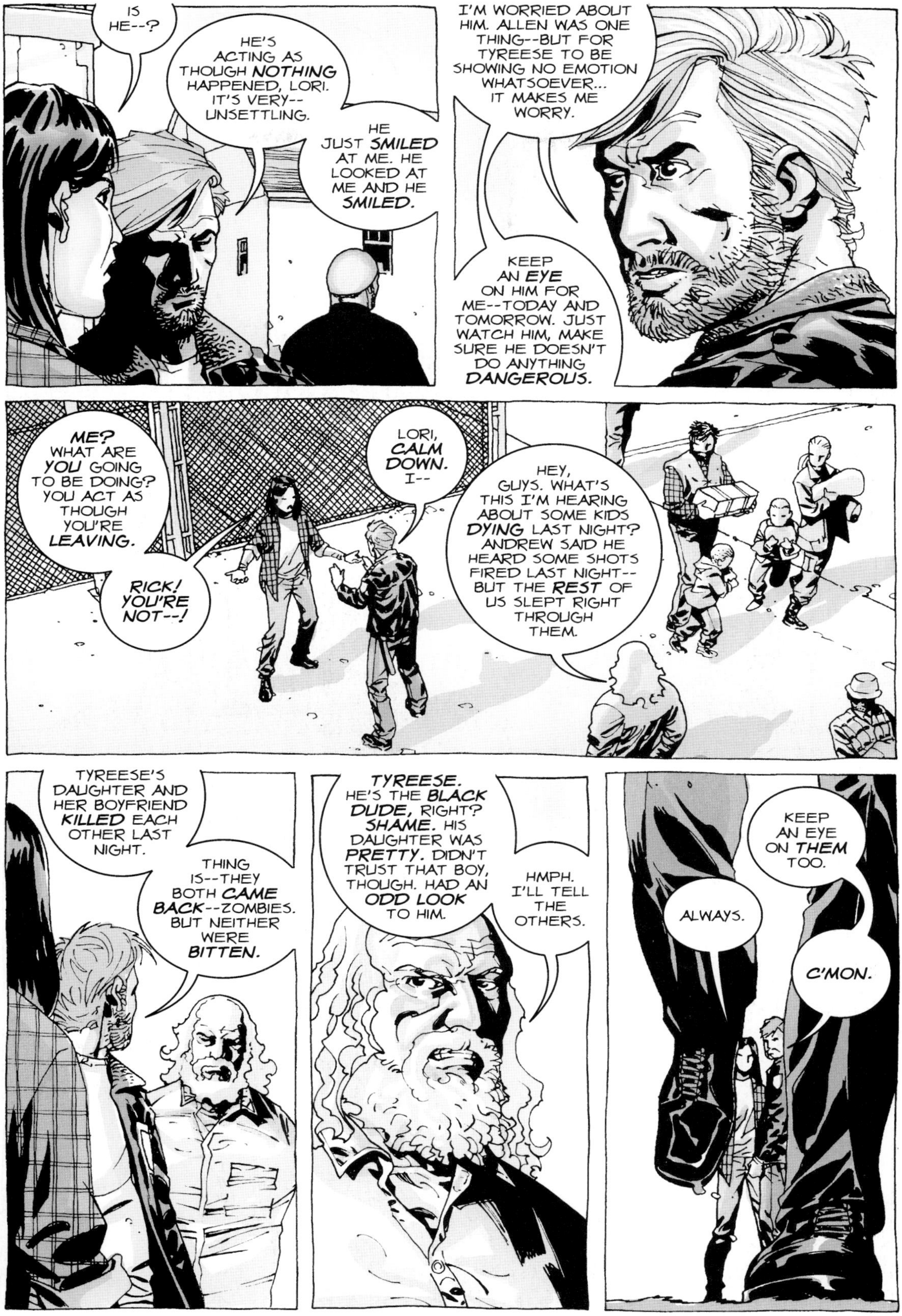
IS HE--?
HE'S ACTING AS THOUGH NOTHING HAPPENED, LORI. IT'S VERY-- UNSETTLING.
HE JUST SMILED AT ME. HE LOOKED AT ME AND HE SMILED.
I'M WORRIED ABOUT HIM. ALLEN WAS ONE THING--BUT FOR TYREESE TO BE SHOWING NO EMOTION WHATSOEVER... IT MAKES ME WORRY.
KEEP AN EYE ON HIM FOR ME--TODAY AND TOMORROW. JUST WATCH HIM, MAKE SURE HE DOESN'T DO ANYTHING DANGEROUS.
ME? WHAT ARE YOU GOING TO BE DOING? YOU ACT AS THOUGH YOU'RE LEAVING.
RICK! YOU'RE NOT--!
LORI, CALM DOWN. I--
HEY, GUYS. WHAT'S THIS I'M HEARING ABOUT SOME KIDS DYING LAST NIGHT? ANDREW SAID HE HEARD SOME SHOTS FIRED LAST NIGHT--BUT THE REST OF US SLEPT RIGHT THROUGH THEM.
TYREESE'S DAUGHTER AND HER BOYFRIEND KILLED EACH OTHER LAST NIGHT.
THING IS--THEY BOTH CAME BACK--ZOMBIES. BUT NEITHER WERE BITTEN.
TYREESE. HE'S THE BLACK DUDE, RIGHT? SHAME. HIS DAUGHTER WAS PRETTY. DIDN'T TRUST THAT BOY, THOUGH. HAD AN ODD LOOK TO HIM.
HMPH. I'LL TELL THE OTHERS.
KEEP AN EYE ON THEM TOO.
ALWAYS.
C'MON.

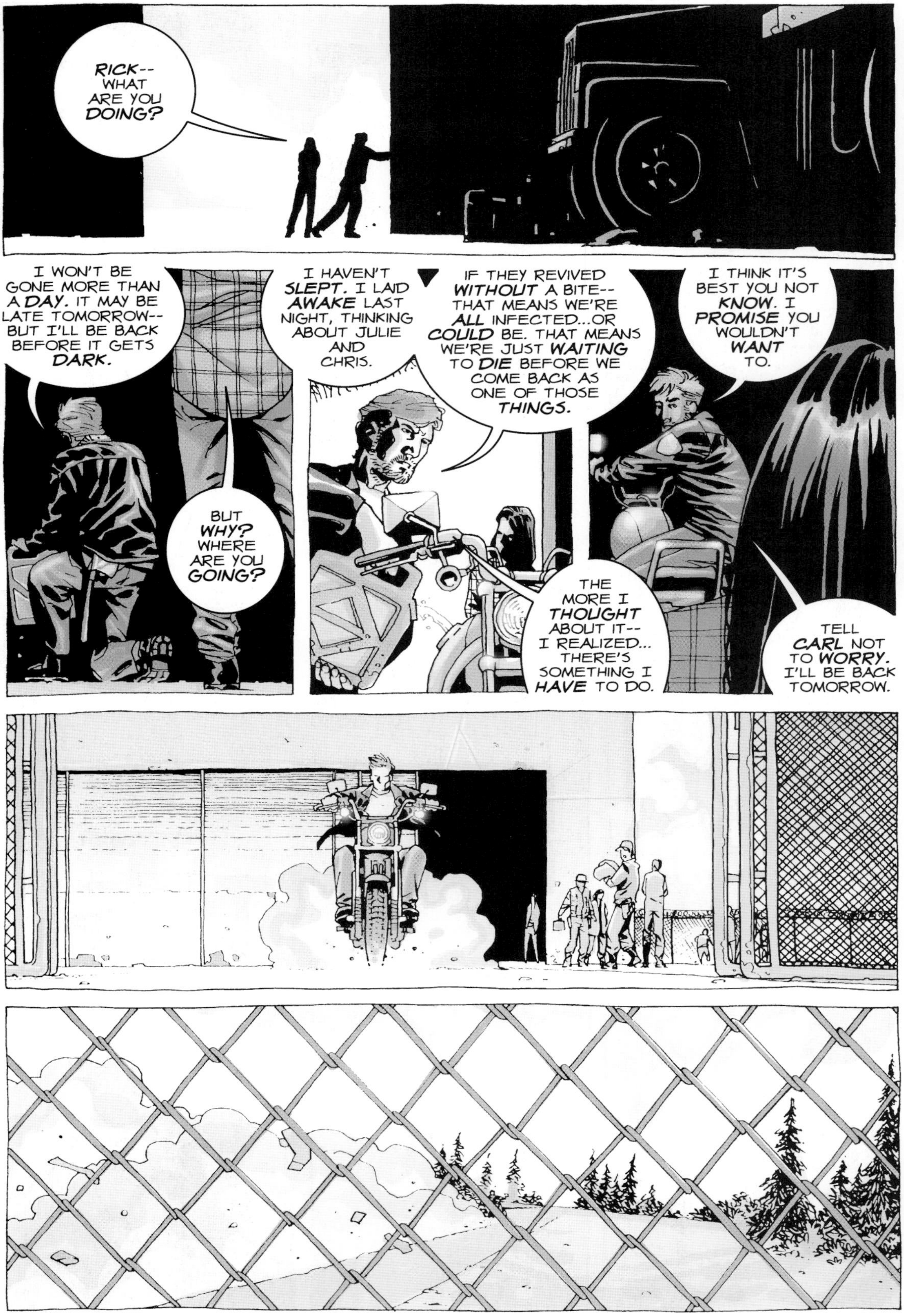
RICK-- WHAT ARE YOU DOING?
I WON'T BE GONE MORE THAN A DAY. IT MAY BE LATE TOMORROW-- BUT I'LL BE BACK BEFORE IT GETS DARK.
BUT WHY? WHERE ARE YOU GOING?
I HAVEN'T SLEPT. I LAID AWAKE LAST NIGHT, THINKING ABOUT JULIE AND CHRIS.
IF THEY REVIVED WITHOUT A BITE-- THAT MEANS WE'RE ALL INFECTED...OR COULD BE. THAT MEANS WE'RE JUST WAITING TO DIE BEFORE WE COME BACK AS ONE OF THOSE THINGS.
THE MORE I THOUGHT ABOUT IT-- I REALIZED... THERE'S SOMETHING I HAVE TO DO.
I THINK IT'S BEST YOU NOT KNOW. I PROMISE YOU WOULDN'T WANT TO.
TELL CARL NOT TO WORRY. I'LL BE BACK TOMORROW.

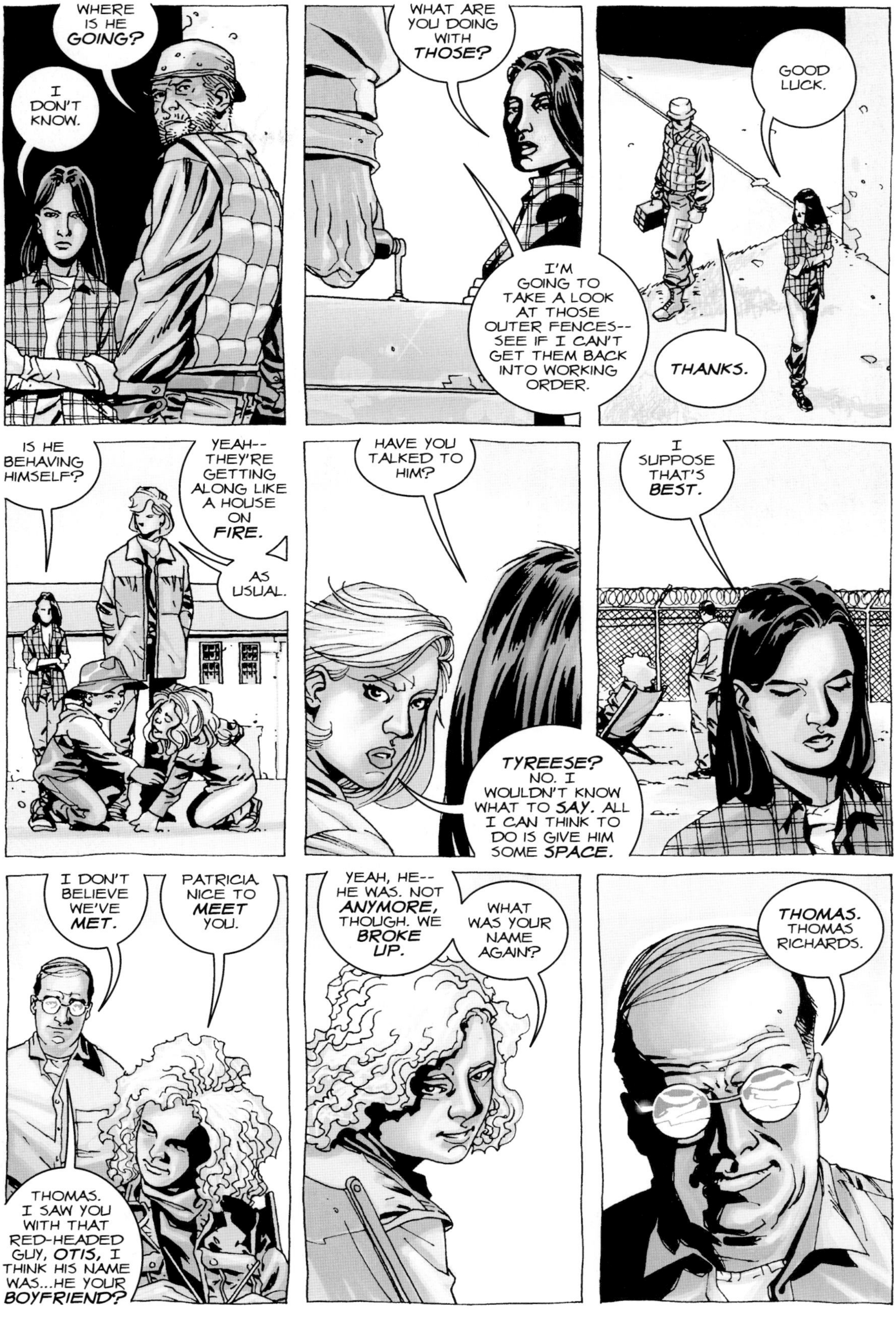
WHERE IS HE GOING?
I DON'T KNOW.
WHAT ARE YOU DOING WITH THOSE?
I'M GOING TO TAKE A LOOK AT THOSE OUTER FENCES-- SEE IF I CAN'T GET THEM BACK INTO WORKING ORDER.
GOOD LUCK.
THANKS.
IS HE BEHAVING HIMSELF?
YEAH-- THEY'RE GETTING ALONG LIKE A HOUSE ON FIRE.
AS USUAL.
HAVE YOU TALKED TO HIM?
TYREESE? NO. I WOULDN'T KNOW WHAT TO SAY. ALL I CAN THINK TO DO IS GIVE HIM SOME SPACE.
I SUPPOSE THAT'S BEST.
I DON'T BELIEVE WE'VE MET.
PATRICIA. NICE TO MEET YOU.
THOMAS. I SAW YOU WITH THAT RED-HEADED GUY, OTIS, I THINK HIS NAME WAS...HE YOUR BOYFRIEND?
YEAH, HE-- HE WAS. NOT ANYMORE, THOUGH. WE BROKE UP.
WHAT WAS YOUR NAME AGAIN?
THOMAS. THOMAS RICHARDS.

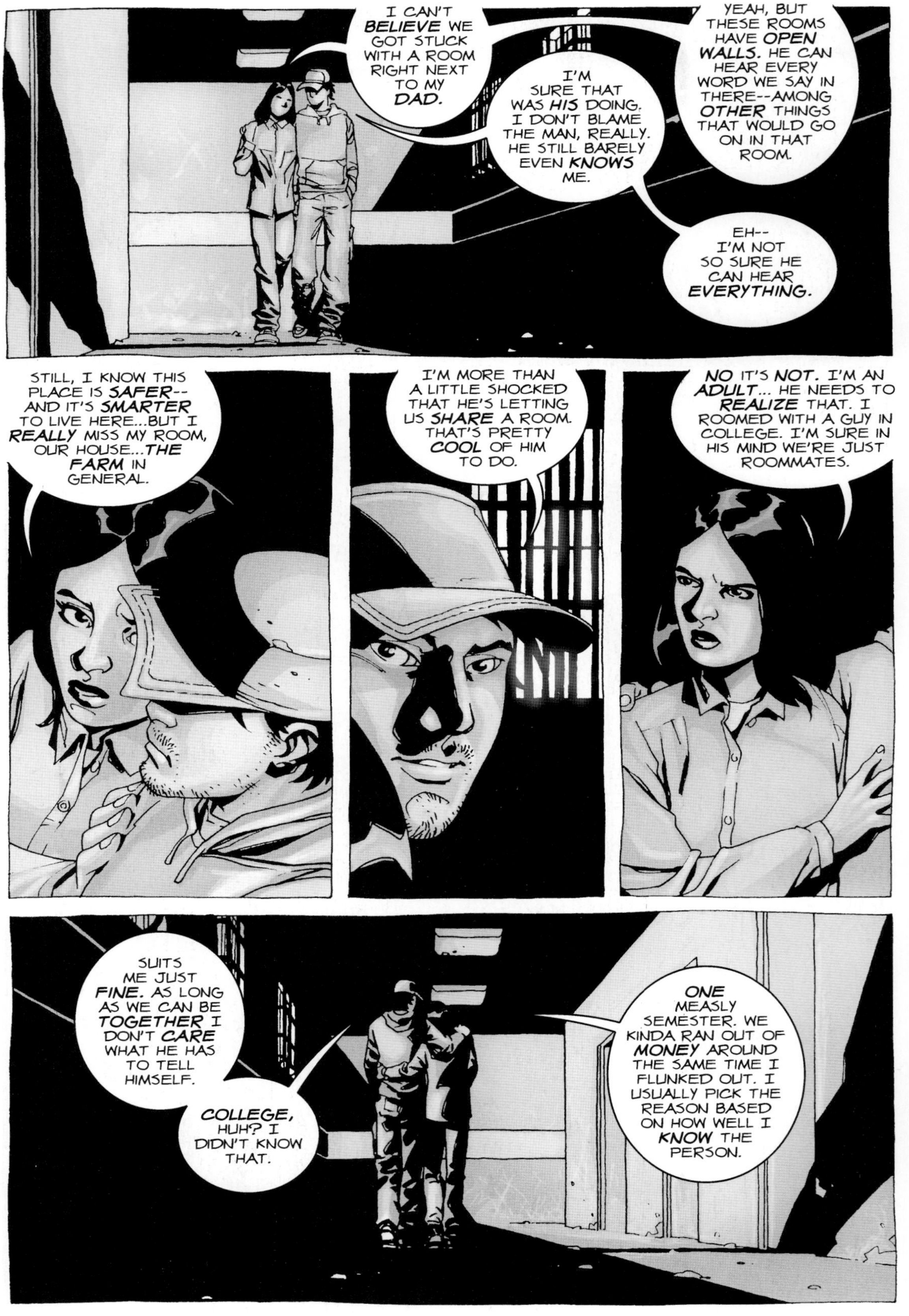
I CAN'T BELIEVE WE GOT STUCK WITH A ROOM RIGHT NEXT TO MY DAD.
I'M SURE THAT WAS HIS DOING. I DON'T BLAME THE MAN, REALLY. HE STILL BARELY EVEN KNOWS ME.
YEAH, BUT THESE ROOMS HAVE OPEN WALLS. HE CAN HEAR EVERY WORD WE SAY IN THERE--AMONG OTHER THINGS THAT WOULD GO ON IN THAT ROOM.
EH-- I'M NOT SO SURE HE CAN HEAR EVERYTHING.
STILL, I KNOW THIS PLACE IS SAFER-- AND IT'S SMARTER TO LIVE HERE...BUT I REALLY MISS MY ROOM, OUR HOUSE...THE FARM IN GENERAL.
I'M MORE THAN A LITTLE SHOCKED THAT HE'S LETTING US SHARE A ROOM. THAT'S PRETTY COOL OF HIM TO DO.
NO IT'S NOT. I'M AN ADULT... HE NEEDS TO REALIZE THAT. I ROOMED WITH A GUY IN COLLEGE. I'M SURE IN HIS MIND WE'RE JUST ROOMMATES.
SUITS ME JUST FINE. AS LONG AS WE CAN BE TOGETHER I DON'T CARE WHAT HE HAS TO TELL HIMSELF.
COLLEGE, HUH? I DIDN'T KNOW THAT.
ONE MEASLY SEMESTER. WE KINDA RAN OUT OF MONEY AROUND THE SAME TIME I FLUNKED OUT. I USUALLY PICK THE REASON BASED ON HOW WELL I KNOW THE PERSON.

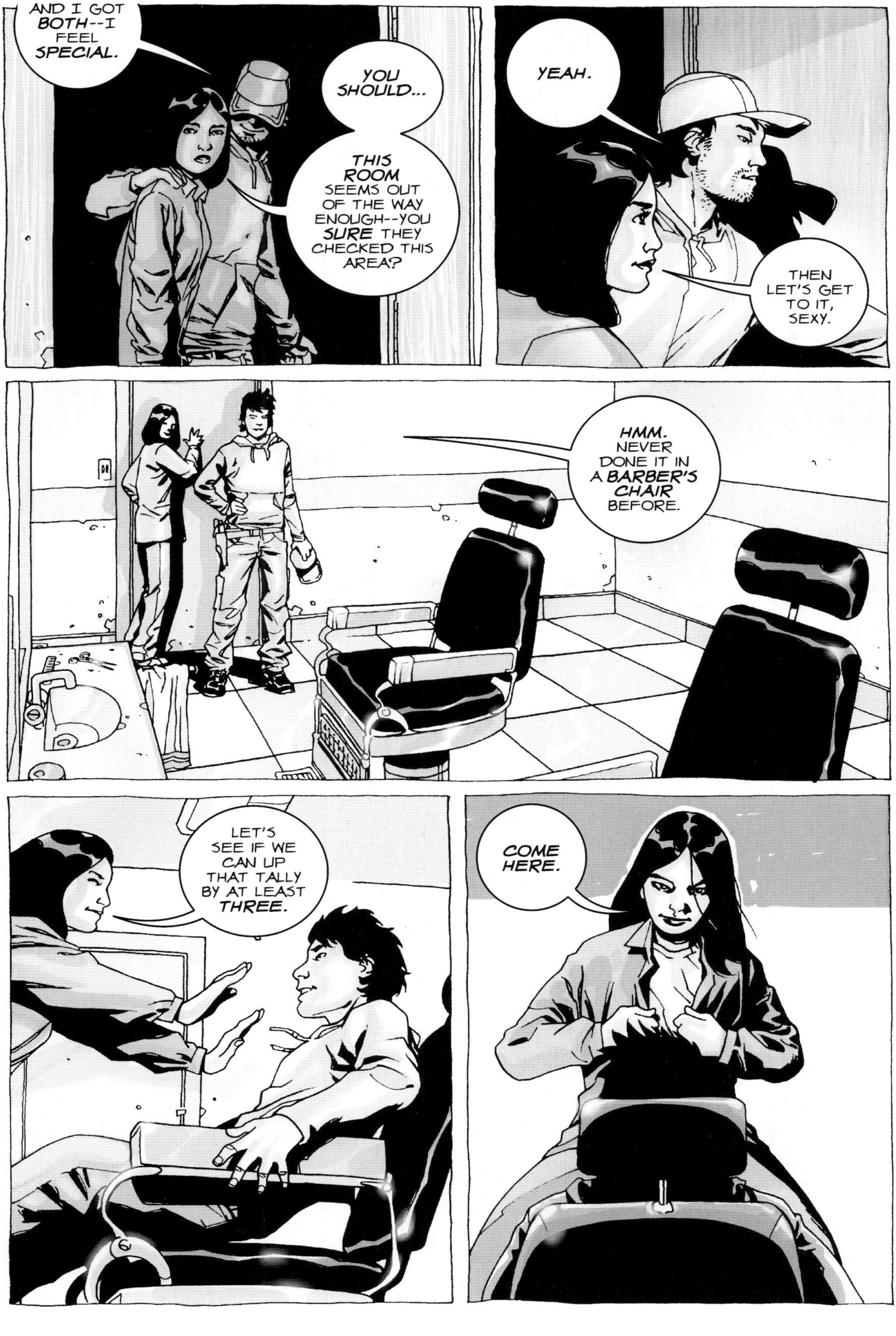
AND I GOT BOTH--I FEEL SPECIAL.
YOU SHOULD...
THIS ROOM SEEMS OUT OF THE WAY ENOUGH--YOU SURE THEY CHECKED THIS AREA?
YEAH.
THEN LET'S GET TO IT, SEXY.
HMM. NEVER DONE IT IN A BARBER'S CHAIR BEFORE.
LET'S SEE IF WE CAN UP THAT TALLY BY AT LEAST THREE.
COME HERE.

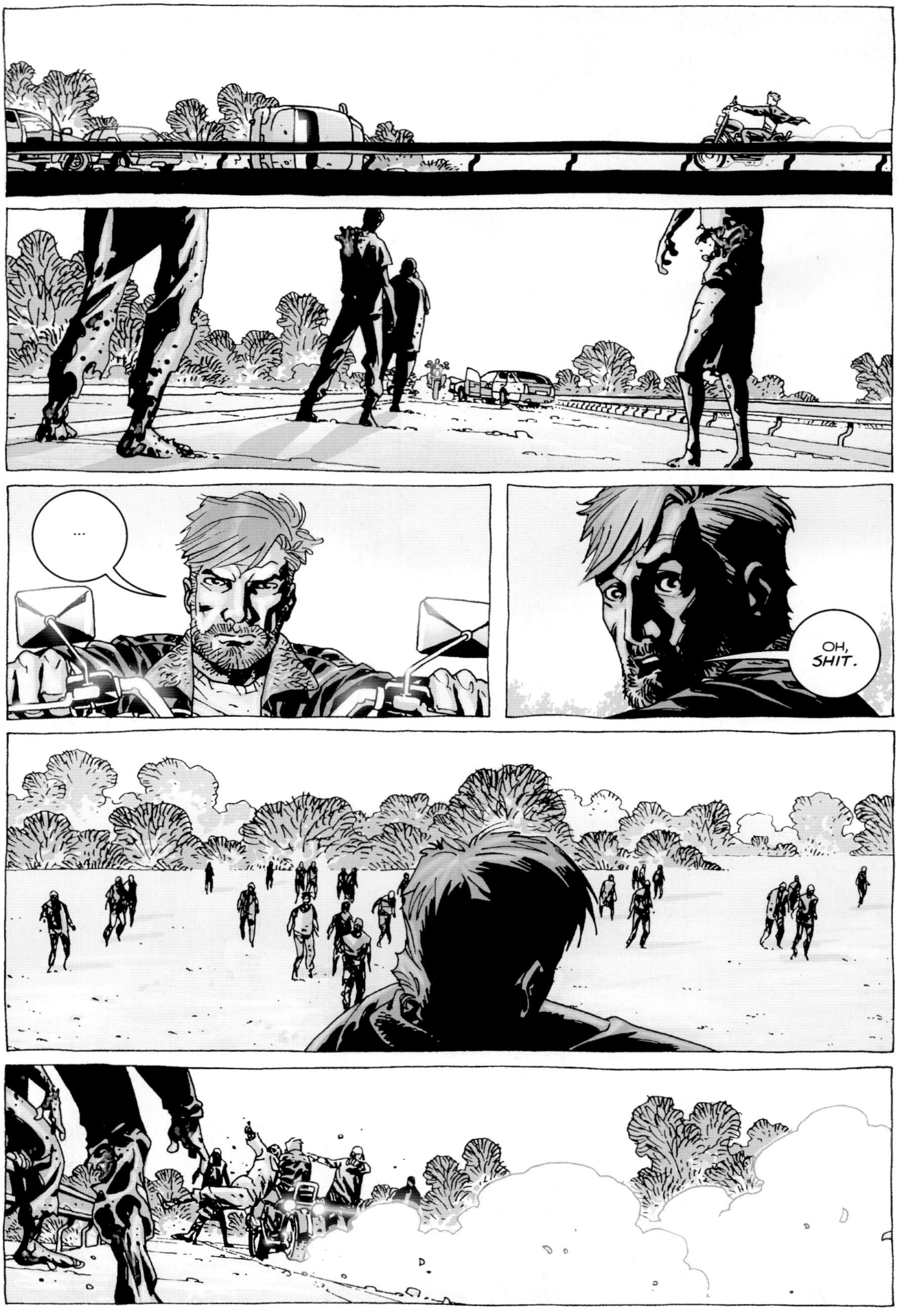
...
OH, SHIT.

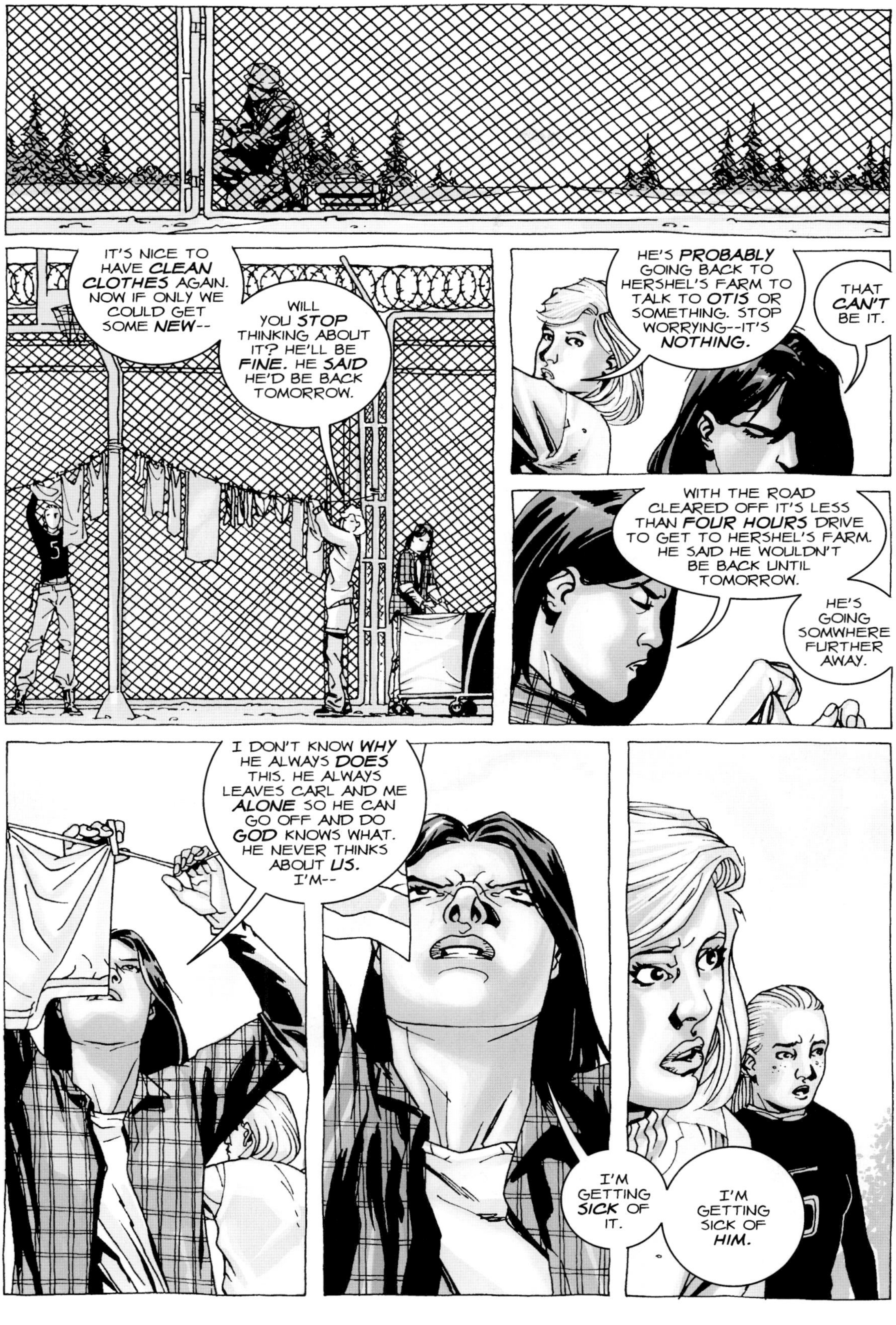
IT'S NICE TO HAVE CLEAN CLOTHES AGAIN. NOW IF ONLY WE COULD GET SOME NEW--
WILL YOU STOP THINKING ABOUT IT? HE'LL BE FINE. HE SAID HE'D BE BACK TOMORROW.
HE'S PROBABLY GOING BACK TO HERSHEL'S FARM TO TALK TO OTIS OR SOMETHING. STOP WORRYING--IT'S NOTHING.
THAT CAN'T BE IT.
WITH THE ROAD CLEARED OFF IT'S LESS THAN FOUR HOURS DRIVE TO GET TO HERSHEL'S FARM. HE SAID HE WOULDN'T BE BACK UNTIL TOMORROW.
HE'S GOING SOMWHERE FURTHER AWAY.
I DON'T KNOW WHY HE ALWAYS DOES THIS. HE ALWAYS LEAVES CARL AND ME ALONE SO HE CAN GO OFF AND DO GOD KNOWS WHAT. HE NEVER THINKS ABOUT US. I'M--
I'M GETTING SICK OF IT.
I'M GETTING SICK OF HIM.

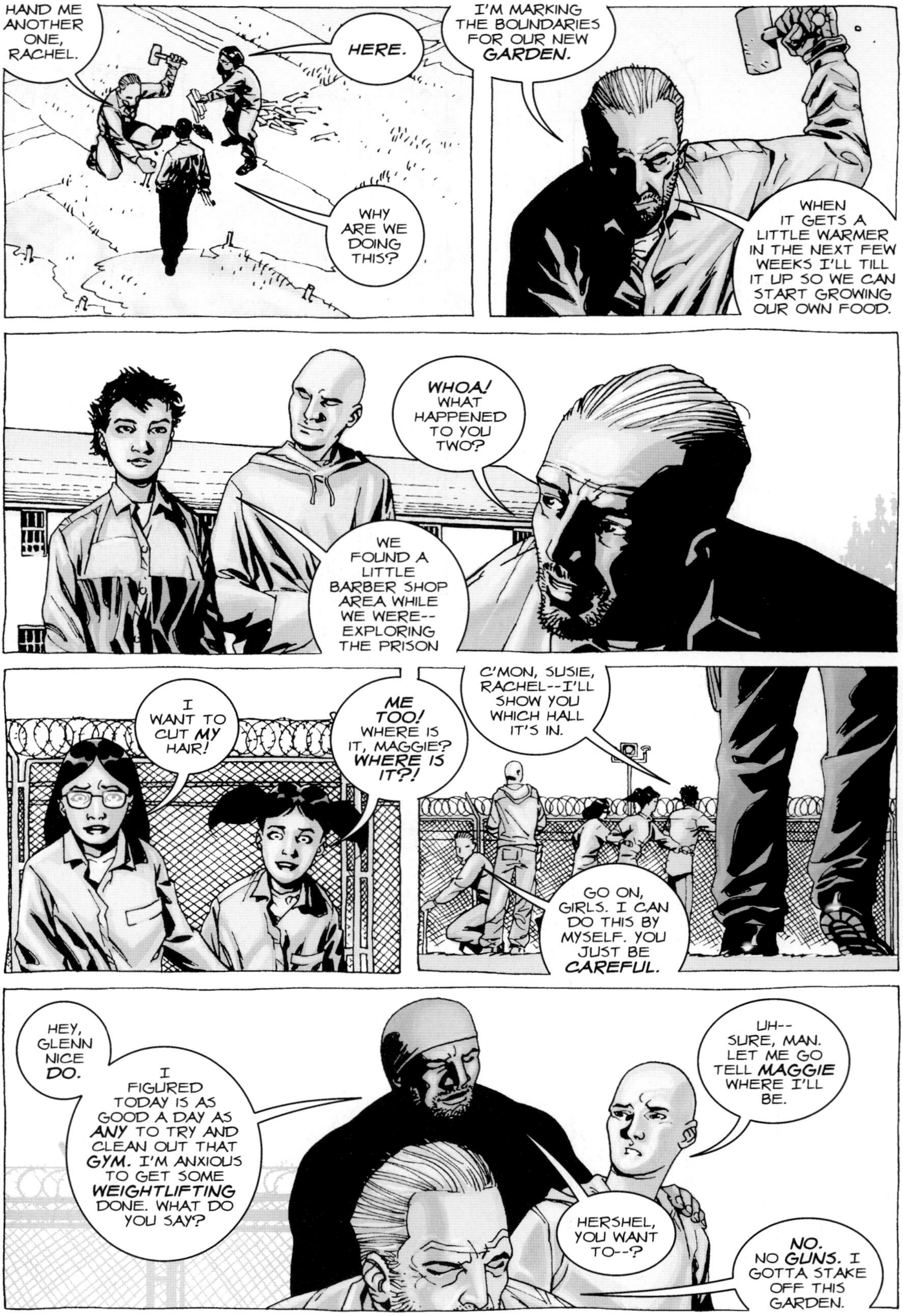

HAND ME ANOTHER ONE, RACHEL.
HERE.
WHY ARE WE DOING THIS?
I'M MARKING THE BOUNDARIES FOR OUR NEW GARDEN.
WHEN IT GETS A LITTLE WARMER IN THE NEXT FEW WEEKS I'LL TILL IT UP SO WE CAN START GROWING OUR OWN FOOD.
WHOA! WHAT HAPPENED TO YOU TWO?
WE FOUND A LITTLE BARBER SHOP AREA WHILE WE WERE-- EXPLORING THE PRISON
I WANT TO CUT MY HAIR!
ME TOO! WHERE IS IT, MAGGIE? WHERE IS IT?!
C'MON, SUSIE, RACHEL--I'LL SHOW YOU WHICH HALL IT'S IN.
GO ON, GIRLS. I CAN DO THIS BY MYSELF. YOU JUST BE CAREFUL.
HEY, GLENN NICE DO.
I FIGURED TODAY IS AS GOOD A DAY AS ANY TO TRY AND CLEAN OUT THAT GYM. I'M ANXIOUS TO GET SOME WEIGHTLIFTING DONE. WHAT DO YOU SAY?
UH-- SURE, MAN. LET ME GO TELL MAGGIE WHERE I'LL BE.
HERSHEL, YOU WANT TO--?
NO. NO GUNS. I GOTTA STAKE OFF THIS GARDEN.

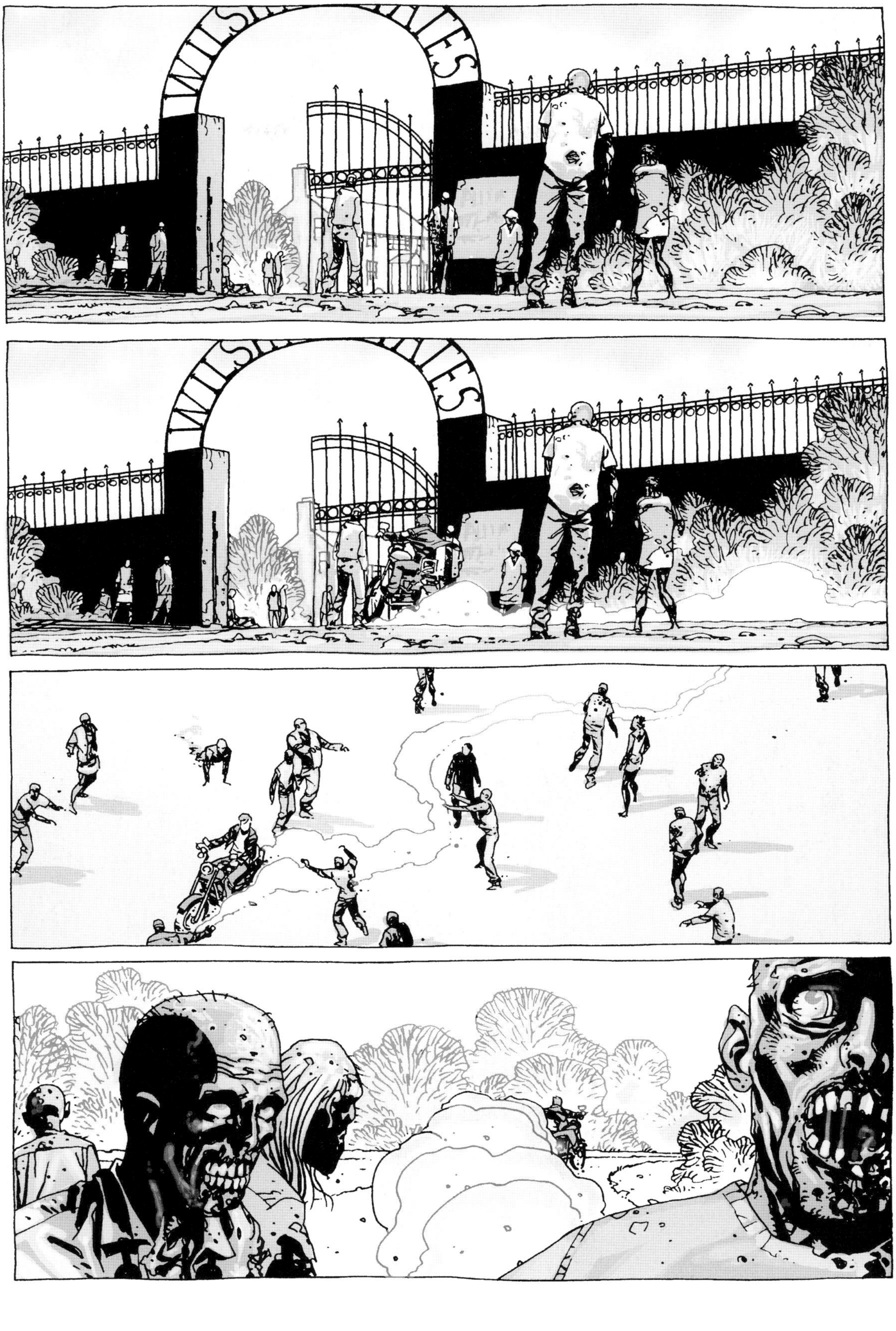

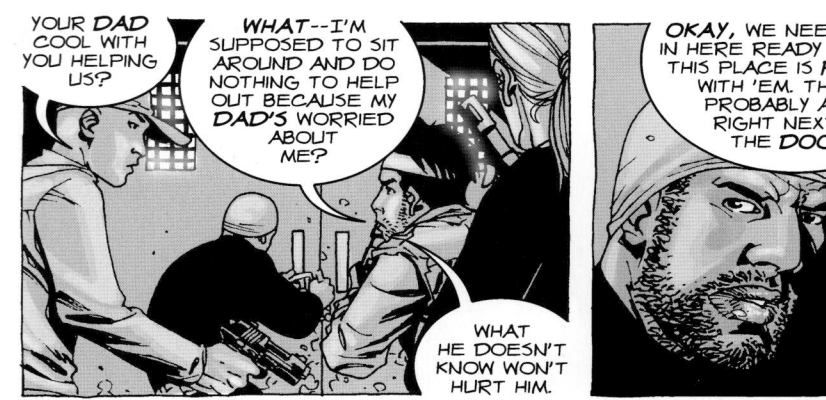

YOUR *DAD* COOL WITH YOU HELPING US?

WHAT--I'M SUPPOSED TO SIT AROUND AND DO NOTHING TO HELP OUT BECAUSE MY *DAD'S* WORRIED ABOUT ME?

WHAT HE DOESN'T KNOW WON'T HURT HIM.

OKAY, WE NEED TO GO IN HERE READY TO *FIRE.* THIS PLACE IS *PACKED* WITH 'EM. THERE'S PROBABLY A FEW RIGHT NEXT TO THE *DOOR.*

I KNOW WE DON'T HAVE MANY *BULLETS* LEFT, SO STAY *CLOSE* TO THE DOOR. IF WE RUN OUT, WE JUST WALK BACK OUT AND LOCK THE DOORS.

UNDERSTOOD?

HERE WE GO.

LET'S CLEAR AN AREA AROUND *US* AND THE *DOOR* FIRST... THEN WORK OUR WAY FORWARD WITHOUT LETTING ANY *PAST* US!

BLAM!

SOUNDS LIKE A *PLAN* TO ME.

BLAM! BLAM!

THROK!

BLAM!

RAARGH!

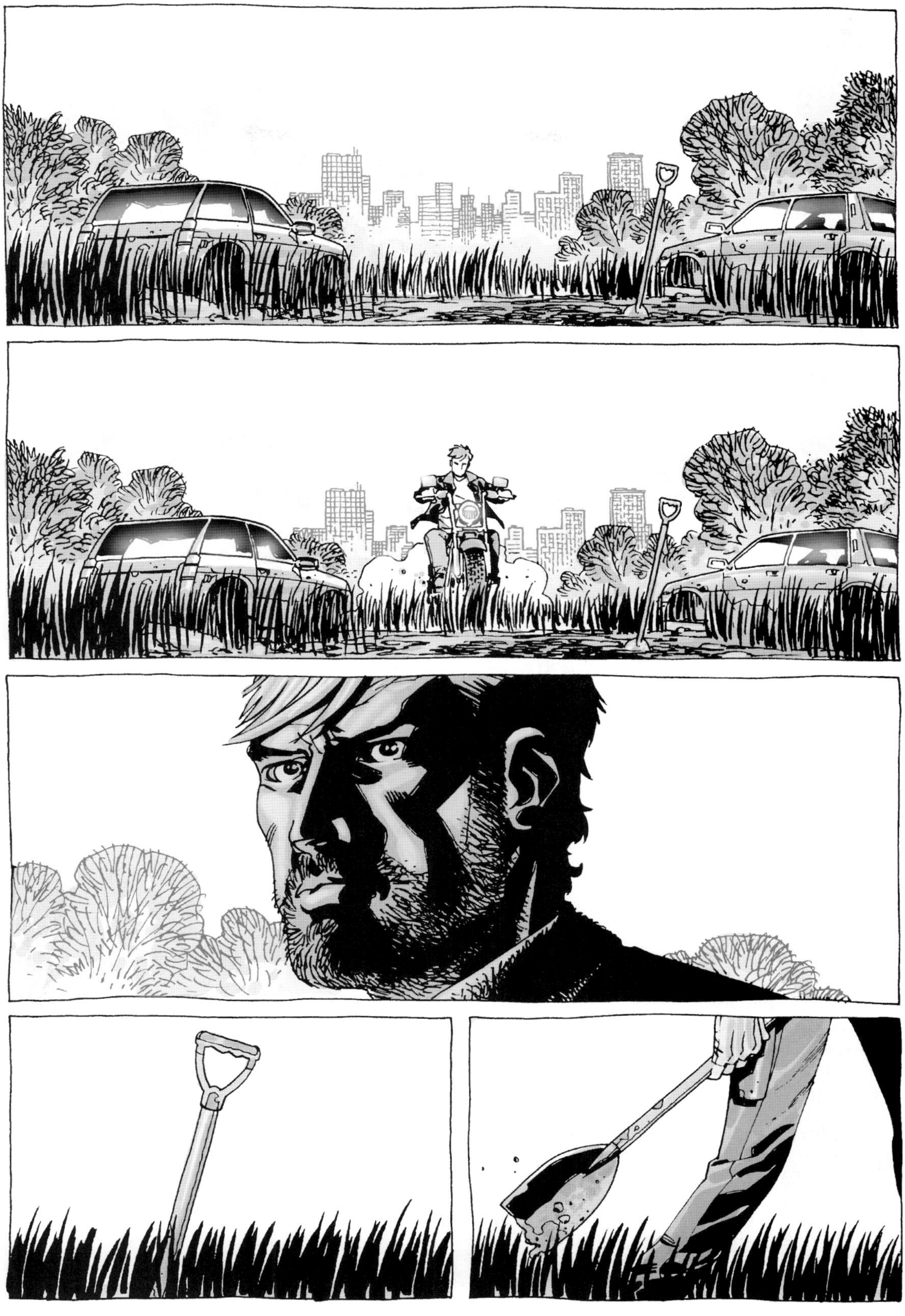

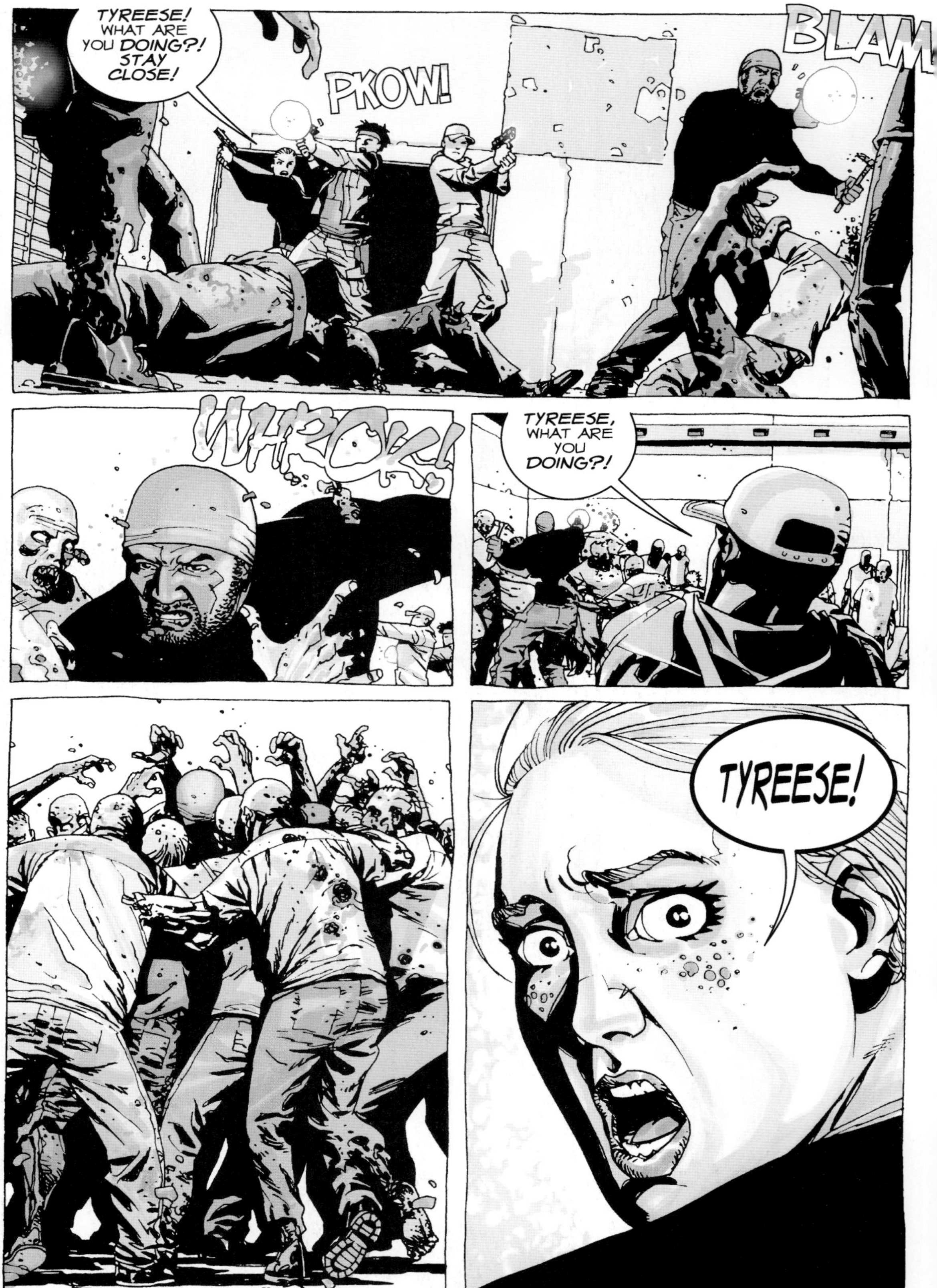
TYREESE! WHAT ARE YOU DOING?! STAY CLOSE!
PKOW!
BLAM
WHROK!
TYREESE, WHAT ARE YOU DOING?!
TYREESE!

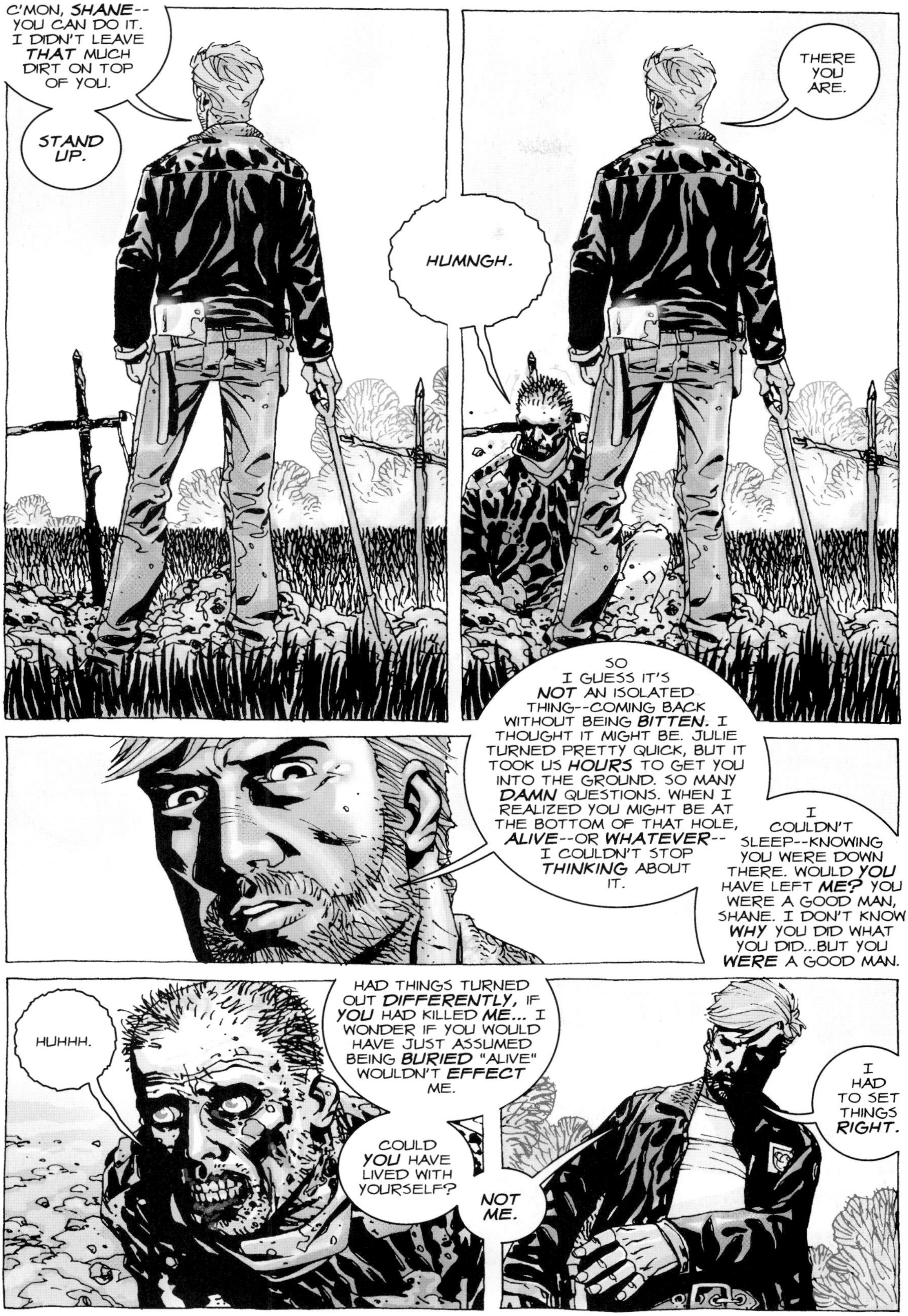
C'MON, SHANE--
YOU CAN DO IT. I DIDN'T LEAVE THAT MUCH DIRT ON TOP OF YOU.
STAND UP.
HUMNGH.
THERE YOU ARE.
SO I GUESS IT'S NOT AN ISOLATED THING--COMING BACK WITHOUT BEING BITTEN. I THOUGHT IT MIGHT BE. JULIE TURNED PRETTY QUICK, BUT IT TOOK US HOURS TO GET YOU INTO THE GROUND. SO MANY DAMN QUESTIONS. WHEN I REALIZED YOU MIGHT BE AT THE BOTTOM OF THAT HOLE, ALIVE--OR WHATEVER-- I COULDN'T STOP THINKING ABOUT IT.
I COULDN'T SLEEP--KNOWING YOU WERE DOWN THERE. WOULD YOU HAVE LEFT ME? YOU WERE A GOOD MAN, SHANE. I DON'T KNOW WHY YOU DID WHAT YOU DID...BUT YOU WERE A GOOD MAN.
HUHHH.
HAD THINGS TURNED OUT DIFFERENTLY, IF YOU HAD KILLED ME... I WONDER IF YOU WOULD HAVE JUST ASSUMED BEING BURIED "ALIVE" WOULDN'T EFFECT ME.
COULD YOU HAVE LIVED WITH YOURSELF?
NOT ME.
I HAD TO SET THINGS RIGHT.

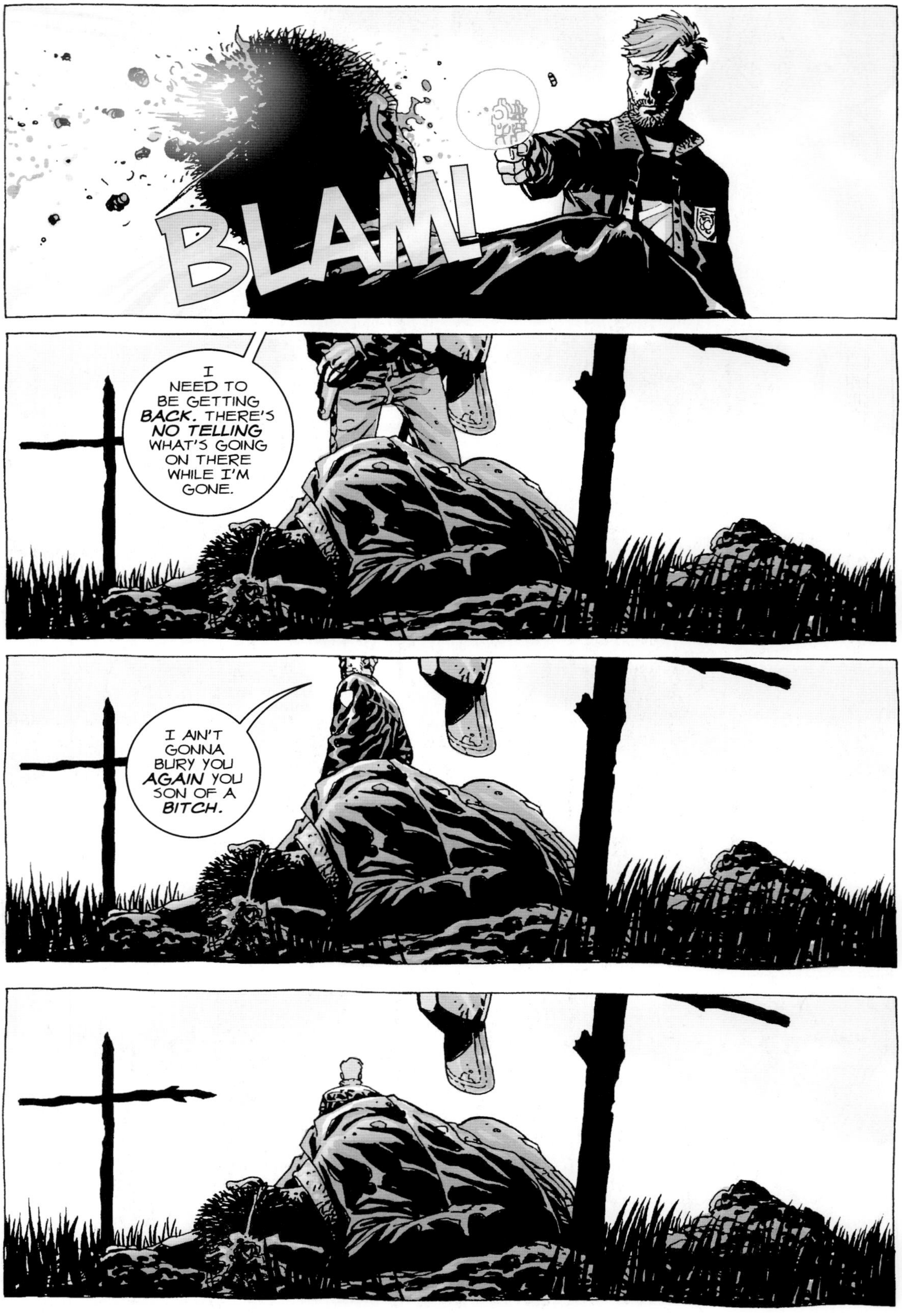
BLAM!
I NEED TO BE GETTING BACK. THERE'S NO TELLING WHAT'S GOING ON THERE WHILE I'M GONE.
I AIN'T GONNA BURY YOU AGAIN YOU SON OF A BITCH.

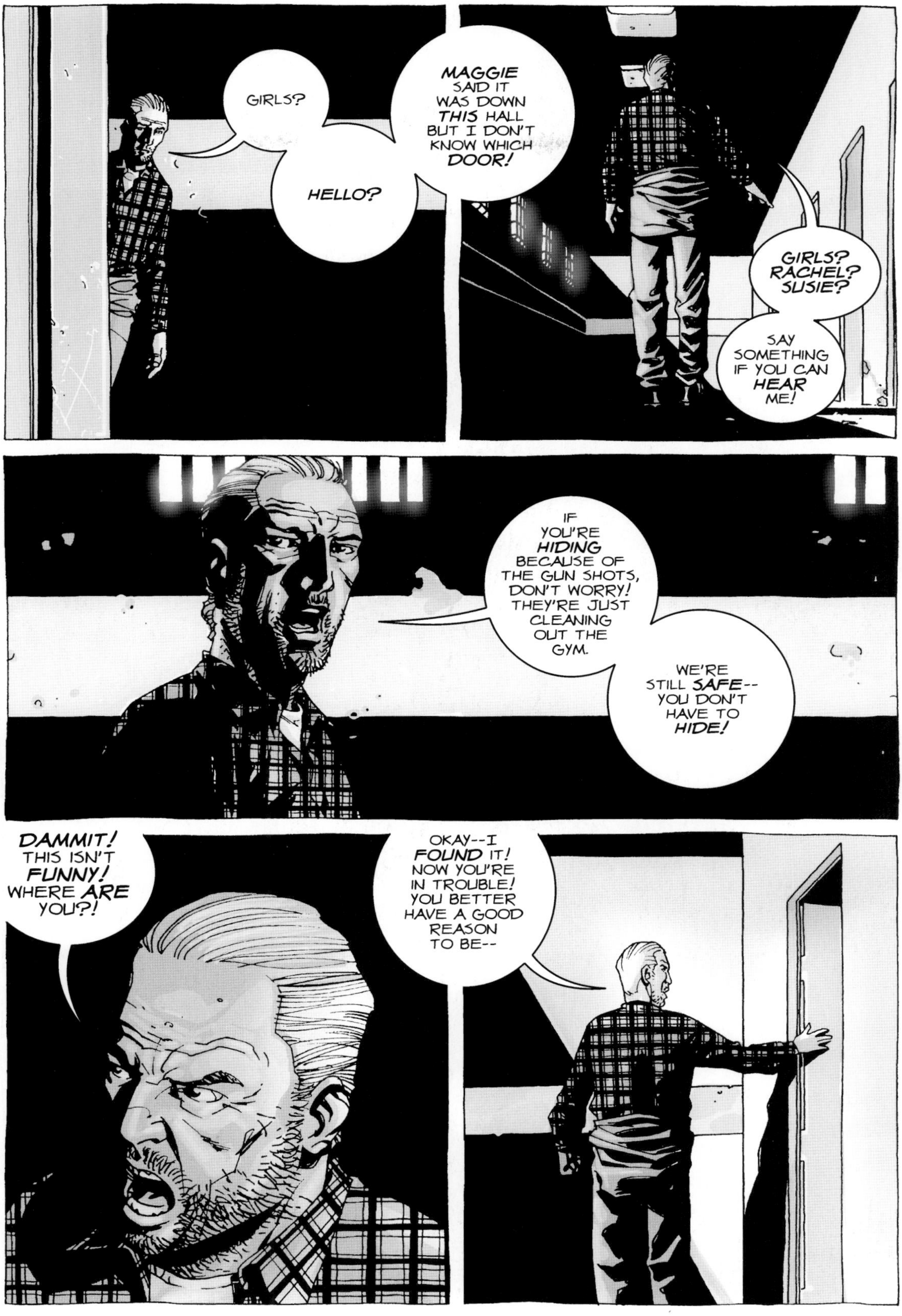
GIRLS?
HELLO?
MAGGIE SAID IT WAS DOWN THIS HALL BUT I DON'T KNOW WHICH DOOR!
GIRLS? RACHEL? SUSIE?
SAY SOMETHING IF YOU CAN HEAR ME!
IF YOU'RE HIDING BECAUSE OF THE GUN SHOTS, DON'T WORRY! THEY'RE JUST CLEANING OUT THE GYM.
WE'RE STILL SAFE-- YOU DON'T HAVE TO HIDE!
DAMMIT! THIS ISN'T FUNNY! WHERE ARE YOU?!
OKAY--I FOUND IT! NOW YOU'RE IN TROUBLE! YOU BETTER HAVE A GOOD REASON TO BE--

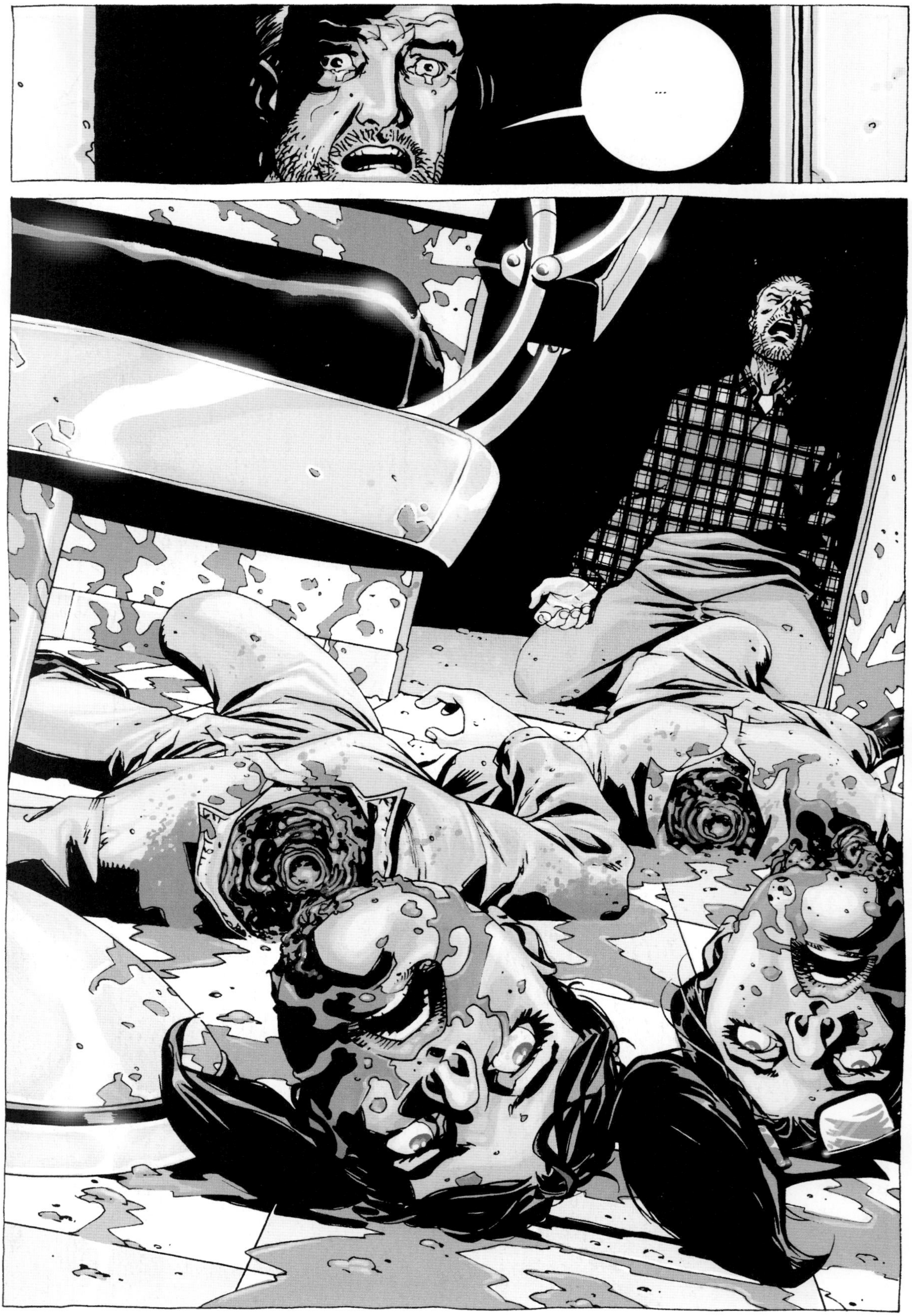
...

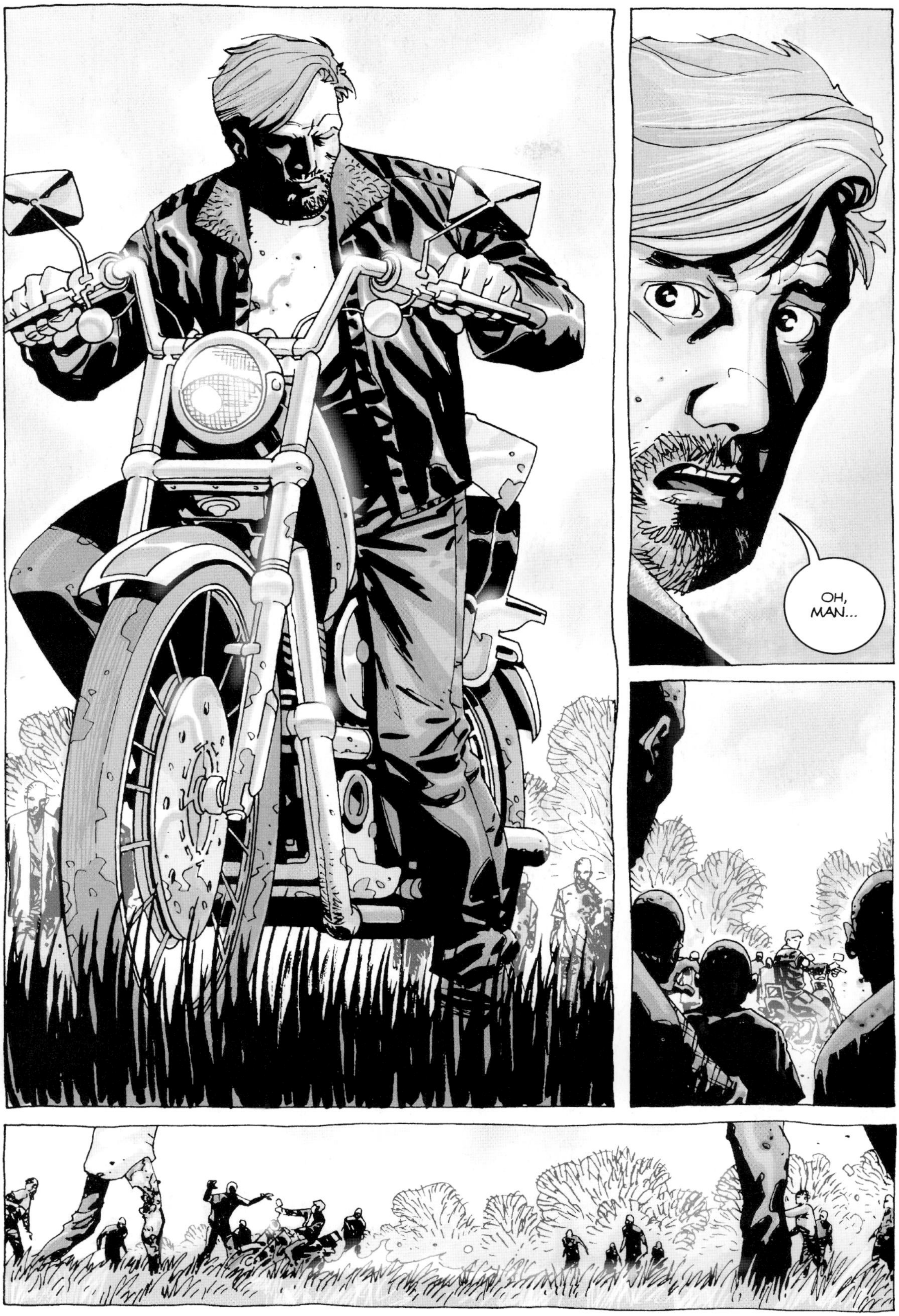
OH, MAN...

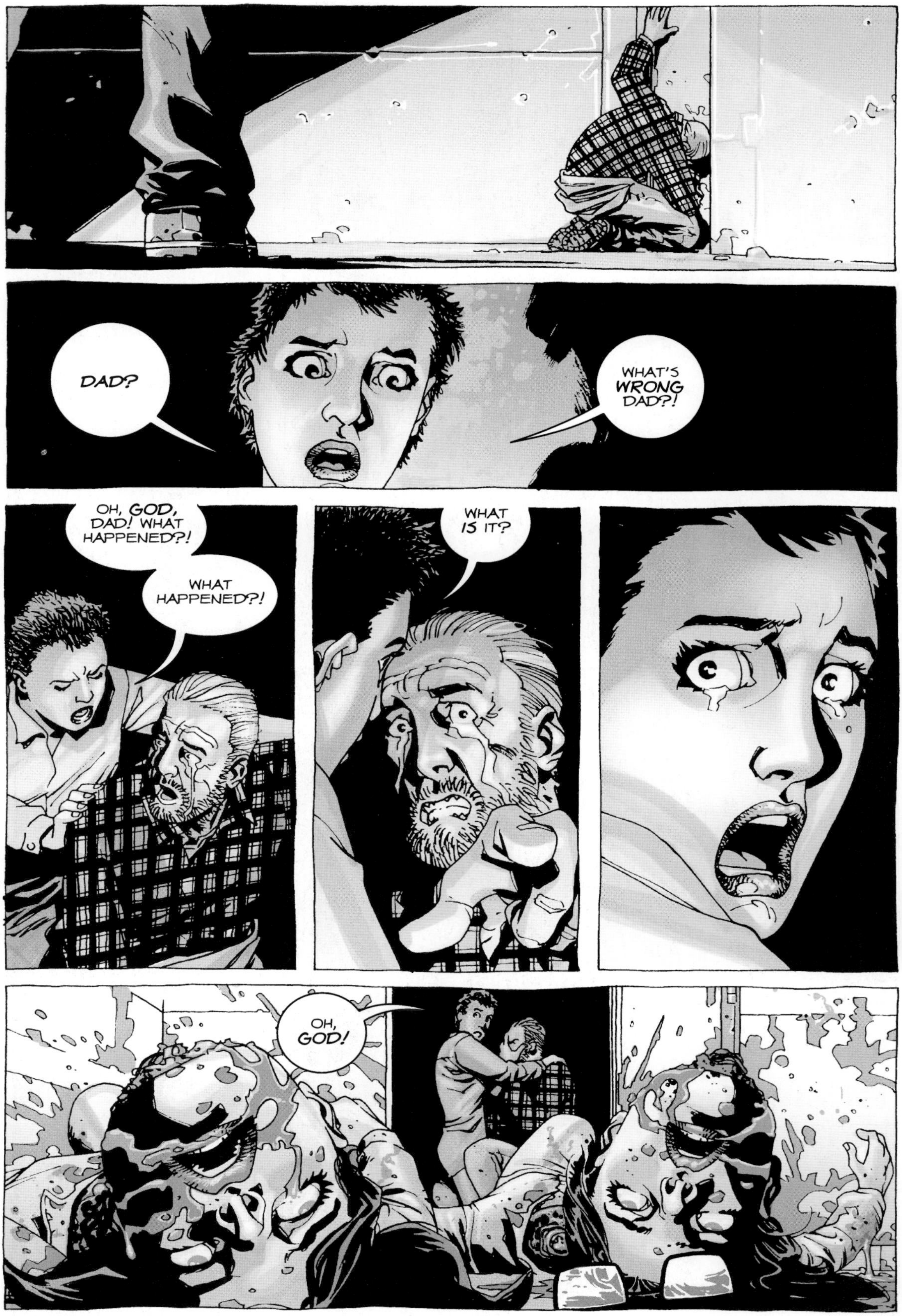
DAD?
WHAT'S WRONG DAD?!
OH, GOD, DAD! WHAT HAPPENED?!
WHAT HAPPENED?!
WHAT IS IT?
OH, GOD!

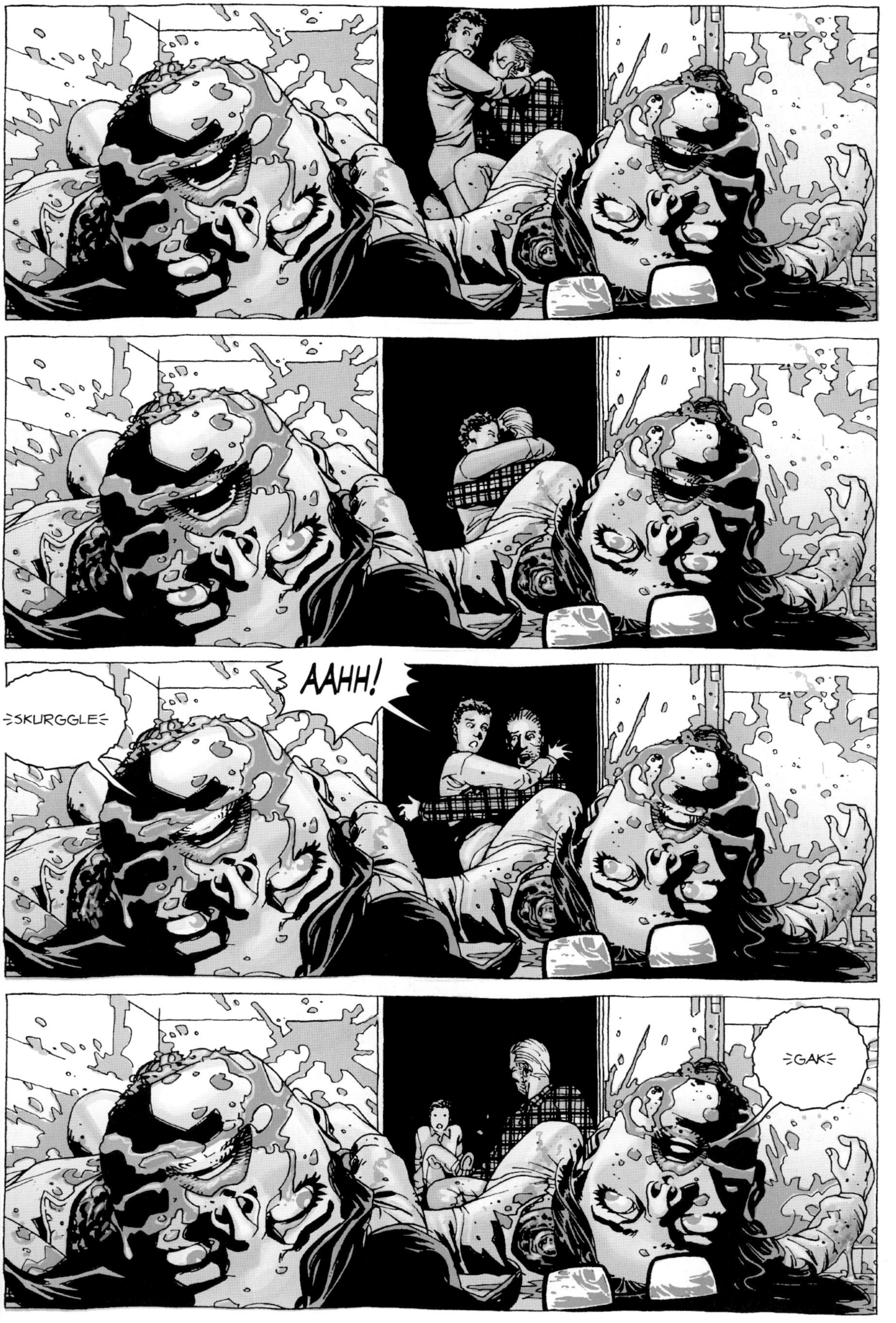
SKURGGLE
AAHH!
GAK

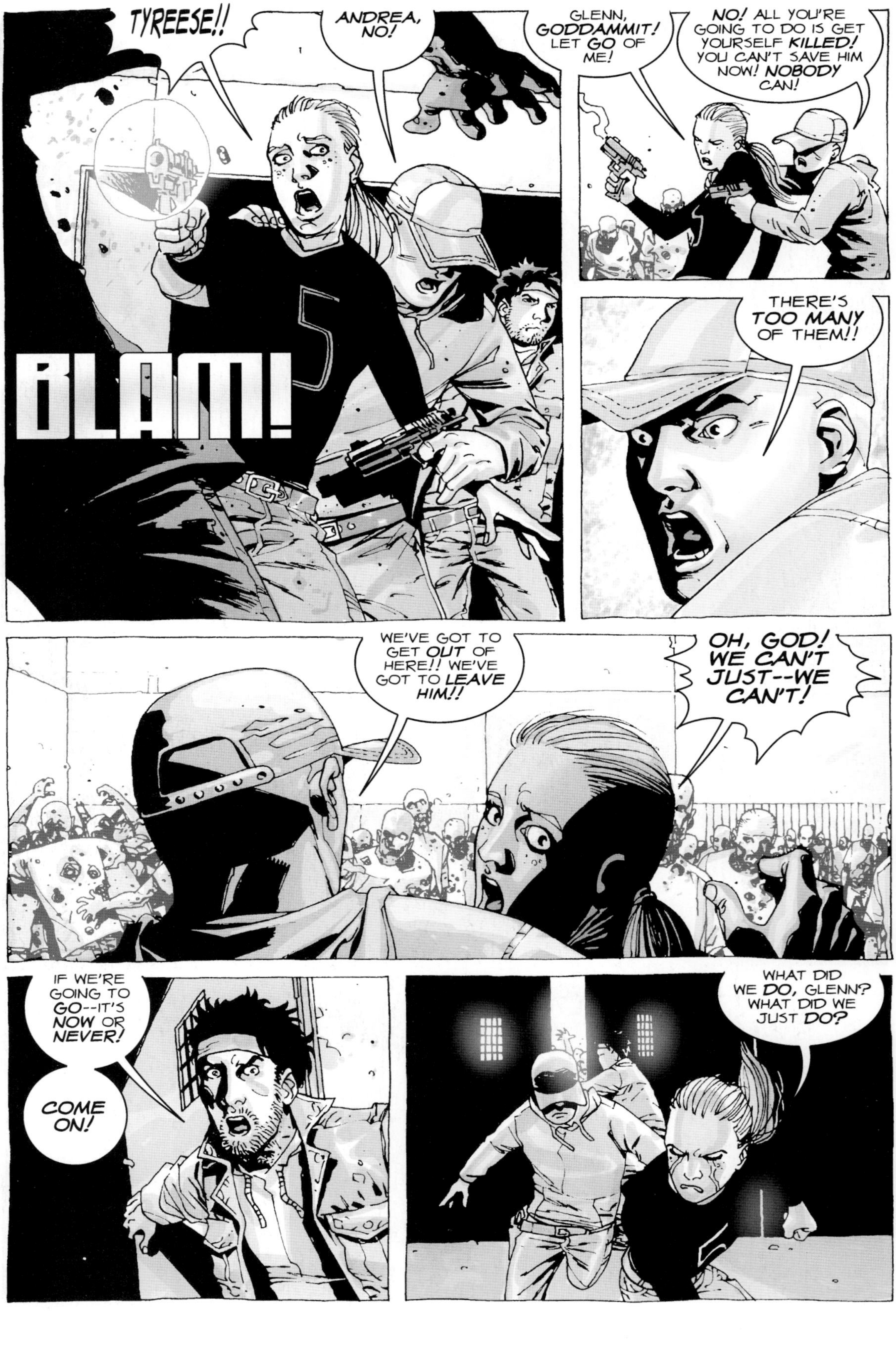
TYREESE!!
ANDREA, NO!
BLAM!
GLENN, GODDAMMIT! LET GO OF ME!
NO! ALL YOU'RE GOING TO DO IS GET YOURSELF KILLED! YOU CAN'T SAVE HIM NOW! NOBODY CAN!
THERE'S TOO MANY OF THEM!!
WE'VE GOT TO GET OUT OF HERE!! WE'VE GOT TO LEAVE HIM!!
OH, GOD! WE CAN'T JUST--WE CAN'T!
IF WE'RE GOING TO GO--IT'S NOW OR NEVER!
COME ON!
WHAT DID WE DO, GLENN? WHAT DID WE JUST DO?

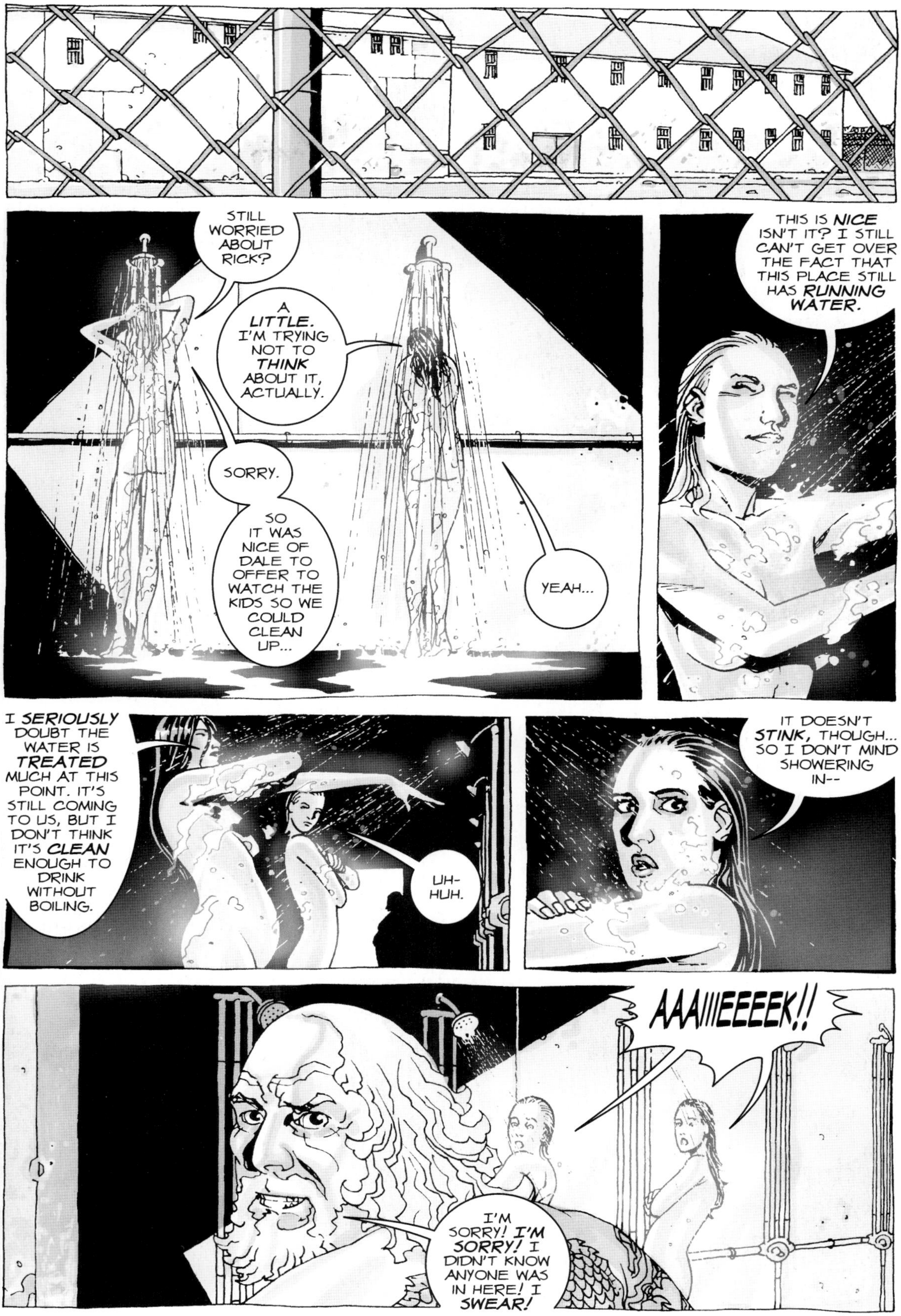
STILL WORRIED ABOUT RICK?
A LITTLE. I'M TRYING NOT TO THINK ABOUT IT, ACTUALLY.
SORRY.
SO IT WAS NICE OF DALE TO OFFER TO WATCH THE KIDS SO WE COULD CLEAN UP...
YEAH...
THIS IS NICE ISN'T IT? I STILL CAN'T GET OVER THE FACT THAT THIS PLACE STILL HAS RUNNING WATER.
I SERIOUSLY DOUBT THE WATER IS TREATED MUCH AT THIS POINT. IT'S STILL COMING TO US, BUT I DON'T THINK IT'S CLEAN ENOUGH TO DRINK WITHOUT BOILING.
UH-HUH.
IT DOESN'T STINK, THOUGH... SO I DON'T MIND SHOWERING IN--
AAAIIIEEEEK!!
I'M SORRY! I'M SORRY! I DIDN'T KNOW ANYONE WAS IN HERE! I SWEAR!

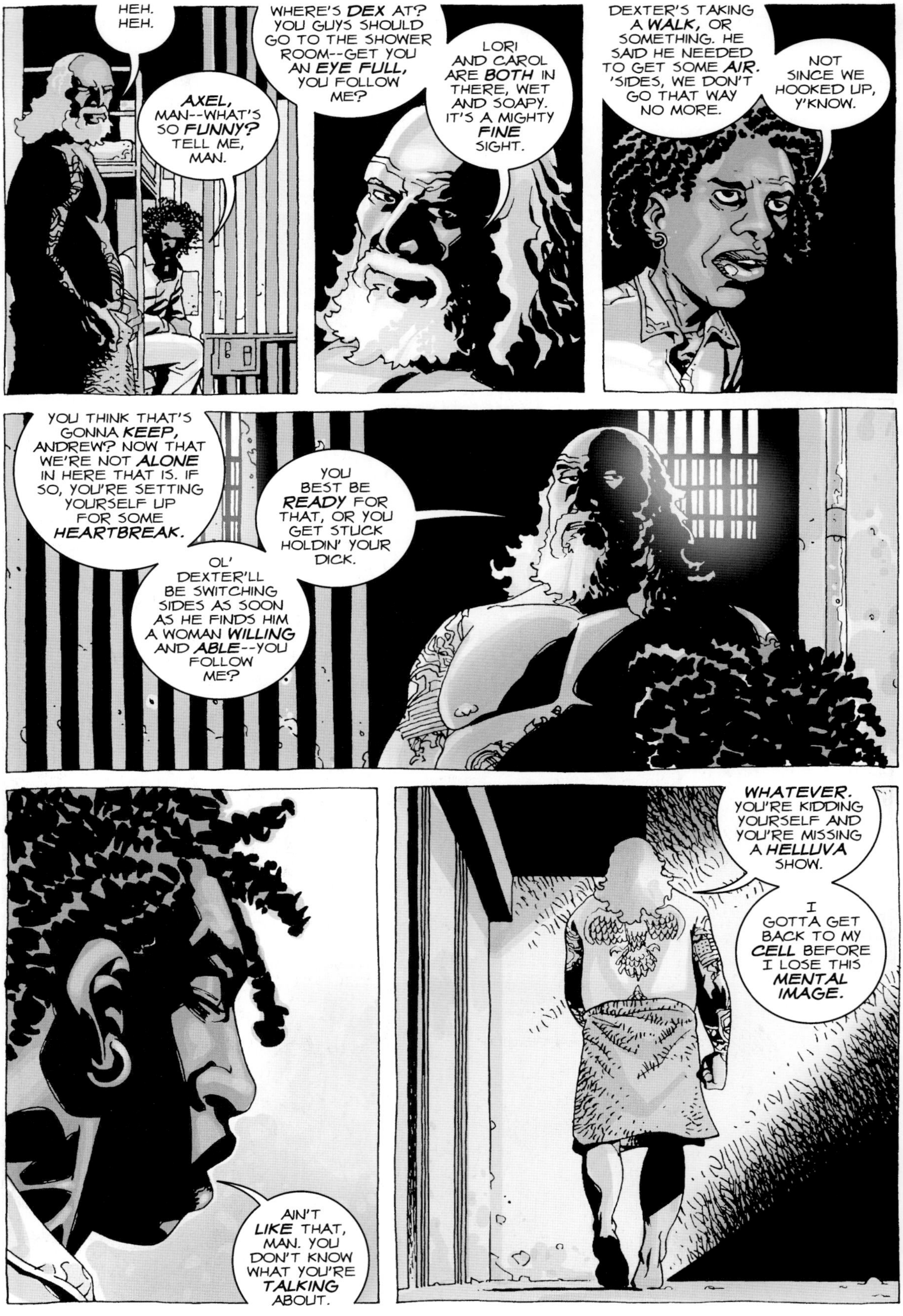
HEH. HEH.
AXEL, MAN--WHAT'S SO FUNNY? TELL ME, MAN.
WHERE'S DEX AT? YOU GUYS SHOULD GO TO THE SHOWER ROOM--GET YOU AN EYE FULL, YOU FOLLOW ME?
LORI AND CAROL ARE BOTH IN THERE, WET AND SOAPY. IT'S A MIGHTY FINE SIGHT.
DEXTER'S TAKING A WALK, OR SOMETHING. HE SAID HE NEEDED TO GET SOME AIR. 'SIDES, WE DON'T GO THAT WAY NO MORE.
NOT SINCE WE HOOKED UP, Y'KNOW.
YOU THINK THAT'S GONNA KEEP, ANDREW? NOW THAT WE'RE NOT ALONE IN HERE THAT IS. IF SO, YOU'RE SETTING YOURSELF UP FOR SOME HEARTBREAK.
YOU BEST BE READY FOR THAT, OR YOU GET STUCK HOLDIN' YOUR DICK.
OL' DEXTER'LL BE SWITCHING SIDES AS SOON AS HE FINDS HIM A WOMAN WILLING AND ABLE--YOU FOLLOW ME?
AIN'T LIKE THAT, MAN. YOU DON'T KNOW WHAT YOU'RE TALKING ABOUT.
WHATEVER. YOU'RE KIDDING YOURSELF AND YOU'RE MISSING A HELLUVA SHOW.
I GOTTA GET BACK TO MY CELL BEFORE I LOSE THIS MENTAL IMAGE.

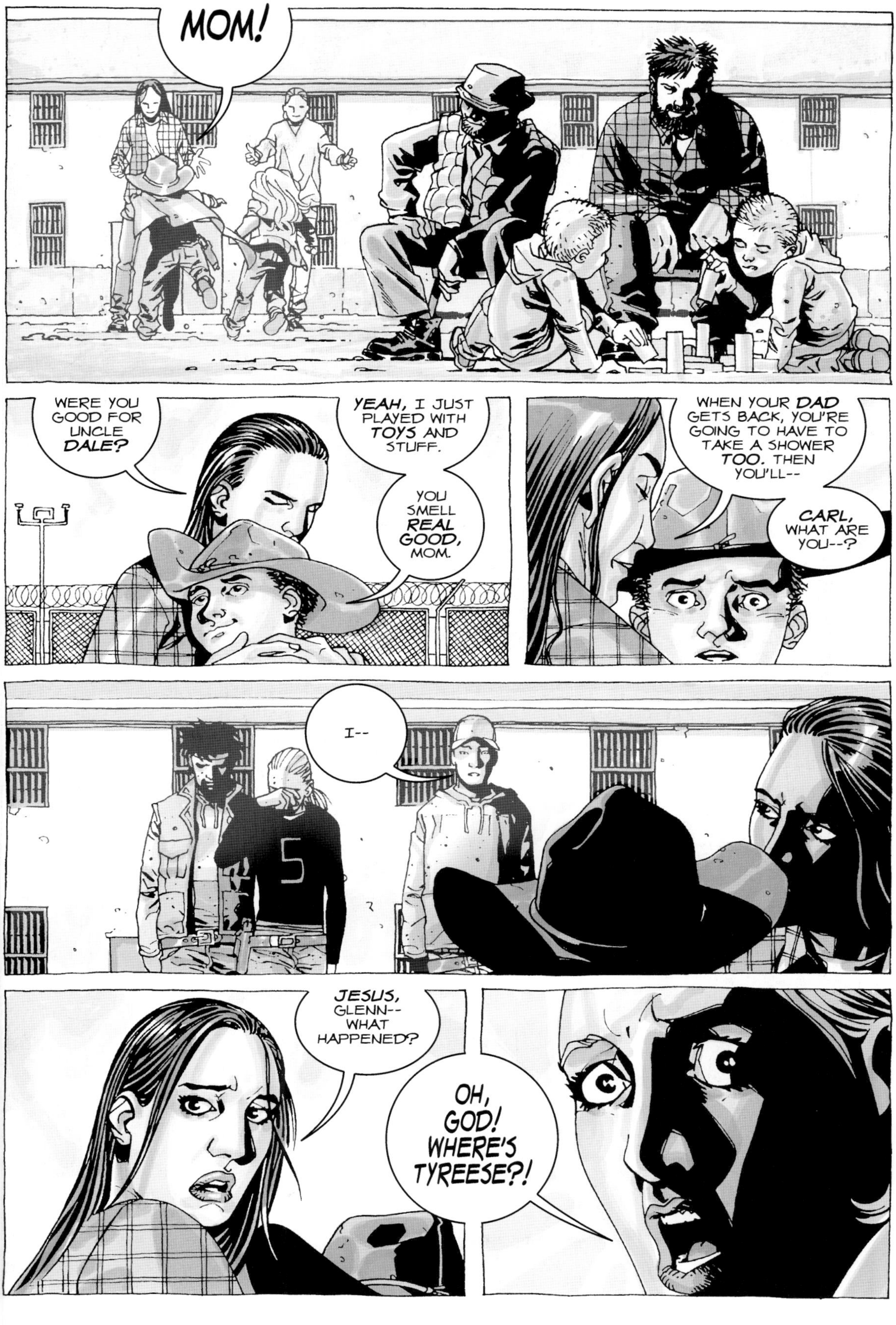
MOM!
WERE YOU GOOD FOR UNCLE DALE?
YEAH, I JUST PLAYED WITH TOYS AND STUFF.
YOU SMELL REAL GOOD, MOM.
WHEN YOUR DAD GETS BACK, YOU'RE GOING TO HAVE TO TAKE A SHOWER TOO. THEN YOU'LL--
CARL, WHAT ARE YOU--?
I--
JESUS, GLENN-- WHAT HAPPENED?
OH, GOD! WHERE'S TYREESE?!

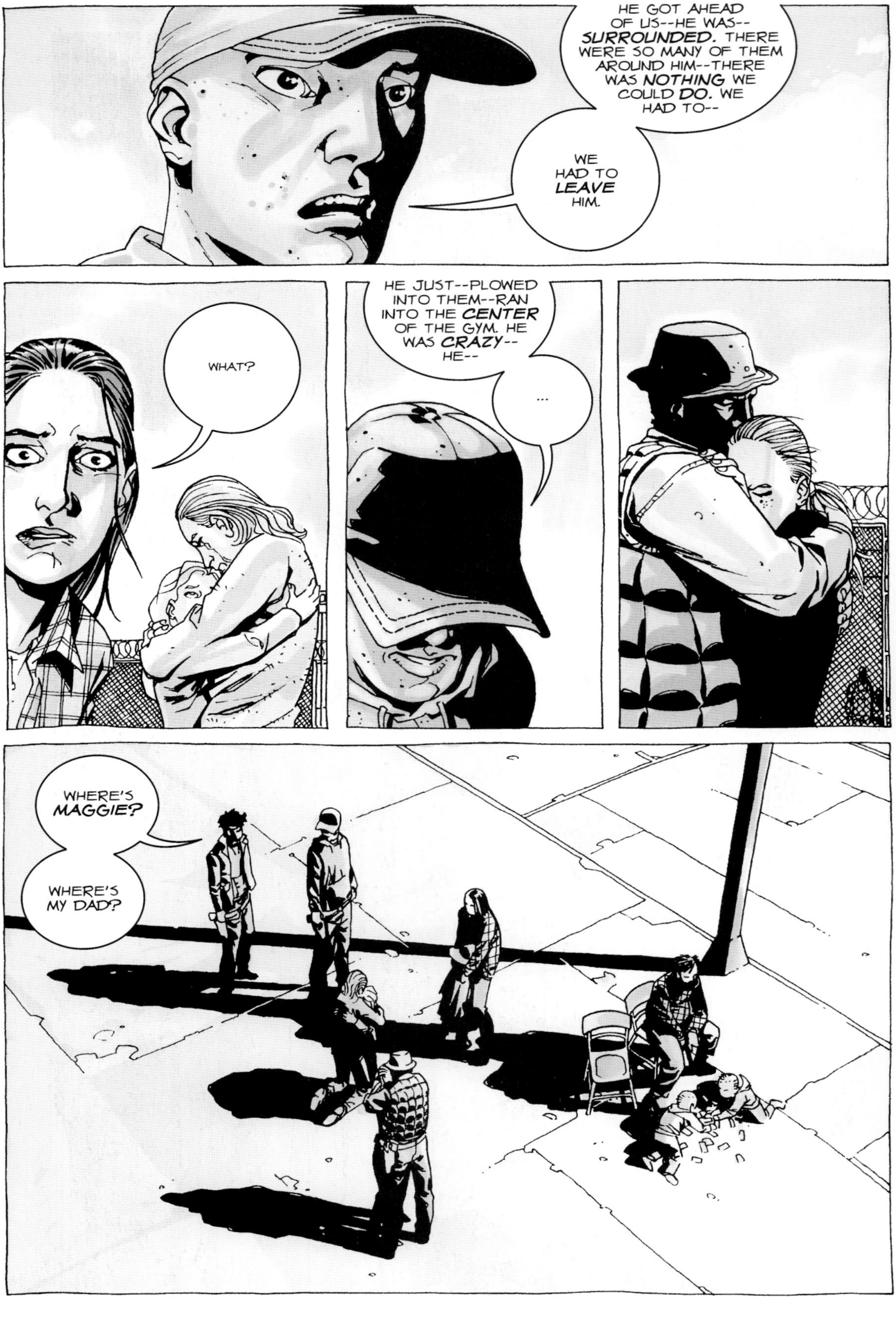
HE GOT AHEAD OF US--HE WAS--SURROUNDED. THERE WERE SO MANY OF THEM AROUND HIM--THERE WAS NOTHING WE COULD DO. WE HAD TO--
WE HAD TO LEAVE HIM.
WHAT?
HE JUST--PLOWED INTO THEM--RAN INTO THE CENTER OF THE GYM. HE WAS CRAZY--HE--
...
WHERE'S MAGGIE?
WHERE'S MY DAD?

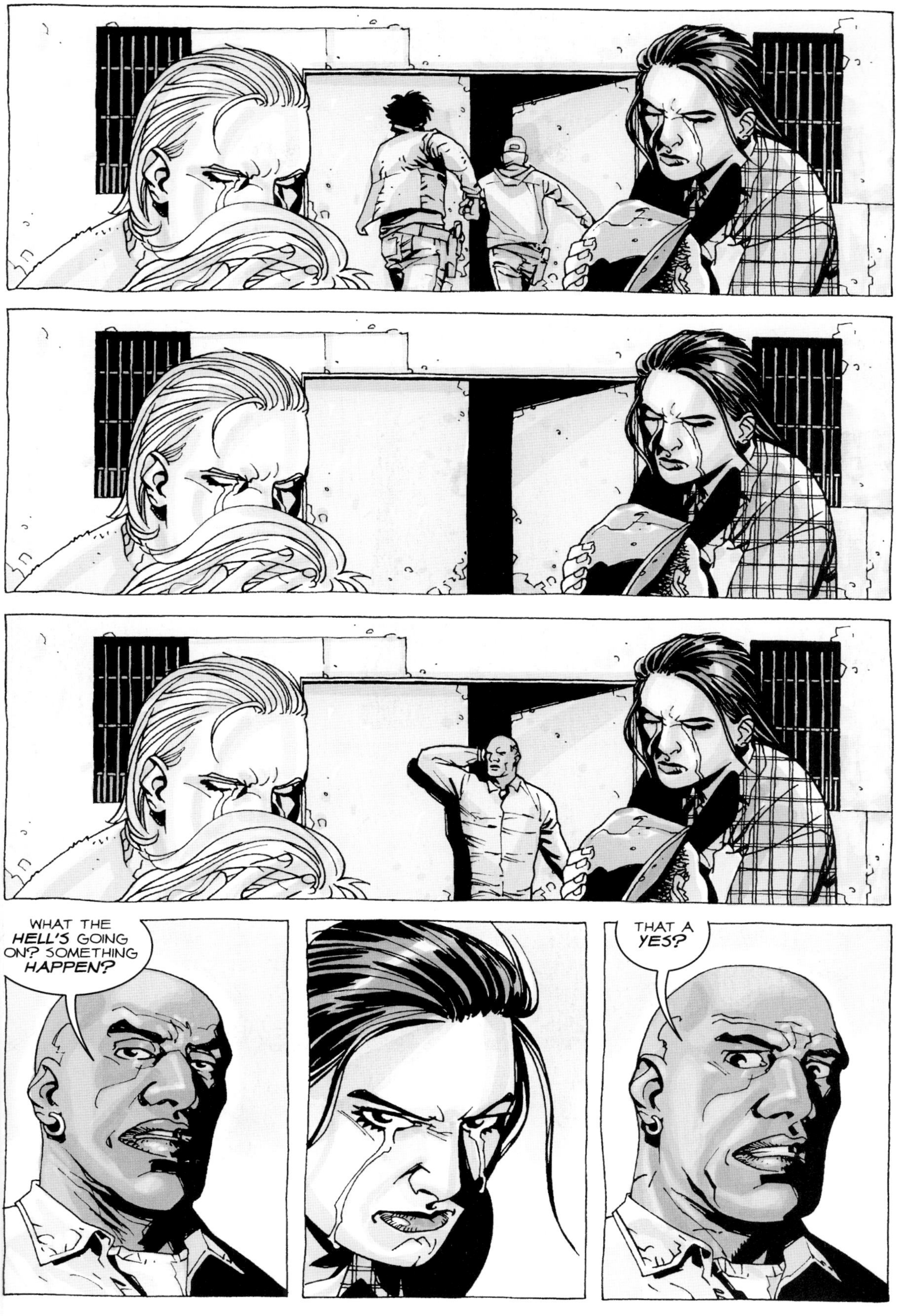
WHAT THE HELL'S GOING ON? SOMETHING HAPPEN?
THAT A YES?

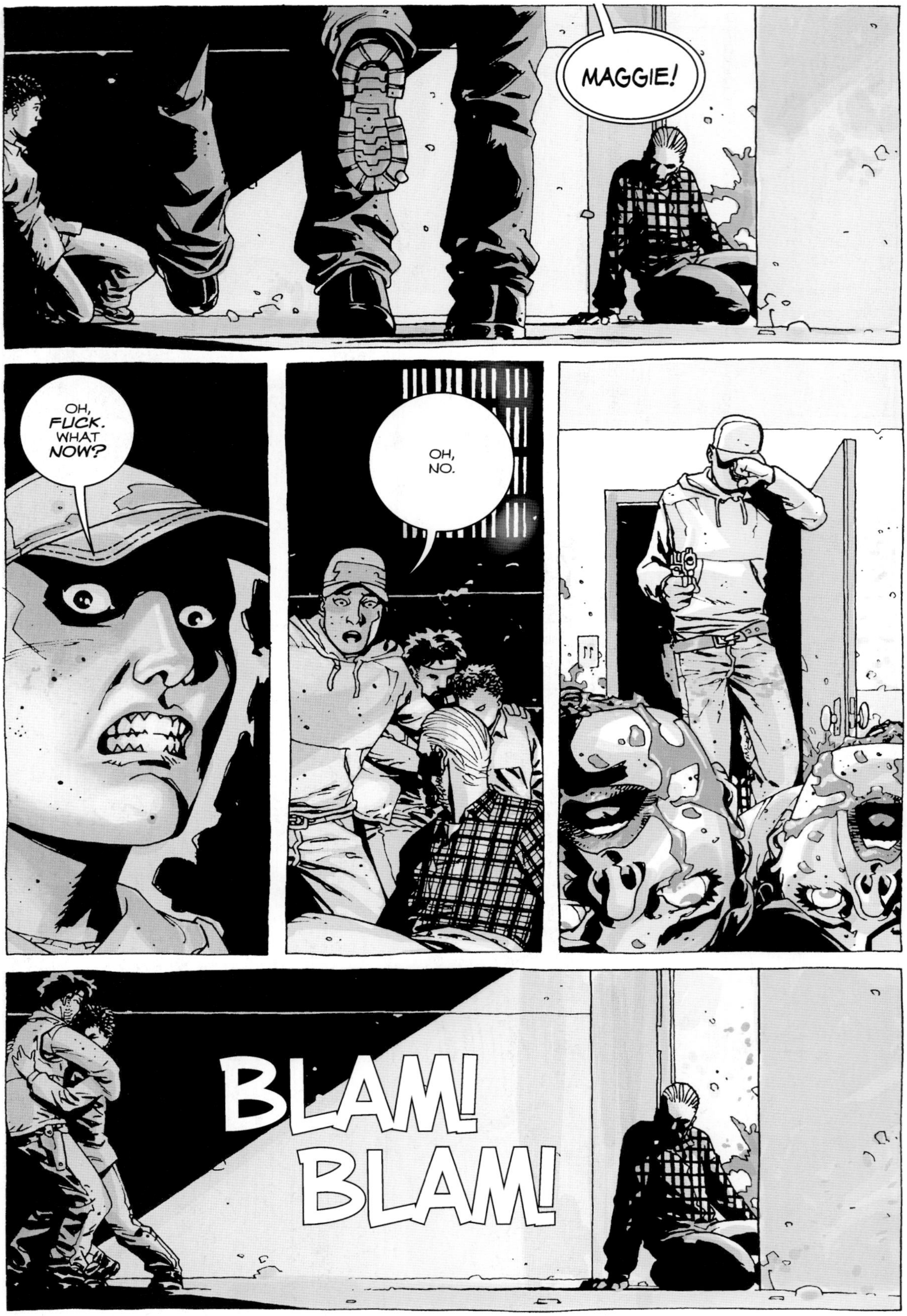
MAGGIE!
OH, FUCK. WHAT NOW?
OH, NO.
BLAM!
BLAM!

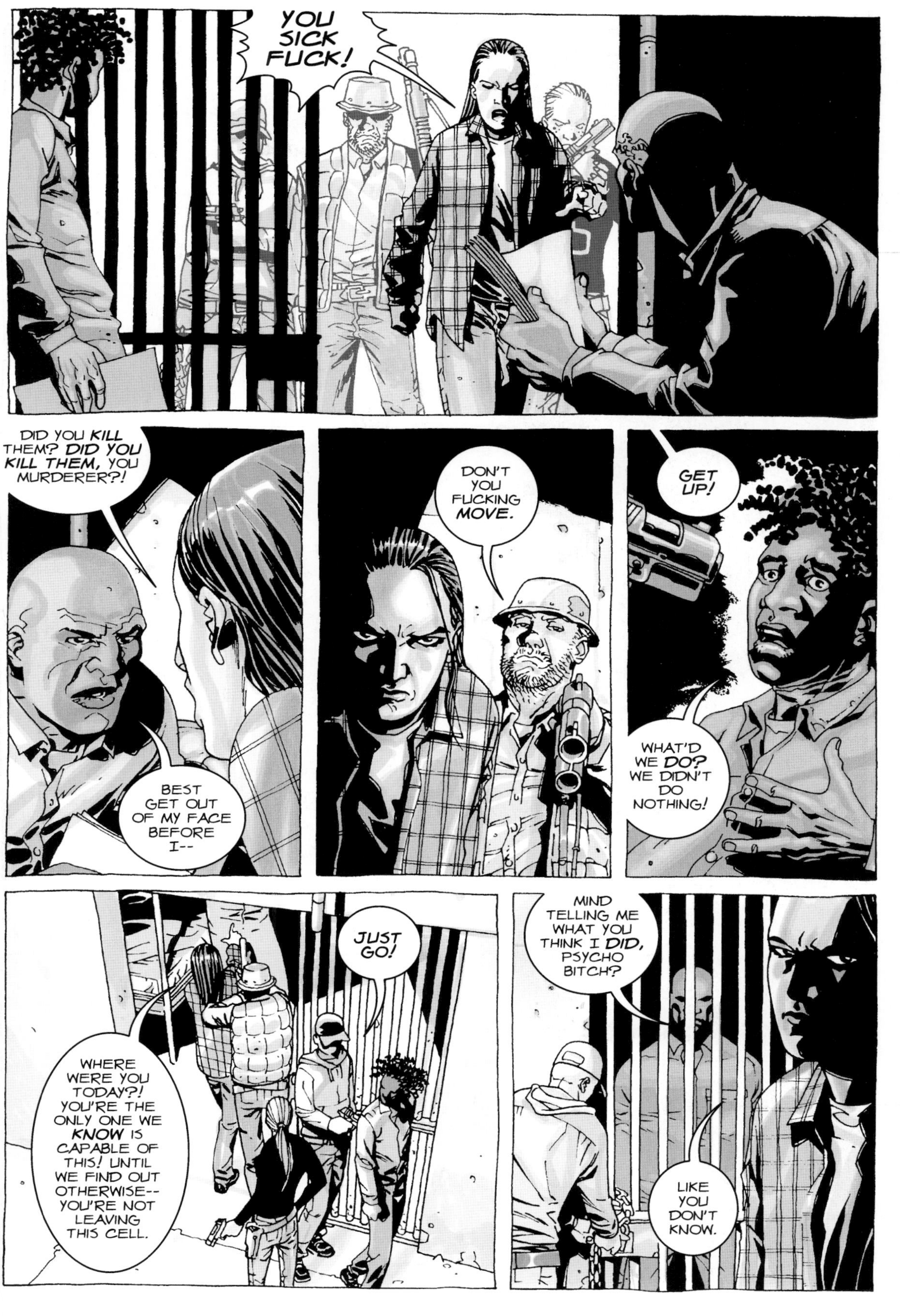
YOU SICK FUCK!
DID YOU KILL THEM? DID YOU KILL THEM, YOU MURDERER?!
BEST GET OUT OF MY FACE BEFORE I--
DON'T YOU FUCKING MOVE.
GET UP!
WHAT'D WE DO? WE DIDN'T DO NOTHING!
JUST GO!
WHERE WERE YOU TODAY?! YOU'RE THE ONLY ONE WE KNOW IS CAPABLE OF THIS! UNTIL WE FIND OUT OTHERWISE-- YOU'RE NOT LEAVING THIS CELL.
MIND TELLING ME WHAT YOU THINK I DID, PSYCHO BITCH?
LIKE YOU DON'T KNOW.

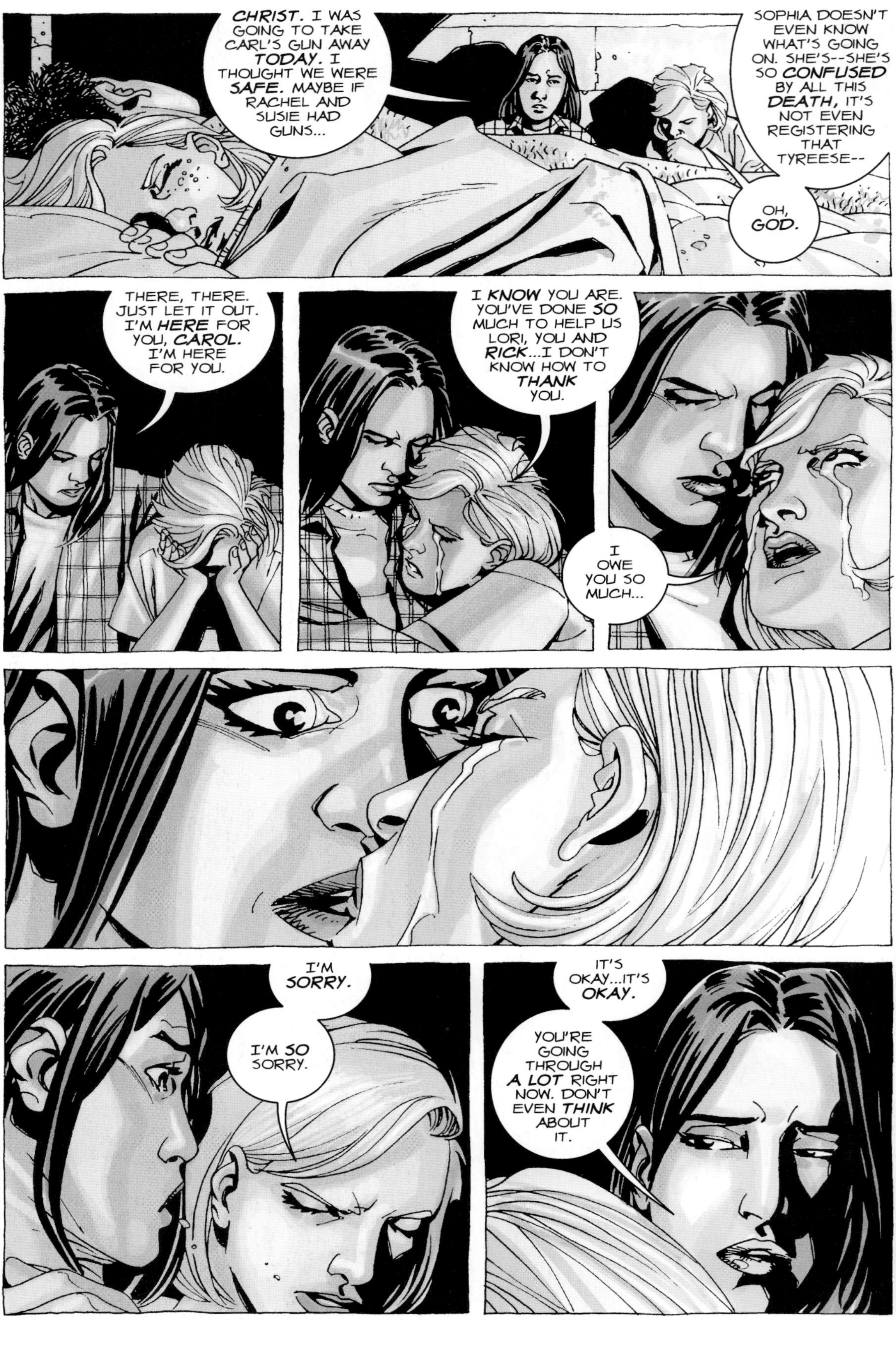
CHRIST. I WAS GOING TO TAKE CARL'S GUN AWAY TODAY. I THOUGHT WE WERE SAFE. MAYBE IF RACHEL AND SUSIE HAD GUNS...
SOPHIA DOESN'T EVEN KNOW WHAT'S GOING ON. SHE'S--SHE'S SO CONFUSED BY ALL THIS DEATH, IT'S NOT EVEN REGISTERING THAT TYREESE--
OH, GOD.
THERE, THERE. JUST LET IT OUT. I'M HERE FOR YOU, CAROL. I'M HERE FOR YOU.
I KNOW YOU ARE. YOU'VE DONE SO MUCH TO HELP US LORI, YOU AND RICK...I DON'T KNOW HOW TO THANK YOU.
I OWE YOU SO MUCH...
I'M SORRY.
I'M SO SORRY.
IT'S OKAY...IT'S OKAY.
YOU'RE GOING THROUGH A LOT RIGHT NOW. DON'T EVEN THINK ABOUT IT.

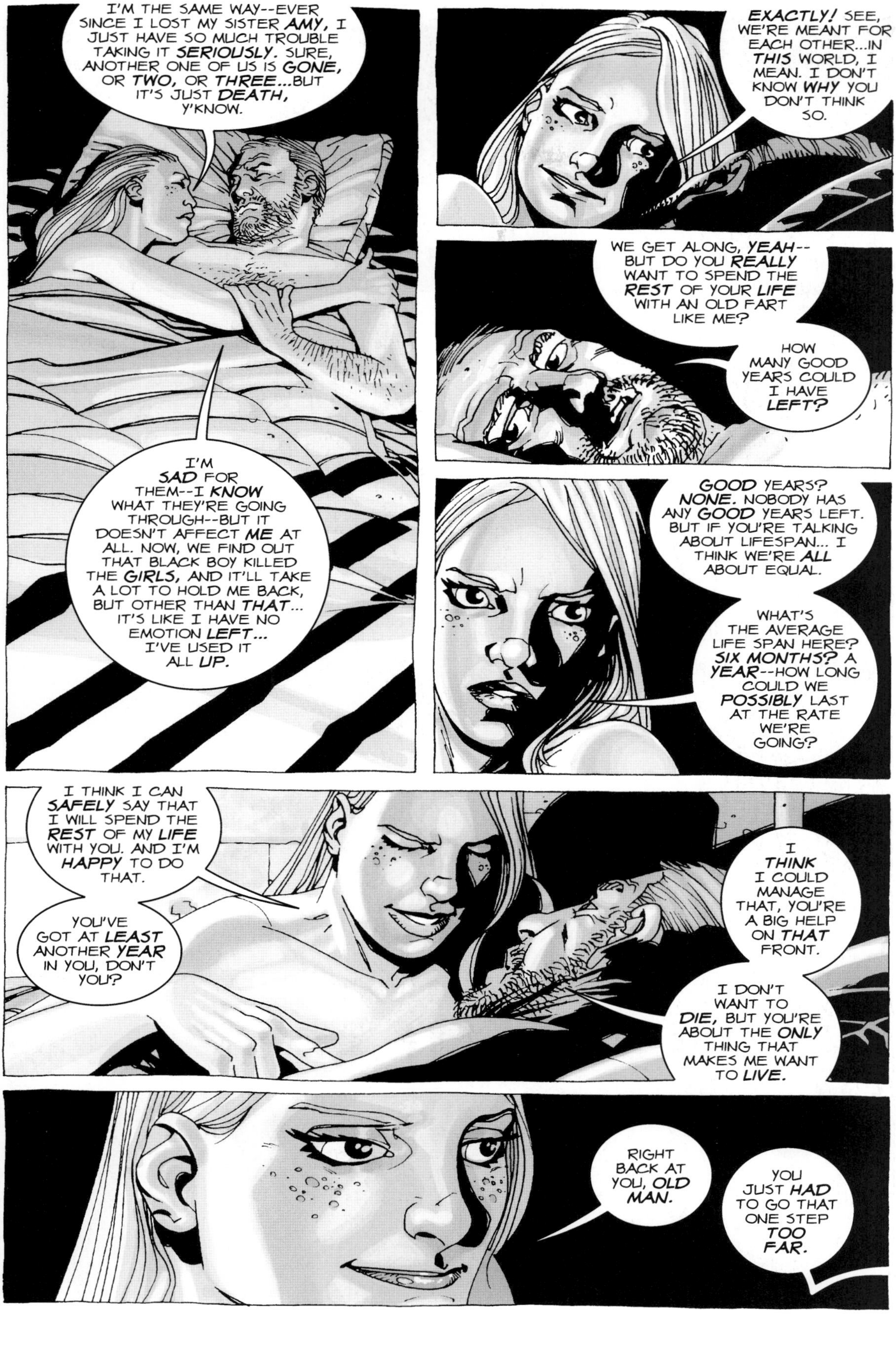
I'M THE SAME WAY--EVER SINCE I LOST MY SISTER AMY, I JUST HAVE SO MUCH TROUBLE TAKING IT SERIOUSLY. SURE, ANOTHER ONE OF US IS GONE, OR TWO, OR THREE...BUT IT'S JUST DEATH, Y'KNOW.
I'M SAD FOR THEM--I KNOW WHAT THEY'RE GOING THROUGH--BUT IT DOESN'T AFFECT ME AT ALL. NOW, WE FIND OUT THAT BLACK BOY KILLED THE GIRLS, AND IT'LL TAKE A LOT TO HOLD ME BACK, BUT OTHER THAN THAT... IT'S LIKE I HAVE NO EMOTION LEFT... I'VE USED IT ALL UP.
EXACTLY! SEE, WE'RE MEANT FOR EACH OTHER...IN THIS WORLD, I MEAN. I DON'T KNOW WHY YOU DON'T THINK SO.
WE GET ALONG, YEAH--BUT DO YOU REALLY WANT TO SPEND THE REST OF YOUR LIFE WITH AN OLD FART LIKE ME?
HOW MANY GOOD YEARS COULD I HAVE LEFT?
GOOD YEARS? NONE. NOBODY HAS ANY GOOD YEARS LEFT. BUT IF YOU'RE TALKING ABOUT LIFESPAN... I THINK WE'RE ALL ABOUT EQUAL.
WHAT'S THE AVERAGE LIFE SPAN HERE? SIX MONTHS? A YEAR--HOW LONG COULD WE POSSIBLY LAST AT THE RATE WE'RE GOING?
I THINK I CAN SAFELY SAY THAT I WILL SPEND THE REST OF MY LIFE WITH YOU. AND I'M HAPPY TO DO THAT.
YOU'VE GOT AT LEAST ANOTHER YEAR IN YOU, DON'T YOU?
I THINK I COULD MANAGE THAT, YOU'RE A BIG HELP ON THAT FRONT.
I DON'T WANT TO DIE, BUT YOU'RE ABOUT THE ONLY THING THAT MAKES ME WANT TO LIVE.
RIGHT BACK AT YOU, OLD MAN.
YOU JUST HAD TO GO THAT ONE STEP TOO FAR.

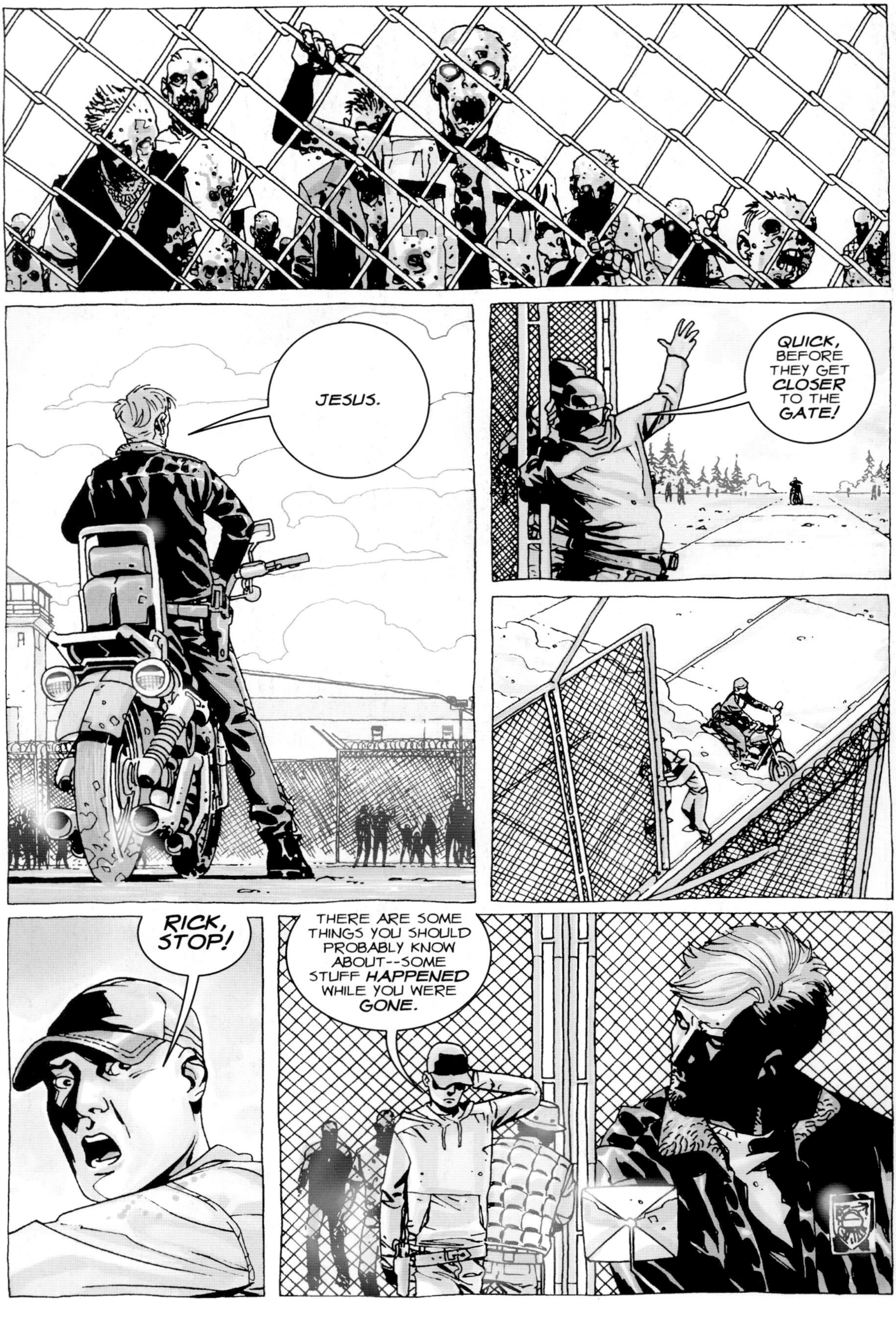
JESUS.
QUICK, BEFORE THEY GET CLOSER TO THE GATE!
RICK, STOP!
THERE ARE SOME THINGS YOU SHOULD PROBABLY KNOW ABOUT--SOME STUFF HAPPENED WHILE YOU WERE GONE.

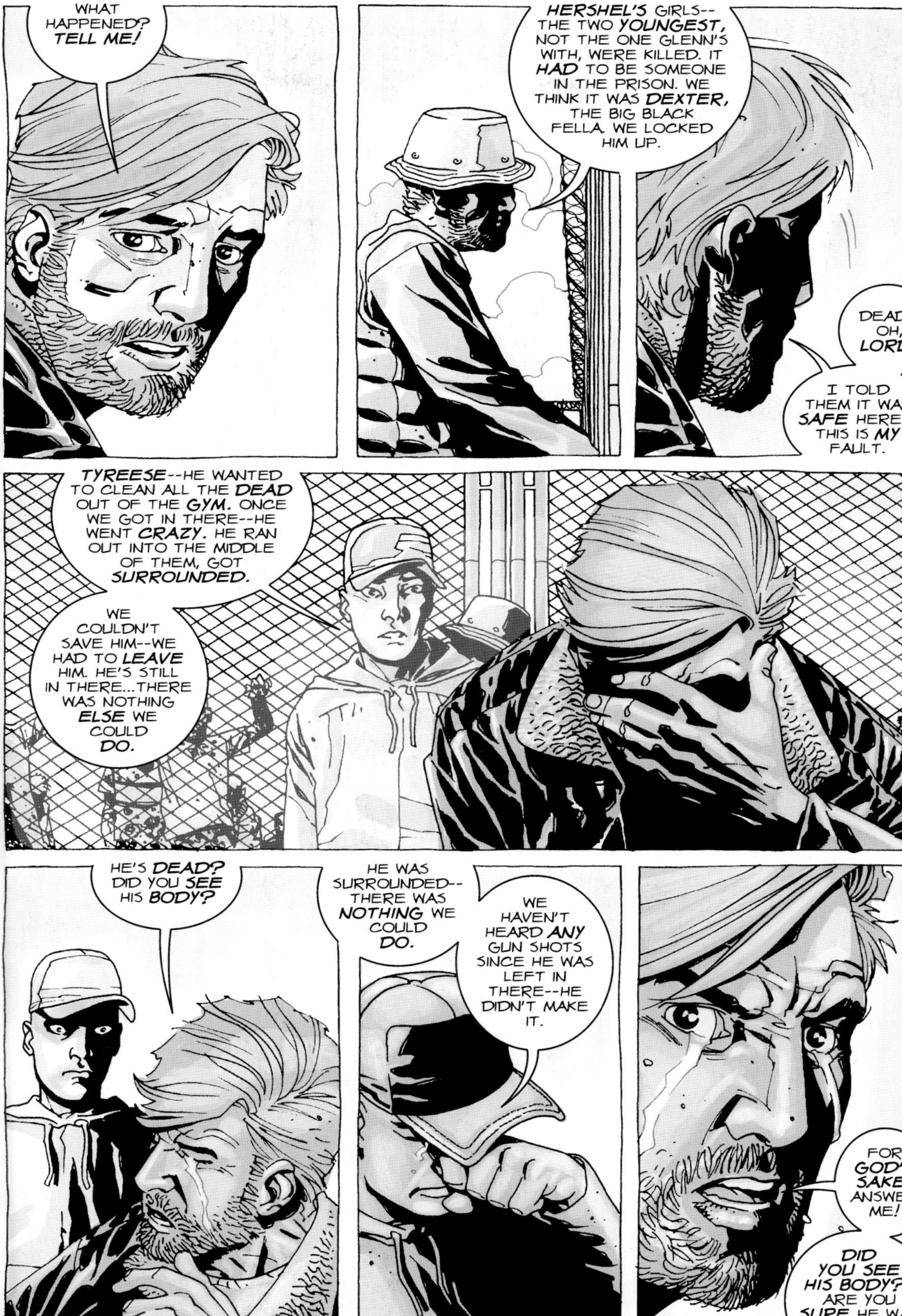
WHAT HAPPENED? TELL ME!
HERSHEL'S GIRLS-- THE TWO YOUNGEST, NOT THE ONE GLENN'S WITH, WERE KILLED. IT HAD TO BE SOMEONE IN THE PRISON. WE THINK IT WAS DEXTER, THE BIG BLACK FELLA WE LOCKED HIM UP.
DEAD? OH, LORD.
I TOLD THEM IT WAS SAFE HERE-- THIS IS MY FAULT.
TYREESE--HE WANTED TO CLEAN ALL THE DEAD OUT OF THE GYM. ONCE WE GOT IN THERE--HE WENT CRAZY. HE RAN OUT INTO THE MIDDLE OF THEM, GOT SURROUNDED.
WE COULDN'T SAVE HIM--WE HAD TO LEAVE HIM. HE'S STILL IN THERE...THERE WAS NOTHING ELSE WE COULD DO.
HE'S DEAD? DID YOU SEE HIS BODY?
HE WAS SURROUNDED-- THERE WAS NOTHING WE COULD DO.
WE HAVEN'T HEARD ANY GUN SHOTS SINCE HE WAS LEFT IN THERE--HE DIDN'T MAKE IT.
FOR GOD'S SAKE, ANSWER ME!
DID YOU SEE HIS BODY?! ARE YOU SURE HE WAS KILLED?!

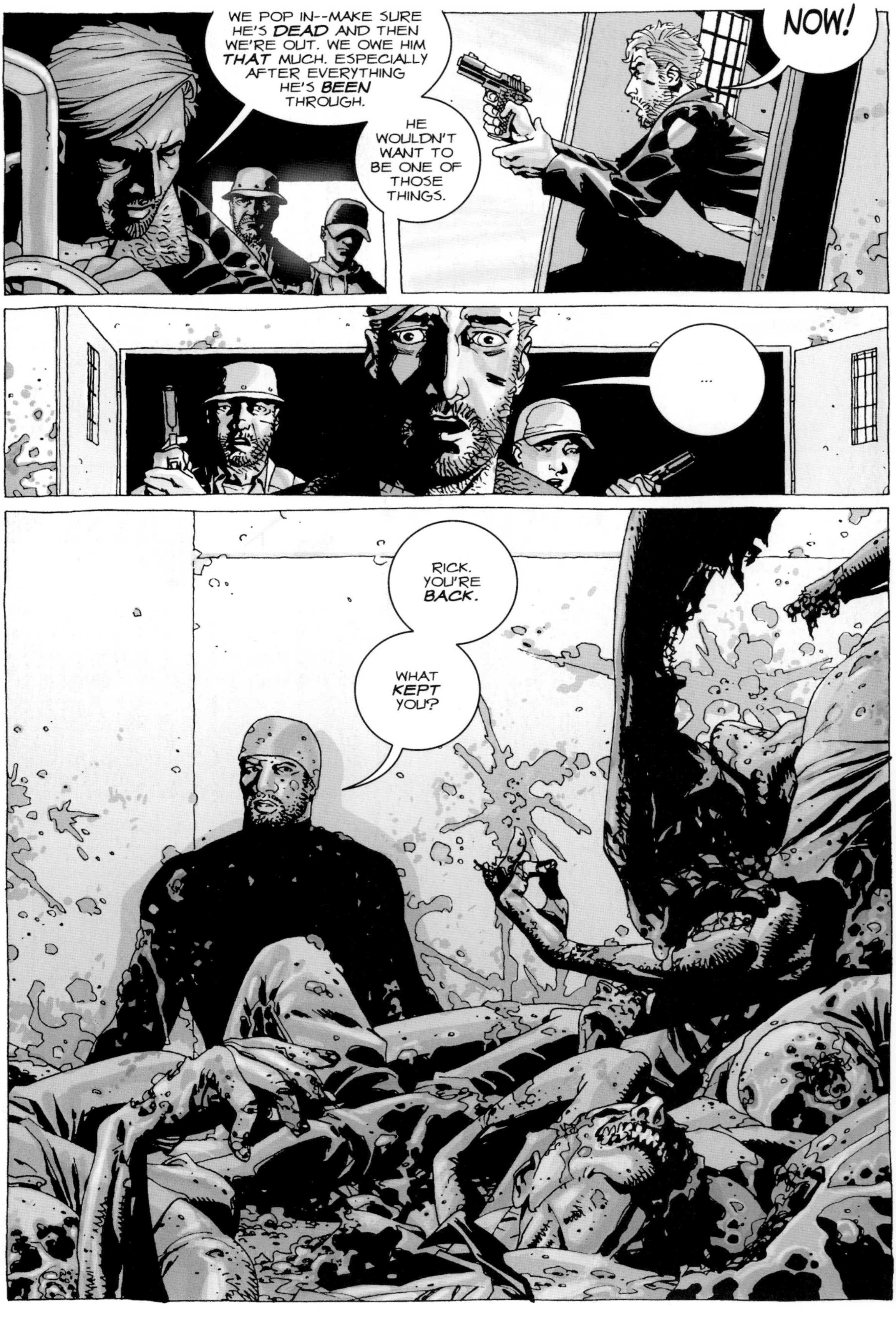
WE POP IN--MAKE SURE HE'S DEAD AND THEN WE'RE OUT. WE OWE HIM THAT MUCH. ESPECIALLY AFTER EVERYTHING HE'S BEEN THROUGH.
HE WOULDN'T WANT TO BE ONE OF THOSE THINGS.
NOW!
...
RICK. YOU'RE BACK.
WHAT KEPT YOU?

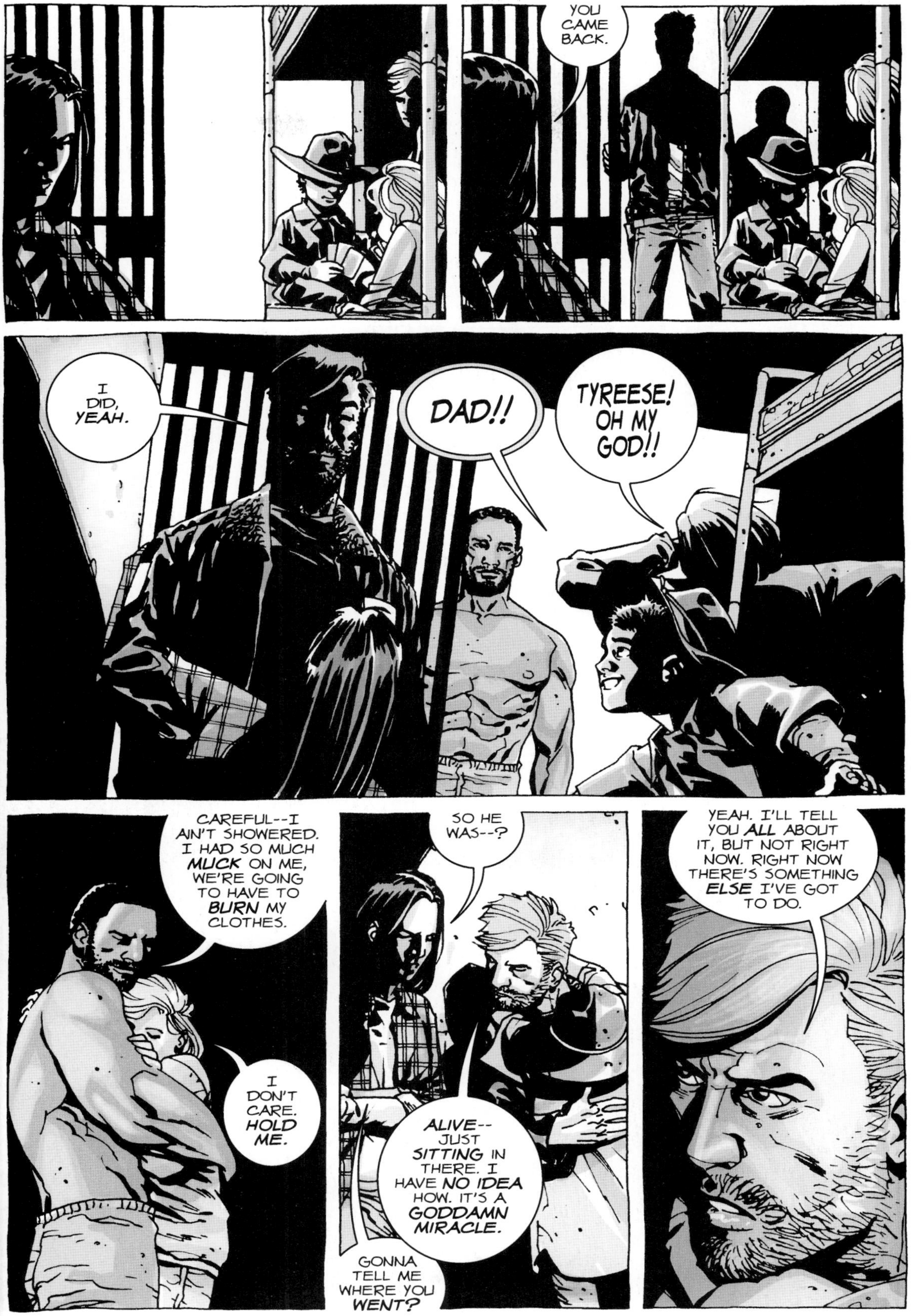
YOU CAME BACK.
I DID, YEAH.
DAD!!
TYREESE! OH MY GOD!!
CAREFUL--I AIN'T SHOWERED. I HAD SO MUCH MUCK ON ME, WE'RE GOING TO HAVE TO BURN MY CLOTHES.
I DON'T CARE. HOLD ME.
SO HE WAS--?
ALIVE--JUST SITTING IN THERE. I HAVE NO IDEA HOW. IT'S A GODDAMN MIRACLE.
GONNA TELL ME WHERE YOU WENT?
YEAH. I'LL TELL YOU ALL ABOUT IT, BUT NOT RIGHT NOW. RIGHT NOW THERE'S SOMETHING ELSE I'VE GOT TO DO.

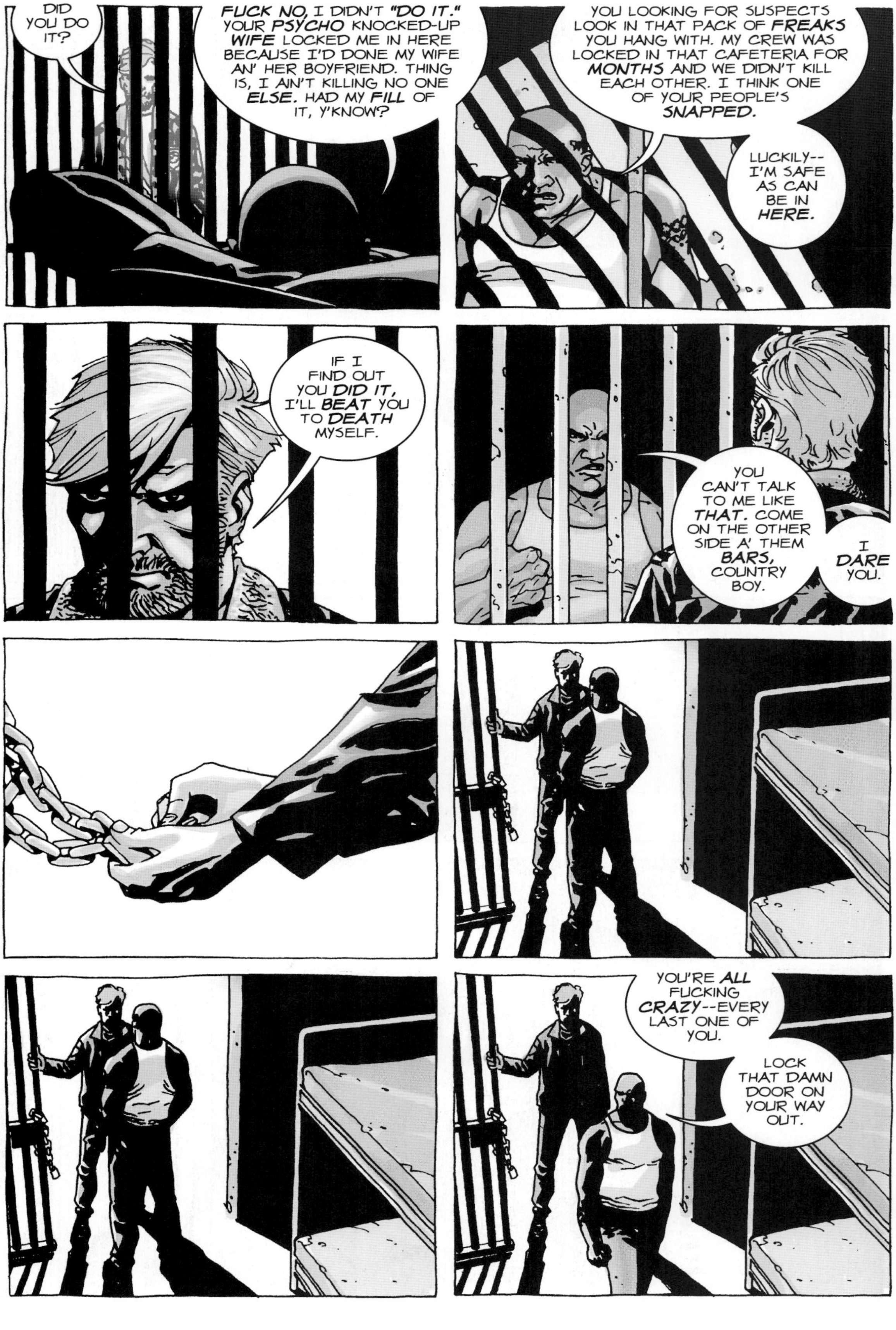
DID YOU DO IT?
FUCK NO, I DIDN'T "DO IT." YOUR PSYCHO KNOCKED-UP WIFE LOCKED ME IN HERE BECAUSE I'D DONE MY WIFE AN' HER BOYFRIEND. THING IS, I AIN'T KILLING NO ONE ELSE. HAD MY FILL OF IT, Y'KNOW?
YOU LOOKING FOR SUSPECTS LOOK IN THAT PACK OF FREAKS YOU HANG WITH. MY CREW WAS LOCKED IN THAT CAFETERIA FOR MONTHS AND WE DIDN'T KILL EACH OTHER. I THINK ONE OF YOUR PEOPLE'S SNAPPED.
LUCKILY-- I'M SAFE AS CAN BE IN HERE.
IF I FIND OUT YOU DID IT, I'LL BEAT YOU TO DEATH MYSELF.
YOU CAN'T TALK TO ME LIKE THAT. COME ON THE OTHER SIDE A' THEM BARS, COUNTRY BOY.
I DARE YOU.
YOU'RE ALL FUCKING CRAZY--EVERY LAST ONE OF YOU.
LOCK THAT DAMN DOOR ON YOUR WAY OUT.

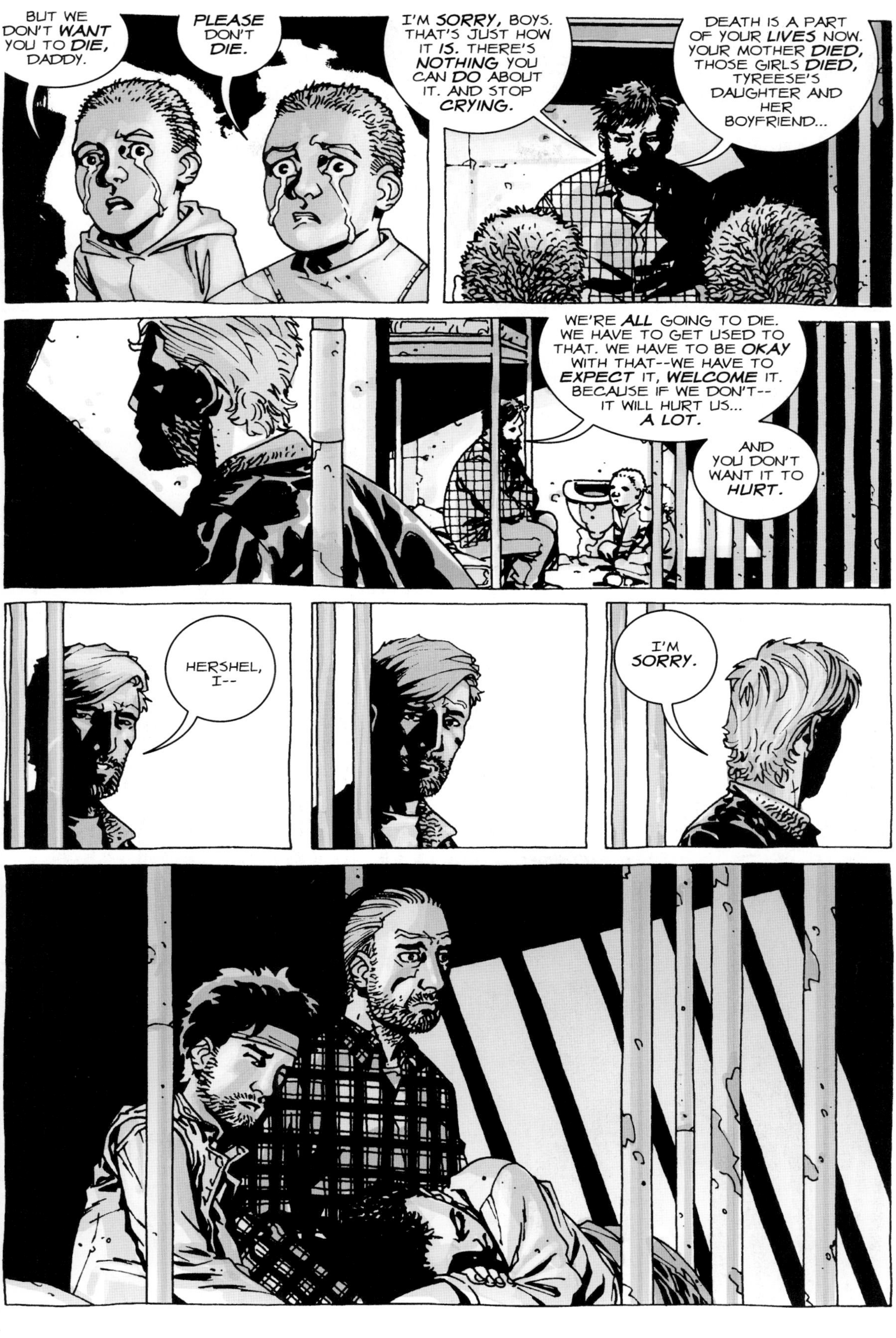
BUT WE DON'T WANT YOU TO DIE, DADDY.
PLEASE DON'T DIE.
I'M SORRY, BOYS. THAT'S JUST HOW IT IS. THERE'S NOTHING YOU CAN DO ABOUT IT. AND STOP CRYING.
DEATH IS A PART OF YOUR LIVES NOW. YOUR MOTHER DIED, THOSE GIRLS DIED, TYREESE'S DAUGHTER AND HER BOYFRIEND...
WE'RE ALL GOING TO DIE. WE HAVE TO GET USED TO THAT. WE HAVE TO BE OKAY WITH THAT--WE HAVE TO EXPECT IT, WELCOME IT. BECAUSE IF WE DON'T-- IT WILL HURT US... A LOT.
AND YOU DON'T WANT IT TO HURT.
HERSHEL, I--
I'M SORRY.

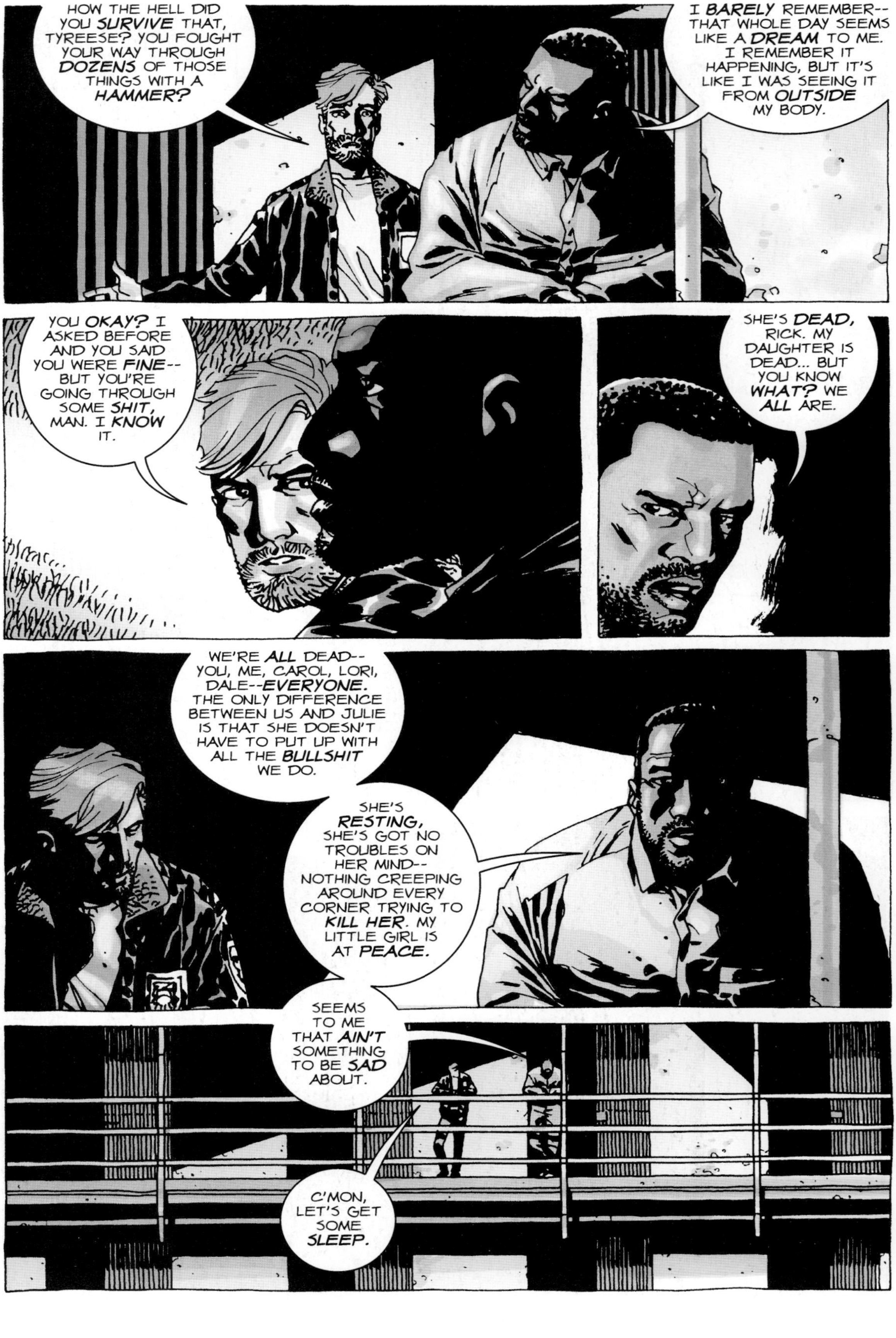
HOW THE HELL DID YOU SURVIVE THAT, TYREESE? YOU FOUGHT YOUR WAY THROUGH DOZENS OF THOSE THINGS WITH A HAMMER?
I BARELY REMEMBER-- THAT WHOLE DAY SEEMS LIKE A DREAM TO ME. I REMEMBER IT HAPPENING, BUT IT'S LIKE I WAS SEEING IT FROM OUTSIDE MY BODY.
YOU OKAY? I ASKED BEFORE AND YOU SAID YOU WERE FINE-- BUT YOU'RE GOING THROUGH SOME SHIT, MAN. I KNOW IT.
SHE'S DEAD, RICK. MY DAUGHTER IS DEAD... BUT YOU KNOW WHAT? WE ALL ARE.
WE'RE ALL DEAD-- YOU, ME, CAROL, LORI, DALE--EVERYONE. THE ONLY DIFFERENCE BETWEEN US AND JULIE IS THAT SHE DOESN'T HAVE TO PUT UP WITH ALL THE BULLSHIT WE DO.
SHE'S RESTING, SHE'S GOT NO TROUBLES ON HER MIND-- NOTHING CREEPING AROUND EVERY CORNER TRYING TO KILL HER. MY LITTLE GIRL IS AT PEACE.
SEEMS TO ME THAT AIN'T SOMETHING TO BE SAD ABOUT.
C'MON, LET'S GET SOME SLEEP.

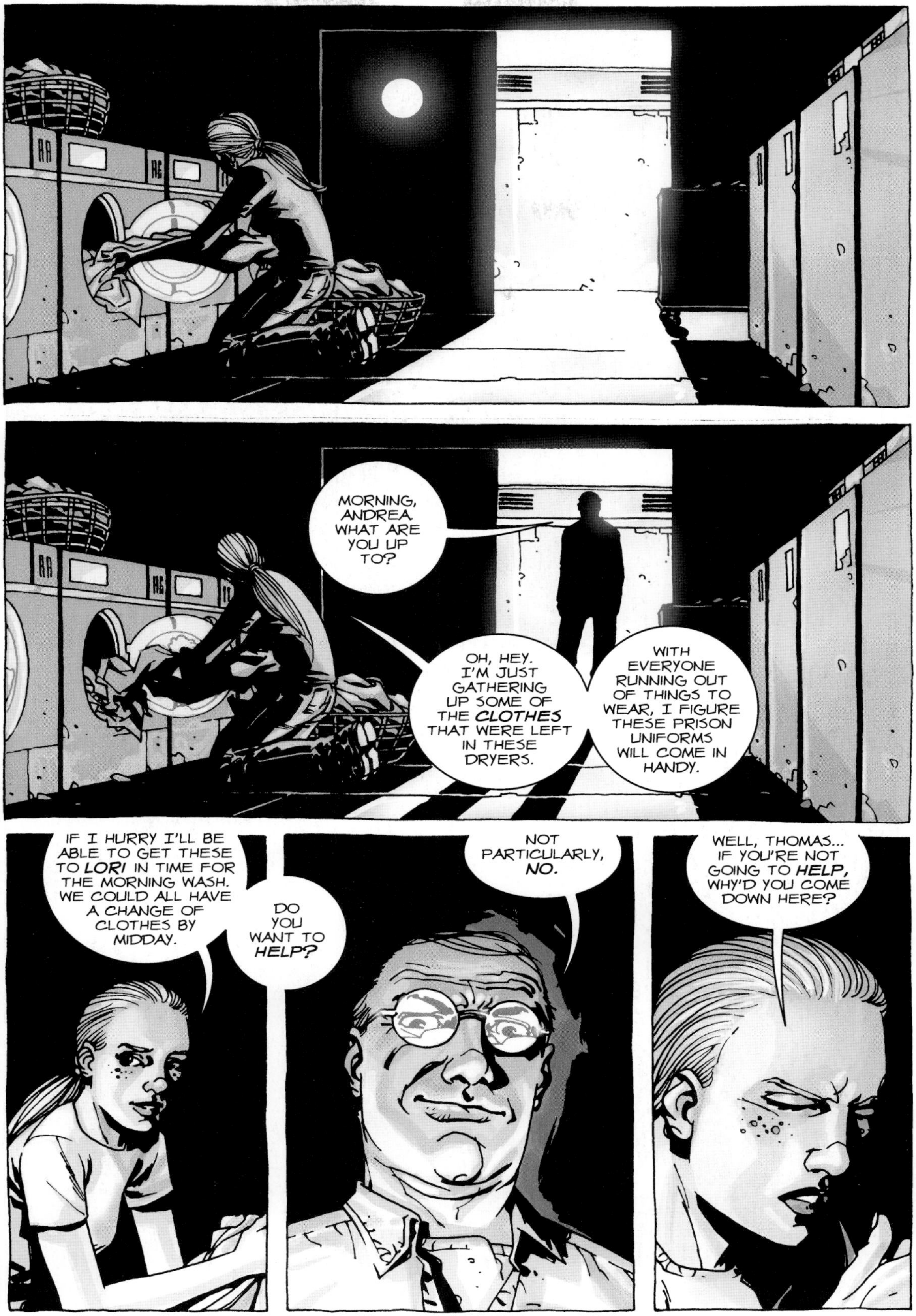
MORNING, ANDREA. WHAT ARE YOU UP TO?
OH, HEY. I'M JUST GATHERING UP SOME OF THE CLOTHES THAT WERE LEFT IN THESE DRYERS.
WITH EVERYONE RUNNING OUT OF THINGS TO WEAR, I FIGURE THESE PRISON UNIFORMS WILL COME IN HANDY.
IF I HURRY I'LL BE ABLE TO GET THESE TO LORI IN TIME FOR THE MORNING WASH. WE COULD ALL HAVE A CHANGE OF CLOTHES BY MIDDAY.
DO YOU WANT TO HELP?
NOT PARTICULARLY, NO.
WELL, THOMAS... IF YOU'RE NOT GOING TO HELP, WHY'D YOU COME DOWN HERE?

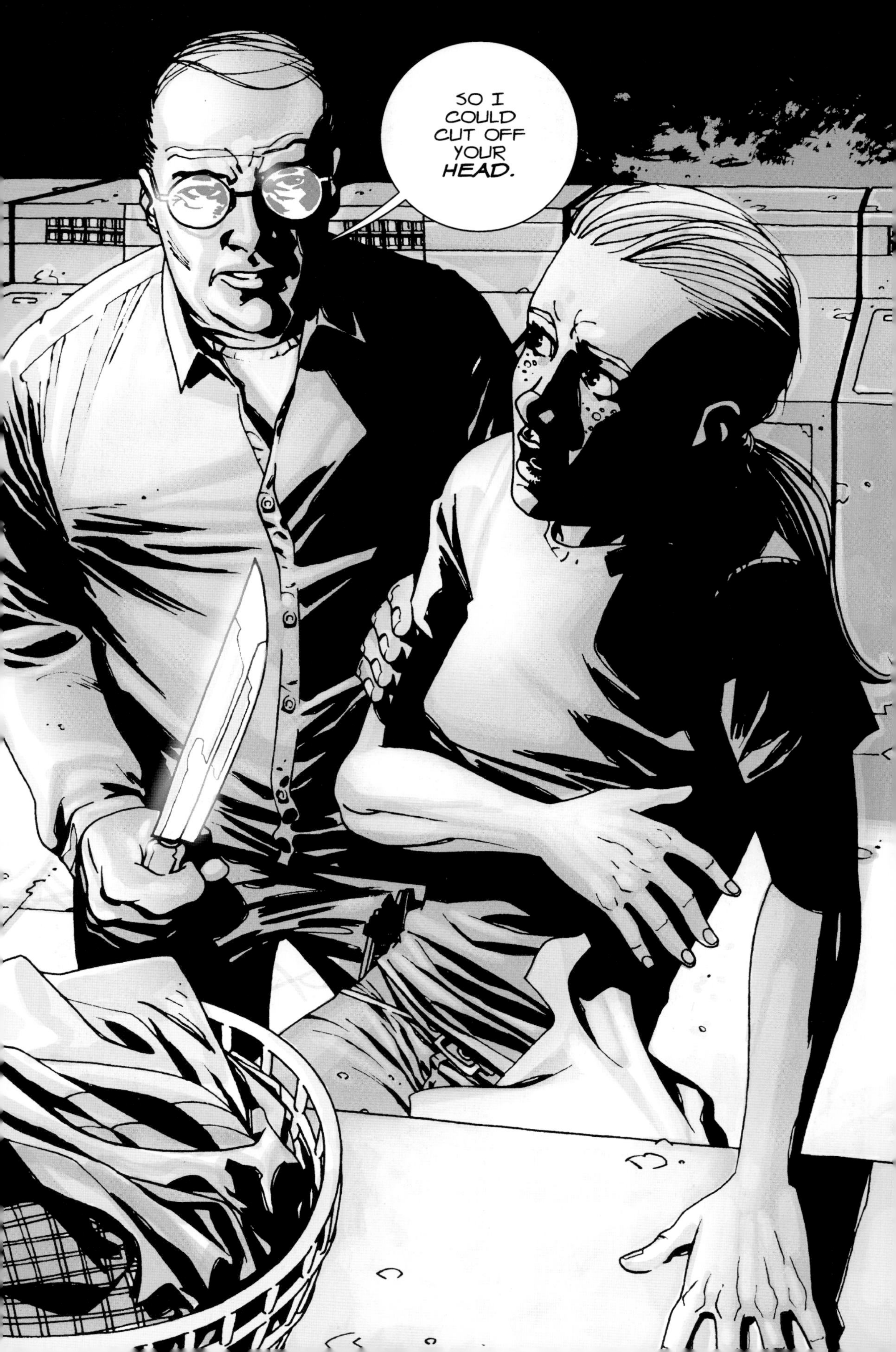
SO I COULD CUT OFF YOUR HEAD.

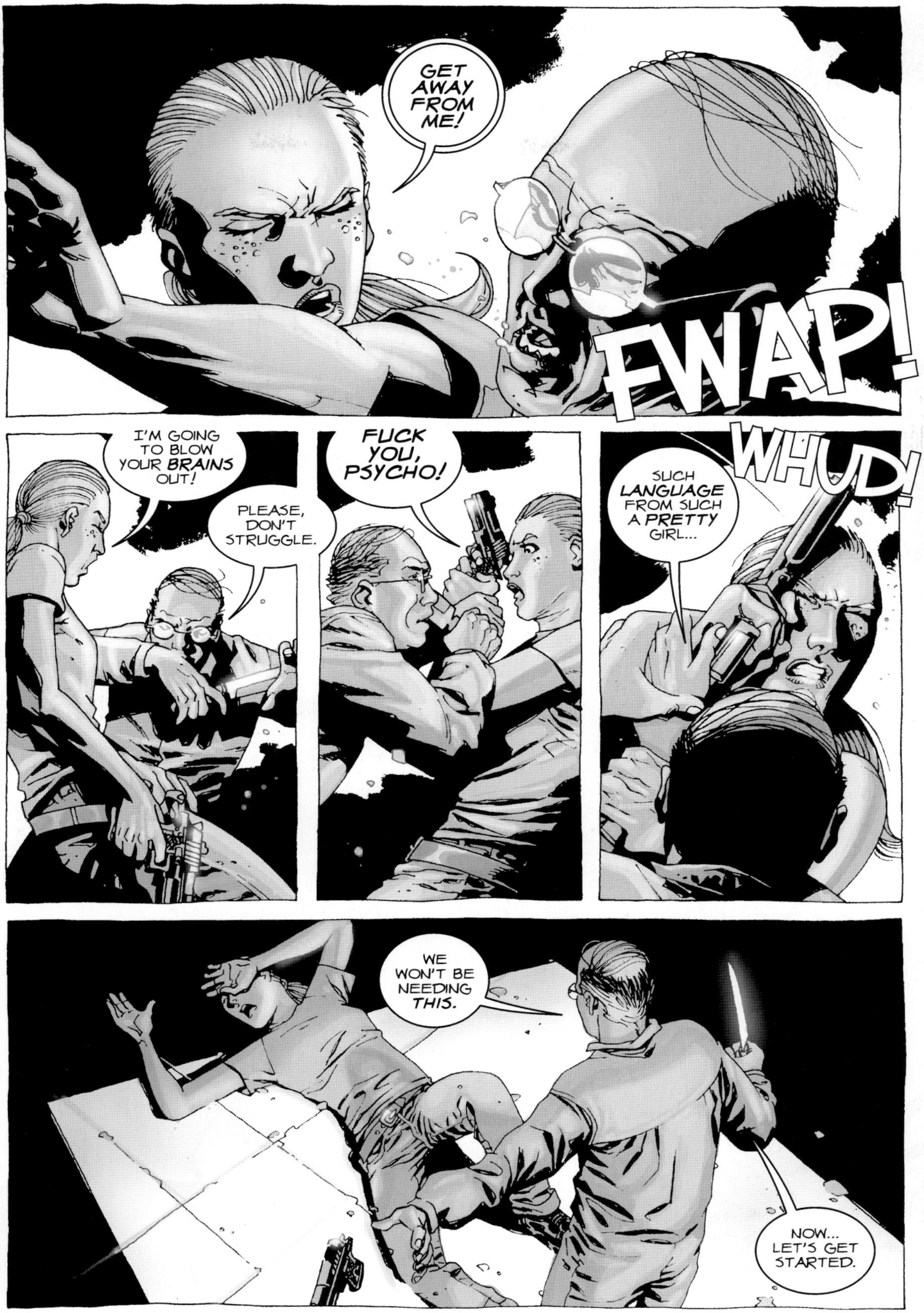
GET AWAY FROM ME!
FWAP!
I'M GOING TO BLOW YOUR BRAINS OUT!
PLEASE, DON'T STRUGGLE.
FUCK YOU, PSYCHO!
WHUD!
SUCH LANGUAGE FROM SUCH A PRETTY GIRL...
WE WON'T BE NEEDING THIS.
NOW... LET'S GET STARTED.

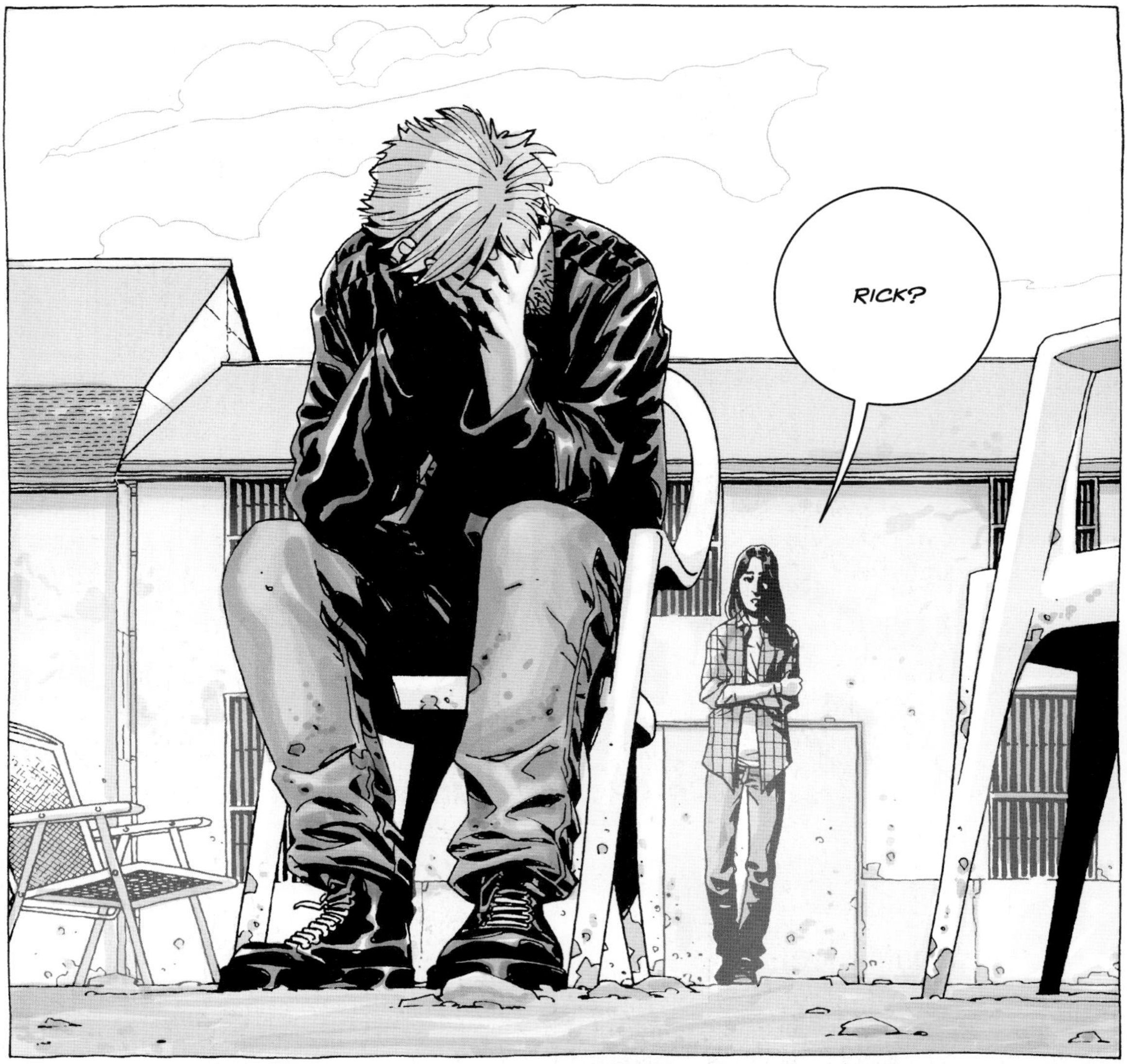
RICK?

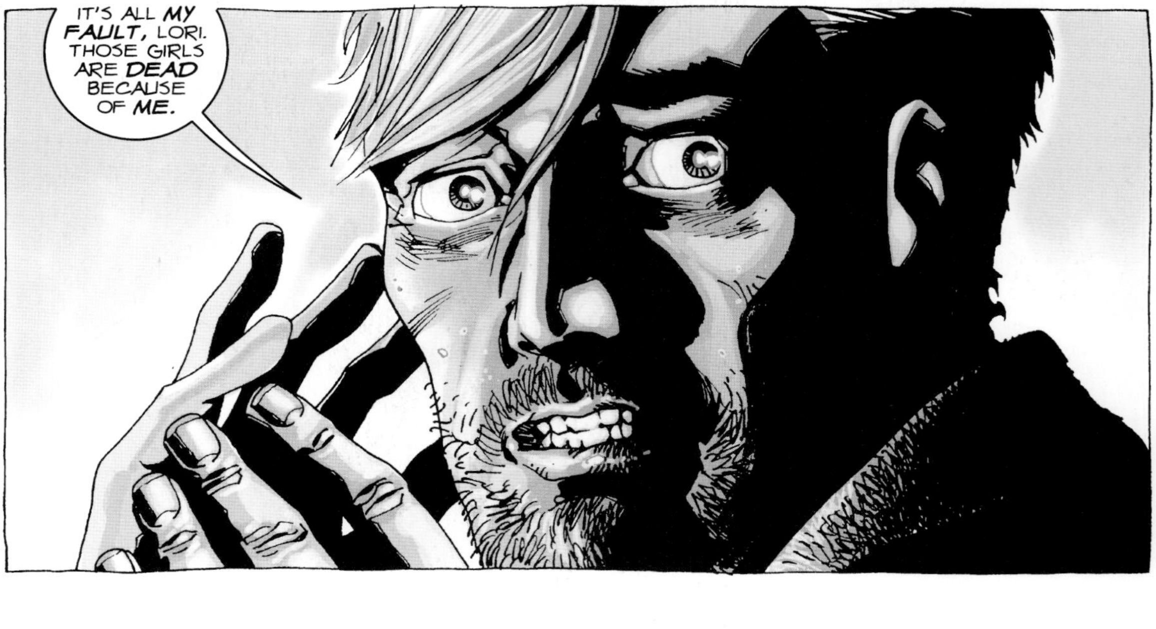
IT'S ALL MY FAULT, LORI. THOSE GIRLS ARE DEAD BECAUSE OF ME.

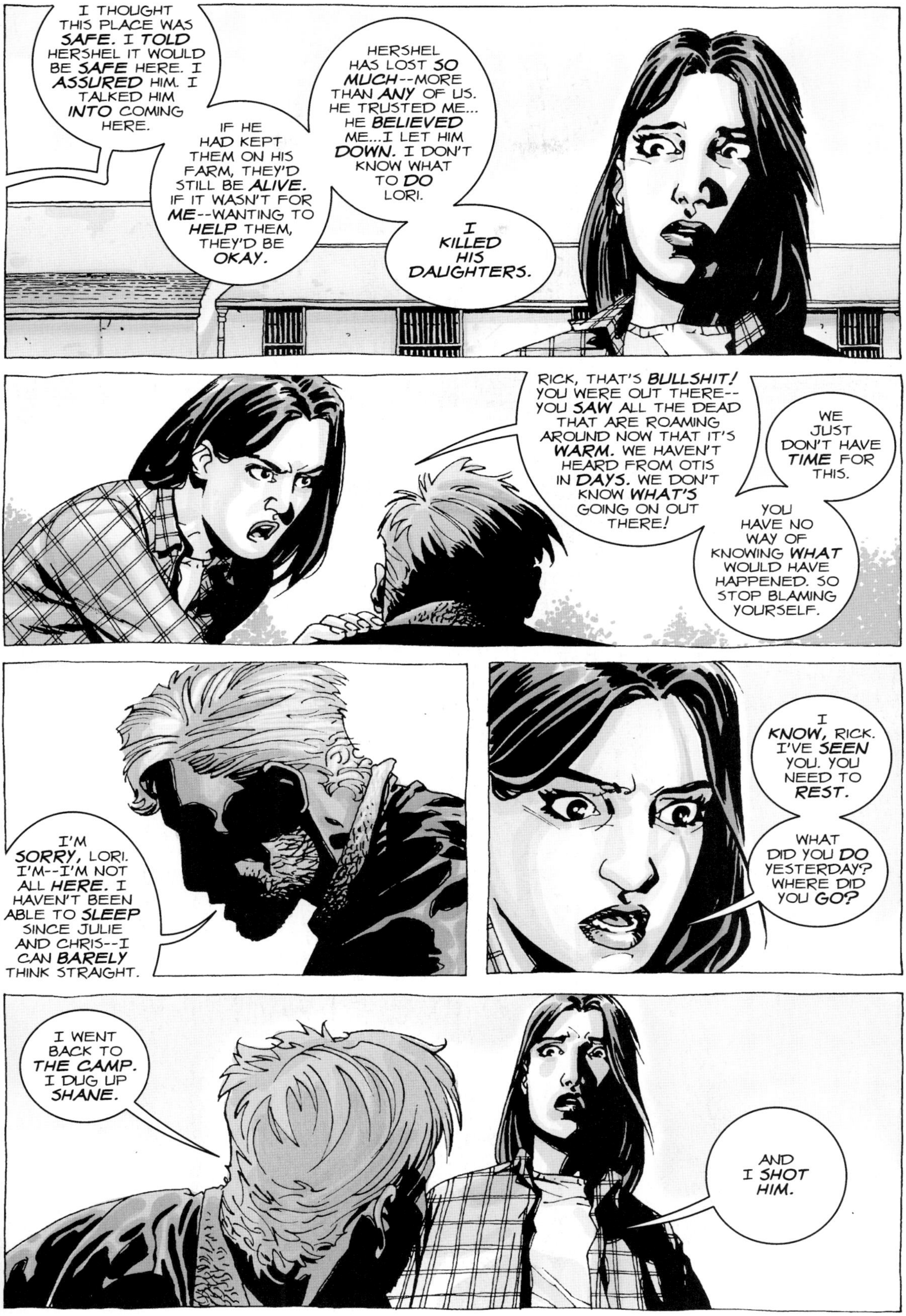
I THOUGHT THIS PLACE WAS SAFE. I TOLD HERSHEL IT WOULD BE SAFE HERE. I ASSURED HIM. I TALKED HIM INTO COMING HERE.
IF HE HAD KEPT THEM ON HIS FARM, THEY'D STILL BE ALIVE. IF IT WASN'T FOR ME--WANTING TO HELP THEM, THEY'D BE OKAY.
HERSHEL HAS LOST SO MUCH--MORE THAN ANY OF US. HE TRUSTED ME... HE BELIEVED ME...I LET HIM DOWN. I DON'T KNOW WHAT TO DO LORI.
I KILLED HIS DAUGHTERS.
RICK, THAT'S BULLSHIT! YOU WERE OUT THERE-- YOU SAW ALL THE DEAD THAT ARE ROAMING AROUND NOW THAT IT'S WARM. WE HAVEN'T HEARD FROM OTIS IN DAYS. WE DON'T KNOW WHAT'S GOING ON OUT THERE!
WE JUST DON'T HAVE TIME FOR THIS.
YOU HAVE NO WAY OF KNOWING WHAT WOULD HAVE HAPPENED. SO STOP BLAMING YOURSELF.
I'M SORRY, LORI. I'M--I'M NOT ALL HERE. I HAVEN'T BEEN ABLE TO SLEEP SINCE JULIE AND CHRIS--I CAN BARELY THINK STRAIGHT.
I KNOW, RICK. I'VE SEEN YOU. YOU NEED TO REST.
WHAT DID YOU DO YESTERDAY? WHERE DID YOU GO?
I WENT BACK TO THE CAMP. I DUG UP SHANE.
AND I SHOT HIM.

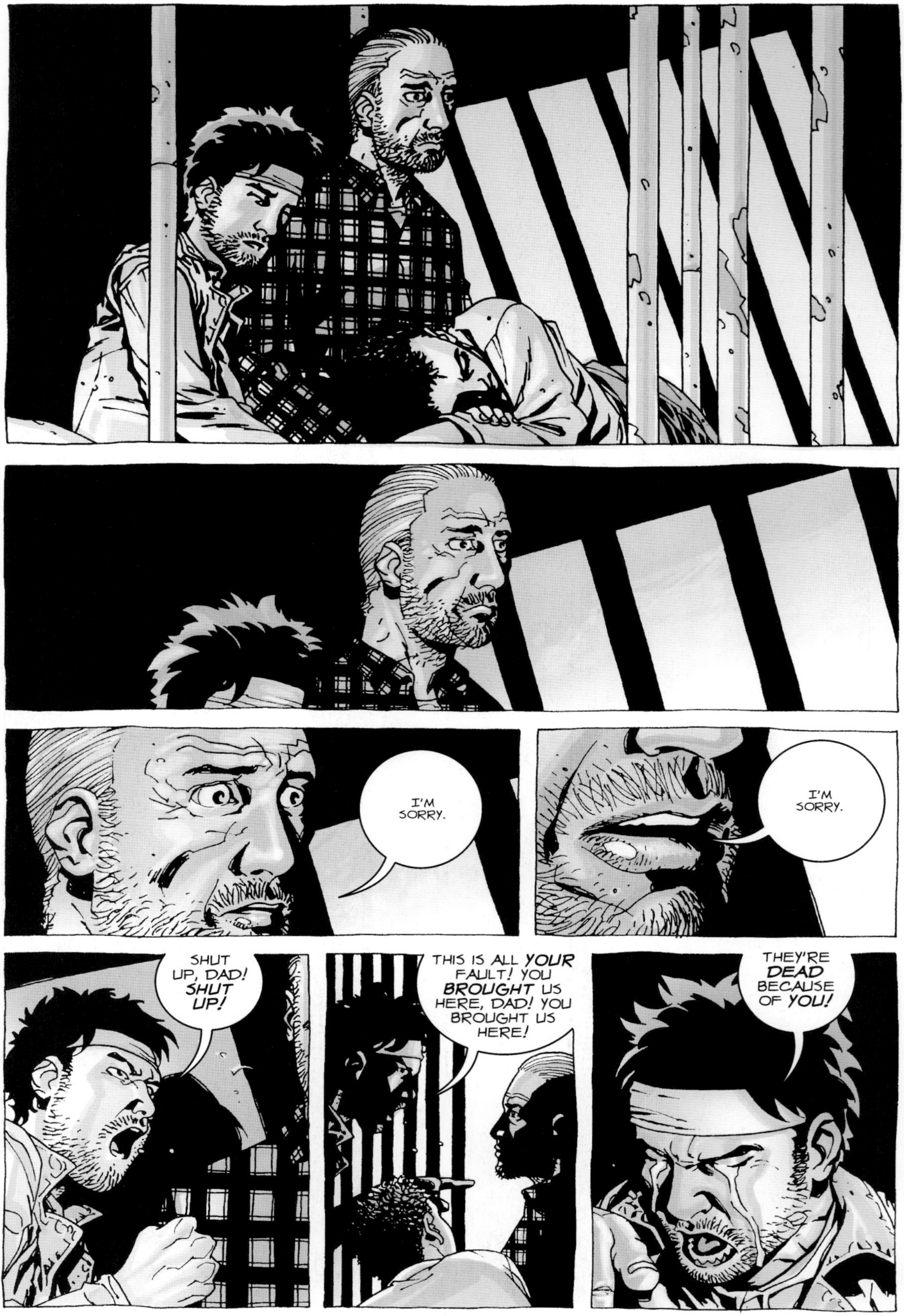
I'M SORRY.
I'M SORRY.
SHUT UP, DAD! SHUT UP!
THIS IS ALL YOUR FAULT! YOU BROUGHT US HERE, DAD! YOU BROUGHT US HERE!
THEY'RE DEAD BECAUSE OF YOU!

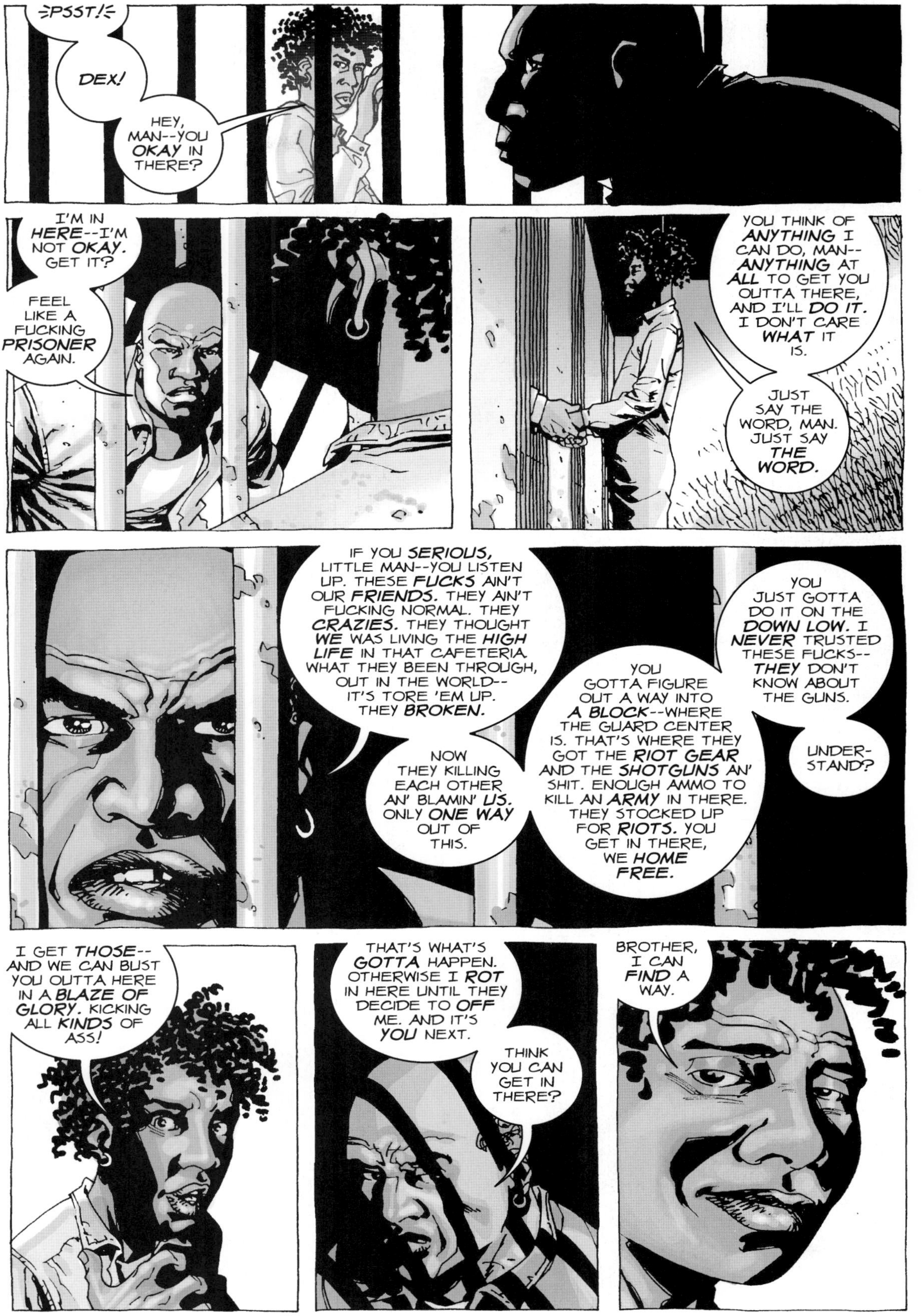
PSST!
DEX!
HEY, MAN--YOU OKAY IN THERE?
I'M IN HERE--I'M NOT OKAY. GET IT?
FEEL LIKE A FUCKING PRISONER AGAIN.
YOU THINK OF ANYTHING I CAN DO, MAN-- ANYTHING AT ALL TO GET YOU OUTTA THERE, AND I'LL DO IT. I DON'T CARE WHAT IT IS.
JUST SAY THE WORD, MAN. JUST SAY THE WORD.
IF YOU SERIOUS, LITTLE MAN--YOU LISTEN UP. THESE FUCKS AIN'T OUR FRIENDS. THEY AIN'T FUCKING NORMAL. THEY CRAZIES. THEY THOUGHT WE WAS LIVING THE HIGH LIFE IN THAT CAFETERIA. WHAT THEY BEEN THROUGH, OUT IN THE WORLD-- IT'S TORE 'EM UP. THEY BROKEN.
NOW THEY KILLING EACH OTHER AN' BLAMIN' US. ONLY ONE WAY OUT OF THIS.
YOU GOTTA FIGURE OUT A WAY INTO A BLOCK--WHERE THE GUARD CENTER IS. THAT'S WHERE THEY GOT THE RIOT GEAR AND THE SHOTGUNS AN' SHIT. ENOUGH AMMO TO KILL AN ARMY IN THERE. THEY STOCKED UP FOR RIOTS. YOU GET IN THERE, WE HOME FREE.
YOU JUST GOTTA DO IT ON THE DOWN LOW. I NEVER TRUSTED THESE FUCKS-- THEY DON'T KNOW ABOUT THE GUNS.
UNDER-STAND?
I GET THOSE-- AND WE CAN BUST YOU OUTTA HERE IN A BLAZE OF GLORY. KICKING ALL KINDS OF ASS!
THAT'S WHAT'S GOTTA HAPPEN. OTHERWISE I ROT IN HERE UNTIL THEY DECIDE TO OFF ME. AND IT'S YOU NEXT.
THINK YOU CAN GET IN THERE?
BROTHER, I CAN FIND A WAY.

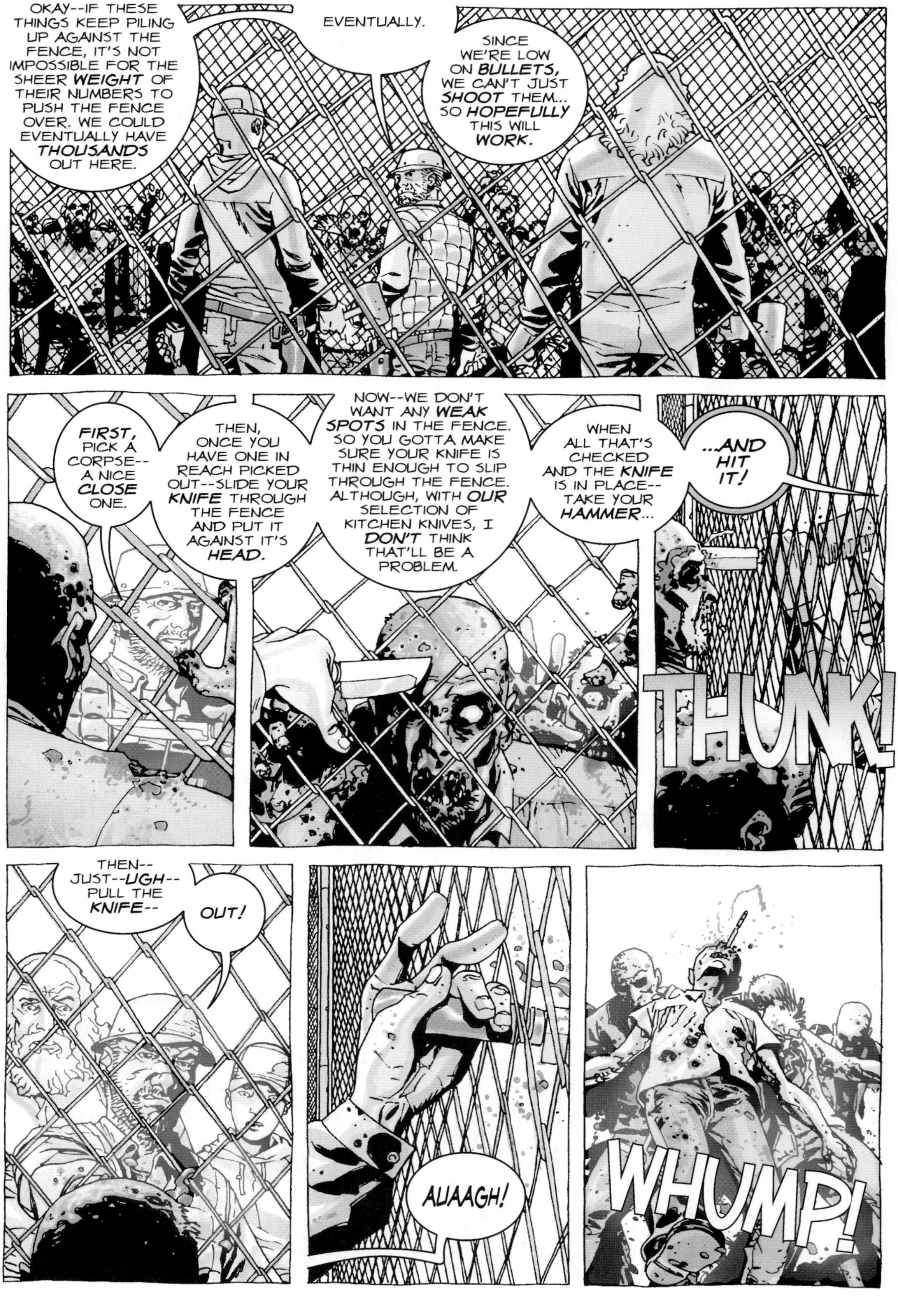
OKAY--IF THESE THINGS KEEP PILING UP AGAINST THE FENCE, IT'S NOT IMPOSSIBLE FOR THE SHEER WEIGHT OF THEIR NUMBERS TO PUSH THE FENCE OVER. WE COULD EVENTUALLY HAVE THOUSANDS OUT HERE.
EVENTUALLY.
SINCE WE'RE LOW ON BULLETS, WE CAN'T JUST SHOOT THEM... SO HOPEFULLY THIS WILL WORK.
FIRST, PICK A CORPSE--A NICE CLOSE ONE.
THEN, ONCE YOU HAVE ONE IN REACH PICKED OUT--SLIDE YOUR KNIFE THROUGH THE FENCE AND PUT IT AGAINST IT'S HEAD.
NOW--WE DON'T WANT ANY WEAK SPOTS IN THE FENCE. SO YOU GOTTA MAKE SURE YOUR KNIFE IS THIN ENOUGH TO SLIP THROUGH THE FENCE. ALTHOUGH, WITH OUR SELECTION OF KITCHEN KNIVES, I DON'T THINK THAT'LL BE A PROBLEM.
WHEN ALL THAT'S CHECKED AND THE KNIFE IS IN PLACE--TAKE YOUR HAMMER...
...AND HIT IT!
THUNK!
THEN--JUST--UGH--PULL THE KNIFE--
OUT!
AUAAGH!
WHUMP!

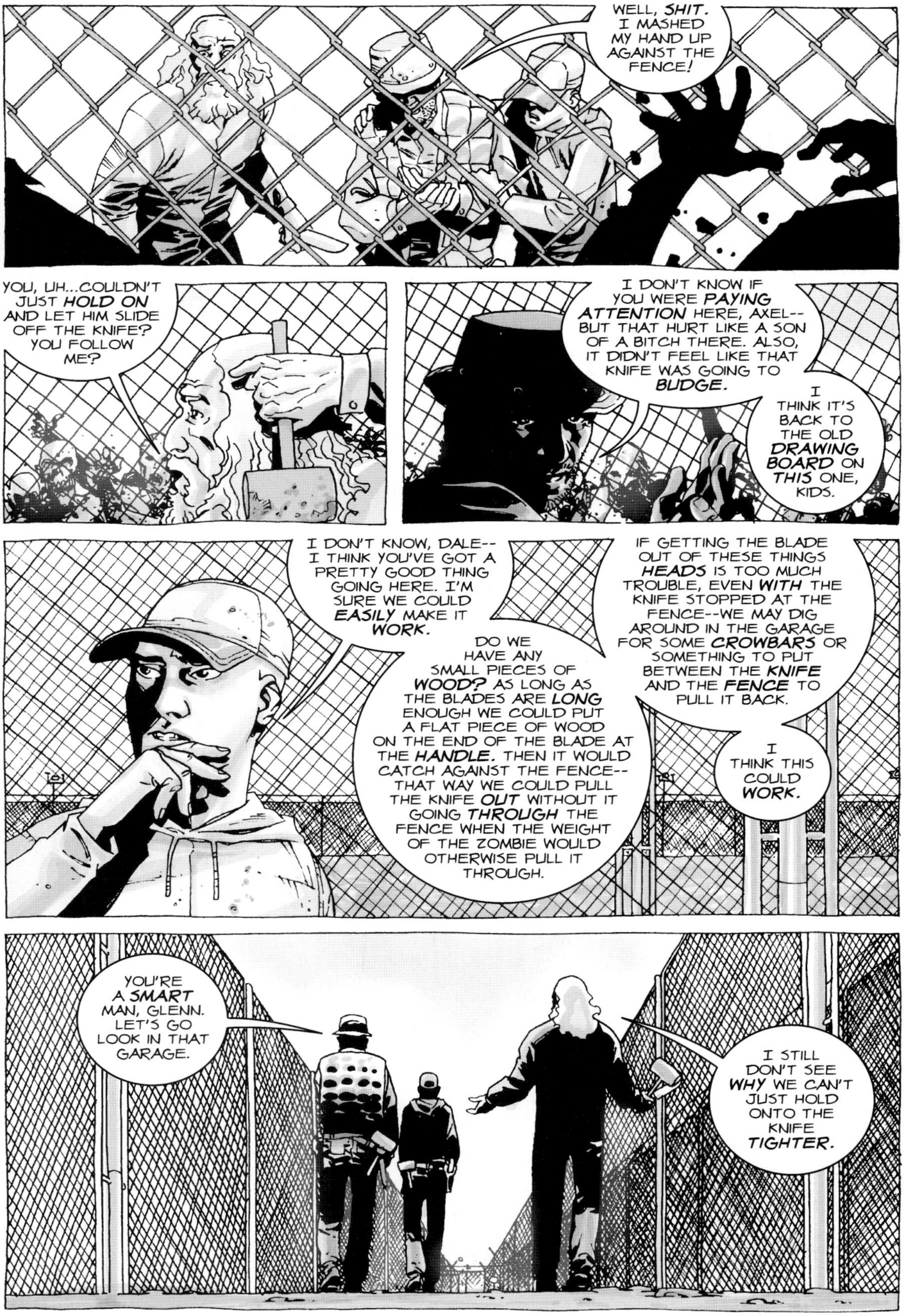

WELL, SHIT. I MASHED MY HAND UP AGAINST THE FENCE!
YOU, UH...COULDN'T JUST HOLD ON AND LET HIM SLIDE OFF THE KNIFE? YOU FOLLOW ME?
I DON'T KNOW IF YOU WERE PAYING ATTENTION HERE, AXEL--BUT THAT HURT LIKE A SON OF A BITCH THERE. ALSO, IT DIDN'T FEEL LIKE THAT KNIFE WAS GOING TO BUDGE.
I THINK IT'S BACK TO THE OLD DRAWING BOARD ON THIS ONE, KIDS.
I DON'T KNOW, DALE--I THINK YOU'VE GOT A PRETTY GOOD THING GOING HERE. I'M SURE WE COULD EASILY MAKE IT WORK.
DO WE HAVE ANY SMALL PIECES OF WOOD? AS LONG AS THE BLADES ARE LONG ENOUGH WE COULD PUT A FLAT PIECE OF WOOD ON THE END OF THE BLADE AT THE HANDLE. THEN IT WOULD CATCH AGAINST THE FENCE--THAT WAY WE COULD PULL THE KNIFE OUT WITHOUT IT GOING THROUGH THE FENCE WHEN THE WEIGHT OF THE ZOMBIE WOULD OTHERWISE PULL IT THROUGH.
IF GETTING THE BLADE OUT OF THESE THINGS HEADS IS TOO MUCH TROUBLE, EVEN WITH THE KNIFE STOPPED AT THE FENCE--WE MAY DIG AROUND IN THE GARAGE FOR SOME CROWBARS OR SOMETHING TO PUT BETWEEN THE KNIFE AND THE FENCE TO PULL IT BACK.
I THINK THIS COULD WORK.
YOU'RE A SMART MAN, GLENN. LET'S GO LOOK IN THAT GARAGE.
I STILL DON'T SEE WHY WE CAN'T JUST HOLD ONTO THE KNIFE TIGHTER.

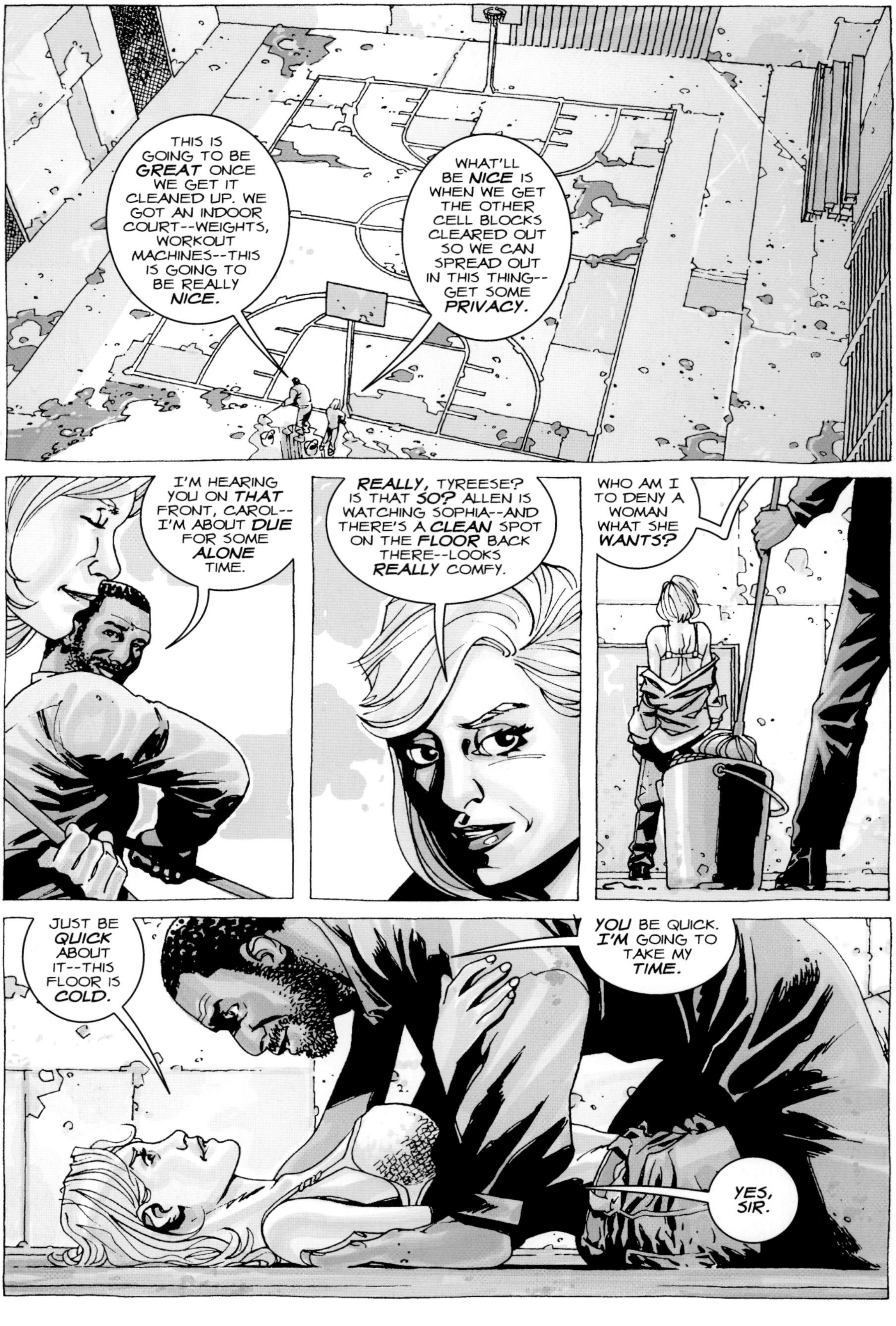
THIS IS GOING TO BE GREAT ONCE WE GET IT CLEANED UP. WE GOT AN INDOOR COURT--WEIGHTS, WORKOUT MACHINES--THIS IS GOING TO BE REALLY NICE.
WHAT'LL BE NICE IS WHEN WE GET THE OTHER CELL BLOCKS CLEARED OUT SO WE CAN SPREAD OUT IN THIS THING--GET SOME PRIVACY.
I'M HEARING YOU ON THAT FRONT, CAROL--I'M ABOUT DUE FOR SOME ALONE TIME.
REALLY, TYREESE? IS THAT SO? ALLEN IS WATCHING SOPHIA--AND THERE'S A CLEAN SPOT ON THE FLOOR BACK THERE--LOOKS REALLY COMFY.
WHO AM I TO DENY A WOMAN WHAT SHE WANTS?
JUST BE QUICK ABOUT IT--THIS FLOOR IS COLD.
YOU BE QUICK. I'M GOING TO TAKE MY TIME.
YES, SIR.

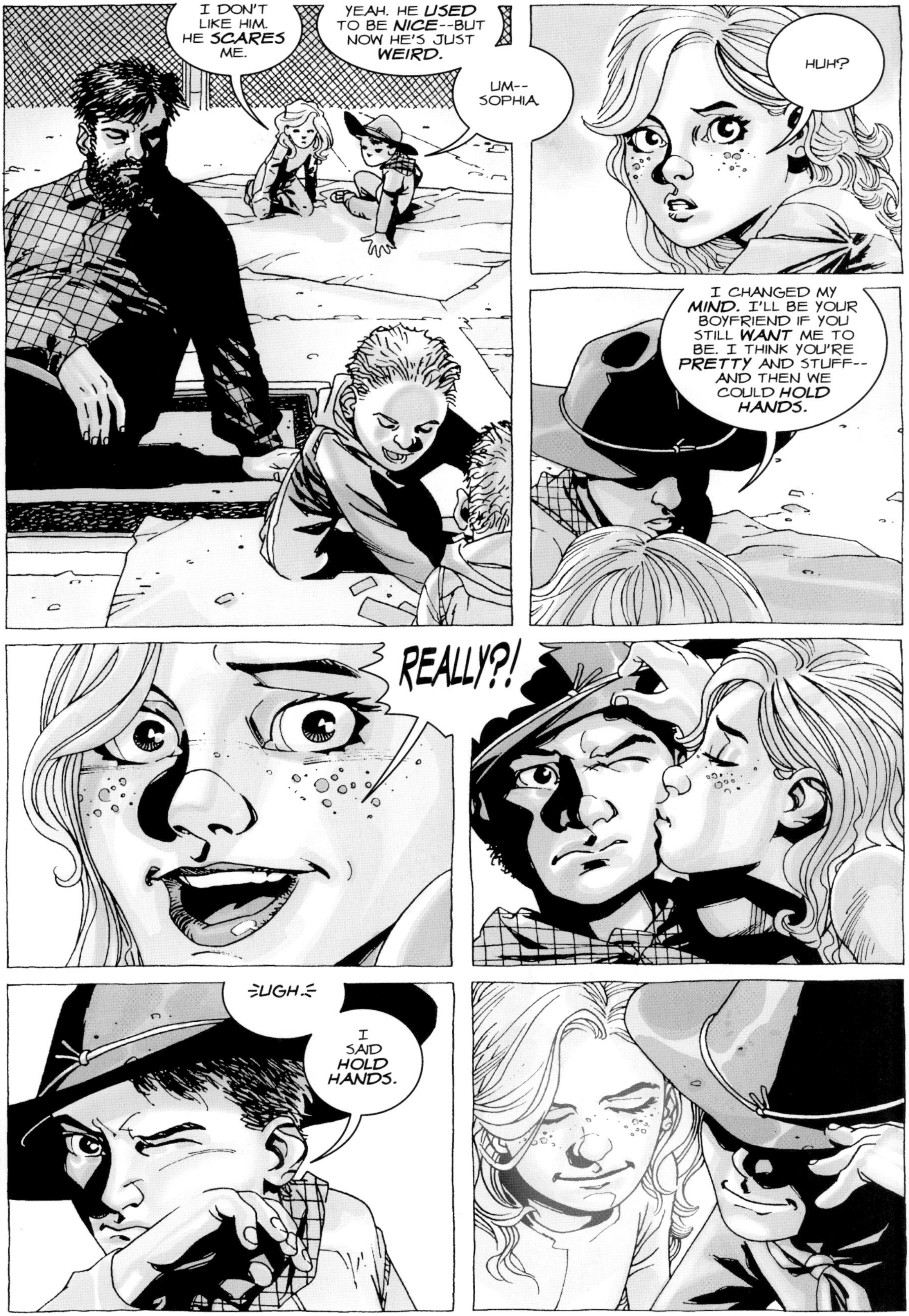
I DON'T LIKE HIM. HE SCARES ME.
YEAH. HE USED TO BE NICE--BUT NOW HE'S JUST WEIRD.
UM-- SOPHIA.
HUH?
I CHANGED MY MIND. I'LL BE YOUR BOYFRIEND IF YOU STILL WANT ME TO BE. I THINK YOU'RE PRETTY AND STUFF-- AND THEN WE COULD HOLD HANDS.
REALLY?!
UGH.
I SAID HOLD HANDS.

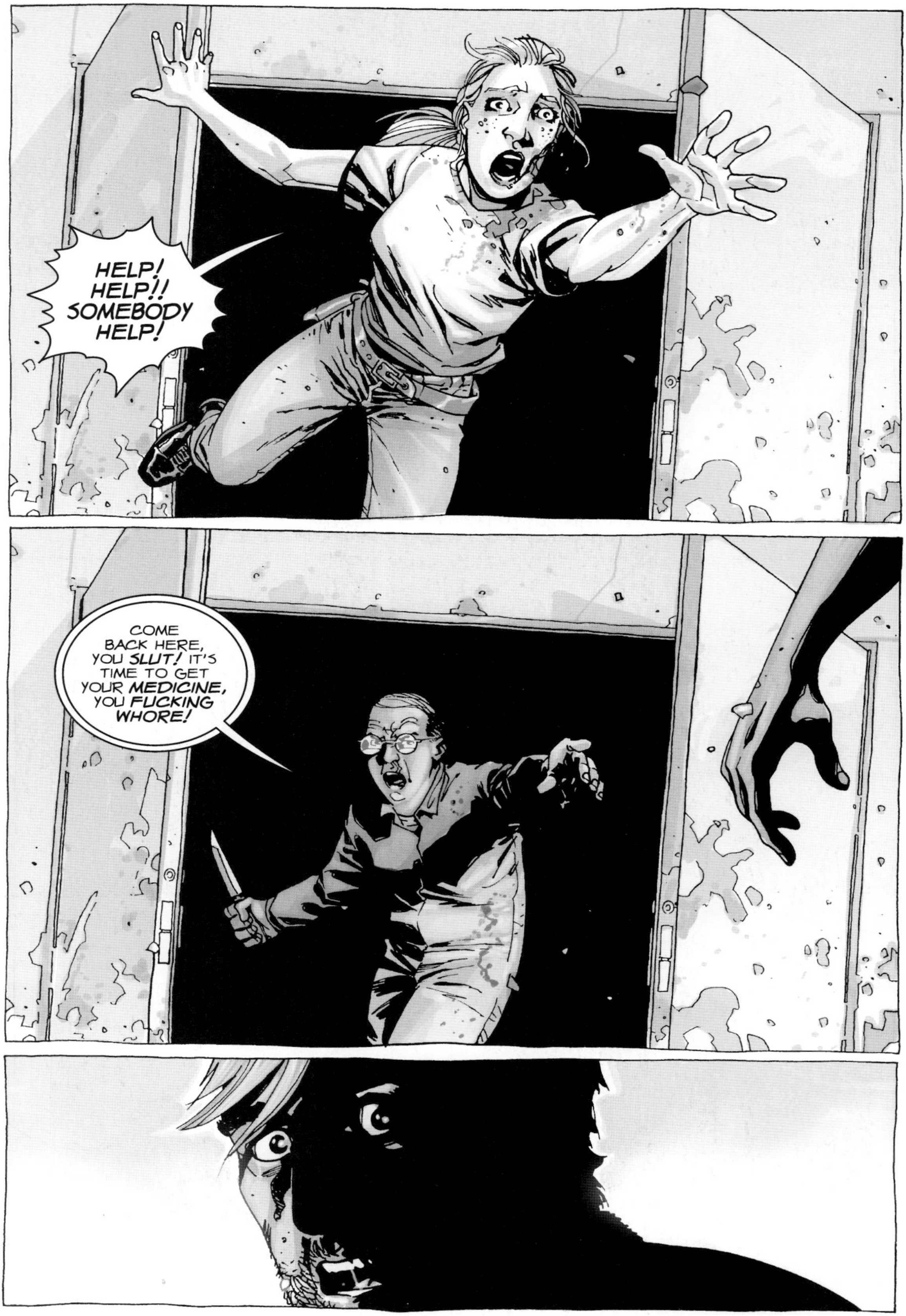
HELP! HELP!! SOMEBODY HELP!
COME BACK HERE, YOU SLUT! IT'S TIME TO GET YOUR MEDICINE, YOU FUCKING WHORE!

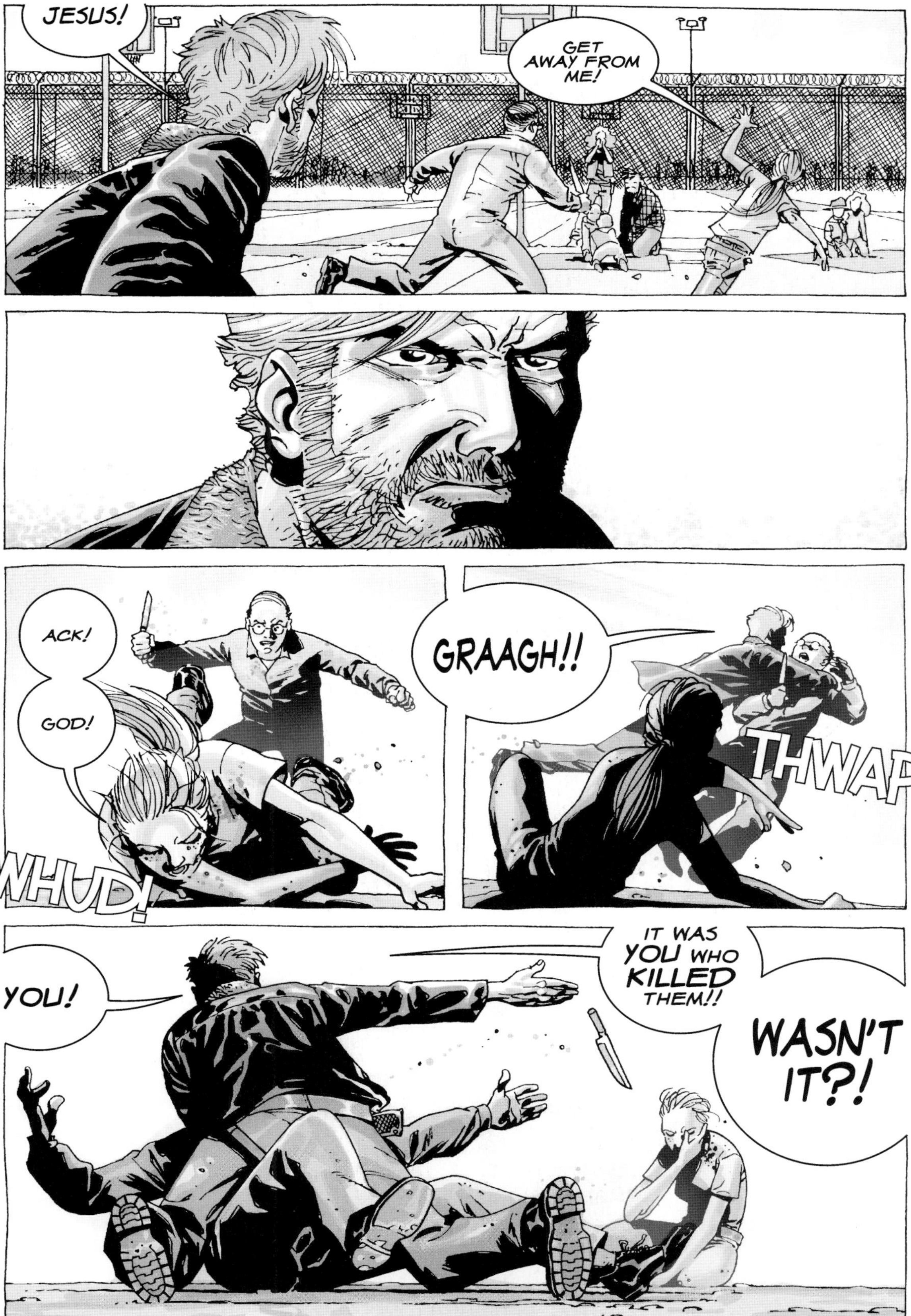
JESUS!
GET AWAY FROM ME!
ACK!
GOD!
WHUD!
GRAAGH!!
THWAP!
YOU!
IT WAS YOU WHO KILLED THEM!!
WASN'T IT?!

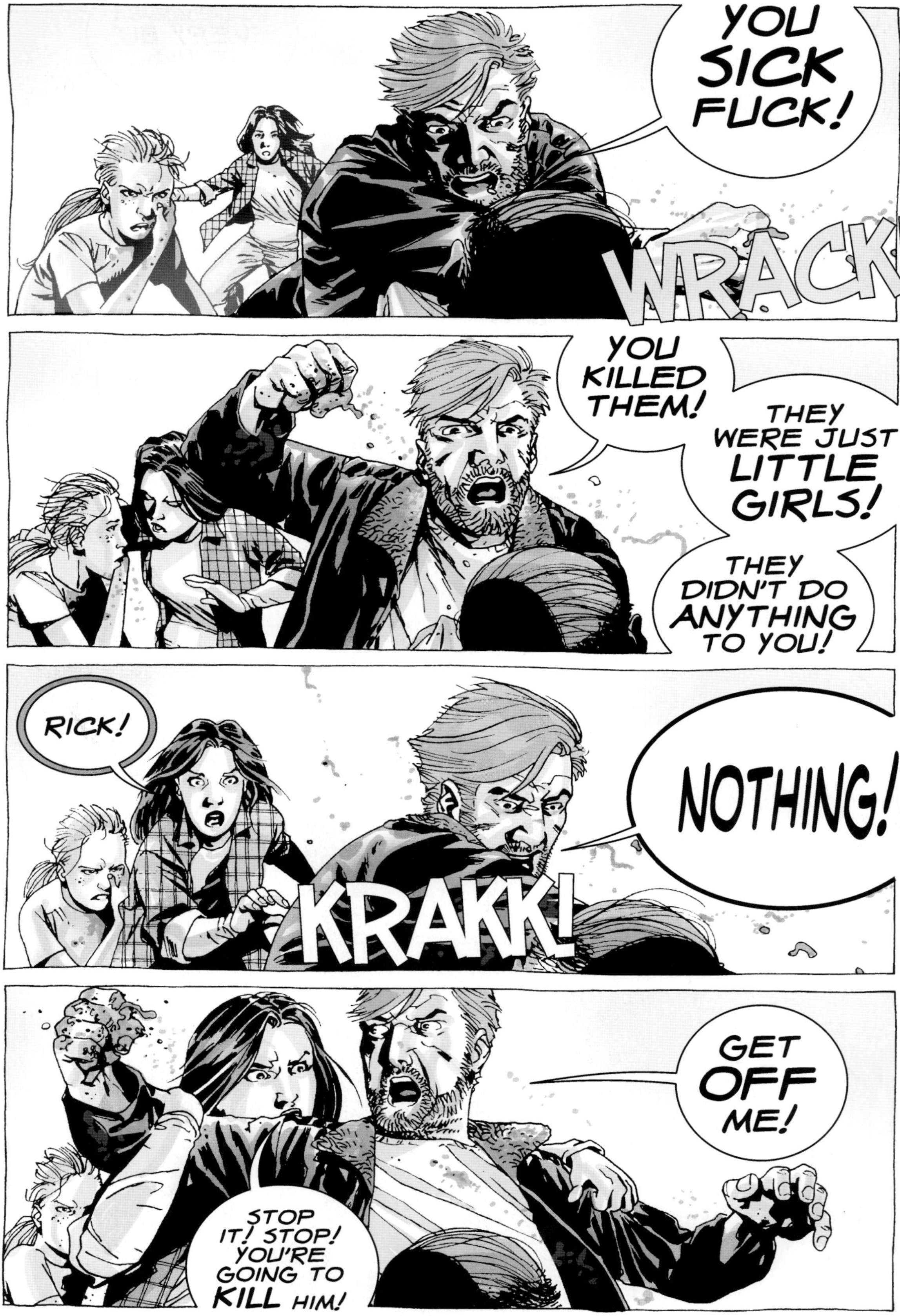
YOU SICK FUCK!
WRACK!
YOU KILLED THEM!
THEY WERE JUST LITTLE GIRLS!
THEY DIDN'T DO ANYTHING TO YOU!
RICK!
NOTHING!
KRAKK!
GET OFF ME!
STOP IT! STOP! YOU'RE GOING TO KILL HIM!

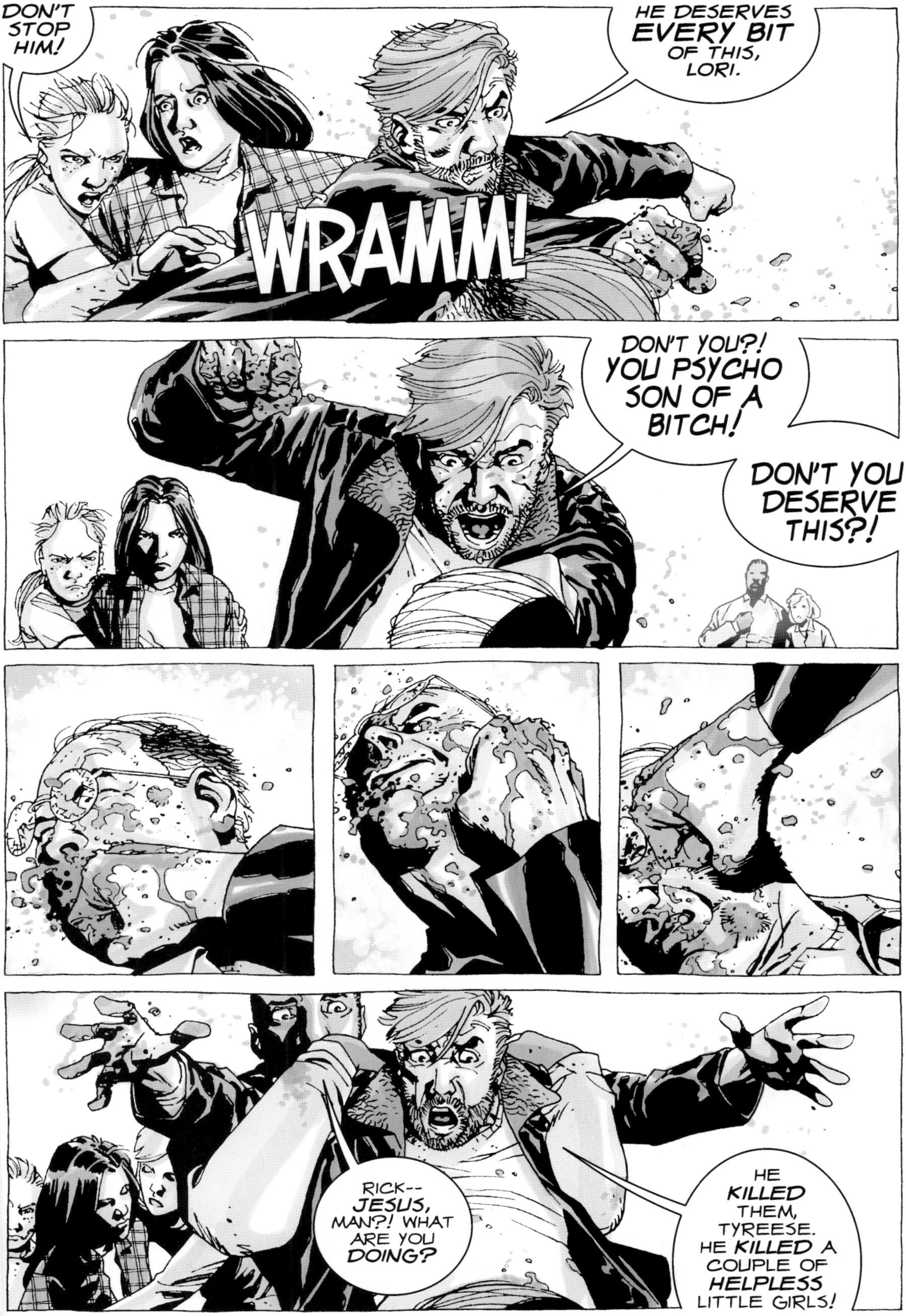
DON'T STOP HIM!
HE DESERVES EVERY BIT OF THIS, LORI.
WRAMM!
DON'T YOU?! YOU PSYCHO SON OF A BITCH!
DON'T YOU DESERVE THIS?!
RICK-- JESUS, MAN?! WHAT ARE YOU DOING?
HE KILLED THEM, TYREESE. HE KILLED A COUPLE OF HELPLESS LITTLE GIRLS!

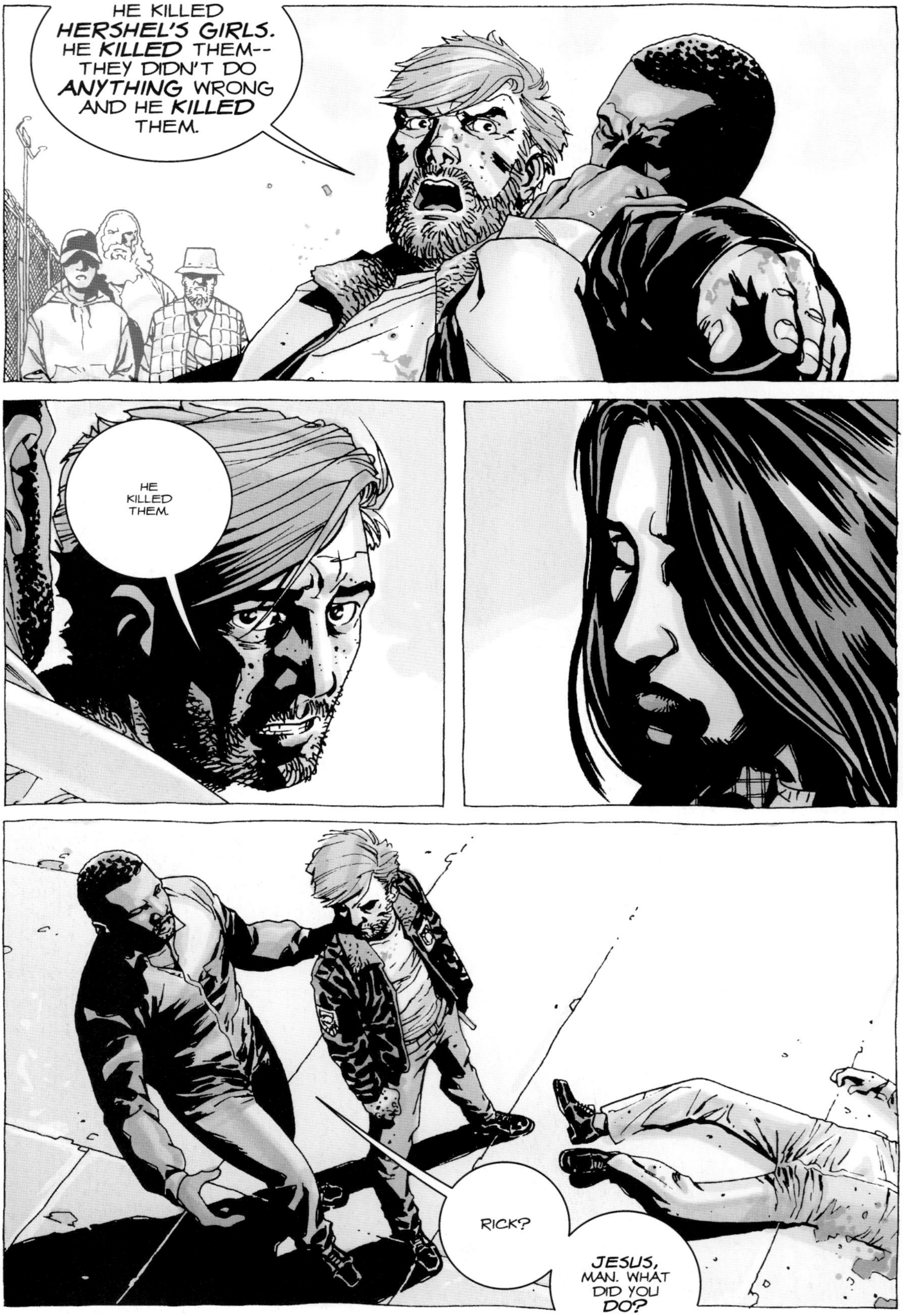
HE KILLED HERSHEL'S GIRLS. HE KILLED THEM-- THEY DIDN'T DO ANYTHING WRONG AND HE KILLED THEM.
HE KILLED THEM.
RICK?
JESUS, MAN. WHAT DID YOU DO?

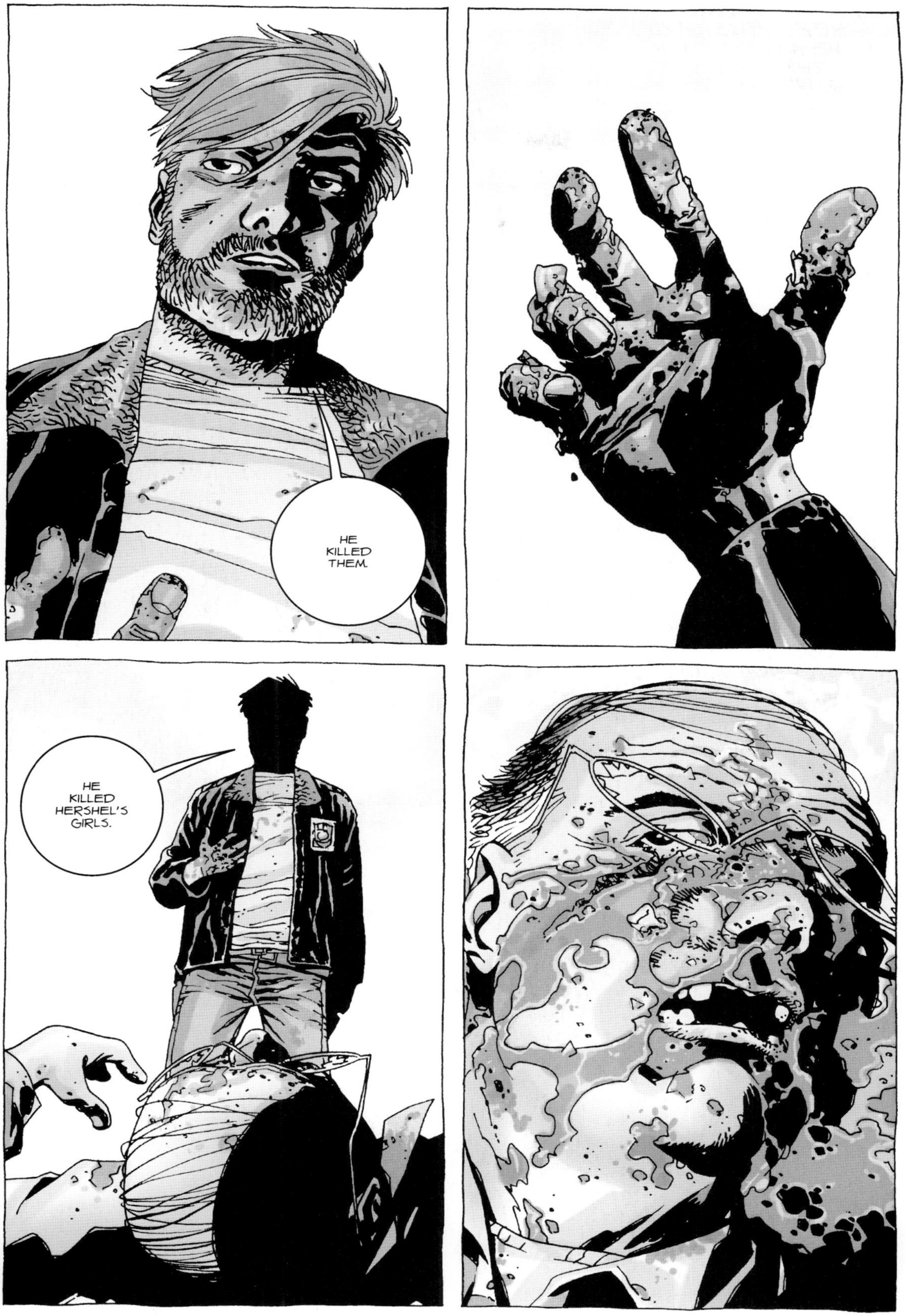
HE KILLED THEM.
HE KILLED HERSHEL'S GIRLS.

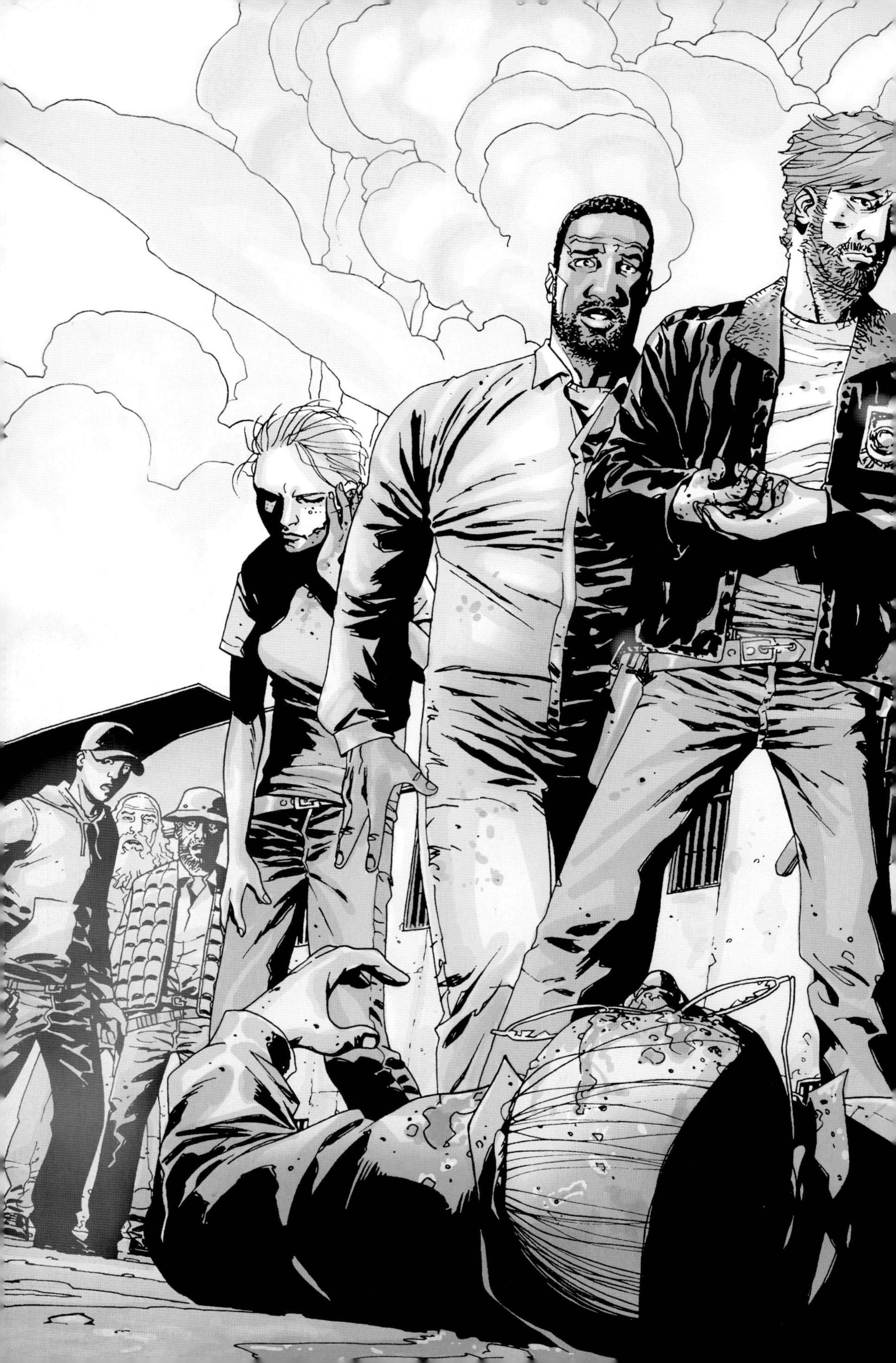

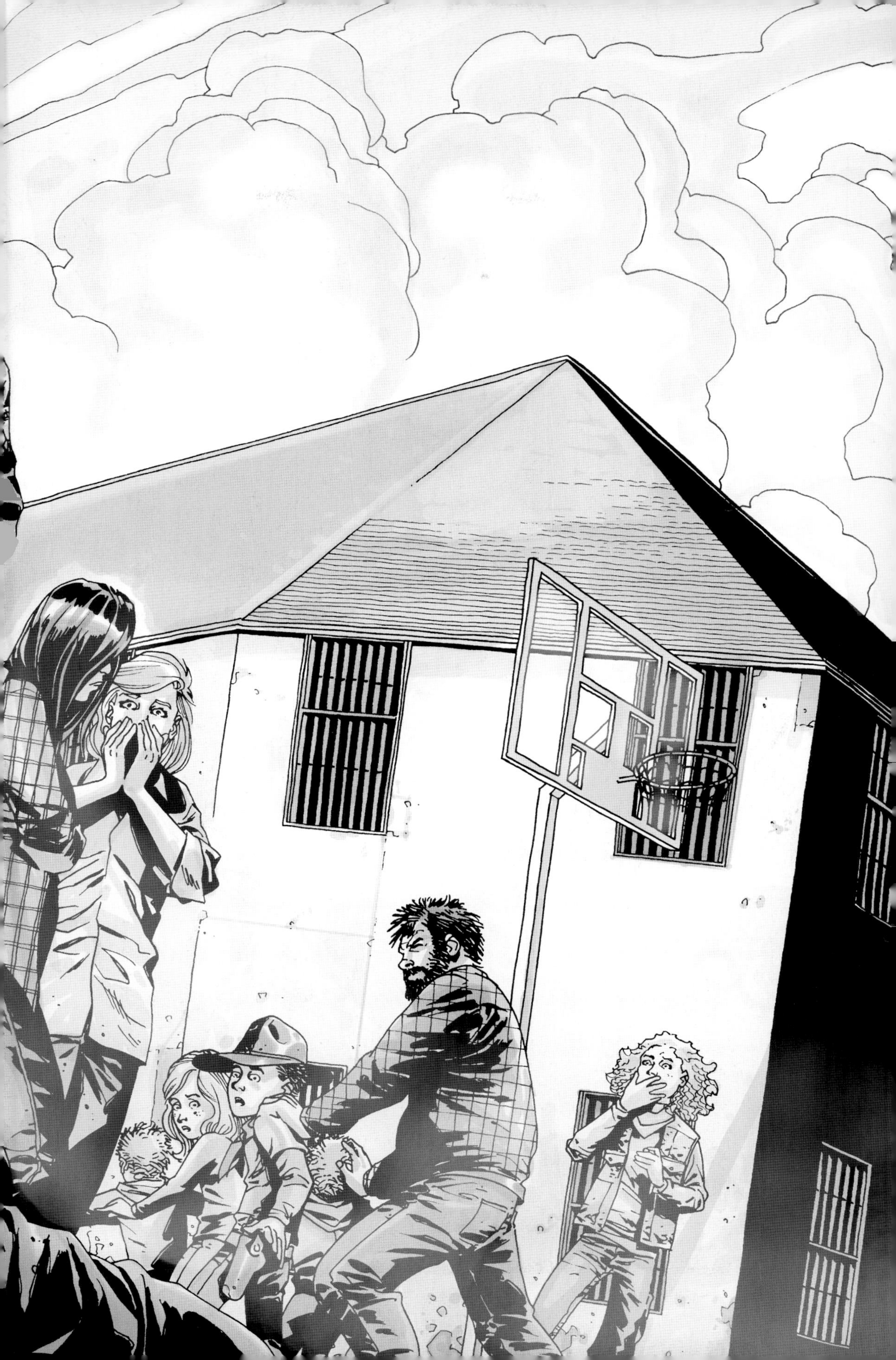

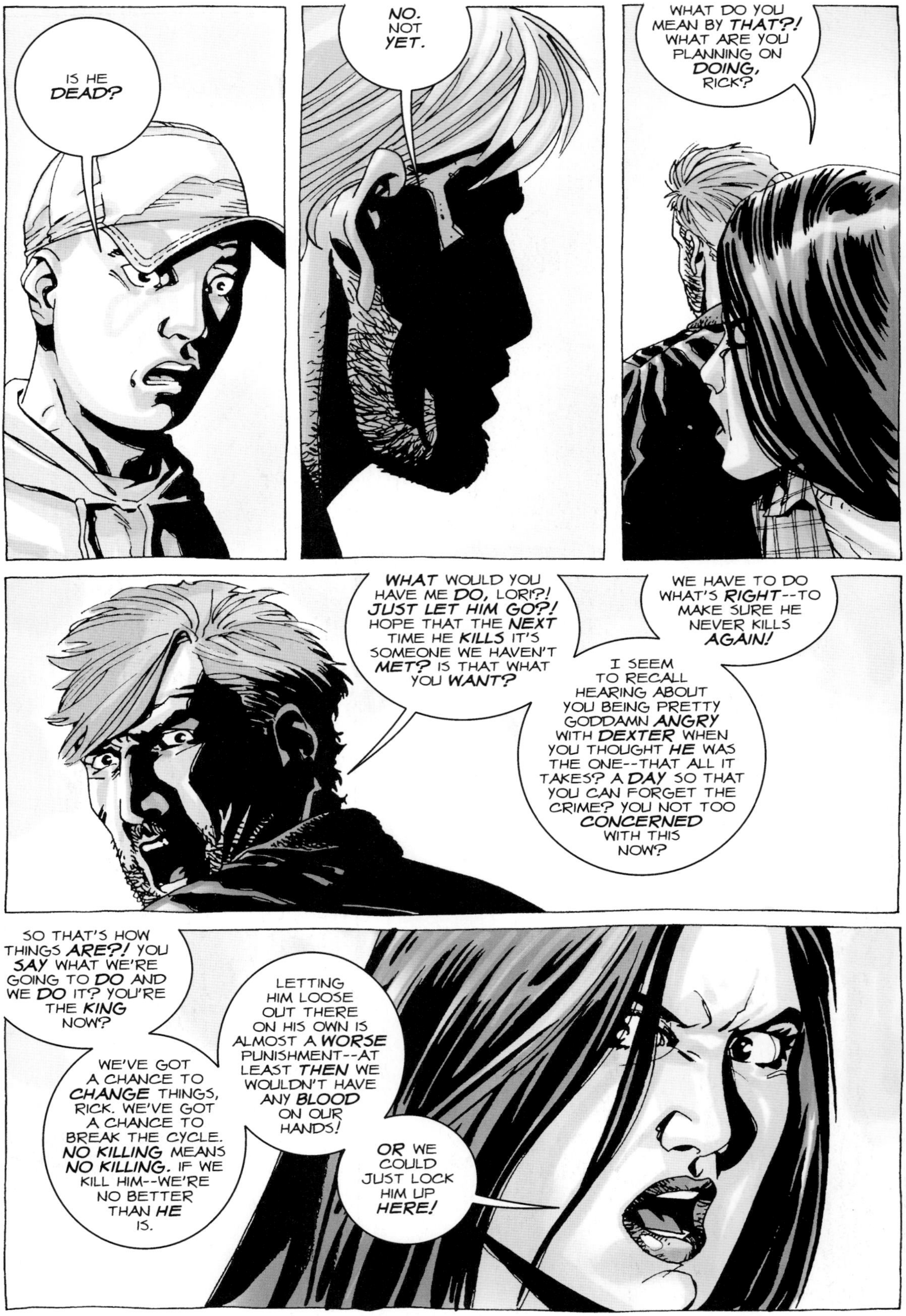
IS HE DEAD?
NO. NOT YET.
WHAT DO YOU MEAN BY THAT?! WHAT ARE YOU PLANNING ON DOING, RICK?
WHAT WOULD YOU HAVE ME DO, LORI?! JUST LET HIM GO?! HOPE THAT THE NEXT TIME HE KILLS IT'S SOMEONE WE HAVEN'T MET? IS THAT WHAT YOU WANT?
WE HAVE TO DO WHAT'S RIGHT--TO MAKE SURE HE NEVER KILLS AGAIN!
I SEEM TO RECALL HEARING ABOUT YOU BEING PRETTY GODDAMN ANGRY WITH DEXTER WHEN YOU THOUGHT HE WAS THE ONE--THAT ALL IT TAKES? A DAY SO THAT YOU CAN FORGET THE CRIME? YOU NOT TOO CONCERNED WITH THIS NOW?
SO THAT'S HOW THINGS ARE?! YOU SAY WHAT WE'RE GOING TO DO AND WE DO IT? YOU'RE THE KING NOW?
WE'VE GOT A CHANCE TO CHANGE THINGS, RICK. WE'VE GOT A CHANCE TO BREAK THE CYCLE. NO KILLING MEANS NO KILLING. IF WE KILL HIM--WE'RE NO BETTER THAN HE IS.
LETTING HIM LOOSE OUT THERE ON HIS OWN IS ALMOST A WORSE PUNISHMENT--AT LEAST THEN WE WOULDN'T HAVE ANY BLOOD ON OUR HANDS!
OR WE COULD JUST LOCK HIM UP HERE!

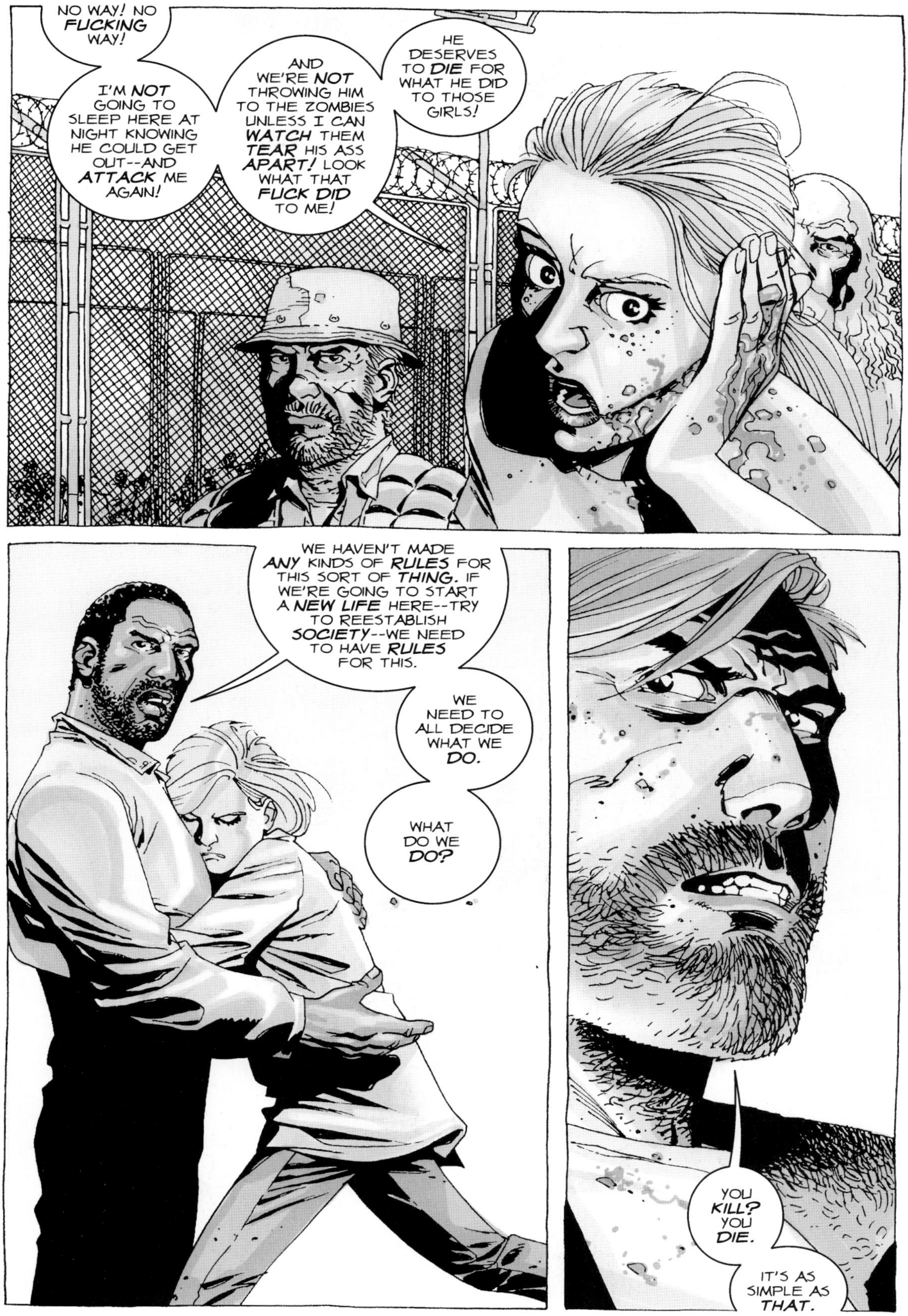

NO WAY! NO FUCKING WAY!
I'M NOT GOING TO SLEEP HERE AT NIGHT KNOWING HE COULD GET OUT--AND ATTACK ME AGAIN!
AND WE'RE NOT THROWING HIM TO THE ZOMBIES UNLESS I CAN WATCH THEM TEAR HIS ASS APART! LOOK WHAT THAT FUCK DID TO ME!
HE DESERVES TO DIE FOR WHAT HE DID TO THOSE GIRLS!
WE HAVEN'T MADE ANY KINDS OF RULES FOR THIS SORT OF THING. IF WE'RE GOING TO START A NEW LIFE HERE--TRY TO REESTABLISH SOCIETY--WE NEED TO HAVE RULES FOR THIS.
WE NEED TO ALL DECIDE WHAT WE DO.
WHAT DO WE DO?
YOU KILL? YOU DIE.
IT'S AS SIMPLE AS THAT.

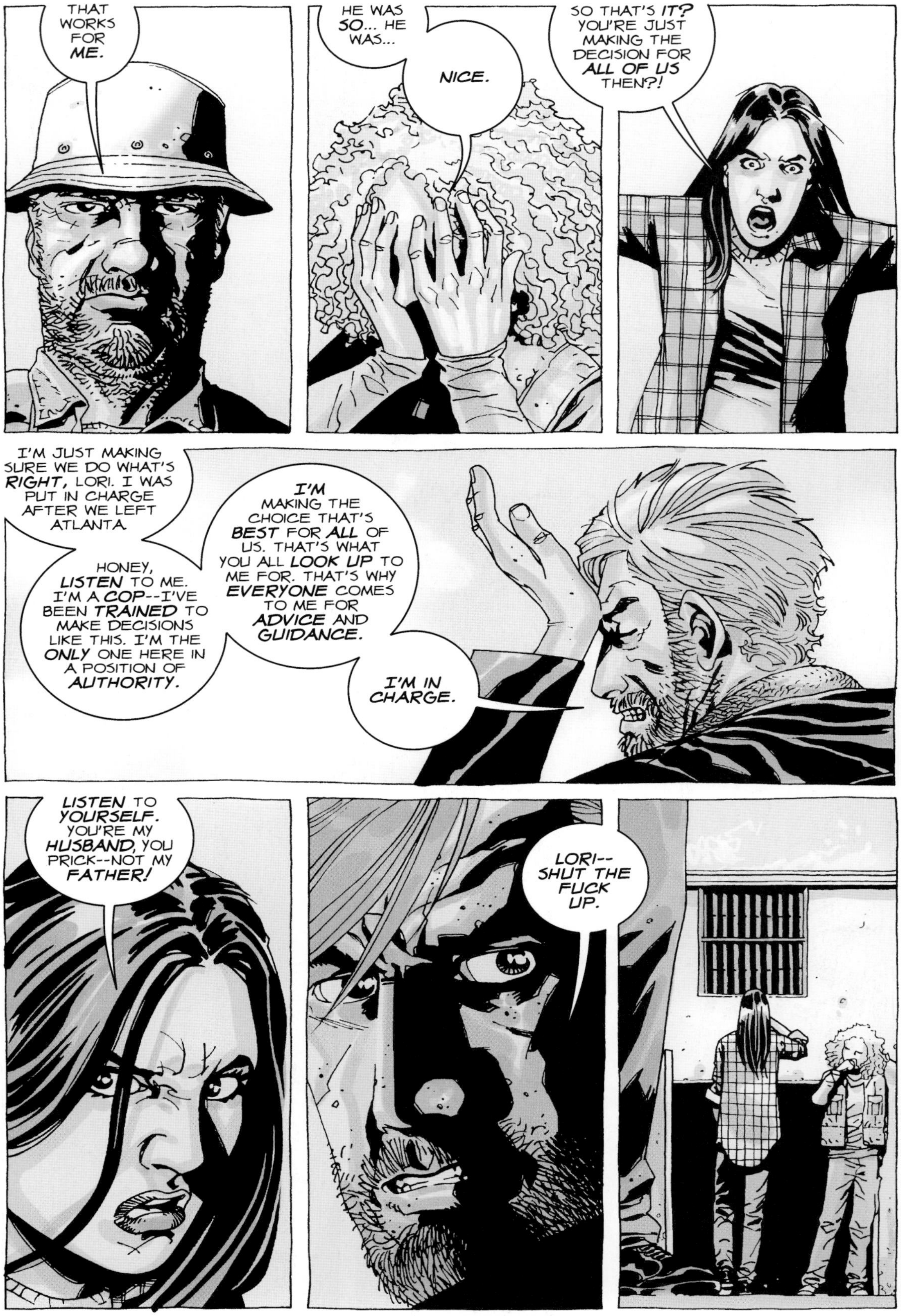
THAT WORKS FOR ME.
HE WAS SO... HE WAS...
NICE.
SO THAT'S IT? YOU'RE JUST MAKING THE DECISION FOR ALL OF US THEN?!
I'M JUST MAKING SURE WE DO WHAT'S RIGHT, LORI. I WAS PUT IN CHARGE AFTER WE LEFT ATLANTA.
HONEY, LISTEN TO ME. I'M A COP--I'VE BEEN TRAINED TO MAKE DECISIONS LIKE THIS. I'M THE ONLY ONE HERE IN A POSITION OF AUTHORITY.
I'M MAKING THE CHOICE THAT'S BEST FOR ALL OF US. THAT'S WHAT YOU ALL LOOK UP TO ME FOR. THAT'S WHY EVERYONE COMES TO ME FOR ADVICE AND GUIDANCE.
I'M IN CHARGE.
LISTEN TO YOURSELF. YOU'RE MY HUSBAND, YOU PRICK--NOT MY FATHER!
LORI-- SHUT THE FUCK UP.

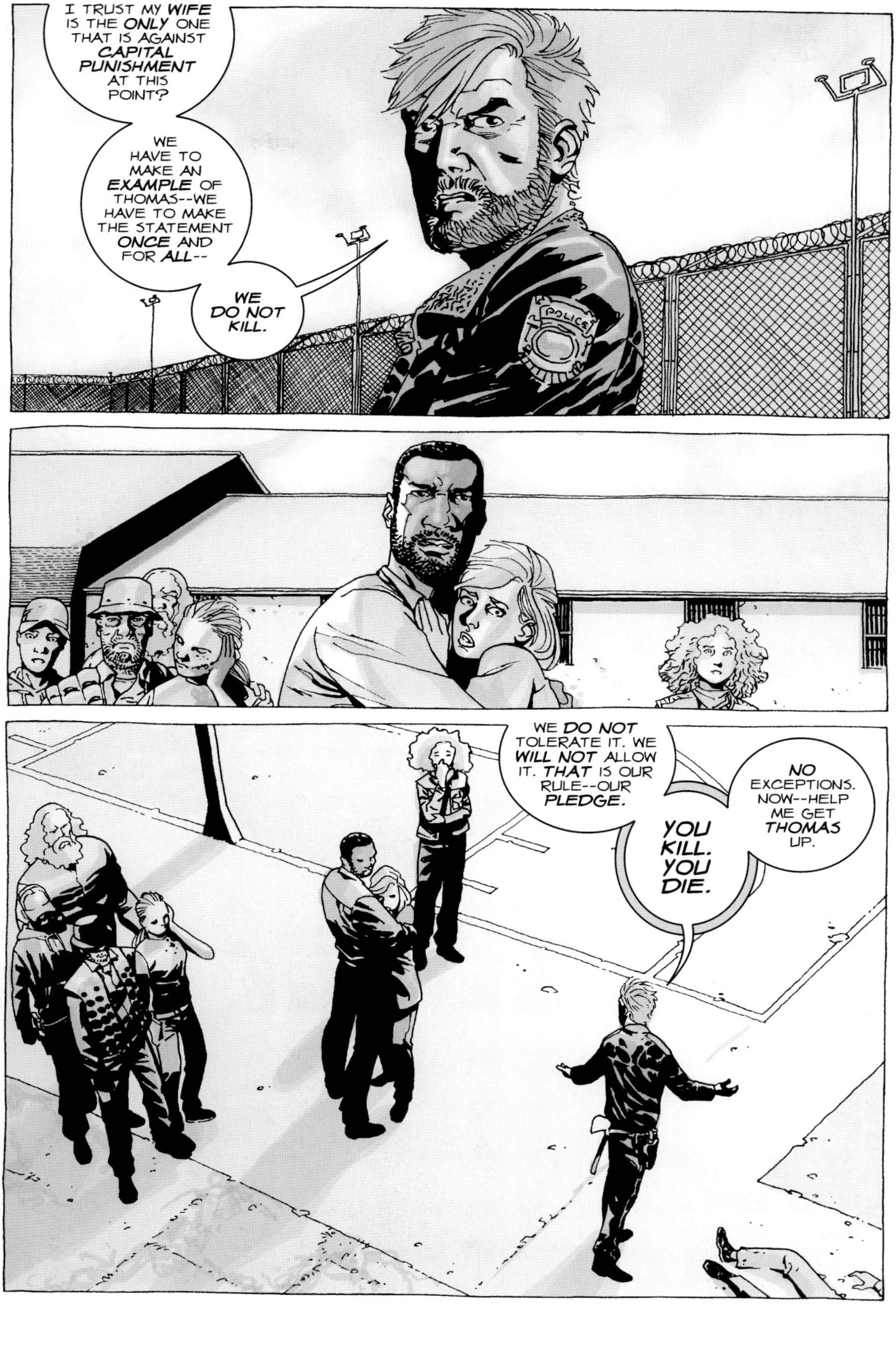
I TRUST MY WIFE IS THE ONLY ONE THAT IS AGAINST CAPITAL PUNISHMENT AT THIS POINT?
WE HAVE TO MAKE AN EXAMPLE OF THOMAS--WE HAVE TO MAKE THE STATEMENT ONCE AND FOR ALL--
WE DO NOT KILL.
WE DO NOT TOLERATE IT. WE WILL NOT ALLOW IT. THAT IS OUR RULE--OUR PLEDGE.
YOU KILL. YOU DIE.
NO EXCEPTIONS. NOW--HELP ME GET THOMAS UP.

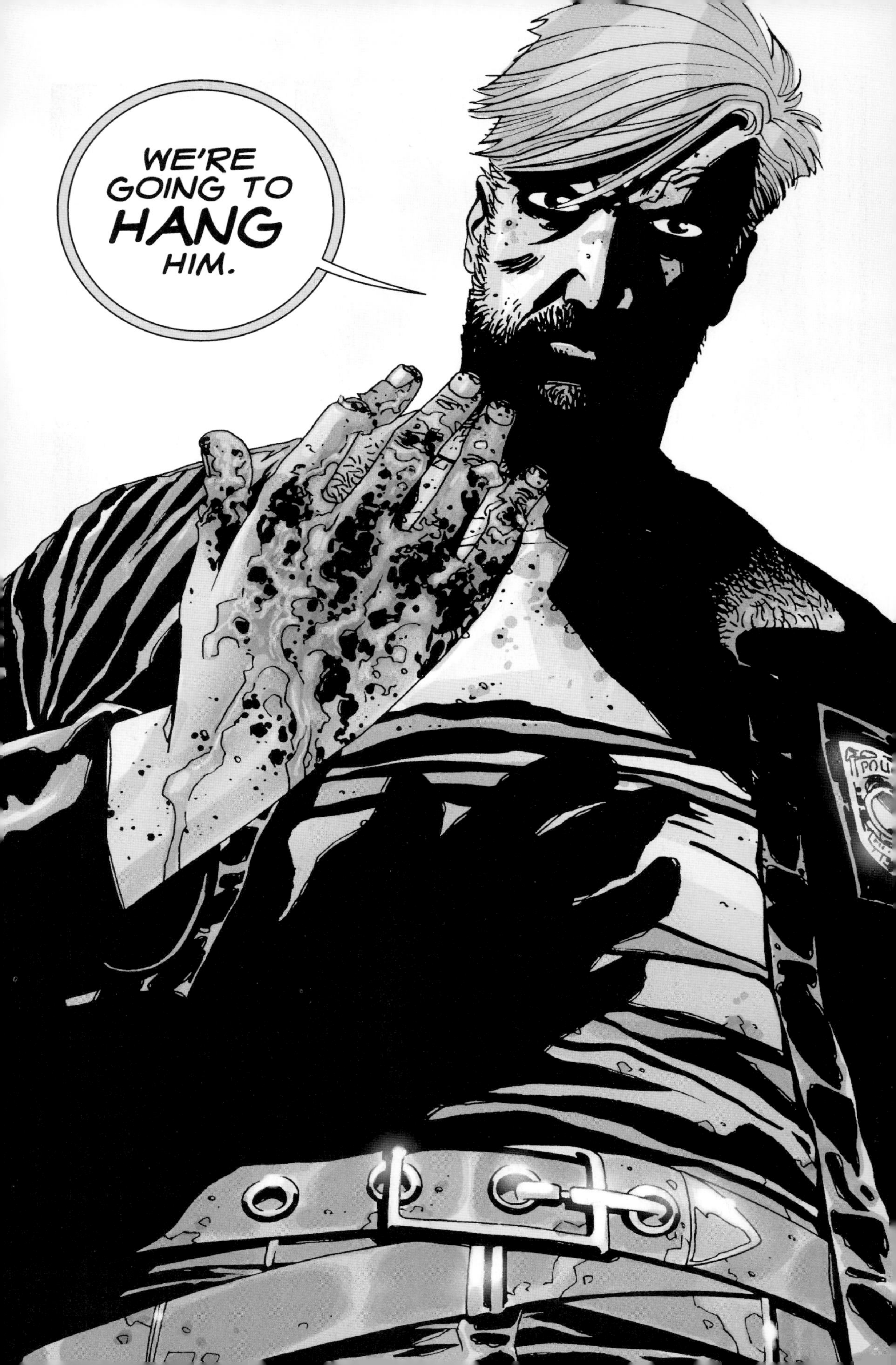
WE'RE GOING TO HANG HIM.

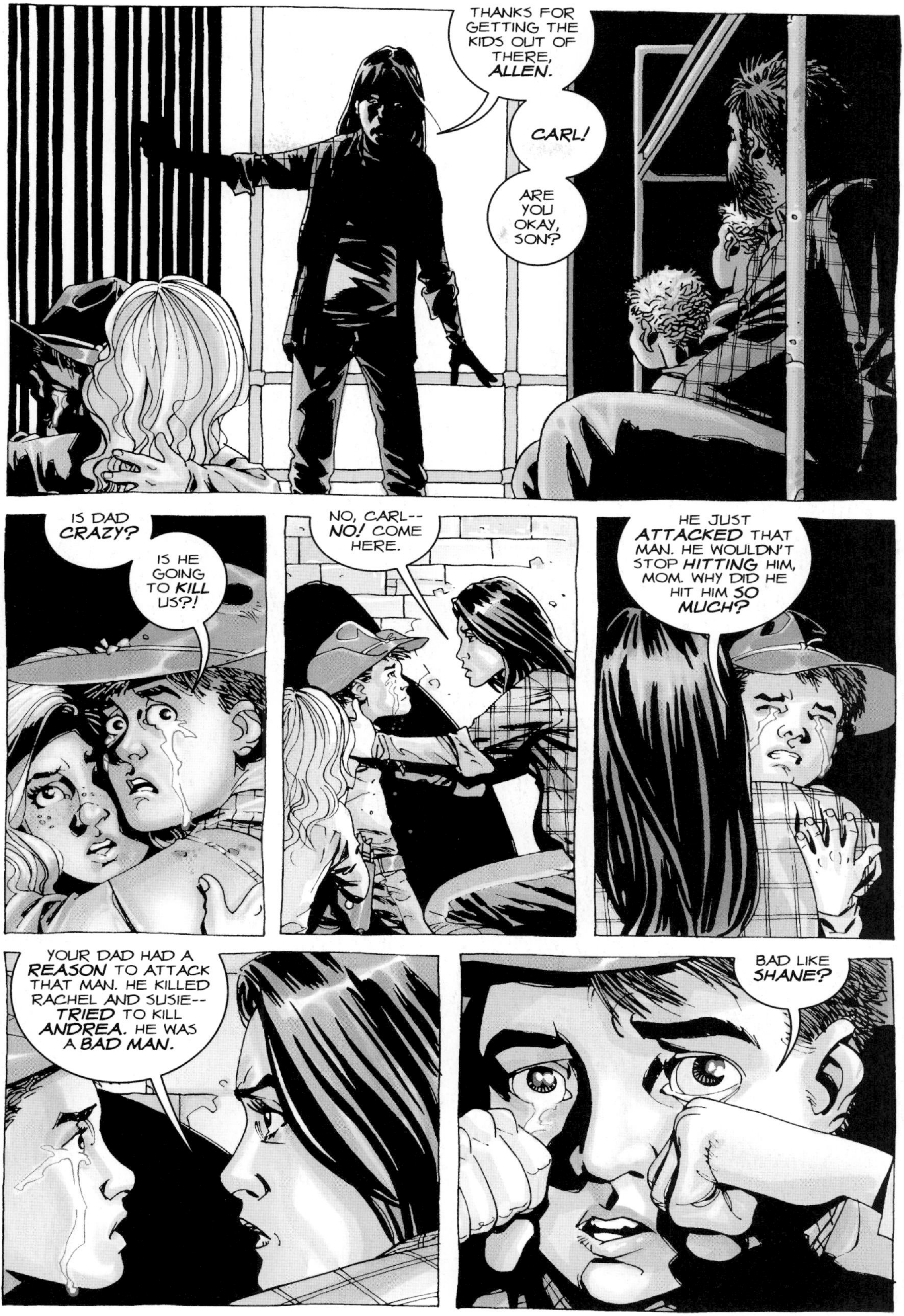
THANKS FOR GETTING THE KIDS OUT OF THERE, ALLEN.
CARL!
ARE YOU OKAY, SON?
IS DAD CRAZY?
IS HE GOING TO KILL US?!
NO, CARL-- NO! COME HERE.
HE JUST ATTACKED THAT MAN. HE WOULDN'T STOP HITTING HIM, MOM. WHY DID HE HIT HIM SO MUCH?
YOUR DAD HAD A REASON TO ATTACK THAT MAN. HE KILLED RACHEL AND SUSIE-- TRIED TO KILL ANDREA. HE WAS A BAD MAN.
BAD LIKE SHANE?

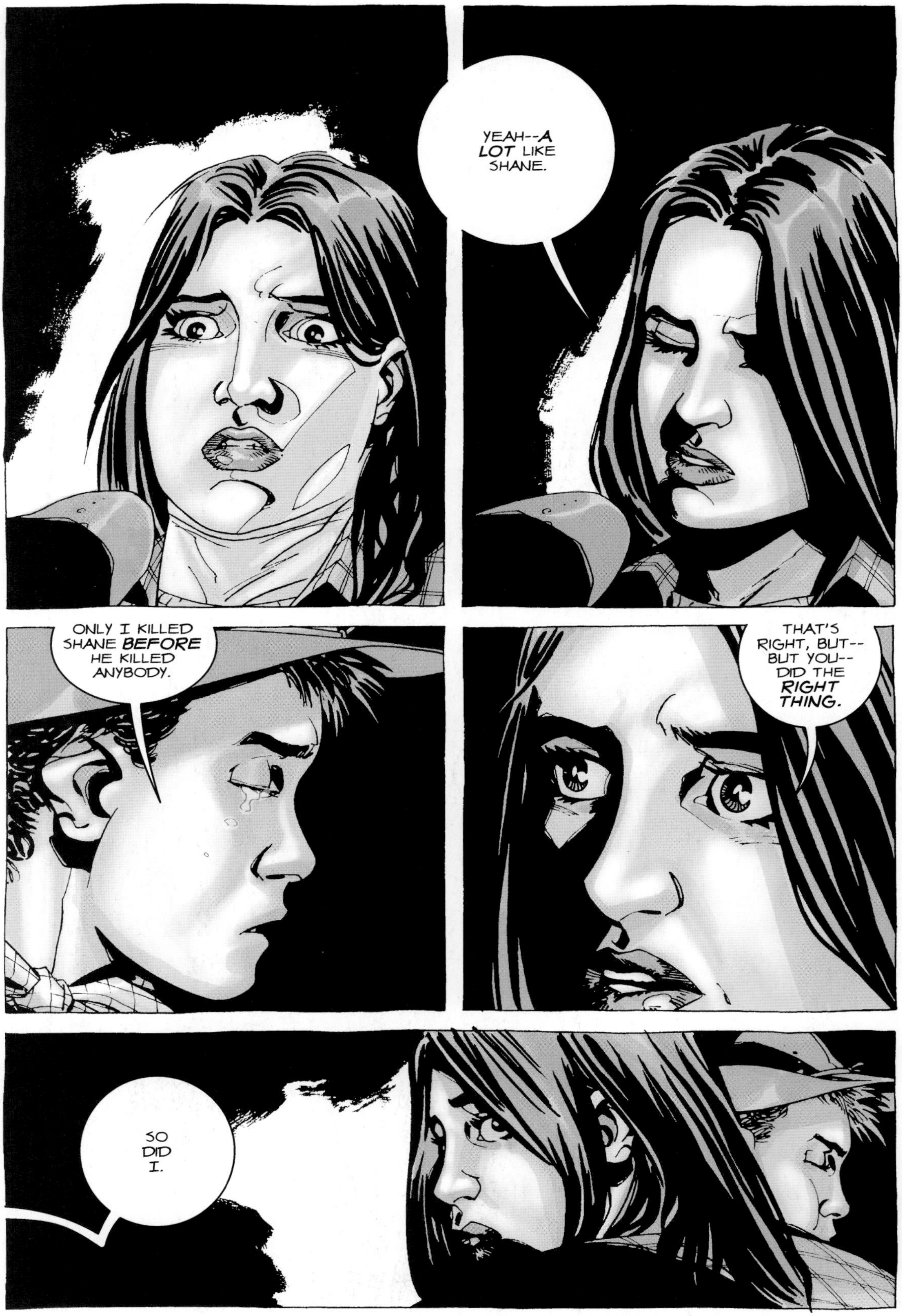
YEAH--A LOT LIKE SHANE.
ONLY I KILLED SHANE BEFORE HE KILLED ANYBODY.
THAT'S RIGHT, BUT--BUT YOU--DID THE RIGHT THING.
SO DID I.

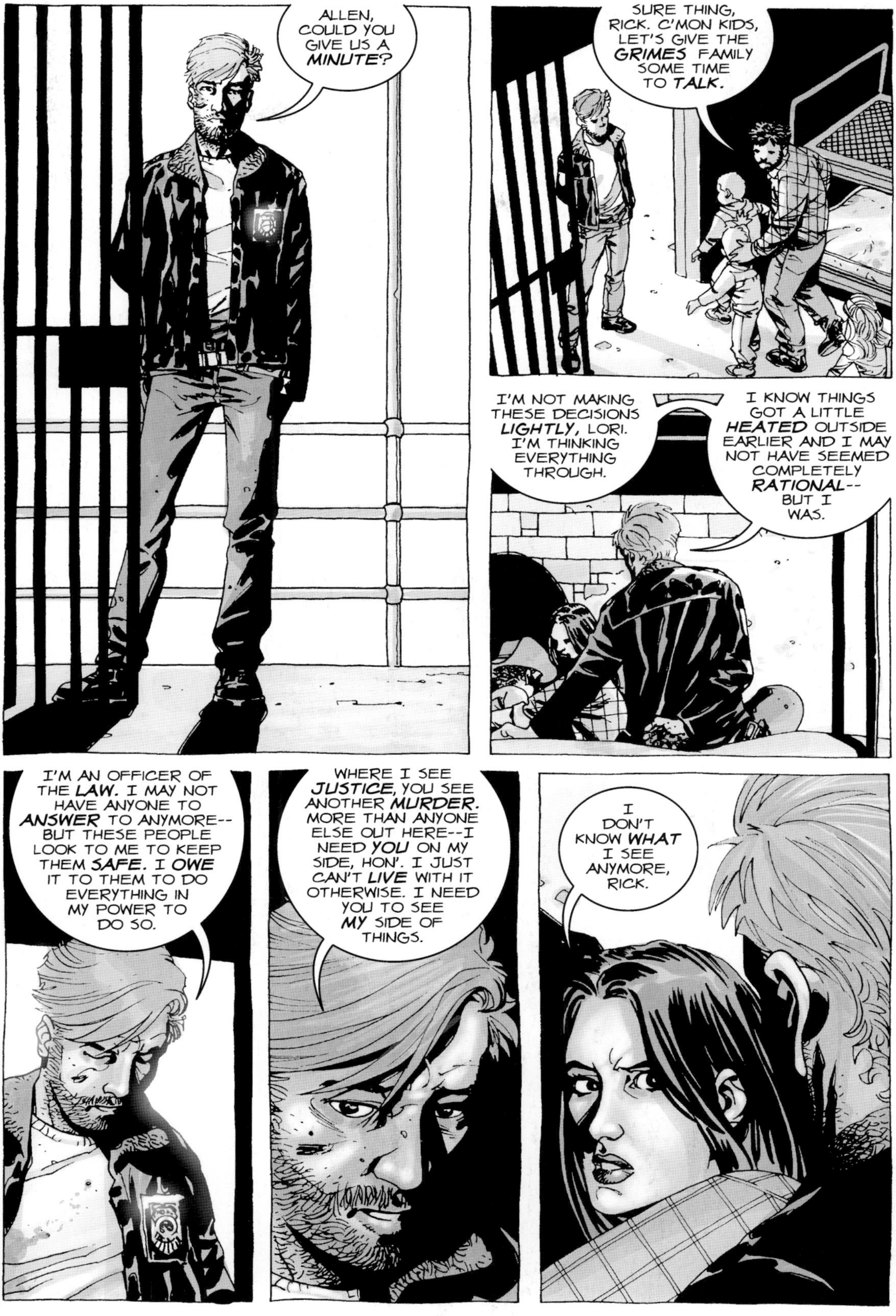
ALLEN, COULD YOU GIVE US A MINUTE?
SURE THING, RICK. C'MON KIDS, LET'S GIVE THE GRIMES FAMILY SOME TIME TO TALK.
I KNOW THINGS GOT A LITTLE HEATED OUTSIDE EARLIER AND I MAY NOT HAVE SEEMED COMPLETELY RATIONAL-- BUT I WAS.
I'M NOT MAKING THESE DECISIONS LIGHTLY, LORI. I'M THINKING EVERYTHING THROUGH.
I'M AN OFFICER OF THE LAW. I MAY NOT HAVE ANYONE TO ANSWER TO ANYMORE-- BUT THESE PEOPLE LOOK TO ME TO KEEP THEM SAFE. I OWE IT TO THEM TO DO EVERYTHING IN MY POWER TO DO SO.
WHERE I SEE JUSTICE, YOU SEE ANOTHER MURDER. MORE THAN ANYONE ELSE OUT HERE--I NEED YOU ON MY SIDE, HON'. I JUST CAN'T LIVE WITH IT OTHERWISE. I NEED YOU TO SEE MY SIDE OF THINGS.
I DON'T KNOW WHAT I SEE ANYMORE, RICK.

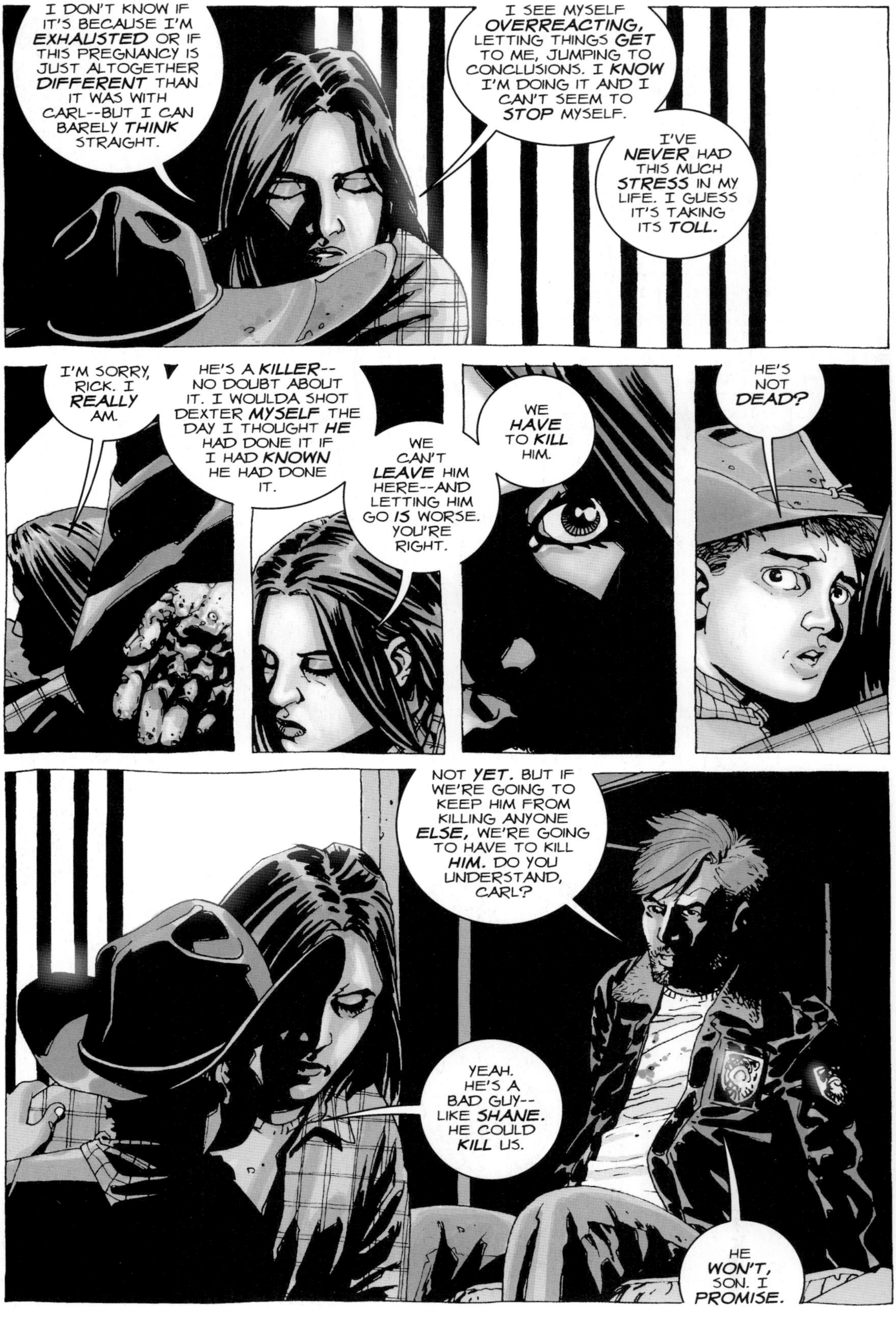
I DON'T KNOW IF IT'S BECAUSE I'M EXHAUSTED OR IF THIS PREGNANCY IS JUST ALTOGETHER DIFFERENT THAN IT WAS WITH CARL--BUT I CAN BARELY THINK STRAIGHT.
I SEE MYSELF OVERREACTING, LETTING THINGS GET TO ME, JUMPING TO CONCLUSIONS. I KNOW I'M DOING IT AND I CAN'T SEEM TO STOP MYSELF.
I'VE NEVER HAD THIS MUCH STRESS IN MY LIFE. I GUESS IT'S TAKING ITS TOLL.
I'M SORRY, RICK. I REALLY AM.
HE'S A KILLER-- NO DOUBT ABOUT IT. I WOULDA SHOT DEXTER MYSELF THE DAY I THOUGHT HE HAD DONE IT IF I HAD KNOWN HE HAD DONE IT.
WE CAN'T LEAVE HIM HERE--AND LETTING HIM GO IS WORSE. YOU'RE RIGHT.
WE HAVE TO KILL HIM.
HE'S NOT DEAD?
NOT YET. BUT IF WE'RE GOING TO KEEP HIM FROM KILLING ANYONE ELSE, WE'RE GOING TO HAVE TO KILL HIM. DO YOU UNDERSTAND, CARL?
YEAH. HE'S A BAD GUY-- LIKE SHANE. HE COULD KILL US.
HE WON'T, SON. I PROMISE.

OKAY--YOU SIT RIGHT THERE. I STILL HAVE THE *FIRST AID* KIT FROM THE *RV.* LET ME GET IT.

HERSHEL'D PROBABLY DO A BETTER JOB PATCHING YOU UP BUT I DON'T THINK HE'S *READY* TO HELP *ANYONE* AFTER WHAT HE JUST WENT THROUGH.

I'M NOT IN TOO GOOD A MOOD *EITHER*--THAT FUCKER *DID* JUST TRY TO *KILL* ME.

JESUS! THIS *FUCKING* HURTS!

LOOK FORWARD--LET ME MAKE SURE I CAN STOP THIS BLEEDING. I THINK MOST OF IT'S *STOPPED* ALREADY. THIS'LL BE *MOSTLY* CLEAN UP.

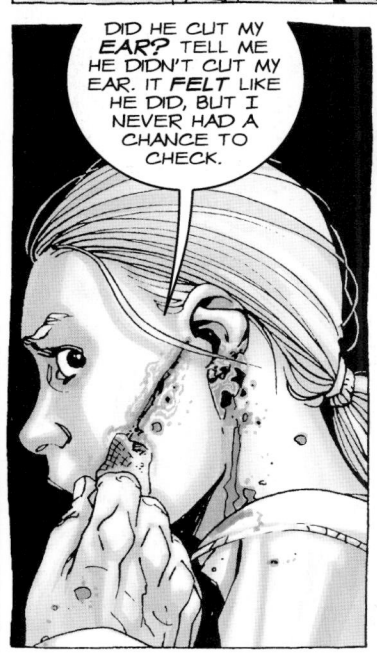

DID HE CUT MY *EAR?* TELL ME HE DIDN'T CUT MY EAR. IT *FELT* LIKE HE DID, BUT I NEVER HAD A CHANCE TO CHECK.

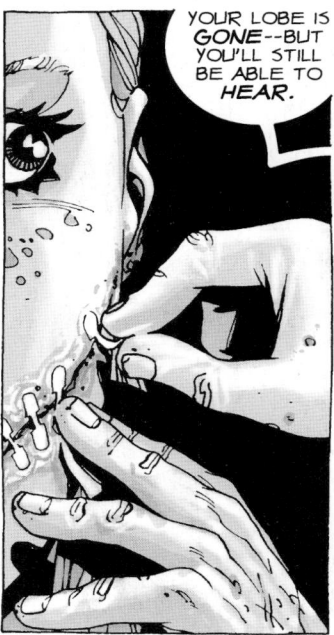

YOUR LOBE IS *GONE*--BUT YOU'LL STILL BE ABLE TO *HEAR.*

I COULDN'T CARE *LESS* ABOUT HEARING. I DON'T WANT TO LOOK LIKE A *FREAK.*

YOU'VE GOT NOTHING TO WORRY ABOUT. YOU'LL BE AS PRETTY AS *EVER*, AS SOON AS WE CLEAN YOU UP.

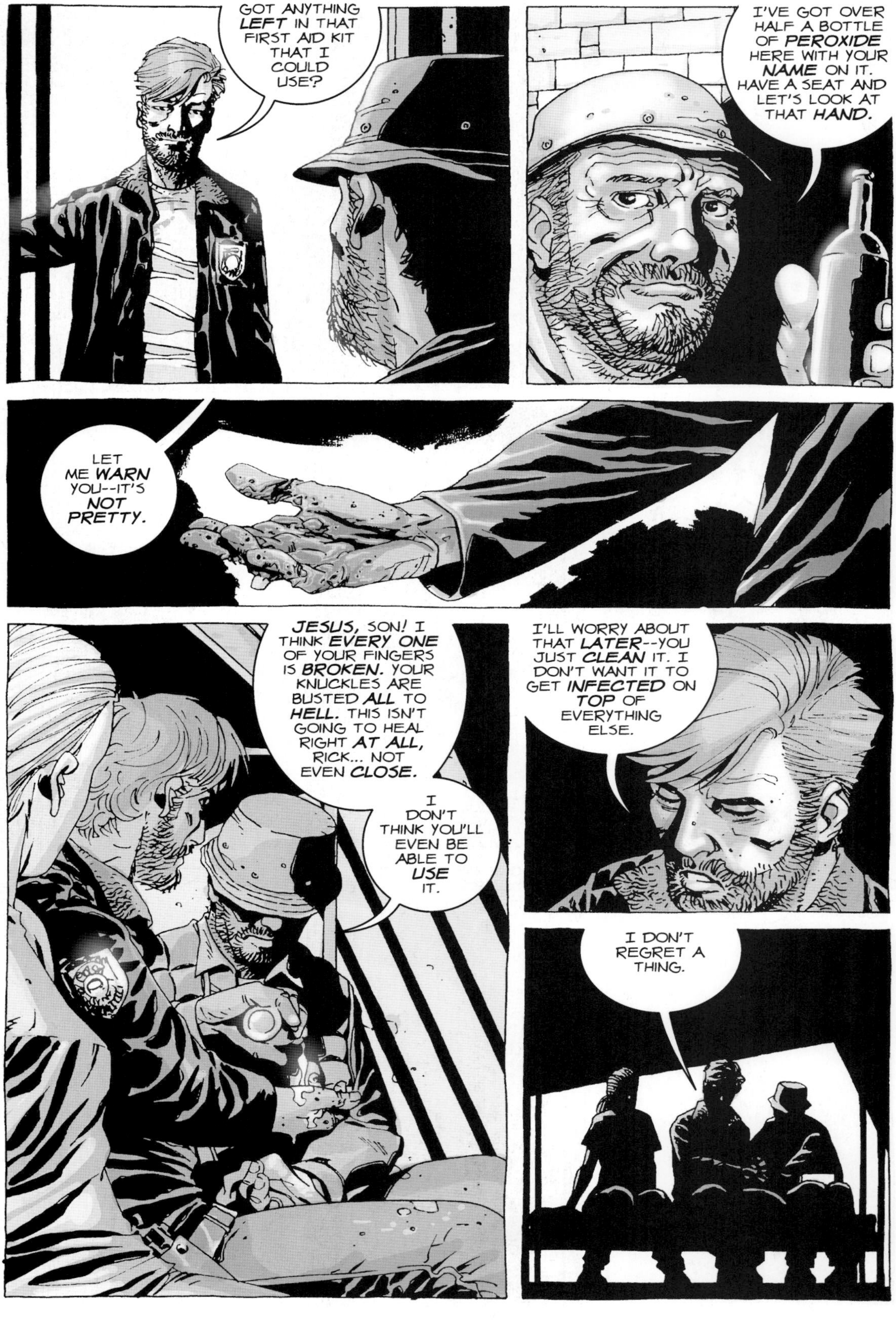
GOT ANYTHING LEFT IN THAT FIRST AID KIT THAT I COULD USE?
I'VE GOT OVER HALF A BOTTLE OF PEROXIDE HERE WITH YOUR NAME ON IT. HAVE A SEAT AND LET'S LOOK AT THAT HAND.
LET ME WARN YOU--IT'S NOT PRETTY.
JESUS, SON! I THINK EVERY ONE OF YOUR FINGERS IS BROKEN. YOUR KNUCKLES ARE BUSTED ALL TO HELL. THIS ISN'T GOING TO HEAL RIGHT AT ALL, RICK... NOT EVEN CLOSE.
I DON'T THINK YOU'LL EVEN BE ABLE TO USE IT.
I'LL WORRY ABOUT THAT LATER--YOU JUST CLEAN IT. I DON'T WANT IT TO GET INFECTED ON TOP OF EVERYTHING ELSE.
I DON'T REGRET A THING.

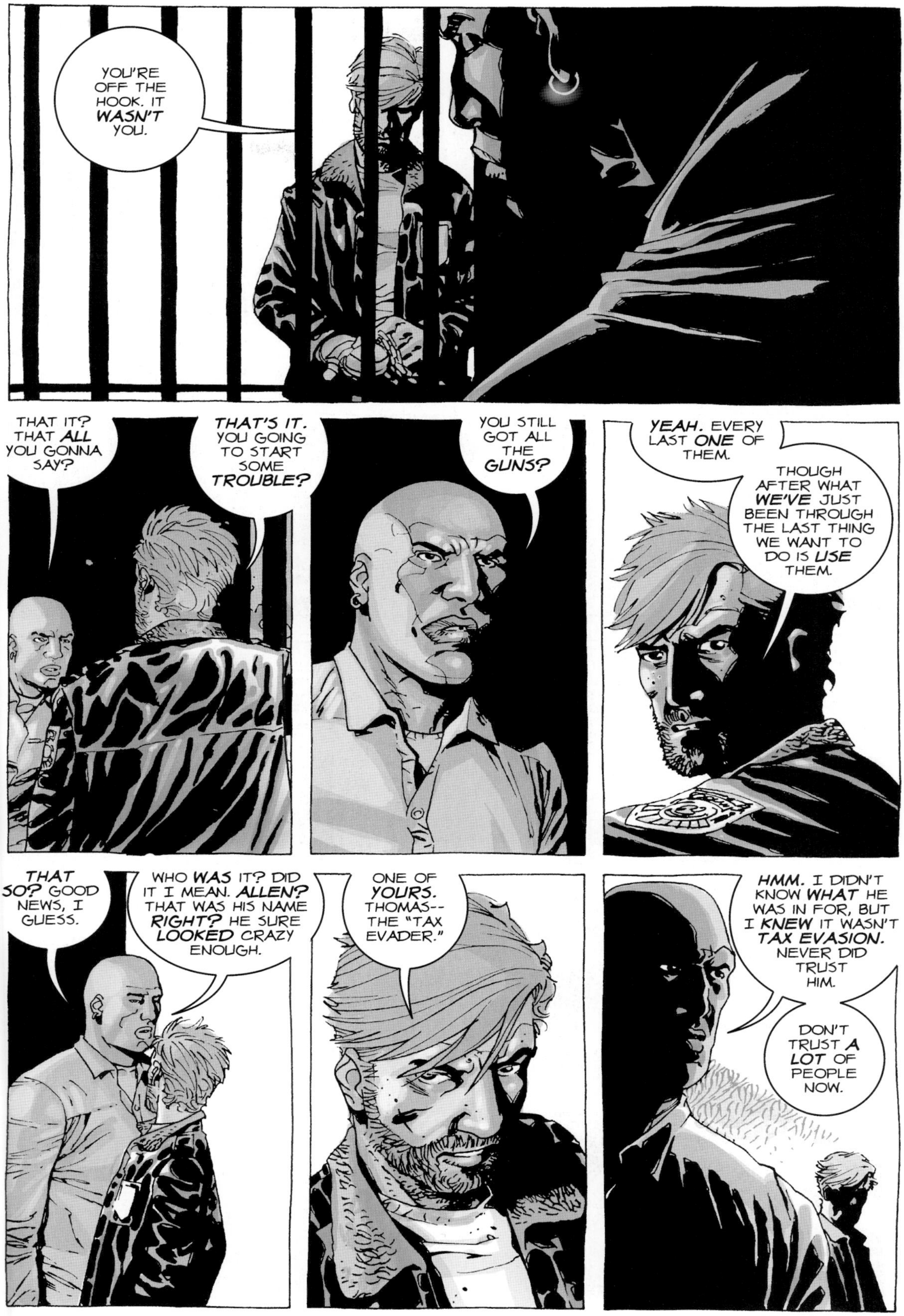
YOU'RE OFF THE HOOK. IT WASN'T YOU.
THAT IT? THAT ALL YOU GONNA SAY?
THAT'S IT. YOU GOING TO START SOME TROUBLE?
YOU STILL GOT ALL THE GUNS?
YEAH. EVERY LAST ONE OF THEM.
THOUGH AFTER WHAT WE'VE JUST BEEN THROUGH THE LAST THING WE WANT TO DO IS USE THEM.
THAT SO? GOOD NEWS, I GUESS.
WHO WAS IT? DID IT I MEAN. ALLEN? THAT WAS HIS NAME RIGHT? HE SURE LOOKED CRAZY ENOUGH.
ONE OF YOURS. THOMAS-- THE "TAX EVADER."
HMM. I DIDN'T KNOW WHAT HE WAS IN FOR, BUT I KNEW IT WASN'T TAX EVASION. NEVER DID TRUST HIM.
DON'T TRUST A LOT OF PEOPLE NOW.

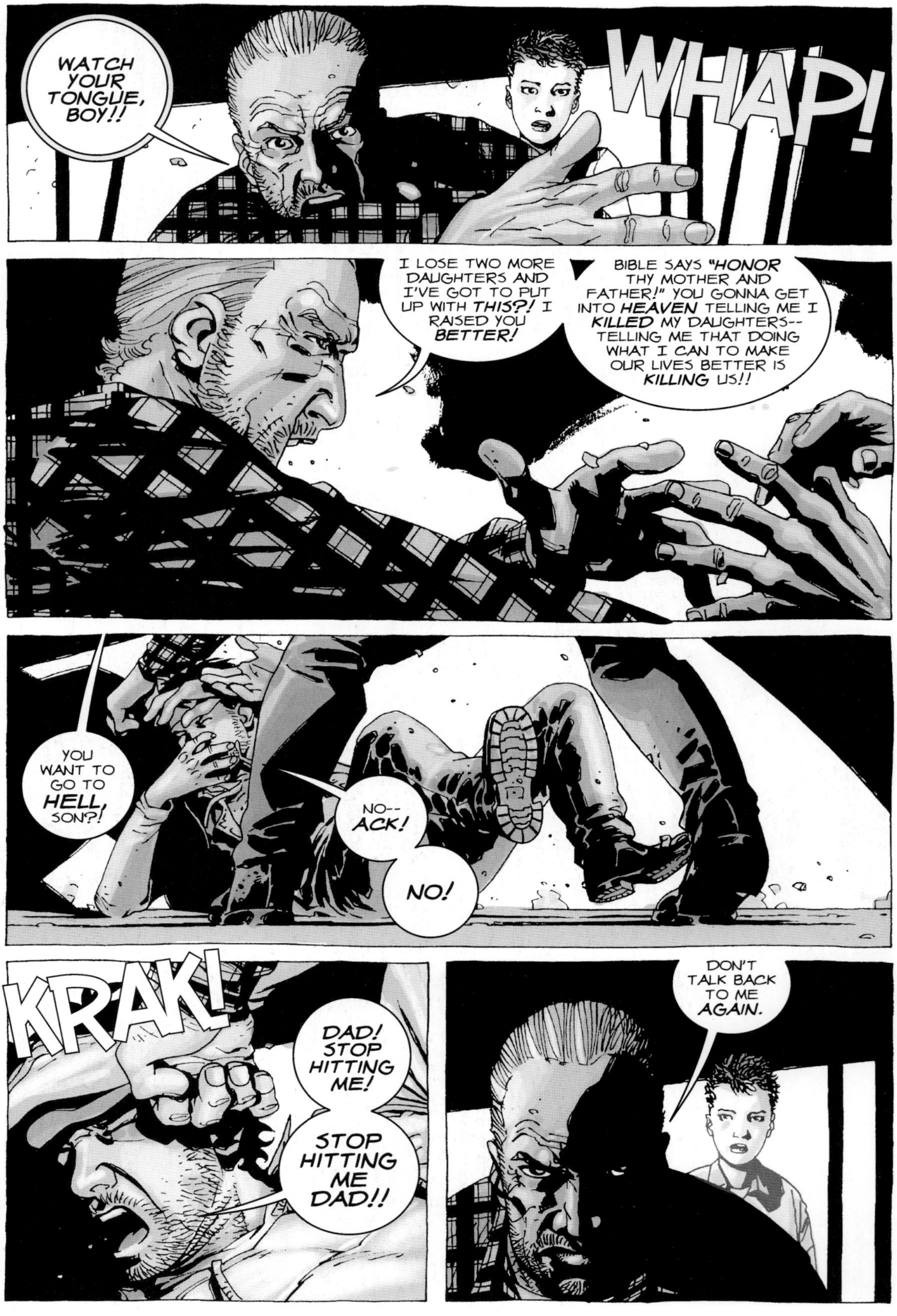
WATCH YOUR TONGUE, BOY!!
WHAP!
I LOSE TWO MORE DAUGHTERS AND I'VE GOT TO PUT UP WITH THIS?! I RAISED YOU BETTER!
BIBLE SAYS "HONOR THY MOTHER AND FATHER!" YOU GONNA GET INTO HEAVEN TELLING ME I KILLED MY DAUGHTERS-- TELLING ME THAT DOING WHAT I CAN TO MAKE OUR LIVES BETTER IS KILLING US!!
YOU WANT TO GO TO HELL, SON?!
NO-- ACK!
NO!
KRAK!
DAD! STOP HITTING ME!
STOP HITTING ME DAD!!
DON'T TALK BACK TO ME AGAIN.

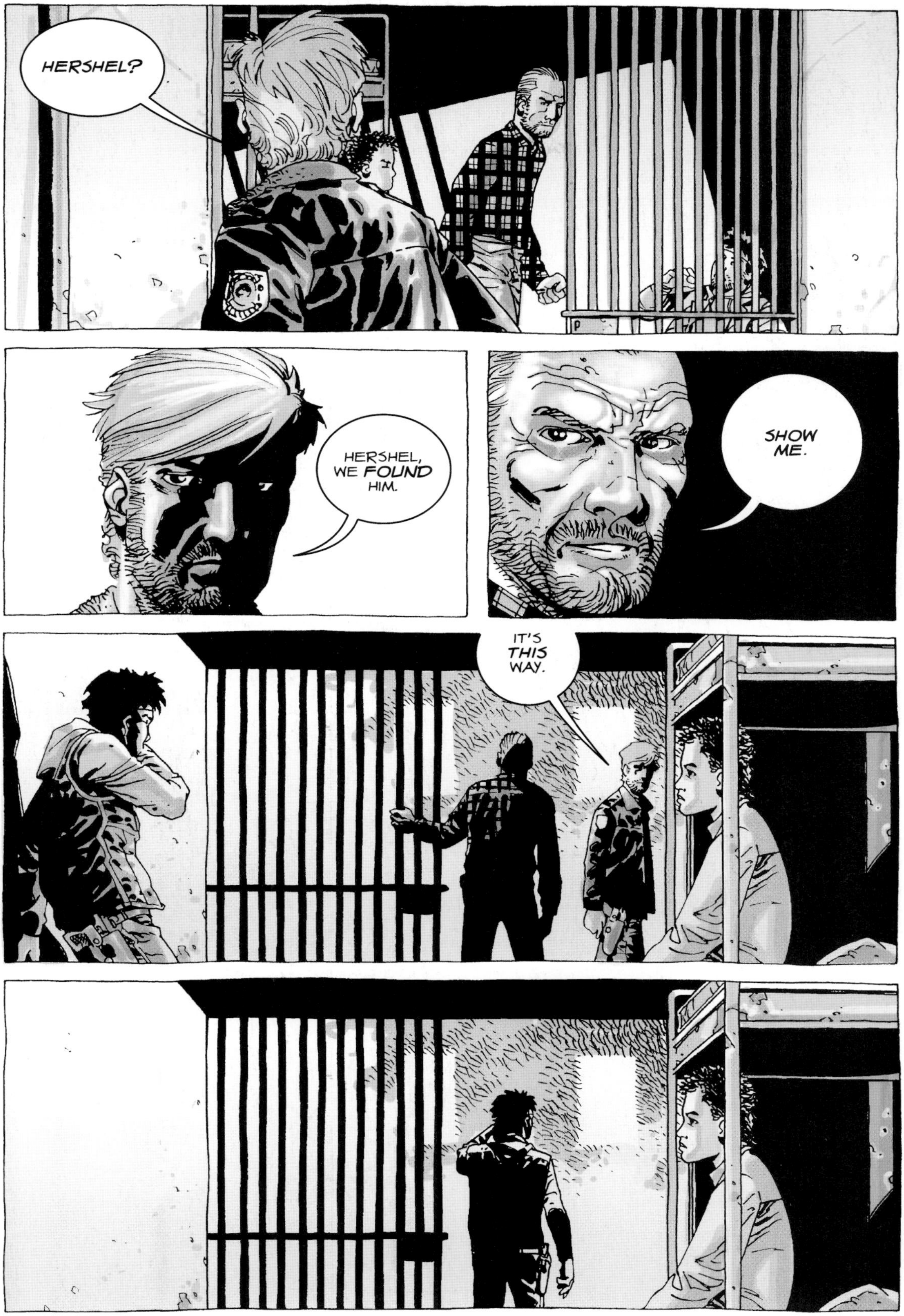
HERSHEL?
HERSHEL, WE FOUND HIM.
SHOW ME.
IT'S THIS WAY.

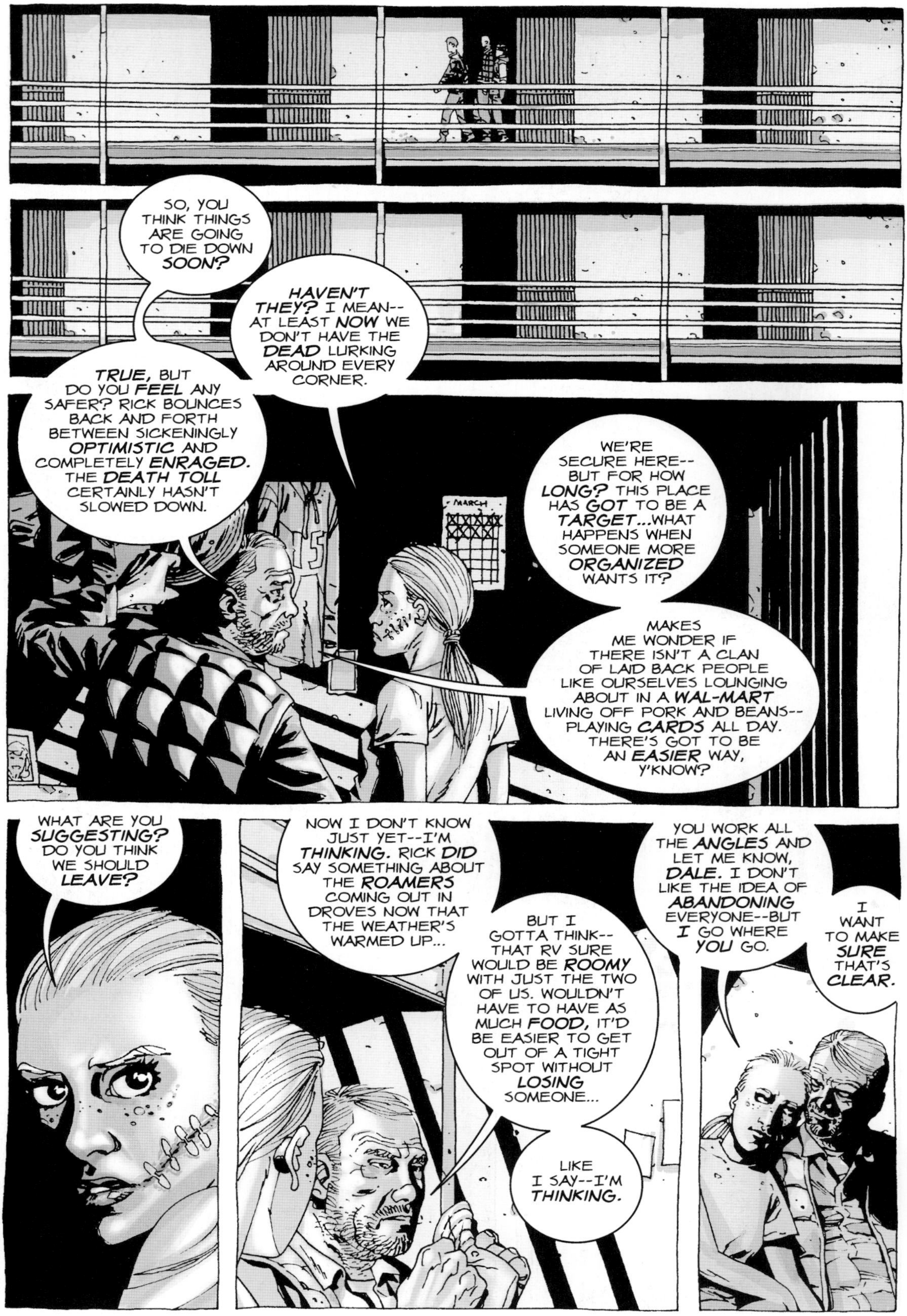
SO, YOU THINK THINGS ARE GOING TO DIE DOWN SOON?
HAVEN'T THEY? I MEAN-- AT LEAST NOW WE DON'T HAVE THE DEAD LURKING AROUND EVERY CORNER.
TRUE, BUT DO YOU FEEL ANY SAFER? RICK BOUNCES BACK AND FORTH BETWEEN SICKENINGLY OPTIMISTIC AND COMPLETELY ENRAGED. THE DEATH TOLL CERTAINLY HASN'T SLOWED DOWN.
WE'RE SECURE HERE-- BUT FOR HOW LONG? THIS PLACE HAS GOT TO BE A TARGET...WHAT HAPPENS WHEN SOMEONE MORE ORGANIZED WANTS IT?
MAKES ME WONDER IF THERE ISN'T A CLAN OF LAID BACK PEOPLE LIKE OURSELVES LOUNGING ABOUT IN A WAL-MART LIVING OFF PORK AND BEANS-- PLAYING CARDS ALL DAY. THERE'S GOT TO BE AN EASIER WAY, Y'KNOW?
WHAT ARE YOU SUGGESTING? DO YOU THINK WE SHOULD LEAVE?
NOW I DON'T KNOW JUST YET--I'M THINKING. RICK DID SAY SOMETHING ABOUT THE ROAMERS COMING OUT IN DROVES NOW THAT THE WEATHER'S WARMED UP...
BUT I GOTTA THINK-- THAT RV SURE WOULD BE ROOMY WITH JUST THE TWO OF US. WOULDN'T HAVE TO HAVE AS MUCH FOOD, IT'D BE EASIER TO GET OUT OF A TIGHT SPOT WITHOUT LOSING SOMEONE...
LIKE I SAY--I'M THINKING.
YOU WORK ALL THE ANGLES AND LET ME KNOW, DALE. I DON'T LIKE THE IDEA OF ABANDONING EVERYONE--BUT I GO WHERE YOU GO.
I WANT TO MAKE SURE THAT'S CLEAR.

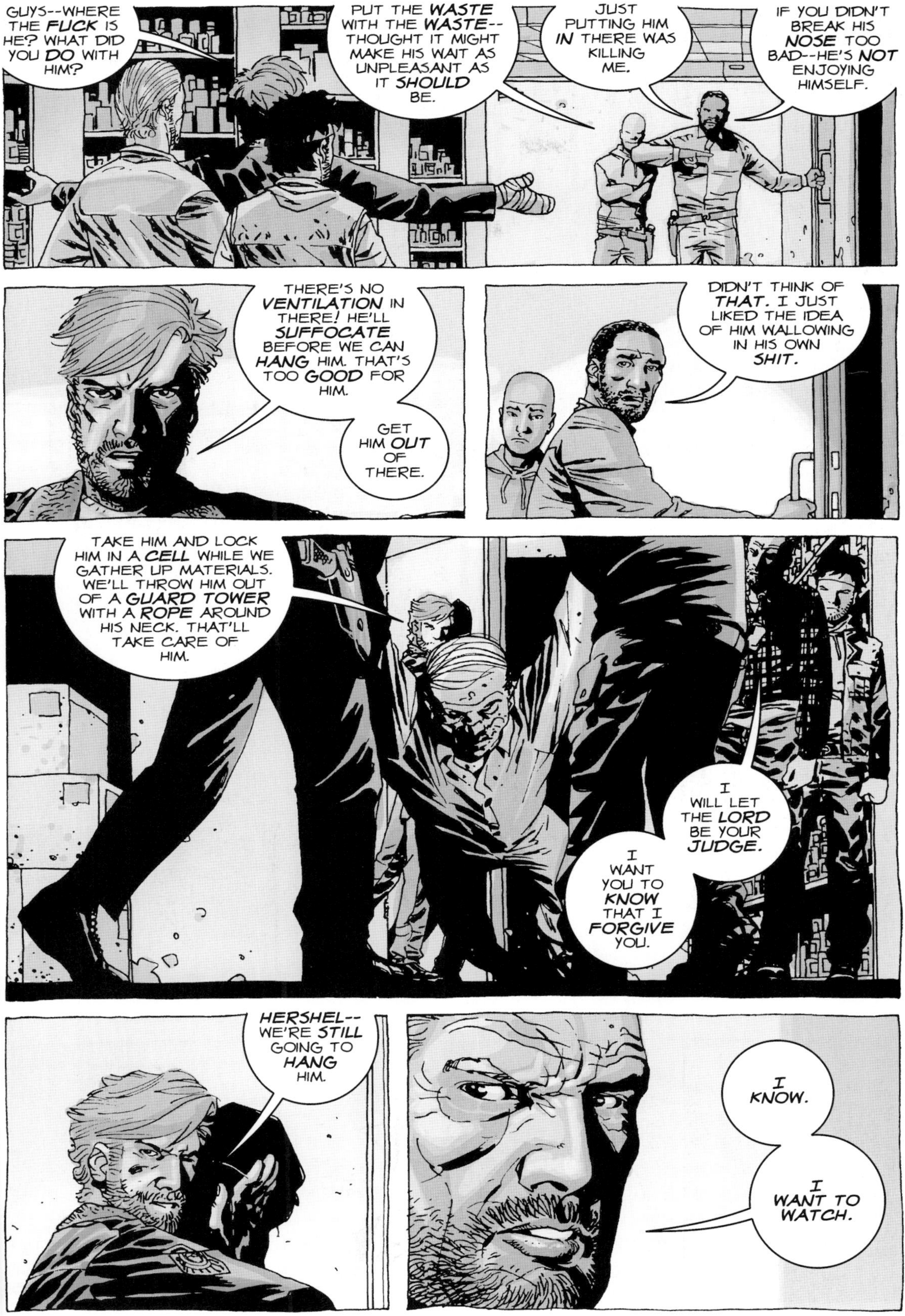
GUYS--WHERE THE FUCK IS HE? WHAT DID YOU DO WITH HIM?
PUT THE WASTE WITH THE WASTE--THOUGHT IT MIGHT MAKE HIS WAIT AS UNPLEASANT AS IT SHOULD BE.
JUST PUTTING HIM IN THERE WAS KILLING ME.
IF YOU DIDN'T BREAK HIS NOSE TOO BAD--HE'S NOT ENJOYING HIMSELF.
THERE'S NO VENTILATION IN THERE! HE'LL SUFFOCATE BEFORE WE CAN HANG HIM. THAT'S TOO GOOD FOR HIM.
GET HIM OUT OF THERE.
DIDN'T THINK OF THAT. I JUST LIKED THE IDEA OF HIM WALLOWING IN HIS OWN SHIT.
TAKE HIM AND LOCK HIM IN A CELL WHILE WE GATHER UP MATERIALS. WE'LL THROW HIM OUT OF A GUARD TOWER WITH A ROPE AROUND HIS NECK. THAT'LL TAKE CARE OF HIM.
I WILL LET THE LORD BE YOUR JUDGE.
I WANT YOU TO KNOW THAT I FORGIVE YOU.
HERSHEL--WE'RE STILL GOING TO HANG HIM.
I KNOW.
I WANT TO WATCH.

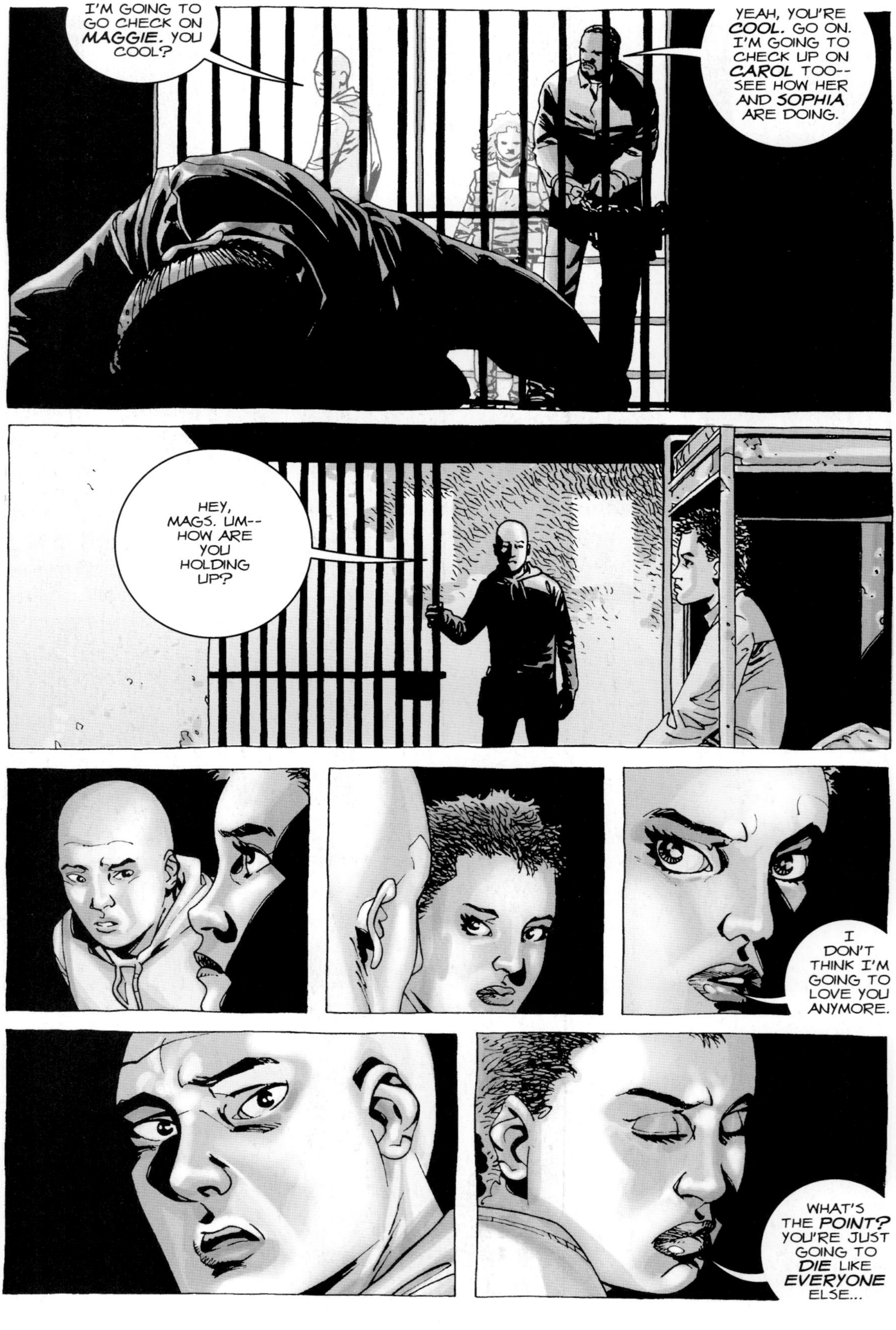
I'M GOING TO GO CHECK ON MAGGIE. YOU COOL?
YEAH, YOU'RE COOL. GO ON. I'M GOING TO CHECK UP ON CAROL TOO-- SEE HOW HER AND SOPHIA ARE DOING.
HEY, MAGS. UM-- HOW ARE YOU HOLDING UP?
I DON'T THINK I'M GOING TO LOVE YOU ANYMORE.
WHAT'S THE POINT? YOU'RE JUST GOING TO DIE LIKE EVERYONE ELSE...

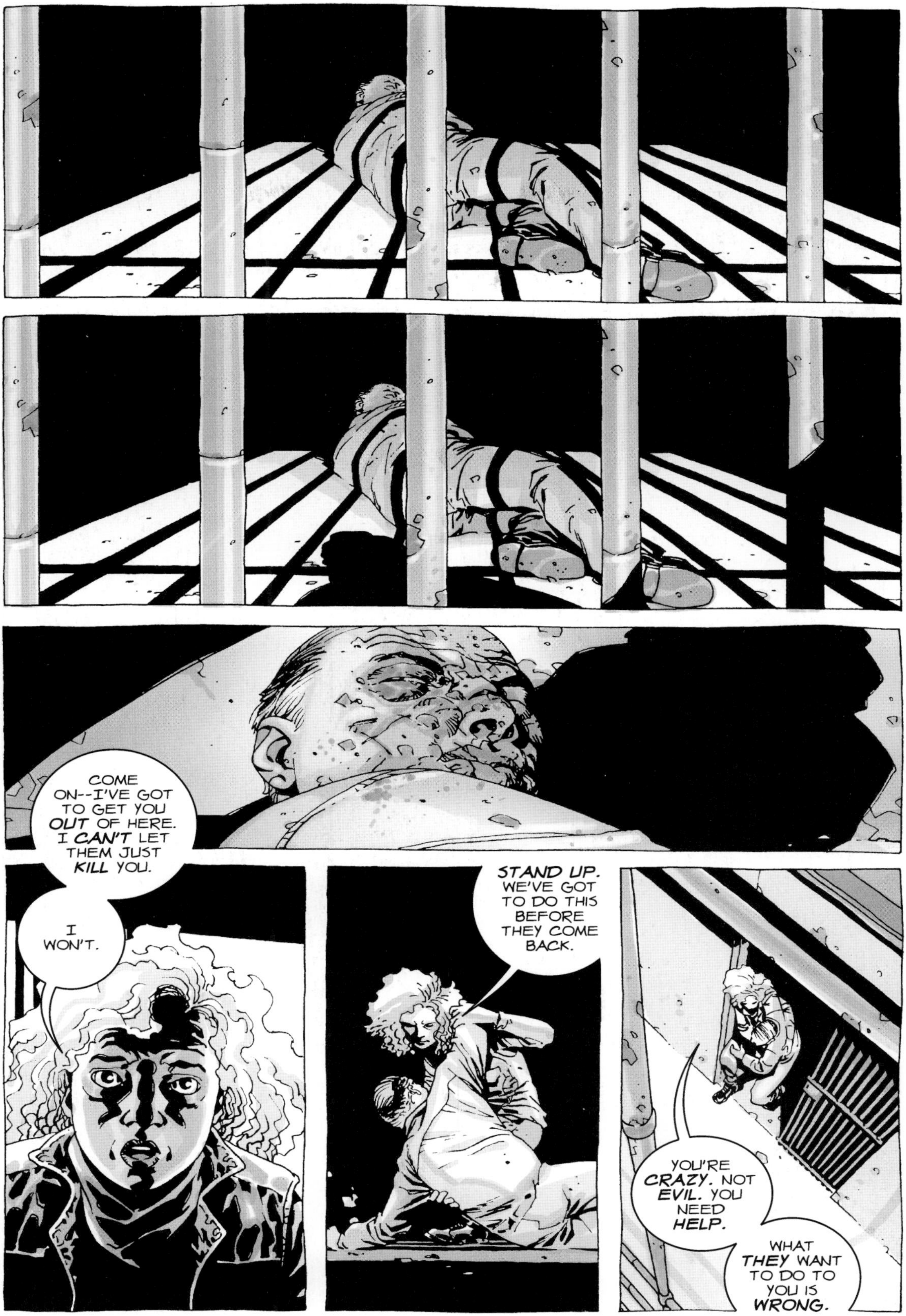
COME ON--I'VE GOT TO GET YOU OUT OF HERE. I CAN'T LET THEM JUST KILL YOU.
I WON'T.
STAND UP. WE'VE GOT TO DO THIS BEFORE THEY COME BACK.
YOU'RE CRAZY. NOT EVIL. YOU NEED HELP.
WHAT THEY WANT TO DO TO YOU IS WRONG.

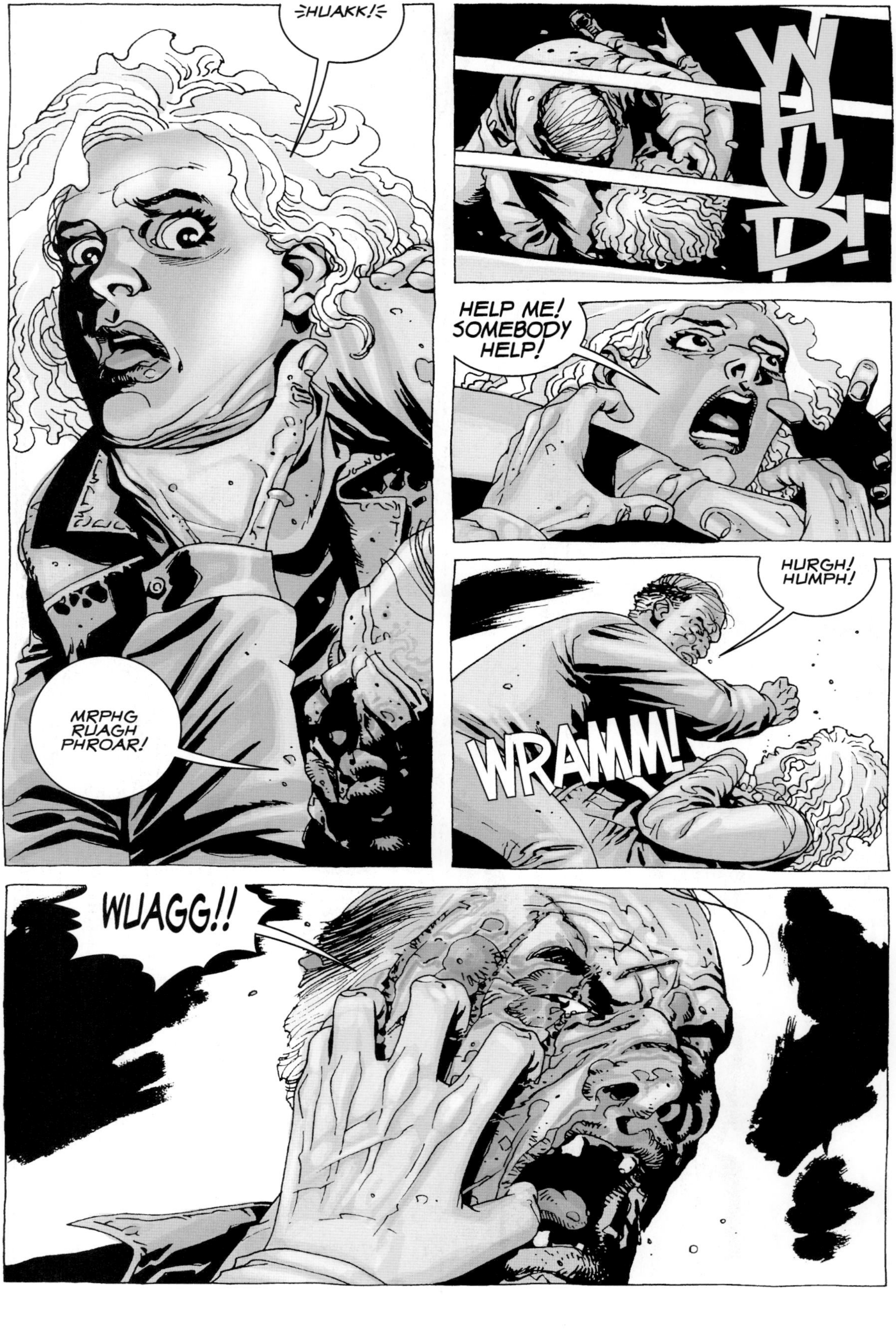
HUAKK!
MRPHG RUAGH PHROAR!
WHUD!
HELP ME! SOMEBODY HELP!
HURGH! HUMPH!
WRAMM!
WUAGG!!

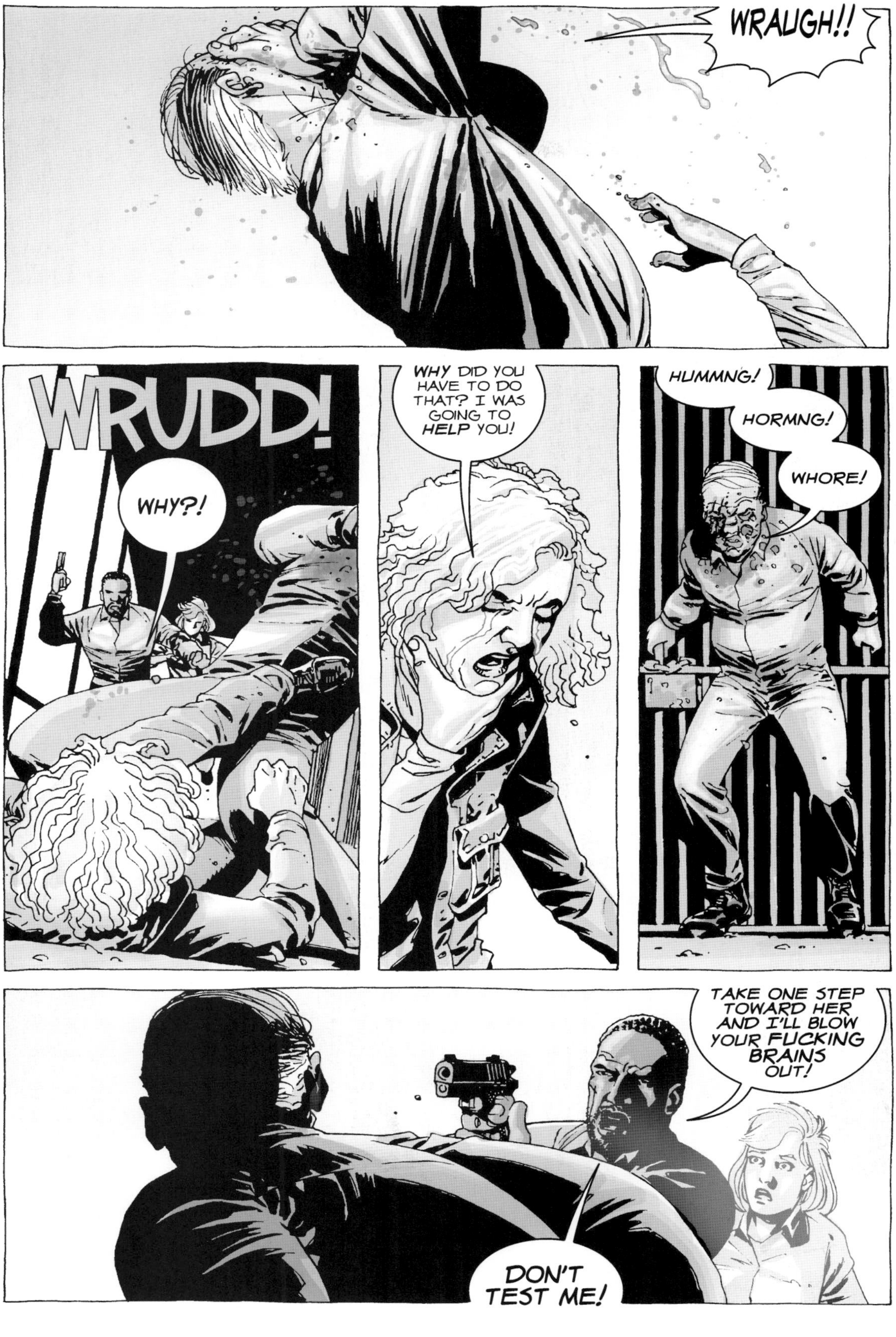
WRAUGH!!
WRUDD!
WHY?!
WHY DID YOU HAVE TO DO THAT? I WAS GOING TO HELP YOU!
HUMMNG!
HORMNG!
WHORE!
TAKE ONE STEP TOWARD HER AND I'LL BLOW YOUR FUCKING BRAINS OUT!
DON'T TEST ME!

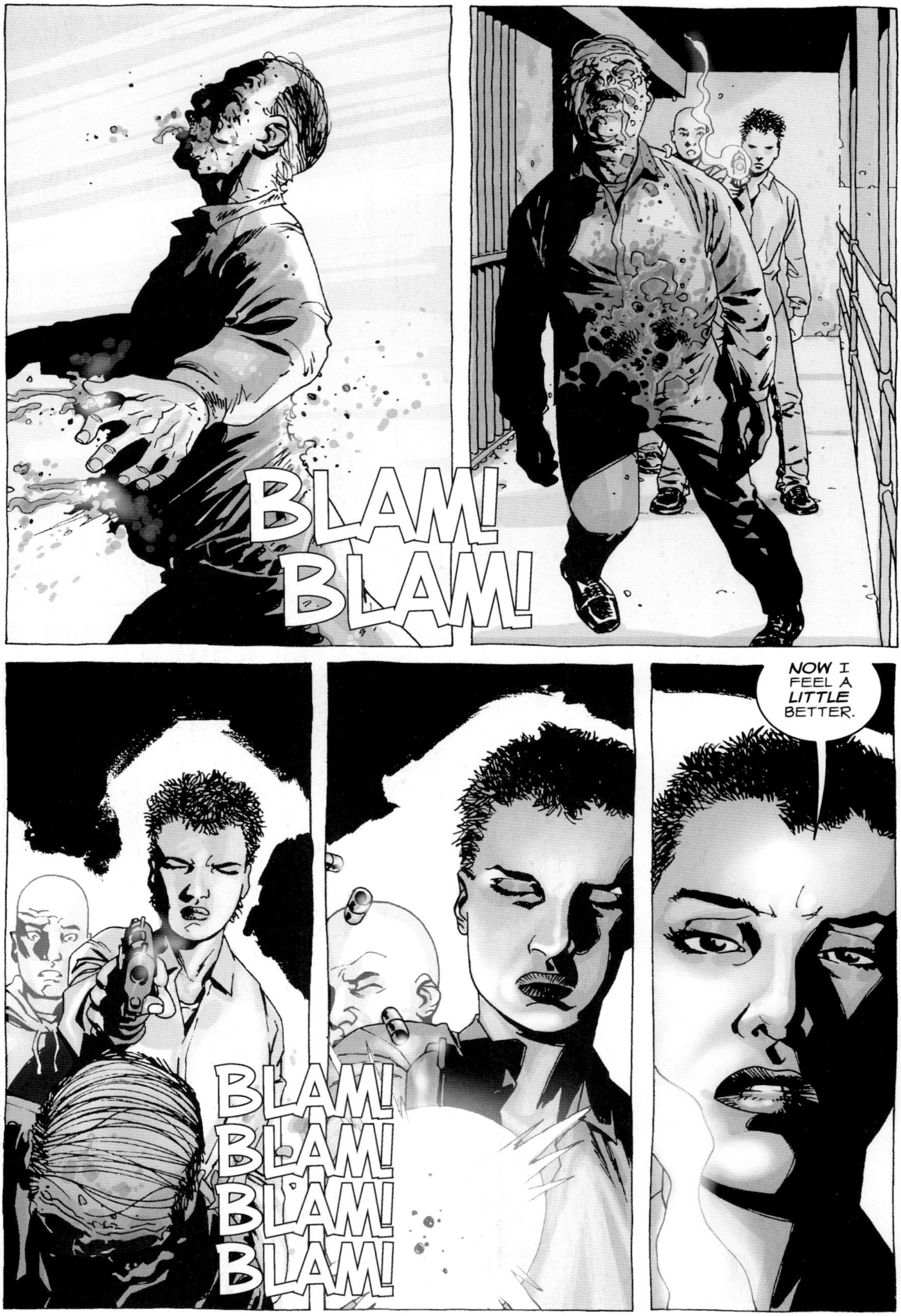
BLAM!
BLAM!
BLAM!
BLAM!
BLAM!
BLAM!
NOW I FEEL A LITTLE BETTER.

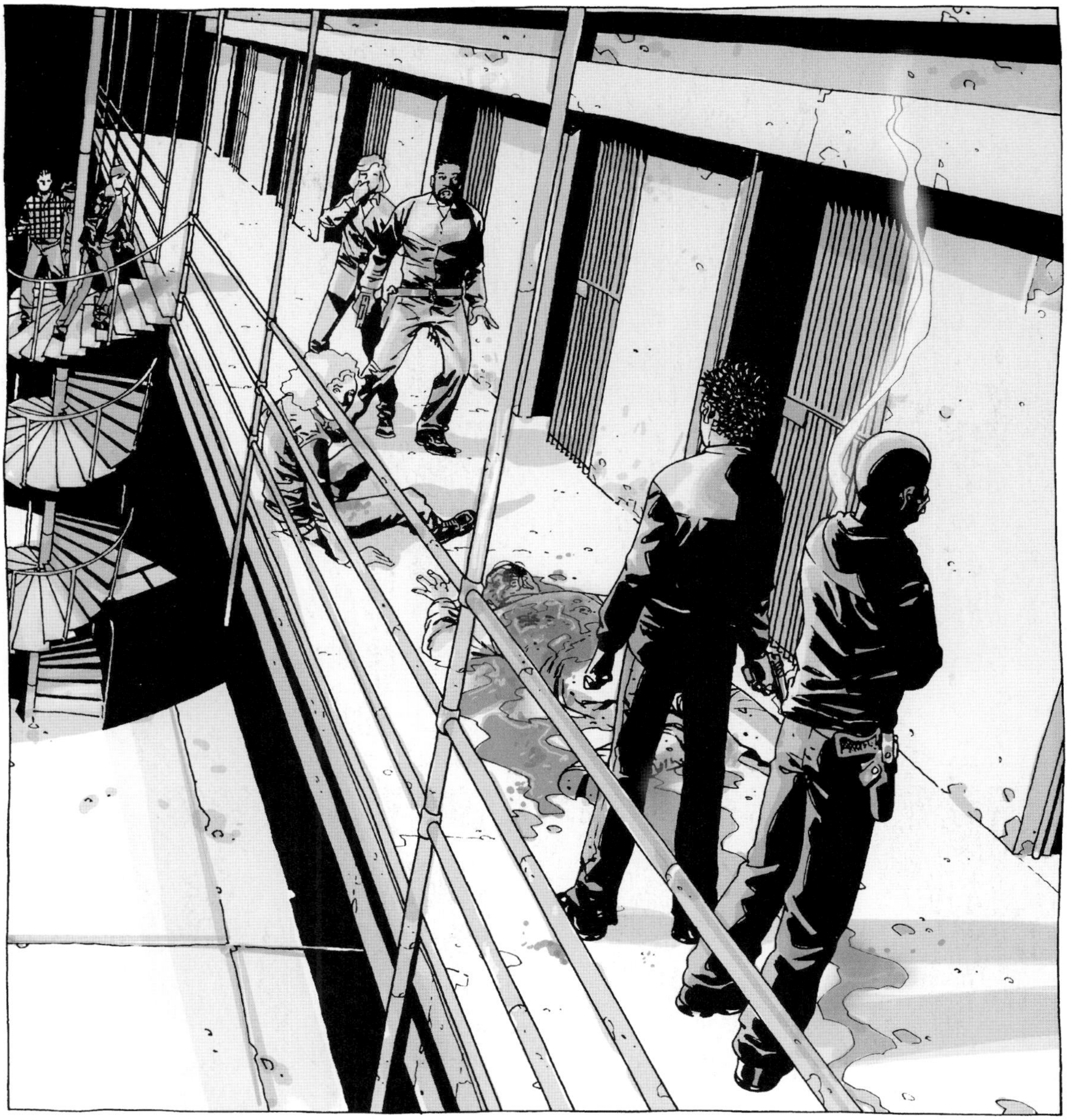

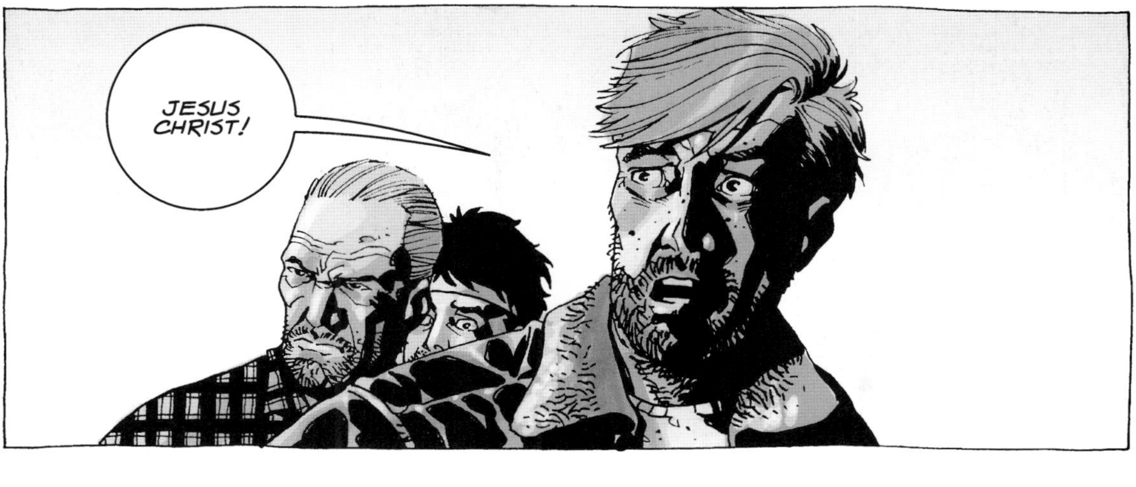
JESUS CHRIST!

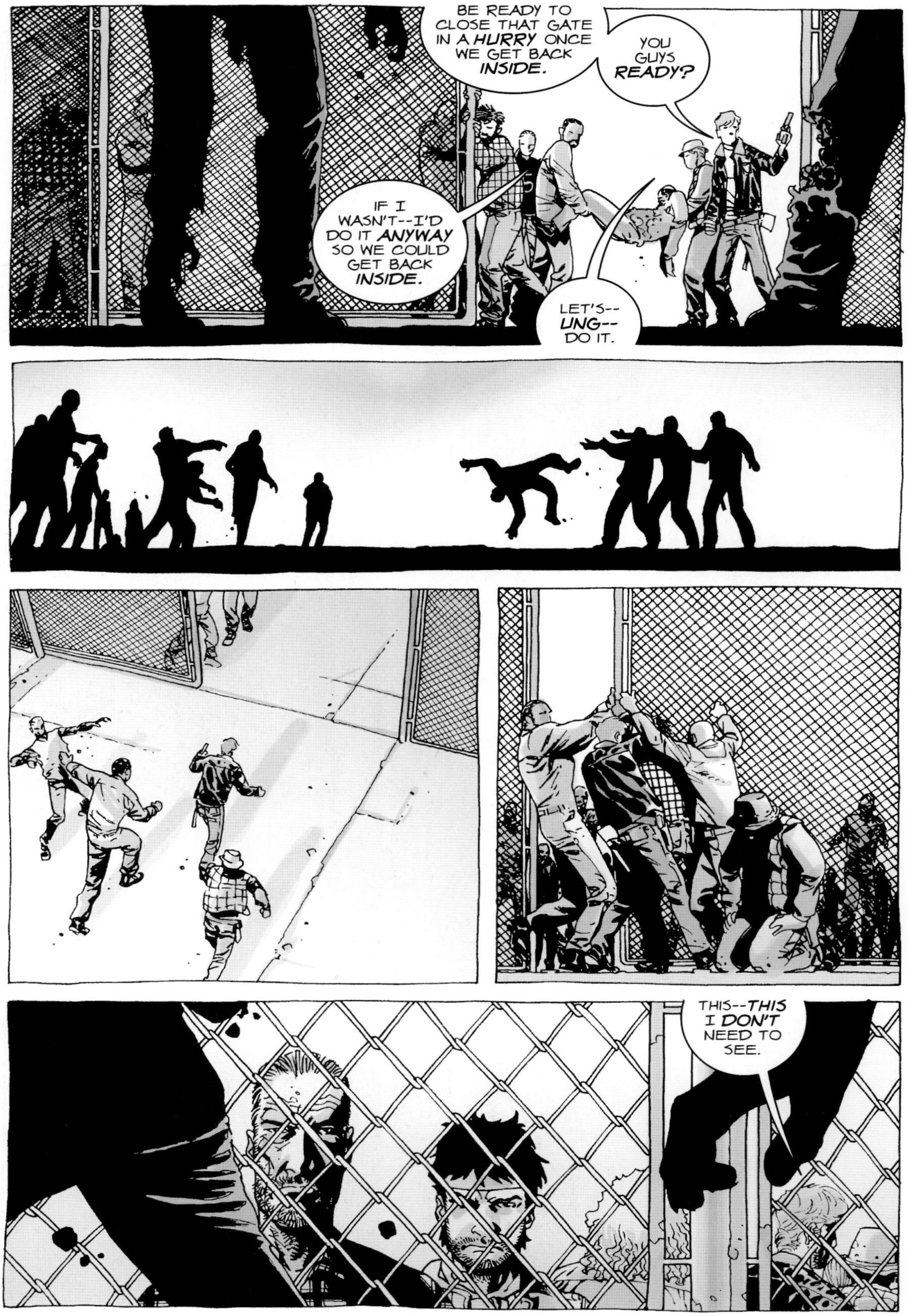
BE READY TO CLOSE THAT GATE IN A *HURRY* ONCE WE GET BACK *INSIDE.*
YOU GUYS *READY?*
IF I WASN'T--I'D DO IT *ANYWAY* SO WE COULD GET BACK *INSIDE.*
LET'S-- *UNG--* DO IT.
THIS--*THIS* I *DON'T* NEED TO SEE.

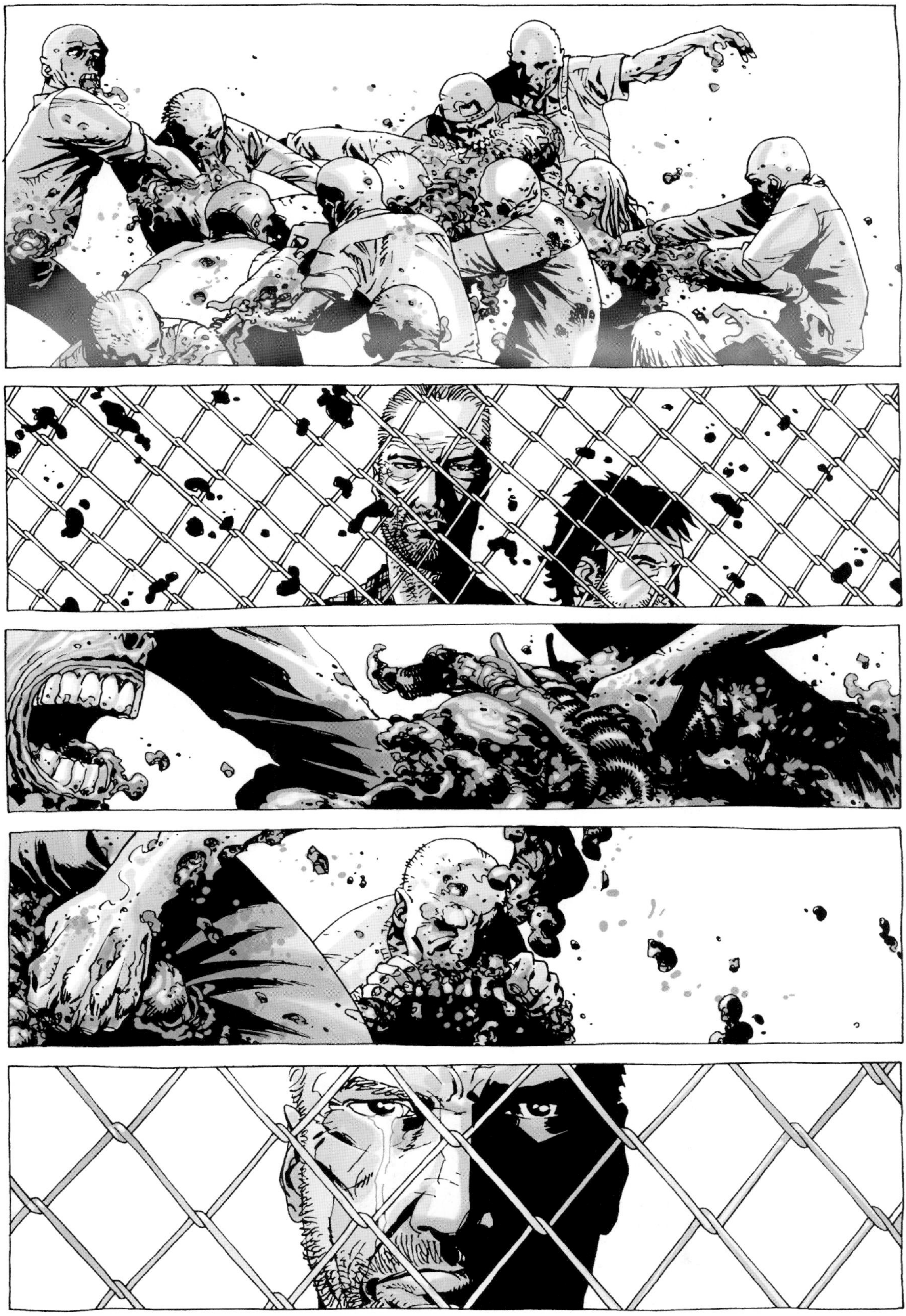

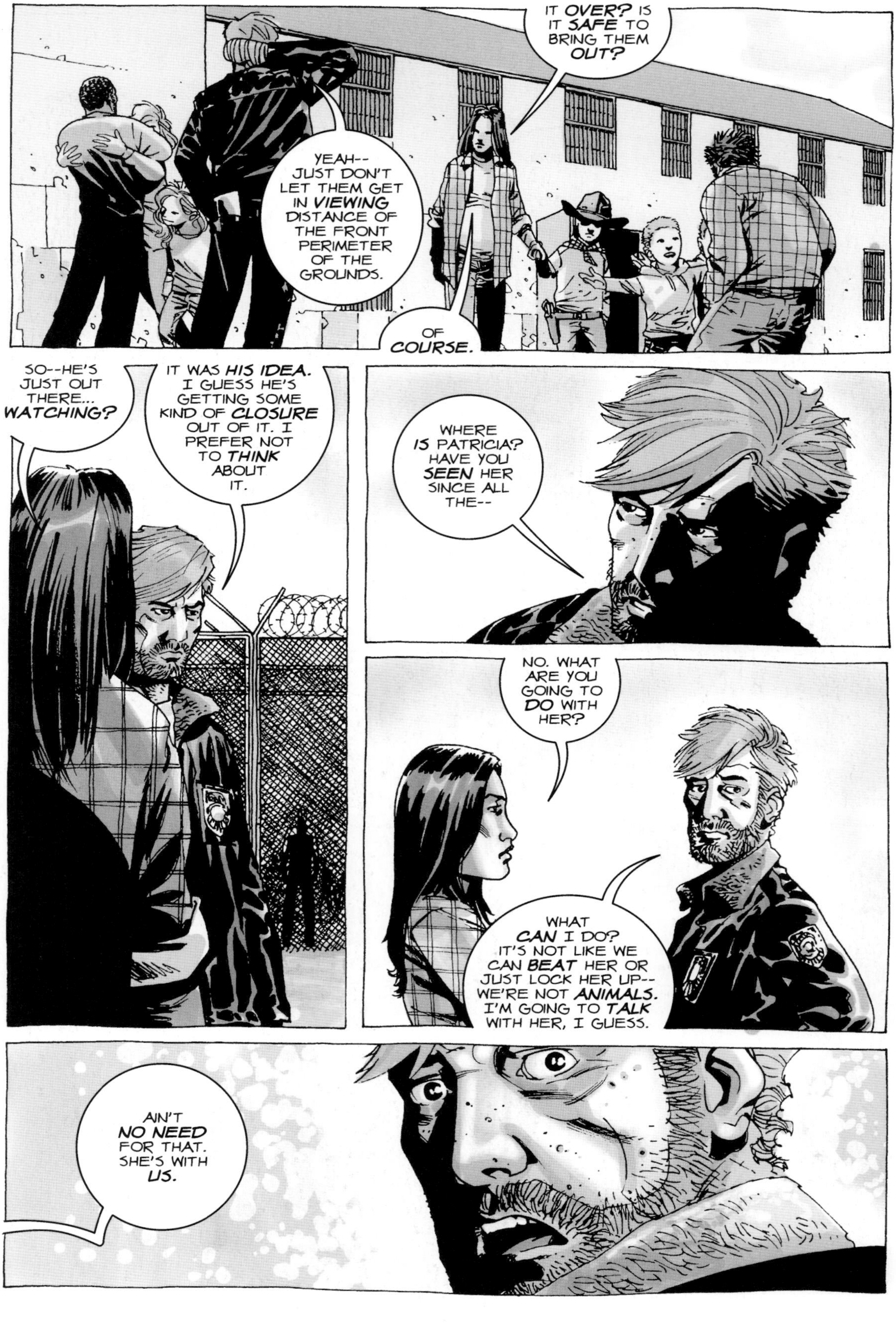
IT OVER? IS IT SAFE TO BRING THEM OUT?
YEAH-- JUST DON'T LET THEM GET IN VIEWING DISTANCE OF THE FRONT PERIMETER OF THE GROUNDS.
OF COURSE.
SO--HE'S JUST OUT THERE... WATCHING?
IT WAS HIS IDEA. I GUESS HE'S GETTING SOME KIND OF CLOSURE OUT OF IT. I PREFER NOT TO THINK ABOUT IT.
WHERE IS PATRICIA? HAVE YOU SEEN HER SINCE ALL THE--
NO. WHAT ARE YOU GOING TO DO WITH HER?
WHAT CAN I DO? IT'S NOT LIKE WE CAN BEAT HER OR JUST LOCK HER UP-- WE'RE NOT ANIMALS. I'M GOING TO TALK WITH HER, I GUESS.
AIN'T NO NEED FOR THAT. SHE'S WITH US.

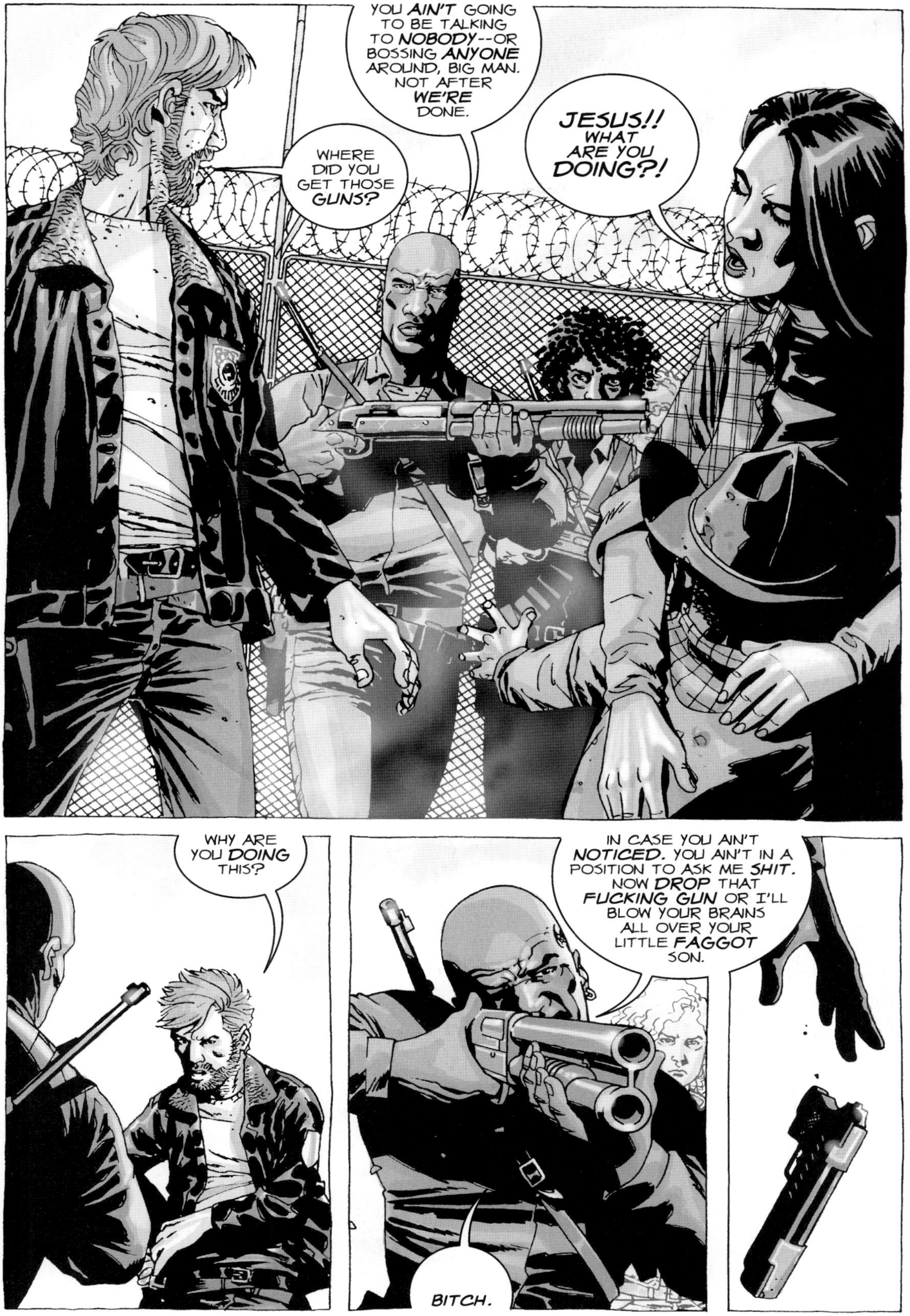
WHERE DID YOU GET THOSE GUNS?
YOU AIN'T GOING TO BE TALKING TO NOBODY--OR BOSSING ANYONE AROUND, BIG MAN. NOT AFTER WE'RE DONE.
JESUS!! WHAT ARE YOU DOING?!
WHY ARE YOU DOING THIS?
IN CASE YOU AIN'T NOTICED. YOU AIN'T IN A POSITION TO ASK ME SHIT. NOW DROP THAT FUCKING GUN OR I'LL BLOW YOUR BRAINS ALL OVER YOUR LITTLE FAGGOT SON.
BITCH.

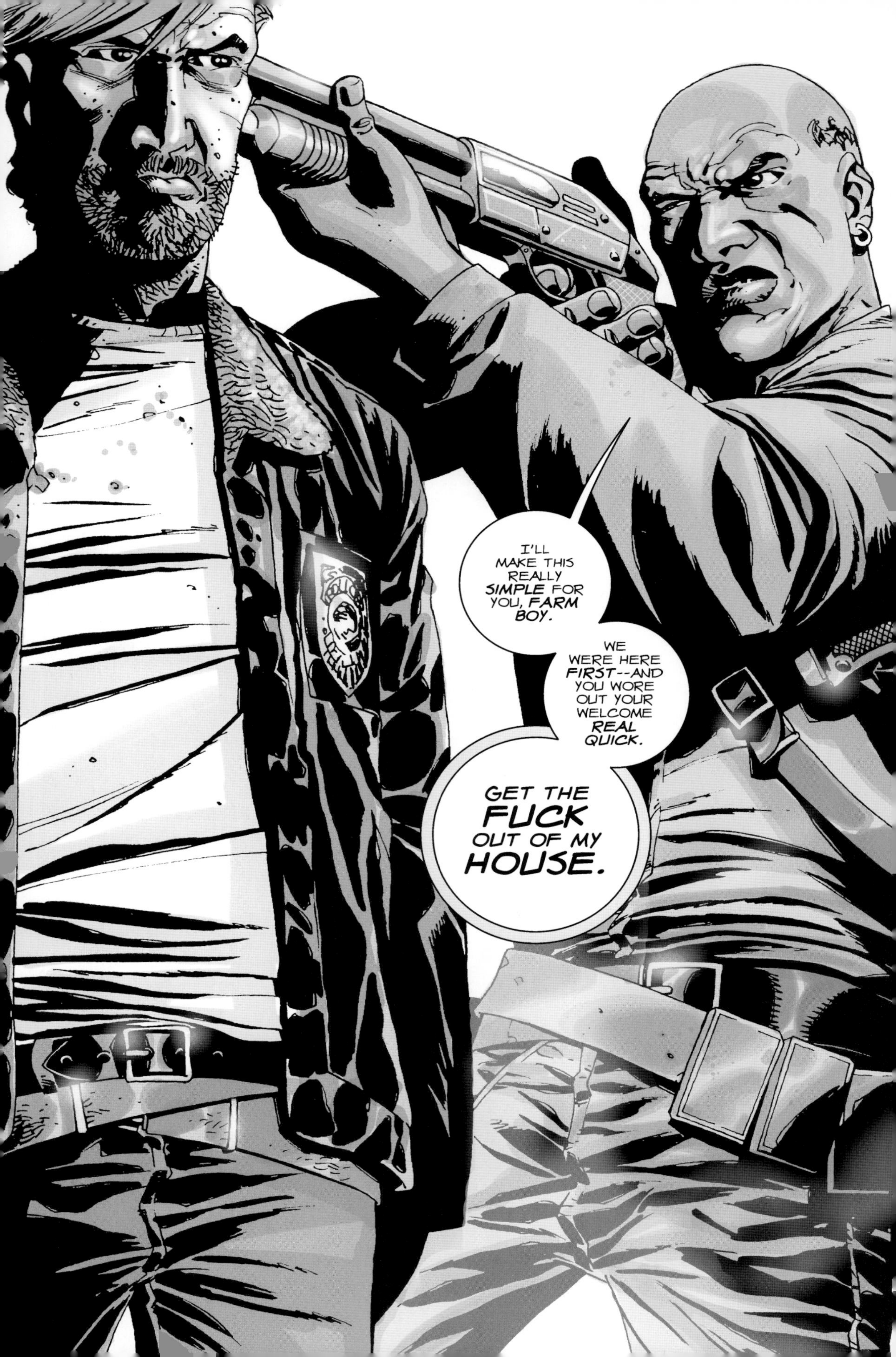
I'LL MAKE THIS REALLY SIMPLE FOR YOU, FARM BOY.
WE WERE HERE FIRST--AND YOU WORE OUT YOUR WELCOME REAL QUICK.
GET THE FUCK OUT OF MY HOUSE.

Chapter Four:
The Heart's Desire

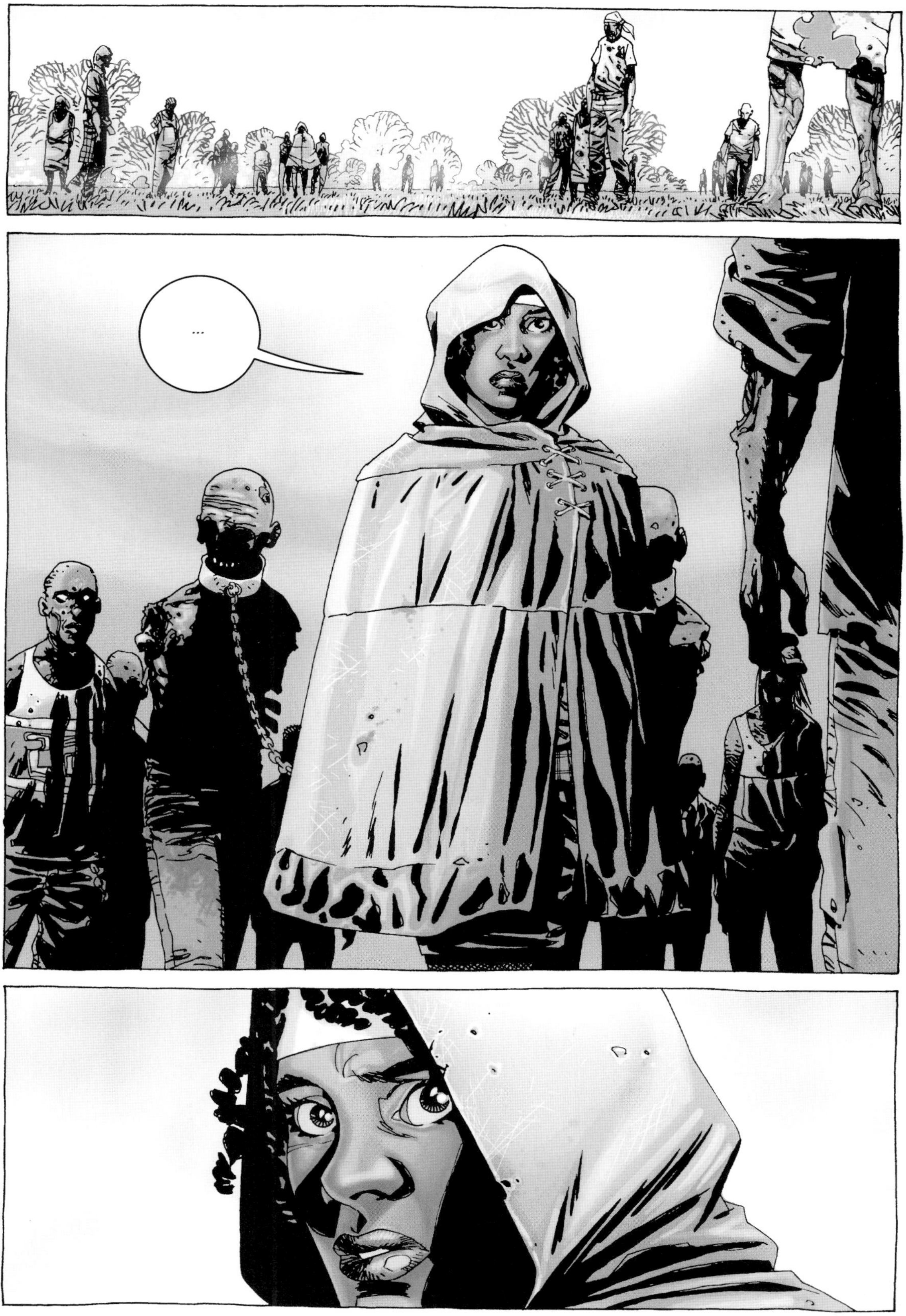
...

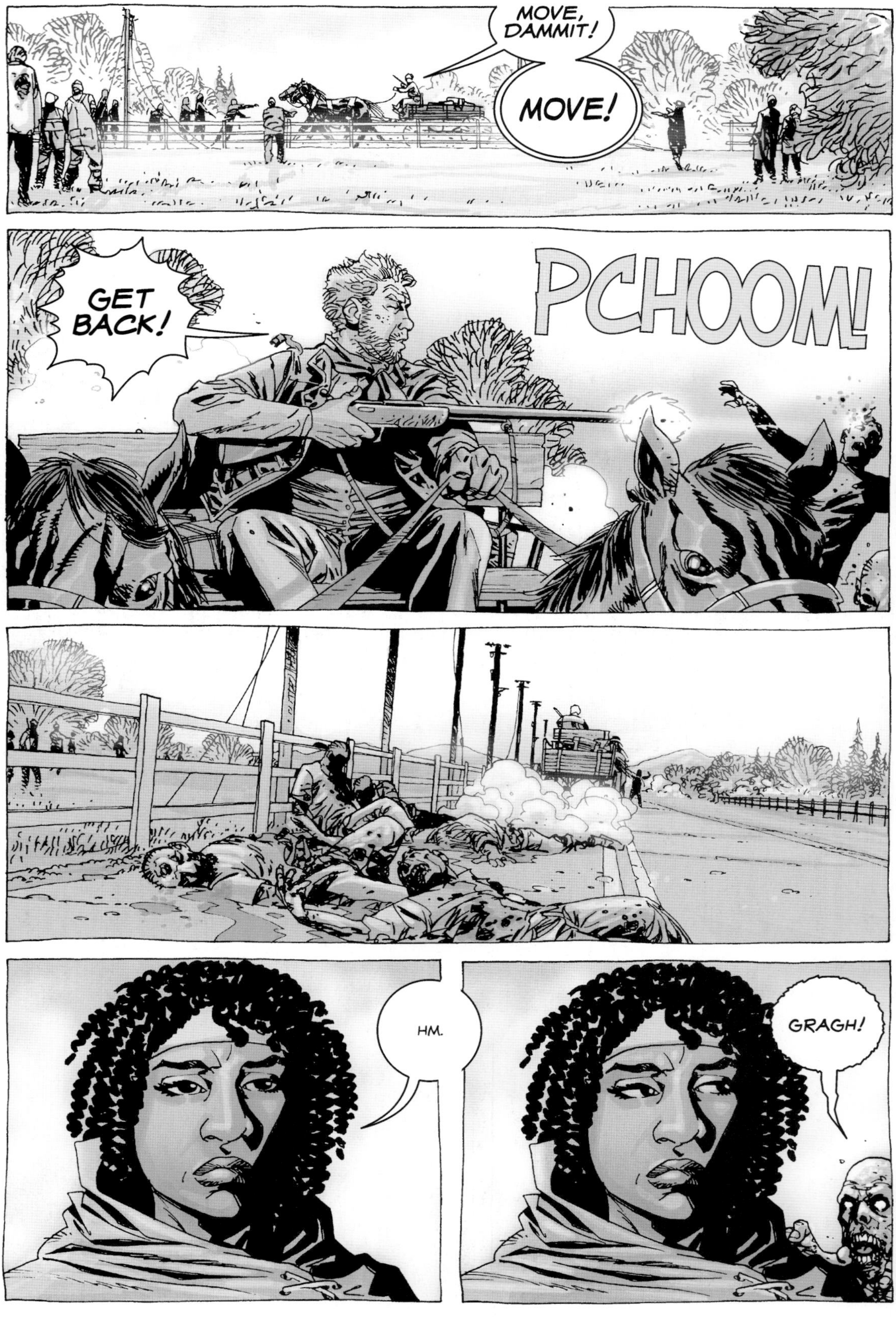
MOVE, DAMMIT!
MOVE!
GET BACK!
PCHOOM!
HM.
GRAGH!

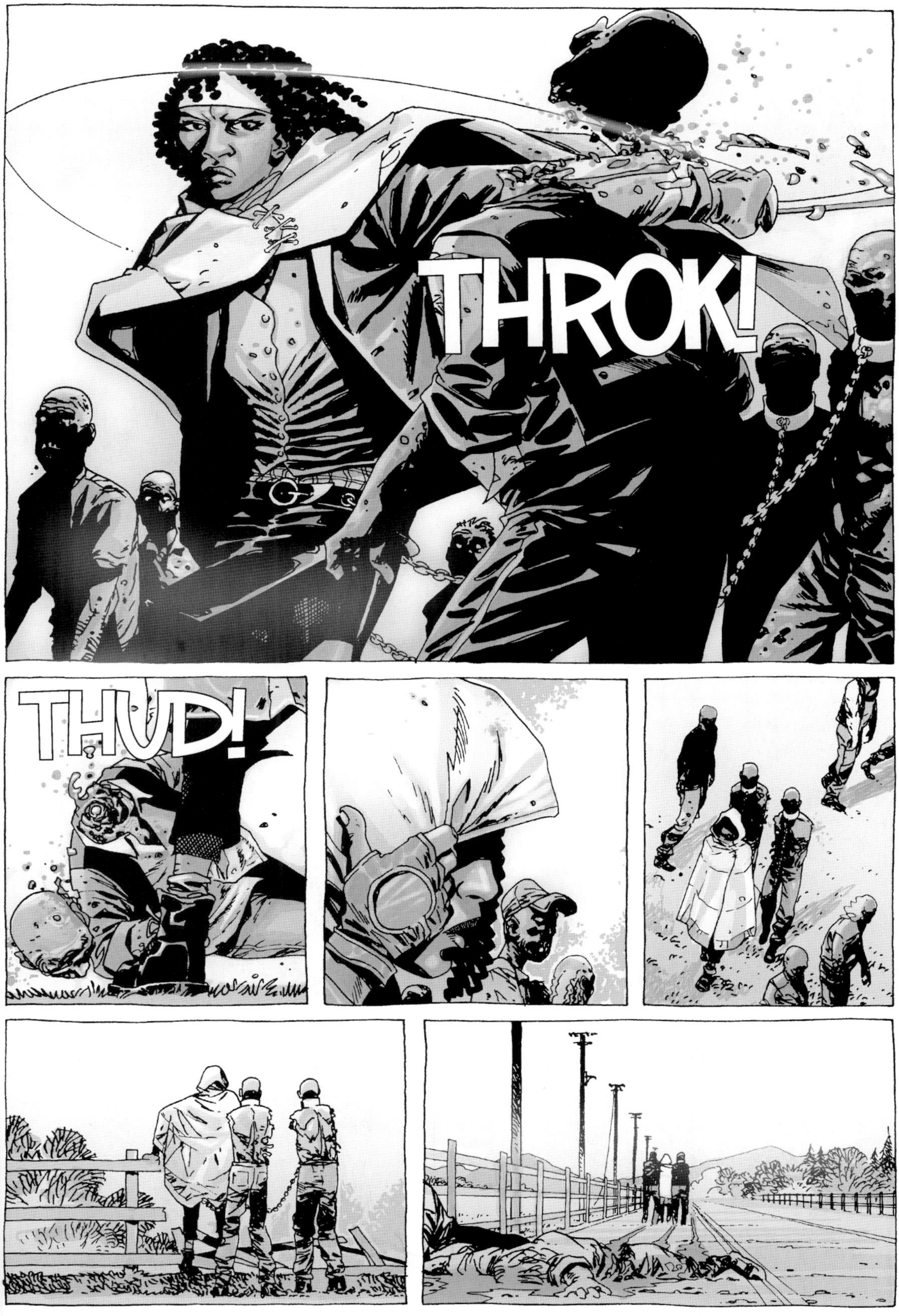
THROK!
THUD!

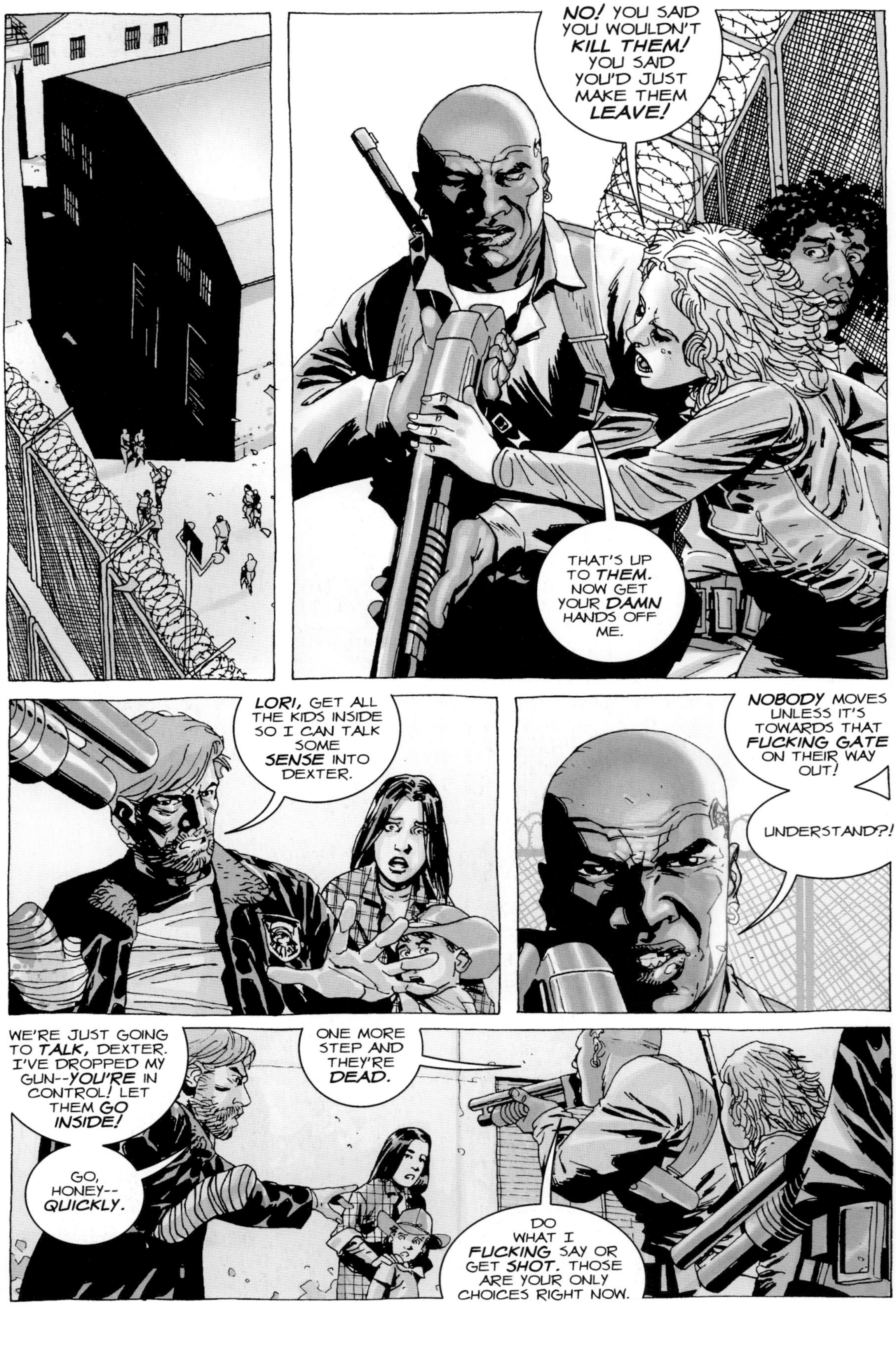
NO! YOU SAID YOU WOULDN'T KILL THEM! YOU SAID YOU'D JUST MAKE THEM LEAVE!
THAT'S UP TO THEM. NOW GET YOUR DAMN HANDS OFF ME.
LORI, GET ALL THE KIDS INSIDE SO I CAN TALK SOME SENSE INTO DEXTER.
NOBODY MOVES UNLESS IT'S TOWARDS THAT FUCKING GATE ON THEIR WAY OUT!
UNDERSTAND?!
WE'RE JUST GOING TO TALK, DEXTER. I'VE DROPPED MY GUN--YOU'RE IN CONTROL! LET THEM GO INSIDE!
GO, HONEY-- QUICKLY.
ONE MORE STEP AND THEY'RE DEAD.
DO WHAT I FUCKING SAY OR GET SHOT. THOSE ARE YOUR ONLY CHOICES RIGHT NOW.

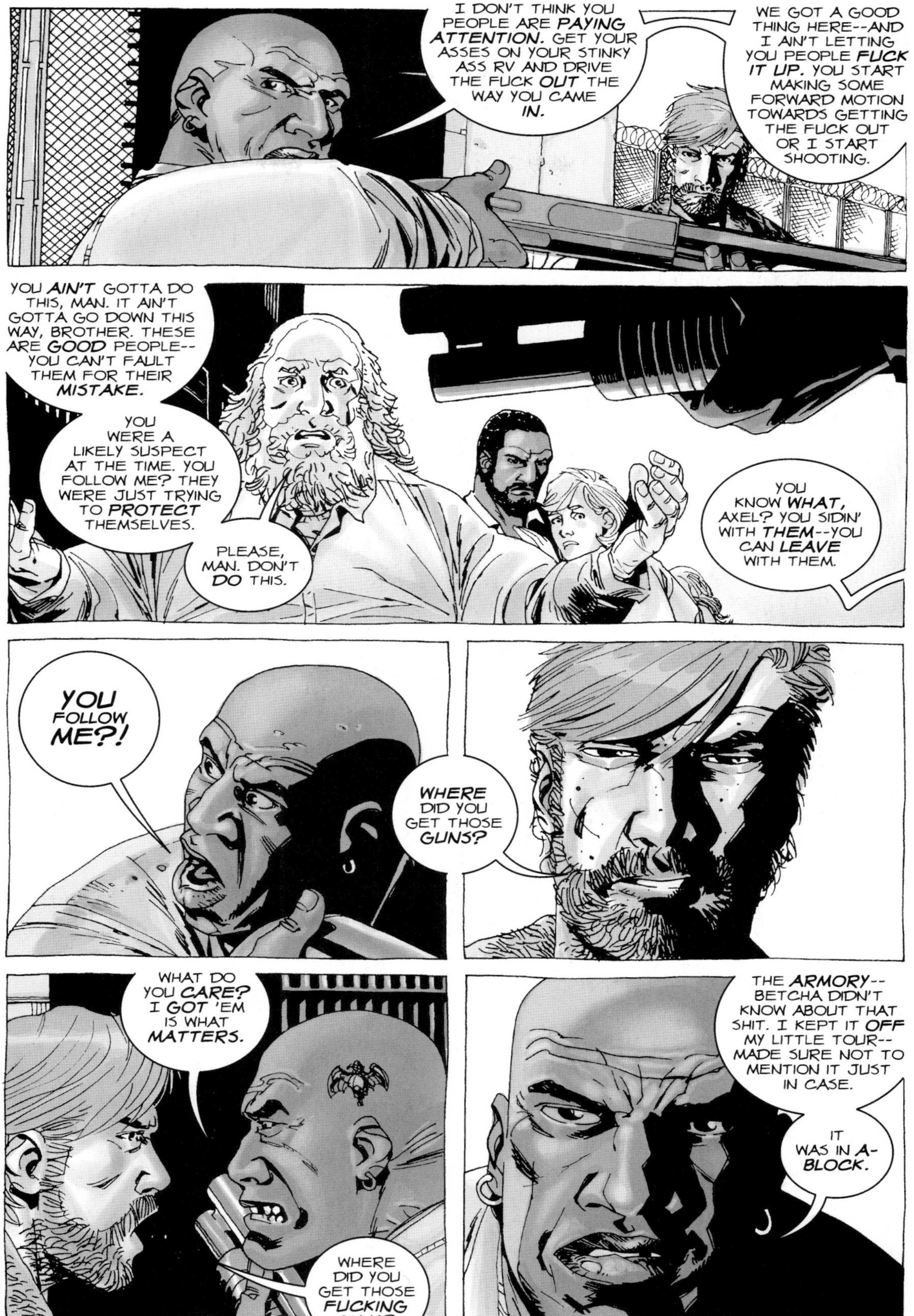
I DON'T THINK YOU PEOPLE ARE PAYING ATTENTION. GET YOUR ASSES ON YOUR STINKY ASS RV AND DRIVE THE FUCK OUT THE WAY YOU CAME IN.
WE GOT A GOOD THING HERE--AND I AIN'T LETTING YOU PEOPLE FUCK IT UP. YOU START MAKING SOME FORWARD MOTION TOWARDS GETTING THE FUCK OUT OR I START SHOOTING.
YOU AIN'T GOTTA DO THIS, MAN. IT AIN'T GOTTA GO DOWN THIS WAY, BROTHER. THESE ARE GOOD PEOPLE-- YOU CAN'T FAULT THEM FOR THEIR MISTAKE.
YOU WERE A LIKELY SUSPECT AT THE TIME. YOU FOLLOW ME? THEY WERE JUST TRYING TO PROTECT THEMSELVES.
PLEASE, MAN. DON'T DO THIS.
YOU KNOW WHAT, AXEL? YOU SIDIN' WITH THEM--YOU CAN LEAVE WITH THEM.
YOU FOLLOW ME?!
WHERE DID YOU GET THOSE GUNS?
WHAT DO YOU CARE? I GOT 'EM IS WHAT MATTERS.
WHERE DID YOU GET THOSE FUCKING GUNS?
THE ARMORY-- BETCHA DIDN'T KNOW ABOUT THAT SHIT. I KEPT IT OFF MY LITTLE TOUR-- MADE SURE NOT TO MENTION IT JUST IN CASE.
IT WAS IN A-BLOCK.

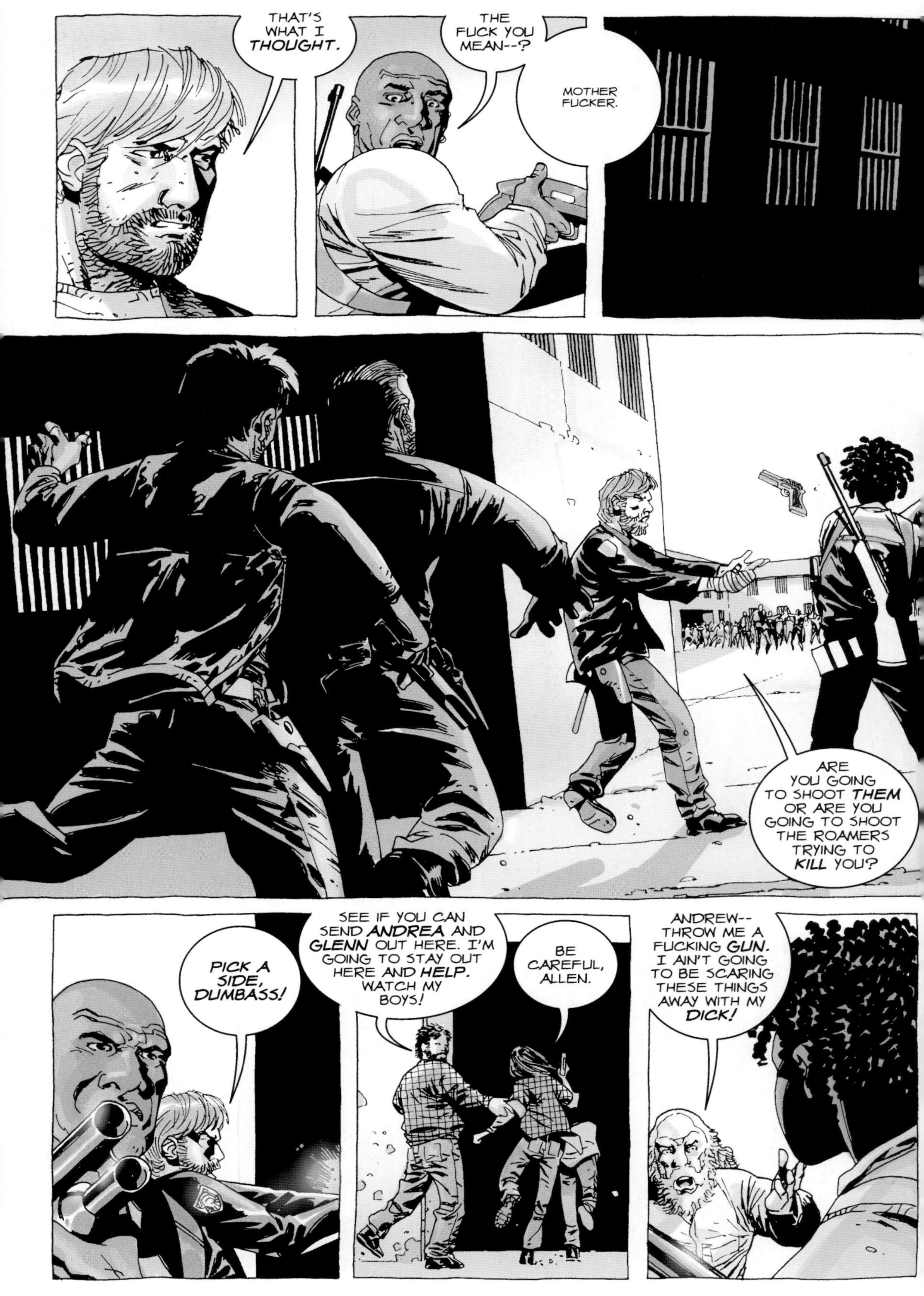

THAT'S WHAT I THOUGHT.
THE FUCK YOU MEAN--?
MOTHER FUCKER.
ARE YOU GOING TO SHOOT THEM OR ARE YOU GOING TO SHOOT THE ROAMERS TRYING TO KILL YOU?
PICK A SIDE, DUMBASS!
SEE IF YOU CAN SEND ANDREA AND GLENN OUT HERE. I'M GOING TO STAY OUT HERE AND HELP. WATCH MY BOYS!
BE CAREFUL, ALLEN.
ANDREW-- THROW ME A FUCKING GUN. I AIN'T GOING TO BE SCARING THESE THINGS AWAY WITH MY DICK!

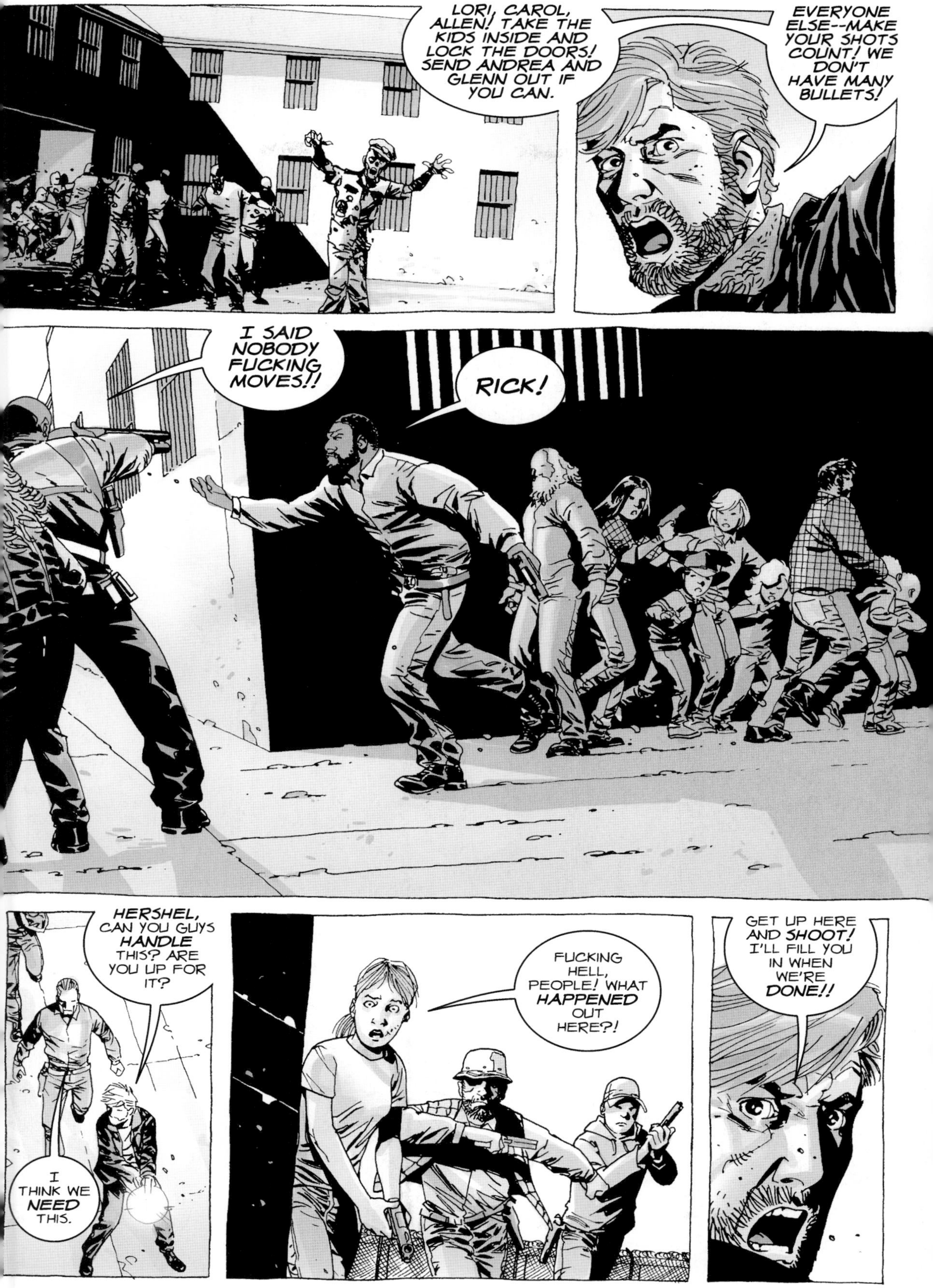
LORI, CAROL, ALLEN! TAKE THE KIDS INSIDE AND LOCK THE DOORS! SEND ANDREA AND GLENN OUT IF YOU CAN.
EVERYONE ELSE--MAKE YOUR SHOTS COUNT! WE DON'T HAVE MANY BULLETS!
I SAID NOBODY FUCKING MOVES!!
RICK!
HERSHEL, CAN YOU GUYS HANDLE THIS? ARE YOU UP FOR IT?
I THINK WE NEED THIS.
FUCKING HELL, PEOPLE! WHAT HAPPENED OUT HERE?!
GET UP HERE AND SHOOT! I'LL FILL YOU IN WHEN WE'RE DONE!!

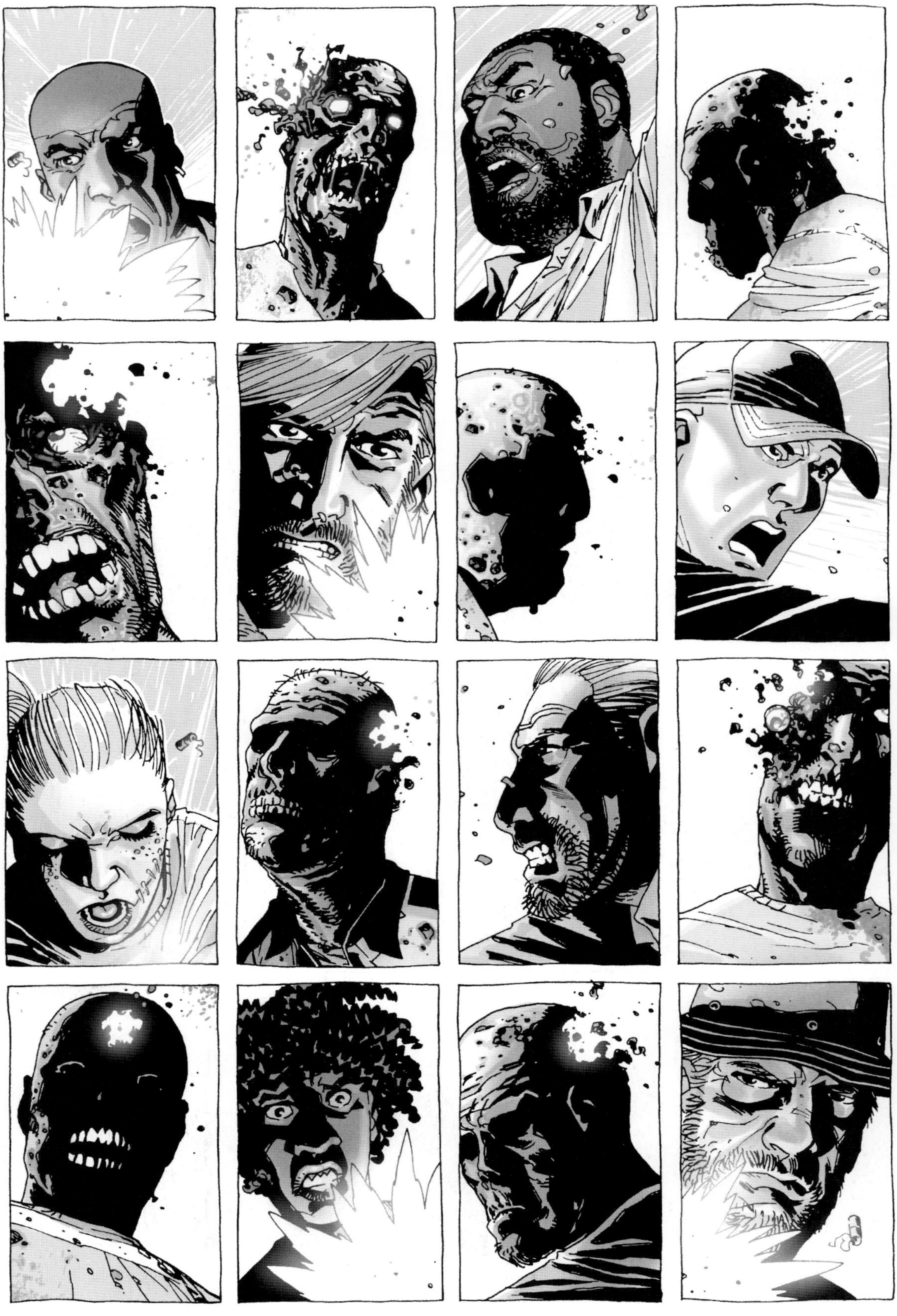

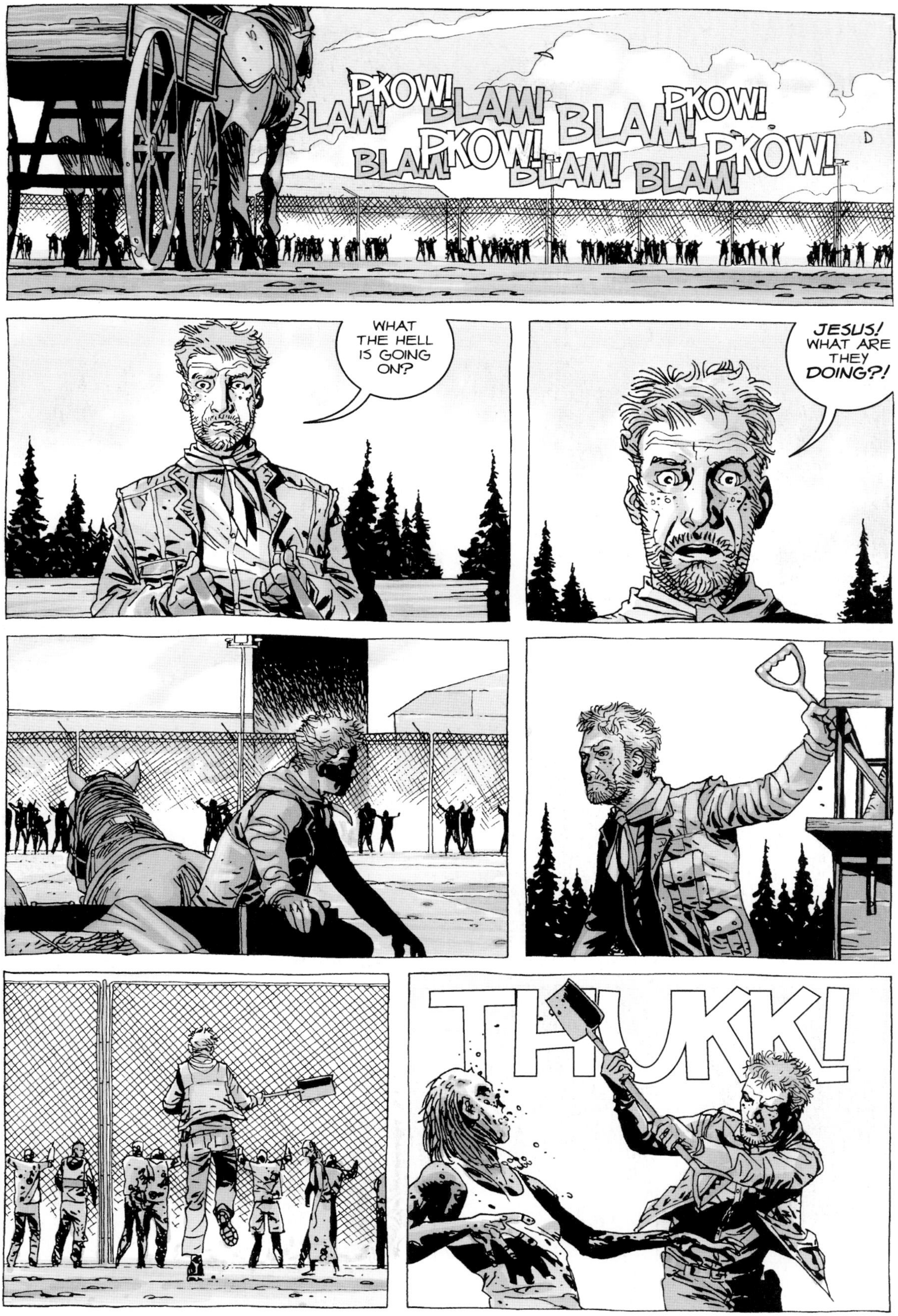
PKOW! BLAM! BLAM! BLAM! PKOW!
BLAM! PKOW! BLAM! BLAM! PKOW!
WHAT THE HELL IS GOING ON?
JESUS! WHAT ARE THEY DOING?!
THUKK!

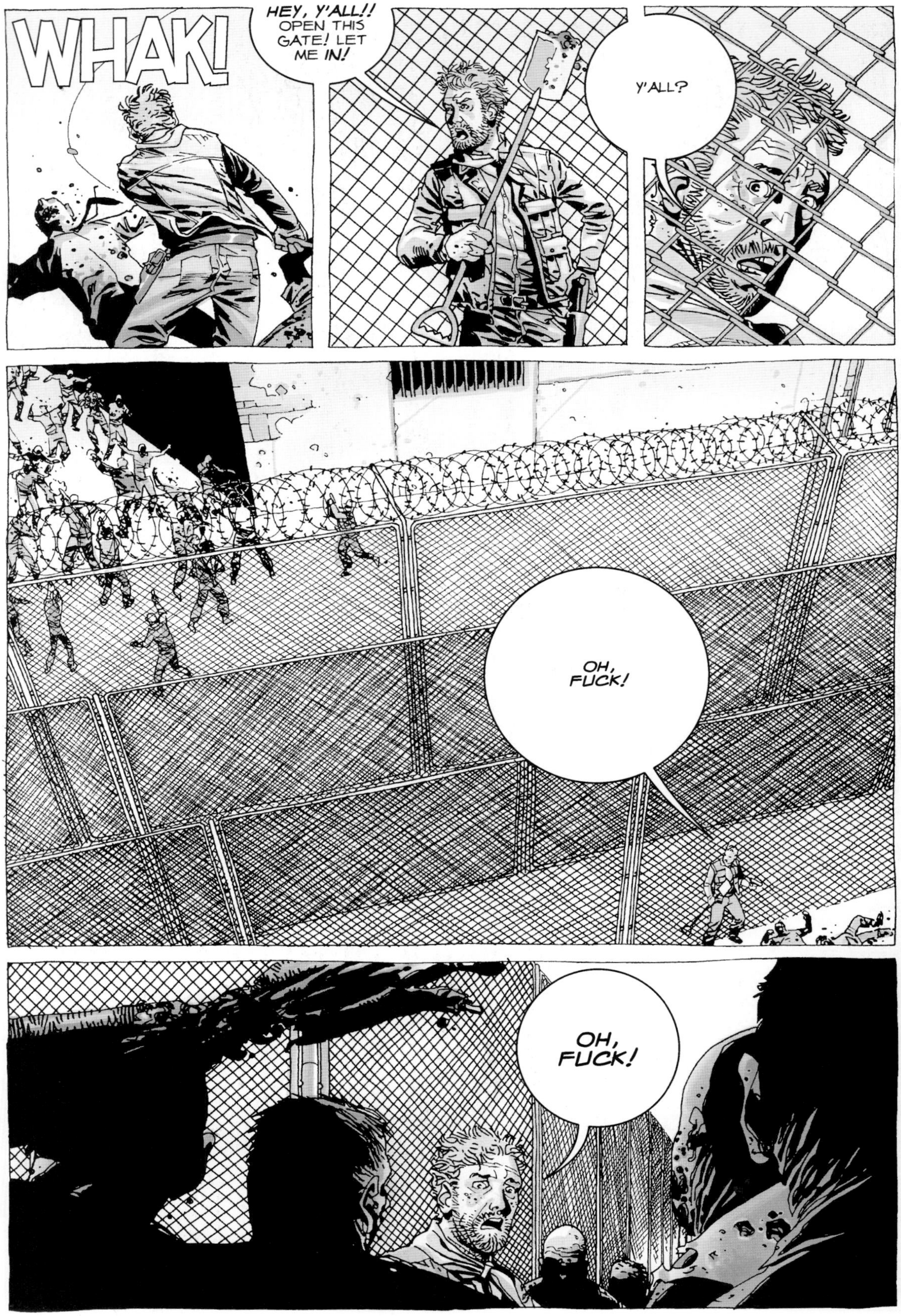
WHAK!
HEY, Y'ALL!! OPEN THIS GATE! LET ME IN!
Y'ALL?
OH, FUCK!
OH, FUCK!

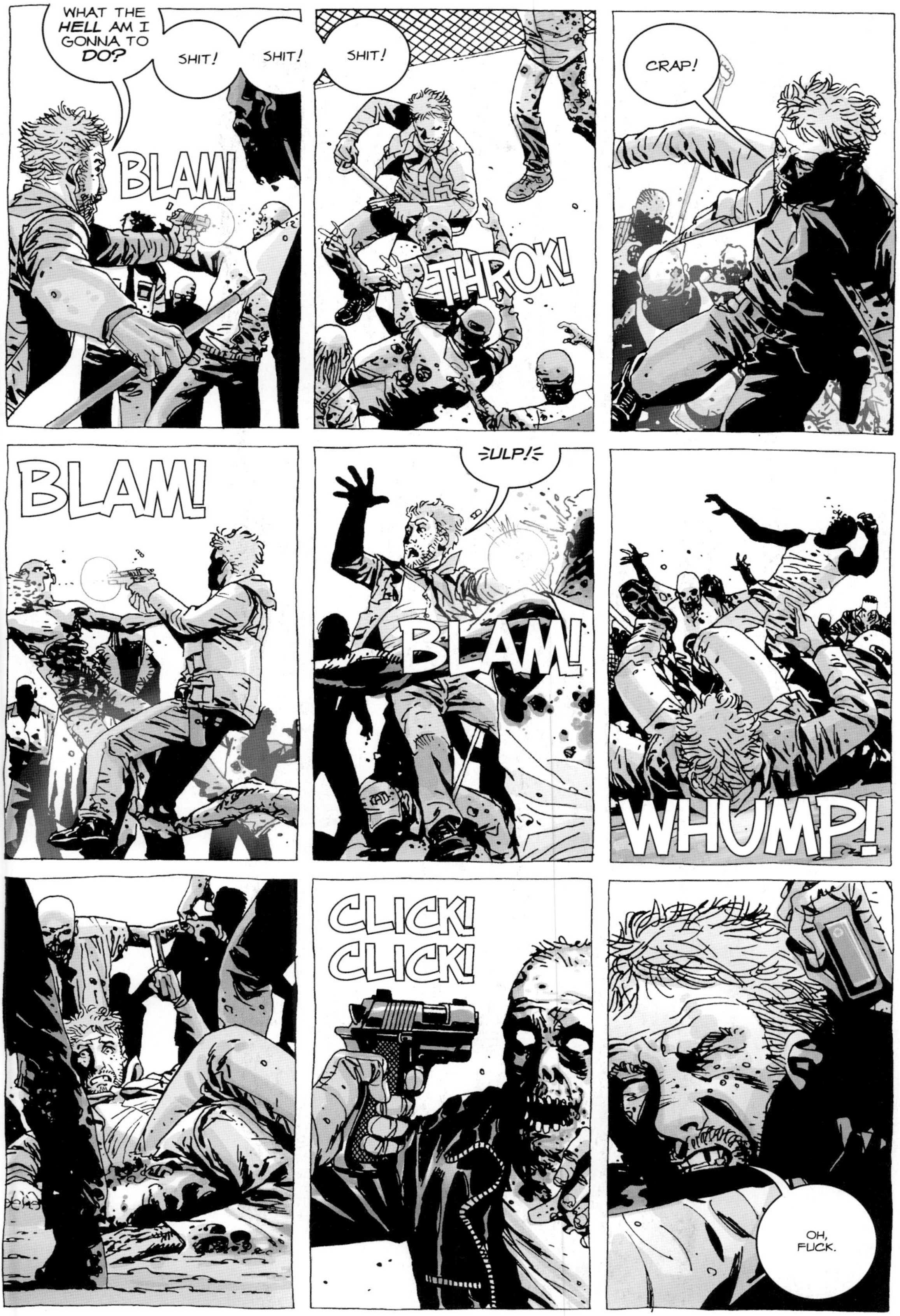
WHAT THE HELL AM I GONNA TO DO?
SHIT!
SHIT!
SHIT!
BLAM!
THROK!
CRAP!
BLAM!
ULP!
BLAM!
WHUMP!
CLICK! CLICK!
OH, FUCK.

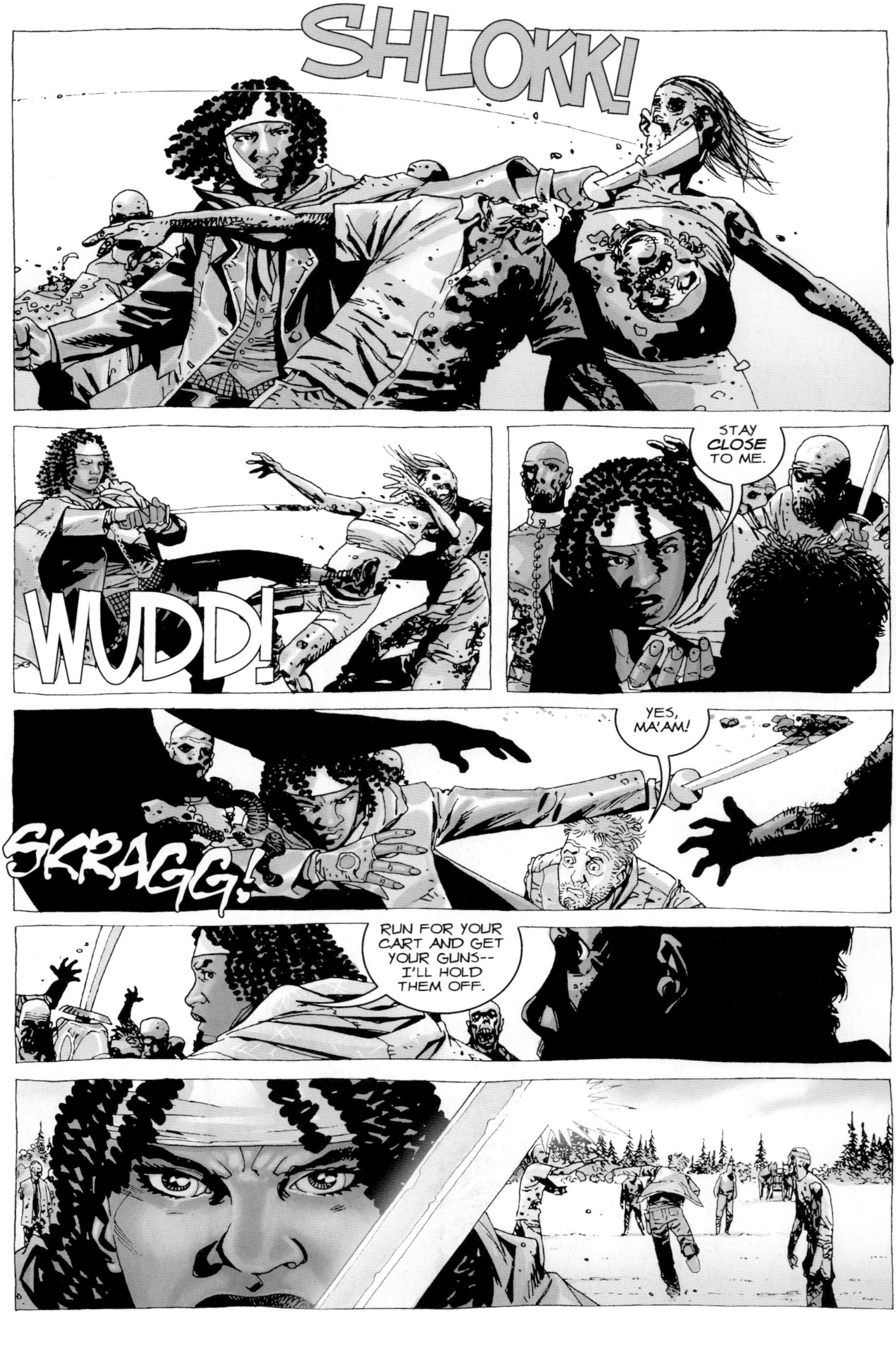
SHLOKK!
WUDD!
STAY CLOSE TO ME.
YES, MA'AM!
SKRAGG!
RUN FOR YOUR CART AND GET YOUR GUNS-- I'LL HOLD THEM OFF.

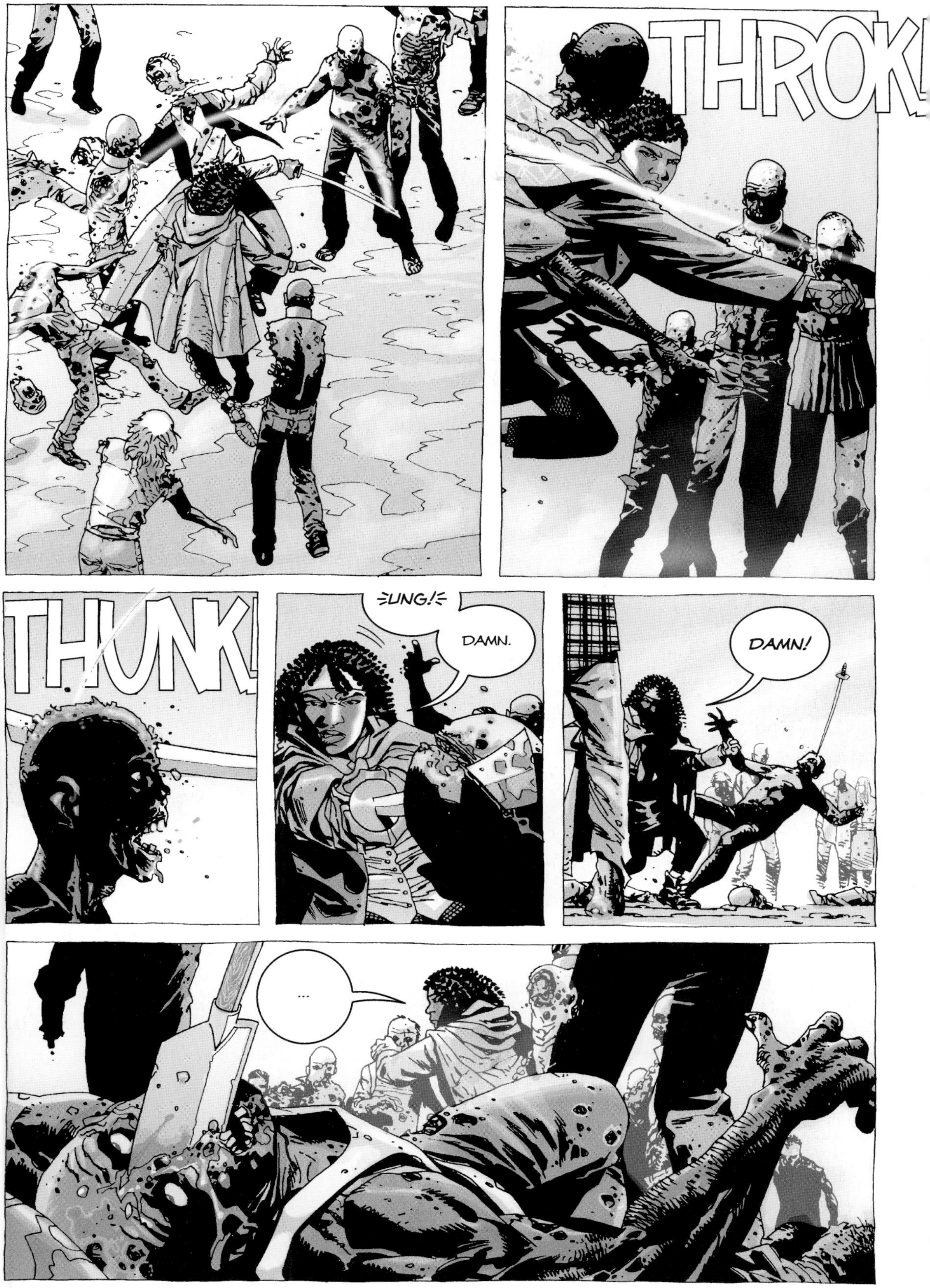
THROK!
THUNK!
UNG!
DAMN.
DAMN!
...

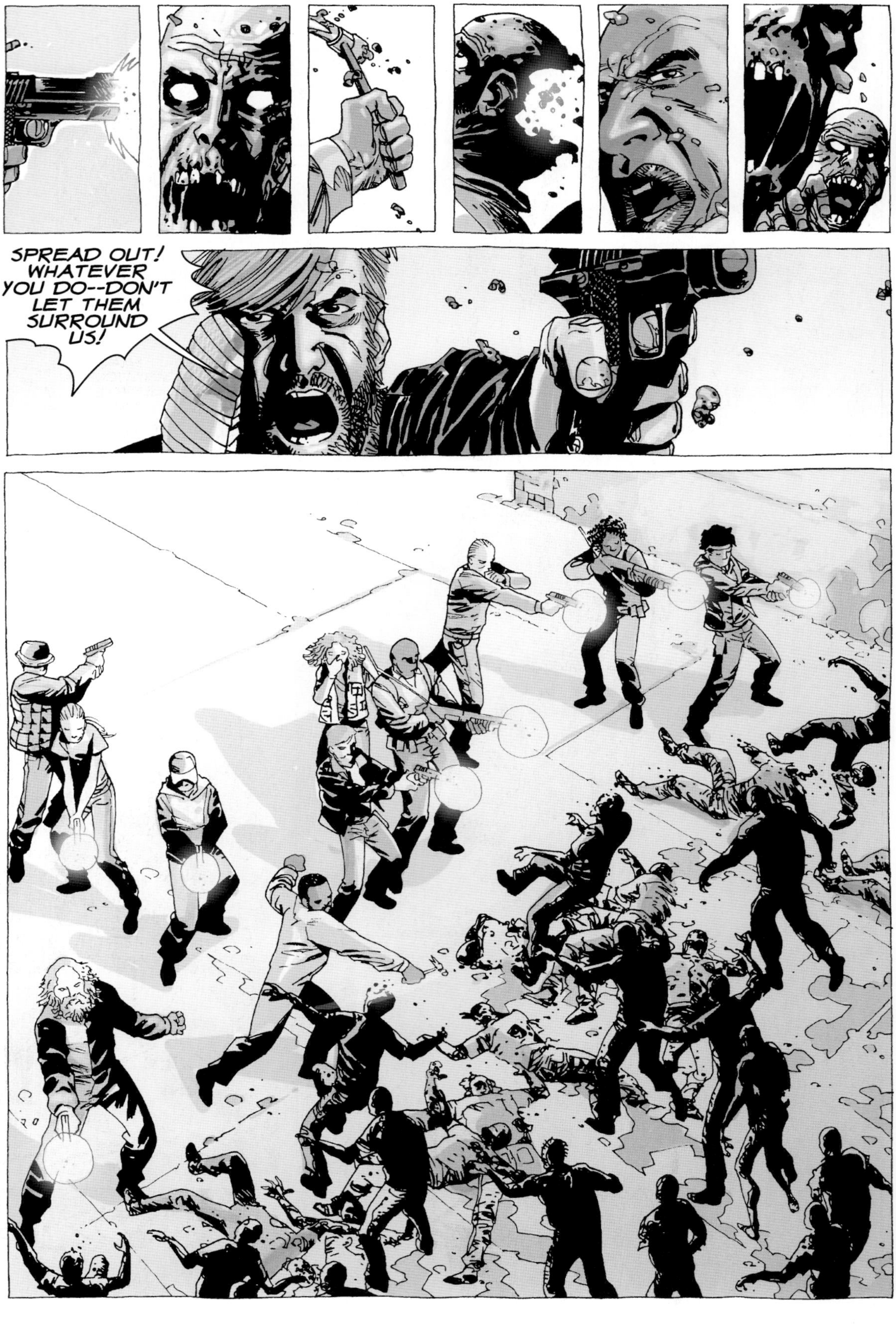
SPREAD OUT! WHATEVER YOU DO--DON'T LET THEM SURROUND US!

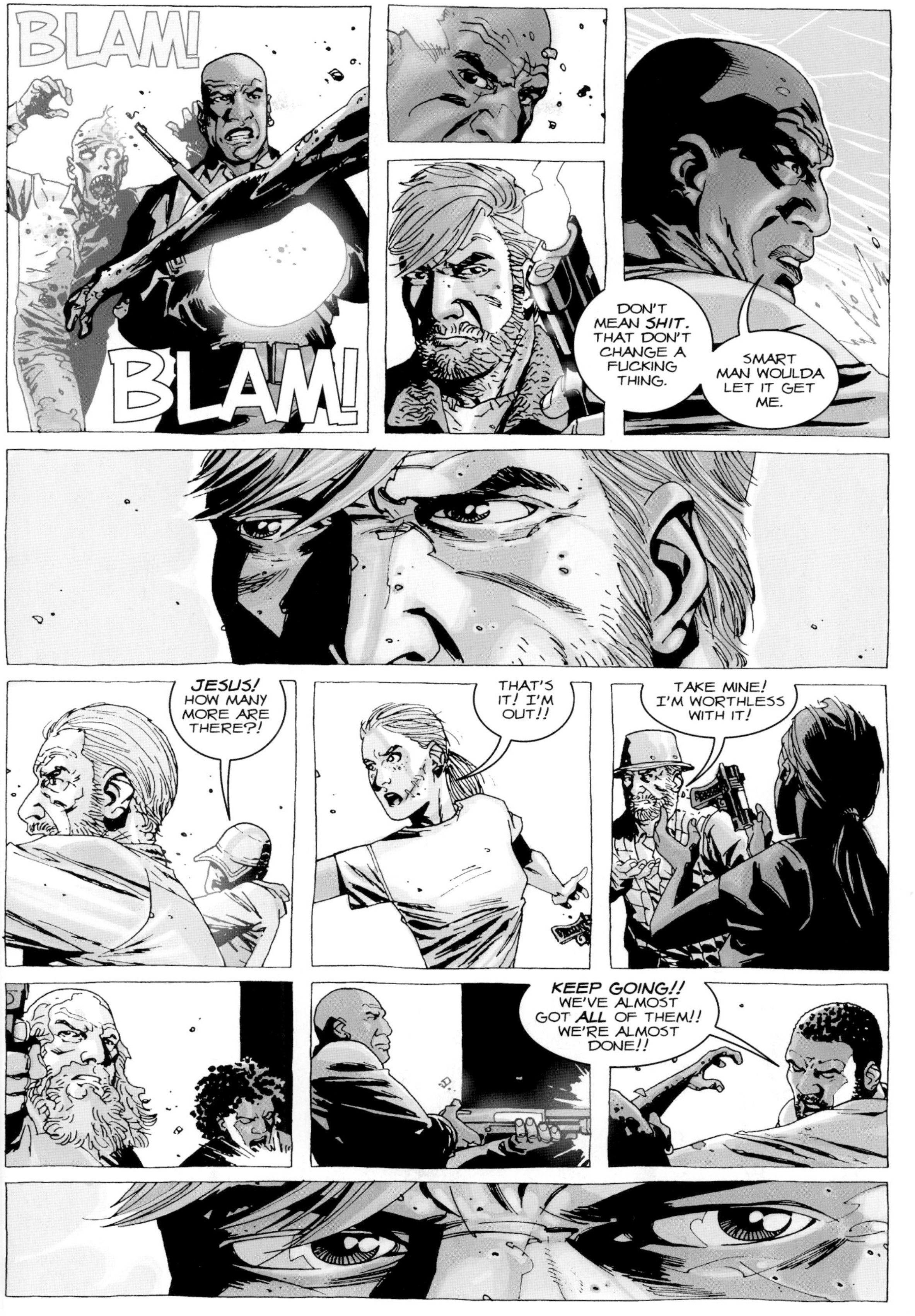
BLAM!
BLAM!
DON'T MEAN SHIT. THAT DON'T CHANGE A FUCKING THING.
SMART MAN WOULDA LET IT GET ME.
JESUS! HOW MANY MORE ARE THERE?!
THAT'S IT! I'M OUT!!
TAKE MINE! I'M WORTHLESS WITH IT!
KEEP GOING!! WE'VE ALMOST GOT ALL OF THEM!! WE'RE ALMOST DONE!!

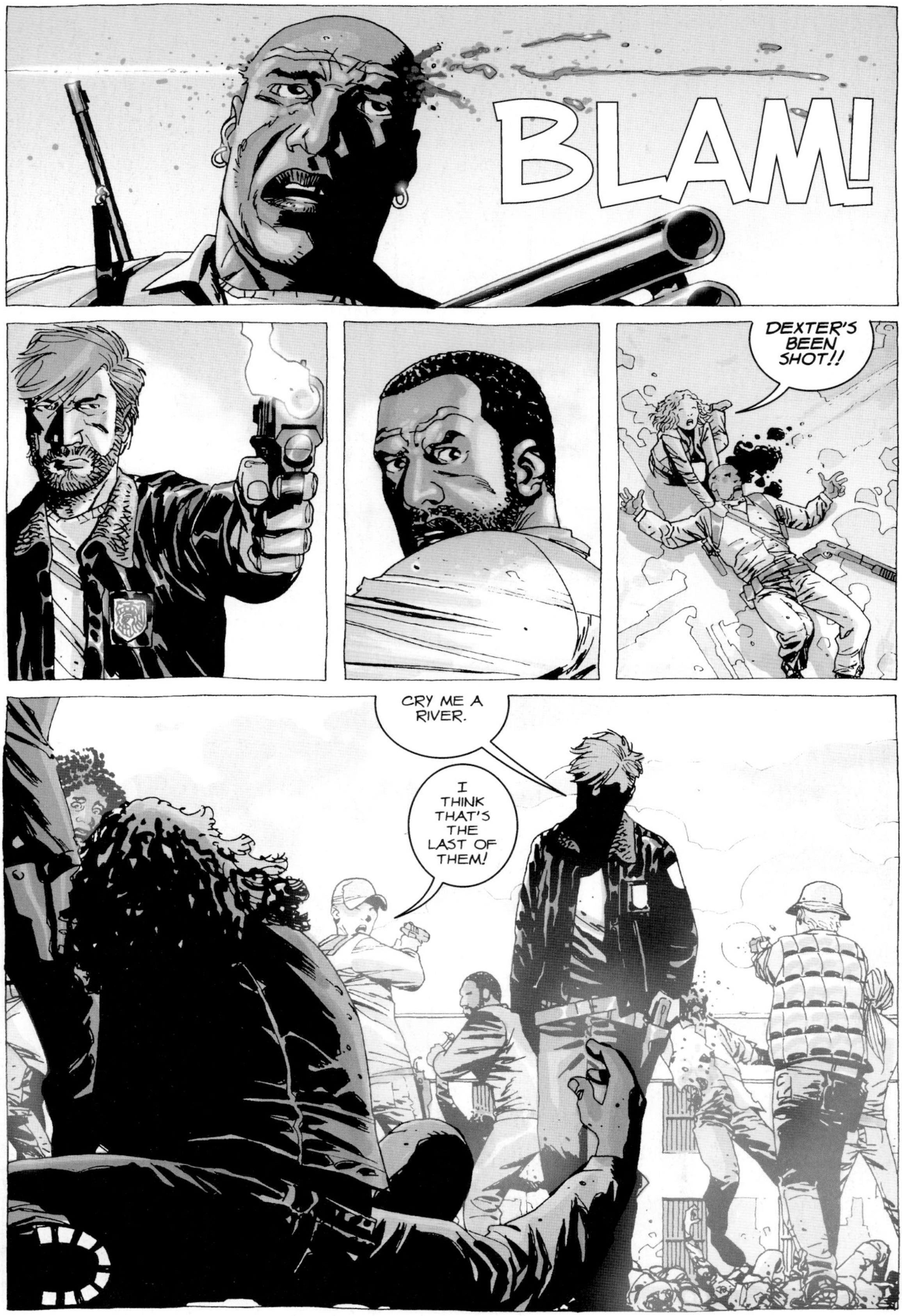
BLAM!
DEXTER'S BEEN SHOT!!
CRY ME A RIVER.
I THINK THAT'S THE LAST OF THEM!

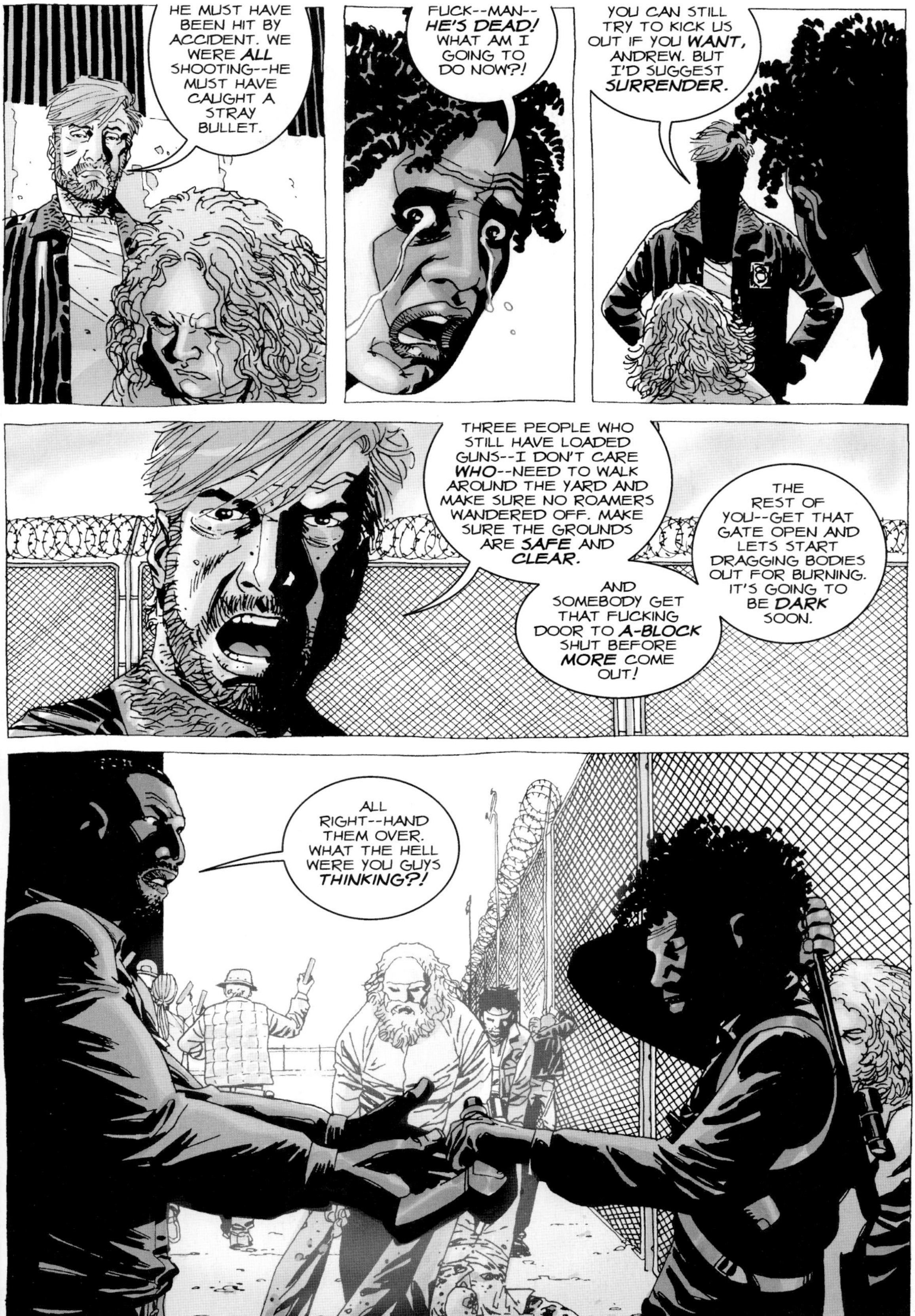
HE MUST HAVE BEEN HIT BY ACCIDENT. WE WERE ALL SHOOTING--HE MUST HAVE CAUGHT A STRAY BULLET.
FUCK--MAN-- HE'S DEAD! WHAT AM I GOING TO DO NOW?!
YOU CAN STILL TRY TO KICK US OUT IF YOU WANT, ANDREW. BUT I'D SUGGEST SURRENDER.
THREE PEOPLE WHO STILL HAVE LOADED GUNS--I DON'T CARE WHO--NEED TO WALK AROUND THE YARD AND MAKE SURE NO ROAMERS WANDERED OFF. MAKE SURE THE GROUNDS ARE SAFE AND CLEAR.
AND SOMEBODY GET THAT FUCKING DOOR TO A-BLOCK SHUT BEFORE MORE COME OUT!
THE REST OF YOU--GET THAT GATE OPEN AND LETS START DRAGGING BODIES OUT FOR BURNING. IT'S GOING TO BE DARK SOON.
ALL RIGHT--HAND THEM OVER. WHAT THE HELL WERE YOU GUYS THINKING?!

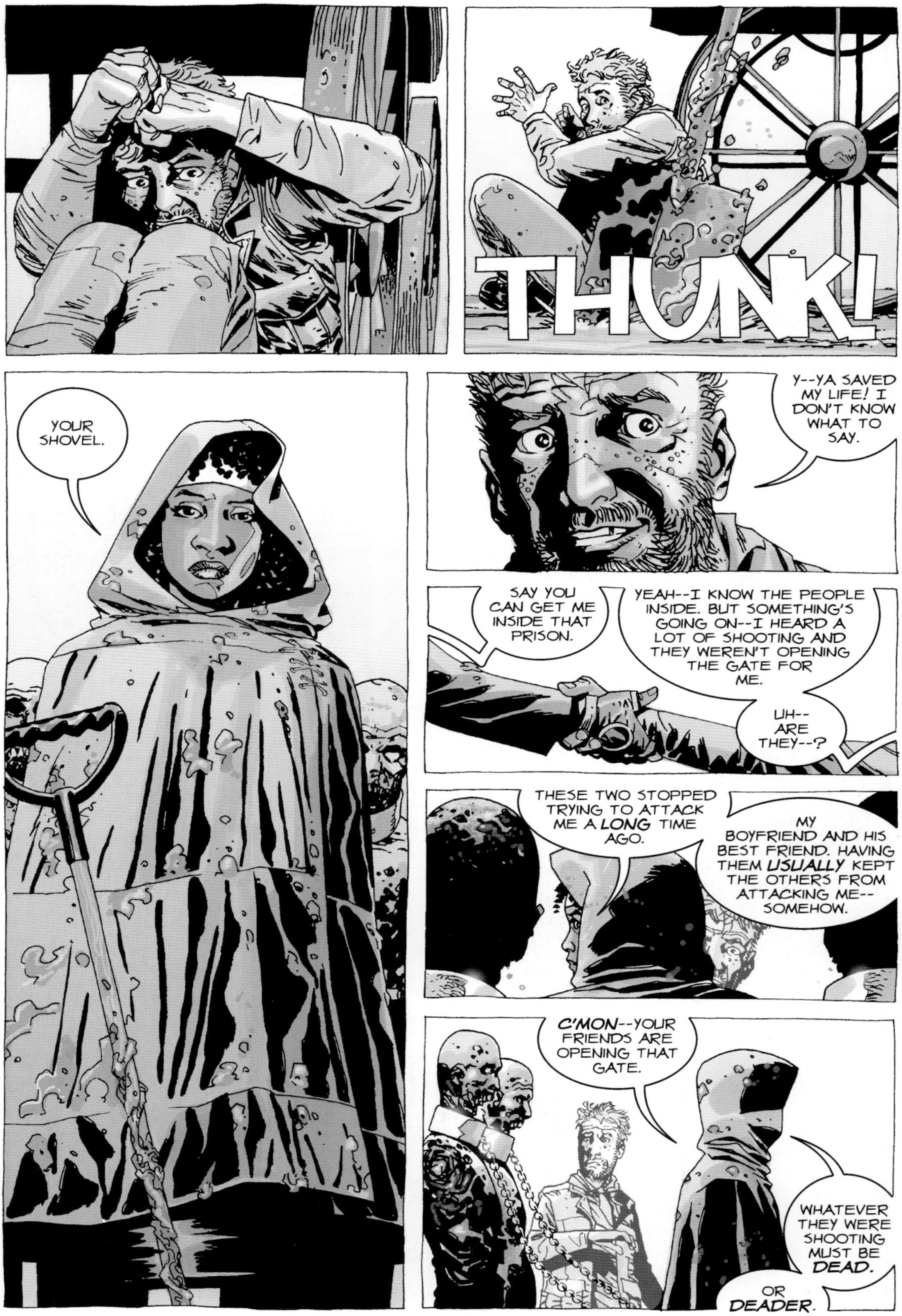
THUNK!
YOUR SHOVEL.
Y--YA SAVED MY LIFE! I DON'T KNOW WHAT TO SAY.
SAY YOU CAN GET ME INSIDE THAT PRISON.
YEAH--I KNOW THE PEOPLE INSIDE. BUT SOMETHING'S GOING ON--I HEARD A LOT OF SHOOTING AND THEY WEREN'T OPENING THE GATE FOR ME.
UH-- ARE THEY--?
THESE TWO STOPPED TRYING TO ATTACK ME A LONG TIME AGO.
MY BOYFRIEND AND HIS BEST FRIEND. HAVING THEM USUALLY KEPT THE OTHERS FROM ATTACKING ME-- SOMEHOW.
C'MON--YOUR FRIENDS ARE OPENING THAT GATE.
WHATEVER THEY WERE SHOOTING MUST BE DEAD.
OR DEADER.

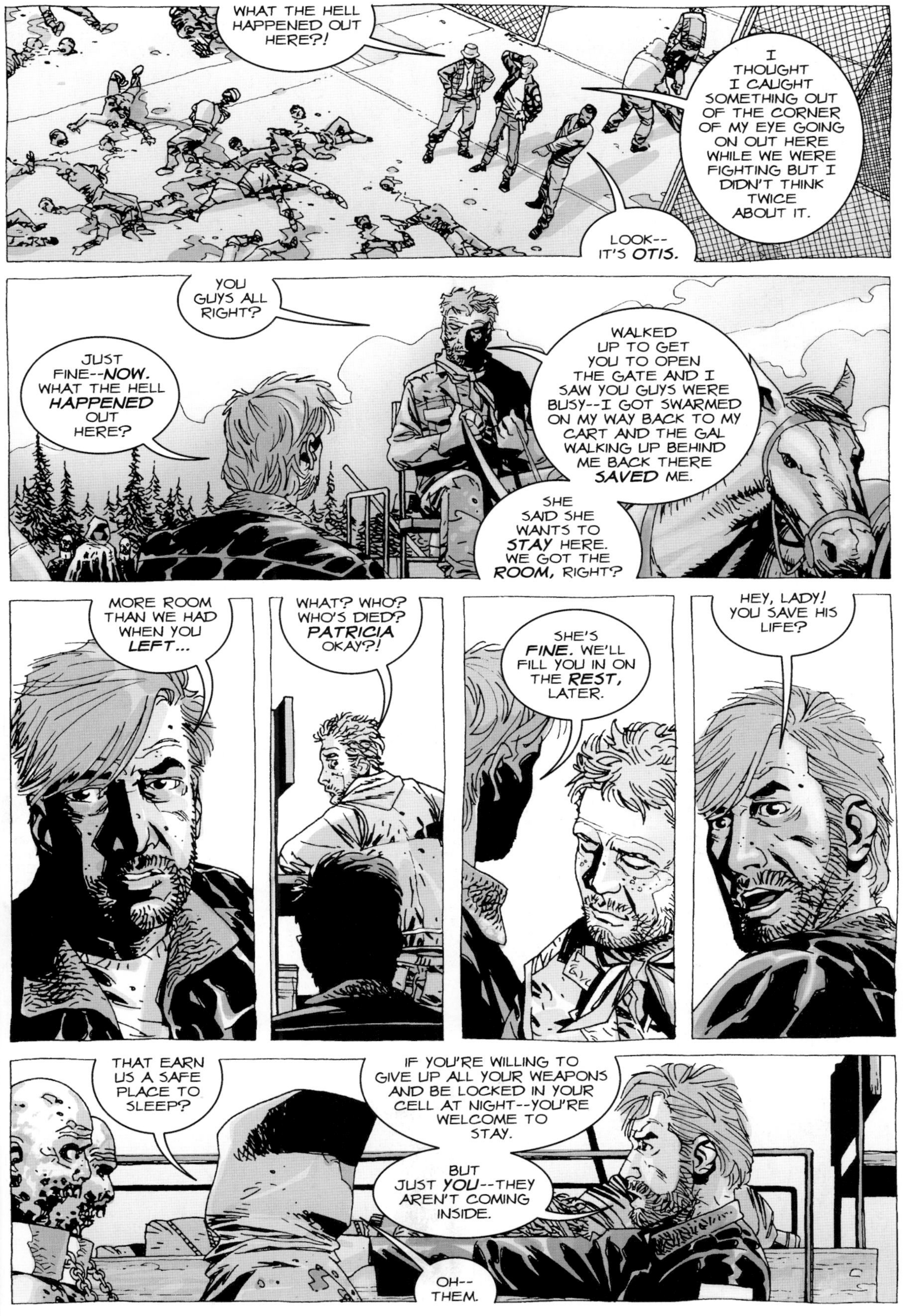
WHAT THE HELL HAPPENED OUT HERE?!
I THOUGHT I CAUGHT SOMETHING OUT OF THE CORNER OF MY EYE GOING ON OUT HERE WHILE WE WERE FIGHTING BUT I DIDN'T THINK TWICE ABOUT IT.
LOOK-- IT'S OTIS.
YOU GUYS ALL RIGHT?
JUST FINE--NOW. WHAT THE HELL HAPPENED OUT HERE?
WALKED UP TO GET YOU TO OPEN THE GATE AND I SAW YOU GUYS WERE BUSY--I GOT SWARMED ON MY WAY BACK TO MY CART AND THE GAL WALKING UP BEHIND ME BACK THERE SAVED ME.
SHE SAID SHE WANTS TO STAY HERE. WE GOT THE ROOM, RIGHT?
MORE ROOM THAN WE HAD WHEN YOU LEFT...
WHAT? WHO? WHO'S DIED? PATRICIA OKAY?!
SHE'S FINE. WE'LL FILL YOU IN ON THE REST, LATER.
HEY, LADY! YOU SAVE HIS LIFE?
THAT EARN US A SAFE PLACE TO SLEEP?
IF YOU'RE WILLING TO GIVE UP ALL YOUR WEAPONS AND BE LOCKED IN YOUR CELL AT NIGHT--YOU'RE WELCOME TO STAY.
BUT JUST YOU--THEY AREN'T COMING INSIDE.
OH-- THEM.

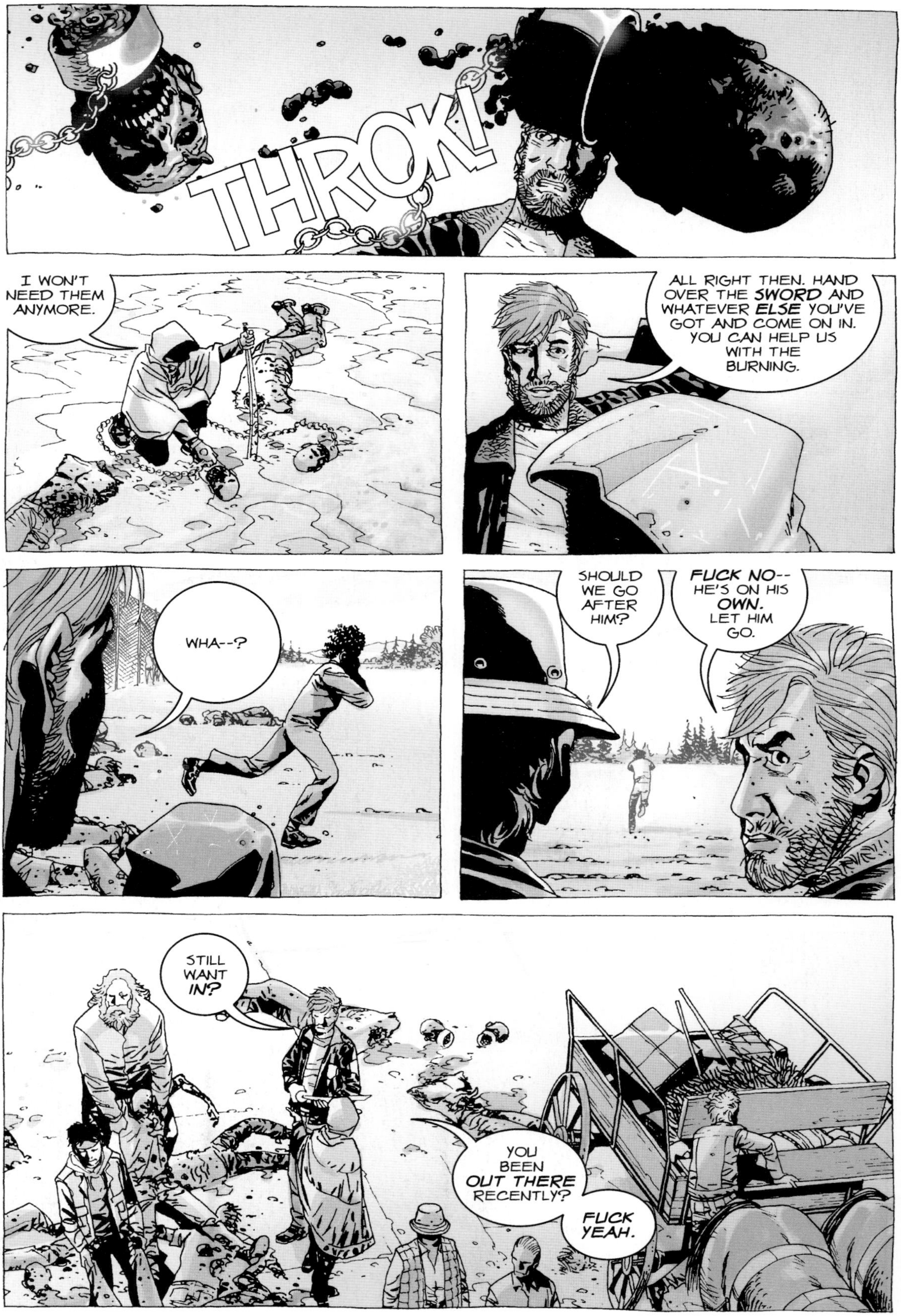
THROK!
I WON'T NEED THEM ANYMORE.
ALL RIGHT THEN. HAND OVER THE SWORD AND WHATEVER ELSE YOU'VE GOT AND COME ON IN. YOU CAN HELP US WITH THE BURNING.
WHA--?
SHOULD WE GO AFTER HIM?
FUCK NO-- HE'S ON HIS OWN. LET HIM GO.
STILL WANT IN?
YOU BEEN OUT THERE RECENTLY?
FUCK YEAH.

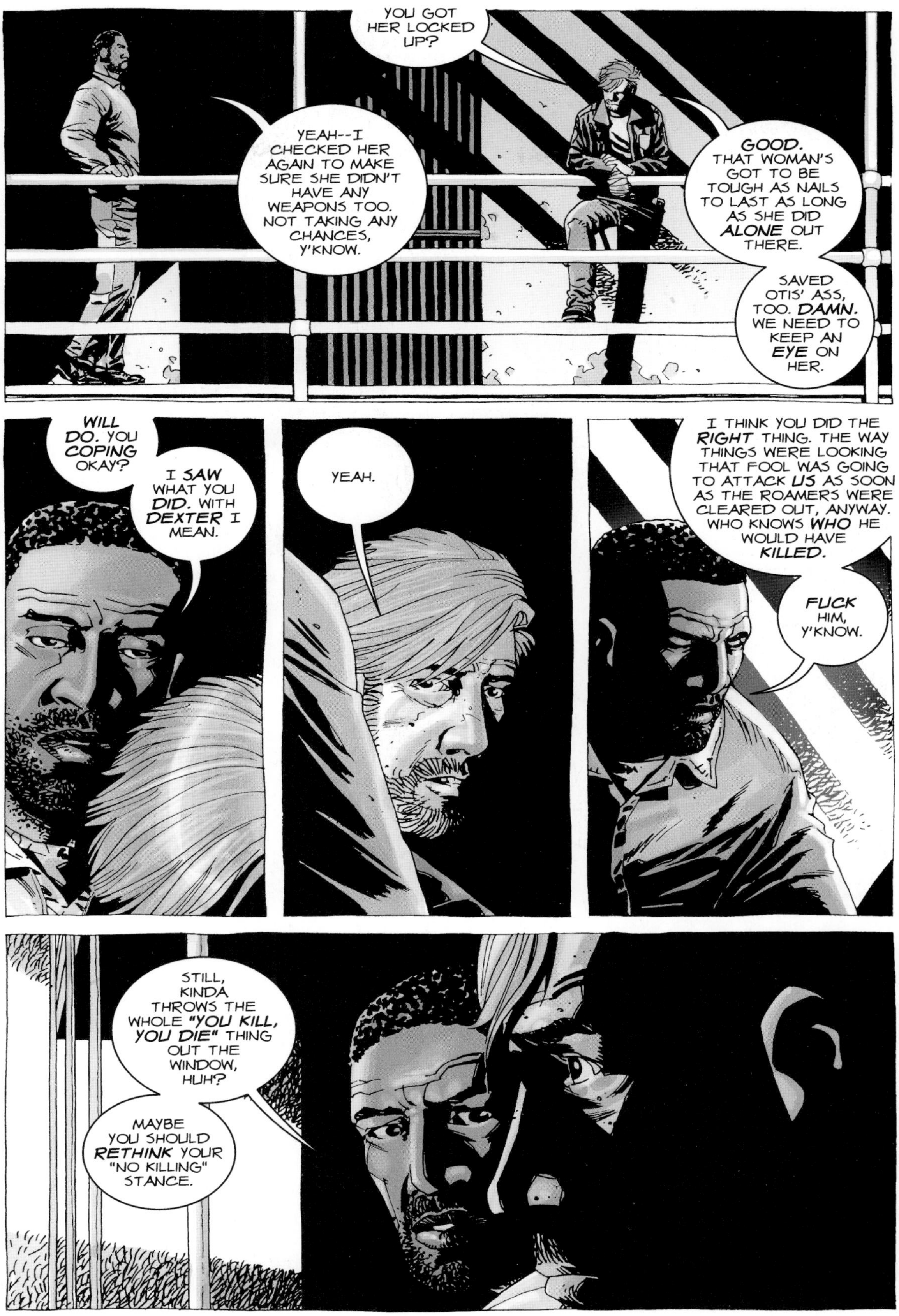
YOU GOT HER LOCKED UP?
YEAH--I CHECKED HER AGAIN TO MAKE SURE SHE DIDN'T HAVE ANY WEAPONS TOO. NOT TAKING ANY CHANCES, Y'KNOW.
GOOD. THAT WOMAN'S GOT TO BE TOUGH AS NAILS TO LAST AS LONG AS SHE DID ALONE OUT THERE.
SAVED OTIS' ASS, TOO. DAMN. WE NEED TO KEEP AN EYE ON HER.
WILL DO. YOU COPING OKAY?
I SAW WHAT YOU DID. WITH DEXTER I MEAN.
YEAH.
I THINK YOU DID THE RIGHT THING. THE WAY THINGS WERE LOOKING THAT FOOL WAS GOING TO ATTACK US AS SOON AS THE ROAMERS WERE CLEARED OUT, ANYWAY. WHO KNOWS WHO HE WOULD HAVE KILLED.
FUCK HIM, Y'KNOW.
STILL, KINDA THROWS THE WHOLE "YOU KILL, YOU DIE" THING OUT THE WINDOW, HUH?
MAYBE YOU SHOULD RETHINK YOUR "NO KILLING" STANCE.

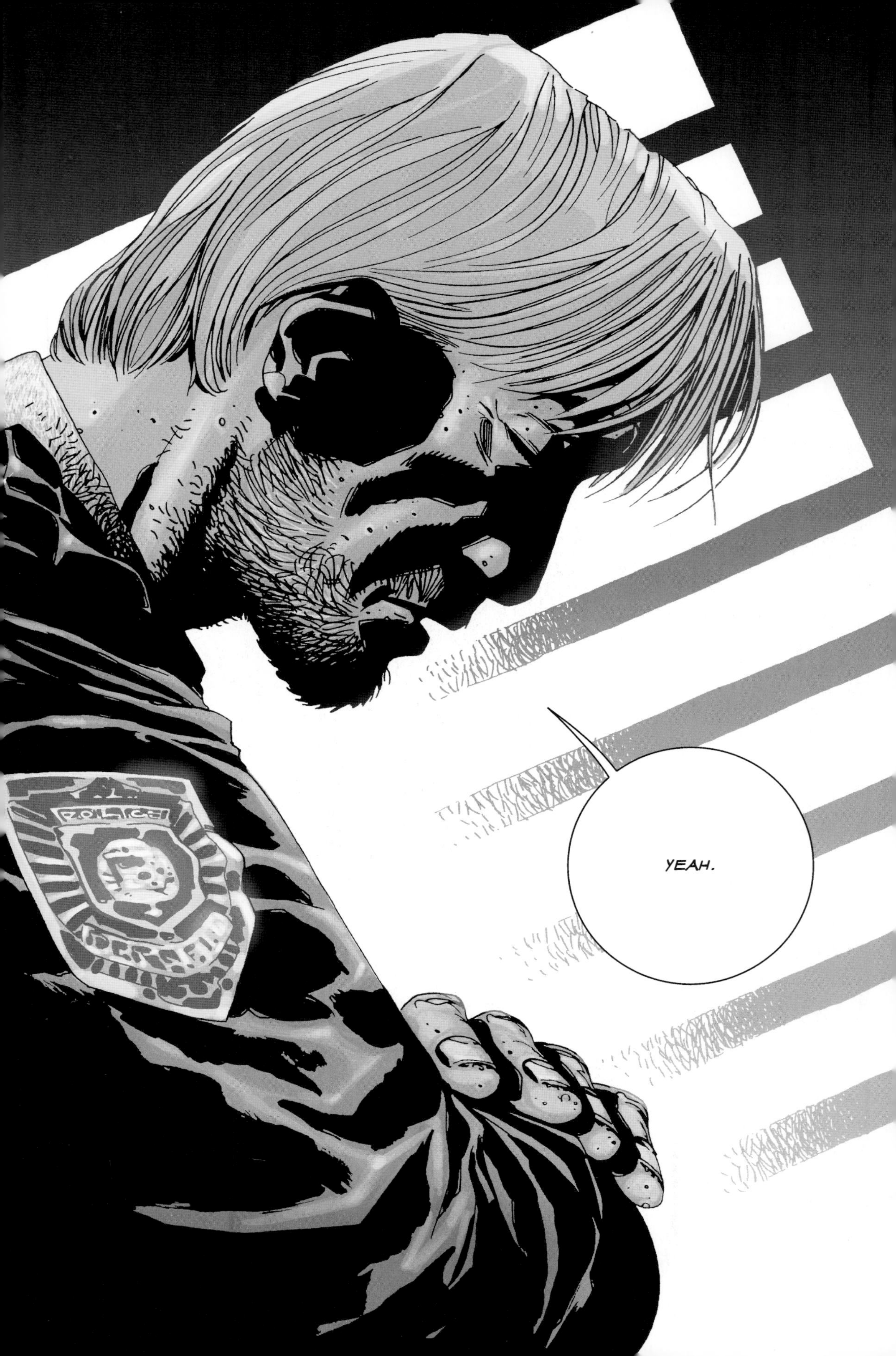
YEAH.

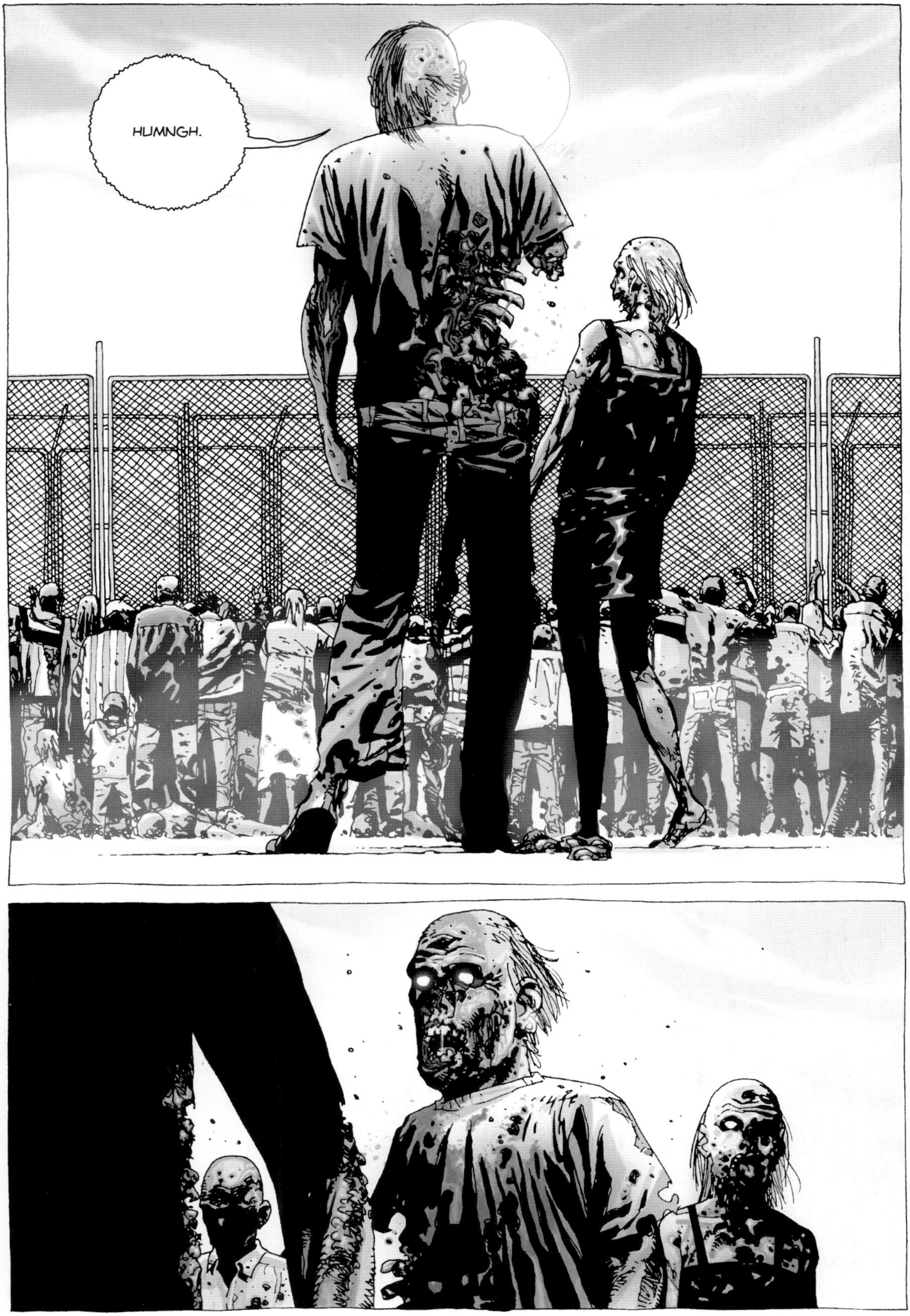
HUMNGH.

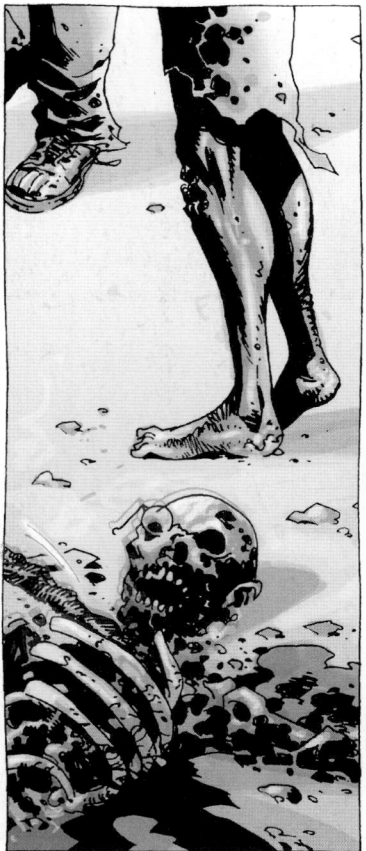

GUH.

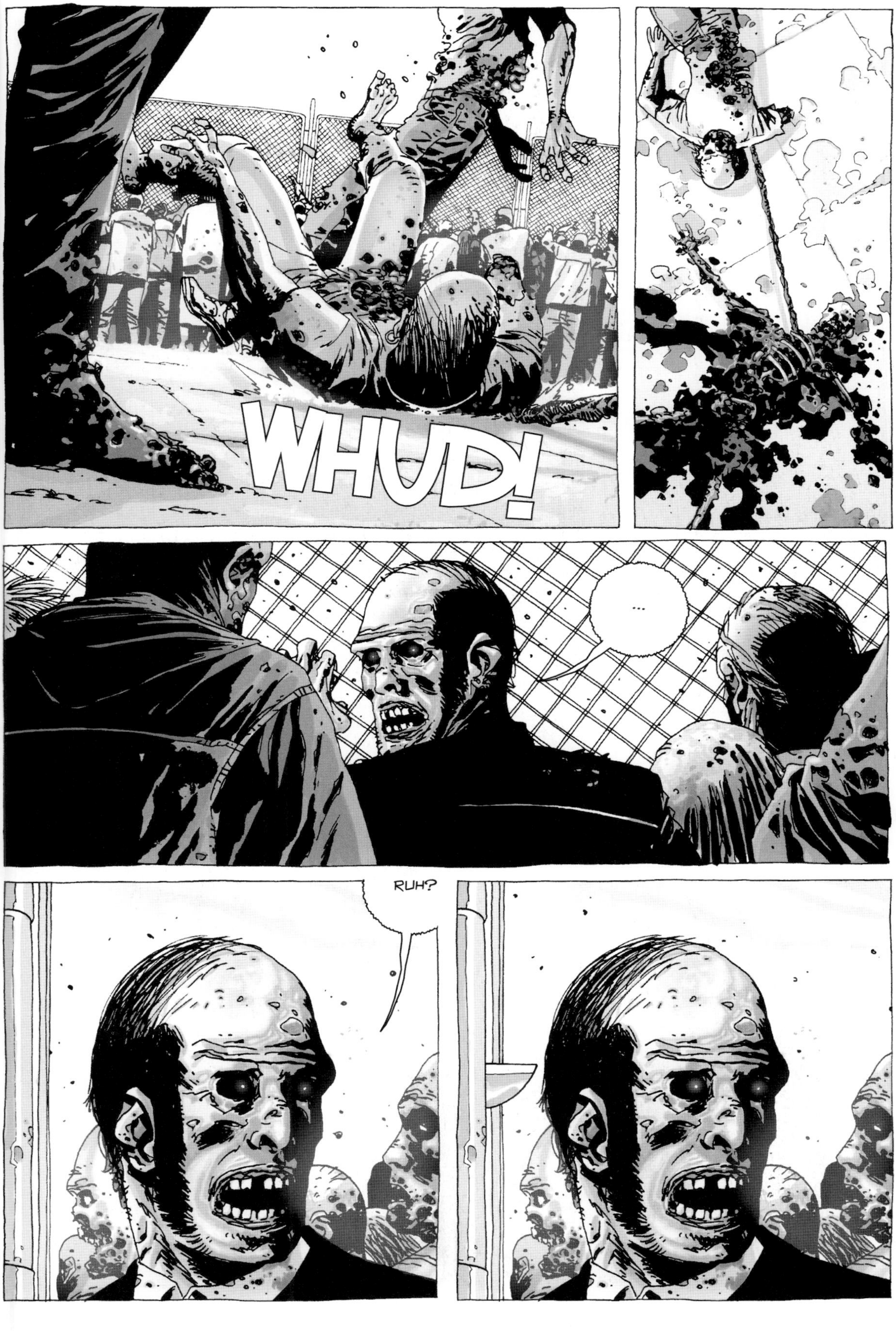
WHUD!
...
RUH?

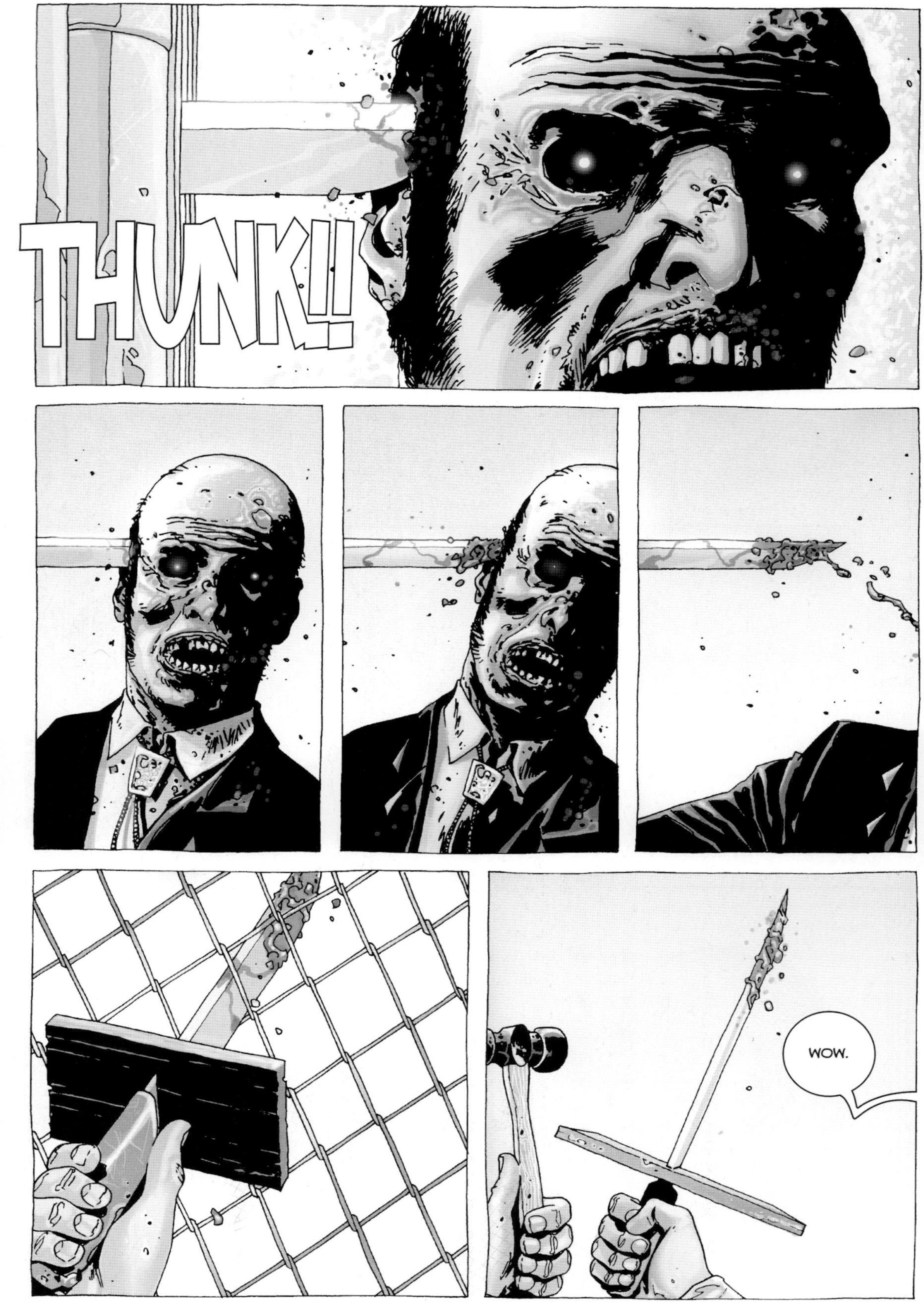
THUNK!!
WOW.

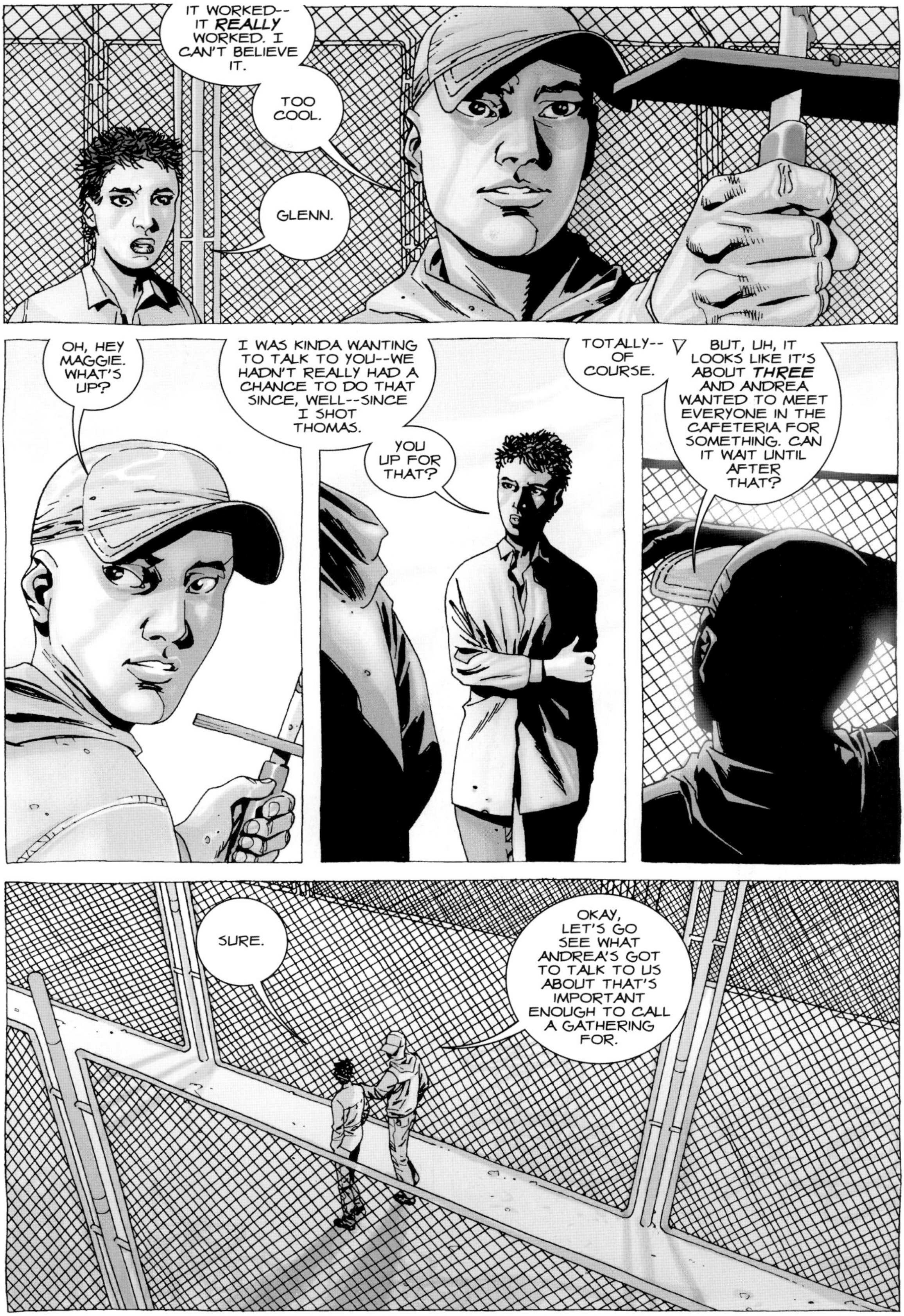
IT WORKED-- IT REALLY WORKED. I CAN'T BELIEVE IT.
TOO COOL.
GLENN.
OH, HEY MAGGIE. WHAT'S UP?
I WAS KINDA WANTING TO TALK TO YOU--WE HADN'T REALLY HAD A CHANCE TO DO THAT SINCE, WELL--SINCE I SHOT THOMAS.
YOU UP FOR THAT?
TOTALLY-- OF COURSE.
BUT, UH, IT LOOKS LIKE IT'S ABOUT THREE AND ANDREA WANTED TO MEET EVERYONE IN THE CAFETERIA FOR SOMETHING. CAN IT WAIT UNTIL AFTER THAT?
SURE.
OKAY, LET'S GO SEE WHAT ANDREA'S GOT TO TALK TO US ABOUT THAT'S IMPORTANT ENOUGH TO CALL A GATHERING FOR.

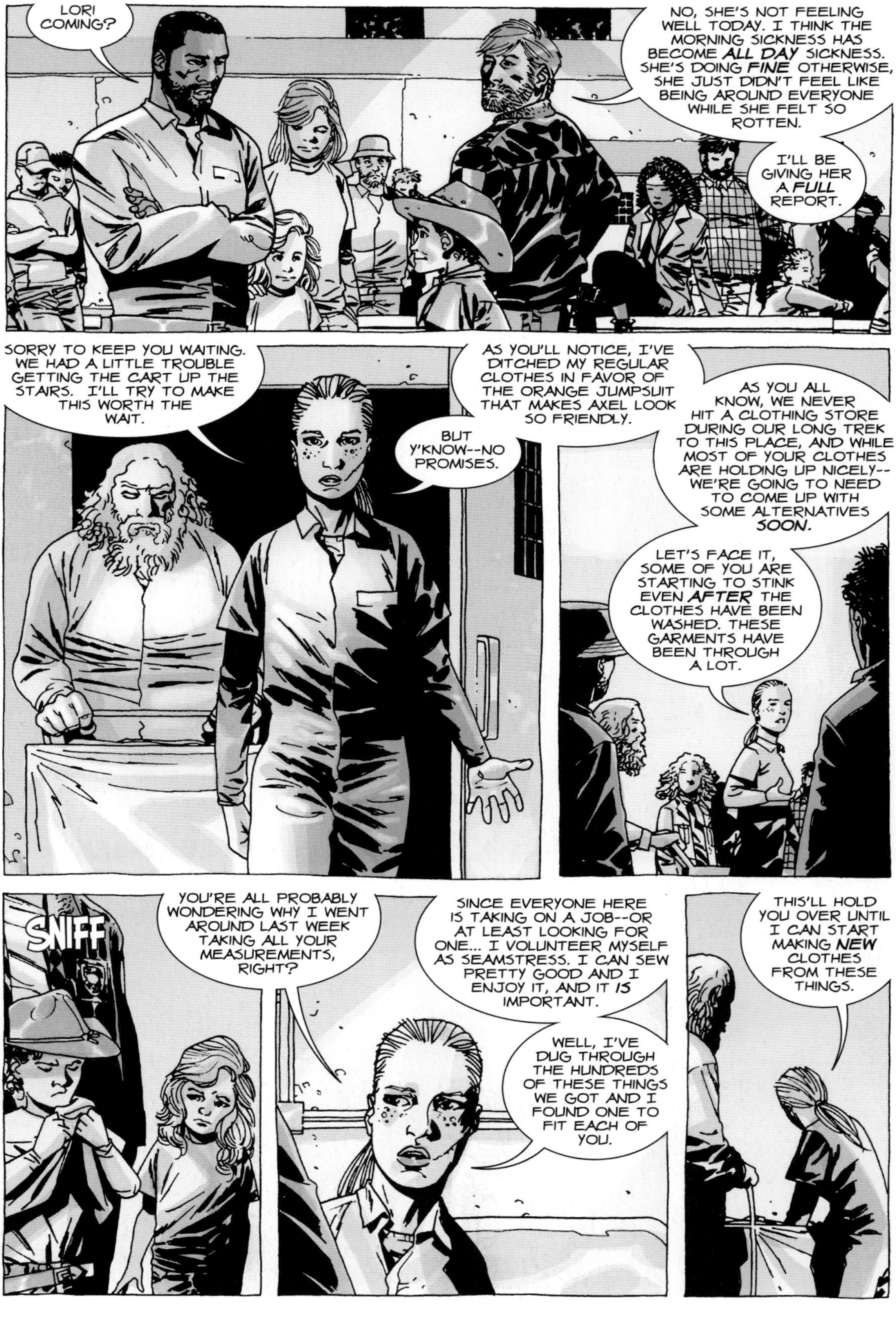
LORI COMING?
NO, SHE'S NOT FEELING WELL TODAY. I THINK THE MORNING SICKNESS HAS BECOME ALL DAY SICKNESS. SHE'S DOING FINE OTHERWISE, SHE JUST DIDN'T FEEL LIKE BEING AROUND EVERYONE WHILE SHE FELT SO ROTTEN.
I'LL BE GIVING HER A FULL REPORT.
SORRY TO KEEP YOU WAITING. WE HAD A LITTLE TROUBLE GETTING THE CART UP THE STAIRS. I'LL TRY TO MAKE THIS WORTH THE WAIT.
BUT Y'KNOW--NO PROMISES.
AS YOU'LL NOTICE, I'VE DITCHED MY REGULAR CLOTHES IN FAVOR OF THE ORANGE JUMPSUIT THAT MAKES AXEL LOOK SO FRIENDLY.
AS YOU ALL KNOW, WE NEVER HIT A CLOTHING STORE DURING OUR LONG TREK TO THIS PLACE, AND WHILE MOST OF YOUR CLOTHES ARE HOLDING UP NICELY-- WE'RE GOING TO NEED TO COME UP WITH SOME ALTERNATIVES SOON.
LET'S FACE IT, SOME OF YOU ARE STARTING TO STINK EVEN AFTER THE CLOTHES HAVE BEEN WASHED. THESE GARMENTS HAVE BEEN THROUGH A LOT.
SNIFF
YOU'RE ALL PROBABLY WONDERING WHY I WENT AROUND LAST WEEK TAKING ALL YOUR MEASUREMENTS, RIGHT?
SINCE EVERYONE HERE IS TAKING ON A JOB--OR AT LEAST LOOKING FOR ONE... I VOLUNTEER MYSELF AS SEAMSTRESS. I CAN SEW PRETTY GOOD AND I ENJOY IT, AND IT IS IMPORTANT.
WELL, I'VE DUG THROUGH THE HUNDREDS OF THESE THINGS WE GOT AND I FOUND ONE TO FIT EACH OF YOU.
THIS'LL HOLD YOU OVER UNTIL I CAN START MAKING NEW CLOTHES FROM THESE THINGS.

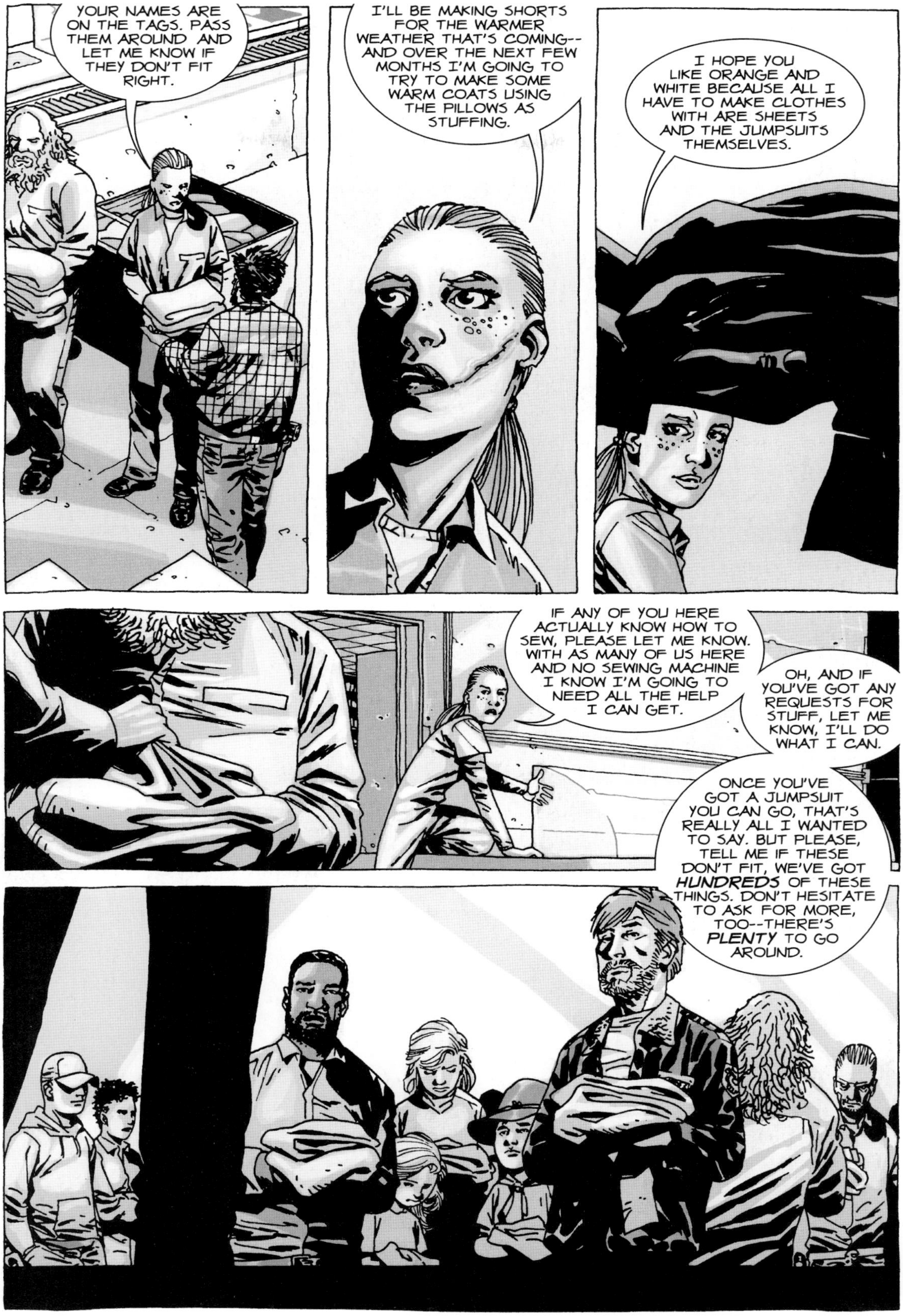
YOUR NAMES ARE ON THE TAGS. PASS THEM AROUND AND LET ME KNOW IF THEY DON'T FIT RIGHT.
I'LL BE MAKING SHORTS FOR THE WARMER WEATHER THAT'S COMING-- AND OVER THE NEXT FEW MONTHS I'M GOING TO TRY TO MAKE SOME WARM COATS USING THE PILLOWS AS STUFFING.
I HOPE YOU LIKE ORANGE AND WHITE BECAUSE ALL I HAVE TO MAKE CLOTHES WITH ARE SHEETS AND THE JUMPSUITS THEMSELVES.
IF ANY OF YOU HERE ACTUALLY KNOW HOW TO SEW, PLEASE LET ME KNOW. WITH AS MANY OF US HERE AND NO SEWING MACHINE I KNOW I'M GOING TO NEED ALL THE HELP I CAN GET.
OH, AND IF YOU'VE GOT ANY REQUESTS FOR STUFF, LET ME KNOW, I'LL DO WHAT I CAN.
ONCE YOU'VE GOT A JUMPSUIT YOU CAN GO, THAT'S REALLY ALL I WANTED TO SAY. BUT PLEASE, TELL ME IF THESE DON'T FIT, WE'VE GOT ***HUNDREDS*** OF THESE THINGS. DON'T HESITATE TO ASK FOR MORE, TOO--THERE'S ***PLENTY*** TO GO AROUND.

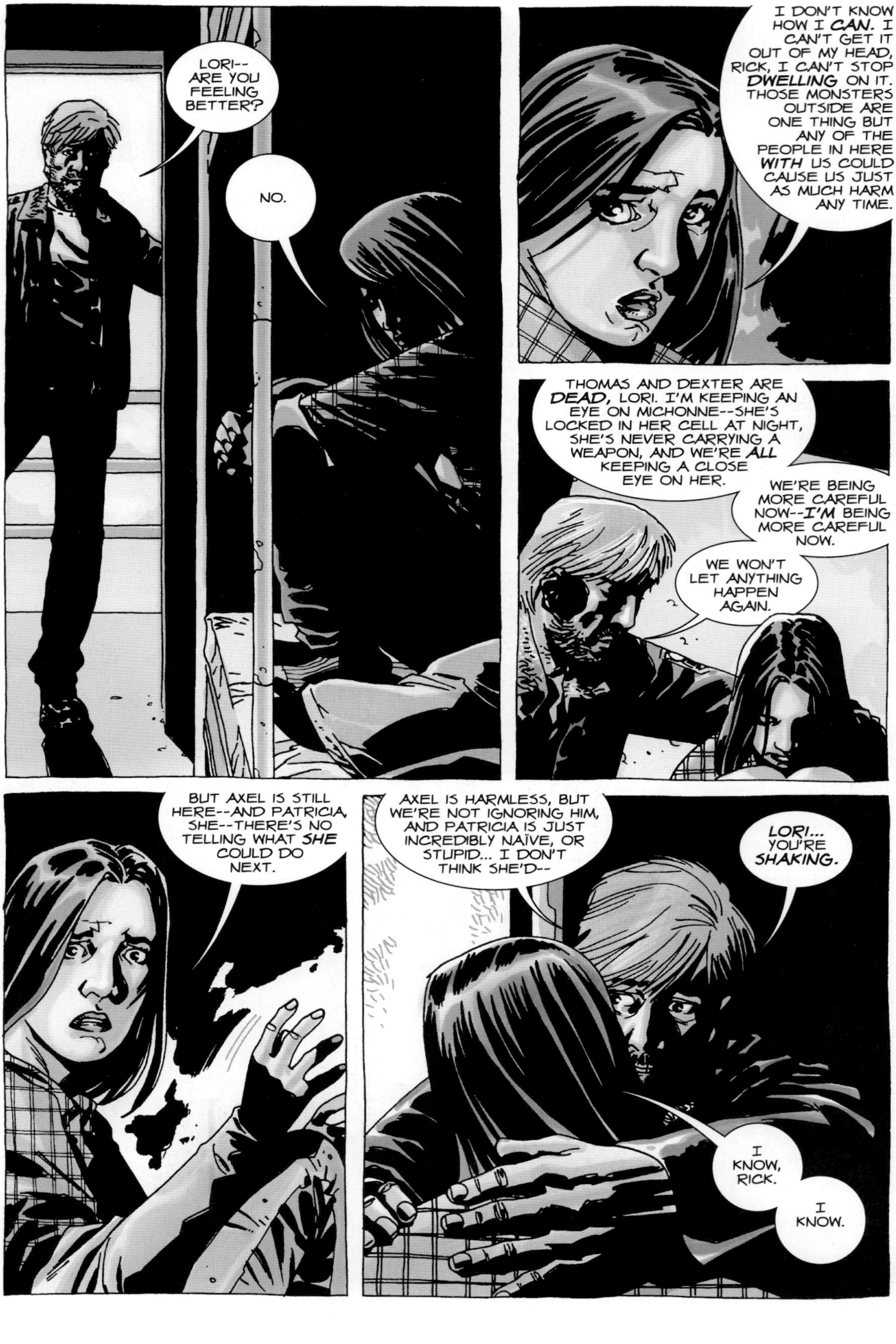
LORI-- ARE YOU FEELING BETTER?
NO.
I DON'T KNOW HOW I CAN. I CAN'T GET IT OUT OF MY HEAD, RICK, I CAN'T STOP DWELLING ON IT. THOSE MONSTERS OUTSIDE ARE ONE THING BUT ANY OF THE PEOPLE IN HERE WITH US COULD CAUSE US JUST AS MUCH HARM ANY TIME.
THOMAS AND DEXTER ARE DEAD, LORI. I'M KEEPING AN EYE ON MICHONNE--SHE'S LOCKED IN HER CELL AT NIGHT, SHE'S NEVER CARRYING A WEAPON, AND WE'RE ALL KEEPING A CLOSE EYE ON HER.
WE'RE BEING MORE CAREFUL NOW--I'M BEING MORE CAREFUL NOW.
WE WON'T LET ANYTHING HAPPEN AGAIN.
BUT AXEL IS STILL HERE--AND PATRICIA, SHE--THERE'S NO TELLING WHAT SHE COULD DO NEXT.
AXEL IS HARMLESS, BUT WE'RE NOT IGNORING HIM, AND PATRICIA IS JUST INCREDIBLY NAÏVE, OR STUPID... I DON'T THINK SHE'D--
LORI... YOU'RE SHAKING.
I KNOW, RICK.
I KNOW.

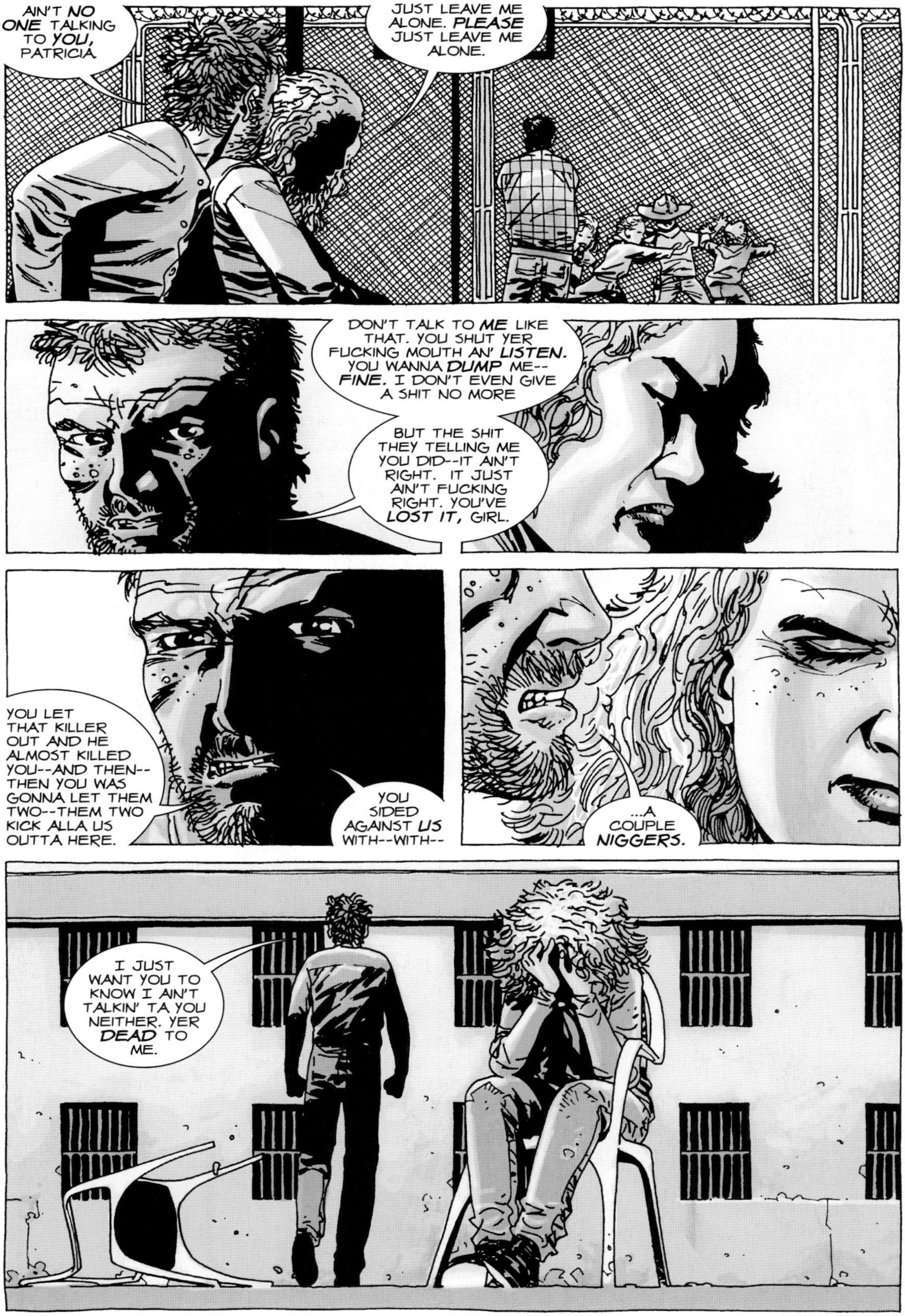

AIN'T NO ONE TALKING TO YOU, PATRICIA.
JUST LEAVE ME ALONE. PLEASE JUST LEAVE ME ALONE.
DON'T TALK TO ME LIKE THAT. YOU SHUT YER FUCKING MOUTH AN' LISTEN. YOU WANNA DUMP ME-- FINE. I DON'T EVEN GIVE A SHIT NO MORE
BUT THE SHIT THEY TELLING ME YOU DID--IT AIN'T RIGHT. IT JUST AIN'T FUCKING RIGHT. YOU'VE LOST IT, GIRL.
YOU LET THAT KILLER OUT AND HE ALMOST KILLED YOU--AND THEN-- THEN YOU WAS GONNA LET THEM TWO--THEM TWO KICK ALLA US OUTTA HERE.
YOU SIDED AGAINST US WITH--WITH--
...A COUPLE NIGGERS.
I JUST WANT YOU TO KNOW I AIN'T TALKIN' TA YOU NEITHER. YER DEAD TO ME.

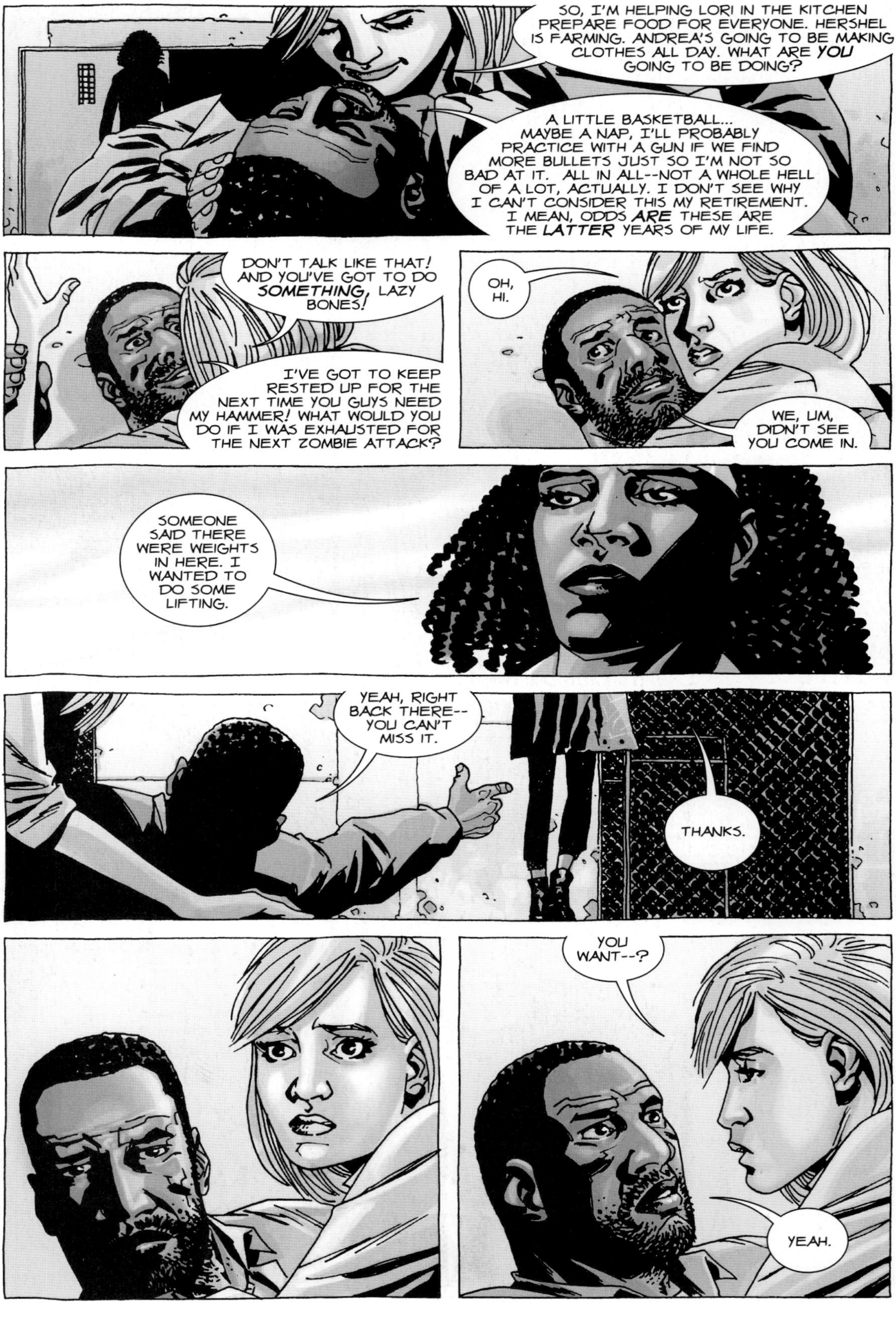

SO, I'M HELPING LORI IN THE KITCHEN PREPARE FOOD FOR EVERYONE. HERSHEL IS FARMING. ANDREA'S GOING TO BE MAKING CLOTHES ALL DAY. WHAT ARE *YOU* GOING TO BE DOING?
A LITTLE BASKETBALL... MAYBE A NAP, I'LL PROBABLY PRACTICE WITH A GUN IF WE FIND MORE BULLETS JUST SO I'M NOT SO BAD AT IT. ALL IN ALL--NOT A WHOLE HELL OF A LOT, ACTUALLY. I DON'T SEE WHY I CAN'T CONSIDER THIS MY RETIREMENT. I MEAN, ODDS *ARE* THESE ARE THE *LATTER* YEARS OF MY LIFE.
DON'T TALK LIKE THAT! AND YOU'VE GOT TO DO *SOMETHING*, LAZY BONES!
I'VE GOT TO KEEP RESTED UP FOR THE NEXT TIME YOU GUYS NEED MY HAMMER! WHAT WOULD YOU DO IF I WAS EXHAUSTED FOR THE NEXT ZOMBIE ATTACK?
OH, HI.
WE, UM, DIDN'T SEE YOU COME IN.
SOMEONE SAID THERE WERE WEIGHTS IN HERE. I WANTED TO DO SOME LIFTING.
YEAH, RIGHT BACK THERE-- YOU CAN'T MISS IT.
THANKS.
YOU WANT--?
YEAH.

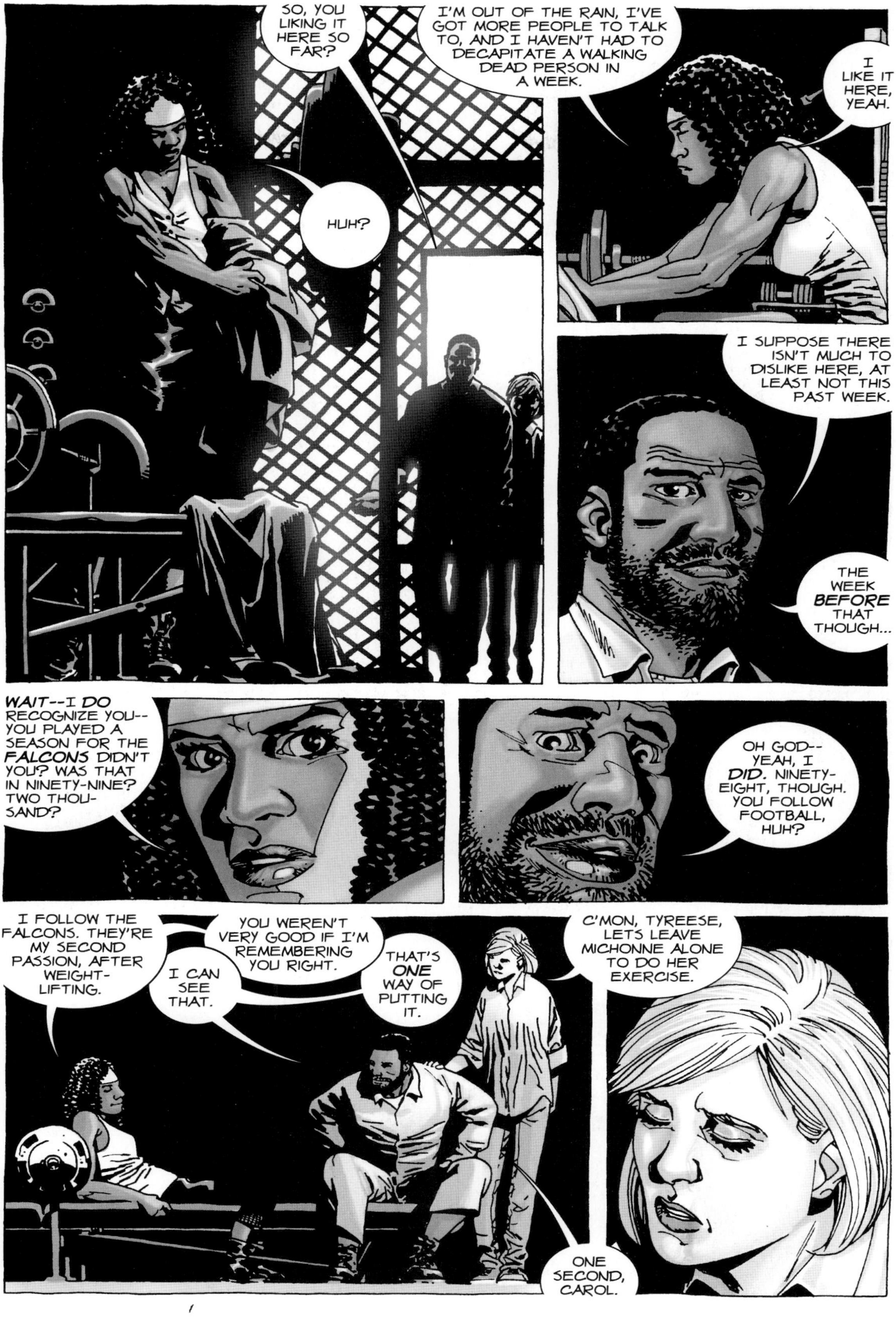
SO, YOU LIKING IT HERE SO FAR?
HUH?
I'M OUT OF THE RAIN, I'VE GOT MORE PEOPLE TO TALK TO, AND I HAVEN'T HAD TO DECAPITATE A WALKING DEAD PERSON IN A WEEK.
I LIKE IT HERE, YEAH.
I SUPPOSE THERE ISN'T MUCH TO DISLIKE HERE, AT LEAST NOT THIS PAST WEEK.
THE WEEK BEFORE THAT THOUGH...
WAIT--I DO RECOGNIZE YOU--YOU PLAYED A SEASON FOR THE FALCONS DIDN'T YOU? WAS THAT IN NINETY-NINE? TWO THOUSAND?
OH GOD--YEAH, I DID. NINETY-EIGHT, THOUGH. YOU FOLLOW FOOTBALL, HUH?
I FOLLOW THE FALCONS. THEY'RE MY SECOND PASSION, AFTER WEIGHT-LIFTING.
I CAN SEE THAT.
YOU WEREN'T VERY GOOD IF I'M REMEMBERING YOU RIGHT.
THAT'S ONE WAY OF PUTTING IT.
C'MON, TYREESE, LETS LEAVE MICHONNE ALONE TO DO HER EXERCISE.
ONE SECOND, CAROL.

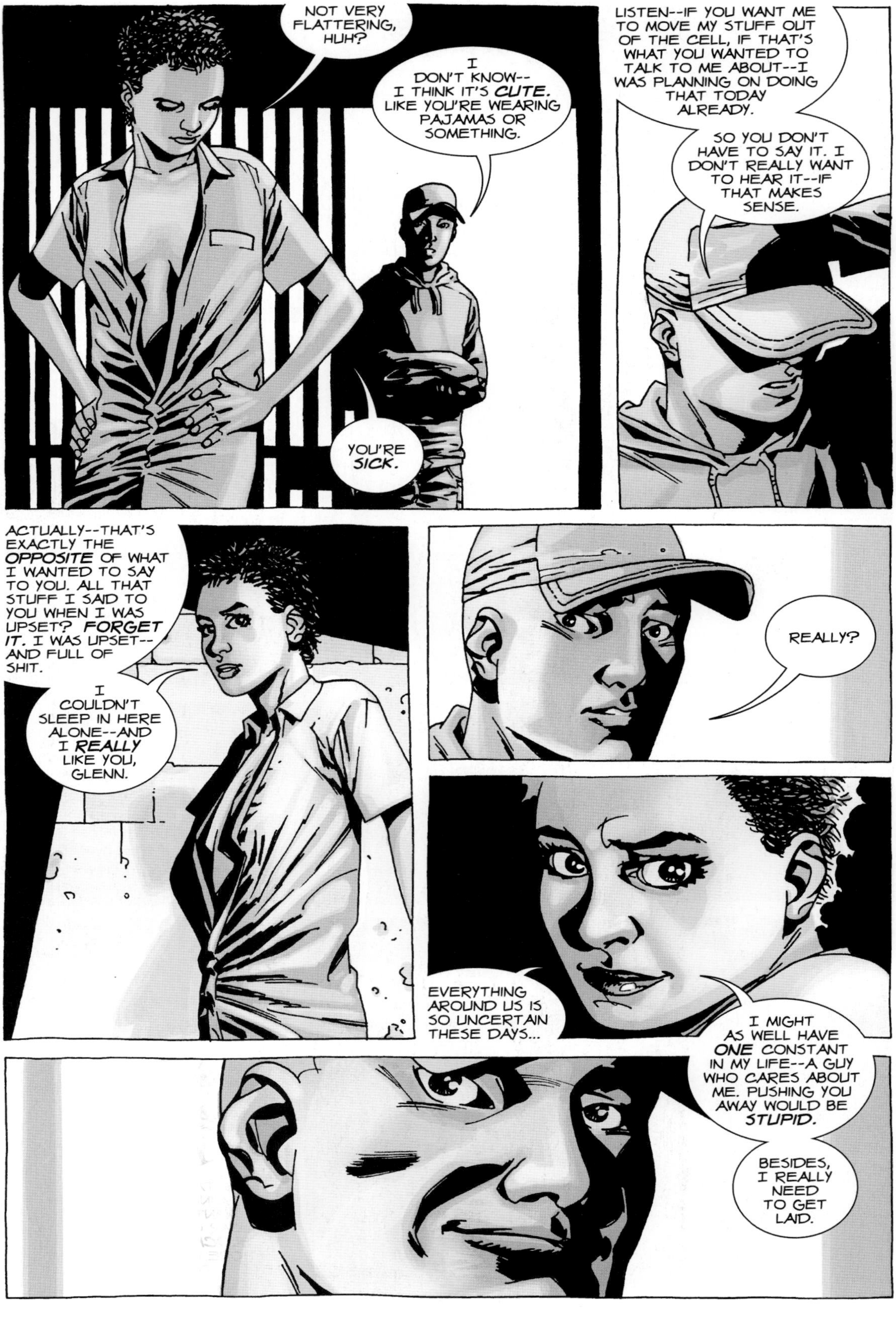
NOT VERY FLATTERING, HUH?
I DON'T KNOW-- I THINK IT'S CUTE. LIKE YOU'RE WEARING PAJAMAS OR SOMETHING.
YOU'RE SICK.
LISTEN--IF YOU WANT ME TO MOVE MY STUFF OUT OF THE CELL, IF THAT'S WHAT YOU WANTED TO TALK TO ME ABOUT--I WAS PLANNING ON DOING THAT TODAY ALREADY.
SO YOU DON'T HAVE TO SAY IT. I DON'T REALLY WANT TO HEAR IT--IF THAT MAKES SENSE.
ACTUALLY--THAT'S EXACTLY THE OPPOSITE OF WHAT I WANTED TO SAY TO YOU. ALL THAT STUFF I SAID TO YOU WHEN I WAS UPSET? FORGET IT. I WAS UPSET-- AND FULL OF SHIT.
I COULDN'T SLEEP IN HERE ALONE--AND I REALLY LIKE YOU, GLENN.
REALLY?
EVERYTHING AROUND US IS SO UNCERTAIN THESE DAYS...
I MIGHT AS WELL HAVE ONE CONSTANT IN MY LIFE--A GUY WHO CARES ABOUT ME. PUSHING YOU AWAY WOULD BE STUPID.
BESIDES, I REALLY NEED TO GET LAID.

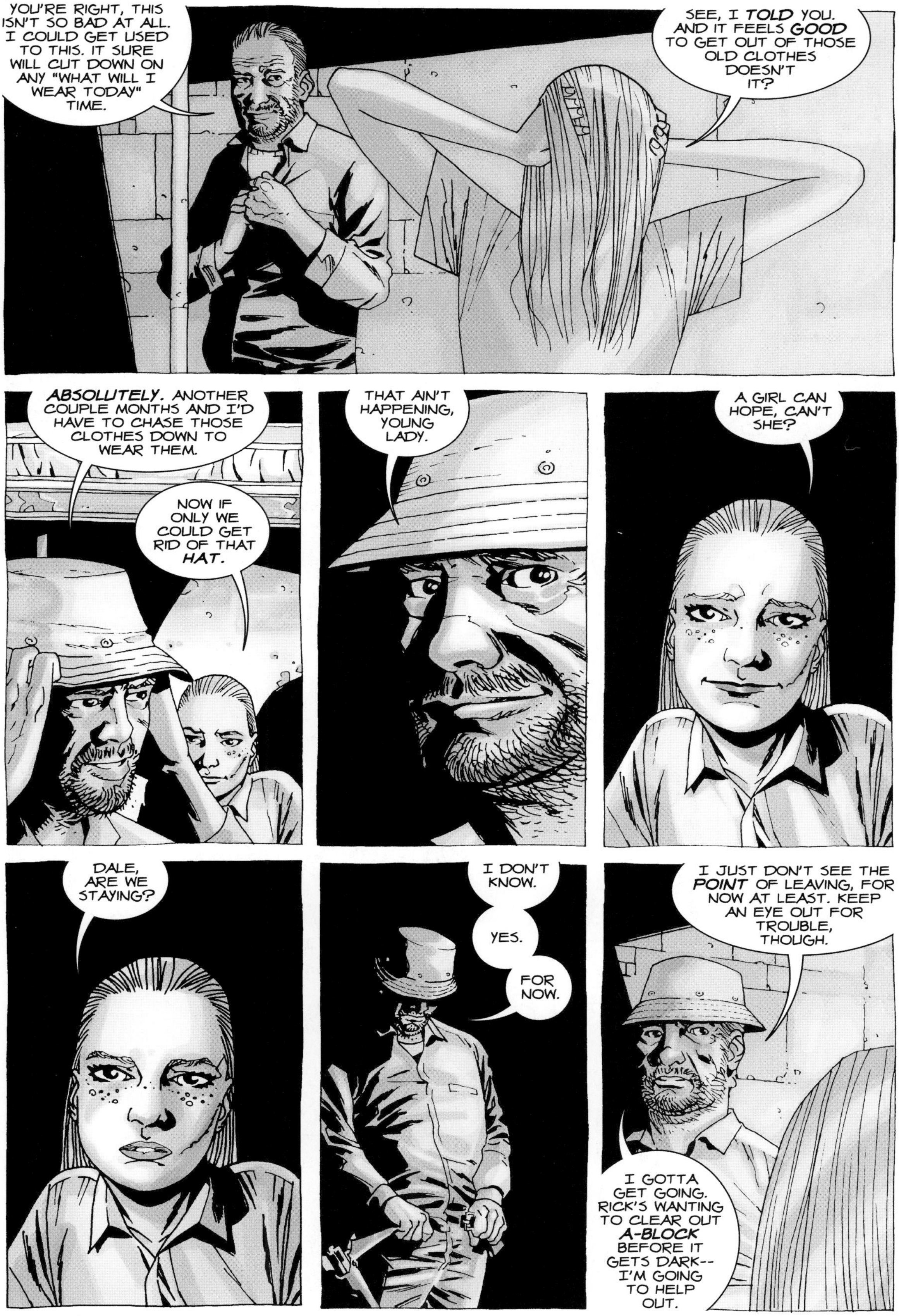
YOU'RE RIGHT, THIS ISN'T SO BAD AT ALL. I COULD GET USED TO THIS. IT SURE WILL CUT DOWN ON ANY "WHAT WILL I WEAR TODAY" TIME.
SEE, I TOLD YOU. AND IT FEELS GOOD TO GET OUT OF THOSE OLD CLOTHES DOESN'T IT?
ABSOLUTELY. ANOTHER COUPLE MONTHS AND I'D HAVE TO CHASE THOSE CLOTHES DOWN TO WEAR THEM.
NOW IF ONLY WE COULD GET RID OF THAT HAT.
THAT AIN'T HAPPENING, YOUNG LADY.
A GIRL CAN HOPE, CAN'T SHE?
DALE, ARE WE STAYING?
I DON'T KNOW.
YES.
FOR NOW.
I JUST DON'T SEE THE POINT OF LEAVING, FOR NOW AT LEAST. KEEP AN EYE OUT FOR TROUBLE, THOUGH.
I GOTTA GET GOING. RICK'S WANTING TO CLEAR OUT A-BLOCK BEFORE IT GETS DARK-- I'M GOING TO HELP OUT.

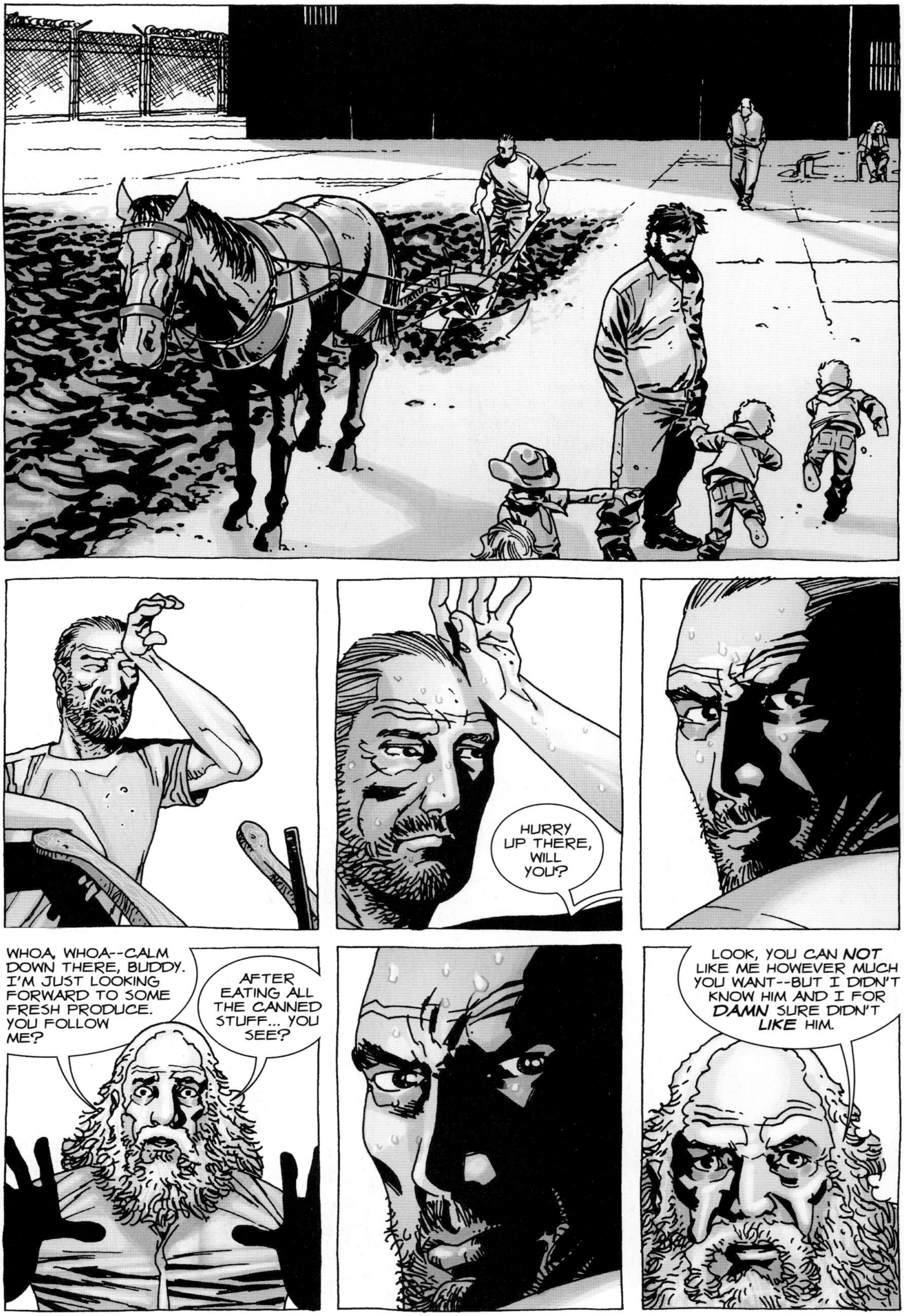
HURRY UP THERE, WILL YOU?
WHOA, WHOA--CALM DOWN THERE, BUDDY. I'M JUST LOOKING FORWARD TO SOME FRESH PRODUCE. YOU FOLLOW ME?
AFTER EATING ALL THE CANNED STUFF... YOU SEE?
LOOK, YOU CAN **NOT** LIKE ME HOWEVER MUCH YOU WANT--BUT I DIDN'T KNOW HIM AND I FOR **DAMN** SURE DIDN'T **LIKE** HIM.

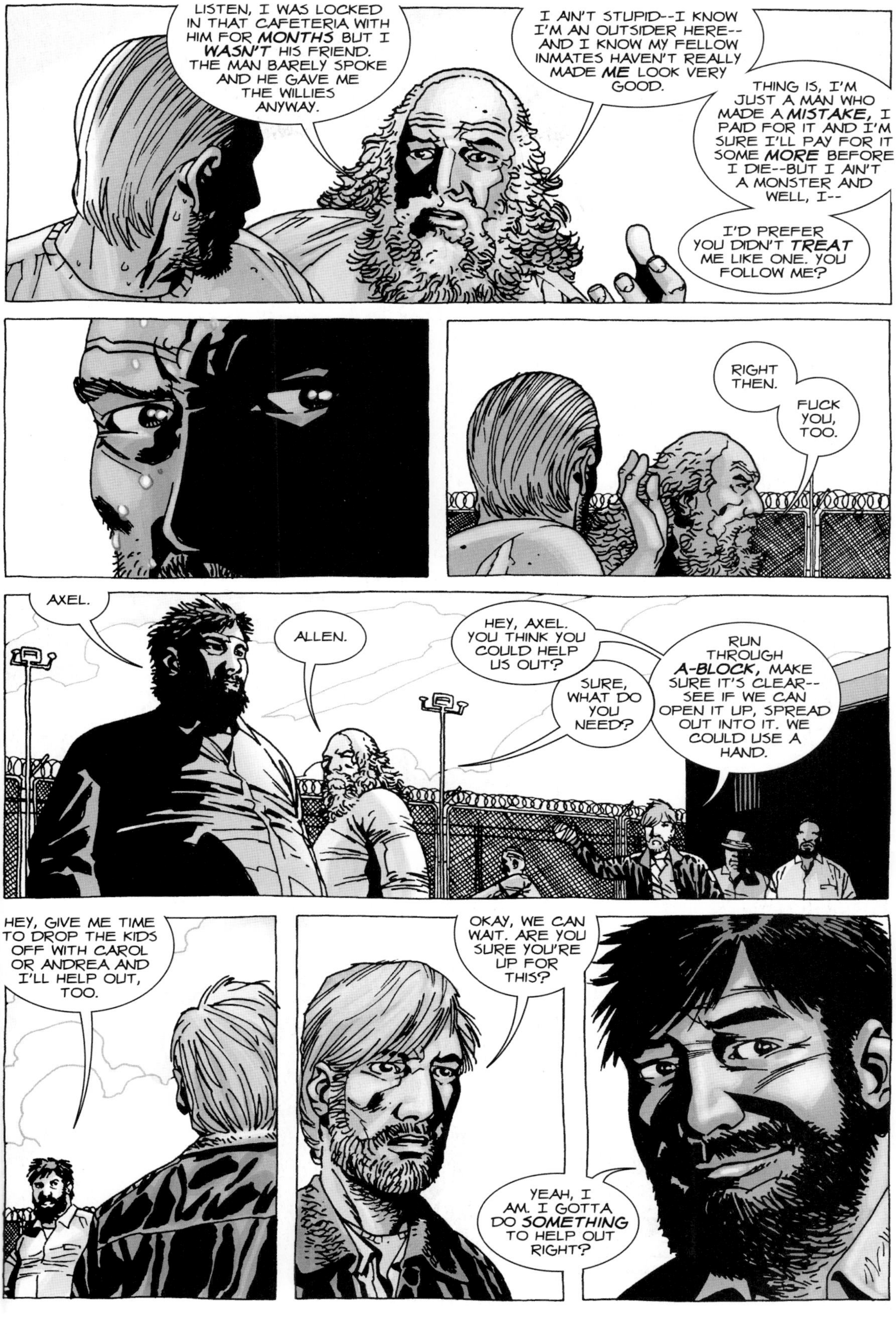

LISTEN, I WAS LOCKED IN THAT CAFETERIA WITH HIM FOR MONTHS BUT I WASN'T HIS FRIEND. THE MAN BARELY SPOKE AND HE GAVE ME THE WILLIES ANYWAY.
I AIN'T STUPID--I KNOW I'M AN OUTSIDER HERE--AND I KNOW MY FELLOW INMATES HAVEN'T REALLY MADE ME LOOK VERY GOOD.
THING IS, I'M JUST A MAN WHO MADE A MISTAKE, I PAID FOR IT AND I'M SURE I'LL PAY FOR IT SOME MORE BEFORE I DIE--BUT I AIN'T A MONSTER AND WELL, I--
I'D PREFER YOU DIDN'T TREAT ME LIKE ONE. YOU FOLLOW ME?
RIGHT THEN.
FUCK YOU, TOO.
AXEL.
ALLEN.
HEY, AXEL. YOU THINK YOU COULD HELP US OUT?
SURE, WHAT DO YOU NEED?
RUN THROUGH A-BLOCK, MAKE SURE IT'S CLEAR--SEE IF WE CAN OPEN IT UP, SPREAD OUT INTO IT. WE COULD USE A HAND.
HEY, GIVE ME TIME TO DROP THE KIDS OFF WITH CAROL OR ANDREA AND I'LL HELP OUT, TOO.
OKAY, WE CAN WAIT. ARE YOU SURE YOU'RE UP FOR THIS?
YEAH, I AM. I GOTTA DO SOMETHING TO HELP OUT RIGHT?

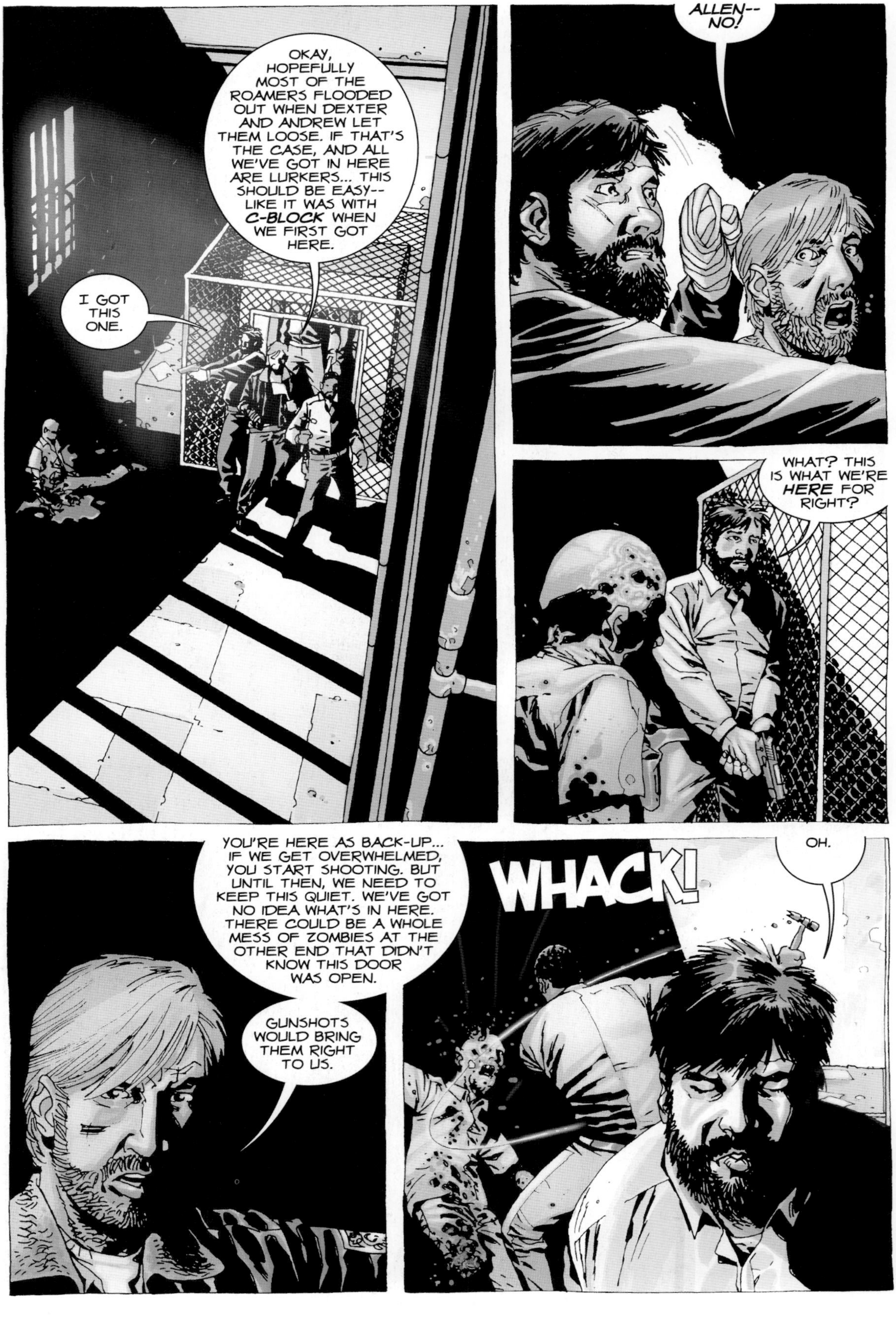
OKAY, HOPEFULLY MOST OF THE ROAMERS FLOODED OUT WHEN DEXTER AND ANDREW LET THEM LOOSE. IF THAT'S THE CASE, AND ALL WE'VE GOT IN HERE ARE LURKERS... THIS SHOULD BE EASY-- LIKE IT WAS WITH C-BLOCK WHEN WE FIRST GOT HERE.
I GOT THIS ONE.
ALLEN-- NO!
WHAT? THIS IS WHAT WE'RE HERE FOR RIGHT?
YOU'RE HERE AS BACK-UP... IF WE GET OVERWHELMED, YOU START SHOOTING. BUT UNTIL THEN, WE NEED TO KEEP THIS QUIET. WE'VE GOT NO IDEA WHAT'S IN HERE. THERE COULD BE A WHOLE MESS OF ZOMBIES AT THE OTHER END THAT DIDN'T KNOW THIS DOOR WAS OPEN.
GUNSHOTS WOULD BRING THEM RIGHT TO US.
WHACK!
OH.

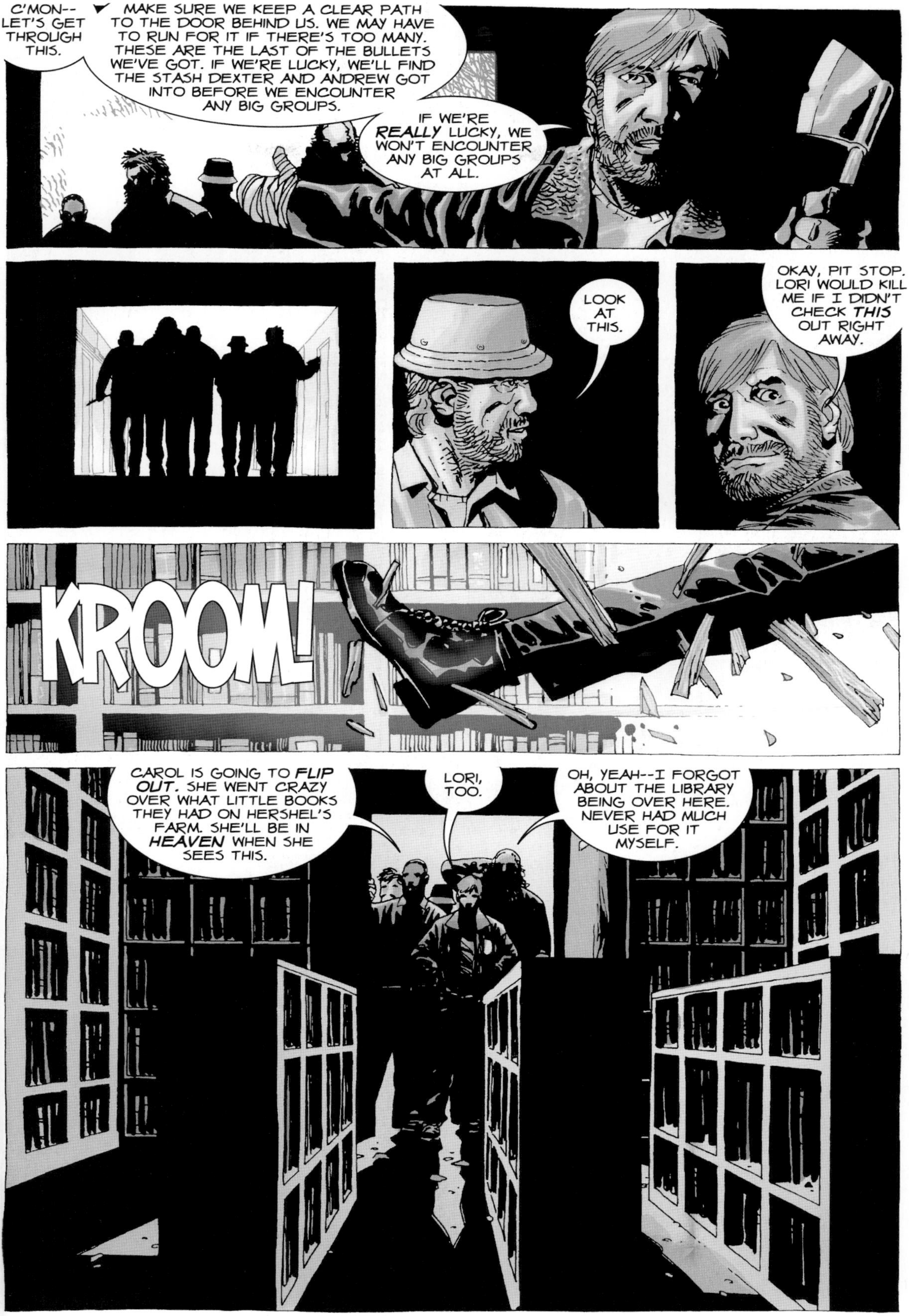
C'MON-- LET'S GET THROUGH THIS.
MAKE SURE WE KEEP A CLEAR PATH TO THE DOOR BEHIND US. WE MAY HAVE TO RUN FOR IT IF THERE'S TOO MANY. THESE ARE THE LAST OF THE BULLETS WE'VE GOT. IF WE'RE LUCKY, WE'LL FIND THE STASH DEXTER AND ANDREW GOT INTO BEFORE WE ENCOUNTER ANY BIG GROUPS.
IF WE'RE *REALLY* LUCKY, WE WON'T ENCOUNTER ANY BIG GROUPS AT ALL.
LOOK AT THIS.
OKAY, PIT STOP. LORI WOULD KILL ME IF I DIDN'T CHECK *THIS* OUT RIGHT AWAY.
KROOM!
CAROL IS GOING TO *FLIP OUT.* SHE WENT CRAZY OVER WHAT LITTLE BOOKS THEY HAD ON HERSHEL'S FARM. SHE'LL BE IN *HEAVEN* WHEN SHE SEES THIS.
LORI, TOO.
OH, YEAH--I FORGOT ABOUT THE LIBRARY BEING OVER HERE. NEVER HAD MUCH USE FOR IT MYSELF.

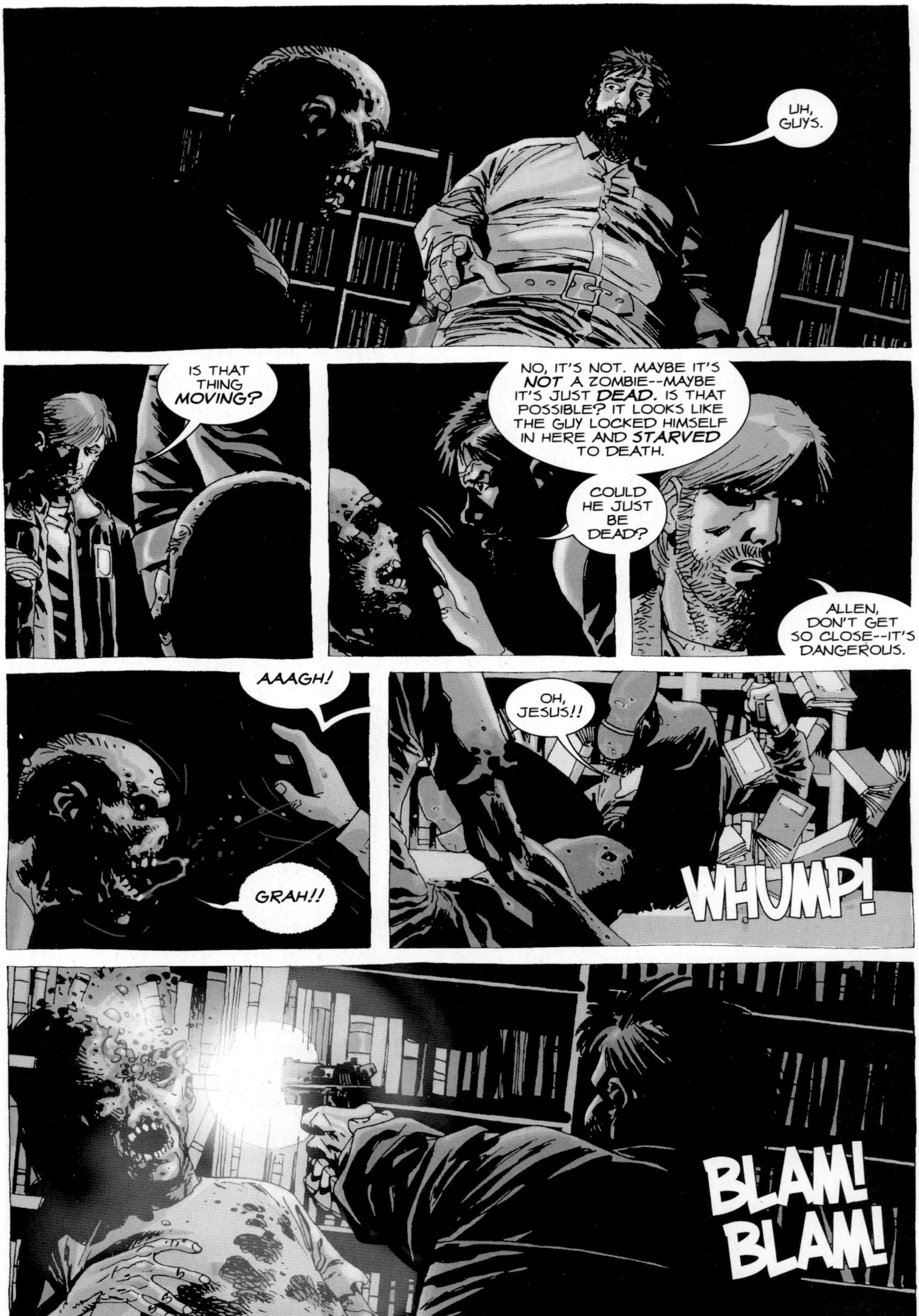

UH, GUYS.
IS THAT THING MOVING?
NO, IT'S NOT. MAYBE IT'S NOT A ZOMBIE--MAYBE IT'S JUST DEAD. IS THAT POSSIBLE? IT LOOKS LIKE THE GUY LOCKED HIMSELF IN HERE AND STARVED TO DEATH.
COULD HE JUST BE DEAD?
ALLEN, DON'T GET SO CLOSE--IT'S DANGEROUS.
AAAGH!
GRAH!!
OH, JESUS!!
WHUMP!
BLAM! BLAM!

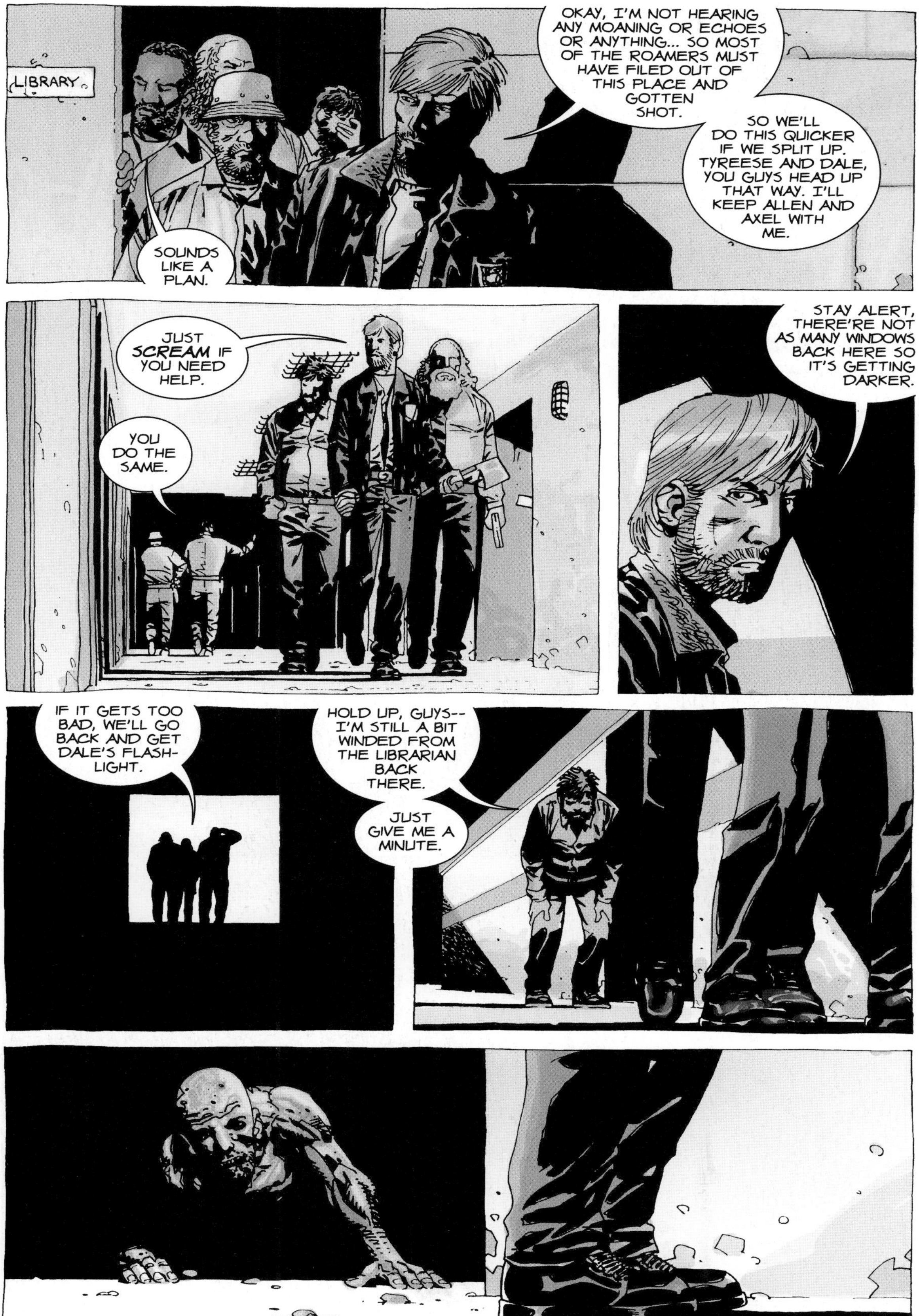
LIBRARY
OKAY, I'M NOT HEARING ANY MOANING OR ECHOES OR ANYTHING... SO MOST OF THE ROAMERS MUST HAVE FILED OUT OF THIS PLACE AND GOTTEN SHOT.
SO WE'LL DO THIS QUICKER IF WE SPLIT UP. TYREESE AND DALE, YOU GUYS HEAD UP THAT WAY. I'LL KEEP ALLEN AND AXEL WITH ME.
SOUNDS LIKE A PLAN.
JUST SCREAM IF YOU NEED HELP.
YOU DO THE SAME.
STAY ALERT, THERE'RE NOT AS MANY WINDOWS BACK HERE SO IT'S GETTING DARKER.
IF IT GETS TOO BAD, WE'LL GO BACK AND GET DALE'S FLASH-LIGHT.
HOLD UP, GUYS-- I'M STILL A BIT WINDED FROM THE LIBRARIAN BACK THERE.
JUST GIVE ME A MINUTE.

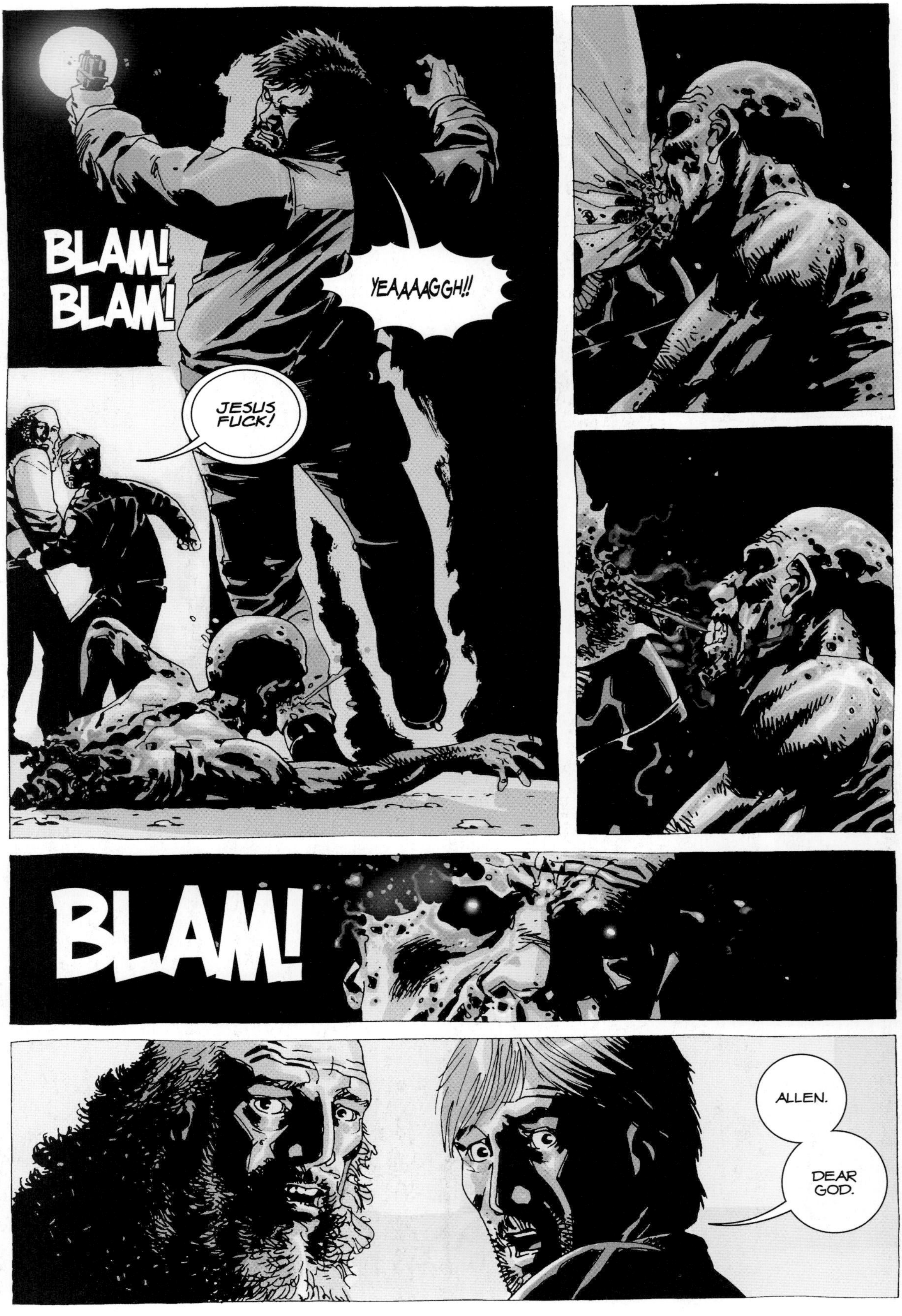
BLAM! BLAM!
YEAAAAGGH!!
JESUS FUCK!
BLAM!
ALLEN.
DEAR GOD.

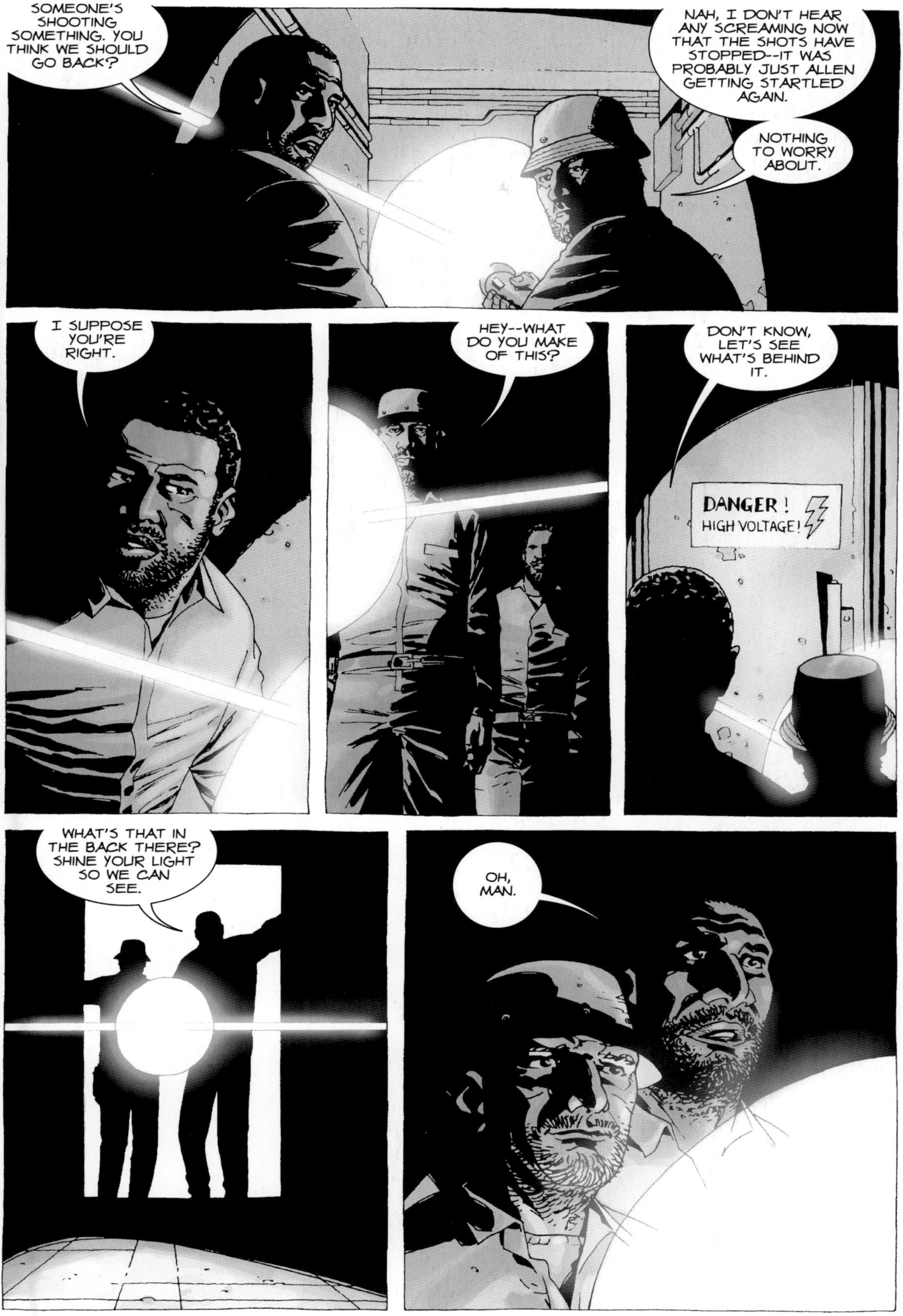
SOMEONE'S SHOOTING SOMETHING. YOU THINK WE SHOULD GO BACK?
NAH, I DON'T HEAR ANY SCREAMING NOW THAT THE SHOTS HAVE STOPPED--IT WAS PROBABLY JUST ALLEN GETTING STARTLED AGAIN.
NOTHING TO WORRY ABOUT.
I SUPPOSE YOU'RE RIGHT.
HEY--WHAT DO YOU MAKE OF THIS?
DON'T KNOW, LET'S SEE WHAT'S BEHIND IT.
DANGER !
HIGH VOLTAGE!
WHAT'S THAT IN THE BACK THERE? SHINE YOUR LIGHT SO WE CAN SEE.
OH, MAN.

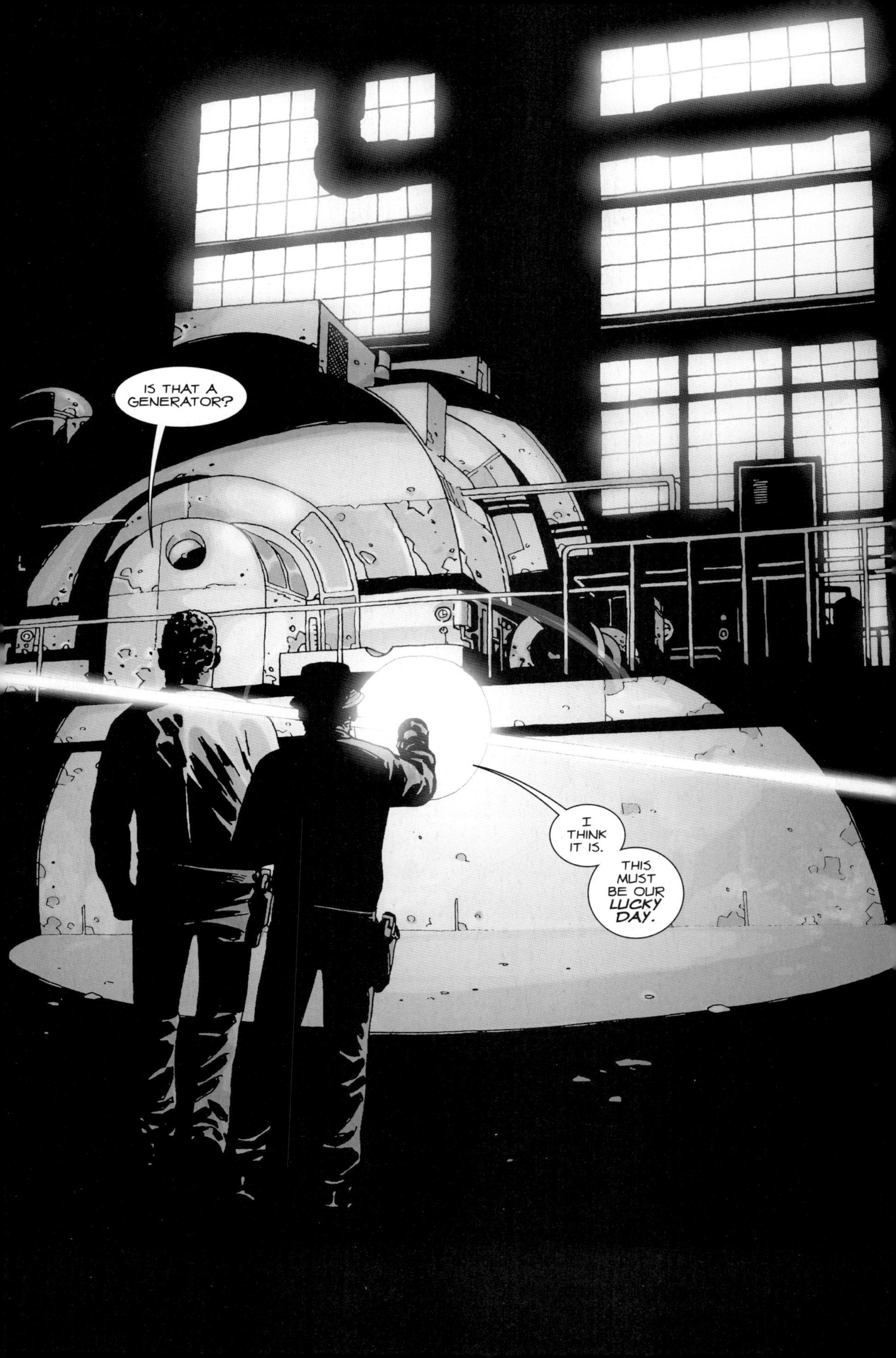
IS THAT A GENERATOR?
I THINK IT IS.
THIS MUST BE OUR *LUCKY DAY*.

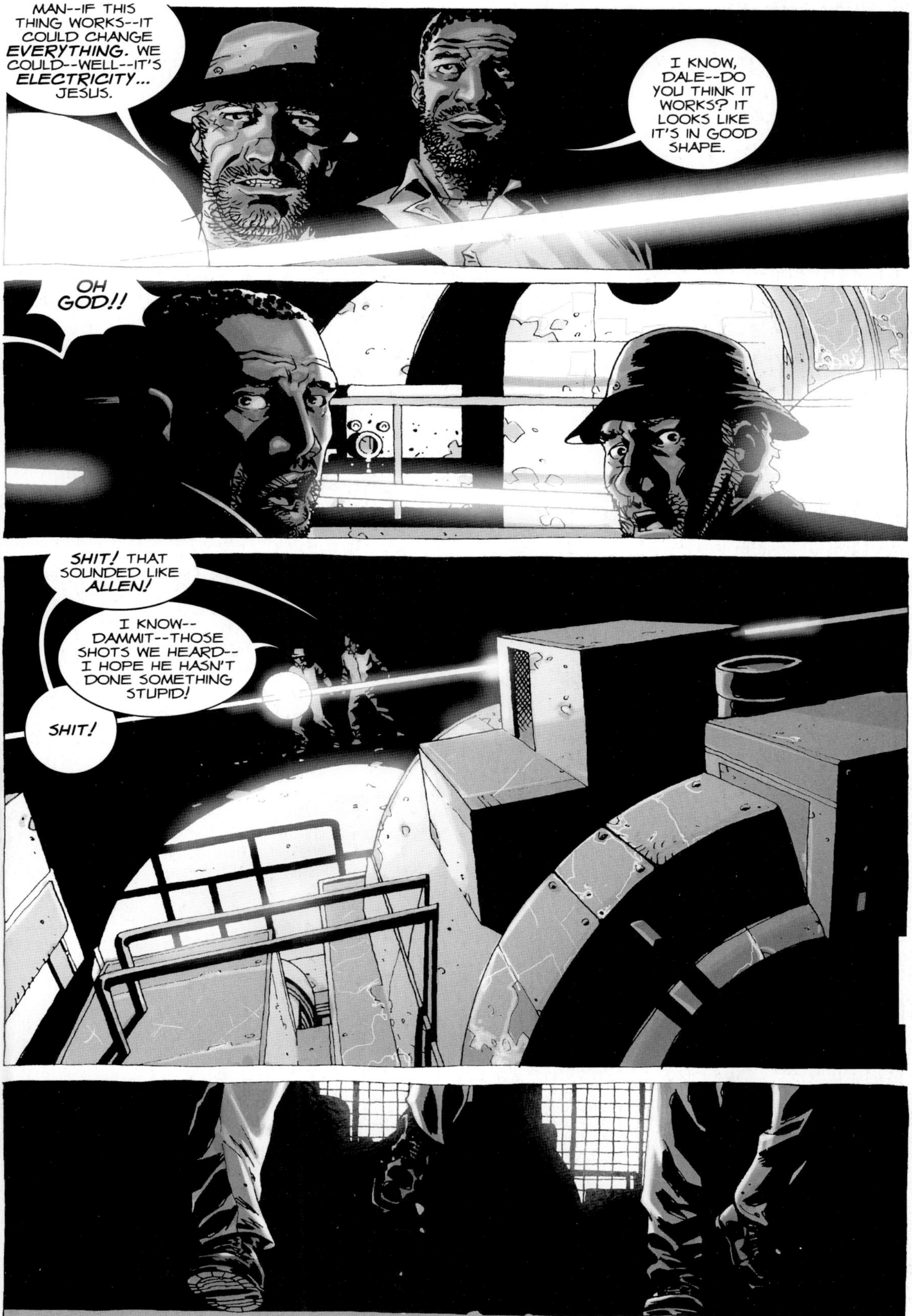

MAN--IF THIS THING WORKS--IT COULD CHANGE EVERYTHING. WE COULD--WELL--IT'S ELECTRICITY... JESUS.
I KNOW, DALE--DO YOU THINK IT WORKS? IT LOOKS LIKE IT'S IN GOOD SHAPE.
OH GOD!!
SHIT! THAT SOUNDED LIKE ALLEN!
I KNOW--DAMMIT--THOSE SHOTS WE HEARD--I HOPE HE HASN'T DONE SOMETHING STUPID!
SHIT!

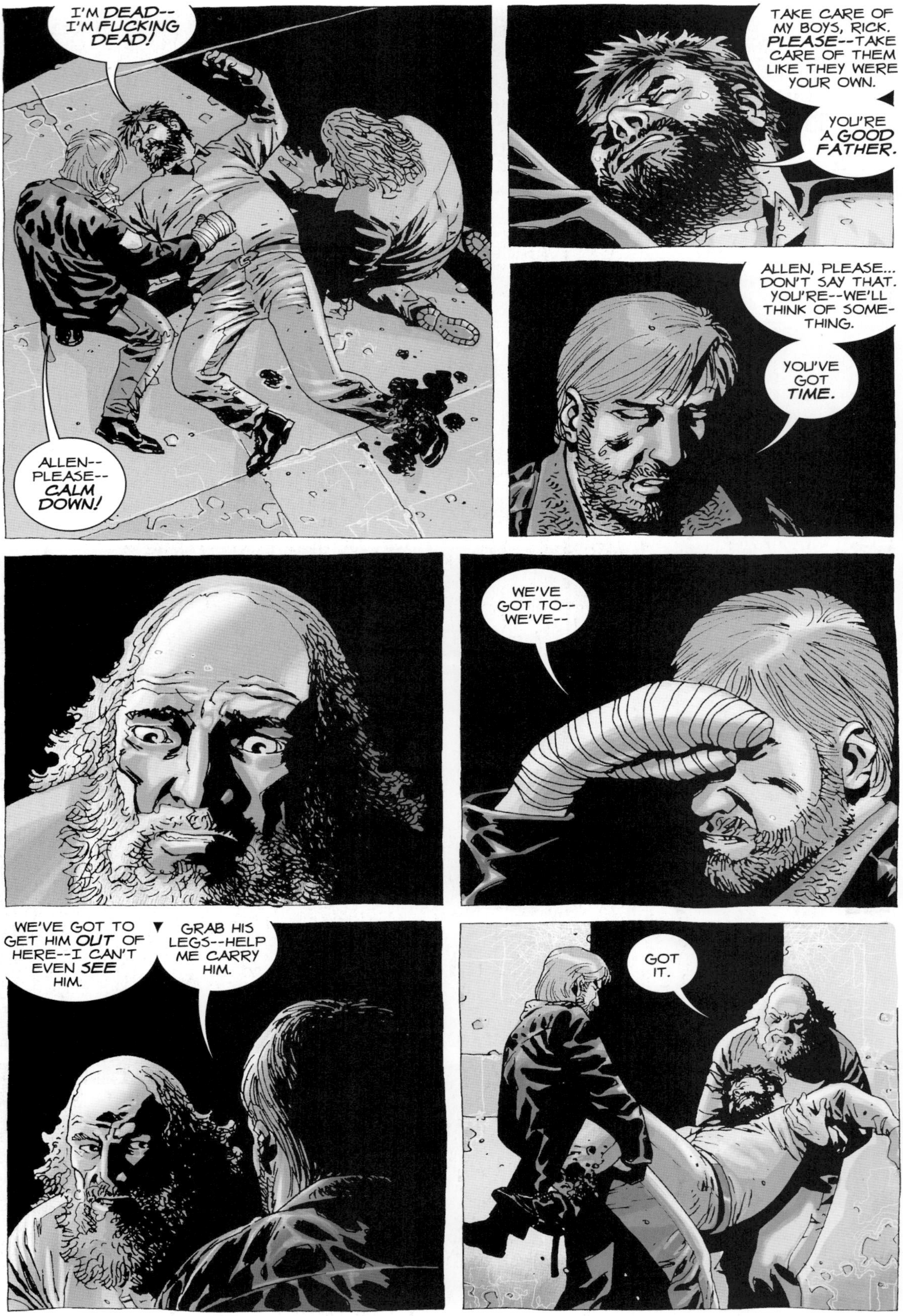
I'M DEAD-- I'M FUCKING DEAD!
ALLEN-- PLEASE-- CALM DOWN!
TAKE CARE OF MY BOYS, RICK. PLEASE--TAKE CARE OF THEM LIKE THEY WERE YOUR OWN.
YOU'RE A GOOD FATHER.
ALLEN, PLEASE... DON'T SAY THAT. YOU'RE--WE'LL THINK OF SOME-THING.
YOU'VE GOT TIME.
WE'VE GOT TO-- WE'VE--
WE'VE GOT TO GET HIM OUT OF HERE--I CAN'T EVEN SEE HIM.
GRAB HIS LEGS--HELP ME CARRY HIM.
GOT IT.

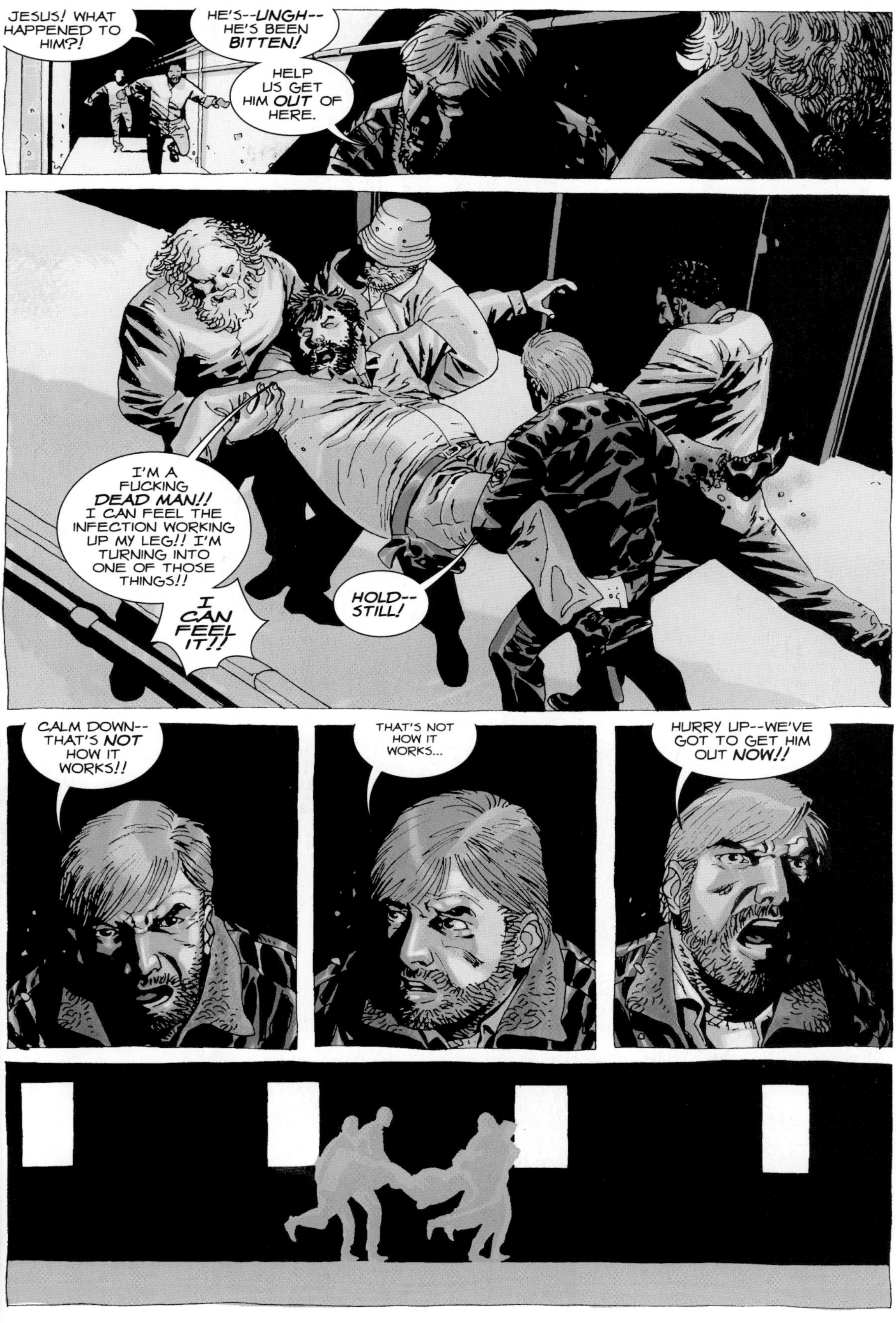
JESUS! WHAT HAPPENED TO HIM?!
HE'S--UNGH-- HE'S BEEN BITTEN!
HELP US GET HIM OUT OF HERE.
I'M A FUCKING DEAD MAN!! I CAN FEEL THE INFECTION WORKING UP MY LEG!! I'M TURNING INTO ONE OF THOSE THINGS!!
I CAN FEEL IT!!
HOLD-- STILL!
CALM DOWN-- THAT'S NOT HOW IT WORKS!!
THAT'S NOT HOW IT WORKS...
HURRY UP--WE'VE GOT TO GET HIM OUT NOW!!

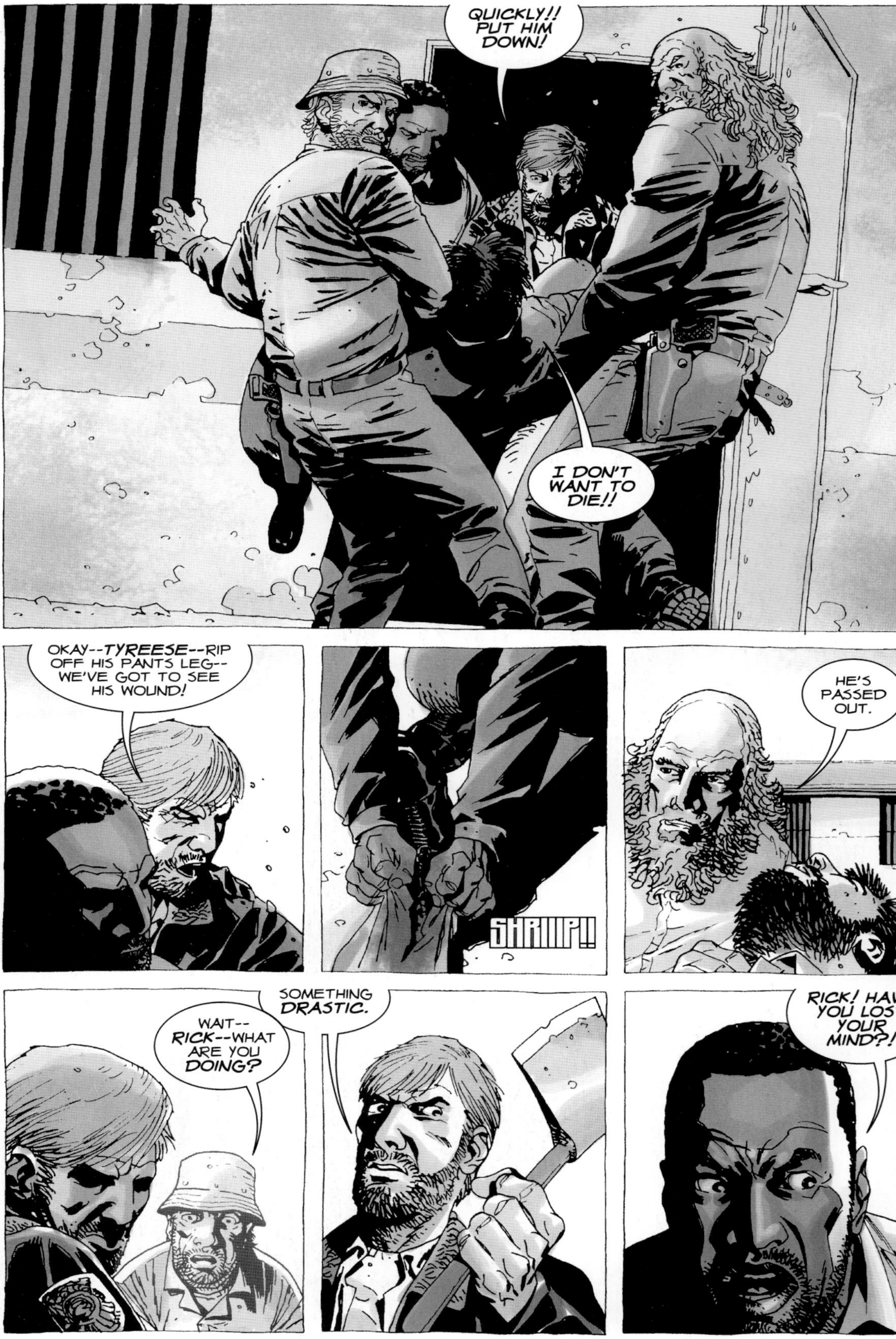
QUICKLY!! PUT HIM DOWN!
I DON'T WANT TO DIE!!
OKAY--TYREESE--RIP OFF HIS PANTS LEG-- WE'VE GOT TO SEE HIS WOUND!
SHRIIIP!!
HE'S PASSED OUT.
WAIT-- RICK--WHAT ARE YOU DOING?
SOMETHING DRASTIC.
RICK! HAVE YOU LOST YOUR MIND?!

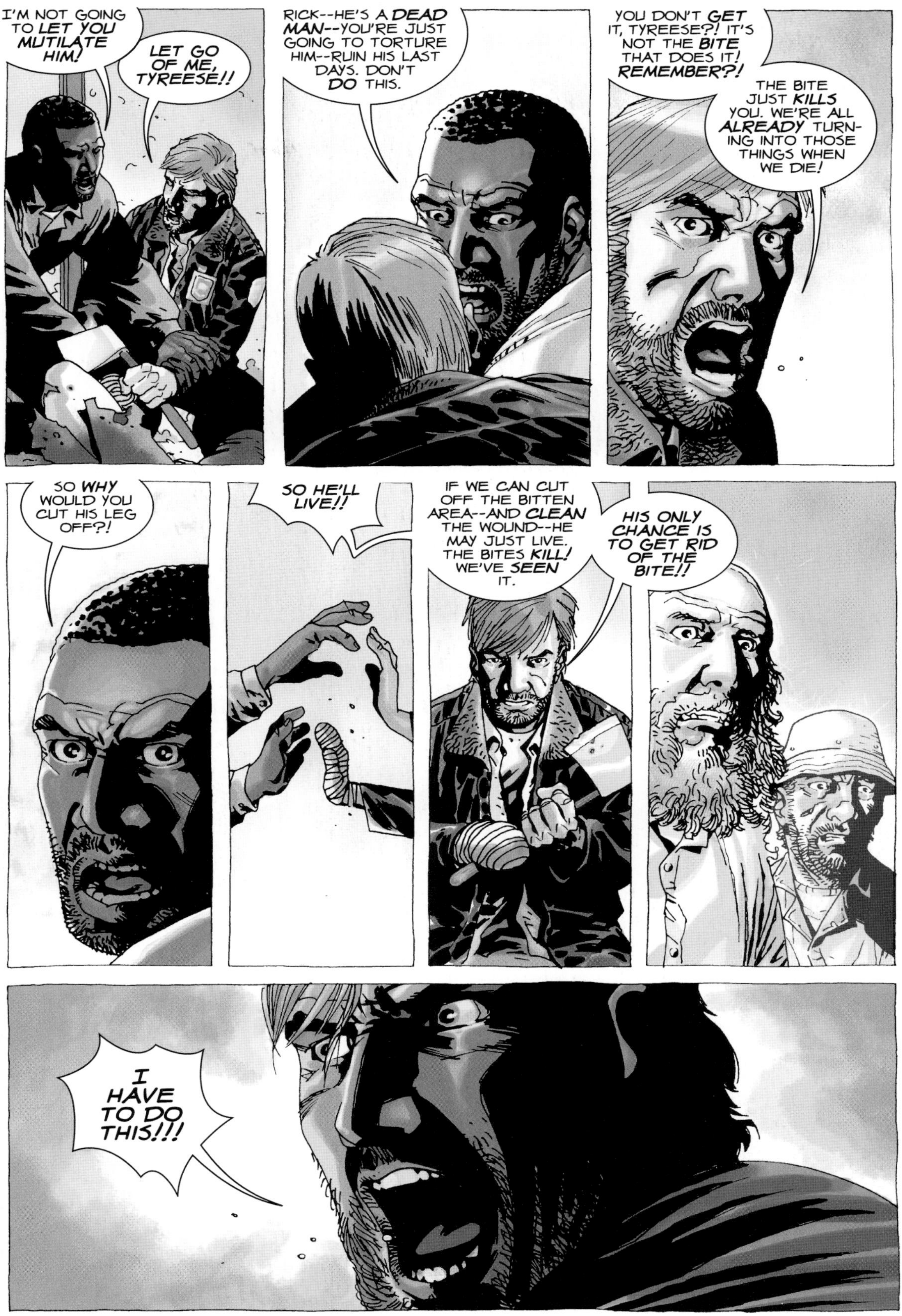
I'M NOT GOING TO LET YOU MUTILATE HIM!
LET GO OF ME, TYREESE!!
RICK--HE'S A DEAD MAN--YOU'RE JUST GOING TO TORTURE HIM--RUIN HIS LAST DAYS. DON'T DO THIS.
YOU DON'T GET IT, TYREESE?! IT'S NOT THE BITE THAT DOES IT! REMEMBER?!
THE BITE JUST KILLS YOU. WE'RE ALL ALREADY TURNING INTO THOSE THINGS WHEN WE DIE!
SO WHY WOULD YOU CUT HIS LEG OFF?!
SO HE'LL LIVE!!
IF WE CAN CUT OFF THE BITTEN AREA--AND CLEAN THE WOUND--HE MAY JUST LIVE. THE BITES KILL! WE'VE SEEN IT.
HIS ONLY CHANCE IS TO GET RID OF THE BITE!!
I HAVE TO DO THIS!!!

DO IT.
I DON'T KNOW...
JUST DO IT.
THUNK!!
THUNK!!
THUNK!
THUNK!
THUNK!
THUNK!!

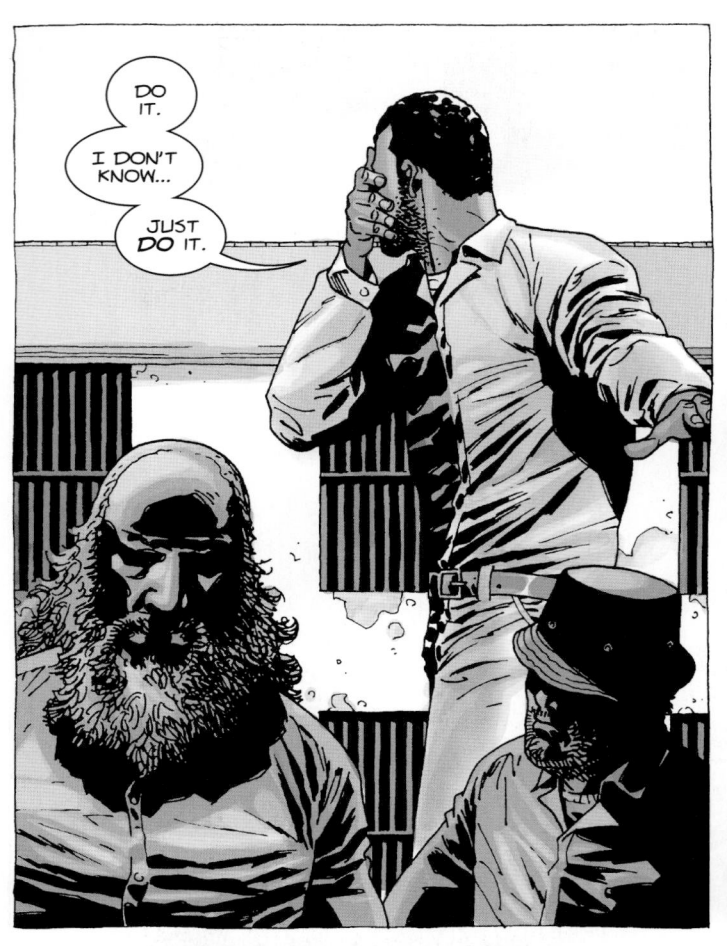

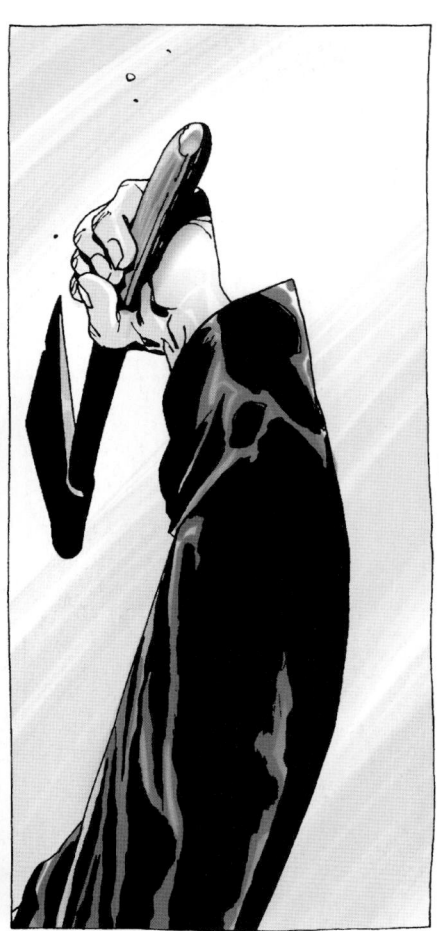

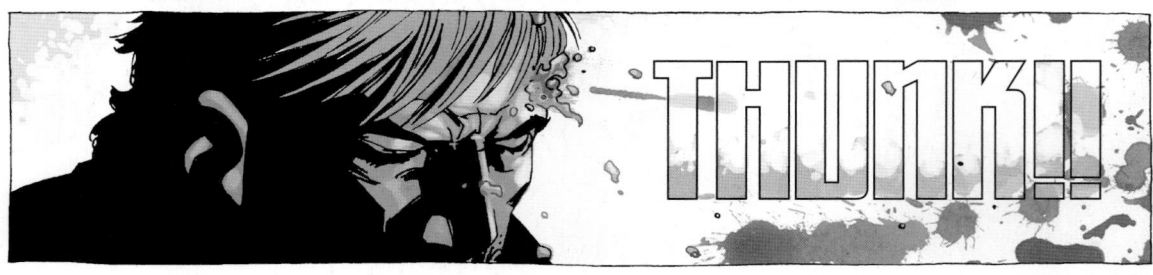

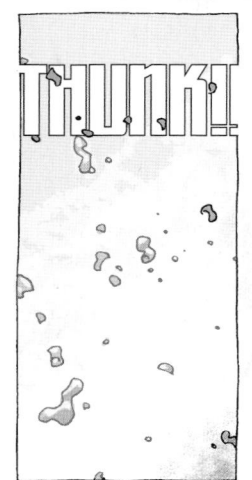

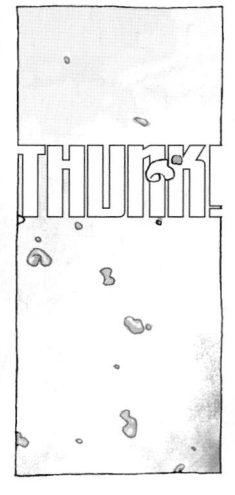

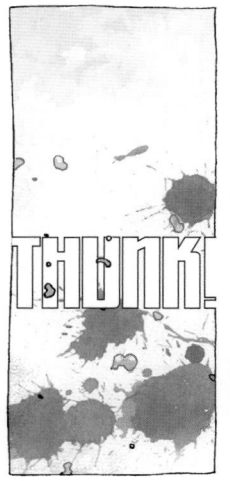

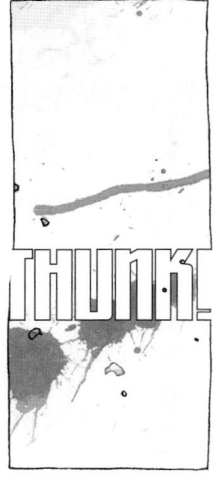

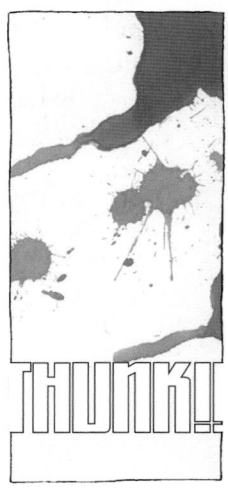

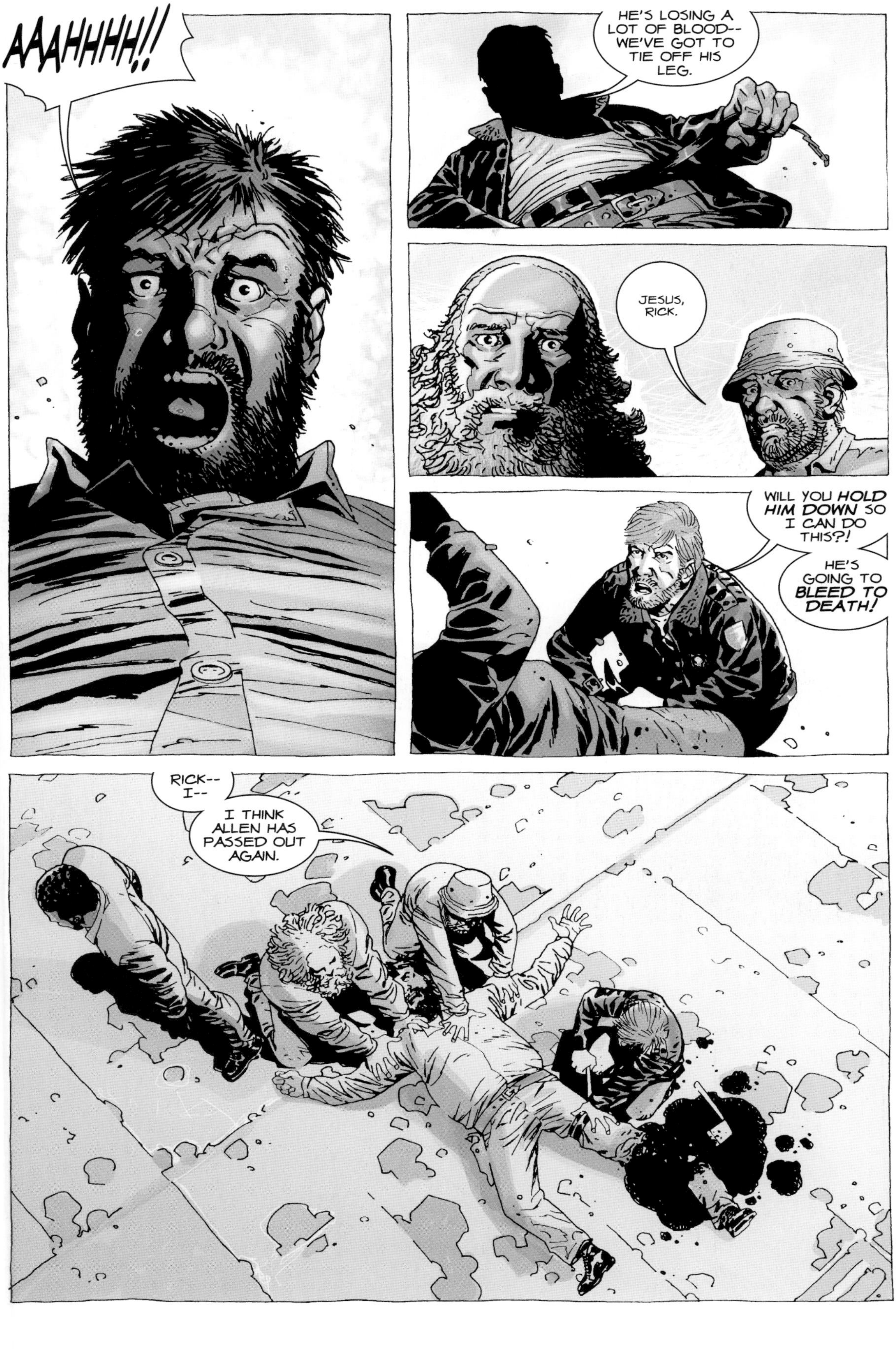
AAAHHHH!!
HE'S LOSING A LOT OF BLOOD-- WE'VE GOT TO TIE OFF HIS LEG.
JESUS, RICK.
WILL YOU HOLD HIM DOWN SO I CAN DO THIS?!
HE'S GOING TO BLEED TO DEATH!
RICK-- I--
I THINK ALLEN HAS PASSED OUT AGAIN.

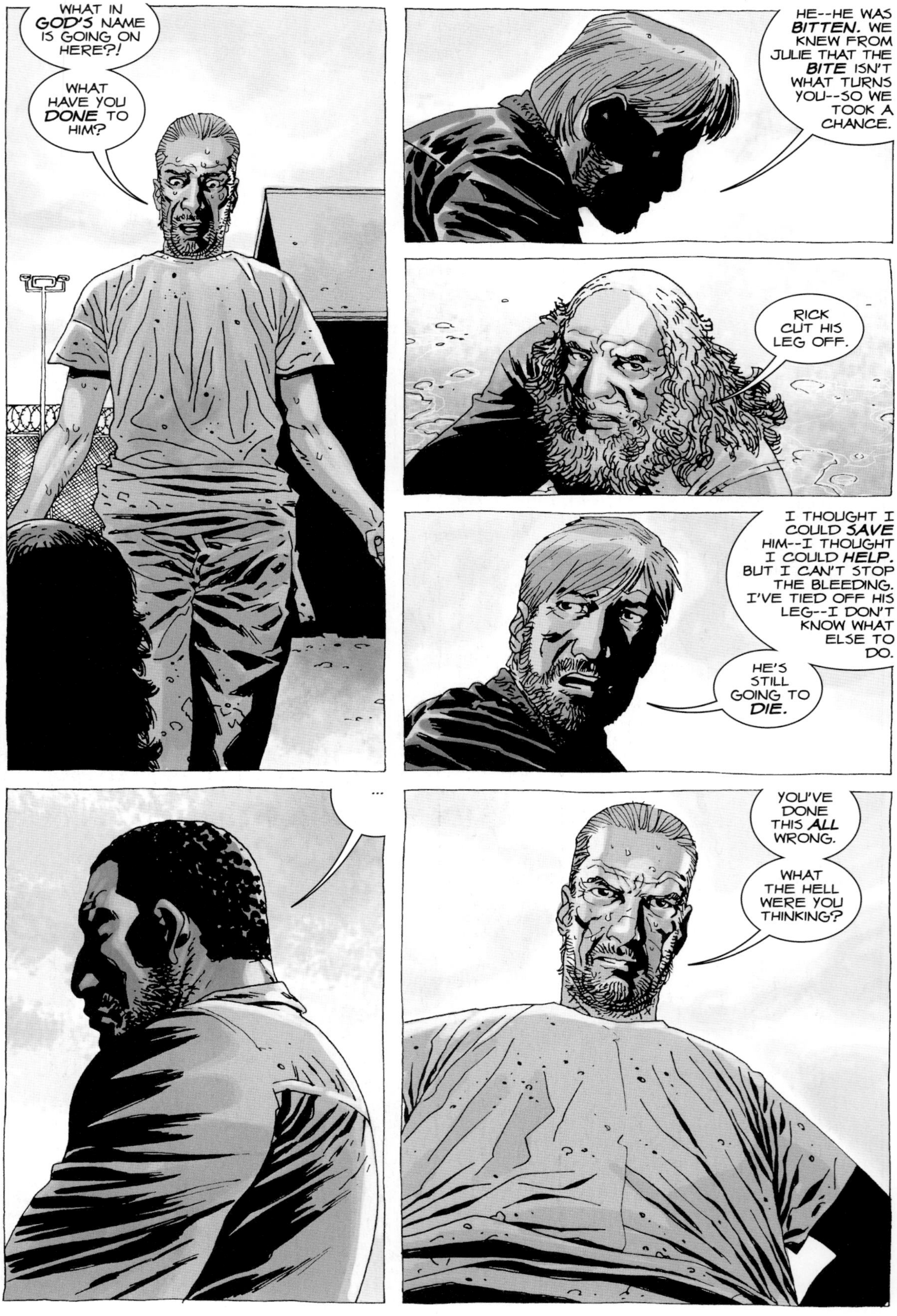
WHAT IN GOD'S NAME IS GOING ON HERE?!
WHAT HAVE YOU DONE TO HIM?
HE--HE WAS BITTEN. WE KNEW FROM JULIE THAT THE BITE ISN'T WHAT TURNS YOU--SO WE TOOK A CHANCE.
RICK CUT HIS LEG OFF.
I THOUGHT I COULD SAVE HIM--I THOUGHT I COULD HELP. BUT I CAN'T STOP THE BLEEDING. I'VE TIED OFF HIS LEG--I DON'T KNOW WHAT ELSE TO DO.
HE'S STILL GOING TO DIE.
...
YOU'VE DONE THIS ALL WRONG.
WHAT THE HELL WERE YOU THINKING?

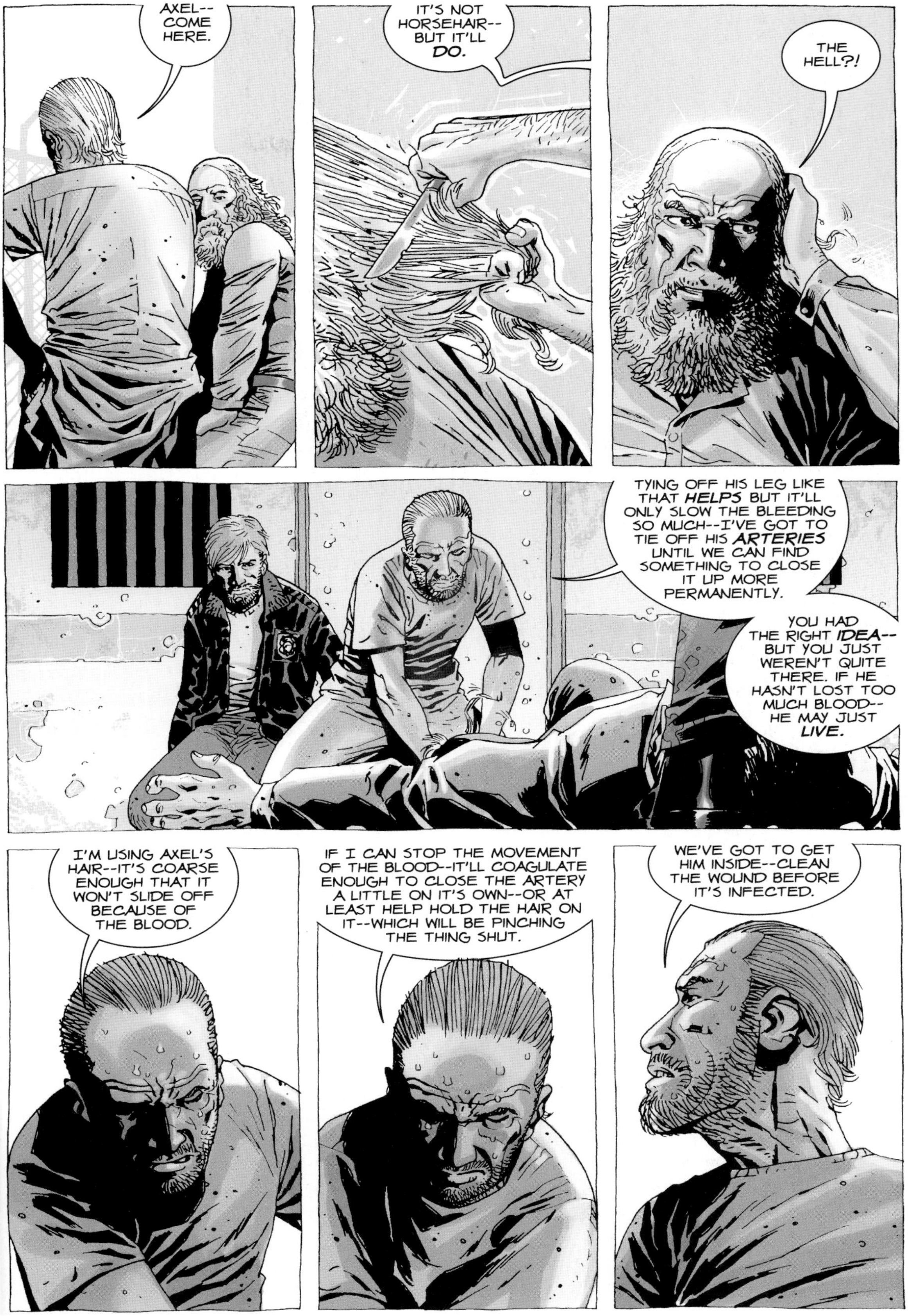
AXEL-- COME HERE.
IT'S NOT HORSEHAIR-- BUT IT'LL DO.
THE HELL?!
TYING OFF HIS LEG LIKE THAT HELPS BUT IT'LL ONLY SLOW THE BLEEDING SO MUCH--I'VE GOT TO TIE OFF HIS ARTERIES UNTIL WE CAN FIND SOMETHING TO CLOSE IT UP MORE PERMANENTLY.
YOU HAD THE RIGHT IDEA-- BUT YOU JUST WEREN'T QUITE THERE. IF HE HASN'T LOST TOO MUCH BLOOD-- HE MAY JUST LIVE.
I'M USING AXEL'S HAIR--IT'S COARSE ENOUGH THAT IT WON'T SLIDE OFF BECAUSE OF THE BLOOD.
IF I CAN STOP THE MOVEMENT OF THE BLOOD--IT'LL COAGULATE ENOUGH TO CLOSE THE ARTERY A LITTLE ON IT'S OWN--OR AT LEAST HELP HOLD THE HAIR ON IT--WHICH WILL BE PINCHING THE THING SHUT.
WE'VE GOT TO GET HIM INSIDE--CLEAN THE WOUND BEFORE IT'S INFECTED.

YOU-- ARE YOU STILL *SCARED* OF THEM?

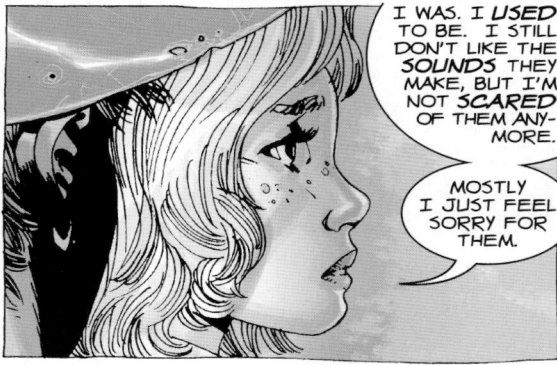

I WAS. I *USED* TO BE. I STILL DON'T LIKE THE *SOUNDS* THEY MAKE, BUT I'M NOT *SCARED* OF THEM ANY-MORE.

MOSTLY I JUST FEEL SORRY FOR THEM.

YOU FEEL *SORRY* FOR THEM?

WHY?

BECAUSE THEY LOOK SO SAD.

DON'T THEY LOOK *SAD* TO YOU?

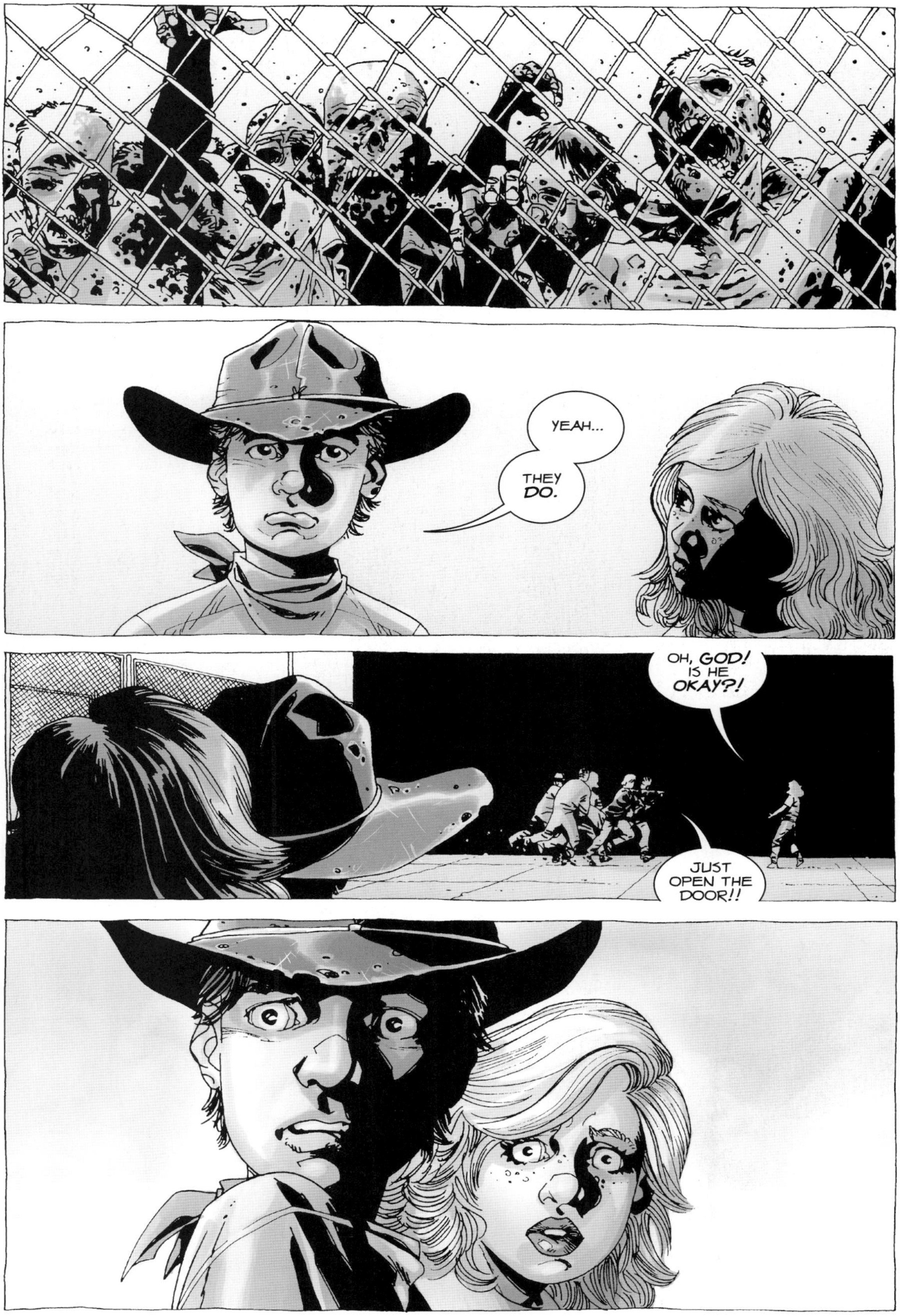
YEAH...
THEY DO.
OH, GOD! IS HE OKAY?!
JUST OPEN THE DOOR!!

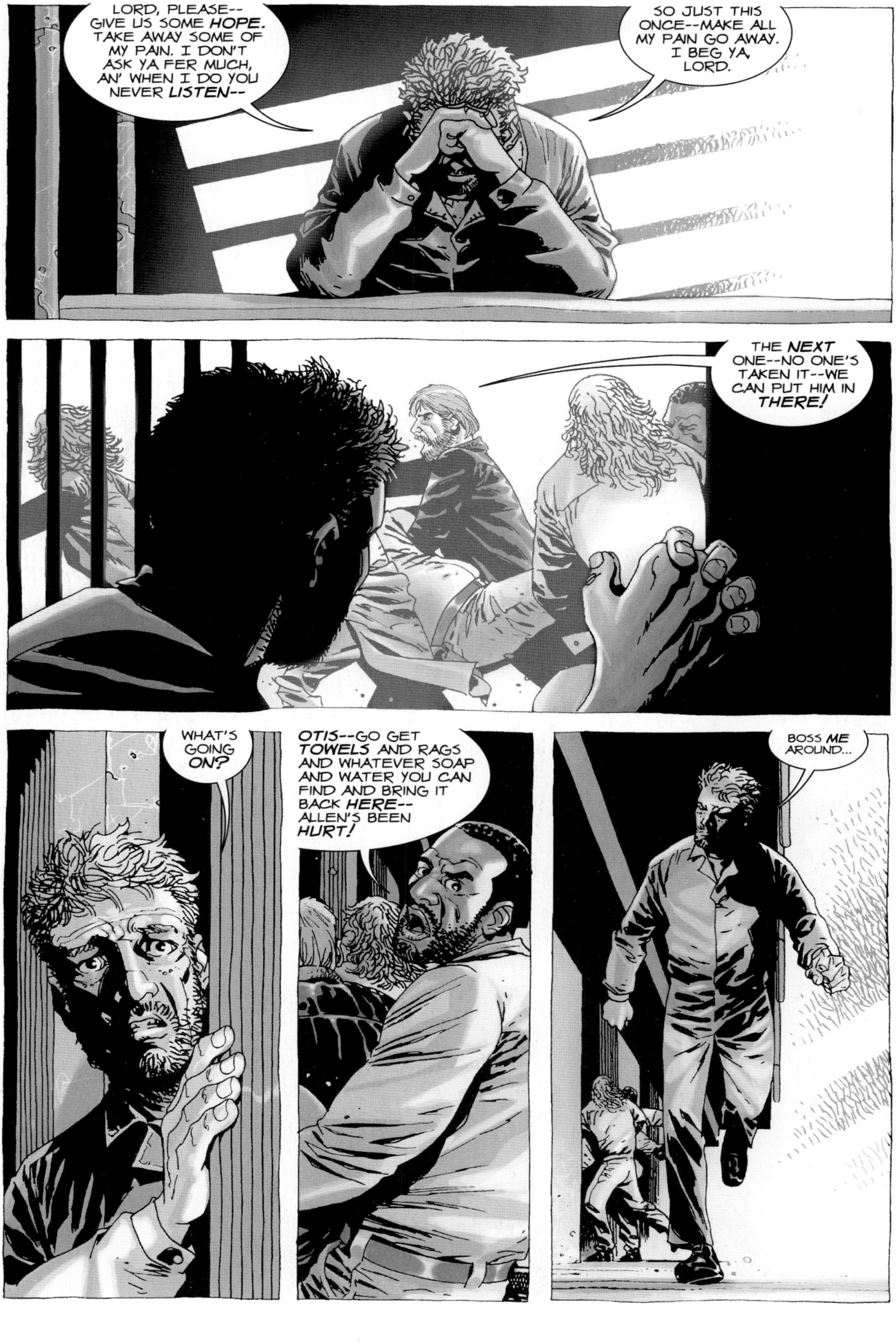
LORD, PLEASE-- GIVE US SOME HOPE. TAKE AWAY SOME OF MY PAIN. I DON'T ASK YA FER MUCH, AN' WHEN I DO YOU NEVER LISTEN--
SO JUST THIS ONCE--MAKE ALL MY PAIN GO AWAY. I BEG YA, LORD.
THE NEXT ONE--NO ONE'S TAKEN IT--WE CAN PUT HIM IN THERE!
WHAT'S GOING ON?
OTIS--GO GET TOWELS AND RAGS AND WHATEVER SOAP AND WATER YOU CAN FIND AND BRING IT BACK HERE-- ALLEN'S BEEN HURT!
BOSS ME AROUND...

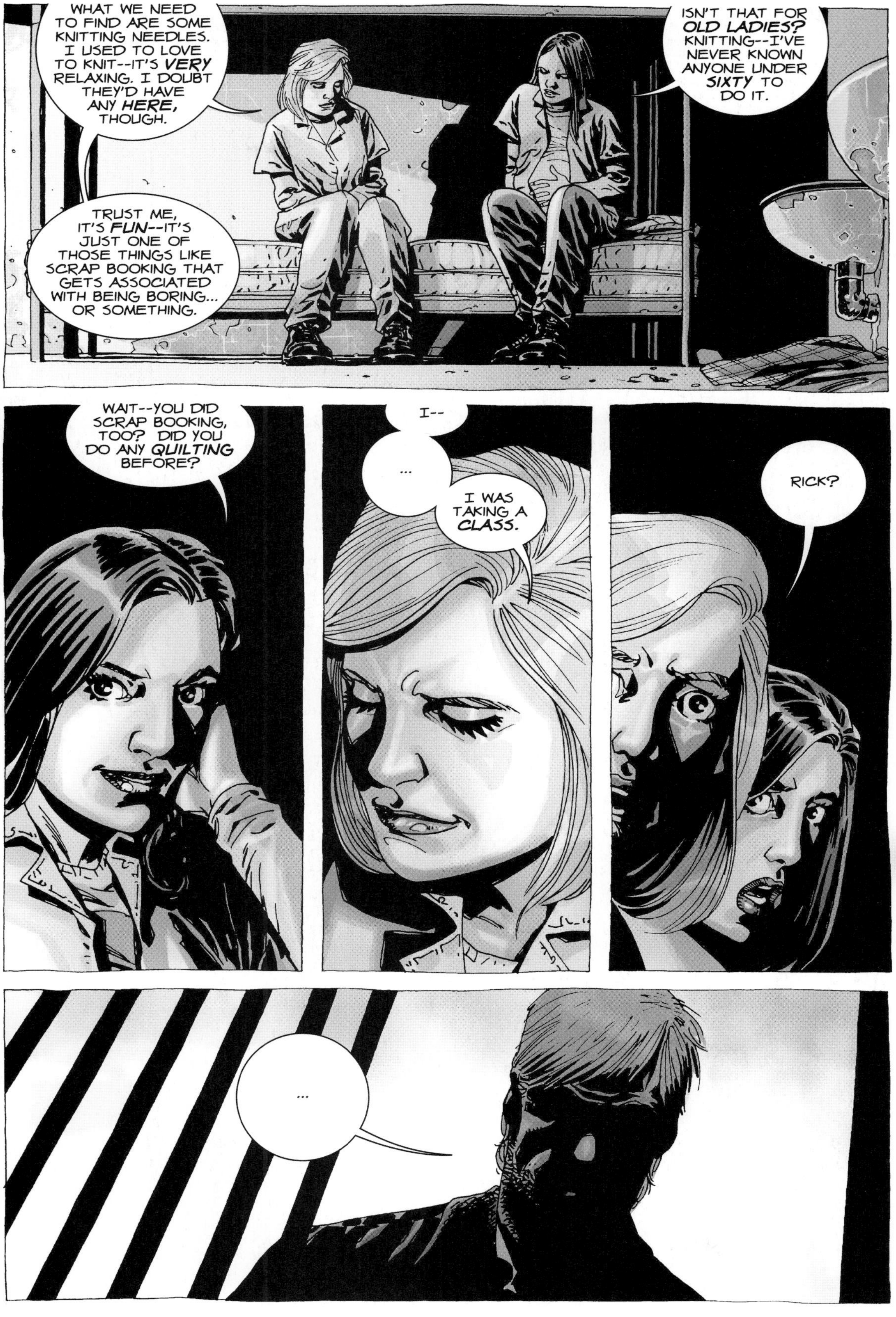
WHAT WE NEED TO FIND ARE SOME KNITTING NEEDLES. I USED TO LOVE TO KNIT--IT'S VERY RELAXING. I DOUBT THEY'D HAVE ANY HERE, THOUGH.
ISN'T THAT FOR OLD LADIES? KNITTING--I'VE NEVER KNOWN ANYONE UNDER SIXTY TO DO IT.
TRUST ME, IT'S FUN--IT'S JUST ONE OF THOSE THINGS LIKE SCRAP BOOKING THAT GETS ASSOCIATED WITH BEING BORING... OR SOMETHING.
WAIT--YOU DID SCRAP BOOKING, TOO? DID YOU DO ANY QUILTING BEFORE?
I--
...
I WAS TAKING A CLASS.
RICK?
...

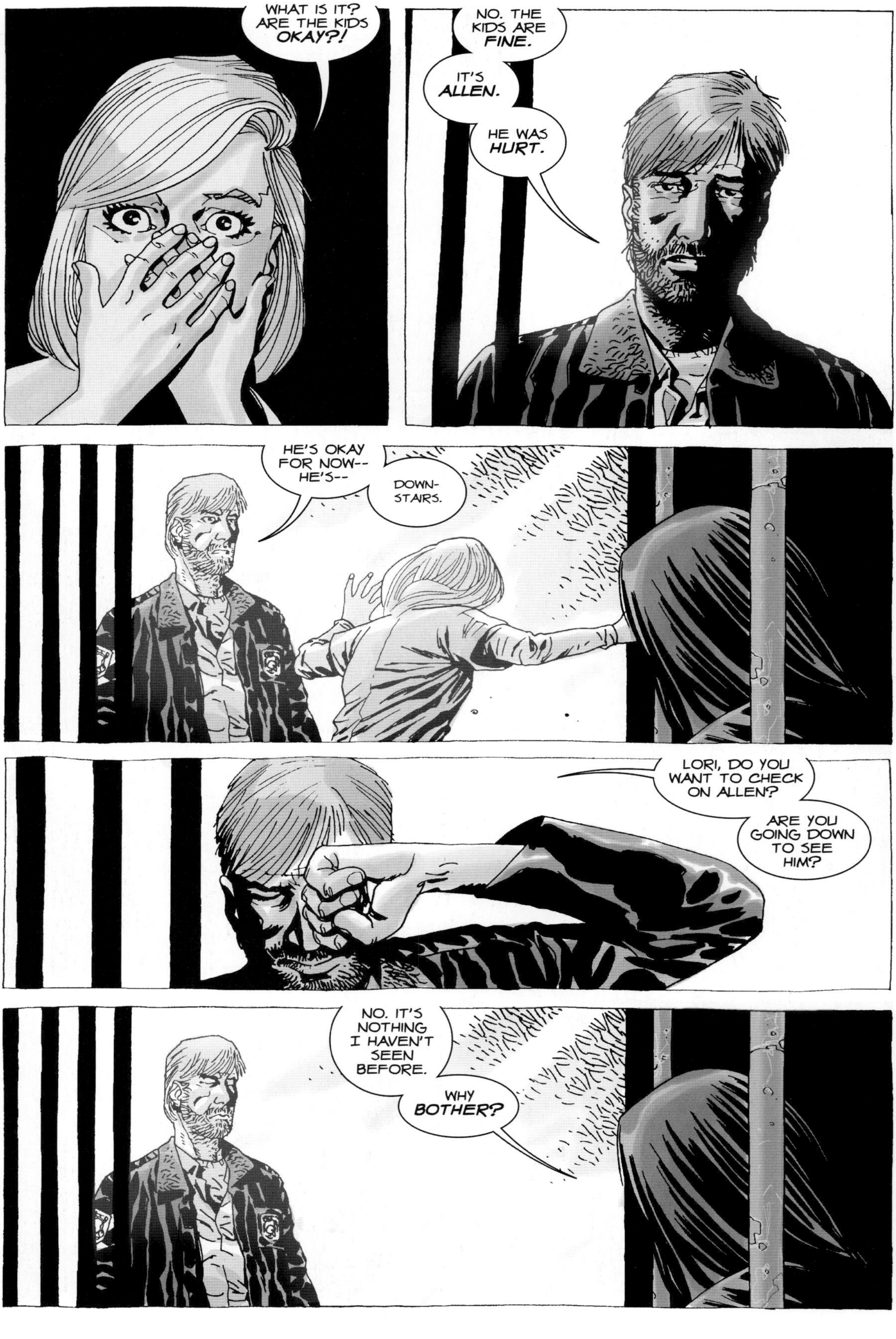
WHAT IS IT? ARE THE KIDS OKAY?!
NO. THE KIDS ARE FINE.
IT'S ALLEN.
HE WAS HURT.
HE'S OKAY FOR NOW-- HE'S--
DOWN-STAIRS.
LORI, DO YOU WANT TO CHECK ON ALLEN?
ARE YOU GOING DOWN TO SEE HIM?
NO. IT'S NOTHING I HAVEN'T SEEN BEFORE.
WHY BOTHER?

YOU HANG IN THERE, ALLEN. YOU'RE GOING TO BE OKAY.
I PROMISE-- YOU'RE GOING TO GET THROUGH THIS.
I--I'M NOT GOING TO MAKE IT.
I'M GOING TO DIE.
DON'T SAY THAT. YOU'RE GOING TO BE FINE.
YOUR SONS ARE HERE-- THEY NEED YOU. YOU'RE GOING TO BE OKAY.
TAKE CARE OF MY BOYS. YOU AND DALE-- YOU TAKE CARE OF THEM LIKE THEY WERE YOUR OWN.
PLEASE.
I WON'T HAVE TO, ALLEN-- LISTEN TO ME.
IS HE OKAY? HOW IS HE DOING?
I--
...
HE'S IN AND OUT-- HE'S LOST A LOT OF BLOOD.
WHAT HAPPENED?

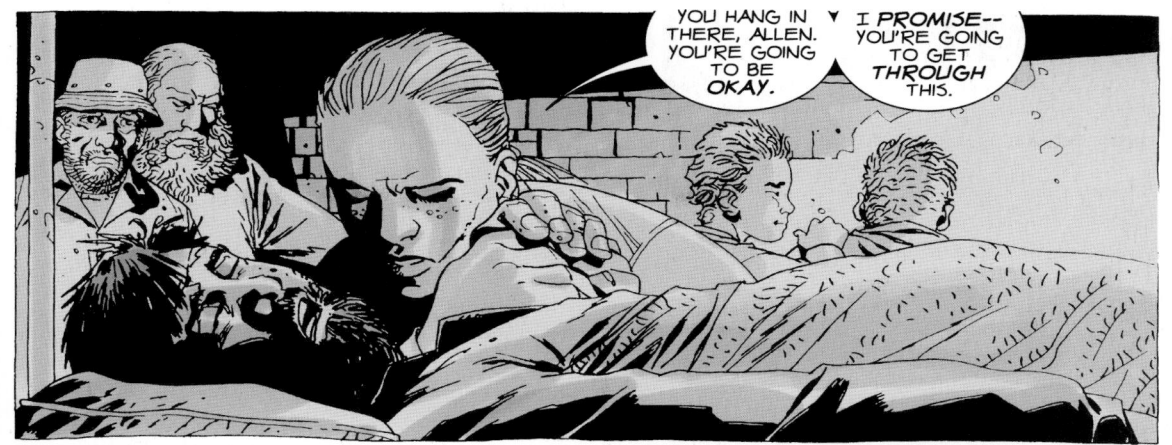

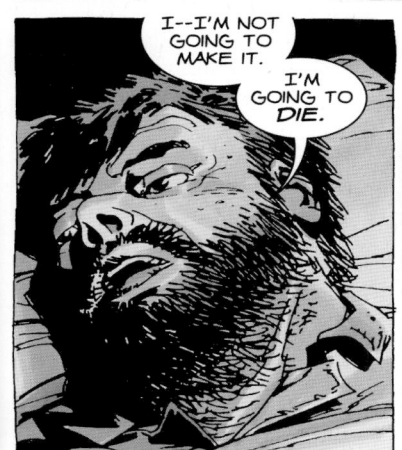

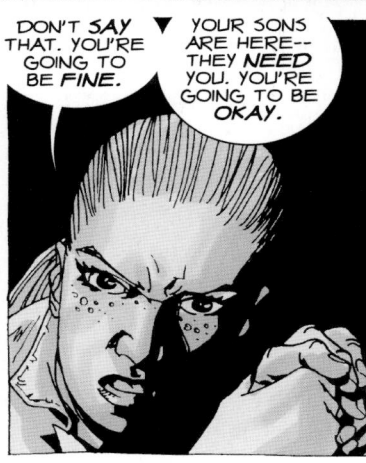

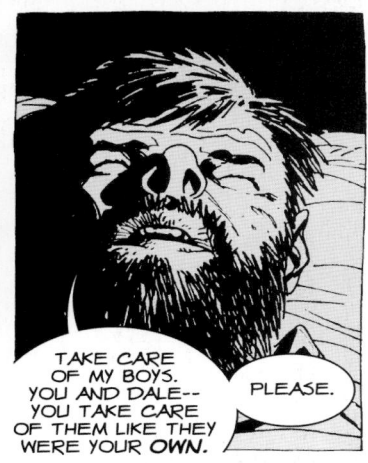

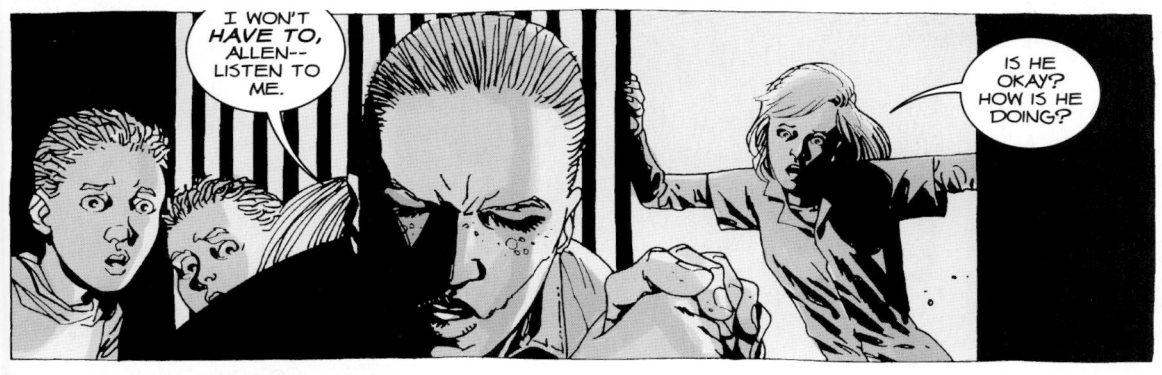

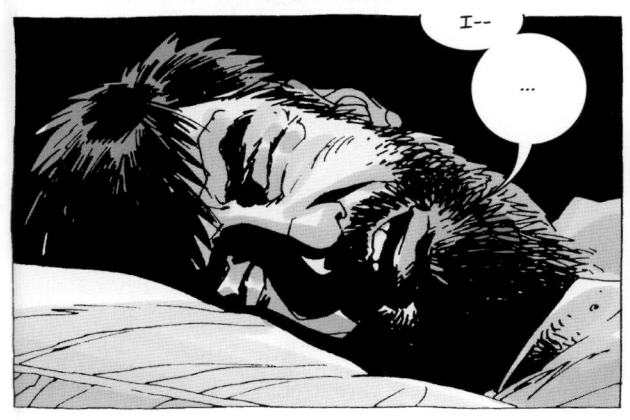

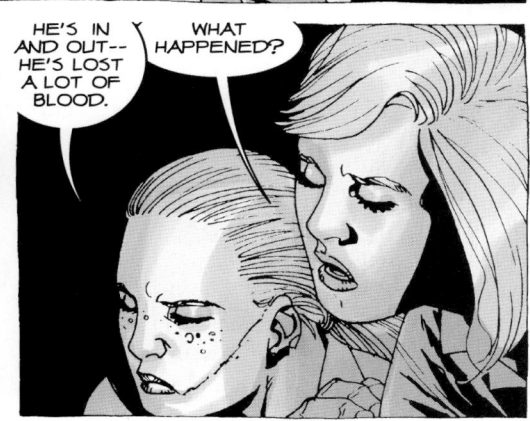

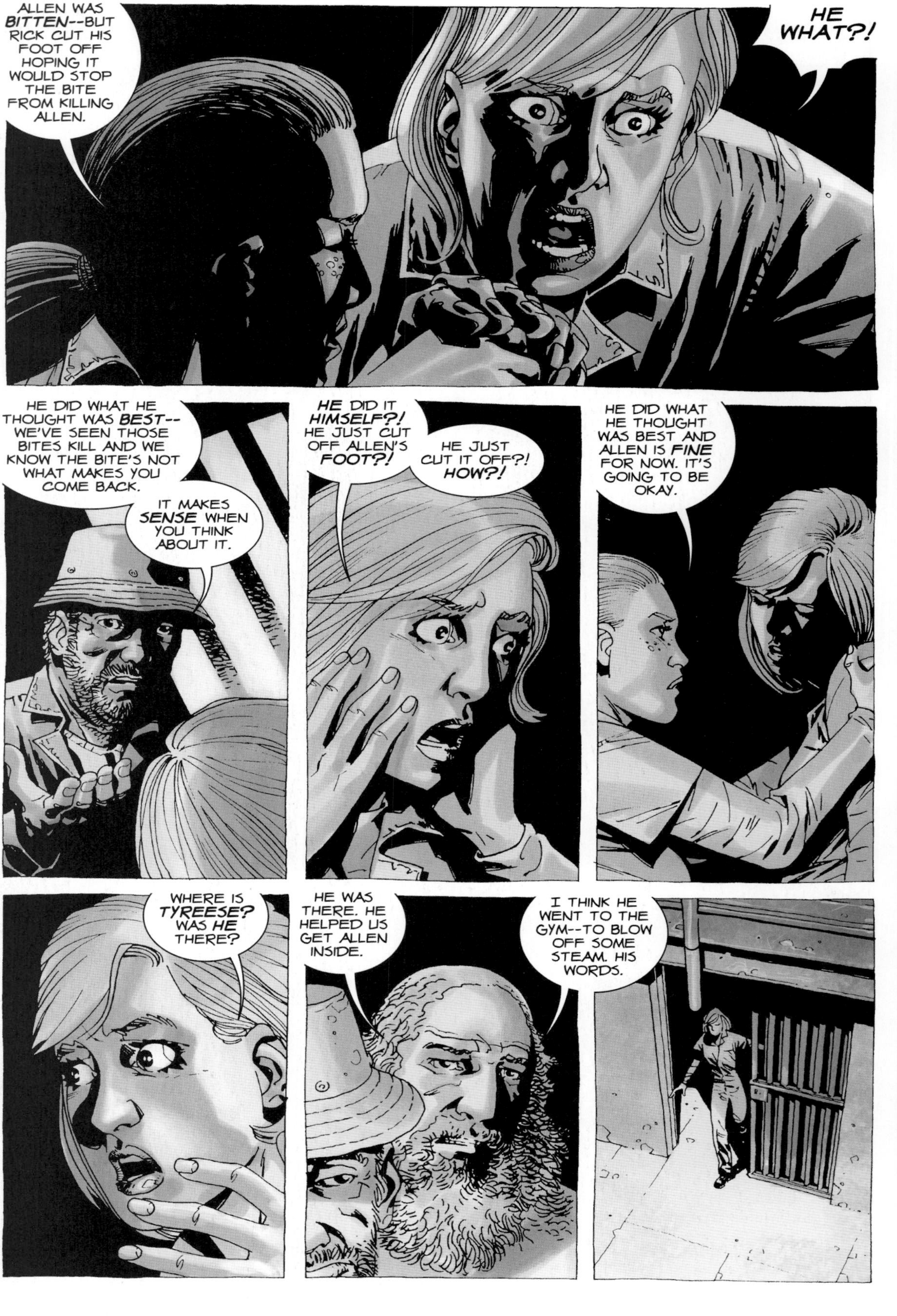
ALLEN WAS BITTEN--BUT RICK CUT HIS FOOT OFF HOPING IT WOULD STOP THE BITE FROM KILLING ALLEN.
HE WHAT?!
HE DID WHAT HE THOUGHT WAS BEST--WE'VE SEEN THOSE BITES KILL AND WE KNOW THE BITE'S NOT WHAT MAKES YOU COME BACK.
IT MAKES SENSE WHEN YOU THINK ABOUT IT.
HE DID IT HIMSELF?! HE JUST CUT OFF ALLEN'S FOOT?!
HE JUST CUT IT OFF?! HOW?!
HE DID WHAT HE THOUGHT WAS BEST AND ALLEN IS FINE FOR NOW. IT'S GOING TO BE OKAY.
WHERE IS TYREESE? WAS HE THERE?
HE WAS THERE. HE HELPED US GET ALLEN INSIDE.
I THINK HE WENT TO THE GYM--TO BLOW OFF SOME STEAM. HIS WORDS.

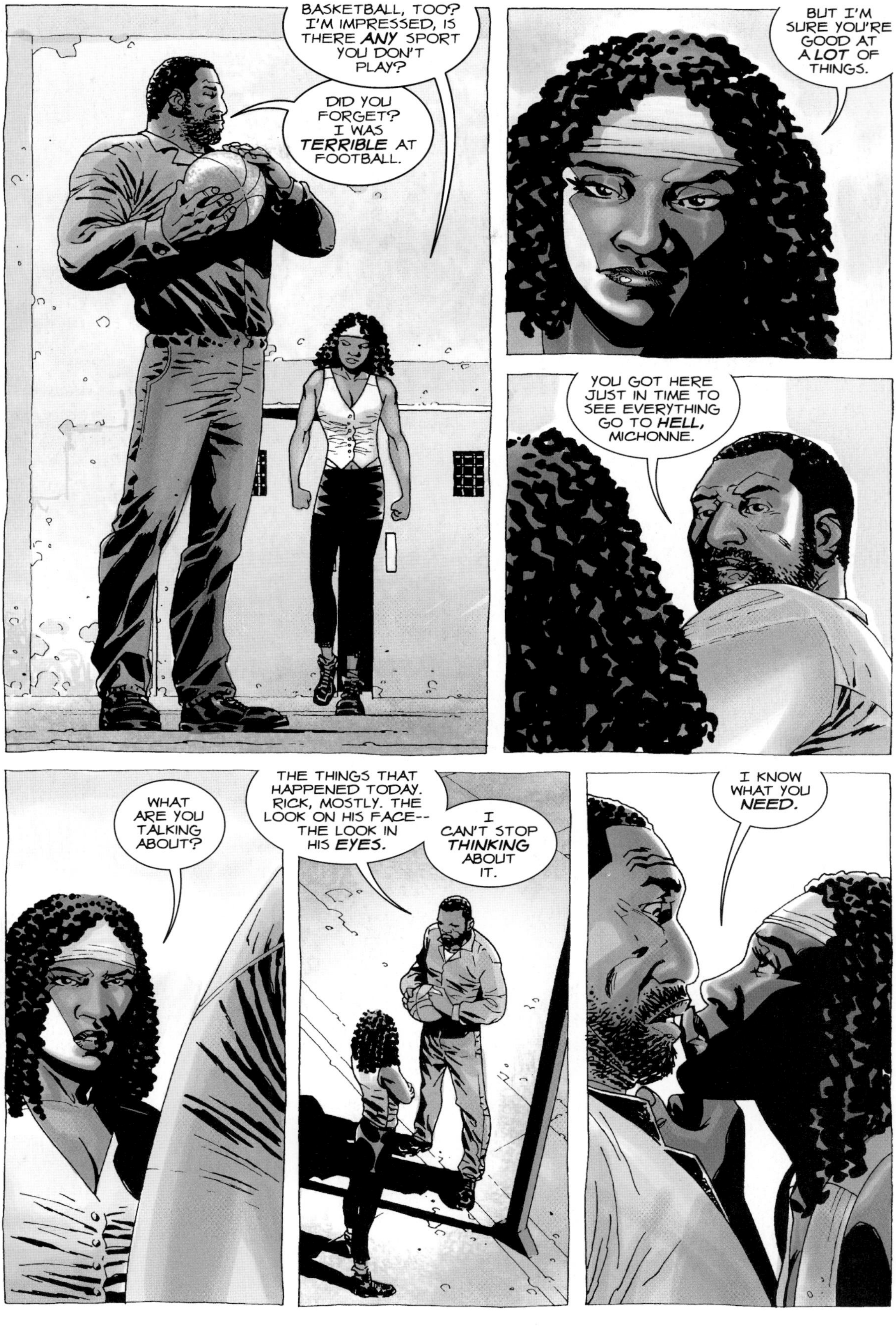
BASKETBALL, TOO? I'M IMPRESSED, IS THERE ANY SPORT YOU DON'T PLAY?
DID YOU FORGET? I WAS TERRIBLE AT FOOTBALL.
BUT I'M SURE YOU'RE GOOD AT A LOT OF THINGS.
YOU GOT HERE JUST IN TIME TO SEE EVERYTHING GO TO HELL, MICHONNE.
WHAT ARE YOU TALKING ABOUT?
THE THINGS THAT HAPPENED TODAY. RICK, MOSTLY. THE LOOK ON HIS FACE-- THE LOOK IN HIS EYES.
I CAN'T STOP THINKING ABOUT IT.
I KNOW WHAT YOU NEED.

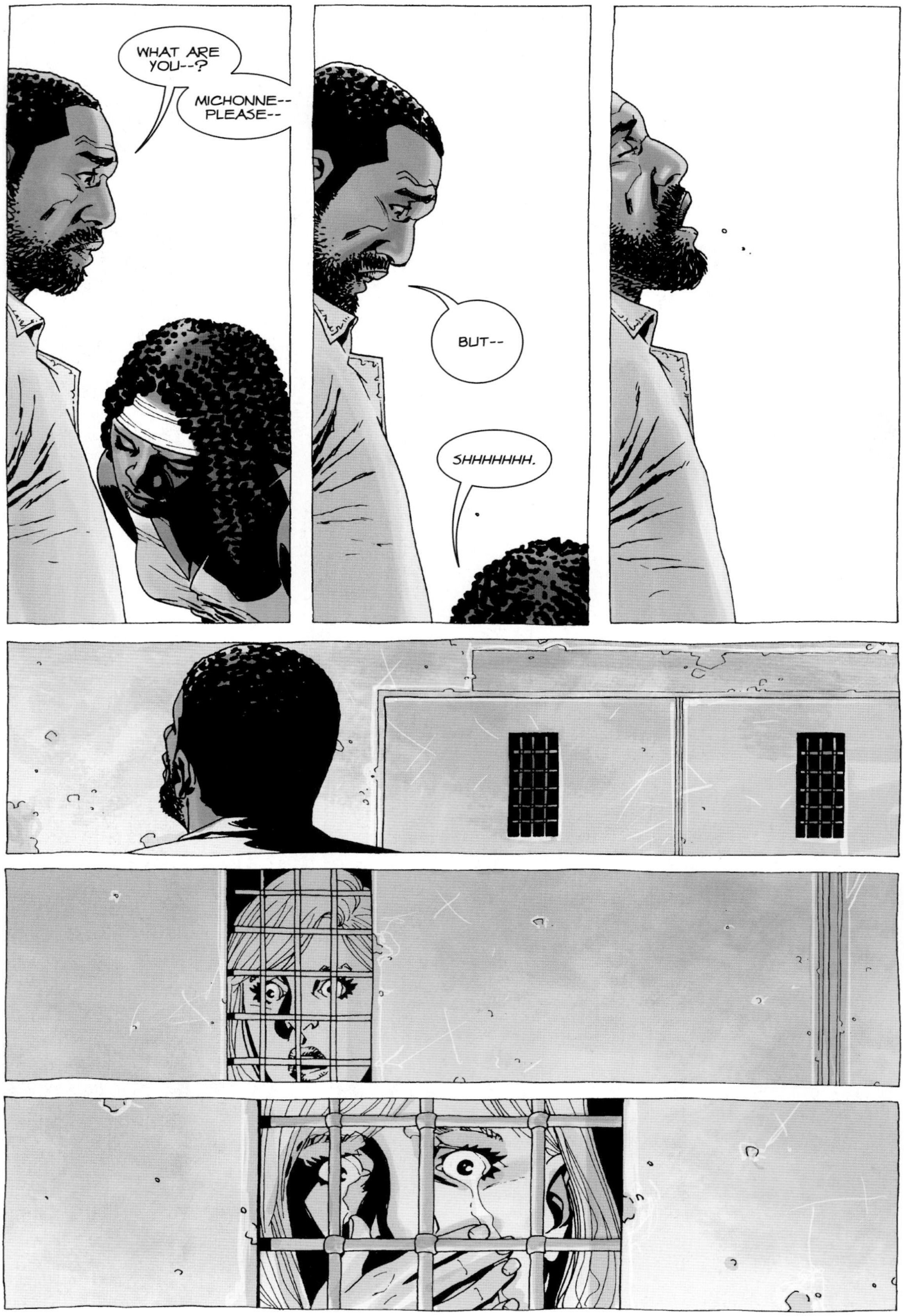
WHAT ARE YOU--?
MICHONNE-- PLEASE--
BUT--
SHHHHHHH.

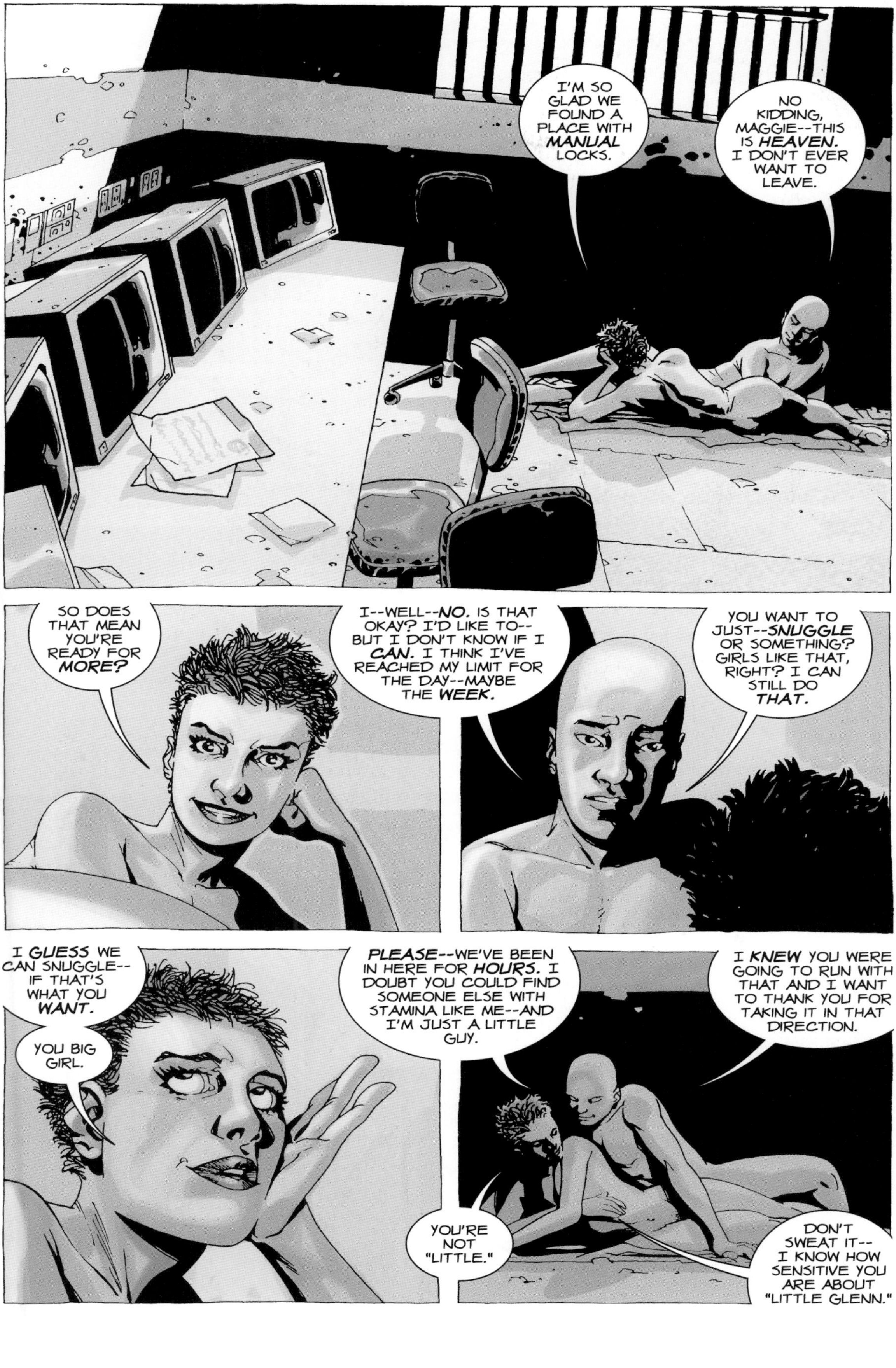
I'M SO GLAD WE FOUND A PLACE WITH MANUAL LOCKS.
NO KIDDING, MAGGIE--THIS IS HEAVEN. I DON'T EVER WANT TO LEAVE.
SO DOES THAT MEAN YOU'RE READY FOR MORE?
I--WELL--NO. IS THAT OKAY? I'D LIKE TO--BUT I DON'T KNOW IF I CAN. I THINK I'VE REACHED MY LIMIT FOR THE DAY--MAYBE THE WEEK.
YOU WANT TO JUST--SNUGGLE OR SOMETHING? GIRLS LIKE THAT, RIGHT? I CAN STILL DO THAT.
I GUESS WE CAN SNUGGLE--IF THAT'S WHAT YOU WANT.
YOU BIG GIRL.
PLEASE--WE'VE BEEN IN HERE FOR HOURS. I DOUBT YOU COULD FIND SOMEONE ELSE WITH STAMINA LIKE ME--AND I'M JUST A LITTLE GUY.
YOU'RE NOT "LITTLE."
I KNEW YOU WERE GOING TO RUN WITH THAT AND I WANT TO THANK YOU FOR TAKING IT IN THAT DIRECTION.
DON'T SWEAT IT--I KNOW HOW SENSITIVE YOU ARE ABOUT "LITTLE GLENN."

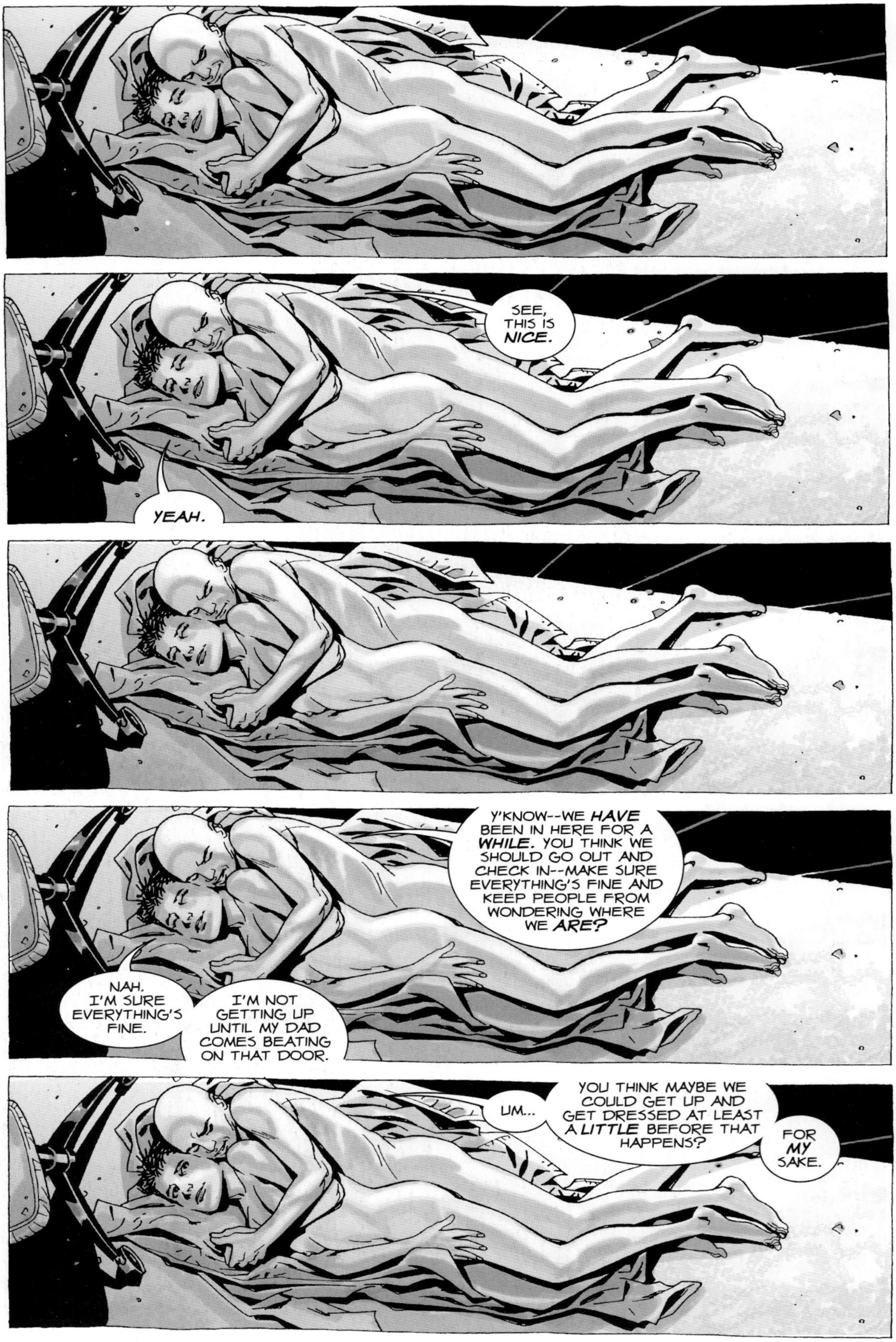

SEE, THIS IS NICE.
YEAH.
Y'KNOW--WE HAVE BEEN IN HERE FOR A WHILE. YOU THINK WE SHOULD GO OUT AND CHECK IN--MAKE SURE EVERYTHING'S FINE AND KEEP PEOPLE FROM WONDERING WHERE WE ARE?
NAH. I'M SURE EVERYTHING'S FINE.
I'M NOT GETTING UP UNTIL MY DAD COMES BEATING ON THAT DOOR.
UM...
YOU THINK MAYBE WE COULD GET UP AND GET DRESSED AT LEAST A LITTLE BEFORE THAT HAPPENS?
FOR MY SAKE.

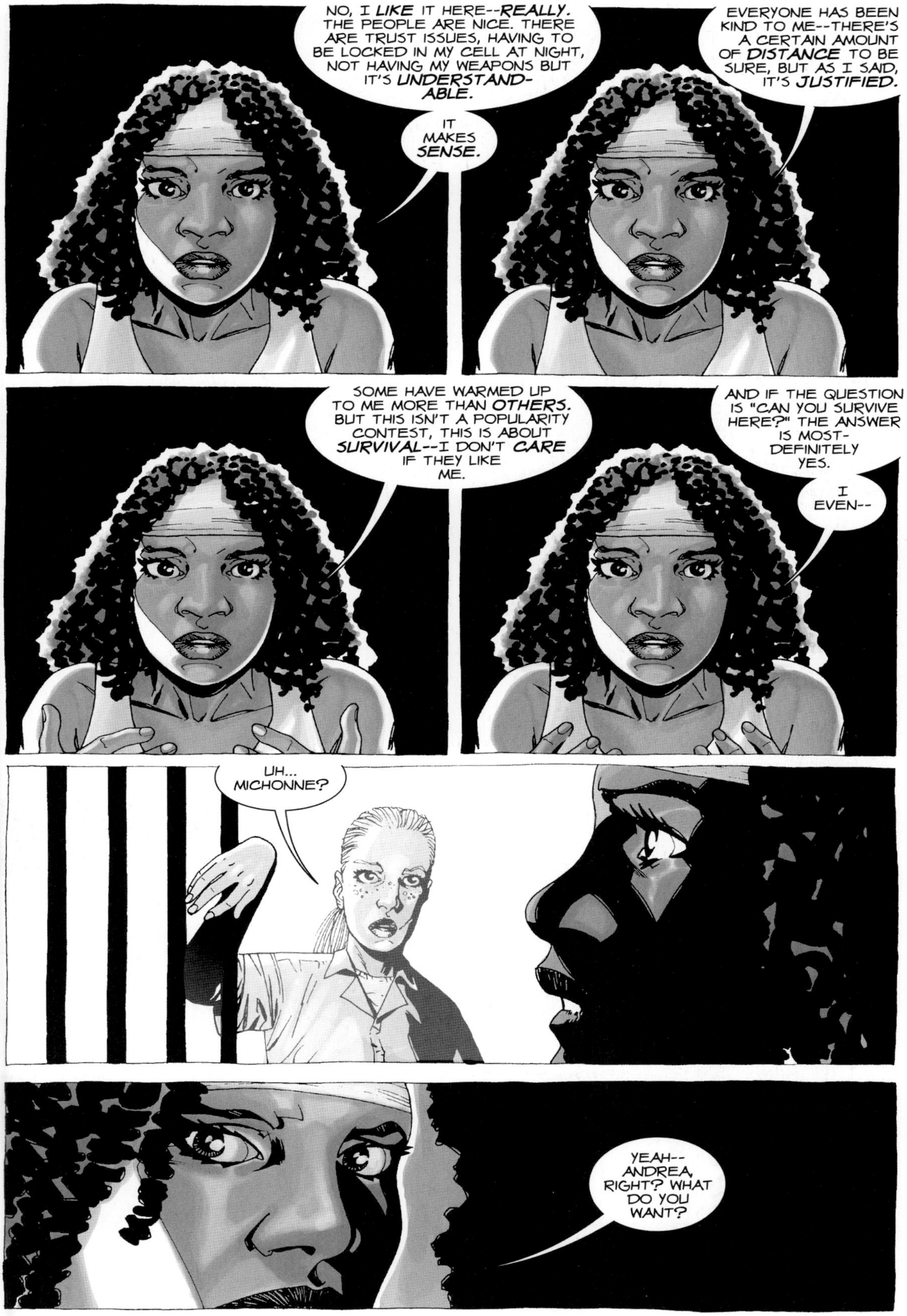
NO, I LIKE IT HERE--REALLY. THE PEOPLE ARE NICE. THERE ARE TRUST ISSUES, HAVING TO BE LOCKED IN MY CELL AT NIGHT, NOT HAVING MY WEAPONS BUT IT'S UNDERSTANDABLE.
IT MAKES SENSE.
EVERYONE HAS BEEN KIND TO ME--THERE'S A CERTAIN AMOUNT OF DISTANCE TO BE SURE, BUT AS I SAID, IT'S JUSTIFIED.
SOME HAVE WARMED UP TO ME MORE THAN OTHERS. BUT THIS ISN'T A POPULARITY CONTEST, THIS IS ABOUT SURVIVAL--I DON'T CARE IF THEY LIKE ME.
AND IF THE QUESTION IS "CAN YOU SURVIVE HERE?" THE ANSWER IS MOST-DEFINITELY YES.
I EVEN--
UH... MICHONNE?
YEAH-- ANDREA, RIGHT? WHAT DO YOU WANT?

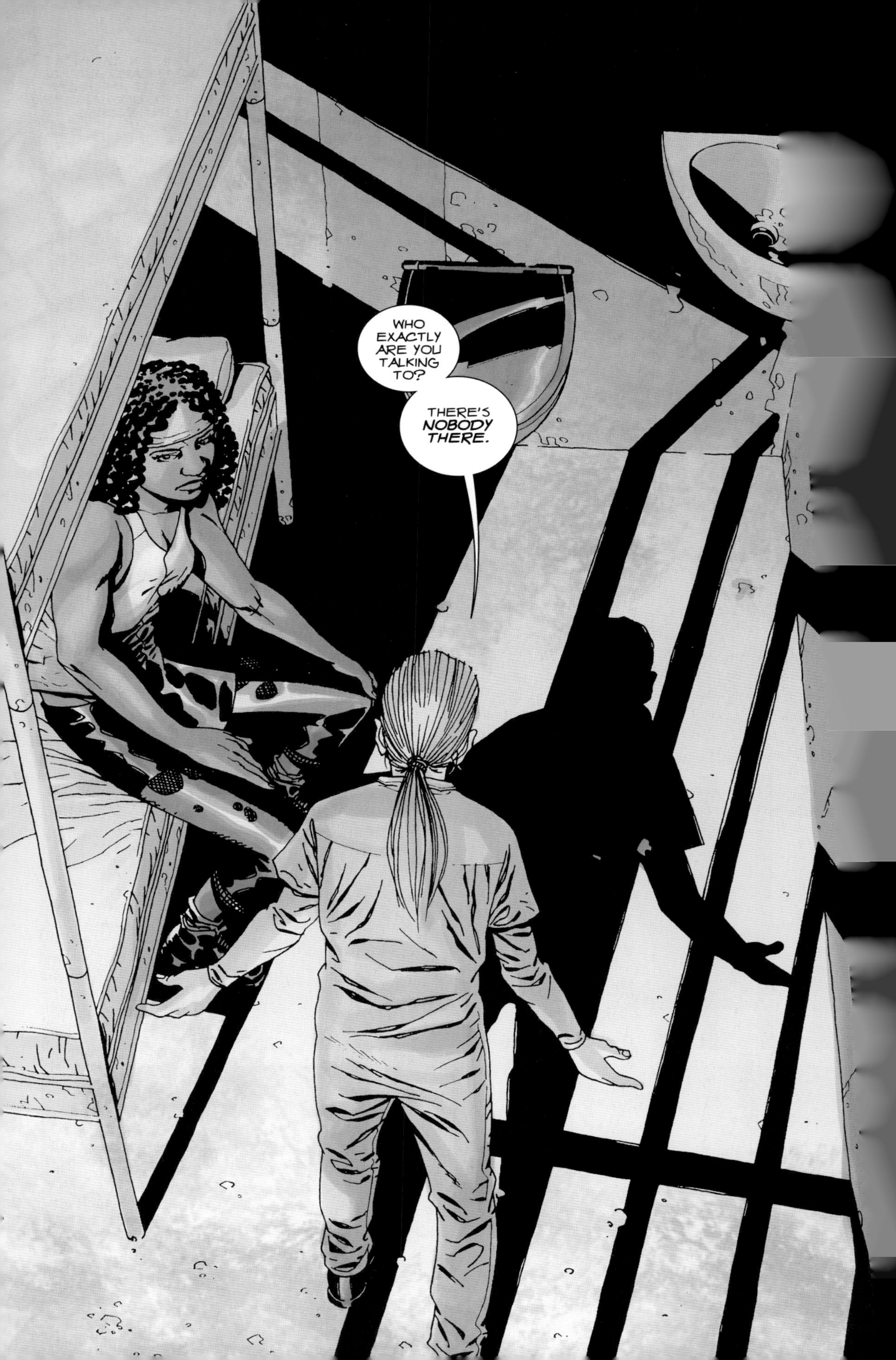
WHO EXACTLY ARE YOU TALKING TO?
THERE'S *NOBODY THERE.*

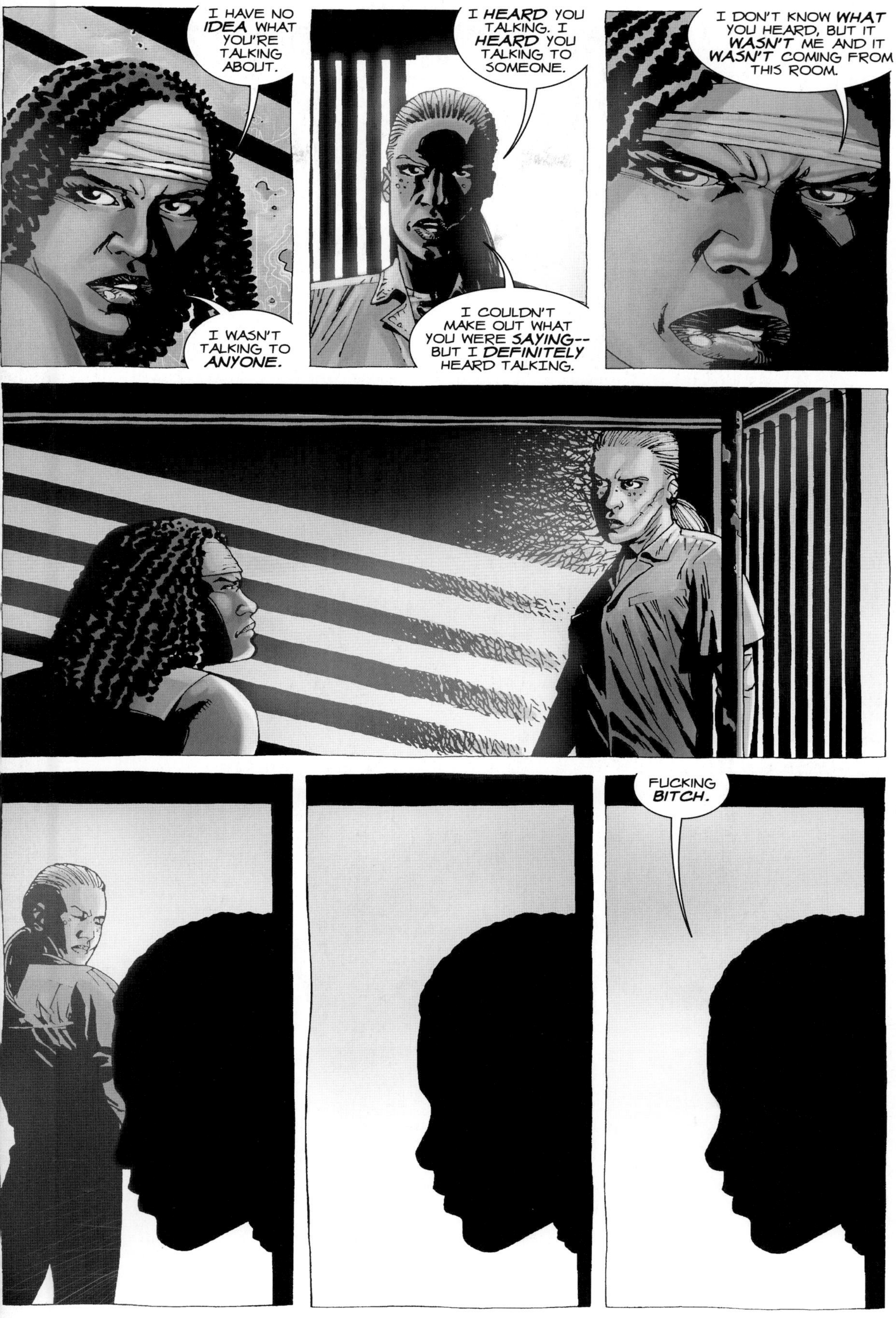
I HAVE NO IDEA WHAT YOU'RE TALKING ABOUT.
I WASN'T TALKING TO ANYONE.
I HEARD YOU TALKING. I HEARD YOU TALKING TO SOMEONE.
I COULDN'T MAKE OUT WHAT YOU WERE SAYING-- BUT I DEFINITELY HEARD TALKING.
I DON'T KNOW WHAT YOU HEARD, BUT IT WASN'T ME AND IT WASN'T COMING FROM THIS ROOM.
FUCKING BITCH.

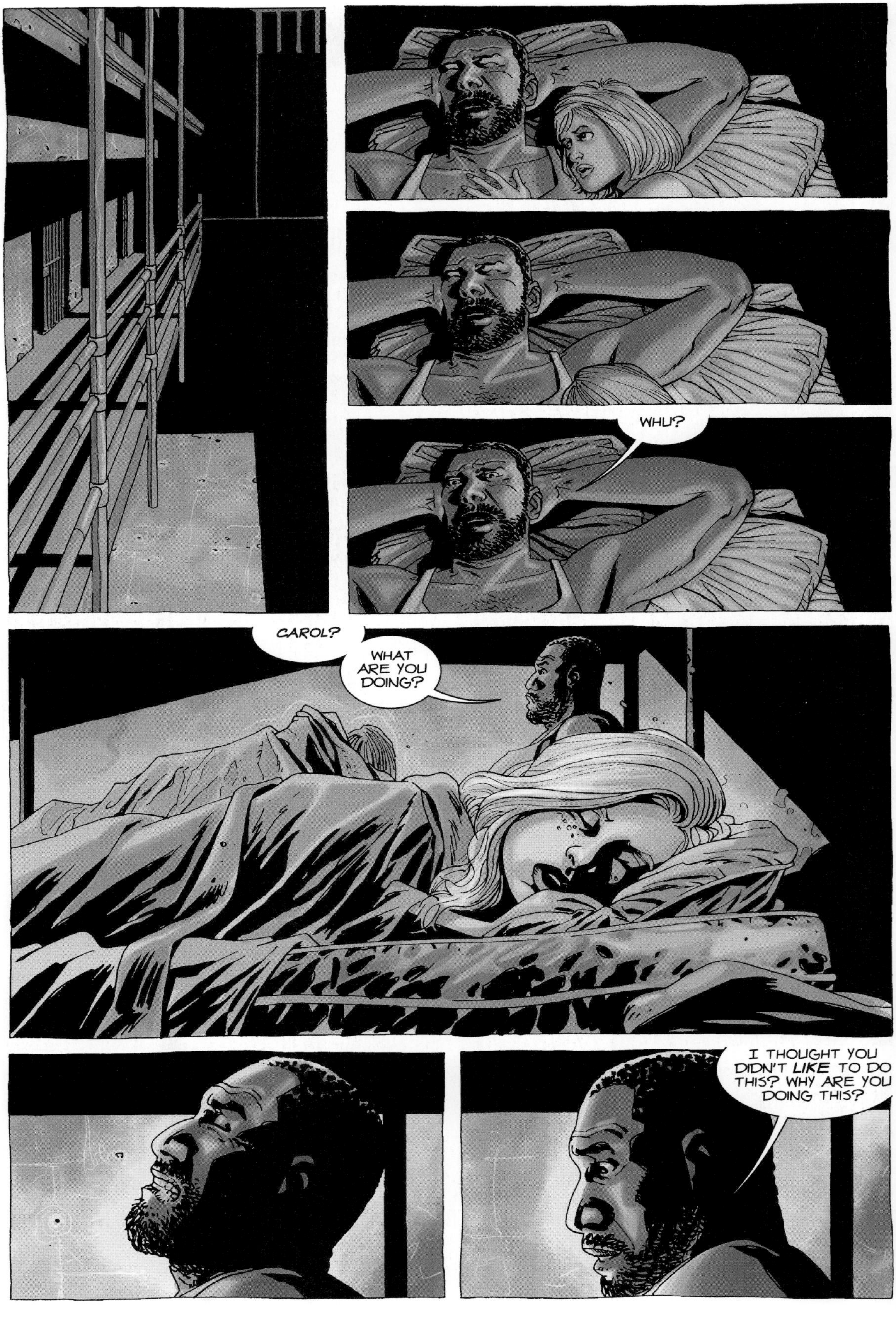
WHU?
CAROL?
WHAT ARE YOU DOING?
I THOUGHT YOU DIDN'T LIKE TO DO THIS? WHY ARE YOU DOING THIS?

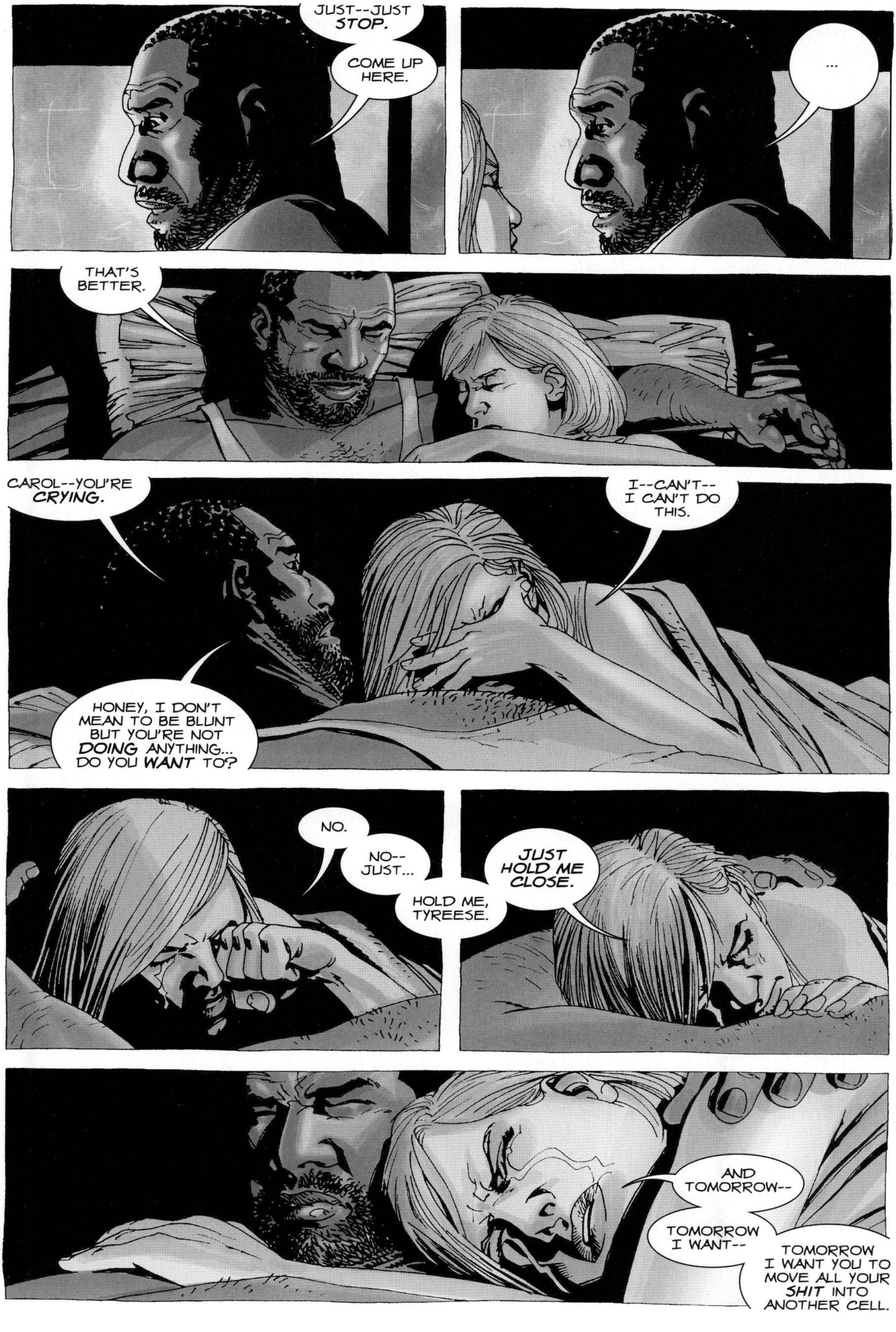
JUST--JUST STOP.
COME UP HERE.
...
THAT'S BETTER.
CAROL--YOU'RE CRYING.
I--CAN'T-- I CAN'T DO THIS.
HONEY, I DON'T MEAN TO BE BLUNT BUT YOU'RE NOT DOING ANYTHING... DO YOU WANT TO?
NO.
NO-- JUST...
HOLD ME, TYREESE.
JUST HOLD ME CLOSE.
AND TOMORROW--
TOMORROW I WANT--
TOMORROW I WANT YOU TO MOVE ALL YOUR SHIT INTO ANOTHER CELL.

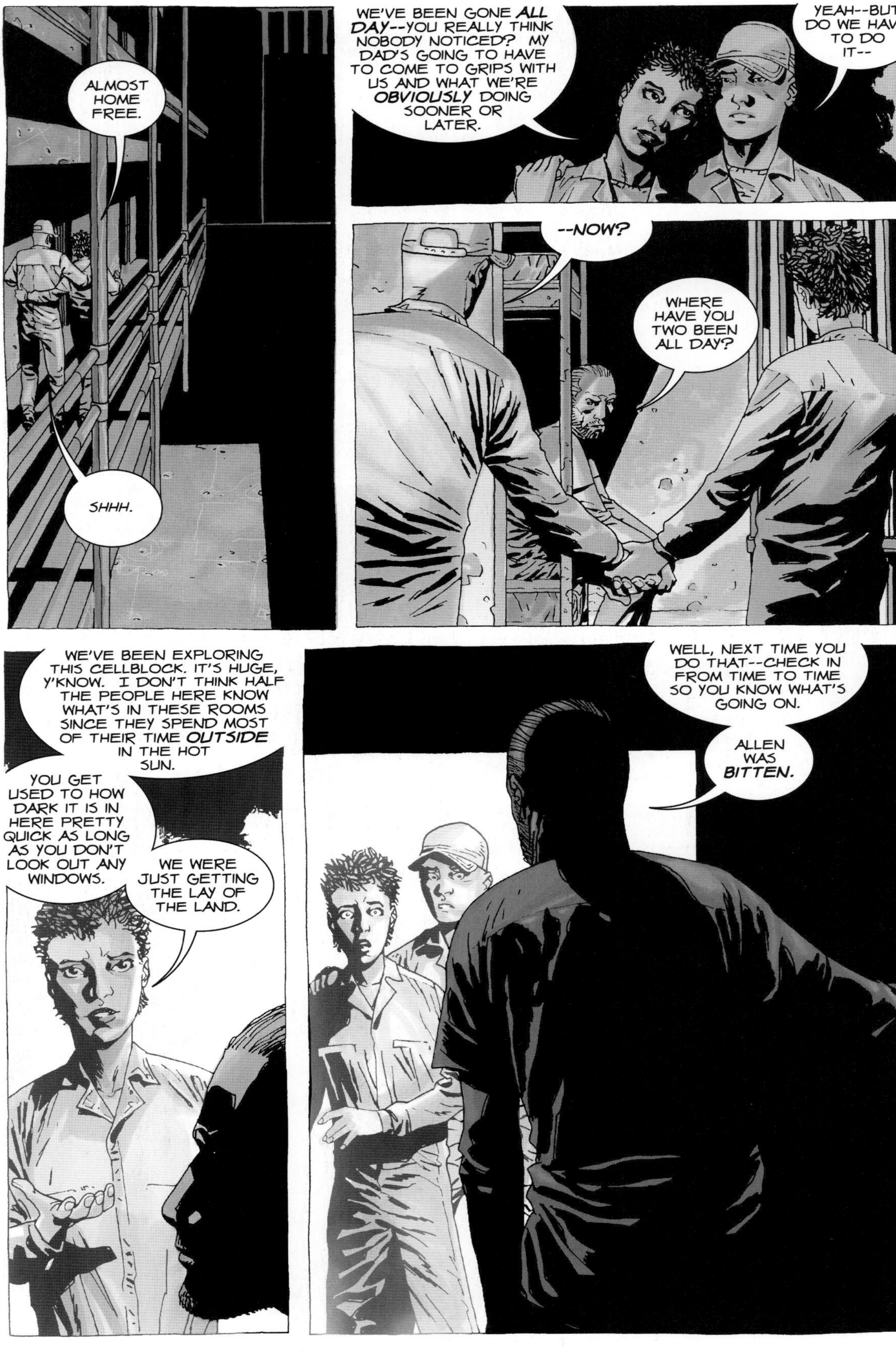
ALMOST HOME FREE.
SHHH.
WE'VE BEEN GONE ALL DAY--YOU REALLY THINK NOBODY NOTICED? MY DAD'S GOING TO HAVE TO COME TO GRIPS WITH US AND WHAT WE'RE OBVIOUSLY DOING SOONER OR LATER.
YEAH--BUT DO WE HAVE TO DO IT--
--NOW?
WHERE HAVE YOU TWO BEEN ALL DAY?
WE'VE BEEN EXPLORING THIS CELLBLOCK. IT'S HUGE, Y'KNOW. I DON'T THINK HALF THE PEOPLE HERE KNOW WHAT'S IN THESE ROOMS SINCE THEY SPEND MOST OF THEIR TIME OUTSIDE IN THE HOT SUN.
YOU GET USED TO HOW DARK IT IS IN HERE PRETTY QUICK AS LONG AS YOU DON'T LOOK OUT ANY WINDOWS.
WE WERE JUST GETTING THE LAY OF THE LAND.
WELL, NEXT TIME YOU DO THAT--CHECK IN FROM TIME TO TIME SO YOU KNOW WHAT'S GOING ON.
ALLEN WAS BITTEN.

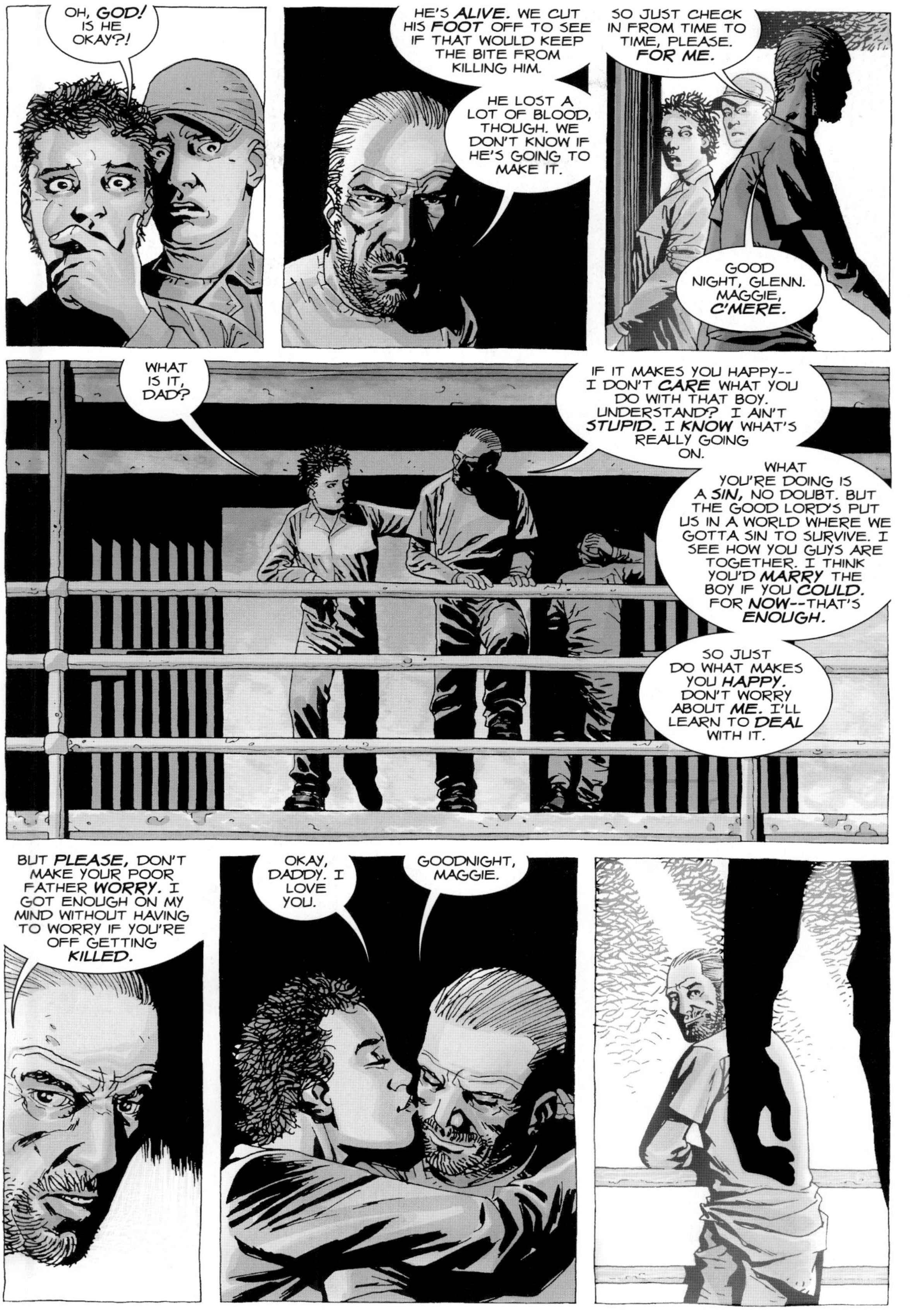
OH, GOD! IS HE OKAY?!
HE'S ALIVE. WE CUT HIS FOOT OFF TO SEE IF THAT WOULD KEEP THE BITE FROM KILLING HIM.
HE LOST A LOT OF BLOOD, THOUGH. WE DON'T KNOW IF HE'S GOING TO MAKE IT.
SO JUST CHECK IN FROM TIME TO TIME, PLEASE. FOR ME.
GOOD NIGHT, GLENN. MAGGIE, C'MERE.
WHAT IS IT, DAD?
IF IT MAKES YOU HAPPY-- I DON'T CARE WHAT YOU DO WITH THAT BOY. UNDERSTAND? I AIN'T STUPID. I KNOW WHAT'S REALLY GOING ON.
WHAT YOU'RE DOING IS A SIN, NO DOUBT. BUT THE GOOD LORD'S PUT US IN A WORLD WHERE WE GOTTA SIN TO SURVIVE. I SEE HOW YOU GUYS ARE TOGETHER. I THINK YOU'D MARRY THE BOY IF YOU COULD. FOR NOW--THAT'S ENOUGH.
SO JUST DO WHAT MAKES YOU HAPPY. DON'T WORRY ABOUT ME. I'LL LEARN TO DEAL WITH IT.
BUT PLEASE, DON'T MAKE YOUR POOR FATHER WORRY. I GOT ENOUGH ON MY MIND WITHOUT HAVING TO WORRY IF YOU'RE OFF GETTING KILLED.
OKAY, DADDY. I LOVE YOU.
GOODNIGHT, MAGGIE.

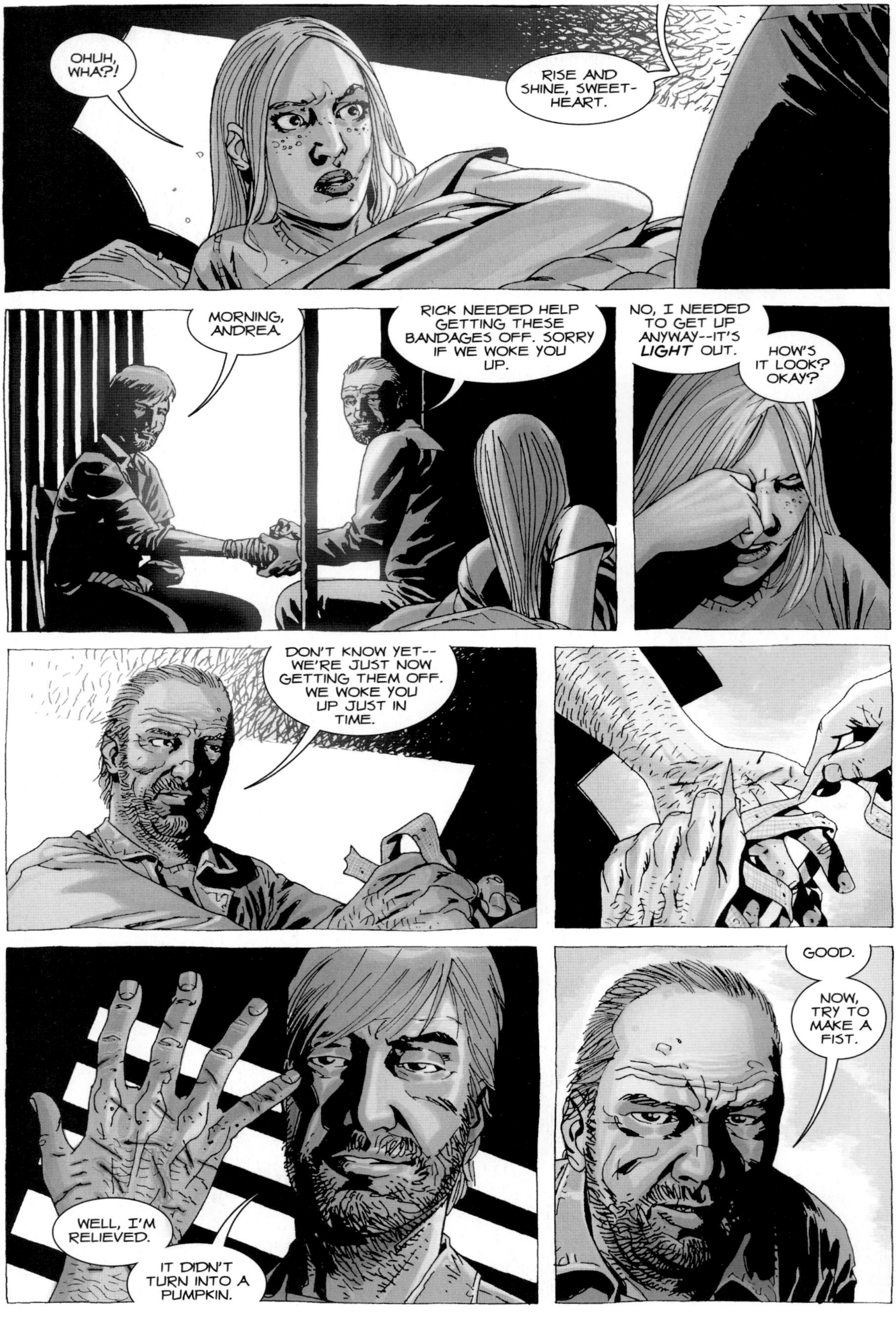
OHUH, WHA?!
RISE AND SHINE, SWEET-HEART.
MORNING, ANDREA.
RICK NEEDED HELP GETTING THESE BANDAGES OFF. SORRY IF WE WOKE YOU UP.
NO, I NEEDED TO GET UP ANYWAY--IT'S LIGHT OUT.
HOW'S IT LOOK? OKAY?
DON'T KNOW YET-- WE'RE JUST NOW GETTING THEM OFF. WE WOKE YOU UP JUST IN TIME.
WELL, I'M RELIEVED.
IT DIDN'T TURN INTO A PUMPKIN.
GOOD.
NOW, TRY TO MAKE A FIST.

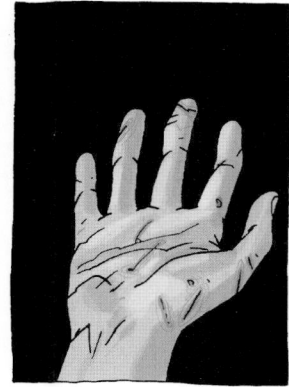

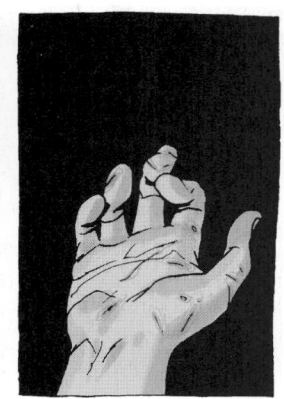

WELL, THAT'S SEEMS TO BE AS *GOOD* AS IT GETS.

FOR *NOW* AT LEAST--IT COULD STILL BE HEALING, AND THE MORE YOU *USE* YOUR HAND THE BETTER IT COULD GET.

IT'S NOT THE END OF THE WORLD.

OH, *REALLY?*

TELL *THAT* TO THE LIVING DEAD OUT *THERE.*

POOR CHOICE OF WORDS.

JUST DON'T BE TOO UPSET OVER THE HAND-- LIKE I SAY, IT SHOULD GET BETTER, WITH TIME. I MEAN, I'M JUST GUESSING HERE-- I'M NO *DOCTOR.*

UNDERSTOOD. WELL, WITH PRACTICE I SHOULD STILL BE ABLE TO FIRE A GUN.

WHAT MORE DO I *NEED* IN THIS DAY AND AGE?

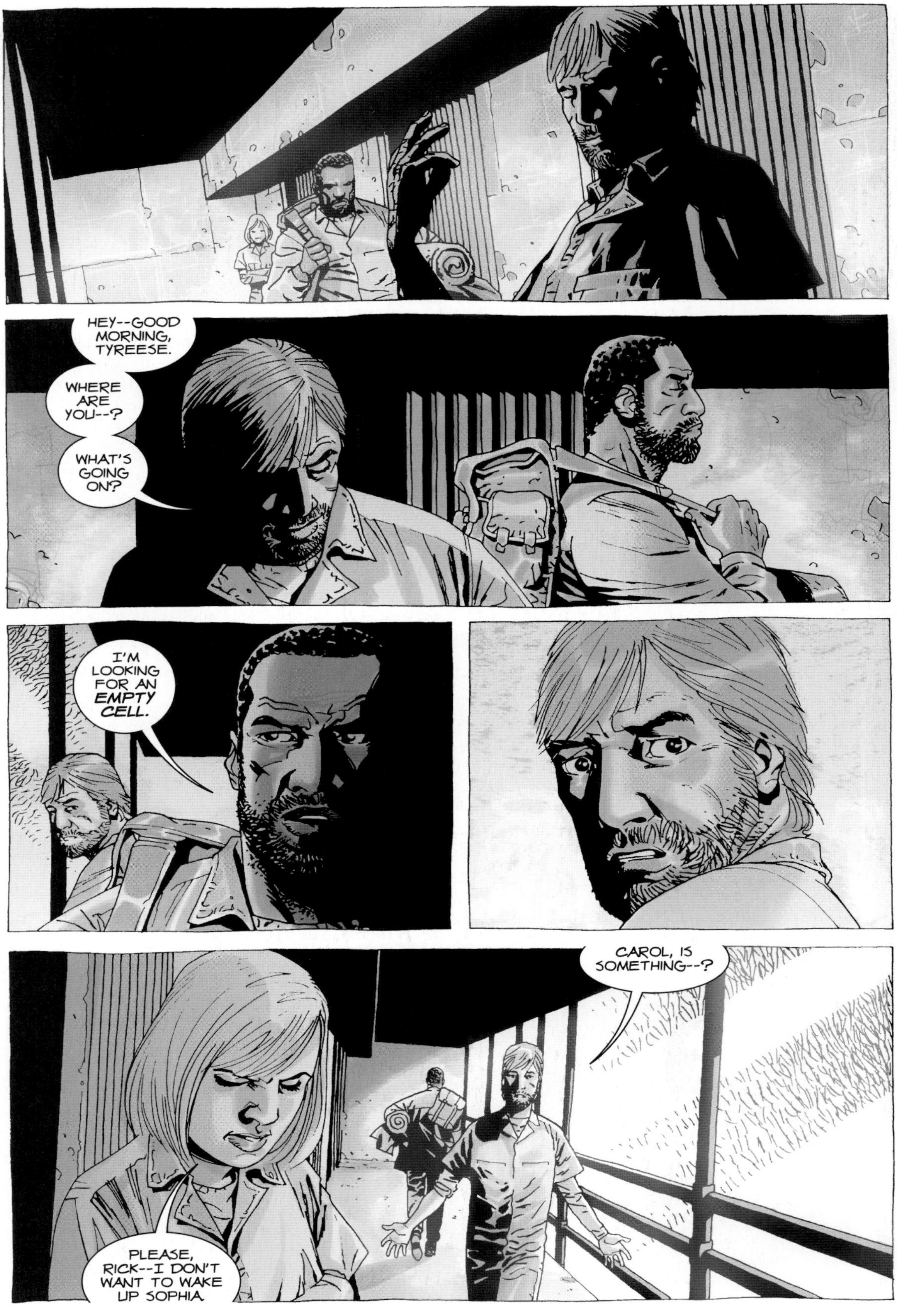
HEY--GOOD MORNING, TYREESE.
WHERE ARE YOU--?
WHAT'S GOING ON?
I'M LOOKING FOR AN *EMPTY CELL.*
CAROL, IS SOMETHING--?
PLEASE, RICK--I DON'T WANT TO WAKE UP SOPHIA.

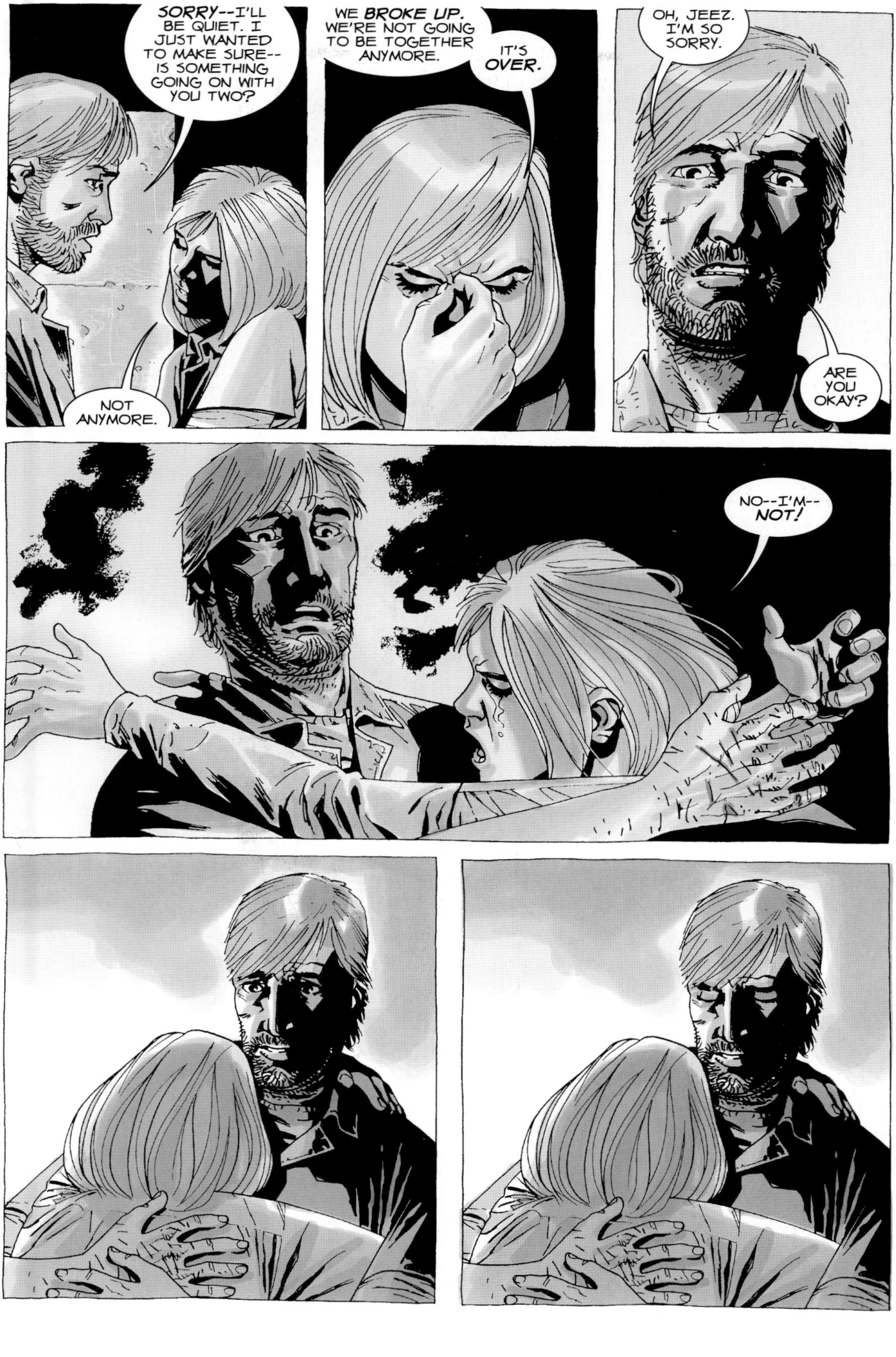
SORRY--I'LL BE QUIET. I JUST WANTED TO MAKE SURE-- IS SOMETHING GOING ON WITH YOU TWO?
NOT ANYMORE.
WE BROKE UP. WE'RE NOT GOING TO BE TOGETHER ANYMORE.
IT'S OVER.
OH, JEEZ. I'M SO SORRY.
ARE YOU OKAY?
NO--I'M--NOT!

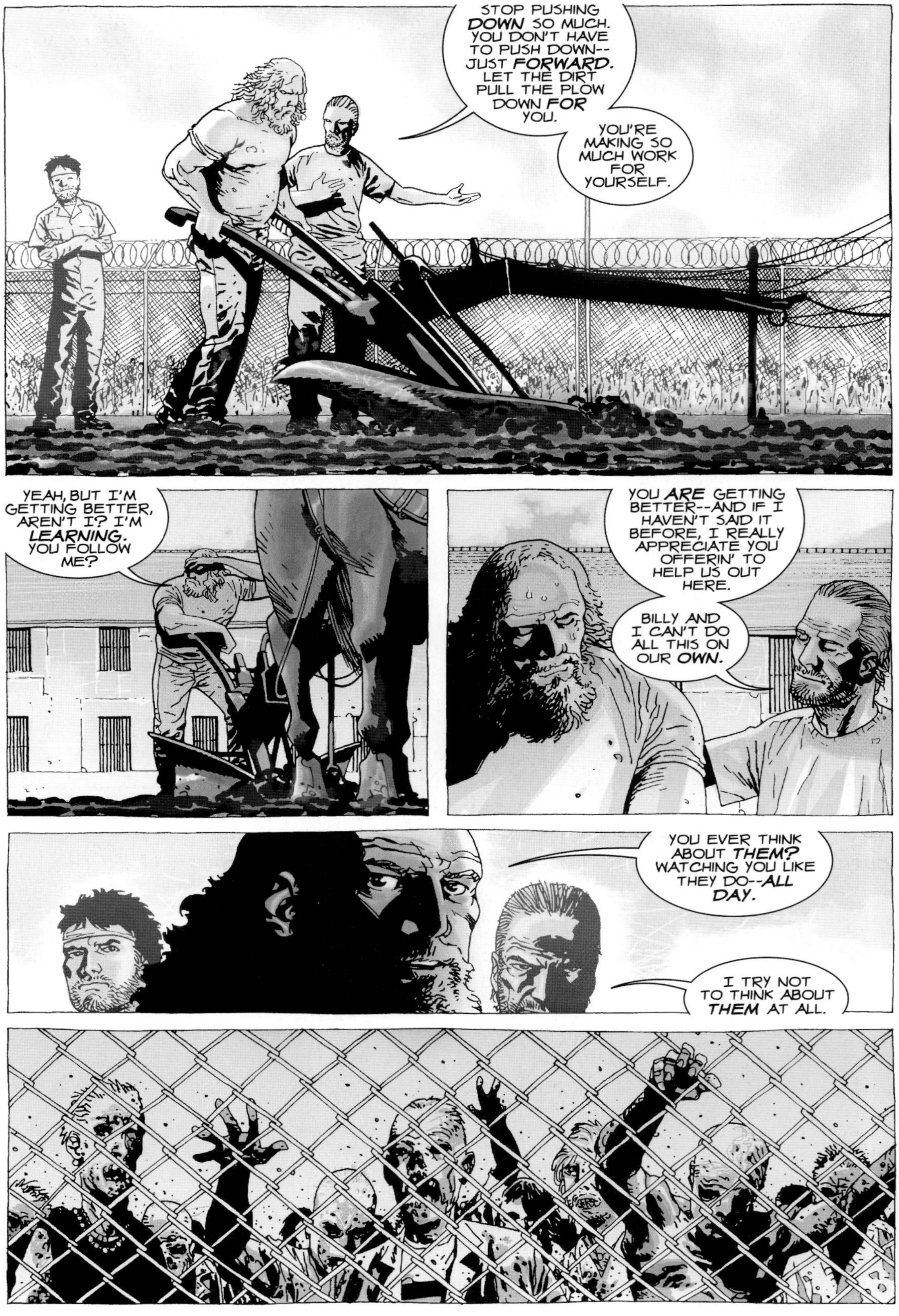
STOP PUSHING DOWN SO MUCH. YOU DON'T HAVE TO PUSH DOWN-- JUST FORWARD. LET THE DIRT PULL THE PLOW DOWN FOR YOU.
YOU'RE MAKING SO MUCH WORK FOR YOURSELF.
YEAH, BUT I'M GETTING BETTER, AREN'T I? I'M LEARNING. YOU FOLLOW ME?
YOU ARE GETTING BETTER--AND IF I HAVEN'T SAID IT BEFORE, I REALLY APPRECIATE YOU OFFERIN' TO HELP US OUT HERE.
BILLY AND I CAN'T DO ALL THIS ON OUR OWN.
YOU EVER THINK ABOUT THEM? WATCHING YOU LIKE THEY DO--ALL DAY.
I TRY NOT TO THINK ABOUT THEM AT ALL.

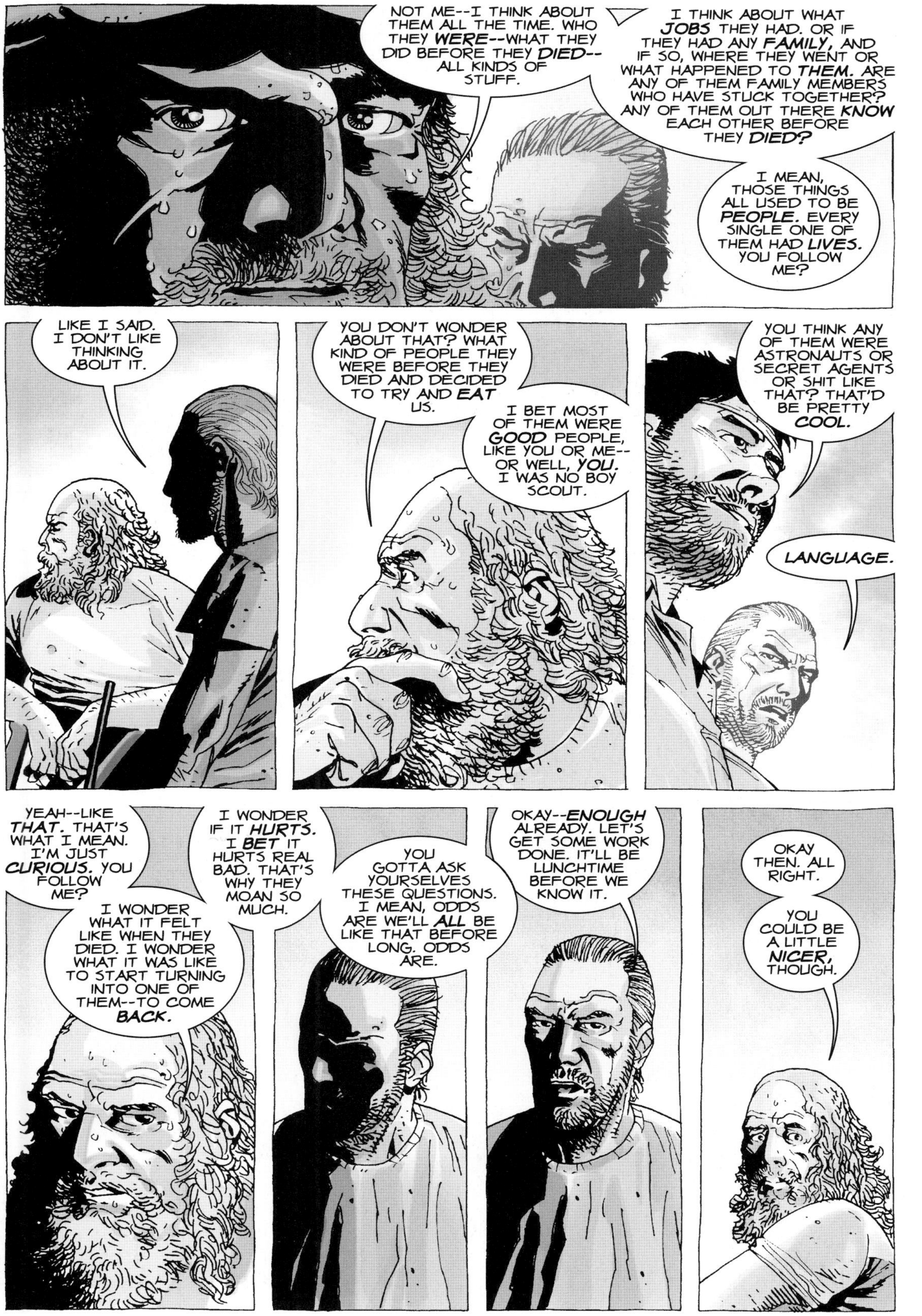
NOT ME--I THINK ABOUT THEM ALL THE TIME. WHO THEY WERE--WHAT THEY DID BEFORE THEY DIED--ALL KINDS OF STUFF.
I THINK ABOUT WHAT JOBS THEY HAD. OR IF THEY HAD ANY FAMILY, AND IF SO, WHERE THEY WENT OR WHAT HAPPENED TO THEM. ARE ANY OF THEM FAMILY MEMBERS WHO HAVE STUCK TOGETHER? ANY OF THEM OUT THERE KNOW EACH OTHER BEFORE THEY DIED?
I MEAN, THOSE THINGS ALL USED TO BE PEOPLE. EVERY SINGLE ONE OF THEM HAD LIVES. YOU FOLLOW ME?
LIKE I SAID. I DON'T LIKE THINKING ABOUT IT.
YOU DON'T WONDER ABOUT THAT? WHAT KIND OF PEOPLE THEY WERE BEFORE THEY DIED AND DECIDED TO TRY AND EAT US.
I BET MOST OF THEM WERE GOOD PEOPLE, LIKE YOU OR ME--OR WELL, YOU. I WAS NO BOY SCOUT.
YOU THINK ANY OF THEM WERE ASTRONAUTS OR SECRET AGENTS OR SHIT LIKE THAT? THAT'D BE PRETTY COOL.
LANGUAGE.
YEAH--LIKE THAT. THAT'S WHAT I MEAN. I'M JUST CURIOUS. YOU FOLLOW ME?
I WONDER WHAT IT FELT LIKE WHEN THEY DIED. I WONDER WHAT IT WAS LIKE TO START TURNING INTO ONE OF THEM--TO COME BACK.
I WONDER IF IT HURTS. I BET IT HURTS REAL BAD. THAT'S WHY THEY MOAN SO MUCH.
YOU GOTTA ASK YOURSELVES THESE QUESTIONS. I MEAN, ODDS ARE WE'LL ALL BE LIKE THAT BEFORE LONG. ODDS ARE.
OKAY--ENOUGH ALREADY. LET'S GET SOME WORK DONE. IT'LL BE LUNCHTIME BEFORE WE KNOW IT.
OKAY THEN. ALL RIGHT.
YOU COULD BE A LITTLE NICER, THOUGH.

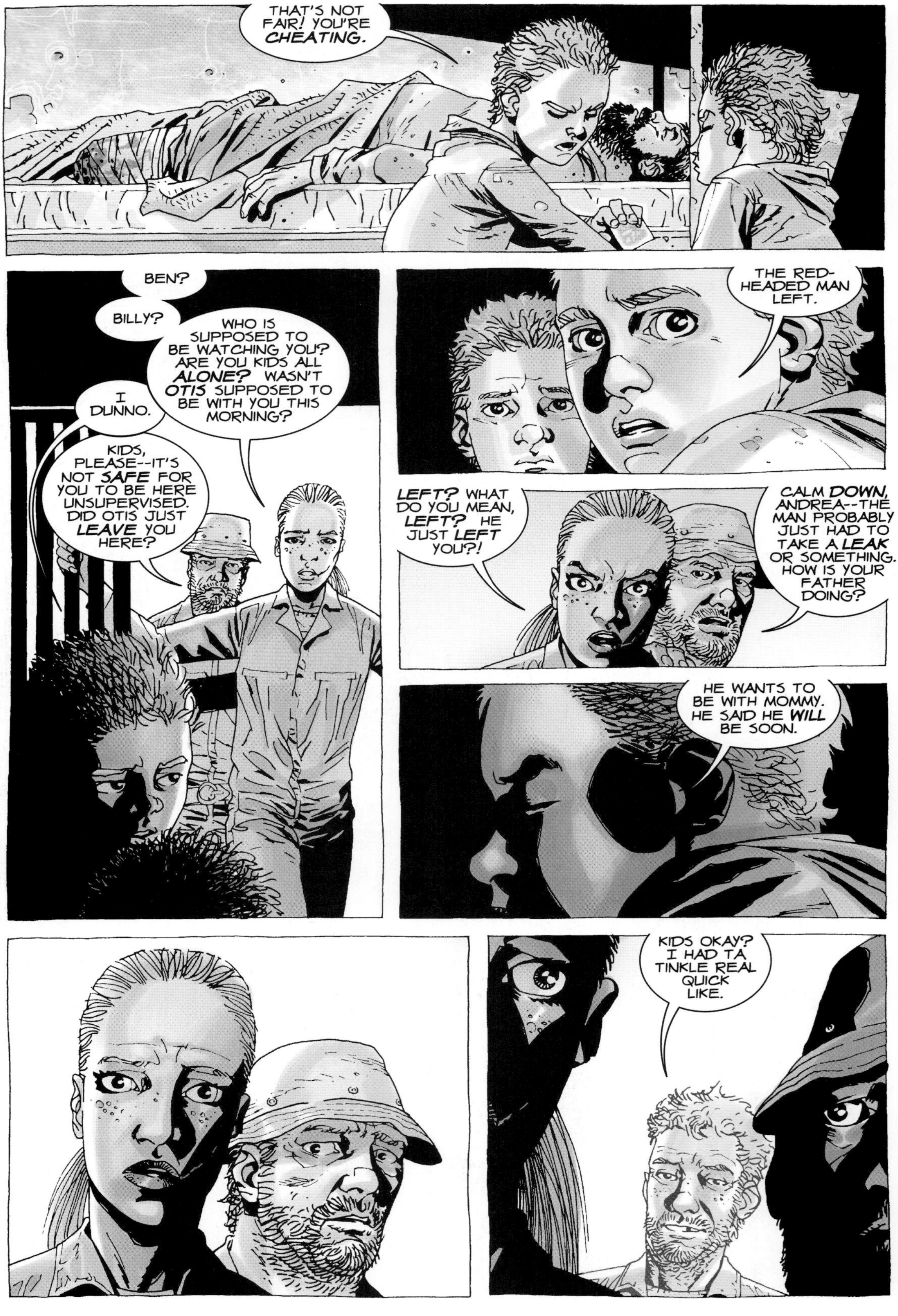
THAT'S NOT FAIR! YOU'RE CHEATING.
BEN?
BILLY?
WHO IS SUPPOSED TO BE WATCHING YOU? ARE YOU KIDS ALL ALONE? WASN'T OTIS SUPPOSED TO BE WITH YOU THIS MORNING?
I DUNNO.
KIDS, PLEASE--IT'S NOT SAFE FOR YOU TO BE HERE UNSUPERVISED. DID OTIS JUST LEAVE YOU HERE?
THE RED-HEADED MAN LEFT.
LEFT? WHAT DO YOU MEAN, LEFT? HE JUST LEFT YOU?!
CALM DOWN, ANDREA--THE MAN PROBABLY JUST HAD TO TAKE A LEAK OR SOMETHING. HOW IS YOUR FATHER DOING?
HE WANTS TO BE WITH MOMMY. HE SAID HE WILL BE SOON.
KIDS OKAY? I HAD TA TINKLE REAL QUICK LIKE.

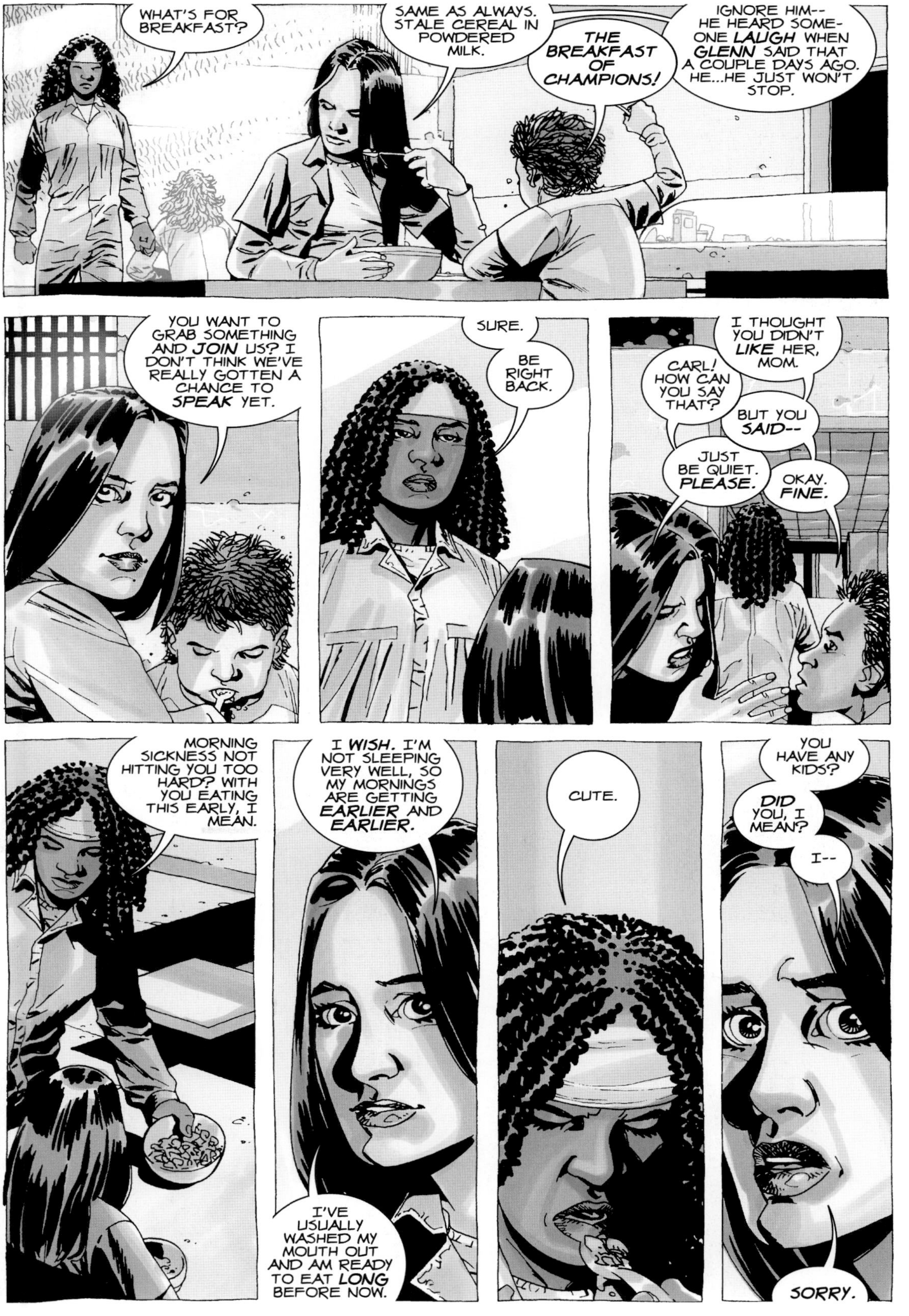
WHAT'S FOR BREAKFAST?
SAME AS ALWAYS. STALE CEREAL IN POWDERED MILK.
THE BREAKFAST OF CHAMPIONS!
IGNORE HIM-- HE HEARD SOME-ONE LAUGH WHEN GLENN SAID THAT A COUPLE DAYS AGO. HE...HE JUST WON'T STOP.
YOU WANT TO GRAB SOMETHING AND JOIN US? I DON'T THINK WE'VE REALLY GOTTEN A CHANCE TO SPEAK YET.
SURE.
BE RIGHT BACK.
I THOUGHT YOU DIDN'T LIKE HER, MOM.
CARL! HOW CAN YOU SAY THAT?
BUT YOU SAID--
JUST BE QUIET. PLEASE.
OKAY. FINE.
MORNING SICKNESS NOT HITTING YOU TOO HARD? WITH YOU EATING THIS EARLY, I MEAN.
I WISH. I'M NOT SLEEPING VERY WELL, SO MY MORNINGS ARE GETTING EARLIER AND EARLIER.
I'VE USUALLY WASHED MY MOUTH OUT AND AM READY TO EAT LONG BEFORE NOW.
CUTE.
YOU HAVE ANY KIDS?
DID YOU, I MEAN?
I--
SORRY.

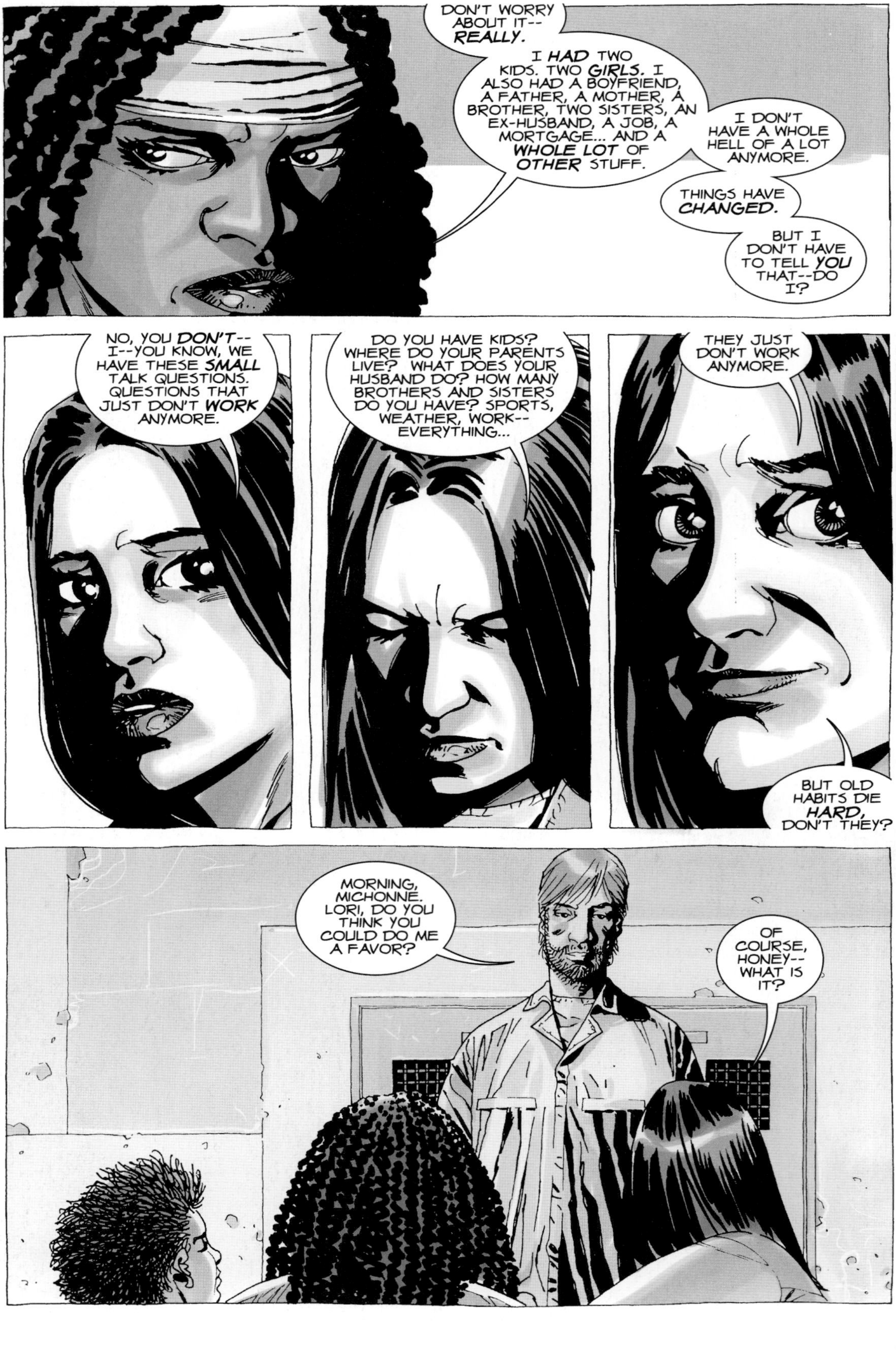
DON'T WORRY ABOUT IT-- REALLY.
I HAD TWO KIDS. TWO GIRLS. I ALSO HAD A BOYFRIEND, A FATHER, A MOTHER, A BROTHER, TWO SISTERS, AN EX-HUSBAND, A JOB, A MORTGAGE... AND A WHOLE LOT OF OTHER STUFF.
I DON'T HAVE A WHOLE HELL OF A LOT ANYMORE.
THINGS HAVE CHANGED.
BUT I DON'T HAVE TO TELL YOU THAT--DO I?
NO, YOU DON'T-- I--YOU KNOW, WE HAVE THESE SMALL TALK QUESTIONS. QUESTIONS THAT JUST DON'T WORK ANYMORE.
DO YOU HAVE KIDS? WHERE DO YOUR PARENTS LIVE? WHAT DOES YOUR HUSBAND DO? HOW MANY BROTHERS AND SISTERS DO YOU HAVE? SPORTS, WEATHER, WORK-- EVERYTHING...
THEY JUST DON'T WORK ANYMORE.
BUT OLD HABITS DIE HARD, DON'T THEY?
MORNING, MICHONNE. LORI, DO YOU THINK YOU COULD DO ME A FAVOR?
OF COURSE, HONEY-- WHAT IS IT?

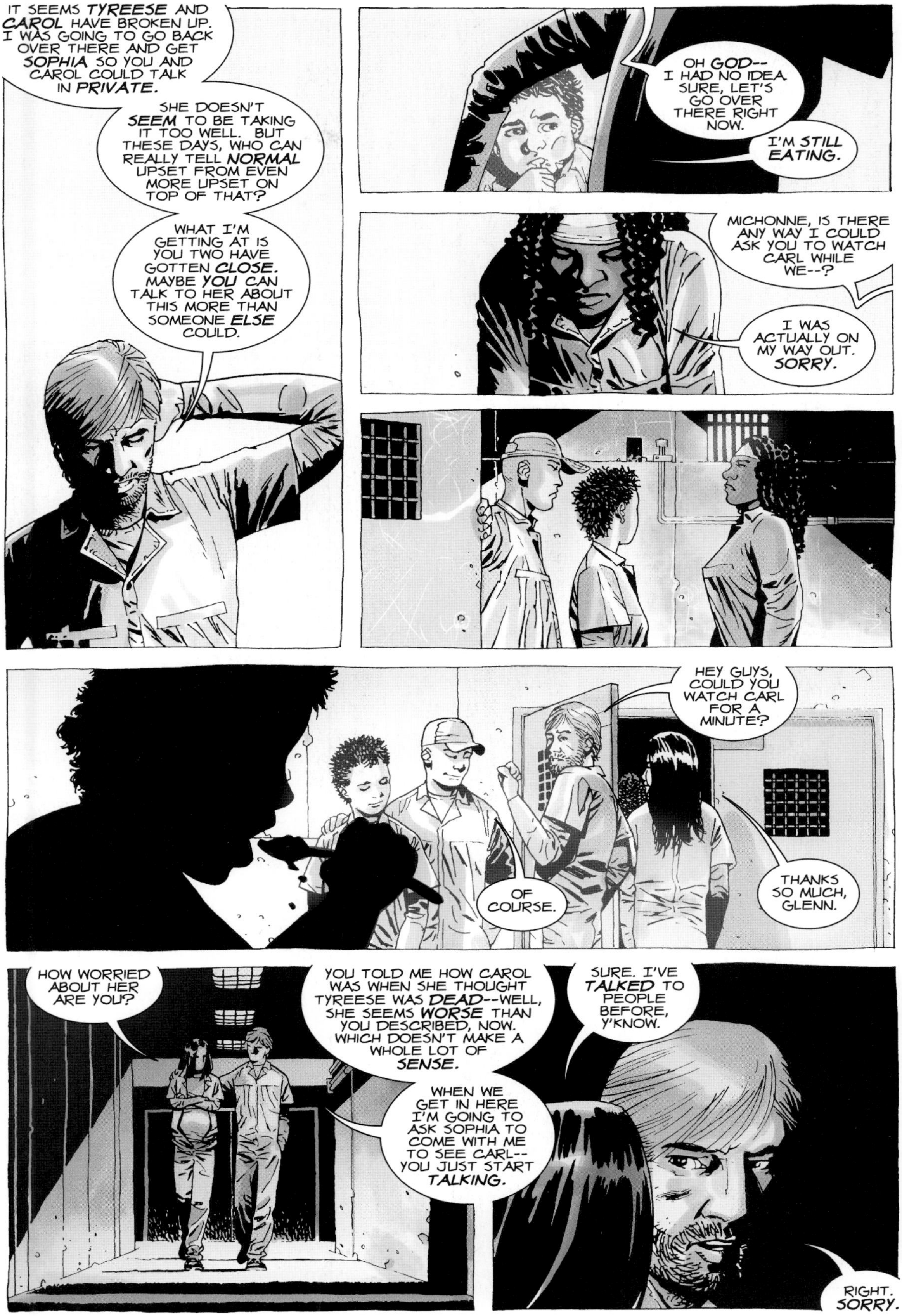
IT SEEMS TYREESE AND CAROL HAVE BROKEN UP. I WAS GOING TO GO BACK OVER THERE AND GET SOPHIA SO YOU AND CAROL COULD TALK IN PRIVATE.
SHE DOESN'T SEEM TO BE TAKING IT TOO WELL. BUT THESE DAYS, WHO CAN REALLY TELL NORMAL UPSET FROM EVEN MORE UPSET ON TOP OF THAT?
WHAT I'M GETTING AT IS YOU TWO HAVE GOTTEN CLOSE. MAYBE YOU CAN TALK TO HER ABOUT THIS MORE THAN SOMEONE ELSE COULD.
OH GOD-- I HAD NO IDEA. SURE, LET'S GO OVER THERE RIGHT NOW.
I'M STILL EATING.
MICHONNE, IS THERE ANY WAY I COULD ASK YOU TO WATCH CARL WHILE WE--?
I WAS ACTUALLY ON MY WAY OUT. SORRY.
HEY GUYS, COULD YOU WATCH CARL WHILE FOR A MINUTE?
OF COURSE.
THANKS SO MUCH, GLENN.
HOW WORRIED ABOUT HER ARE YOU?
YOU TOLD ME HOW CAROL WAS WHEN SHE THOUGHT TYREESE WAS DEAD--WELL, SHE SEEMS WORSE THAN YOU DESCRIBED, NOW. WHICH DOESN'T MAKE A WHOLE LOT OF SENSE.
WHEN WE GET IN HERE I'M GOING TO ASK SOPHIA TO COME WITH ME TO SEE CARL-- YOU JUST START TALKING.
SURE. I'VE TALKED TO PEOPLE BEFORE, Y'KNOW.
RIGHT. SORRY.

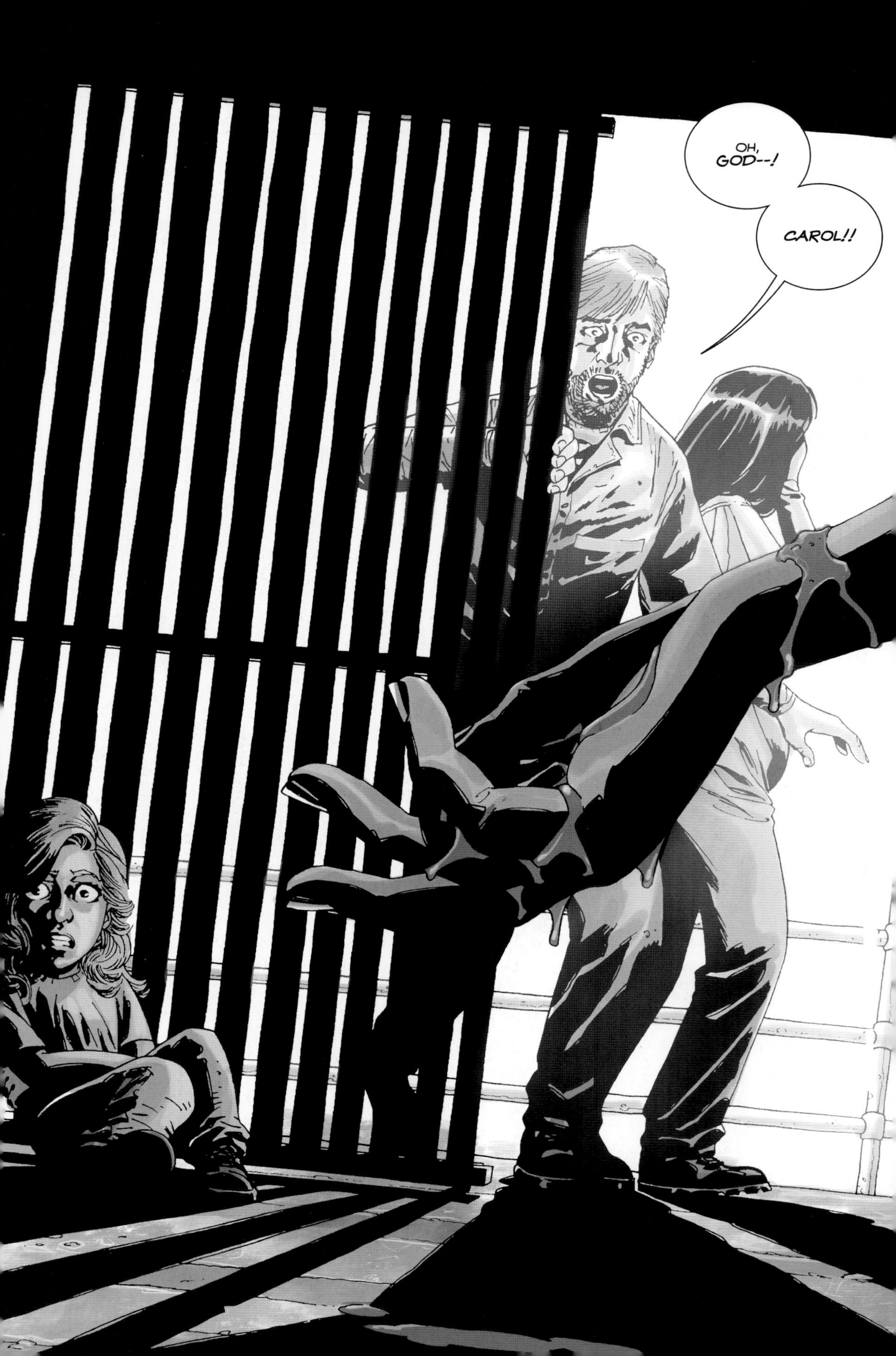
OH, GOD--!
CAROL!!

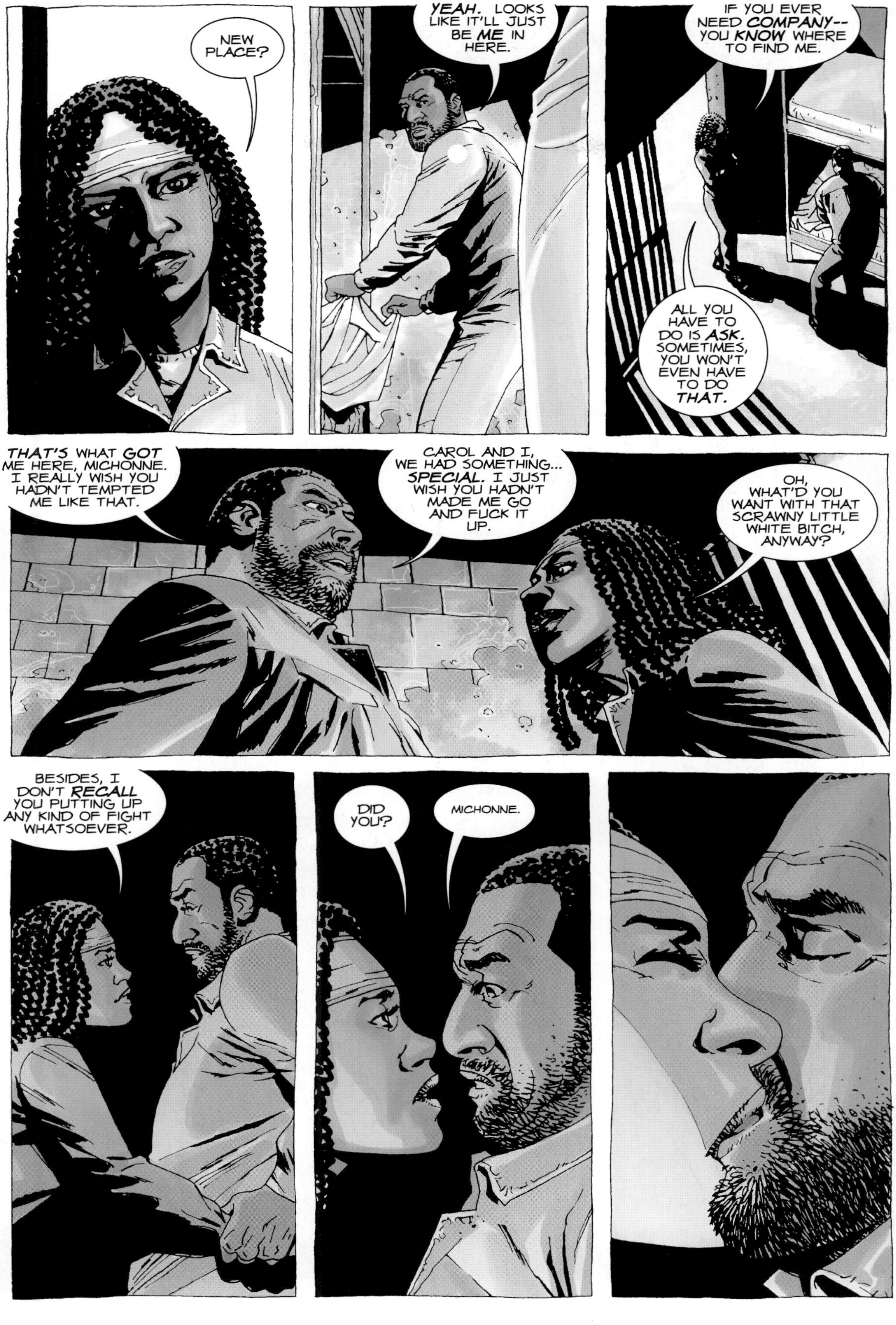
NEW PLACE?
YEAH. LOOKS LIKE IT'LL JUST BE ME IN HERE.
IF YOU EVER NEED COMPANY-- YOU KNOW WHERE TO FIND ME.
ALL YOU HAVE TO DO IS ASK. SOMETIMES, YOU WON'T EVEN HAVE TO DO THAT.
THAT'S WHAT GOT ME HERE, MICHONNE. I REALLY WISH YOU HADN'T TEMPTED ME LIKE THAT.
CAROL AND I, WE HAD SOMETHING... SPECIAL. I JUST WISH YOU HADN'T MADE ME GO AND FUCK IT UP.
OH, WHAT'D YOU WANT WITH THAT SCRAWNY LITTLE WHITE BITCH, ANYWAY?
BESIDES, I DON'T RECALL YOU PUTTING UP ANY KIND OF FIGHT WHATSOEVER.
DID YOU?
MICHONNE.

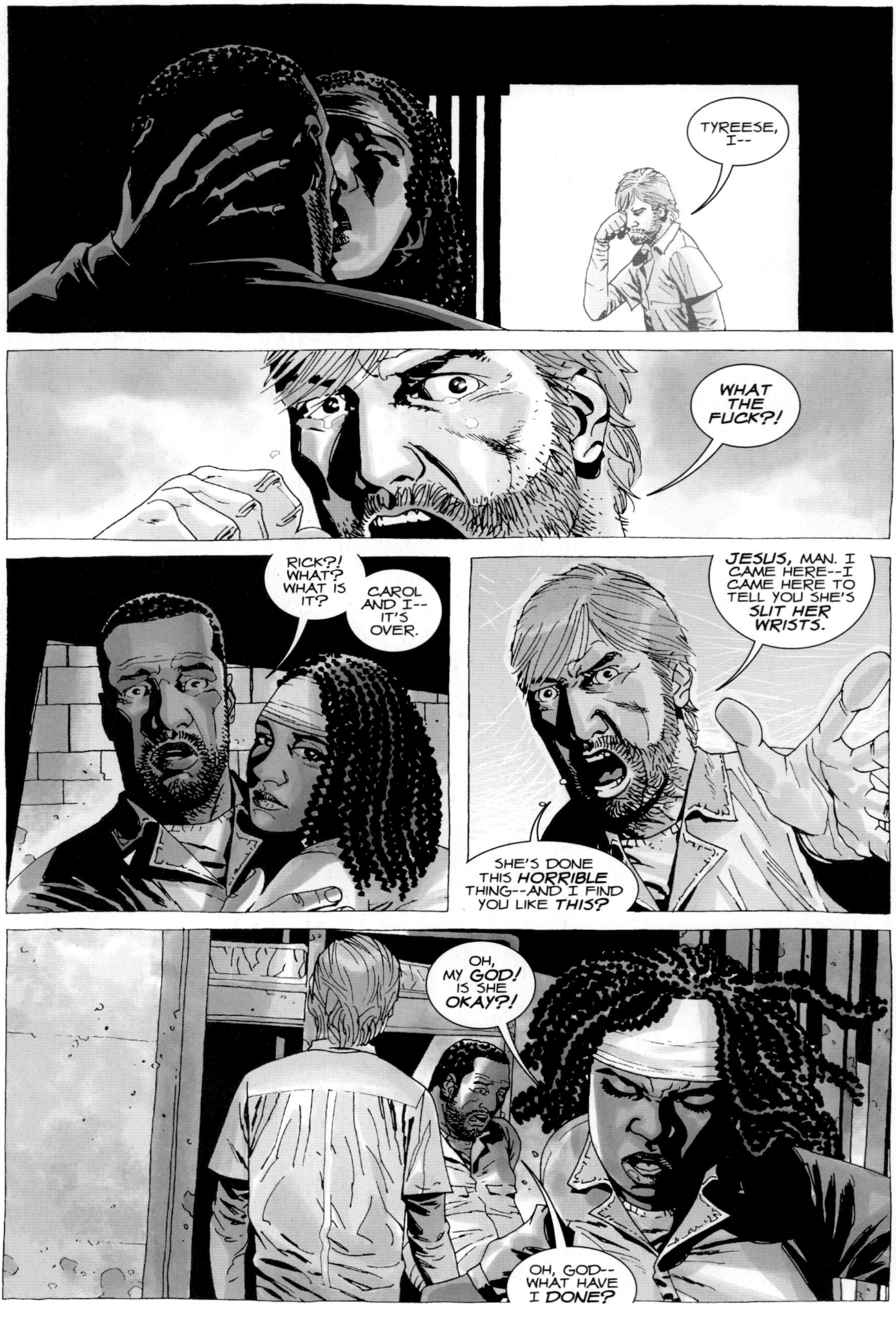
TYREESE, I--
WHAT THE FUCK?!
RICK?! WHAT? WHAT IS IT?
CAROL AND I-- IT'S OVER.
JESUS, MAN. I CAME HERE--I CAME HERE TO TELL YOU SHE'S SLIT HER WRISTS.
SHE'S DONE THIS HORRIBLE THING--AND I FIND YOU LIKE THIS?
OH, MY GOD! IS SHE OKAY?!
OH, GOD-- WHAT HAVE I DONE?

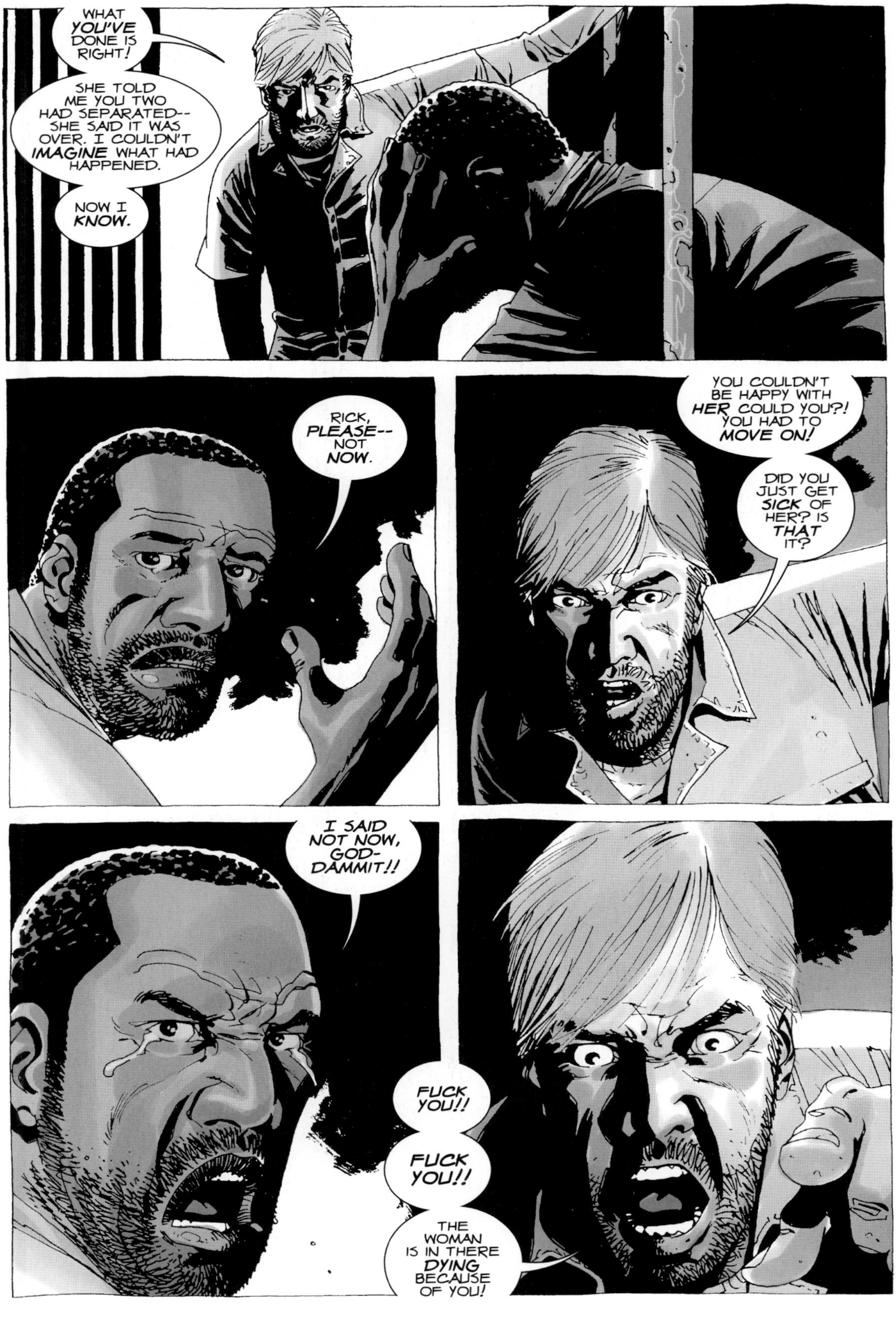
WHAT YOU'VE DONE IS RIGHT!
SHE TOLD ME YOU TWO HAD SEPARATED-- SHE SAID IT WAS OVER. I COULDN'T IMAGINE WHAT HAD HAPPENED.
NOW I KNOW.
RICK, PLEASE-- NOT NOW.
YOU COULDN'T BE HAPPY WITH HER COULD YOU?! YOU HAD TO MOVE ON!
DID YOU JUST GET SICK OF HER? IS THAT IT?
I SAID NOT NOW, GOD-DAMMIT!!
FUCK YOU!!
FUCK YOU!!
THE WOMAN IS IN THERE DYING BECAUSE OF YOU!

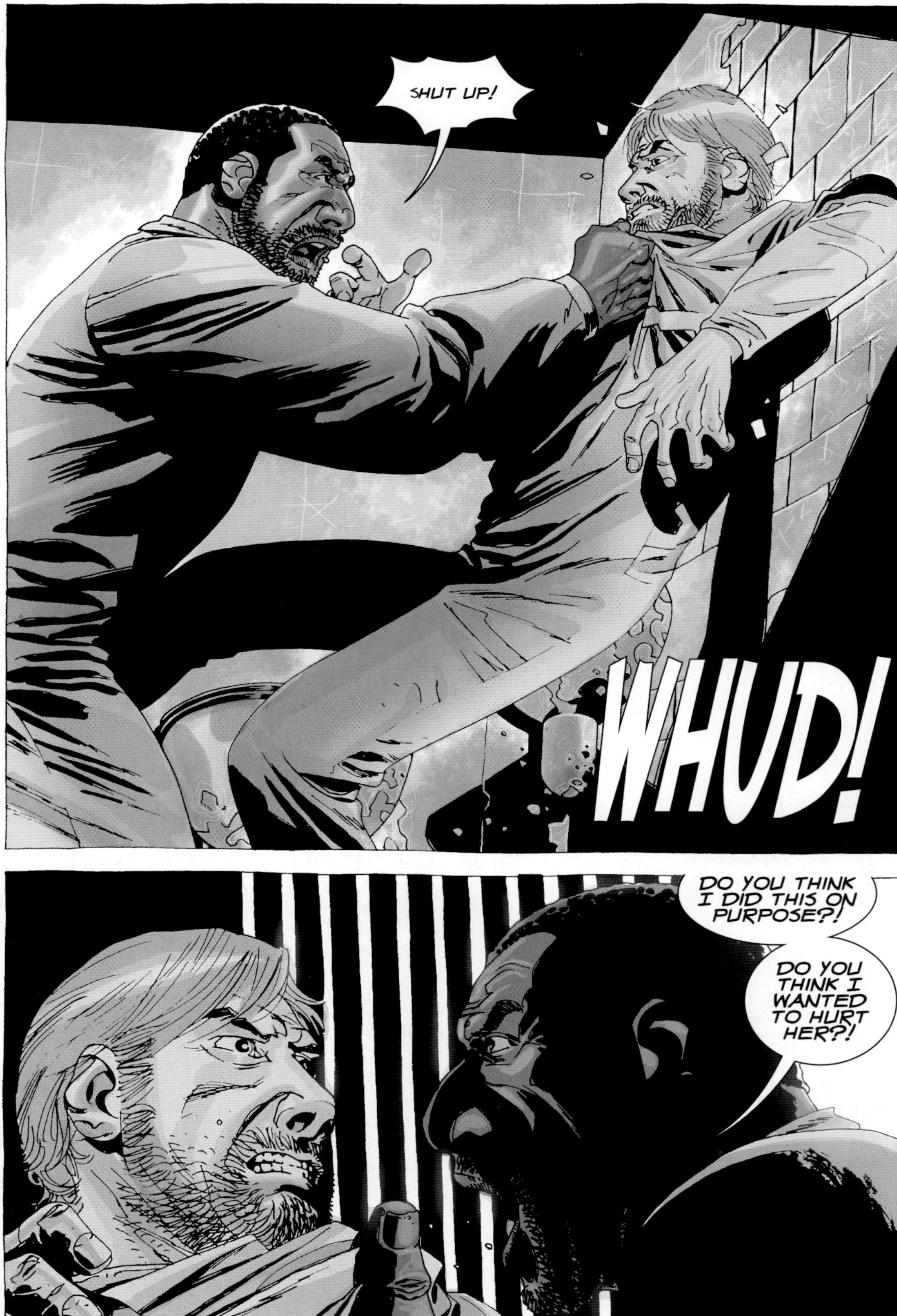
SHUT UP!
WHUD!
DO YOU THINK I DID THIS ON PURPOSE?!
DO YOU THINK I WANTED TO HURT HER?!

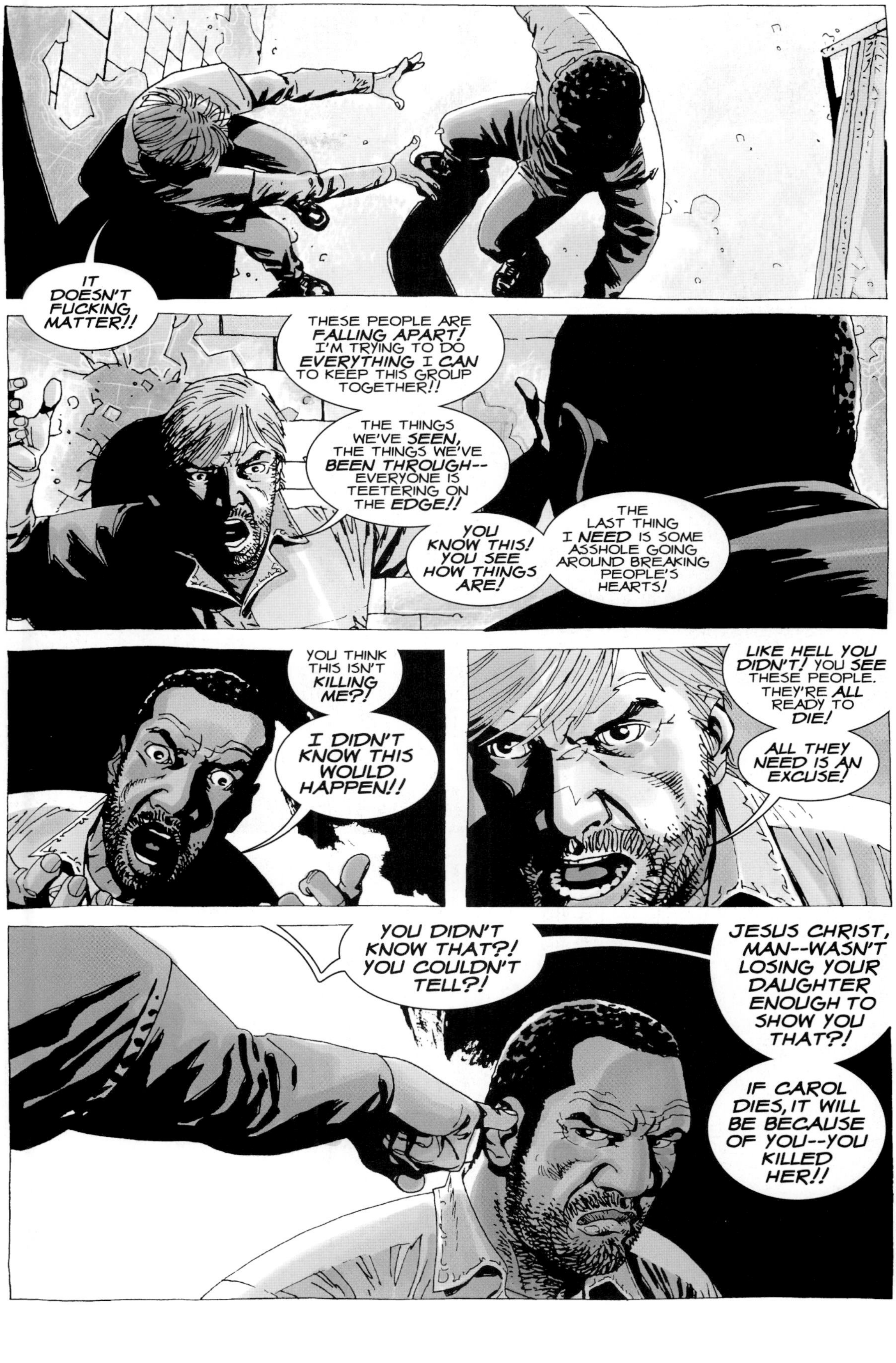
IT DOESN'T FUCKING MATTER!!
THESE PEOPLE ARE FALLING APART! I'M TRYING TO DO EVERYTHING I CAN TO KEEP THIS GROUP TOGETHER!!
THE THINGS WE'VE SEEN, THE THINGS WE'VE BEEN THROUGH-- EVERYONE IS TEETERING ON THE EDGE!!
YOU KNOW THIS! YOU SEE HOW THINGS ARE!
THE LAST THING I NEED IS SOME ASSHOLE GOING AROUND BREAKING PEOPLE'S HEARTS!
YOU THINK THIS ISN'T KILLING ME?!
I DIDN'T KNOW THIS WOULD HAPPEN!!
LIKE HELL YOU DIDN'T! YOU SEE THESE PEOPLE. THEY'RE ALL READY TO DIE!
ALL THEY NEED IS AN EXCUSE!
YOU DIDN'T KNOW THAT?! YOU COULDN'T TELL?!
JESUS CHRIST, MAN--WASN'T LOSING YOUR DAUGHTER ENOUGH TO SHOW YOU THAT?!
IF CAROL DIES, IT WILL BE BECAUSE OF YOU--YOU KILLED HER!!

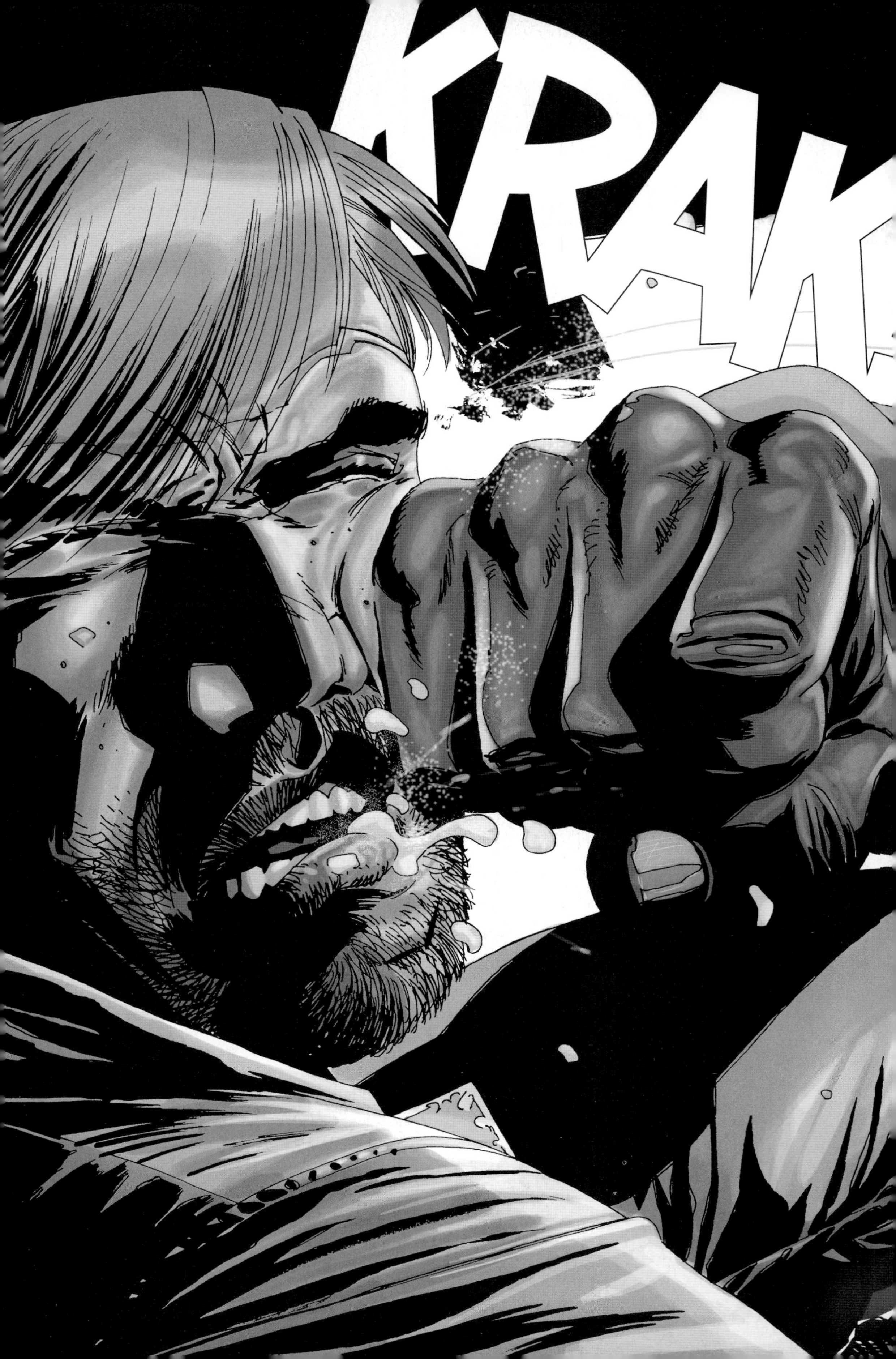
KRAK

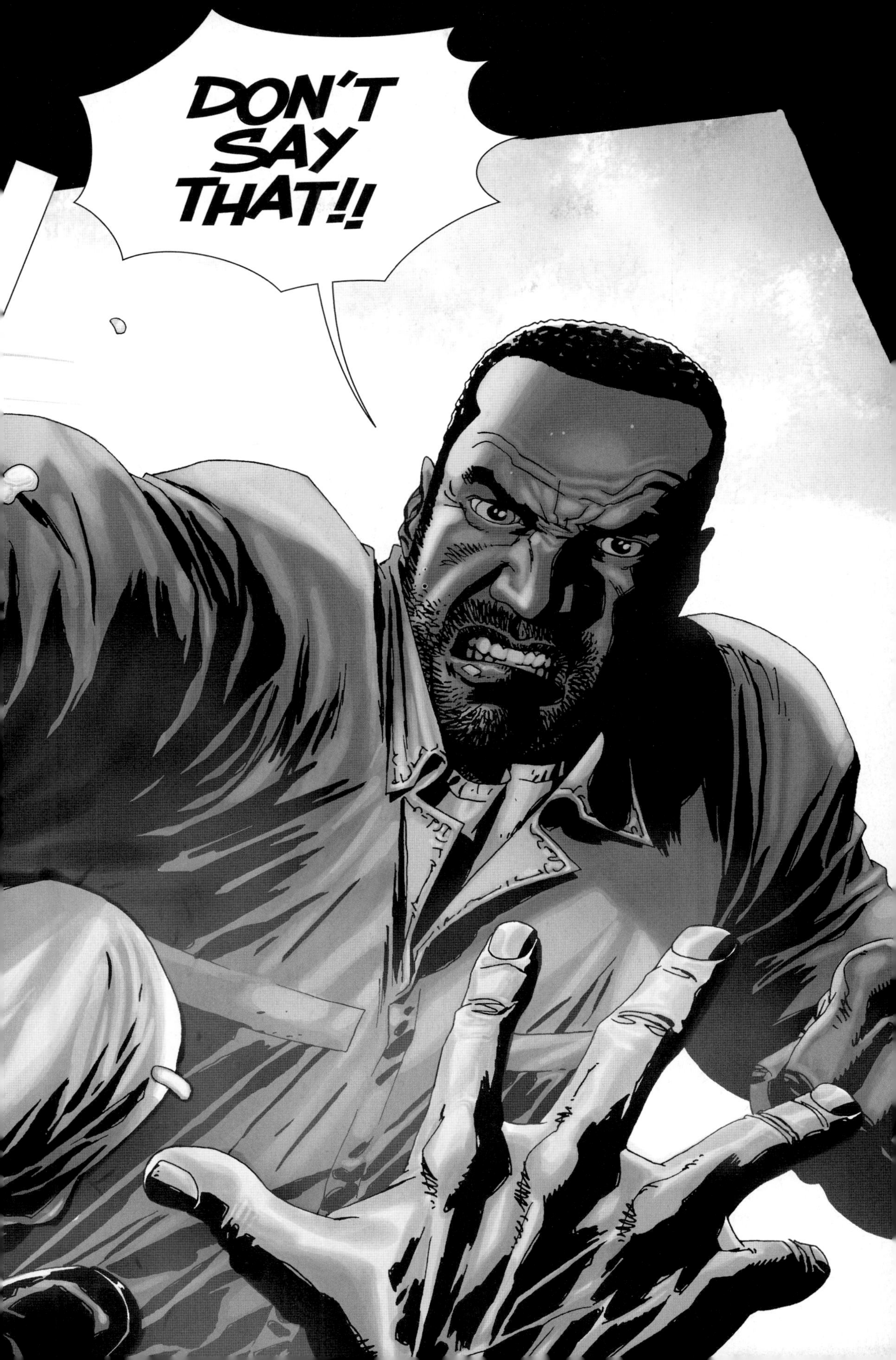
DON'T SAY THAT!!

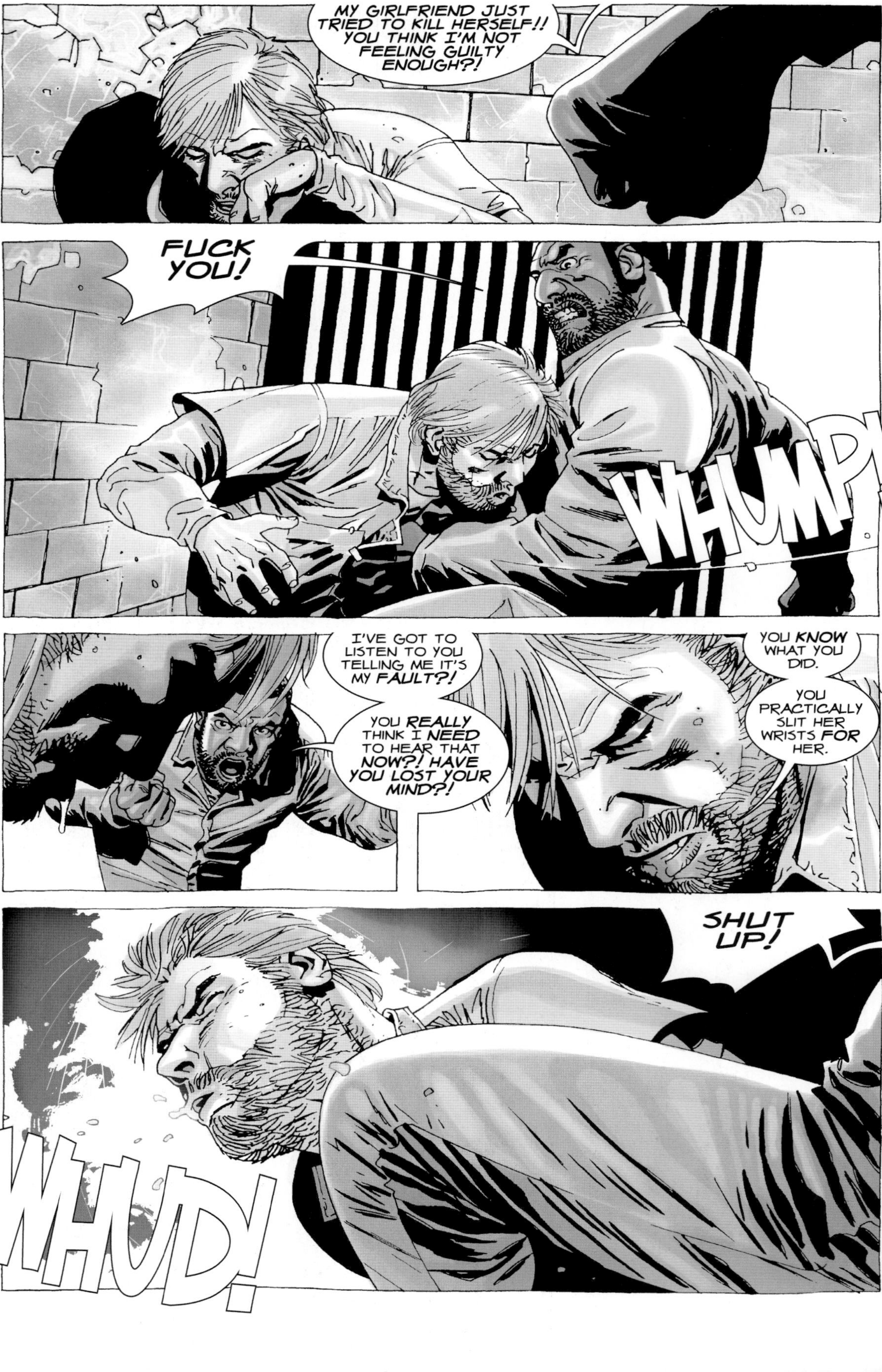
MY GIRLFRIEND JUST TRIED TO KILL HERSELF!! YOU THINK I'M NOT FEELING GUILTY ENOUGH?!
FUCK YOU!
WHUMP!
I'VE GOT TO LISTEN TO YOU TELLING ME IT'S MY FAULT?!
YOU REALLY THINK I NEED TO HEAR THAT NOW?! HAVE YOU LOST YOUR MIND?!
YOU KNOW WHAT YOU DID.
YOU PRACTICALLY SLIT HER WRISTS FOR HER.
SHUT UP!
WHUD!

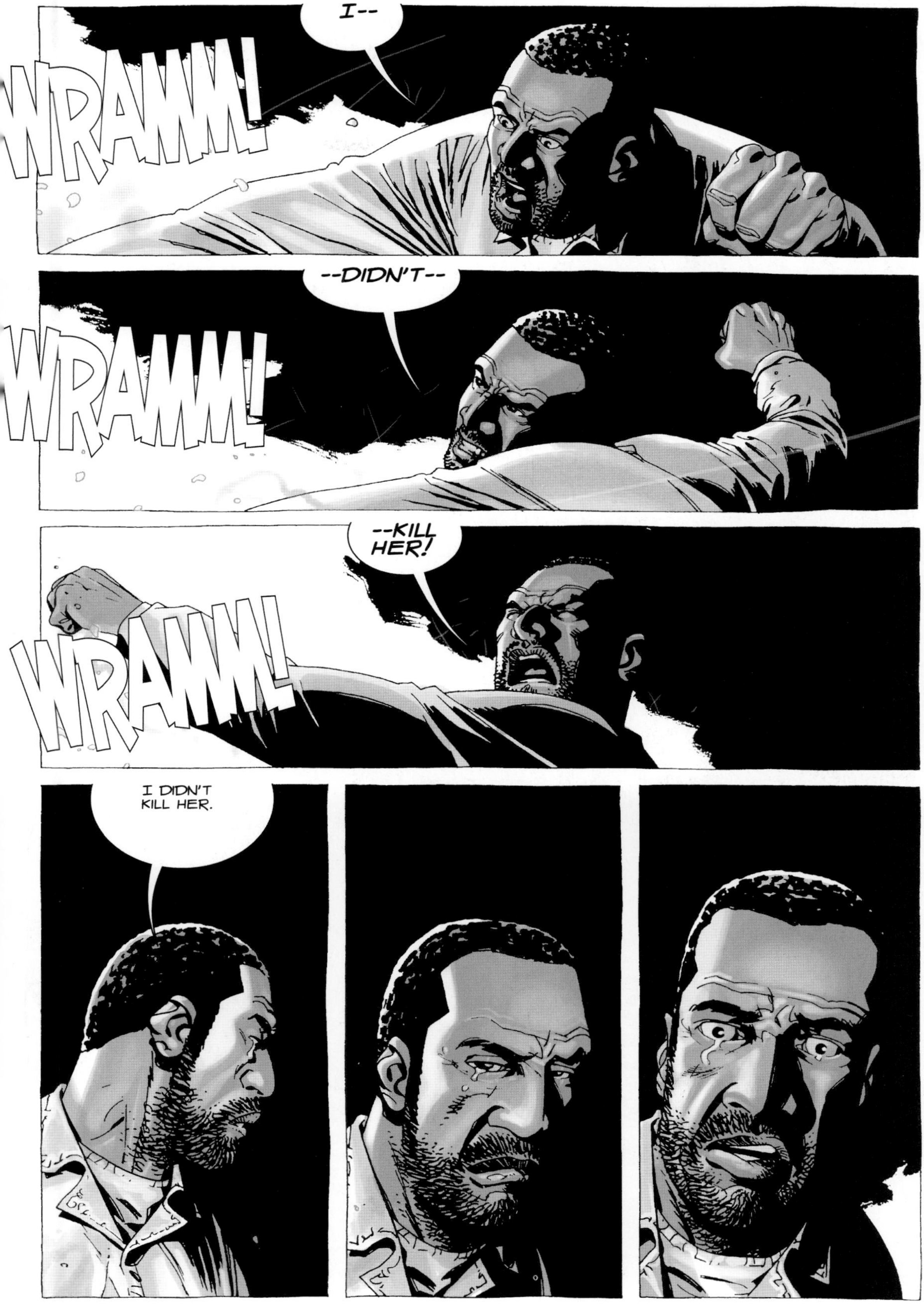
I--
WRAMM!
--DIDN'T--
WRAMM!
--KILL HER!
WRAMM!
I DIDN'T KILL HER.

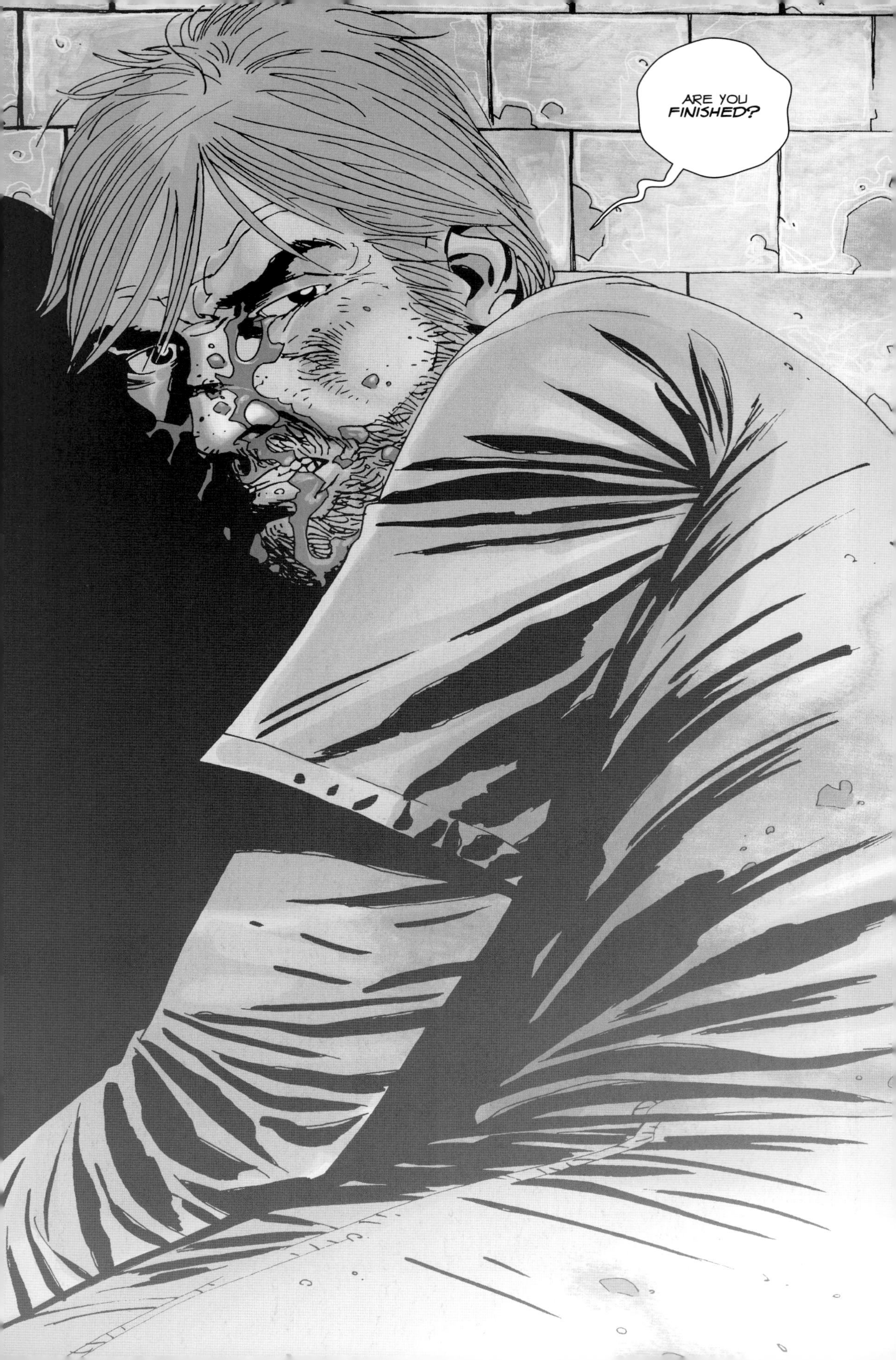
ARE YOU FINISHED?

GET IT THROUGH YOUR HEAD. IF CAROL DIES--IT'S YOUR FAULT. I WANT YOU TO REALIZE THAT NEXT TIME YOU'RE FUCKING "LADY MYSTERIOUS."

AND CALM THE FUCK DOWN. TRUTH GETTING TO YOU?!

DON'T FUCKING HIT ME AGAIN!

YOU'RE INSANE. YOU HAVE LOST YOUR MIND.

ME?! YOU THINK I'VE LOST IT!! YOU THINK I'M BLOCKING OUT WHAT HAPPENED BETWEEN YOU AND CHRIS IN THE SHOWERS?!

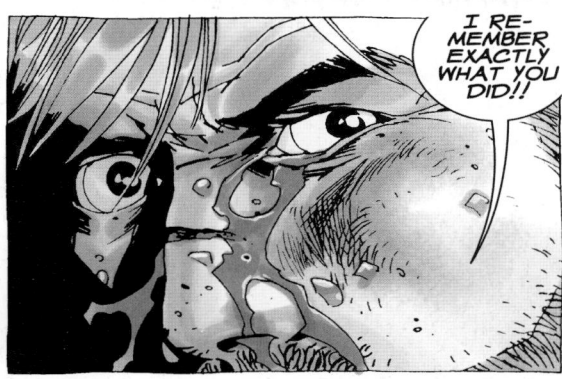

I RE-MEMBER EXACTLY WHAT YOU DID!!

YEAH-- I KILLED CHRIS-- FINE--

I MURDERED HIM IN COLD BLOOD!

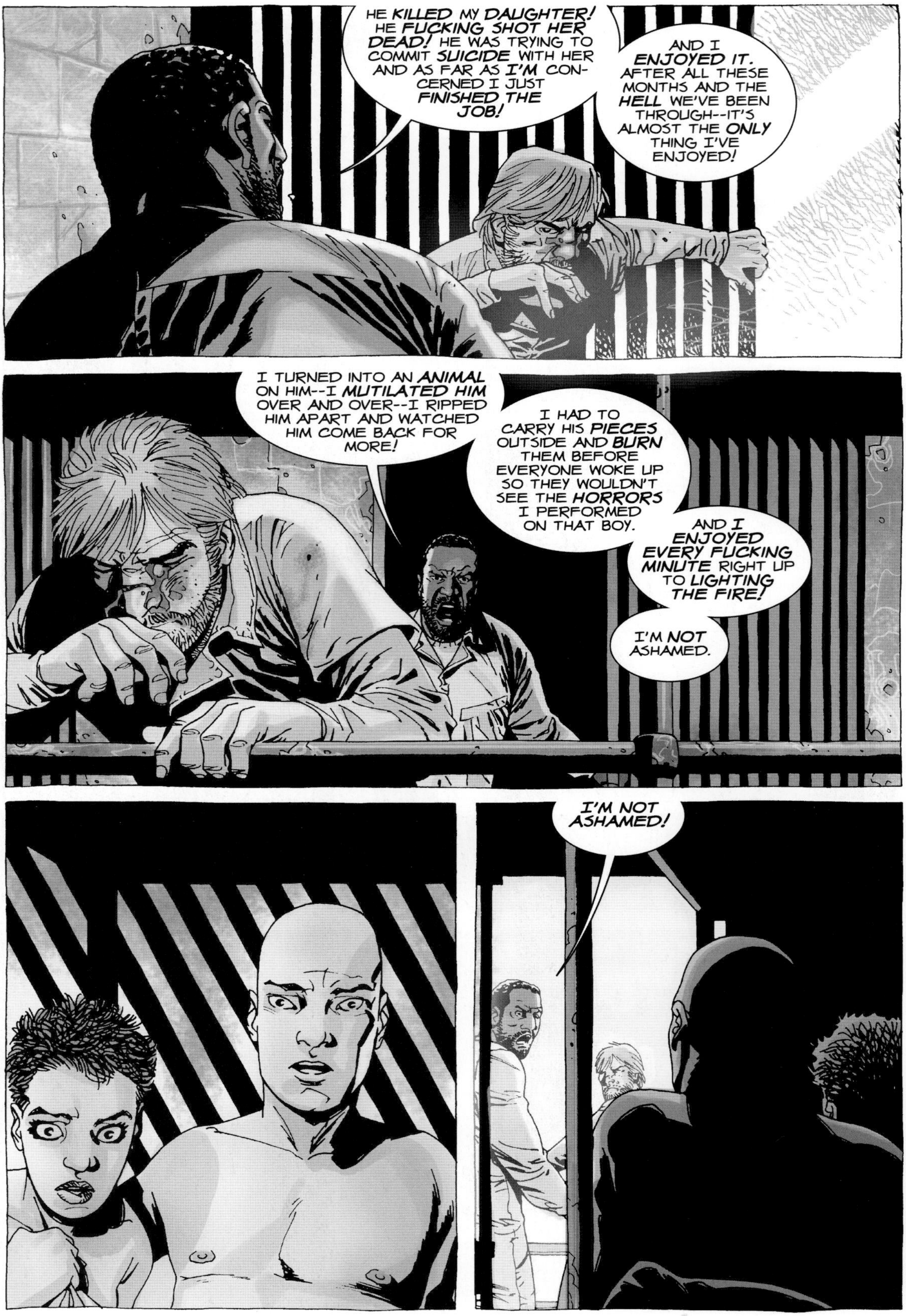
HE KILLED MY DAUGHTER! HE FUCKING SHOT HER DEAD! HE WAS TRYING TO COMMIT SUICIDE WITH HER AND AS FAR AS I'M CONCERNED I JUST FINISHED THE JOB!
AND I ENJOYED IT. AFTER ALL THESE MONTHS AND THE HELL WE'VE BEEN THROUGH--IT'S ALMOST THE ONLY THING I'VE ENJOYED!
I TURNED INTO AN ANIMAL ON HIM--I MUTILATED HIM OVER AND OVER--I RIPPED HIM APART AND WATCHED HIM COME BACK FOR MORE!
I HAD TO CARRY HIS PIECES OUTSIDE AND BURN THEM BEFORE EVERYONE WOKE UP SO THEY WOULDN'T SEE THE HORRORS I PERFORMED ON THAT BOY.
AND I ENJOYED EVERY FUCKING MINUTE RIGHT UP TO LIGHTING THE FIRE!
I'M NOT ASHAMED.
I'M NOT ASHAMED!

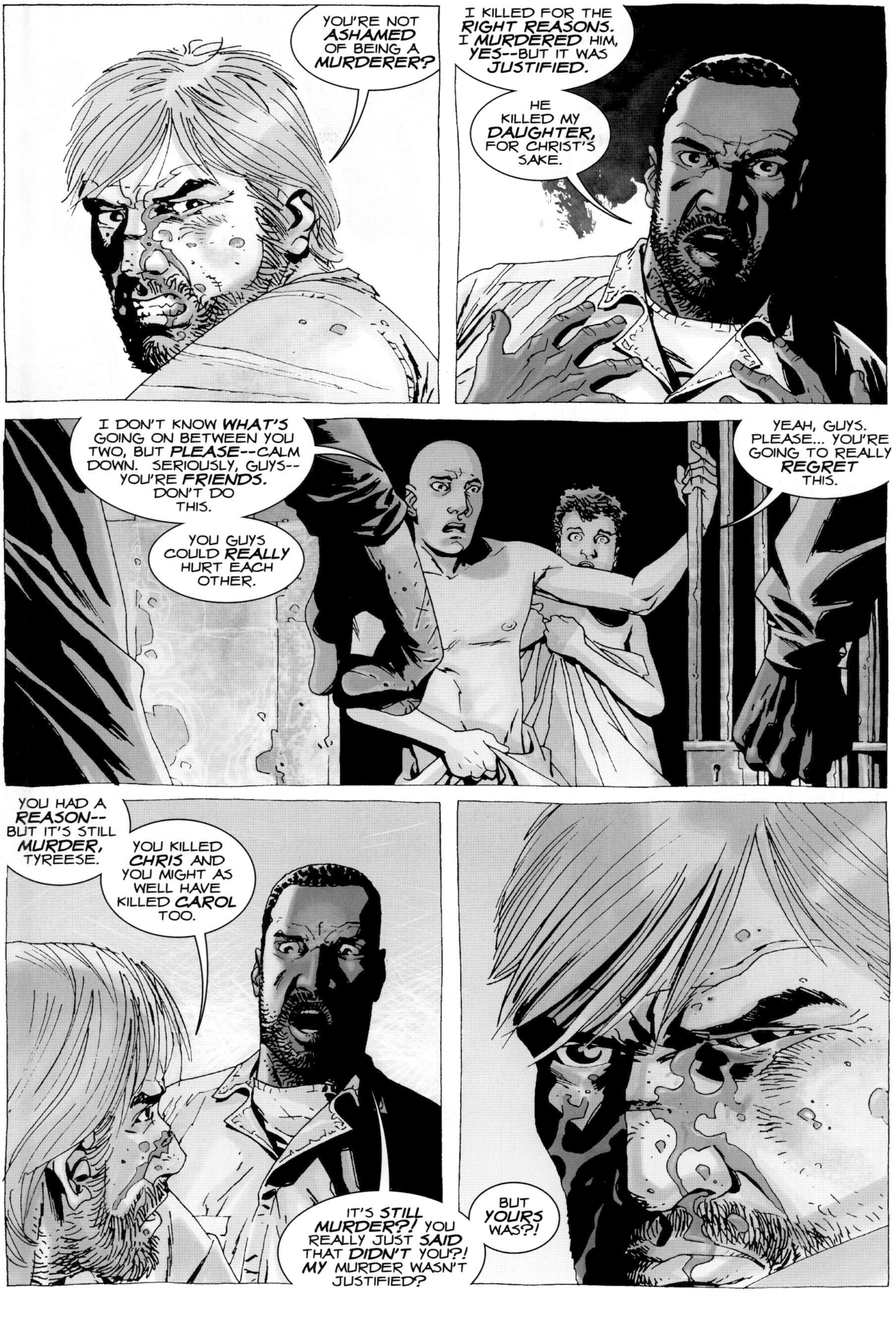

YOU'RE NOT ASHAMED OF BEING A MURDERER?
I KILLED FOR THE RIGHT REASONS. I MURDERED HIM, YES--BUT IT WAS JUSTIFIED.
HE KILLED MY DAUGHTER, FOR CHRIST'S SAKE.
I DON'T KNOW WHAT'S GOING ON BETWEEN YOU TWO, BUT PLEASE--CALM DOWN. SERIOUSLY, GUYS--YOU'RE FRIENDS. DON'T DO THIS.
YOU GUYS COULD REALLY HURT EACH OTHER.
YEAH, GUYS. PLEASE... YOU'RE GOING TO REALLY REGRET THIS.
YOU HAD A REASON--BUT IT'S STILL MURDER, TYREESE.
YOU KILLED CHRIS AND YOU MIGHT AS WELL HAVE KILLED CAROL TOO.
IT'S STILL MURDER?! YOU REALLY JUST SAID THAT DIDN'T YOU?! MY MURDER WASN'T JUSTIFIED?
BUT YOURS WAS?!

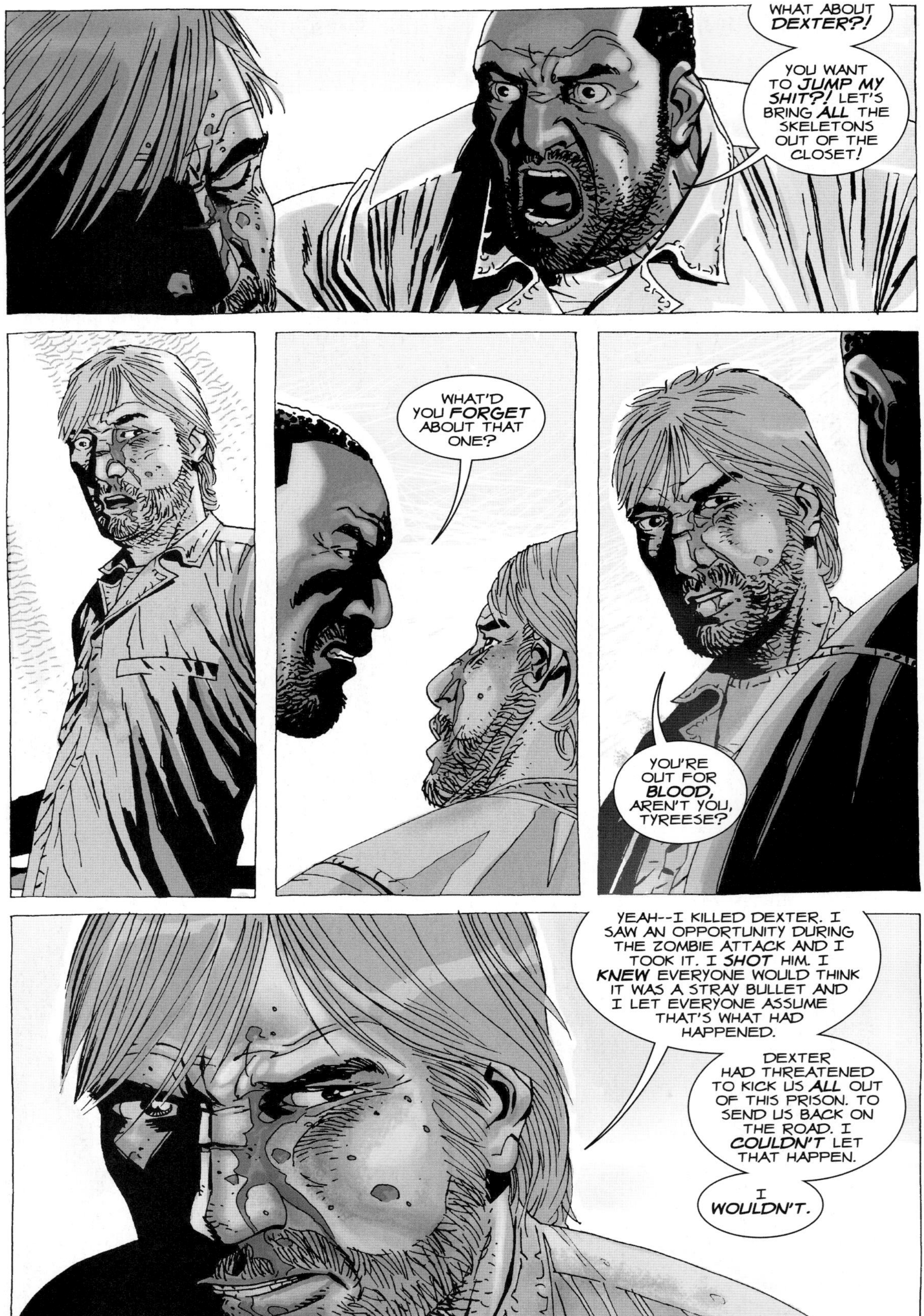
WHAT ABOUT DEXTER?!
YOU WANT TO JUMP MY SHIT?! LET'S BRING ALL THE SKELETONS OUT OF THE CLOSET!
WHAT'D YOU FORGET ABOUT THAT ONE?
YOU'RE OUT FOR BLOOD, AREN'T YOU, TYREESE?
YEAH--I KILLED DEXTER. I SAW AN OPPORTUNITY DURING THE ZOMBIE ATTACK AND I TOOK IT. I SHOT HIM. I KNEW EVERYONE WOULD THINK IT WAS A STRAY BULLET AND I LET EVERYONE ASSUME THAT'S WHAT HAD HAPPENED.
DEXTER HAD THREATENED TO KICK US ALL OUT OF THIS PRISON. TO SEND US BACK ON THE ROAD. I COULDN'T LET THAT HAPPEN.
I WOULDN'T.

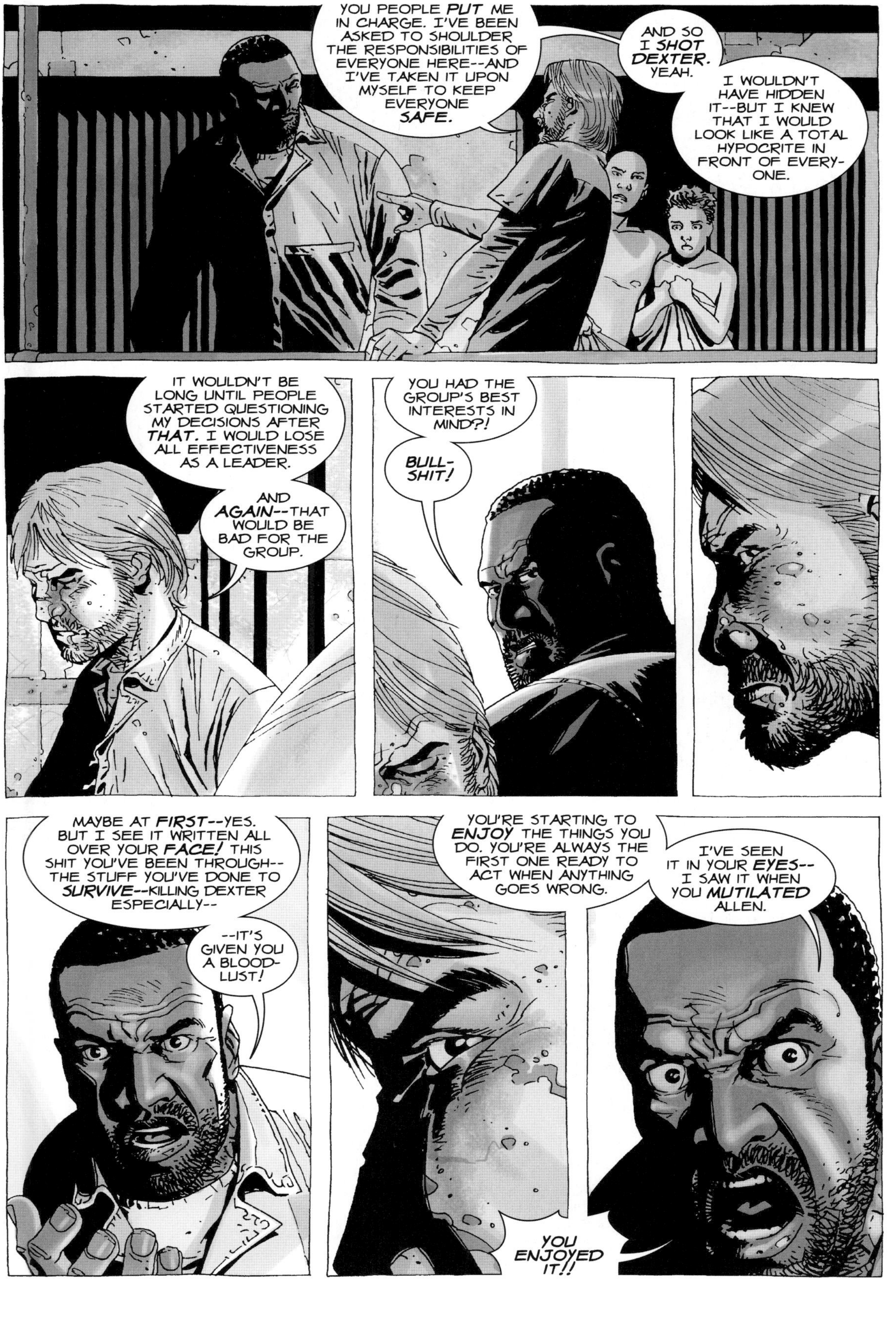
YOU PEOPLE PUT ME IN CHARGE. I'VE BEEN ASKED TO SHOULDER THE RESPONSIBILITIES OF EVERYONE HERE--AND I'VE TAKEN IT UPON MYSELF TO KEEP EVERYONE SAFE.
AND SO I SHOT DEXTER. YEAH.
I WOULDN'T HAVE HIDDEN IT--BUT I KNEW THAT I WOULD LOOK LIKE A TOTAL HYPOCRITE IN FRONT OF EVERY-ONE.
IT WOULDN'T BE LONG UNTIL PEOPLE STARTED QUESTIONING MY DECISIONS AFTER THAT. I WOULD LOSE ALL EFFECTIVENESS AS A LEADER.
AND AGAIN--THAT WOULD BE BAD FOR THE GROUP.
YOU HAD THE GROUP'S BEST INTERESTS IN MIND?!
BULL-SHIT!
MAYBE AT FIRST--YES. BUT I SEE IT WRITTEN ALL OVER YOUR FACE! THIS SHIT YOU'VE BEEN THROUGH--THE STUFF YOU'VE DONE TO SURVIVE--KILLING DEXTER ESPECIALLY--
--IT'S GIVEN YOU A BLOOD-LUST!
YOU'RE STARTING TO ENJOY THE THINGS YOU DO. YOU'RE ALWAYS THE FIRST ONE READY TO ACT WHEN ANYTHING GOES WRONG.
I'VE SEEN IT IN YOUR EYES--I SAW IT WHEN YOU MUTILATED ALLEN.
YOU ENJOYED IT!!

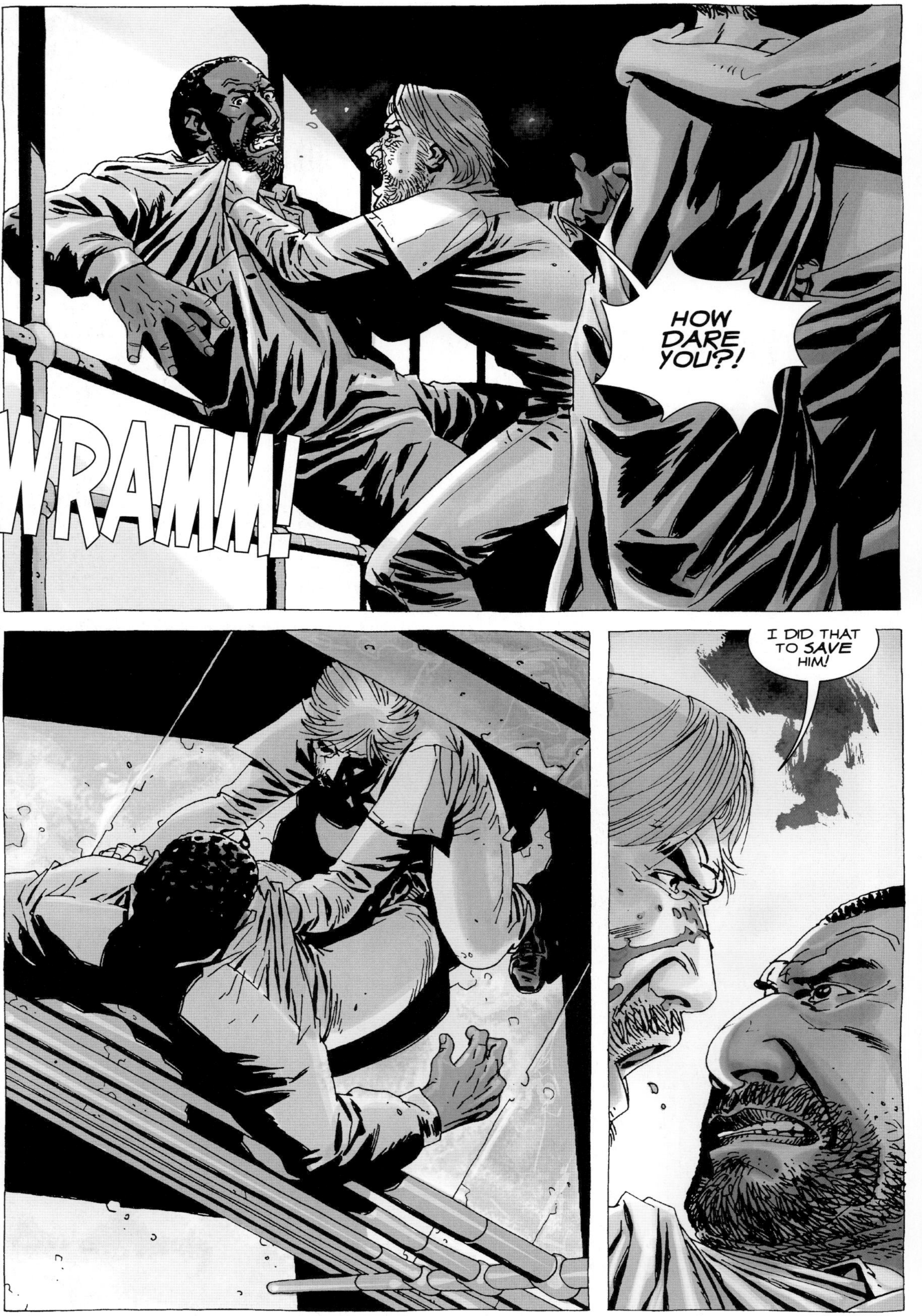
HOW DARE YOU?!
WRAMM!
I DID THAT TO SAVE HIM!

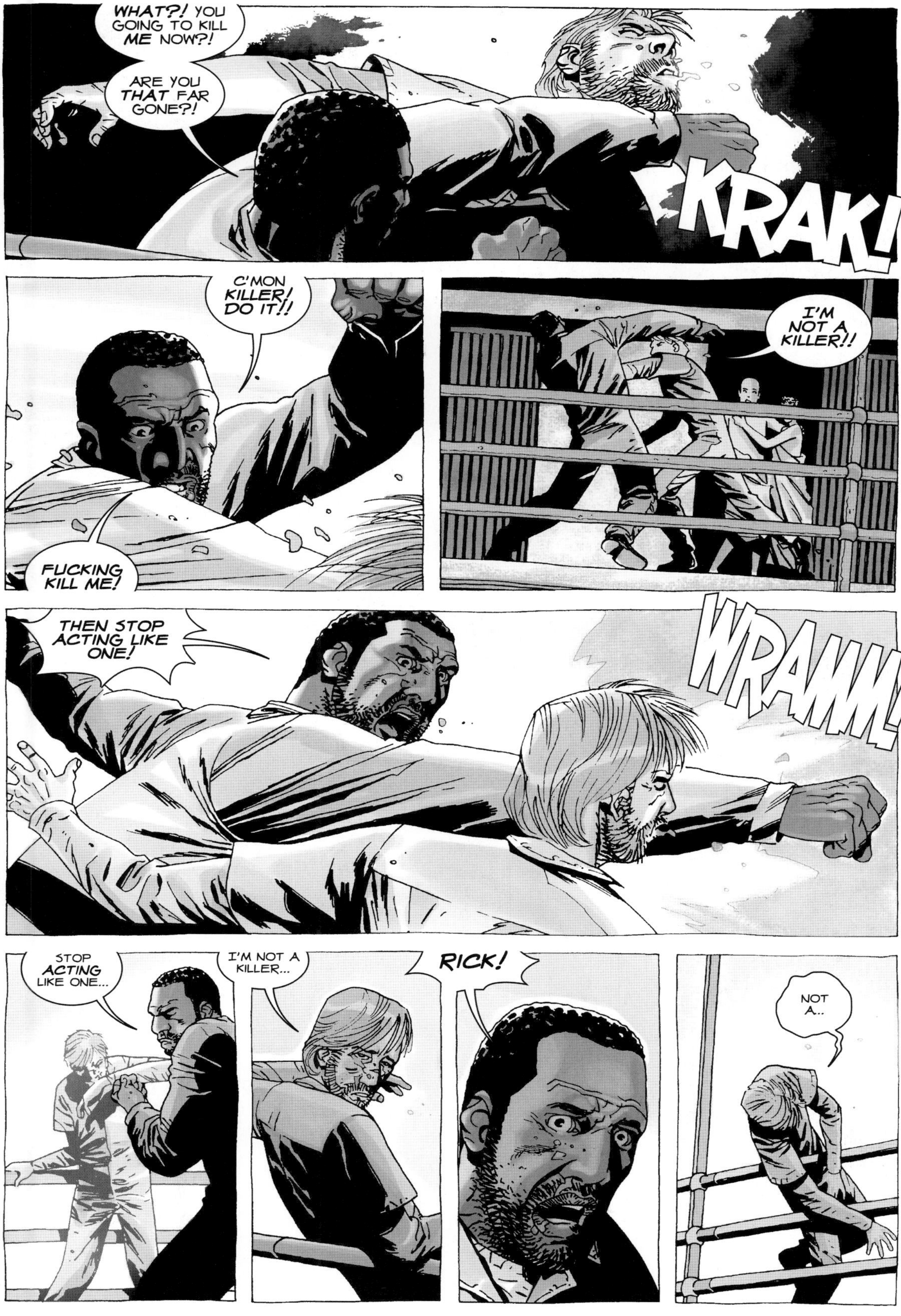
WHAT?! YOU GOING TO KILL ME NOW?!
ARE YOU THAT FAR GONE?!
KRAK!
C'MON KILLER! DO IT!!
FUCKING KILL ME!
I'M NOT A KILLER!!
THEN STOP ACTING LIKE ONE!
WRAMM!
STOP ACTING LIKE ONE...
I'M NOT A KILLER...
RICK!
NOT A...

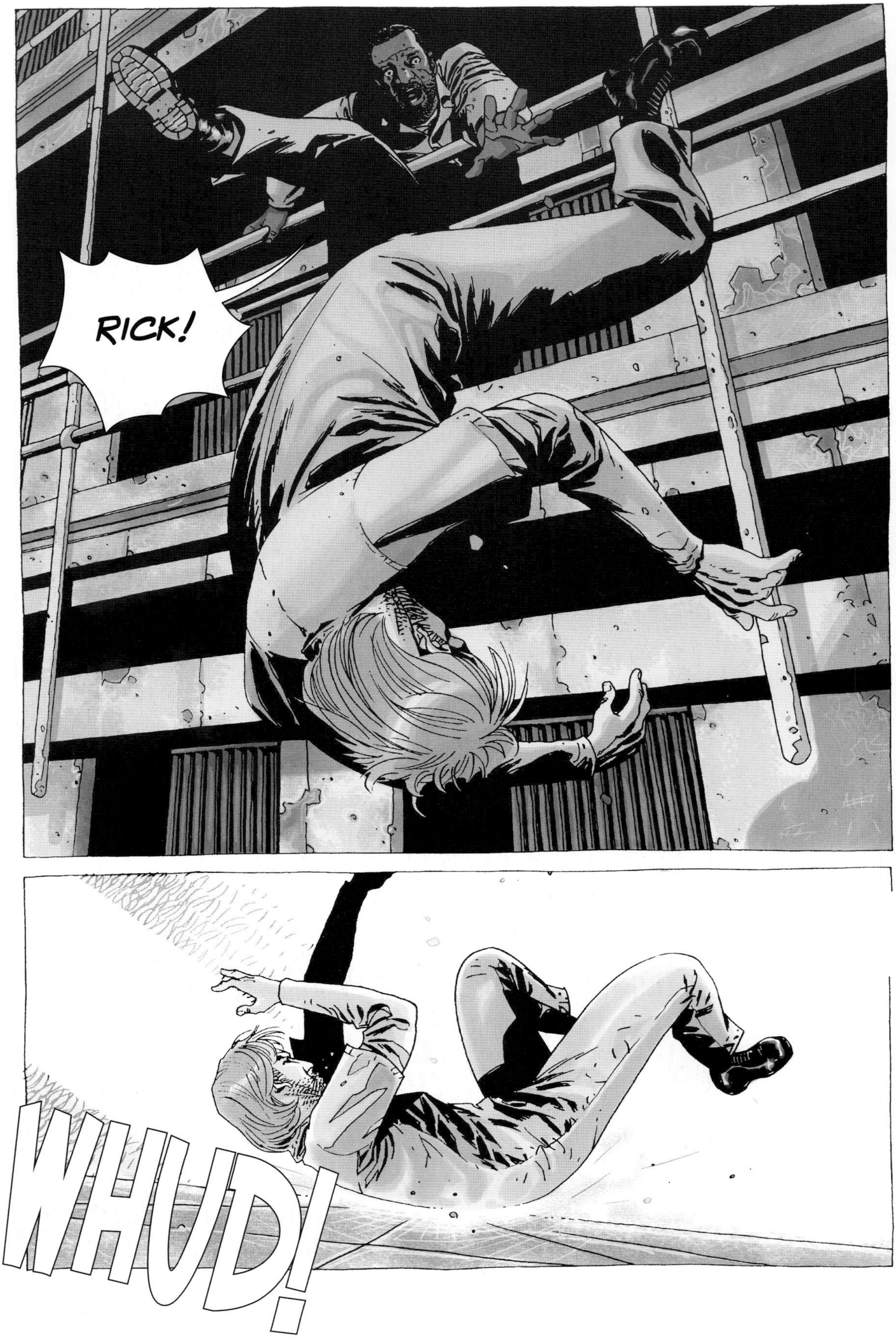
RICK!
WHUD!

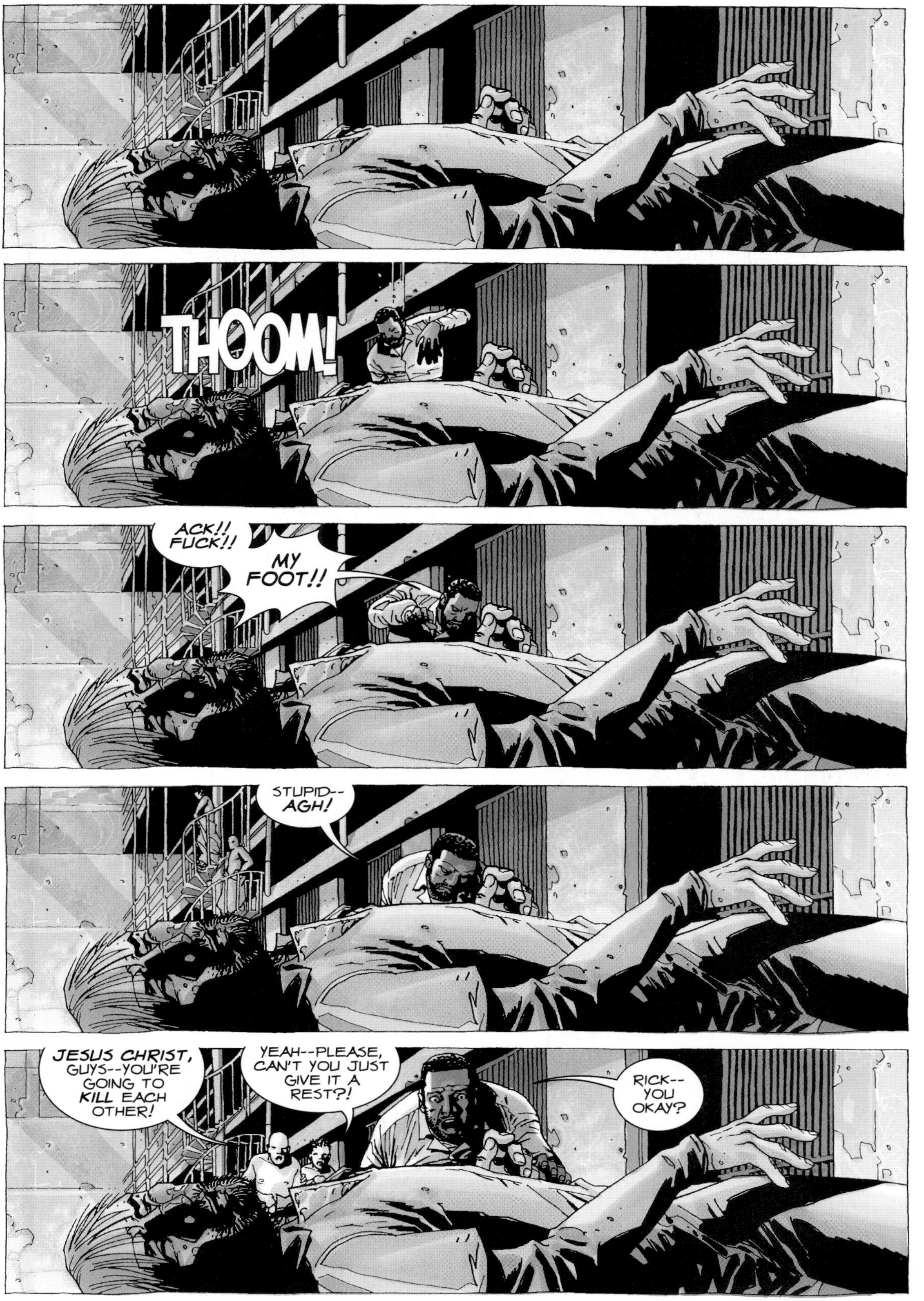
THOOM!
ACK!! FUCK!!
MY FOOT!!
STUPID-- AGH!
JESUS CHRIST, GUYS--YOU'RE GOING TO KILL EACH OTHER!
YEAH--PLEASE, CAN'T YOU JUST GIVE IT A REST?!
RICK-- YOU OKAY?

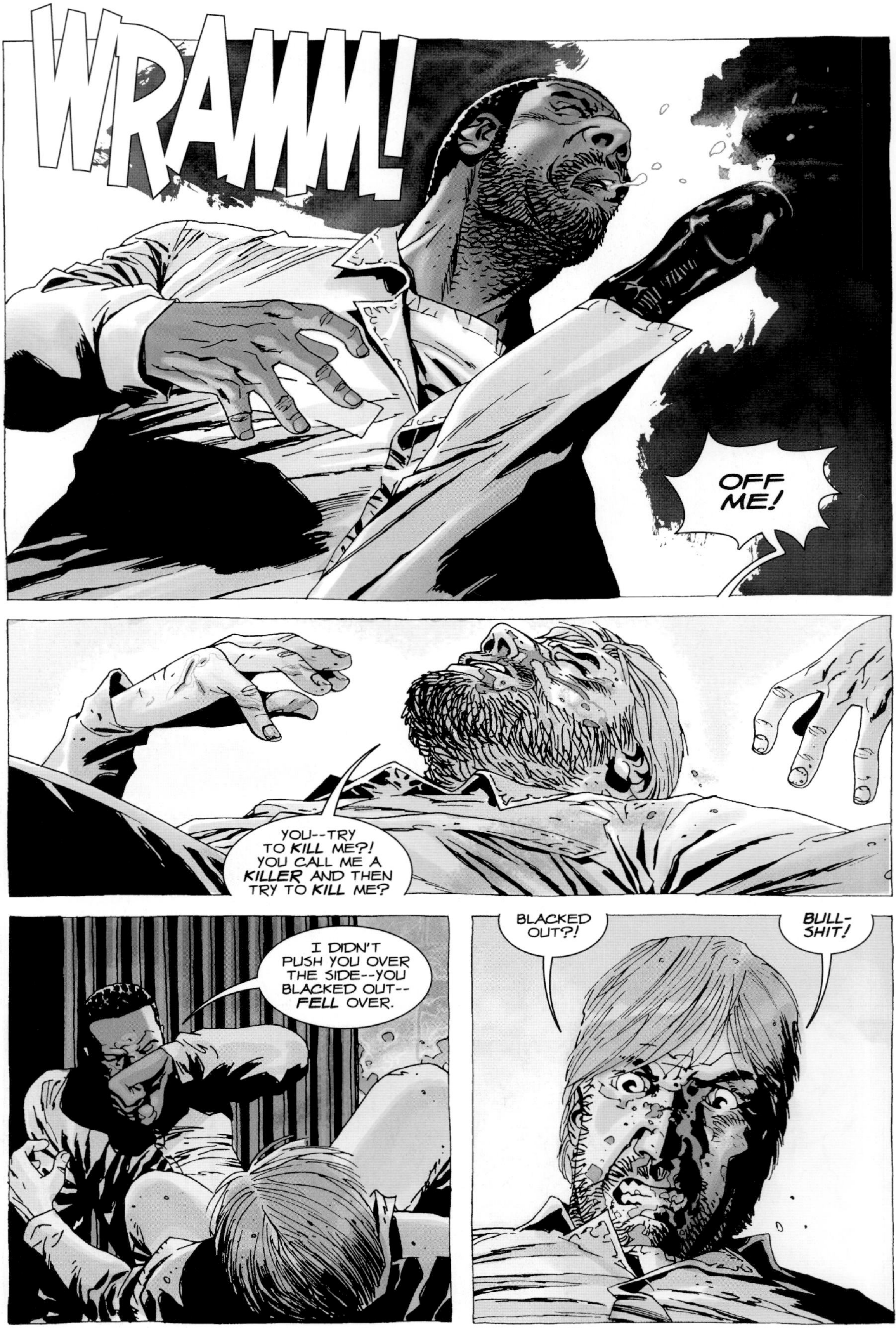
WRAMM!
OFF ME!
YOU--TRY TO KILL ME?! YOU CALL ME A KILLER AND THEN TRY TO KILL ME?
I DIDN'T PUSH YOU OVER THE SIDE--YOU BLACKED OUT-- FELL OVER.
BLACKED OUT?!
BULL-SHIT!

FINE--YOU DON'T BELIEVE ME? HIT ME AGAIN. GO AHEAD!
I CAN'T.
FUCK THIS.
DON'T EVEN THINK ABOUT GETTING UP--I'M NOT THROUGH WITH YOU YET.
GUYS...
JESUS.
RICK!

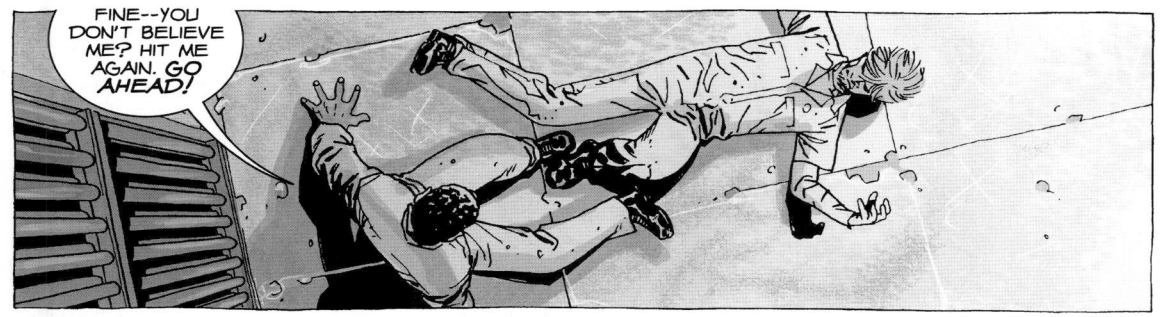

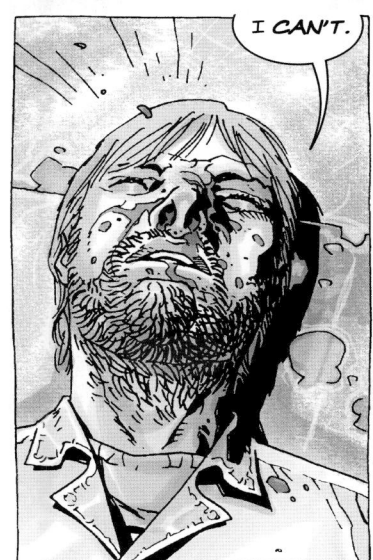

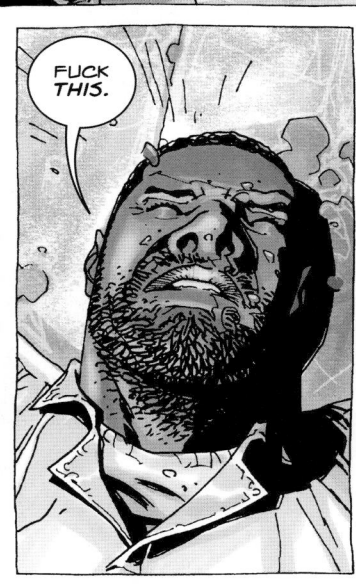

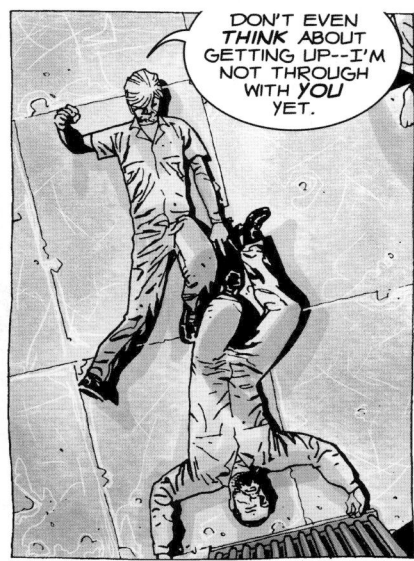

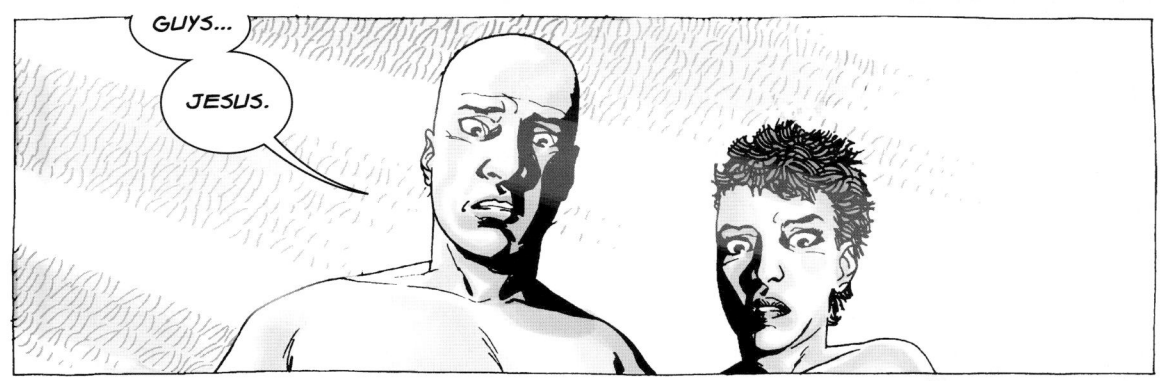

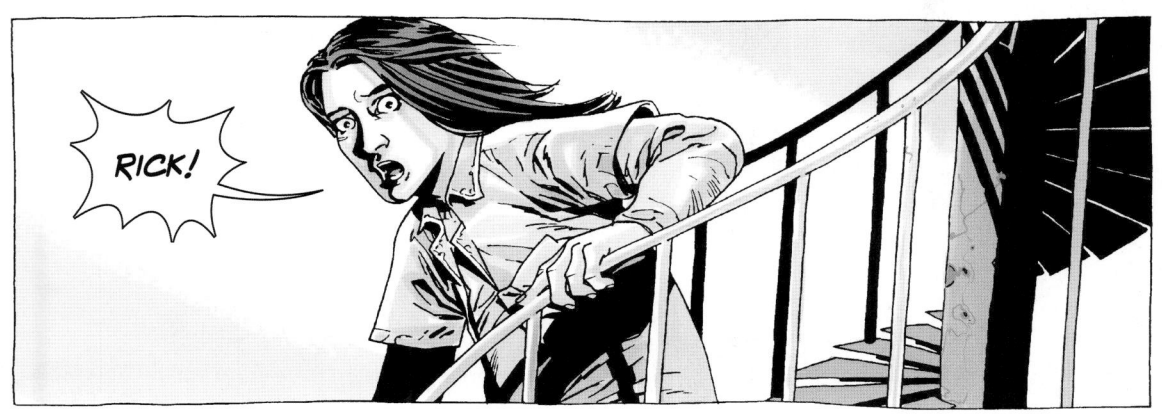

WHAT HAPPENED?

THEY HAD A FIGHT.

OH MY GOD-- IS ANYTHING BROKEN?

I DON'T KNOW.

FEELS LIKE EVERYTHING IS.

CAN YOU STAND? WE NEED TO GET YOU TO A BED.

DON'T KNOW.

SHIT!

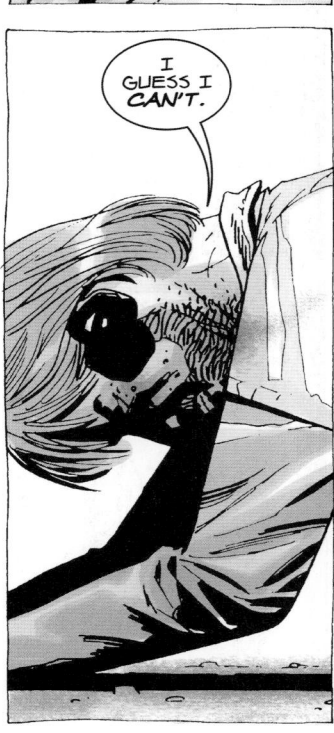

I GUESS I CAN'T.

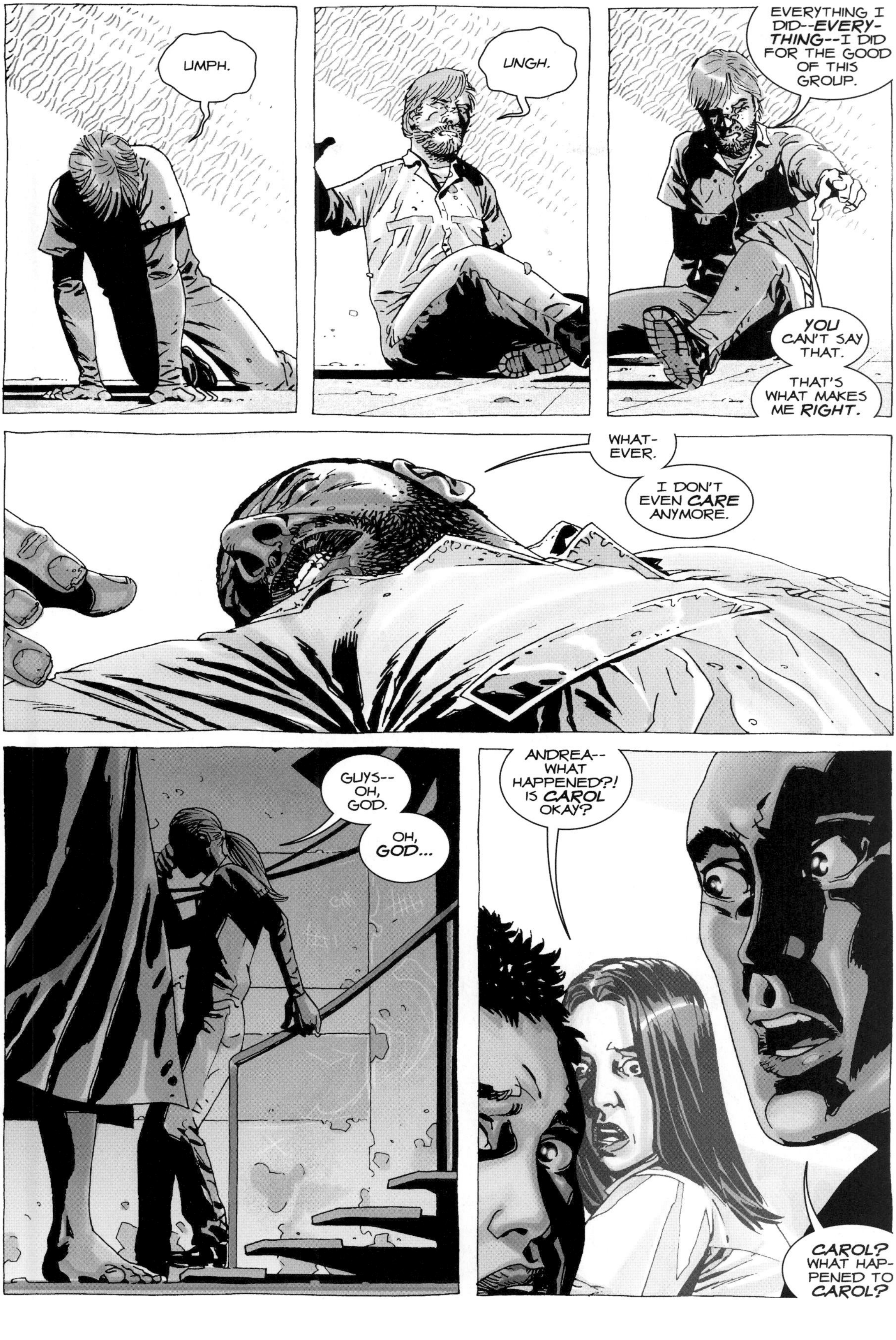
UMPH.
UNGH.
EVERYTHING I DID--EVERY-THING--I DID FOR THE GOOD OF THIS GROUP.
YOU CAN'T SAY THAT.
THAT'S WHAT MAKES ME RIGHT.
WHAT-EVER.
I DON'T EVEN CARE ANYMORE.
GUYS--OH, GOD.
OH, GOD...
ANDREA--WHAT HAPPENED?! IS CAROL OKAY?
CAROL? WHAT HAP-PENED TO CAROL?

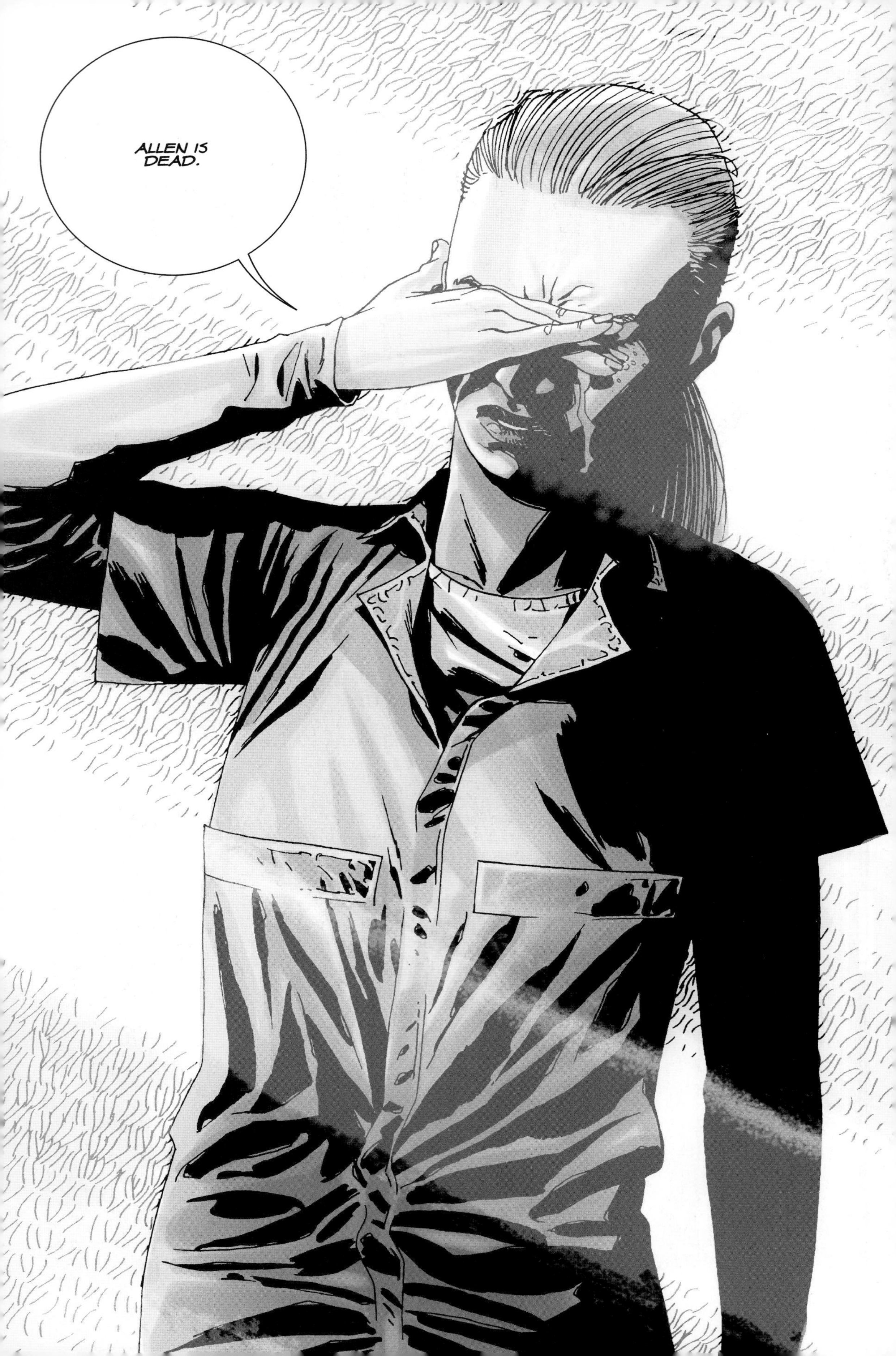
ALLEN IS DEAD.

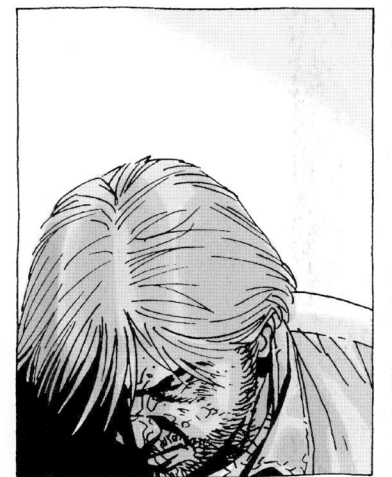

I'LL SHOOT HIM. I DON'T WANT ANYONE ELSE TO HAVE TO DO IT.

UNLESS YOU THINK I'D ENJOY THAT TOO MUCH...

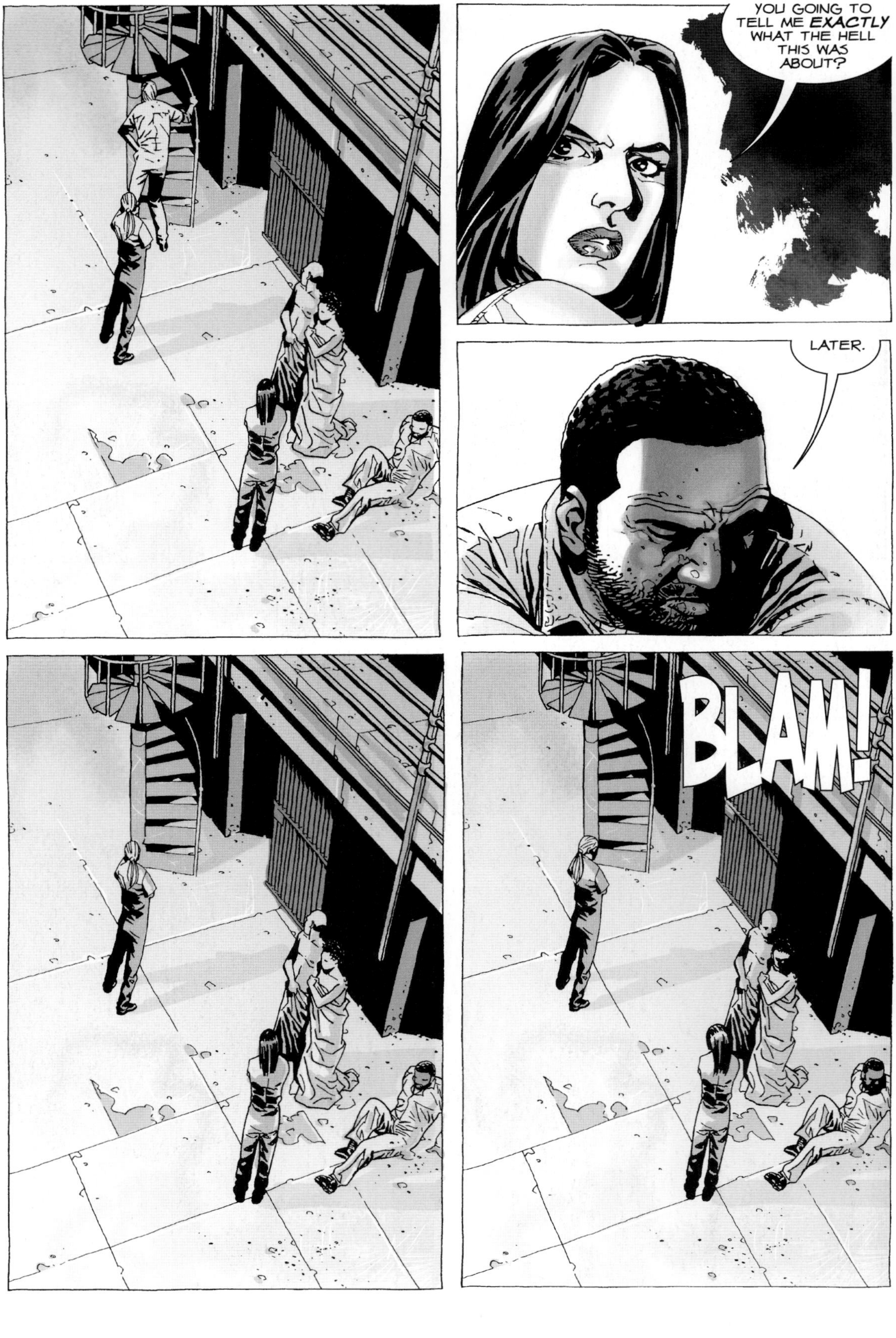
YOU GOING TO TELL ME EXACTLY WHAT THE HELL THIS WAS ABOUT?
LATER.
BLAM!

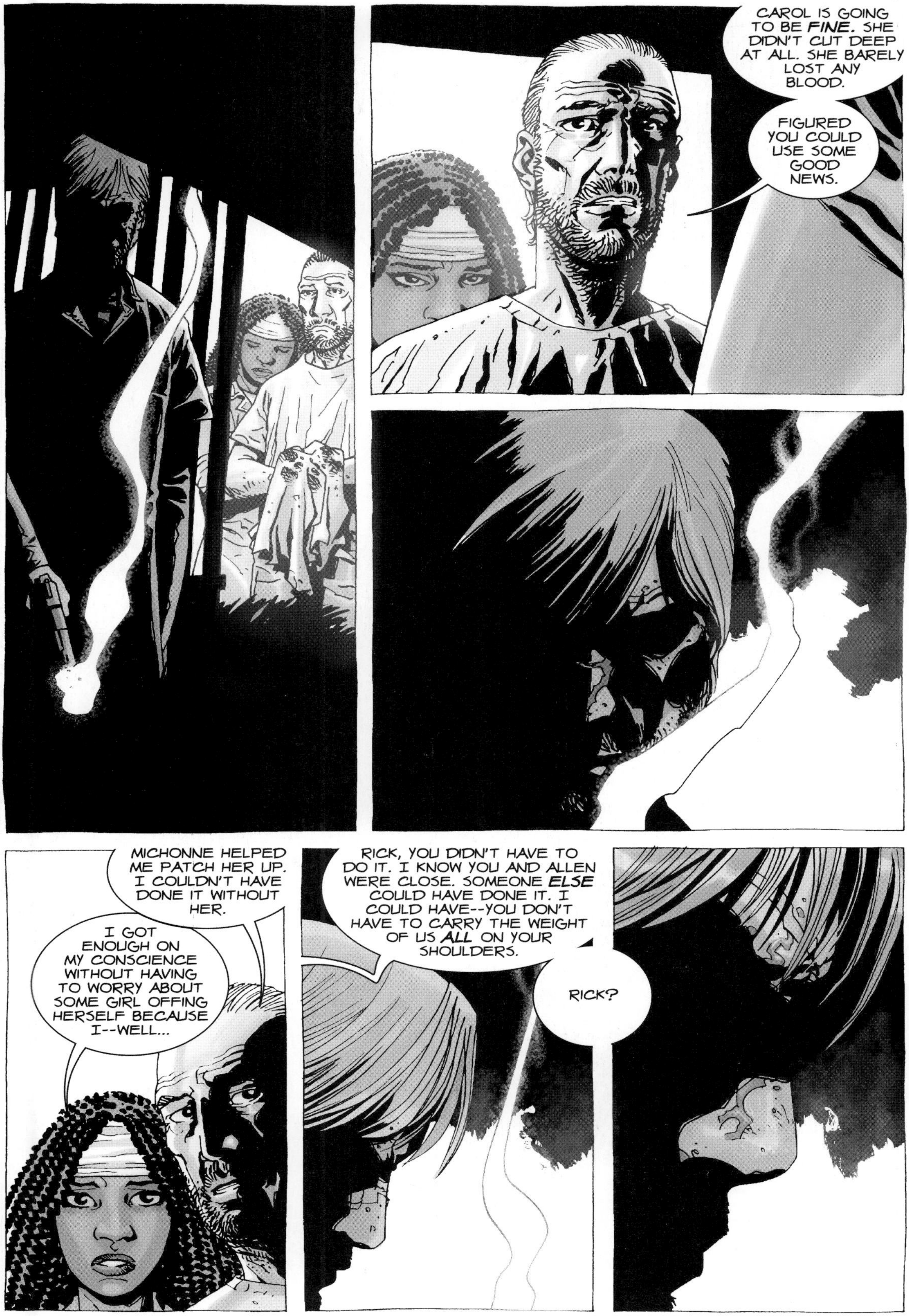
CAROL IS GOING TO BE FINE. SHE DIDN'T CUT DEEP AT ALL. SHE BARELY LOST ANY BLOOD.
FIGURED YOU COULD USE SOME GOOD NEWS.
MICHONNE HELPED ME PATCH HER UP. I COULDN'T HAVE DONE IT WITHOUT HER.
I GOT ENOUGH ON MY CONSCIENCE WITHOUT HAVING TO WORRY ABOUT SOME GIRL OFFING HERSELF BECAUSE I--WELL...
RICK, YOU DIDN'T HAVE TO DO IT. I KNOW YOU AND ALLEN WERE CLOSE. SOMEONE ELSE COULD HAVE DONE IT. I COULD HAVE--YOU DON'T HAVE TO CARRY THE WEIGHT OF US ALL ON YOUR SHOULDERS.
RICK?

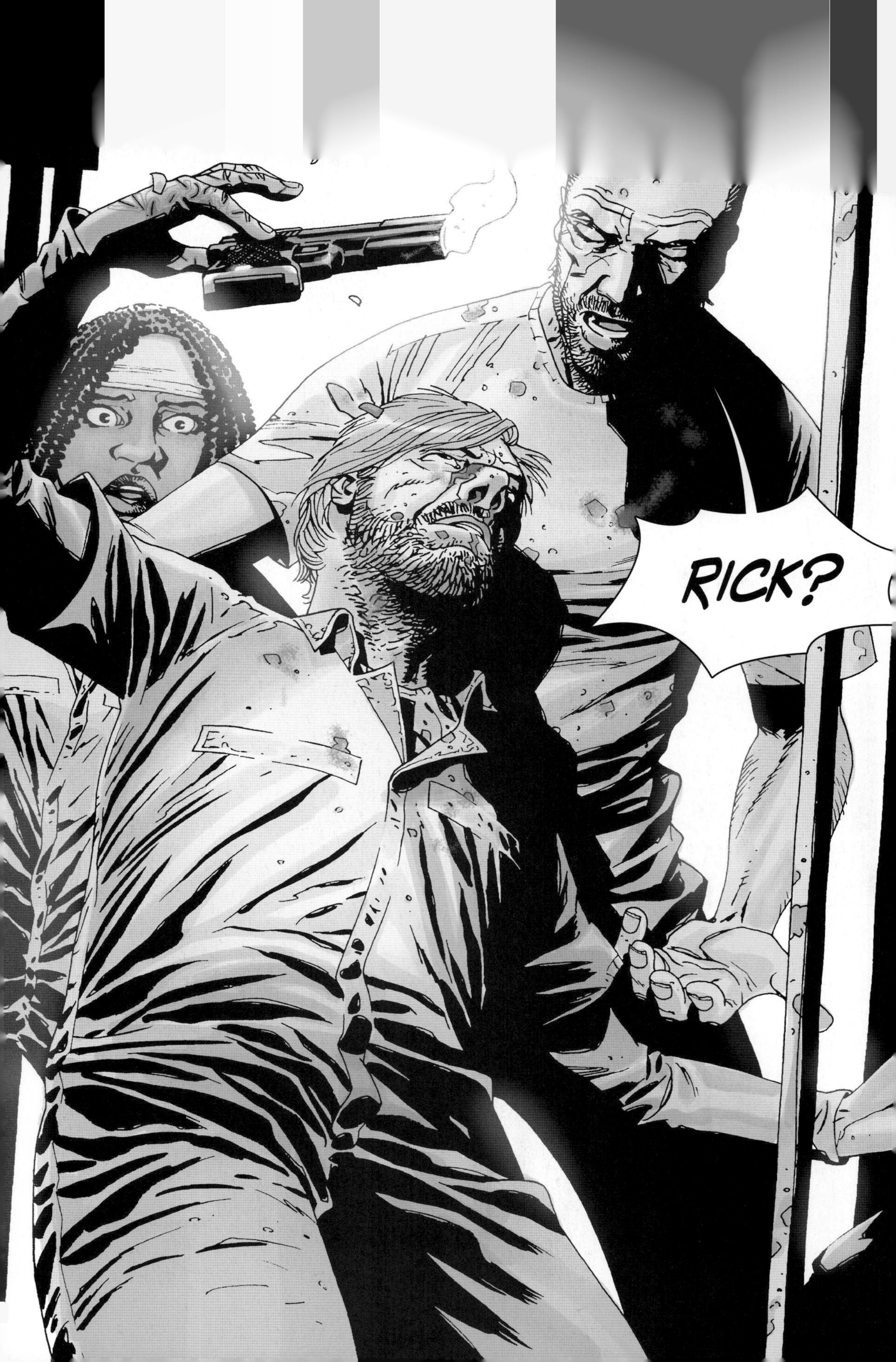
RICK?

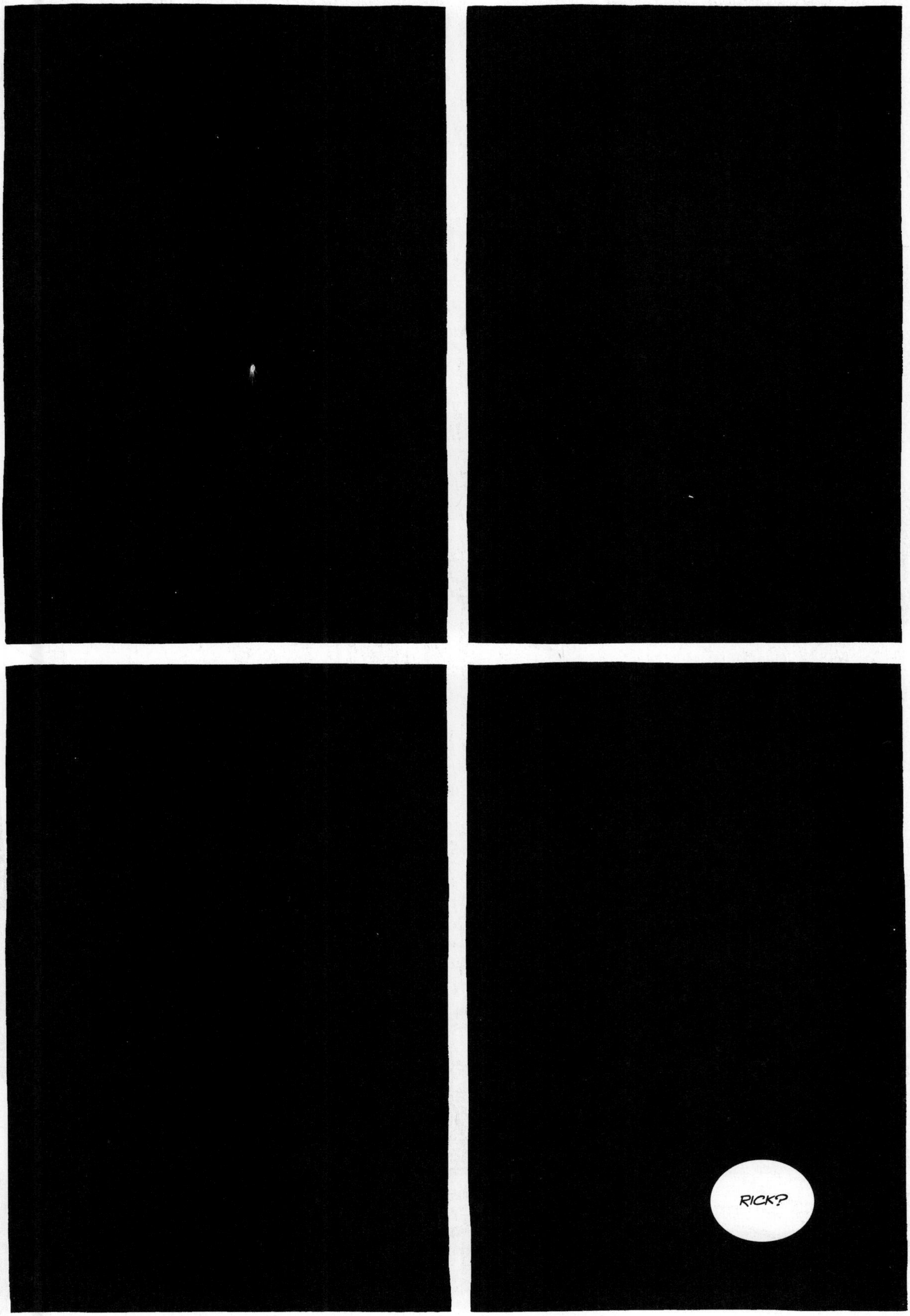
RICK?

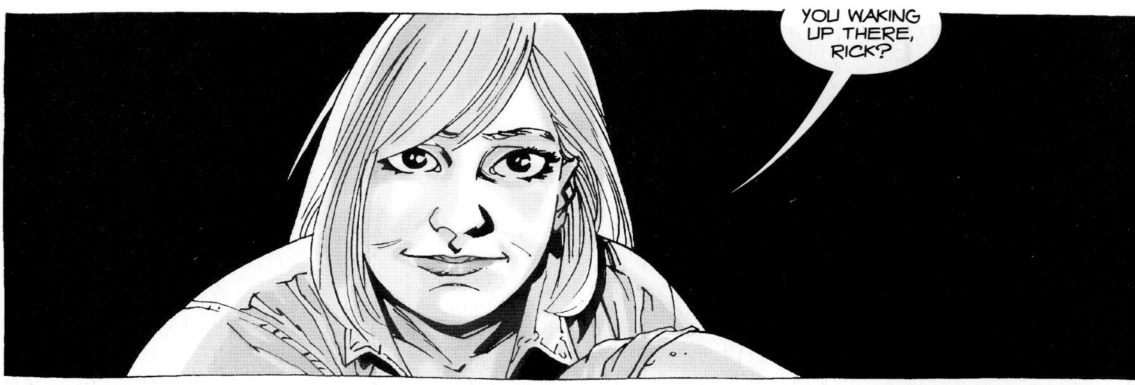
YOU WAKING UP THERE, RICK?

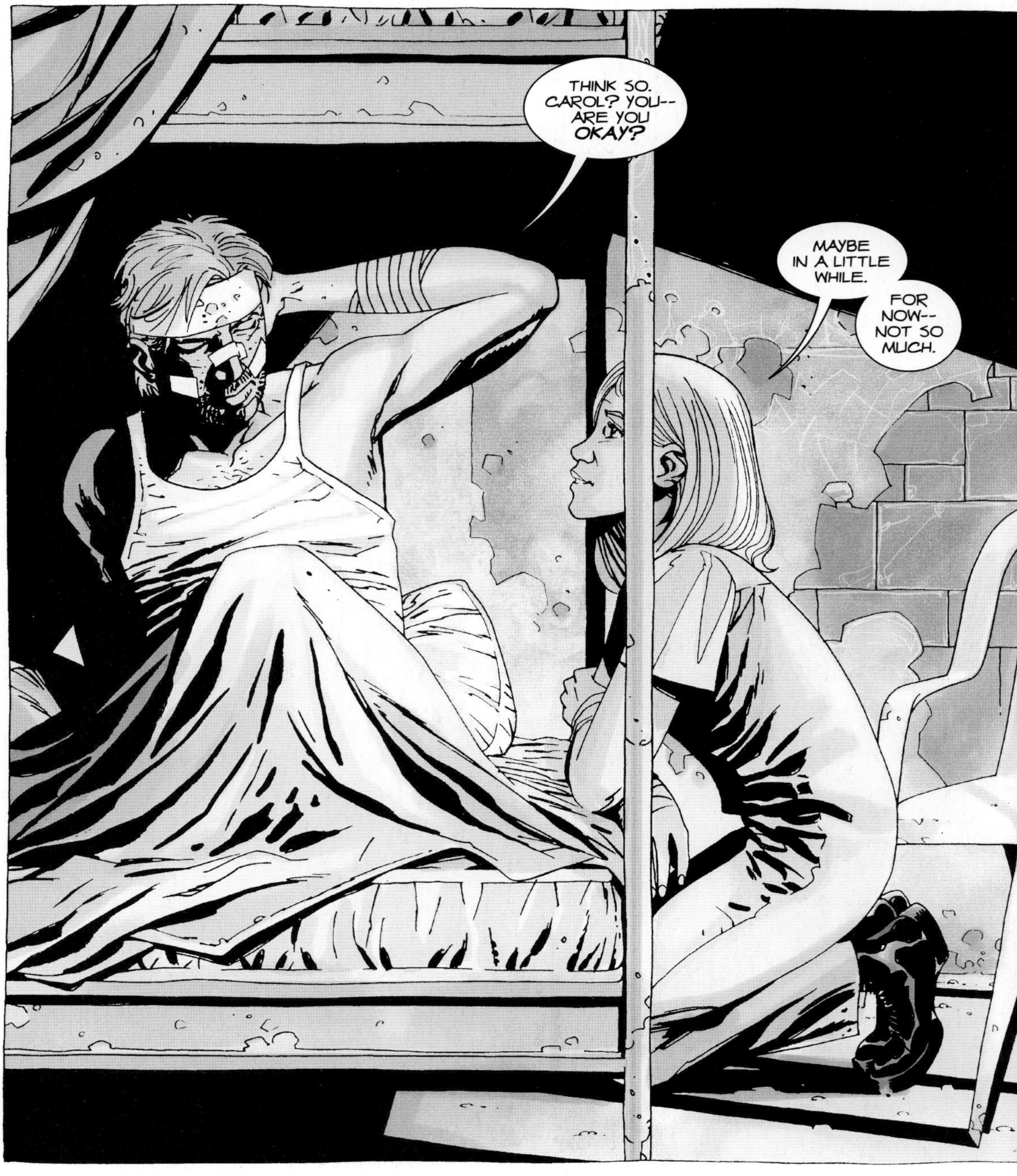
THINK SO. CAROL? YOU-- ARE YOU OKAY?
MAYBE IN A LITTLE WHILE.
FOR NOW-- NOT SO MUCH.

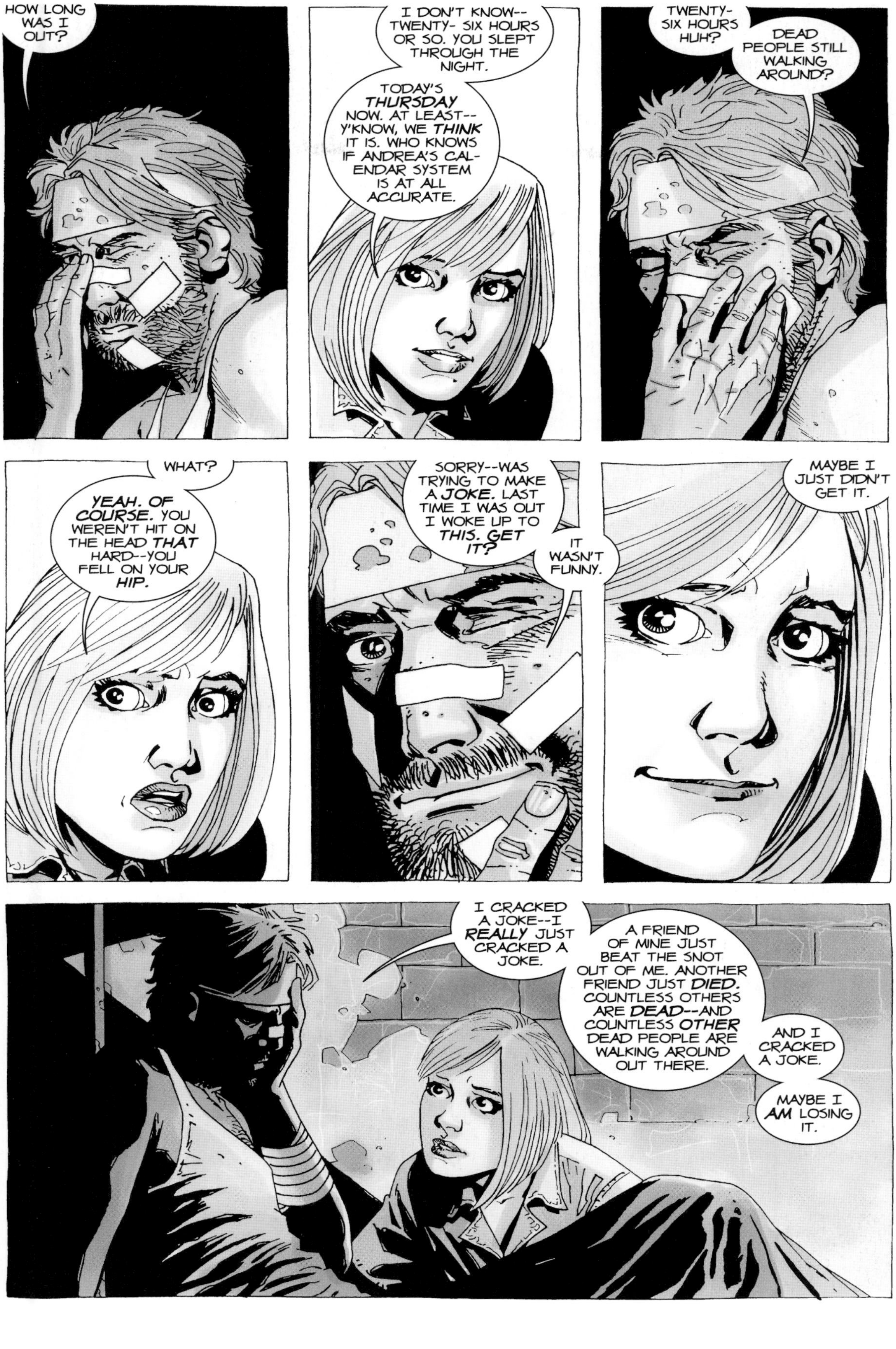

HOW LONG WAS I OUT?
I DON'T KNOW-- TWENTY- SIX HOURS OR SO. YOU SLEPT THROUGH THE NIGHT.
TODAY'S THURSDAY NOW. AT LEAST-- Y'KNOW, WE THINK IT IS. WHO KNOWS IF ANDREA'S CAL- ENDAR SYSTEM IS AT ALL ACCURATE.
TWENTY- SIX HOURS HUH?
DEAD PEOPLE STILL WALKING AROUND?
WHAT?
YEAH. OF COURSE. YOU WEREN'T HIT ON THE HEAD THAT HARD--YOU FELL ON YOUR HIP.
SORRY--WAS TRYING TO MAKE A JOKE. LAST TIME I WAS OUT I WOKE UP TO THIS. GET IT?
IT WASN'T FUNNY.
MAYBE I JUST DIDN'T GET IT.
I CRACKED A JOKE--I REALLY JUST CRACKED A JOKE.
A FRIEND OF MINE JUST BEAT THE SNOT OUT OF ME. ANOTHER FRIEND JUST DIED. COUNTLESS OTHERS ARE DEAD--AND COUNTLESS OTHER DEAD PEOPLE ARE WALKING AROUND OUT THERE.
AND I CRACKED A JOKE.
MAYBE I AM LOSING IT.

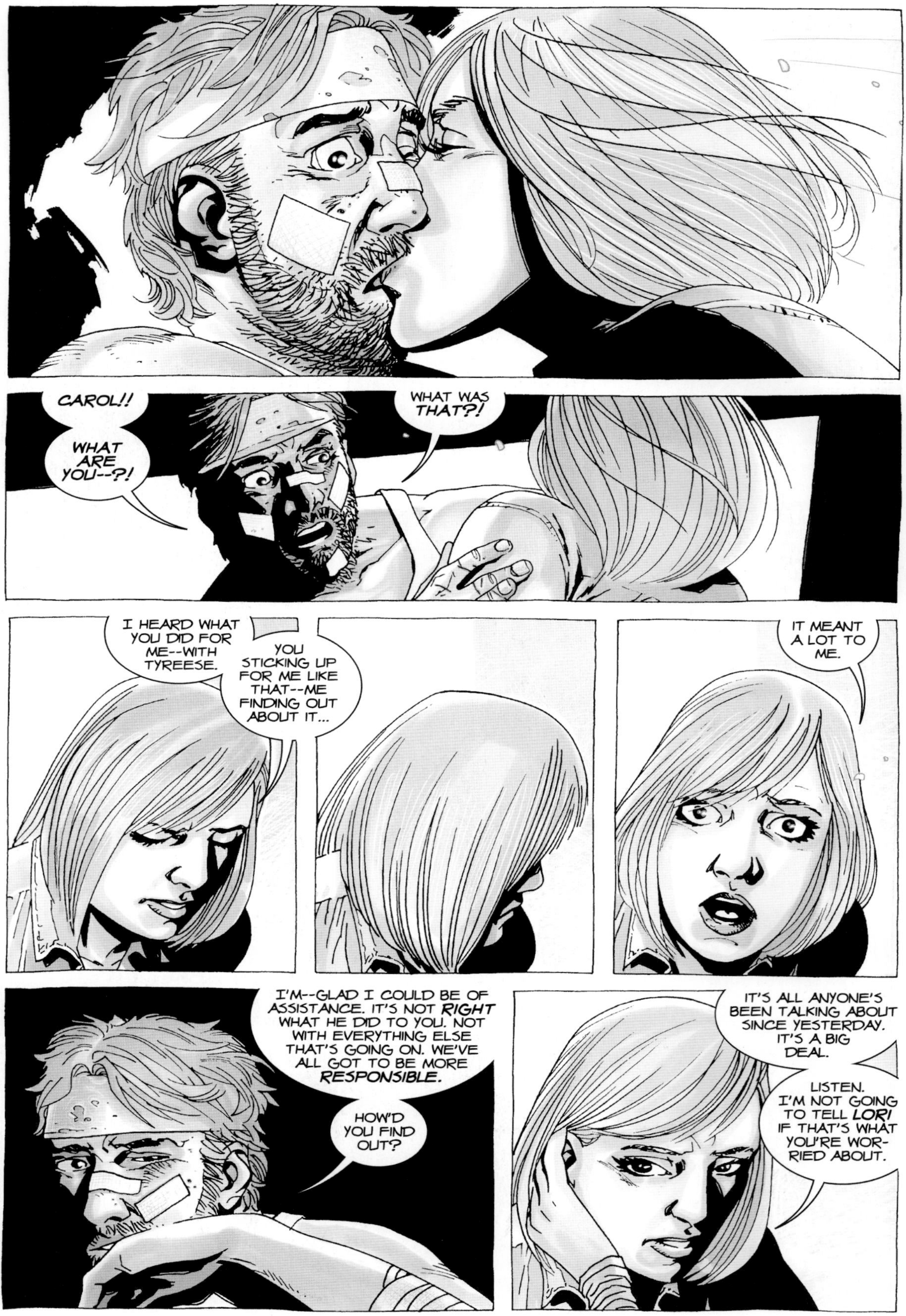
CAROL!!
WHAT ARE YOU--?!
WHAT WAS THAT?!
I HEARD WHAT YOU DID FOR ME--WITH TYREESE.
YOU STICKING UP FOR ME LIKE THAT--ME FINDING OUT ABOUT IT...
IT MEANT A LOT TO ME.
I'M--GLAD I COULD BE OF ASSISTANCE. IT'S NOT RIGHT WHAT HE DID TO YOU. NOT WITH EVERYTHING ELSE THAT'S GOING ON. WE'VE ALL GOT TO BE MORE RESPONSIBLE.
HOW'D YOU FIND OUT?
IT'S ALL ANYONE'S BEEN TALKING ABOUT SINCE YESTERDAY. IT'S A BIG DEAL.
LISTEN. I'M NOT GOING TO TELL LORI IF THAT'S WHAT YOU'RE WORRIED ABOUT.

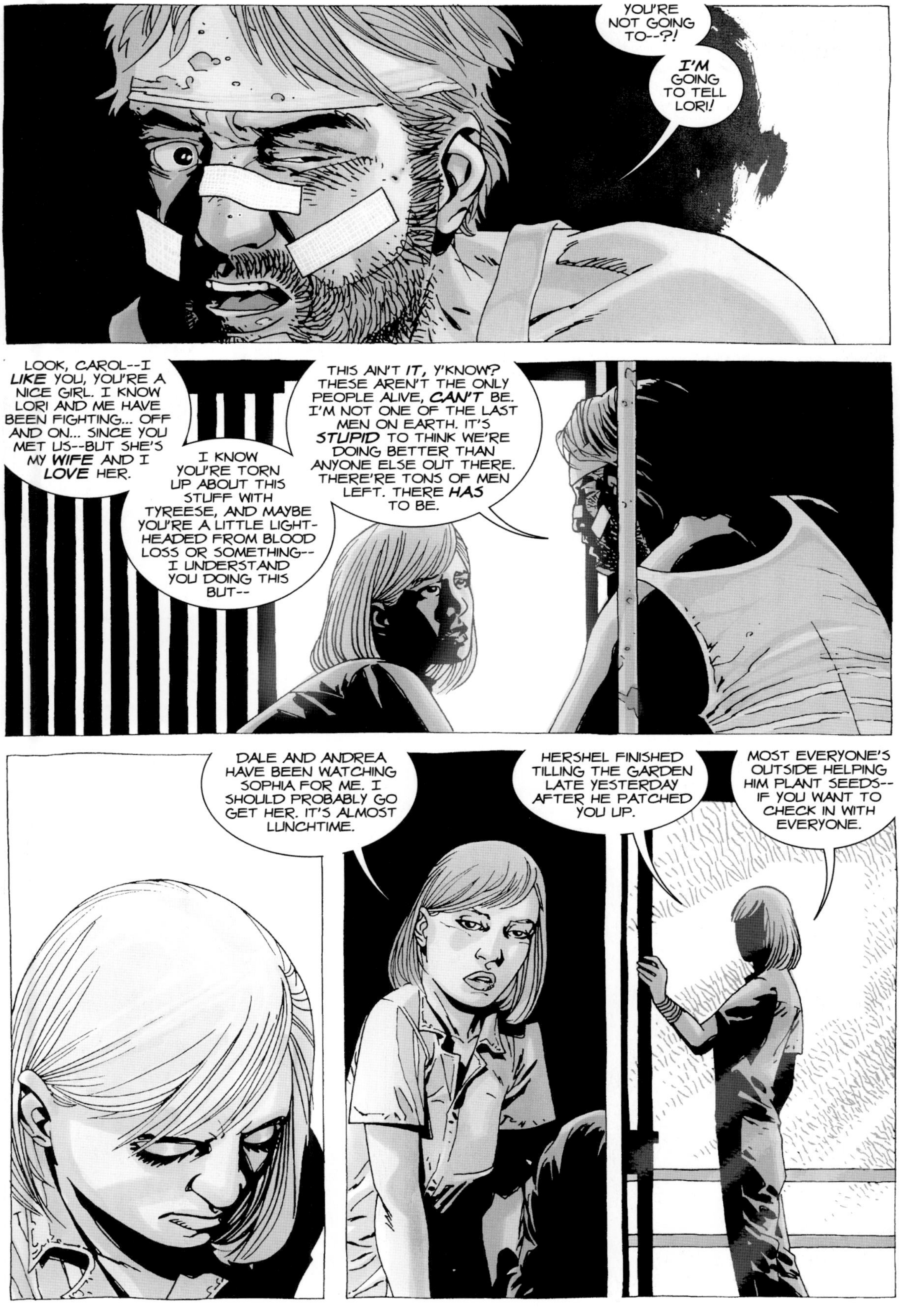
YOU'RE NOT GOING TO--?!
I'M GOING TO TELL LORI!
LOOK, CAROL--I LIKE YOU, YOU'RE A NICE GIRL. I KNOW LORI AND ME HAVE BEEN FIGHTING... OFF AND ON... SINCE YOU MET US--BUT SHE'S MY WIFE AND I LOVE HER.
I KNOW YOU'RE TORN UP ABOUT THIS STUFF WITH TYREESE, AND MAYBE YOU'RE A LITTLE LIGHT-HEADED FROM BLOOD LOSS OR SOMETHING-- I UNDERSTAND YOU DOING THIS BUT--
THIS AIN'T IT, Y'KNOW? THESE AREN'T THE ONLY PEOPLE ALIVE, CAN'T BE. I'M NOT ONE OF THE LAST MEN ON EARTH. IT'S STUPID TO THINK WE'RE DOING BETTER THAN ANYONE ELSE OUT THERE. THERE'RE TONS OF MEN LEFT. THERE HAS TO BE.
DALE AND ANDREA HAVE BEEN WATCHING SOPHIA FOR ME. I SHOULD PROBABLY GO GET HER. IT'S ALMOST LUNCHTIME.
HERSHEL FINISHED TILLING THE GARDEN LATE YESTERDAY AFTER HE PATCHED YOU UP.
MOST EVERYONE'S OUTSIDE HELPING HIM PLANT SEEDS-- IF YOU WANT TO CHECK IN WITH EVERYONE.

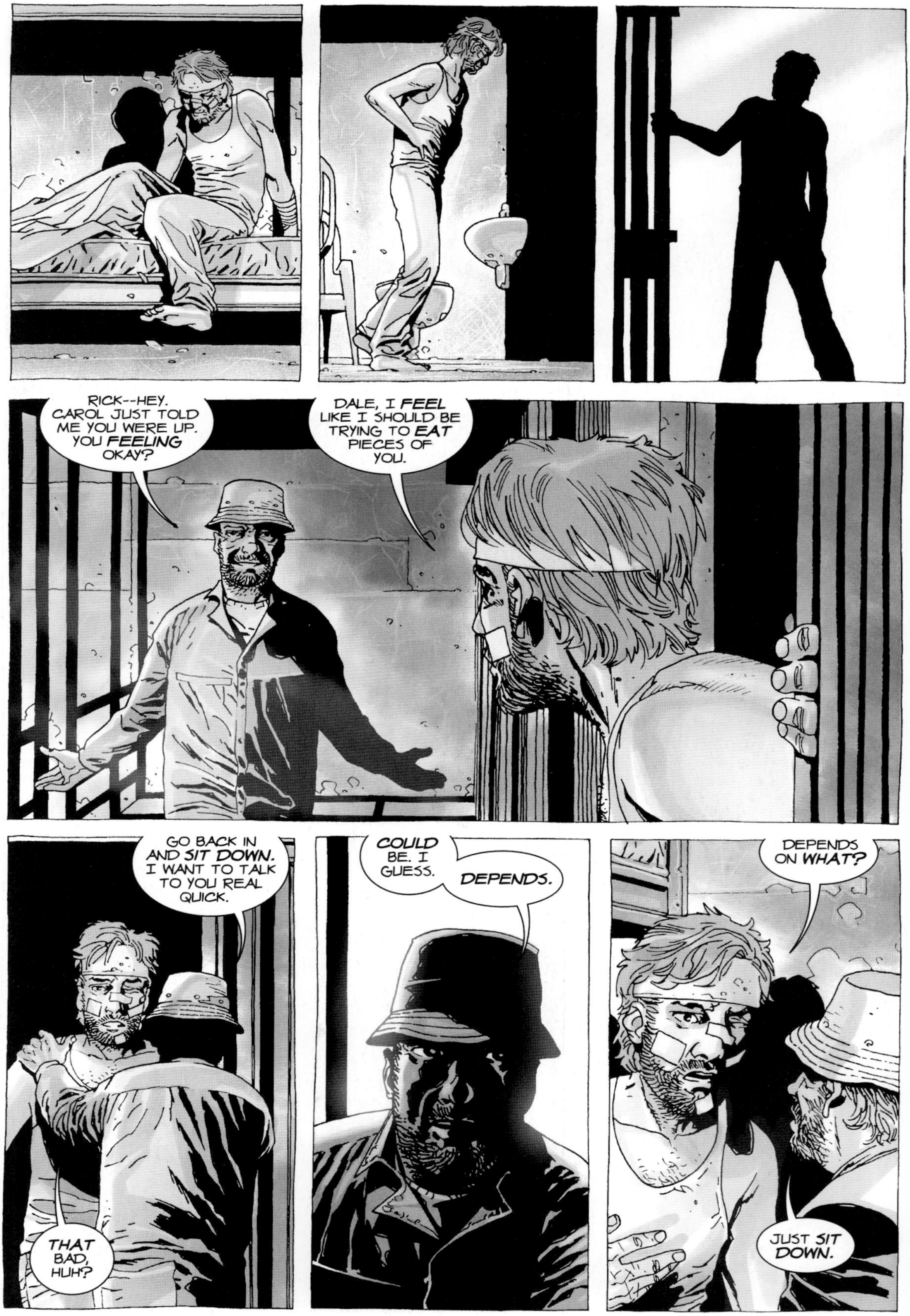
RICK--HEY. CAROL JUST TOLD ME YOU WERE UP. YOU FEELING OKAY?
DALE, I FEEL LIKE I SHOULD BE TRYING TO EAT PIECES OF YOU.
GO BACK IN AND SIT DOWN. I WANT TO TALK TO YOU REAL QUICK.
THAT BAD, HUH?
COULD BE. I GUESS.
DEPENDS.
DEPENDS ON WHAT?
JUST SIT DOWN.

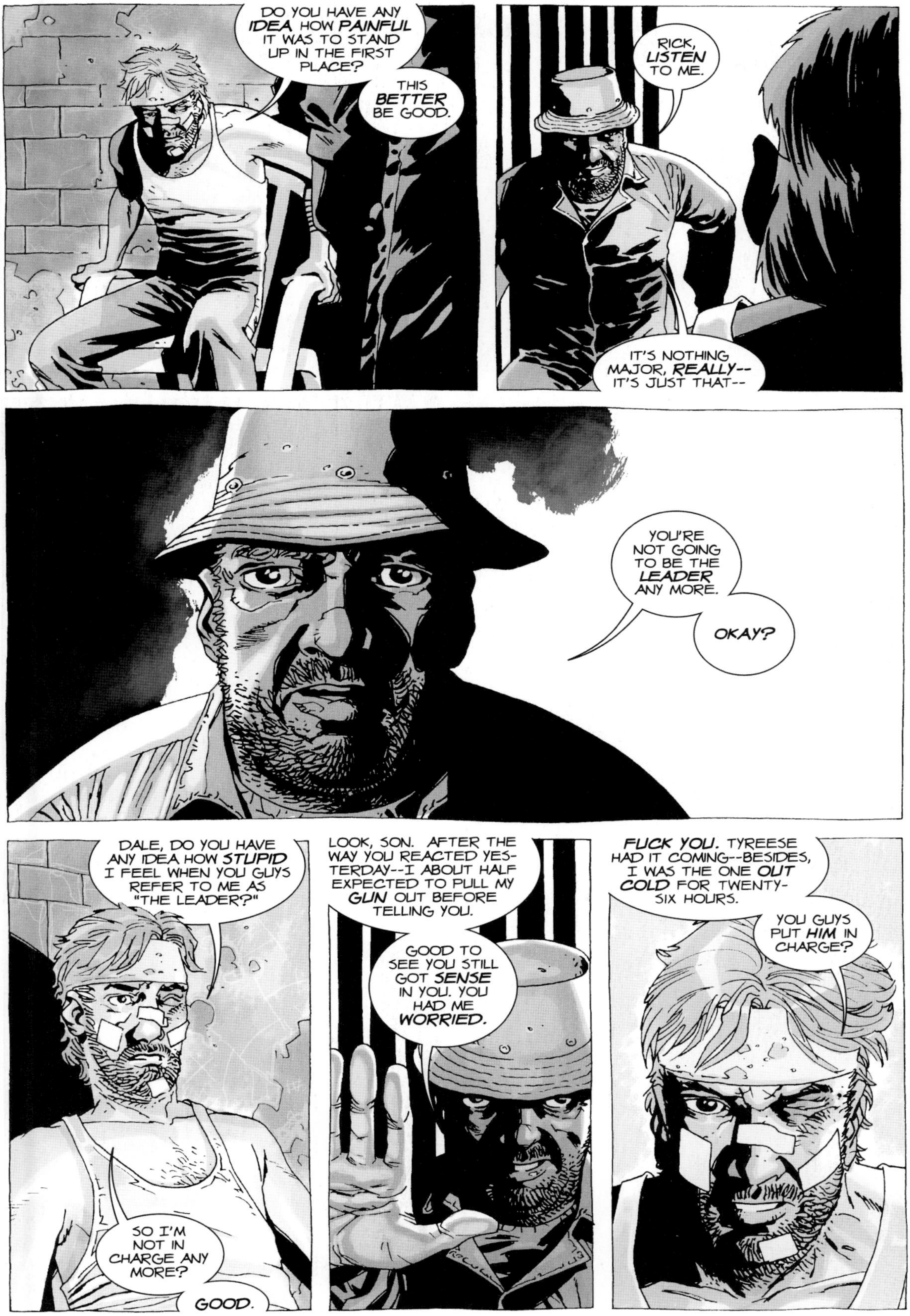
DO YOU HAVE ANY IDEA HOW PAINFUL IT WAS TO STAND UP IN THE FIRST PLACE?
THIS BETTER BE GOOD.
RICK, LISTEN TO ME.
IT'S NOTHING MAJOR, REALLY-- IT'S JUST THAT--
YOU'RE NOT GOING TO BE THE LEADER ANY MORE.
OKAY?
DALE, DO YOU HAVE ANY IDEA HOW STUPID I FEEL WHEN YOU GUYS REFER TO ME AS "THE LEADER?"
SO I'M NOT IN CHARGE ANY MORE?
GOOD.
LOOK, SON. AFTER THE WAY YOU REACTED YES-TERDAY--I ABOUT HALF EXPECTED TO PULL MY GUN OUT BEFORE TELLING YOU.
GOOD TO SEE YOU STILL GOT SENSE IN YOU. YOU HAD ME WORRIED.
FUCK YOU. TYREESE HAD IT COMING--BESIDES, I WAS THE ONE OUT COLD FOR TWENTY-SIX HOURS.
YOU GUYS PUT HIM IN CHARGE?

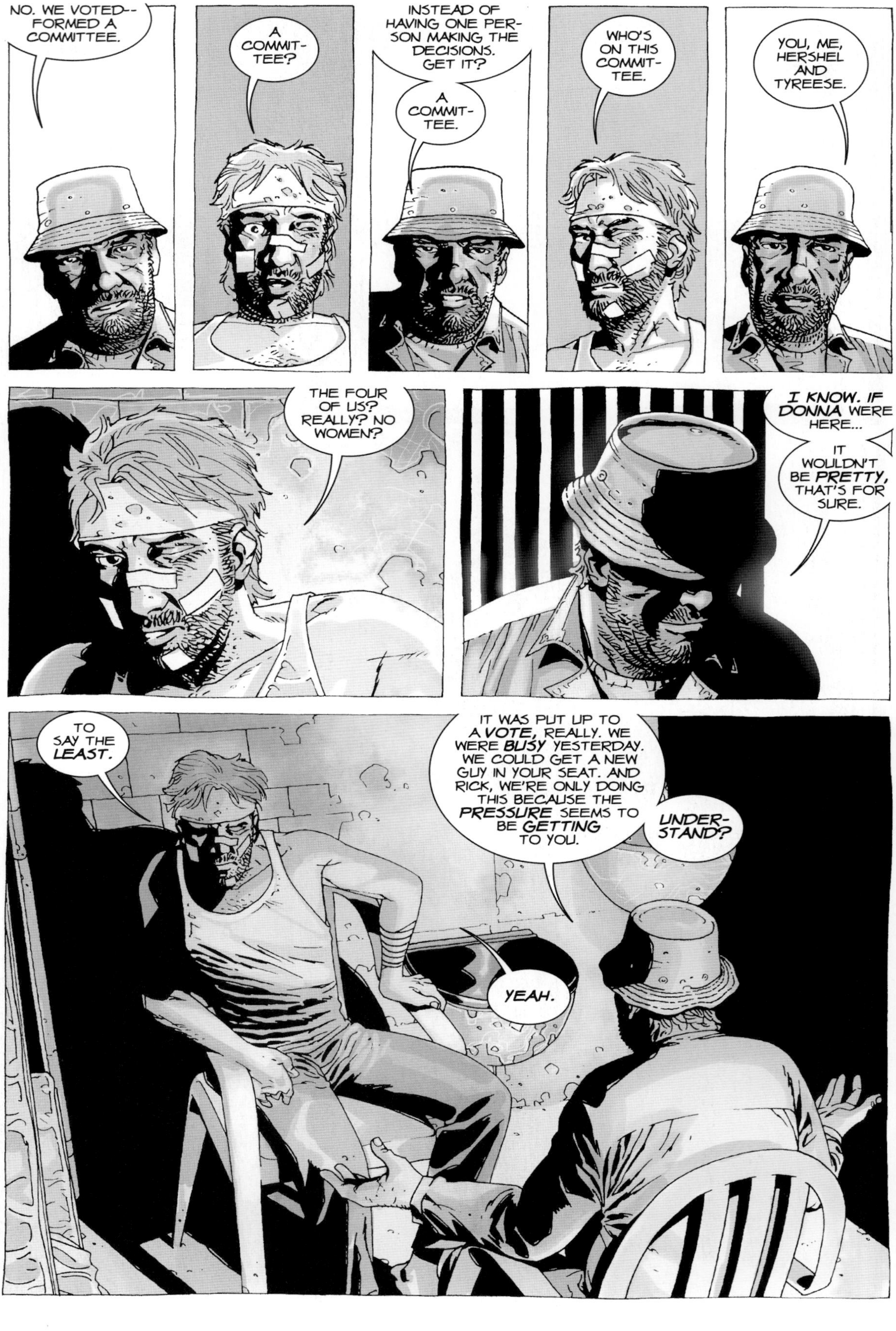
NO. WE VOTED-- FORMED A COMMITTEE.
A COMMIT-TEE?
INSTEAD OF HAVING ONE PER-SON MAKING THE DECISIONS. GET IT?
A COMMIT-TEE.
WHO'S ON THIS COMMIT-TEE.
YOU, ME, HERSHEL AND TYREESE.
THE FOUR OF US? REALLY? NO WOMEN?
I KNOW. IF DONNA WERE HERE...
IT WOULDN'T BE PRETTY, THAT'S FOR SURE.
TO SAY THE LEAST.
IT WAS PUT UP TO A VOTE, REALLY. WE WERE BUSY YESTERDAY. WE COULD GET A NEW GUY IN YOUR SEAT. AND RICK, WE'RE ONLY DOING THIS BECAUSE THE PRESSURE SEEMS TO BE GETTING TO YOU.
UNDER-STAND?
YEAH.

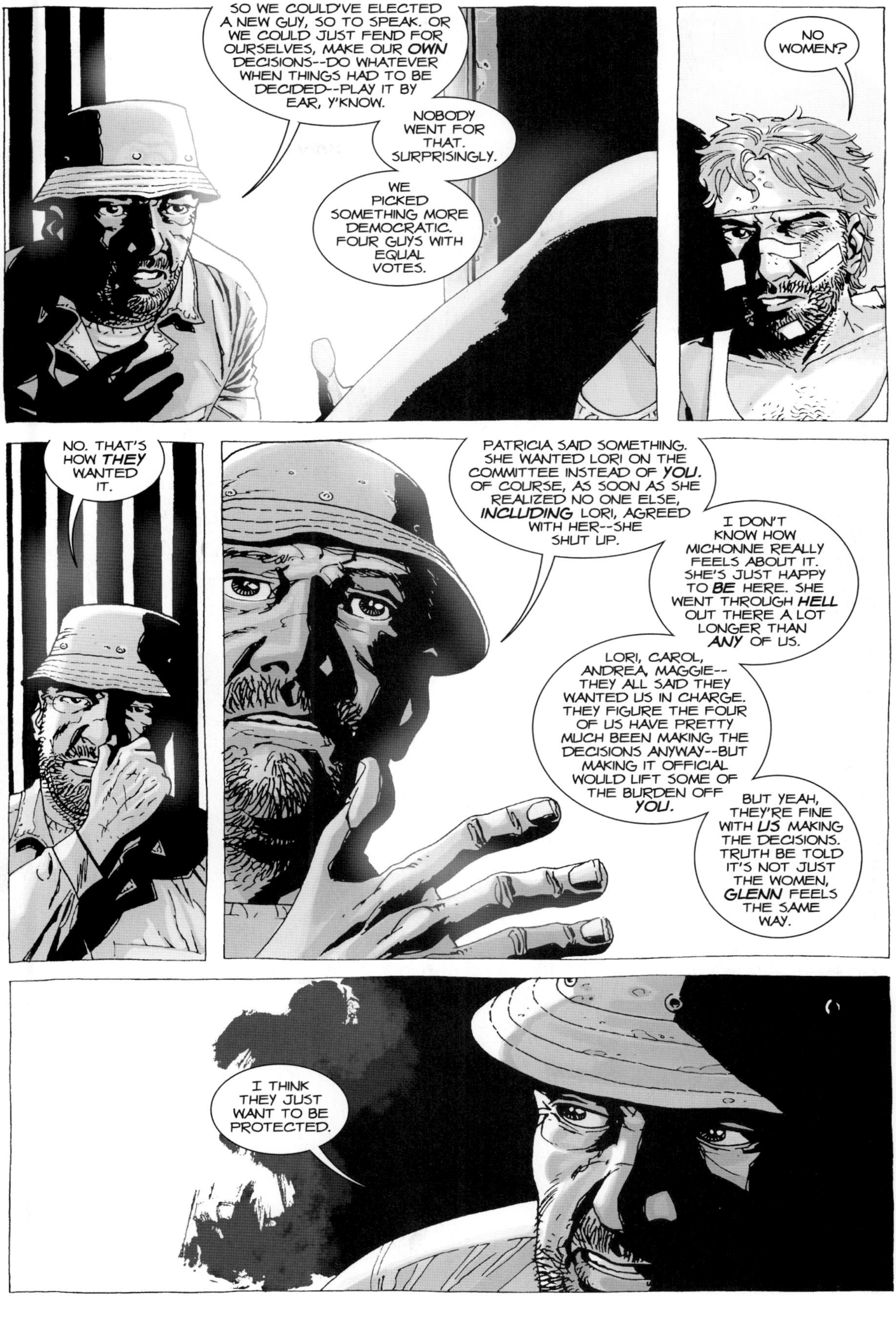
SO WE COULD'VE ELECTED A NEW GUY, SO TO SPEAK. OR WE COULD JUST FEND FOR OURSELVES, MAKE OUR OWN DECISIONS--DO WHATEVER WHEN THINGS HAD TO BE DECIDED--PLAY IT BY EAR, Y'KNOW.
NOBODY WENT FOR THAT. SURPRISINGLY.
WE PICKED SOMETHING MORE DEMOCRATIC. FOUR GUYS WITH EQUAL VOTES.
NO WOMEN?
NO. THAT'S HOW THEY WANTED IT.
PATRICIA SAID SOMETHING. SHE WANTED LORI ON THE COMMITTEE INSTEAD OF YOU. OF COURSE, AS SOON AS SHE REALIZED NO ONE ELSE, INCLUDING LORI, AGREED WITH HER--SHE SHUT UP.
I DON'T KNOW HOW MICHONNE REALLY FEELS ABOUT IT. SHE'S JUST HAPPY TO BE HERE. SHE WENT THROUGH HELL OUT THERE A LOT LONGER THAN ANY OF US.
LORI, CAROL, ANDREA, MAGGIE--THEY ALL SAID THEY WANTED US IN CHARGE. THEY FIGURE THE FOUR OF US HAVE PRETTY MUCH BEEN MAKING THE DECISIONS ANYWAY--BUT MAKING IT OFFICIAL WOULD LIFT SOME OF THE BURDEN OFF YOU.
BUT YEAH, THEY'RE FINE WITH US MAKING THE DECISIONS. TRUTH BE TOLD IT'S NOT JUST THE WOMEN, GLENN FEELS THE SAME WAY.
I THINK THEY JUST WANT TO BE PROTECTED.

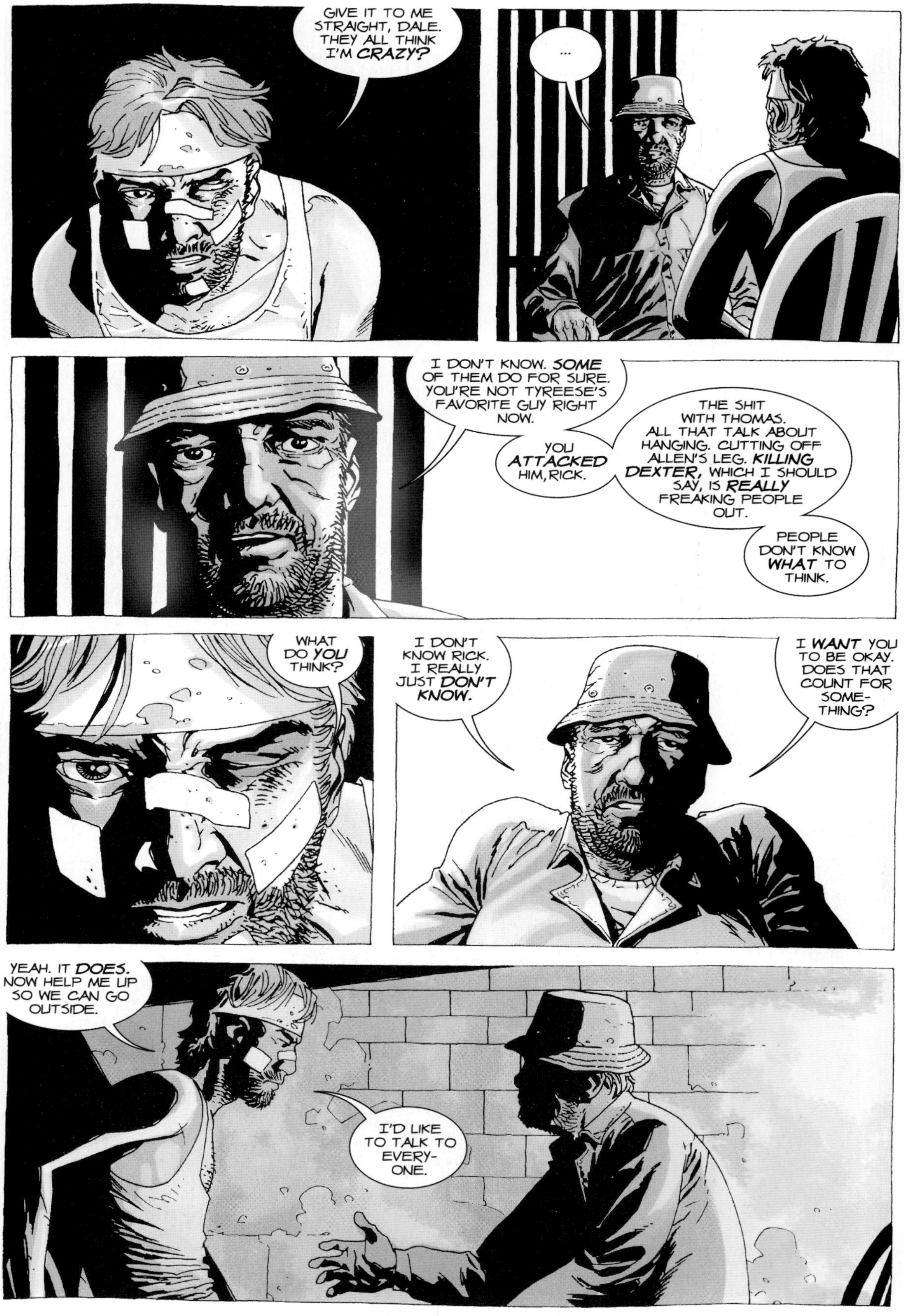
GIVE IT TO ME STRAIGHT, DALE. THEY ALL THINK I'M CRAZY?
...
I DON'T KNOW. SOME OF THEM DO FOR SURE. YOU'RE NOT TYREESE'S FAVORITE GUY RIGHT NOW.
YOU ATTACKED HIM, RICK.
THE SHIT WITH THOMAS. ALL THAT TALK ABOUT HANGING. CUTTING OFF ALLEN'S LEG. KILLING DEXTER, WHICH I SHOULD SAY, IS REALLY FREAKING PEOPLE OUT.
PEOPLE DON'T KNOW WHAT TO THINK.
WHAT DO YOU THINK?
I DON'T KNOW RICK. I REALLY JUST DON'T KNOW.
I WANT YOU TO BE OKAY. DOES THAT COUNT FOR SOME-THING?
YEAH. IT DOES. NOW HELP ME UP SO WE CAN GO OUTSIDE.
I'D LIKE TO TALK TO EVERY-ONE.

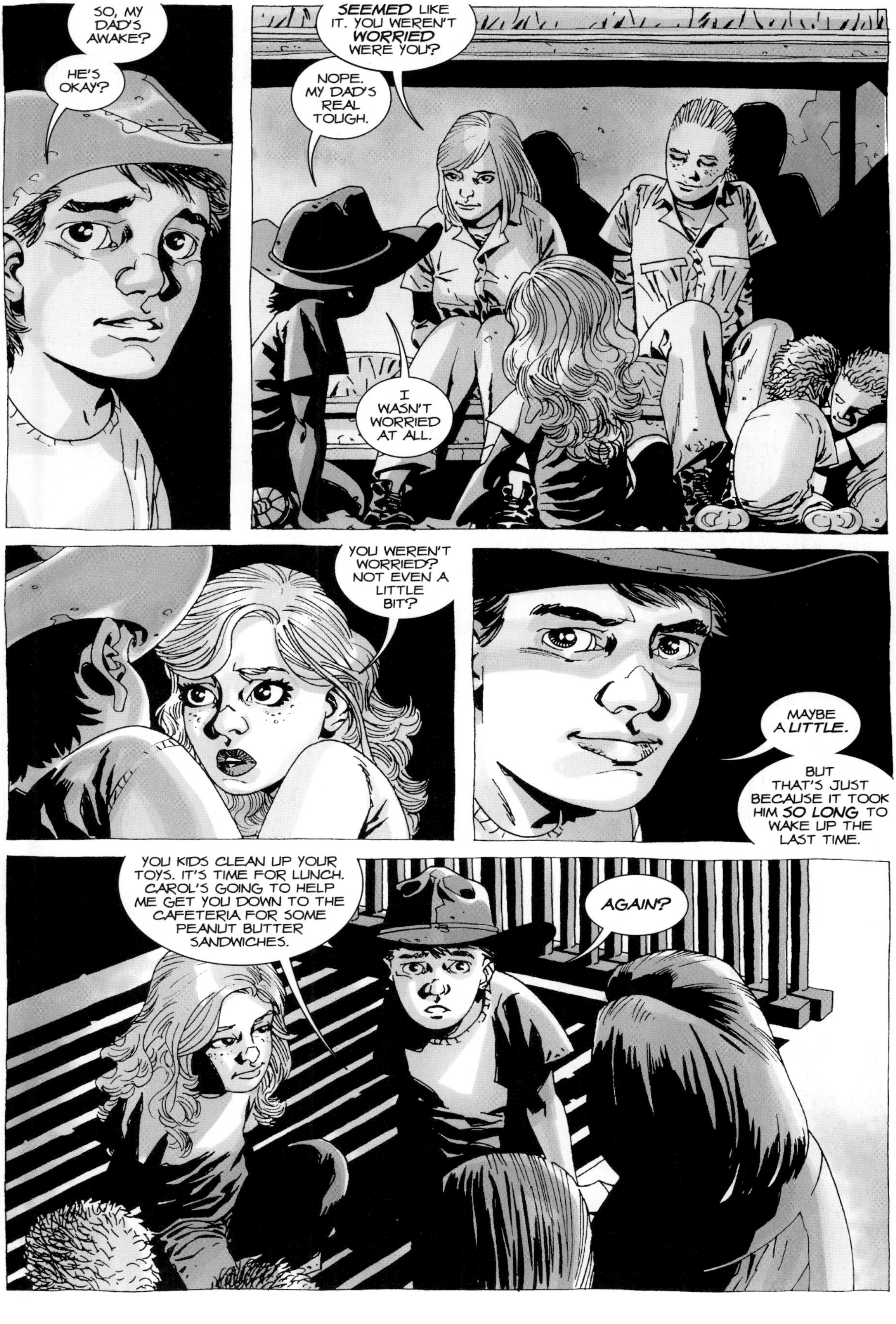
SO, MY DAD'S AWAKE?
HE'S OKAY?
SEEMED LIKE IT. YOU WEREN'T WORRIED WERE YOU?
NOPE. MY DAD'S REAL TOUGH.
I WASN'T WORRIED AT ALL.
YOU WEREN'T WORRIED? NOT EVEN A LITTLE BIT?
MAYBE A LITTLE.
BUT THAT'S JUST BECAUSE IT TOOK HIM SO LONG TO WAKE UP THE LAST TIME.
YOU KIDS CLEAN UP YOUR TOYS. IT'S TIME FOR LUNCH. CAROL'S GOING TO HELP ME GET YOU DOWN TO THE CAFETERIA FOR SOME PEANUT BUTTER SANDWICHES.
AGAIN?

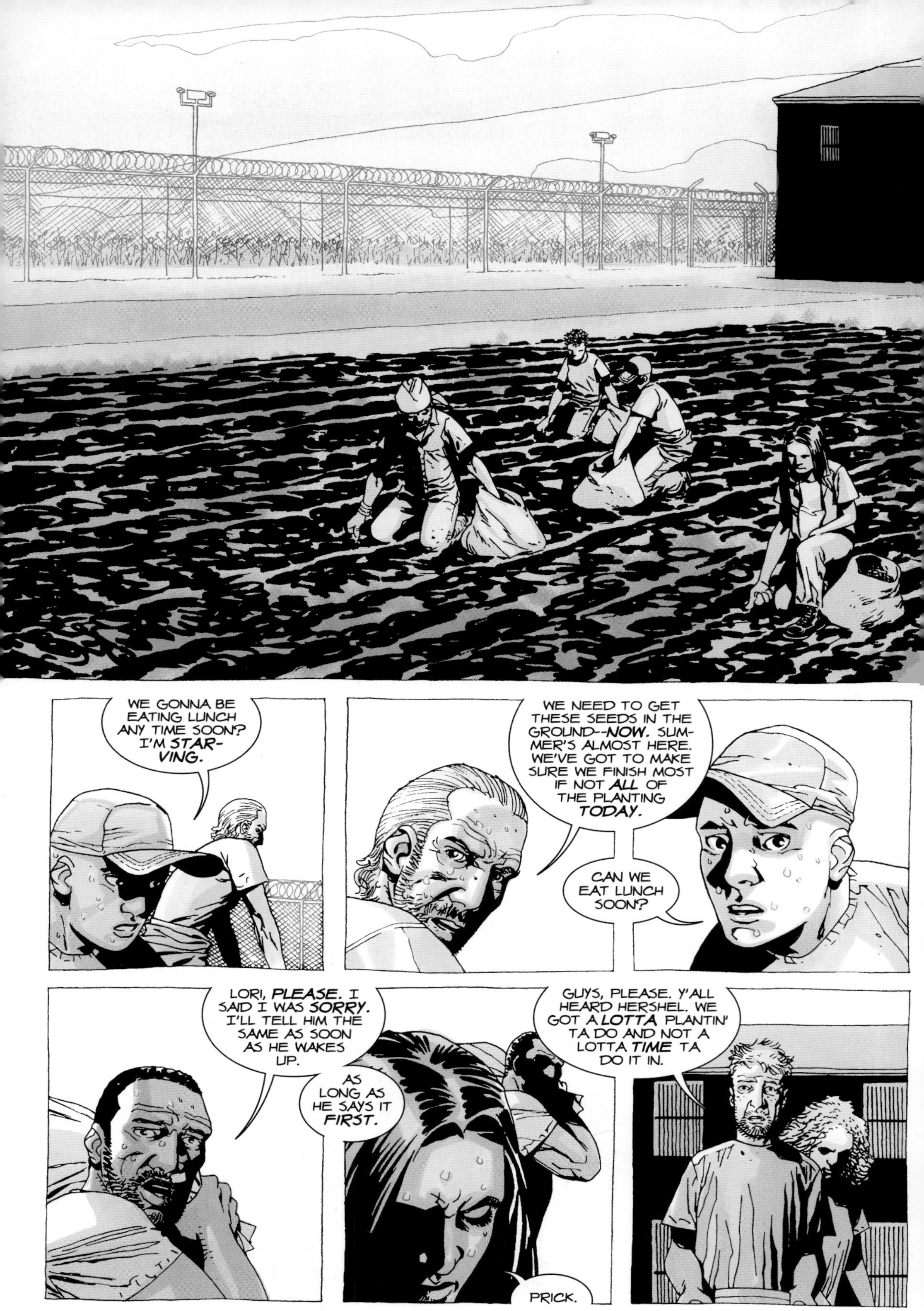
WE GONNA BE EATING LUNCH ANY TIME SOON? I'M STAR-VING.
WE NEED TO GET THESE SEEDS IN THE GROUND--NOW. SUMMER'S ALMOST HERE. WE'VE GOT TO MAKE SURE WE FINISH MOST IF NOT ALL OF THE PLANTING TODAY.
CAN WE EAT LUNCH SOON?
LORI, PLEASE. I SAID I WAS SORRY. I'LL TELL HIM THE SAME AS SOON AS HE WAKES UP.
AS LONG AS HE SAYS IT FIRST.
PRICK.
GUYS, PLEASE. Y'ALL HEARD HERSHEL. WE GOT A LOTTA PLANTIN' TA DO AND NOT A LOTTA TIME TA DO IT IN.

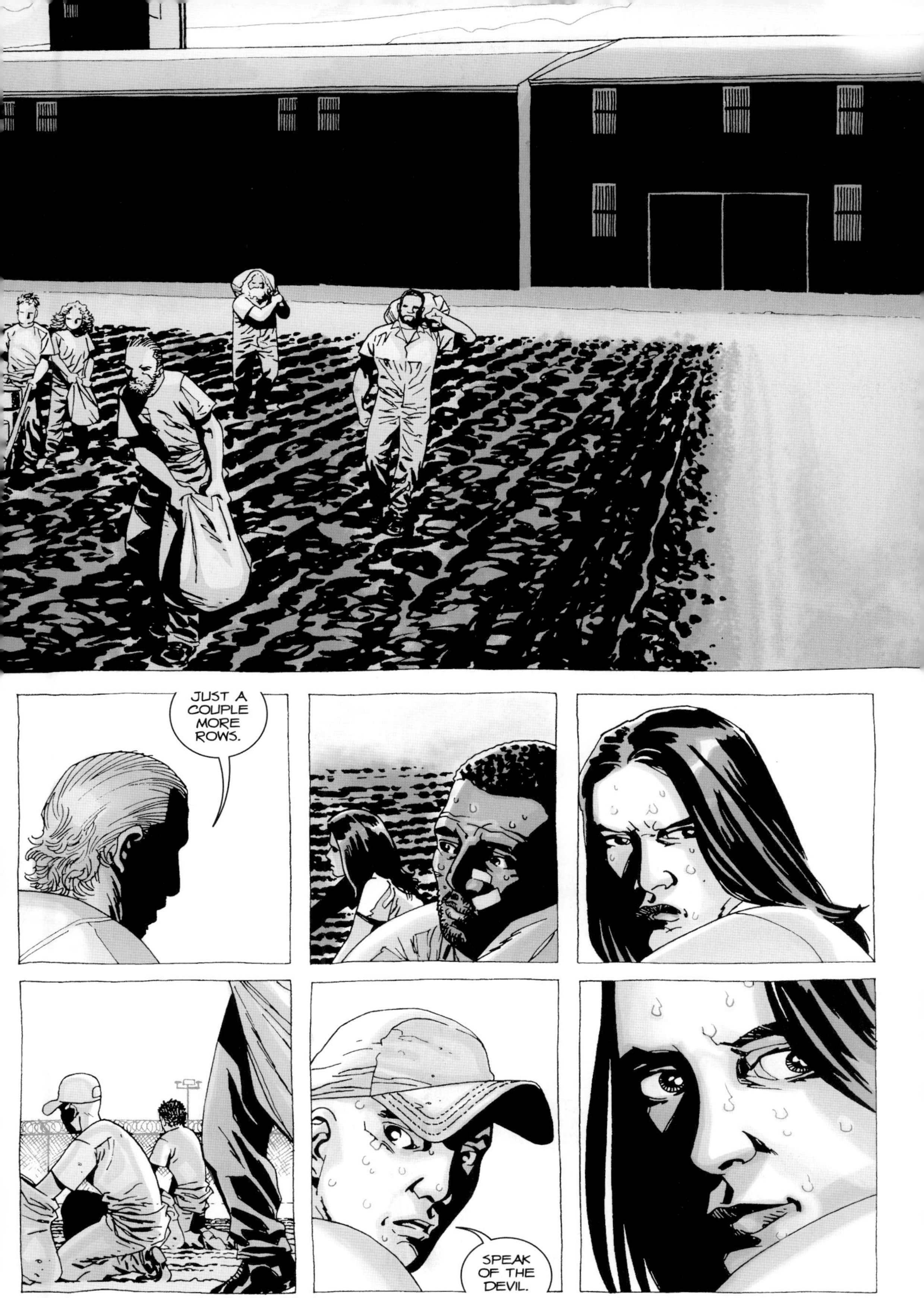
JUST A COUPLE MORE ROWS.
SPEAK OF THE DEVIL.

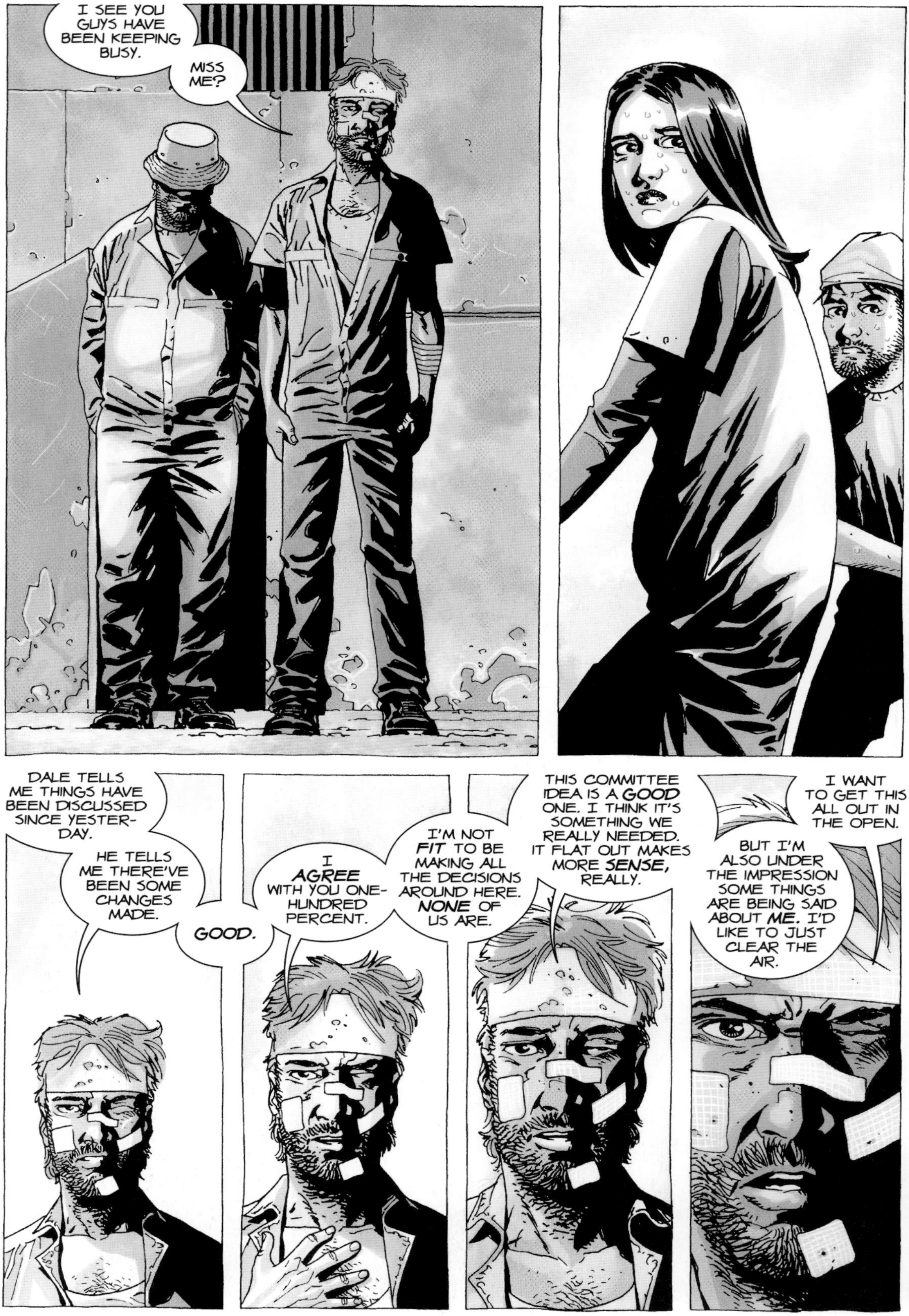
I SEE YOU GUYS HAVE BEEN KEEPING BUSY.
MISS ME?
DALE TELLS ME THINGS HAVE BEEN DISCUSSED SINCE YESTER-DAY.
HE TELLS ME THERE'VE BEEN SOME CHANGES MADE.
GOOD.
I AGREE WITH YOU ONE-HUNDRED PERCENT.
I'M NOT FIT TO BE MAKING ALL THE DECISIONS AROUND HERE. NONE OF US ARE.
THIS COMMITTEE IDEA IS A GOOD ONE. I THINK IT'S SOMETHING WE REALLY NEEDED. IT FLAT OUT MAKES MORE SENSE, REALLY.
I WANT TO GET THIS ALL OUT IN THE OPEN.
BUT I'M ALSO UNDER THE IMPRESSION SOME THINGS ARE BEING SAID ABOUT ME. I'D LIKE TO JUST CLEAR THE AIR.

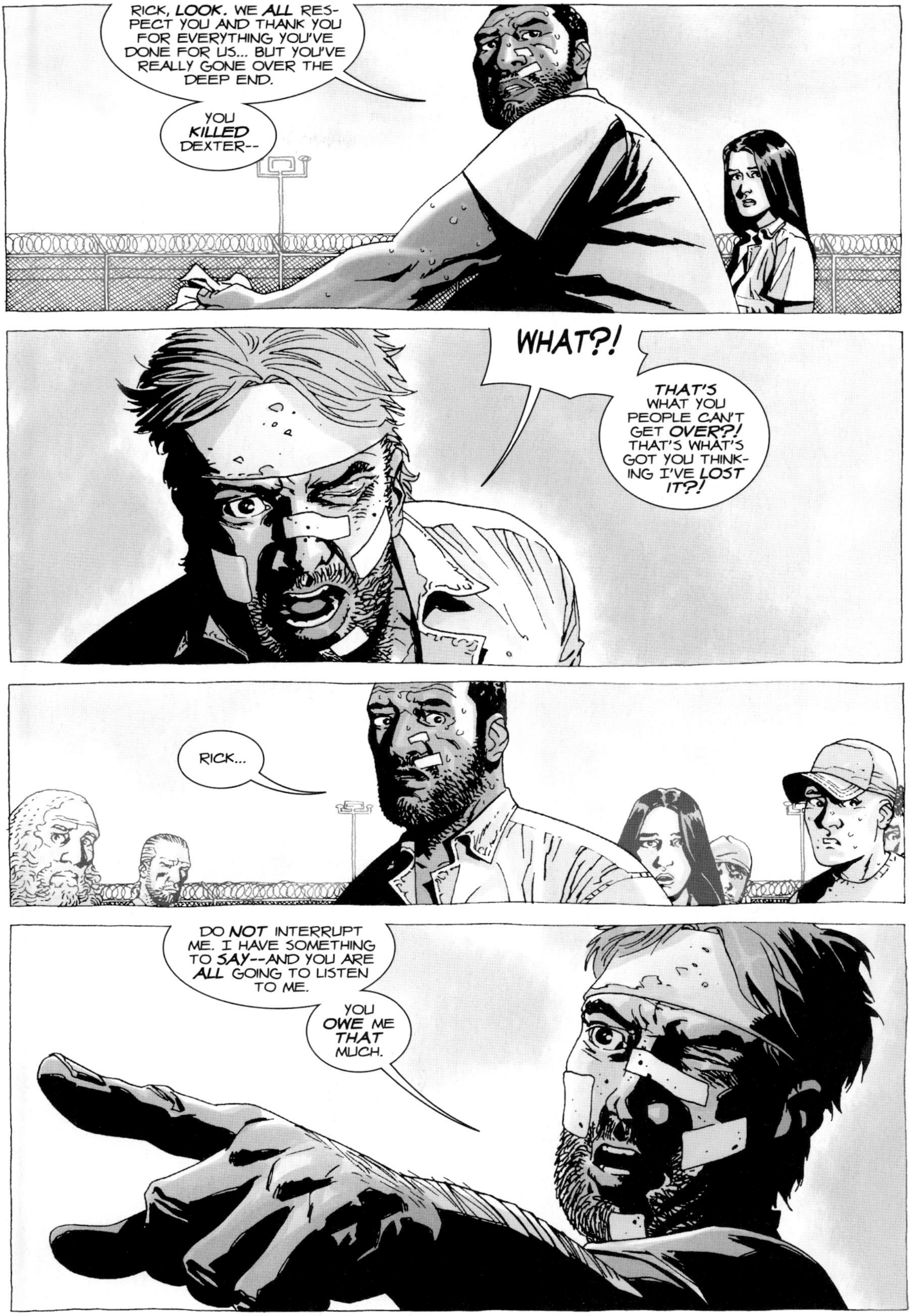
RICK, LOOK. WE ALL RESPECT YOU AND THANK YOU FOR EVERYTHING YOU'VE DONE FOR US... BUT YOU'VE REALLY GONE OVER THE DEEP END.
YOU KILLED DEXTER--
WHAT?!
THAT'S WHAT YOU PEOPLE CAN'T GET OVER?! THAT'S WHAT'S GOT YOU THINKING I'VE LOST IT?!
RICK...
DO NOT INTERRUPT ME. I HAVE SOMETHING TO SAY--AND YOU ARE ALL GOING TO LISTEN TO ME.
YOU OWE ME THAT MUCH.

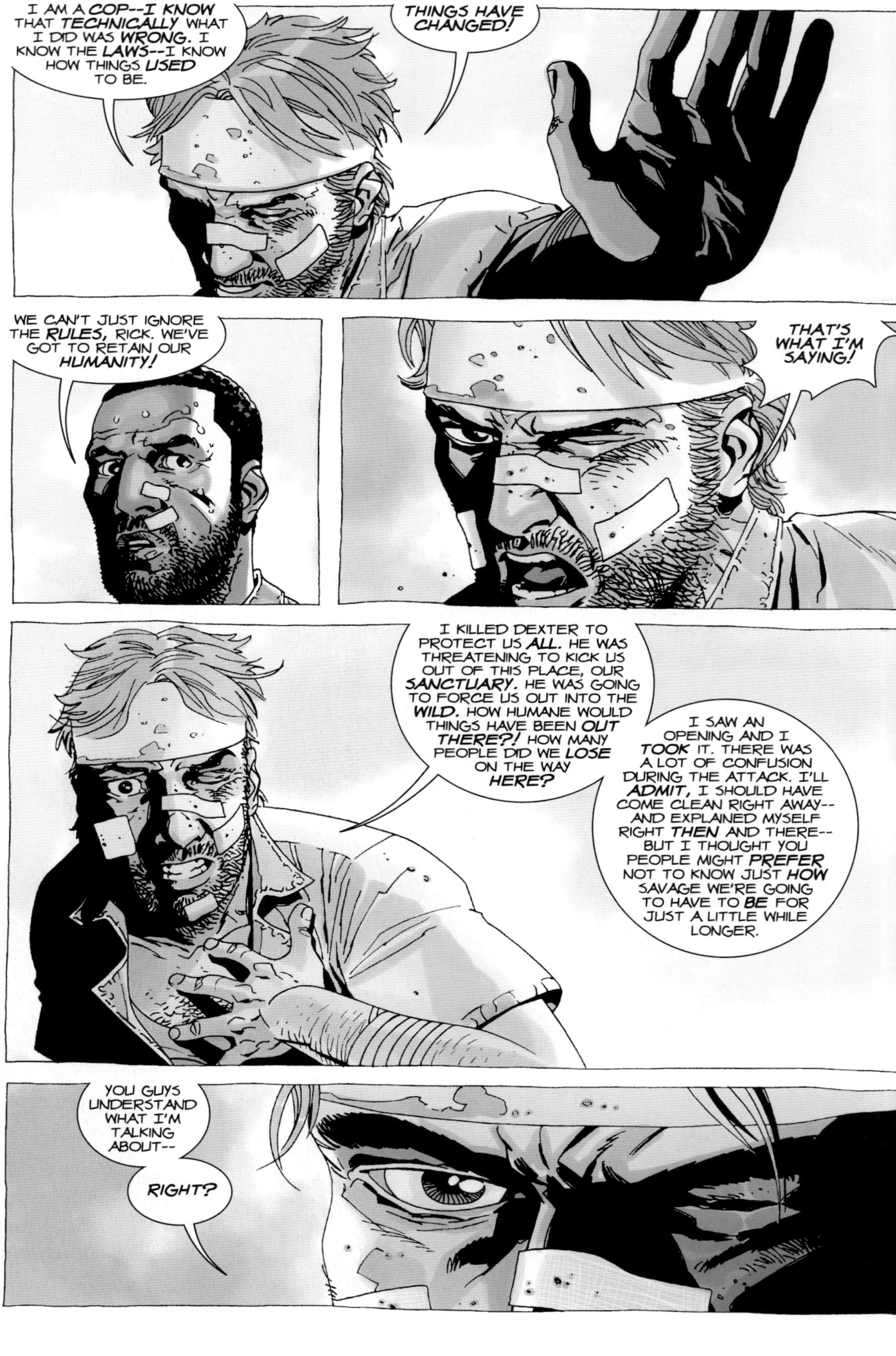

I AM A COP--I KNOW THAT TECHNICALLY WHAT I DID WAS WRONG. I KNOW THE LAWS--I KNOW HOW THINGS USED TO BE.
THINGS HAVE CHANGED!
WE CAN'T JUST IGNORE THE RULES, RICK. WE'VE GOT TO RETAIN OUR HUMANITY!
THAT'S WHAT I'M SAYING!
I KILLED DEXTER TO PROTECT US ALL. HE WAS THREATENING TO KICK US OUT OF THIS PLACE, OUR SANCTUARY. HE WAS GOING TO FORCE US OUT INTO THE WILD. HOW HUMANE WOULD THINGS HAVE BEEN OUT THERE?! HOW MANY PEOPLE DID WE LOSE ON THE WAY HERE?
I SAW AN OPENING AND I TOOK IT. THERE WAS A LOT OF CONFUSION DURING THE ATTACK. I'LL ADMIT, I SHOULD HAVE COME CLEAN RIGHT AWAY-- AND EXPLAINED MYSELF RIGHT THEN AND THERE-- BUT I THOUGHT YOU PEOPLE MIGHT PREFER NOT TO KNOW JUST HOW SAVAGE WE'RE GOING TO HAVE TO BE FOR JUST A LITTLE WHILE LONGER.
YOU GUYS UNDERSTAND WHAT I'M TALKING ABOUT--
RIGHT?

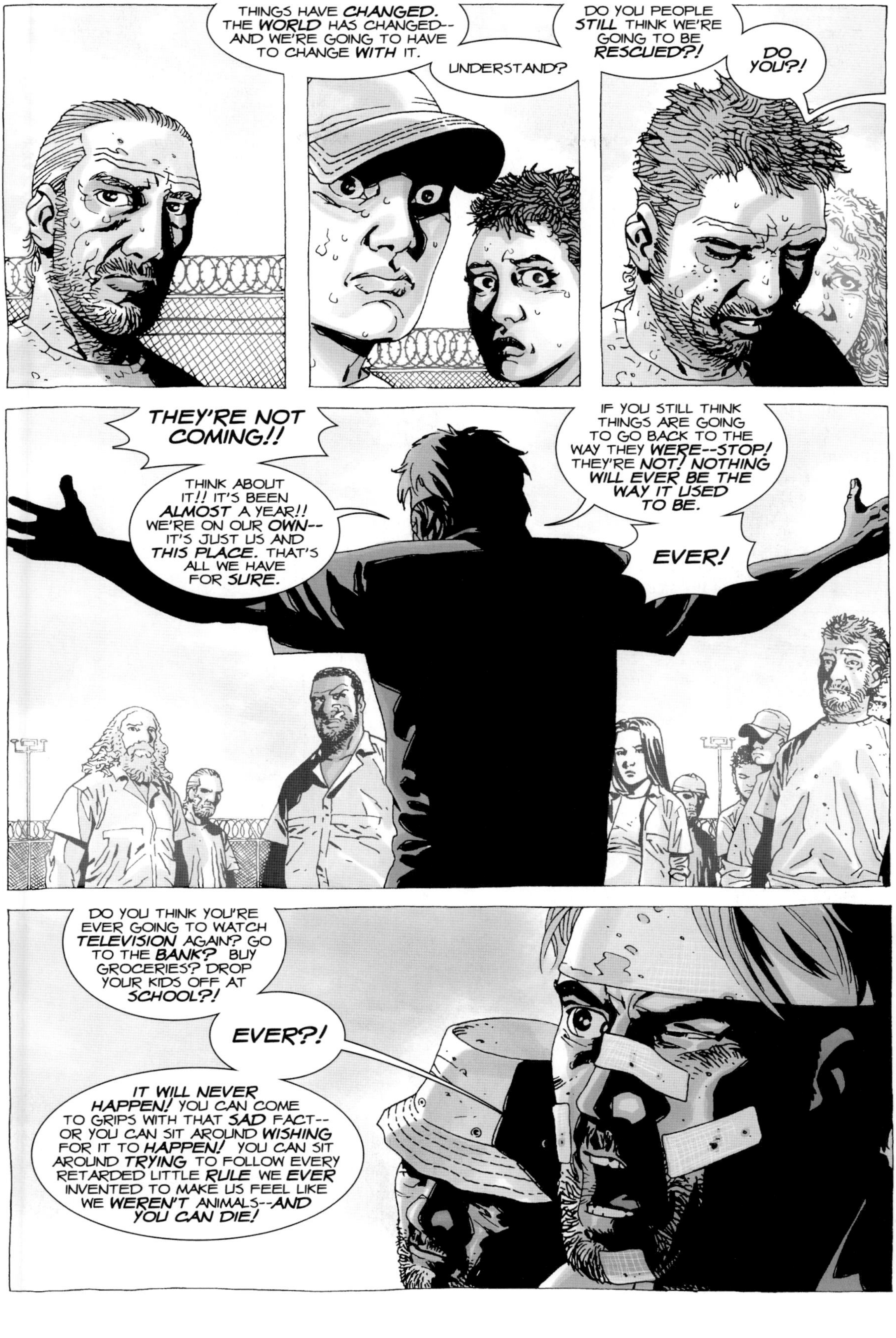
THINGS HAVE CHANGED. THE WORLD HAS CHANGED-- AND WE'RE GOING TO HAVE TO CHANGE WITH IT.
UNDERSTAND?
DO YOU PEOPLE STILL THINK WE'RE GOING TO BE RESCUED?!
DO YOU?!
THEY'RE NOT COMING!!
THINK ABOUT IT!! IT'S BEEN ALMOST A YEAR!! WE'RE ON OUR OWN-- IT'S JUST US AND THIS PLACE. THAT'S ALL WE HAVE FOR SURE.
IF YOU STILL THINK THINGS ARE GOING TO GO BACK TO THE WAY THEY WERE--STOP! THEY'RE NOT! NOTHING WILL EVER BE THE WAY IT USED TO BE.
EVER!
DO YOU THINK YOU'RE EVER GOING TO WATCH TELEVISION AGAIN? GO TO THE BANK? BUY GROCERIES? DROP YOUR KIDS OFF AT SCHOOL?!
EVER?!
IT WILL NEVER HAPPEN! YOU CAN COME TO GRIPS WITH THAT SAD FACT-- OR YOU CAN SIT AROUND WISHING FOR IT TO HAPPEN! YOU CAN SIT AROUND TRYING TO FOLLOW EVERY RETARDED LITTLE RULE WE EVER INVENTED TO MAKE US FEEL LIKE WE WEREN'T ANIMALS--AND YOU CAN DIE!

WE WILL *CHANGE!* WE WILL *EVOLVE.* WE'LL MAKE *NEW* RULES--WE'LL STILL BE *HUMANE* AND *KIND* AND WE'LL STILL *CARE* FOR EACH OTHER.

BUT WHEN THE TIME COMES-- WE *HAVE* TO BE PREPARED TO DO *WHATEVER* IT TAKES TO *KEEP* US *SAFE.*

WHAT- EVER IT TAKES!

"YOU KILL--YOU *DIE.*"

THAT WAS PROBABLY THE MOST NAIVE THING I'VE *EVER* SAID.

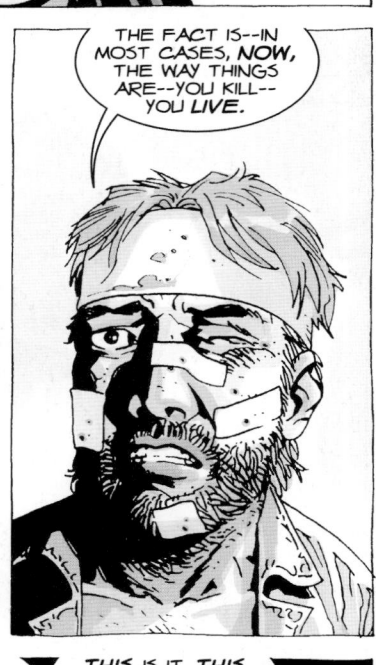

THE FACT IS--IN MOST CASES, *NOW,* THE WAY THINGS ARE--YOU KILL-- YOU *LIVE.*

WE HAVE TO *ADAPT* TO THIS WORLD IF WE ARE GOING TO SURVIVE. HAVE I GONE A LITTLE *CRAZY? MAYBE--* BUT SO HAS THE WORLD.

YOU DON'T WANT ME TO BE THE LEADER? *FINE.* I DON'T *CARE.* I'M *HAPPY* TO BE WITHOUT THE PRESSURE. I WILL TELL YOU THIS RIGHT NOW, THOUGH.

I WILL DO *WHATEVER* I HAVE TO DO TO KEEP US SAFE. *WHATEVER* IT IS--I WILL DO IT.

IF YOU WANT TO STOP BUTTING HEADS WITH ME--IF YOU WANT TO GET ON THE SAME PAGE WITH ME--*UNDER- STAND THAT.*

BUT YOU *HAVE* TO STOP THE CHARADE-- YOU'VE *GOT* TO STOP FOOLING YOURSELVES.

THIS IS IT. *THIS* IS OUR LIFE. WE'RE NOT *WAITING* HERE. WE'RE NOT BIDING OUR TIME--WAITING FOR WHAT COMES *NEXT.* OR WAITING TO BE RES- CUED!

THIS IS WHAT WE *HAVE!* THIS IS ALL WE'LL *EVER* HAVE.

IF YOU WANT TO MAKE THINGS BETTER, MAKE *THIS* PLACE BETTER. WE HAVE TO COME TO GRIPS WITH THAT.

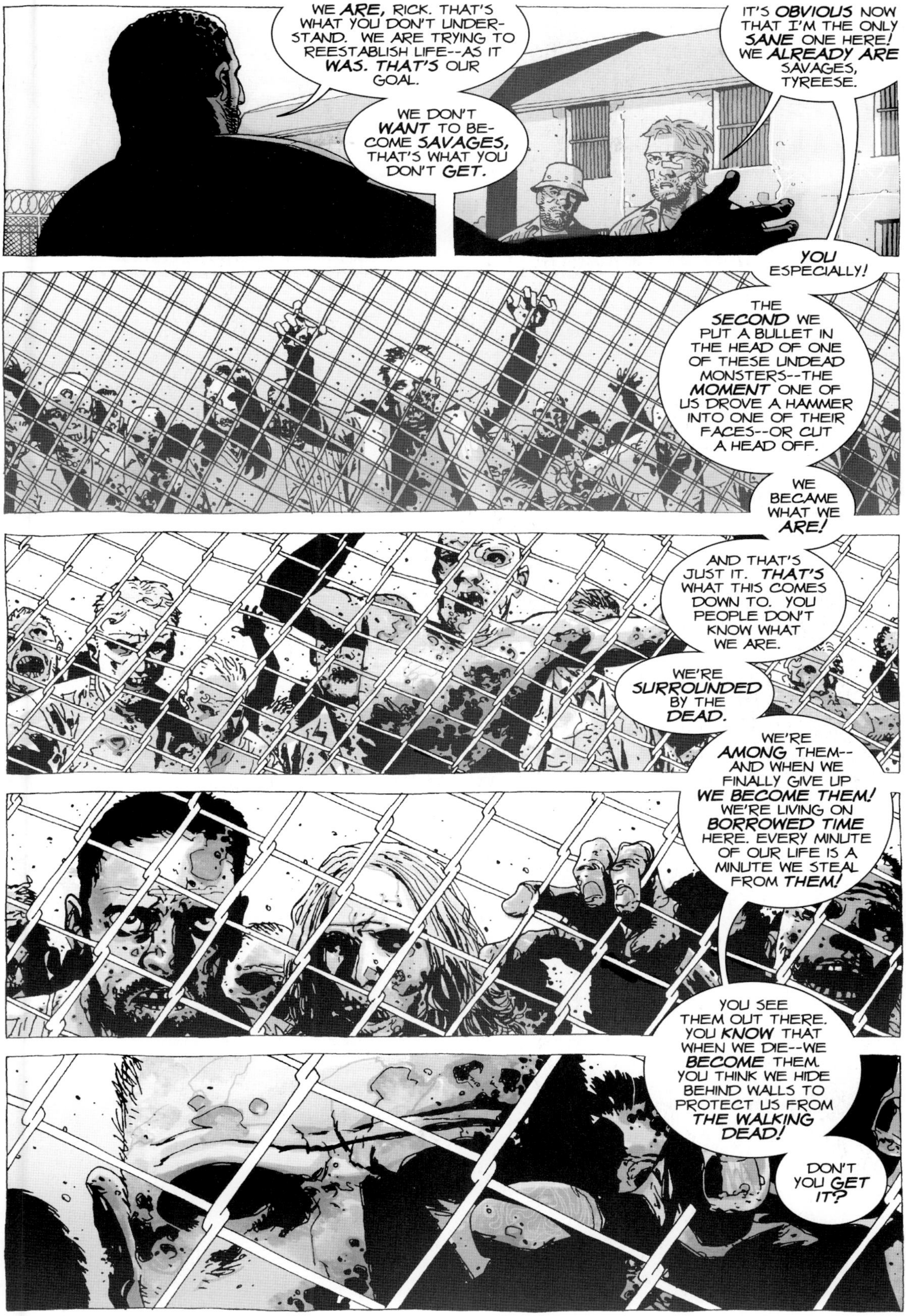
WE ARE, RICK. THAT'S WHAT YOU DON'T UNDER-STAND. WE ARE TRYING TO REESTABLISH LIFE--AS IT WAS. THAT'S OUR GOAL.
WE DON'T WANT TO BE-COME SAVAGES, THAT'S WHAT YOU DON'T GET.
IT'S OBVIOUS NOW THAT I'M THE ONLY SANE ONE HERE! WE ALREADY ARE SAVAGES, TYREESE.
YOU ESPECIALLY!
THE SECOND WE PUT A BULLET IN THE HEAD OF ONE OF THESE UNDEAD MONSTERS--THE MOMENT ONE OF US DROVE A HAMMER INTO ONE OF THEIR FACES--OR CUT A HEAD OFF.
WE BECAME WHAT WE ARE!
AND THAT'S JUST IT. THAT'S WHAT THIS COMES DOWN TO. YOU PEOPLE DON'T KNOW WHAT WE ARE.
WE'RE SURROUNDED BY THE DEAD.
WE'RE AMONG THEM--AND WHEN WE FINALLY GIVE UP WE BECOME THEM! WE'RE LIVING ON BORROWED TIME HERE. EVERY MINUTE OF OUR LIFE IS A MINUTE WE STEAL FROM THEM!
YOU SEE THEM OUT THERE. YOU KNOW THAT WHEN WE DIE--WE BECOME THEM. YOU THINK WE HIDE BEHIND WALLS TO PROTECT US FROM THE WALKING DEAD!
DON'T YOU GET IT?

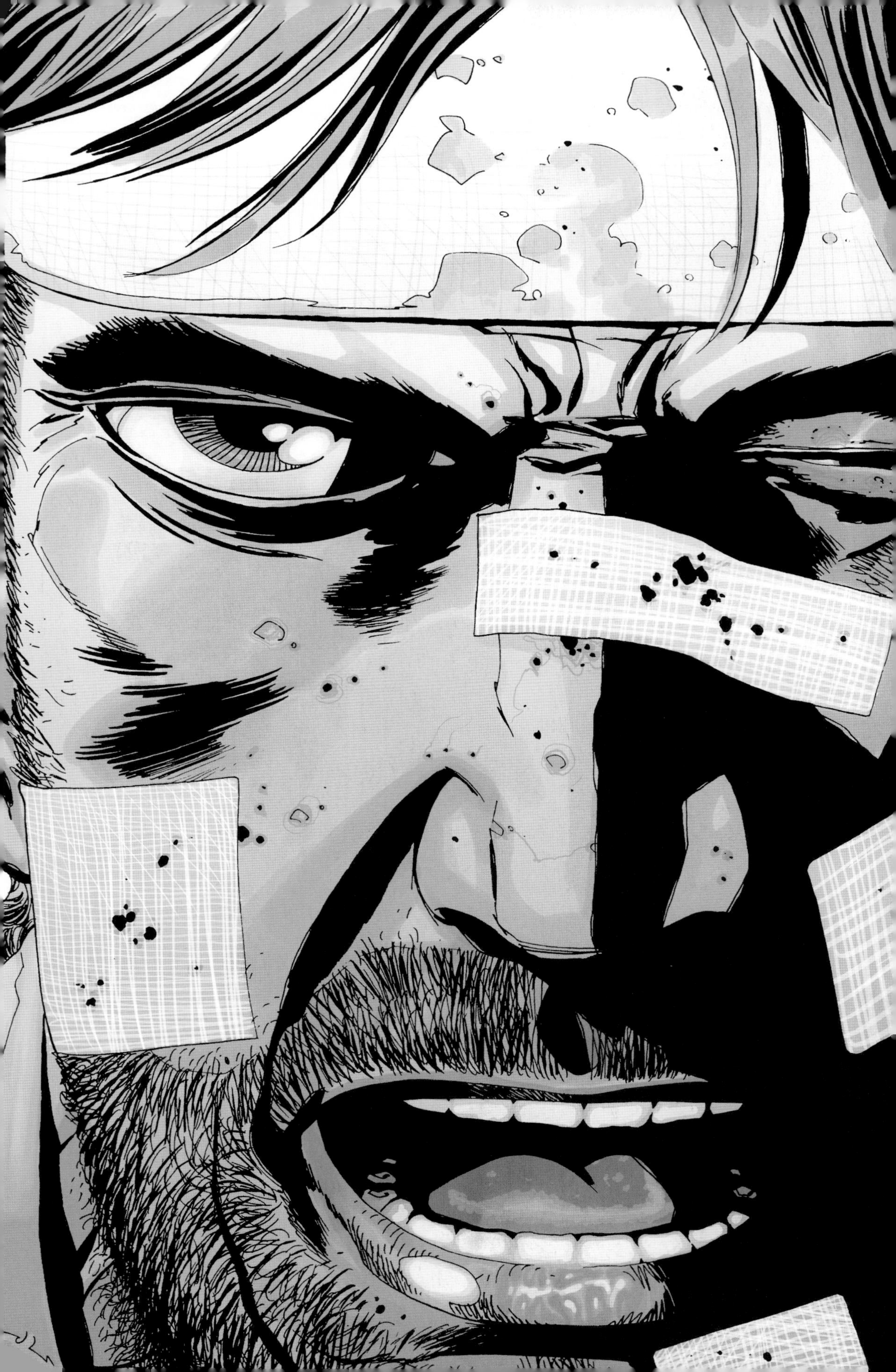

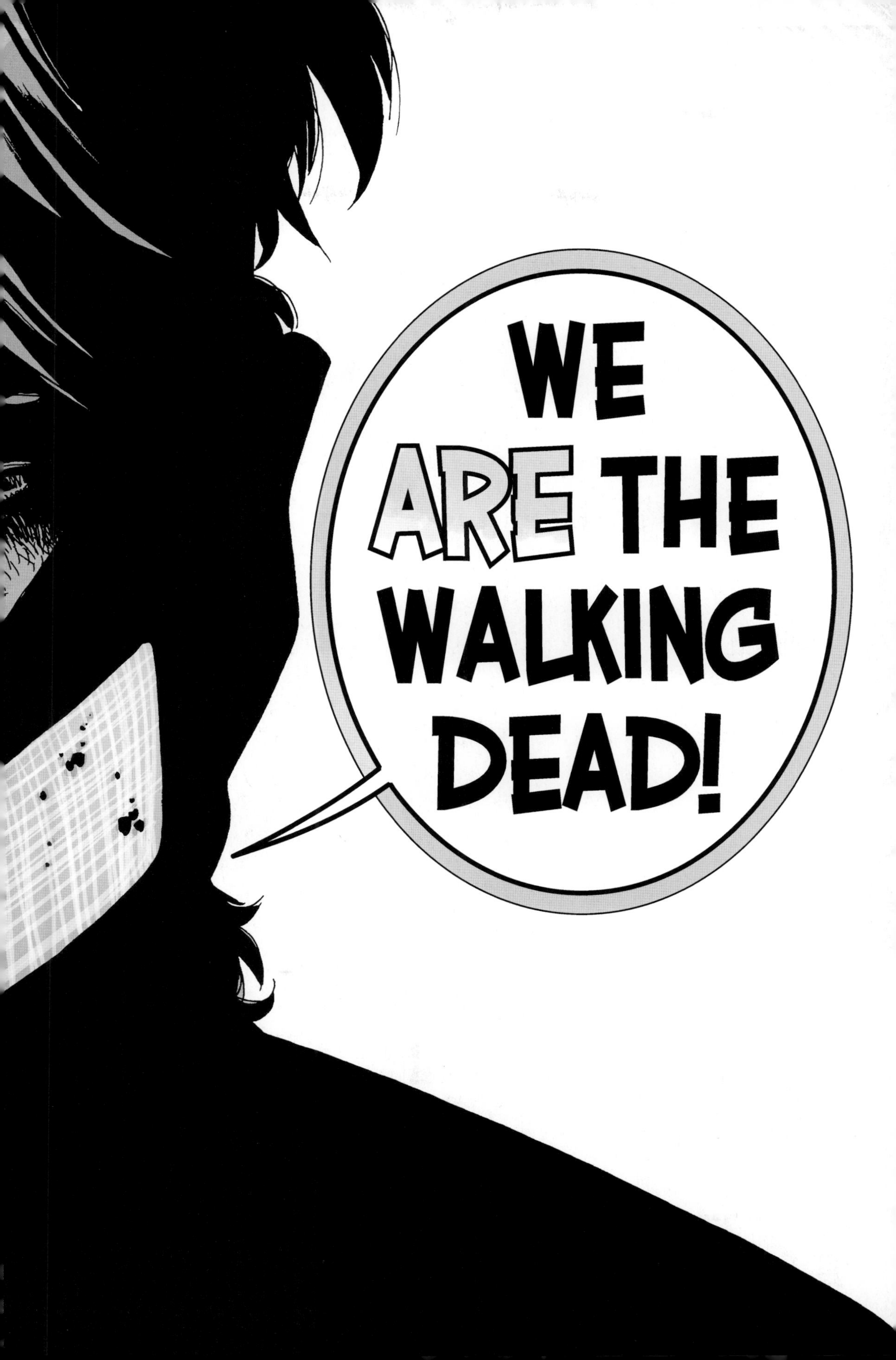
WE ARE THE WALKING DEAD!

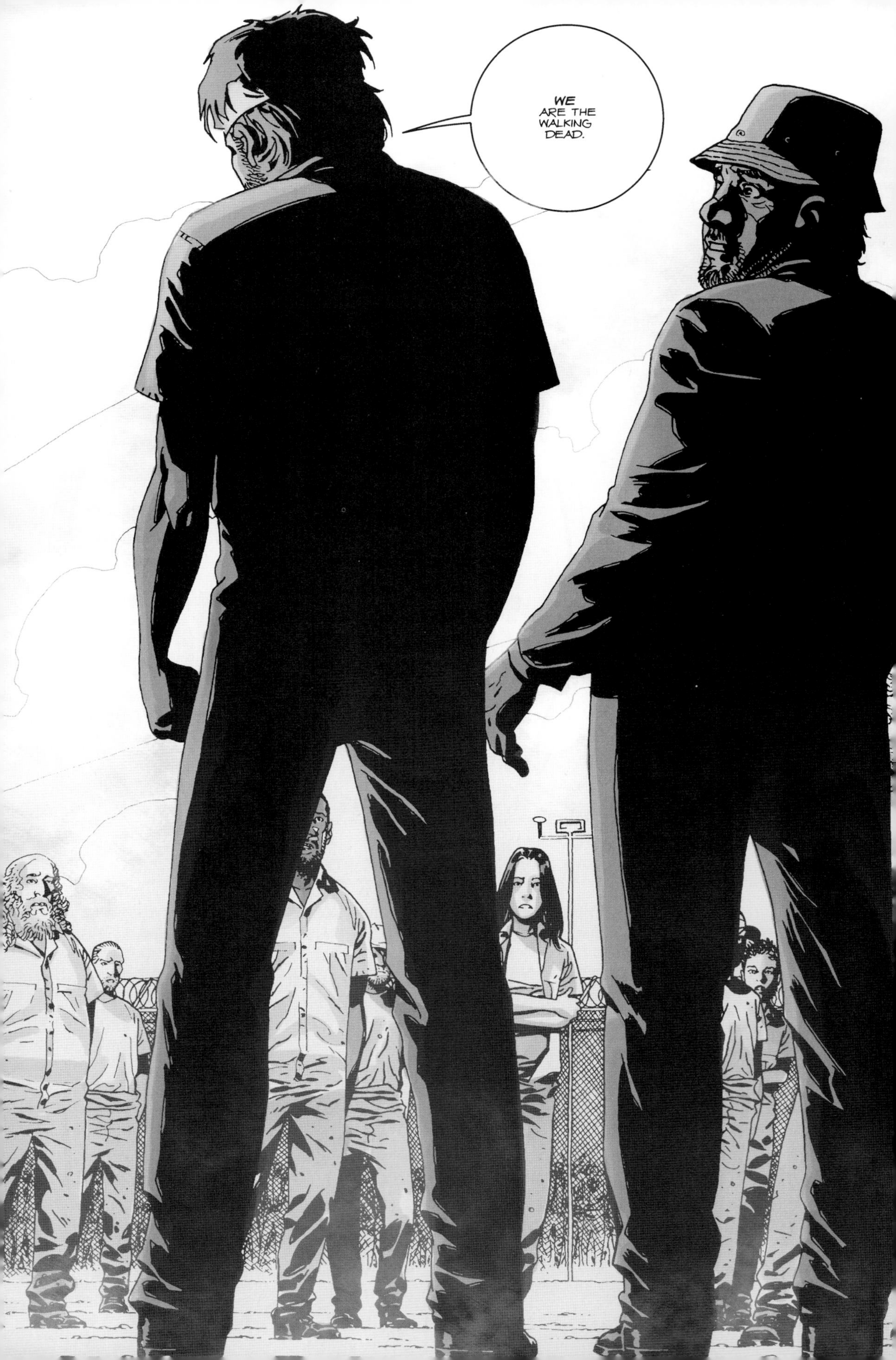
WE ARE THE WALKING DEAD.

Chapter Five:
The Best Defense

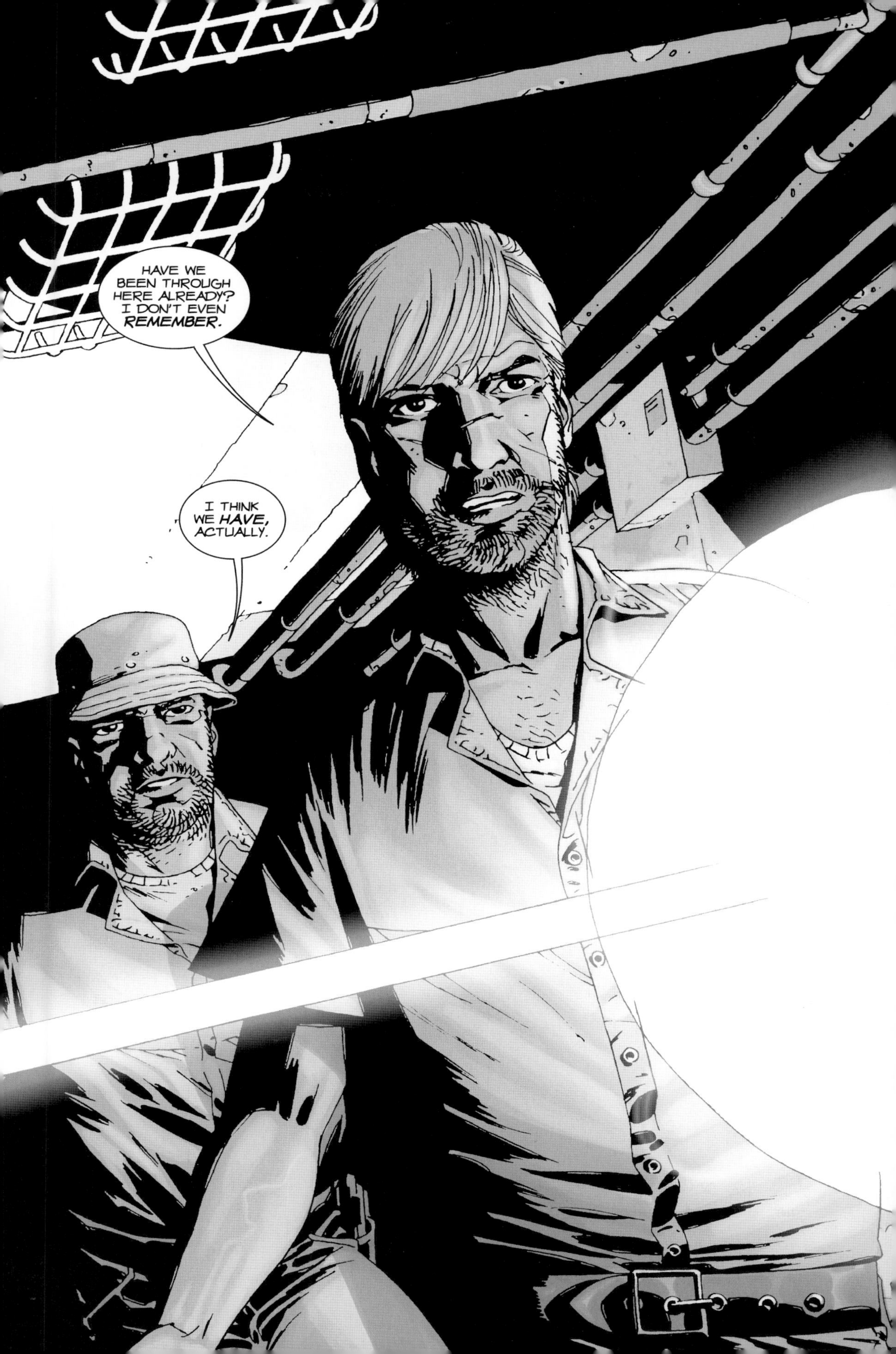
HAVE WE BEEN THROUGH HERE ALREADY? I DON'T EVEN REMEMBER.
I THINK WE HAVE, ACTUALLY.

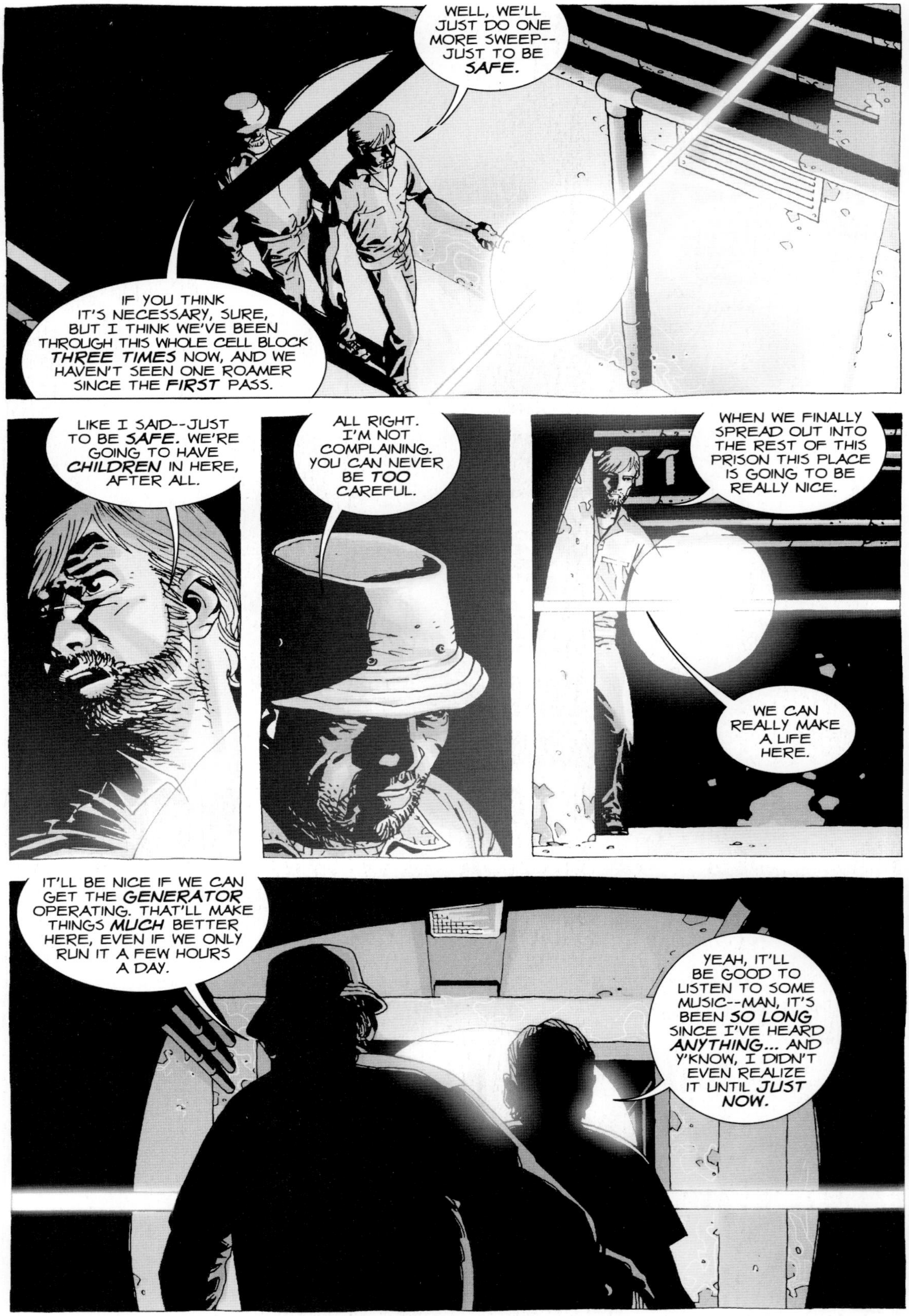
WELL, WE'LL JUST DO ONE MORE SWEEP-- JUST TO BE SAFE.
IF YOU THINK IT'S NECESSARY, SURE, BUT I THINK WE'VE BEEN THROUGH THIS WHOLE CELL BLOCK THREE TIMES NOW, AND WE HAVEN'T SEEN ONE ROAMER SINCE THE FIRST PASS.
LIKE I SAID--JUST TO BE SAFE. WE'RE GOING TO HAVE CHILDREN IN HERE, AFTER ALL.
ALL RIGHT. I'M NOT COMPLAINING. YOU CAN NEVER BE TOO CAREFUL.
WHEN WE FINALLY SPREAD OUT INTO THE REST OF THIS PRISON THIS PLACE IS GOING TO BE REALLY NICE.
WE CAN REALLY MAKE A LIFE HERE.
IT'LL BE NICE IF WE CAN GET THE GENERATOR OPERATING. THAT'LL MAKE THINGS MUCH BETTER HERE, EVEN IF WE ONLY RUN IT A FEW HOURS A DAY.
YEAH, IT'LL BE GOOD TO LISTEN TO SOME MUSIC--MAN, IT'S BEEN SO LONG SINCE I'VE HEARD ANYTHING... AND Y'KNOW, I DIDN'T EVEN REALIZE IT UNTIL JUST NOW.

YOU'VE HAD A *LOT* ON YOUR MIND FOR A *LONG* TIME. IT'S UNDERSTANDABLE.

YOU KNOW WHAT I'VE BEEN THINKING ABOUT A LOT LATELY? *MORGAN* AND... JEEZ, I DON'T EVEN REMEMBER HIS SON'S *NAME*. I THINK IT WAS DAVID... BUT I'M NOT SURE.

WHO?

THEY WERE STAYING IN THE HOUSE NEXT TO MINE IN CYNTHIANA--THE TOWN WE LIVED IN BEFORE. IT WAS MORGAN AND HIS SON, WHATEVER HIS NAME WAS, STAYING IN THIS PLACE, ALL BY THEMSELVES.

THEY HAD DECIDED *NOT* TO TRY AND MAKE IT TO A LARGE CITY, THEY WERE JUST GOING TO STAY PUT, FEND FOR THEMSELVES. WHICH AS IT TURNS OUT WAS *REALLY* DAMN SMART.

I WONDER ABOUT THEM-- I WONDER IF THEY'RE STILL OUT THERE.

THAT WAS OVER HALF A YEAR AGO... SO WHO *KNOWS*.

YEAH-- YOU'RE RI--

KRIK

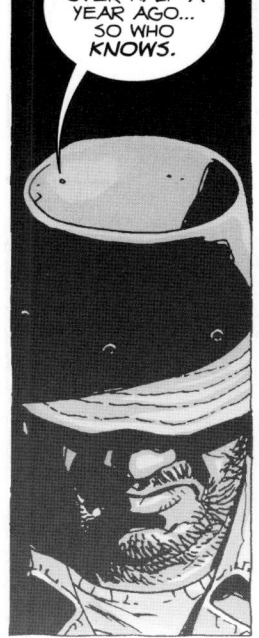

I'M GOING TO SWING AROUND THE CORNER TO SEE WHAT IT IS-- YOU BE READY TO FIRE.

RIGHT.

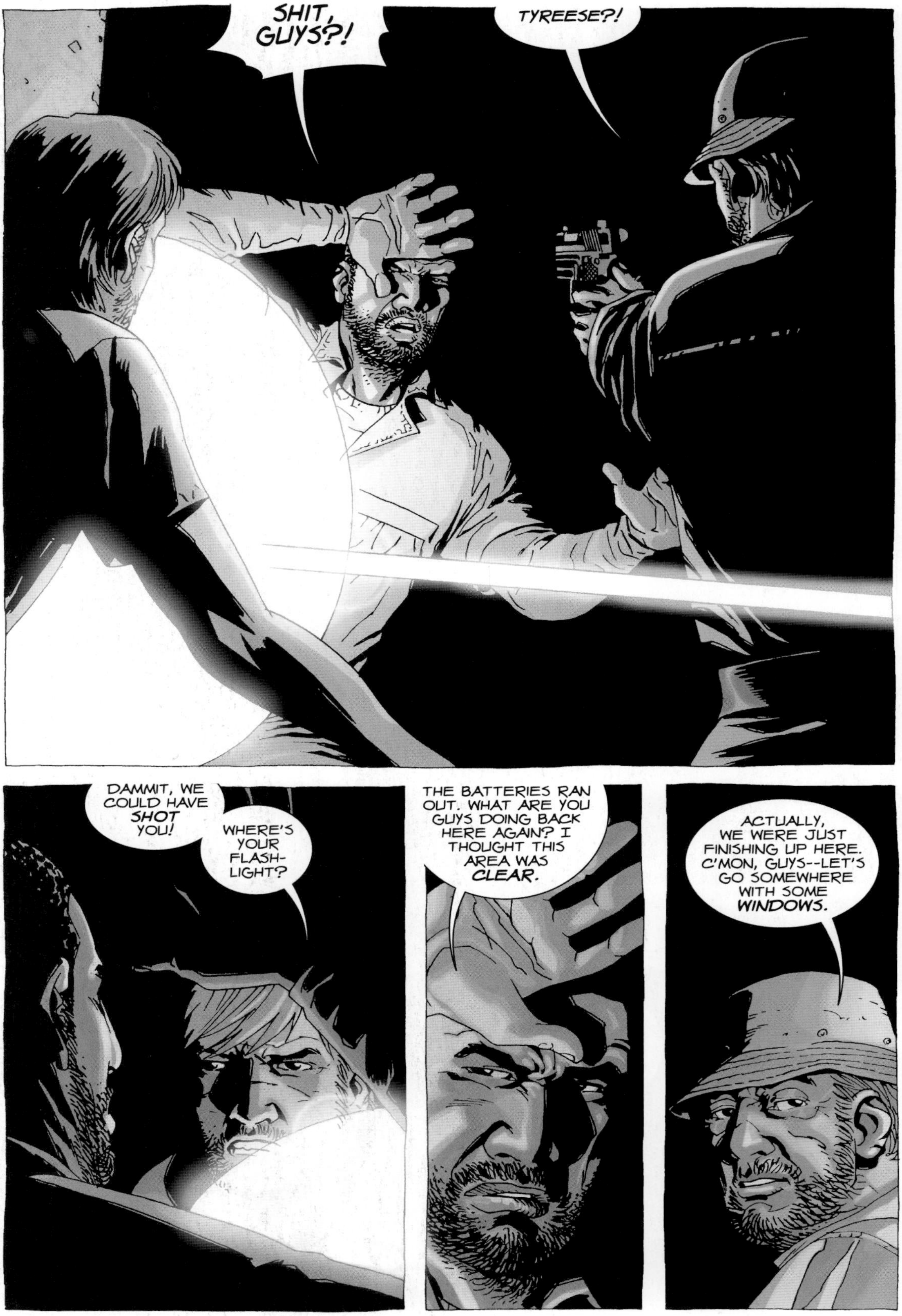

SHIT, GUYS?!
TYREESE?!
DAMMIT, WE COULD HAVE SHOT YOU!
WHERE'S YOUR FLASH-LIGHT?
THE BATTERIES RAN OUT. WHAT ARE YOU GUYS DOING BACK HERE AGAIN? I THOUGHT THIS AREA WAS CLEAR.
ACTUALLY, WE WERE JUST FINISHING UP HERE. C'MON, GUYS--LET'S GO SOMEWHERE WITH SOME WINDOWS.

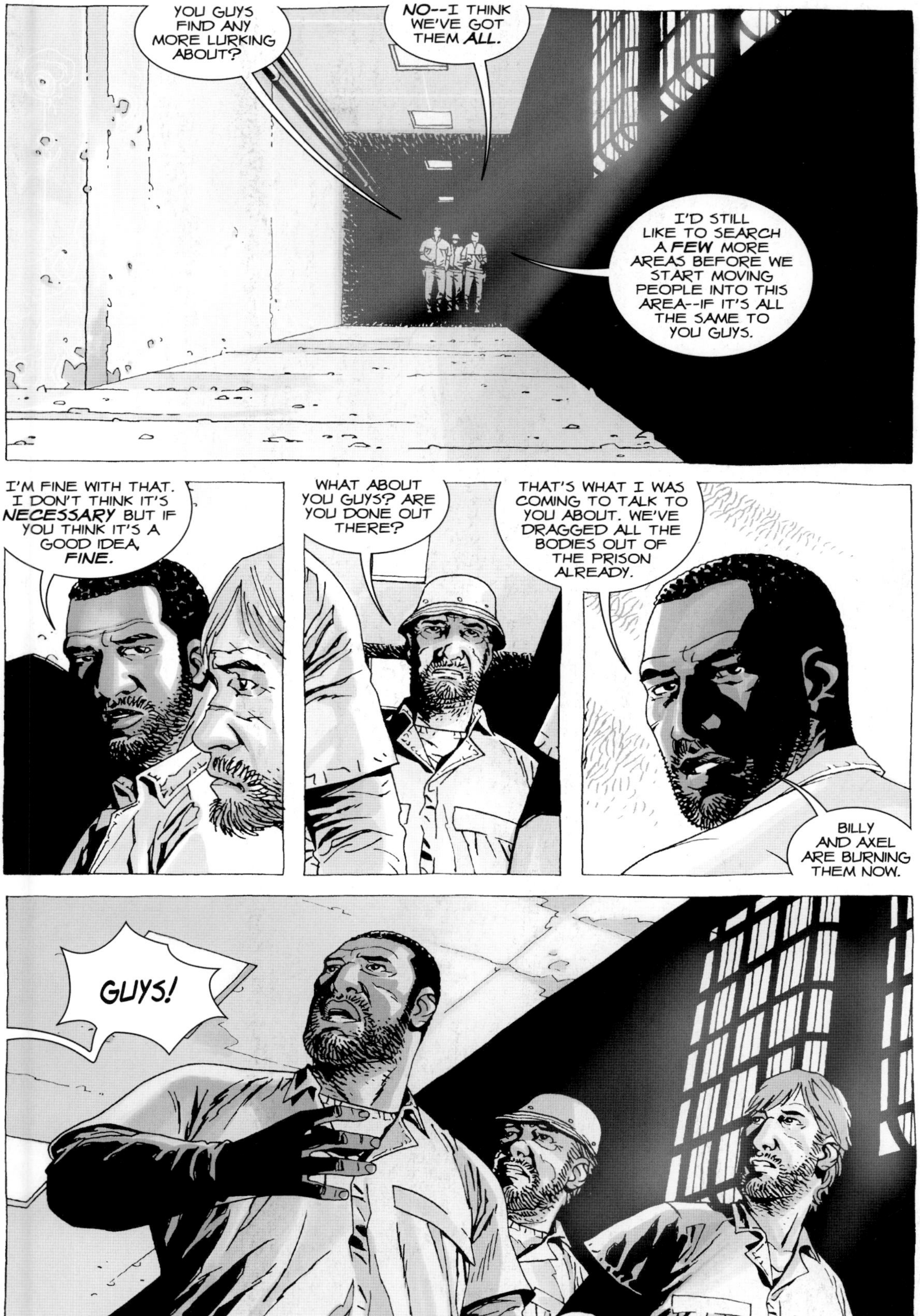
YOU GUYS FIND ANY MORE LURKING ABOUT?
NO--I THINK WE'VE GOT THEM ALL.
I'D STILL LIKE TO SEARCH A FEW MORE AREAS BEFORE WE START MOVING PEOPLE INTO THIS AREA--IF IT'S ALL THE SAME TO YOU GUYS.
I'M FINE WITH THAT. I DON'T THINK IT'S NECESSARY BUT IF YOU THINK IT'S A GOOD IDEA, FINE.
WHAT ABOUT YOU GUYS? ARE YOU DONE OUT THERE?
THAT'S WHAT I WAS COMING TO TALK TO YOU ABOUT. WE'VE DRAGGED ALL THE BODIES OUT OF THE PRISON ALREADY.
BILLY AND AXEL ARE BURNING THEM NOW.
GUYS!

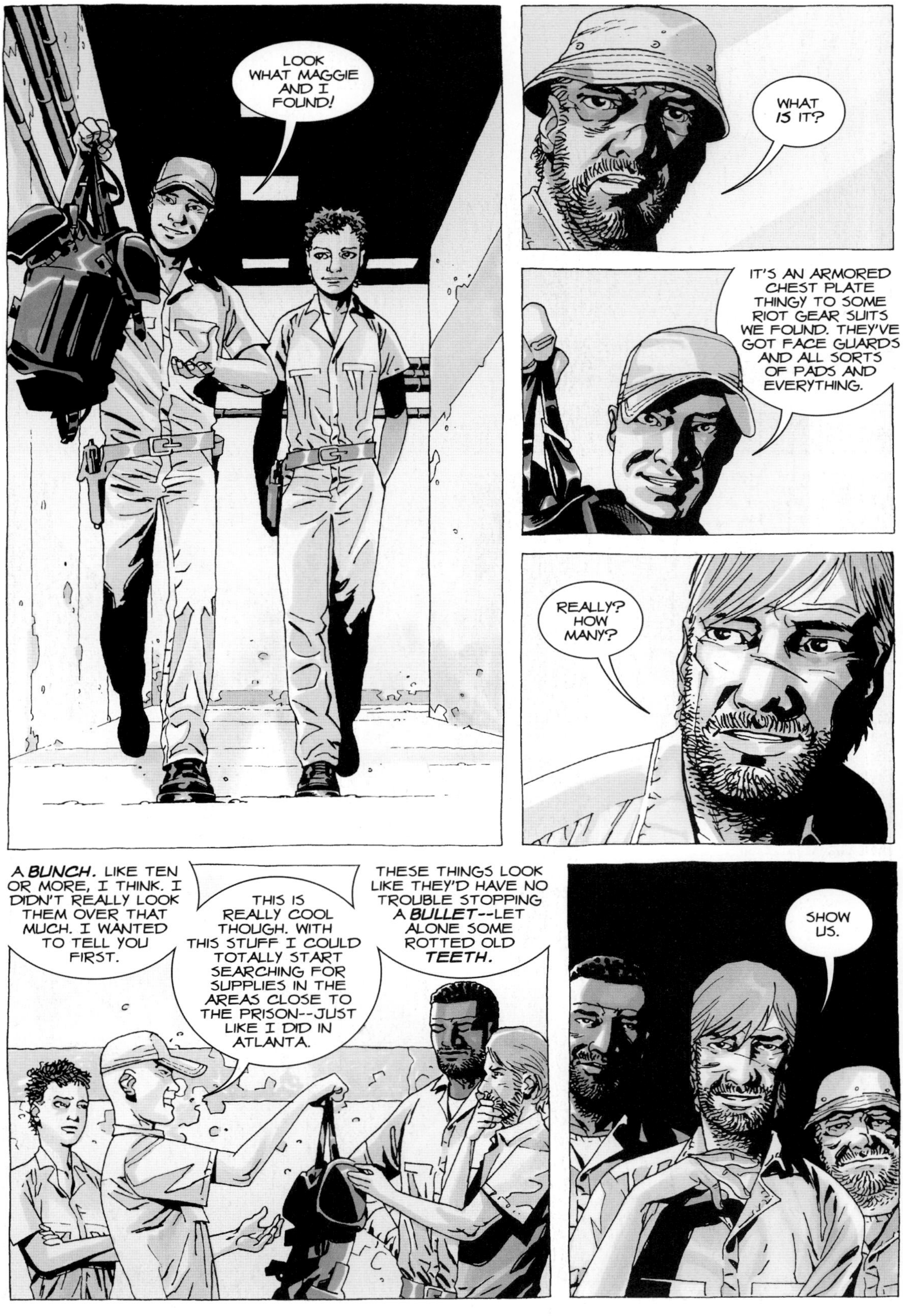
LOOK WHAT MAGGIE AND I FOUND!
WHAT IS IT?
IT'S AN ARMORED CHEST PLATE THINGY TO SOME RIOT GEAR SUITS WE FOUND. THEY'VE GOT FACE GUARDS AND ALL SORTS OF PADS AND EVERYTHING.
REALLY? HOW MANY?
A BUNCH. LIKE TEN OR MORE, I THINK. I DIDN'T REALLY LOOK THEM OVER THAT MUCH. I WANTED TO TELL YOU FIRST.
THIS IS REALLY COOL THOUGH. WITH THIS STUFF I COULD TOTALLY START SEARCHING FOR SUPPLIES IN THE AREAS CLOSE TO THE PRISON--JUST LIKE I DID IN ATLANTA.
THESE THINGS LOOK LIKE THEY'D HAVE NO TROUBLE STOPPING A BULLET--LET ALONE SOME ROTTED OLD TEETH.
SHOW US.

THERE'S NO WINDOWS SO IT'S PRETTY DARK IN HERE. I IMAGINE THEY HAD TO KEEP THIS ROOM *SECURE,* WITH THE PRISONERS AROUND AND ALL.

I THINK IT'S EVEN IN AN AREA THE PRISONERS WEREN'T ALLOWED TO GO IN. IT'S RIGHT NEXT TO THE WARDEN'S OFFICE.

WHICH, BY THE WAY-- THERE'S A *COUCH* IN THERE THAT'S WAY MORE COMFORTABLE THAN ANY OF THE *BEDS* WE'VE BEEN SLEEPING ON.

WAY MORE COMFORTABLE.

THANKS. I DON'T EVEN WANT TO STAND *NEXT* TO THAT COUCH, NOW.

DEXTER AND ANDREW MUST HAVE GOTTEN UP HERE IN A *HURRY,* MOSTLY IN THE *DARK.* MAYBE DEXTER HAD A PLAN TO BREAK INTO THIS PLACE ALREADY.

OTHERWISE, I DON'T SEE *HOW* HE COULD HAVE GOTTEN INSIDE HERE AND OUT LIKE HE DID, WITHOUT GETTING ATTACKED BY ONE OF THE ROAMERS.

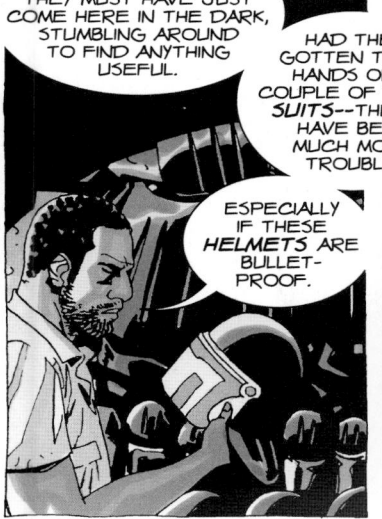

THEY MUST HAVE JUST COME HERE IN THE DARK, STUMBLING AROUND TO FIND ANYTHING USEFUL.

HAD THEY GOTTEN THEIR HANDS ON A COUPLE OF THESE *SUITS*--THEY'D HAVE BEEN MUCH MORE TROUBLE.

ESPECIALLY IF THESE *HELMETS* ARE BULLET-PROOF.

YEAH.

RIGHT.

OKAY GUYS-- LOOKS LIKE THE PRISON IS *CLEAR.* LET'S GET OUT OF HERE.

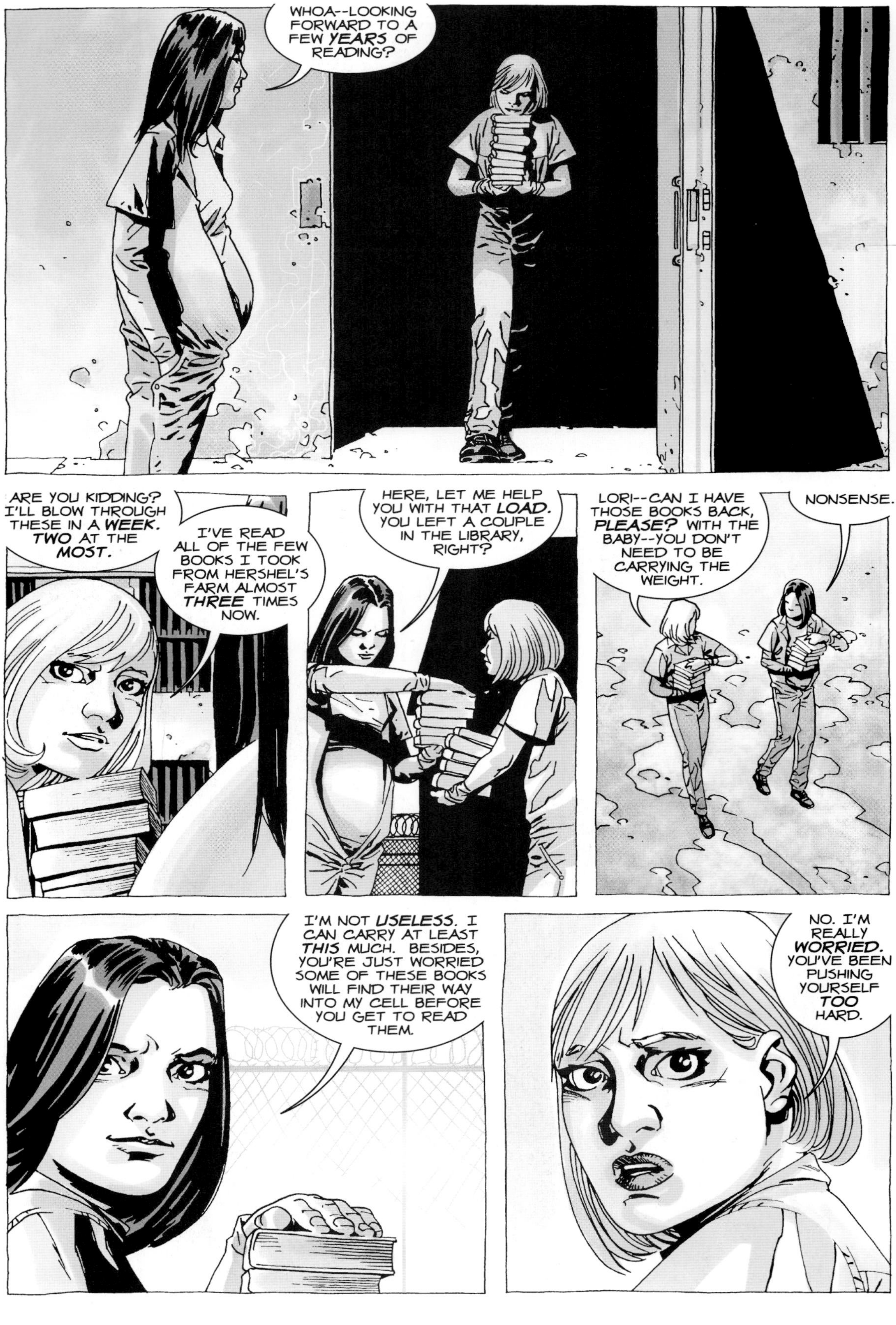
WHOA--LOOKING FORWARD TO A FEW YEARS OF READING?
ARE YOU KIDDING? I'LL BLOW THROUGH THESE IN A WEEK. TWO AT THE MOST.
I'VE READ ALL OF THE FEW BOOKS I TOOK FROM HERSHEL'S FARM ALMOST THREE TIMES NOW.
HERE, LET ME HELP YOU WITH THAT LOAD. YOU LEFT A COUPLE IN THE LIBRARY, RIGHT?
LORI--CAN I HAVE THOSE BOOKS BACK, PLEASE? WITH THE BABY--YOU DON'T NEED TO BE CARRYING THE WEIGHT.
NONSENSE.
I'M NOT USELESS. I CAN CARRY AT LEAST THIS MUCH. BESIDES, YOU'RE JUST WORRIED SOME OF THESE BOOKS WILL FIND THEIR WAY INTO MY CELL BEFORE YOU GET TO READ THEM.
NO. I'M REALLY WORRIED. YOU'VE BEEN PUSHING YOURSELF TOO HARD.

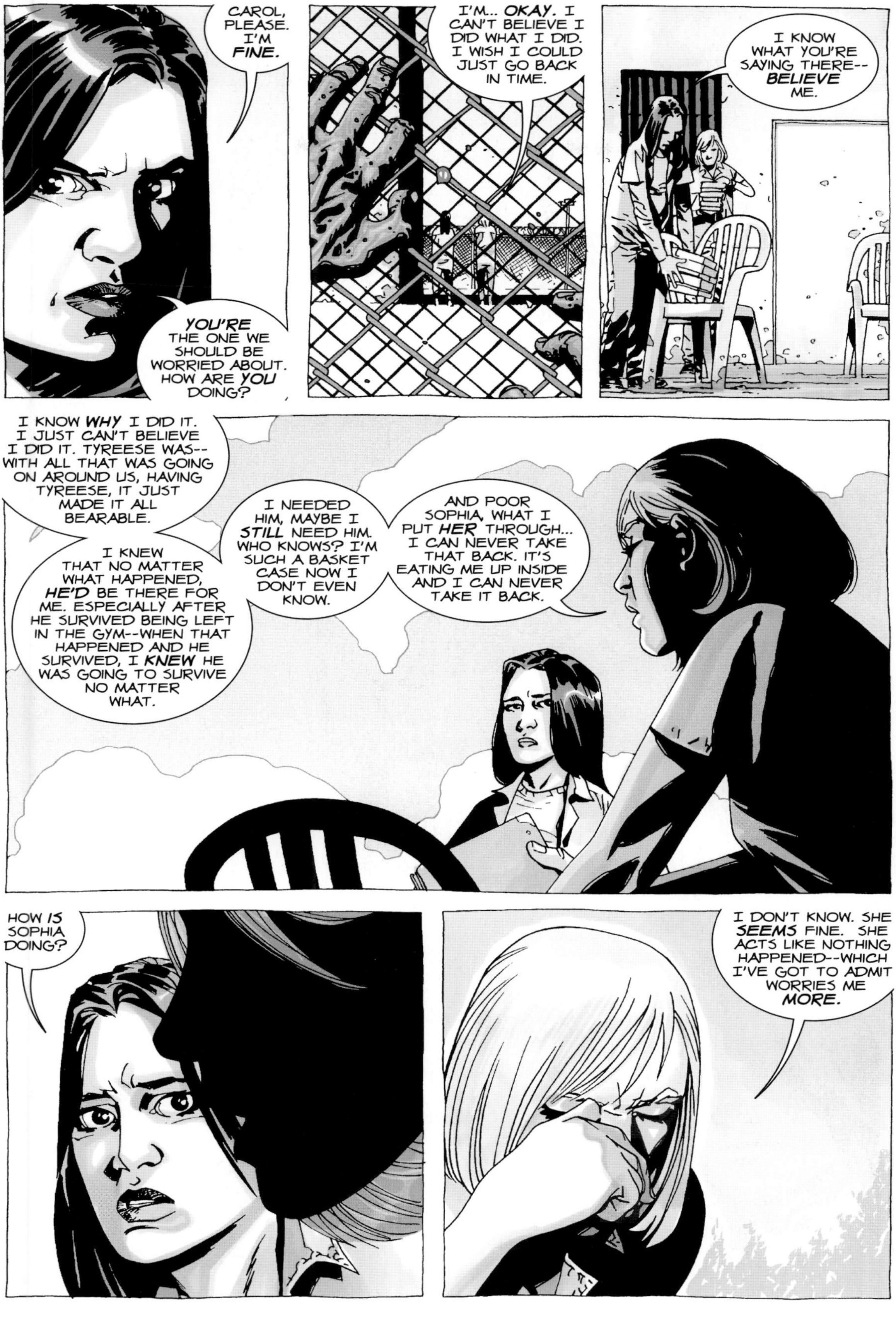
CAROL, PLEASE. I'M FINE.
YOU'RE THE ONE WE SHOULD BE WORRIED ABOUT. HOW ARE YOU DOING?
I'M... OKAY. I CAN'T BELIEVE I DID WHAT I DID. I WISH I COULD JUST GO BACK IN TIME.
I KNOW WHAT YOU'RE SAYING THERE-- BELIEVE ME.
I KNOW WHY I DID IT. I JUST CAN'T BELIEVE I DID IT. TYREESE WAS-- WITH ALL THAT WAS GOING ON AROUND US, HAVING TYREESE, IT JUST MADE IT ALL BEARABLE.
I KNEW THAT NO MATTER WHAT HAPPENED, HE'D BE THERE FOR ME. ESPECIALLY AFTER HE SURVIVED BEING LEFT IN THE GYM--WHEN THAT HAPPENED AND HE SURVIVED, I KNEW HE WAS GOING TO SURVIVE NO MATTER WHAT.
I NEEDED HIM, MAYBE I STILL NEED HIM. WHO KNOWS? I'M SUCH A BASKET CASE NOW I DON'T EVEN KNOW.
AND POOR SOPHIA, WHAT I PUT HER THROUGH... I CAN NEVER TAKE THAT BACK. IT'S EATING ME UP INSIDE AND I CAN NEVER TAKE IT BACK.
HOW IS SOPHIA DOING?
I DON'T KNOW. SHE SEEMS FINE. SHE ACTS LIKE NOTHING HAPPENED--WHICH I'VE GOT TO ADMIT WORRIES ME MORE.

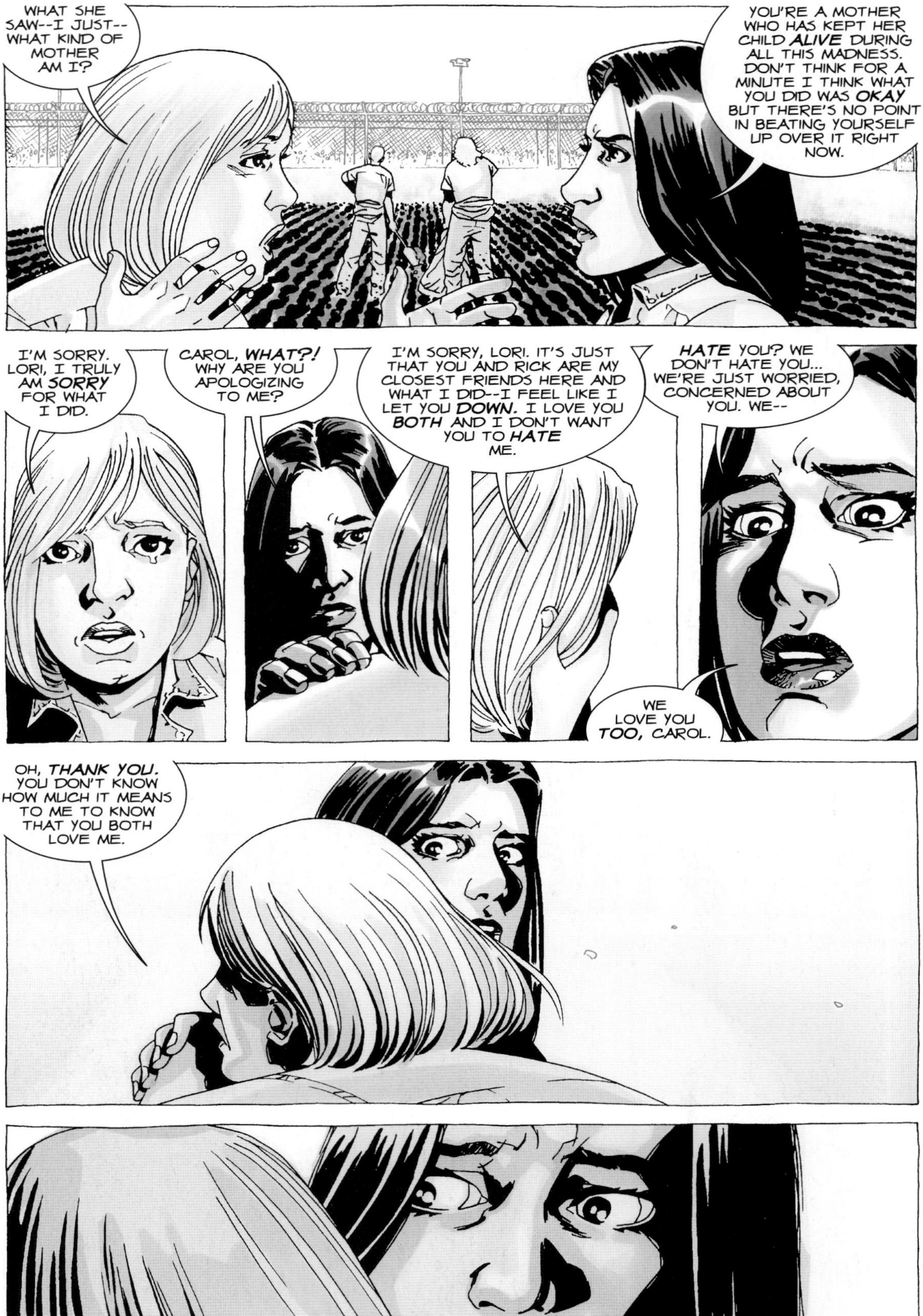
WHAT SHE SAW--I JUST-- WHAT KIND OF MOTHER AM I?
YOU'RE A MOTHER WHO HAS KEPT HER CHILD ALIVE DURING ALL THIS MADNESS. DON'T THINK FOR A MINUTE I THINK WHAT YOU DID WAS OKAY BUT THERE'S NO POINT IN BEATING YOURSELF UP OVER IT RIGHT NOW.
I'M SORRY. LORI, I TRULY AM SORRY FOR WHAT I DID.
CAROL, WHAT?! WHY ARE YOU APOLOGIZING TO ME?
I'M SORRY, LORI. IT'S JUST THAT YOU AND RICK ARE MY CLOSEST FRIENDS HERE AND WHAT I DID--I FEEL LIKE I LET YOU DOWN. I LOVE YOU BOTH AND I DON'T WANT YOU TO HATE ME.
HATE YOU? WE DON'T HATE YOU... WE'RE JUST WORRIED, CONCERNED ABOUT YOU. WE--
WE LOVE YOU TOO, CAROL.
OH, THANK YOU. YOU DON'T KNOW HOW MUCH IT MEANS TO ME TO KNOW THAT YOU BOTH LOVE ME.

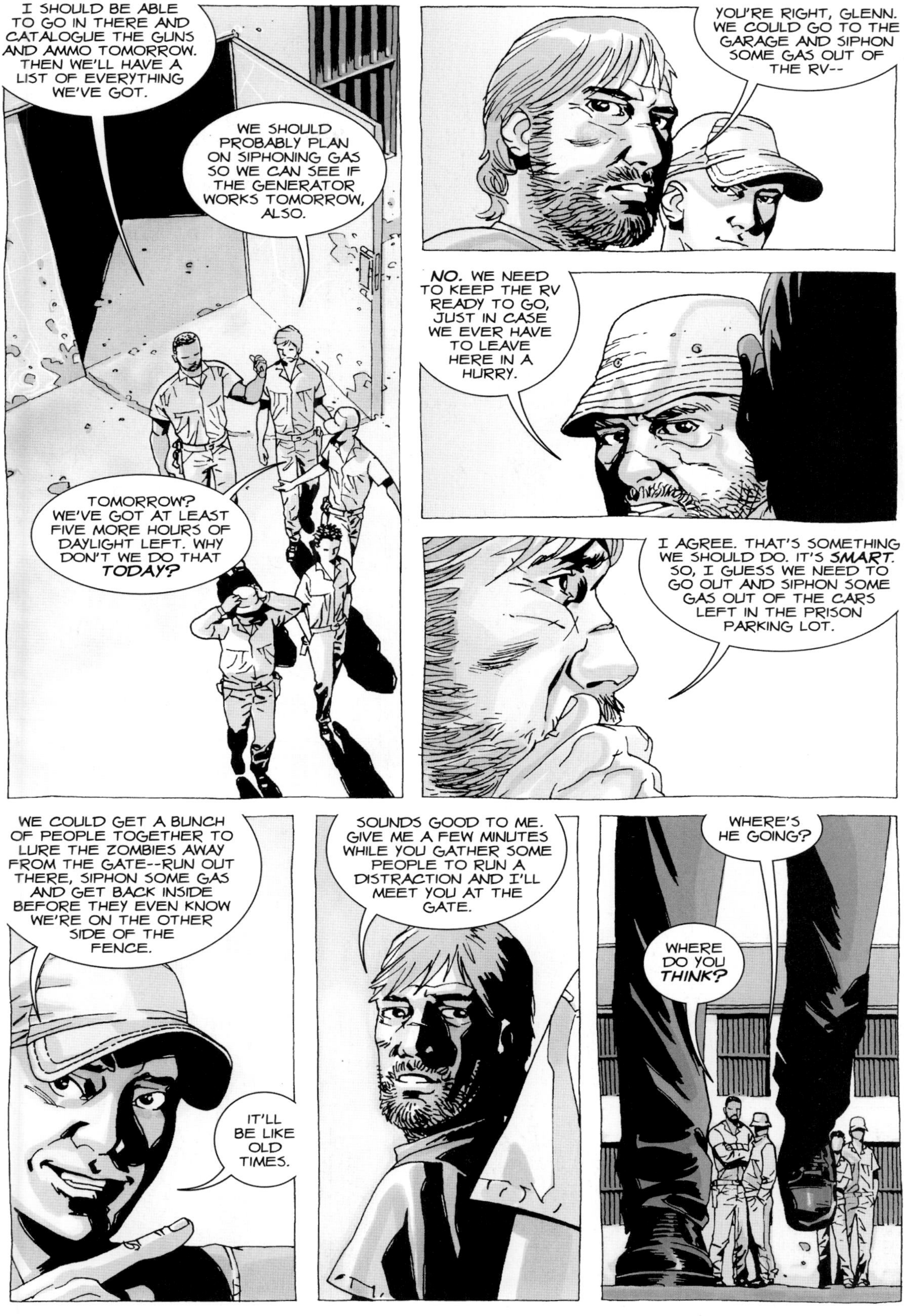
I SHOULD BE ABLE TO GO IN THERE AND CATALOGUE THE GUNS AND AMMO TOMORROW. THEN WE'LL HAVE A LIST OF EVERYTHING WE'VE GOT.
WE SHOULD PROBABLY PLAN ON SIPHONING GAS SO WE CAN SEE IF THE GENERATOR WORKS TOMORROW, ALSO.
TOMORROW? WE'VE GOT AT LEAST FIVE MORE HOURS OF DAYLIGHT LEFT. WHY DON'T WE DO THAT TODAY?
YOU'RE RIGHT, GLENN. WE COULD GO TO THE GARAGE AND SIPHON SOME GAS OUT OF THE RV--
NO. WE NEED TO KEEP THE RV READY TO GO, JUST IN CASE WE EVER HAVE TO LEAVE HERE IN A HURRY.
I AGREE. THAT'S SOMETHING WE SHOULD DO. IT'S SMART. SO, I GUESS WE NEED TO GO OUT AND SIPHON SOME GAS OUT OF THE CARS LEFT IN THE PRISON PARKING LOT.
WE COULD GET A BUNCH OF PEOPLE TOGETHER TO LURE THE ZOMBIES AWAY FROM THE GATE--RUN OUT THERE, SIPHON SOME GAS AND GET BACK INSIDE BEFORE THEY EVEN KNOW WE'RE ON THE OTHER SIDE OF THE FENCE.
IT'LL BE LIKE OLD TIMES.
SOUNDS GOOD TO ME. GIVE ME A FEW MINUTES WHILE YOU GATHER SOME PEOPLE TO RUN A DISTRACTION AND I'LL MEET YOU AT THE GATE.
WHERE'S HE GOING?
WHERE DO YOU THINK?

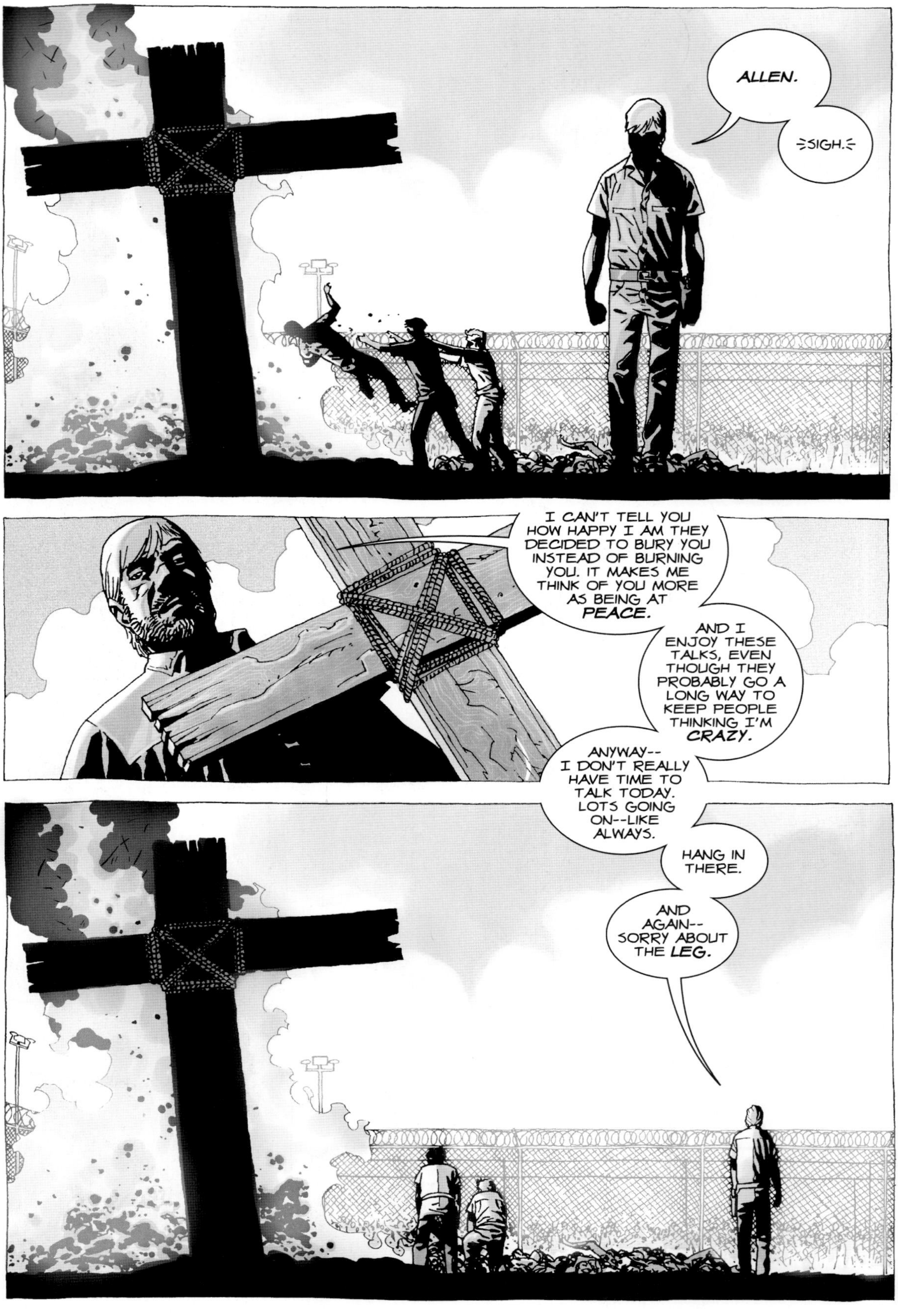
ALLEN.
SIGH.
I CAN'T TELL YOU HOW HAPPY I AM THEY DECIDED TO BURY YOU INSTEAD OF BURNING YOU. IT MAKES ME THINK OF YOU MORE AS BEING AT PEACE.
AND I ENJOY THESE TALKS, EVEN THOUGH THEY PROBABLY GO A LONG WAY TO KEEP PEOPLE THINKING I'M CRAZY.
ANYWAY-- I DON'T REALLY HAVE TIME TO TALK TODAY. LOTS GOING ON--LIKE ALWAYS.
HANG IN THERE.
AND AGAIN-- SORRY ABOUT THE LEG.

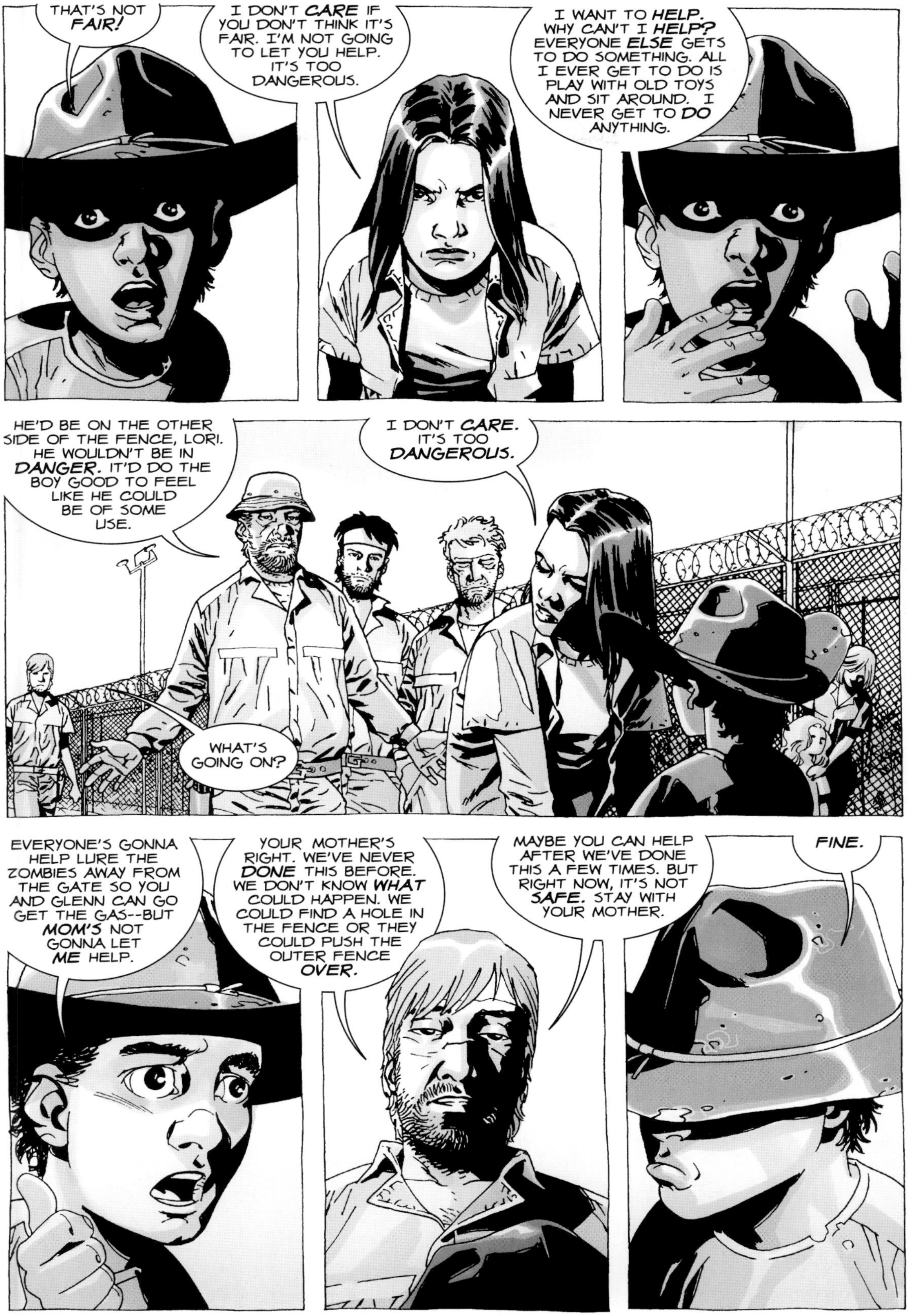
THAT'S NOT FAIR!
I DON'T CARE IF YOU DON'T THINK IT'S FAIR. I'M NOT GOING TO LET YOU HELP. IT'S TOO DANGEROUS.
I WANT TO HELP. WHY CAN'T I HELP? EVERYONE ELSE GETS TO DO SOMETHING. ALL I EVER GET TO DO IS PLAY WITH OLD TOYS AND SIT AROUND. I NEVER GET TO DO ANYTHING.
HE'D BE ON THE OTHER SIDE OF THE FENCE, LORI. HE WOULDN'T BE IN DANGER. IT'D DO THE BOY GOOD TO FEEL LIKE HE COULD BE OF SOME USE.
I DON'T CARE. IT'S TOO DANGEROUS.
WHAT'S GOING ON?
EVERYONE'S GONNA HELP LURE THE ZOMBIES AWAY FROM THE GATE SO YOU AND GLENN CAN GO GET THE GAS--BUT MOM'S NOT GONNA LET ME HELP.
YOUR MOTHER'S RIGHT. WE'VE NEVER DONE THIS BEFORE. WE DON'T KNOW WHAT COULD HAPPEN. WE COULD FIND A HOLE IN THE FENCE OR THEY COULD PUSH THE OUTER FENCE OVER.
MAYBE YOU CAN HELP AFTER WE'VE DONE THIS A FEW TIMES. BUT RIGHT NOW, IT'S NOT SAFE. STAY WITH YOUR MOTHER.
FINE.

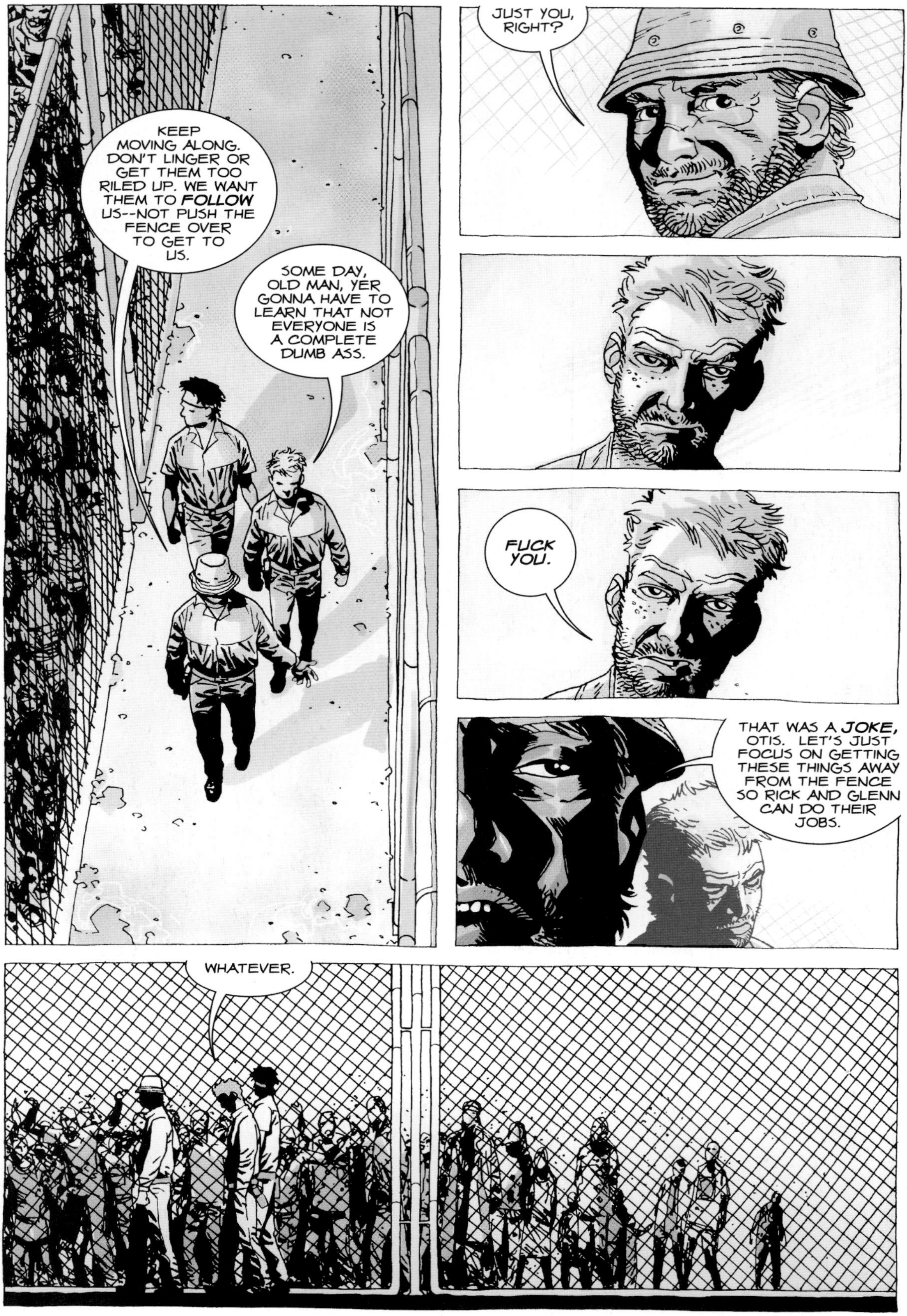
KEEP MOVING ALONG. DON'T LINGER OR GET THEM TOO RILED UP. WE WANT THEM TO FOLLOW US--NOT PUSH THE FENCE OVER TO GET TO US.
SOME DAY, OLD MAN, YER GONNA HAVE TO LEARN THAT NOT EVERYONE IS A COMPLETE DUMB ASS.
JUST YOU, RIGHT?
FUCK YOU.
THAT WAS A JOKE, OTIS. LET'S JUST FOCUS ON GETTING THESE THINGS AWAY FROM THE FENCE SO RICK AND GLENN CAN DO THEIR JOBS.
WHATEVER.

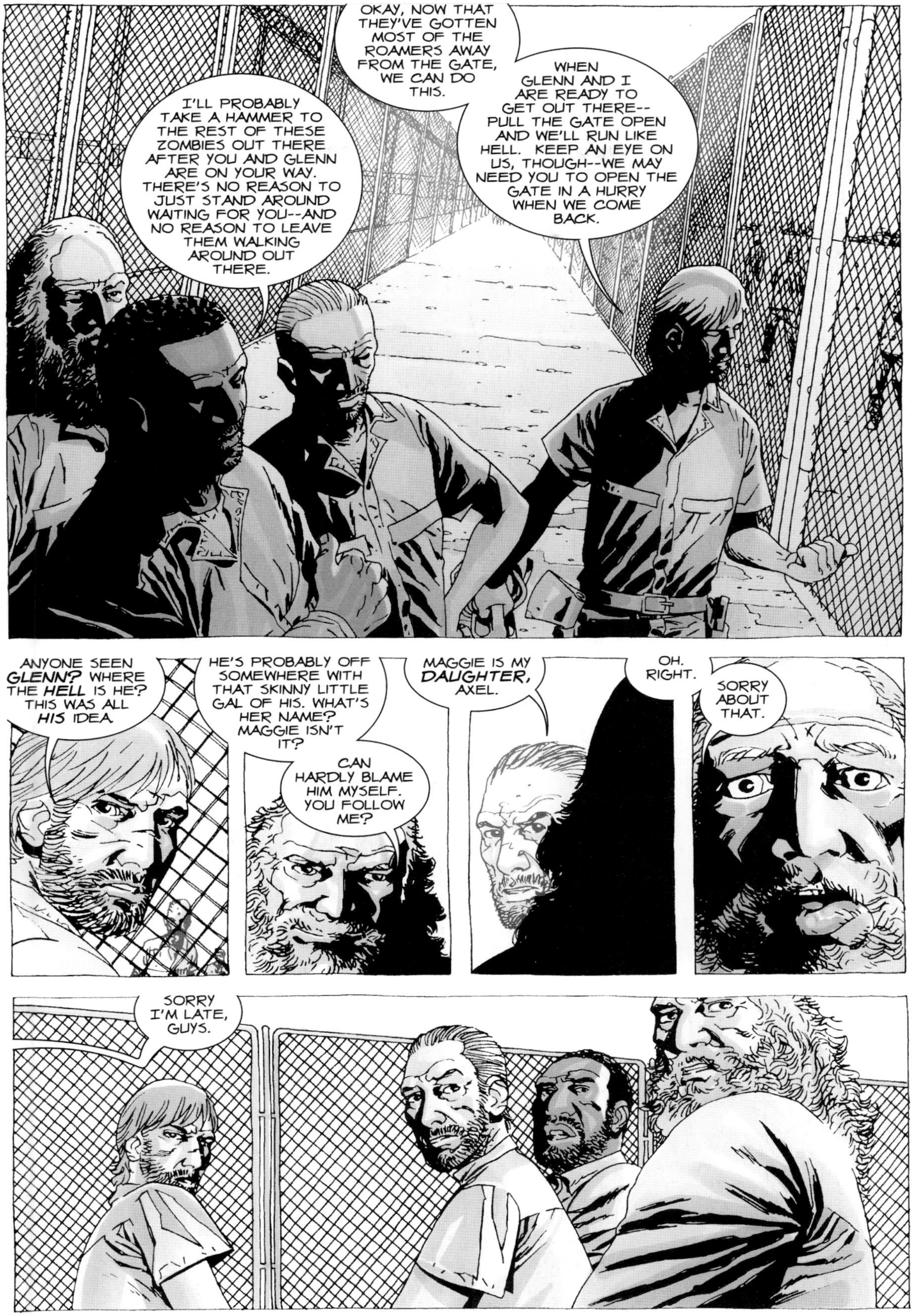
OKAY, NOW THAT THEY'VE GOTTEN MOST OF THE ROAMERS AWAY FROM THE GATE, WE CAN DO THIS.
WHEN GLENN AND I ARE READY TO GET OUT THERE-- PULL THE GATE OPEN AND WE'LL RUN LIKE HELL. KEEP AN EYE ON US, THOUGH--WE MAY NEED YOU TO OPEN THE GATE IN A HURRY WHEN WE COME BACK.
I'LL PROBABLY TAKE A HAMMER TO THE REST OF THESE ZOMBIES OUT THERE AFTER YOU AND GLENN ARE ON YOUR WAY. THERE'S NO REASON TO JUST STAND AROUND WAITING FOR YOU--AND NO REASON TO LEAVE THEM WALKING AROUND OUT THERE.
ANYONE SEEN GLENN? WHERE THE HELL IS HE? THIS WAS ALL HIS IDEA.
HE'S PROBABLY OFF SOMEWHERE WITH THAT SKINNY LITTLE GAL OF HIS. WHAT'S HER NAME? MAGGIE ISN'T IT?
CAN HARDLY BLAME HIM MYSELF. YOU FOLLOW ME?
MAGGIE IS MY DAUGHTER, AXEL.
OH. RIGHT.
SORRY ABOUT THAT.
SORRY I'M LATE, GUYS.

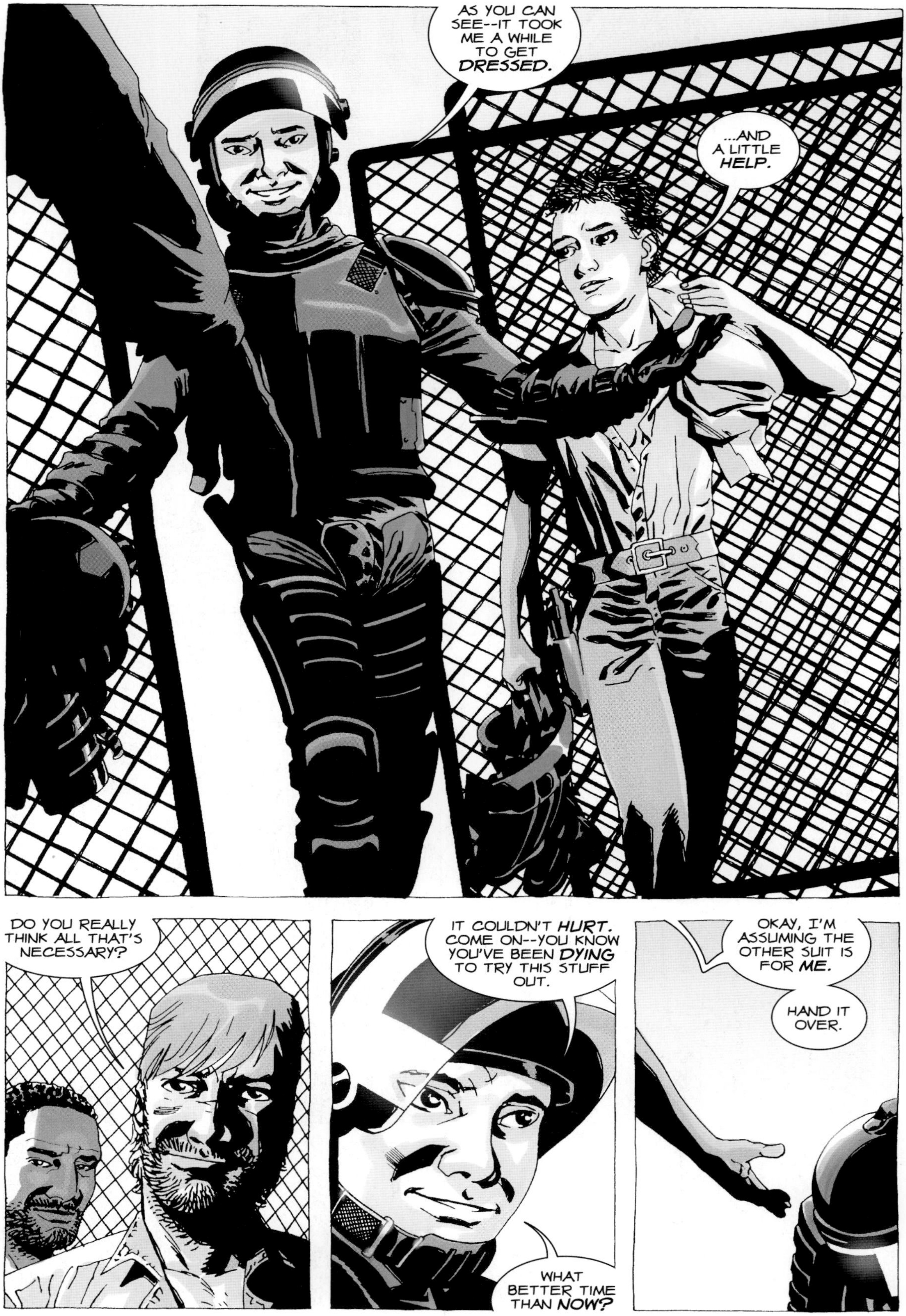
AS YOU CAN SEE--IT TOOK ME A WHILE TO GET DRESSED.
...AND A LITTLE HELP.
DO YOU REALLY THINK ALL THAT'S NECESSARY?
IT COULDN'T HURT. COME ON--YOU KNOW YOU'VE BEEN DYING TO TRY THIS STUFF OUT.
WHAT BETTER TIME THAN NOW?
OKAY, I'M ASSUMING THE OTHER SUIT IS FOR ME.
HAND IT OVER.

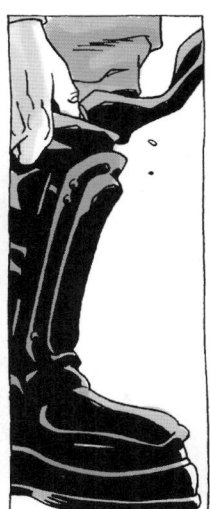
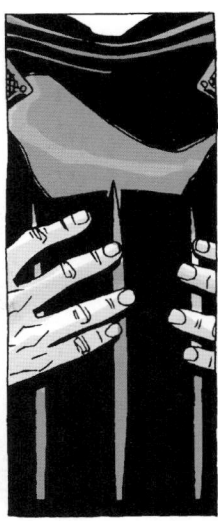

LOOKING *GOOD*, DUDE.

Y'KNOW, THEY HAD A BUNCH OF THESE UP THERE WITH THE SUITS. MIGHT BE USEFUL IF WE NEED TO BASH IN SOME HEADS WITHOUT DRAWING ATTENTION TO US WITH GUNFIRE.

I'LL STICK WITH MY AXE, THANK YOU VERY MUCH. I'VE GOTTEN USED TO USING IT IN MY *LEFT* HAND.

CAN'T DO MUCH OF ANYTHING DEADLY WITH THE RIGHT JUST YET, EXCEPT WAIL ON PEOPLE.

YOU GUYS READY?

JUST SAY THE WORD.

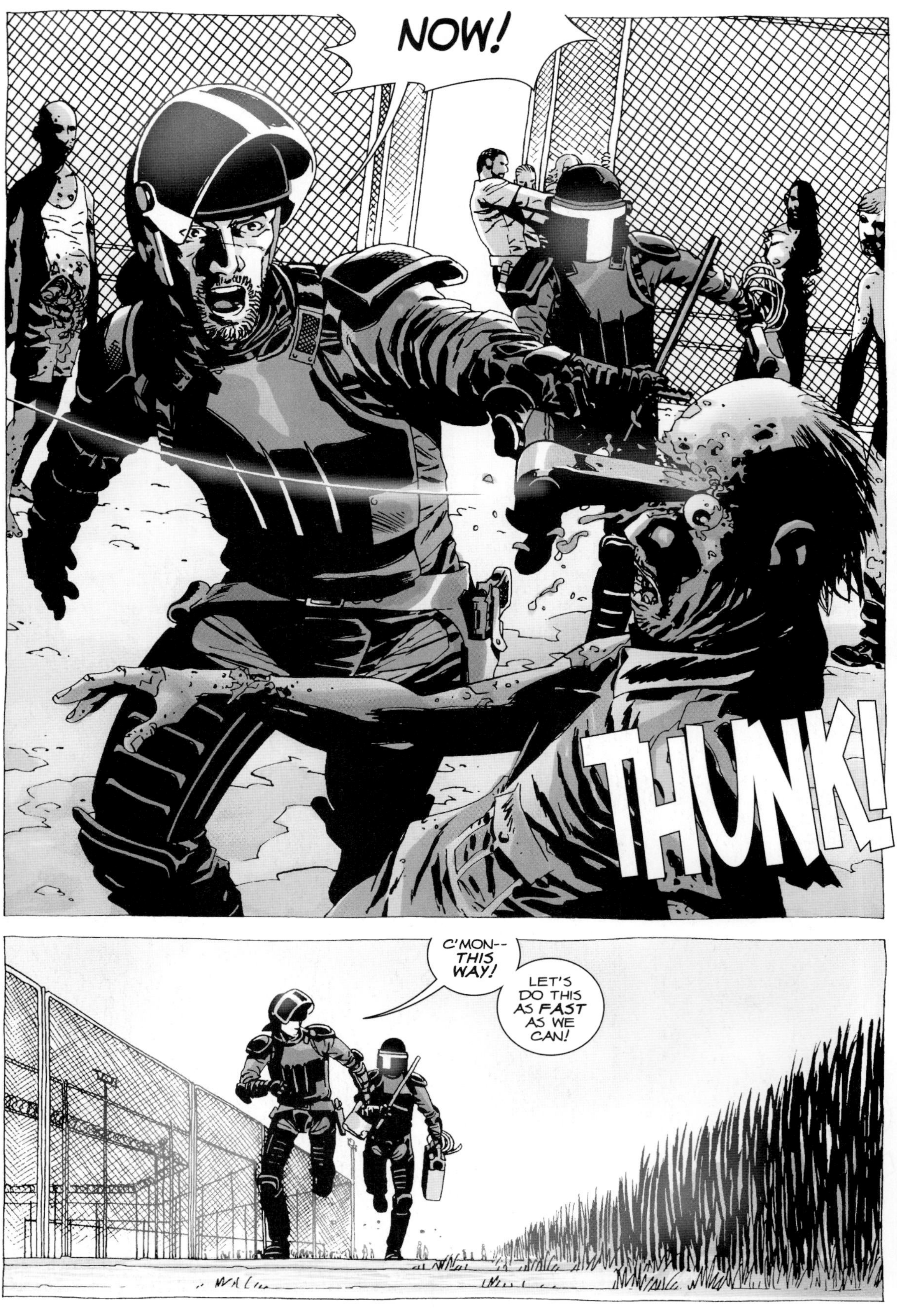
NOW!
THUNK!
C'MON-- THIS WAY!
LET'S DO THIS AS FAST AS WE CAN!

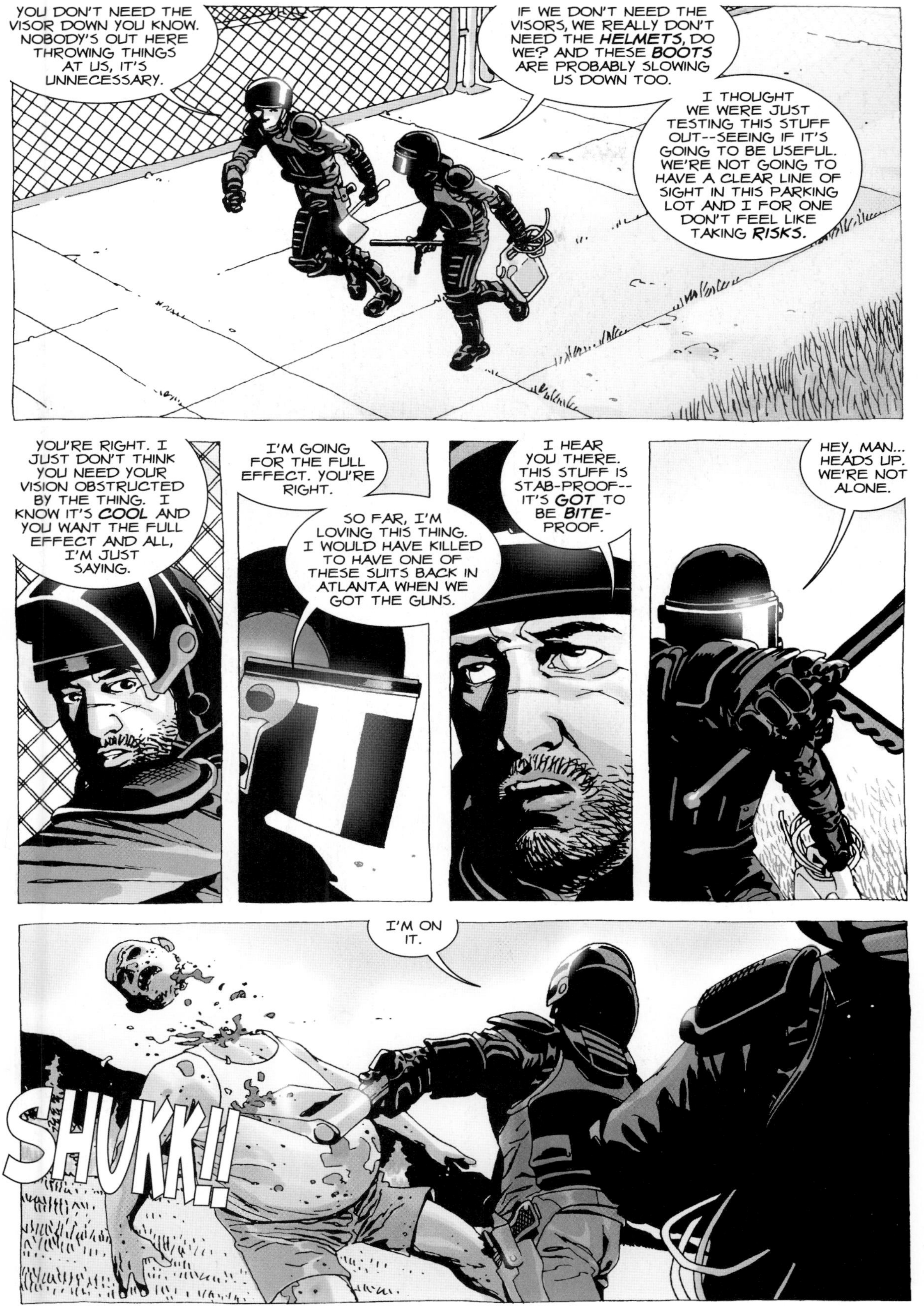
YOU DON'T NEED THE VISOR DOWN YOU KNOW. NOBODY'S OUT HERE THROWING THINGS AT US, IT'S UNNECESSARY.
IF WE DON'T NEED THE VISORS, WE REALLY DON'T NEED THE HELMETS, DO WE? AND THESE BOOTS ARE PROBABLY SLOWING US DOWN TOO.
I THOUGHT WE WERE JUST TESTING THIS STUFF OUT--SEEING IF IT'S GOING TO BE USEFUL. WE'RE NOT GOING TO HAVE A CLEAR LINE OF SIGHT IN THIS PARKING LOT AND I FOR ONE DON'T FEEL LIKE TAKING RISKS.
YOU'RE RIGHT. I JUST DON'T THINK YOU NEED YOUR VISION OBSTRUCTED BY THE THING. I KNOW IT'S COOL AND YOU WANT THE FULL EFFECT AND ALL, I'M JUST SAYING.
I'M GOING FOR THE FULL EFFECT. YOU'RE RIGHT.
SO FAR, I'M LOVING THIS THING. I WOULD HAVE KILLED TO HAVE ONE OF THESE SUITS BACK IN ATLANTA WHEN WE GOT THE GUNS.
I HEAR YOU THERE. THIS STUFF IS STAB-PROOF-- IT'S GOT TO BE BITE-PROOF.
HEY, MAN... HEADS UP. WE'RE NOT ALONE.
I'M ON IT.
SHUKK!!

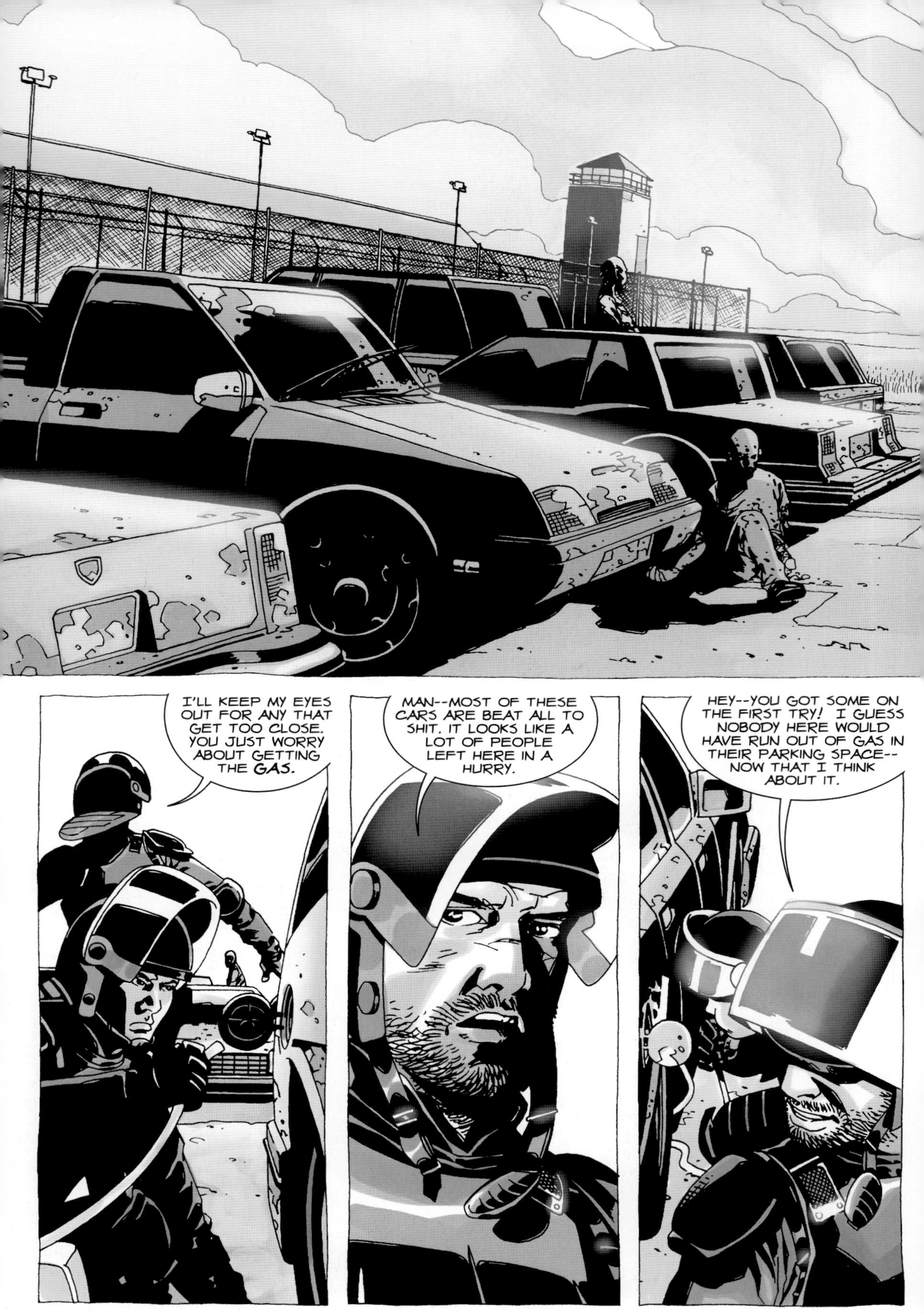
I'LL KEEP MY EYES OUT FOR ANY THAT GET TOO CLOSE. YOU JUST WORRY ABOUT GETTING THE GAS.
MAN--MOST OF THESE CARS ARE BEAT ALL TO SHIT. IT LOOKS LIKE A LOT OF PEOPLE LEFT HERE IN A HURRY.
HEY--YOU GOT SOME ON THE FIRST TRY! I GUESS NOBODY HERE WOULD HAVE RUN OUT OF GAS IN THEIR PARKING SPACE-- NOW THAT I THINK ABOUT IT.

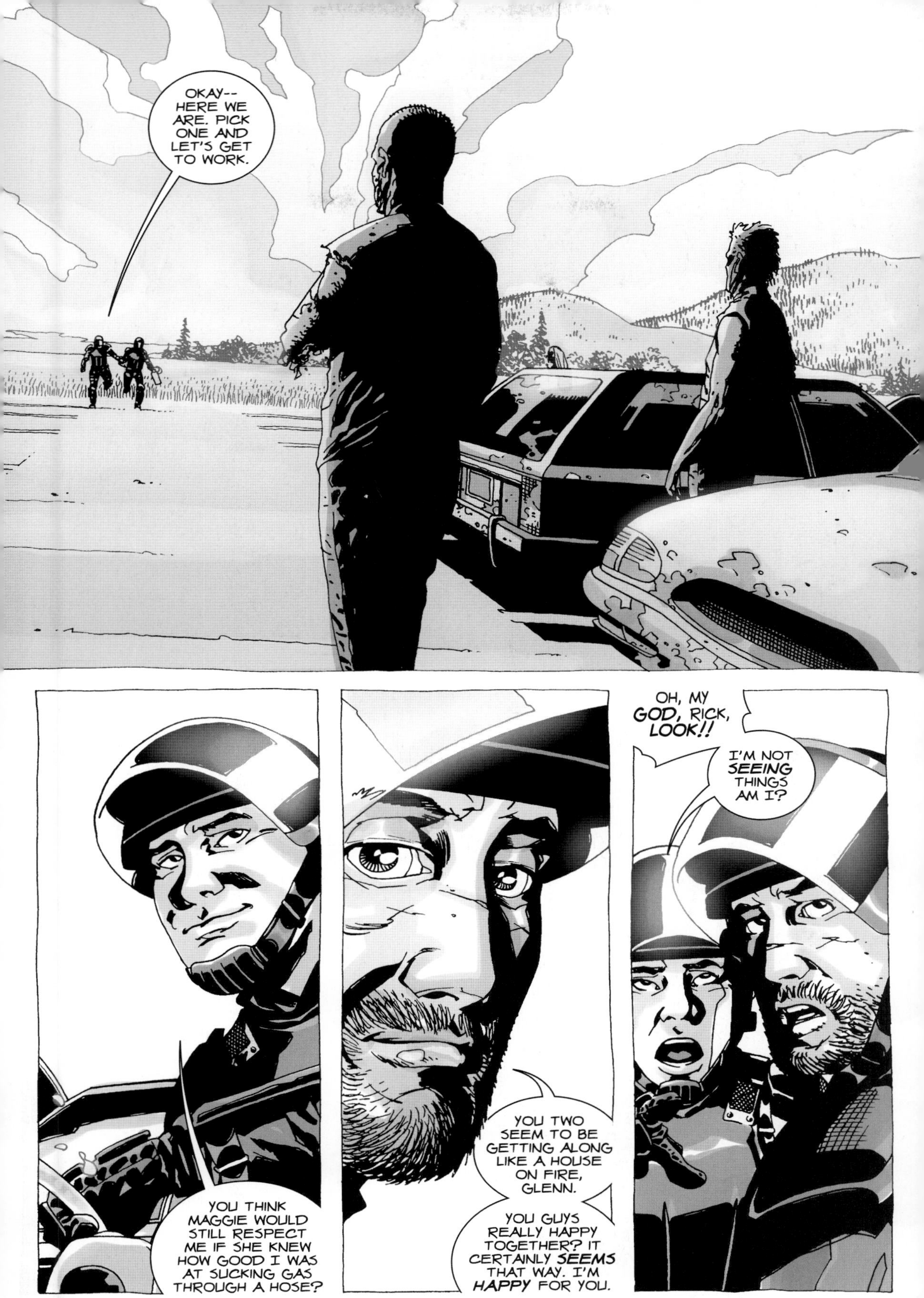
OKAY-- HERE WE ARE. PICK ONE AND LET'S GET TO WORK.
YOU THINK MAGGIE WOULD STILL RESPECT ME IF SHE KNEW HOW GOOD I WAS AT SUCKING GAS THROUGH A HOSE?
YOU TWO SEEM TO BE GETTING ALONG LIKE A HOUSE ON FIRE, GLENN.
YOU GUYS REALLY HAPPY TOGETHER? IT CERTAINLY SEEMS THAT WAY. I'M HAPPY FOR YOU.
OH, MY GOD, RICK, LOOK!!
I'M NOT SEEING THINGS AM I?

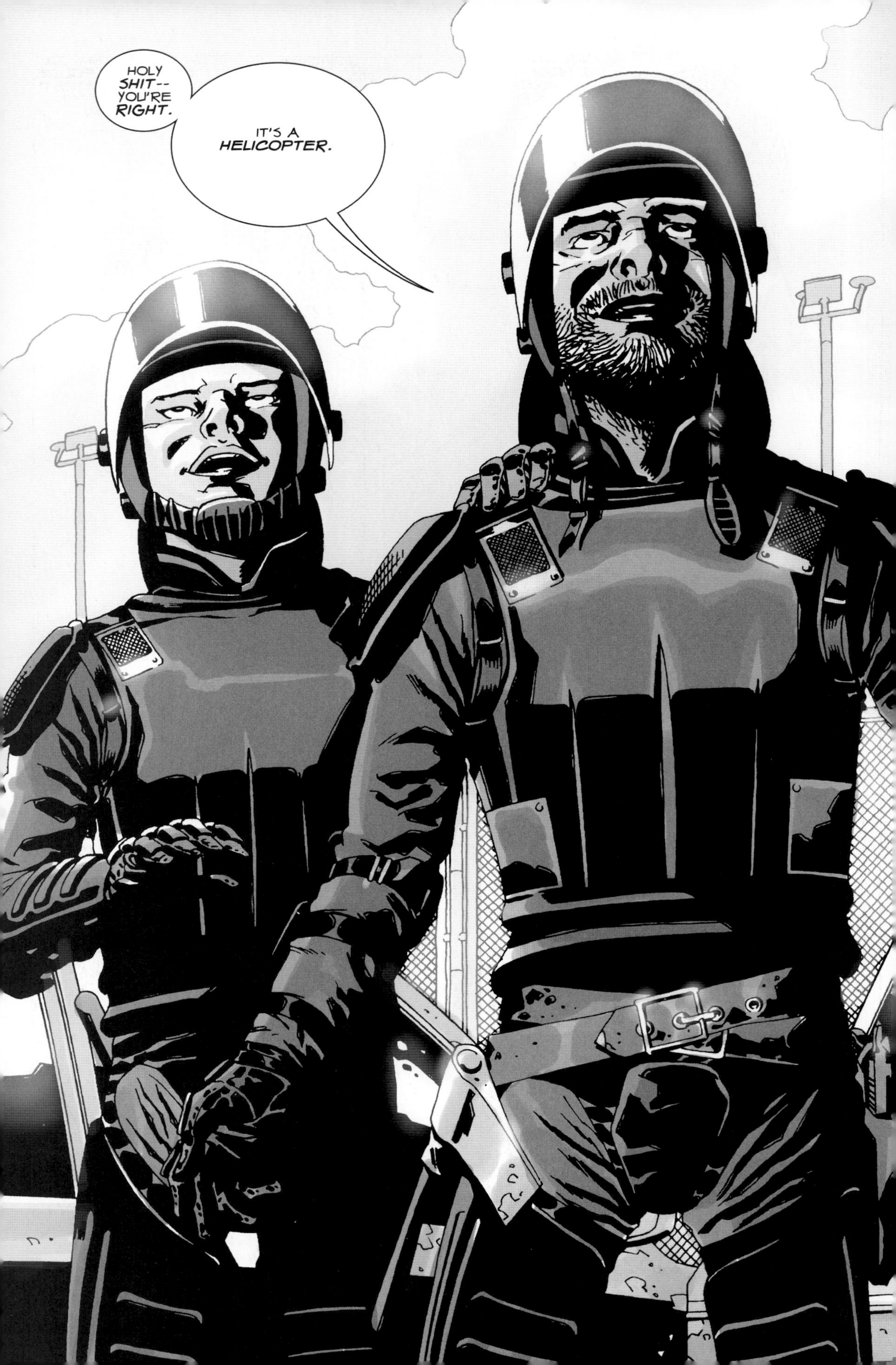

HOLY SHIT-- YOU'RE RIGHT.
IT'S A HELICOPTER.

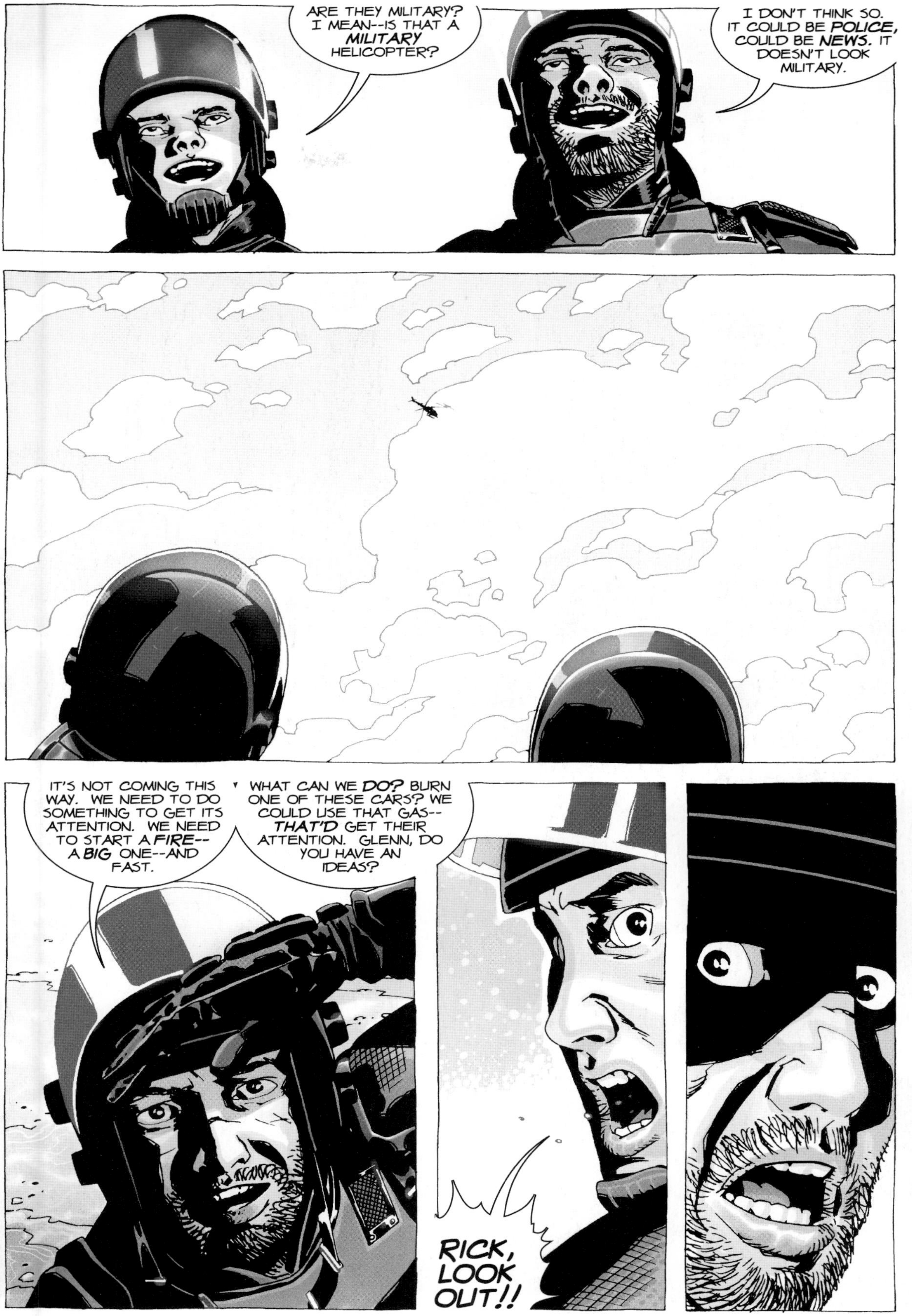
ARE THEY MILITARY? I MEAN--IS THAT A MILITARY HELICOPTER?
I DON'T THINK SO. IT COULD BE POLICE, COULD BE NEWS. IT DOESN'T LOOK MILITARY.
IT'S NOT COMING THIS WAY. WE NEED TO DO SOMETHING TO GET ITS ATTENTION. WE NEED TO START A FIRE-- A BIG ONE--AND FAST.
WHAT CAN WE DO? BURN ONE OF THESE CARS? WE COULD USE THAT GAS-- THAT'D GET THEIR ATTENTION. GLENN, DO YOU HAVE AN IDEAS?
RICK, LOOK OUT!!

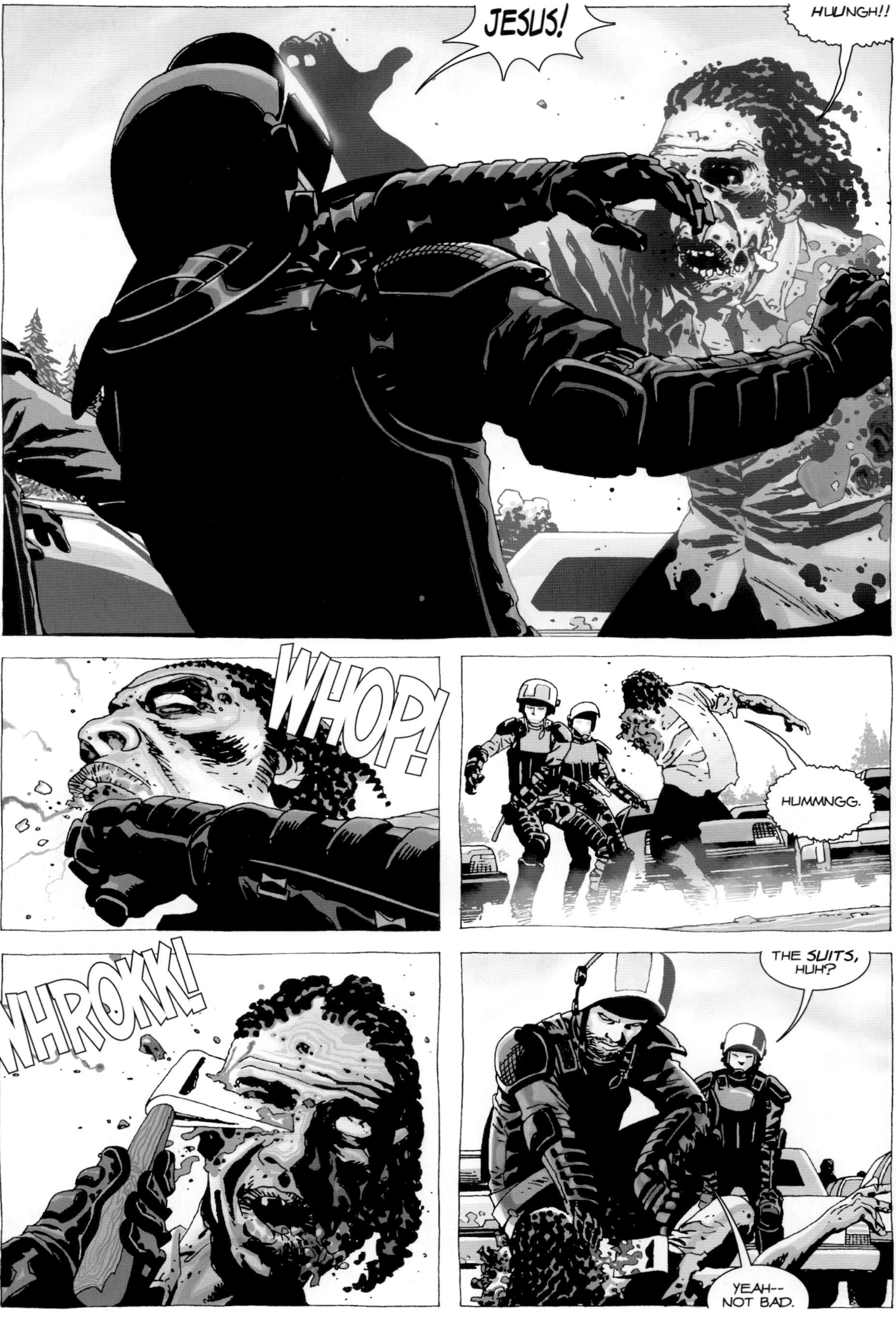
JESUS!
HUUNGH!!
WHOP!
HUMMNGG.
WHROKK!
THE SUITS, HUH?
YEAH-- NOT BAD.

WAIT--WHERE'D THE COPTER GO? WHERE IS IT?

THERE!

OH, SHIT--IS IT LANDING?

NO--I THINK IT'S CRASHING!

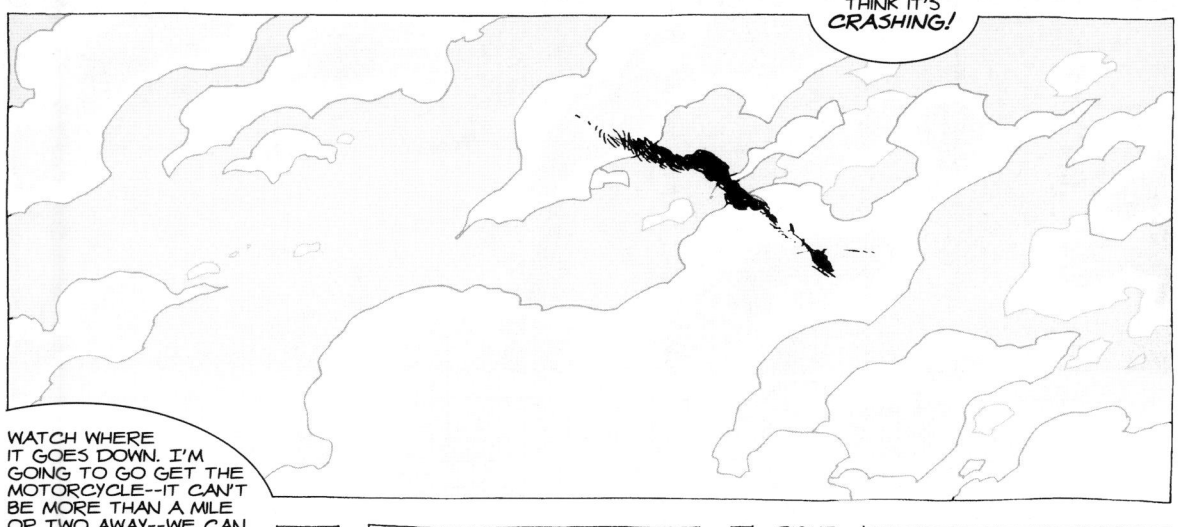

WATCH WHERE IT GOES DOWN. I'M GOING TO GO GET THE MOTORCYCLE--IT CAN'T BE MORE THAN A MILE OR TWO AWAY--WE CAN RIDE THAT OVER TO WHERE IT CRASHES. WE NEED TO FIND OUT WHO THESE PEOPLE ARE.

WE NEED TO KNOW WHERE THEY CAME FROM.

JUST GO TELL THEM WHERE WE'RE GOING WHILE I GET ONE OF THESE CARS STARTED. IF THERE ARE ANY SURVIVORS WE CAN'T TAKE THEM BACK HERE ON A MOTORCYCLE.

RIGHT.

GOOD THINKING.

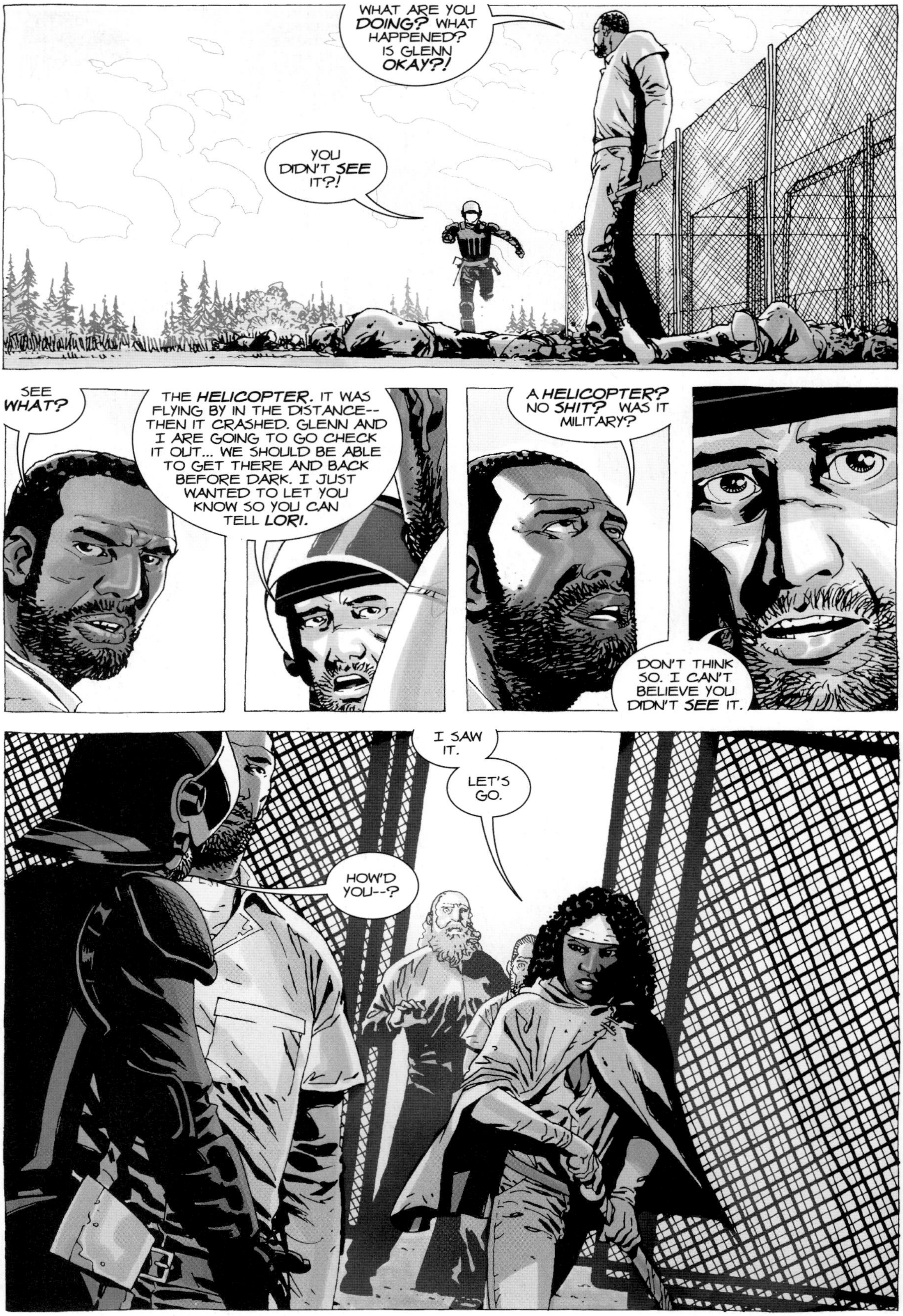
WHAT ARE YOU DOING? WHAT HAPPENED? IS GLENN OKAY?!
YOU DIDN'T SEE IT?!
SEE WHAT?
THE HELICOPTER. IT WAS FLYING BY IN THE DISTANCE-- THEN IT CRASHED. GLENN AND I ARE GOING TO GO CHECK IT OUT... WE SHOULD BE ABLE TO GET THERE AND BACK BEFORE DARK. I JUST WANTED TO LET YOU KNOW SO YOU CAN TELL LORI.
A HELICOPTER? NO SHIT? WAS IT MILITARY?
DON'T THINK SO. I CAN'T BELIEVE YOU DIDN'T SEE IT.
I SAW IT.
LET'S GO.
HOW'D YOU--?

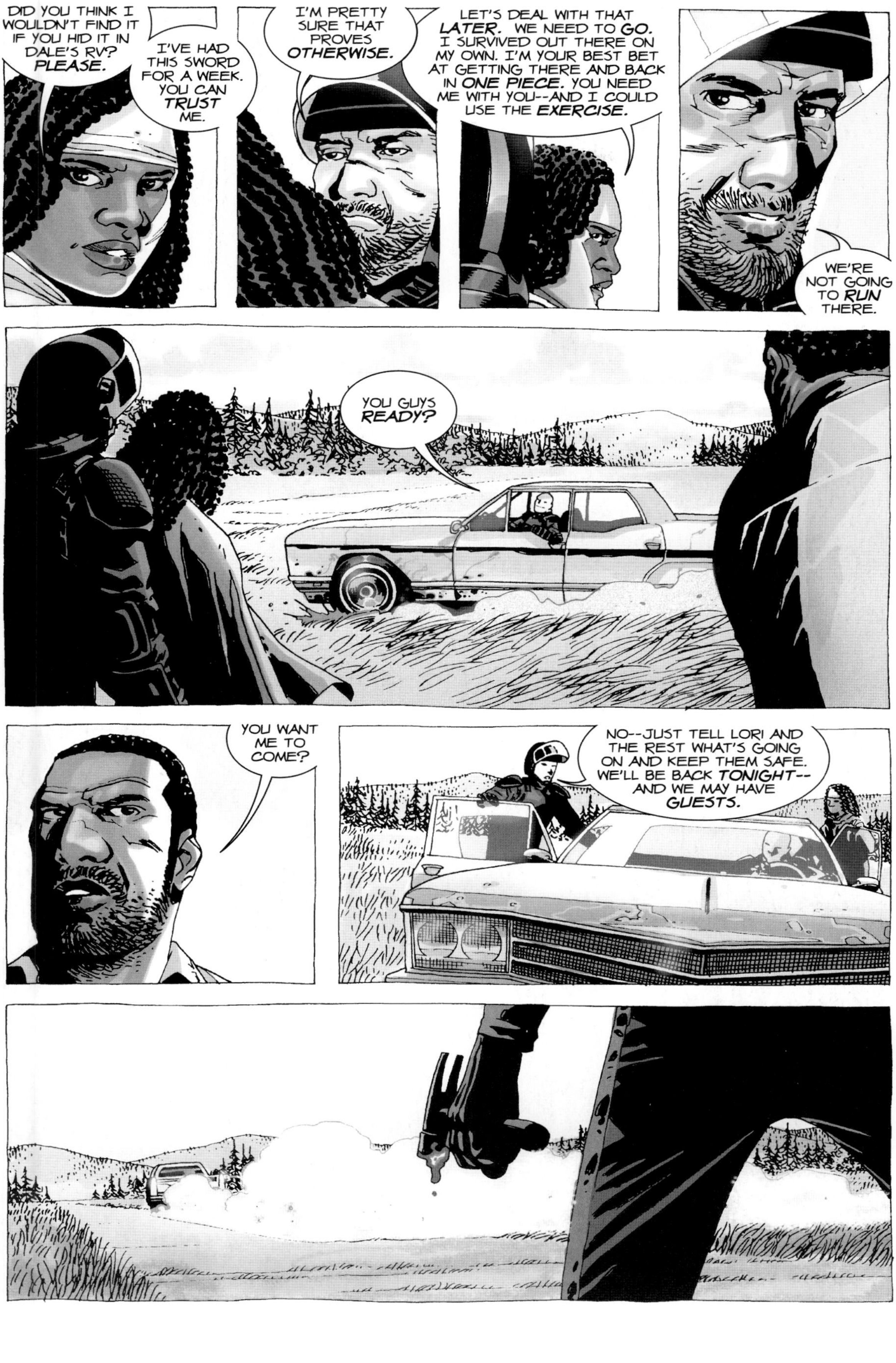
DID YOU THINK I WOULDN'T FIND IT IF YOU HID IT IN DALE'S RV? PLEASE.
I'VE HAD THIS SWORD FOR A WEEK. YOU CAN TRUST ME.
I'M PRETTY SURE THAT PROVES OTHERWISE.
LET'S DEAL WITH THAT LATER. WE NEED TO GO. I SURVIVED OUT THERE ON MY OWN. I'M YOUR BEST BET AT GETTING THERE AND BACK IN ONE PIECE. YOU NEED ME WITH YOU--AND I COULD USE THE EXERCISE.
WE'RE NOT GOING TO RUN THERE.
YOU GUYS READY?
YOU WANT ME TO COME?
NO--JUST TELL LORI AND THE REST WHAT'S GOING ON AND KEEP THEM SAFE. WE'LL BE BACK TONIGHT-- AND WE MAY HAVE GUESTS.

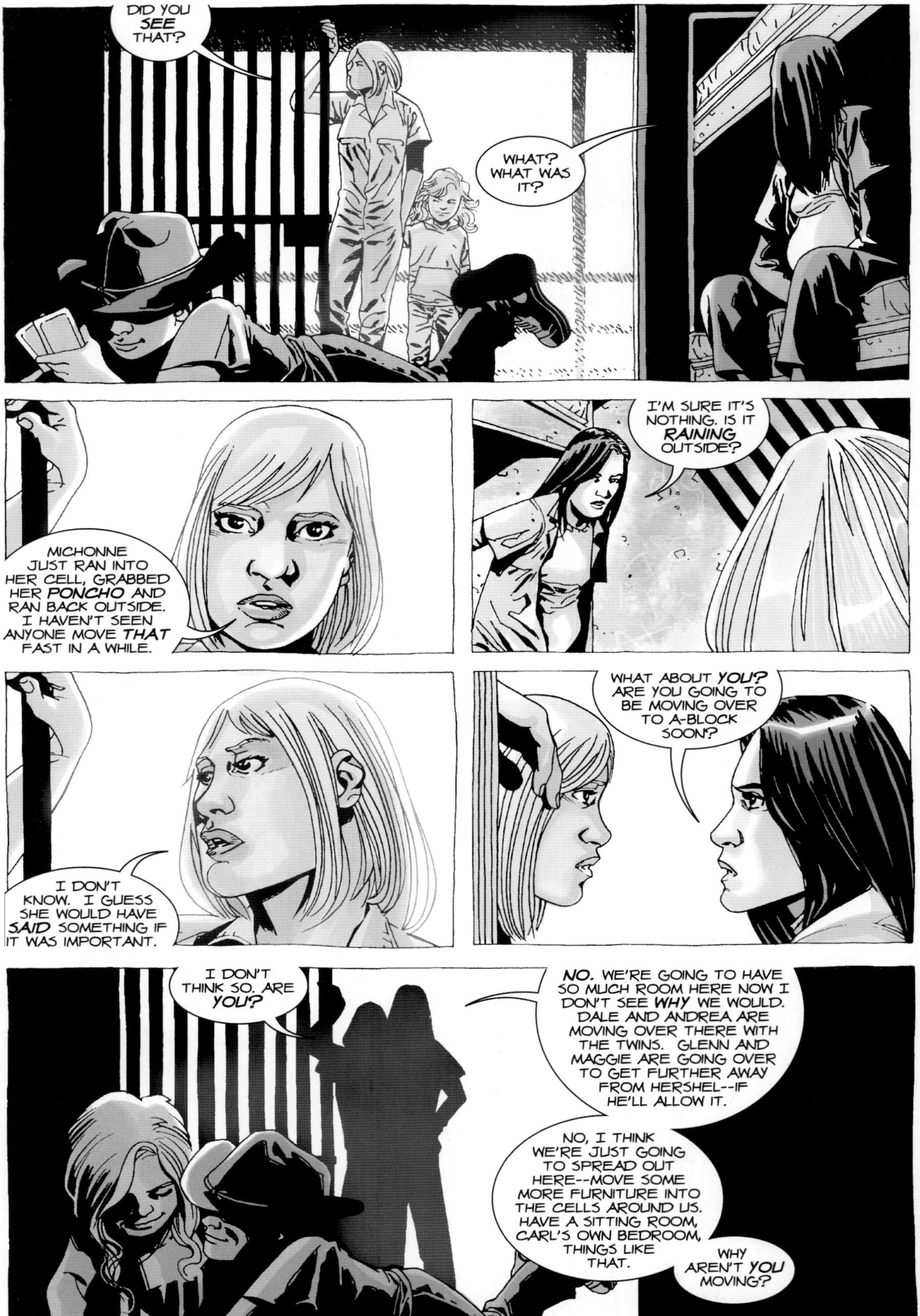

DID YOU SEE THAT?
WHAT? WHAT WAS IT?
MICHONNE JUST RAN INTO HER CELL, GRABBED HER PONCHO AND RAN BACK OUTSIDE. I HAVEN'T SEEN ANYONE MOVE THAT FAST IN A WHILE.
I'M SURE IT'S NOTHING. IS IT RAINING OUTSIDE?
I DON'T KNOW. I GUESS SHE WOULD HAVE SAID SOMETHING IF IT WAS IMPORTANT.
WHAT ABOUT YOU? ARE YOU GOING TO BE MOVING OVER TO A-BLOCK SOON?
I DON'T THINK SO. ARE YOU?
NO. WE'RE GOING TO HAVE SO MUCH ROOM HERE NOW I DON'T SEE WHY WE WOULD. DALE AND ANDREA ARE MOVING OVER THERE WITH THE TWINS. GLENN AND MAGGIE ARE GOING OVER TO GET FURTHER AWAY FROM HERSHEL--IF HE'LL ALLOW IT.
NO, I THINK WE'RE JUST GOING TO SPREAD OUT HERE--MOVE SOME MORE FURNITURE INTO THE CELLS AROUND US. HAVE A SITTING ROOM, CARL'S OWN BEDROOM, THINGS LIKE THAT.
WHY AREN'T YOU MOVING?

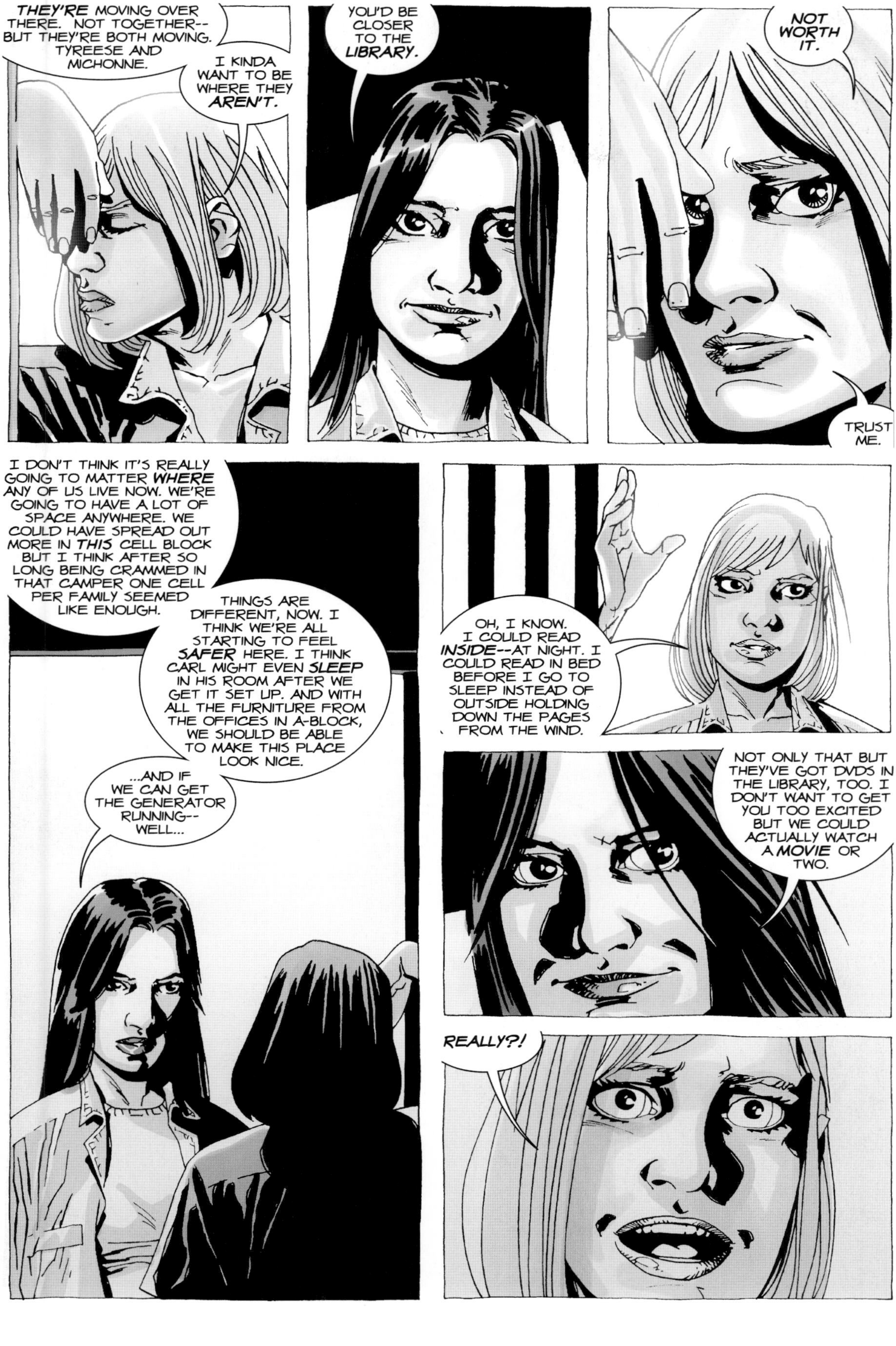
THEY'RE MOVING OVER THERE. NOT TOGETHER-- BUT THEY'RE BOTH MOVING. TYREESE AND MICHONNE.
I KINDA WANT TO BE WHERE THEY AREN'T.
YOU'D BE CLOSER TO THE LIBRARY.
NOT WORTH IT.
TRUST ME.
I DON'T THINK IT'S REALLY GOING TO MATTER WHERE ANY OF US LIVE NOW. WE'RE GOING TO HAVE A LOT OF SPACE ANYWHERE. WE COULD HAVE SPREAD OUT MORE IN THIS CELL BLOCK BUT I THINK AFTER SO LONG BEING CRAMMED IN THAT CAMPER ONE CELL PER FAMILY SEEMED LIKE ENOUGH.
THINGS ARE DIFFERENT, NOW. I THINK WE'RE ALL STARTING TO FEEL SAFER HERE. I THINK CARL MIGHT EVEN SLEEP IN HIS ROOM AFTER WE GET IT SET UP. AND WITH ALL THE FURNITURE FROM THE OFFICES IN A-BLOCK, WE SHOULD BE ABLE TO MAKE THIS PLACE LOOK NICE.
...AND IF WE CAN GET THE GENERATOR RUNNING-- WELL...
OH, I KNOW. I COULD READ INSIDE--AT NIGHT. I COULD READ IN BED BEFORE I GO TO SLEEP INSTEAD OF OUTSIDE HOLDING DOWN THE PAGES FROM THE WIND.
NOT ONLY THAT BUT THEY'VE GOT DVDS IN THE LIBRARY, TOO. I DON'T WANT TO GET YOU TOO EXCITED BUT WE COULD ACTUALLY WATCH A MOVIE OR TWO.
REALLY?!

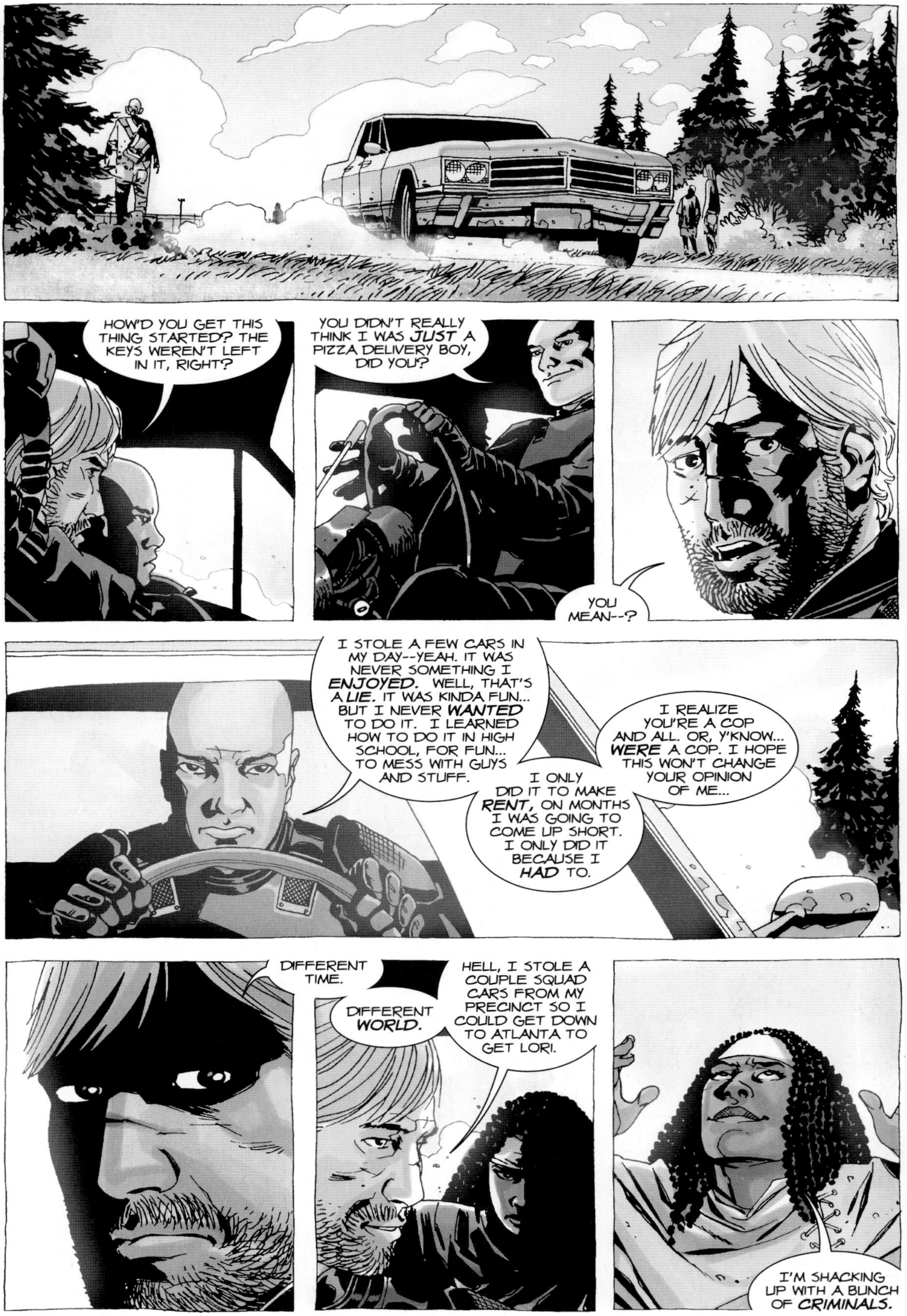
HOW'D YOU GET THIS THING STARTED? THE KEYS WEREN'T LEFT IN IT, RIGHT?
YOU DIDN'T REALLY THINK I WAS *JUST* A PIZZA DELIVERY BOY, DID YOU?
YOU MEAN--?
I STOLE A FEW CARS IN MY DAY--YEAH. IT WAS NEVER SOMETHING I ***ENJOYED.*** WELL, THAT'S A ***LIE.*** IT WAS KINDA FUN... BUT I NEVER ***WANTED*** TO DO IT. I LEARNED HOW TO DO IT IN HIGH SCHOOL, FOR FUN... TO MESS WITH GUYS AND STUFF.
I ONLY DID IT TO MAKE ***RENT,*** ON MONTHS I WAS GOING TO COME UP SHORT. I ONLY DID IT BECAUSE I ***HAD*** TO.
I REALIZE YOU'RE A COP AND ALL. OR, Y'KNOW... ***WERE*** A COP. I HOPE THIS WON'T CHANGE YOUR OPINION OF ME...
DIFFERENT TIME.
DIFFERENT ***WORLD.***
HELL, I STOLE A COUPLE SQUAD CARS FROM MY PRECINCT SO I COULD GET DOWN TO ATLANTA TO GET LORI.
I'M SHACKING UP WITH A BUNCH OF ***CRIMINALS.***

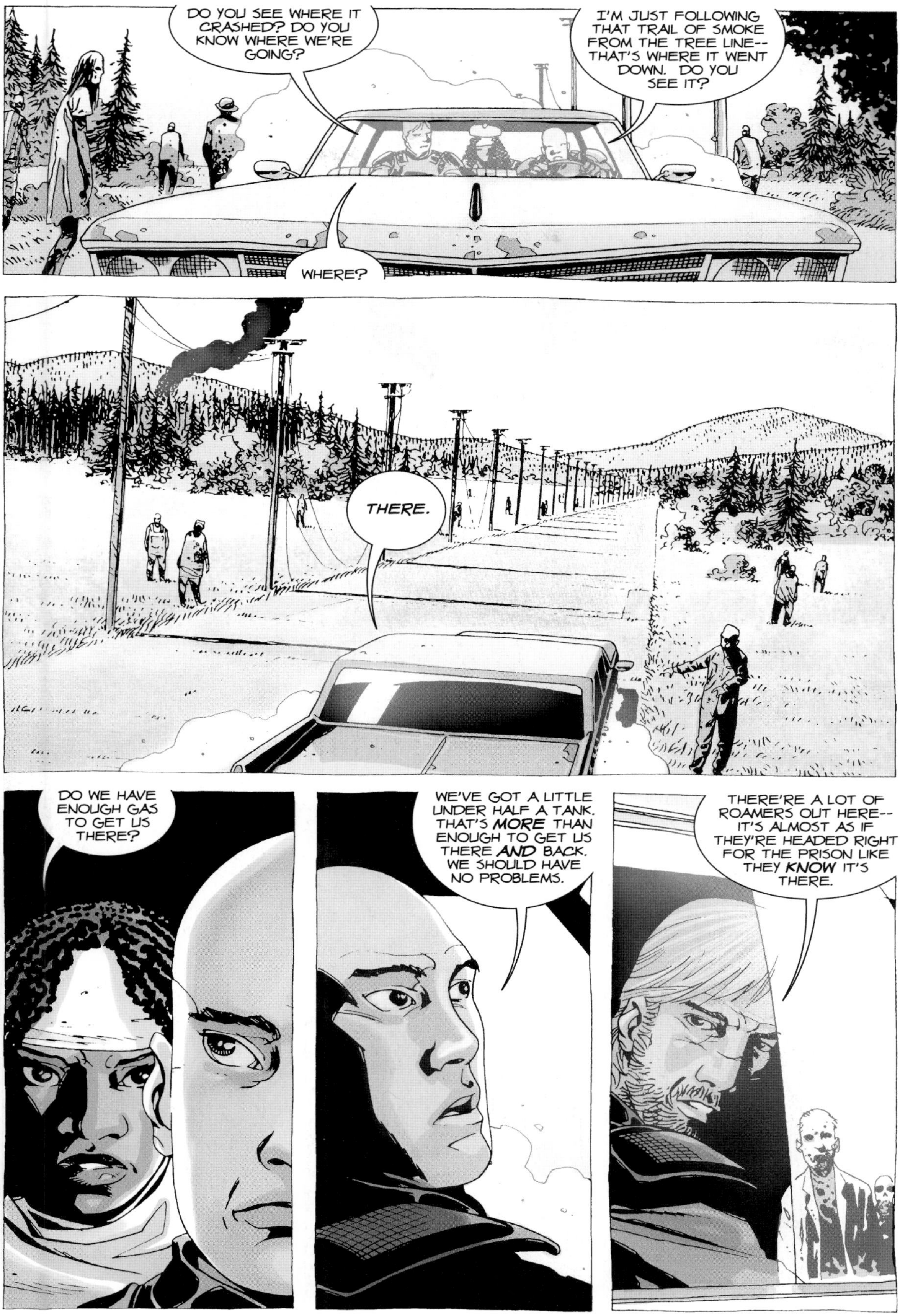
DO YOU SEE WHERE IT CRASHED? DO YOU KNOW WHERE WE'RE GOING?
I'M JUST FOLLOWING THAT TRAIL OF SMOKE FROM THE TREE LINE-- THAT'S WHERE IT WENT DOWN. DO YOU SEE IT?
WHERE?
THERE.
DO WE HAVE ENOUGH GAS TO GET US THERE?
WE'VE GOT A LITTLE UNDER HALF A TANK. THAT'S MORE THAN ENOUGH TO GET US THERE AND BACK. WE SHOULD HAVE NO PROBLEMS.
THERE'RE A LOT OF ROAMERS OUT HERE-- IT'S ALMOST AS IF THEY'RE HEADED RIGHT FOR THE PRISON LIKE THEY KNOW IT'S THERE.

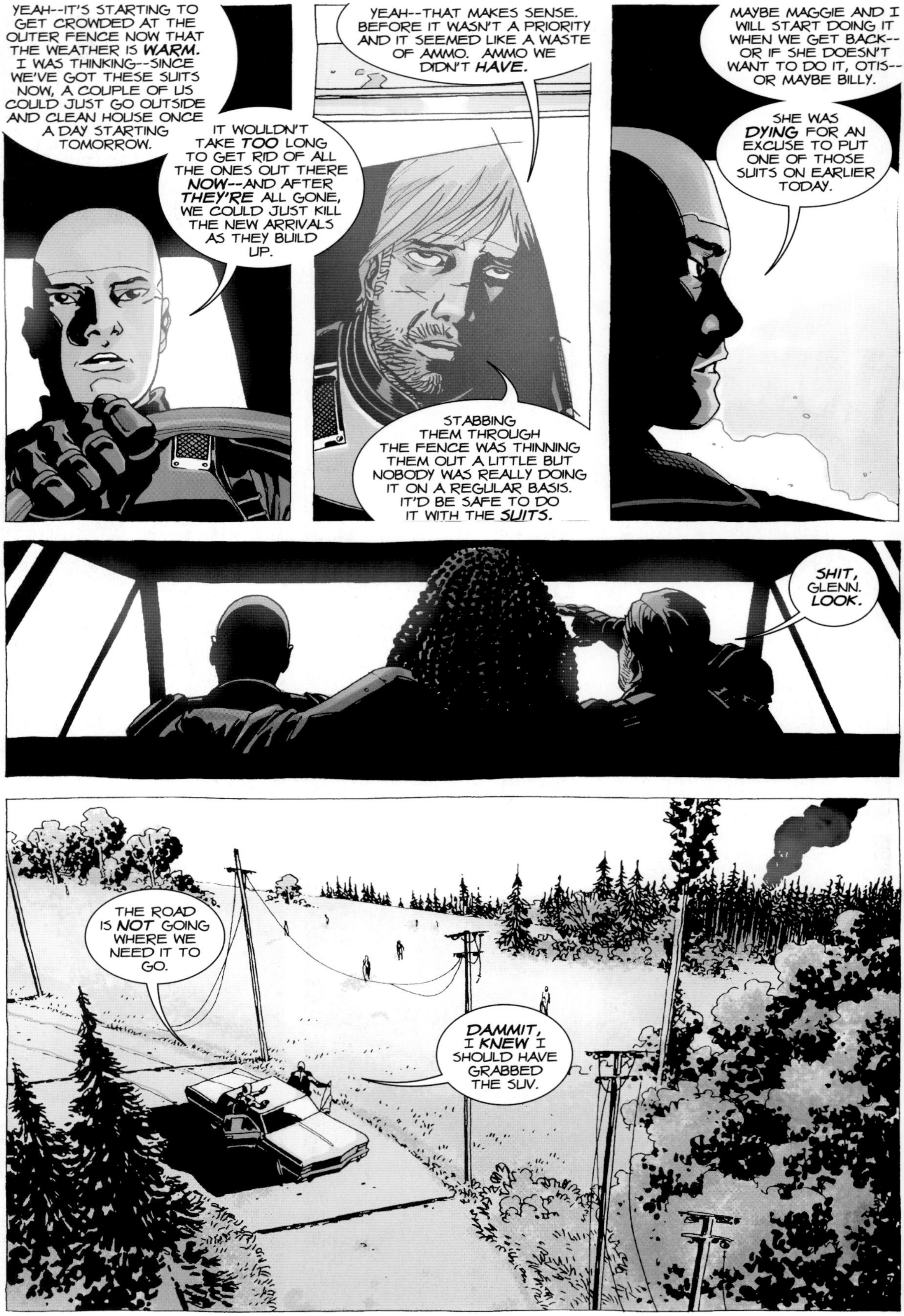
YEAH--IT'S STARTING TO GET CROWDED AT THE OUTER FENCE NOW THAT THE WEATHER IS WARM. I WAS THINKING--SINCE WE'VE GOT THESE SUITS NOW, A COUPLE OF US COULD JUST GO OUTSIDE AND CLEAN HOUSE ONCE A DAY STARTING TOMORROW.
IT WOULDN'T TAKE TOO LONG TO GET RID OF ALL THE ONES OUT THERE NOW--AND AFTER THEY'RE ALL GONE, WE COULD JUST KILL THE NEW ARRIVALS AS THEY BUILD UP.
YEAH--THAT MAKES SENSE. BEFORE IT WASN'T A PRIORITY AND IT SEEMED LIKE A WASTE OF AMMO. AMMO WE DIDN'T HAVE.
STABBING THEM THROUGH THE FENCE WAS THINNING THEM OUT A LITTLE BUT NOBODY WAS REALLY DOING IT ON A REGULAR BASIS. IT'D BE SAFE TO DO IT WITH THE SUITS.
MAYBE MAGGIE AND I WILL START DOING IT WHEN WE GET BACK--OR IF SHE DOESN'T WANT TO DO IT, OTIS--OR MAYBE BILLY.
SHE WAS DYING FOR AN EXCUSE TO PUT ONE OF THOSE SUITS ON EARLIER TODAY.
SHIT, GLENN. LOOK.
THE ROAD IS NOT GOING WHERE WE NEED IT TO GO.
DAMMIT, I KNEW I SHOULD HAVE GRABBED THE SUV.

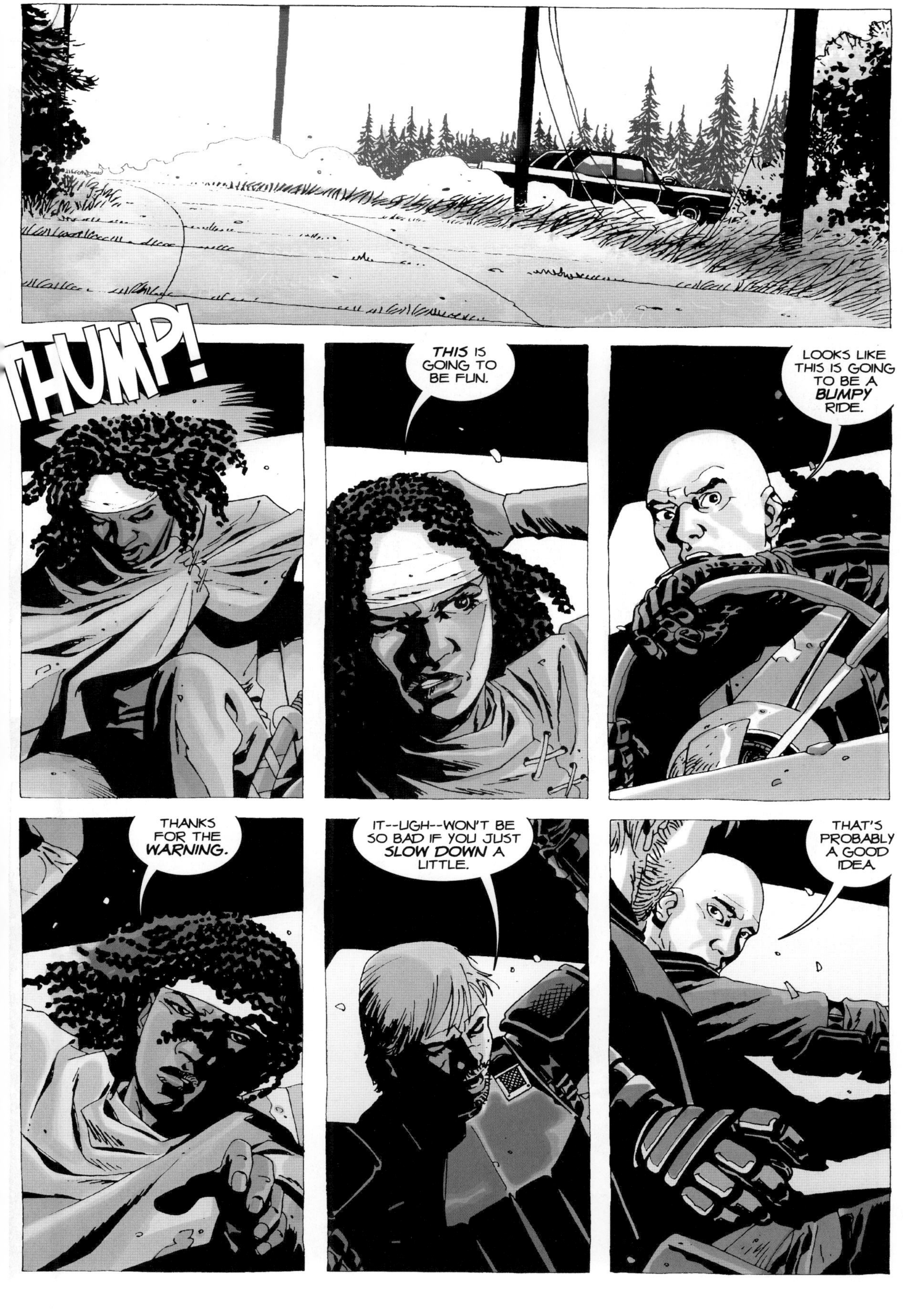

THUMP!
THIS IS GOING TO BE FUN.
LOOKS LIKE THIS IS GOING TO BE A BUMPY RIDE.
THANKS FOR THE WARNING.
IT--UGH--WON'T BE SO BAD IF YOU JUST SLOW DOWN A LITTLE.
THAT'S PROBABLY A GOOD IDEA

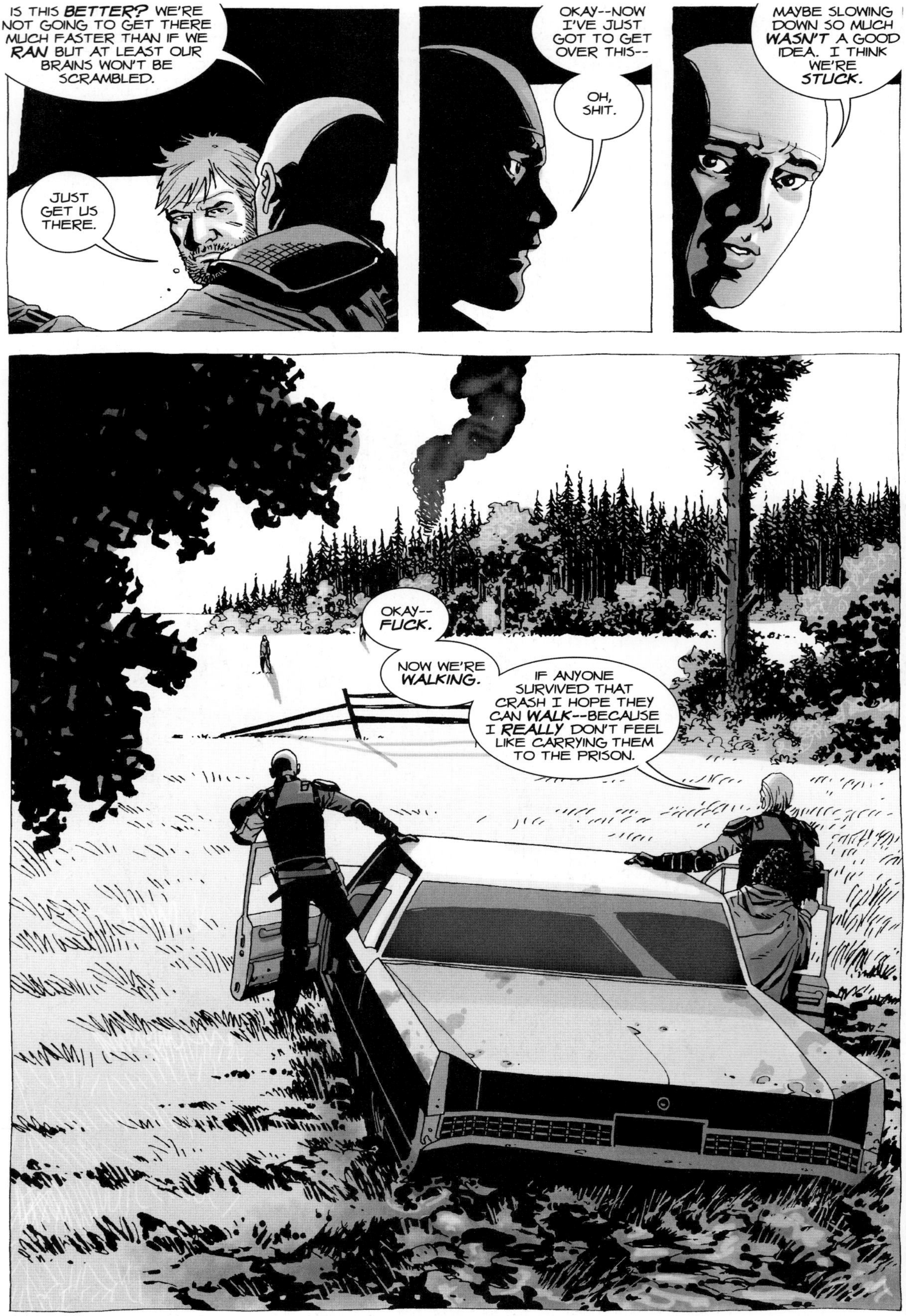
IS THIS BETTER? WE'RE NOT GOING TO GET THERE MUCH FASTER THAN IF WE RAN BUT AT LEAST OUR BRAINS WON'T BE SCRAMBLED.
JUST GET US THERE.
OKAY--NOW I'VE JUST GOT TO GET OVER THIS--
OH, SHIT.
MAYBE SLOWING DOWN SO MUCH WASN'T A GOOD IDEA. I THINK WE'RE STUCK.
OKAY-- FUCK.
NOW WE'RE WALKING.
IF ANYONE SURVIVED THAT CRASH I HOPE THEY CAN WALK--BECAUSE I REALLY DON'T FEEL LIKE CARRYING THEM TO THE PRISON.

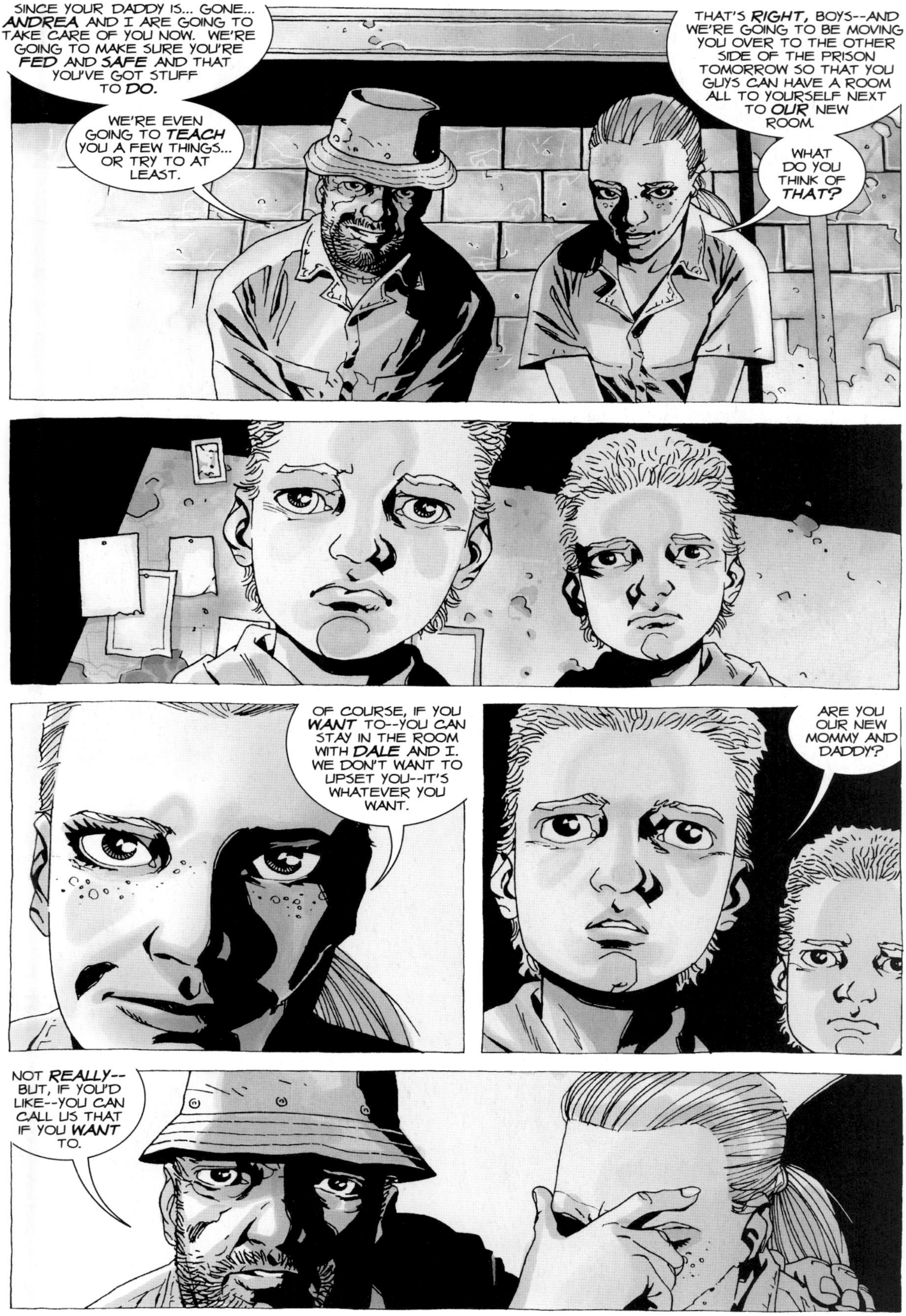
SINCE YOUR DADDY IS... GONE... ANDREA AND I ARE GOING TO TAKE CARE OF YOU NOW. WE'RE GOING TO MAKE SURE YOU'RE FED AND SAFE AND THAT YOU'VE GOT STUFF TO DO.
WE'RE EVEN GOING TO TEACH YOU A FEW THINGS... OR TRY TO AT LEAST.
THAT'S RIGHT, BOYS--AND WE'RE GOING TO BE MOVING YOU OVER TO THE OTHER SIDE OF THE PRISON TOMORROW SO THAT YOU GUYS CAN HAVE A ROOM ALL TO YOURSELF NEXT TO OUR NEW ROOM.
WHAT DO YOU THINK OF THAT?
OF COURSE, IF YOU WANT TO--YOU CAN STAY IN THE ROOM WITH DALE AND I. WE DON'T WANT TO UPSET YOU--IT'S WHATEVER YOU WANT.
ARE YOU OUR NEW MOMMY AND DADDY?
NOT REALLY--BUT, IF YOU'D LIKE--YOU CAN CALL US THAT IF YOU WANT TO.

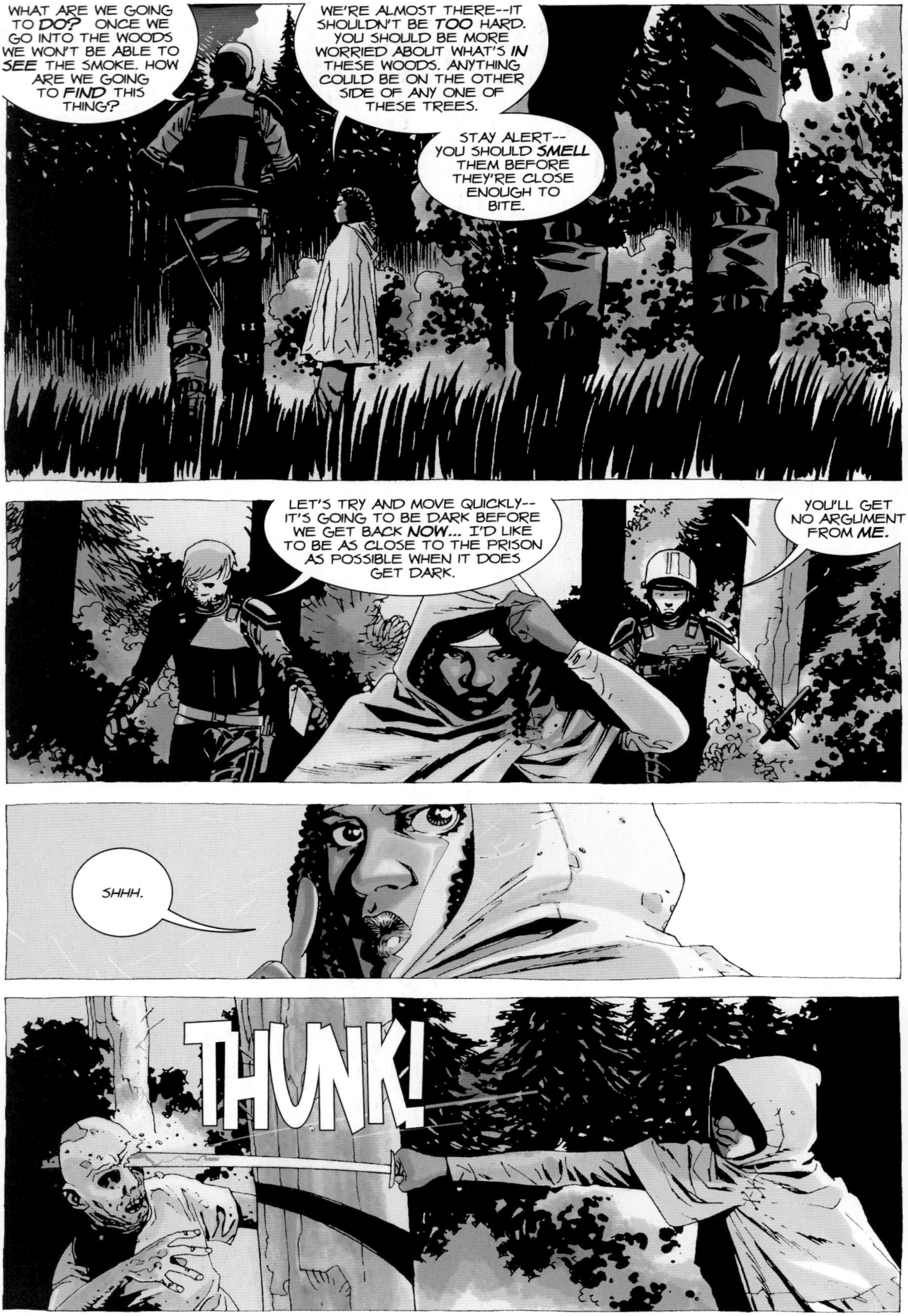
WHAT ARE WE GOING TO DO? ONCE WE GO INTO THE WOODS WE WON'T BE ABLE TO SEE THE SMOKE. HOW ARE WE GOING TO FIND THIS THING?
WE'RE ALMOST THERE--IT SHOULDN'T BE TOO HARD. YOU SHOULD BE MORE WORRIED ABOUT WHAT'S IN THESE WOODS. ANYTHING COULD BE ON THE OTHER SIDE OF ANY ONE OF THESE TREES.
STAY ALERT-- YOU SHOULD SMELL THEM BEFORE THEY'RE CLOSE ENOUGH TO BITE.
LET'S TRY AND MOVE QUICKLY-- IT'S GOING TO BE DARK BEFORE WE GET BACK NOW... I'D LIKE TO BE AS CLOSE TO THE PRISON AS POSSIBLE WHEN IT DOES GET DARK.
YOU'LL GET NO ARGUMENT FROM ME.
SHHH.
THUNK!

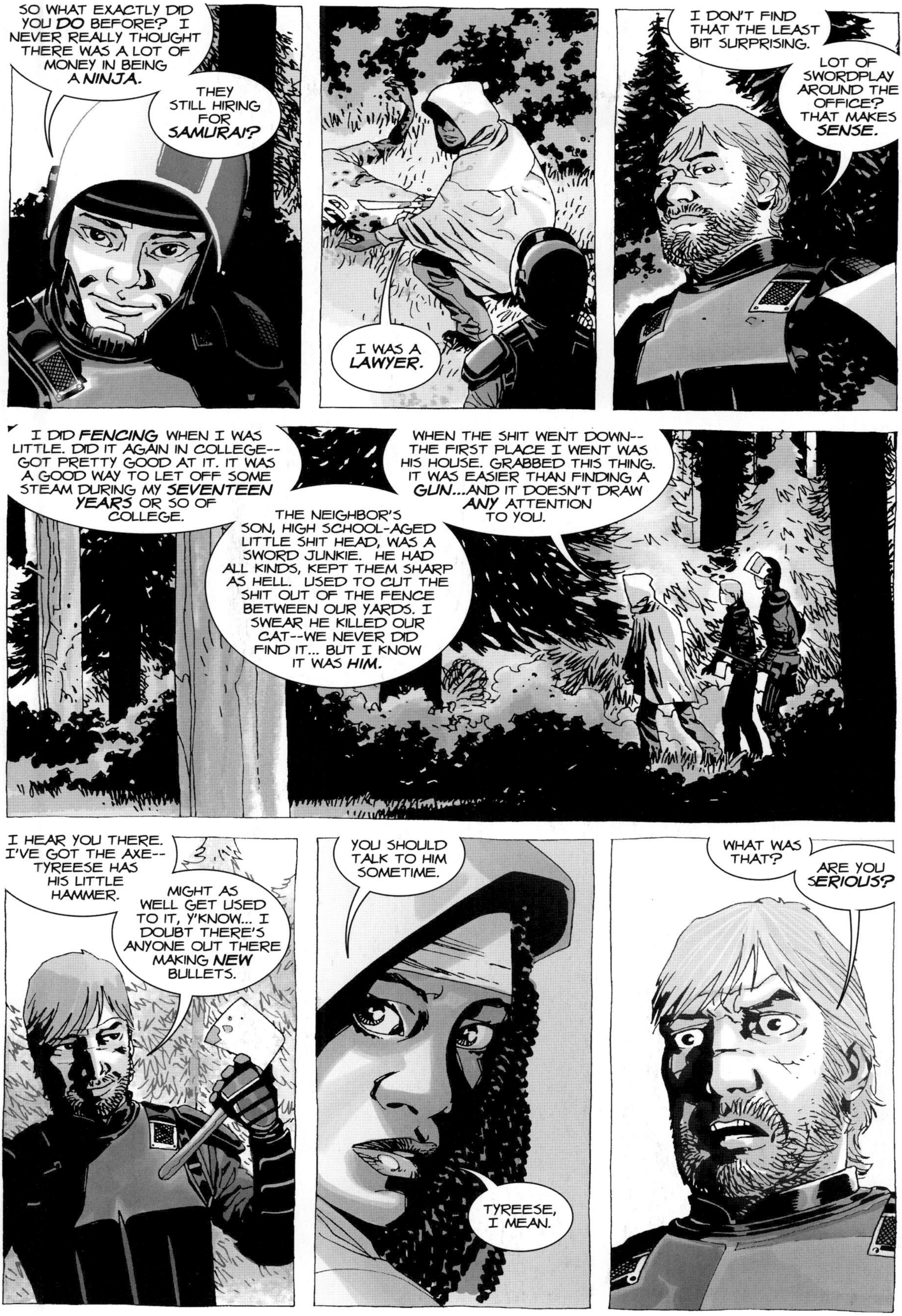
SO WHAT EXACTLY DID YOU DO BEFORE? I NEVER REALLY THOUGHT THERE WAS A LOT OF MONEY IN BEING A NINJA.
THEY STILL HIRING FOR SAMURAI?
I WAS A LAWYER.
I DON'T FIND THAT THE LEAST BIT SURPRISING.
LOT OF SWORDPLAY AROUND THE OFFICE? THAT MAKES SENSE.
I DID FENCING WHEN I WAS LITTLE. DID IT AGAIN IN COLLEGE-- GOT PRETTY GOOD AT IT. IT WAS A GOOD WAY TO LET OFF SOME STEAM DURING MY SEVENTEEN YEARS OR SO OF COLLEGE.
THE NEIGHBOR'S SON, HIGH SCHOOL-AGED LITTLE SHIT HEAD, WAS A SWORD JUNKIE. HE HAD ALL KINDS, KEPT THEM SHARP AS HELL. USED TO CUT THE SHIT OUT OF THE FENCE BETWEEN OUR YARDS. I SWEAR HE KILLED OUR CAT--WE NEVER DID FIND IT... BUT I KNOW IT WAS HIM.
WHEN THE SHIT WENT DOWN-- THE FIRST PLACE I WENT WAS HIS HOUSE. GRABBED THIS THING. IT WAS EASIER THAN FINDING A GUN...AND IT DOESN'T DRAW ANY ATTENTION TO YOU.
I HEAR YOU THERE. I'VE GOT THE AXE-- TYREESE HAS HIS LITTLE HAMMER.
MIGHT AS WELL GET USED TO IT, Y'KNOW... I DOUBT THERE'S ANYONE OUT THERE MAKING NEW BULLETS.
YOU SHOULD TALK TO HIM SOMETIME.
TYREESE, I MEAN.
WHAT WAS THAT?
ARE YOU SERIOUS?

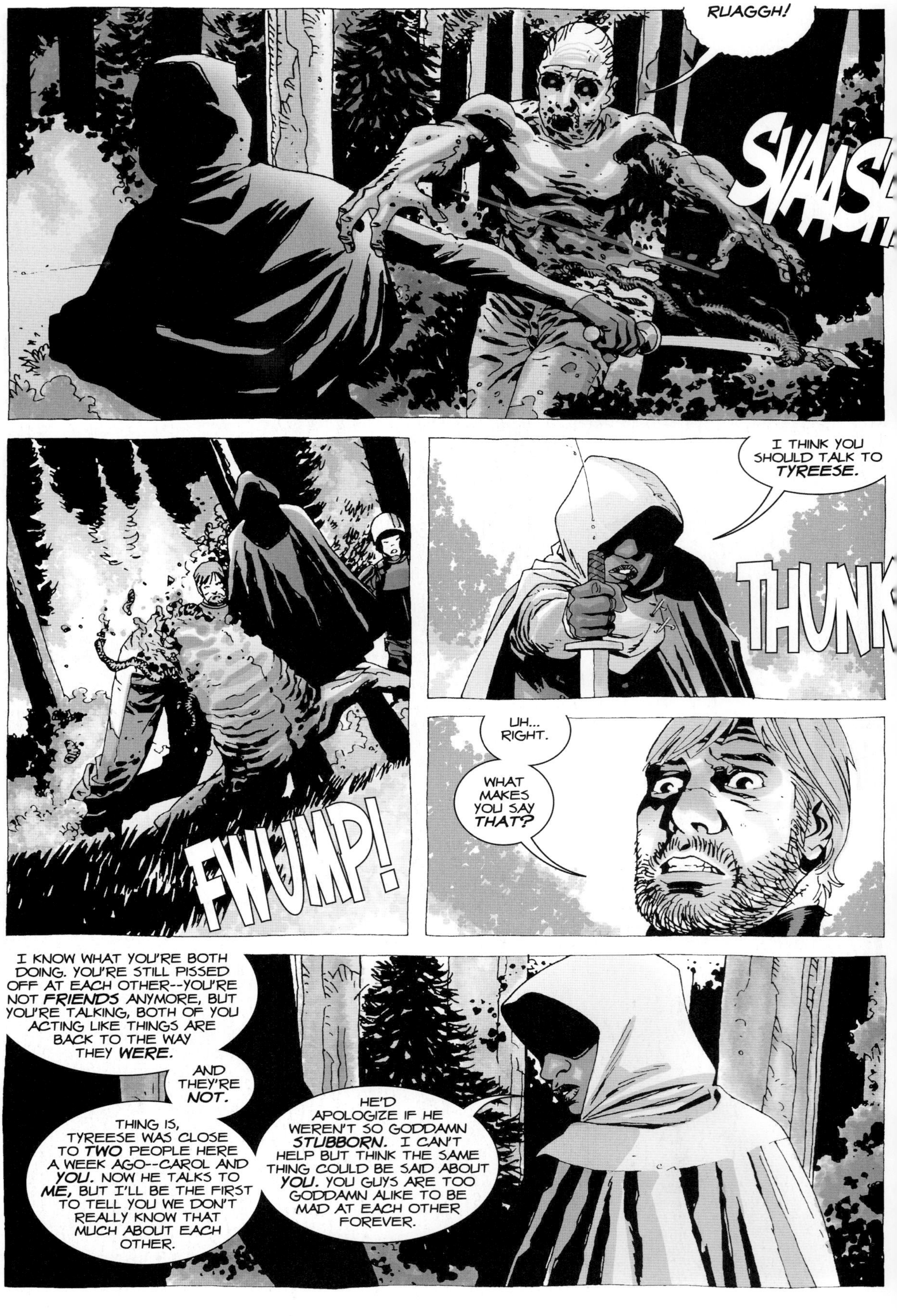
RUAGGH!
SVAASH
FWUMP!
I THINK YOU SHOULD TALK TO TYREESE.
THUNK
UH... RIGHT.
WHAT MAKES YOU SAY THAT?
I KNOW WHAT YOU'RE BOTH DOING. YOU'RE STILL PISSED OFF AT EACH OTHER--YOU'RE NOT FRIENDS ANYMORE, BUT YOU'RE TALKING, BOTH OF YOU ACTING LIKE THINGS ARE BACK TO THE WAY THEY WERE.
AND THEY'RE NOT.
THING IS, TYREESE WAS CLOSE TO TWO PEOPLE HERE A WEEK AGO--CAROL AND YOU. NOW HE TALKS TO ME, BUT I'LL BE THE FIRST TO TELL YOU WE DON'T REALLY KNOW THAT MUCH ABOUT EACH OTHER.
HE'D APOLOGIZE IF HE WEREN'T SO GODDAMN STUBBORN. I CAN'T HELP BUT THINK THE SAME THING COULD BE SAID ABOUT YOU. YOU GUYS ARE TOO GODDAMN ALIKE TO BE MAD AT EACH OTHER FOREVER.

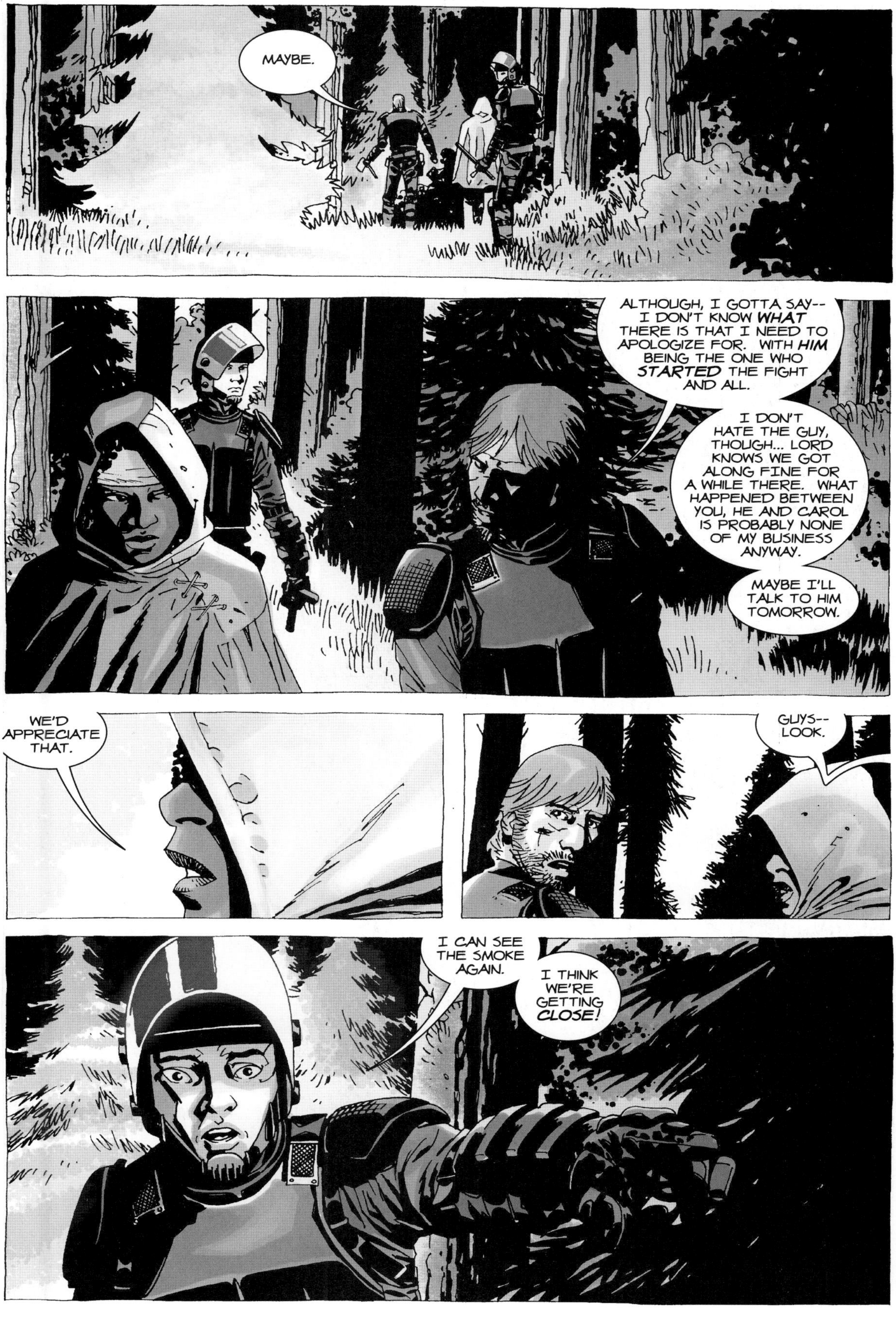
MAYBE.
ALTHOUGH, I GOTTA SAY-- I DON'T KNOW WHAT THERE IS THAT I NEED TO APOLOGIZE FOR. WITH HIM BEING THE ONE WHO STARTED THE FIGHT AND ALL.
I DON'T HATE THE GUY, THOUGH... LORD KNOWS WE GOT ALONG FINE FOR A WHILE THERE. WHAT HAPPENED BETWEEN YOU, HE AND CAROL IS PROBABLY NONE OF MY BUSINESS ANYWAY.
MAYBE I'LL TALK TO HIM TOMORROW.
WE'D APPRECIATE THAT.
GUYS-- LOOK.
I CAN SEE THE SMOKE AGAIN.
I THINK WE'RE GETTING CLOSE!

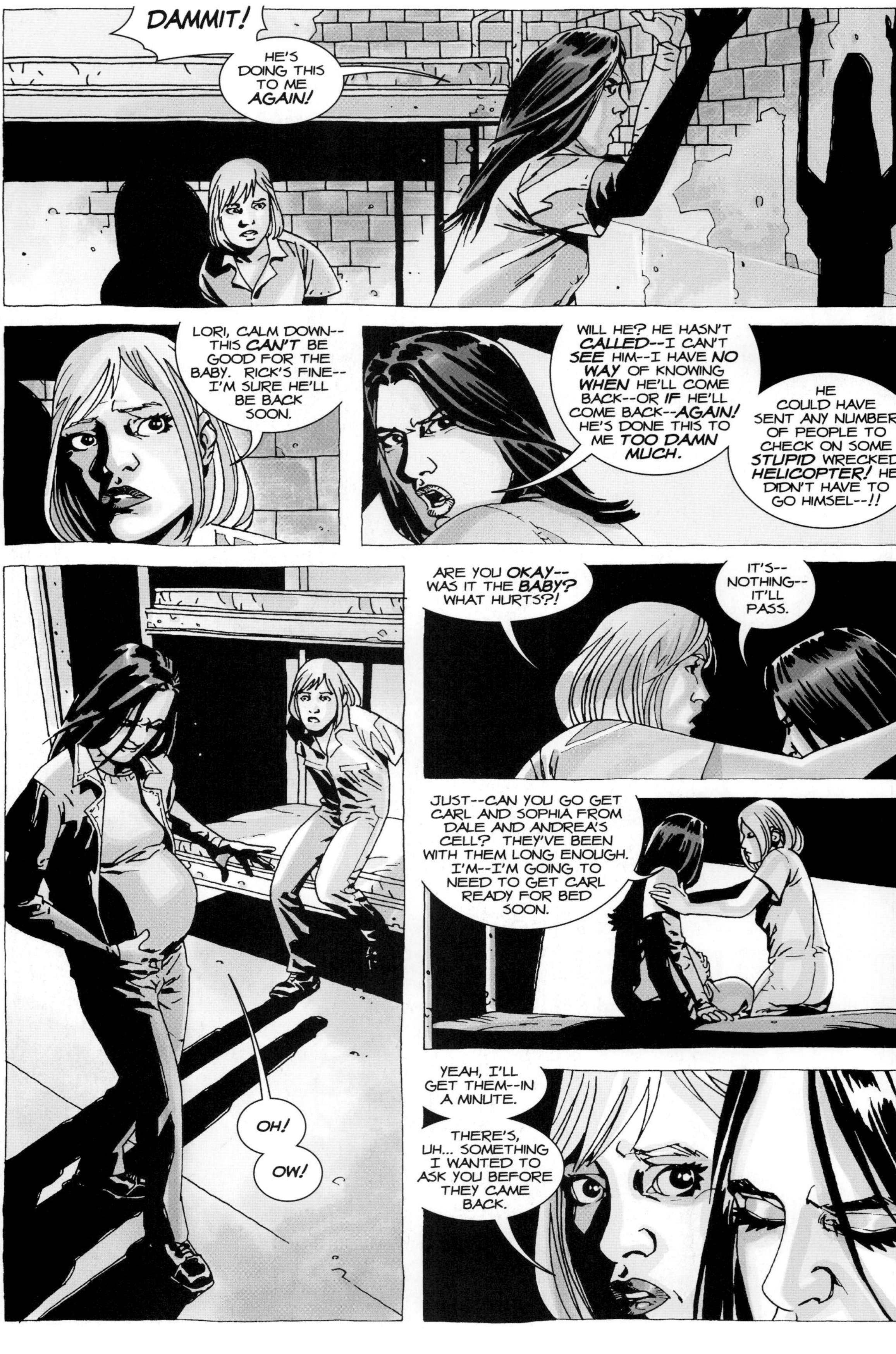
DAMMIT!
HE'S DOING THIS TO ME AGAIN!
LORI, CALM DOWN-- THIS CAN'T BE GOOD FOR THE BABY. RICK'S FINE-- I'M SURE HE'LL BE BACK SOON.
WILL HE? HE HASN'T CALLED--I CAN'T SEE HIM--I HAVE NO WAY OF KNOWING WHEN HE'LL COME BACK--OR IF HE'LL COME BACK--AGAIN! HE'S DONE THIS TO ME TOO DAMN MUCH.
HE COULD HAVE SENT ANY NUMBER OF PEOPLE TO CHECK ON SOME STUPID WRECKED HELICOPTER! HE DIDN'T HAVE TO GO HIMSEL--!!
OH!
OW!
ARE YOU OKAY-- WAS IT THE BABY? WHAT HURTS?!
IT'S-- NOTHING-- IT'LL PASS.
JUST--CAN YOU GO GET CARL AND SOPHIA FROM DALE AND ANDREA'S CELL? THEY'VE BEEN WITH THEM LONG ENOUGH. I'M--I'M GOING TO NEED TO GET CARL READY FOR BED SOON.
YEAH, I'LL GET THEM--IN A MINUTE.
THERE'S, UH... SOMETHING I WANTED TO ASK YOU BEFORE THEY CAME BACK.

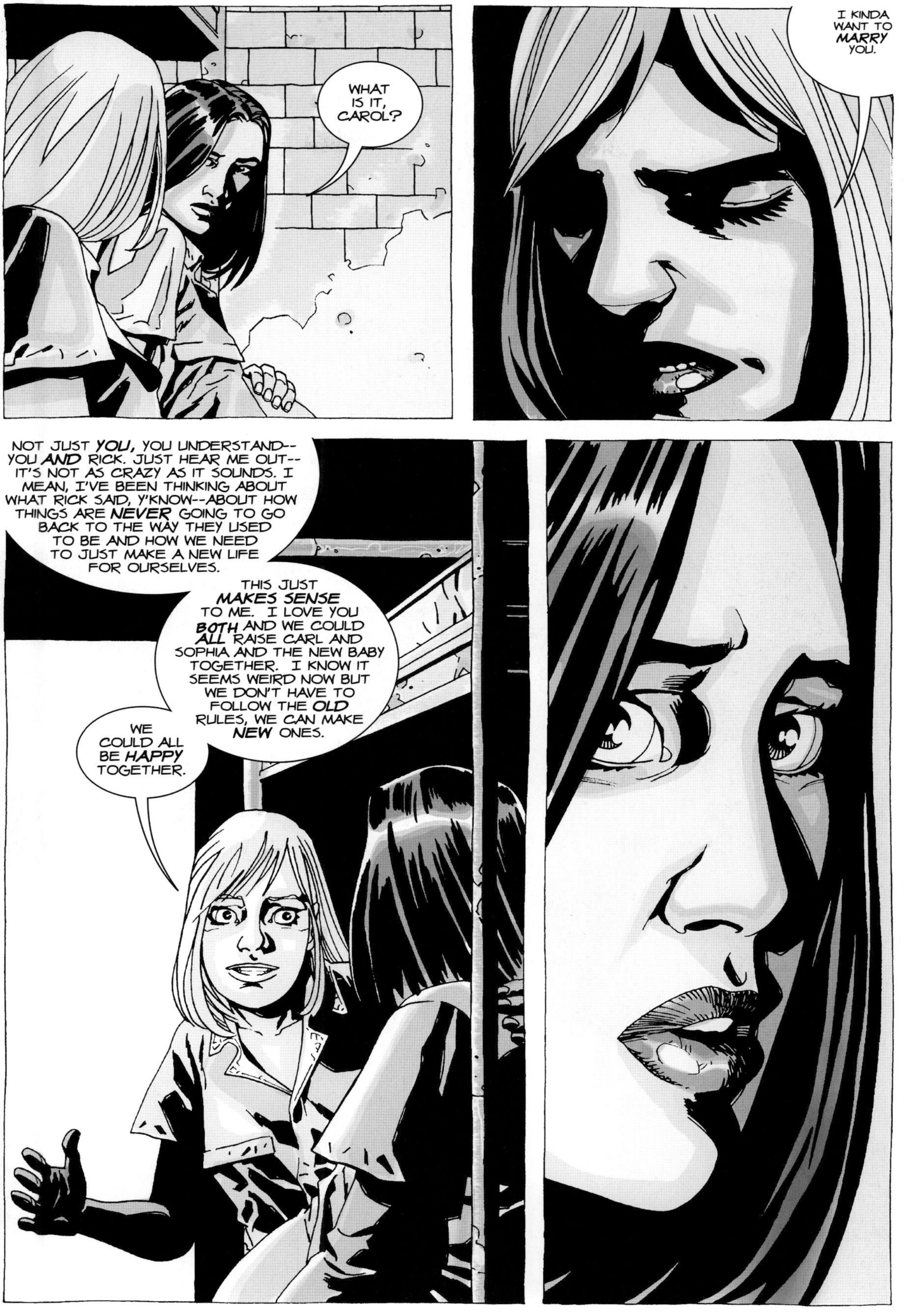
WHAT IS IT, CAROL?
I KINDA WANT TO MARRY YOU.
NOT JUST YOU, YOU UNDERSTAND-- YOU AND RICK. JUST HEAR ME OUT-- IT'S NOT AS CRAZY AS IT SOUNDS. I MEAN, I'VE BEEN THINKING ABOUT WHAT RICK SAID, Y'KNOW--ABOUT HOW THINGS ARE NEVER GOING TO GO BACK TO THE WAY THEY USED TO BE AND HOW WE NEED TO JUST MAKE A NEW LIFE FOR OURSELVES.
THIS JUST MAKES SENSE TO ME. I LOVE YOU BOTH AND WE COULD ALL RAISE CARL AND SOPHIA AND THE NEW BABY TOGETHER. I KNOW IT SEEMS WEIRD NOW BUT WE DON'T HAVE TO FOLLOW THE OLD RULES, WE CAN MAKE NEW ONES.
WE COULD ALL BE HAPPY TOGETHER.

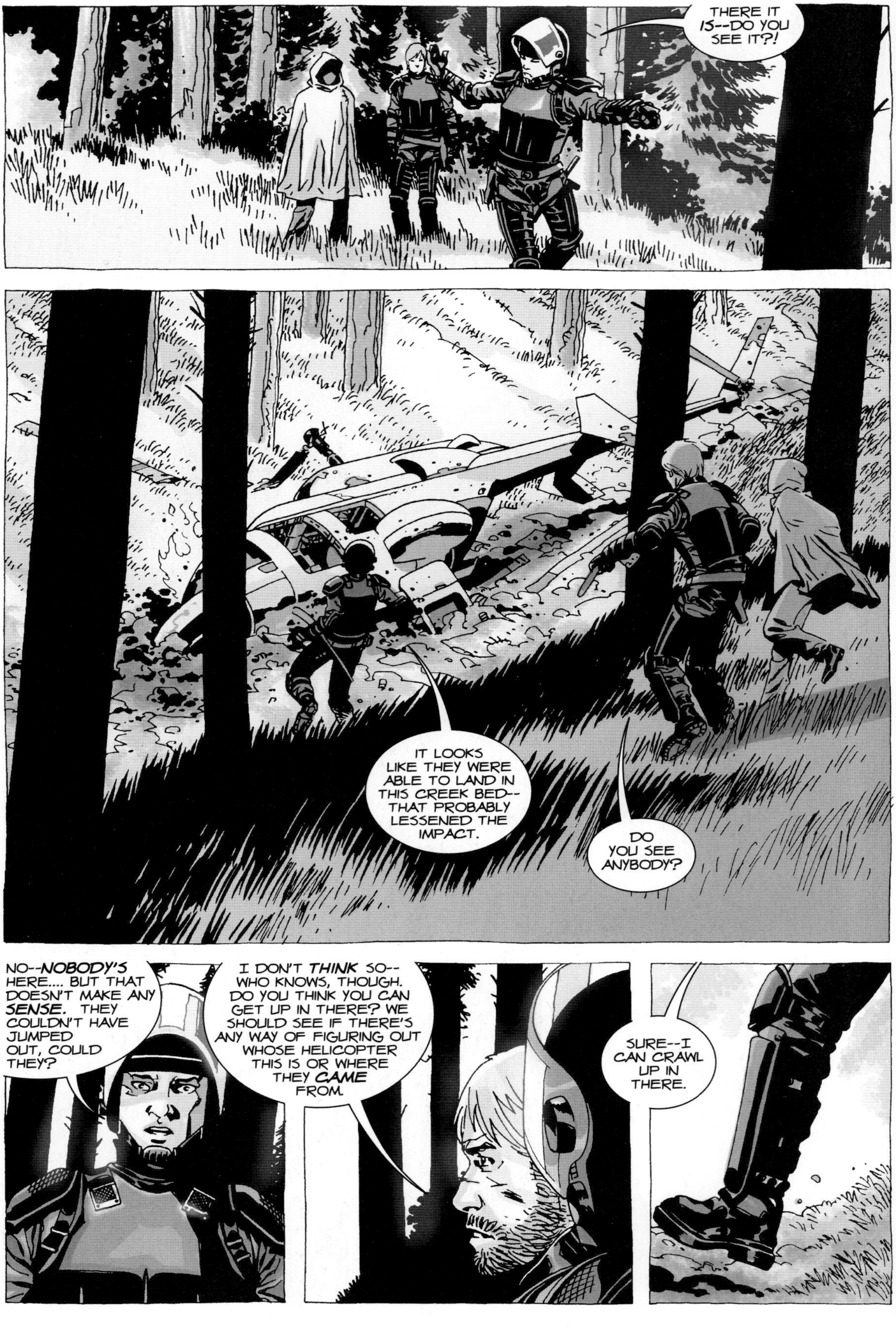
THERE IT IS--DO YOU SEE IT?!
IT LOOKS LIKE THEY WERE ABLE TO LAND IN THIS CREEK BED--THAT PROBABLY LESSENED THE IMPACT.
DO YOU SEE ANYBODY?
NO--NOBODY'S HERE.... BUT THAT DOESN'T MAKE ANY SENSE. THEY COULDN'T HAVE JUMPED OUT, COULD THEY?
I DON'T THINK SO--WHO KNOWS, THOUGH. DO YOU THINK YOU CAN GET UP IN THERE? WE SHOULD SEE IF THERE'S ANY WAY OF FIGURING OUT WHOSE HELICOPTER THIS IS OR WHERE THEY CAME FROM.
SURE--I CAN CRAWL UP IN THERE.

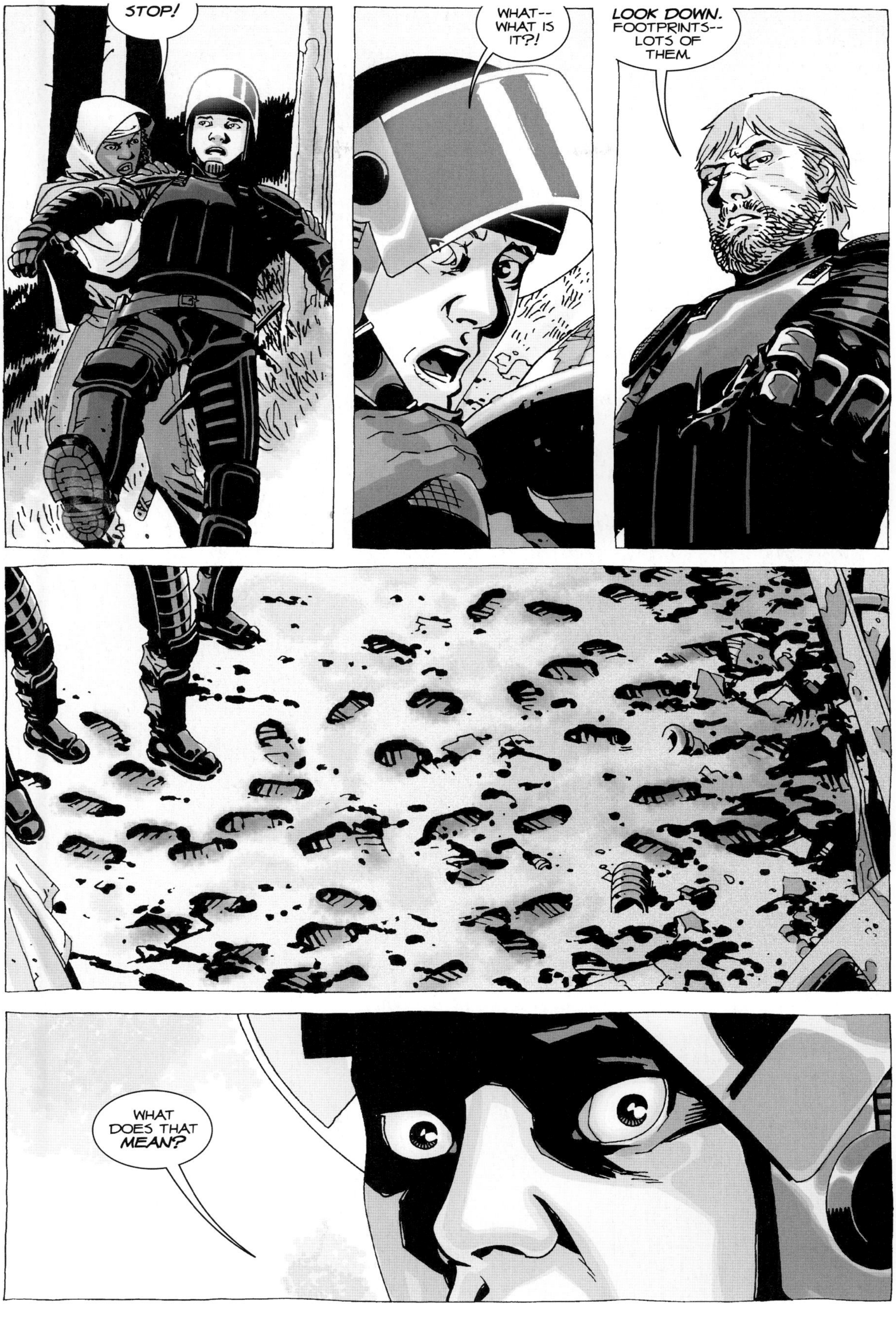
STOP!
WHAT--
WHAT IS
IT?!
LOOK DOWN.
FOOTPRINTS--
LOTS OF
THEM.
WHAT
DOES THAT
MEAN?

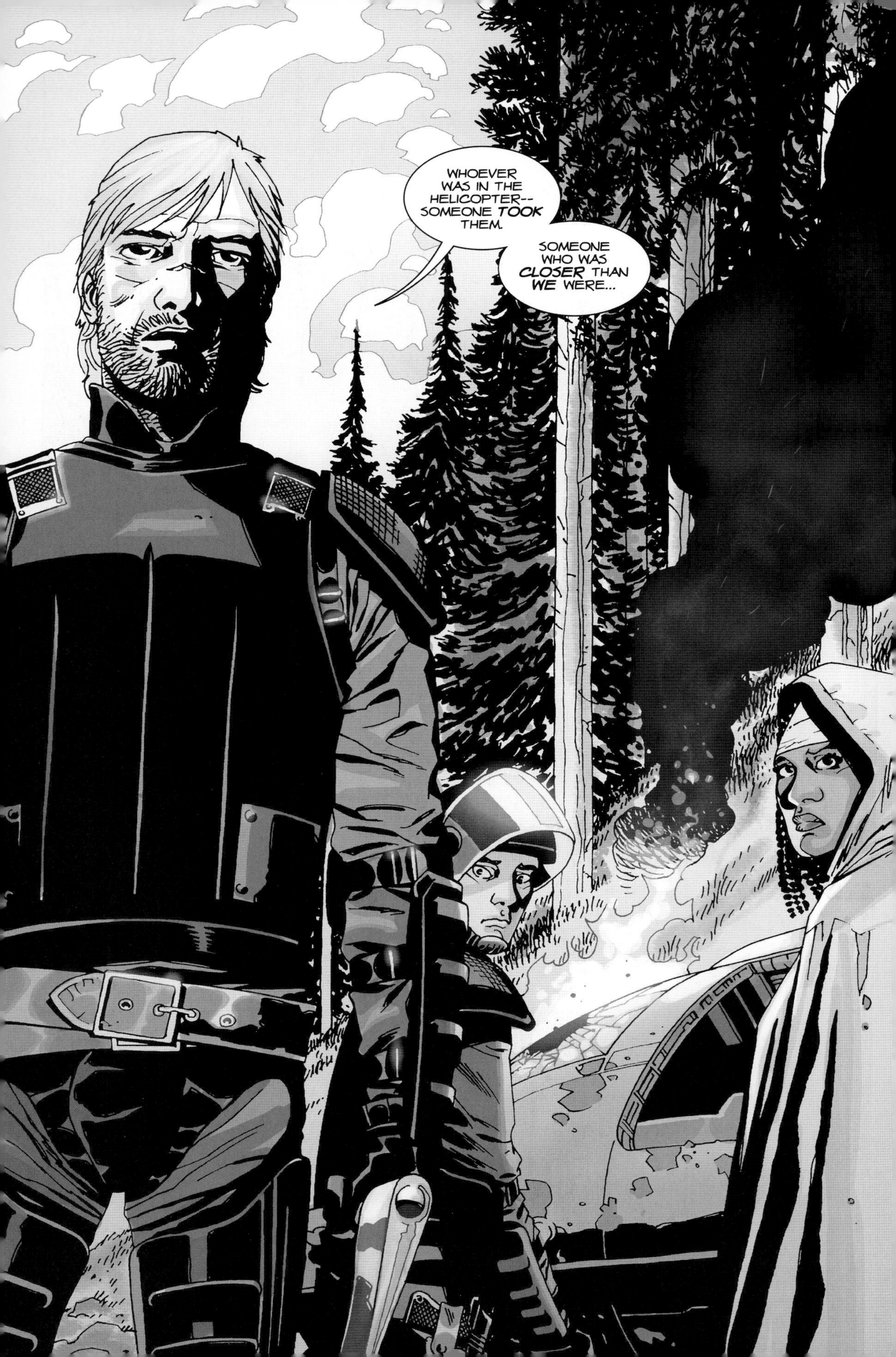
WHOEVER WAS IN THE HELICOPTER-- SOMEONE TOOK THEM.
SOMEONE WHO WAS CLOSER THAN WE WERE...

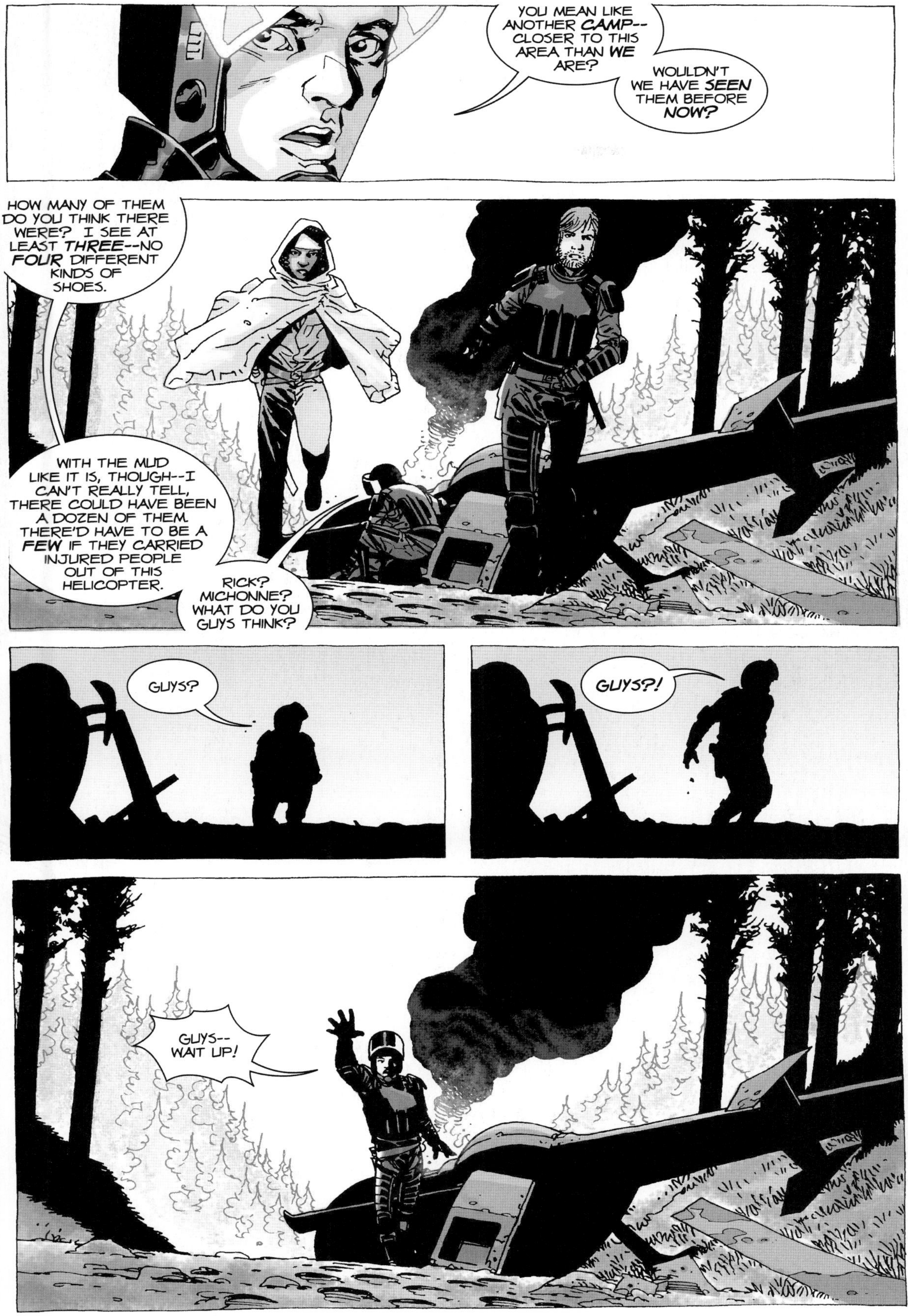
YOU MEAN LIKE ANOTHER CAMP-- CLOSER TO THIS AREA THAN WE ARE?
WOULDN'T WE HAVE SEEN THEM BEFORE NOW?
HOW MANY OF THEM DO YOU THINK THERE WERE? I SEE AT LEAST THREE--NO FOUR DIFFERENT KINDS OF SHOES.
WITH THE MUD LIKE IT IS, THOUGH--I CAN'T REALLY TELL, THERE COULD HAVE BEEN A DOZEN OF THEM. THERE'D HAVE TO BE A FEW IF THEY CARRIED INJURED PEOPLE OUT OF THIS HELICOPTER.
RICK? MICHONNE? WHAT DO YOU GUYS THINK?
GUYS?
GUYS?!
GUYS-- WAIT UP!

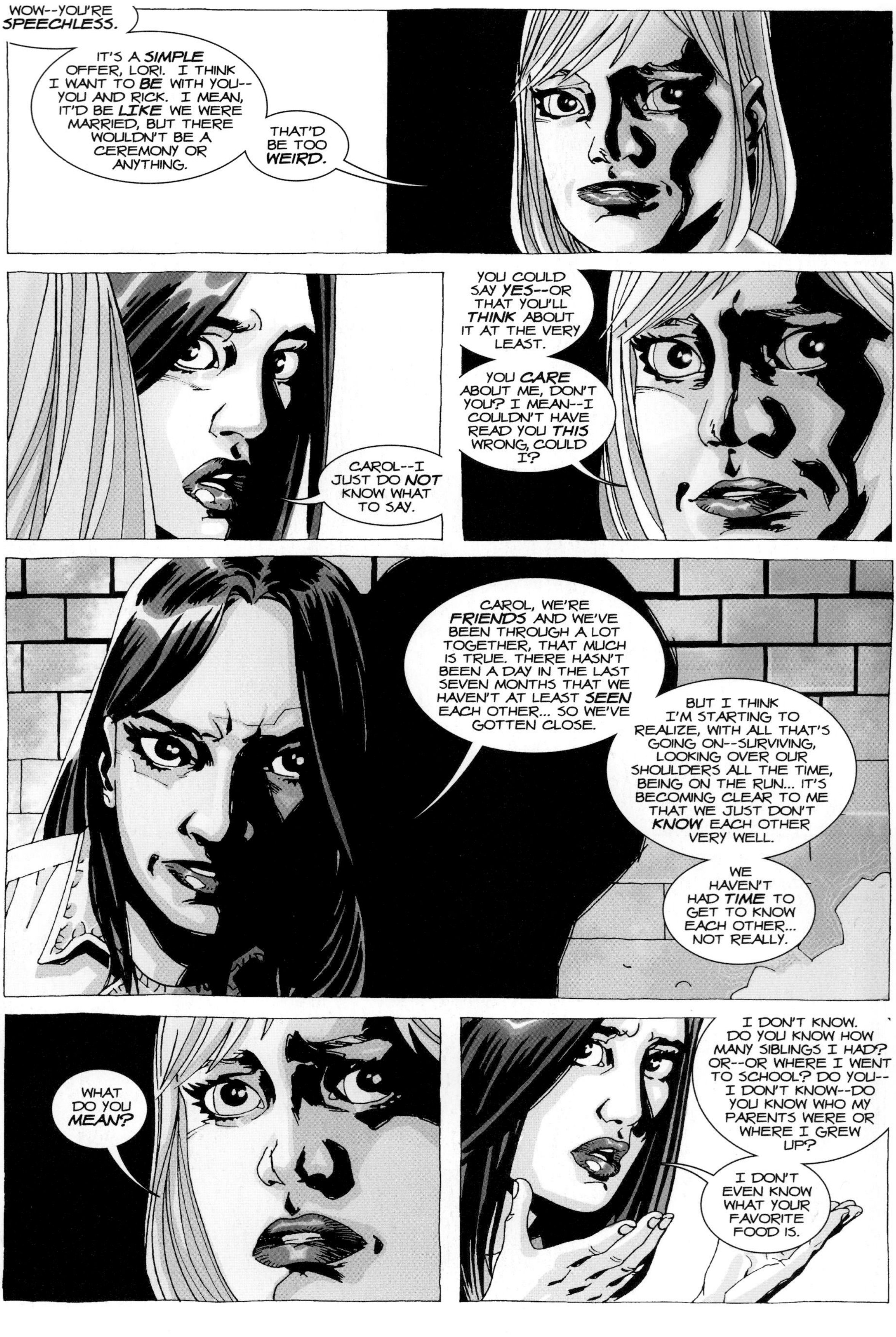
WOW--YOU'RE SPEECHLESS.
IT'S A SIMPLE OFFER, LORI. I THINK I WANT TO BE WITH YOU-- YOU AND RICK. I MEAN, IT'D BE LIKE WE WERE MARRIED, BUT THERE WOULDN'T BE A CEREMONY OR ANYTHING.
THAT'D BE TOO WEIRD.
CAROL--I JUST DO NOT KNOW WHAT TO SAY.
YOU COULD SAY YES--OR THAT YOU'LL THINK ABOUT IT AT THE VERY LEAST.
YOU CARE ABOUT ME, DON'T YOU? I MEAN--I COULDN'T HAVE READ YOU THIS WRONG, COULD I?
CAROL, WE'RE FRIENDS AND WE'VE BEEN THROUGH A LOT TOGETHER, THAT MUCH IS TRUE. THERE HASN'T BEEN A DAY IN THE LAST SEVEN MONTHS THAT WE HAVEN'T AT LEAST SEEN EACH OTHER... SO WE'VE GOTTEN CLOSE.
BUT I THINK I'M STARTING TO REALIZE, WITH ALL THAT'S GOING ON--SURVIVING, LOOKING OVER OUR SHOULDERS ALL THE TIME, BEING ON THE RUN... IT'S BECOMING CLEAR TO ME THAT WE JUST DON'T KNOW EACH OTHER VERY WELL.
WE HAVEN'T HAD TIME TO GET TO KNOW EACH OTHER... NOT REALLY.
WHAT DO YOU MEAN?
I DON'T KNOW. DO YOU KNOW HOW MANY SIBLINGS I HAD? OR--OR WHERE I WENT TO SCHOOL? DO YOU-- I DON'T KNOW--DO YOU KNOW WHO MY PARENTS WERE OR WHERE I GREW UP?
I DON'T EVEN KNOW WHAT YOUR FAVORITE FOOD IS.

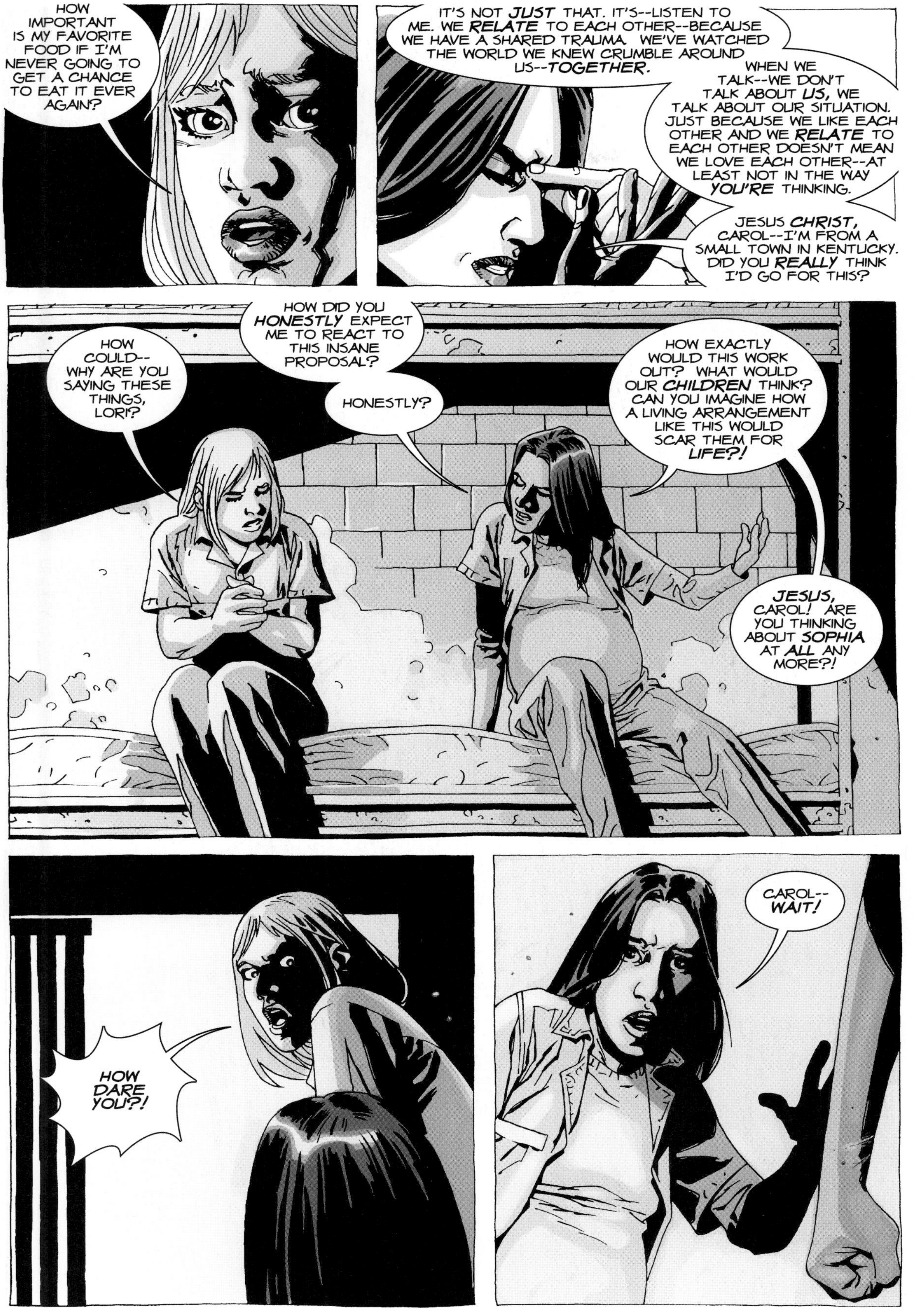
HOW IMPORTANT IS MY FAVORITE FOOD IF I'M NEVER GOING TO GET A CHANCE TO EAT IT EVER AGAIN?
IT'S NOT JUST THAT. IT'S--LISTEN TO ME. WE RELATE TO EACH OTHER--BECAUSE WE HAVE A SHARED TRAUMA. WE'VE WATCHED THE WORLD WE KNEW CRUMBLE AROUND US--TOGETHER.
WHEN WE TALK--WE DON'T TALK ABOUT US, WE TALK ABOUT OUR SITUATION. JUST BECAUSE WE LIKE EACH OTHER AND WE RELATE TO EACH OTHER DOESN'T MEAN WE LOVE EACH OTHER--AT LEAST NOT IN THE WAY YOU'RE THINKING.
JESUS CHRIST, CAROL--I'M FROM A SMALL TOWN IN KENTUCKY. DID YOU REALLY THINK I'D GO FOR THIS?
HOW COULD-- WHY ARE YOU SAYING THESE THINGS, LORI?
HOW DID YOU HONESTLY EXPECT ME TO REACT TO THIS INSANE PROPOSAL?
HONESTLY?
HOW EXACTLY WOULD THIS WORK OUT? WHAT WOULD OUR CHILDREN THINK? CAN YOU IMAGINE HOW A LIVING ARRANGEMENT LIKE THIS WOULD SCAR THEM FOR LIFE?!
JESUS, CAROL! ARE YOU THINKING ABOUT SOPHIA AT ALL ANY MORE?!
HOW DARE YOU?!
CAROL-- WAIT!

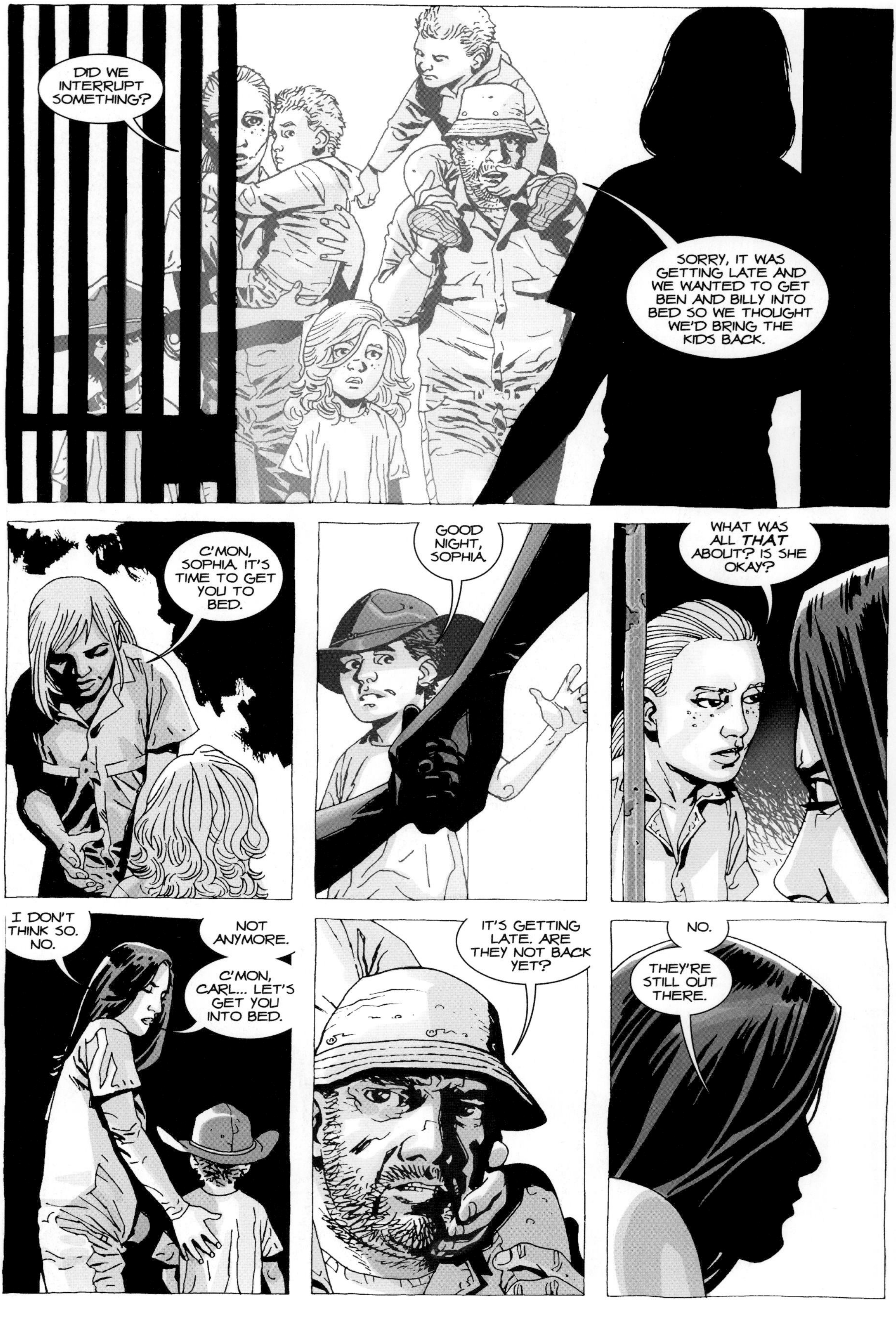
DID WE INTERRUPT SOMETHING?
SORRY, IT WAS GETTING LATE AND WE WANTED TO GET BEN AND BILLY INTO BED SO WE THOUGHT WE'D BRING THE KIDS BACK.
C'MON, SOPHIA. IT'S TIME TO GET YOU TO BED.
GOOD NIGHT, SOPHIA.
WHAT WAS ALL THAT ABOUT? IS SHE OKAY?
I DON'T THINK SO. NO.
NOT ANYMORE.
C'MON, CARL... LET'S GET YOU INTO BED.
IT'S GETTING LATE. ARE THEY NOT BACK YET?
NO.
THEY'RE STILL OUT THERE.

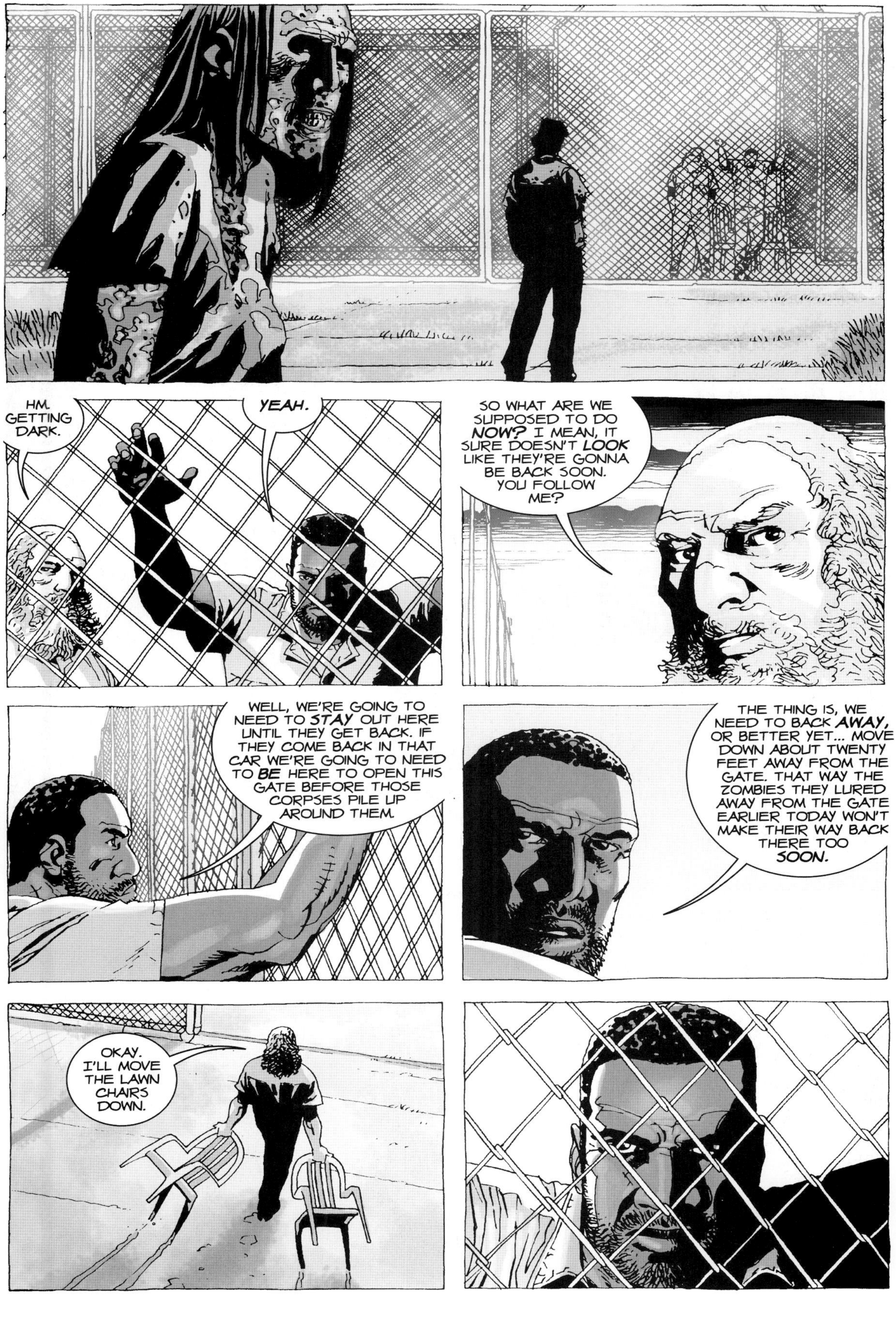
HM. GETTING DARK.
YEAH.
SO WHAT ARE WE SUPPOSED TO DO NOW? I MEAN, IT SURE DOESN'T LOOK LIKE THEY'RE GONNA BE BACK SOON. YOU FOLLOW ME?
WELL, WE'RE GOING TO NEED TO STAY OUT HERE UNTIL THEY GET BACK. IF THEY COME BACK IN THAT CAR WE'RE GOING TO NEED TO BE HERE TO OPEN THIS GATE BEFORE THOSE CORPSES PILE UP AROUND THEM.
THE THING IS, WE NEED TO BACK AWAY, OR BETTER YET... MOVE DOWN ABOUT TWENTY FEET AWAY FROM THE GATE. THAT WAY THE ZOMBIES THEY LURED AWAY FROM THE GATE EARLIER TODAY WON'T MAKE THEIR WAY BACK THERE TOO SOON.
OKAY. I'LL MOVE THE LAWN CHAIRS DOWN.

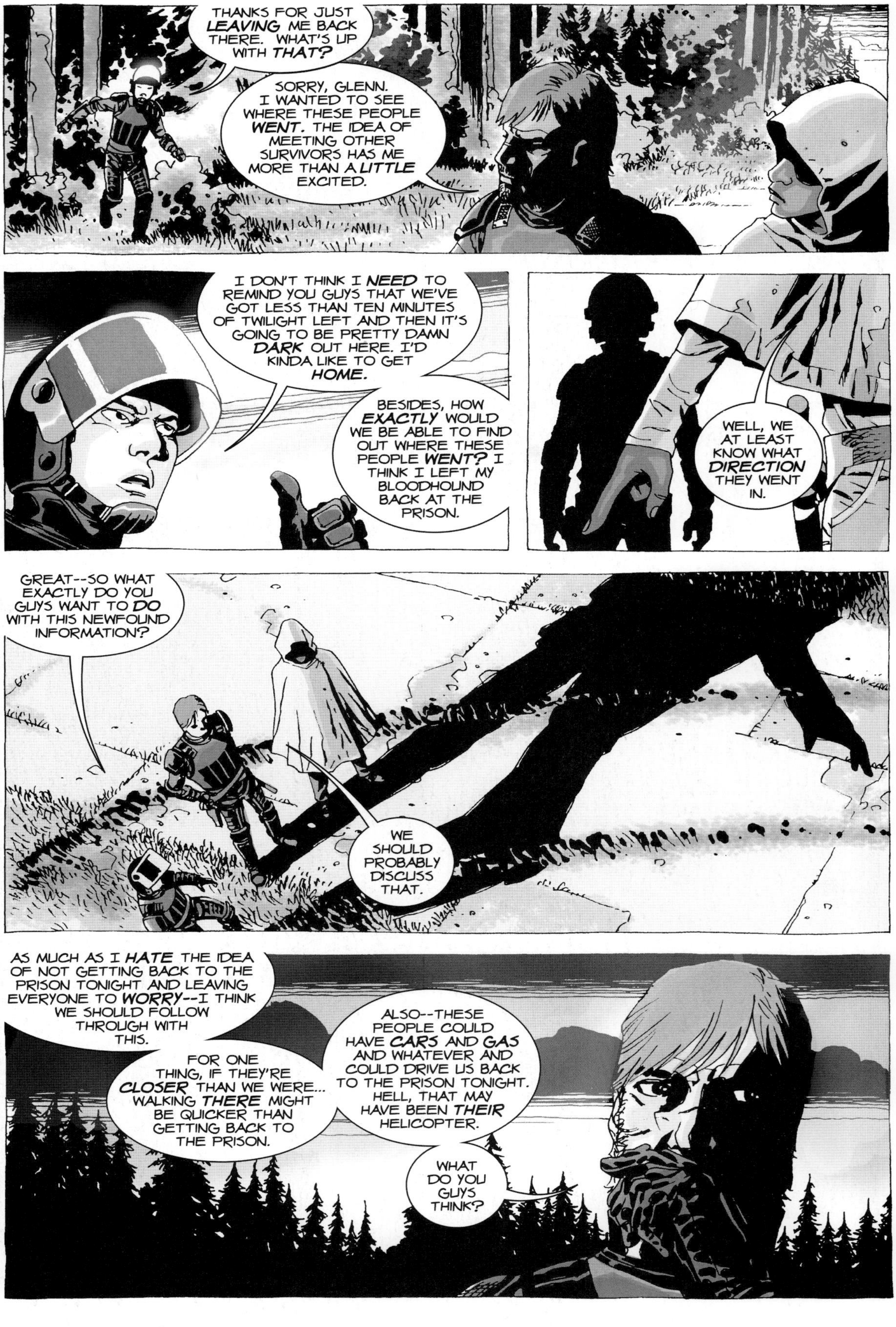
THANKS FOR JUST LEAVING ME BACK THERE. WHAT'S UP WITH THAT?
SORRY, GLENN. I WANTED TO SEE WHERE THESE PEOPLE WENT. THE IDEA OF MEETING OTHER SURVIVORS HAS ME MORE THAN A LITTLE EXCITED.
I DON'T THINK I NEED TO REMIND YOU GUYS THAT WE'VE GOT LESS THAN TEN MINUTES OF TWILIGHT LEFT AND THEN IT'S GOING TO BE PRETTY DAMN DARK OUT HERE. I'D KINDA LIKE TO GET HOME.
BESIDES, HOW EXACTLY WOULD WE BE ABLE TO FIND OUT WHERE THESE PEOPLE WENT? I THINK I LEFT MY BLOODHOUND BACK AT THE PRISON.
WELL, WE AT LEAST KNOW WHAT DIRECTION THEY WENT IN.
GREAT--SO WHAT EXACTLY DO YOU GUYS WANT TO DO WITH THIS NEWFOUND INFORMATION?
WE SHOULD PROBABLY DISCUSS THAT.
AS MUCH AS I HATE THE IDEA OF NOT GETTING BACK TO THE PRISON TONIGHT AND LEAVING EVERYONE TO WORRY--I THINK WE SHOULD FOLLOW THROUGH WITH THIS.
FOR ONE THING, IF THEY'RE CLOSER THAN WE WERE... WALKING THERE MIGHT BE QUICKER THAN GETTING BACK TO THE PRISON.
ALSO--THESE PEOPLE COULD HAVE CARS AND GAS AND WHATEVER AND COULD DRIVE US BACK TO THE PRISON TONIGHT. HELL, THAT MAY HAVE BEEN THEIR HELICOPTER.
WHAT DO YOU GUYS THINK?

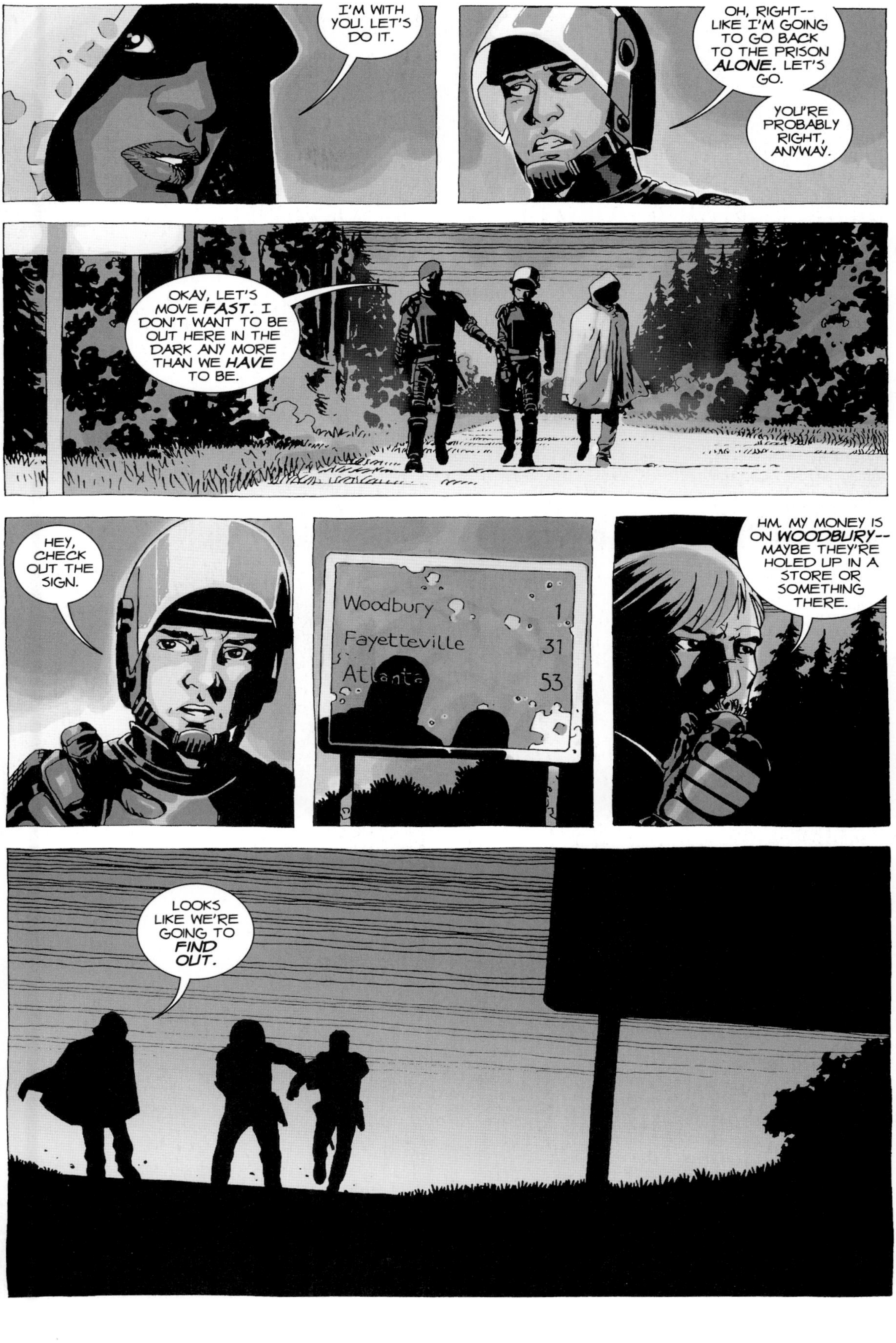
I'M WITH YOU. LET'S DO IT.
OH, RIGHT-- LIKE I'M GOING TO GO BACK TO THE PRISON ALONE. LET'S GO.
YOU'RE PROBABLY RIGHT, ANYWAY.
OKAY, LET'S MOVE FAST. I DON'T WANT TO BE OUT HERE IN THE DARK ANY MORE THAN WE HAVE TO BE.
HEY, CHECK OUT THE SIGN.
Woodbury 1
Fayetteville 31
Atlanta 53
HM. MY MONEY IS ON WOODBURY-- MAYBE THEY'RE HOLED UP IN A STORE OR SOMETHING THERE.
LOOKS LIKE WE'RE GOING TO FIND OUT.

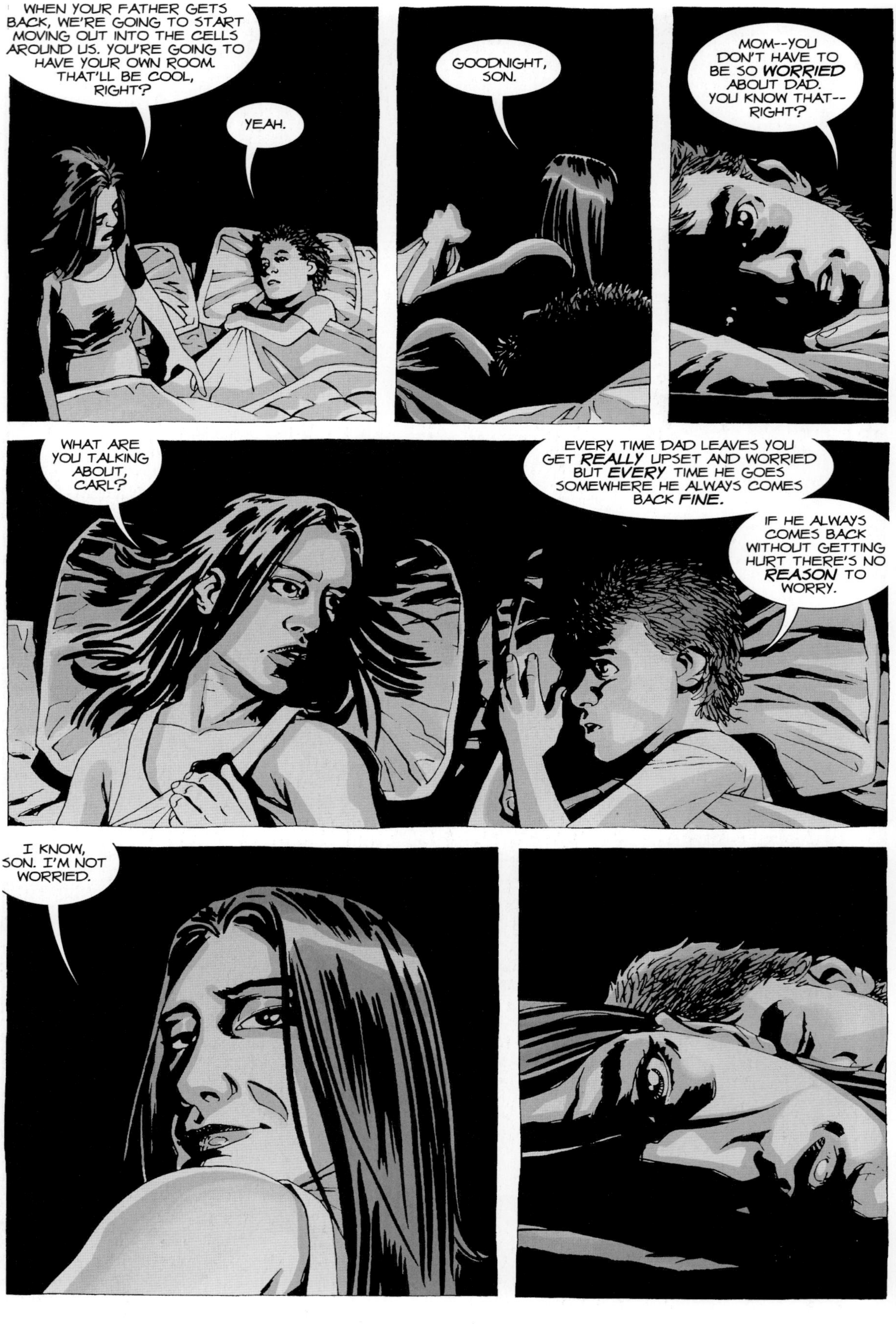
WHEN YOUR FATHER GETS BACK, WE'RE GOING TO START MOVING OUT INTO THE CELLS AROUND US. YOU'RE GOING TO HAVE YOUR OWN ROOM. THAT'LL BE COOL, RIGHT?
YEAH.
GOODNIGHT, SON.
MOM--YOU DON'T HAVE TO BE SO WORRIED ABOUT DAD. YOU KNOW THAT--RIGHT?
WHAT ARE YOU TALKING ABOUT, CARL?
EVERY TIME DAD LEAVES YOU GET REALLY UPSET AND WORRIED BUT EVERY TIME HE GOES SOMEWHERE HE ALWAYS COMES BACK FINE.
IF HE ALWAYS COMES BACK WITHOUT GETTING HURT THERE'S NO REASON TO WORRY.
I KNOW, SON. I'M NOT WORRIED.

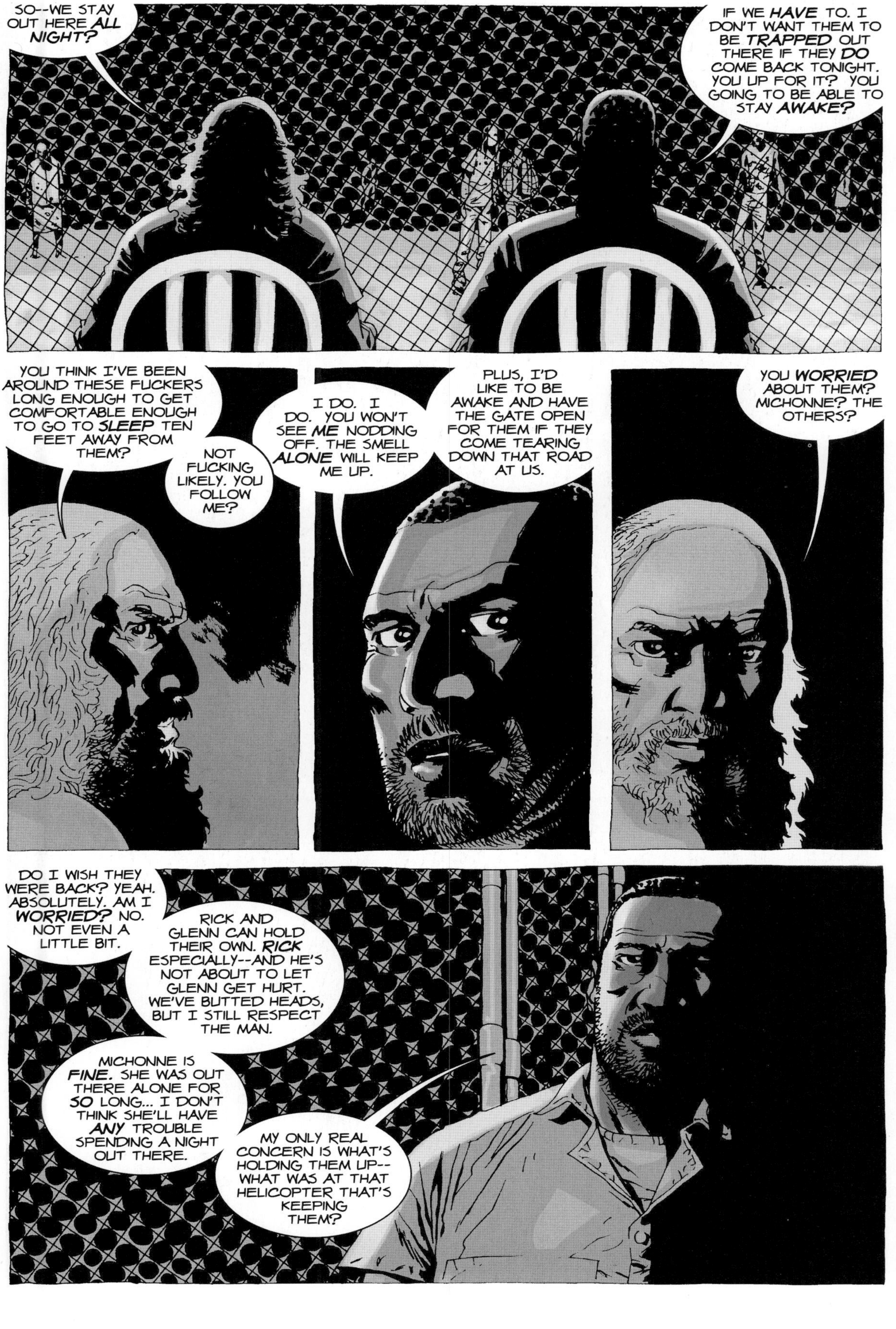
SO--WE STAY OUT HERE ALL NIGHT?
IF WE HAVE TO. I DON'T WANT THEM TO BE TRAPPED OUT THERE IF THEY DO COME BACK TONIGHT. YOU UP FOR IT? YOU GOING TO BE ABLE TO STAY AWAKE?
YOU THINK I'VE BEEN AROUND THESE FUCKERS LONG ENOUGH TO GET COMFORTABLE ENOUGH TO GO TO SLEEP TEN FEET AWAY FROM THEM?
NOT FUCKING LIKELY. YOU FOLLOW ME?
I DO. I DO. YOU WON'T SEE ME NODDING OFF. THE SMELL ALONE WILL KEEP ME UP.
PLUS, I'D LIKE TO BE AWAKE AND HAVE THE GATE OPEN FOR THEM IF THEY COME TEARING DOWN THAT ROAD AT US.
YOU WORRIED ABOUT THEM? MICHONNE? THE OTHERS?
DO I WISH THEY WERE BACK? YEAH. ABSOLUTELY. AM I WORRIED? NO. NOT EVEN A LITTLE BIT.
RICK AND GLENN CAN HOLD THEIR OWN. RICK ESPECIALLY--AND HE'S NOT ABOUT TO LET GLENN GET HURT. WE'VE BUTTED HEADS, BUT I STILL RESPECT THE MAN.
MICHONNE IS FINE. SHE WAS OUT THERE ALONE FOR SO LONG... I DON'T THINK SHE'LL HAVE ANY TROUBLE SPENDING A NIGHT OUT THERE.
MY ONLY REAL CONCERN IS WHAT'S HOLDING THEM UP--WHAT WAS AT THAT HELICOPTER THAT'S KEEPING THEM?

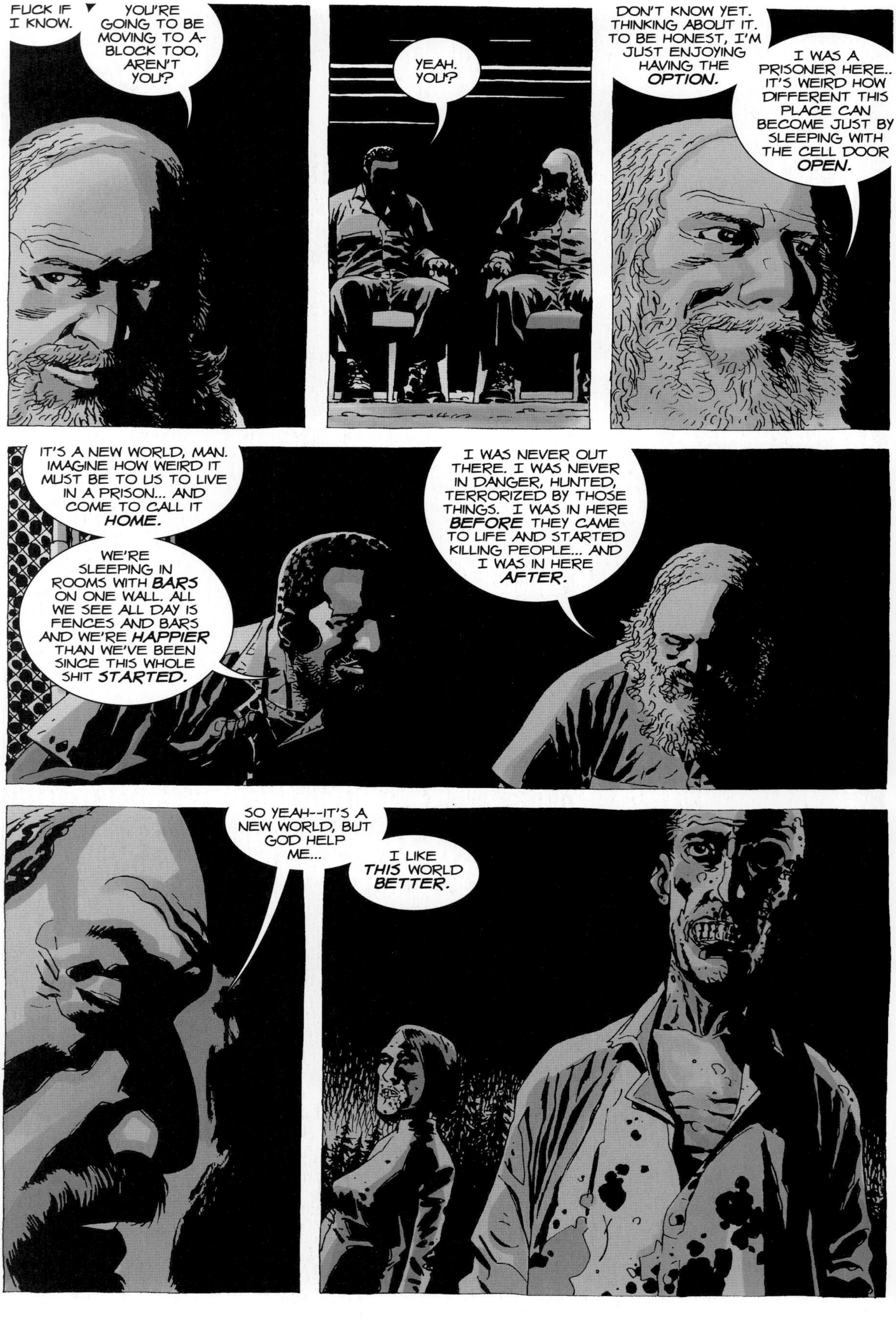
FUCK IF I KNOW.
YOU'RE GOING TO BE MOVING TO A-BLOCK TOO, AREN'T YOU?
YEAH. YOU?
DON'T KNOW YET. THINKING ABOUT IT. TO BE HONEST, I'M JUST ENJOYING HAVING THE OPTION.
I WAS A PRISONER HERE.. IT'S WEIRD HOW DIFFERENT THIS PLACE CAN BECOME JUST BY SLEEPING WITH THE CELL DOOR OPEN.
IT'S A NEW WORLD, MAN. IMAGINE HOW WEIRD IT MUST BE TO US TO LIVE IN A PRISON... AND COME TO CALL IT HOME.
WE'RE SLEEPING IN ROOMS WITH BARS ON ONE WALL. ALL WE SEE ALL DAY IS FENCES AND BARS AND WE'RE HAPPIER THAN WE'VE BEEN SINCE THIS WHOLE SHIT STARTED.
I WAS NEVER OUT THERE. I WAS NEVER IN DANGER, HUNTED, TERRORIZED BY THOSE THINGS. I WAS IN HERE BEFORE THEY CAME TO LIFE AND STARTED KILLING PEOPLE... AND I WAS IN HERE AFTER.
SO YEAH--IT'S A NEW WORLD, BUT GOD HELP ME...
I LIKE THIS WORLD BETTER.

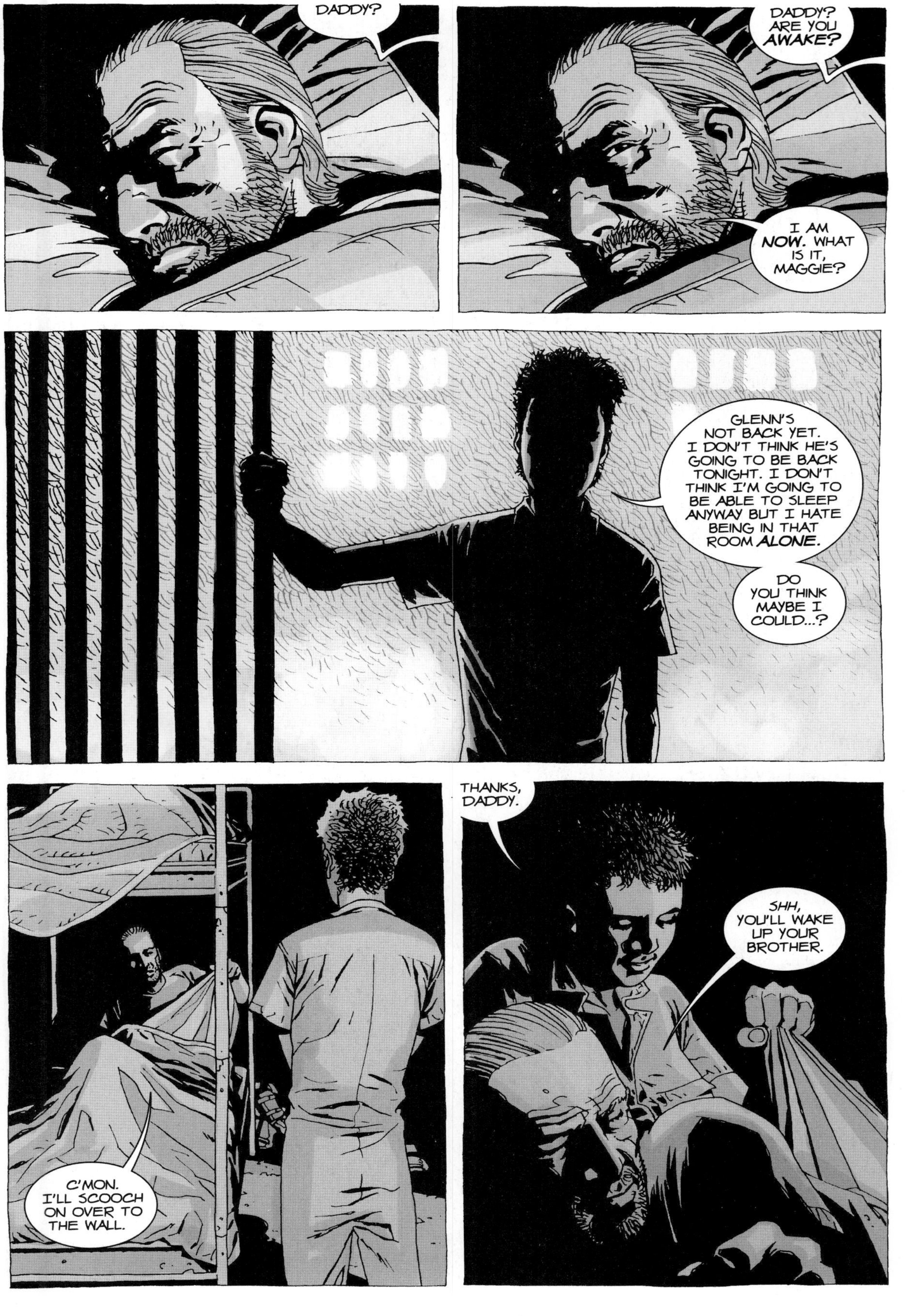
DADDY?
DADDY? ARE YOU AWAKE?
I AM NOW. WHAT IS IT, MAGGIE?
GLENN'S NOT BACK YET. I DON'T THINK HE'S GOING TO BE BACK TONIGHT. I DON'T THINK I'M GOING TO BE ABLE TO SLEEP ANYWAY BUT I HATE BEING IN THAT ROOM ALONE.
DO YOU THINK MAYBE I COULD...?
C'MON. I'LL SCOOCH ON OVER TO THE WALL.
THANKS, DADDY.
SHH, YOU'LL WAKE UP YOUR BROTHER.

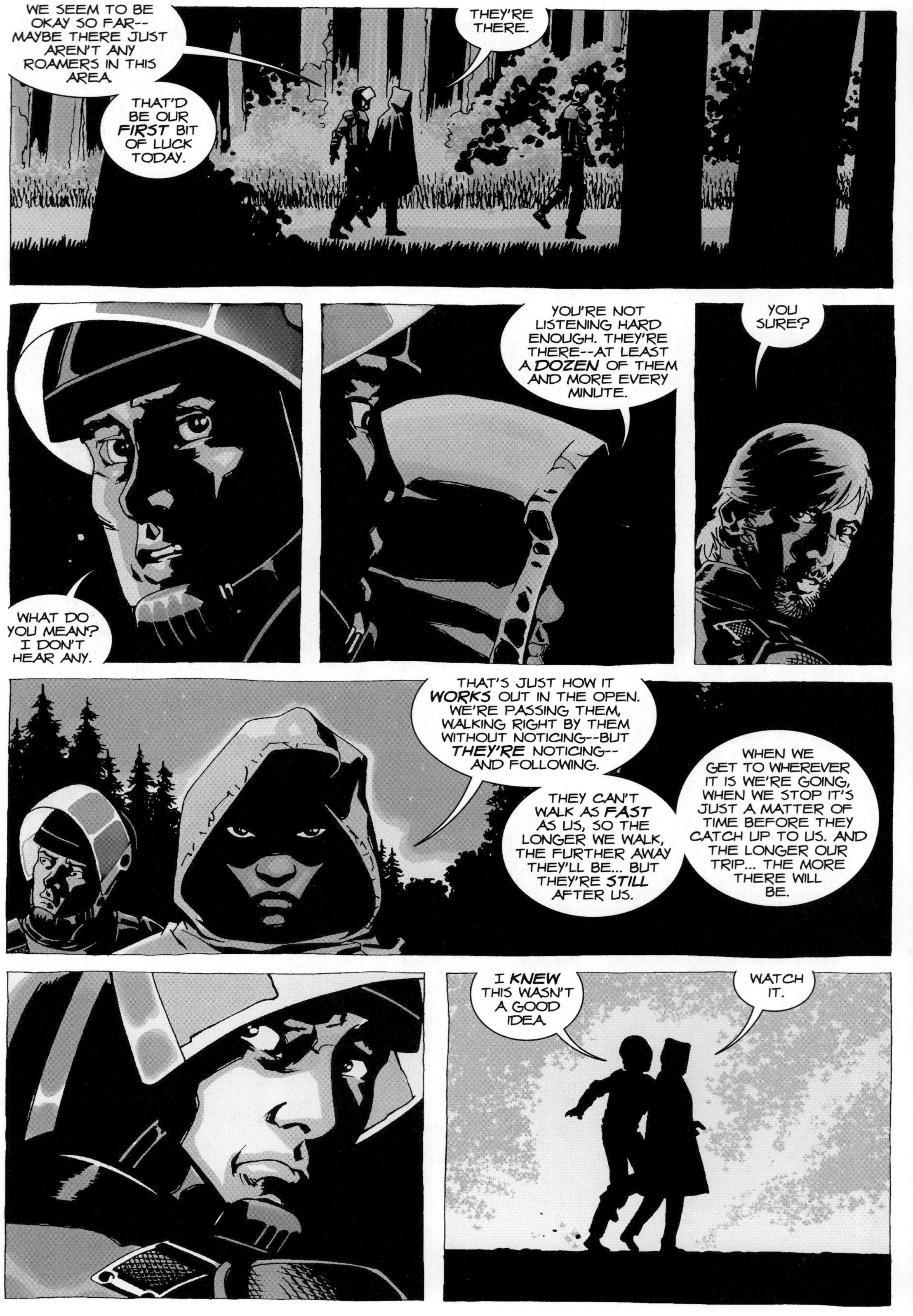
WE SEEM TO BE OKAY SO FAR-- MAYBE THERE JUST AREN'T ANY ROAMERS IN THIS AREA.
THAT'D BE OUR FIRST BIT OF LUCK TODAY.
THEY'RE THERE.
WHAT DO YOU MEAN? I DON'T HEAR ANY.
YOU'RE NOT LISTENING HARD ENOUGH. THEY'RE THERE--AT LEAST A DOZEN OF THEM AND MORE EVERY MINUTE.
YOU SURE?
THAT'S JUST HOW IT WORKS OUT IN THE OPEN. WE'RE PASSING THEM, WALKING RIGHT BY THEM WITHOUT NOTICING--BUT THEY'RE NOTICING-- AND FOLLOWING.
THEY CAN'T WALK AS FAST AS US, SO THE LONGER WE WALK, THE FURTHER AWAY THEY'LL BE... BUT THEY'RE STILL AFTER US.
WHEN WE GET TO WHEREVER IT IS WE'RE GOING, WHEN WE STOP IT'S JUST A MATTER OF TIME BEFORE THEY CATCH UP TO US. AND THE LONGER OUR TRIP... THE MORE THERE WILL BE.
I KNEW THIS WASN'T A GOOD IDEA.
WATCH IT.

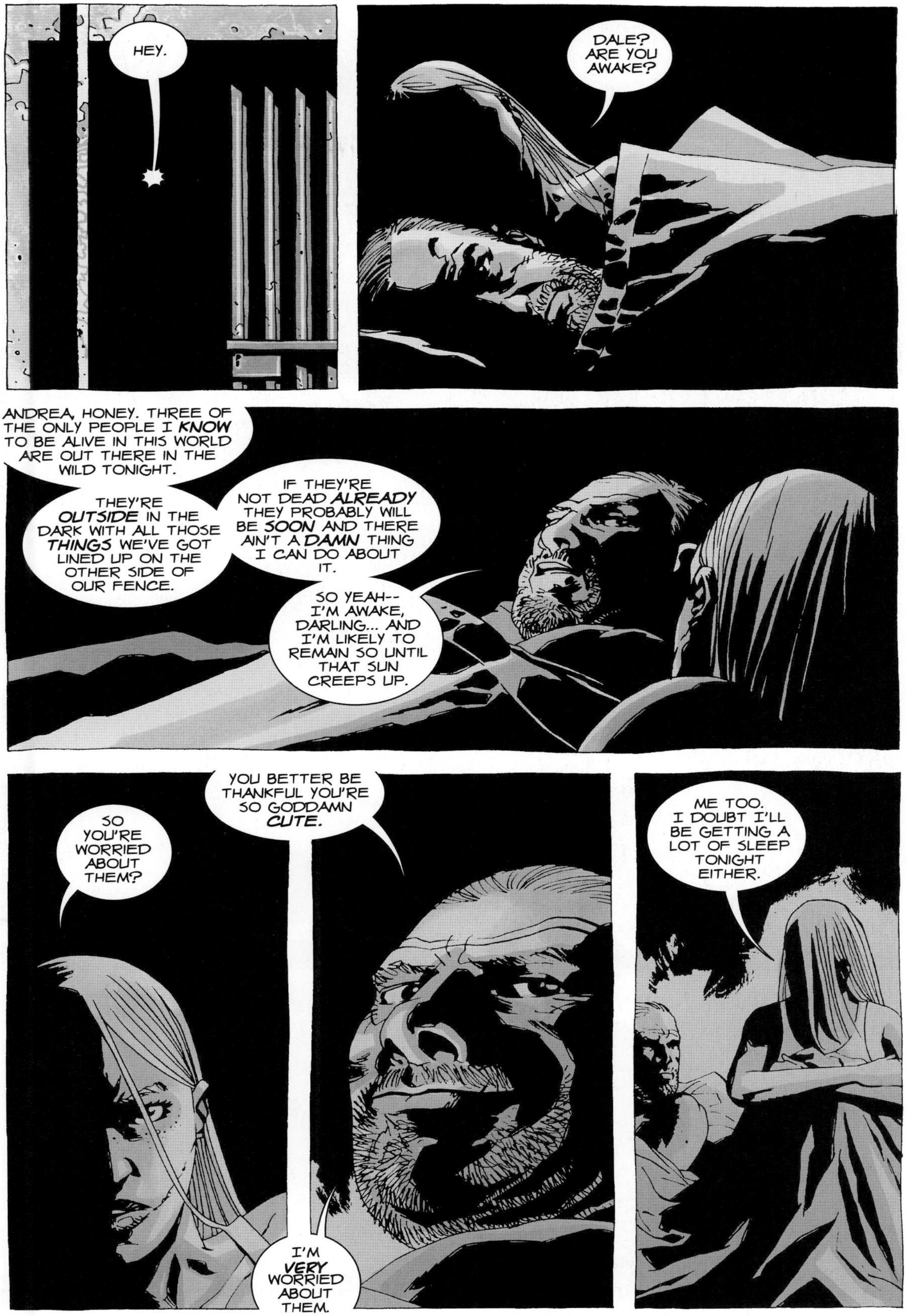
HEY.
DALE? ARE YOU AWAKE?
ANDREA, HONEY. THREE OF THE ONLY PEOPLE I KNOW TO BE ALIVE IN THIS WORLD ARE OUT THERE IN THE WILD TONIGHT.
THEY'RE OUTSIDE IN THE DARK WITH ALL THOSE THINGS WE'VE GOT LINED UP ON THE OTHER SIDE OF OUR FENCE.
IF THEY'RE NOT DEAD ALREADY THEY PROBABLY WILL BE SOON AND THERE AIN'T A DAMN THING I CAN DO ABOUT IT.
SO YEAH-- I'M AWAKE, DARLING... AND I'M LIKELY TO REMAIN SO UNTIL THAT SUN CREEPS UP.
SO YOU'RE WORRIED ABOUT THEM?
YOU BETTER BE THANKFUL YOU'RE SO GODDAMN CUTE.
I'M VERY WORRIED ABOUT THEM.
ME TOO. I DOUBT I'LL BE GETTING A LOT OF SLEEP TONIGHT EITHER.

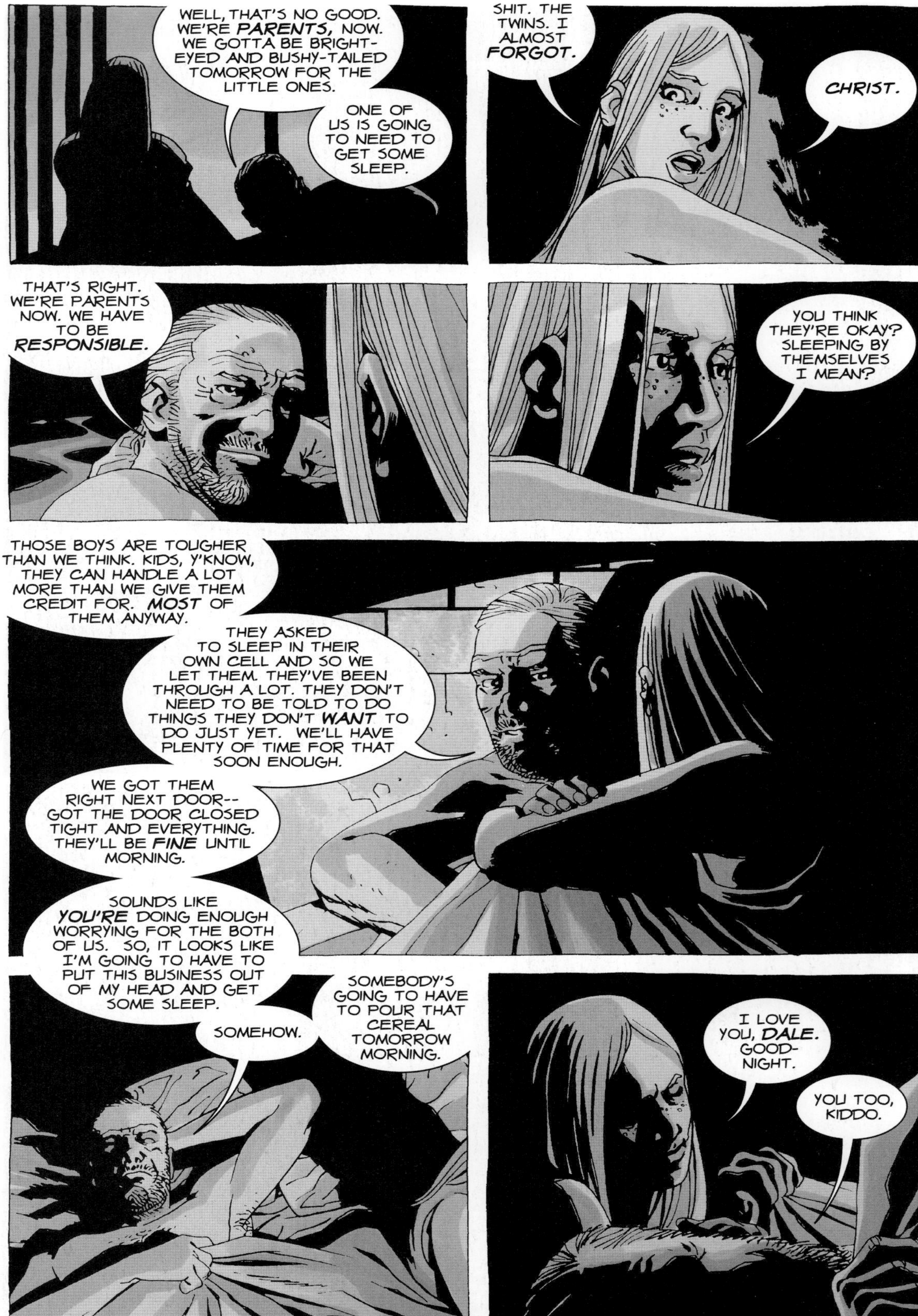
WELL, THAT'S NO GOOD. WE'RE PARENTS, NOW. WE GOTTA BE BRIGHT-EYED AND BUSHY-TAILED TOMORROW FOR THE LITTLE ONES.
ONE OF US IS GOING TO NEED TO GET SOME SLEEP.
SHIT. THE TWINS. I ALMOST FORGOT.
CHRIST.
THAT'S RIGHT. WE'RE PARENTS NOW. WE HAVE TO BE RESPONSIBLE.
YOU THINK THEY'RE OKAY? SLEEPING BY THEMSELVES I MEAN?
THOSE BOYS ARE TOUGHER THAN WE THINK. KIDS, Y'KNOW, THEY CAN HANDLE A LOT MORE THAN WE GIVE THEM CREDIT FOR. MOST OF THEM ANYWAY.
THEY ASKED TO SLEEP IN THEIR OWN CELL AND SO WE LET THEM. THEY'VE BEEN THROUGH A LOT. THEY DON'T NEED TO BE TOLD TO DO THINGS THEY DON'T WANT TO DO JUST YET. WE'LL HAVE PLENTY OF TIME FOR THAT SOON ENOUGH.
WE GOT THEM RIGHT NEXT DOOR-- GOT THE DOOR CLOSED TIGHT AND EVERYTHING. THEY'LL BE FINE UNTIL MORNING.
SOUNDS LIKE YOU'RE DOING ENOUGH WORRYING FOR THE BOTH OF US. SO, IT LOOKS LIKE I'M GOING TO HAVE TO PUT THIS BUSINESS OUT OF MY HEAD AND GET SOME SLEEP.
SOMEHOW.
SOMEBODY'S GOING TO HAVE TO POUR THAT CEREAL TOMORROW MORNING.
I LOVE YOU, DALE. GOOD-NIGHT.
YOU TOO, KIDDO.

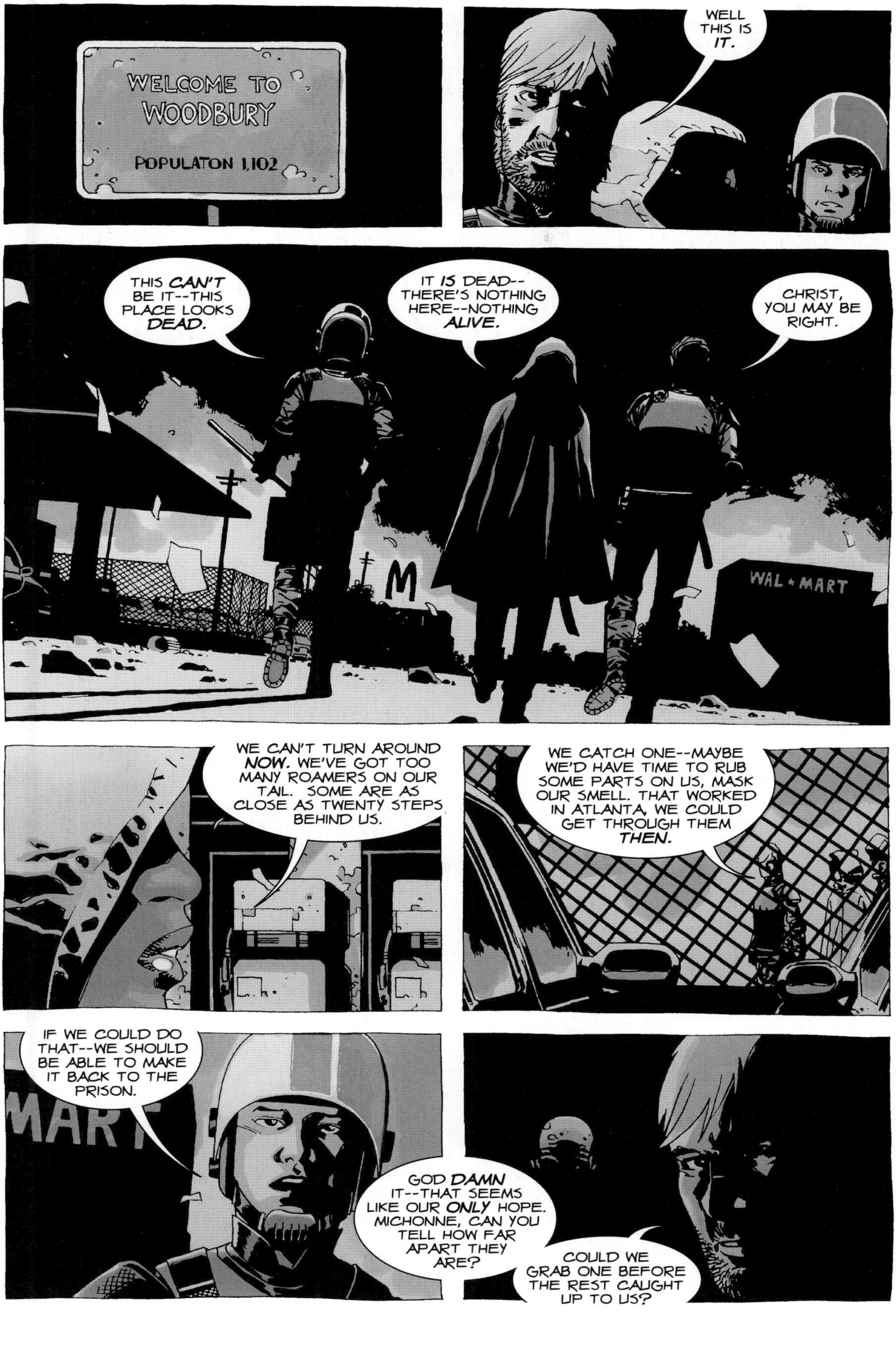
WELCOME TO WOODBURY
POPULATON 1,102
WELL THIS IS IT.
THIS CAN'T BE IT--THIS PLACE LOOKS DEAD.
IT IS DEAD--THERE'S NOTHING HERE--NOTHING ALIVE.
CHRIST, YOU MAY BE RIGHT.
M
WAL★MART
WE CAN'T TURN AROUND NOW. WE'VE GOT TOO MANY ROAMERS ON OUR TAIL. SOME ARE AS CLOSE AS TWENTY STEPS BEHIND US.
WE CATCH ONE--MAYBE WE'D HAVE TIME TO RUB SOME PARTS ON US, MASK OUR SMELL. THAT WORKED IN ATLANTA, WE COULD GET THROUGH THEM THEN.
IF WE COULD DO THAT--WE SHOULD BE ABLE TO MAKE IT BACK TO THE PRISON.
MART
GOD DAMN IT--THAT SEEMS LIKE OUR ONLY HOPE. MICHONNE, CAN YOU TELL HOW FAR APART THEY ARE?
COULD WE GRAB ONE BEFORE THE REST CAUGHT UP TO US?

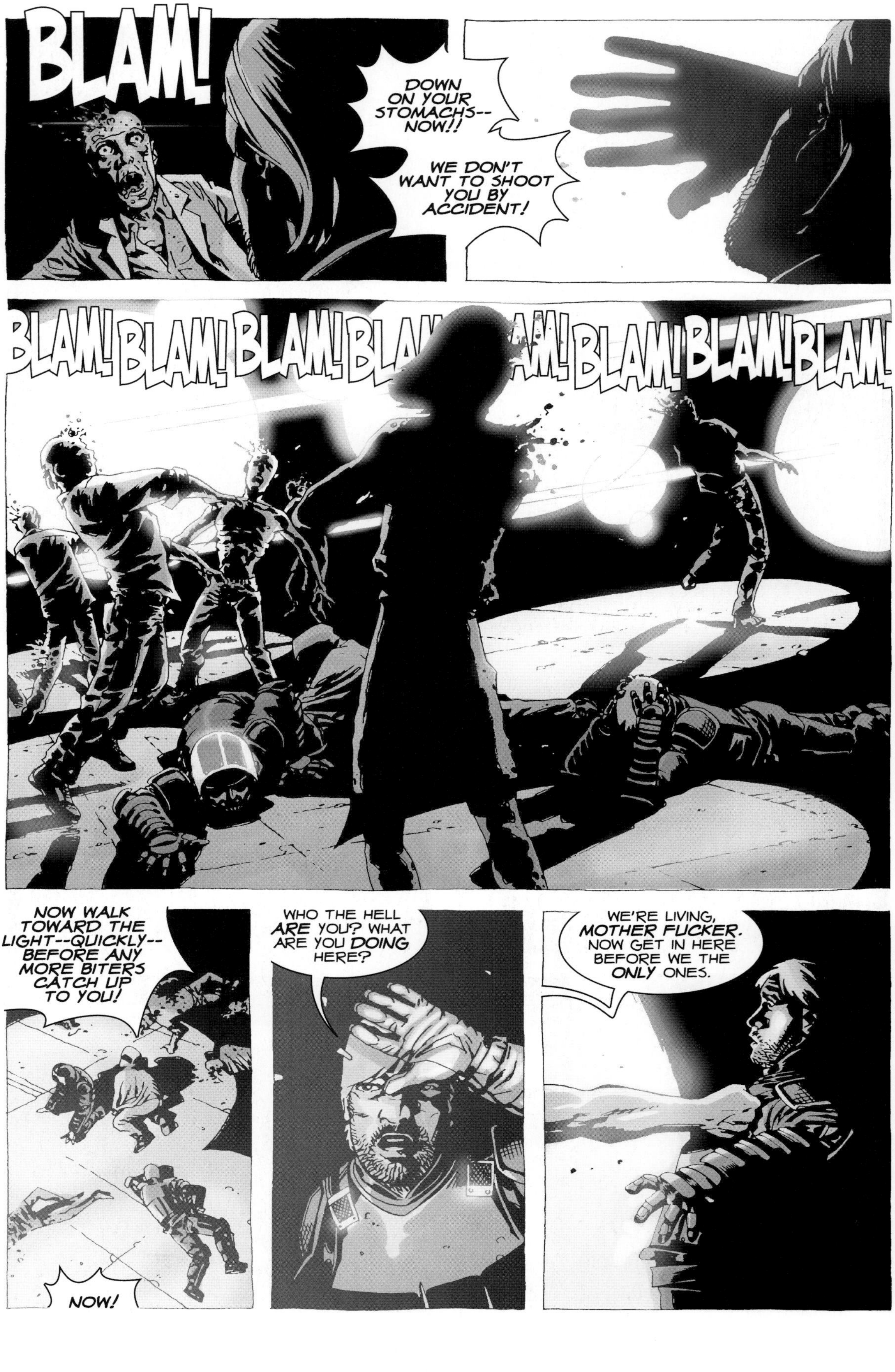
BLAM!
DOWN ON YOUR STOMACHS-- NOW!!
WE DON'T WANT TO SHOOT YOU BY ACCIDENT!
BLAM! BLAM! BLAM! BLAM! BLAM! BLAM! BLAM! BLAM!
NOW WALK TOWARD THE LIGHT--QUICKLY-- BEFORE ANY MORE BITERS CATCH UP TO YOU!
NOW!
WHO THE HELL ARE YOU? WHAT ARE YOU DOING HERE?
WE'RE LIVING, MOTHER FUCKER. NOW GET IN HERE BEFORE WE THE ONLY ONES.

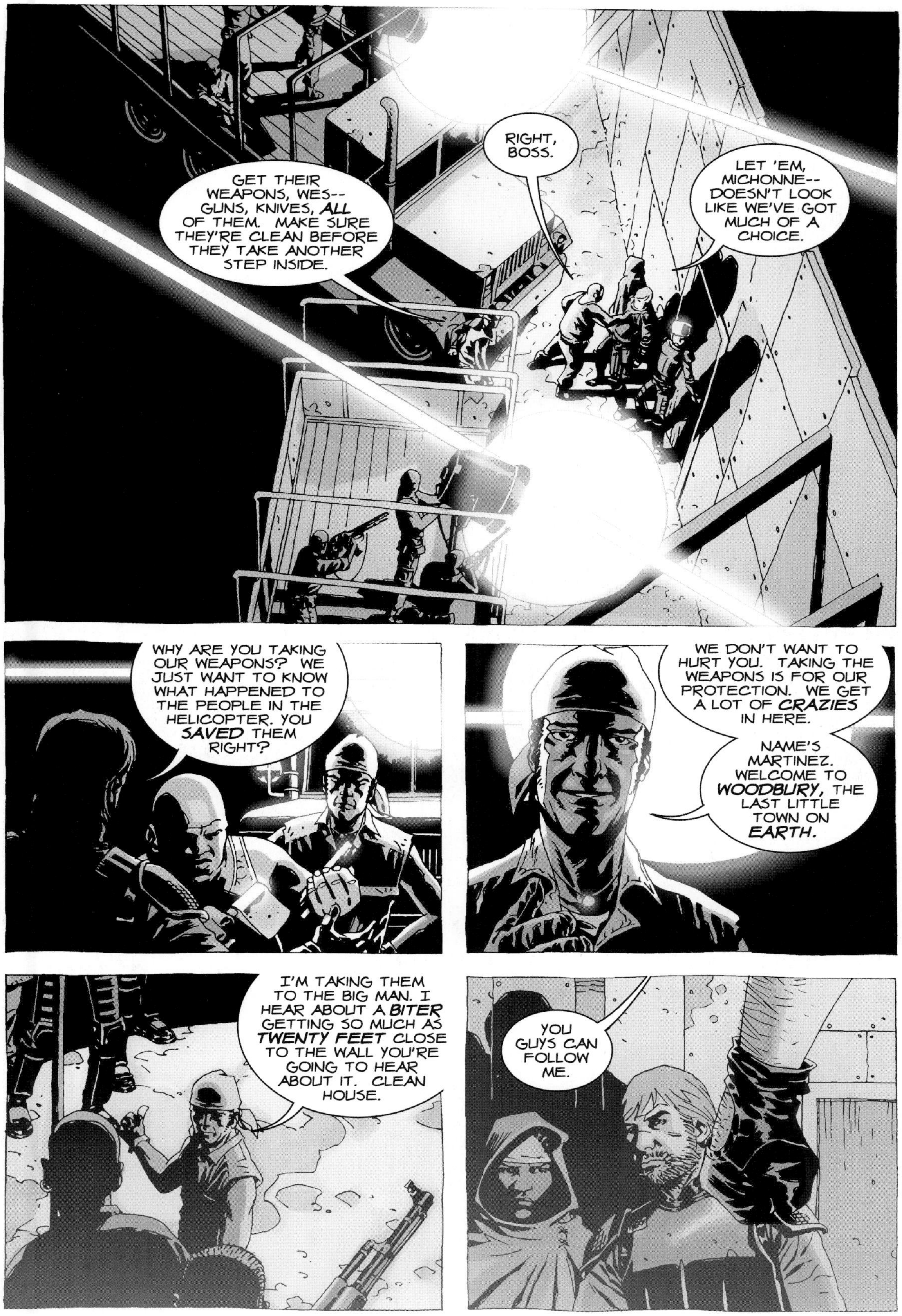
GET THEIR WEAPONS, WES-- GUNS, KNIVES, ALL OF THEM. MAKE SURE THEY'RE CLEAN BEFORE THEY TAKE ANOTHER STEP INSIDE.
RIGHT, BOSS.
LET 'EM, MICHONNE-- DOESN'T LOOK LIKE WE'VE GOT MUCH OF A CHOICE.
WHY ARE YOU TAKING OUR WEAPONS? WE JUST WANT TO KNOW WHAT HAPPENED TO THE PEOPLE IN THE HELICOPTER. YOU SAVED THEM RIGHT?
WE DON'T WANT TO HURT YOU. TAKING THE WEAPONS IS FOR OUR PROTECTION. WE GET A LOT OF CRAZIES IN HERE.
NAME'S MARTINEZ. WELCOME TO WOODBURY, THE LAST LITTLE TOWN ON EARTH.
I'M TAKING THEM TO THE BIG MAN. I HEAR ABOUT A BITER GETTING SO MUCH AS TWENTY FEET CLOSE TO THE WALL YOU'RE GOING TO HEAR ABOUT IT. CLEAN HOUSE.
YOU GUYS CAN FOLLOW ME.

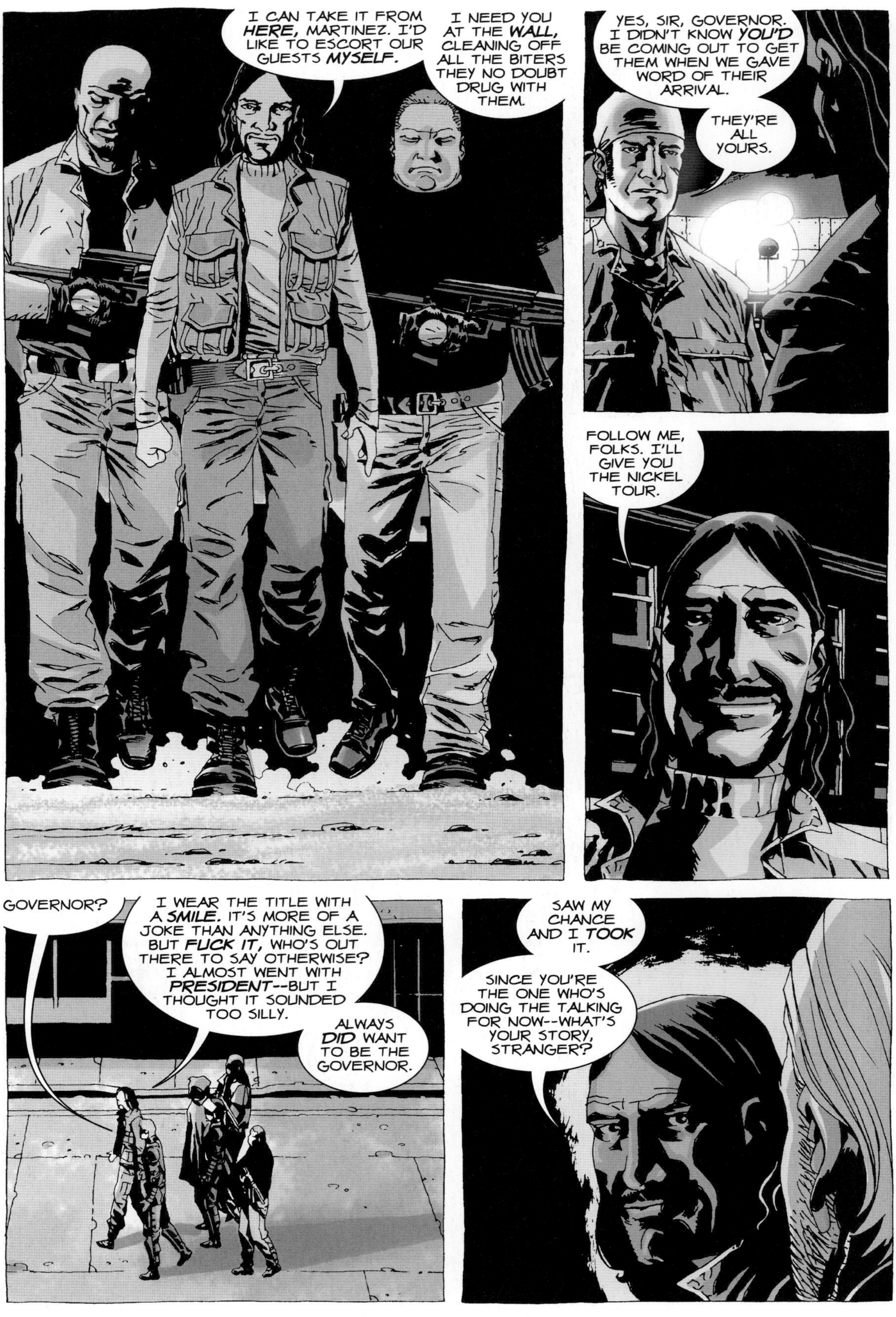
I CAN TAKE IT FROM HERE, MARTINEZ. I'D LIKE TO ESCORT OUR GUESTS MYSELF.
I NEED YOU AT THE WALL, CLEANING OFF ALL THE BITERS THEY NO DOUBT DRUG WITH THEM.
YES, SIR, GOVERNOR. I DIDN'T KNOW YOU'D BE COMING OUT TO GET THEM WHEN WE GAVE WORD OF THEIR ARRIVAL.
THEY'RE ALL YOURS.
FOLLOW ME, FOLKS. I'LL GIVE YOU THE NICKEL TOUR.
GOVERNOR?
I WEAR THE TITLE WITH A SMILE. IT'S MORE OF A JOKE THAN ANYTHING ELSE. BUT FUCK IT, WHO'S OUT THERE TO SAY OTHERWISE? I ALMOST WENT WITH PRESIDENT--BUT I THOUGHT IT SOUNDED TOO SILLY.
ALWAYS DID WANT TO BE THE GOVERNOR.
SAW MY CHANCE AND I TOOK IT.
SINCE YOU'RE THE ONE WHO'S DOING THE TALKING FOR NOW--WHAT'S YOUR STORY, STRANGER?

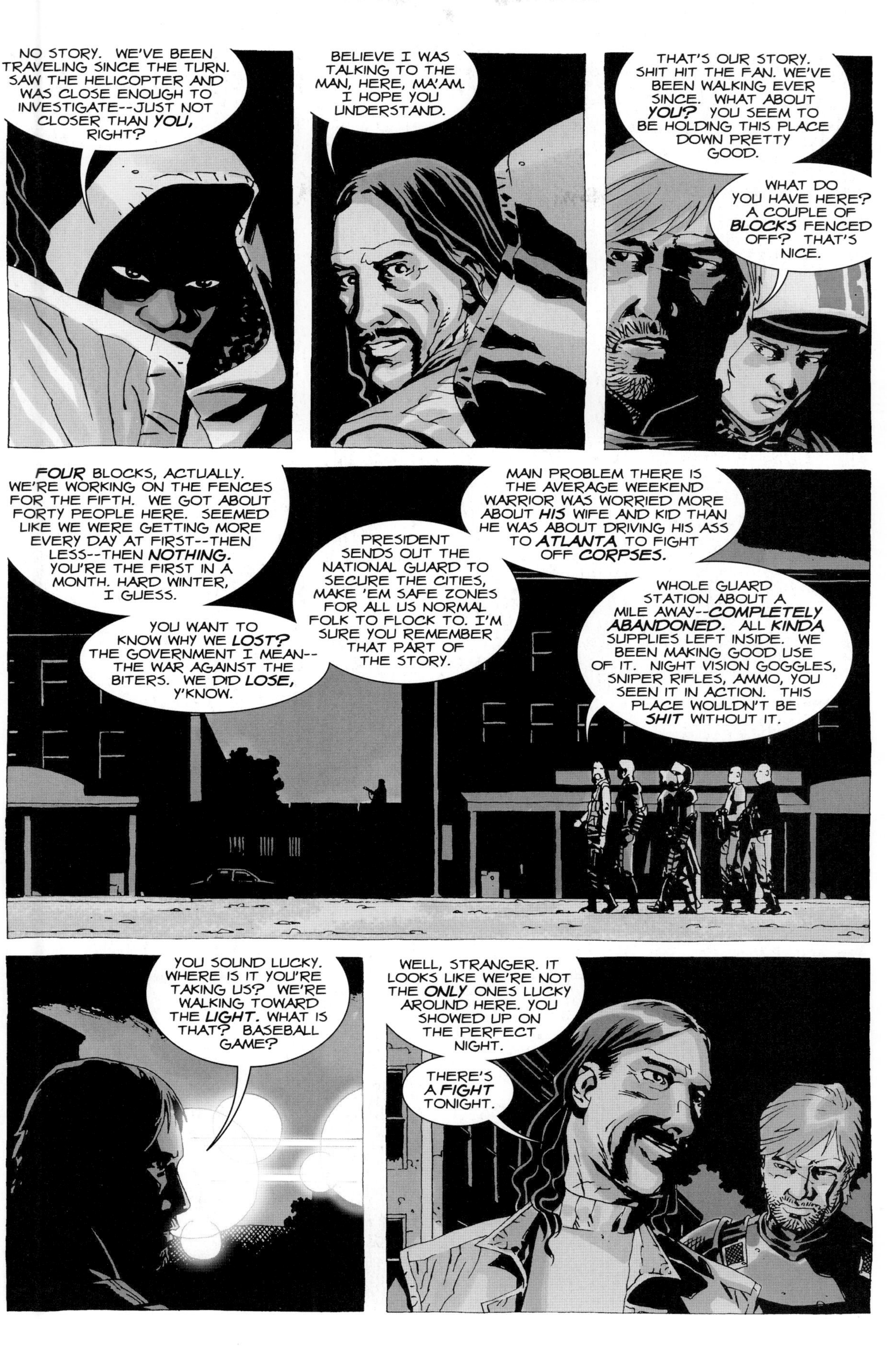
NO STORY. WE'VE BEEN TRAVELING SINCE THE TURN. SAW THE HELICOPTER AND WAS CLOSE ENOUGH TO INVESTIGATE--JUST NOT CLOSER THAN YOU, RIGHT?
BELIEVE I WAS TALKING TO THE MAN, HERE, MA'AM. I HOPE YOU UNDERSTAND.
THAT'S OUR STORY. SHIT HIT THE FAN. WE'VE BEEN WALKING EVER SINCE. WHAT ABOUT YOU? YOU SEEM TO BE HOLDING THIS PLACE DOWN PRETTY GOOD.
WHAT DO YOU HAVE HERE? A COUPLE OF BLOCKS FENCED OFF? THAT'S NICE.
FOUR BLOCKS, ACTUALLY. WE'RE WORKING ON THE FENCES FOR THE FIFTH. WE GOT ABOUT FORTY PEOPLE HERE. SEEMED LIKE WE WERE GETTING MORE EVERY DAY AT FIRST--THEN LESS--THEN NOTHING. YOU'RE THE FIRST IN A MONTH. HARD WINTER, I GUESS.
YOU WANT TO KNOW WHY WE LOST? THE GOVERNMENT I MEAN-- THE WAR AGAINST THE BITERS. WE DID LOSE, Y'KNOW.
PRESIDENT SENDS OUT THE NATIONAL GUARD TO SECURE THE CITIES, MAKE 'EM SAFE ZONES FOR ALL US NORMAL FOLK TO FLOCK TO. I'M SURE YOU REMEMBER THAT PART OF THE STORY.
MAIN PROBLEM THERE IS THE AVERAGE WEEKEND WARRIOR WAS WORRIED MORE ABOUT HIS WIFE AND KID THAN HE WAS ABOUT DRIVING HIS ASS TO ATLANTA TO FIGHT OFF CORPSES.
WHOLE GUARD STATION ABOUT A MILE AWAY--COMPLETELY ABANDONED. ALL KINDA SUPPLIES LEFT INSIDE. WE BEEN MAKING GOOD USE OF IT. NIGHT VISION GOGGLES, SNIPER RIFLES, AMMO, YOU SEEN IT IN ACTION. THIS PLACE WOULDN'T BE SHIT WITHOUT IT.
YOU SOUND LUCKY. WHERE IS IT YOU'RE TAKING US? WE'RE WALKING TOWARD THE LIGHT. WHAT IS THAT? BASEBALL GAME?
WELL, STRANGER. IT LOOKS LIKE WE'RE NOT THE ONLY ONES LUCKY AROUND HERE. YOU SHOWED UP ON THE PERFECT NIGHT.
THERE'S A FIGHT TONIGHT.

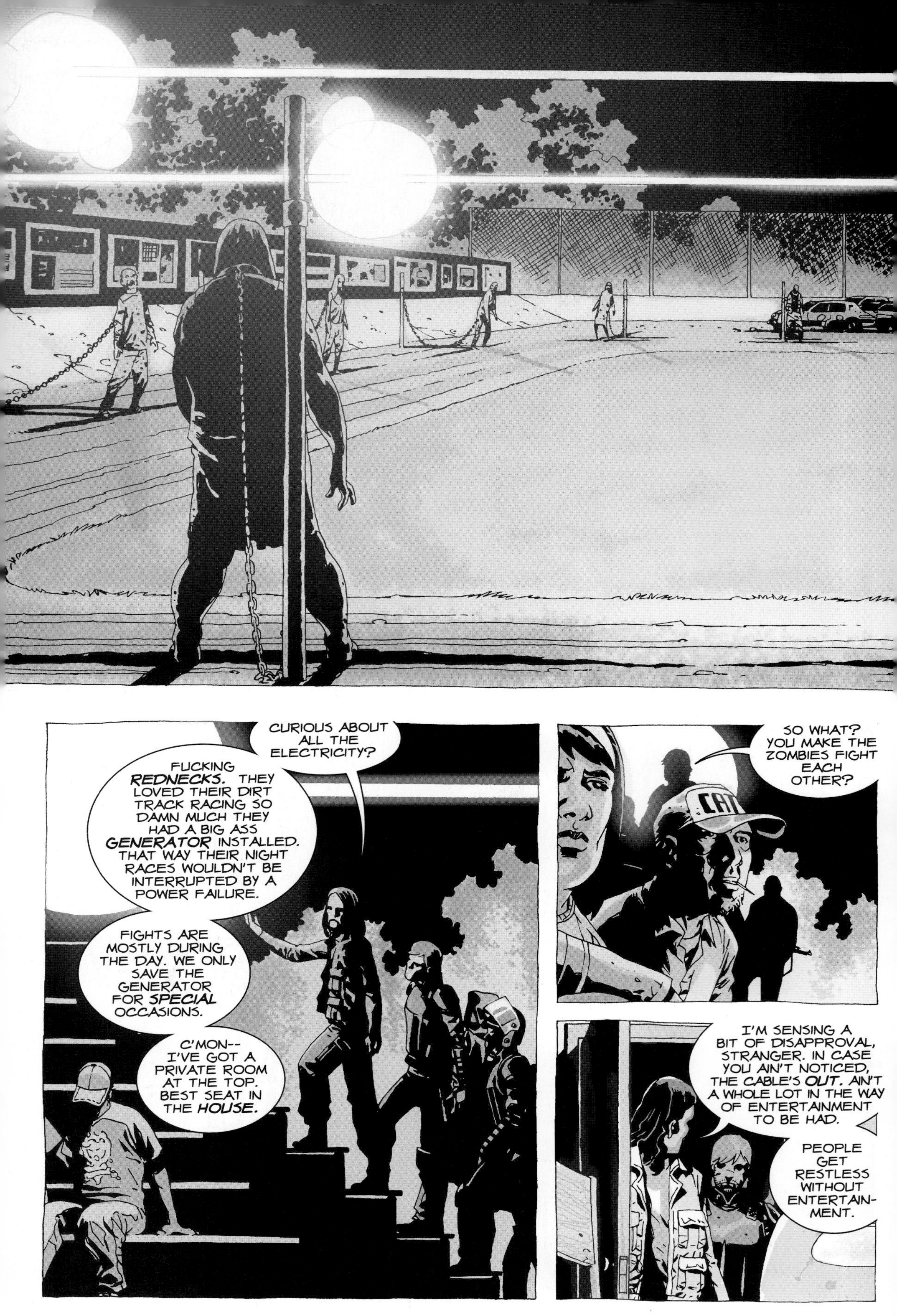
CURIOUS ABOUT ALL THE ELECTRICITY?
FUCKING REDNECKS. THEY LOVED THEIR DIRT TRACK RACING SO DAMN MUCH THEY HAD A BIG ASS GENERATOR INSTALLED. THAT WAY THEIR NIGHT RACES WOULDN'T BE INTERRUPTED BY A POWER FAILURE.
FIGHTS ARE MOSTLY DURING THE DAY. WE ONLY SAVE THE GENERATOR FOR SPECIAL OCCASIONS.
C'MON-- I'VE GOT A PRIVATE ROOM AT THE TOP. BEST SEAT IN THE HOUSE.
SO WHAT? YOU MAKE THE ZOMBIES FIGHT EACH OTHER?
CAT
I'M SENSING A BIT OF DISAPPROVAL, STRANGER. IN CASE YOU AIN'T NOTICED, THE CABLE'S OUT. AIN'T A WHOLE LOT IN THE WAY OF ENTERTAINMENT TO BE HAD.
PEOPLE GET RESTLESS WITHOUT ENTERTAIN-MENT.

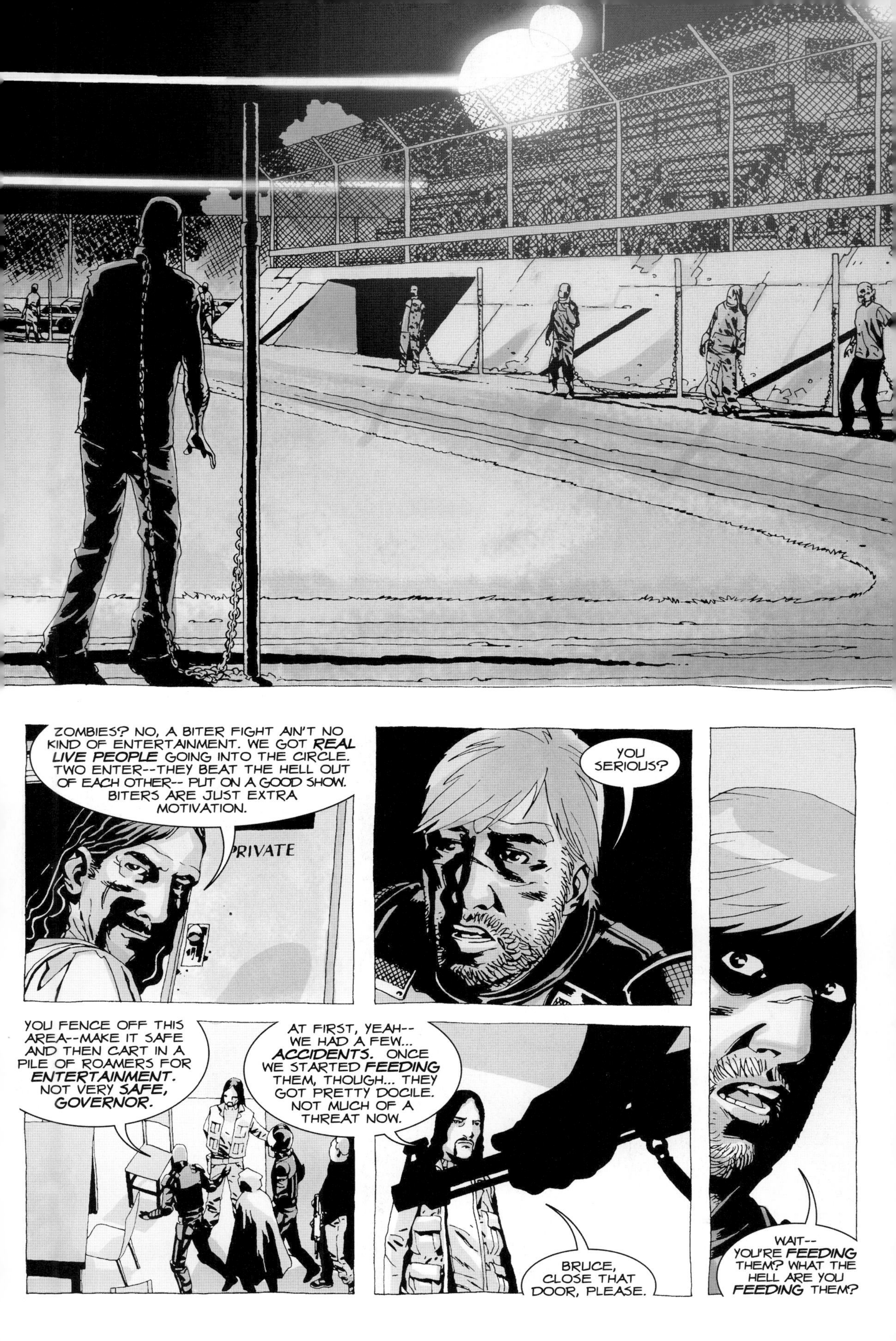
ZOMBIES? NO, A BITER FIGHT AIN'T NO KIND OF ENTERTAINMENT. WE GOT REAL LIVE PEOPLE GOING INTO THE CIRCLE. TWO ENTER--THEY BEAT THE HELL OUT OF EACH OTHER-- PUT ON A GOOD SHOW. BITERS ARE JUST EXTRA MOTIVATION.
PRIVATE
YOU SERIOUS?
YOU FENCE OFF THIS AREA--MAKE IT SAFE AND THEN CART IN A PILE OF ROAMERS FOR ENTERTAINMENT. NOT VERY SAFE, GOVERNOR.
AT FIRST, YEAH-- WE HAD A FEW... ACCIDENTS. ONCE WE STARTED FEEDING THEM, THOUGH... THEY GOT PRETTY DOCILE. NOT MUCH OF A THREAT NOW.
BRUCE, CLOSE THAT DOOR, PLEASE.
WAIT-- YOU'RE FEEDING THEM? WHAT THE HELL ARE YOU FEEDING THEM?

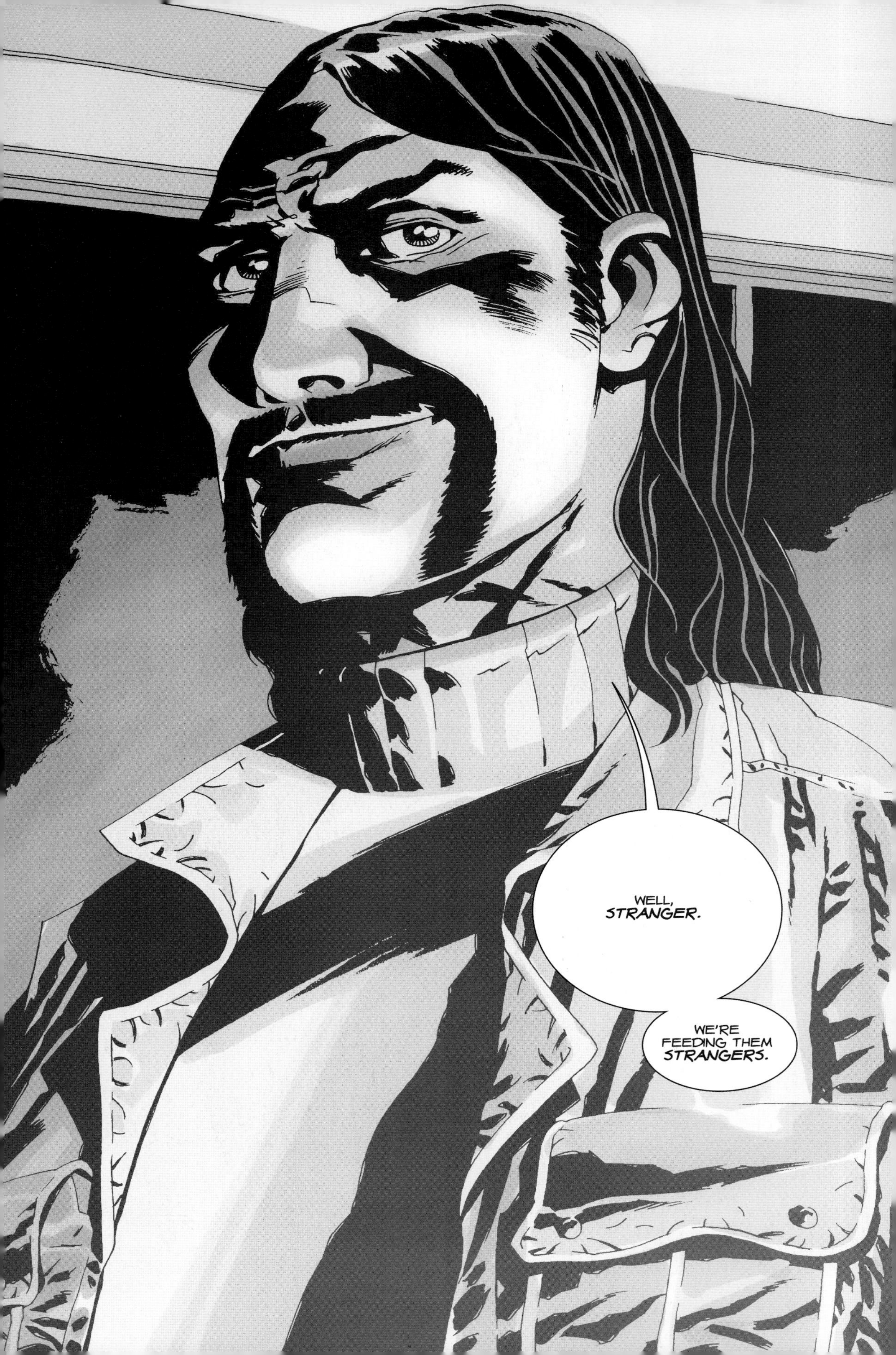
WELL, STRANGER.
WE'RE FEEDING THEM STRANGERS.

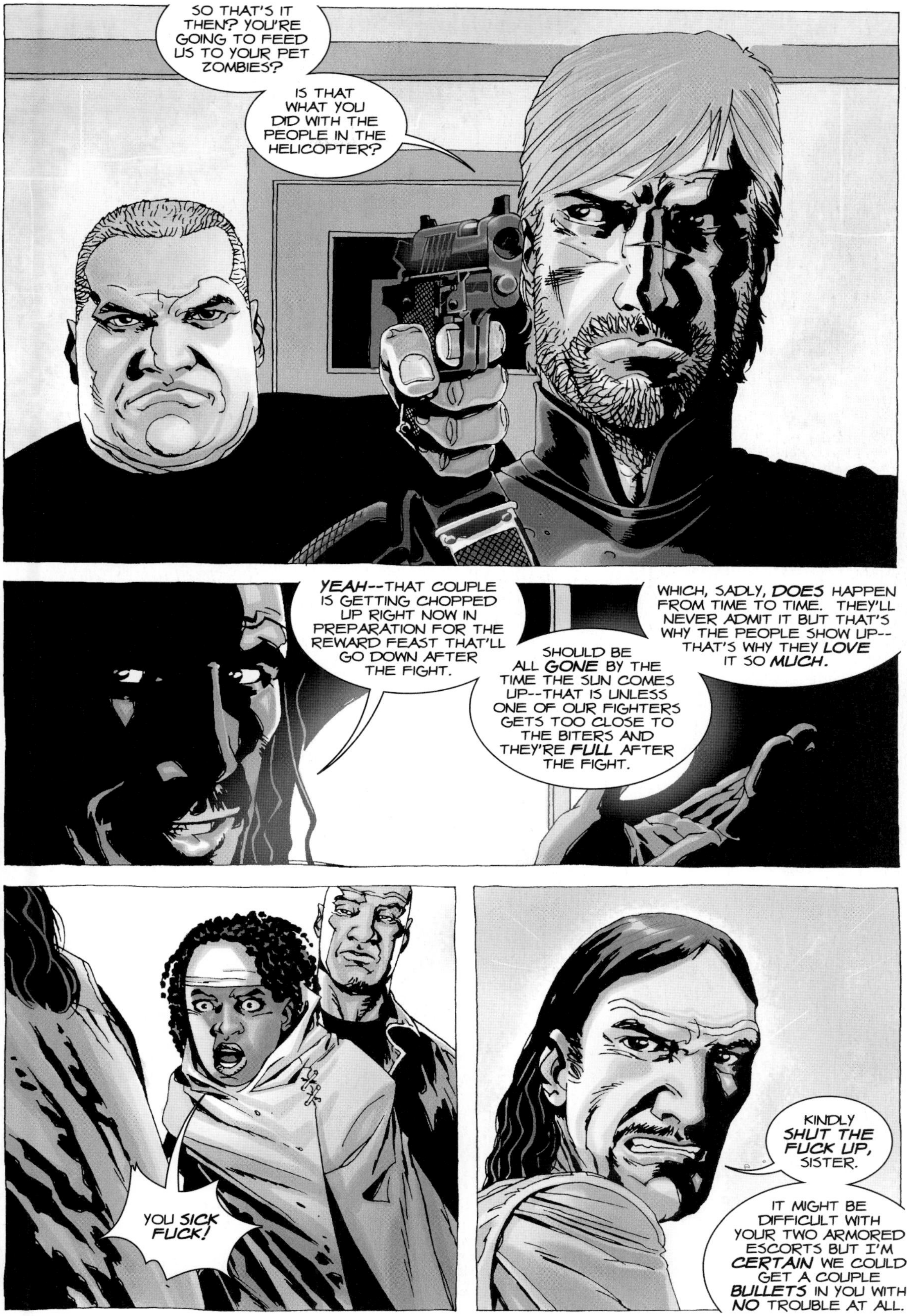
SO THAT'S IT THEN? YOU'RE GOING TO FEED US TO YOUR PET ZOMBIES?
IS THAT WHAT YOU DID WITH THE PEOPLE IN THE HELICOPTER?
YEAH--THAT COUPLE IS GETTING CHOPPED UP RIGHT NOW IN PREPARATION FOR THE REWARD FEAST THAT'LL GO DOWN AFTER THE FIGHT.
SHOULD BE ALL GONE BY THE TIME THE SUN COMES UP--THAT IS UNLESS ONE OF OUR FIGHTERS GETS TOO CLOSE TO THE BITERS AND THEY'RE FULL AFTER THE FIGHT.
WHICH, SADLY, DOES HAPPEN FROM TIME TO TIME. THEY'LL NEVER ADMIT IT BUT THAT'S WHY THE PEOPLE SHOW UP-- THAT'S WHY THEY LOVE IT SO MUCH.
YOU SICK FUCK!
KINDLY SHUT THE FUCK UP, SISTER.
IT MIGHT BE DIFFICULT WITH YOUR TWO ARMORED ESCORTS BUT I'M CERTAIN WE COULD GET A COUPLE BULLETS IN YOU WITH NO TROUBLE AT ALL.

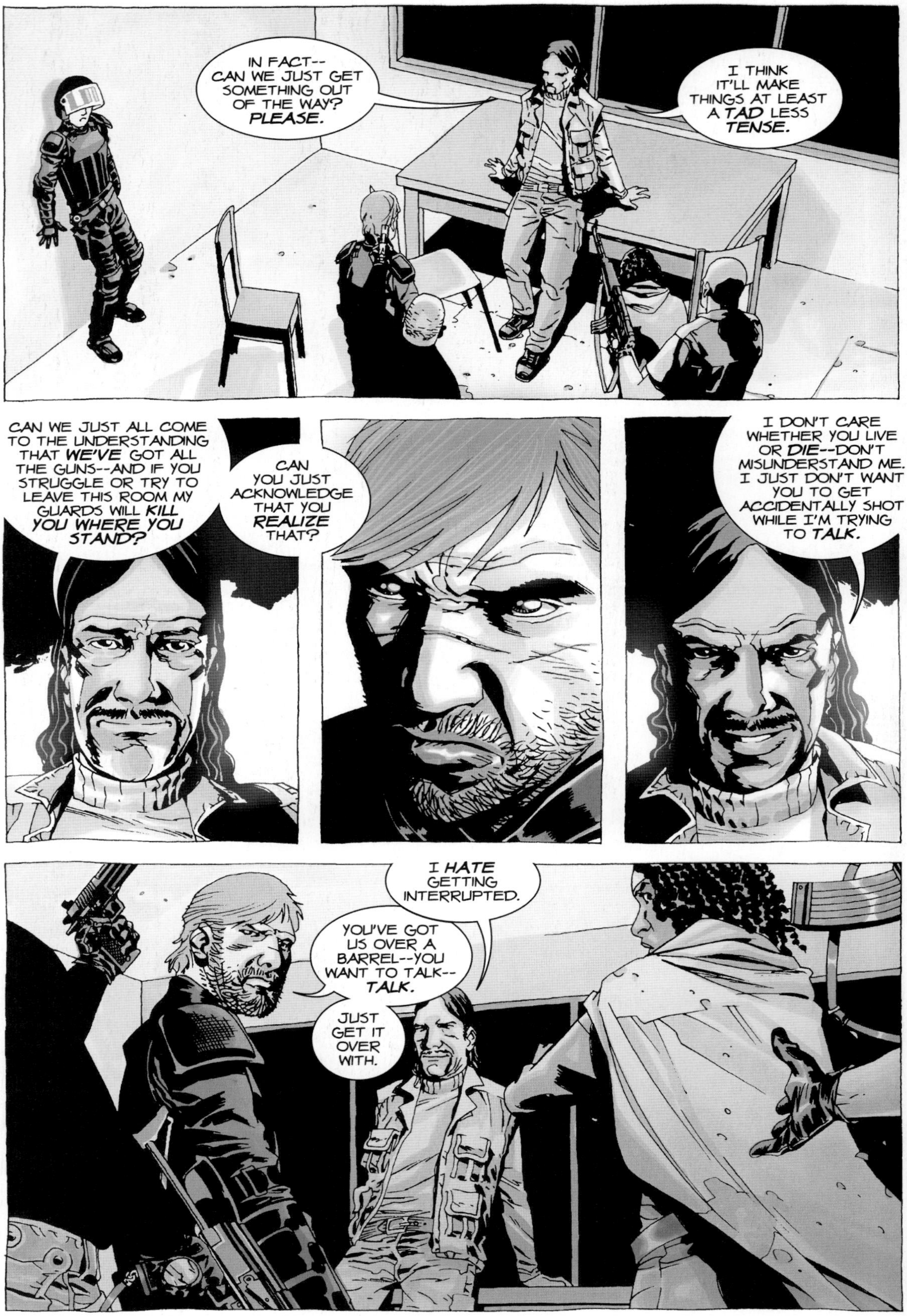
IN FACT-- CAN WE JUST GET SOMETHING OUT OF THE WAY? PLEASE.
I THINK IT'LL MAKE THINGS AT LEAST A TAD LESS TENSE.
CAN WE JUST ALL COME TO THE UNDERSTANDING THAT WE'VE GOT ALL THE GUNS--AND IF YOU STRUGGLE OR TRY TO LEAVE THIS ROOM MY GUARDS WILL KILL YOU WHERE YOU STAND?
CAN YOU JUST ACKNOWLEDGE THAT YOU REALIZE THAT?
I DON'T CARE WHETHER YOU LIVE OR DIE--DON'T MISUNDERSTAND ME. I JUST DON'T WANT YOU TO GET ACCIDENTALLY SHOT WHILE I'M TRYING TO TALK.
I HATE GETTING INTERRUPTED.
YOU'VE GOT US OVER A BARREL--YOU WANT TO TALK-- TALK.
JUST GET IT OVER WITH.

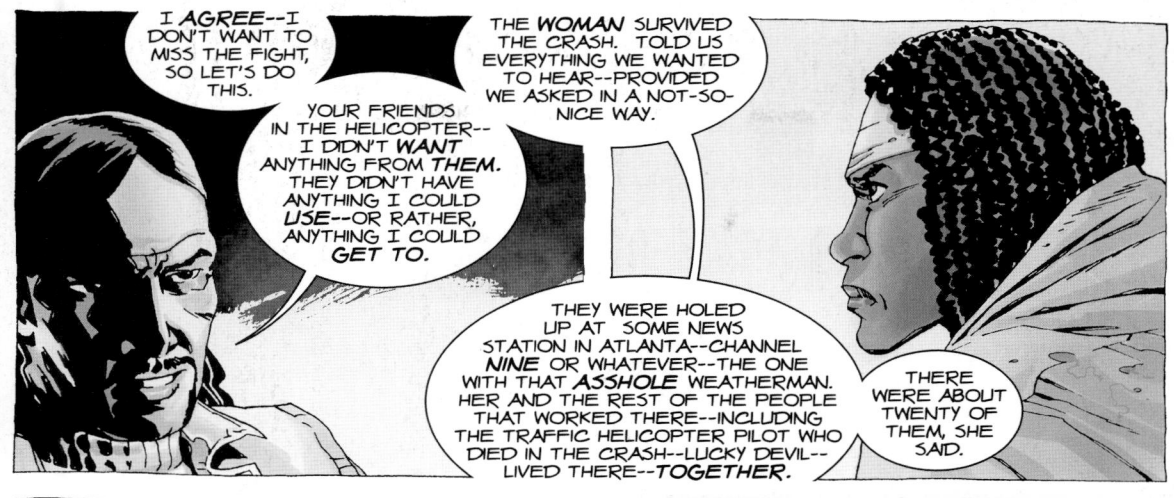

I *AGREE*--I DON'T WANT TO MISS THE FIGHT, SO LET'S DO THIS.

YOUR FRIENDS IN THE HELICOPTER-- I DIDN'T *WANT* ANYTHING FROM *THEM.* THEY DIDN'T HAVE ANYTHING I COULD *USE*--OR RATHER, ANYTHING I COULD *GET TO.*

THE *WOMAN* SURVIVED THE CRASH. TOLD US EVERYTHING WE WANTED TO HEAR--PROVIDED WE ASKED IN A NOT-SO-NICE WAY.

THEY WERE HOLED UP AT SOME NEWS STATION IN ATLANTA--CHANNEL *NINE* OR WHATEVER--THE ONE WITH THAT *ASSHOLE* WEATHERMAN. HER AND THE REST OF THE PEOPLE THAT WORKED THERE--INCLUDING THE TRAFFIC HELICOPTER PILOT WHO DIED IN THE CRASH--LUCKY DEVIL-- LIVED THERE--*TOGETHER.*

THERE WERE ABOUT TWENTY OF THEM, SHE SAID.

THEY *TURNED* ON EACH OTHER--RAN OUT OF FOOD--*SOMETHING*-- STARTING *KILLING* EACH OTHER. OUR LADY AND THE PILOT GOT OUT--BUT SOME SICK FUCK *SABOTAGED* THE HELICOPTER'S ENGINE.

SEEMS HE WANTED TO MAKE SURE NOBODY LEFT *WITHOUT* HIM.

THERE'S A *LESSON* THERE. YOU GOTTA KEEP PEOPLE *OCCUPIED* OR THEY'LL *TURN* ON YOU. *READING* AND *FUCKING* WILL ONLY KEEP PEOPLE BUSY FOR *SO LONG.* EVENTUALLY THERE'S GOTTA BE SOMETHING *ELSE.*

HENCE OUR LITTLE SPORTING EVENT HERE.

BUT ENOUGH ABOUT *THAT*--FOR NOW. THERE'RE *PLENTY* OF THINGS I'D LIKE TO HAVE IN THAT BUILDING-- THE *CHANNEL NINE* BUILDING... BUT IN THE CENTER OF ATLANTA-- BITERVILLE--AIN'T *NO WAY* I'M GOING TO GET TO IT.

SO THEY GET FED TO THE BITERS. I MEAN, SOMEBODY'S GOTTA BE--WHY NOT *THEM?*

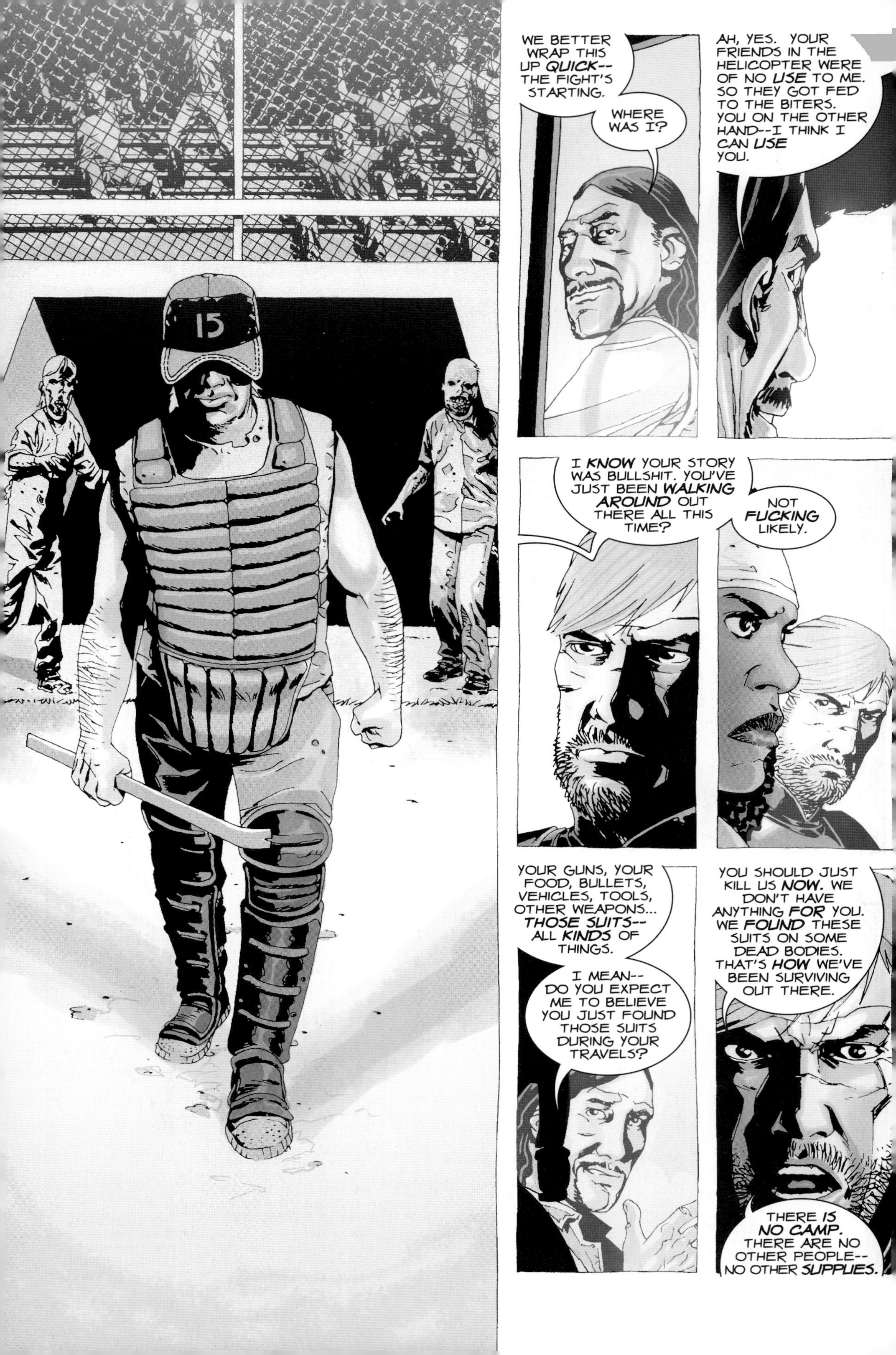
WE BETTER WRAP THIS UP QUICK-- THE FIGHT'S STARTING.
WHERE WAS I?
AH, YES. YOUR FRIENDS IN THE HELICOPTER WERE OF NO USE TO ME. SO THEY GOT FED TO THE BITERS. YOU ON THE OTHER HAND--I THINK I CAN USE YOU.
I KNOW YOUR STORY WAS BULLSHIT. YOU'VE JUST BEEN WALKING AROUND OUT THERE ALL THIS TIME?
NOT FUCKING LIKELY.
YOUR GUNS, YOUR FOOD, BULLETS, VEHICLES, TOOLS, OTHER WEAPONS... THOSE SUITS-- ALL KINDS OF THINGS.
I MEAN-- DO YOU EXPECT ME TO BELIEVE YOU JUST FOUND THOSE SUITS DURING YOUR TRAVELS?
YOU SHOULD JUST KILL US NOW. WE DON'T HAVE ANYTHING FOR YOU. WE FOUND THESE SUITS ON SOME DEAD BODIES. THAT'S HOW WE'VE BEEN SURVIVING OUT THERE.
THERE IS NO CAMP. THERE ARE NO OTHER PEOPLE-- NO OTHER SUPPLIES.
15

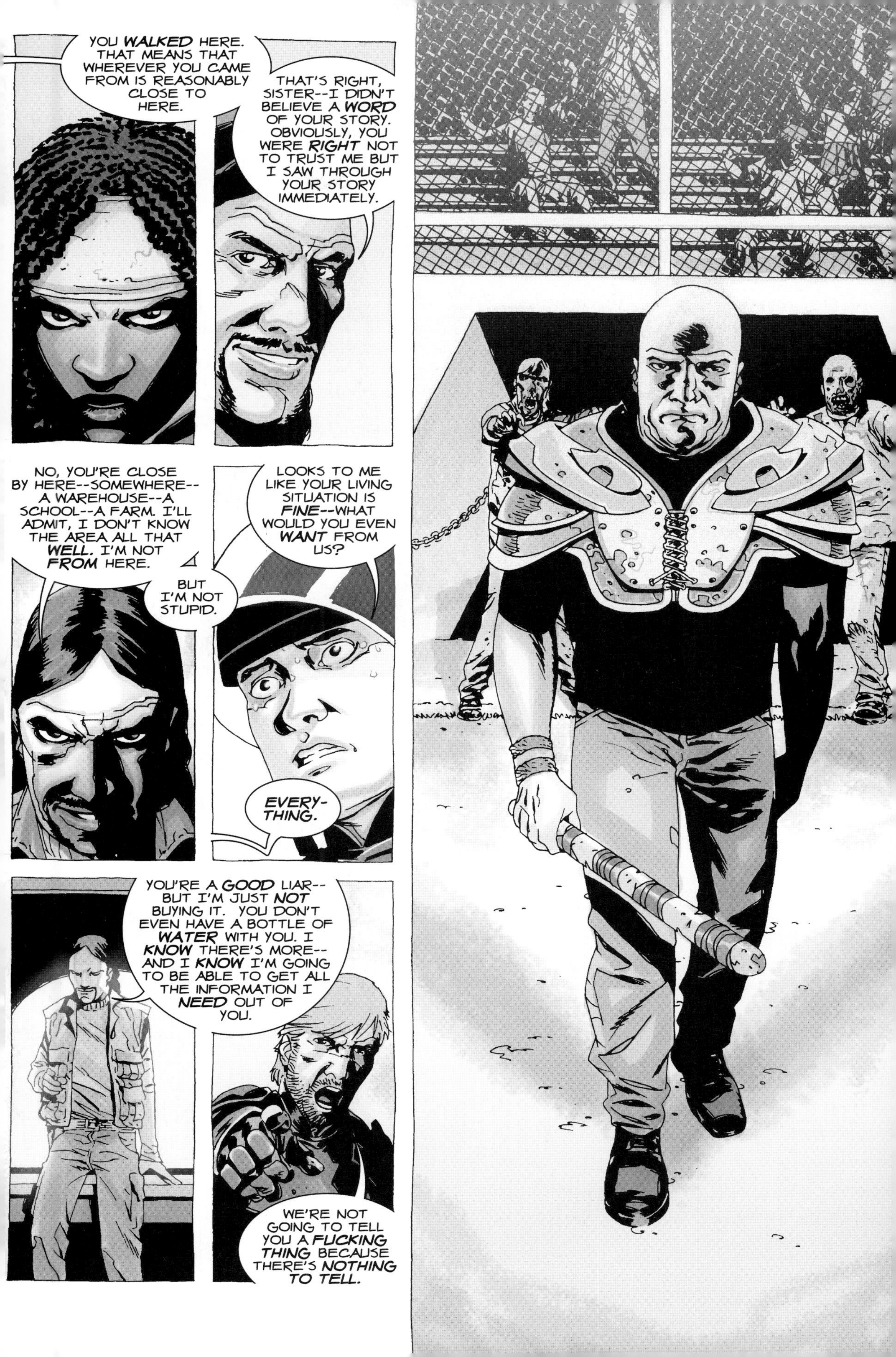
YOU WALKED HERE. THAT MEANS THAT WHEREVER YOU CAME FROM IS REASONABLY CLOSE TO HERE.
THAT'S RIGHT, SISTER--I DIDN'T BELIEVE A WORD OF YOUR STORY. OBVIOUSLY, YOU WERE RIGHT NOT TO TRUST ME BUT I SAW THROUGH YOUR STORY IMMEDIATELY.
NO, YOU'RE CLOSE BY HERE--SOMEWHERE--A WAREHOUSE--A SCHOOL--A FARM. I'LL ADMIT, I DON'T KNOW THE AREA ALL THAT WELL. I'M NOT FROM HERE.
BUT I'M NOT STUPID.
LOOKS TO ME LIKE YOUR LIVING SITUATION IS FINE--WHAT WOULD YOU EVEN WANT FROM US?
EVERY-THING.
YOU'RE A GOOD LIAR--BUT I'M JUST NOT BUYING IT. YOU DON'T EVEN HAVE A BOTTLE OF WATER WITH YOU. I KNOW THERE'S MORE--AND I KNOW I'M GOING TO BE ABLE TO GET ALL THE INFORMATION I NEED OUT OF YOU.
WE'RE NOT GOING TO TELL YOU A FUCKING THING BECAUSE THERE'S NOTHING TO TELL.

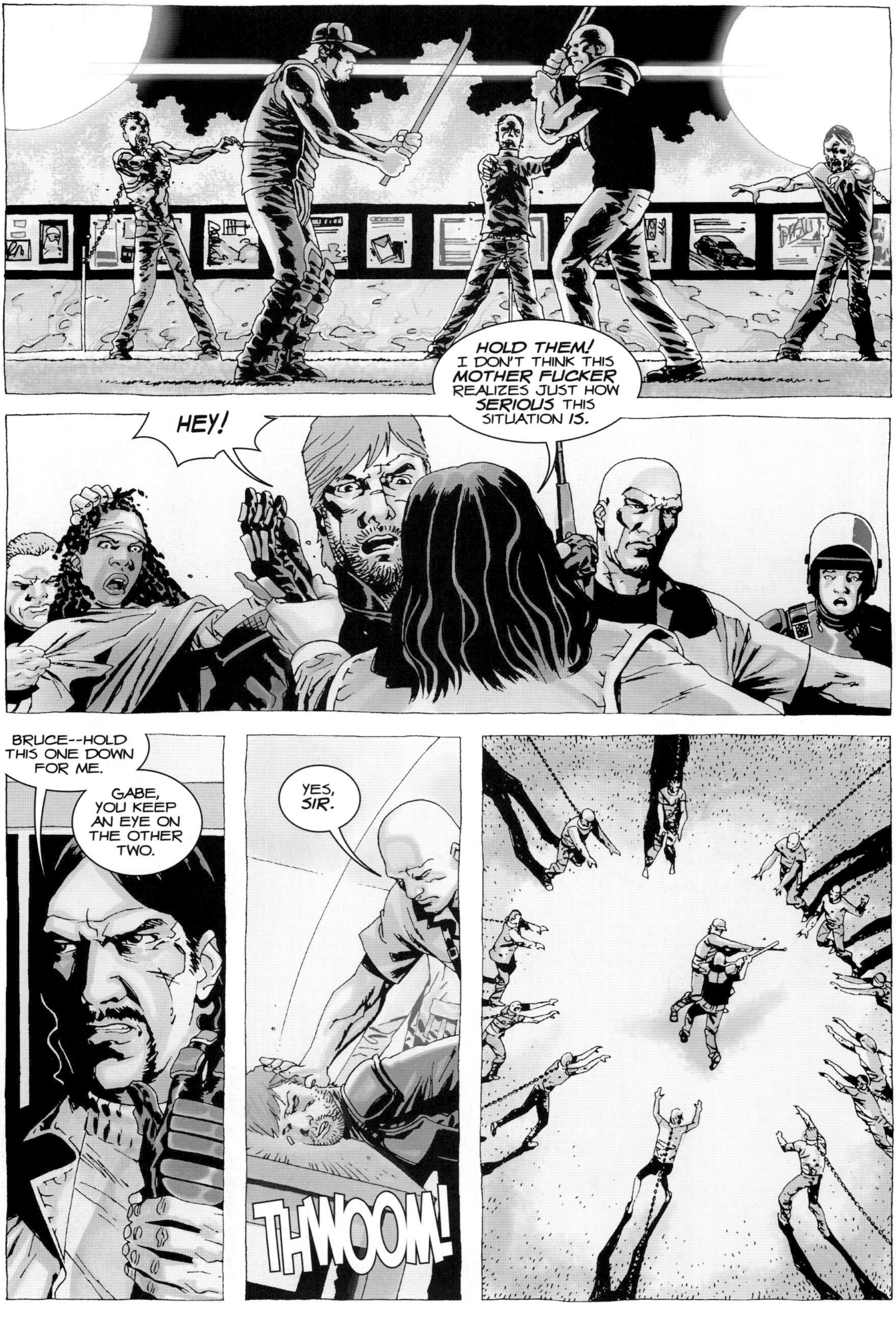
HOLD THEM! I DON'T THINK THIS MOTHER FUCKER REALIZES JUST HOW SERIOUS THIS SITUATION IS.
HEY!
BRUCE--HOLD THIS ONE DOWN FOR ME.
GABE, YOU KEEP AN EYE ON THE OTHER TWO.
YES, SIR.
THWOOM!

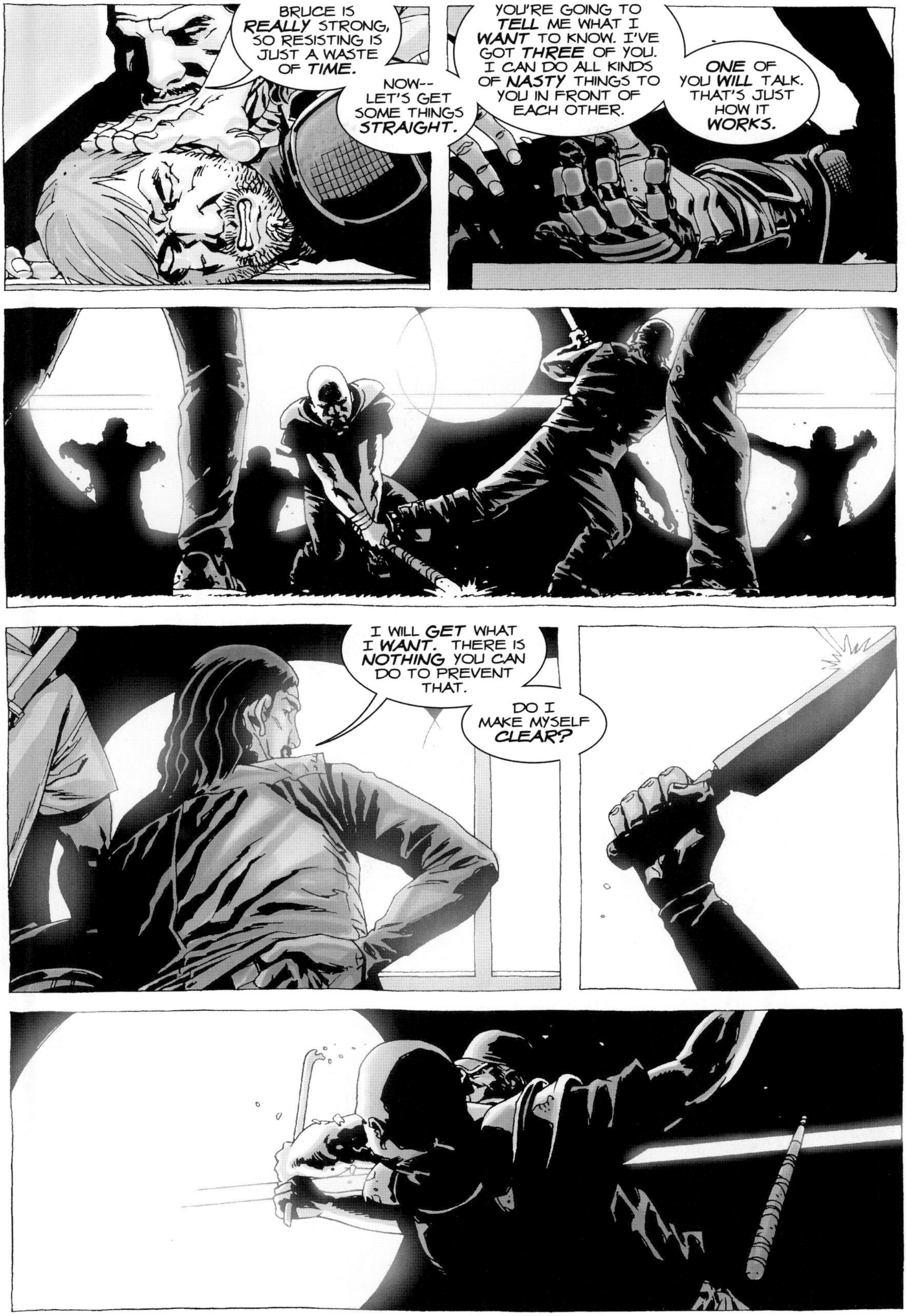
BRUCE IS REALLY STRONG, SO RESISTING IS JUST A WASTE OF TIME.
NOW-- LET'S GET SOME THINGS STRAIGHT.
YOU'RE GOING TO TELL ME WHAT I WANT TO KNOW. I'VE GOT THREE OF YOU. I CAN DO ALL KINDS OF NASTY THINGS TO YOU IN FRONT OF EACH OTHER.
ONE OF YOU WILL TALK. THAT'S JUST HOW IT WORKS.
I WILL GET WHAT I WANT. THERE IS NOTHING YOU CAN DO TO PREVENT THAT.
DO I MAKE MYSELF CLEAR?

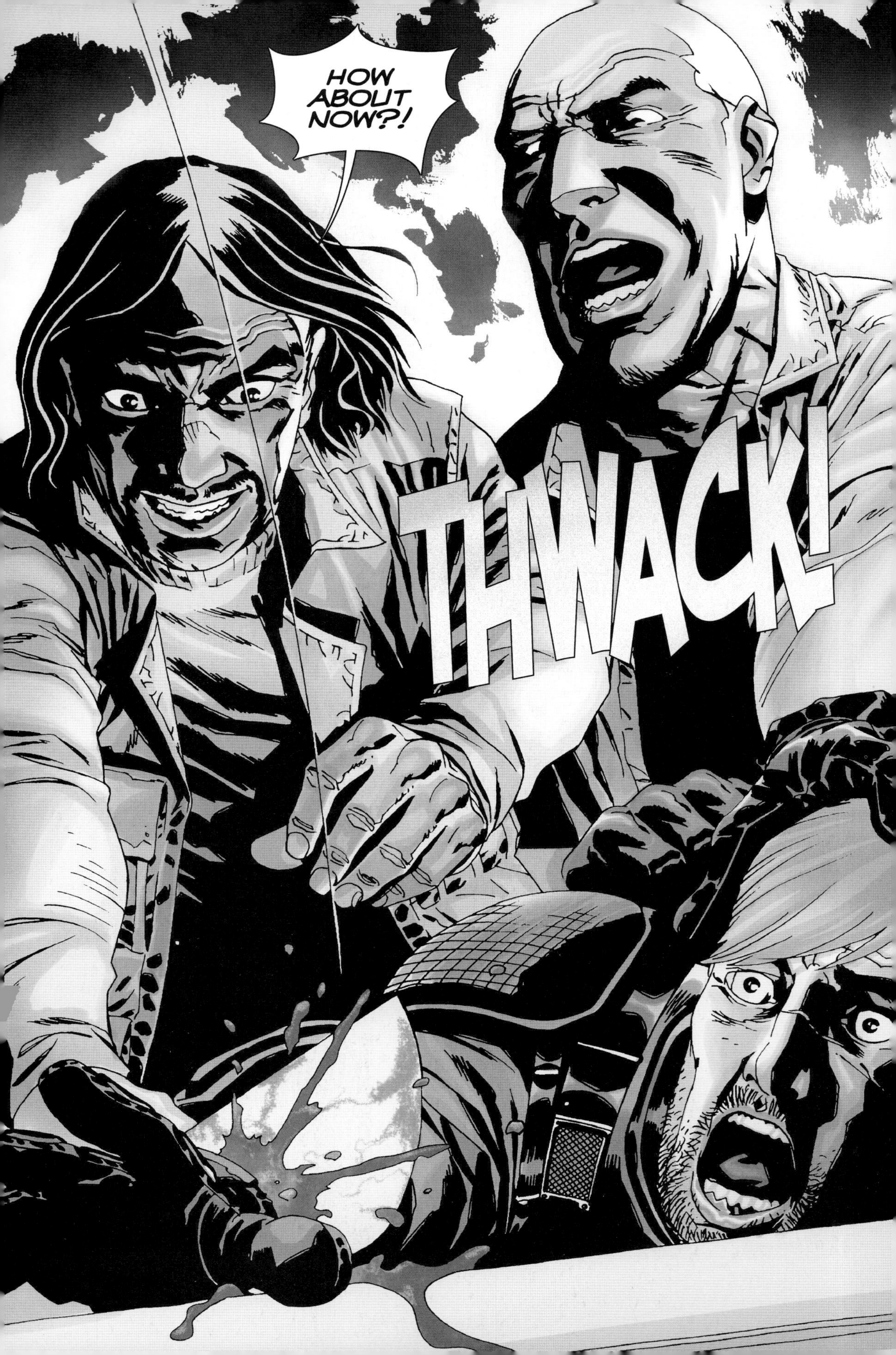
HOW ABOUT NOW?!
THWACK!

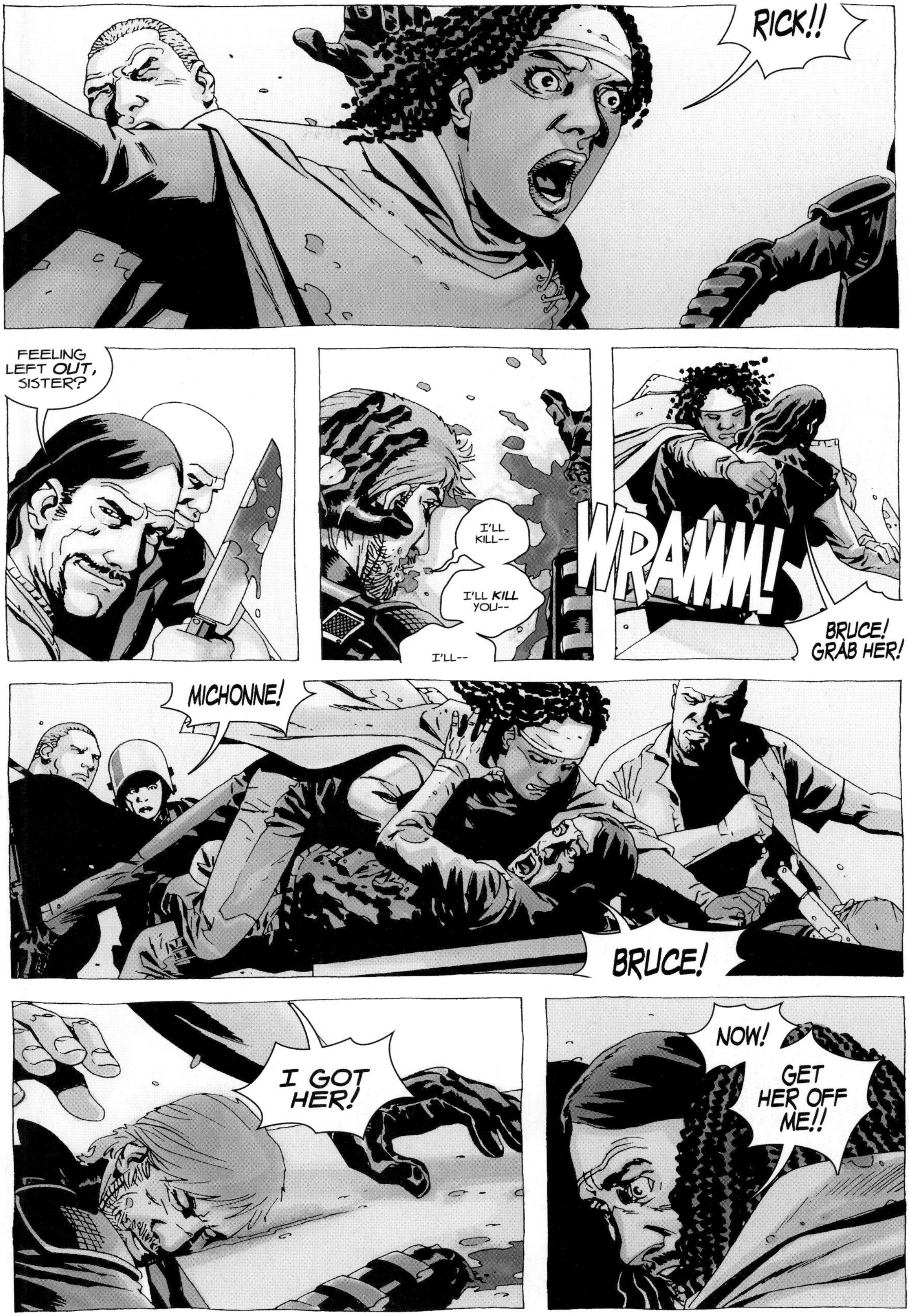
RICK!!
FEELING LEFT OUT, SISTER?
I'LL KILL--
I'LL KILL YOU--
I'LL--
WRAMM!
BRUCE! GRAB HER!
MICHONNE!
BRUCE!
I GOT HER!
NOW!
GET HER OFF ME!!

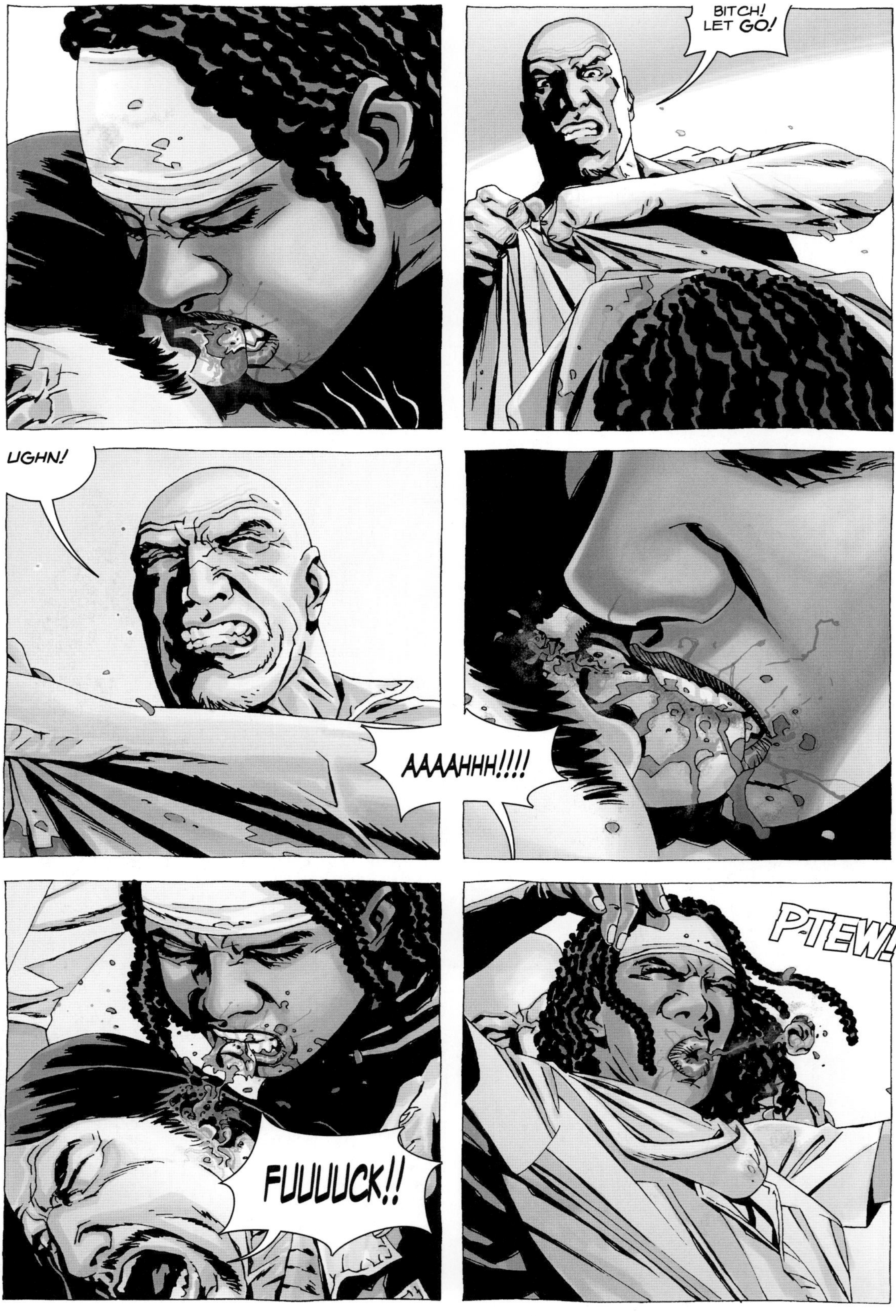

BITCH! LET GO!
UGHN!
AAAAHHH!!!!
FUUUUCK!!
P-TEW!

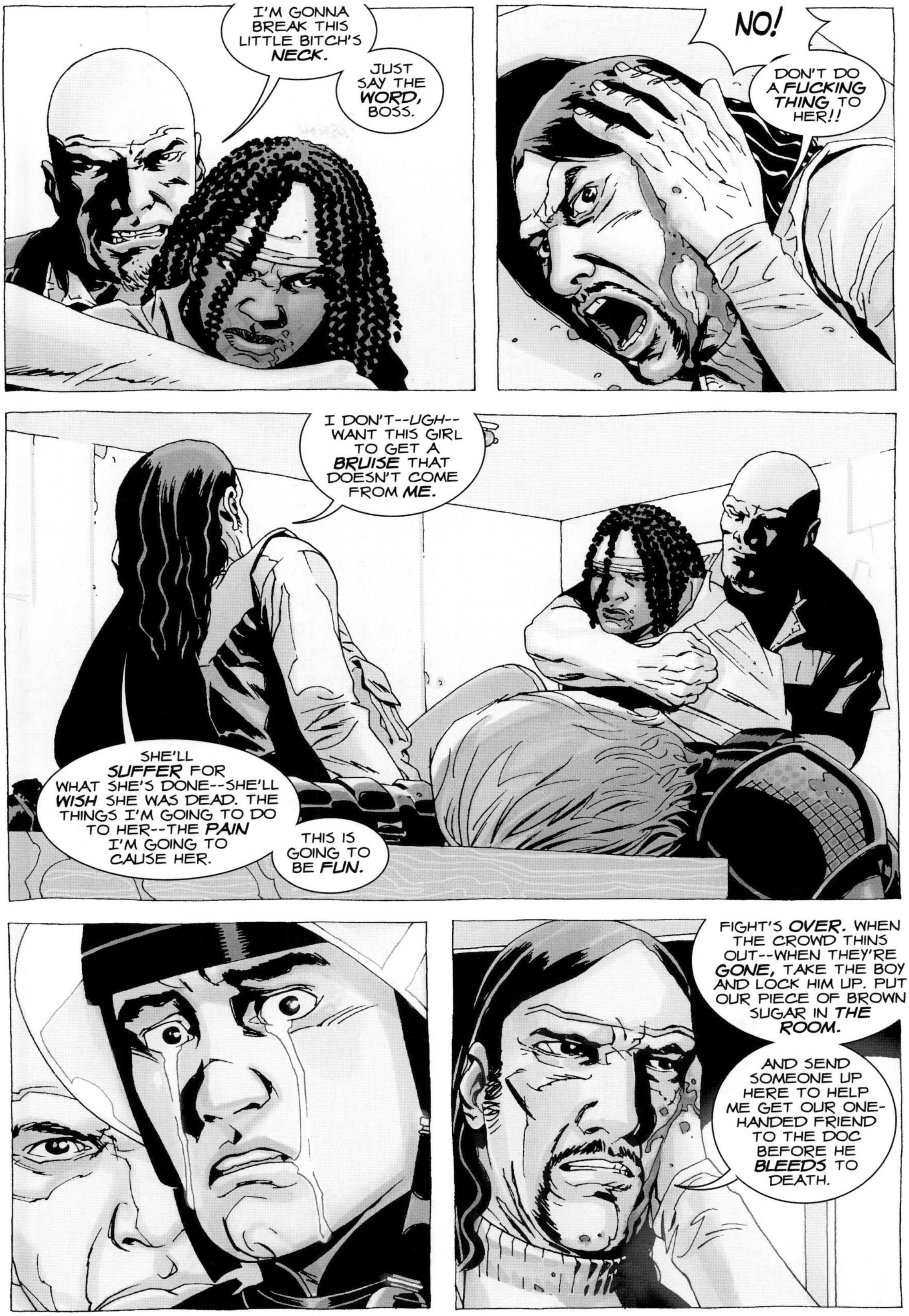
I'M GONNA BREAK THIS LITTLE BITCH'S NECK.
JUST SAY THE WORD, BOSS.
NO!
DON'T DO A FUCKING THING TO HER!!
I DON'T--UGH--WANT THIS GIRL TO GET A BRUISE THAT DOESN'T COME FROM ME.
SHE'LL SUFFER FOR WHAT SHE'S DONE--SHE'LL WISH SHE WAS DEAD. THE THINGS I'M GOING TO DO TO HER--THE PAIN I'M GOING TO CAUSE HER.
THIS IS GOING TO BE FUN.
FIGHT'S OVER. WHEN THE CROWD THINS OUT--WHEN THEY'RE GONE, TAKE THE BOY AND LOCK HIM UP. PUT OUR PIECE OF BROWN SUGAR IN THE ROOM.
AND SEND SOMEONE UP HERE TO HELP ME GET OUR ONE-HANDED FRIEND TO THE DOC BEFORE HE BLEEDS TO DEATH.

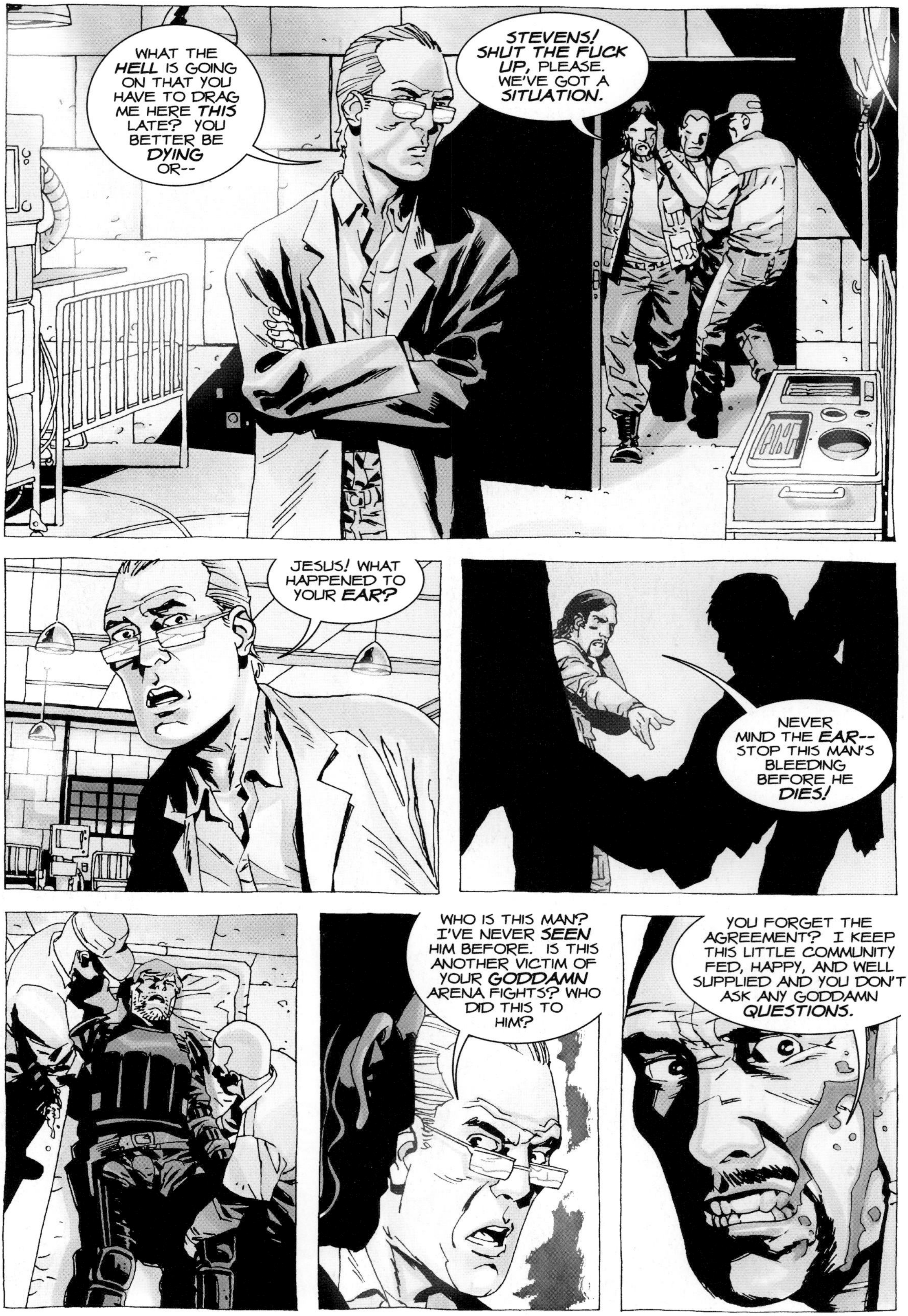
WHAT THE HELL IS GOING ON THAT YOU HAVE TO DRAG ME HERE THIS LATE? YOU BETTER BE DYING OR--
STEVENS! SHUT THE FUCK UP, PLEASE. WE'VE GOT A SITUATION.
JESUS! WHAT HAPPENED TO YOUR EAR?
NEVER MIND THE EAR-- STOP THIS MAN'S BLEEDING BEFORE HE DIES!
WHO IS THIS MAN? I'VE NEVER SEEN HIM BEFORE. IS THIS ANOTHER VICTIM OF YOUR GODDAMN ARENA FIGHTS? WHO DID THIS TO HIM?
YOU FORGET THE AGREEMENT? I KEEP THIS LITTLE COMMUNITY FED, HAPPY, AND WELL SUPPLIED AND YOU DON'T ASK ANY GODDAMN QUESTIONS.

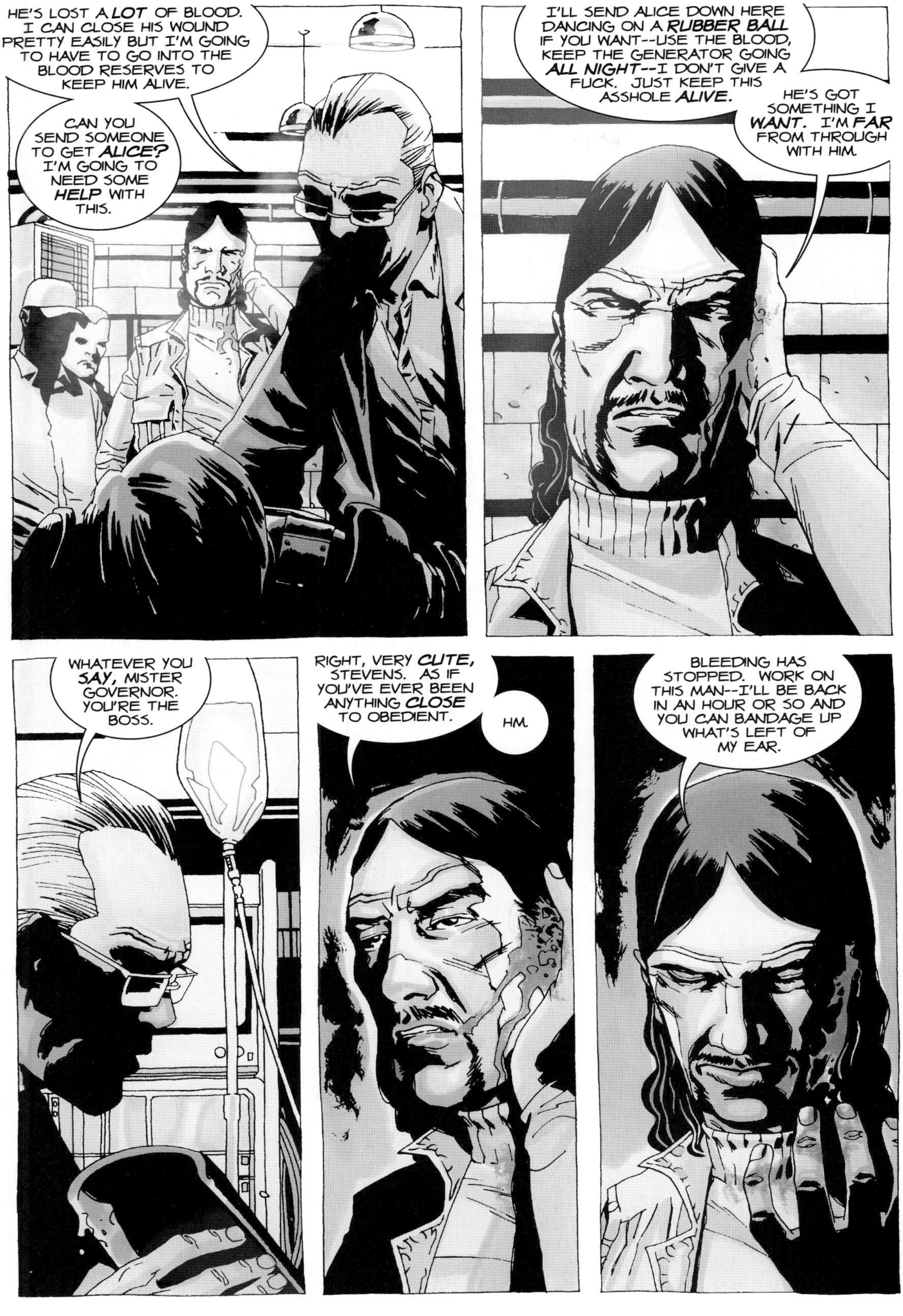
HE'S LOST A LOT OF BLOOD. I CAN CLOSE HIS WOUND PRETTY EASILY BUT I'M GOING TO HAVE TO GO INTO THE BLOOD RESERVES TO KEEP HIM ALIVE.
CAN YOU SEND SOMEONE TO GET ALICE? I'M GOING TO NEED SOME HELP WITH THIS.
I'LL SEND ALICE DOWN HERE DANCING ON A RUBBER BALL IF YOU WANT--USE THE BLOOD, KEEP THE GENERATOR GOING ALL NIGHT--I DON'T GIVE A FUCK. JUST KEEP THIS ASSHOLE ALIVE.
HE'S GOT SOMETHING I WANT. I'M FAR FROM THROUGH WITH HIM.
WHATEVER YOU SAY, MISTER GOVERNOR. YOU'RE THE BOSS.
RIGHT, VERY CUTE, STEVENS. AS IF YOU'VE EVER BEEN ANYTHING CLOSE TO OBEDIENT.
HM.
BLEEDING HAS STOPPED. WORK ON THIS MAN--I'LL BE BACK IN AN HOUR OR SO AND YOU CAN BANDAGE UP WHAT'S LEFT OF MY EAR.

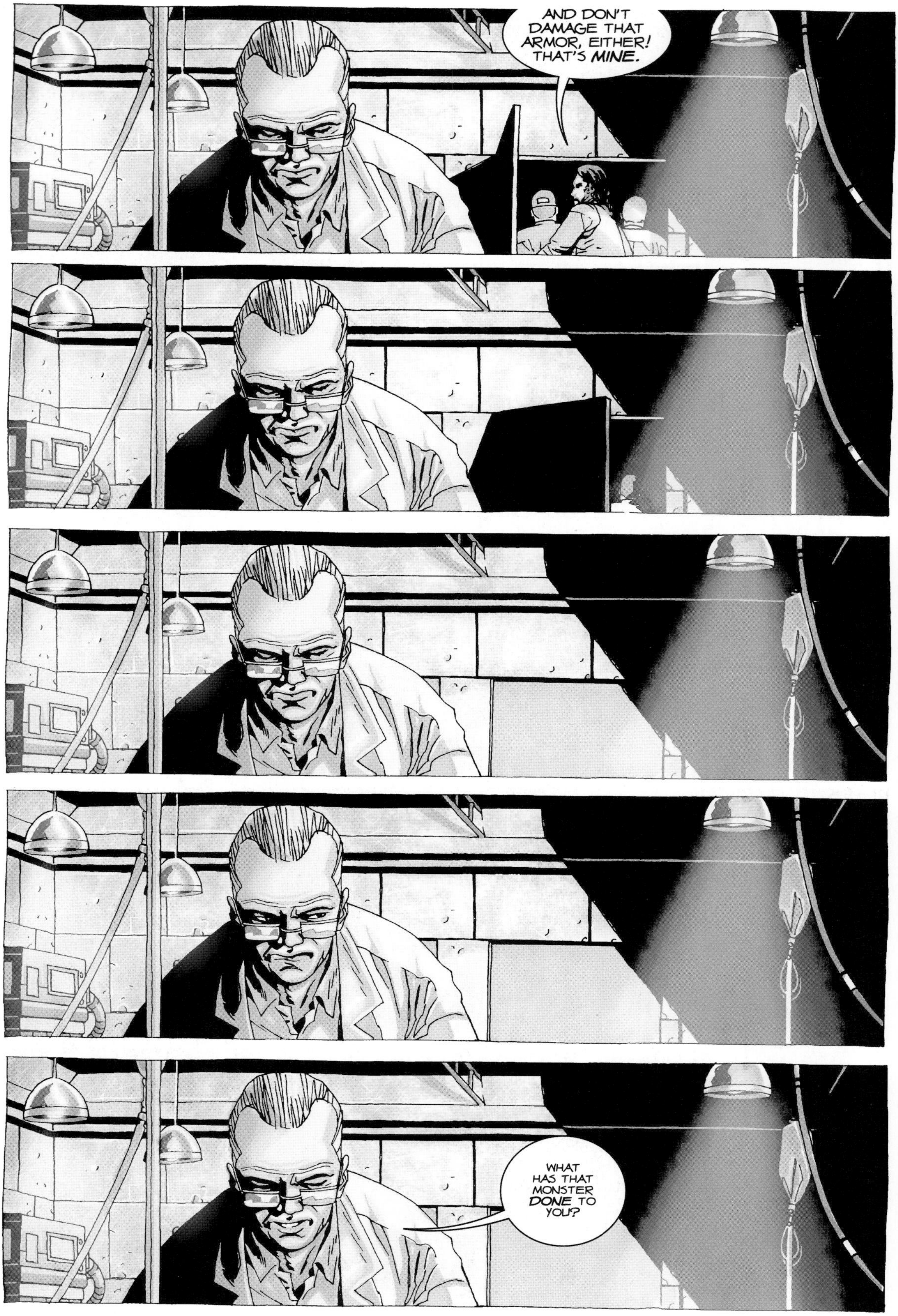
AND DON'T DAMAGE THAT ARMOR, EITHER! THAT'S MINE.
WHAT HAS THAT MONSTER DONE TO YOU?

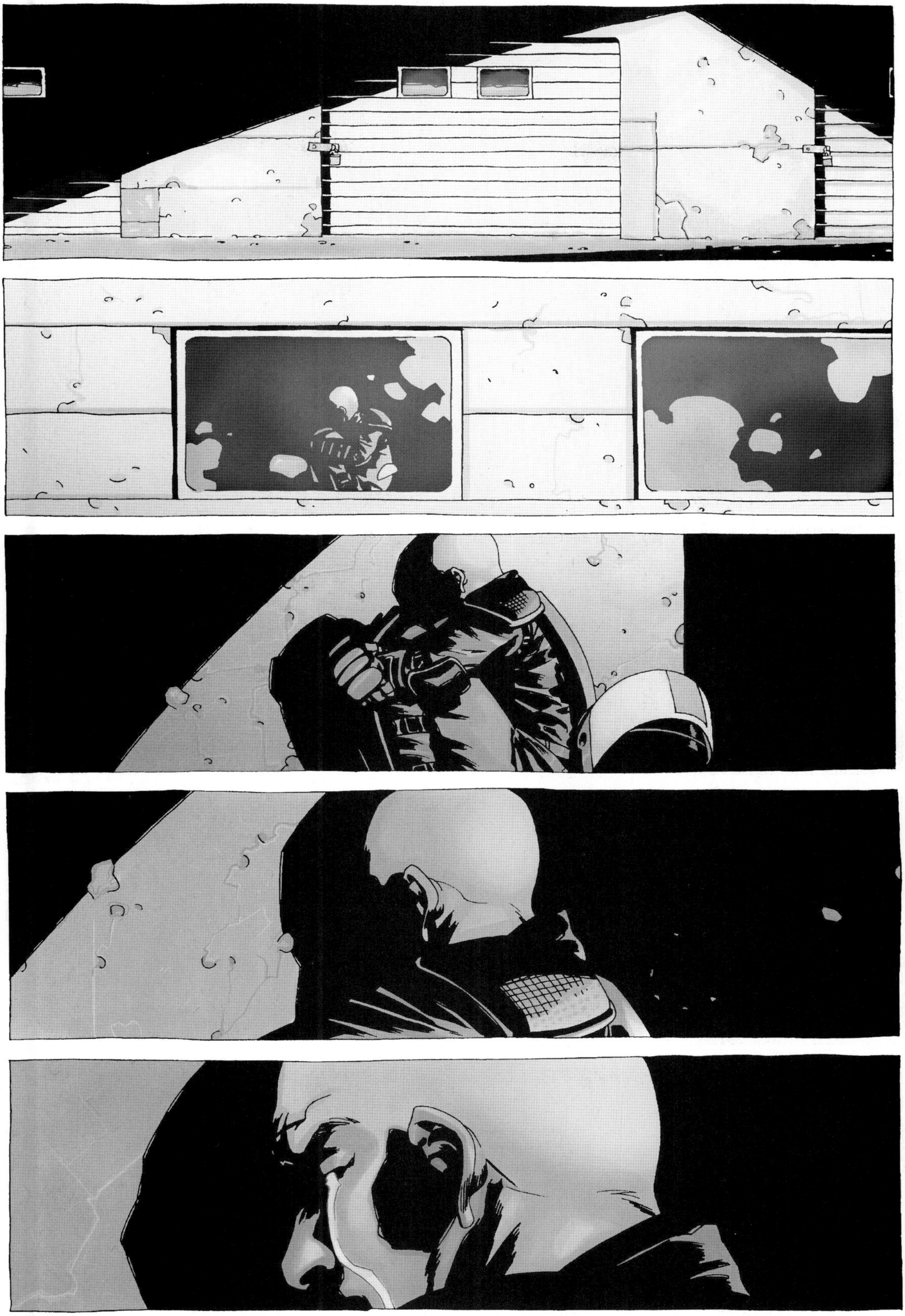

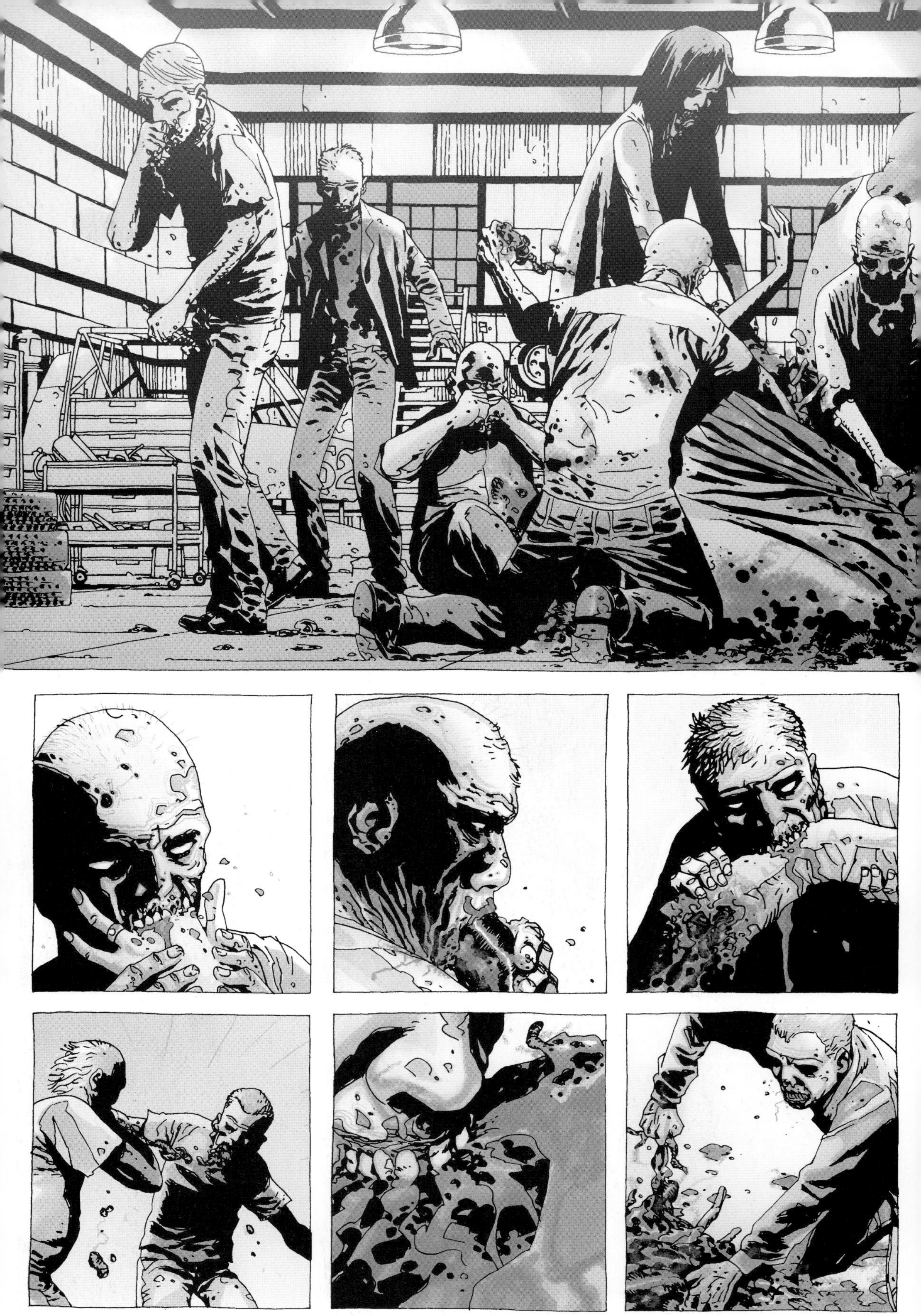

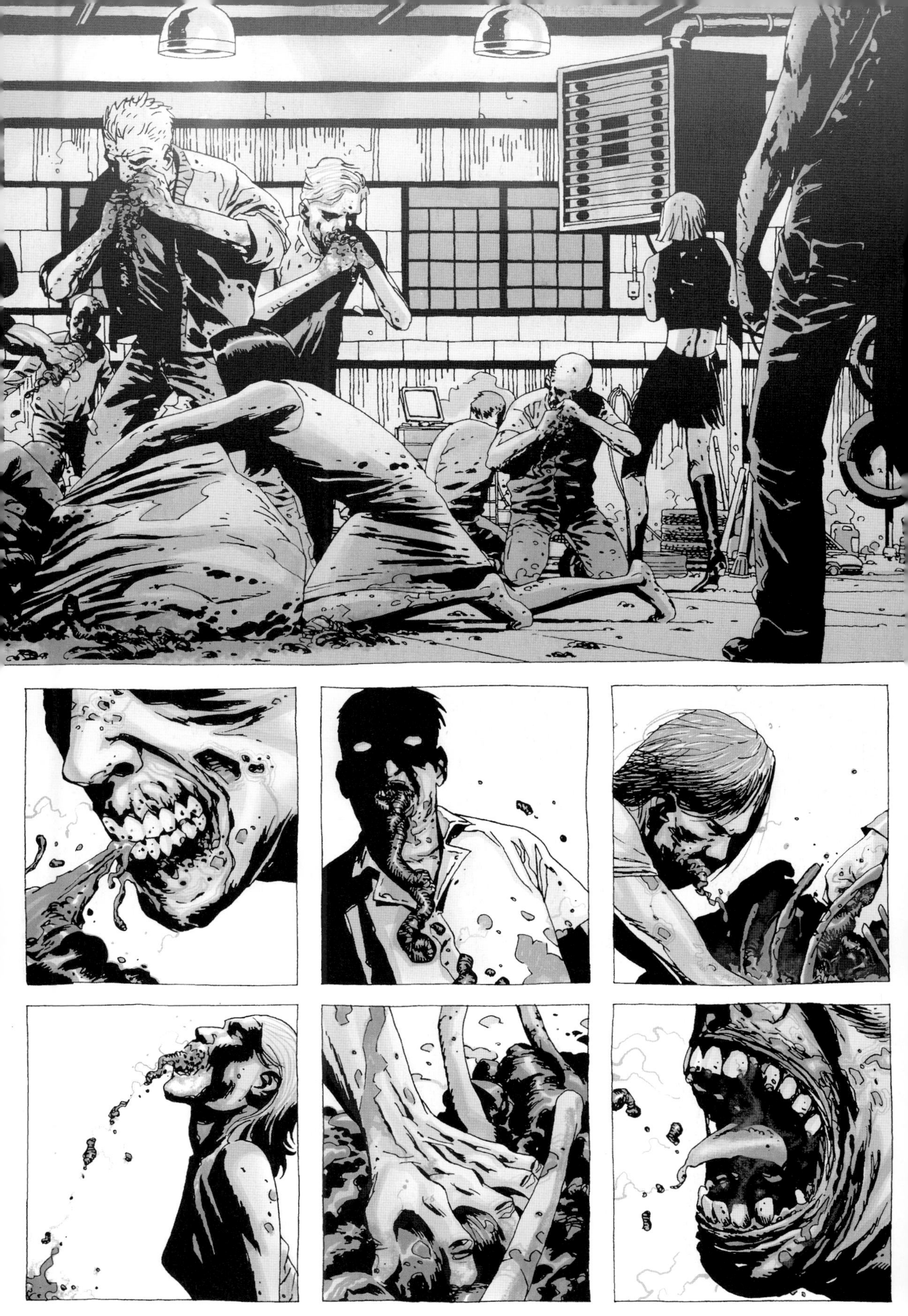

SIR?

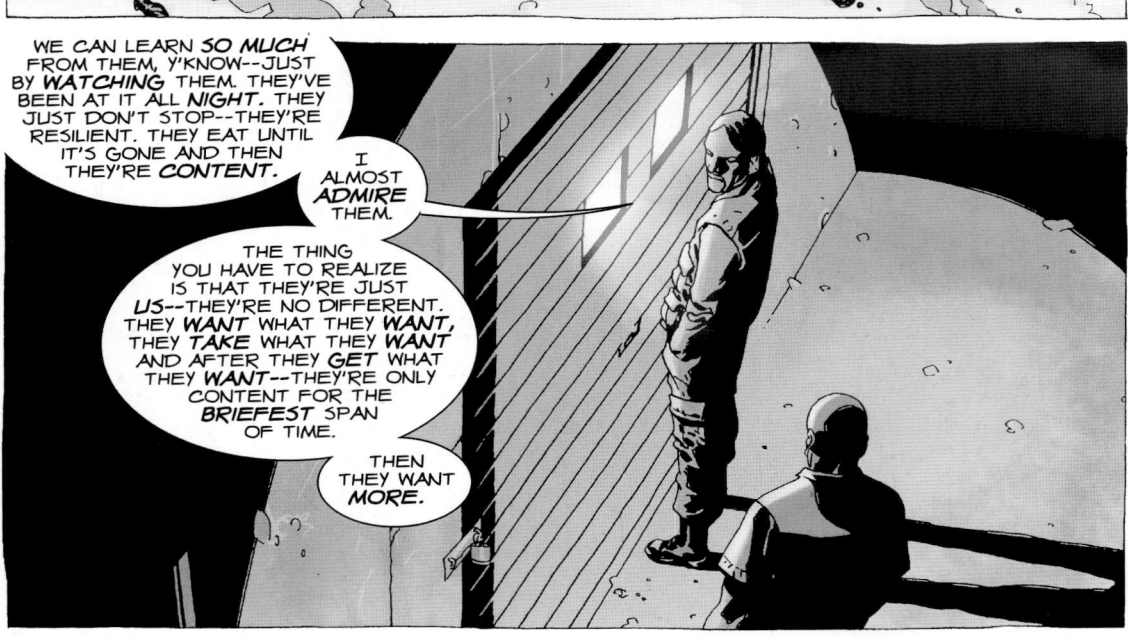

WE CAN LEARN *SO MUCH* FROM THEM, Y'KNOW--JUST BY *WATCHING* THEM. THEY'VE BEEN AT IT ALL *NIGHT*. THEY JUST DON'T STOP--THEY'RE RESILIENT. THEY EAT UNTIL IT'S GONE AND THEN THEY'RE *CONTENT*.

I ALMOST *ADMIRE* THEM.

THE THING YOU HAVE TO REALIZE IS THAT THEY'RE JUST *US*--THEY'RE NO DIFFERENT. THEY *WANT* WHAT THEY *WANT*, THEY *TAKE* WHAT THEY *WANT* AND AFTER THEY *GET* WHAT THEY *WANT*--THEY'RE ONLY CONTENT FOR THE *BRIEFEST* SPAN OF TIME.

THEN THEY WANT *MORE*.

WHAT IS IT *YOU* WANT? CAN'T YOU SEE I'M *BUSY*?

YOU WANTED ME TO COME GET YOU WHEN THE WOMAN CALMED DOWN.

SHE'S CALMED DOWN... FOR THE MOST PART.

OH--THEN WHAT ARE WE *WAITING* FOR?

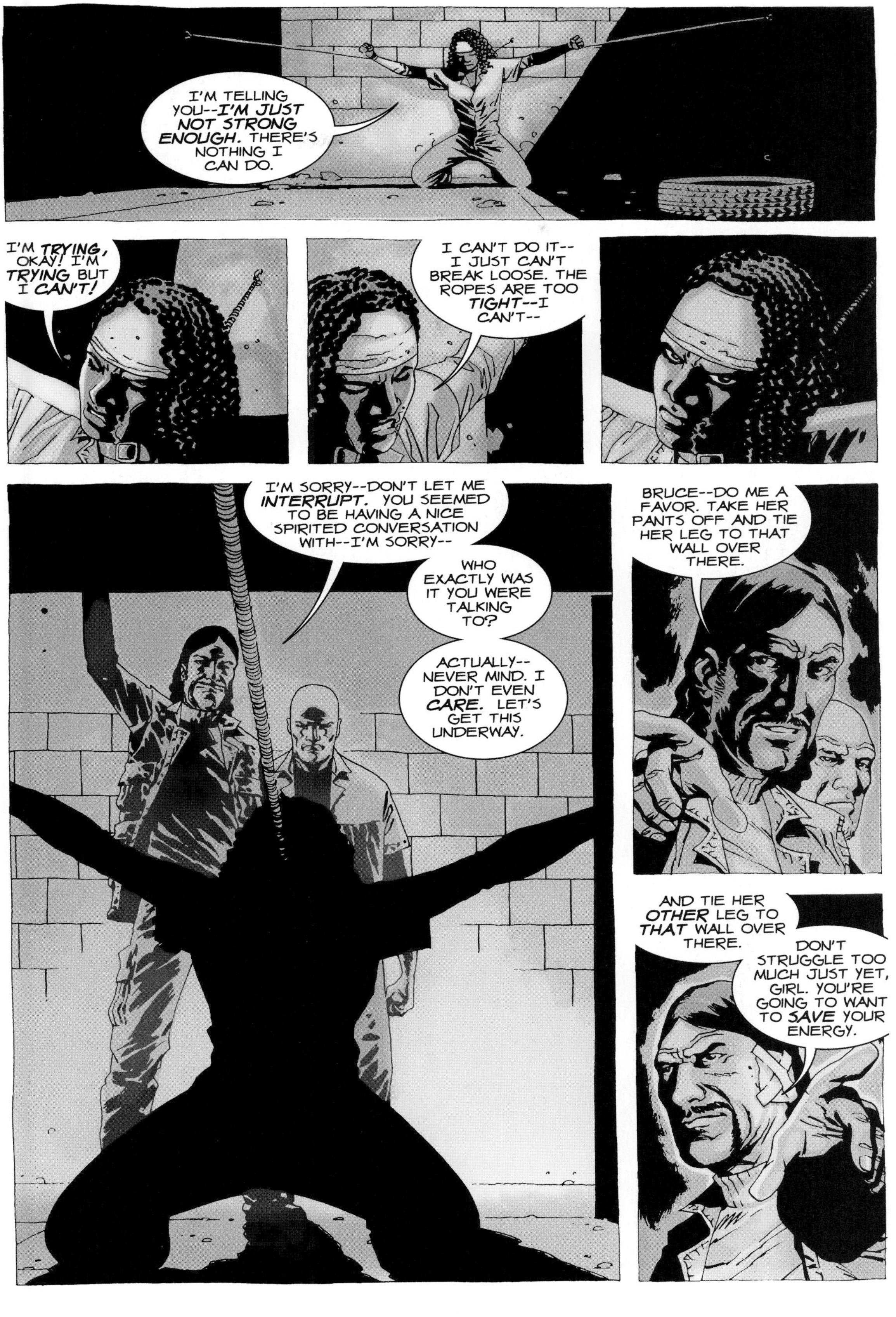
I'M TELLING YOU--I'M JUST NOT STRONG ENOUGH. THERE'S NOTHING I CAN DO.
I'M TRYING, OKAY! I'M TRYING BUT I CAN'T!
I CAN'T DO IT-- I JUST CAN'T BREAK LOOSE. THE ROPES ARE TOO TIGHT--I CAN'T--
I'M SORRY--DON'T LET ME INTERRUPT. YOU SEEMED TO BE HAVING A NICE SPIRITED CONVERSATION WITH--I'M SORRY--
WHO EXACTLY WAS IT YOU WERE TALKING TO?
ACTUALLY-- NEVER MIND. I DON'T EVEN CARE. LET'S GET THIS UNDERWAY.
BRUCE--DO ME A FAVOR. TAKE HER PANTS OFF AND TIE HER LEG TO THAT WALL OVER THERE.
AND TIE HER OTHER LEG TO THAT WALL OVER THERE.
DON'T STRUGGLE TOO MUCH JUST YET, GIRL. YOU'RE GOING TO WANT TO SAVE YOUR ENERGY.

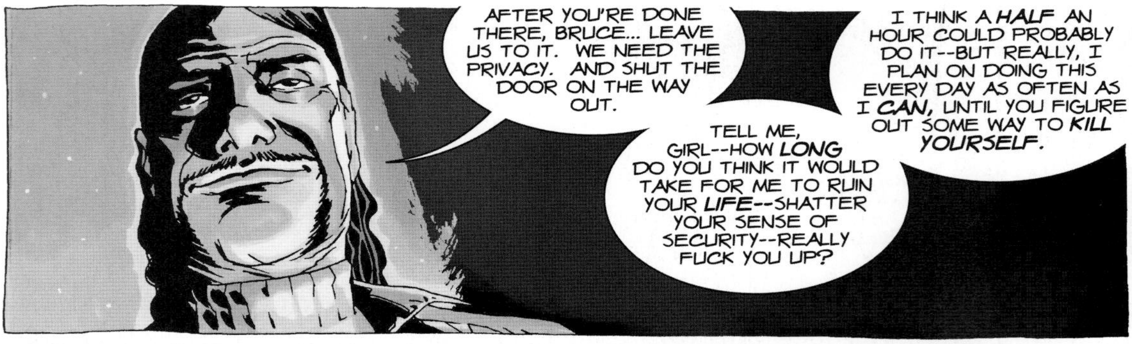
AFTER YOU'RE DONE THERE, BRUCE... LEAVE US TO IT. WE NEED THE PRIVACY. AND SHUT THE DOOR ON THE WAY OUT.
TELL ME, GIRL--HOW *LONG* DO YOU THINK IT WOULD TAKE FOR ME TO RUIN YOUR *LIFE*--SHATTER YOUR SENSE OF SECURITY--REALLY FUCK YOU UP?
I THINK A *HALF* AN HOUR COULD PROBABLY DO IT--BUT REALLY, I PLAN ON DOING THIS EVERY DAY AS OFTEN AS I *CAN,* UNTIL YOU FIGURE OUT SOME WAY TO *KILL YOURSELF.*
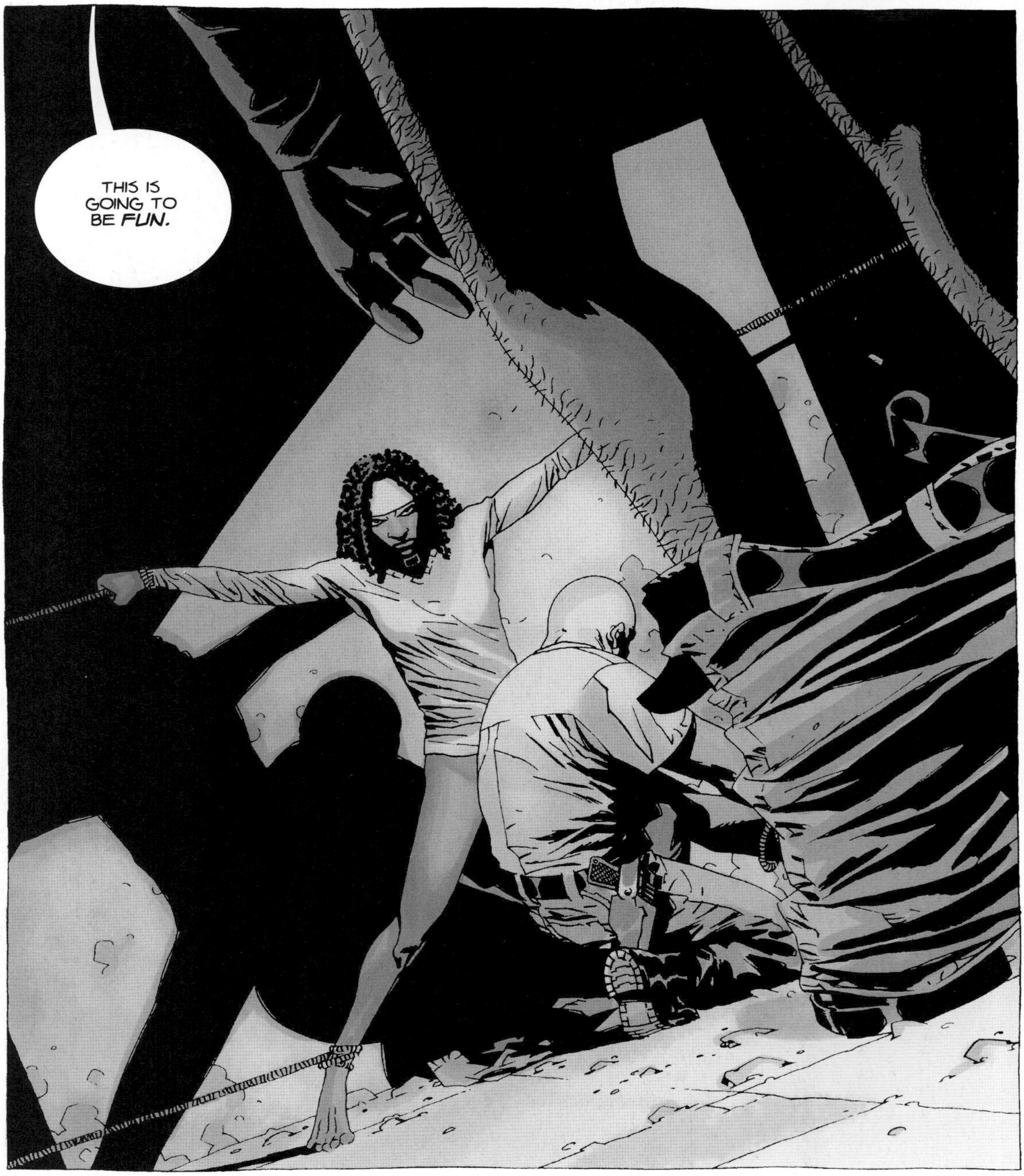
THIS IS GOING TO BE *FUN.*

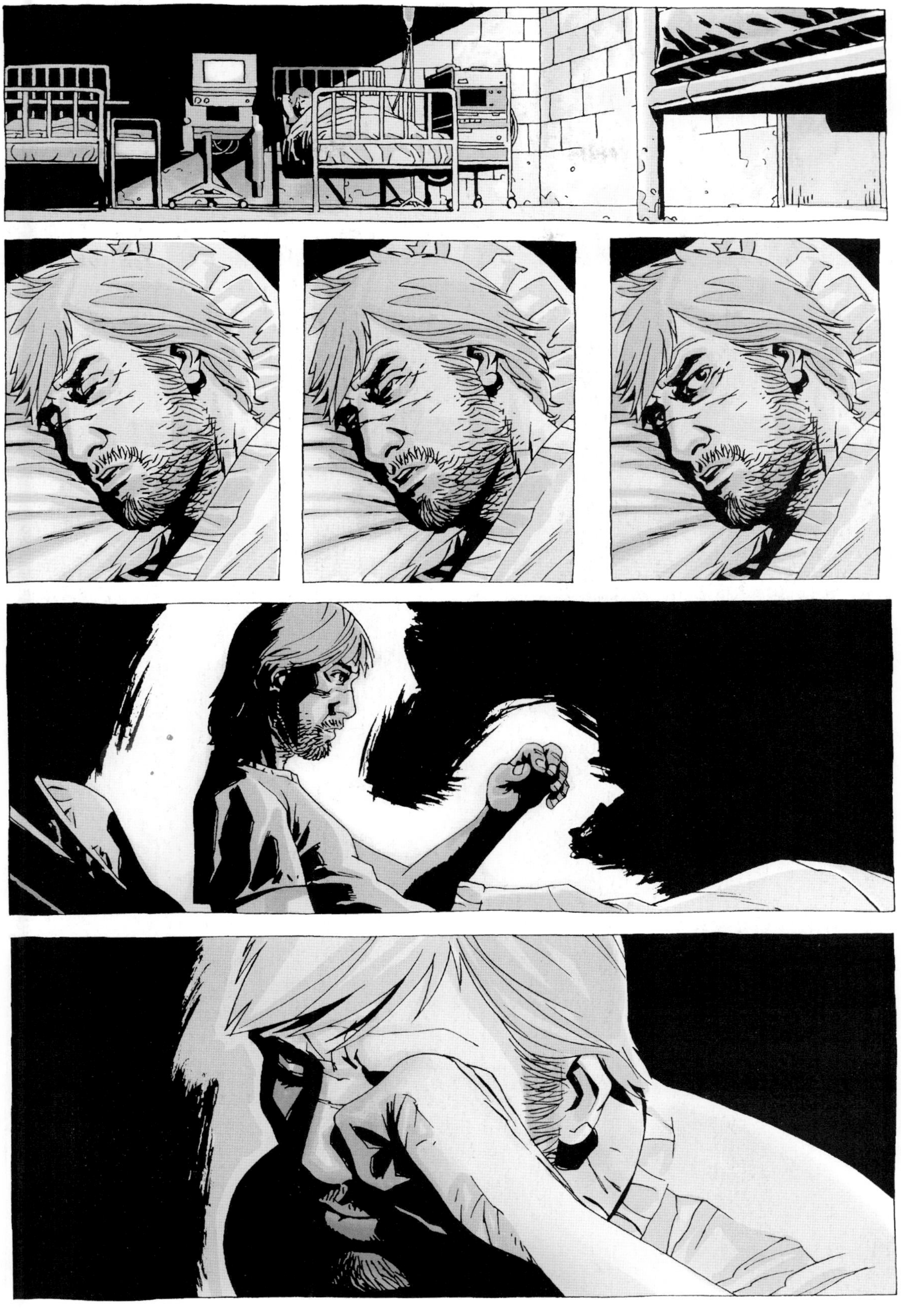

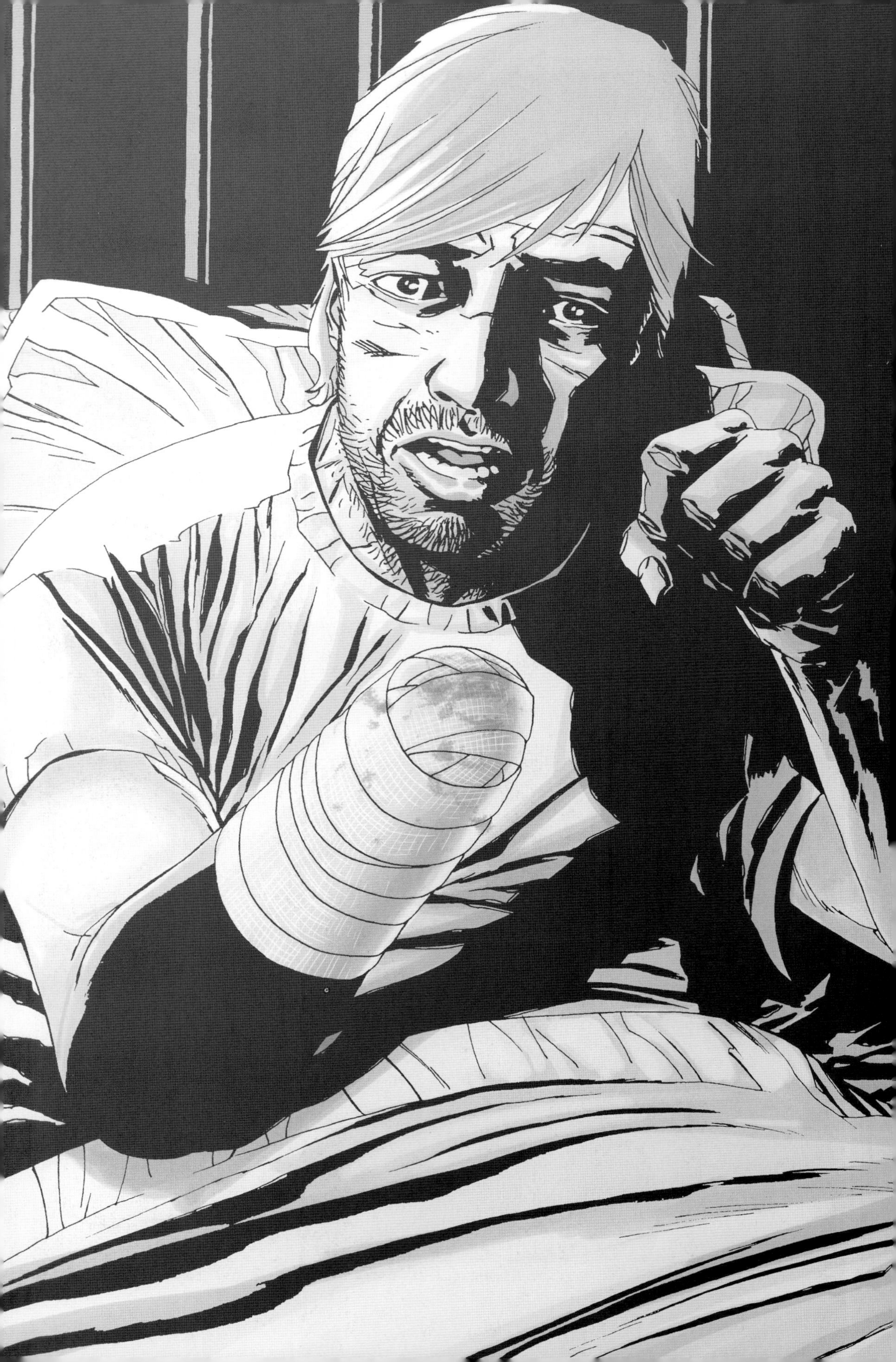

HU-- UNGH.

≈HUFF≈

≈HUFF≈

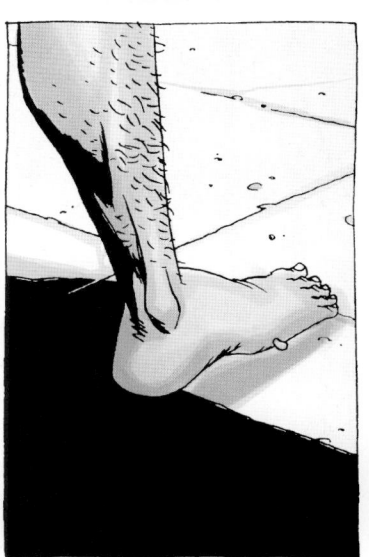

...

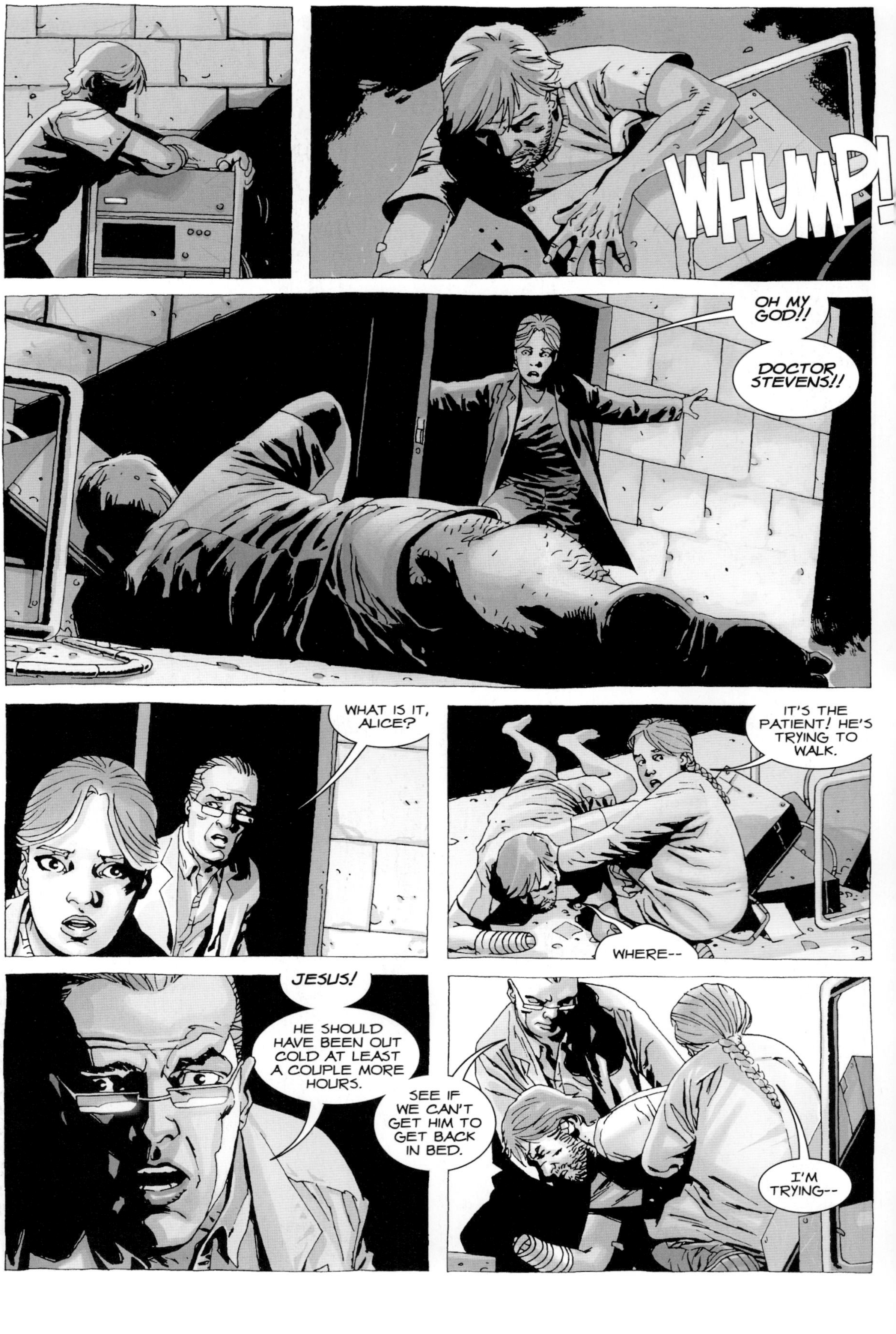
WHUMP!
OH MY GOD!!
DOCTOR STEVENS!!
WHAT IS IT, ALICE?
IT'S THE PATIENT! HE'S TRYING TO WALK.
WHERE--
JESUS!
HE SHOULD HAVE BEEN OUT COLD AT LEAST A COUPLE MORE HOURS.
SEE IF WE CAN'T GET HIM TO GET BACK IN BED.
I'M TRYING--

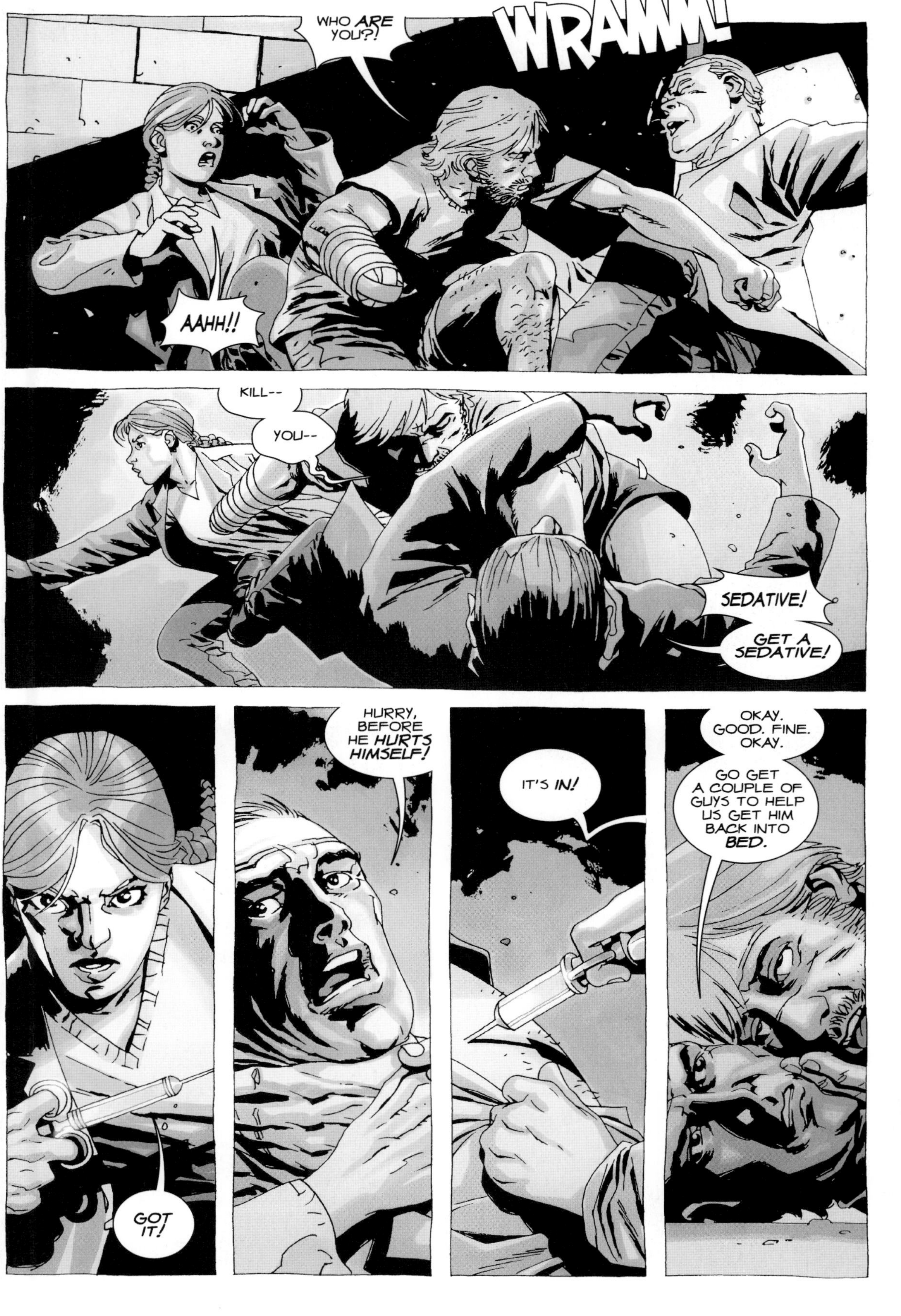
WHO ARE YOU?!
WRAMM!
AAHH!!
KILL--
YOU--
SEDATIVE!
GET A SEDATIVE!
GOT IT!
HURRY, BEFORE HE HURTS HIMSELF!
IT'S IN!
OKAY. GOOD. FINE. OKAY.
GO GET A COUPLE OF GUYS TO HELP US GET HIM BACK INTO BED.

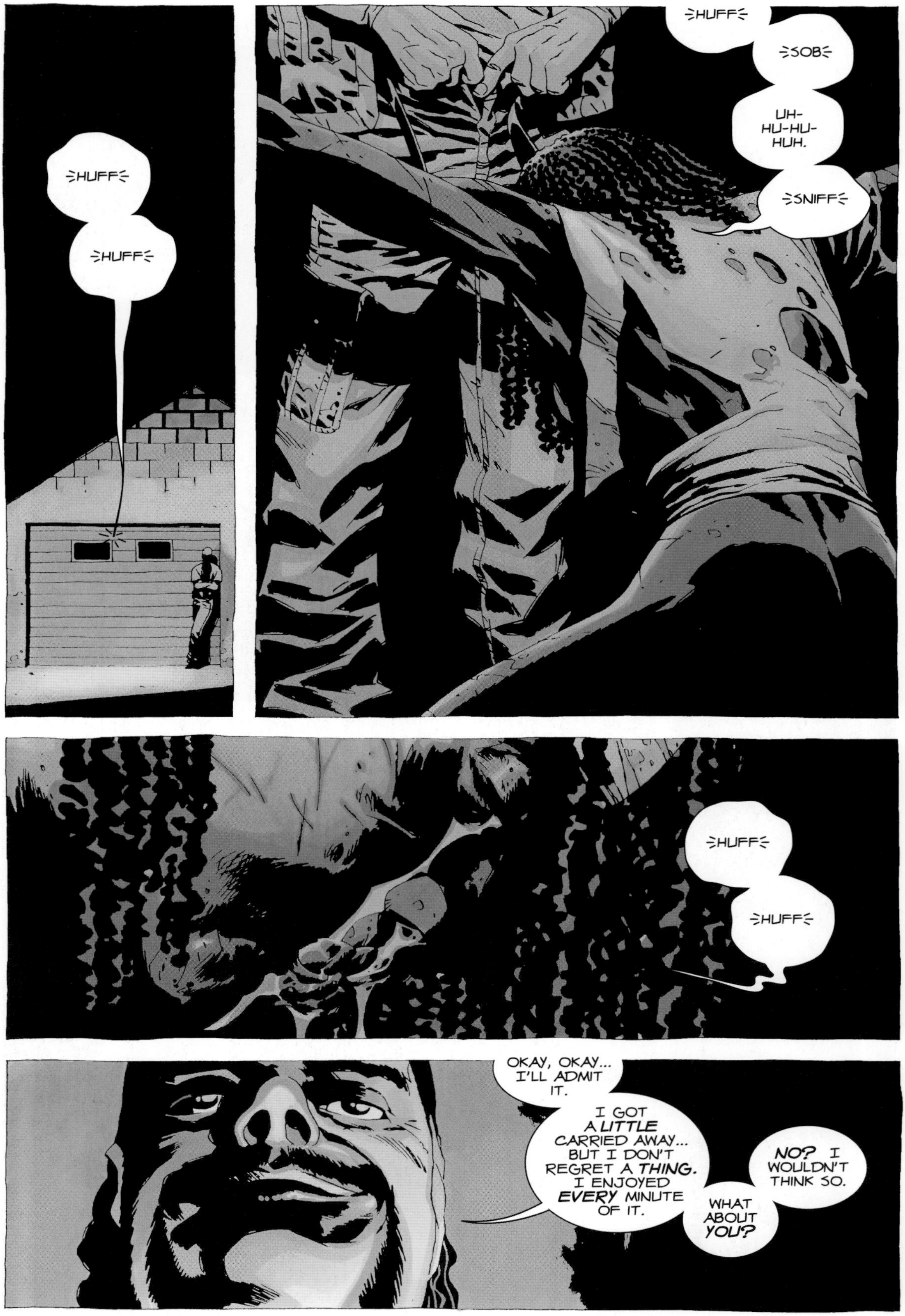

HUFF
HUFF
HUFF
SOB
UH-HU-HU-HUH.
SNIFF
HUFF
HUFF
OKAY, OKAY... I'LL ADMIT IT.
I GOT A LITTLE CARRIED AWAY... BUT I DON'T REGRET A THING. I ENJOYED EVERY MINUTE OF IT.
WHAT ABOUT YOU?
NO? I WOULDN'T THINK SO.

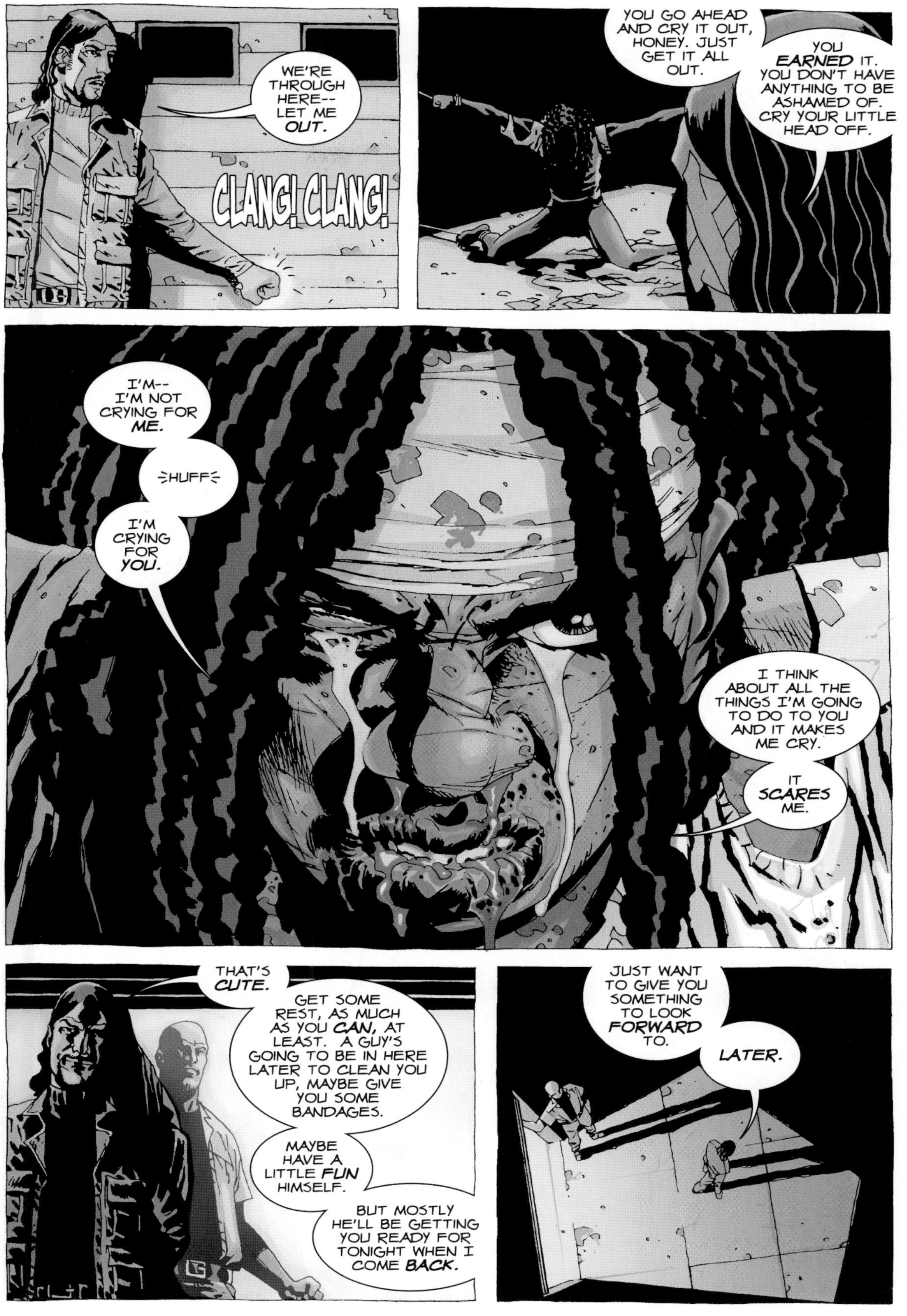
WE'RE THROUGH HERE-- LET ME OUT.
CLANG! CLANG!
YOU GO AHEAD AND CRY IT OUT, HONEY. JUST GET IT ALL OUT.
YOU EARNED IT. YOU DON'T HAVE ANYTHING TO BE ASHAMED OF. CRY YOUR LITTLE HEAD OFF.
I'M-- I'M NOT CRYING FOR ME.
HUFF
I'M CRYING FOR YOU.
I THINK ABOUT ALL THE THINGS I'M GOING TO DO TO YOU AND IT MAKES ME CRY.
IT SCARES ME.
THAT'S CUTE.
GET SOME REST, AS MUCH AS YOU CAN, AT LEAST. A GUY'S GOING TO BE IN HERE LATER TO CLEAN YOU UP, MAYBE GIVE YOU SOME BANDAGES.
MAYBE HAVE A LITTLE FUN HIMSELF.
BUT MOSTLY HE'LL BE GETTING YOU READY FOR TONIGHT WHEN I COME BACK.
JUST WANT TO GIVE YOU SOMETHING TO LOOK FORWARD TO.
LATER.

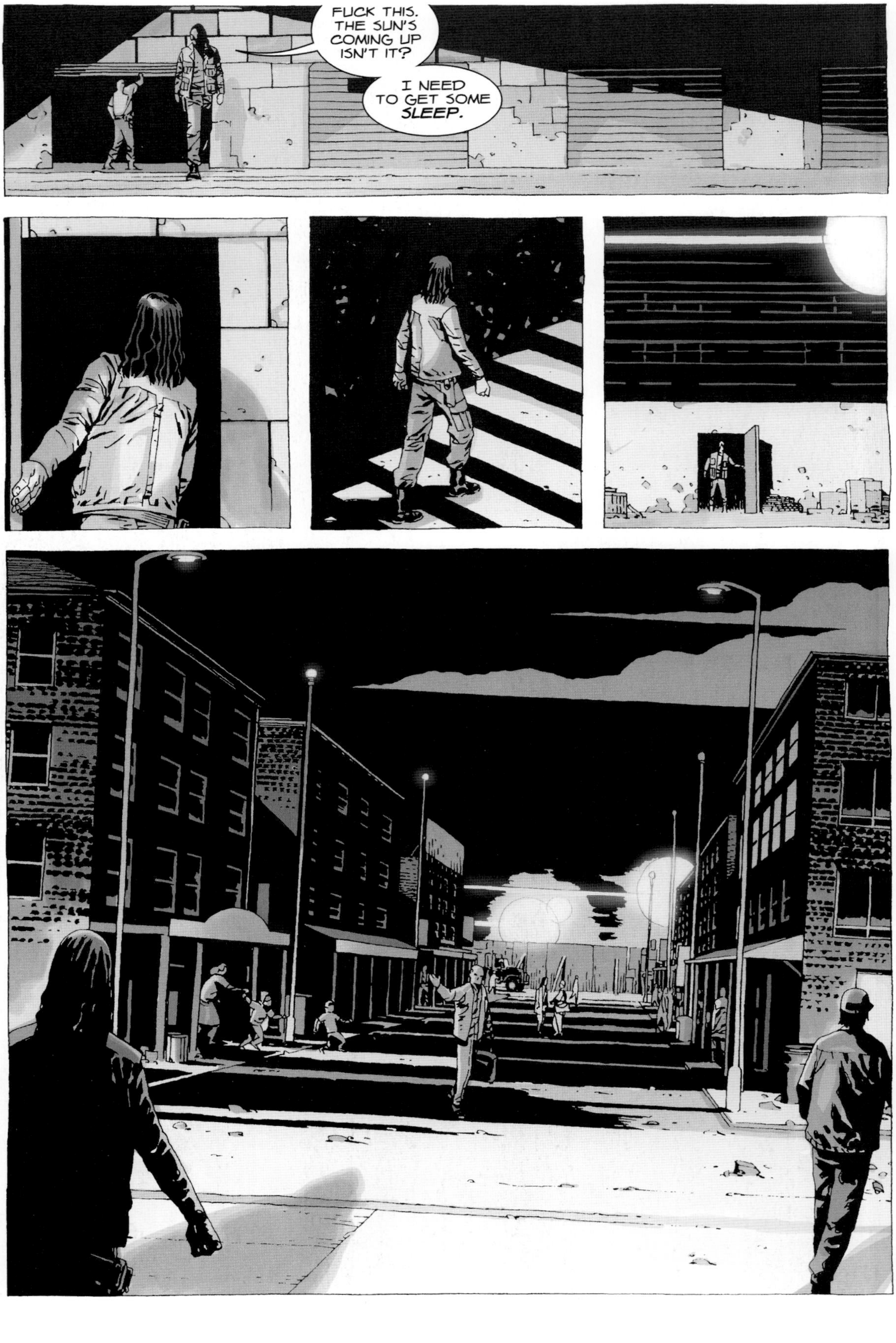
FUCK THIS. THE SUN'S COMING UP ISN'T IT?
I NEED TO GET SOME SLEEP.

KIDS, PLEASE--I TOLD YOU TO STOP RUNNING.

MORNING.

MORNING, GOVERNOR.

YOU KIDS SLOW DOWN, NOW. LISTEN TO YOUR MOTHER.

OKAY.

BOB, PLEASE. GO GET YOU SOME FOOD. I HATE TO SEE YOU WASTING AWAY LIKE THIS.

WE GOT RID OF THE BARTER SYSTEM. THEY'LL JUST GIVE YOU SOMETHING.

FINE, OKAY. IF IT'LL GET MOTHER HEN OFF MY BACK.

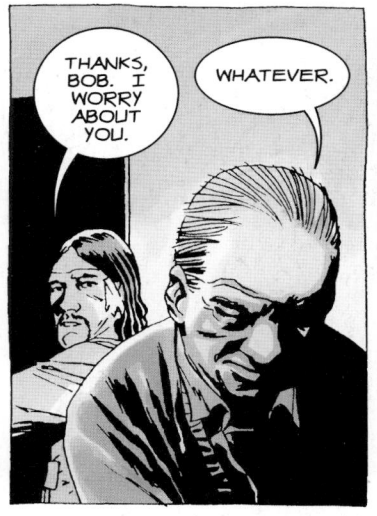

THANKS, BOB. I WORRY ABOUT YOU.

WHATEVER.

I KNOW, I KNOW... SORRY I WAS OUT SO LATE... OR EARLY, DEPENDING ON HOW YOU LOOK AT IT.

ROAARGH!

WRAMM!!

BEHAVE YOURSELF, GODDAMN IT!

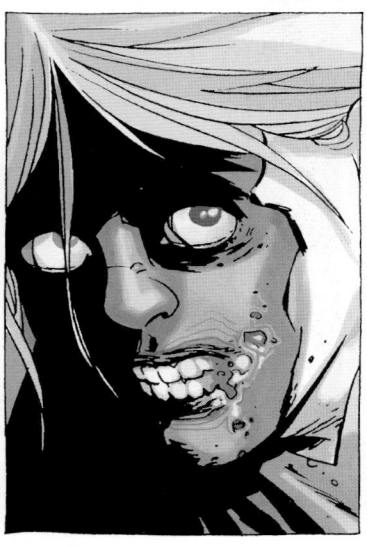

I'M SORRY, HONEY. WHAT'S GOT YOU SO UPSET?

YOU HAVEN'T TRIED TO ATTACK ME IN MONTHS.

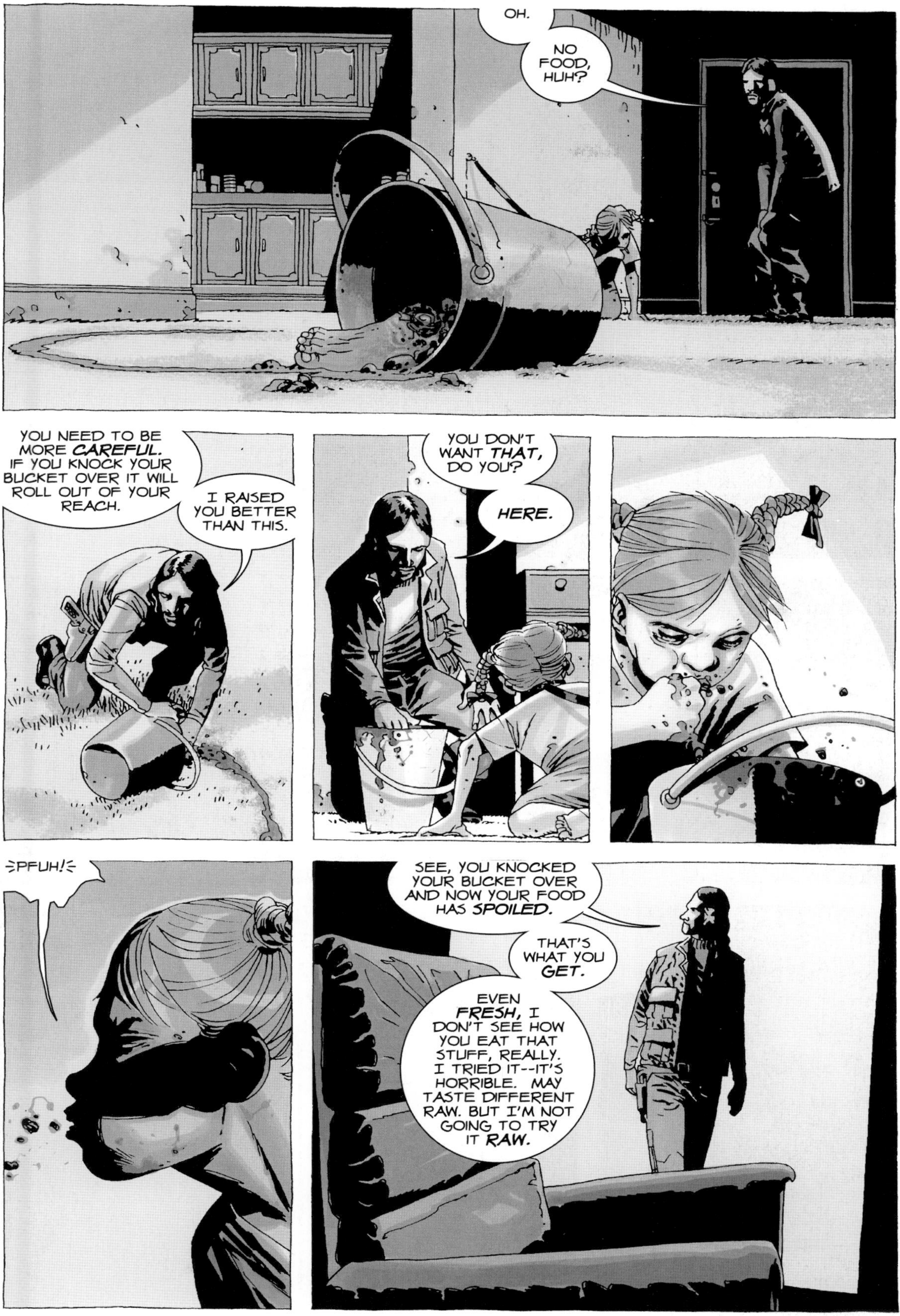
OH.
NO FOOD, HUH?
YOU NEED TO BE MORE CAREFUL. IF YOU KNOCK YOUR BUCKET OVER IT WILL ROLL OUT OF YOUR REACH.
I RAISED YOU BETTER THAN THIS.
YOU DON'T WANT THAT, DO YOU?
HERE.
PFUH!
SEE, YOU KNOCKED YOUR BUCKET OVER AND NOW YOUR FOOD HAS SPOILED.
THAT'S WHAT YOU GET.
EVEN FRESH, I DON'T SEE HOW YOU EAT THAT STUFF, REALLY. I TRIED IT--IT'S HORRIBLE. MAY TASTE DIFFERENT RAW. BUT I'M NOT GOING TO TRY IT RAW.

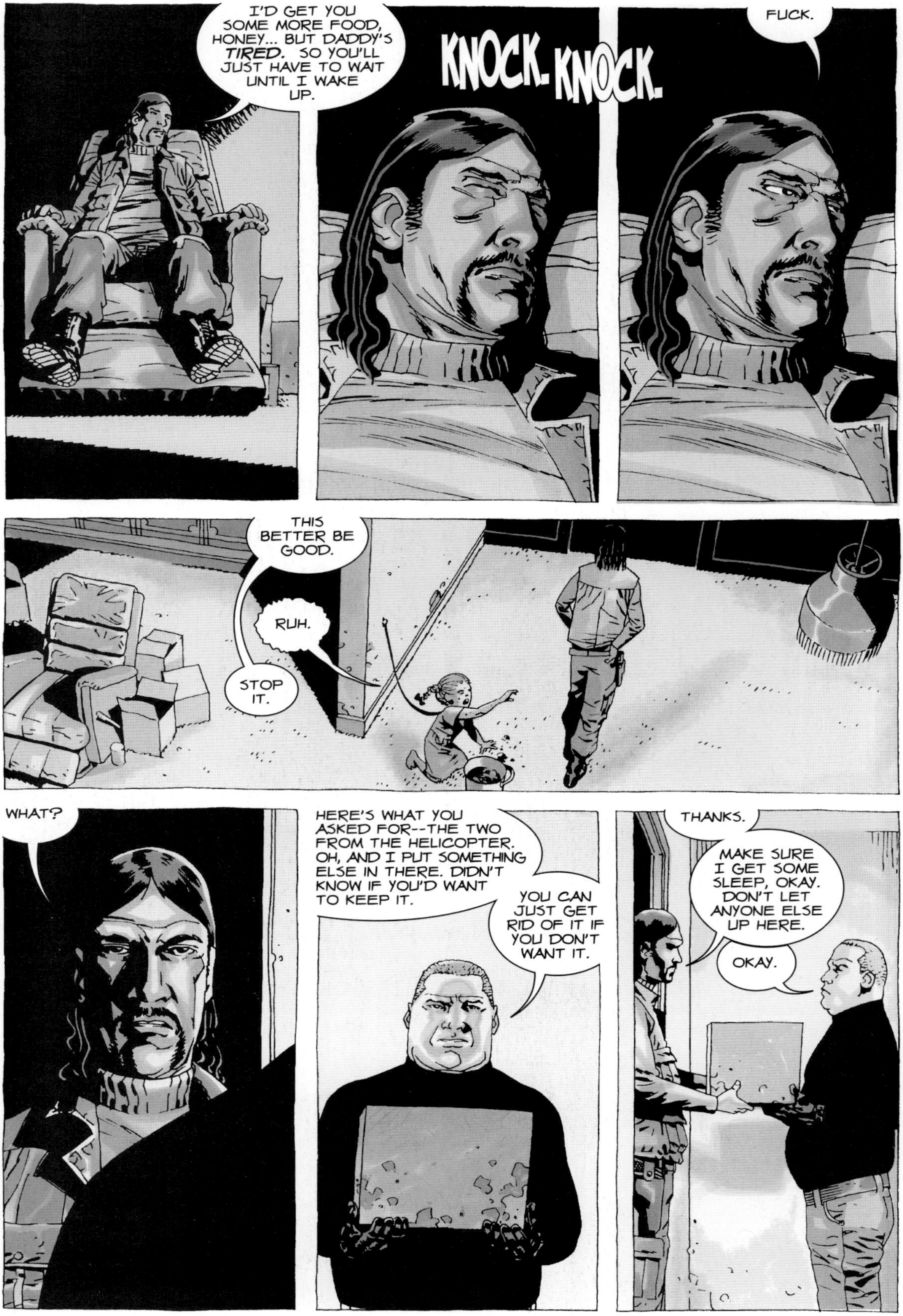
I'D GET YOU SOME MORE FOOD, HONEY... BUT DADDY'S *TIRED.* SO YOU'LL JUST HAVE TO WAIT UNTIL I WAKE UP.
KNOCK. KNOCK.
FUCK.
THIS BETTER BE GOOD.
RUH.
STOP IT.
WHAT?
HERE'S WHAT YOU ASKED FOR--THE TWO FROM THE HELICOPTER. OH, AND I PUT SOMETHING ELSE IN THERE. DIDN'T KNOW IF YOU'D WANT TO KEEP IT.
YOU CAN JUST GET RID OF IT IF YOU DON'T WANT IT.
THANKS.
MAKE SURE I GET SOME SLEEP, OKAY. DON'T LET ANYONE ELSE UP HERE.
OKAY.

NO. THIS ISN'T FOR *YOU.*

WELL...

...I SUPPOSE YOU CAN HAVE *THIS.*

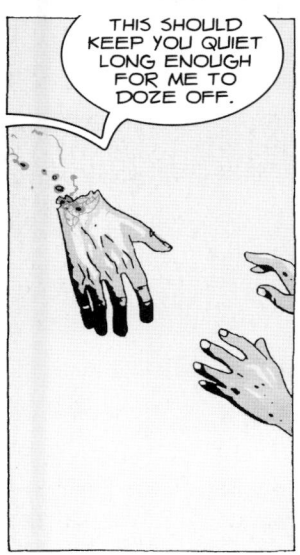

THIS SHOULD KEEP YOU QUIET LONG ENOUGH FOR ME TO DOZE OFF.

YOU GUYS HAVE GOT GUESTS-- NEW NEIGHBORS, ACTUALLY.

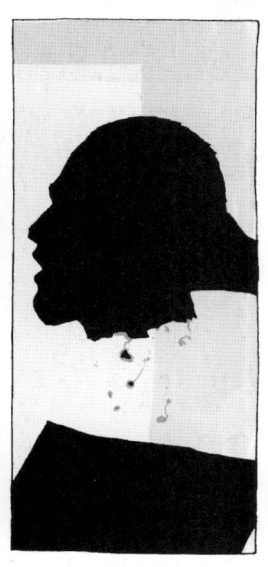

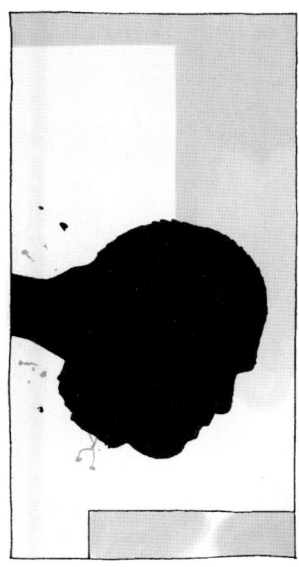

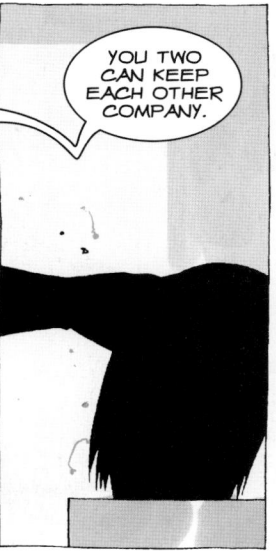

YOU TWO CAN KEEP EACH OTHER COMPANY.

GOTTA GET OFF MY FEET...

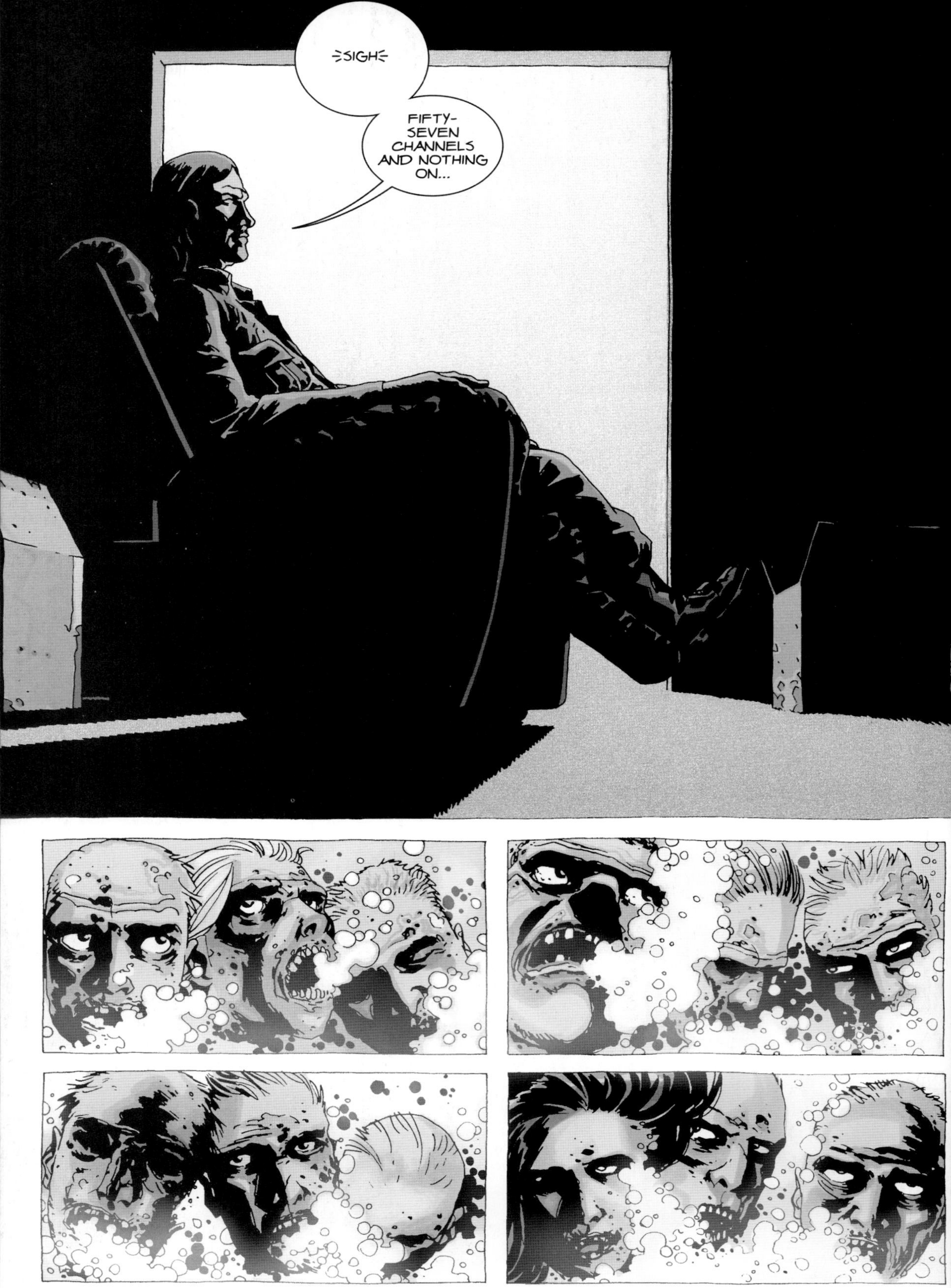
=SIGH=
FIFTY-SEVEN CHANNELS AND NOTHING ON...

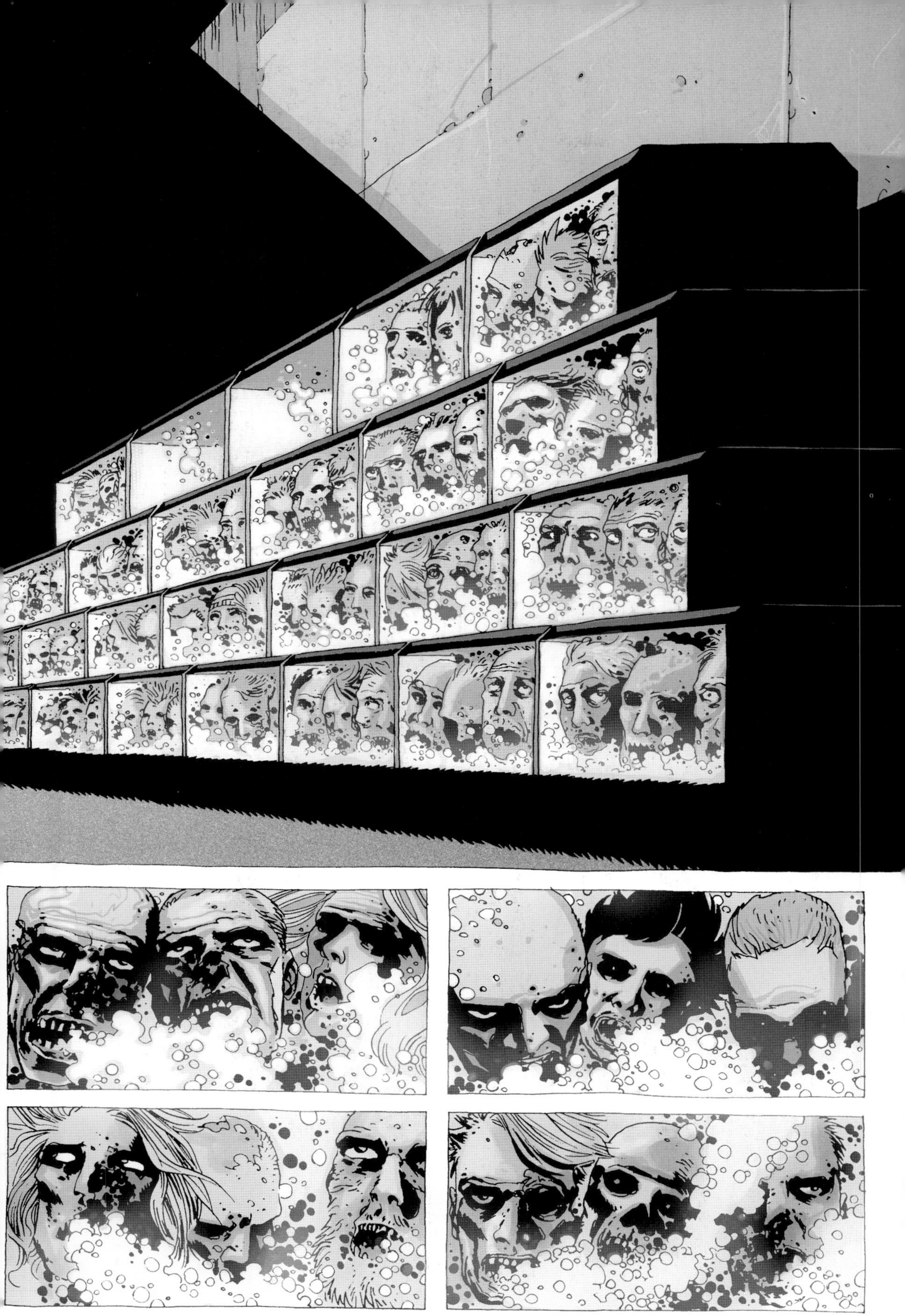

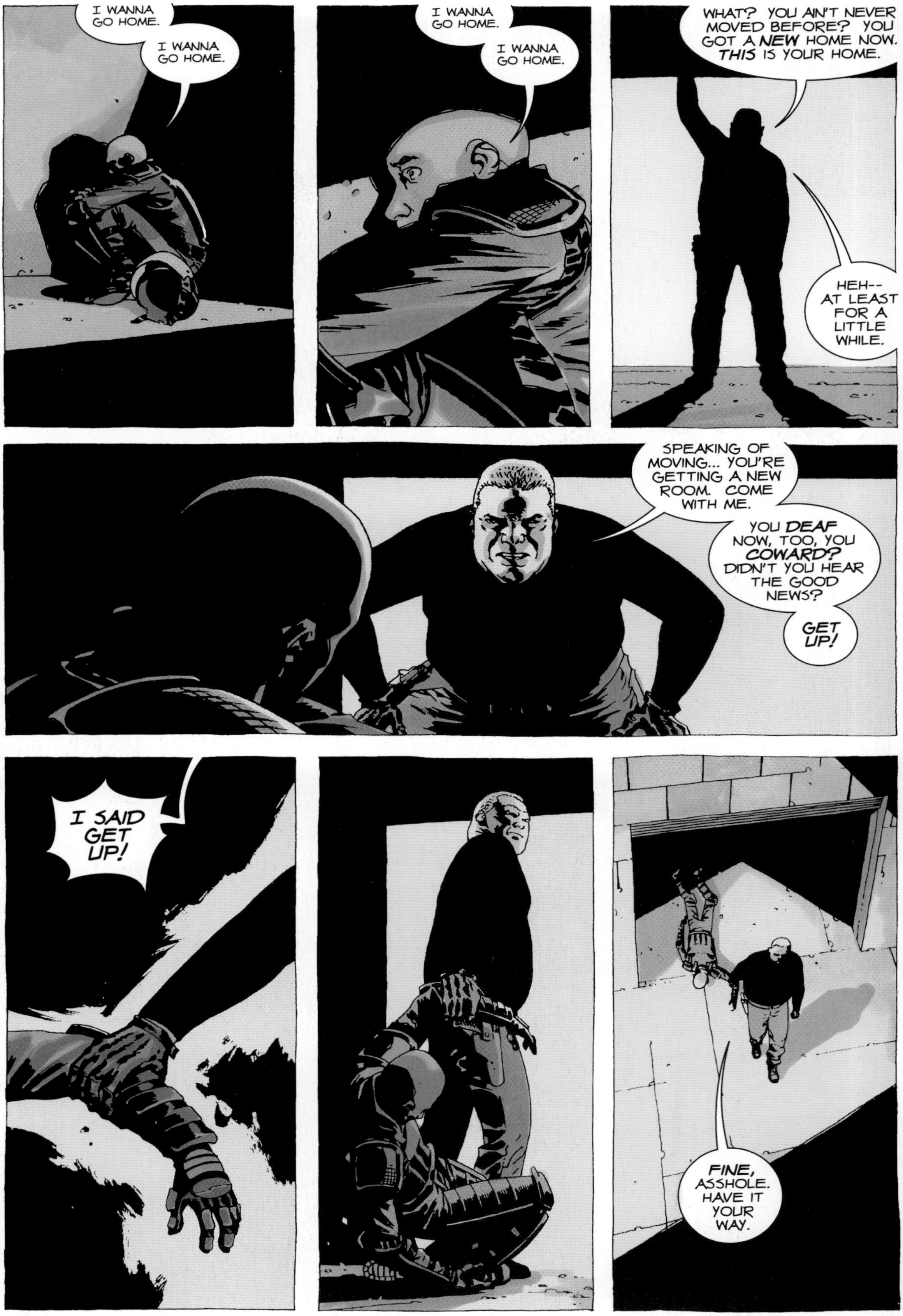
I WANNA GO HOME.
I WANNA GO HOME.
I WANNA GO HOME.
I WANNA GO HOME.
WHAT? YOU AIN'T NEVER MOVED BEFORE? YOU GOT A NEW HOME NOW. THIS IS YOUR HOME.
HEH-- AT LEAST FOR A LITTLE WHILE.
SPEAKING OF MOVING... YOU'RE GETTING A NEW ROOM. COME WITH ME.
YOU DEAF NOW, TOO, YOU COWARD? DIDN'T YOU HEAR THE GOOD NEWS?
GET UP!
I SAID GET UP!
FINE, ASSHOLE. HAVE IT YOUR WAY.

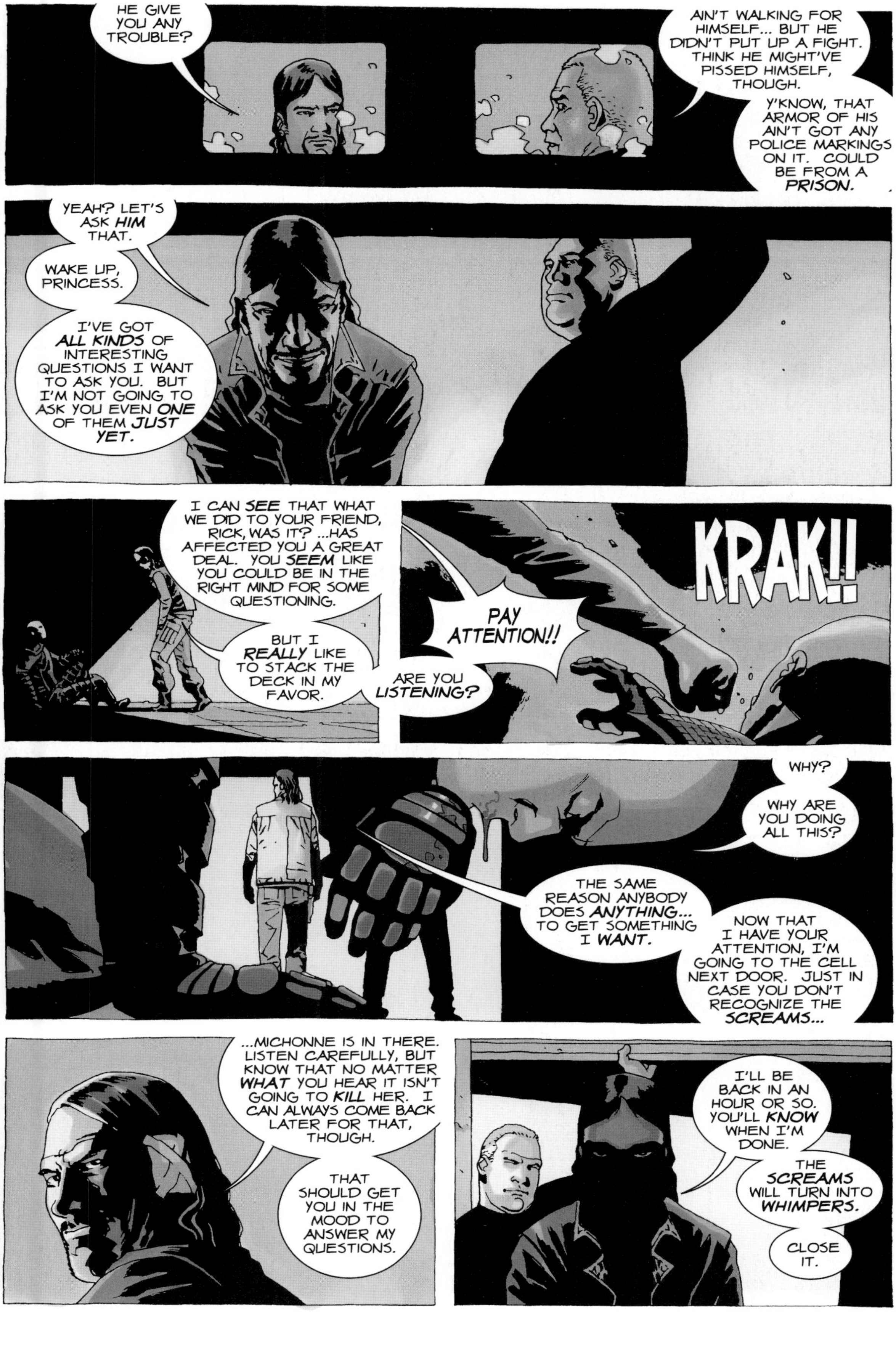
HE GIVE YOU ANY TROUBLE?
AIN'T WALKING FOR HIMSELF... BUT HE DIDN'T PUT UP A FIGHT. THINK HE MIGHT'VE PISSED HIMSELF, THOUGH.
Y'KNOW, THAT ARMOR OF HIS AIN'T GOT ANY POLICE MARKINGS ON IT. COULD BE FROM A PRISON.
YEAH? LET'S ASK HIM THAT.
WAKE UP, PRINCESS.
I'VE GOT ALL KINDS OF INTERESTING QUESTIONS I WANT TO ASK YOU. BUT I'M NOT GOING TO ASK YOU EVEN ONE OF THEM JUST YET.
I CAN SEE THAT WHAT WE DID TO YOUR FRIEND, RICK, WAS IT? ...HAS AFFECTED YOU A GREAT DEAL. YOU SEEM LIKE YOU COULD BE IN THE RIGHT MIND FOR SOME QUESTIONING.
BUT I REALLY LIKE TO STACK THE DECK IN MY FAVOR.
KRAK!!
PAY ATTENTION!!
ARE YOU LISTENING?
WHY?
WHY ARE YOU DOING ALL THIS?
THE SAME REASON ANYBODY DOES ANYTHING... TO GET SOMETHING I WANT.
NOW THAT I HAVE YOUR ATTENTION, I'M GOING TO THE CELL NEXT DOOR. JUST IN CASE YOU DON'T RECOGNIZE THE SCREAMS...
...MICHONNE IS IN THERE. LISTEN CAREFULLY, BUT KNOW THAT NO MATTER WHAT YOU HEAR IT ISN'T GOING TO KILL HER. I CAN ALWAYS COME BACK LATER FOR THAT, THOUGH.
THAT SHOULD GET YOU IN THE MOOD TO ANSWER MY QUESTIONS.
I'LL BE BACK IN AN HOUR OR SO. YOU'LL KNOW WHEN I'M DONE.
THE SCREAMS WILL TURN INTO WHIMPERS.
CLOSE IT.

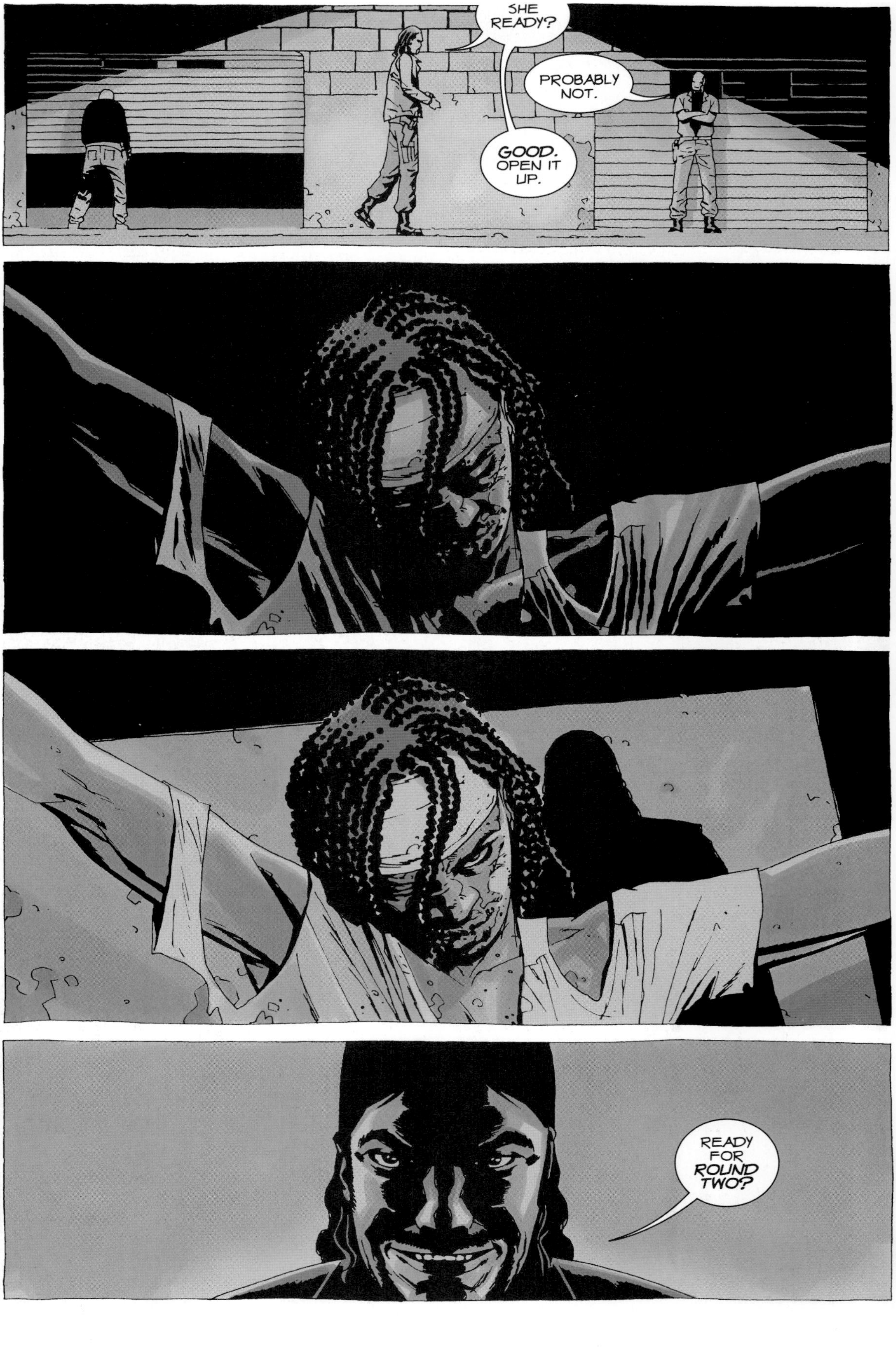
SHE READY?
PROBABLY NOT.
GOOD. OPEN IT UP.
READY FOR ROUND TWO?

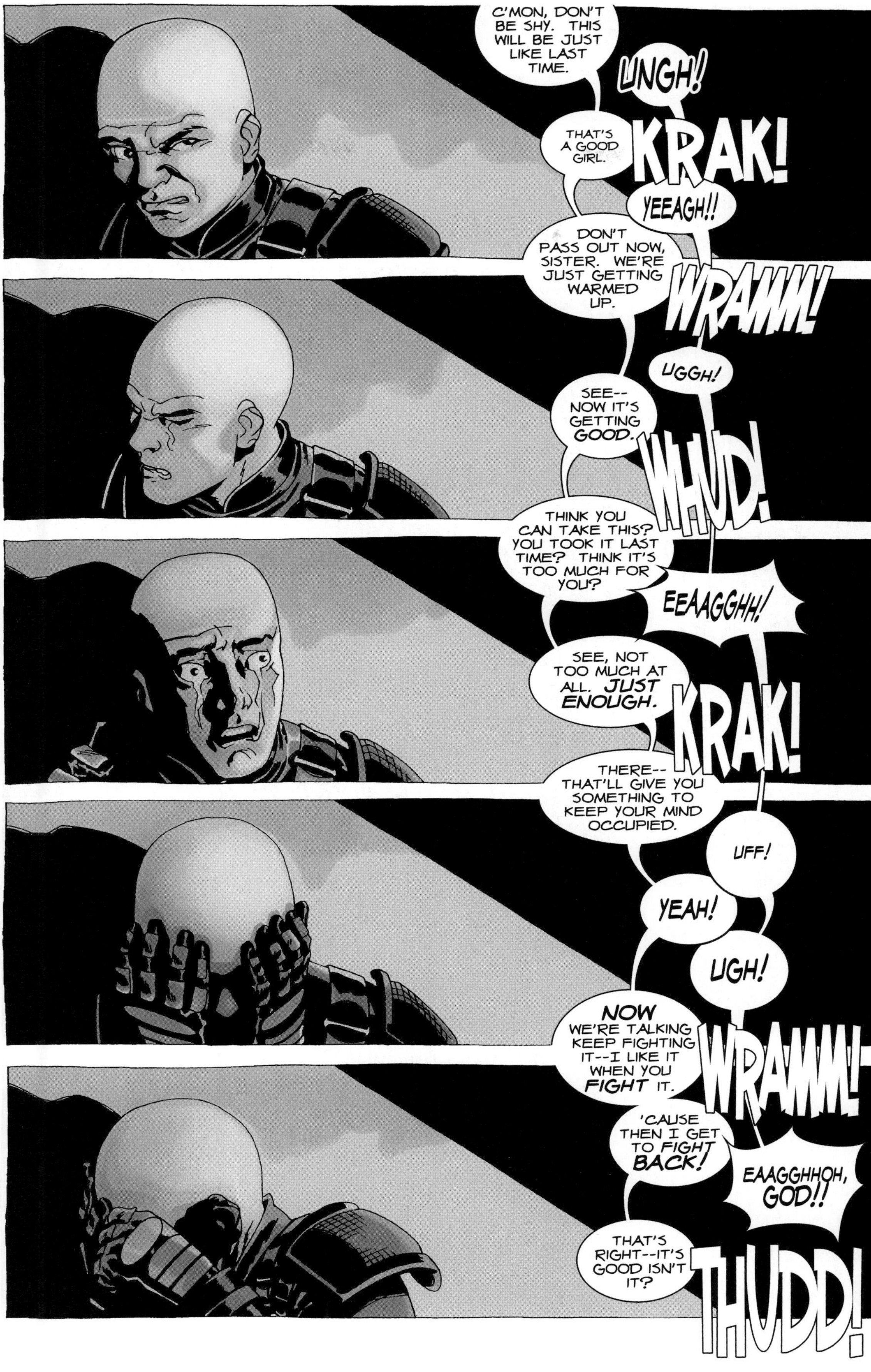

C'MON, DON'T BE SHY. THIS WILL BE JUST LIKE LAST TIME.
UNGH!
THAT'S A GOOD GIRL.
KRAK!
YEEAGH!!
DON'T PASS OUT NOW, SISTER. WE'RE JUST GETTING WARMED UP.
WRAMM!
UGGH!
SEE--NOW IT'S GETTING GOOD.
WHUD!
THINK YOU CAN TAKE THIS? YOU TOOK IT LAST TIME? THINK IT'S TOO MUCH FOR YOU?
EEAAGGHH!
SEE, NOT TOO MUCH AT ALL. JUST ENOUGH.
KRAK!
THERE--THAT'LL GIVE YOU SOMETHING TO KEEP YOUR MIND OCCUPIED.
UFF!
YEAH!
UGH!
NOW WE'RE TALKING KEEP FIGHTING IT--I LIKE IT WHEN YOU FIGHT IT.
WRAMM!
'CAUSE THEN I GET TO FIGHT BACK!
EAAGGHHOH, GOD!!
THAT'S RIGHT--IT'S GOOD ISN'T IT?
THUDD!

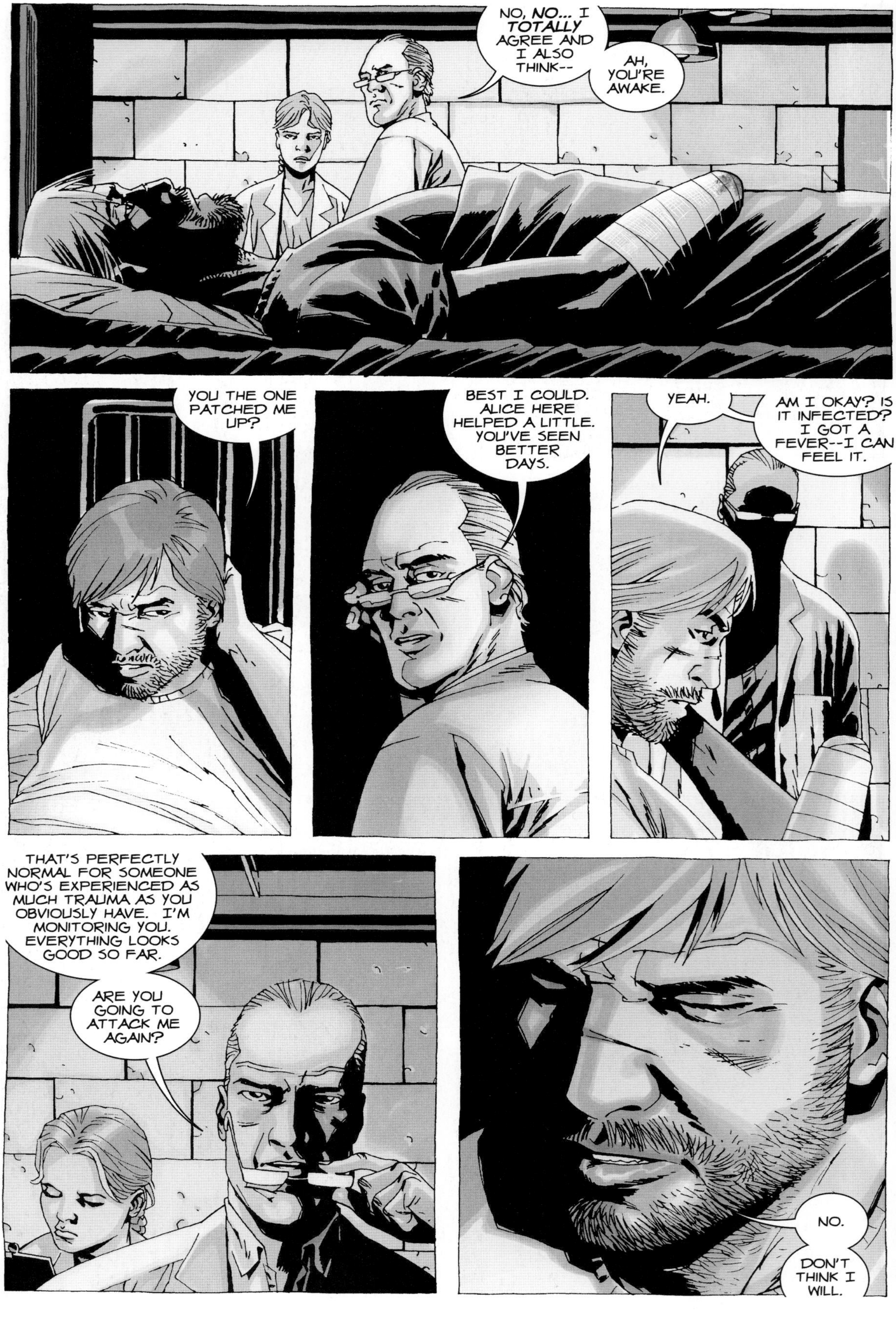
NO, *NO*... I *TOTALLY* AGREE AND I ALSO THINK--
AH, YOU'RE AWAKE.
YOU THE ONE PATCHED ME UP?
BEST I COULD. ALICE HERE HELPED A LITTLE. YOU'VE SEEN BETTER DAYS.
YEAH.
AM I OKAY? IS IT INFECTED? I GOT A FEVER--I CAN FEEL IT.
THAT'S PERFECTLY NORMAL FOR SOMEONE WHO'S EXPERIENCED AS MUCH TRAUMA AS YOU OBVIOUSLY HAVE. I'M MONITORING YOU. EVERYTHING LOOKS GOOD SO FAR.
ARE YOU GOING TO ATTACK ME AGAIN?
NO.
DON'T THINK I WILL.

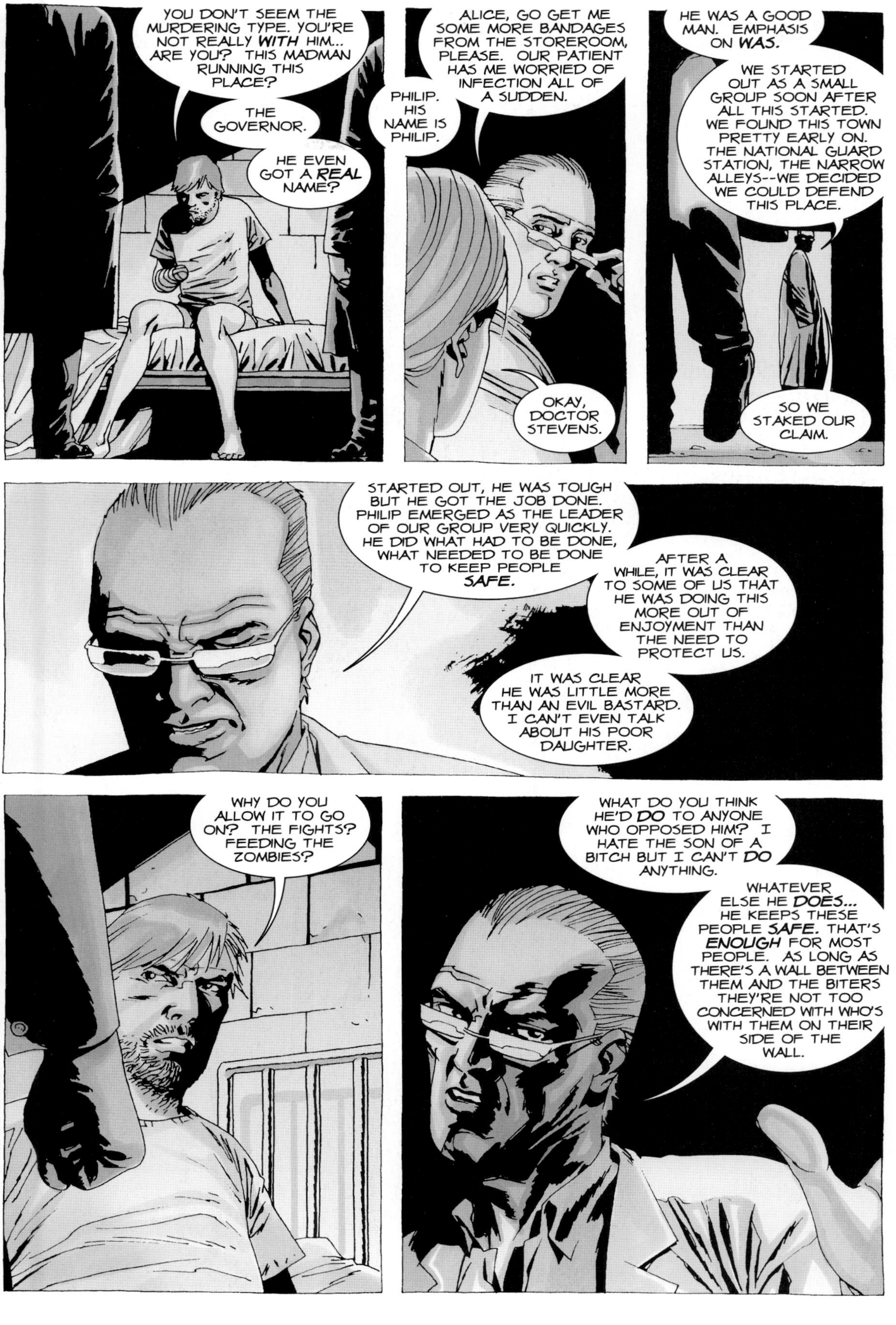

YOU DON'T SEEM THE MURDERING TYPE. YOU'RE NOT REALLY WITH HIM... ARE YOU? THIS MADMAN RUNNING THIS PLACE?
THE GOVERNOR.
HE EVEN GOT A REAL NAME?
PHILIP. HIS NAME IS PHILIP.
ALICE, GO GET ME SOME MORE BANDAGES FROM THE STOREROOM, PLEASE. OUR PATIENT HAS ME WORRIED OF INFECTION ALL OF A SUDDEN.
OKAY, DOCTOR STEVENS.
HE WAS A GOOD MAN. EMPHASIS ON WAS.
WE STARTED OUT AS A SMALL GROUP SOON AFTER ALL THIS STARTED. WE FOUND THIS TOWN PRETTY EARLY ON. THE NATIONAL GUARD STATION, THE NARROW ALLEYS--WE DECIDED WE COULD DEFEND THIS PLACE.
SO WE STAKED OUR CLAIM.
STARTED OUT, HE WAS TOUGH BUT HE GOT THE JOB DONE. PHILIP EMERGED AS THE LEADER OF OUR GROUP VERY QUICKLY. HE DID WHAT HAD TO BE DONE, WHAT NEEDED TO BE DONE TO KEEP PEOPLE SAFE.
AFTER A WHILE, IT WAS CLEAR TO SOME OF US THAT HE WAS DOING THIS MORE OUT OF ENJOYMENT THAN THE NEED TO PROTECT US.
IT WAS CLEAR HE WAS LITTLE MORE THAN AN EVIL BASTARD. I CAN'T EVEN TALK ABOUT HIS POOR DAUGHTER.
WHY DO YOU ALLOW IT TO GO ON? THE FIGHTS? FEEDING THE ZOMBIES?
WHAT DO YOU THINK HE'D DO TO ANYONE WHO OPPOSED HIM? I HATE THE SON OF A BITCH BUT I CAN'T DO ANYTHING.
WHATEVER ELSE HE DOES... HE KEEPS THESE PEOPLE SAFE. THAT'S ENOUGH FOR MOST PEOPLE. AS LONG AS THERE'S A WALL BETWEEN THEM AND THE BITERS THEY'RE NOT TOO CONCERNED WITH WHO'S WITH THEM ON THEIR SIDE OF THE WALL.

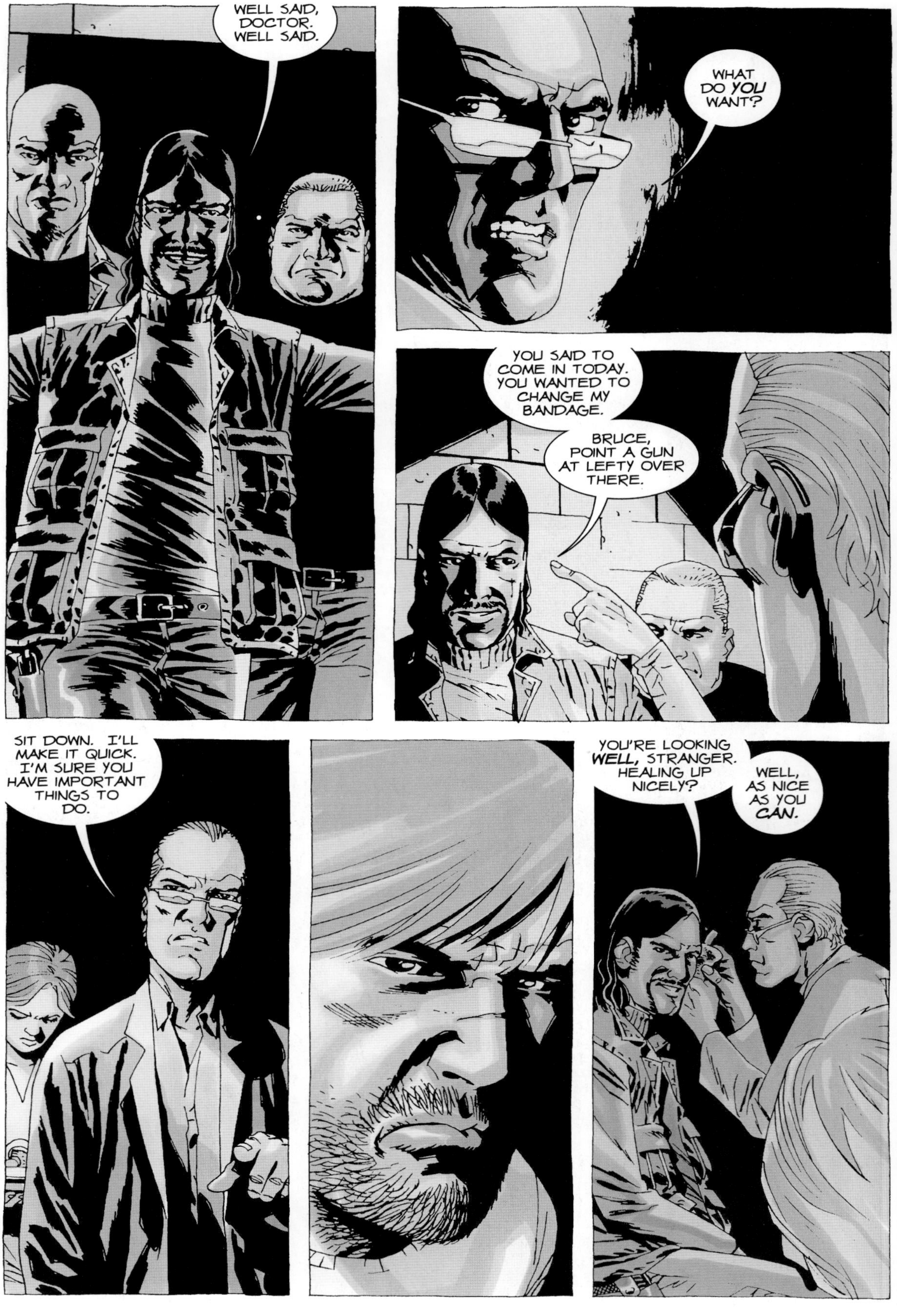
WELL SAID, DOCTOR. WELL SAID.
WHAT DO YOU WANT?
YOU SAID TO COME IN TODAY. YOU WANTED TO CHANGE MY BANDAGE.
BRUCE, POINT A GUN AT LEFTY OVER THERE.
SIT DOWN. I'LL MAKE IT QUICK. I'M SURE YOU HAVE IMPORTANT THINGS TO DO.
YOU'RE LOOKING WELL, STRANGER. HEALING UP NICELY?
WELL, AS NICE AS YOU CAN.

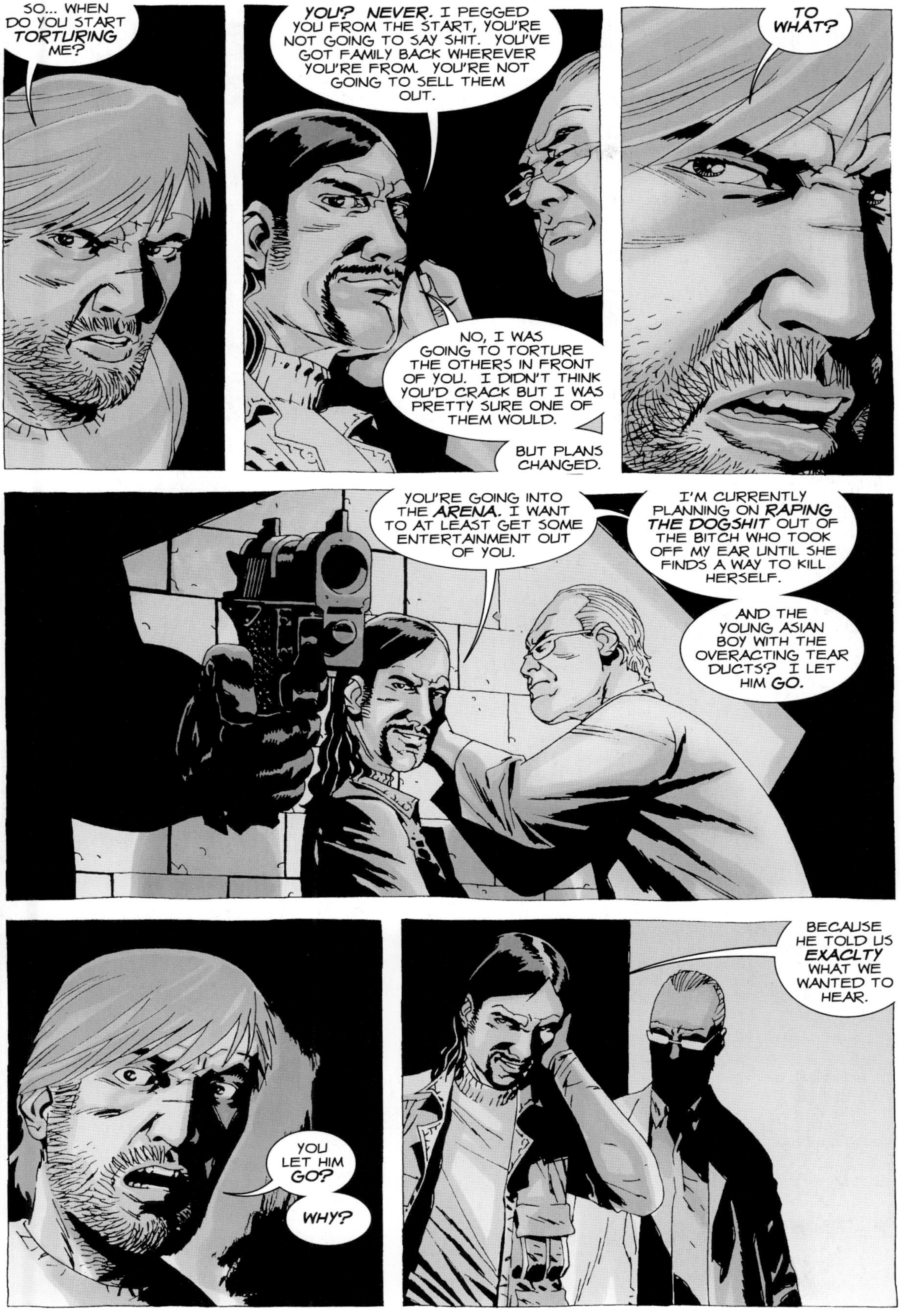

SO... WHEN DO YOU START TORTURING ME?
YOU? NEVER. I PEGGED YOU FROM THE START, YOU'RE NOT GOING TO SAY SHIT. YOU'VE GOT FAMILY BACK WHEREVER YOU'RE FROM. YOU'RE NOT GOING TO SELL THEM OUT.
NO, I WAS GOING TO TORTURE THE OTHERS IN FRONT OF YOU. I DIDN'T THINK YOU'D CRACK BUT I WAS PRETTY SURE ONE OF THEM WOULD.
BUT PLANS CHANGED.
TO WHAT?
YOU'RE GOING INTO THE ARENA. I WANT TO AT LEAST GET SOME ENTERTAINMENT OUT OF YOU.
I'M CURRENTLY PLANNING ON RAPING THE DOGSHIT OUT OF THE BITCH WHO TOOK OFF MY EAR UNTIL SHE FINDS A WAY TO KILL HERSELF.
AND THE YOUNG ASIAN BOY WITH THE OVERACTING TEAR DUCTS? I LET HIM GO.
YOU LET HIM GO?
WHY?
BECAUSE HE TOLD US EXACLTY WHAT WE WANTED TO HEAR.

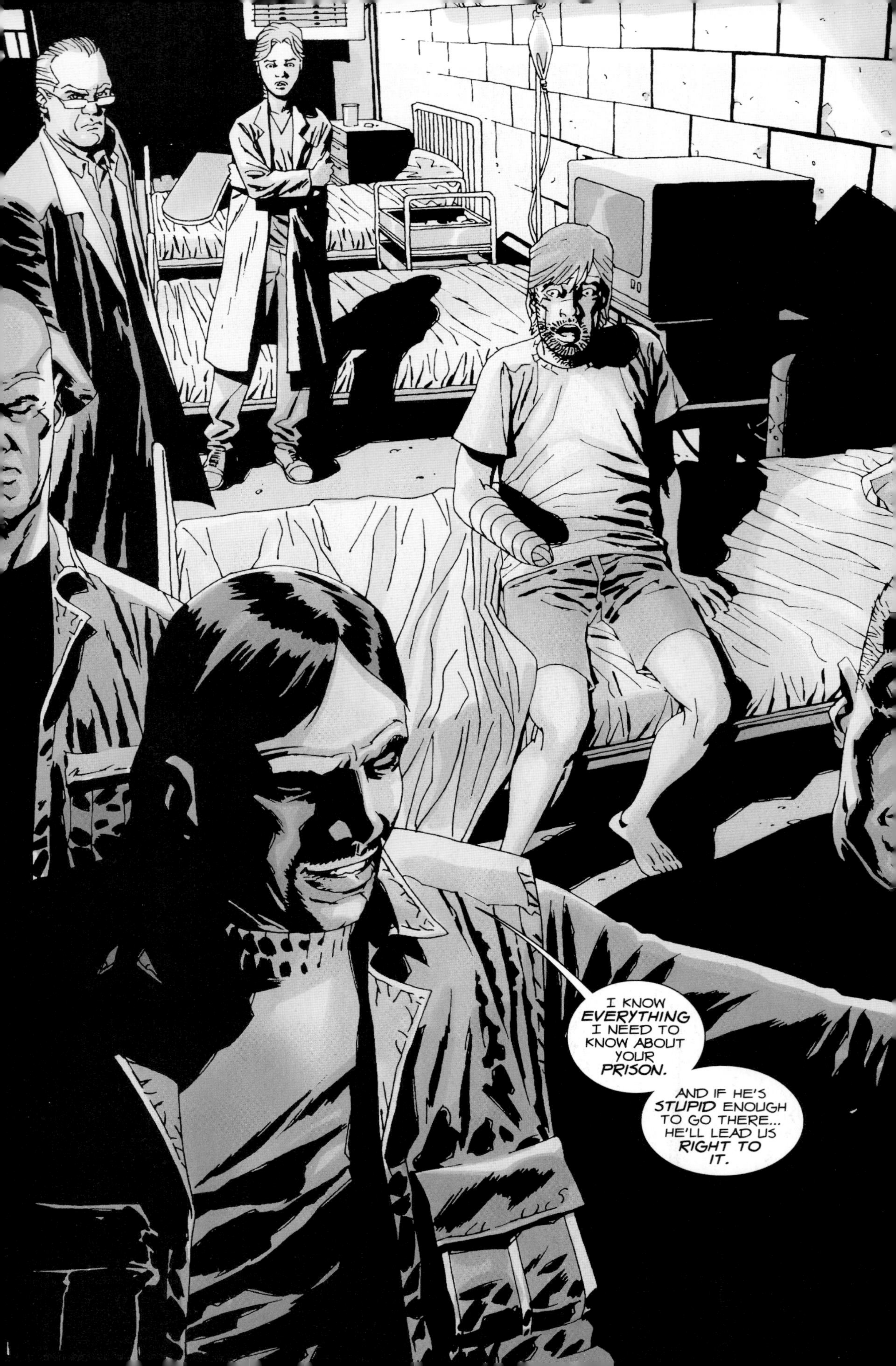

I KNOW EVERYTHING I NEED TO KNOW ABOUT YOUR PRISON.
AND IF HE'S STUPID ENOUGH TO GO THERE... HE'LL LEAD US RIGHT TO IT.

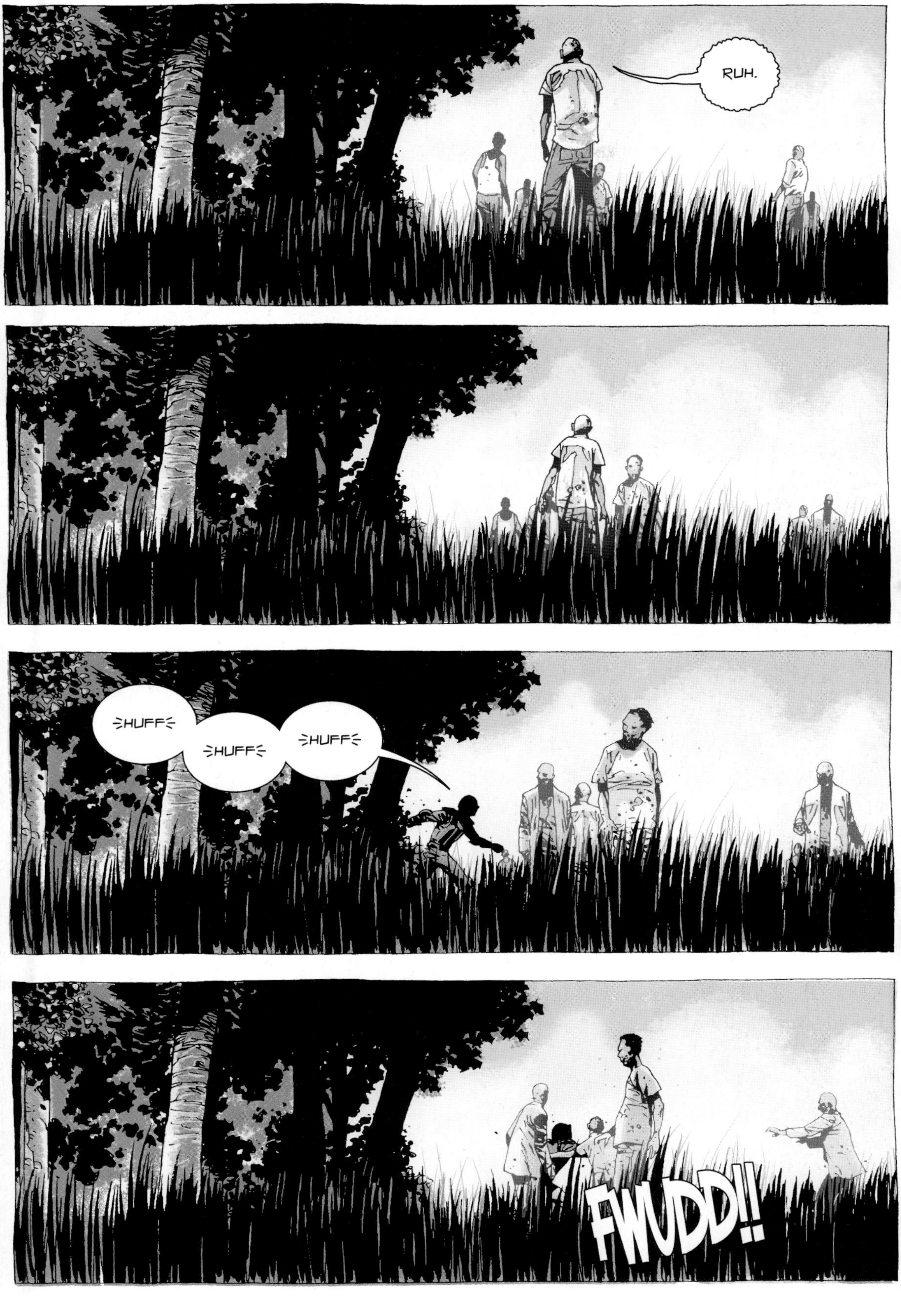
RUH.
HUFF
HUFF
HUFF
FWUDD!!

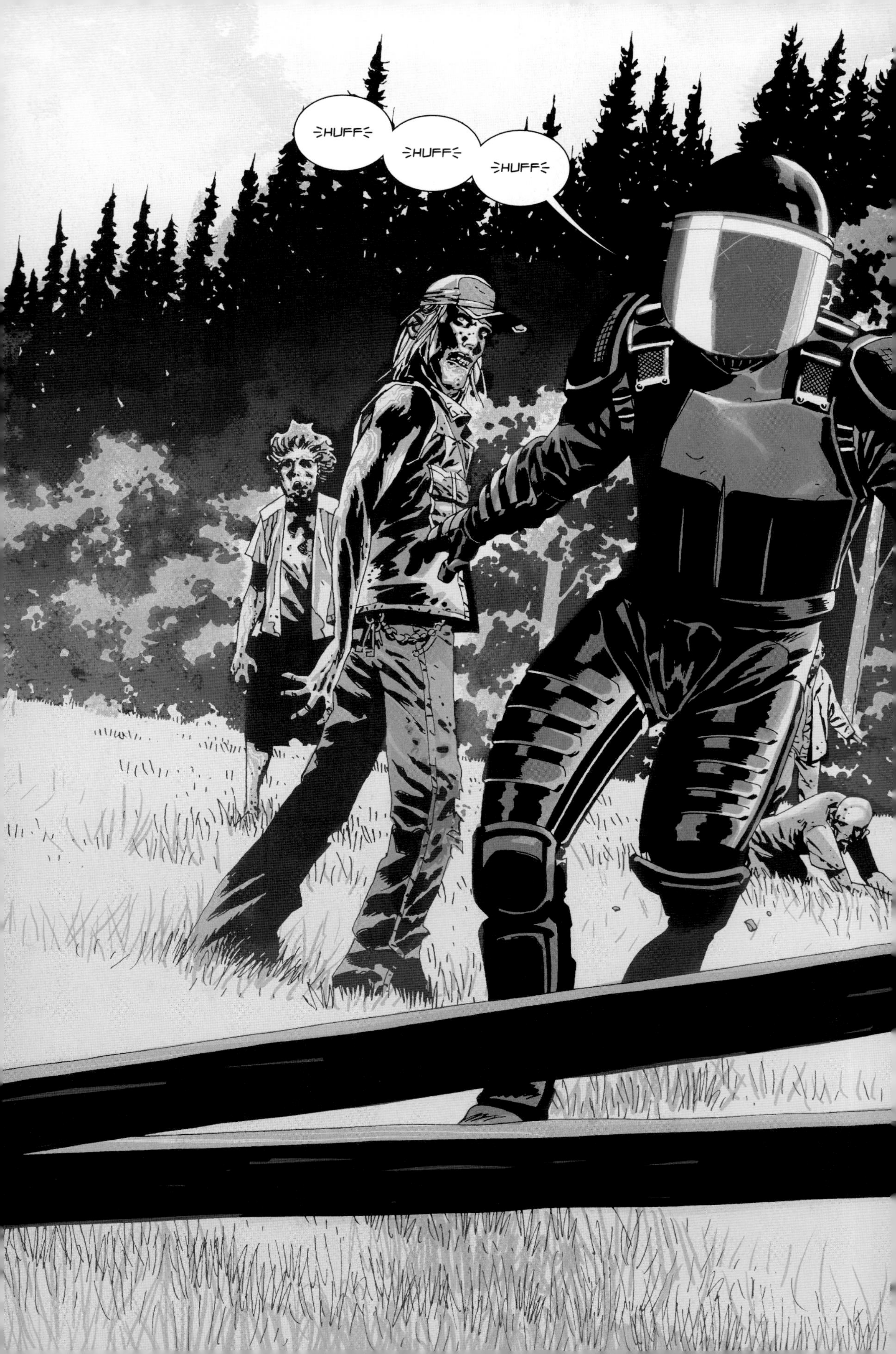
HUFF
HUFF
HUFF

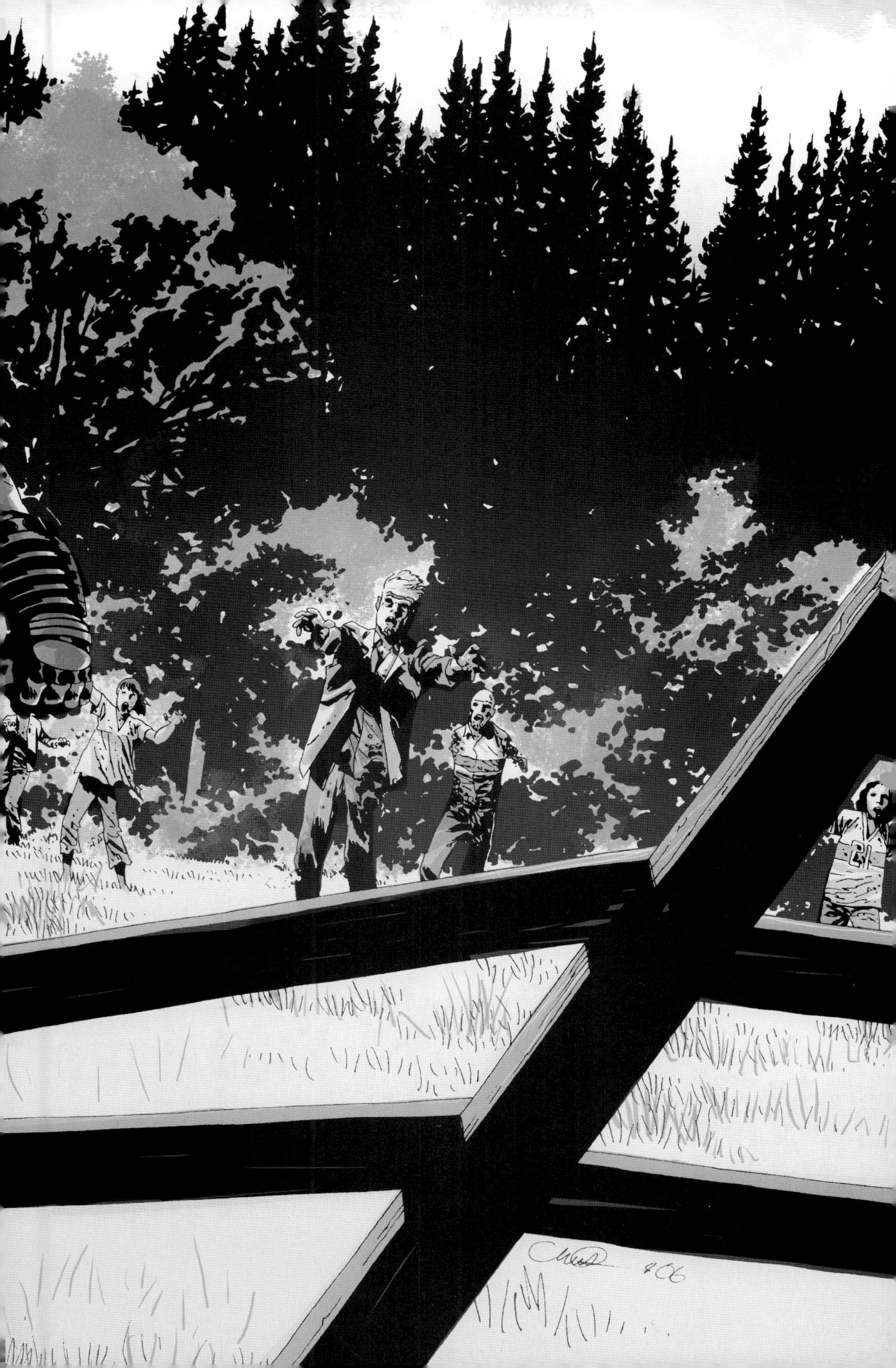

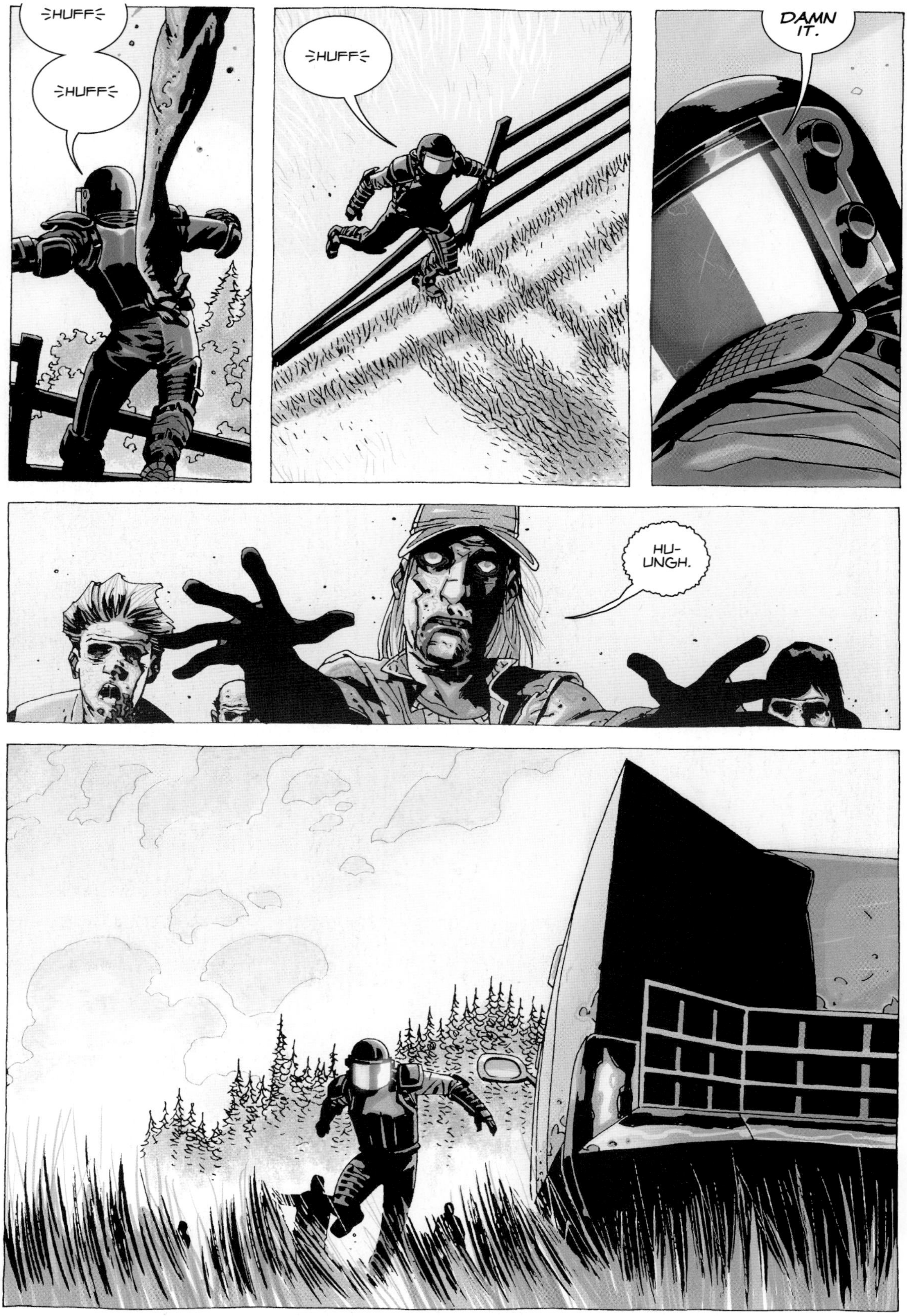

HUFF
HUFF
HUFF
DAMN IT.
HU-UNGH.

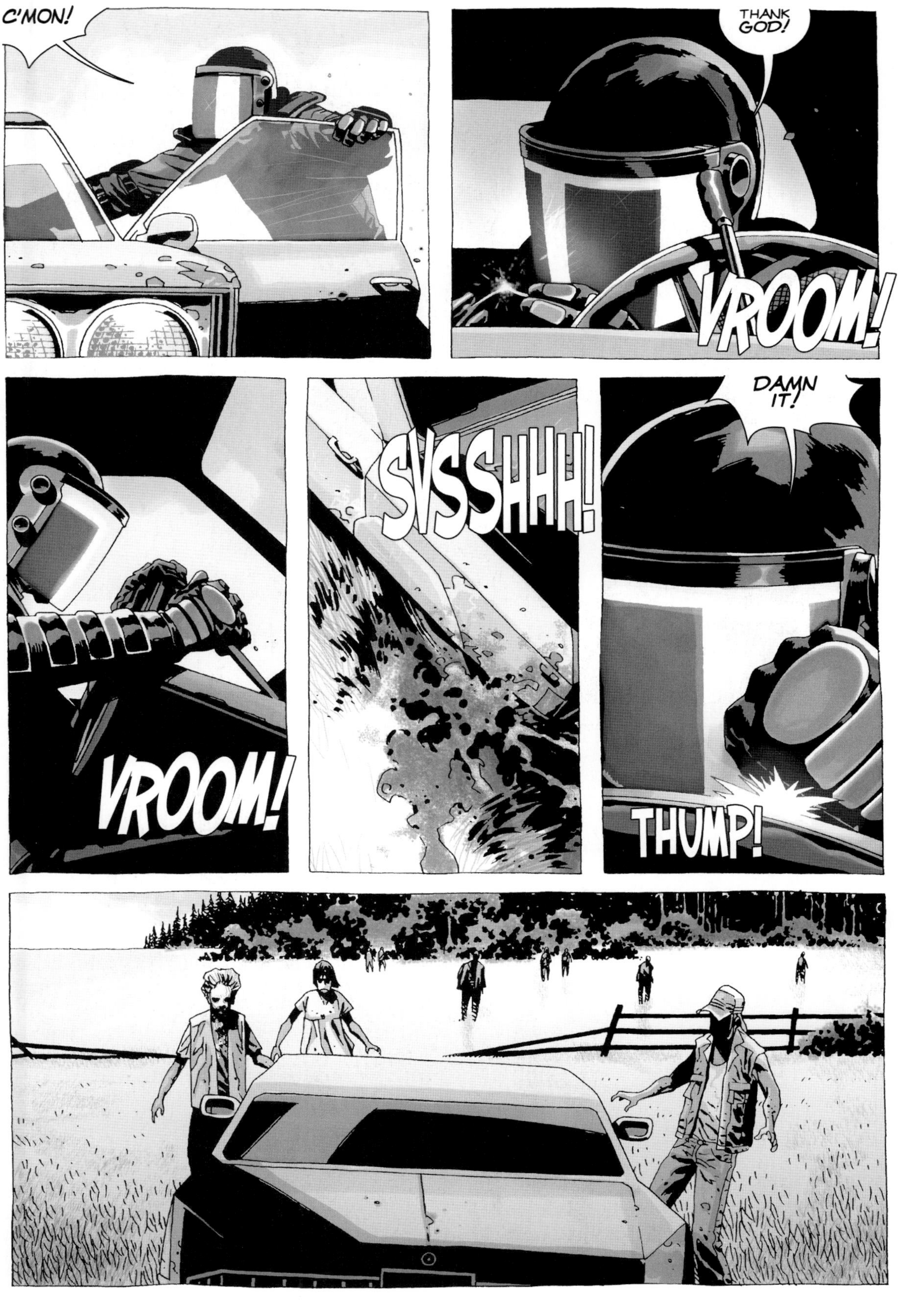
C'MON!
THANK GOD!
VROOM!
VROOM!
SVSSHHH!
DAMN IT!
THUMP!

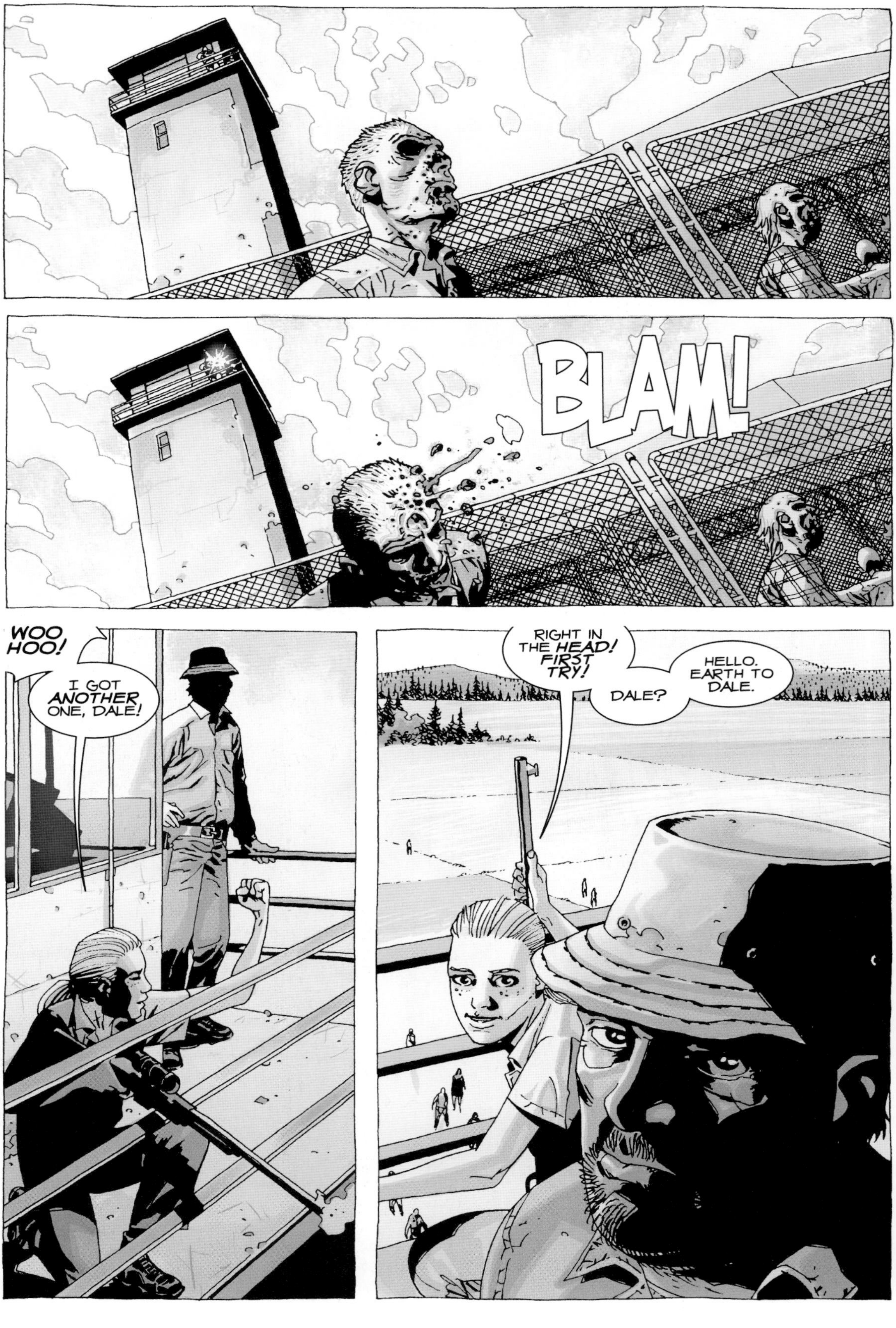
BLAM!
WOO HOO!
I GOT ANOTHER ONE, DALE!
RIGHT IN THE HEAD! FIRST TRY!
DALE?
HELLO. EARTH TO DALE.

PLEASE, HONEY. THEY'RE EITHER GONNA COME BACK, OR THEY'RE *NOT*. I'M WORRIED ABOUT THEM, TOO, I *AM*, BUT WATCHING THE HORIZON ALL DAY ISN'T GOING TO BRING THEM BACK *FASTER*.

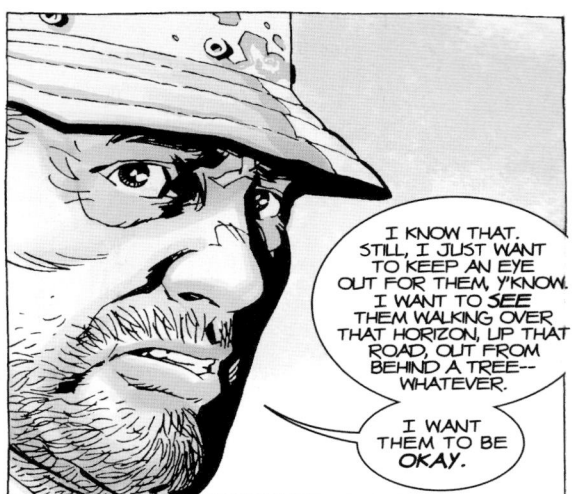

I KNOW THAT. STILL, I JUST WANT TO KEEP AN EYE OUT FOR THEM, Y'KNOW. I WANT TO *SEE* THEM WALKING OVER THAT HORIZON, UP THAT ROAD, OUT FROM BEHIND A TREE-- WHATEVER.

I WANT THEM TO BE *OKAY*.

YOU'RE GOING TO BE OKAY, RIGHT? IF THEY *DON'T* COME BACK, I MEAN. I'M KINDA DEPENDING ON YOU. THE TWINS, TOO--AND HELL, THE WHOLE GROUP, REALLY.

YEAH, I'M *FINE*. I LOST MY *WIFE* TO THOSE MONSTERS. COMPARED TO *THAT* I BARELY EVEN *KNOW* THESE PEOPLE.

I'LL-- I'LL HOLD TOGETHER, DARLING. DON'T YOU WORRY.

HERE, SEE IF YOU CAN PICK OFF THAT ONE DOWN THERE-- HE LOOKS LIKE A NASTY ONE.

OH, YOU THINK I CAN'T DO IT?

IN ONE SHOT? I DON'T KNOW. WE'LL JUST HAVE TO *SEE*, WON'T WE?

HE GOT **CARROTS** IN THIS HERE GARDEN? I **LOVE** ME SOME CARROTS.

I THINK HE'S GOT A WHOLE LOTTA STUFF HERE. I WASN'T REALLY PAYING ATTENTION WHEN WE PLANTED THE STUFF. VEGETABLES ARE ALL THE **SAME** TO ME. FRUITS TOO.

I SWEAR I'D HOP THAT FENCE RIGHT NOW IF I KNEW THERE WAS A **CANDY BAR** WITHIN WALKING DISTANCE.

STALE ONES, EVEN.

I COULD GO FOR A CANDY BAR RIGHT ABOUT NOW. I THINK THEY HAD SOME IN THE PRISON BUT AXEL AND THEM **OTHERS** ATE 'EM ALL BEFORE WE SHOWED UP.

FUCKERS.

FUCKERS.

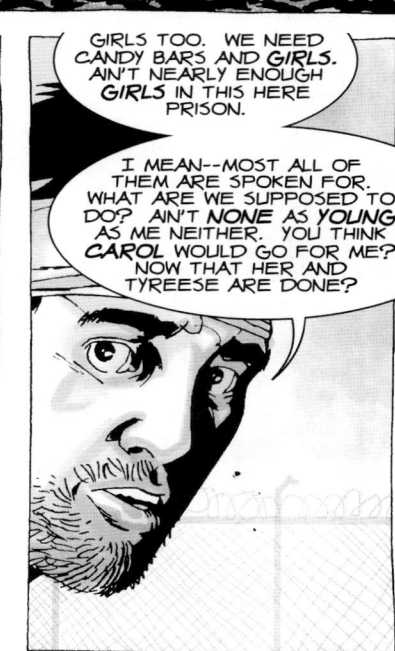

GIRLS TOO. WE NEED CANDY BARS AND **GIRLS**. AIN'T NEARLY ENOUGH **GIRLS** IN THIS HERE PRISON.

I MEAN--MOST ALL OF THEM ARE SPOKEN FOR. WHAT ARE WE SUPPOSED TO DO? AIN'T **NONE** AS **YOUNG** AS ME NEITHER. YOU THINK **CAROL** WOULD GO FOR ME? NOW THAT HER AND TYREESE ARE DONE?

LITTLE BOY LIKE YOU?

NOT **LIKELY**.

MAYBE IF I GROW A MUSTACHE...

SURE. THEN, INSTEAD OF LOOKIN' LIKE A LITTLE BOY... YOU'LL LOOK LIKE A LITTLE BOY...

WITH A **MUSTACHE**.

'SIDES, YOU BEEN NURSIN' THAT STUBBLE FOR **MONTHS**, HOW YOU EXPECT TO TURN THAT INTO A **MUSTACHE**?

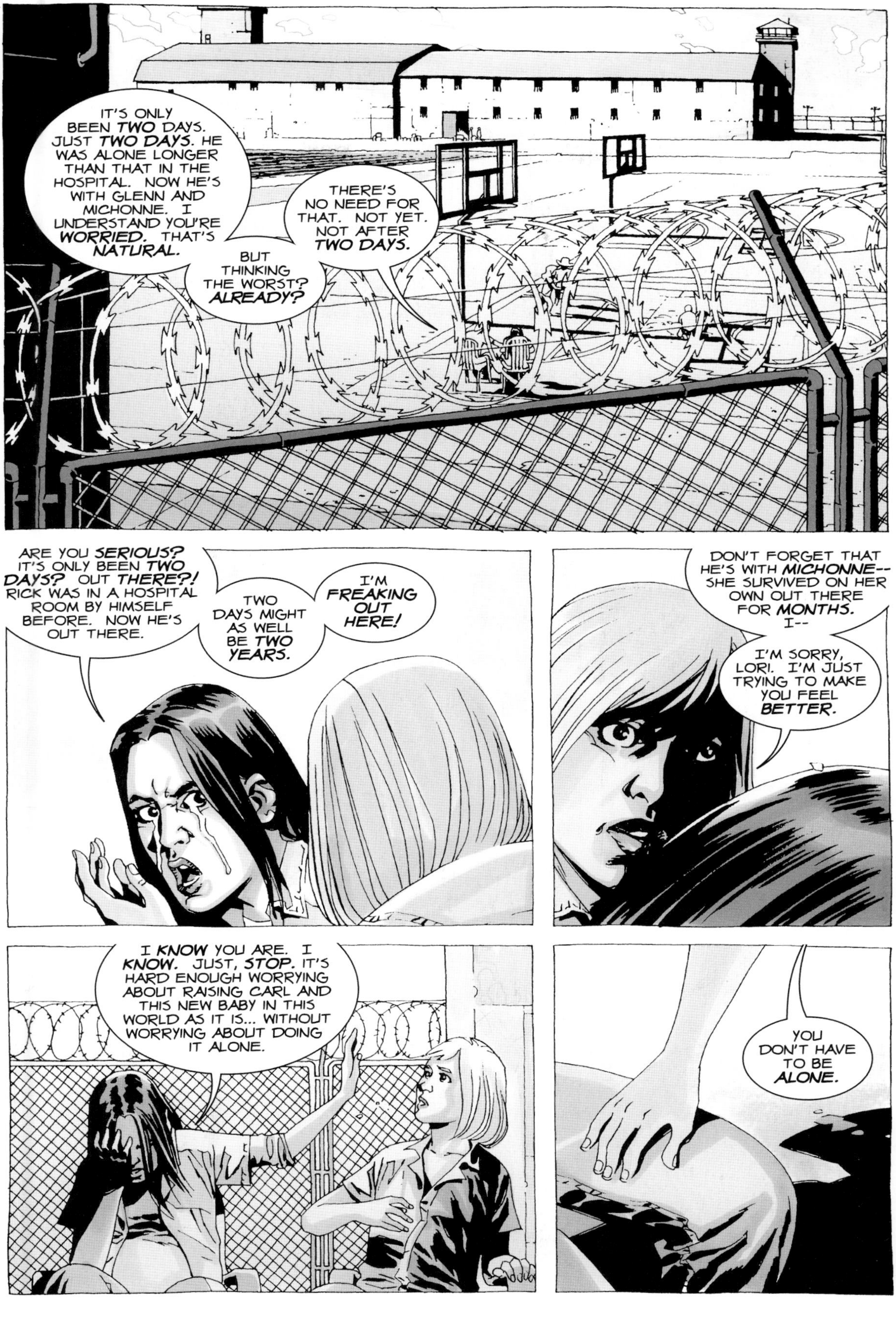

IT'S ONLY BEEN *TWO* DAYS. JUST *TWO DAYS.* HE WAS ALONE LONGER THAN THAT IN THE HOSPITAL. NOW HE'S WITH GLENN AND MICHONNE. I UNDERSTAND YOU'RE *WORRIED.* THAT'S *NATURAL.*

THERE'S NO NEED FOR THAT. NOT YET. NOT AFTER *TWO DAYS.*

BUT THINKING THE WORST? *ALREADY?*

ARE YOU *SERIOUS?* IT'S ONLY BEEN *TWO DAYS?* OUT *THERE?!* RICK WAS IN A HOSPITAL ROOM BY HIMSELF BEFORE. NOW HE'S OUT THERE.

TWO DAYS MIGHT AS WELL BE *TWO YEARS.*

I'M *FREAKING OUT* HERE!

DON'T FORGET THAT HE'S WITH *MICHONNE*-- SHE SURVIVED ON HER OWN OUT THERE FOR *MONTHS.* I--

I'M SORRY, LORI. I'M JUST TRYING TO MAKE YOU FEEL *BETTER.*

I *KNOW* YOU ARE. I *KNOW.* JUST, *STOP.* IT'S HARD ENOUGH WORRYING ABOUT RAISING CARL AND THIS NEW BABY IN THIS WORLD AS IT IS... WITHOUT WORRYING ABOUT DOING IT ALONE.

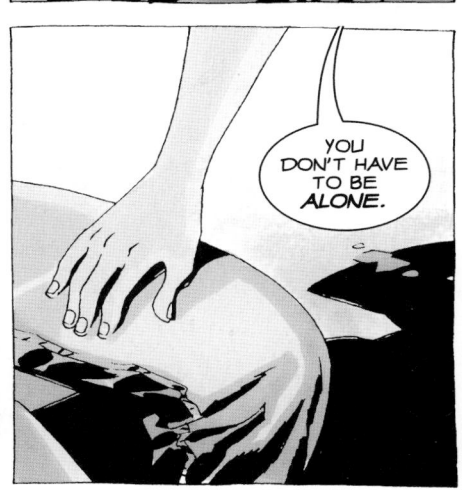

YOU DON'T HAVE TO BE *ALONE.*

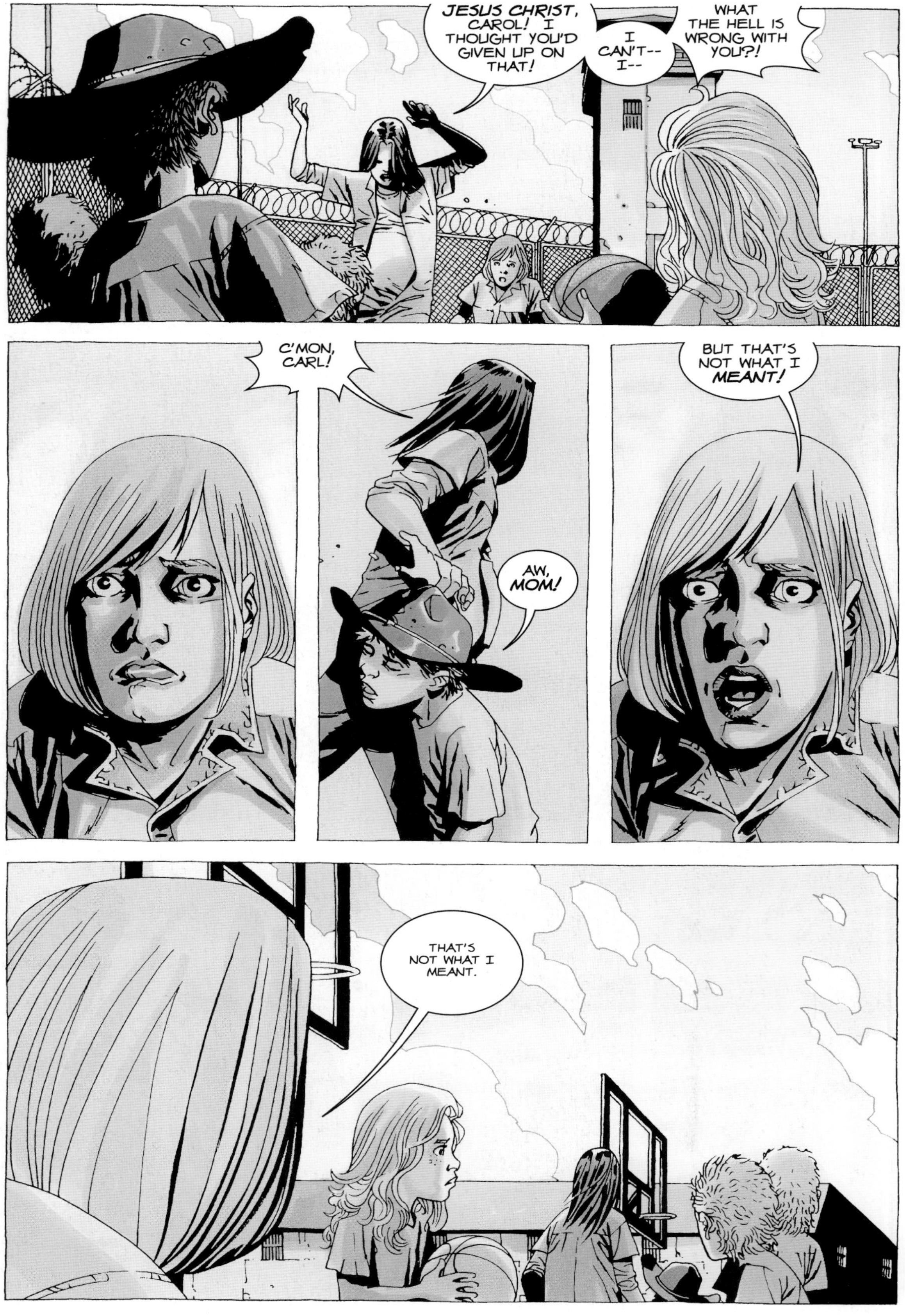
JESUS CHRIST, CAROL! I THOUGHT YOU'D GIVEN UP ON THAT!
I CAN'T-- I--
WHAT THE HELL IS WRONG WITH YOU?!
C'MON, CARL!
AW, MOM!
BUT THAT'S NOT WHAT I MEANT!
THAT'S NOT WHAT I MEANT.

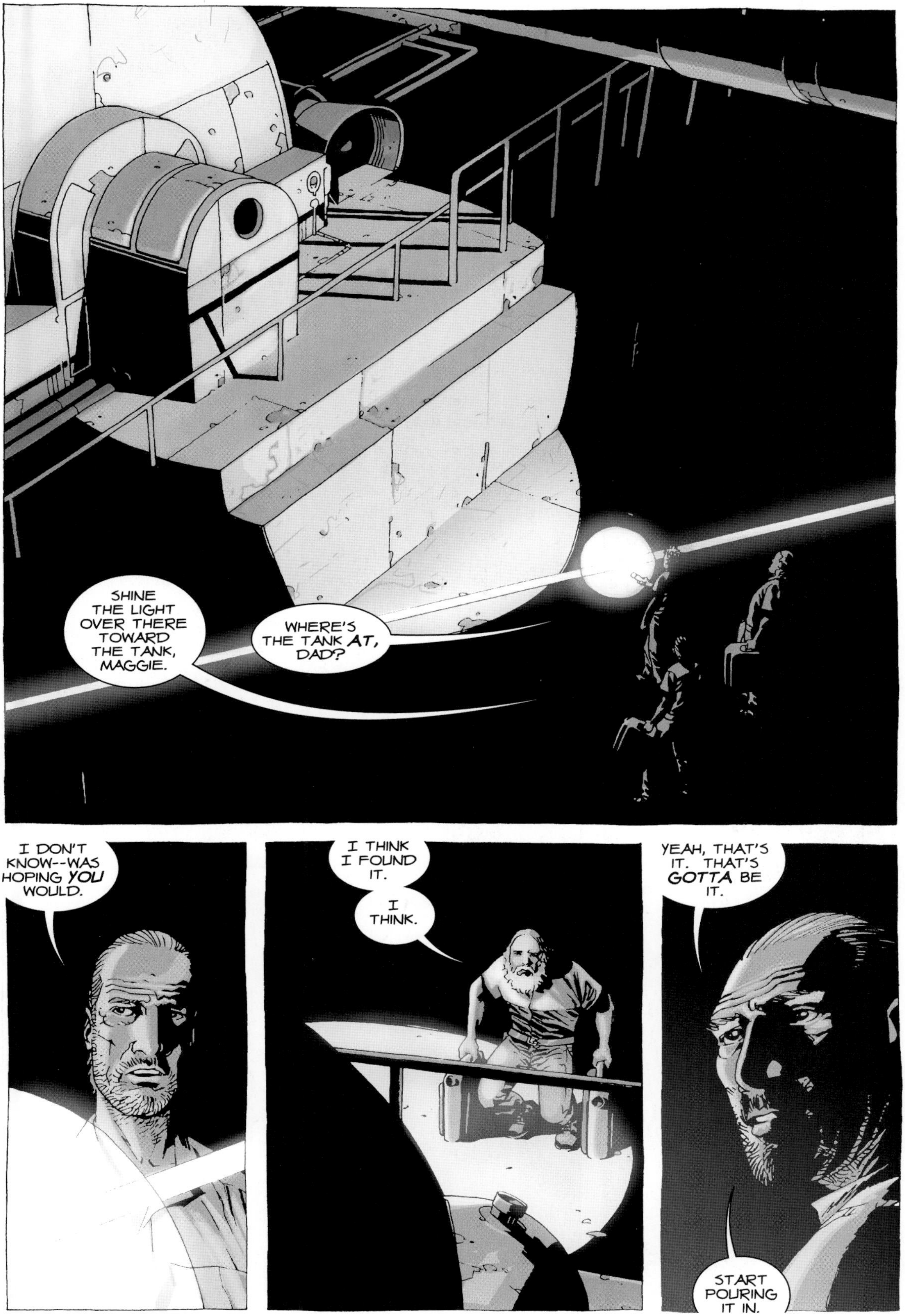
SHINE THE LIGHT OVER THERE TOWARD THE TANK, MAGGIE.
WHERE'S THE TANK *AT*, DAD?
I DON'T KNOW--WAS HOPING *YOU* WOULD.
I THINK I FOUND IT.
I THINK.
YEAH, THAT'S IT. THAT'S *GOTTA* BE IT.
START POURING IT IN.

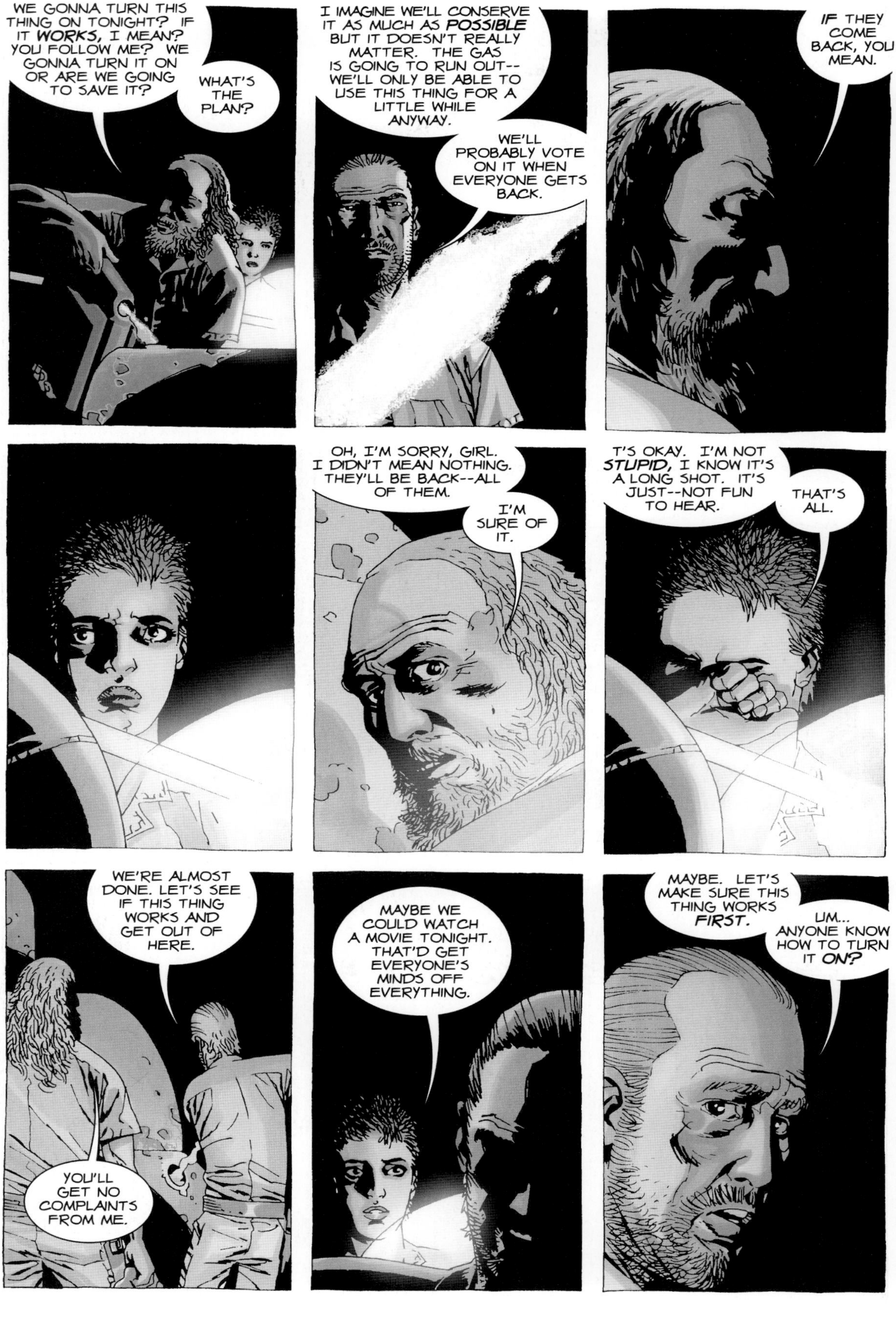
WE GONNA TURN THIS THING ON TONIGHT? IF IT WORKS, I MEAN? YOU FOLLOW ME? WE GONNA TURN IT ON OR ARE WE GOING TO SAVE IT?
WHAT'S THE PLAN?
I IMAGINE WE'LL CONSERVE IT AS MUCH AS POSSIBLE BUT IT DOESN'T REALLY MATTER. THE GAS IS GOING TO RUN OUT-- WE'LL ONLY BE ABLE TO USE THIS THING FOR A LITTLE WHILE ANYWAY.
WE'LL PROBABLY VOTE ON IT WHEN EVERYONE GETS BACK.
IF THEY COME BACK, YOU MEAN.
OH, I'M SORRY, GIRL. I DIDN'T MEAN NOTHING. THEY'LL BE BACK--ALL OF THEM.
I'M SURE OF IT.
T'S OKAY. I'M NOT STUPID, I KNOW IT'S A LONG SHOT. IT'S JUST--NOT FUN TO HEAR.
THAT'S ALL.
WE'RE ALMOST DONE. LET'S SEE IF THIS THING WORKS AND GET OUT OF HERE.
YOU'LL GET NO COMPLAINTS FROM ME.
MAYBE WE COULD WATCH A MOVIE TONIGHT. THAT'D GET EVERYONE'S MINDS OFF EVERYTHING.
MAYBE. LET'S MAKE SURE THIS THING WORKS FIRST.
UM... ANYONE KNOW HOW TO TURN IT ON?

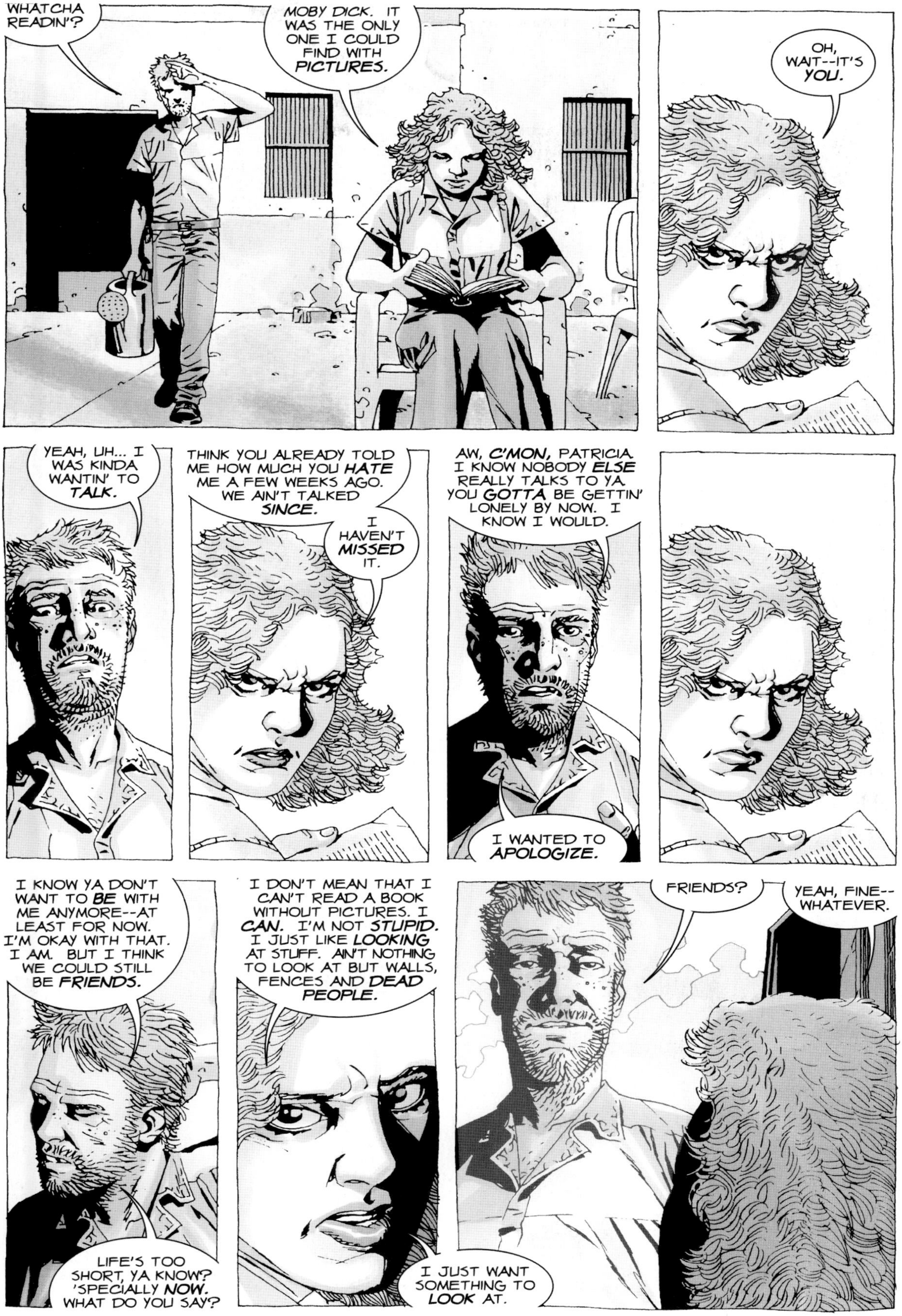
WHATCHA READIN'?
MOBY DICK. IT WAS THE ONLY ONE I COULD FIND WITH PICTURES.
OH, WAIT--IT'S YOU.
YEAH, UH... I WAS KINDA WANTIN' TO TALK.
THINK YOU ALREADY TOLD ME HOW MUCH YOU HATE ME A FEW WEEKS AGO. WE AIN'T TALKED SINCE.
I HAVEN'T MISSED IT.
AW, C'MON, PATRICIA. I KNOW NOBODY ELSE REALLY TALKS TO YA. YOU GOTTA BE GETTIN' LONELY BY NOW. I KNOW I WOULD.
I WANTED TO APOLOGIZE.
I KNOW YA DON'T WANT TO BE WITH ME ANYMORE--AT LEAST FOR NOW. I'M OKAY WITH THAT. I AM. BUT I THINK WE COULD STILL BE FRIENDS.
LIFE'S TOO SHORT, YA KNOW? 'SPECIALLY NOW. WHAT DO YOU SAY?
I DON'T MEAN THAT I CAN'T READ A BOOK WITHOUT PICTURES. I CAN. I'M NOT STUPID. I JUST LIKE LOOKING AT STUFF. AIN'T NOTHING TO LOOK AT BUT WALLS, FENCES AND DEAD PEOPLE.
I JUST WANT SOMETHING TO LOOK AT.
FRIENDS?
YEAH, FINE--WHATEVER.

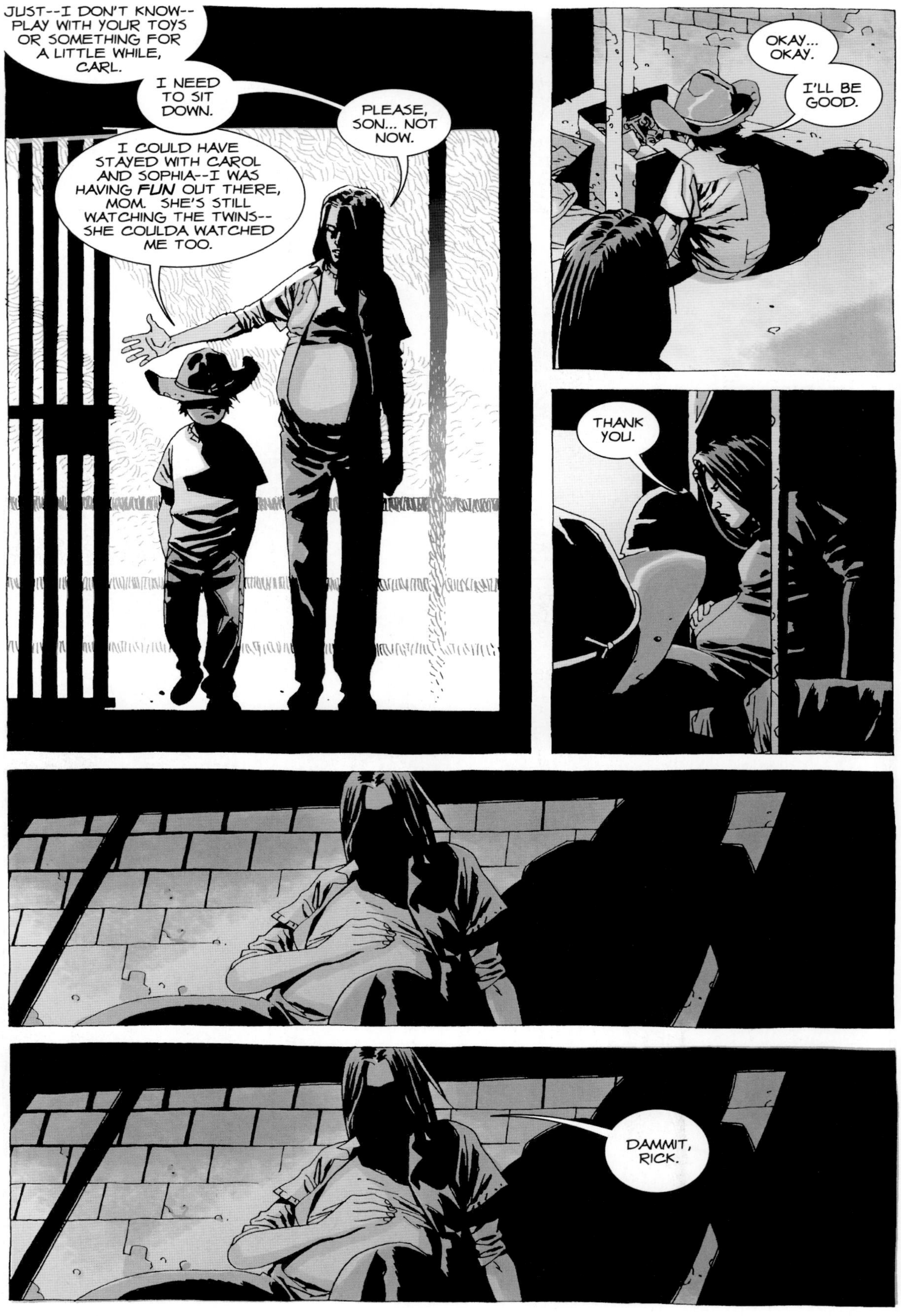
JUST--I DON'T KNOW-- PLAY WITH YOUR TOYS OR SOMETHING FOR A LITTLE WHILE, CARL.
I NEED TO SIT DOWN.
I COULD HAVE STAYED WITH CAROL AND SOPHIA--I WAS HAVING FUN OUT THERE, MOM. SHE'S STILL WATCHING THE TWINS-- SHE COULDA WATCHED ME TOO.
PLEASE, SON... NOT NOW.
OKAY... OKAY.
I'LL BE GOOD.
THANK YOU.
DAMMIT, RICK.

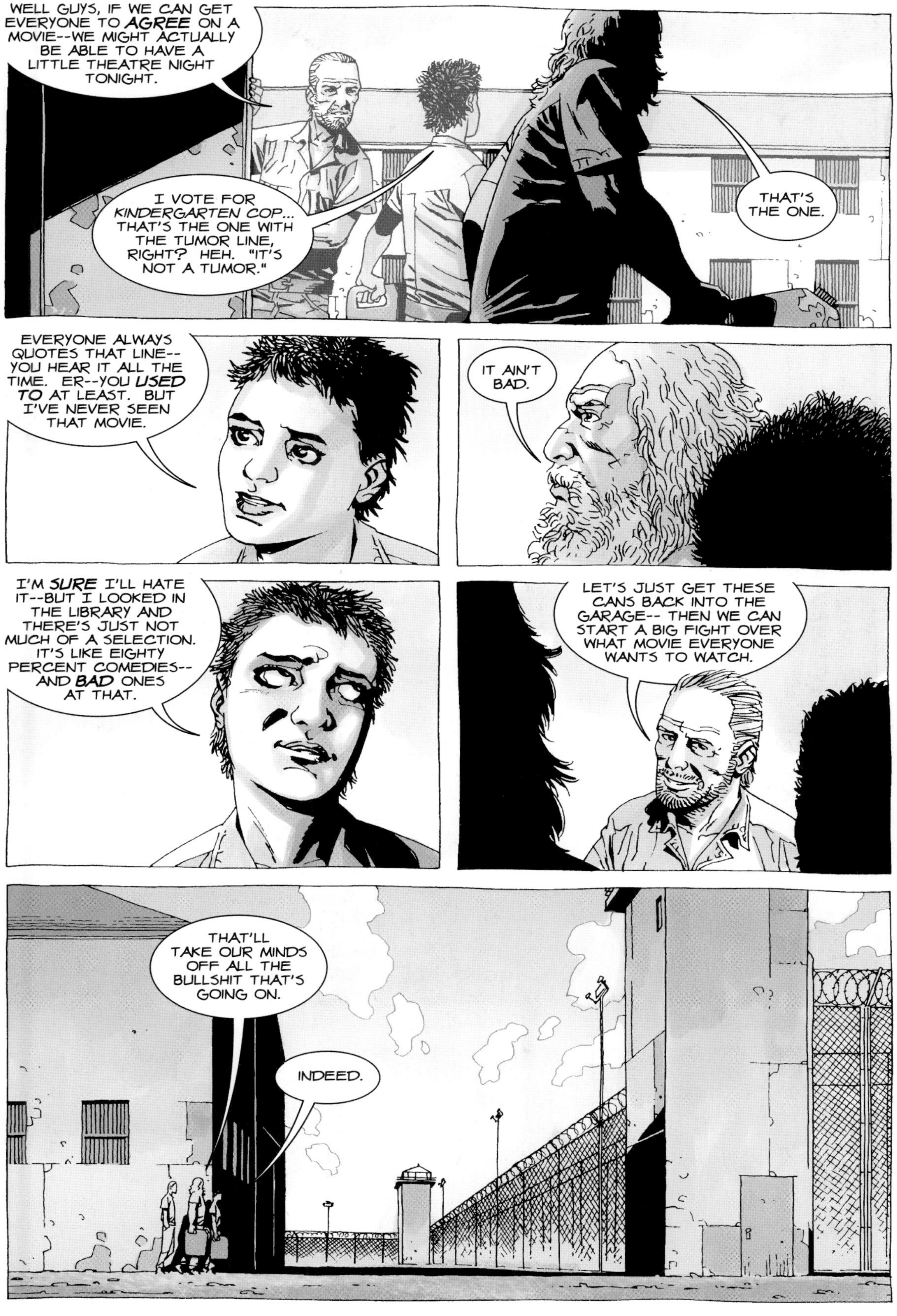
WELL GUYS, IF WE CAN GET EVERYONE TO AGREE ON A MOVIE--WE MIGHT ACTUALLY BE ABLE TO HAVE A LITTLE THEATRE NIGHT TONIGHT.
I VOTE FOR KINDERGARTEN COP... THAT'S THE ONE WITH THE TUMOR LINE, RIGHT? HEH. "IT'S NOT A TUMOR."
THAT'S THE ONE.
EVERYONE ALWAYS QUOTES THAT LINE--YOU HEAR IT ALL THE TIME. ER--YOU USED TO AT LEAST. BUT I'VE NEVER SEEN THAT MOVIE.
IT AIN'T BAD.
I'M SURE I'LL HATE IT--BUT I LOOKED IN THE LIBRARY AND THERE'S JUST NOT MUCH OF A SELECTION. IT'S LIKE EIGHTY PERCENT COMEDIES--AND BAD ONES AT THAT.
LET'S JUST GET THESE CANS BACK INTO THE GARAGE-- THEN WE CAN START A BIG FIGHT OVER WHAT MOVIE EVERYONE WANTS TO WATCH.
THAT'LL TAKE OUR MINDS OFF ALL THE BULLSHIT THAT'S GOING ON.
INDEED.

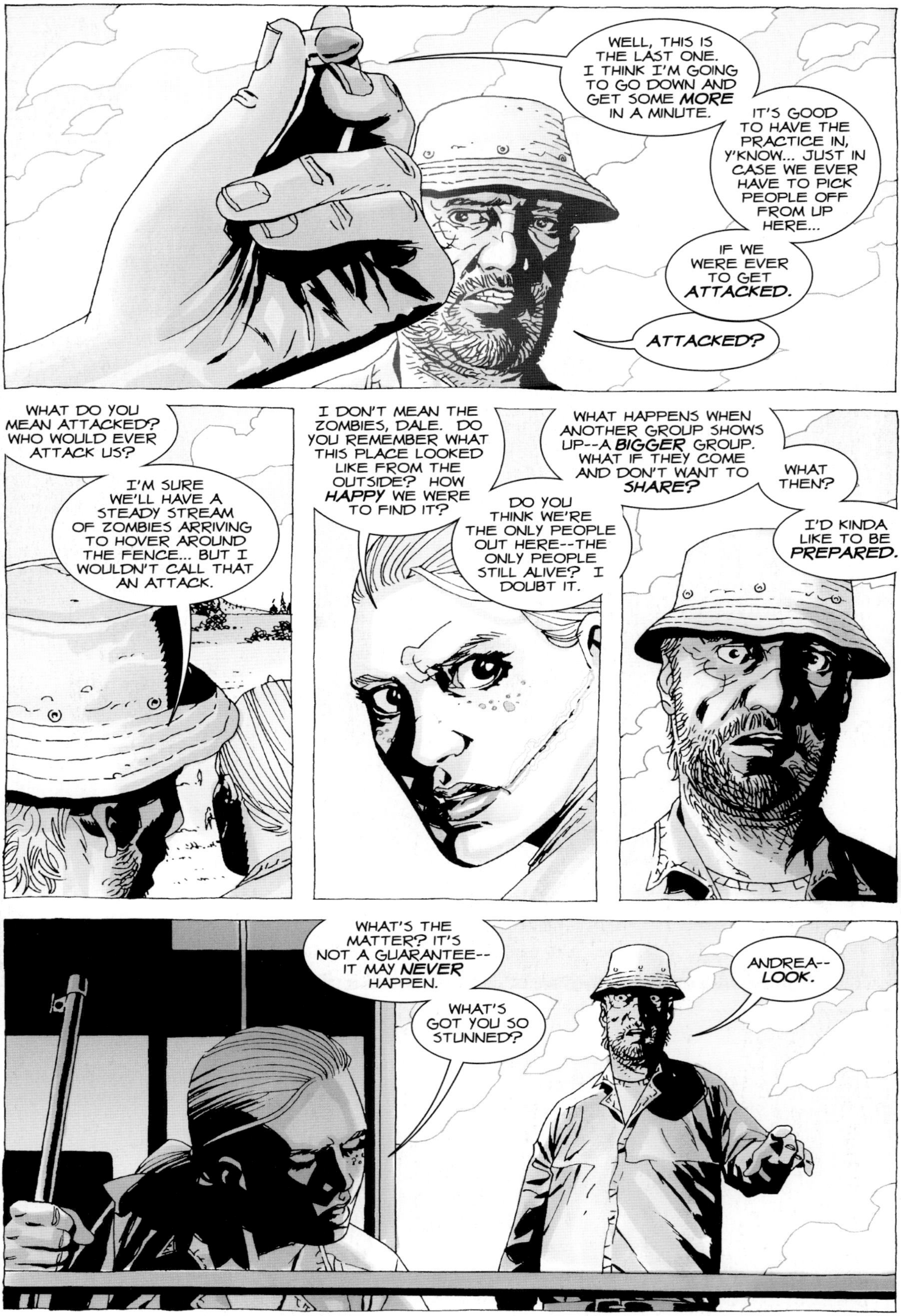
WELL, THIS IS THE LAST ONE. I THINK I'M GOING TO GO DOWN AND GET SOME **MORE** IN A MINUTE.
IT'S GOOD TO HAVE THE PRACTICE IN, Y'KNOW... JUST IN CASE WE EVER HAVE TO PICK PEOPLE OFF FROM UP HERE...
IF WE WERE EVER TO GET **ATTACKED.**
ATTACKED?
WHAT DO YOU MEAN ATTACKED? WHO WOULD EVER ATTACK US?
I'M SURE WE'LL HAVE A STEADY STREAM OF ZOMBIES ARRIVING TO HOVER AROUND THE FENCE... BUT I WOULDN'T CALL THAT AN ATTACK.
I DON'T MEAN THE ZOMBIES, DALE. DO YOU REMEMBER WHAT THIS PLACE LOOKED LIKE FROM THE OUTSIDE? HOW **HAPPY** WE WERE TO FIND IT?
DO YOU THINK WE'RE THE ONLY PEOPLE OUT HERE--THE ONLY PEOPLE STILL ALIVE? I DOUBT IT.
WHAT HAPPENS WHEN ANOTHER GROUP SHOWS UP--A **BIGGER** GROUP. WHAT IF THEY COME AND DON'T WANT TO **SHARE?**
WHAT THEN?
I'D KINDA LIKE TO BE **PREPARED.**
WHAT'S THE MATTER? IT'S NOT A GUARANTEE-- IT MAY **NEVER** HAPPEN.
WHAT'S GOT YOU SO STUNNED?
ANDREA-- **LOOK.**

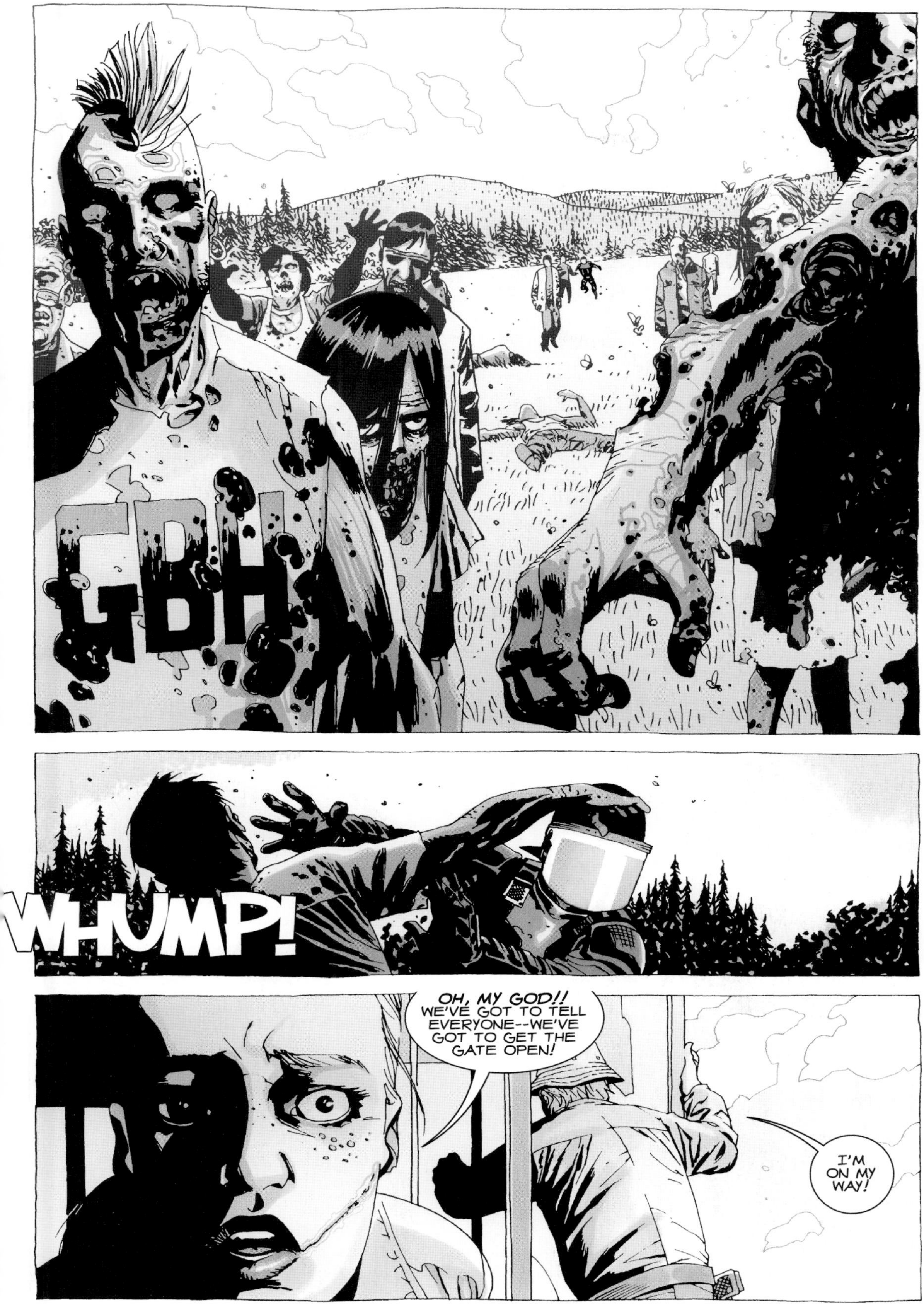
GBH
WHUMP!
OH, MY GOD!! WE'VE GOT TO TELL EVERYONE--WE'VE GOT TO GET THE GATE OPEN!
I'M ON MY WAY!

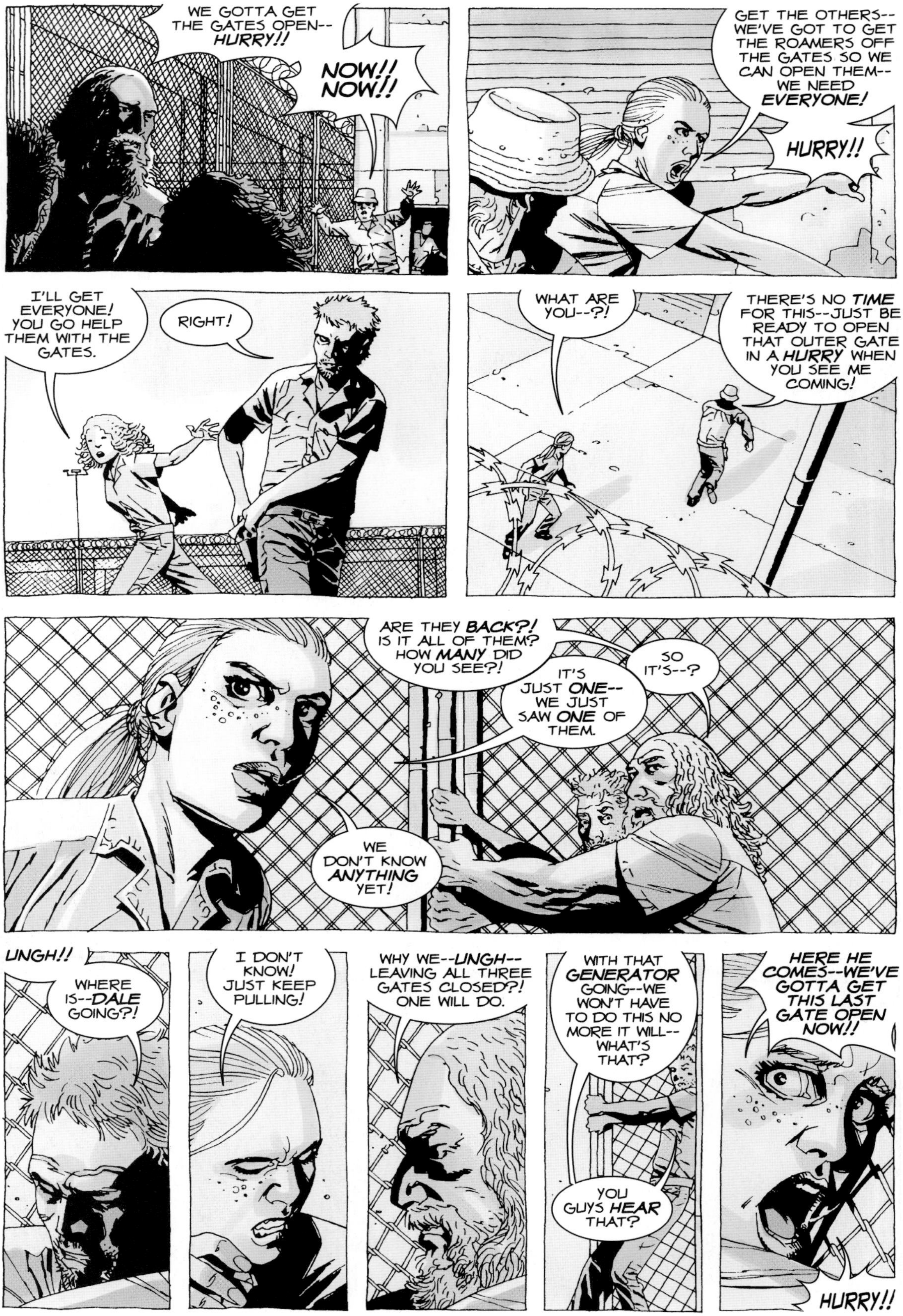
WE GOTTA GET THE GATES OPEN-- HURRY!!
NOW!! NOW!!
GET THE OTHERS-- WE'VE GOT TO GET THE ROAMERS OFF THE GATES SO WE CAN OPEN THEM-- WE NEED EVERYONE!
HURRY!!
I'LL GET EVERYONE! YOU GO HELP THEM WITH THE GATES.
RIGHT!
WHAT ARE YOU--?!
THERE'S NO TIME FOR THIS--JUST BE READY TO OPEN THAT OUTER GATE IN A HURRY WHEN YOU SEE ME COMING!
ARE THEY BACK?! IS IT ALL OF THEM? HOW MANY DID YOU SEE?!
SO IT'S--?
IT'S JUST ONE-- WE JUST SAW ONE OF THEM.
WE DON'T KNOW ANYTHING YET!
UNGH!!
WHERE IS--DALE GOING?!
I DON'T KNOW! JUST KEEP PULLING!
WHY WE--UNGH-- LEAVING ALL THREE GATES CLOSED?! ONE WILL DO.
WITH THAT GENERATOR GOING--WE WON'T HAVE TO DO THIS NO MORE IT WILL-- WHAT'S THAT?
YOU GUYS HEAR THAT?
HERE HE COMES--WE'VE GOTTA GET THIS LAST GATE OPEN NOW!!
HURRY!!

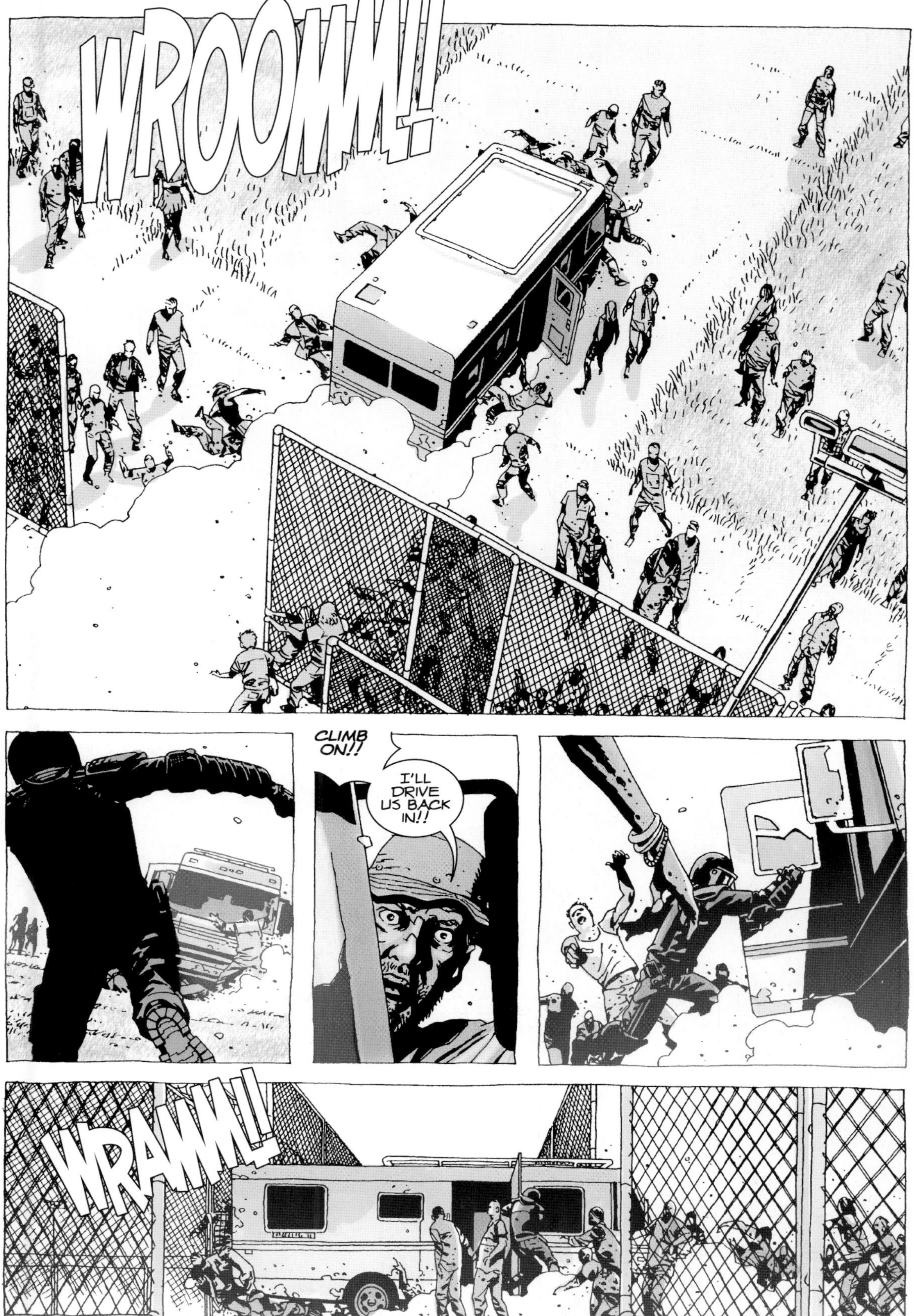
WROOMM!!
CLIMB ON!!
I'LL DRIVE US BACK IN!!
WRAMM!!

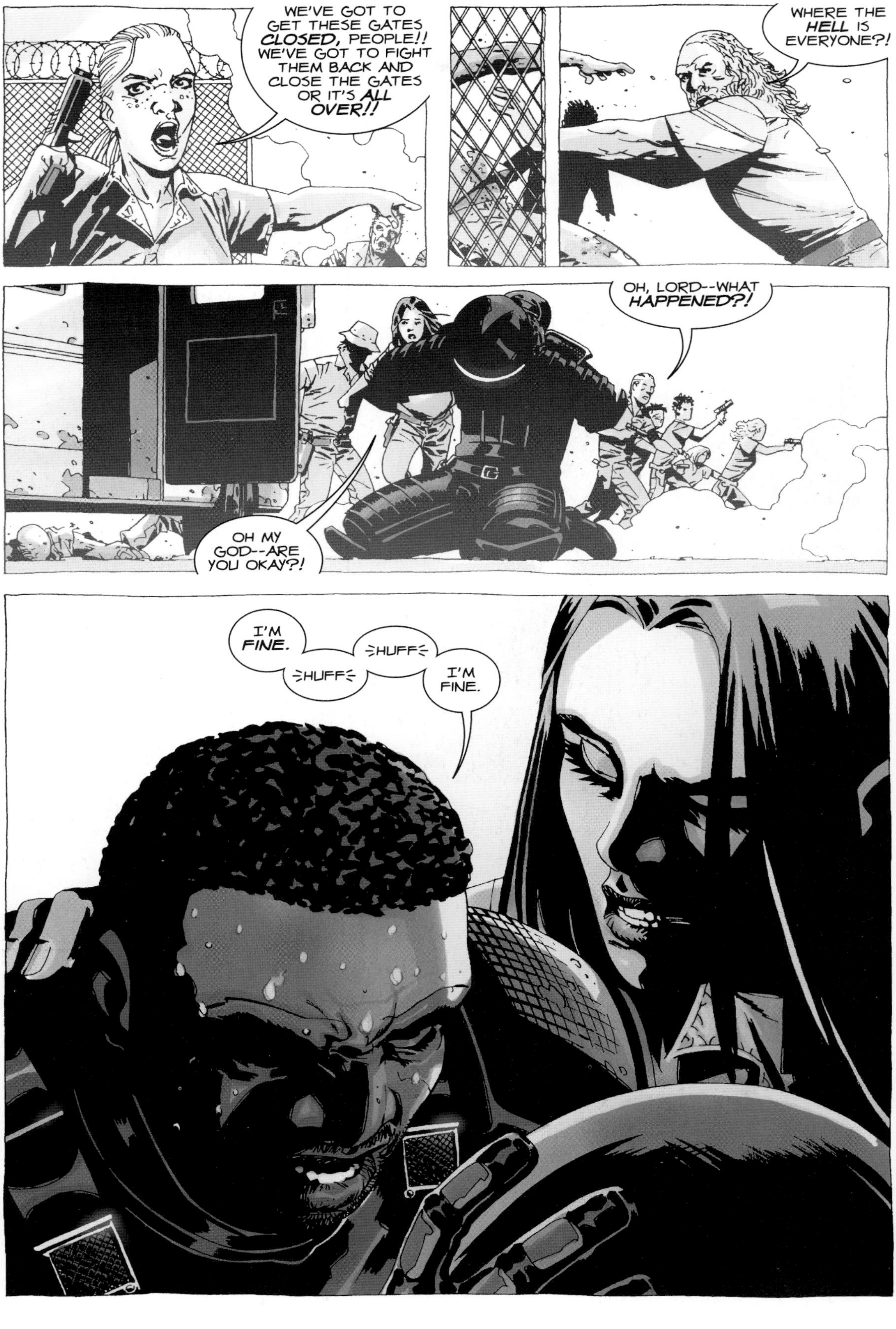
WE'VE GOT TO GET THESE GATES CLOSED, PEOPLE!! WE'VE GOT TO FIGHT THEM BACK AND CLOSE THE GATES OR IT'S ALL OVER!!
WHERE THE HELL IS EVERYONE?!
OH, LORD--WHAT HAPPENED?!
OH MY GOD--ARE YOU OKAY?!
I'M FINE.
HUFF
HUFF
I'M FINE.

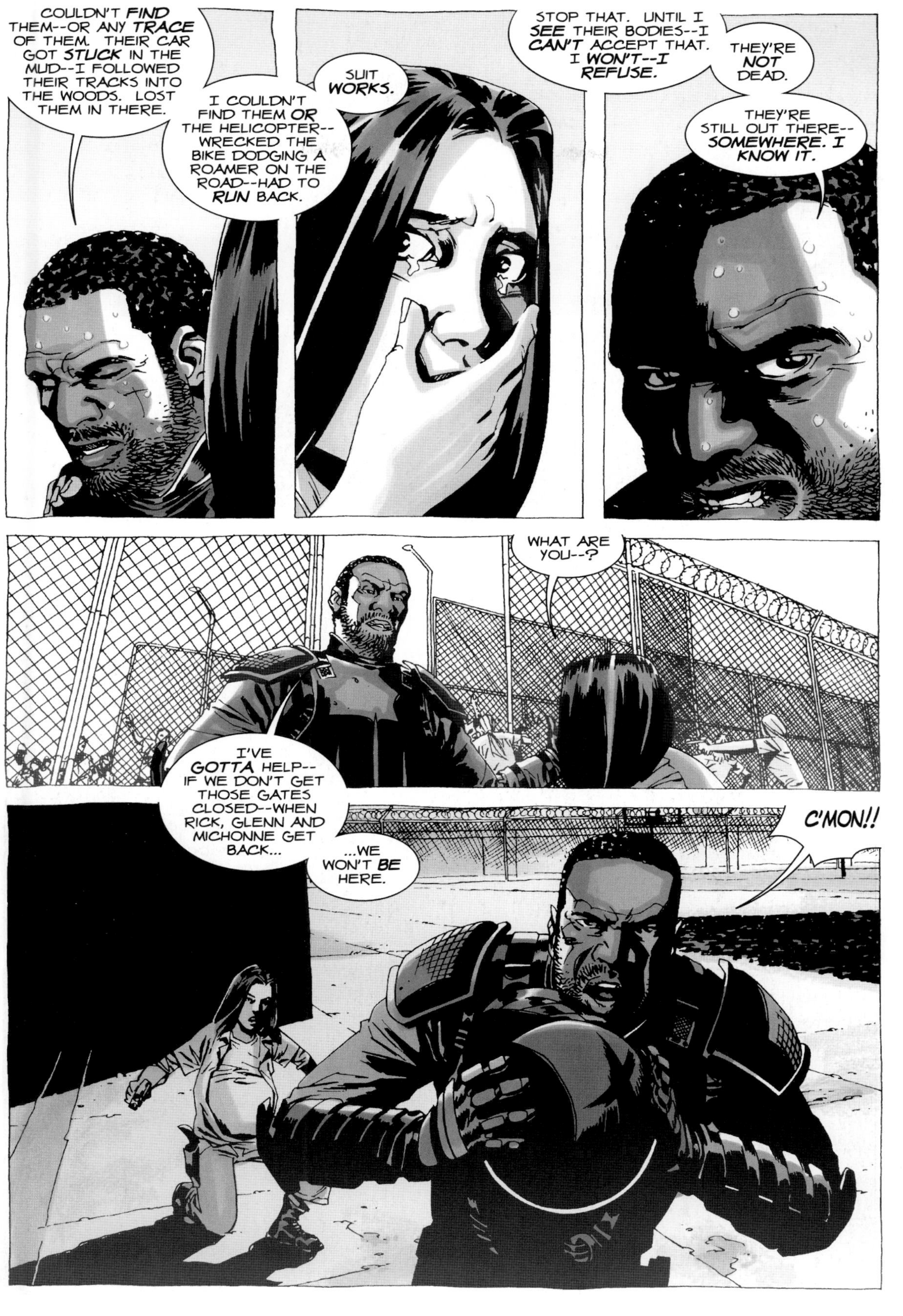

COULDN'T FIND THEM--OR ANY TRACE OF THEM. THEIR CAR GOT STUCK IN THE MUD--I FOLLOWED THEIR TRACKS INTO THE WOODS. LOST THEM IN THERE.
I COULDN'T FIND THEM OR THE HELICOPTER-- WRECKED THE BIKE DODGING A ROAMER ON THE ROAD--HAD TO RUN BACK.
SUIT WORKS.
STOP THAT. UNTIL I SEE THEIR BODIES--I CAN'T ACCEPT THAT. I WON'T--I REFUSE.
THEY'RE NOT DEAD.
THEY'RE STILL OUT THERE-- SOMEWHERE. I KNOW IT.
WHAT ARE YOU--?
I'VE GOTTA HELP-- IF WE DON'T GET THOSE GATES CLOSED--WHEN RICK, GLENN AND MICHONNE GET BACK...
...WE WON'T BE HERE.
C'MON!!

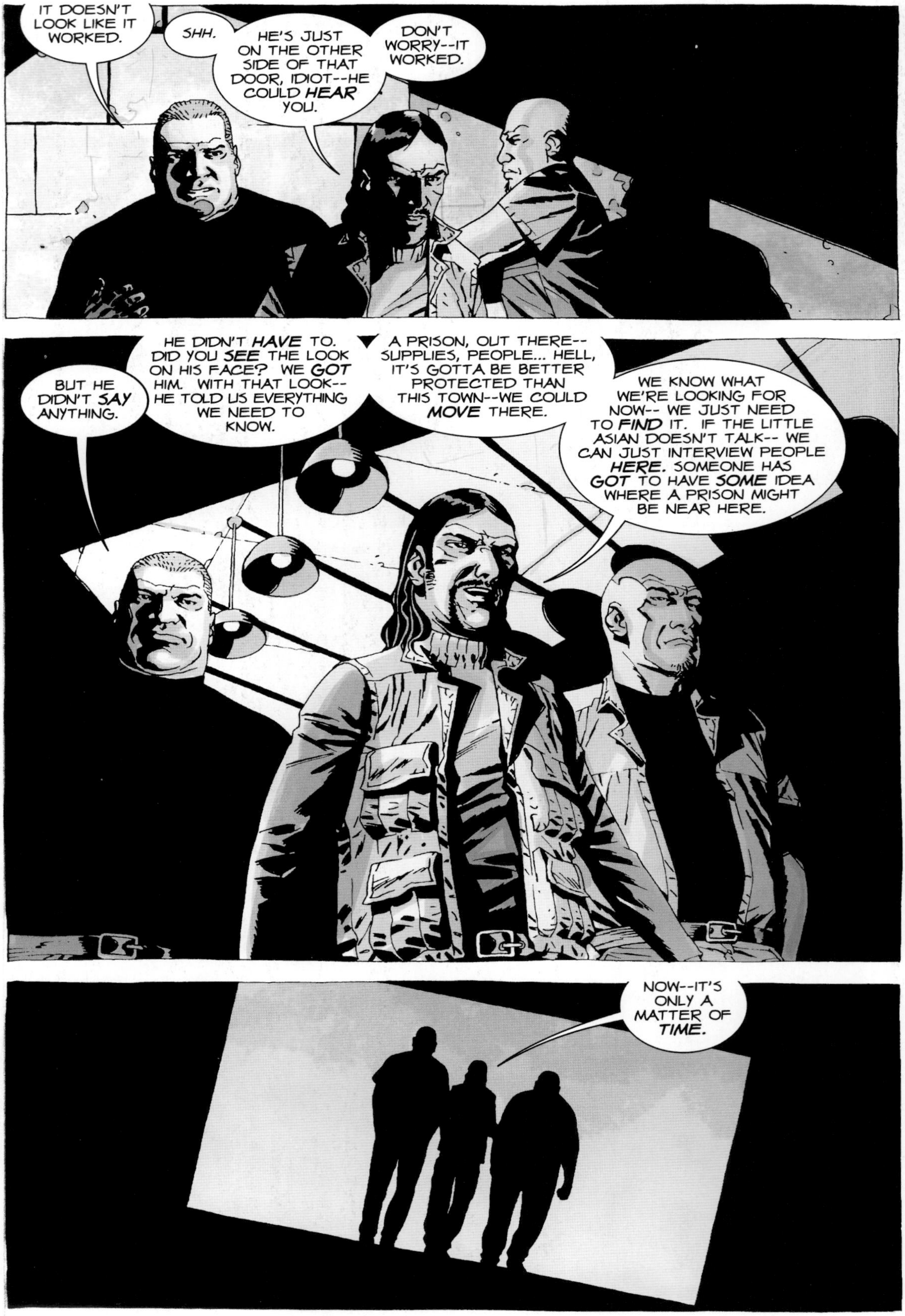
IT DOESN'T LOOK LIKE IT WORKED.
SHH.
HE'S JUST ON THE OTHER SIDE OF THAT DOOR, IDIOT--HE COULD HEAR YOU.
DON'T WORRY--IT WORKED.
BUT HE DIDN'T SAY ANYTHING.
HE DIDN'T HAVE TO. DID YOU SEE THE LOOK ON HIS FACE? WE GOT HIM. WITH THAT LOOK--HE TOLD US EVERYTHING WE NEED TO KNOW.
A PRISON, OUT THERE--SUPPLIES, PEOPLE... HELL, IT'S GOTTA BE BETTER PROTECTED THAN THIS TOWN--WE COULD MOVE THERE.
WE KNOW WHAT WE'RE LOOKING FOR NOW-- WE JUST NEED TO FIND IT. IF THE LITTLE ASIAN DOESN'T TALK-- WE CAN JUST INTERVIEW PEOPLE HERE. SOMEONE HAS GOT TO HAVE SOME IDEA WHERE A PRISON MIGHT BE NEAR HERE.
NOW--IT'S ONLY A MATTER OF TIME.

Chapter Six:
This Sorrowful Life

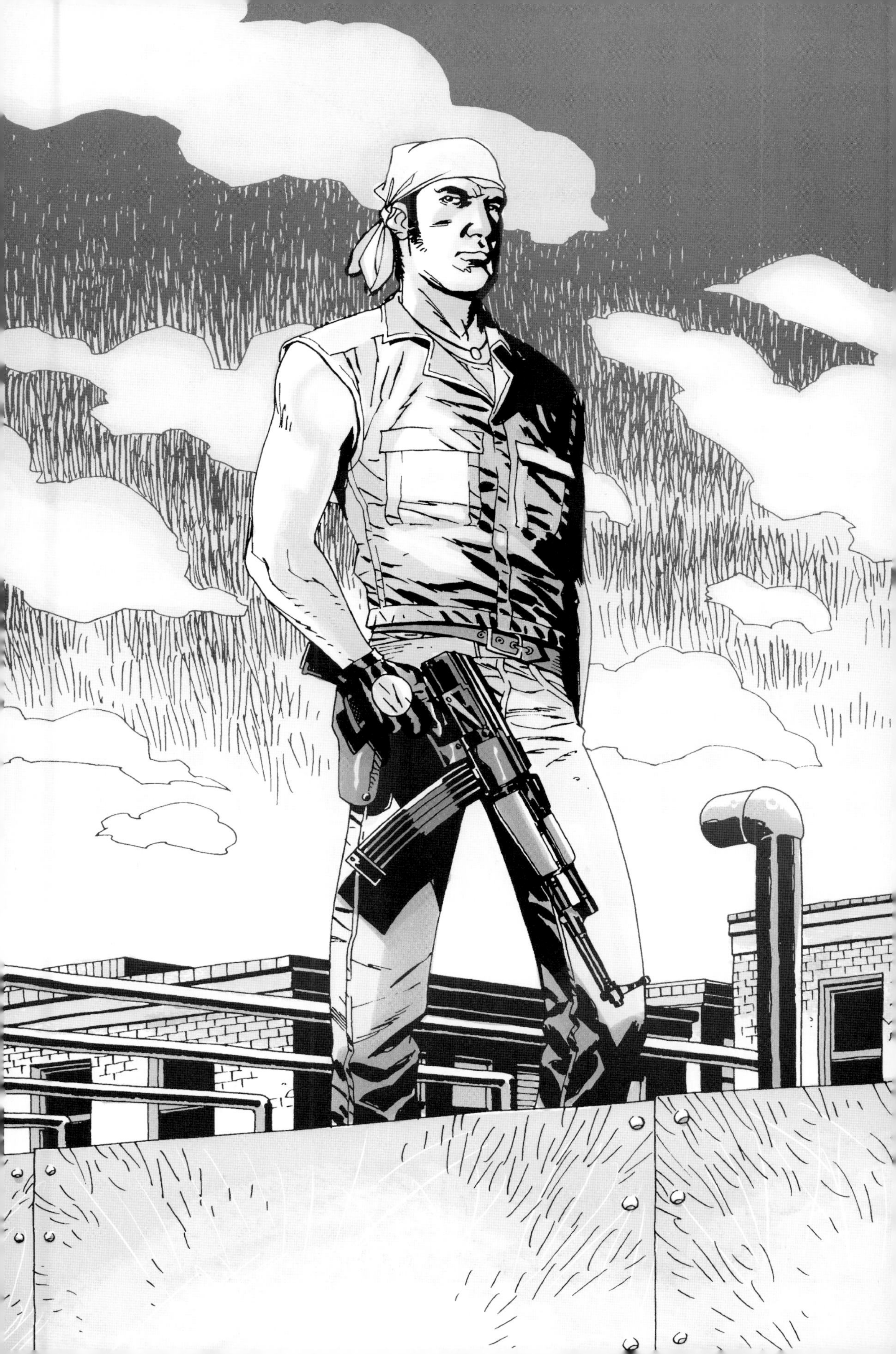

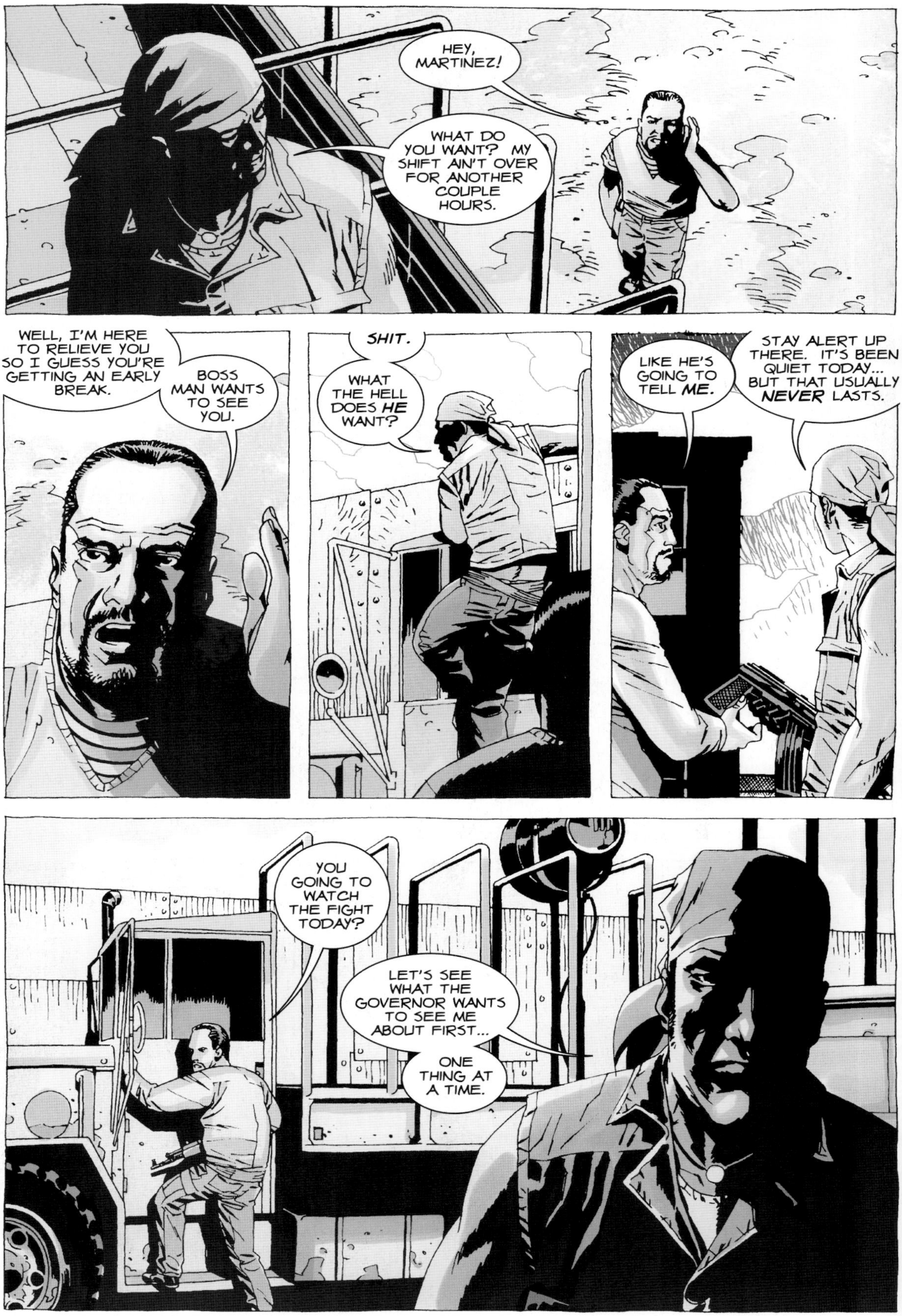
HEY, MARTINEZ!
WHAT DO YOU WANT? MY SHIFT AIN'T OVER FOR ANOTHER COUPLE HOURS.
WELL, I'M HERE TO RELIEVE YOU SO I GUESS YOU'RE GETTING AN EARLY BREAK.
BOSS MAN WANTS TO SEE YOU.
SHIT.
WHAT THE HELL DOES HE WANT?
LIKE HE'S GOING TO TELL ME.
STAY ALERT UP THERE. IT'S BEEN QUIET TODAY... BUT THAT USUALLY NEVER LASTS.
YOU GOING TO WATCH THE FIGHT TODAY?
LET'S SEE WHAT THE GOVERNOR WANTS TO SEE ME ABOUT FIRST...
ONE THING AT A TIME.

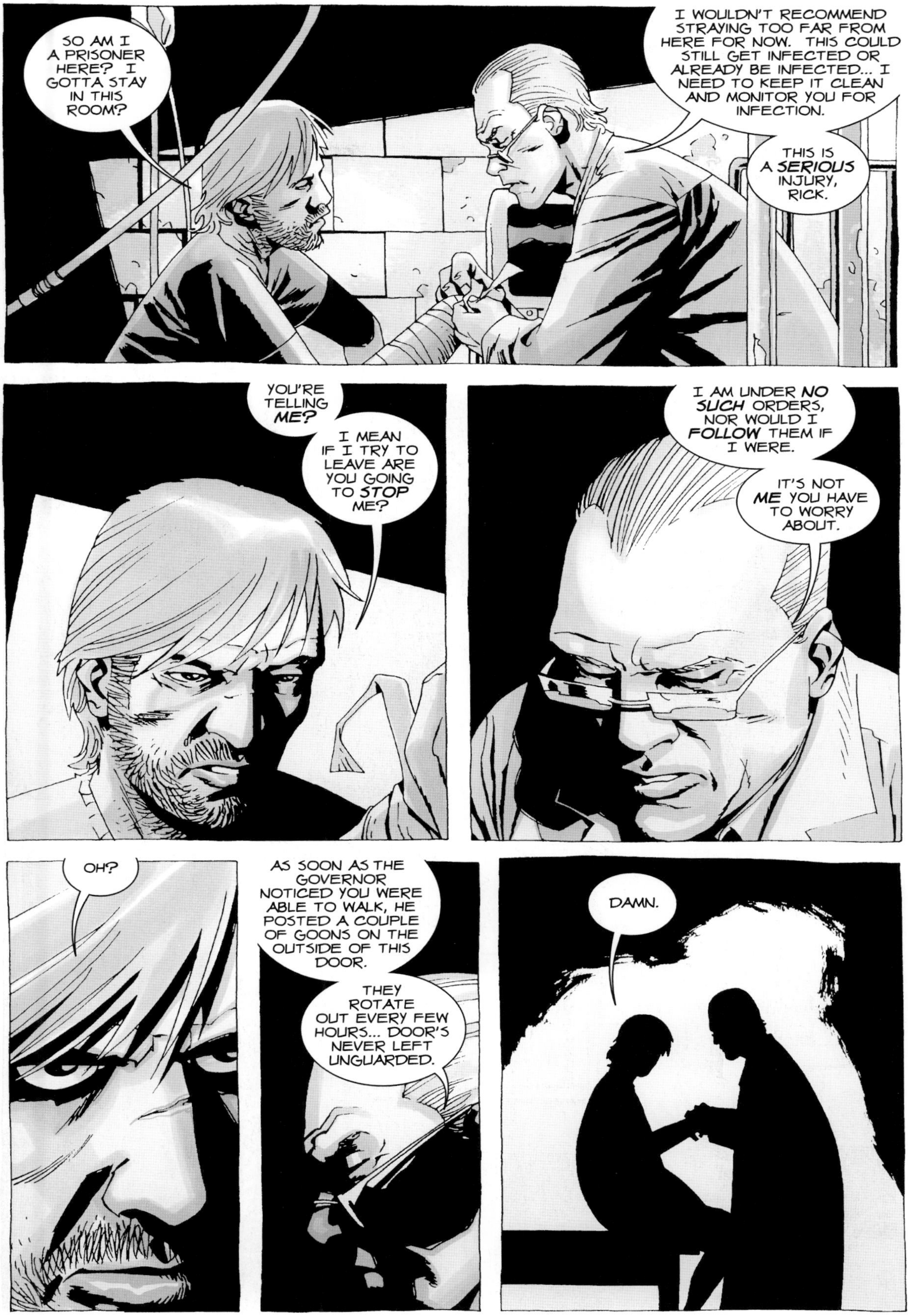
SO AM I A PRISONER HERE? I GOTTA STAY IN THIS ROOM?
I WOULDN'T RECOMMEND STRAYING TOO FAR FROM HERE FOR NOW. THIS COULD STILL GET INFECTED OR ALREADY BE INFECTED... I NEED TO KEEP IT CLEAN AND MONITOR YOU FOR INFECTION.
THIS IS A SERIOUS INJURY, RICK.
YOU'RE TELLING ME?
I MEAN IF I TRY TO LEAVE ARE YOU GOING TO STOP ME?
I AM UNDER NO SUCH ORDERS, NOR WOULD I FOLLOW THEM IF I WERE.
IT'S NOT ME YOU HAVE TO WORRY ABOUT.
OH?
AS SOON AS THE GOVERNOR NOTICED YOU WERE ABLE TO WALK, HE POSTED A COUPLE OF GOONS ON THE OUTSIDE OF THIS DOOR.
THEY ROTATE OUT EVERY FEW HOURS... DOOR'S NEVER LEFT UNGUARDED.
DAMN.

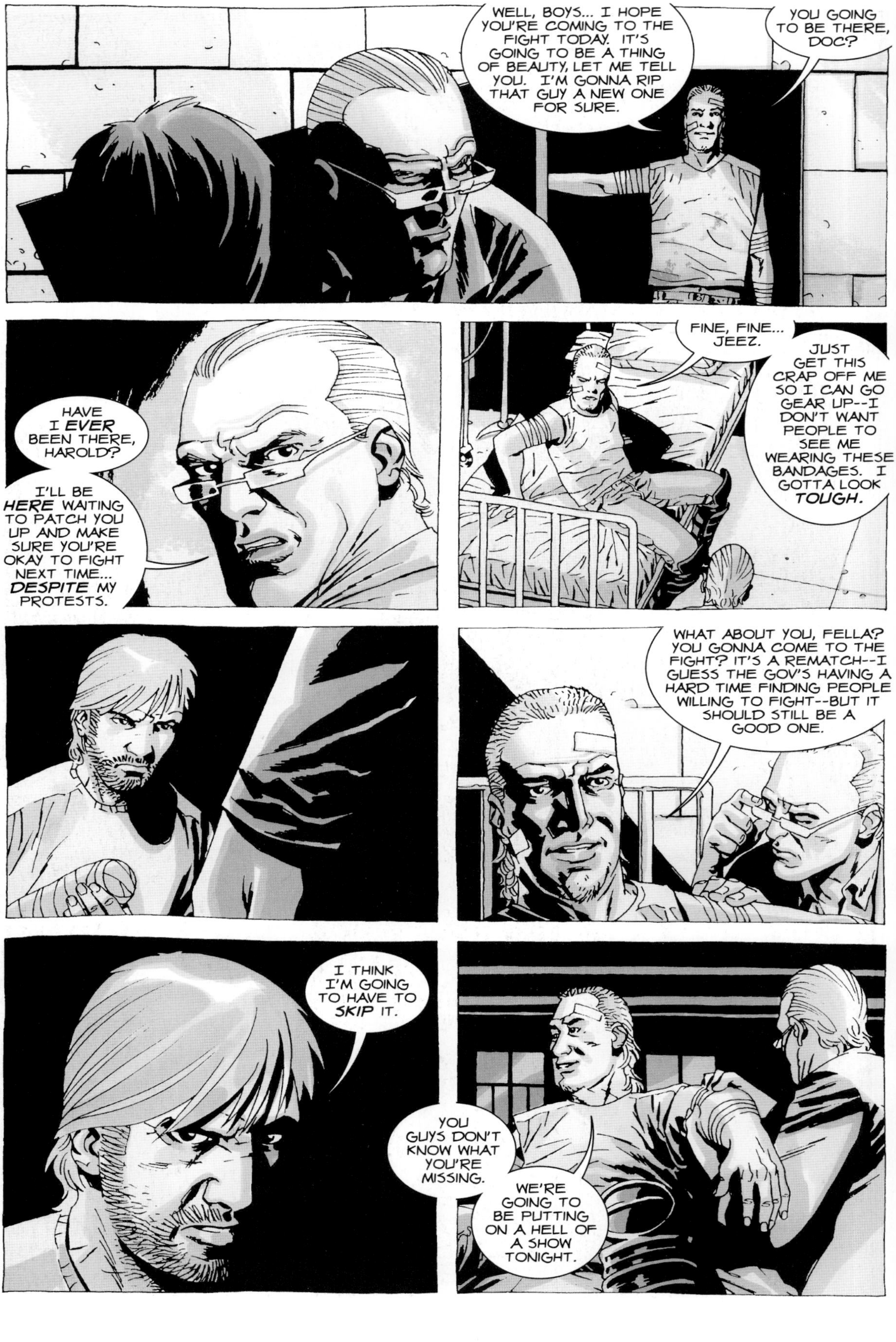
WELL, BOYS... I HOPE YOU'RE COMING TO THE FIGHT TODAY. IT'S GOING TO BE A THING OF BEAUTY, LET ME TELL YOU. I'M GONNA RIP THAT GUY A NEW ONE FOR SURE.
YOU GOING TO BE THERE, DOC?
HAVE I EVER BEEN THERE, HAROLD?
I'LL BE HERE WAITING TO PATCH YOU UP AND MAKE SURE YOU'RE OKAY TO FIGHT NEXT TIME... DESPITE MY PROTESTS.
FINE, FINE... JEEZ.
JUST GET THIS CRAP OFF ME SO I CAN GO GEAR UP--I DON'T WANT PEOPLE TO SEE ME WEARING THESE BANDAGES. I GOTTA LOOK TOUGH.
WHAT ABOUT YOU, FELLA? YOU GONNA COME TO THE FIGHT? IT'S A REMATCH--I GUESS THE GOV'S HAVING A HARD TIME FINDING PEOPLE WILLING TO FIGHT--BUT IT SHOULD STILL BE A GOOD ONE.
I THINK I'M GOING TO HAVE TO SKIP IT.
YOU GUYS DON'T KNOW WHAT YOU'RE MISSING.
WE'RE GOING TO BE PUTTING ON A HELL OF A SHOW TONIGHT.

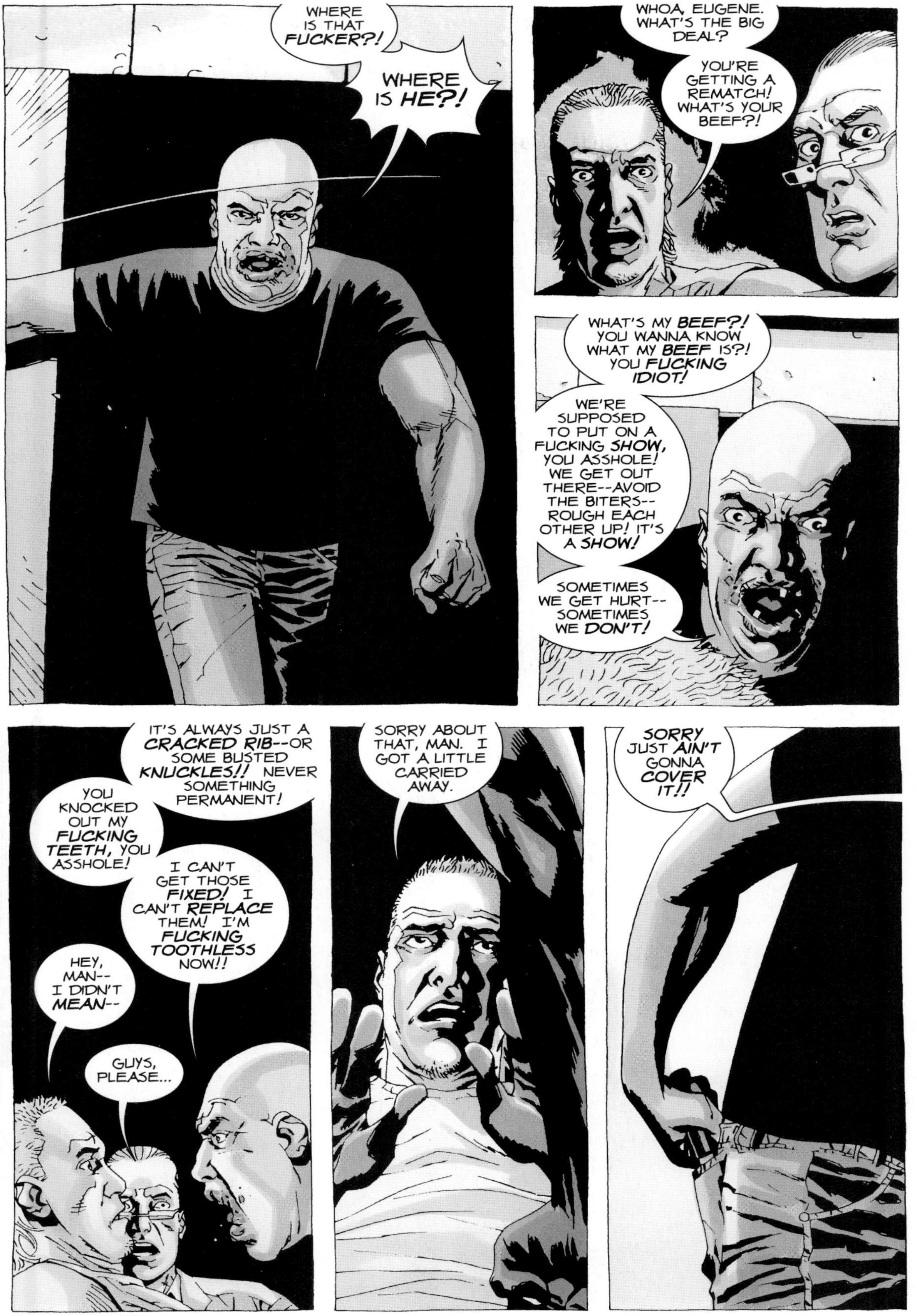
WHERE IS THAT FUCKER?!
WHERE IS HE?!
WHOA, EUGENE. WHAT'S THE BIG DEAL?
YOU'RE GETTING A REMATCH! WHAT'S YOUR BEEF?!
WHAT'S MY BEEF?! YOU WANNA KNOW WHAT MY BEEF IS?! YOU FUCKING IDIOT!
WE'RE SUPPOSED TO PUT ON A FUCKING SHOW, YOU ASSHOLE! WE GET OUT THERE--AVOID THE BITERS--ROUGH EACH OTHER UP! IT'S A SHOW!
SOMETIMES WE GET HURT--SOMETIMES WE DON'T!
IT'S ALWAYS JUST A CRACKED RIB--OR SOME BUSTED KNUCKLES!! NEVER SOMETHING PERMANENT!
YOU KNOCKED OUT MY FUCKING TEETH, YOU ASSHOLE!
I CAN'T GET THOSE FIXED! I CAN'T REPLACE THEM! I'M FUCKING TOOTHLESS NOW!!
HEY, MAN-- I DIDN'T MEAN--
GUYS, PLEASE...
SORRY ABOUT THAT, MAN. I GOT A LITTLE CARRIED AWAY.
SORRY JUST AIN'T GONNA COVER IT!!

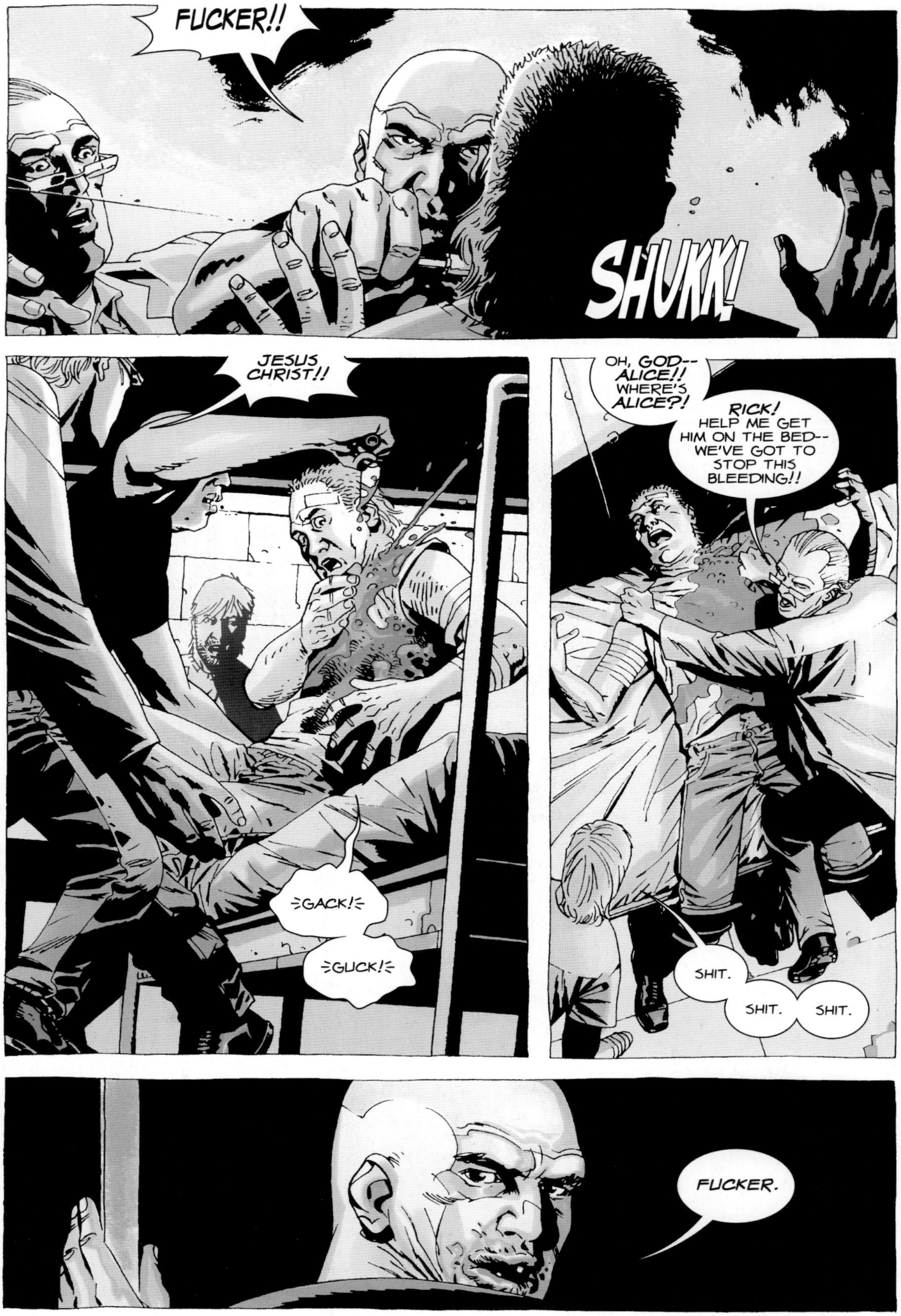
FUCKER!!
SHUKK!
JESUS CHRIST!!
GACK!
GUCK!
OH, GOD-- ALICE!! WHERE'S ALICE?!
RICK! HELP ME GET HIM ON THE BED-- WE'VE GOT TO STOP THIS BLEEDING!!
SHIT.
SHIT.
SHIT.
FUCKER.

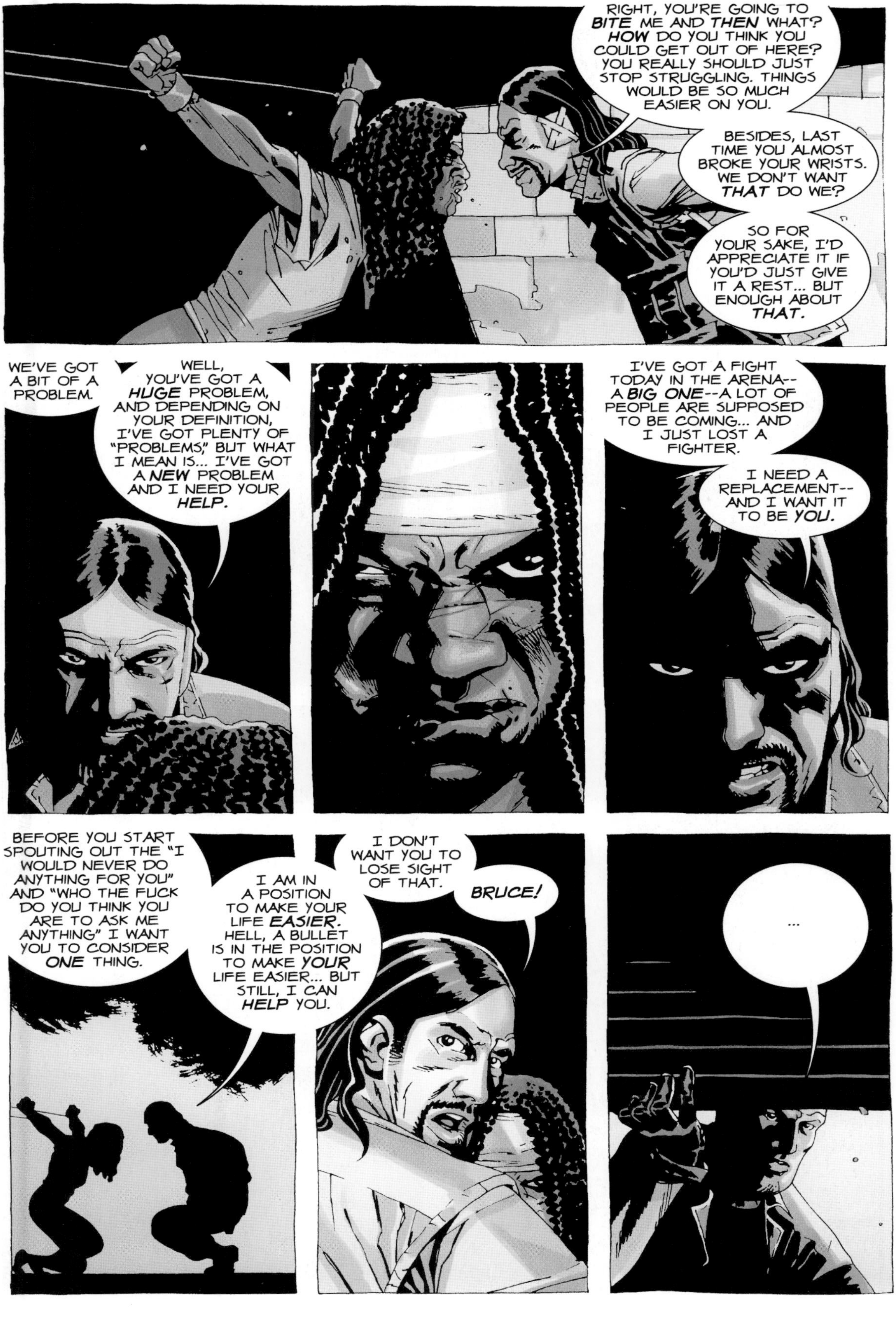
RIGHT, YOU'RE GOING TO BITE ME AND THEN WHAT? HOW DO YOU THINK YOU COULD GET OUT OF HERE? YOU REALLY SHOULD JUST STOP STRUGGLING. THINGS WOULD BE SO MUCH EASIER ON YOU.
BESIDES, LAST TIME YOU ALMOST BROKE YOUR WRISTS. WE DON'T WANT THAT DO WE?
SO FOR YOUR SAKE, I'D APPRECIATE IT IF YOU'D JUST GIVE IT A REST... BUT ENOUGH ABOUT THAT.
WE'VE GOT A BIT OF A PROBLEM.
WELL, YOU'VE GOT A HUGE PROBLEM, AND DEPENDING ON YOUR DEFINITION, I'VE GOT PLENTY OF "PROBLEMS," BUT WHAT I MEAN IS... I'VE GOT A NEW PROBLEM AND I NEED YOUR HELP.
I'VE GOT A FIGHT TODAY IN THE ARENA-- A BIG ONE--A LOT OF PEOPLE ARE SUPPOSED TO BE COMING... AND I JUST LOST A FIGHTER.
I NEED A REPLACEMENT-- AND I WANT IT TO BE YOU.
BEFORE YOU START SPOUTING OUT THE "I WOULD NEVER DO ANYTHING FOR YOU" AND "WHO THE FUCK DO YOU THINK YOU ARE TO ASK ME ANYTHING" I WANT YOU TO CONSIDER ONE THING.
I AM IN A POSITION TO MAKE YOUR LIFE EASIER. HELL, A BULLET IS IN THE POSITION TO MAKE YOUR LIFE EASIER... BUT STILL, I CAN HELP YOU.
I DON'T WANT YOU TO LOSE SIGHT OF THAT.
BRUCE!
...

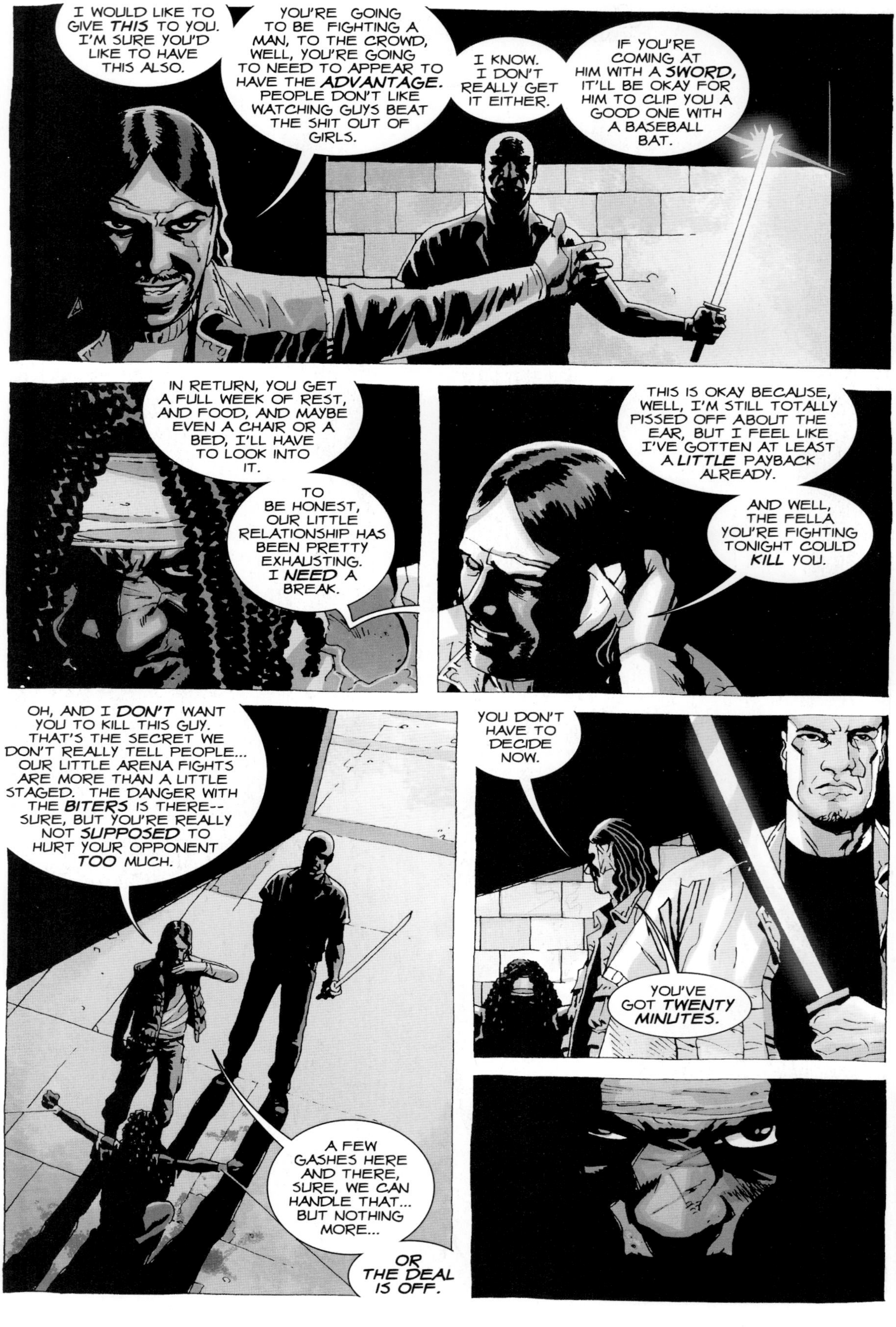
I WOULD LIKE TO GIVE THIS TO YOU. I'M SURE YOU'D LIKE TO HAVE THIS ALSO.
YOU'RE GOING TO BE FIGHTING A MAN, TO THE CROWD, WELL, YOU'RE GOING TO NEED TO APPEAR TO HAVE THE ADVANTAGE. PEOPLE DON'T LIKE WATCHING GUYS BEAT THE SHIT OUT OF GIRLS.
I KNOW. I DON'T REALLY GET IT EITHER.
IF YOU'RE COMING AT HIM WITH A SWORD, IT'LL BE OKAY FOR HIM TO CLIP YOU A GOOD ONE WITH A BASEBALL BAT.
IN RETURN, YOU GET A FULL WEEK OF REST, AND FOOD, AND MAYBE EVEN A CHAIR OR A BED, I'LL HAVE TO LOOK INTO IT.
TO BE HONEST, OUR LITTLE RELATIONSHIP HAS BEEN PRETTY EXHAUSTING. I NEED A BREAK.
THIS IS OKAY BECAUSE, WELL, I'M STILL TOTALLY PISSED OFF ABOUT THE EAR, BUT I FEEL LIKE I'VE GOTTEN AT LEAST A LITTLE PAYBACK ALREADY.
AND WELL, THE FELLA YOU'RE FIGHTING TONIGHT COULD KILL YOU.
OH, AND I DON'T WANT YOU TO KILL THIS GUY. THAT'S THE SECRET WE DON'T REALLY TELL PEOPLE... OUR LITTLE ARENA FIGHTS ARE MORE THAN A LITTLE STAGED. THE DANGER WITH THE BITERS IS THERE-- SURE, BUT YOU'RE REALLY NOT SUPPOSED TO HURT YOUR OPPONENT TOO MUCH.
A FEW GASHES HERE AND THERE, SURE, WE CAN HANDLE THAT... BUT NOTHING MORE...
OR THE DEAL IS OFF.
YOU DON'T HAVE TO DECIDE NOW.
YOU'VE GOT TWENTY MINUTES.

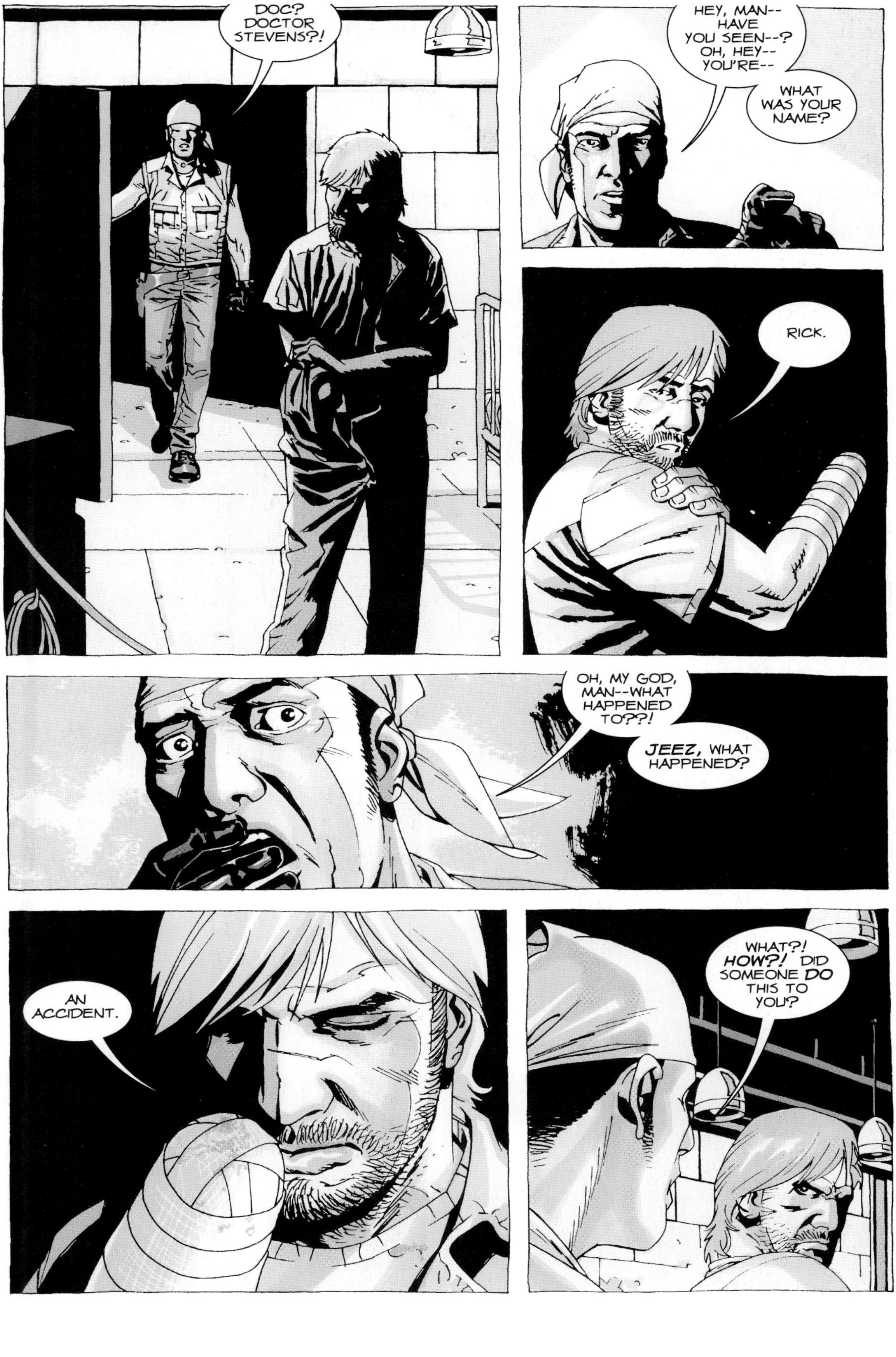
DOC? DOCTOR STEVENS?!
HEY, MAN-- HAVE YOU SEEN--? OH, HEY-- YOU'RE--
WHAT WAS YOUR NAME?
RICK.
OH, MY GOD, MAN--WHAT HAPPENED TO??!
JEEZ, WHAT HAPPENED?
AN ACCIDENT.
WHAT?! HOW?! DID SOMEONE DO THIS TO YOU?

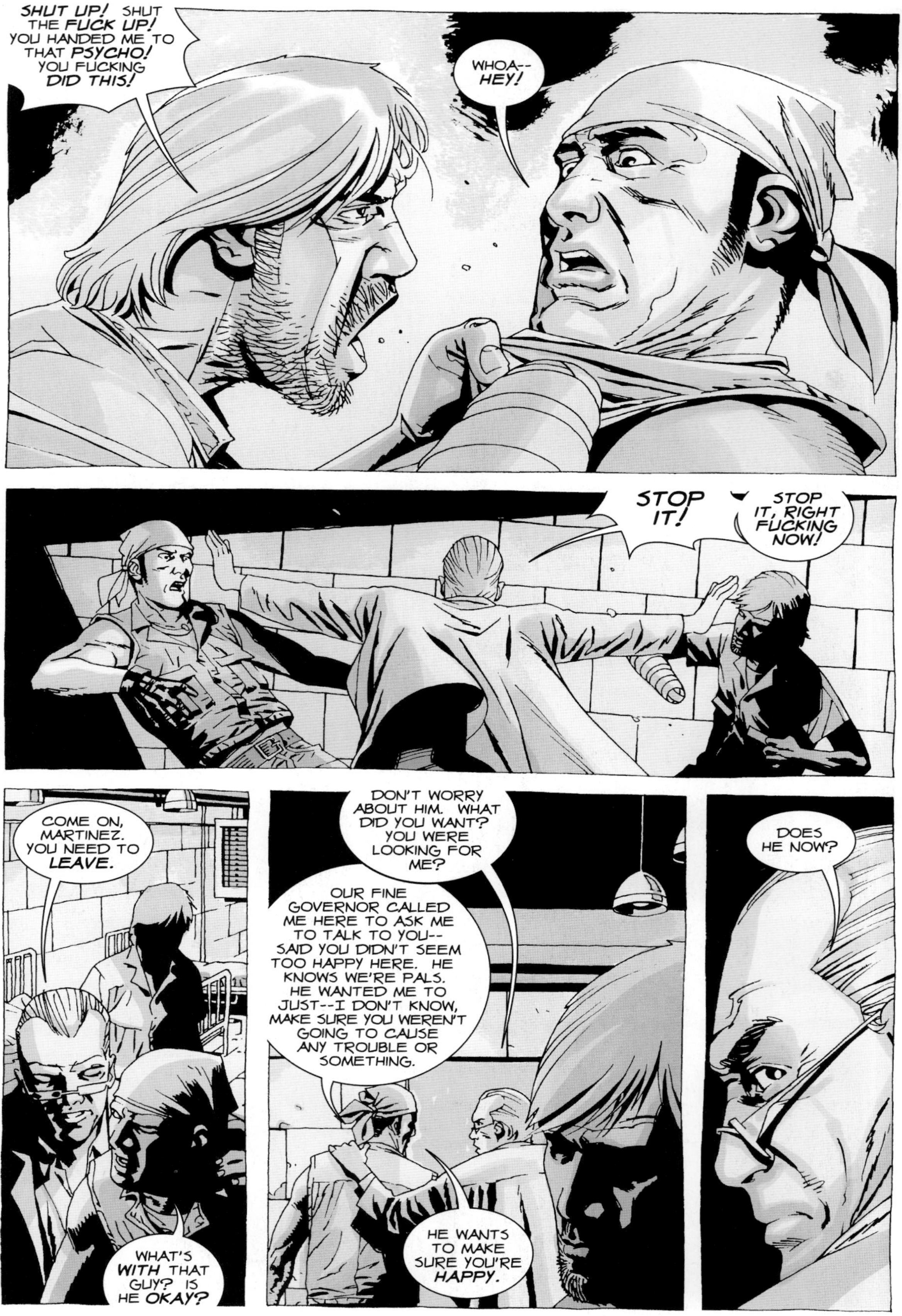
SHUT UP! SHUT THE FUCK UP! YOU HANDED ME TO THAT PSYCHO! YOU FUCKING DID THIS!
WHOA-- HEY!
STOP IT!
STOP IT, RIGHT FUCKING NOW!
COME ON, MARTINEZ. YOU NEED TO LEAVE.
WHAT'S WITH THAT GUY? IS HE OKAY?
DON'T WORRY ABOUT HIM. WHAT DID YOU WANT? YOU WERE LOOKING FOR ME?
OUR FINE GOVERNOR CALLED ME HERE TO ASK ME TO TALK TO YOU-- SAID YOU DIDN'T SEEM TOO HAPPY HERE. HE KNOWS WE'RE PALS. HE WANTED ME TO JUST--I DON'T KNOW, MAKE SURE YOU WEREN'T GOING TO CAUSE ANY TROUBLE OR SOMETHING.
HE WANTS TO MAKE SURE YOU'RE HAPPY.
DOES HE NOW?

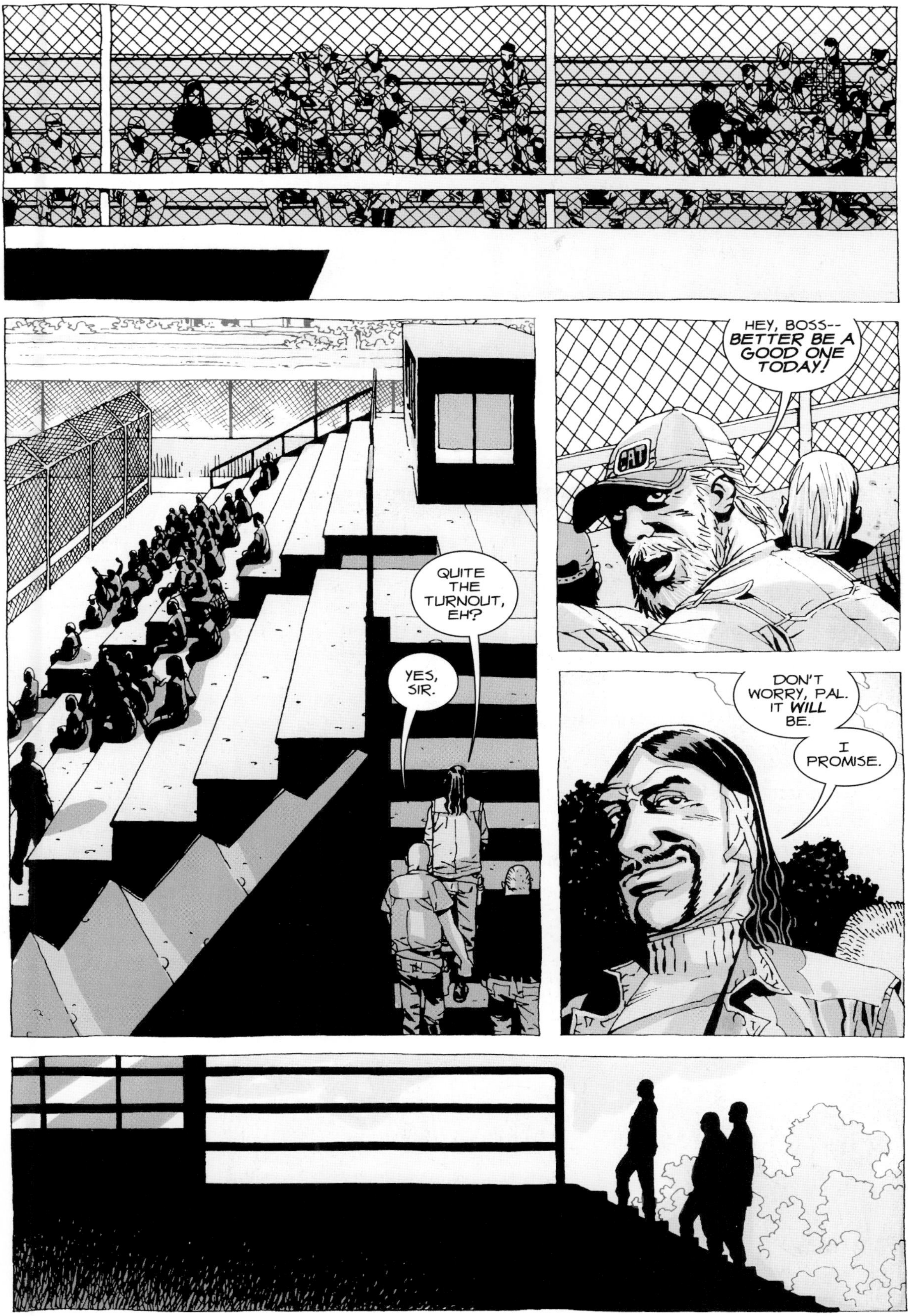
QUITE THE TURNOUT, EH?
YES, SIR.
HEY, BOSS-- BETTER BE A GOOD ONE TODAY!
DON'T WORRY, PAL. IT WILL BE.
I PROMISE.

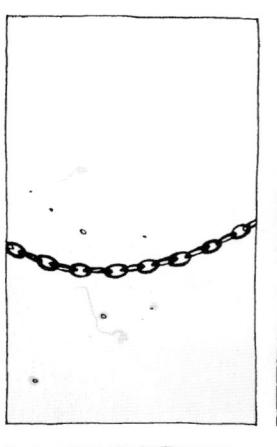

YOU SURE ABOUT THIS, BOSS?

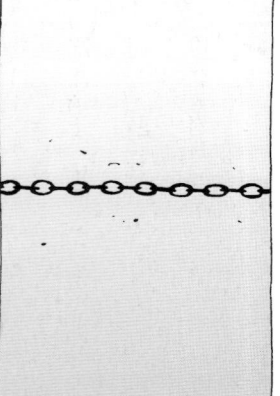

THIS IS GOING TO BE GOOD.

THE CHANCE TO SEE THIS BITCH TAKE A BEATING WITHOUT *ME* BREAKING A SWEAT?

YEAH-- I THINK IT'S A GOOD MOVE.

HERE WE GO.

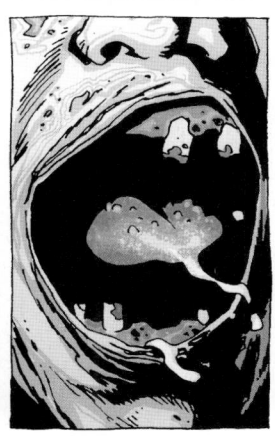

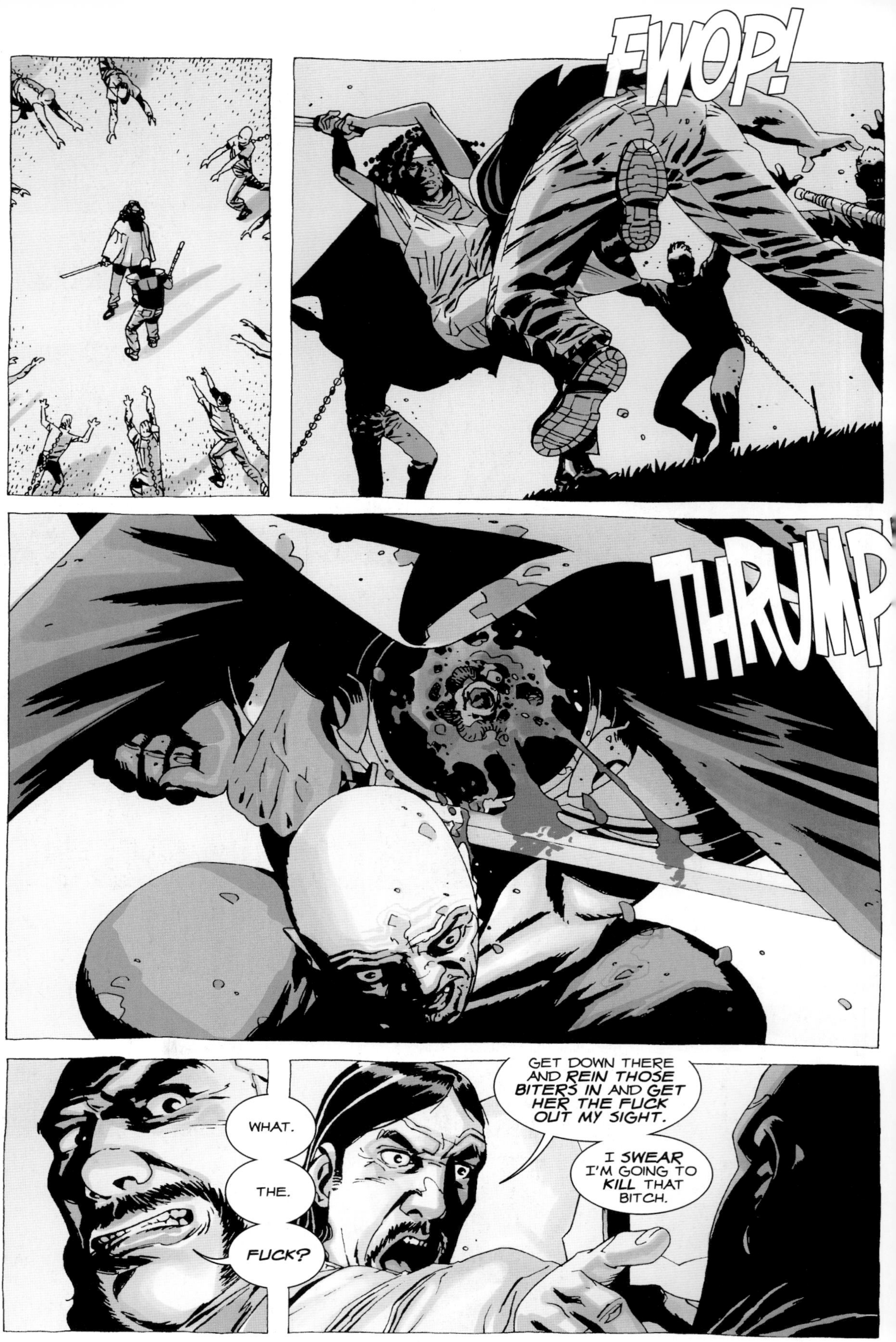
FWOP!
THRUMP
WHAT.
THE.
FUCK?
GET DOWN THERE AND REIN THOSE BITERS IN AND GET HER THE FUCK OUT MY SIGHT.
I SWEAR I'M GOING TO KILL THAT BITCH.

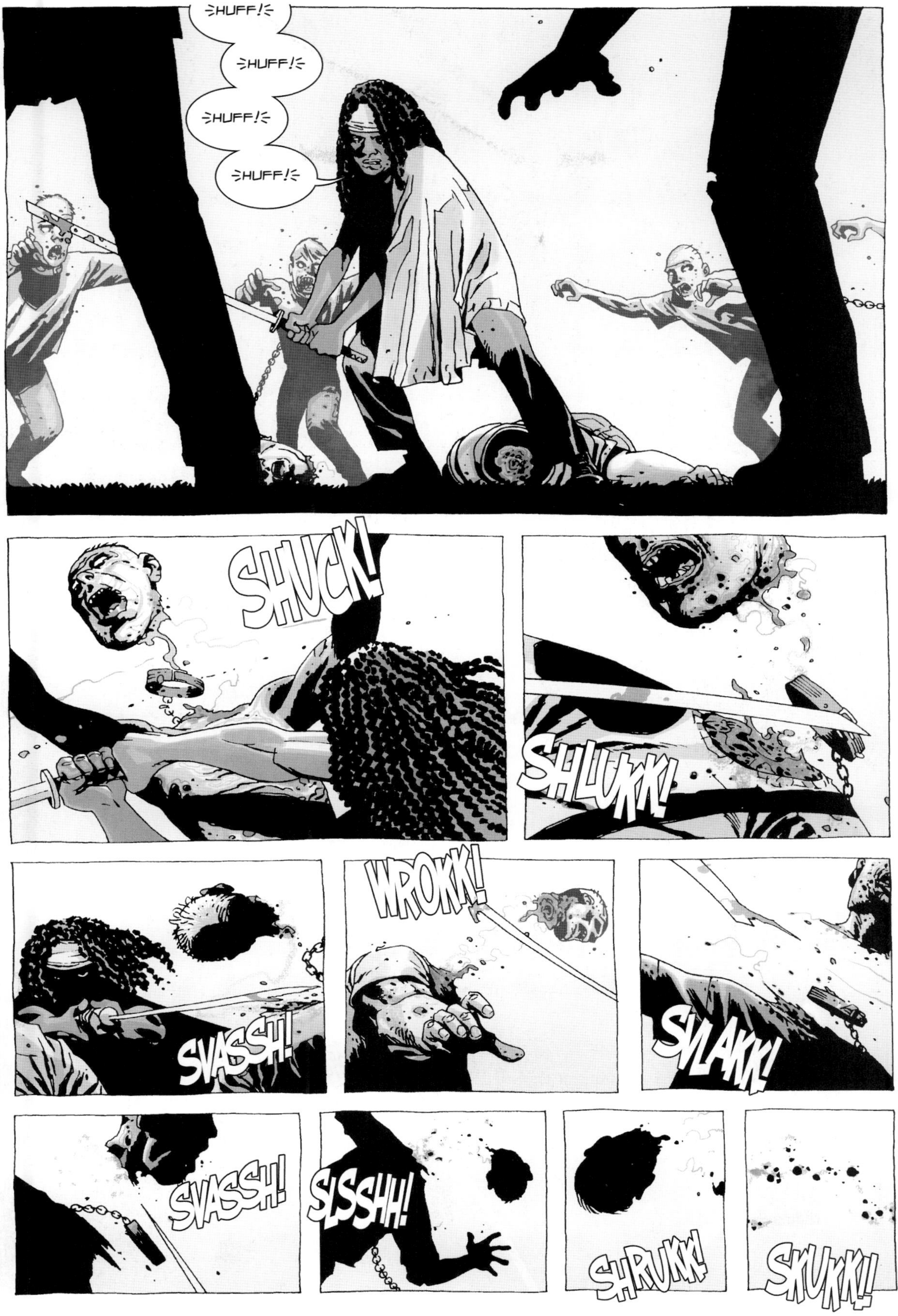
HUFF!
HUFF!
HUFF!
HUFF!
SHUCK!
SHLUKK!
SVASSH!
WROKK!
SVLAKK!
SVASSH!
SLSSHH!
SHRUKK!
SKUKK!!

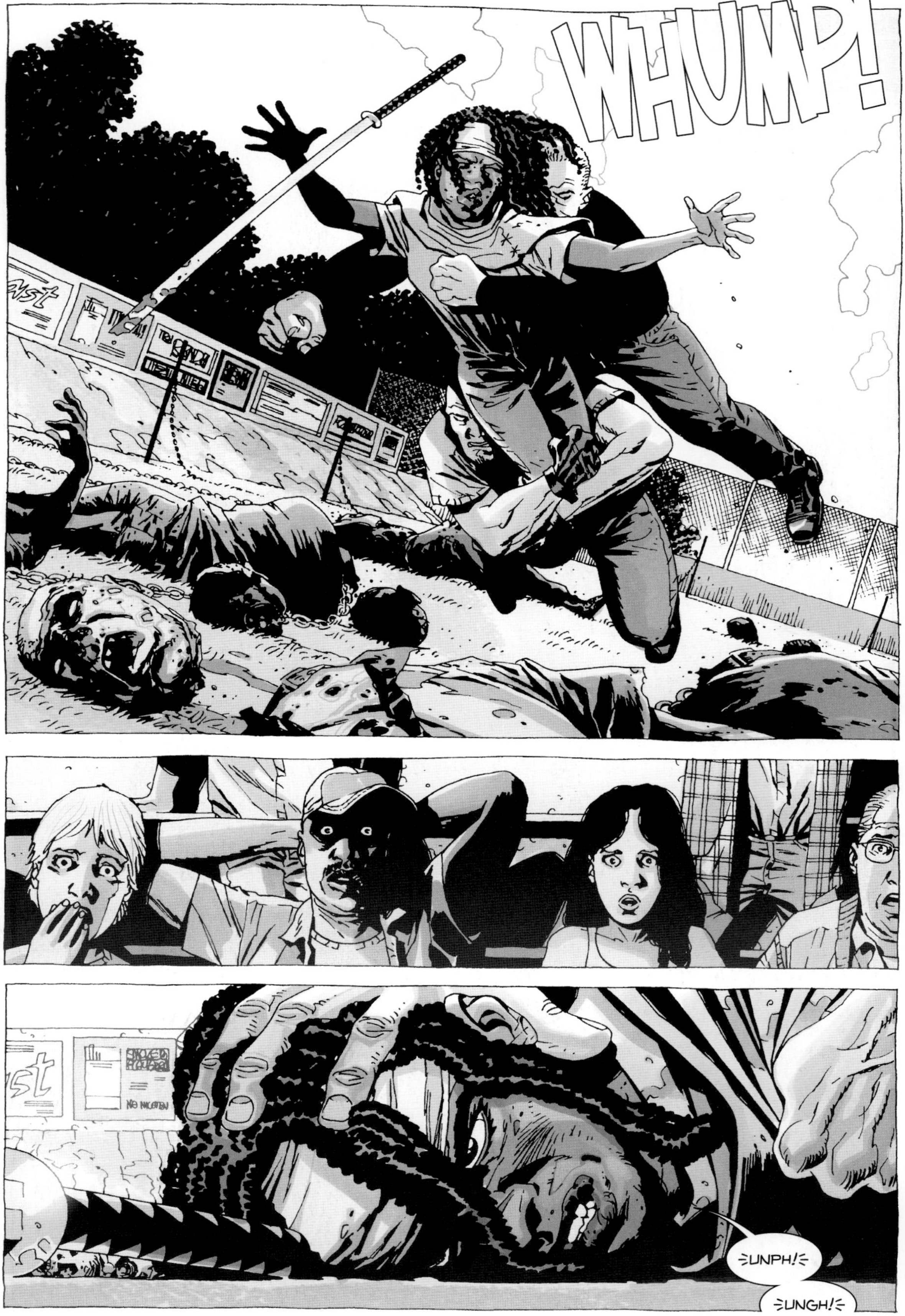
WHUMP!
UNPH!
UNGH!

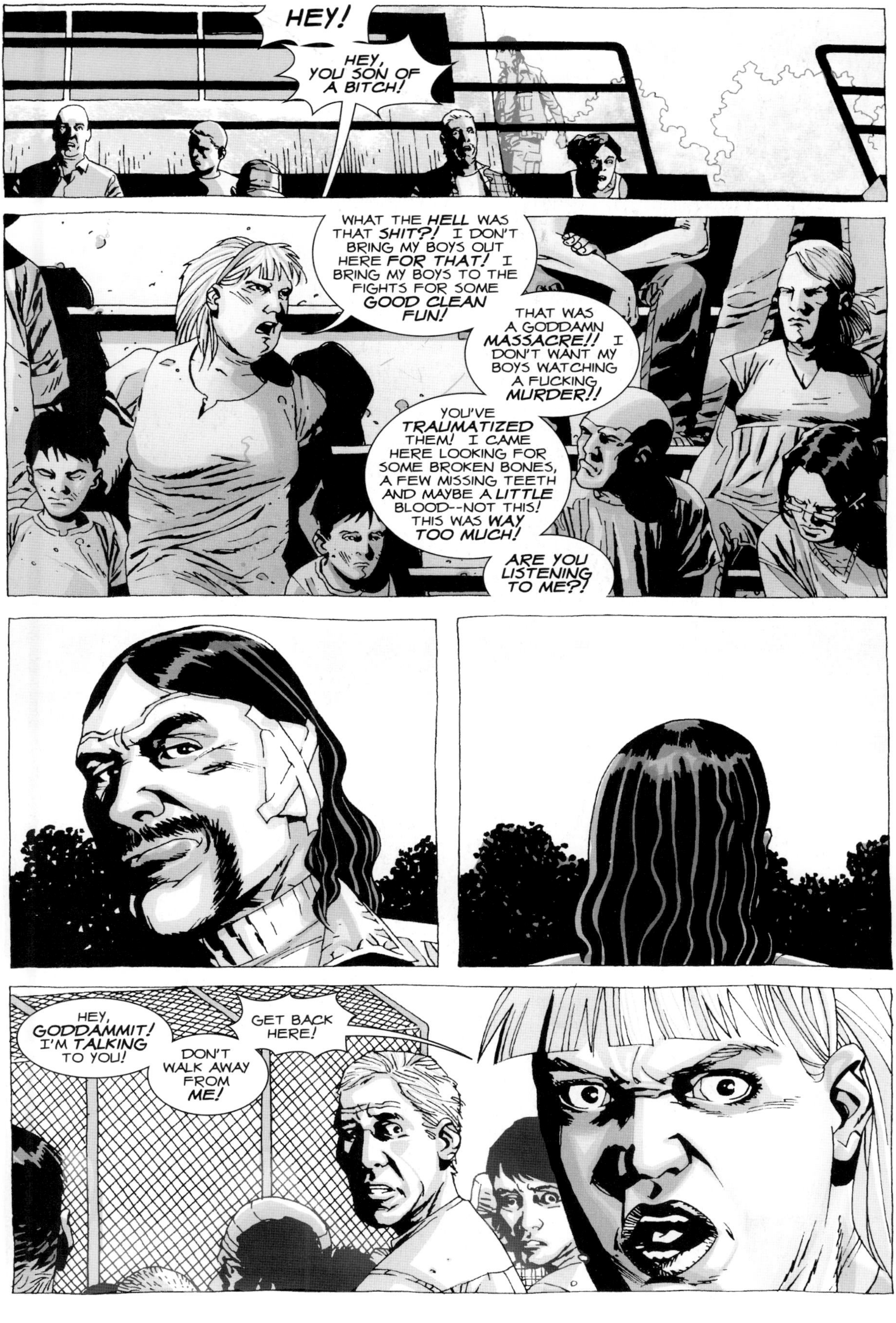
HEY!
HEY, YOU SON OF A BITCH!
WHAT THE HELL WAS THAT SHIT?! I DON'T BRING MY BOYS OUT HERE FOR THAT! I BRING MY BOYS TO THE FIGHTS FOR SOME GOOD CLEAN FUN!
THAT WAS A GODDAMN MASSACRE!! I DON'T WANT MY BOYS WATCHING A FUCKING MURDER!!
YOU'VE TRAUMATIZED THEM! I CAME HERE LOOKING FOR SOME BROKEN BONES, A FEW MISSING TEETH AND MAYBE A LITTLE BLOOD--NOT THIS! THIS WAS WAY TOO MUCH!
ARE YOU LISTENING TO ME?!
HEY, GODDAMMIT! I'M TALKING TO YOU!
GET BACK HERE!
DON'T WALK AWAY FROM ME!

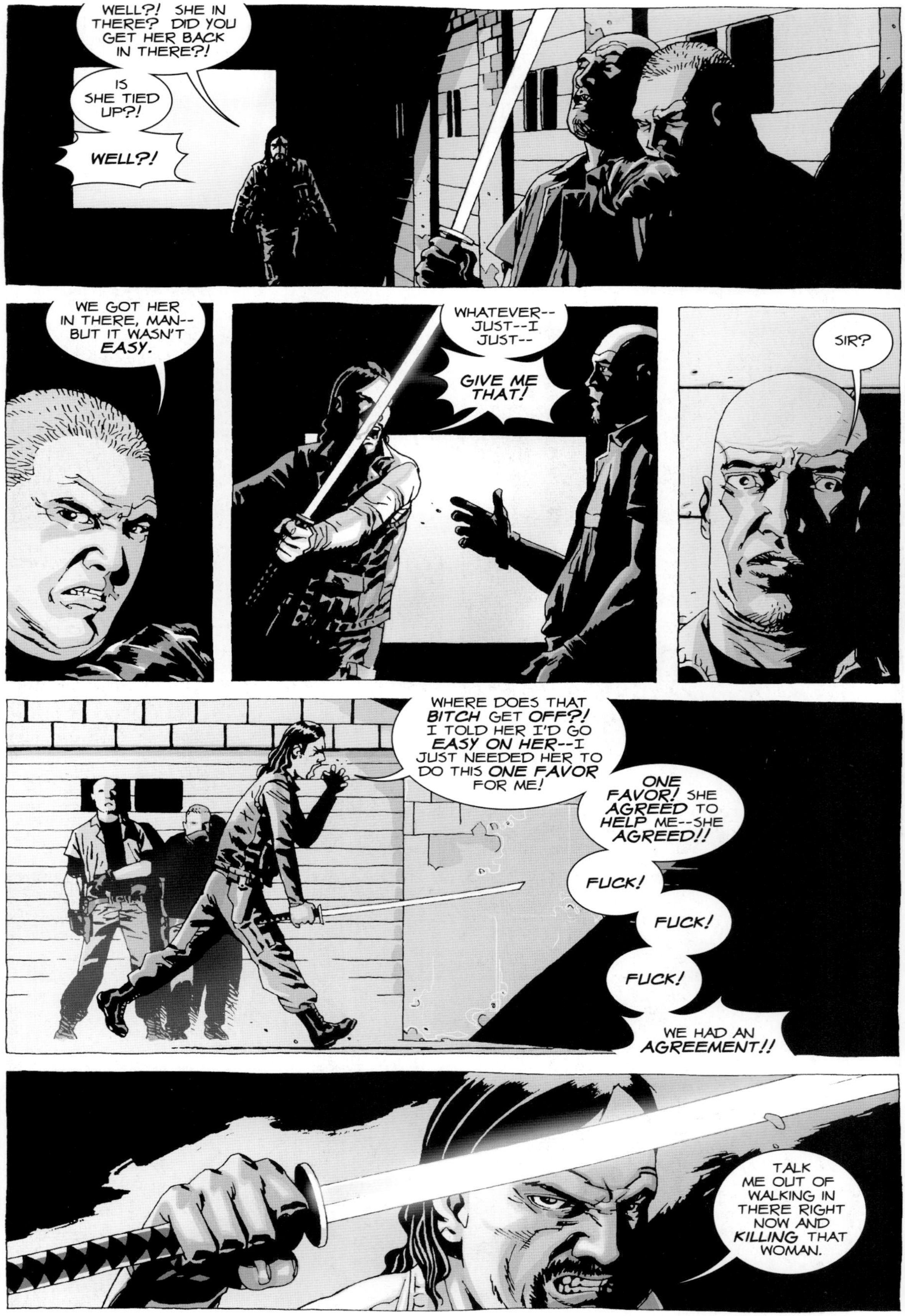
WELL?! SHE IN THERE? DID YOU GET HER BACK IN THERE?!
IS SHE TIED UP?!
WELL?!
WE GOT HER IN THERE, MAN-- BUT IT WASN'T EASY.
WHATEVER-- JUST--I JUST--
GIVE ME THAT!
SIR?
WHERE DOES THAT BITCH GET OFF?! I TOLD HER I'D GO EASY ON HER--I JUST NEEDED HER TO DO THIS ONE FAVOR FOR ME!
ONE FAVOR! SHE AGREED TO HELP ME--SHE AGREED!!
FUCK!
FUCK!
FUCK!
WE HAD AN AGREEMENT!!
TALK ME OUT OF WALKING IN THERE RIGHT NOW AND KILLING THAT WOMAN.

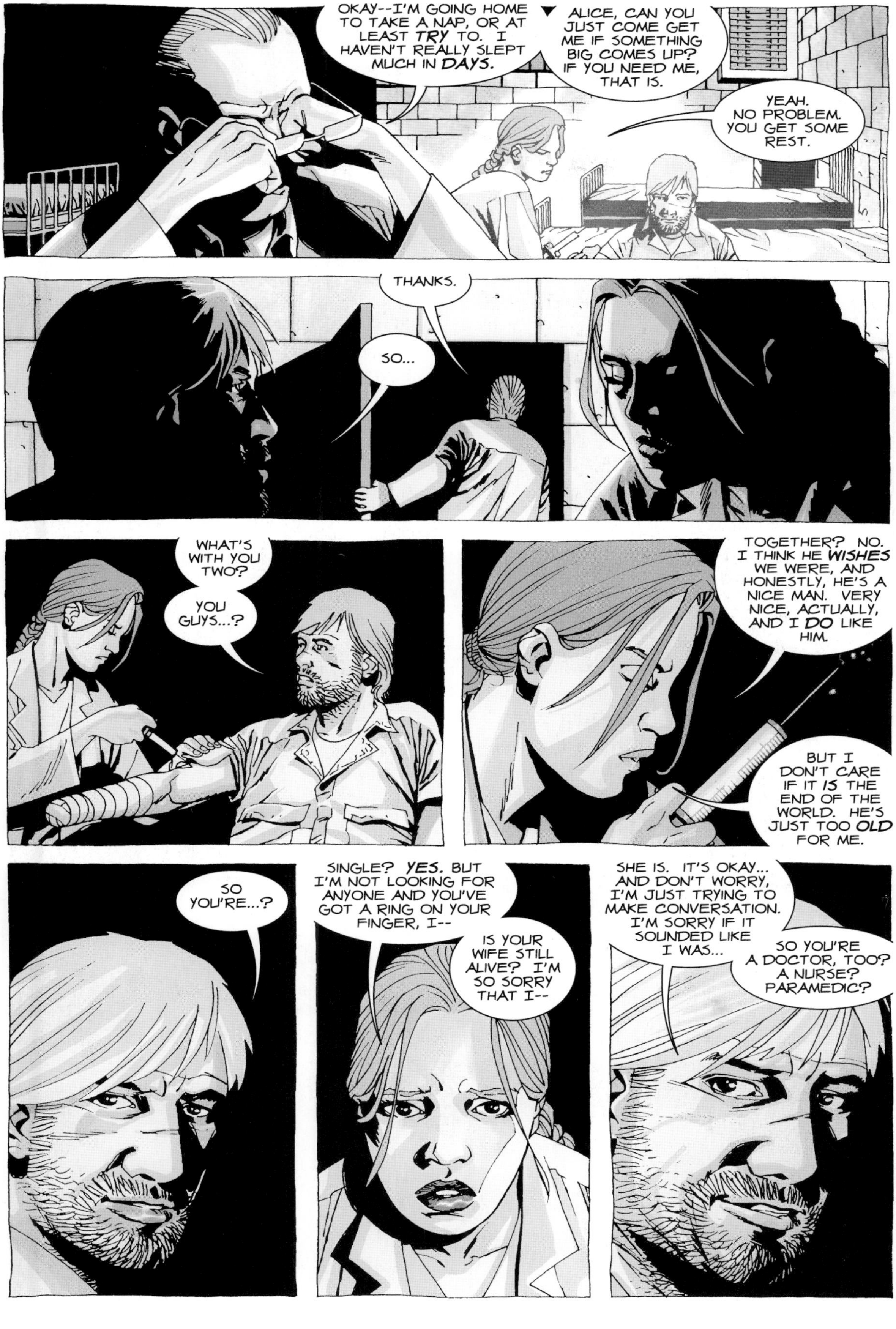
OKAY--I'M GOING HOME TO TAKE A NAP, OR AT LEAST TRY TO. I HAVEN'T REALLY SLEPT MUCH IN DAYS.
ALICE, CAN YOU JUST COME GET ME IF SOMETHING BIG COMES UP? IF YOU NEED ME, THAT IS.
YEAH. NO PROBLEM. YOU GET SOME REST.
THANKS.
SO...
WHAT'S WITH YOU TWO?
YOU GUYS...?
TOGETHER? NO. I THINK HE WISHES WE WERE, AND HONESTLY, HE'S A NICE MAN. VERY NICE, ACTUALLY, AND I DO LIKE HIM.
BUT I DON'T CARE IF IT IS THE END OF THE WORLD. HE'S JUST TOO OLD FOR ME.
SO YOU'RE...?
SINGLE? YES. BUT I'M NOT LOOKING FOR ANYONE AND YOU'VE GOT A RING ON YOUR FINGER, I--
IS YOUR WIFE STILL ALIVE? I'M SO SORRY THAT I--
SHE IS. IT'S OKAY... AND DON'T WORRY, I'M JUST TRYING TO MAKE CONVERSATION. I'M SORRY IF IT SOUNDED LIKE I WAS...
SO YOU'RE A DOCTOR, TOO? A NURSE? PARAMEDIC?

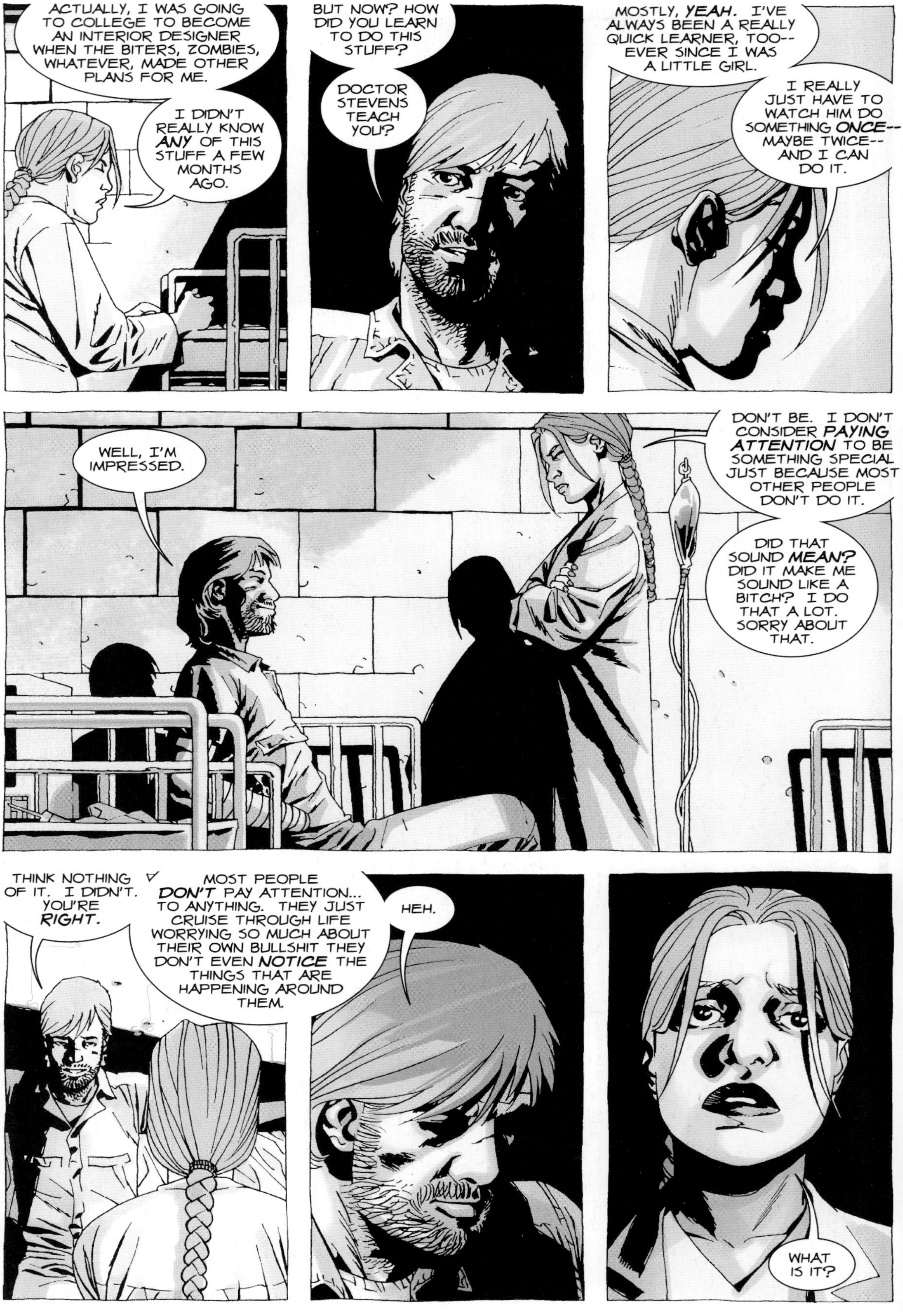
ACTUALLY, I WAS GOING TO COLLEGE TO BECOME AN INTERIOR DESIGNER WHEN THE BITERS, ZOMBIES, WHATEVER, MADE OTHER PLANS FOR ME.
I DIDN'T REALLY KNOW ANY OF THIS STUFF A FEW MONTHS AGO.
BUT NOW? HOW DID YOU LEARN TO DO THIS STUFF?
DOCTOR STEVENS TEACH YOU?
MOSTLY, YEAH. I'VE ALWAYS BEEN A REALLY QUICK LEARNER, TOO-- EVER SINCE I WAS A LITTLE GIRL.
I REALLY JUST HAVE TO WATCH HIM DO SOMETHING ONCE-- MAYBE TWICE-- AND I CAN DO IT.
WELL, I'M IMPRESSED.
DON'T BE. I DON'T CONSIDER PAYING ATTENTION TO BE SOMETHING SPECIAL JUST BECAUSE MOST OTHER PEOPLE DON'T DO IT.
DID THAT SOUND MEAN? DID IT MAKE ME SOUND LIKE A BITCH? I DO THAT A LOT. SORRY ABOUT THAT.
THINK NOTHING OF IT. I DIDN'T. YOU'RE RIGHT.
MOST PEOPLE DON'T PAY ATTENTION... TO ANYTHING. THEY JUST CRUISE THROUGH LIFE WORRYING SO MUCH ABOUT THEIR OWN BULLSHIT THEY DON'T EVEN NOTICE THE THINGS THAT ARE HAPPENING AROUND THEM.
HEH.
WHAT IS IT?

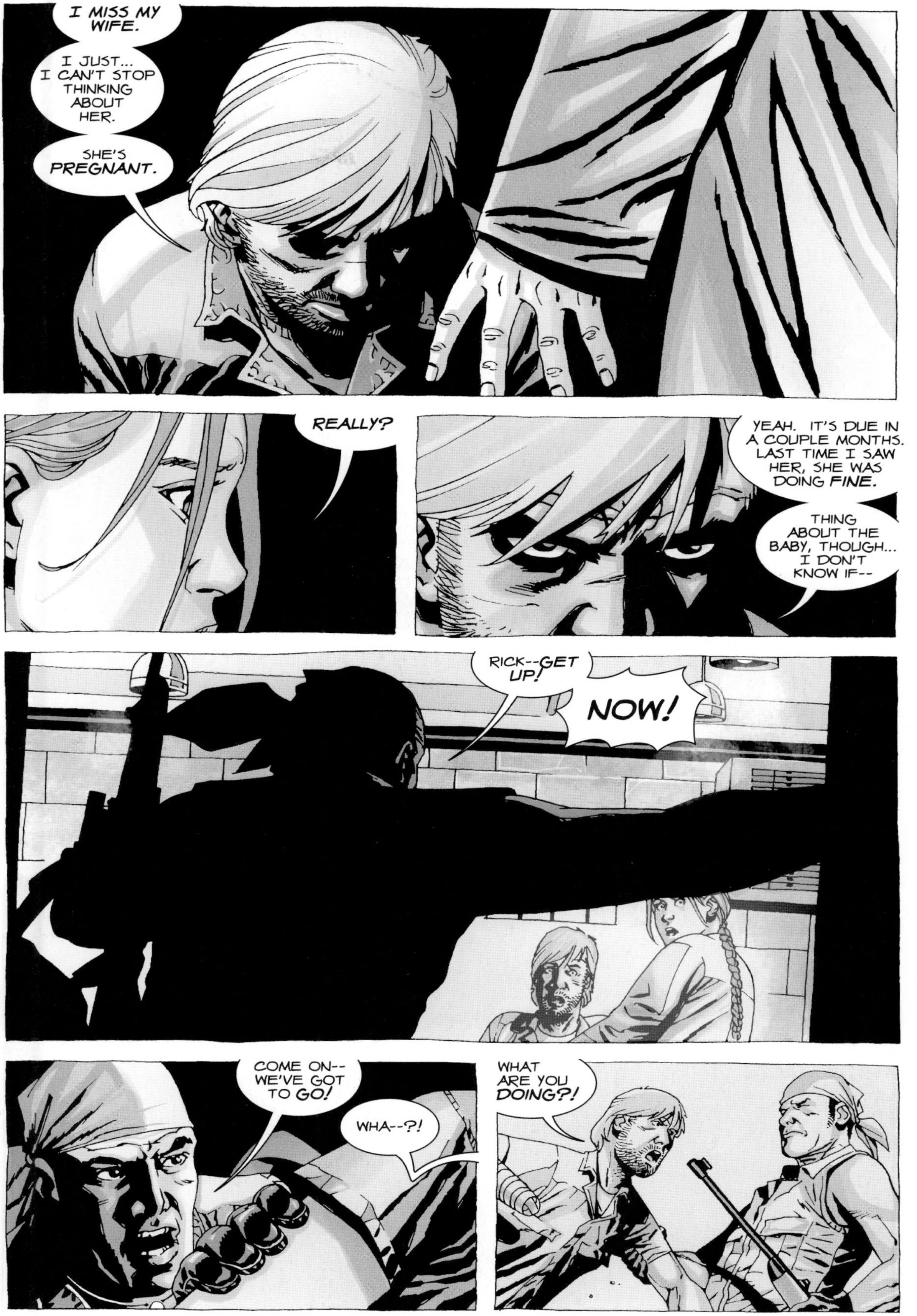
I MISS MY WIFE.
I JUST... I CAN'T STOP THINKING ABOUT HER.
SHE'S PREGNANT.
REALLY?
YEAH. IT'S DUE IN A COUPLE MONTHS. LAST TIME I SAW HER, SHE WAS DOING FINE.
THING ABOUT THE BABY, THOUGH... I DON'T KNOW IF--
RICK--GET UP!
NOW!
COME ON-- WE'VE GOT TO GO!
WHA--?!
WHAT ARE YOU DOING?!

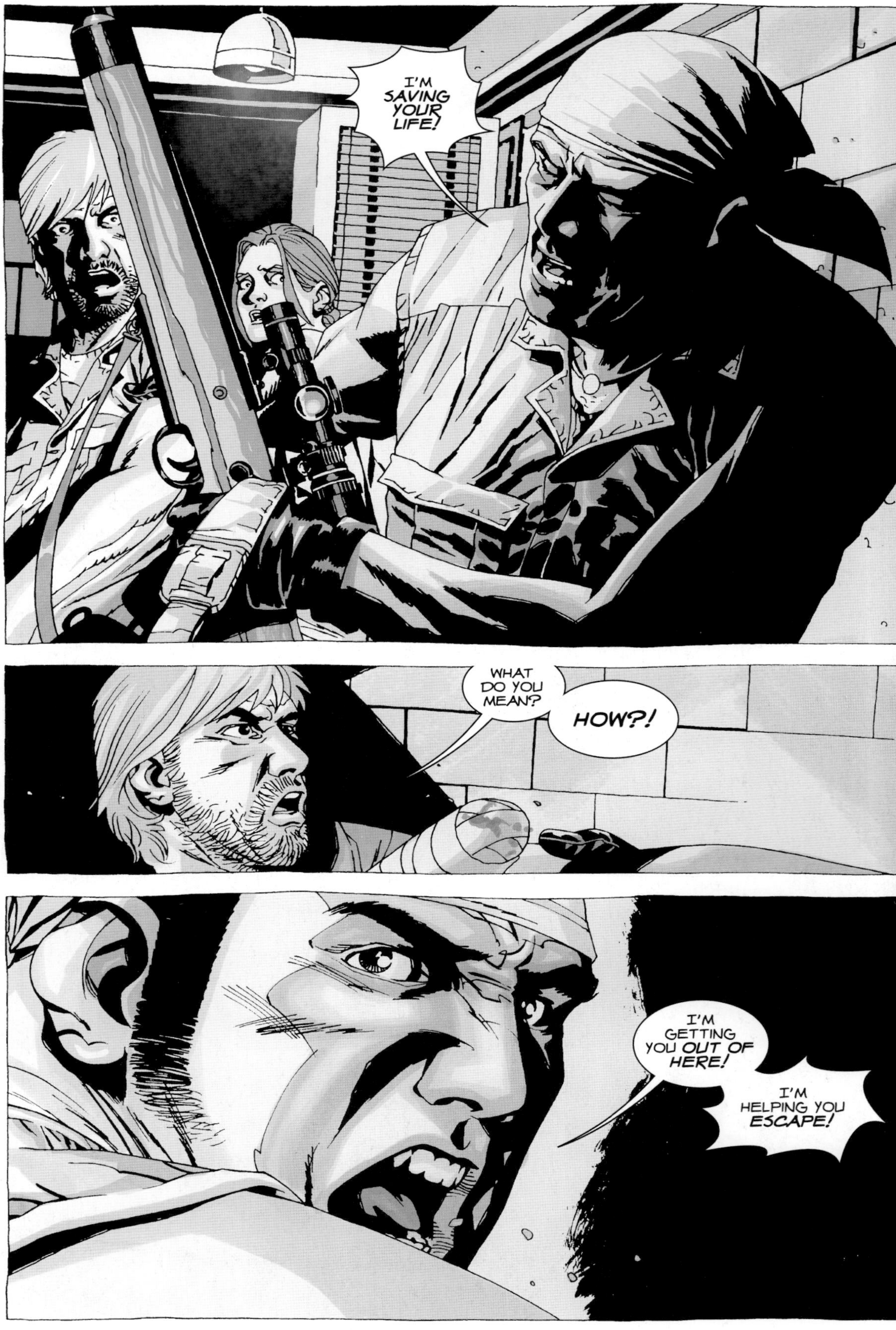
I'M SAVING YOUR LIFE!
WHAT DO YOU MEAN?
HOW?!
I'M GETTING YOU OUT OF HERE!
I'M HELPING YOU ESCAPE!

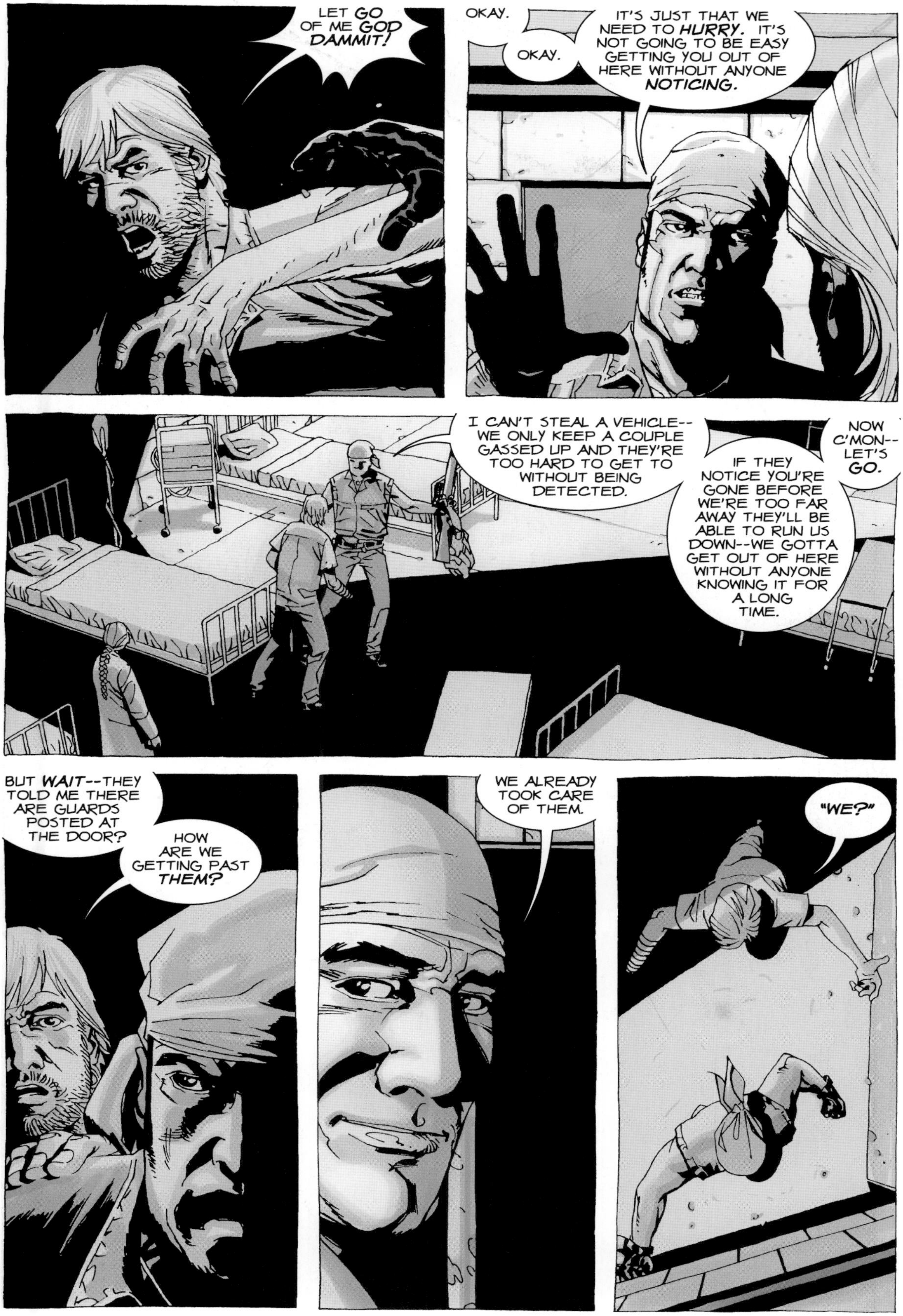
LET GO OF ME GOD DAMMIT!
OKAY.
OKAY.
IT'S JUST THAT WE NEED TO HURRY. IT'S NOT GOING TO BE EASY GETTING YOU OUT OF HERE WITHOUT ANYONE NOTICING.
I CAN'T STEAL A VEHICLE-- WE ONLY KEEP A COUPLE GASSED UP AND THEY'RE TOO HARD TO GET TO WITHOUT BEING DETECTED.
IF THEY NOTICE YOU'RE GONE BEFORE WE'RE TOO FAR AWAY THEY'LL BE ABLE TO RUN US DOWN--WE GOTTA GET OUT OF HERE WITHOUT ANYONE KNOWING IT FOR A LONG TIME.
NOW C'MON-- LET'S GO.
BUT WAIT--THEY TOLD ME THERE ARE GUARDS POSTED AT THE DOOR?
HOW ARE WE GETTING PAST THEM?
WE ALREADY TOOK CARE OF THEM.
"WE?"

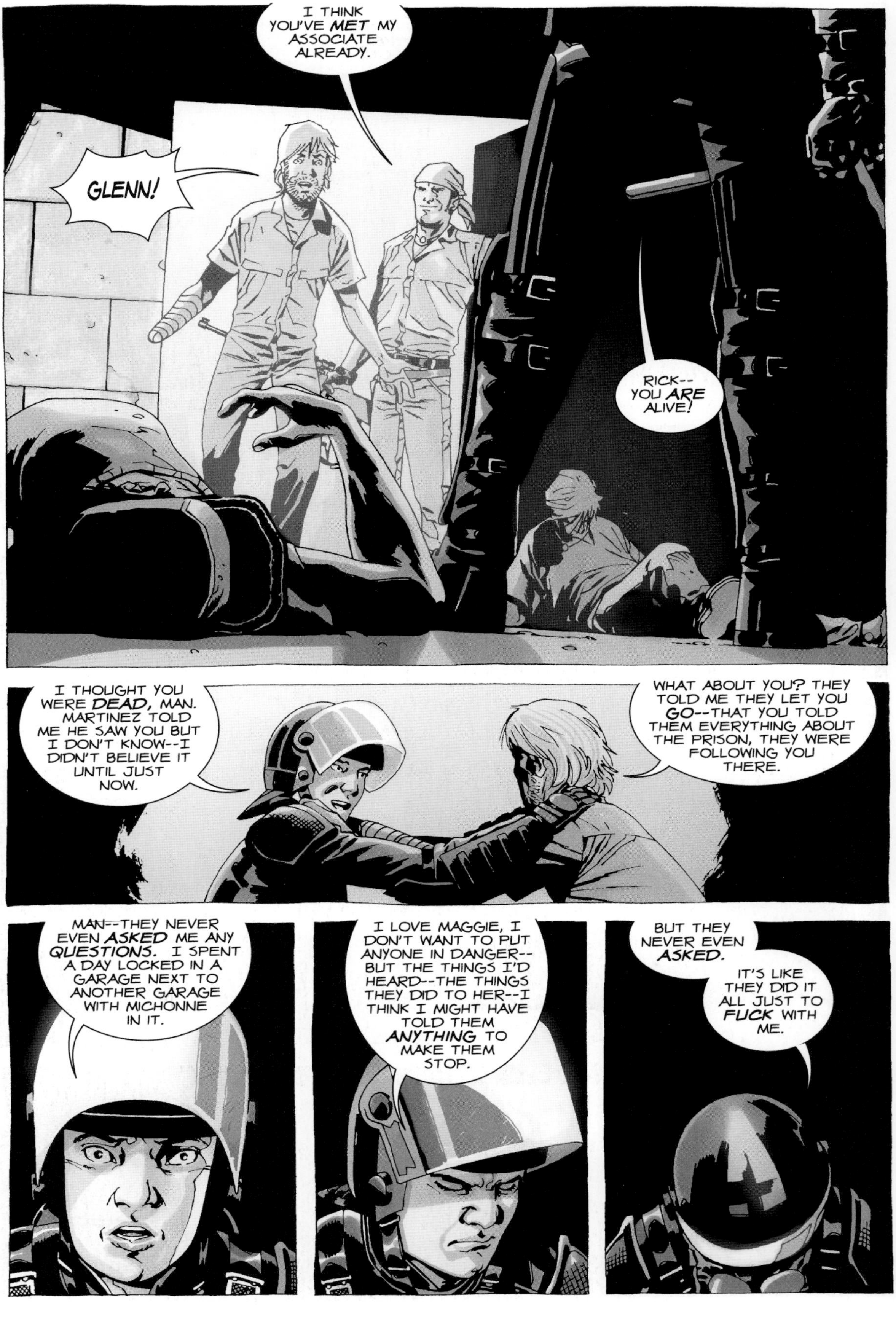
I THINK YOU'VE MET MY ASSOCIATE ALREADY.
GLENN!
RICK-- YOU ARE ALIVE!
I THOUGHT YOU WERE DEAD, MAN. MARTINEZ TOLD ME HE SAW YOU BUT I DON'T KNOW--I DIDN'T BELIEVE IT UNTIL JUST NOW.
WHAT ABOUT YOU? THEY TOLD ME THEY LET YOU GO--THAT YOU TOLD THEM EVERYTHING ABOUT THE PRISON, THEY WERE FOLLOWING YOU THERE.
MAN--THEY NEVER EVEN ASKED ME ANY QUESTIONS. I SPENT A DAY LOCKED IN A GARAGE NEXT TO ANOTHER GARAGE WITH MICHONNE IN IT.
I LOVE MAGGIE, I DON'T WANT TO PUT ANYONE IN DANGER-- BUT THE THINGS I'D HEARD--THE THINGS THEY DID TO HER--I THINK I MIGHT HAVE TOLD THEM ANYTHING TO MAKE THEM STOP.
BUT THEY NEVER EVEN ASKED.
IT'S LIKE THEY DID IT ALL JUST TO FUCK WITH ME.

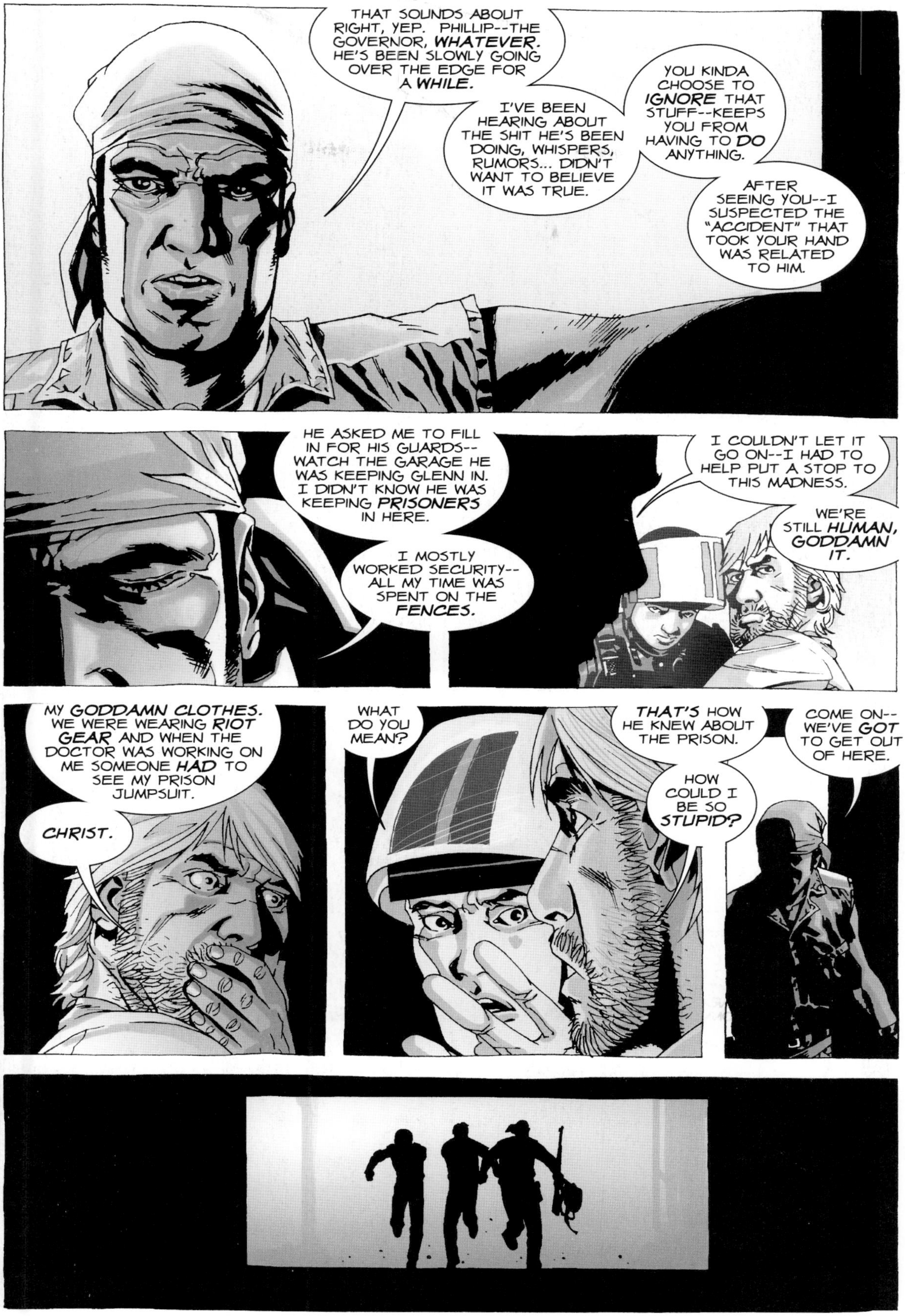
THAT SOUNDS ABOUT RIGHT, YEP. PHILLIP--THE GOVERNOR, WHATEVER. HE'S BEEN SLOWLY GOING OVER THE EDGE FOR A WHILE.
I'VE BEEN HEARING ABOUT THE SHIT HE'S BEEN DOING, WHISPERS, RUMORS... DIDN'T WANT TO BELIEVE IT WAS TRUE.
YOU KINDA CHOOSE TO IGNORE THAT STUFF--KEEPS YOU FROM HAVING TO DO ANYTHING.
AFTER SEEING YOU--I SUSPECTED THE "ACCIDENT" THAT TOOK YOUR HAND WAS RELATED TO HIM.
HE ASKED ME TO FILL IN FOR HIS GUARDS--WATCH THE GARAGE HE WAS KEEPING GLENN IN. I DIDN'T KNOW HE WAS KEEPING PRISONERS IN HERE.
I MOSTLY WORKED SECURITY--ALL MY TIME WAS SPENT ON THE FENCES.
I COULDN'T LET IT GO ON--I HAD TO HELP PUT A STOP TO THIS MADNESS.
WE'RE STILL HUMAN, GODDAMN IT.
MY GODDAMN CLOTHES. WE WERE WEARING RIOT GEAR AND WHEN THE DOCTOR WAS WORKING ON ME SOMEONE HAD TO SEE MY PRISON JUMPSUIT.
CHRIST.
WHAT DO YOU MEAN?
THAT'S HOW HE KNEW ABOUT THE PRISON.
HOW COULD I BE SO STUPID?
COME ON--WE'VE GOT TO GET OUT OF HERE.

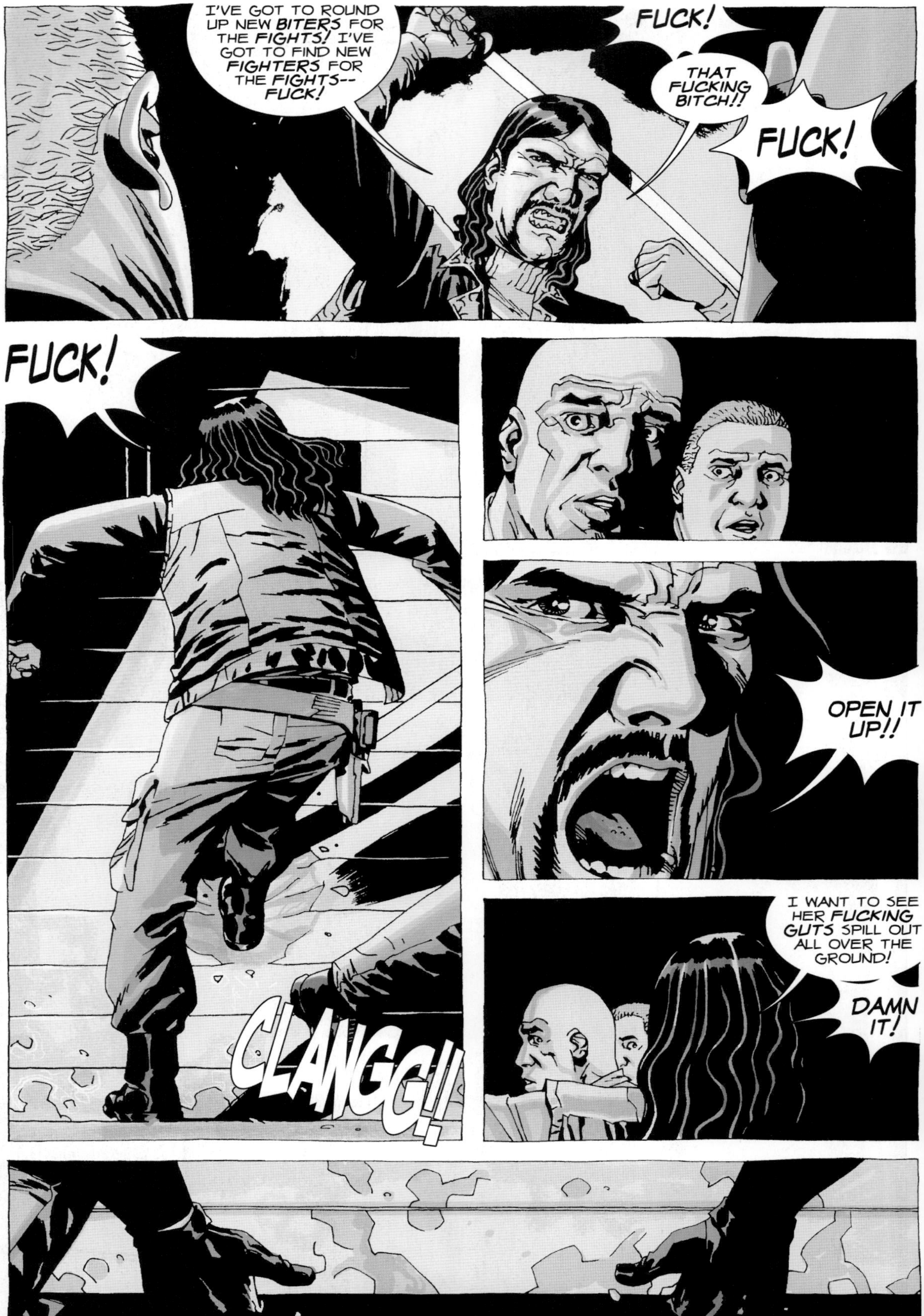
I'VE GOT TO ROUND UP NEW BITERS FOR THE FIGHTS! I'VE GOT TO FIND NEW FIGHTERS FOR THE FIGHTS-- FUCK!
FUCK!
THAT FUCKING BITCH!!
FUCK!
FUCK!
CLANGG!!
OPEN IT UP!!
I WANT TO SEE HER FUCKING GUTS SPILL OUT ALL OVER THE GROUND!
DAMN IT!

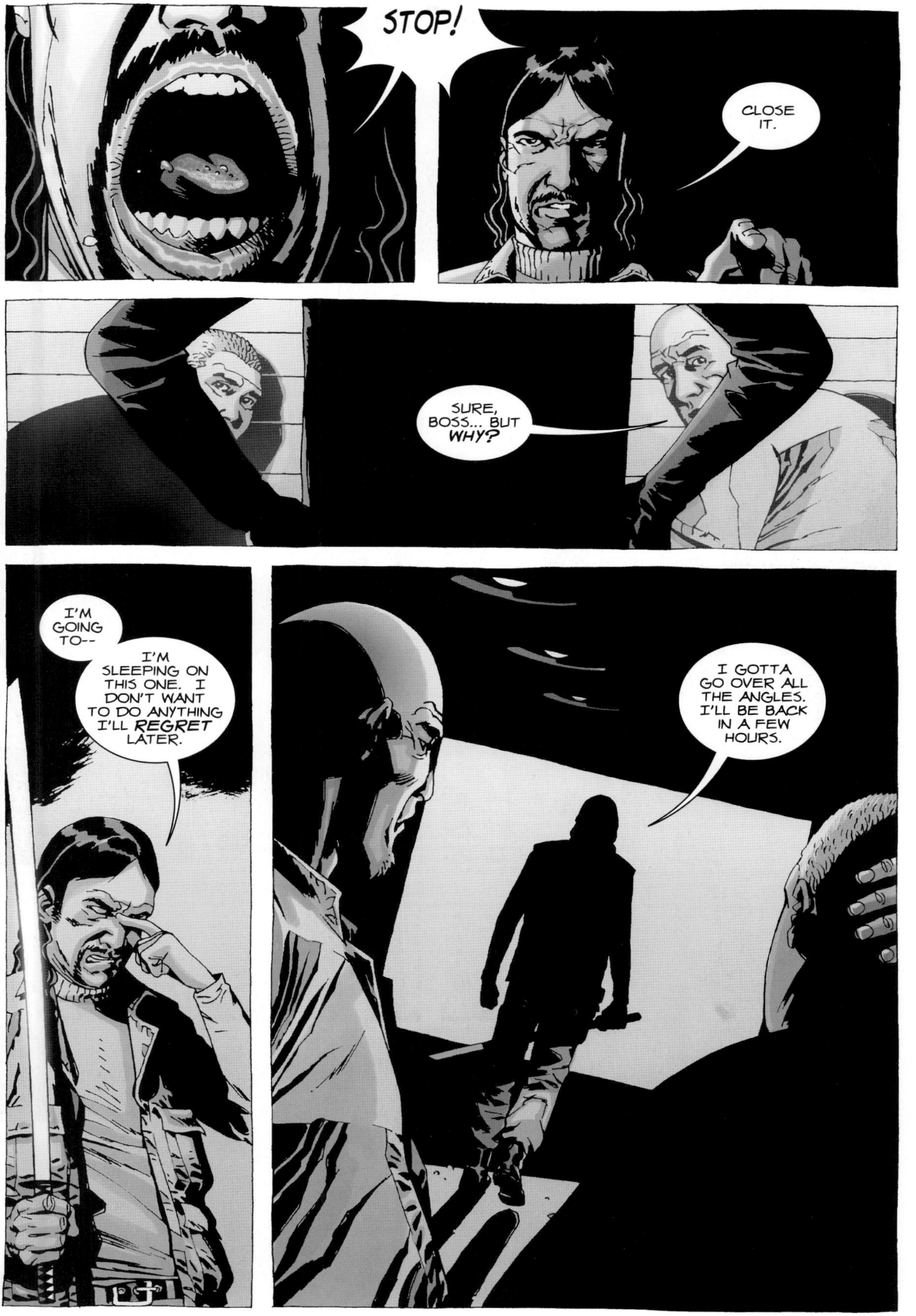
STOP!
CLOSE IT.
SURE, BOSS... BUT WHY?
I'M GOING TO--
I'M SLEEPING ON THIS ONE. I DON'T WANT TO DO ANYTHING I'LL REGRET LATER.
I GOTTA GO OVER ALL THE ANGLES. I'LL BE BACK IN A FEW HOURS.

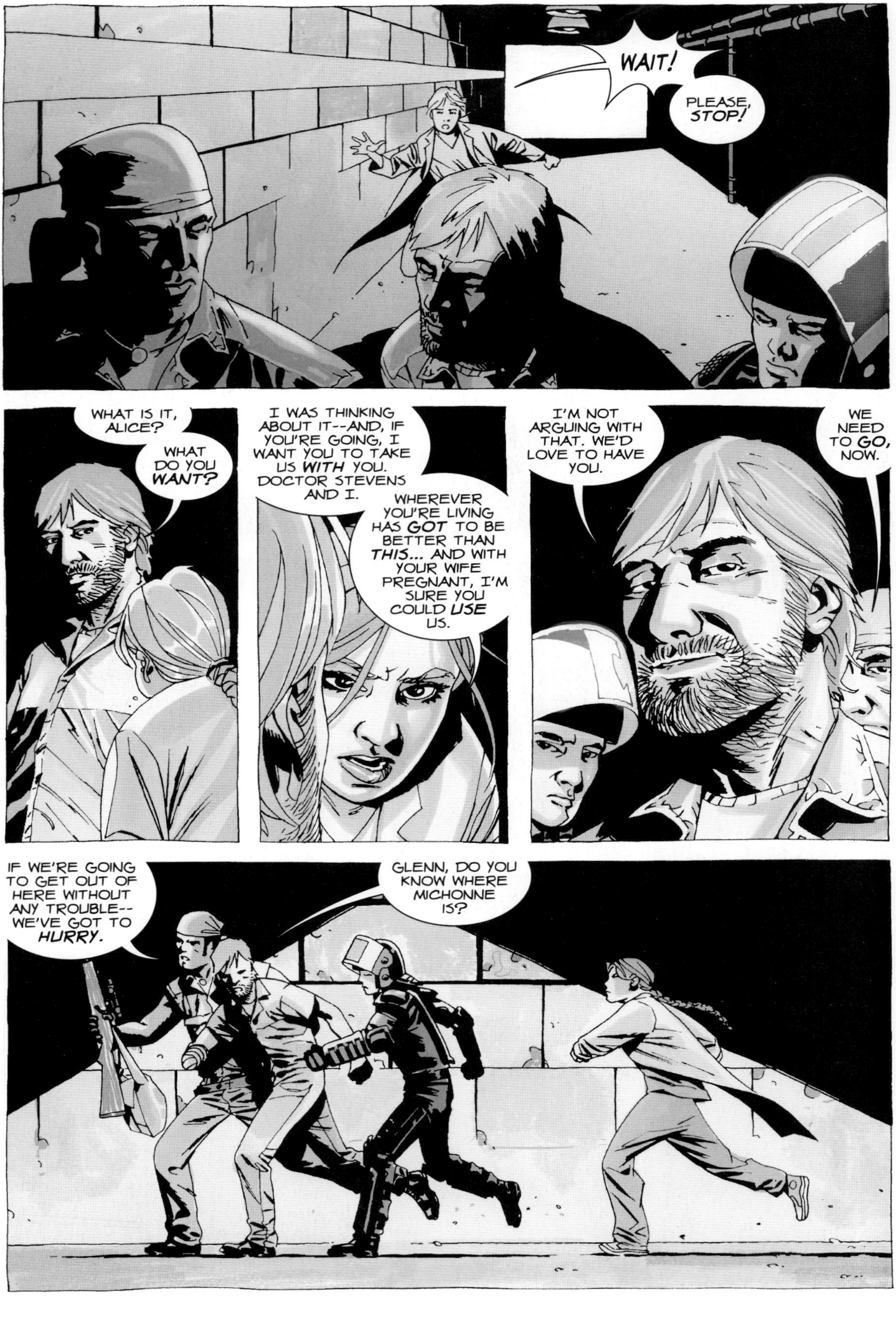
WAIT!
PLEASE, STOP!
WHAT IS IT, ALICE?
WHAT DO YOU WANT?
I WAS THINKING ABOUT IT--AND, IF YOU'RE GOING, I WANT YOU TO TAKE US WITH YOU. DOCTOR STEVENS AND I.
WHEREVER YOU'RE LIVING HAS GOT TO BE BETTER THAN THIS... AND WITH YOUR WIFE PREGNANT, I'M SURE YOU COULD USE US.
I'M NOT ARGUING WITH THAT. WE'D LOVE TO HAVE YOU.
WE NEED TO GO, NOW.
IF WE'RE GOING TO GET OUT OF HERE WITHOUT ANY TROUBLE-- WE'VE GOT TO HURRY.
GLENN, DO YOU KNOW WHERE MICHONNE IS?

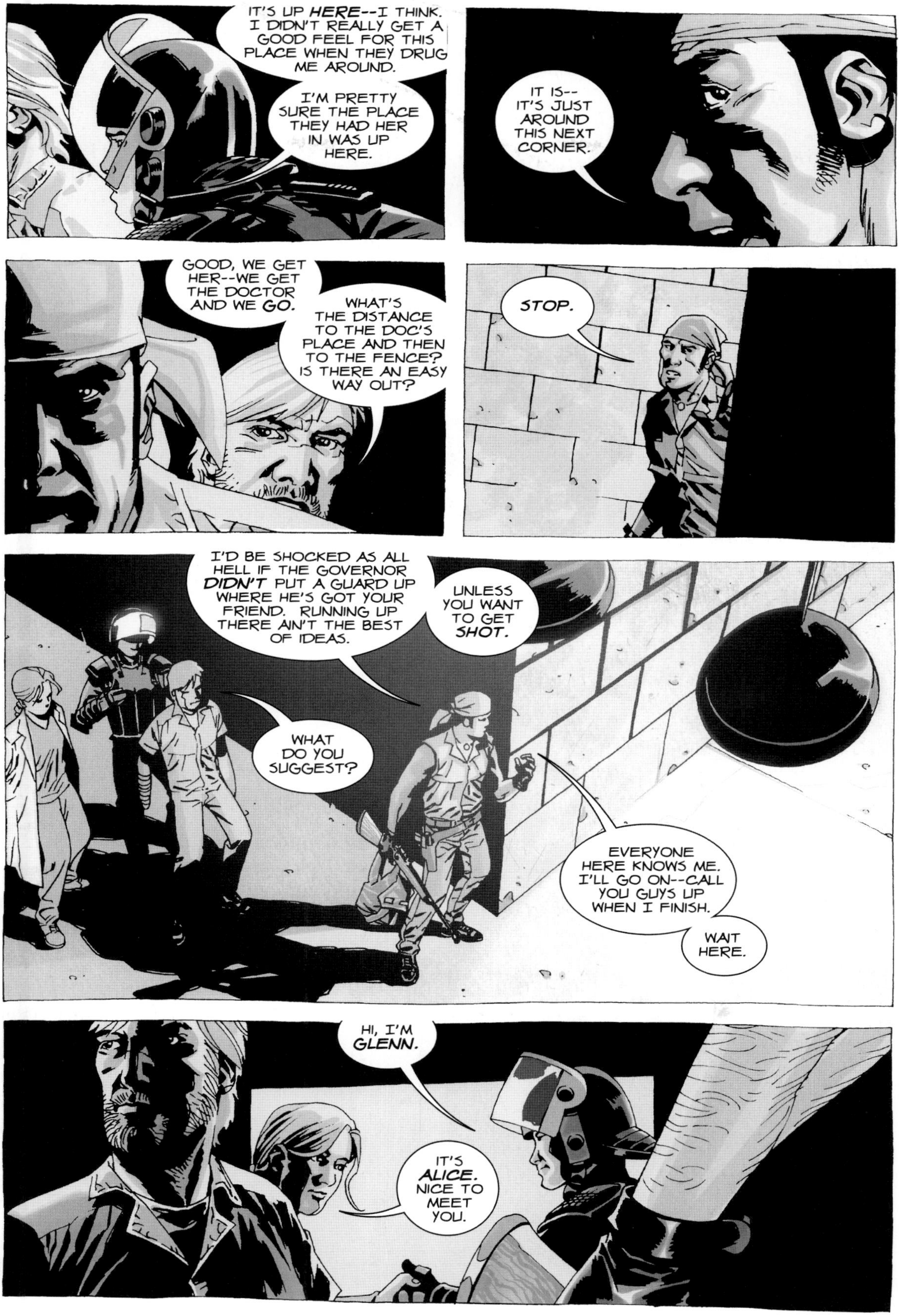
IT'S UP HERE--I THINK. I DIDN'T REALLY GET A GOOD FEEL FOR THIS PLACE WHEN THEY DRUG ME AROUND.
I'M PRETTY SURE THE PLACE THEY HAD HER IN WAS UP HERE.
IT IS-- IT'S JUST AROUND THIS NEXT CORNER.
GOOD, WE GET HER--WE GET THE DOCTOR AND WE GO.
WHAT'S THE DISTANCE TO THE DOC'S PLACE AND THEN TO THE FENCE? IS THERE AN EASY WAY OUT?
STOP.
I'D BE SHOCKED AS ALL HELL IF THE GOVERNOR DIDN'T PUT A GUARD UP WHERE HE'S GOT YOUR FRIEND. RUNNING UP THERE AIN'T THE BEST OF IDEAS.
UNLESS YOU WANT TO GET SHOT.
WHAT DO YOU SUGGEST?
EVERYONE HERE KNOWS ME. I'LL GO ON--CALL YOU GUYS UP WHEN I FINISH.
WAIT HERE.
HI, I'M GLENN.
IT'S ALICE. NICE TO MEET YOU.

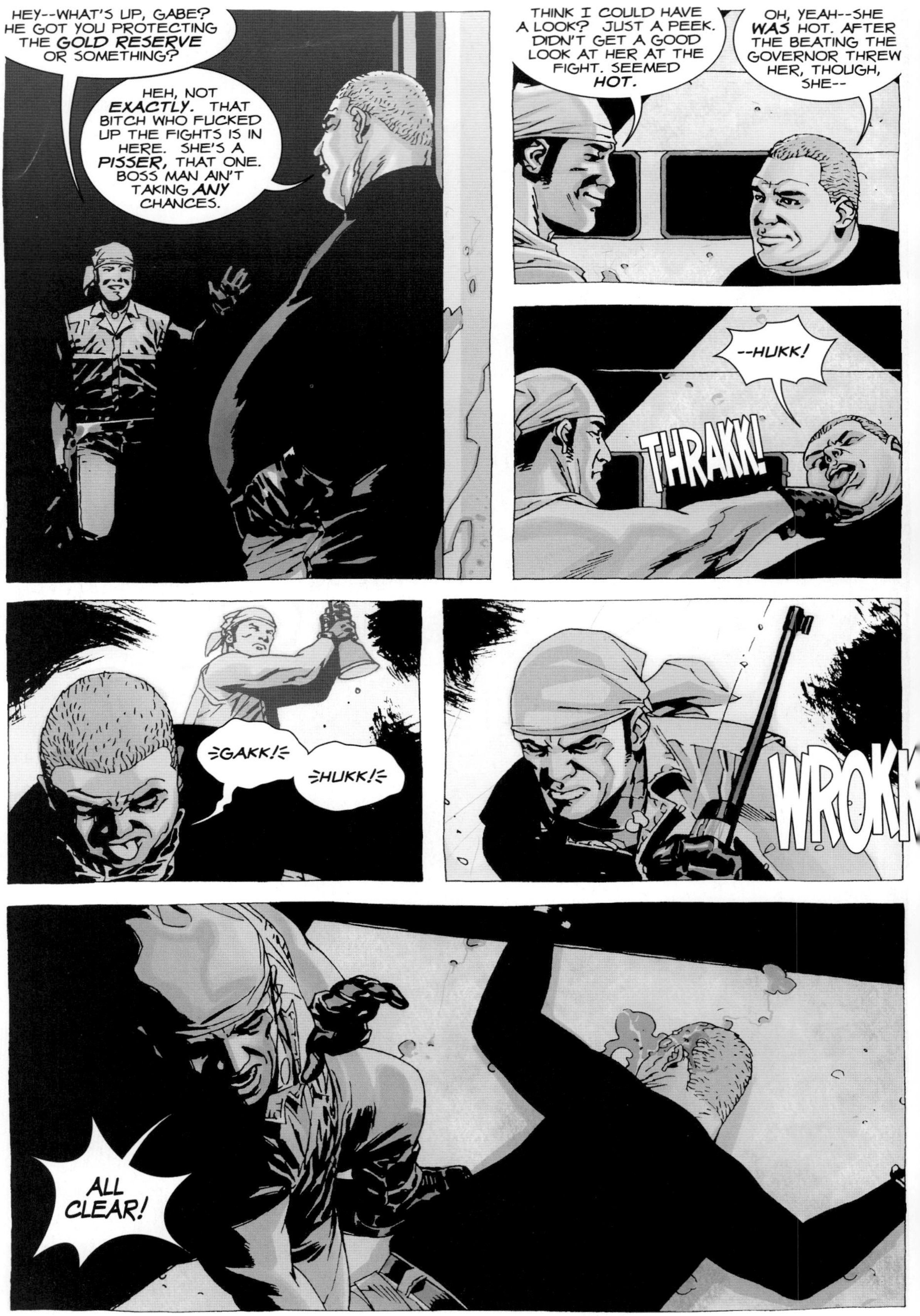

HEY--WHAT'S UP, GABE? HE GOT YOU PROTECTING THE GOLD RESERVE OR SOMETHING?
HEH, NOT EXACTLY. THAT BITCH WHO FUCKED UP THE FIGHTS IS IN HERE. SHE'S A PISSER, THAT ONE. BOSS MAN AIN'T TAKING ANY CHANCES.
THINK I COULD HAVE A LOOK? JUST A PEEK. DIDN'T GET A GOOD LOOK AT HER AT THE FIGHT. SEEMED HOT.
OH, YEAH--SHE WAS HOT. AFTER THE BEATING THE GOVERNOR THREW HER, THOUGH, SHE--
--HUKK!
THRAKK!
GAKK!
HUKK!
WROKK
ALL CLEAR!

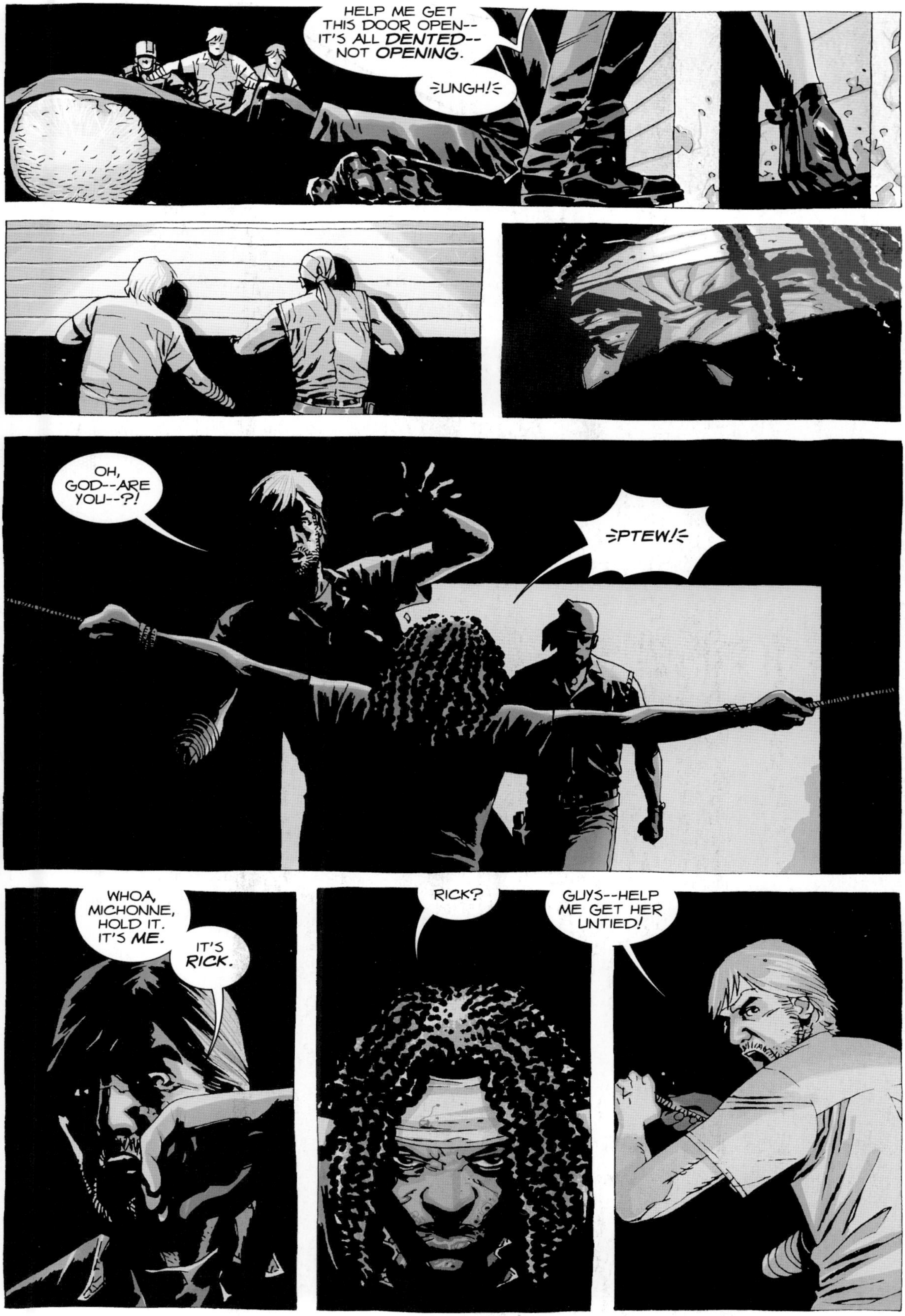
HELP ME GET THIS DOOR OPEN-- IT'S ALL DENTED-- NOT OPENING.
=UNGH!=
OH, GOD--ARE YOU--?!
=PTEW!=
WHOA, MICHONNE, HOLD IT. IT'S ME.
IT'S RICK.
RICK?
GUYS--HELP ME GET HER UNTIED!

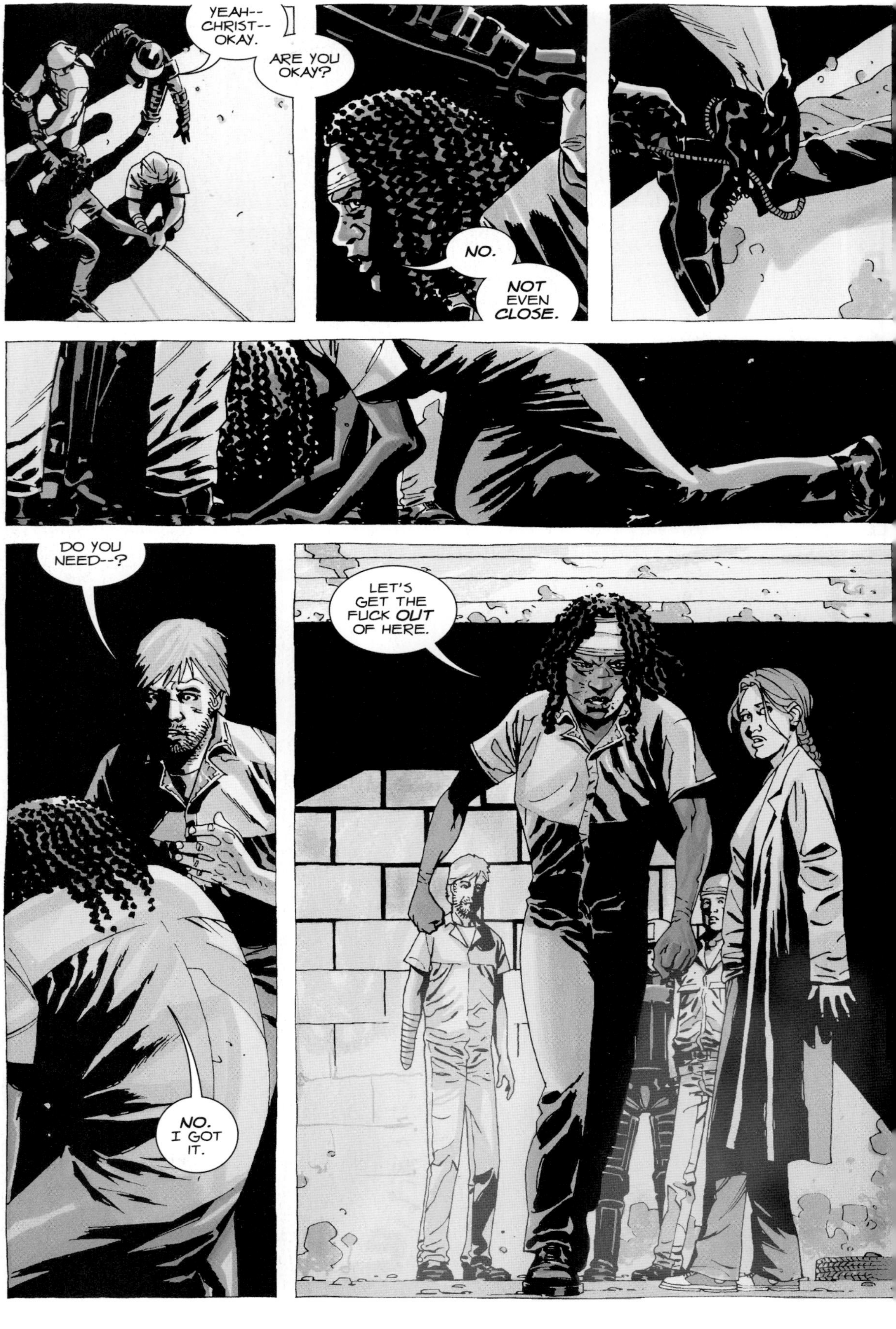
YEAH-- CHRIST-- OKAY.
ARE YOU OKAY?
NO.
NOT EVEN CLOSE.
DO YOU NEED--?
NO. I GOT IT.
LET'S GET THE FUCK OUT OF HERE.

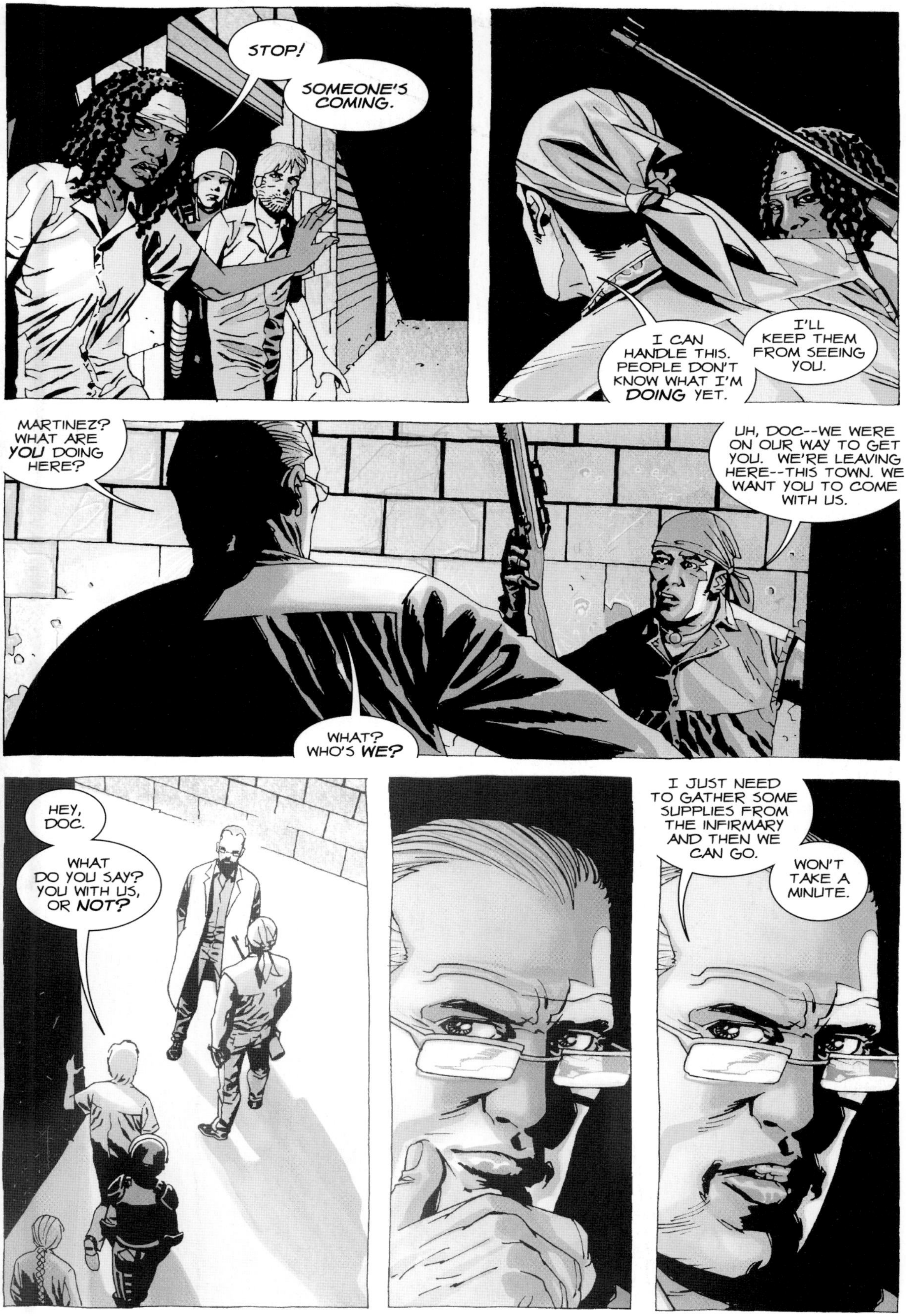
STOP!
SOMEONE'S COMING.
I CAN HANDLE THIS. PEOPLE DON'T KNOW WHAT I'M DOING YET.
I'LL KEEP THEM FROM SEEING YOU.
MARTINEZ? WHAT ARE YOU DOING HERE?
UH, DOC--WE WERE ON OUR WAY TO GET YOU. WE'RE LEAVING HERE--THIS TOWN. WE WANT YOU TO COME WITH US.
WHAT? WHO'S WE?
HEY, DOC.
WHAT DO YOU SAY? YOU WITH US, OR NOT?
I JUST NEED TO GATHER SOME SUPPLIES FROM THE INFIRMARY AND THEN WE CAN GO.
WON'T TAKE A MINUTE.

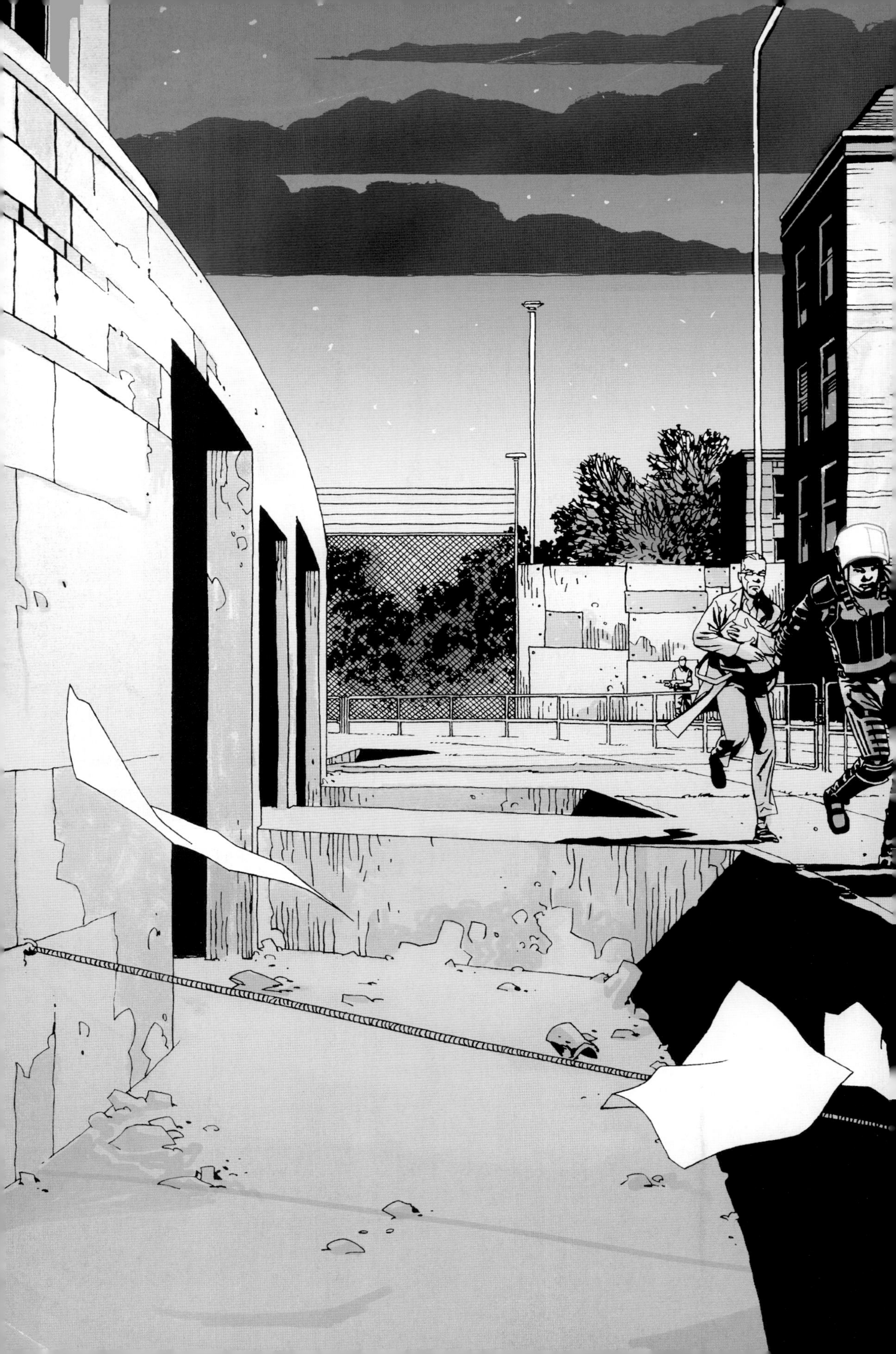

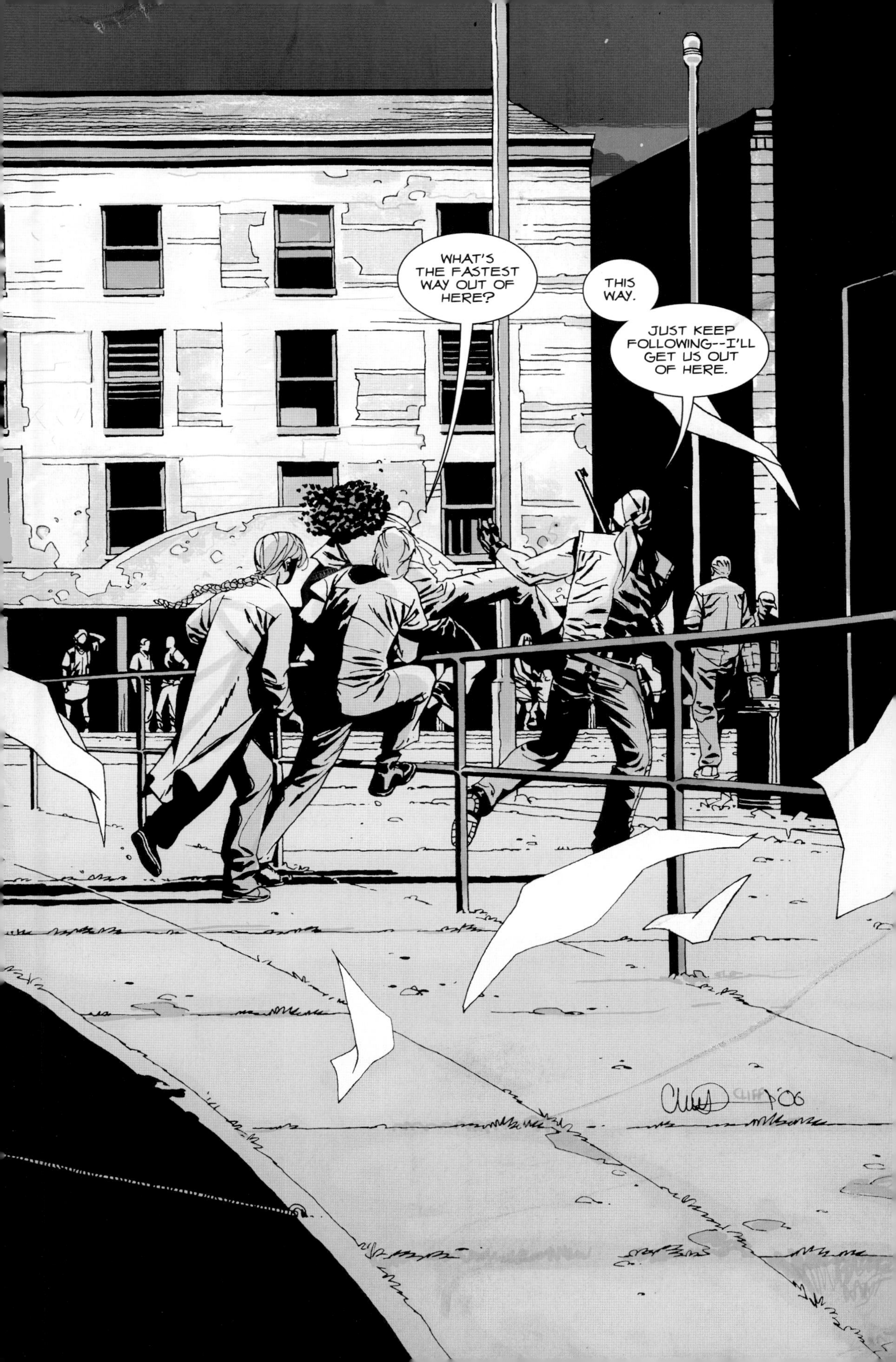
WHAT'S THE FASTEST WAY OUT OF HERE?
THIS WAY.
JUST KEEP FOLLOWING--I'LL GET US OUT OF HERE.
CLIFF '06

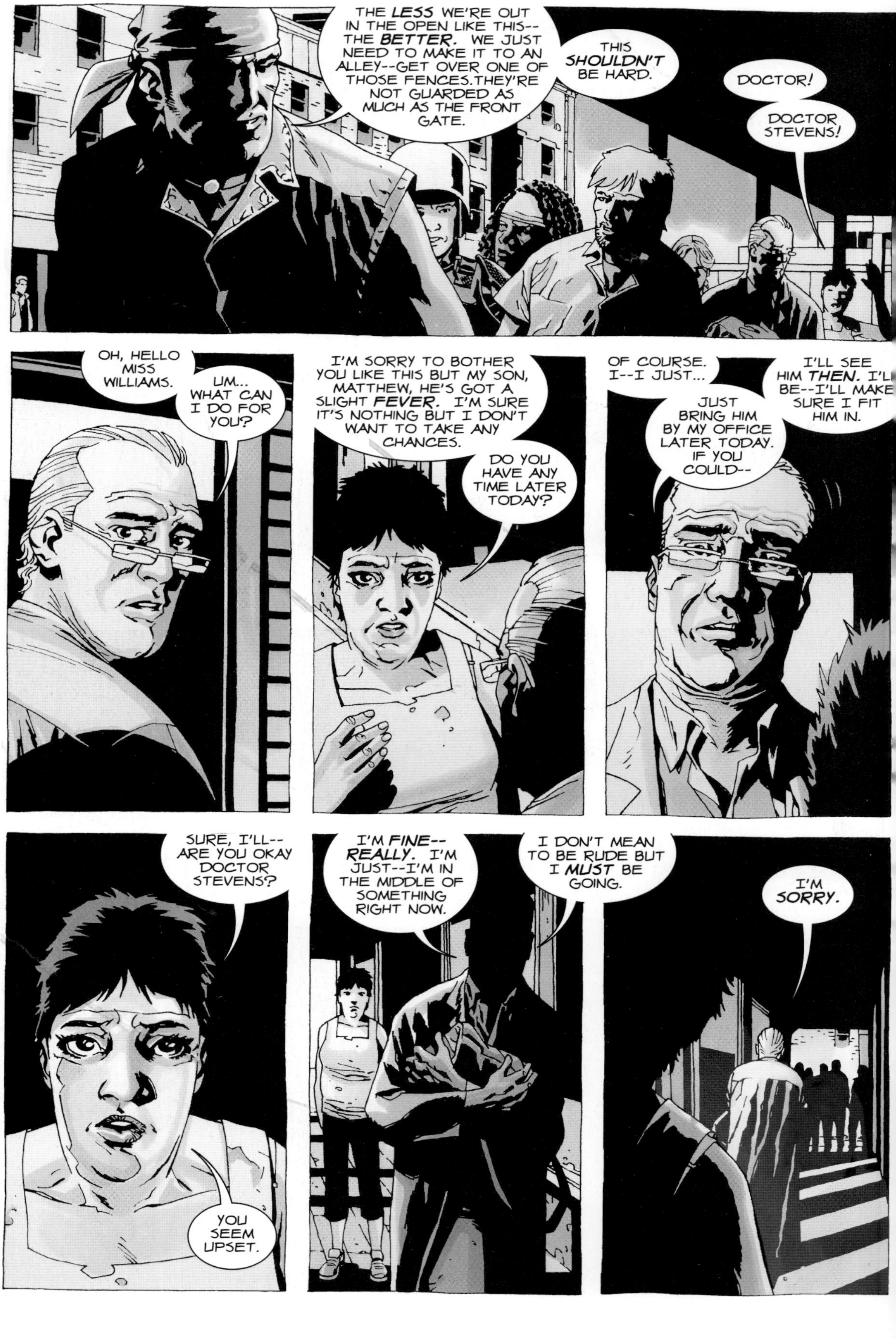
THE LESS WE'RE OUT IN THE OPEN LIKE THIS-- THE BETTER. WE JUST NEED TO MAKE IT TO AN ALLEY--GET OVER ONE OF THOSE FENCES. THEY'RE NOT GUARDED AS MUCH AS THE FRONT GATE.
THIS SHOULDN'T BE HARD.
DOCTOR!
DOCTOR STEVENS!
OH, HELLO MISS WILLIAMS.
UM... WHAT CAN I DO FOR YOU?
I'M SORRY TO BOTHER YOU LIKE THIS BUT MY SON, MATTHEW, HE'S GOT A SLIGHT FEVER. I'M SURE IT'S NOTHING BUT I DON'T WANT TO TAKE ANY CHANCES.
DO YOU HAVE ANY TIME LATER TODAY?
OF COURSE. I--I JUST...
JUST BRING HIM BY MY OFFICE LATER TODAY. IF YOU COULD--
I'LL SEE HIM THEN. I'LL BE--I'LL MAKE SURE I FIT HIM IN.
SURE, I'LL-- ARE YOU OKAY DOCTOR STEVENS?
YOU SEEM UPSET.
I'M FINE-- REALLY. I'M JUST--I'M IN THE MIDDLE OF SOMETHING RIGHT NOW.
I DON'T MEAN TO BE RUDE BUT I MUST BE GOING.
I'M SORRY.

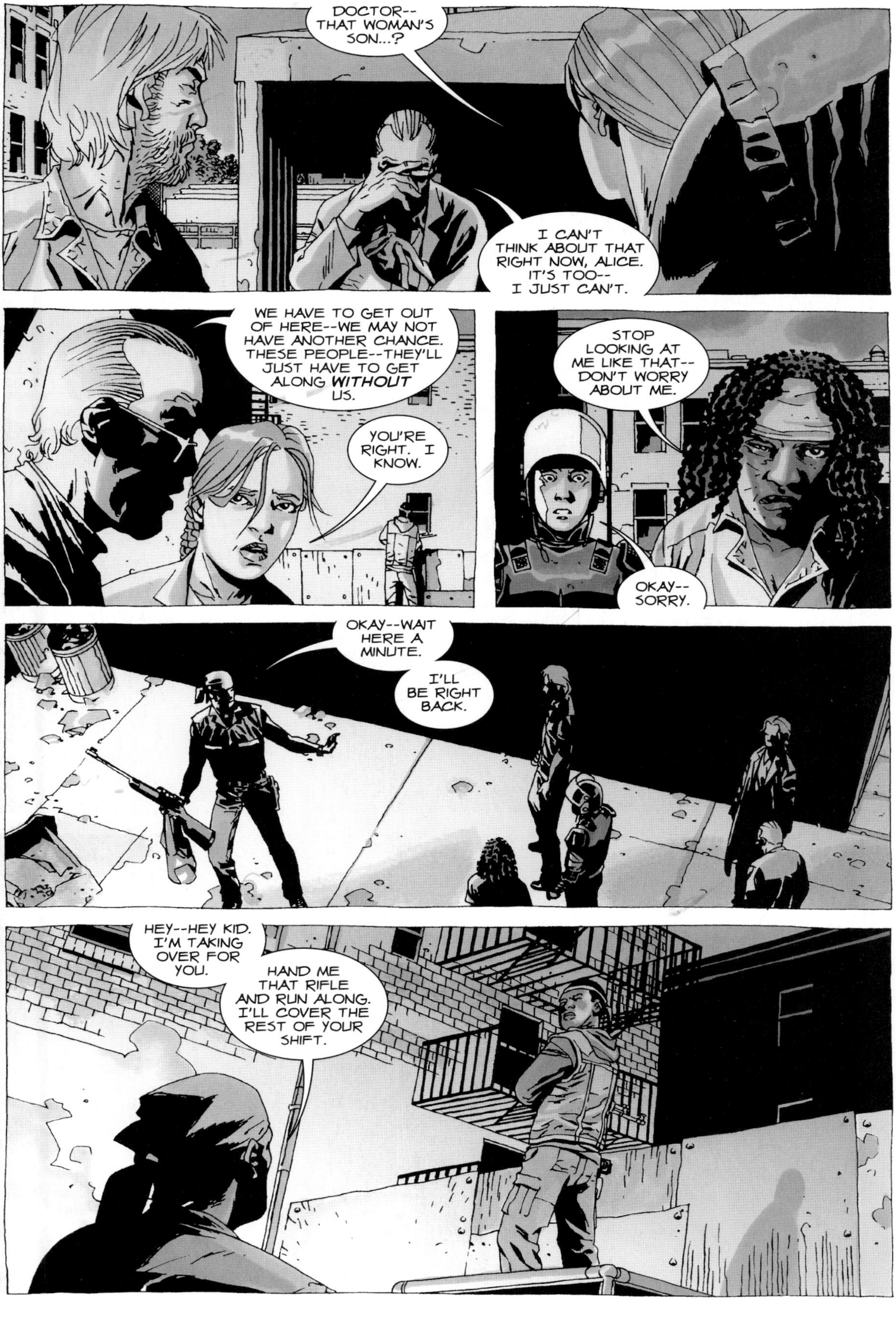
DOCTOR-- THAT WOMAN'S SON...?
I CAN'T THINK ABOUT THAT RIGHT NOW, ALICE. IT'S TOO-- I JUST CAN'T.
WE HAVE TO GET OUT OF HERE--WE MAY NOT HAVE ANOTHER CHANCE. THESE PEOPLE--THEY'LL JUST HAVE TO GET ALONG *WITHOUT* US.
YOU'RE RIGHT. I KNOW.
STOP LOOKING AT ME LIKE THAT-- DON'T WORRY ABOUT ME.
OKAY-- SORRY.
OKAY--WAIT HERE A MINUTE.
I'LL BE RIGHT BACK.
HEY--HEY KID. I'M TAKING OVER FOR YOU.
HAND ME THAT RIFLE AND RUN ALONG. I'LL COVER THE REST OF YOUR SHIFT.

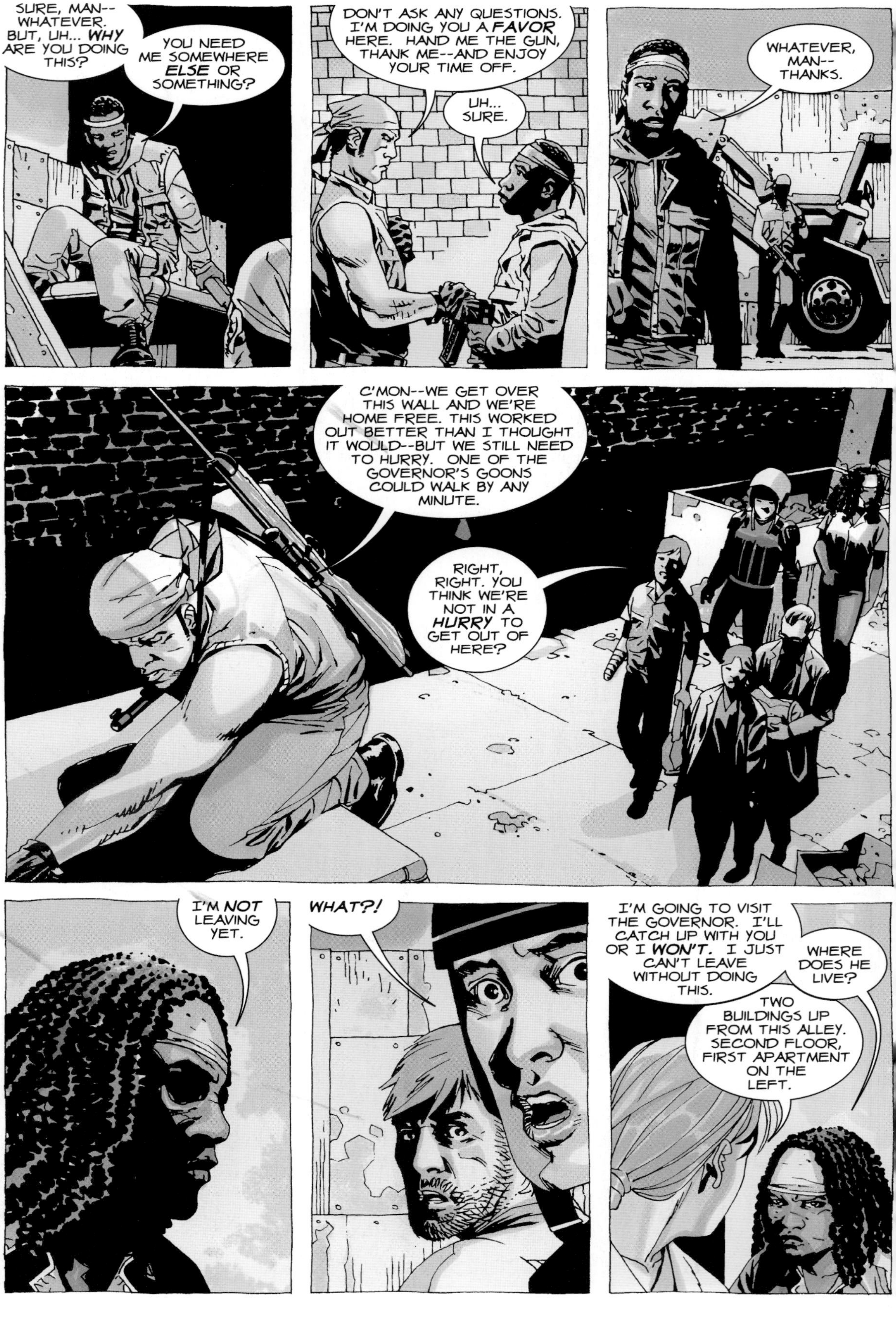
SURE, MAN--WHATEVER. BUT, UH... WHY ARE YOU DOING THIS?
YOU NEED ME SOMEWHERE ELSE OR SOMETHING?
DON'T ASK ANY QUESTIONS. I'M DOING YOU A FAVOR HERE. HAND ME THE GUN, THANK ME--AND ENJOY YOUR TIME OFF.
UH... SURE.
WHATEVER, MAN--THANKS.
C'MON--WE GET OVER THIS WALL AND WE'RE HOME FREE. THIS WORKED OUT BETTER THAN I THOUGHT IT WOULD--BUT WE STILL NEED TO HURRY. ONE OF THE GOVERNOR'S GOONS COULD WALK BY ANY MINUTE.
RIGHT, RIGHT. YOU THINK WE'RE NOT IN A HURRY TO GET OUT OF HERE?
I'M NOT LEAVING YET.
WHAT?!
I'M GOING TO VISIT THE GOVERNOR. I'LL CATCH UP WITH YOU OR I WON'T. I JUST CAN'T LEAVE WITHOUT DOING THIS.
WHERE DOES HE LIVE?
TWO BUILDINGS UP FROM THIS ALLEY. SECOND FLOOR, FIRST APARTMENT ON THE LEFT.

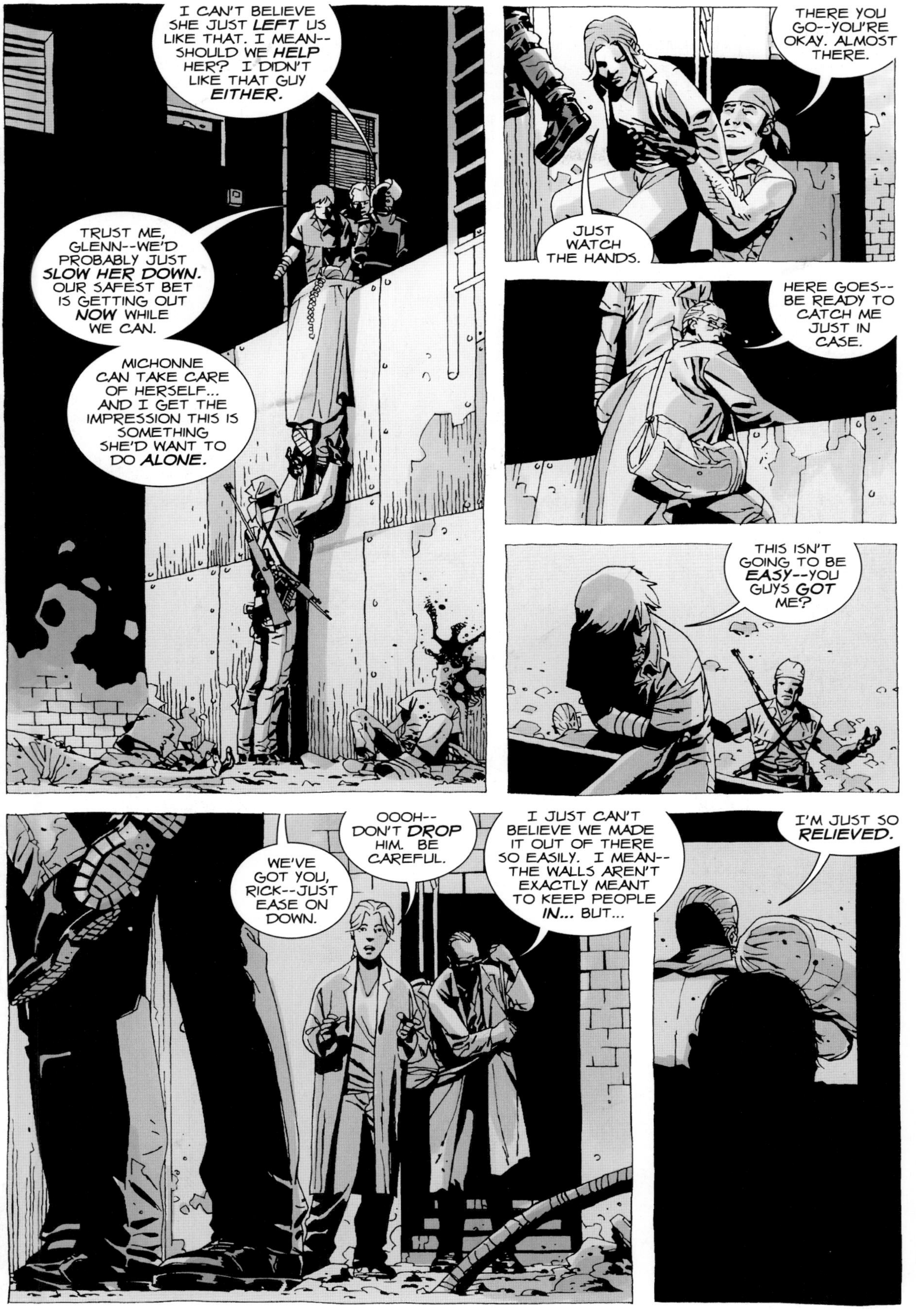
I CAN'T BELIEVE SHE JUST LEFT US LIKE THAT. I MEAN--SHOULD WE HELP HER? I DIDN'T LIKE THAT GUY EITHER.
TRUST ME, GLENN--WE'D PROBABLY JUST SLOW HER DOWN. OUR SAFEST BET IS GETTING OUT NOW WHILE WE CAN.
MICHONNE CAN TAKE CARE OF HERSELF... AND I GET THE IMPRESSION THIS IS SOMETHING SHE'D WANT TO DO ALONE.
THERE YOU GO--YOU'RE OKAY. ALMOST THERE.
JUST WATCH THE HANDS.
HERE GOES--BE READY TO CATCH ME JUST IN CASE.
THIS ISN'T GOING TO BE EASY--YOU GUYS GOT ME?
WE'VE GOT YOU, RICK--JUST EASE ON DOWN.
OOOH--DON'T DROP HIM. BE CAREFUL.
I JUST CAN'T BELIEVE WE MADE IT OUT OF THERE SO EASILY. I MEAN--THE WALLS AREN'T EXACTLY MEANT TO KEEP PEOPLE IN... BUT...
I'M JUST SO RELIEVED.

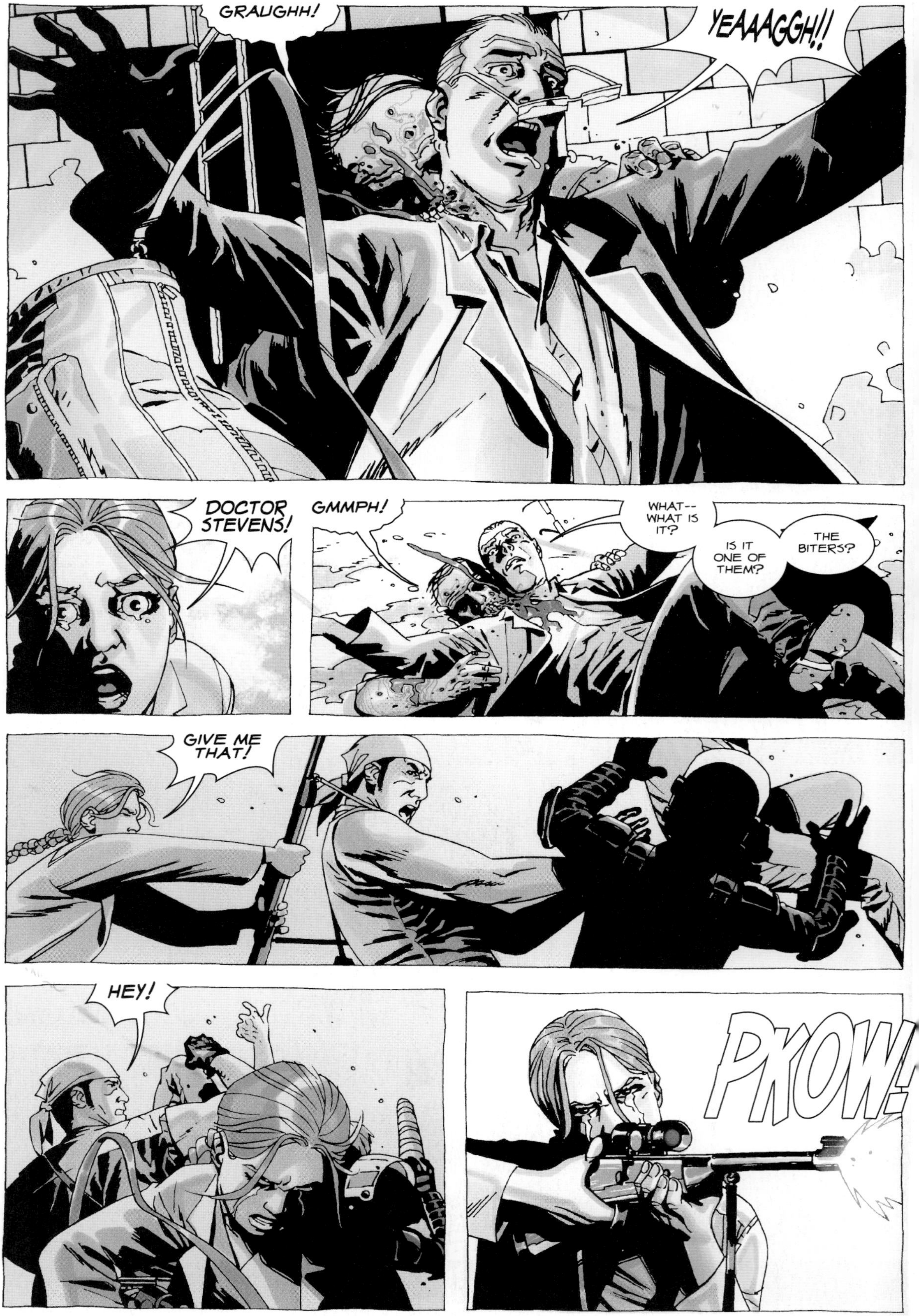
GRAUGHH!
YEAAAGGH!!
DOCTOR STEVENS!
GMMPH!
WHAT-- WHAT IS IT?
IS IT ONE OF THEM?
THE BITERS?
GIVE ME THAT!
HEY!
PKOW!

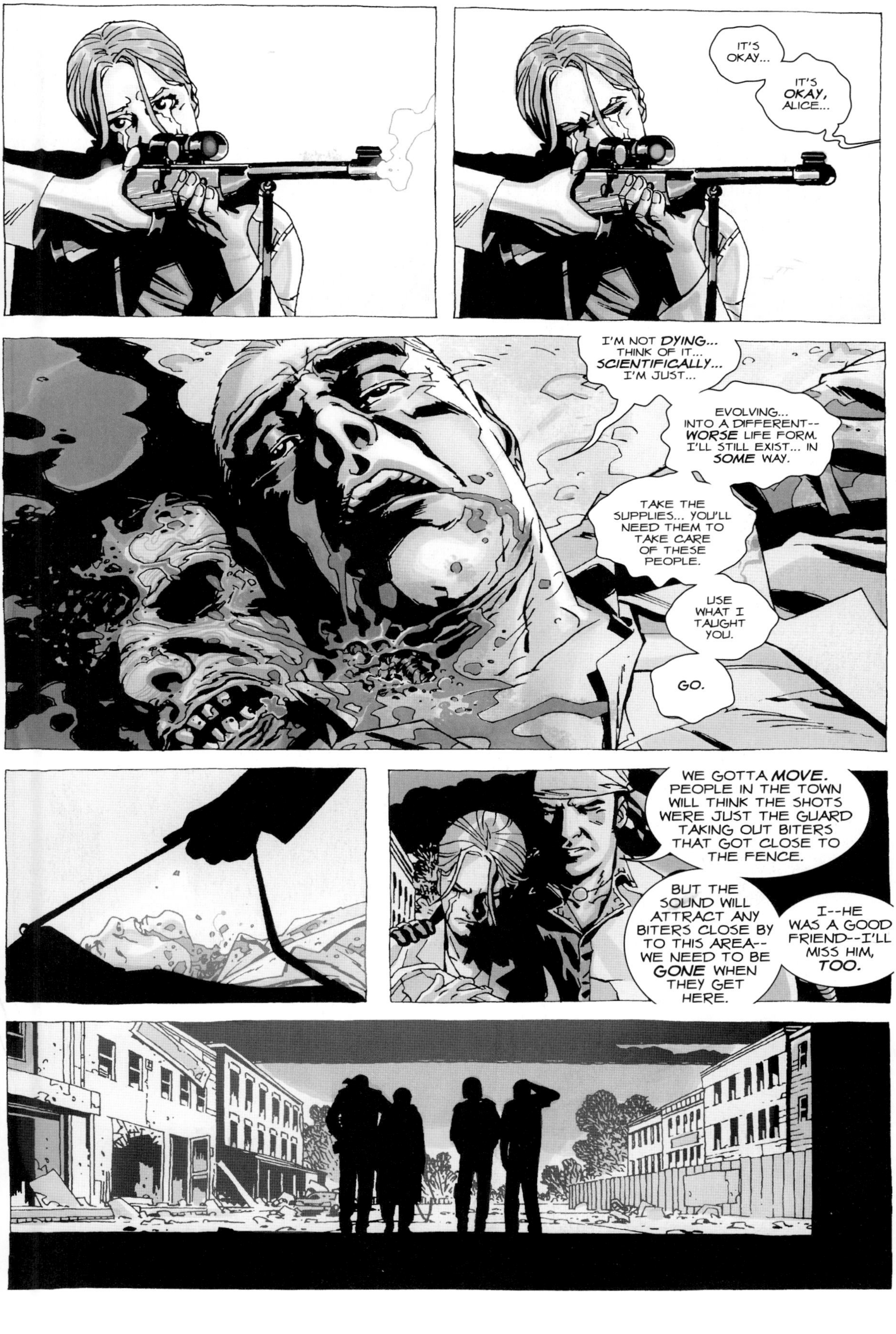
IT'S OKAY...
IT'S OKAY, ALICE...
I'M NOT DYING... THINK OF IT... SCIENTIFICALLY... I'M JUST...
EVOLVING... INTO A DIFFERENT-- WORSE LIFE FORM. I'LL STILL EXIST... IN SOME WAY.
TAKE THE SUPPLIES... YOU'LL NEED THEM TO TAKE CARE OF THESE PEOPLE.
USE WHAT I TAUGHT YOU.
GO.
WE GOTTA MOVE. PEOPLE IN THE TOWN WILL THINK THE SHOTS WERE JUST THE GUARD TAKING OUT BITERS THAT GOT CLOSE TO THE FENCE.
BUT THE SOUND WILL ATTRACT ANY BITERS CLOSE BY TO THIS AREA-- WE NEED TO BE GONE WHEN THEY GET HERE.
I--HE WAS A GOOD FRIEND--I'LL MISS HIM, TOO.

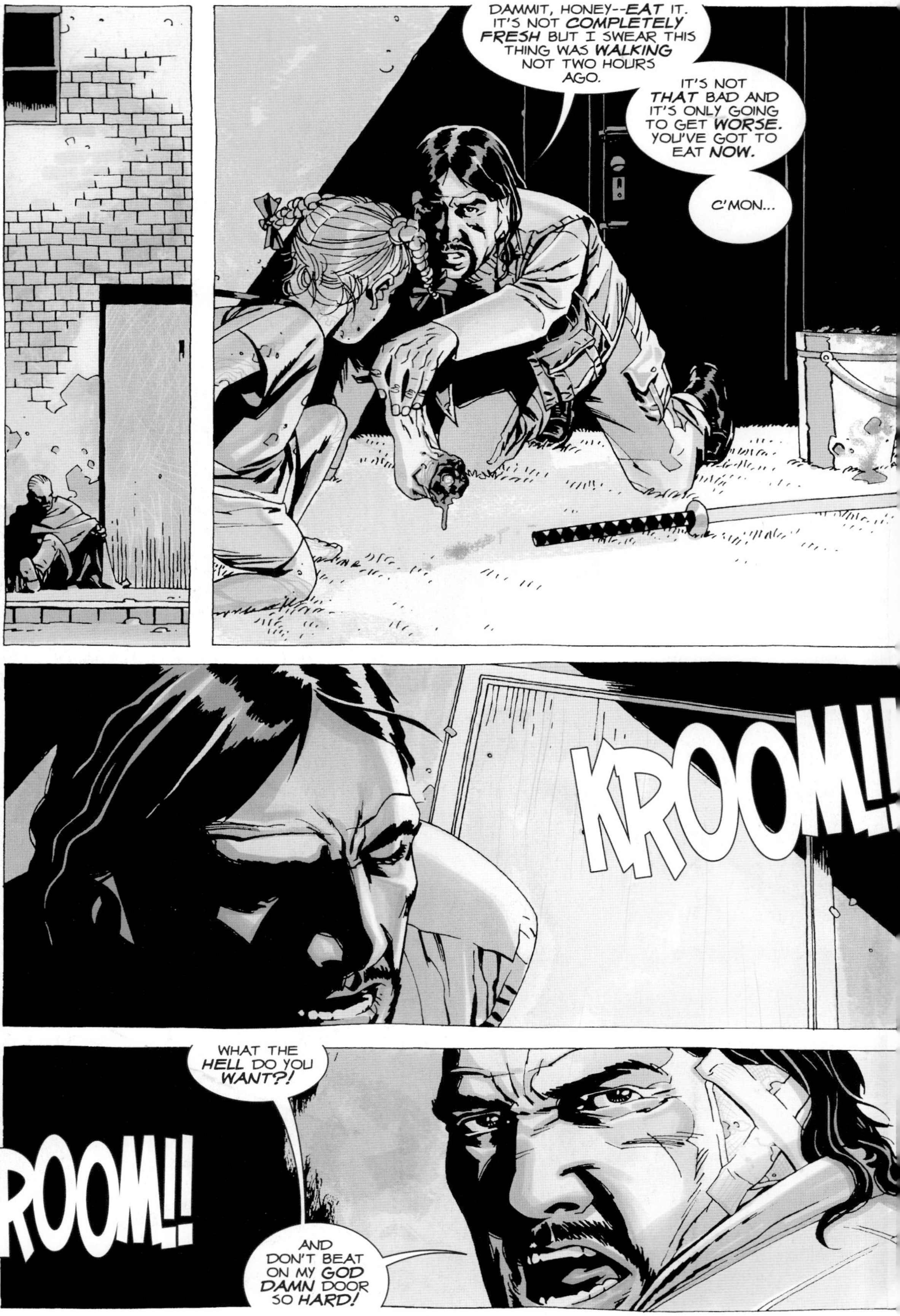

DAMMIT, HONEY--EAT IT. IT'S NOT COMPLETELY FRESH BUT I SWEAR THIS THING WAS WALKING NOT TWO HOURS AGO.
IT'S NOT THAT BAD AND IT'S ONLY GOING TO GET WORSE. YOU'VE GOT TO EAT NOW.
C'MON...
KROOM!!
WHAT THE HELL DO YOU WANT?!
KROOM!!
AND DON'T BEAT ON MY GOD DAMN DOOR SO HARD!

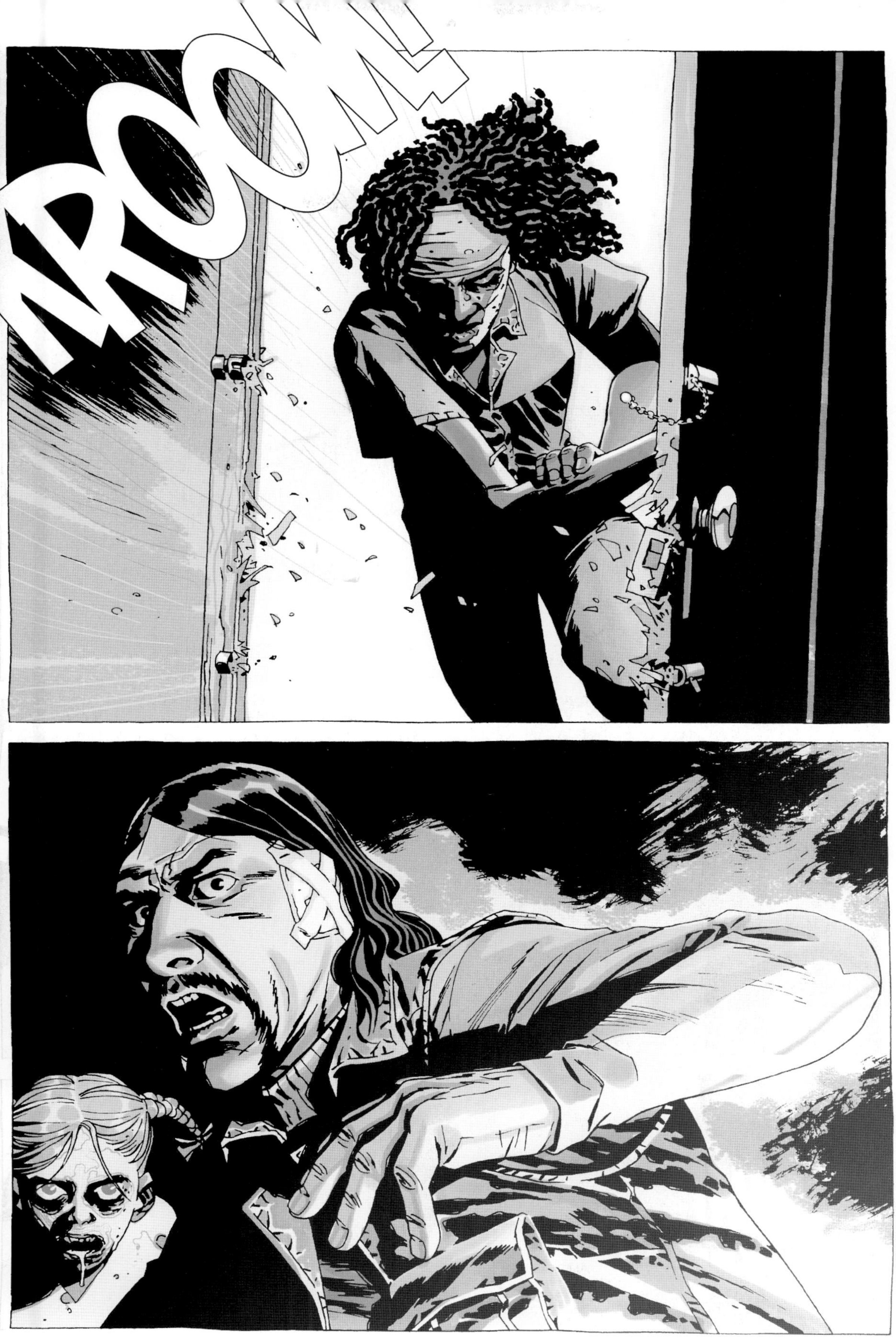
VROOM!

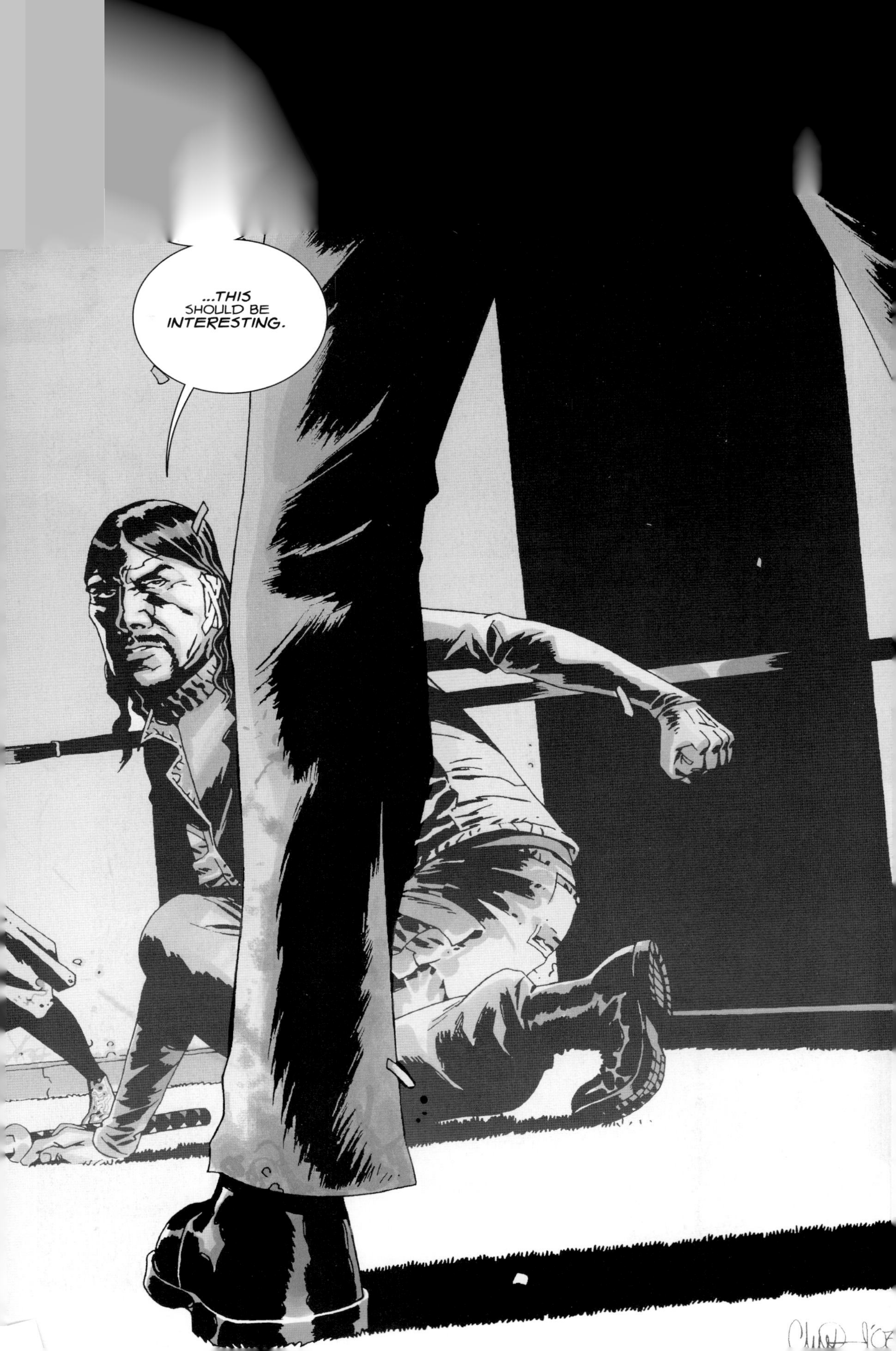
...THIS SHOULD BE INTERESTING.

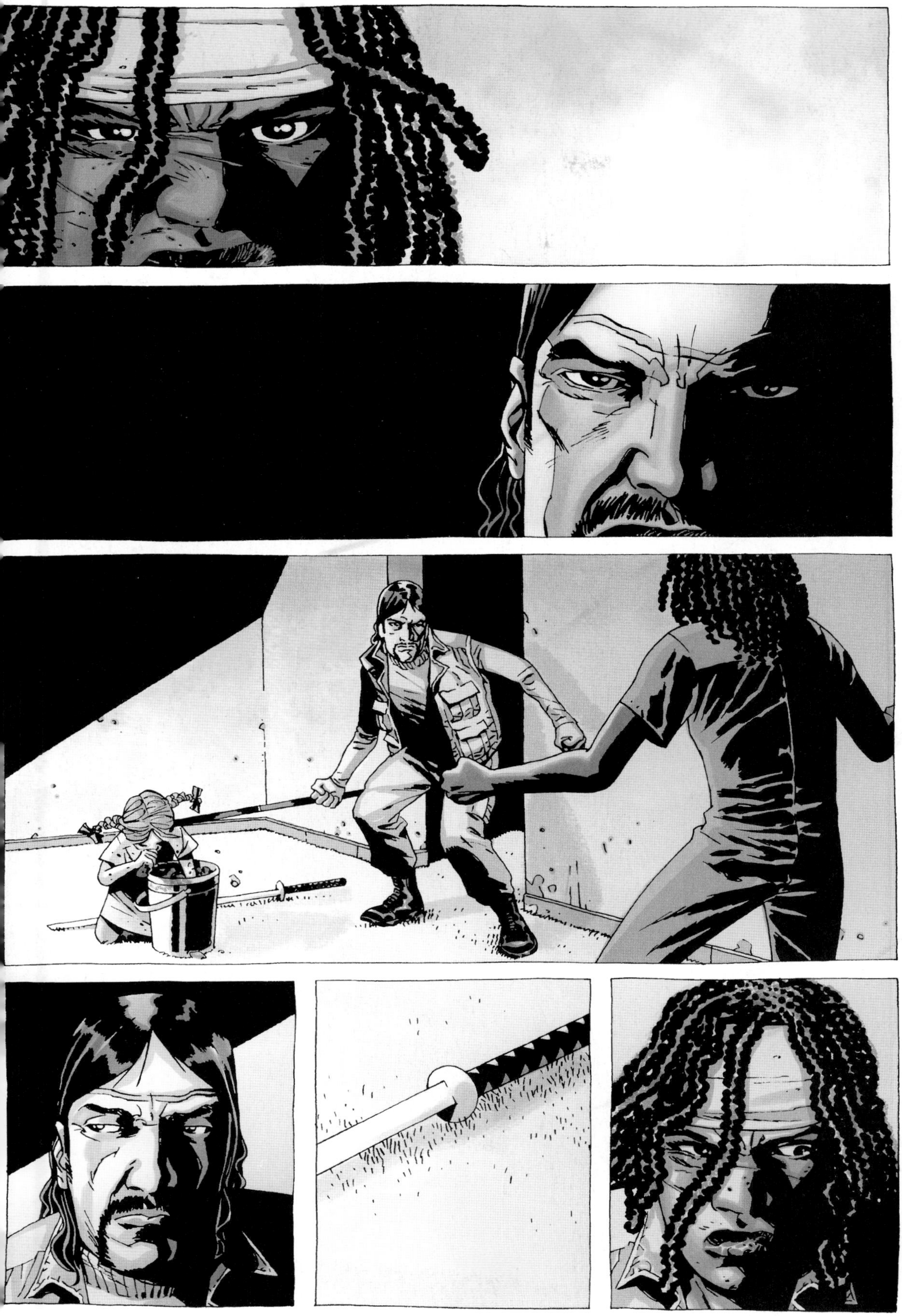

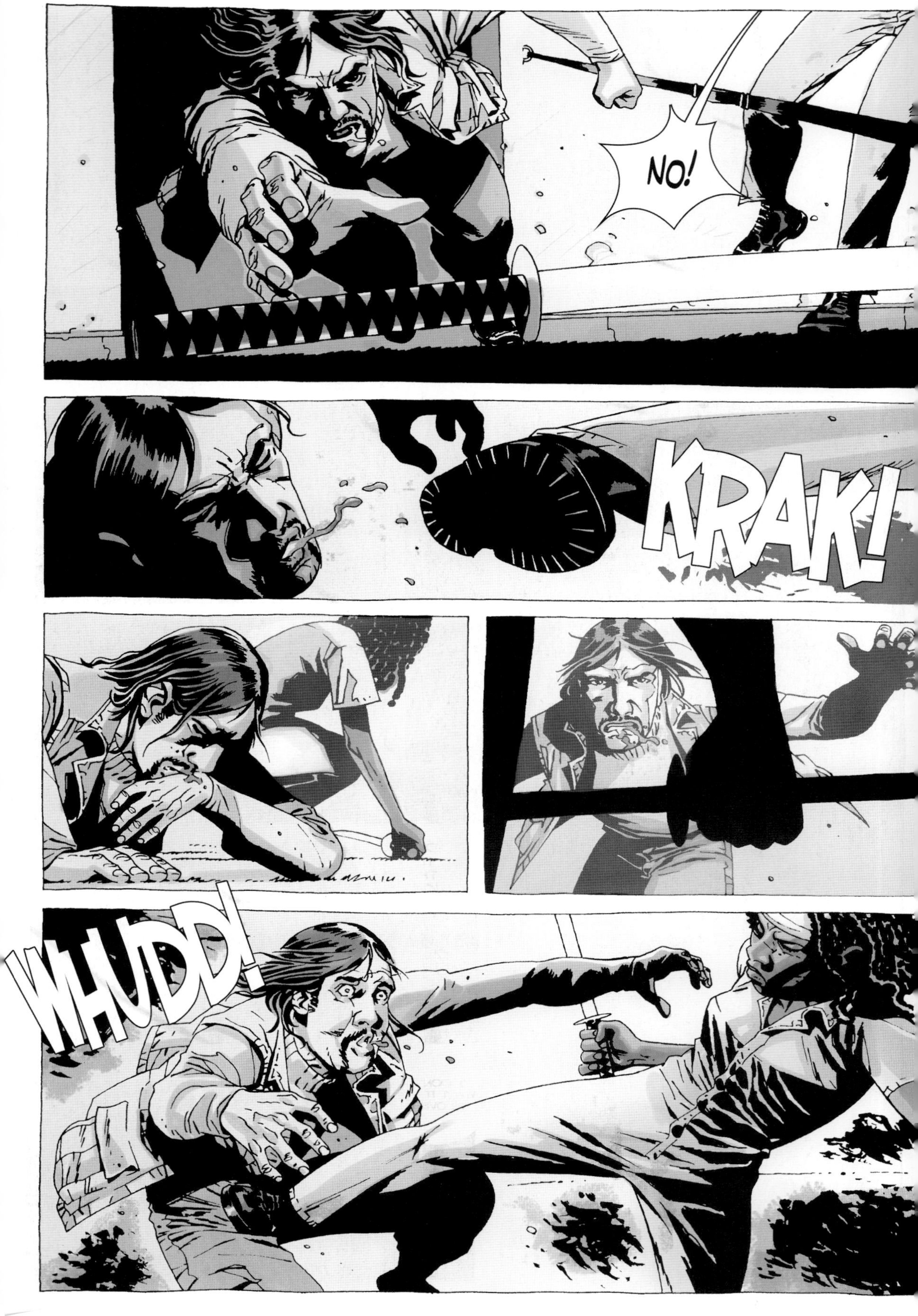
NO!
KRAK!
WHUDD!

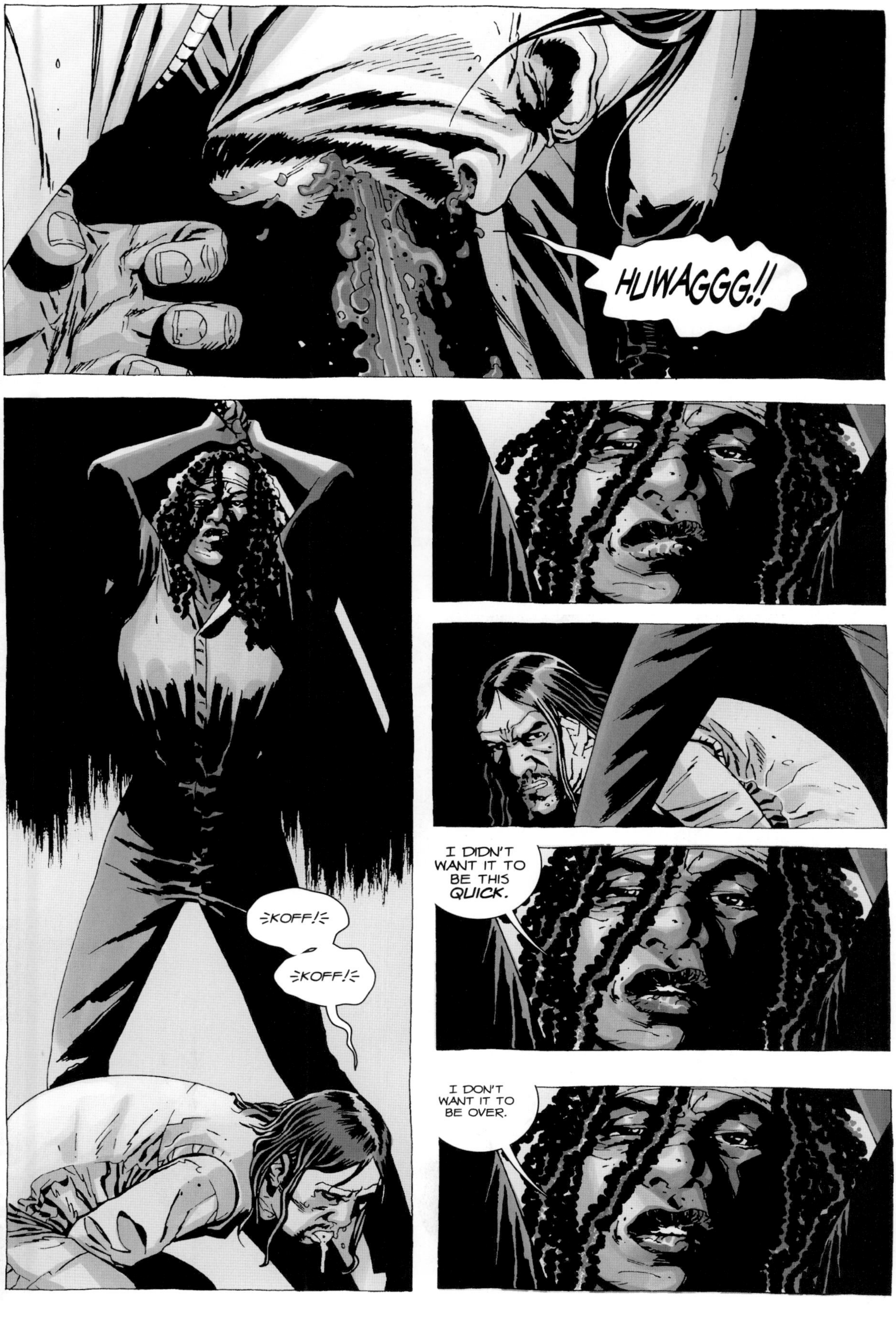
HUWAGGG!!
KOFF!
KOFF!
I DIDN'T WANT IT TO BE THIS QUICK.
I DON'T WANT IT TO BE OVER.

WHUMP

WHUDD!

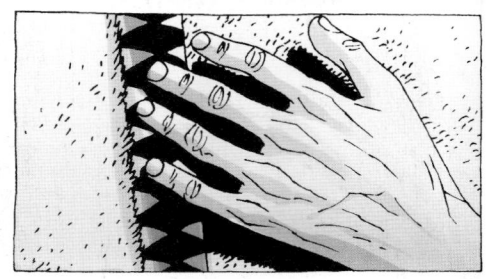

HRRKK!!

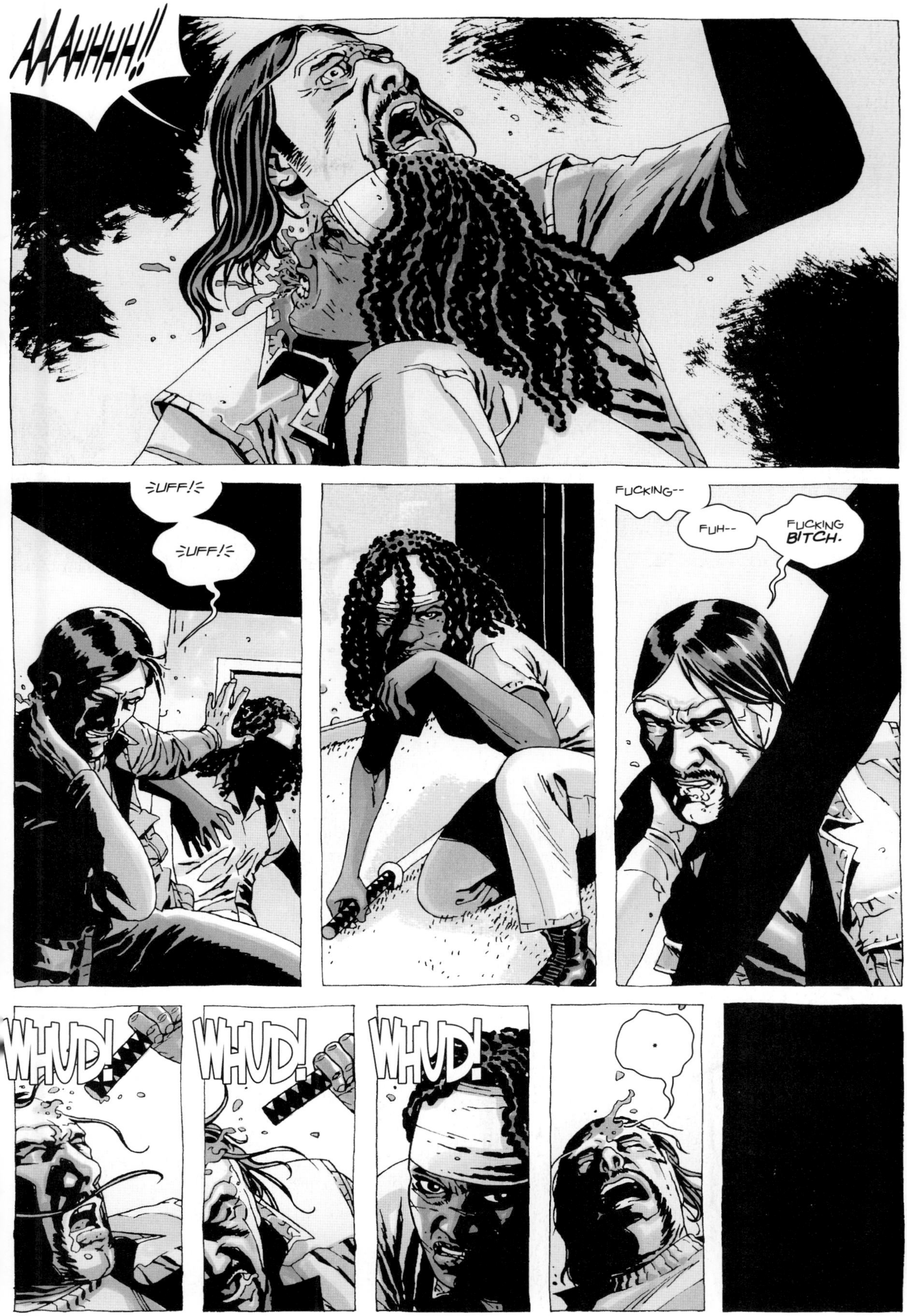
AAAHHHH!!
UFF!
UFF!
FUCKING--
FUH--
FUCKING BITCH.
WHUD!
WHUD!
WHUD!
.

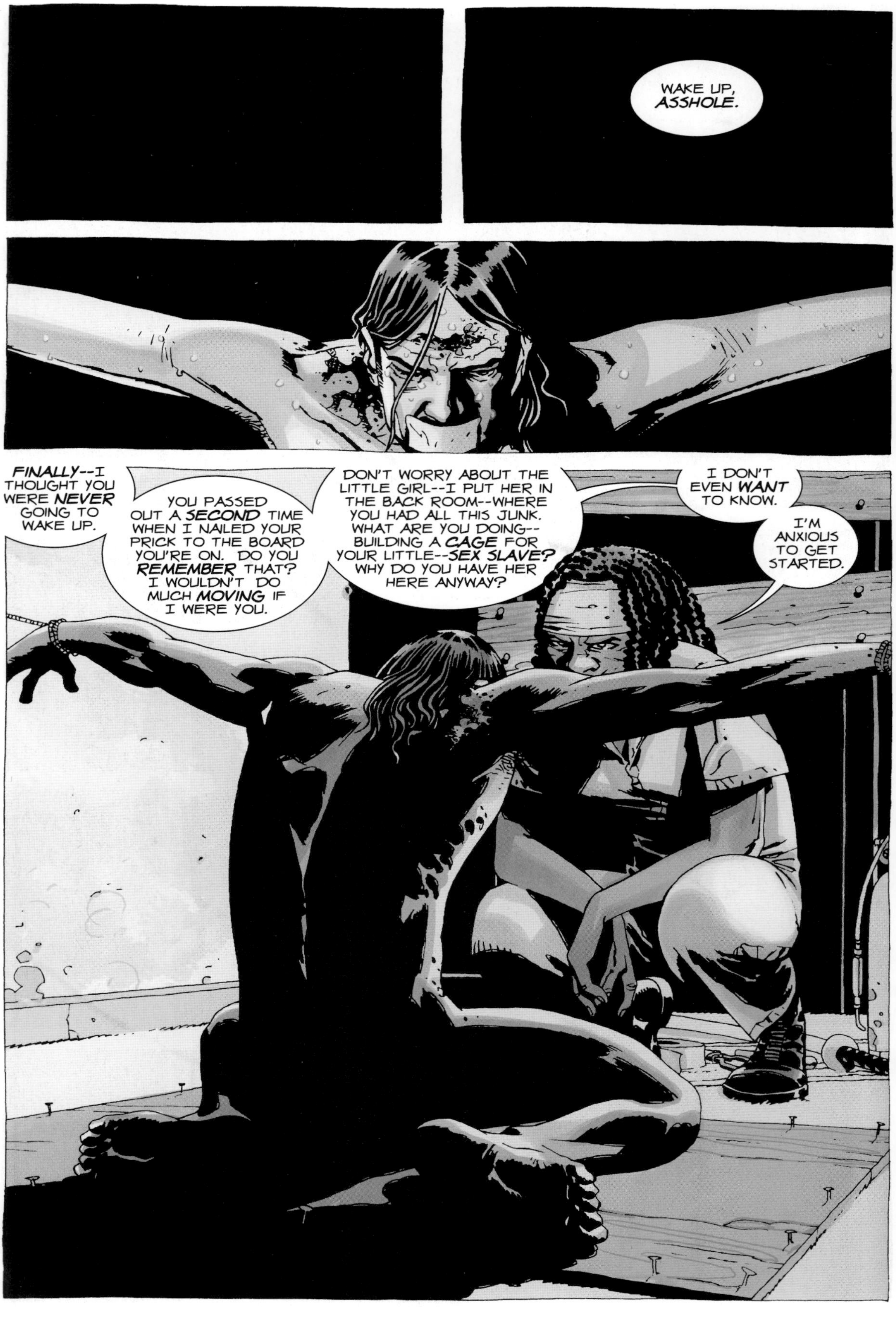
WAKE UP, ASSHOLE.
FINALLY--I THOUGHT YOU WERE NEVER GOING TO WAKE UP.
YOU PASSED OUT A SECOND TIME WHEN I NAILED YOUR PRICK TO THE BOARD YOU'RE ON. DO YOU REMEMBER THAT? I WOULDN'T DO MUCH MOVING IF I WERE YOU.
DON'T WORRY ABOUT THE LITTLE GIRL--I PUT HER IN THE BACK ROOM--WHERE YOU HAD ALL THIS JUNK. WHAT ARE YOU DOING--BUILDING A CAGE FOR YOUR LITTLE--SEX SLAVE? WHY DO YOU HAVE HER HERE ANYWAY?
I DON'T EVEN WANT TO KNOW.
I'M ANXIOUS TO GET STARTED.

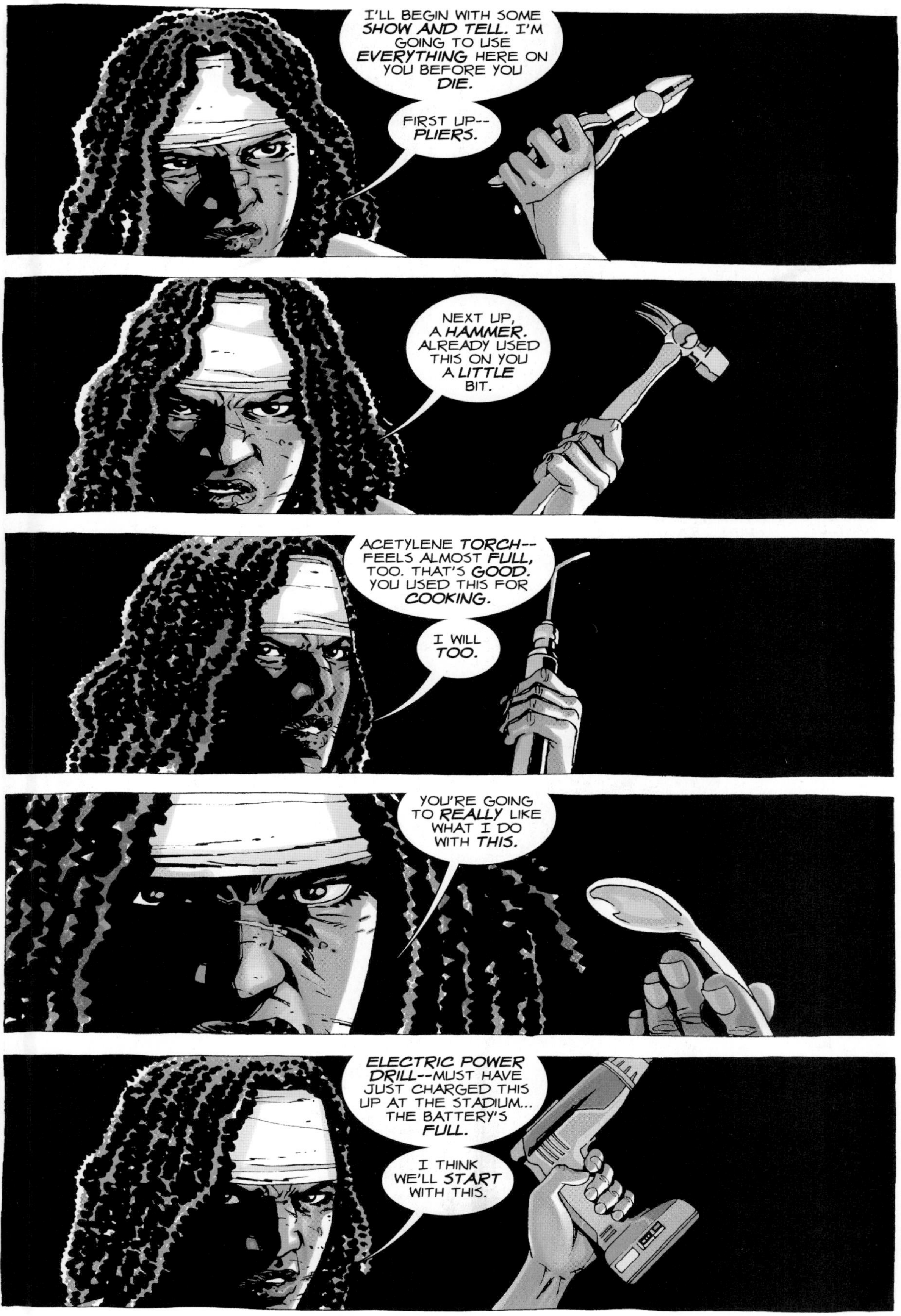
I'LL BEGIN WITH SOME SHOW AND TELL. I'M GOING TO USE EVERYTHING HERE ON YOU BEFORE YOU DIE.
FIRST UP-- PLIERS.
NEXT UP, A HAMMER. ALREADY USED THIS ON YOU A LITTLE BIT.
ACETYLENE TORCH-- FEELS ALMOST FULL, TOO. THAT'S GOOD. YOU USED THIS FOR COOKING.
I WILL TOO.
YOU'RE GOING TO REALLY LIKE WHAT I DO WITH THIS.
ELECTRIC POWER DRILL--MUST HAVE JUST CHARGED THIS UP AT THE STADIUM... THE BATTERY'S FULL.
I THINK WE'LL START WITH THIS.

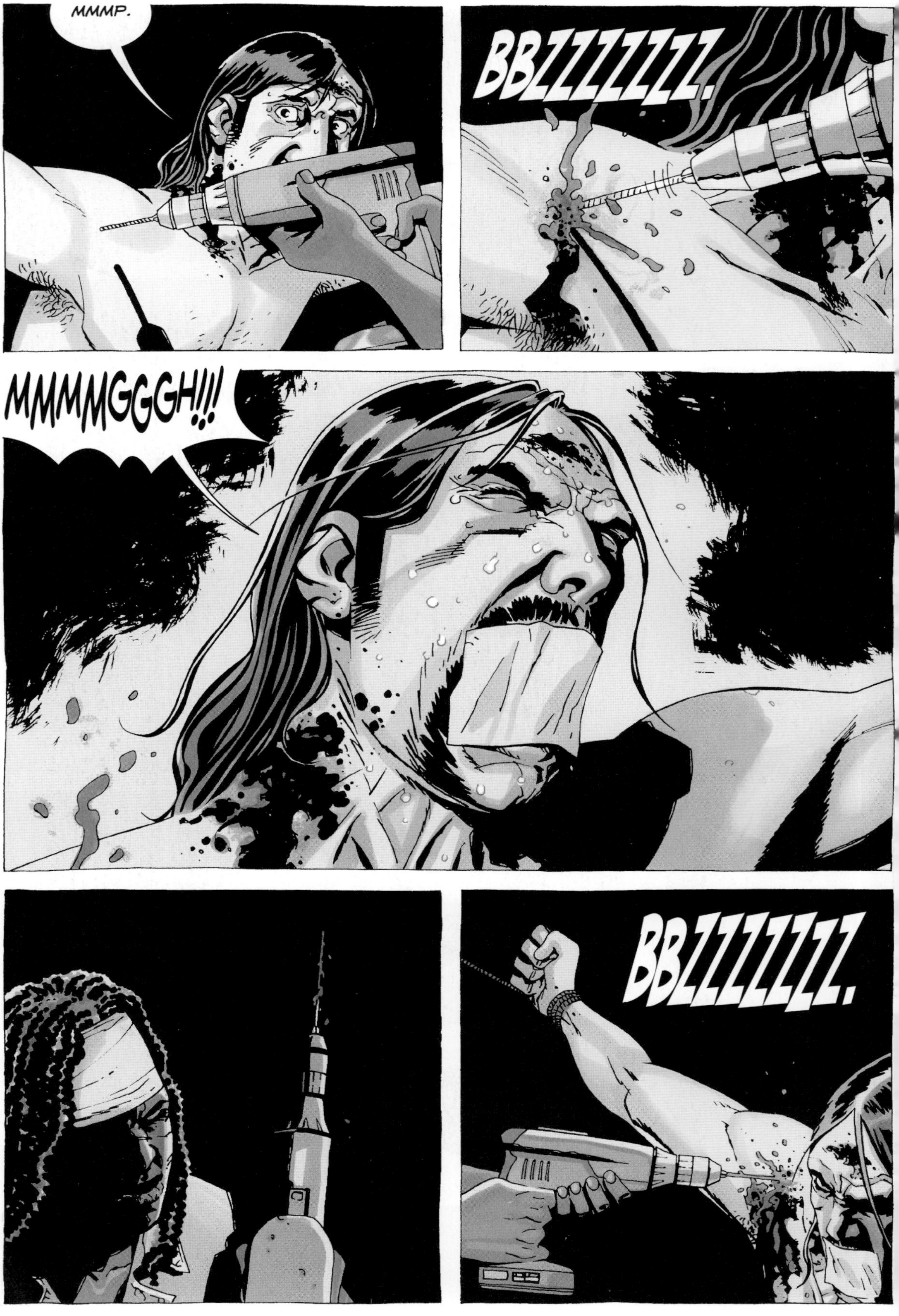
MMMP.
BBZZZZZZZZ.
MMMMGGGH!!!
BBZZZZZZZ.

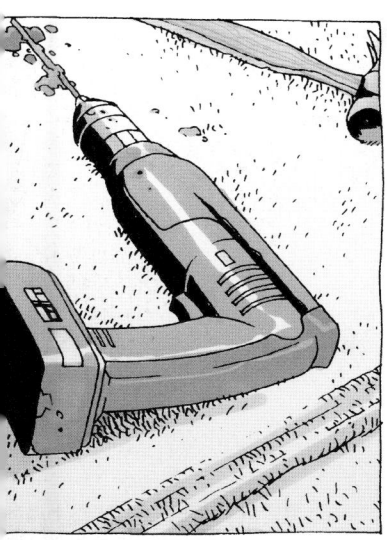

WACK!

WAKE UP!

YOU'RE GOING TO LOVE THIS.

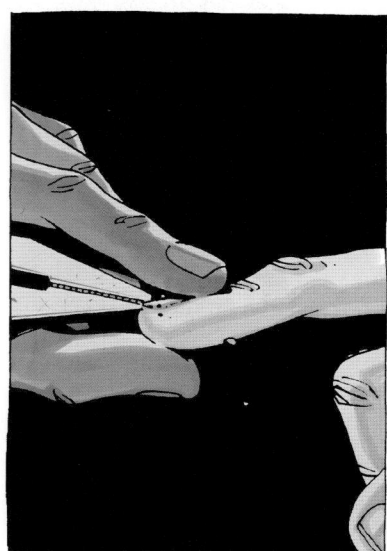

SHRKK!

MMUURGGH!

SKRRK!

MRRGH!

SHKK!

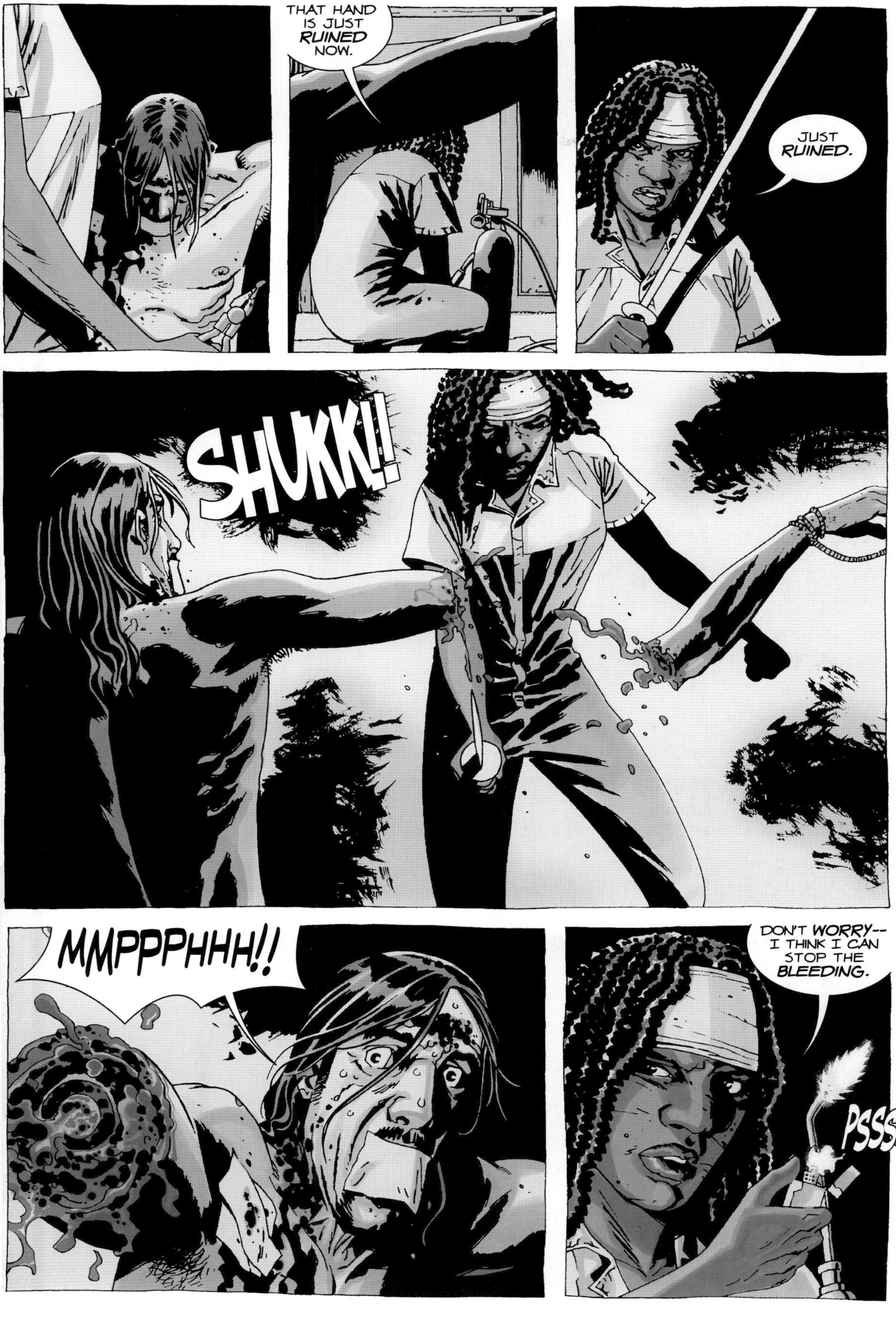
THAT HAND IS JUST RUINED NOW.
JUST RUINED.
SHUKK!!
MMPPPHHH!!
DON'T WORRY-- I THINK I CAN STOP THE BLEEDING.
PSSSH!

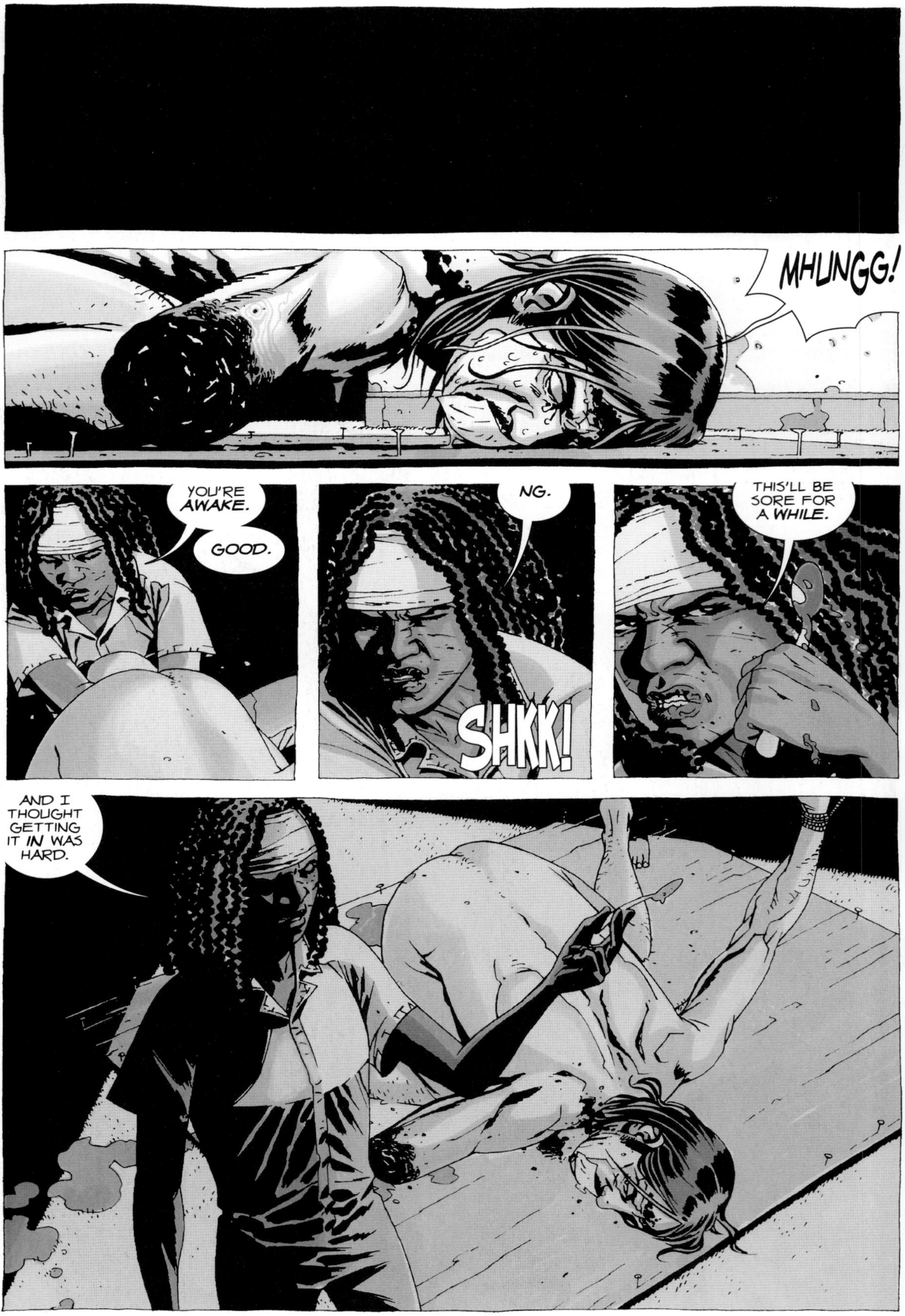
MHUNGG!
YOU'RE AWAKE.
GOOD.
NG.
SHKK!
THIS'LL BE SORE FOR A WHILE.
AND I THOUGHT GETTING IT IN WAS HARD.

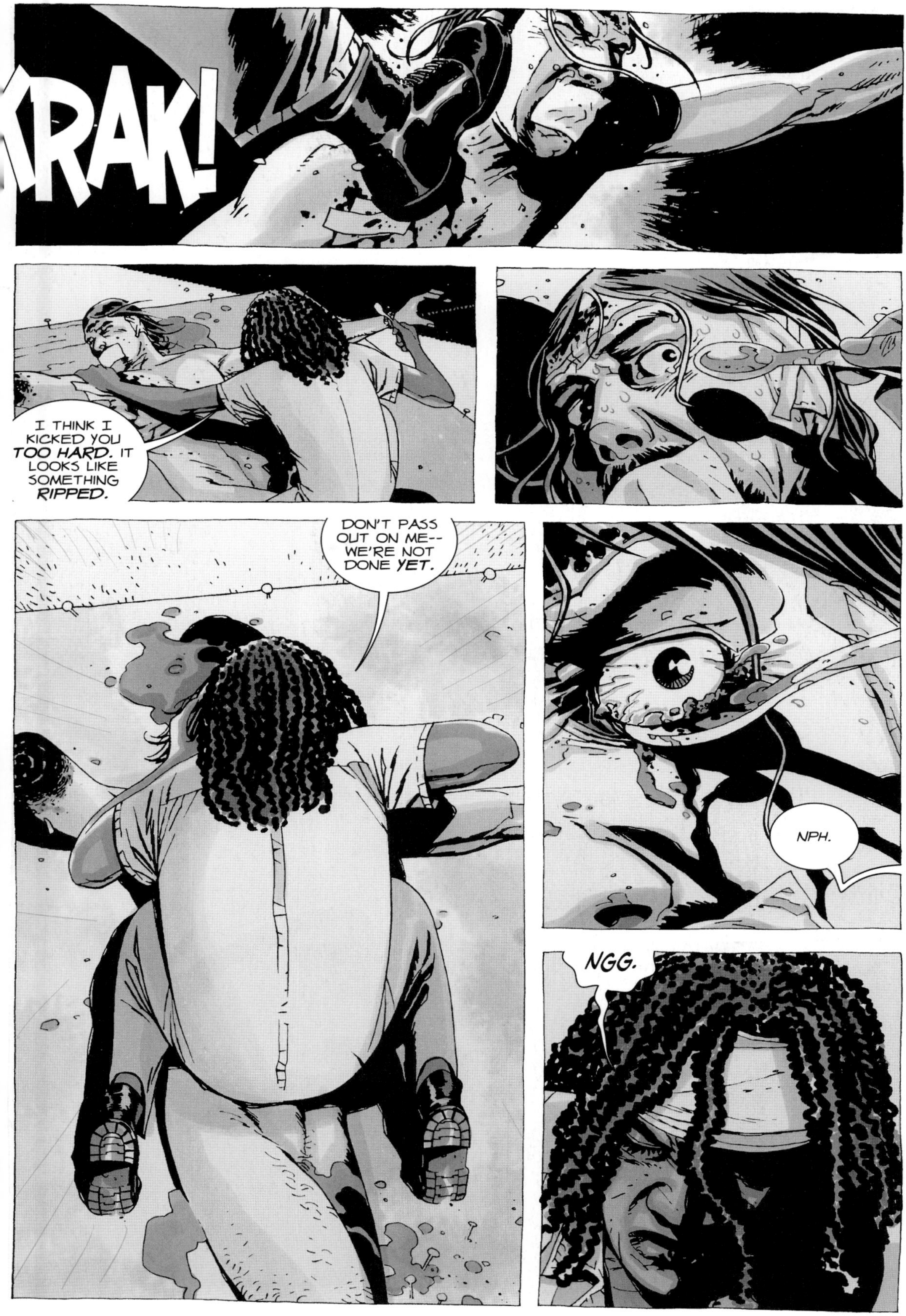
KRAK!
I THINK I KICKED YOU TOO HARD. IT LOOKS LIKE SOMETHING RIPPED.
DON'T PASS OUT ON ME-- WE'RE NOT DONE YET.
NPH.
NGG.

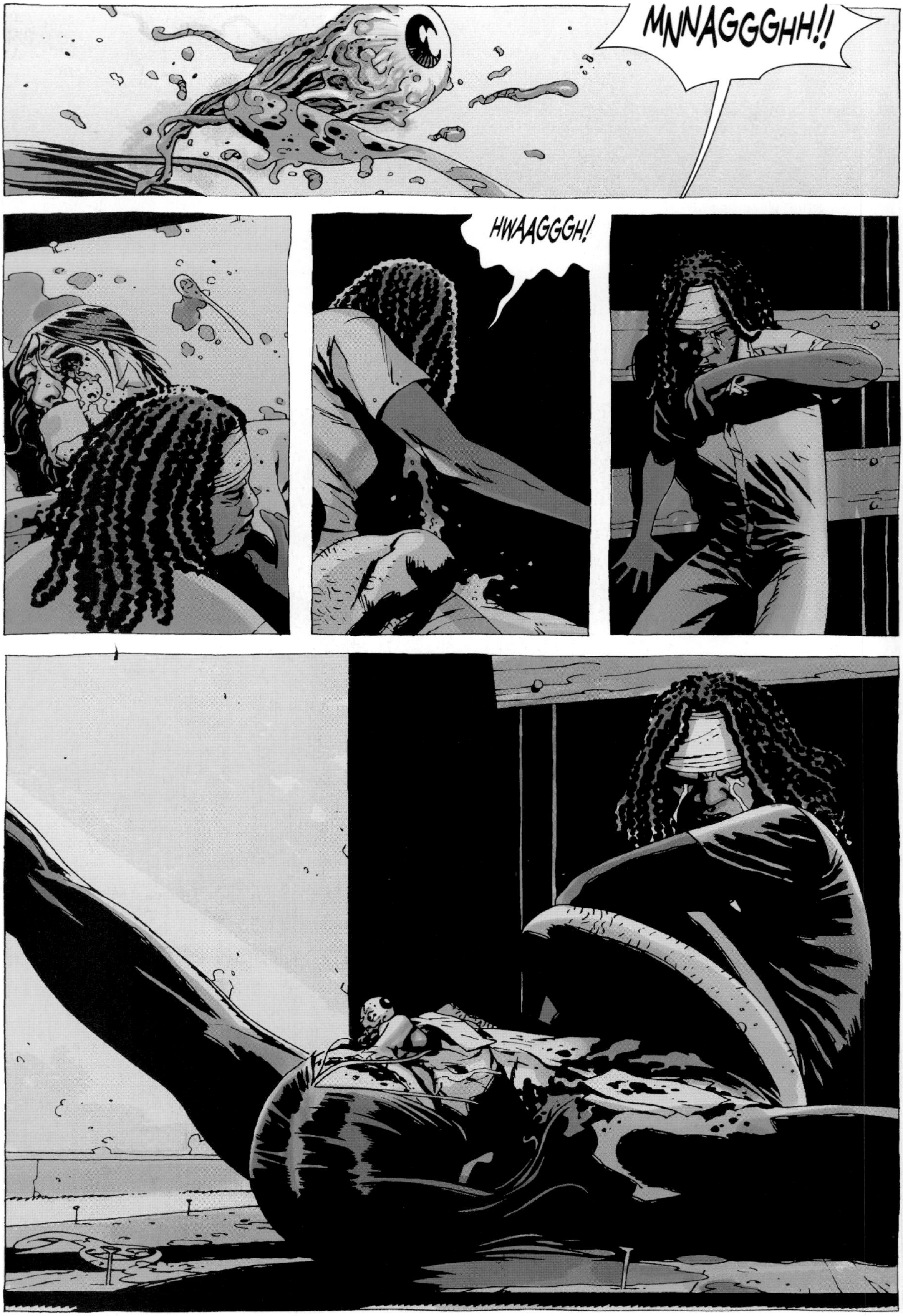
MNNAGGGHH!!
HWAAGGGH!

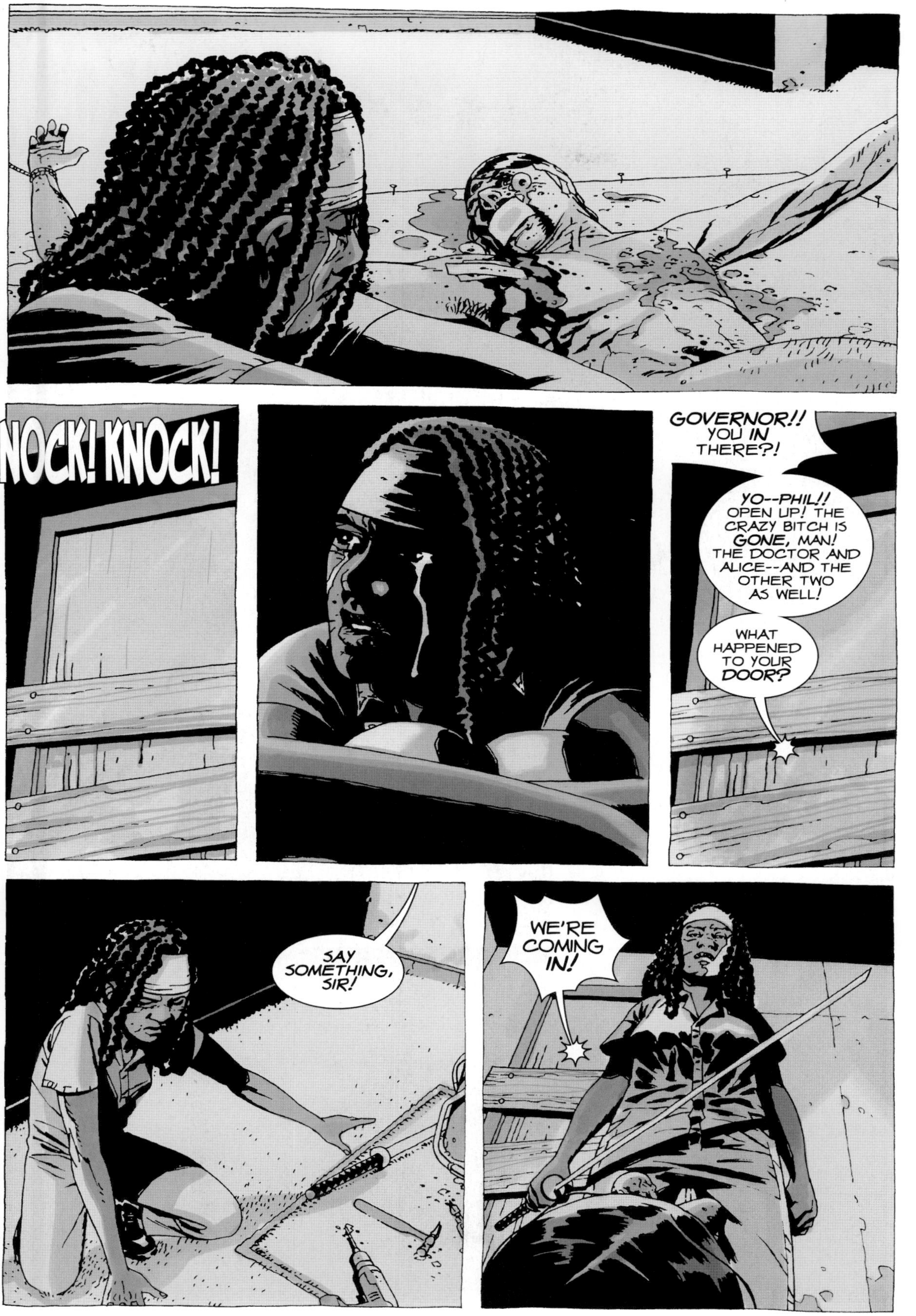

NOCK! KNOCK!
GOVERNOR!! YOU IN THERE?!
YO--PHIL!! OPEN UP! THE CRAZY BITCH IS GONE, MAN! THE DOCTOR AND ALICE--AND THE OTHER TWO AS WELL!
WHAT HAPPENED TO YOUR DOOR?
SAY SOMETHING, SIR!
WE'RE COMING IN!

LOOKS LIKE WHAT'S LEFT OF THAT THING *COULD* POSSIBLY *HEAL* IF YOU SURVIVE THIS.

AND WE *WOULDN'T* WANT *THAT.*

SHKK!

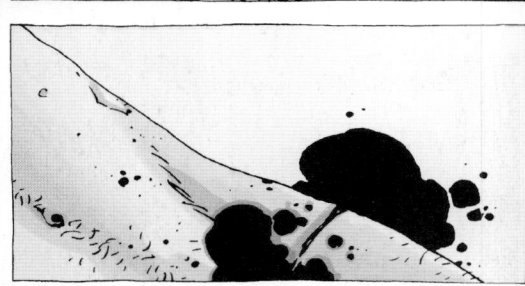

KROOM!

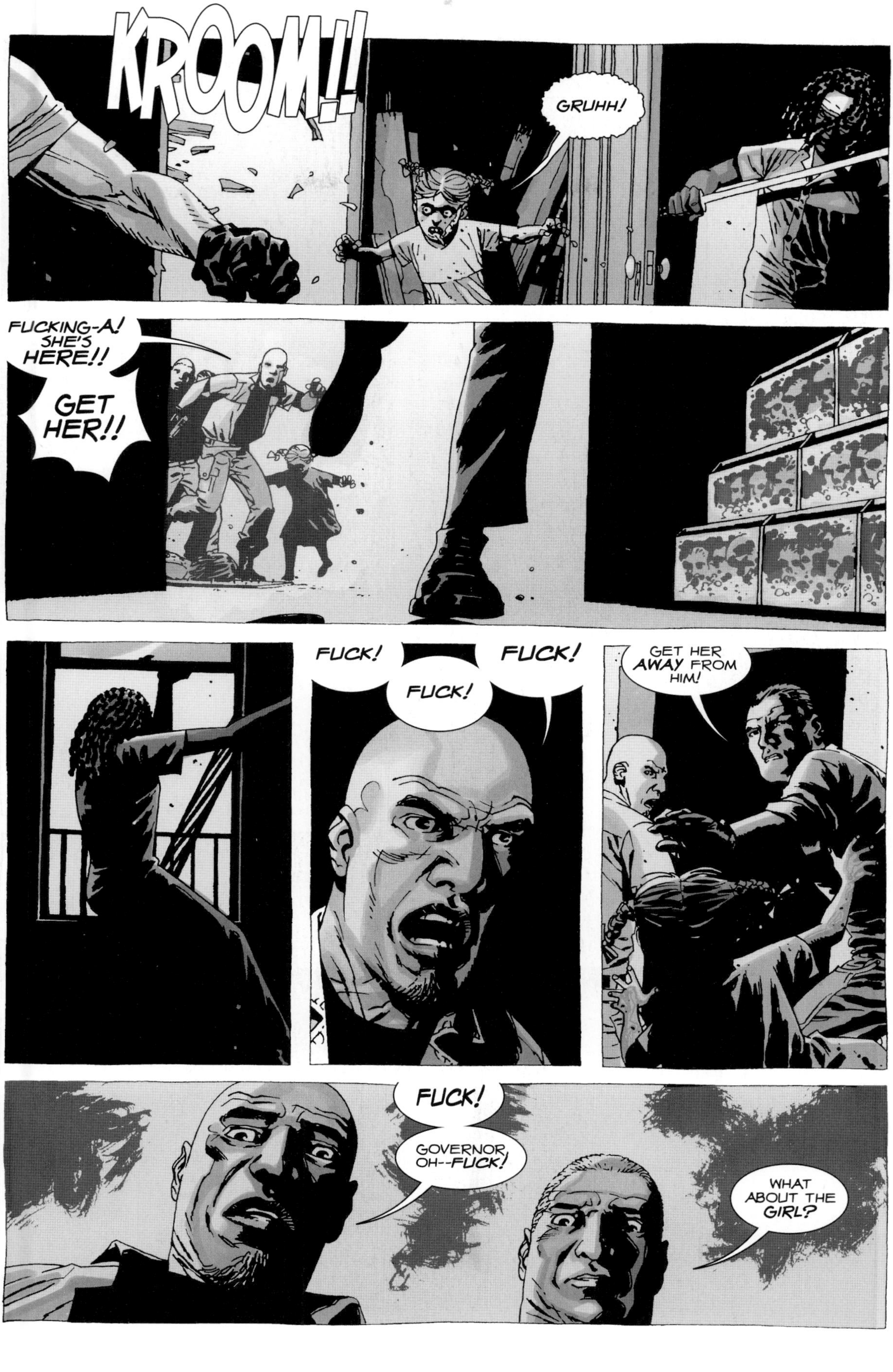
KROOM!!
GRUHH!
FUCKING-A! SHE'S HERE!!
GET HER!!
FUCK!
FUCK!
FUCK!
GET HER AWAY FROM HIM!
FUCK!
GOVERNOR, OH--FUCK!
WHAT ABOUT THE GIRL?

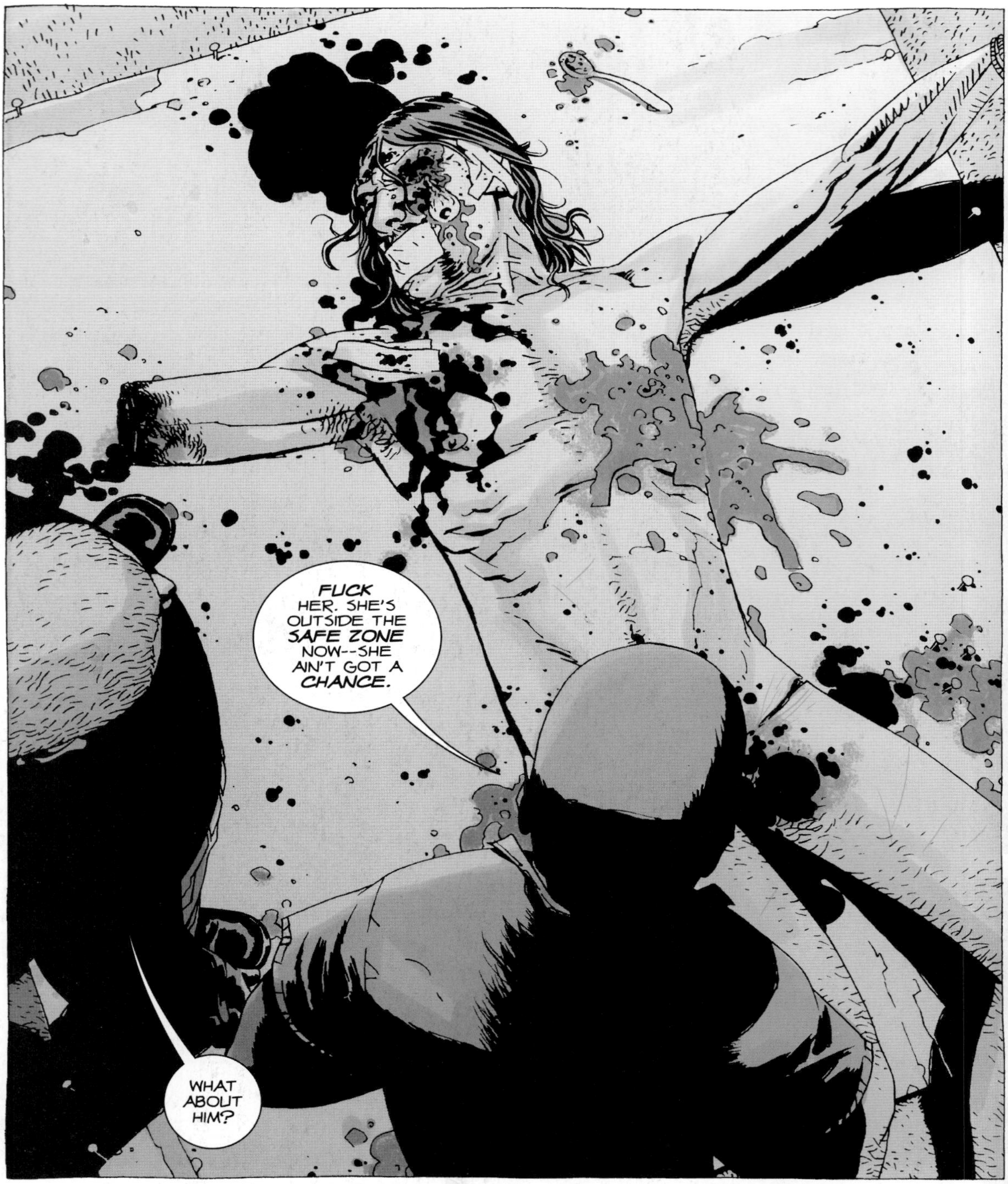
FUCK HER. SHE'S OUTSIDE THE SAFE ZONE NOW--SHE AIN'T GOT A CHANCE.
WHAT ABOUT HIM?
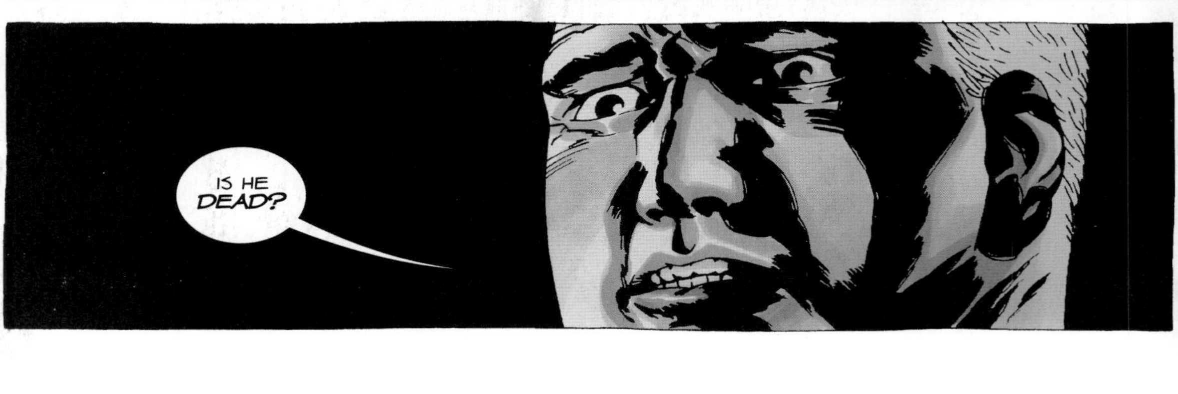
IS HE DEAD?

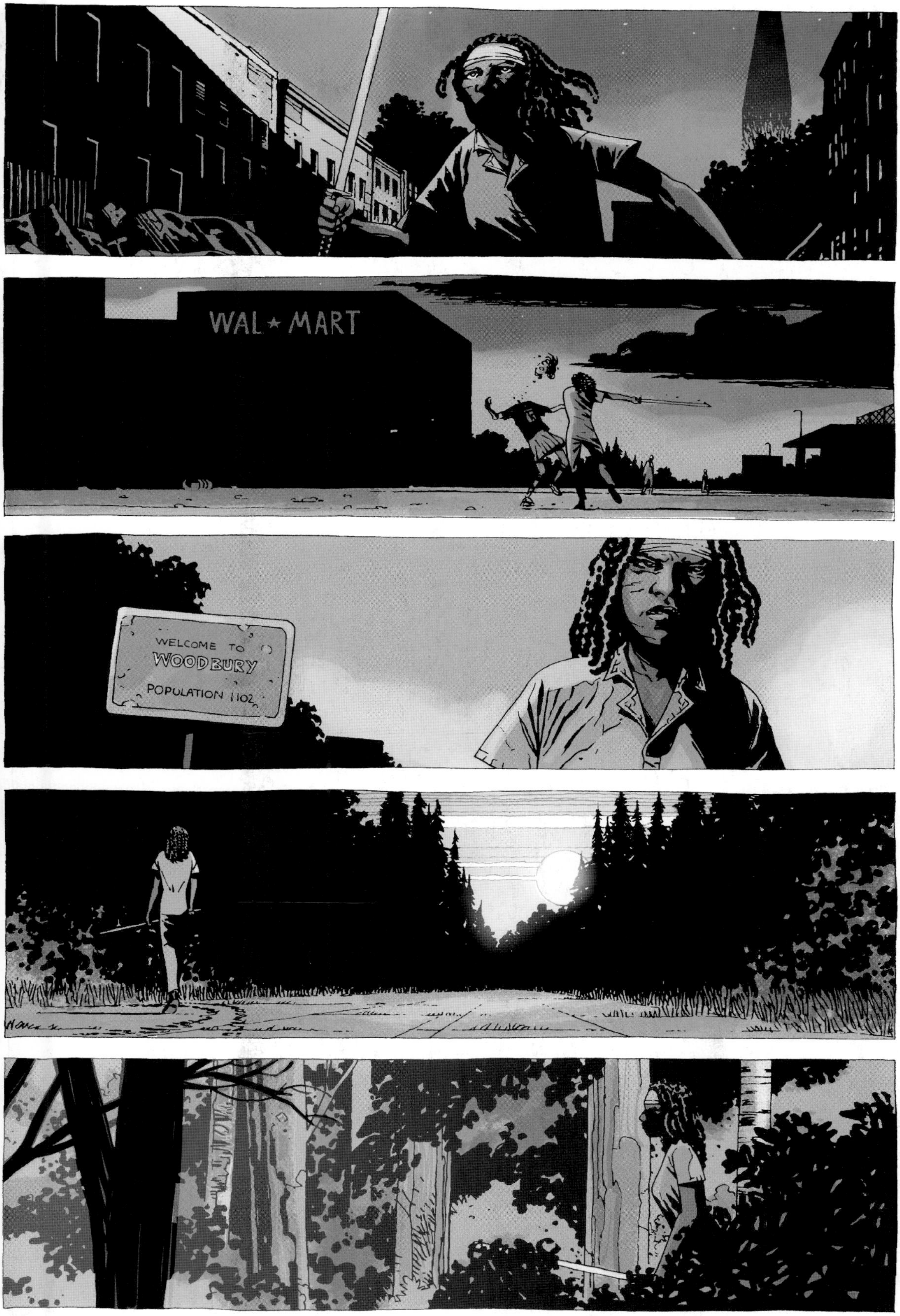
WAL★MART
WELCOME TO
WOODBURY
POPULATION 1102

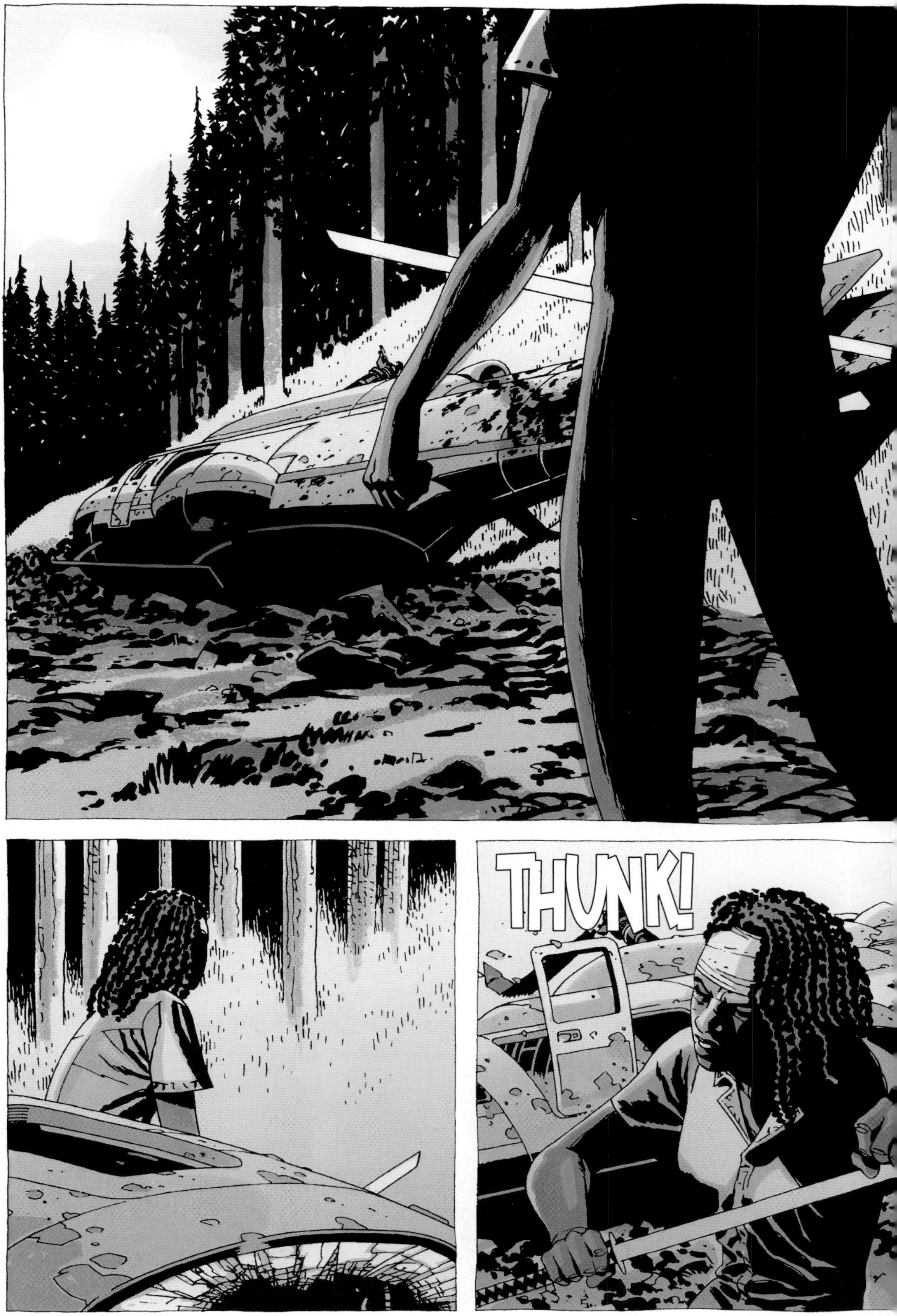
THUNK!

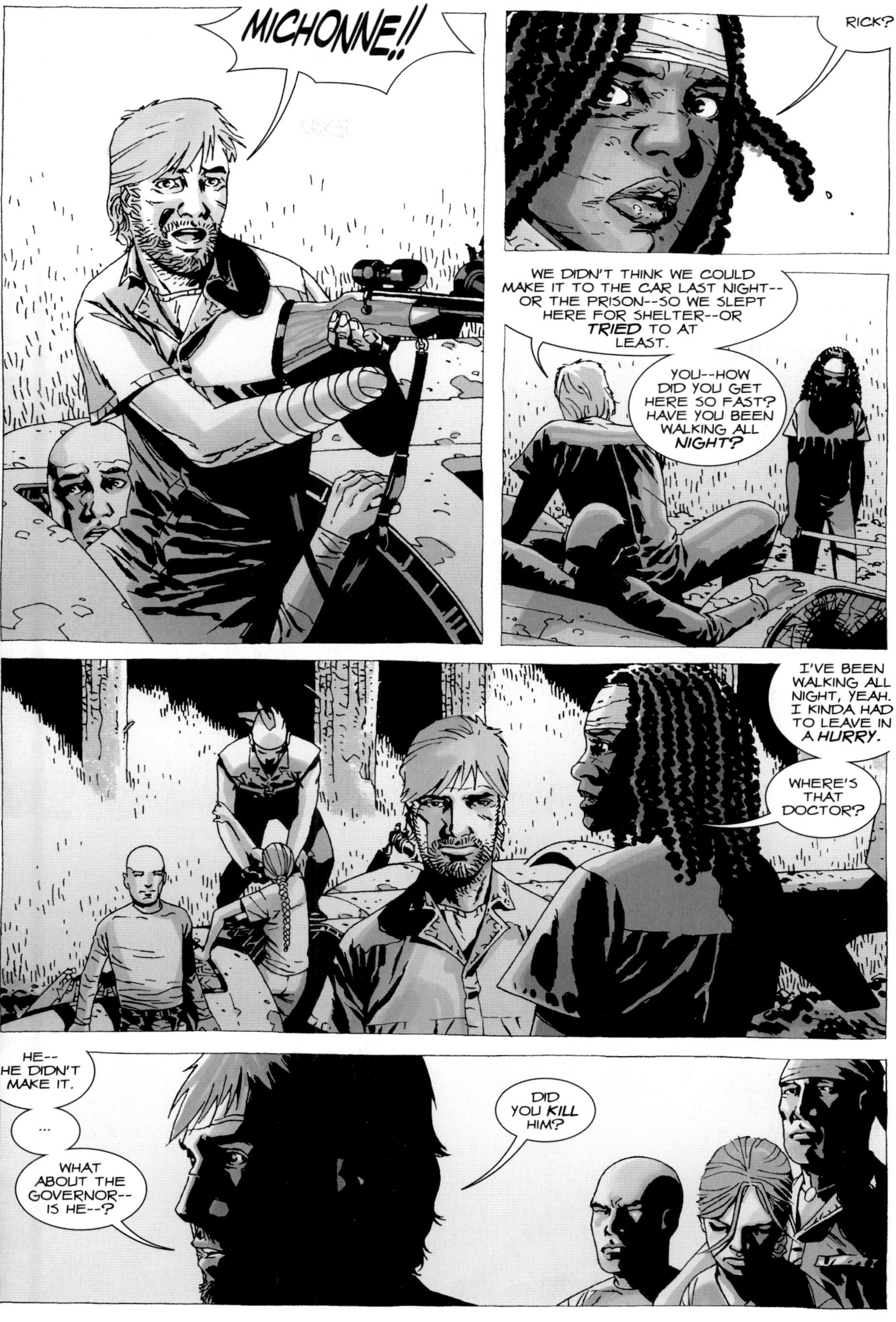
MICHONNE!!
RICK?
WE DIDN'T THINK WE COULD MAKE IT TO THE CAR LAST NIGHT--OR THE PRISON--SO WE SLEPT HERE FOR SHELTER--OR TRIED TO AT LEAST.
YOU--HOW DID YOU GET HERE SO FAST? HAVE YOU BEEN WALKING ALL NIGHT?
I'VE BEEN WALKING ALL NIGHT, YEAH. I KINDA HAD TO LEAVE IN A HURRY.
WHERE'S THAT DOCTOR?
HE--HE DIDN'T MAKE IT.
...
WHAT ABOUT THE GOVERNOR--IS HE--?
DID YOU KILL HIM?

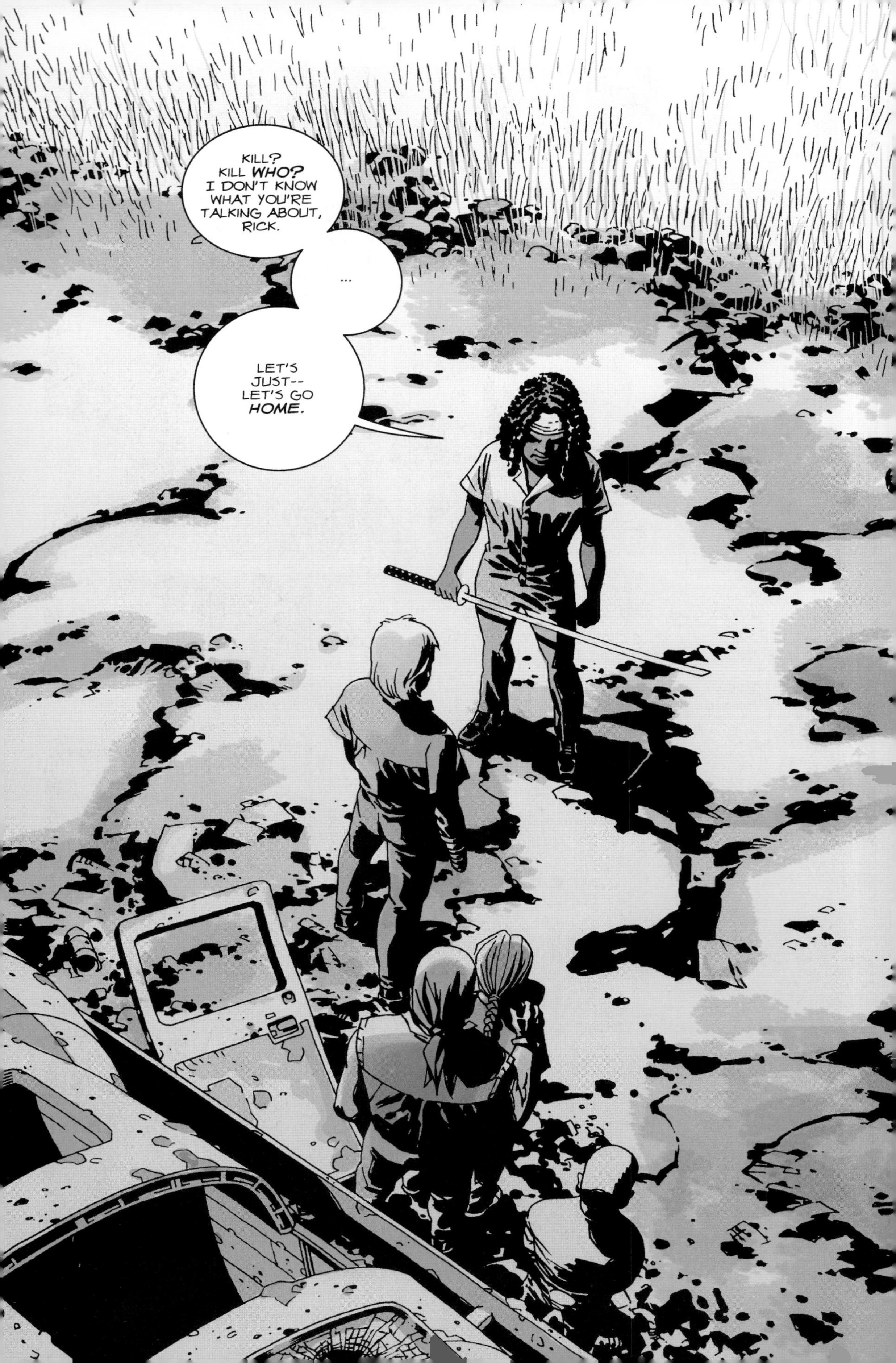
KILL? KILL WHO? I DON'T KNOW WHAT YOU'RE TALKING ABOUT, RICK.
...
LET'S JUST-- LET'S GO HOME.

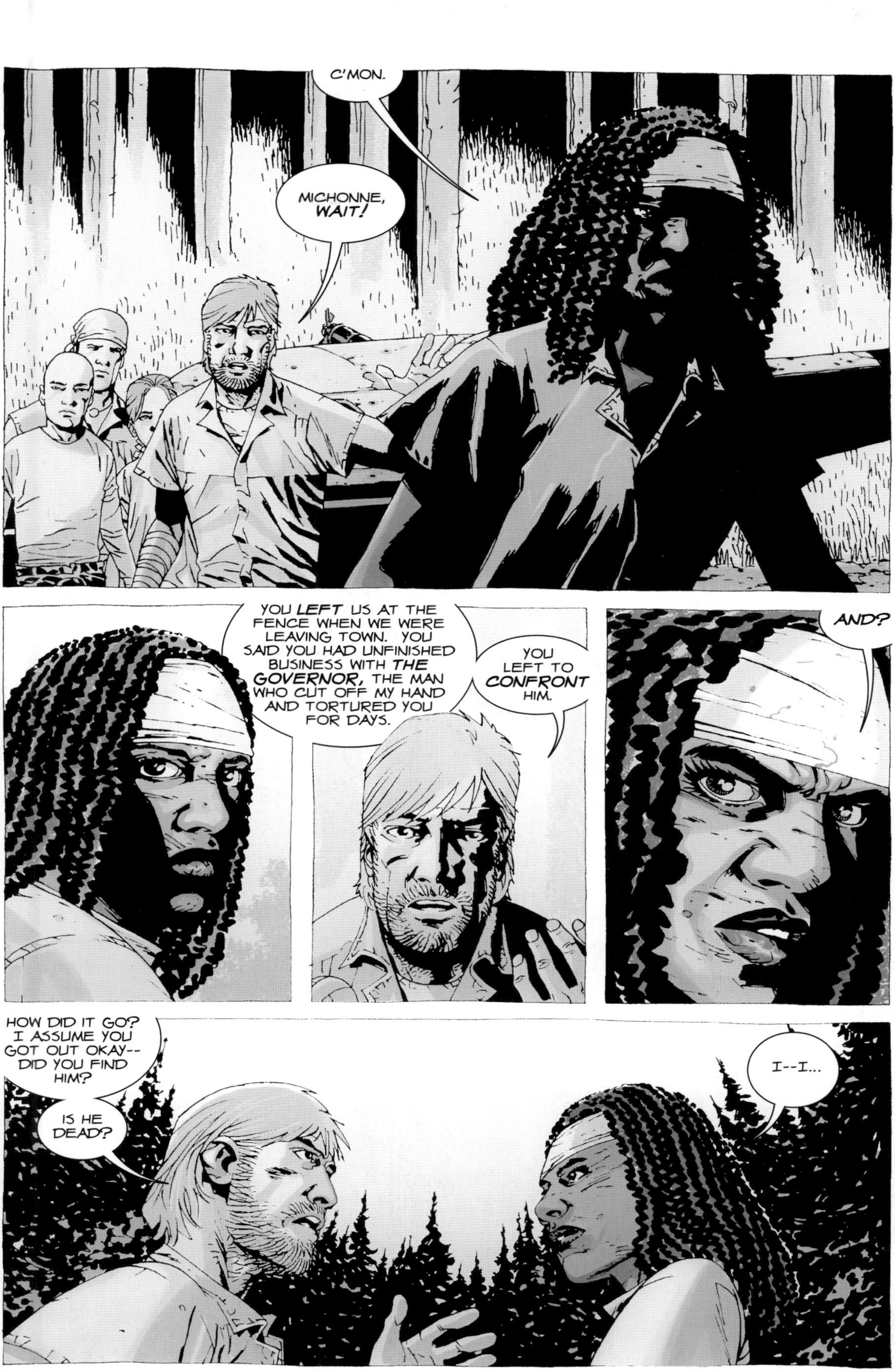
C'MON.
MICHONNE, WAIT!
YOU LEFT US AT THE FENCE WHEN WE WERE LEAVING TOWN. YOU SAID YOU HAD UNFINISHED BUSINESS WITH THE GOVERNOR, THE MAN WHO CUT OFF MY HAND AND TORTURED YOU FOR DAYS.
YOU LEFT TO CONFRONT HIM.
AND?
HOW DID IT GO? I ASSUME YOU GOT OUT OKAY-- DID YOU FIND HIM?
IS HE DEAD?
I--I...

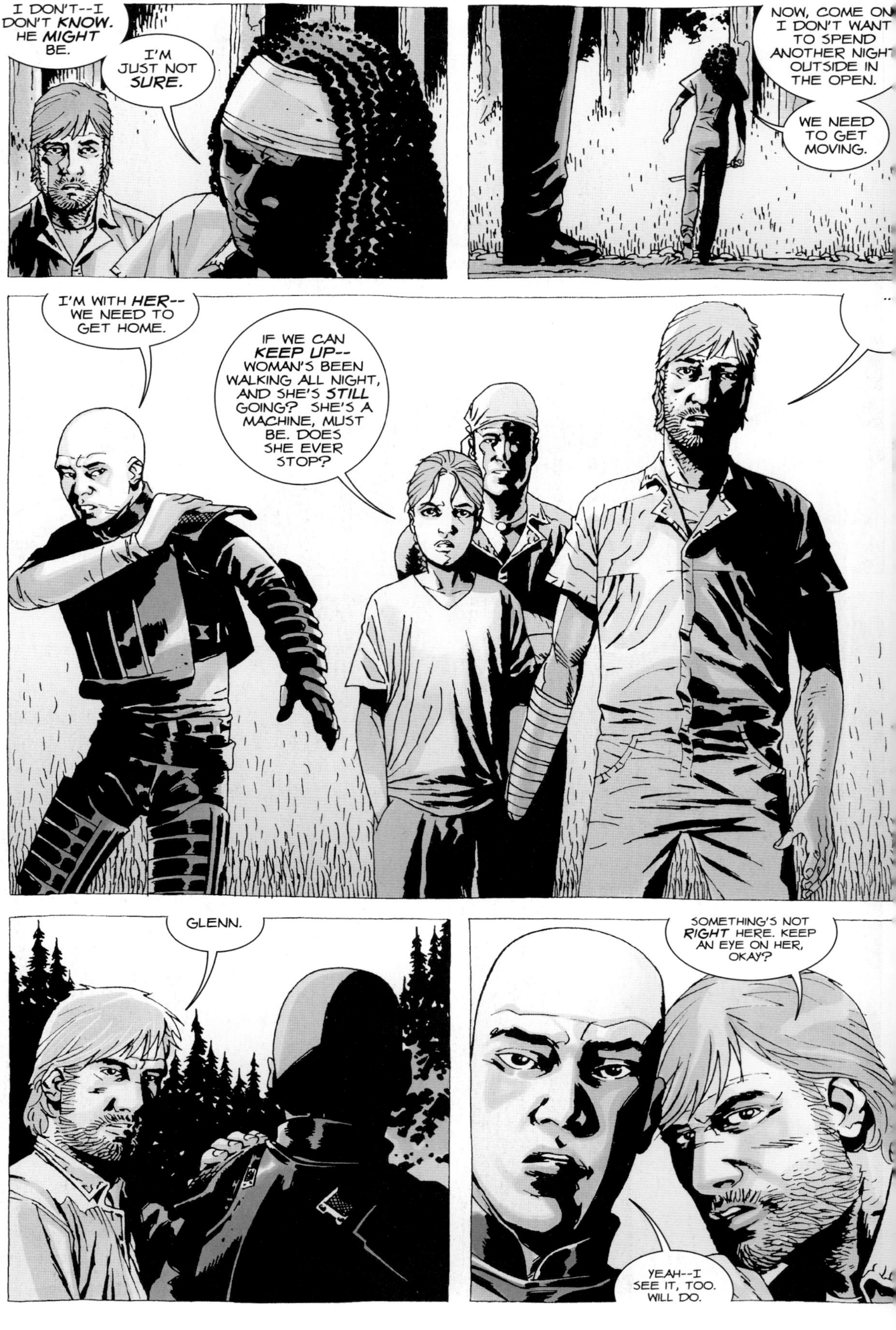
I DON'T--I DON'T KNOW. HE MIGHT BE.
I'M JUST NOT SURE.
NOW, COME ON I DON'T WANT TO SPEND ANOTHER NIGHT OUTSIDE IN THE OPEN.
WE NEED TO GET MOVING.
I'M WITH HER-- WE NEED TO GET HOME.
IF WE CAN KEEP UP-- WOMAN'S BEEN WALKING ALL NIGHT, AND SHE'S STILL GOING? SHE'S A MACHINE, MUST BE. DOES SHE EVER STOP?
GLENN.
SOMETHING'S NOT RIGHT HERE. KEEP AN EYE ON HER, OKAY?
YEAH--I SEE IT, TOO. WILL DO.

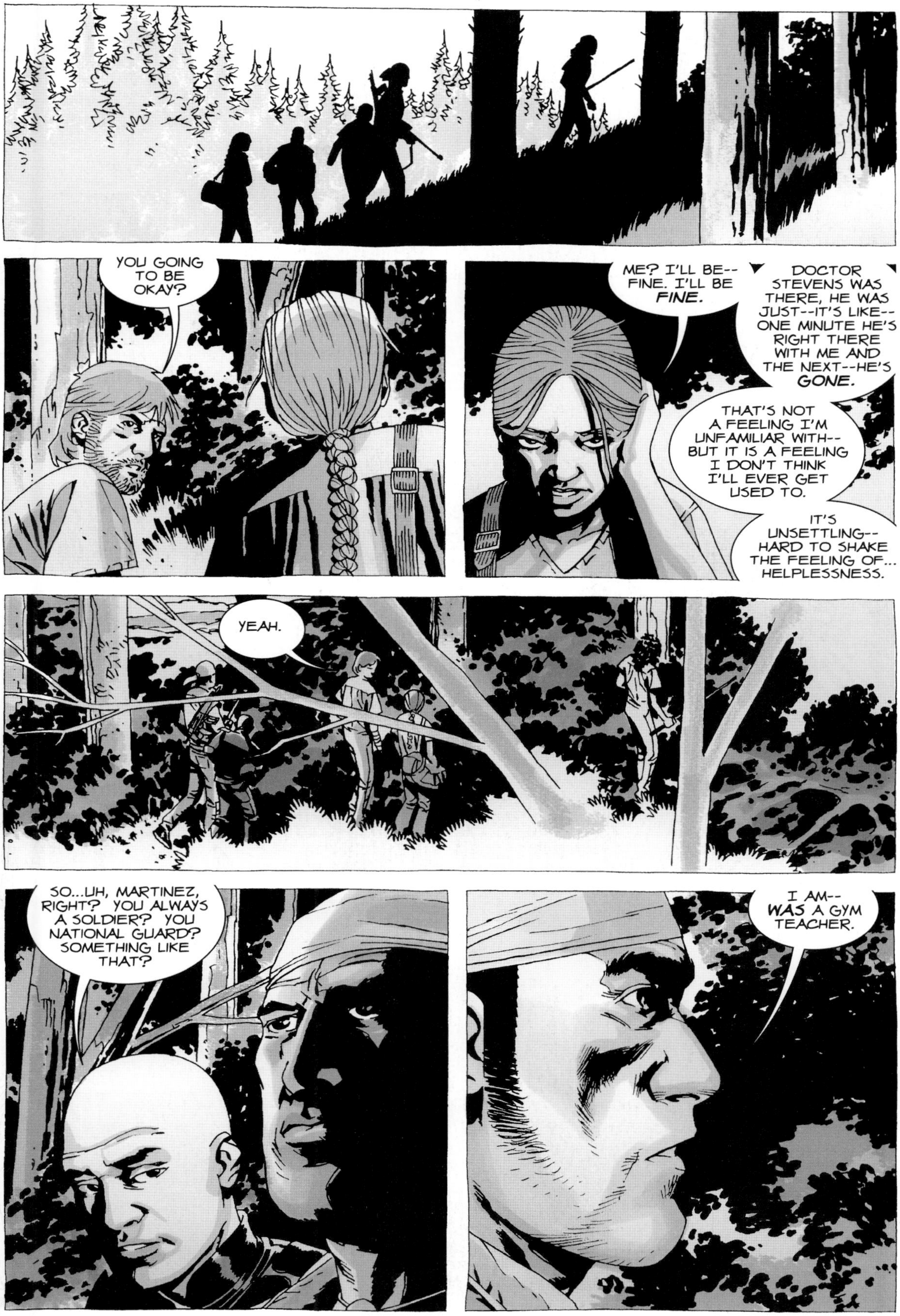
YOU GOING TO BE OKAY?
ME? I'LL BE-- FINE. I'LL BE FINE.
DOCTOR STEVENS WAS THERE, HE WAS JUST--IT'S LIKE-- ONE MINUTE HE'S RIGHT THERE WITH ME AND THE NEXT--HE'S GONE.
THAT'S NOT A FEELING I'M UNFAMILIAR WITH-- BUT IT IS A FEELING I DON'T THINK I'LL EVER GET USED TO.
IT'S UNSETTLING-- HARD TO SHAKE THE FEELING OF... HELPLESSNESS.
YEAH.
SO...UH, MARTINEZ, RIGHT? YOU ALWAYS A SOLDIER? YOU NATIONAL GUARD? SOMETHING LIKE THAT?
I AM-- WAS A GYM TEACHER.

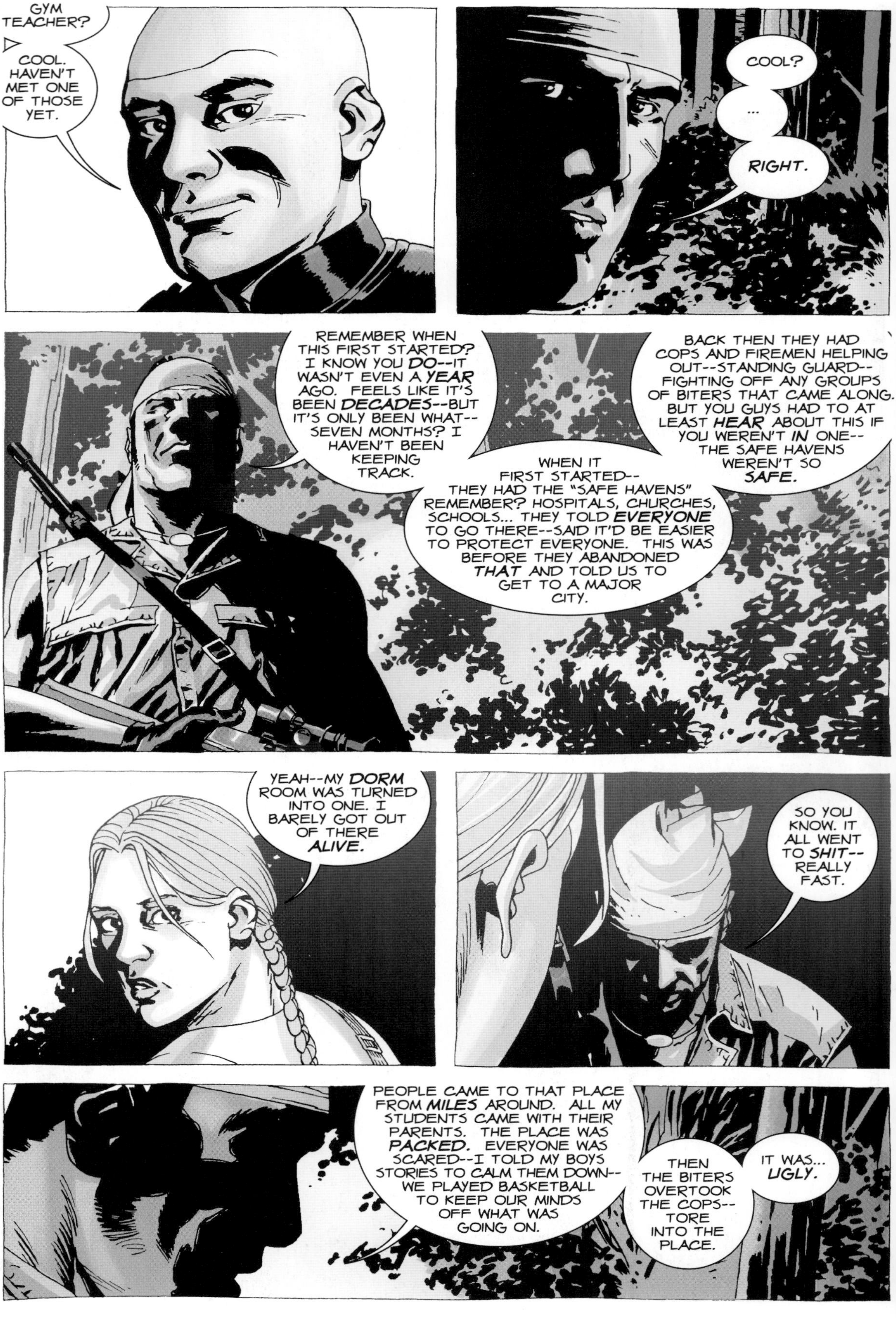
GYM TEACHER?
COOL. HAVEN'T MET ONE OF THOSE YET.
COOL?
...
RIGHT.
REMEMBER WHEN THIS FIRST STARTED? I KNOW YOU DO--IT WASN'T EVEN A YEAR AGO. FEELS LIKE IT'S BEEN DECADES--BUT IT'S ONLY BEEN WHAT--SEVEN MONTHS? I HAVEN'T BEEN KEEPING TRACK.
WHEN IT FIRST STARTED--THEY HAD THE "SAFE HAVENS" REMEMBER? HOSPITALS, CHURCHES, SCHOOLS... THEY TOLD EVERYONE TO GO THERE--SAID IT'D BE EASIER TO PROTECT EVERYONE. THIS WAS BEFORE THEY ABANDONED THAT AND TOLD US TO GET TO A MAJOR CITY.
BACK THEN THEY HAD COPS AND FIREMEN HELPING OUT--STANDING GUARD--FIGHTING OFF ANY GROUPS OF BITERS THAT CAME ALONG. BUT YOU GUYS HAD TO AT LEAST HEAR ABOUT THIS IF YOU WEREN'T IN ONE--THE SAFE HAVENS WEREN'T SO SAFE.
YEAH--MY DORM ROOM WAS TURNED INTO ONE. I BARELY GOT OUT OF THERE ALIVE.
SO YOU KNOW. IT ALL WENT TO SHIT--REALLY FAST.
PEOPLE CAME TO THAT PLACE FROM MILES AROUND. ALL MY STUDENTS CAME WITH THEIR PARENTS. THE PLACE WAS PACKED. EVERYONE WAS SCARED--I TOLD MY BOYS STORIES TO CALM THEM DOWN--WE PLAYED BASKETBALL TO KEEP OUR MINDS OFF WHAT WAS GOING ON.
THEN THE BITERS OVERTOOK THE COPS--TORE INTO THE PLACE.
IT WAS... UGLY.

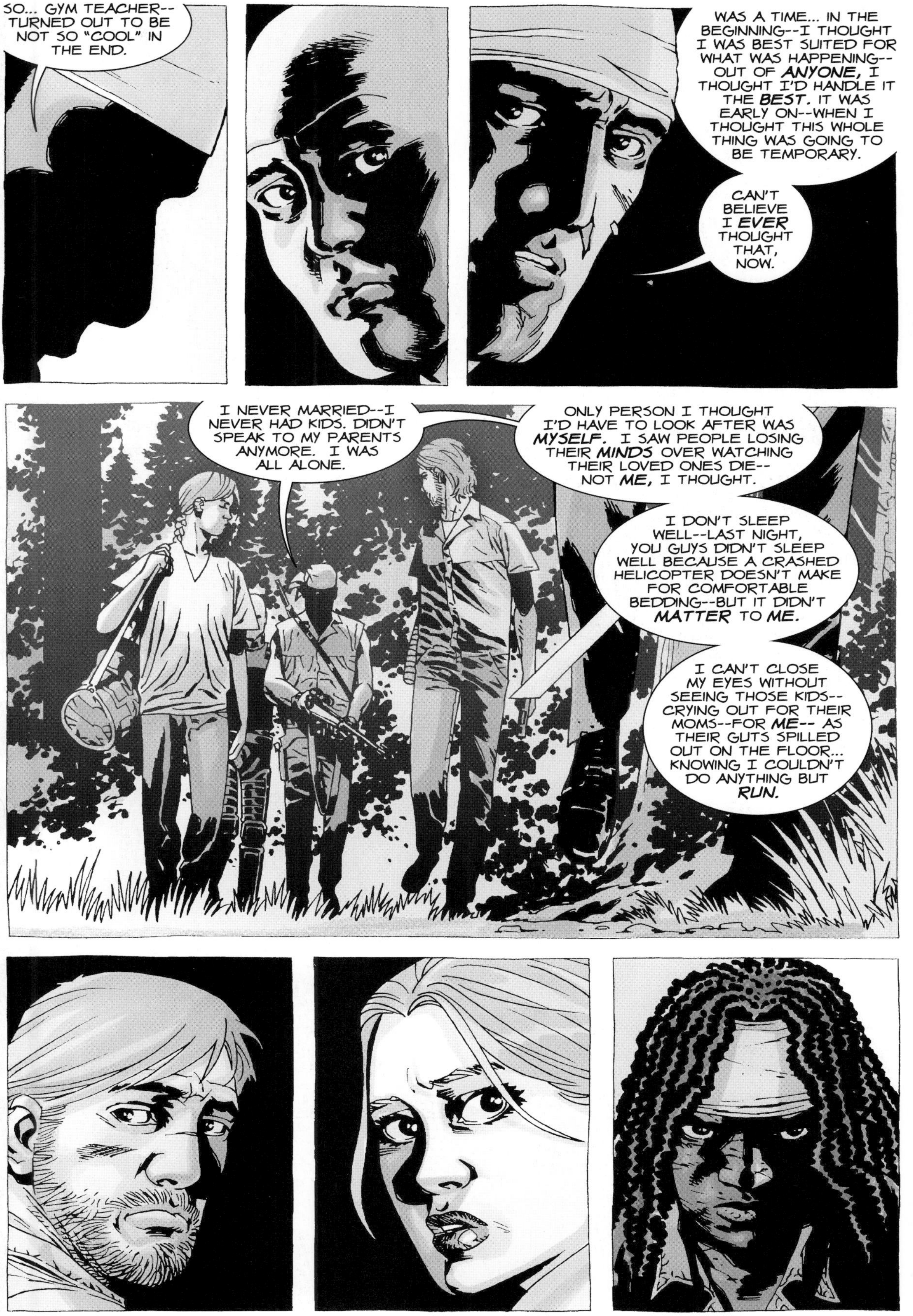
SO... GYM TEACHER-- TURNED OUT TO BE NOT SO "COOL" IN THE END.
WAS A TIME... IN THE BEGINNING--I THOUGHT I WAS BEST SUITED FOR WHAT WAS HAPPENING-- OUT OF ANYONE, I THOUGHT I'D HANDLE IT THE BEST. IT WAS EARLY ON--WHEN I THOUGHT THIS WHOLE THING WAS GOING TO BE TEMPORARY.
CAN'T BELIEVE I EVER THOUGHT THAT, NOW.
I NEVER MARRIED--I NEVER HAD KIDS. DIDN'T SPEAK TO MY PARENTS ANYMORE. I WAS ALL ALONE.
ONLY PERSON I THOUGHT I'D HAVE TO LOOK AFTER WAS MYSELF. I SAW PEOPLE LOSING THEIR MINDS OVER WATCHING THEIR LOVED ONES DIE-- NOT ME, I THOUGHT.
I DON'T SLEEP WELL--LAST NIGHT, YOU GUYS DIDN'T SLEEP WELL BECAUSE A CRASHED HELICOPTER DOESN'T MAKE FOR COMFORTABLE BEDDING--BUT IT DIDN'T MATTER TO ME.
I CAN'T CLOSE MY EYES WITHOUT SEEING THOSE KIDS-- CRYING OUT FOR THEIR MOMS--FOR ME-- AS THEIR GUTS SPILLED OUT ON THE FLOOR... KNOWING I COULDN'T DO ANYTHING BUT RUN.

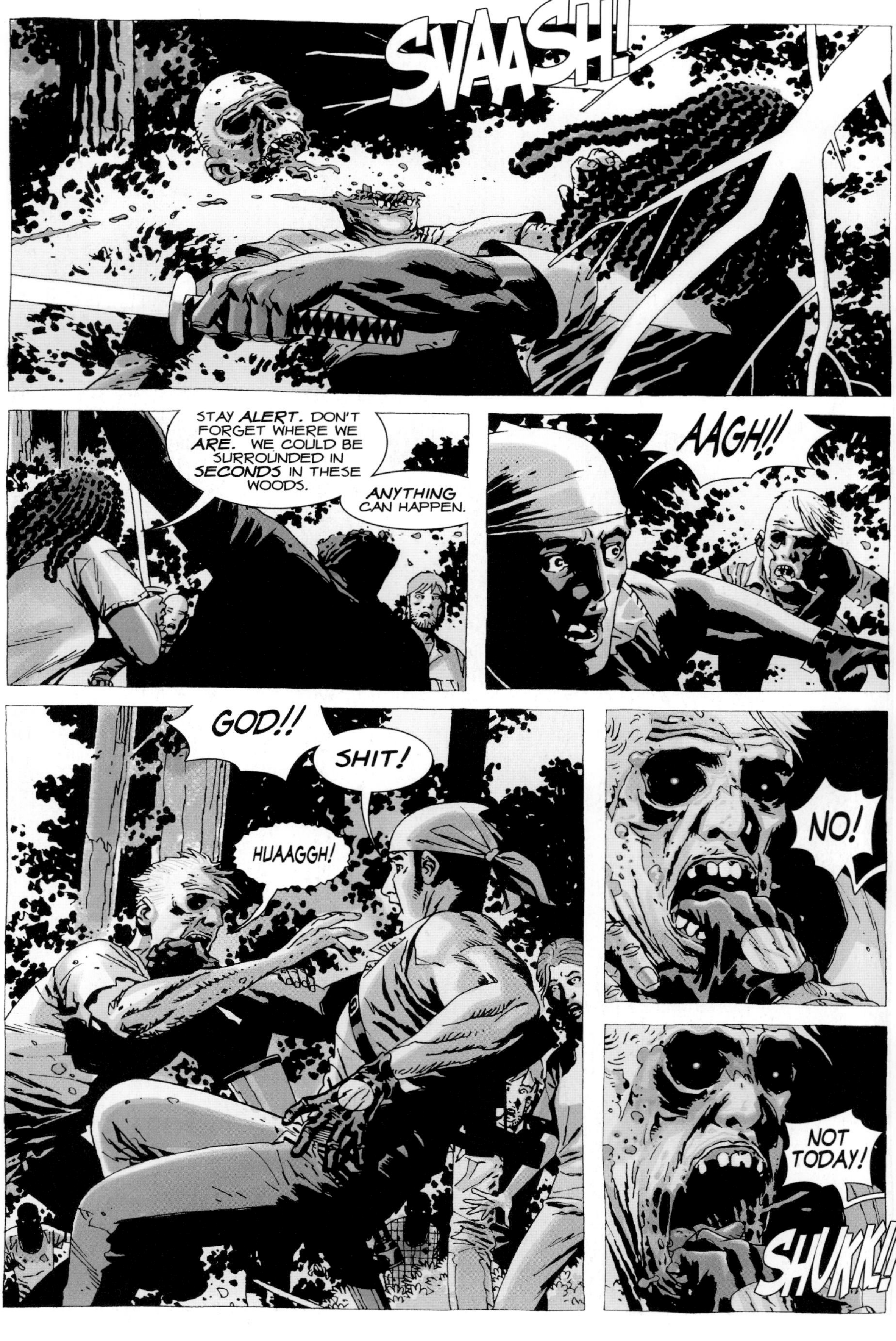
SVAASH!
STAY ALERT. DON'T FORGET WHERE WE ARE. WE COULD BE SURROUNDED IN SECONDS IN THESE WOODS.
ANYTHING CAN HAPPEN.
AAGH!!
GOD!!
SHIT!
HUAAGGH!
NO!
NOT TODAY!
SHUKK!!

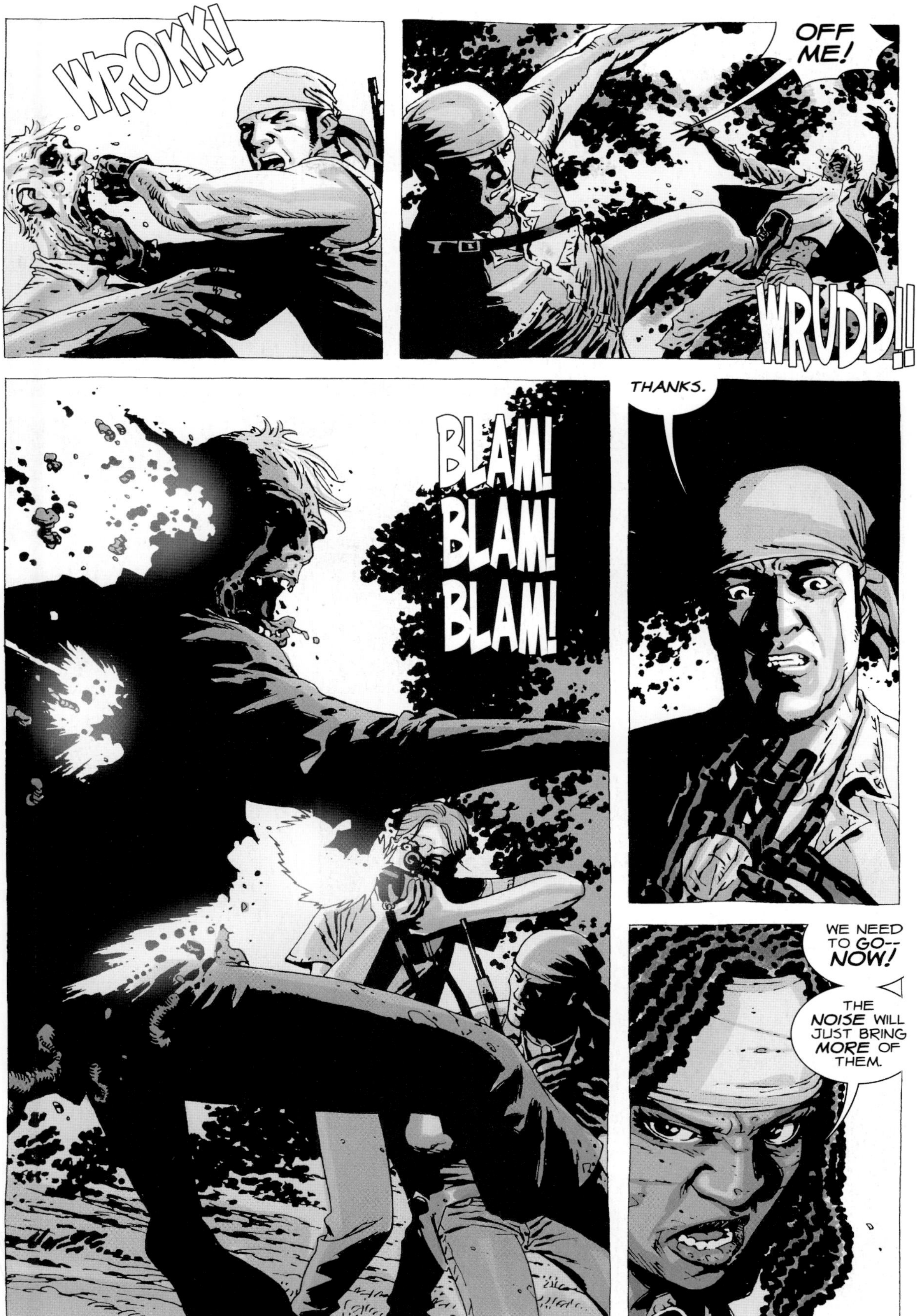
WROKK!
OFF ME!
WRUDD!!
BLAM! BLAM! BLAM!
THANKS.
WE NEED TO GO-- NOW!
THE NOISE WILL JUST BRING MORE OF THEM.

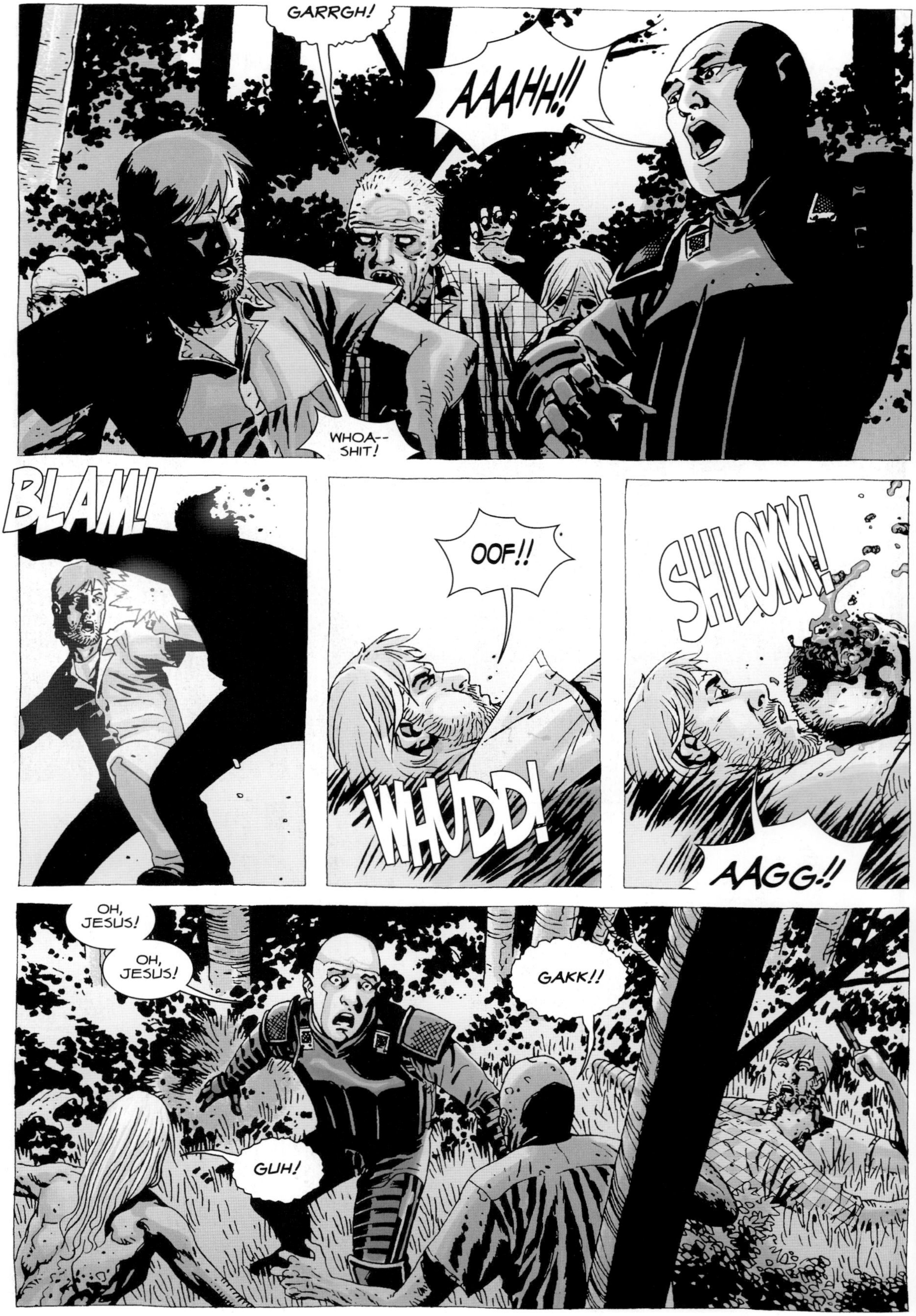
GARRGH!
AAAHH!!
WHOA-- SHIT!
BLAM!
OOF!!
WHUDD!
SHLOKK!
AAGG!!
OH, JESUS!
OH, JESUS!
GAKK!!
GUH!

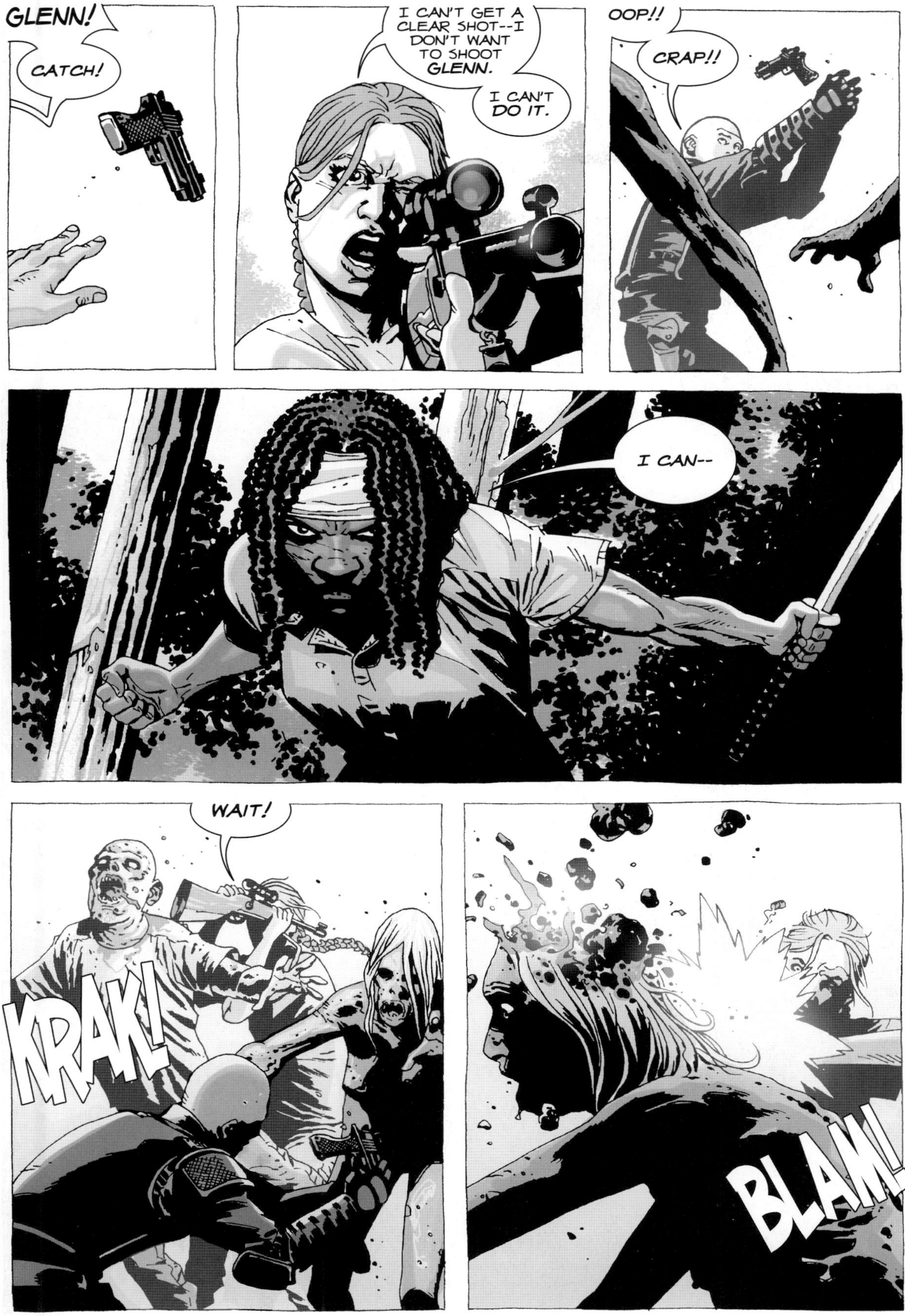
GLENN!
CATCH!
I CAN'T GET A CLEAR SHOT--I DON'T WANT TO SHOOT GLENN.
I CAN'T DO IT.
OOP!!
CRAP!!
I CAN--
WAIT!
KRAK!
BLAM!

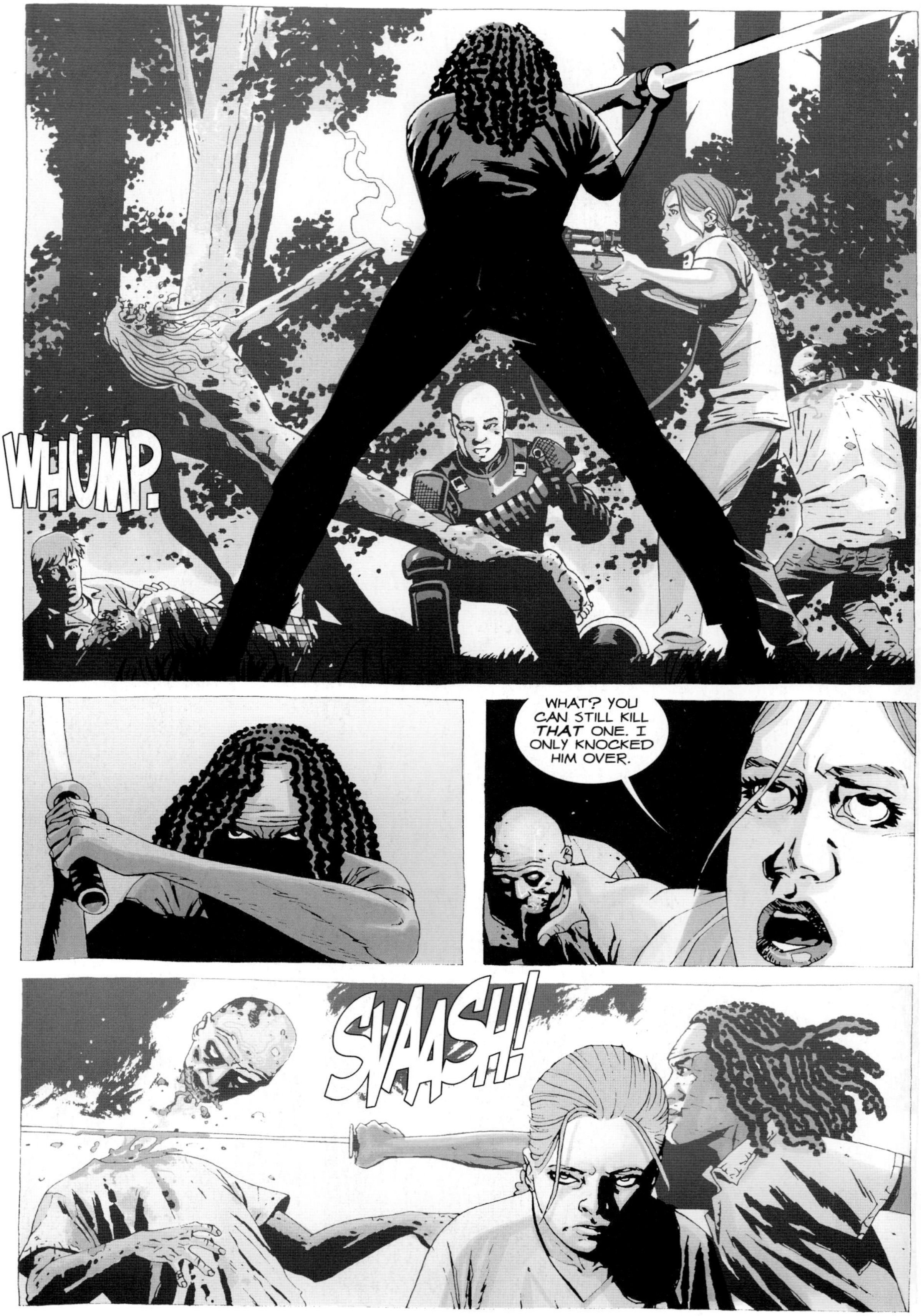
WHUMP.
WHAT? YOU CAN STILL KILL *THAT* ONE. I ONLY KNOCKED HIM OVER.
SVAASH!

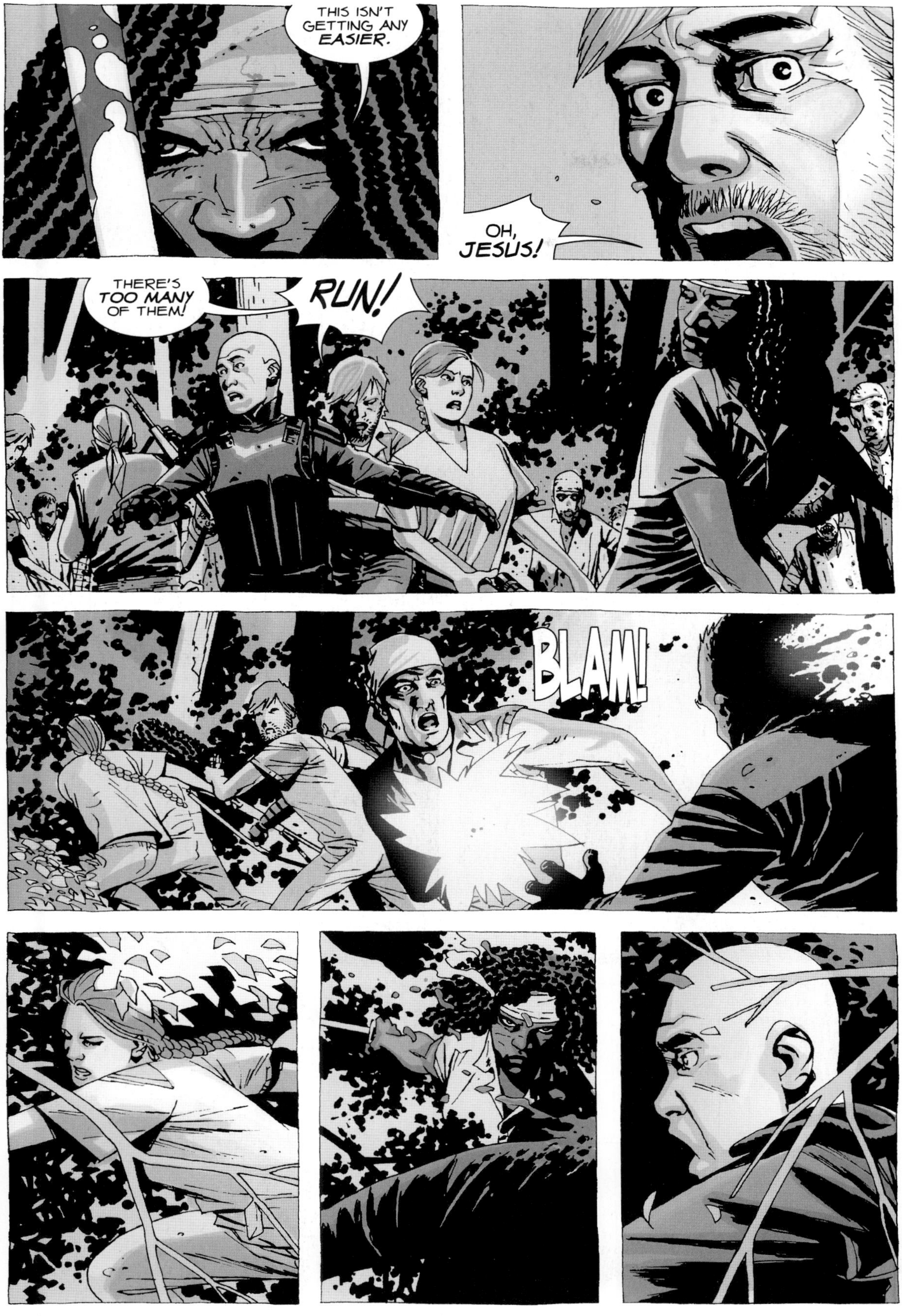
THIS ISN'T GETTING ANY EASIER.
OH, JESUS!
THERE'S TOO MANY OF THEM!
RUN!
BLAM!

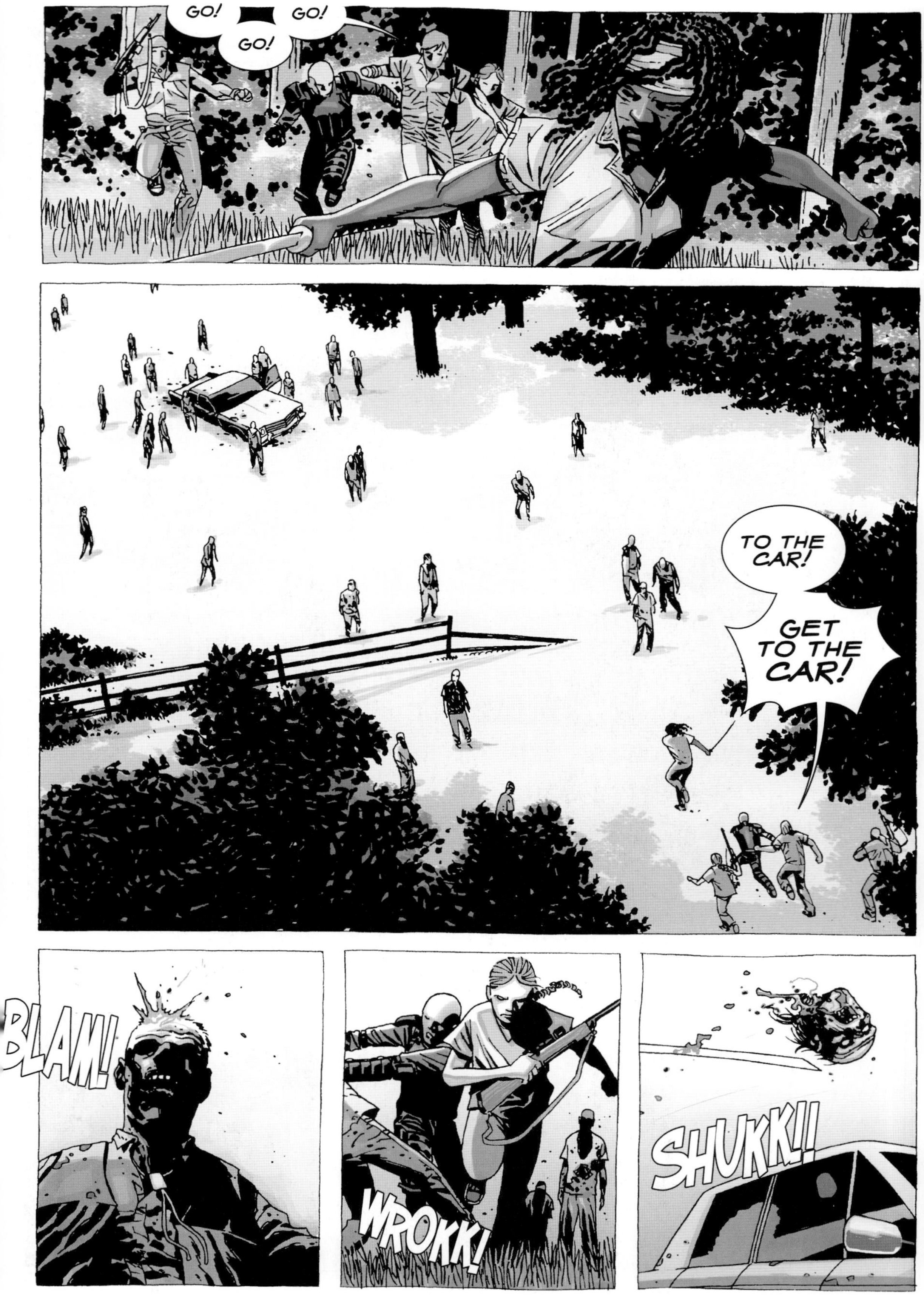
GO! GO! GO!
TO THE CAR!
GET TO THE CAR!
BLAM!
WROKK!
SHUKK!!

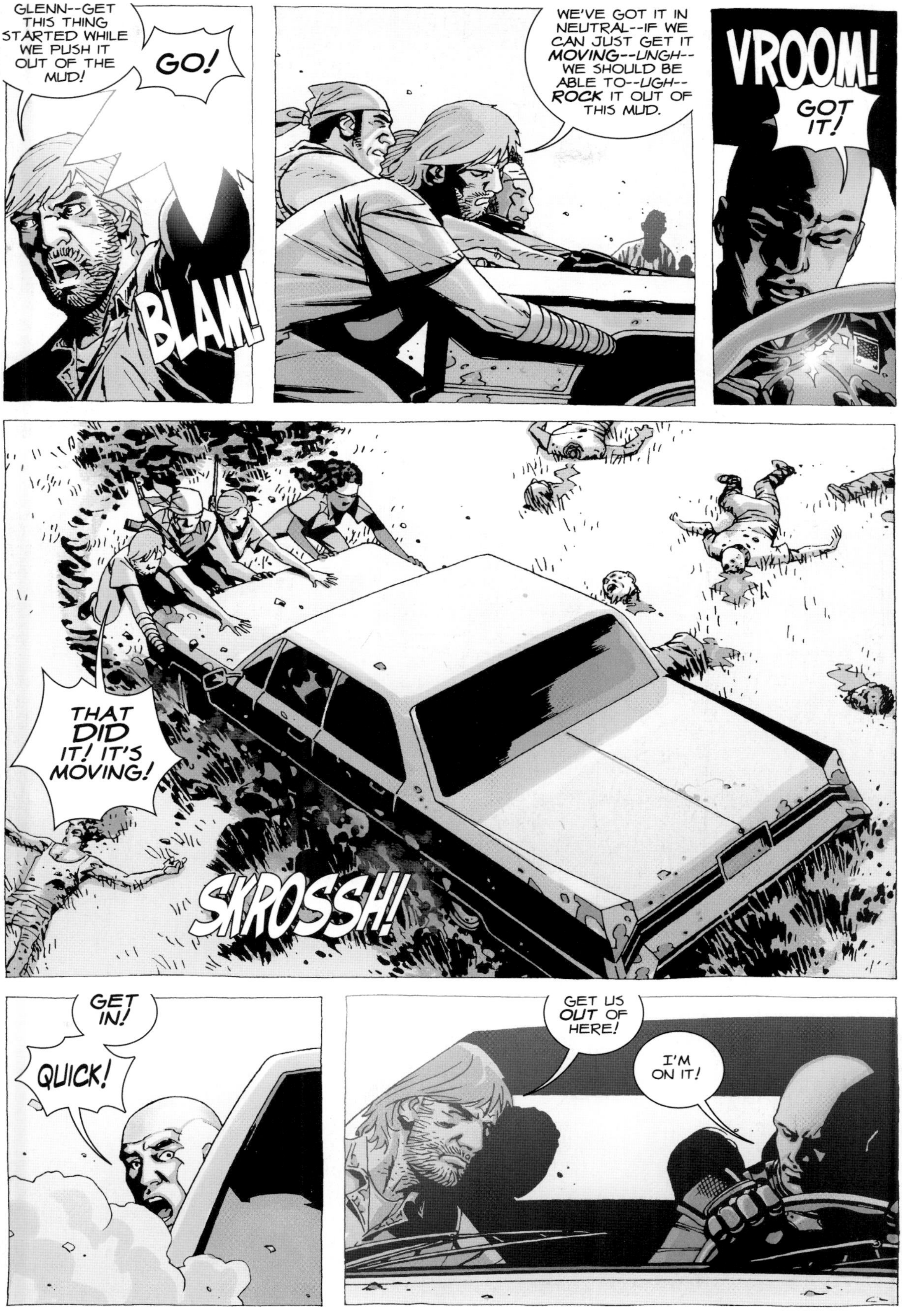
GLENN--GET THIS THING STARTED WHILE WE PUSH IT OUT OF THE MUD!
GO!
BLAM!
WE'VE GOT IT IN NEUTRAL--IF WE CAN JUST GET IT MOVING--UNGH--WE SHOULD BE ABLE TO--UGH--ROCK IT OUT OF THIS MUD.
VROOM!
GOT IT!
THAT DID IT! IT'S MOVING!
SKROSSH!
GET IN!
QUICK!
GET US OUT OF HERE!
I'M ON IT!

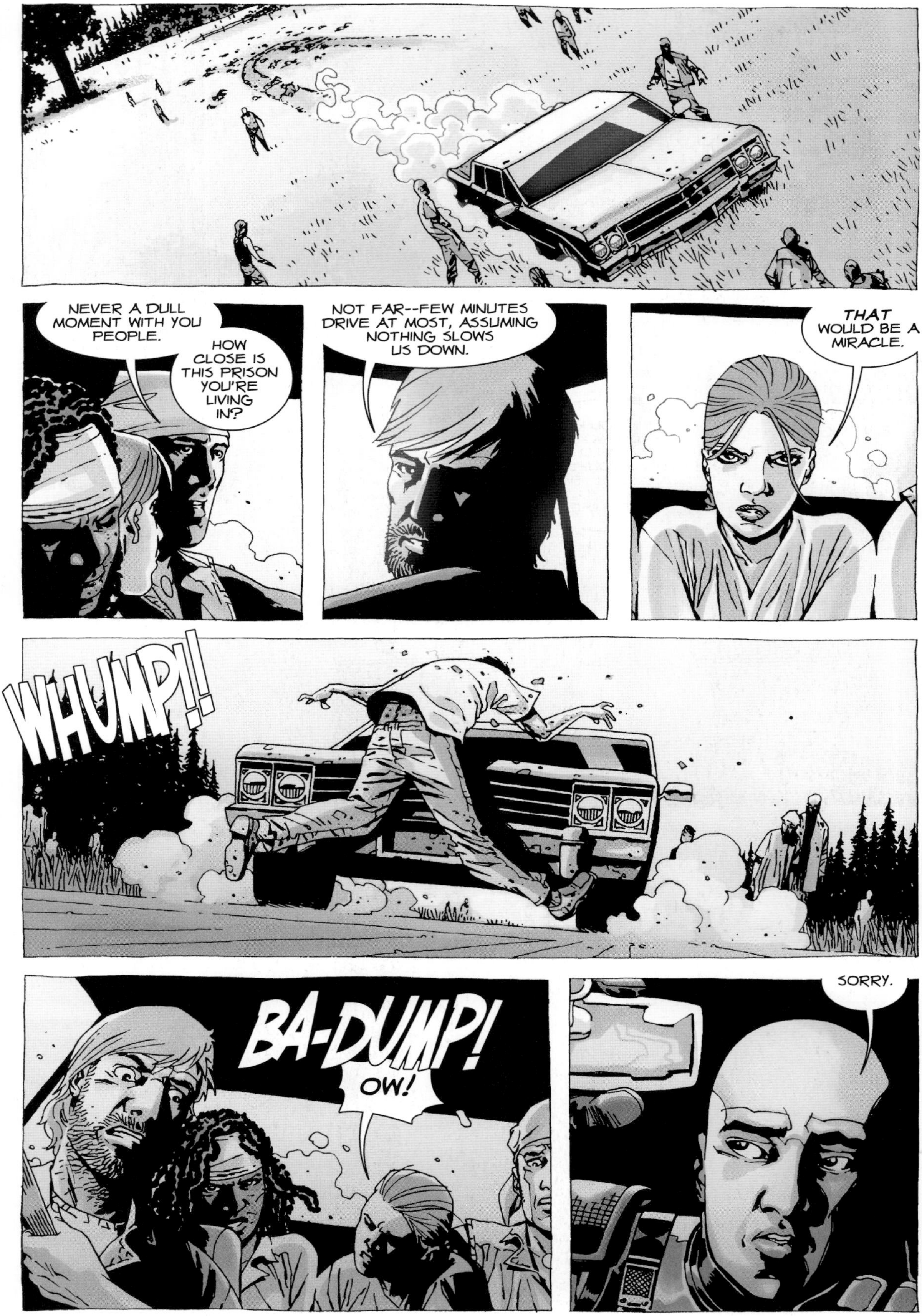
NEVER A DULL MOMENT WITH YOU PEOPLE.
HOW CLOSE IS THIS PRISON YOU'RE LIVING IN?
NOT FAR--FEW MINUTES DRIVE AT MOST, ASSUMING NOTHING SLOWS US DOWN.
THAT WOULD BE A MIRACLE.
WHUMP!!
BA-DUMP!
OW!
SORRY.

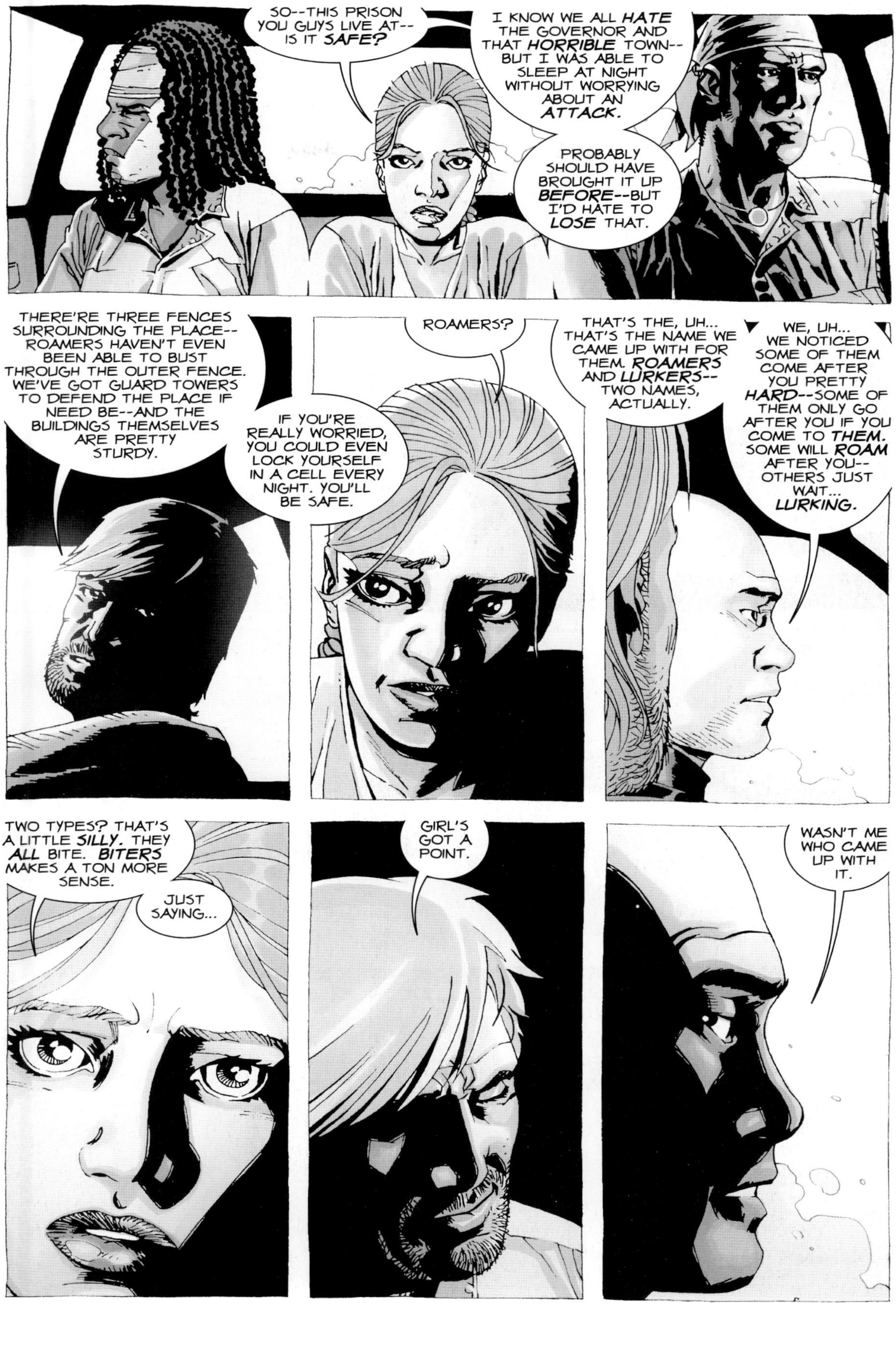
SO--THIS PRISON YOU GUYS LIVE AT--IS IT SAFE?
I KNOW WE ALL HATE THE GOVERNOR AND THAT HORRIBLE TOWN--BUT I WAS ABLE TO SLEEP AT NIGHT WITHOUT WORRYING ABOUT AN ATTACK.
PROBABLY SHOULD HAVE BROUGHT IT UP BEFORE--BUT I'D HATE TO LOSE THAT.
THERE'RE THREE FENCES SURROUNDING THE PLACE--ROAMERS HAVEN'T EVEN BEEN ABLE TO BUST THROUGH THE OUTER FENCE. WE'VE GOT GUARD TOWERS TO DEFEND THE PLACE IF NEED BE--AND THE BUILDINGS THEMSELVES ARE PRETTY STURDY.
IF YOU'RE REALLY WORRIED, YOU COULD EVEN LOCK YOURSELF IN A CELL EVERY NIGHT. YOU'LL BE SAFE.
ROAMERS?
THAT'S THE, UH... THAT'S THE NAME WE CAME UP WITH FOR THEM. ROAMERS AND LURKERS--TWO NAMES, ACTUALLY.
WE, UH... WE NOTICED SOME OF THEM COME AFTER YOU PRETTY HARD--SOME OF THEM ONLY GO AFTER YOU IF YOU COME TO THEM. SOME WILL ROAM AFTER YOU--OTHERS JUST WAIT... LURKING.
TWO TYPES? THAT'S A LITTLE SILLY. THEY ALL BITE. BITERS MAKES A TON MORE SENSE.
JUST SAYING...
GIRL'S GOT A POINT.
WASN'T ME WHO CAME UP WITH IT.

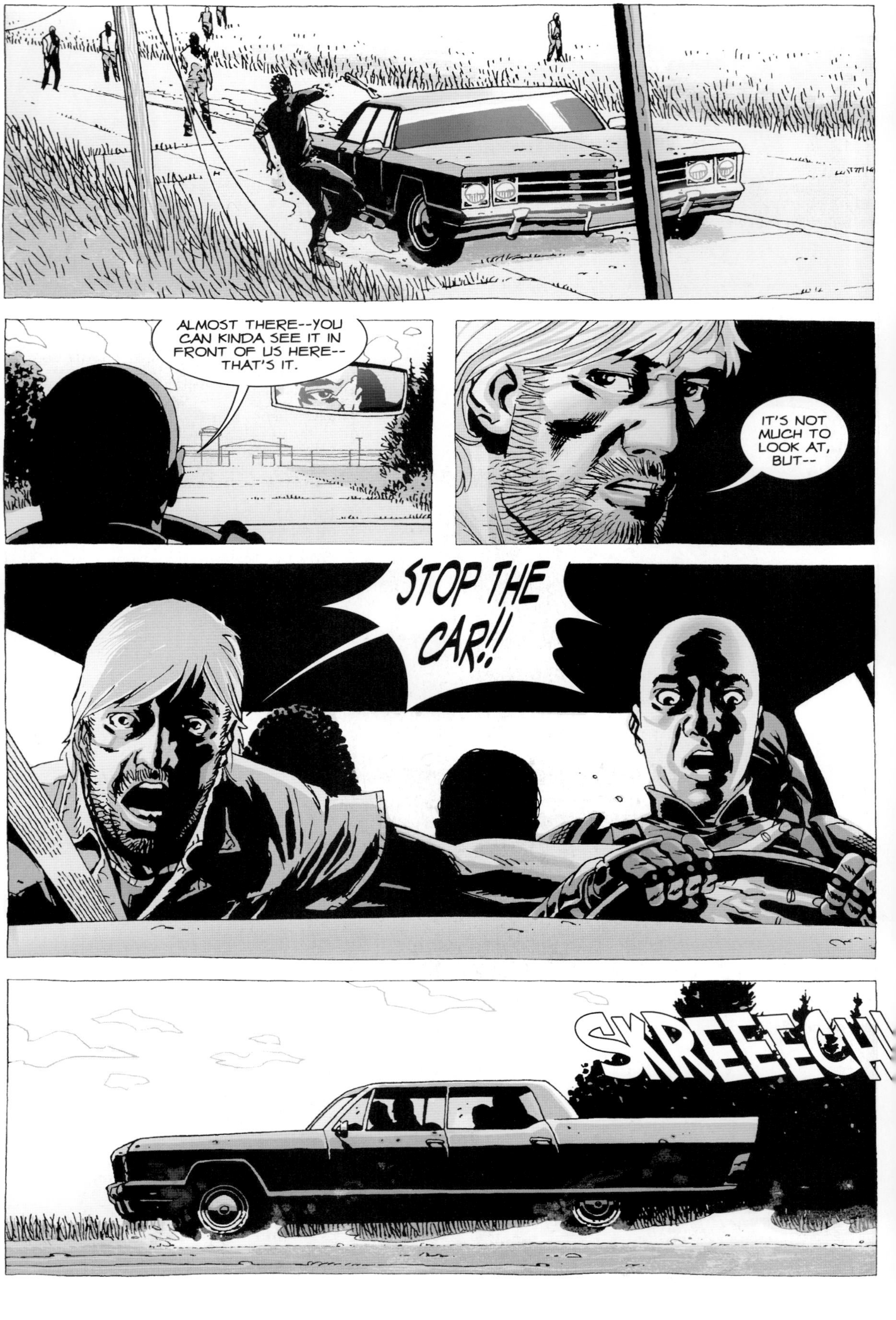
ALMOST THERE--YOU CAN KINDA SEE IT IN FRONT OF US HERE--THAT'S IT.
IT'S NOT MUCH TO LOOK AT, BUT--
STOP THE CAR!!
SKREEEECH

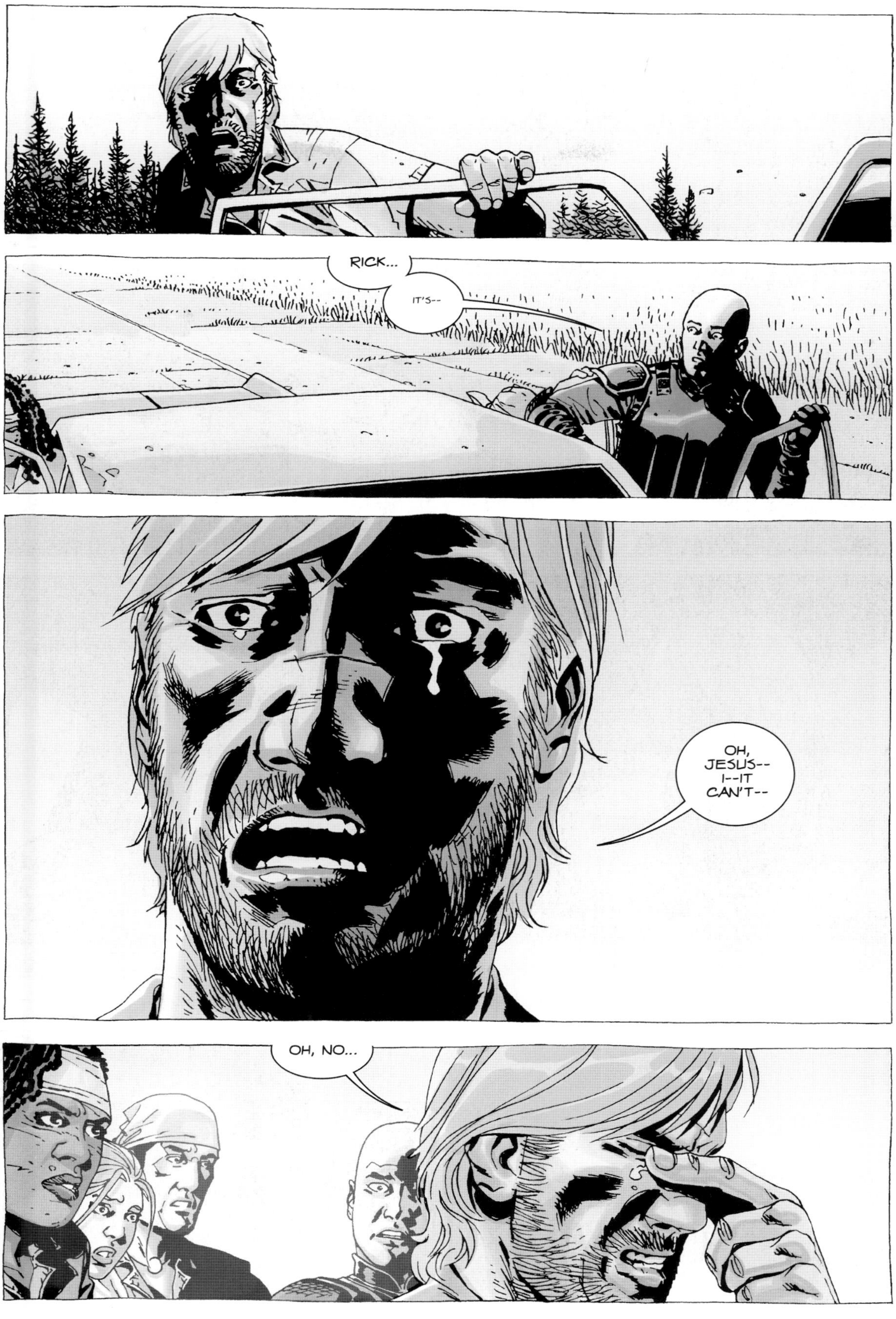
RICK...
IT'S--
OH, JESUS-- I--IT CAN'T--
OH, NO...

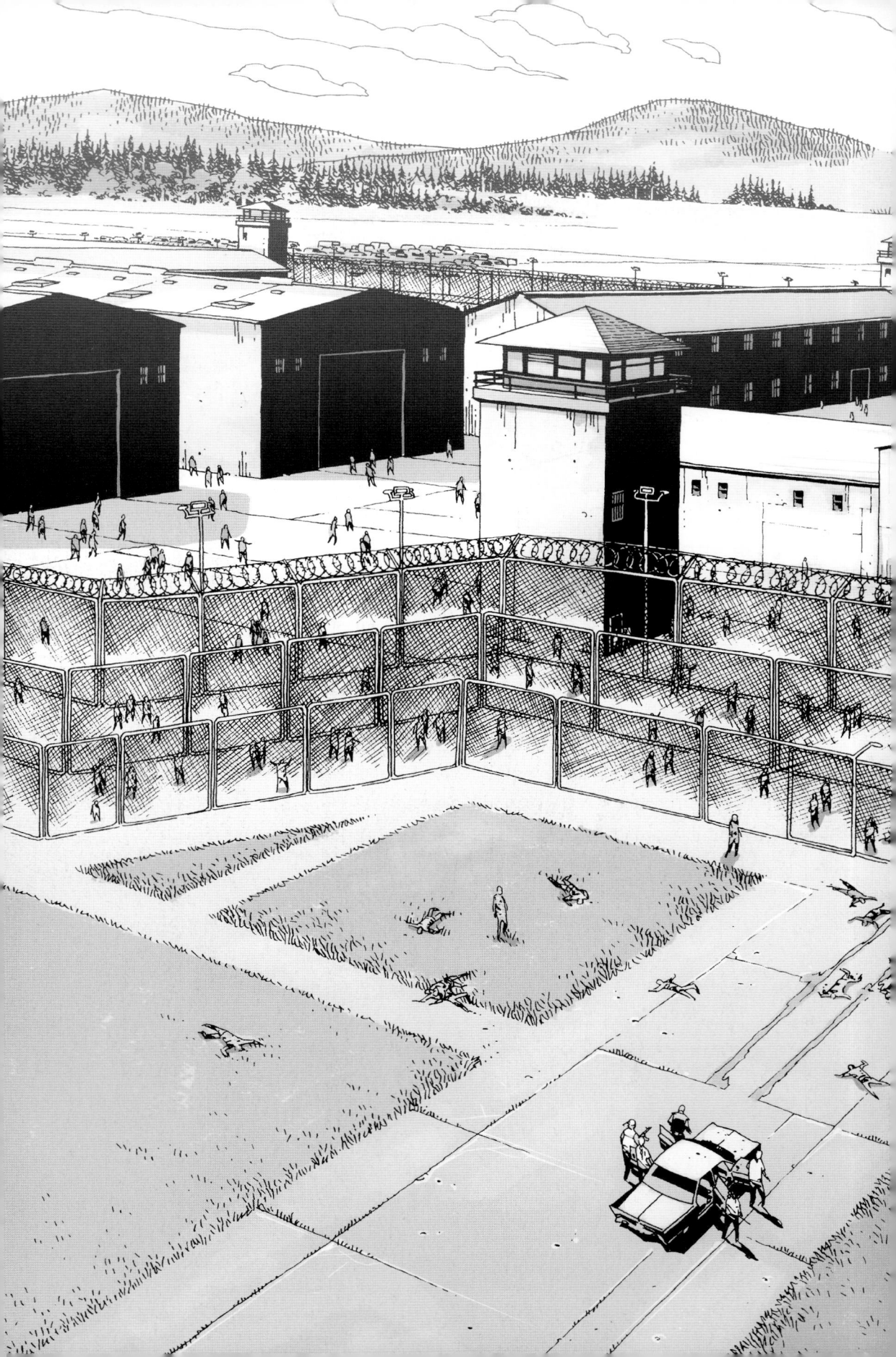

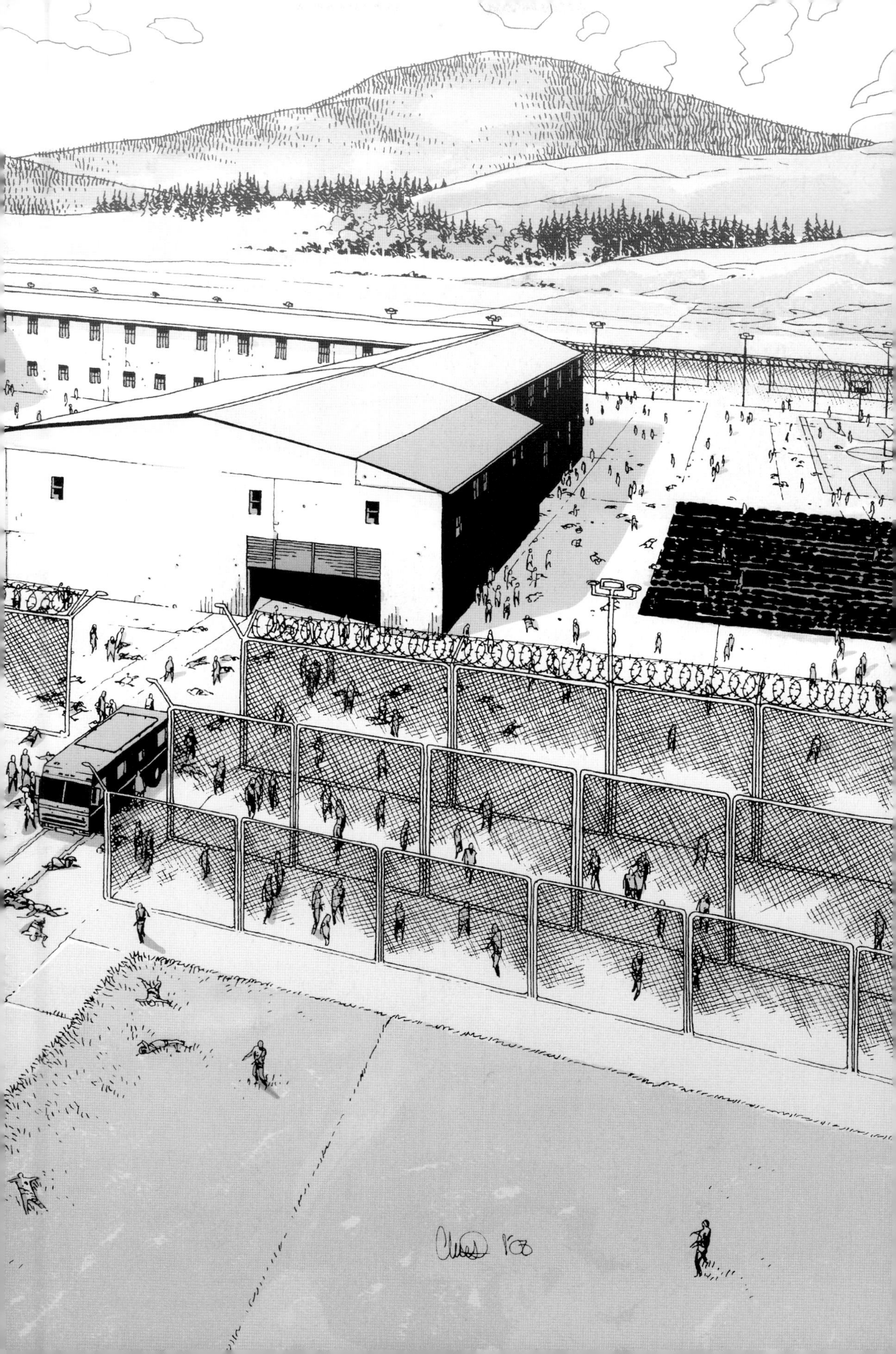

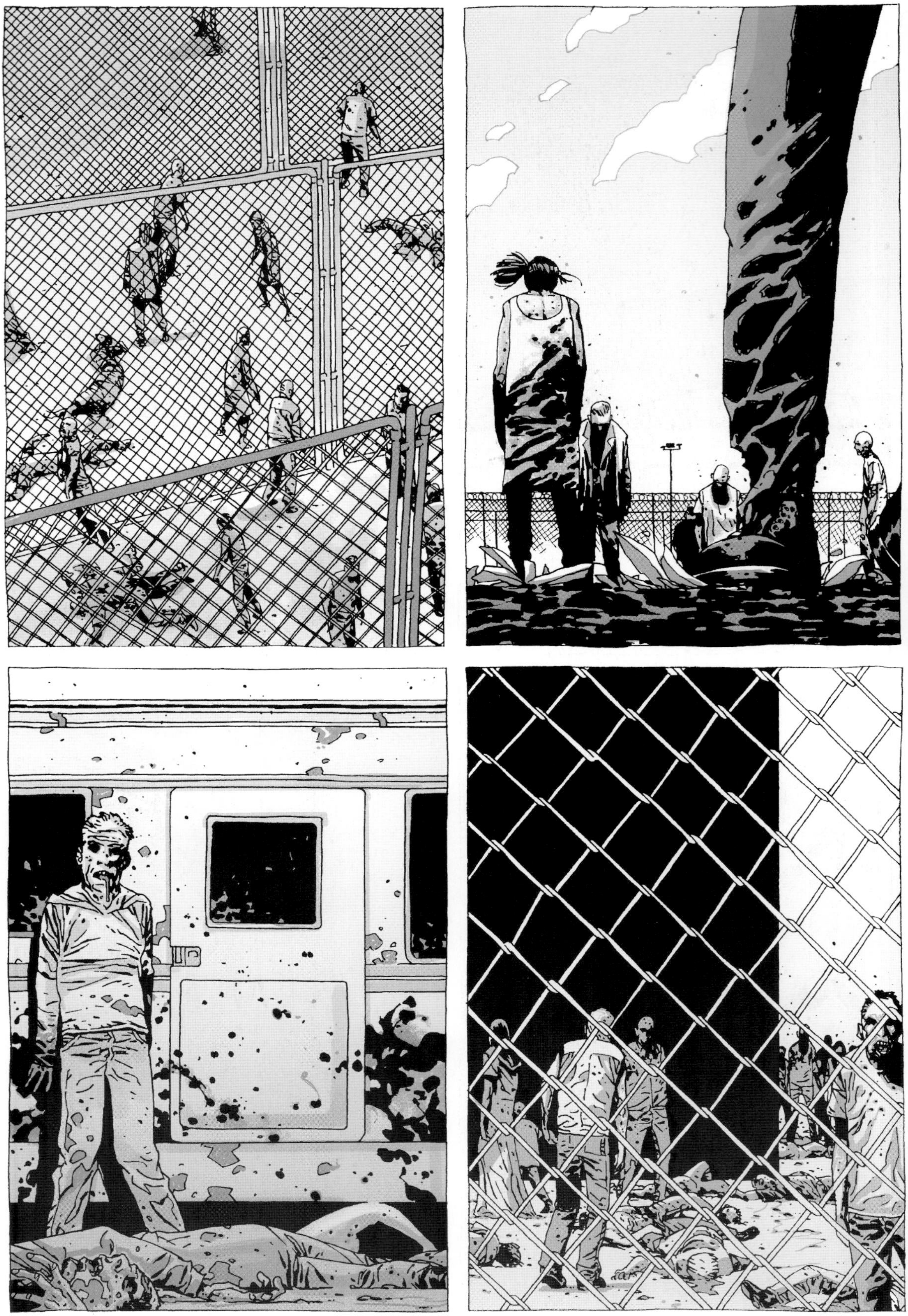

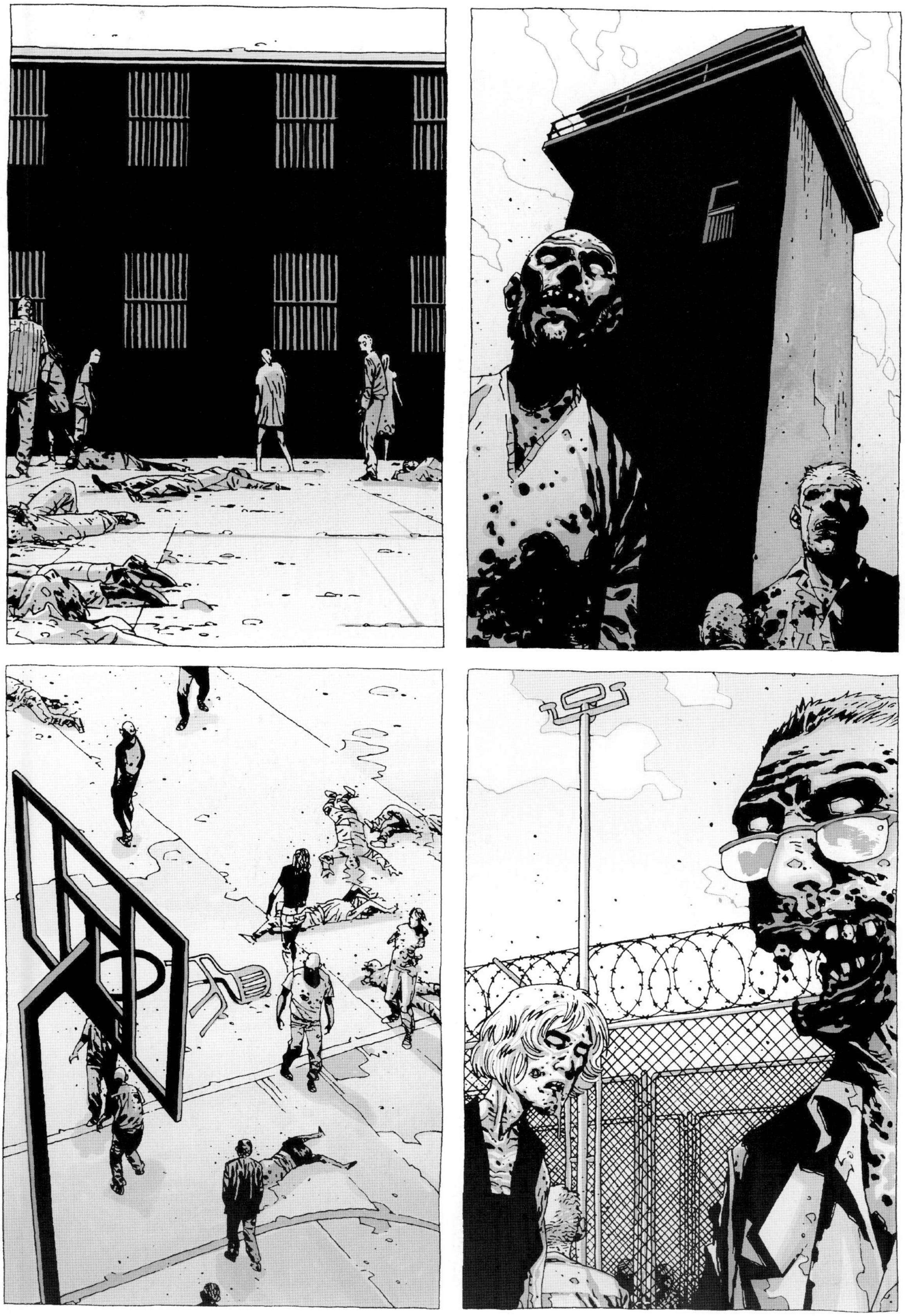

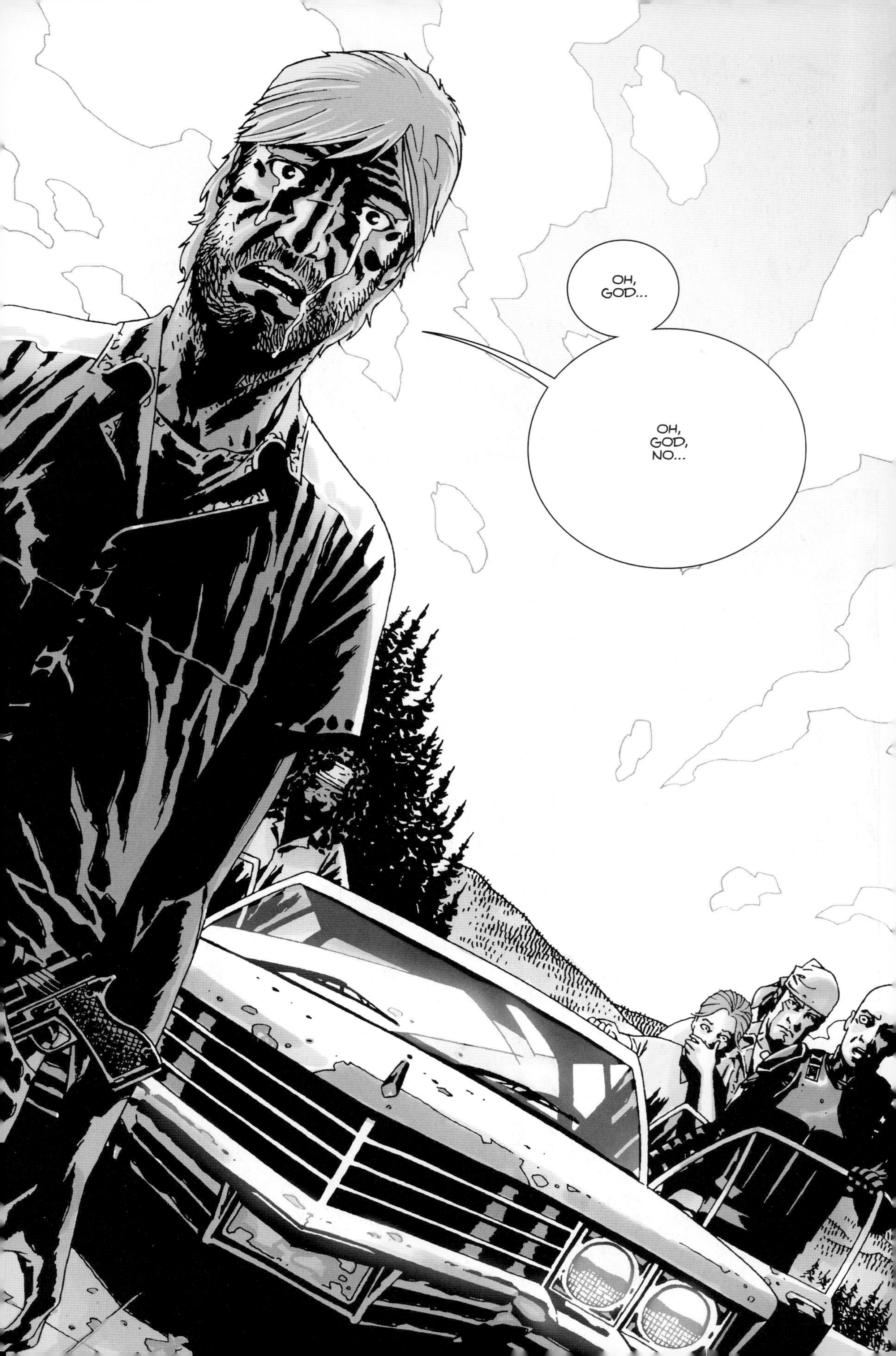
OH, GOD...
OH, GOD, NO...

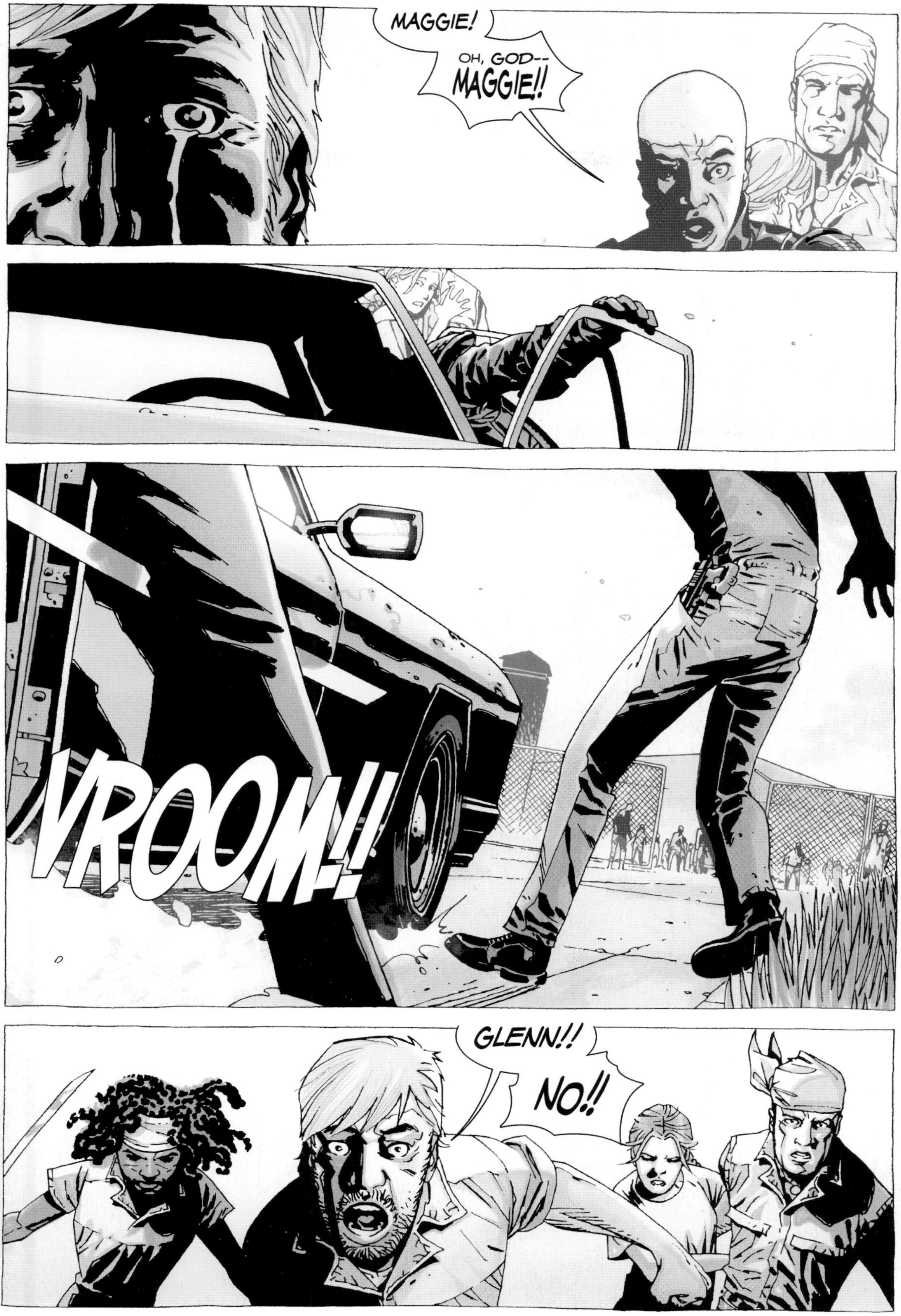
MAGGIE!
OH, GOD-- MAGGIE!!
VROOM!!
GLENN!!
NO!!

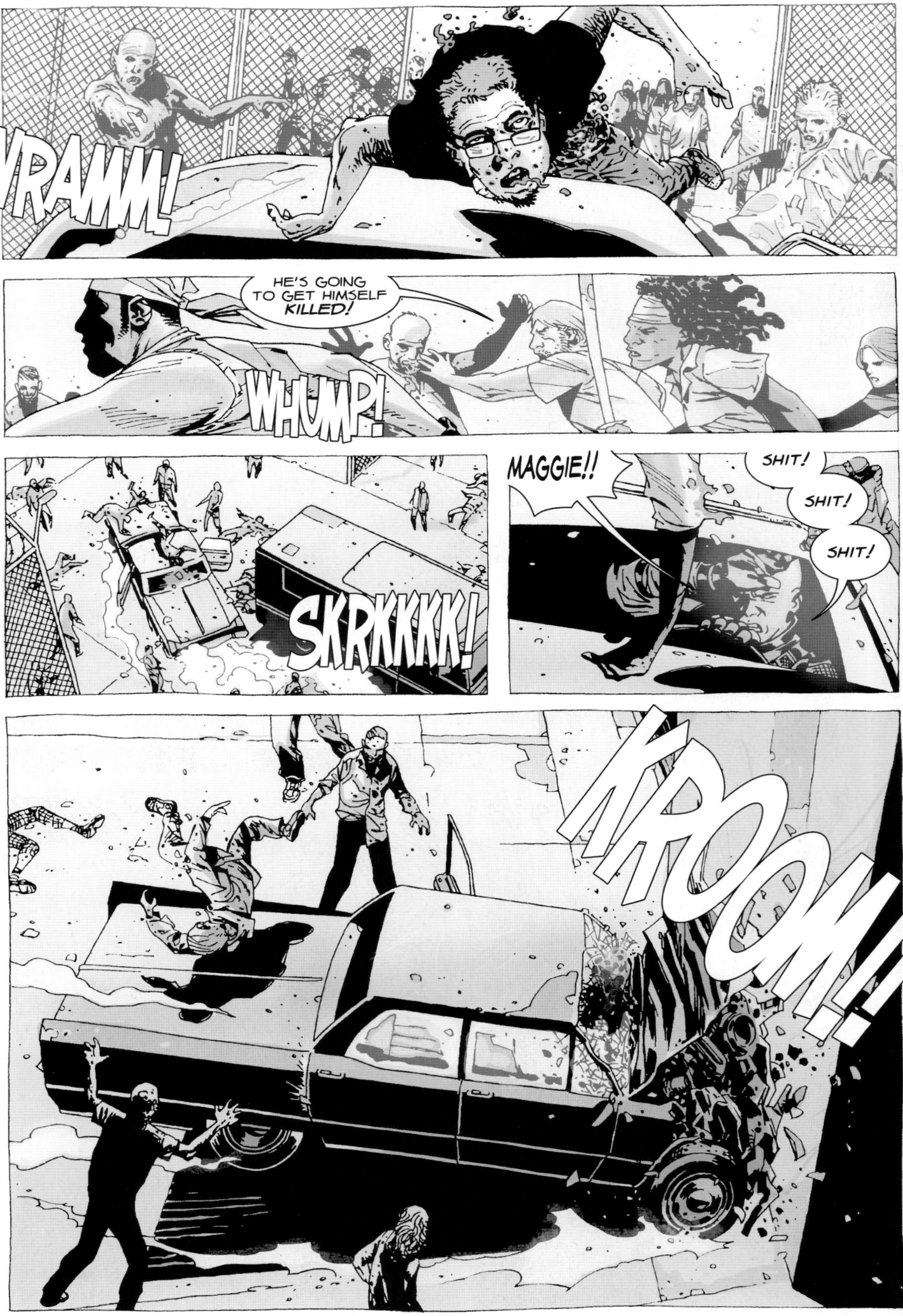
WRAMM!
HE'S GOING TO GET HIMSELF KILLED!
WHUMP!
SKRKKKK!
MAGGIE!!
SHIT!
SHIT!
SHIT!
KROOOM!!!

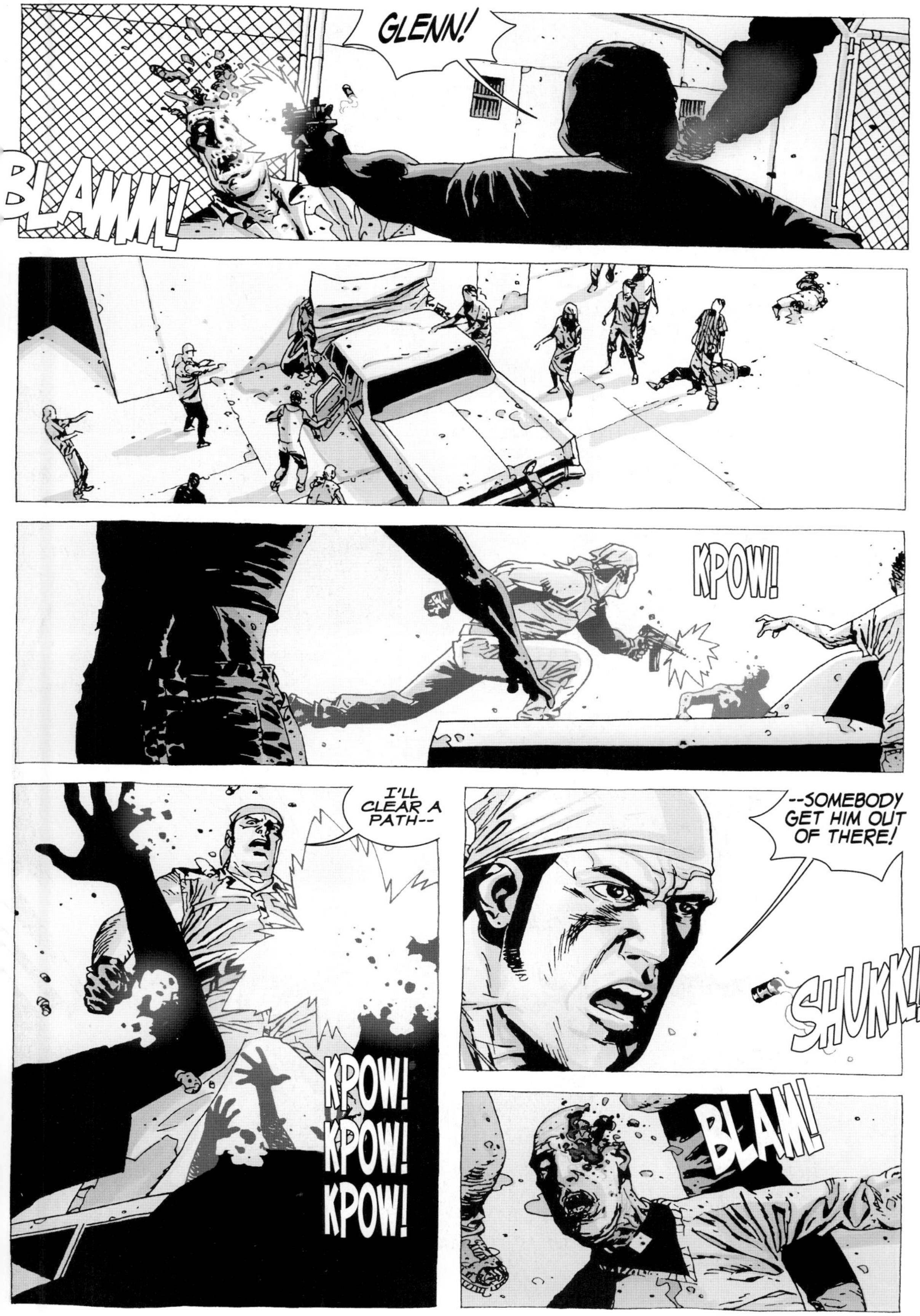
GLENN!
BLAMM!
KPOW!
I'LL CLEAR A PATH--
KPOW!
KPOW!
KPOW!
--SOMEBODY GET HIM OUT OF THERE!
SHUKK!!
BLAM!

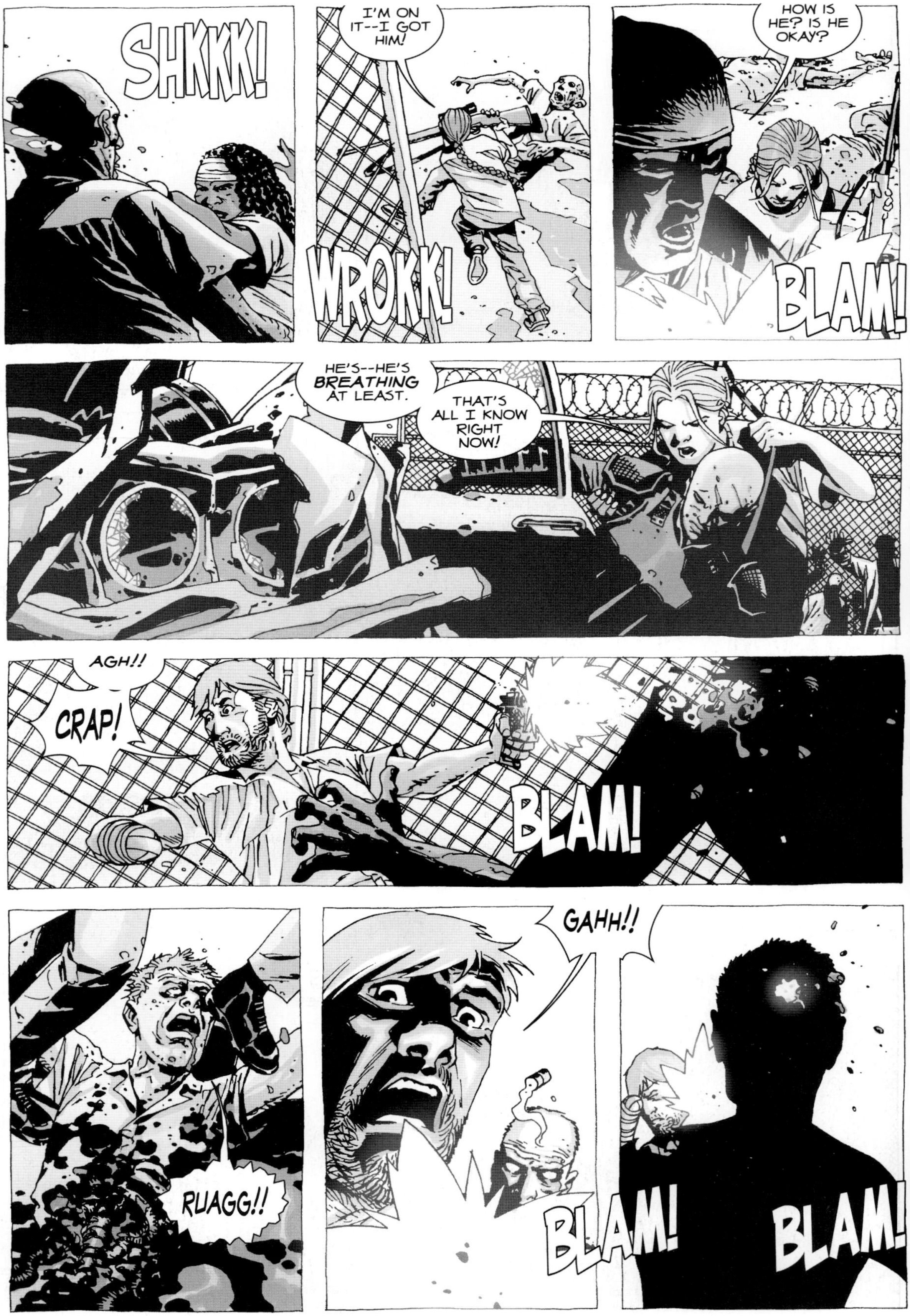
SHKKK!
I'M ON IT--I GOT HIM!
WROKK!
HOW IS HE? IS HE OKAY?
BLAM!
HE'S--HE'S BREATHING AT LEAST.
THAT'S ALL I KNOW RIGHT NOW!
AGH!!
CRAP!
BLAM!
RUAGG!!
GAHH!!
BLAM!
BLAM!

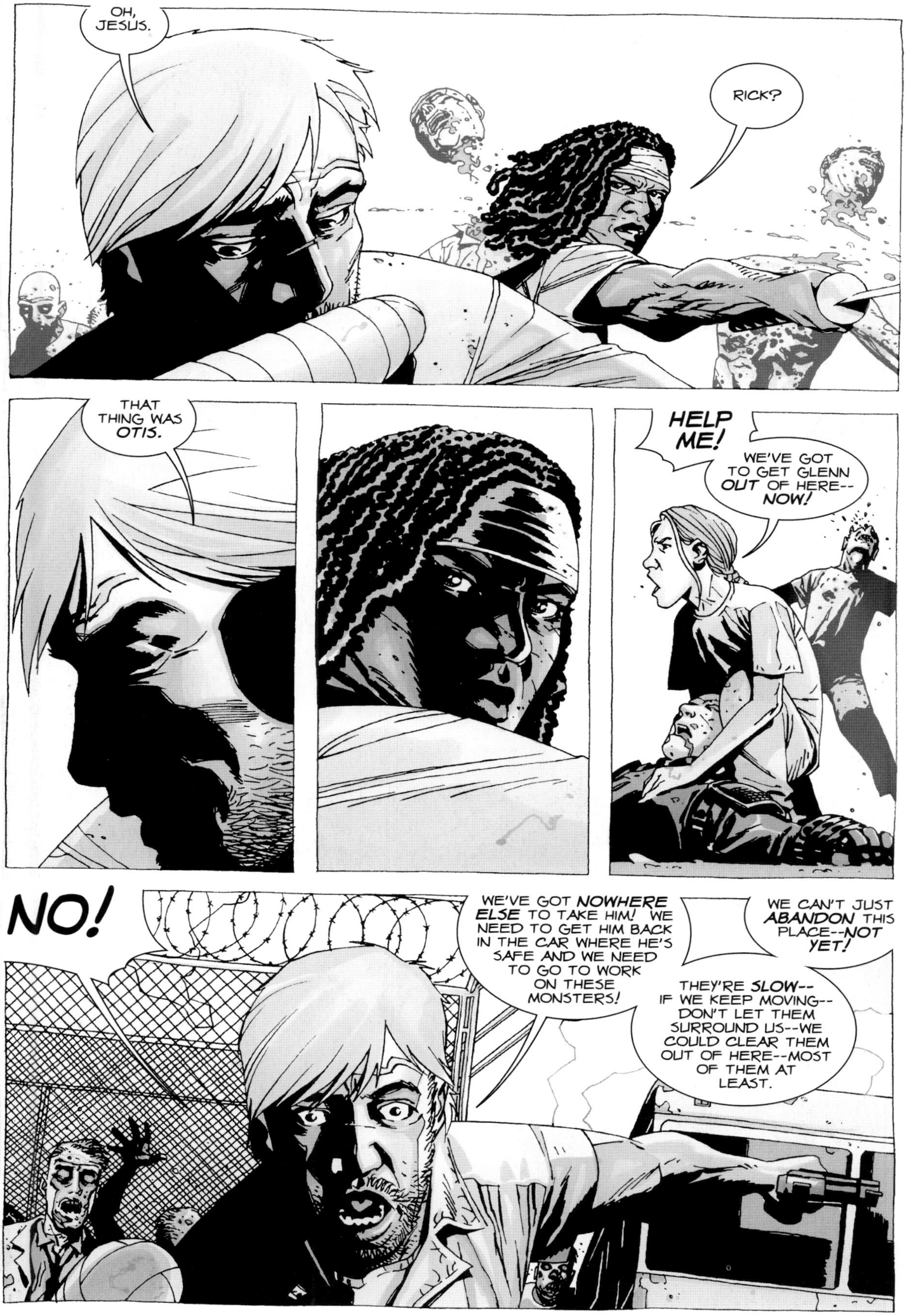
OH, JESUS.
RICK?
THAT THING WAS OTIS.
HELP ME!
WE'VE GOT TO GET GLENN OUT OF HERE-- NOW!
NO!
WE'VE GOT NOWHERE ELSE TO TAKE HIM! WE NEED TO GET HIM BACK IN THE CAR WHERE HE'S SAFE AND WE NEED TO GO TO WORK ON THESE MONSTERS!
WE CAN'T JUST ABANDON THIS PLACE--NOT YET!
THEY'RE SLOW-- IF WE KEEP MOVING-- DON'T LET THEM SURROUND US--WE COULD CLEAR THEM OUT OF HERE--MOST OF THEM AT LEAST.

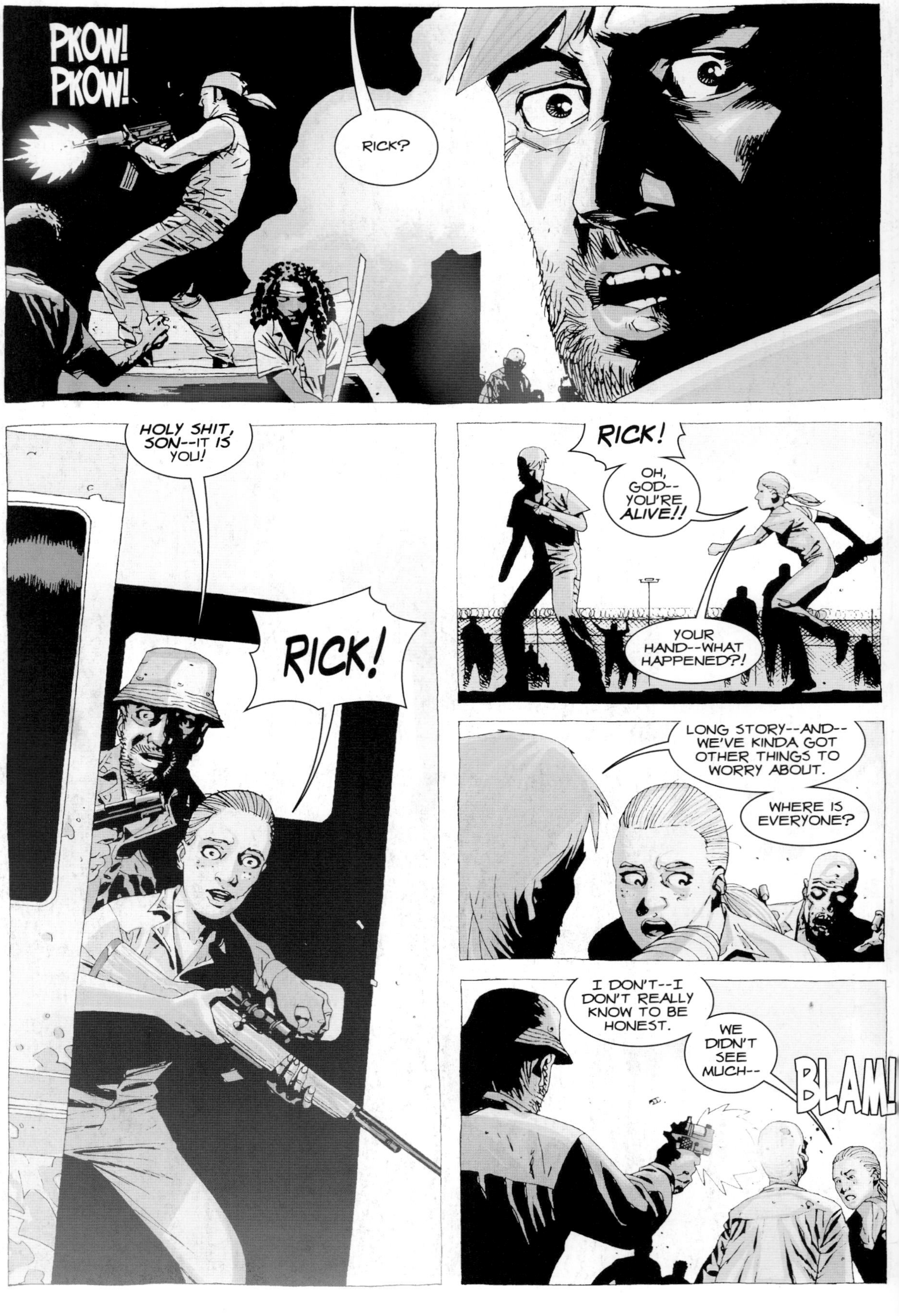
PKOW! PKOW!
RICK?
HOLY SHIT, SON--IT IS YOU!
RICK!
RICK!
OH, GOD--YOU'RE ALIVE!!
YOUR HAND--WHAT HAPPENED?!
LONG STORY--AND--WE'VE KINDA GOT OTHER THINGS TO WORRY ABOUT.
WHERE IS EVERYONE?
I DON'T--I DON'T REALLY KNOW TO BE HONEST.
WE DIDN'T SEE MUCH--
BLAM!

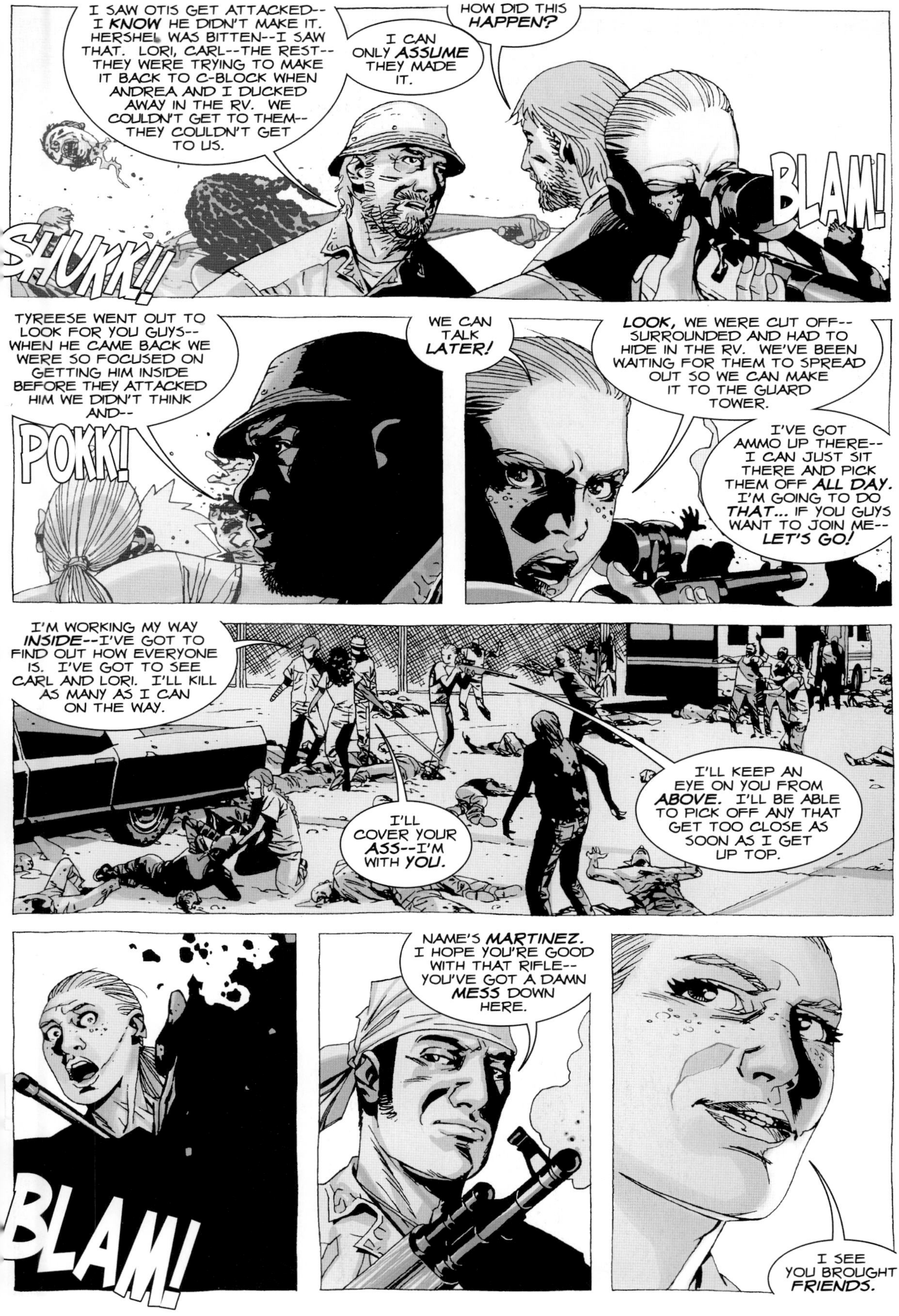
I SAW OTIS GET ATTACKED-- I KNOW HE DIDN'T MAKE IT. HERSHEL WAS BITTEN--I SAW THAT. LORI, CARL--THE REST-- THEY WERE TRYING TO MAKE IT BACK TO C-BLOCK WHEN ANDREA AND I DUCKED AWAY IN THE RV. WE COULDN'T GET TO THEM-- THEY COULDN'T GET TO US.
I CAN ONLY ASSUME THEY MADE IT.
HOW DID THIS HAPPEN?
SHUKK!!
BLAM!
TYREESE WENT OUT TO LOOK FOR YOU GUYS-- WHEN HE CAME BACK WE WERE SO FOCUSED ON GETTING HIM INSIDE BEFORE THEY ATTACKED HIM WE DIDN'T THINK AND--
POKK!
WE CAN TALK LATER!
LOOK, WE WERE CUT OFF-- SURROUNDED AND HAD TO HIDE IN THE RV. WE'VE BEEN WAITING FOR THEM TO SPREAD OUT SO WE CAN MAKE IT TO THE GUARD TOWER.
I'VE GOT AMMO UP THERE-- I CAN JUST SIT THERE AND PICK THEM OFF ALL DAY. I'M GOING TO DO THAT... IF YOU GUYS WANT TO JOIN ME-- LET'S GO!
I'M WORKING MY WAY INSIDE--I'VE GOT TO FIND OUT HOW EVERYONE IS. I'VE GOT TO SEE CARL AND LORI. I'LL KILL AS MANY AS I CAN ON THE WAY.
I'LL COVER YOUR ASS--I'M WITH YOU.
I'LL KEEP AN EYE ON YOU FROM ABOVE. I'LL BE ABLE TO PICK OFF ANY THAT GET TOO CLOSE AS SOON AS I GET UP TOP.
BLAM!
NAME'S MARTINEZ. I HOPE YOU'RE GOOD WITH THAT RIFLE-- YOU'VE GOT A DAMN MESS DOWN HERE.
I SEE YOU BROUGHT FRIENDS.

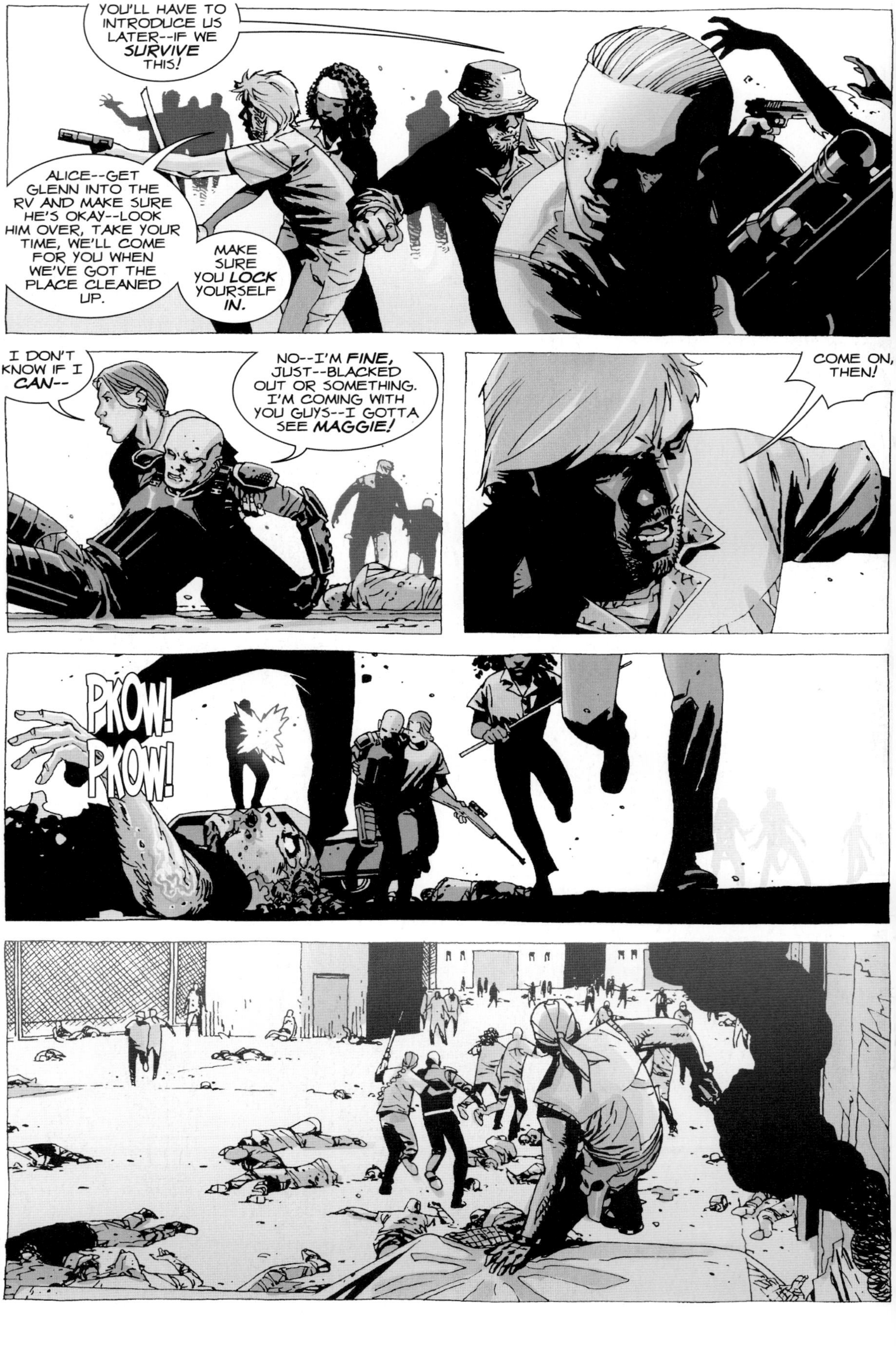
YOU'LL HAVE TO INTRODUCE US LATER--IF WE SURVIVE THIS!
ALICE--GET GLENN INTO THE RV AND MAKE SURE HE'S OKAY--LOOK HIM OVER, TAKE YOUR TIME, WE'LL COME FOR YOU WHEN WE'VE GOT THE PLACE CLEANED UP.
MAKE SURE YOU LOCK YOURSELF IN.
I DON'T KNOW IF I CAN--
NO--I'M FINE, JUST--BLACKED OUT OR SOMETHING. I'M COMING WITH YOU GUYS--I GOTTA SEE MAGGIE!
COME ON, THEN!
PKOW! PKOW!

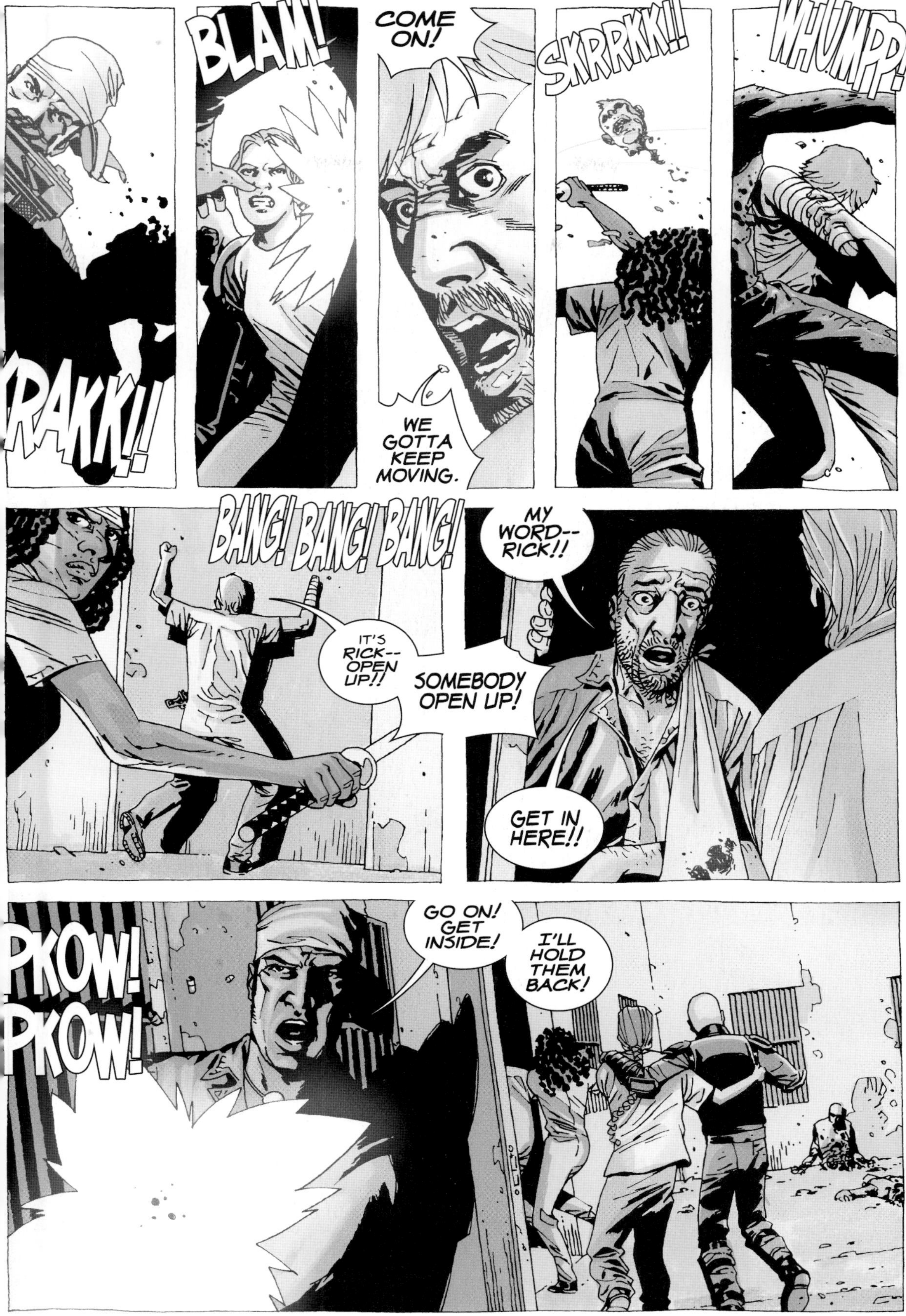
RAKK!!
BLAM!
COME ON!
WE GOTTA KEEP MOVING.
SKRRKK!!
WHUMPP!
BANG! BANG! BANG!
IT'S RICK-- OPEN UP!!
SOMEBODY OPEN UP!
MY WORD-- RICK!!
GET IN HERE!!
PKOW! PKOW!
GO ON! GET INSIDE!
I'LL HOLD THEM BACK!

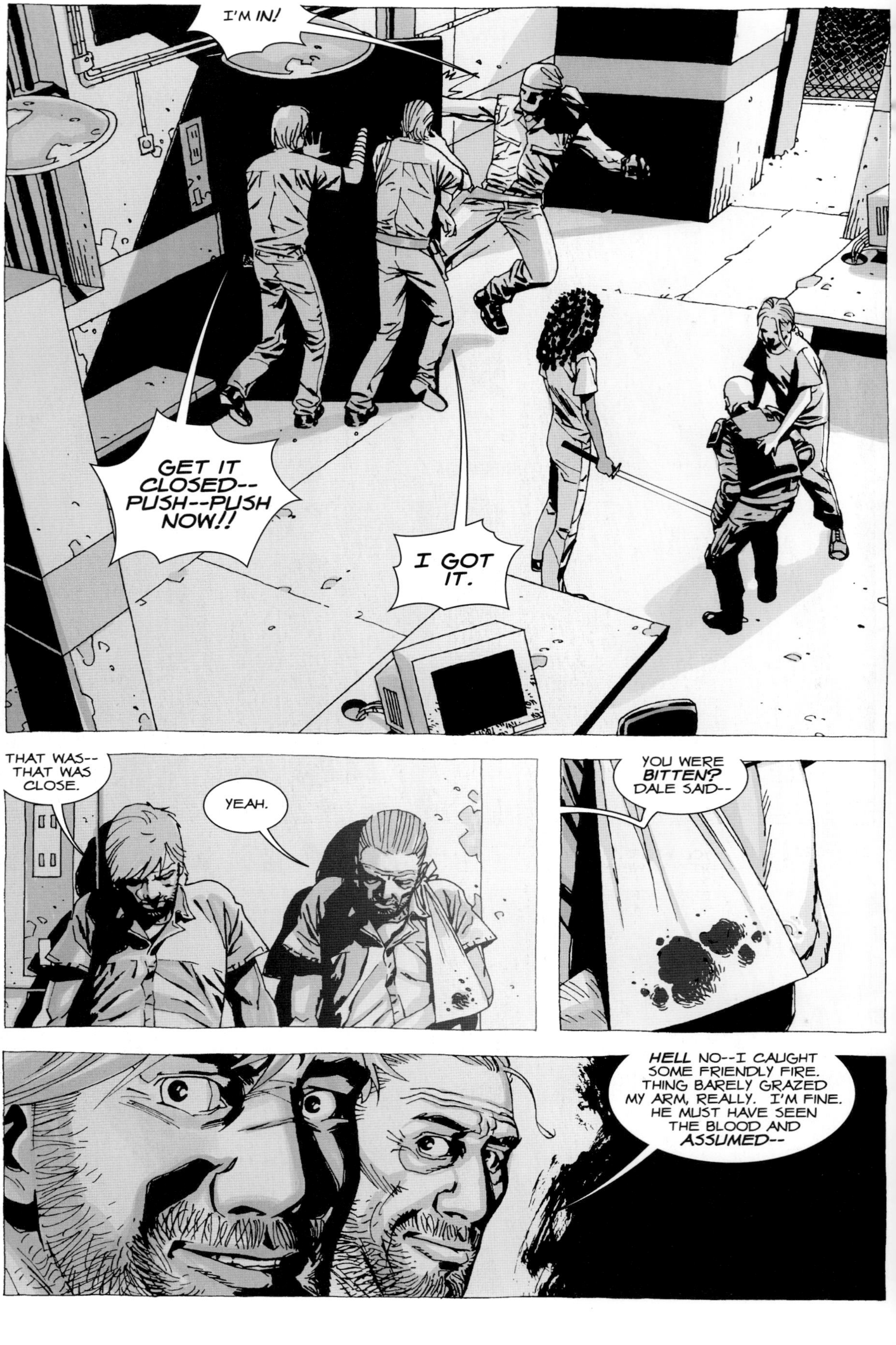

I'M IN!
GET IT CLOSED-- PUSH--PUSH NOW!!
I GOT IT.
THAT WAS-- THAT WAS CLOSE.
YEAH.
YOU WERE BITTEN? DALE SAID--
HELL NO--I CAUGHT SOME FRIENDLY FIRE. THING BARELY GRAZED MY ARM, REALLY. I'M FINE. HE MUST HAVE SEEN THE BLOOD AND ASSUMED--

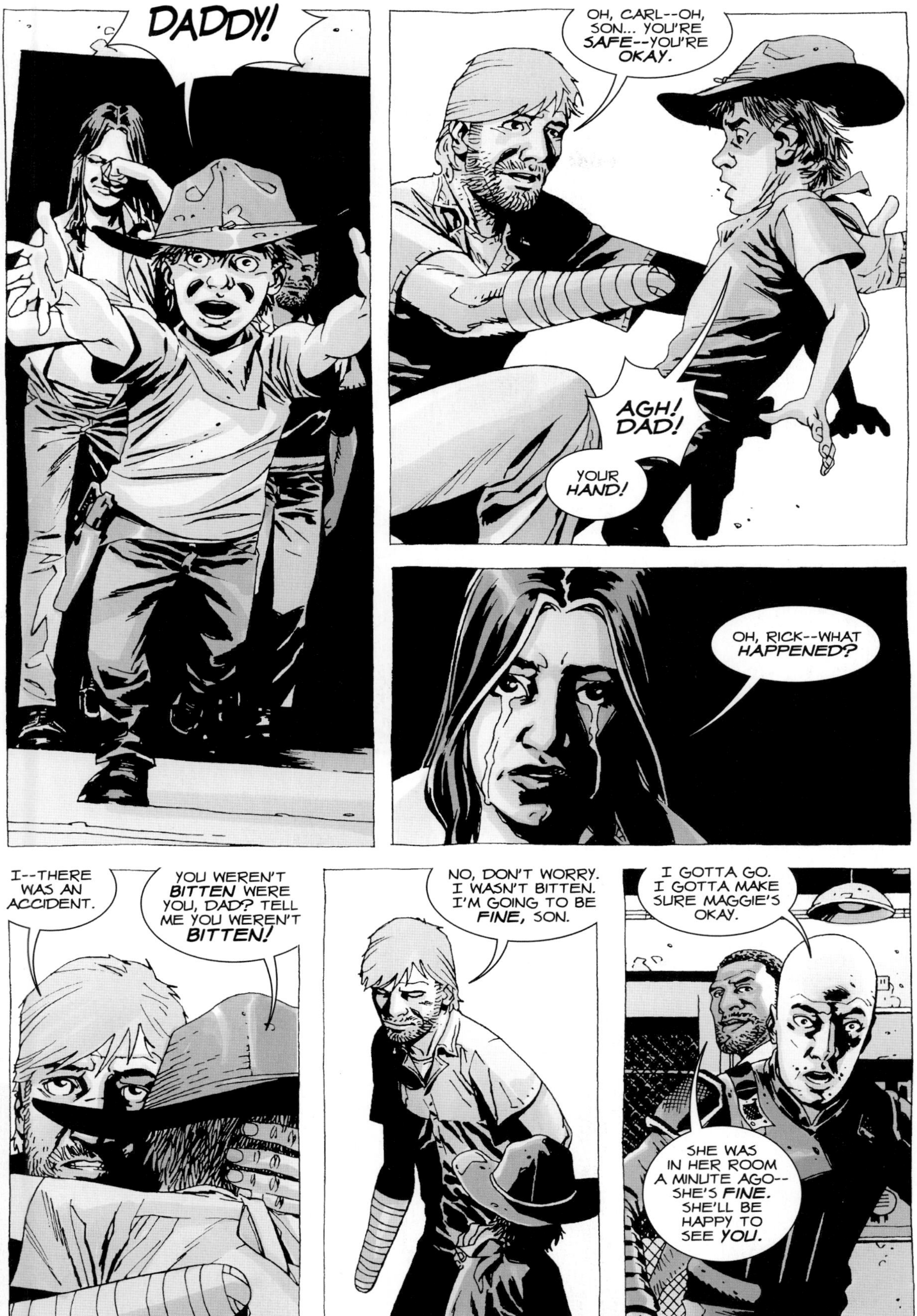
DADDY!
OH, CARL--OH, SON... YOU'RE SAFE--YOU'RE OKAY.
AGH! DAD!
YOUR HAND!
OH, RICK--WHAT HAPPENED?
I--THERE WAS AN ACCIDENT.
YOU WEREN'T BITTEN WERE YOU, DAD? TELL ME YOU WEREN'T BITTEN!
NO, DON'T WORRY. I WASN'T BITTEN. I'M GOING TO BE FINE, SON.
I GOTTA GO. I GOTTA MAKE SURE MAGGIE'S OKAY.
SHE WAS IN HER ROOM A MINUTE AGO--SHE'S FINE. SHE'LL BE HAPPY TO SEE YOU.

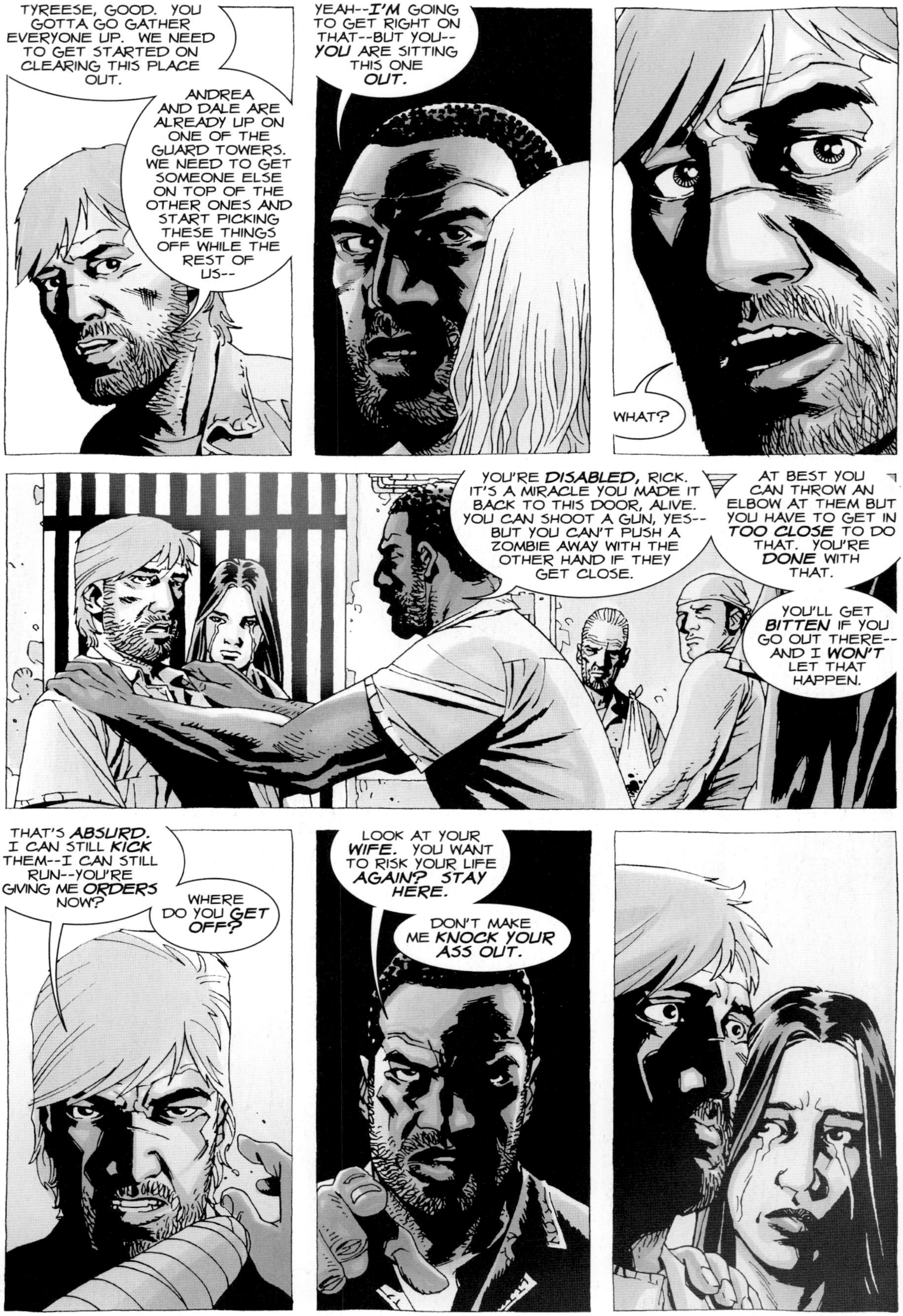
TYREESE, GOOD. YOU GOTTA GO GATHER EVERYONE UP. WE NEED TO GET STARTED ON CLEARING THIS PLACE OUT.
ANDREA AND DALE ARE ALREADY UP ON ONE OF THE GUARD TOWERS. WE NEED TO GET SOMEONE ELSE ON TOP OF THE OTHER ONES AND START PICKING THESE THINGS OFF WHILE THE REST OF US--
YEAH--I'M GOING TO GET RIGHT ON THAT--BUT YOU--YOU ARE SITTING THIS ONE OUT.
WHAT?
YOU'RE DISABLED, RICK. IT'S A MIRACLE YOU MADE IT BACK TO THIS DOOR, ALIVE. YOU CAN SHOOT A GUN, YES--BUT YOU CAN'T PUSH A ZOMBIE AWAY WITH THE OTHER HAND IF THEY GET CLOSE.
AT BEST YOU CAN THROW AN ELBOW AT THEM BUT YOU HAVE TO GET IN TOO CLOSE TO DO THAT. YOU'RE DONE WITH THAT.
YOU'LL GET BITTEN IF YOU GO OUT THERE--AND I WON'T LET THAT HAPPEN.
THAT'S ABSURD. I CAN STILL KICK THEM--I CAN STILL RUN--YOU'RE GIVING ME ORDERS NOW?
WHERE DO YOU GET OFF?
LOOK AT YOUR WIFE. YOU WANT TO RISK YOUR LIFE AGAIN? STAY HERE.
DON'T MAKE ME KNOCK YOUR ASS OUT.

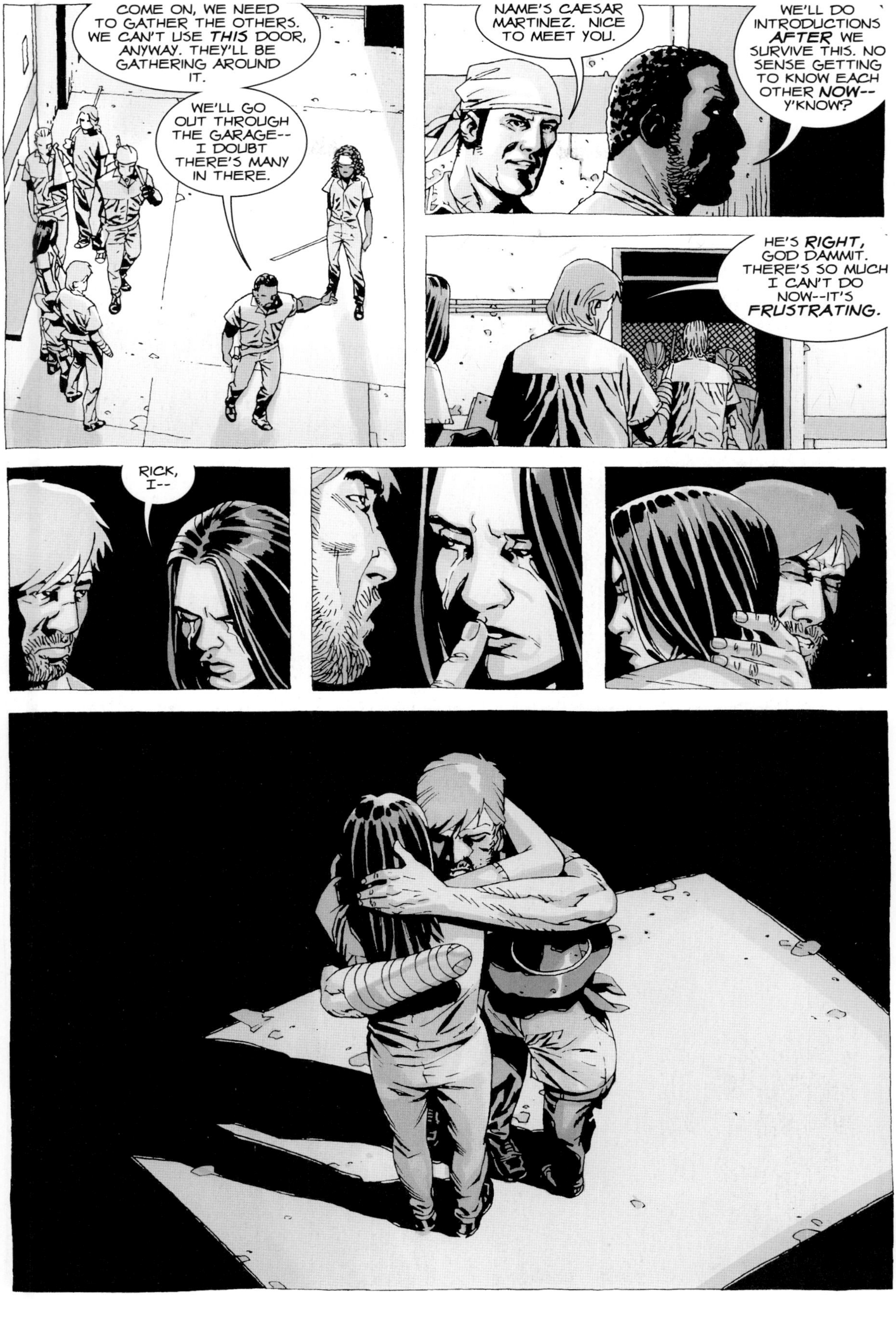

COME ON, WE NEED TO GATHER THE OTHERS. WE CAN'T USE *THIS* DOOR, ANYWAY. THEY'LL BE GATHERING AROUND IT.
WE'LL GO OUT THROUGH THE GARAGE-- I DOUBT THERE'S MANY IN THERE.
NAME'S CAESAR MARTINEZ. NICE TO MEET YOU.
WE'LL DO INTRODUCTIONS *AFTER* WE SURVIVE THIS. NO SENSE GETTING TO KNOW EACH OTHER *NOW*-- Y'KNOW?
HE'S *RIGHT*, GOD DAMMIT. THERE'S SO MUCH I CAN'T DO NOW--IT'S *FRUSTRATING*.
RICK, I--

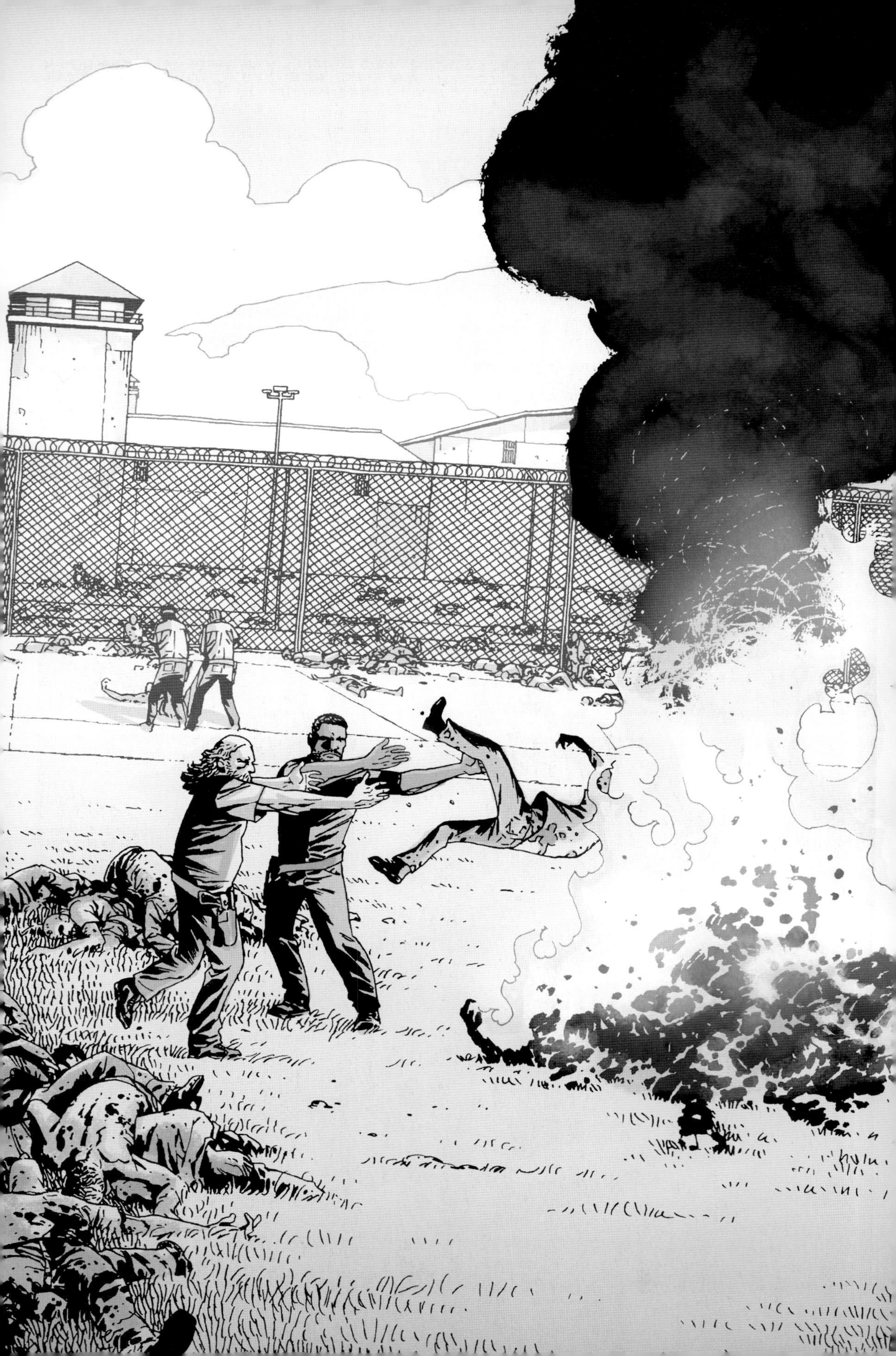

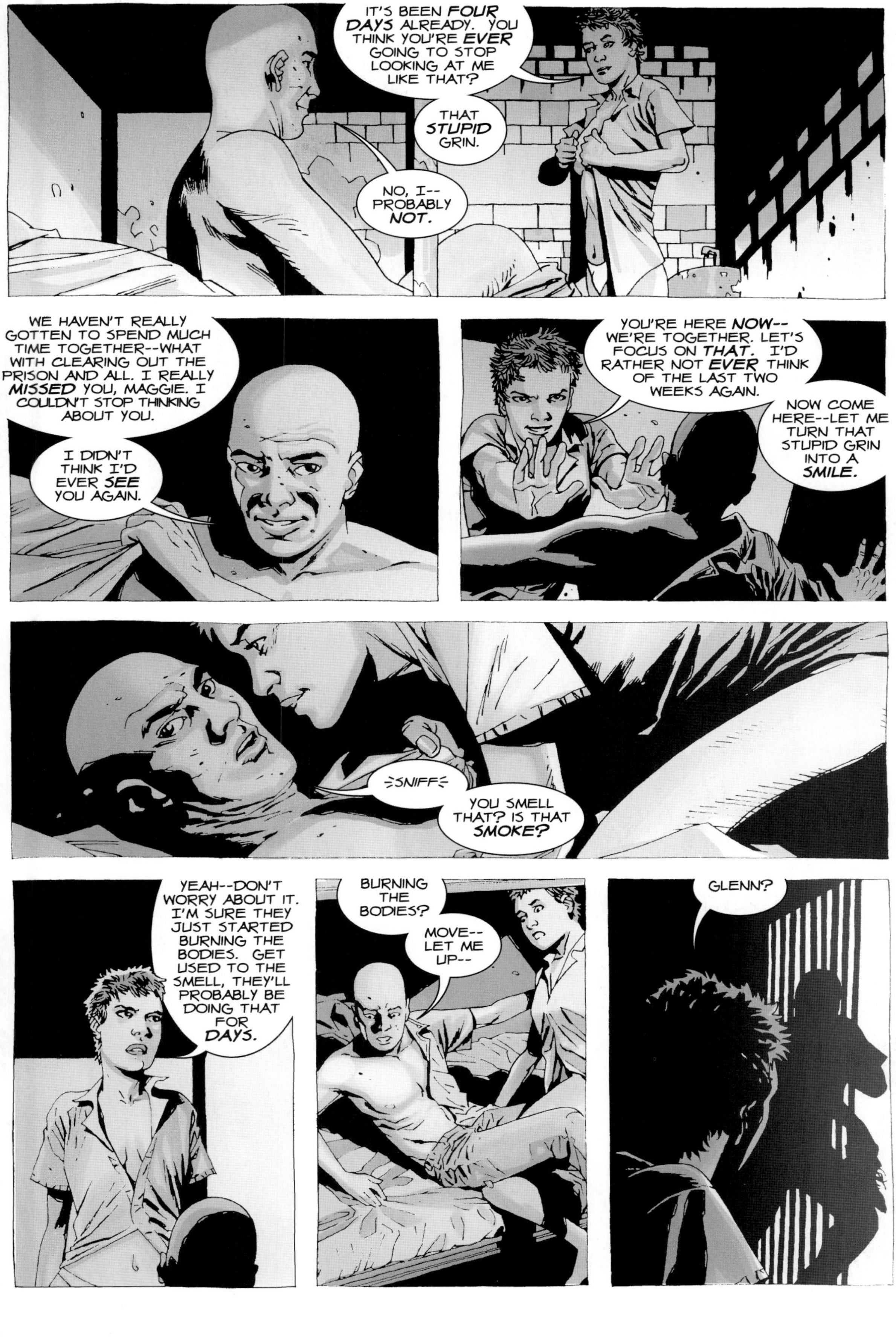
IT'S BEEN FOUR DAYS ALREADY. YOU THINK YOU'RE EVER GOING TO STOP LOOKING AT ME LIKE THAT?
THAT STUPID GRIN.
NO, I-- PROBABLY NOT.
WE HAVEN'T REALLY GOTTEN TO SPEND MUCH TIME TOGETHER--WHAT WITH CLEARING OUT THE PRISON AND ALL. I REALLY MISSED YOU, MAGGIE. I COULDN'T STOP THINKING ABOUT YOU.
I DIDN'T THINK I'D EVER SEE YOU AGAIN.
YOU'RE HERE NOW-- WE'RE TOGETHER. LET'S FOCUS ON THAT. I'D RATHER NOT EVER THINK OF THE LAST TWO WEEKS AGAIN.
NOW COME HERE--LET ME TURN THAT STUPID GRIN INTO A SMILE.
SNIFF
YOU SMELL THAT? IS THAT SMOKE?
YEAH--DON'T WORRY ABOUT IT. I'M SURE THEY JUST STARTED BURNING THE BODIES. GET USED TO THE SMELL, THEY'LL PROBABLY BE DOING THAT FOR DAYS.
BURNING THE BODIES?
MOVE-- LET ME UP--
GLENN?

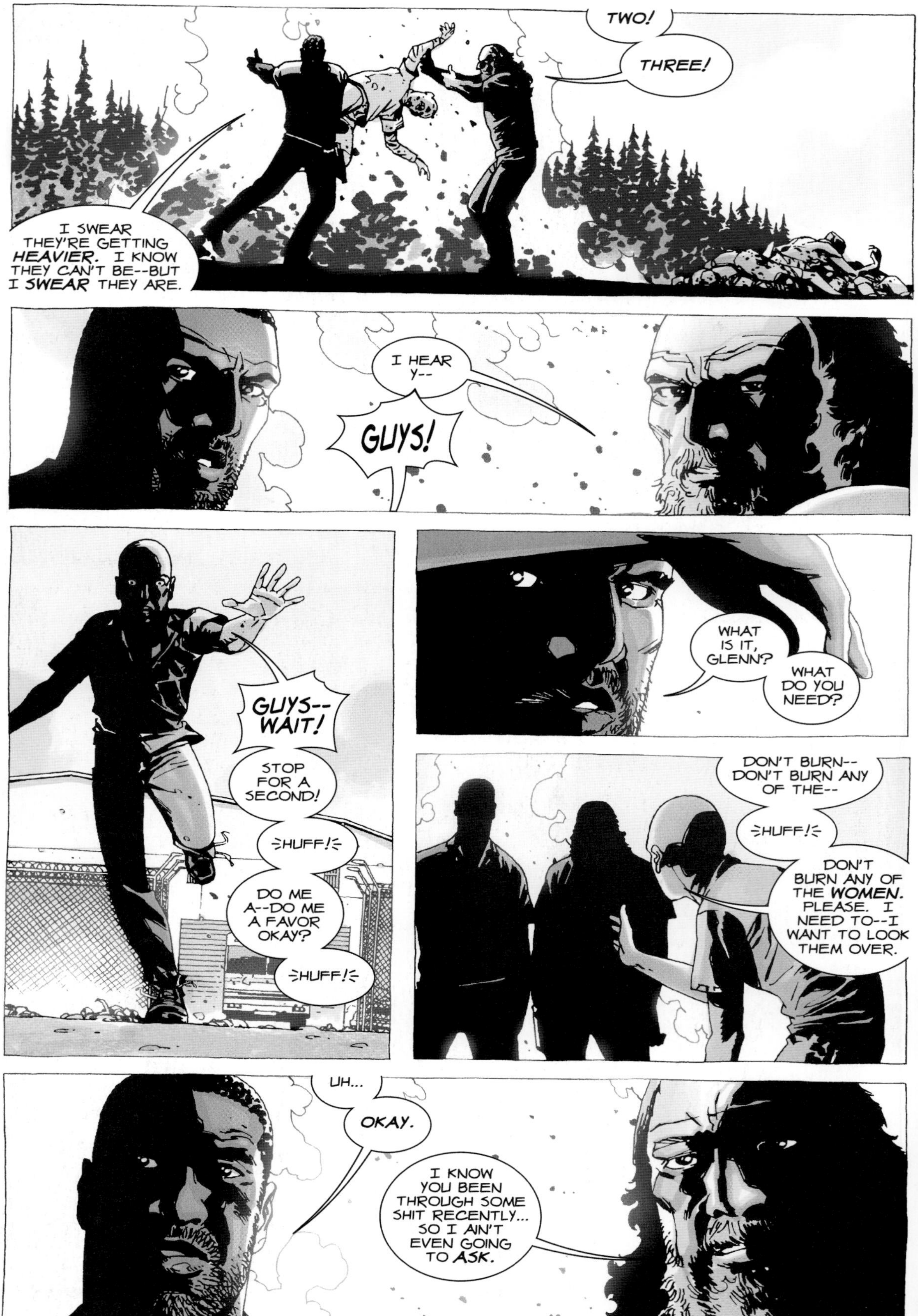
TWO!
THREE!
I SWEAR THEY'RE GETTING HEAVIER. I KNOW THEY CAN'T BE--BUT I SWEAR THEY ARE.
I HEAR Y--
GUYS!
GUYS-- WAIT!
STOP FOR A SECOND!
HUFF!
DO ME A--DO ME A FAVOR OKAY?
HUFF!
WHAT IS IT, GLENN?
WHAT DO YOU NEED?
DON'T BURN-- DON'T BURN ANY OF THE--
HUFF!
DON'T BURN ANY OF THE WOMEN. PLEASE. I NEED TO--I WANT TO LOOK THEM OVER.
UH...
OKAY.
I KNOW YOU BEEN THROUGH SOME SHIT RECENTLY... SO I AIN'T EVEN GOING TO ASK.

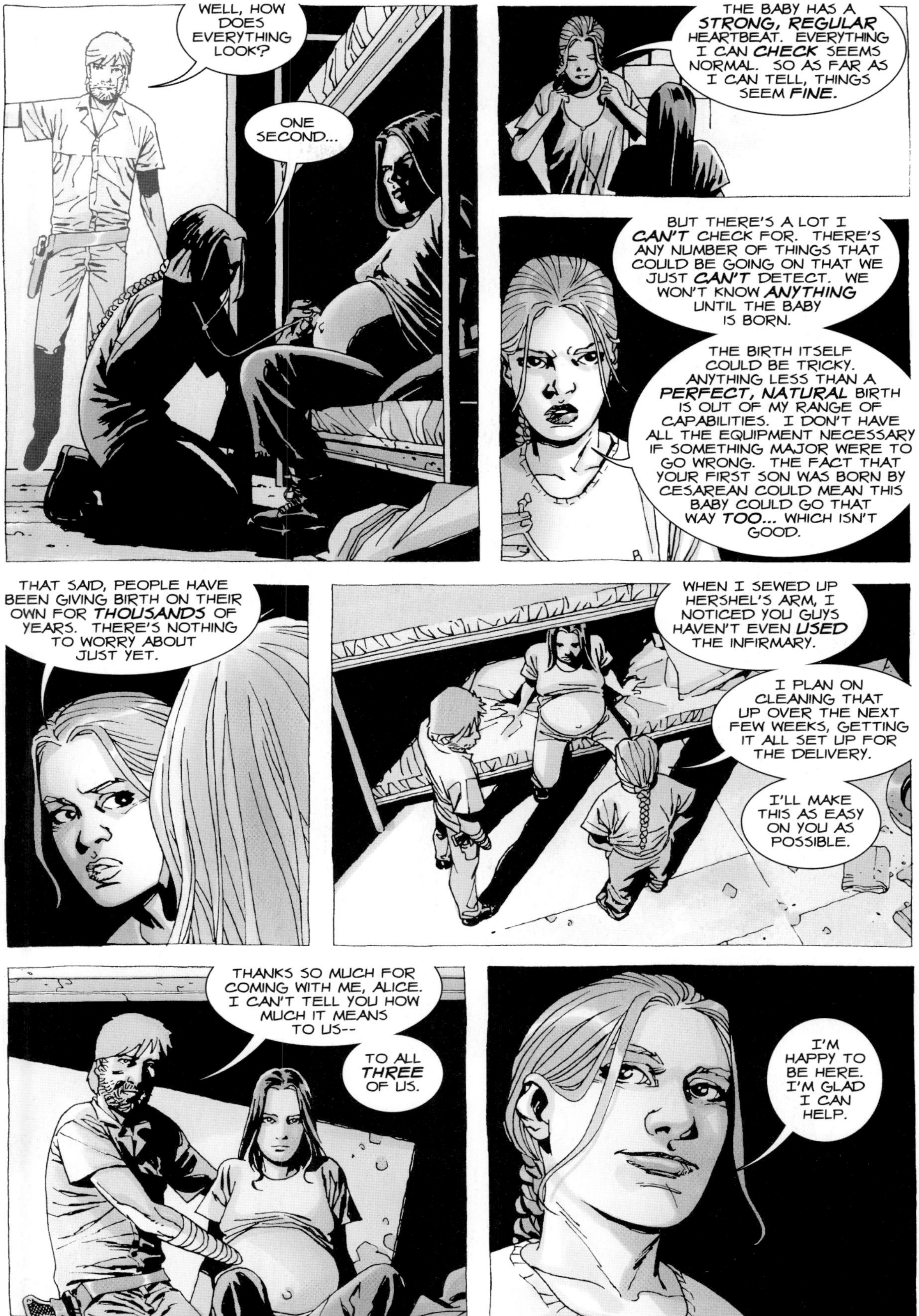
WELL, HOW DOES EVERYTHING LOOK?
ONE SECOND...
THE BABY HAS A STRONG, REGULAR HEARTBEAT. EVERYTHING I CAN CHECK SEEMS NORMAL. SO AS FAR AS I CAN TELL, THINGS SEEM FINE.
BUT THERE'S A LOT I CAN'T CHECK FOR. THERE'S ANY NUMBER OF THINGS THAT COULD BE GOING ON THAT WE JUST CAN'T DETECT. WE WON'T KNOW ANYTHING UNTIL THE BABY IS BORN.
THE BIRTH ITSELF COULD BE TRICKY. ANYTHING LESS THAN A PERFECT, NATURAL BIRTH IS OUT OF MY RANGE OF CAPABILITIES. I DON'T HAVE ALL THE EQUIPMENT NECESSARY IF SOMETHING MAJOR WERE TO GO WRONG. THE FACT THAT YOUR FIRST SON WAS BORN BY CESAREAN COULD MEAN THIS BABY COULD GO THAT WAY TOO... WHICH ISN'T GOOD.
THAT SAID, PEOPLE HAVE BEEN GIVING BIRTH ON THEIR OWN FOR THOUSANDS OF YEARS. THERE'S NOTHING TO WORRY ABOUT JUST YET.
WHEN I SEWED UP HERSHEL'S ARM, I NOTICED YOU GUYS HAVEN'T EVEN USED THE INFIRMARY.
I PLAN ON CLEANING THAT UP OVER THE NEXT FEW WEEKS, GETTING IT ALL SET UP FOR THE DELIVERY.
I'LL MAKE THIS AS EASY ON YOU AS POSSIBLE.
THANKS SO MUCH FOR COMING WITH ME, ALICE. I CAN'T TELL YOU HOW MUCH IT MEANS TO US--
TO ALL THREE OF US.
I'M HAPPY TO BE HERE. I'M GLAD I CAN HELP.

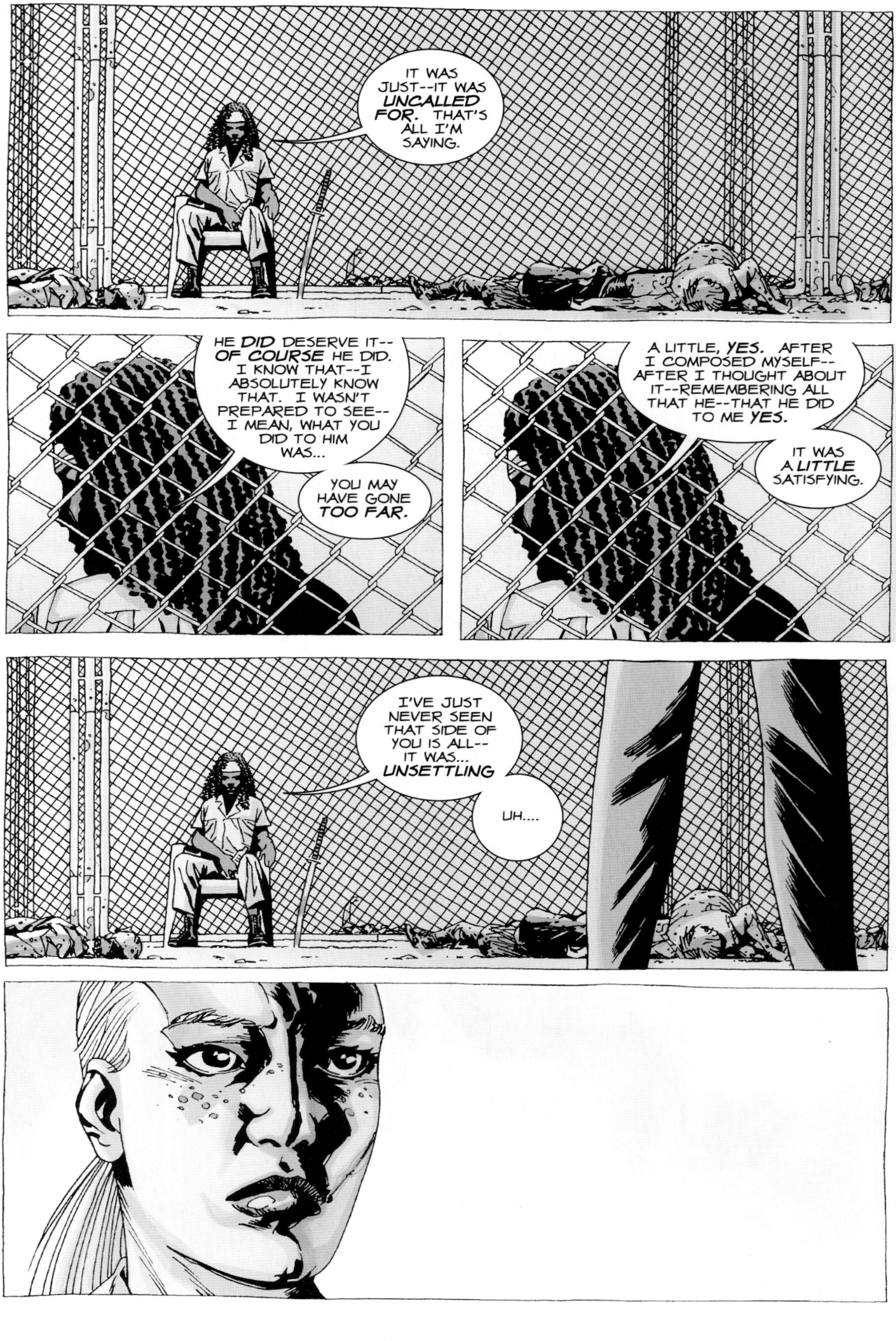
IT WAS JUST--IT WAS UNCALLED FOR. THAT'S ALL I'M SAYING.
HE DID DESERVE IT--OF COURSE HE DID. I KNOW THAT--I ABSOLUTELY KNOW THAT. I WASN'T PREPARED TO SEE--I MEAN, WHAT YOU DID TO HIM WAS...
YOU MAY HAVE GONE TOO FAR.
A LITTLE, YES. AFTER I COMPOSED MYSELF--AFTER I THOUGHT ABOUT IT--REMEMBERING ALL THAT HE--THAT HE DID TO ME YES.
IT WAS A LITTLE SATISFYING.
I'VE JUST NEVER SEEN THAT SIDE OF YOU IS ALL--IT WAS... UNSETTLING
UH....

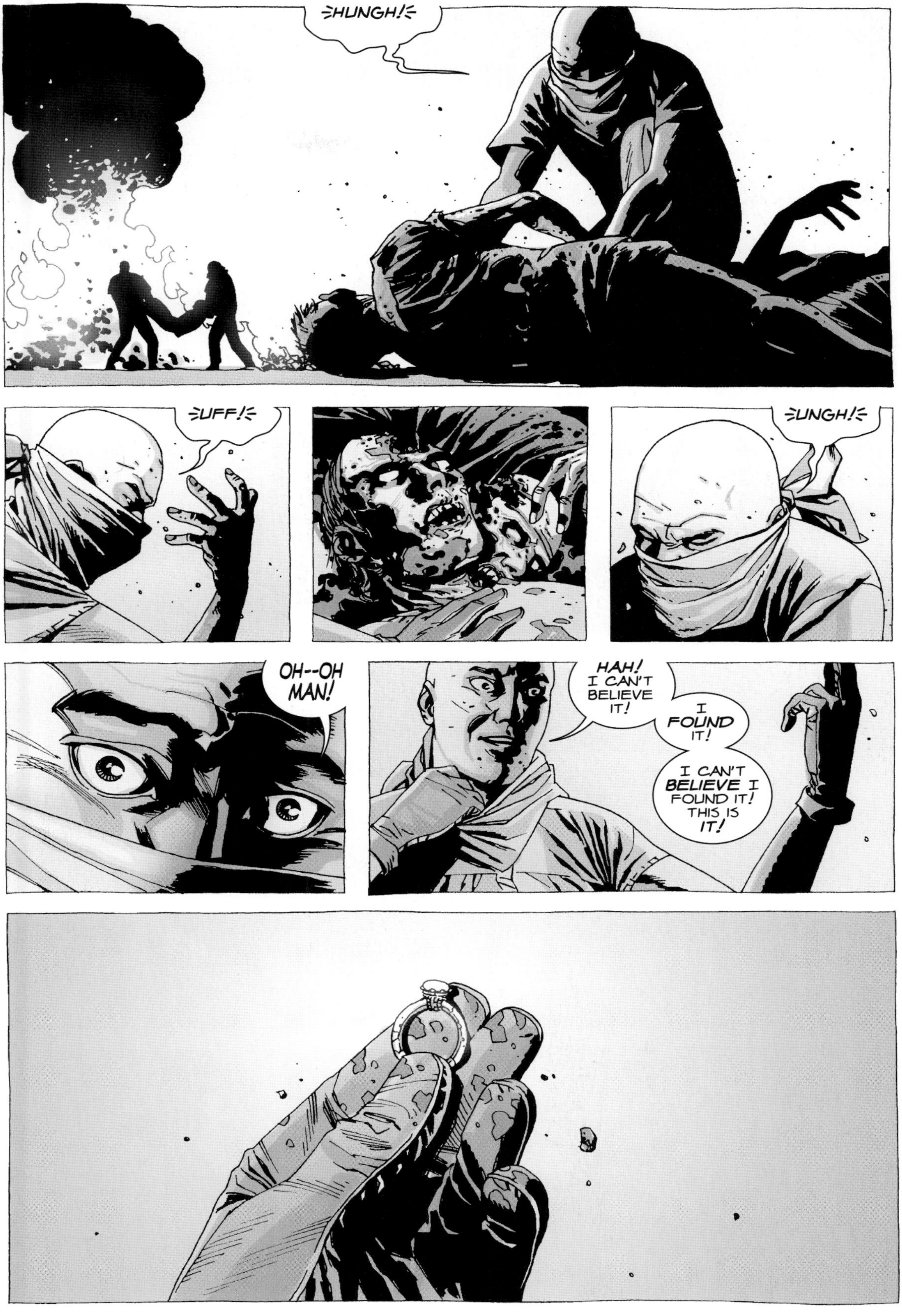

=HUNGH!=
=UFF!=
=UNGH!=
OH--OH MAN!
HAH! I CAN'T BELIEVE IT!
I FOUND IT!
I CAN'T BELIEVE I FOUND IT! THIS IS IT!

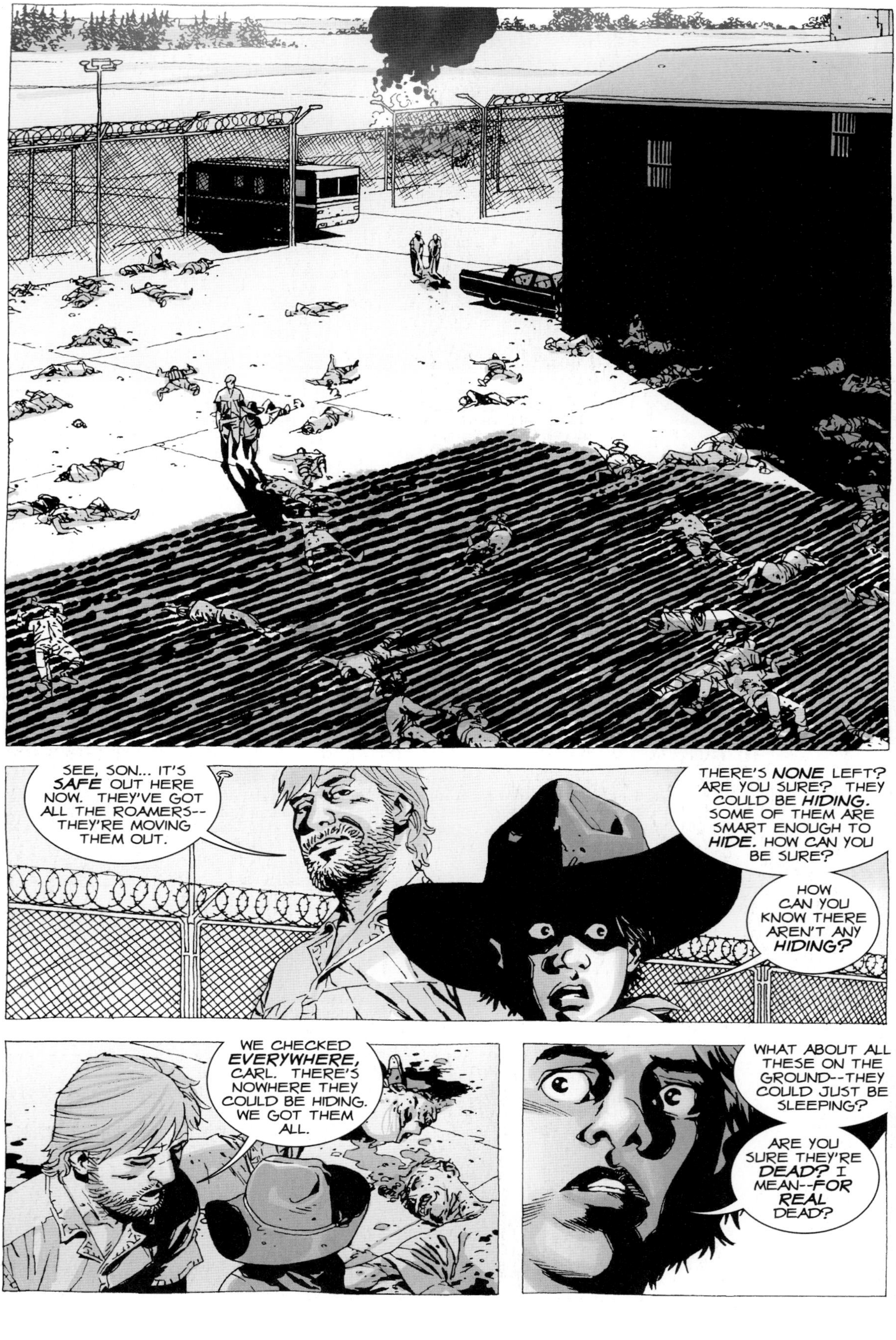
SEE, SON... IT'S SAFE OUT HERE NOW. THEY'VE GOT ALL THE ROAMERS-- THEY'RE MOVING THEM OUT.
THERE'S NONE LEFT? ARE YOU SURE? THEY COULD BE HIDING. SOME OF THEM ARE SMART ENOUGH TO HIDE. HOW CAN YOU BE SURE?
HOW CAN YOU KNOW THERE AREN'T ANY HIDING?
WE CHECKED EVERYWHERE, CARL. THERE'S NOWHERE THEY COULD BE HIDING. WE GOT THEM ALL.
WHAT ABOUT ALL THESE ON THE GROUND--THEY COULD JUST BE SLEEPING?
ARE YOU SURE THEY'RE DEAD? I MEAN--FOR REAL DEAD?

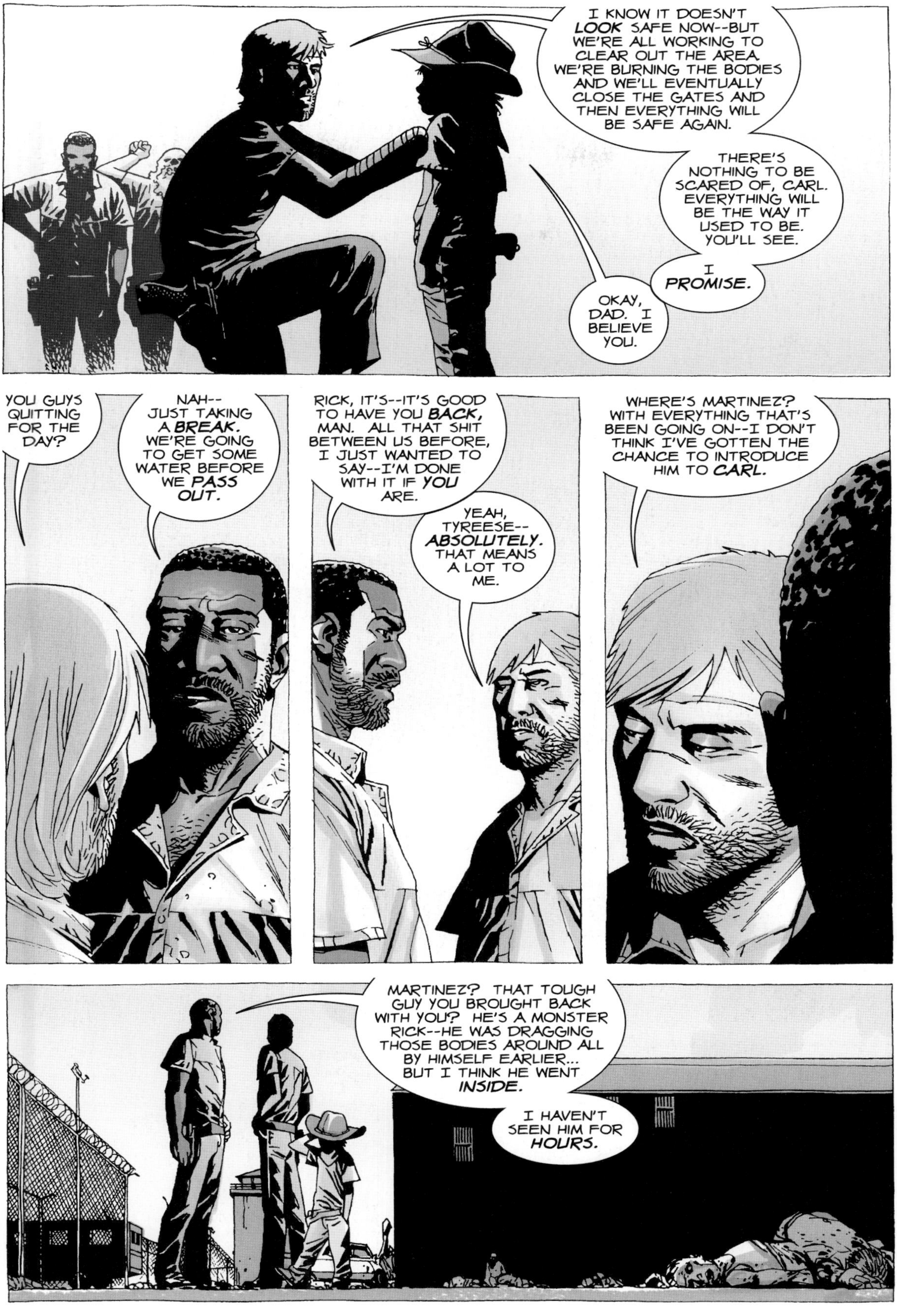
I KNOW IT DOESN'T LOOK SAFE NOW--BUT WE'RE ALL WORKING TO CLEAR OUT THE AREA. WE'RE BURNING THE BODIES AND WE'LL EVENTUALLY CLOSE THE GATES AND THEN EVERYTHING WILL BE SAFE AGAIN.
THERE'S NOTHING TO BE SCARED OF, CARL. EVERYTHING WILL BE THE WAY IT USED TO BE. YOU'LL SEE.
I PROMISE.
OKAY, DAD. I BELIEVE YOU.
YOU GUYS QUITTING FOR THE DAY?
NAH-- JUST TAKING A BREAK. WE'RE GOING TO GET SOME WATER BEFORE WE PASS OUT.
RICK, IT'S--IT'S GOOD TO HAVE YOU BACK, MAN. ALL THAT SHIT BETWEEN US BEFORE, I JUST WANTED TO SAY--I'M DONE WITH IT IF YOU ARE.
YEAH, TYREESE-- ABSOLUTELY. THAT MEANS A LOT TO ME.
WHERE'S MARTINEZ? WITH EVERYTHING THAT'S BEEN GOING ON--I DON'T THINK I'VE GOTTEN THE CHANCE TO INTRODUCE HIM TO CARL.
MARTINEZ? THAT TOUGH GUY YOU BROUGHT BACK WITH YOU? HE'S A MONSTER RICK--HE WAS DRAGGING THOSE BODIES AROUND ALL BY HIMSELF EARLIER... BUT I THINK HE WENT INSIDE.
I HAVEN'T SEEN HIM FOR HOURS.

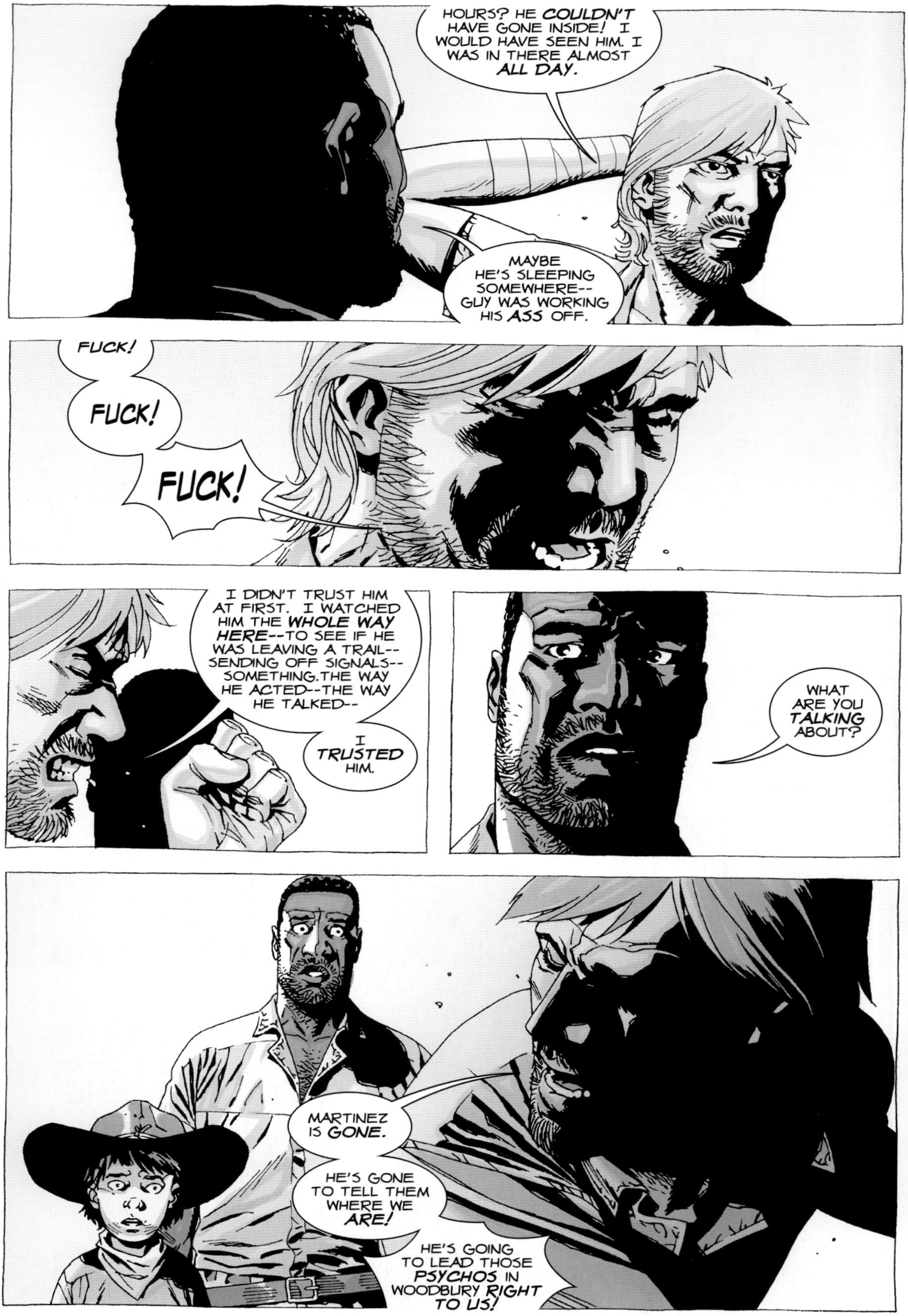
HOURS? HE COULDN'T HAVE GONE INSIDE! I WOULD HAVE SEEN HIM. I WAS IN THERE ALMOST ALL DAY.
MAYBE HE'S SLEEPING SOMEWHERE-- GUY WAS WORKING HIS ASS OFF.
FUCK!
FUCK!
FUCK!
I DIDN'T TRUST HIM AT FIRST. I WATCHED HIM THE WHOLE WAY HERE--TO SEE IF HE WAS LEAVING A TRAIL-- SENDING OFF SIGNALS-- SOMETHING. THE WAY HE ACTED--THE WAY HE TALKED--
I TRUSTED HIM.
WHAT ARE YOU TALKING ABOUT?
MARTINEZ IS GONE.
HE'S GONE TO TELL THEM WHERE WE ARE!
HE'S GOING TO LEAD THOSE PSYCHOS IN WOODBURY RIGHT TO US!

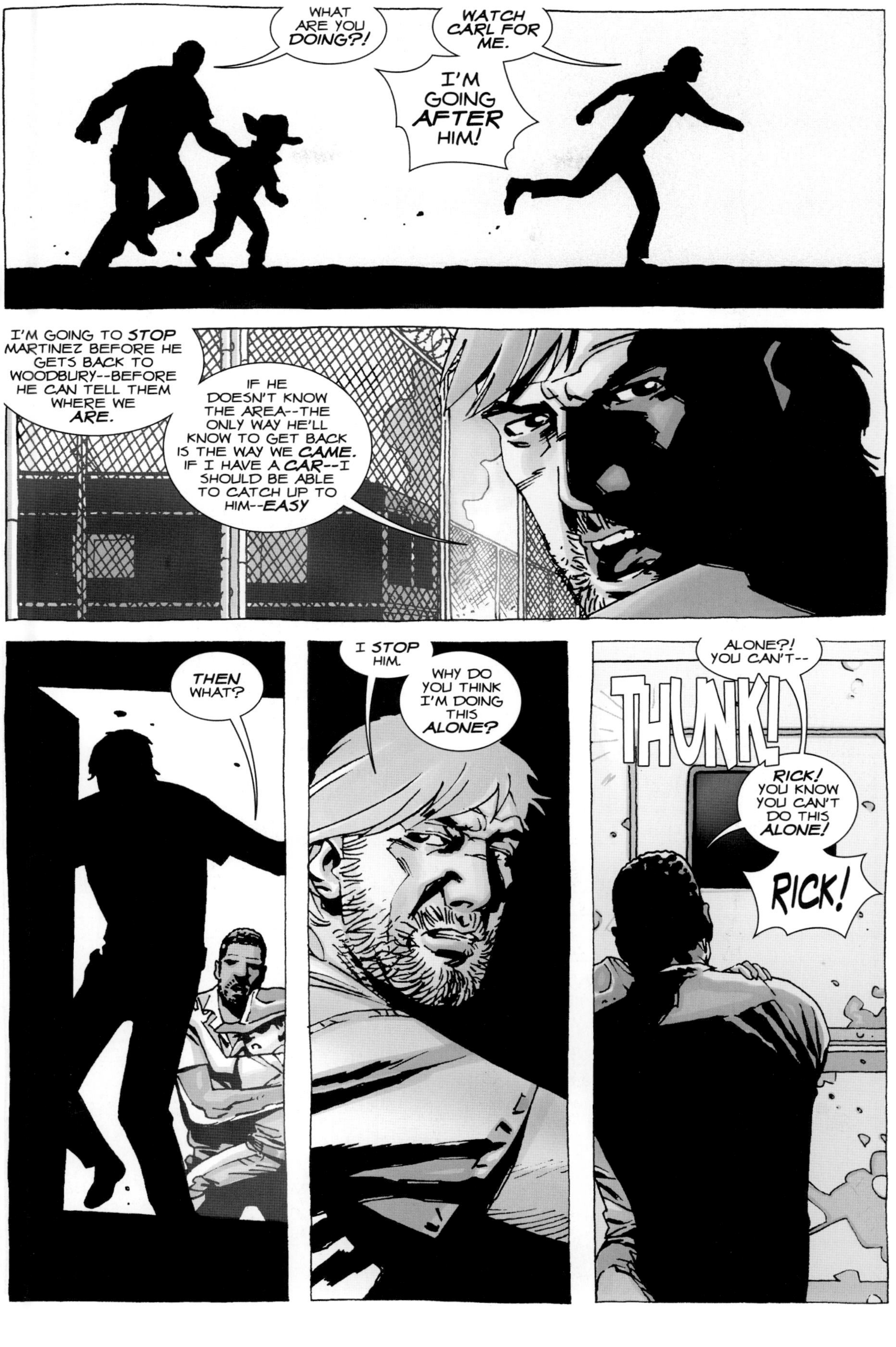
WHAT ARE YOU DOING?!
WATCH CARL FOR ME.
I'M GOING AFTER HIM!
I'M GOING TO STOP MARTINEZ BEFORE HE GETS BACK TO WOODBURY--BEFORE HE CAN TELL THEM WHERE WE ARE.
IF HE DOESN'T KNOW THE AREA--THE ONLY WAY HE'LL KNOW TO GET BACK IS THE WAY WE CAME. IF I HAVE A CAR--I SHOULD BE ABLE TO CATCH UP TO HIM--EASY
THEN WHAT?
I STOP HIM.
WHY DO YOU THINK I'M DOING THIS ALONE?
ALONE?! YOU CAN'T--
THUNK!
RICK! YOU KNOW YOU CAN'T DO THIS ALONE!
RICK!

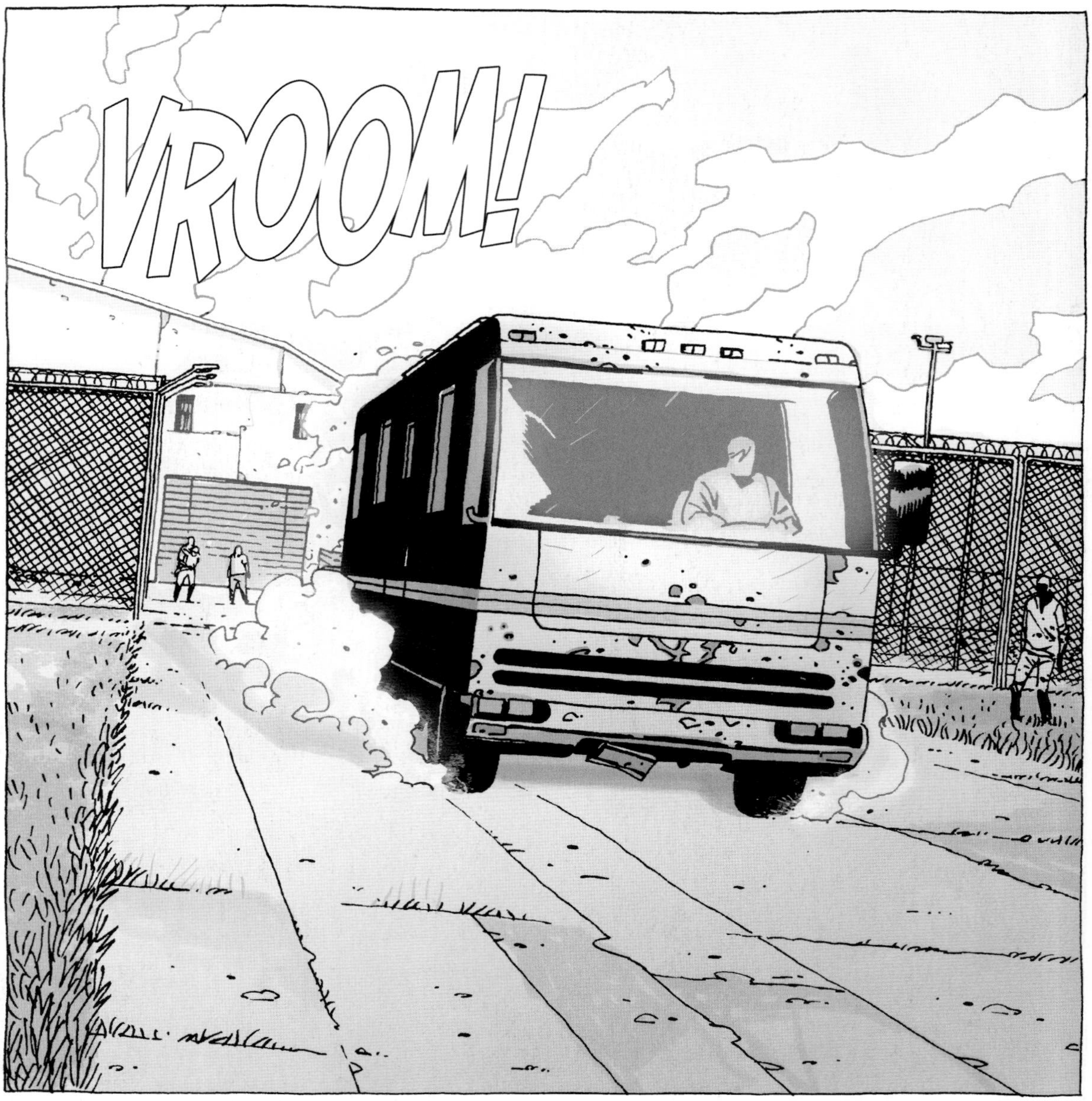
VROOM!

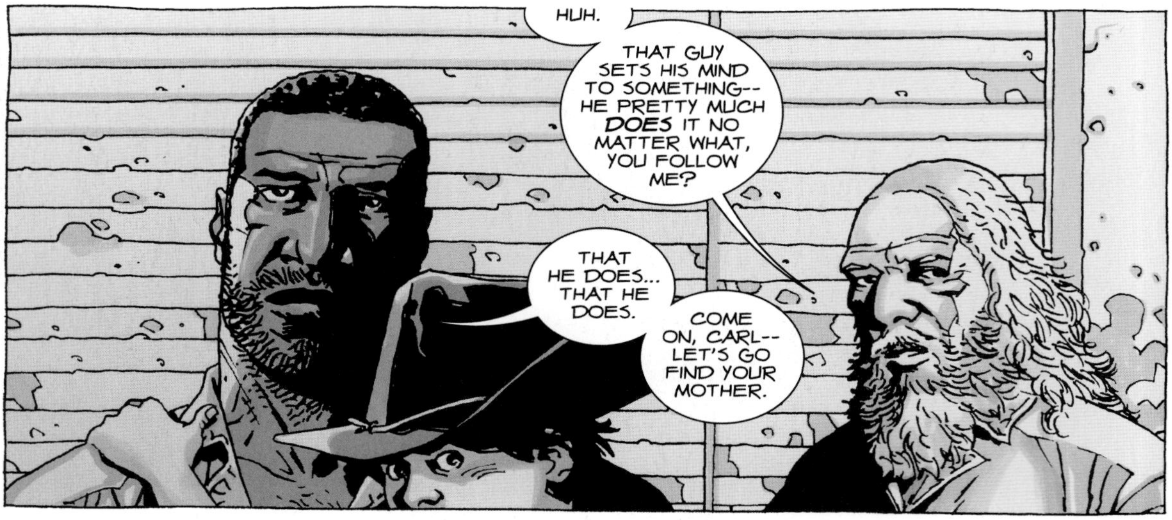
HUH.
THAT GUY SETS HIS MIND TO SOMETHING-- HE PRETTY MUCH DOES IT NO MATTER WHAT, YOU FOLLOW ME?
THAT HE DOES... THAT HE DOES.
COME ON, CARL-- LET'S GO FIND YOUR MOTHER.

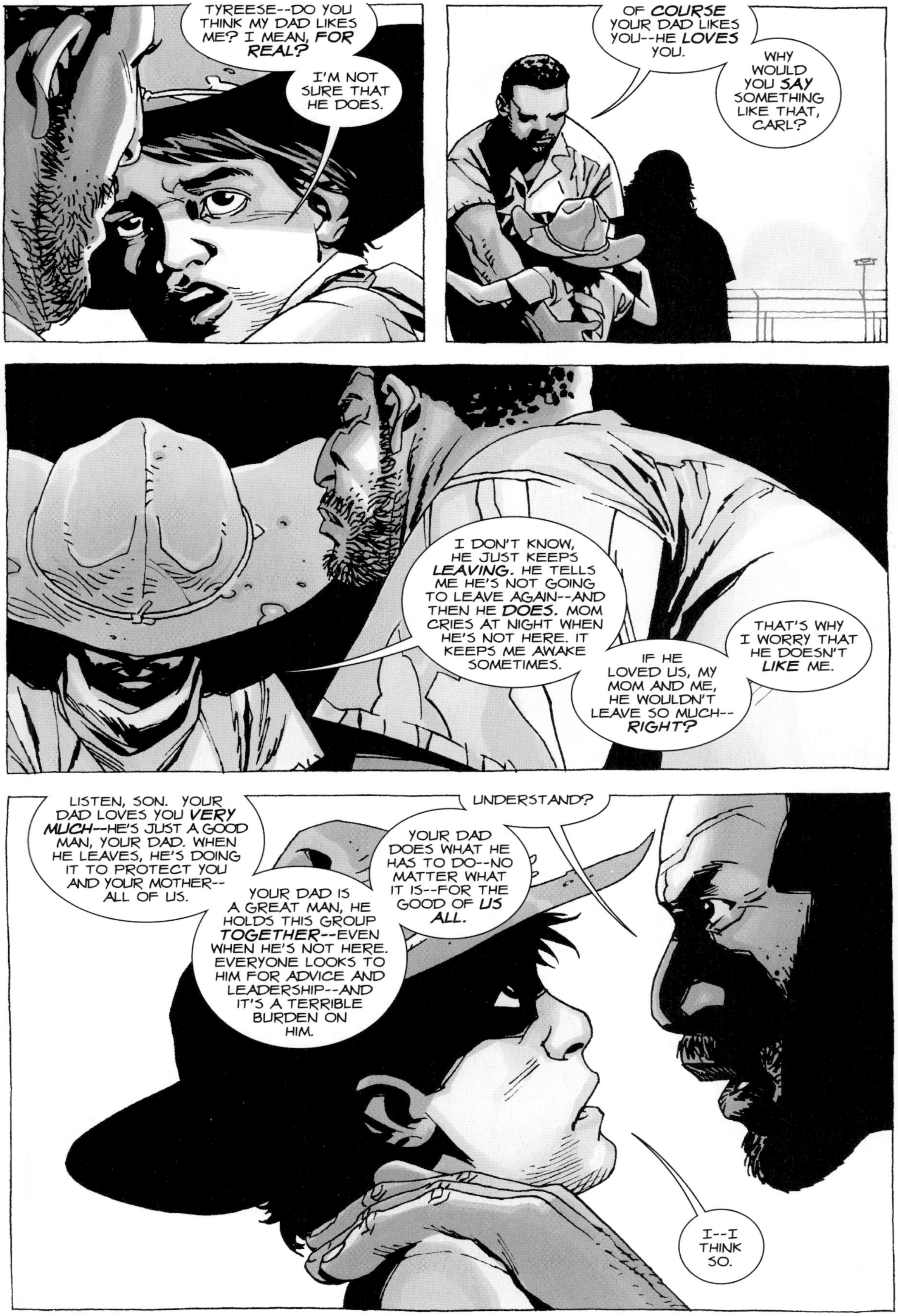
TYREESE--DO YOU THINK MY DAD LIKES ME? I MEAN, FOR REAL?
I'M NOT SURE THAT HE DOES.
OF COURSE YOUR DAD LIKES YOU--HE LOVES YOU.
WHY WOULD YOU SAY SOMETHING LIKE THAT, CARL?
I DON'T KNOW, HE JUST KEEPS LEAVING. HE TELLS ME HE'S NOT GOING TO LEAVE AGAIN--AND THEN HE DOES. MOM CRIES AT NIGHT WHEN HE'S NOT HERE. IT KEEPS ME AWAKE SOMETIMES.
IF HE LOVED US, MY MOM AND ME, HE WOULDN'T LEAVE SO MUCH--RIGHT?
THAT'S WHY I WORRY THAT HE DOESN'T LIKE ME.
LISTEN, SON. YOUR DAD LOVES YOU VERY MUCH--HE'S JUST A GOOD MAN, YOUR DAD. WHEN HE LEAVES, HE'S DOING IT TO PROTECT YOU AND YOUR MOTHER--ALL OF US.
YOUR DAD IS A GREAT MAN, HE HOLDS THIS GROUP TOGETHER--EVEN WHEN HE'S NOT HERE. EVERYONE LOOKS TO HIM FOR ADVICE AND LEADERSHIP--AND IT'S A TERRIBLE BURDEN ON HIM.
YOUR DAD DOES WHAT HE HAS TO DO--NO MATTER WHAT IT IS--FOR THE GOOD OF US ALL.
UNDERSTAND?
I--I THINK SO.

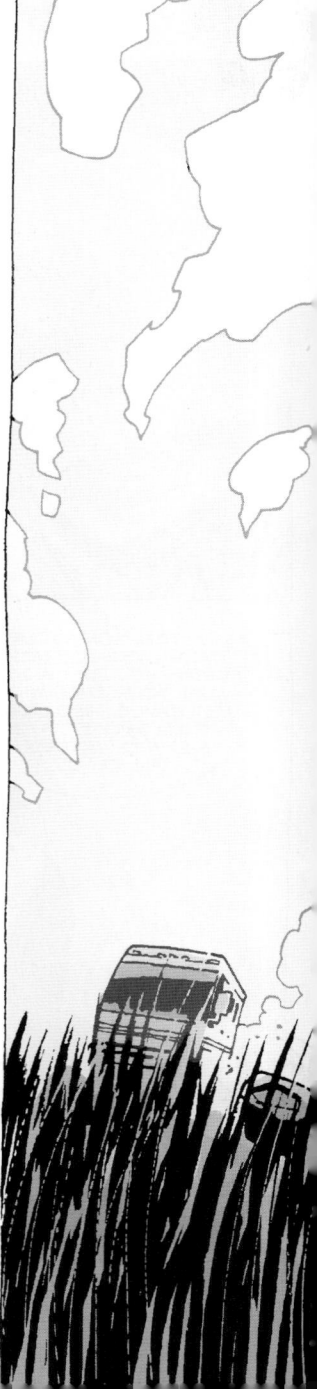

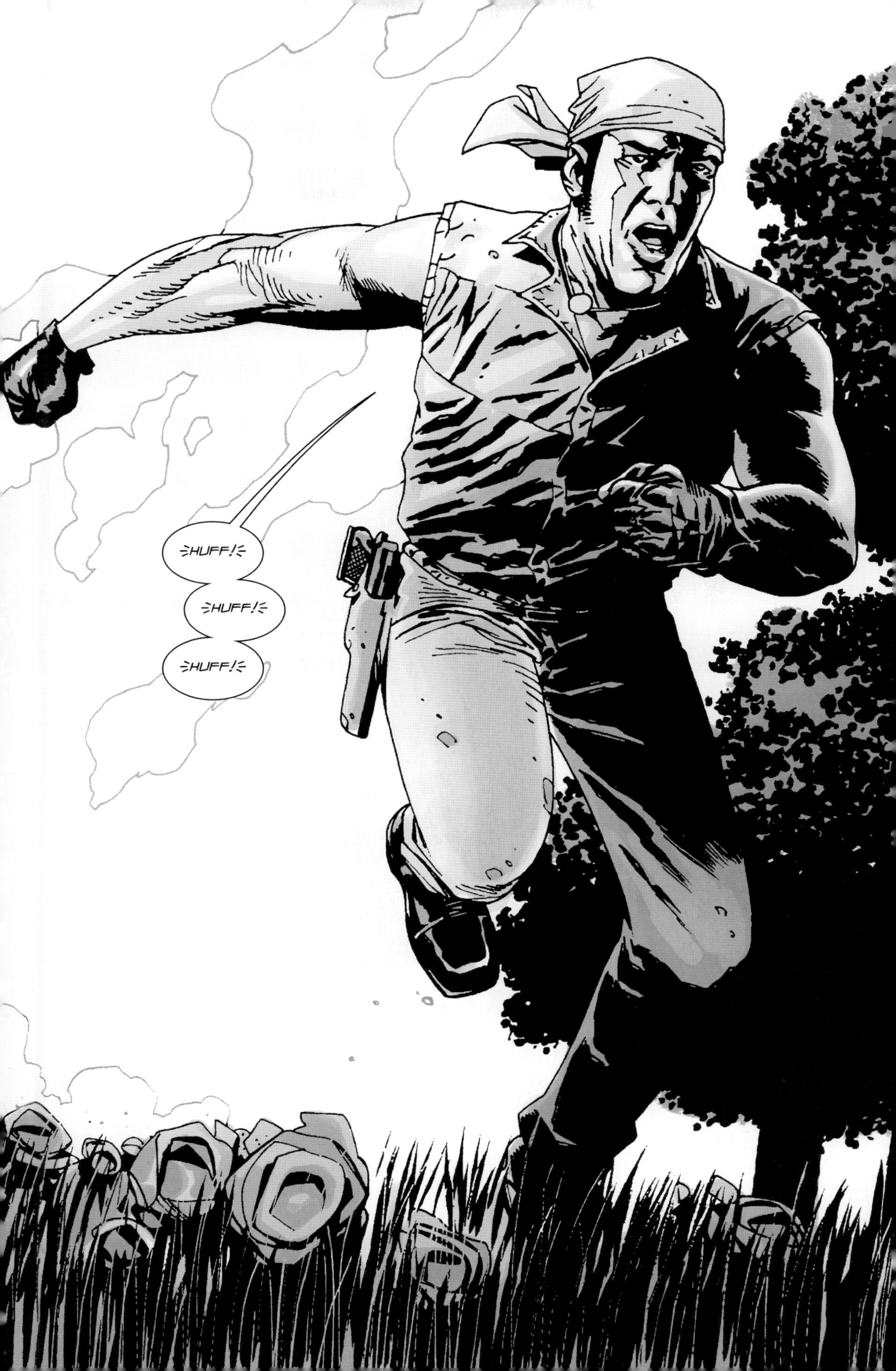
HUFF!
HUFF!
HUFF!

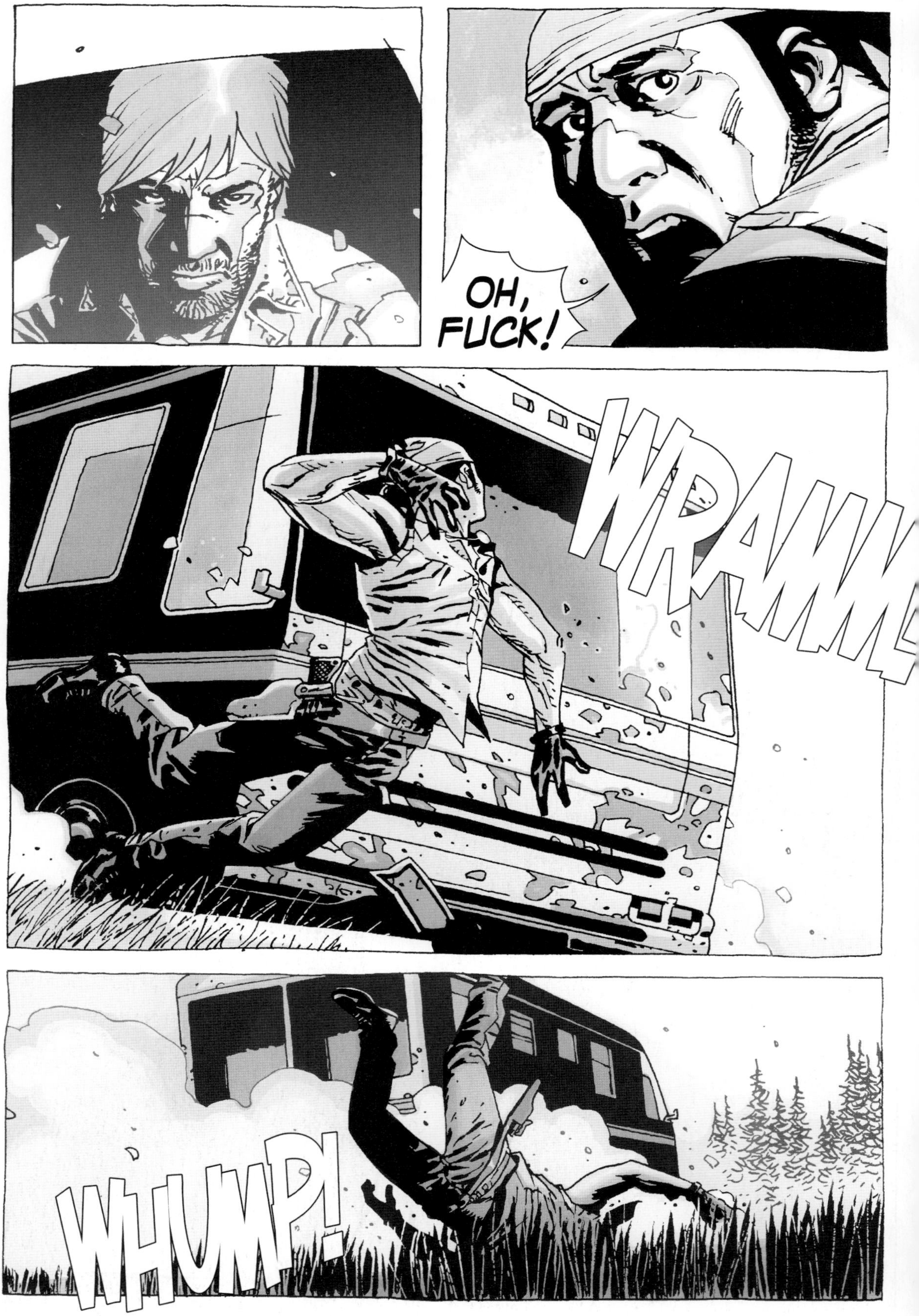
OH, FUCK!
WRAMM
WHUMP!

CRAZY... FUCKER. CAN'T... MOVE.

CRAZY.

TRYING TO... TRYING TO KILL ME. CAN'T--

KILL ME...

YOU WERE GOING TO LEAD THEM RIGHT TO US?! YOU WERE GOING TO BETRAY US ALL?! PUT US ALL IN DANGER--MY FAMILY IN DANGER?!

YOU WERE GOING TO BETRAY US?!

WROKK!

YOU SELFISH PIECE OF SHIT. YOU'VE GOT THE--ROOM--THE SUPPLIES FOR EVERYONE IN WOODBURY--THE WHOLE DAMN TOWN!

EVERYONE.

=KOFF!=

=KOFF!=

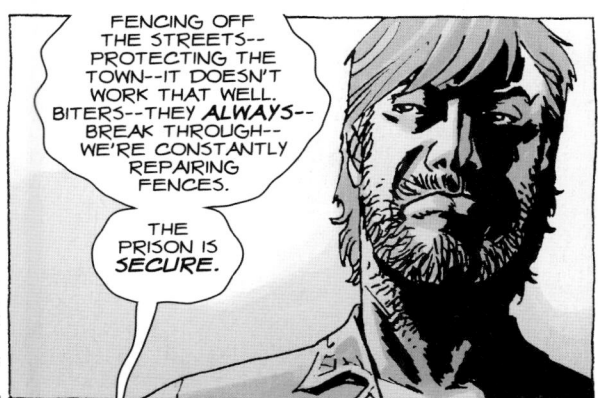

FENCING OFF THE STREETS-- PROTECTING THE TOWN--IT DOESN'T WORK THAT WELL. BITERS--THEY ALWAYS-- BREAK THROUGH-- WE'RE CONSTANTLY REPAIRING FENCES.

THE PRISON IS SECURE.

MY PEOPLE DESERVE TO BE SAFE, TOO.

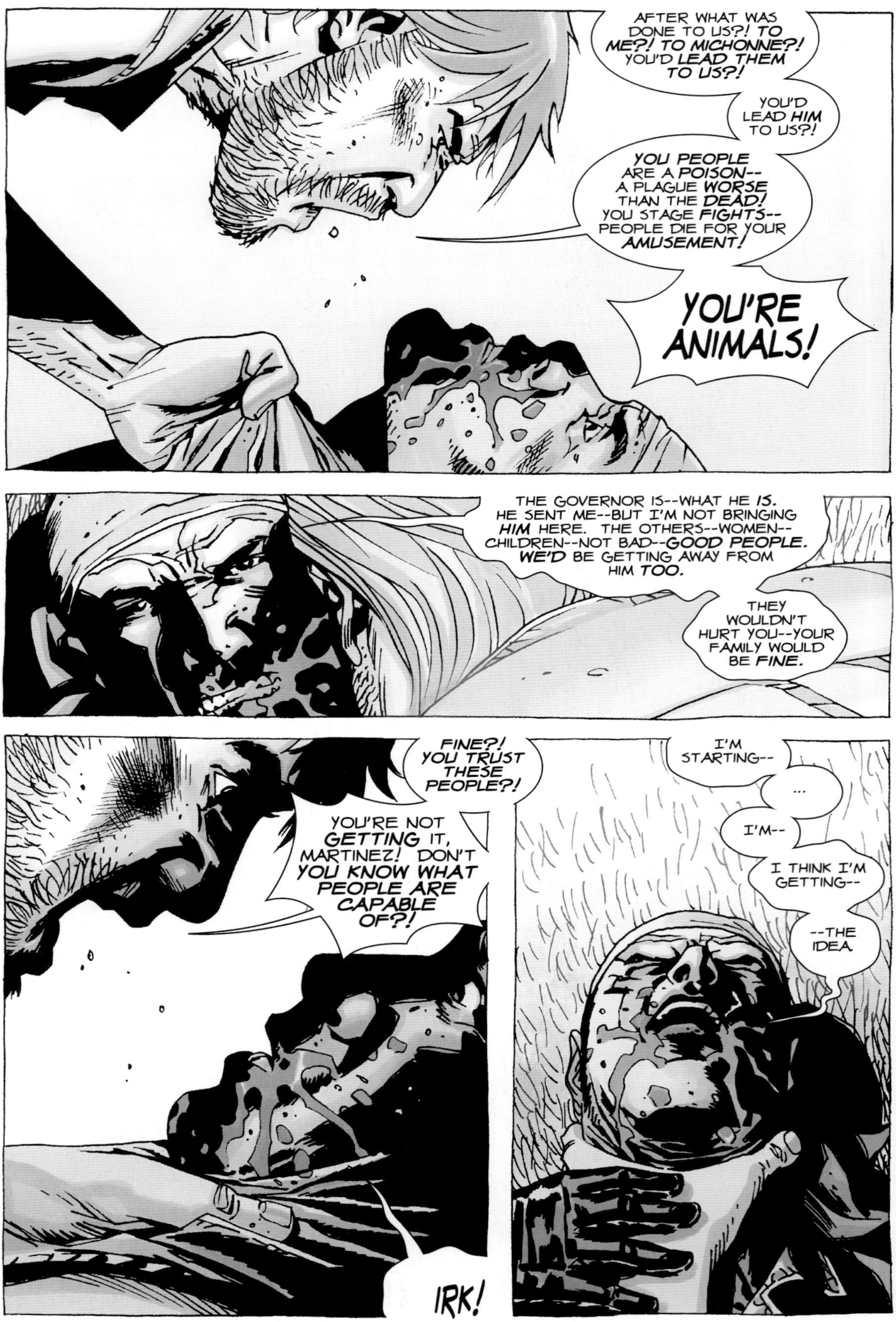
AFTER WHAT WAS DONE TO US?! TO ME?! TO MICHONNE?! YOU'D LEAD THEM TO US?!
YOU'D LEAD HIM TO US?!
YOU PEOPLE ARE A POISON-- A PLAGUE WORSE THAN THE DEAD! YOU STAGE FIGHTS-- PEOPLE DIE FOR YOUR AMUSEMENT!
YOU'RE ANIMALS!
THE GOVERNOR IS--WHAT HE IS. HE SENT ME--BUT I'M NOT BRINGING HIM HERE. THE OTHERS--WOMEN--CHILDREN--NOT BAD--GOOD PEOPLE. WE'D BE GETTING AWAY FROM HIM TOO.
THEY WOULDN'T HURT YOU--YOUR FAMILY WOULD BE FINE.
FINE?! YOU TRUST THESE PEOPLE?!
YOU'RE NOT GETTING IT, MARTINEZ! DON'T YOU KNOW WHAT PEOPLE ARE CAPABLE OF?!
IRK!
I'M STARTING--
...
I'M--
I THINK I'M GETTING--
--THE IDEA.

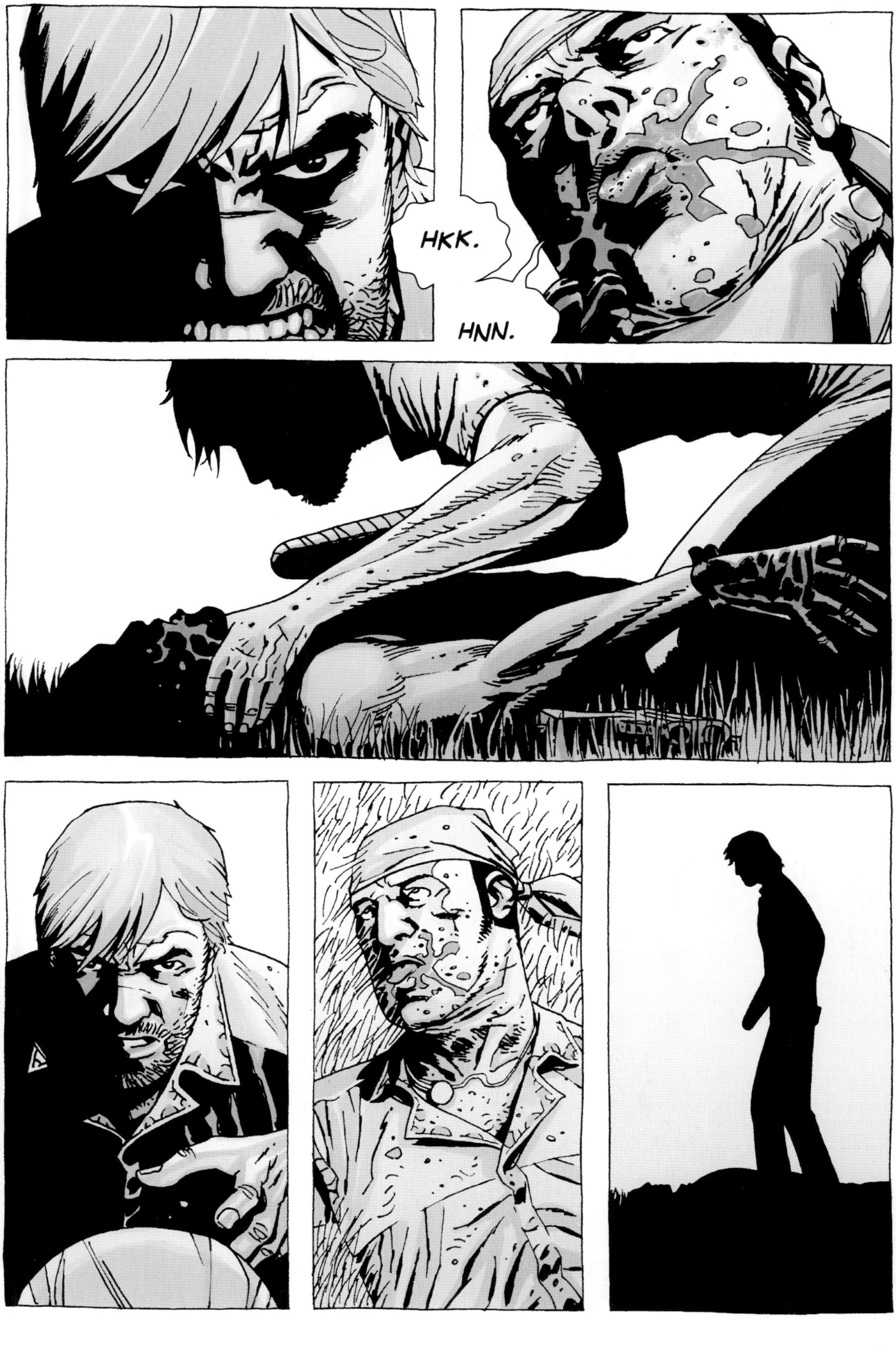
HKK.
HNN.

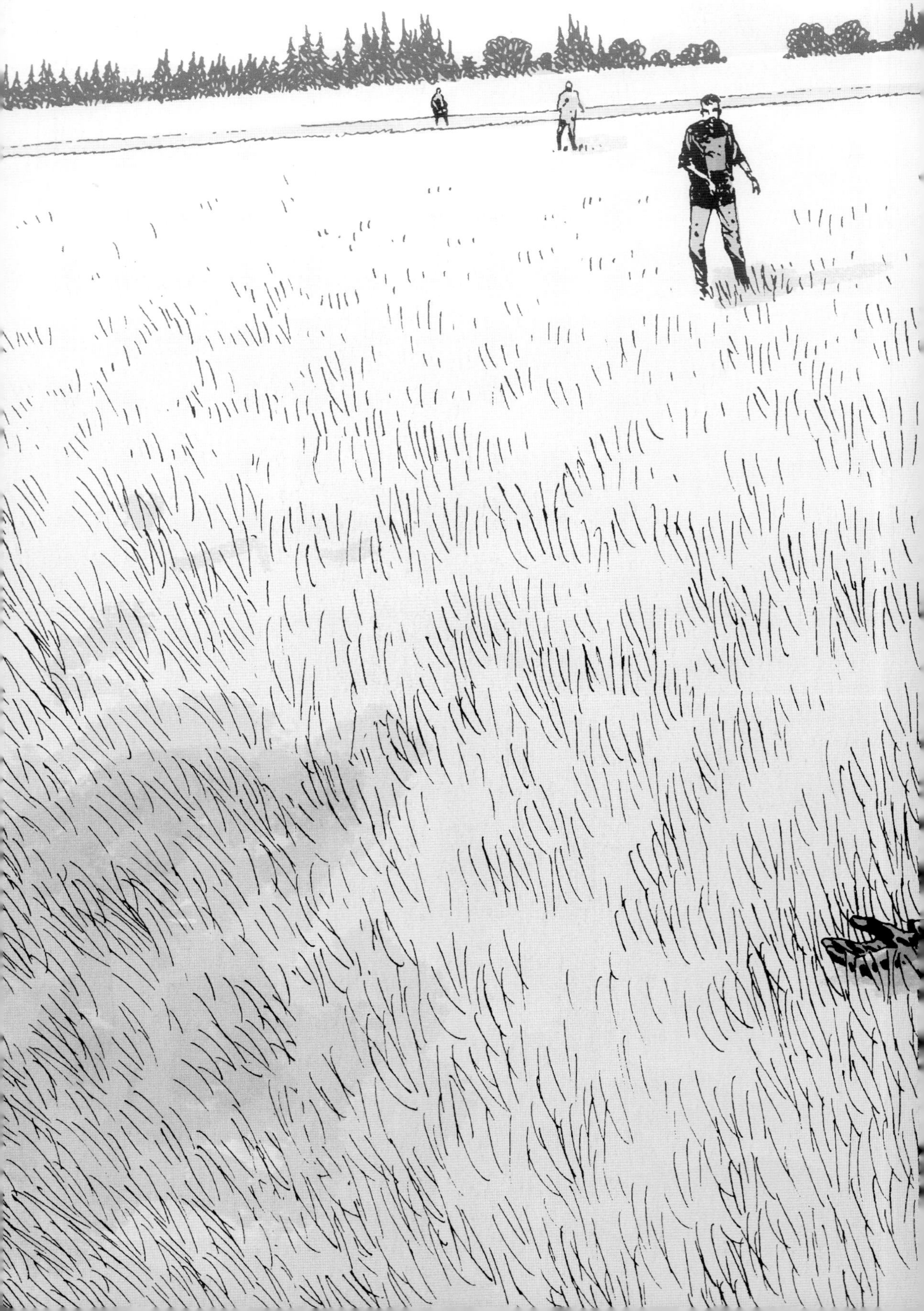

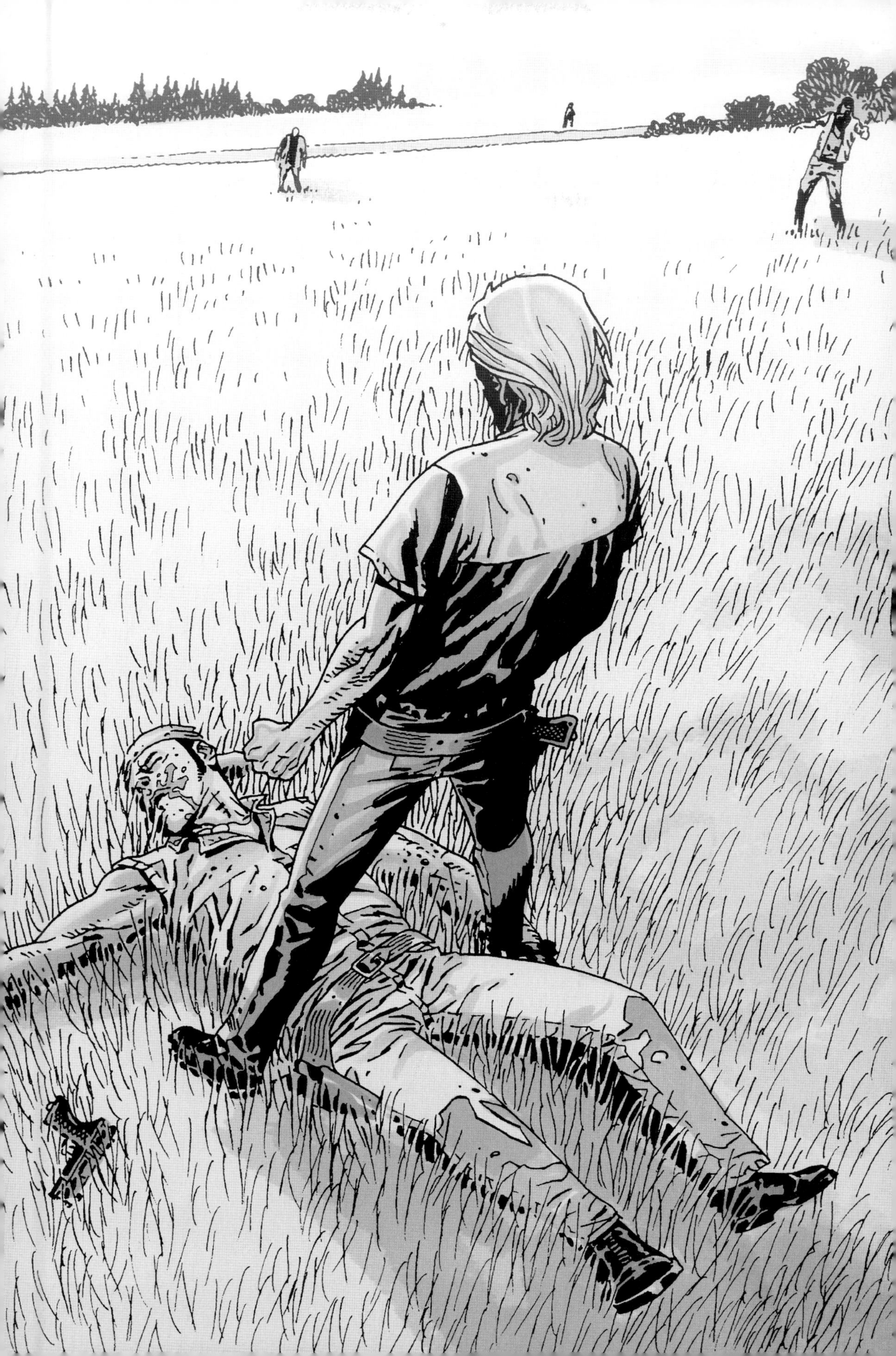

WORRIED?

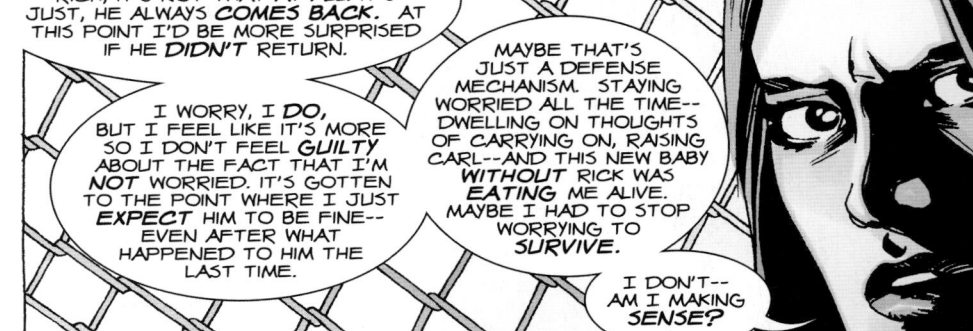

ME? NOT *ANYMORE.* NOT NOW.

I THINK I WORRY MORE ABOUT BEING ABLE TO STAND UP IN THE MORNING... WITHOUT FALLING BACK ON THE BED, AT LEAST.

IT'S NOT THAT I CARE *LESS* ABOUT RICK, IT'S NOT THAT AT ALL. IT'S JUST, HE ALWAYS *COMES BACK.* AT THIS POINT I'D BE MORE SURPRISED IF HE *DIDN'T* RETURN.

I WORRY, I *DO,* BUT I FEEL LIKE IT'S MORE SO I DON'T FEEL *GUILTY* ABOUT THE FACT THAT I'M *NOT* WORRIED. IT'S GOTTEN TO THE POINT WHERE I JUST *EXPECT* HIM TO BE FINE-- EVEN AFTER WHAT HAPPENED TO HIM THE LAST TIME.

MAYBE THAT'S JUST A DEFENSE MECHANISM. STAYING WORRIED ALL THE TIME-- DWELLING ON THOUGHTS OF CARRYING ON, RAISING CARL--AND THIS NEW BABY *WITHOUT* RICK WAS *EATING* ME ALIVE. MAYBE I HAD TO STOP WORRYING TO *SURVIVE.*

I DON'T-- AM I MAKING *SENSE?*

MAKING SENSE? I DON'T KNOW. IT ALL SEEMS REASONABLE TO *ME.*

BUT THE WORLD AIN'T EXACTLY FULL OF THINGS THAT MAKE SENSE ANYMORE NOW IS IT?

WHEN DID IT *EVER?*

YEAH.

MAYBE WE WERE JUST *FOOLING OURSELVES* UNTIL SOMETHING HAPPENED THAT WAS BIG ENOUGH TO MAKE US STOP AND REALIZE HOW *CRAZY* OUR WORLD REALLY IS.

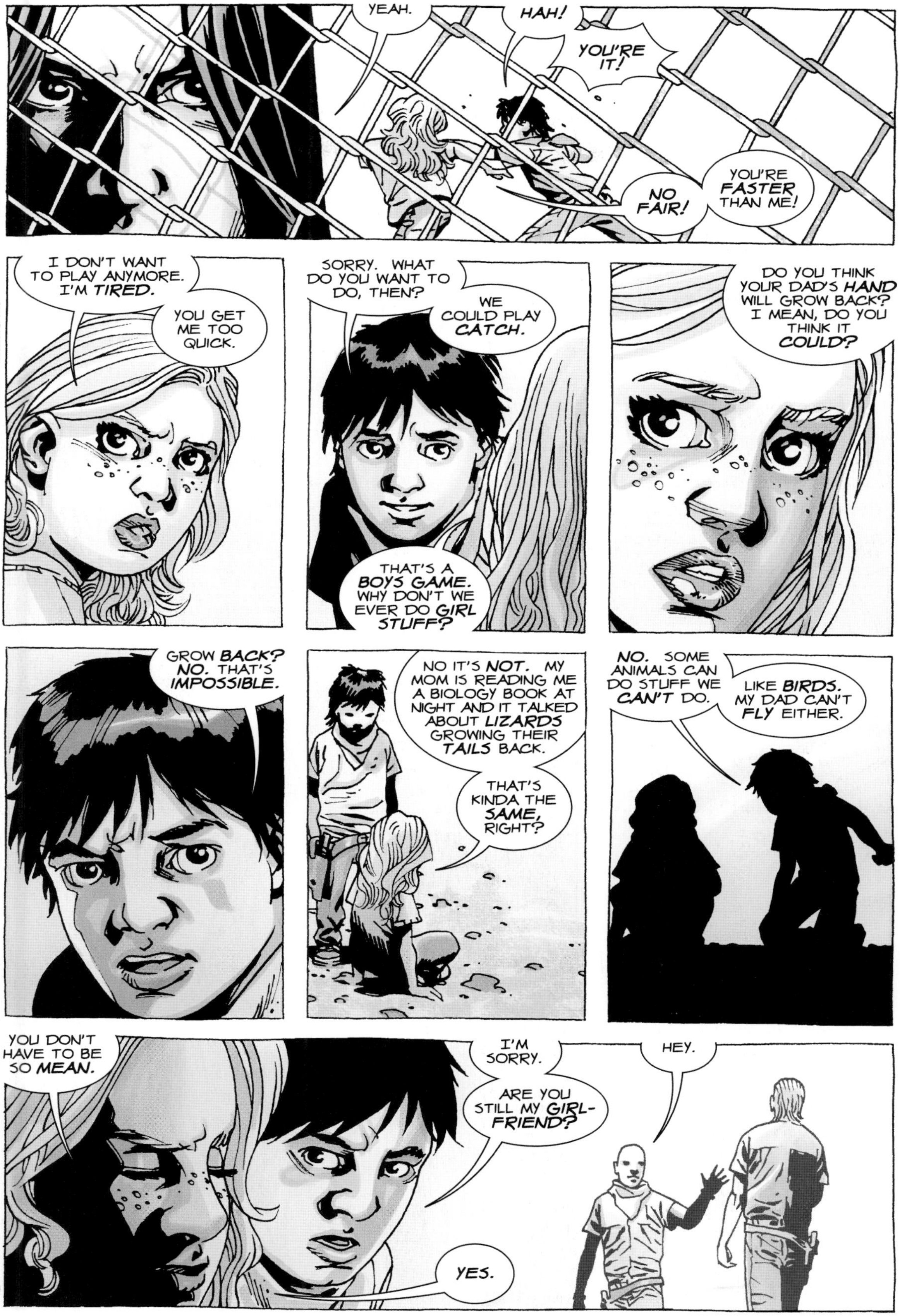
YEAH.
HAH!
YOU'RE IT!
NO FAIR!
YOU'RE FASTER THAN ME!
I DON'T WANT TO PLAY ANYMORE. I'M TIRED.
YOU GET ME TOO QUICK.
SORRY. WHAT DO YOU WANT TO DO, THEN?
WE COULD PLAY CATCH.
THAT'S A BOYS GAME. WHY DON'T WE EVER DO GIRL STUFF?
DO YOU THINK YOUR DAD'S HAND WILL GROW BACK? I MEAN, DO YOU THINK IT COULD?
GROW BACK? NO. THAT'S IMPOSSIBLE.
NO IT'S NOT. MY MOM IS READING ME A BIOLOGY BOOK AT NIGHT AND IT TALKED ABOUT LIZARDS GROWING THEIR TAILS BACK.
THAT'S KINDA THE SAME, RIGHT?
NO. SOME ANIMALS CAN DO STUFF WE CAN'T DO.
LIKE BIRDS. MY DAD CAN'T FLY EITHER.
YOU DON'T HAVE TO BE SO MEAN.
I'M SORRY.
ARE YOU STILL MY GIRL-FRIEND?
YES.
HEY.

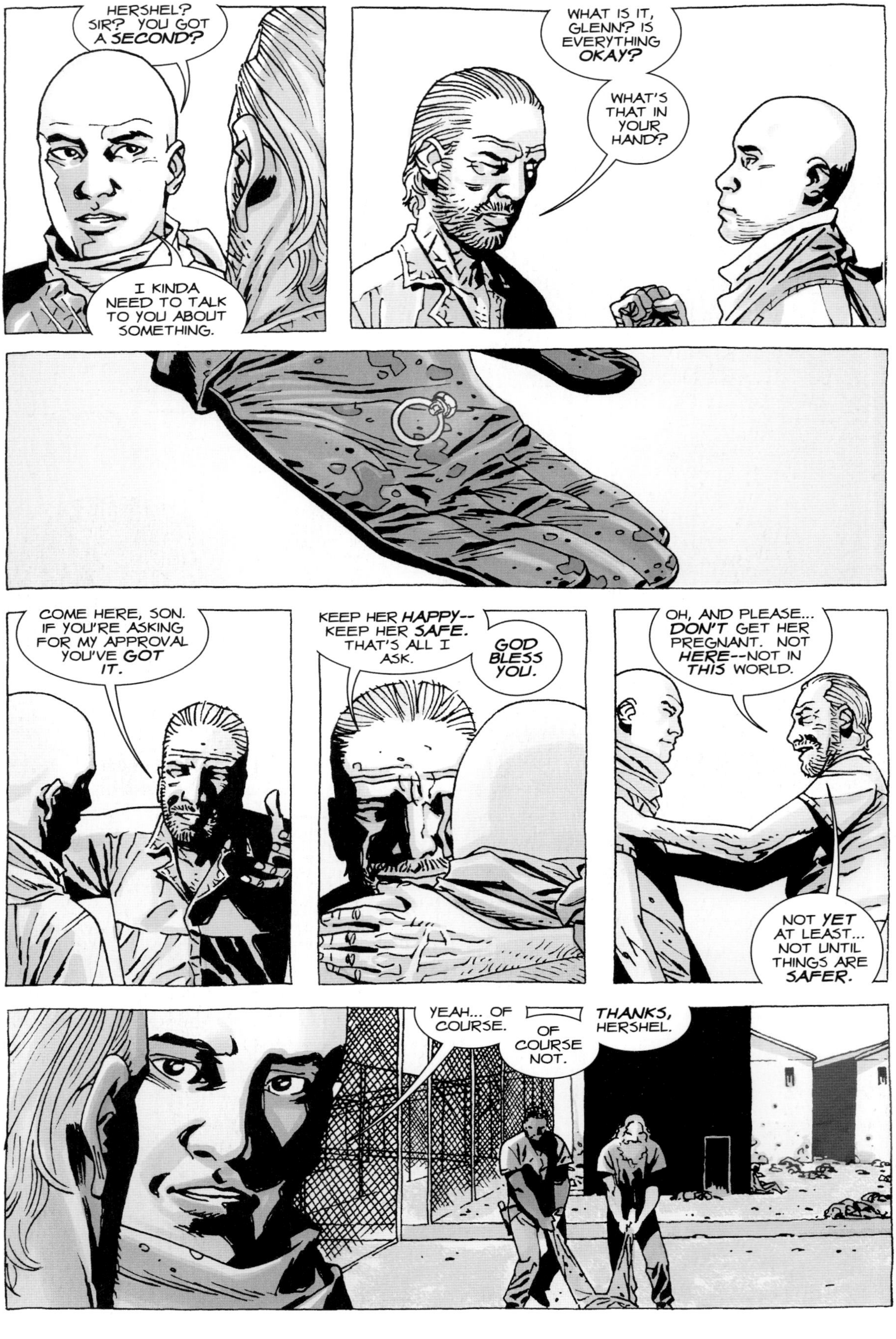
HERSHEL? SIR? YOU GOT A SECOND?
I KINDA NEED TO TALK TO YOU ABOUT SOMETHING.
WHAT IS IT, GLENN? IS EVERYTHING OKAY?
WHAT'S THAT IN YOUR HAND?
COME HERE, SON. IF YOU'RE ASKING FOR MY APPROVAL YOU'VE GOT IT.
KEEP HER HAPPY-- KEEP HER SAFE. THAT'S ALL I ASK.
GOD BLESS YOU.
OH, AND PLEASE... DON'T GET HER PREGNANT. NOT HERE--NOT IN THIS WORLD.
NOT YET AT LEAST... NOT UNTIL THINGS ARE SAFER.
YEAH... OF COURSE.
OF COURSE NOT.
THANKS, HERSHEL.

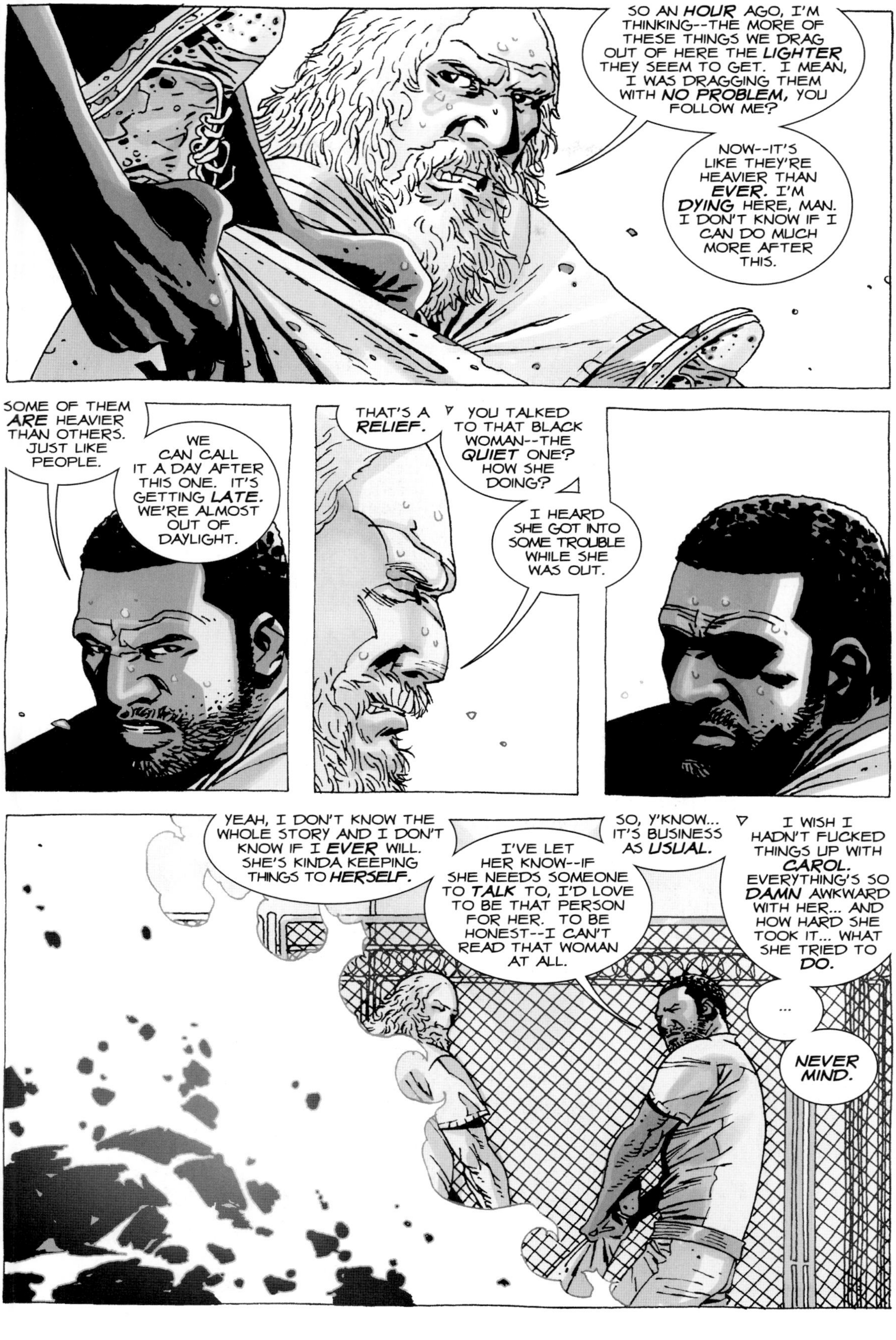
SO AN HOUR AGO, I'M THINKING--THE MORE OF THESE THINGS WE DRAG OUT OF HERE THE LIGHTER THEY SEEM TO GET. I MEAN, I WAS DRAGGING THEM WITH NO PROBLEM, YOU FOLLOW ME?
NOW--IT'S LIKE THEY'RE HEAVIER THAN EVER. I'M DYING HERE, MAN. I DON'T KNOW IF I CAN DO MUCH MORE AFTER THIS.
SOME OF THEM ARE HEAVIER THAN OTHERS. JUST LIKE PEOPLE.
WE CAN CALL IT A DAY AFTER THIS ONE. IT'S GETTING LATE. WE'RE ALMOST OUT OF DAYLIGHT.
THAT'S A RELIEF.
YOU TALKED TO THAT BLACK WOMAN--THE QUIET ONE? HOW SHE DOING?
I HEARD SHE GOT INTO SOME TROUBLE WHILE SHE WAS OUT.
YEAH, I DON'T KNOW THE WHOLE STORY AND I DON'T KNOW IF I EVER WILL. SHE'S KINDA KEEPING THINGS TO HERSELF.
I'VE LET HER KNOW--IF SHE NEEDS SOMEONE TO TALK TO, I'D LOVE TO BE THAT PERSON FOR HER. TO BE HONEST--I CAN'T READ THAT WOMAN AT ALL.
SO, Y'KNOW... IT'S BUSINESS AS USUAL.
I WISH I HADN'T FUCKED THINGS UP WITH CAROL. EVERYTHING'S SO DAMN AWKWARD WITH HER... AND HOW HARD SHE TOOK IT... WHAT SHE TRIED TO DO.
...
NEVER MIND.

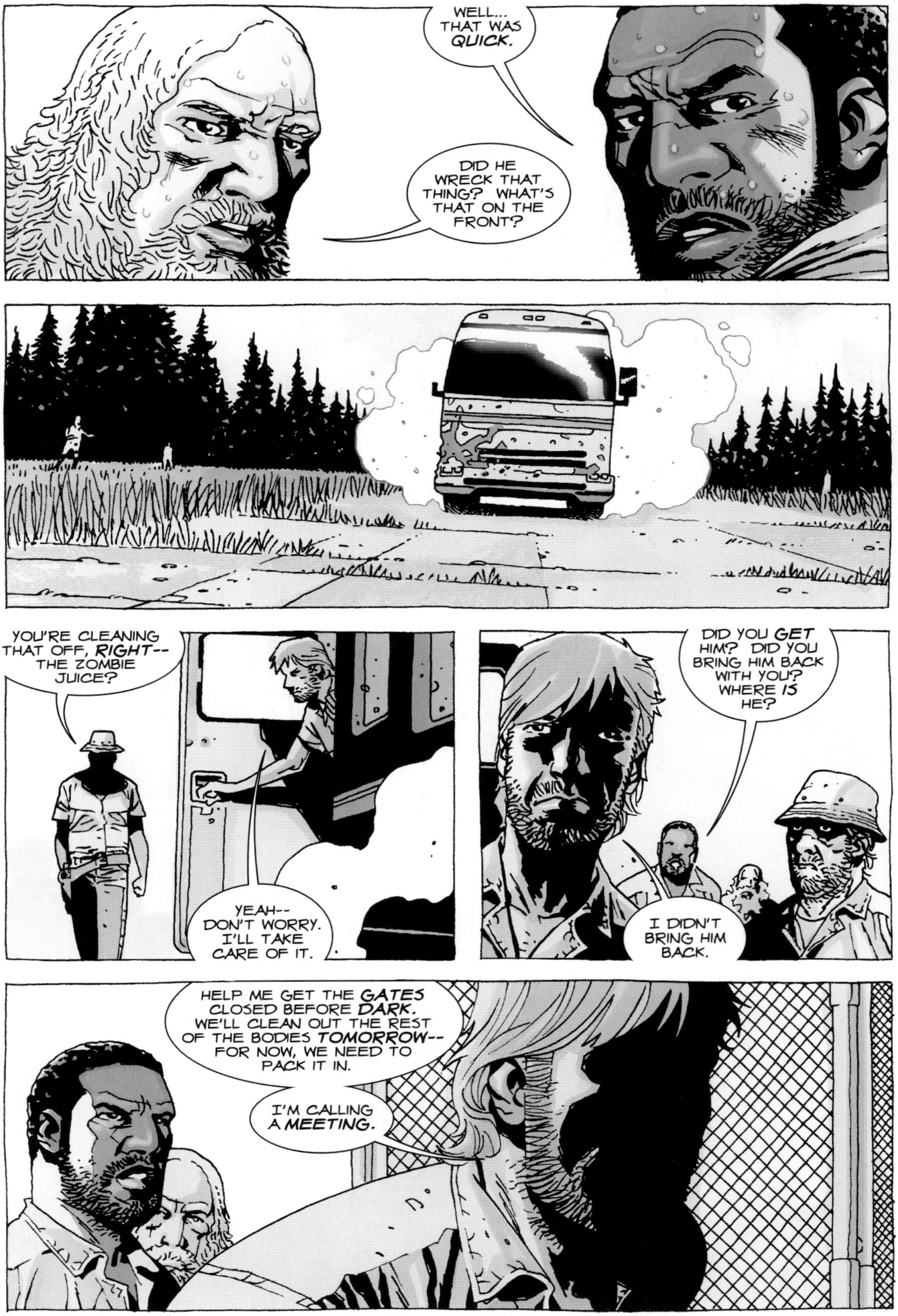
WELL... THAT WAS QUICK.
DID HE WRECK THAT THING? WHAT'S THAT ON THE FRONT?
YOU'RE CLEANING THAT OFF, RIGHT-- THE ZOMBIE JUICE?
YEAH-- DON'T WORRY. I'LL TAKE CARE OF IT.
DID YOU GET HIM? DID YOU BRING HIM BACK WITH YOU? WHERE IS HE?
I DIDN'T BRING HIM BACK.
HELP ME GET THE GATES CLOSED BEFORE DARK. WE'LL CLEAN OUT THE REST OF THE BODIES TOMORROW-- FOR NOW, WE NEED TO PACK IT IN.
I'M CALLING A MEETING.

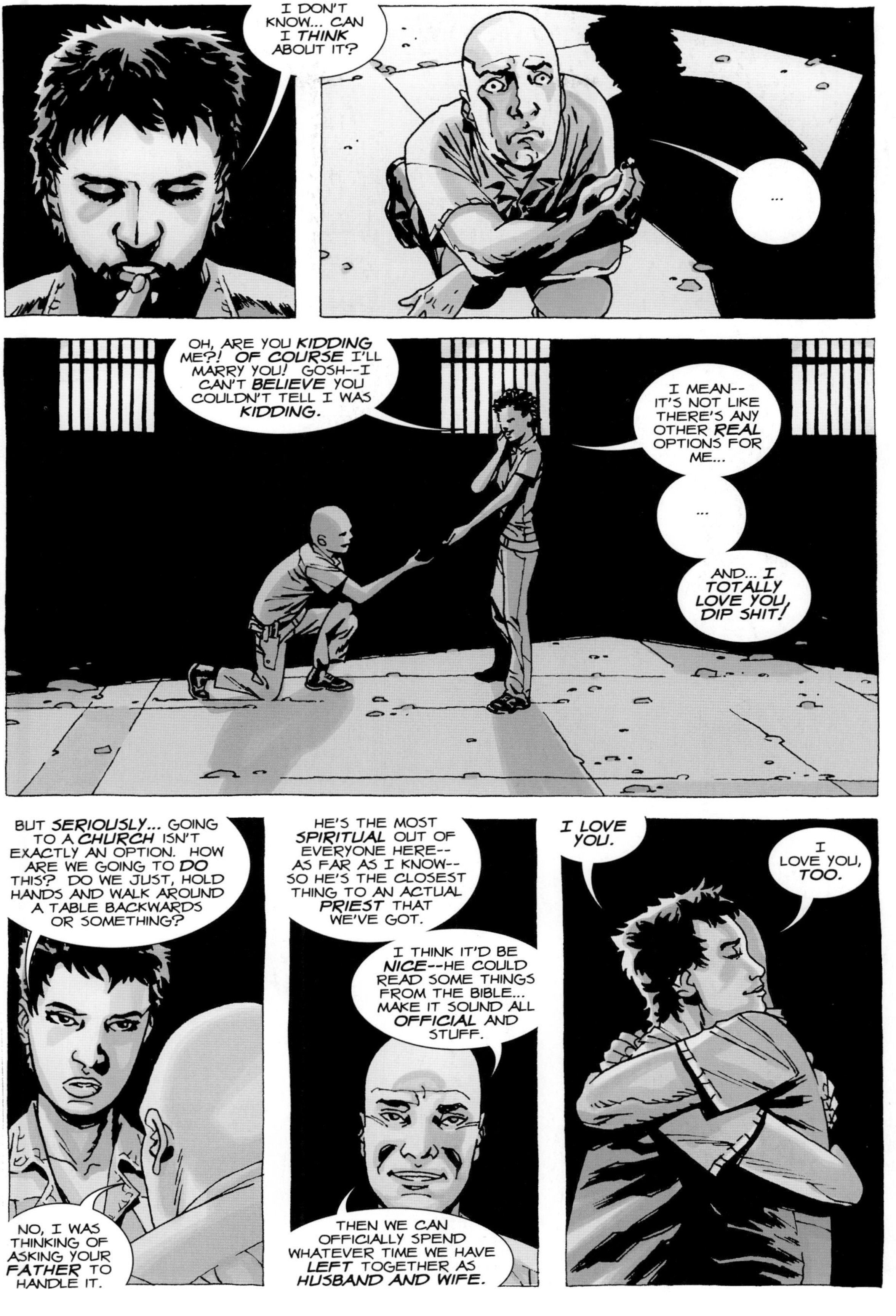

I DON'T KNOW... CAN I THINK ABOUT IT?
...
OH, ARE YOU KIDDING ME?! OF COURSE I'LL MARRY YOU! GOSH--I CAN'T BELIEVE YOU COULDN'T TELL I WAS KIDDING.
I MEAN-- IT'S NOT LIKE THERE'S ANY OTHER REAL OPTIONS FOR ME...
...
AND... I TOTALLY LOVE YOU, DIP SHIT!
BUT SERIOUSLY... GOING TO A CHURCH ISN'T EXACTLY AN OPTION. HOW ARE WE GOING TO DO THIS? DO WE JUST, HOLD HANDS AND WALK AROUND A TABLE BACKWARDS OR SOMETHING?
NO, I WAS THINKING OF ASKING YOUR FATHER TO HANDLE IT.
HE'S THE MOST SPIRITUAL OUT OF EVERYONE HERE-- AS FAR AS I KNOW-- SO HE'S THE CLOSEST THING TO AN ACTUAL PRIEST THAT WE'VE GOT.
I THINK IT'D BE NICE--HE COULD READ SOME THINGS FROM THE BIBLE... MAKE IT SOUND ALL OFFICIAL AND STUFF.
THEN WE CAN OFFICIALLY SPEND WHATEVER TIME WE HAVE LEFT TOGETHER AS HUSBAND AND WIFE.
I LOVE YOU.
I LOVE YOU, TOO.

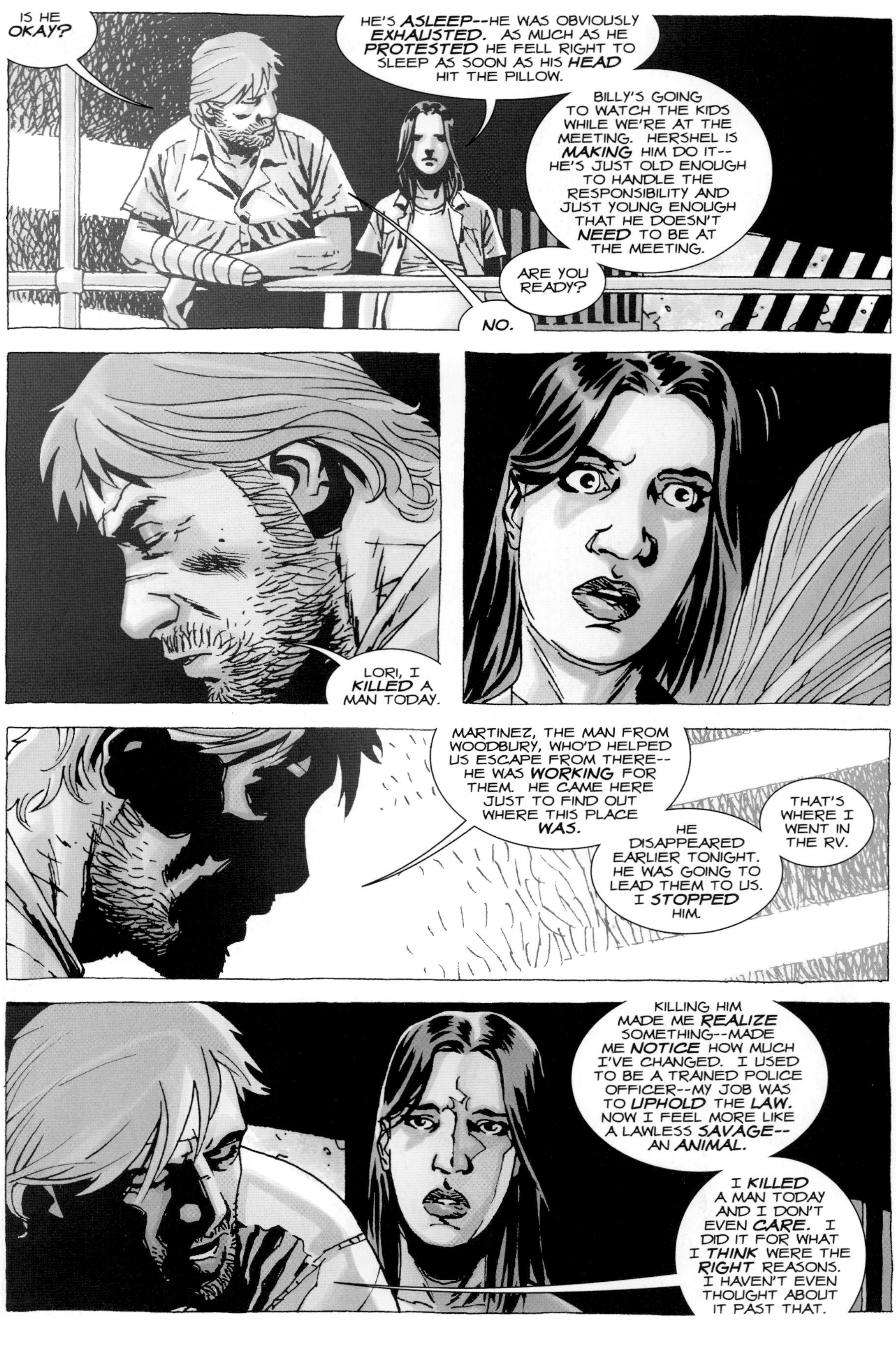

IS HE OKAY?
HE'S ASLEEP--HE WAS OBVIOUSLY EXHAUSTED. AS MUCH AS HE PROTESTED HE FELL RIGHT TO SLEEP AS SOON AS HIS HEAD HIT THE PILLOW.
BILLY'S GOING TO WATCH THE KIDS WHILE WE'RE AT THE MEETING. HERSHEL IS MAKING HIM DO IT--HE'S JUST OLD ENOUGH TO HANDLE THE RESPONSIBILITY AND JUST YOUNG ENOUGH THAT HE DOESN'T NEED TO BE AT THE MEETING.
ARE YOU READY?
NO.
LORI, I KILLED A MAN TODAY.
MARTINEZ, THE MAN FROM WOODBURY, WHO'D HELPED US ESCAPE FROM THERE--HE WAS WORKING FOR THEM. HE CAME HERE JUST TO FIND OUT WHERE THIS PLACE WAS.
HE DISAPPEARED EARLIER TONIGHT. HE WAS GOING TO LEAD THEM TO US. I STOPPED HIM.
THAT'S WHERE I WENT IN THE RV.
KILLING HIM MADE ME REALIZE SOMETHING--MADE ME NOTICE HOW MUCH I'VE CHANGED. I USED TO BE A TRAINED POLICE OFFICER--MY JOB WAS TO UPHOLD THE LAW. NOW I FEEL MORE LIKE A LAWLESS SAVAGE--AN ANIMAL.
I KILLED A MAN TODAY AND I DON'T EVEN CARE. I DID IT FOR WHAT I THINK WERE THE RIGHT REASONS. I HAVEN'T EVEN THOUGHT ABOUT IT PAST THAT.

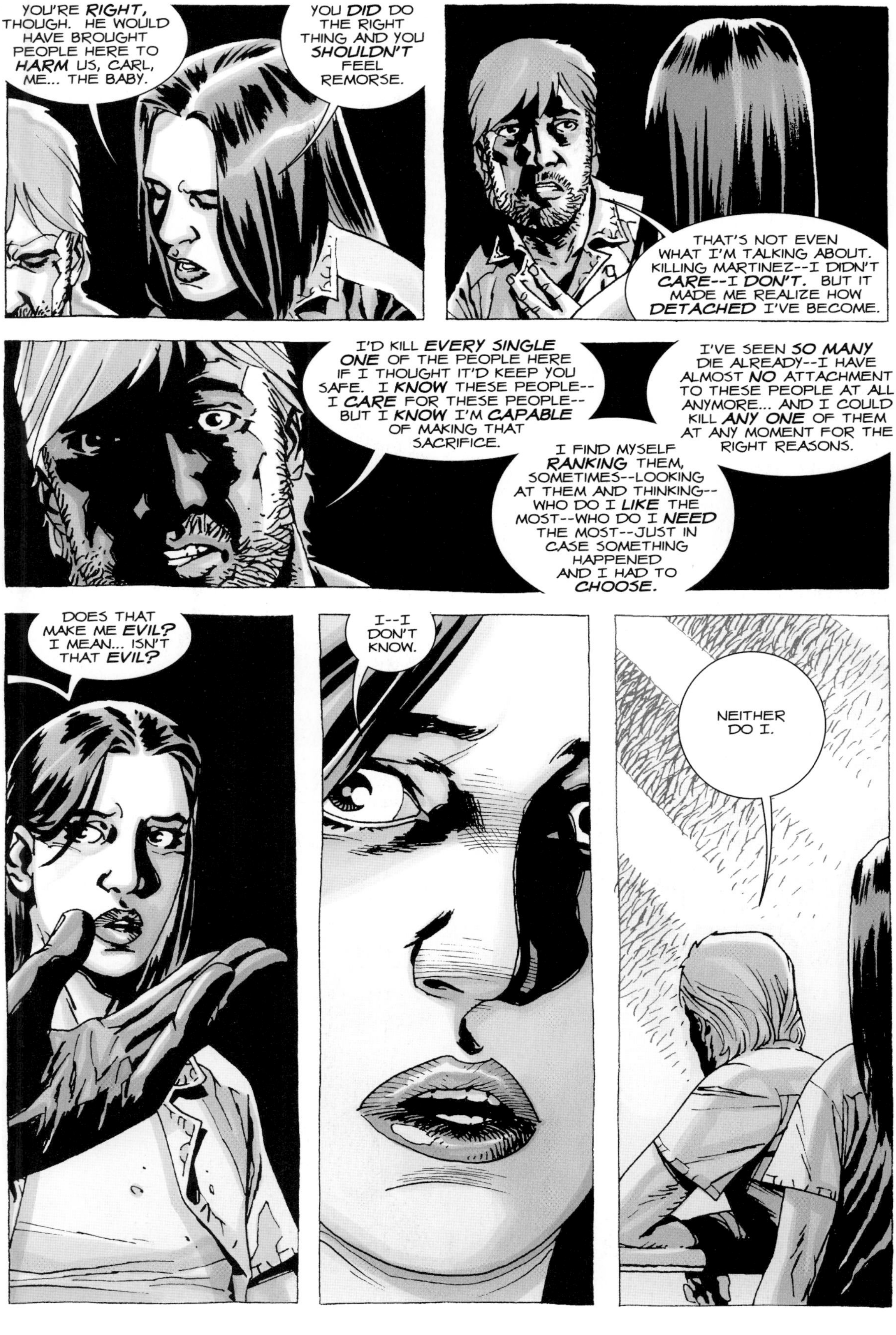
YOU'RE RIGHT, THOUGH. HE WOULD HAVE BROUGHT PEOPLE HERE TO HARM US, CARL, ME... THE BABY.
YOU DID DO THE RIGHT THING AND YOU SHOULDN'T FEEL REMORSE.
THAT'S NOT EVEN WHAT I'M TALKING ABOUT. KILLING MARTINEZ--I DIDN'T CARE--I DON'T. BUT IT MADE ME REALIZE HOW DETACHED I'VE BECOME.
I'D KILL EVERY SINGLE ONE OF THE PEOPLE HERE IF I THOUGHT IT'D KEEP YOU SAFE. I KNOW THESE PEOPLE--I CARE FOR THESE PEOPLE--BUT I KNOW I'M CAPABLE OF MAKING THAT SACRIFICE.
I'VE SEEN SO MANY DIE ALREADY--I HAVE ALMOST NO ATTACHMENT TO THESE PEOPLE AT ALL ANYMORE... AND I COULD KILL ANY ONE OF THEM AT ANY MOMENT FOR THE RIGHT REASONS.
I FIND MYSELF RANKING THEM, SOMETIMES--LOOKING AT THEM AND THINKING--WHO DO I LIKE THE MOST--WHO DO I NEED THE MOST--JUST IN CASE SOMETHING HAPPENED AND I HAD TO CHOOSE.
DOES THAT MAKE ME EVIL? I MEAN... ISN'T THAT EVIL?
I--I DON'T KNOW.
NEITHER DO I.

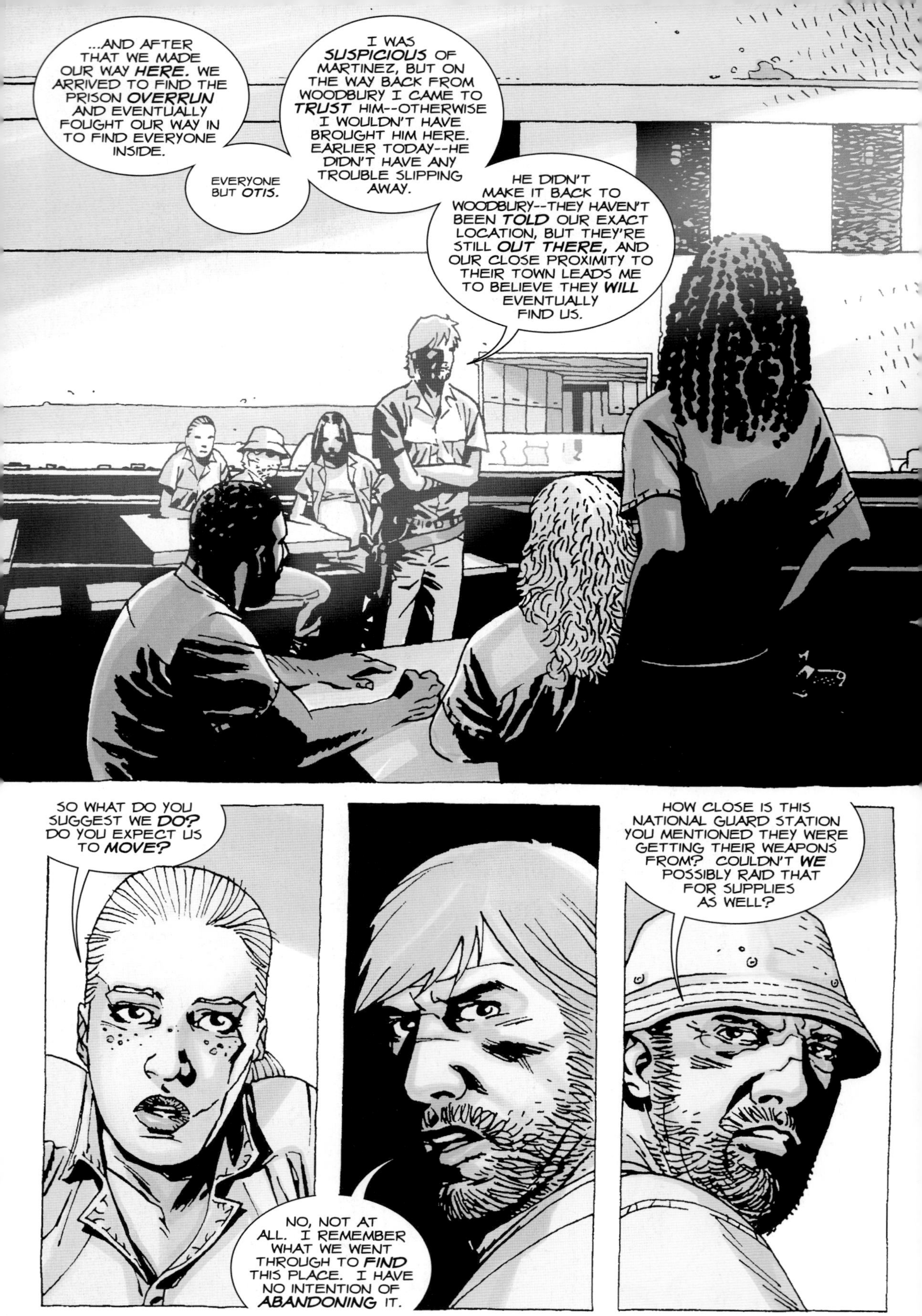
...AND AFTER THAT WE MADE OUR WAY HERE. WE ARRIVED TO FIND THE PRISON OVERRUN AND EVENTUALLY FOUGHT OUR WAY IN TO FIND EVERYONE INSIDE.
EVERYONE BUT OTIS.
I WAS SUSPICIOUS OF MARTINEZ, BUT ON THE WAY BACK FROM WOODBURY I CAME TO TRUST HIM--OTHERWISE I WOULDN'T HAVE BROUGHT HIM HERE. EARLIER TODAY--HE DIDN'T HAVE ANY TROUBLE SLIPPING AWAY.
HE DIDN'T MAKE IT BACK TO WOODBURY--THEY HAVEN'T BEEN TOLD OUR EXACT LOCATION, BUT THEY'RE STILL OUT THERE, AND OUR CLOSE PROXIMITY TO THEIR TOWN LEADS ME TO BELIEVE THEY WILL EVENTUALLY FIND US.
SO WHAT DO YOU SUGGEST WE DO? DO YOU EXPECT US TO MOVE?
NO, NOT AT ALL. I REMEMBER WHAT WE WENT THROUGH TO FIND THIS PLACE. I HAVE NO INTENTION OF ABANDONING IT.
HOW CLOSE IS THIS NATIONAL GUARD STATION YOU MENTIONED THEY WERE GETTING THEIR WEAPONS FROM? COULDN'T WE POSSIBLY RAID THAT FOR SUPPLIES AS WELL?

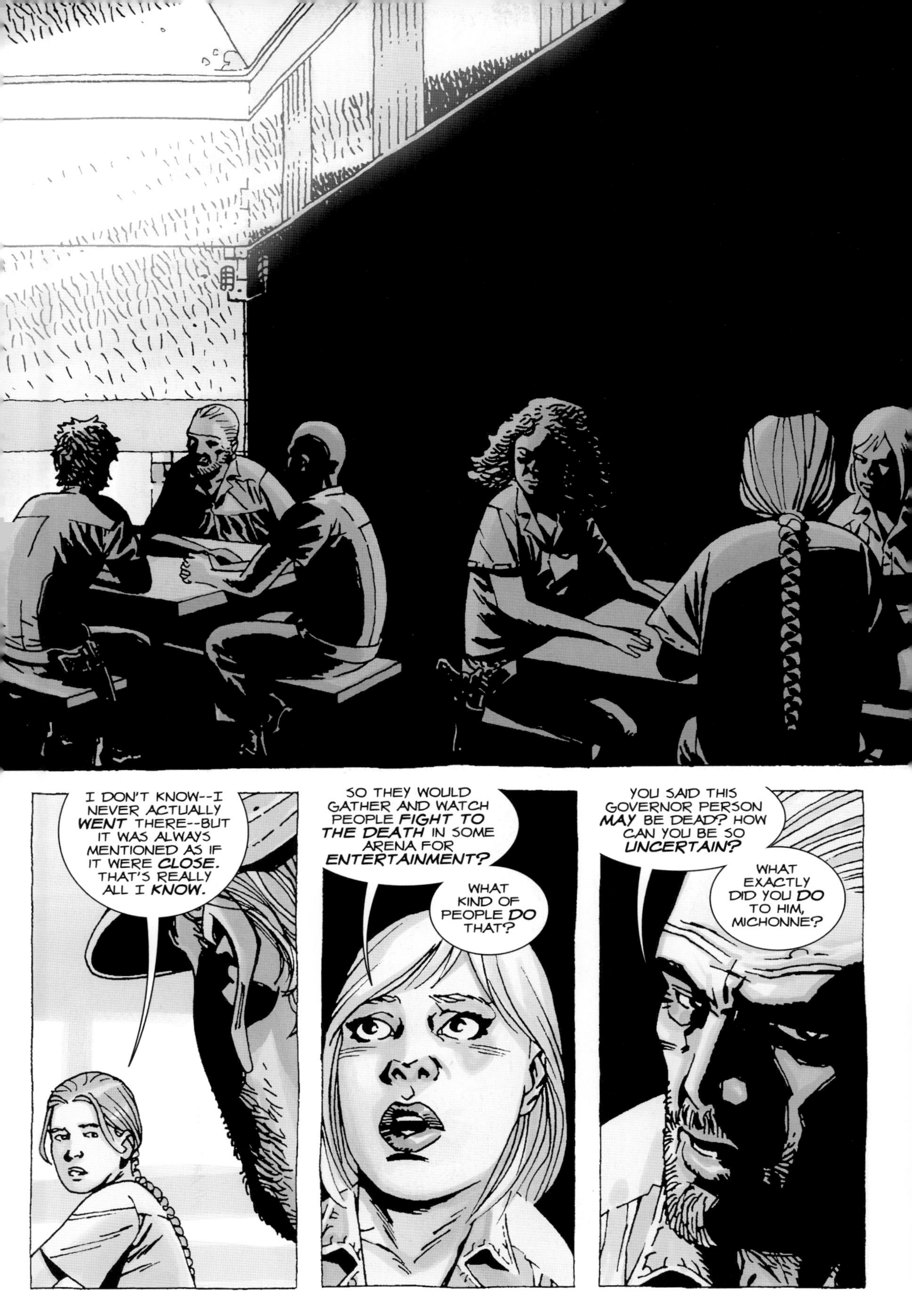
I DON'T KNOW--I NEVER ACTUALLY WENT THERE--BUT IT WAS ALWAYS MENTIONED AS IF IT WERE CLOSE. THAT'S REALLY ALL I KNOW.
SO THEY WOULD GATHER AND WATCH PEOPLE FIGHT TO THE DEATH IN SOME ARENA FOR ENTERTAINMENT?
WHAT KIND OF PEOPLE DO THAT?
YOU SAID THIS GOVERNOR PERSON MAY BE DEAD? HOW CAN YOU BE SO UNCERTAIN?
WHAT EXACTLY DID YOU DO TO HIM, MICHONNE?

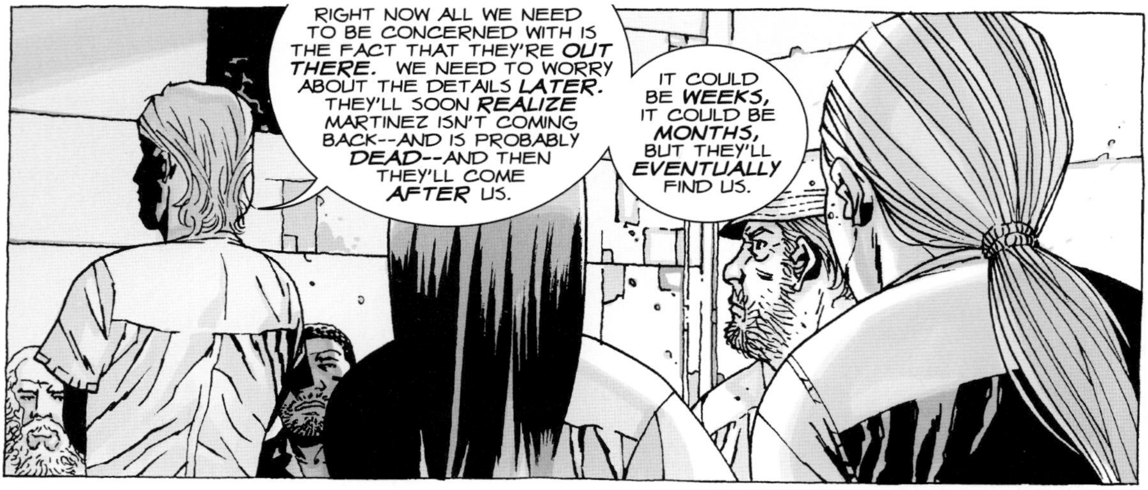
RIGHT NOW ALL WE NEED TO BE CONCERNED WITH IS THE FACT THAT THEY'RE OUT THERE. WE NEED TO WORRY ABOUT THE DETAILS LATER. THEY'LL SOON REALIZE MARTINEZ ISN'T COMING BACK--AND IS PROBABLY DEAD--AND THEN THEY'LL COME AFTER US.
IT COULD BE WEEKS, IT COULD BE MONTHS, BUT THEY'LL EVENTUALLY FIND US.

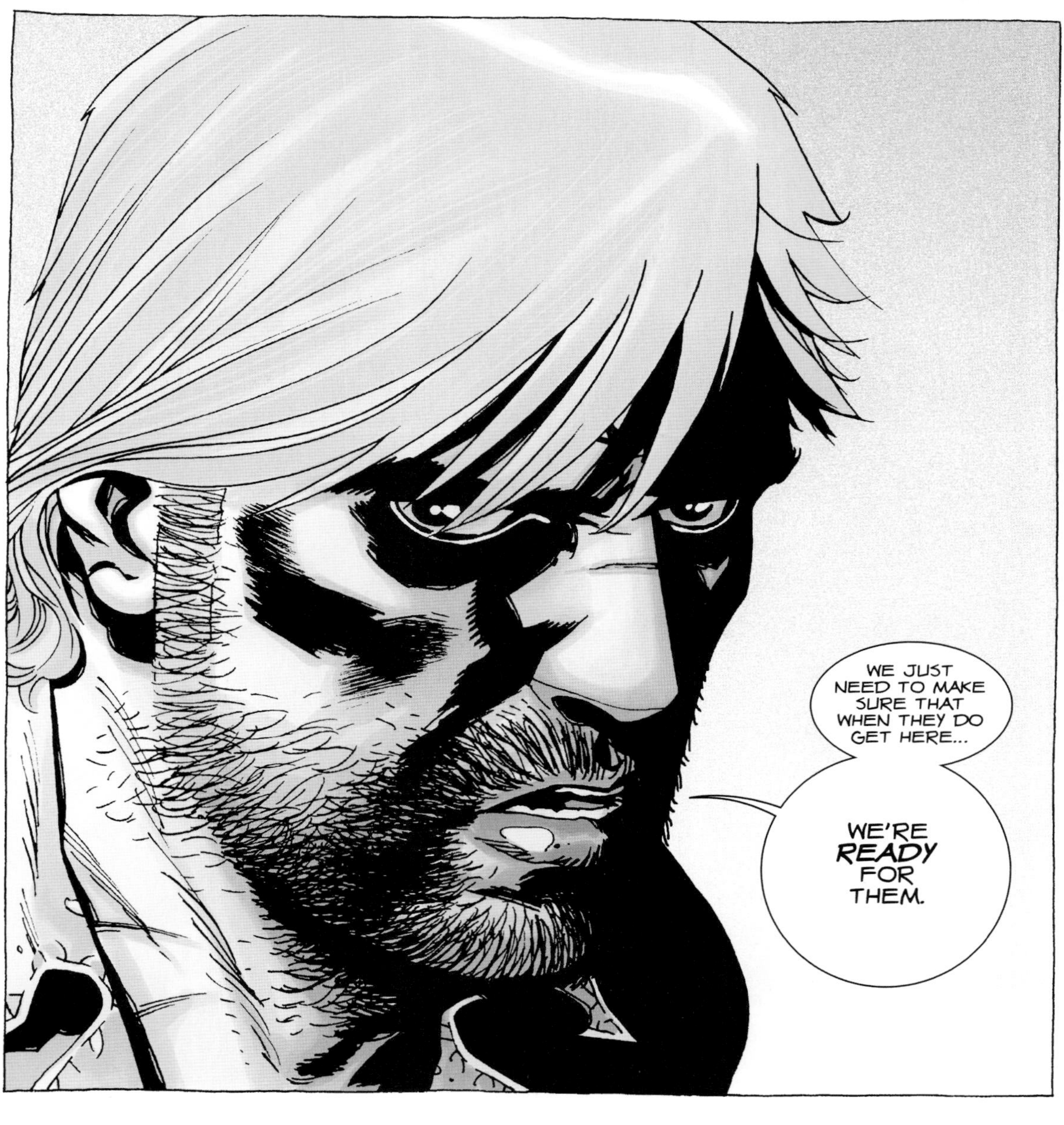
WE JUST NEED TO MAKE SURE THAT WHEN THEY DO GET HERE...
WE'RE READY FOR THEM.

Chapter Seven:
The Calm Before

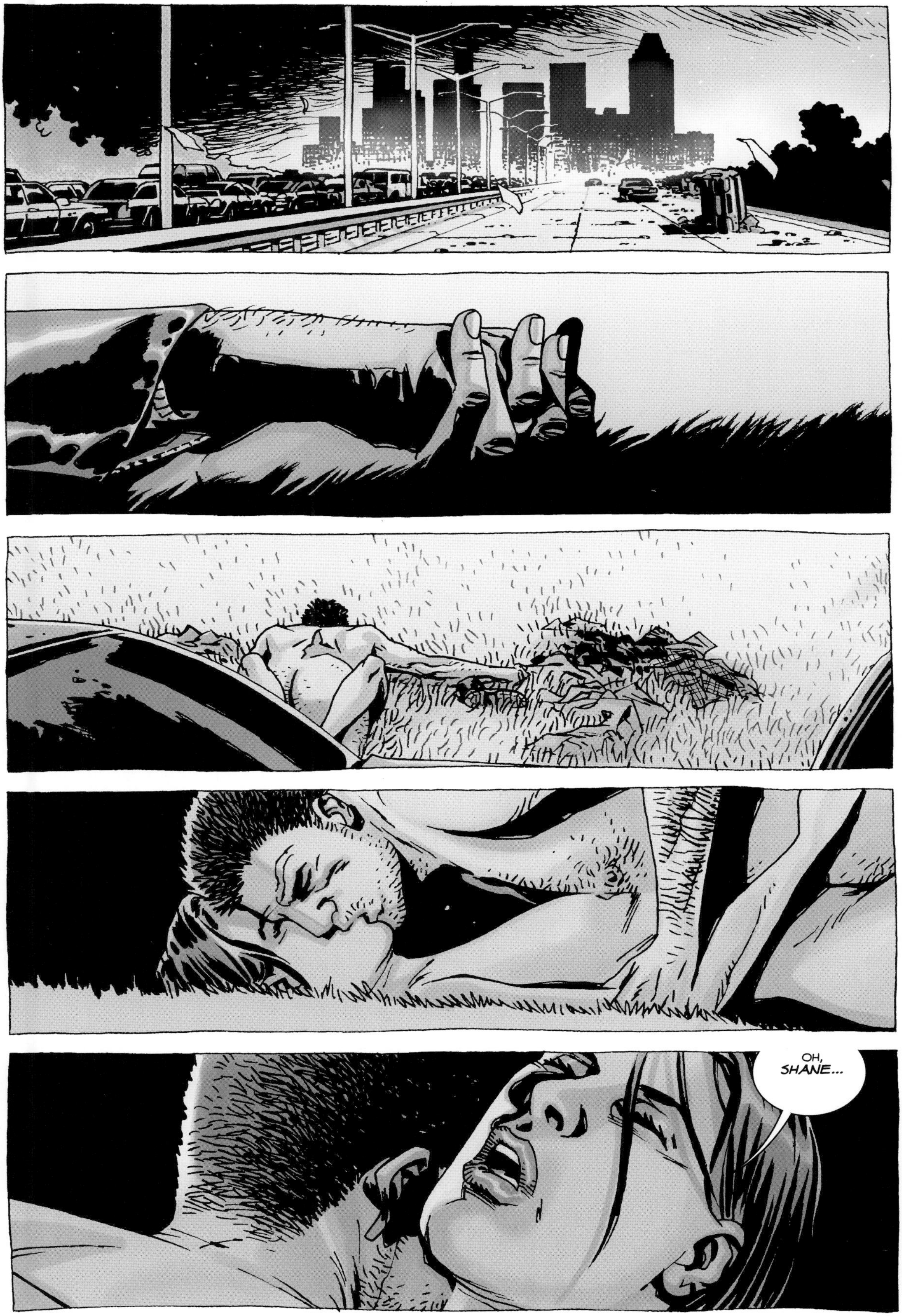

OH, SHANE...

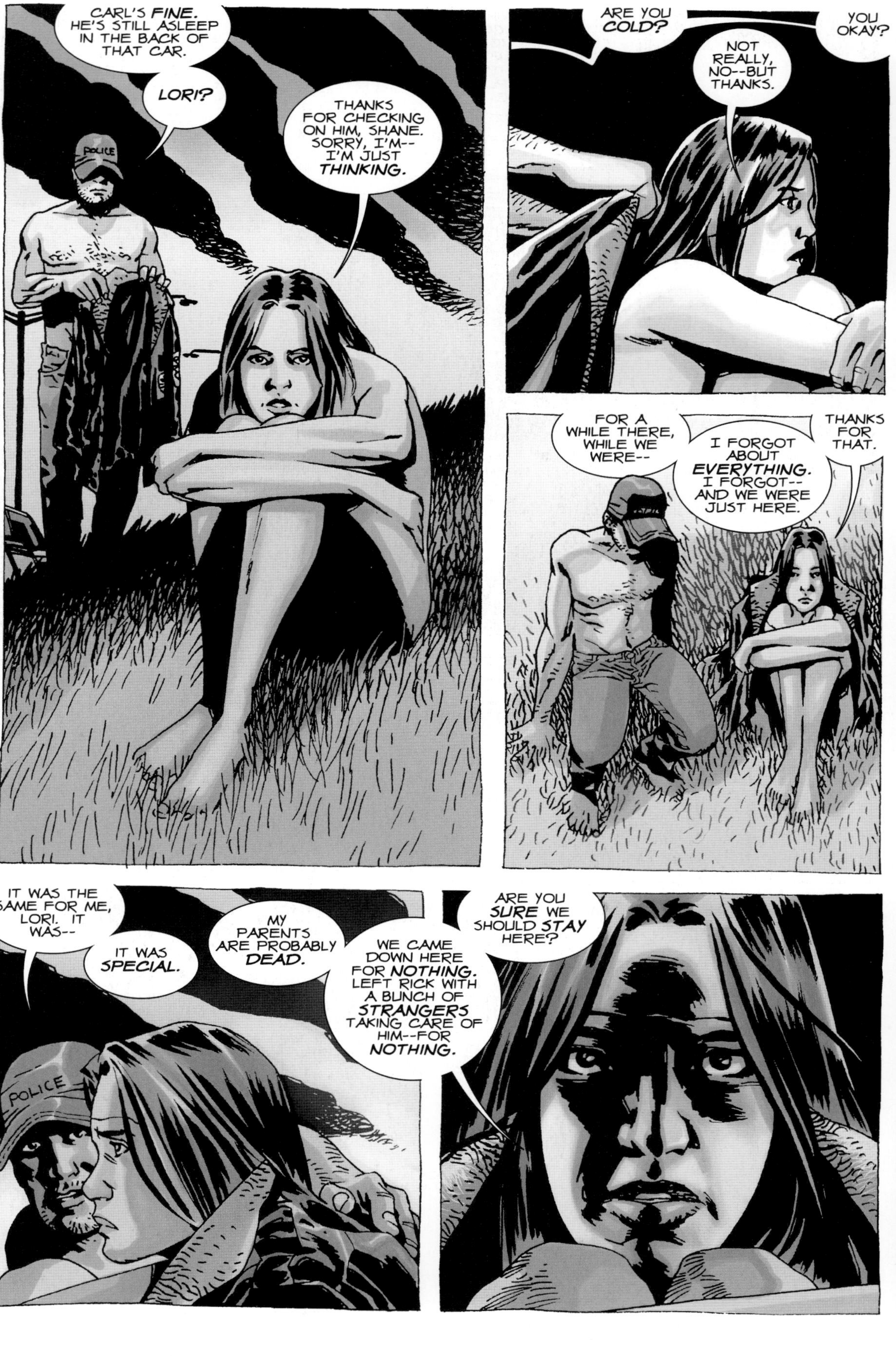

CARL'S FINE. HE'S STILL ASLEEP IN THE BACK OF THAT CAR.
LORI?
THANKS FOR CHECKING ON HIM, SHANE. SORRY, I'M-- I'M JUST THINKING.
ARE YOU COLD?
YOU OKAY?
NOT REALLY, NO--BUT THANKS.
FOR A WHILE THERE, WHILE WE WERE--
I FORGOT ABOUT EVERYTHING. I FORGOT-- AND WE WERE JUST HERE.
THANKS FOR THAT.
IT WAS THE SAME FOR ME, LORI. IT WAS--
IT WAS SPECIAL.
MY PARENTS ARE PROBABLY DEAD.
WE CAME DOWN HERE FOR NOTHING. LEFT RICK WITH A BUNCH OF STRANGERS TAKING CARE OF HIM--FOR NOTHING.
ARE YOU SURE WE SHOULD STAY HERE?

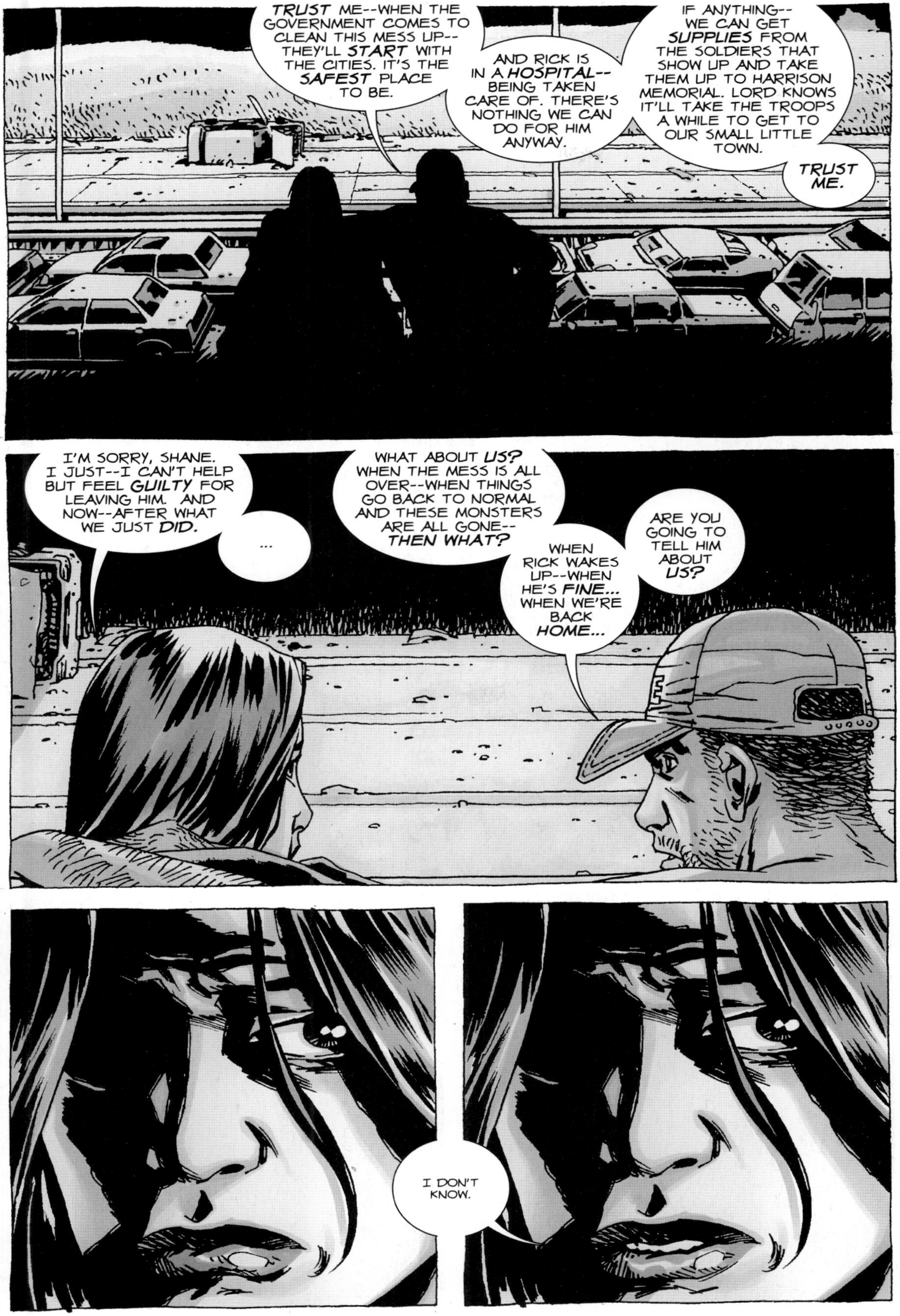
TRUST ME--WHEN THE GOVERNMENT COMES TO CLEAN THIS MESS UP--THEY'LL START WITH THE CITIES. IT'S THE SAFEST PLACE TO BE.
AND RICK IS IN A HOSPITAL--BEING TAKEN CARE OF. THERE'S NOTHING WE CAN DO FOR HIM ANYWAY.
IF ANYTHING--WE CAN GET SUPPLIES FROM THE SOLDIERS THAT SHOW UP AND TAKE THEM UP TO HARRISON MEMORIAL. LORD KNOWS IT'LL TAKE THE TROOPS A WHILE TO GET TO OUR SMALL LITTLE TOWN.
TRUST ME.
I'M SORRY, SHANE. I JUST--I CAN'T HELP BUT FEEL GUILTY FOR LEAVING HIM. AND NOW--AFTER WHAT WE JUST DID.
...
WHAT ABOUT US? WHEN THE MESS IS ALL OVER--WHEN THINGS GO BACK TO NORMAL AND THESE MONSTERS ARE ALL GONE--THEN WHAT?
WHEN RICK WAKES UP--WHEN HE'S FINE... WHEN WE'RE BACK HOME...
ARE YOU GOING TO TELL HIM ABOUT US?
I DON'T KNOW.

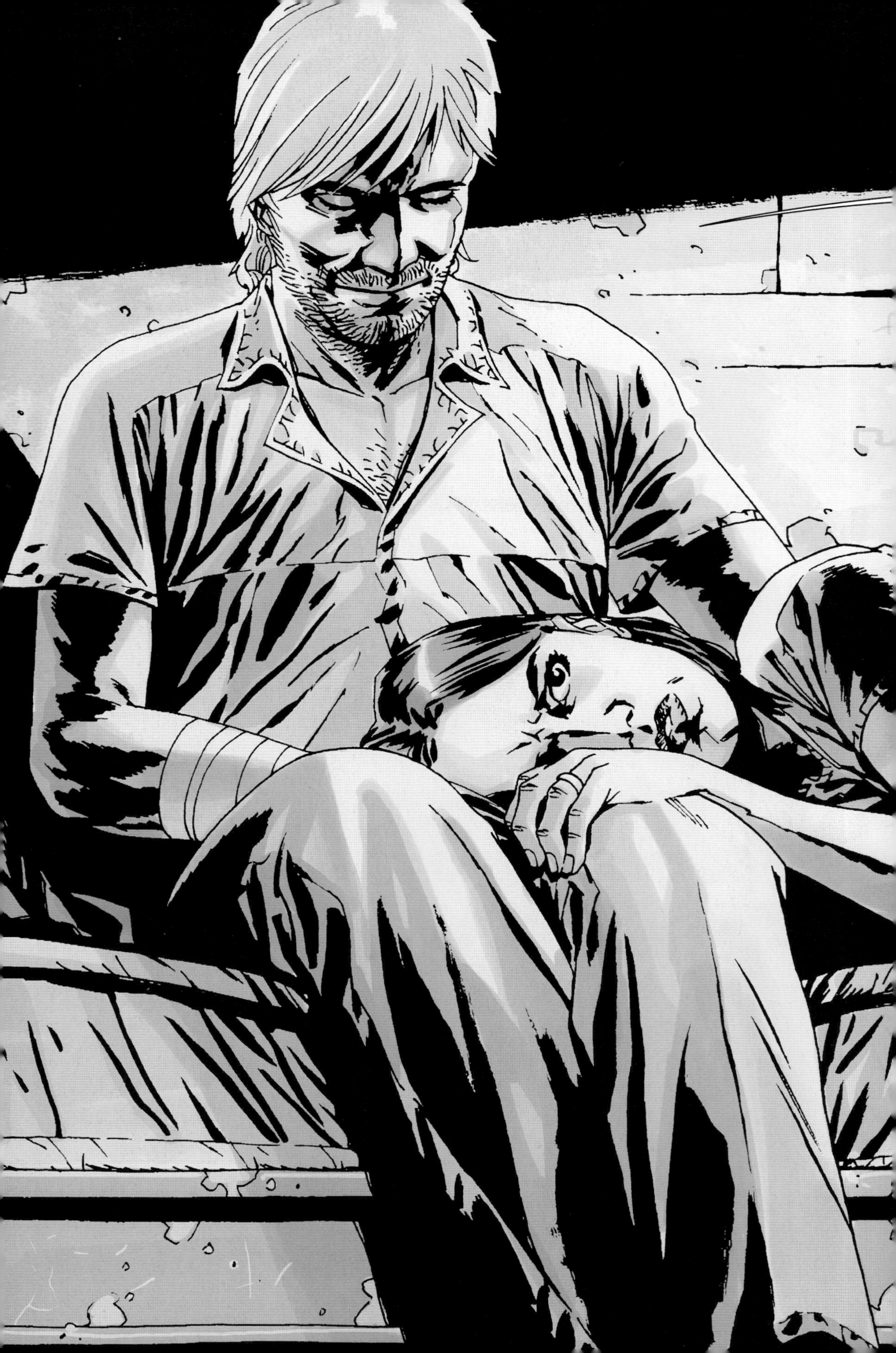

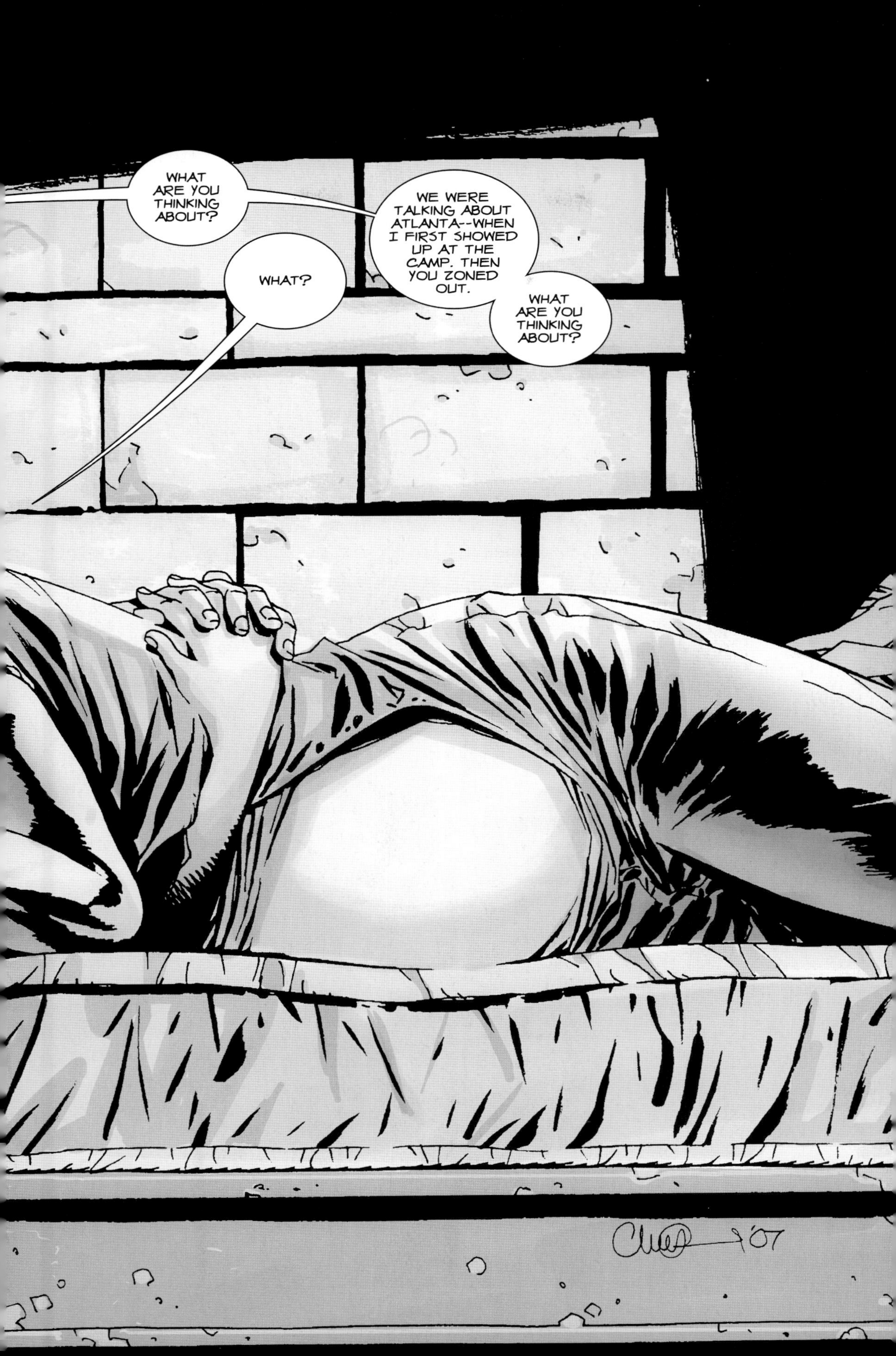
WHAT ARE YOU THINKING ABOUT?
WE WERE TALKING ABOUT ATLANTA--WHEN I FIRST SHOWED UP AT THE CAMP. THEN YOU ZONED OUT.
WHAT?
WHAT ARE YOU THINKING ABOUT?

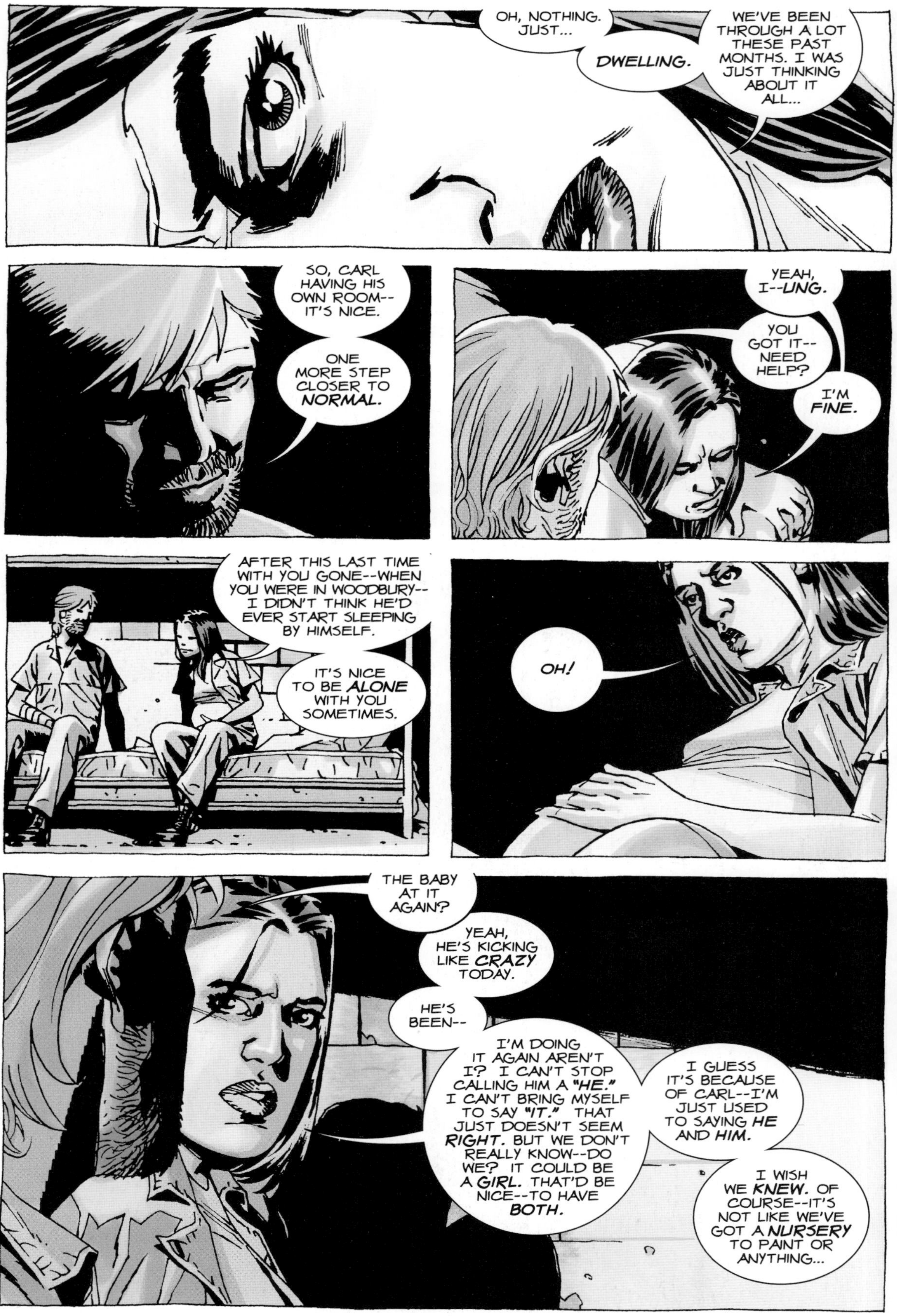
OH, NOTHING. JUST...
DWELLING.
WE'VE BEEN THROUGH A LOT THESE PAST MONTHS. I WAS JUST THINKING ABOUT IT ALL...
SO, CARL HAVING HIS OWN ROOM-- IT'S NICE.
ONE MORE STEP CLOSER TO NORMAL.
YEAH, I--UNG.
YOU GOT IT-- NEED HELP?
I'M FINE.
AFTER THIS LAST TIME WITH YOU GONE--WHEN YOU WERE IN WOODBURY-- I DIDN'T THINK HE'D EVER START SLEEPING BY HIMSELF.
IT'S NICE TO BE ALONE WITH YOU SOMETIMES.
OH!
THE BABY AT IT AGAIN?
YEAH, HE'S KICKING LIKE CRAZY TODAY.
HE'S BEEN--
I'M DOING IT AGAIN AREN'T I? I CAN'T STOP CALLING HIM A "HE." I CAN'T BRING MYSELF TO SAY "IT." THAT JUST DOESN'T SEEM RIGHT. BUT WE DON'T REALLY KNOW--DO WE? IT COULD BE A GIRL. THAT'D BE NICE--TO HAVE BOTH.
I GUESS IT'S BECAUSE OF CARL--I'M JUST USED TO SAYING HE AND HIM.
I WISH WE KNEW. OF COURSE--IT'S NOT LIKE WE'VE GOT A NURSERY TO PAINT OR ANYTHING...

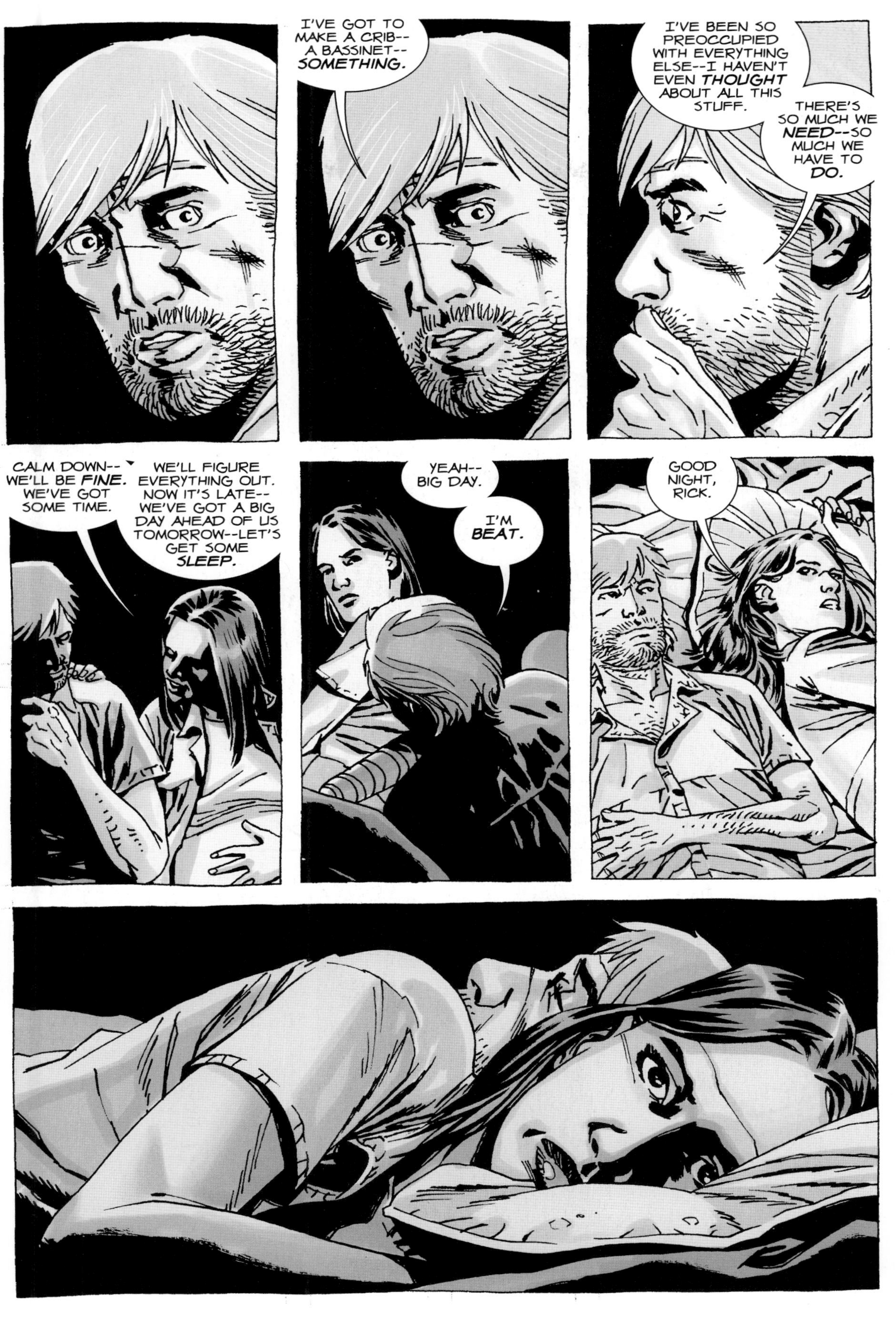
I'VE GOT TO MAKE A CRIB--A BASSINET--SOMETHING.
I'VE BEEN SO PREOCCUPIED WITH EVERYTHING ELSE--I HAVEN'T EVEN THOUGHT ABOUT ALL THIS STUFF.
THERE'S SO MUCH WE NEED--SO MUCH WE HAVE TO DO.
CALM DOWN--WE'LL BE FINE. WE'VE GOT SOME TIME.
WE'LL FIGURE EVERYTHING OUT. NOW IT'S LATE--WE'VE GOT A BIG DAY AHEAD OF US TOMORROW--LET'S GET SOME SLEEP.
YEAH--BIG DAY.
I'M BEAT.
GOOD NIGHT, RICK.

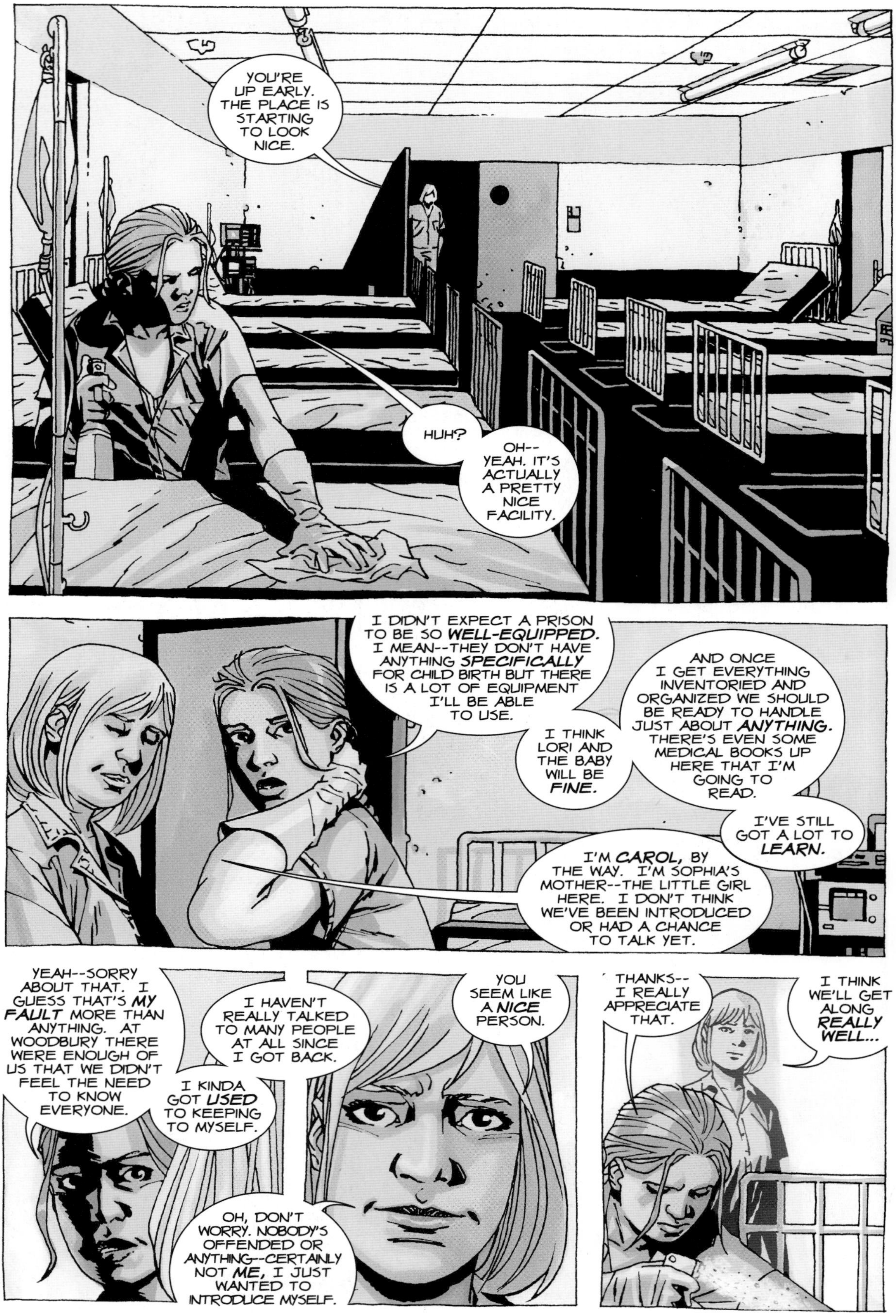
YOU'RE UP EARLY. THE PLACE IS STARTING TO LOOK NICE.
HUH?
OH-- YEAH. IT'S ACTUALLY A PRETTY NICE FACILITY.
I DIDN'T EXPECT A PRISON TO BE SO WELL-EQUIPPED. I MEAN--THEY DON'T HAVE ANYTHING SPECIFICALLY FOR CHILD BIRTH BUT THERE IS A LOT OF EQUIPMENT I'LL BE ABLE TO USE.
I THINK LORI AND THE BABY WILL BE FINE.
AND ONCE I GET EVERYTHING INVENTORIED AND ORGANIZED WE SHOULD BE READY TO HANDLE JUST ABOUT ANYTHING. THERE'S EVEN SOME MEDICAL BOOKS UP HERE THAT I'M GOING TO READ.
I'VE STILL GOT A LOT TO LEARN.
I'M CAROL, BY THE WAY. I'M SOPHIA'S MOTHER--THE LITTLE GIRL HERE. I DON'T THINK WE'VE BEEN INTRODUCED OR HAD A CHANCE TO TALK YET.
YEAH--SORRY ABOUT THAT. I GUESS THAT'S MY FAULT MORE THAN ANYTHING. AT WOODBURY THERE WERE ENOUGH OF US THAT WE DIDN'T FEEL THE NEED TO KNOW EVERYONE.
I HAVEN'T REALLY TALKED TO MANY PEOPLE AT ALL SINCE I GOT BACK.
I KINDA GOT USED TO KEEPING TO MYSELF.
OH, DON'T WORRY. NOBODY'S OFFENDED OR ANYTHING--CERTAINLY NOT ME, I JUST WANTED TO INTRODUCE MYSELF.
YOU SEEM LIKE A NICE PERSON.
THANKS-- I REALLY APPRECIATE THAT.
I THINK WE'LL GET ALONG REALLY WELL...

YOU DECENT, PATRICIA?

DECENT *ENOUGH.* COME ON IN.

YOU OKAY? I JUST WANTED TO CHECK ON YOU. WE HAVEN'T REALLY TALKED IN A WHILE.

YOU ALL RIGHT?

SURE, BILLY. I'M JUST THINKING ABOUT OTIS. WASN'T MUCH FUSS MADE OVER HIS DEATH--I GUESS PEOPLE ARE JUST GETTING *USED* TO IT. STILL--IT'S A *SHAME.*

HE WAS A COMPLETE *PRICK* MOST OF THE TIME--BUT HE WAS THE CLOSEST THING I HAD TO A *FRIEND* OUT HERE.

I'M SORRY FOR THAT. MY DAD, ME--MAGGIE. WE WERE, LIKE EVERYONE ELSE, MAD ABOUT YOU PULLING THAT SHIT WITH THOSE PRISONERS, BUT WE *ALL* DONE SOMETHING WE AIN'T PROUD OF. NOBODY'S PERFECT.

WE'RE STILL YOUR FRIENDS. I'LL TRY TO START ACTING LIKE IT.

YOU'RE COMING TO MY SISTER'S WEDDING, RIGHT?

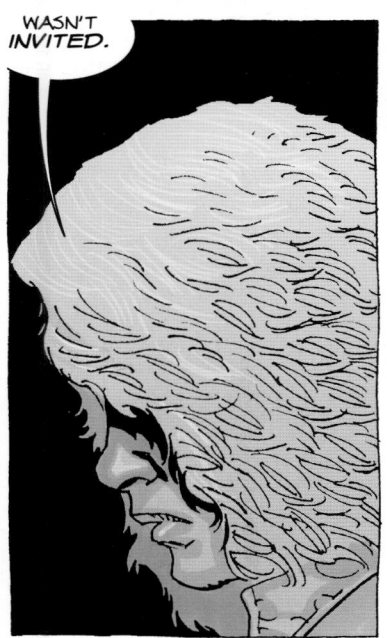

WASN'T *INVITED.*

I WASN'T INVITED *EITHER* BUT I'M GONNA BE THERE. I THINK PEOPLE ARE JUST ASSUMING EVERYONE'S COMING.

WEREN'T NO INVITATIONS *MADE,* Y'KNOW? SO--YOU WANT TO COME? I KNOW MAGGIE'D WANT YOU THERE-- WAS A TIME YOU WAS LIKE A MOM--OR AT LEAST AN OLDER *SISTER* TO HER.

I DON'T KNOW.

WHEN IS IT?

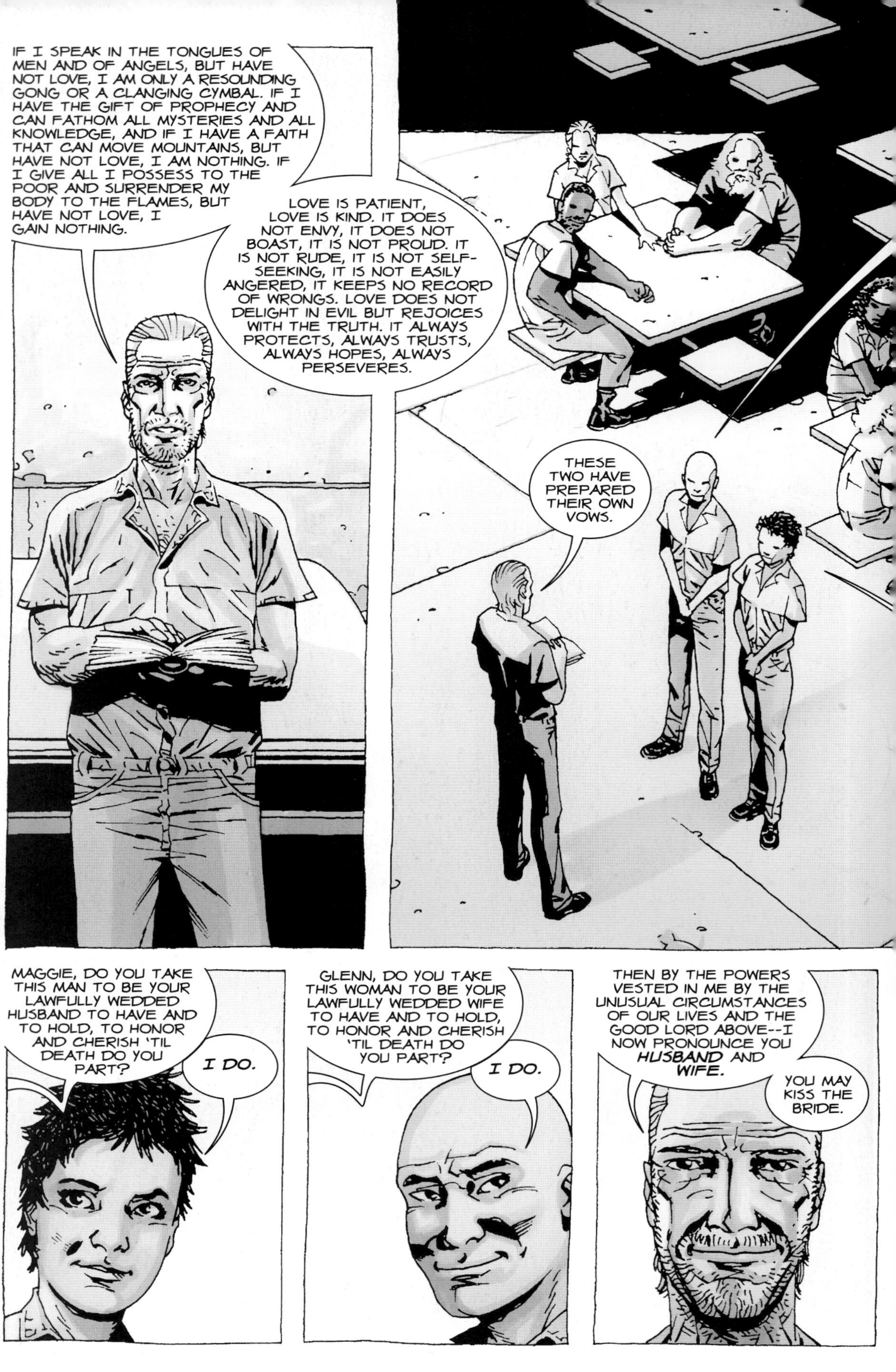
IF I SPEAK IN THE TONGUES OF MEN AND OF ANGELS, BUT HAVE NOT LOVE, I AM ONLY A RESOUNDING GONG OR A CLANGING CYMBAL. IF I HAVE THE GIFT OF PROPHECY AND CAN FATHOM ALL MYSTERIES AND ALL KNOWLEDGE, AND IF I HAVE A FAITH THAT CAN MOVE MOUNTAINS, BUT HAVE NOT LOVE, I AM NOTHING. IF I GIVE ALL I POSSESS TO THE POOR AND SURRENDER MY BODY TO THE FLAMES, BUT HAVE NOT LOVE, I GAIN NOTHING.
LOVE IS PATIENT, LOVE IS KIND. IT DOES NOT ENVY, IT DOES NOT BOAST, IT IS NOT PROUD. IT IS NOT RUDE, IT IS NOT SELF-SEEKING, IT IS NOT EASILY ANGERED, IT KEEPS NO RECORD OF WRONGS. LOVE DOES NOT DELIGHT IN EVIL BUT REJOICES WITH THE TRUTH. IT ALWAYS PROTECTS, ALWAYS TRUSTS, ALWAYS HOPES, ALWAYS PERSEVERES.
THESE TWO HAVE PREPARED THEIR OWN VOWS.
MAGGIE, DO YOU TAKE THIS MAN TO BE YOUR LAWFULLY WEDDED HUSBAND TO HAVE AND TO HOLD, TO HONOR AND CHERISH 'TIL DEATH DO YOU PART?
I DO.
GLENN, DO YOU TAKE THIS WOMAN TO BE YOUR LAWFULLY WEDDED WIFE TO HAVE AND TO HOLD, TO HONOR AND CHERISH 'TIL DEATH DO YOU PART?
I DO.
THEN BY THE POWERS VESTED IN ME BY THE UNUSUAL CIRCUMSTANCES OF OUR LIVES AND THE GOOD LORD ABOVE--I NOW PRONOUNCE YOU HUSBAND AND WIFE.
YOU MAY KISS THE BRIDE.

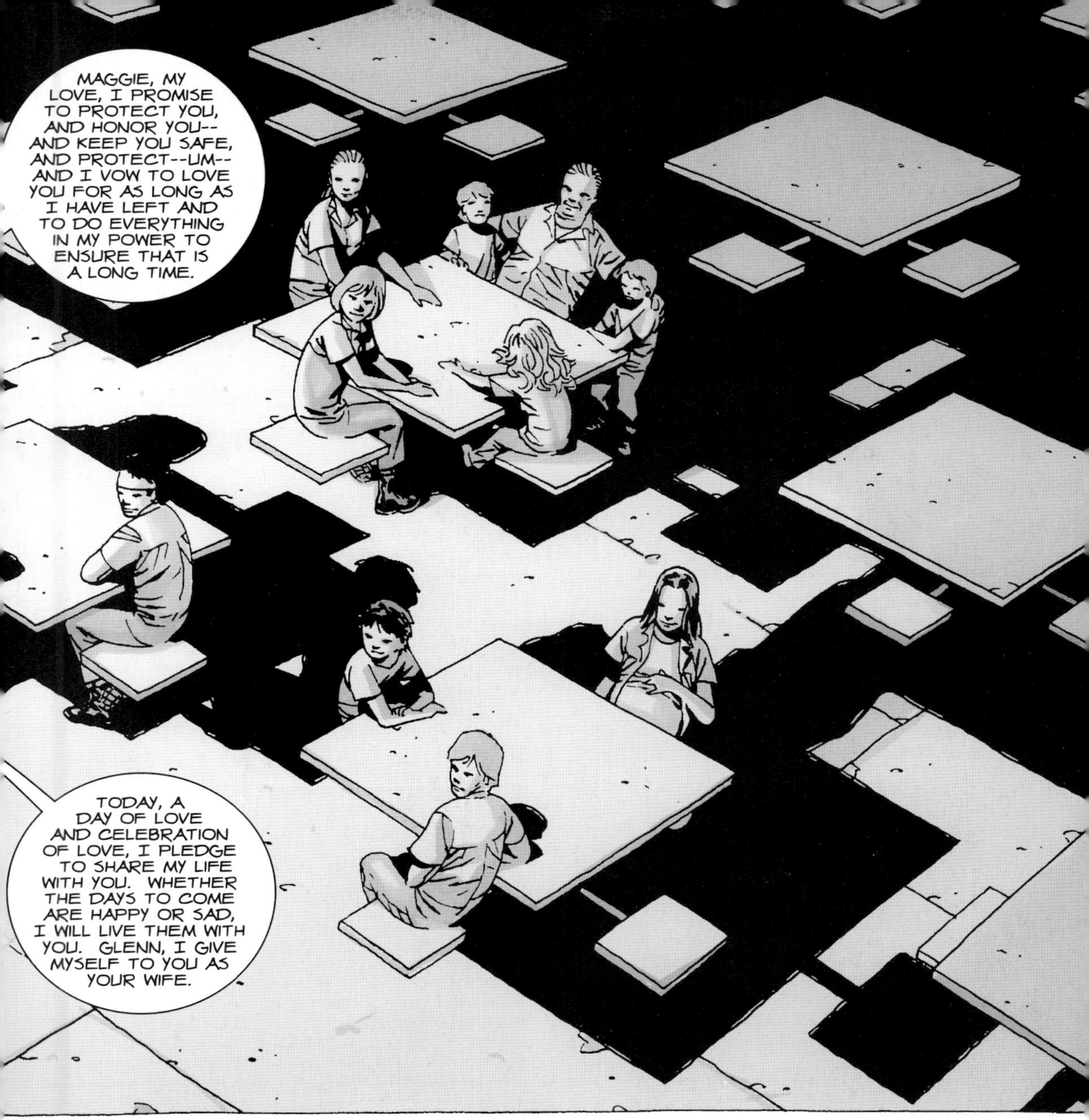
MAGGIE, MY LOVE, I PROMISE TO PROTECT YOU, AND HONOR YOU-- AND KEEP YOU SAFE, AND PROTECT--UM-- AND I VOW TO LOVE YOU FOR AS LONG AS I HAVE LEFT AND TO DO EVERYTHING IN MY POWER TO ENSURE THAT IS A LONG TIME.
TODAY, A DAY OF LOVE AND CELEBRATION OF LOVE, I PLEDGE TO SHARE MY LIFE WITH YOU. WHETHER THE DAYS TO COME ARE HAPPY OR SAD, I WILL LIVE THEM WITH YOU. GLENN, I GIVE MYSELF TO YOU AS YOUR WIFE.

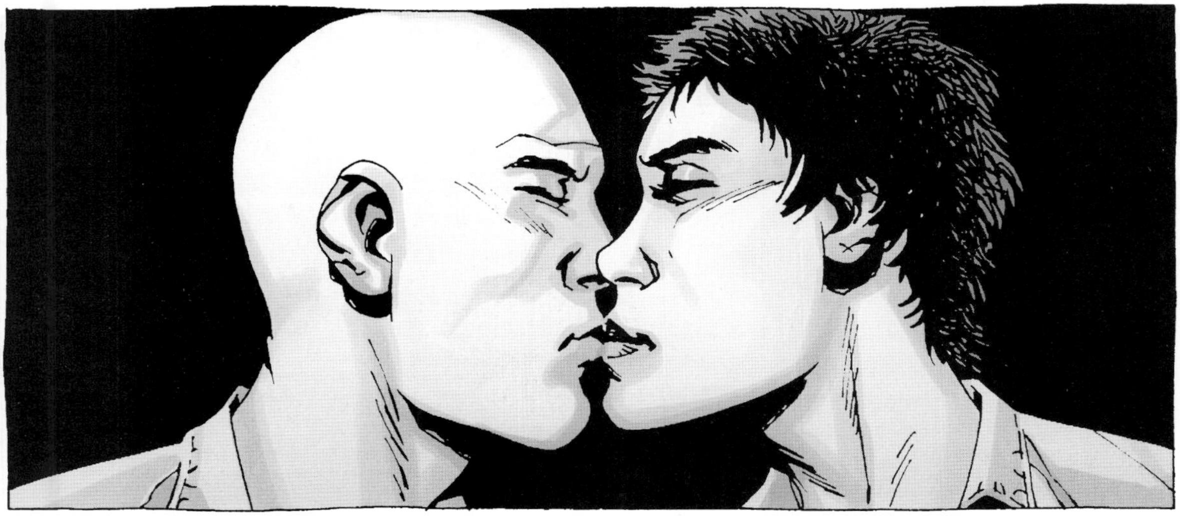

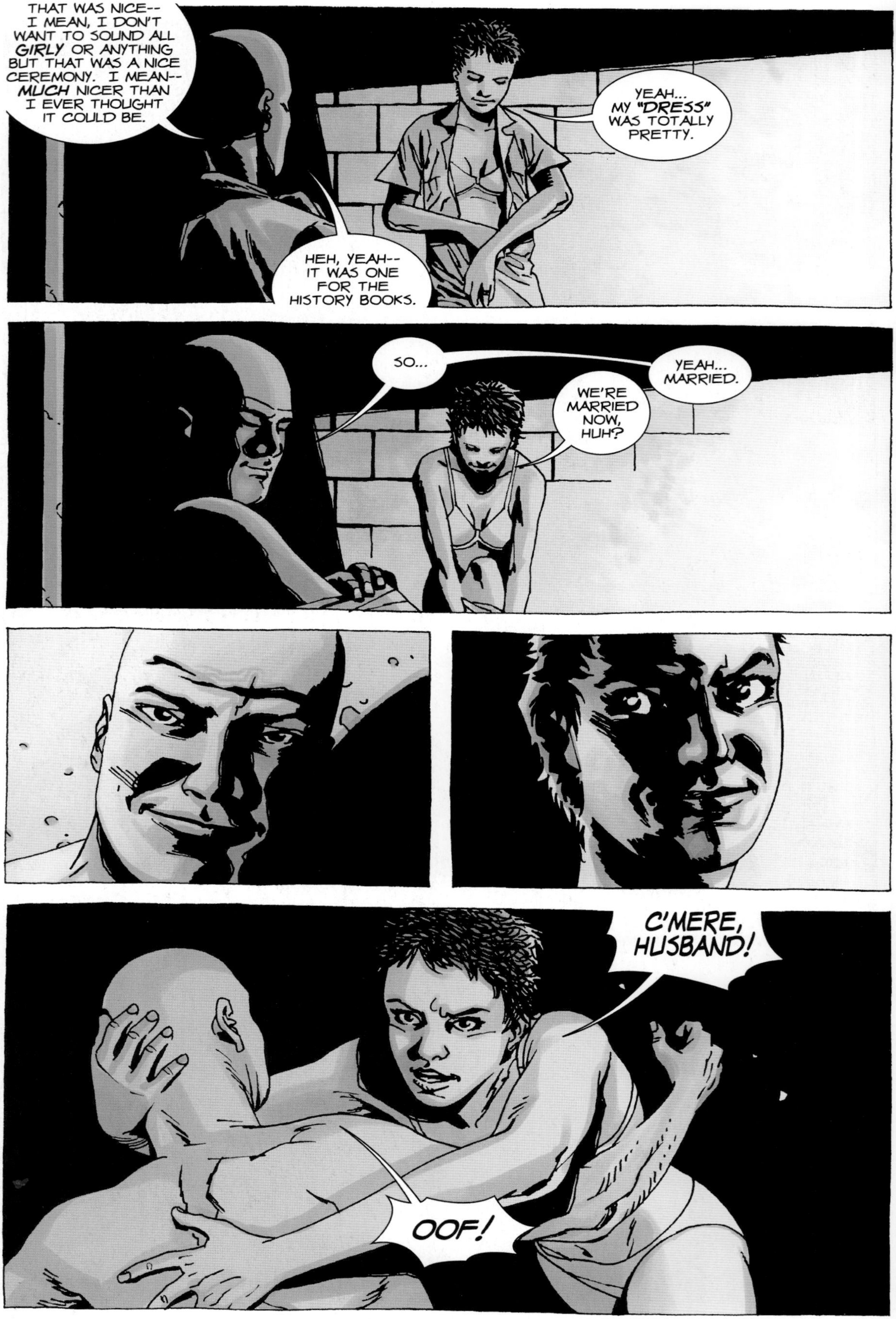
THAT WAS NICE-- I MEAN, I DON'T WANT TO SOUND ALL GIRLY OR ANYTHING BUT THAT WAS A NICE CEREMONY. I MEAN-- MUCH NICER THAN I EVER THOUGHT IT COULD BE.
YEAH... MY "DRESS" WAS TOTALLY PRETTY.
HEH, YEAH-- IT WAS ONE FOR THE HISTORY BOOKS.
SO...
YEAH... MARRIED.
WE'RE MARRIED NOW, HUH?
C'MERE, HUSBAND!
OOF!

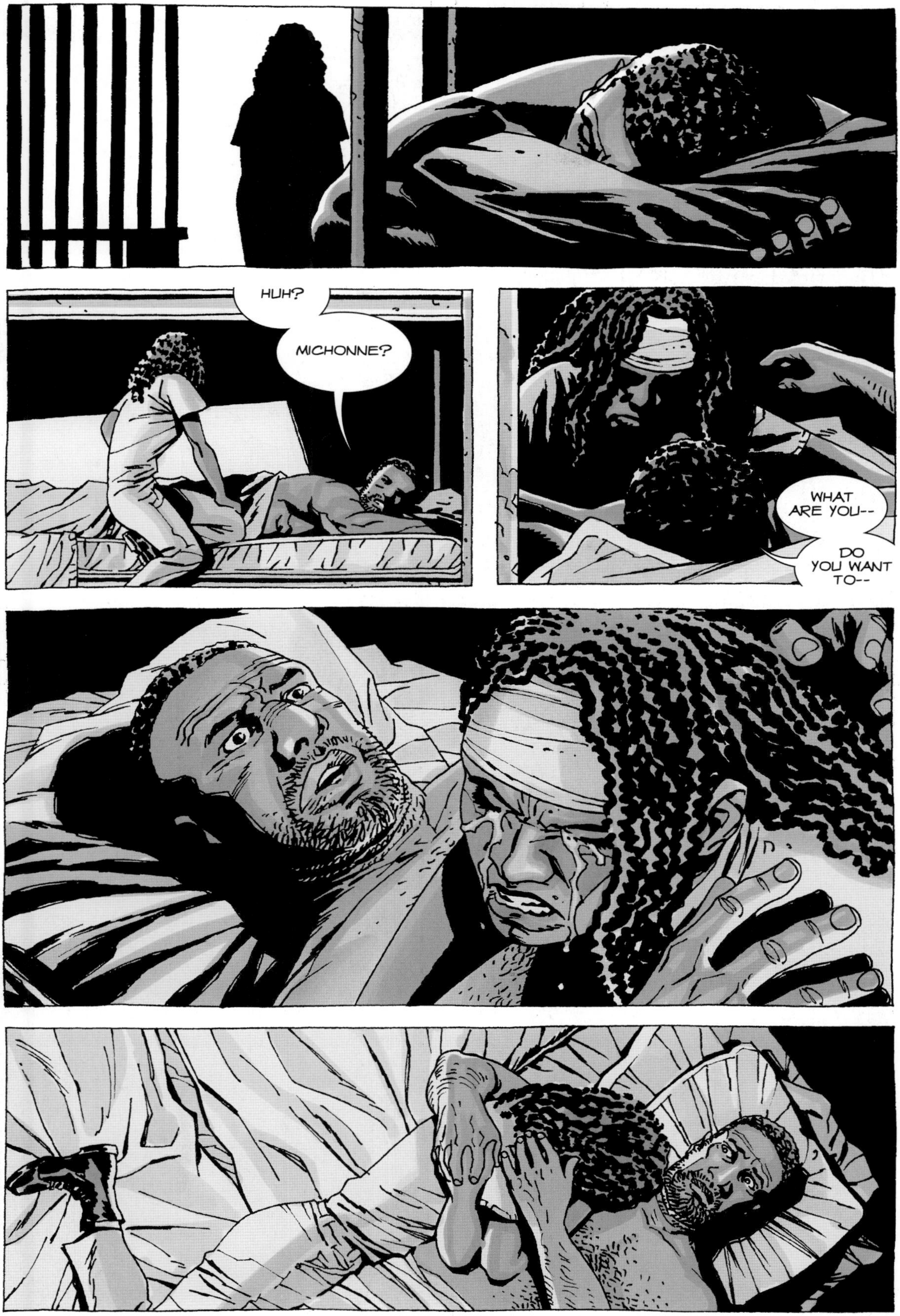
HUH?
MICHONNE?
WHAT ARE YOU--
DO YOU WANT TO--

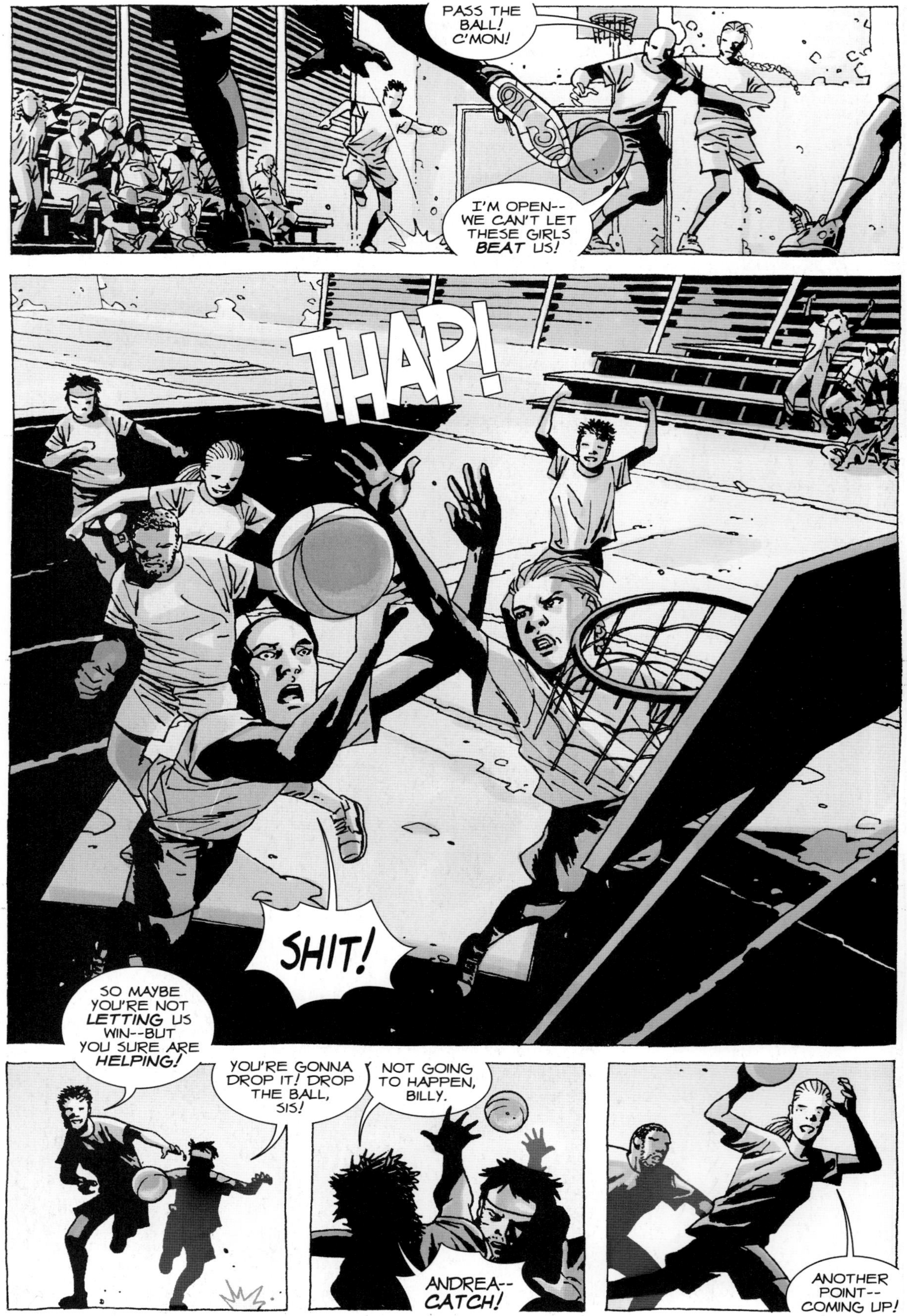
PASS THE BALL! C'MON!
I'M OPEN-- WE CAN'T LET THESE GIRLS BEAT US!
THAP!
SHIT!
SO MAYBE YOU'RE NOT LETTING US WIN--BUT YOU SURE ARE HELPING!
YOU'RE GONNA DROP IT! DROP THE BALL, SIS!
NOT GOING TO HAPPEN, BILLY.
ANDREA-- CATCH!
ANOTHER POINT-- COMING UP!

GO GIRLS!! GO!! YOU CAN DO IT!! BEAT THEM! BEAT THEM!!

SHE FOUND MORE CLOTHES. THAT'S WHERE THEY GOT THE SHORTS AND THE T-SHIRTS. THE PRISON KEPT ATHLETIC WEAR FOR THE INMATES TOO. THEY'VE GOT SWEATPANTS AND STUFF ALSO.

GOOD, GOD.

OH, YEAH?

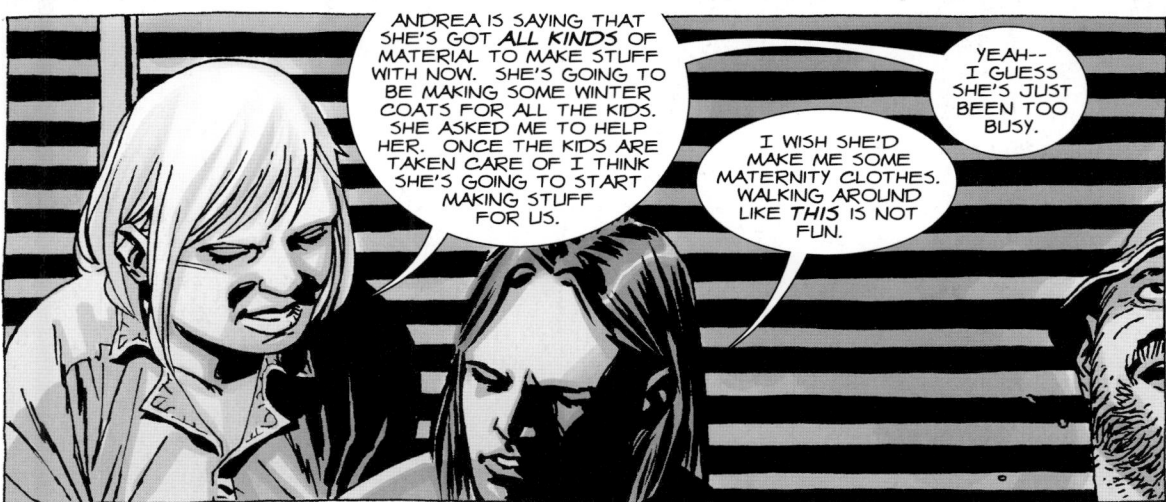

ANDREA IS SAYING THAT SHE'S GOT ALL KINDS OF MATERIAL TO MAKE STUFF WITH NOW. SHE'S GOING TO BE MAKING SOME WINTER COATS FOR ALL THE KIDS. SHE ASKED ME TO HELP HER. ONCE THE KIDS ARE TAKEN CARE OF I THINK SHE'S GOING TO START MAKING STUFF FOR US.

I WISH SHE'D MAKE ME SOME MATERNITY CLOTHES. WALKING AROUND LIKE THIS IS NOT FUN.

YEAH-- I GUESS SHE'S JUST BEEN TOO BUSY.

WHY AREN'T YOU PLAYING, DAD? YOU'D REALLY KICK THEIR BUTTS.

OH. I FORGOT.

SORRY.

IT'S OKAY, SON. DON'T LET IT UPSET YOU. I'M FINE WITH IT. DON'T LET IT MAKE YOU FEEL UNCOMFORTABLE.

IT'S JUST A BIG BOO-BOO.

OKAY, DAD.

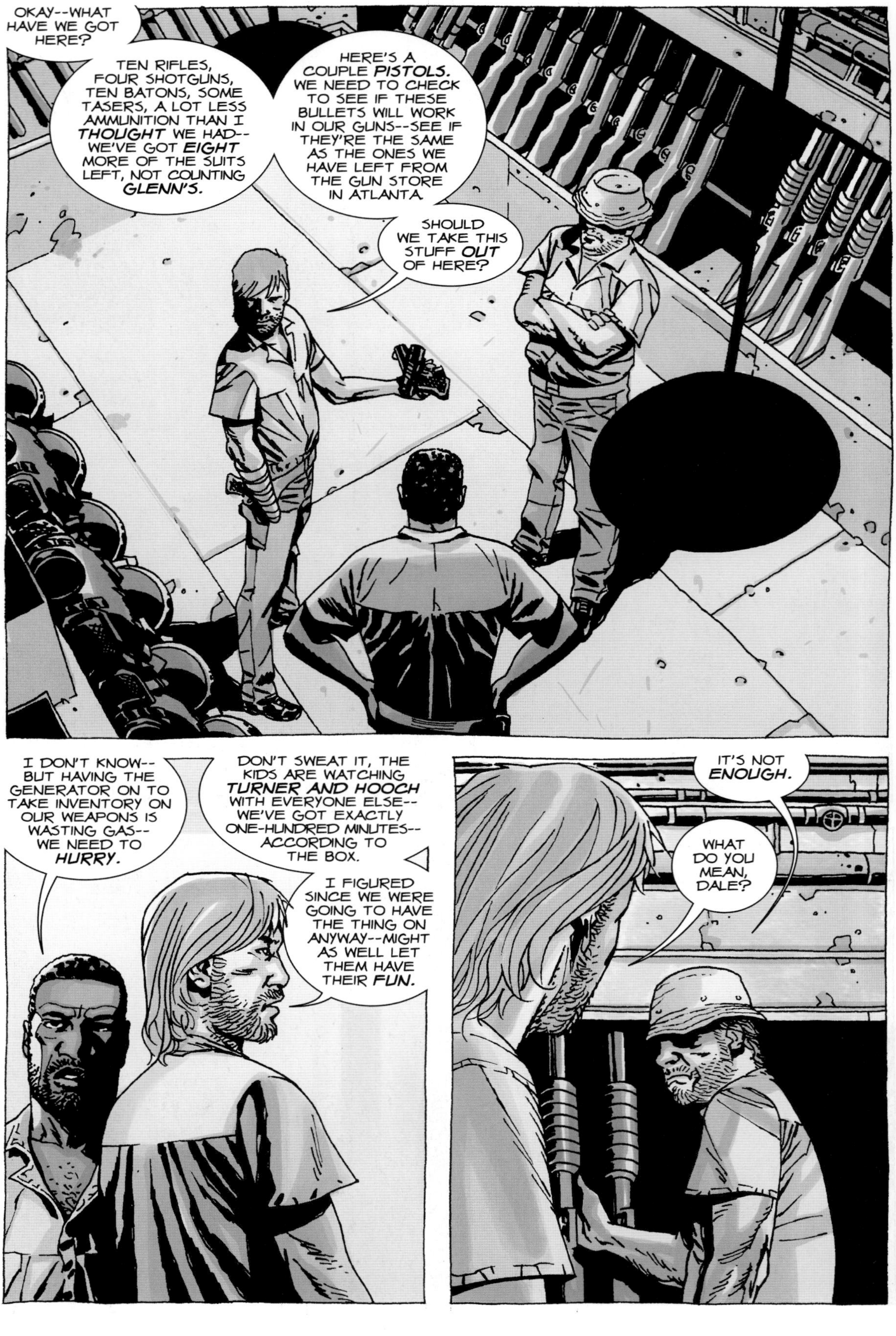
OKAY--WHAT HAVE WE GOT HERE?
TEN RIFLES, FOUR SHOTGUNS, TEN BATONS, SOME TASERS, A LOT LESS AMMUNITION THAN I THOUGHT WE HAD-- WE'VE GOT EIGHT MORE OF THE SUITS LEFT, NOT COUNTING GLENN'S.
HERE'S A COUPLE PISTOLS. WE NEED TO CHECK TO SEE IF THESE BULLETS WILL WORK IN OUR GUNS--SEE IF THEY'RE THE SAME AS THE ONES WE HAVE LEFT FROM THE GUN STORE IN ATLANTA.
SHOULD WE TAKE THIS STUFF OUT OF HERE?
I DON'T KNOW-- BUT HAVING THE GENERATOR ON TO TAKE INVENTORY ON OUR WEAPONS IS WASTING GAS-- WE NEED TO HURRY.
DON'T SWEAT IT, THE KIDS ARE WATCHING TURNER AND HOOCH WITH EVERYONE ELSE-- WE'VE GOT EXACTLY ONE-HUNDRED MINUTES-- ACCORDING TO THE BOX.
I FIGURED SINCE WE WERE GOING TO HAVE THE THING ON ANYWAY--MIGHT AS WELL LET THEM HAVE THEIR FUN.
IT'S NOT ENOUGH.
WHAT DO YOU MEAN, DALE?

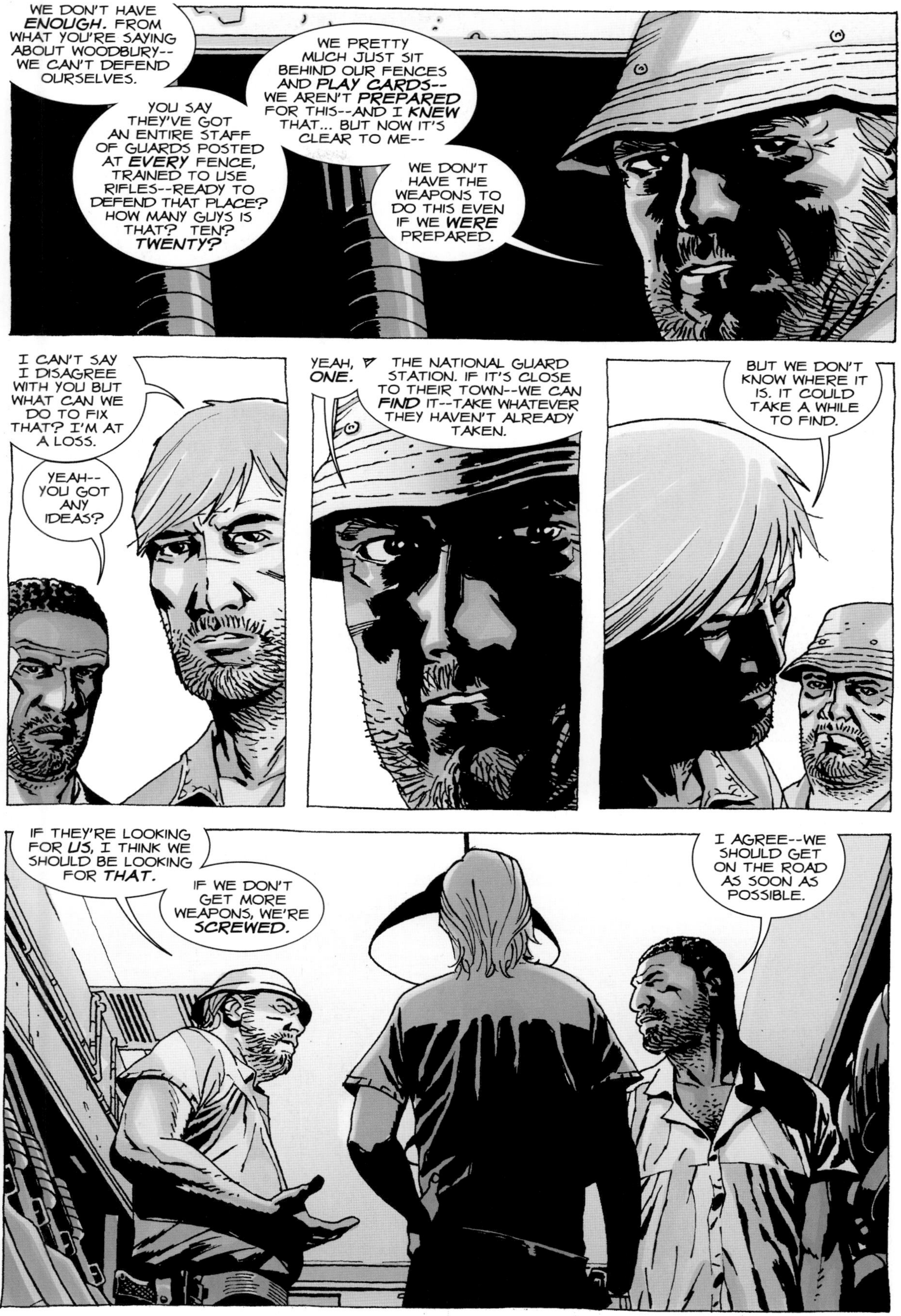
WE DON'T HAVE ENOUGH. FROM WHAT YOU'RE SAYING ABOUT WOODBURY-- WE CAN'T DEFEND OURSELVES.
YOU SAY THEY'VE GOT AN ENTIRE STAFF OF GUARDS POSTED AT EVERY FENCE, TRAINED TO USE RIFLES--READY TO DEFEND THAT PLACE? HOW MANY GUYS IS THAT? TEN? TWENTY?
WE PRETTY MUCH JUST SIT BEHIND OUR FENCES AND PLAY CARDS-- WE AREN'T PREPARED FOR THIS--AND I KNEW THAT... BUT NOW IT'S CLEAR TO ME--
WE DON'T HAVE THE WEAPONS TO DO THIS EVEN IF WE WERE PREPARED.
I CAN'T SAY I DISAGREE WITH YOU BUT WHAT CAN WE DO TO FIX THAT? I'M AT A LOSS.
YEAH-- YOU GOT ANY IDEAS?
YEAH, ONE.
THE NATIONAL GUARD STATION. IF IT'S CLOSE TO THEIR TOWN--WE CAN FIND IT--TAKE WHATEVER THEY HAVEN'T ALREADY TAKEN.
BUT WE DON'T KNOW WHERE IT IS. IT COULD TAKE A WHILE TO FIND.
IF THEY'RE LOOKING FOR US, I THINK WE SHOULD BE LOOKING FOR THAT.
IF WE DON'T GET MORE WEAPONS, WE'RE SCREWED.
I AGREE--WE SHOULD GET ON THE ROAD AS SOON AS POSSIBLE.

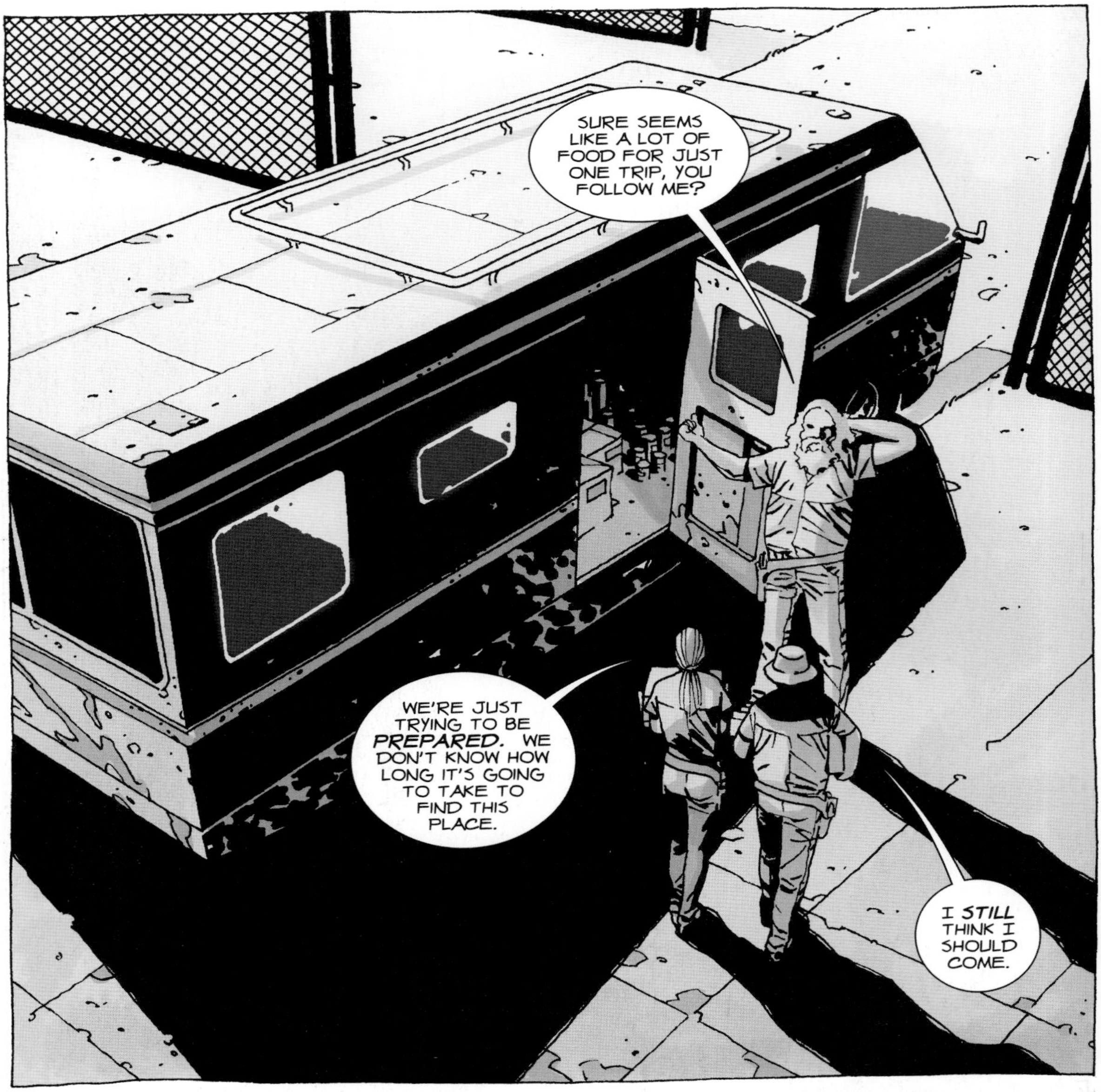
SURE SEEMS LIKE A LOT OF FOOD FOR JUST ONE TRIP, YOU FOLLOW ME?
WE'RE JUST TRYING TO BE PREPARED. WE DON'T KNOW HOW LONG IT'S GOING TO TAKE TO FIND THIS PLACE.
I STILL THINK I SHOULD COME.

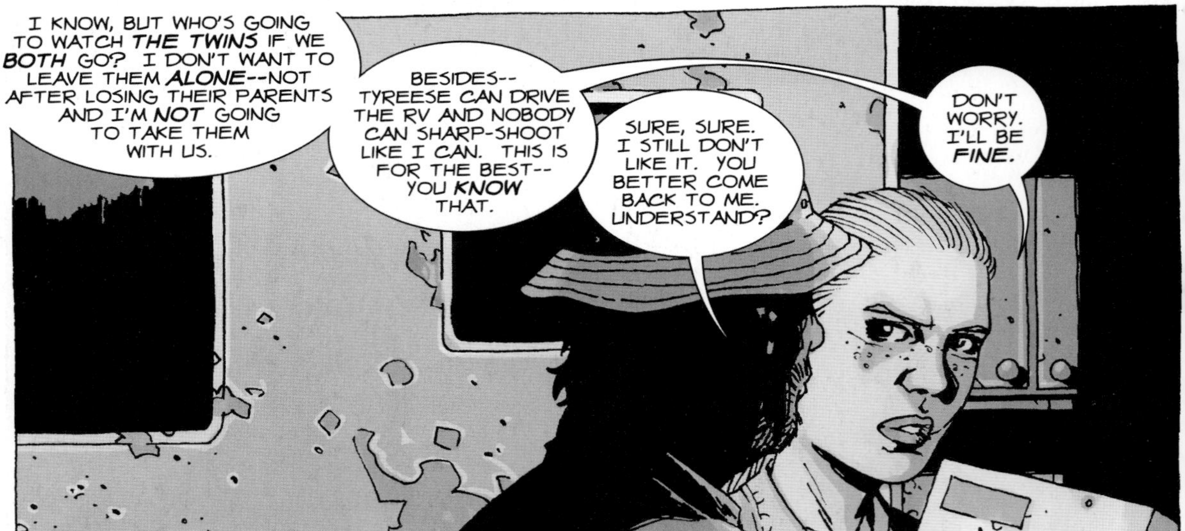
I KNOW, BUT WHO'S GOING TO WATCH THE TWINS IF WE BOTH GO? I DON'T WANT TO LEAVE THEM ALONE--NOT AFTER LOSING THEIR PARENTS AND I'M NOT GOING TO TAKE THEM WITH US.
BESIDES-- TYREESE CAN DRIVE THE RV AND NOBODY CAN SHARP-SHOOT LIKE I CAN. THIS IS FOR THE BEST-- YOU KNOW THAT.
SURE, SURE. I STILL DON'T LIKE IT. YOU BETTER COME BACK TO ME. UNDERSTAND?
DON'T WORRY. I'LL BE FINE.

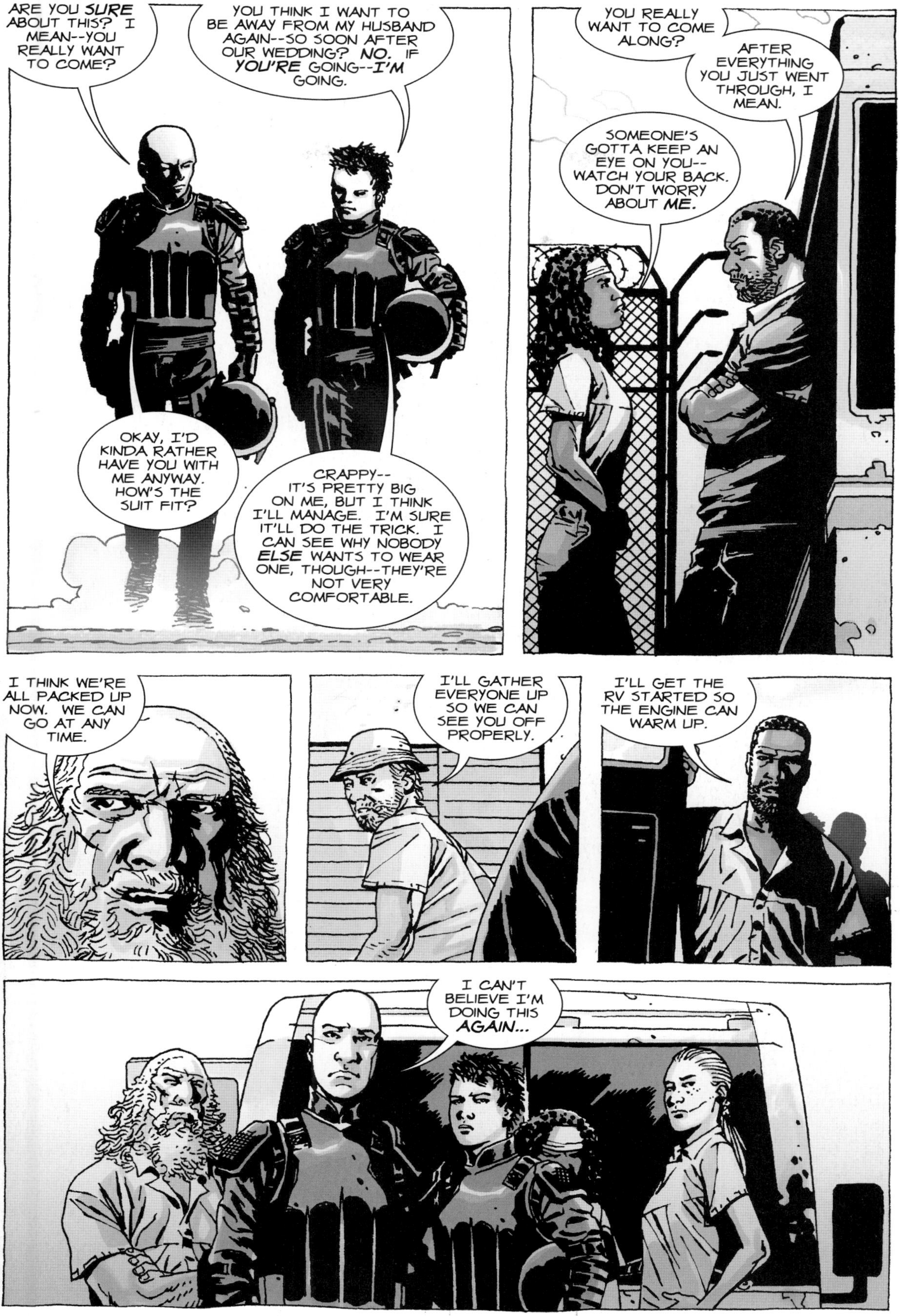

ARE YOU SURE ABOUT THIS? I MEAN--YOU REALLY WANT TO COME?
YOU THINK I WANT TO BE AWAY FROM MY HUSBAND AGAIN--SO SOON AFTER OUR WEDDING? NO. IF YOU'RE GOING--I'M GOING.
OKAY, I'D KINDA RATHER HAVE YOU WITH ME ANYWAY. HOW'S THE SUIT FIT?
CRAPPY-- IT'S PRETTY BIG ON ME, BUT I THINK I'LL MANAGE. I'M SURE IT'LL DO THE TRICK. I CAN SEE WHY NOBODY ELSE WANTS TO WEAR ONE, THOUGH--THEY'RE NOT VERY COMFORTABLE.
YOU REALLY WANT TO COME ALONG?
AFTER EVERYTHING YOU JUST WENT THROUGH, I MEAN.
SOMEONE'S GOTTA KEEP AN EYE ON YOU-- WATCH YOUR BACK. DON'T WORRY ABOUT ME.
I THINK WE'RE ALL PACKED UP NOW. WE CAN GO AT ANY TIME.
I'LL GATHER EVERYONE UP SO WE CAN SEE YOU OFF PROPERLY.
I'LL GET THE RV STARTED SO THE ENGINE CAN WARM UP.
I CAN'T BELIEVE I'M DOING THIS AGAIN...

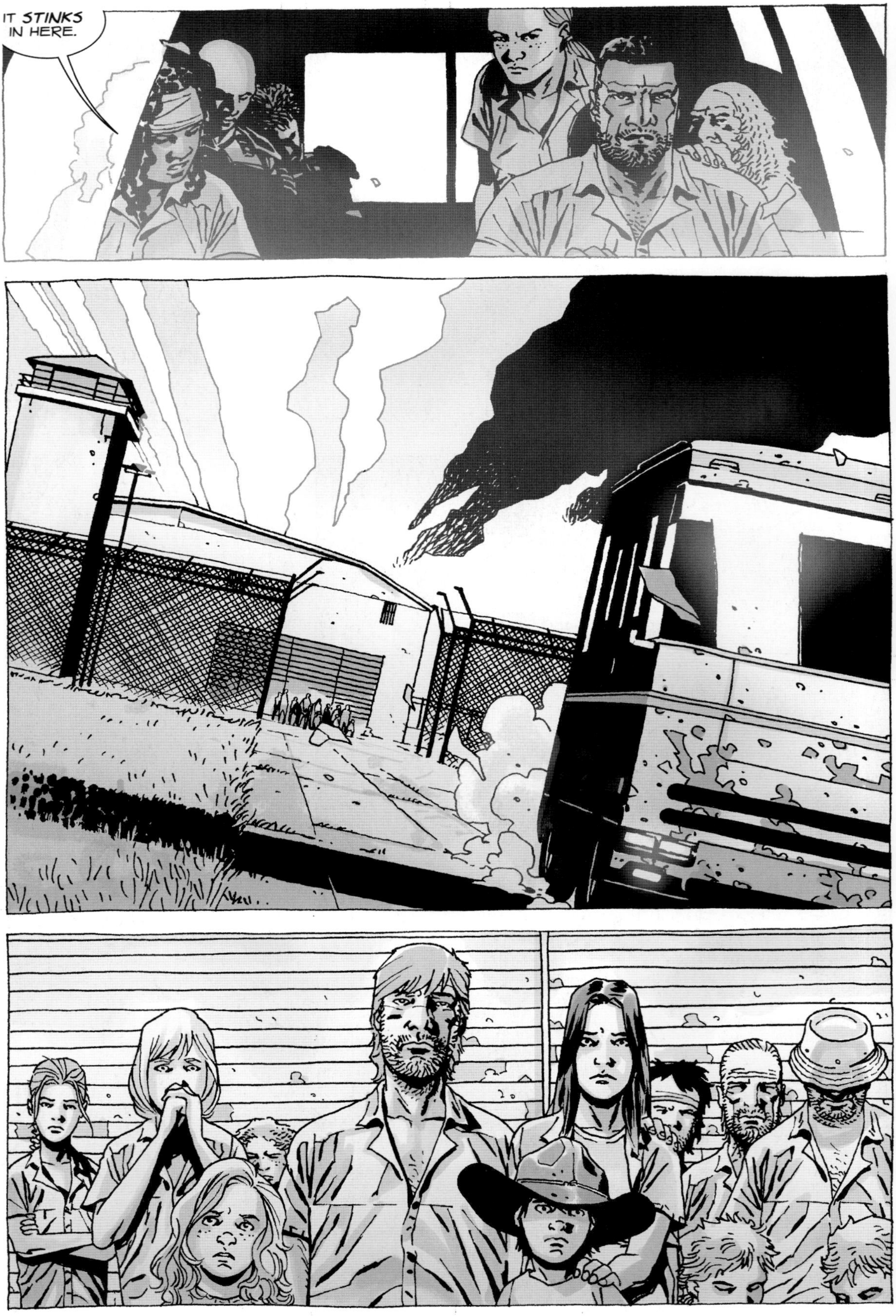
IT STINKS IN HERE.

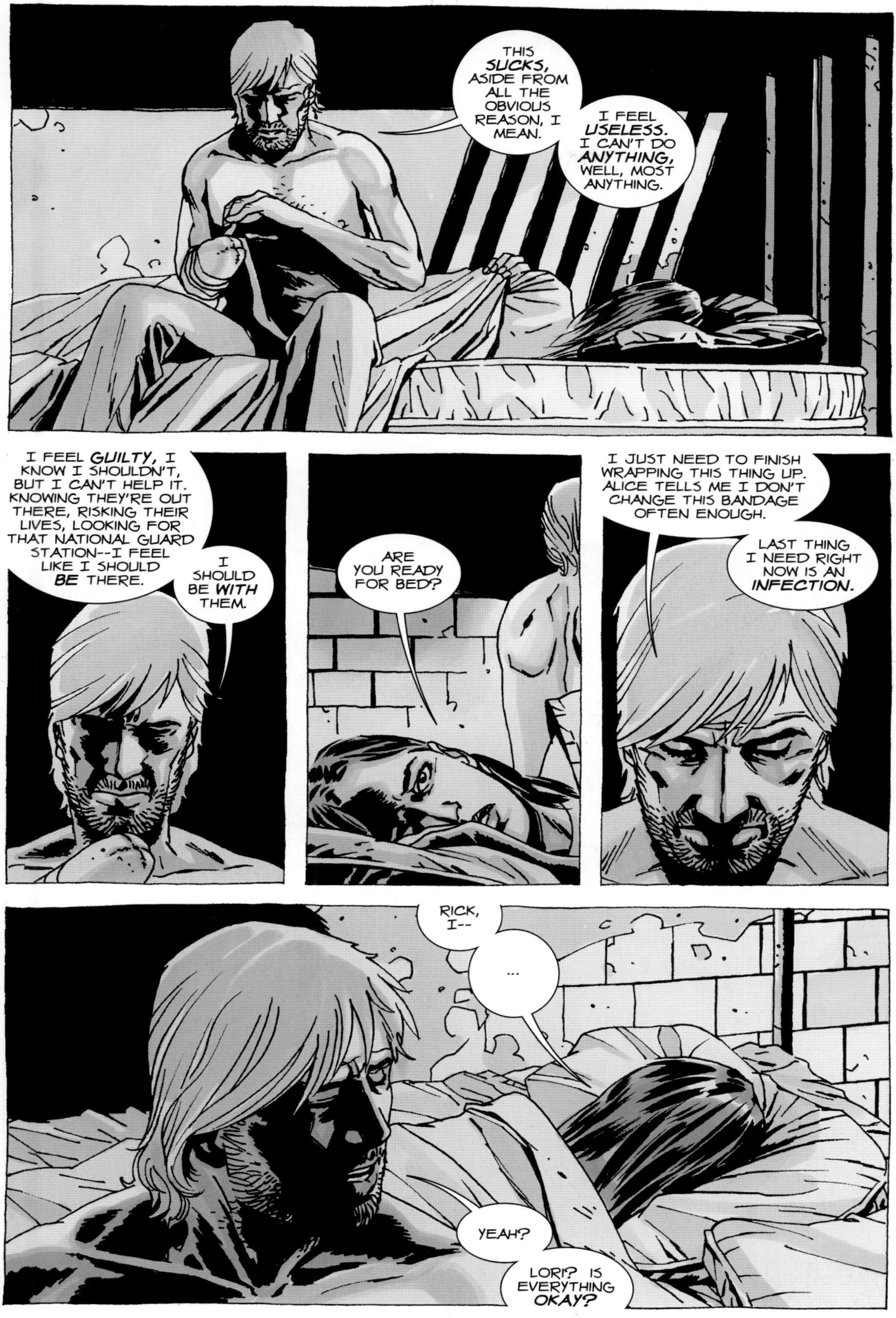
THIS SUCKS, ASIDE FROM ALL THE OBVIOUS REASON, I MEAN.
I FEEL USELESS. I CAN'T DO ANYTHING, WELL, MOST ANYTHING.
I FEEL GUILTY, I KNOW I SHOULDN'T, BUT I CAN'T HELP IT. KNOWING THEY'RE OUT THERE, RISKING THEIR LIVES, LOOKING FOR THAT NATIONAL GUARD STATION--I FEEL LIKE I SHOULD BE THERE.
I SHOULD BE WITH THEM.
ARE YOU READY FOR BED?
I JUST NEED TO FINISH WRAPPING THIS THING UP. ALICE TELLS ME I DON'T CHANGE THIS BANDAGE OFTEN ENOUGH.
LAST THING I NEED RIGHT NOW IS AN INFECTION.
RICK, I--
...
YEAH?
LORI? IS EVERYTHING OKAY?

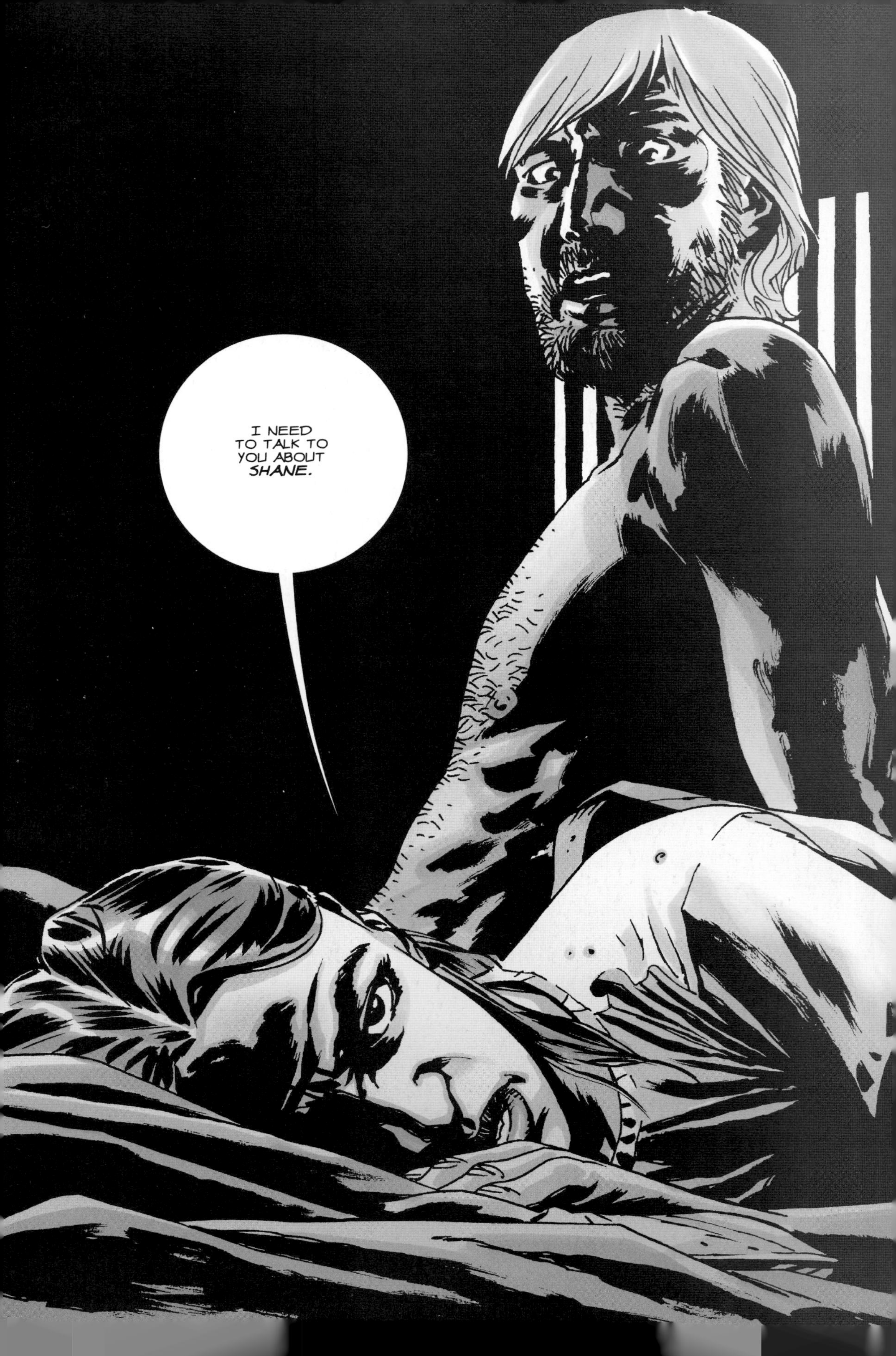
I NEED TO TALK TO YOU ABOUT SHANE.

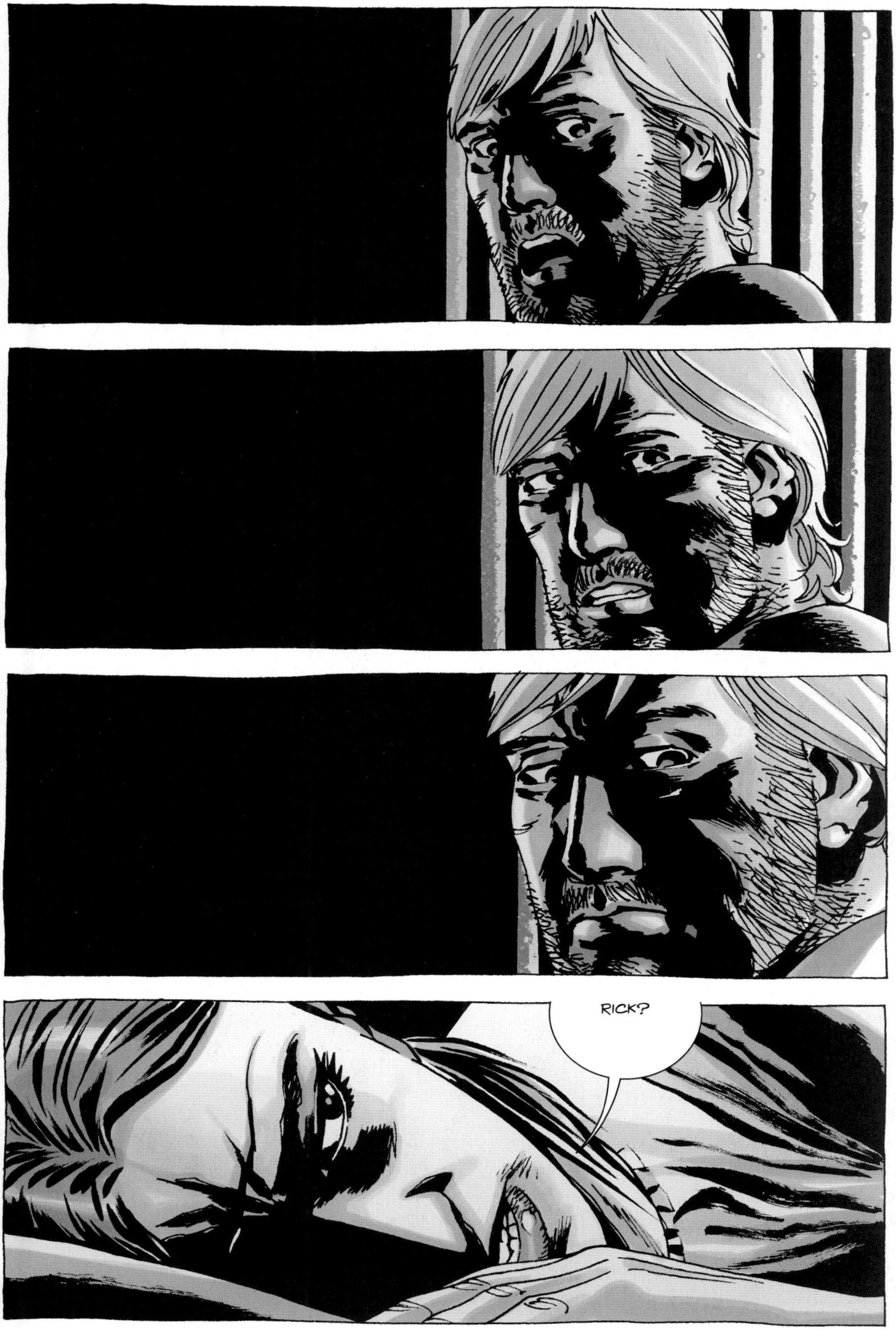
RICK?

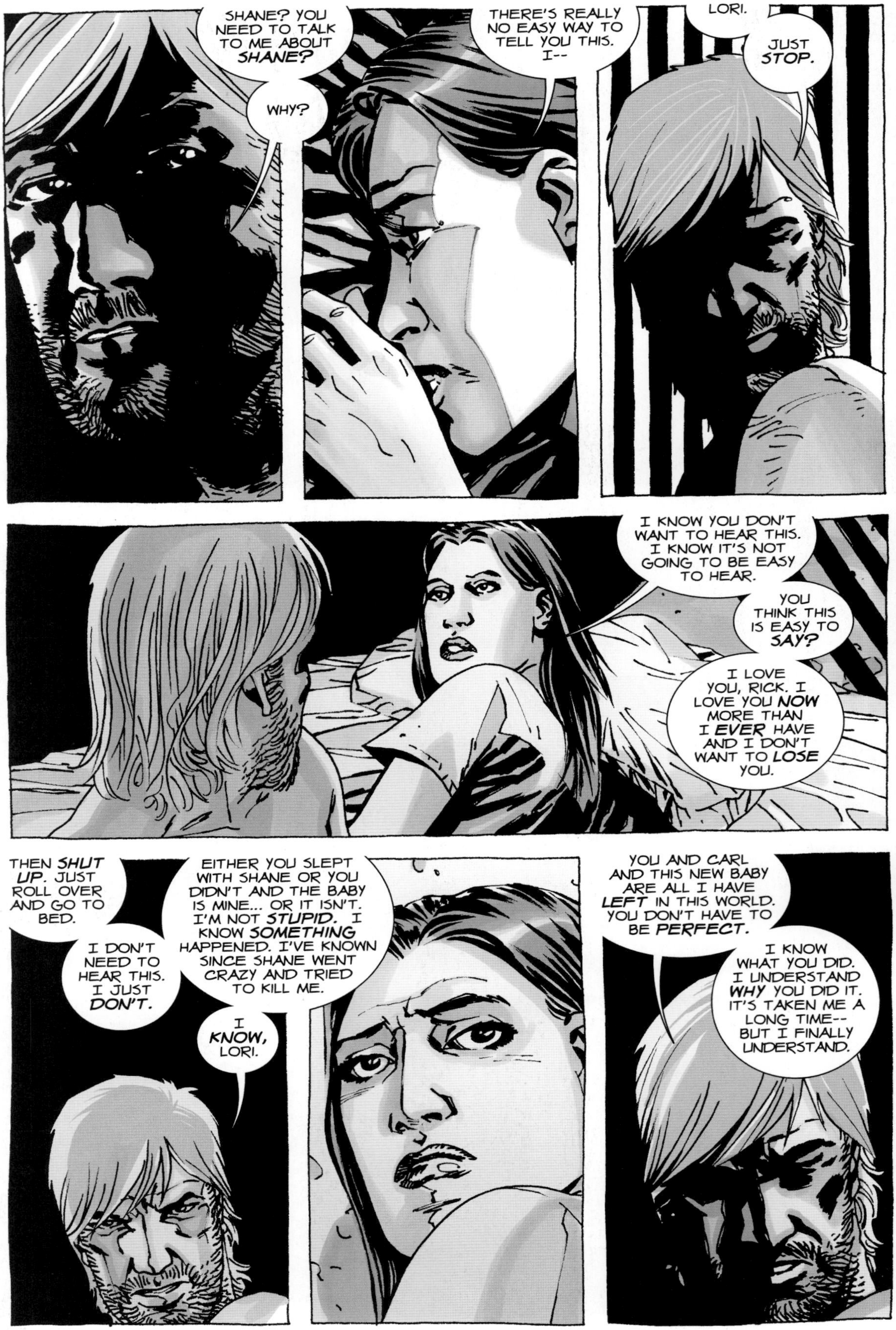

SHANE? YOU NEED TO TALK TO ME ABOUT SHANE?
WHY?
THERE'S REALLY NO EASY WAY TO TELL YOU THIS. I--
LORI.
JUST STOP.
I KNOW YOU DON'T WANT TO HEAR THIS. I KNOW IT'S NOT GOING TO BE EASY TO HEAR.
YOU THINK THIS IS EASY TO SAY?
I LOVE YOU, RICK. I LOVE YOU NOW MORE THAN I EVER HAVE AND I DON'T WANT TO LOSE YOU.
THEN SHUT UP. JUST ROLL OVER AND GO TO BED.
I DON'T NEED TO HEAR THIS. I JUST DON'T.
EITHER YOU SLEPT WITH SHANE OR YOU DIDN'T AND THE BABY IS MINE... OR IT ISN'T. I'M NOT STUPID. I KNOW SOMETHING HAPPENED. I'VE KNOWN SINCE SHANE WENT CRAZY AND TRIED TO KILL ME.
I KNOW, LORI.
YOU AND CARL AND THIS NEW BABY ARE ALL I HAVE LEFT IN THIS WORLD. YOU DON'T HAVE TO BE PERFECT.
I KNOW WHAT YOU DID. I UNDERSTAND WHY YOU DID IT. IT'S TAKEN ME A LONG TIME-- BUT I FINALLY UNDERSTAND.

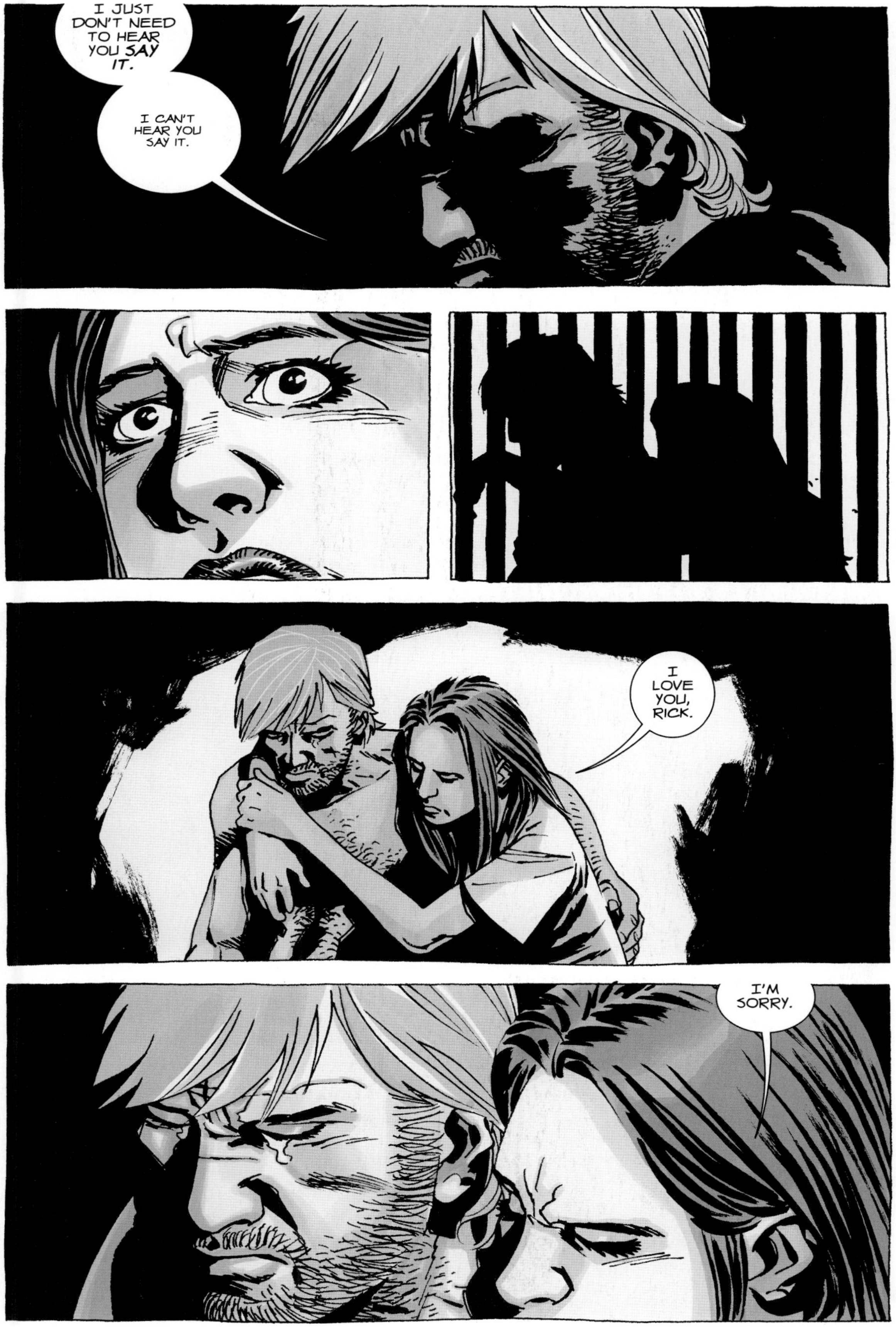
I JUST DON'T NEED TO HEAR YOU SAY IT.
I CAN'T HEAR YOU SAY IT.
I LOVE YOU, RICK.
I'M SORRY.

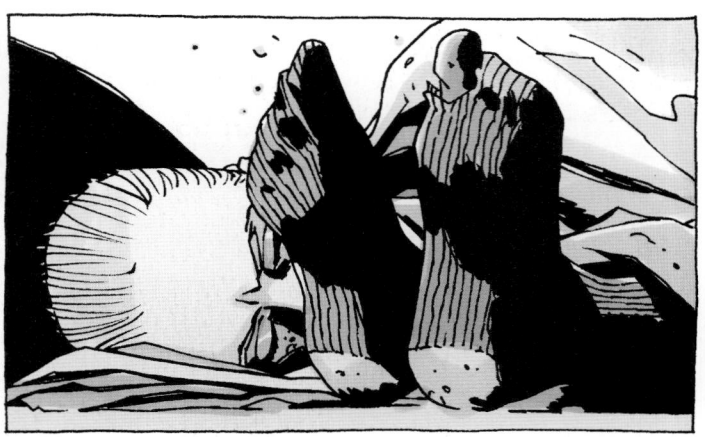

YEAGGH!

EW!

EW!

EW!

HUNGH?

NOW I REMEMBER WHY I HATED LIVING IN THIS RV SO DAMN MUCH.

OH GOOD--YOU'RE AWAKE. I WANTED TO TAKE A QUICK SNOOZE BEFORE WE HIT THE ROAD. YOU FOLLOW ME?

I'M BEAT.

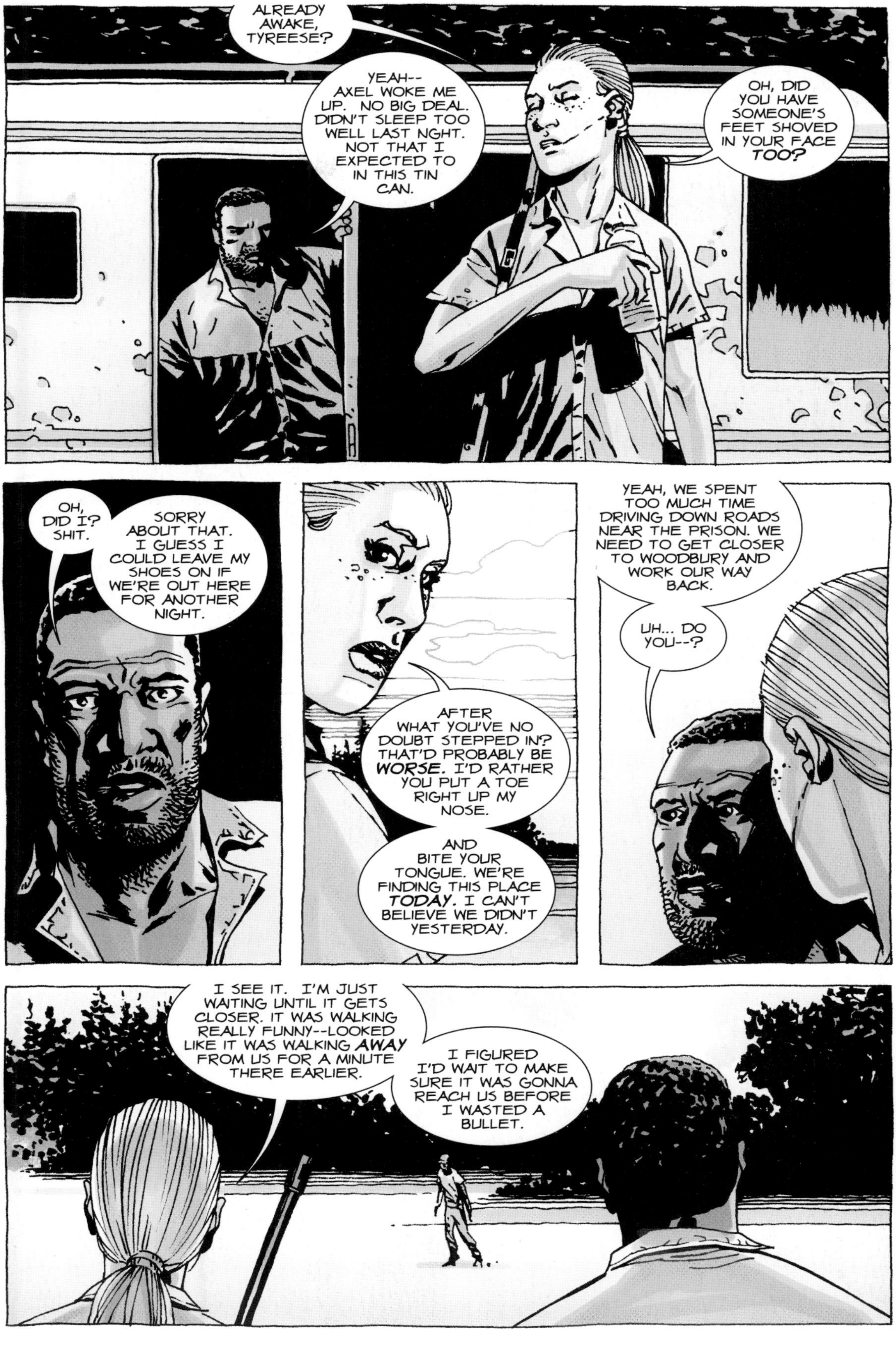

ALREADY AWAKE, TYREESE?
YEAH-- AXEL WOKE ME UP. NO BIG DEAL. DIDN'T SLEEP TOO WELL LAST NGHT. NOT THAT I EXPECTED TO IN THIS TIN CAN.
OH, DID YOU HAVE SOMEONE'S FEET SHOVED IN YOUR FACE TOO?
OH, DID I? SHIT.
SORRY ABOUT THAT. I GUESS I COULD LEAVE MY SHOES ON IF WE'RE OUT HERE FOR ANOTHER NIGHT.
AFTER WHAT YOU'VE NO DOUBT STEPPED IN? THAT'D PROBABLY BE WORSE. I'D RATHER YOU PUT A TOE RIGHT UP MY NOSE.
AND BITE YOUR TONGUE. WE'RE FINDING THIS PLACE TODAY. I CAN'T BELIEVE WE DIDN'T YESTERDAY.
YEAH, WE SPENT TOO MUCH TIME DRIVING DOWN ROADS NEAR THE PRISON. WE NEED TO GET CLOSER TO WOODBURY AND WORK OUR WAY BACK.
UH... DO YOU--?
I SEE IT. I'M JUST WAITING UNTIL IT GETS CLOSER. IT WAS WALKING REALLY FUNNY--LOOKED LIKE IT WAS WALKING AWAY FROM US FOR A MINUTE THERE EARLIER.
I FIGURED I'D WAIT TO MAKE SURE IT WAS GONNA REACH US BEFORE I WASTED A BULLET.

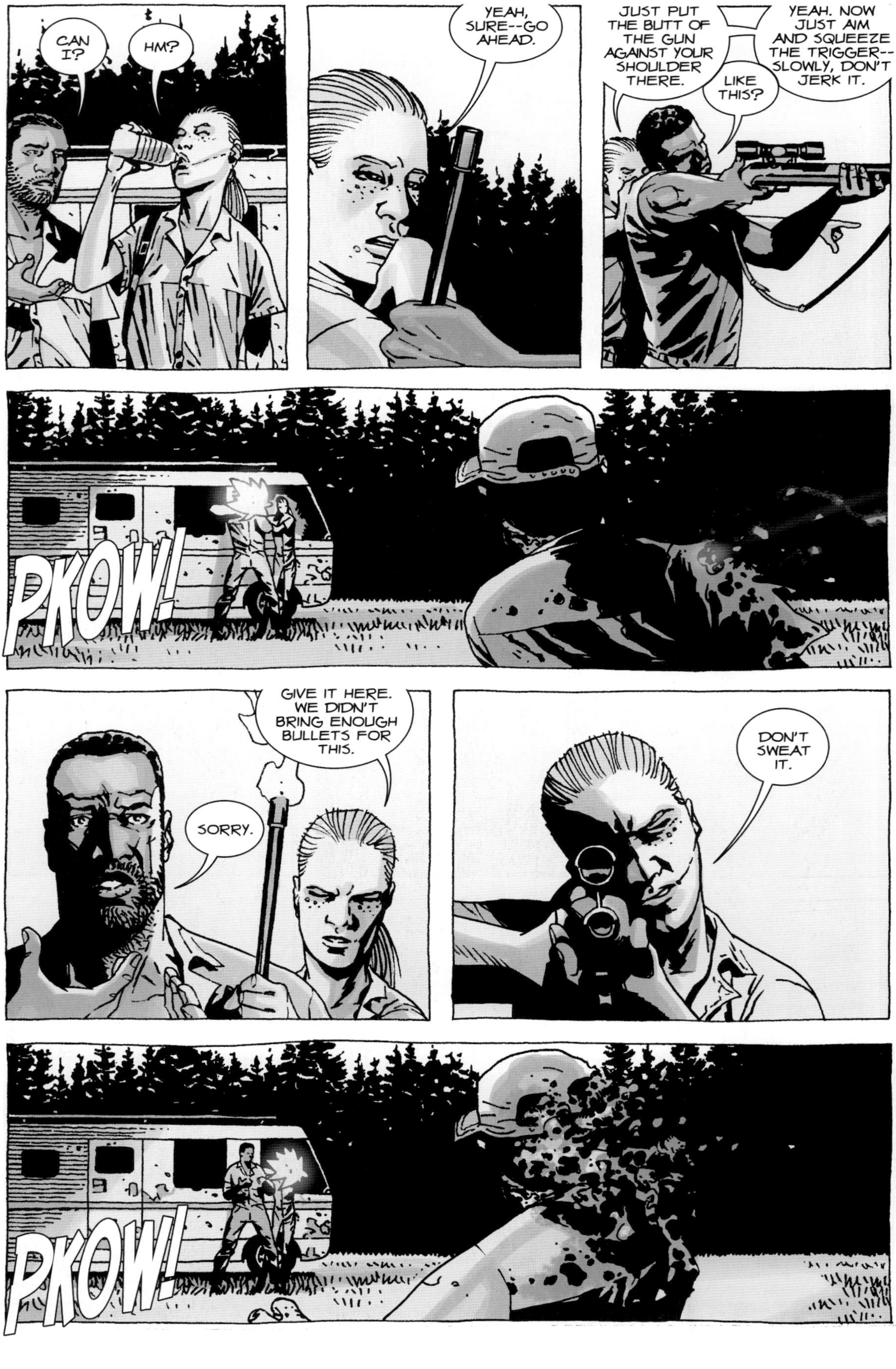
CAN I?
HM?
YEAH, SURE--GO AHEAD.
JUST PUT THE BUTT OF THE GUN AGAINST YOUR SHOULDER THERE.
LIKE THIS?
YEAH. NOW JUST AIM AND SQUEEZE THE TRIGGER--SLOWLY, DON'T JERK IT.
PKOW!
GIVE IT HERE. WE DIDN'T BRING ENOUGH BULLETS FOR THIS.
SORRY.
DON'T SWEAT IT.
PKOW!

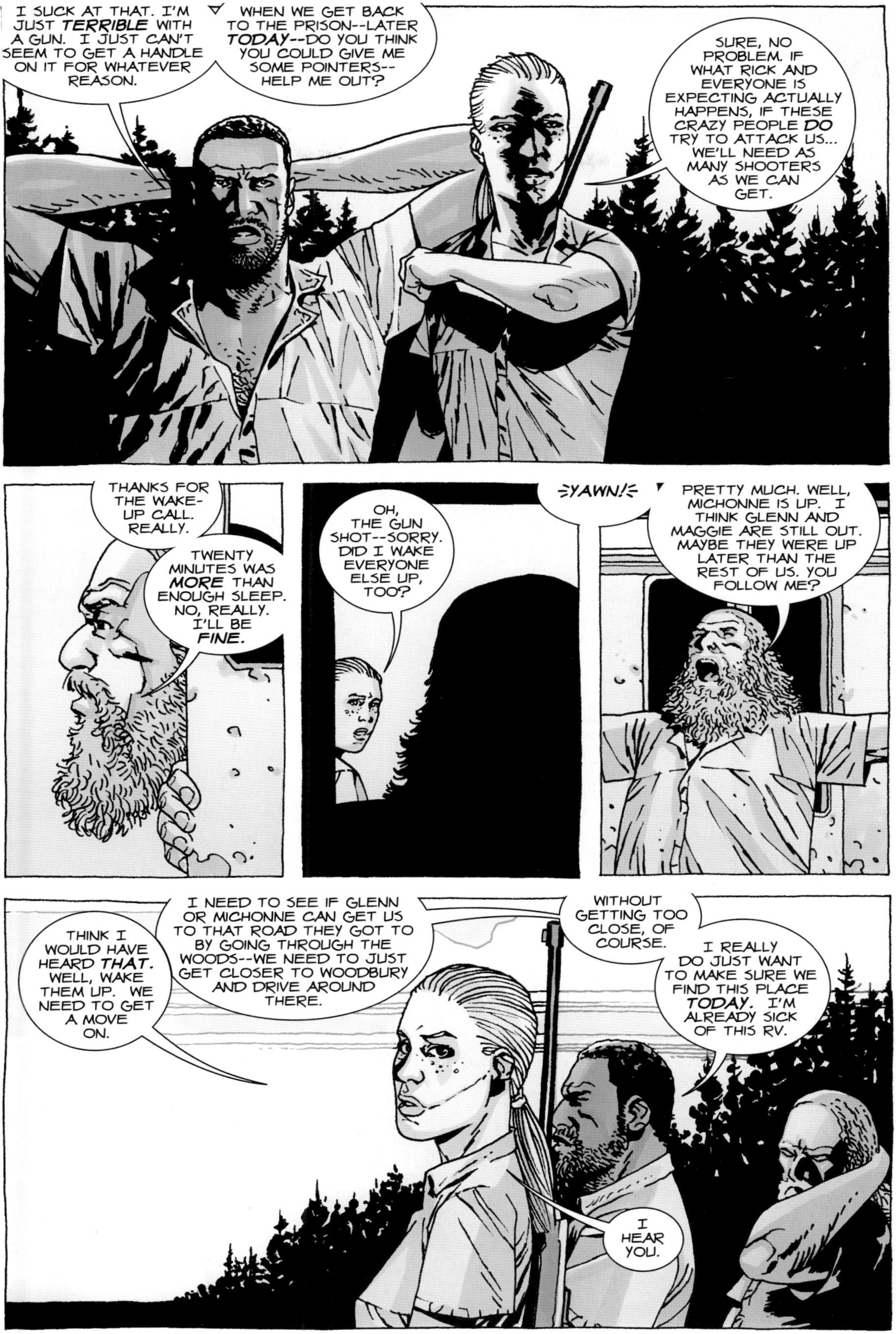
I SUCK AT THAT. I'M JUST TERRIBLE WITH A GUN. I JUST CAN'T SEEM TO GET A HANDLE ON IT FOR WHATEVER REASON.
WHEN WE GET BACK TO THE PRISON--LATER TODAY--DO YOU THINK YOU COULD GIVE ME SOME POINTERS--HELP ME OUT?
SURE, NO PROBLEM. IF WHAT RICK AND EVERYONE IS EXPECTING ACTUALLY HAPPENS, IF THESE CRAZY PEOPLE DO TRY TO ATTACK US... WE'LL NEED AS MANY SHOOTERS AS WE CAN GET.
THANKS FOR THE WAKE-UP CALL. REALLY.
TWENTY MINUTES WAS MORE THAN ENOUGH SLEEP. NO, REALLY. I'LL BE FINE.
OH, THE GUN SHOT--SORRY. DID I WAKE EVERYONE ELSE UP, TOO?
YAWN!
PRETTY MUCH. WELL, MICHONNE IS UP. I THINK GLENN AND MAGGIE ARE STILL OUT. MAYBE THEY WERE UP LATER THAN THE REST OF US. YOU FOLLOW ME?
THINK I WOULD HAVE HEARD THAT. WELL, WAKE THEM UP. WE NEED TO GET A MOVE ON.
I NEED TO SEE IF GLENN OR MICHONNE CAN GET US TO THAT ROAD THEY GOT TO BY GOING THROUGH THE WOODS--WE NEED TO JUST GET CLOSER TO WOODBURY AND DRIVE AROUND THERE.
WITHOUT GETTING TOO CLOSE, OF COURSE.
I REALLY DO JUST WANT TO MAKE SURE WE FIND THIS PLACE TODAY. I'M ALREADY SICK OF THIS RV.
I HEAR YOU.

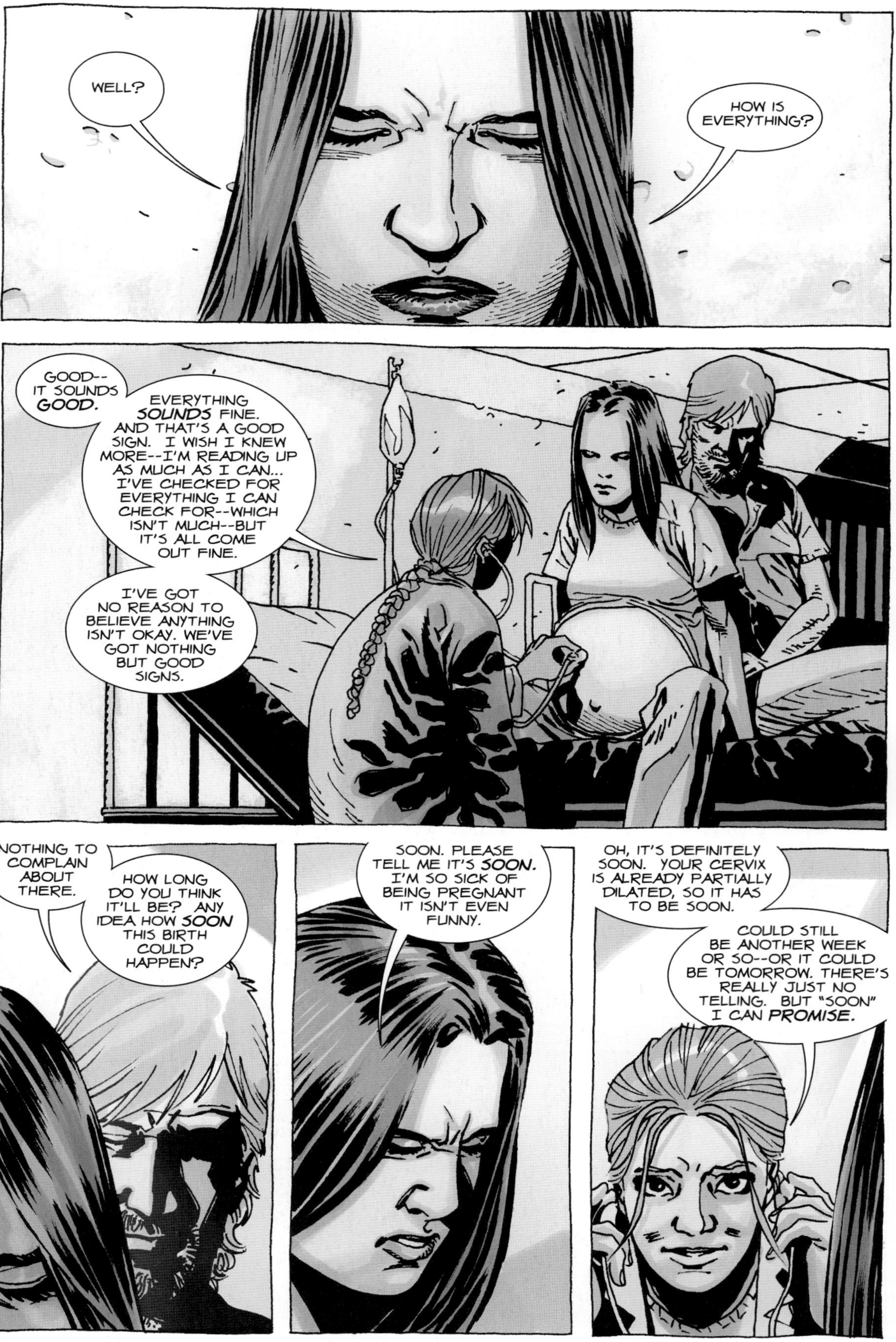
WELL?
HOW IS EVERYTHING?
GOOD-- IT SOUNDS GOOD.
EVERYTHING SOUNDS FINE. AND THAT'S A GOOD SIGN. I WISH I KNEW MORE--I'M READING UP AS MUCH AS I CAN... I'VE CHECKED FOR EVERYTHING I CAN CHECK FOR--WHICH ISN'T MUCH--BUT IT'S ALL COME OUT FINE.
I'VE GOT NO REASON TO BELIEVE ANYTHING ISN'T OKAY. WE'VE GOT NOTHING BUT GOOD SIGNS.
NOTHING TO COMPLAIN ABOUT THERE.
HOW LONG DO YOU THINK IT'LL BE? ANY IDEA HOW SOON THIS BIRTH COULD HAPPEN?
SOON. PLEASE TELL ME IT'S SOON. I'M SO SICK OF BEING PREGNANT IT ISN'T EVEN FUNNY.
OH, IT'S DEFINITELY SOON. YOUR CERVIX IS ALREADY PARTIALLY DILATED, SO IT HAS TO BE SOON.
COULD STILL BE ANOTHER WEEK OR SO--OR IT COULD BE TOMORROW. THERE'S REALLY JUST NO TELLING. BUT "SOON" I CAN PROMISE.

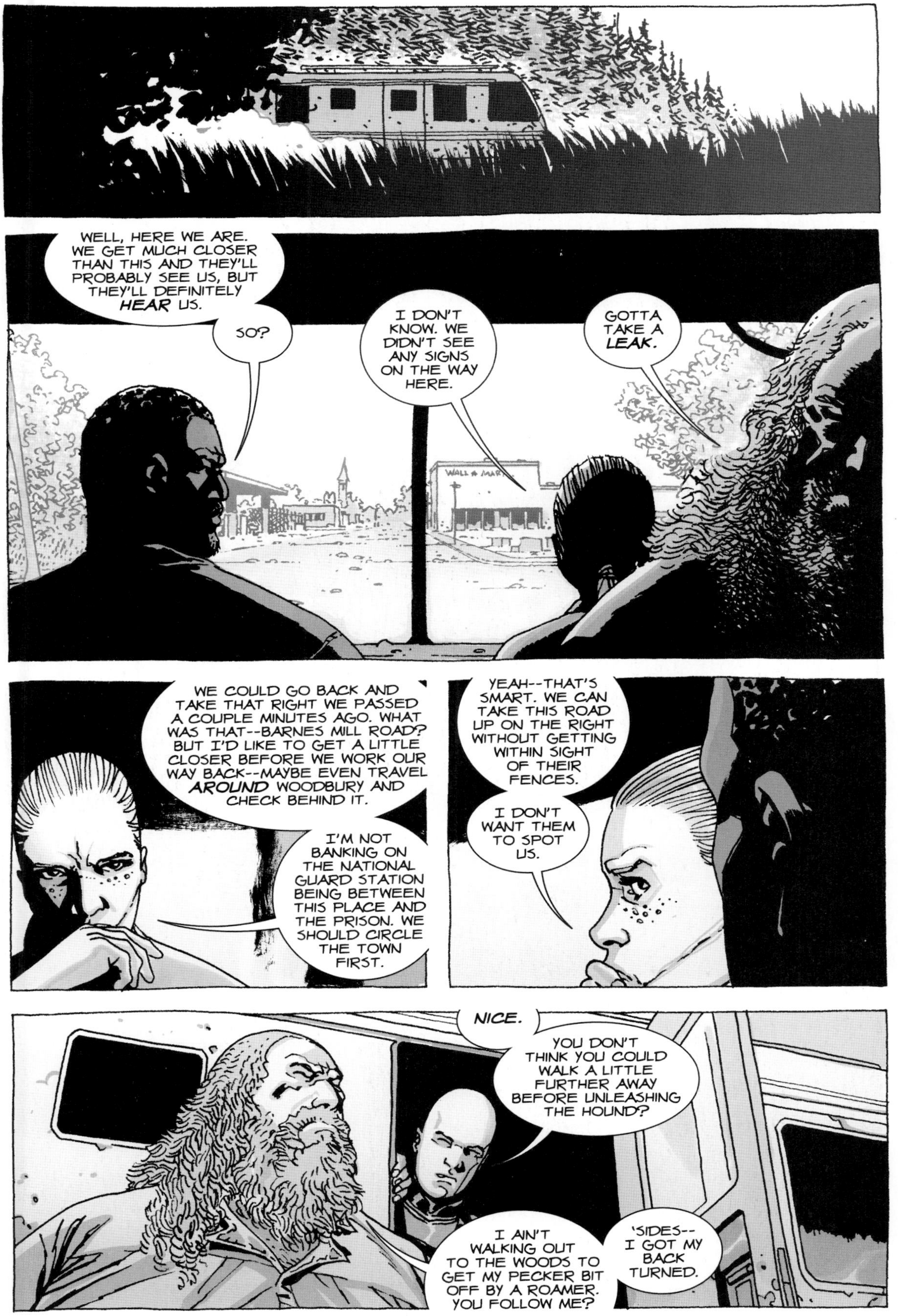
WELL, HERE WE ARE. WE GET MUCH CLOSER THAN THIS AND THEY'LL PROBABLY SEE US, BUT THEY'LL DEFINITELY HEAR US.
SO?
I DON'T KNOW. WE DIDN'T SEE ANY SIGNS ON THE WAY HERE.
GOTTA TAKE A LEAK.
WALL ✱ MART
WE COULD GO BACK AND TAKE THAT RIGHT WE PASSED A COUPLE MINUTES AGO. WHAT WAS THAT--BARNES MILL ROAD? BUT I'D LIKE TO GET A LITTLE CLOSER BEFORE WE WORK OUR WAY BACK--MAYBE EVEN TRAVEL AROUND WOODBURY AND CHECK BEHIND IT.
I'M NOT BANKING ON THE NATIONAL GUARD STATION BEING BETWEEN THIS PLACE AND THE PRISON. WE SHOULD CIRCLE THE TOWN FIRST.
YEAH--THAT'S SMART. WE CAN TAKE THIS ROAD UP ON THE RIGHT WITHOUT GETTING WITHIN SIGHT OF THEIR FENCES.
I DON'T WANT THEM TO SPOT US.
NICE.
YOU DON'T THINK YOU COULD WALK A LITTLE FURTHER AWAY BEFORE UNLEASHING THE HOUND?
I AIN'T WALKING OUT TO THE WOODS TO GET MY PECKER BIT OFF BY A ROAMER. YOU FOLLOW ME?
'SIDES-- I GOT MY BACK TURNED.

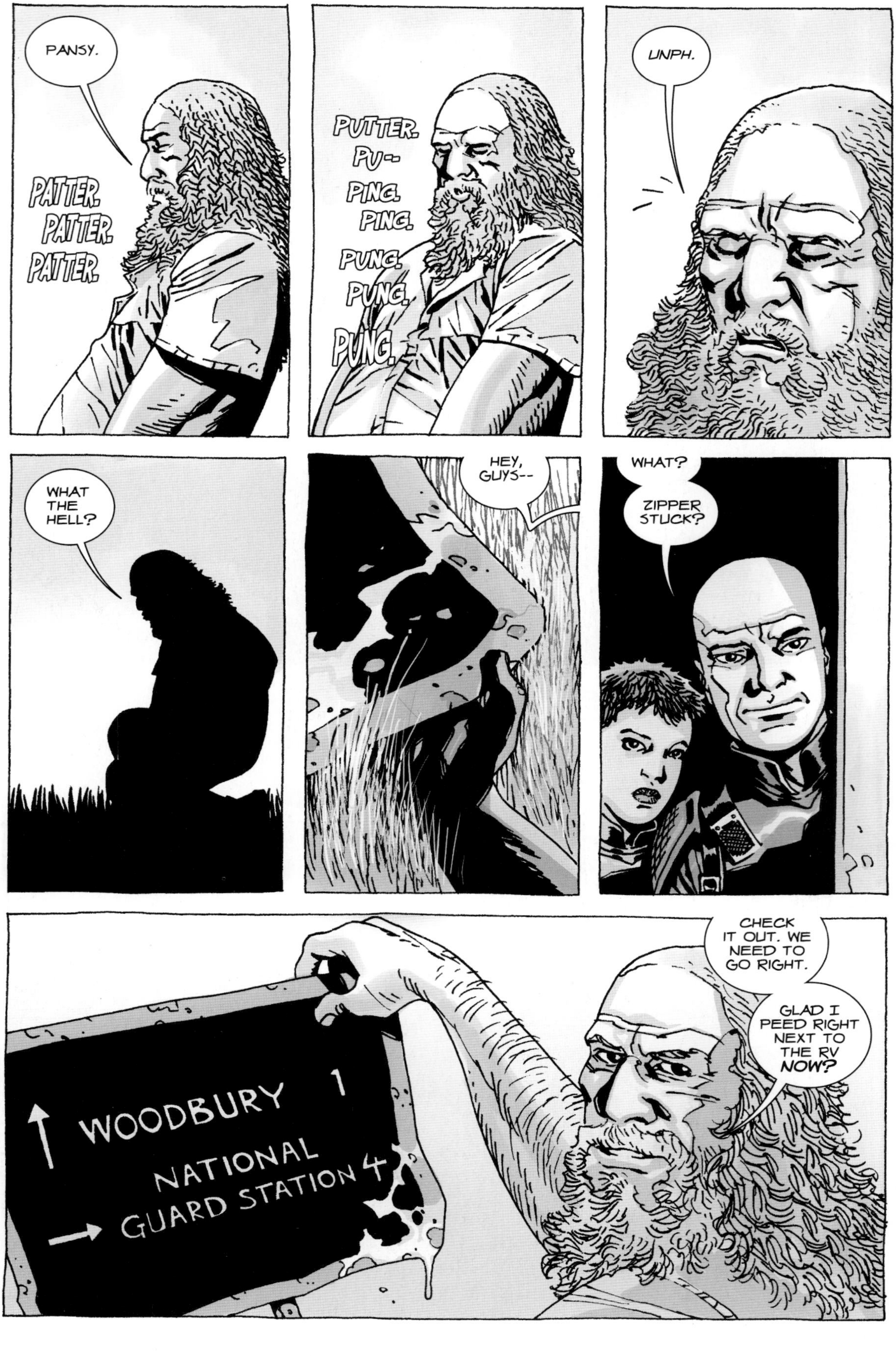
PANSY.
PATTER. PATTER. PATTER.
PUTTER. PU-- PING. PING. PUNG. PUNG. PUNG.
UNPH.
WHAT THE HELL?
HEY, GUYS--
WHAT?
ZIPPER STUCK?
WOODBURY 1
NATIONAL GUARD STATION 4
CHECK IT OUT. WE NEED TO GO RIGHT.
GLAD I PEED RIGHT NEXT TO THE RV NOW?

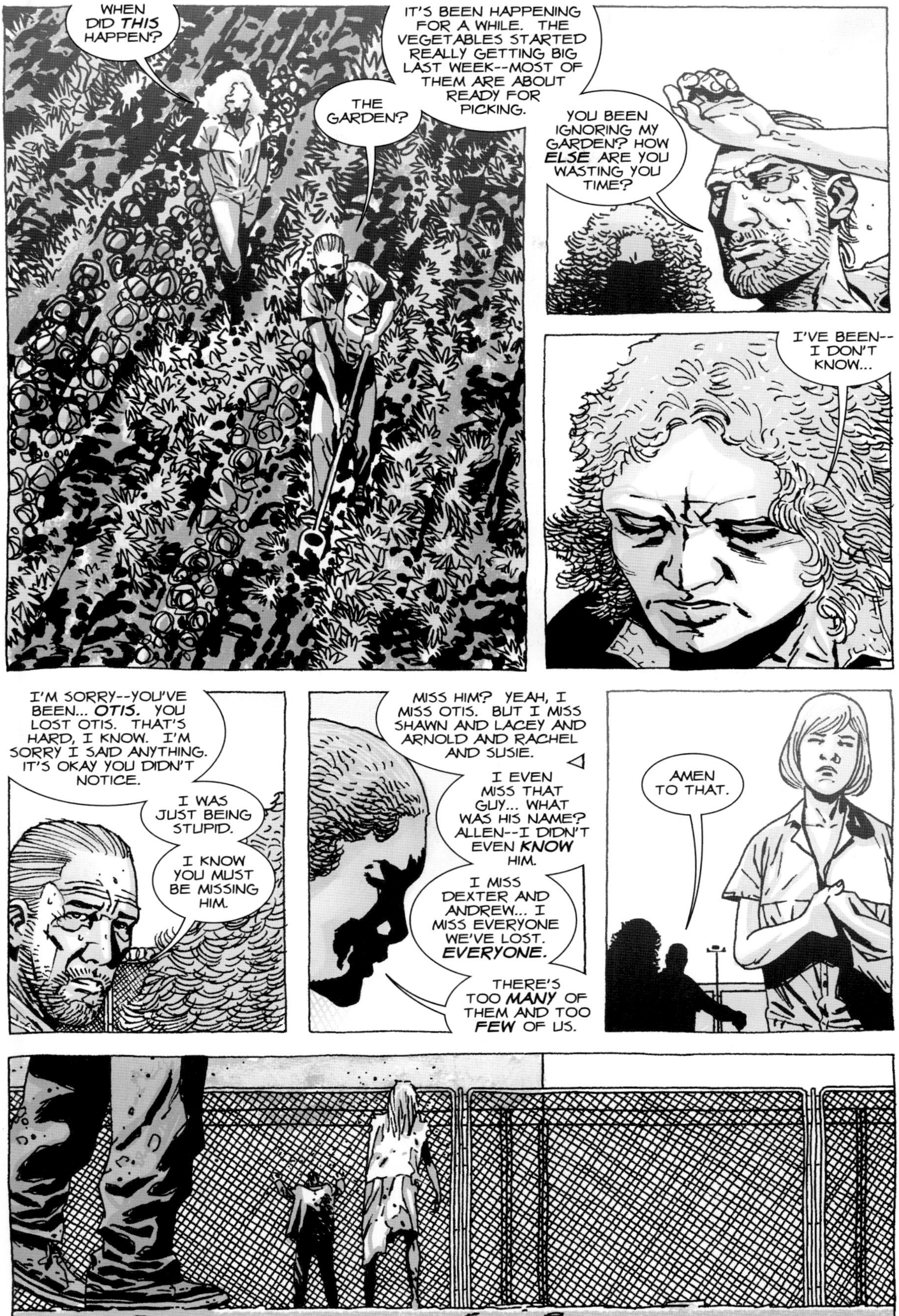
WHEN DID THIS HAPPEN?
THE GARDEN?
IT'S BEEN HAPPENING FOR A WHILE. THE VEGETABLES STARTED REALLY GETTING BIG LAST WEEK--MOST OF THEM ARE ABOUT READY FOR PICKING.
YOU BEEN IGNORING MY GARDEN? HOW ELSE ARE YOU WASTING YOU TIME?
I'VE BEEN-- I DON'T KNOW...
I'M SORRY--YOU'VE BEEN... OTIS. YOU LOST OTIS. THAT'S HARD, I KNOW. I'M SORRY I SAID ANYTHING. IT'S OKAY YOU DIDN'T NOTICE.
I WAS JUST BEING STUPID.
I KNOW YOU MUST BE MISSING HIM.
MISS HIM? YEAH, I MISS OTIS. BUT I MISS SHAWN AND LACEY AND ARNOLD AND RACHEL AND SUSIE.
I EVEN MISS THAT GUY... WHAT WAS HIS NAME? ALLEN--I DIDN'T EVEN KNOW HIM.
I MISS DEXTER AND ANDREW... I MISS EVERYONE WE'VE LOST. EVERYONE.
THERE'S TOO MANY OF THEM AND TOO FEW OF US.
AMEN TO THAT.

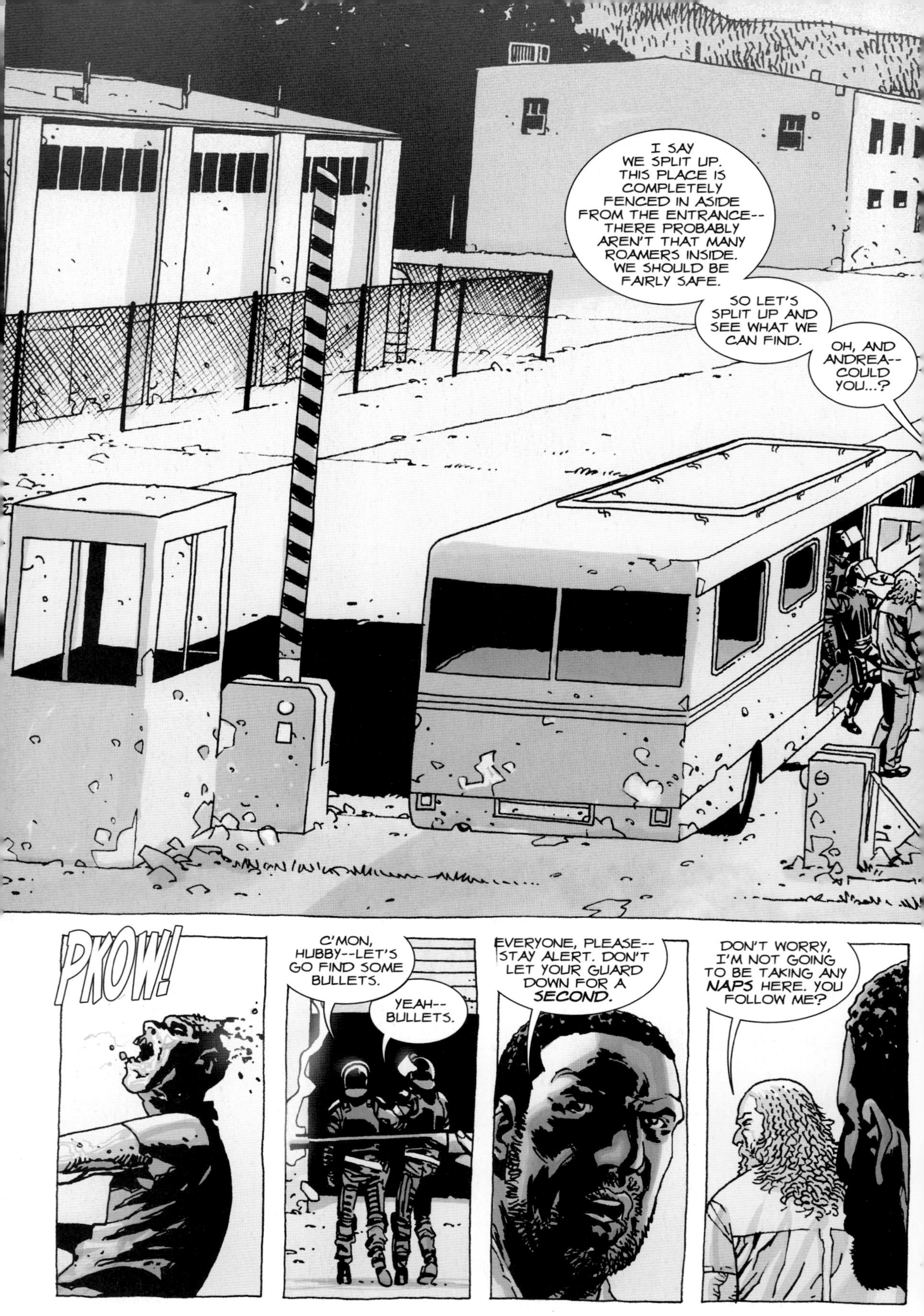
I SAY WE SPLIT UP. THIS PLACE IS COMPLETELY FENCED IN ASIDE FROM THE ENTRANCE-- THERE PROBABLY AREN'T THAT MANY ROAMERS INSIDE. WE SHOULD BE FAIRLY SAFE.
SO LET'S SPLIT UP AND SEE WHAT WE CAN FIND.
OH, AND ANDREA-- COULD YOU...?
PKOW!
C'MON, HUBBY--LET'S GO FIND SOME BULLETS.
YEAH-- BULLETS.
EVERYONE, PLEASE-- STAY ALERT. DON'T LET YOUR GUARD DOWN FOR A SECOND.
DON'T WORRY, I'M NOT GOING TO BE TAKING ANY NAPS HERE. YOU FOLLOW ME?

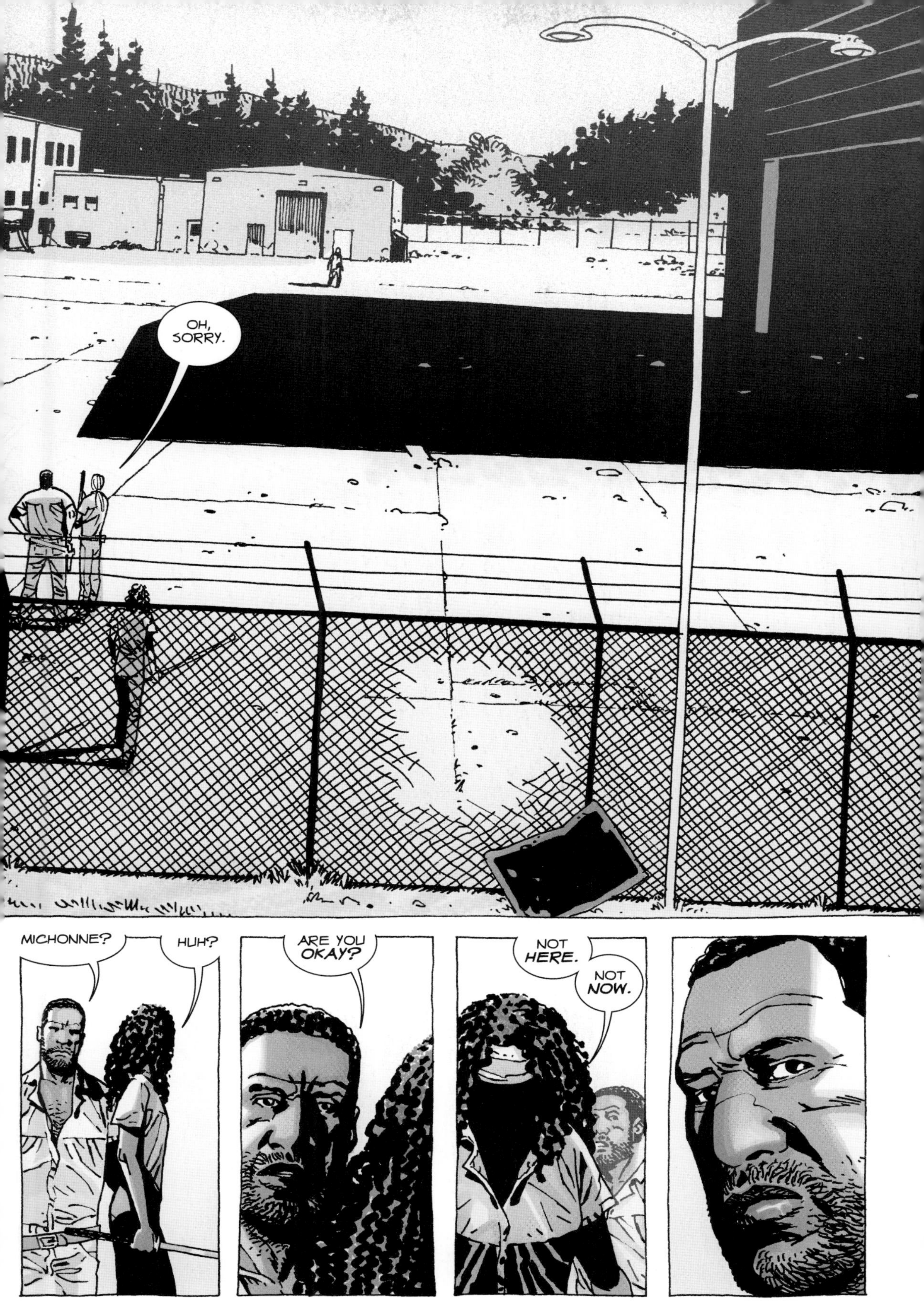
OH, SORRY.
MICHONNE?
HUH?
ARE YOU OKAY?
NOT HERE.
NOT NOW.

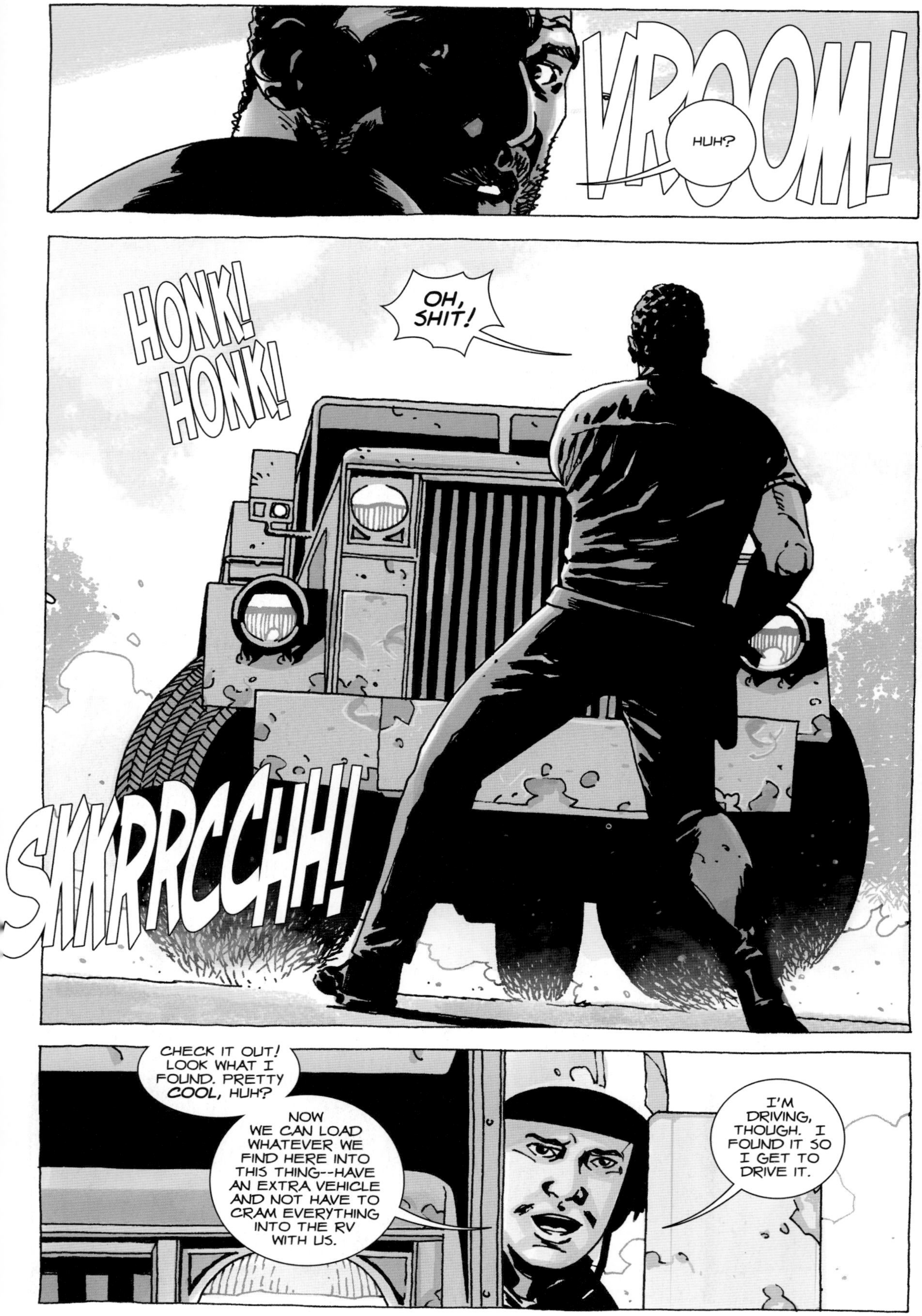
VROOM!
HUH?
HONK! HONK!
OH, SHIT!
SKKRRCCHH!
CHECK IT OUT! LOOK WHAT I FOUND. PRETTY COOL, HUH?
NOW WE CAN LOAD WHATEVER WE FIND HERE INTO THIS THING--HAVE AN EXTRA VEHICLE AND NOT HAVE TO CRAM EVERYTHING INTO THE RV WITH US.
I'M DRIVING, THOUGH. I FOUND IT SO I GET TO DRIVE IT.

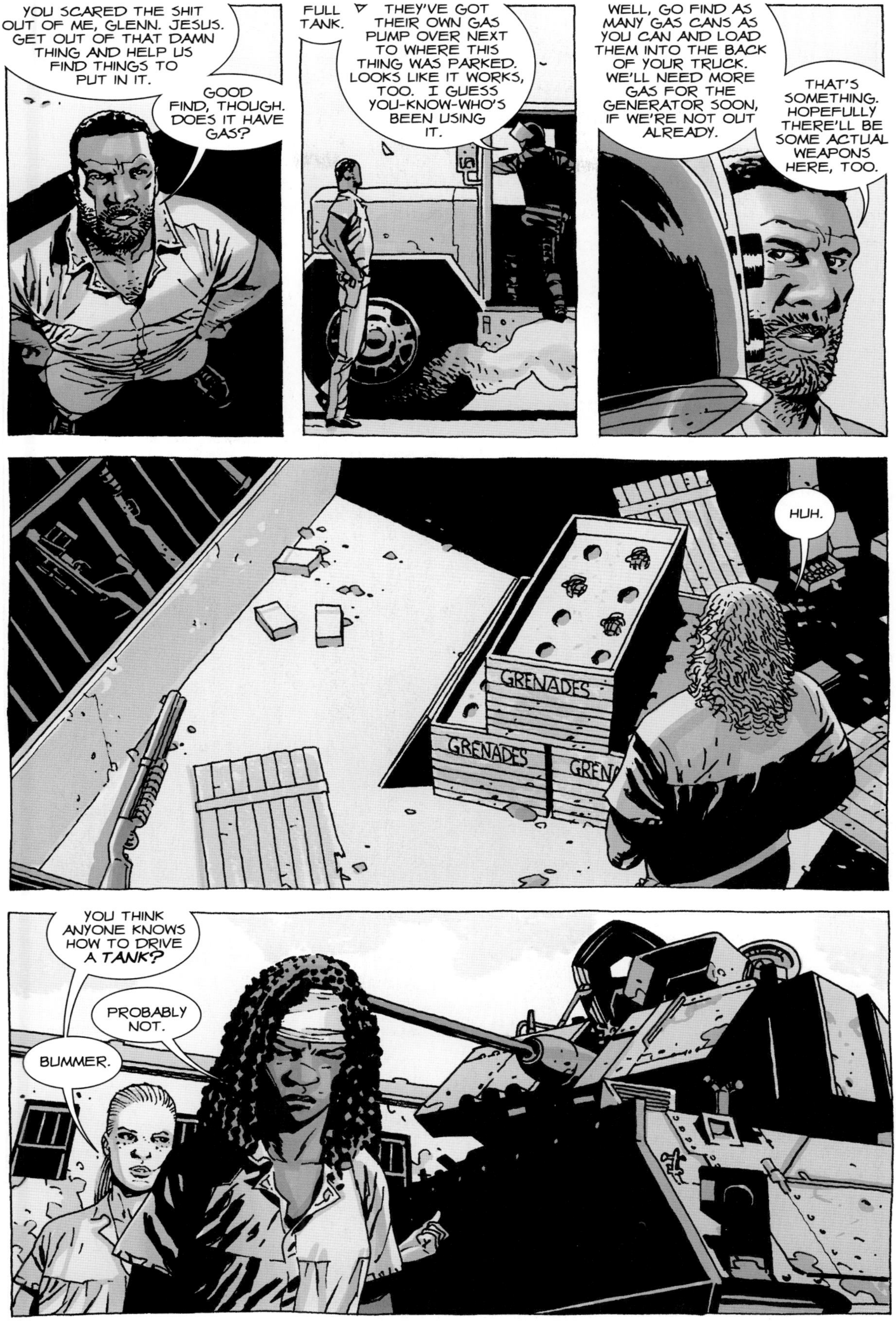

YOU SCARED THE SHIT OUT OF ME, GLENN. JESUS. GET OUT OF THAT DAMN THING AND HELP US FIND THINGS TO PUT IN IT.
GOOD FIND, THOUGH. DOES IT HAVE GAS?
FULL TANK.
THEY'VE GOT THEIR OWN GAS PUMP OVER NEXT TO WHERE THIS THING WAS PARKED. LOOKS LIKE IT WORKS, TOO. I GUESS YOU-KNOW-WHO'S BEEN USING IT.
WELL, GO FIND AS MANY GAS CANS AS YOU CAN AND LOAD THEM INTO THE BACK OF YOUR TRUCK. WE'LL NEED MORE GAS FOR THE GENERATOR SOON, IF WE'RE NOT OUT ALREADY.
THAT'S SOMETHING. HOPEFULLY THERE'LL BE SOME ACTUAL WEAPONS HERE, TOO.
HUH.
GRENADES
GRENADES
GRENA
YOU THINK ANYONE KNOWS HOW TO DRIVE A *TANK?*
PROBABLY NOT.
BUMMER.

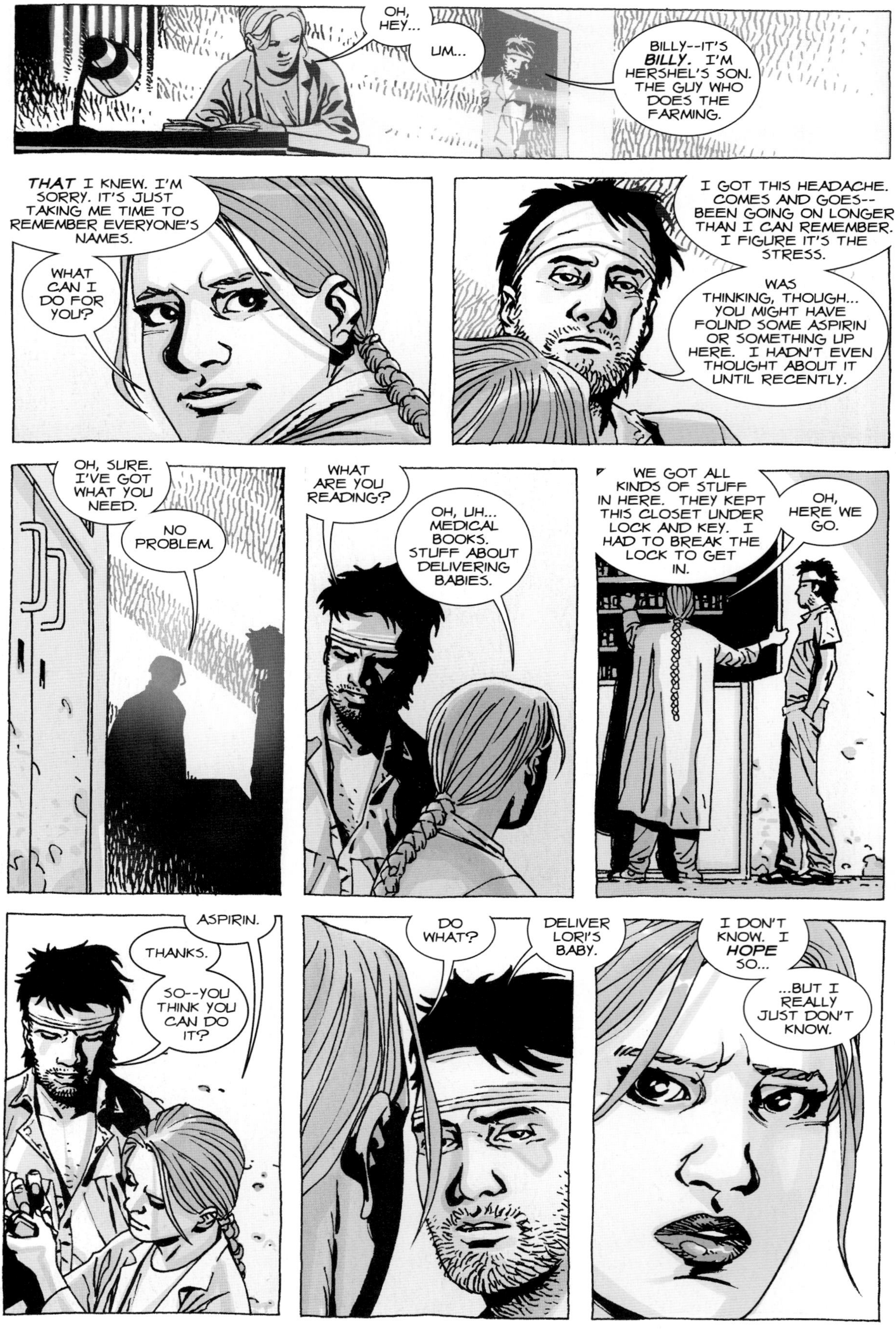
OH, HEY...
UM...
BILLY--IT'S BILLY. I'M HERSHEL'S SON. THE GUY WHO DOES THE FARMING.
THAT I KNEW. I'M SORRY. IT'S JUST TAKING ME TIME TO REMEMBER EVERYONE'S NAMES.
WHAT CAN I DO FOR YOU?
I GOT THIS HEADACHE. COMES AND GOES-- BEEN GOING ON LONGER THAN I CAN REMEMBER. I FIGURE IT'S THE STRESS.
WAS THINKING, THOUGH... YOU MIGHT HAVE FOUND SOME ASPIRIN OR SOMETHING UP HERE. I HADN'T EVEN THOUGHT ABOUT IT UNTIL RECENTLY.
OH, SURE. I'VE GOT WHAT YOU NEED.
NO PROBLEM.
WHAT ARE YOU READING?
OH, UH... MEDICAL BOOKS. STUFF ABOUT DELIVERING BABIES.
WE GOT ALL KINDS OF STUFF IN HERE. THEY KEPT THIS CLOSET UNDER LOCK AND KEY. I HAD TO BREAK THE LOCK TO GET IN.
OH, HERE WE GO.
ASPIRIN.
THANKS.
SO--YOU THINK YOU CAN DO IT?
DO WHAT?
DELIVER LORI'S BABY.
I DON'T KNOW. I HOPE SO...
...BUT I REALLY JUST DON'T KNOW.

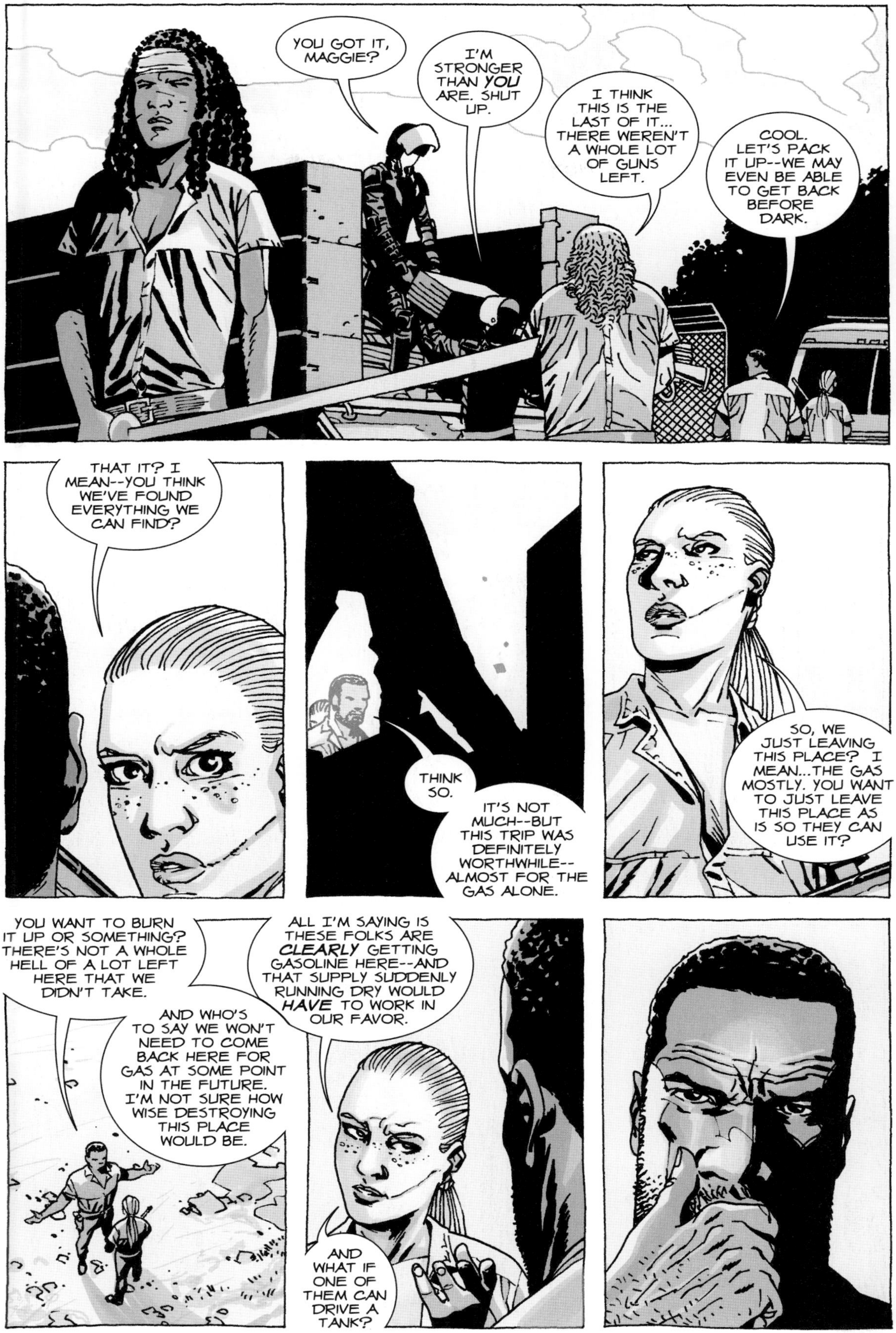

YOU GOT IT, MAGGIE?
I'M STRONGER THAN YOU ARE. SHUT UP.
I THINK THIS IS THE LAST OF IT... THERE WEREN'T A WHOLE LOT OF GUNS LEFT.
COOL. LET'S PACK IT UP--WE MAY EVEN BE ABLE TO GET BACK BEFORE DARK.
THAT IT? I MEAN--YOU THINK WE'VE FOUND EVERYTHING WE CAN FIND?
THINK SO.
IT'S NOT MUCH--BUT THIS TRIP WAS DEFINITELY WORTHWHILE--ALMOST FOR THE GAS ALONE.
SO, WE JUST LEAVING THIS PLACE? I MEAN...THE GAS MOSTLY. YOU WANT TO JUST LEAVE THIS PLACE AS IS SO THEY CAN USE IT?
YOU WANT TO BURN IT UP OR SOMETHING? THERE'S NOT A WHOLE HELL OF A LOT LEFT HERE THAT WE DIDN'T TAKE.
AND WHO'S TO SAY WE WON'T NEED TO COME BACK HERE FOR GAS AT SOME POINT IN THE FUTURE. I'M NOT SURE HOW WISE DESTROYING THIS PLACE WOULD BE.
ALL I'M SAYING IS THESE FOLKS ARE CLEARLY GETTING GASOLINE HERE--AND THAT SUPPLY SUDDENLY RUNNING DRY WOULD HAVE TO WORK IN OUR FAVOR.
AND WHAT IF ONE OF THEM CAN DRIVE A TANK?

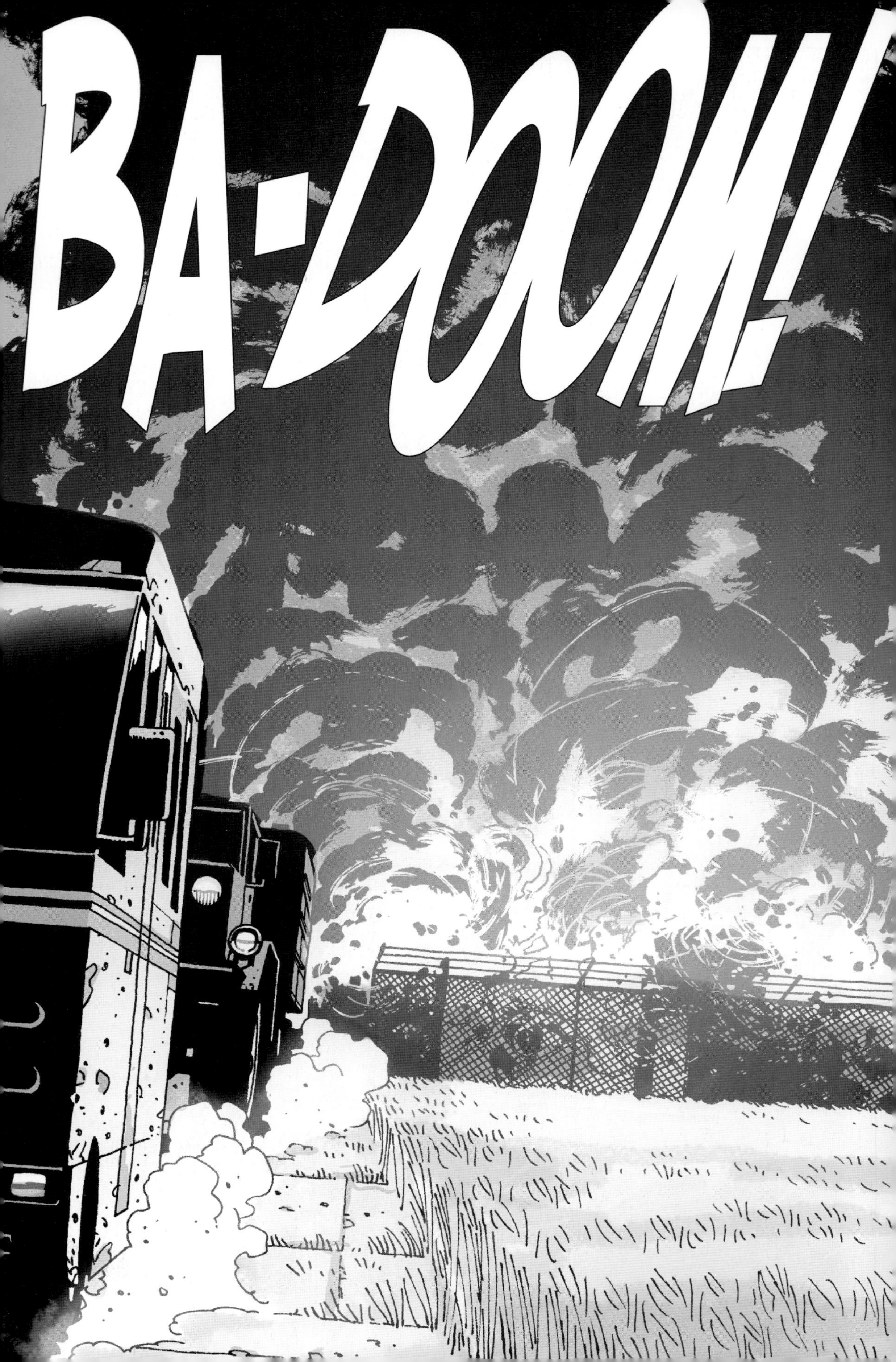
BA-DOOM!

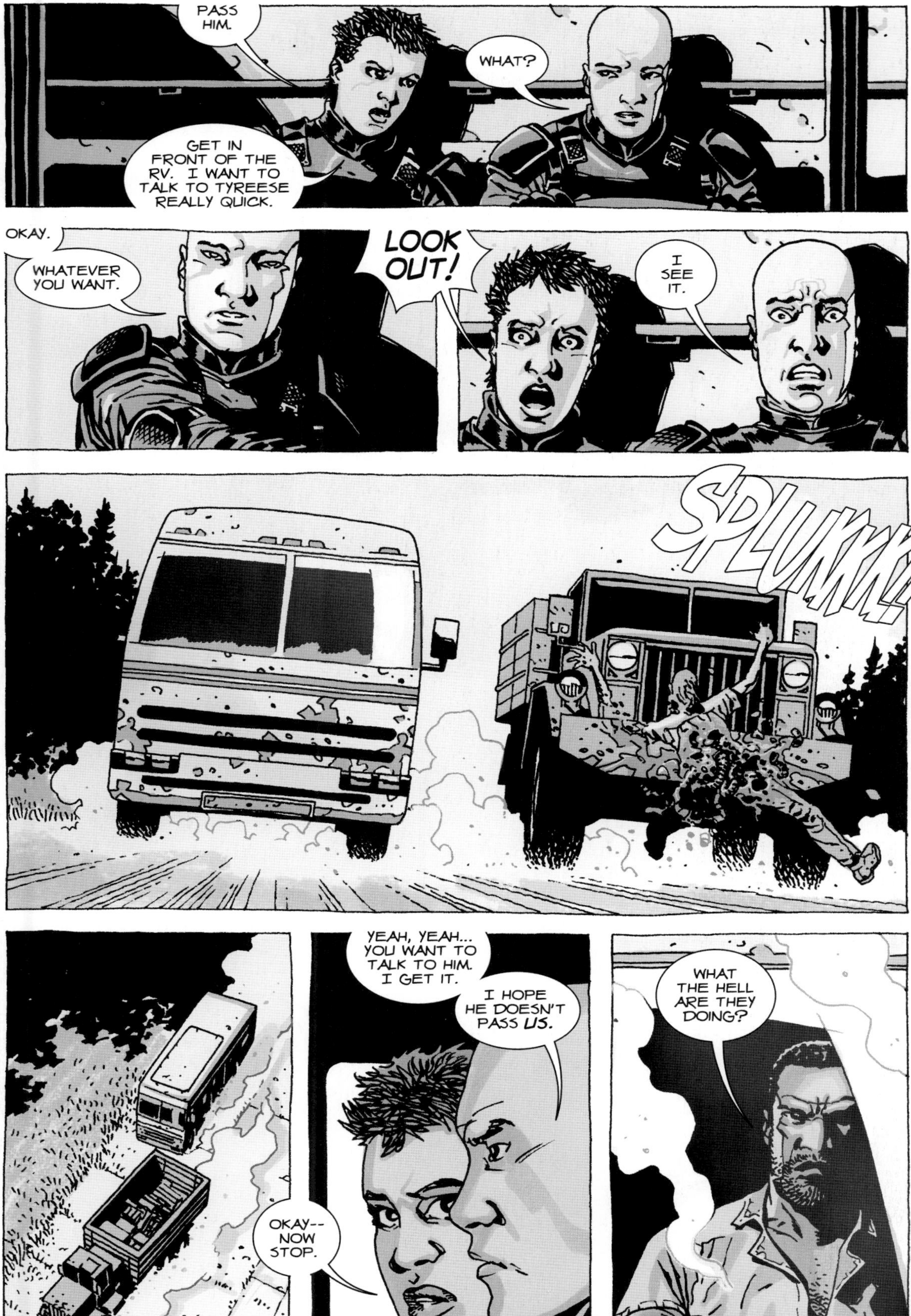
PASS HIM.
WHAT?
GET IN FRONT OF THE RV. I WANT TO TALK TO TYREESE REALLY QUICK.
OKAY.
WHATEVER YOU WANT.
LOOK OUT!
I SEE IT.
SPLUKKK!!
YEAH, YEAH... YOU WANT TO TALK TO HIM. I GET IT.
I HOPE HE DOESN'T PASS US.
OKAY-- NOW STOP.
WHAT THE HELL ARE THEY DOING?

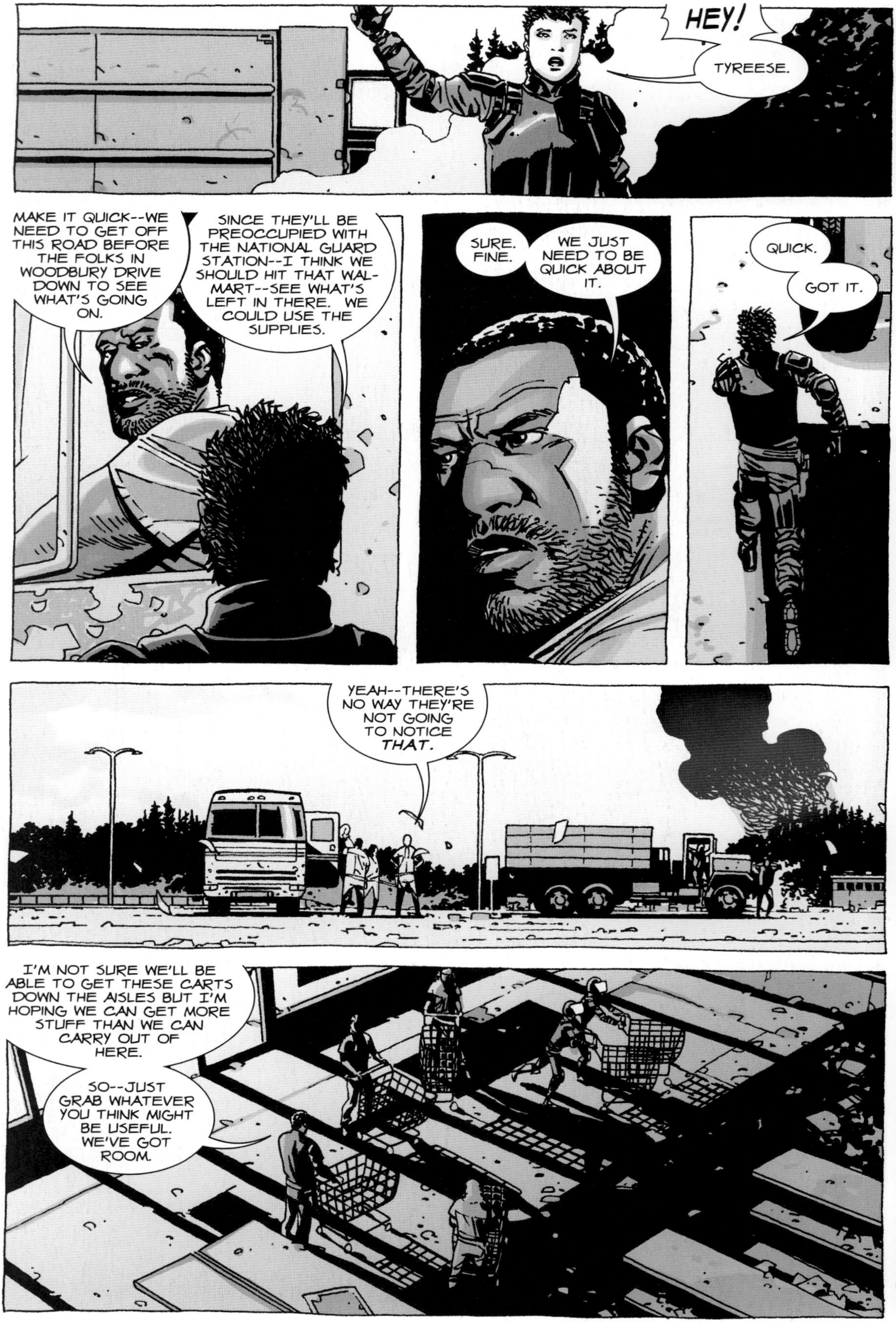
HEY!
TYREESE.
MAKE IT QUICK--WE NEED TO GET OFF THIS ROAD BEFORE THE FOLKS IN WOODBURY DRIVE DOWN TO SEE WHAT'S GOING ON.
SINCE THEY'LL BE PREOCCUPIED WITH THE NATIONAL GUARD STATION--I THINK WE SHOULD HIT THAT WAL-MART--SEE WHAT'S LEFT IN THERE. WE COULD USE THE SUPPLIES.
SURE. FINE.
WE JUST NEED TO BE QUICK ABOUT IT.
QUICK.
GOT IT.
YEAH--THERE'S NO WAY THEY'RE NOT GOING TO NOTICE *THAT.*
I'M NOT SURE WE'LL BE ABLE TO GET THESE CARTS DOWN THE AISLES BUT I'M HOPING WE CAN GET MORE STUFF THAN WE CAN CARRY OUT OF HERE.
SO--JUST GRAB WHATEVER YOU THINK MIGHT BE USEFUL. WE'VE GOT ROOM.

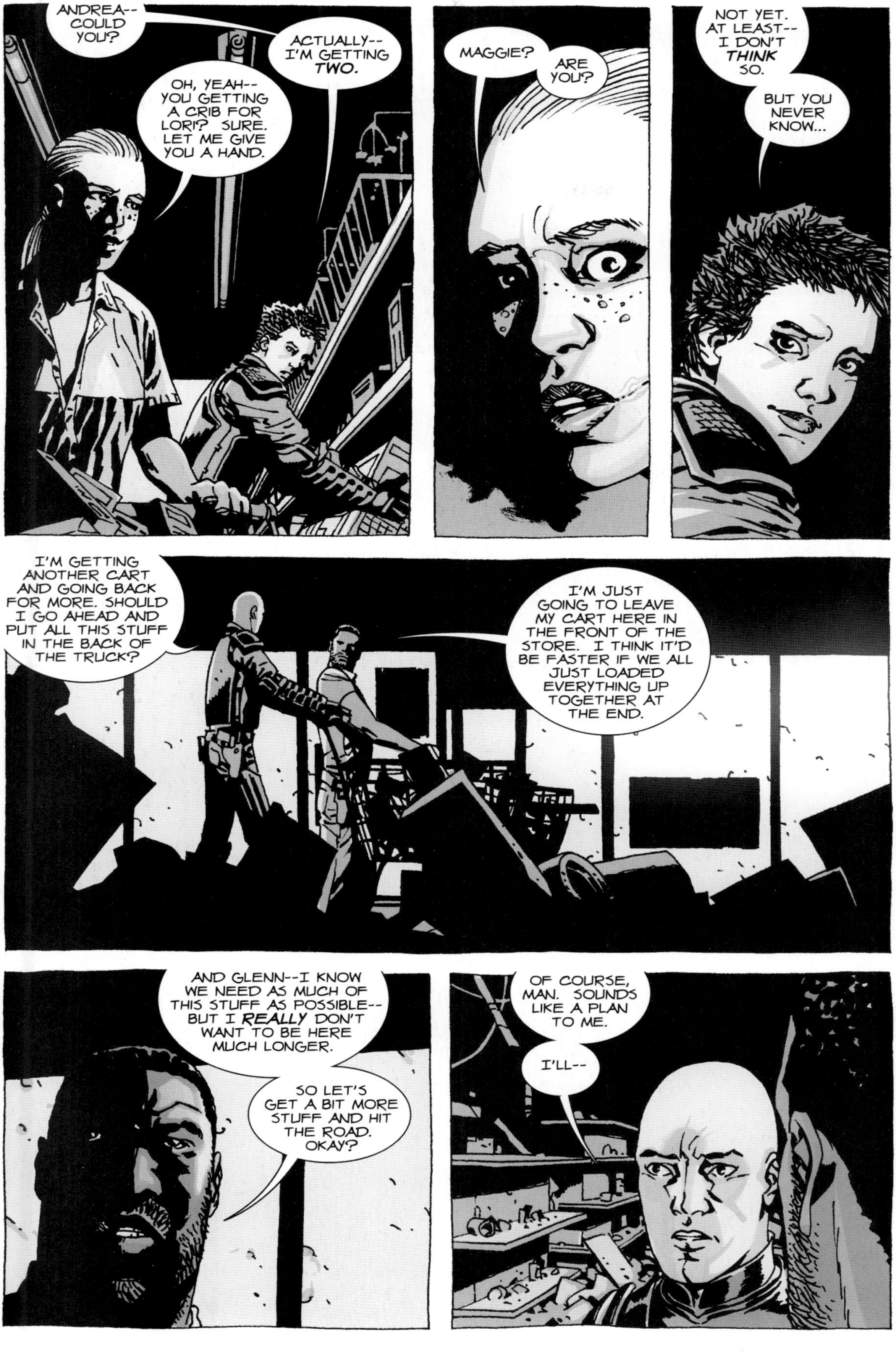
ANDREA-- COULD YOU?
ACTUALLY-- I'M GETTING TWO.
OH, YEAH-- YOU GETTING A CRIB FOR LORI? SURE. LET ME GIVE YOU A HAND.
MAGGIE?
ARE YOU?
NOT YET. AT LEAST-- I DON'T THINK SO.
BUT YOU NEVER KNOW...
I'M GETTING ANOTHER CART AND GOING BACK FOR MORE. SHOULD I GO AHEAD AND PUT ALL THIS STUFF IN THE BACK OF THE TRUCK?
I'M JUST GOING TO LEAVE MY CART HERE IN THE FRONT OF THE STORE. I THINK IT'D BE FASTER IF WE ALL JUST LOADED EVERYTHING UP TOGETHER AT THE END.
AND GLENN--I KNOW WE NEED AS MUCH OF THIS STUFF AS POSSIBLE-- BUT I REALLY DON'T WANT TO BE HERE MUCH LONGER.
SO LET'S GET A BIT MORE STUFF AND HIT THE ROAD. OKAY?
OF COURSE, MAN. SOUNDS LIKE A PLAN TO ME.
I'LL--

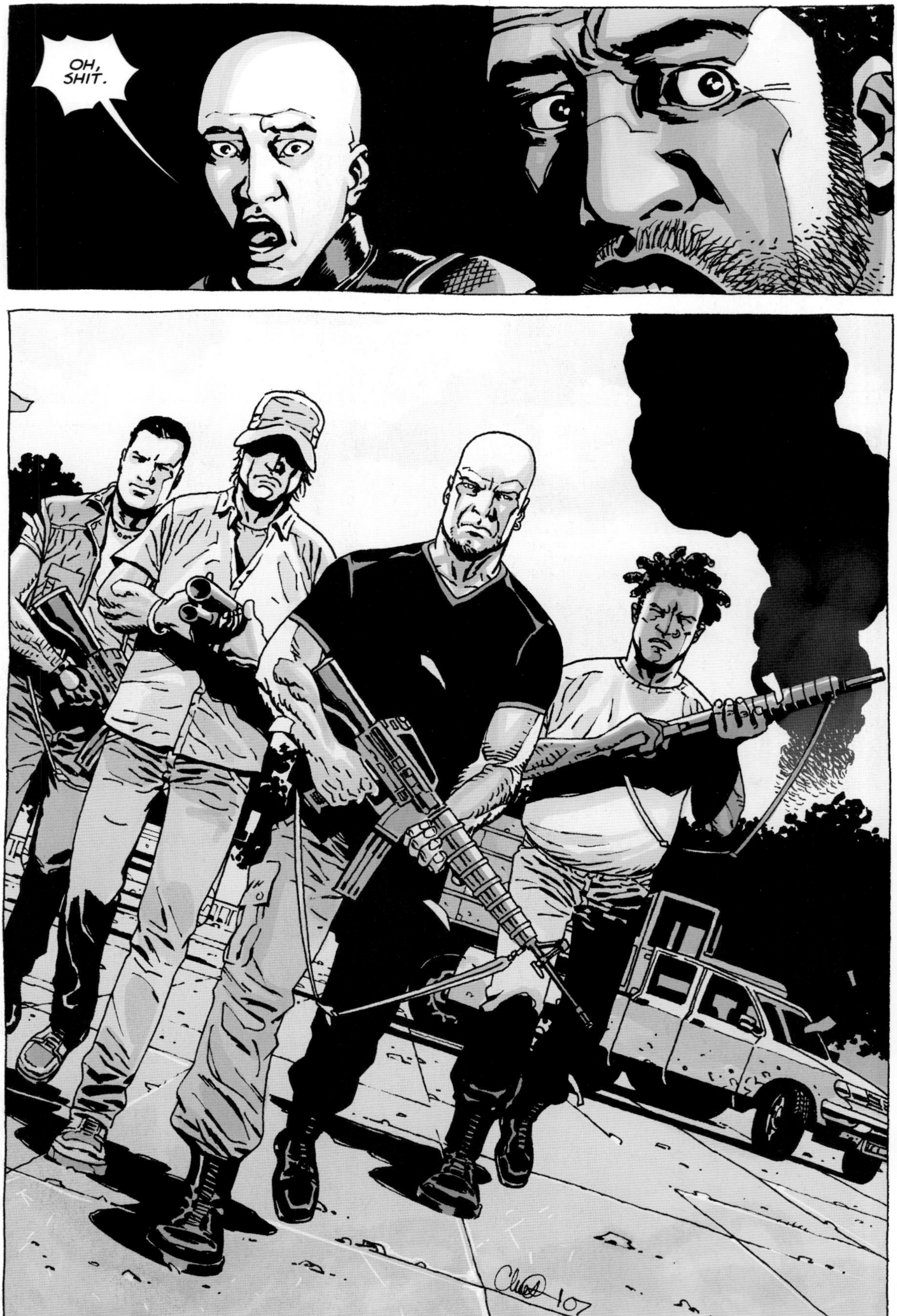
OH, SHIT.

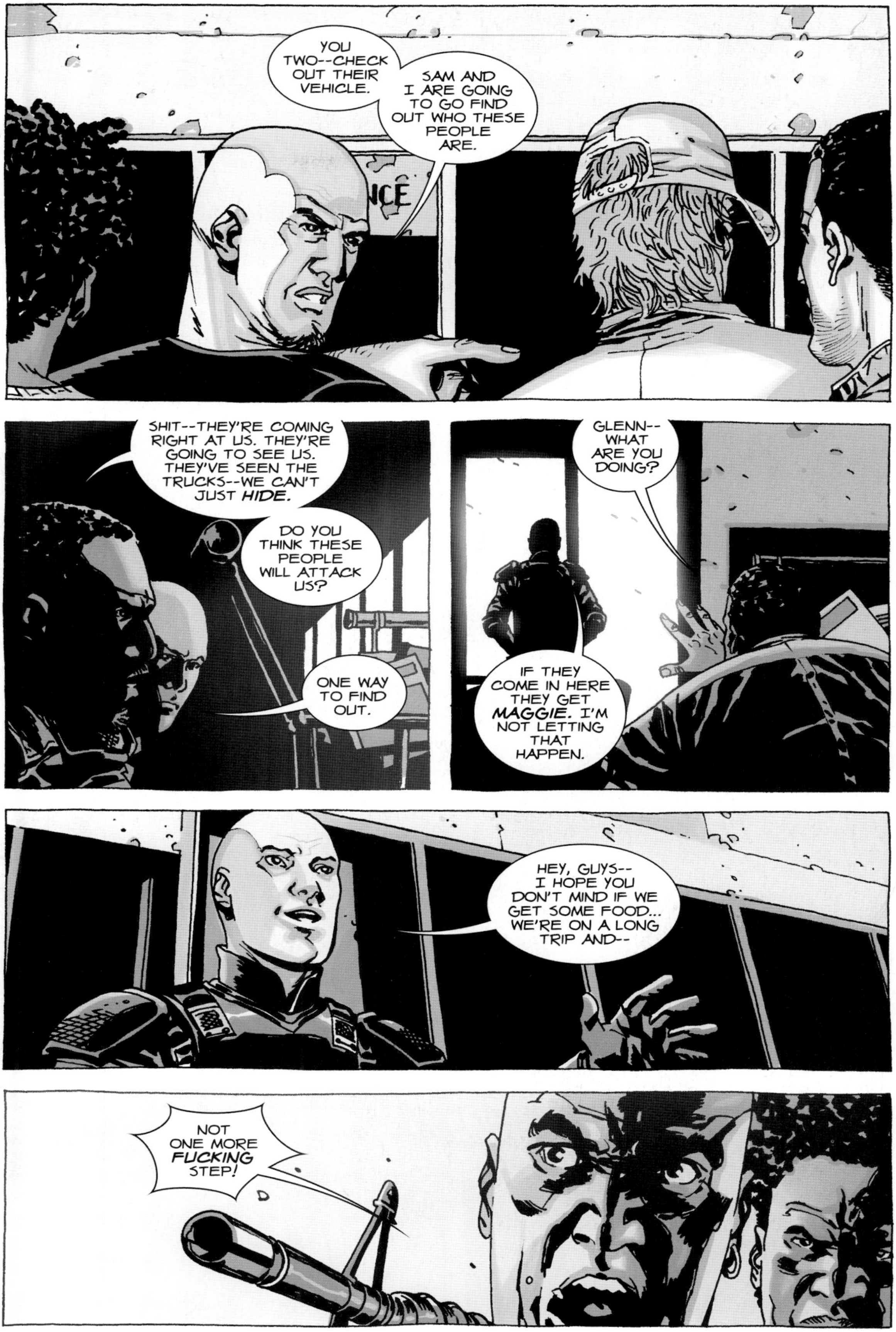
YOU TWO--CHECK OUT THEIR VEHICLE.
SAM AND I ARE GOING TO GO FIND OUT WHO THESE PEOPLE ARE.
SHIT--THEY'RE COMING RIGHT AT US. THEY'RE GOING TO SEE US. THEY'VE SEEN THE TRUCKS--WE CAN'T JUST HIDE.
DO YOU THINK THESE PEOPLE WILL ATTACK US?
ONE WAY TO FIND OUT.
GLENN--WHAT ARE YOU DOING?
IF THEY COME IN HERE THEY GET MAGGIE. I'M NOT LETTING THAT HAPPEN.
HEY, GUYS-- I HOPE YOU DON'T MIND IF WE GET SOME FOOD... WE'RE ON A LONG TRIP AND--
NOT ONE MORE FUCKING STEP!

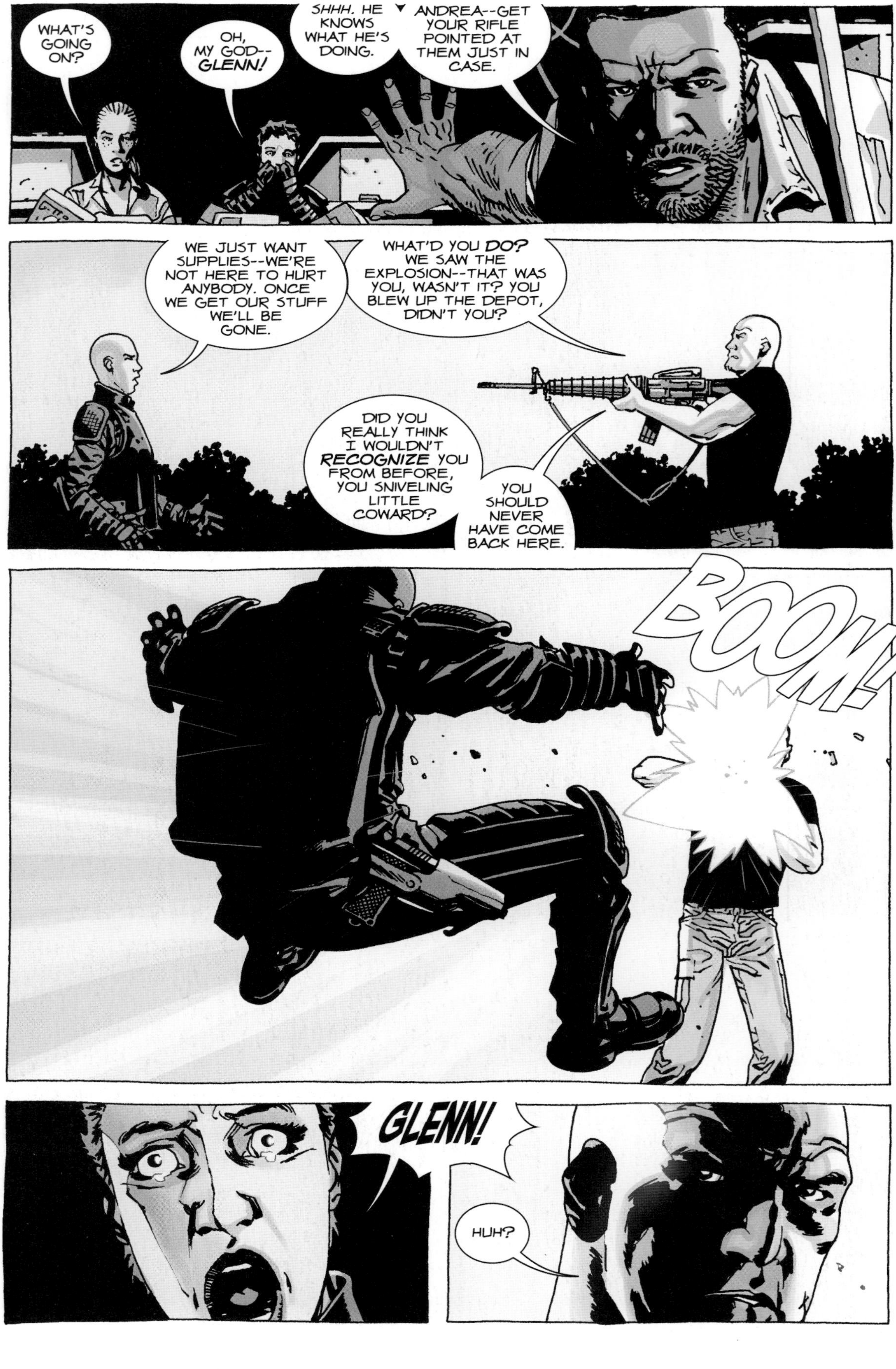
WHAT'S GOING ON?
OH, MY GOD-- GLENN!
SHHH. HE KNOWS WHAT HE'S DOING.
ANDREA--GET YOUR RIFLE POINTED AT THEM JUST IN CASE.
WE JUST WANT SUPPLIES--WE'RE NOT HERE TO HURT ANYBODY. ONCE WE GET OUR STUFF WE'LL BE GONE.
WHAT'D YOU DO? WE SAW THE EXPLOSION--THAT WAS YOU, WASN'T IT? YOU BLEW UP THE DEPOT, DIDN'T YOU?
DID YOU REALLY THINK I WOULDN'T RECOGNIZE YOU FROM BEFORE, YOU SNIVELING LITTLE COWARD?
YOU SHOULD NEVER HAVE COME BACK HERE.
BOOM!
GLENN!
HUH?

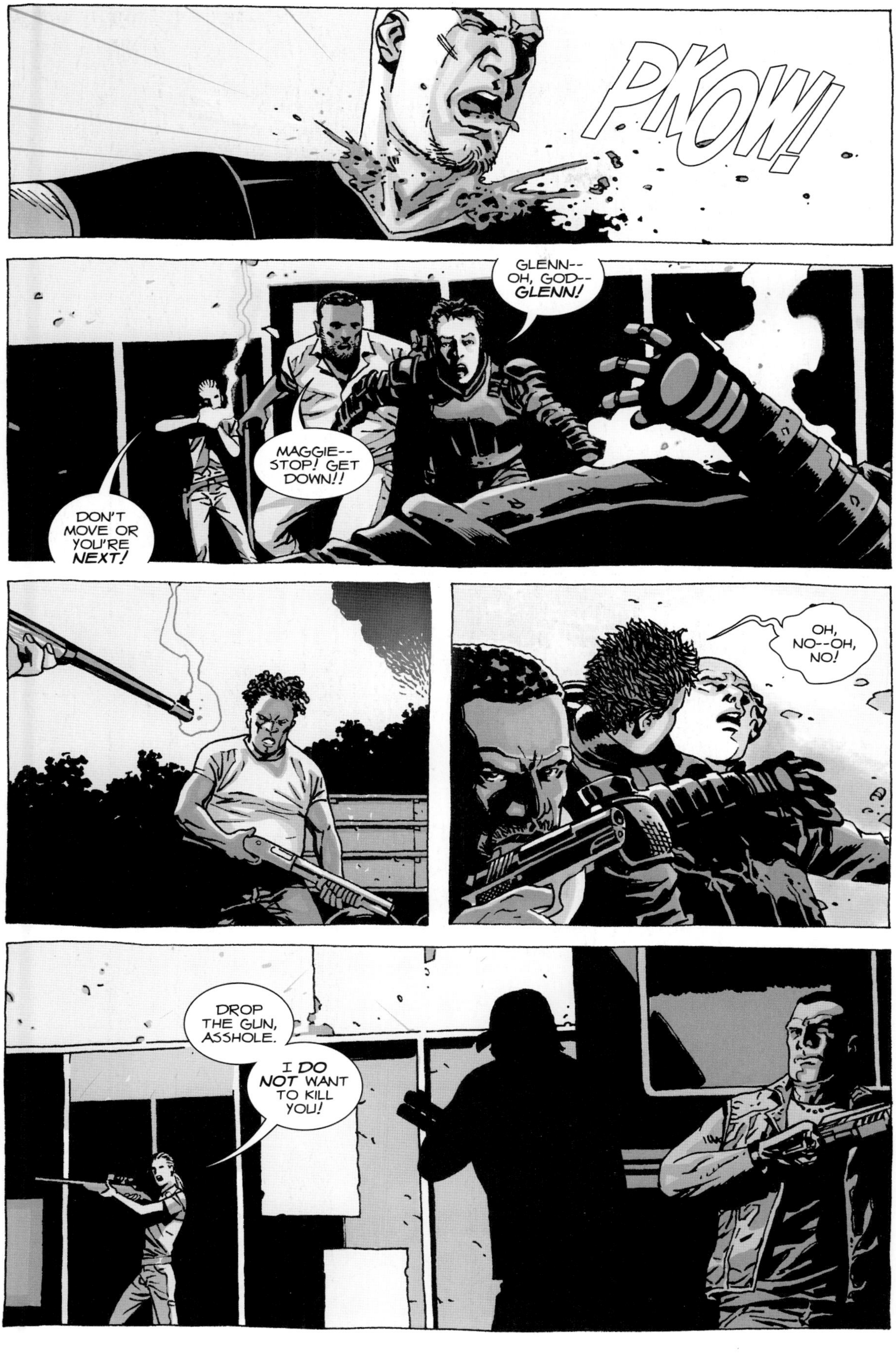
P'KOW!
GLENN-- OH, GOD-- GLENN!
MAGGIE-- STOP! GET DOWN!!
DON'T MOVE OR YOU'RE NEXT!
OH, NO--OH, NO!
DROP THE GUN, ASSHOLE.
I DO NOT WANT TO KILL YOU!

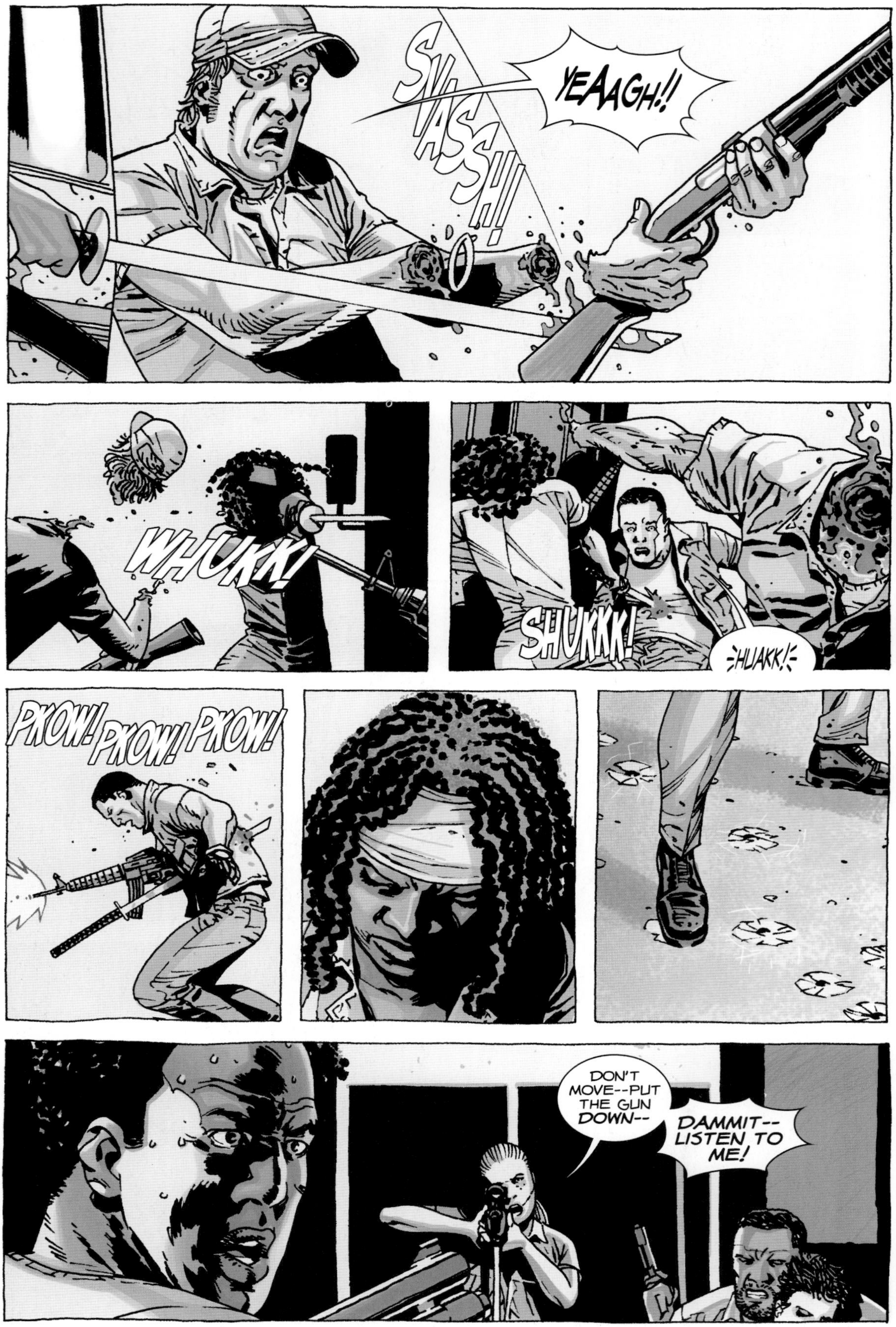

YEAAGH!!
SWASSH!!
WHUKK!
SHUKKK!
HUAKK!
PKOW! PKOW! PKOW!
DON'T MOVE--PUT THE GUN DOWN--
DAMMIT-- LISTEN TO ME!

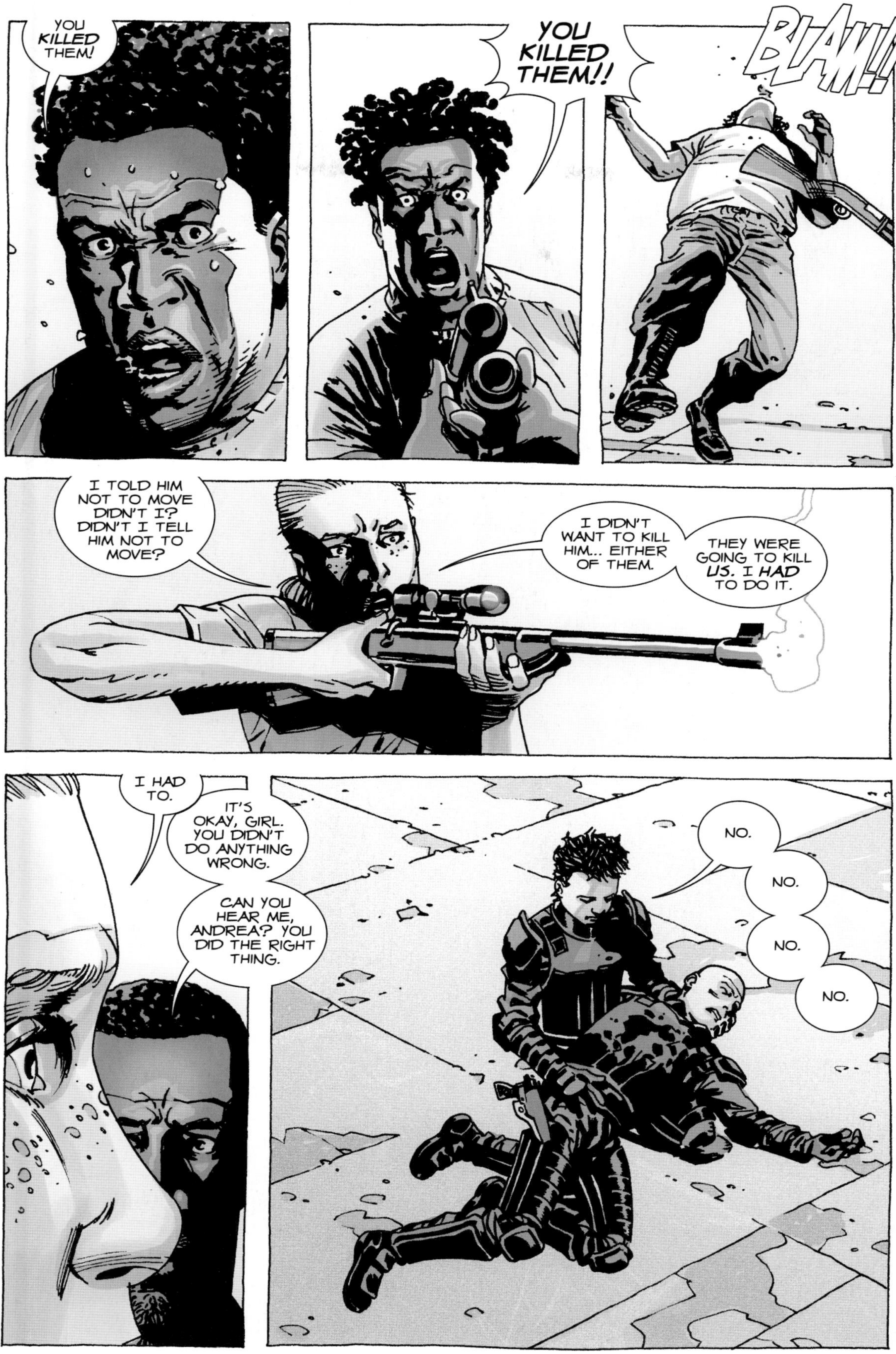
YOU KILLED THEM!
YOU KILLED THEM!!
BLAM!!
I TOLD HIM NOT TO MOVE DIDN'T I? DIDN'T I TELL HIM NOT TO MOVE?
I DIDN'T WANT TO KILL HIM... EITHER OF THEM.
THEY WERE GOING TO KILL US. I HAD TO DO IT.
I HAD TO.
IT'S OKAY, GIRL. YOU DIDN'T DO ANYTHING WRONG.
CAN YOU HEAR ME, ANDREA? YOU DID THE RIGHT THING.
NO.
NO.
NO.
NO.

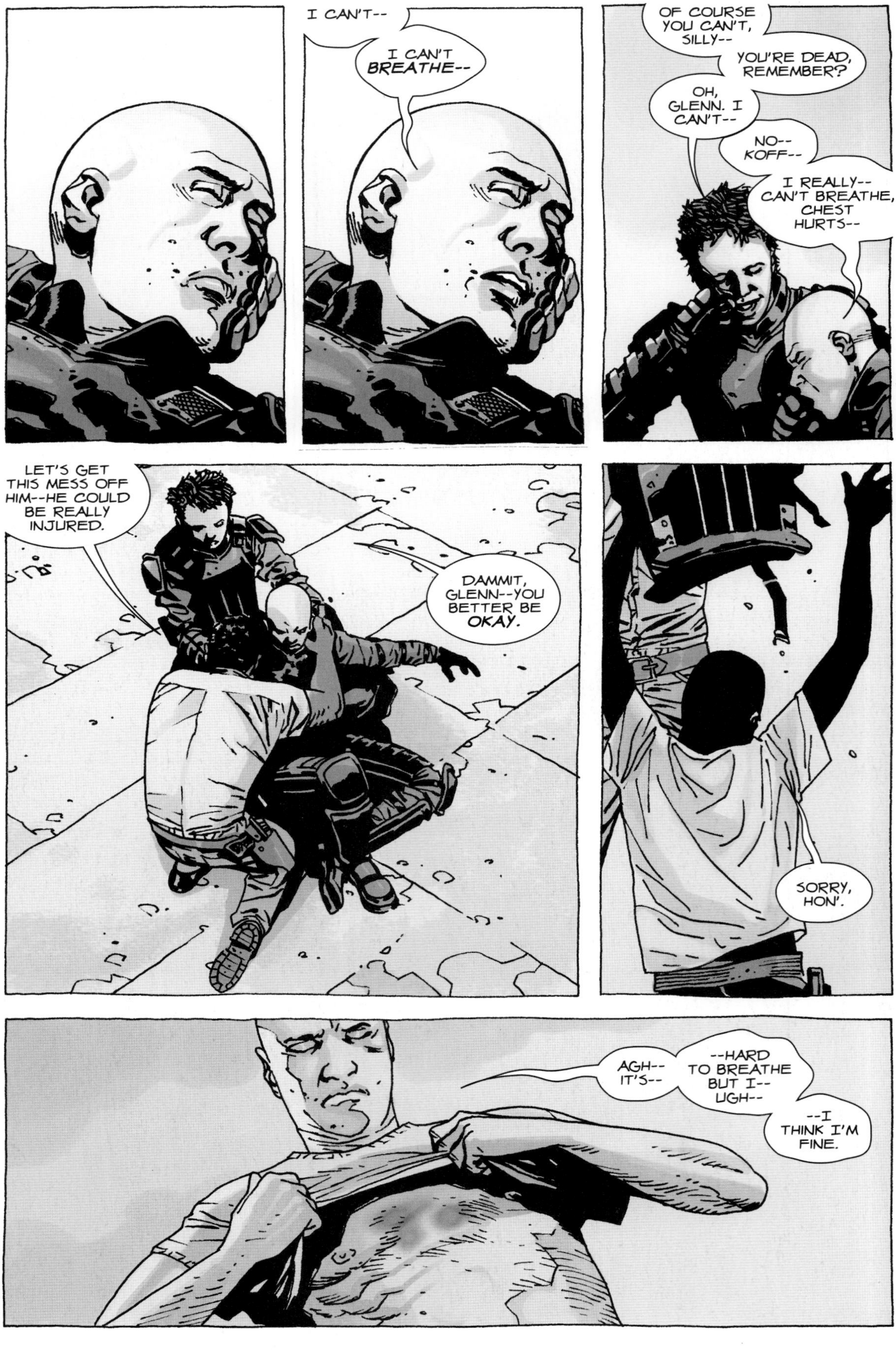
I CAN'T--
I CAN'T BREATHE--
OF COURSE YOU CAN'T, SILLY--
YOU'RE DEAD, REMEMBER?
OH, GLENN. I CAN'T--
NO-- KOFF--
I REALLY-- CAN'T BREATHE, CHEST HURTS--
LET'S GET THIS MESS OFF HIM--HE COULD BE REALLY INJURED.
DAMMIT, GLENN--YOU BETTER BE OKAY.
SORRY, HON'.
AGH-- IT'S--
--HARD TO BREATHE BUT I-- UGH--
--I THINK I'M FINE.

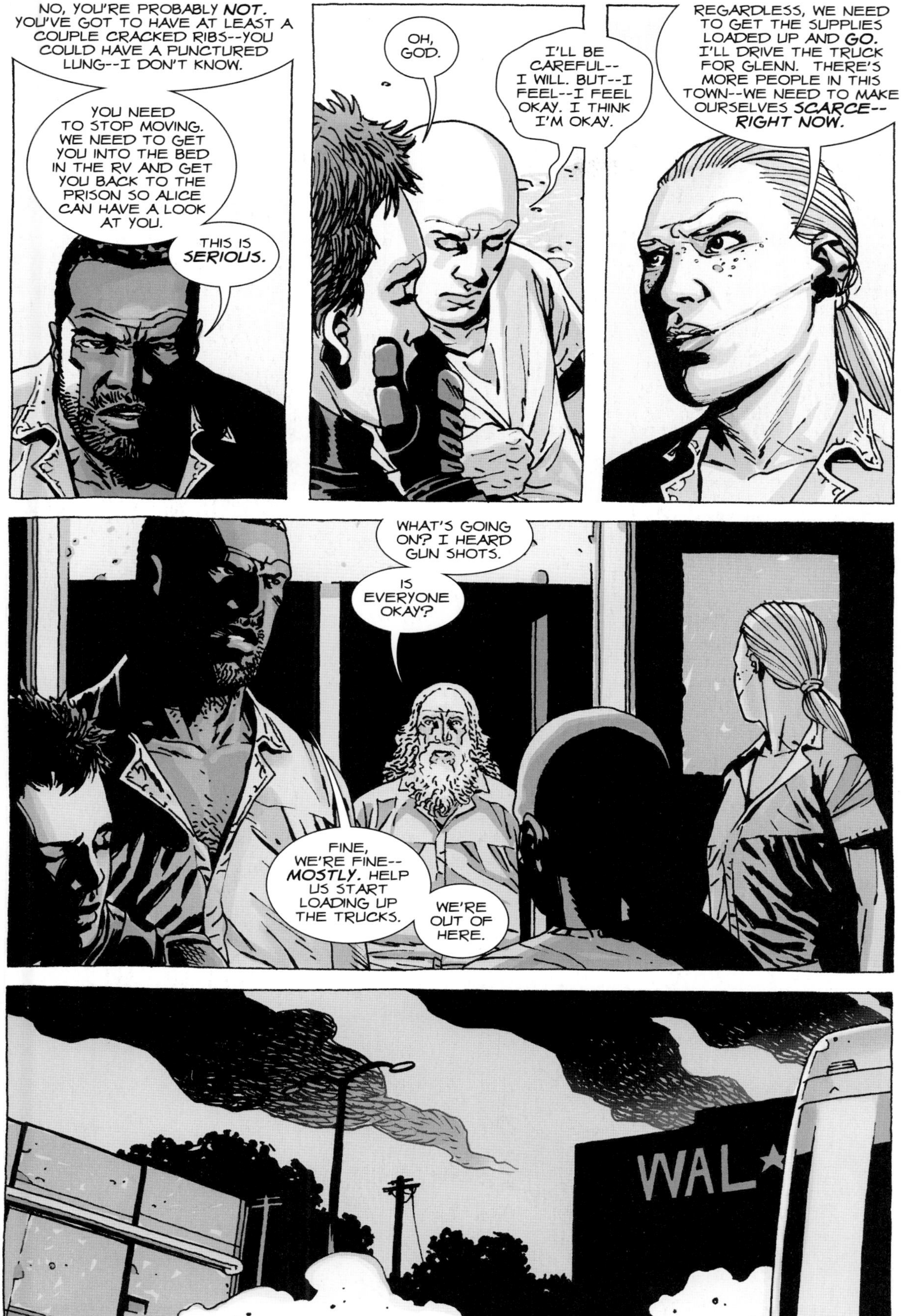
NO, YOU'RE PROBABLY NOT. YOU'VE GOT TO HAVE AT LEAST A COUPLE CRACKED RIBS--YOU COULD HAVE A PUNCTURED LUNG--I DON'T KNOW.
YOU NEED TO STOP MOVING. WE NEED TO GET YOU INTO THE BED IN THE RV AND GET YOU BACK TO THE PRISON SO ALICE CAN HAVE A LOOK AT YOU.
THIS IS SERIOUS.
OH, GOD.
I'LL BE CAREFUL-- I WILL. BUT--I FEEL--I FEEL OKAY. I THINK I'M OKAY.
REGARDLESS, WE NEED TO GET THE SUPPLIES LOADED UP AND GO. I'LL DRIVE THE TRUCK FOR GLENN. THERE'S MORE PEOPLE IN THIS TOWN--WE NEED TO MAKE OURSELVES SCARCE-- RIGHT NOW.
WHAT'S GOING ON? I HEARD GUN SHOTS.
IS EVERYONE OKAY?
FINE, WE'RE FINE-- MOSTLY. HELP US START LOADING UP THE TRUCKS.
WE'RE OUT OF HERE.
WAL★

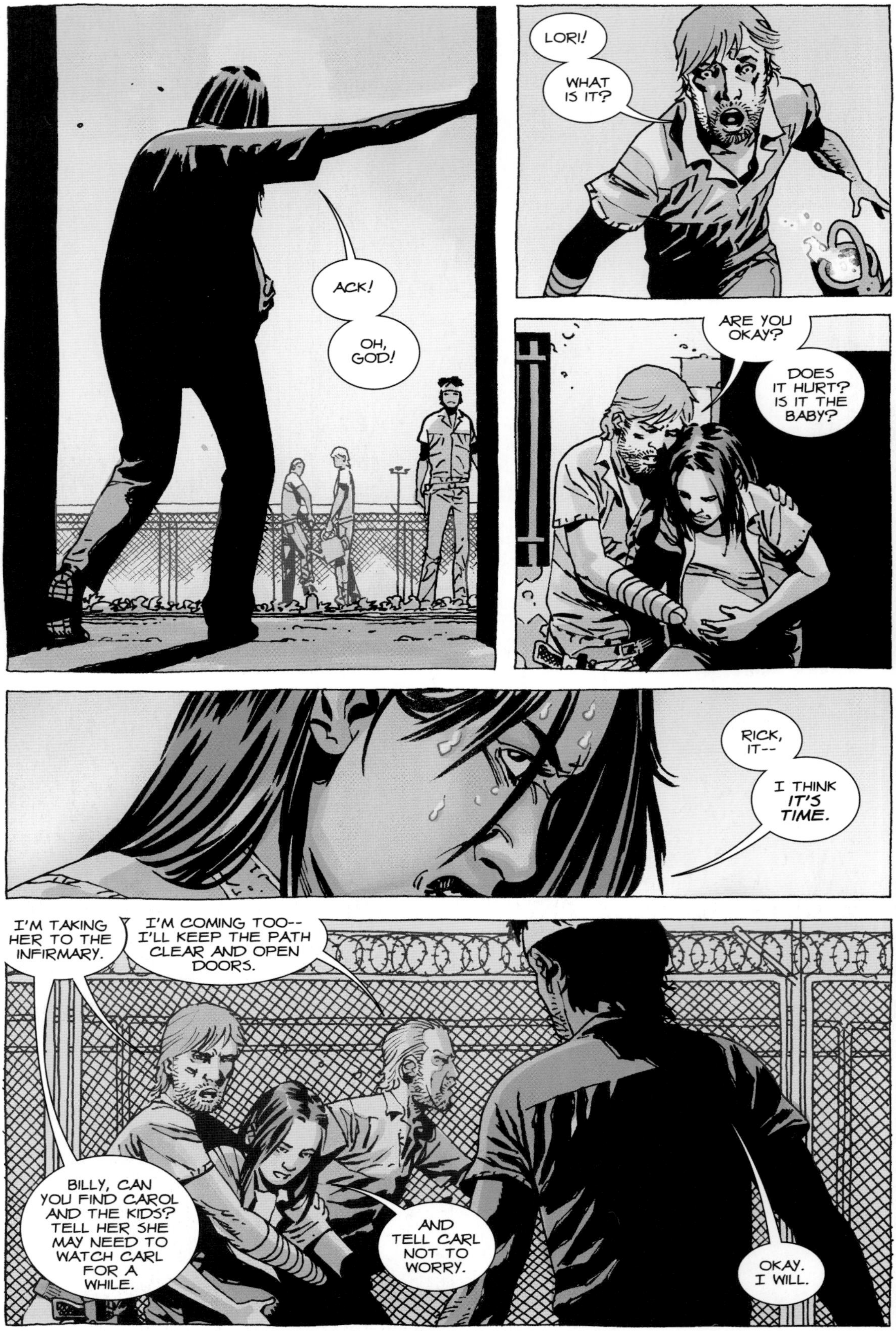
ACK!
OH, GOD!
LORI!
WHAT IS IT?
ARE YOU OKAY?
DOES IT HURT? IS IT THE BABY?
RICK, IT--
I THINK *IT'S TIME.*
I'M TAKING HER TO THE INFIRMARY.
I'M COMING TOO-- I'LL KEEP THE PATH CLEAR AND OPEN DOORS.
BILLY, CAN YOU FIND CAROL AND THE KIDS? TELL HER SHE MAY NEED TO WATCH CARL FOR A WHILE.
AND TELL CARL NOT TO WORRY.
OKAY. I WILL.

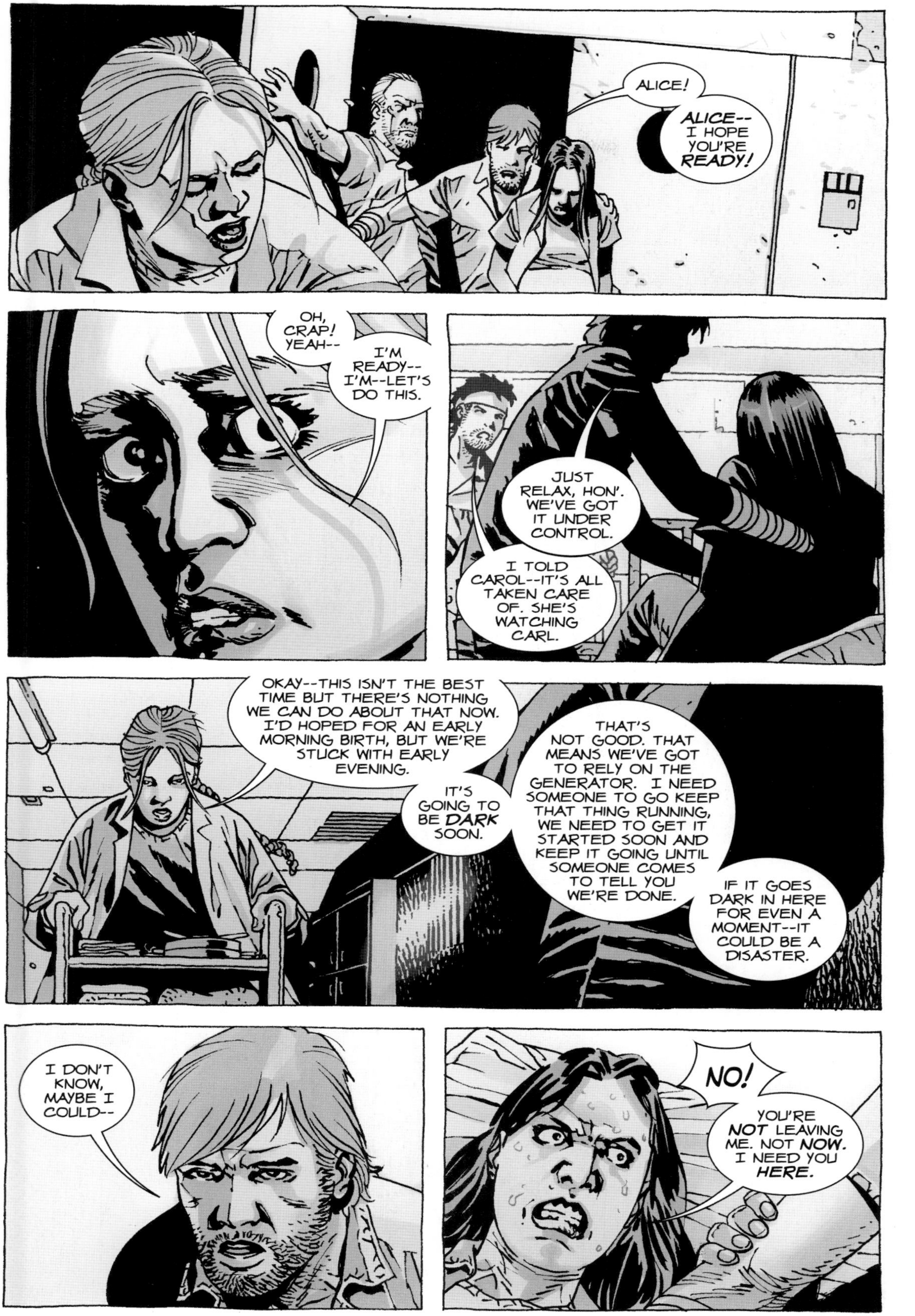

ALICE!
ALICE-- I HOPE YOU'RE READY!
OH, CRAP! YEAH--
I'M READY-- I'M--LET'S DO THIS.
JUST RELAX, HON'. WE'VE GOT IT UNDER CONTROL.
I TOLD CAROL--IT'S ALL TAKEN CARE OF. SHE'S WATCHING CARL.
OKAY--THIS ISN'T THE BEST TIME BUT THERE'S NOTHING WE CAN DO ABOUT THAT NOW. I'D HOPED FOR AN EARLY MORNING BIRTH, BUT WE'RE STUCK WITH EARLY EVENING.
IT'S GOING TO BE DARK SOON.
THAT'S NOT GOOD. THAT MEANS WE'VE GOT TO RELY ON THE GENERATOR. I NEED SOMEONE TO GO KEEP THAT THING RUNNING, WE NEED TO GET IT STARTED SOON AND KEEP IT GOING UNTIL SOMEONE COMES TO TELL YOU WE'RE DONE.
IF IT GOES DARK IN HERE FOR EVEN A MOMENT--IT COULD BE A DISASTER.
I DON'T KNOW, MAYBE I COULD--
NO!
YOU'RE NOT LEAVING ME. NOT NOW. I NEED YOU HERE.

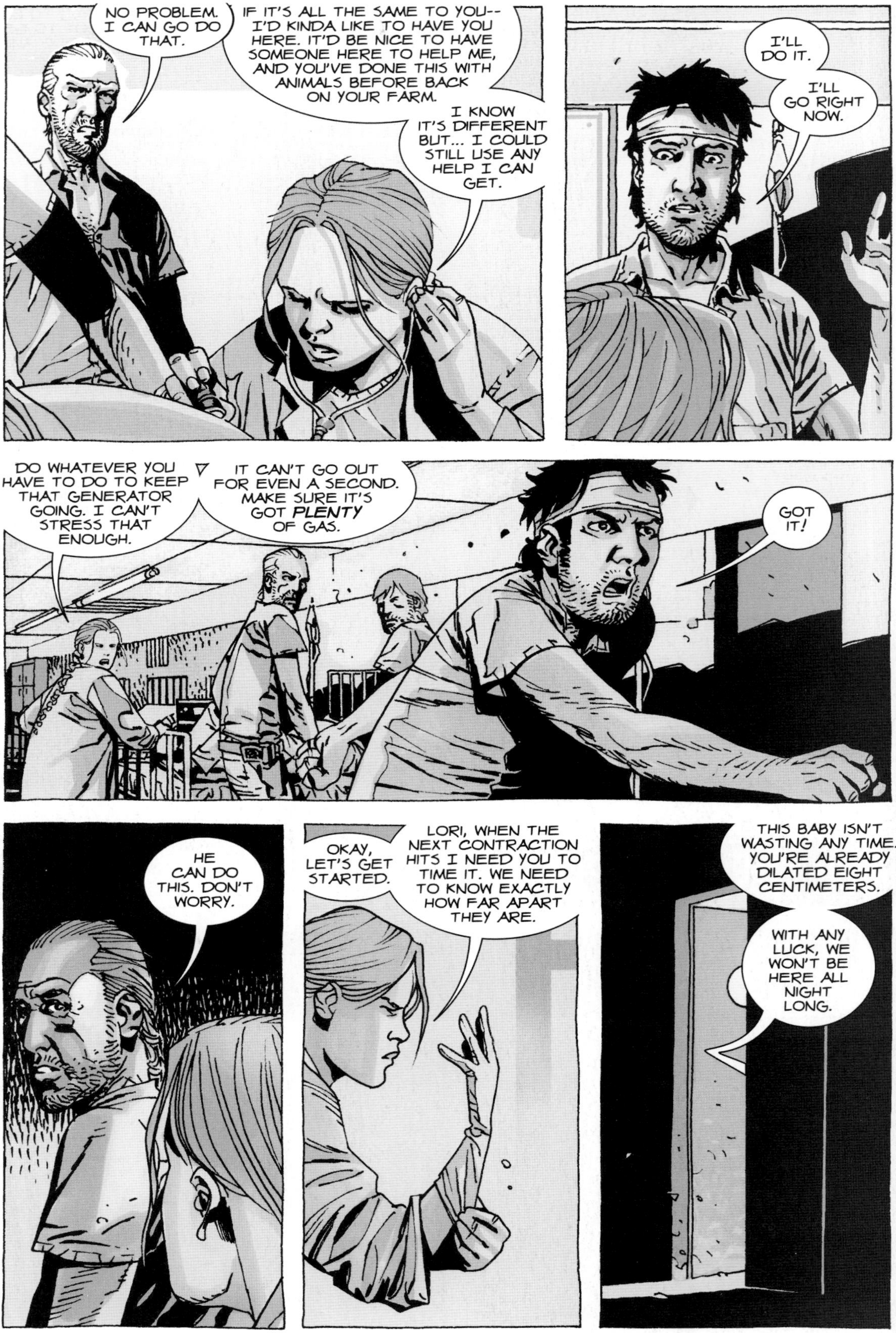
NO PROBLEM. I CAN GO DO THAT.
IF IT'S ALL THE SAME TO YOU-- I'D KINDA LIKE TO HAVE YOU HERE. IT'D BE NICE TO HAVE SOMEONE HERE TO HELP ME, AND YOU'VE DONE THIS WITH ANIMALS BEFORE BACK ON YOUR FARM.
I KNOW IT'S DIFFERENT BUT... I COULD STILL USE ANY HELP I CAN GET.
I'LL DO IT.
I'LL GO RIGHT NOW.
DO WHATEVER YOU HAVE TO DO TO KEEP THAT GENERATOR GOING. I CAN'T STRESS THAT ENOUGH.
IT CAN'T GO OUT FOR EVEN A SECOND. MAKE SURE IT'S GOT PLENTY OF GAS.
GOT IT!
HE CAN DO THIS. DON'T WORRY.
OKAY, LET'S GET STARTED.
LORI, WHEN THE NEXT CONTRACTION HITS I NEED YOU TO TIME IT. WE NEED TO KNOW EXACTLY HOW FAR APART THEY ARE.
THIS BABY ISN'T WASTING ANY TIME. YOU'RE ALREADY DILATED EIGHT CENTIMETERS.
WITH ANY LUCK, WE WON'T BE HERE ALL NIGHT LONG.

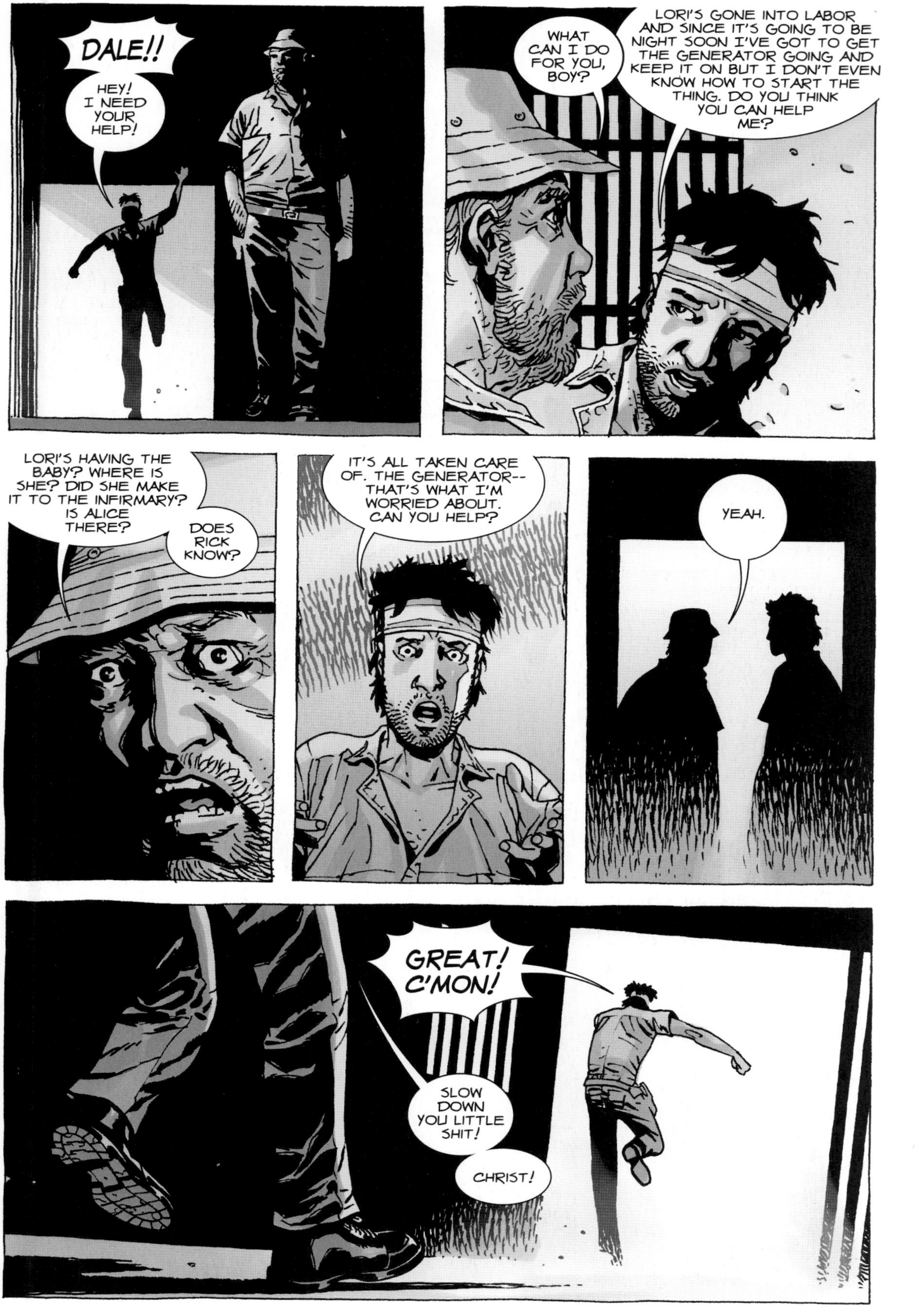
DALE!!
HEY! I NEED YOUR HELP!
WHAT CAN I DO FOR YOU, BOY?
LORI'S GONE INTO LABOR AND SINCE IT'S GOING TO BE NIGHT SOON I'VE GOT TO GET THE GENERATOR GOING AND KEEP IT ON BUT I DON'T EVEN KNOW HOW TO START THE THING. DO YOU THINK YOU CAN HELP ME?
LORI'S HAVING THE BABY? WHERE IS SHE? DID SHE MAKE IT TO THE INFIRMARY? IS ALICE THERE?
DOES RICK KNOW?
IT'S ALL TAKEN CARE OF. THE GENERATOR-- THAT'S WHAT I'M WORRIED ABOUT. CAN YOU HELP?
YEAH.
GREAT! C'MON!
SLOW DOWN YOU LITTLE SHIT!
CHRIST!

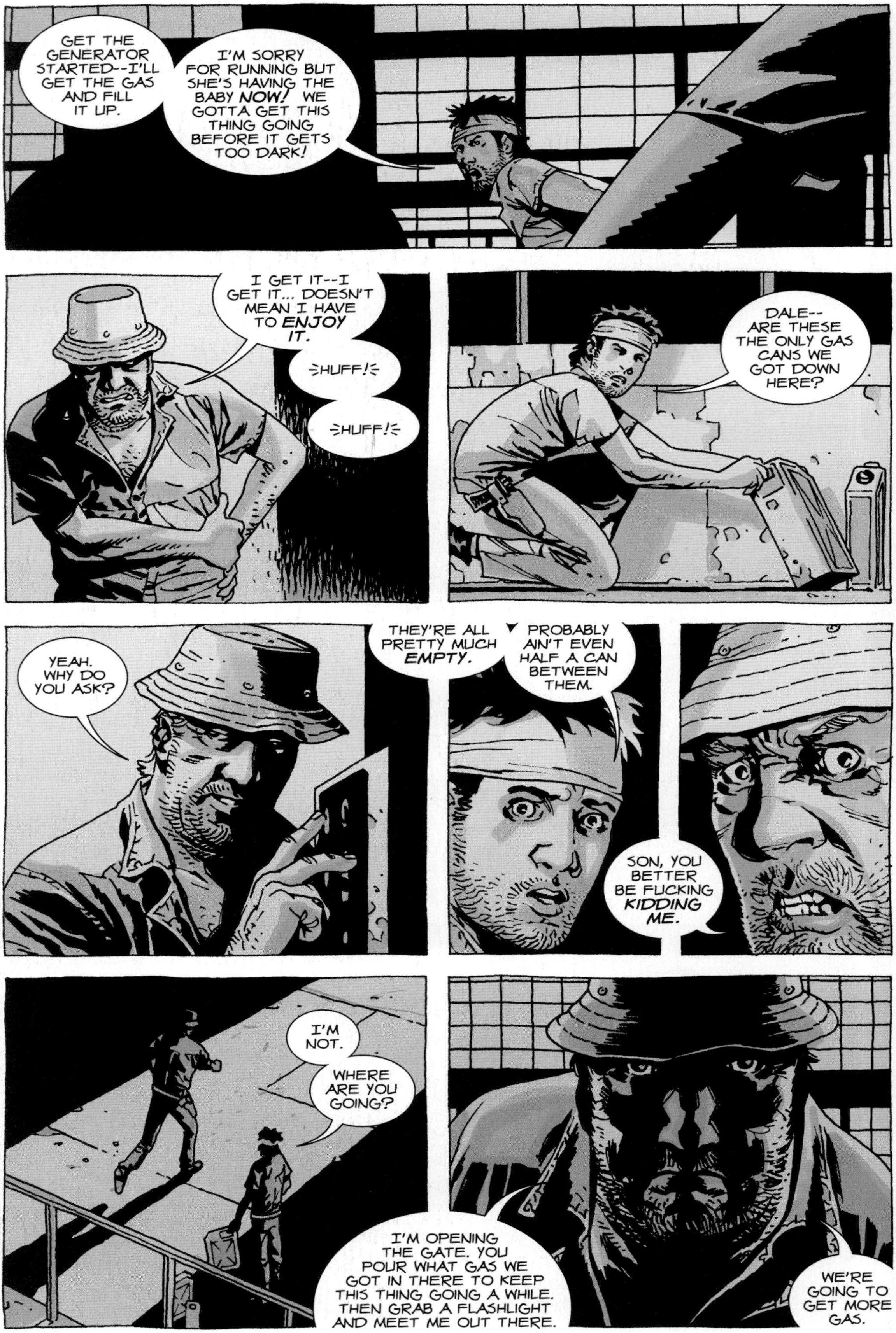
GET THE GENERATOR STARTED--I'LL GET THE GAS AND FILL IT UP.
I'M SORRY FOR RUNNING BUT SHE'S HAVING THE BABY NOW! WE GOTTA GET THIS THING GOING BEFORE IT GETS TOO DARK!
I GET IT--I GET IT... DOESN'T MEAN I HAVE TO ENJOY IT.
HUFF!
HUFF!
DALE-- ARE THESE THE ONLY GAS CANS WE GOT DOWN HERE?
YEAH. WHY DO YOU ASK?
THEY'RE ALL PRETTY MUCH EMPTY.
PROBABLY AIN'T EVEN HALF A CAN BETWEEN THEM.
SON, YOU BETTER BE FUCKING KIDDING ME.
I'M NOT.
WHERE ARE YOU GOING?
I'M OPENING THE GATE. YOU POUR WHAT GAS WE GOT IN THERE TO KEEP THIS THING GOING A WHILE. THEN GRAB A FLASHLIGHT AND MEET ME OUT THERE.
WE'RE GOING TO GET MORE GAS.

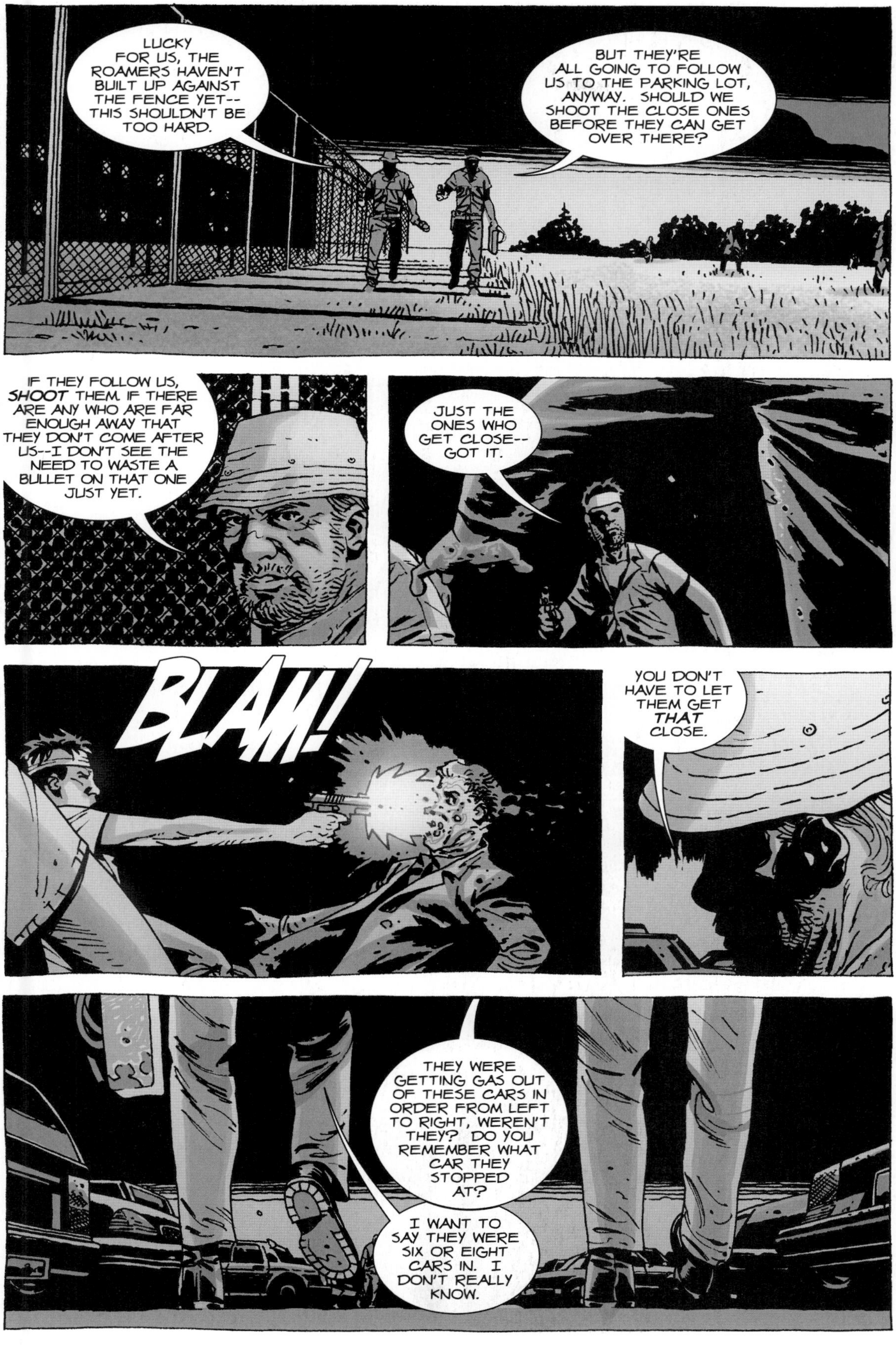
LUCKY FOR US, THE ROAMERS HAVEN'T BUILT UP AGAINST THE FENCE YET-- THIS SHOULDN'T BE TOO HARD.
BUT THEY'RE ALL GOING TO FOLLOW US TO THE PARKING LOT, ANYWAY. SHOULD WE SHOOT THE CLOSE ONES BEFORE THEY CAN GET OVER THERE?
IF THEY FOLLOW US, SHOOT THEM. IF THERE ARE ANY WHO ARE FAR ENOUGH AWAY THAT THEY DON'T COME AFTER US--I DON'T SEE THE NEED TO WASTE A BULLET ON THAT ONE JUST YET.
JUST THE ONES WHO GET CLOSE-- GOT IT.
BLAM!
YOU DON'T HAVE TO LET THEM GET THAT CLOSE.
THEY WERE GETTING GAS OUT OF THESE CARS IN ORDER FROM LEFT TO RIGHT, WEREN'T THEY? DO YOU REMEMBER WHAT CAR THEY STOPPED AT?
I WANT TO SAY THEY WERE SIX OR EIGHT CARS IN. I DON'T REALLY KNOW.

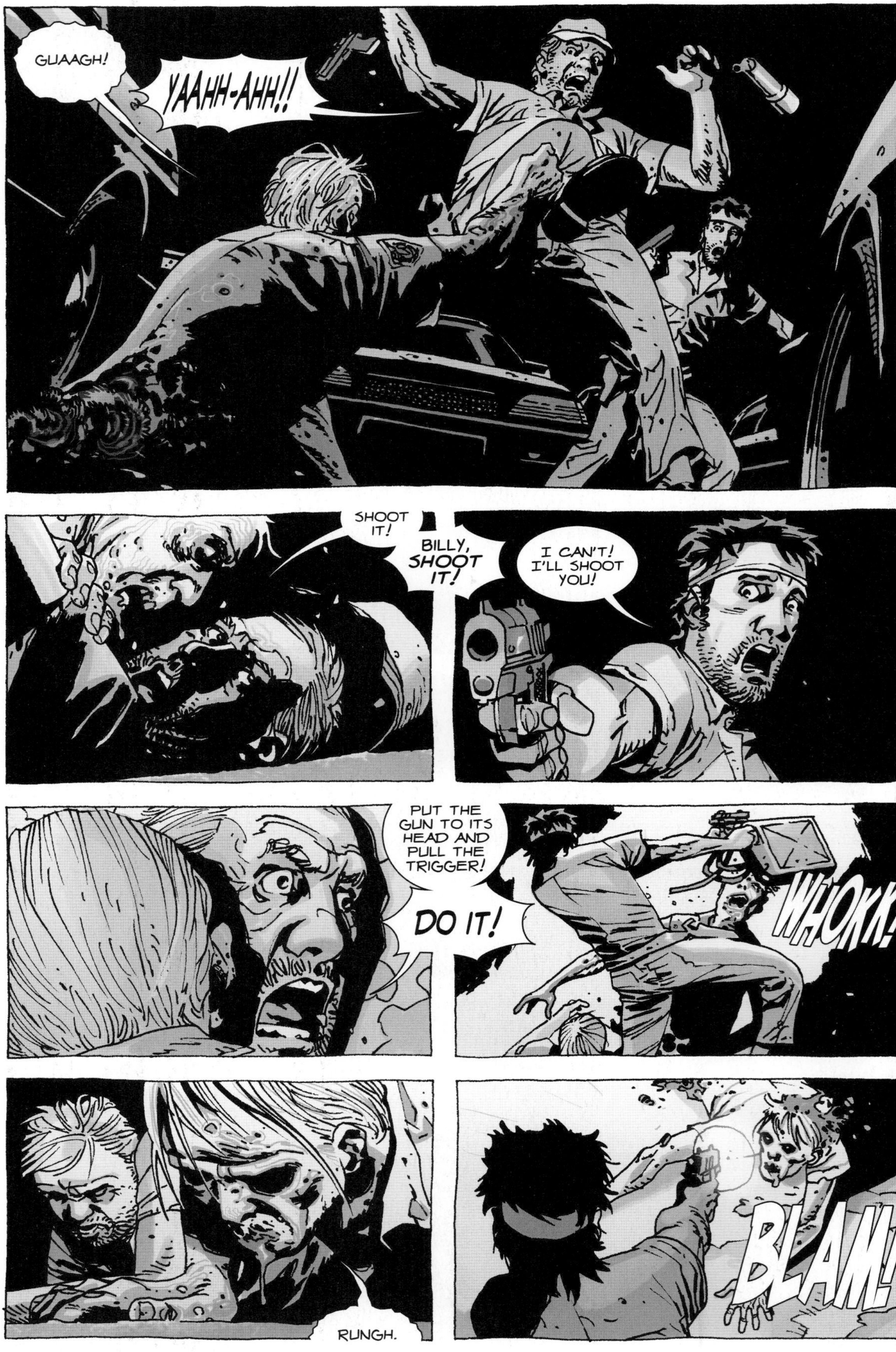
GUAAGH!
YAAHH-AHH!!
SHOOT IT!
BILLY, SHOOT IT!
I CAN'T! I'LL SHOOT YOU!
PUT THE GUN TO ITS HEAD AND PULL THE TRIGGER!
DO IT!
WHOKK!
RUNGH.
BLAM!

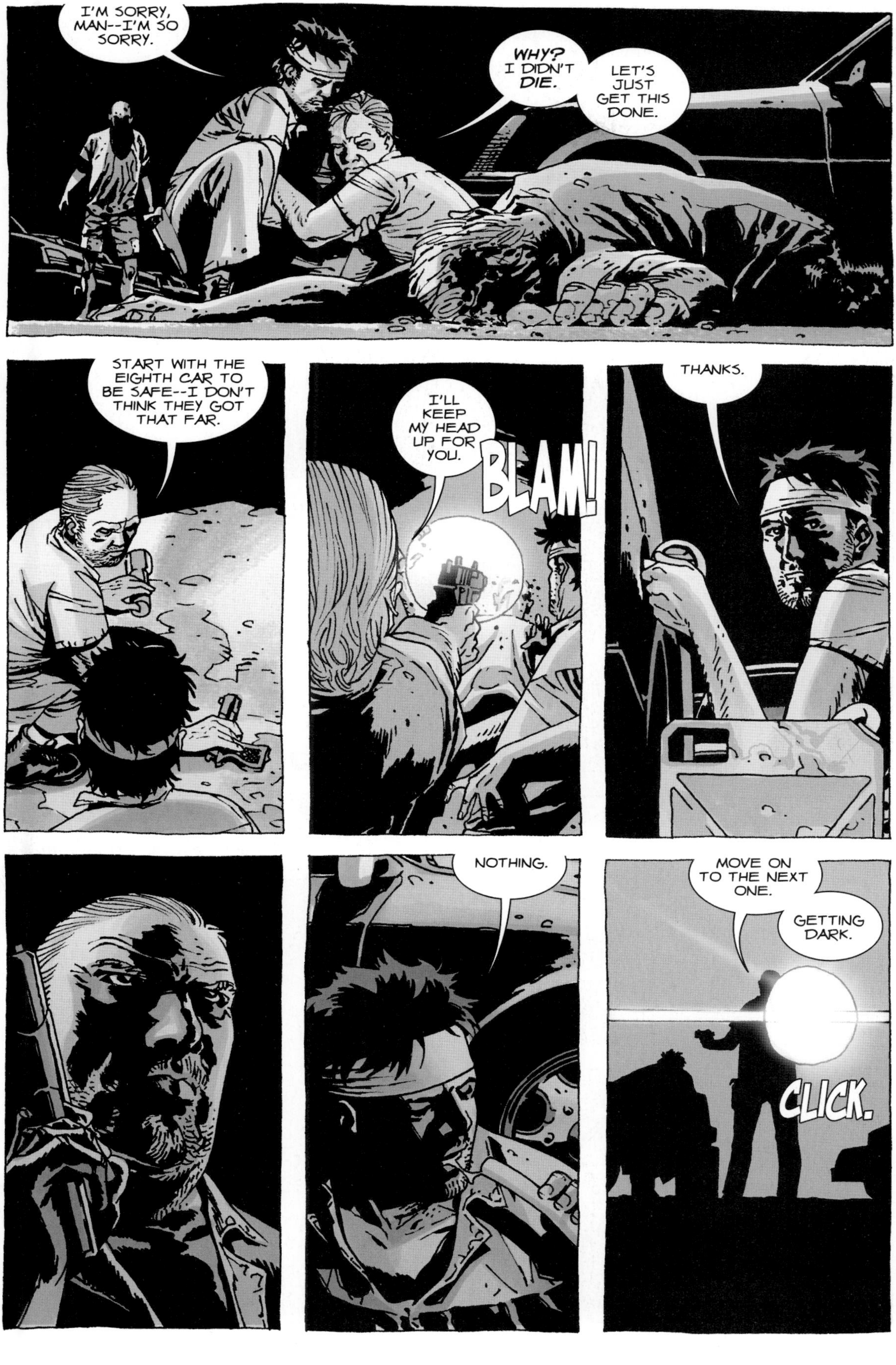
I'M SORRY, MAN--I'M SO SORRY.
WHY? I DIDN'T DIE.
LET'S JUST GET THIS DONE.
START WITH THE EIGHTH CAR TO BE SAFE--I DON'T THINK THEY GOT THAT FAR.
I'LL KEEP MY HEAD UP FOR YOU.
BLAM!
THANKS.
NOTHING.
MOVE ON TO THE NEXT ONE.
GETTING DARK.
CLICK.

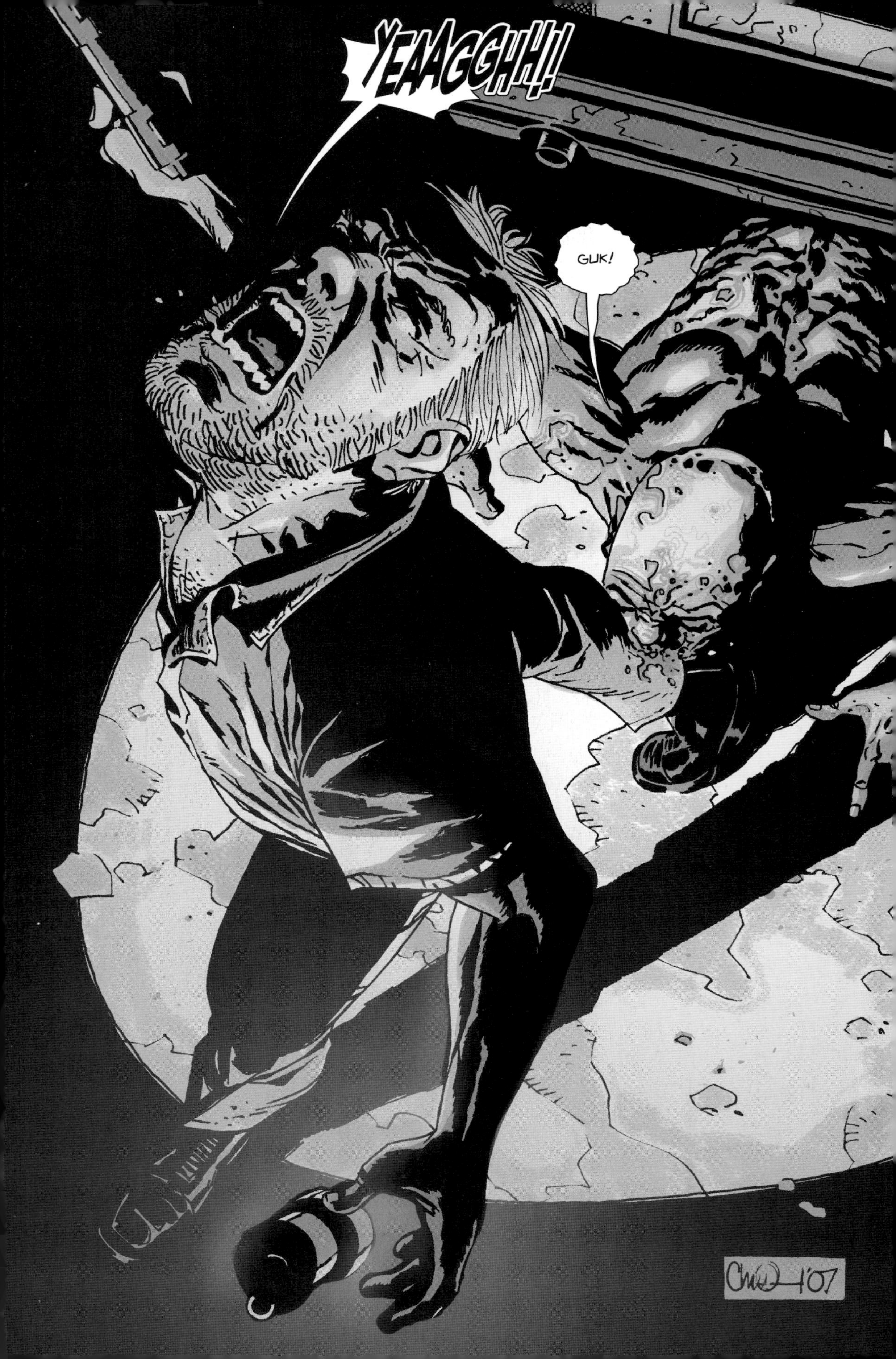
YEAAGGHH!!
GUK!

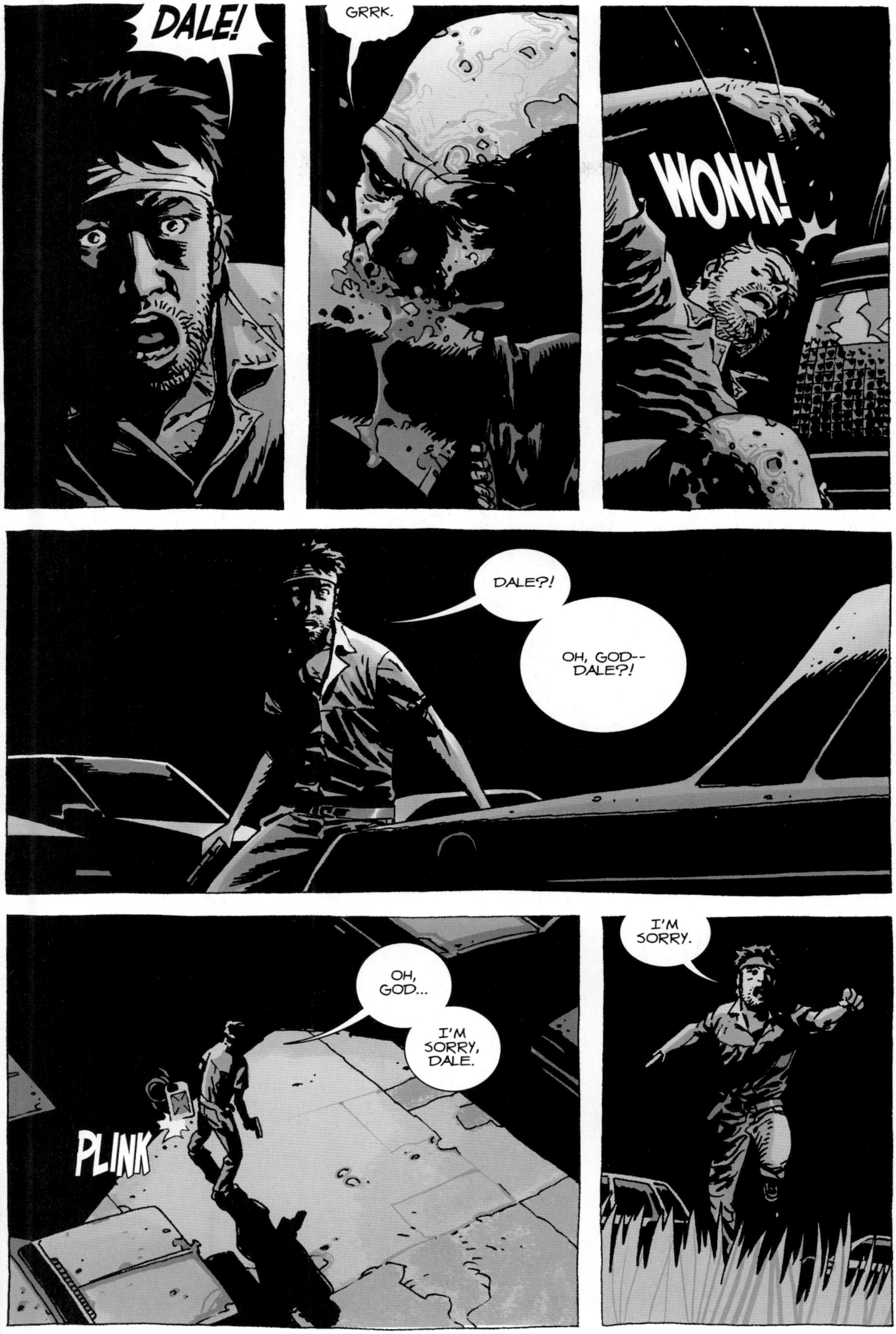
DALE!
GRRK.
WONK!
DALE?!
OH, GOD--
DALE?!
OH, GOD...
I'M SORRY, DALE.
PLINK
I'M SORRY.

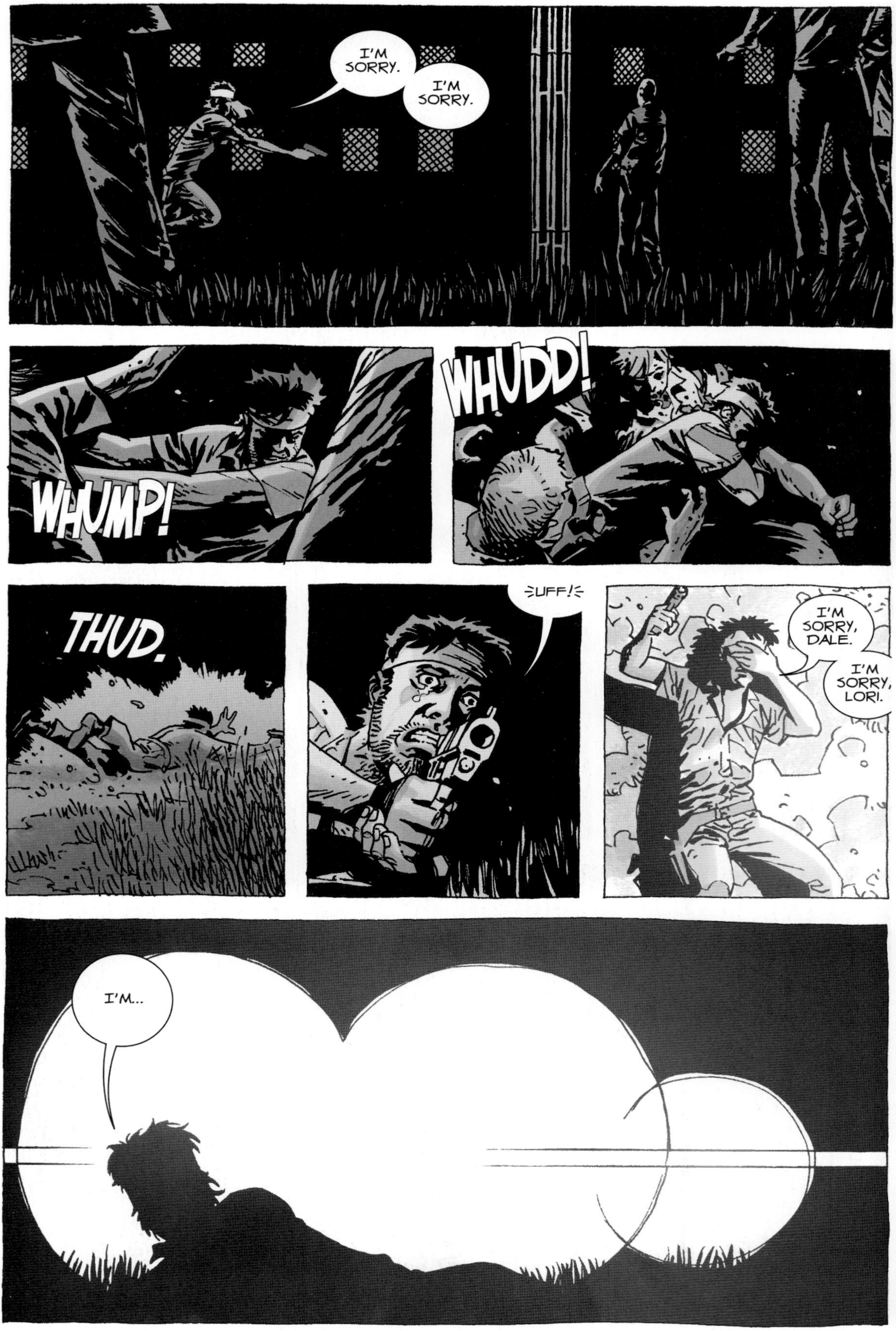
I'M SORRY.
I'M SORRY.
WHUMP!
WHUDD!
THUD.
UFF!
I'M SORRY, DALE.
I'M SORRY, LORI.
I'M...

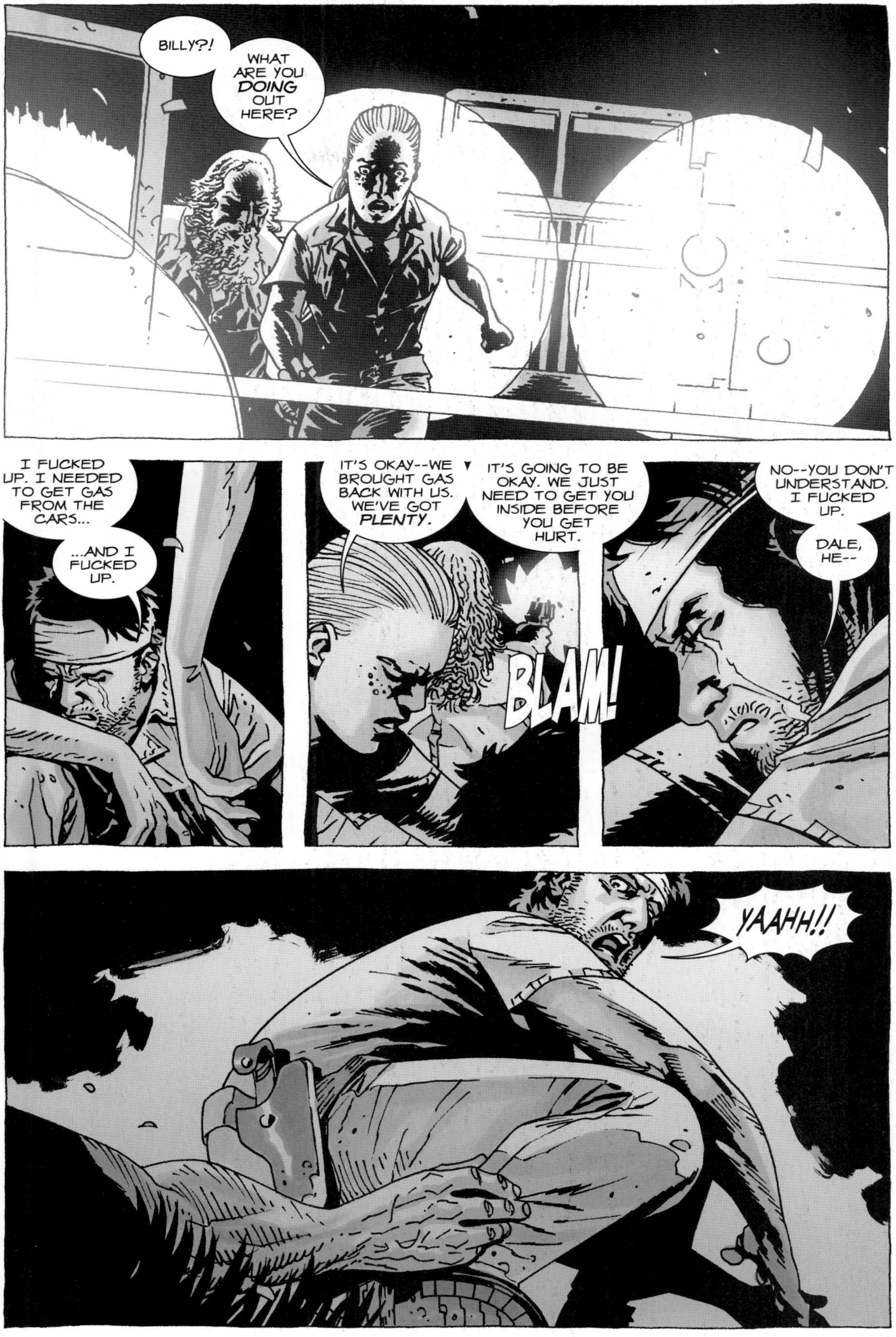
BILLY?!
WHAT ARE YOU DOING OUT HERE?
I FUCKED UP. I NEEDED TO GET GAS FROM THE CARS...
...AND I FUCKED UP.
IT'S OKAY--WE BROUGHT GAS BACK WITH US. WE'VE GOT PLENTY.
IT'S GOING TO BE OKAY. WE JUST NEED TO GET YOU INSIDE BEFORE YOU GET HURT.
BLAM!
NO--YOU DON'T UNDERSTAND. I FUCKED UP.
DALE, HE--
YAAHH!!

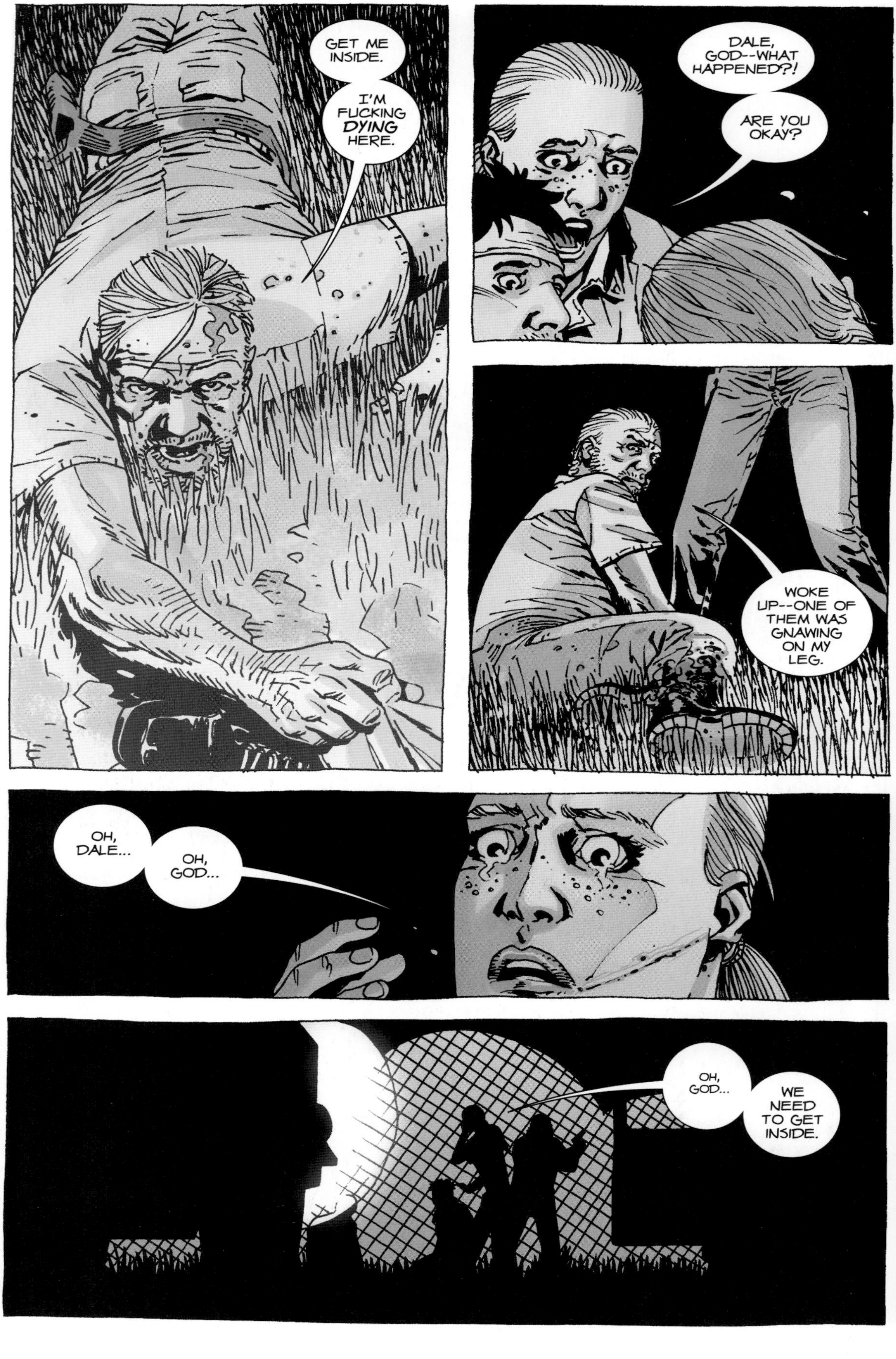
GET ME INSIDE.
I'M FUCKING DYING HERE.
DALE, GOD--WHAT HAPPENED?!
ARE YOU OKAY?
WOKE UP--ONE OF THEM WAS GNAWING ON MY LEG.
OH, DALE...
OH, GOD...
OH, GOD...
WE NEED TO GET INSIDE.

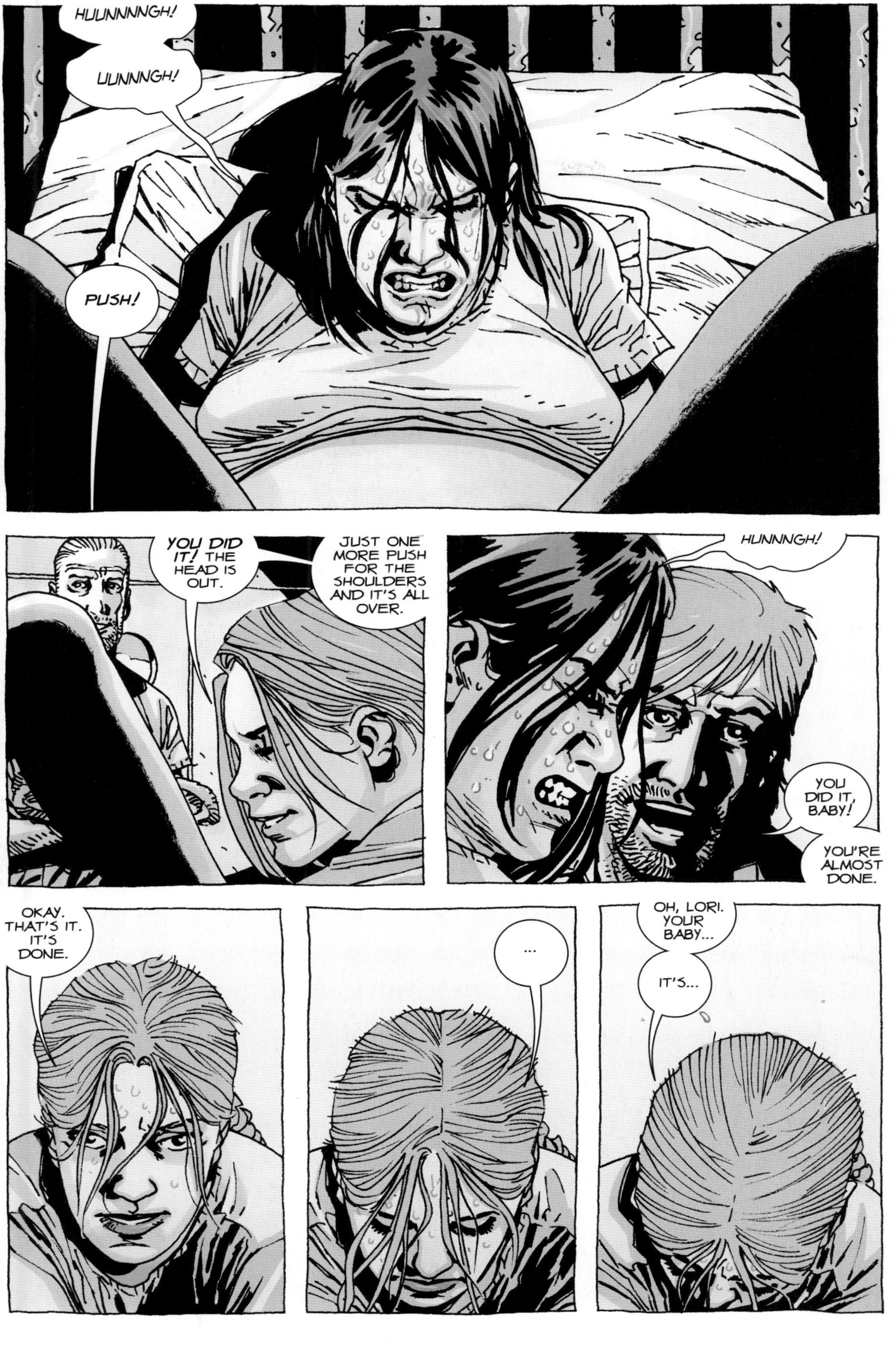
HUUNNNNGH!
UUNNNGH!
PUSH!
YOU DID IT! THE HEAD IS OUT.
JUST ONE MORE PUSH FOR THE SHOULDERS AND IT'S ALL OVER.
HUNNNGH!
YOU DID IT, BABY!
YOU'RE ALMOST DONE.
OKAY. THAT'S IT. IT'S DONE.
...
OH, LORI. YOUR BABY...
IT'S...

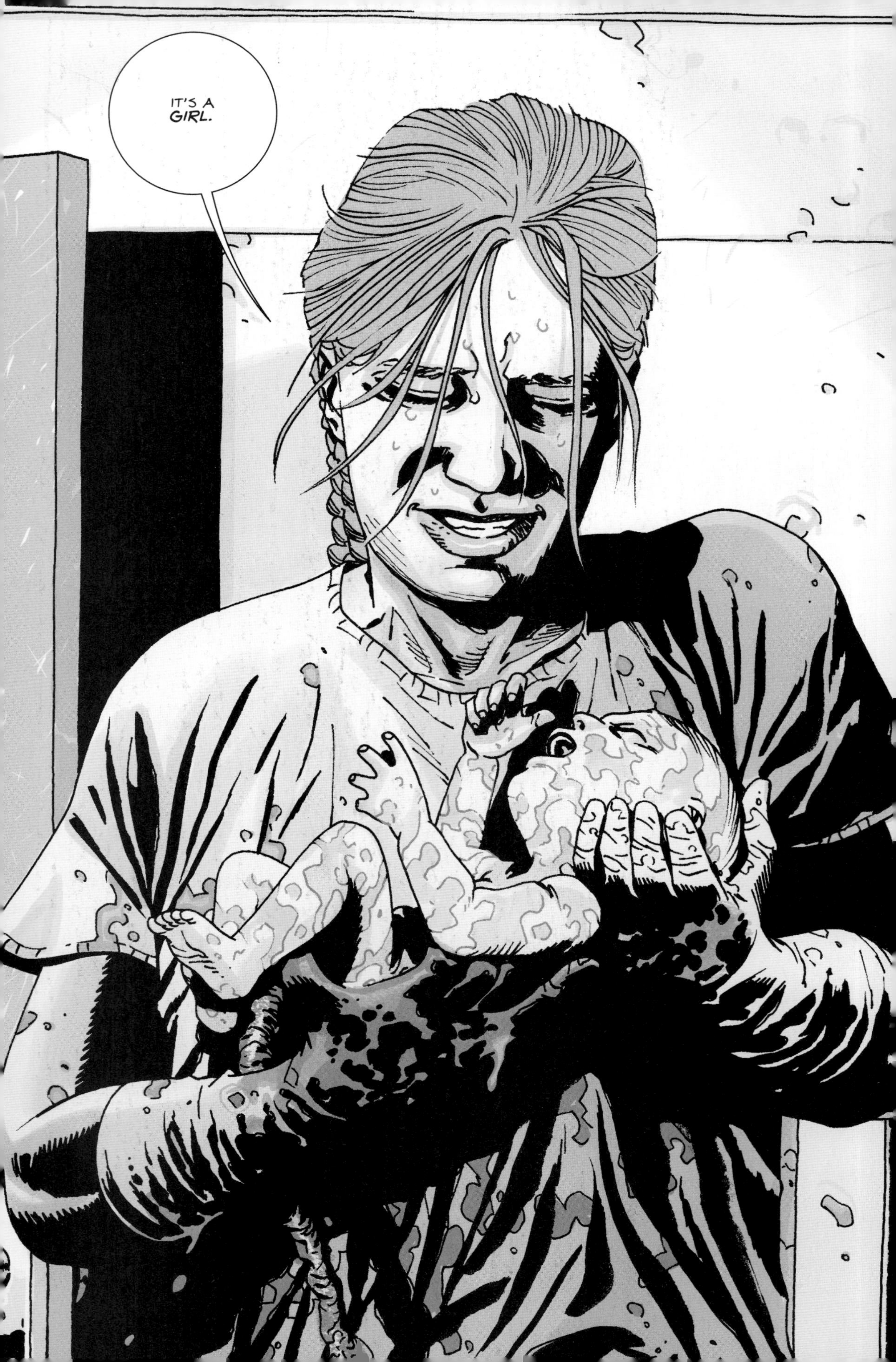
IT'S A GIRL.

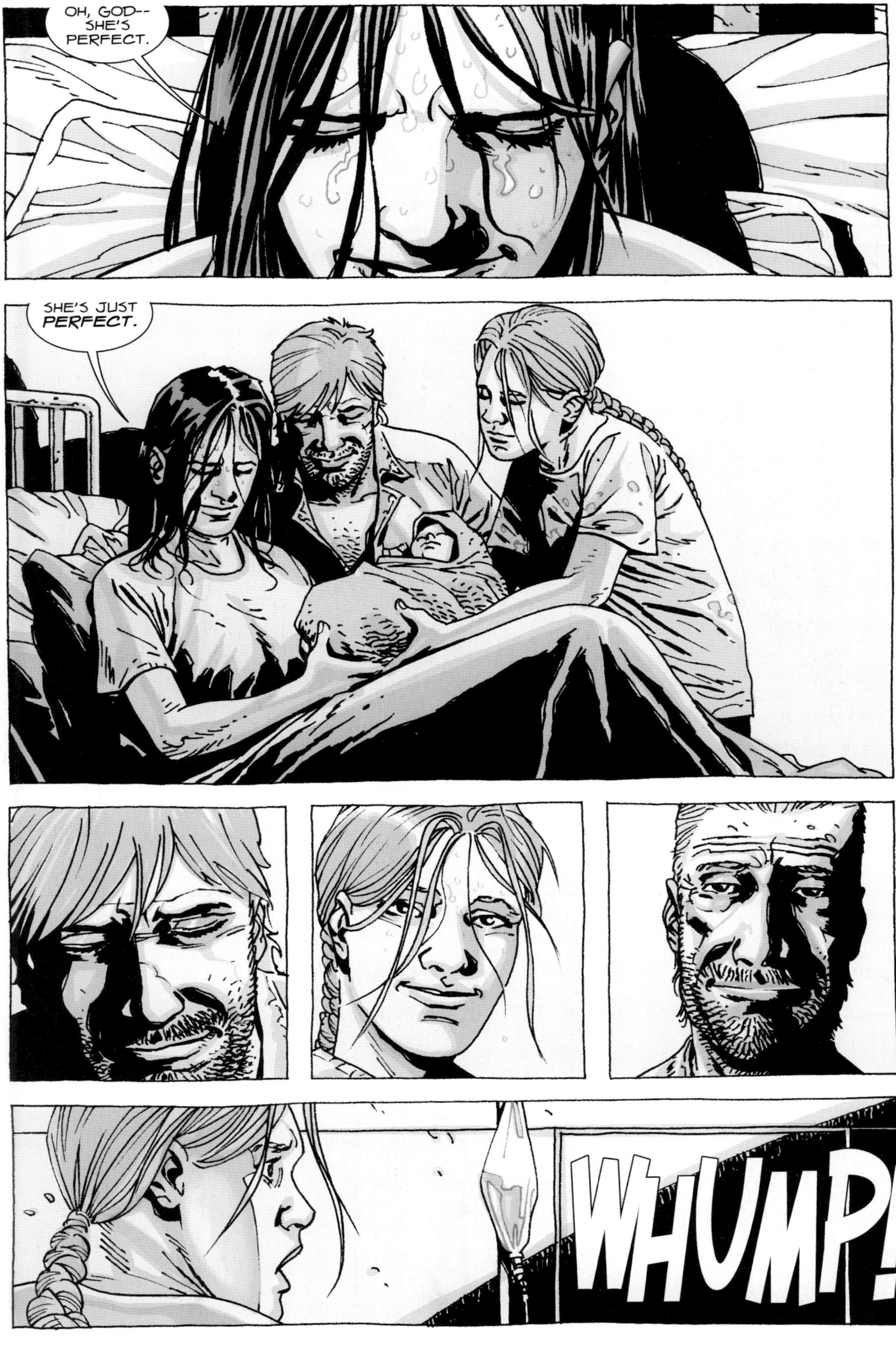
OH, GOD-- SHE'S PERFECT.
SHE'S JUST *PERFECT*.
WHUMP!

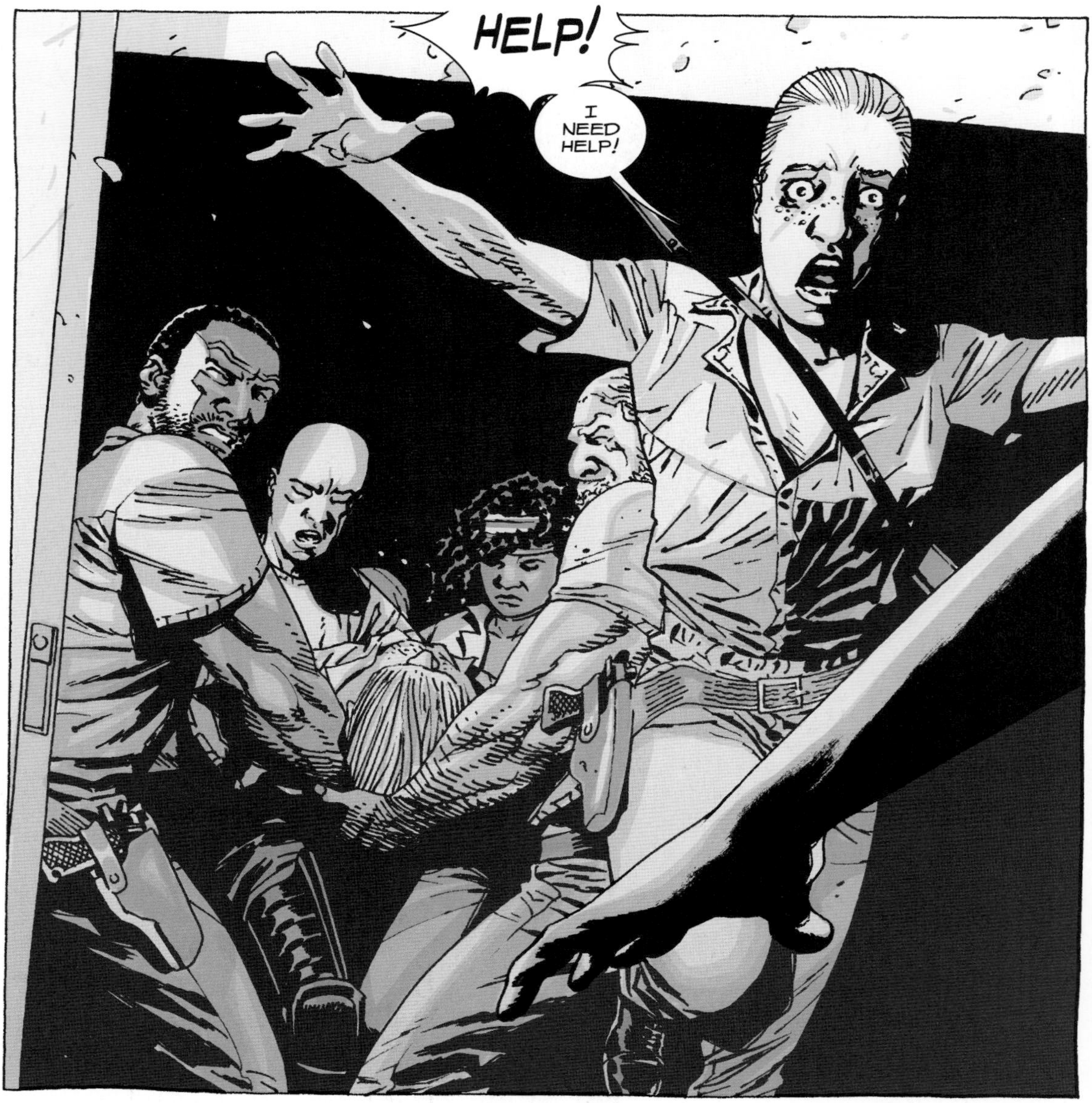
HELP!
I NEED HELP!

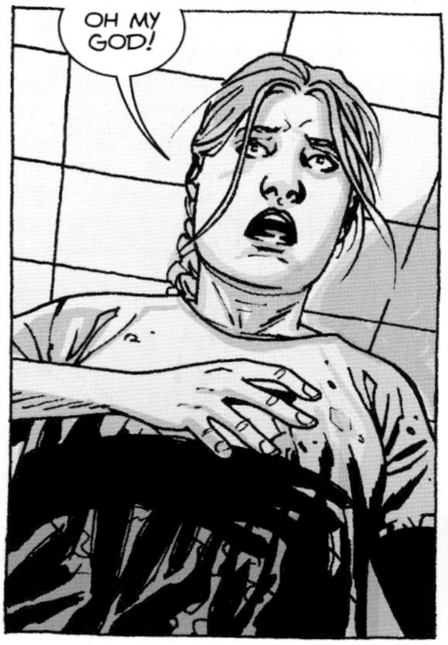
OH MY GOD!

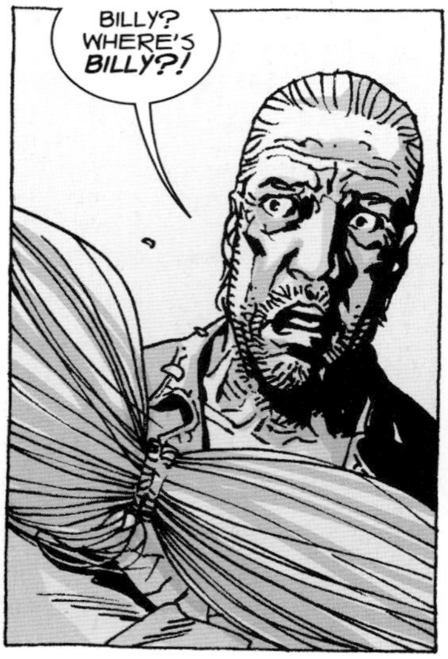
BILLY? WHERE'S BILLY?!

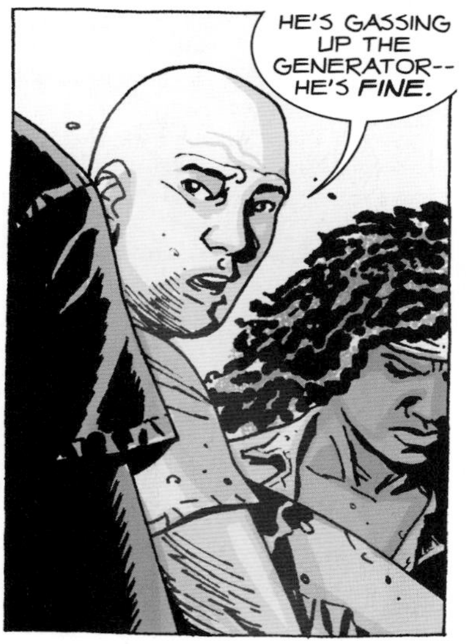
HE'S GASSING UP THE GENERATOR-- HE'S FINE.

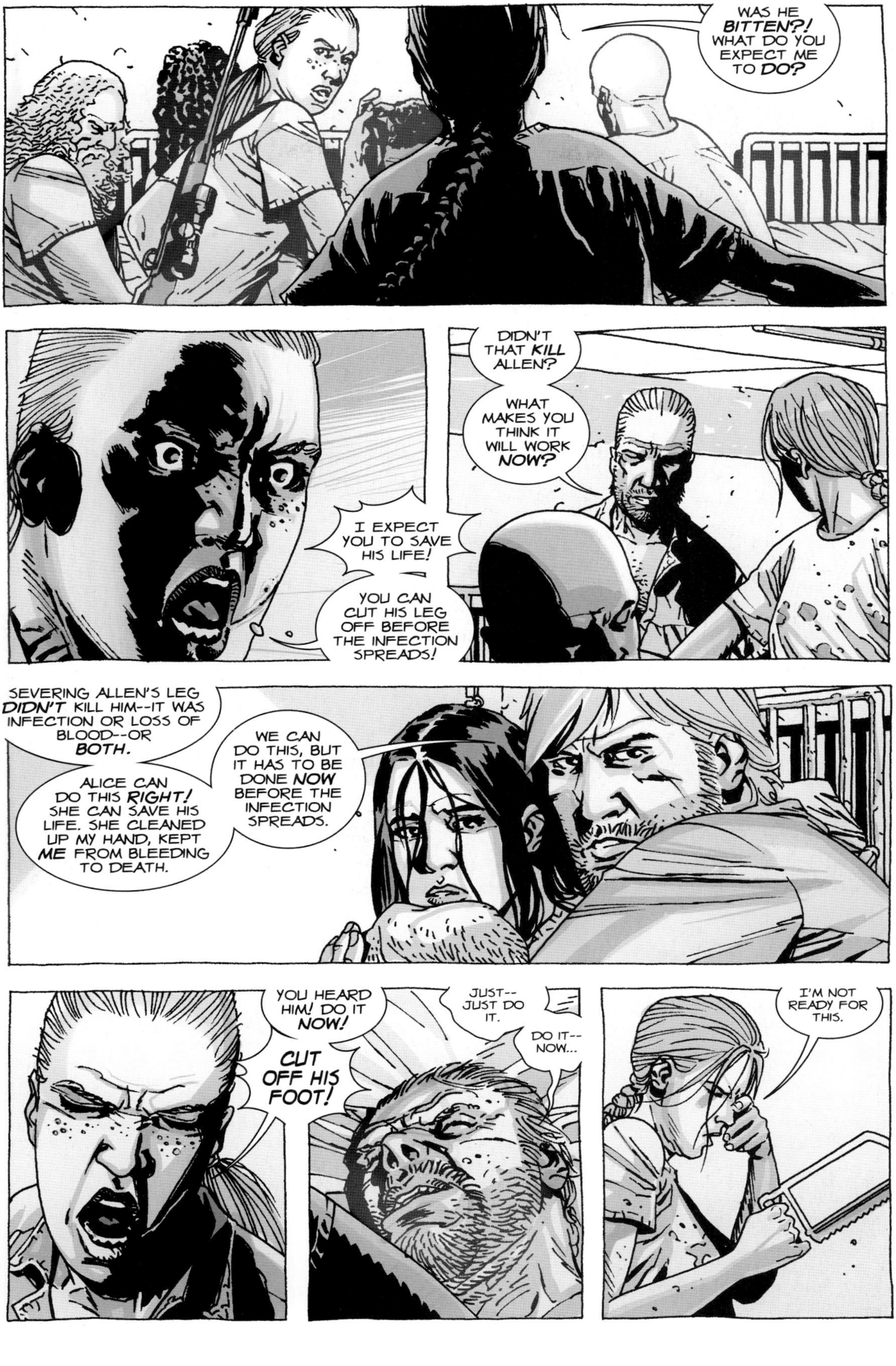

WAS HE BITTEN?! WHAT DO YOU EXPECT ME TO DO?
DIDN'T THAT KILL ALLEN?
WHAT MAKES YOU THINK IT WILL WORK NOW?
I EXPECT YOU TO SAVE HIS LIFE!
YOU CAN CUT HIS LEG OFF BEFORE THE INFECTION SPREADS!
SEVERING ALLEN'S LEG DIDN'T KILL HIM--IT WAS INFECTION OR LOSS OF BLOOD--OR BOTH.
ALICE CAN DO THIS RIGHT! SHE CAN SAVE HIS LIFE. SHE CLEANED UP MY HAND, KEPT ME FROM BLEEDING TO DEATH.
WE CAN DO THIS, BUT IT HAS TO BE DONE NOW BEFORE THE INFECTION SPREADS.
YOU HEARD HIM! DO IT NOW!
CUT OFF HIS FOOT!
JUST-- JUST DO IT.
DO IT-- NOW...
I'M NOT READY FOR THIS.

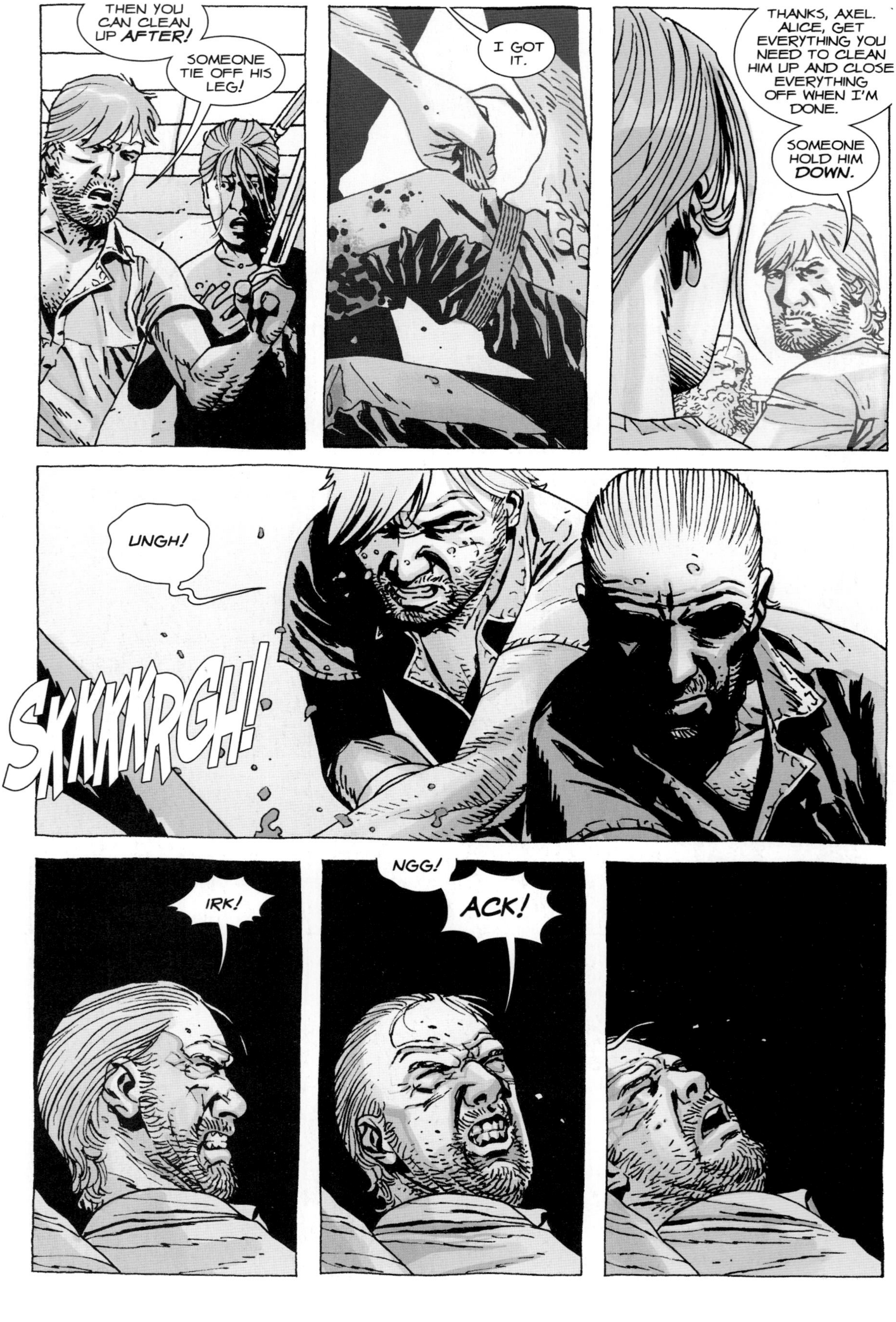

THEN YOU CAN CLEAN UP AFTER!
SOMEONE TIE OFF HIS LEG!
I GOT IT.
THANKS, AXEL. ALICE, GET EVERYTHING YOU NEED TO CLEAN HIM UP AND CLOSE EVERYTHING OFF WHEN I'M DONE.
SOMEONE HOLD HIM DOWN.
UNGH!
SKKKKRGH!
IRK!
NGG!
ACK!

DALE, OH GOD!!

IS HE *BREATHING?!*

HE'S BREATHING. HE'S FINE.

HE JUST PASSED OUT.

IT'S DONE.

ALL YOURS.

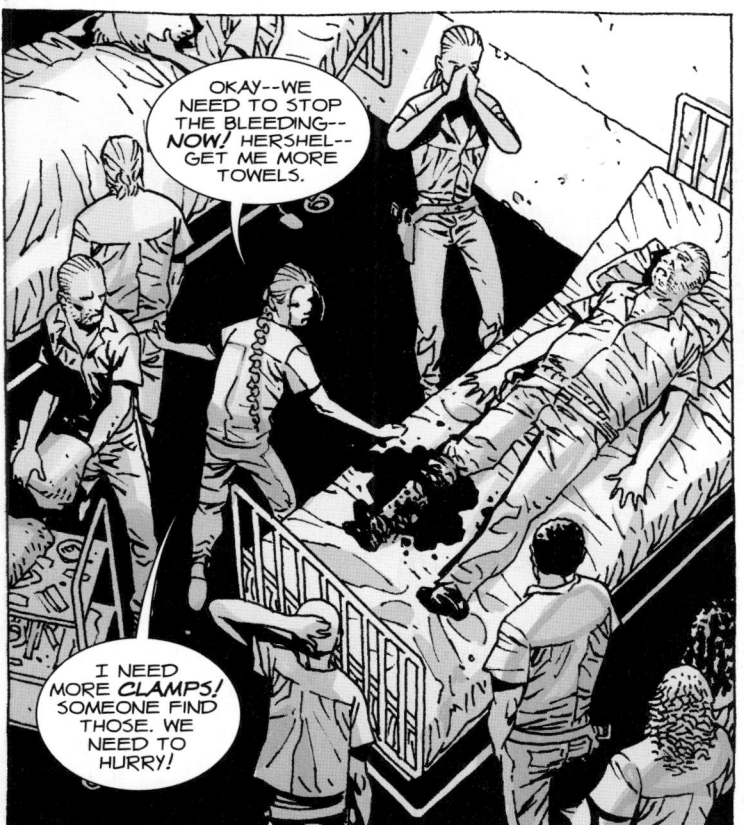

OKAY--WE NEED TO STOP THE BLEEDING-- *NOW!* HERSHEL-- GET ME MORE TOWELS.

I NEED MORE *CLAMPS!* SOMEONE FIND THOSE. WE NEED TO HURRY!

THIS WORLD...

THIS *FUCKING* WORLD...

...

I THINK WE SHOULD NAME HER *JUDITH.*

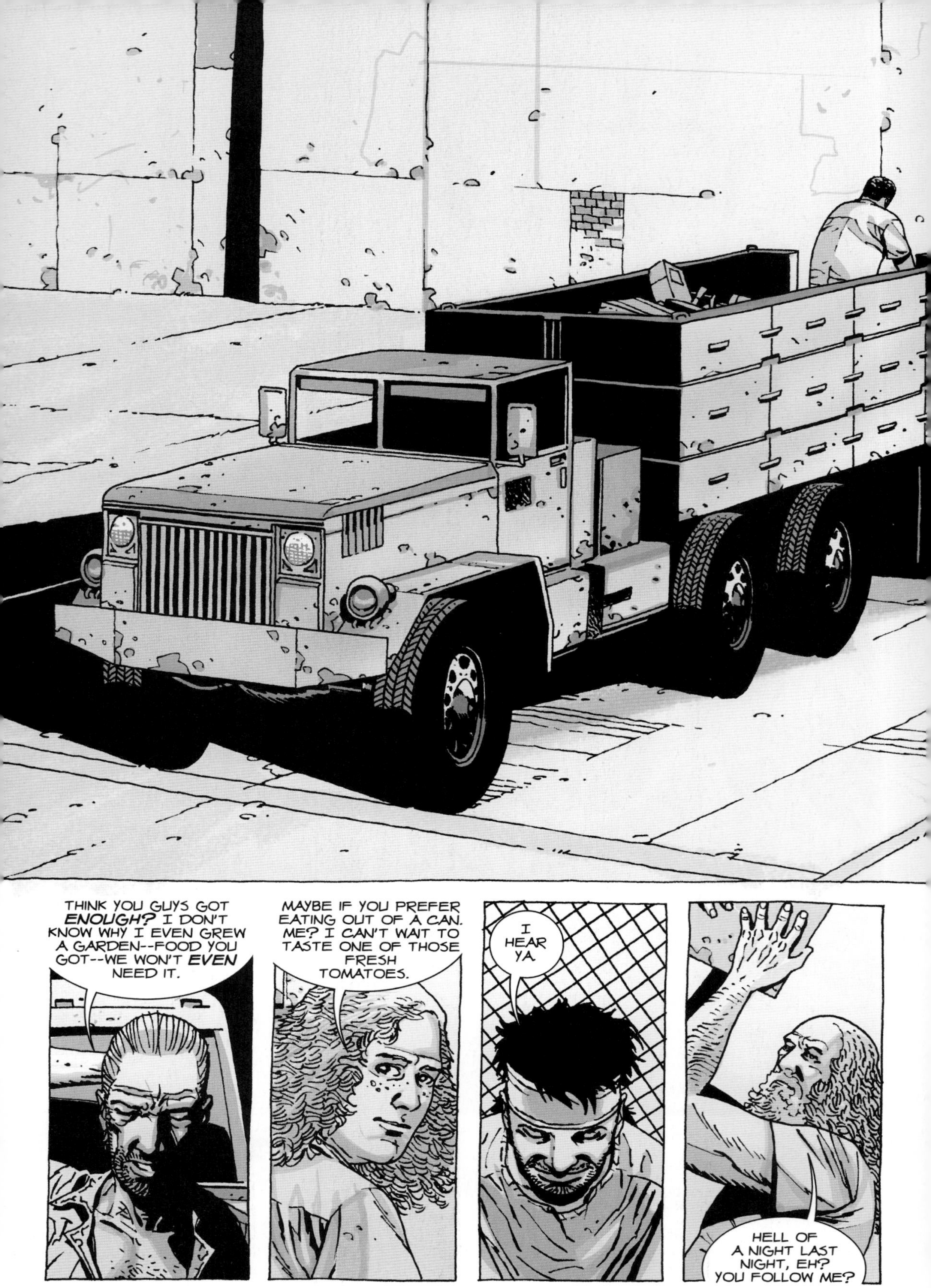
THINK YOU GUYS GOT ENOUGH? I DON'T KNOW WHY I EVEN GREW A GARDEN--FOOD YOU GOT--WE WON'T EVEN NEED IT.
MAYBE IF YOU PREFER EATING OUT OF A CAN. ME? I CAN'T WAIT TO TASTE ONE OF THOSE FRESH TOMATOES.
I HEAR YA.
HELL OF A NIGHT LAST NIGHT, EH? YOU FOLLOW ME?

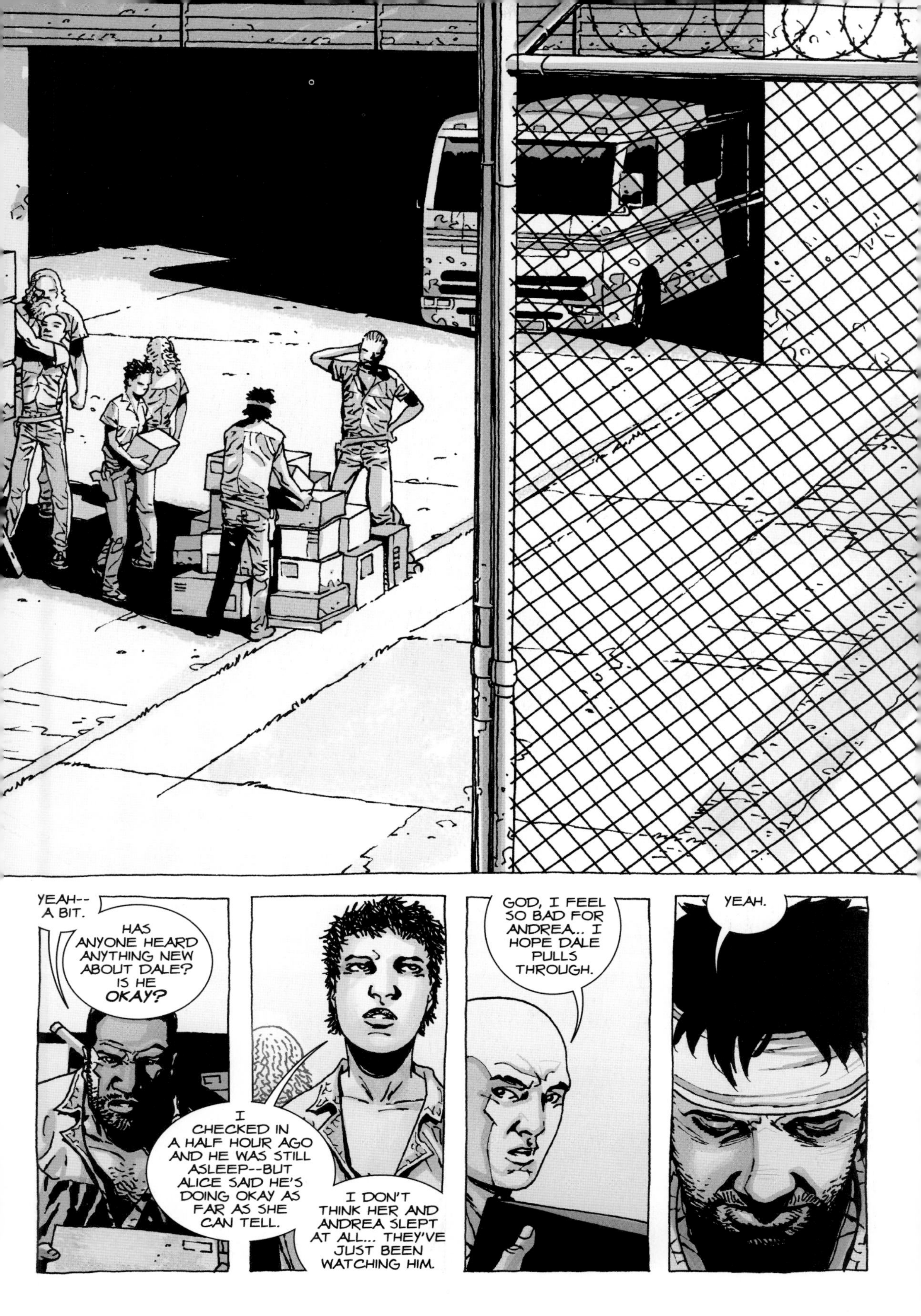
HAS ANYONE HEARD ANYTHING NEW ABOUT DALE? IS HE OKAY?
YEAH-- A BIT.
I CHECKED IN A HALF HOUR AGO AND HE WAS STILL ASLEEP--BUT ALICE SAID HE'S DOING OKAY AS FAR AS SHE CAN TELL.
I DON'T THINK HER AND ANDREA SLEPT AT ALL... THEY'VE JUST BEEN WATCHING HIM.
GOD, I FEEL SO BAD FOR ANDREA.. I HOPE DALE PULLS THROUGH.
YEAH.

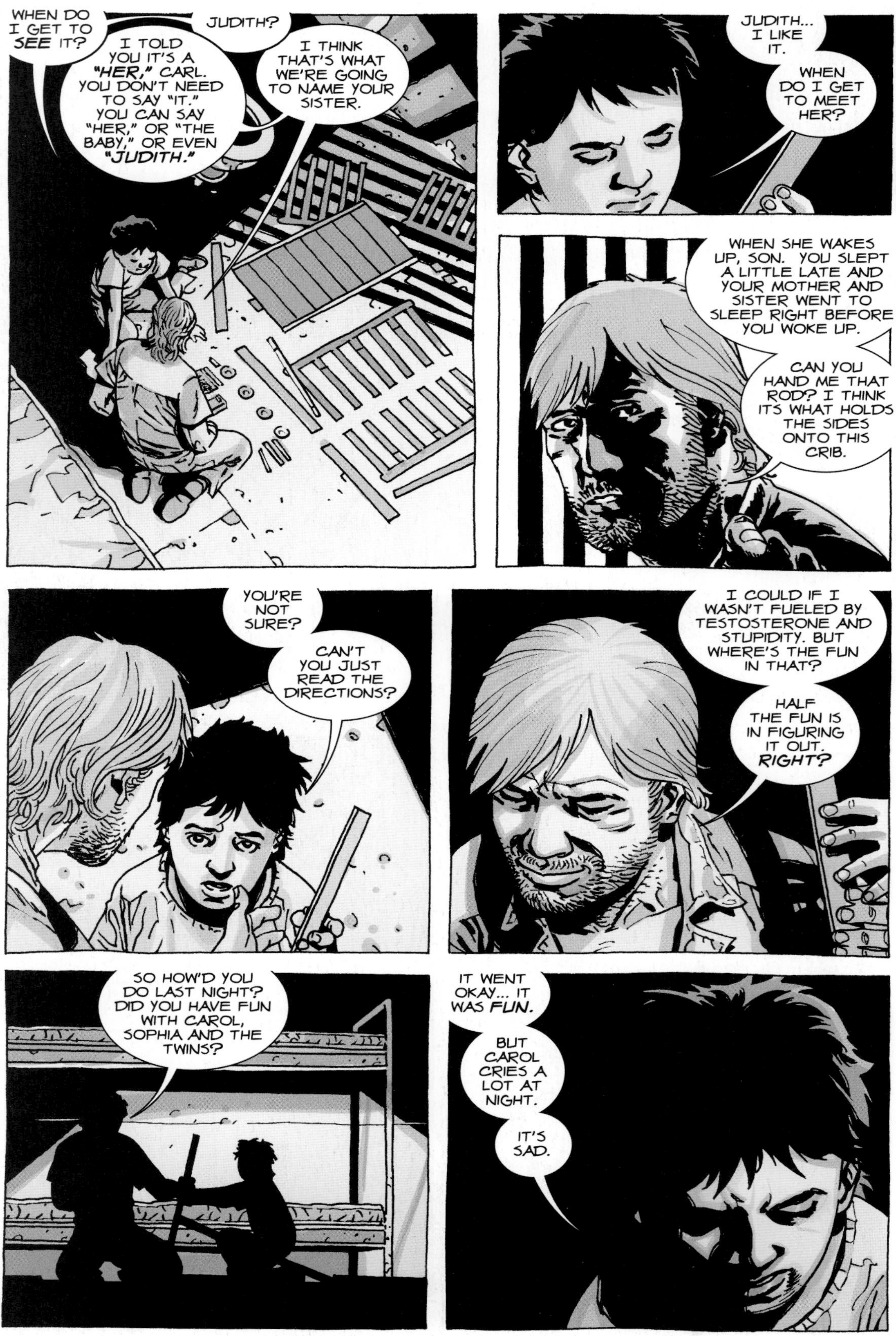
WHEN DO I GET TO SEE IT?
JUDITH?
I TOLD YOU IT'S A "HER," CARL. YOU DON'T NEED TO SAY "IT." YOU CAN SAY "HER," OR "THE BABY," OR EVEN "JUDITH."
I THINK THAT'S WHAT WE'RE GOING TO NAME YOUR SISTER.
JUDITH... I LIKE IT.
WHEN DO I GET TO MEET HER?
WHEN SHE WAKES UP, SON. YOU SLEPT A LITTLE LATE AND YOUR MOTHER AND SISTER WENT TO SLEEP RIGHT BEFORE YOU WOKE UP.
CAN YOU HAND ME THAT ROD? I THINK ITS WHAT HOLDS THE SIDES ONTO THIS CRIB.
YOU'RE NOT SURE?
CAN'T YOU JUST READ THE DIRECTIONS?
I COULD IF I WASN'T FUELED BY TESTOSTERONE AND STUPIDITY. BUT WHERE'S THE FUN IN THAT?
HALF THE FUN IS IN FIGURING IT OUT. RIGHT?
SO HOW'D YOU DO LAST NIGHT? DID YOU HAVE FUN WITH CAROL, SOPHIA AND THE TWINS?
IT WENT OKAY... IT WAS FUN.
BUT CAROL CRIES A LOT AT NIGHT.
IT'S SAD.

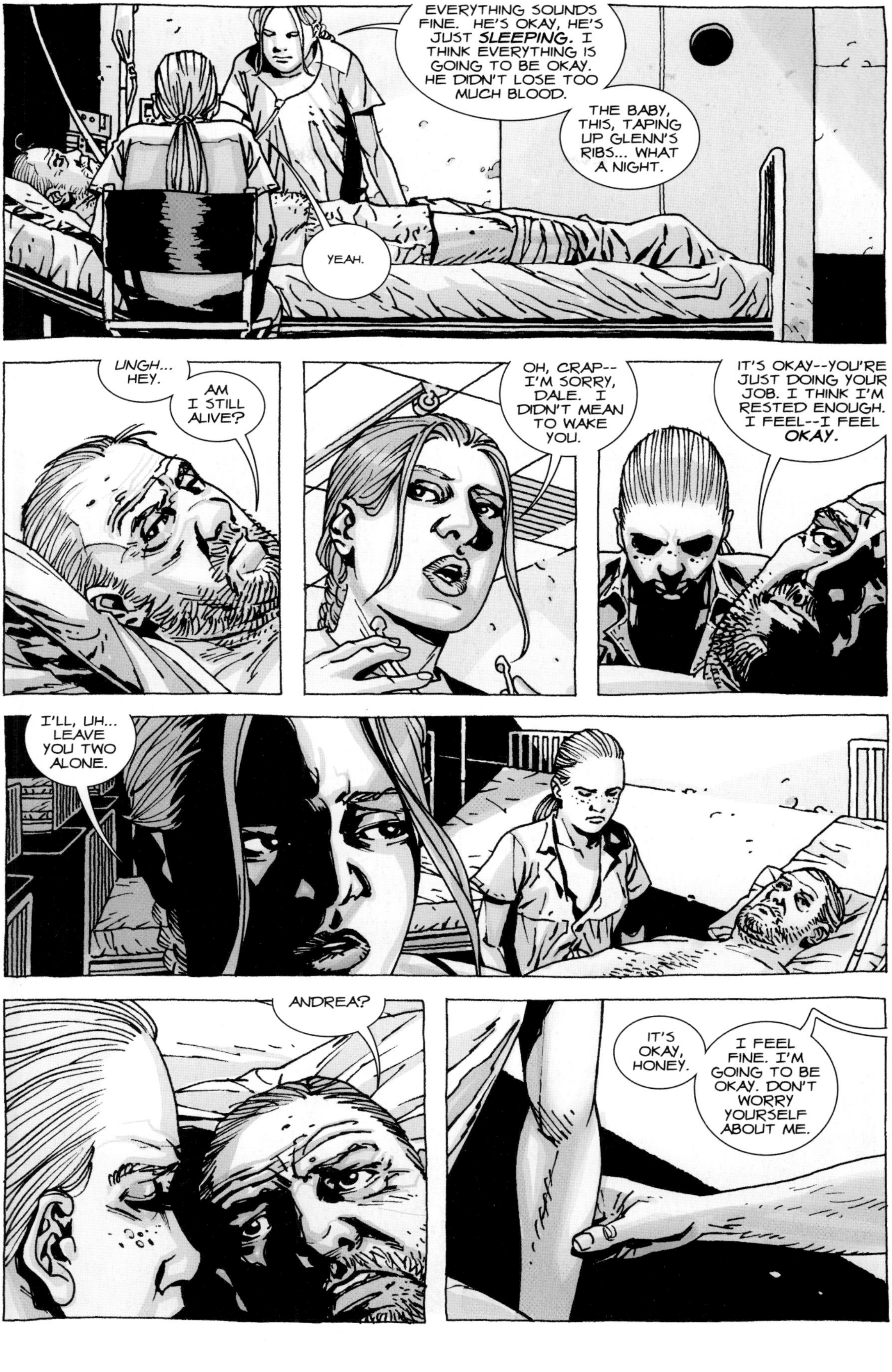
EVERYTHING SOUNDS FINE. HE'S OKAY, HE'S JUST SLEEPING. I THINK EVERYTHING IS GOING TO BE OKAY. HE DIDN'T LOSE TOO MUCH BLOOD.
THE BABY, THIS, TAPING UP GLENN'S RIBS... WHAT A NIGHT.
YEAH.
UNGH... HEY.
AM I STILL ALIVE?
OH, CRAP-- I'M SORRY, DALE. I DIDN'T MEAN TO WAKE YOU.
IT'S OKAY--YOU'RE JUST DOING YOUR JOB. I THINK I'M RESTED ENOUGH. I FEEL--I FEEL OKAY.
I'LL, UH... LEAVE YOU TWO ALONE.
ANDREA?
IT'S OKAY, HONEY.
I FEEL FINE. I'M GOING TO BE OKAY. DON'T WORRY YOURSELF ABOUT ME.

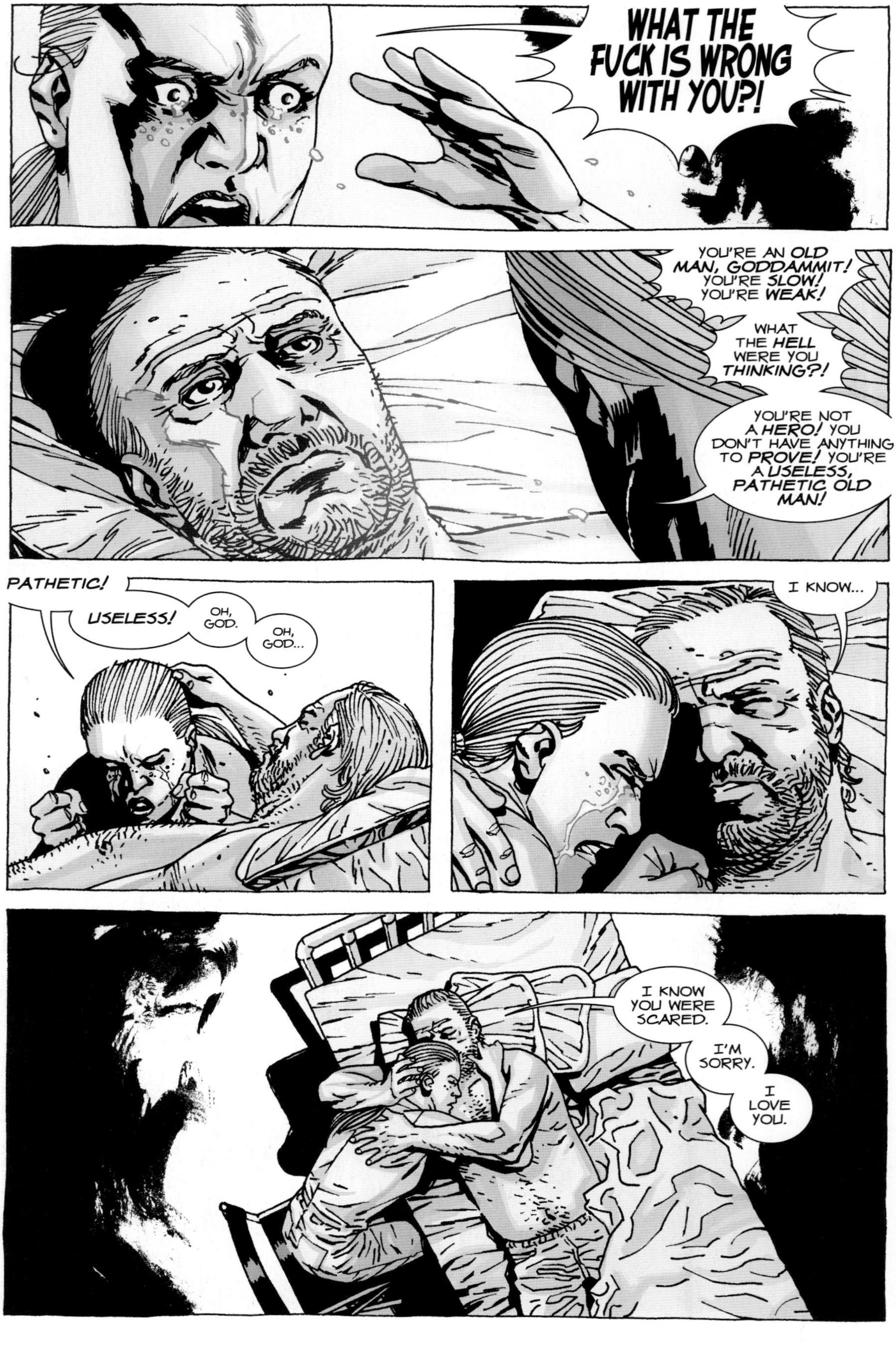
WHAT THE FUCK IS WRONG WITH YOU?!
YOU'RE AN OLD MAN, GODDAMMIT! YOU'RE SLOW! YOU'RE WEAK!
WHAT THE HELL WERE YOU THINKING?!
YOU'RE NOT A HERO! YOU DON'T HAVE ANYTHING TO PROVE! YOU'RE A USELESS, PATHETIC OLD MAN!
PATHETIC!
USELESS!
OH, GOD.
OH, GOD...
I KNOW...
I KNOW YOU WERE SCARED.
I'M SORRY.
I LOVE YOU.

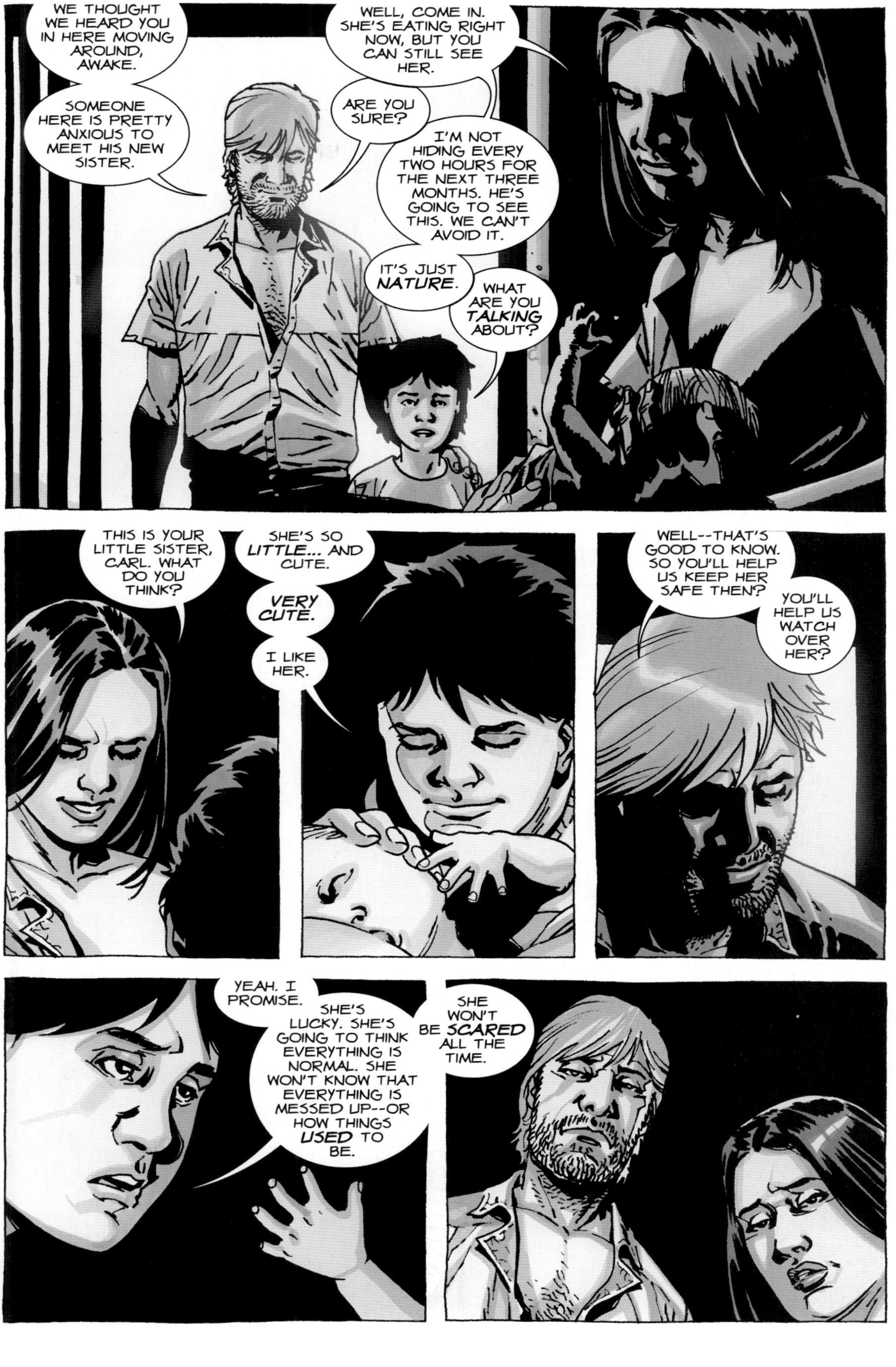
WE THOUGHT WE HEARD YOU IN HERE MOVING AROUND, AWAKE.
SOMEONE HERE IS PRETTY ANXIOUS TO MEET HIS NEW SISTER.
WELL, COME IN. SHE'S EATING RIGHT NOW, BUT YOU CAN STILL SEE HER.
ARE YOU SURE?
I'M NOT HIDING EVERY TWO HOURS FOR THE NEXT THREE MONTHS. HE'S GOING TO SEE THIS. WE CAN'T AVOID IT.
IT'S JUST NATURE.
WHAT ARE YOU TALKING ABOUT?
THIS IS YOUR LITTLE SISTER, CARL. WHAT DO YOU THINK?
SHE'S SO LITTLE... AND CUTE.
VERY CUTE.
I LIKE HER.
WELL--THAT'S GOOD TO KNOW. SO YOU'LL HELP US KEEP HER SAFE THEN?
YOU'LL HELP US WATCH OVER HER?
YEAH. I PROMISE.
SHE'S LUCKY. SHE'S GOING TO THINK EVERYTHING IS NORMAL. SHE WON'T KNOW THAT EVERYTHING IS MESSED UP--OR HOW THINGS USED TO BE.
SHE WON'T BE SCARED ALL THE TIME.

I'M SWEATING BUCKETS OUT HERE. YOU FOLLOW ME?

ACCORDING TO ANDREA'S CALENDAR-- IF THAT'S AT ALL ACCURATE ANYMORE... IT'S EARLY JULY.

FEELS LIKE *AUGUST* TO ME.

FEELS LIKE *HELL.*

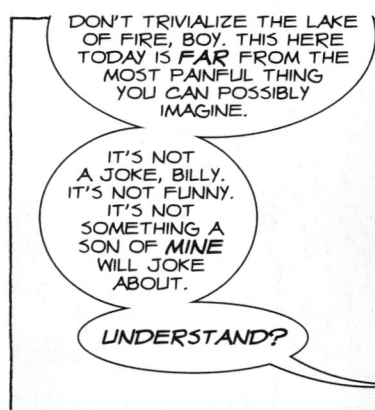

DON'T TRIVIALIZE THE LAKE OF FIRE, BOY. THIS HERE TODAY IS *FAR* FROM THE MOST PAINFUL THING YOU CAN POSSIBLY IMAGINE.

IT'S NOT A JOKE, BILLY. IT'S NOT FUNNY. IT'S NOT SOMETHING A SON OF *MINE* WILL JOKE ABOUT.

UNDERSTAND?

UH, Y--YEAH, DAD.

SORRY.

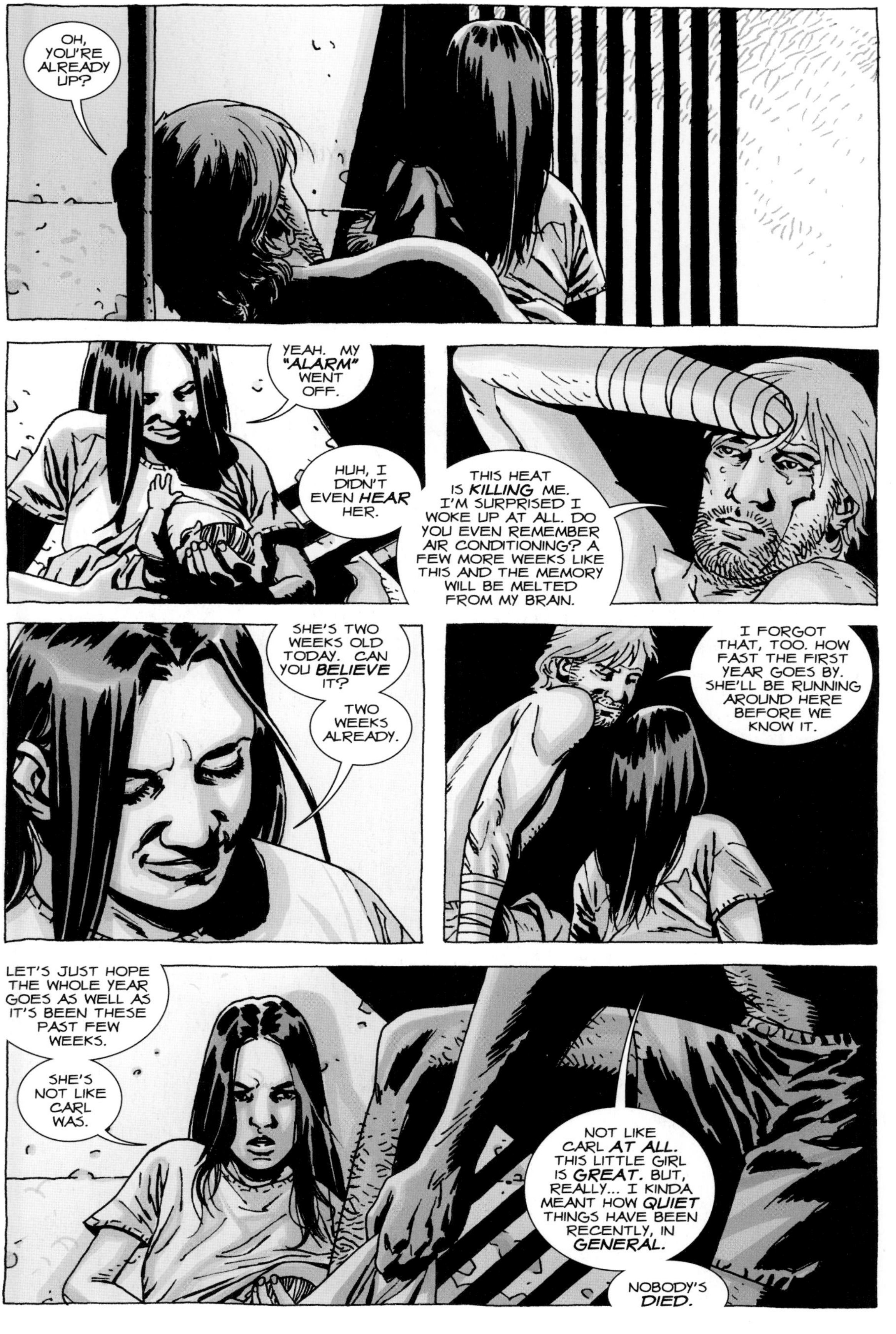
OH, YOU'RE ALREADY UP?
YEAH. MY "ALARM" WENT OFF.
HUH, I DIDN'T EVEN HEAR HER.
THIS HEAT IS KILLING ME. I'M SURPRISED I WOKE UP AT ALL. DO YOU EVEN REMEMBER AIR CONDITIONING? A FEW MORE WEEKS LIKE THIS AND THE MEMORY WILL BE MELTED FROM MY BRAIN.
SHE'S TWO WEEKS OLD TODAY. CAN YOU BELIEVE IT?
TWO WEEKS ALREADY.
I FORGOT THAT, TOO. HOW FAST THE FIRST YEAR GOES BY. SHE'LL BE RUNNING AROUND HERE BEFORE WE KNOW IT.
LET'S JUST HOPE THE WHOLE YEAR GOES AS WELL AS IT'S BEEN THESE PAST FEW WEEKS.
SHE'S NOT LIKE CARL WAS.
NOT LIKE CARL AT ALL. THIS LITTLE GIRL IS GREAT. BUT, REALLY... I KINDA MEANT HOW QUIET THINGS HAVE BEEN RECENTLY, IN GENERAL.
NOBODY'S DIED.

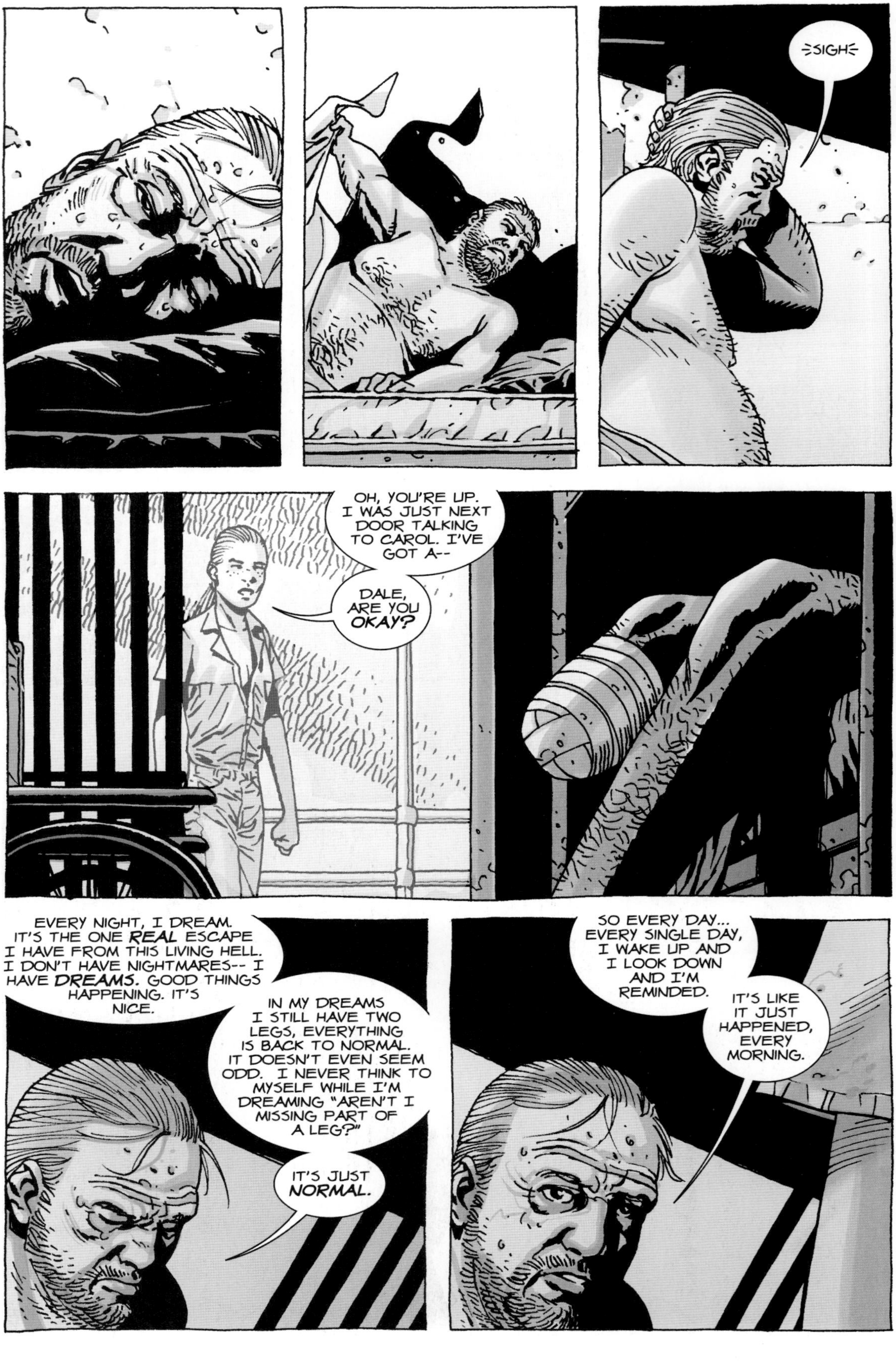

SIGH
OH, YOU'RE UP. I WAS JUST NEXT DOOR TALKING TO CAROL. I'VE GOT A--
DALE, ARE YOU OKAY?
EVERY NIGHT, I DREAM. IT'S THE ONE REAL ESCAPE I HAVE FROM THIS LIVING HELL. I DON'T HAVE NIGHTMARES-- I HAVE DREAMS. GOOD THINGS HAPPENING. IT'S NICE.
IN MY DREAMS I STILL HAVE TWO LEGS, EVERYTHING IS BACK TO NORMAL. IT DOESN'T EVEN SEEM ODD. I NEVER THINK TO MYSELF WHILE I'M DREAMING "AREN'T I MISSING PART OF A LEG?"
IT'S JUST NORMAL.
SO EVERY DAY... EVERY SINGLE DAY, I WAKE UP AND I LOOK DOWN AND I'M REMINDED.
IT'S LIKE IT JUST HAPPENED, EVERY MORNING.

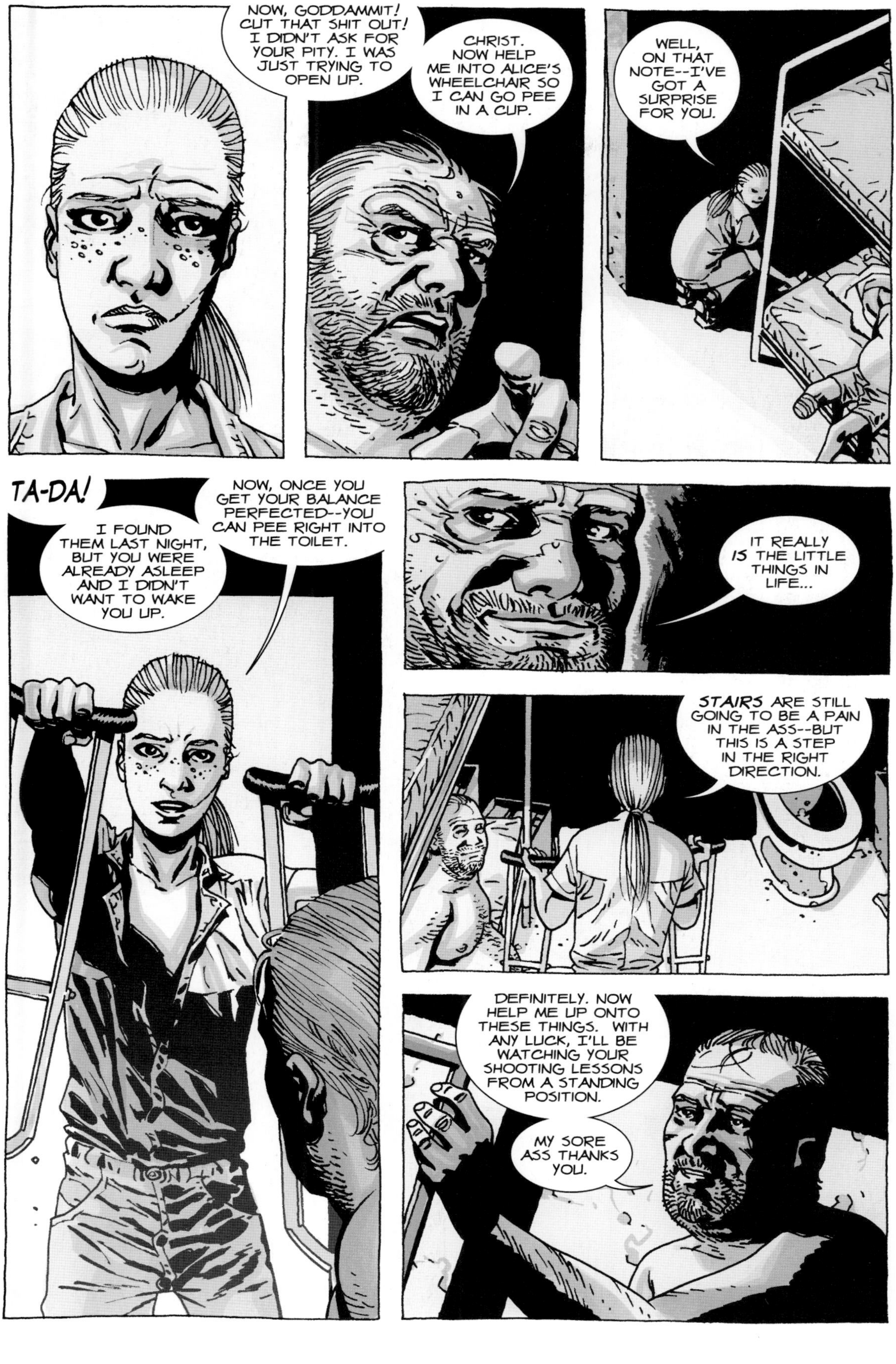
NOW, GODDAMMIT! CUT THAT SHIT OUT! I DIDN'T ASK FOR YOUR PITY. I WAS JUST TRYING TO OPEN UP.
CHRIST. NOW HELP ME INTO ALICE'S WHEELCHAIR SO I CAN GO PEE IN A CUP.
WELL, ON THAT NOTE--I'VE GOT A SURPRISE FOR YOU.
TA-DA!
I FOUND THEM LAST NIGHT, BUT YOU WERE ALREADY ASLEEP AND I DIDN'T WANT TO WAKE YOU UP.
NOW, ONCE YOU GET YOUR BALANCE PERFECTED--YOU CAN PEE RIGHT INTO THE TOILET.
IT REALLY *IS* THE LITTLE THINGS IN LIFE...
STAIRS ARE STILL GOING TO BE A PAIN IN THE ASS--BUT THIS IS A STEP IN THE RIGHT DIRECTION.
DEFINITELY. NOW HELP ME UP ONTO THESE THINGS. WITH ANY LUCK, I'LL BE WATCHING YOUR SHOOTING LESSONS FROM A STANDING POSITION.
MY SORE ASS THANKS YOU.

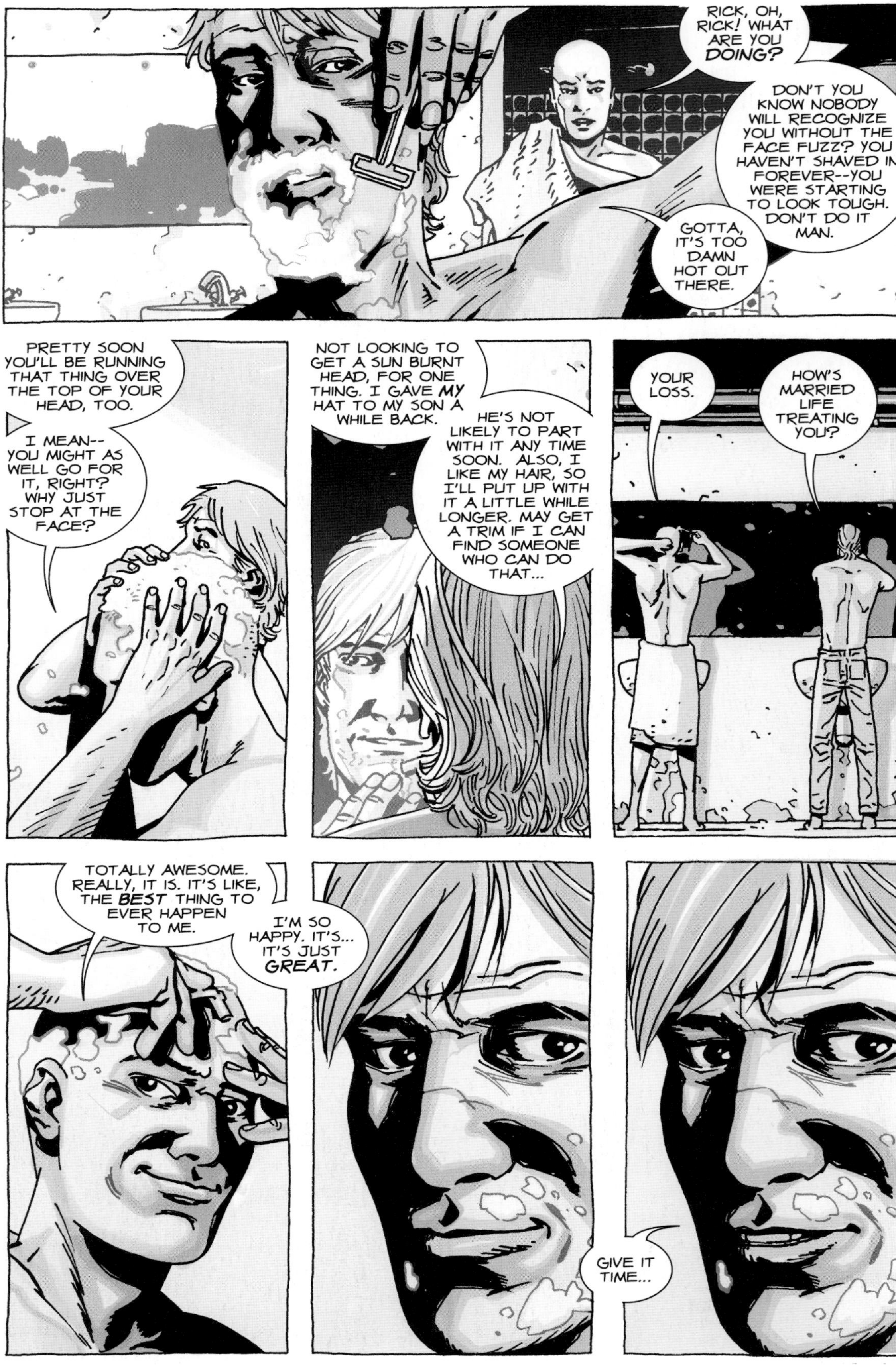
RICK, OH, RICK! WHAT ARE YOU DOING?
DON'T YOU KNOW NOBODY WILL RECOGNIZE YOU WITHOUT THE FACE FUZZ? YOU HAVEN'T SHAVED IN FOREVER--YOU WERE STARTING TO LOOK TOUGH. DON'T DO IT MAN.
GOTTA, IT'S TOO DAMN HOT OUT THERE.
PRETTY SOON YOU'LL BE RUNNING THAT THING OVER THE TOP OF YOUR HEAD, TOO.
I MEAN-- YOU MIGHT AS WELL GO FOR IT, RIGHT? WHY JUST STOP AT THE FACE?
NOT LOOKING TO GET A SUN BURNT HEAD, FOR ONE THING. I GAVE MY HAT TO MY SON A WHILE BACK.
HE'S NOT LIKELY TO PART WITH IT ANY TIME SOON. ALSO, I LIKE MY HAIR, SO I'LL PUT UP WITH IT A LITTLE WHILE LONGER. MAY GET A TRIM IF I CAN FIND SOMEONE WHO CAN DO THAT...
YOUR LOSS.
HOW'S MARRIED LIFE TREATING YOU?
TOTALLY AWESOME. REALLY, IT IS. IT'S LIKE, THE BEST THING TO EVER HAPPEN TO ME.
I'M SO HAPPY. IT'S... IT'S JUST GREAT.
GIVE IT TIME...

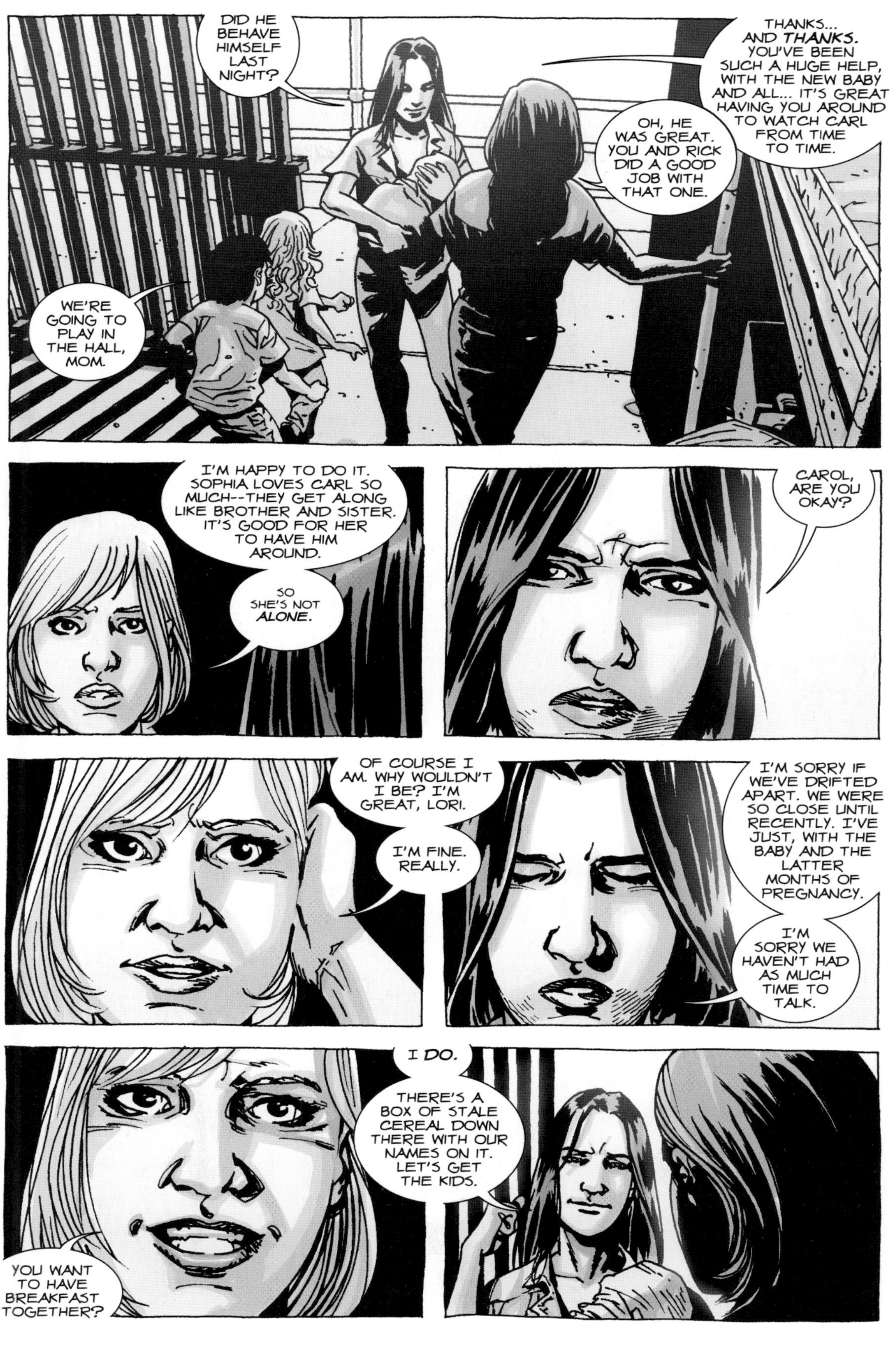
DID HE BEHAVE HIMSELF LAST NIGHT?
THANKS... AND THANKS. YOU'VE BEEN SUCH A HUGE HELP, WITH THE NEW BABY AND ALL... IT'S GREAT HAVING YOU AROUND TO WATCH CARL FROM TIME TO TIME.
OH, HE WAS GREAT. YOU AND RICK DID A GOOD JOB WITH THAT ONE.
WE'RE GOING TO PLAY IN THE HALL, MOM.
I'M HAPPY TO DO IT. SOPHIA LOVES CARL SO MUCH--THEY GET ALONG LIKE BROTHER AND SISTER. IT'S GOOD FOR HER TO HAVE HIM AROUND.
SO SHE'S NOT ALONE.
CAROL, ARE YOU OKAY?
OF COURSE I AM. WHY WOULDN'T I BE? I'M GREAT, LORI.
I'M FINE. REALLY.
I'M SORRY IF WE'VE DRIFTED APART. WE WERE SO CLOSE UNTIL RECENTLY. I'VE JUST, WITH THE BABY AND THE LATTER MONTHS OF PREGNANCY.
I'M SORRY WE HAVEN'T HAD AS MUCH TIME TO TALK.
YOU WANT TO HAVE BREAKFAST TOGETHER?
I DO.
THERE'S A BOX OF STALE CEREAL DOWN THERE WITH OUR NAMES ON IT. LET'S GET THE KIDS.

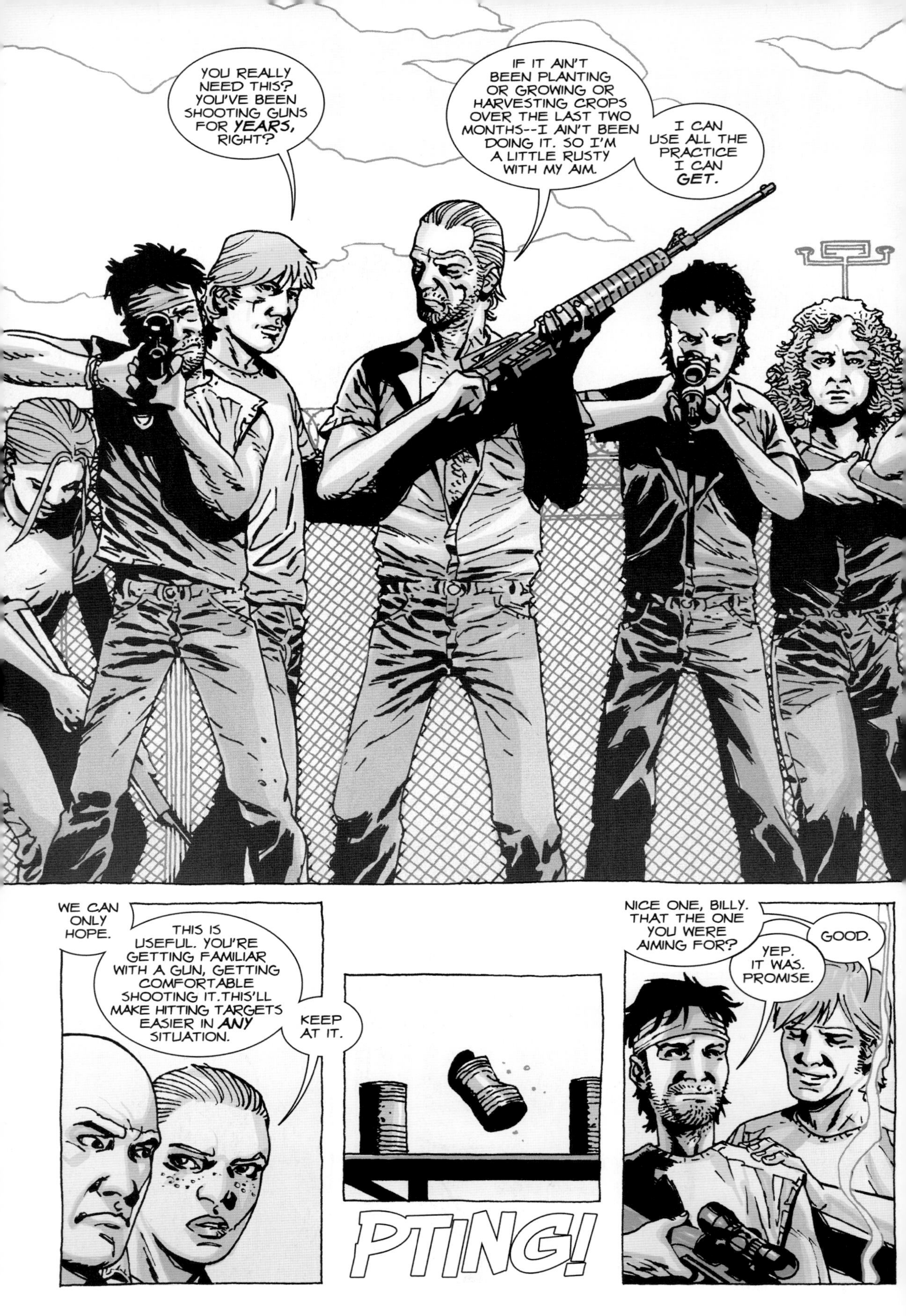
YOU REALLY NEED THIS? YOU'VE BEEN SHOOTING GUNS FOR *YEARS*, RIGHT?
IF IT AIN'T BEEN PLANTING OR GROWING OR HARVESTING CROPS OVER THE LAST TWO MONTHS--I AIN'T BEEN DOING IT. SO I'M A LITTLE RUSTY WITH MY AIM.
I CAN USE ALL THE PRACTICE I CAN *GET*.
WE CAN ONLY HOPE.
THIS IS USEFUL. YOU'RE GETTING FAMILIAR WITH A GUN, GETTING COMFORTABLE SHOOTING IT. THIS'LL MAKE HITTING TARGETS EASIER IN *ANY* SITUATION.
KEEP AT IT.
PTING!
NICE ONE, BILLY. THAT THE ONE YOU WERE AIMING FOR?
YEP. IT WAS. PROMISE.
GOOD.

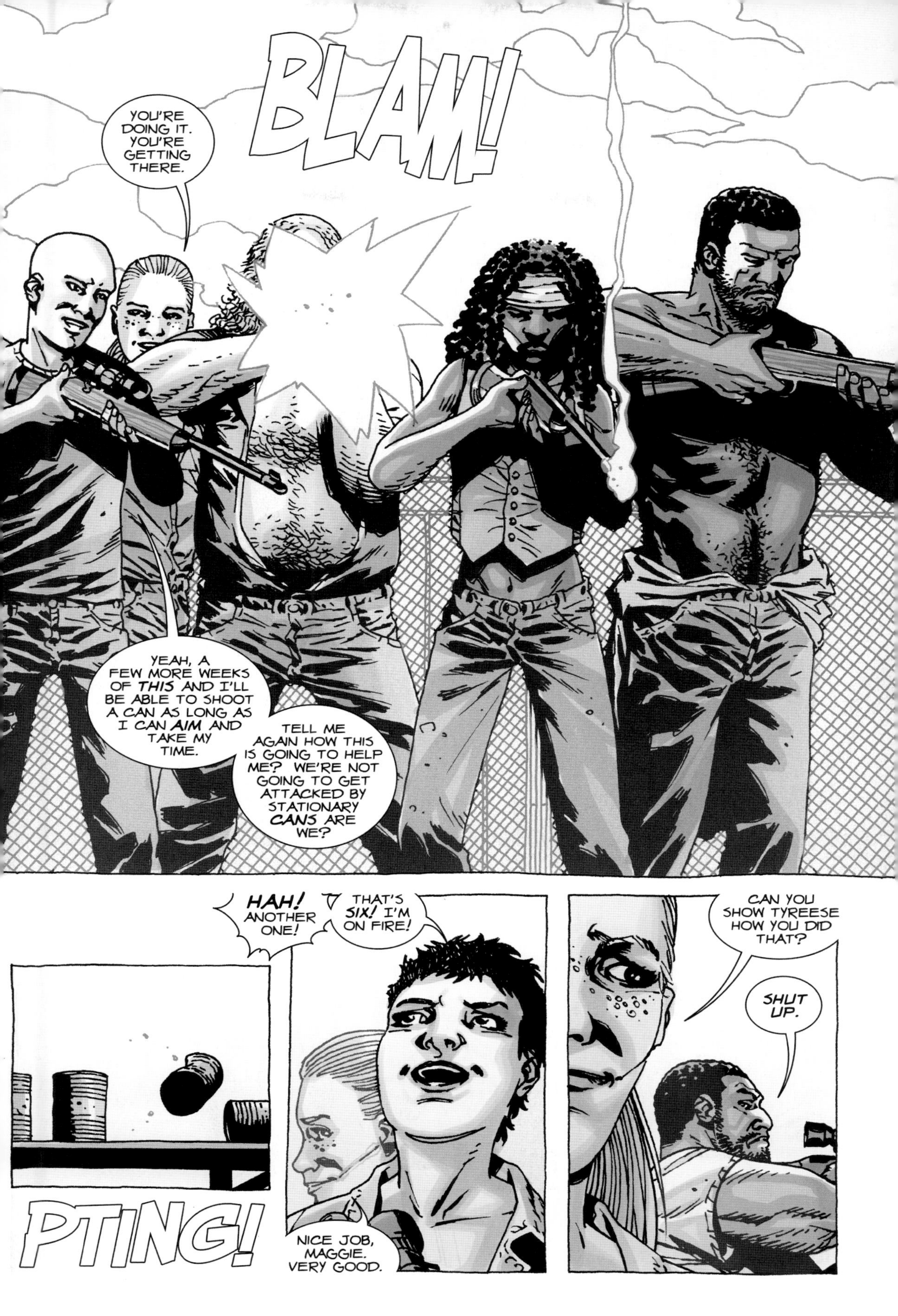
BLAM!
YOU'RE DOING IT. YOU'RE GETTING THERE.
YEAH, A FEW MORE WEEKS OF THIS AND I'LL BE ABLE TO SHOOT A CAN AS LONG AS I CAN AIM AND TAKE MY TIME.
TELL ME AGAIN HOW THIS IS GOING TO HELP ME? WE'RE NOT GOING TO GET ATTACKED BY STATIONARY CANS ARE WE?
HAH! ANOTHER ONE!
PTING!
THAT'S SIX! I'M ON FIRE!
NICE JOB, MAGGIE. VERY GOOD.
CAN YOU SHOW TYREESE HOW YOU DID THAT?
SHUT UP.

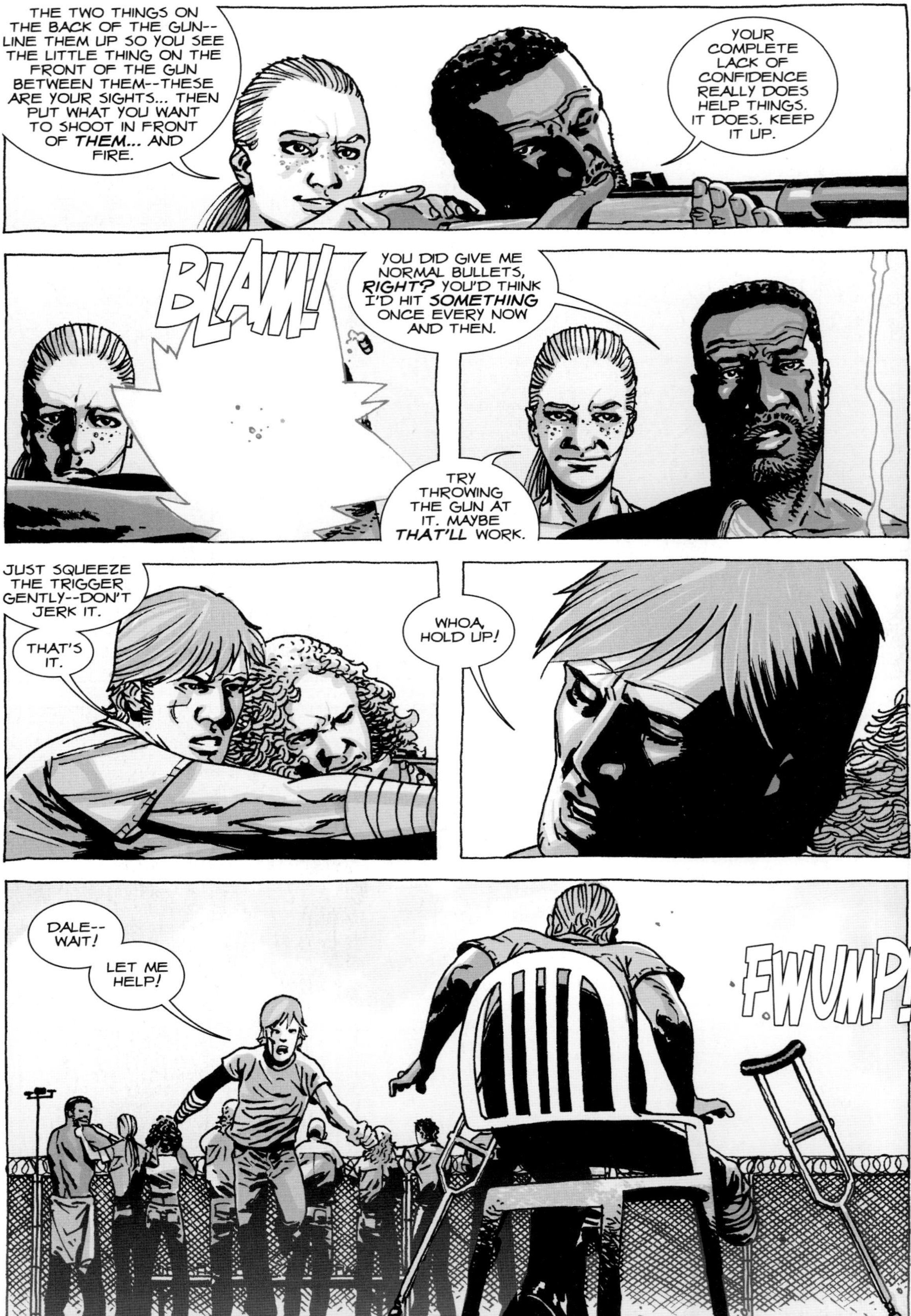
THE TWO THINGS ON THE BACK OF THE GUN-- LINE THEM UP SO YOU SEE THE LITTLE THING ON THE FRONT OF THE GUN BETWEEN THEM--THESE ARE YOUR SIGHTS... THEN PUT WHAT YOU WANT TO SHOOT IN FRONT OF THEM... AND FIRE.
YOUR COMPLETE LACK OF CONFIDENCE REALLY DOES HELP THINGS. IT DOES. KEEP IT UP.
BLAM!
YOU DID GIVE ME NORMAL BULLETS, RIGHT? YOU'D THINK I'D HIT SOMETHING ONCE EVERY NOW AND THEN.
TRY THROWING THE GUN AT IT. MAYBE THAT'LL WORK.
JUST SQUEEZE THE TRIGGER GENTLY--DON'T JERK IT.
THAT'S IT.
WHOA, HOLD UP!
DALE-- WAIT!
LET ME HELP!
FWUMP!

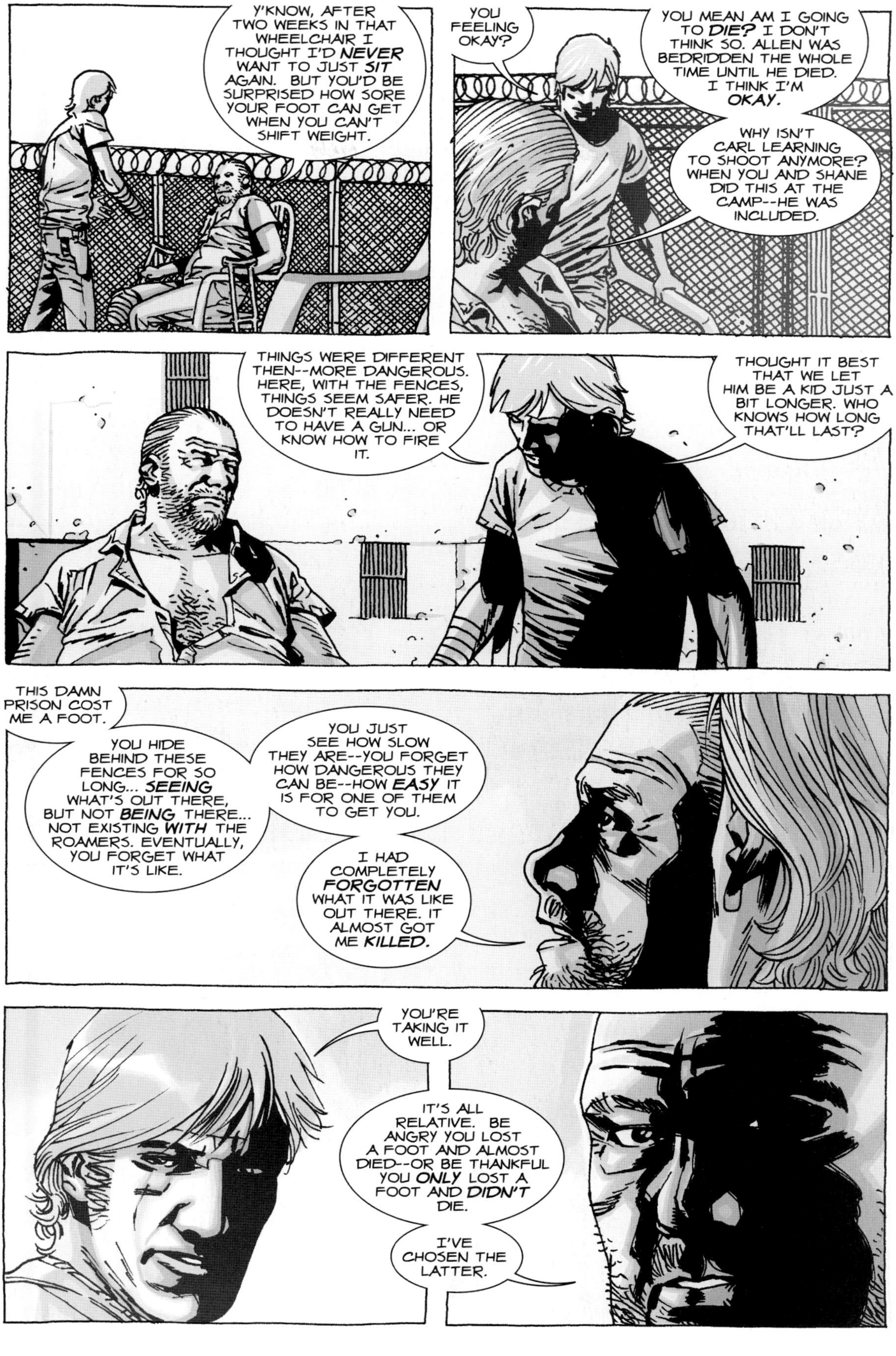
Y'KNOW, AFTER TWO WEEKS IN THAT WHEELCHAIR I THOUGHT I'D NEVER WANT TO JUST SIT AGAIN. BUT YOU'D BE SURPRISED HOW SORE YOUR FOOT CAN GET WHEN YOU CAN'T SHIFT WEIGHT.
YOU FEELING OKAY?
YOU MEAN AM I GOING TO DIE? I DON'T THINK SO. ALLEN WAS BEDRIDDEN THE WHOLE TIME UNTIL HE DIED. I THINK I'M OKAY.
WHY ISN'T CARL LEARNING TO SHOOT ANYMORE? WHEN YOU AND SHANE DID THIS AT THE CAMP--HE WAS INCLUDED.
THINGS WERE DIFFERENT THEN--MORE DANGEROUS. HERE, WITH THE FENCES, THINGS SEEM SAFER. HE DOESN'T REALLY NEED TO HAVE A GUN... OR KNOW HOW TO FIRE IT.
THOUGHT IT BEST THAT WE LET HIM BE A KID JUST A BIT LONGER. WHO KNOWS HOW LONG THAT'LL LAST?
THIS DAMN PRISON COST ME A FOOT.
YOU HIDE BEHIND THESE FENCES FOR SO LONG... SEEING WHAT'S OUT THERE, BUT NOT BEING THERE... NOT EXISTING WITH THE ROAMERS. EVENTUALLY, YOU FORGET WHAT IT'S LIKE.
YOU JUST SEE HOW SLOW THEY ARE--YOU FORGET HOW DANGEROUS THEY CAN BE--HOW EASY IT IS FOR ONE OF THEM TO GET YOU.
I HAD COMPLETELY FORGOTTEN WHAT IT WAS LIKE OUT THERE. IT ALMOST GOT ME KILLED.
YOU'RE TAKING IT WELL.
IT'S ALL RELATIVE. BE ANGRY YOU LOST A FOOT AND ALMOST DIED--OR BE THANKFUL YOU ONLY LOST A FOOT AND DIDN'T DIE.
I'VE CHOSEN THE LATTER.

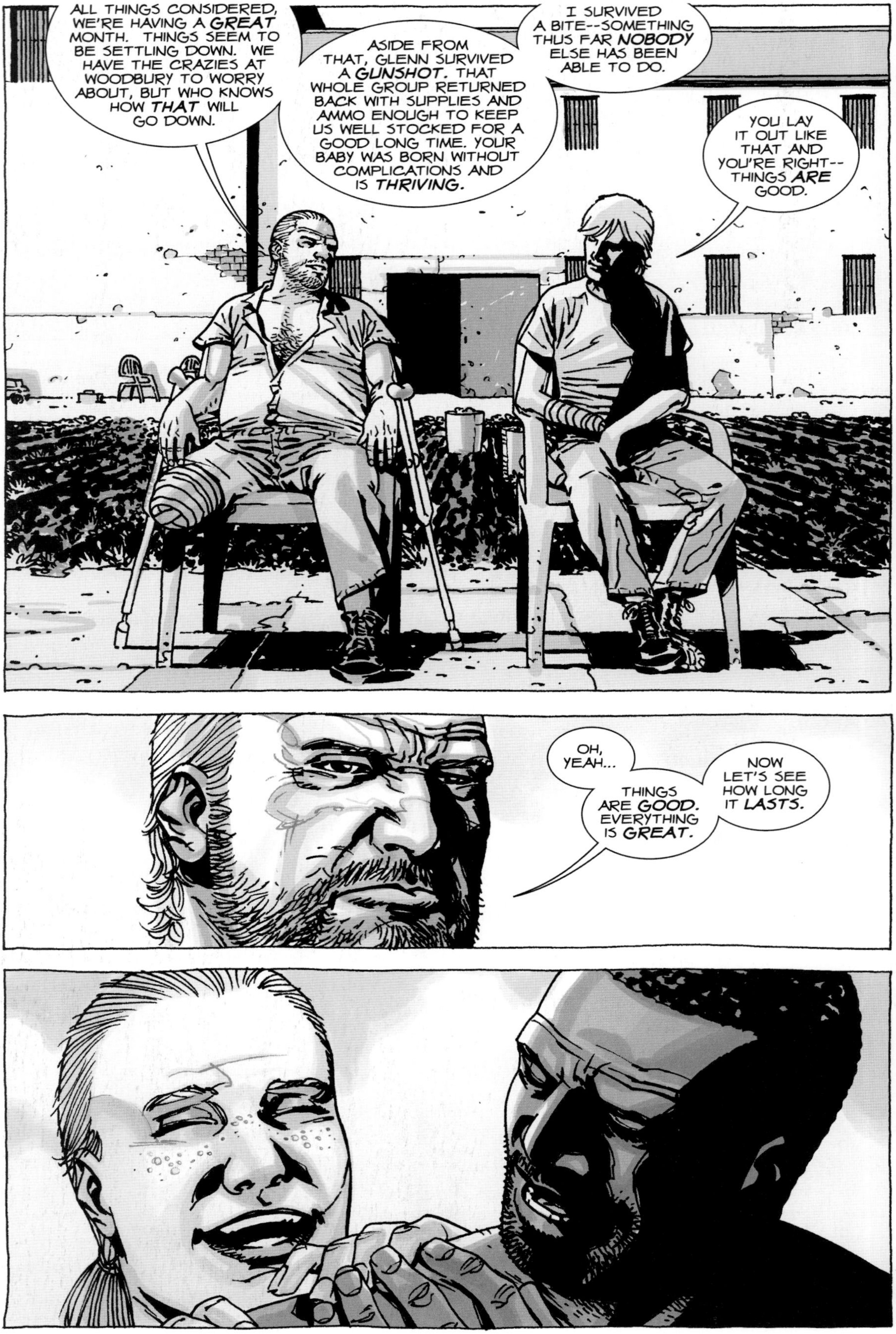
ALL THINGS CONSIDERED, WE'RE HAVING A GREAT MONTH. THINGS SEEM TO BE SETTLING DOWN. WE HAVE THE CRAZIES AT WOODBURY TO WORRY ABOUT, BUT WHO KNOWS HOW THAT WILL GO DOWN.
ASIDE FROM THAT, GLENN SURVIVED A GUNSHOT. THAT WHOLE GROUP RETURNED BACK WITH SUPPLIES AND AMMO ENOUGH TO KEEP US WELL STOCKED FOR A GOOD LONG TIME. YOUR BABY WAS BORN WITHOUT COMPLICATIONS AND IS THRIVING.
I SURVIVED A BITE--SOMETHING THUS FAR NOBODY ELSE HAS BEEN ABLE TO DO.
YOU LAY IT OUT LIKE THAT AND YOU'RE RIGHT-- THINGS ARE GOOD.
OH, YEAH...
THINGS ARE GOOD. EVERYTHING IS GREAT.
NOW LET'S SEE HOW LONG IT LASTS.

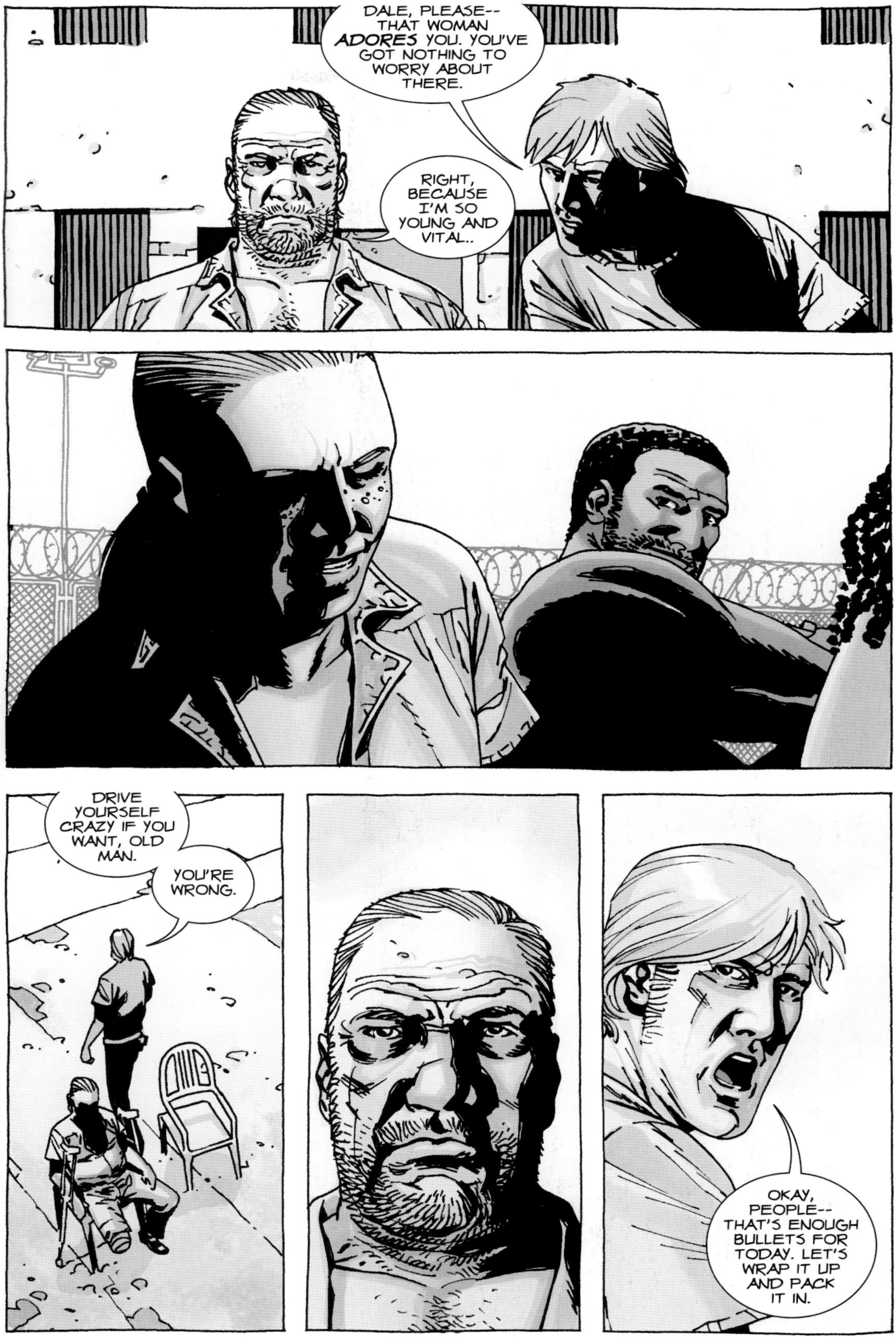
DALE, PLEASE-- THAT WOMAN ADORES YOU. YOU'VE GOT NOTHING TO WORRY ABOUT THERE.
RIGHT, BECAUSE I'M SO YOUNG AND VITAL..
DRIVE YOURSELF CRAZY IF YOU WANT, OLD MAN.
YOU'RE WRONG.
OKAY, PEOPLE-- THAT'S ENOUGH BULLETS FOR TODAY. LET'S WRAP IT UP AND PACK IT IN.

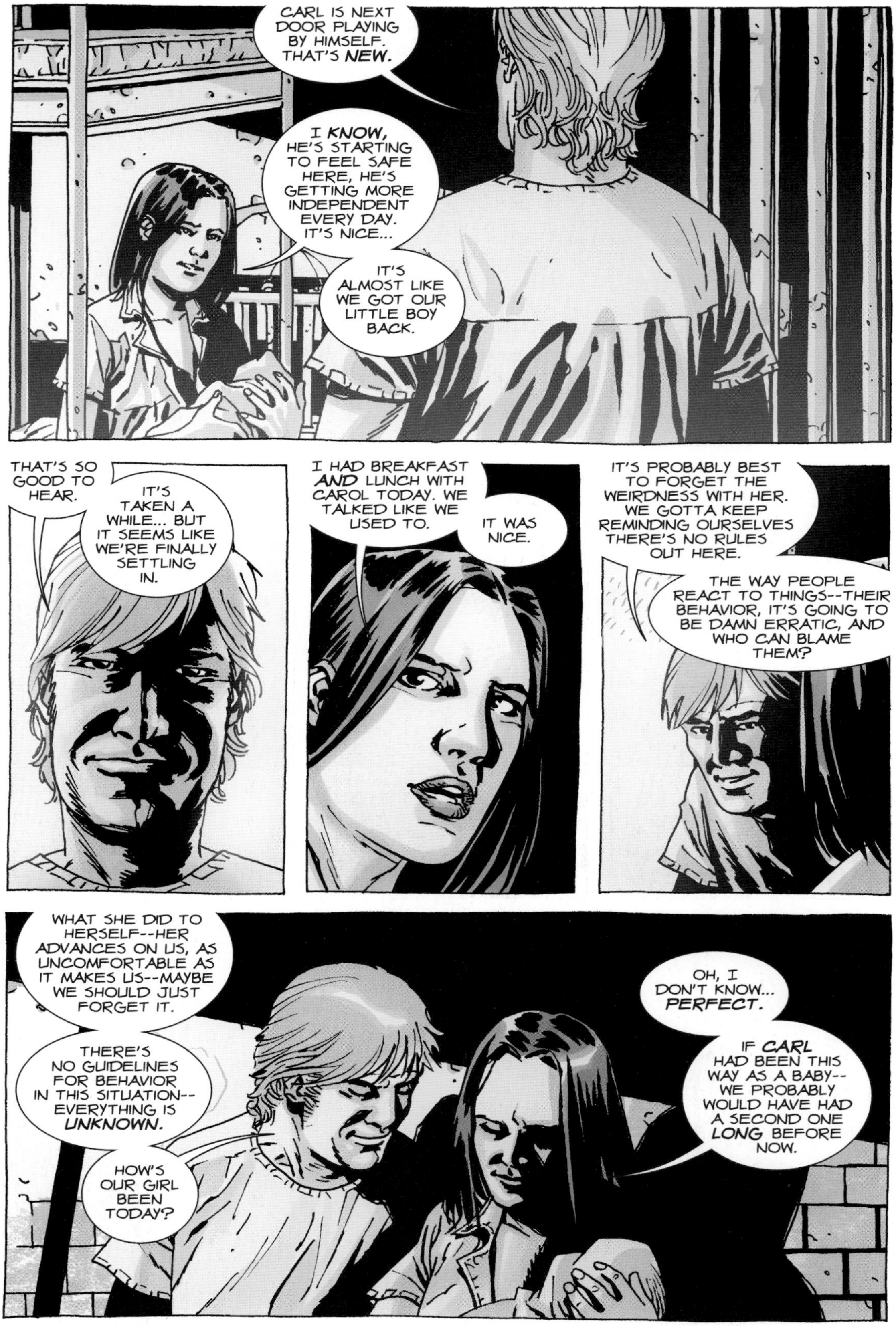
CARL IS NEXT DOOR PLAYING BY HIMSELF. THAT'S NEW.
I KNOW, HE'S STARTING TO FEEL SAFE HERE, HE'S GETTING MORE INDEPENDENT EVERY DAY. IT'S NICE...
IT'S ALMOST LIKE WE GOT OUR LITTLE BOY BACK.
THAT'S SO GOOD TO HEAR.
IT'S TAKEN A WHILE... BUT IT SEEMS LIKE WE'RE FINALLY SETTLING IN.
I HAD BREAKFAST AND LUNCH WITH CAROL TODAY. WE TALKED LIKE WE USED TO.
IT WAS NICE.
IT'S PROBABLY BEST TO FORGET THE WEIRDNESS WITH HER. WE GOTTA KEEP REMINDING OURSELVES THERE'S NO RULES OUT HERE.
THE WAY PEOPLE REACT TO THINGS--THEIR BEHAVIOR, IT'S GOING TO BE DAMN ERRATIC, AND WHO CAN BLAME THEM?
WHAT SHE DID TO HERSELF--HER ADVANCES ON US, AS UNCOMFORTABLE AS IT MAKES US--MAYBE WE SHOULD JUST FORGET IT.
THERE'S NO GUIDELINES FOR BEHAVIOR IN THIS SITUATION--EVERYTHING IS UNKNOWN.
HOW'S OUR GIRL BEEN TODAY?
OH, I DON'T KNOW... PERFECT.
IF CARL HAD BEEN THIS WAY AS A BABY--WE PROBABLY WOULD HAVE HAD A SECOND ONE LONG BEFORE NOW.

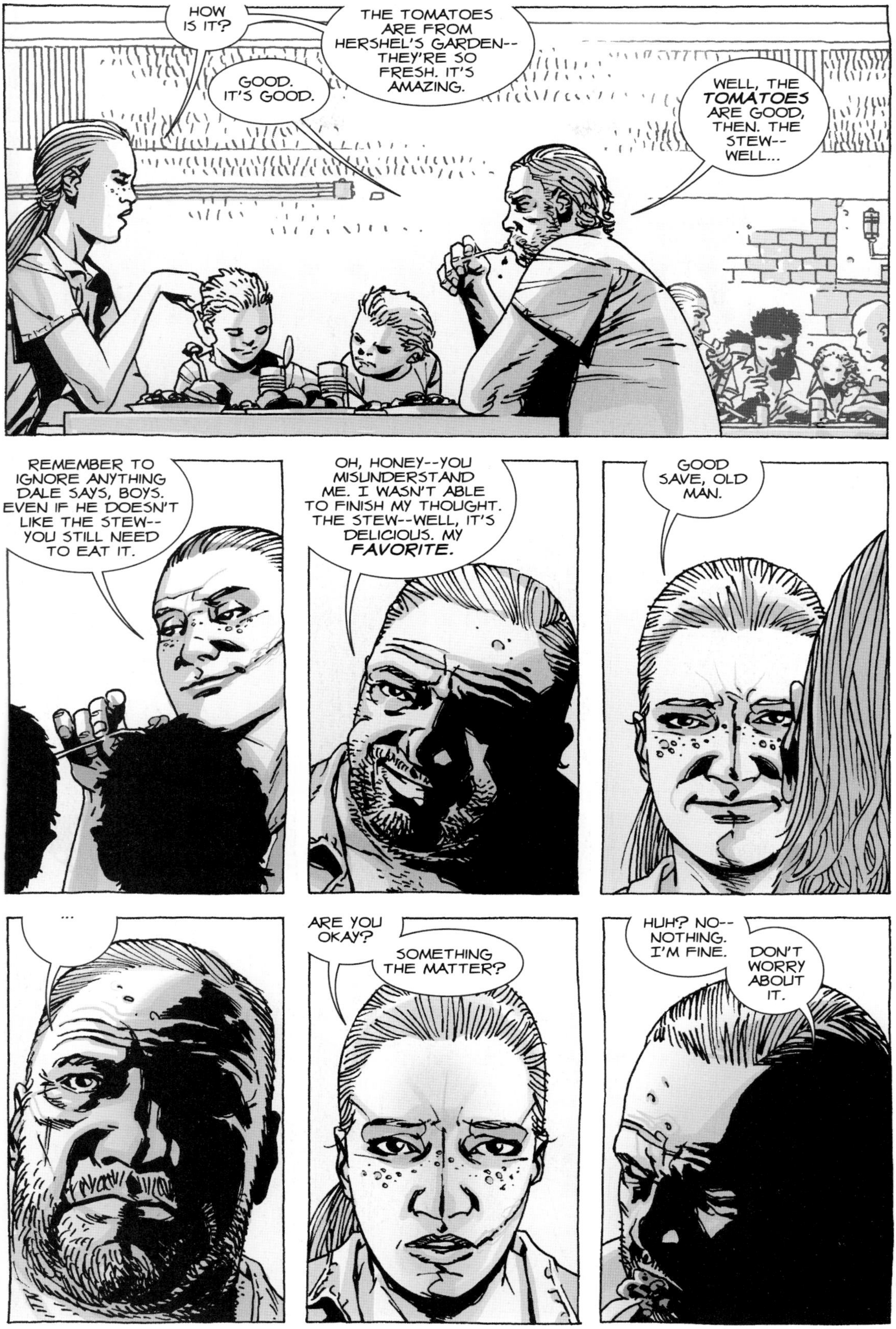
HOW IS IT?
THE TOMATOES ARE FROM HERSHEL'S GARDEN-- THEY'RE SO FRESH. IT'S AMAZING.
GOOD. IT'S GOOD.
WELL, THE *TOMATOES* ARE GOOD, THEN. THE STEW-- WELL...
REMEMBER TO IGNORE ANYTHING DALE SAYS, BOYS. EVEN IF HE DOESN'T LIKE THE STEW-- YOU STILL NEED TO EAT IT.
OH, HONEY--YOU MISUNDERSTAND ME. I WASN'T ABLE TO FINISH MY THOUGHT. THE STEW--WELL, IT'S DELICIOUS. MY *FAVORITE.*
GOOD SAVE, OLD MAN.
...
ARE YOU OKAY?
SOMETHING THE MATTER?
HUH? NO-- NOTHING. I'M FINE.
DON'T WORRY ABOUT IT.

YOU KNOW... PEOPLE ARE STARTING TO TALK.

ABOUT US HAVING **SEX?**

KINDA, BUT NOT EXACTLY. THE CRIB, THEY'RE TALKING ABOUT WHY WE GOT THE CRIB. ANDREA'S PRACTICALLY **EXPECTING** AN ANNOUNCEMENT.

PEOPLE THINK YOU'RE PREGNANT? **ALREADY?**

WELL--I **COULD** BE.

NO YOU COULDN'T BE. I'M CAREFUL.

WHY?

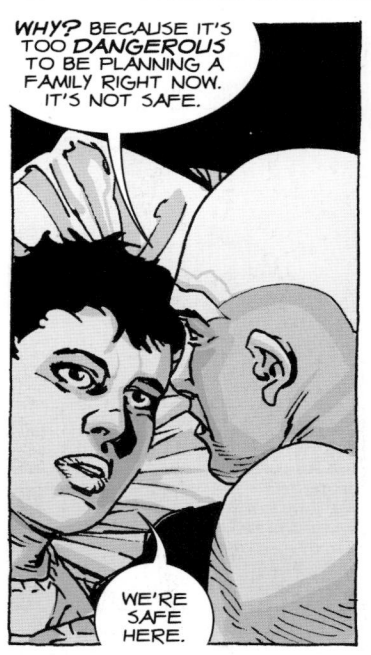

WHY? BECAUSE IT'S TOO **DANGEROUS** TO BE PLANNING A FAMILY RIGHT NOW. IT'S NOT SAFE.

WE'RE SAFE HERE.

WHAT IF THIS IS THE SAFEST PLACE OUT THERE? WHAT IF THIS IS IT FOR US? SHOULD WE JUST **NOT** START A FAMILY?

I DON'T KNOW IF I WANT TO DENY MYSELF THAT JUST BECAUSE I'M SCARED. SHOULD WE JUST **NEVER** HAVE KIDS?

I DON'T KNOW... I JUST DON'T KNOW.

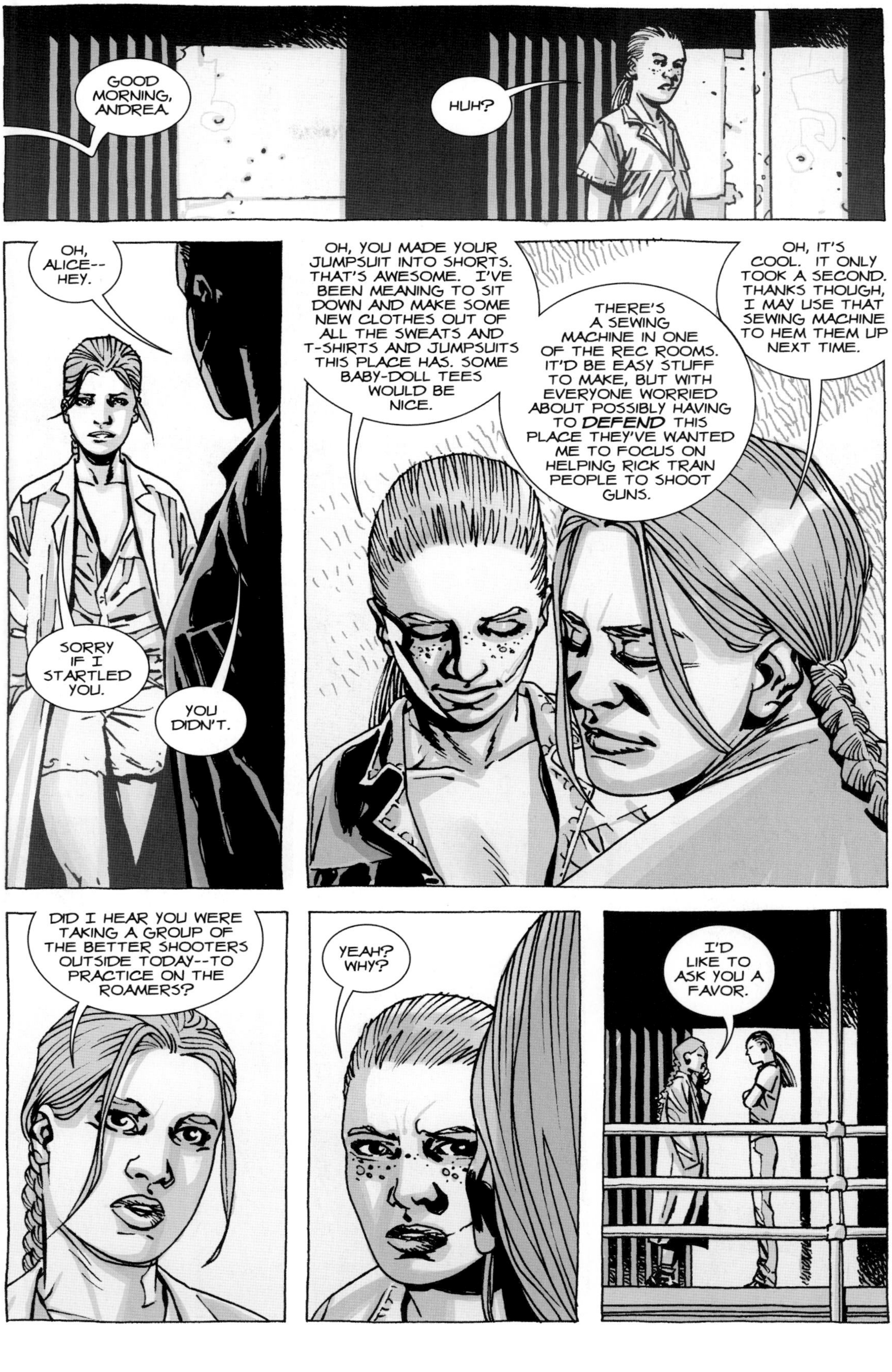
GOOD MORNING, ANDREA
HUH?
OH, ALICE-- HEY.
SORRY IF I STARTLED YOU.
YOU DIDN'T.
OH, YOU MADE YOUR JUMPSUIT INTO SHORTS. THAT'S AWESOME. I'VE BEEN MEANING TO SIT DOWN AND MAKE SOME NEW CLOTHES OUT OF ALL THE SWEATS AND T-SHIRTS AND JUMPSUITS THIS PLACE HAS. SOME BABY-DOLL TEES WOULD BE NICE.
THERE'S A SEWING MACHINE IN ONE OF THE REC ROOMS. IT'D BE EASY STUFF TO MAKE, BUT WITH EVERYONE WORRIED ABOUT POSSIBLY HAVING TO DEFEND THIS PLACE THEY'VE WANTED ME TO FOCUS ON HELPING RICK TRAIN PEOPLE TO SHOOT GUNS.
OH, IT'S COOL. IT ONLY TOOK A SECOND. THANKS THOUGH, I MAY USE THAT SEWING MACHINE TO HEM THEM UP NEXT TIME.
DID I HEAR YOU WERE TAKING A GROUP OF THE BETTER SHOOTERS OUTSIDE TODAY--TO PRACTICE ON THE ROAMERS?
YEAH? WHY?
I'D LIKE TO ASK YOU A FAVOR.

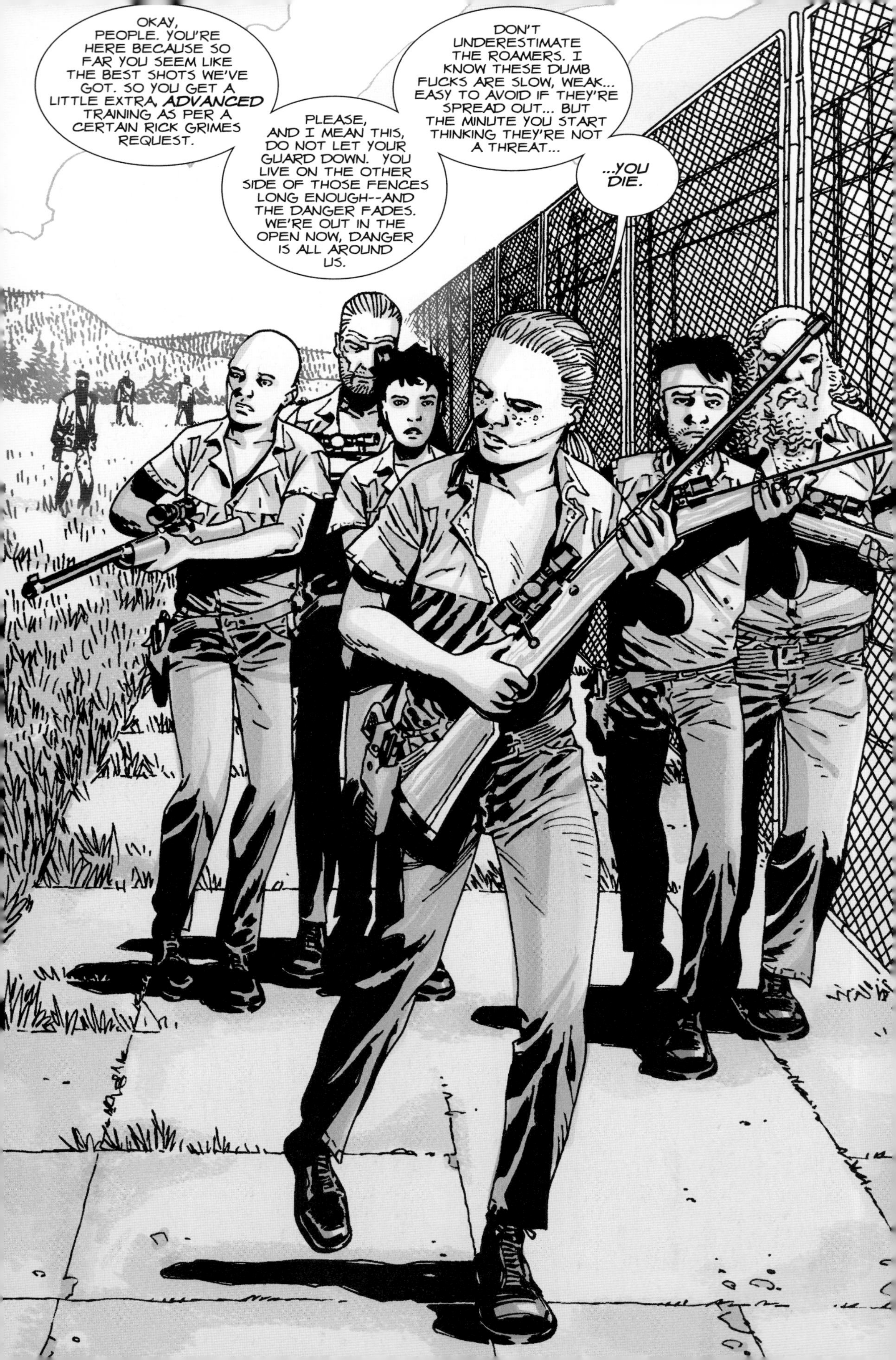
OKAY, PEOPLE. YOU'RE HERE BECAUSE SO FAR YOU SEEM LIKE THE BEST SHOTS WE'VE GOT. SO YOU GET A LITTLE EXTRA, ADVANCED TRAINING AS PER A CERTAIN RICK GRIMES REQUEST.
PLEASE, AND I MEAN THIS, DO NOT LET YOUR GUARD DOWN. YOU LIVE ON THE OTHER SIDE OF THOSE FENCES LONG ENOUGH--AND THE DANGER FADES. WE'RE OUT IN THE OPEN NOW, DANGER IS ALL AROUND US.
DON'T UNDERESTIMATE THE ROAMERS. I KNOW THESE DUMB FUCKS ARE SLOW, WEAK... EASY TO AVOID IF THEY'RE SPREAD OUT... BUT THE MINUTE YOU START THINKING THEY'RE NOT A THREAT...
...YOU DIE.

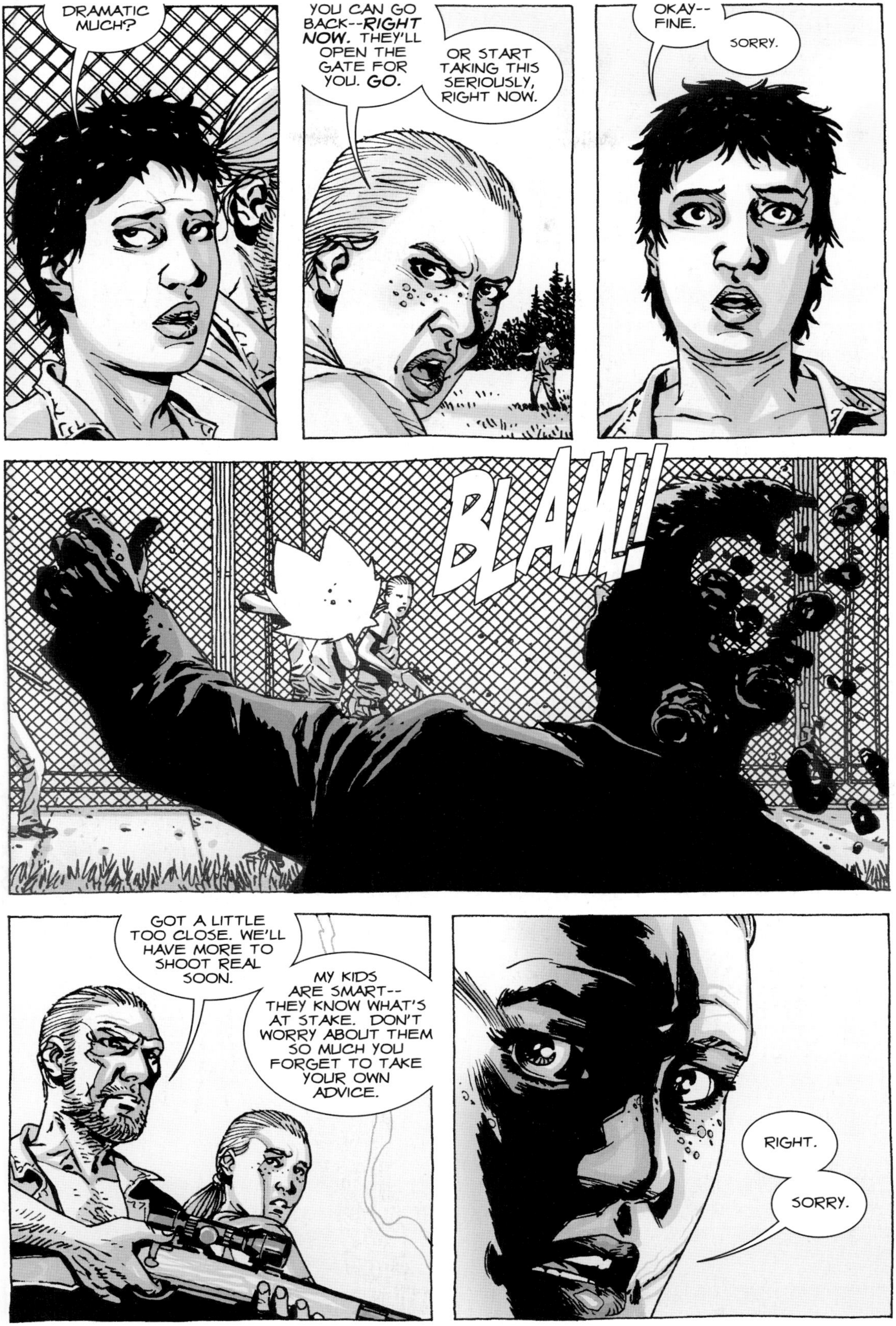
DRAMATIC MUCH?
YOU CAN GO BACK--**RIGHT NOW.** THEY'LL OPEN THE GATE FOR YOU. **GO.**
OR START TAKING THIS SERIOUSLY, RIGHT NOW.
OKAY-- FINE.
SORRY.
BLAM!!
GOT A LITTLE TOO CLOSE. WE'LL HAVE MORE TO SHOOT REAL SOON.
MY KIDS ARE SMART-- THEY KNOW WHAT'S AT STAKE. DON'T WORRY ABOUT THEM SO MUCH YOU FORGET TO TAKE YOUR OWN ADVICE.
RIGHT.
SORRY.

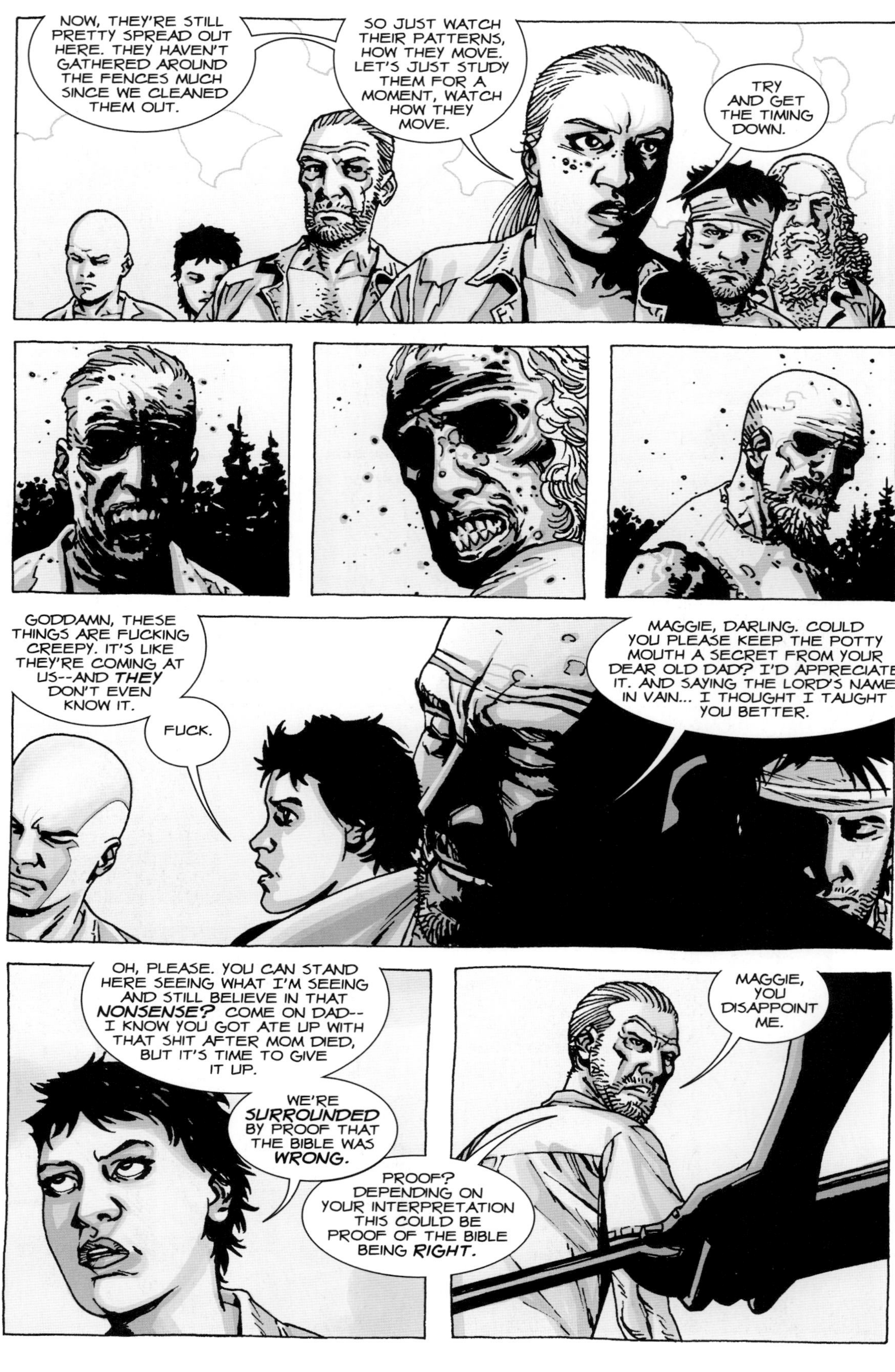
NOW, THEY'RE STILL PRETTY SPREAD OUT HERE. THEY HAVEN'T GATHERED AROUND THE FENCES MUCH SINCE WE CLEANED THEM OUT.
SO JUST WATCH THEIR PATTERNS, HOW THEY MOVE. LET'S JUST STUDY THEM FOR A MOMENT, WATCH HOW THEY MOVE.
TRY AND GET THE TIMING DOWN.
GODDAMN, THESE THINGS ARE FUCKING CREEPY. IT'S LIKE THEY'RE COMING AT US--AND THEY DON'T EVEN KNOW IT.
FUCK.
MAGGIE, DARLING. COULD YOU PLEASE KEEP THE POTTY MOUTH A SECRET FROM YOUR DEAR OLD DAD? I'D APPRECIATE IT. AND SAYING THE LORD'S NAME IN VAIN... I THOUGHT I TAUGHT YOU BETTER.
OH, PLEASE. YOU CAN STAND HERE SEEING WHAT I'M SEEING AND STILL BELIEVE IN THAT NONSENSE? COME ON DAD-- I KNOW YOU GOT ATE UP WITH THAT SHIT AFTER MOM DIED, BUT IT'S TIME TO GIVE IT UP.
WE'RE SURROUNDED BY PROOF THAT THE BIBLE WAS WRONG.
PROOF? DEPENDING ON YOUR INTERPRETATION THIS COULD BE PROOF OF THE BIBLE BEING RIGHT.
MAGGIE, YOU DISAPPOINT ME.

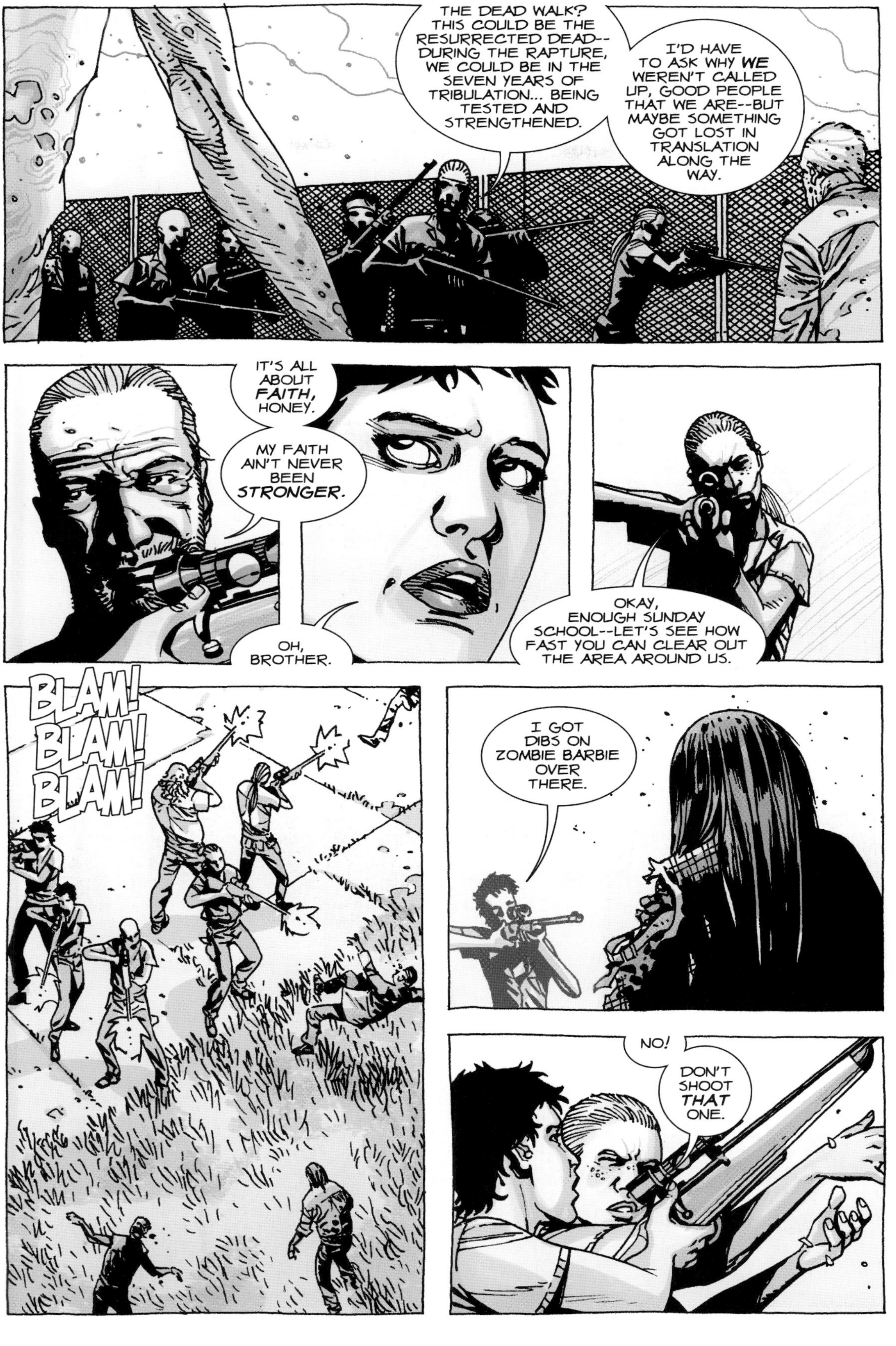
THE DEAD WALK? THIS COULD BE THE RESURRECTED DEAD-- DURING THE RAPTURE, WE COULD BE IN THE SEVEN YEARS OF TRIBULATION... BEING TESTED AND STRENGTHENED.
I'D HAVE TO ASK WHY WE WEREN'T CALLED UP, GOOD PEOPLE THAT WE ARE--BUT MAYBE SOMETHING GOT LOST IN TRANSLATION ALONG THE WAY.
IT'S ALL ABOUT FAITH, HONEY.
MY FAITH AIN'T NEVER BEEN STRONGER.
OH, BROTHER.
OKAY, ENOUGH SUNDAY SCHOOL--LET'S SEE HOW FAST YOU CAN CLEAR OUT THE AREA AROUND US.
BLAM! BLAM! BLAM!
I GOT DIBS ON ZOMBIE BARBIE OVER THERE.
NO!
DON'T SHOOT THAT ONE.

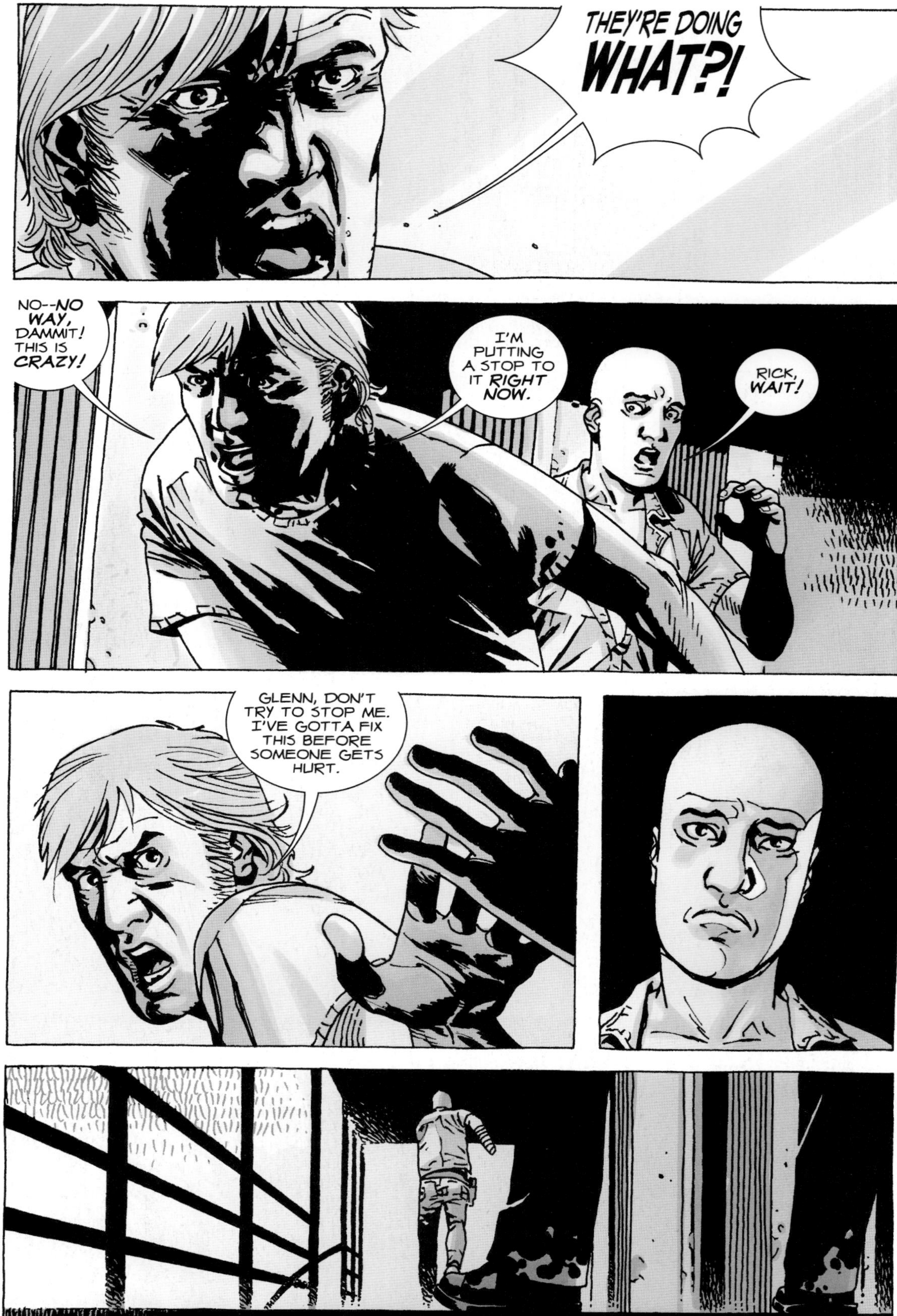
THEY'RE DOING WHAT?!
NO--NO WAY, DAMMIT! THIS IS CRAZY!
I'M PUTTING A STOP TO IT RIGHT NOW.
RICK, WAIT!
GLENN, DON'T TRY TO STOP ME. I'VE GOTTA FIX THIS BEFORE SOMEONE GETS HURT.

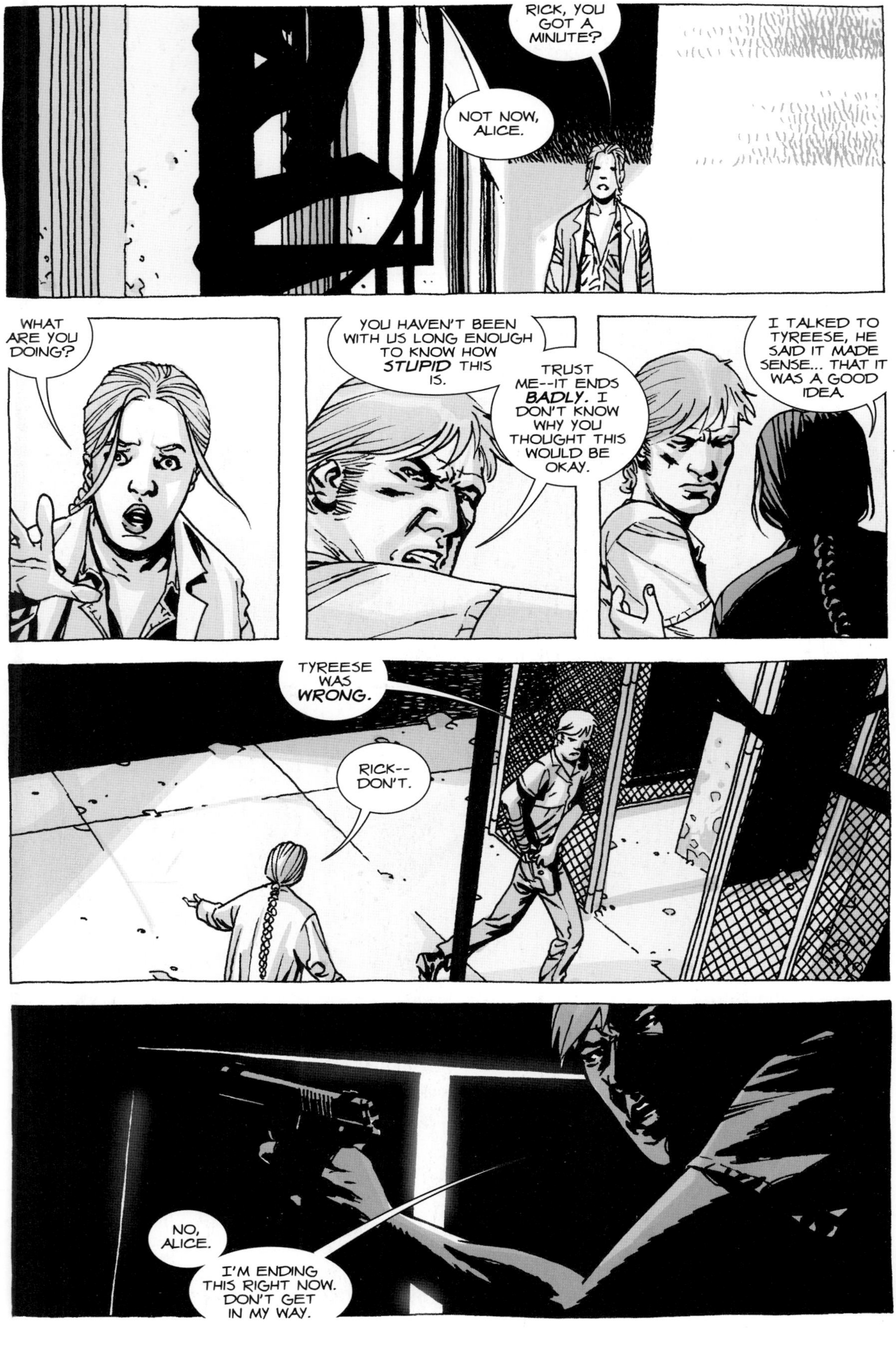
RICK, YOU GOT A MINUTE?
NOT NOW, ALICE.
WHAT ARE YOU DOING?
YOU HAVEN'T BEEN WITH US LONG ENOUGH TO KNOW HOW STUPID THIS IS.
TRUST ME--IT ENDS BADLY. I DON'T KNOW WHY YOU THOUGHT THIS WOULD BE OKAY.
I TALKED TO TYREESE, HE SAID IT MADE SENSE... THAT IT WAS A GOOD IDEA.
TYREESE WAS WRONG.
RICK-- DON'T.
NO, ALICE.
I'M ENDING THIS RIGHT NOW. DON'T GET IN MY WAY.

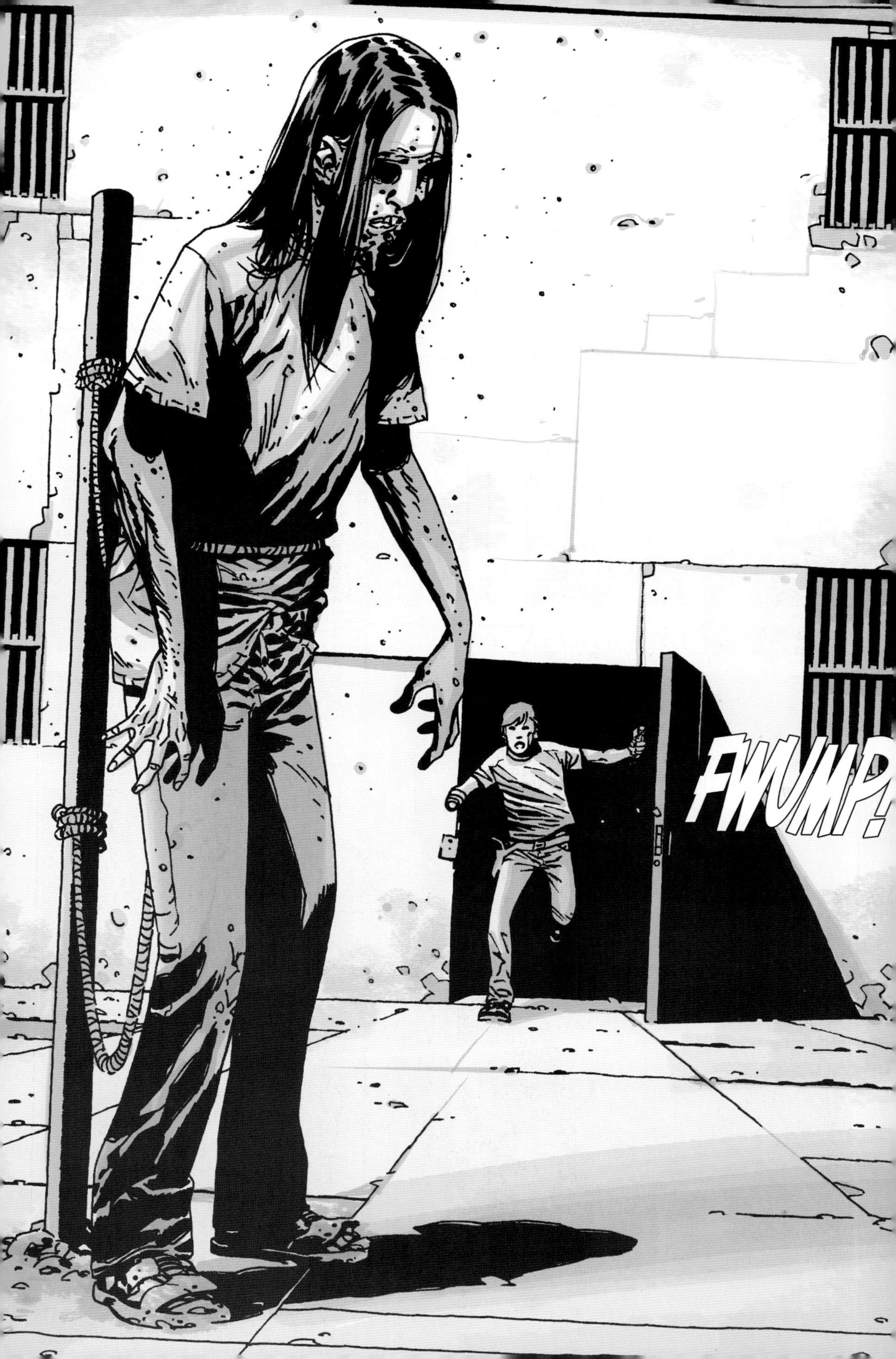
FWUMP!

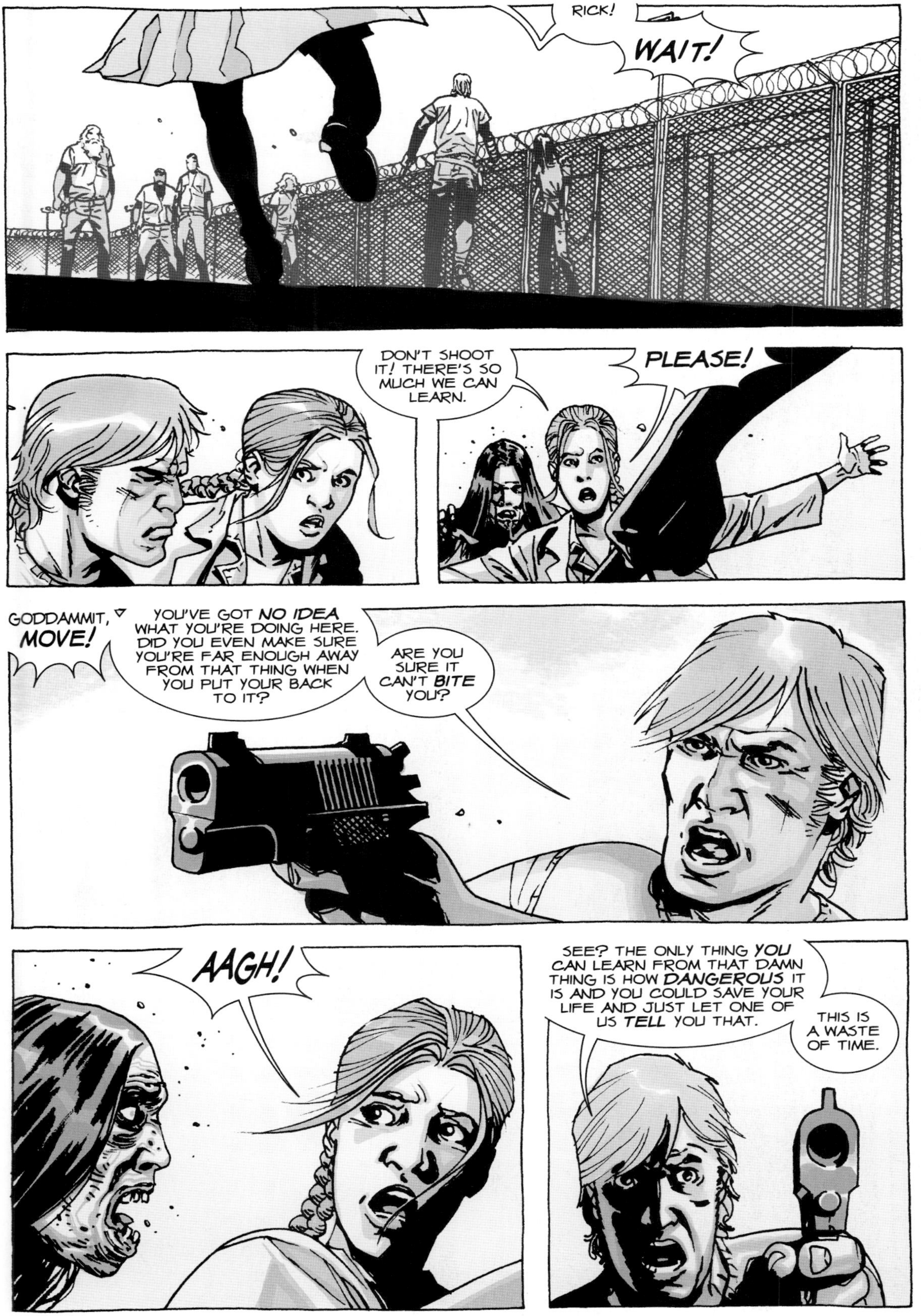
RICK!
WAIT!
DON'T SHOOT IT! THERE'S SO MUCH WE CAN LEARN.
PLEASE!
GODDAMMIT, MOVE!
YOU'VE GOT NO IDEA WHAT YOU'RE DOING HERE. DID YOU EVEN MAKE SURE YOU'RE FAR ENOUGH AWAY FROM THAT THING WHEN YOU PUT YOUR BACK TO IT?
ARE YOU SURE IT CAN'T BITE YOU?
AAGH!
SEE? THE ONLY THING YOU CAN LEARN FROM THAT DAMN THING IS HOW DANGEROUS IT IS AND YOU COULD SAVE YOUR LIFE AND JUST LET ONE OF US TELL YOU THAT.
THIS IS A WASTE OF TIME.

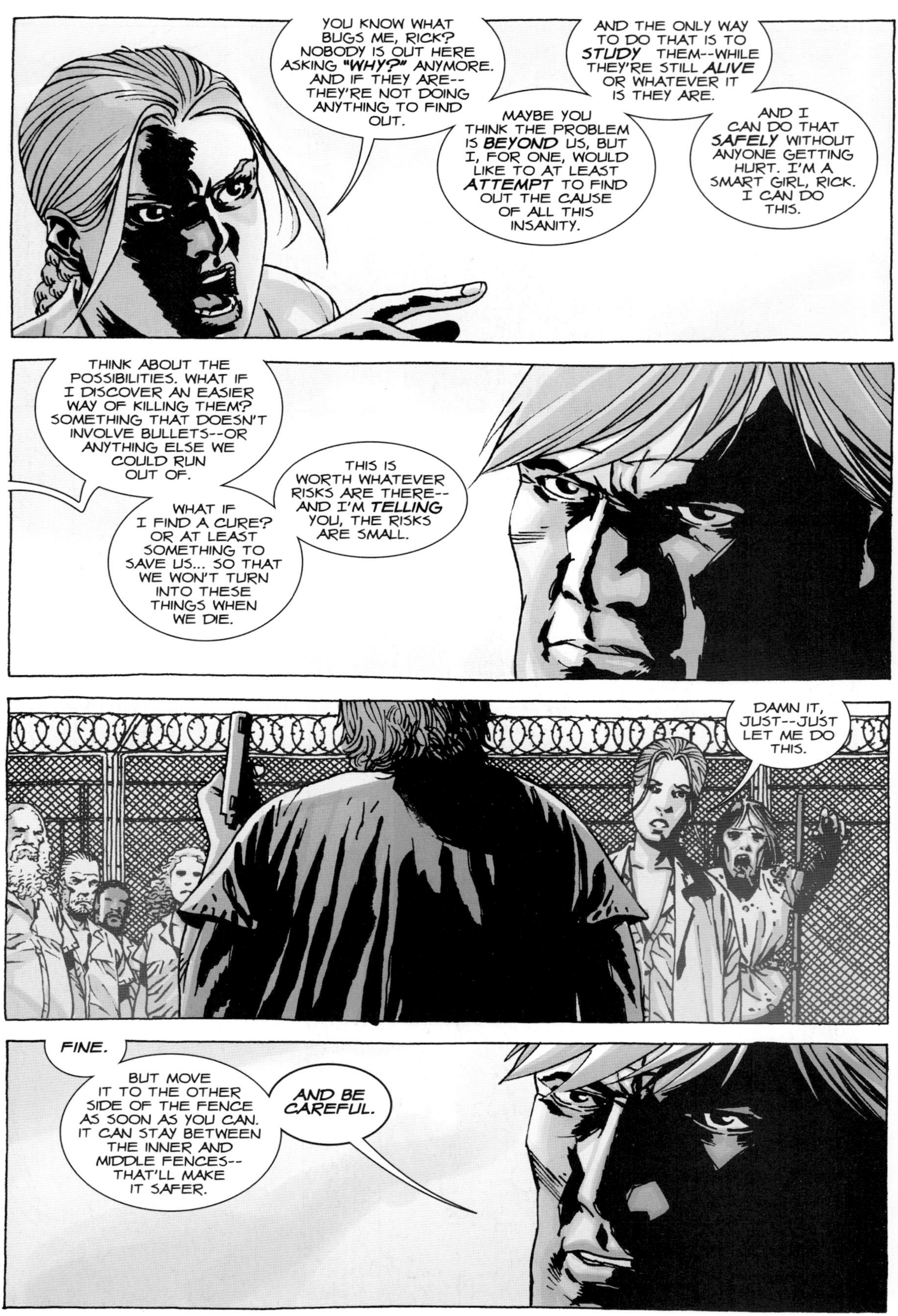
YOU KNOW WHAT BUGS ME, RICK? NOBODY IS OUT HERE ASKING "WHY?" ANYMORE. AND IF THEY ARE-- THEY'RE NOT DOING ANYTHING TO FIND OUT.
MAYBE YOU THINK THE PROBLEM IS BEYOND US, BUT I, FOR ONE, WOULD LIKE TO AT LEAST ATTEMPT TO FIND OUT THE CAUSE OF ALL THIS INSANITY.
AND THE ONLY WAY TO DO THAT IS TO STUDY THEM--WHILE THEY'RE STILL ALIVE OR WHATEVER IT IS THEY ARE.
AND I CAN DO THAT SAFELY WITHOUT ANYONE GETTING HURT. I'M A SMART GIRL, RICK. I CAN DO THIS.
THINK ABOUT THE POSSIBILITIES. WHAT IF I DISCOVER AN EASIER WAY OF KILLING THEM? SOMETHING THAT DOESN'T INVOLVE BULLETS--OR ANYTHING ELSE WE COULD RUN OUT OF.
WHAT IF I FIND A CURE? OR AT LEAST SOMETHING TO SAVE US... SO THAT WE WON'T TURN INTO THESE THINGS WHEN WE DIE.
THIS IS WORTH WHATEVER RISKS ARE THERE-- AND I'M TELLING YOU, THE RISKS ARE SMALL.
DAMN IT, JUST--JUST LET ME DO THIS.
FINE.
BUT MOVE IT TO THE OTHER SIDE OF THE FENCE AS SOON AS YOU CAN. IT CAN STAY BETWEEN THE INNER AND MIDDLE FENCES-- THAT'LL MAKE IT SAFER.
AND BE CAREFUL.

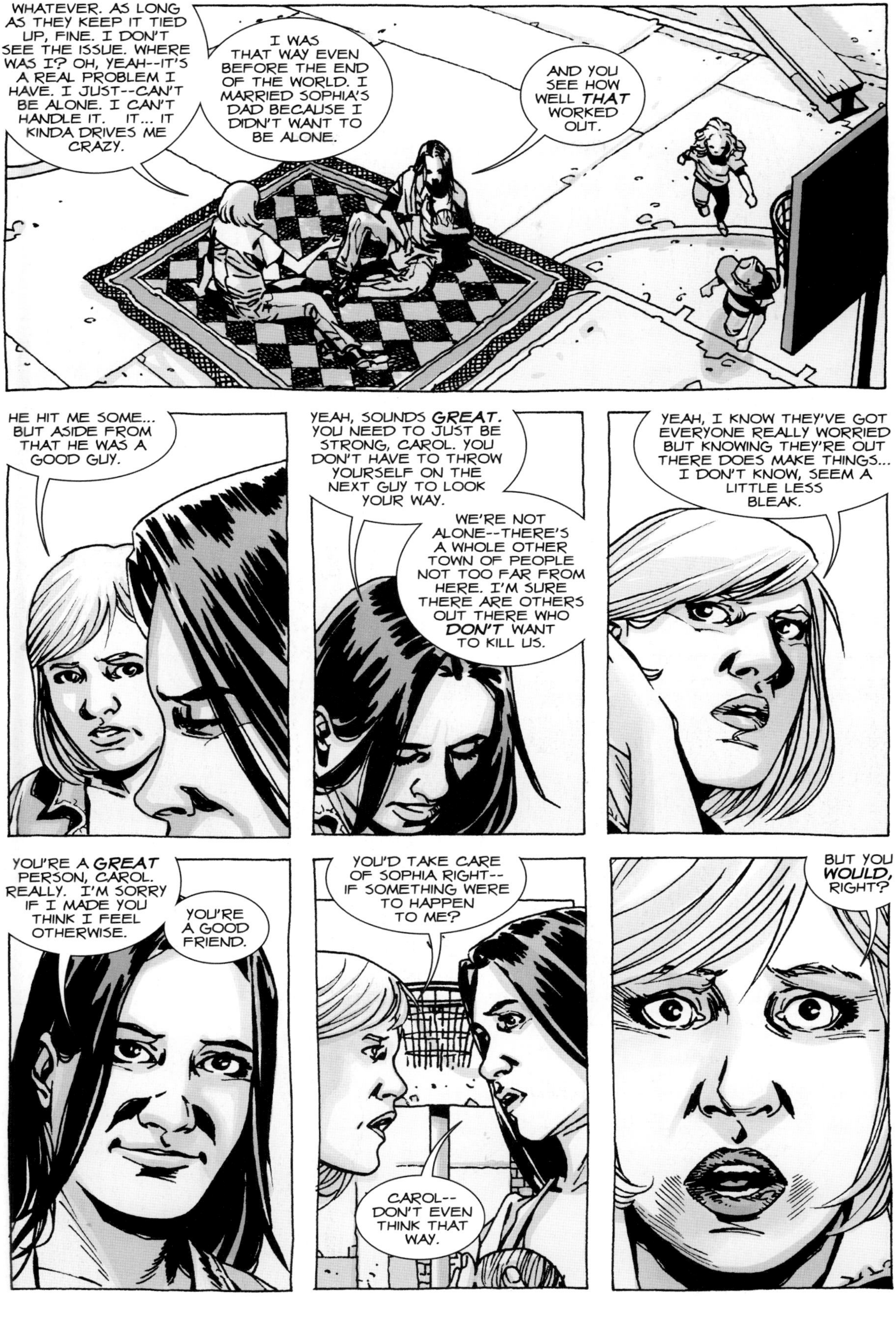
WHATEVER. AS LONG AS THEY KEEP IT TIED UP, FINE. I DON'T SEE THE ISSUE. WHERE WAS I? OH, YEAH--IT'S A REAL PROBLEM I HAVE. I JUST--CAN'T BE ALONE. I CAN'T HANDLE IT. IT... IT KINDA DRIVES ME CRAZY.
I WAS THAT WAY EVEN BEFORE THE END OF THE WORLD. I MARRIED SOPHIA'S DAD BECAUSE I DIDN'T WANT TO BE ALONE.
AND YOU SEE HOW WELL THAT WORKED OUT.
HE HIT ME SOME... BUT ASIDE FROM THAT HE WAS A GOOD GUY.
YEAH, SOUNDS GREAT. YOU NEED TO JUST BE STRONG, CAROL. YOU DON'T HAVE TO THROW YOURSELF ON THE NEXT GUY TO LOOK YOUR WAY.
WE'RE NOT ALONE--THERE'S A WHOLE OTHER TOWN OF PEOPLE NOT TOO FAR FROM HERE. I'M SURE THERE ARE OTHERS OUT THERE WHO DON'T WANT TO KILL US.
YEAH, I KNOW THEY'VE GOT EVERYONE REALLY WORRIED BUT KNOWING THEY'RE OUT THERE DOES MAKE THINGS... I DON'T KNOW, SEEM A LITTLE LESS BLEAK.
YOU'RE A GREAT PERSON, CAROL. REALLY. I'M SORRY IF I MADE YOU THINK I FEEL OTHERWISE.
YOU'RE A GOOD FRIEND.
YOU'D TAKE CARE OF SOPHIA RIGHT-- IF SOMETHING WERE TO HAPPEN TO ME?
CAROL-- DON'T EVEN THINK THAT WAY.
BUT YOU WOULD, RIGHT?

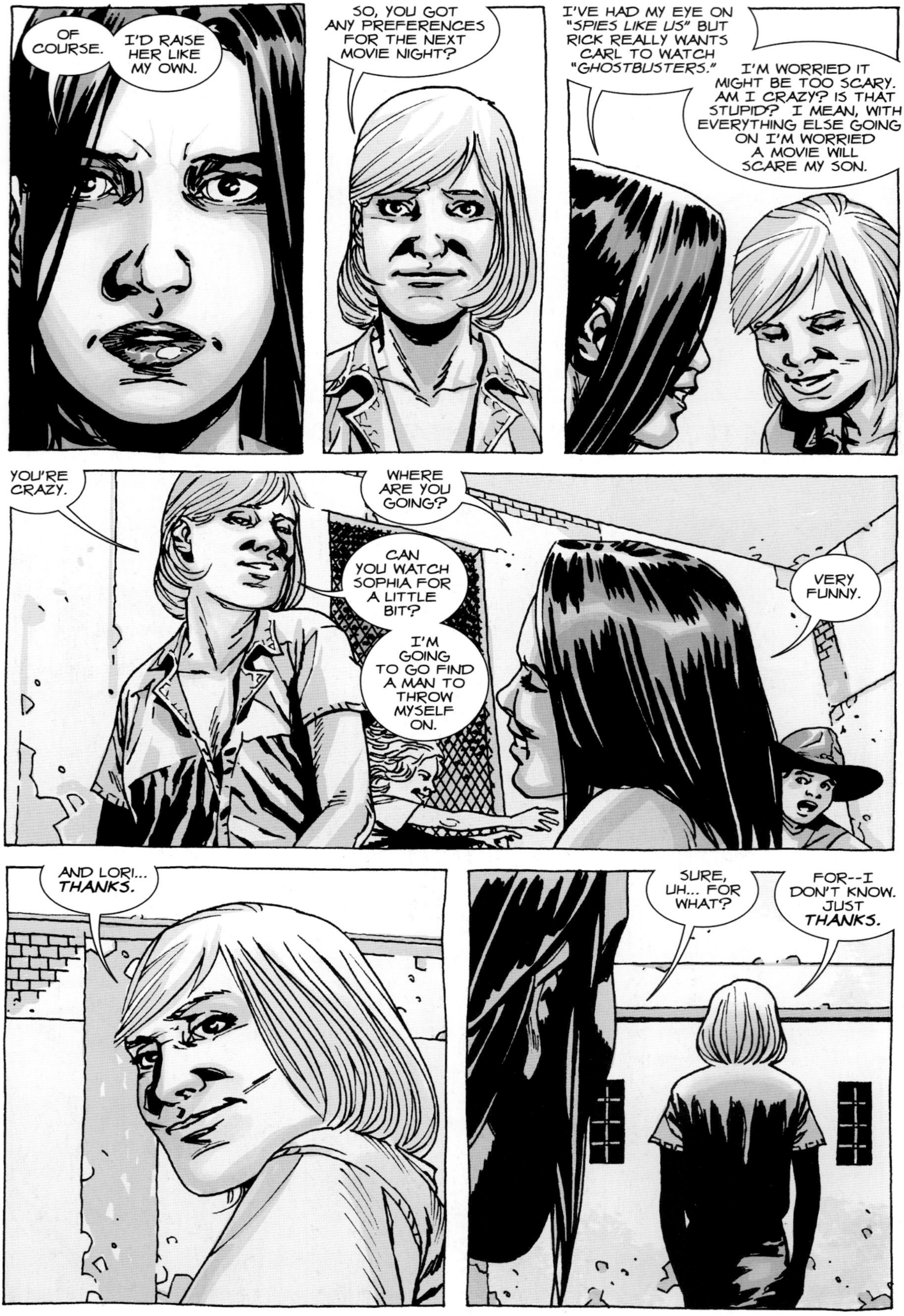
OF COURSE.
I'D RAISE HER LIKE MY OWN.
SO, YOU GOT ANY PREFERENCES FOR THE NEXT MOVIE NIGHT?
I'VE HAD MY EYE ON "*SPIES LIKE US*" BUT RICK REALLY WANTS CARL TO WATCH "*GHOSTBUSTERS.*"
I'M WORRIED IT MIGHT BE TOO SCARY. AM I CRAZY? IS THAT STUPID? I MEAN, WITH EVERYTHING ELSE GOING ON I'M WORRIED A MOVIE WILL SCARE MY SON.
YOU'RE CRAZY.
WHERE ARE YOU GOING?
CAN YOU WATCH SOPHIA FOR A LITTLE BIT?
I'M GOING TO GO FIND A MAN TO THROW MYSELF ON.
VERY FUNNY.
AND LORI... ***THANKS.***
SURE, UH... FOR WHAT?
FOR--I DON'T KNOW. JUST ***THANKS.***

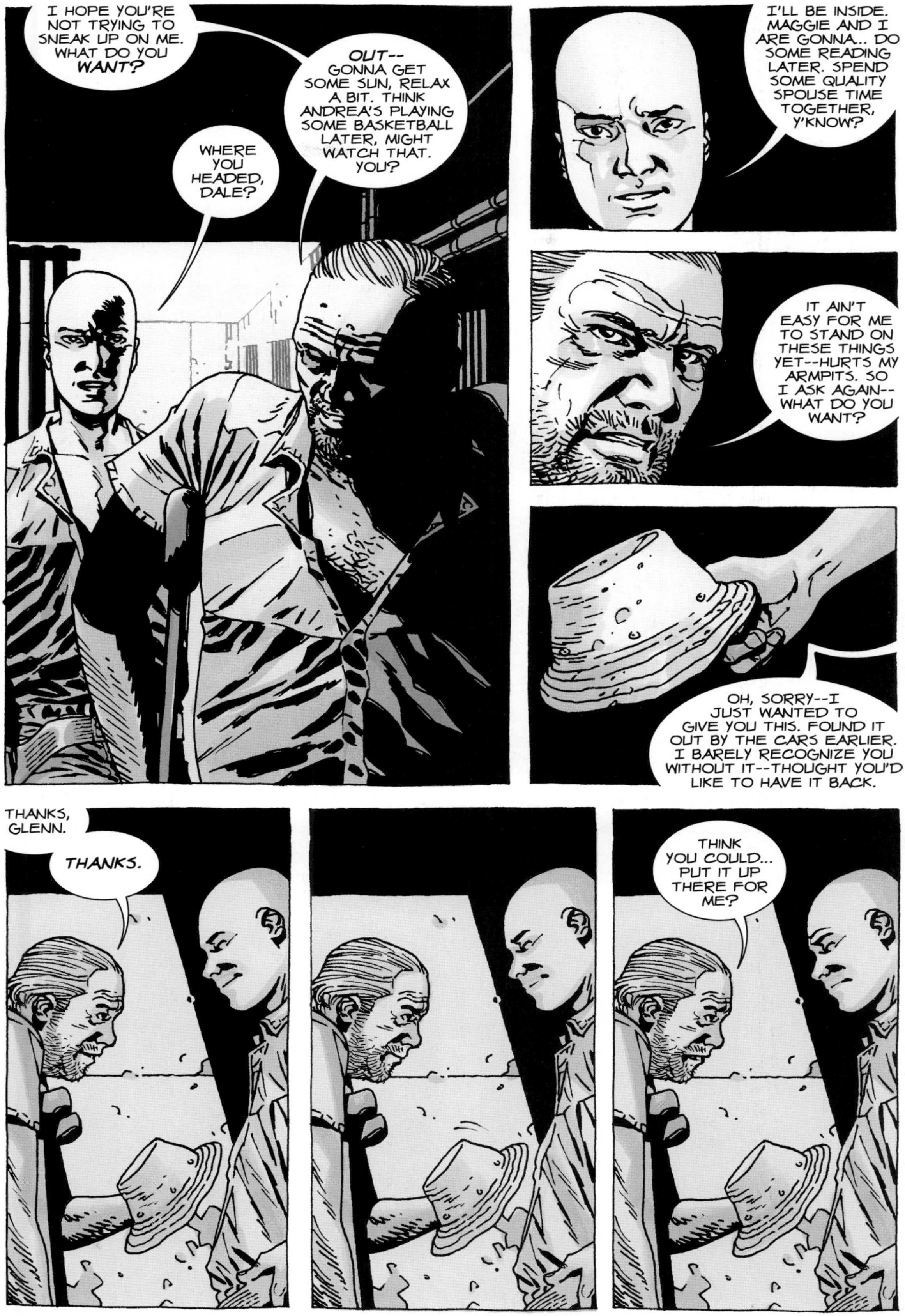
I HOPE YOU'RE NOT TRYING TO SNEAK UP ON ME. WHAT DO YOU *WANT?*
WHERE YOU HEADED, DALE?
OUT-- GONNA GET SOME SUN, RELAX A BIT. THINK ANDREA'S PLAYING SOME BASKETBALL LATER, MIGHT WATCH THAT. YOU?
I'LL BE INSIDE. MAGGIE AND I ARE GONNA.. DO SOME READING LATER. SPEND SOME QUALITY SPOUSE TIME TOGETHER, Y'KNOW?
IT AIN'T EASY FOR ME TO STAND ON THESE THINGS YET--HURTS MY ARMPITS. SO I ASK AGAIN-- WHAT DO YOU WANT?
OH, SORRY--I JUST WANTED TO GIVE YOU THIS. FOUND IT OUT BY THE CARS EARLIER. I BARELY RECOGNIZE YOU WITHOUT IT--THOUGHT YOU'D LIKE TO HAVE IT BACK.
THANKS, GLENN.
THANKS.
THINK YOU COULD... PUT IT UP THERE FOR ME?

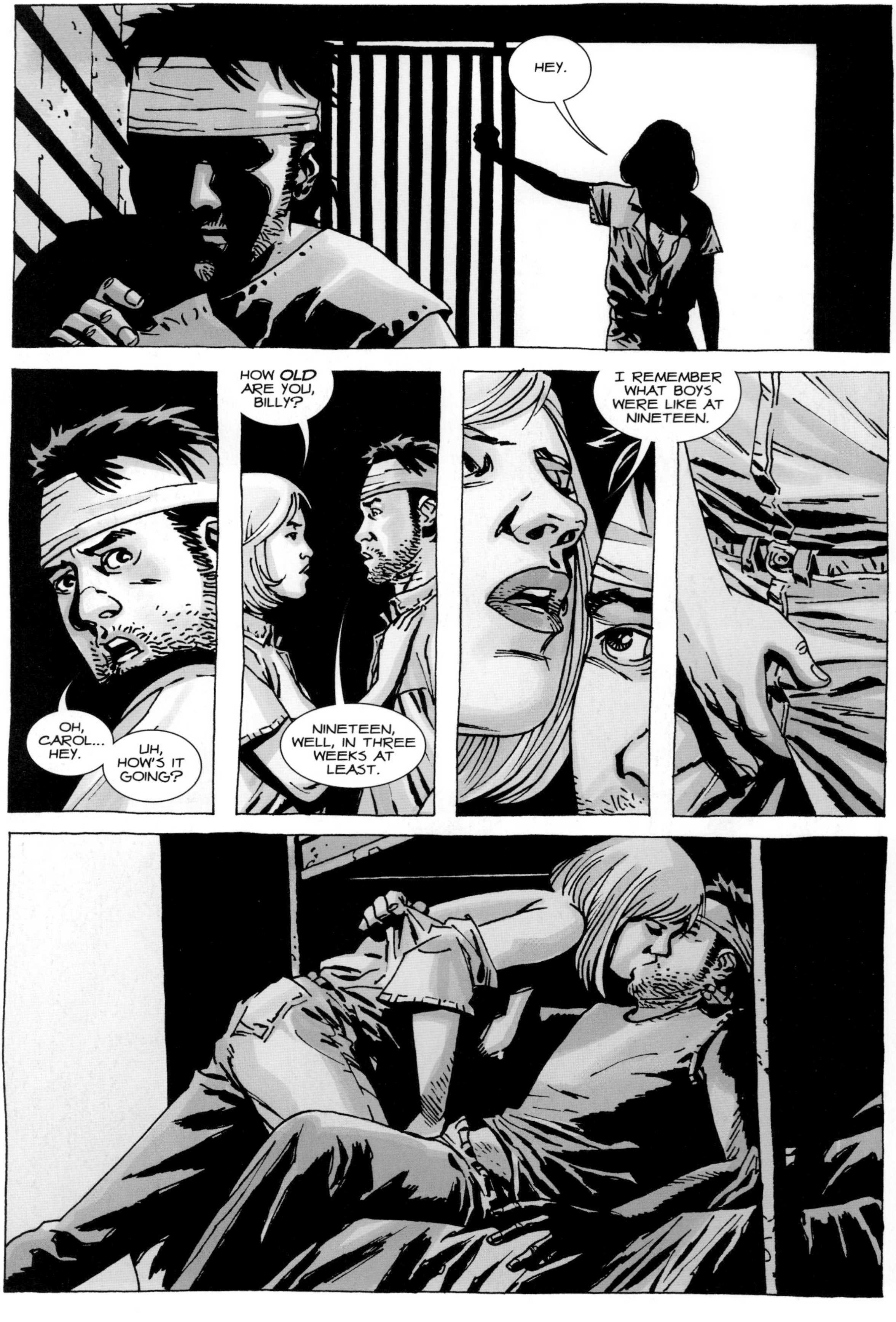
HEY.
OH, CAROL... HEY.
UH, HOW'S IT GOING?
HOW OLD ARE YOU, BILLY?
NINETEEN, WELL, IN THREE WEEKS AT LEAST.
I REMEMBER WHAT BOYS WERE LIKE AT NINETEEN.

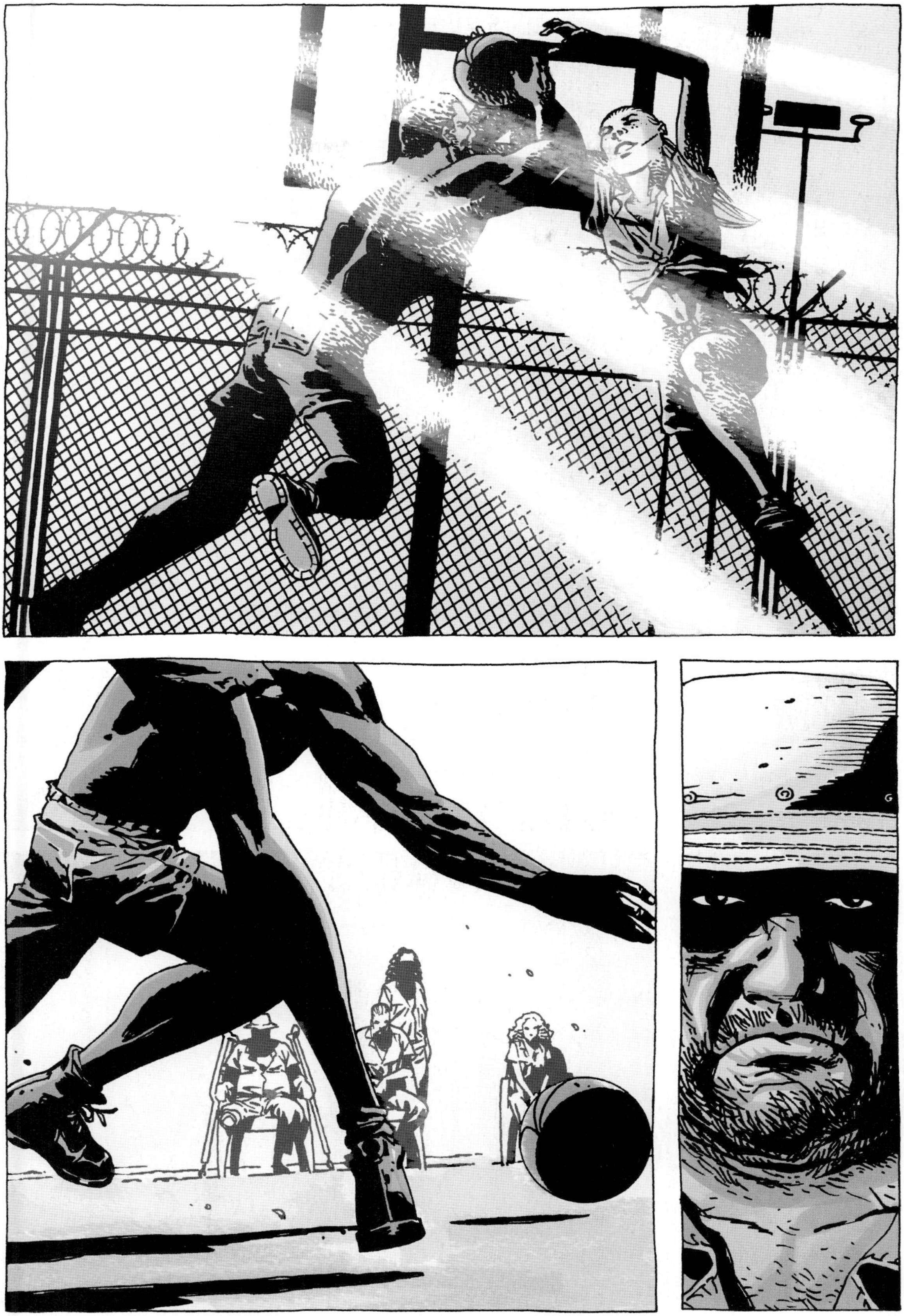

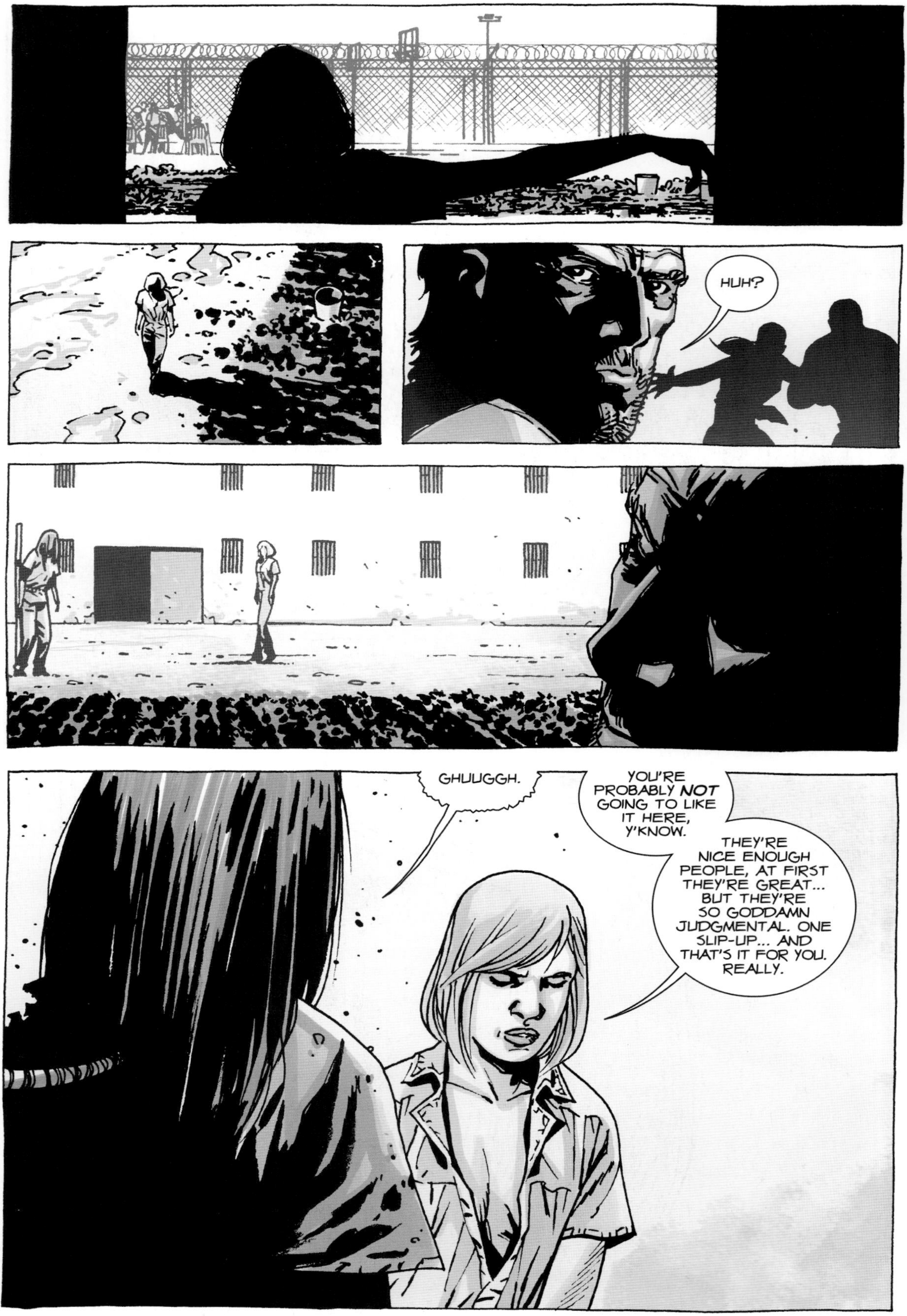
HUH?
GHUUGGH.
YOU'RE PROBABLY NOT GOING TO LIKE IT HERE, Y'KNOW.
THEY'RE NICE ENOUGH PEOPLE, AT FIRST THEY'RE GREAT... BUT THEY'RE SO GODDAMN JUDGMENTAL. ONE SLIP-UP... AND THAT'S IT FOR YOU. REALLY.

I TRIED TO KILL MYSELF. I DID. IT DIDN'T WORK, OBVIOUSLY, BUT I TRIED. THEY WON'T LET ME FORGET IT. SINCE THEN, I CAN SEE IT IN THEIR EYES-- THEY'VE LOST RESPECT FOR ME. **ALL** OF THEM.

EVEN MY BEST FRIEND.

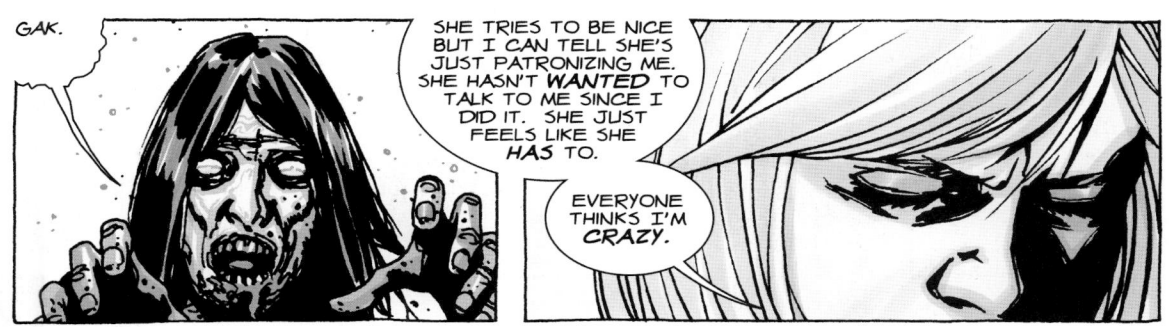

GAK.

SHE TRIES TO BE NICE BUT I CAN TELL SHE'S JUST PATRONIZING ME. SHE HASN'T **WANTED** TO TALK TO ME SINCE I DID IT. SHE JUST FEELS LIKE SHE **HAS** TO.

EVERYONE THINKS I'M **CRAZY**.

I DON'T REALLY HAVE ANYONE TO TALK TO, SO I FIGURED I'D INTRODUCE MYSELF. I'M CAROL.

I THINK I'LL JUST TALK TO **YOU** FROM NOW ON. YOU LISTEN, YOU DON'T SEEM TO JUDGE ME. THAT'S REALLY IMPORTANT IN A FRIENDSHIP, Y'KNOW. NOT JUDGING PEOPLE.

I REALLY HOPE YOU **LIKE** ME.

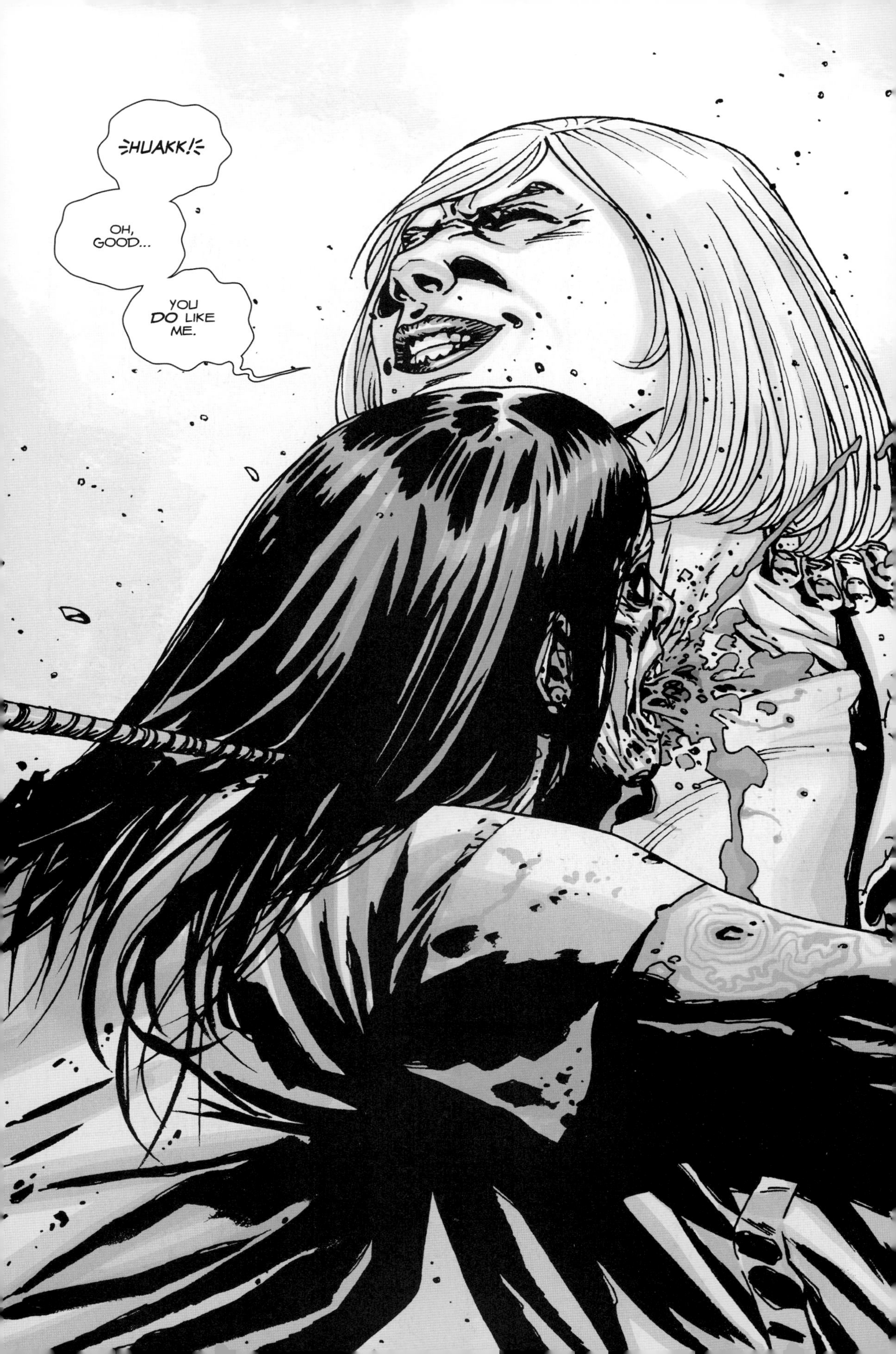

HUAKK!
OH, GOOD...
YOU DO LIKE ME.

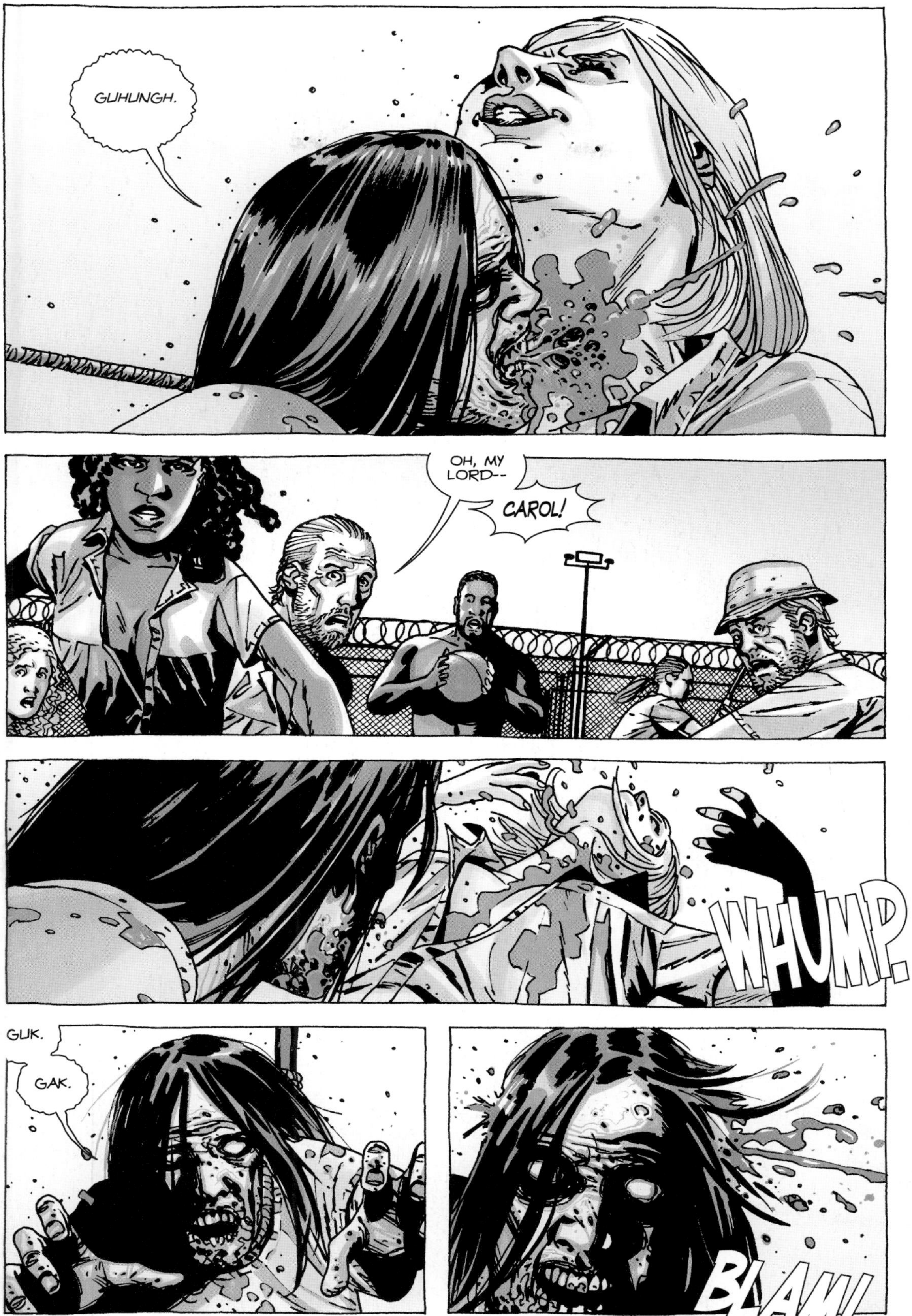
GUHUNGH.
OH, MY LORD--
CAROL!
WHUMP.
GUK.
GAK.
BLAM!

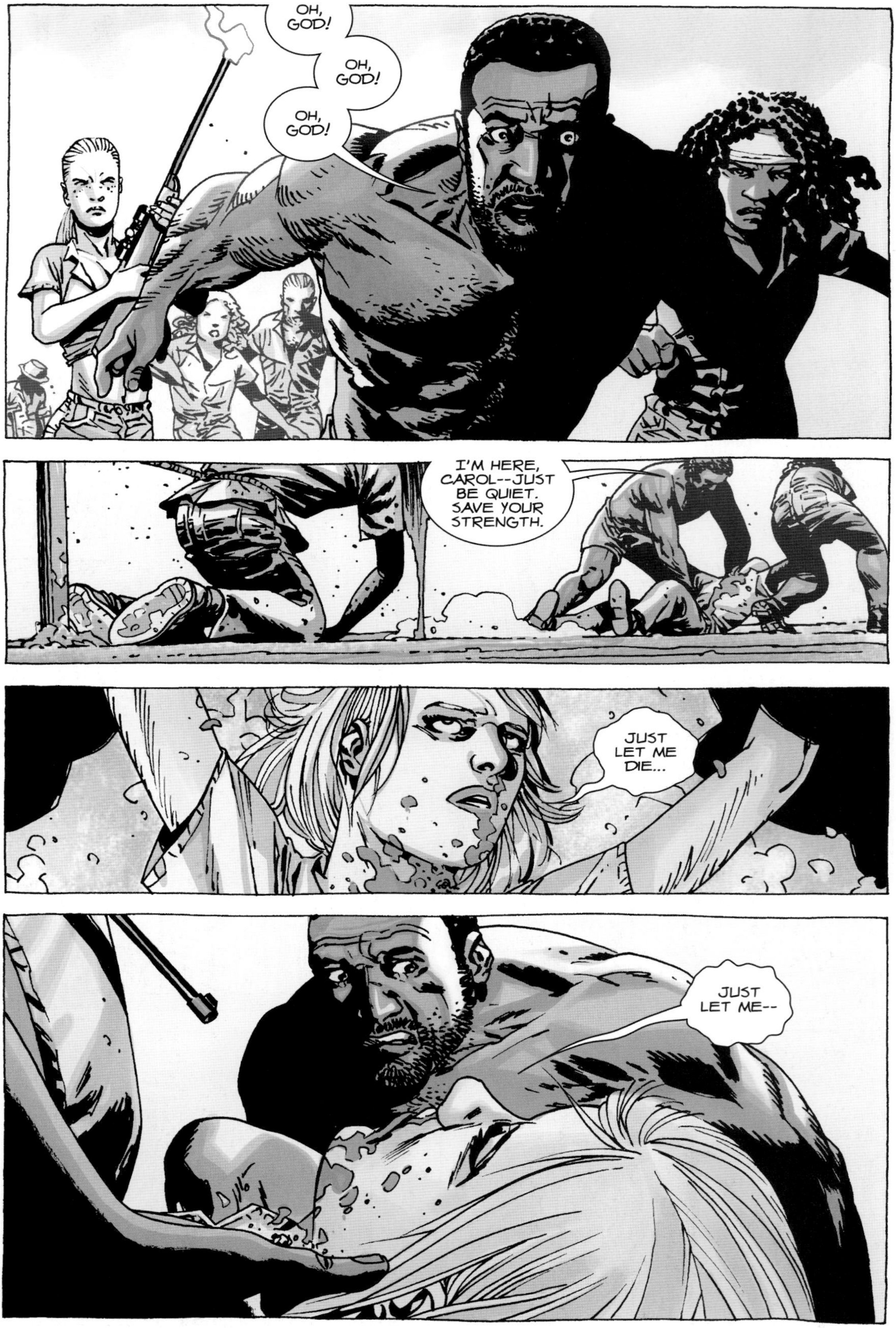
OH, GOD!
OH, GOD!
OH, GOD!
I'M HERE, CAROL--JUST BE QUIET. SAVE YOUR STRENGTH.
JUST LET ME DIE...
JUST LET ME--

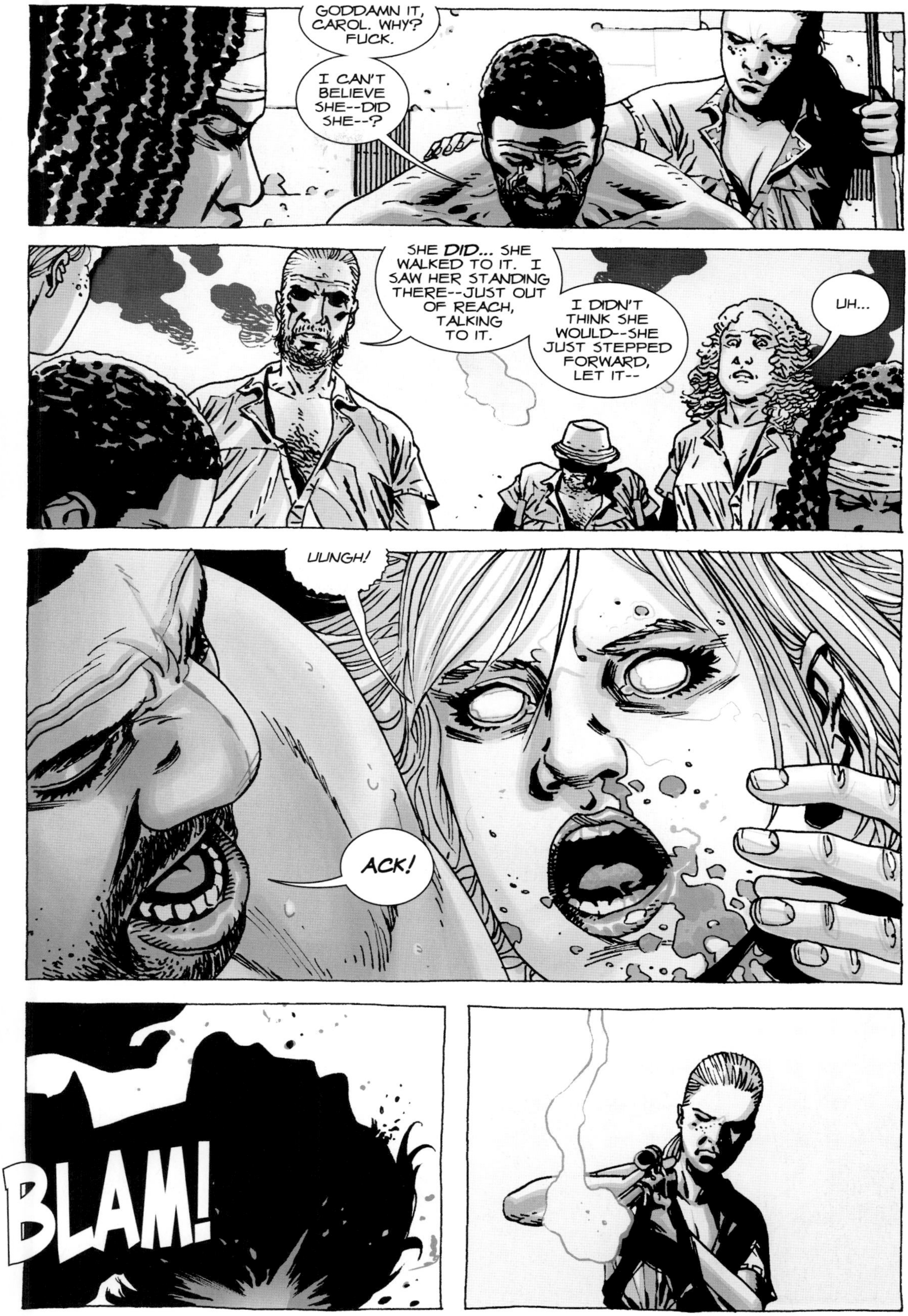
GODDAMN IT, CAROL. WHY? FUCK.
I CAN'T BELIEVE SHE--DID SHE--?
SHE *DID*... SHE WALKED TO IT. I SAW HER STANDING THERE--JUST OUT OF REACH, TALKING TO IT.
I DIDN'T THINK SHE WOULD--SHE JUST STEPPED FORWARD, LET IT--
UH...
UUNGH!
ACK!
BLAM!

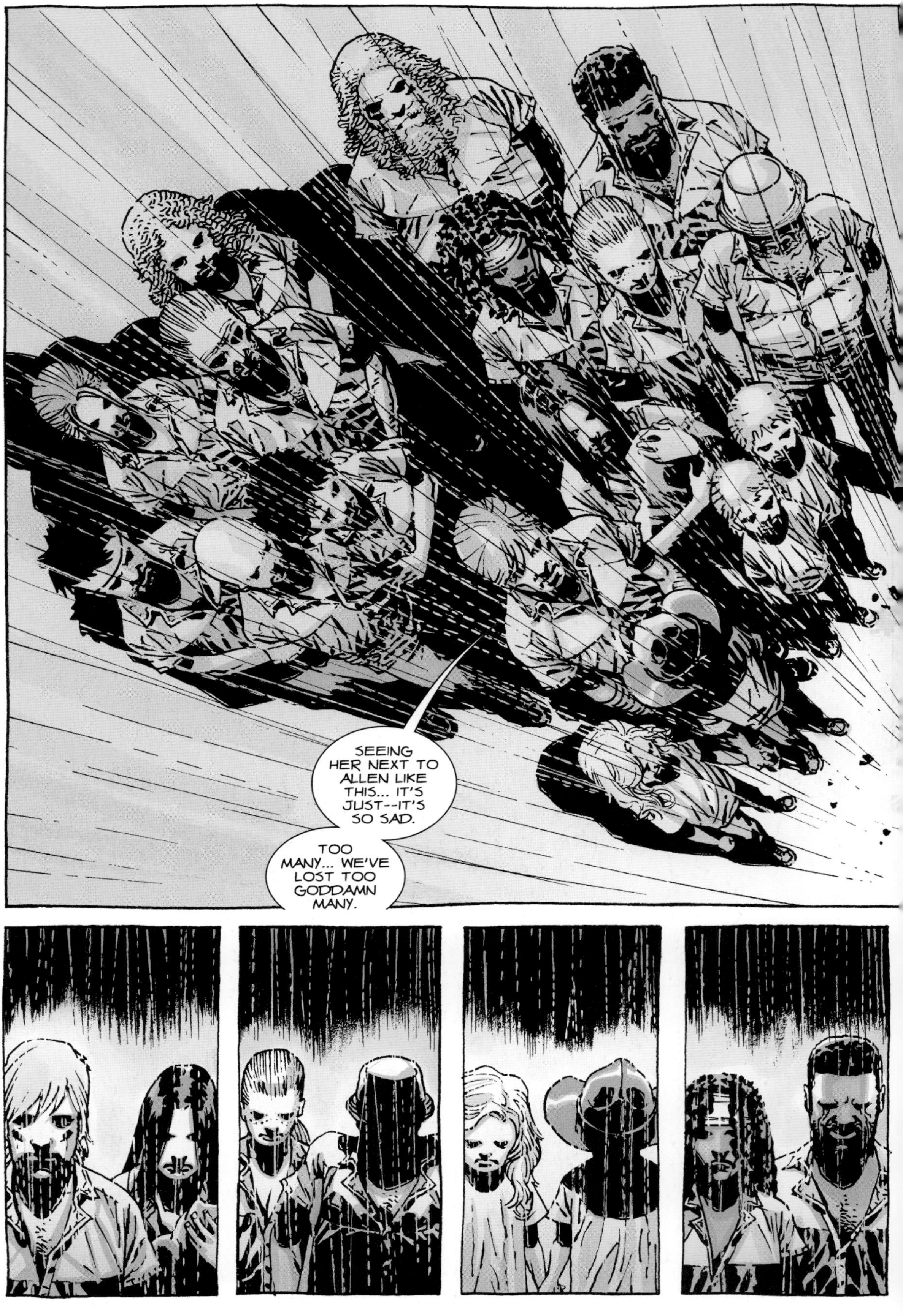
SEEING HER NEXT TO ALLEN LIKE THIS... IT'S JUST--IT'S SO SAD.
TOO MANY... WE'VE LOST TOO GODDAMN MANY.

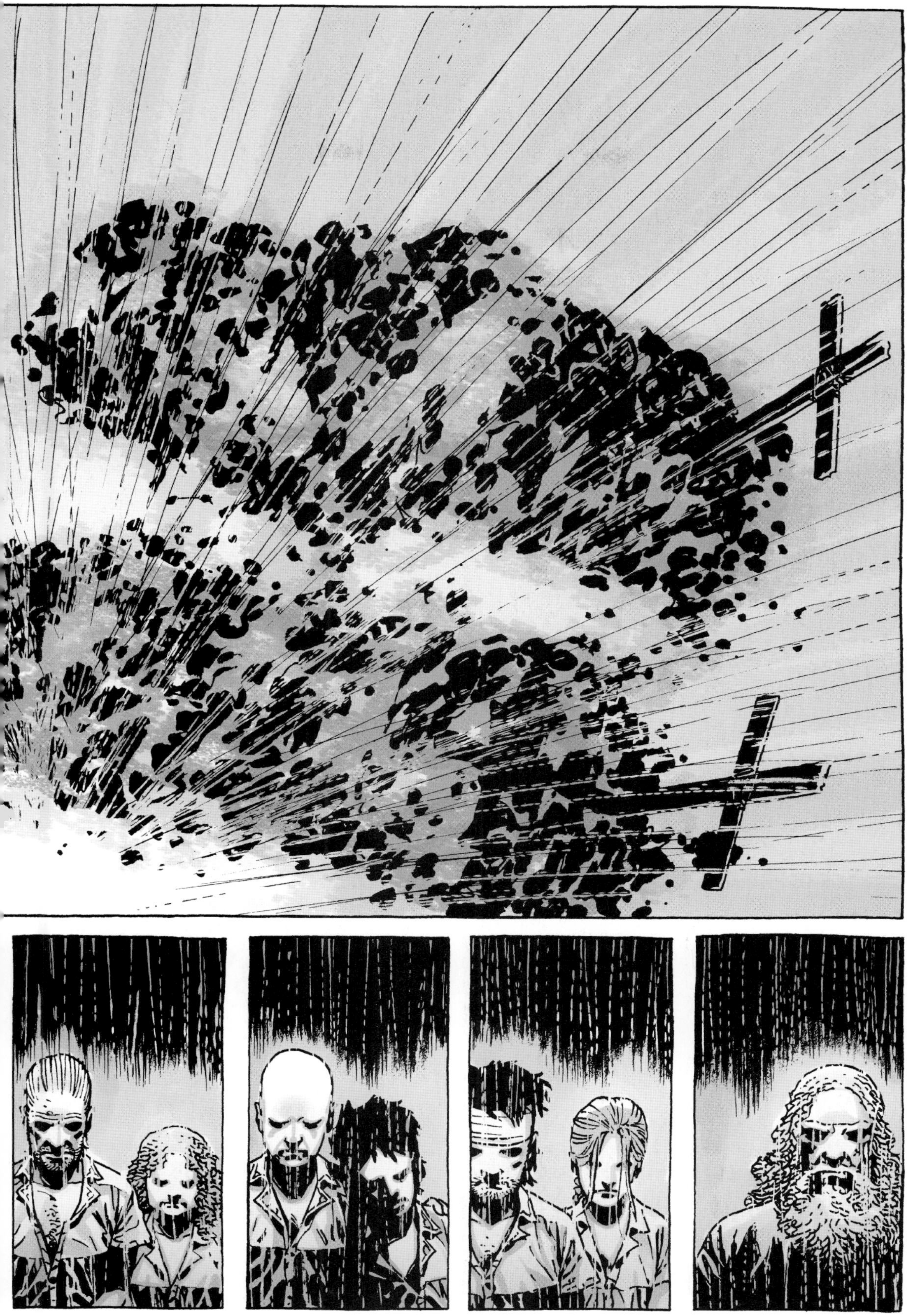

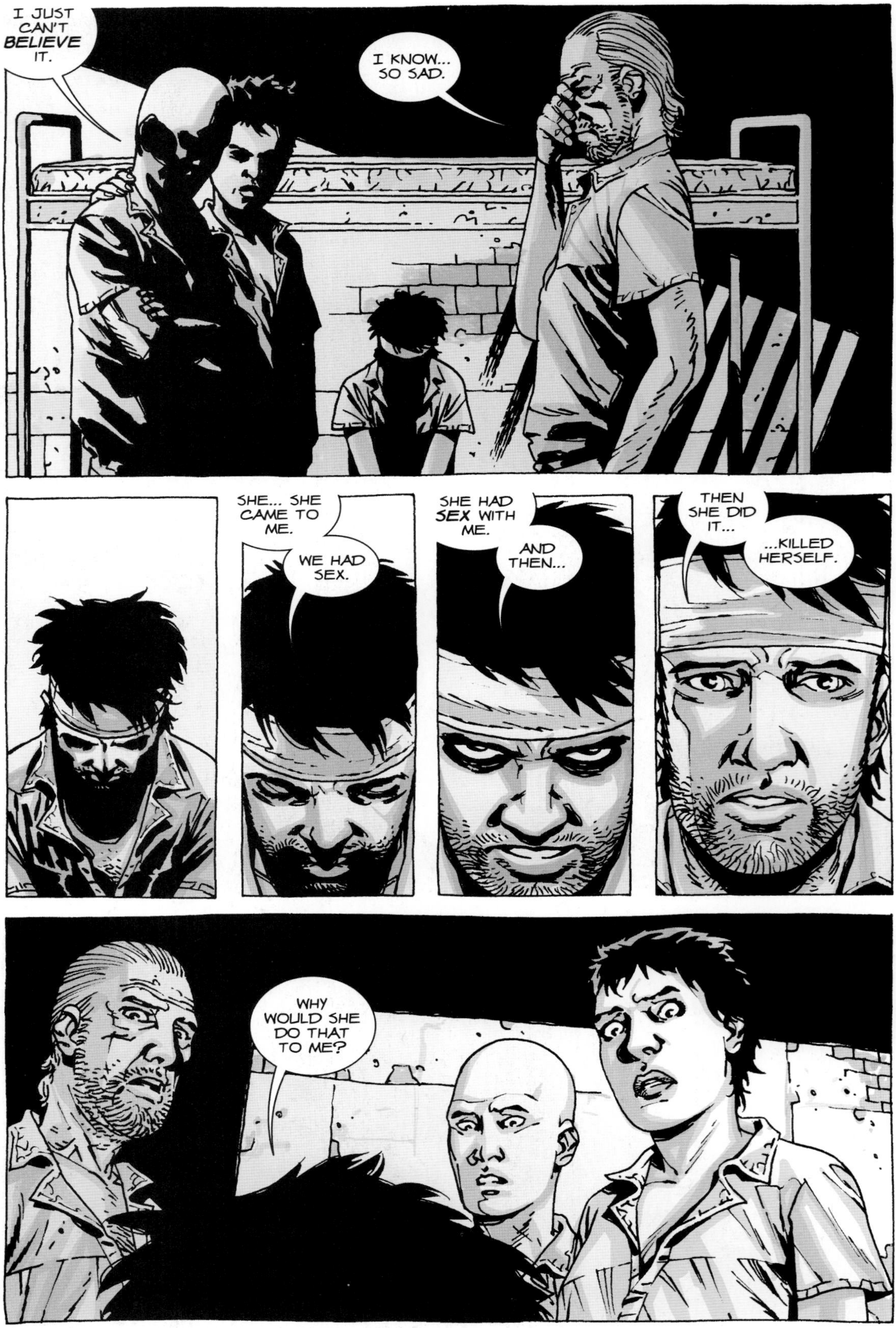
I JUST CAN'T BELIEVE IT.
I KNOW... SO SAD.
SHE... SHE CAME TO ME.
WE HAD SEX.
SHE HAD SEX WITH ME.
AND THEN...
THEN SHE DID IT...
...KILLED HERSELF.
WHY WOULD SHE DO THAT TO ME?

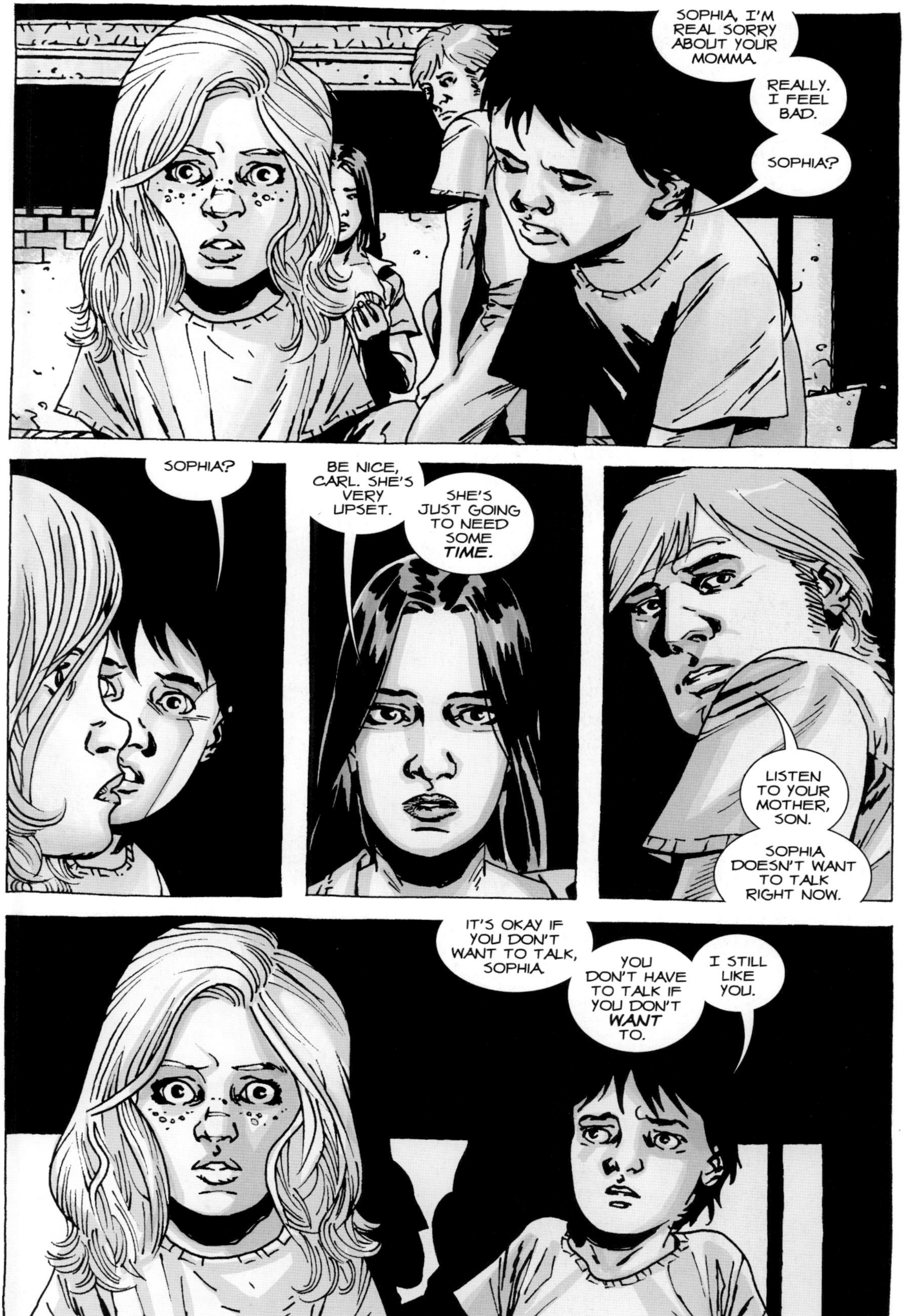
SOPHIA, I'M REAL SORRY ABOUT YOUR MOMMA.
REALLY. I FEEL BAD.
SOPHIA?
SOPHIA?
BE NICE, CARL. SHE'S VERY UPSET.
SHE'S JUST GOING TO NEED SOME *TIME.*
LISTEN TO YOUR MOTHER, SON.
SOPHIA DOESN'T WANT TO TALK RIGHT NOW.
IT'S OKAY IF YOU DON'T WANT TO TALK, SOPHIA.
YOU DON'T HAVE TO TALK IF YOU DON'T *WANT* TO.
I STILL LIKE YOU.

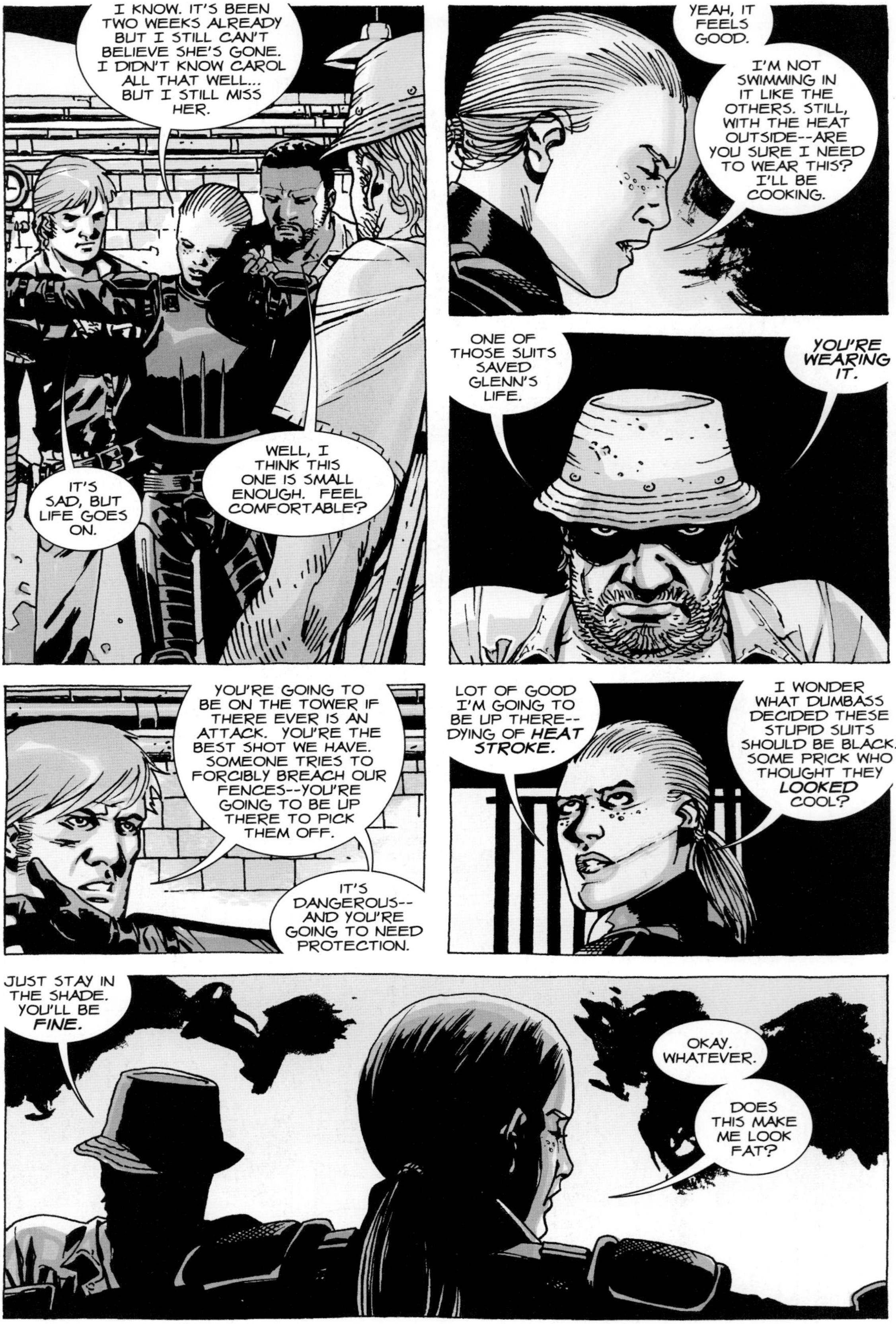
I KNOW. IT'S BEEN TWO WEEKS ALREADY BUT I STILL CAN'T BELIEVE SHE'S GONE. I DIDN'T KNOW CAROL ALL THAT WELL... BUT I STILL MISS HER.
IT'S SAD, BUT LIFE GOES ON.
WELL, I THINK THIS ONE IS SMALL ENOUGH. FEEL COMFORTABLE?
YEAH, IT FEELS GOOD.
I'M NOT SWIMMING IN IT LIKE THE OTHERS. STILL, WITH THE HEAT OUTSIDE--ARE YOU SURE I NEED TO WEAR THIS? I'LL BE COOKING.
ONE OF THOSE SUITS SAVED GLENN'S LIFE.
YOU'RE WEARING IT.
YOU'RE GOING TO BE ON THE TOWER IF THERE EVER IS AN ATTACK. YOU'RE THE BEST SHOT WE HAVE. SOMEONE TRIES TO FORCIBLY BREACH OUR FENCES--YOU'RE GOING TO BE UP THERE TO PICK THEM OFF.
IT'S DANGEROUS--AND YOU'RE GOING TO NEED PROTECTION.
LOT OF GOOD I'M GOING TO BE UP THERE--DYING OF HEAT STROKE.
I WONDER WHAT DUMBASS DECIDED THESE STUPID SUITS SHOULD BE BLACK. SOME PRICK WHO THOUGHT THEY LOOKED COOL?
JUST STAY IN THE SHADE. YOU'LL BE FINE.
OKAY. WHATEVER.
DOES THIS MAKE ME LOOK FAT?

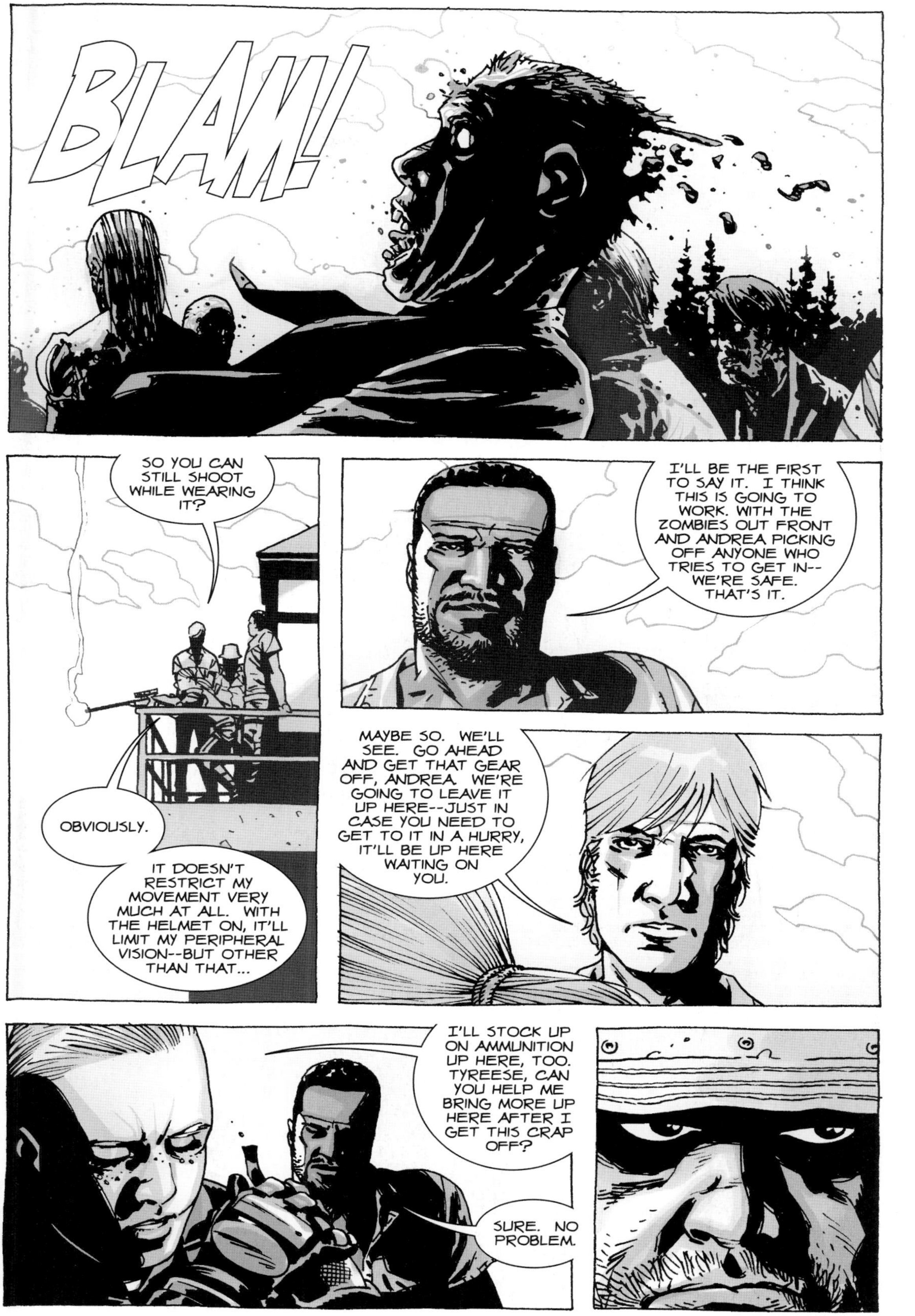
BLAM!
SO YOU CAN STILL SHOOT WHILE WEARING IT?
OBVIOUSLY.
IT DOESN'T RESTRICT MY MOVEMENT VERY MUCH AT ALL. WITH THE HELMET ON, IT'LL LIMIT MY PERIPHERAL VISION--BUT OTHER THAN THAT...
I'LL BE THE FIRST TO SAY IT. I THINK THIS IS GOING TO WORK. WITH THE ZOMBIES OUT FRONT AND ANDREA PICKING OFF ANYONE WHO TRIES TO GET IN-- WE'RE SAFE. THAT'S IT.
MAYBE SO. WE'LL SEE. GO AHEAD AND GET THAT GEAR OFF, ANDREA. WE'RE GOING TO LEAVE IT UP HERE--JUST IN CASE YOU NEED TO GET TO IT IN A HURRY, IT'LL BE UP HERE WAITING ON YOU.
I'LL STOCK UP ON AMMUNITION UP HERE, TOO. TYREESE, CAN YOU HELP ME BRING MORE UP HERE AFTER I GET THIS CRAP OFF?
SURE. NO PROBLEM.

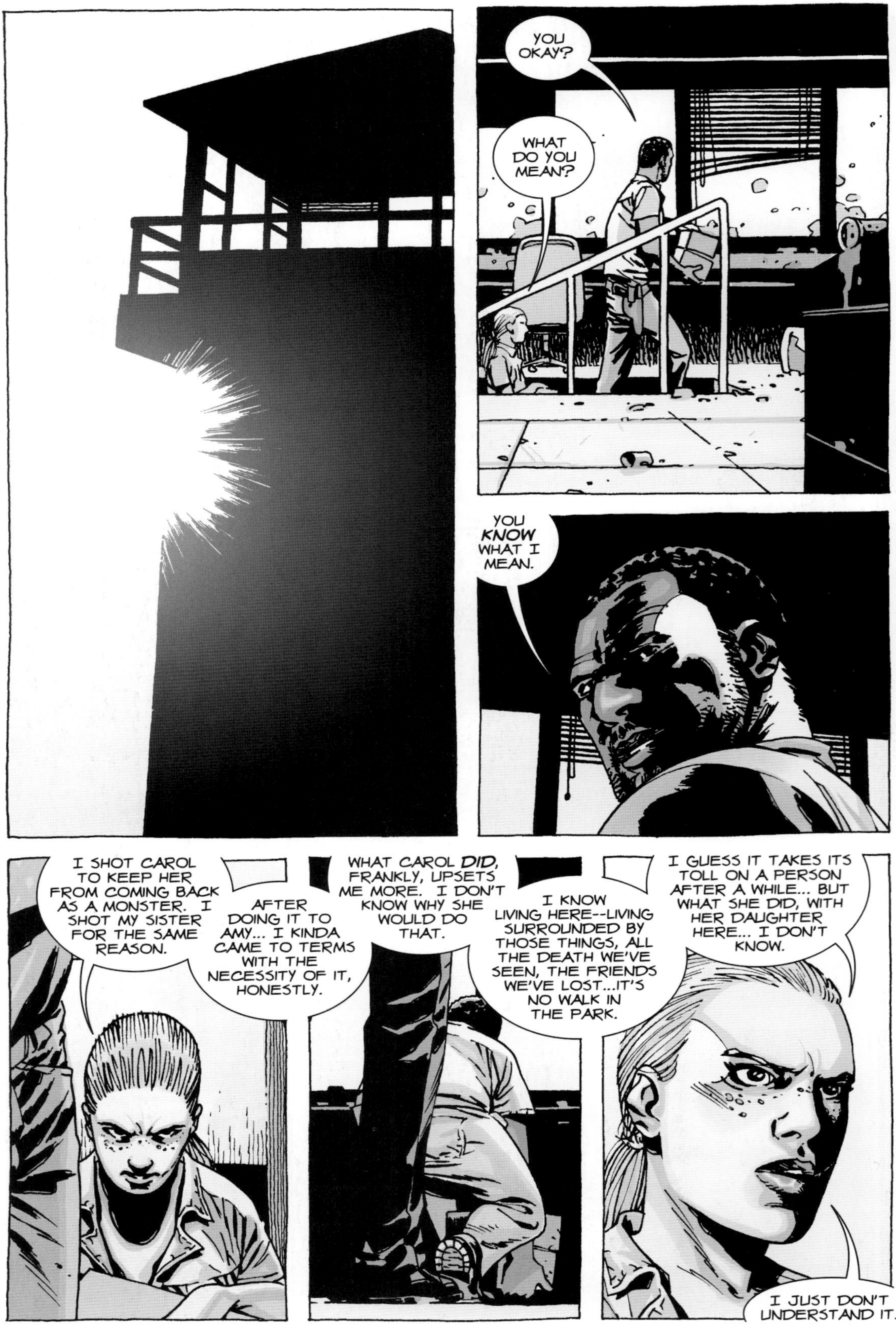
YOU OKAY?
WHAT DO YOU MEAN?
YOU KNOW WHAT I MEAN.
I SHOT CAROL TO KEEP HER FROM COMING BACK AS A MONSTER. I SHOT MY SISTER FOR THE SAME REASON.
AFTER DOING IT TO AMY... I KINDA CAME TO TERMS WITH THE NECESSITY OF IT, HONESTLY.
WHAT CAROL DID, FRANKLY, UPSETS ME MORE. I DON'T KNOW WHY SHE WOULD DO THAT.
I KNOW LIVING HERE--LIVING SURROUNDED BY THOSE THINGS, ALL THE DEATH WE'VE SEEN, THE FRIENDS WE'VE LOST...IT'S NO WALK IN THE PARK.
I GUESS IT TAKES ITS TOLL ON A PERSON AFTER A WHILE... BUT WHAT SHE DID, WITH HER DAUGHTER HERE... I DON'T KNOW.
I JUST DON'T UNDERSTAND IT.

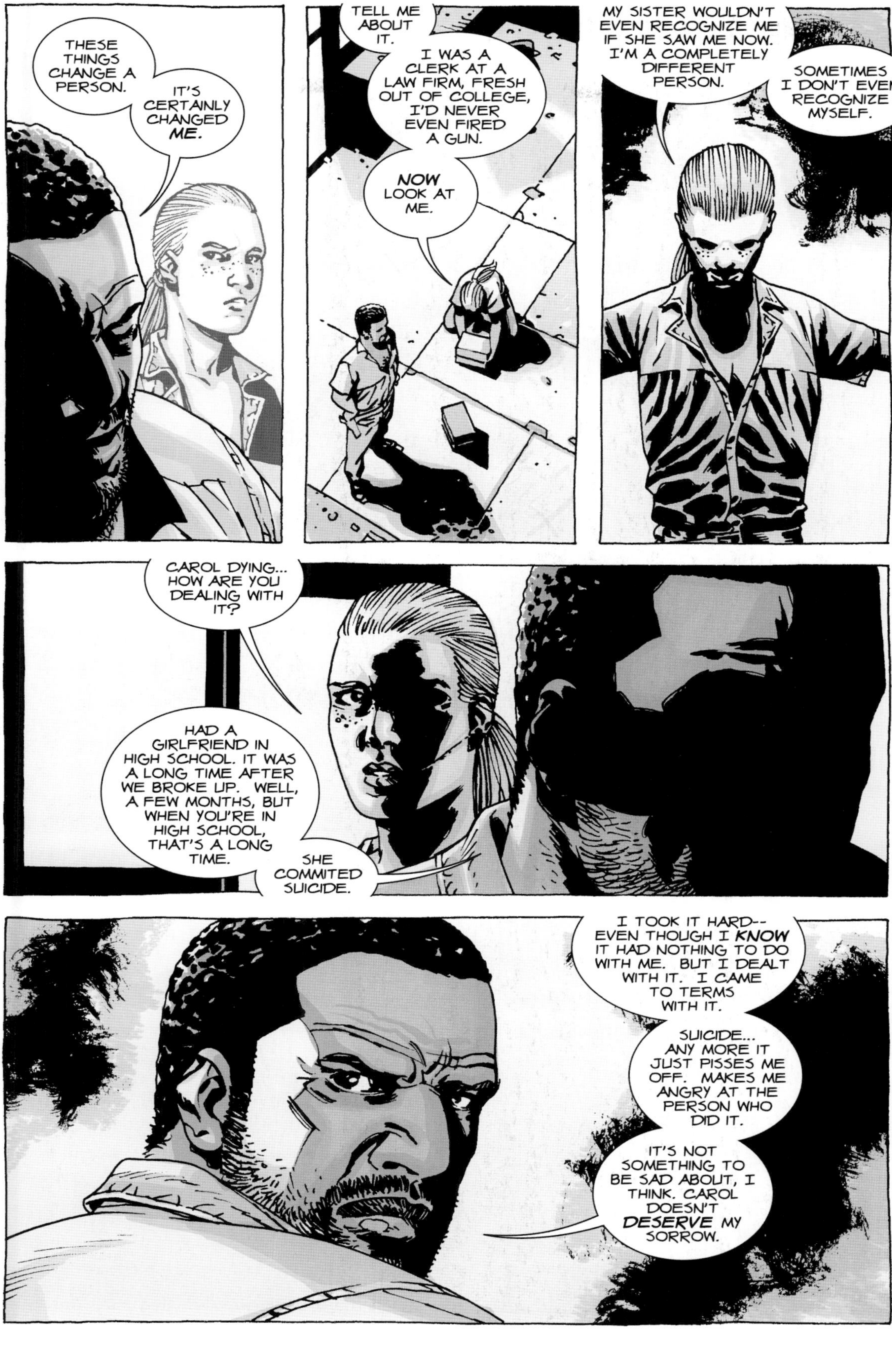
THESE THINGS CHANGE A PERSON.
IT'S CERTAINLY CHANGED ME.
TELL ME ABOUT IT.
I WAS A CLERK AT A LAW FIRM, FRESH OUT OF COLLEGE, I'D NEVER EVEN FIRED A GUN.
NOW LOOK AT ME.
MY SISTER WOULDN'T EVEN RECOGNIZE ME IF SHE SAW ME NOW. I'M A COMPLETELY DIFFERENT PERSON.
SOMETIMES I DON'T EVEN RECOGNIZE MYSELF.
CAROL DYING... HOW ARE YOU DEALING WITH IT?
HAD A GIRLFRIEND IN HIGH SCHOOL. IT WAS A LONG TIME AFTER WE BROKE UP. WELL, A FEW MONTHS, BUT WHEN YOU'RE IN HIGH SCHOOL, THAT'S A LONG TIME.
SHE COMMITED SUICIDE.
I TOOK IT HARD-- EVEN THOUGH I KNOW IT HAD NOTHING TO DO WITH ME. BUT I DEALT WITH IT. I CAME TO TERMS WITH IT.
SUICIDE... ANY MORE IT JUST PISSES ME OFF. MAKES ME ANGRY AT THE PERSON WHO DID IT.
IT'S NOT SOMETHING TO BE SAD ABOUT, I THINK. CAROL DOESN'T DESERVE MY SORROW.

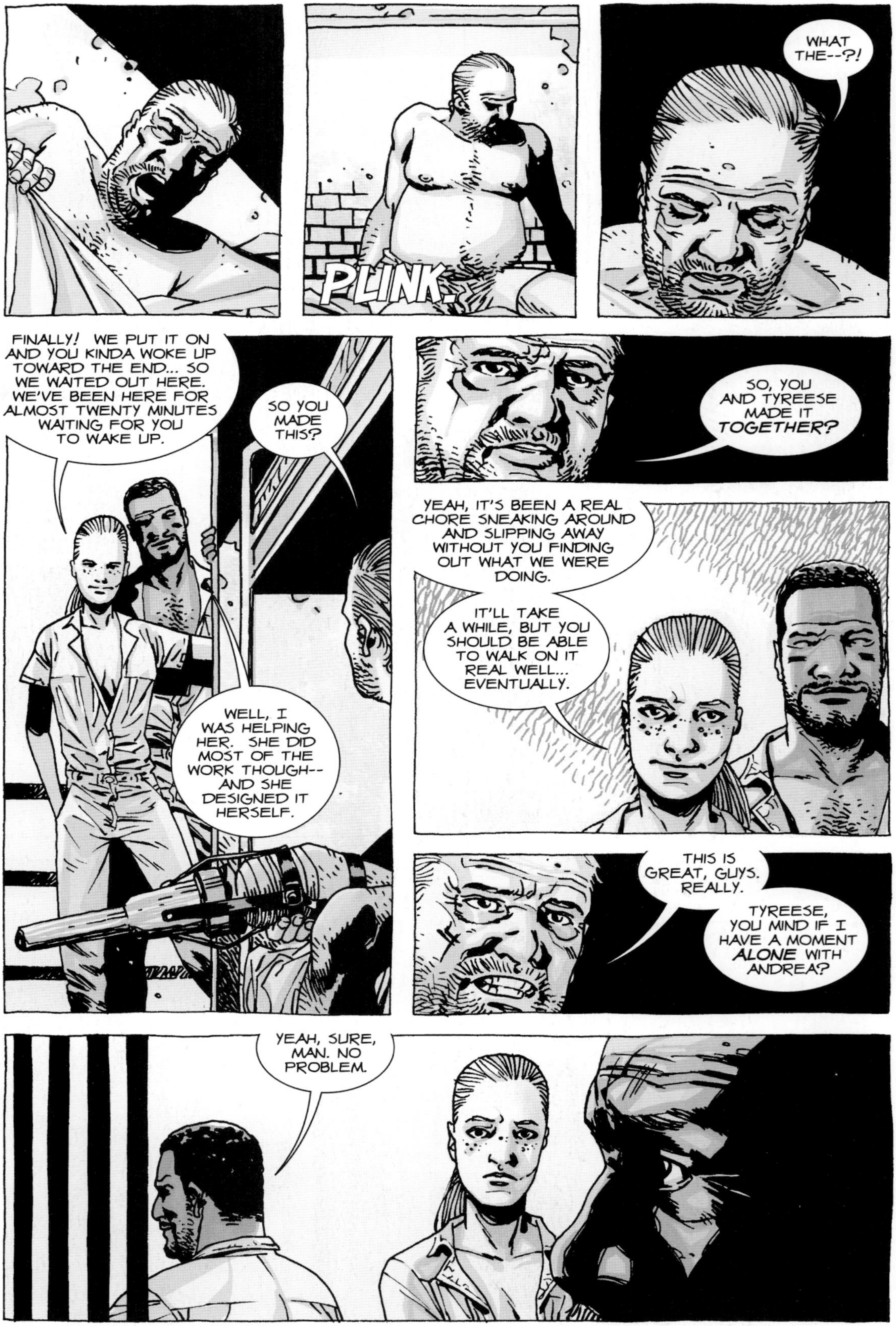

PLINK.
WHAT THE--?!
FINALLY! WE PUT IT ON AND YOU KINDA WOKE UP TOWARD THE END... SO WE WAITED OUT HERE. WE'VE BEEN HERE FOR ALMOST TWENTY MINUTES WAITING FOR YOU TO WAKE UP.
SO YOU MADE THIS?
WELL, I WAS HELPING HER. SHE DID MOST OF THE WORK THOUGH-- AND SHE DESIGNED IT HERSELF.
SO, YOU AND TYREESE MADE IT TOGETHER?
YEAH, IT'S BEEN A REAL CHORE SNEAKING AROUND AND SLIPPING AWAY WITHOUT YOU FINDING OUT WHAT WE WERE DOING.
IT'LL TAKE A WHILE, BUT YOU SHOULD BE ABLE TO WALK ON IT REAL WELL... EVENTUALLY.
THIS IS GREAT, GUYS. REALLY.
TYREESE, YOU MIND IF I HAVE A MOMENT ALONE WITH ANDREA?
YEAH, SURE, MAN. NO PROBLEM.

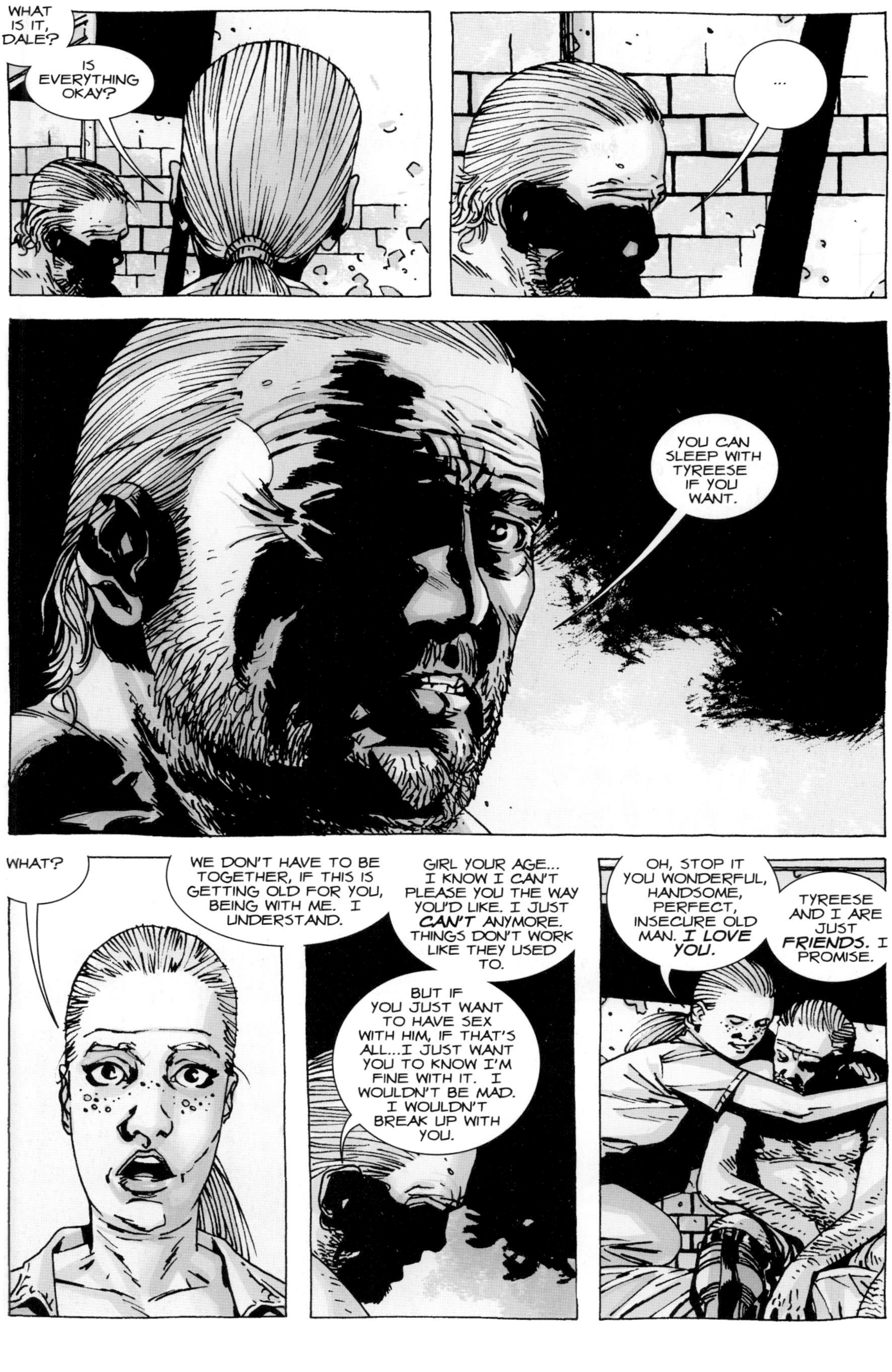
WHAT IS IT, DALE?
IS EVERYTHING OKAY?
...
YOU CAN SLEEP WITH TYREESE IF YOU WANT.
WHAT?
WE DON'T HAVE TO BE TOGETHER, IF THIS IS GETTING OLD FOR YOU, BEING WITH ME. I UNDERSTAND.
GIRL YOUR AGE... I KNOW I CAN'T PLEASE YOU THE WAY YOU'D LIKE. I JUST CAN'T ANYMORE. THINGS DON'T WORK LIKE THEY USED TO.
BUT IF YOU JUST WANT TO HAVE SEX WITH HIM, IF THAT'S ALL...I JUST WANT YOU TO KNOW I'M FINE WITH IT. I WOULDN'T BE MAD. I WOULDN'T BREAK UP WITH YOU.
OH, STOP IT YOU WONDERFUL, HANDSOME, PERFECT, INSECURE OLD MAN. I LOVE YOU.
TYREESE AND I ARE JUST FRIENDS. I PROMISE.

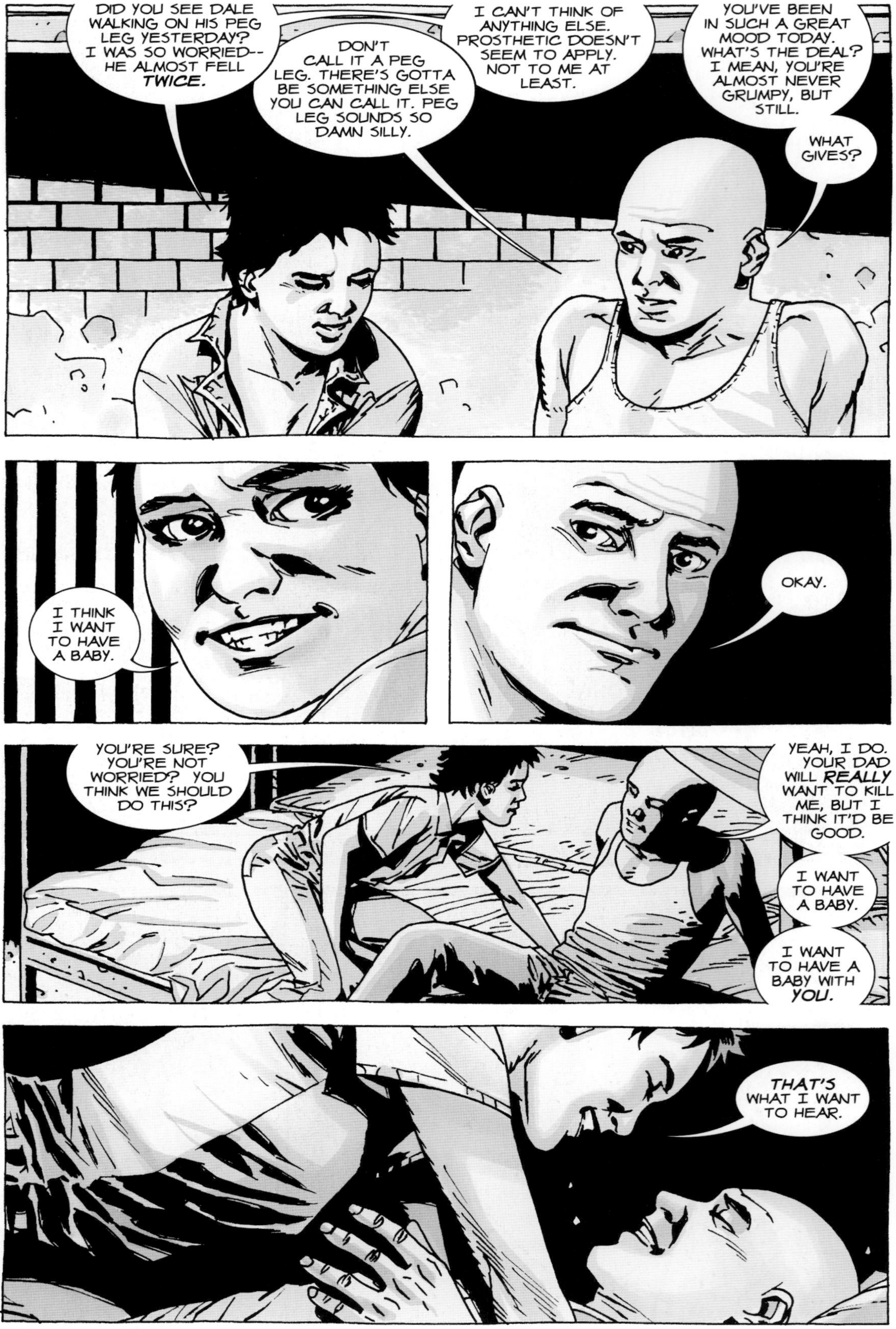
DID YOU SEE DALE WALKING ON HIS PEG LEG YESTERDAY? I WAS SO WORRIED-- HE ALMOST FELL TWICE.
DON'T CALL IT A PEG LEG. THERE'S GOTTA BE SOMETHING ELSE YOU CAN CALL IT. PEG LEG SOUNDS SO DAMN SILLY.
I CAN'T THINK OF ANYTHING ELSE. PROSTHETIC DOESN'T SEEM TO APPLY. NOT TO ME AT LEAST.
YOU'VE BEEN IN SUCH A GREAT MOOD TODAY. WHAT'S THE DEAL? I MEAN, YOU'RE ALMOST NEVER GRUMPY, BUT STILL.
WHAT GIVES?
I THINK I WANT TO HAVE A BABY.
OKAY.
YOU'RE SURE? YOU'RE NOT WORRIED? YOU THINK WE SHOULD DO THIS?
YEAH, I DO. YOUR DAD WILL REALLY WANT TO KILL ME, BUT I THINK IT'D BE GOOD.
I WANT TO HAVE A BABY.
I WANT TO HAVE A BABY WITH YOU.
THAT'S WHAT I WANT TO HEAR.

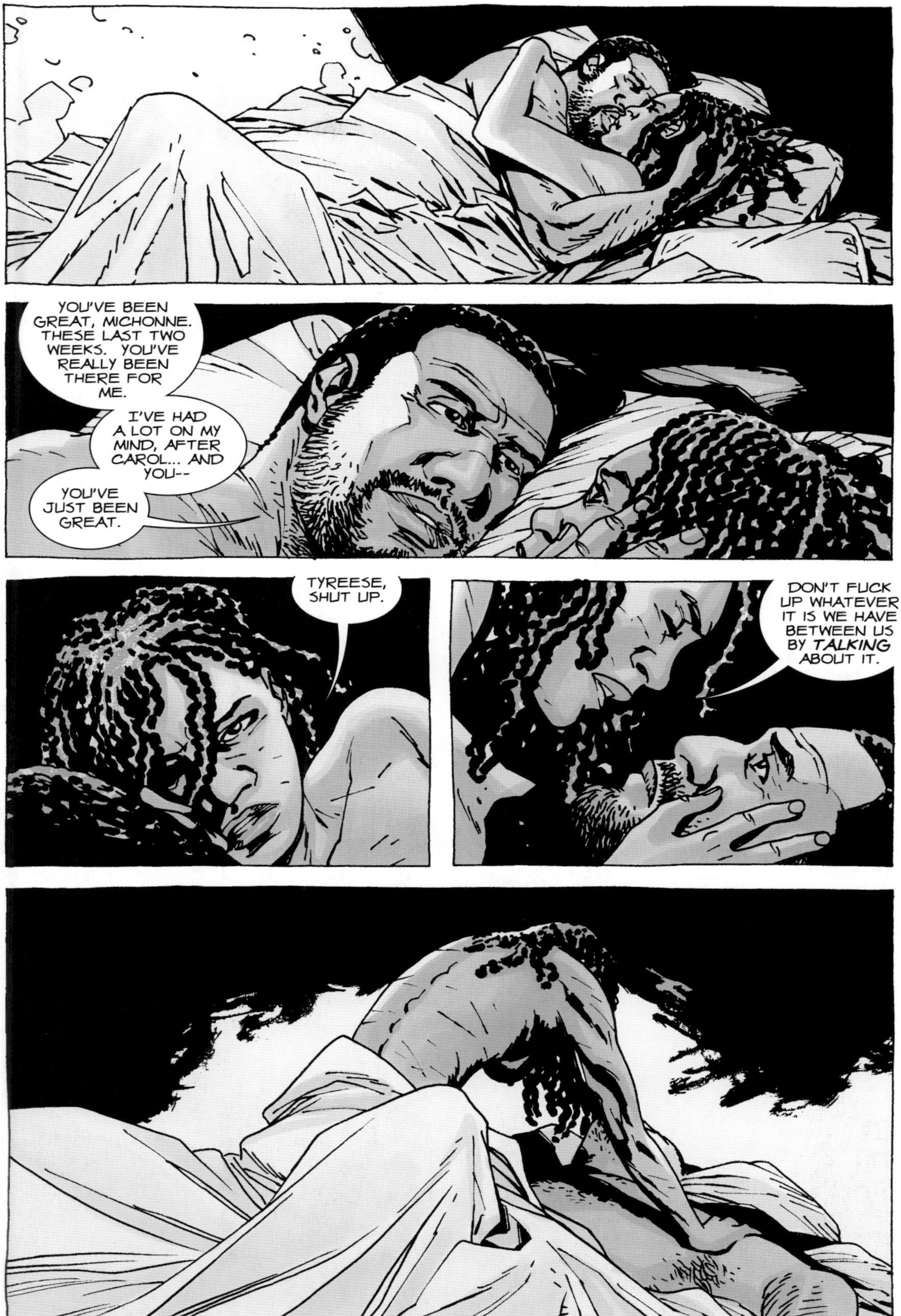
YOU'VE BEEN GREAT, MICHONNE. THESE LAST TWO WEEKS. YOU'VE REALLY BEEN THERE FOR ME.
I'VE HAD A LOT ON MY MIND, AFTER CAROL... AND YOU--
YOU'VE JUST BEEN GREAT.
TYREESE, SHUT UP.
DON'T FUCK UP WHATEVER IT IS WE HAVE BETWEEN US BY TALKING ABOUT IT.

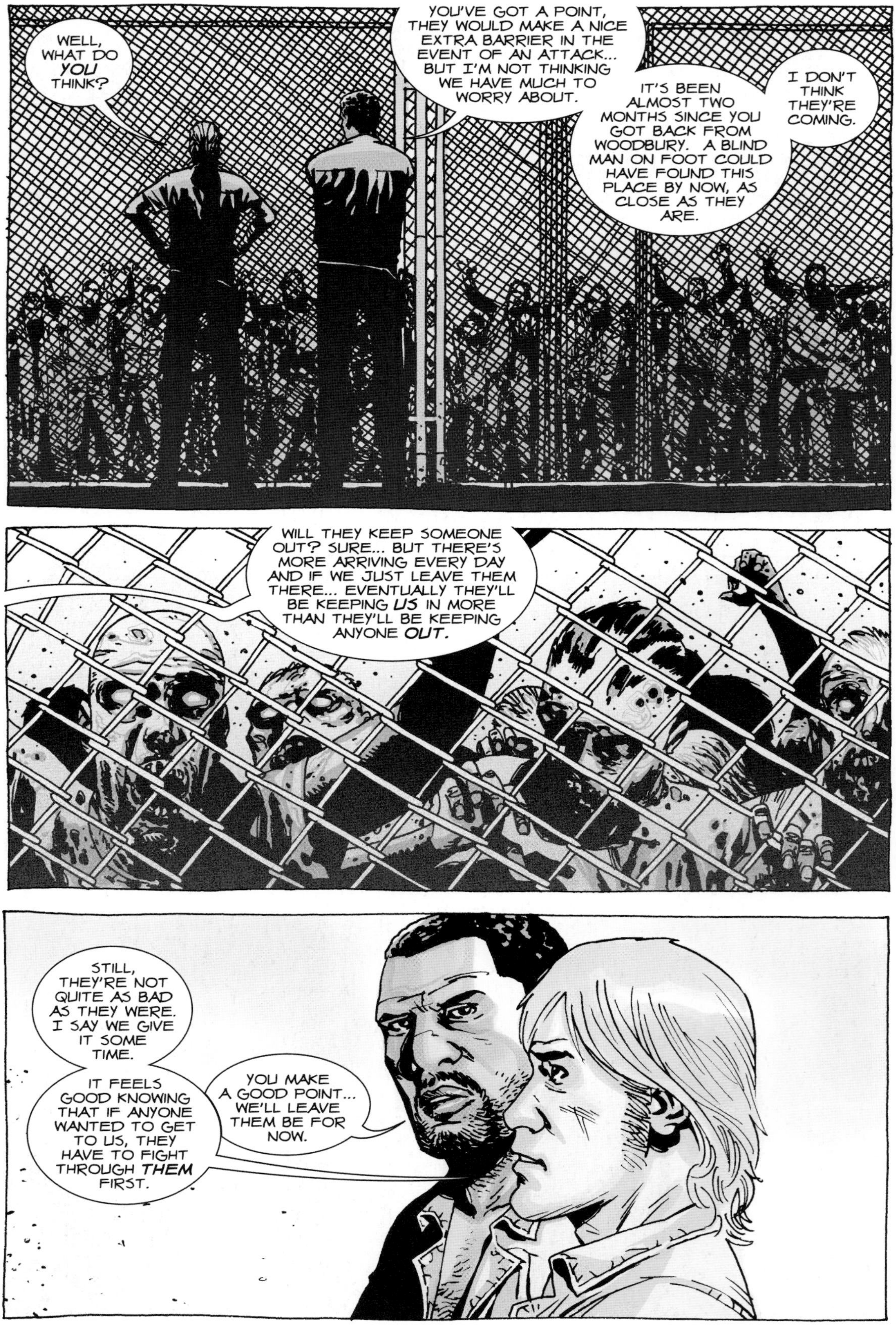
WELL, WHAT DO YOU THINK?
YOU'VE GOT A POINT, THEY WOULD MAKE A NICE EXTRA BARRIER IN THE EVENT OF AN ATTACK... BUT I'M NOT THINKING WE HAVE MUCH TO WORRY ABOUT.
IT'S BEEN ALMOST TWO MONTHS SINCE YOU GOT BACK FROM WOODBURY. A BLIND MAN ON FOOT COULD HAVE FOUND THIS PLACE BY NOW, AS CLOSE AS THEY ARE.
I DON'T THINK THEY'RE COMING.
WILL THEY KEEP SOMEONE OUT? SURE... BUT THERE'S MORE ARRIVING EVERY DAY AND IF WE JUST LEAVE THEM THERE... EVENTUALLY THEY'LL BE KEEPING US IN MORE THAN THEY'LL BE KEEPING ANYONE OUT.
STILL, THEY'RE NOT QUITE AS BAD AS THEY WERE. I SAY WE GIVE IT SOME TIME.
IT FEELS GOOD KNOWING THAT IF ANYONE WANTED TO GET TO US, THEY HAVE TO FIGHT THROUGH THEM FIRST.
YOU MAKE A GOOD POINT... WE'LL LEAVE THEM BE FOR NOW.

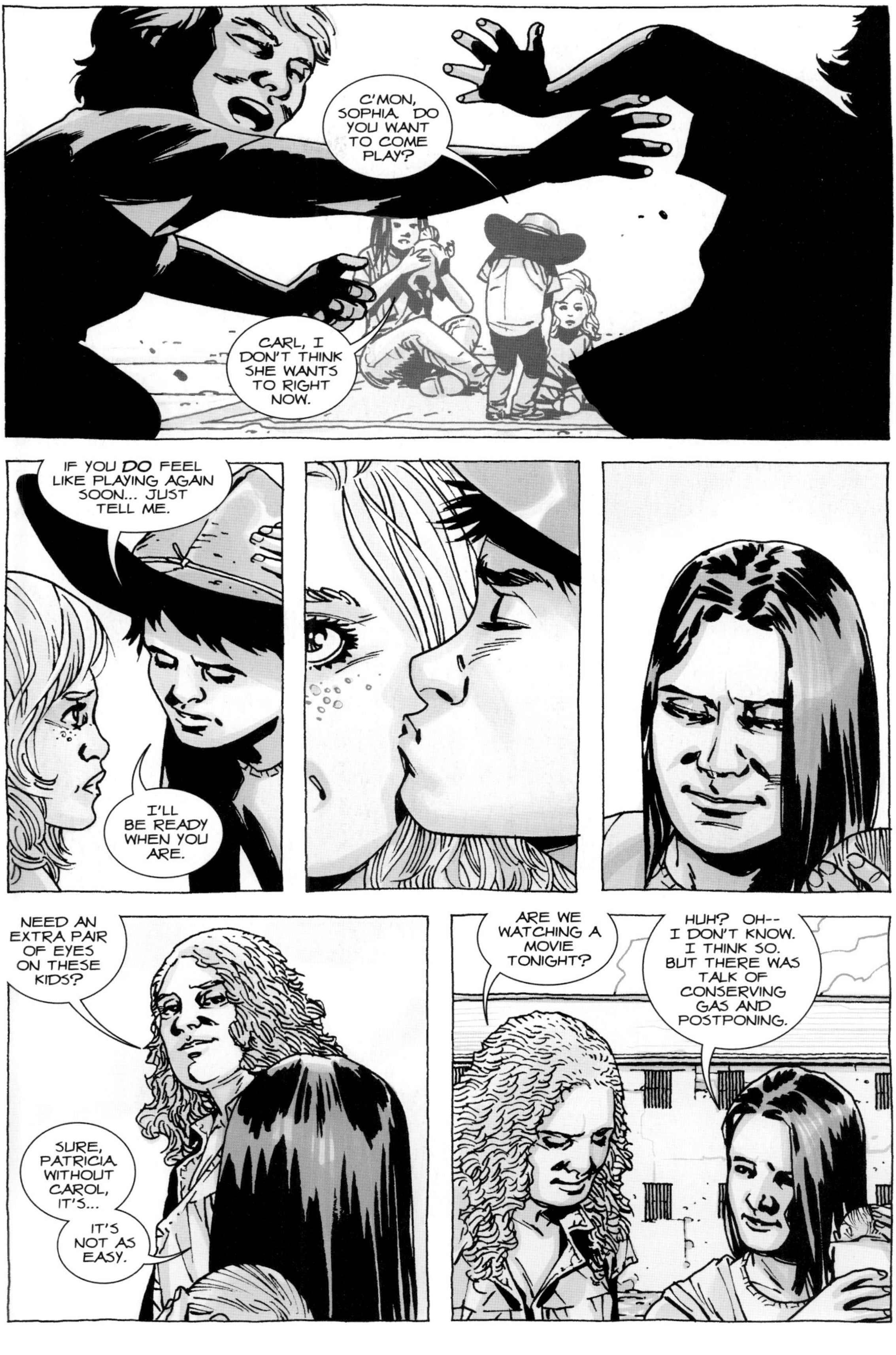
C'MON, SOPHIA. DO YOU WANT TO COME PLAY?
CARL, I DON'T THINK SHE WANTS TO RIGHT NOW.
IF YOU DO FEEL LIKE PLAYING AGAIN SOON... JUST TELL ME.
I'LL BE READY WHEN YOU ARE.
NEED AN EXTRA PAIR OF EYES ON THESE KIDS?
SURE, PATRICIA. WITHOUT CAROL, IT'S...
IT'S NOT AS EASY.
ARE WE WATCHING A MOVIE TONIGHT?
HUH? OH-- I DON'T KNOW. I THINK SO. BUT THERE WAS TALK OF CONSERVING GAS AND POSTPONING.

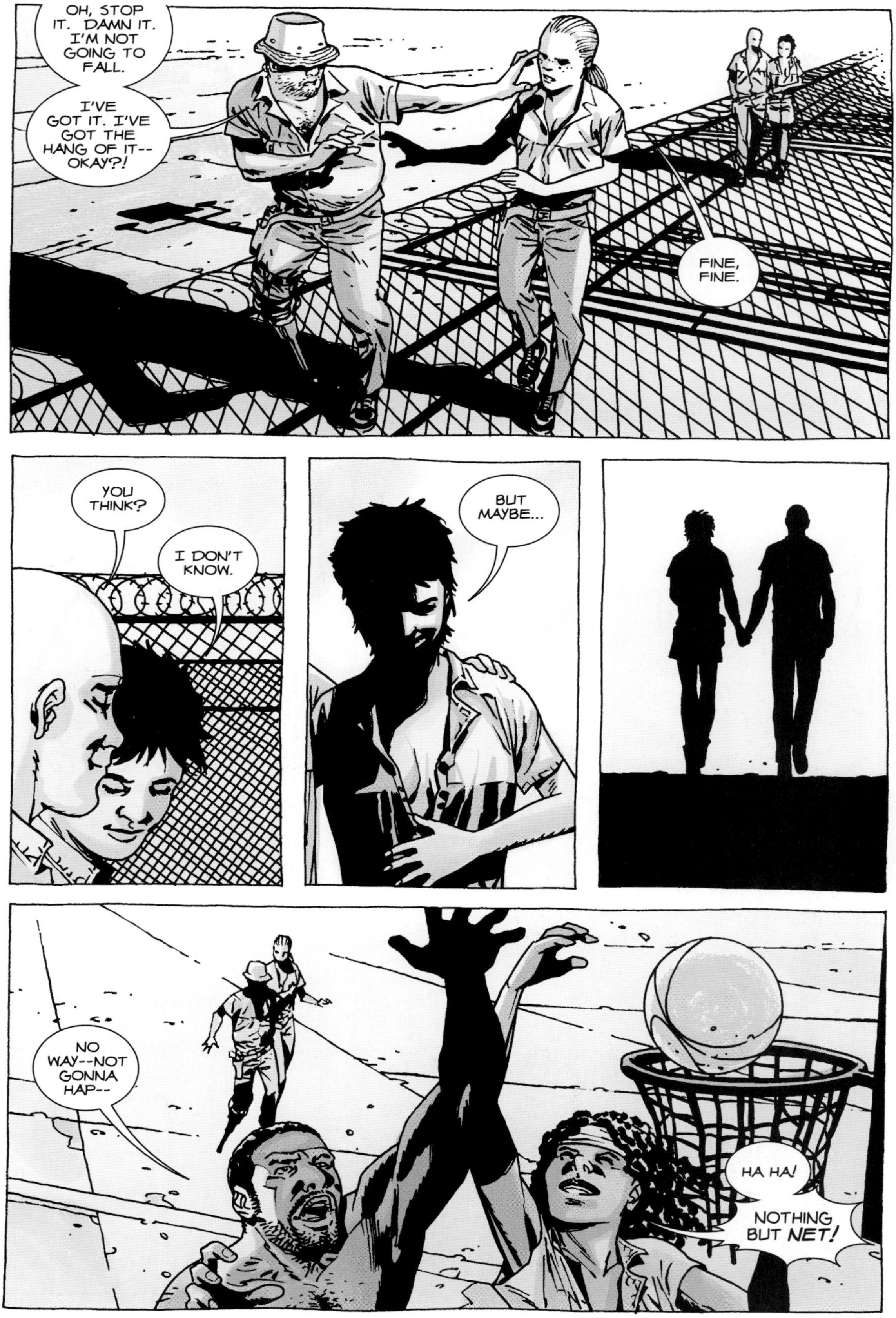
OH, STOP IT. DAMN IT. I'M NOT GOING TO FALL.
I'VE GOT IT. I'VE GOT THE HANG OF IT--OKAY?!
FINE, FINE.
YOU THINK?
I DON'T KNOW.
BUT MAYBE...
NO WAY--NOT GONNA HAP--
HA HA!
NOTHING BUT NET!

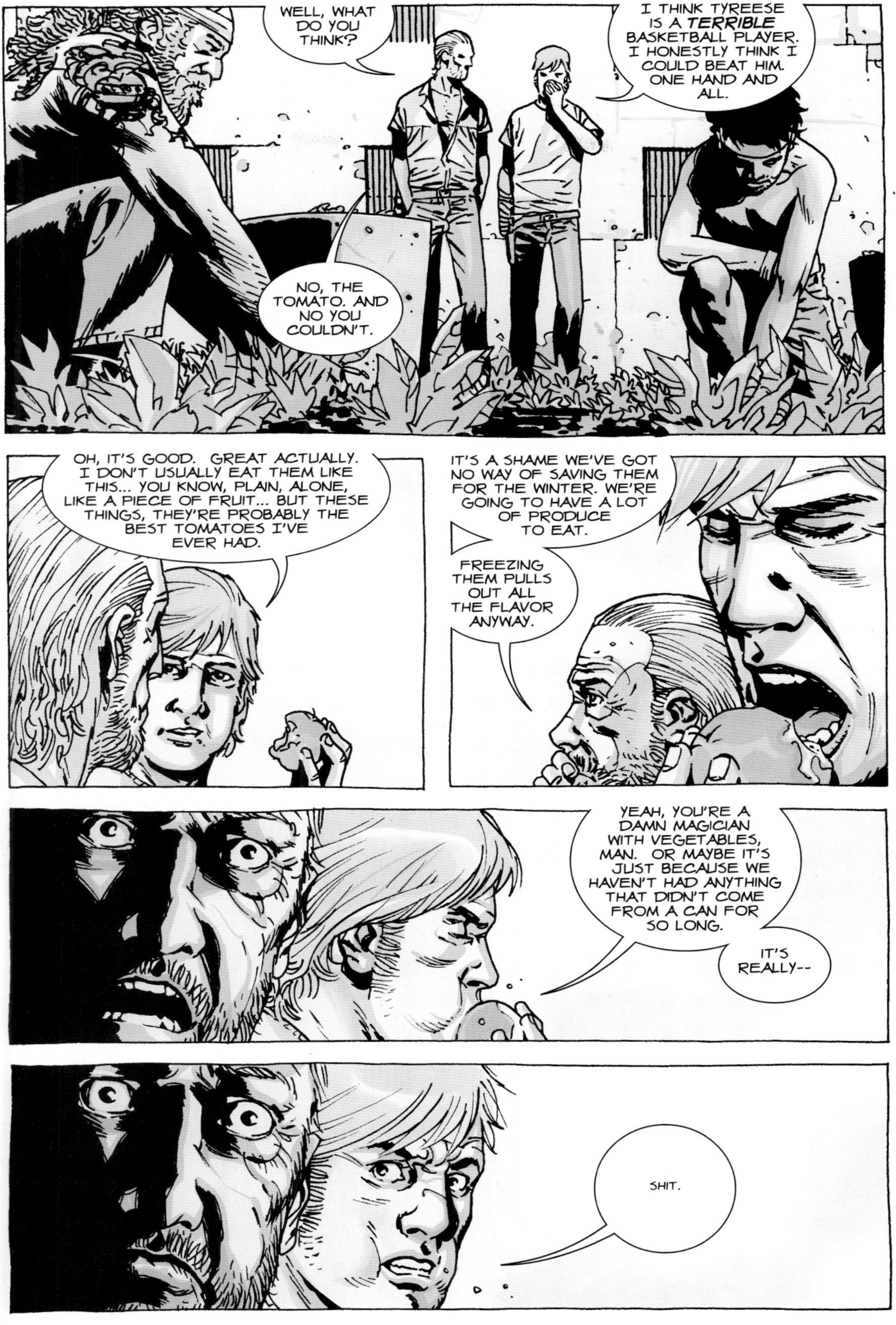
WELL, WHAT DO YOU THINK?
I THINK TYREESE IS A TERRIBLE BASKETBALL PLAYER. I HONESTLY THINK I COULD BEAT HIM. ONE HAND AND ALL.
NO, THE TOMATO. AND NO YOU COULDN'T.
OH, IT'S GOOD. GREAT ACTUALLY. I DON'T USUALLY EAT THEM LIKE THIS... YOU KNOW, PLAIN, ALONE, LIKE A PIECE OF FRUIT... BUT THESE THINGS, THEY'RE PROBABLY THE BEST TOMATOES I'VE EVER HAD.
IT'S A SHAME WE'VE GOT NO WAY OF SAVING THEM FOR THE WINTER. WE'RE GOING TO HAVE A LOT OF PRODUCE TO EAT.
FREEZING THEM PULLS OUT ALL THE FLAVOR ANYWAY.
YEAH, YOU'RE A DAMN MAGICIAN WITH VEGETABLES, MAN. OR MAYBE IT'S JUST BECAUSE WE HAVEN'T HAD ANYTHING THAT DIDN'T COME FROM A CAN FOR SO LONG.
IT'S REALLY--
SHIT.

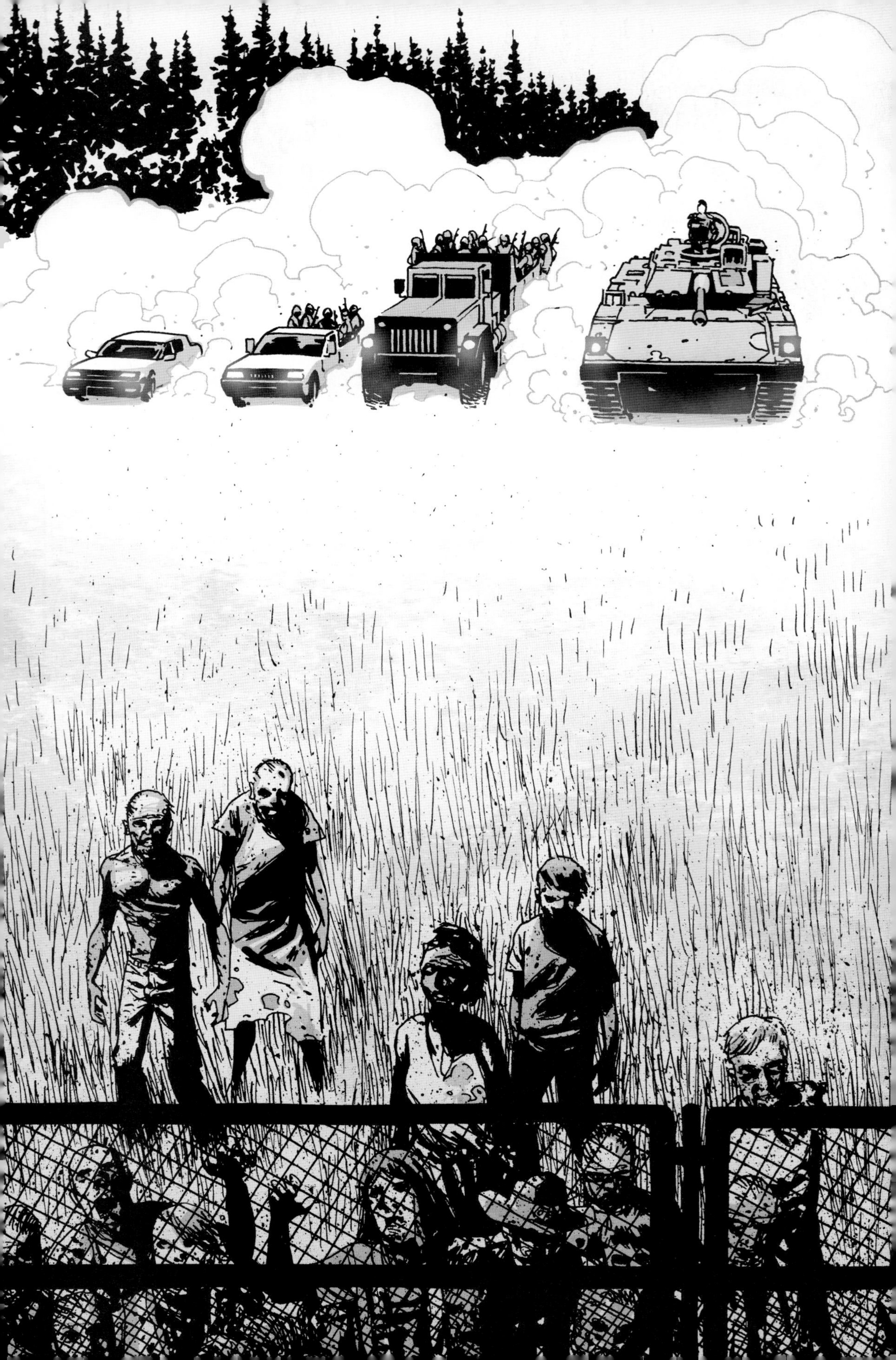

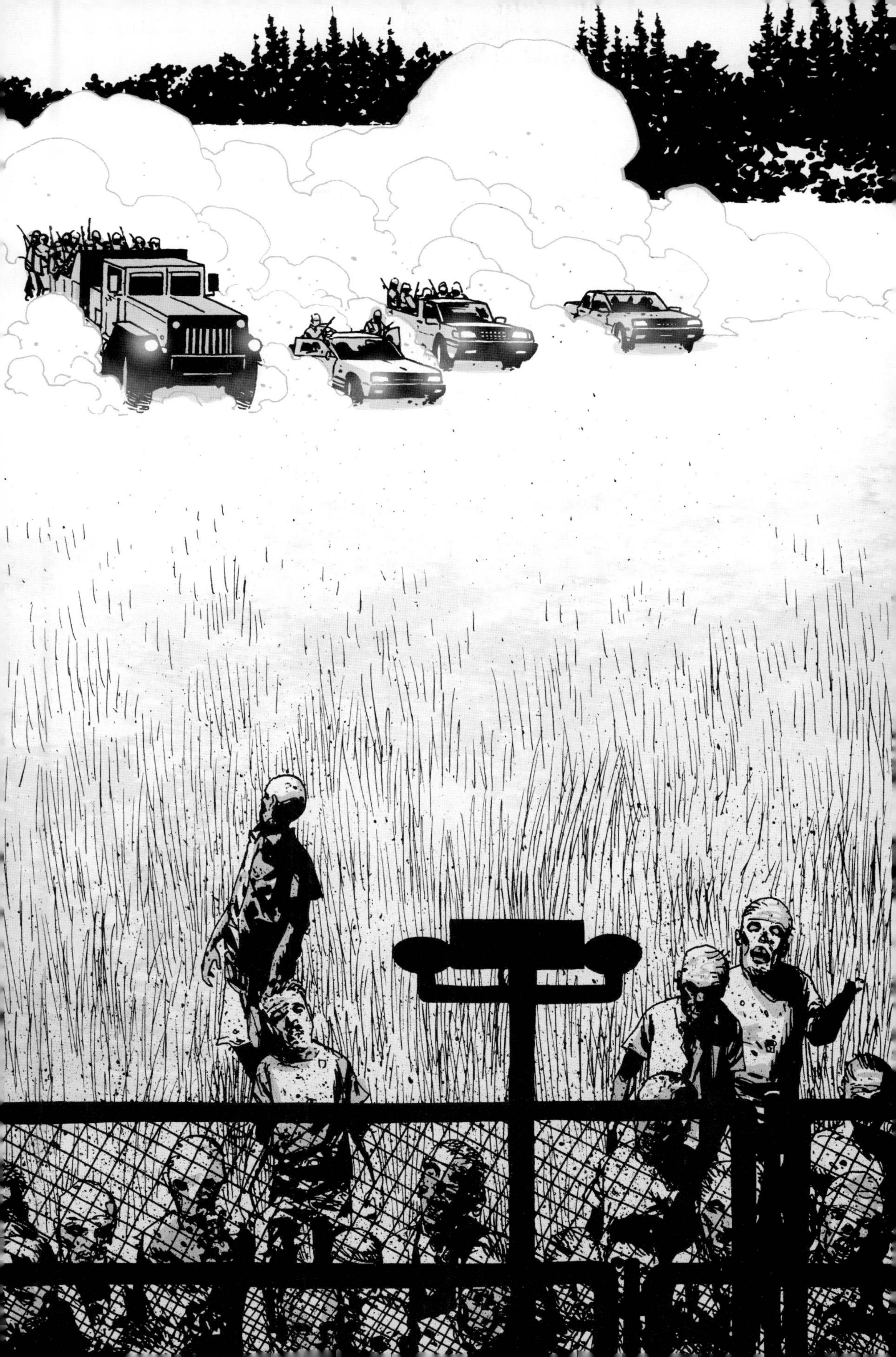

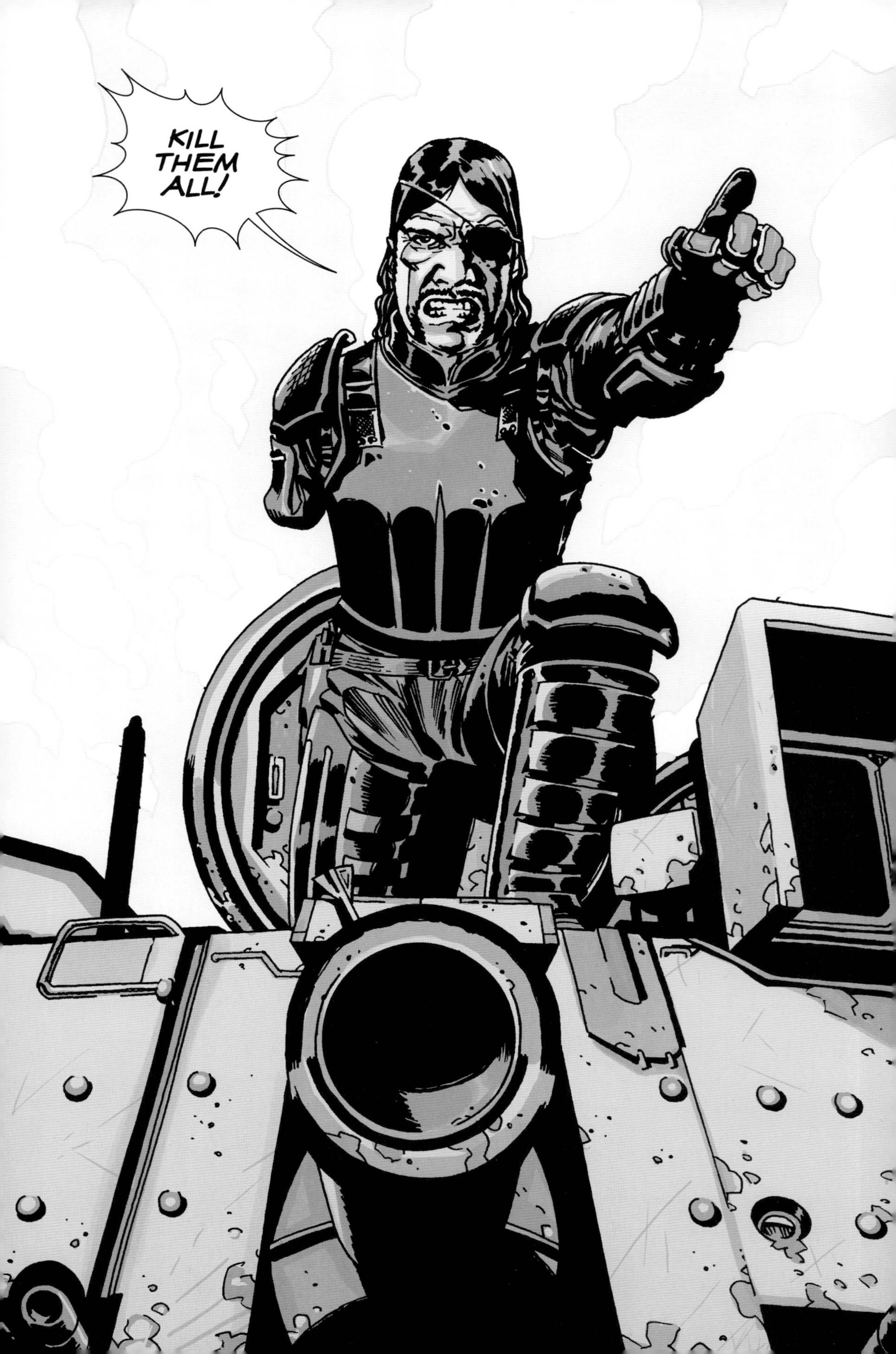
KILL THEM ALL!

Chapter Eight:
Made To Suffer

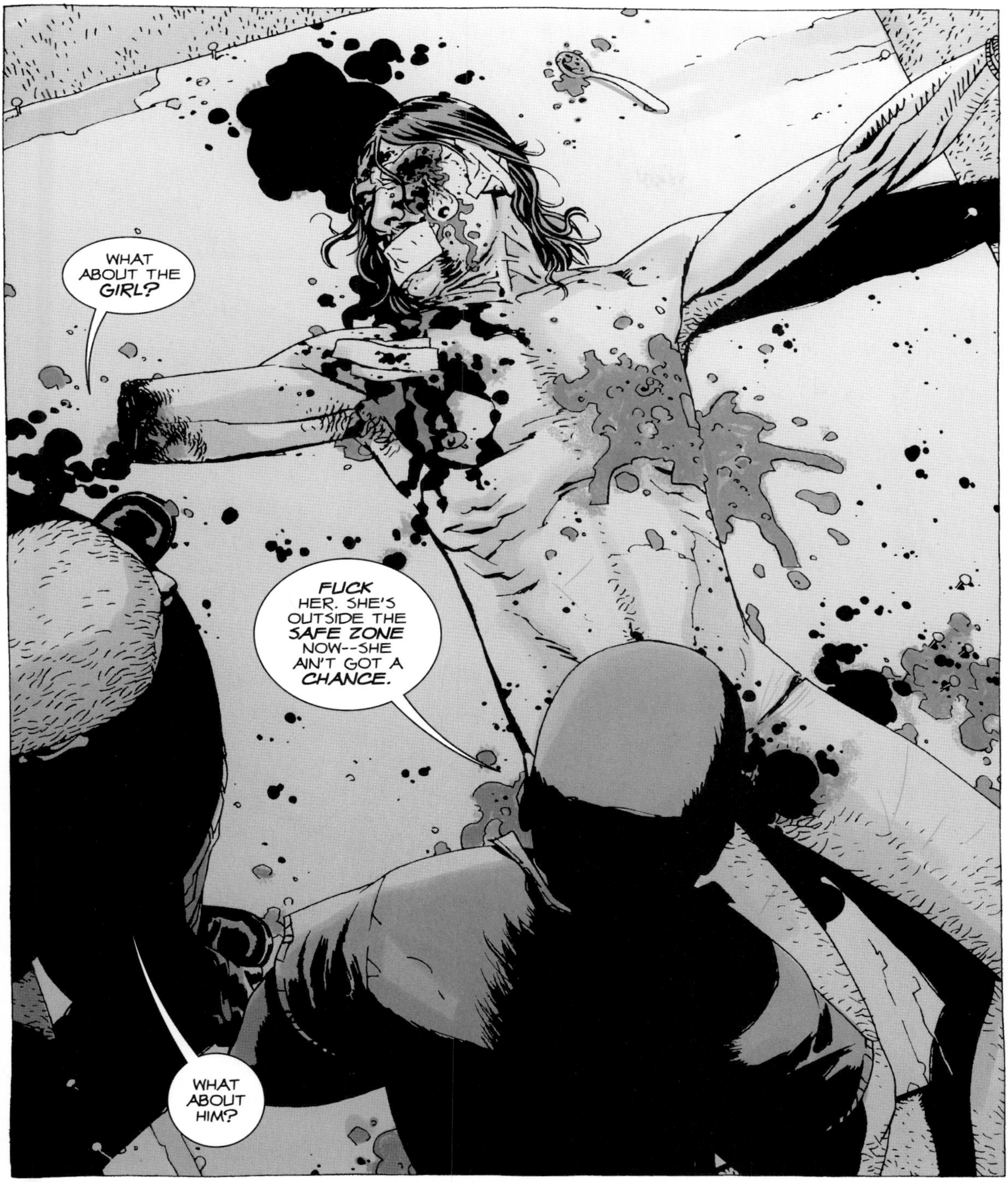
WHAT ABOUT THE GIRL?
FUCK HER. SHE'S OUTSIDE THE SAFE ZONE NOW--SHE AIN'T GOT A CHANCE.
WHAT ABOUT HIM?

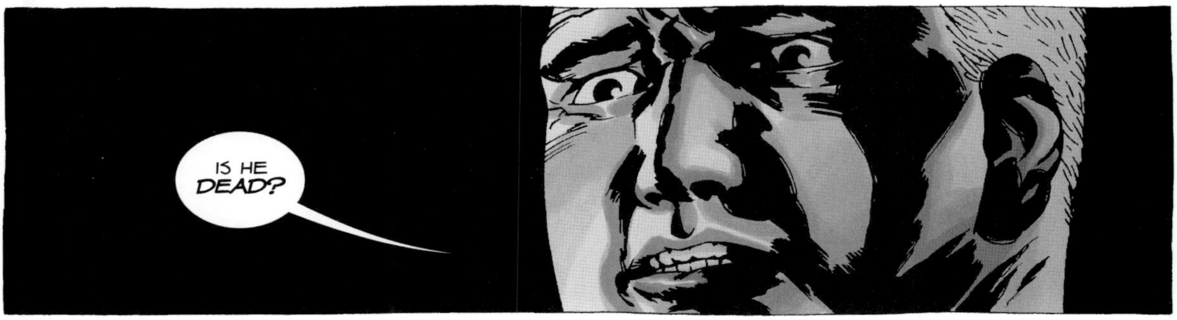
IS HE DEAD?

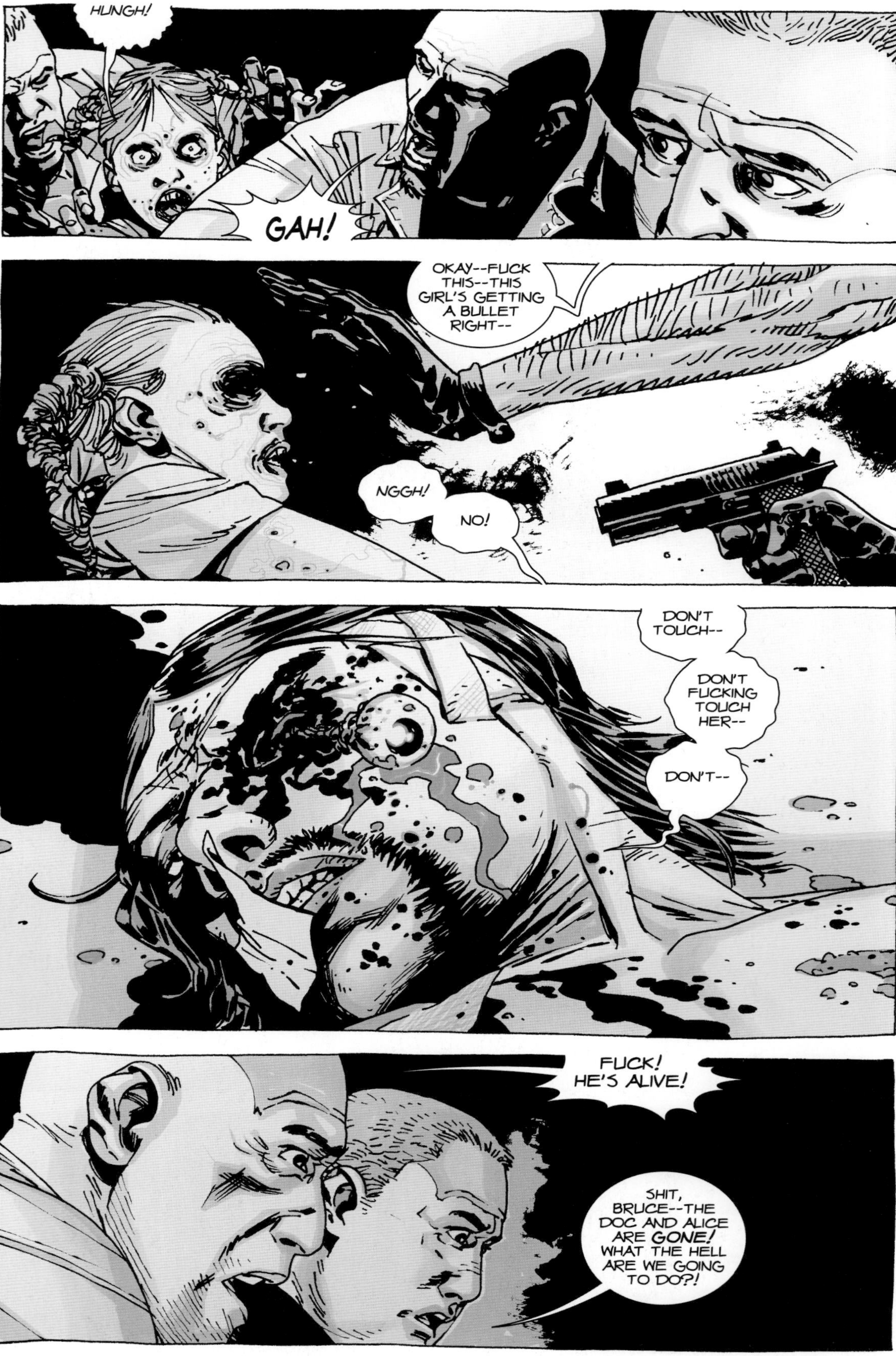
HUNGH!
GAH!
OKAY--FUCK THIS--THIS GIRL'S GETTING A BULLET RIGHT--
NGGH!
NO!
DON'T TOUCH--
DON'T FUCKING TOUCH HER--
DON'T--
FUCK! HE'S ALIVE!
SHIT, BRUCE--THE DOC AND ALICE ARE **GONE!** WHAT THE HELL ARE WE GOING TO DO?!

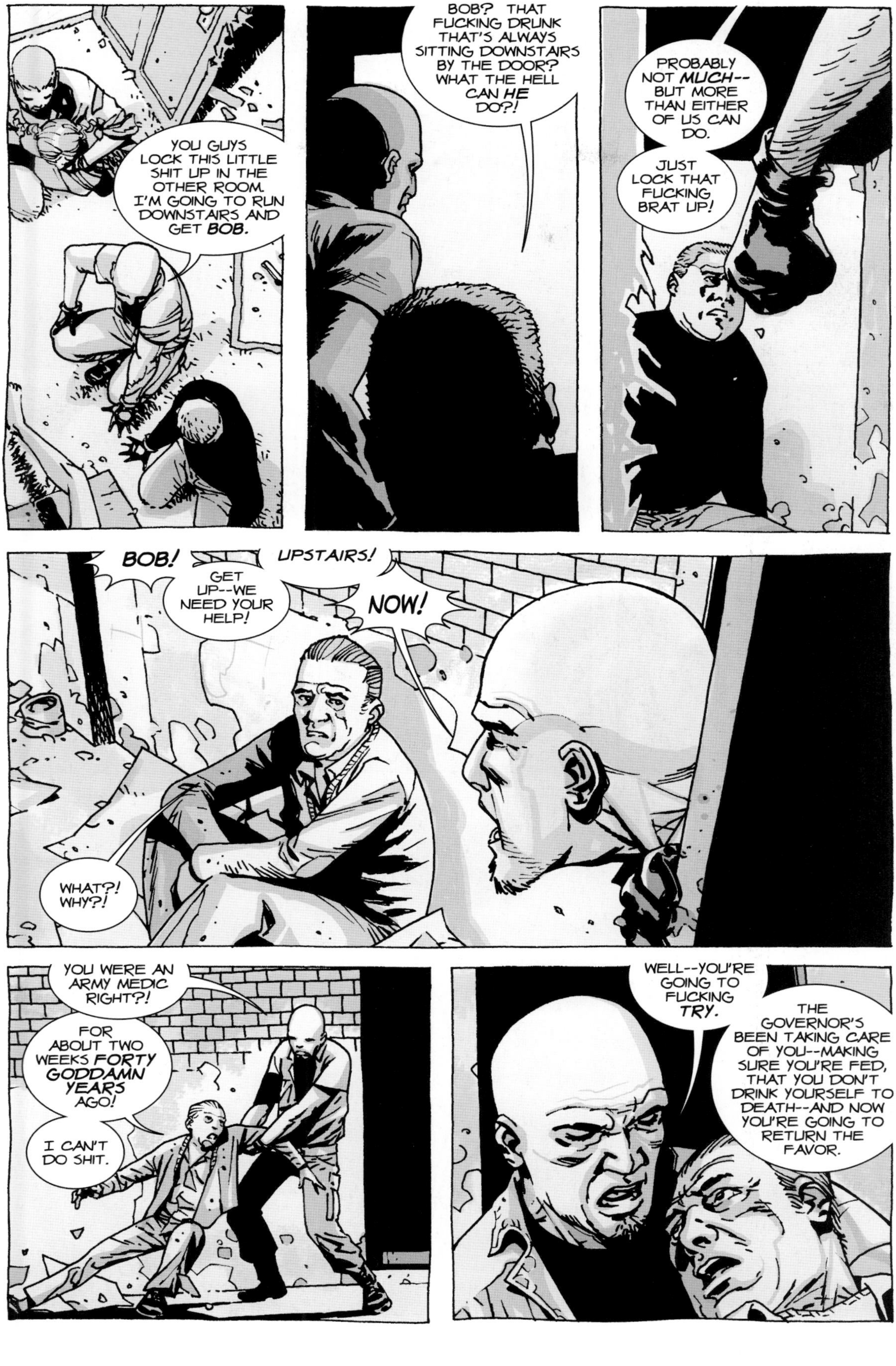
YOU GUYS LOCK THIS LITTLE SHIT UP IN THE OTHER ROOM. I'M GOING TO RUN DOWNSTAIRS AND GET BOB.
BOB? THAT FUCKING DRUNK THAT'S ALWAYS SITTING DOWNSTAIRS BY THE DOOR? WHAT THE HELL CAN HE DO?!
PROBABLY NOT MUCH-- BUT MORE THAN EITHER OF US CAN DO.
JUST LOCK THAT FUCKING BRAT UP!
BOB!
GET UP--WE NEED YOUR HELP!
UPSTAIRS!
NOW!
WHAT?! WHY?!
YOU WERE AN ARMY MEDIC RIGHT?!
FOR ABOUT TWO WEEKS FORTY GODDAMN YEARS AGO!
I CAN'T DO SHIT.
WELL--YOU'RE GOING TO FUCKING TRY.
THE GOVERNOR'S BEEN TAKING CARE OF YOU--MAKING SURE YOU'RE FED, THAT YOU DON'T DRINK YOURSELF TO DEATH--AND NOW YOU'RE GOING TO RETURN THE FAVOR.

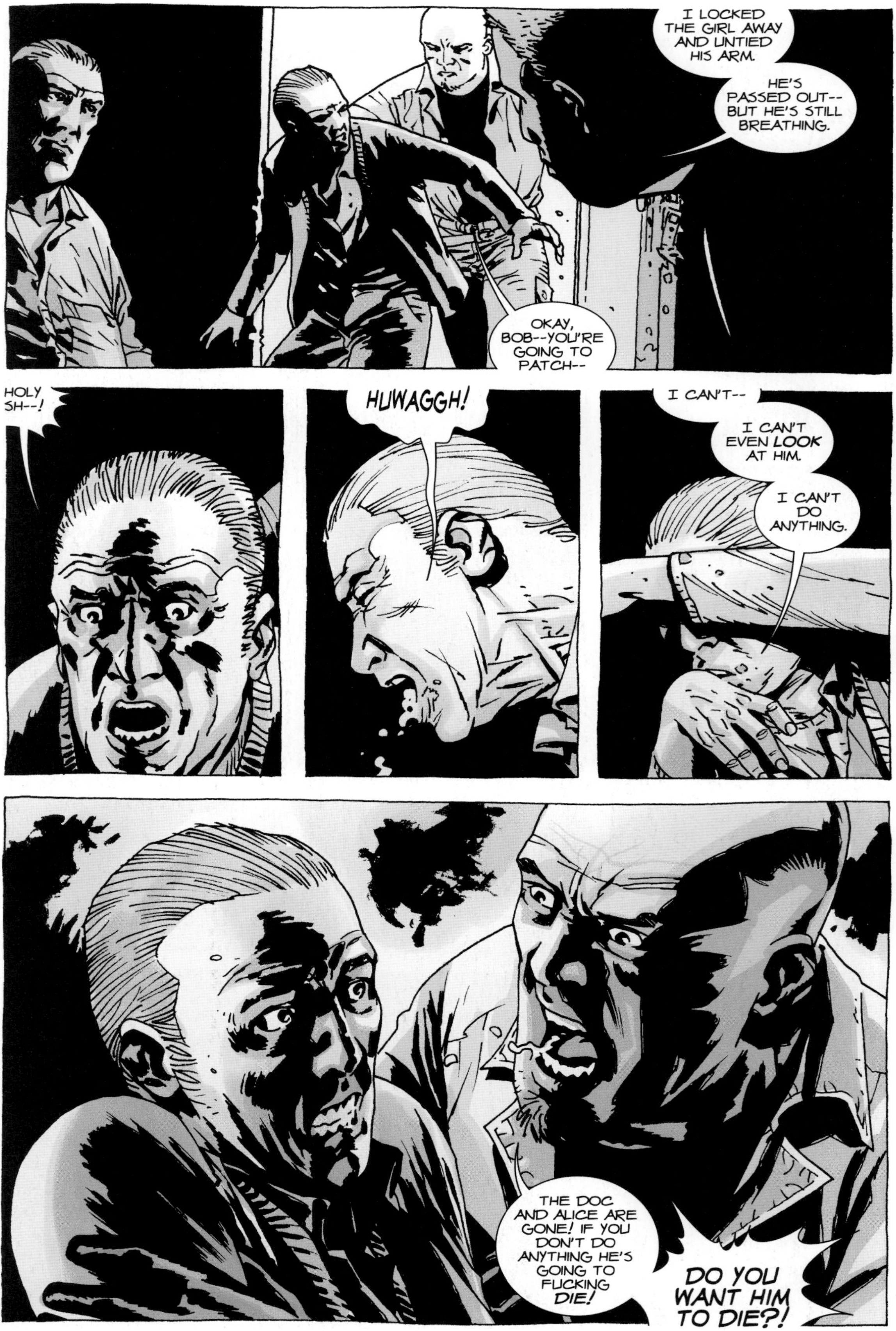
I LOCKED THE GIRL AWAY AND UNTIED HIS ARM.
HE'S PASSED OUT--BUT HE'S STILL BREATHING.
OKAY, BOB--YOU'RE GOING TO PATCH--
HOLY SH--!
HUWAGGH!
I CAN'T--
I CAN'T EVEN LOOK AT HIM.
I CAN'T DO ANYTHING.
THE DOC AND ALICE ARE GONE! IF YOU DON'T DO ANYTHING HE'S GOING TO FUCKING DIE!
DO YOU WANT HIM TO DIE?!

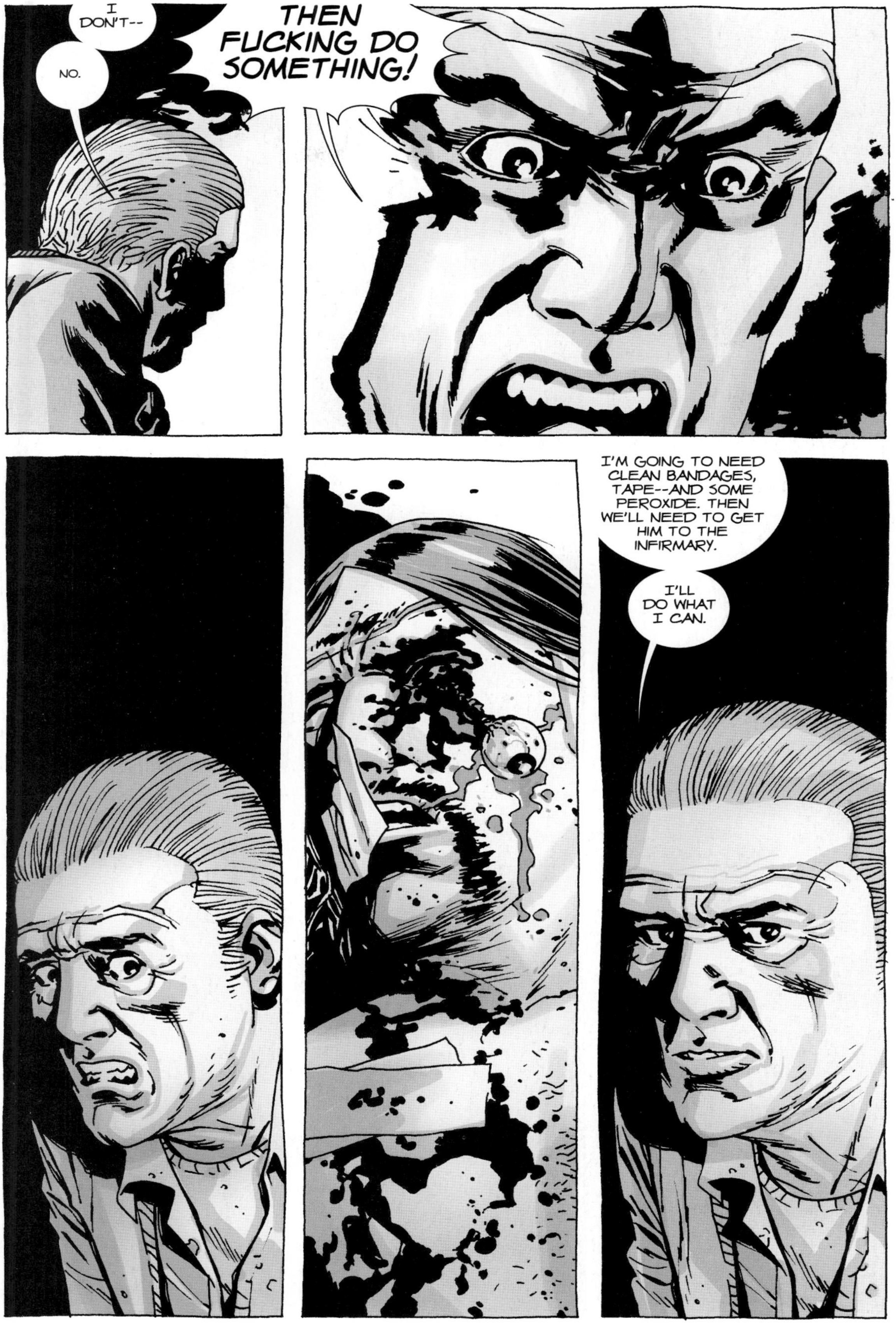
I DON'T--
NO.
THEN FUCKING DO SOMETHING!
I'M GOING TO NEED CLEAN BANDAGES, TAPE--AND SOME PEROXIDE. THEN WE'LL NEED TO GET HIM TO THE INFIRMARY.
I'LL DO WHAT I CAN.

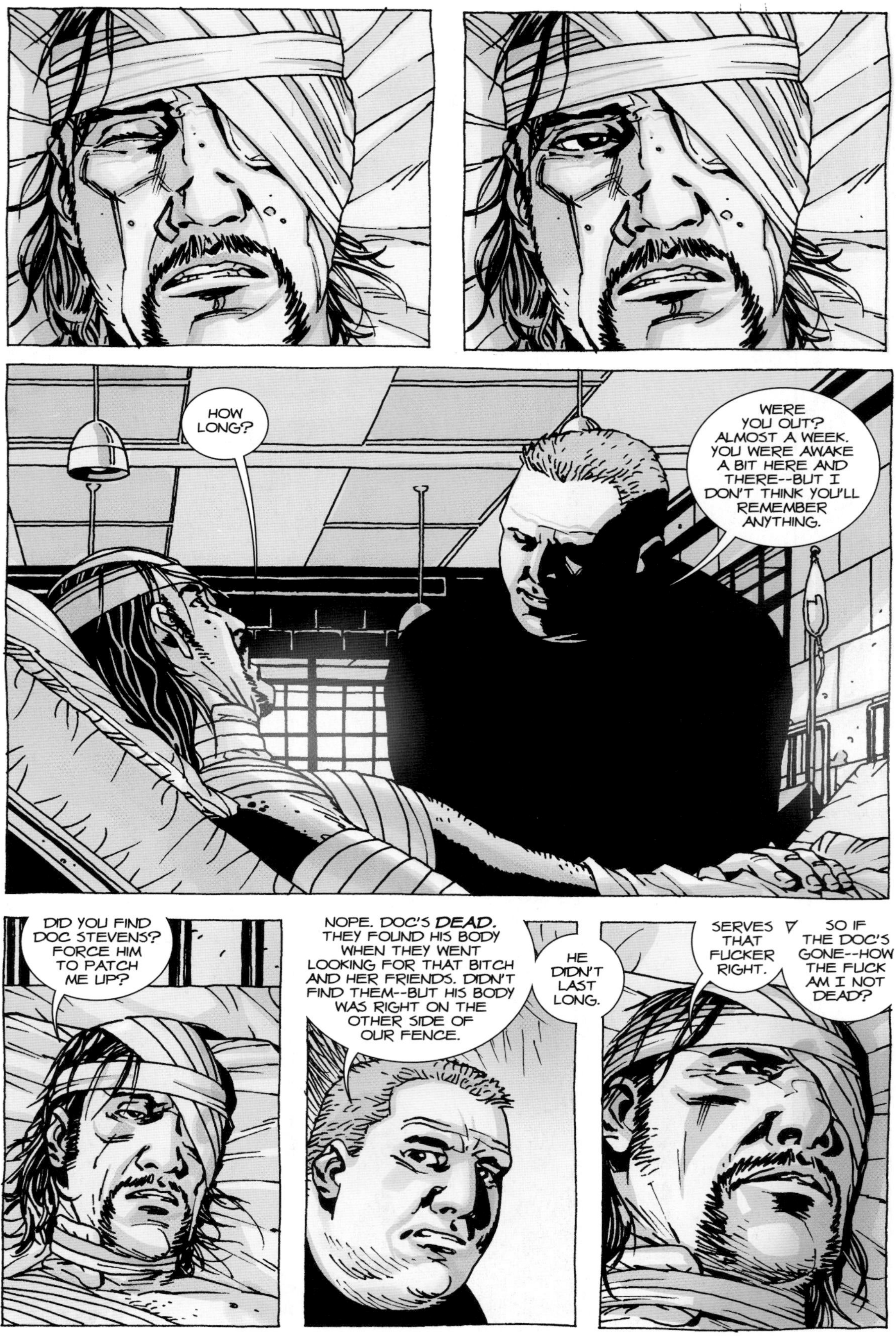
HOW LONG?
WERE YOU OUT? ALMOST A WEEK. YOU WERE AWAKE A BIT HERE AND THERE--BUT I DON'T THINK YOU'LL REMEMBER ANYTHING.
DID YOU FIND DOC STEVENS? FORCE HIM TO PATCH ME UP?
NOPE. DOC'S *DEAD.* THEY FOUND HIS BODY WHEN THEY WENT LOOKING FOR THAT BITCH AND HER FRIENDS. DIDN'T FIND THEM--BUT HIS BODY WAS RIGHT ON THE OTHER SIDE OF OUR FENCE.
HE DIDN'T LAST LONG.
SERVES THAT FUCKER RIGHT.
SO IF THE DOC'S GONE--HOW THE FUCK AM I NOT DEAD?

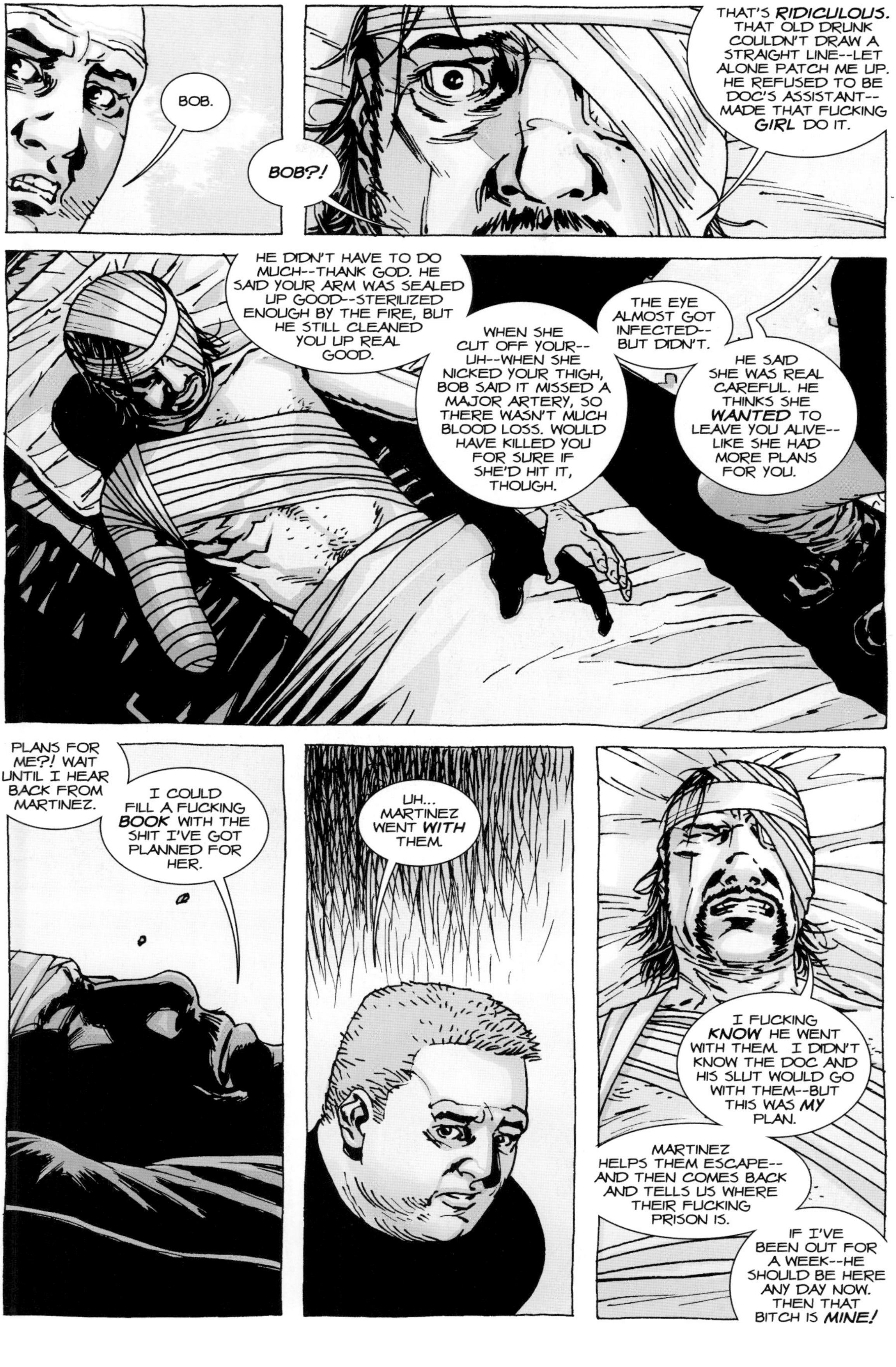
BOB.
BOB?!
THAT'S RIDICULOUS. THAT OLD DRUNK COULDN'T DRAW A STRAIGHT LINE--LET ALONE PATCH ME UP. HE REFUSED TO BE DOC'S ASSISTANT--MADE THAT FUCKING GIRL DO IT.
HE DIDN'T HAVE TO DO MUCH--THANK GOD. HE SAID YOUR ARM WAS SEALED UP GOOD--STERILIZED ENOUGH BY THE FIRE, BUT HE STILL CLEANED YOU UP REAL GOOD.
WHEN SHE CUT OFF YOUR-- UH--WHEN SHE NICKED YOUR THIGH, BOB SAID IT MISSED A MAJOR ARTERY, SO THERE WASN'T MUCH BLOOD LOSS. WOULD HAVE KILLED YOU FOR SURE IF SHE'D HIT IT, THOUGH.
THE EYE ALMOST GOT INFECTED-- BUT DIDN'T.
HE SAID SHE WAS REAL CAREFUL. HE THINKS SHE WANTED TO LEAVE YOU ALIVE-- LIKE SHE HAD MORE PLANS FOR YOU.
PLANS FOR ME?! WAIT UNTIL I HEAR BACK FROM MARTINEZ.
I COULD FILL A FUCKING BOOK WITH THE SHIT I'VE GOT PLANNED FOR HER.
UH... MARTINEZ WENT WITH THEM.
I FUCKING KNOW HE WENT WITH THEM. I DIDN'T KNOW THE DOC AND HIS SLUT WOULD GO WITH THEM--BUT THIS WAS MY PLAN.
MARTINEZ HELPS THEM ESCAPE-- AND THEN COMES BACK AND TELLS US WHERE THEIR FUCKING PRISON IS.
IF I'VE BEEN OUT FOR A WEEK--HE SHOULD BE HERE ANY DAY NOW. THEN THAT BITCH IS MINE!

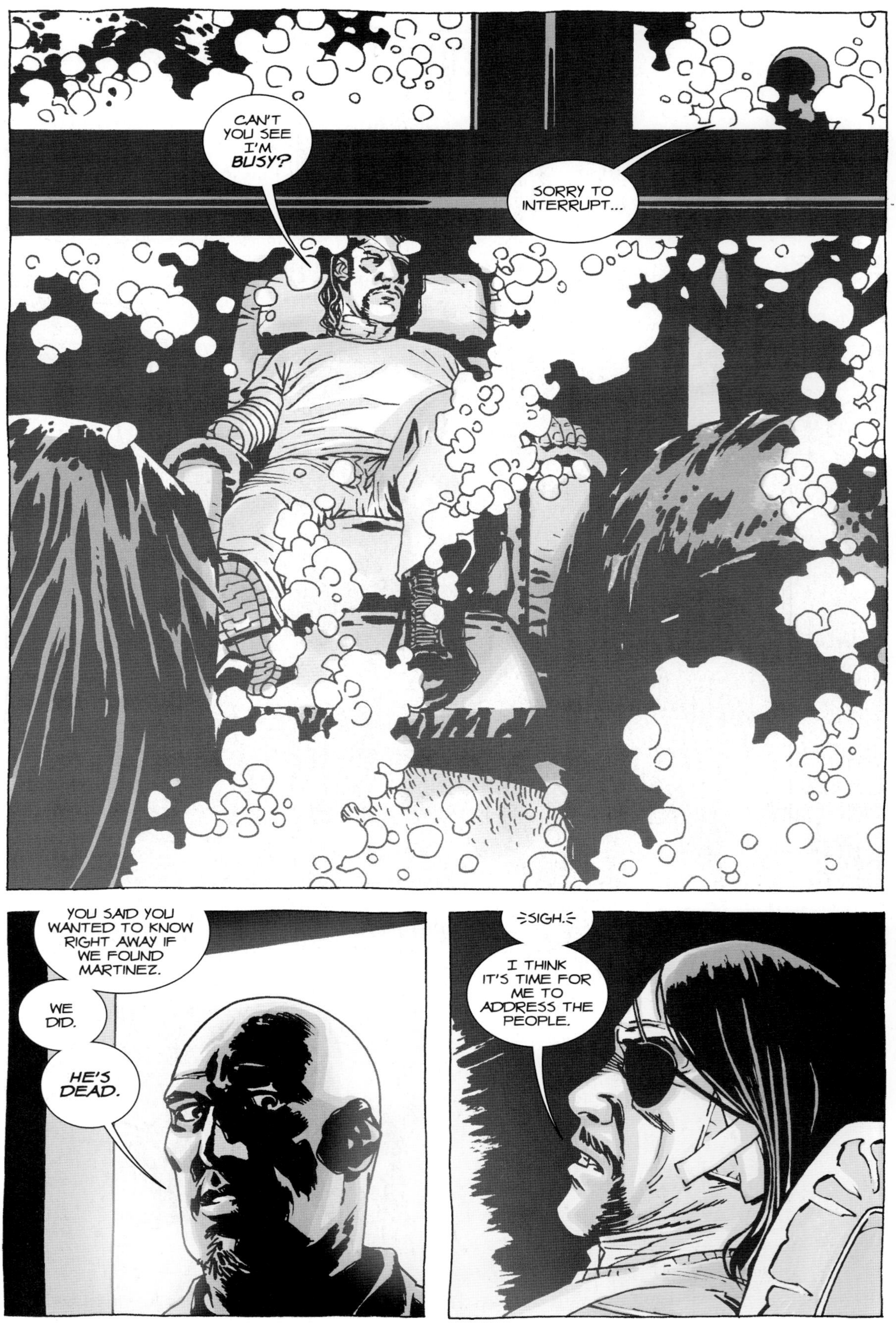
CAN'T YOU SEE I'M BUSY?
SORRY TO INTERRUPT...
YOU SAID YOU WANTED TO KNOW RIGHT AWAY IF WE FOUND MARTINEZ.
WE DID.
HE'S DEAD.
SIGH.
I THINK IT'S TIME FOR ME TO ADDRESS THE PEOPLE.

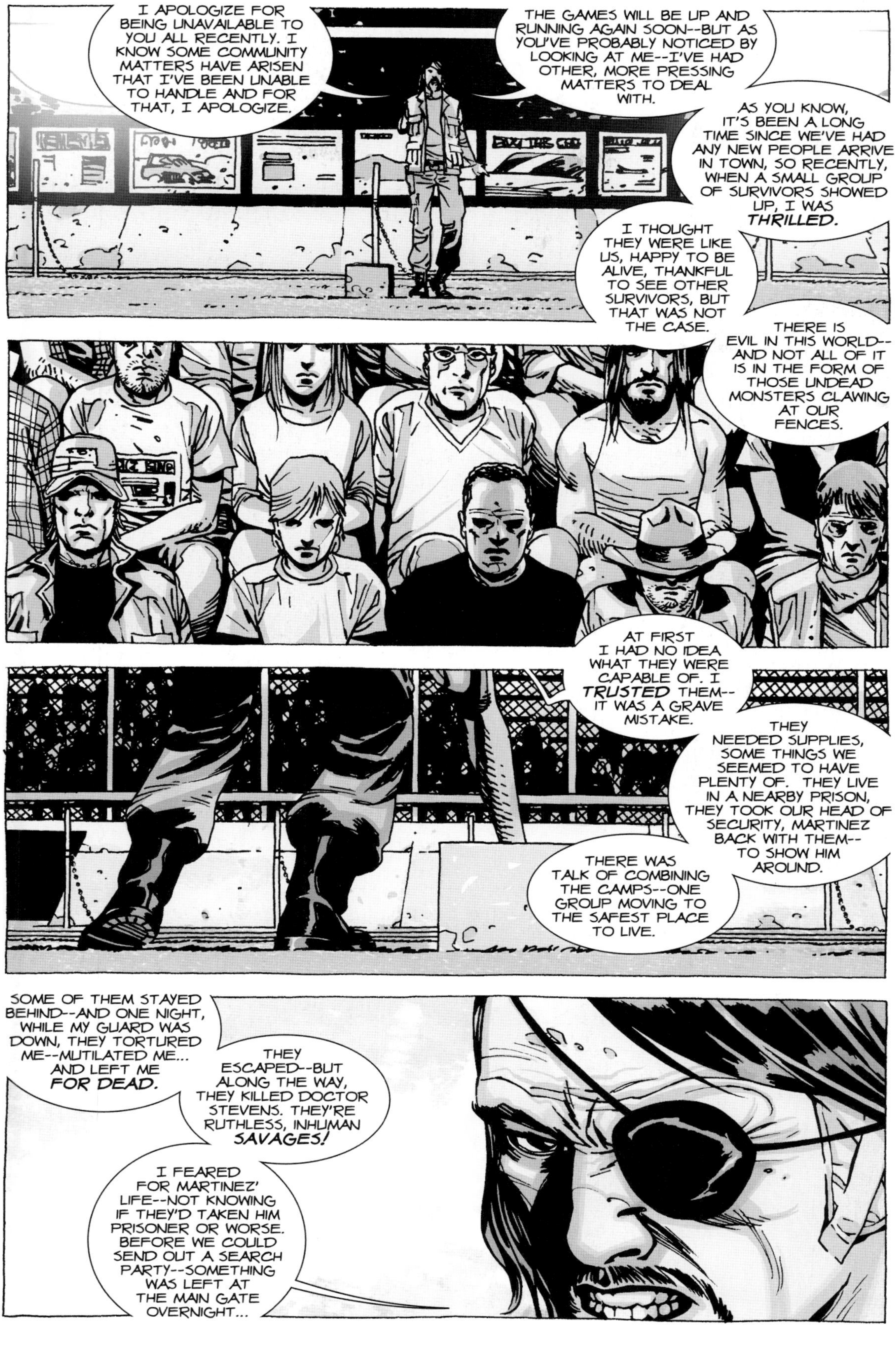
I APOLOGIZE FOR BEING UNAVAILABLE TO YOU ALL RECENTLY. I KNOW SOME COMMUNITY MATTERS HAVE ARISEN THAT I'VE BEEN UNABLE TO HANDLE AND FOR THAT, I APOLOGIZE.
THE GAMES WILL BE UP AND RUNNING AGAIN SOON--BUT AS YOU'VE PROBABLY NOTICED BY LOOKING AT ME--I'VE HAD OTHER, MORE PRESSING MATTERS TO DEAL WITH.
AS YOU KNOW, IT'S BEEN A LONG TIME SINCE WE'VE HAD ANY NEW PEOPLE ARRIVE IN TOWN, SO RECENTLY, WHEN A SMALL GROUP OF SURVIVORS SHOWED UP, I WAS THRILLED.
I THOUGHT THEY WERE LIKE US, HAPPY TO BE ALIVE, THANKFUL TO SEE OTHER SURVIVORS, BUT THAT WAS NOT THE CASE.
THERE IS EVIL IN THIS WORLD--AND NOT ALL OF IT IS IN THE FORM OF THOSE UNDEAD MONSTERS CLAWING AT OUR FENCES.
AT FIRST I HAD NO IDEA WHAT THEY WERE CAPABLE OF. I TRUSTED THEM--IT WAS A GRAVE MISTAKE.
THEY NEEDED SUPPLIES, SOME THINGS WE SEEMED TO HAVE PLENTY OF. THEY LIVE IN A NEARBY PRISON, THEY TOOK OUR HEAD OF SECURITY, MARTINEZ BACK WITH THEM--TO SHOW HIM AROUND.
THERE WAS TALK OF COMBINING THE CAMPS--ONE GROUP MOVING TO THE SAFEST PLACE TO LIVE.
SOME OF THEM STAYED BEHIND--AND ONE NIGHT, WHILE MY GUARD WAS DOWN, THEY TORTURED ME--MUTILATED ME... AND LEFT ME FOR DEAD.
THEY ESCAPED--BUT ALONG THE WAY, THEY KILLED DOCTOR STEVENS. THEY'RE RUTHLESS, INHUMAN SAVAGES!
I FEARED FOR MARTINEZ' LIFE--NOT KNOWING IF THEY'D TAKEN HIM PRISONER OR WORSE. BEFORE WE COULD SEND OUT A SEARCH PARTY--SOMETHING WAS LEFT AT THE MAIN GATE OVERNIGHT...

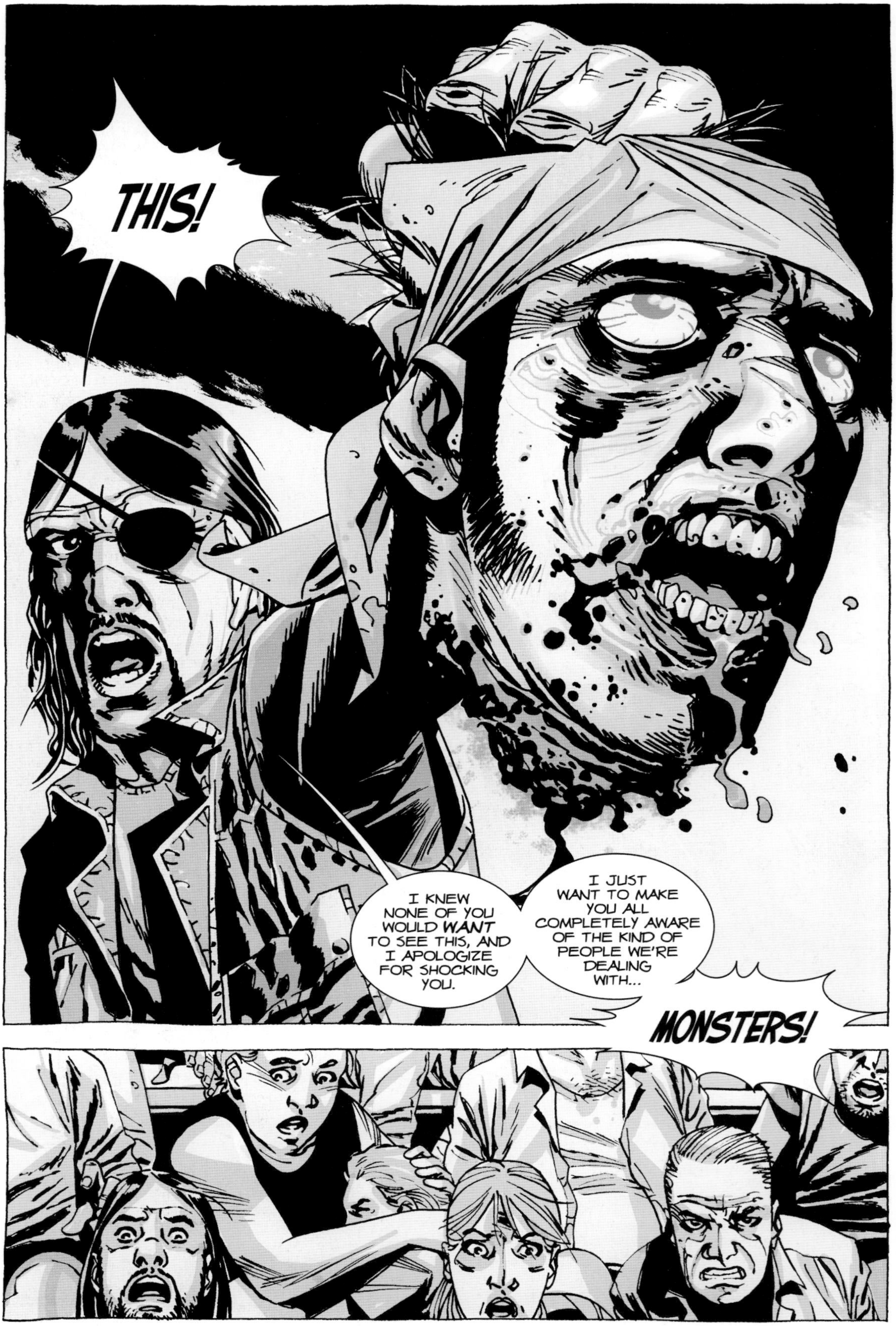
THIS!
I KNEW NONE OF YOU WOULD WANT TO SEE THIS, AND I APOLOGIZE FOR SHOCKING YOU.
I JUST WANT TO MAKE YOU ALL COMPLETELY AWARE OF THE KIND OF PEOPLE WE'RE DEALING WITH...
MONSTERS!

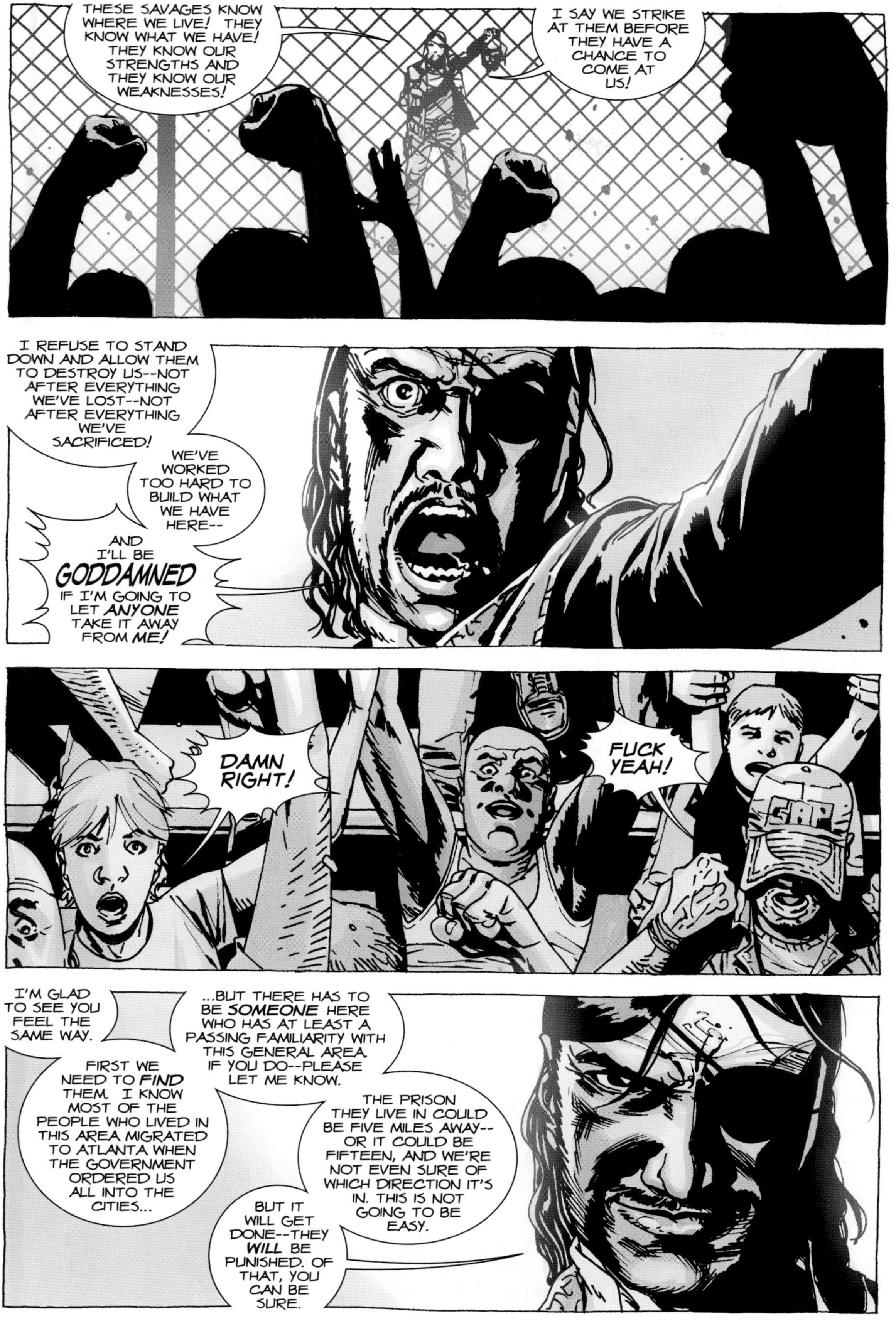
THESE SAVAGES KNOW WHERE WE LIVE! THEY KNOW WHAT WE HAVE! THEY KNOW OUR STRENGTHS AND THEY KNOW OUR WEAKNESSES!
I SAY WE STRIKE AT THEM BEFORE THEY HAVE A CHANCE TO COME AT US!
I REFUSE TO STAND DOWN AND ALLOW THEM TO DESTROY US--NOT AFTER EVERYTHING WE'VE LOST--NOT AFTER EVERYTHING WE'VE SACRIFICED!
WE'VE WORKED TOO HARD TO BUILD WHAT WE HAVE HERE--
AND I'LL BE GODDAMNED IF I'M GOING TO LET ANYONE TAKE IT AWAY FROM ME!
DAMN RIGHT!
FUCK YEAH!
I'M GLAD TO SEE YOU FEEL THE SAME WAY.
FIRST WE NEED TO FIND THEM. I KNOW MOST OF THE PEOPLE WHO LIVED IN THIS AREA MIGRATED TO ATLANTA WHEN THE GOVERNMENT ORDERED US ALL INTO THE CITIES...
...BUT THERE HAS TO BE SOMEONE HERE WHO HAS AT LEAST A PASSING FAMILIARITY WITH THIS GENERAL AREA. IF YOU DO--PLEASE LET ME KNOW.
THE PRISON THEY LIVE IN COULD BE FIVE MILES AWAY--OR IT COULD BE FIFTEEN, AND WE'RE NOT EVEN SURE OF WHICH DIRECTION IT'S IN. THIS IS NOT GOING TO BE EASY.
BUT IT WILL GET DONE--THEY WILL BE PUNISHED. OF THAT, YOU CAN BE SURE.

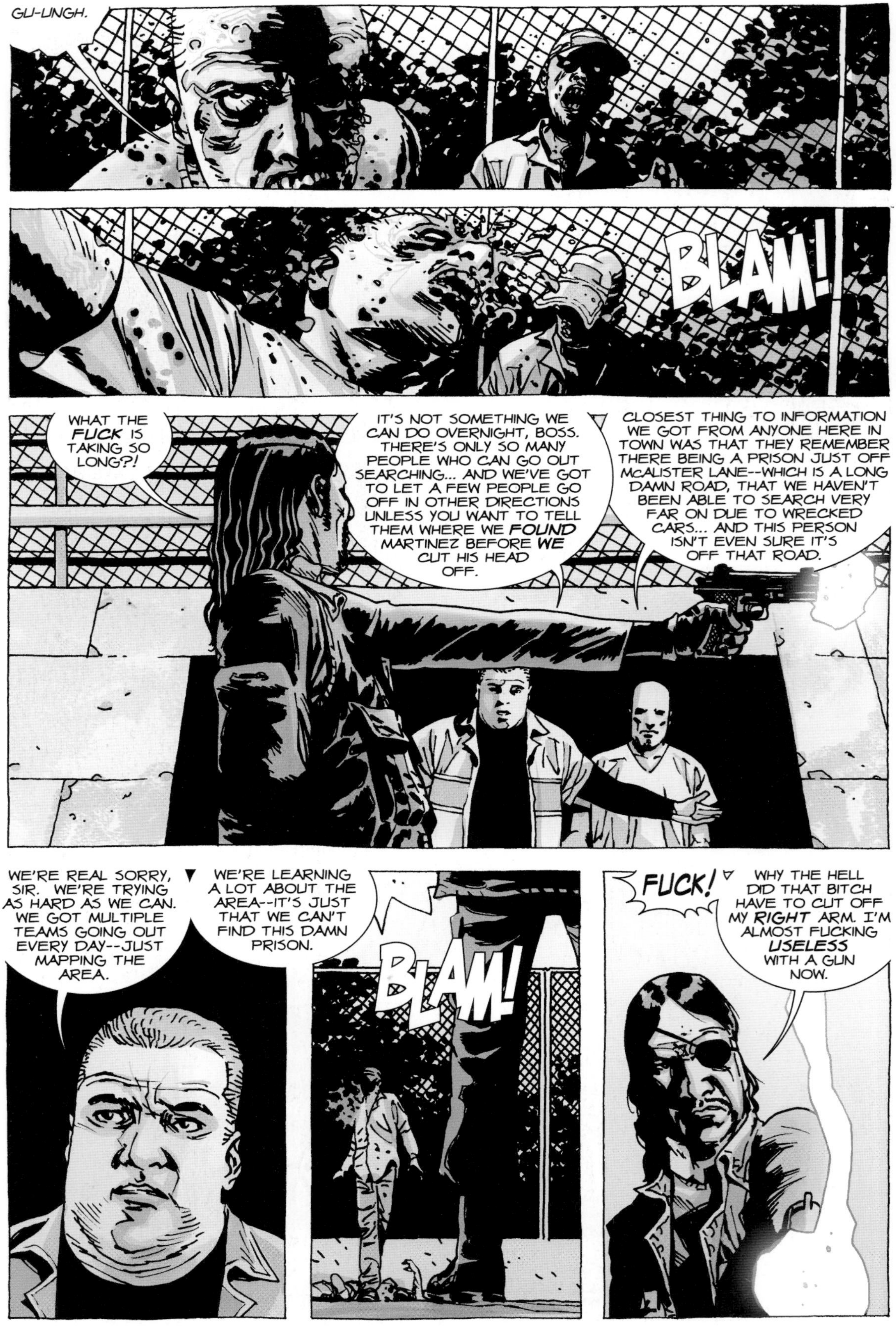
GU-UNGH.
BLAM!
WHAT THE FUCK IS TAKING SO LONG?!
IT'S NOT SOMETHING WE CAN DO OVERNIGHT, BOSS. THERE'S ONLY SO MANY PEOPLE WHO CAN GO OUT SEARCHING... AND WE'VE GOT TO LET A FEW PEOPLE GO OFF IN OTHER DIRECTIONS UNLESS YOU WANT TO TELL THEM WHERE WE FOUND MARTINEZ BEFORE WE CUT HIS HEAD OFF.
CLOSEST THING TO INFORMATION WE GOT FROM ANYONE HERE IN TOWN WAS THAT THEY REMEMBER THERE BEING A PRISON JUST OFF McALISTER LANE--WHICH IS A LONG DAMN ROAD, THAT WE HAVEN'T BEEN ABLE TO SEARCH VERY FAR ON DUE TO WRECKED CARS... AND THIS PERSON ISN'T EVEN SURE IT'S OFF THAT ROAD.
WE'RE REAL SORRY, SIR. WE'RE TRYING AS HARD AS WE CAN. WE GOT MULTIPLE TEAMS GOING OUT EVERY DAY--JUST MAPPING THE AREA.
WE'RE LEARNING A LOT ABOUT THE AREA--IT'S JUST THAT WE CAN'T FIND THIS DAMN PRISON.
BLAM!
FUCK!
WHY THE HELL DID THAT BITCH HAVE TO CUT OFF MY RIGHT ARM. I'M ALMOST FUCKING USELESS WITH A GUN NOW.

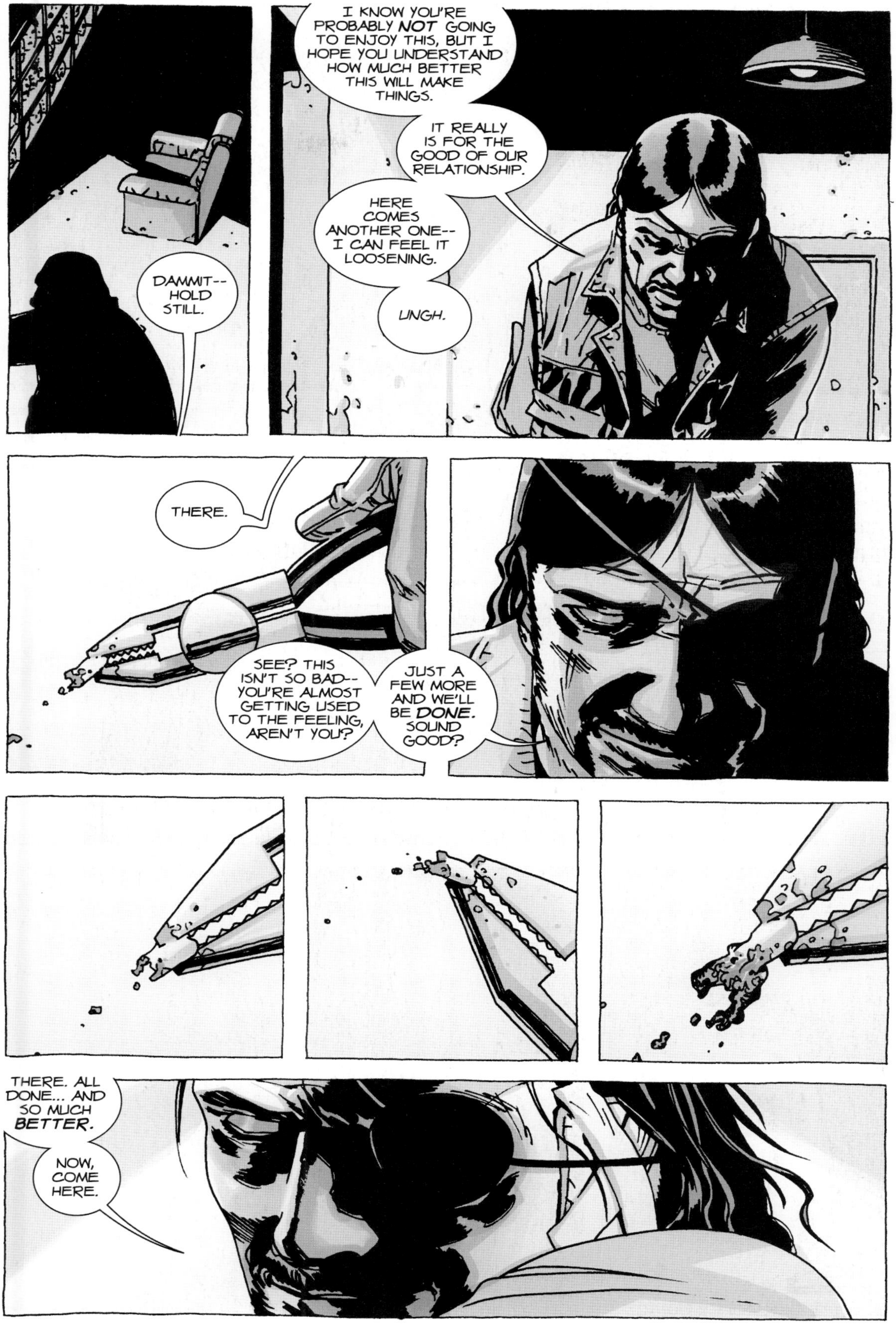
DAMMIT-- HOLD STILL.
I KNOW YOU'RE PROBABLY NOT GOING TO ENJOY THIS, BUT I HOPE YOU UNDERSTAND HOW MUCH BETTER THIS WILL MAKE THINGS.
IT REALLY IS FOR THE GOOD OF OUR RELATIONSHIP.
HERE COMES ANOTHER ONE-- I CAN FEEL IT LOOSENING.
UNGH.
THERE.
SEE? THIS ISN'T SO BAD-- YOU'RE ALMOST GETTING USED TO THE FEELING, AREN'T YOU?
JUST A FEW MORE AND WE'LL BE DONE. SOUND GOOD?
THERE. ALL DONE... AND SO MUCH BETTER.
NOW, COME HERE.

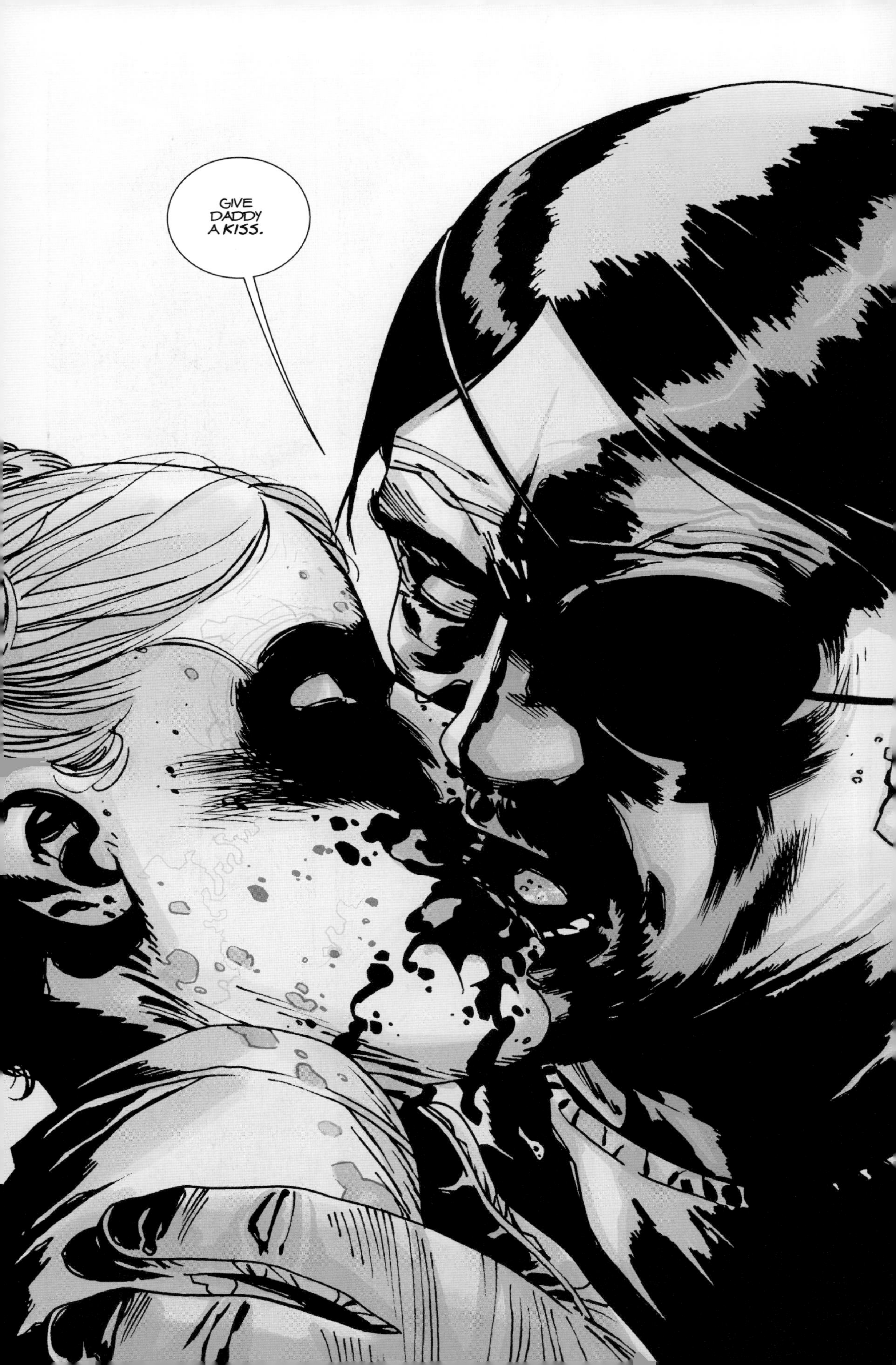
GIVE DADDY A KISS.

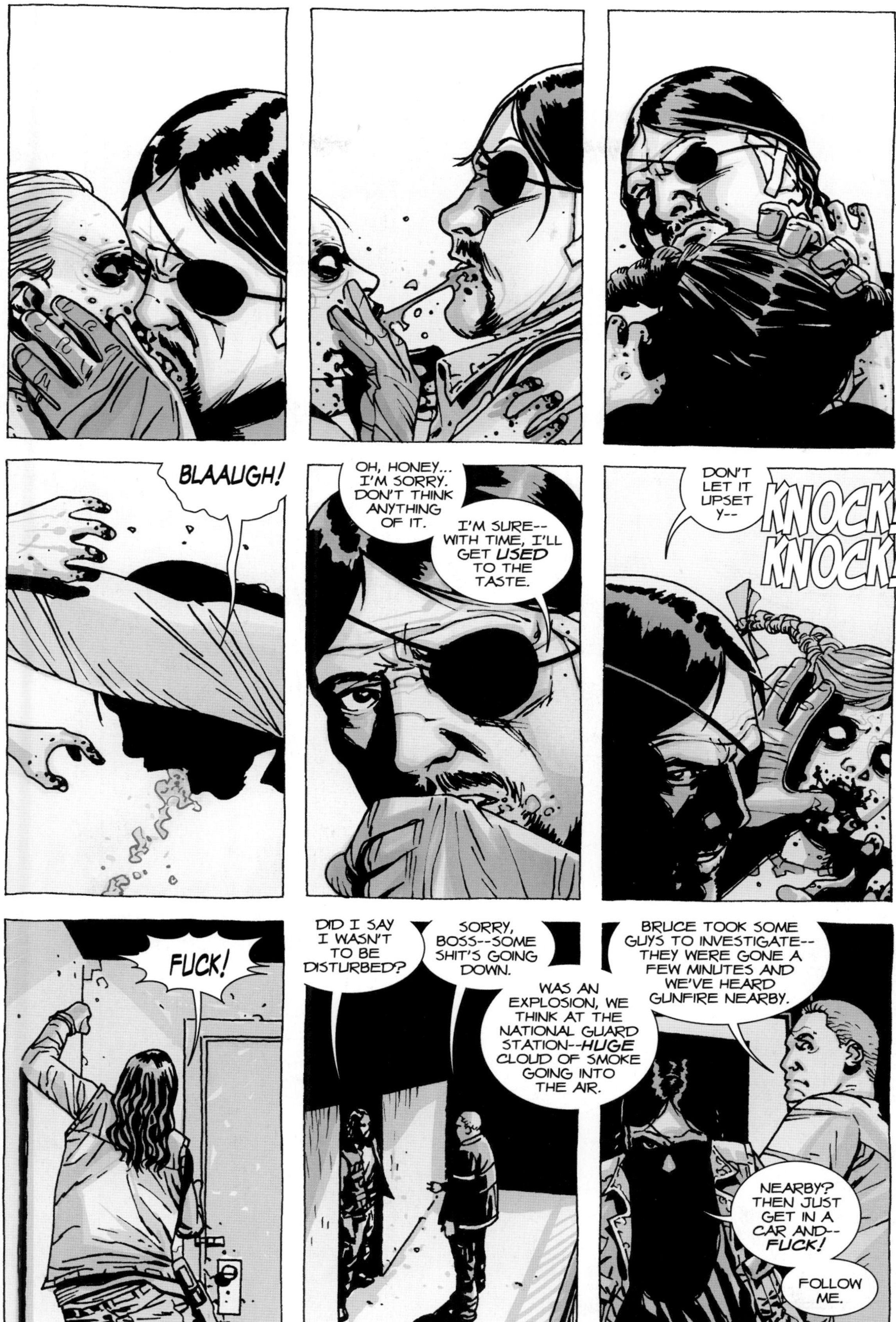
BLAAUGH!
OH, HONEY... I'M SORRY. DON'T THINK ANYTHING OF IT.
I'M SURE-- WITH TIME, I'LL GET USED TO THE TASTE.
DON'T LET IT UPSET Y--
KNOCK! KNOCK!
FUCK!
DID I SAY I WASN'T TO BE DISTURBED?
SORRY, BOSS--SOME SHIT'S GOING DOWN.
WAS AN EXPLOSION, WE THINK AT THE NATIONAL GUARD STATION--HUGE CLOUD OF SMOKE GOING INTO THE AIR.
BRUCE TOOK SOME GUYS TO INVESTIGATE-- THEY WERE GONE A FEW MINUTES AND WE'VE HEARD GUNFIRE NEARBY.
NEARBY? THEN JUST GET IN A CAR AND-- FUCK!
FOLLOW ME.

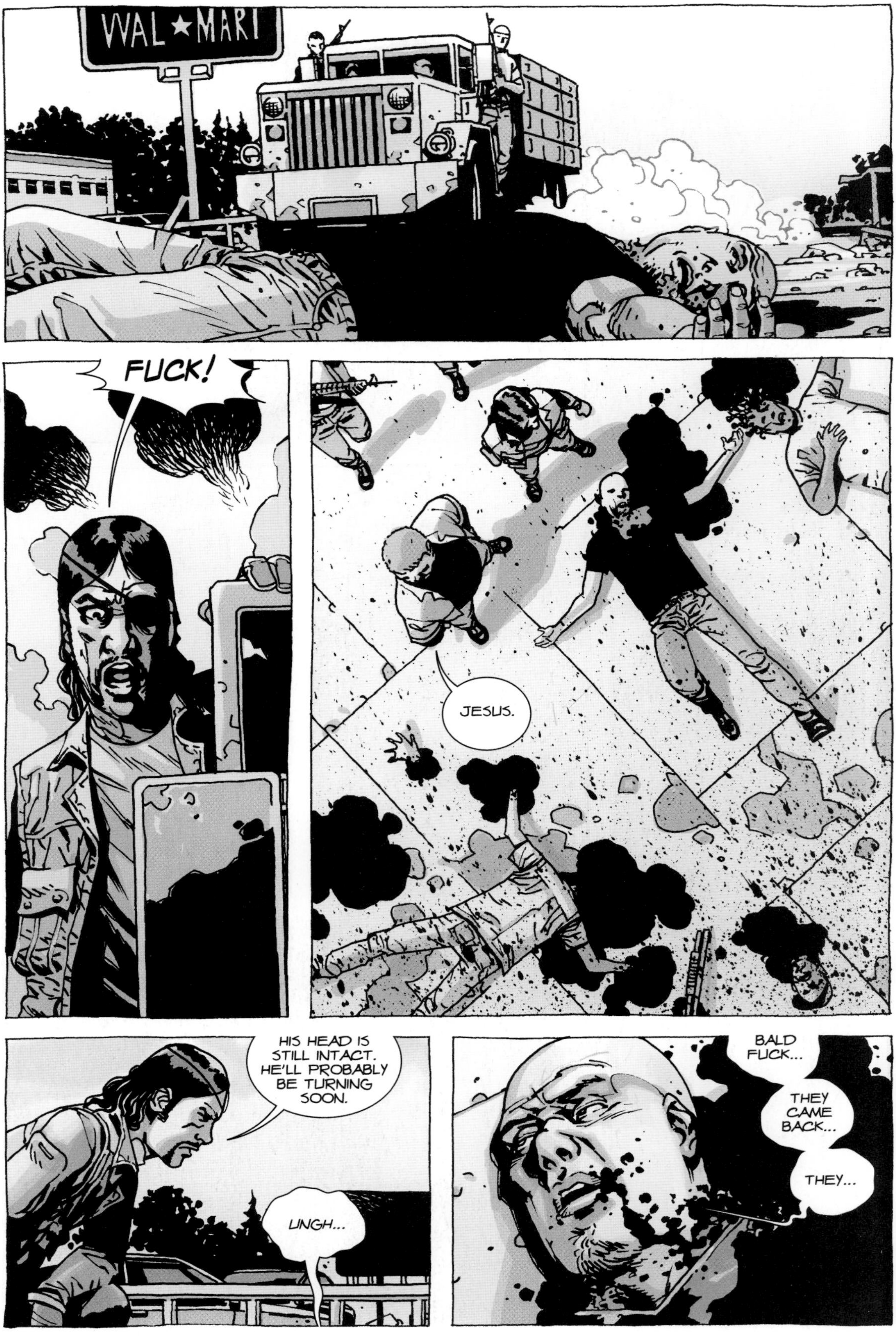
WAL★MART
FUCK!
JESUS.
HIS HEAD IS STILL INTACT. HE'LL PROBABLY BE TURNING SOON.
UNGH...
BALD FUCK...
THEY CAME BACK...
THEY...

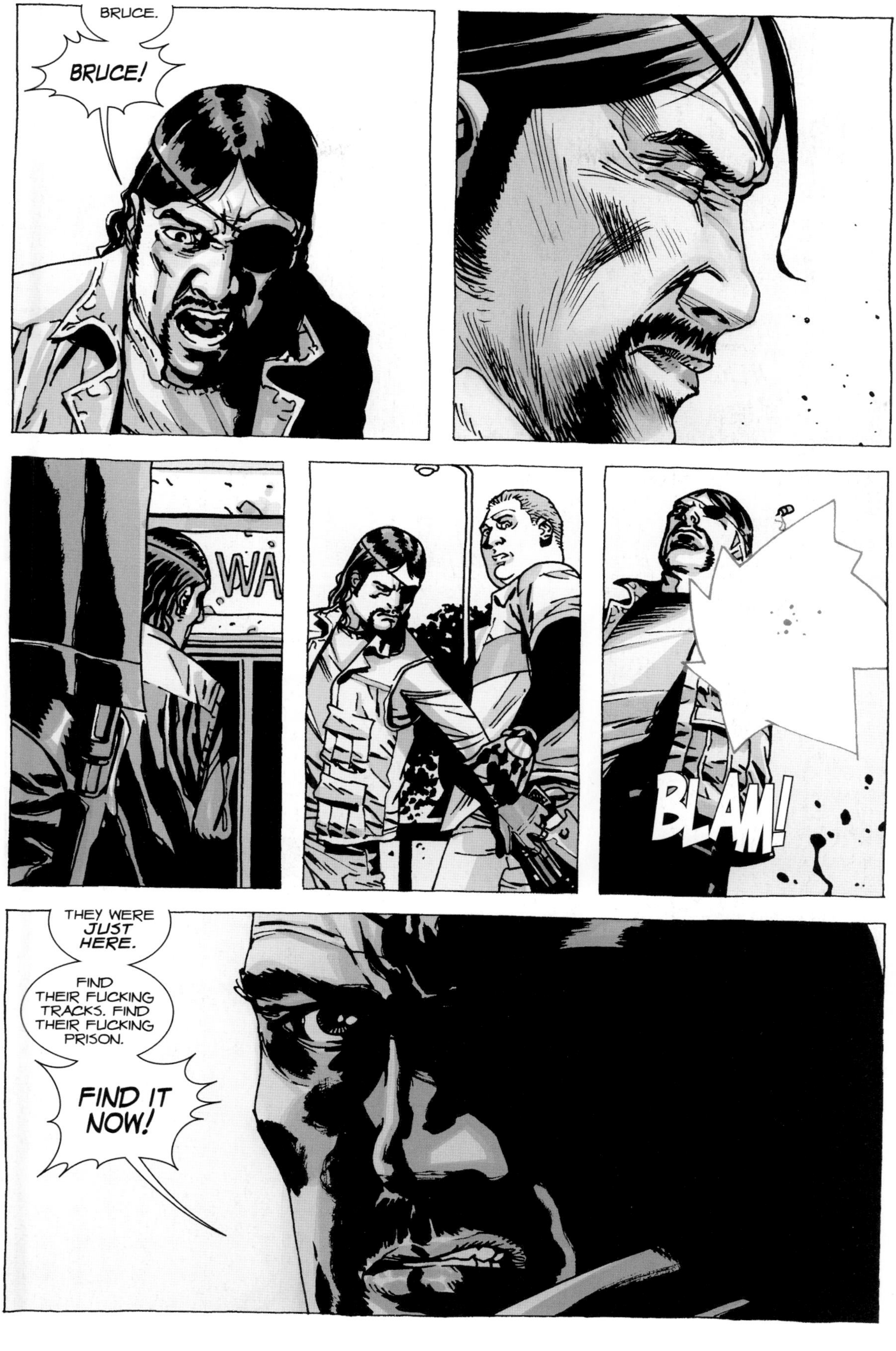
BRUCE.
BRUCE!
WA
BLAM!
THEY WERE JUST HERE.
FIND THEIR FUCKING TRACKS. FIND THEIR FUCKING PRISON.
FIND IT NOW!

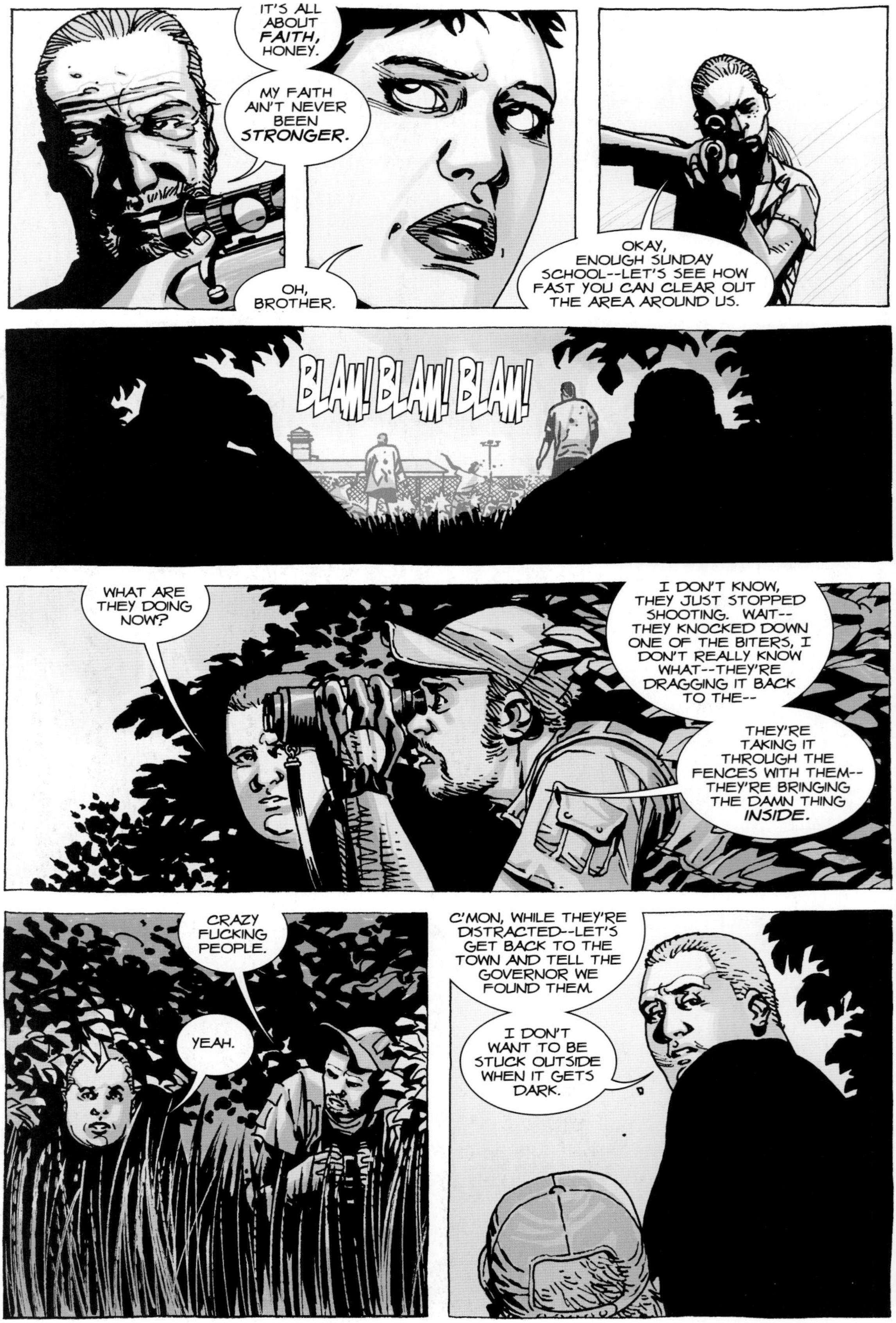
IT'S ALL ABOUT FAITH, HONEY.
MY FAITH AIN'T NEVER BEEN STRONGER.
OH, BROTHER.
OKAY, ENOUGH SUNDAY SCHOOL--LET'S SEE HOW FAST YOU CAN CLEAR OUT THE AREA AROUND US.
BLAM! BLAM! BLAM!
WHAT ARE THEY DOING NOW?
I DON'T KNOW, THEY JUST STOPPED SHOOTING. WAIT-- THEY KNOCKED DOWN ONE OF THE BITERS, I DON'T REALLY KNOW WHAT--THEY'RE DRAGGING IT BACK TO THE--
THEY'RE TAKING IT THROUGH THE FENCES WITH THEM-- THEY'RE BRINGING THE DAMN THING INSIDE.
CRAZY FUCKING PEOPLE.
YEAH.
C'MON, WHILE THEY'RE DISTRACTED--LET'S GET BACK TO THE TOWN AND TELL THE GOVERNOR WE FOUND THEM.
I DON'T WANT TO BE STUCK OUTSIDE WHEN IT GETS DARK.

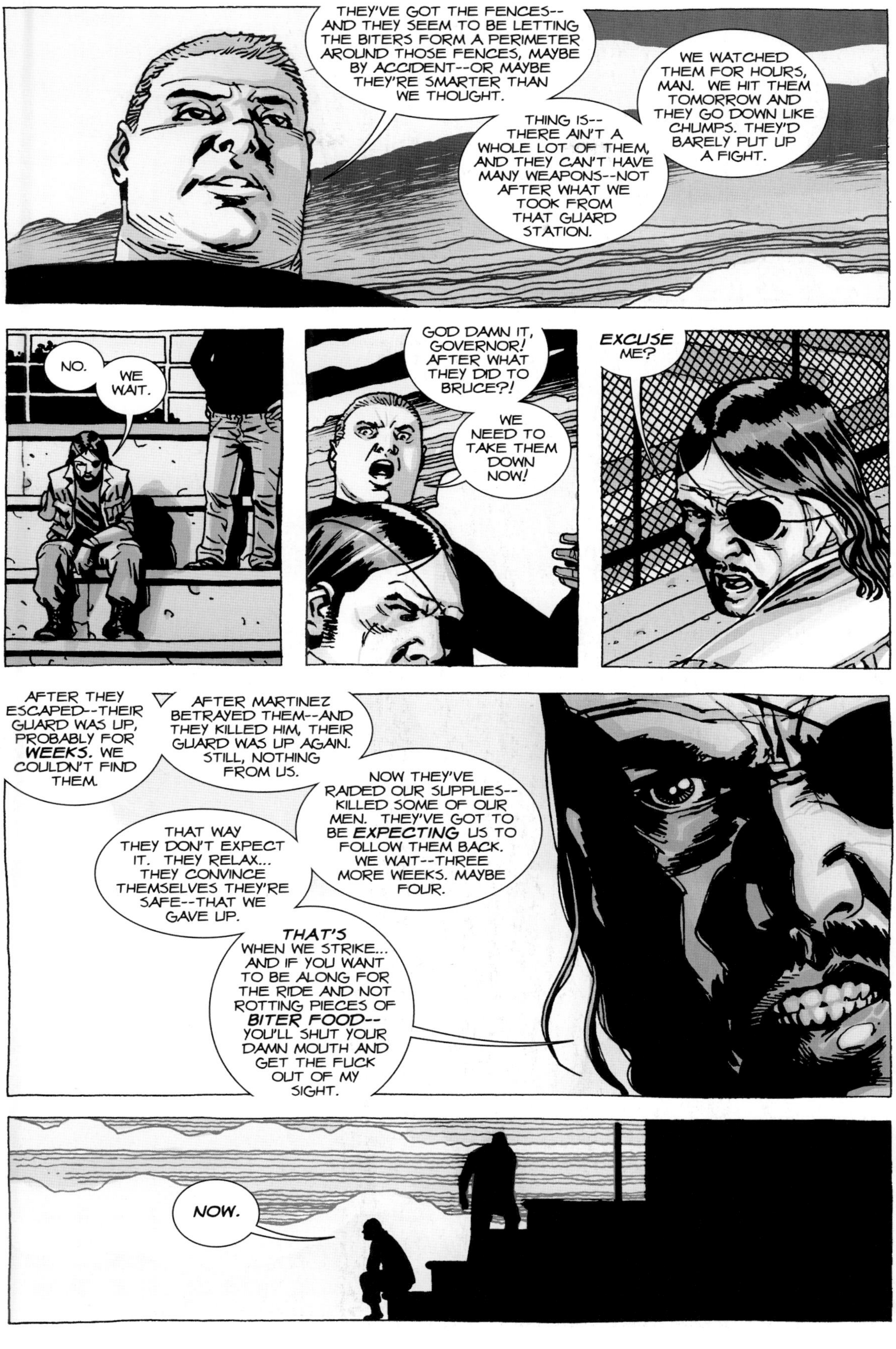
THEY'VE GOT THE FENCES-- AND THEY SEEM TO BE LETTING THE BITERS FORM A PERIMETER AROUND THOSE FENCES, MAYBE BY ACCIDENT--OR MAYBE THEY'RE SMARTER THAN WE THOUGHT.
THING IS-- THERE AIN'T A WHOLE LOT OF THEM, AND THEY CAN'T HAVE MANY WEAPONS--NOT AFTER WHAT WE TOOK FROM THAT GUARD STATION.
WE WATCHED THEM FOR HOURS, MAN. WE HIT THEM TOMORROW AND THEY GO DOWN LIKE CHUMPS. THEY'D BARELY PUT UP A FIGHT.
NO.
WE WAIT.
GOD DAMN IT, GOVERNOR! AFTER WHAT THEY DID TO BRUCE?!
WE NEED TO TAKE THEM DOWN NOW!
EXCUSE ME?
AFTER THEY ESCAPED--THEIR GUARD WAS UP, PROBABLY FOR WEEKS. WE COULDN'T FIND THEM.
AFTER MARTINEZ BETRAYED THEM--AND THEY KILLED HIM, THEIR GUARD WAS UP AGAIN. STILL, NOTHING FROM US.
NOW THEY'VE RAIDED OUR SUPPLIES-- KILLED SOME OF OUR MEN. THEY'VE GOT TO BE EXPECTING US TO FOLLOW THEM BACK. WE WAIT--THREE MORE WEEKS. MAYBE FOUR.
THAT WAY THEY DON'T EXPECT IT. THEY RELAX... THEY CONVINCE THEMSELVES THEY'RE SAFE--THAT WE GAVE UP.
THAT'S WHEN WE STRIKE... AND IF YOU WANT TO BE ALONG FOR THE RIDE AND NOT ROTTING PIECES OF BITER FOOD-- YOU'LL SHUT YOUR DAMN MOUTH AND GET THE FUCK OUT OF MY SIGHT.
NOW.

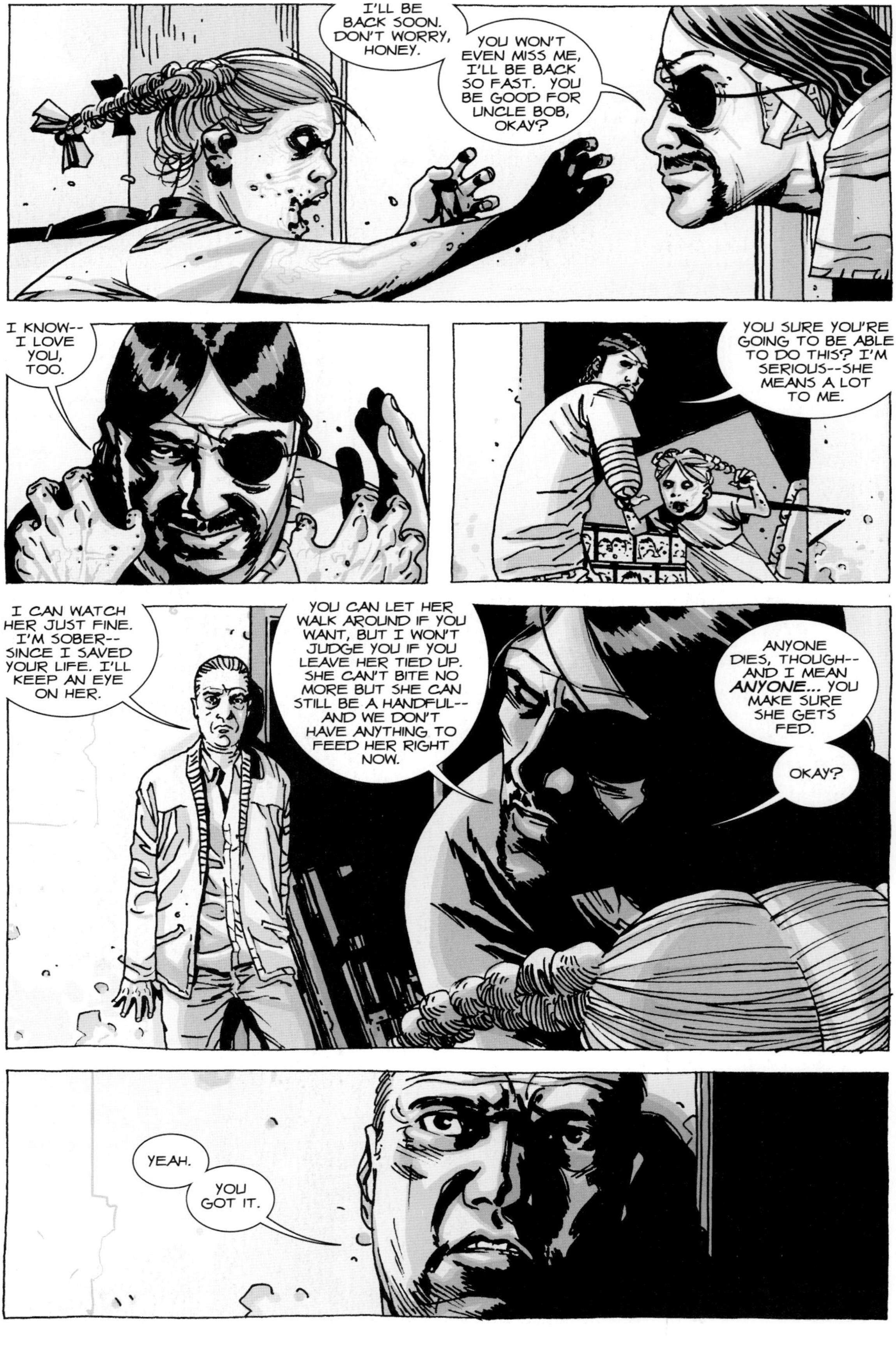
I'LL BE BACK SOON. DON'T WORRY, HONEY.
YOU WON'T EVEN MISS ME, I'LL BE BACK SO FAST. YOU BE GOOD FOR UNCLE BOB, OKAY?
I KNOW-- I LOVE YOU, TOO.
YOU SURE YOU'RE GOING TO BE ABLE TO DO THIS? I'M SERIOUS--SHE MEANS A LOT TO ME.
I CAN WATCH HER JUST FINE. I'M SOBER-- SINCE I SAVED YOUR LIFE. I'LL KEEP AN EYE ON HER.
YOU CAN LET HER WALK AROUND IF YOU WANT, BUT I WON'T JUDGE YOU IF YOU LEAVE HER TIED UP. SHE CAN'T BITE NO MORE BUT SHE CAN STILL BE A HANDFUL-- AND WE DON'T HAVE ANYTHING TO FEED HER RIGHT NOW.
ANYONE DIES, THOUGH-- AND I MEAN ANYONE... YOU MAKE SURE SHE GETS FED.
OKAY?
YEAH.
YOU GOT IT.

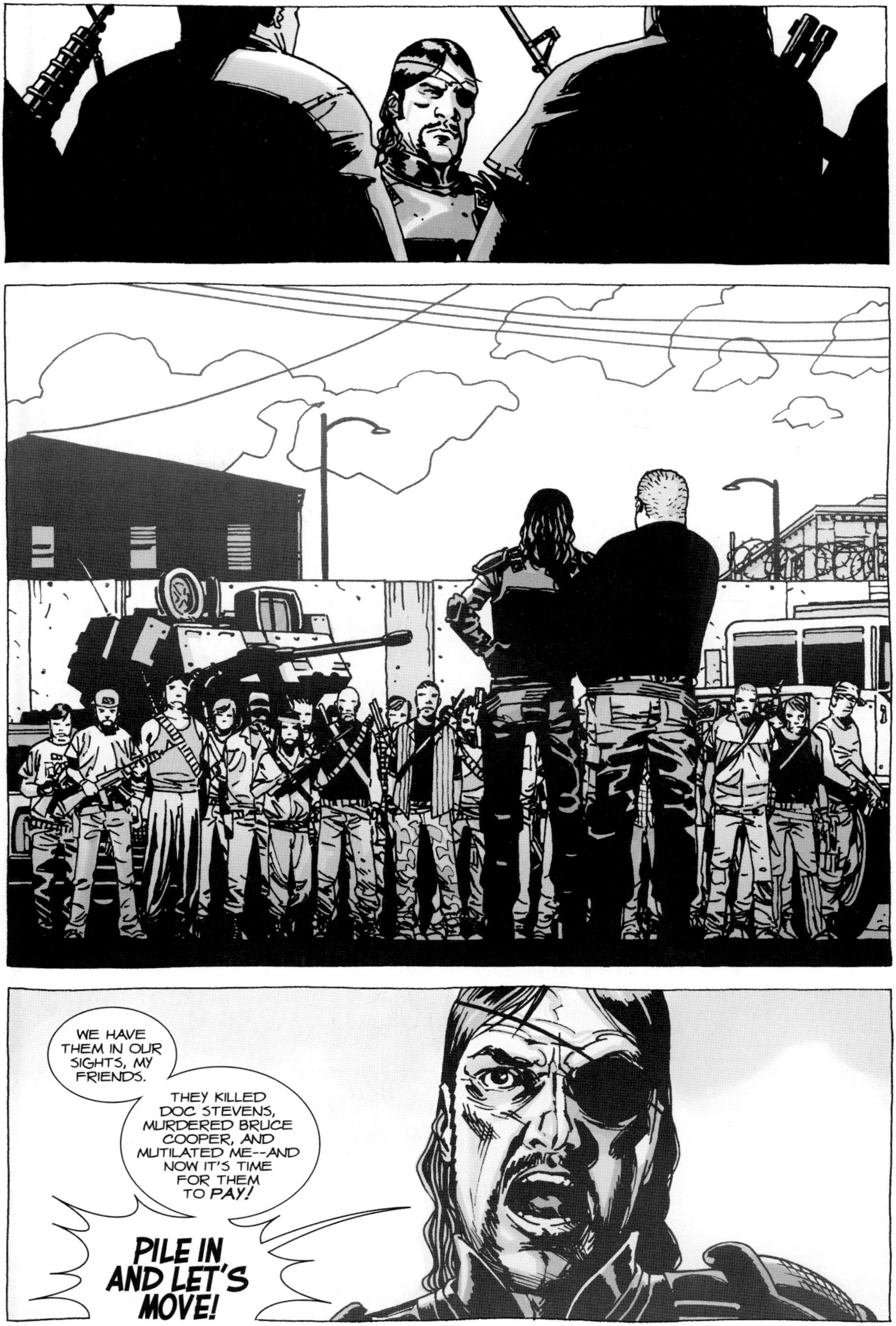
WE HAVE THEM IN OUR SIGHTS, MY FRIENDS.
THEY KILLED DOC STEVENS, MURDERED BRUCE COOPER, AND MUTILATED ME--AND NOW IT'S TIME FOR THEM TO PAY!
PILE IN AND LET'S MOVE!

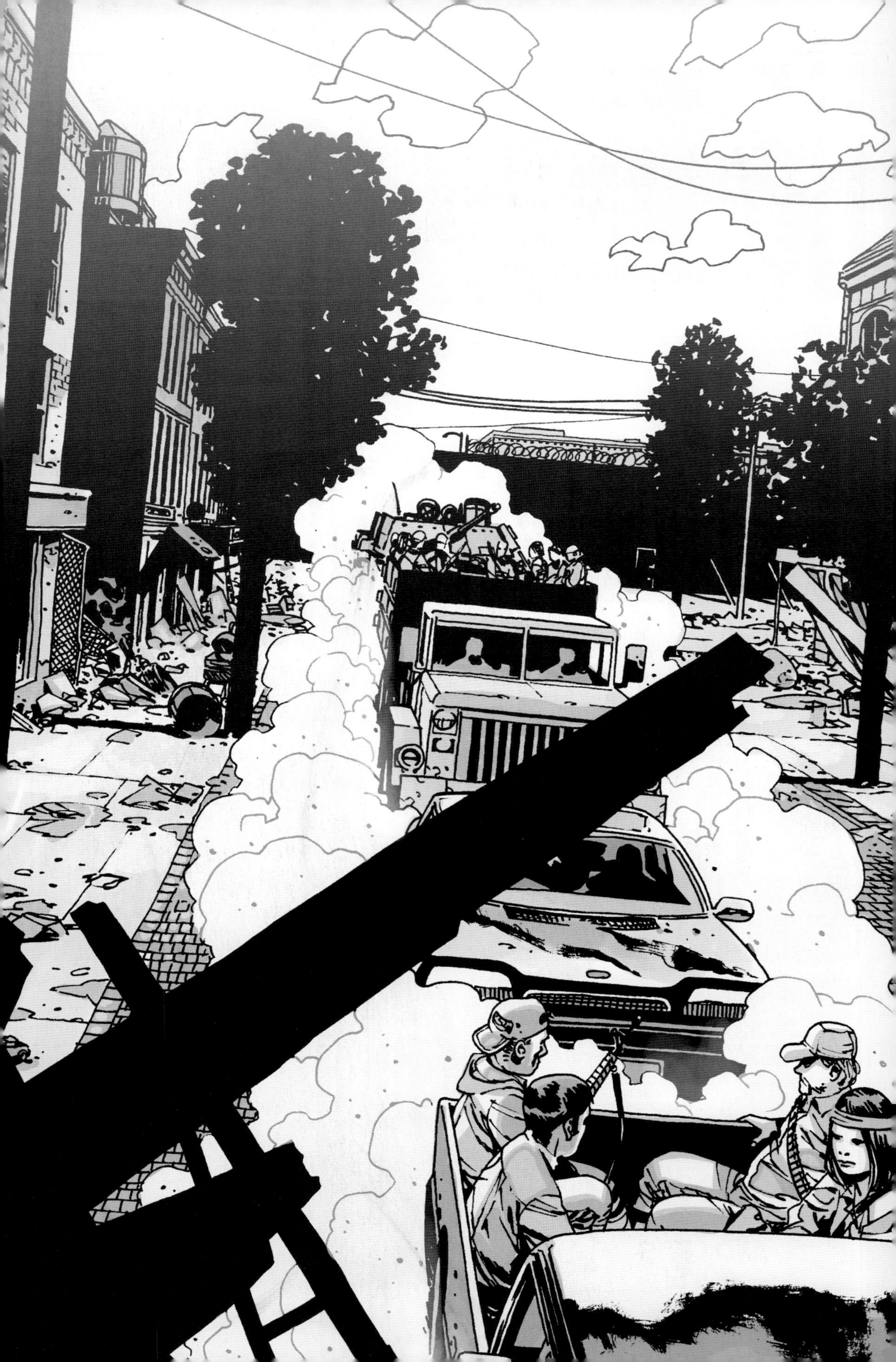

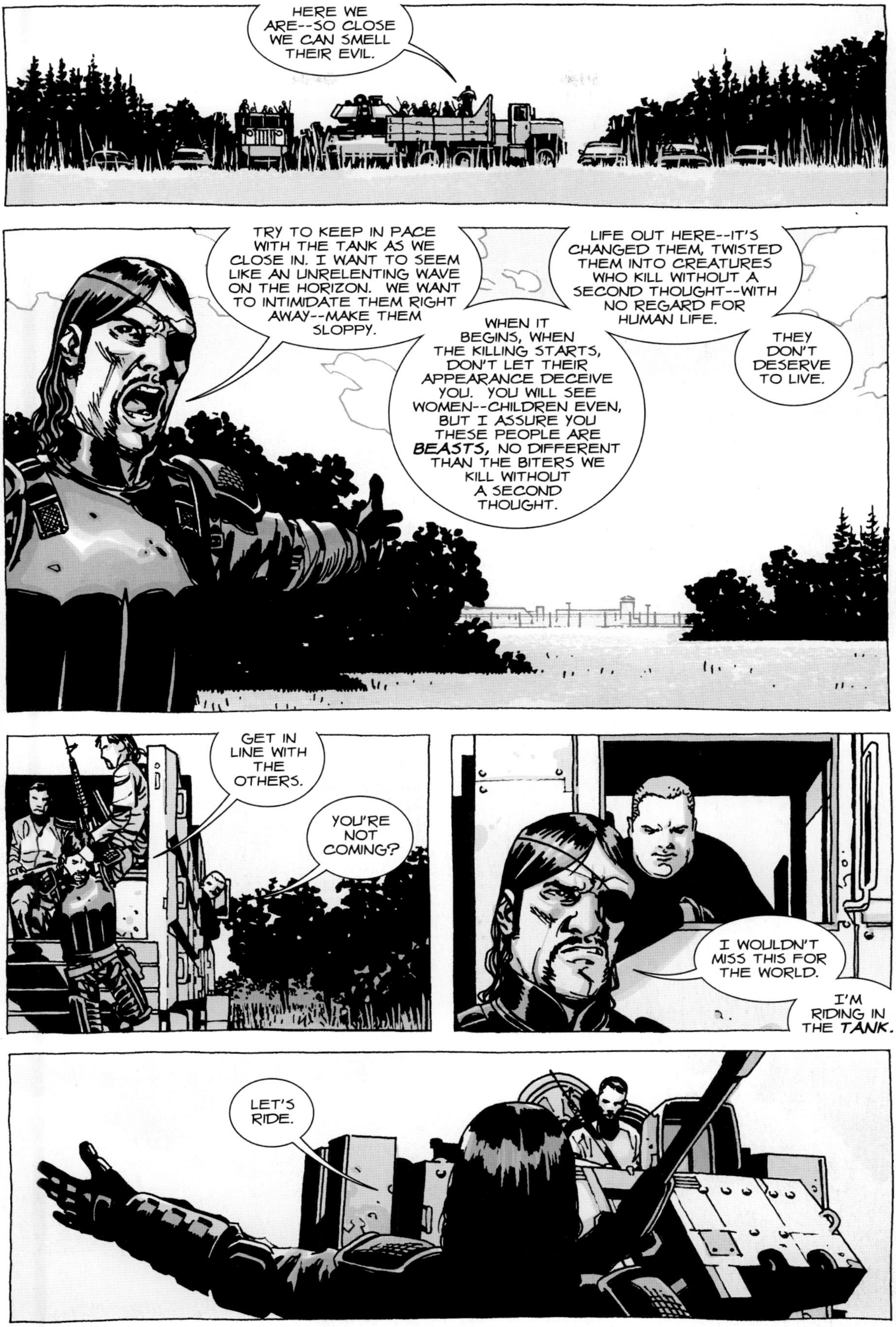
HERE WE ARE--SO CLOSE WE CAN SMELL THEIR EVIL.
TRY TO KEEP IN PACE WITH THE TANK AS WE CLOSE IN. I WANT TO SEEM LIKE AN UNRELENTING WAVE ON THE HORIZON. WE WANT TO INTIMIDATE THEM RIGHT AWAY--MAKE THEM SLOPPY.
WHEN IT BEGINS, WHEN THE KILLING STARTS, DON'T LET THEIR APPEARANCE DECEIVE YOU. YOU WILL SEE WOMEN--CHILDREN EVEN, BUT I ASSURE YOU THESE PEOPLE ARE *BEASTS,* NO DIFFERENT THAN THE BITERS WE KILL WITHOUT A SECOND THOUGHT.
LIFE OUT HERE--IT'S CHANGED THEM, TWISTED THEM INTO CREATURES WHO KILL WITHOUT A SECOND THOUGHT--WITH NO REGARD FOR HUMAN LIFE.
THEY DON'T DESERVE TO LIVE.
GET IN LINE WITH THE OTHERS.
YOU'RE NOT COMING?
I WOULDN'T MISS THIS FOR THE WORLD.
I'M RIDING IN THE *TANK.*
LET'S RIDE.

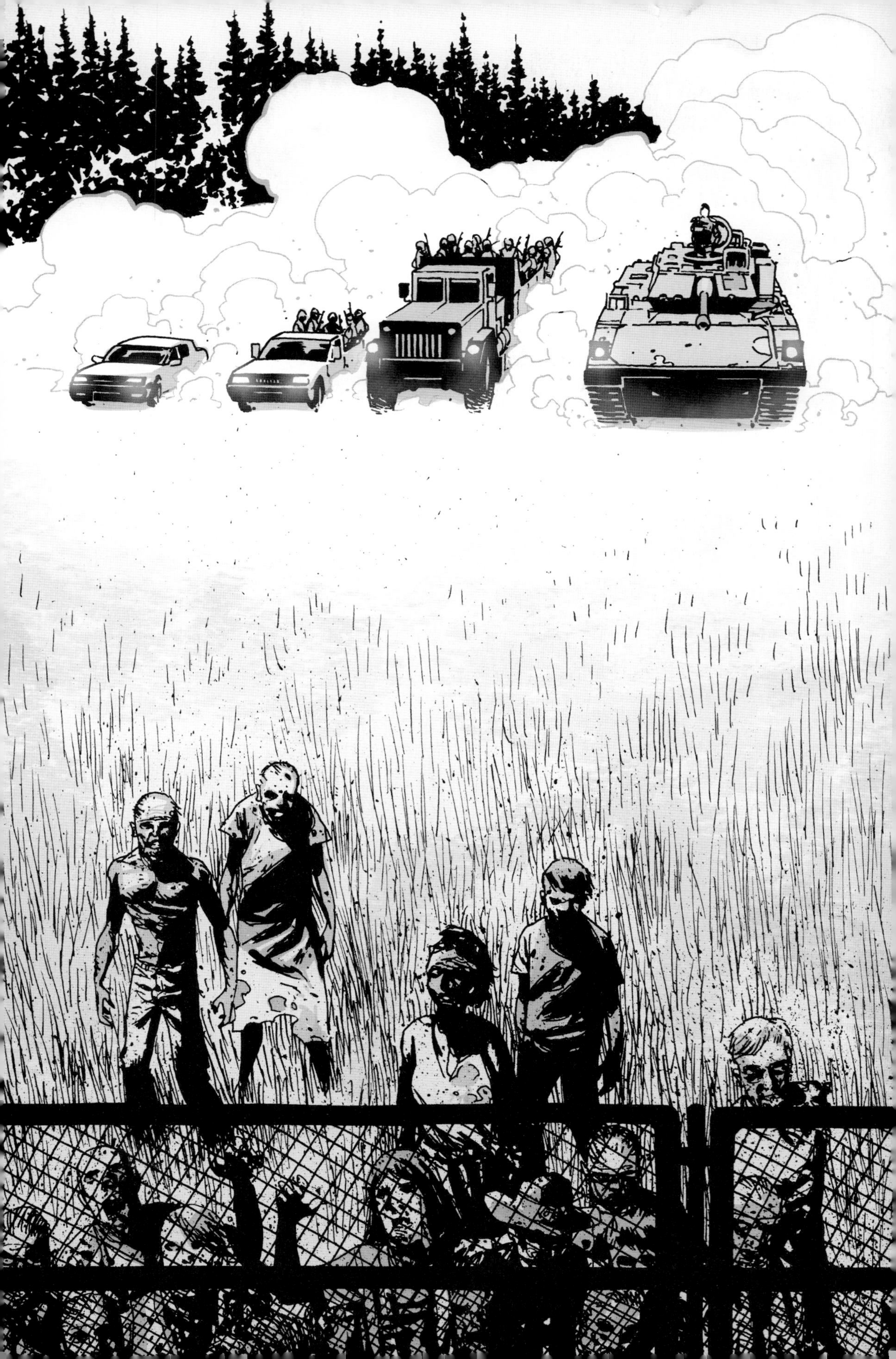

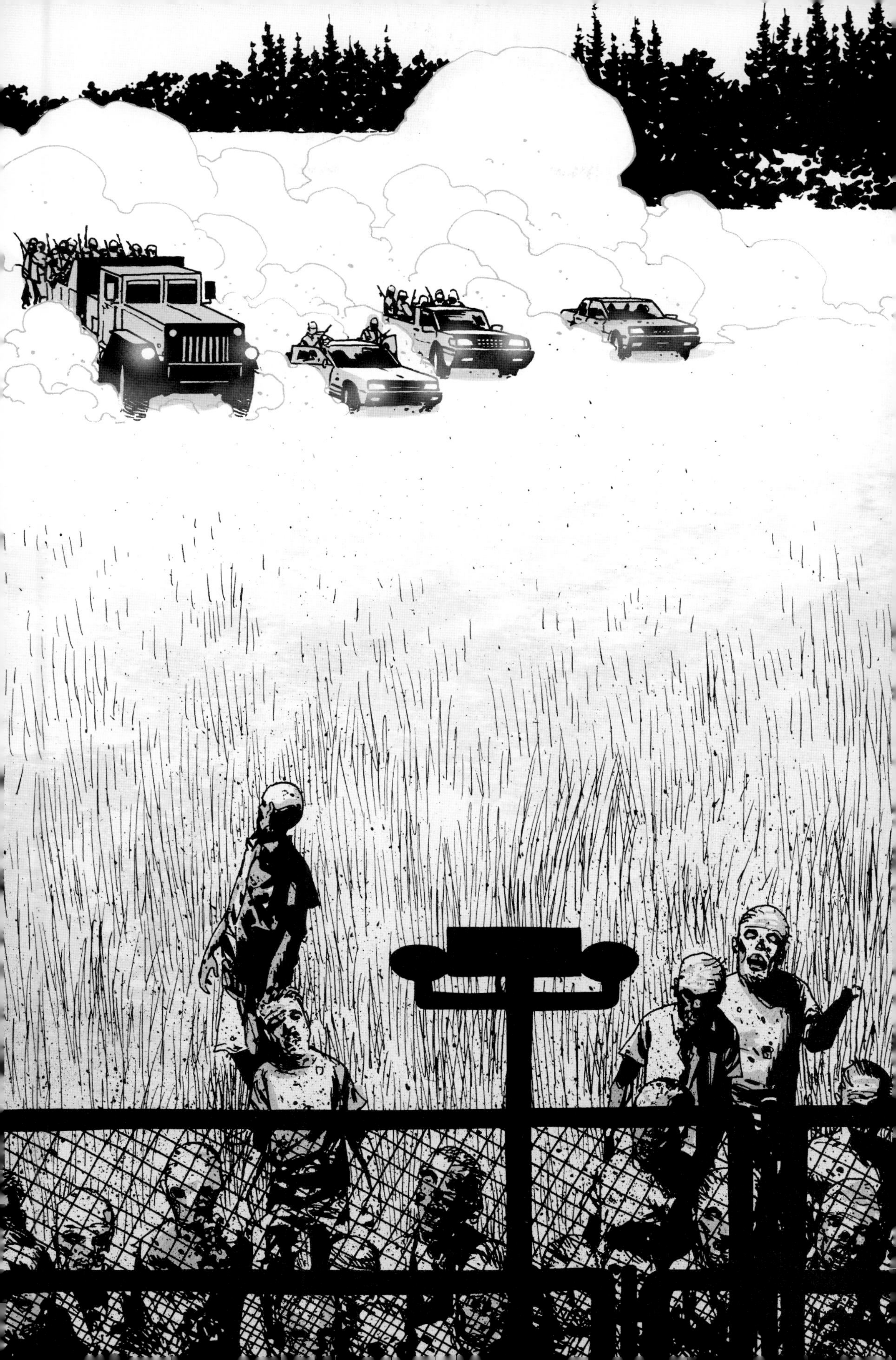

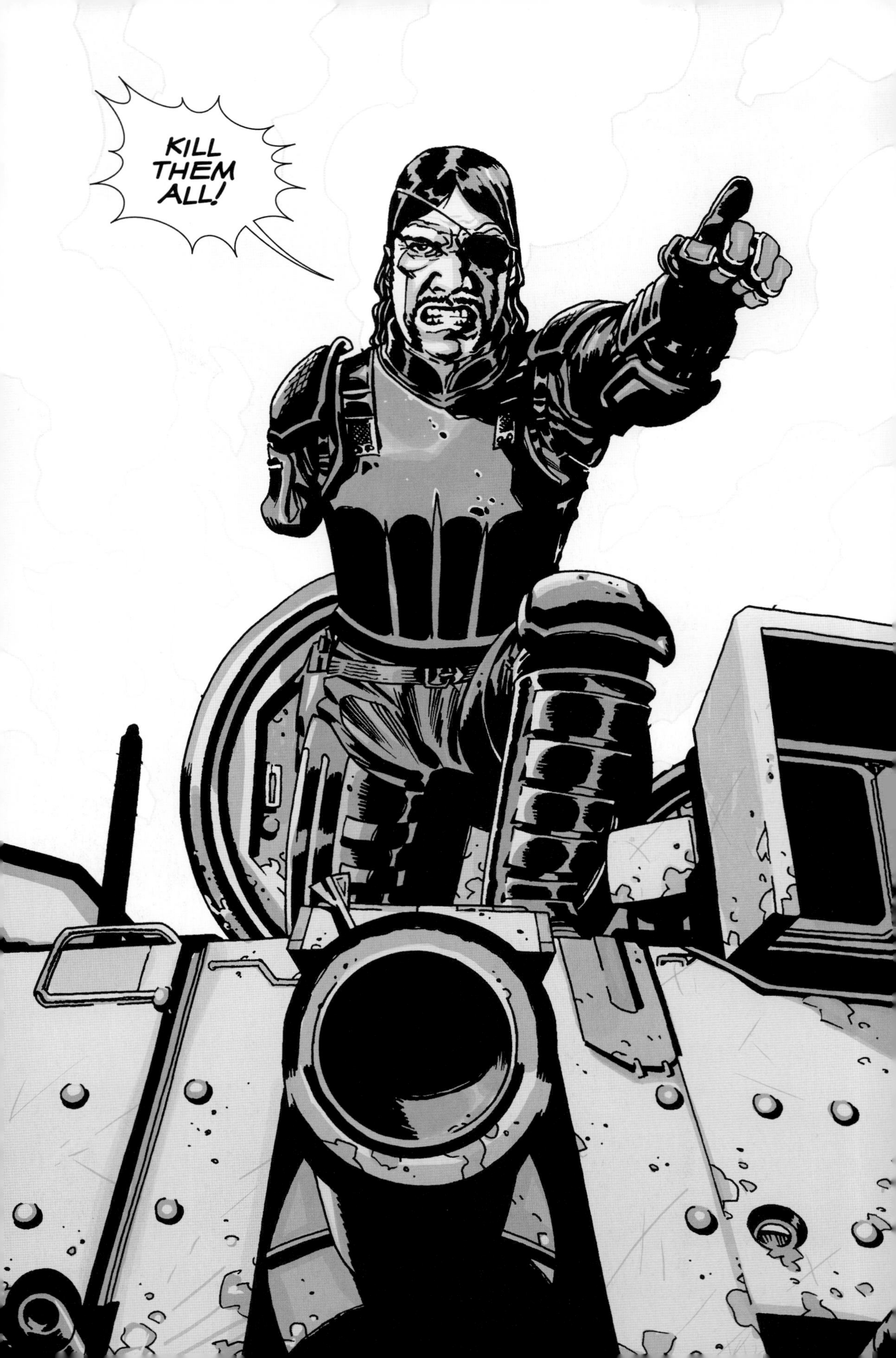
KILL THEM ALL!

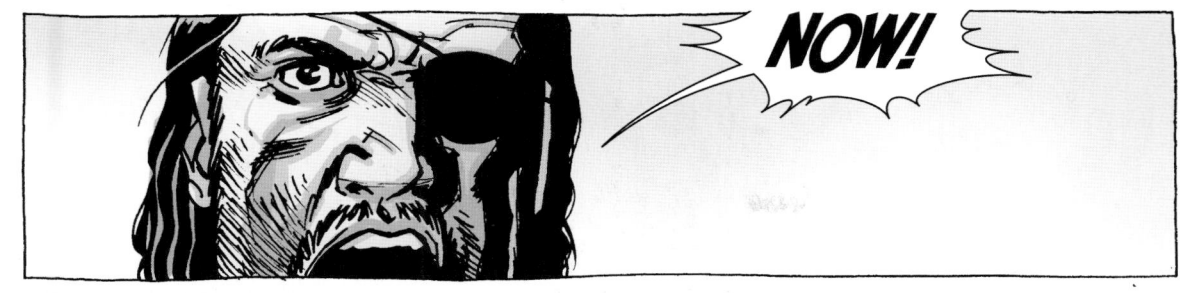

NOW!

BLAM! BLAM!
BLAM! BLAM!

BLAM! BLAM! BLAM! BLAM!

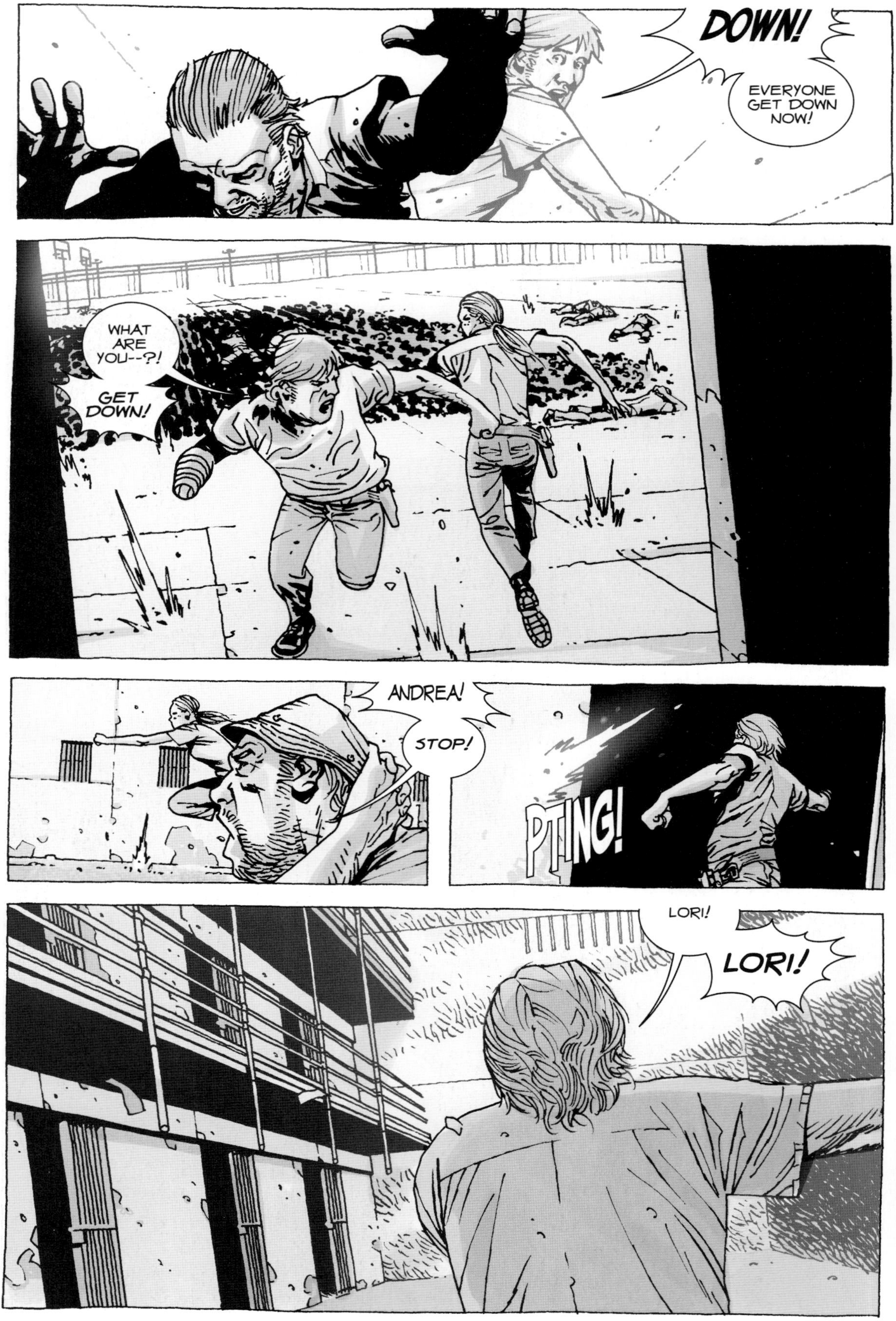
DOWN!
EVERYONE GET DOWN NOW!
WHAT ARE YOU--?!
GET DOWN!
ANDREA!
STOP!
PTING!
LORI!
LORI!

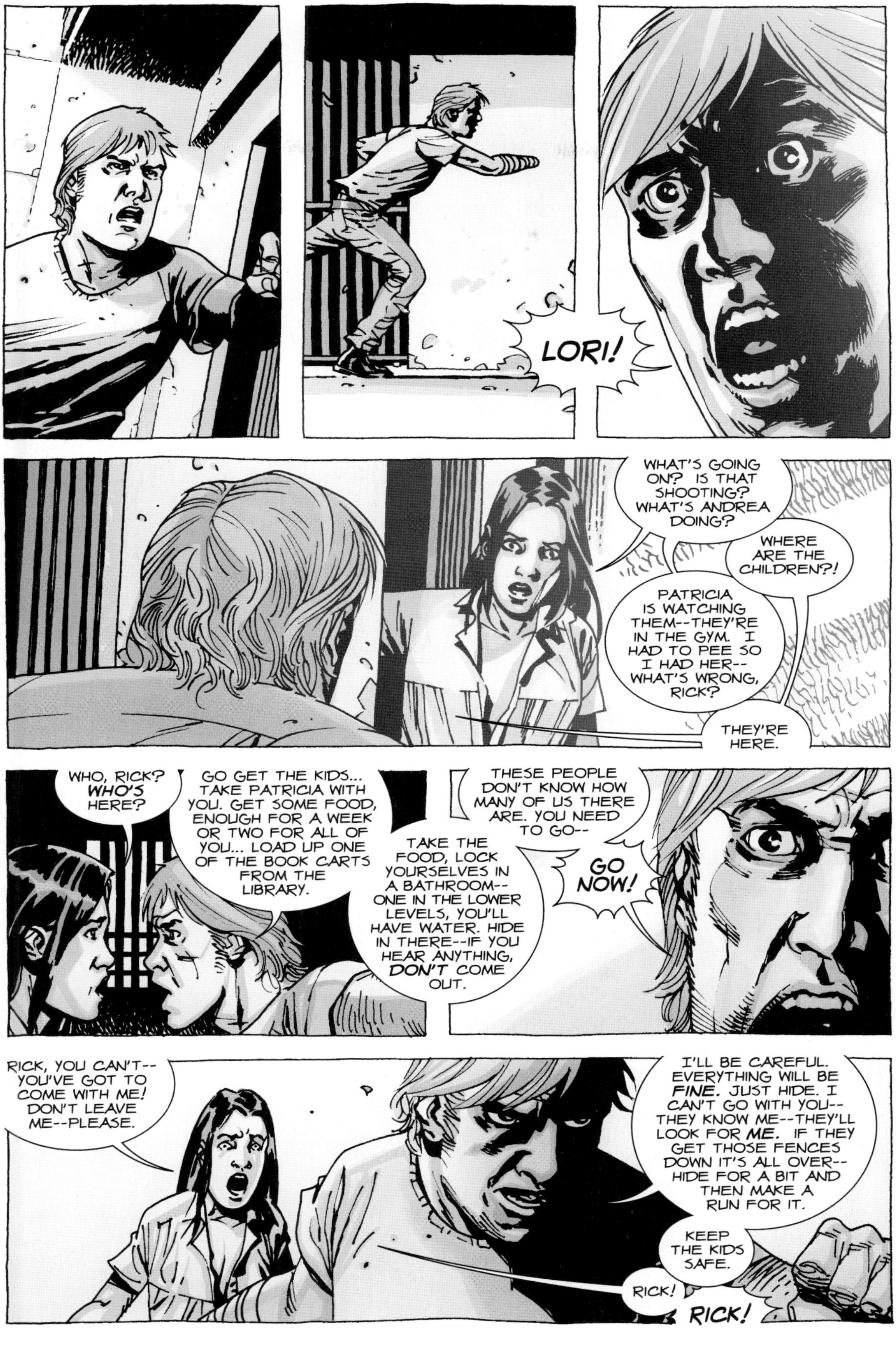
LORI!
WHAT'S GOING ON? IS THAT SHOOTING? WHAT'S ANDREA DOING?
WHERE ARE THE CHILDREN?!
PATRICIA IS WATCHING THEM--THEY'RE IN THE GYM. I HAD TO PEE SO I HAD HER-- WHAT'S WRONG, RICK?
THEY'RE HERE.
WHO, RICK? WHO'S HERE?
GO GET THE KIDS... TAKE PATRICIA WITH YOU. GET SOME FOOD, ENOUGH FOR A WEEK OR TWO FOR ALL OF YOU... LOAD UP ONE OF THE BOOK CARTS FROM THE LIBRARY.
TAKE THE FOOD, LOCK YOURSELVES IN A BATHROOM-- ONE IN THE LOWER LEVELS, YOU'LL HAVE WATER. HIDE IN THERE--IF YOU HEAR ANYTHING, DON'T COME OUT.
THESE PEOPLE DON'T KNOW HOW MANY OF US THERE ARE. YOU NEED TO GO--
GO NOW!
RICK, YOU CAN'T-- YOU'VE GOT TO COME WITH ME! DON'T LEAVE ME--PLEASE.
I'LL BE CAREFUL. EVERYTHING WILL BE FINE. JUST HIDE. I CAN'T GO WITH YOU-- THEY KNOW ME--THEY'LL LOOK FOR ME. IF THEY GET THOSE FENCES DOWN IT'S ALL OVER-- HIDE FOR A BIT AND THEN MAKE A RUN FOR IT.
KEEP THE KIDS SAFE.
RICK!
RICK!

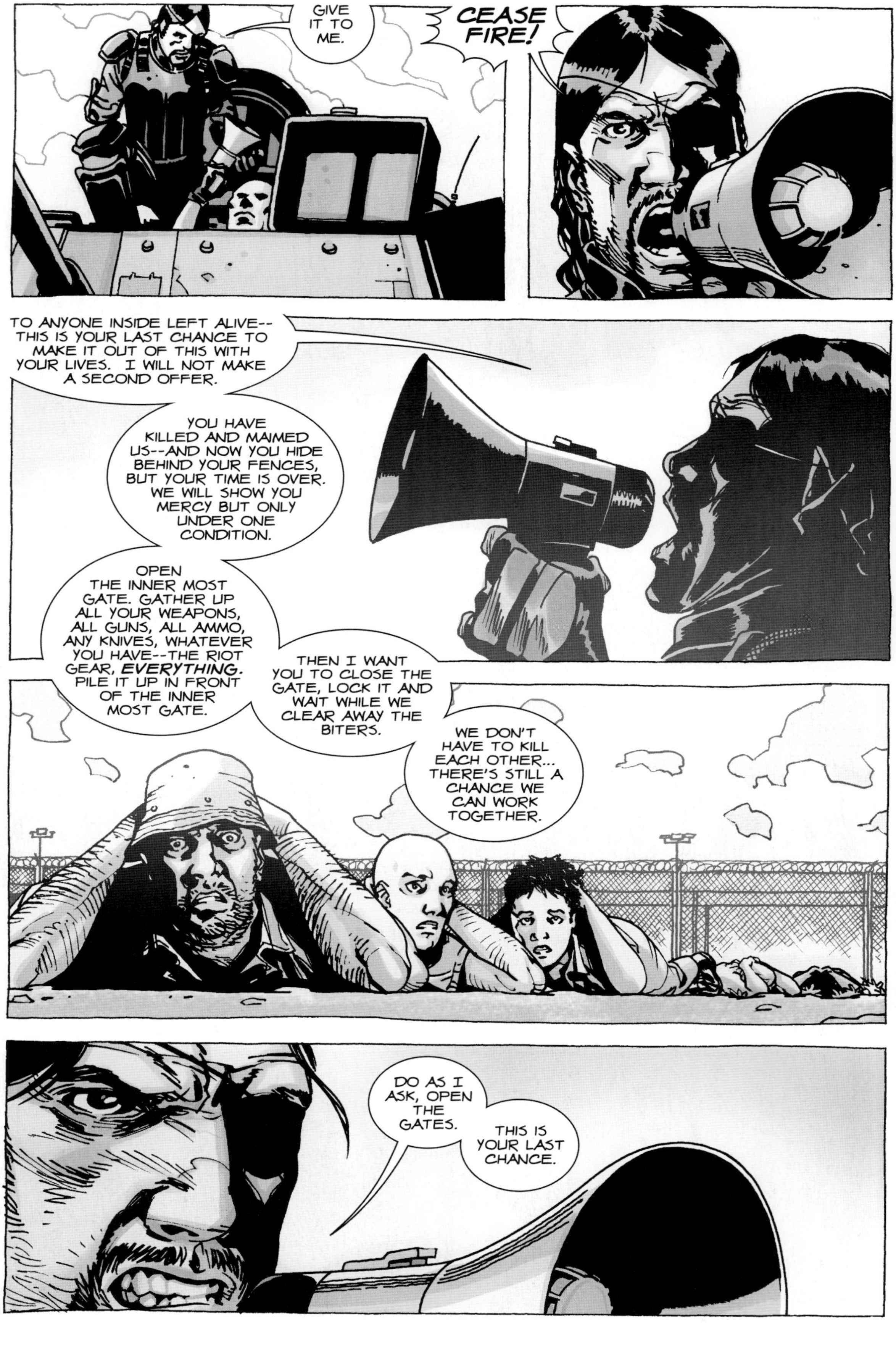
GIVE IT TO ME.
CEASE FIRE!
TO ANYONE INSIDE LEFT ALIVE--THIS IS YOUR LAST CHANCE TO MAKE IT OUT OF THIS WITH YOUR LIVES. I WILL NOT MAKE A SECOND OFFER.
YOU HAVE KILLED AND MAIMED US--AND NOW YOU HIDE BEHIND YOUR FENCES, BUT YOUR TIME IS OVER. WE WILL SHOW YOU MERCY BUT ONLY UNDER ONE CONDITION.
OPEN THE INNER MOST GATE. GATHER UP ALL YOUR WEAPONS, ALL GUNS, ALL AMMO, ANY KNIVES, WHATEVER YOU HAVE--THE RIOT GEAR, EVERYTHING. PILE IT UP IN FRONT OF THE INNER MOST GATE.
THEN I WANT YOU TO CLOSE THE GATE, LOCK IT AND WAIT WHILE WE CLEAR AWAY THE BITERS.
WE DON'T HAVE TO KILL EACH OTHER... THERE'S STILL A CHANCE WE CAN WORK TOGETHER.
DO AS I ASK, OPEN THE GATES.
THIS IS YOUR LAST CHANCE.

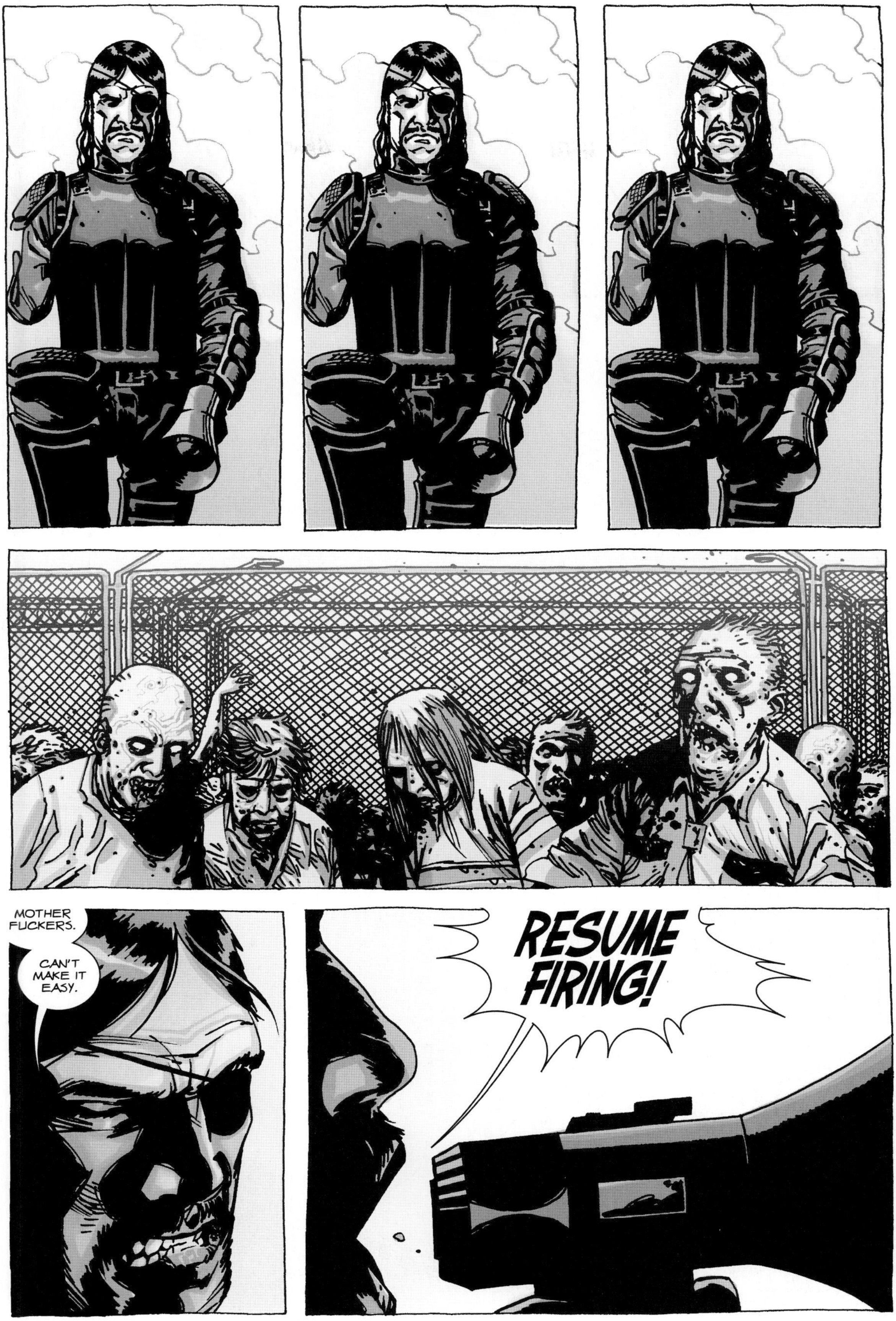
MOTHER FUCKERS.
CAN'T MAKE IT EASY.
RESUME FIRING!

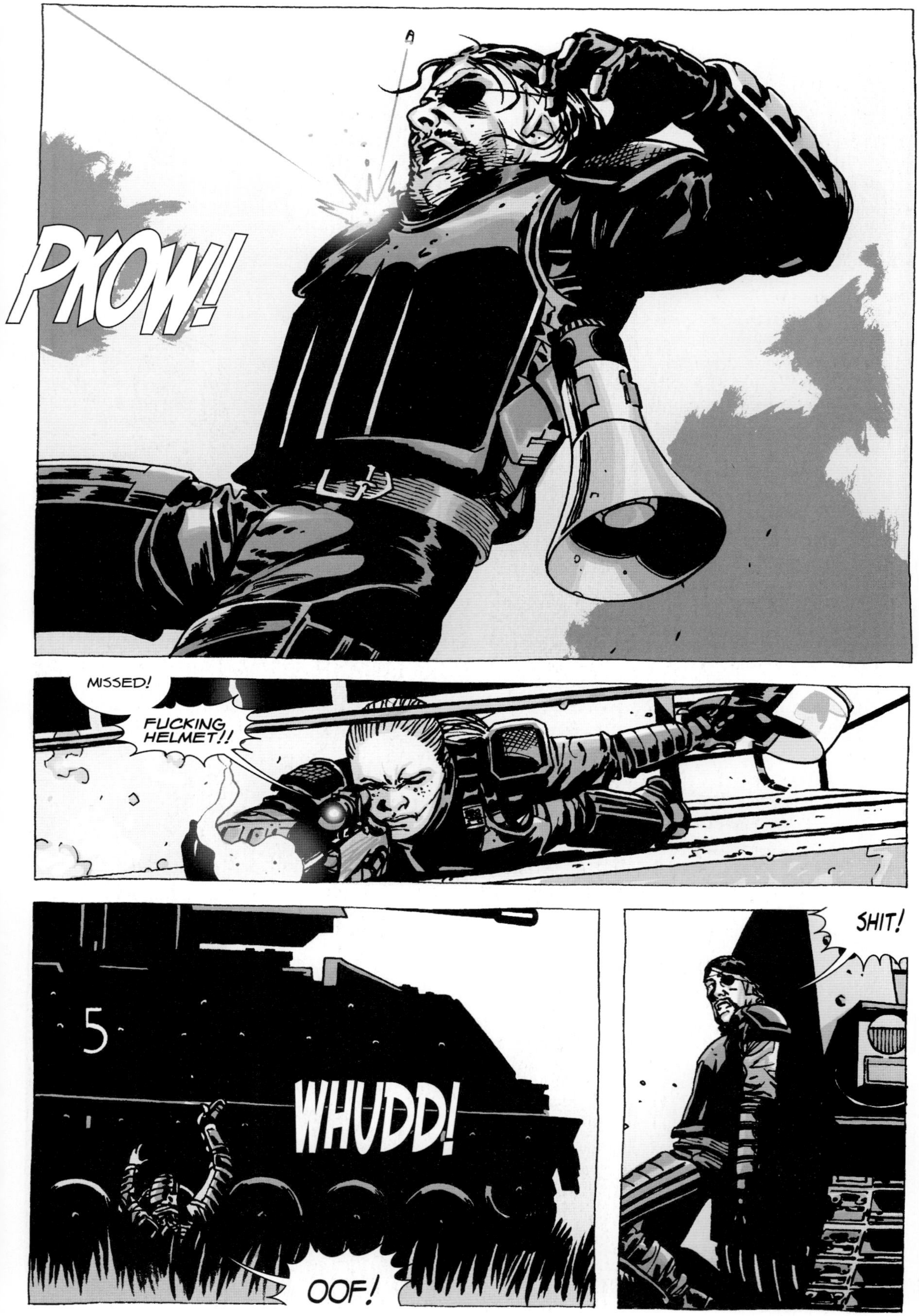
PKOW!
MISSED!
FUCKING HELMET!!
5
WHUDD!
OOF!
SHIT!

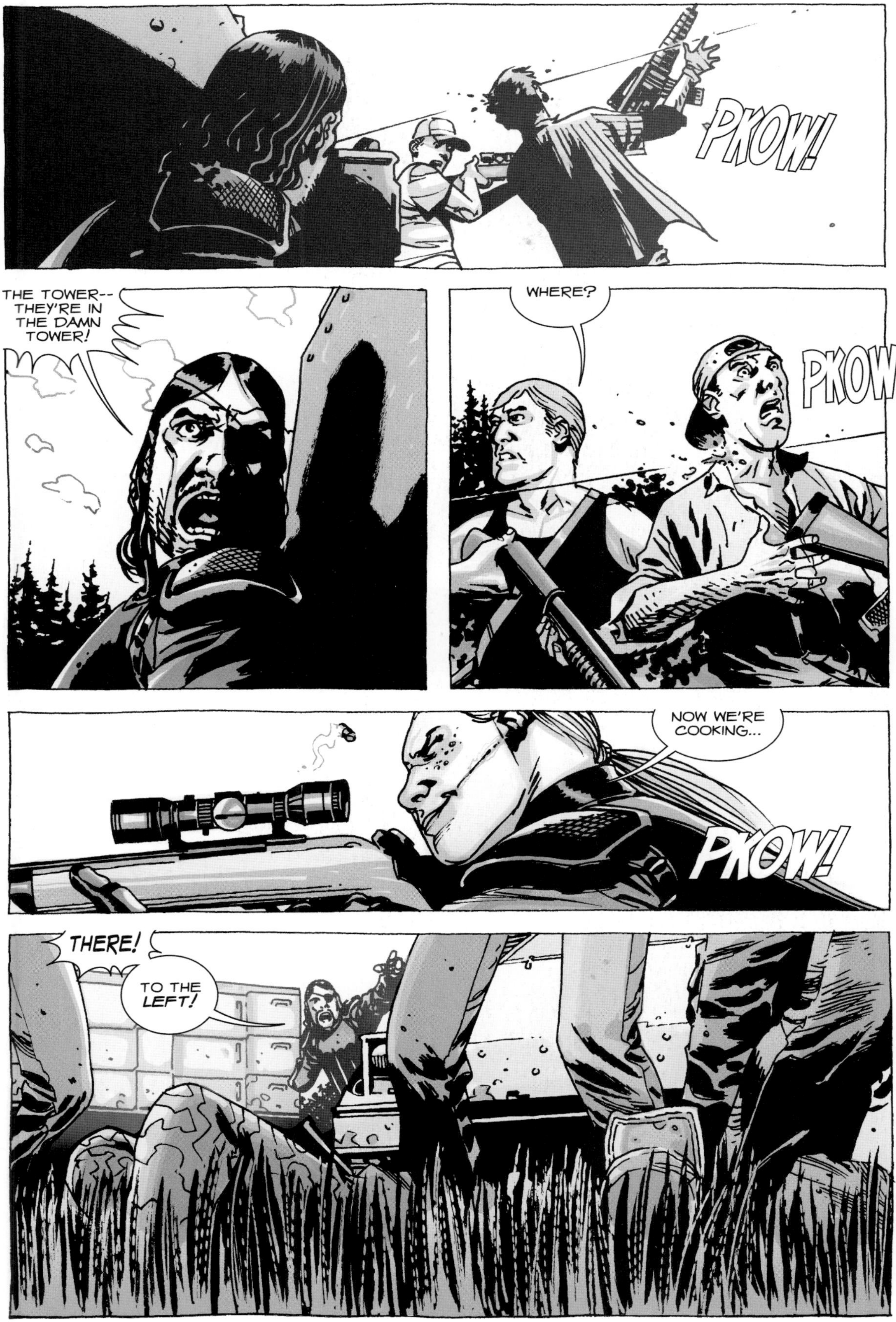
PKOW!
THE TOWER-- THEY'RE IN THE DAMN TOWER!
WHERE?
PKOW!
NOW WE'RE COOKING...
PKOW!
THERE!
TO THE LEFT!

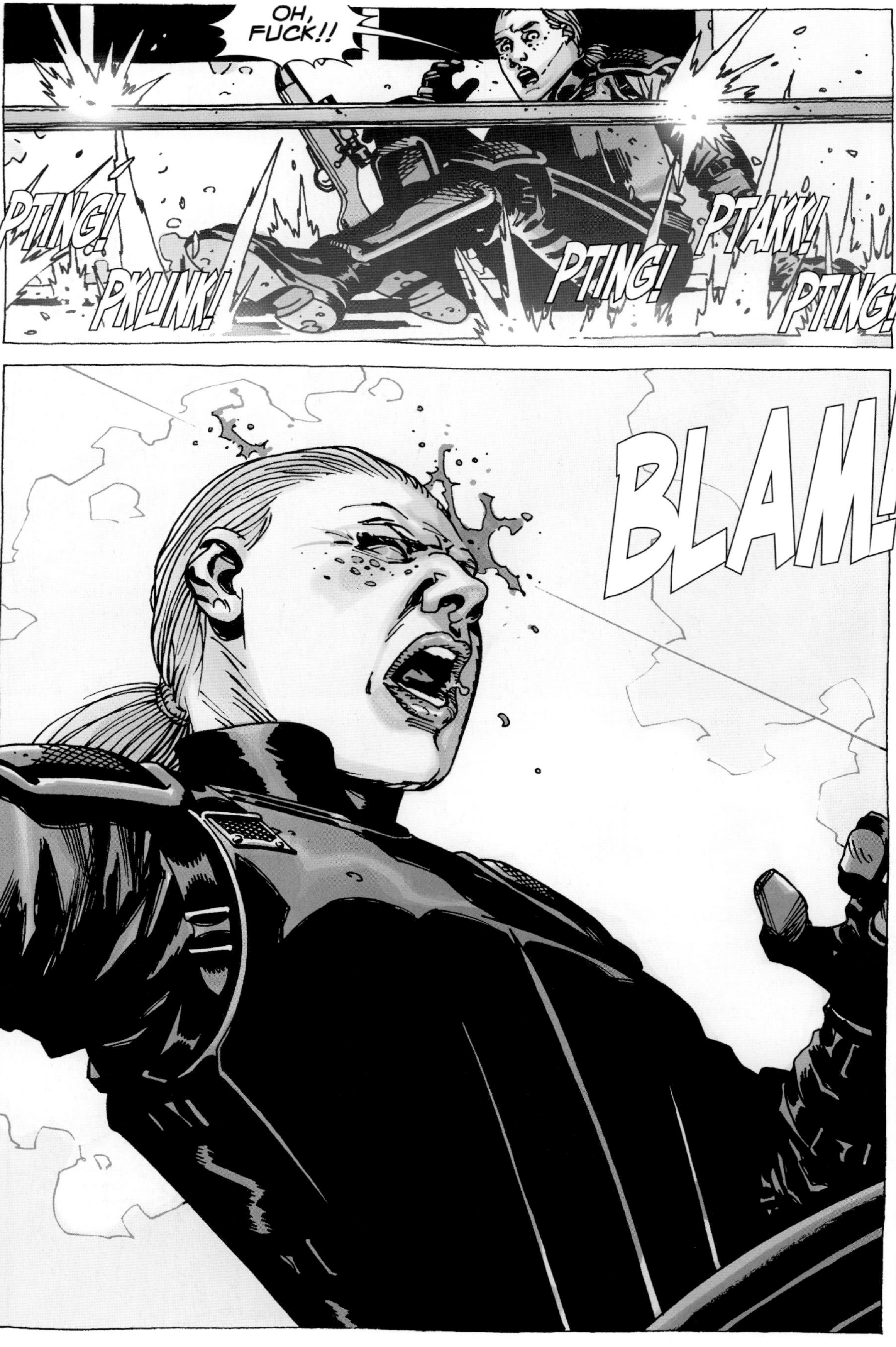
OH, FUCK!!
PTING!
PKUNK!
PTING!
PTAKK!
PTING!
BLAM!

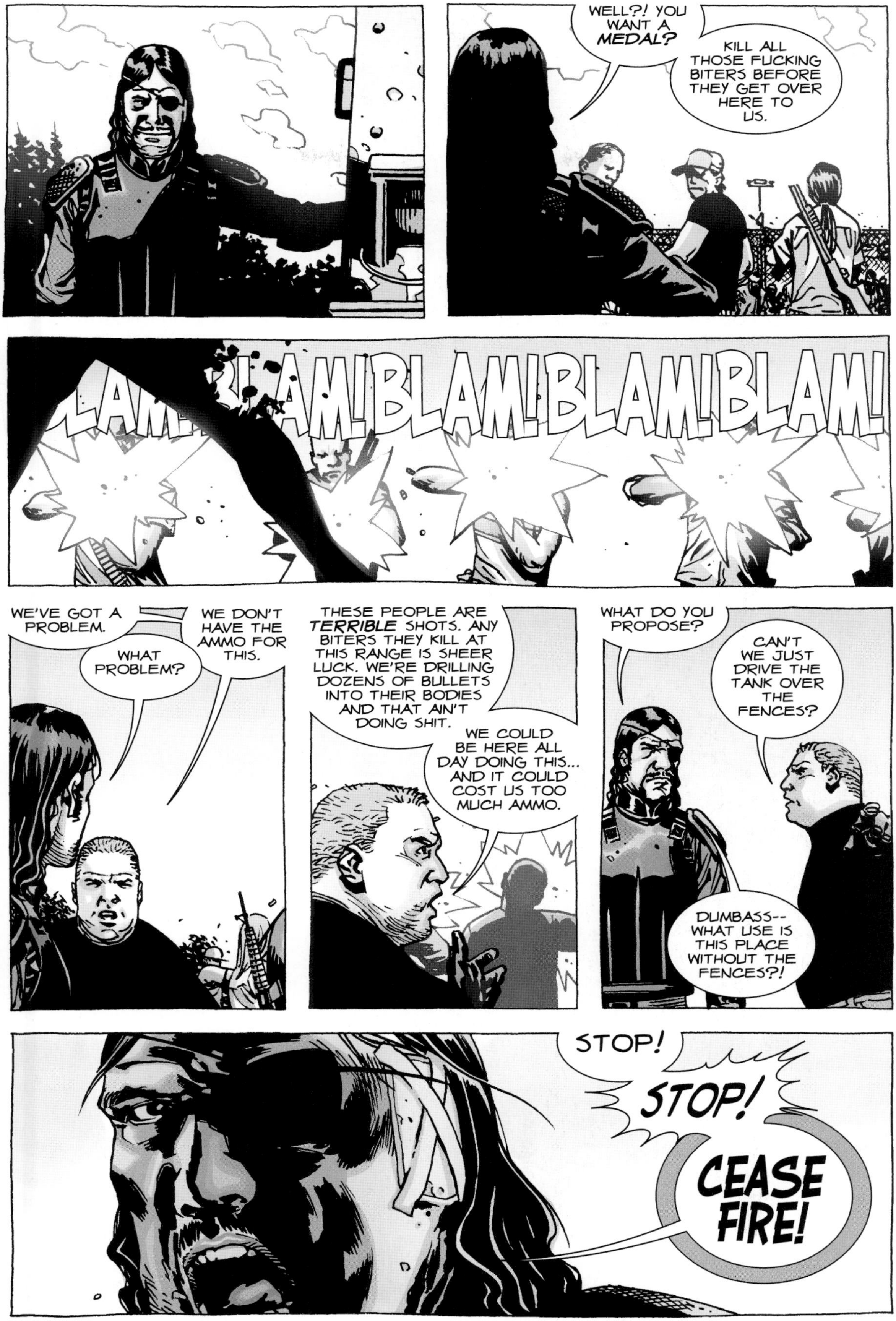
WELL?! YOU WANT A MEDAL?
KILL ALL THOSE FUCKING BITERS BEFORE THEY GET OVER HERE TO US.
BLAM! BLAM! BLAM! BLAM! BLAM!
WE'VE GOT A PROBLEM.
WHAT PROBLEM?
WE DON'T HAVE THE AMMO FOR THIS.
THESE PEOPLE ARE TERRIBLE SHOTS. ANY BITERS THEY KILL AT THIS RANGE IS SHEER LUCK. WE'RE DRILLING DOZENS OF BULLETS INTO THEIR BODIES AND THAT AIN'T DOING SHIT.
WE COULD BE HERE ALL DAY DOING THIS... AND IT COULD COST US TOO MUCH AMMO.
WHAT DO YOU PROPOSE?
CAN'T WE JUST DRIVE THE TANK OVER THE FENCES?
DUMBASS-- WHAT USE IS THIS PLACE WITHOUT THE FENCES?!
STOP!
STOP!
CEASE FIRE!

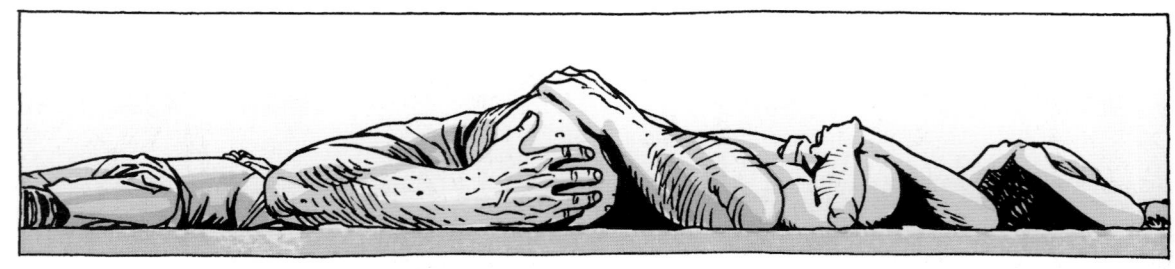

THEY STOPPED.

SHOULD WE STAY DOWN? WHAT DO WE DO?

STAY DOWN. CRAWL CLOSE-- WE GOTTA WORK THIS OUT.

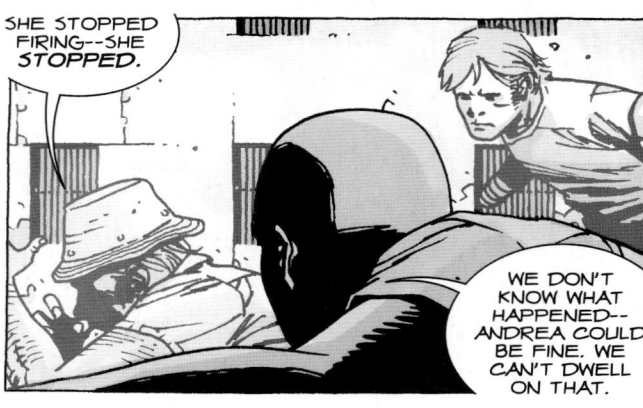

SHE STOPPED FIRING--SHE STOPPED.

WE DON'T KNOW WHAT HAPPENED-- ANDREA COULD BE FINE. WE CAN'T DWELL ON THAT.

THEY STOPPED FIRING... WHAT SHOULD WE DO?

WE SHOULD RUN! WE GOTTA MAKE A RUN FOR IT. THEY DON'T HAVE ALL SIDES OF THE PRISON COVERED-- WE COULD STILL GET OUT!

NO!

THEY COULD HAVE PLANNED FOR THAT. WE'RE SAFEST HERE. WE'RE NOT GOING ANYWHERE.

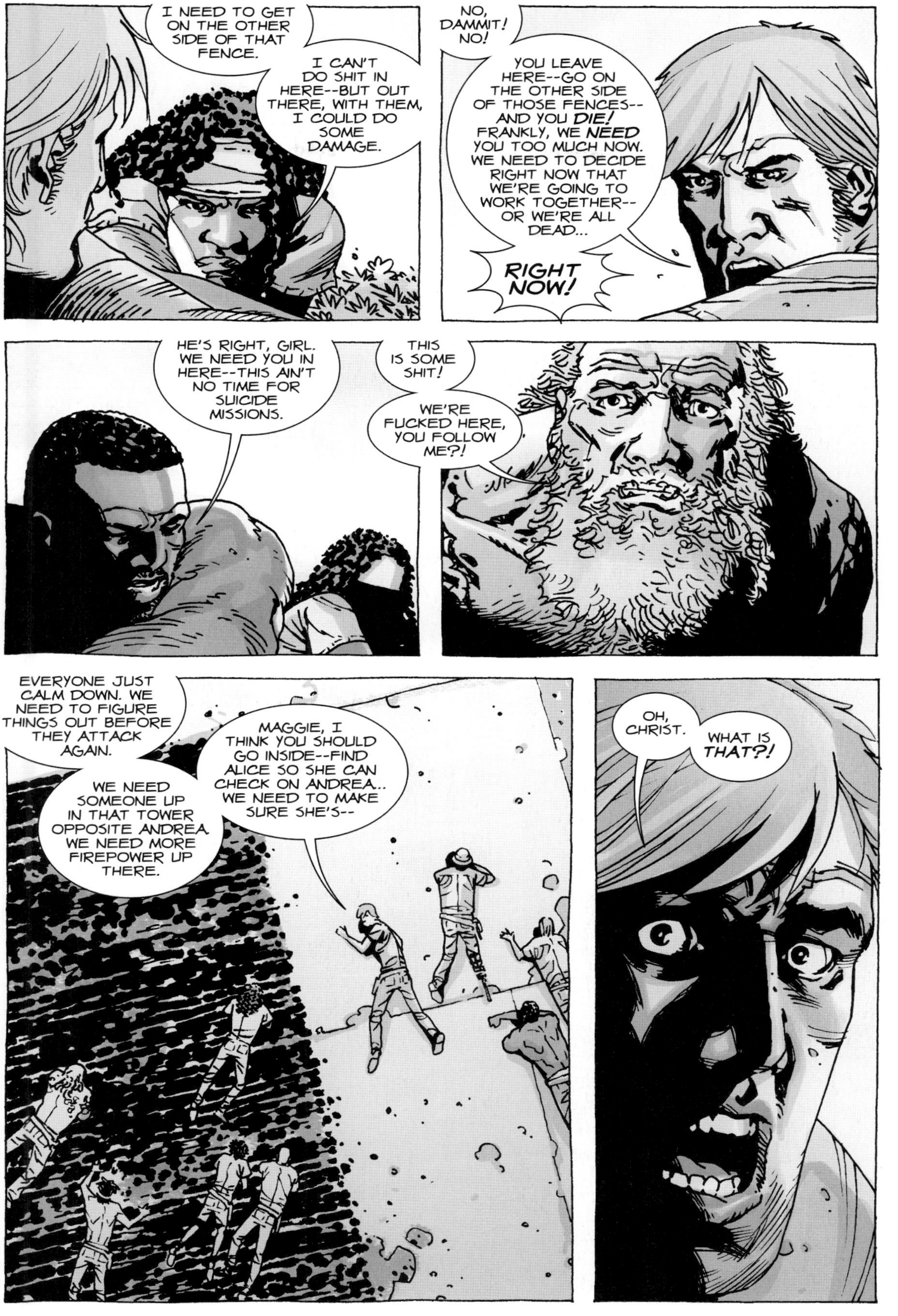
I NEED TO GET ON THE OTHER SIDE OF THAT FENCE.
I CAN'T DO SHIT IN HERE--BUT OUT THERE, WITH THEM, I COULD DO SOME DAMAGE.
NO, DAMMIT! NO!
YOU LEAVE HERE--GO ON THE OTHER SIDE OF THOSE FENCES--AND YOU DIE! FRANKLY, WE NEED YOU TOO MUCH NOW. WE NEED TO DECIDE RIGHT NOW THAT WE'RE GOING TO WORK TOGETHER--OR WE'RE ALL DEAD...
RIGHT NOW!
HE'S RIGHT, GIRL. WE NEED YOU IN HERE--THIS AIN'T NO TIME FOR SUICIDE MISSIONS.
THIS IS SOME SHIT!
WE'RE FUCKED HERE, YOU FOLLOW ME?!
EVERYONE JUST CALM DOWN. WE NEED TO FIGURE THINGS OUT BEFORE THEY ATTACK AGAIN.
WE NEED SOMEONE UP IN THAT TOWER OPPOSITE ANDREA. WE NEED MORE FIREPOWER UP THERE.
MAGGIE, I THINK YOU SHOULD GO INSIDE--FIND ALICE SO SHE CAN CHECK ON ANDREA.. WE NEED TO MAKE SURE SHE'S--
OH, CHRIST.
WHAT IS THAT?!

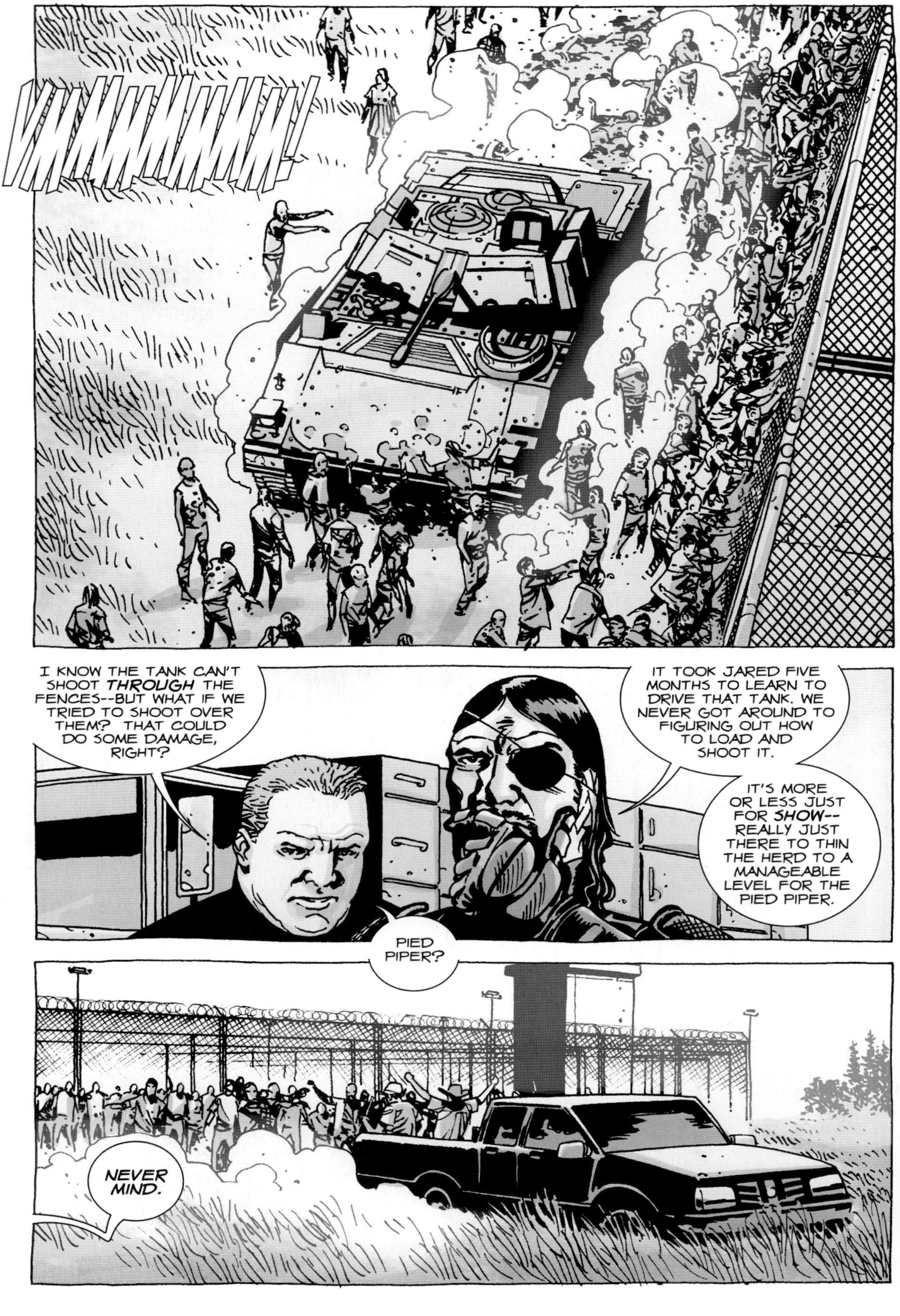
I KNOW THE TANK CAN'T SHOOT THROUGH THE FENCES--BUT WHAT IF WE TRIED TO SHOOT OVER THEM? THAT COULD DO SOME DAMAGE, RIGHT?
IT TOOK JARED FIVE MONTHS TO LEARN TO DRIVE THAT TANK. WE NEVER GOT AROUND TO FIGURING OUT HOW TO LOAD AND SHOOT IT.
IT'S MORE OR LESS JUST FOR SHOW-- REALLY JUST THERE TO THIN THE HERD TO A MANAGEABLE LEVEL FOR THE PIED PIPER.
PIED PIPER?
NEVER MIND.

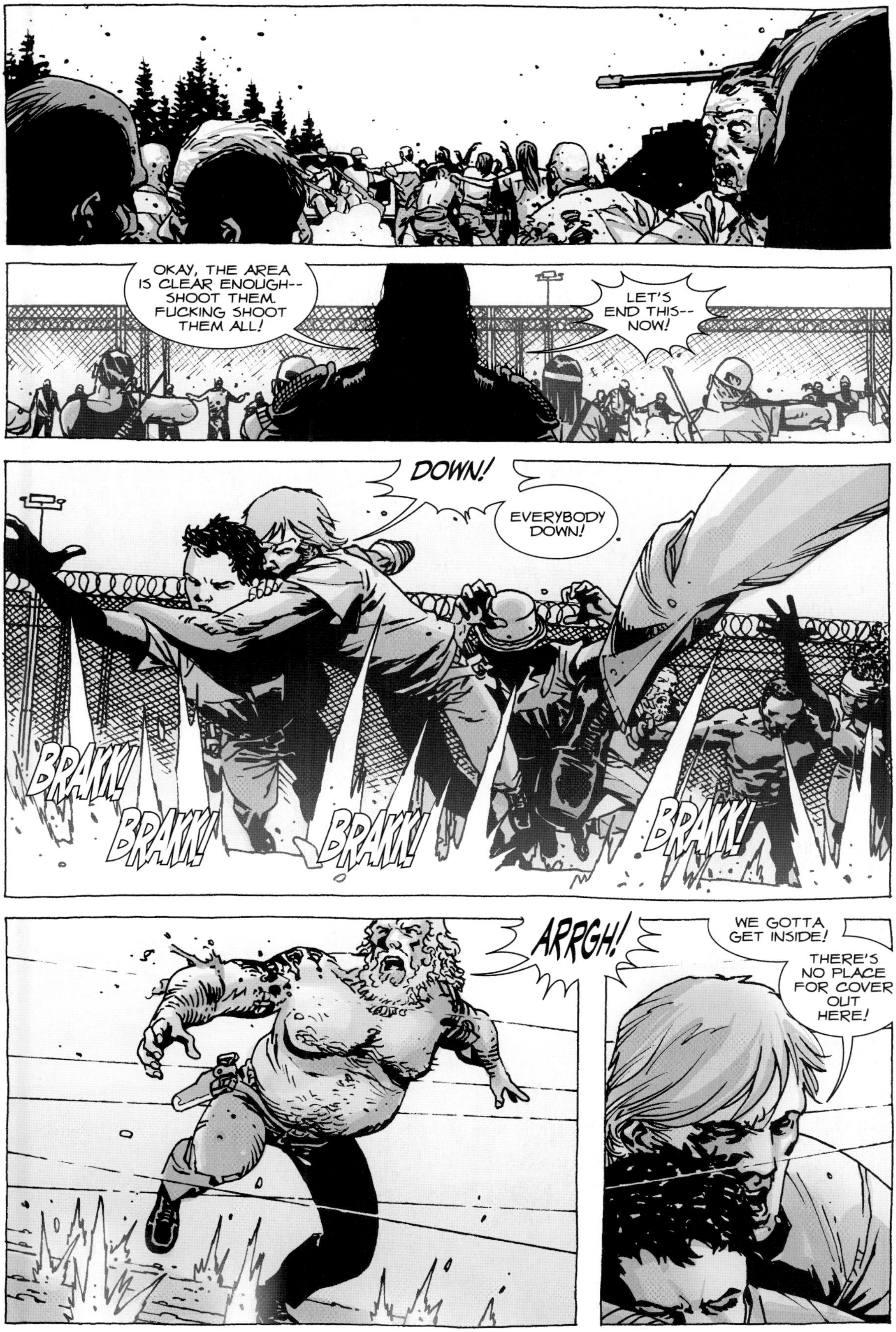
OKAY, THE AREA IS CLEAR ENOUGH-- SHOOT THEM. FUCKING SHOOT THEM ALL!
LET'S END THIS-- NOW!
DOWN!
EVERYBODY DOWN!
BRAKK!
BRAKK!
BRAKK!
BRAKK!
ARRGH!
WE GOTTA GET INSIDE!
THERE'S NO PLACE FOR COVER OUT HERE!

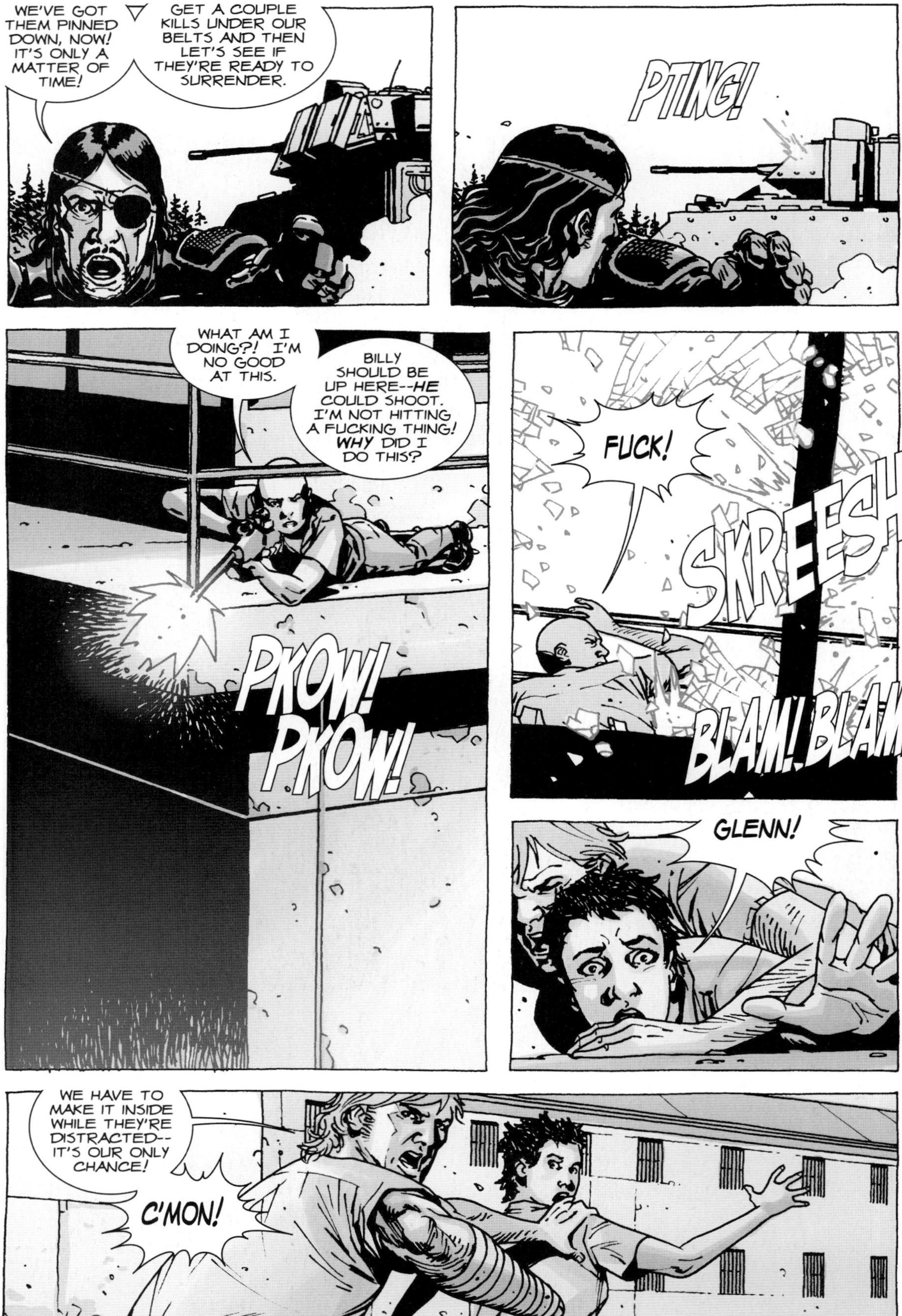
WE'VE GOT THEM PINNED DOWN, NOW! IT'S ONLY A MATTER OF TIME!
GET A COUPLE KILLS UNDER OUR BELTS AND THEN LET'S SEE IF THEY'RE READY TO SURRENDER.
PTING!
WHAT AM I DOING?! I'M NO GOOD AT THIS.
BILLY SHOULD BE UP HERE--HE COULD SHOOT. I'M NOT HITTING A FUCKING THING! WHY DID I DO THIS?
PKOW! PKOW!
FUCK!
SKREESH!
BLAM! BLAM!
GLENN!
WE HAVE TO MAKE IT INSIDE WHILE THEY'RE DISTRACTED-- IT'S OUR ONLY CHANCE!
C'MON!

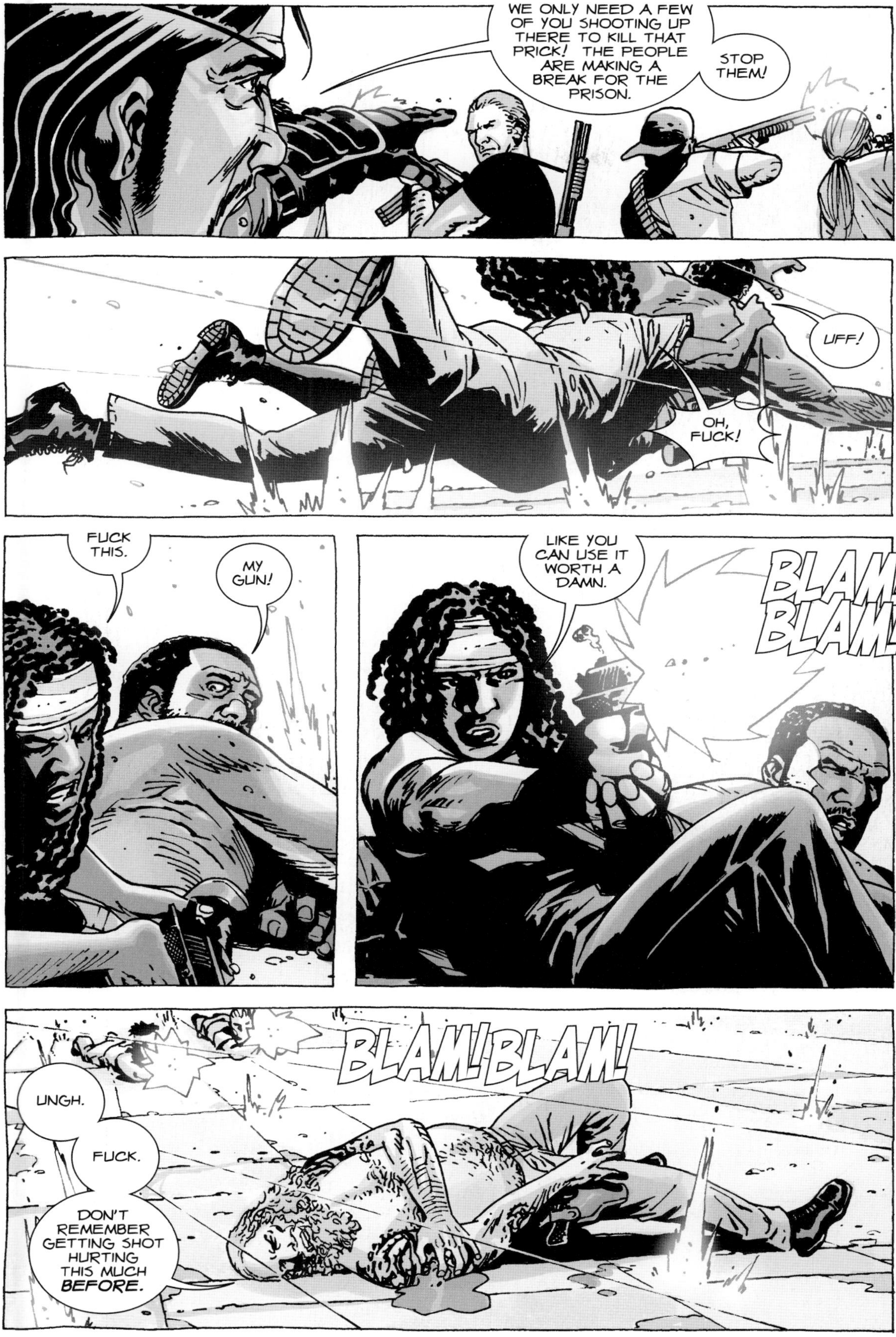
WE ONLY NEED A FEW OF YOU SHOOTING UP THERE TO KILL THAT PRICK! THE PEOPLE ARE MAKING A BREAK FOR THE PRISON.
STOP THEM!
UFF!
OH, FUCK!
FUCK THIS.
MY GUN!
LIKE YOU CAN USE IT WORTH A DAMN.
BLAM! BLAM!
BLAM! BLAM!
UNGH.
FUCK.
DON'T REMEMBER GETTING SHOT HURTING THIS MUCH *BEFORE*.

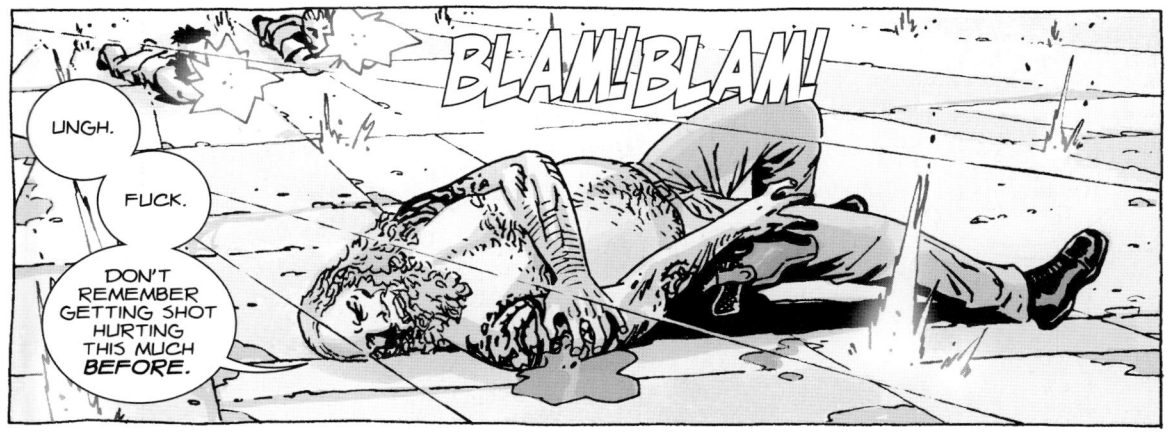

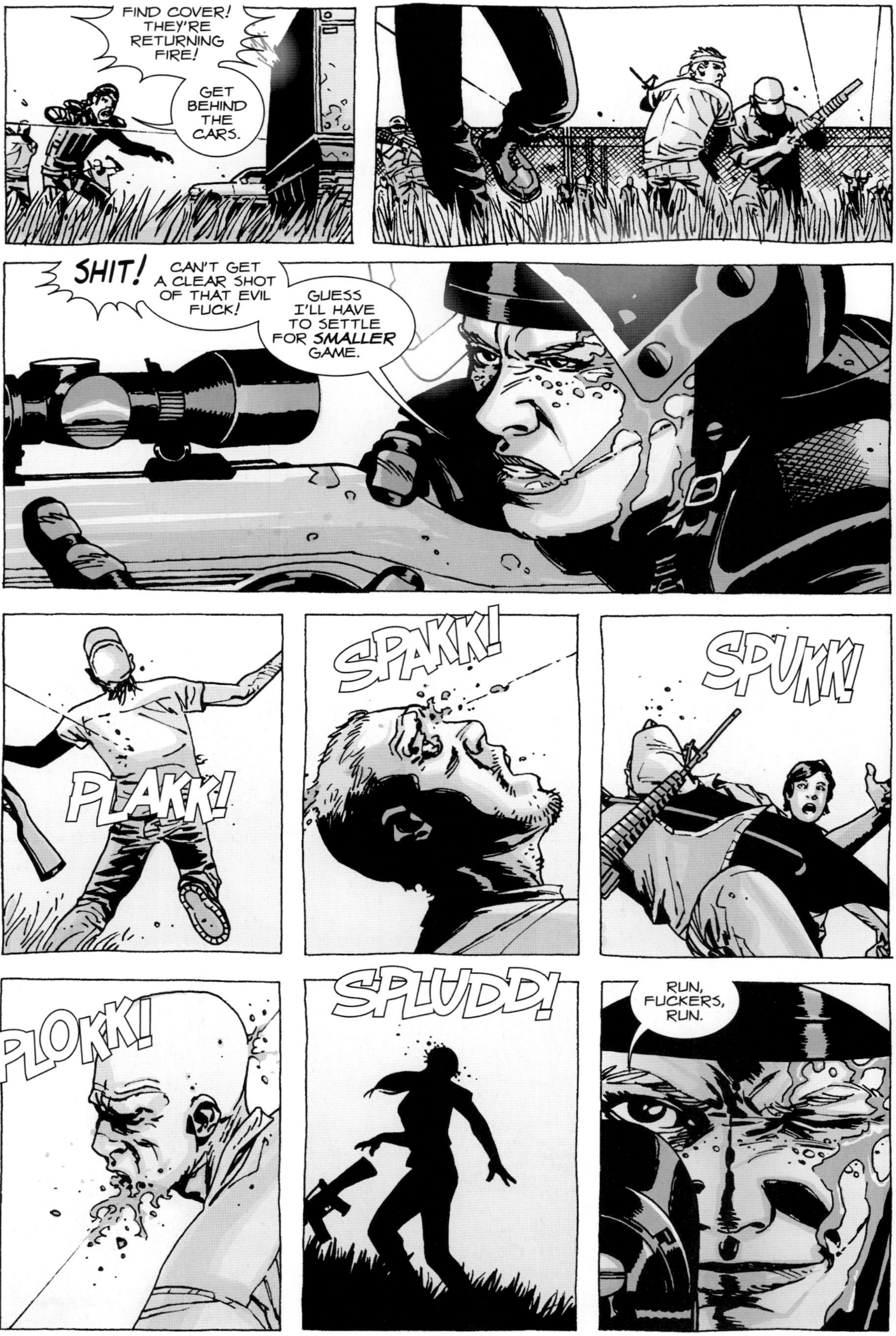

FIND COVER! THEY'RE RETURNING FIRE!
GET BEHIND THE CARS.
SHIT!
CAN'T GET A CLEAR SHOT OF THAT EVIL FUCK!
GUESS I'LL HAVE TO SETTLE FOR SMALLER GAME.
PLAKK!
SPAKK!
SPUKK!
PLOKK!
SPLUDD!
RUN, FUCKERS, RUN.

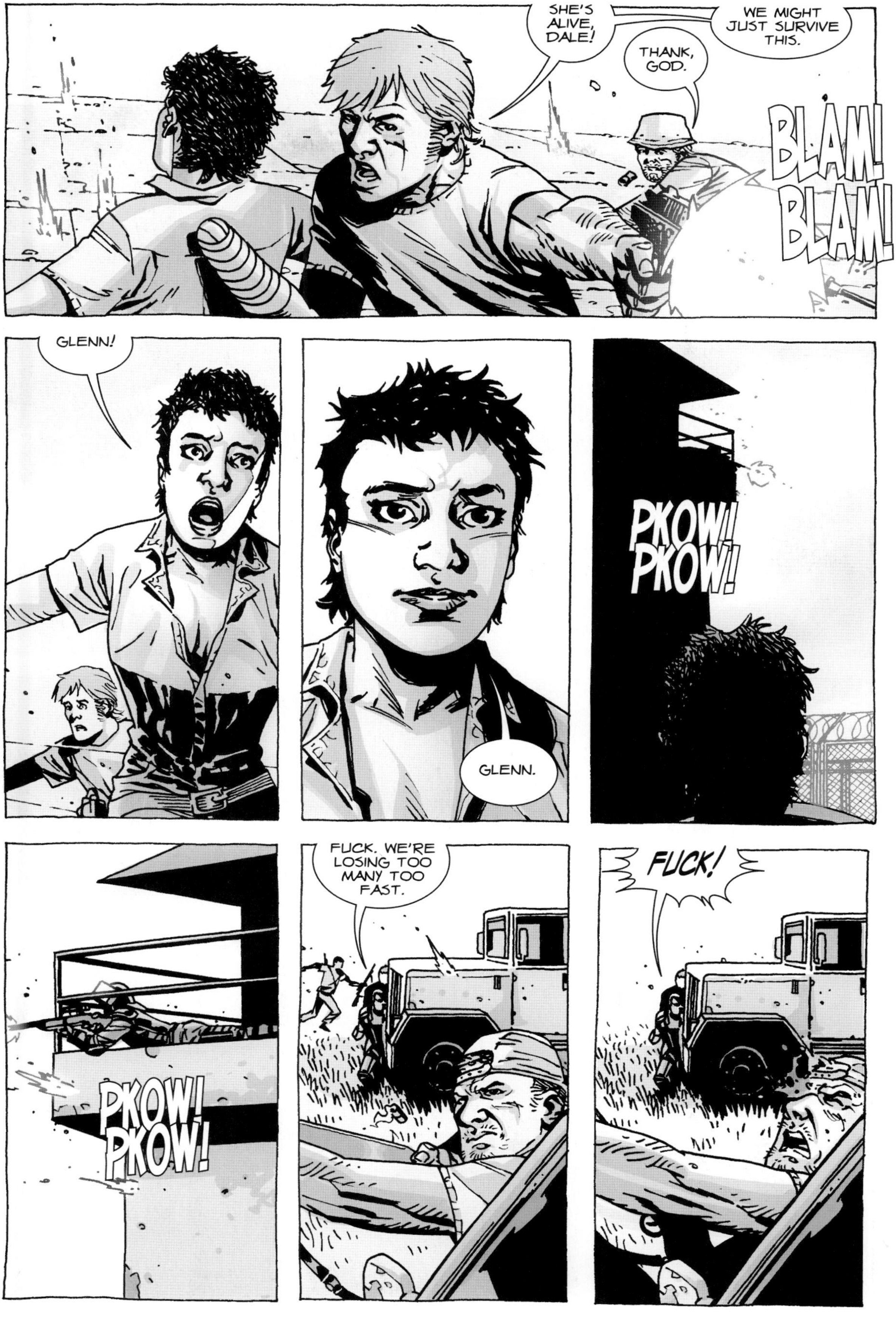
SHE'S ALIVE, DALE!
THANK, GOD.
WE MIGHT JUST SURVIVE THIS.
BLAM! BLAM!
GLENN!
GLENN.
PKOW! PKOW!
PKOW! PKOW!
FUCK. WE'RE LOSING TOO MANY TOO FAST.
FUCK!

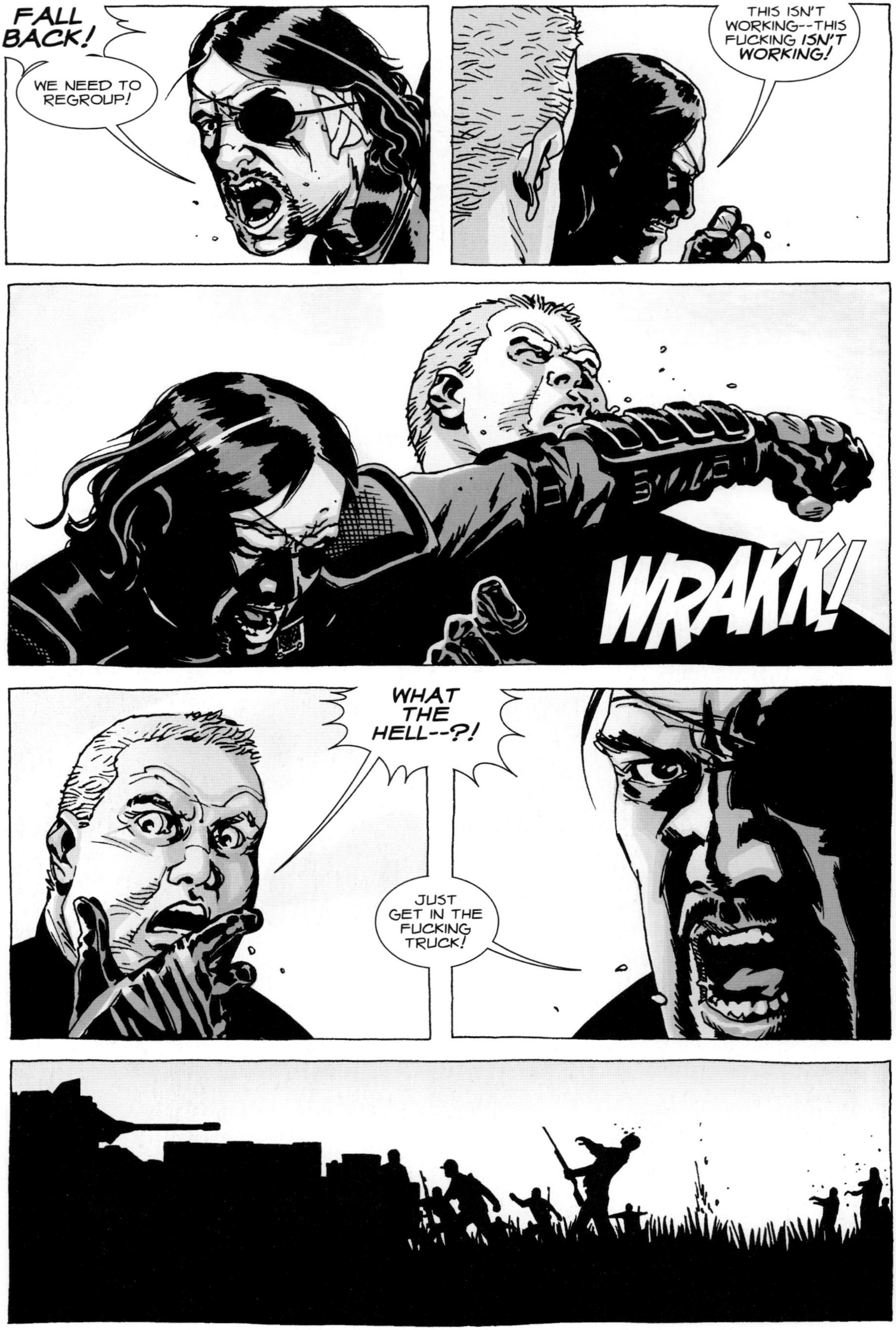
FALL BACK!
WE NEED TO REGROUP!
THIS ISN'T WORKING--THIS FUCKING ISN'T WORKING!
WRAKK!
WHAT THE HELL--?!
JUST GET IN THE FUCKING TRUCK!

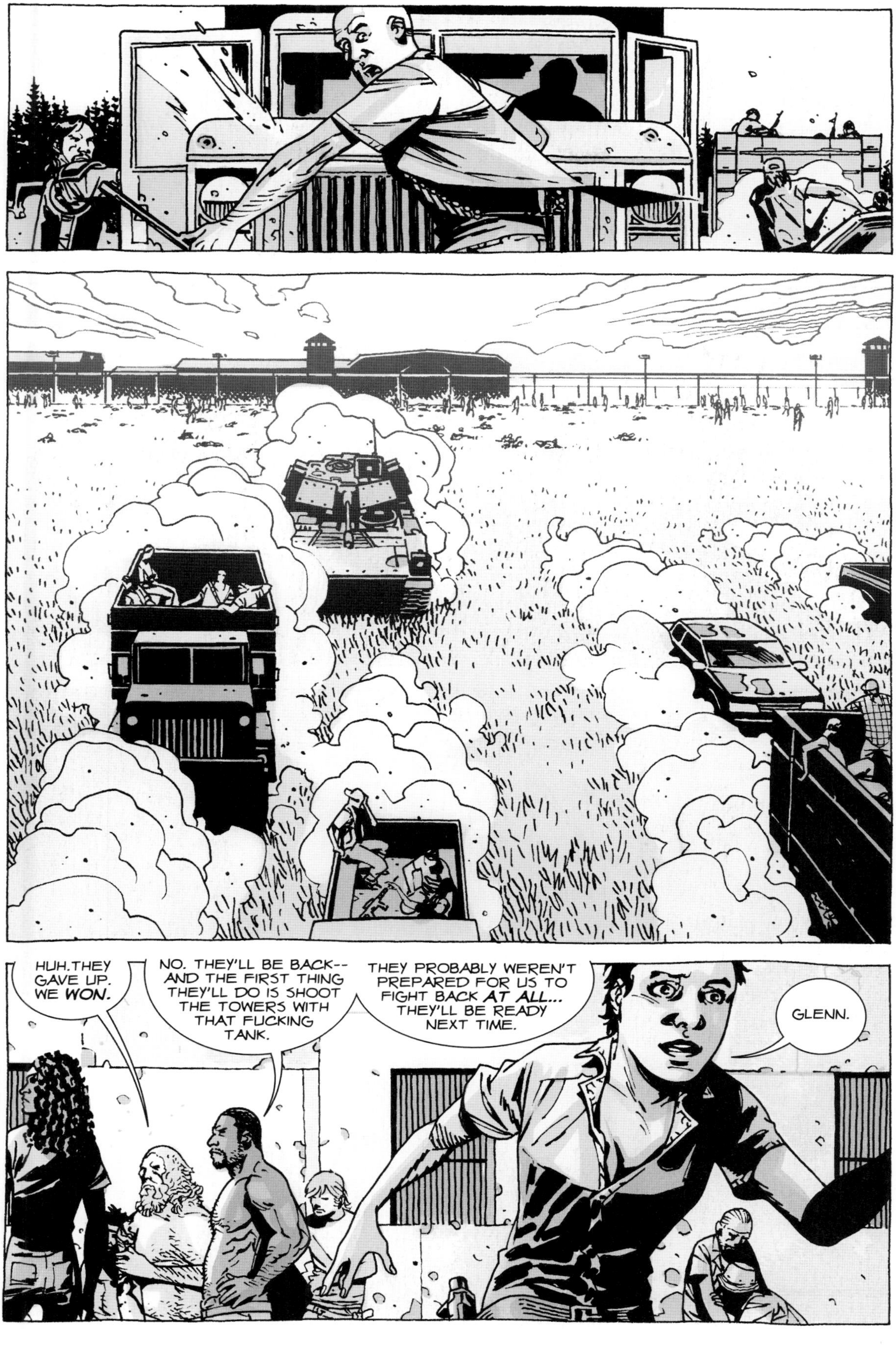
HUH. THEY GAVE UP. WE **WON.**
NO. THEY'LL BE BACK-- AND THE FIRST THING THEY'LL DO IS SHOOT THE TOWERS WITH THAT FUCKING TANK.
THEY PROBABLY WEREN'T PREPARED FOR US TO FIGHT BACK **AT ALL...** THEY'LL BE READY NEXT TIME.
GLENN.

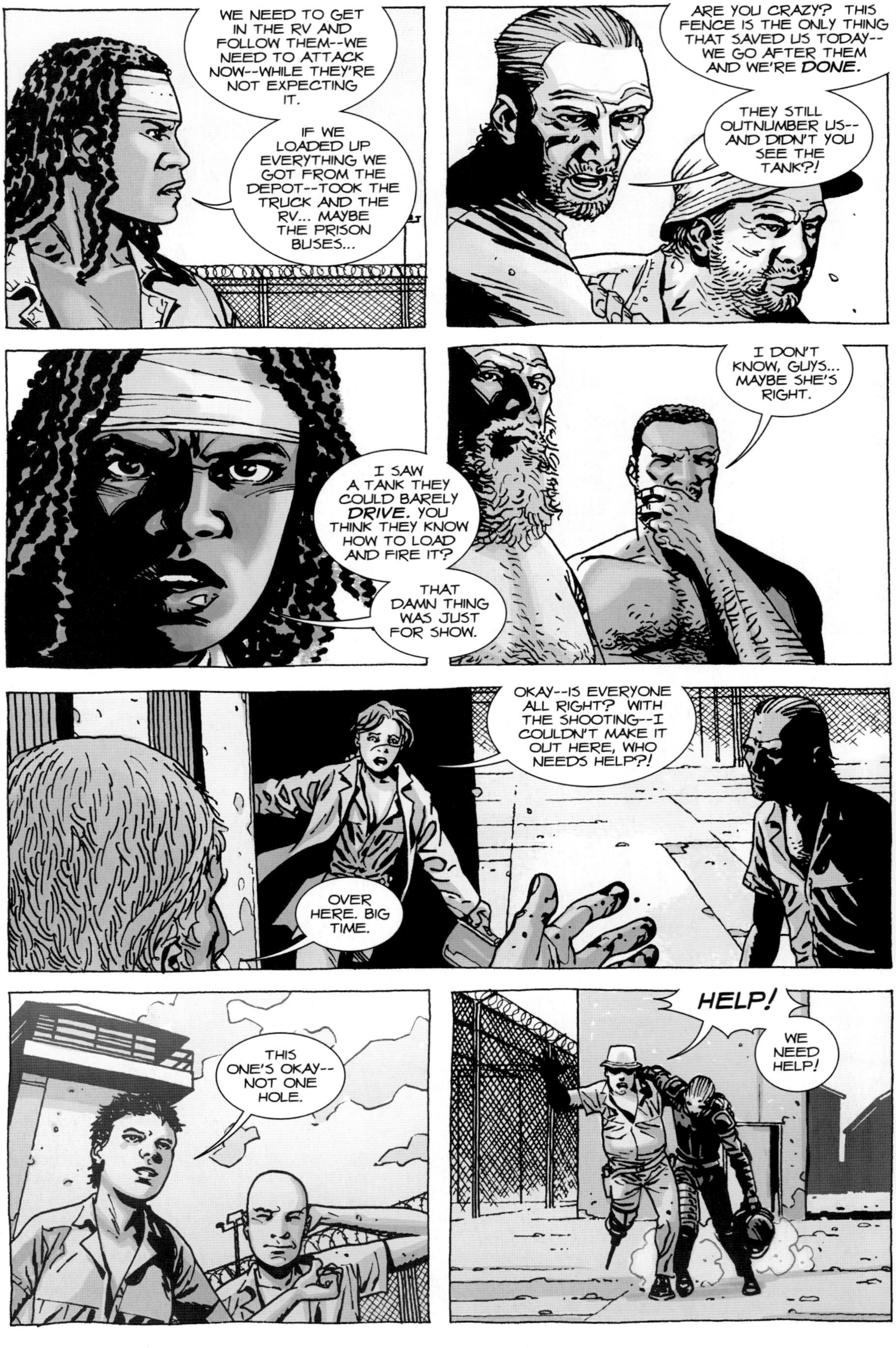
WE NEED TO GET IN THE RV AND FOLLOW THEM--WE NEED TO ATTACK NOW--WHILE THEY'RE NOT EXPECTING IT.
IF WE LOADED UP EVERYTHING WE GOT FROM THE DEPOT--TOOK THE TRUCK AND THE RV... MAYBE THE PRISON BUSES...
ARE YOU CRAZY? THIS FENCE IS THE ONLY THING THAT SAVED US TODAY-- WE GO AFTER THEM AND WE'RE DONE.
THEY STILL OUTNUMBER US-- AND DIDN'T YOU SEE THE TANK?!
I SAW A TANK THEY COULD BARELY DRIVE. YOU THINK THEY KNOW HOW TO LOAD AND FIRE IT?
THAT DAMN THING WAS JUST FOR SHOW.
I DON'T KNOW, GUYS... MAYBE SHE'S RIGHT.
OKAY--IS EVERYONE ALL RIGHT? WITH THE SHOOTING--I COULDN'T MAKE IT OUT HERE, WHO NEEDS HELP?!
OVER HERE. BIG TIME.
THIS ONE'S OKAY-- NOT ONE HOLE.
HELP!
WE NEED HELP!

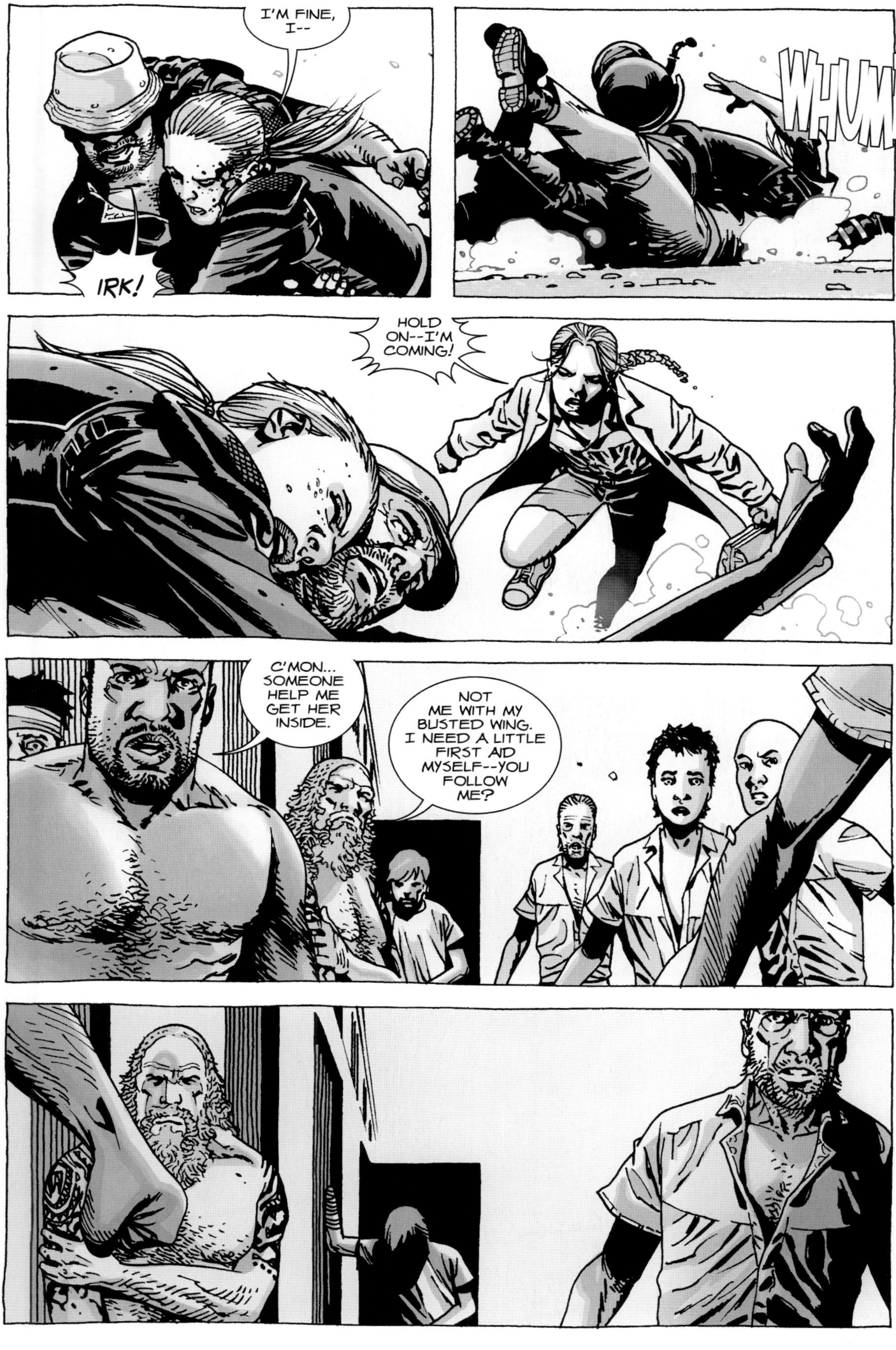
I'M FINE, I--
IRK!
WHUMP!
HOLD ON--I'M COMING!
C'MON... SOMEONE HELP ME GET HER INSIDE.
NOT ME WITH MY BUSTED WING. I NEED A LITTLE FIRST AID MYSELF--YOU FOLLOW ME?

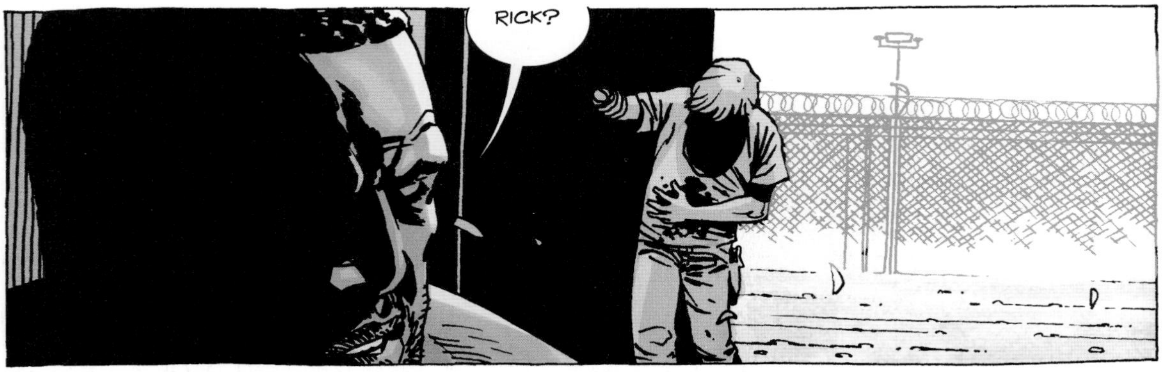
RICK?

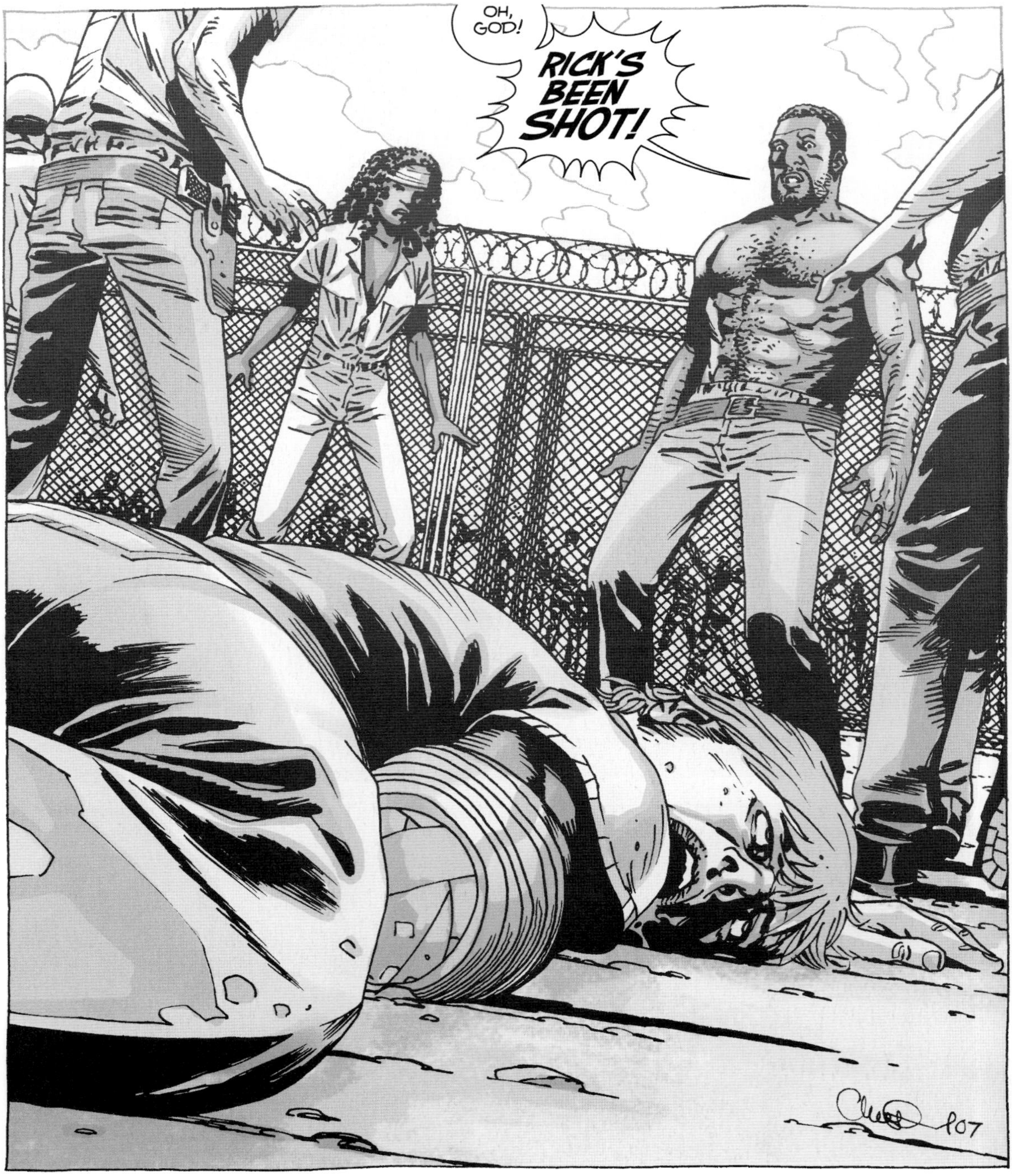
OH, GOD!
RICK'S BEEN SHOT!

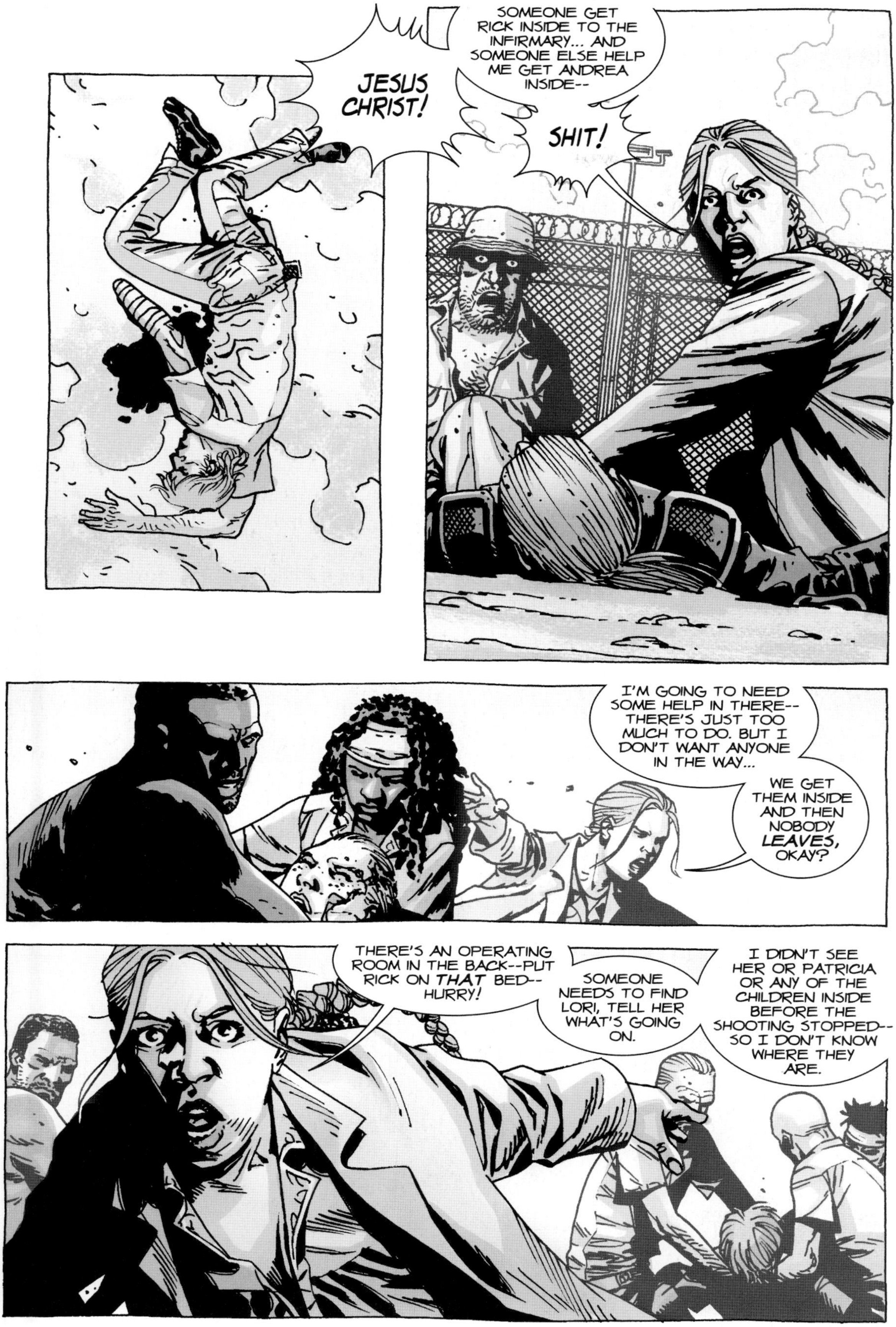
JESUS CHRIST!
SOMEONE GET RICK INSIDE TO THE INFIRMARY... AND SOMEONE ELSE HELP ME GET ANDREA INSIDE--
SHIT!
I'M GOING TO NEED SOME HELP IN THERE-- THERE'S JUST TOO MUCH TO DO. BUT I DON'T WANT ANYONE IN THE WAY...
WE GET THEM INSIDE AND THEN NOBODY LEAVES, OKAY?
THERE'S AN OPERATING ROOM IN THE BACK--PUT RICK ON THAT BED-- HURRY!
SOMEONE NEEDS TO FIND LORI, TELL HER WHAT'S GOING ON.
I DIDN'T SEE HER OR PATRICIA OR ANY OF THE CHILDREN INSIDE BEFORE THE SHOOTING STOPPED-- SO I DON'T KNOW WHERE THEY ARE.

HUGHN?

CRAP.

DID WE WIN?

NOT YET--YOU HAVEN'T BEEN OUT LONG, A LITTLE OVER AN HOUR, MAYBE AN HOUR AND A HALF.

YOU WEREN'T HURT TOO BAD. THE BULLET REALLY JUST SCRAPED THE SIDE OF YOUR SKULL--CUT A NICE GROOVE IN IT BUT DIDN'T CRACK IT.

YOU'LL HAVE A HELL OF A SCAR, HAIR WON'T GROW BACK IN PLACES--BUT YOU'RE GOING TO BE FINE. YOU BARELY LOST ANY BLOOD, NOT ENOUGH TO CAUSE ANY COMPLICATIONS.

YOU'RE GOING TO BE *FINE*.

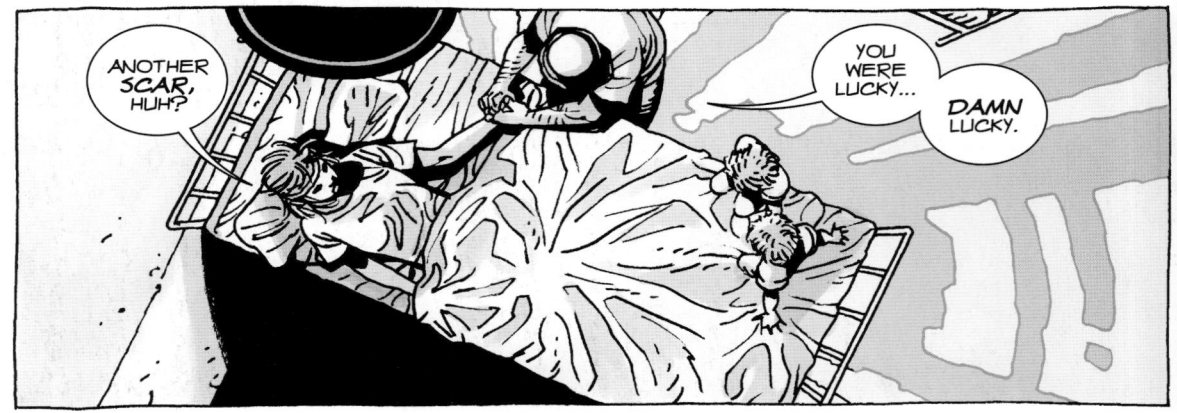

ANOTHER *SCAR*, HUH?

YOU WERE LUCKY...

DAMN LUCKY.

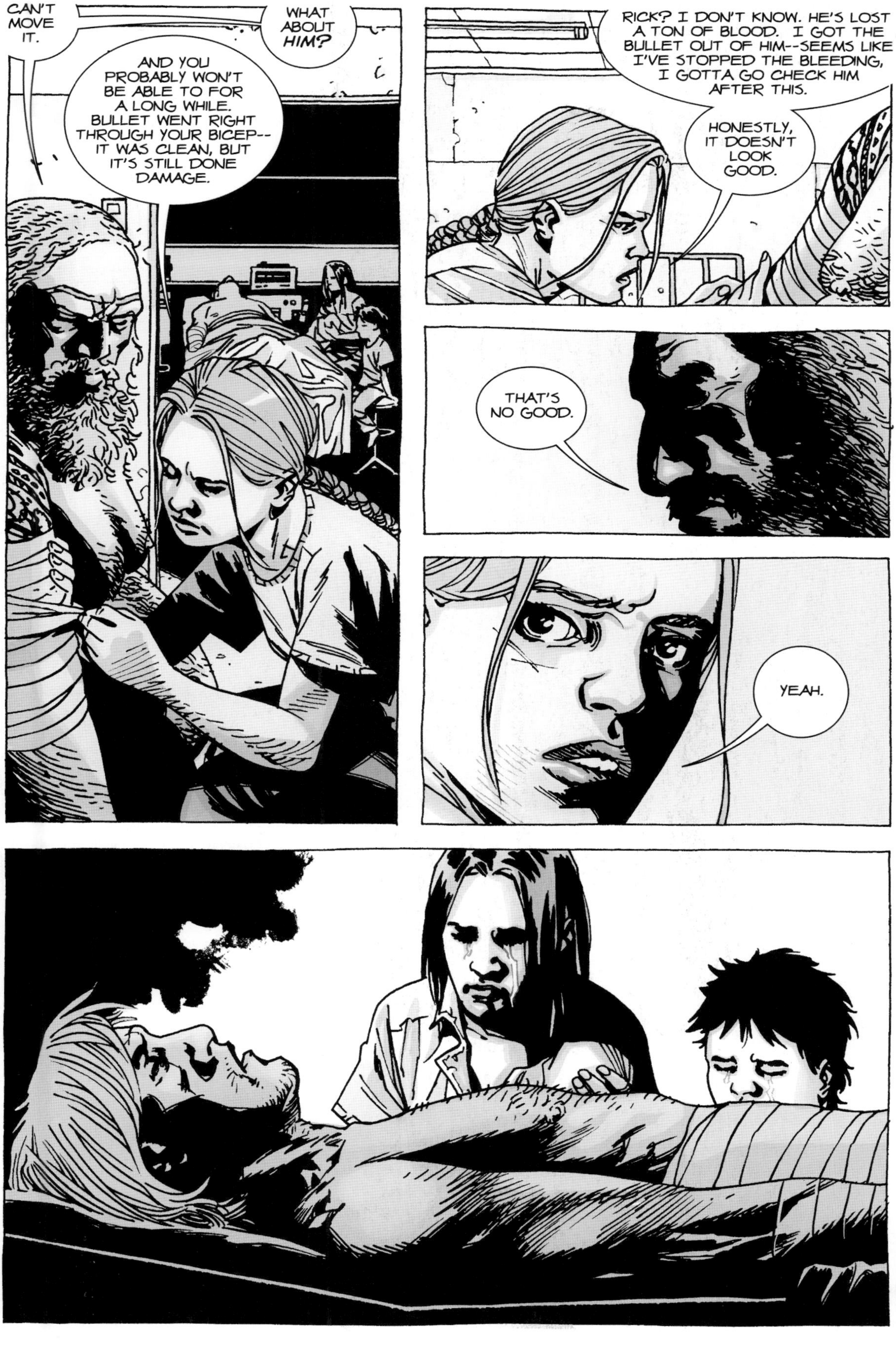
CAN'T MOVE IT.
WHAT ABOUT HIM?
AND YOU PROBABLY WON'T BE ABLE TO FOR A LONG WHILE. BULLET WENT RIGHT THROUGH YOUR BICEP-- IT WAS CLEAN, BUT IT'S STILL DONE DAMAGE.
RICK? I DON'T KNOW. HE'S LOST A TON OF BLOOD. I GOT THE BULLET OUT OF HIM--SEEMS LIKE I'VE STOPPED THE BLEEDING, I GOTTA GO CHECK HIM AFTER THIS.
HONESTLY, IT DOESN'T LOOK GOOD.
THAT'S NO GOOD.
YEAH.

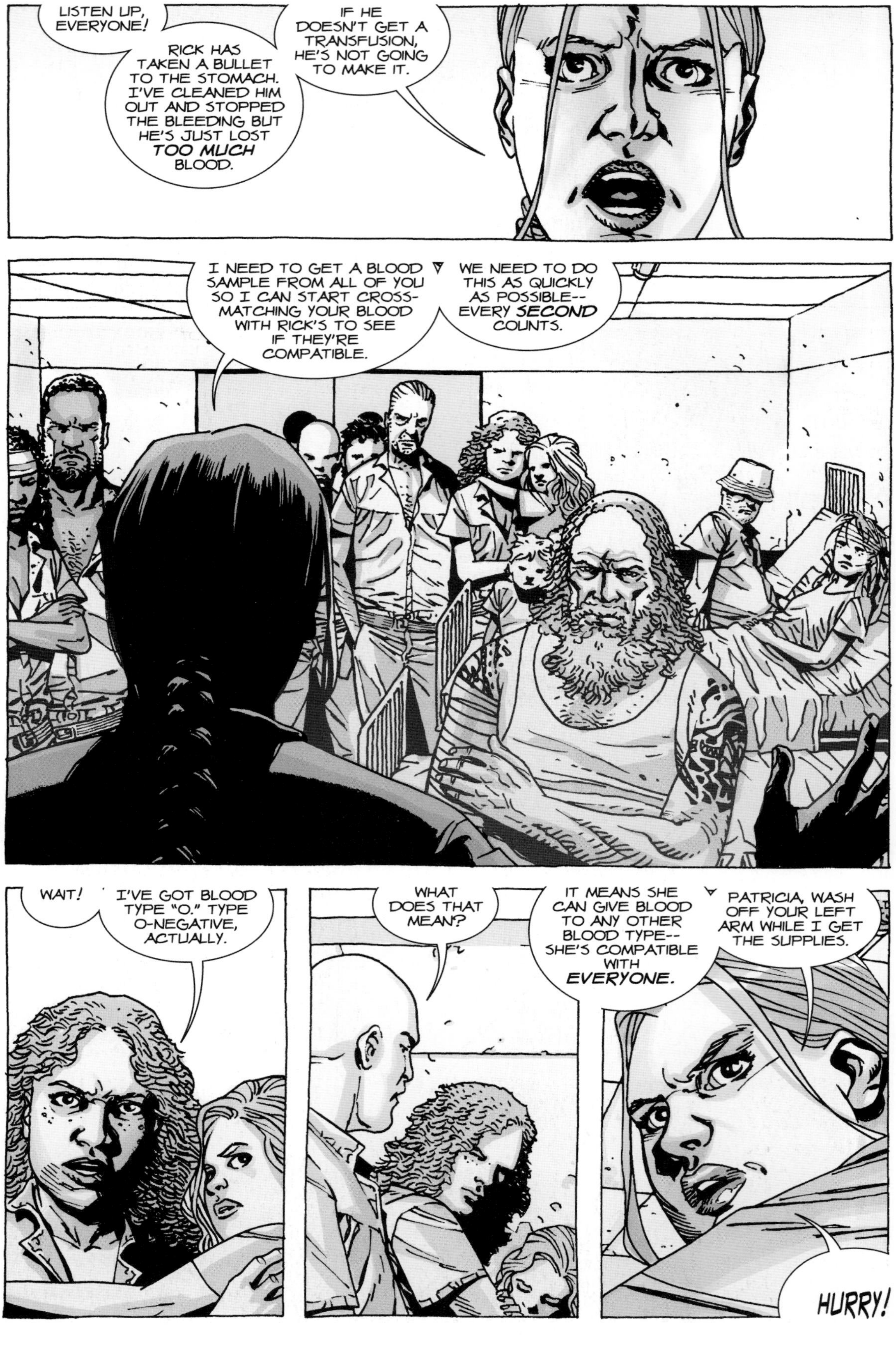
LISTEN UP, EVERYONE!
RICK HAS TAKEN A BULLET TO THE STOMACH. I'VE CLEANED HIM OUT AND STOPPED THE BLEEDING BUT HE'S JUST LOST TOO MUCH BLOOD.
IF HE DOESN'T GET A TRANSFUSION, HE'S NOT GOING TO MAKE IT.
I NEED TO GET A BLOOD SAMPLE FROM ALL OF YOU SO I CAN START CROSS-MATCHING YOUR BLOOD WITH RICK'S TO SEE IF THEY'RE COMPATIBLE.
WE NEED TO DO THIS AS QUICKLY AS POSSIBLE-- EVERY SECOND COUNTS.
WAIT!
I'VE GOT BLOOD TYPE "O." TYPE O-NEGATIVE, ACTUALLY.
WHAT DOES THAT MEAN?
IT MEANS SHE CAN GIVE BLOOD TO ANY OTHER BLOOD TYPE-- SHE'S COMPATIBLE WITH EVERYONE.
PATRICIA, WASH OFF YOUR LEFT ARM WHILE I GET THE SUPPLIES.
HURRY!

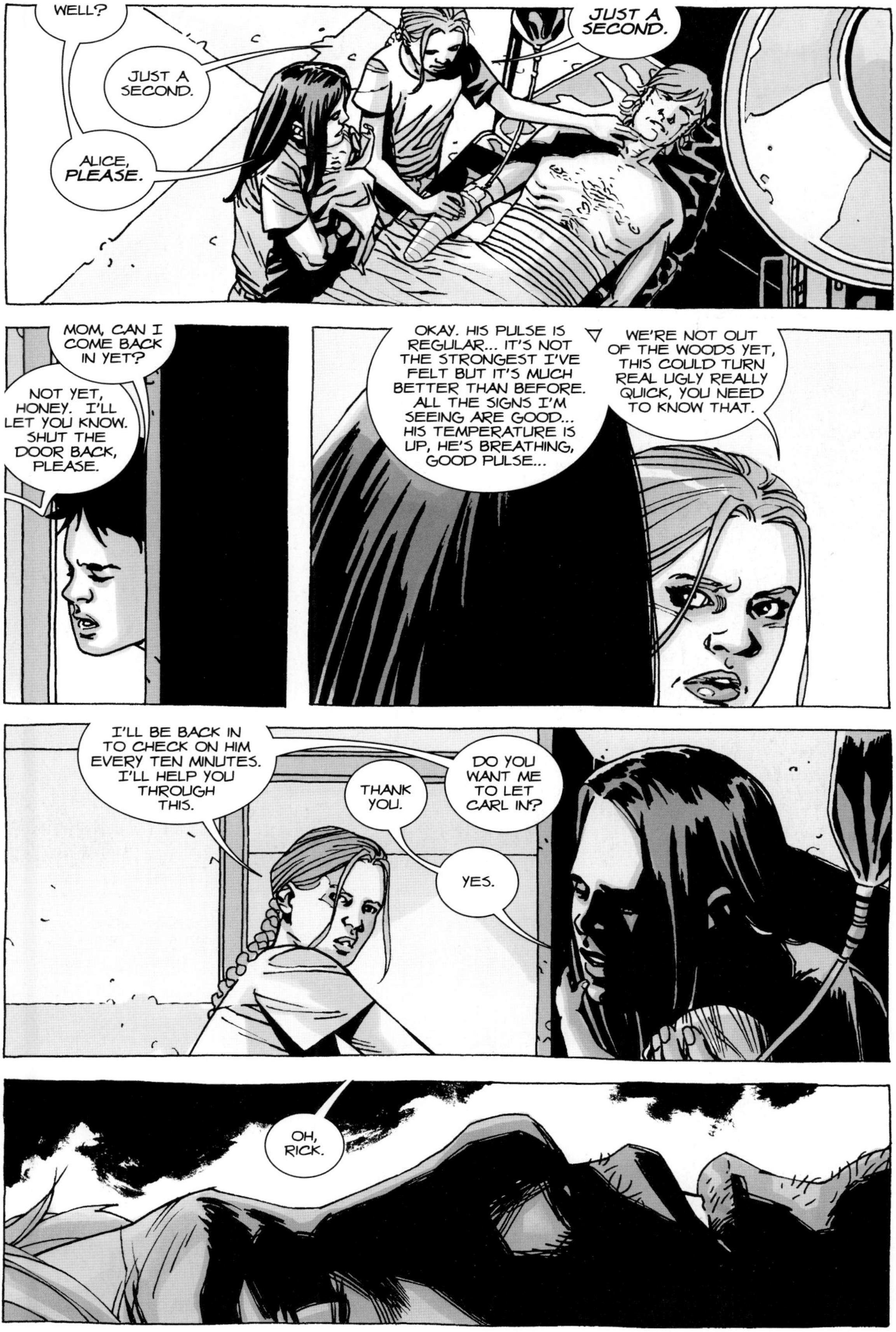
WELL?
JUST A SECOND.
ALICE, *PLEASE.*
JUST A SECOND.
MOM, CAN I COME BACK IN YET?
NOT YET, HONEY. I'LL LET YOU KNOW. SHUT THE DOOR BACK, PLEASE.
OKAY. HIS PULSE IS REGULAR... IT'S NOT THE STRONGEST I'VE FELT BUT IT'S MUCH BETTER THAN BEFORE. ALL THE SIGNS I'M SEEING ARE GOOD... HIS TEMPERATURE IS UP, HE'S BREATHING, GOOD PULSE...
WE'RE NOT OUT OF THE WOODS YET, THIS COULD TURN REAL UGLY REALLY QUICK, YOU NEED TO KNOW THAT.
I'LL BE BACK IN TO CHECK ON HIM EVERY TEN MINUTES. I'LL HELP YOU THROUGH THIS.
THANK YOU.
DO YOU WANT ME TO LET CARL IN?
YES.
OH, RICK.

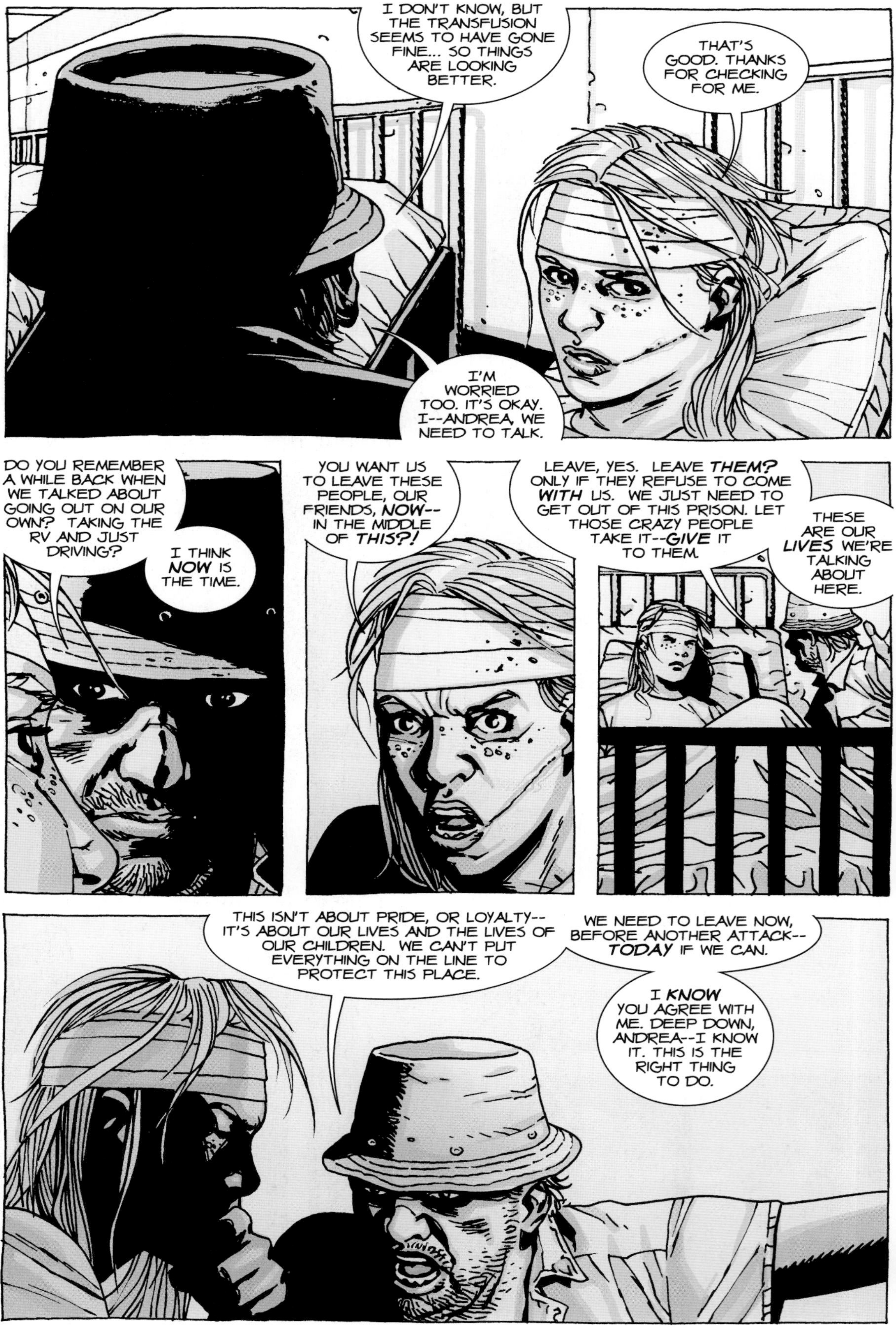
I DON'T KNOW, BUT THE TRANSFUSION SEEMS TO HAVE GONE FINE... SO THINGS ARE LOOKING BETTER.
THAT'S GOOD. THANKS FOR CHECKING FOR ME.
I'M WORRIED TOO. IT'S OKAY. I--ANDREA, WE NEED TO TALK.
DO YOU REMEMBER A WHILE BACK WHEN WE TALKED ABOUT GOING OUT ON OUR OWN? TAKING THE RV AND JUST DRIVING?
I THINK NOW IS THE TIME.
YOU WANT US TO LEAVE THESE PEOPLE, OUR FRIENDS, NOW-- IN THE MIDDLE OF THIS?!
LEAVE, YES. LEAVE THEM? ONLY IF THEY REFUSE TO COME WITH US. WE JUST NEED TO GET OUT OF THIS PRISON. LET THOSE CRAZY PEOPLE TAKE IT--GIVE IT TO THEM.
THESE ARE OUR LIVES WE'RE TALKING ABOUT HERE.
THIS ISN'T ABOUT PRIDE, OR LOYALTY-- IT'S ABOUT OUR LIVES AND THE LIVES OF OUR CHILDREN. WE CAN'T PUT EVERYTHING ON THE LINE TO PROTECT THIS PLACE.
WE NEED TO LEAVE NOW, BEFORE ANOTHER ATTACK-- TODAY IF WE CAN.
I KNOW YOU AGREE WITH ME. DEEP DOWN, ANDREA--I KNOW IT. THIS IS THE RIGHT THING TO DO.

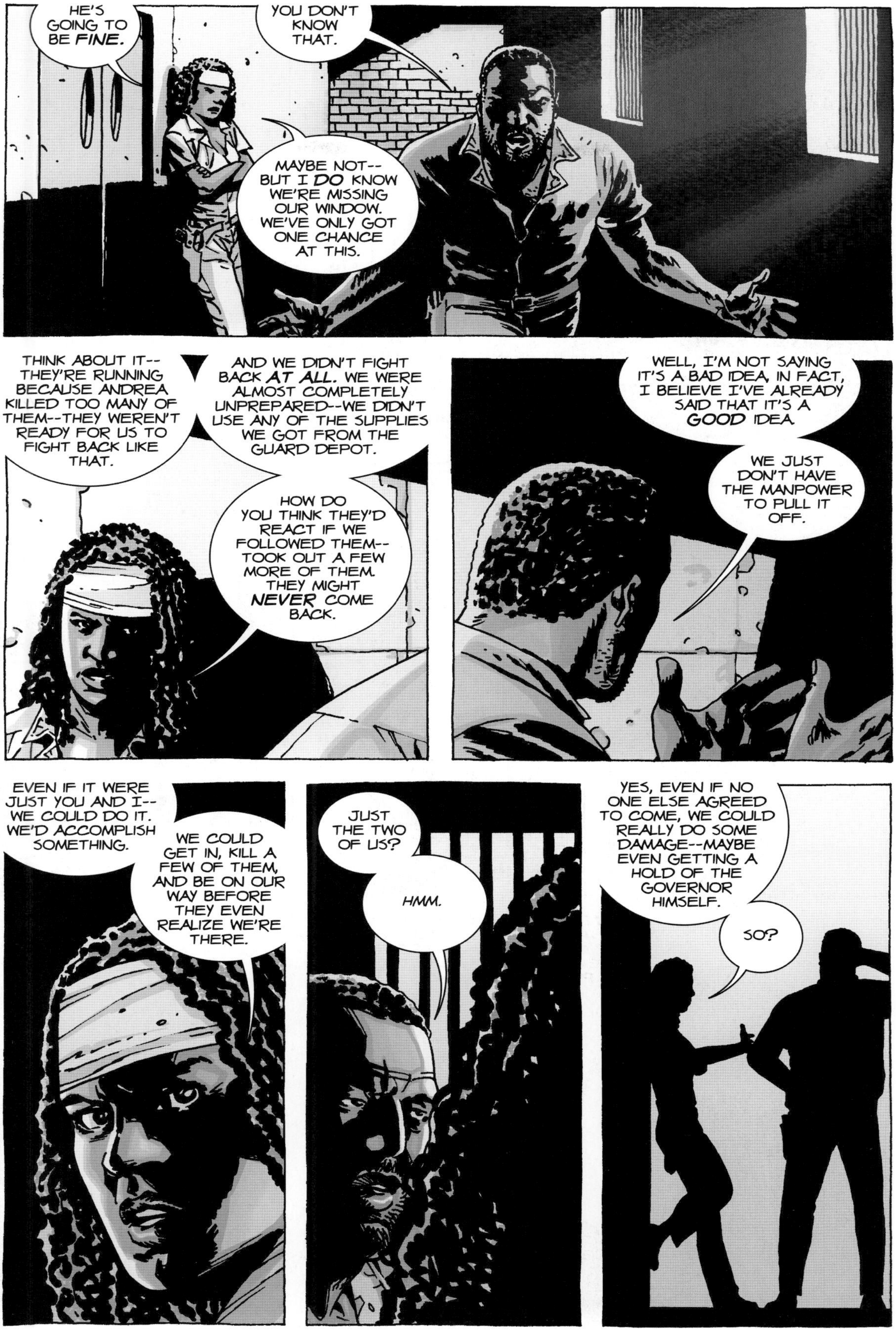
HE'S GOING TO BE FINE.
YOU DON'T KNOW THAT.
MAYBE NOT--BUT I DO KNOW WE'RE MISSING OUR WINDOW. WE'VE ONLY GOT ONE CHANCE AT THIS.
THINK ABOUT IT--THEY'RE RUNNING BECAUSE ANDREA KILLED TOO MANY OF THEM--THEY WEREN'T READY FOR US TO FIGHT BACK LIKE THAT.
AND WE DIDN'T FIGHT BACK AT ALL. WE WERE ALMOST COMPLETELY UNPREPARED--WE DIDN'T USE ANY OF THE SUPPLIES WE GOT FROM THE GUARD DEPOT.
HOW DO YOU THINK THEY'D REACT IF WE FOLLOWED THEM--TOOK OUT A FEW MORE OF THEM. THEY MIGHT NEVER COME BACK.
WELL, I'M NOT SAYING IT'S A BAD IDEA, IN FACT, I BELIEVE I'VE ALREADY SAID THAT IT'S A GOOD IDEA.
WE JUST DON'T HAVE THE MANPOWER TO PULL IT OFF.
EVEN IF IT WERE JUST YOU AND I--WE COULD DO IT. WE'D ACCOMPLISH SOMETHING.
WE COULD GET IN, KILL A FEW OF THEM, AND BE ON OUR WAY BEFORE THEY EVEN REALIZE WE'RE THERE.
JUST THE TWO OF US?
HMM.
YES, EVEN IF NO ONE ELSE AGREED TO COME, WE COULD REALLY DO SOME DAMAGE--MAYBE EVEN GETTING A HOLD OF THE GOVERNOR HIMSELF.
SO?

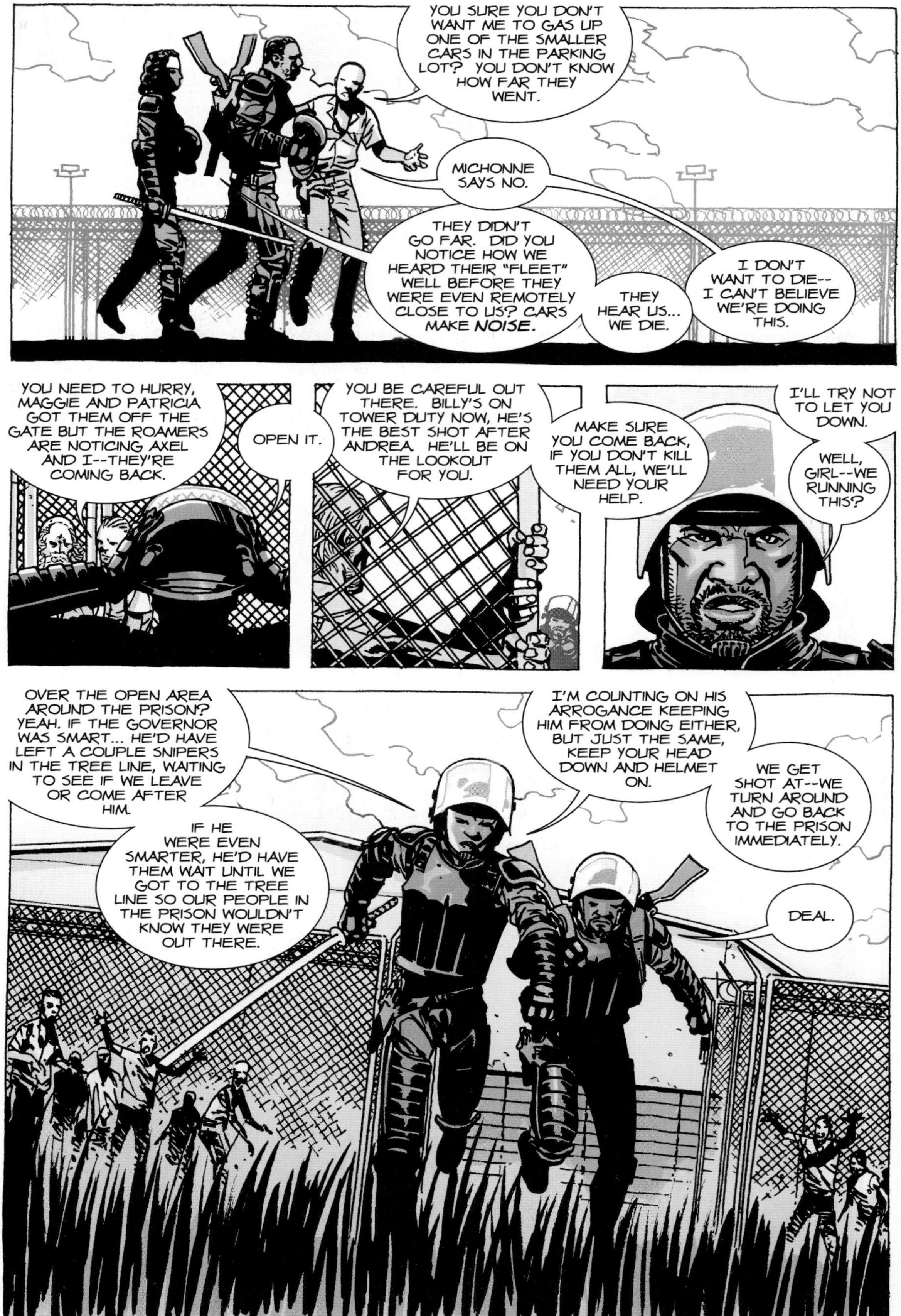
YOU SURE YOU DON'T WANT ME TO GAS UP ONE OF THE SMALLER CARS IN THE PARKING LOT? YOU DON'T KNOW HOW FAR THEY WENT.
MICHONNE SAYS NO.
THEY DIDN'T GO FAR. DID YOU NOTICE HOW WE HEARD THEIR "FLEET" WELL BEFORE THEY WERE EVEN REMOTELY CLOSE TO US? CARS MAKE NOISE.
THEY HEAR US... WE DIE.
I DON'T WANT TO DIE-- I CAN'T BELIEVE WE'RE DOING THIS.
YOU NEED TO HURRY, MAGGIE AND PATRICIA GOT THEM OFF THE GATE BUT THE ROAMERS ARE NOTICING AXEL AND I--THEY'RE COMING BACK.
OPEN IT.
YOU BE CAREFUL OUT THERE. BILLY'S ON TOWER DUTY NOW, HE'S THE BEST SHOT AFTER ANDREA. HE'LL BE ON THE LOOKOUT FOR YOU.
MAKE SURE YOU COME BACK, IF YOU DON'T KILL THEM ALL, WE'LL NEED YOUR HELP.
I'LL TRY NOT TO LET YOU DOWN.
WELL, GIRL--WE RUNNING THIS?
OVER THE OPEN AREA AROUND THE PRISON? YEAH. IF THE GOVERNOR WAS SMART... HE'D HAVE LEFT A COUPLE SNIPERS IN THE TREE LINE, WAITING TO SEE IF WE LEAVE OR COME AFTER HIM.
IF HE WERE EVEN SMARTER, HE'D HAVE THEM WAIT UNTIL WE GOT TO THE TREE LINE SO OUR PEOPLE IN THE PRISON WOULDN'T KNOW THEY WERE OUT THERE.
I'M COUNTING ON HIS ARROGANCE KEEPING HIM FROM DOING EITHER, BUT JUST THE SAME, KEEP YOUR HEAD DOWN AND HELMET ON.
WE GET SHOT AT--WE TURN AROUND AND GO BACK TO THE PRISON IMMEDIATELY.
DEAL.

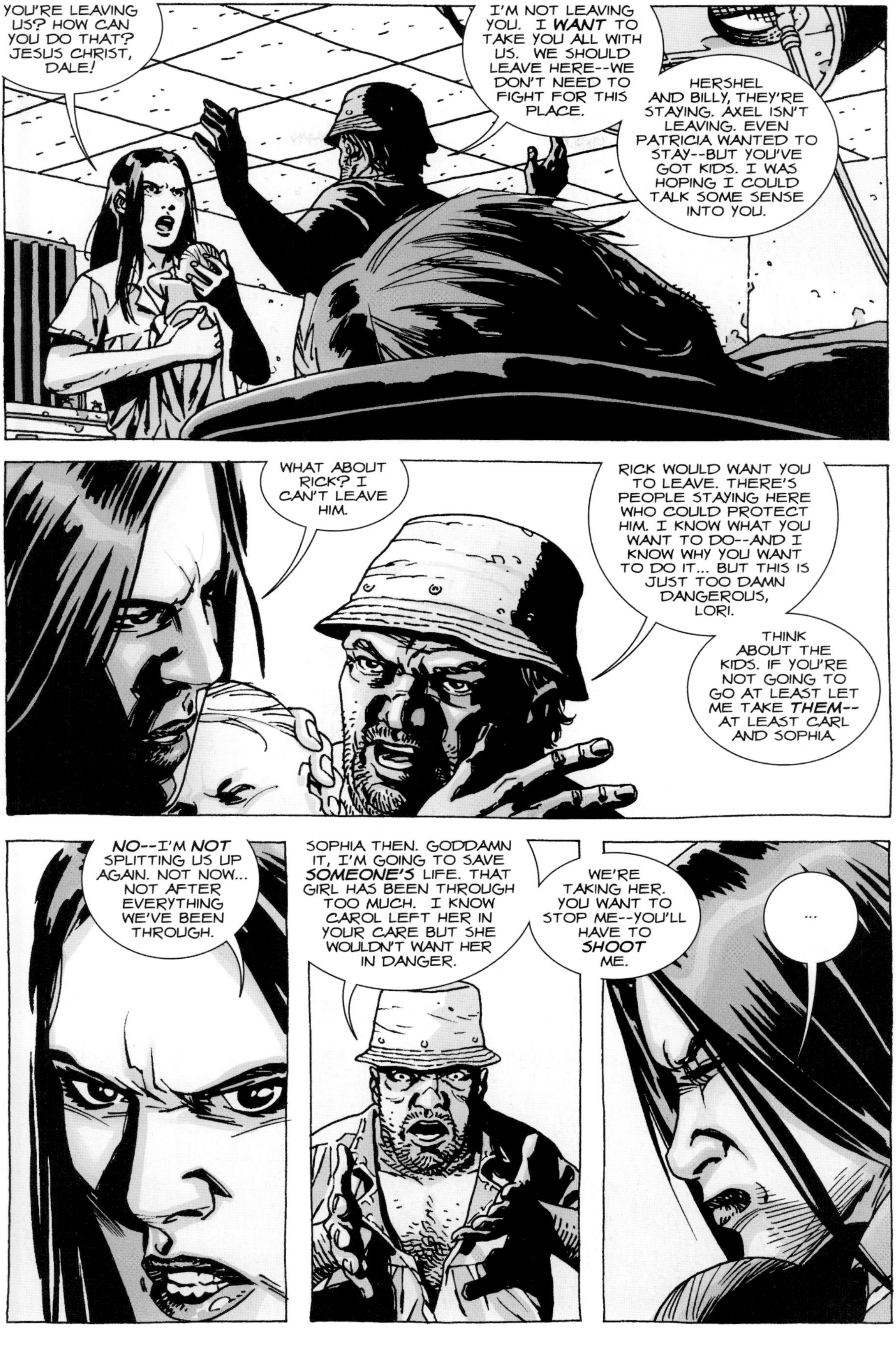
YOU'RE LEAVING US? HOW CAN YOU DO THAT? JESUS CHRIST, DALE!
I'M NOT LEAVING YOU. I WANT TO TAKE YOU ALL WITH US. WE SHOULD LEAVE HERE--WE DON'T NEED TO FIGHT FOR THIS PLACE.
HERSHEL AND BILLY, THEY'RE STAYING. AXEL ISN'T LEAVING. EVEN PATRICIA WANTED TO STAY--BUT YOU'VE GOT KIDS. I WAS HOPING I COULD TALK SOME SENSE INTO YOU.
WHAT ABOUT RICK? I CAN'T LEAVE HIM.
RICK WOULD WANT YOU TO LEAVE. THERE'S PEOPLE STAYING HERE WHO COULD PROTECT HIM. I KNOW WHAT YOU WANT TO DO--AND I KNOW WHY YOU WANT TO DO IT... BUT THIS IS JUST TOO DAMN DANGEROUS, LORI.
THINK ABOUT THE KIDS. IF YOU'RE NOT GOING TO GO AT LEAST LET ME TAKE THEM--AT LEAST CARL AND SOPHIA.
NO--I'M NOT SPLITTING US UP AGAIN. NOT NOW... NOT AFTER EVERYTHING WE'VE BEEN THROUGH.
SOPHIA THEN. GODDAMN IT, I'M GOING TO SAVE SOMEONE'S LIFE. THAT GIRL HAS BEEN THROUGH TOO MUCH. I KNOW CAROL LEFT HER IN YOUR CARE BUT SHE WOULDN'T WANT HER IN DANGER.
WE'RE TAKING HER. YOU WANT TO STOP ME--YOU'LL HAVE TO SHOOT ME.
...

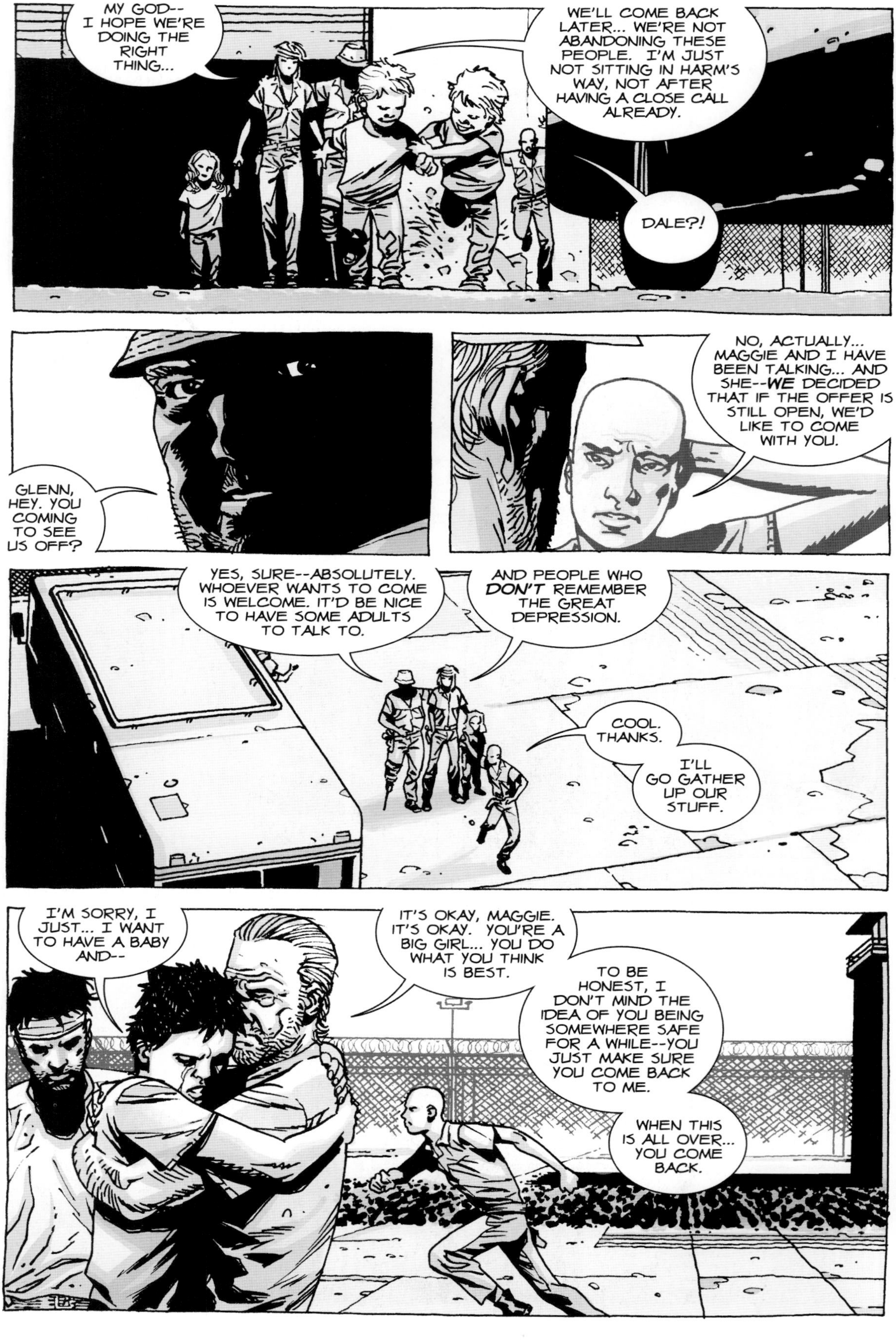
MY GOD-- I HOPE WE'RE DOING THE RIGHT THING...
WE'LL COME BACK LATER... WE'RE NOT ABANDONING THESE PEOPLE. I'M JUST NOT SITTING IN HARM'S WAY, NOT AFTER HAVING A CLOSE CALL ALREADY.
DALE?!
GLENN, HEY. YOU COMING TO SEE US OFF?
NO, ACTUALLY... MAGGIE AND I HAVE BEEN TALKING... AND SHE--WE DECIDED THAT IF THE OFFER IS STILL OPEN, WE'D LIKE TO COME WITH YOU.
YES, SURE--ABSOLUTELY. WHOEVER WANTS TO COME IS WELCOME. IT'D BE NICE TO HAVE SOME ADULTS TO TALK TO.
AND PEOPLE WHO DON'T REMEMBER THE GREAT DEPRESSION.
COOL. THANKS.
I'LL GO GATHER UP OUR STUFF.
I'M SORRY, I JUST... I WANT TO HAVE A BABY AND--
IT'S OKAY, MAGGIE. IT'S OKAY. YOU'RE A BIG GIRL... YOU DO WHAT YOU THINK IS BEST.
TO BE HONEST, I DON'T MIND THE IDEA OF YOU BEING SOMEWHERE SAFE FOR A WHILE--YOU JUST MAKE SURE YOU COME BACK TO ME.
WHEN THIS IS ALL OVER... YOU COME BACK.

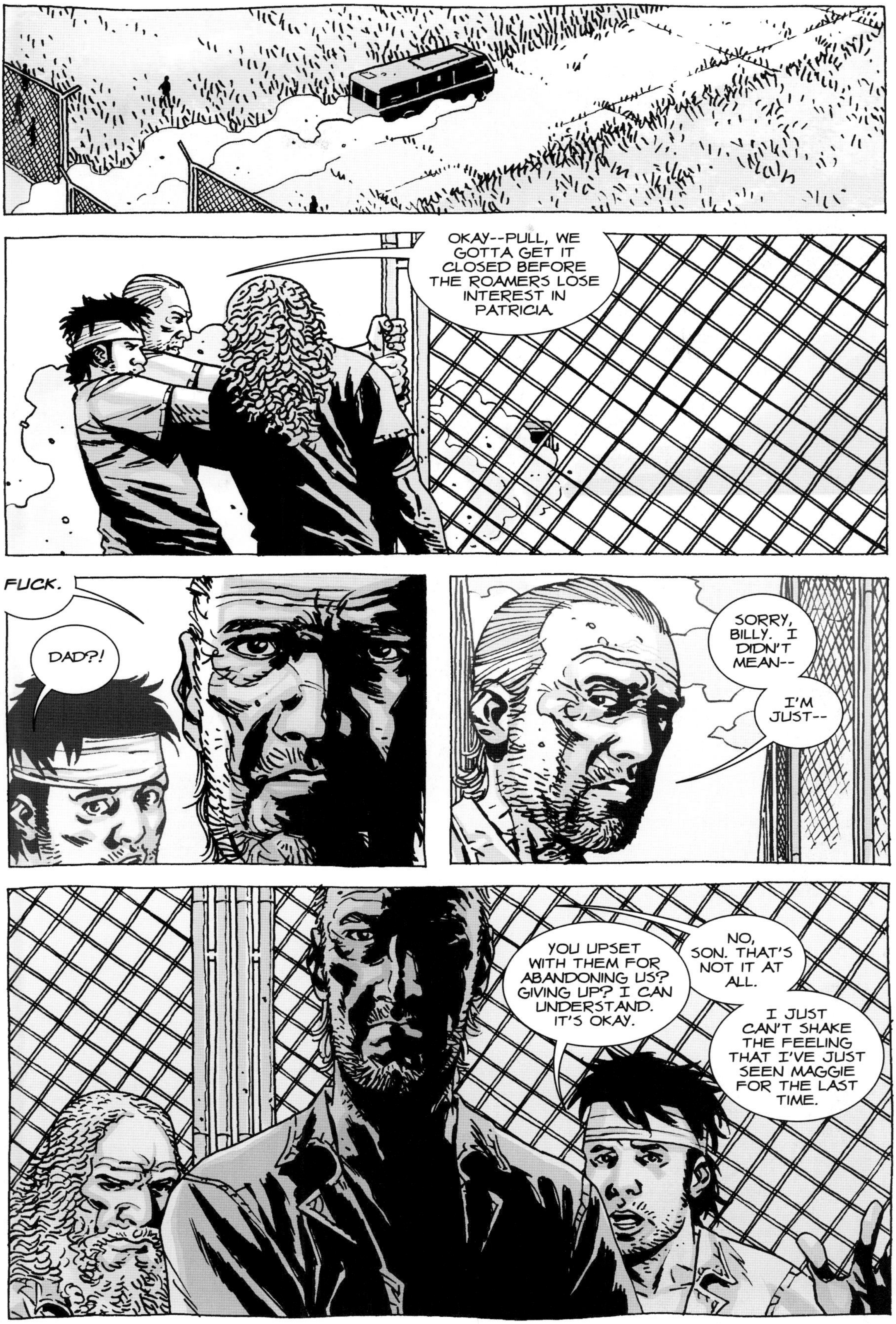
OKAY--PULL, WE GOTTA GET IT CLOSED BEFORE THE ROAMERS LOSE INTEREST IN PATRICIA.
FUCK.
DAD?!
SORRY, BILLY. I DIDN'T MEAN--
I'M JUST--
YOU UPSET WITH THEM FOR ABANDONING US? GIVING UP? I CAN UNDERSTAND. IT'S OKAY.
NO, SON. THAT'S NOT IT AT ALL.
I JUST CAN'T SHAKE THE FEELING THAT I'VE JUST SEEN MAGGIE FOR THE LAST TIME.

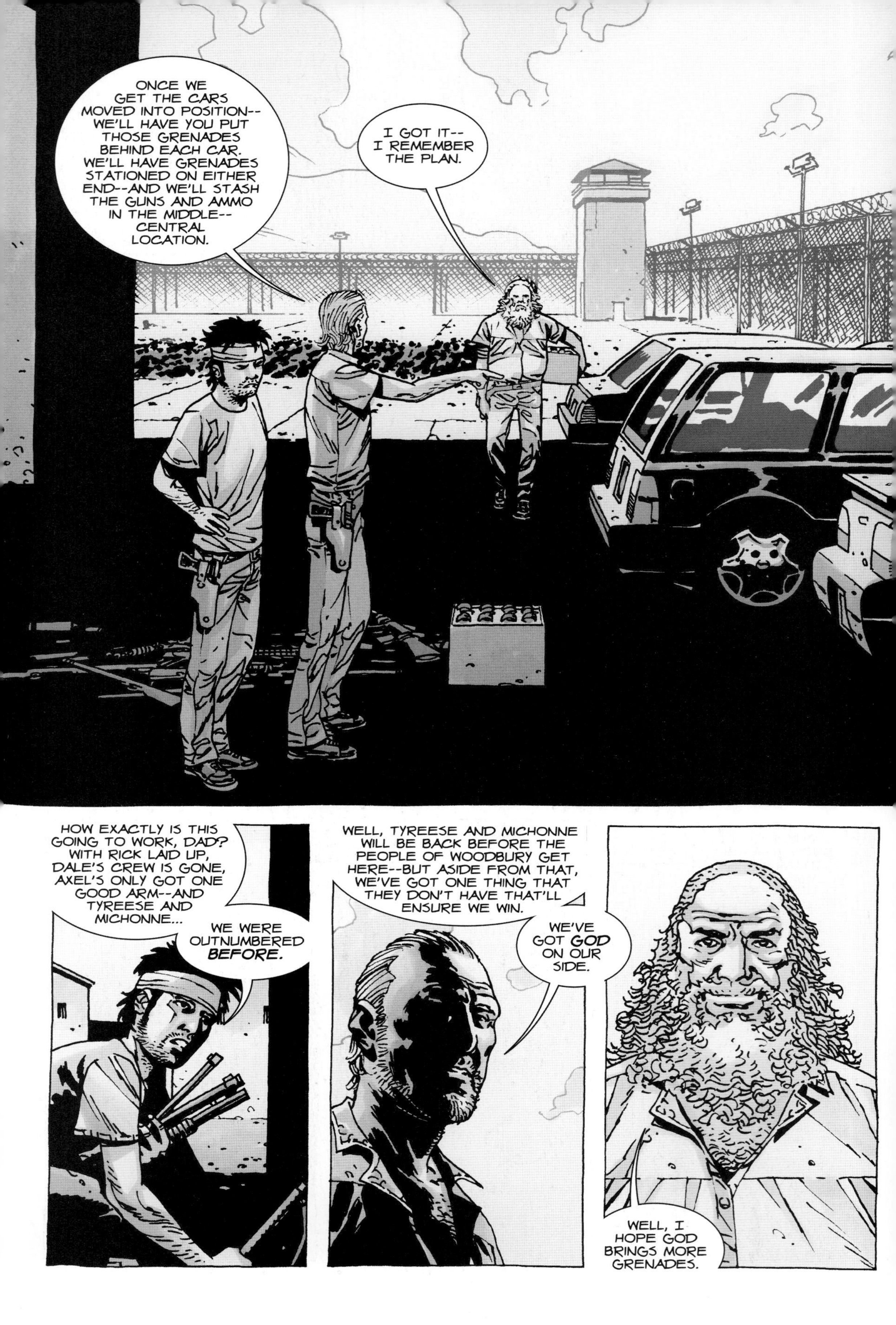
ONCE WE GET THE CARS MOVED INTO POSITION-- WE'LL HAVE YOU PUT THOSE GRENADES BEHIND EACH CAR. WE'LL HAVE GRENADES STATIONED ON EITHER END--AND WE'LL STASH THE GUNS AND AMMO IN THE MIDDLE-- CENTRAL LOCATION.
I GOT IT-- I REMEMBER THE PLAN.
HOW EXACTLY IS THIS GOING TO WORK, DAD? WITH RICK LAID UP, DALE'S CREW IS GONE, AXEL'S ONLY GOT ONE GOOD ARM--AND TYREESE AND MICHONNE...
WE WERE OUTNUMBERED *BEFORE.*
WELL, TYREESE AND MICHONNE WILL BE BACK BEFORE THE PEOPLE OF WOODBURY GET HERE--BUT ASIDE FROM THAT, WE'VE GOT ONE THING THAT THEY DON'T HAVE THAT'LL ENSURE WE WIN.
WE'VE GOT *GOD* ON OUR SIDE.
WELL, I HOPE GOD BRINGS MORE GRENADES.

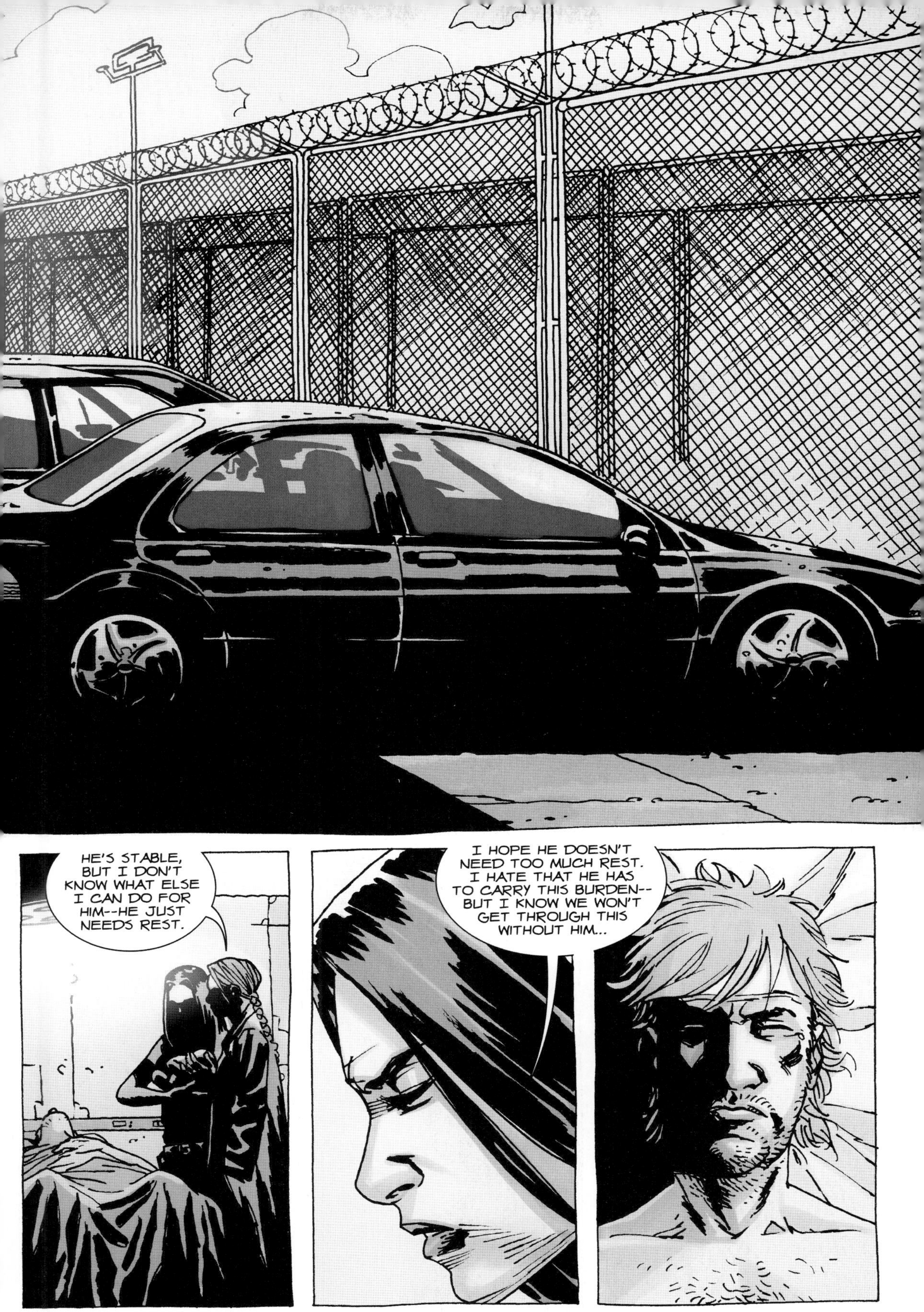
HE'S STABLE, BUT I DON'T KNOW WHAT ELSE I CAN DO FOR HIM--HE JUST NEEDS REST.
I HOPE HE DOESN'T NEED TOO MUCH REST. I HATE THAT HE HAS TO CARRY THIS BURDEN-- BUT I KNOW WE WON'T GET THROUGH THIS WITHOUT HIM...

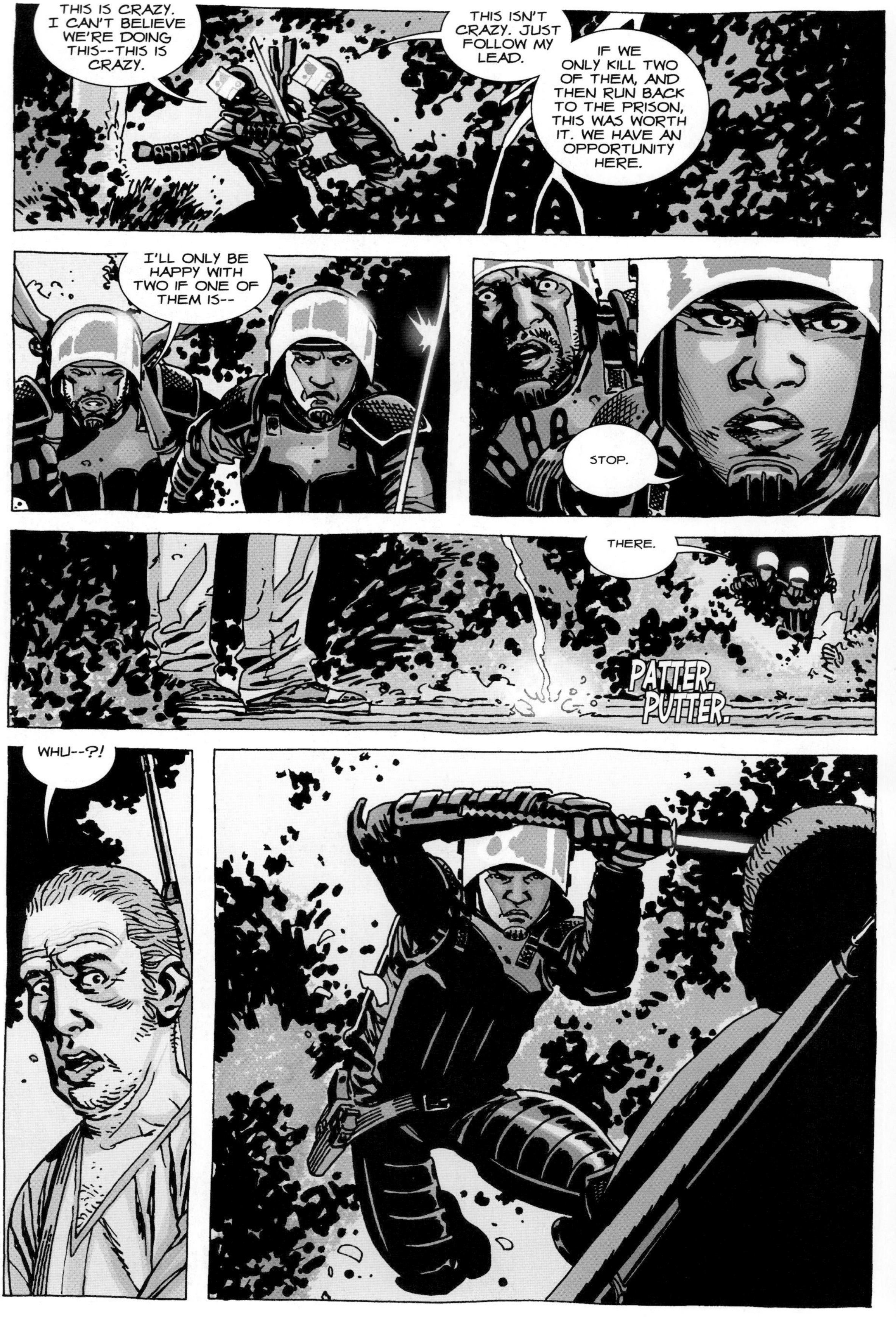
THIS IS CRAZY. I CAN'T BELIEVE WE'RE DOING THIS--THIS IS CRAZY.
THIS ISN'T CRAZY. JUST FOLLOW MY LEAD.
IF WE ONLY KILL TWO OF THEM, AND THEN RUN BACK TO THE PRISON, THIS WAS WORTH IT. WE HAVE AN OPPORTUNITY HERE.
I'LL ONLY BE HAPPY WITH TWO IF ONE OF THEM IS--
STOP.
THERE.
PATTER. PUTTER.
WHU--?!

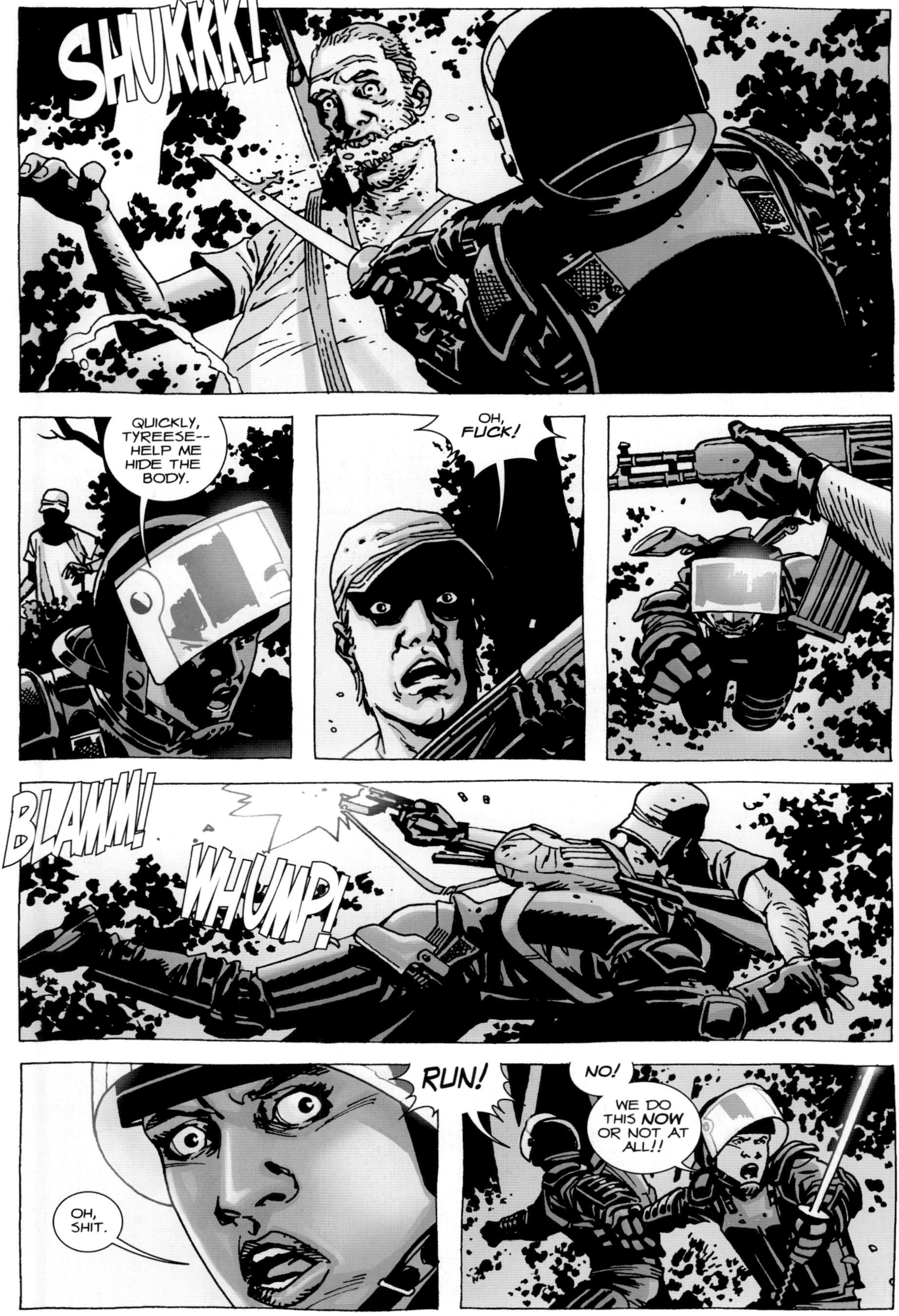
SHUKKK!
QUICKLY, TYREESE-- HELP ME HIDE THE BODY.
OH, FUCK!
BLAMM!
WHUMP!
RUN!
OH, SHIT.
NO!
WE DO THIS NOW OR NOT AT ALL!!

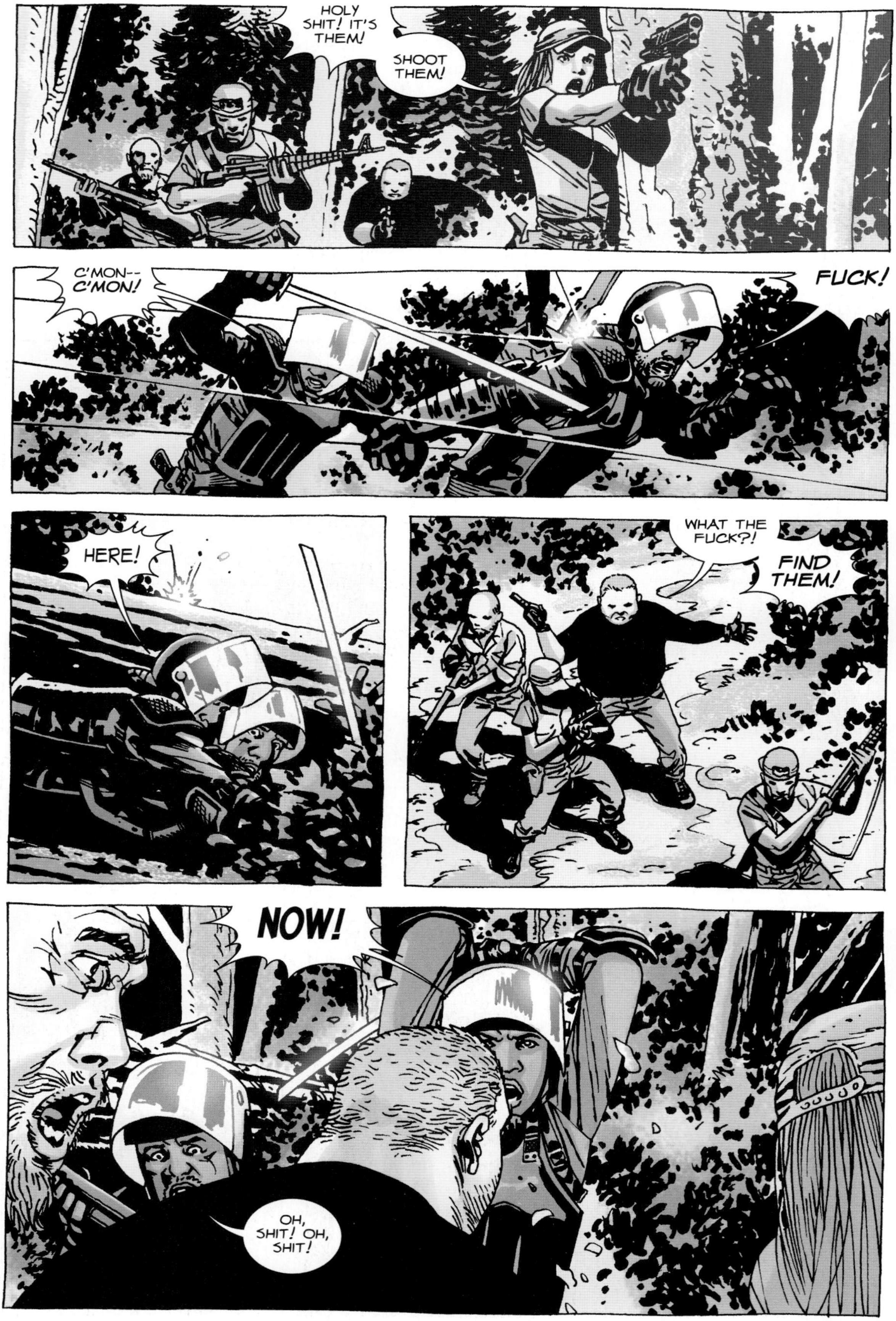

HOLY SHIT! IT'S THEM!
SHOOT THEM!
C'MON-- C'MON!
FUCK!
HERE!
WHAT THE FUCK?!
FIND THEM!
NOW!
OH, SHIT! OH, SHIT!

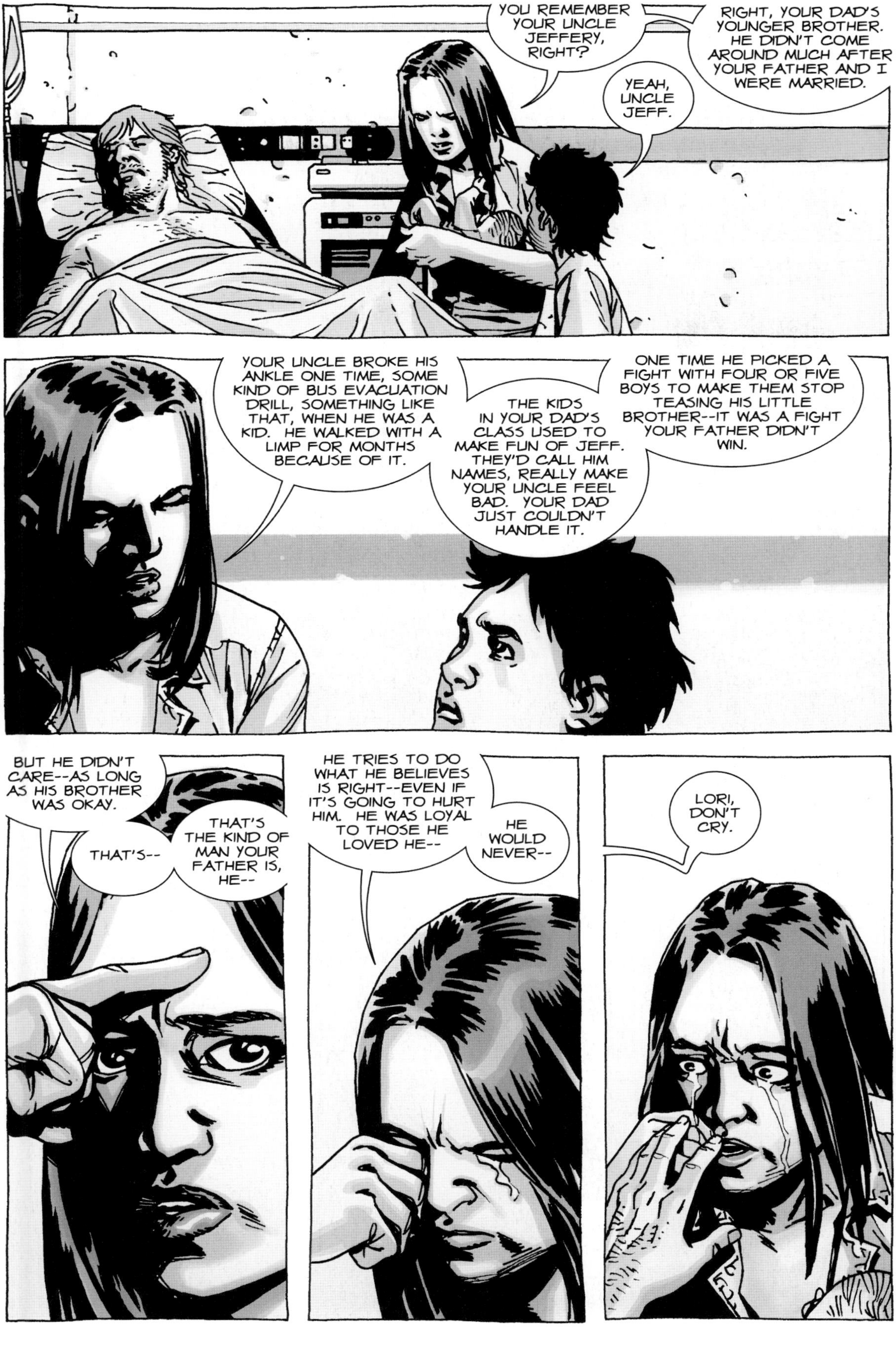
YOU REMEMBER YOUR UNCLE JEFFERY, RIGHT?
YEAH, UNCLE JEFF.
RIGHT, YOUR DAD'S YOUNGER BROTHER. HE DIDN'T COME AROUND MUCH AFTER YOUR FATHER AND I WERE MARRIED.
YOUR UNCLE BROKE HIS ANKLE ONE TIME, SOME KIND OF BUS EVACUATION DRILL, SOMETHING LIKE THAT, WHEN HE WAS A KID. HE WALKED WITH A LIMP FOR MONTHS BECAUSE OF IT.
THE KIDS IN YOUR DAD'S CLASS USED TO MAKE FUN OF JEFF. THEY'D CALL HIM NAMES, REALLY MAKE YOUR UNCLE FEEL BAD. YOUR DAD JUST COULDN'T HANDLE IT.
ONE TIME HE PICKED A FIGHT WITH FOUR OR FIVE BOYS TO MAKE THEM STOP TEASING HIS LITTLE BROTHER--IT WAS A FIGHT YOUR FATHER DIDN'T WIN.
BUT HE DIDN'T CARE--AS LONG AS HIS BROTHER WAS OKAY.
THAT'S--
THAT'S THE KIND OF MAN YOUR FATHER IS, HE--
HE TRIES TO DO WHAT HE BELIEVES IS RIGHT--EVEN IF IT'S GOING TO HURT HIM. HE WAS LOYAL TO THOSE HE LOVED HE--
HE WOULD NEVER--
LORI, DON'T CRY.

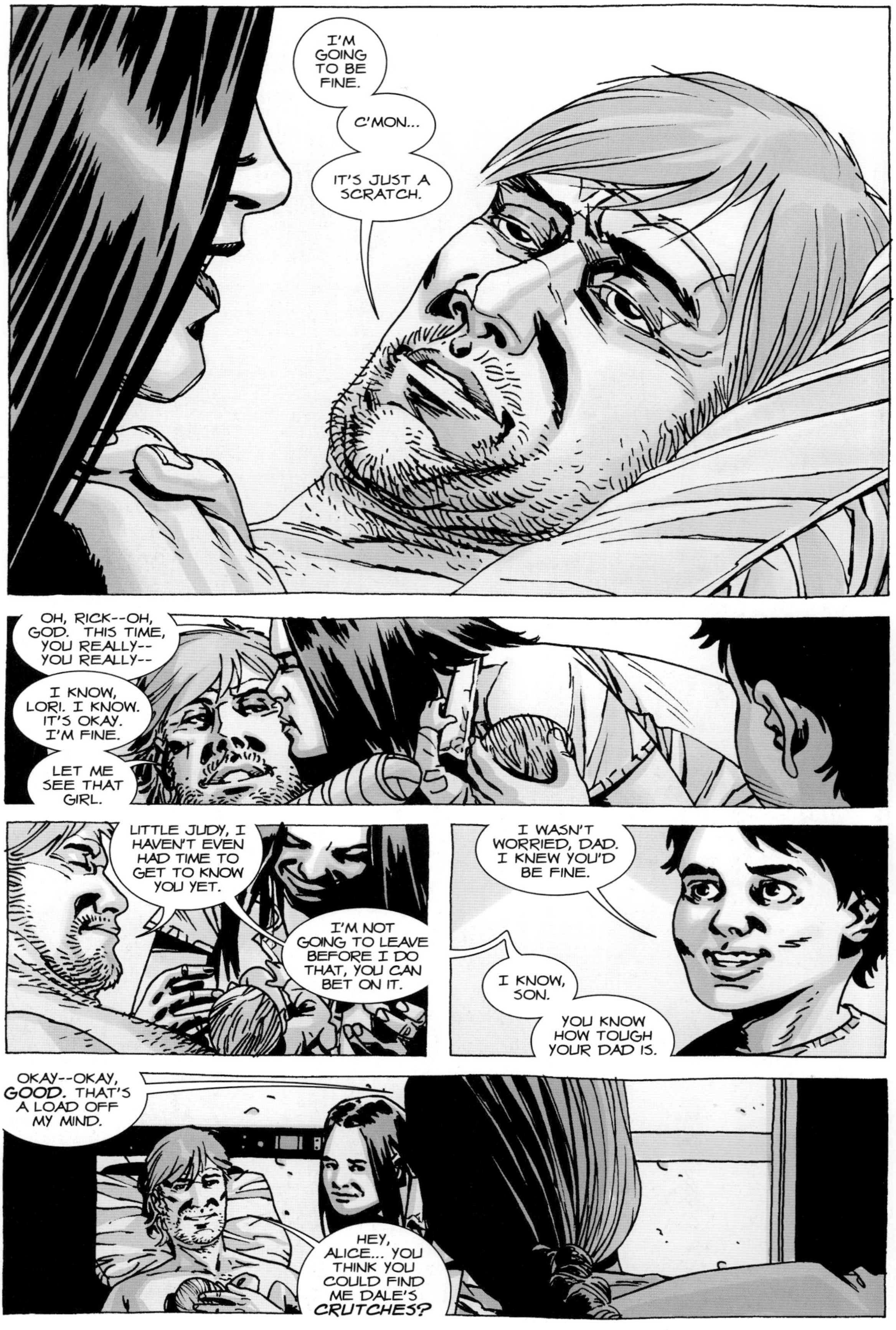
I'M GOING TO BE FINE.
C'MON...
IT'S JUST A SCRATCH.
OH, RICK--OH, GOD. THIS TIME, YOU REALLY-- YOU REALLY--
I KNOW, LORI. I KNOW. IT'S OKAY. I'M FINE.
LET ME SEE THAT GIRL.
LITTLE JUDY, I HAVEN'T EVEN HAD TIME TO GET TO KNOW YOU YET.
I'M NOT GOING TO LEAVE BEFORE I DO THAT, YOU CAN BET ON IT.
I WASN'T WORRIED, DAD. I KNEW YOU'D BE FINE.
I KNOW, SON.
YOU KNOW HOW TOUGH YOUR DAD IS.
OKAY--OKAY, GOOD. THAT'S A LOAD OFF MY MIND.
HEY, ALICE... YOU THINK YOU COULD FIND ME DALE'S CRUTCHES?

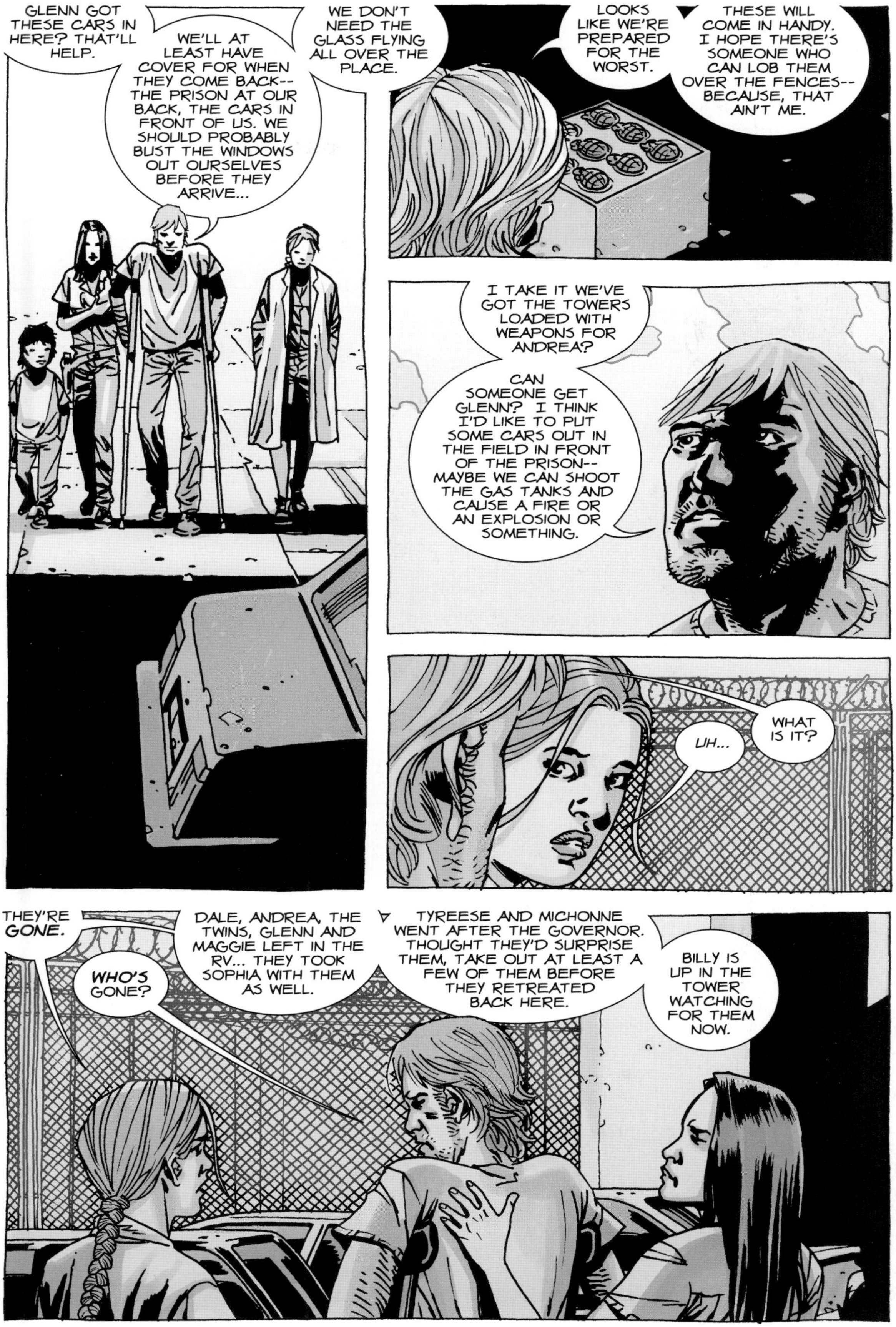
GLENN GOT THESE CARS IN HERE? THAT'LL HELP.
WE'LL AT LEAST HAVE COVER FOR WHEN THEY COME BACK-- THE PRISON AT OUR BACK, THE CARS IN FRONT OF US. WE SHOULD PROBABLY BUST THE WINDOWS OUT OURSELVES BEFORE THEY ARRIVE...
WE DON'T NEED THE GLASS FLYING ALL OVER THE PLACE.
LOOKS LIKE WE'RE PREPARED FOR THE WORST.
THESE WILL COME IN HANDY. I HOPE THERE'S SOMEONE WHO CAN LOB THEM OVER THE FENCES-- BECAUSE, THAT AIN'T ME.
I TAKE IT WE'VE GOT THE TOWERS LOADED WITH WEAPONS FOR ANDREA?
CAN SOMEONE GET GLENN? I THINK I'D LIKE TO PUT SOME CARS OUT IN THE FIELD IN FRONT OF THE PRISON-- MAYBE WE CAN SHOOT THE GAS TANKS AND CAUSE A FIRE OR AN EXPLOSION OR SOMETHING.
WHAT IS IT?
UH...
THEY'RE *GONE*.
WHO'S GONE?
DALE, ANDREA, THE TWINS, GLENN AND MAGGIE LEFT IN THE RV... THEY TOOK SOPHIA WITH THEM AS WELL.
TYREESE AND MICHONNE WENT AFTER THE GOVERNOR. THOUGHT THEY'D SURPRISE THEM, TAKE OUT AT LEAST A FEW OF THEM BEFORE THEY RETREATED BACK HERE.
BILLY IS UP IN THE TOWER WATCHING FOR THEM NOW.

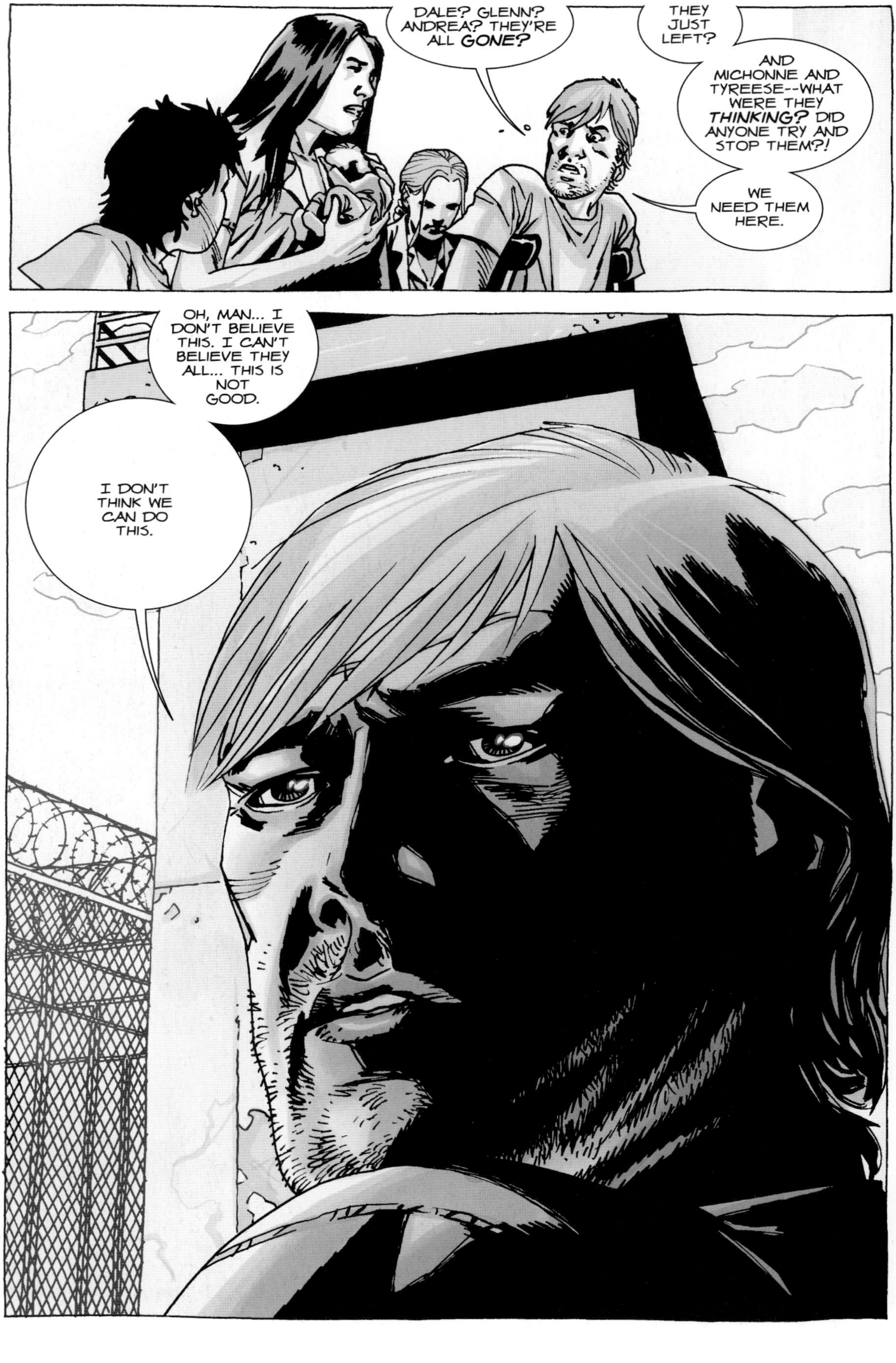
DALE? GLENN? ANDREA? THEY'RE ALL GONE?
THEY JUST LEFT?
AND MICHONNE AND TYREESE--WHAT WERE THEY THINKING? DID ANYONE TRY AND STOP THEM?!
WE NEED THEM HERE.
OH, MAN... I DON'T BELIEVE THIS. I CAN'T BELIEVE THEY ALL... THIS IS NOT GOOD.
I DON'T THINK WE CAN DO THIS.

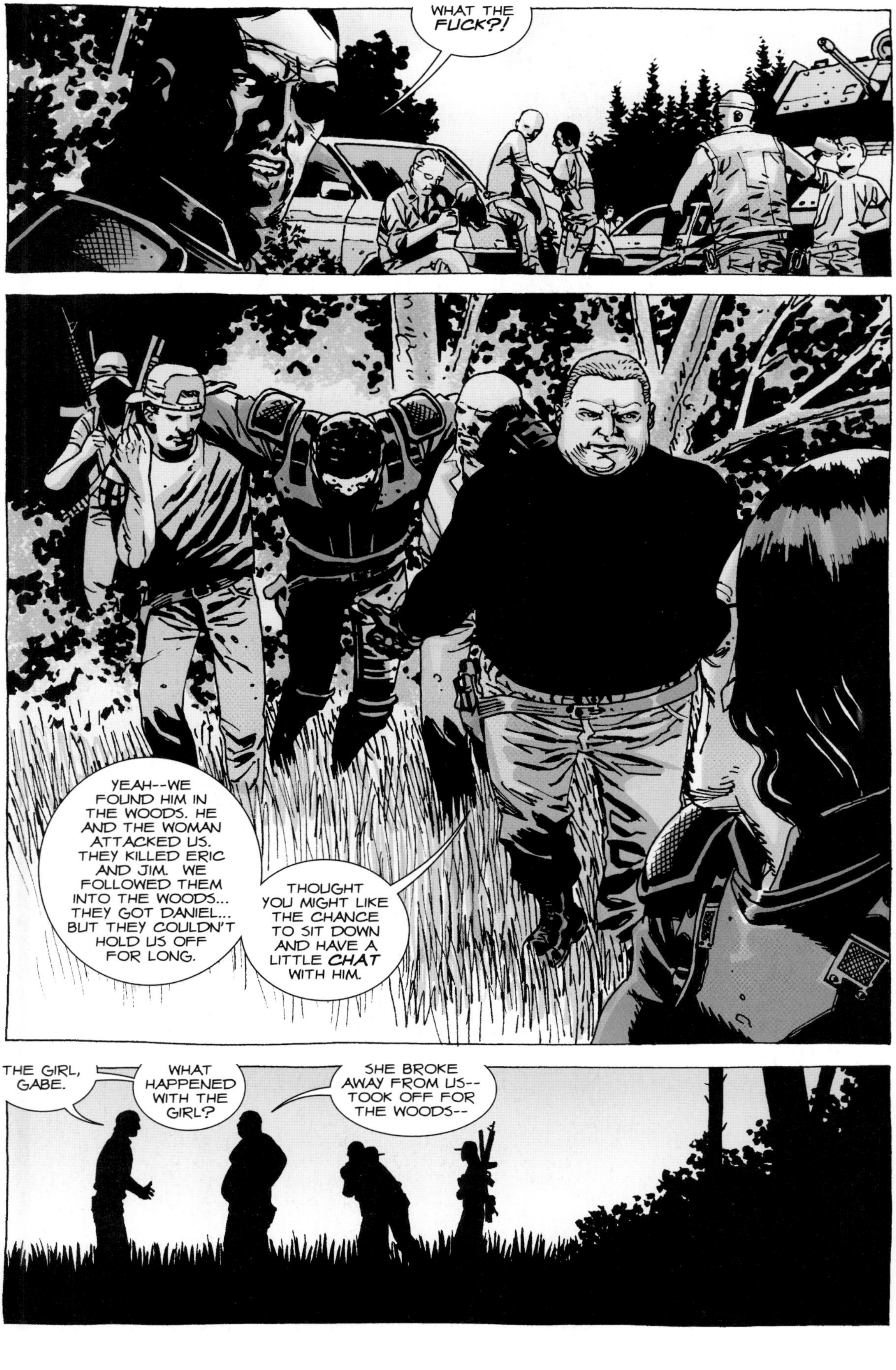
WHAT THE FUCK?!
YEAH--WE FOUND HIM IN THE WOODS. HE AND THE WOMAN ATTACKED US. THEY KILLED ERIC AND JIM. WE FOLLOWED THEM INTO THE WOODS... THEY GOT DANIEL... BUT THEY COULDN'T HOLD US OFF FOR LONG.
THOUGHT YOU MIGHT LIKE THE CHANCE TO SIT DOWN AND HAVE A LITTLE CHAT WITH HIM.
THE GIRL, GABE.
WHAT HAPPENED WITH THE GIRL?
SHE BROKE AWAY FROM US-- TOOK OFF FOR THE WOODS--

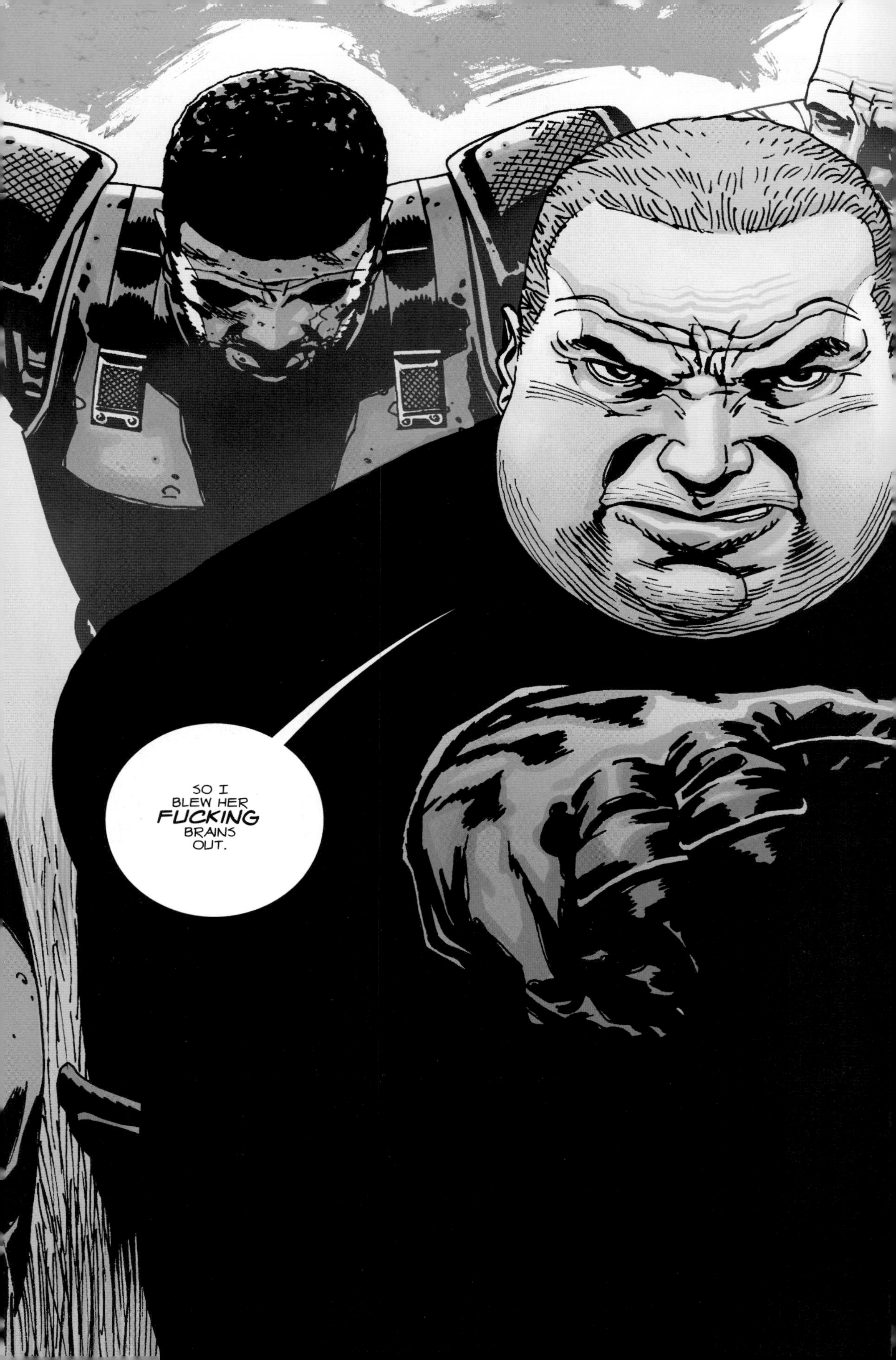
SO I BLEW HER FUCKING BRAINS OUT.

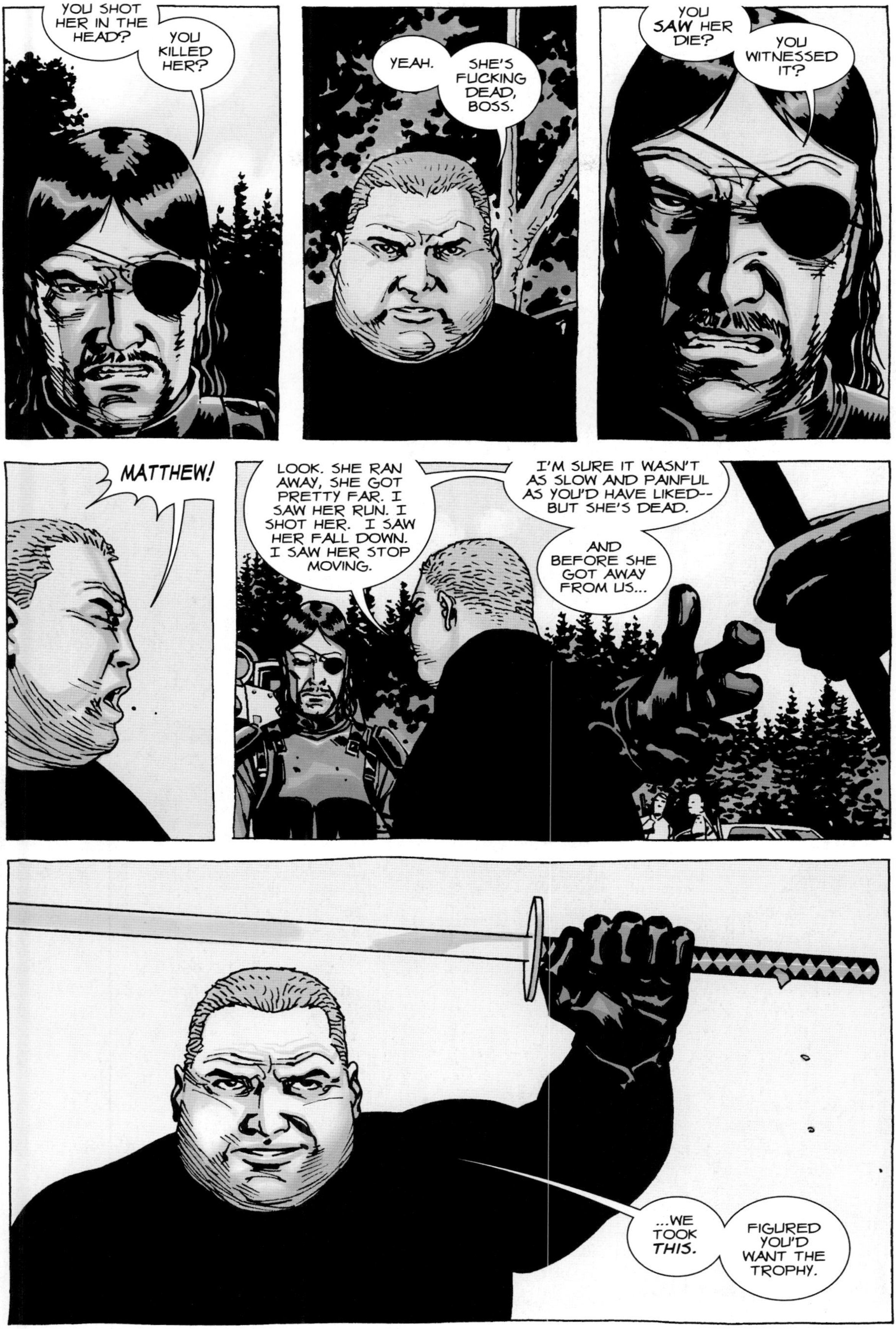
YOU SHOT HER IN THE HEAD?
YOU KILLED HER?
YEAH.
SHE'S FUCKING DEAD, BOSS.
YOU SAW HER DIE?
YOU WITNESSED IT?
MATTHEW!
LOOK. SHE RAN AWAY, SHE GOT PRETTY FAR. I SAW HER RUN. I SHOT HER. I SAW HER FALL DOWN. I SAW HER STOP MOVING.
I'M SURE IT WASN'T AS SLOW AND PAINFUL AS YOU'D HAVE LIKED-- BUT SHE'S DEAD.
AND BEFORE SHE GOT AWAY FROM US...
...WE TOOK THIS.
FIGURED YOU'D WANT THE TROPHY.

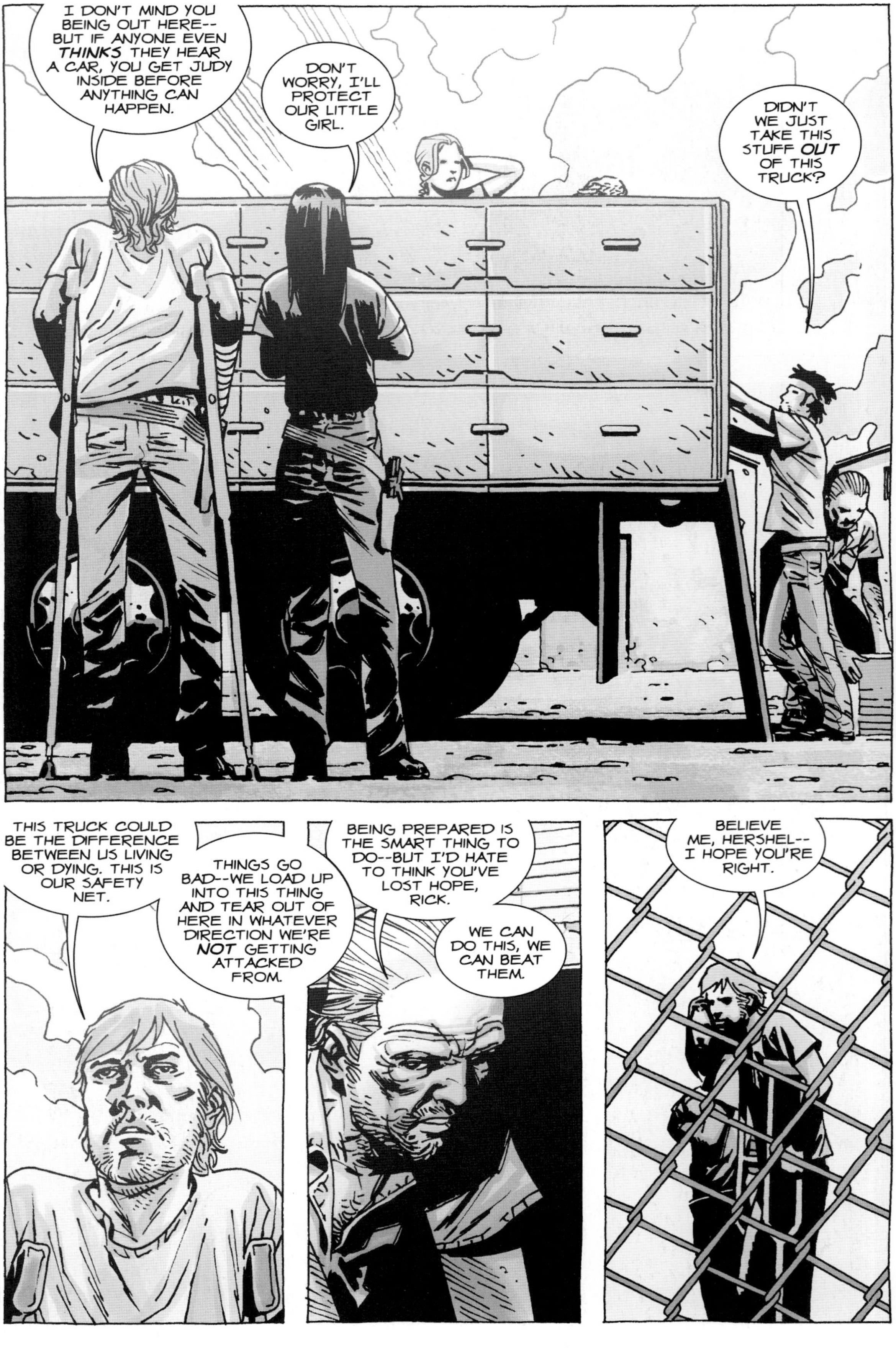
I DON'T MIND YOU BEING OUT HERE-- BUT IF ANYONE EVEN THINKS THEY HEAR A CAR, YOU GET JUDY INSIDE BEFORE ANYTHING CAN HAPPEN.
DON'T WORRY, I'LL PROTECT OUR LITTLE GIRL.
DIDN'T WE JUST TAKE THIS STUFF OUT OF THIS TRUCK?
THIS TRUCK COULD BE THE DIFFERENCE BETWEEN US LIVING OR DYING. THIS IS OUR SAFETY NET.
THINGS GO BAD--WE LOAD UP INTO THIS THING AND TEAR OUT OF HERE IN WHATEVER DIRECTION WE'RE NOT GETTING ATTACKED FROM.
BEING PREPARED IS THE SMART THING TO DO--BUT I'D HATE TO THINK YOU'VE LOST HOPE, RICK.
WE CAN DO THIS, WE CAN BEAT THEM.
BELIEVE ME, HERSHEL-- I HOPE YOU'RE RIGHT.

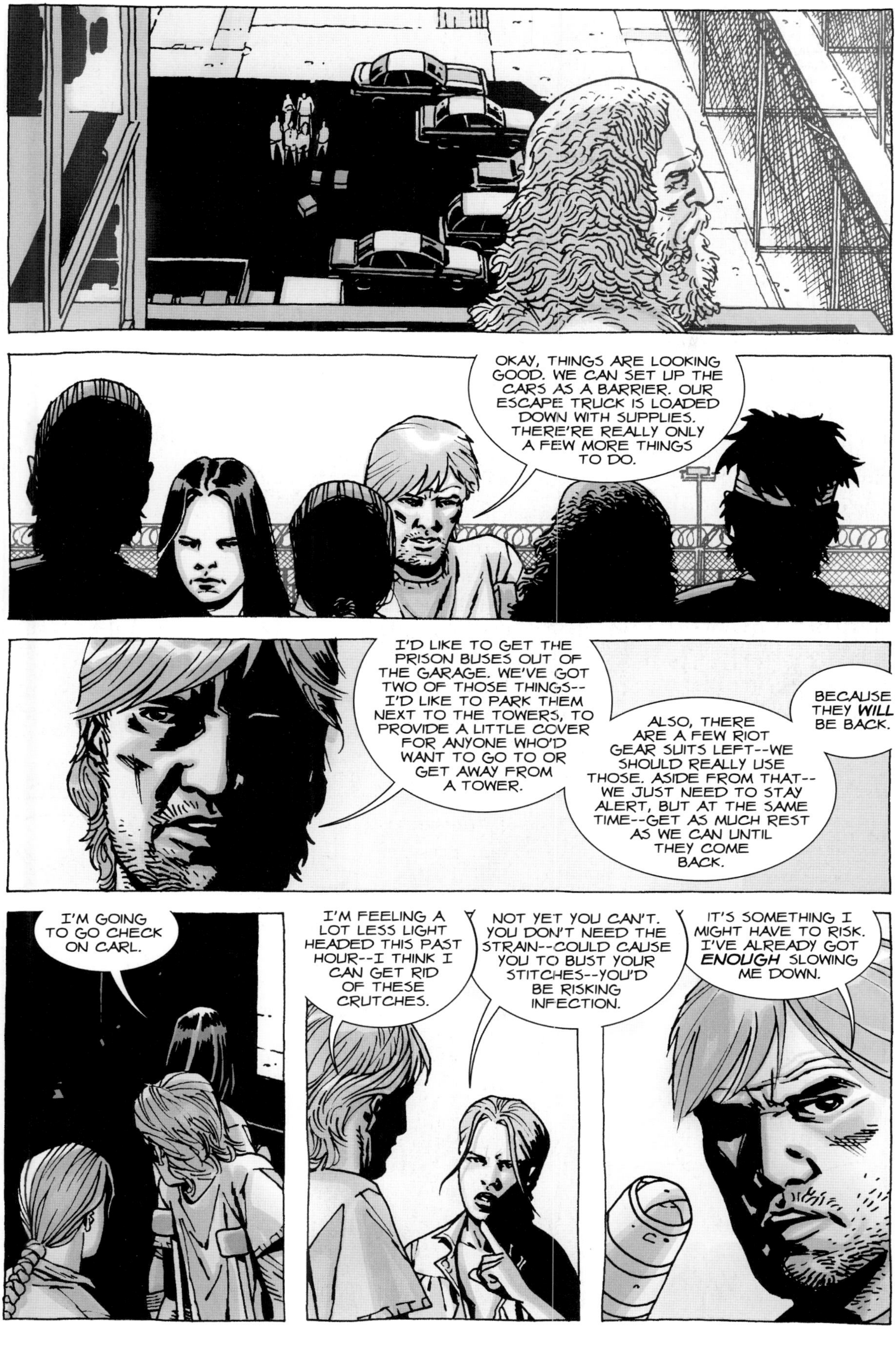
OKAY, THINGS ARE LOOKING GOOD. WE CAN SET UP THE CARS AS A BARRIER. OUR ESCAPE TRUCK IS LOADED DOWN WITH SUPPLIES. THERE'RE REALLY ONLY A FEW MORE THINGS TO DO.
I'D LIKE TO GET THE PRISON BUSES OUT OF THE GARAGE. WE'VE GOT TWO OF THOSE THINGS-- I'D LIKE TO PARK THEM NEXT TO THE TOWERS, TO PROVIDE A LITTLE COVER FOR ANYONE WHO'D WANT TO GO TO OR GET AWAY FROM A TOWER.
ALSO, THERE ARE A FEW RIOT GEAR SUITS LEFT--WE SHOULD REALLY USE THOSE. ASIDE FROM THAT-- WE JUST NEED TO STAY ALERT, BUT AT THE SAME TIME--GET AS MUCH REST AS WE CAN UNTIL THEY COME BACK.
BECAUSE THEY ***WILL*** BE BACK.
I'M GOING TO GO CHECK ON CARL.
I'M FEELING A LOT LESS LIGHT HEADED THIS PAST HOUR--I THINK I CAN GET RID OF THESE CRUTCHES.
NOT YET YOU CAN'T. YOU DON'T NEED THE STRAIN--COULD CAUSE YOU TO BUST YOUR STITCHES--YOU'D BE RISKING INFECTION.
IT'S SOMETHING I MIGHT HAVE TO RISK. I'VE ALREADY GOT ***ENOUGH*** SLOWING ME DOWN.

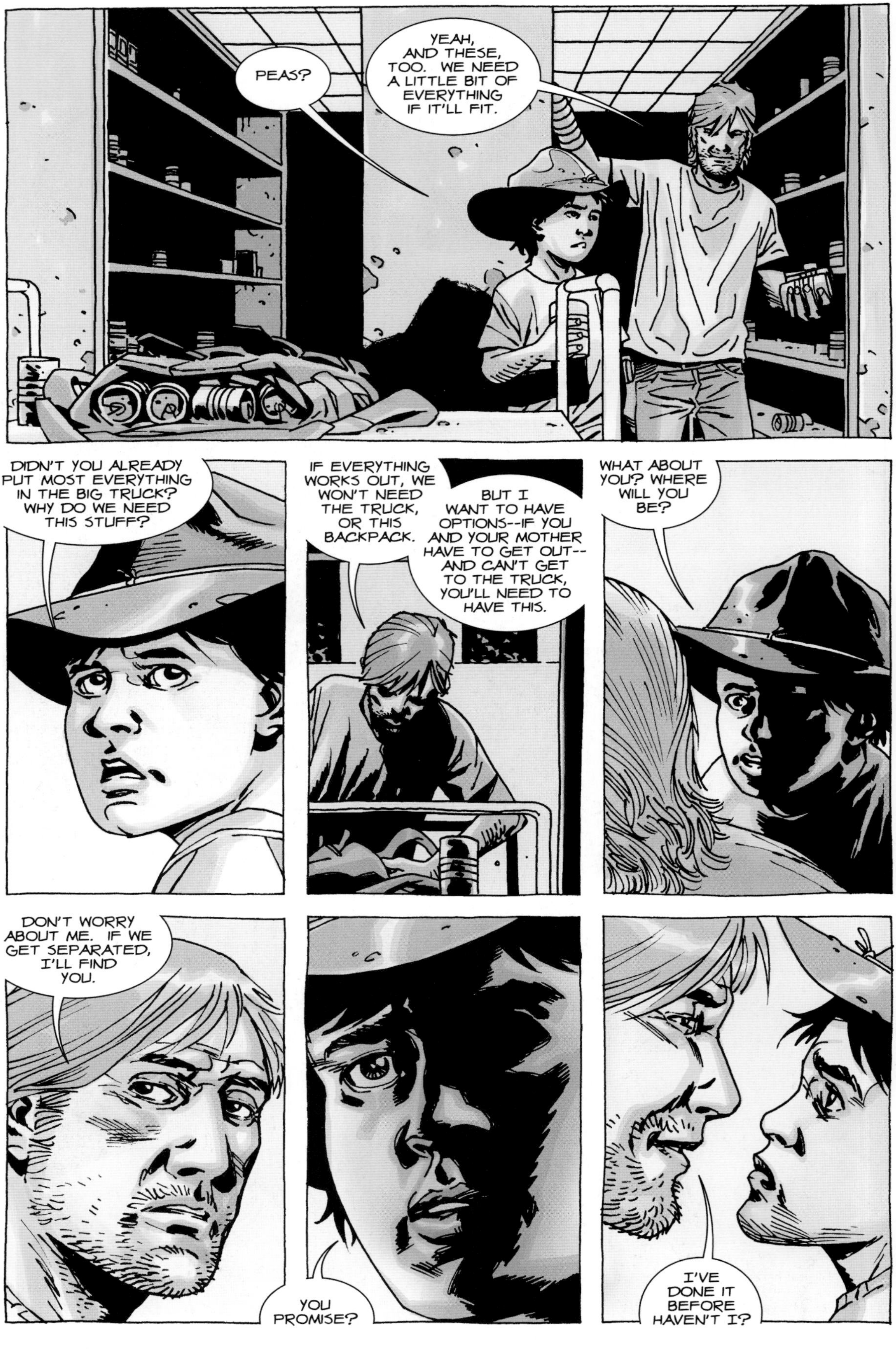
PEAS?
YEAH, AND THESE, TOO. WE NEED A LITTLE BIT OF EVERYTHING IF IT'LL FIT.
DIDN'T YOU ALREADY PUT MOST EVERYTHING IN THE BIG TRUCK? WHY DO WE NEED THIS STUFF?
IF EVERYTHING WORKS OUT, WE WON'T NEED THE TRUCK, OR THIS BACKPACK.
BUT I WANT TO HAVE OPTIONS--IF YOU AND YOUR MOTHER HAVE TO GET OUT-- AND CAN'T GET TO THE TRUCK, YOU'LL NEED TO HAVE THIS.
WHAT ABOUT YOU? WHERE WILL YOU BE?
DON'T WORRY ABOUT ME. IF WE GET SEPARATED, I'LL FIND YOU.
YOU PROMISE?
I'VE DONE IT BEFORE HAVEN'T I?

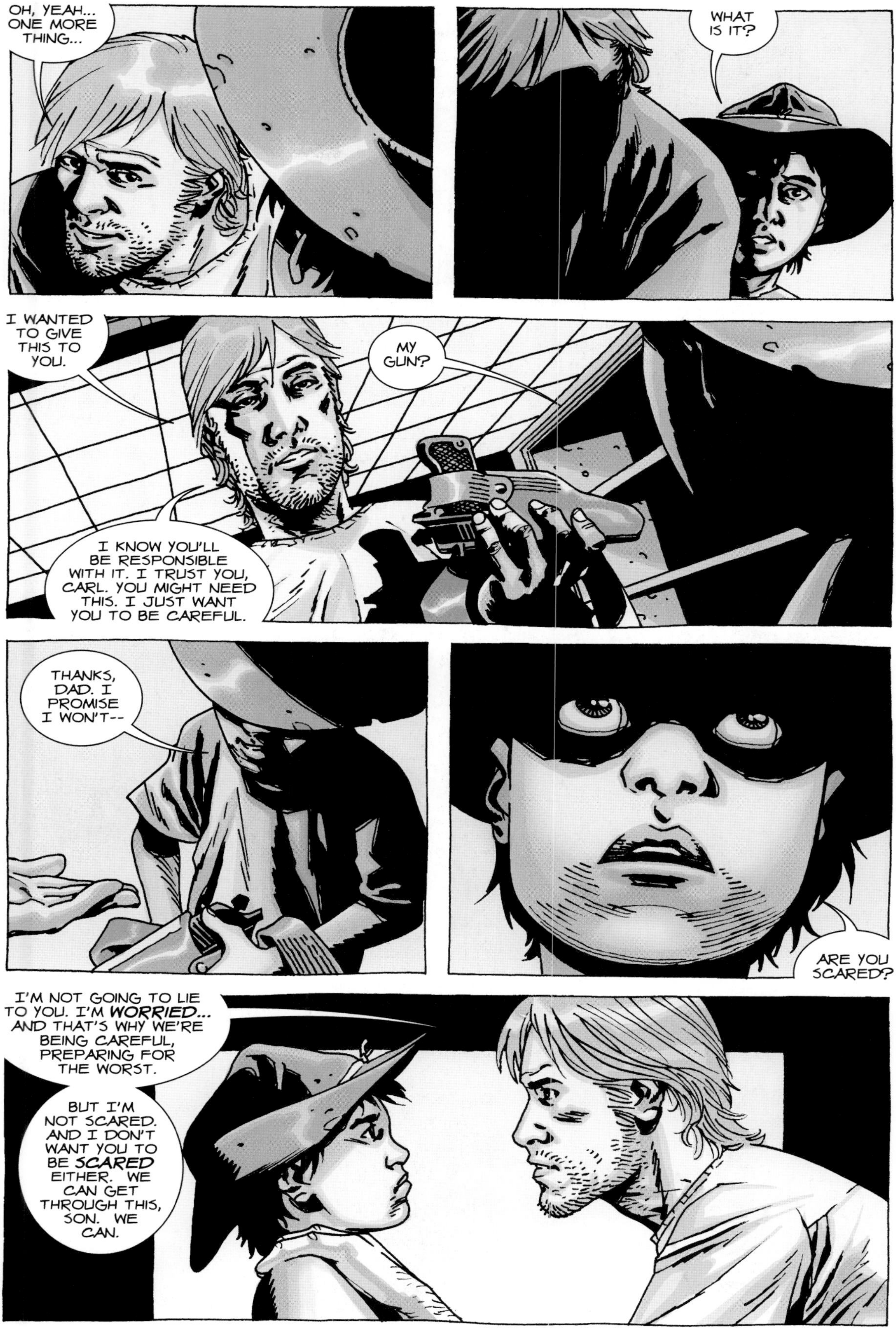
OH, YEAH... ONE MORE THING...
WHAT IS IT?
I WANTED TO GIVE THIS TO YOU.
MY GUN?
I KNOW YOU'LL BE RESPONSIBLE WITH IT. I TRUST YOU, CARL. YOU MIGHT NEED THIS. I JUST WANT YOU TO BE CAREFUL.
THANKS, DAD. I PROMISE I WON'T--
ARE YOU SCARED?
I'M NOT GOING TO LIE TO YOU. I'M WORRIED... AND THAT'S WHY WE'RE BEING CAREFUL, PREPARING FOR THE WORST.
BUT I'M NOT SCARED. AND I DON'T WANT YOU TO BE SCARED EITHER. WE CAN GET THROUGH THIS, SON. WE CAN.

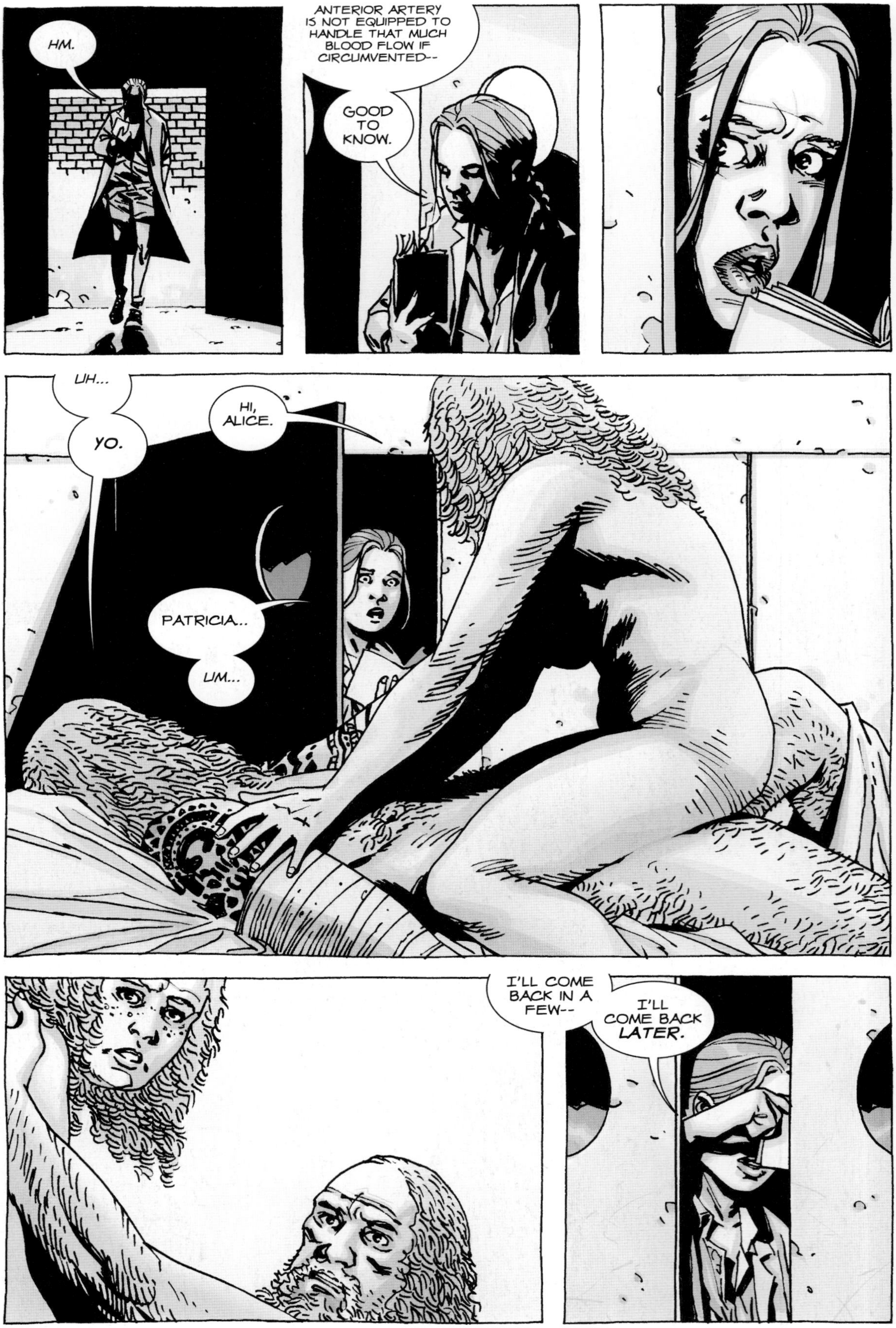
HM.
ANTERIOR ARTERY IS NOT EQUIPPED TO HANDLE THAT MUCH BLOOD FLOW IF CIRCUMVENTED--
GOOD TO KNOW.
UH...
YO.
HI, ALICE.
PATRICIA..
UM...
I'LL COME BACK IN A FEW--
I'LL COME BACK LATER.

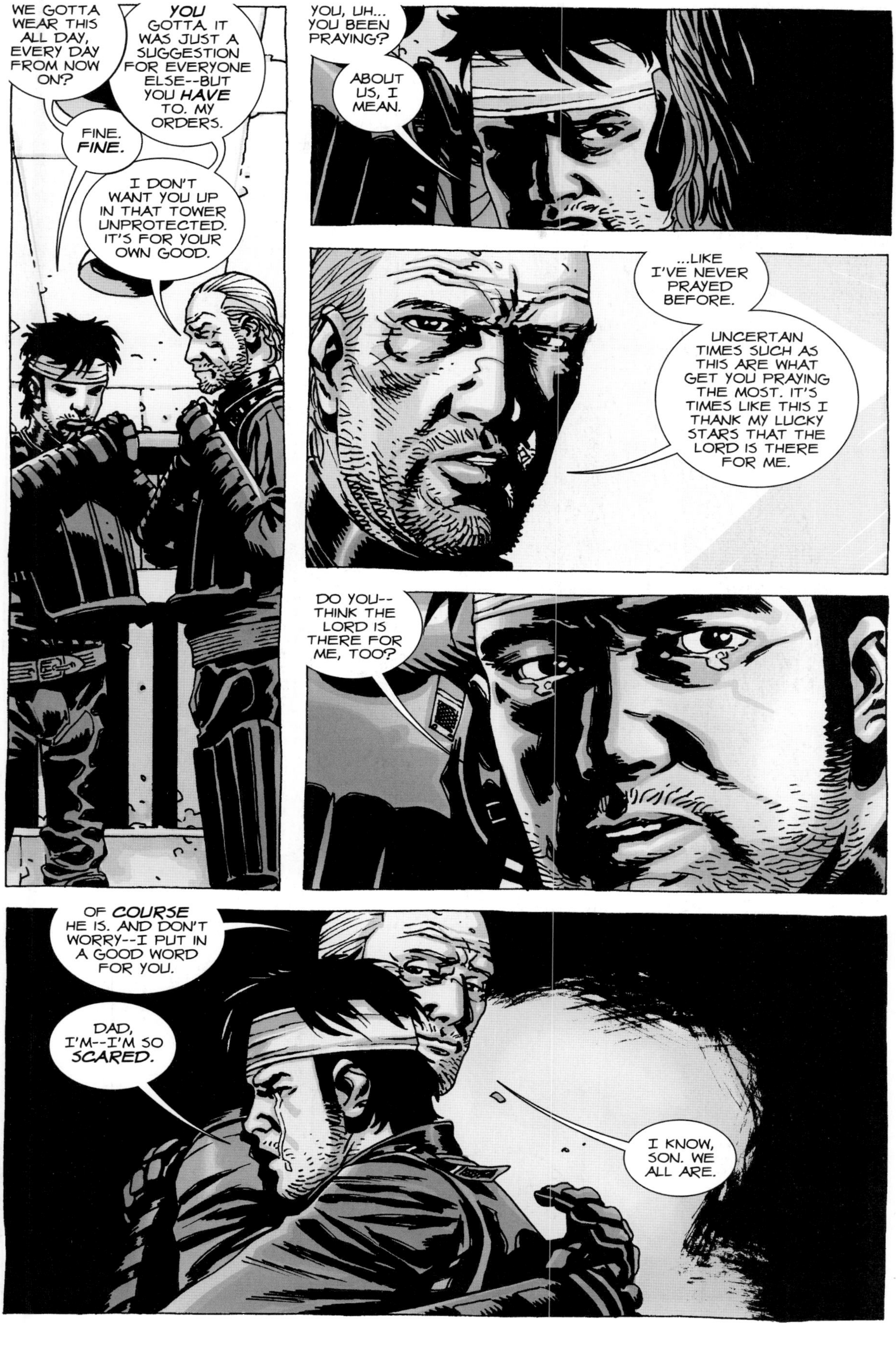
WE GOTTA WEAR THIS ALL DAY, EVERY DAY FROM NOW ON?
YOU GOTTA. IT WAS JUST A SUGGESTION FOR EVERYONE ELSE--BUT YOU HAVE TO. MY ORDERS.
FINE. FINE.
I DON'T WANT YOU UP IN THAT TOWER UNPROTECTED. IT'S FOR YOUR OWN GOOD.
YOU, UH... YOU BEEN PRAYING?
ABOUT US, I MEAN.
...LIKE I'VE NEVER PRAYED BEFORE.
UNCERTAIN TIMES SUCH AS THIS ARE WHAT GET YOU PRAYING THE MOST. IT'S TIMES LIKE THIS I THANK MY LUCKY STARS THAT THE LORD IS THERE FOR ME.
DO YOU-- THINK THE LORD IS THERE FOR ME, TOO?
OF COURSE HE IS. AND DON'T WORRY--I PUT IN A GOOD WORD FOR YOU.
DAD, I'M--I'M SO SCARED.
I KNOW, SON. WE ALL ARE.

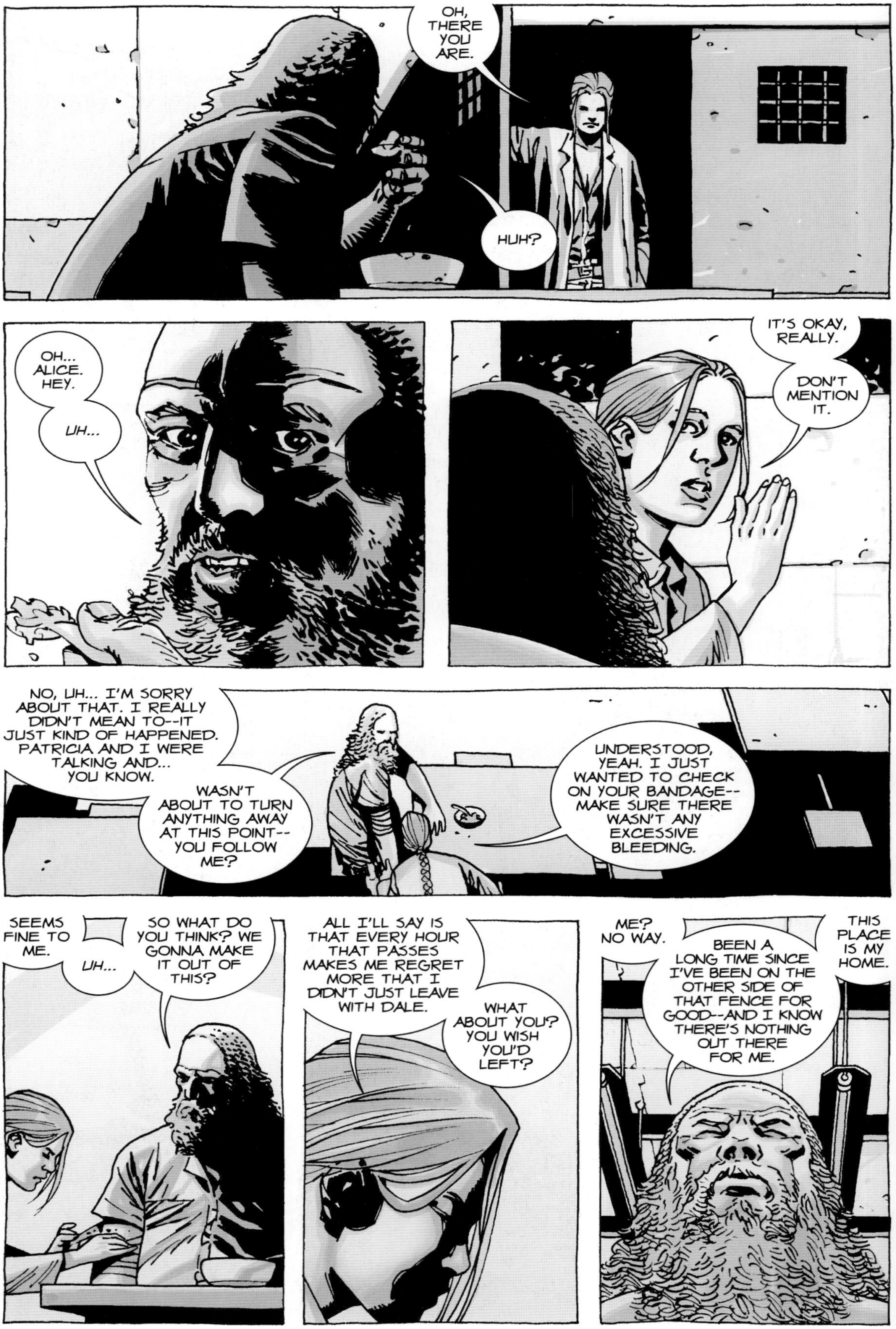
OH, THERE YOU ARE.
HUH?
OH... ALICE. HEY.
UH...
IT'S OKAY, REALLY.
DON'T MENTION IT.
NO, UH... I'M SORRY ABOUT THAT. I REALLY DIDN'T MEAN TO--IT JUST KIND OF HAPPENED. PATRICIA AND I WERE TALKING AND... YOU KNOW.
WASN'T ABOUT TO TURN ANYTHING AWAY AT THIS POINT--YOU FOLLOW ME?
UNDERSTOOD, YEAH. I JUST WANTED TO CHECK ON YOUR BANDAGE--MAKE SURE THERE WASN'T ANY EXCESSIVE BLEEDING.
SEEMS FINE TO ME.
UH...
SO WHAT DO YOU THINK? WE GONNA MAKE IT OUT OF THIS?
ALL I'LL SAY IS THAT EVERY HOUR THAT PASSES MAKES ME REGRET MORE THAT I DIDN'T JUST LEAVE WITH DALE.
WHAT ABOUT YOU? YOU WISH YOU'D LEFT?
ME? NO WAY.
THIS PLACE IS MY HOME.
BEEN A LONG TIME SINCE I'VE BEEN ON THE OTHER SIDE OF THAT FENCE FOR GOOD--AND I KNOW THERE'S NOTHING OUT THERE FOR ME.

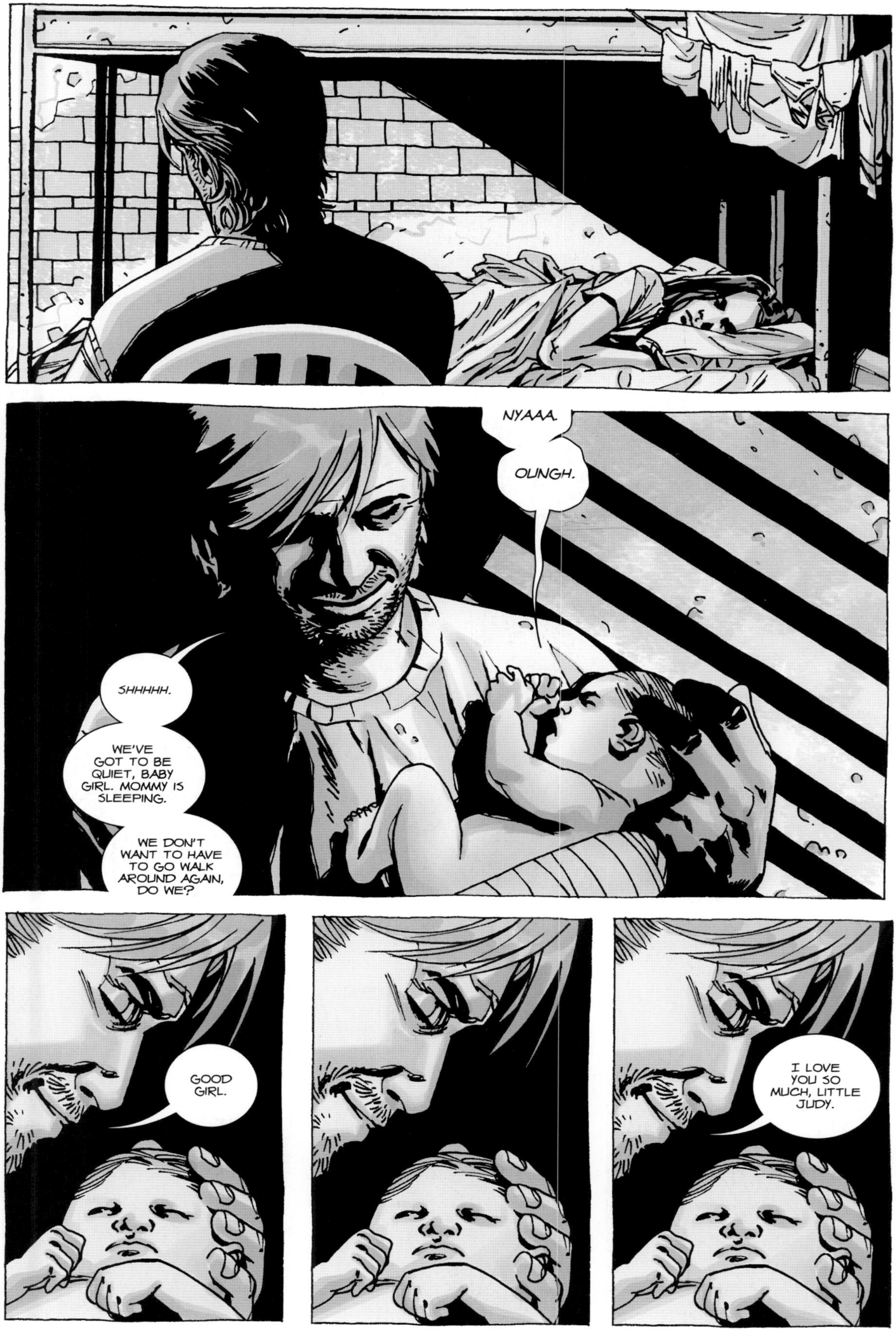
NYAAA.
OUNGH.
SHHHHH.
WE'VE GOT TO BE QUIET, BABY GIRL. MOMMY IS SLEEPING.
WE DON'T WANT TO HAVE TO GO WALK AROUND AGAIN, DO WE?
GOOD GIRL.
I LOVE YOU SO MUCH, LITTLE JUDY.

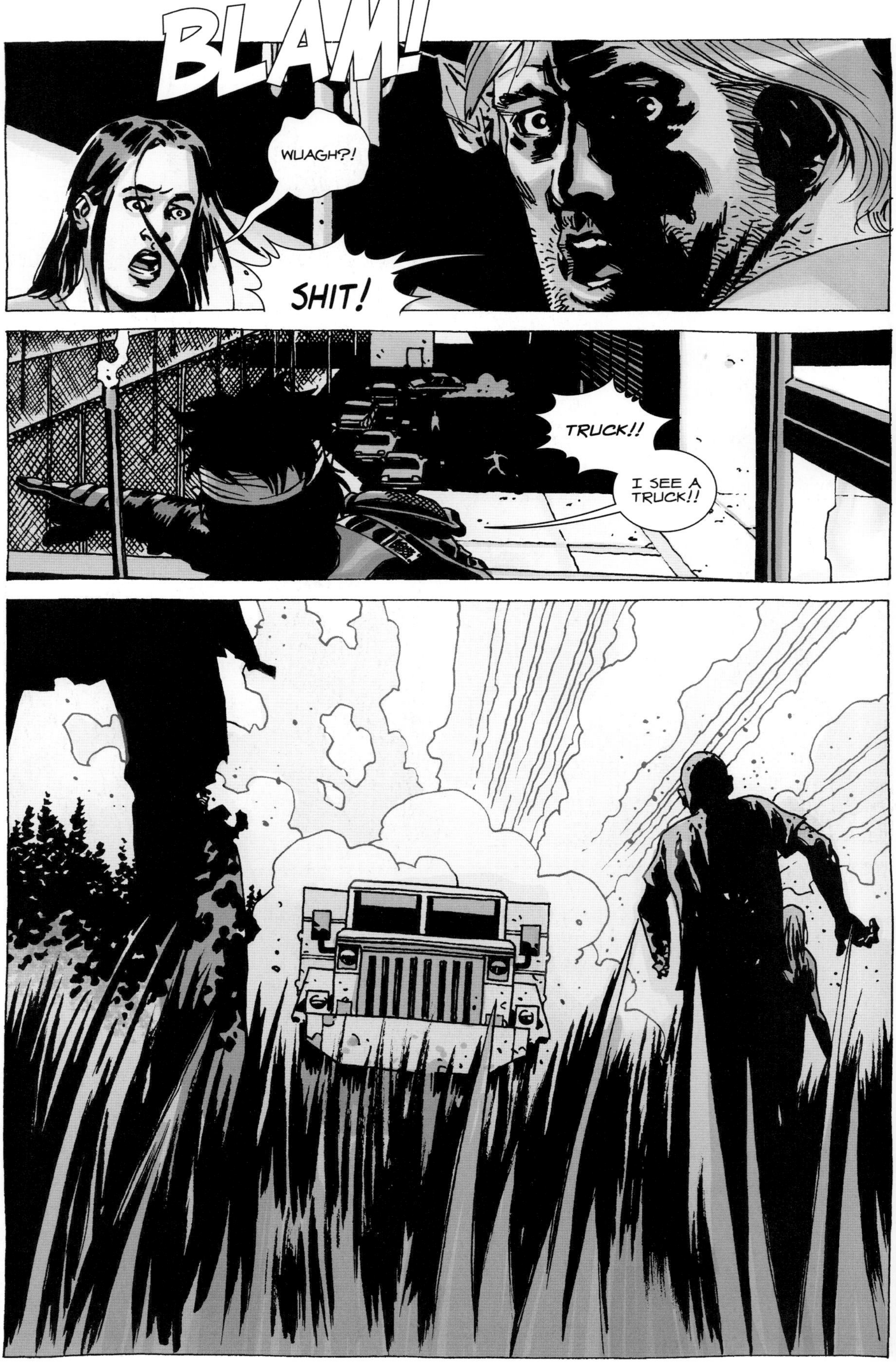
BLAM!
WUAGH?!
SHIT!
TRUCK!!
I SEE A TRUCK!!

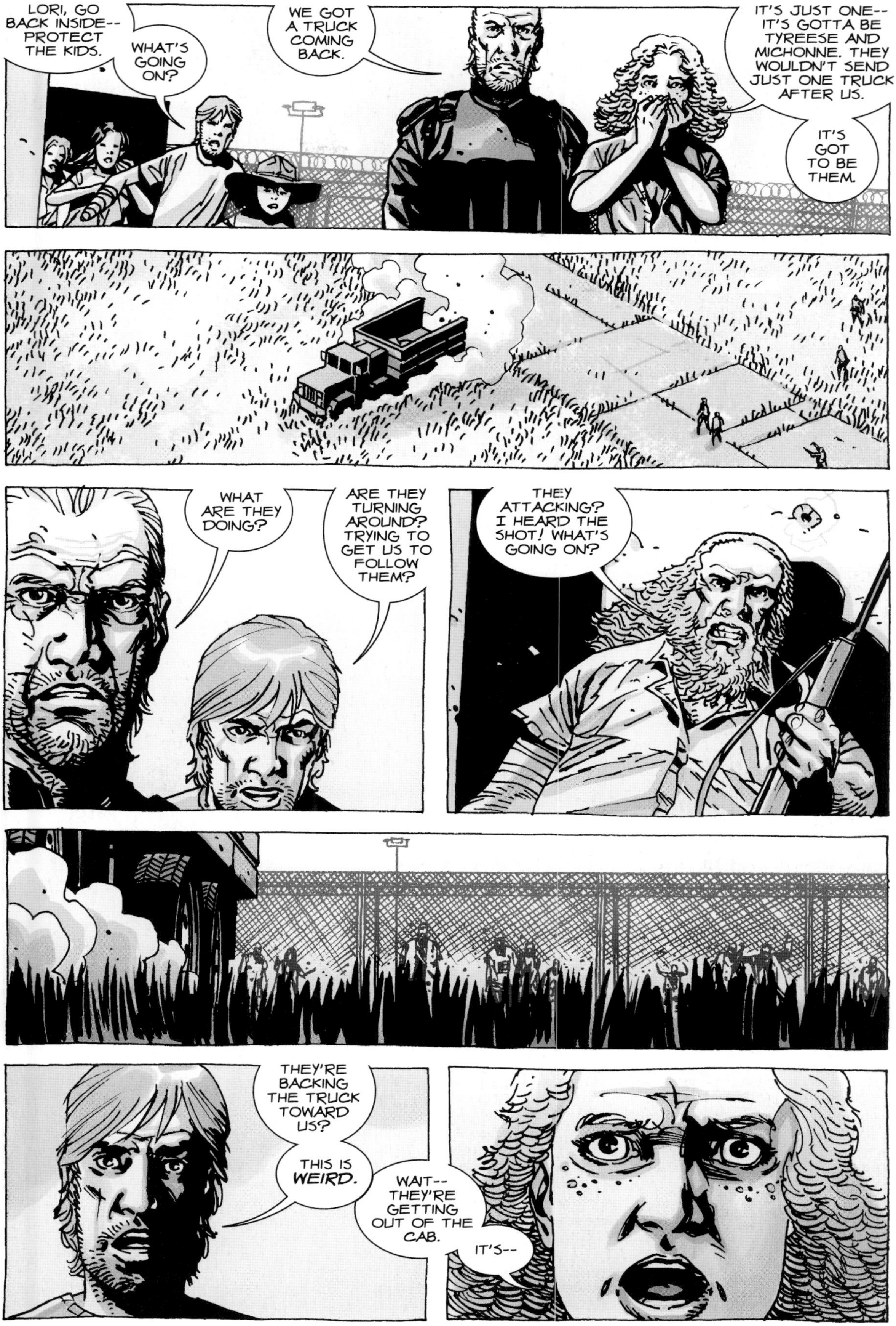
LORI, GO BACK INSIDE-- PROTECT THE KIDS.
WHAT'S GOING ON?
WE GOT A TRUCK COMING BACK.
IT'S JUST ONE-- IT'S GOTTA BE TYREESE AND MICHONNE. THEY WOULDN'T SEND JUST ONE TRUCK AFTER US.
IT'S GOT TO BE THEM.
WHAT ARE THEY DOING?
ARE THEY TURNING AROUND? TRYING TO GET US TO FOLLOW THEM?
THEY ATTACKING? I HEARD THE SHOT! WHAT'S GOING ON?
THEY'RE BACKING THE TRUCK TOWARD US?
THIS IS WEIRD.
WAIT-- THEY'RE GETTING OUT OF THE CAB.
IT'S--

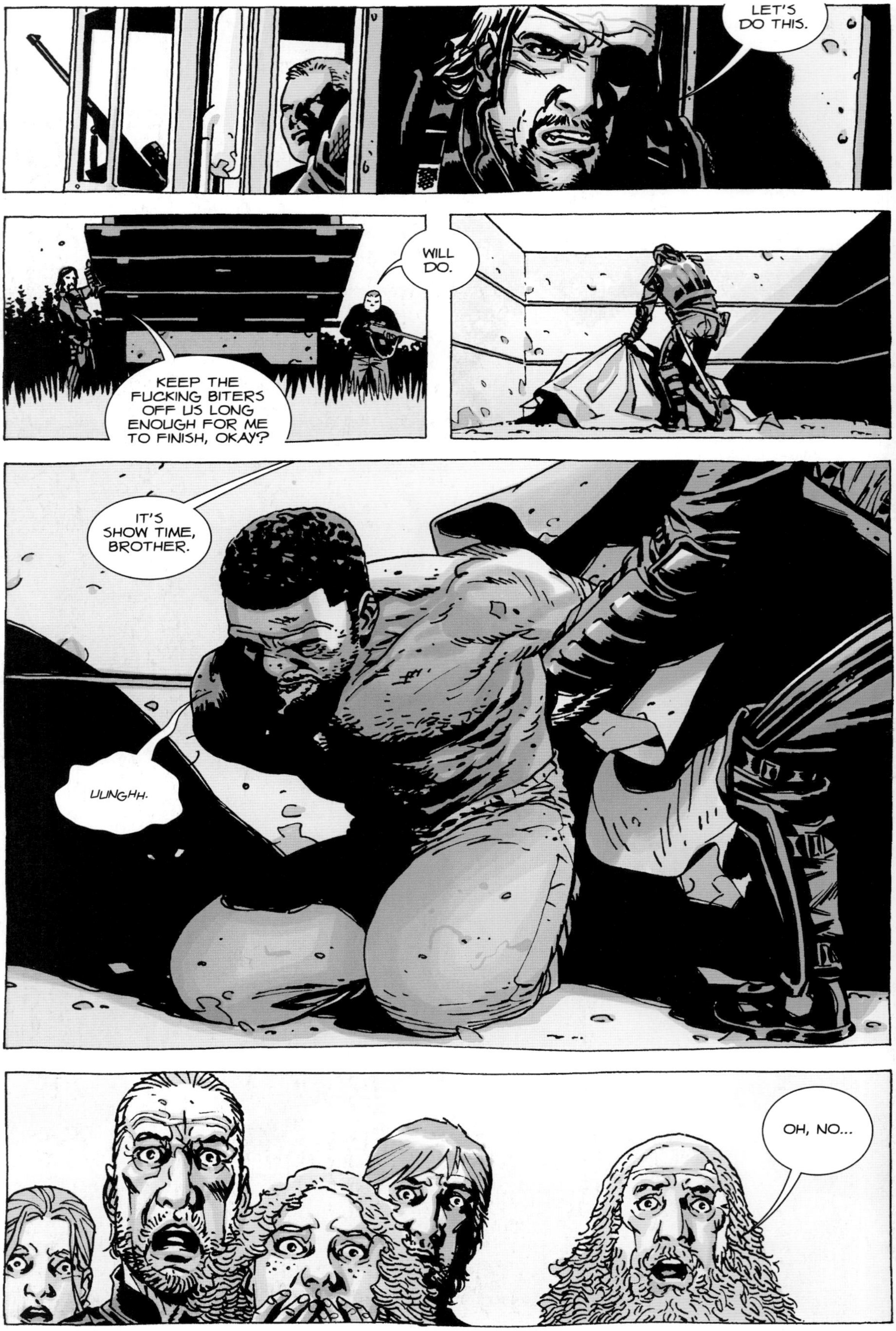
LET'S DO THIS.
KEEP THE FUCKING BITERS OFF US LONG ENOUGH FOR ME TO FINISH, OKAY?
WILL DO.
IT'S SHOW TIME, BROTHER.
UUNGHH.
OH, NO...

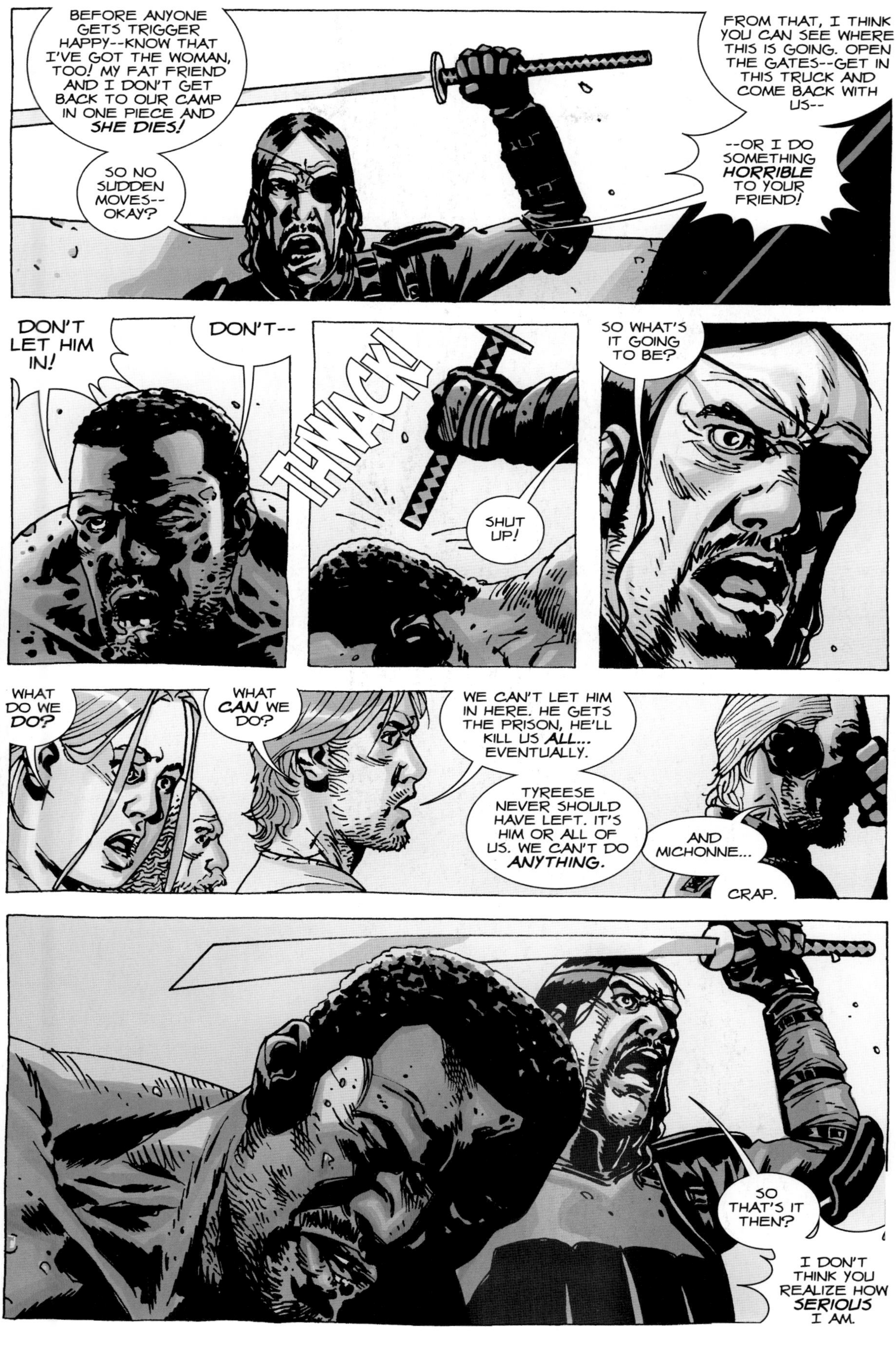
BEFORE ANYONE GETS TRIGGER HAPPY--KNOW THAT I'VE GOT THE WOMAN, TOO! MY FAT FRIEND AND I DON'T GET BACK TO OUR CAMP IN ONE PIECE AND SHE DIES!
SO NO SUDDEN MOVES--OKAY?
FROM THAT, I THINK YOU CAN SEE WHERE THIS IS GOING. OPEN THE GATES--GET IN THIS TRUCK AND COME BACK WITH US--
--OR I DO SOMETHING HORRIBLE TO YOUR FRIEND!
DON'T LET HIM IN!
DON'T--
THWACK!
SHUT UP!
SO WHAT'S IT GOING TO BE?
WHAT DO WE DO?
WHAT CAN WE DO?
WE CAN'T LET HIM IN HERE. HE GETS THE PRISON, HE'LL KILL US ALL... EVENTUALLY.
TYREESE NEVER SHOULD HAVE LEFT. IT'S HIM OR ALL OF US. WE CAN'T DO ANYTHING.
AND MICHONNE...
CRAP.
SO THAT'S IT THEN?
I DON'T THINK YOU REALIZE HOW SERIOUS I AM.

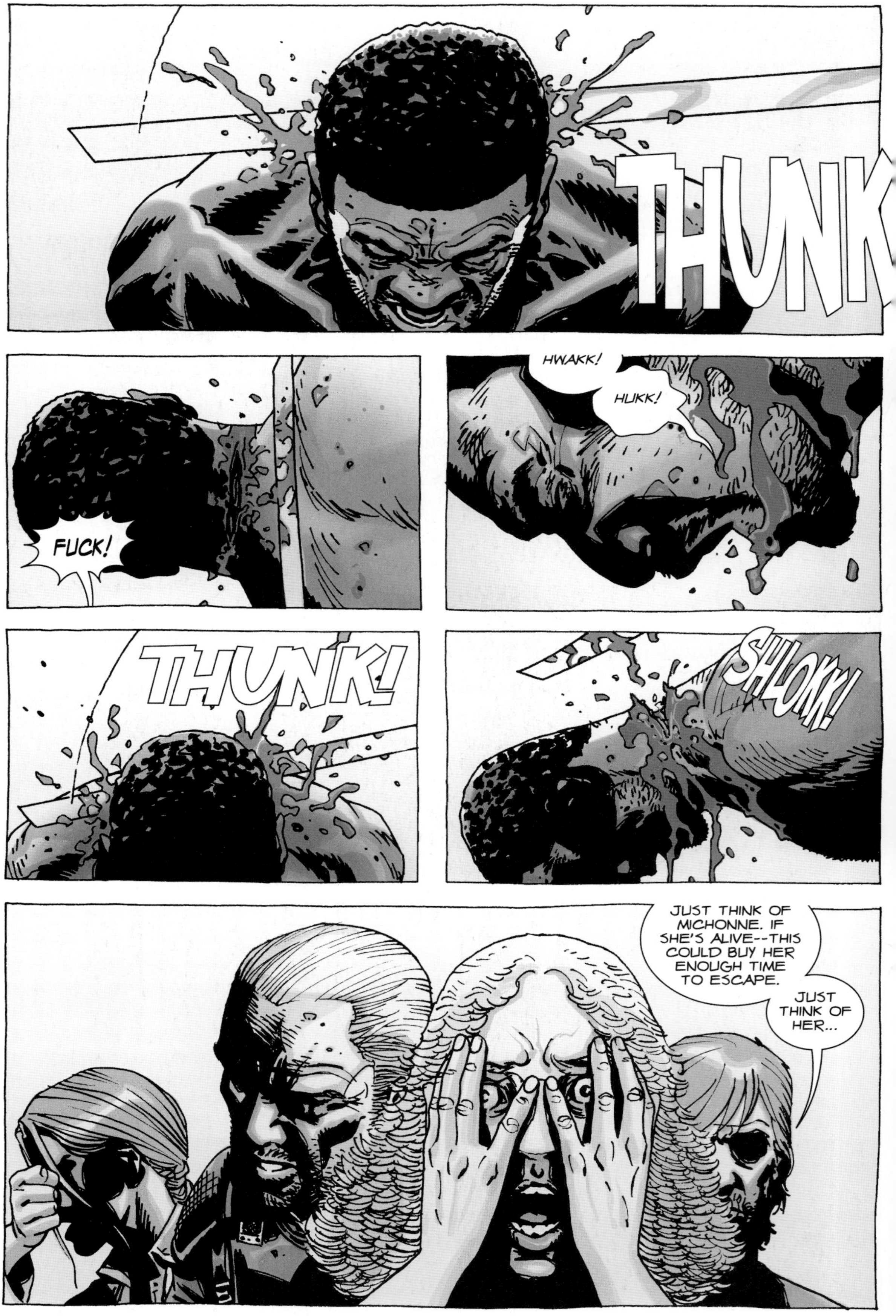
THUNK
FUCK!
HWAKK!
HUKK!
THUNK!
SHLOKK!
JUST THINK OF MICHONNE. IF SHE'S ALIVE--THIS COULD BUY HER ENOUGH TIME TO ESCAPE.
JUST THINK OF HER...

SHUKK!!

WHUMP!

THUNK!

THUNK!

THUNK!

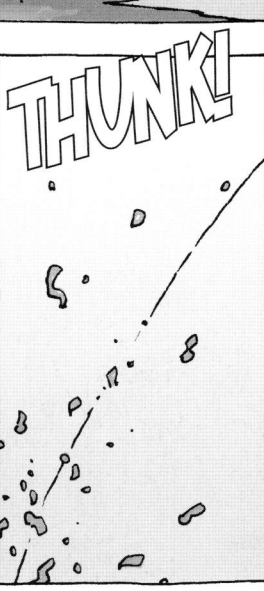

=HUFF!=

=HUFF!=

=HUFF!=

WROK!

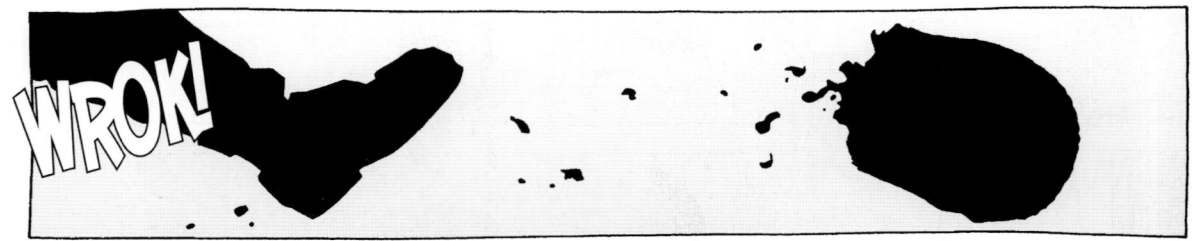

LEAVE HIM FOR THE BITERS. LET'S ROLL BEFORE THEY GET TOO CLOSE-- OR BEFORE ONE OF THESE SHELL-SHOCKED FUCKS DECIDES TO FIRE A GUN.

WHUMP!

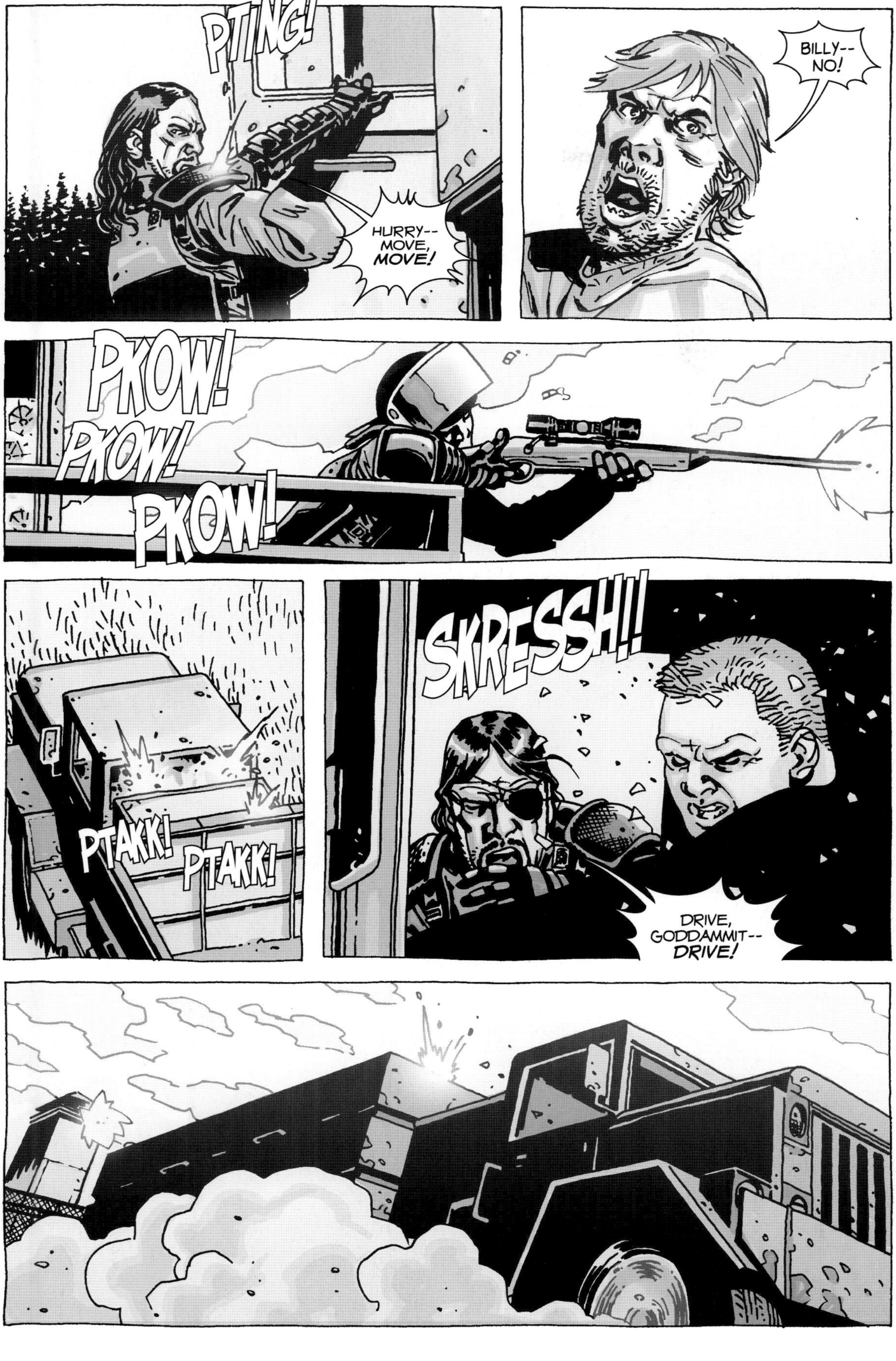
PTING!
HURRY--
MOVE,
MOVE!
BILLY--
NO!
PKOW!
PKOW!
PKOW!
PTAKK!
PTAKK!
SKRESSH!!
DRIVE,
GODDAMMIT--
DRIVE!

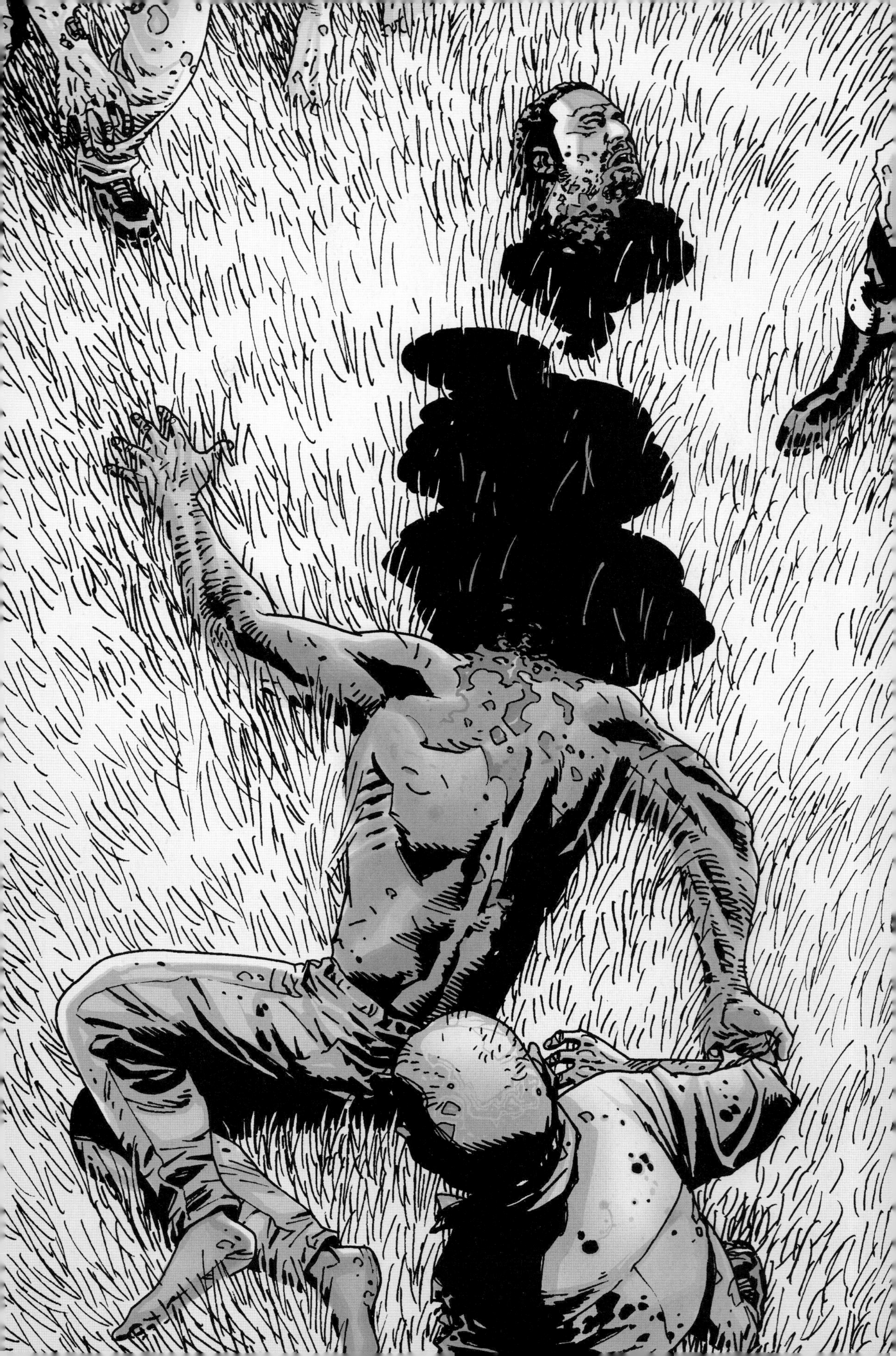

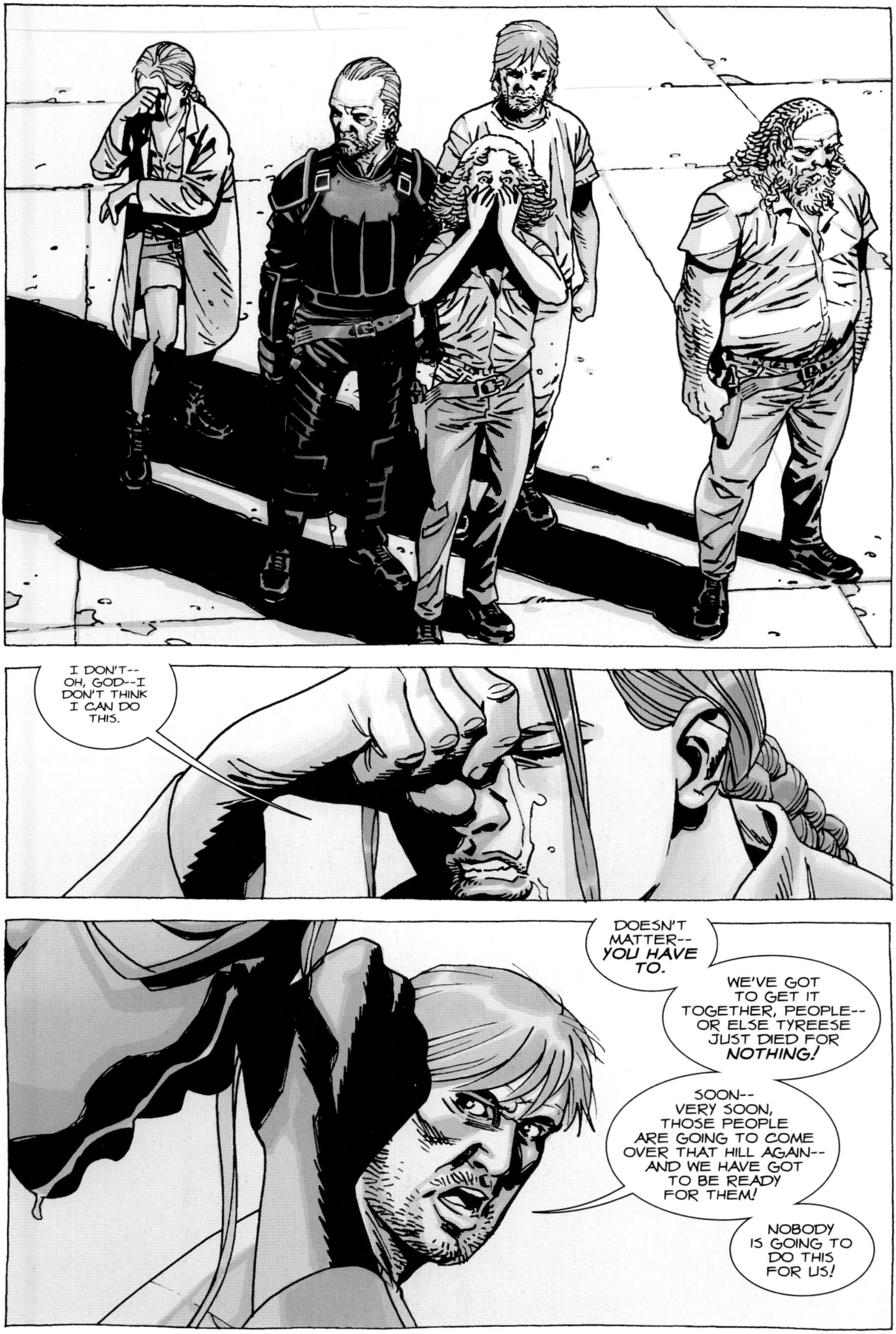
I DON'T-- OH, GOD--I DON'T THINK I CAN DO THIS.
DOESN'T MATTER-- YOU HAVE TO.
WE'VE GOT TO GET IT TOGETHER, PEOPLE-- OR ELSE TYREESE JUST DIED FOR NOTHING!
SOON-- VERY SOON, THOSE PEOPLE ARE GOING TO COME OVER THAT HILL AGAIN-- AND WE HAVE GOT TO BE READY FOR THEM!
NOBODY IS GOING TO DO THIS FOR US!

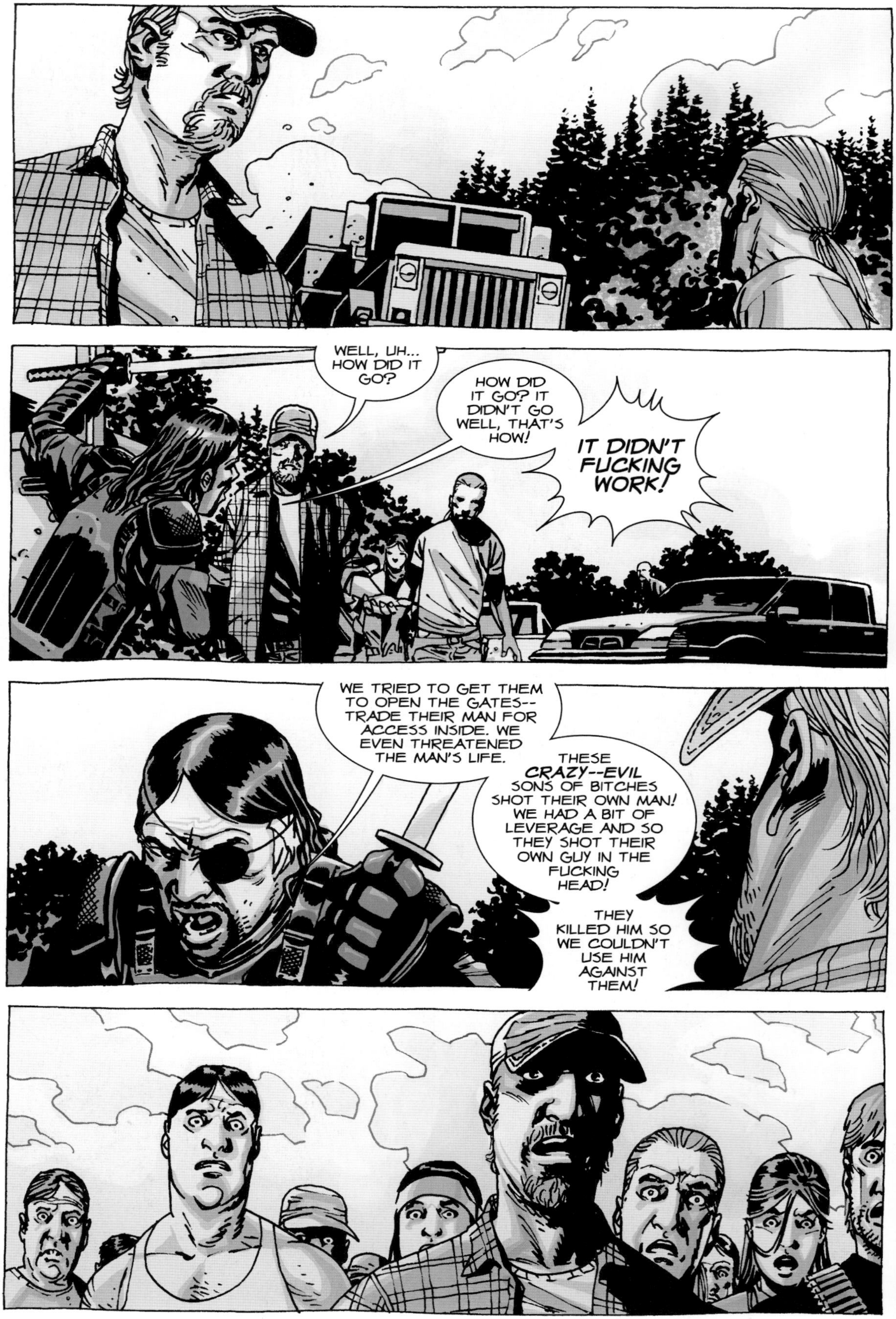
WELL, UH... HOW DID IT GO?
HOW DID IT GO? IT DIDN'T GO WELL, THAT'S HOW!
IT DIDN'T FUCKING WORK!
WE TRIED TO GET THEM TO OPEN THE GATES-- TRADE THEIR MAN FOR ACCESS INSIDE. WE EVEN THREATENED THE MAN'S LIFE.
THESE CRAZY--EVIL SONS OF BITCHES SHOT THEIR OWN MAN! WE HAD A BIT OF LEVERAGE AND SO THEY SHOT THEIR OWN GUY IN THE FUCKING HEAD!
THEY KILLED HIM SO WE COULDN'T USE HIM AGAINST THEM!

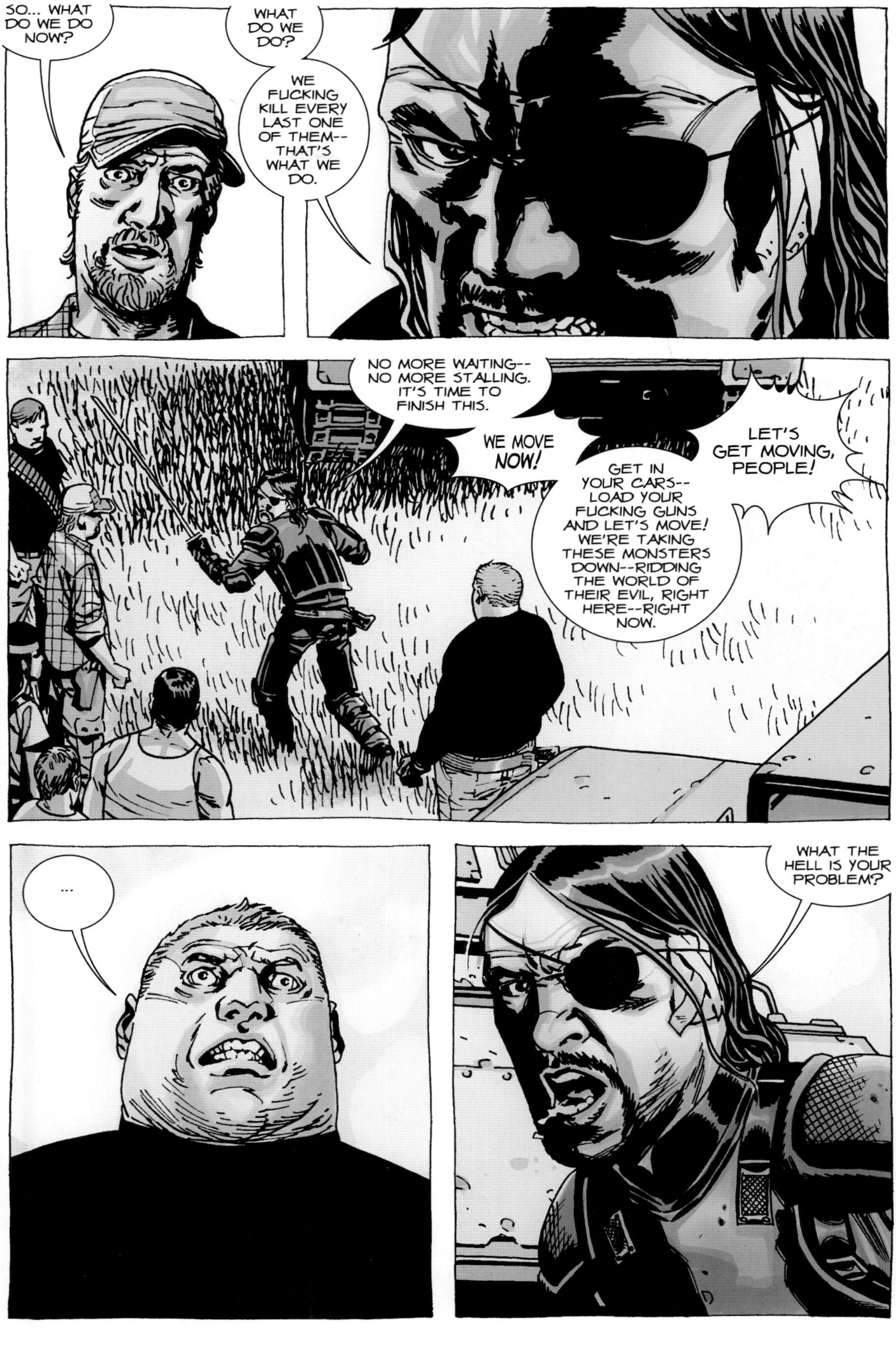
SO... WHAT DO WE DO NOW?
WHAT DO WE DO?
WE FUCKING KILL EVERY LAST ONE OF THEM-- THAT'S WHAT WE DO.
NO MORE WAITING-- NO MORE STALLING. IT'S TIME TO FINISH THIS.
WE MOVE NOW!
GET IN YOUR CARS-- LOAD YOUR FUCKING GUNS AND LET'S MOVE! WE'RE TAKING THESE MONSTERS DOWN--RIDDING THE WORLD OF THEIR EVIL, RIGHT HERE--RIGHT NOW.
LET'S GET MOVING, PEOPLE!
...
WHAT THE HELL IS YOUR PROBLEM?

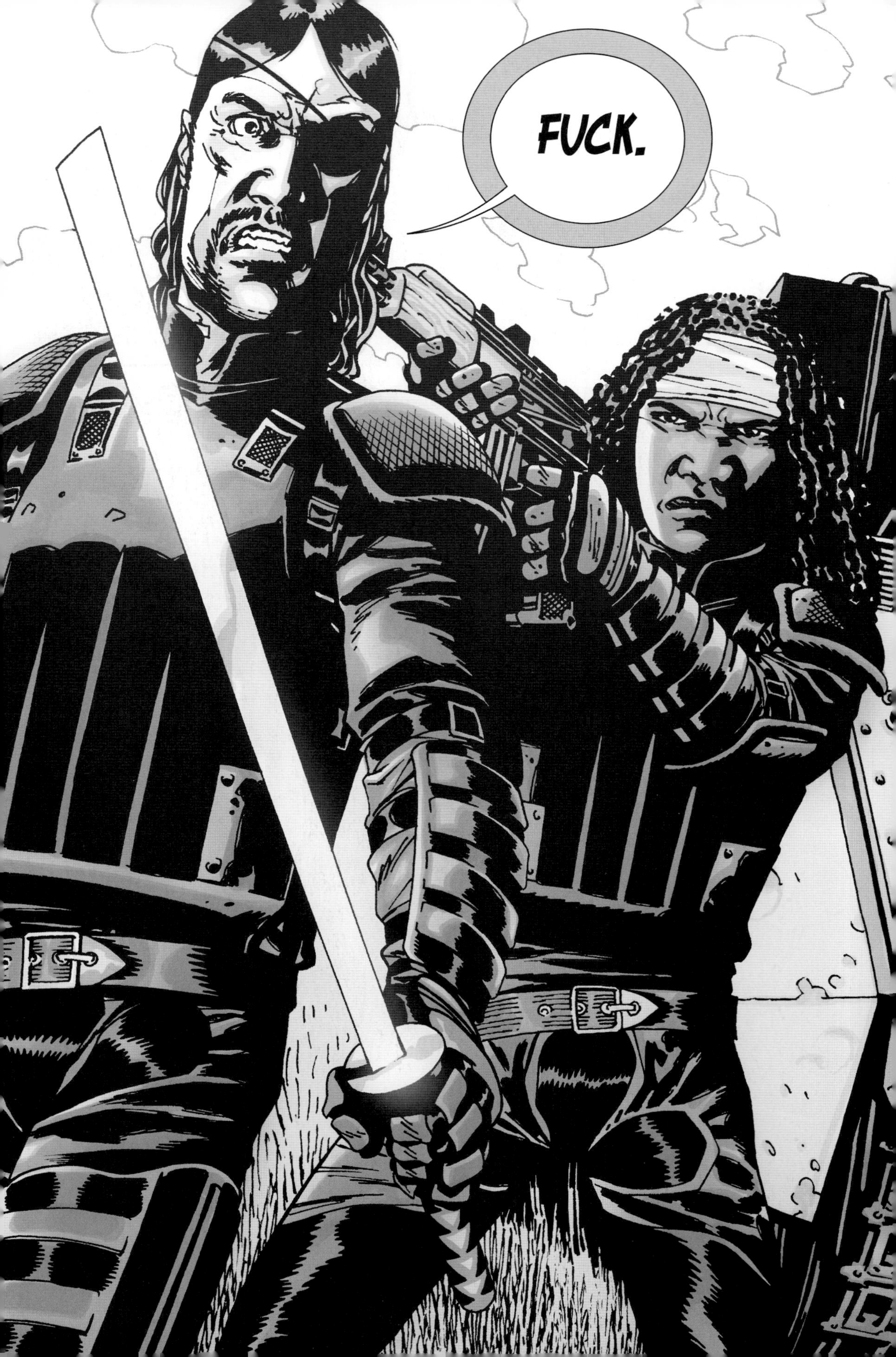
FUCK.

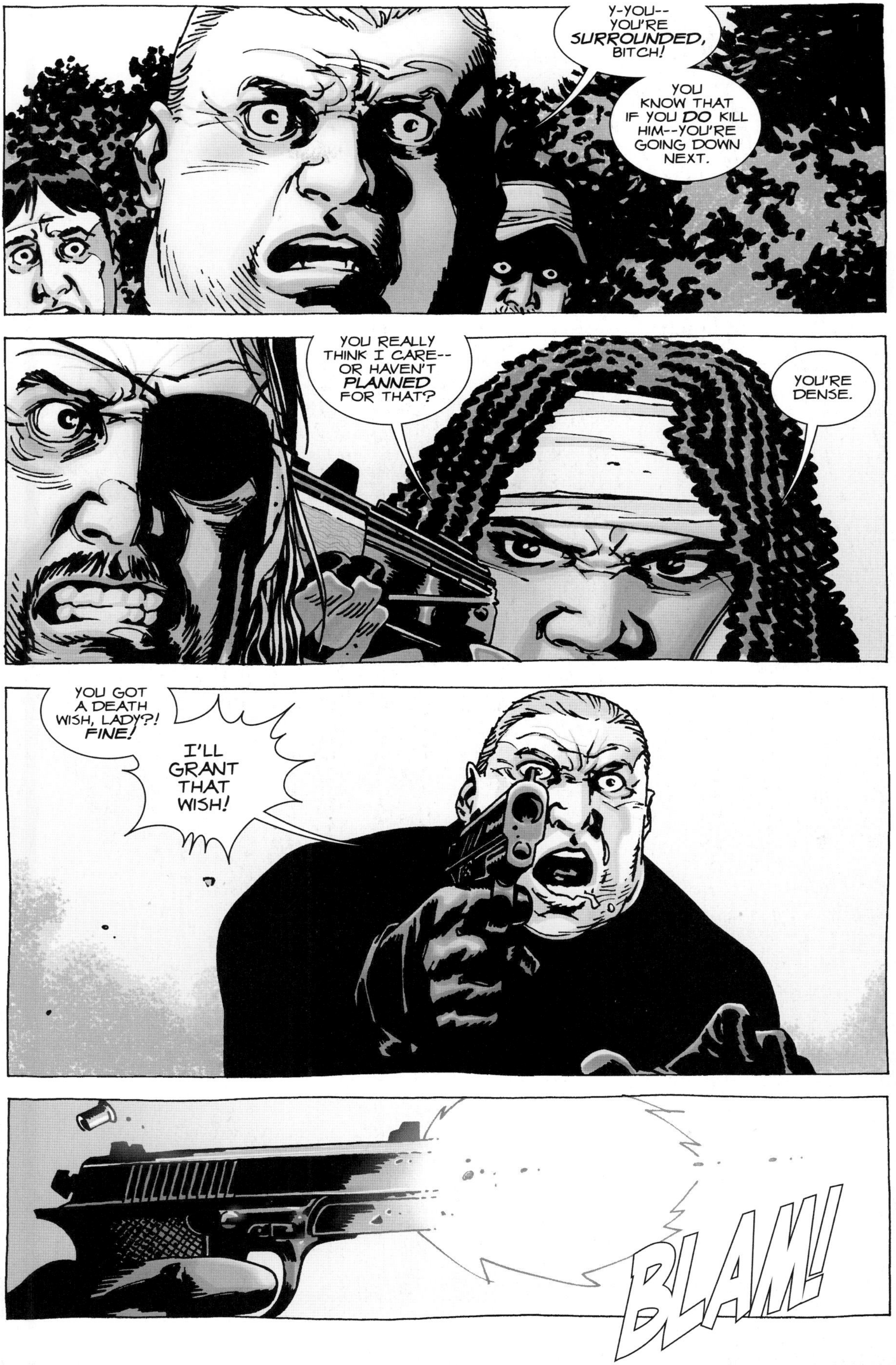
Y-YOU-- YOU'RE SURROUNDED, BITCH!
YOU KNOW THAT IF YOU DO KILL HIM--YOU'RE GOING DOWN NEXT.
YOU REALLY THINK I CARE-- OR HAVEN'T PLANNED FOR THAT?
YOU'RE DENSE.
YOU GOT A DEATH WISH, LADY?! FINE!
I'LL GRANT THAT WISH!
BLAM!

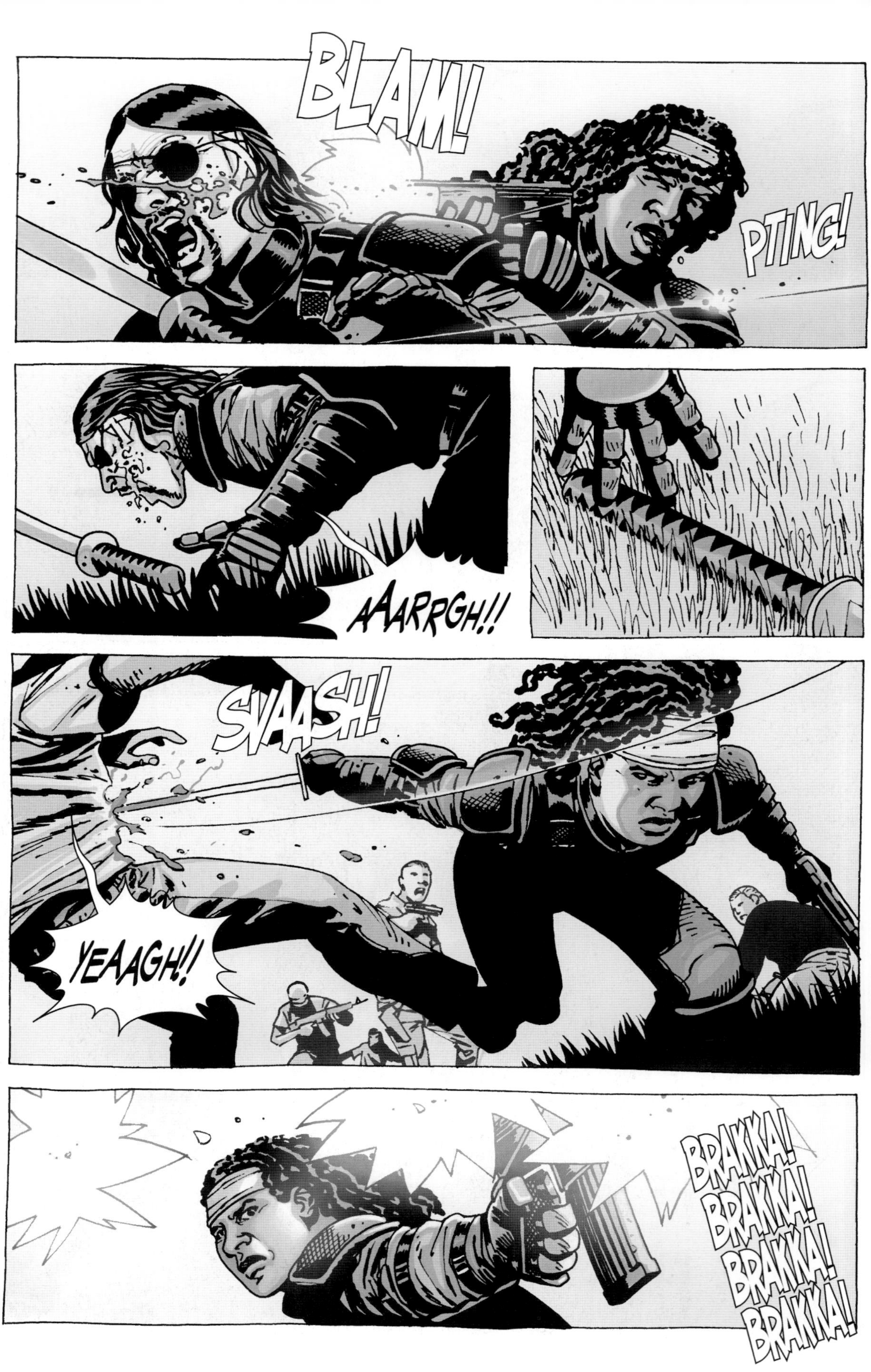
BLAM!
PTING!
AAARRGH!!
SVAASH!
YEAAGH!!
BRAKKA!
BRAKKA!
BRAKKA!
BRAKKA!

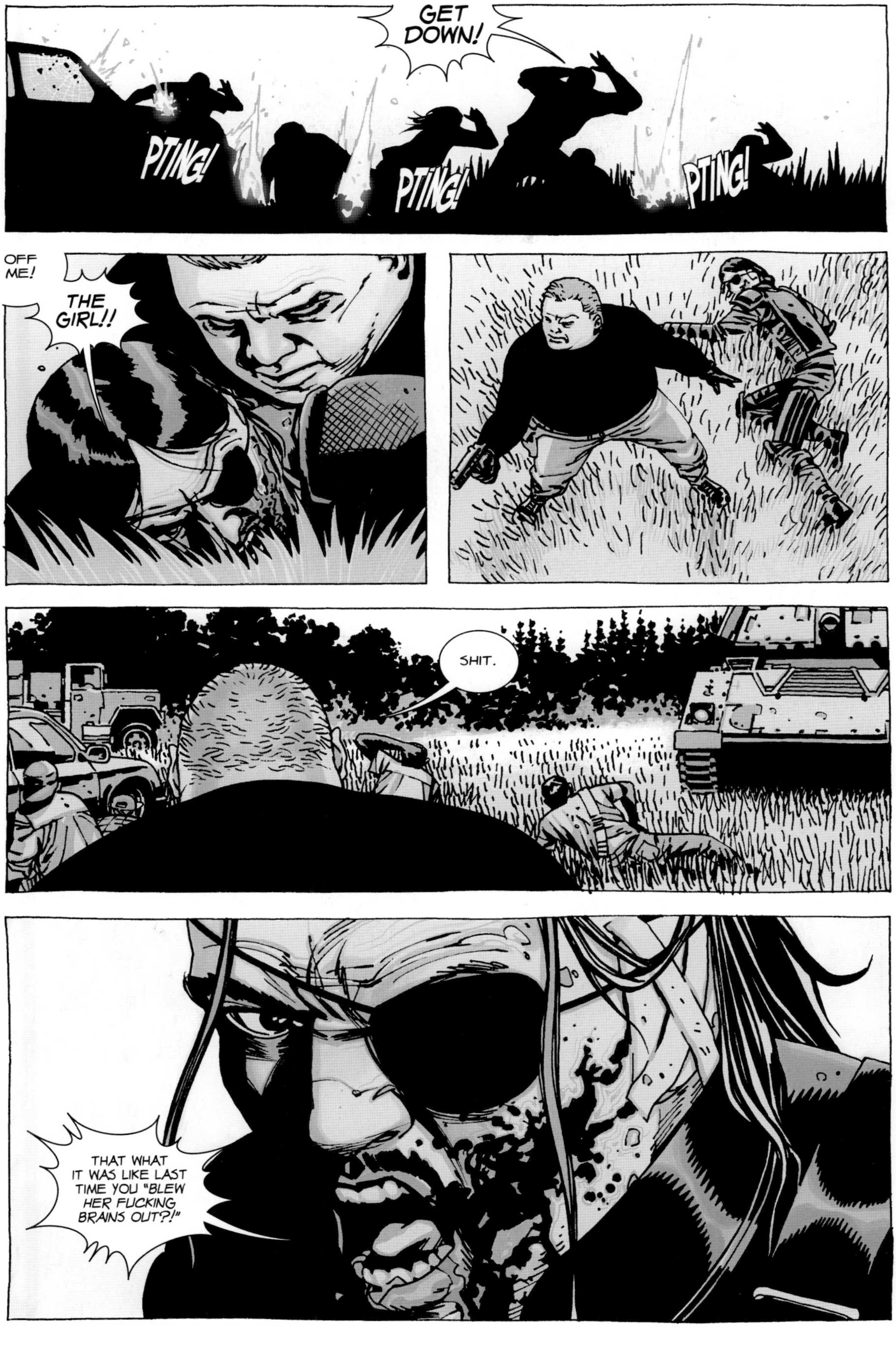
GET DOWN!
PTING!
PTING!
PTING!
OFF ME!
THE GIRL!!
SHIT.
THAT WHAT IT WAS LIKE LAST TIME YOU "BLEW HER FUCKING BRAINS OUT?!"

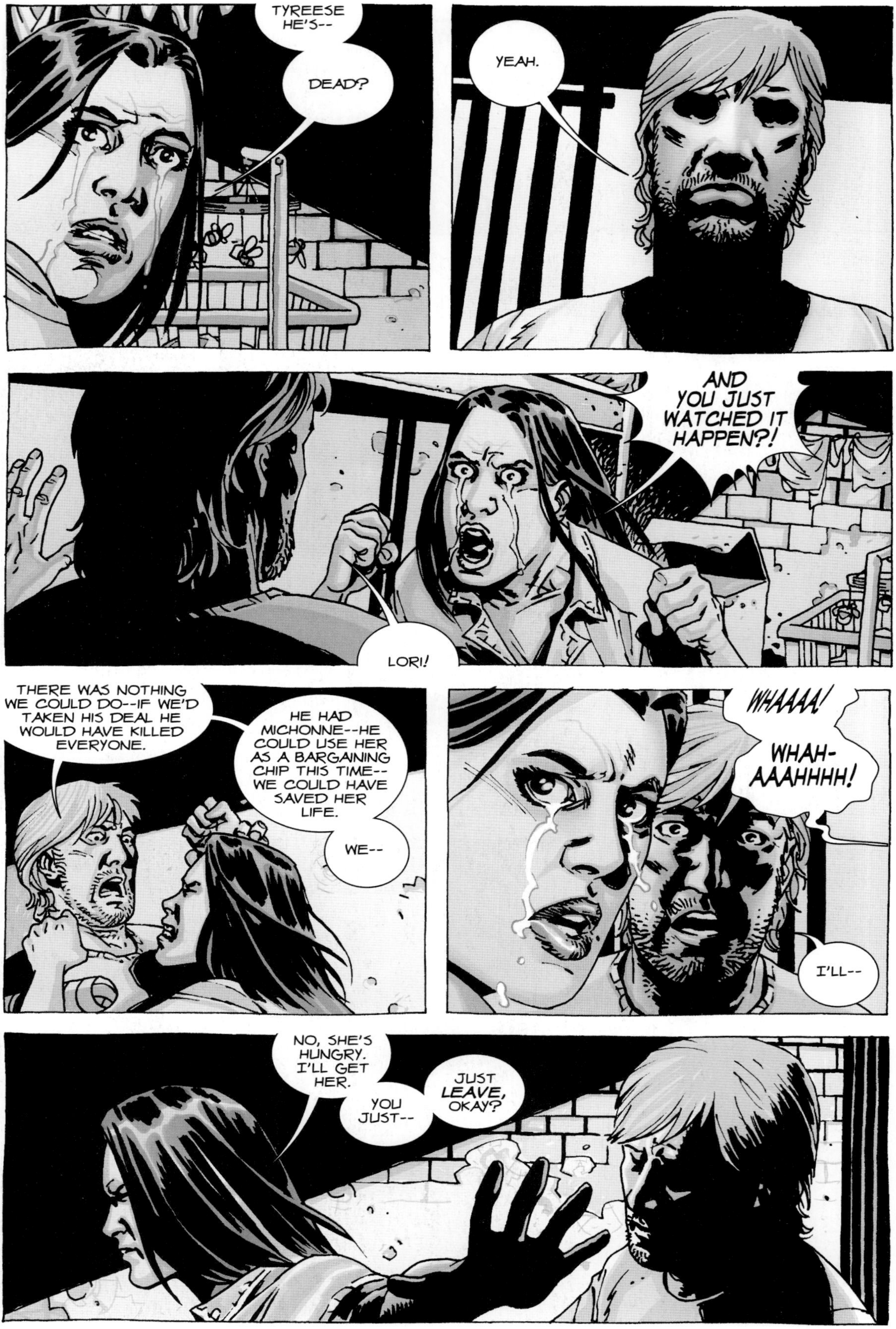
TYREESE HE'S--
DEAD?
YEAH.
AND YOU JUST WATCHED IT HAPPEN?!
LORI!
THERE WAS NOTHING WE COULD DO--IF WE'D TAKEN HIS DEAL HE WOULD HAVE KILLED EVERYONE.
HE HAD MICHONNE--HE COULD USE HER AS A BARGAINING CHIP THIS TIME--WE COULD HAVE SAVED HER LIFE.
WE--
WHAAAA!
WHAH-AAAHHHH!
I'LL--
NO, SHE'S HUNGRY. I'LL GET HER.
YOU JUST--
JUST LEAVE, OKAY?

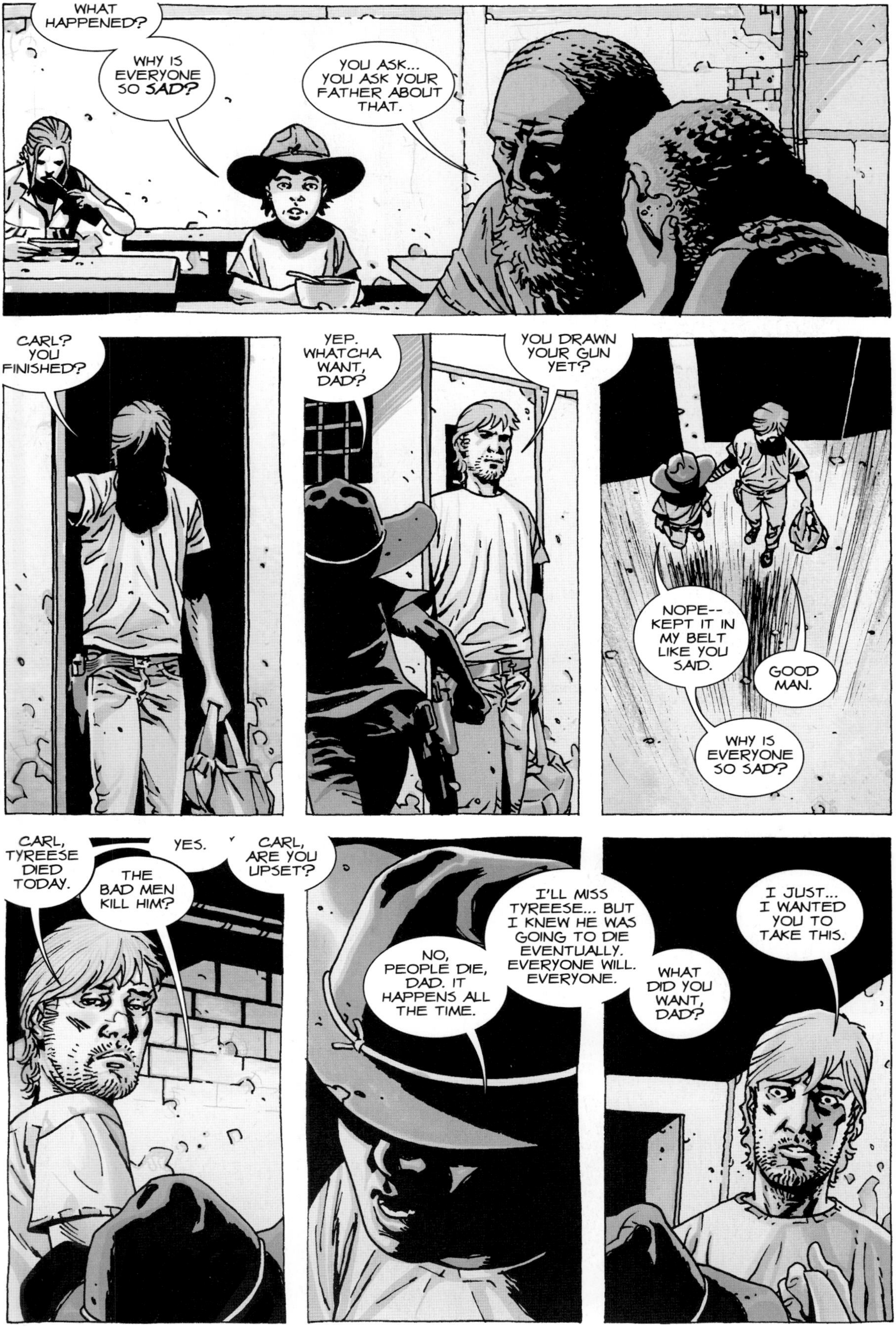
WHAT HAPPENED?
WHY IS EVERYONE SO *SAD?*
YOU ASK... YOU ASK YOUR FATHER ABOUT THAT.
CARL? YOU FINISHED?
YEP. WHATCHA WANT, DAD?
YOU DRAWN YOUR GUN YET?
NOPE-- KEPT IT IN MY BELT LIKE YOU SAID.
GOOD MAN.
WHY IS EVERYONE SO SAD?
CARL, TYREESE DIED TODAY.
THE BAD MEN KILL HIM?
YES.
CARL, ARE YOU UPSET?
NO, PEOPLE DIE, DAD. IT HAPPENS ALL THE TIME.
I'LL MISS TYREESE... BUT I KNEW HE WAS GOING TO DIE EVENTUALLY. EVERYONE WILL. EVERYONE.
WHAT DID YOU WANT, DAD?
I JUST... I WANTED YOU TO TAKE THIS.

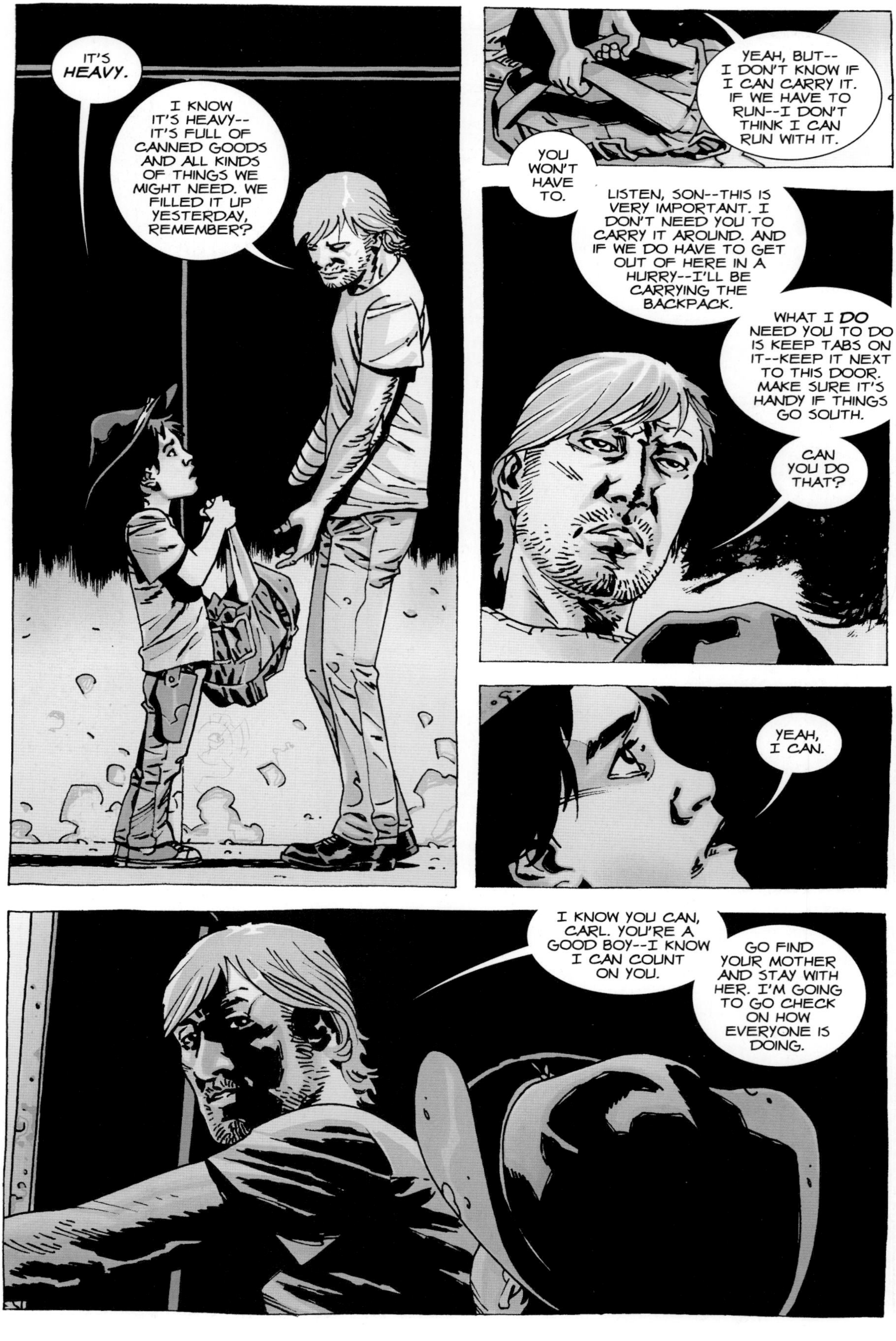
IT'S HEAVY.
I KNOW IT'S HEAVY-- IT'S FULL OF CANNED GOODS AND ALL KINDS OF THINGS WE MIGHT NEED. WE FILLED IT UP YESTERDAY, REMEMBER?
YEAH, BUT-- I DON'T KNOW IF I CAN CARRY IT. IF WE HAVE TO RUN--I DON'T THINK I CAN RUN WITH IT.
YOU WON'T HAVE TO.
LISTEN, SON--THIS IS VERY IMPORTANT. I DON'T NEED YOU TO CARRY IT AROUND. AND IF WE DO HAVE TO GET OUT OF HERE IN A HURRY--I'LL BE CARRYING THE BACKPACK.
WHAT I DO NEED YOU TO DO IS KEEP TABS ON IT--KEEP IT NEXT TO THIS DOOR. MAKE SURE IT'S HANDY IF THINGS GO SOUTH.
CAN YOU DO THAT?
YEAH, I CAN.
I KNOW YOU CAN, CARL. YOU'RE A GOOD BOY--I KNOW I CAN COUNT ON YOU.
GO FIND YOUR MOTHER AND STAY WITH HER. I'M GOING TO GO CHECK ON HOW EVERYONE IS DOING.

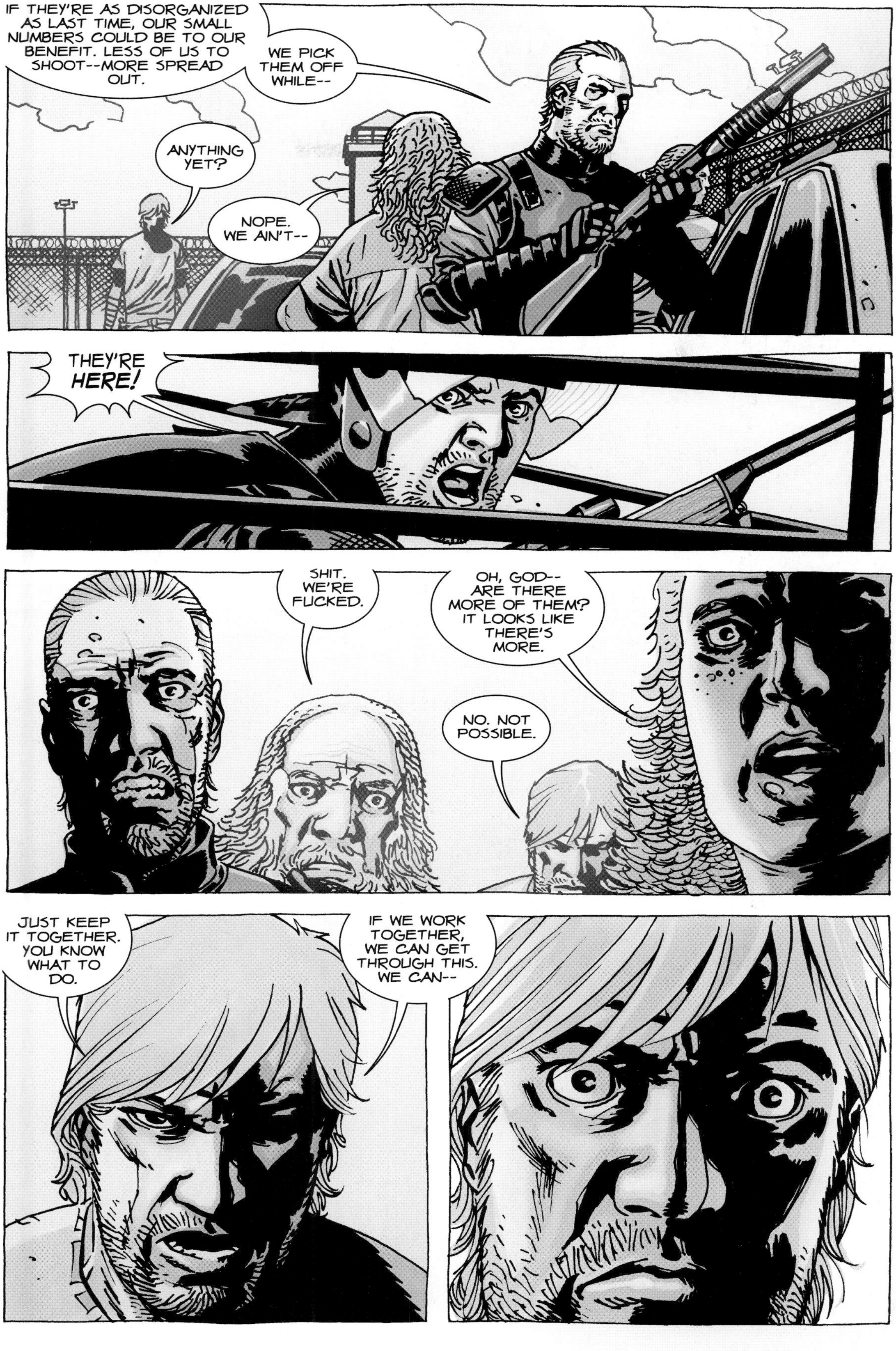
IF THEY'RE AS DISORGANIZED AS LAST TIME, OUR SMALL NUMBERS COULD BE TO OUR BENEFIT. LESS OF US TO SHOOT--MORE SPREAD OUT.
WE PICK THEM OFF WHILE--
ANYTHING YET?
NOPE. WE AIN'T--
THEY'RE HERE!
SHIT. WE'RE FUCKED.
OH, GOD-- ARE THERE MORE OF THEM? IT LOOKS LIKE THERE'S MORE.
NO. NOT POSSIBLE.
JUST KEEP IT TOGETHER. YOU KNOW WHAT TO DO.
IF WE WORK TOGETHER, WE CAN GET THROUGH THIS. WE CAN--

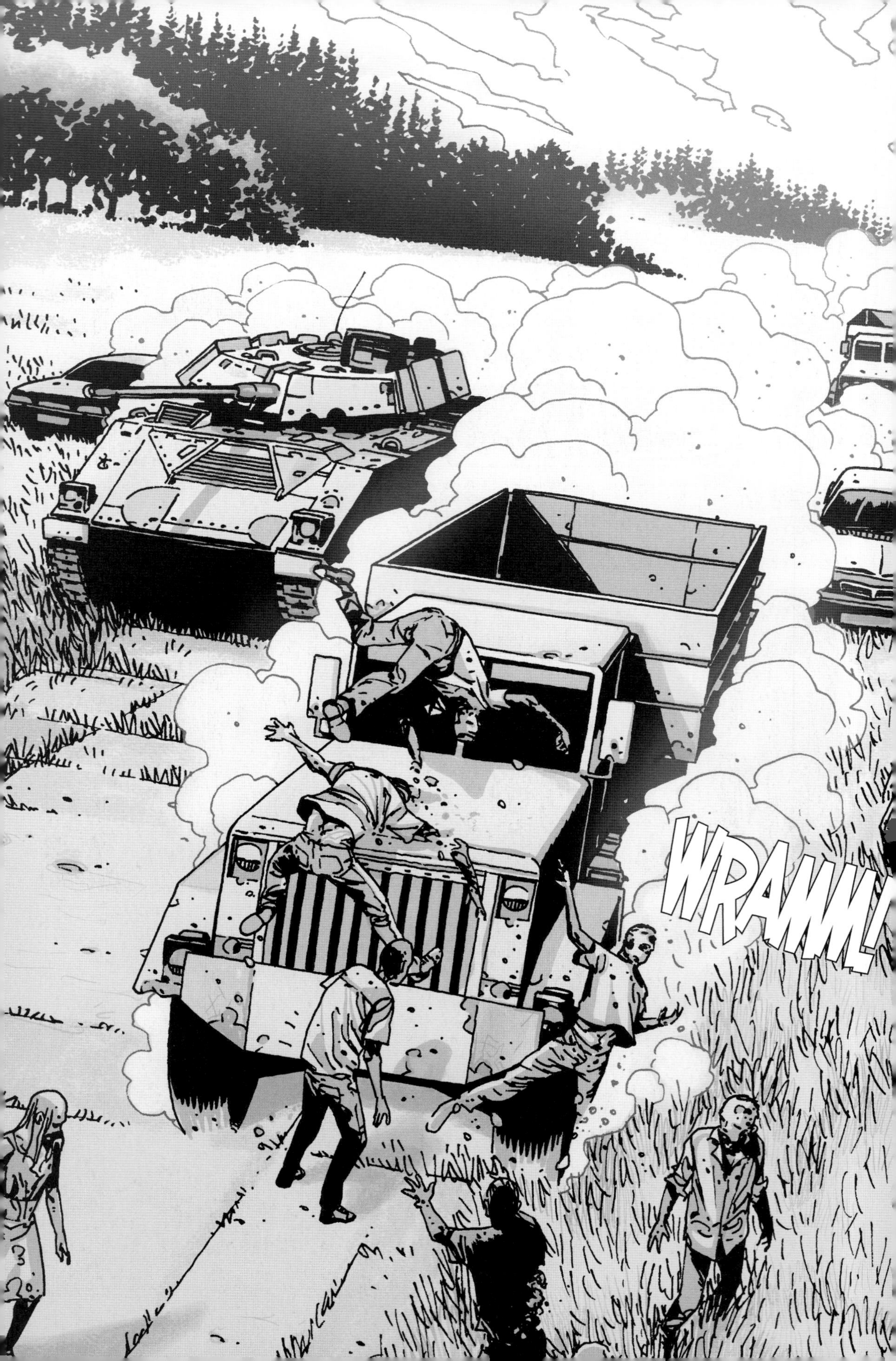
WRAMM!

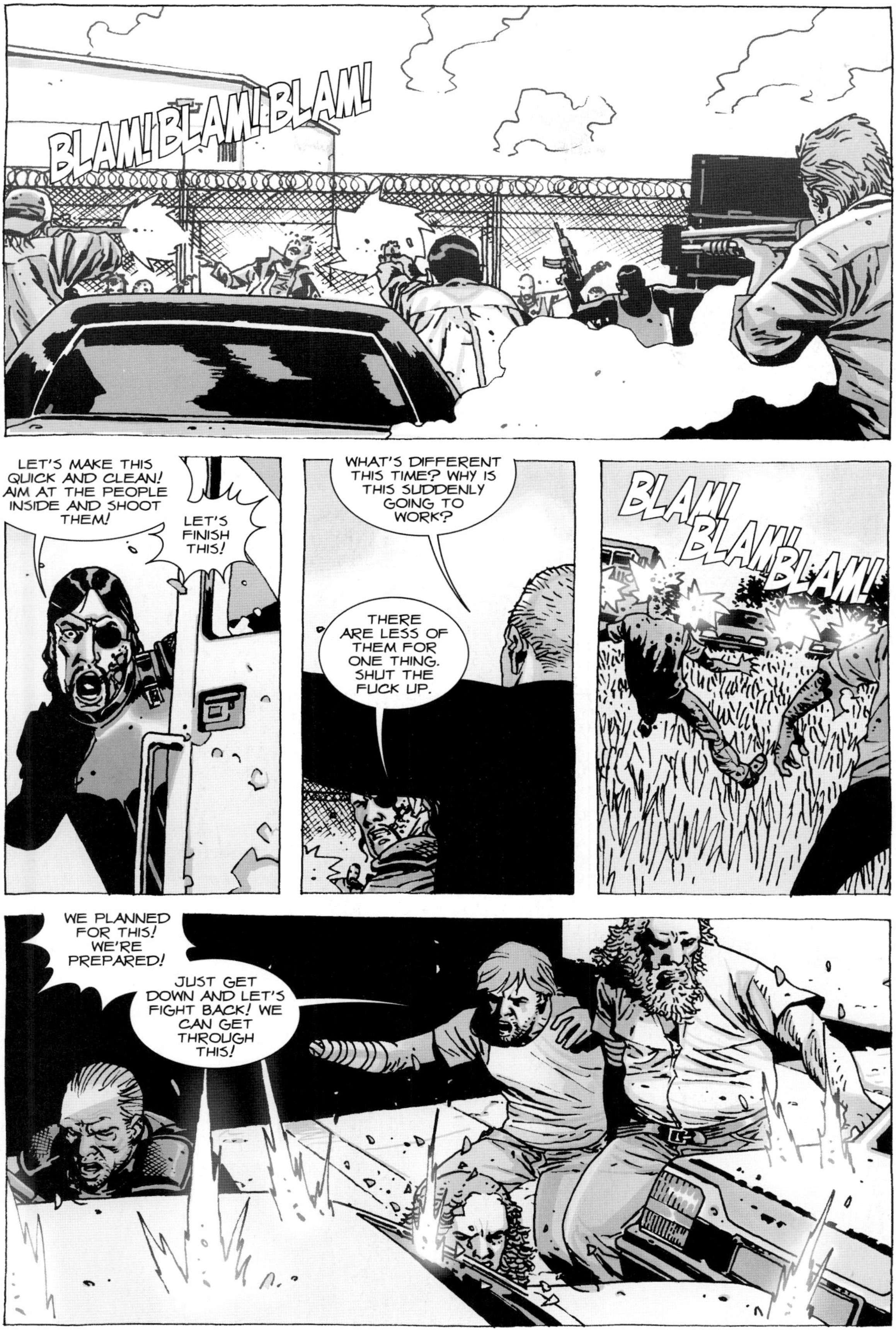
BLAM! BLAM! BLAM!
LET'S MAKE THIS QUICK AND CLEAN! AIM AT THE PEOPLE INSIDE AND SHOOT THEM!
LET'S FINISH THIS!
WHAT'S DIFFERENT THIS TIME? WHY IS THIS SUDDENLY GOING TO WORK?
THERE ARE LESS OF THEM FOR ONE THING. SHUT THE FUCK UP.
BLAM! BLAM! BLAM!
WE PLANNED FOR THIS! WE'RE PREPARED!
JUST GET DOWN AND LET'S FIGHT BACK! WE CAN GET THROUGH THIS!

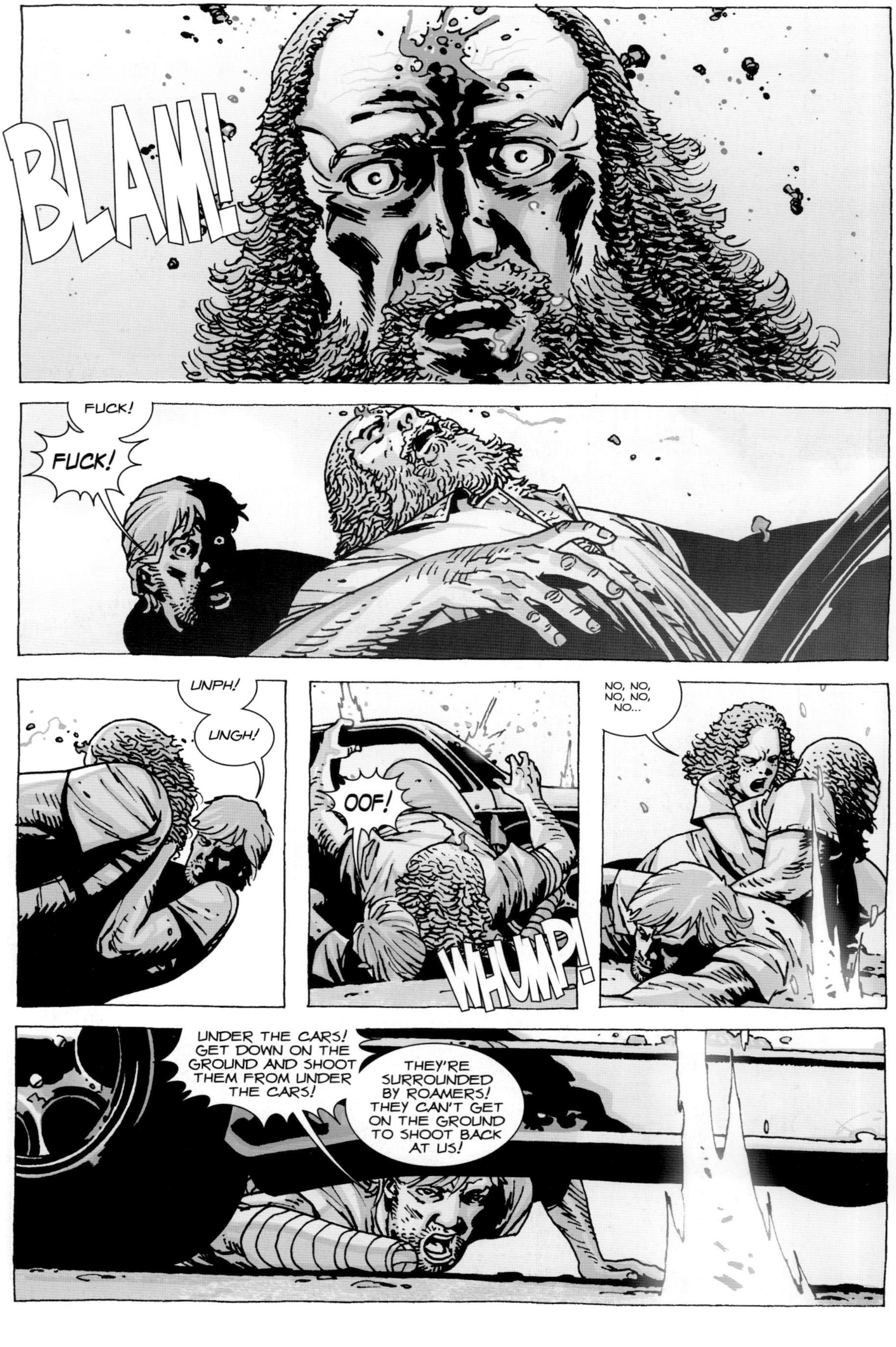
BLAM!
FUCK!
FUCK!
UNPH!
UNGH!
OOF!
WHUMP!
NO, NO, NO, NO, NO...
UNDER THE CARS! GET DOWN ON THE GROUND AND SHOOT THEM FROM UNDER THE CARS!
THEY'RE SURROUNDED BY ROAMERS! THEY CAN'T GET ON THE GROUND TO SHOOT BACK AT US!

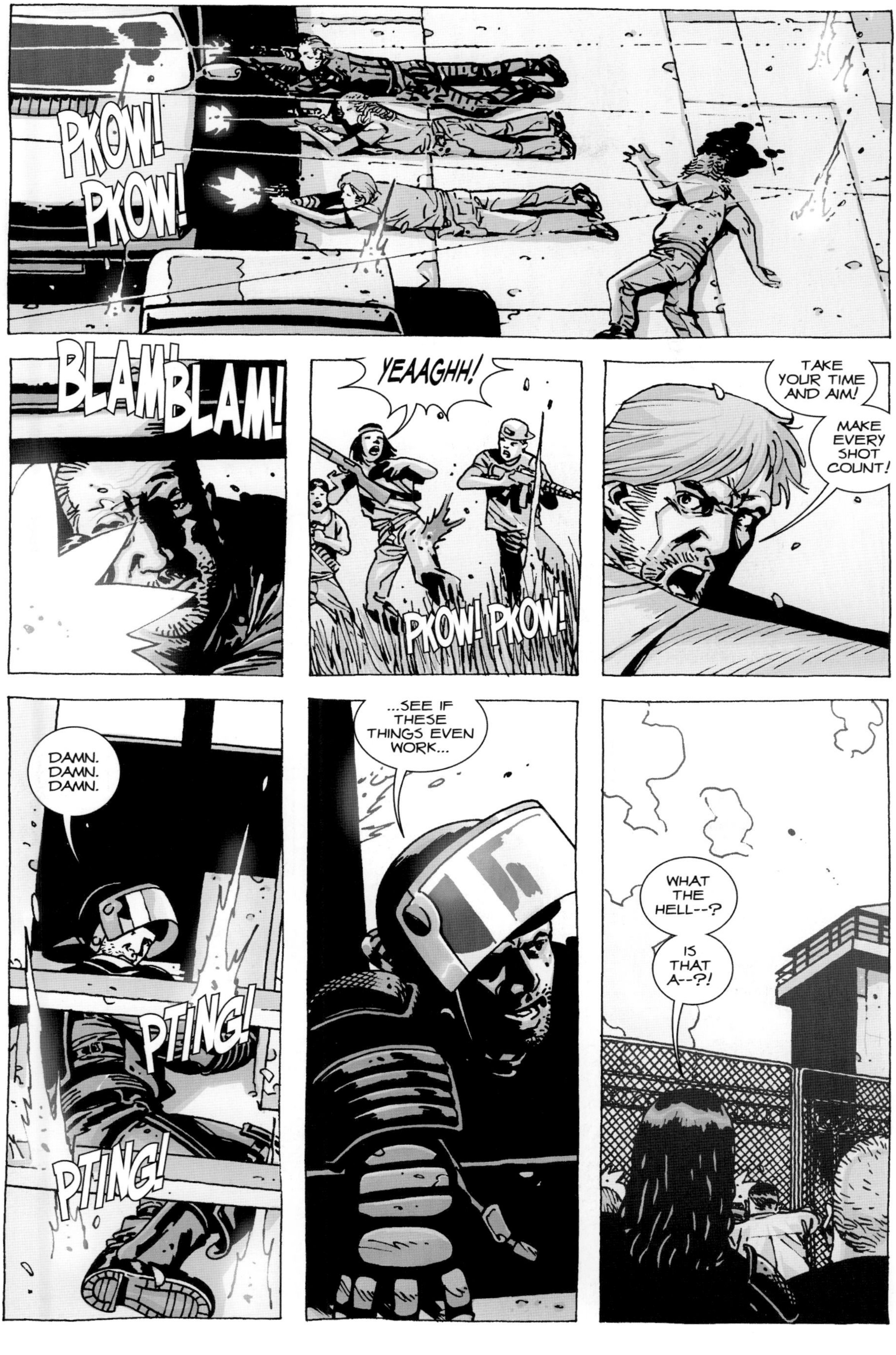
PKOW!
PKOW!
BLAM! BLAM!
YEAAGHH!
PKOW! PKOW!
TAKE YOUR TIME AND AIM!
MAKE EVERY SHOT COUNT!
DAMN. DAMN. DAMN.
PTING!
PTING!
...SEE IF THESE THINGS EVEN WORK...
WHAT THE HELL--?
IS THAT A--?!

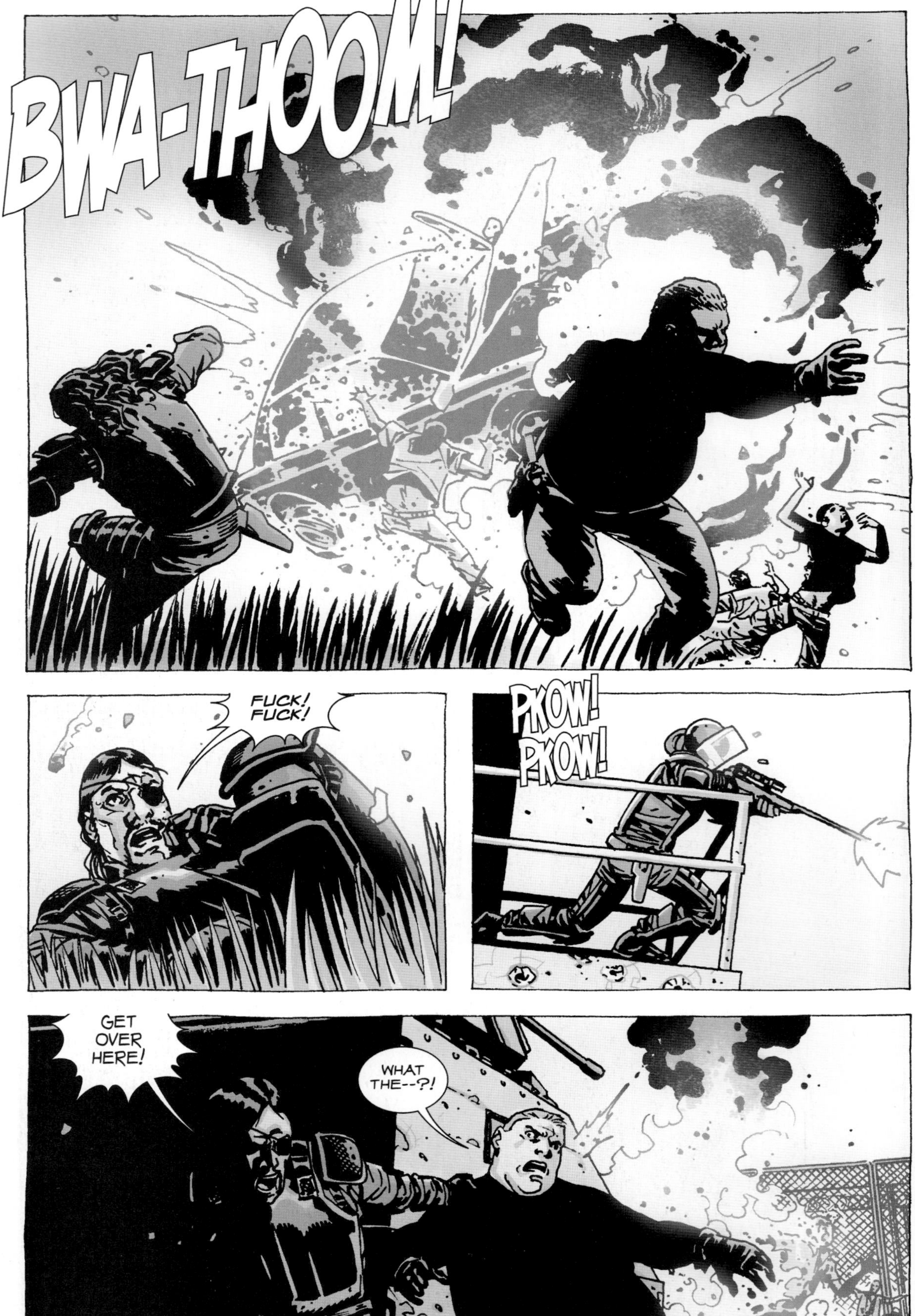
BWA-THOOM!
FUCK! FUCK!
PKOW! PKOW!
GET OVER HERE!
WHAT THE--?!

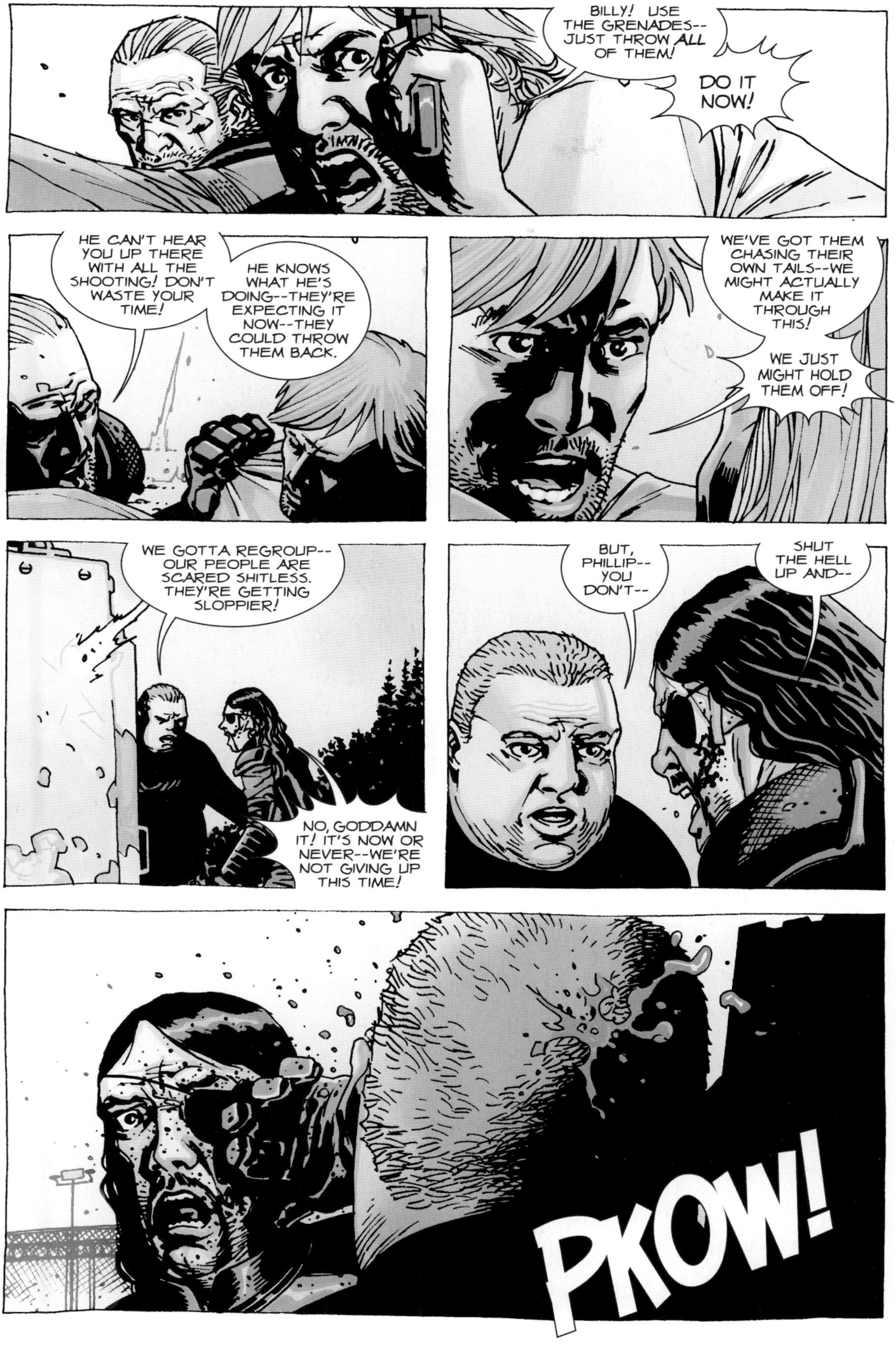
BILLY! USE THE GRENADES--JUST THROW ALL OF THEM!
DO IT NOW!
HE CAN'T HEAR YOU UP THERE WITH ALL THE SHOOTING! DON'T WASTE YOUR TIME!
HE KNOWS WHAT HE'S DOING--THEY'RE EXPECTING IT NOW--THEY COULD THROW THEM BACK.
WE'VE GOT THEM CHASING THEIR OWN TAILS--WE MIGHT ACTUALLY MAKE IT THROUGH THIS!
WE JUST MIGHT HOLD THEM OFF!
WE GOTTA REGROUP--OUR PEOPLE ARE SCARED SHITLESS. THEY'RE GETTING SLOPPIER!
NO, GODDAMN IT! IT'S NOW OR NEVER--WE'RE NOT GIVING UP THIS TIME!
BUT, PHILLIP--YOU DON'T--
SHUT THE HELL UP AND--
PKOW!

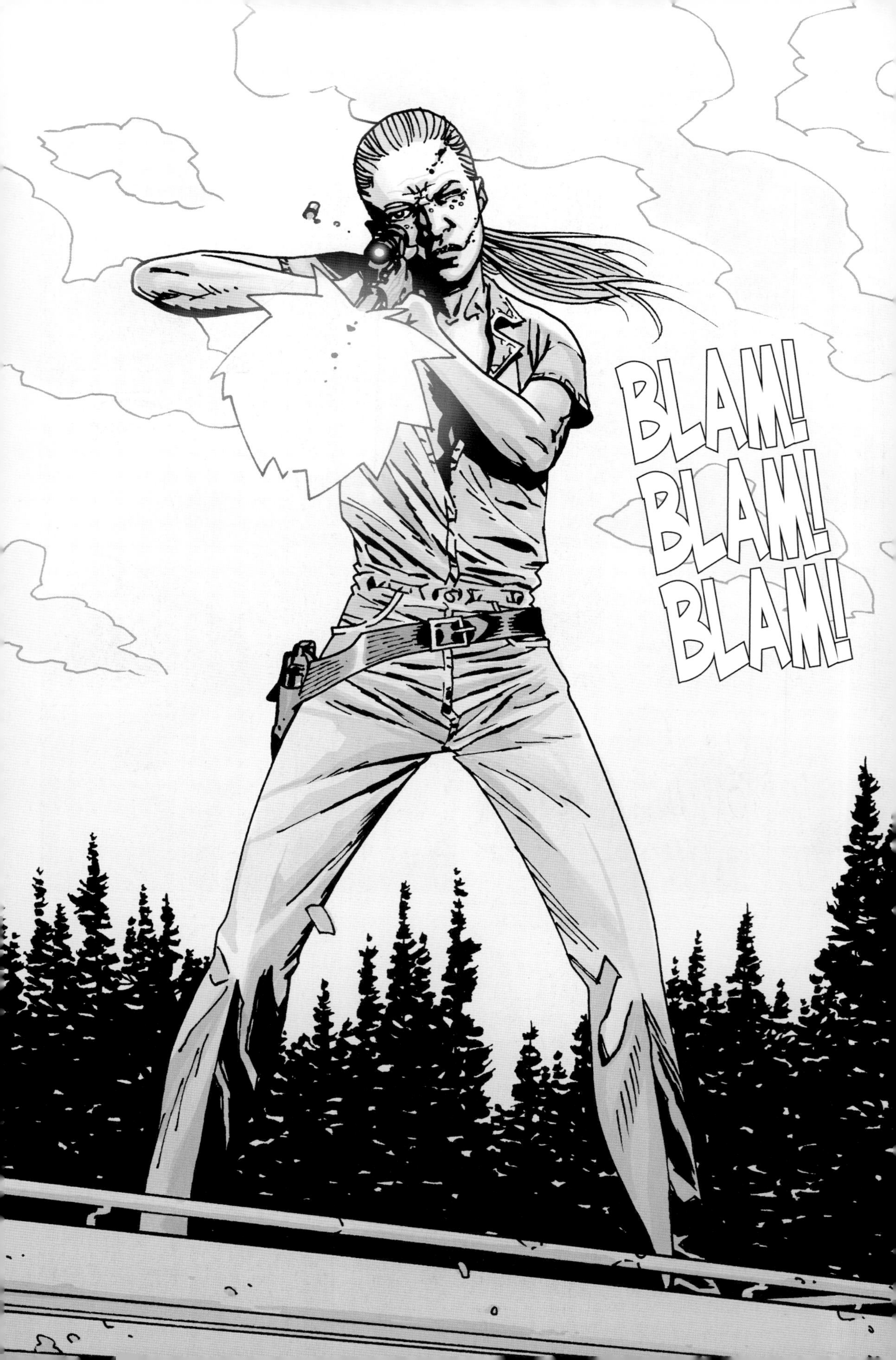
BLAM!
BLAM!
BLAM!

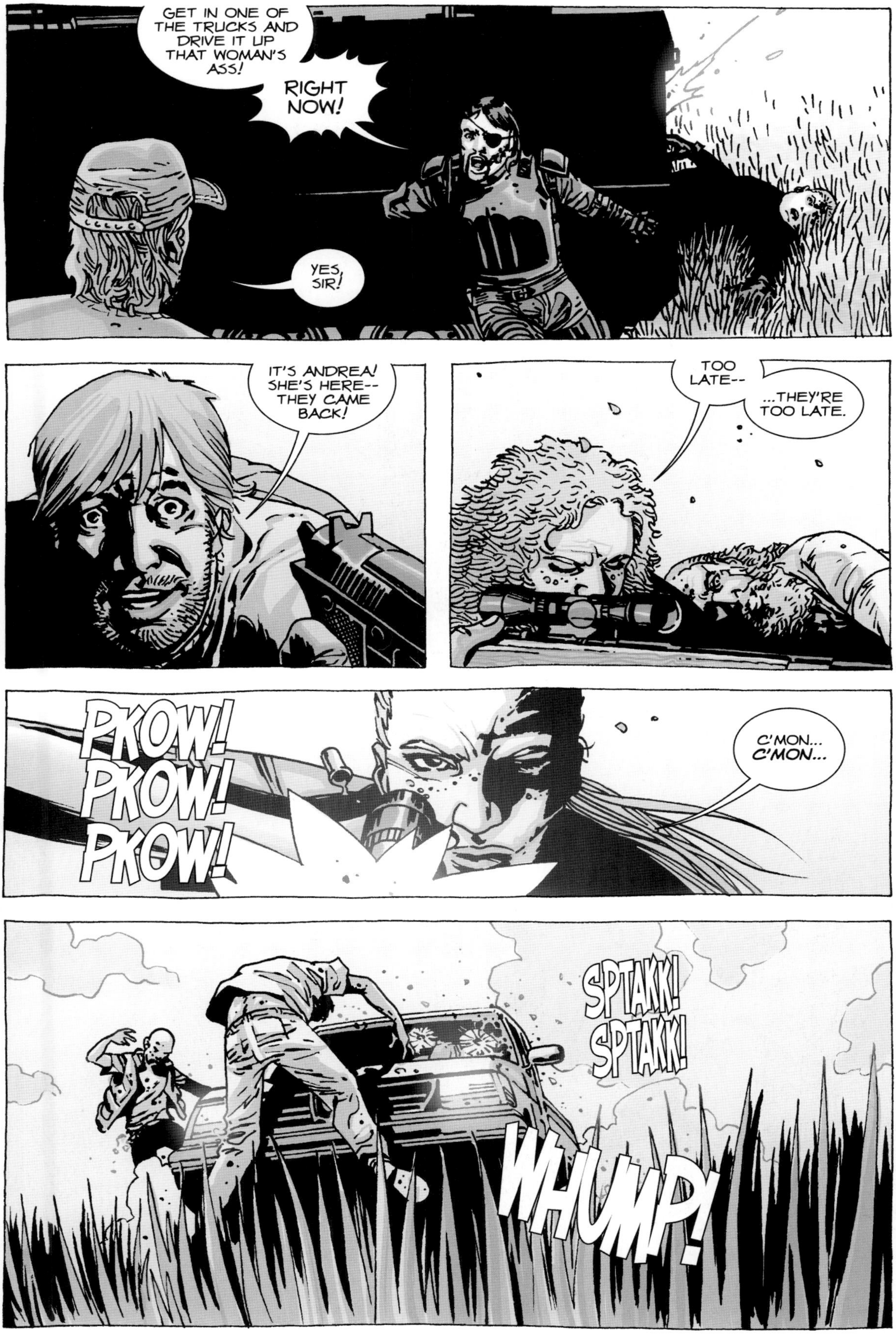
GET IN ONE OF THE TRUCKS AND DRIVE IT UP THAT WOMAN'S ASS!
RIGHT NOW!
YES, SIR!
IT'S ANDREA! SHE'S HERE-- THEY CAME BACK!
TOO LATE--
...THEY'RE TOO LATE.
PKOW! PKOW! PKOW!
C'MON... C'MON...
SPTAKK! SPTAKK!
WHUMP!

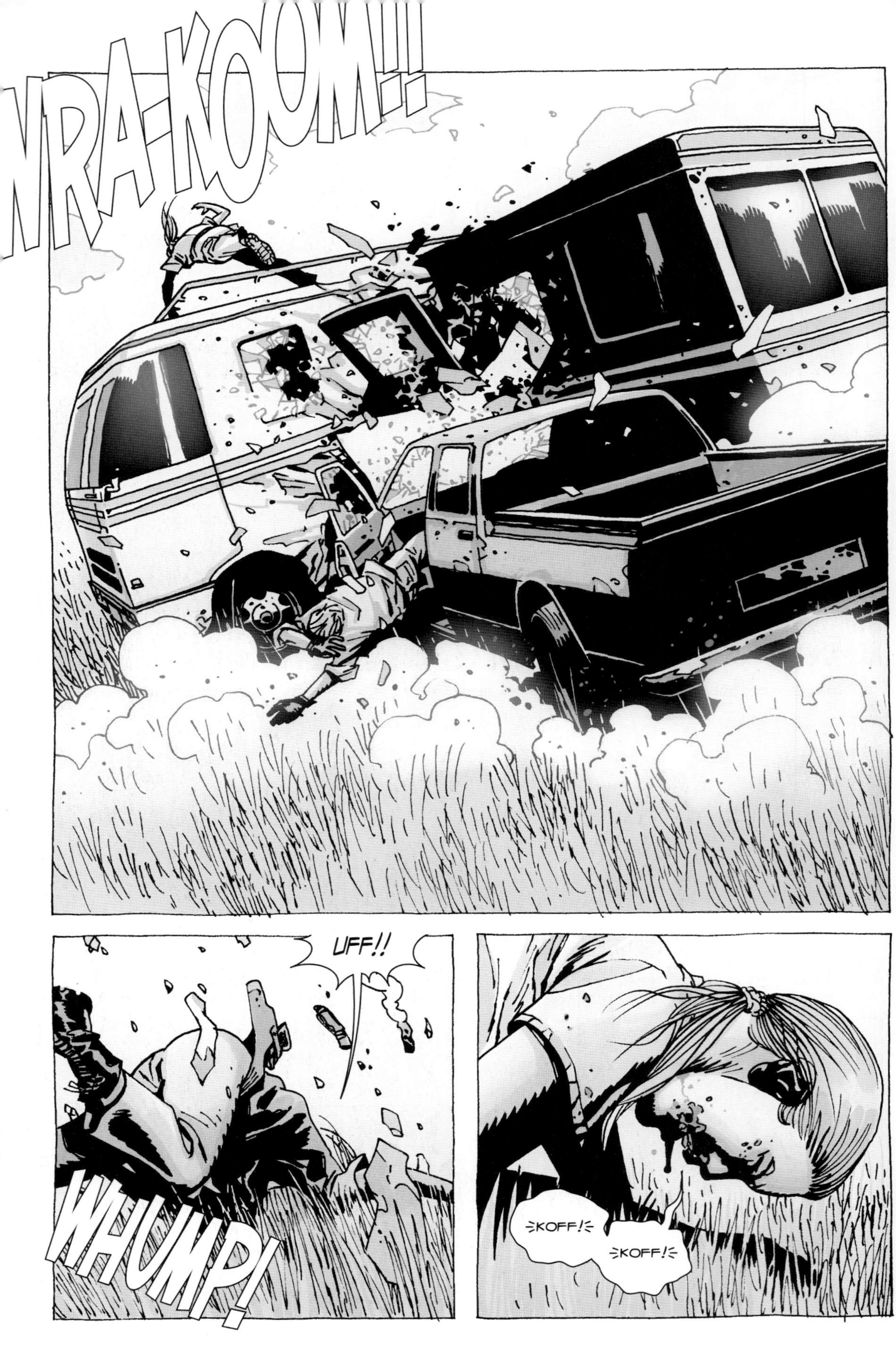
WRA-KOOM!!!
UFF!!
WHUMP!
KOFF!
KOFF!

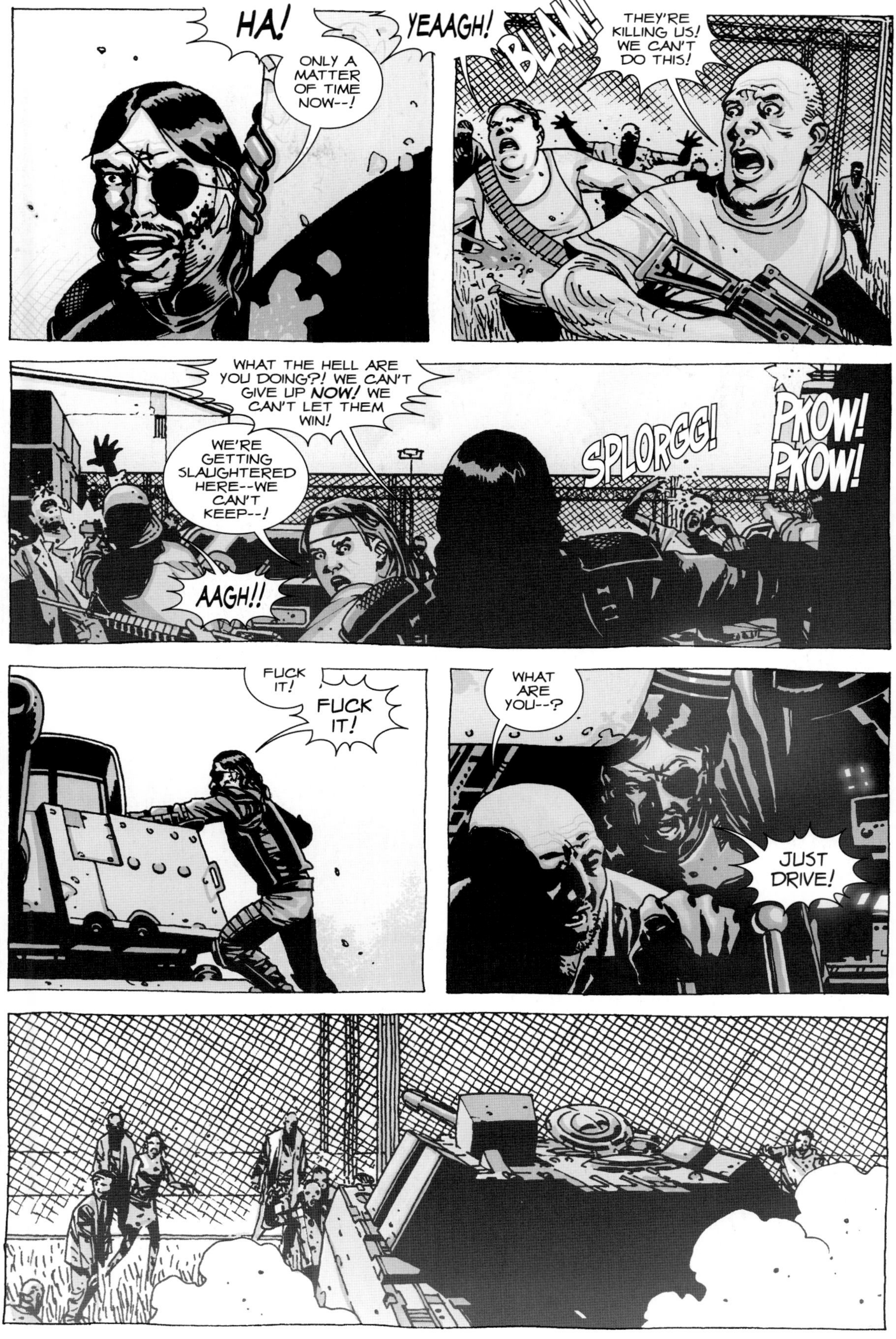
HA!
ONLY A MATTER OF TIME NOW--!
YEAAAGH!
BLAM!
THEY'RE KILLING US! WE CAN'T DO THIS!
WHAT THE HELL ARE YOU DOING?! WE CAN'T GIVE UP NOW! WE CAN'T LET THEM WIN!
WE'RE GETTING SLAUGHTERED HERE--WE CAN'T KEEP--!
AAGH!!
SPLORGG!
PKOW! PKOW!
FUCK IT!
FUCK IT!
WHAT ARE YOU--?
JUST DRIVE!

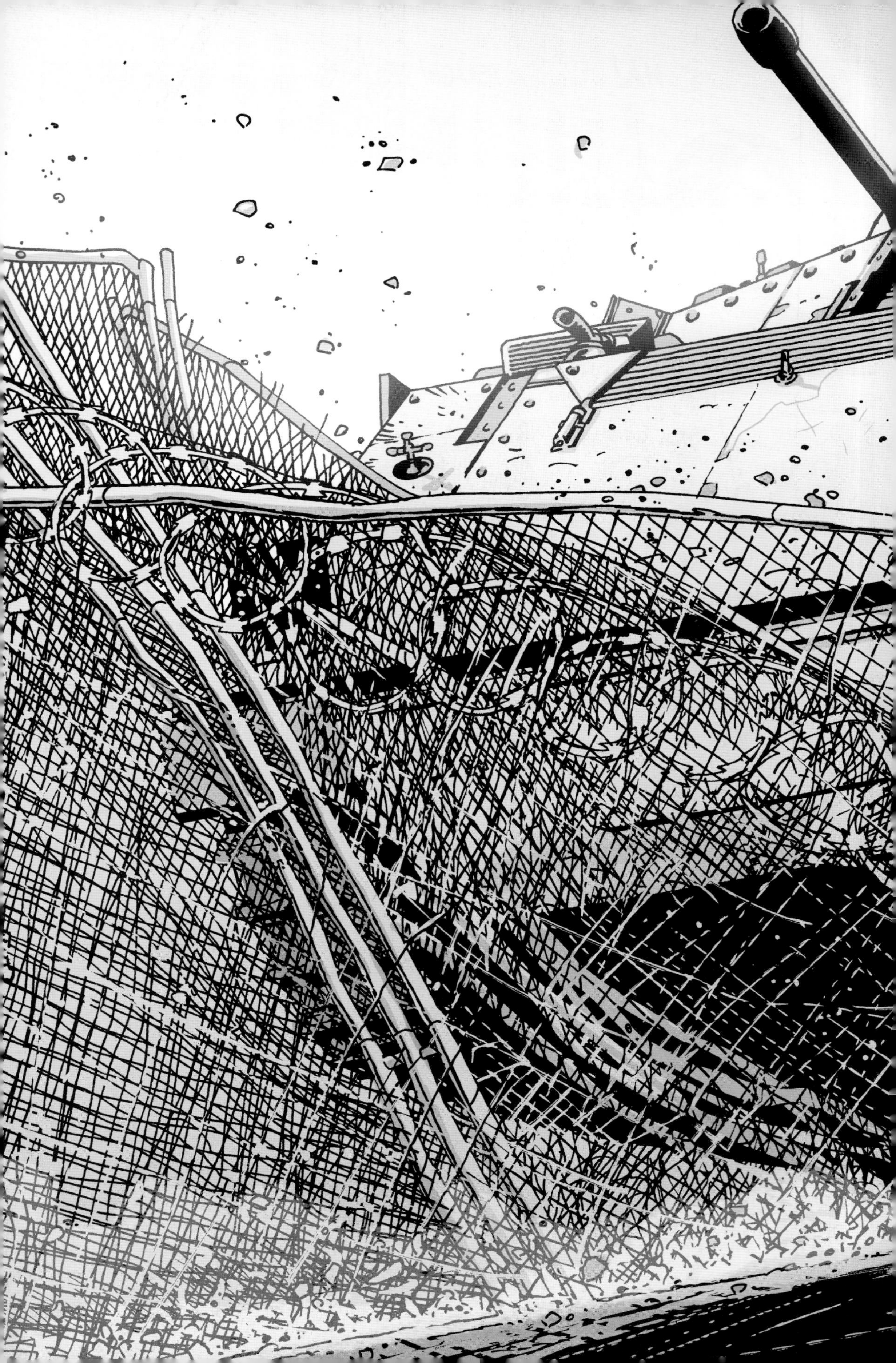

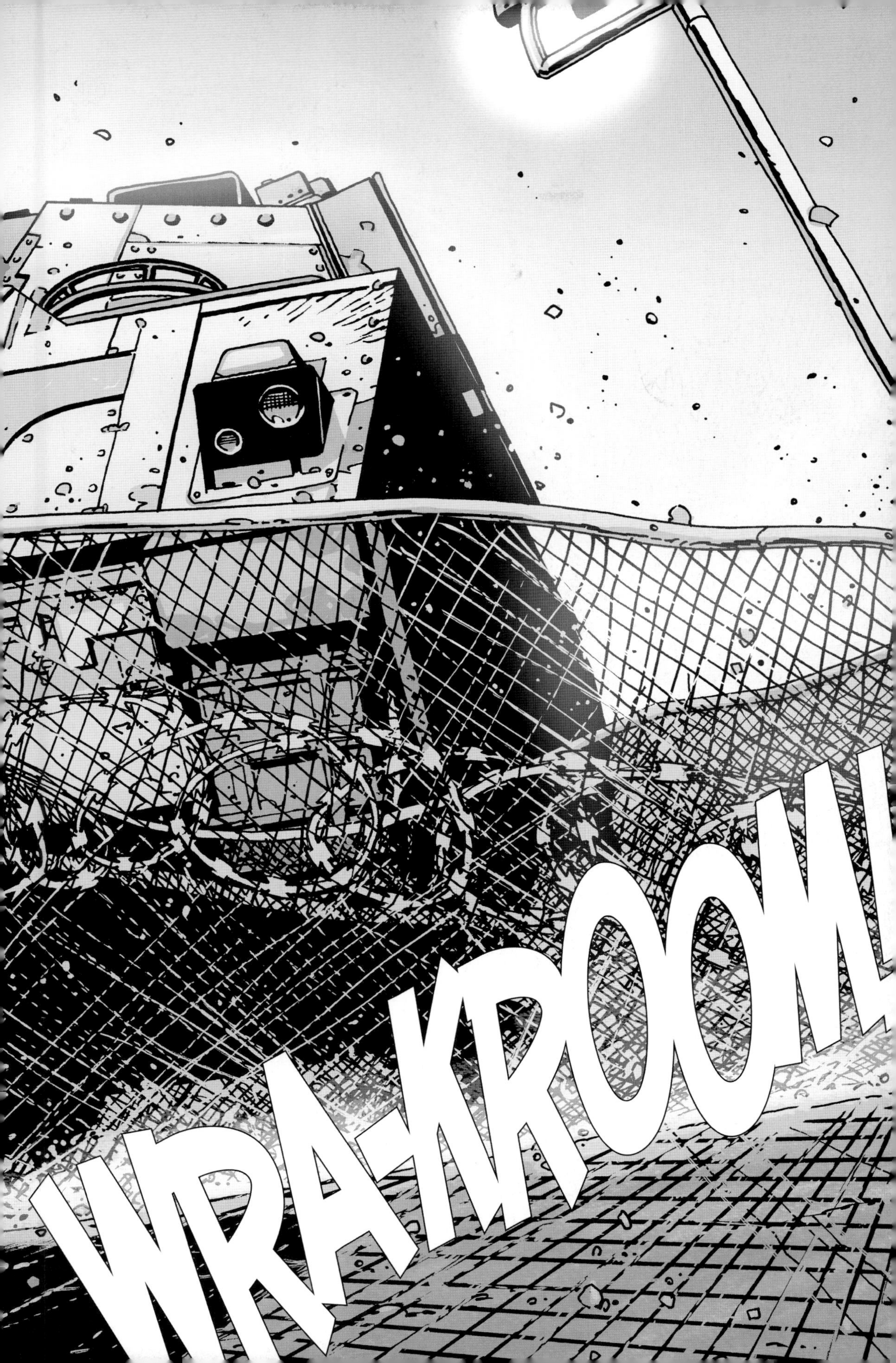
WRA-KROOM!

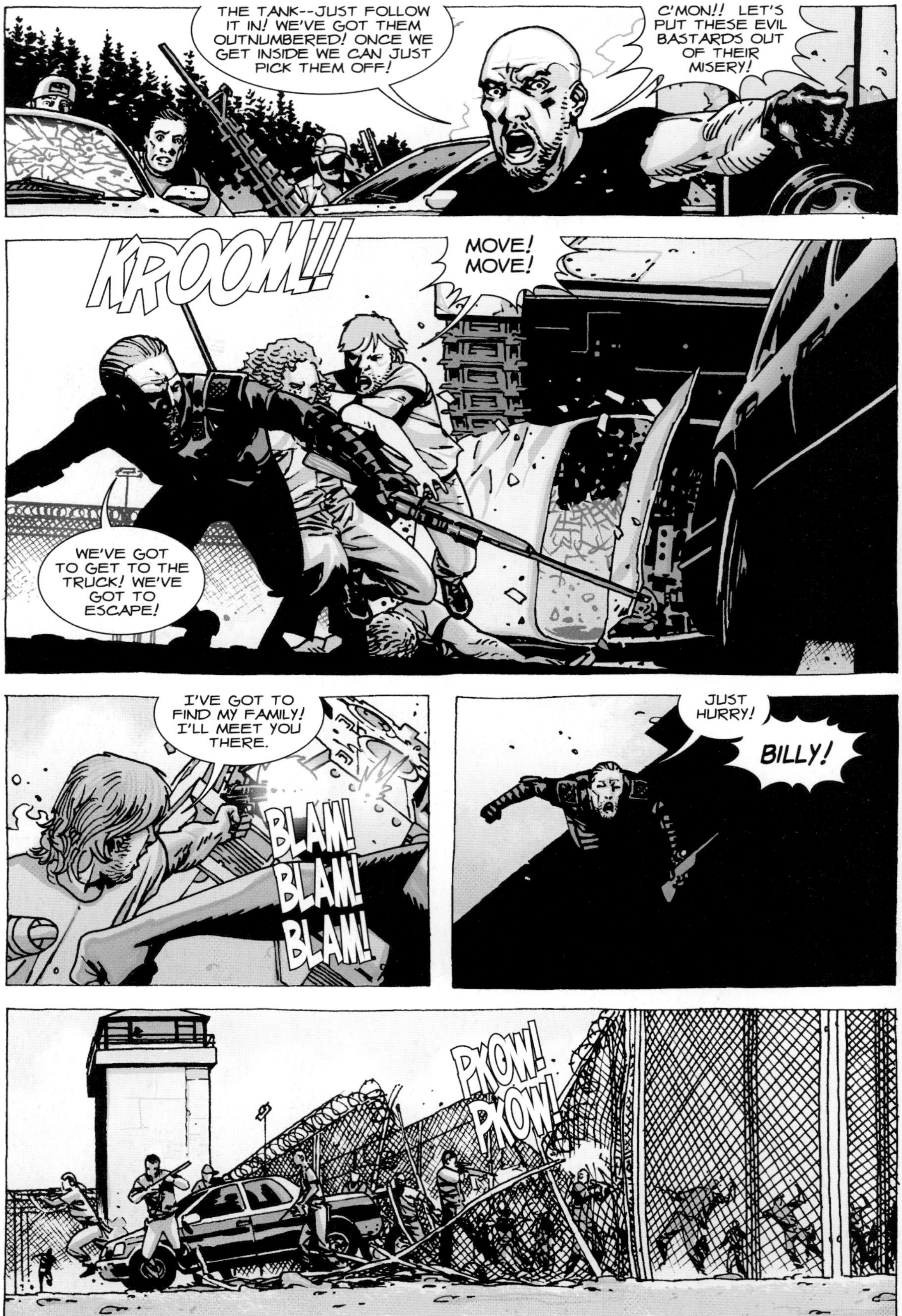
THE TANK--JUST FOLLOW IT IN! WE'VE GOT THEM OUTNUMBERED! ONCE WE GET INSIDE WE CAN JUST PICK THEM OFF!
C'MON!! LET'S PUT THESE EVIL BASTARDS OUT OF THEIR MISERY!
KROOM!!
MOVE! MOVE!
WE'VE GOT TO GET TO THE TRUCK! WE'VE GOT TO ESCAPE!
I'VE GOT TO FIND MY FAMILY! I'LL MEET YOU THERE.
BLAM! BLAM! BLAM!
JUST HURRY!
BILLY!
PKOW! PKOW!

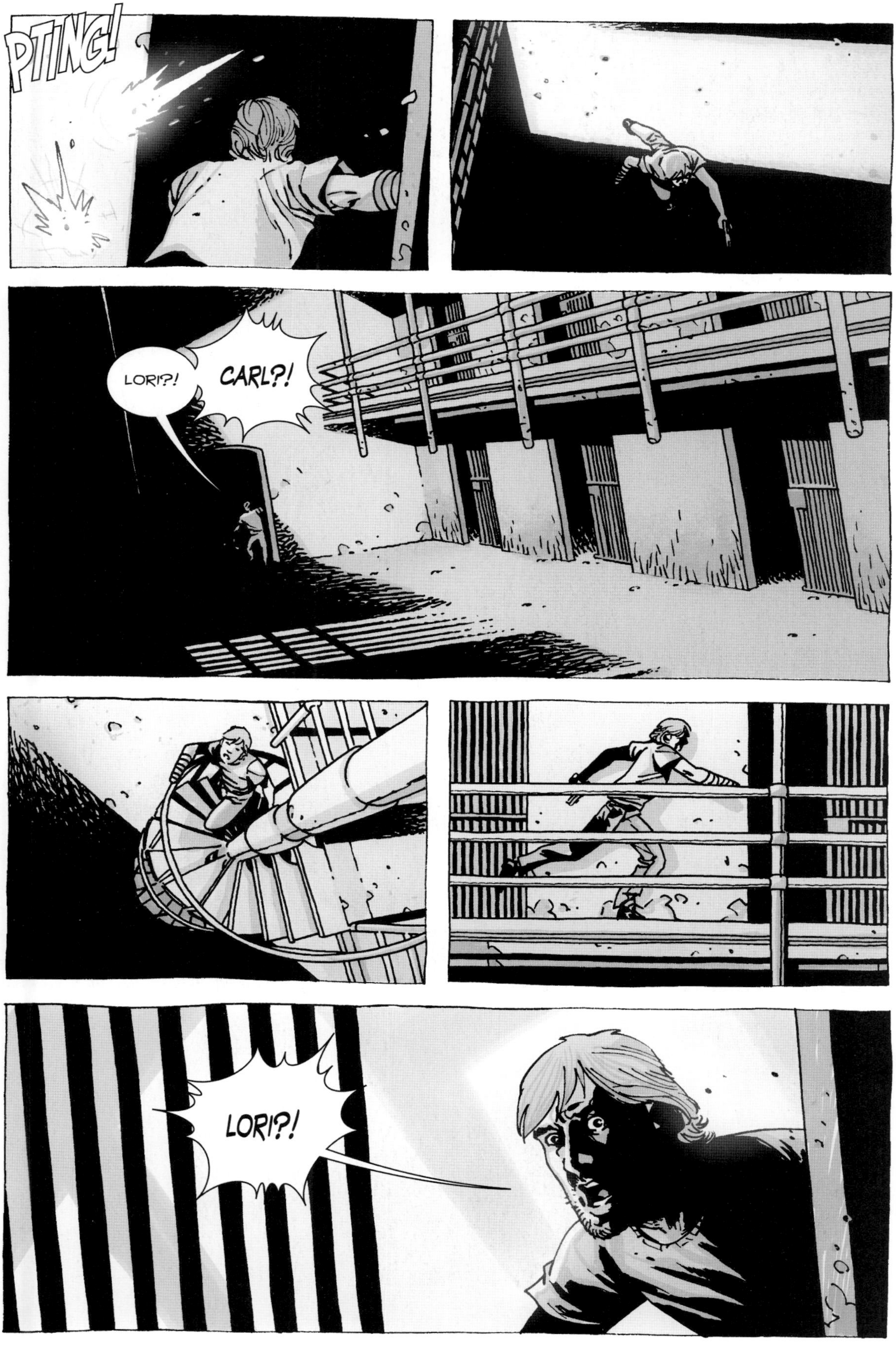

PTING!
LORI?!
CARL?!
LORI?!

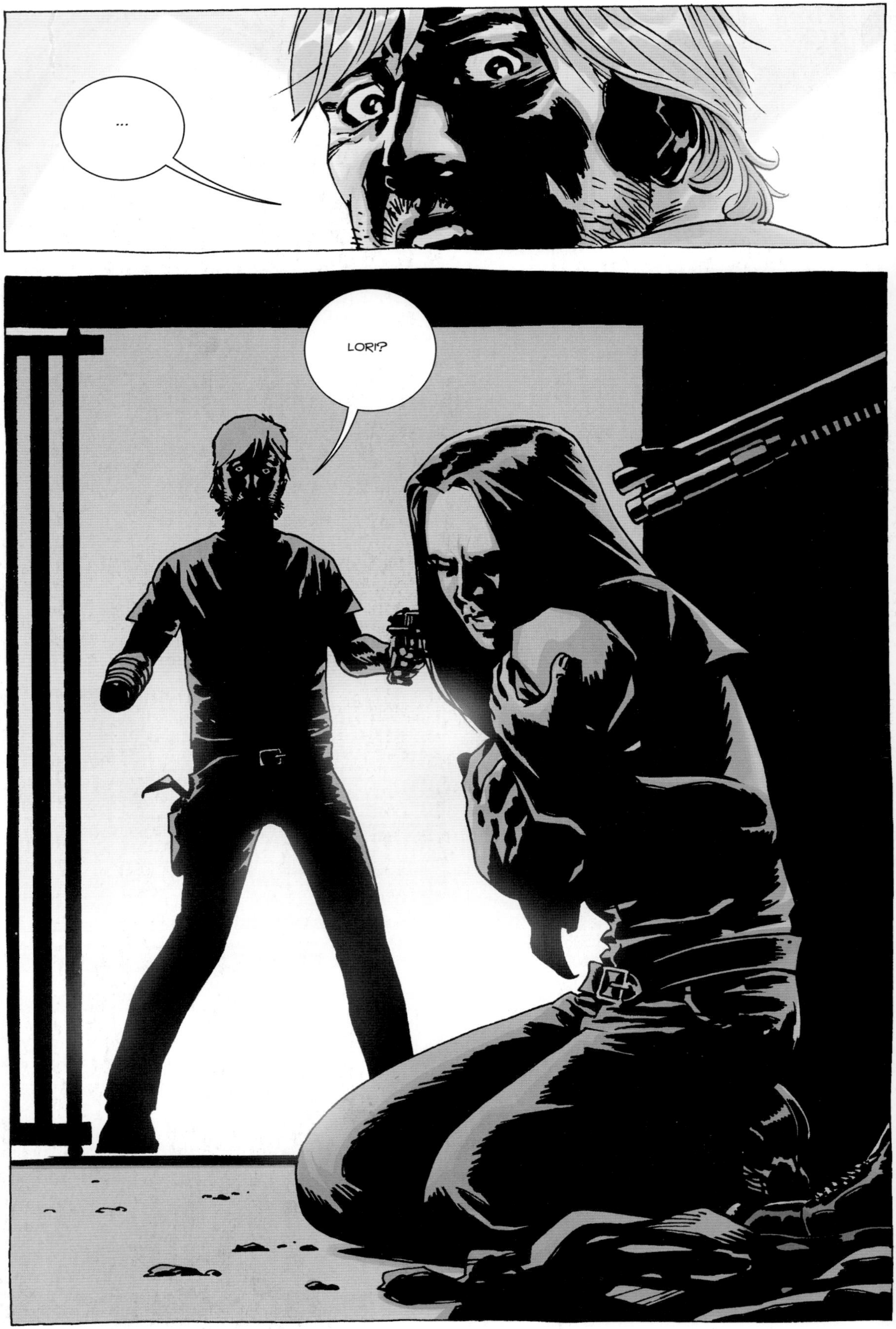
...
LORI!?

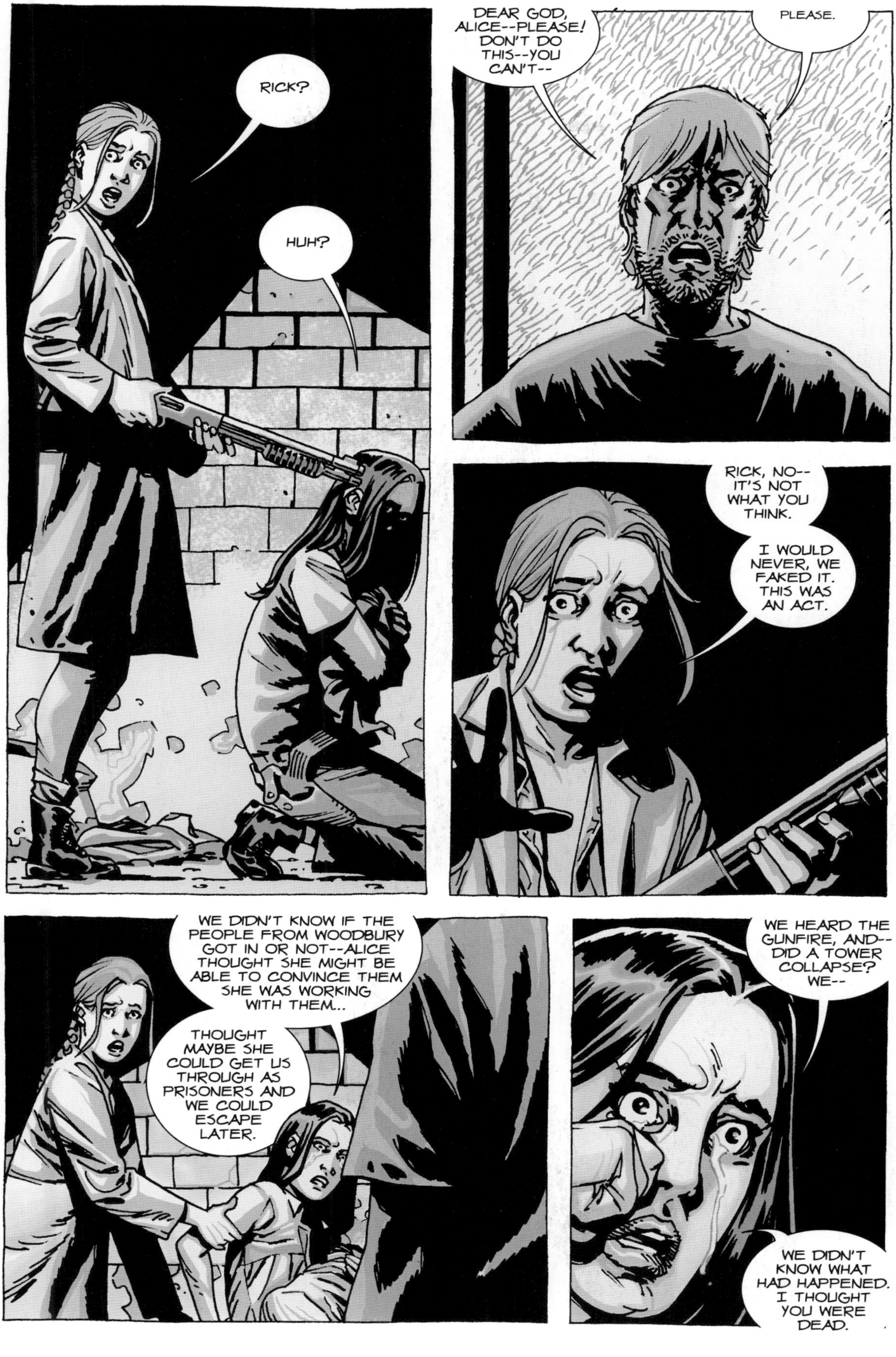
RICK?
HUH?
DEAR GOD, ALICE--PLEASE! DON'T DO THIS--YOU CAN'T--
PLEASE.
RICK, NO-- IT'S NOT WHAT YOU THINK.
I WOULD NEVER, WE FAKED IT. THIS WAS AN ACT.
WE DIDN'T KNOW IF THE PEOPLE FROM WOODBURY GOT IN OR NOT--ALICE THOUGHT SHE MIGHT BE ABLE TO CONVINCE THEM SHE WAS WORKING WITH THEM...
THOUGHT MAYBE SHE COULD GET US THROUGH AS PRISONERS AND WE COULD ESCAPE LATER.
WE HEARD THE GUNFIRE, AND-- DID A TOWER COLLAPSE? WE--
WE DIDN'T KNOW WHAT HAD HAPPENED. I THOUGHT YOU WERE DEAD.

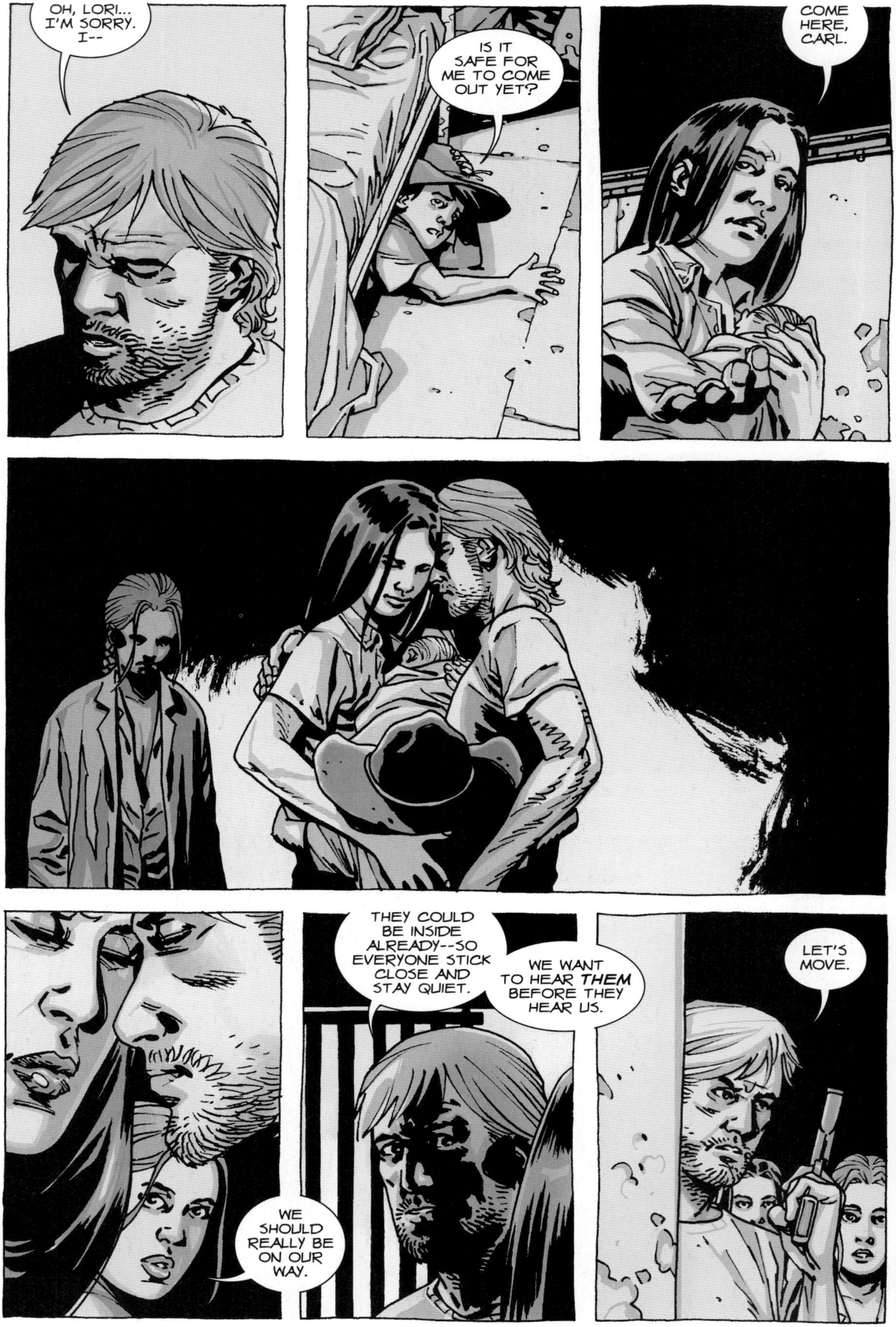
OH, LORI... I'M SORRY. I--
IS IT SAFE FOR ME TO COME OUT YET?
COME HERE, CARL.
WE SHOULD REALLY BE ON OUR WAY.
THEY COULD BE INSIDE ALREADY--SO EVERYONE STICK CLOSE AND STAY QUIET.
WE WANT TO HEAR *THEM* BEFORE THEY HEAR US.
LET'S MOVE.

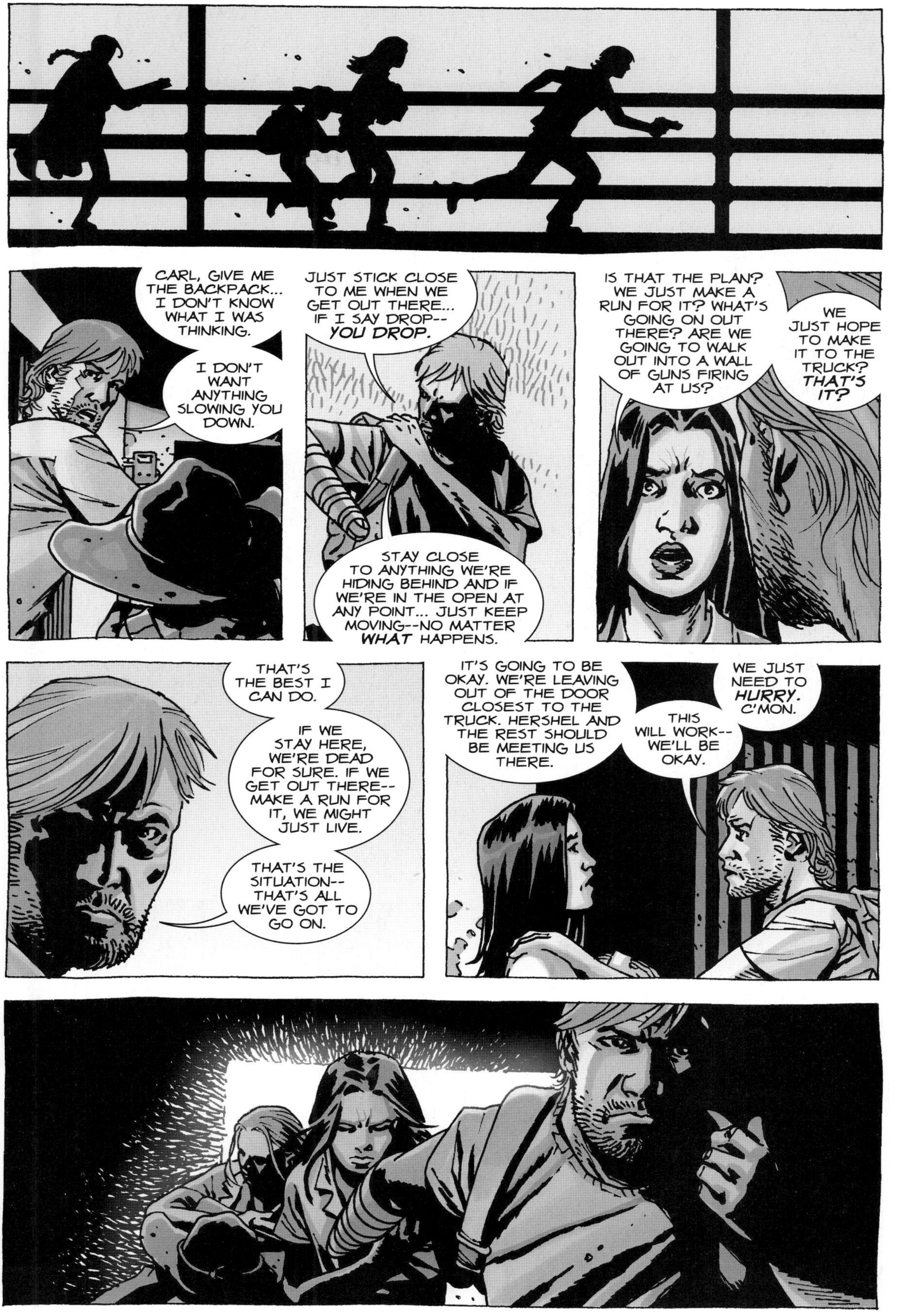
CARL, GIVE ME THE BACKPACK... I DON'T KNOW WHAT I WAS THINKING.
I DON'T WANT ANYTHING SLOWING YOU DOWN.
JUST STICK CLOSE TO ME WHEN WE GET OUT THERE... IF I SAY DROP-- YOU DROP.
STAY CLOSE TO ANYTHING WE'RE HIDING BEHIND AND IF WE'RE IN THE OPEN AT ANY POINT... JUST KEEP MOVING--NO MATTER WHAT HAPPENS.
IS THAT THE PLAN? WE JUST MAKE A RUN FOR IT? WHAT'S GOING ON OUT THERE? ARE WE GOING TO WALK OUT INTO A WALL OF GUNS FIRING AT US?
WE JUST HOPE TO MAKE IT TO THE TRUCK? THAT'S IT?
THAT'S THE BEST I CAN DO.
IF WE STAY HERE, WE'RE DEAD FOR SURE. IF WE GET OUT THERE-- MAKE A RUN FOR IT, WE MIGHT JUST LIVE.
THAT'S THE SITUATION-- THAT'S ALL WE'VE GOT TO GO ON.
IT'S GOING TO BE OKAY. WE'RE LEAVING OUT OF THE DOOR CLOSEST TO THE TRUCK. HERSHEL AND THE REST SHOULD BE MEETING US THERE.
THIS WILL WORK-- WE'LL BE OKAY.
WE JUST NEED TO HURRY. C'MON.

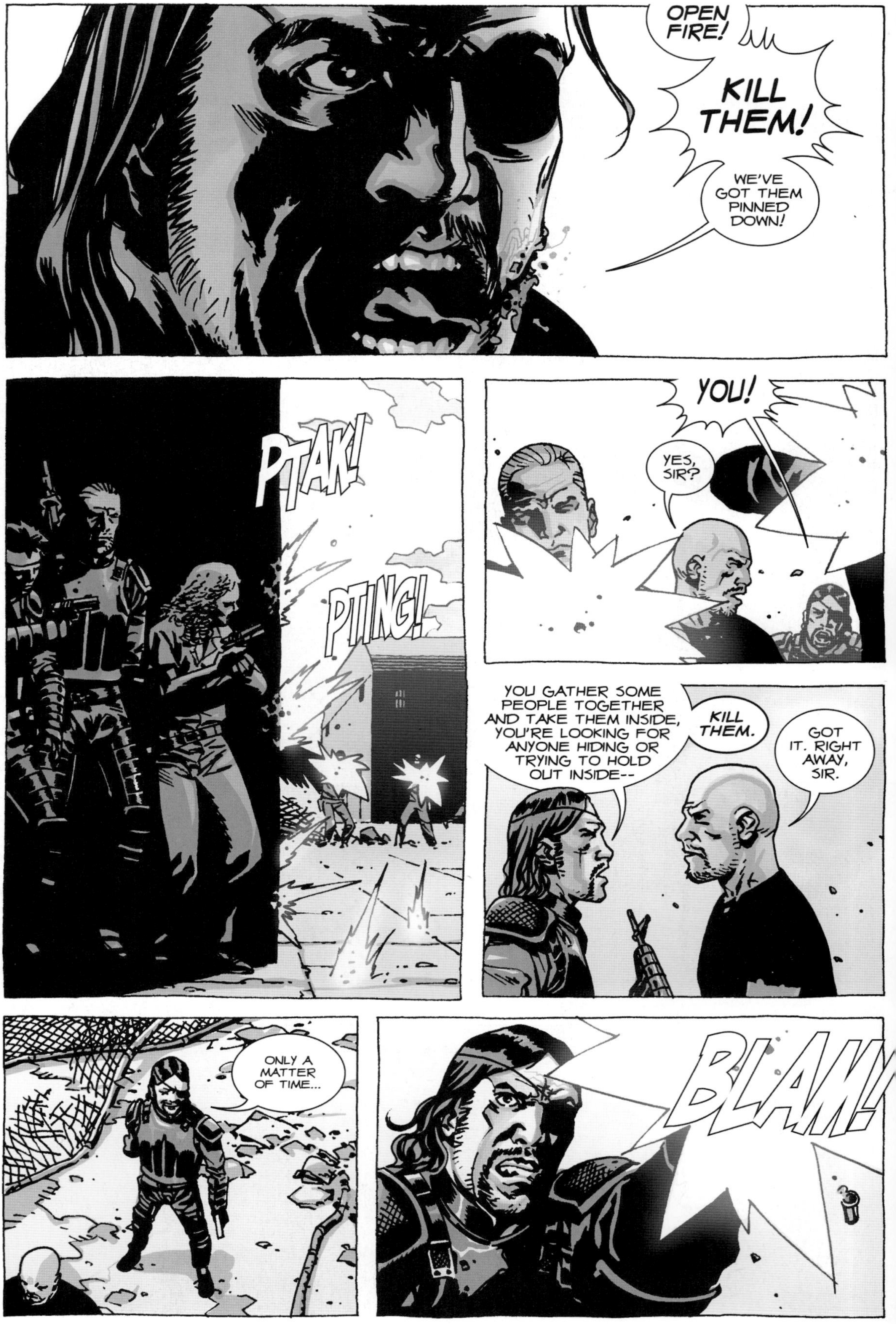
OPEN FIRE!
KILL THEM!
WE'VE GOT THEM PINNED DOWN!
PTAK!
PTING!
YOU!
YES, SIR?
YOU GATHER SOME PEOPLE TOGETHER AND TAKE THEM INSIDE, YOU'RE LOOKING FOR ANYONE HIDING OR TRYING TO HOLD OUT INSIDE--
KILL THEM.
GOT IT. RIGHT AWAY, SIR.
ONLY A MATTER OF TIME...
BLAM!

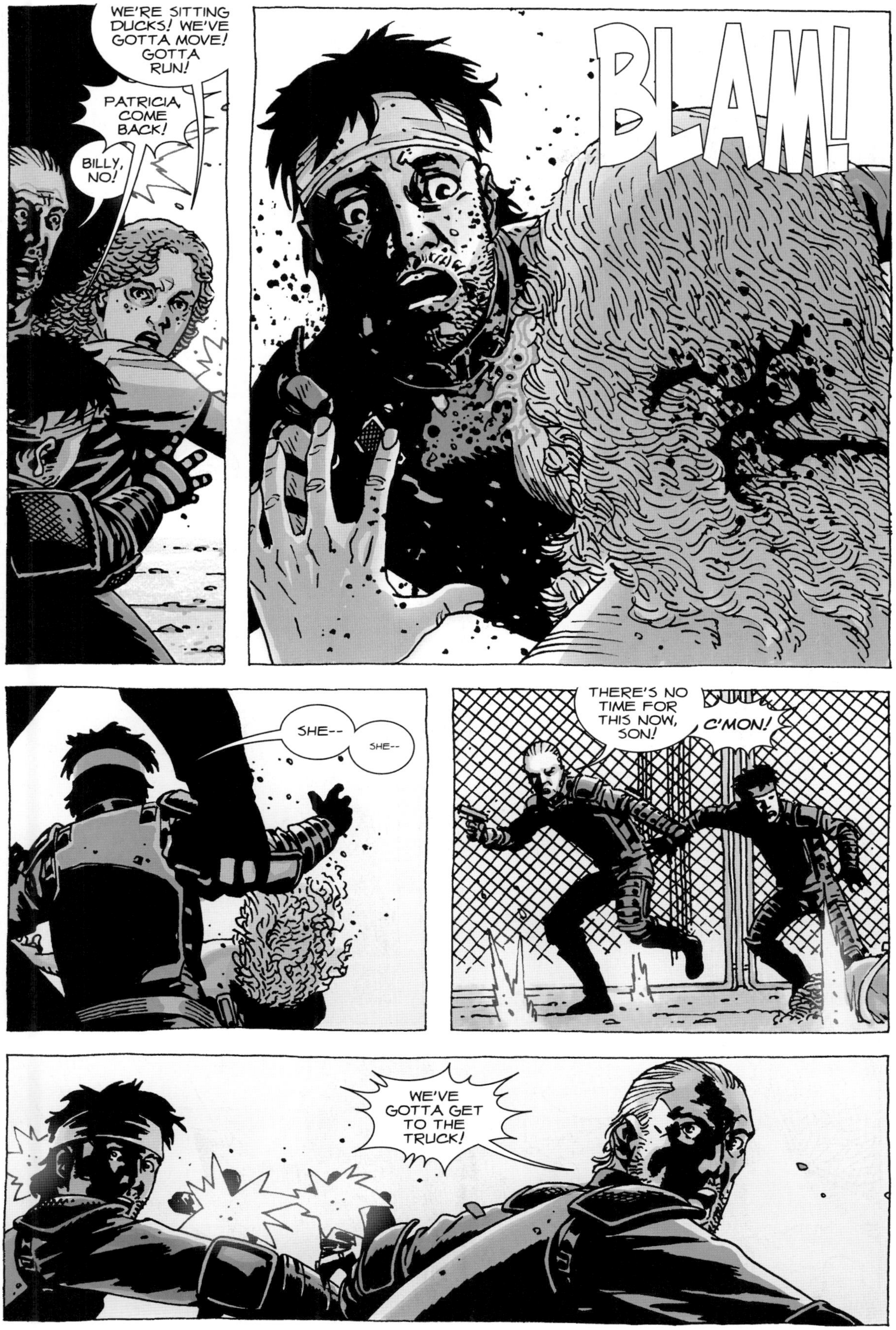
WE'RE SITTING DUCKS! WE'VE GOTTA MOVE! GOTTA RUN!
PATRICIA, COME BACK!
BILLY, NO!
BLAM!
SHE--
SHE--
THERE'S NO TIME FOR THIS NOW, SON!
C'MON!
WE'VE GOTTA GET TO THE TRUCK!

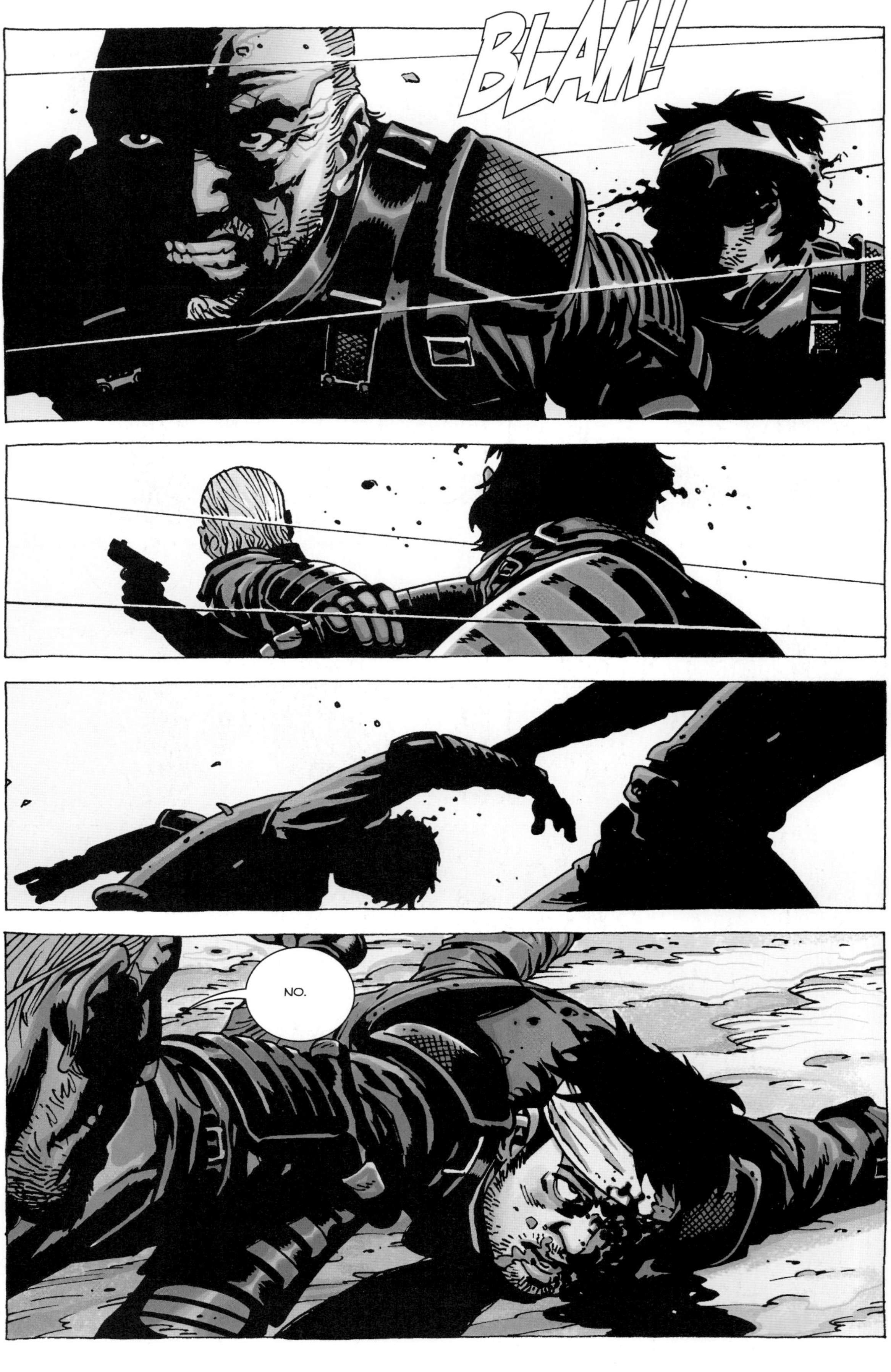
BLAM!
NO.

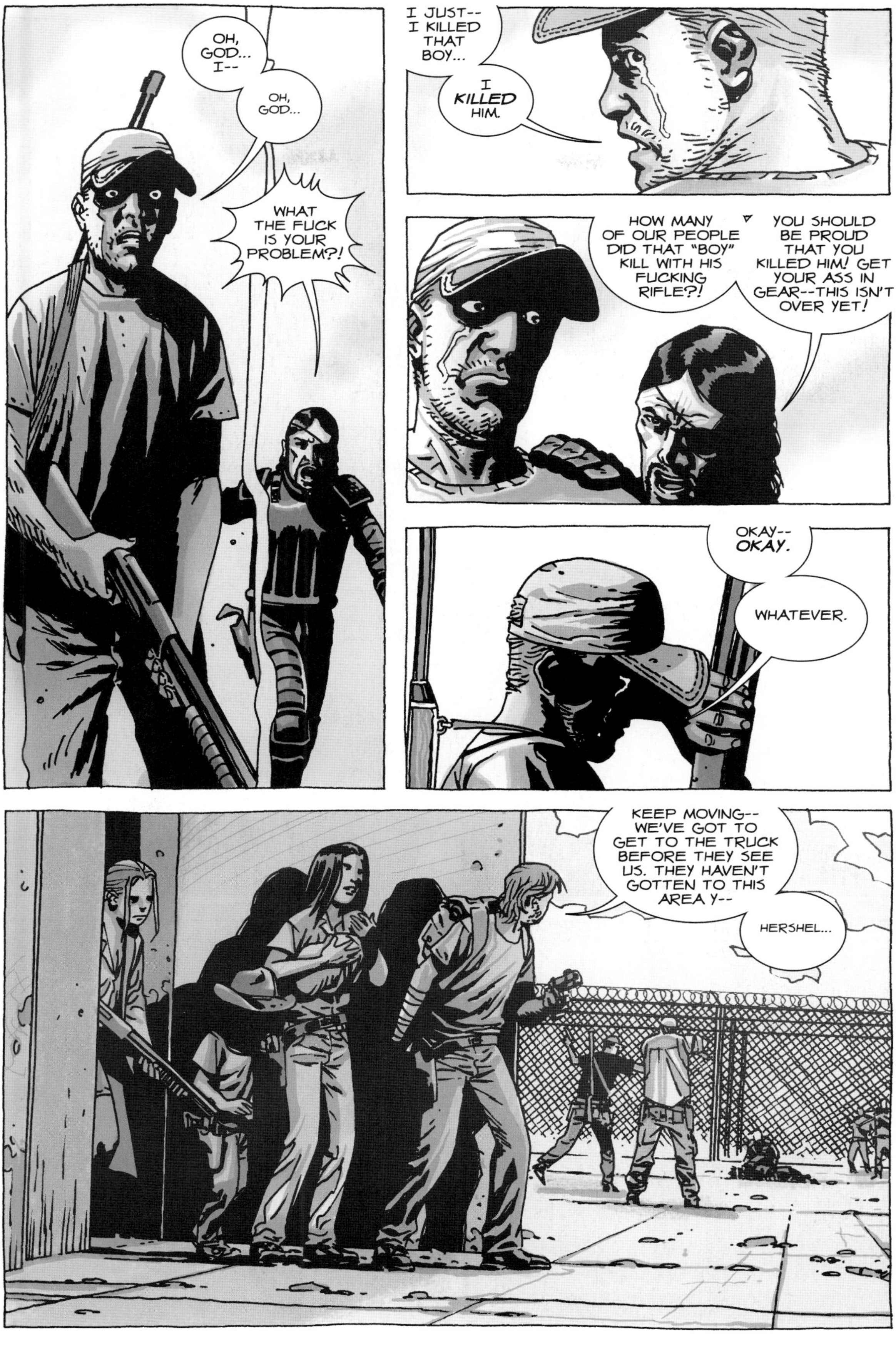
OH, GOD... I--
OH, GOD...
WHAT THE FUCK IS YOUR PROBLEM?!
I JUST-- I KILLED THAT BOY...
I *KILLED* HIM.
HOW MANY OF OUR PEOPLE DID THAT "BOY" KILL WITH HIS FUCKING RIFLE?!
YOU SHOULD BE PROUD THAT YOU KILLED HIM! GET YOUR ASS IN GEAR--THIS ISN'T OVER YET!
OKAY-- *OKAY.*
WHATEVER.
KEEP MOVING-- WE'VE GOT TO GET TO THE TRUCK BEFORE THEY SEE US. THEY HAVEN'T GOTTEN TO THIS AREA Y--
HERSHEL...

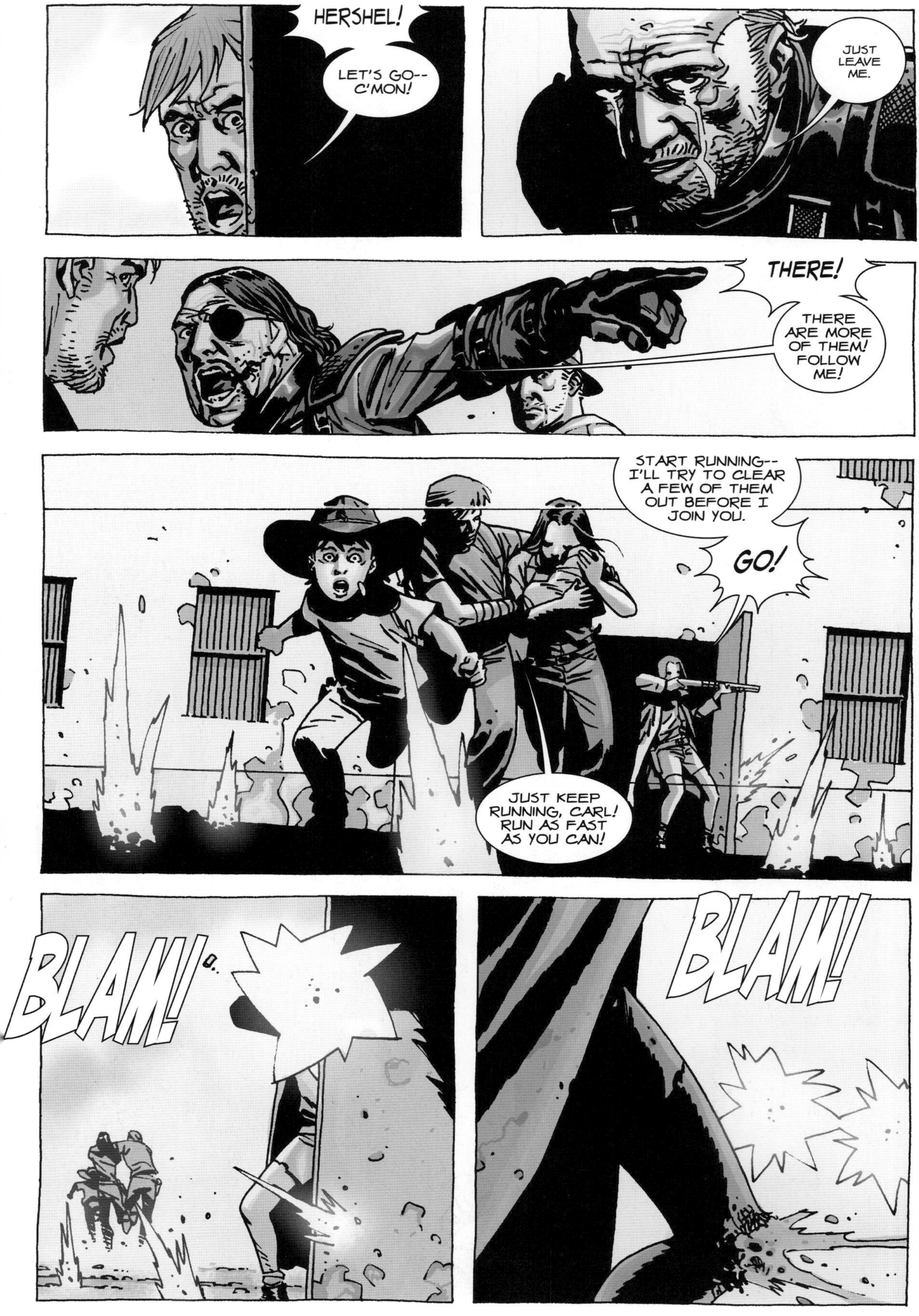
HERSHEL!
LET'S GO-- C'MON!
JUST LEAVE ME.
THERE!
THERE ARE MORE OF THEM! FOLLOW ME!
START RUNNING-- I'LL TRY TO CLEAR A FEW OF THEM OUT BEFORE I JOIN YOU.
GO!
JUST KEEP RUNNING, CARL! RUN AS FAST AS YOU CAN!
BLAM!
BLAM!

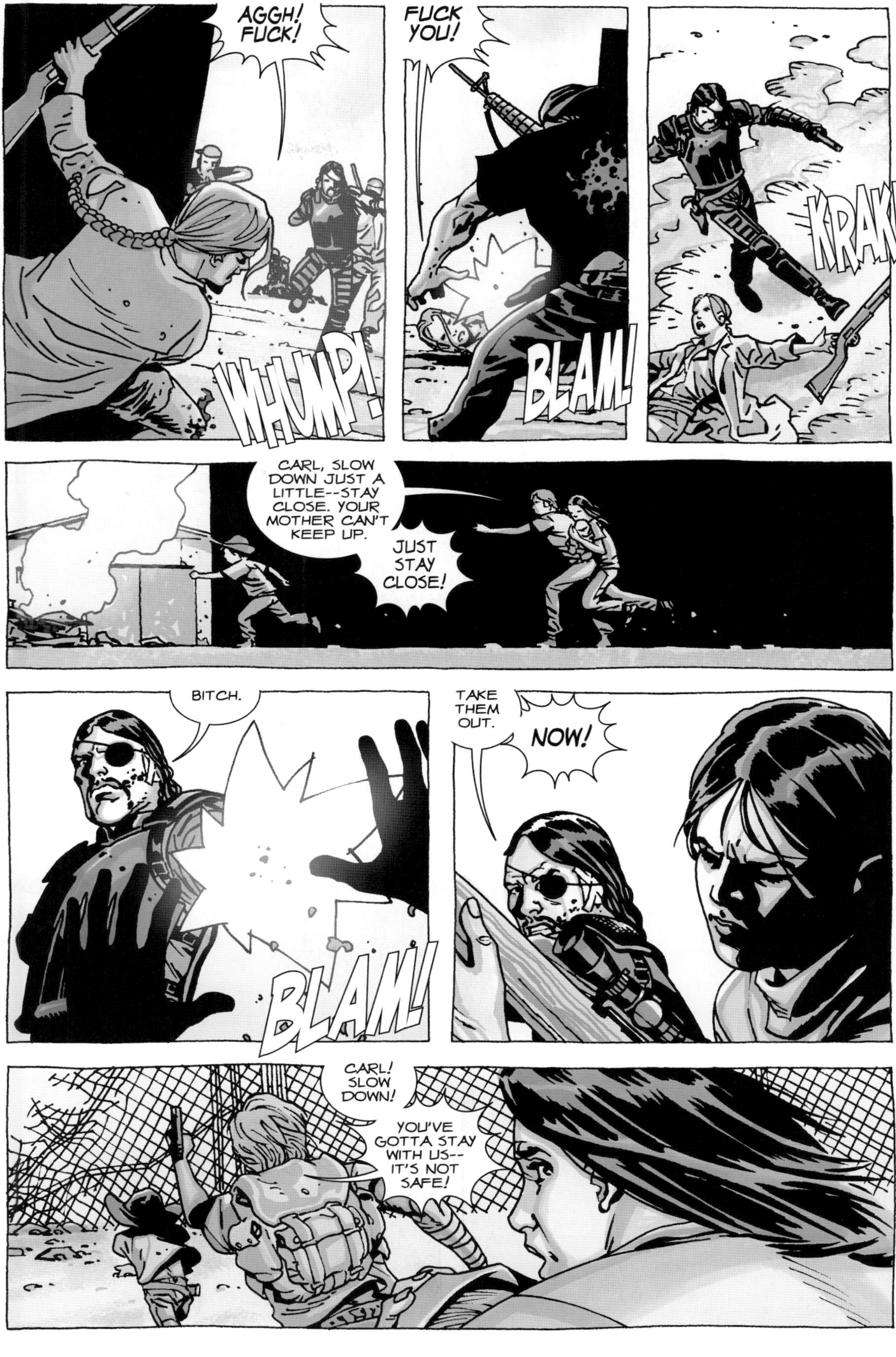
AGGH! FUCK!
WHUMP!
FUCK YOU!
BLAM!
KRAK!
CARL, SLOW DOWN JUST A LITTLE--STAY CLOSE. YOUR MOTHER CAN'T KEEP UP.
JUST STAY CLOSE!
BITCH.
BLAM!
TAKE THEM OUT.
NOW!
CARL! SLOW DOWN!
YOU'VE GOTTA STAY WITH US-- IT'S NOT SAFE!

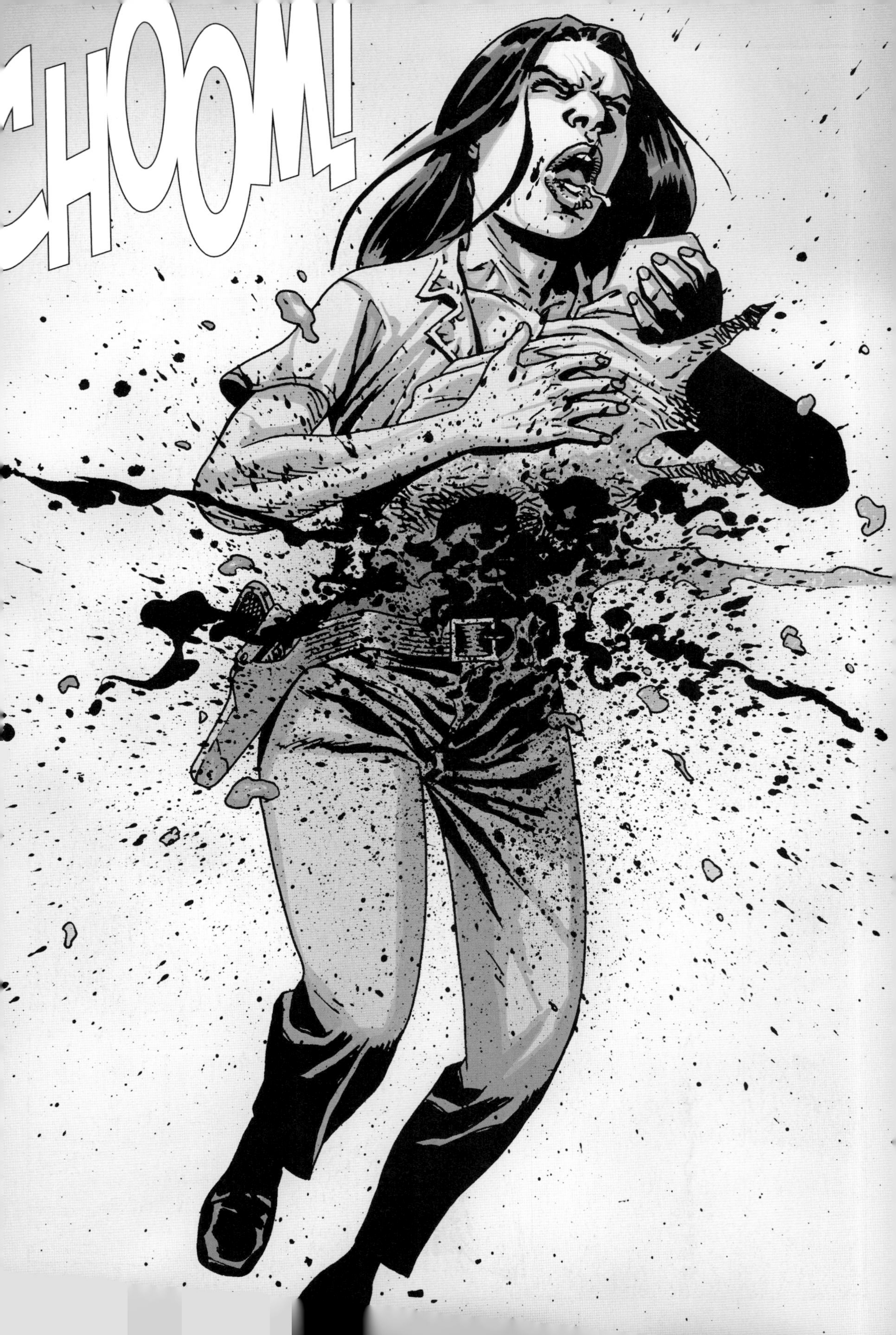
CHOOM!

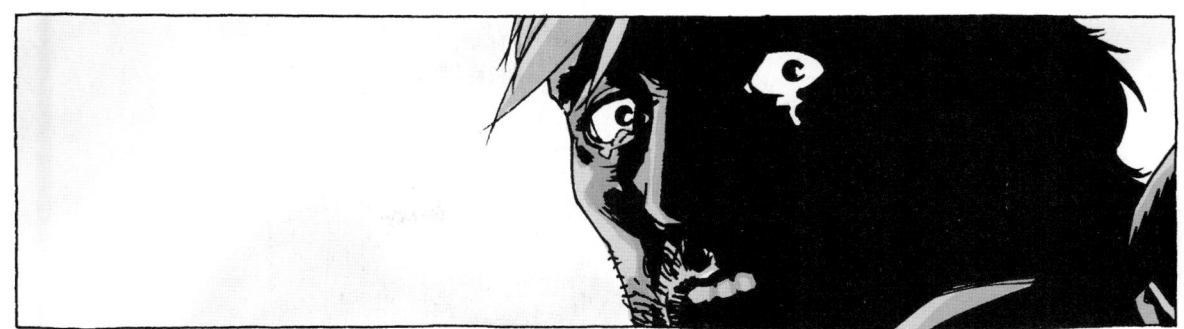

DON'T LOOK BACK, CARL! DON'T--

JUST KEEP RUNNING!

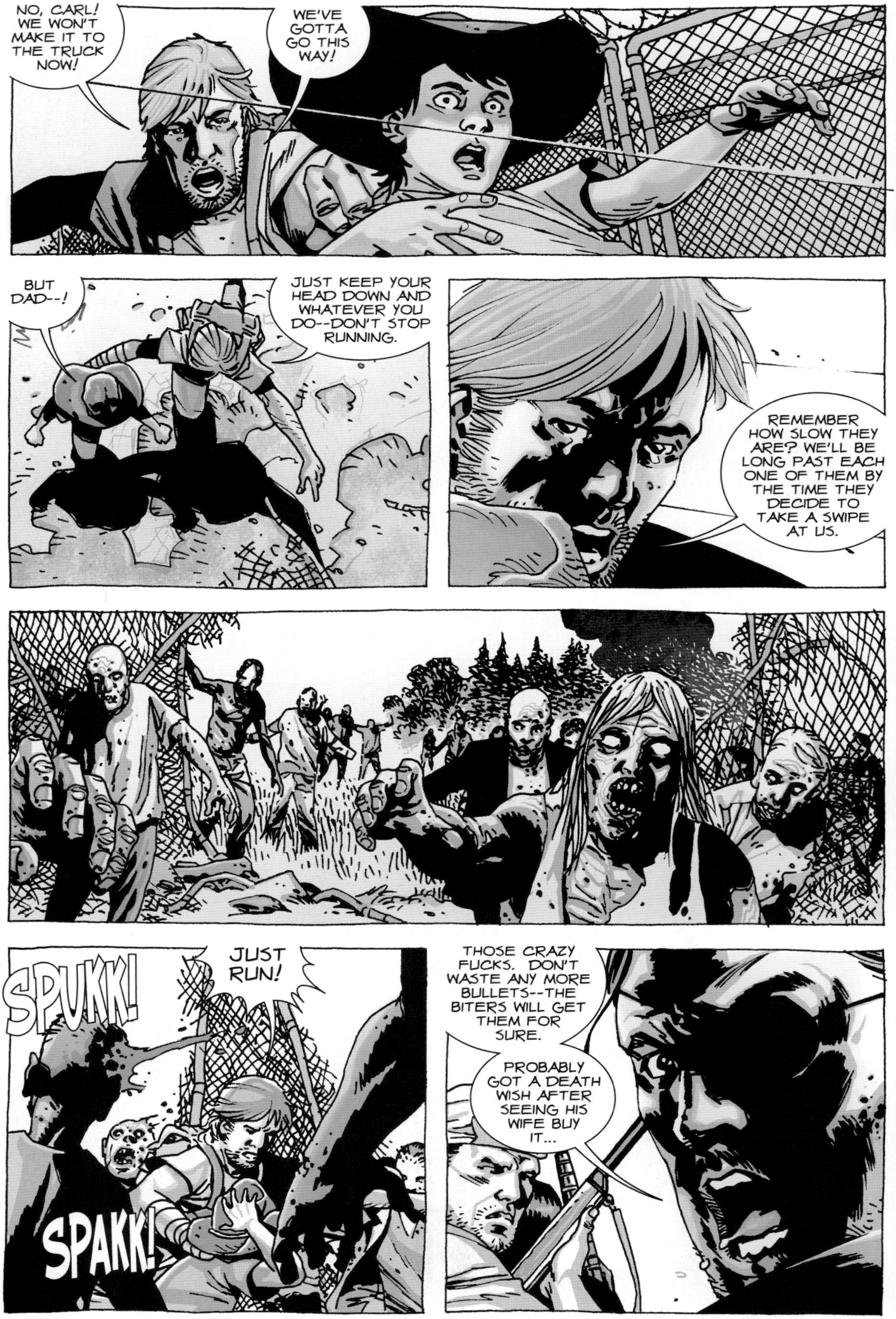
NO, CARL! WE WON'T MAKE IT TO THE TRUCK NOW!
WE'VE GOTTA GO THIS WAY!
BUT DAD--!
JUST KEEP YOUR HEAD DOWN AND WHATEVER YOU DO--DON'T STOP RUNNING.
REMEMBER HOW SLOW THEY ARE? WE'LL BE LONG PAST EACH ONE OF THEM BY THE TIME THEY DECIDE TO TAKE A SWIPE AT US.
SPUKK!
JUST RUN!
SPAKK!
THOSE CRAZY FUCKS. DON'T WASTE ANY MORE BULLETS--THE BITERS WILL GET THEM FOR SURE.
PROBABLY GOT A DEATH WISH AFTER SEEING HIS WIFE BUY IT...

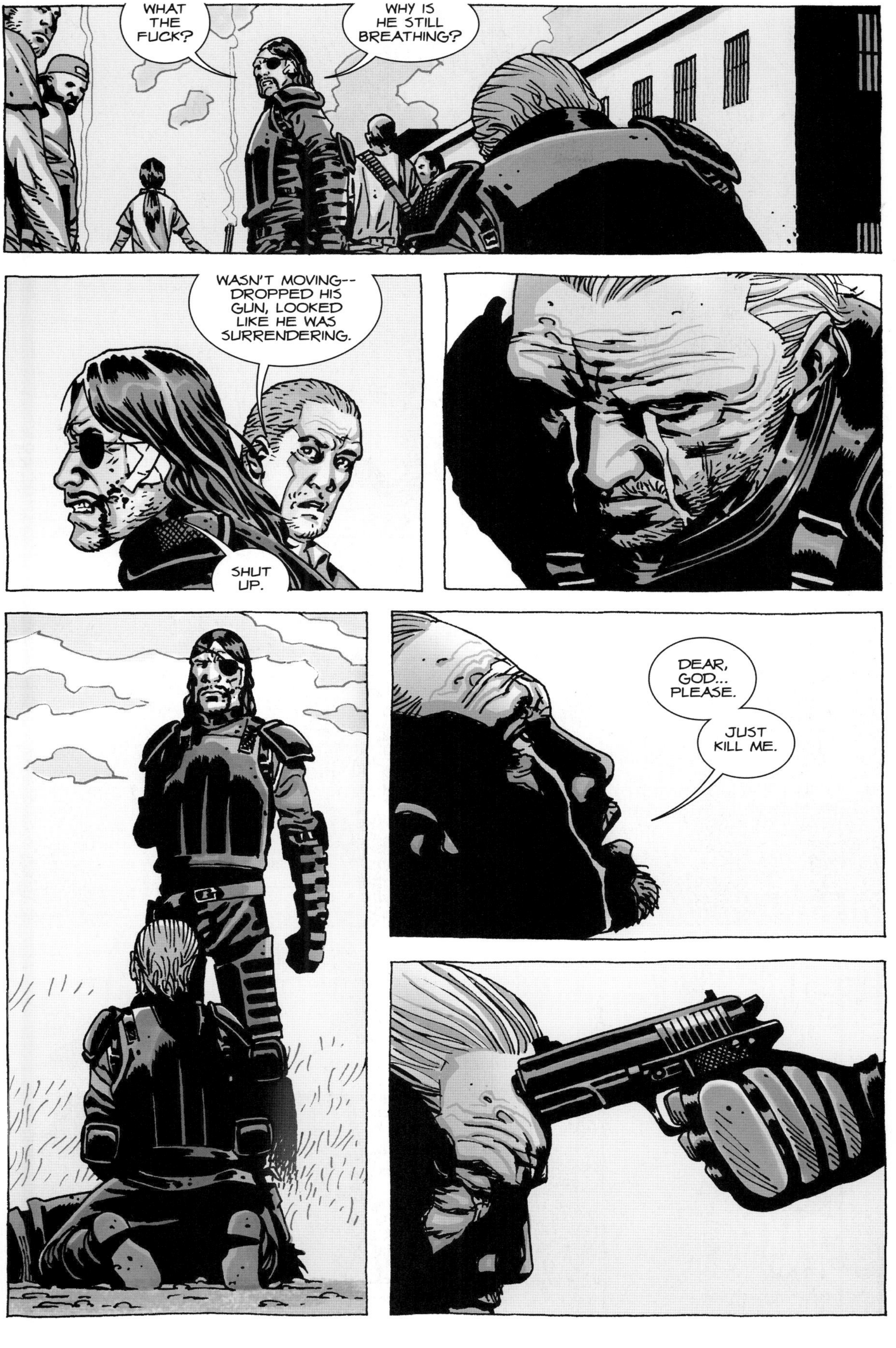
WHAT THE FUCK?
WHY IS HE STILL BREATHING?
WASN'T MOVING-- DROPPED HIS GUN, LOOKED LIKE HE WAS SURRENDERING.
SHUT UP.
DEAR, GOD... PLEASE.
JUST KILL ME.

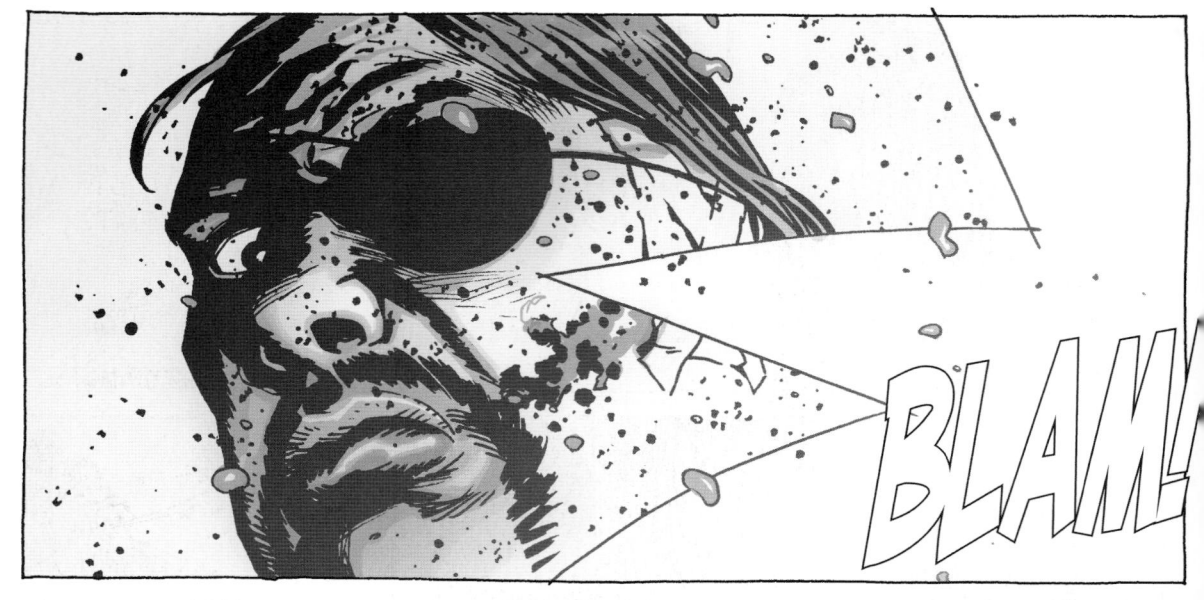

OH,
GOD...

OH, GOD!
OH, GOD!

WHAT THE
FUCK IS *HER*
PROBLEM?!

WHAT THE
FUCK IS
WRONG WITH
YOU?!

YOU
MONSTER...

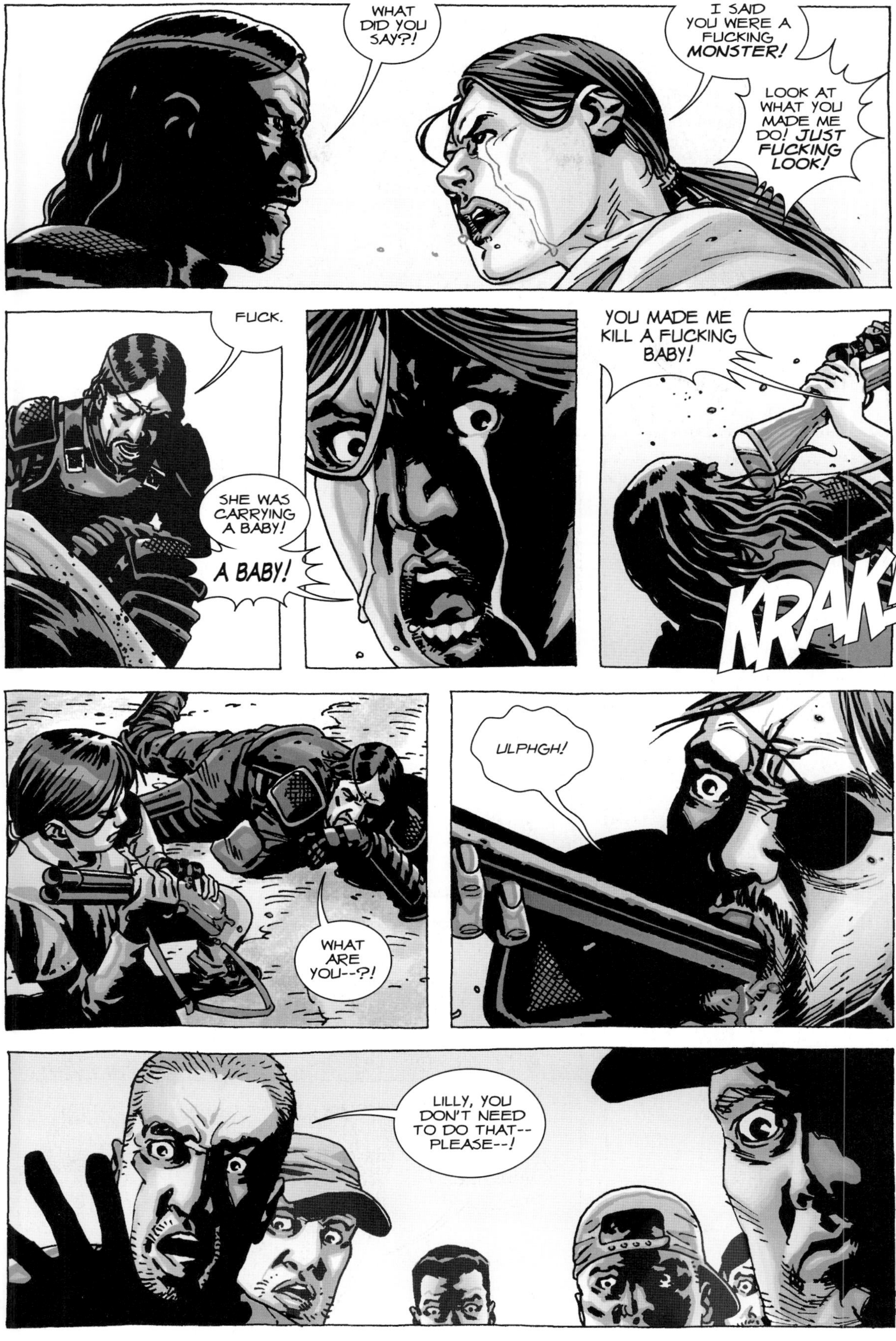

WHAT DID YOU SAY?!
I SAID YOU WERE A FUCKING MONSTER!
LOOK AT WHAT YOU MADE ME DO! JUST FUCKING LOOK!
FUCK.
SHE WAS CARRYING A BABY!
A BABY!
YOU MADE ME KILL A FUCKING BABY!
KRAK!
WHAT ARE YOU--?!
ULPHGH!
LILLY, YOU DON'T NEED TO DO THAT-- PLEASE--!

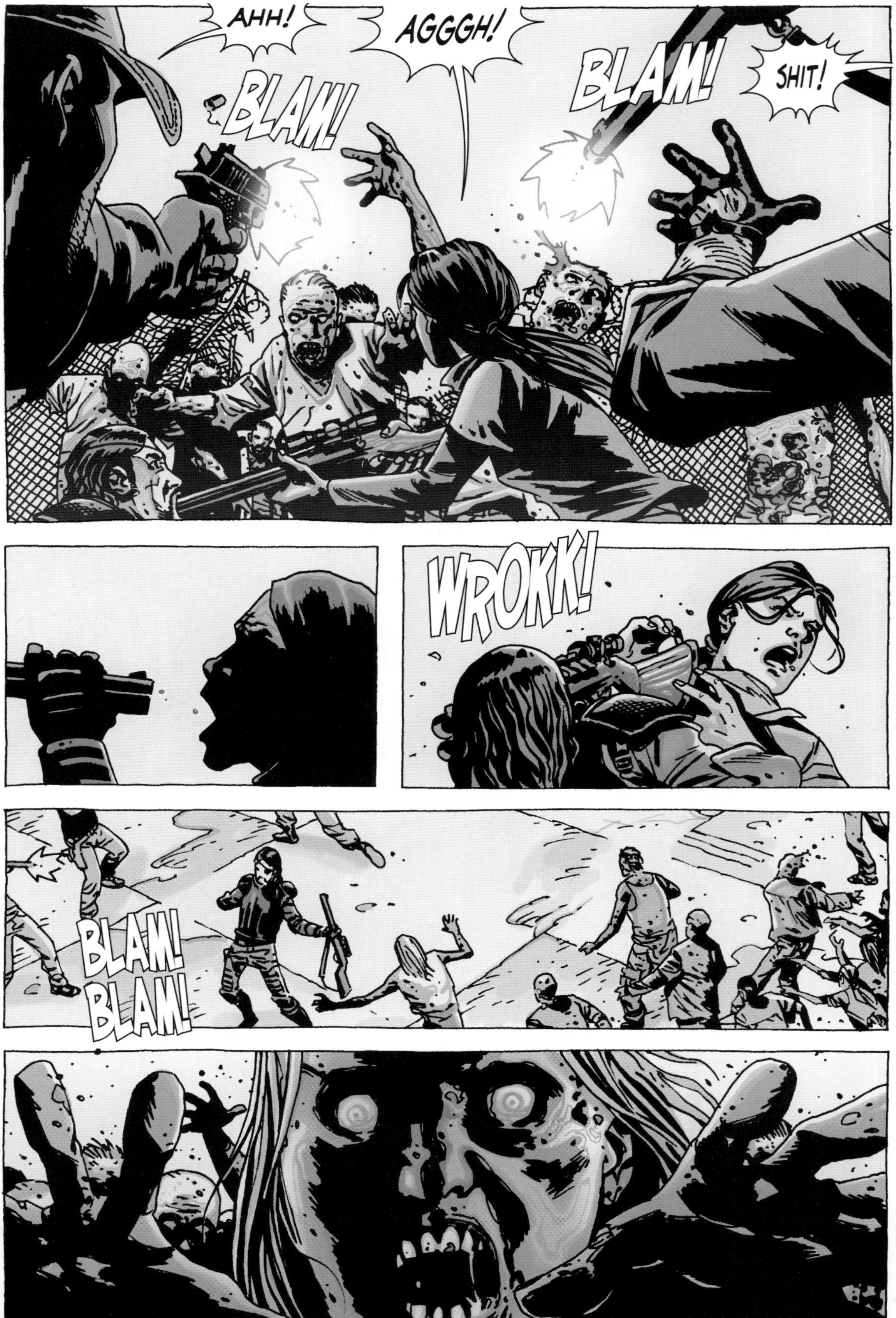
AHH!
AGGGH!
BLAM!
BLAM!
SHIT!
WROKK!
BLAM! BLAM!

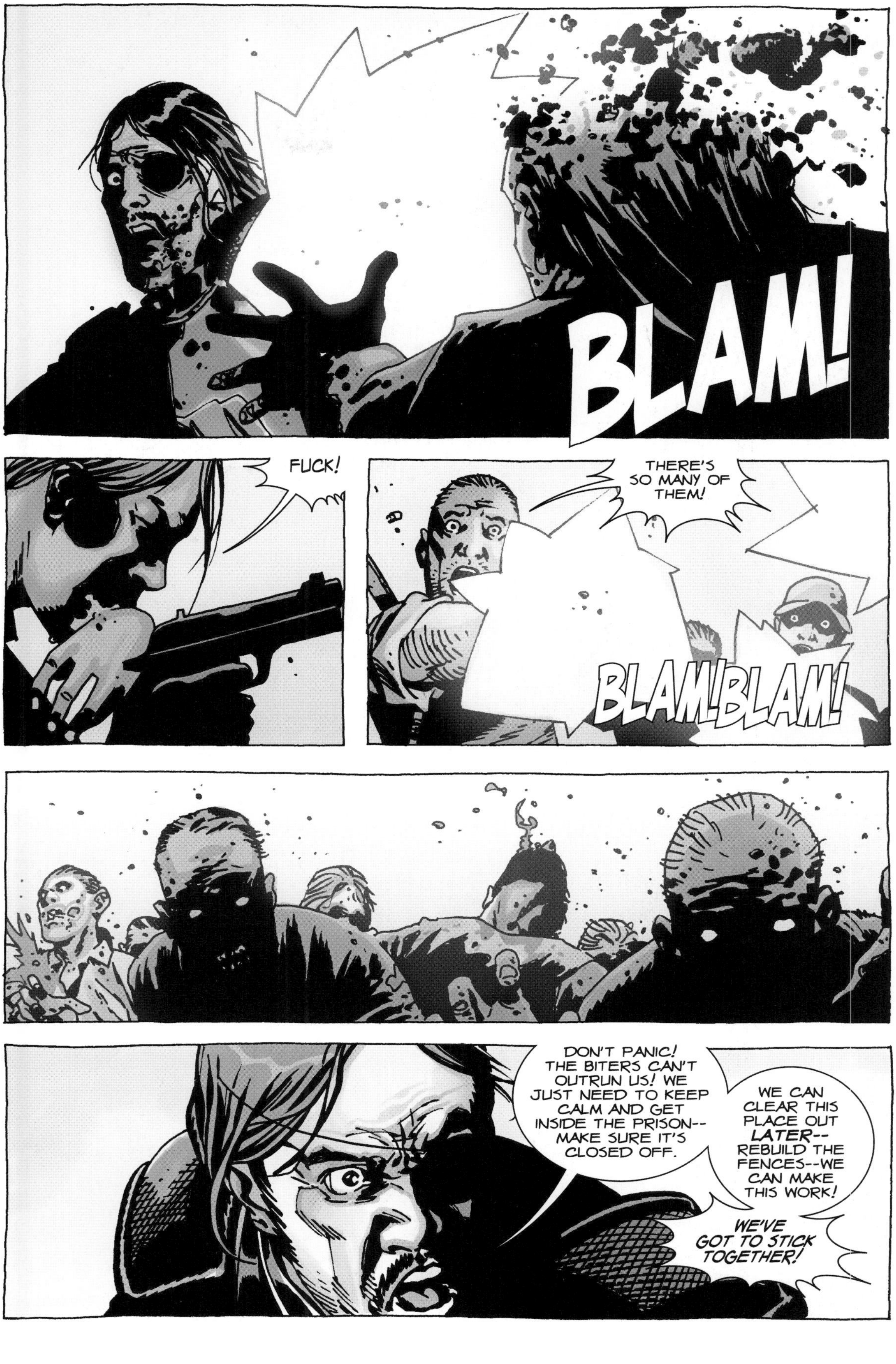
BLAM!
FUCK!
THERE'S SO MANY OF THEM!
BLAM! BLAM!
DON'T PANIC! THE BITERS CAN'T OUTRUN US! WE JUST NEED TO KEEP CALM AND GET INSIDE THE PRISON--MAKE SURE IT'S CLOSED OFF.
WE CAN CLEAR THIS PLACE OUT LATER--REBUILD THE FENCES--WE CAN MAKE THIS WORK!
WE'VE GOT TO STICK TOGETHER!

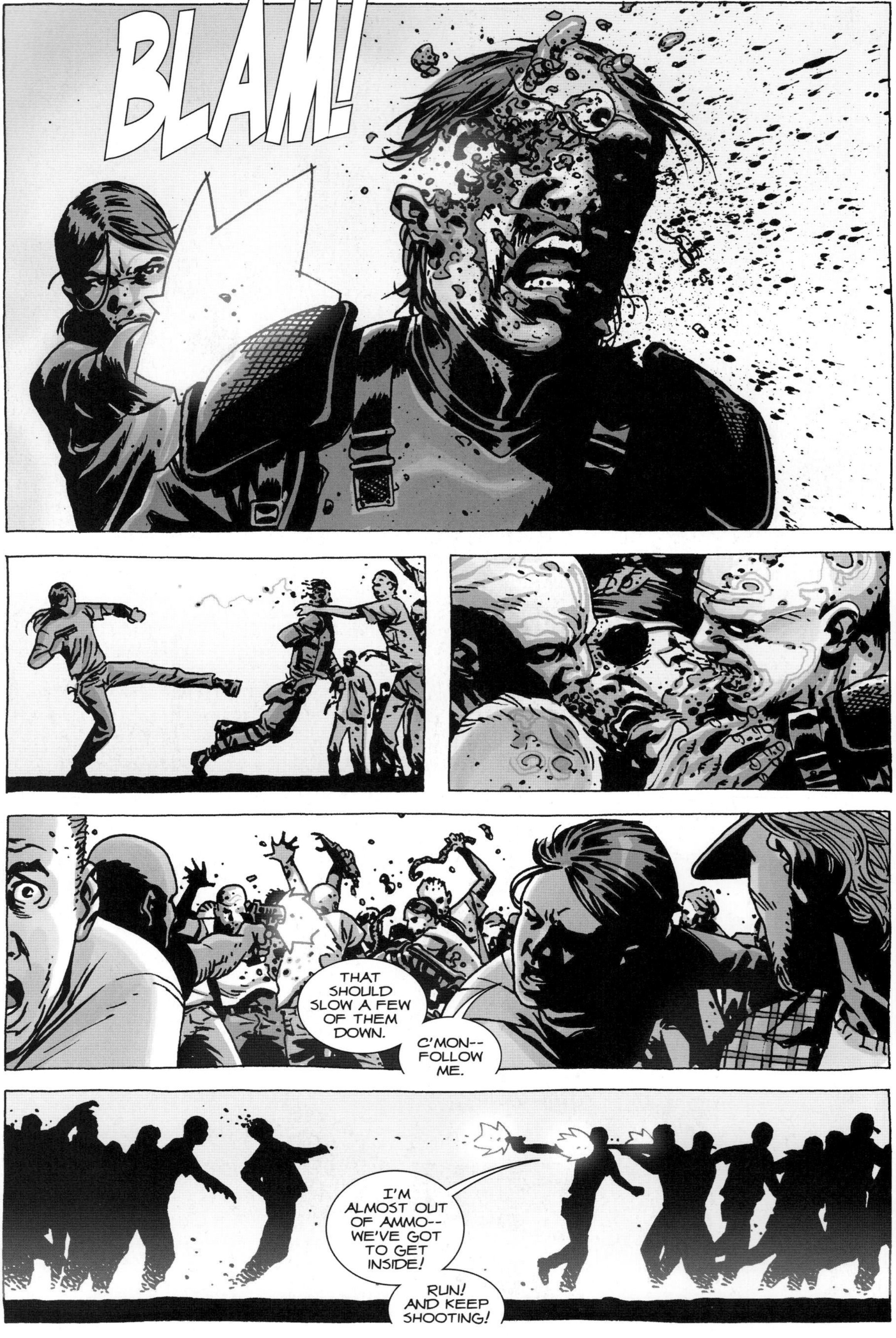
BLAM!
THAT SHOULD SLOW A FEW OF THEM DOWN.
C'MON-- FOLLOW ME.
I'M ALMOST OUT OF AMMO-- WE'VE GOT TO GET INSIDE!
RUN! AND KEEP SHOOTING!

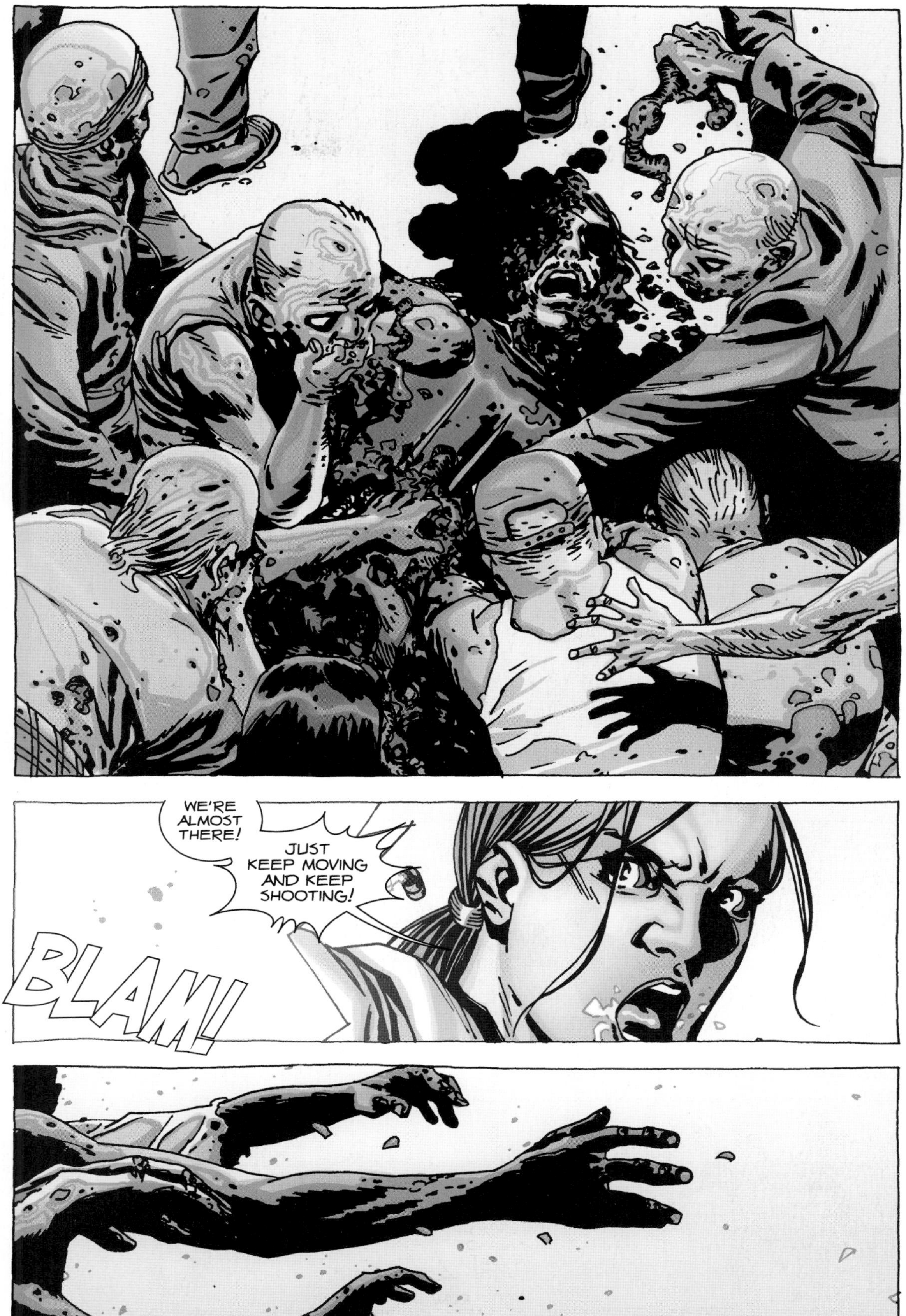
WE'RE ALMOST THERE!
JUST KEEP MOVING AND KEEP SHOOTING!
BLAM!

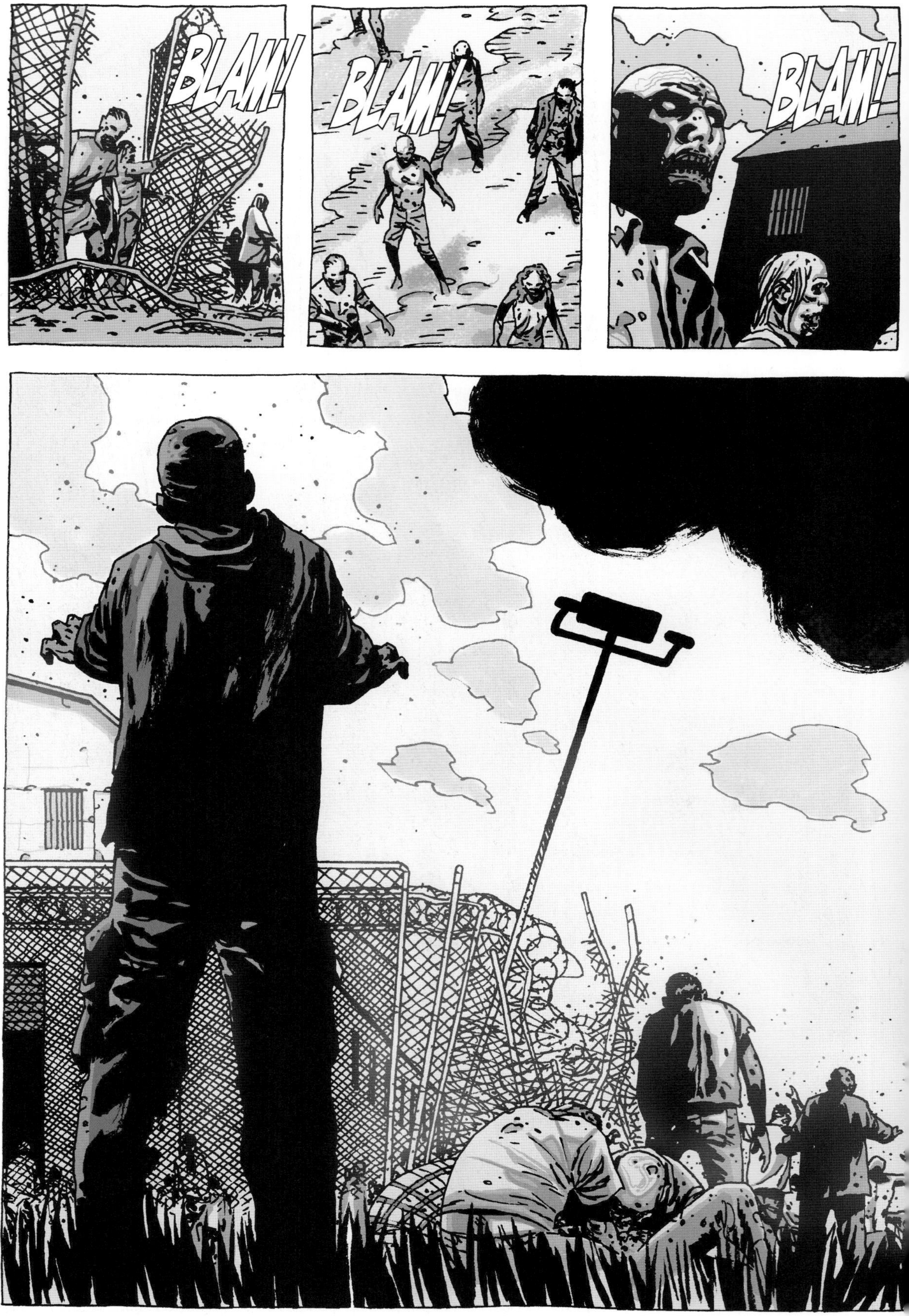
BLAM!
BLAM!
BLAM!

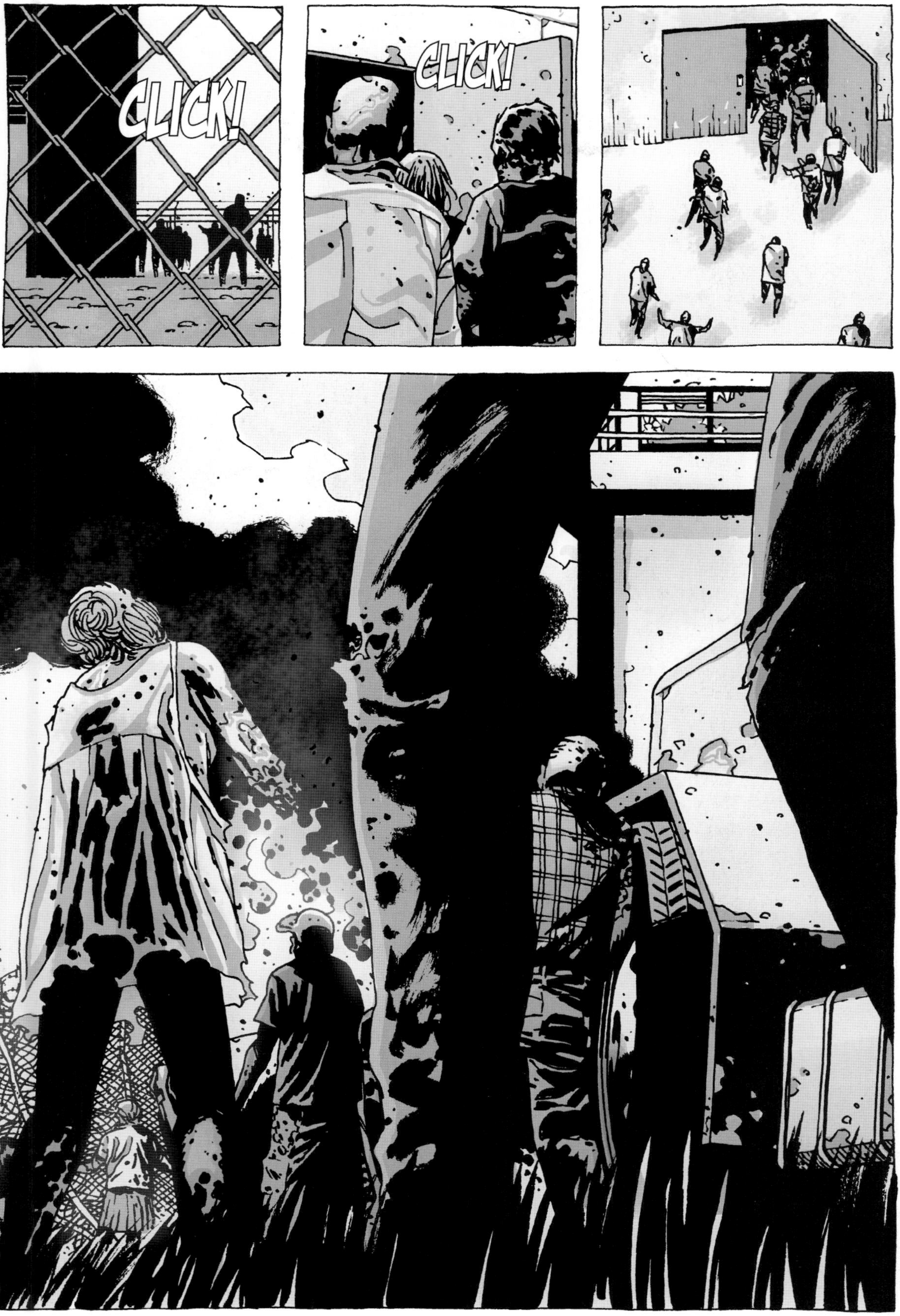
CLICK!
CLICK!

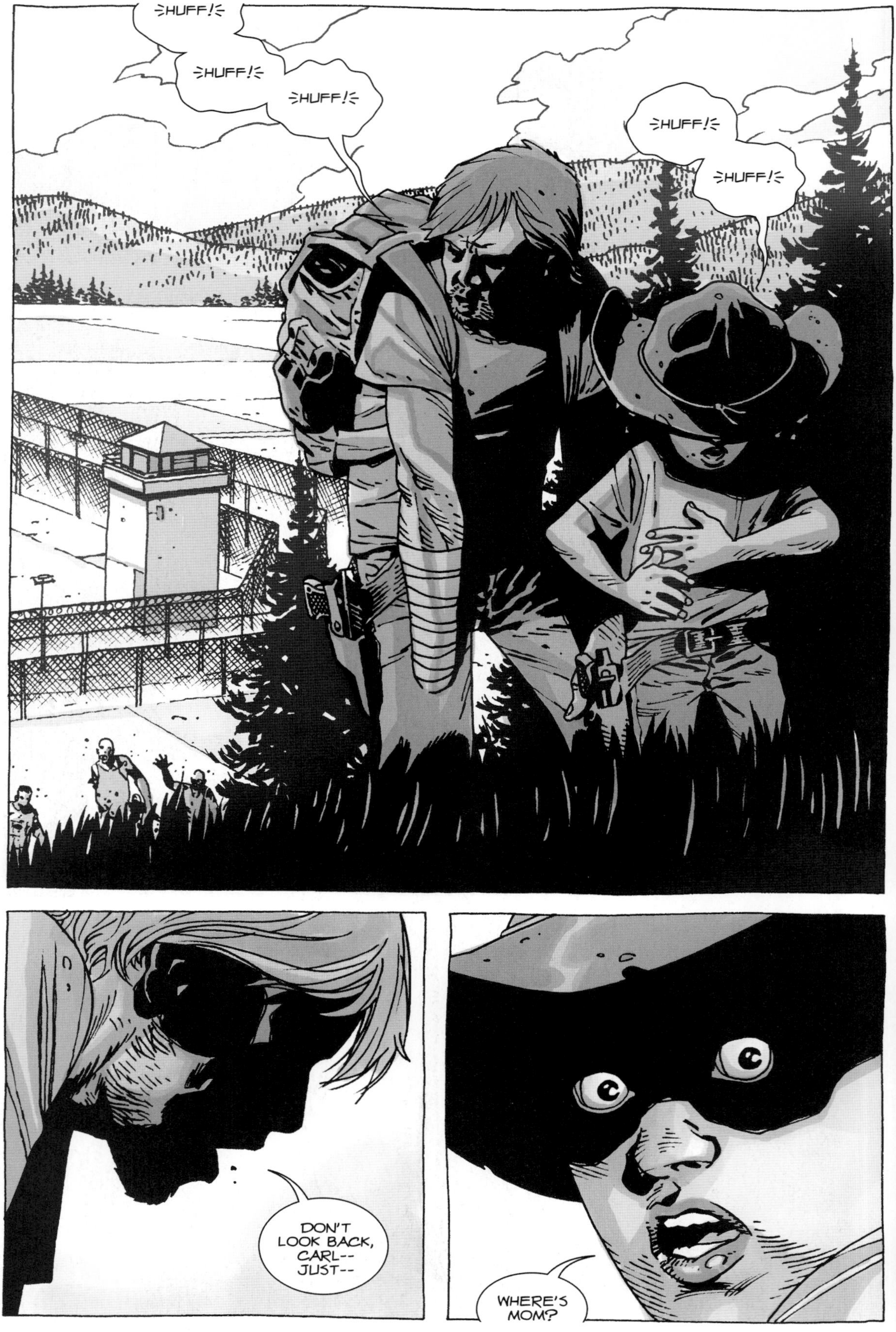
HUFF!
HUFF!
HUFF!
HUFF!
HUFF!
DON'T LOOK BACK, CARL-- JUST--
WHERE'S MOM?

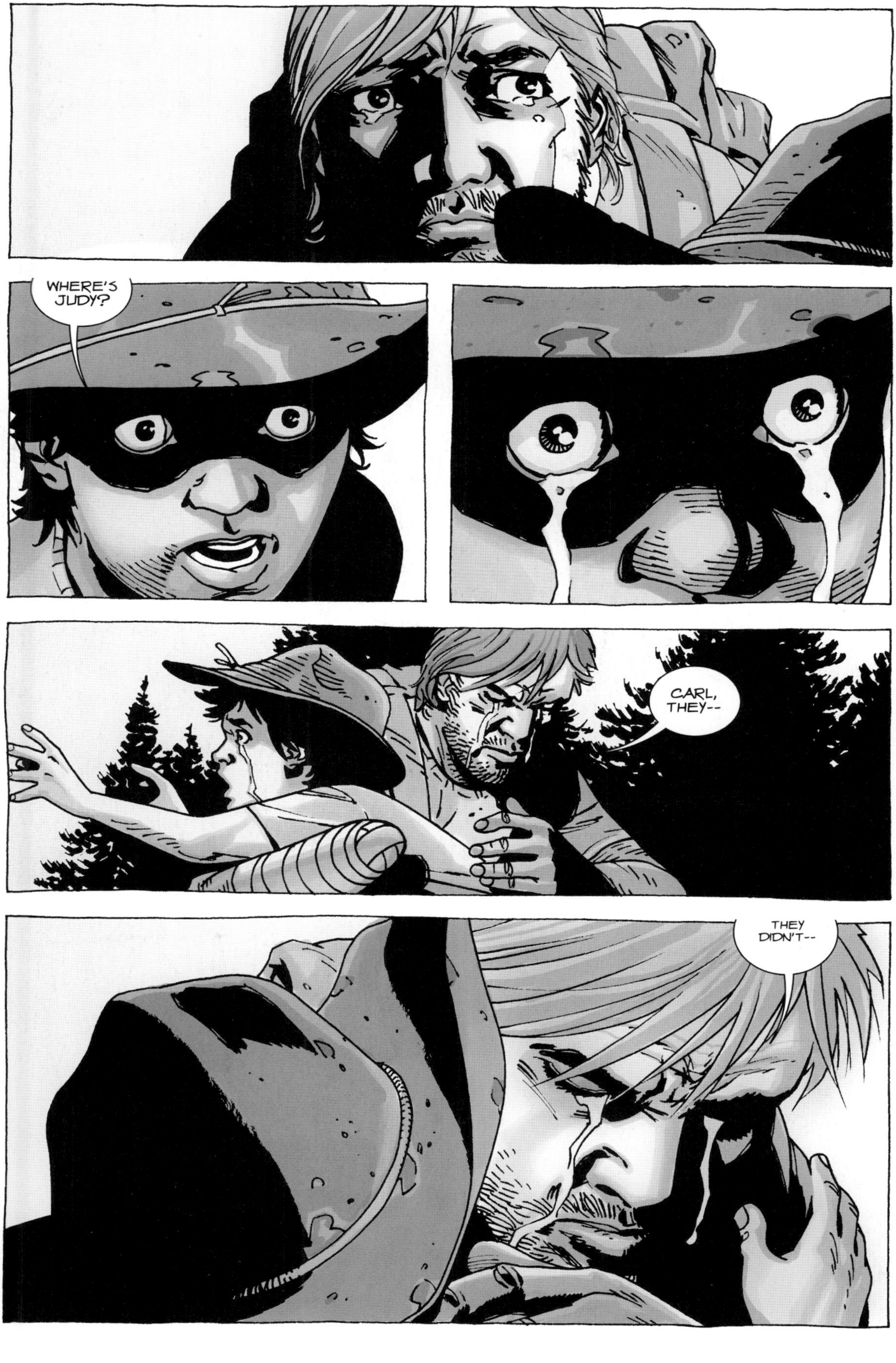
WHERE'S JUDY?
CARL, THEY--
THEY DIDN'T--

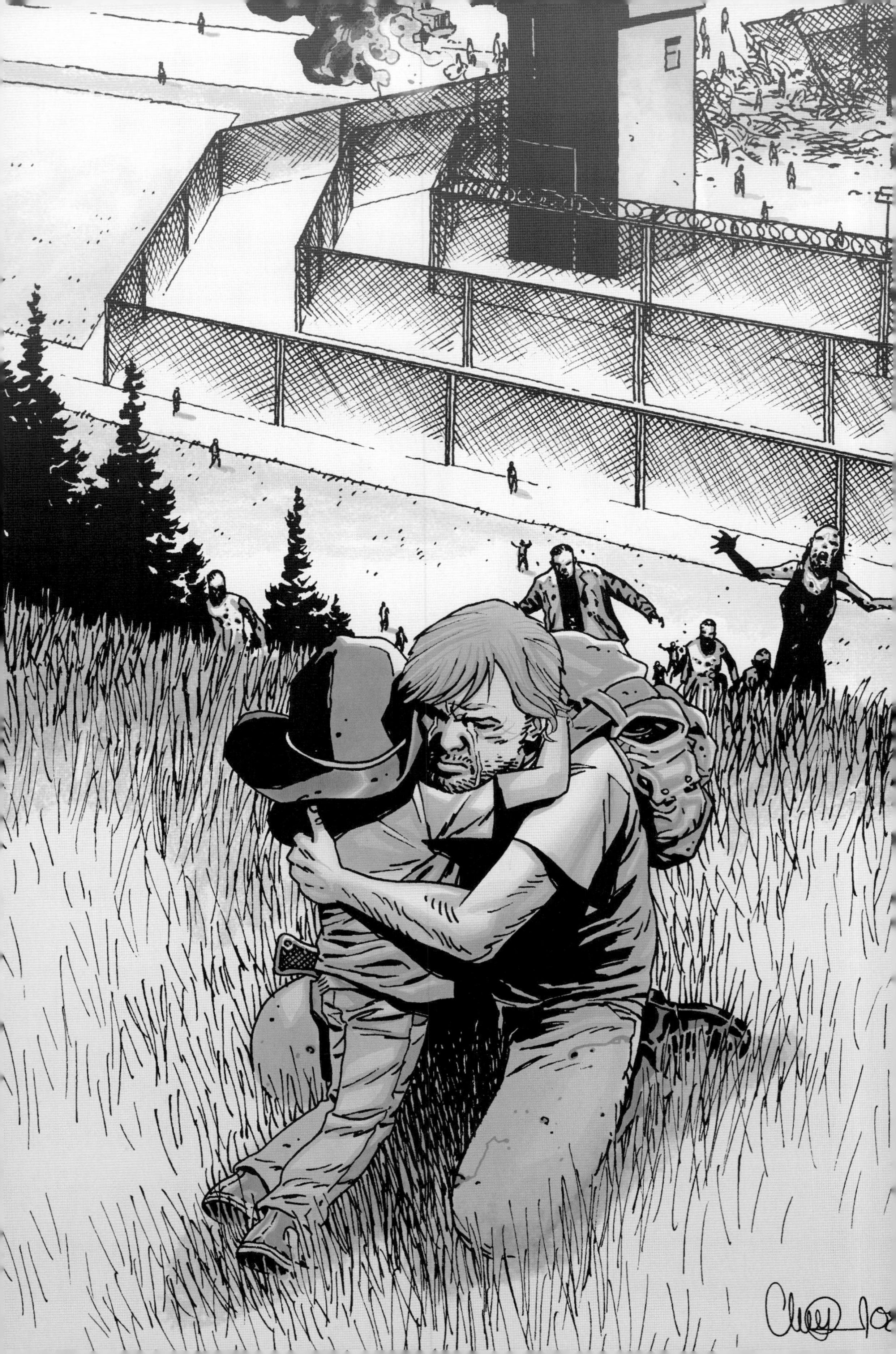

to be continued...

On the following pages you'll find a short story Charlie Adlard, Cliff Rathburn and I did for the Image Comics Holiday Special in 2005.

It features Morgan and Duane, the father and son from issue #1 of this series. For those keeping track, it takes place around the same time as issue #7 (the beginning of chapter two). I've been itching to get back to these two since issue #1 and regretting that it took so long... but here they are. We might just see them again at some point.

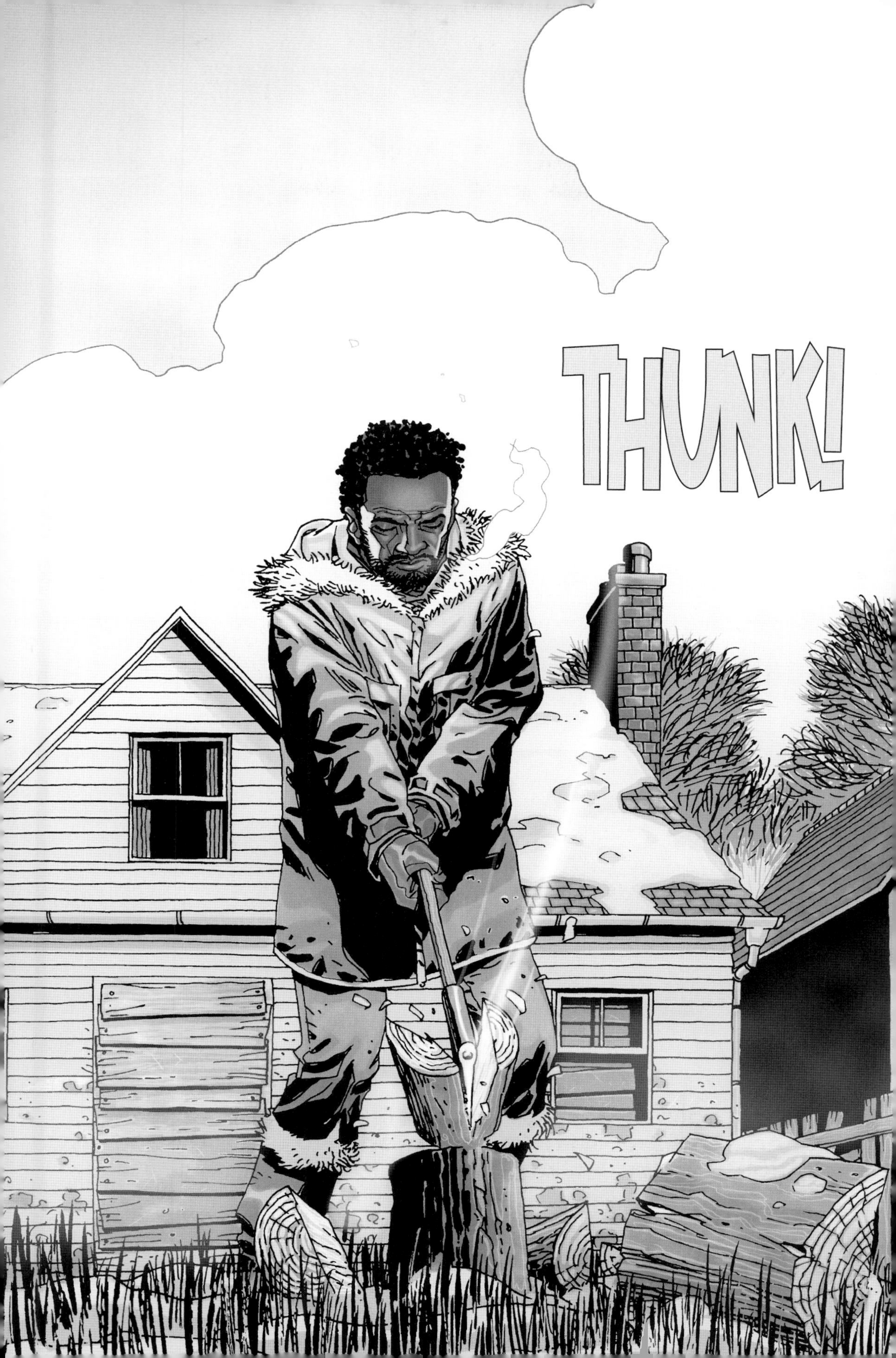
THUNK!

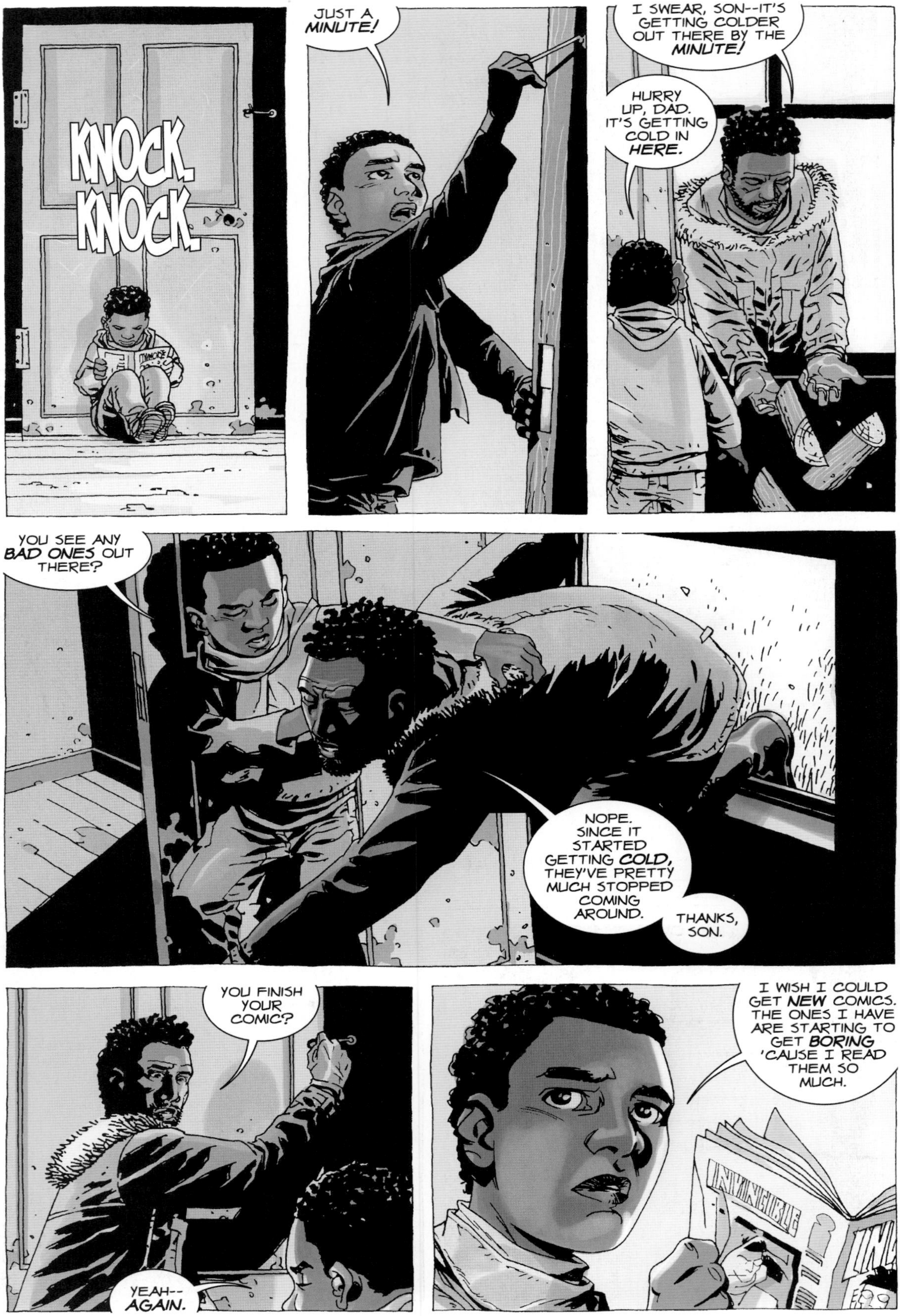
KNOCK KNOCK
JUST A MINUTE!
I SWEAR, SON--IT'S GETTING COLDER OUT THERE BY THE MINUTE!
HURRY UP, DAD. IT'S GETTING COLD IN HERE.
YOU SEE ANY BAD ONES OUT THERE?
NOPE. SINCE IT STARTED GETTING COLD, THEY'VE PRETTY MUCH STOPPED COMING AROUND.
THANKS, SON.
YOU FINISH YOUR COMIC?
YEAH-- AGAIN.
I WISH I COULD GET NEW COMICS. THE ONES I HAVE ARE STARTING TO GET BORING 'CAUSE I READ THEM SO MUCH.
INVINCIBLE

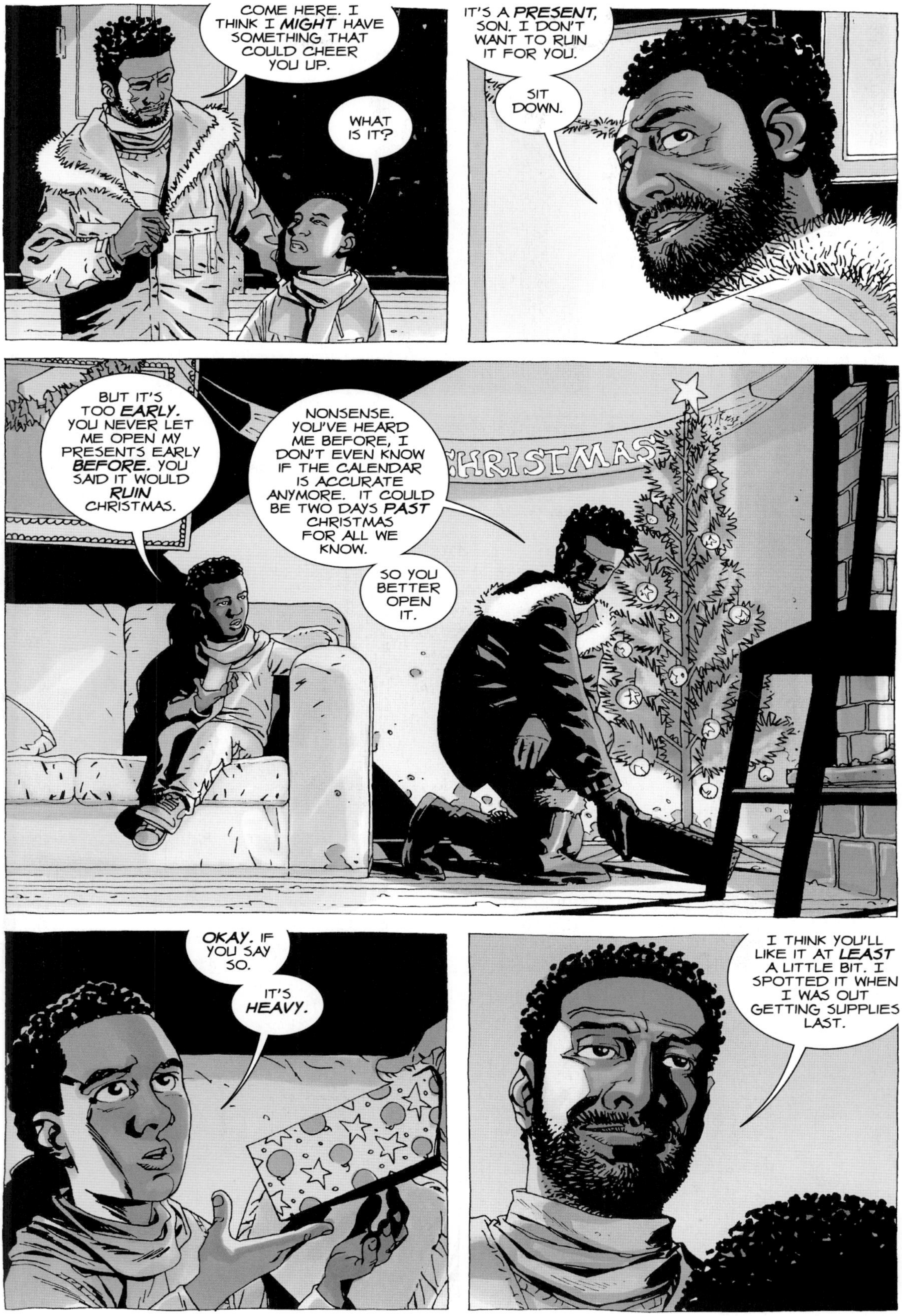
COME HERE. I THINK I *MIGHT* HAVE SOMETHING THAT COULD CHEER YOU UP.
WHAT IS IT?
IT'S A *PRESENT*, SON. I DON'T WANT TO RUIN IT FOR YOU.
SIT DOWN.
BUT IT'S TOO *EARLY*. YOU NEVER LET ME OPEN MY PRESENTS EARLY *BEFORE*. YOU SAID IT WOULD *RUIN* CHRISTMAS.
NONSENSE. YOU'VE HEARD ME BEFORE, I DON'T EVEN KNOW IF THE CALENDAR IS ACCURATE ANYMORE. IT COULD BE TWO DAYS *PAST* CHRISTMAS FOR ALL WE KNOW.
SO YOU BETTER OPEN IT.
OKAY. IF YOU SAY SO.
IT'S *HEAVY*.
I THINK YOU'LL LIKE IT AT *LEAST* A LITTLE BIT. I SPOTTED IT WHEN I WAS OUT GETTING SUPPLIES LAST.

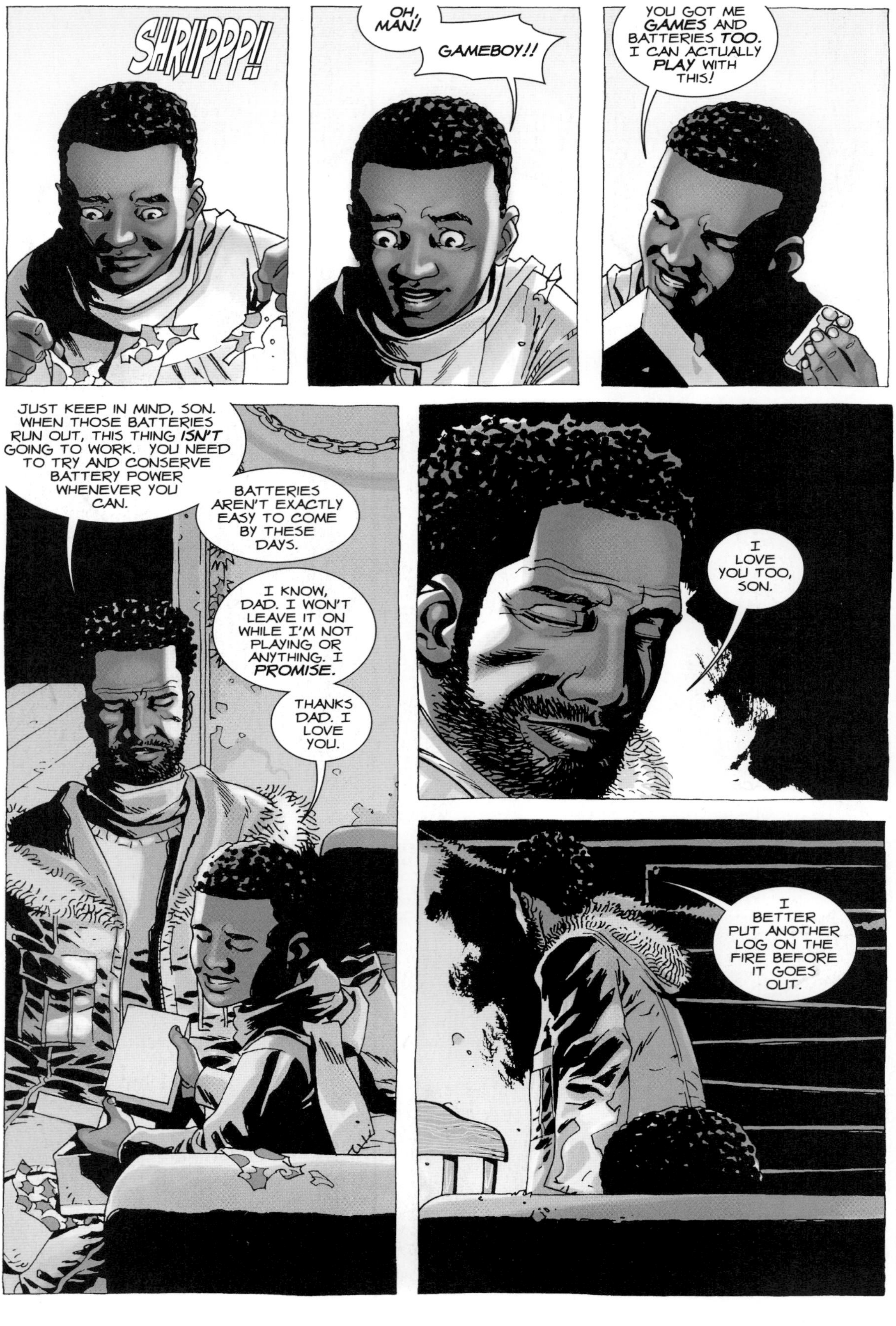
SHRIPPP!!
OH, MAN!
GAMEBOY!!
YOU GOT ME GAMES AND BATTERIES TOO. I CAN ACTUALLY PLAY WITH THIS!
JUST KEEP IN MIND, SON. WHEN THOSE BATTERIES RUN OUT, THIS THING ISN'T GOING TO WORK. YOU NEED TO TRY AND CONSERVE BATTERY POWER WHENEVER YOU CAN.
BATTERIES AREN'T EXACTLY EASY TO COME BY THESE DAYS.
I KNOW, DAD. I WON'T LEAVE IT ON WHILE I'M NOT PLAYING OR ANYTHING. I PROMISE.
THANKS DAD. I LOVE YOU.
I LOVE YOU TOO, SON.
I BETTER PUT ANOTHER LOG ON THE FIRE BEFORE IT GOES OUT.

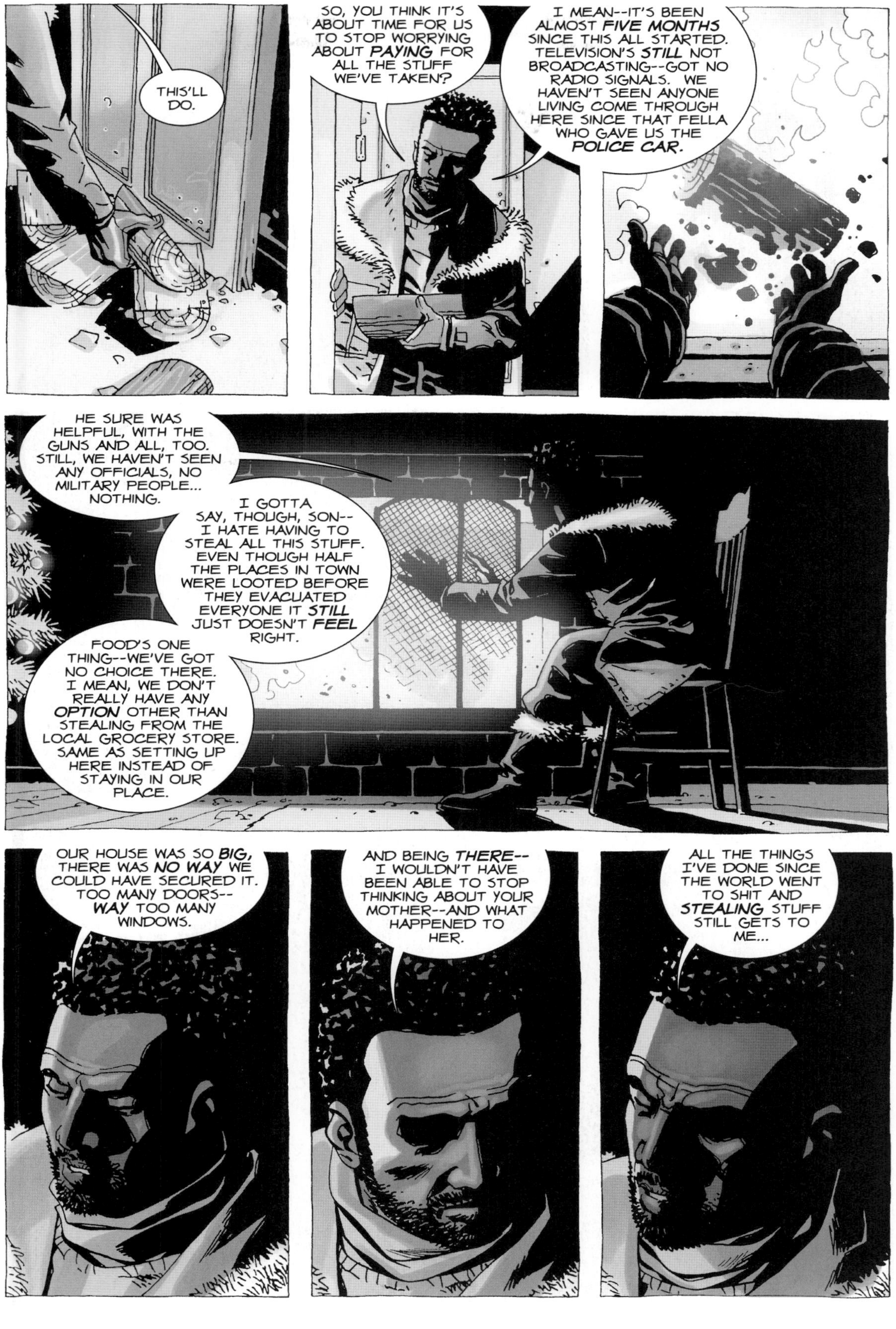
THIS'LL DO.
SO, YOU THINK IT'S ABOUT TIME FOR US TO STOP WORRYING ABOUT PAYING FOR ALL THE STUFF WE'VE TAKEN?
I MEAN--IT'S BEEN ALMOST FIVE MONTHS SINCE THIS ALL STARTED. TELEVISION'S STILL NOT BROADCASTING--GOT NO RADIO SIGNALS. WE HAVEN'T SEEN ANYONE LIVING COME THROUGH HERE SINCE THAT FELLA WHO GAVE US THE POLICE CAR.
HE SURE WAS HELPFUL, WITH THE GUNS AND ALL, TOO. STILL, WE HAVEN'T SEEN ANY OFFICIALS, NO MILITARY PEOPLE... NOTHING.
I GOTTA SAY, THOUGH, SON-- I HATE HAVING TO STEAL ALL THIS STUFF. EVEN THOUGH HALF THE PLACES IN TOWN WERE LOOTED BEFORE THEY EVACUATED EVERYONE IT STILL JUST DOESN'T FEEL RIGHT.
FOOD'S ONE THING--WE'VE GOT NO CHOICE THERE. I MEAN, WE DON'T REALLY HAVE ANY OPTION OTHER THAN STEALING FROM THE LOCAL GROCERY STORE. SAME AS SETTING UP HERE INSTEAD OF STAYING IN OUR PLACE.
OUR HOUSE WAS SO BIG, THERE WAS NO WAY WE COULD HAVE SECURED IT. TOO MANY DOORS-- WAY TOO MANY WINDOWS.
AND BEING THERE-- I WOULDN'T HAVE BEEN ABLE TO STOP THINKING ABOUT YOUR MOTHER--AND WHAT HAPPENED TO HER.
ALL THE THINGS I'VE DONE SINCE THE WORLD WENT TO SHIT AND STEALING STUFF STILL GETS TO ME...

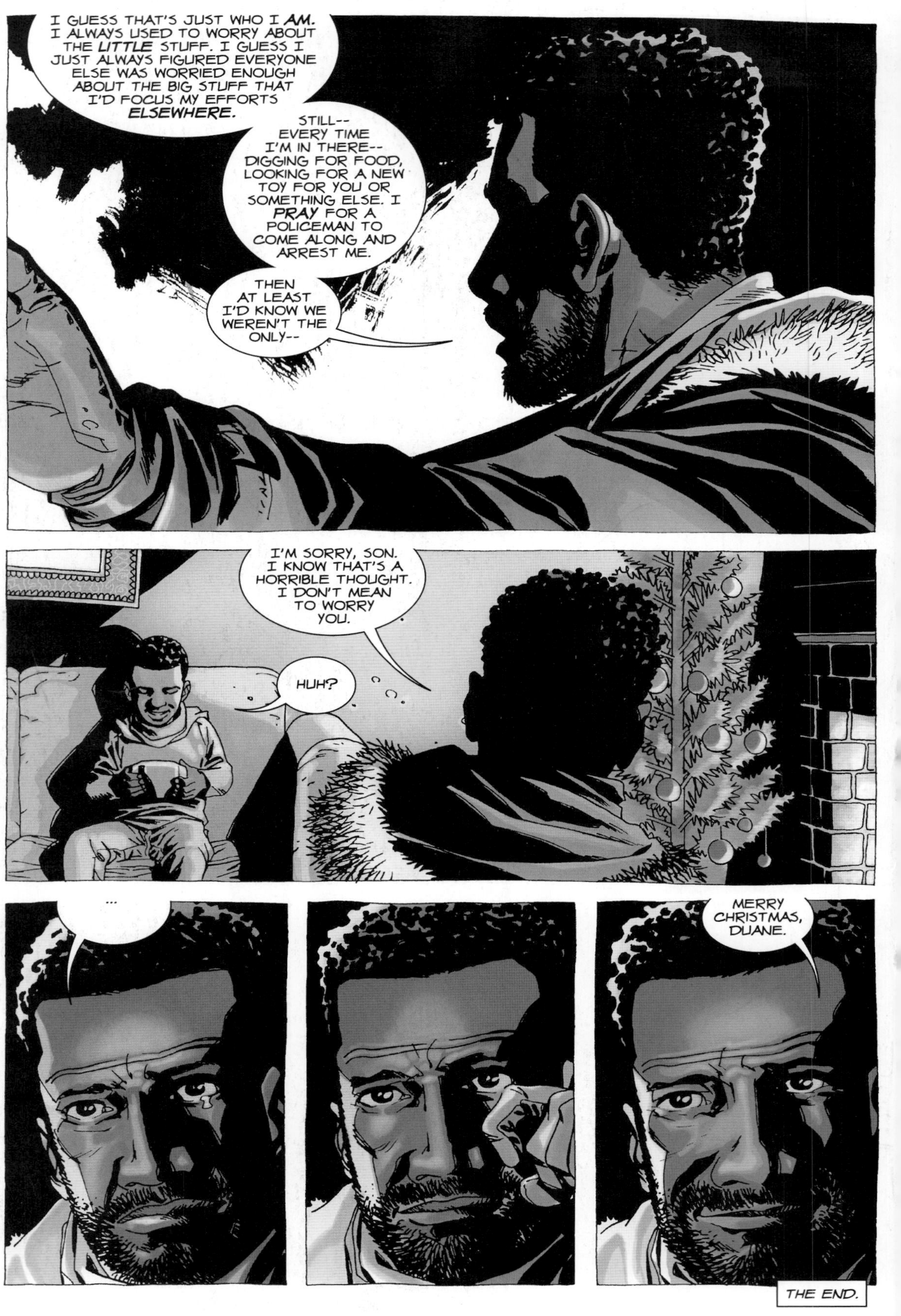
I GUESS THAT'S JUST WHO I *AM*. I ALWAYS USED TO WORRY ABOUT THE *LITTLE* STUFF. I GUESS I JUST ALWAYS FIGURED EVERYONE ELSE WAS WORRIED ENOUGH ABOUT THE BIG STUFF THAT I'D FOCUS MY EFFORTS *ELSEWHERE.*
STILL-- EVERY TIME I'M IN THERE-- DIGGING FOR FOOD, LOOKING FOR A NEW TOY FOR YOU OR SOMETHING ELSE. I *PRAY* FOR A POLICEMAN TO COME ALONG AND ARREST ME.
THEN AT LEAST I'D KNOW WE WEREN'T THE ONLY--
I'M SORRY, SON. I KNOW THAT'S A HORRIBLE THOUGHT. I DON'T MEAN TO WORRY YOU.
HUH?
...
MERRY CHRISTMAS, DUANE.
THE END.